The Rats Came Back

The Rats Came Back

Story by Ross Seidel
Illustrations by Rudolf Kurz

Annick Press Ltd. • Toronto • New York

©1995 Ross Seidel (text)
©1995 Rudolf Kurz (art)
Design by Rudolf Kurz
Cover design by Sheryl Shapiro

Annick Press Ltd.

Annick Press gratefully acknowledges the support of the
Canada Council and the Ontario Arts Council.

Canadian Cataloguing in Publication Data

Seidel, Ross
    The rats came back

ISBN 1-55037-403-6 (bound) ISBN 1-55037-402-8 (pbk.)

I. Kurz, Rudolf. II. Title.

PS8587.E54R38 1995   jC813'.54   C95-931196-3
PZ7.S45Ra 1995

The art in this book was rendered in watercolours.
The text was typeset in Century Oldstyle.

Distributed in Canada by: Published in the U.S.A. by Annick Press (U.S.) Ltd.
Firefly Books Ltd.   Distributed in the U.S.A. by:
250 Sparks Avenue   Firefly Books (U.S.) Inc.
Willowdale, ON   P.O. Box 1338
M2H 2S4   Ellicott Station
                                     Buffalo, NY 14205

∞ Printed on acid-free paper.

Printed and bound in Canada by
Friesens, Altona, Manitoba

For my parents,
and for
all parents.
— Ross Seidel

To Catherine,
Elizabeth
and Oliver,
with love
— Rudolf Kurz

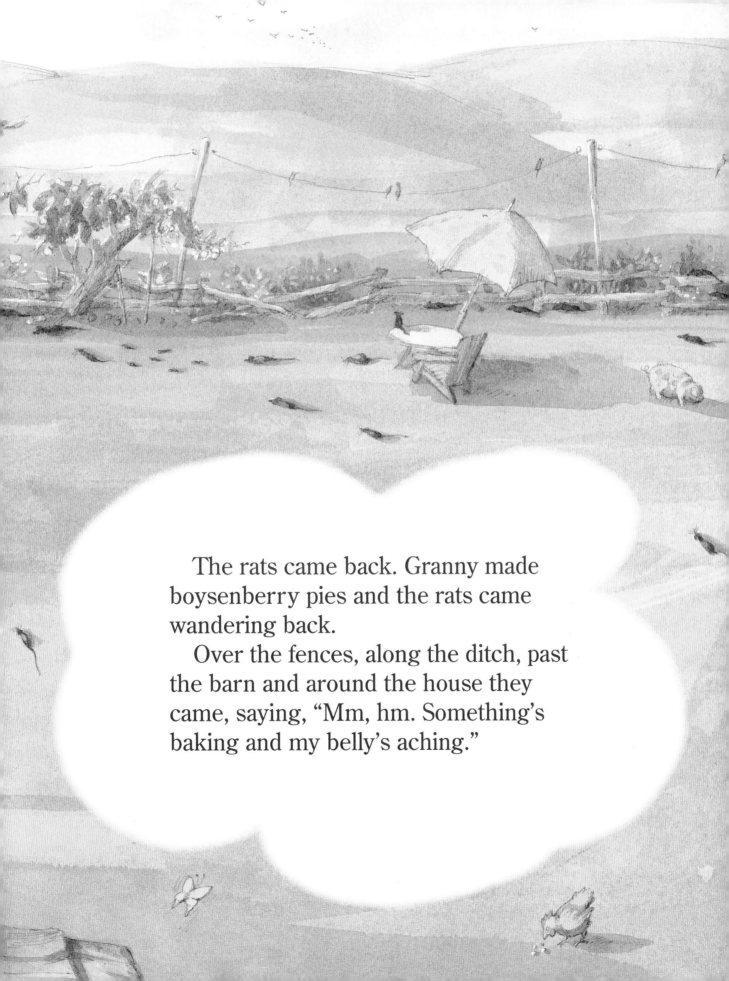

The rats came back. Granny made boysenberry pies and the rats came wandering back.

Over the fences, along the ditch, past the barn and around the house they came, saying, "Mm, hm. Something's baking and my belly's aching."

Up the rickety stairs of Granny's house they quietly crept. Around the verandah they tiptoed.

"Shh," one rat said. "Listen."

"Kkaahh wwhhheewww," the rats heard. "Kaahh wwhheewww."

"What's that?"

"It's Granny. She's having a nap!"

"Hee, hee, hee," the rats giggled.

Then, soft as a whisper, the rats scurried under the buckled back door, through the broken basement windows and down the long tattered hallway into Granny's kitchen.

"Mm," they said as they peeked through the oven door.

Meanwhile, Granny was still curled up in her rocking chair, snoring away. "Kahkahkah wwhheeww," she went. "Kahkahkah wwhheeww."

In the huge oven the sixteen boysenberry pies were just beginning to brown.

"Come on, let's eat! I'm starving!" one rat grumbled—a grumble so loud that it woke Granny. She sat up and saw the rats.

"You little rascals!" she shouted, grabbing her broom. "You're back! You're back!"

"Yes'm," the rats answered in chorus.

"Then pitter-patter, let's get at 'er!" Granny said.

Well. Out of the baskets and pails came brooms and brushes, mops and sponges, saws and hammers, ratchets and rulers, and nails and glue.

Then up the walls, down the stairs, and across
the ceiling the rats scattered, to all the places
Granny couldn't get to.

Rats were cleaning the chandeliers, fixing cracks in the ceiling, mopping up spider webs and repairing broken windows. There were rats painting and polishing, plastering and perfuming and hanging upside down, right side up, inside, outside, every which side, in Granny's old, old house.

And while all the cleaning and painting and polishing was going on, Granny was keeping her eyes on the pies so that they wouldn't burn.

Goodness me, those rats were handy. It didn't take them long to make Granny's house look sparkling new.

After they were done, they put away their brooms and brushes, their mops and sponges, saws and hammers and ratchets and rulers. Then off came their gloves, their polka-dotted toques and their dirty coveralls. And into the shower they jumped.

Meanwhile, Granny laid the table with her
long, white, embroidered tablecloth, finest china
and favourite coloured candles. Then, one by
one, she slid the sixteen boysenberry pies out of
the oven and onto the counter while the rats
seated themselves around the table.

Now all that needed to be done was to eat those sixteen boysenberry pies.

Well, those hungry rats— they certainly took care

of

that.

Travelling to Latin America?

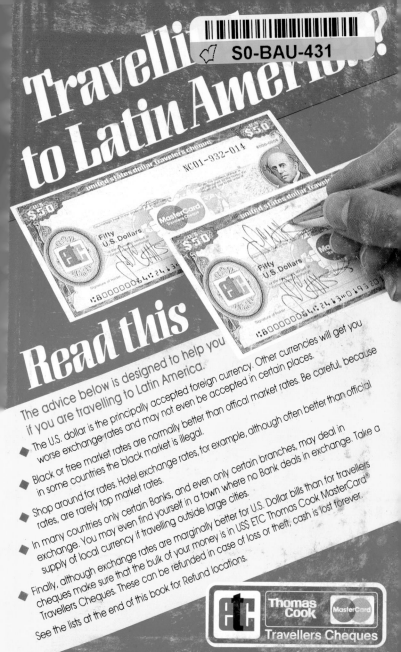

Read this

The advice below is designed to help you if you are travelling to Latin America.

- The U.S. dollar is the principally accepted foreign currency. Other currencies will get you worse exchange rates and may not even be accepted in certain places. Be careful, because in some countries the black market is illegal.

- Black or free market rates are normally better than offical market rates.

- Shop around for rates. Hotel exchange rates, for example, although often better than official rates, are rarely top market rates.

- In many countries only certain Banks, and even only certain branches, may deal in exchange. You may even find yourself in a town where no Bank deals in exchange. Take a supply of local currency if travelling outside large cities.

- Finally, although exchange rates are marginally better for U.S. Dollar bills than for travellers cheques make sure that the bulk of your money is in US$ ETC Thomas Cook MasterCard® Travellers Cheques. These can be refunded in case of loss or theft, cash is lost forever. See the lists at the end of this book for Refund locations.

Mexico City — | — Rio de Janeiro
Caracas — | — Bogota
Lima — | — Santiago
San Juan — | — Havana
Asuncion — | — Sao Paolo
Panama City — | — Quito
San Jose — | — Guayaquil
Buenos Aires — | — Santo Domingo
Managua — | — Guatemala
Montevideo — |

THE HOTTEST IN LATIN AMERICA.

Iberia gives you the hottest all-round service to Latin America.

With more flights to more places than any other airline. Plus a network of internal flights.

Iberia Preference Class, the hottest business class, means seat selection

when you book, separate check-in desks, through check-in to final destination, and exclusive lounges at most airports.

In flight, seating in a separate cabin offers the comfort and space of traditional first class: on our 747s you'll be right up-front, and only two abreast. The service is distinguished by impeccable attention to detail–there's even an on board library.

Ask your business travel agent to book the hottest service to Latin America.

IBERIA
AIRLINES OF SPAIN
WARM TO THE EXPERIENCE.

London 01-437 5622; Manchester 061-436 6444; Birmingham 021-643 1953; Glasgow 041-248 6581; Dublin 0001 779846.

1990
SOUTH AMERICAN HANDBOOK
SIXTY SIXTH EDITION

Editor
Ben Box

Associate Editor
Joyce Candy

"Travel, in the younger sort, is a part of
education; in the elder, a part of experience.
He that travelleth into a country before he hath
some entrance into the language, goeth to
school, and not to travel."

Francis Bacon, Essays: Of Travel.

TRADE & TRAVEL
PUBLICATIONS

TRADE & TRAVEL PUBLICATIONS LTD
5 PRINCE'S BUILDINGS
GEORGE STREET
BATH ENGLAND
TEL. 0225 469141
FAX 0225 462921

66th annual edition, published September 1989

ISBN 0 900751 29 0

Published in the United States of America and Canada by
Prentice Hall Trade
Division of Simon & Schuster Inc.
15 Columbus Circle
New York, NY 10023.

In North America, ISBN 0-13-823550-3

COVER

The jaguar is the largest of the South American "big cats". A dweller of
the Amazon and Central American forests, especially near the rivers,
jaguars can cover short distances with devasting speed and are good
swimmers. As hunters, jaguars have few equals. Their natural cunning,
versatility, power and speed enable them to catch turtles, fish, and baby
cayman crocodiles as well as land based mammals like capybara, a sort
of giant guinea pig which is the world's largest rodent.

More heavily built than the leopards of Africa and Asia, jaguars are
adult and able to breed at the age of three. A litter usually consists of
two cubs but some females may have up to four cubs in one litter.

The world's first jaguar reserve was set aside in 1986 as part of the
Cockscomb Basin Forest Reserve in Belize.

Cover illustration by Carl Melegari.
Photoset by Nuffield Press Ltd, Oxford;
printed and bound in Great Britain by Richard Clay Ltd., Bungay, Suffolk.

CONTENTS

PREFACE

It is with a sense of deep loss that we announce the death of John Brooks, editor of *The South American Handbook* since 1972. He died unexpectedly of cancer on February 8, 1989. As a prefix to the tribute to him which appears elsewhere in this edition, it must be said here that any user of this or subsequent editions will be sharing John Brooks' enjoyment in, and his concerns for, Latin America. His goal, as editor, was the annual improvement of the *Handbook* and the extension of its services to readers. At the beginning of a new decade, we look forward to pursuing these aims with vigour. In this way, the book will serve as a memorial to him.

It transpired that the trip he made with his wife, Sylvia, to Peru in September/October 1988 was his last to the continent. Even with the considerable assistance of Foptur and others (to whom acknowledgements are made at the end of the Peru chapter), they were struck by the difficulties at present facing that country. This impression has been reinforced by many readers' letters and by subsequent events (including the murder of a Welsh hiker in May 1989) which have led a number of foreign embassies to advise their citizens to avoid Peru. Nevertheless these and the other regional problems (political, economic, social and environmental) do not alter the philosophy of the *Handbook*. To understand Latin America you must experience it, and your experience will be enhanced by an awareness of the historical and geographical context in which it is set.

A second announcement has to be made: after 18 years working with *The South American Handbook* (14 as associate editor), Joyce Candy is retiring. Her contribution to the marketing and selling advertising space has been incalculable, but it is chiefly through her that readers who write to the book feel that they are part of an extended family. Without the personal attention she has always given each letter, travellers would not have recognized the high value which we place on their information. This is a unique tradition which we shall be glad to continue. Joyce will be much missed, but, on behalf of all who have had the pleasure to correspond with her, we wish her a happy retirement.

John Brooks' death caused the postponement of the some of the planned improvements for this edition, notably the completion of the extension of our map coverage (although 30 new maps have been added) and a complete overhaul of certain country chapters. However, other major plans have been realized. Readers will notice that *The South American Handbook* no longer contains the anglophone, French, or Dutch West Indies. This section is now incorporated in a companion volume, *The Caribbean Islands Handbook*, the first edition of which is published simultaneously with this one. The Hispanic Caribbean islands will appear in both books. In the course of a research trip for *The Caribbean Islands Handbook* by Ben Box in October/November 1988, much important information was gathered, and hospitality received, in Cuba, Haiti and the Dominican Republic (specific thanks are given in those sections).

We are very pleased to include in these pages a thorough revision by Kevin Healey of the section on Baja California, much needed in view of the popularity of the peninsula among North Americans, especially motorists. The Falklands Islands/Islas Malvinas chapter has been rewritten by Wayne Bernhardson; the growth in wildlife tours to the islands makes this a very welcome improvement. Also, Dr. David Snashall has kindly updated the Health Information chapter.

Again this year it is our pleasant duty to thank all the correspondents who have written in with corrections and additions for the text; all are mentioned in the acknowledgements sections after each chapter. Thanks are also due to Simon Ellis for updating Costa Rica and the Central American air routes, John Lewis for hotel information from around the region, Sarah Cameron, our economics editor, for bringing the economy sections up to date, and Maxine Reeder and her colleagues at Baseline Creative for their dedicated work on the maps. For their invaluable assistance in subediting portions of the text at short notice, we are indebted to Janet Krengel and Sandy and María Luisa Campbell. In this regard we are deeply grateful to Sylvia Brooks, who helped with the subediting at a most difficult time. To her and her family, we offer our very best wishes.

The Editor

OUR NEW EDITOR

The Publishers are pleased to announce the appointment of Ben Box as Editor of *The South American Handbook*, who becomes the book's 6th Editor, since W.H. Koebel published his extraordinary *Anglo-South American Handbook* in 1921.

1924 saw the first edition of the retitled *South American Handbook*, laid out to a new format and sold at the reduced price of seven shillings and six pence to "extend its sphere of usefulness" beyond the commercial sector which had hitherto provided the main readership.

The 1990 Edition is the 66th in an unbroken sequence of annually updated editions since 1924—each new issue striving to improve on the previous one.

Ben Box is no stranger to Latin America or to *The South American Handbook*, having edited much of the last seven editions under John Brooks' editorship.

He obtained a BA Honours degree in Spanish, with certificate in Portuguese from the University of Southampton and a PhD in Medieval Hispanic and Portuguese Studies from the University of London.

He has travelled extensively through the Caribbean and Latin America and in addition to being the Editor of *The South American Handbook* and Trade & Travel's new *Caribbean Islands Handbook*, works as a freelance writer on Hispanic and Latin American affairs. He has contributed to the London *Times*, *Observer* and *Independent* newspapers as well as the *Encyclopaedia Britannica* and *International Yearbook* and *Statesmen's Who's Who*. He is author of a critical guide to Gabriel García Márquez' novel *El coronel no tiene quien le escriba* (published by Grant and Cutler Ltd, London).

We wish Ben much happiness and satisfaction in his work with the Handbook which he intends to continue in the best traditions of his predecessors.

JOHN BROOKS

John Brooks died suddenly in February 1989. The following is an extract of a tribute paid by the publishers at the John Brooks Memorial held at Canning House, London on 4th May 1989.

John Brooks was appointed editor of *The South American Handbook* in 1972 with the 1973 book his first edition. John Dawson of the printers Dawson & Goodall decided to buy the title from the Royal Mail Company, knowing much about printing but nothing about publishing in general and South America in particular.

He chose someone who was not only a genuine expert on Latin America, but who was also an inspired editor. John Brooks already knew of the book, having used it when he lived in Brazil in the 60's.

It fell to him to reorganize the *Handbook* totally; a herculean task. He built a team of sub-editors from among his colleagues at Lloyds Bank, both in the Economics Department and also in South America. He quickly established his own editorial style—something which has often been understated. Despite its cramped looks, it takes a gifted editor with a firm command of the English language to get 1.1 million words into a manageable format.

From the start, he recognised that the key to success lay with what he consistently referred to as "Our Readers". Under his editorship, the correspondence has increased to the 600+ lengthy letters for the 1990 edition. It is this above all else which has allowed the *Handbook* to react quickly to the changing needs of travellers. He instituted the idea of printing their names at the end of each chapter.

In all of this, his overall aim was to guarantee that the practical nature of the *Handbook* continued. He naturally slanted it towards the budget traveller and in particular he felt it important to help young people with little money to get around and learn about people and countries.

He believed that the *Handbook* should be neither political nor opinionated, despite his own personal views. On the rare occasions when he felt a comment was required, it was almost invariably to ensure that the opposite view was given in order to give a balanced approach. This is not to say that his own preferences are not in evidence—breakfast is one of the most used words in the *Handbook* (quickly followed by puddings)!

He also recognised the failings of the *Handbook*—and strove each year to improve on them. To a certain extent, he sought to cover these failings by attempting to make the *Handbook* a good read (something which is commented on regularly by the readers) and his dry wit constantly shines through the text.

We are glad that he considered the 1989 edition to be one of the most complete and "best yet". Despite the constantly good reviews, John's natural modesty never allowed him to become conceited. On his travels to the continent, his wife Sylvia at his side, he rarely owned up to being the editor. The tragedy of his death is that he had so much more to offer. We were already planning to produce other titles with him.

He wrote in his first preface that he was proud of being associated with the *Handbook*. We in Bath were certainly proud of being associated with a fine editor.

HOW TO USE THIS HANDBOOK

The South American Handbook is the most complete and up-to-date package of information for independent travellers on Latin America, the Hispanic Caribbean and Haiti currently in print. Its text of over a million words is updated every year for the new edition which is published on 1 September. The text is based on the Editors' personal travels, contributions from national tourist authorities, notes from correspondents living in the countries we cover, detailed material and maps which Handbook users send us, and the extensive sources of information on Latin America available in London and elsewhere.

Editorial Logic Users of the Handbook will find that we employ a logical system of arrangement, which we believe is the most useful for travellers. The capital city is (with one exception, dictated by geography—Chile) the first place covered in detail. The territory is then divided into subsections which are numbered on the country contents and map as well as in the text. In the subsections, towns appear in sequence along a route, which falls within the natural geography of the region. The routes cover the most interesting places to visit and do not necessarily constitute the shortest possible distance from A to B. Details are also given of any interesting excursions or other sights that are off the route. Travellers can therefore plan their own itineraries according to the time available, and their own special interests.

Cross Referencing and Indexing There is a complete index of place names, organized in country sections, at the end of the book.

To make it easier for Readers to find their way around the text, we have a comprehensive system of cross-references. For ease of use, the "see page" entry has been highlighted in heavier type. On the page referred to, you will find the entry again emphasised in some form of heavier type.

Maps The South American Handbook maps within the text are undergoing a programme of updating, improvement and expansion. By the 1991 edition there will be some 150 maps. Three types are used:

A. Country Maps These appear at the start of each country chapter and show main access routes (not necessarily major roads in all cases), main towns, and divisions of the country as described in the text. These divisions are numbered on the map, in the country's contents list and at the text divisions in the chapter. The numbers are not recommendations as to which parts of the country are most interesting to visit, they are only for easy identification.

B. Regional Maps By the 1991 edition, each subsection of the country listed in the country contents will have its own regional map. These give extra information on a more detailed scale and show the main physical features, towns, means of communication and points of interest.

C. City and Town Maps Generally these are detailed maps of town centres, showing means of access to bus and railway stations and airports. The main streets are indicated by means of a numbered key.

Roads —————	Capital Cities ■SANTIAGO
Railways ┼┼┼┼┼┼┼┼┼┼	Cities/Towns ●córdoba
Trails/Paths/Tracks – – – –	Archaeological sites ▲
Rivers RÍO ARUÑA	Mountains ⌒
Ferries	Streets SAN MARTÍN
Waterfall ⟋⟋⟍	Parks
Barrier Reef ~ ~ ~	Train station T
Borders —————	Bus Station B
Country Subdivisions /////////	Airport ✈
Metropolitan areas ▨	Key Numbers 6
Major Highway ⟨══════⟩	

Introduction and Hints This first section in the book gives information and hints that apply generally to all the countries we cover on

- Travel to and in Latin America
- money
- law enforcement
- security
- travelling with children
- camping
- language

- photography
- surface transport
- hitch-hiking
- motoring and motorcycling
- hiking and trekking
- river boats
- cycling

Health Information This major section by Dr David Snashall of St Thomas's Hospital Medical School, London, gives details of the health risks common in Latin America and the Caribbean, and the sensible precautions travellers should take to combat them.

Country Sections Information is set out country by country in a constant sequence as follows:

- List of contents
- Description of physical geography
  - people
  - history
  - present form of government
- Survey of Cities, Towns and places of interest
  - things to do
  - things worth seeing
  - where to stay
  - eating out
  - services for visitors
- Economic report
- Information for visitors
  - how to get there
  - what documents are necessary

clothing
food
health precautions
the best time for visiting
currency regulations
other essential information

All those readers who have written with valuable updating material are listed with thanks at the end of each chapter.

Hotels and Restaurants In large cities, lists of hotels and restaurants include only those establishments for which positive recommendations have been received. In smaller towns, these lists contain both the favourable recommendations and others. In general, restaurants are grouped by neighbourhood and by type of cuisine.

Prices Our hotel price ranges, for double rooms with taxes and service charges but without meals unless stated, are unchanged from last year. The complete range remains as follows:

L—Over US$70	**A**—US$45-70	**B**—US$30-45
C—US$20-30	**D**—US$12-20	**E**—US$5-12
F—US$2-5	**G**—Up to US$2	

Other abbreviations used in the book (apart from p.p. = per person; a/c = air conditioned; rec. = recommended; T = telephone) should be self-explanatory.

Our warmest thanks are also due to the following who have responded so generously to our request for maps and whose kindness may not have been acknowledged elsewhere in this edition: Julian Anderson (Buenos Aires), Dale Bedford (Auckland 9), Henry Z.M. Corman (Halifax, N.S.), Richard Davies (Great Bookham, Sy.) a most useful contribution, Aldo Lazo Del Carpio (Lima) and Huberth Monge (Costa Rican National Parks Service SPN).

We are also grateful to those travellers, listed below, who have sent us important information for the "Introduction and Hints" section which follows: Martin R. Eayrs (Buenos Aires), Ian Atkinson (Upton-on-Severn), Michel Banz (Farum, Dmk), Justin Bell (Bath), Christopher Canaday (Salinas, CA), Jim Cilch (USPCV, CR), Patrick Cleary and Margaret Lloyd (Cranbrook, Kent), Jane Coburn and Philip Barnes (Thirroul, NSW), Roger Davison and Jane Eccles (London W3), Nick De Smith and Minnie Lamplugh (Tunbridge Wells), G. Van Dulken (Emsworth, Hants.), Paul Eaton (Victoria, BC), Eva Ekelund and Jim Lindsay (Stockholm), Fred and Marianne Emery (London SE26), Margaret and Martin Evans (Brighton), Jorge Fernández Umpiérrez (Lima), John Fitzpatrick (Bern), Henri and Nicki Hendriksen (North Ryde, NSW), Don Hoyle (London EC2), Simon Jeffreys (Peterborough), Danièle Lamarche (London E1), Annette Lees and Shane Wright (Whakatane, NZ), R.W. Le Sueur (Jersey), Paul Living (Reading), Elaine and George McClellan (Danville, CA), Stryker McGuire and Julie Jedamus (Ashfield, Mass.), Christoph Müller (Zürich 8004), Karl Olson (New York), Lars Østenuind (Copenhagen), Michael Ridley (S. Croydon), Arno Schmid (Hamburg 71), Florian Schulz (Berlin 27), Stanis Smith (Burnaby, BC), Ann Sorrel (Newark, NJ), Jens Stockmarr and Dorte Dahl Johansen (Hellerup, Dmk.), Christian Stolte (Winsen, W.Ger.), Dag Tangen (Oslo 2) and John Walker.

WARNING: Whilst every endeavour is made to ensure that the facts printed in this book are correct at the time of going to press, travellers are cautioned to obtain authoritative advice from consulates, airlines, etc. concerning current travel and visa requirements and conditions before embarkation. The publishers cannot accept legal responsibility for errors, however caused, which are printed in this book.

INTRODUCTION AND HINTS

Travel to and in Latin America   All the main airlines plying to each country are given in the "Information for Visitors" sections, together with any shipping lines that still carry passengers. Airlines will only allow a certain weight of luggage without a surcharge; this is normally 30 kg. for first class and 20 kg. for business and economy classes, but these limits are often not strictly enforced when it is known that the plane is not going to be full. On the other hand, weight limits for internal flights are often lower; best to enquire beforehand.

Chris Parrott, of Journey Latin America, has told us:

1. Generally it is cheaper to fly from London rather than a point in Europe to South American destinations.

2. There are no "charters" as such (but see para. 8 on next page), though most airlines offer discounted fares of one sort or another on scheduled flights. These are not offered by the airlines direct to the public, but through agencies who specialize in this type of fare*. The very busy seasons are as follows: all of Mexico and Central and South America; Dec.7—Jan. 15. Peru/Ecuador/Colombia/Venezuela/Central America/ Mexico July 10—Sept.10. If you intend travelling during those times, book as far ahead as possible.

3. Other fares fall into three groups, and are all on scheduled services:
   A. Student (or Under 26) fares. Some airlines are flexible on the age limit, others strict. One way and returns available, or "Open Jaws" (see below). NB Some student tickets carry standby status only, and should be avoided in the busy seasons (see above).
   B. Excursion (return) fares with restricted validity e.g. 10-35 days, 14-90 days, 5-60 days. These are fixed date tickets where the dates of travel cannot be changed after issue of ticket.
   C. Yearly fares: these may be bought on a one-way or return basis, and usually the returns can be issued with the return date left open. You must, however, fix the route.

4. For people intending to travel a linear route and return from a different point from that which they entered, there are "Open Jaws" fares, which are available on student or yearly fares, or occasionally on excursion fares.

5. Many of these fares require a change of plane at an intermediate point, and a stopover may be permitted, or even obligatory, depending on schedules. Simply because a flight stops at a given airport does not mean you can break your journey there—the airline must have traffic rights to pick up or set down passengers between points A and B before it will be permitted. This is where dealing with a specialized agency (like Journey Latin America!) will really pay dividends. There are dozens of agencies that offer the simple returns to Rio or Lima at roughly the same (discounted) fare. On multi-stop itineraries, the specialized agencies can often save clients hundreds of pounds.

6. Although it's a little more complicated, it's possible to sell tickets in London for travel originating in South America at substantially cheaper fares than those available locally. This is useful for the traveller who doesn't know where he will end up, or who plans to travel for more than a year. But a oneway ticket from South America is more expensive than a oneway in the other direction, so it's always best to buy a return. (I have heard of travellers buying an unused return seat on French charter flights—they're advertised in the small ads in some of the cheap hotels in Lima—and the charter company doesn't seem to mind who sits in the seat; very hit and miss though).

---

*In London, these include Trailfinders, 48 Earl's Court Road, London W8 6EJ. (T 01-938 3366): Melia Travel Ltd., 12 Dover Street, London W1X 4NS (T 01-491 3881), Steamond Ltd., 23 Eccleston Street, London SW1W 9LX (T 01-730 8646); Transatlantic Wings, 70 Pembroke Road, London W.8. (T 01-602 4021); and **Journey Latin America**, 16 Devonshire Road, Chiswick, London W4 2HD (T 01-747 3108). (Ed.)

7. Certain South American countries impose local tax on flights originating there. Among these are Uruguay, Peru, Ecuador, Colombia and Mexico. This often applies if you happen to have bought a ticket, say, London—Rio—Santiago—Lima—Los Angeles and then on to Australia. Depending on the way it's issued the passenger could get charged tax on all the sectors from Lima onwards.

8. There are several cheap French charters to Mexico, Guatemala, Colombia, Ecuador, Peru, Bolivia and the southern countries, but no-one in the UK sells them. Try: Uniclam-Voyages, 63 rue Monsieur-le Prince, 75006 Paris. A cheap Swiss charter firm is Sindbad, 3 Schoffelgasse, 8025 Zürich. It is reported that Aeroflot flies cheaply between Frankfurt and Luxembourg, and Lima. There are some special fares available on scheduled flights from Dublin. Líneas Aéreas Paraguayas flies weekly between Frankfurt, Brussels and Asunción and have one fare for all S. American destinations, including changes and "Open Jaws" journeys, of about US$900 from Brussels.

9. If you buy discounted air tickets *always* check the reservation with the airline concerned to make sure the flight still exists. Also remember the IATA airlines' schedules change in March and October each year, so if you're going to be away a long time it's best to leave return flight coupons open.

Purchaseable only in the USA and still one of the cheapest ways of flying around the continent, AeroPerú's "Around South America Airpass" offers a 45-day return ticket to Miami for US$759. It includes Lima and six other South American cities, plus discounted flights within Peru.

N.B. At the time of going to press, there was some doubt over the future of Eastern Airlines' services to the region. We retain them in the text in the hope that the company's problems are solved satisfactorily.

Beware buying tickets from the general sales agents in Europe of minor South American airlines. They are sometimes incorrectly made out and therefore impossible to transfer or cash in. If you buy internal airline tickets in South American countries you may find cash refunds difficult to get if you change your plans: better to change your ticket for a different one. On the other hand you can save money by buying tickets in a country with a black exchange market, for local currency, for flights on its national airline. Overbooking by Latin American airlines is very common (largely due to repeated block bookings by travel agents, which everyone knows will not be used), so always reconfirm the next stage of your flight within 72 hours of your intended departure. And it does no harm to reconfirm yet again in the last 24 hours, just to show them you mean it, and turn up for the flight in good time (at least 2 hours before departure).

We advise people who travel the cheap way in Latin America to pay for all transport as they go along, and not in advance. This advice does not apply to people on a tight schedule: paying as you go along may save money, but it is likely to waste your time somewhat. The one exception to this general principle is in transatlantic flights; here money is saved by booking as far as possible in one operation.

The national airlines of Argentina, Bolivia, Brazil, Chile, Colombia and Venezuela operate schemes for unlimited travel within those countries at a set price. See the respective country sections.

There is also an "Amerailpass", giving unlimited travel on the railways of Argentina, Bolivia, Brazil, Chile, Paraguay and Uruguay, which can be bought for 16 (US$120), 23 (US$140), 30 (US$175) or 60 (US$260) days. Payment must be in US dollars, so the savings may not be that great. Details in the paragraphs on rail travel under the principal cities, but remember that railway services are being progressively withdrawn. *Warning:* Not all railway staff know about the pass.

Warning   Many countries in Latin America are reluctant to let travellers enter their territory if they do not already have onward or return tickets. (Look under "Information for Visitors" sections for the countries you intend to visit.) The purchase of a Miscellaneous Charges Order (open ticket) from an IATA airline for (say) US$100 will satisfy this requirement in many but not all countries; it is valid for 12 months, can be exchanged for a ticket, or cashed at the airline offices in the country of issue. (The onward ticket requirement does not apply to travellers with their own vehicles.) If you have no onward ticket, a consular letter verifying a statement from your bank at home, giving details of your account with them, might be helpful.

Money is best carried in US dollar travellers' cheques (denominations of US$50 and US$100 are preferable, though one does need a few of US$20) or cash. Sterling and other currencies are not recommended. Travellers' cheques are convenient but they attract thieves (though refunds can of course be arranged) and you will find that they are more difficult than dollar bills to change in small towns. Though the risk of loss is greater, many travellers take part of their funds in US dollar notes; better rates can usually be obtained for them. Low-value US dollar bills are very useful for shopping: shopkeepers and exchange shops (*casas de cambio*) tend to give better exchange rates than hotels or banks. The better hotels will normally change travellers' cheques for their guests (often at a rather poor rate), but if you're travelling on the cheap it is essential to keep in funds; watch weekends and public holidays carefully and never run out of local currency. Take plenty of local currency, in small denominations, when making trips into the interior. Spread your money around your person: less chance of thieves finding it all.

American Express (Amex), Carte Blanche and Diners Club credit cards are useful, and so are those of the Visa and Master Charge groups. Conceal them very carefully (*not* under the insole of a shoe, however: that may render them unusable!), and make sure you know the correct procedure if they are lost or stolen. We advise using credit cards only for dollar transactions, or in countries where there is no black market exchange rate. Remember that credit card transactions are always at an officially recognized rate of exchange (sometimes, if there are several, the least favourable one); you may find it much cheaper to pay cash and get the parallel rate. Note that the Eurocard/Eurocheque system is virtually unknown in Latin America. For credit card security, insist that imprints are made in your presence and that any imprints incorrectly completed should be torn into tiny pieces. Also destroy the carbon papers after the form is completed (signatures can be copied from them).

We recommend in general the use of American Express or Thomas Cook US$ travellers' cheques, but should point out that less commission is often charged on Citibank or Bank of America cheques, if they are cashed at Latin American branches of those banks. These cheques are always accepted by banks, even though they may not be as well known outside banks as those of American Express or Thomas Cook. It is a good idea to take two kinds of cheque: if large numbers of one kind have recently been forged or stolen, making people suspicious, it is unlikely to have happened simultaneously with the other kind. Several banks charge a high fixed commission for changing travellers' cheques—sometimes as much as US$5-10 a cheque—because they don't really want to be bothered. Exchange houses (*casas de cambio*) are usually much better for this service. Some establishments may ask to see the customer's record of purchase before accepting travellers' cheques.

In those countries where there is a black market, find out how much of their currency you are allowed to take in, and *buy before you enter*, preferably in a big city where banks are unlikely to make a charge on the transaction. (In small places the bank may charge up to 50 cents on a 10-dollar travellers' cheque.) There is always an active (but illegal) black market in local currency in all those countries that have no free exchange; it is, however, not illegal to buy currency outside the country you are about to enter, up to any limit that may be imposed. The City of London currency dealers are worth checking with: some find themselves overloaded from time to time with exotic currencies they can't get rid of, and let them go at a large discount. Check in the publication *Banknotes of the World* (the dealers usually have it for consultation) that the notes you are being offered are still current, however.

N.B. If you are having additional sums of money sent out during a tour of Latin America, try to have it sent to one of the countries where you can easily exchange dollar travellers' cheques for dollars cash; at present these are Bolivia, Chile, Ecuador and Uruguay. These countries are also good for getting US$ travellers cheques for a Eurocheque or Amex card, and for buying other Latin American currencies at favourable rates. In many countries, one can get at least US$500 in Amex travellers' cheques on the American Express card (US$1,000 on the gold card): quite the easiest way of adding to one's funds. Remember that a transfer of funds, even by telex, can take several days, and charges can be high; a recommended method is, before leaving, to find out which local bank is correspondent to your bank at home, then when you need funds, telex your own bank and ask them to telex the money to the local bank (confirming by air mail). It is possible to obtain money within hours by this method.

Whenever you leave a country, sell any local currency before leaving, because the further away you get, the less the value of a country's money.

Americans (we are told) should know that if they run out of funds they can expect no help from the US Embassy or Consul other than a referral to some welfare organization.

Passports   Remember that Latin Americans, especially officials, are very document-minded. You should always carry your passport in a safe place about your person, or if not going far, leave it in the hotel safe. If staying in a country for several weeks, it is worth while registering at your Embassy or Consulate. Then, if your passport is stolen, the process of replacing it is simplified and speeded up. Keeping photocopies of essential documents, and some additional passport-sized photographs, is recommended

Remember that it is your responsibility to ensure that your passport is stamped in and out when you cross frontiers. The absence of entry and exit stamps can cause serious difficulties: seek out the proper migration offices if the stamping process is not carried out as you cross.

Identity and Membership Cards   Membership cards of British, European and US motoring organizations have been found useful for discounts off hotel charges, car rentals, maps, towing charges, etc. Student cards must carry a photograph if they are to be of any use in Latin America for discounts. (If you describe yourself as a student on your tourist card you may be able to get discounts, even if you haven't a student card.). Business people should carry a good supply of visiting cards, which are essential for good business relations in Latin America.

Law Enforcement Whereas in Europe and North America we are accustomed to law enforcement on a systematic basis, in general, enforcement in Latin America is achieved by periodic campaigns. The most typical is a round-up of criminals in the cities just before Christmas. In December, therefore, you may well be asked for identification at any time, and if you cannot produce it, you will be jailed. At first sight, on arrival, it may seem that you can flout the law with impunity, because everybody else is obviously doing so. If a visitor is jailed his friends should take him food every day. This is especially important for people on a diet, such as diabetics. It must also be borne in mind that in the event of a vehicle accident in which anyone is injured, all drivers involved are automatically detained until blame has been established, and this does not usually take less than two weeks. Sometimes these problems can be avoided by offering a bribe, but this, naturally, is illegal and may be extremely dangerous. Imported cigarettes from airport duty-free shops are very much appreciated by customs officials.

Never offer a bribe unless you are fully conversant with the customs of the country. (In Chile, for instance, it would land you in serious trouble if you tried to bribe a *carabinero*.) Wait until the official makes the suggestion, or offer money in some form which is apparently not bribery, e.g. "In our country we have a system of on-the-spot fines. Is there a similar system here?" Do not assume that an official who accepts a bribe is prepared to do anything else that is illegal. You bribe him to persuade him to do his job, or to persuade him not to do it, or to do it more quickly, or more slowly. You do not bribe him to do something which is against the law. The mere suggestion would make him very upset.

Security Try and look as little like a tourist as possible, especially in poor areas of cities. Most crime is opportunistic so if you are aware of the dangers, act confidently and use your common sense you will lessen many of the risks. The following tips, all endorsed by travellers, are meant to forewarn, but not alarm, you. Keep all documents secure; hide your main cash supply in different places or under your clothes (extra pockets sewn inside shirts and trousers, moneybelts, neck or leg pouches, and elasticated support bandages for keeping money and cheques above the elbow or below the knee have been repeatedly recommended—the last by John Hatt in *The Tropical Traveller*). Keep cameras in bags (preferably with a chain or wire in the strap to defeat the slasher) or briefcases; take spare spectacles (eyeglasses); don't wear wrist-watches (unless they're digital—too cheap and plentiful to attract thieves nowadays) or jewellery. If you wear a shoulder-bag in a market, carry it in front of you. Backpacks are vulnerable to slashers: a good idea is to cover with a sack with maybe a layer of wire netting between. Use a pack which is lockable at its base.

Ignore mustard smearers and paint or shampoo sprayers, and strangers' remarks like "what's that on your shoulder?" or "have you seen that dirt on your shoe?". Furthermore, don't bend over to pick up money or other items in the street. These are all ruses intended to distract your attention and make you easy for an accomplice to steal from. If someone follows you when you're in the street, let him catch up with you and "give him the eye".

Be wary of "plainclothes policemen"; insist on seeing identification and on going to the police station by main roads. Do not hand over your identification (or money—which he should not need to see anyway) until you are at the station. Be even more suspicious if he seeks confirmation of his status from a passer-by. If attacked, remember your assailants may well be armed, and try not to resist.

It is best, if you can trust your hotel, to leave any valuables you don't need in safe-deposit there, when sightseeing locally. If you don't trust the hotel, lock everything in your pack and secure that in your room (some people take eyelet-screws for padlocking cupboards or drawers). If you lose valuables, always report to police and note details of report—for insurance purposes.

When you have all your luggage with you at a bus or railway station, be especially careful: don't get into arguments—or even conversations—with any locals if you can help it, and lock all the items together with a chain or cable if you are waiting for some time. Take a taxi between airport/bus station/railway station and hotel, if you can possibly afford it. Avoid night buses; never arrive at night; and watch your belongings whether they are stowed inside or outside the cabin. Finally, never accept food, drink, sweets or cigarettes from unknown fellow-travellers on buses or trains. They may be drugged, and you would wake up hours later without your belongings. In this connection, never accept a bar drink from an opened bottle (unless you can see that that bottle is in general use): always have it uncapped in front of you.

A last point, from Canadian film-maker Russ Bentley: a courteous, friendly manner of speaking, including to beggars and market vendors, may avoid your being "set up" for robbery or assault. For specific local problems, see under the individual countries in the text.

Hotels   A cheap but not bad hotel might be in the region of US$5 a night in Argentina, Mexico or Brazil, but is less in the Andean countries. For the indigent, it is a good idea to ask for a boarding house—*casa de huéspedes, hospedaje, pensión, casa familial* or *residencial*, according to country; they are normally to be found in abundance near bus and railway stations and markets. There are often great seasonal variations in hotel prices in resorts. Remember, cheaper hotels don't always supply soap, towels and toilet paper. A useful tip: ask the Hertz employee at the airport for advice when you arrive—as long as he's not busy.

Warning   The electric showers used in innumerable cheap hotels are extremely dangerous. If you can't avoid using them, check the wiring for obvious flaws and try not to touch the rose while it is producing hot water.

Youth Hostels   Organizations affiliated to the Youth Hostels movement exist in Argentina, Brazil, Colombia, Chile, Mexico, Peru and Uruguay. There are associate organizations in Costa Rica, Guatemala and Ecuador. Further information in the country sections and from the IYHA.

Meals   In all countries except Brazil and Chile (where cold meats, cheese, eggs, fruit etc. generally figure) breakfast usually means coffee or tea with rolls and butter, and anything more is charged extra. There is a paragraph on each nation's food under "Information for Visitors". For reliable cheap meals, look in and near the markets and eat what the locals are eating, making sure that you can see it being cooked.

Travelling with Children   We are grateful to Tim and Arlene Frost, of New Zealand, for the following notes:

People contemplating overland travel in South America with children should remember that a lot of time can be spent waiting for buses, trains, and especially for aeroplanes. On bus journeys, if the children are good at amusing themselves, or can readily sleep while travelling, the problems can be considerably lessened. Travel on trains, while not as fast or at times as comfortable as buses, allows more scope for moving about. Some trains provide tables between seats, so that games can be played.

Food can be a problem if the children are not adaptable. It is easier to take biscuits, drinks, bread etc. with you on longer trips than to rely on meal stops where the food may not be to taste. A small immersion heater and jug for making hot drinks is invaluable, but remember that electric current varies. Try and get a dual-voltage one (110v and 220v).

Fares: On all long-distance buses you pay for each seat, and there are no half-fares if the children occupy a seat each. For shorter trips it is cheaper, if less comfortable, to seat small children on your knee. Often there are spare seats which children can occupy after tickets have been collected. In city and local excursion buses, small children generally do not pay a fare, but are not entitled to a seat when paying customers are standing. On sightseeing tours you should *always* bargain for a family rate—often children can go free. (In trains, reductions for children are general, but not universal.)

All civil airlines charge half for children under 12, but some military services don't have half-fares, or have younger age limits. Children's fares on Lloyd Aéreo Boliviano are considerably more than half, and there is only a 7kg. baggage allowance. (LAB also checks children's ages on passports.)

Hotels: In all hotels, bargain for rates. If charges are per person, always insist that two children will occupy one bed only, therefore counting as one tariff. If rates are per bed, the same applies. In either case you can almost always get a reduced rate at cheaper hotels. (In restaurants, you can normally buy children's helpings, or divide one full-size helping between two children.)

Generally, travel with children presents no special problems—in fact the path is often smoother for family groups. Officials tend to be more amenable where children are concerned. Moreover, even thieves and pickpockets seem to have some of the traditional respect for families, and may leave you alone because of it!

Camping There is a growing network of organized campsites, to which reference is made in the text immediately below hotel lists, under each town. If there is no organized site in town, a football pitch or gravel pit might serve. Géraldine des Cressonnières, of Linkebeek, Belgium, gives the following rules for "wild" camping: (1) arrive in daylight; (2) ask permission to camp from the parish priest, or the fire chief, or the police, or a farmer regarding his own property; (3) never ask a group of people— especially young people; (4) never camp on a beach (because of sandflies and thieves). If you can't get information from anyone, camp in a spot where you can't be seen from the nearest inhabited place.

Gas cylinders and bottles are usually exchangeable, but if not can be recharged; specify whether you use butane or propane. (Liquid fuels are readily available.) The Camping Clube do Brasil gives 50% discounts to holders of international campers' cards.

Souvenirs Remember that these can almost invariably be bought more cheaply away from the capital, though the choice may be less wide. Bargaining seems to be the general rule in most countries' street markets. Visitors should remember that souvenirs made from endangered species, for example, sea-turtle shells, may not be imported into their home countries, and are advised to ask the responsible government agency at home for a complete list of the endangered species concerned.

If British travellers have no space in their luggage, they might like to remember Tumi, the Latin American Craft Centre, at 23 Chalk Farm Road, London NW1 (T 01-485 4152) and 2 New Bond Street Place, Bath (T 0225 62367), who specialize in Mexican and Andean products. There are similar shops in the USA; one good one is on the ground floor of Citicorp Center, Lexington Avenue and 53rd Street, New York.

Mail Postal services in most countries are not very efficient, and pilfering is frequent. All mail, especially packages, should be registered. Some travellers recommend that mail should be sent to one's Embassy (or, if a cardholder, American Express agent) rather than to the Poste Restante (*Lista de Correos*) department of a country's Post Office. Some Embassies and post offices, however, do not keep mail for more than a month. If there seems to be no mail at the Lista under the initial letter of your surname, ask them to look under the initial of your forename or your middle name. For the smallest risk of misunderstanding, use title, initial and surname only. (If you're a British male, and all else fails, ask them to look under "E" for "Esquire"!—Geoffrey van Dulken.)

Travellers' Appearance There is a natural prejudice in all countries against travellers who ignore personal hygiene and have a generally dirty and unkempt appearance. Most Latin Americans, if they can afford it, devote great care to their clothes and appearance; it is appreciated if visitors do likewise. The general prejudice previously reported against backpacks has virtually disappeared, unless carried by those whom officials identify as "hippies". (Remember, however, that backpacks are much easier to pilfer from or slash than conventional luggage; an electric motor-cycle alarm—or a flour sack with a layer of wire mesh inside—might stop this.) One tip we have received; young people of informal dress and life-style may find it advantageous to procure a letter from someone in an official position testifying to their good character, on official-looking notepaper. John Oliver, of Durban, tells us that a photograph of a pretty blonde young woman inside one's passport can have a similar salutary effect on Latin American officials!

Some countries have laws or prejudices against the wearing by civilians of army-surplus clothing. In many places there is also a prejudice against shorts, which are only appropriate on the beach, or for jogging, or for sports and games. A medium weight shawl with some wool content is recommended for women: it can double as pillow, light blanket, bathrobe or sunscreen as required.

Drugs Users of drugs, even of soft ones, without medical prescription should be particularly careful, as some countries impose heavy penalties— up to ten years' imprisonment—for even the simple possession of such substances. In this connection, the planting of drugs on travellers—by traffickers or the police—is not unknown. If offered drugs on the street, make no response at all and keep walking. Note that people who roll their own cigarettes are often suspected of carrying drugs and subjected to intensive searches. Advisable to stick to commercial brands of cigarettes—but better still not to smoke at all.

Toilets Many of the cheapest hotels in the poorer areas, also restaurants and bars, have inadequate water supplies. This may mean that used toilet paper should not be flushed down the pan, but placed in the receptacle provided. This is not very sanitary, of course, but a blocked pan or drain is infinitely more of a health risk.

Cockroaches These are ubiquitous and unpleasant, but not dangerous. Take some insecticide powder if staying in cheap hotels; Baygon (Bayer) has been recommended. Stuff toilet paper in any holes in walls that you may suspect of being parts of cockroach runs.

Language Without some knowledge of Spanish you can become very frustrated and feel helpless in many situations. English is absolutely useless off the beaten track. Some initial study, to get you up to a basic Spanish vocabulary of 500 words or so, and a pocket dictionary and phrase-book, are most strongly recommended: your pleasure will be doubled if you can talk to the locals. Not all the locals speak Spanish, of course; apart from Brazil's Portuguese, you will find that some Indians in the more remote highland parts of Bolivia, Guatemala and Peru, and lowland Indians in Amazonia, speak only their indigenous languages, though there will usually be at least one person in each village who can speak Spanish.

The basic Spanish of Hispanic America is that of south-western Spain, with soft "c's" and "z's" pronounced as "s", and not as "th" as in the other parts of Spain. Castilian Spanish is readily understood, but is not appreciated when spoken by non-Spaniards; try and learn the basic Latin American pronunciation. There are several regional variations in pronunciation, particularly in the River Plate countries, which are noted in the Argentine section "Information for Visitors". Differences in vocabulary also exist, both between peninsular Spanish and Latin American Spanish, and between the usages of the different countries.

If you are going to Brazil, you should learn some Portuguese. Spanish is not adequate: you may be understood but you will probably not be able to understand the answers.

Courtesy Remember that politeness—even a little ceremoniousness—is much appreciated. In this connection professional or business cards are useful (and have even been known to secure for their owners discount prices in hotels). Michael Davison makes the following suggestions: men should always remove any headgear and say "con permiso" ("com licença" in Brazil) when entering offices, and be prepared to shake hands (this is much commoner in Latin America than in Europe or North America); always say "Buenos días" or "Buenas tardes" ("Bom dia" or "Boa tarde" in Brazil) and wait for a reply before proceeding further; in a word, don't rush them! Always remember that the traveller from abroad has enjoyed greater advantages in life than most Latin American minor officials, and should be friendly and courteous in consequence. N. F. Hawkes adds: never be impatient or criticize situations in public: the officials may know more English than you think and they can certainly interpret gestures and facial expressions. Be judicious about discussing politics with strangers (especially in Guatemala, Honduras and El Salvador). Politeness can be a liability, however, in some situations; most Latin Americans are disorderly queuers. Russ Bentley stresses that politeness and friendliness, with small useful gifts for children such as pencils and scratchpads, not only increase the pleasure of one's trip, but may well improve one's personal security.

Moira Chubb, from New Zealand, suggests that if you are a guest and are offered food that arouses your suspicions, the only courteous way out is to feign an allergy or a stomach ailment.

Explorers The South American Explorers' Club is at Avenida Portugal 146 (Casilla 3714), Lima, Peru (Telephone: 31-44-80), with a new office also in Quito (1989). (For further details see under Lima, **page 733**, and Quito.) Large-scale topographical maps are usually obtainable from a country's Instituto Geográfico Militar or equivalent, on production of the price and your passport.

Wildlife Wildlife lovers might like to know about Kilverstone Wildlife Park, Thetford, Norfolk, IP24 2RL, England. This is a private zoo, open to the public, which specializes in Latin American fauna and is helping to preserve species threatened with extinction, by breeding and returning them to their native habitat.

Photography Take as much film in from home as you can; it is expensive in most places, though not in Venezuela. Some travellers have advised against mailing exposed films home; better to take them with you. The postal authorities may use less sensitive equipment for X-ray screening than the airports do.

Dan Buck and Anne Meadows write: A note on developing film in South America. Black and white is a problem. Often it is shoddily machine-processed and the negatives are ruined. Ask the store if you can see an example of their laboratory's work and if they hand-develop.

Jeremy Till and Sarah Wigglesworth suggest that exposed film can be protected in humid areas by putting it in a balloon and tying a knot.

A professional, John Burke, writes: "I used Agfa and Kodak for colour slides, all of which have come out true from Caracas to Arica. Suggest keep film on concrete floor. One canned reel was kept after use in refrigerator (for six weeks) before coming home from Lima and has been processed okay. At all costs avoid photographing shadows in the tropics, including shaded side of a person's face; they come out jet-black. Also avoid lens-hood, if possible; it tends to flatten colours. I used no lens other than ultra-violet. No special attention is needed when photographing high altitude areas like Bogotá, Cuzco or La Paz, when it is cloudy—if anything, the lens can be opened half a stop more than meter reads. (It may well be different in bright sunlight.) In Lima suggest photography between time morning cloud clears and about 1100, and again after 1600. In April 0800-0930 is perfect. Officials tend to be officious and suspicious about photography of what they consider to be super-strategic areas (like a patch of desert near Tacna and the planning ministry in Caracas!). I was always in the fortunate position of being able to quell them with letters from higher authority, but the average tourist might come unstuck."

Surface Transport   The continent has a growing road system for motor traffic, with frequent bus services. The buses are often comfortable; Brazil, Chile and Venezuela are the best; Ecuador is quite good; the other Andean countries are a long way behind, because of difficulties of terrain. Some services in Mexico and Central America are excellent. In mountainous country, however, do not expect buses to get to their destination, after long journeys, anywhere near on time. When the journey takes more than 3 or 4 hours, meal stops at country inns or bars, good and bad, are the rule. See what the locals are eating—and buy likewise, or make sure you're stocked up well on food and drink at the start. For drinks, stick to bottled water or soft drinks or coffee (black). The food sold by vendors at bus stops may be all right: watch if locals are buying, though unpeeled fruit is of course reliable. (See above on **Security** in buses.)

In most countries trains are slower than buses. They do tend, however, to provide finer scenery, and you can normally see much more wildlife than from the road—it is less disturbed by one or two trains a day than by the more frequent road traffic.

Hitch-hiking   This custom is increasing in Latin America, and travellers have reported considerable success in virtually all countries. Neatness of appearance certainly helps. Argentina, Brazil, Chile, Costa Rica, Ecuador, Panama and Venezuela are reported as good; Peru and Bolivia less so ("paying trucks" recommended here). If trying to hitchhike away from main roads and in sparsely-populated areas, however, allow plenty of time.

Joanna Codrington writes: Hitch-hiking in Latin America is reasonably safe and straightforward for males and couples, provided one speaks some Spanish/Portuguese. In Peru and Bolivia there is little private transport and trucks charge about ⅔ the equivalent fare. But elsewhere cars and trucks will carry you free of charge, and will generally treat you as their guests. It is a most enjoyable mode of transport—a good way to meet the local people, to improve one's languages and to learn about the country. Truck drivers in particular are often well versed in things of interest one is passing, e.g. crops and industries.

Here are a few general hints: in remoter parts, make enquiries first about the volume of traffic on the road. On long journeys, set out at crack of dawn, which is when trucks usually leave. They tend to go longer distances than cars.

And now, here are some guidelines for females hitching alone. You must remember the cultural differences, i.e. a local woman travelling in such a fashion would undoubtedly be of dubious moral status. Problems can arise through a genuine misunderstanding. Careful steering of the conversation to illustrate one's reasons for travelling alone is useful and can prevent the necessity of copious explanations later on. Also, probe your driver to find out as much as you can about him and his circumstances. Problems virtually never occur during daylight; so, if possible, plan your journey accordingly. If you should be in a vehicle after dark (it will probably be a truck) it is best not to talk, and perhaps to turn up the music so the driver can forget your presence. If the journey does entail a night, be a bit discriminating about your driver; the unshaven, barbaric sort should be avoided. Also, notice if the driver has a bed, so you can sleep on the seats. Discuss sleeping arrangements before night-time.

Overall, be friendly so that the driver enjoys having you with him, and let him feel that you trust him completely. Though, of course, be careful not to overdo it; you will soon work out the right balance. Should things go awry, the worst that is likely to happen is that you will be turfed out, and may suffer a consequent draughty night.

Motoring   The car freely crosses international frontiers without payment of customs duties provided it is eventually returned to its country of origin. In Central America, this is controlled by an entry made in your passport. In South America, it is controlled by a separate document, the *Carnet* *de Passages en Douanes* or *Libreta de Pasos por Aduana*, which is obtainable at the automobile touring club in the country where the vehicle is registered, and must be stamped at both sides of each frontier. Failure to obtain a stamp will result in your being turned back, perhaps after driving as much as 200 km., so it is important to find the Customs Office (*Aduana—Alfândega* in Brazil) in order to avoid this inconvenience; it may be at the border or in the town nearest the border. (N.B. Since the AAA stopped issuing *Carnets de Passages*, and since the AA charges two-and-a-half times the maximum estimated duty which may be levied on the vehicle, check if you can purchase the *carnet* in country of entry; e.g. it costs US$200 in Venezuela.) Most countries have special (and cheaper) arrangements for motorists visiting neighbouring countries only. Difficulties have been experienced in entering Peru: check with Peruvian Consulate before setting out.

A separate insurance policy has to be issued in each country if a claim is to be legally payable in the country where an accident occurs. Companies with the necessary international connections include American International Underwriters, Guardian Royal Exchange Assurance, AFIA and Saint Paul. Give them at least four months' notice of your requirements. Remember that in many countries third-party insurance for drivers may not be compulsory, or if compulsory, not enforced; you may have no claim on the other driver after an accident, except through the courts—a time-consuming exercise. If you are injured in an accident, people may refuse to take you to hospital; if you are found dead on arrival they could be jailed until it is proved that they were not responsible for the accident. An additional reason for always driving carefully.

The normal saloon car reaches most destinations of interest to the tourist. High ground clearance is useful for badly surfaced or unsurfaced roads. In some places, service is not available for sophisticated items like automatic transmission, electronic ignition and fuel injection, so the simpler the car the better. Unleaded petrol (gasoline) is not available except in parts of Mexico. It's an advantage if you can sleep comfortably in it; hence the liking for minibuses such as the VW (which can be "Africanized" by the makers, with protective grills and additional cranked exhaust pipe added and a converter for high altitudes; there is also a good VW service network throughout the continent). Four-wheel-drive utility vehicles are useful for the back country; on the other hand, luggage cannot be hidden, as in the boot of a car, so the contents are more susceptible to theft. Consider installing a large trunk for your bags.

Theft of all vehicles is common. Apply at least two anti-theft devices when parked, even in car parks, and remove easily detachable items such as hub-caps, mirrors and windscreen wipers. At least one locking wheel nut per wheel is useful. A policy of insurance may not satisfactorily solve the problem of a car stolen outside its country of origin. There will be a delay of at least a month in paying the claim, and the sum insured may be inadequate if the theft occurs in a country where cars are more expensive than in the country of origin. Import duty becomes payable on the stolen car, and again on any car bought for the return trip home. If, on the other hand, a cash settlement is made, there may be difficulties with exchange control. The same is largely true if a vehicle becomes a total loss in an accident.

Spare fuel should be in steel, not plastic, cans. You won't have travelled far before the plastic can will spring a leak, and there is danger of a spark from static electricity igniting the petrol when pouring. (In Venezuela, it is illegal to carry petrol from a garage in a can without a permit from the police, and this can only be obtained after paying a fine of Bs 500 for running out of fuel.) In remote areas, gas stations (few and far between, so keep well topped up) are unmarked. Look for a building with empty oil drums outside or ask. In this connection, it is wise to carry a funnel and/or hose to help fill the tank; often in rural areas there are no pumps and fuel must be taken from a drum. An in-line fuel filter is an advantage. (In Mexico, there are not many gas stations on main roads: you need to look in the villages off the road.—Ed.)

If the motor is not to fail at high altitudes, the spark must be advanced and cold spark plugs changed for hot; alternatively, take sets of smaller carburettor jets for use at altitude, which is a more fuel-economic solution. You can reduce the risk of a broken windscreen on gravel roads by not following closely behind other vehicles, and reducing speed when other vehicles (especially trucks with double rear wheels) are passing. (Wire over-screens are available in some cities, such as Buenos Aires.) A reversing light is needed for driving on narrow mountain roads at night or in narrow unlit tunnels built on curves. Landslides are frequent in the mountains in the rainy season. Keep enough reserve of fuel to be able to turn back, and take warm clothes and food in case you are delayed a day or so. Take plenty of water (for radiator and yourself). The car is liable to be searched for arms and drugs with some frequency in certain areas.

In addition to the normal spares carried, fan belt, spark plugs etc., the more adventurous driver needs a spade, tow cable, planks for placing under the wheels when stuck in dust or sand, filters for fuel, air, water and oil, light bulbs, wiper blades, spare parts for the suspension and steering, jump leads in case of battery failure, extra battery as back-up, and either an extra spare wheel or repair patches, air pump and valve screw. Help to repair a tyre is sometimes only available if you can provide these items yourself. An emergency fan belt which can be fitted without the use of tools is available from Flexicorn Ltd, North Wing Mills, Bradford BD1 4EP, England.

If you are not a mechanic, or don't have one with you, try to get to know the general look of your engine so that at least you'll know after a repair if anything looks unfamiliar, and always get on chatty terms with the mechanics when you're having anything done to the car.

Make a check list to ensure you have everything before you start each journey. The list is also useful for establishing what it is essential to replace after the theft of a car's contents. If you carry a cooler for food and drink, any official on the highway who spots it is likely to ask for refreshments, so take plenty or you may end up with none for yourself.

Finally, overland motorists would be very well advised to read *Overland and Beyond*, by Theresa and Jonathan Hewat, who motored round the world over 3½ years in a VW minibus. The revised and expanded 5th edition, published by Roger Lascelles, 3 Holland Park Mansions, 16 Holland Park Gardens, London W14 8DY, contains a wealth of good sense on all aspects of overland motoring. Another book containing much practical information on South American motoring conditions and requirements, as well as being a travelogue, is *Driving to Heaven*, by Derek Stansfield (available from Remous Ltd, Wyvern Building, North Street, Milborne Port, Sherborne, Dorset, DT9 5EP, UK, or from the author, 13, The Meads, Milborne Port, Sherborne, DT9 5DS, £8.95 incl. postage and packing).

If driving and camping, the purchase of a 12-volt low-consumption neon light will add greatly to convenience.

If travelling from Europe with a car, do not sail to Panama if you are going south. You will still have the Darién Gap to negotiate. Much better to take the ship to Curaçao, where there is a car ferry to Venezuela. If shipping a car further south, Montevideo has much less bureaucracy and paperwork than any Argentine or Brazilian port. In any event you need a *Carnet de Passages* and an International Certificate of Registration.

Motorcycling   Charles and Lucia Newall write: Motorcycling in South America is a great adventure, exhausting sometimes but not beyond the capacity of any experienced rider.

Machine: The bike should be tough and simple and capable of handling dirt roads if you plan on going into the Andes. If riding solo a large 4-stroke trail bike, e.g. Honda or Yamaha 500, would be ideal; if carrying a passenger a larger machine might be needed. We used an 800cc BMW road bike which handled a variety of conditions with ease.

Preparations: Fit a handlebar windscreen rather than a large touring fairing, which will hamper low-speed handling and complicate shipping from Panama. Standard air filters should be replaced by cleanable types e.g. K and N. You may need to carry a set of smaller carburettor jets to adapt the engine for high altitudes; chech with the manufacturer.

The standard rear suspension on motorcycles may give trouble if you are going to travel on unmade roads; again, check with the manufacturer. If so, fit high-quality replacement units (Konis) with springs matched for the weight carried.

The luggage panniers and rack should be very robust; distribute the weight of luggage around the bike rather than just piling it on the back. A fuel range of about 250 (400 km.) miles is useful and also the ability to run on 80-octane fuel.

Spares: A modern well-maintained machine shouldn't need any major repairs on a 25,000-mile trip. Take the usual consumables with you, such as plugs, points, filters, bulbs, chains, tubes and a set of cables; add to this any other parts which might be weak points on your machine. If possible, take spare tyres. Make arrangements to have parts sent out from home if you need anything unusual; a parts book and a good manual are invaluable. Find out how to service your machine and carry the correct tools. (Local mechanics are very good at making do without the proper parts.)

Clothes: Your clothing should keep you comfortable from 20° to 85°F and include a tough waterproof outer layer complete with overboots and overgloves.

Security: Security is not a problem; use a strong chain and lock. Hotel owners are very helpful and good about letting you bring your machine inside, but don't leave a loaded machine unattended. In general much safer than taking night buses or trains; cheaper too.

Documents: Passports, international driving licences, *Carnet de Passages*, or *Libreta de Paso*, motoring association membership card (for discounts etc.), registration certificate, Hoja de Ruta required in Bolivia. A letter from your Embassy, saying that you are a bona-fide tourist and have no intention of selling your bike, is very useful.

Shipping: It is much easier to fly a motorcycle from Panama than a car. SAM and Copa, space permitting, will take bikes in the baggage holds of their 737s. (It cost us US$130 for a 200-kilo machine.) For the adventurous, possibility of taking small boats down to Turbo, but at the high risk of losing the machine.

Warnings: Do not try to ride the Andean roads in the rainy season as conditions are very dangerous, with muddy roads and deep river fords. Do not attempt to take a bike through the Darién Gap.

Hiking and Trekking Hilary Bradt, the well-known trekker, author and publisher, writes: A network of paths and tracks covers much of Central and South America and is in constant use by the local people. In countries with a large Indian population—Guatemala, Ecuador, Peru and Bolivia, for instance—you can walk just about anywhere, but in the more European countries, such as Costa Rica, Venezuela, Chile, and Argentina, you must usually limit yourself to the many excellent national parks with hiking trails. Most Central and South American countries have an Instituto Geográfico Militar which sells topographical maps, scale 1:100,000 or 1:50,000. The physical features shown on these are usually accurate; the trails and place names less so. National Parks offices also sell maps.

Hiking and backpacking should not be approached casually. Even if you only plan to be out a couple of hours you should have comfortable, safe footwear and a daypack to carry your sweater and waterproof. At high altitudes the difference in temperature between sun and shade is remarkable. The longer trips mentioned in this book require basic backpacking equipment. Essential items are: backpack with frame, sleeping bag, closed cell foam mat for insulation, stove, tent or tarpaulin, dried food (not tins), water bottle, compass. Some but not all of these things are available in South America.

When planning treks in the Andes you should be aware of the effects and dangers of acute mountain sickness, and cerebral and pulmonary oedema (see Health Information, **page 28**). These can be avoided by spending a few days acclimatizing to the altitude before starting your walk, and by climbing slowly. Otherwise there are fewer dangers than in most cities. Hikers have little to fear from the animal kingdom apart from insects (although it's best to avoid actually stepping on a snake), and robbery and assault are very rare. You are much more of a threat to the environment than vice versa. Leave no evidence of your passing; don't litter and don't give gratuitous presents of sweets or money to rural villagers. Respect their system of reciprocity; if they give you hospitality or food, then is the time to reciprocate with presents.

Maps Those from the Institutos Geográficos Militares in the capitals (see above) are often the only good maps available in Latin Amercica. It is therfore wise to get as many as possible in your home country before leaving, especially if travelling by land. A recommended series of general maps is that published by International Travel Map Productions (ITM), PO Box 2290, Vancouver BC, V6B 2WF, Canada, compiled with historical notes, by Kevin Healey. Available are South America North East and North West (both 1:4,000,000), Central America (1:1,800,000), the Yucatán (1:1,000,000) and Baja California (1:1,000,000).

Other Books We should mention the Bradts' "Backpacking Guide Series" published by Bradt Enterprises, 41 Nortoft Road, Chalfont St. Peter, Bucks, SL9 0LA, UK., and 95 Harvey Street, Cambridge, MA 02140, USA. They give detailed descriptions of hiking trails (mentioned in our country "Information for Visitors" sections) and much fascinating information, with many illustrations, in the following volumes: *Mexico and Central America; Venezuela, Colombia and Ecuador; Peru and Bolivia; Chile and Argentina, plus the Falkland Islands; Climbing and Hiking in Ecuador; South America, River Trips.* (2 volumes). (The Bradts also sell other trail guides, and import trekking and topographical maps from South America, including the ITM series.) *South America on a Shoestring*, by Geoff Crowther (Lonely Planet Publications) has been recommended repeatedly for the quality of its maps. Lonely Planet's growing number of individual country guides have also been praised.

Another very useful book, highly recommended, aimed specifically at the budget traveller is *The Tropical Traveller*, by John Hatt (Pan Books, 2nd edition, 1985).

River Transport Geoffrey Dempsey has sent us the following note, with particular reference to Amazonia:

Because expanding air services have captured the lucrative end of the passenger market, passenger services on the rivers are in decline. Worst hit have been the upper reaches; rivers like the Ucayali in Peru, but the trend is apparent throughout the region. The situation has been aggravated for the casual traveller by a new generation of purpose-built tugs (all engine-room and bridge) that can handle up to a dozen freight barges but have no passenger accommodation. In Peru passenger boats must now supplement incomes by carrying cargo, and this lengthens their journey cycle. In the face of long delays, travellers might consider shorter "legs" involving more frequent changes of boat; though the more local the service, the slower and more uncomfortable it will be.

Hammocks, mosquito nets (not always good quality), plastic containers for water storage, kettles and cooking utensils can be purchased in any sizeable riverside town, as well as tinned food such as sardines, meat loaf, frankfurters, ham and fruit. Fresh bread, cake, eggs, fruit—papayas, bananas, pineapples, oranges etc.—are available in most villages. Cabin bunks are provided with thin mattresses but these are often foul. Replacements can be bought locally but rolls of plastic foam that can be cut to size are also available and much cheaper. Eye-screws for securing washing lines and mosquito nets are useful, and tall passengers who are not taking a hammock and who may find insufficient headroom on some boats should consider a camp-chair. The writer yearned for a cushion.

Cycling Hallam Murray writes: At first glance a bicycle may not appear to be the most obvious vehicle for a major journey, but given ample time and reasonable energy it most certainly is the best. It can be ridden, carried by almost every other form of transport from an aeroplane to a canoe, and can even be lifted across one's shoulders over short distances. We rode over 2,000 miles in the Andes, on unpaved roads which would have defeated even the most robust car or truck. Often we were envied by travellers using more orthodox transport, for we were able to explore the remoter regions and to meet people who were not normally in contact with tourists. To add to this we had virtually no transport costs.

Choosing a Bicycle: A thoroughly robust machine is a must. The Dawes Super Galaxy is ideal, with its indestructible frame of Reynolds 531 tubing and wide ratioed gears. It is essential that all parts conform to an accepted international specification to facilitate replacement (e.g. threads, wheels, spokes and gears). For approaching US$600 it is possible to buy such a machine. (A mountain or "all-terrain" bicycle, such as those made in Peru by Goliat, is a good alternative to a touring machine brought from home. The best Goliat model sells for about US$500).

Equipment for 2 Bicycles: A small, comprehensive tool kit (to include block and chain rivet removers and a spoke key), 2 spare tyres, 4 inner tubes, puncture repair kit with plenty of extra patches and glue, 4 brake blocks, set of brake and gear cables, 12 spokes, replacement set of nuts and bolts, selection of ball bearings, oil, grease, 2 pumps, a mileometer, a loud bell, a long case-hardened steel chain and secure lock.

Luggage: Strong back panniers, such as the Karrimor Iberian. Handlebar bags. Adhesive carpet tape is a must for protecting vulnerable parts of panniers which are easily frayed (e.g. where panniers rub against luggage rack). We carried a load of 23 kg. per bicycle and this was not excessive. Our most vital equipment included tent, sleeping bags, Optimus petrol stove (an absolute must—light and efficient), plastic survival bag for storing luggage at night when camping out (almost every night), 4 elastic "spiders", 4 one-litre water bottles, compass, altimeter, Swiss Army knife, torch, comprehensive medical kit, money belts, small presents such as postcards of home, balloons etc. Sunhats protect against hours of ferocious tropical sun.

Vital Tips: Always buy the highest quality equipment before you set out. In Europe and North America we are spoilt by quality. In the developing world, many indigenous manufactured goods are shoddy and rarely last.

Give the bicycle a thorough daily check for loose nuts and bolts and bearings. See that all parts run smoothly. Always camp out of sight of a road. Remember that thieves are attracted to towns and cities, so when sight-seeing, try to leave your bicycle with someone such as a café owner. Country people are invariably more honest than town folk and are usually friendly and very inquisitive. However, don't take unnecessary risks; always see that the bicycle is secure. In remoter regions the dogs are vicious; carry a stick to frighten them off. Keep to the small roads wherever possible. The traffic on some sections of the main roads can be a nightmare. Most towns have a bicycle shop of some description, but it is best to do your own repairs and adjustments. In an emergency it's amazing how one can improvise with wire, string, nuts and bolts! Richard's Bicycle Book makes essential reading for even the most mechanically minded. (Bicycle repair shops in Argentina, S Brazil, Chile and Uruguay are reported to be good, with foreign components widely available in Uruguay and Chile.)

Travel to the USA Until July 1988 all foreigners (except Canadians) needed visas to enter the USA. Despite subsequent relaxations of visa requirements for British air travellers with round-trip tickets to the USA, it is advisable to have a visa to allow entry by land, or on airlines from South and Central America which are not "participating carriers" on the Visa Waiver scheme. If you are thinking of travelling via the USA, or of visiting the USA after Latin America, you are strongly advised to get your visa from a US Consulate in your own country, not while travelling. If you wish to visit a little-known part of the USA (and W Canada), David Stanley's *Alaska-Yukon Handbook* (Chico, CA 96927, Moon Publications), 230 pages, will be of the very greatest use. It costs only US$8 (book postage anywhere).

Final Hints Everybody has his/her own list. Items most often mentioned include a small portable stove (liquid fuel is more readily available than gas—though the latter is becoming more common—and you need a combination canteen to go with it), air cushions for slatted seats, strong shoes (and remember that footwear over 9½ English size, or 42 European size, is difficult to obtain in

Latin America except Argentina and Brazil), money-belt or neck pouch, obtainable from Journey Latin America (address on **page 12**); a small first-aid kit and handbook, rubber window wedges, fully waterproof top clothing, wax earplugs and airline-type eye mask to help you sleep in noisy and poorly curtained hotel rooms, rubber-thong Japanese-type sandals (flip-flops), a polyethylene sheet 2 x 1 metres to cover possibly infested beds and train floors and shelter your luggage, polyethylene bags of varying sizes, a toilet bag you can tie round your waist, a sheet sleeping-bag and pillow-case, a mosquito net (or a hammock with a fitted net), a clothes line, a nailbrush (useful for scrubbing dirt off clothes as well as off oneself), mosquito coils, a vacuum flask, a water bottle, a small dual-voltage immersion heater, a small dual-voltage (or battery-driven) electric fan, tea bags, a light nylon waterproof shopping bag, a universal bath-and basin-plug of the flanged type that will fit any waste-pipe (or improvise one from a sheet of thick rubber), string, electrical insulating tape, large penknife preferably with tin and bottle openers, scissors and corkscrew—the famous Swiss Army range has been repeatedly recommended, collapsible drinking beaker, electric motor-cycle alarm for luggage protection, a flour sack and roll of wire mesh for ditto, alarm clock or watch, candle, torch (flashlight)—especially one that will clip on to a pocket or belt, small transistor radio or battery cassette-player (Walkman type) with earphones, pocket calculator, an adaptor and flex to enable you to take power from an electric-light socket (the Edison screw type is the most commonly used), a padlock for the doors of the cheapest and most casual hotels, spare chain-lengths and padlock for securing luggage to bed or bus/train seat. Small coins, postage stamps, visiting cards and postcards of views from your own country to give away as souvenirs to friendly locals. Useful medicaments are given at the end of the "Health Information" section (**page 35**); to these might be added some lip salve ("Lypsil" has been recommended), and pre-moistened wipes (such as "Wet Ones"). Always carry toilet paper. Women travelling alone may find it useful to wear a wedding ring. Extra passport photos may be useful, also photocopies of essential documents (passport, credit cards, air tickets). **Never** carry firearms. Their possession could land you in serious trouble.

Be careful when asking directions. Women probably know more about the neighbourhood; men about more distant locations. Policemen are often helpful. However, many Latin Americans will give you the wrong answer rather than admit they do not know; this may be partly because they fear losing face, but is also because they like to please. You are more likely to get reliable information if you carefully refrain from asking leading questions.

Lastly, a good principle is to take half the clothes (trousers with plenty of pockets are very useful), and twice the money, that you think you will need.

HEALTH
INFORMATION

The following information has been very kindly compiled for us by Dr. David Snashall, who is presently Senior Lecturer in Occupational Health at St. Thomas's Hospital Medical School in London. He has travelled extensively in Central and South America, worked in Peru and in East Africa and keeps in close touch with developments in preventative and tropical medicine. We incorporate also some welcome observations on the text by Dr. C. J. Schofield, editor of Parasitology Today. The publishers have every confidence that the following information is correct, but cannot assume any direct responsibility in this connection.

THE TRAVELLER to Latin America is inevitably exposed to health risks not encountered in Britain or the USA, especially if he spends time in the tropical regions. Epidemic diseases have been largely brought under control by vaccination programmes and public sanitation but, in rural areas, the latter is rudimentary and the chances of contracting infections of various sorts are much higher than at home.

There are English-speaking doctors in most major cities. If you fall ill the best plan may be to attend the out-patient department of a local hospital or contact your Embassy representative for the name of a reputable doctor. (We give the names of hospitals and some recommended doctors in the main city sections.— Ed.) Medical practices vary from those at home but remember they have particular experience in dealing with locally-occurring diseases.

Self-medication is undesirable except for minor complaints but may be forced on you by circumstances. Whatever the circumstances, be wary of medicines prescribed for you by pharmacists; many are poorly trained and unscrupulous enough to sell you potentially dangerous drugs or old stock they want to get rid of. The large number of pharmacies throughout Latin America is a considerable surprise to most people, as is the range of medicines you can purchase over the counter. There is a tendency towards over-prescription of drug mixtures and in general this should be resisted. Many drugs are manufactured under licence from American or European companies so the trade names may be familiar to you. This means that you do not need to carry a whole chest of medicines, but remember that the shelf-life of some items, especially vaccines and antibiotics, is markedly reduced in tropical conditions. Buy your supplies at the better outlets where they have refrigerators, even though it is more expensive. Check the expiry date of all preparations you buy.

Immigration officials sometimes confiscate scheduled drugs (Lomotil is an example) if they are not accompanied by a doctor's prescription.

With the following precautions and advice, you should keep as healthy as usual. Make local enquiries about health risks if you are apprehensive and take the general advice of European or North American families who have lived or are living in the country.

Before you go   take out medical insurance. You should have a dental check-up, obtain a spare glasses prescription and, if you suffer from a chronic illness (such as diabetes, high blood pressure, ear or sinus troubles, cardiopulmonary disease or a nervous disorder) arrange for a check-up with your doctor, who can at the same time provide you with a letter explaining the details of your disability, if possible in English and Spanish (or Portuguese for Brazil). Check current practice in malaria prophylaxis (prevention).

Inoculations Smallpox vaccination is no longer required anywhere in the world. Cholera vaccination is not required for Latin America. The following vaccinations are recommended:

Yellow fever: this is a live vaccine not to be given to children under nine months of age or persons allergic to eggs. Immunity lasts ten years. An international certificate of yellow fever vaccination will be given and should be kept because it is sometimes asked for.
Typhoid (monovalent): one dose followed by a booster in a month's time; Immunity from this course lasts two to three years.
Poliomyelitis: this is a live vaccine generally given orally and a full course consists of three doses with a booster in tropical regions every three to five years.
Tetanus: one dose should be given with a booster (vital) at six weeks and another at six months, and ten-yearly boosters thereafter are recommended.

Children should, in addition, be properly protected against diphtheria, and against pertussis (whooping cough) and measles, both of which tend to be more serious infections than at home. Measles, mumps and rubella vaccine is now widely available but those teenage girls who have not had rubella (German measles) should be tested and vaccinated. Consult your doctor for advice on tuberculosis inoculation: the disease is still widespread.

Infectious Hepatitis (jaundice) is endemic throughout Latin America and seems to be frequently caught by travellers. The main symptoms are pains in the stomach, lack of appetite, lassitude, and the typical yellow colour of the skin. Medically speaking there are two different types, the less serious but more common is hepatitis A, for which the best protection is the careful preparation of food, the avoidance of contaminated drinking water and scrupulous attention to toilet hygiene. Human normal immunoglobulin (gamma globulin) confers considerable protection against the disease and is particularly useful in epidemics; it should be obtained from a reputable source and is certainly useful for travellers who intend to live rough: they should have a shot before leaving and have it repeated every six months. The dose is 250 mg under 10 years of age and 750 mg above. The dose of gamma globulin depends on the concentration of the particular preparation used, so the manufacturer's advice should be taken. A smaller dose than usual can be given if exposure is for one or two months only.
    The other, more serious, version is hepatitis B which is acquired usually by injections with unclean needles, blood transfusions, as a sexually transmitted disease and possibly by insect bites. This disease can be effectively prevented by a specific vaccination requiring three shots over six months before travelling but this is quite expensive. If you have had jaundice in the past it would be worthwhile having a blood test to see if you are immune to either of the two types because this might avoid the neccessity for vaccination or gamma globulin.
If at a particular occupational risk (e.g. zoologists or veterinarians), or in the case of epidemics, there are vaccines against other diseases such as rabies.

Aids in South America is increasing in its prevalence, as in most countries, but is still largely confined to the well known high risk sections of the population, i.e. homosexual men, intravenous drug abusers, prostitutes and children of infected mothers. The main risk to travellers is from casual sex in the main cities, and the same precautions should be taken as when encountering any sexually transmitted disease. The AIDS virus (HIV) can be passed via unsterilized needles which have been previously used to inject an HIV positive patient, but the risk of this is very small indeed. It would however be sensible to check that needles have been properly sterilised or disposable needles used. Be wary of carrying disposable needles yourself: customs officials find them suspicious. The risk of receiving a blood transfusion with blood infected with the HIV virus is greater than from dirty needles because of the amount of fluid exchanged. Supplies of blood for transfusion should now be screened for HIV in all reputable hospitals so again the risk must be very small indeed. Catching the AIDS virus does not usually produce an illness in itself; the only way to be sure if you feel you have been put at risk is to have a blood test for HIV antibodies on your return to a place where there are reliable laboratory facilities. The test does not become positive for many weeks. Presently the higher risks are probably in Brazil and the West Indies.

Common Problems, some of which will almost certainly be encountered, are:

Heat and Cold   Full acclimatization to high temperatures takes about two weeks and during this period it is normal to feel relatively apathetic, especially if the relative humidity is high. Drink plenty of water (up to 15 litres a day are required when working physically hard in the tropics), use salt on your food and avoid extreme exertion. Tepid showers are more cooling than hot or cold ones. Large hats do not cool you down, but do prevent sunburn. Remember that, especially in the highlands, there can be a large and sudden drop in temperature between sun and shade and between night and day, so dress accordingly. Warm jackets and woollens are essential after dark at high altitude.

Altitude   Acute mountain sickness or *soroche* can strike from about 3,000 metres upwards. It is more likely to affect those who ascend rapidly (e.g. by plane) and those who over-exert themselves. Teenagers are particularly prone. Past experience is not always a good guide: the author, having spent years in Peru travelling constantly between sea level and very high altitude, never suffered the slightest symptoms, then was severely affected climbing Kilimanjaro in Tanzania.

On reaching heights above 3,000 metres, heart pounding and shortness of breath, especially on exertion, are almost universal and a normal response to the lack of oxygen in the air. *Soroche* takes a few hours or days to come on and presents with headache, lassitude, dizziness, loss of appetite, nausea and vomiting. Insomnia is common and often associated with a suffocating feeling when lying in bed. Keen observers may note their breathing tends to wax and wane at night and their face tends to be puffy in the mornings—this is all part of the syndrome. The treatment is rest, pain killers (preferably not aspirin-based) for the headache and anti-sickness pills for vomiting. Oxygen may help at very high altitudes. Various local panaceas ("Coramina glucosada", "Effortil", "Micoren") have their advocates and *mate de coca* (an infusion of coca leaves, widely available) certainly alleviates some of the symptoms. (The drug acetazolamide (Diamox) is said to facilitate acclimatization to altitude; detailed information is available from the Mountain Medicine Centre, c/o Dr. Charles Clarke, Dept. of Neurological Sciences, St. Bartholomew's Hospital, 38 Little Britain, London EC1A 7BE.—Ed.)

On arrival at places over 3,000 metres, a few hours' rest in a chair and avoidance of alcohol, cigarettes and heavy food will go a long way towards preventing *soroche*. Should the symptoms be severe and prolonged it is best to descend to lower altitude and re-ascend slowly or in stages. If this is impossible because of shortage of time or if the likelihood of acute mountain sickness is high then the drug Acetazoleamide (Diamox) can be used as a preventative and continued during the ascent. There is good evidence of the value of this drug in the prevention of *soroche* but some people do experience funny side effects. The usual dose is 500 mg of the slow-release preparation each night, starting the night before ascending above 3,000 metres.

Other problems experienced at high altitude are sunburn, excessively dry air causing skin cracking, sore eyes (it may be wise to leave your contact lenses out) and stuffy noses. It is unwise to ascend to high altitude if you are pregnant, especially in the first 3 months, or if you have any history of heart, lung or blood disease, including sickle-cell.

There is a further, albeit rare, hazard due to rapid ascent to high altitude called acute pulmonary oedema. The condition can affect mountaineers; but also occurs in Andean natives returning from a period at the coast. The condition comes on quite rapidly with breathlessness, noisy breathing, cough, blueness of the lips and frothing at the mouth. Anybody developing this must be brought down as soon as possible, given oxygen and taken to hospital.

Rapid descent from high places will aggravate sinus and middle ear infections, and make bad teeth ache painfully. The same problems are sometimes experienced during descent at the end of a flight.

Despite these various hazards (mostly preventable) of high-altitude travel, many people find the environment healthier and more invigorating than at sea-level.

Intestinal Upsets Practically nobody escapes this one, so be prepared for it. Most of the time it is due to the insanitary preparation of food. Don't eat uncooked fish or vegetables, fruit with the skin on (always peel your fruit yourself), food that is exposed to flies, or salads. Tap water is rarely safe outside the major cities, especially in the rainy season, and stream water is often contaminated by communities living surprisingly high in the mountains. Filtered or bottled (make sure it is opened in your presence—Ed.) water is usually available and safe. If your hotel has a central hot-water supply, this is safe to drink after cooling. Ice for drinks should be made from boiled water but rarely is, so stand your glass on the ice cubes rather than putting them in the drink. Dirty water should first be strained through a filter bag (available from camping shops) and then boiled or treated. Water in general can be rendered safe in the following ways: boil for 5 minutes at sea level, longer at higher altitudes; or add three drops of household bleach to 1 pint of water and leave for 15 minutes; or add 1 drop of tincture of iodine to 1 pint of water and leave for 3 minutes. Commercial water-sterilizing tablets are available, for instance Sterotabs from Boots, England.

Fresh, unpasteurized milk is a source of food poisoning germs, tuberculosis and brucellosis. This applies equally to ice-cream, yoghurt and cheese made from unpasteurized milk. Fresh milk can be rendered safe by heating it to 62°C for 30 minutes followed by rapid cooling, or by boiling it. Matured or processed cheeses are safer than fresh varieties. Heat-treated (UHT), pasteurized or sterilized milk is becoming more available.

The most effective treatment for simple diarrhoea is rest and plenty to drink. Seek medical advice, however, if there is no improvement after three days. Much of the exhaustion of travellers' diarrhoea derives from the dehydration: water and salts are lost from the body and are not replaced. This can be remedied by proprietary preparations of salts which are dissolved in water, e.g. Electrosol (Macarthys) Dioralyte (Armour) Rehidrat (Searle) or ask for "suero oral" at a pharmacy or health centre. Marsha Stuart, of Save the Children, Westport, Conn. states that adding ½ teaspoon of salt (3.5g) and 4 tablespoons of sugar (40 g) to a litre of pure water makes a perfectly good substitute for the proprietary preparations. If rest is not possible, or the lavatory is full of other people with the same trouble, or if the stomach cramps are particularly bad, then the following drugs may help:

Loperamide (Imodium, Janssen, or Arret) up to eight capsules a day. This is now available in the UK without prescription.
Diaphenoxylate with atropine (Lomotil, Searle) up to 16 tablets in any 24 hours, but do *not* use for simple diarrhoea, only to relieve cramps and never in children.
Codeine phosphate 30 mg. One tablet every 4 hours.
Kaolin and morphine or Paregoric, as directed by the pharmacist.
Severe vomiting may be calmed by metoclopramide (Maxolon, Beechams; Primperan, Berk) 10 mg. tablet or injection every 8 hours, but not more frequently.

The vast majority of cases of diarrhoea and/or vomiting are due to microbial infections of the bowel plus an effect from strange food and drink. They represent no more than a temporary inconvenience which you learn to live with and need no special treatment. Fortunately, as you get accustomed to Latin American germs, the attacks become less frequent and you can be more daring in your eating habits.

If, in addition to cramps and diarrhoea, you pass blood in the bowel motion, have severe abdominal pain, fever and feel really terrible, you may well have dysentery and a doctor should be consulted at once. If this is not possible, the recommended treatment for bacillary dysentery is Tetracycline or Ampicillin 500 mg. every 6 hours plus replacement of water and salts. If you catch amoebic dysentery, which has rather similar symptoms, do not try to cure yourself but put yourself in proper medical hands; the treatment can be complex and self-medication may just damp down the symptoms with the risk of serious liver involvement later on.

There are many travellers' tales about special diets, herbal medicines and the consumption of vast quantities of yoghurt as an aid to rehabilitating one's bowels after such attacks. None of them has proved to be useful, in contrast to the widespread success of oral rehydration (water and salt replenishment by mouth) in thousands of children seriously ill with diarrhoea throughout the third world. There is some evidence that alcohol and milk products can prolong diarrhoea so these are best avoided after an attack.

Enterovioform (Ciba), "Mexaform" in Latin America, can have serious side effects (nerve damage, especially to the eyes) if taken for long periods. The active agent, diodochlor-hydroxy-quinoline, is used in many antidiarrhoeals sold in Peru and Ecuador. If it is impossible to control the source of your food and you are likely to be far from medical attention (such as on Amazonian river trips) it is justifiable to take diloxanide furoate (Furamide) 500 mg. daily *plus* a sulphonamide drug e.g. Phthalylsulphathiazole (Thalazole, May & Baker) 500 mg. twice daily. Many businessmen and, for example, athletes who are on short visits of great importance take Streptotriad (May & Baker) one tablet twice daily to prevent diarrhoea and this has been proved to be effective.

Paradoxically, constipation is also common, probably induced by dietary change, inadequate fluid intake in hot places and long bus journeys. Simple laxatives are useful in the short term (the Editor recommends Sennacot) and bulky foods such as maize, beans and plenty of fruit are also useful.

Insects These can be a great nuisance, especially in the tropics, and some, of course, are carriers of serious diseases. The best way of keeping them away at night is to sleep off the ground with a mosquito net and to burn mosquito coils containing pyrethrum. The best way to use insecticide aerosol sprays is to spray the room thoroughly in all areas and then shut the door for a while, re-entering when the smell has dispersed. Tablets of insecticide are also available which, when placed on a heated mat plugged into a wall socket, fill the room with insecticide fumes in the same way. The best repellants contain di-ethyl-meta-toluamide (DET) or di-methyl phthalate—sold as "Deet", "Six-Twelve Plus", "Off", "Boots' Liquid Insect Repellant", "Autan", "Flypel". Liquid is best for arms and face (care around eyes) and aerosol spray for clothes and ankles to deter chiggers, mites and ticks. Liquid DET suspended in water can be used to impregnate cotton clothes and mosquito nets.

If you are bitten, itching may be relieved by baking-soda baths, anti-histamine tablets (care with alcohol or driving), corticosteroid creams (great care—never use if any hint of sepsis) or by judicious scratching. Calamine lotion and cream have limited effectiveness and antihistamine creams (e.g. Antihisan, May & Baker) have a tendency to cause skin allergies and are, therefore, not generally recommended.

Bites which become infected (commonly in the tropics) should be treated with a local antiseptic or antibiotic cream, such as Cetrimide BP (Savlon, ICI) as should infected scratches.

Skin infestations with body lice (crabs) and scabies are, unfortunately, easy to pick up. Use gamma benzene hexachloride for lice and benzene benzoate solution for scabies. Crotamiton cream (Eurax, Geigy) alleviates itching and also kills a number of skin parasites. Malathion lotion 5% (Prioderm) kills lice effectively, but do not use the toxic agricultural insecticide Malathion.

In remote grassland or jungle areas, insect larvae such as that of the bot-fly, which burrow into the flesh, are best removed by covering the breathing hole in your skin with vaseline, then a circular piece of adhesive tape with more vaseline round the edges. If this is allowed to dry well, with no lymph leaking out round the edges, you will be able to squeeze the maggot out next day. The condition is identifiable by a clear hole in the middle of a growing boil or pimple.

Malaria in South America is theoretically confined to coastal and jungle zones but is now on the increase again. Mosquitoes do not thrive above 2,500 metres so you are safe at altitude. There are different varieties of malaria, some resistant to the normal drugs. Make local enquiries if you intend to visit possibly infected zones and use one of the following prophylactic regimes. Start taking the tablets a few days before exposure and continue to take them for six weeks after leaving the malarial zone. Remember to give the drugs to babies and children also. Opinion varies on the precise drugs and dosage to be used for protection; all the drugs may have some side effects, and it is important to balance the risk of catching the disease against the albeit rare side effects. The increasing complexity of the subject as the malarial parasite becomes immune to the new generation of drugs has made concentration on the physical prevention of being bitten by mosquitoes more important, i.e. the use of long-sleeved shirts/blouses and long trousers, repellants and nets.

Prophylactic regimes:

Proguanil (Paludrine ICI) 100 mg, 2 tablets daily
or Chloroquine (Avlochlor, ICI; Nivaquine, May & Baker; Resochin, Bayer; Aralen 300 mg base (2 tablets) weekly (alternatively Amodiaquine can be substituted for Chloroquine).
    Where there is a high risk of chloroquine-resistant falciparum malaria:
either take Chloroquine prophylaxis (as above) and carry Fansidar (Roche) for treatment.
or add Maloprin (Wellcome) 1 tablet per week to your routine Chloroquine prophylaxis.

You can catch malaria even when sticking to the above rules, although it is unlikely. If you do develop symptoms (high fever, shivering, headache, sometimes diarrhoea) seek medical advice immediately. If this is not possible, and there is a great likelihood of malaria, the *treatment* is:

Normal types: Chloroquine, a single dose of 4 tablets (600mg) followed by two tablets (300 mg) in 6 hours and 300 mg each day following.
Falciparum type or type in doubt: Fansidar, single dose of 3 tablets. (We have been told that this drug does not combine well with alcohol, so best to avoid drinking during treatment period.)

If Falciparum type malaria is definitely diagnosed, it is wise to get to a good hospital as the treatment can be complex and the illness very serious.
    Pregnant women are particularly prone to malaria and should stick to Proguanil as a prophylactic. Chloroquine may cause eye damage if taken over a long period. The safety of Fansidar has been questioned and, at the time of writing, it is not recommended for prophylaxis.

Chagas' Disease (South American Trypanosomiasis) is a chronic disease, very rarely caught by travellers, but very difficult to treat. It is transmitted by the simultaneous biting and excreting of the Reduvid bug (Triatoma or Rhodinius), also known as the *vinchuca*, or *barbeiro*. Somewhat resembling a small cockroach, this nocturnal "kissing bug" lives in poor adobe houses with dirt floors often frequented by oppossums. If you cannot avoid such accommodation, sleep off the floor with a candle lit, use a mosquito net and wash any bites thoroughly with soap and water, or a disinfectant.

Sunburn The burning power of the tropical sun, especially at high altitude, is phenomenal. Always wear a wide-brimmed hat and use some form of suncream lotion on untanned skin. Normal temperate-zone suntan lotions (protection factor up to 7) are not much good; you need to use the types designed specifically for the tropics, or for mountaineers or skiers, with a protection factor between 7 and 15. These are often not available in South America; a reasonable substitute is zinc oxide ointment. Glare from the sun can cause conjunctivitis, so wear sunglasses. especially on tropical beaches, where high protection-factor sunscreen cream should also be used.

Snakebite If you are unlucky enough to be bitten by a venomous snake, spider, scorpion or sea creature, try (within limits) to catch the animal for identification. The reactions to be expected are: fright, swelling, pain and bruising around the bite, soreness of the regional lymph glands, nausea, vomiting and fever. If any of the following symptoms supervene, get the victim to a doctor without delay: numbness and tingling of the face, muscular spasms, convulsion, shortness of breath and haemorrhage. The tiny coral snake, with red, black and white bands, is the most dangerous, but is very timid.

Commercial snakebite kits are available, but only useful for the specific type of snake for which they are designed. The serum has to be given intravenously so is not much good unless you have had some practice at making injections into veins. If the bite is on a limb, immobilize the limb and apply a tight bandage between the bite and the body, releasing it for 90 seconds every 15 minutes. Reassurance of the bitten person is very important because death from snakebite is very rare. Do not slash the bite area and try to suck out the poison because this sort of heroism does more harm than good. Hospitals usually hold stocks of snake bite serum. Best precaution: don't walk in snake territory with bare feet or sandals—wear proper shoes or boots.

Spiders and Scorpions   These may be found in the more basic hotels in the Andean countries. If bitten by *Latrodectus* or *Loxosceles* spiders, or stung by scorpions, rest and take plenty of fluids, and call a doctor. Precaution: keep beds away from the walls, and look inside shoes in morning.

Other Afflictions   Remember that **rabies** is endemic throughout Latin America so avoid dogs that are behaving strangely, and cover your toes at night to foil the vampire bats, which also carry the disease. If you are bitten, try to have the animal captured for observation and see a doctor at once. Treatment with human diploid vaccine is now extremely effective and worth seeking out if the likelihood of having contracted rabies is high.

Dengue fever has made its appearance in southern Mexico and the lower-lying parts of Central America; also in Brazil. No treatment: you must just avoid mosquito bites.

Typhus can still occur, carried by ticks. There is usually a reaction at the site of the bite and a fever: seek medical advice.

Intestinal worms are common, and the more serious ones such as **hookworm** can be contracted from walking barefoot on infested earth or beaches. Various other tropical diseases can be caught in jungle areas, usually transmitted by biting insects; they are often related to African diseases and were probably introduced by the slave trade from Africa.

Onchocerciasis (river-blindness), carried by blackflies, is found in parts of Mexico and Venezuela. Cutaneous **leishmaniasis** (Espundia) is carried by sandflies and causes a sore that won't heal; wearing long trousers and long-sleeved shirt in inectious areas helps one to avoid the fly. Epidemics of meningitis occur from time to time. Be careful about swimming in piranha- (or caribe-) infested rivers. It is a good idea not to swim naked: the candiru fish can follow urine currents and become lodged in body orifices; swimwear offers some protection.

Dangerous animals   Apart from mosquitoes, the most dangerous animals are men, be they bandits or behind steering wheels. Think carefully about violent confrontations and wear a seatbelt, if you are lucky enough to have one available to you.

Prickly heat, a very common itchy rash, is avoided by frequent washing and by wearing loose clothing. Cured by allowing skin to dry off through use of powder, and spending 2 nights in an air-conditioned hotel! **Athlete's foot** and other fungal infections are best treated with Tinaderm.

When you return home, remember to take your anti-malarial tablets for 6 weeks. Thousands of people develop malaria after tropical holidays because they do not take this precaution and some of them die, because it is not realized at home that they are suffering from malaria. If you have had attacks of diarrhoea, it is worth having a stool specimen tested in case you may have picked up amoebic dysentery. If you have been living in the bush, a blood test may be worthwhile to detect worms and other parasites.

Basic supplies   The following items you may find useful to take with you from home:

Sunglasses.

Suntan cream.

Insect repellant, flea powder, mosquito net and coils.

Tampons (they can be bought in the main cities), and contraceptives (not easy to obtain everywhere).

Water-sterilizing tablets, e.g. Sterotabs (Boots), Globaline, Puritabs (Kirby & Co. Ltd.).

Antimalarials.

Anti-infective ointment, e.g. Savlon (ICI).

Dusting powder for feet, e.g. Tinaderm (Glaxo), Desenex.

Travel-sickness pills, e.g. Dramamine (Searle), Gravol (Carter-Wallace).

Antacids, e.g. Maalox.

("Tiger balm", an apparently all-purpose remedy, recommended by two overland travellers from New Zealand).

Antidiarrheals, e.g. Lomotil (Searle), Imodium (Janssen) or Arret. (Charcoal tablets are useful for minor stomach ailments.)

First-aid kit.

The following organizations give information regarding well-trained, English-speaking physicians in Latin America:

International Association for Medical Assistance to Travellers, 745 Fifth Avenue, New York 10022.

Intermedic, 777 Third Avenue, New York 10017 (Tel.: 212-486-8974).

Information regarding country-by-country malaria risk can be obtained from the World Health Organization (WHO), or the Ross Institute, London School of Hygiene and Tropical Medicine, Keppel Street, London WC1E 7HT, which publishes a book strongly recommended, entitled *Preservation of Personal Health in Warm Climates*. Medical Advisory Services for Travellers Abroad (Masta), at the Keppel Street address above, prepares health briefs on every country for a fee.

The new edition of *Travellers' Health: How to Stay Healthy Abroad*, edited by Dr. Richard Dawood (Oxford University Press, 1989, paperback, £5.95), has been fully revised and updated, and will even help you survive travel closer to home. We strongly recommend this book, especially to the intrepid travellers who go to the more out-of-the-way places.

ARGENTINA

Maps: Country map, 38; Buenos Aires and surroundings, 44; Buenos Aires detail, 46; North-West Argentina, 70; Córdoba, 72; Tucumán, 79; Salta, 83; Andean Churches, 92; Mendoza, 98; North-East Argentina, 112; Iguazú Falls, 124; Bariloche, 129; Patagonia, 142; Ushuaia, 158.

ARGENTINA is the second largest country in area and third in population in South America. It covers an area of 2,807,560 square km., or 29% of the area of Europe; it is 3,460 km. long from N to S and is, in places, 1,580 km. wide. The population is about 32 million. Apart from the estuary of the Río de la Plata its coast line is 2,575 km. long. Its western frontier runs along the crest of the high Andes, a formidable barrier between it and Chile. Its neighbours to the N are Bolivia and Paraguay and (in the NE) Brazil. To the E is Uruguay. Its far southern limit is the Beagle Channel. The area figures exclude the sector of Antarctica claimed by Argentina.

Argentina is enormously varied both in its types of land and its climates. Geographers usually recognize four main physical areas: the Andes, the North and Mesopotamia, the Pampas, and Patagonia.

The first division, the Andes, includes the whole length of the Cordilleras, low and deeply glaciated in the Patagonian S, high and dry in the prolongation into NW Argentina of the Bolivian Altiplano, the high plateau. S of this is the very parched desert and mountain region S of Tucumán and W of Córdoba. The oases strung along the eastern foot of the Andes—Jujuy, Salta, Tucumán, Catamarca, La Rioja, San Juan, Mendoza and San Rafael—were the first places to be colonized by the Spaniards.

The second division, the North and Mesopotamia, contains the vast forested plains of the Chaco, and the floodplain and gently rolling land known as the Argentine Mesopotamia lying between the rivers Paraná and Uruguay. The Province of Misiones in the NE is actually on the great Paraná plateau. These plains cover 582,750 square km.

The third division, the flat rich pampa, takes up the heart of the land. These vast lands lie S of the Chaco, E of the Andes, W of the Atlantic and the Río Paraná and N of the Río Colorado. The eastern part, which receives more rain, is usually called the Humid Pampa, and the western part the Dry Pampa. The Pampas stretch for hundreds of km. in almost unrelieved flatness and cover some 650,000 square km.

ARGENTINA

1 Buenos Aires and the Pampas.
2 The Córdoba Region.
3 Santiago del Estero, Tucumán, Salta & Jujuy.
4 The Cuyo Region: over the Andes to Chile.
5 North of Mendoza.
6 The Chaco.
7 Mesopotamia.
8 The Iguazú Falls.
9 The Lake District.
10 Patagonia.
11 Tierra del Fuego.

The final division is Patagonia, the area S of the Río Colorado—a land of arid, wind-swept plateaux cut across by ravines. In the deep S the wind is wilder and more continuous. There is no real summer, but to compensate for this the winters are rarely severe. Patagonia has about 780,000 square km.

Three-quarters of Argentina's territory cannot be cultivated without irrigation but only 400,000 hectares are artificially watered.

History of Settlement and Economic Growth   When, in the early 16th century, the first white men came to Argentina, the native Indians had already halted the Inca drive southwards from Peru through Bolivia into northern Argentina. The Spaniard Juan de Solís landed on the shores of the Plata estuary in 1516, but he was killed and the expedition failed. Magellan touched at the estuary four years later, but turned southwards to make his way into the Pacific. In 1527 both Sebastian Cabot and his rival Diego García sailed into the estuary and up the Paraná and the Paraguay. They formed a small settlement, Sancti Spiritus, at the junction of the Caraña and Coronda rivers near their confluence with the Paraná, but it was wiped out by the Indians about two years later and Cabot and García returned to Spain. Eight years later, in 1535, Pedro de Mendoza, with a large force well supplied with equipment and horses, founded a settlement at Buenos Aires. The natives soon made it too hot for him; the settlement was abandoned and Mendoza returned home, but not before sending Juan de Ayolas with a small force up the Paraná. Ayolas set off for Peru, already conquered by Pizarro, leaving Irala in charge. It is not known for certain what happened to Ayolas, but in 1537 Irala and his men settled at Asunción, in Paraguay, where the natives were friendly. There were no further expeditions from Spain to colonize what is now called Argentina, and it was not until 1573 that the settlement at Asunción sent forces S to establish Santa Fe and not until June 11, 1580 that Juan de Garay refounded the settlement at Buenos Aires. It was only under his successor, Hernando Arias de Saavedra (1592-1614), that the new colony became secure.

In the meantime there had been successful expeditions into Argentina both from Peru and Chile—the first, from Peru, as early as 1543. These expeditions led, in the latter half of the 16th century, to the foundation at the eastern foot of the Andes of the oldest towns in Argentina: Santiago del Estero, Tucumán, Córdoba, Salta, La Rioja and Jujuy by Spaniards from Peru following the old Inca road, and San Juan, Mendoza, and San Luis by those from Chile, across the Andes. Peru was given the viceroyalty over all the Spanish possessions in South America in 1543.

For 270 years after its foundation Buenos Aires was of little importance. Spanish stress was upon Lima, and Lima did not send its treasures home by way of Buenos Aires but through Panama and the Caribbean. Buenos Aires was not allowed by Spain to take part in any overseas trade until 1778; its population then was only 24,203. It was merely a military outpost for Spain to confront the Portuguese outpost at Colonia, across the estuary, and lived, in the main, by smuggling. Even when in 1776 the Viceroyalty of Río de la Plata was formed, it made little difference to Buenos Aires as a capital, for its control of the *cabildos* (town councils) in distant towns was very tenuous. When the British, following Spain's alliance with Napoleon, attacked Buenos Aires in 1806 and again in 1807 before being repulsed by local levies, there was no inkling of its future potential. But the defeat of these attacks, known as the Reconquista, had one important result: a great increase in the confidence of the *porteños* (the name given to those born in Buenos Aires) to deal with all comers, including the mother-country, whose restrictions were increasingly unpopular. On May 25, 1810, the *cabildo* of Buenos Aires deposed the viceroy and announced that it was governing henceforth on behalf of King Ferdinand VII, then a captive of Napoleon. Six years later, when Buenos Aires was threatened by invasion from Peru and blockaded by a Spanish fleet in the River Plate, a national congress held at Tucumán declared independence on July 9, 1816. The declaration was given reality by the genius and devotion of José de San Martín, who boldly marched an Argentine army across the Andes to free Chile, and (with the help of Lord

Cochrane, commander of the Chilean Navy), embarked his forces for Peru, where he captured Lima, the first step in the liberation of Peru.

When San Martín returned home, it was to find the country rent by conflict between the central government and the provinces. Disillusioned, he retired to France. The internal conflict was to last a long time. On the one hand stood the Unitarist party, bent on central control; on the other the Federalist party, insisting on local autonomy. The latter had for members the great *caudillos*, the large landowners backed by the *gauchos*, suspicious of the cities. One of their leaders, Juan Manuel de Rosas, took control of the country in 1829. During his second term as Governor of Buenos Aires he asked for and was given extraordinary powers. The result was a 17-year reign of terror. His rule was an international scandal, and when he began a blockade of Asunción in 1845, Britain and France promptly countered with a three-year blockade of Buenos Aires. But in 1851 Justo José de Urquiza, Governor of Entre Ríos, one of his old henchmen, organized a triple *entente* of Brazil, Uruguay, and the Argentine opposition to overthrow him. He was defeated in 1852 at Caseros, a few km. from Buenos Aires, and fled to England, where he farmed quietly for 25 years, dying at Southampton.

Rosas had started his career as a Federalist; once in power he was a Unitarist. His downfall meant the triumph of federalism. In 1853 a federal system was finally incorporated in the constitution, but the old quarrel had not been solved. In 1859, when the constitution was ratified, the capital was moved to Paraná, the province of Buenos Aires seceded, and Buenos Aires, under Bartolomé Mitre, was defeated by the federal forces under Urquiza. Two years later Buenos Aires again fought the country, and this time it won. Once again it became the seat of the federal government, with Bartolomé Mitre as its first constitutional president. (It was during his term that the Triple Alliance of Argentina, Brazil, and Uruguay defeated Francisco Solano López of Paraguay.) There was another political flare-up of the old quarrel in 1880, ending in the humiliation of Buenos Aires, which then ceased to be the capital of its province; a new provincial capital was founded at La Plata, 56 km. to the SE. At that time a young colonel, Julio A. Roca, was finally subduing all the Indian tribes of the pampas and the S. This was an event which was to make possible the final supremacy of Buenos Aires over all rivals.

Politically Argentina was a constitutional republic with a very restricted suffrage up to the passage in 1912 of the Sáenz Peña law, which established universal manhood suffrage. From 1916 to 1930 the Unión Cívica Radical (founded in 1890) held power, under the leadership of Hipólito Yrigoyen and Marcelo T. de Alvear, but lost it to the military uprising of 1930. Though seriously affected by the world depression of the 1930s, Argentina's rich soil and educated population had made it one of the ten wealthiest countries in the world, but this wealth was most unevenly distributed, and the political methods followed by the conservatives and their military associates in the 1930s denied the middle and working classes any effective share in their own country's wealth and government. In 1943 came another military coup, which had a distinctly fascist tinge; in 1946 emerged, as President, **Gen. Juan Domingo Perón (see also page 43)**, who based his power on an alliance between the army and labour; his contacts with labour were greatly assisted by his charismatic wife Eva (since commemorated in the rock-opera "Evita") and the living conditions of the workers were greatly improved—but at the expense of the economic state of the country. By the time a military coup unseated Perón in 1955 serious harm had been done; ever since, Argentina has been struggling to recover its lost economic health.

The Transformation of the Pampas   The pampas, the economic heart of the country, extend fanwise from Buenos Aires for a distance of between 550 and 650 km. Apart from three groups of *sierras* or low hills near Córdoba, Tandil and Bahía Blanca, the surface seems an endless flat monotony, relieved occasionally, in the SW, by sand dunes. There are few rivers. Drinking water is pumped to the surface from a depth of from 30 to 150 metres by the windpumps which are such a prominent feature of the landscape. There are no trees other than those that have been planted, except in the *monte* of the W. But there is, in most years, ample rainfall. It is greatest at Rosario, where it is about 1,020 mm., and evenly distributed throughout the year. The further S from Rosario, the less the rain. At Buenos Aires it is about 940 mm.; it drops to 535 at Bahía Blanca, and is only 400 along the boundary of the Humid Pampa. The further from Rosario, too, the more the rainfall is concentrated during the summer. Over the whole of the pampa the summers are hot, the winters mild, but there is a large climatic difference between various regions: at Rosario the growing season between frosts is about 300 days; at Bahía Blanca it falls to 145 days.

When the Spanish arrived in Argentina the pampas were an area of tall coarse grasses. The cattle and horses they brought with them were soon to roam wild and in time transformed the Indian's way of life. The only part of the pampa occupied by the settlers was the so-called Rim, between the Río Salado, S of the capital, and the Paraná-Plata rivers. Here, in large *estancias*, cattle, horses and mules in great herds roamed the open range. There was a line of forts along the Río Salado: a not very effective protection against marauding Indians. The Spaniards had also brought European grasses with them; these soon supplanted the coarse native grasses, and formed a green carpet surface which stopped abruptly at the Río Salado.

The *estancia* owners and their dependent *gauchos* were in no sense an agricultural people, but towards the end of the 18th century, tenants—to the great contempt of both *estanciero* and *gaucho*—began to plant wheat in the valleys along the Paraná-Plata shore. The fall of Rosas in 1852, and the constitution of 1853, made it possible for Argentina to take a leap forward, but it must be remembered that its civilized population at that time was only 1,200,000.

The rapidly rising population of Europe during the latter half of the 19th century and the consequent demand for cheap food was the spur that impelled Argentina (as it did the United States and Canada) to occupy its grasslands and take to agriculture. This was made possible by the new techniques already developed: agricultural machinery, barbed wire, well-drilling machines and windpumps, roads and railways, and ocean-going steamships. Roads were, and are, a difficulty in the Argentine pampa; the soil lacks gravel or stones to surface the roads, and dirt roads become a quagmire in wet weather and a fume of dust in the dry. Railways, on the other hand, were simple and cheap to build. The system grew as need arose and capital (mostly from Britain) became available. The lines in the pampa radiate out fanwise (with intricate inter-communication) from the ports of Buenos Aires, Rosario, Santa Fe and Bahía Blanca. Argentina, unlike most other countries, had extensive railways before a road system was built.

The occupation of the pampa was made finally possible by a war against the Indians in 1878-83 which virtually exterminated them. Many of the officers in that campaign were given gifts of land of more than 40,000 hectares each. The pampa had passed into private hands on the old traditional pattern of large estates.

Cattle products—hides, tallow, and salt beef—had been the mainstay of Argentine overseas trade during the whole of the colonial period. In the early 19th century wool challenged the supremacy of cattle. The occupation of the grasslands did not, at first, alter the complexion of the foreign trade; it merely increased its volume. In 1877, however, the first ship with refrigeration chambers made it possible to send frozen beef to England, but the meat of the scrub cattle was too strong for English taste. As a result, pedigree bulls were imported from England and the upgrading of the herds began. The same process was applied to sheep. But the improved herds could only flourish where there were no ticks—prevalent in the N—and throve best where forage crops were available. Argentina adopted as its main forage crop alfalfa (lucerne), a plant like clover which proved extremely suitable on the pampa. It has since been supplemented with barley, oats, rye and particularly maize and sorghums.

A striking thing about the Pampas is the bird life. Flamingoes rise in a pink and white cloud, heron egrets gleam white against the blue sky, pink spoonbills dig in the mud and rheas stalk in the distance. Most fascinating are the oven birds, the *horneros,* which build oven-shaped nests six times as big as themselves on the top of telegraph and fence posts.

To sum up, the transformation of the pampa has had two profound effects. Because its newly-created riches flowed out and its needs flowed in mainly through Buenos Aires, that port grew from comparative insignificance into one of the great cities in the world. Also, the transformation of the Humid Pampa led, through immigration, to a vast predominance of the European strain. The first immigrants settled NW of Santa Fe in 1856. Between 1857 and 1930 total immigration was over six million, almost all from Europe. The process has continued; Italians have been by far the most numerous, followed by Spaniards, and then, far behind, groups of other Europeans and Latin Americans. British and North Americans normally came as stockbreeders, technicians and business executives.

The Argentine People   In the Federal Capital and Province of Buenos Aires, where almost 40% of the population lives, the people are almost exclusively of European origin. In the far northern provinces, colonized from neighbouring countries, at least half the people are *mestizos* though they form less than 2% of the population of the whole country. In the highlands of the NW and in the Chaco, there are still a few pure-blooded Indians.

In 1987 the population was 32.0 million. Some 85% are urban and 40% live in cities of 100,000 or more. Population growth: 1.6%; urban growth, 2.0%. Death rate per thousand: 8.7; infantile mortality per thousand live births, 36; birth rate, 24.6. It is estimated that 12.8% are foreign born and generally of European origin. About 95% can read and write.

Not surprisingly, the traditional image of the Argentine is that of the *gaucho; gauchismo* has been a powerful influence in literature, sociology and folklore, and is celebrated each year in the week before the "Day of Tradition", November 10.

Argentina is also celebrated for the tango, a dance that had its origins in the less desirable districts of Buenos Aires in the 1880s, and became accepted among respectable Argentines after being introduced to W.Europe (particularly France) and re-exported to Argentina in the early years of this century.

Communications   Argentina has only four good seaports: Buenos Aires, La Plata, Rosario and Bahía Blanca. The two great rivers flowing southward into the Plate, the Paraná and the Uruguay, are not very reliable shipping routes. The Colorado and the Negro rivers in northern Patagonia are navigable by small vessels only. Internal air services are highly developed.

Most of Argentina is served by about 140,000 km. of road, but only 30% are paved and a further 25% improved. Even so, the network carries 80% of freight tonnage and 82% of medium and long-distance passengers. The 43,100 km. of railway line, owned mostly by British companies until they were taken over by the State in 1948, carry less than 10% of passengers and freight, and are very heavily subsidized.

Political System The form of government has traditionally been a representative, republican federal system. By the 1853 Constitution (amended in 1880) the country is divided into a Federal Capital (the city of Buenos Aires), 22 Provinces and the National Territory of Tierra del Fuego, Antarctica and South Atlantic Islands. Each Province has its own Senate and Chamber of Deputies. The municipal government of the Federal Capital is exercised by a Mayor appointed by the President with the approval of the Senate.

Recent History After an uneasy alternation of three military and two constitutional regimes between 1955 and 1973, **Gen. Juan Domingo Perón (see page 41)** again became President in October 1973, but died on July 1, 1974, leaving the Presidency to his widow, Vice-President María Estela Martínez de Perón. A chaotic political situation, of which a high level of violence (including guerrilla warfare) was a regrettable feature, followed his death; by March 1976 conditions in the country, both of violence and of economic crisis, had deteriorated to the point when the military felt again obliged to intervene. Sra. de Perón was deposed from the Presidency by a military junta, led by Gen. Jorge Videla, and guerrilla warfare and the other features of dissidence were repressed with great brutality: about 9,000 people (according to official statistics; human rights organizations believe the total at least doubles this) disappeared without trace during the so-called "dirty war". General Videla was appointed President in 1978 by the military leaders, for a three-year term. His nominated successor, General Roberto Viola, took over as President for three years in March, 1981 but was replaced by General Leopoldo Galtieri in December 1981. The latter was in turn replaced in June 1982 by General (ret.) Reynaldo Bignone. Confidence in the military began to ebb when their economic policies began to go sour in 1980. In 1982-83 pressure for a democratic restoration grew apace particularly after the South Atlantic conflict in 1982. General elections were held on October 30, 1983 and the Unión Cívica Radical was victorious, winning the Presidency and an absolute majority in the Chamber of Deputies, with 52% of the vote. Accordingly, Dr. Raúl Alfonsín, its candidate, assumed the Presidency on December 10, 1983. During 1985 Generals Videla, Viola and Galtieri were sentenced to long terms of imprisonment for their parts in the "dirty war". The 1987 mid-term legislative elections resulted in the loss of the UCR majority in the Chamber, although they remained the largest party. The Partido Justicialista (Peronists) were the largest party in the Senate. Presidential elections held on May 14, 1989, were won by a 10% margin by Sr. Carlos Menem of the Peronist party.

BUENOS AIRES AND THE PAMPAS (1)

The pampa is little more than a fifth of the total area of the country, but 35% of the people live in Greater Buenos Aires and 32% in the Pampas outside Buenos Aires. The Pampa area has 70% of all the railways, 86% of the land used for cereals and linseed, 65% of the cattle, 40% of the sheep, 77% of the pigs, and nearly 90% of the industrial production.

The River Plate, or Río de la Plata, on which Buenos Aires lies, is not a river but an estuary or great basin, 160 km. long and from 37 to 90 km. wide, into which flow the Rivers Paraná and Uruguay and their tributaries. It is muddy and shallow and the passage of ocean vessels is only made possible by continuous dredging. The tides are of little importance, for there is only a 1.2 metre rise and fall at spring tides. The depth of water is determined by the direction of the wind and the flow of the Paraná and Uruguay rivers.

Buenos Aires, the capital, spreads over some 200 square km. The population of the Federal Capital itself is about 3,323,000, but the population of greater Buenos Aires (including the suburbs in the province of Buenos Aires) is already estimated at 12.6 millions.

BUENOS AIRES
AND THE PAMPAS

BUENOS AIRES

| **T** stations |
| **1** Retiro |
| **2** Lacroze |
| **3** Once |
| **4** Constitución |
| **5** Buenos Aires |

NB. In spite of its name (good air), extreme humidity and unusual pollen conditions can affect asthma sufferers if they stay over an extended period of time (i.e. after a month or so).

Buenos Aires has been virtually rebuilt since the beginning of this century and very few of the old buildings are left. In the centre, which has maintained the original lay-out since its foundation, the streets are often very narrow and are mostly one-way.

The heart of the city, now as in colonial days, is the Plaza de Mayo, with the historic Cabildo, the Town Hall, where the movement for independence from Spain was first planned; the pink Casa Rosada (Presidential Palace); the City Hall; and the Cathedral, where San Martín, the father of Argentine independence, is buried. (For a note on the Mothers of the Plaza de Mayo, **see page 50**). Within a few blocks are the fashionable church of Nuestra Señora de la Merced, the National Library and the main banks and business houses.

Running W from the Plaza, the Avenida de Mayo leads 1½ km. to the Congress building in the Plaza del Congreso. Halfway it crosses the wide Avenida Nueve de Julio. A tall obelisk commemorating the 400th anniversary of the city's founding stands at its centre in the Plaza de la República, surrounded by sloping lawns. The Av. Nueve de Julio itself, one of the widest in the world, consists of three carriageways separated by wide grass borders. In the N the Av. Nueve de Julio meets the Avenida Libertador, the principal way out of the city to the N and W.

N of the Plaza de Mayo is the shopping, theatre and commercial area. The city's traditional shopping centre, Calle Florida (with excellent newsstands), is in this district. This is the popular down-town meeting place, particularly in the late afternoon; it is reserved for pedestrians only and the buskers in the 500 block are worth visiting. Another shopping street is Avenida Santa Fe, which crosses Florida at the Plaza San Martín; it has become as touristy and as expensive as Florida. Avenida Corrientes is the entertainment centre, a street of theatres, restaurants, cafés and night life. Close by, in Calle Lavalle (part reserved to pedestrians) and in nearby streets, there are numerous cinemas and many good and reasonable restaurants.

A broad avenue, Paseo Colón, runs S to the waterfront and the picturesque old port district known as the Boca (now very touristy), where the Riachuelo flows into the Plata (reached by bus 152 from Av. L. N. Alem, or bus 29 from Plaza de Mayo, in the centre, US$0.10). It was here, near Parque Lezama, that Pedro de Mendoza founded the first Buenos Aires. For a tour of the Boca, start at Plaza Vuelta de Rocha, near Av. Pedro de Mendoza and Dr Del Valle Iberlucea, then walk up Caminito, the little pedestrian street used as a theatre and an art market. Visit the Museo de Bellas Artes de la Boca (**see page 49**). The Boca, mostly Italian, has its own distinctive life, but the area, with the adjacent industrial and meat-packing suburb of Avellaneda across the high Avellaneda bridge, is now dirty and run down, and assaults are frequent. Calle Brasil leads from this area to the far side of the docks and the spacious Avenida Costanera which runs along the river front. Here are bathing places (Balneario Municipal), gardens, many restaurants and public concerts: a pleasant place on a hot summer's day but overcrowded on Sundays and holidays. (The food at the outdoor restaurants is now said to be reliable, particularly barbecues; reached by 33 bus from Retiro Station or Av. L.N. Alem.) Bathing in the River Plate is no longer allowed; the water is heavily polluted.

One of the few places which still have late colonial and Rosista buildings is the *barrio* of San Telmo, S of Plaza de Mayo, centred on Plaza Dorrego along the slope which marks the old beach of the River Plate. It is a recognized artistic centre, with plenty of cafés and a pleasant atmosphere; and there is a regular Saturday and Sunday morning antiques market at the Plaza Dorrego (**see page 54**). The 29 bus connects the Boca with San Telmo, and passes the end of Calle Florida, the shopping street.

The theatre retains its hold on the people of Buenos Aires. About 20 commercial theatres play the year round. Recommended is the Teatro Liceo.

BUENOS AIRES CENTRE

There are many amateur theatres. You are advised to book as early as possible for a seat at a concert, ballet, or opera.

Principal Public Buildings

Casa de Gobierno on the E side of the Plaza de Mayo, and called the Casa Rosada because it is pink, contains the offices of the President of the Republic. (The Foreign Minister's offices are at the Palacio de San Martín, Plaza San Martín). The Casa Rosada is notable for its statuary, the rich furnishing of its halls and for its libraries, but it is not at present possible to visit the interior. The Museo de los Presidentes is on the lower floors (see under **Museums**).

The **Cabildo** on the W side of the same Plaza, the old town hall, was put up in 1711 but has been rebuilt several times. Its original structure, fittings and furniture were replaced in 1940 and it was declared a national monument; it is guarded by soldiers in the red and blue uniform of San Martín's grenadiers. See under **Museums**.

Old Congress Hall on the S of the Square, built 1863, is a National Monument. It has been encircled and built over by a palatial bank building. Open Thursday.

Congress Hall (Palacio del Congreso) to the SW at the far end of Avenida de Mayo, of great size and in Greco-Roman architecture, is the seat of the legislature. It contains the Senate and the Chamber of Deputies. There is limited accommodation for the public at the sittings. It is open from 1700 onwards. Queue in front of desk assigned for minor parties, there they take your passport and give you a ticket for your seat and a pink slip to reclaim your passport. You may stay as long as you wish, but must remain seated.

Teatro Colón, one of the world's great opera houses, overlooks Avenida 9 de Julio, with its main entrance on Libertad, between Tucumán and Viamonte. The Colón's interior is resplendent with red plush and gilt; the stage is huge, and salons, dressing rooms and banquet halls are equally sumptuous. Open daily to visitors 1200-1800 (but not always), free guided tours every half hour (English/German, six a day on the hour, US$1), book in advance (closed Jan.-Feb., so check, T 35-5414/15/16). Male visitors must wear jacket and tie to gala performances, but dress smartly anyway. Tickets, sold three days before performance, on the Calle Tucumán side of the theatre. The season (cheapest seat about US$25) runs from April to early December, and there are concert performances most days.

The **Bolsa de Comercio,** built in 1916, a handsome building in Calle 25 de Mayo, corner Sarmiento, contains a stock exchange, a grain market and a general produce market.

Churches

All historic churches are open 1630-1900; some at 0900-1100 also.

The **Cathedral,** Rivadavia 437, on the N of Plaza de Mayo is flanked by the former residence of the Archbishop. On this site was built the first church in Buenos Aires, which after reconstruction in 1677 collapsed in 1753 and the rebuilding was not completed until 1823. The eighteenth century towers were never rebuilt, so that the architectural proportions have suffered. A frieze upon the Greek façade represents Joseph and his brethren. The tomb (1878) of the Liberator, General José de San Martín, is imposing.

The **Church of San Ignacio de Loyola,** at Calles Alsina and Bolívar 225, founded in 1710, is the oldest Colonial building in Buenos Aires. It has two lofty towers. The **San Francisco,** Calles Alsina and Defensa, controlled by the Franciscan Order, was inaugurated in 1754 and given a new façade in 1808.

La Merced, Calles Juan D. Perón (Cangallo) and Reconquista 207, was founded 1604 and rebuilt 1732. One of the altars has a wooden figure of Our Lord, carved during the 18th century by an Indian in Misiones. It has one of the best organs in the country, and one of the few fine carillons of bells in Buenos Aires.

Key to Map of Buenos Aires
1. Plaza de Mayo; 2. Plaza del Congreso; 3. Plaza de la República, and Obelisk; 4. Plaza San Martín; 5. Plaza de la Fuerza Aérea; 6. Parque Lezama; 7. Plaza Constitución; 8. Plaza Lavalle; 9. Plaza Libertad; 10. Parque Colón; 11. Plaza Dorrego; 12. Cathedral; 13. San Ignacio de Loyola; 14. San Francisco; 15. Cabildo and Museum; 16. Casa Rosada and Museo de los Presidentes; 17. City Hall; 18. Congress; 19. Teatro Colón; 20. Museo Histórico Nacional; 21. Museo de la Ciudad; 22. Teatro Municipal General San Martín and Museo Municipal de Arte Moderno; 23. "Presidente Sarmiento" museum ship; 24. Museo Nacional Ferroviario at Retiro Station; 25. Central Post Office; 26 National Tourist Office (3 locations); 27. Buenos Aires Municipal Tourist Office; 28. Railway booking and information office.

Santo Domingo, on Defensa and Av. Belgrano, was founded in 1756. During the British attack on Buenos Aires in 1806 some of Whitelocke's soldiers took refuge in the church. The local forces bombarded it (some of the hits can still be seen on one of the towers); the British capitulated and their regimental colours were preserved in the church. Adjoining is the Salón Belgraniano (with relics of General Belgrano and much colonial furniture). There are summer evening concerts in the church; check times.

El Pilar, Junín 1904, is a jewel of colonial architecture dating from 1717, in a delightful setting of public gardens. An exceptionally fine wooden image of San Pedro de Alcántara, attributed to the famous 17th century Spanish sculptor Alonso Cano, is preserved in a side chapel on the left. It has a huge, unusual graveyard.

Visitors may like to know about the following religious establishments: The **Holy Cross,** Calle Estados Unidos 3150, established by the Passionists. **St. John's Cathedral** (Anglican), 25 de Mayo 282 (service Sun. at 1000), was built half at the expense of the British Government and dedicated in 1831. **St. Paul's, St. Peter's, St. Michael and All Angels** and **St. Saviour's** are Anglican places of worship in the suburbs. **St. Andrew's,** Calle Belgrano 579, is one of the 8 Scottish Presbyterian churches. The **American Church,** Corrientes 718, is Methodist, built in 1863. Service at 1100. **First Methodist** (American) Church, Av. Santa Fe 839, Acassuso.

German Evangelical Church, Esmeralda 162. **Synagogues** Anshe Galitzia at Uriburu 234; Temple at Alvear 1222. **Swedish Church,** Azopardo 1422.

The **Armenian Cathedral** of St. Gregory the Illuminator at the Armenian Centre, and the **Russian Orthodox Cathedral** of The Holy Trinity (Parque Lezama) are interesting.

The **Cemetery of Recoleta,** entrance at Junín 1822 near Museo de Bellas Artes (see below), is one of the sights of Buenos Aires (open 0700-1800). Evita Perón is now buried there; her tomb is now marked besides the inscription, Familia Duarte—guards will point out the grave. "A Doric portico gives on to the main, paved, cypress-lined avenue of a little city of the dead. At the end of the avenue there is a great bronze statue of the resurrected Saviour; on either side, hard up against each other, like houses in a street, there are the family vaults of the Argentine patricians. Every possible style of architecture is represented." G. S. Fraser, in *News from Latin America.* Bus 17 on Esmeralda, to Recoleta, then 10 mins. walk. On Sundays there is a good craft market near the entrance. A new cultural centre has been opened alongside the Recoleta cemetery: exhibitions, concerts, films. Another well known cemetery is that of La Chacarita, reached by Subte to the Federico Lacroze station, which has the much-visited, lovingly-tended tombs of Juan Perón and Carlos Gardel, the tango singer.

Museums, Libraries, Art Exhibitions, etc.

Note: Most museums close on Monday, and in January and most of February for summer holidays. State museums and parks are free on Wednesdays. Check opening hours with Tourist Office.

Museo de los Presidentes (basement of Casa Rosada), Hipólito Irigoyen 218. Historical memorabilia, particularly of former Presidents.
Museo de Bellas Artes (National Gallery), Avenida Libertador 1473. In addition to a fine collection of European works, particularly strong in the 19th century French school, there are paintings representing the conquest of Mexico, executed 300 or 400 years ago, many good Argentine works, and wooden carvings from the Argentine hinterland. Open Tues.-Sun. (free Thurs.), 0900-1245, 1500-1845. Entrance US$2. Warmly rec.
The **National Museum of the Decorative Arts** is at Av. Libertador 1902. The building is shared with the **Museo Nacional de Arte Oriental;** both are open Wed.-Mon., 1500-1900.
Biblioteca Nacional (The National Library). Calle México 566, founded in 1810, moved here in 1902. About 500,000 volumes and 10,000 manuscripts.
Museo Histórico Nacional, Defensa 1600. Trophies and mementoes of historical events. Here are San Martín's uniforms, a replica of his famous sabre, and the original furniture and door of the house in which he died at Boulogne. Open Tues.-Fri. and Sunday, 1500-1900. Entrance US$0.10.
Museo de la Ciudad, Alsina 412, open Mon.-Fri., 1100-1900, Sat., 1600-2000. Permanent exhibition of architectural and urban development exhibits, special exhibitions changed every two months, and a reference library open to the public.
Museo y Biblioteca Mitre, San Martín 336, preserves intact the household of President Bartolomé Mitre. Open 1500-1700.
Museo de Ciencias Naturales at Avenida Angel Gallardo 490, facing Parque Centenario. It houses palaeontological, zoological, mineralogical, botanical, archaeological and marine sections. Open Tues., Thurs., Sun. 1400-1800, US$0.20. Library, Mon.-Fri., 1100-1700.
Museo Municipal de Arte Moderno (Tues.-Sun. 1600-2000) at Avenida Corrientes 1530, and **Museo Municipal de Artes Plásticas Eduardo Sivori** (Tues.-Sun. 1600-2000) at Centro Cultural de Recoleta, Junín 1930, where there are also a cinema, a theatre, and the **Museo de Artes Visuales,** Tues.-Fri. 1600-2000. Free entry on Wed. 19th century and contemporary Argentine painting.

Museo de Bellas Artes de Boca, Pedro de Mendoza 1835, Boca, has many works on local life, entrance free.

Centro Cultural Las Malvinas, Florida 853, stages many art exhibitions by Argentine and foreign artists.

Museo de Motivos Populares Argentinos José Hernández, Av. Libertador 2373, Gaucho collection, open Tues.-Sun., 1400-1800.

Museo del Instituto Nacional Sanmartino, Sánchez de Bustamante and Av. A. M. de Aguado; Mon.-Fri. 0900-1200 and 1400-1700; Sat., Sun. 1400-1700.

Museo de Arte Español Enrique Larreta, Juramento 2291, in Belgrano. 1500-1945. Closed Thurs. The home of the writer Larreta. Also **Biblioteca Alfonso El Sabio**, Mon.-Fri., 1500-1930.

Museo de Cabildo y Revolución de Mayo, Bolívar 65, is the old Cabildo building, converted into a museum in 1940. It contains paintings, documents, furniture, etc., recording the May 1810 revolution, and memorabilia of the 1806 British attack. Entry US$0.33. Open Wed.-Sun., 1500-1900. Library, Mon.-Fri., 1100-1900.

Museo de Arte Hispanoamericano Isaac Fernández Blanco, Suipacha 1422. Contains a most interesting and valuable collection of colonial art, especially silver, in a small colonial mansion. Open Tues.-Sun., 1400-1900, admission US$0.35. Thursdays free. Latin American art and history library at Suipacha 1444 nearby, 0900-1900, Mon.-Fri.

Museo y Biblioteca Ricardo Rojas, Charcas 2837, open Wednesdays and Fridays 1500-1800, US$0.10. The famous writer Rojas lived in this beautiful colonial house for several decades. It contains his library, souvenirs of his travels, and many intriguing literary and historical curios.

Numismatic Museum; fascinating, well kept, little known, at the Banco Central in San Martín, overlooks central foyer, ask guard for directions.

"Presidente Sarmiento", Dársena Norte, a sailing ship used as a naval training ship until 1987; now a museum. Open daily 1000-2100, US$0.40. The corvette **"Uruguay",** tied up by the Boca bridge, is a museum of Antarctica, open Sat. and Sun. 1300-1800, US$0.40.

Bank of London and South America (now Lloyds Bank (BLSA)), Bartolomé Mitre and Reconquista, has a miniature museum on its fifth floor. Open during banking hours; the building, designed by SEPRA (Santiago Sánchez Elia, Federico Peralta Ramos, and Alfredo Agostini) and completed in 1963 is worth seeing for itself. Next door is the **Banco de Córdoba,** designed by the brilliant Córdoba architect Miguel Angel Roca, completed in the early 1970s.

Museo Nacional de Aeronáutica, Av. Costanera Rafael Obligado, next to Jorge Newbery airport, Thurs., Sat. and Sun., 1600-1900. Many civil and military aircraft.

Museo Nacional Ferroviario, Av. Libertador 405, in Retiro station. Mon.-Fri., 0900-1800, free. Archives 1100-1800. For railway fans; no photographing.

Museo Botánico, Las Heras 4102 and Malabia 2690. Open 0800-1200 and 1400-1800, Mon.-Fri. Herbarium pleasant. Some 1,000 cats in residence.

Museo de la Dirección Nacional del Antártico, Angel Gallardo 470, Tues., Thurs. and Sun., 1400-1800. Dioramas.

Museo del Teatro Colón, Tucumán 1161. Mon.-Fri. 1200-1800. Documents and objects related to the theatre. Closed 1987 for refurbishing.

Museo Histórico Saavedra, Crisólogo Larralde (Republiquetas) 6309. Wed.-Fri., 1400-1800; Sat., 1800-2200; Sun., 1500-1900. City history from the eighteenth century. Free on Wed.

Yuchán Centro de Artesanía Aborigen, Defensa 788, has many interesting native artefacts on view, for sale.

Federal Police Museum San Martín 353, 7th floor, worth visiting, small entrance fee. The interesting forensic part can only be seen if you offer a police, medical or journalist's identification.

Museo Internacional de Caricatura y Humorismo, Lima 1037, open Fri., 1700-2100 only, originals of cartoons and caricatures of 20th century, but small international section, admission US$0.05.

Museo de Armas, Maipú y Santa Fe. Open 1500-1900 daily, US$0.15. All kinds of weaponry.

Parks and Squares

Parque Lezama, Calles Defensa and Brasil, originally one of the most beautiful in the city, has been somewhat vandalized. Very lively on Sunday. It has an imposing statue of Pedro de Mendoza, the founder of the original city in 1535. The tradition is that the first founding took place on this spot. The Museo Histórico Nacional **(see page 48)** is in the park.

The **Palermo Parks** with their magnificent avenues are the city's Bois de Boulogne. They are famous for their rose garden, Andalusian Patio, Japanese garden with fish to feed (admission US$0.05) and the Hipódromo Argentino, the Palermo race course, with seats for 45,000. Opposite the parks are the Botanical and Zoological Gardens (the Palermo Zoo and Japanese Garden are closed on Mondays). Nearby are the Municipal Golf Club, Buenos Aires Lawn Tennis Club, riding clubs and polo field, and the popular Club de Gimnasia y Esgrima (Athletic and Fencing Club). The **Planetarium** (just off Belisario Roldán, in the Park), is open Sat. and Sun. only (March-Nov., 1630, 1800, 1930, Dec.-Feb., 1800, 1930, 2100), entry US$0.22. The official name of the Palermo parks is the Parque Tres de Febrero. Reached by Subte line D. The **Show Grounds** of the

Argentine Rural Society, on a site next to Palermo Park, stage the Annual Livestock Exhibition in July.

There is another large and modern race course (one of the best of its kind) with grass track at San Isidro, 25 minutes from the city centre by train or road. The meetings alternate with those at Palermo. There are Saturday and Sunday races throughout the year, and upon all holidays other than May 25 and July 9. Betting is by totalizator only.

The **Municipal Botanical Gardens,** Santa Fe 3951, entrance from Plaza Italia (take Subte, line D), contain characteristic specimens of the world's vegetation. The trees proper to the several provinces of Argentina are brought together in one section. The Gardens are full of stray cats, fed regularly by benevolent local residents. The **Zoo** is next to the Botanical Gardens; rather run down, though several of the animals, such as the Patagonian *mara* (a local short-eared hare), are permitted to roam where they will. The enclosures are mostly very small and many animals look unhappy.

The new **Costanera Sur Wildlife Reserve**, S of the city along the River Plate (entrance at Av. España y Brasil), has several coypu and many types of birds. It opens at 0800 but much can be seen from the road before then. For details, contact Fundacíon Vida Silvestre, Defensa 251, 6°piso, 1075 Bs. As., T 331-4864.

Plazas   The most interesting is the Plaza de Mayo, containing so many public buildings, where the **Mothers of the Plaza de Mayo** still march, Thursdays at 1530, in remembrance of their children who disappeared during the crisis of the 1970s. Others are the Plaza San Martín, with a monument to San Martín in the centre; the former Plaza Británica, now known as the Plaza de la Fuerza Aérea, with the clock tower presented by British and Anglo-Argentine residents, "a florid Victorian sentinel, royal crest upon its bosom" (frequently vandalized); the Plaza Lavalle, which has secondhand bookstalls at the Calle Lavalle end; the Plaza del Congreso, the largest in the city, with a waterfall, floodlit at 2145. There is also the great Plaza de la República, with a 67-metre obelisk at the junction between the Diagonal Norte and the Avenida Corrientes.

Hotels   The Dirección de Turismo fixes maximum and minimum rates for 1, 2 and 3-star hotels, guest houses and inns, but there have been complaints that at 3 stars and below the ratings do not provide very useful guidance. Four and five-star hotels are free to apply any rate they wish. The rates can be taken only as an indication especially since, above 2 stars, hotels charge at the parallel exchange rate, adjusting tariffs daily. All hotels, guest houses, inns and camping sites are graded by the number of beds available, and the services supplied.

Most if not all of the hotels listed below include a continental breakfast in the price. Many of the cheaper hotels in the central area give large reductions on the daily rate for long stays.

Name	Address	Single	Double	Star Grading
Panamericano	Carlos Pellegrini 525	110	125	5
Plaza	Plaza San Martín	95	115	5
Elevage	Maipú 960	145	170	5
Bauen	Callao 346	120	130	5
Libertador	Av. Córdoba y Maipú	97	120	5
Sheraton	San Martín 1225	160	185	5
Claridge	Tucumán 535	115	135	5
Regente Palace	Suipacha 964	90	105	4
Gran Colón	Pellegrini 507	126	144	4
Bizonte Palace	M.T. de Alvear y Suipacha	65	70	4
Bizonte	Paraguay 1207	65	70	4
El Conquistador	Suipacha 948	85	99	4
Las Américas	Libertad 1020	105	120	4
Principado	Paraguay 481	90	105	4
Gran Buenos Aires	M.T. de Alvear (ex-Charcas) 767	77	102	4
Gran King	Lavalle 560	72	82	4
Continental	Diagonal Norte 725	68	85	4
Lancaster	Av. Córdoba 405	72	96	4
Lafayette	Reconquista 546	90	106	4
City	Bolívar 160	60	93	4
Crillón	Av. Santa Fe 796	76	102	4
Carsson	Viamonte 650	72	95	4
Salles	Cerrito 208	75	102	4
Rochester	Esmeralda 542	65	75	4
Sheltown	M.T. de Alvear (ex-Charcas) 742	42	55	4
República	Cerrito 370	69	93	4
Los Dos Chinos	Brasil 780	57	60	4
Gran Dorá	Maipú 963	66	88	4
Torre	Corrientes 6800	36	50	4
Wilton Palace	Callas 1162	58	72	4

Other hotels: An older hotel is the *Alvear Palace*, Av. Alvear 1891, T 41-4031 (near Recoleta), with roof garden, shopping gallery, good. C price range, *Ayamitre*, Ayacucho y Bartolomé Mitre, 2 blocks from Congreso Subte station, pleasant; *Orly*, Paraguay 474, good position, helpful, has some rooms for 4; *Bristol*, Cerrito 286; *Concorde*, 25 de Mayo 630, excellent, a/c, comfortable, rec.; *Savoy*, Av. Callao 181, friendly and helpful.

D range: *San Antonio*, Paraguay 372, with bath, nice atmosphere, clean; *Eibar*, Florida 328, breakfast included, quiet, friendly, helpful, rec.; *Tucumán Palace*, Tucumán 384, moderate, front rooms noisy; *Regis*, Lavalle 813, good value, nice atmosphere; *Novus*, Sarmiento 631 (near Plaza de Mayo), rec. *Orleans*, Callao 465, clean, small rooms (some F), safe and friendly; *Sarmiento Palace*, on Sarmiento nr. Corrientes, incl. breakfast, very clean, very friendly, highly rec. *Astoria*, Av. de Mayo 916, friendly, very clean; *Chile*, Av. de Mayo 1297, will mind luggage; *Viamonte*, Viamonte 833, clean and helpful; *Florida House*, Florida 527, comfortable, hot shower, friendly, a little noisy, but quiet interior rooms available, safe-deposit, rec.; *Camino Real*, Maipú 572, pleasant, clean, central; *Don Juan*, Calle Dr Finochitto 842, rec. *Super*, Gallo nr Av. Santa Fe (Subte D, Agüero), out of centre, a/c, pleasant.

E range: *Tres Sargentos*, Tres Sargentos 345, clean, dark rooms; *Frossard*, Tucumán 686, inexpensive, hot showers, but not quiet; *Mediterráneo*, Rodríguez Peña 152, "friendly, safe, clean but noisy"; *Apolo*, Tucumán 951, friendly, central; *O'Rei*, Lavalle 733, with bath, clean, friendly; *Acapulco*, Lavalle 472, hot-shower (cheaper without bathroom), friendly, convenient; *Odeón*, Esmeralda 368 with Corrientes, clean, friendly; *Parada*, Rivadavia 1291, hot showers, central, friendly; *Gran Vedra*, Av. de Mayo 1350, good value, rec.; *De Mayo*, Av. de Mayo 776, central and friendly; *Novel*, Av. de Mayo 915, good; *La Argentina*, Av. de Mayo 860, with bath, friendly, central, rec.; *Concorde*, 25 de Mayo 630, more expensive with TV and fridge, helpful; *Central Córdoba*, San Martín 1021, safe and friendly, cheaper on 4th floor, rec.; *Sportsman*, Rivadavia 1426, clean, old fashioned, cheaper without bath, rec.; *Cecil*, Av. de Mayo 1239, front noisy, inside rooms windowless, but clean and friendly; *Mundial*, Av. de Mayo 1298, with bath, clean, comfortable; *Suipacha Palace*, Suipacha 18, clean, spacious, charming; *Petit Hotel Goya*, Suipacha 748, noisy, some rooms small and dark, but very central; *Phoenix*, San Martín 780, with bath, clean, large rooms, use of kitchen, rec.; *Majéstica*, Libertad 121, colonial, very clean, friendly; *Uruguay*, Tacuari 83, central, clean, friendly, good value, rec.; *Hispano Argentino*, Lima Oeste 1483, some rooms with bath, clean, quiet, convenient; *Victoria*, Chacabuco 726, clean and cheap, use of kitchens; *Brisas*, Tacuari 1621, bath, etc., clean; *Varela*, Estados Unidos 324 (San Telmo), pleasant; *Ecuador*, Adolfo Alsina 2820, nr. Plaza Once, rec.; *Roxy*, Santiago del Estero 1677 (cheaper per week's stay), hot water, close to cheap restaurants. *Gran Vía*, Sarmiento 1450, T 40-5763, with bath, clean, friendly.

F range: *Aguila*, J. D. Perón (Cangallo) 1554, clean; *Mediterráneo*, Rodríguez Peña 159 basic, central, helpful, safe, clean; *Vila Seca*, Av.de Mayo 776, friendly; *Mendoza*, 25 de Mayo 674, dirty, friendly, cheap, hot shower, many similar in same street; *Ocean*, Maipú 907, reasonable, with bath, cheaper in triple rooms; *Maipú*, Maipú 735, often crowded, clean, friendly, basic, T 322-5142; *Auzmendi*, Tacuari 242, F, with or without bath, basic, safe, clean; *Gran España*, Tacuari 80, T 30-5541, private bath, hot water, central heating; *La Giralda*, Tacuari 17, clean, cheap, unfriendly; *Central*, Alsina 1693, friendly and clean; *Ostende*, Sarmiento y Talcahuano, very cheap; *De France*, San José 9 near Sáenz Peña Subte, clean, hot water; *Patagones*, B. de Yrigoyen 1692, T 28-6775, friendly, safe to leave luggage, rec.; *Cibelles*, Virrey Cevallos, 2 blocks from Congreso, T 37-3143, with bath, safe (next to police HQ). *Bolívar*, in Bolívar (San Telmo), with bath, clean; *Youth Hostel*, Brasil 675 near Constitución station, T 362-9133, F with YHA card. Women should be aware that they could attract unwelcome attention near Constitución station as prostitutes operate there. Otherwise, this area is a short walk to centre and convenient for boats to Uruguay and trains to the N.

One can rent flats on a daily basis in *Edificios Esmeralda,* Marcelo T. de Alvear (ex-Charcas) 842, T 31-3929, US$20-30 for two a day, cleaning included. Facilities for up to 6 persons. Weekly renting at *Edificio Charcas*, M.T. de Alvear 776, US$128 d for one room per week, rec. (visiting singers at the Colón often stay there). Also *Aspen Apartment Hotel*, Esmeralda 933; *Edificio Lemonde*, San Martín 839, rec., US$750 a month; *Residencial Trianon*, Callao y Alvear, 3-bed apartment US$80 a night. Rooms in private house, E, at Cochabamba 771 (San Telmo) owned by Elizabeth Miles, T 27-5839.

NB All the rates quoted are subject to alteration and it should be noted that for the most part they are the basic or minimum rates, inclusive of tax. Check when booking into a hotel whether breakfast is included or not. International telephone calls from hotels may incur a 40%-50% commission in addition to government tax of about the same amount. Tokens can be obtained and the call made from a public telephone box. International calls can be made from the central office on the corner of Maipú and Corrientes, about US$1 a minute.

Hotels with red-green lights or marked *Albergue Transitorio* are hotels for homeless lovers.

Tips In spite of the high service charge it is customary to tip 10% of the total bill; porters at hotels expect a tip—about US$0.50 per day of stay or service rendered. Hairdressers expect 10% of the bill, cinema ushers about US$0.20.

Electric Current 220 volts, 50 cycles, A.C., European Continental-type plugs in old buildings,

Australian 3-pin flat-type in the new. Adaptors can be purchased locally for either type (i.e. from new 3-pin to old 2-pin and vice-versa).

Camping Closest camp site to the city is about 12 km. out to the SW; information on all sites is available from the Automóvil Club Argentino. Those travelling by car might try at the German Sports Club, Sociedad Alemana de Gimnasia, 9 de Julio and Av. Márquez, Villa Ballester, 30 km. N of centre, cheap, or free. Easy to reach by Línea Suárez bus 90, get off at Chilavert.

Sleeping bags and tents direct from the factory at Acoyte 1622, T 855-0619, English, German spoken, reasonable prices, open 0800-1200, 1430-1900, Saturday 0900-1300. Camping gas available at América Pesca, Alfredo Pollini Alvear 1461.

Restaurants "The Buenos Aires Herald" publishes a handy *Guide to Good Eating in Buenos Aires* (with a guide to local wines) by Derek Foster. Eating out in Buenos Aires is very good, and cheap by international standards: you should be able to get a steak dinner with wine for about US$7-8. David Mackintosh tells us that five of the best restaurants are: *Catalinas*, Reconquista 875 (very expensive though—US$25 p.p.); *Francis Malman*, Honduras 4963; *Blabs*, Florida 325; *Au Bec Fin*, Vicente López 1825; and *Montmartre*, Av. Libertador 3302, La Lucila. Other excellent restaurants include *Clark's*, Sarmiento 645, in old English outfitter's shop (also at Junín 1777), well cooked food, US$15 p.p.; *La Emiliana*, Av. Corrientes 1443, good; *London Grill*, Reconquista 435, about US$12 p.p. *Lo Prete*, Luis S. Peña 749; *El Imparcial*, H. Irigoyen 1201, first-class service (Spanish); *Escorpión*, Av. Montes de Oca y Uspallata, good food and service; *La Veda*, Florida 1, excellent food on fixed-price menu and good tango show; *Maxim's* on Paraguay, between Florida and Esmeralda and *Pippo's*, Paraná 356, near corner with Montevideo, and Corrientes near Montevideo (specializes in pasta and meat) and reasonably priced. *El Figón de Bonilla*, rustic style, Junín 1721, and Av. L.N. Alem between Tucumán and Viamonte, good. For roast chicken try *Pepito*, on Uruguay, between Corrientes and Sarmiento. *Le Coq Hardi*, Av. Tres Sargentos 496, corner with San Martín, food, service and atmosphere highly rec., first class; *El Ceibal*, food from the NE, at Pueyrredón and Las Heras, distinguished, expensive; *Irish Pub-Downton Matias*, San Martín 979, lunch only.

Alexandra (English, now expensive), San Martín 780. Typical Argentine restaurants: *La Estancia*, Lavalle 941, popular with business people, excellent grills and service (US$12-14); other "business" restaurants, *ABC*, Lavalle 54-5, traditional (US$8-10); *El Faisán*, Corrientes 260, and *Bolsa de Comercio*, 25 de Mayo 359, downstairs at the Stock Exchange. *La Cabaña*, Entre Ríos 436, old tavern style, US$25-30. The typical parrilla (mixed grill) is a speciality of *Tranquera*, in Palermo Park. Also in Palermo are *La Placita*, on Plaza Recado (5-6 blocks from Subte D, Plaza Italia station) fine atmosphere and good food; and *Mama Liberata*, Cabildo 3800, excellent Italian. *Chiquín*, Juan D. Perón (Cangallo) 920, is a well-known traditional restaurant. *Viga*, J.D. Perón 1116, excellent value, meal with milanesa for US$3. *Los Troncos*, Suipacha 732, good grills. *Yapeyú*, Maipú 389, rec. as good value and friendly; *El Fogón de Martín Fierro*, Palermo, highly rec., huge barbecue; *Don Pipón*, Esmeralda 521, huge cheap grills; ditto at *Mercado del Puerto*, Av. Córdoba 518, warmly rec. *El Suiza*, Viamonte y Reconquista, typical and reasonable, rec.; *Otto's*, on Lavalle 893, rec. There are good restaurants all along Calles Lavalle and Maipú, serving full meals at US$3-5. *Hunter's Place*, Lavalle 445, good. *Los Inmortales*, Lavalle 746, is highly rec.; there are other locations. Some serve *à la carte* dishes which are plentiful (US$ 5 each, upwards), and are open from 1500-2000 when most other restaurants are closed. *Ligure*, Juncal 855, rec.; Italian restaurant on *Sheraton* hotel, meal for US$6, good service; huge steaks at *La Dora*, Av. Leandro N.Alem, near *Sheraton*. *Veracruz*, Uruguay 538, also rec. There are also several economical restaurants along Florida. *La Blanca*, Tucumán and Florida, good and cheap; also *La Chacra* Av. Córdoba 941, huge portions, US$15-18, used by Lufthansa staff; *Mesón Español*, Av. Caseros 1750, good food and very good show of folk music. *Rocinante*, Carlos Pellegrini 715, diagonally opposite Teatro Colón, rec. as delicious and not expensive; nearby is *Posta del Gaucho*, Pellegrini 625, very good, accepts Visa. Other restaurants near the Colón are *Hamburgo*, Carlos Pellegrini 581; *El Quijote*, at No. 663; *Don Luis*, Viamonte 1169; and *Zum Edelweiss*, Libertad 431, not cheap but good. *Pichín No 1* or *No 2*, Paraná and Sarmiento, for gigantic asado de tira; *La Auténtica Banderita*, Moreno 1100, excellent meat dishes; *La Rural*, Suipacha 453, rec., parrillada for US$17, bife de lomo US$4; *El Pulpo*, Tucumán and Reconquista, great variety of sea-food, big portions, moderate prices, highly rec. *El Pescadito*, P. de Mendoza 1483, rec. for pasta and sea-food. *Hispano*, Rivadavia 1200, reasonable, good sea-food. Several good restaurants on Defensa, between Alsina and Plaza de Mayo. *El Repecho de San Telmo*, Carlos Calvo 242, excellent, expensive, reserve in advance. *El Comité*, Carlos Calvo 375, very good, not too dear; *Hippopotamus*, Junín 1787, nouvelle cuisine and good nightclub. Several good places near entrance to Recoleta cemetery: *Norte*, Junín 1767, good food, reasonable prices; *Munich Recoleta*, Junín 1871, good; *Montevideo 352* (address as name), parrillada, good and cheap; *Café Victoria*, Roberto M. Ortiz 1865, typical of the Recoleta area. *Nazarenas*, L. N. Alem (North), good for beef, cheap, excellent atmosphere, rec. The Costanera along the river front is lined with little eating places: *El Rancho Inn* is best, try also *Happenings* and *Los Años Locos*. *Delta Queen* in this area is a floating restaurant in an old, Mississippi-style riverboat, good but expensive. Good snacks all day and night at Retiro and Constitución railway termini, also at *La Escalerita*, Lavalle 717. *La Cautiva*, Sucre 1546, typical local game dishes. *City Grill*, San Martín and Av. Córdoba, good steaks with salad and wine; Swedish food at *Swedish Club*, Tacuari 147, open to non-members. Hungarian, *Budapest*, 25 de Mayo 690, cheap. *Florida Grill*, at Florida 122, standing-only steak restaurant, excellent value; *Chez Moi*, Av. San Juan 1223 (T 270890), French, and Iranian food on Fri. and Sat. lunch, reservations necessary. *La Mosca Blanca*, right hand side of Retiro station, very good and busy; *El Tronio*, Reconquista 918, is very cheap and good. *El Jocoso*, reasonable, at Corrientes and Callao. *La Pipeta*, a little cheaper, very good, at San Martín and Lavalle.

Vegetarian restaurants, *Grannix*, Florida 126 and 461, plenty of cheap food, open lunchtime Mon.-Fri. *Ratatouille*, Sarmiento 1802, excellent value. Natural food shop and restaurant, Córdoba 1599 with Montevideo, rec.; *Tamborá*, Pasaje del Carmen 768 (off Córdoba 1600 block); *Hindú*, Mendoza 2175 (closed Sun., Mon.); *Sai Kai*, Suipacha 920 (lunch only, closed weekend); *Sr. Sol*, Billingshurst 1070 (p.m. except Sat., Sun., lunch also, closed Mon.); *Yin Yang*, Paraná 868 (health-food shop too, lunch only, closed Sun.); *Manantial*, Montevideo 560 (closed Sun.). *La Esquina de las Flores*, Montevideo and Córdoba, excellent value, also good health-food shop. *Verde Esmeralda*, Esmeralda (nr. Av. Corrientes); *El Jardín*, Suipacha 429 and Lavalle 835 (in arcade), 1st floor, rec.; US$3 complete meal, take-away also; *La Huerta*, Paraguay 445, T 311-0470, macrobiotic, rec.; *La Huerta II*, Lavalle 895 y Suipacha, 2nd floor, all you can eat for US$3; *Nueva Era*, Maipú 650, 2nd floor, good value.

Chung Kin, Calle Paraguay, near Maipú, Chinese, set lunch, US$2; *Oriente*, also Chinese, Maipú 512, good; *Nuevo Kow Loon*, also Maipú, excellent and reasonable; *Macau*, Suipacha 477, good Chinese buffet; *China*, Paraná 342, rec.; *El Balcón*, Carlos Pellegrini 525 (Hotel Panamericano), Japanese, very good. *Pumper-nic* is a chain of rather pricey fast food restaurants. *El Pasatiempo*, cheap and good, on Belgrano, near station, rec.; *Manolito's*, Piedras 566, *Barcito*, Piedras 554, and *Parrilla*, Piedras 442, provide cheap meals, and so does *Restaurant Bar Salamanca*, at back of Galería de las Américas, Suipacha 927, platos del día for US$1.50. *Pizzería Los Idolos*, Suipacha 436, said to be the best pizzeria in the city. *Lois*, across from *Hotel Orly* on Paraguay, near San Martín, is busy and good, with excellent food moderately priced, as is *Juvenas* near the same hotel for stand-up lunches. Two other cheap, good ones are *Los Teatros*, Talcahuano 354 (live music 2300-0100, open 24 hrs.) and *Pipón*, Av. de Mayo 1253. *Kentucky Fried Chicken*, Roberto M. Ortiz 1815, Paseo de la Recoleta. For quick cheap snacks the markets are rec., e.g. El Retiro market on the 900 block of Av. Libertador. Stalls of the Cooperadora de Acción Social offer cheap snacks, and can be found in several public areas, e.g. near the Recoleta. The snack bars in underground stations are also cheap; also *Hogar Obrero*, Rivadavia y Esmeraldas, US$0.65 for full meal (but not too good).

Typical Boca restaurant: *Spadavecchia*, Necochea 1180, set menu with wine US$8, seats some 500 people, dancing. There are several others in the same street. They all serve antipasto, pasta and chicken; no point in looking for beef here. All bands are loud; offputting for those with sensitive ears. Nearby is *Restaurant Napolitano*, which serves excellent set lunches of seafood (US$10 for 2), good atmosphere and young wine. Try a family restaurant at corner of Necochea and Suárez known as *Cantina Los Tres Amigos*; live music from 2130, complete meal with wine under US$6 each, excellent, about 4 blocks from commercial centre. The seafood restaurant *La Barca*, on river bank near Avellaneda bridge, US$16 for 2, rec.; also rec. for seafood and good value, *Viejo Puente*, Almirante Brown 1499.

Tea Rooms, Cafés and Bars *Richmond*, Florida 468 between Lavalle and Corrientes (chess played between 1200-2400); *La Estrella* and *El Reloj*, Lavalle and Maipú; *Queen Bess*, Santa Fe 868; well-known are the *Confitería Suiza*, Tucumán 753, and the *Florida Garden* at Florida and Paraguay. *Café El Convento de San Telmo*, Bolívar with Humberto 1°, good coffee, cakes and atmosphere. *En El Patio*, Paraguay 886, very pleasant. *Exedra* at Carlos Pellegrini and Av. Córdoba and many on Av. Libertador in the Palermo area, such as *Round Point*, *Café Tabac*, are fashionable. *Caffé Piazza*, Rivadavia 1400 block opp. Plaza Lorea, exellent coffee, pretty setting. The more bohemian side of the city's intellectual life is centred on Avenida Corrientes, between Cerrito and Callao, where there are many bars and coffee shops, such as *La Paz* (open very late). *Siglo XIX* on Suipacha, rec. for traditional atmosphere; *El Molino*, Rivadavia and Callao, popular with politicians, nr. Congress, Belle Epoque décor, frequent art sales. Excellent ice-cream at *Freddo*, Ayacucho y Quintana. On Lavalle there are *whiskerías* and *cervecerías* where one can have either coffee or exotic drinks, *Bar Suárez*, Lavalle and Maipú, is a good place to watch the world go by. *Café Mozart*, Reconquista 1050, offers variety of music (US$5) along with tea and snacks. *Bar-baro*, cosmopolitan, Tres Sargentos and San Martín. *Bar Rua Nova*, corner of Chacabuco and Av. de Mayo, cheap snacks. *Arrayanes*, Córdoba and San Martín, open Sunday. *Young Men's Bar*, Córdoba and Esmeralda. *Barila*, Santa Fe 2375, has excellent confectionery. *Café Tortoni*, Av. de Mayo 829-35, a haunt of artists, very elegant, over 100 years old, interesting *peña* evenings of poetry and music. Good local atmosphere in bars along Pasaje Bollini. *Bar Verona* in the Boca. Watch whisky prices in bars: much higher than in restaurants.

Night Clubs and Folklore *Michelangelo*, impressive setting, restaurant and nightclub in an old converted monastery, US$20 each, including cover charges and first drink, good show, Balcarce 433, go at about 2300 on Fri.; *Hippopotamus*, Junín 1787, also good restaurant and night club; *Karim*, Carlos Pellegrini y Av. Santa Fe, good; *Caño 14*, Talcahuano 975, *El Viejo Almacén*, Independencia and Balcarce, tango shows at 2230 and 0115, rec. but touristy, (entrance US$25—no dancing for guests); nearby are *Casablanca*, Balcarce 668, and

Taconeando, San Lorenzo and Balcarce 725, tango shows, entrance US$10, more authentic, rec. *La Casa del Cantor*, P.Gollena 603. *El Rancho Ochoa*, Catamarca 999, has a good show and a reasonable meal. The best affordable tango bars are in the Boca, but it is apparently becoming increasingly difficult to find authentic tango for locals; most are tourist-oriented. One recommended place is *Italia Unita* in the 2300 block of J.D. Perón. Recommended night club/discos include *Le Club*, small and exclusive, Quintana 111; *Dimensión*, new and large but pleasant, Av. Córdoba 3653; *Paladium*, "extravagant", on Reconquista next to *Pumper-nic* restaurant. Three gay discos: *Contramano* (the best), Rodrgúez Peña 1082; *Bunker*, Anchorena 1170; *Area*, Junín y Santa Fe.

Bars and restaurants in San Telmo district, with live music (usually beginning 2330-2400, Fri., Sat., Sun., cover charge US$2): *Jazz y Pop*, Venezuela y Chacabuco; *Jazz Café*, Chile 400; *Players*, Humberto I° 528 (piano bar); *La Peluquería*, Bolívar, nr. Carlos Calvo (Samba).

Cultural Events The Luna Park stadium holds pop/jazz concerts. Teatro Alvear has free concerts Tuesday afternoons, usually Orquesta de Tango de Bs. As. Teatro Municipal General San Martín, Av. Corrientes 1530, organizes many cultural activities of which quite a few are free of charge; the theatre's Sala Leopoldo Lugones shows international classic films, US$0.75 Sat.-Sun. Free concerts at ProMusica music shop, Florida 638; schedule in window. Centro Cultural General San Martín, Sarmiento 1551, and the Centro Cultural de Buenos Aires, Junín 1930, next to the Recoleta cemetery, have many free activities. Theatre ticket agency, La Cartelera, Lavalle 828. Look for details in main newspapers.

Cinemas Many, centred on Lavalle and nearby blocks. The selection of films is as good as anywhere else in the world. Films are now shown uncensored. Cost per ticket, US$2, best booked early afternoon to ensure good seats. Reductions on Mon., Tues. and Wed. to US$1.50 unless they are holidays or the days just before holidays. Tickets obtainable, sometimes cheaper, from ticket agencies (*carteleras*), such as the one in the gallery at Maipú y Lavalle. Most foreign films are shown with subtitles, but dubbing increasingly used for major box-office successes. Free films at Asociación Bancaria, Sarmiento 337/341, T 313-9306/312-5011/17; old films at Ciné en el Teatro Hebraíco, Sarmiento 2255, and at Sarmiento 2150, T 48-2170, US$1. On Sat. nights many central cinemas have *transnoches*, late shows starting at 0100.

Markets Sunday markets for souvenirs, antiques, etc.: **Plaza Dorrego (San Telmo)** with food, dancers, buskers, Saturday and Sunday 0900-1300, on Humberto 1° and Defensa (only "antiques"). Also Feria de Las Artes (Fri., 1400-1700) on Defensa and Alsina. Saturday craft, jewellery, etc. market, 1000-1800, at Av. Santa Fe, Plaza Italia (Subte D). At Parque Rivadavia, Rivadavia 4900, around the *ombú* tree, stamps and coins, Sun. 0900-1300, Plazoleta Primera Junta, Rivadavia and Centenera, books and magazines, Sat. 1200-2000, Sun. 1000-2000. Plazoleta Santa Fe, Santa Fe and Uriarte (Palermo) old books and magazines, same times as Primera Junta, and again, plastic arts in the Caminito (Boca) section. Auction sales: some bargains at weekday p.m. auctions, Edificio de Ventas, Banco de la Ciudad de Buenos Aires, Esmeralda 660. Souvenirs can be found in area around San Martín and Paraguay (not markets). Once market is "cheap and cheerful, with many bargains."

Shopping Visit the branches of H. Stern, for fine jewellery at the Sheraton and Plaza Hotels, and at the International Airport. Kelly's, Paraguay 431, has a very large selection of Argentine handicrafts in wool, leather, wood, etc. Excellent leatherwork at LYK, Paraguay y Maipú. Artesanías Argentinas, at Montevideo 1360 and Córdoba 770, a non-profitmaking organization selling handicrafts (clothing, weaving, basketware, wooden goods etc.) all with certificate of origin; also Matra, Defensa 372, and the handicrafts centre at Defensa 788, 1st floor. Apart from shops on Florida and Santa Fe (especially between 1000 and 2000), Av. Corrientes has many shops for men's clothes between 600 and 1000 blocks, and the shops on Arenales N of Av. Santa Fe, and on Av. Alvear on the way to Recoleta, have been recommended. Av. Cabildo in Belgrano district can be reached by 152 bus from Retiro for good shopping between 1600 and 2800 blocks. Many boutiques and places for casual clothes in Martínez suburb. The Mercado de Abasto, originally built in 1893, at Avs. Corrientes, Anchorena, Lavalle and Agüero, has been reopened as a commercial, cultural and entertainment centre. There is a new shopping mall, Bullrich Patio, on Av. Libertador y Carlos Pellegrini.

Bookshops Acme Agency, Suipacha 245; ABC, Av. Córdoba 685 (good selection of second-hand and new English books) and Av. Libertador 13777 in Martínez suburb. Librería Rodríguez, Sarmiento 835, good selection of English books and magazines; French bookshop at Calle Rivadavia 743; Librería Goethe, Corrientes 366 and Librería Henschel, Reconquista 533, both have good selection of secondhand German books. Italian books at Librería Leonardo, Av. Córdoba 335, also (with newspapers and magazines) La Viscontea, Libertad 1067. Secondhand/exchange inside shopping arcade under Av. 9 de Julio at the Obelisco—good stock and prices. Good bookshop at Florida 340, El Ateneo, and Atlántida. Kel Ediciones, Talcahuano 1063, and Laprida 2488 in Florida suburb, also maintain a good stock of English books. Prices at Harrods on Florida are lower than most. Second-hand English language books from British and American Benevolent Society (BABS); look in *Buenos Aires Herald* for address, which changes often.

Libraries   Harrods (2nd floor), on Florida, US$6 a month; Cultura Inglesa, Suipacha 1333 (for members only). See also **Addresses** below. Foreign newspapers at newsstands along Florida.

Laundry   Tintorería Japonesa, in centre at 25 de Mayo 689, good. Tintorería Constitución, Av. Santiago del Estero 1572. Laundry at Esmeralda 1077 takes 2 hrs. Many dry cleaners, efficient and friendly. Several launderettes, e.g. Marcelo T. de Alvear 2018, in centre, US$1.50 wash and dry; Junín 15 with Rivadavia, Mon.-Sat. 0800-2100; Junín 529 with Lavalle; Lavarap, US$0.50 wash, same for drying, Paraguay 888 with Suipacha San Martín with Córdoba, Arenales 894, and many other sites; Marva, Juan D. Perón (Cangallo) 2000 with Ayacucho. Typical charge: US$2 for 6 kg. wash.

Camera Repairs and Film Developing   Film developing to international standards, Photo Farben, Alvarez Thomas 871 (films delivered by 1100 developed by 1600); Profesional Color, Perú 913, 24 hrs., good, expensive, slides 45-min. development process, colour photos 24 hrs., good, cheap. Kodak, Paraná 515, good and cheap developing. Fotospeed, Av. Santa Fe 4838 (20% discount to SAHB owners!) for quality 2-hour service. Camera repairs: Casa Schwarz, Perú 989, international brands; Golden Lab, Lavalle 630, good prices for film; Horacio Calvo, Río bamba 183, all brands and variety of rare accessories.

Taxis   are painted yellow and black, and carry *Taxi* flags. About US$1 per km.; meters show the number of "points" (zones) crossed, *not* the fare in australes, which is shown on a chart held by the driver. A charge is made for each piece of hand baggage. Tips not necessary. Beware of overcharging especially late at night. Check the notes you offer the driver; they have been known to switch a low-value note for your high one and demand the balance. Fares double for journey outside city limit (Av. General Paz).

Car Hire   Cars for hire, expensive, can be got through hotel reception clerks. Use of Avis Car Credit card with central billing in one's home country is possible. Traffic drives on the right. Driving in Buenos Aires is no problem, provided you have eyes in the back of your head and good nerves. Avis agency in the *Sheraton Hotel* (vehicles reported not well serviced); A1 International, M.T. de Alvear 680, T 32-9475/76, 31-0247, Renault 12 US$300 a week + US$24 insurance, unlimited mileage, both have branches in all main cities. Hertz in Buenos Aires and Bariloche. If you want to travel to another country you need a special authorization from the car hire company.

Local Bus   services (*colectivos*) cover a very wide radius, and are clean, frequent, efficient and very fast. The basic fare is about US$0.20. **NB.** The number of the bus is not sufficient indication of destination, as each number has a variety of routes. Look for the little plaques displayed in the driver's window. A guide to all routes is available at newsstands.

Tram   A green and white old-fashioned street car operates on Sat. 1500-2000 and Sun. 1000-1200, 1500-2000 (not Easter Sun.), free, from Emilio Mitre and Directorio (Emilio Mitre Subte), and from near Primera Junta Subte. Operated by Asociación de los Amigos del Tranvía.

Underground Railways ("Subte")   Five lines link the outer parts of the City to the centre. "A" line runs under Calle Rivadavia, from Plaza de Mayo up to Primera Junta. "B" line from central Post Office, Avenida L. N. Alem, under Av. Corrientes to Federico Lacroze railway station. "C" line links Plaza Constitución with the Retiro railway station, and provides connections with all the other lines. "D" line runs from Plaza de Mayo, under the Diagonal Norte, Córdoba and Santa Fe to Palermo. "E" line runs from Plaza de Mayo through San Juan to Avs. Directorio and José María Moreno. The fare is about US$0.10, the same for any direct trip or combination between lines; tokens must be bought at booking offices (*boleterías*); buy a few in advance to save time. System operates 0530-0130. Some stations on lines C and D have some very fine tile-work. Backpacks and luggage allowed. Beware bag- and jewellery-snatchers and pickpockets. The tourist office gives out a map, which can also be bought on station platforms with a booklet giving bus schedules.

Sports   Association and rugby football are both played to a very high standard. Entry to the River Plate Stadium (bus 130) for match, US$3 (enclosure); matches Sun. 1600, Wed. evenings. Ice-hockey is becoming popular. Cricket is not unknown. Polo is played from Oct. to Dec.; a visit to the national finals at Palermo in Nov. is recommended. The Tigre Boat Club, founded in 1888, is open to British or American visitors for a small fee and a limited period. The leading golf clubs are the Hurlingham, Ranelagh, Ituzaingó, Lomas, San Andrés, San Isidro, Sáenz Peña, Olivos, Jockey, Campos Argentinos and Hindú Country Club; visitors wishing to play should bring handicap certificate and make telephone booking. Weekend play possible only with a member. Good hotels may be able to make special arrangements. Tennis and squash are popular: there are 5 squash clubs.

Gambling   Weekly lotteries. Football pools, known as *Prode*.

Chess   Club Argentino de Ajedrez, Paraguay 1858, open daily, arrive after 2000; special tournament every Sat., 1800. High standards.

Exchange   Only official exchange rates available from banks, most of which charge very high commission. Lloyds Bank (BLSA) Ltd, corner of Reconquista and Bartolomé Mitre. It has 12 other branches in the city, and 10 others in Greater Buenos Aires. Royal Bank of Canada, corner of Florida and J. D. Perón (Cangallo); branch at Av. Callao 291. Citibank, B. Mitre 502; branch at Florida 746. First National Bank of Boston, Florida 99. Bank of America, J. D. Perón (Cangallo) and San Martín changes Bank of America traveller's cheques a.m. only, into US$ at very high commission; branch at Paraguay 901 doesn't take American Express or Thomas Cook cheques. Banco Holandés Unido, Florida 359. Deutsche Bank, Bmé. Mitre and Reconquista. Open 1000-1600 (exchange operations up to 1300 only), Mon.-Fri. Banco de la Provincia de Buenos Aires, San Martín, close to Plaza de Mayo, both advance cash on Visa Card.

There are many exchange shops, and increasing numbers deal in travellers' cheques; most are concentrated around San Martín and Corrientes; open from 0900 to 1630, Mon.-Fri. and on Sats., 0900-1200, in rotation. City Service Travel, Florida 890, 4th floor (T 312-8416), is the American Express Agency (for mail), but if you want emergency cash or travellers' cheques from a personal cheque backed by your Amex card, go to Banco de Galicia, J.D. Perón 407, 4th floor, 1000-1500; American Express main office: corner of Av. Libertador and Carlos Pelligrini, Mon.-Fri. 0900-1800, T 312-1661. Impossible to get money on American Express card at the Amex office, but try office at *Hotel Plaza*, Mon.-Fri. 0800-2000, Sat. Exchange shops offer the parallel rate for cash, but prefer not to deal in travellers' cheques. Some exchange shops, *e.g.* Forexcambio, M.T. de Alvear 566, or Exprinter, San Martín 176, will change US$ Amex cheques into US$ cash at 1% commission, Banco Velox for 1½ % and several will do it for 2 % or 3 % . If all *cambios* closed, try Olympia leather shop on Tucumán between Florida and San Martín. There is no service charge on notes, only on cheques. Many exchange shops ask for receipt of purchase of cheques, and practices vary all the time. Major credit cards widely accepted.

Warning Street crime is on the increase. Be particularly careful of bagsnatching gangs in parks and in the Subte: they are not violent, but particularly skilful. Also changing money on the street is fraught with difficulties: stick to the *cambios*.

Clubs The American, English and German Clubs (addresses below) take temporary members and have reciprocal arrangements with many clubs in USA and UK.

Addresses
Argentine Association of English Culture, Suipacha 1333.
American Club, Viamonte 1133, facing Colón Theatre.
American Women's Club, Av. Córdoba 632, 11° piso.
Australian Embassy, Av. Santa Fe 846 (Swissair Building). T 312-6841.
Austrian Embassy, French 3671. T 802-7095/6.
Bolivian Consulate, Belgrano 1670, 2nd floor, open 0900-1400.
Brazilian Consulate, Pellegrini 1363, 5th floor, open Mon.-Fri., 1000-1800. (Easier to get a Brazilian visa from this consulate than in Montevideo; 2-day wait at latter.) T 394-5620.
British Chamber of Commerce, Av. Corrientes 457.
British Community Council, 25 de Mayo 444.
British Interests Section of Swiss Embassy, Luis Agote 2412/52 (near corner Pueyrredón & Guido), Casilla de Correos 2050. T 803-7071, open 0915-1215, 1415-1615.
British Hospital, Perdriel 74. T 23-1081, US$6 a visit. Cheap dental treatment at Av. Caseros y Perdriel 76.
Comisión Nacional de Museos y Monumentos y Lugares Históricos, Av. de Mayo 556; professional archaeology institute.
English Club, 25 de Mayo 581. T 311-9121. Temporary membership available to British business visitors.
French Embassy, Av. Santa Fe 846, 5° piso.
West German Embassy, Villanueva 1055, Belgrano. T 771-5054/9.
German Hospital, Pueyrredón 1658, between C. Berruti and C. Juncal. T 821-4083.
Goethe Institut, Av. Corrientes 311, near Goethe bookshop, German library (open 1300-1800 exc. Wed.) and newspapers, free German films shown. Nearby is the German Club, Corrientes 327.
Irish Embassy, Av. Santa Fe 782, 7th floor, 1059 Buenos Aires. T 44-9987 No visa needed.
Italian Embassy, Billinghurst 2577, consulate at M.T. de Alvear 1149.
Netherlands Embassy, Maipú 66, 1084 Buenos Aires. T 33-6066.
Paraguayan Consulate, Maipú 464, 3rd floor, 0900-1300. T 392-6535.
Peruvian Consulate, Av. Corrientes 330, 2nd floor, open 0900-1300. Tel.:311-3374.
Uruguayan Consulate, Ayacucho 1616, open 1000-1800. Tel.:821-6031.
Salvation Army, Rivadavia 3255.
St. Andrew's Society, Perú 352.
South African Embassy, Marcelo T. de Alvear 590,8° piso. T 311-8991.
Spanish Embassy, Mariscal Ramón Castilla 2720, esq. Av. del Libertador 2075.
Swedish Embassy, Corrientes 310, 3° piso, T 311-3088.
Swedish Club, Tacuari 147.
Swiss Embassy, Av. Santa Fe 846, 12° piso. T 311-6491. Open 0900-1200. (See also British Interests Section above).
USA Chamber of Commerce, Diagonal Norte 567.

US Embassy and Consulate General, Colombia 4300, Palermo. T 774-7611.
US Embassy Residence, Av. Libertador 3502.
US Information Library (Biblioteca Lincoln), Florida 935. Reference library, free, take passport (closed Wed., Sat., Sun.).
Youth Hostel Association—information for all South America; Talcahuano 214, 2° "6" piso T 45-1001 (post code: 1013 Buenos Aires). Buenos Aires hostel at Brasil 675. **N.B.** A YHA card in Argentina costs US$12. Secretariat open Mon.-Fri. 1300-2000. (There are very few hostels near road S from Buenos Aires on Route 3.)
YMCA (Central), Reconquista 439.
YWCA, Tucumán 844.
Municipality, Av. de Mayo 525, facing Plaza de Mayo.
Central Police Station, Moreno 1550. T 38-8041. (Emergency, T 101).
Migraciones (Immigration), Antártida Argentina 1365.

Urgent Medical Service (day and night) (Casualty ward: *Sala de guardia*). T 34-4001/4. The British and German hospitals (see above list) maintain first-aid centres (*centros asistenciales*) as do the other main hospitals. If affected by pollen, asthma sufferers can receive excellent free treatment at the University Hospital de Clínicas José San Martín, Córdoba 2351.

Inoculations Centro Médico Rivadavia, S. de Bustamante 2531, Mon.-Fri., 0730-1900, or Sanidad de Puerto, Mon. and Thurs., 0800-1200, at Av. Ing. Huergo 690, free, bus 20 from Retiro, no appointment required (typhus, cholera, Mon./Thurs. 0800-1200; yellow fever, Thurs. 1400-1600). Hospital Rivadavia, Calles Las Heras y Tagle, for polio inoculation. Free. Centro de Inmunización reported not to give vaccinations any more.

General Post Office (Correo Central), corner of Sarmiento and L.N. Alem. Poste Restante (US$0.30 per letter). State Railways Building, Av. Maipú 4, in the Puerto Nuevo district; open 0800-2000 except on Sundays and national holidays. Centro Postal Internacional, for parcels over 1 kg., at Av. Antártida Argentina, near Retiro station, open 1100 to 1700. KLM (Florida 989) has a special air mail service.

Cables and Telephones Entel on Av. Corrientes, near corner of Calle Maipú, public telex in basement; alternatively in Central Post Office, Leandro N. Alem 300, also telex. Another office at San Martín 322. There are Entel offices for international calls and cables in Retiro and Once stations, open 7 days, 0700-2400. Entel also on Agüero/Las Heras. Calls are cheaper after 1800. *Fichas* (tokens) for calls in the city cost US$0.10, obtained at newspaper stalls and Entel offices.

Language Schools which teach English to Argentines are: International House, Larrea 1333, and the Victoria School of English, Uruguay 782, both British-owned and -run. Masters, Av. de Mayo 791; Berlitz, Av. de Mayo 847 (low rates of pay); Central Consultaret de Personal, Lavalle 1290 (office at 1103); Pullmen, Santiago del Estero 324. Before being allowed to teach, you must have a work permit; if unsure of your papers, ask at Migraciones (address above). Spanish classes at Inlingua, Av. Corrientes y Callao, at Victoria School (see above) and at Interact, Ramón Freire 1047, T 562-8776.

Tourist Information National office at Santa Fe 883 with masses of maps and literature, and said to change money. Open 1000-1700, Mon.-Fri.; T 312-5611, 312-5621. Has addresses of campsites throughout Argentina, and laundromats in Buenos Aires. There are also branches at either end of Calle Florida (Mon.-Fri., 0900-2000, Sat., 0900-1900), less useful, and an office on 1st floor of Retiro bus station, with free city maps. There are also helpful *Casas de Turismo* for most provinces (open Mon.-Fri. usually, 1200-1900, depending on office, check); on Callao are Buenos Aires (no. 237), Córdoba (332), Chaco (322), La Rioja (755), Mendoza (445). Río Negro, Tucumán 1920; Chubut, Paraguay 876; Entre Ríos, Carlos Pellegrini 547; Formosa, H. Irigoyen 1429; Jujuy, Santa Fe 967; Misiones, Santa Fe 983; Neuquén, J. D. Perón (Cangallo) 687; Salta, Diagonal Norte (Roque Sáenz Peña) 91-3; Santa Cruz, Córdoba 1345, 14th floor, Catamarca, Córdoba 2080; Corrientes, San Martín 333; La Pampa, Suipacha 346; San Juan, Maipú 331; Santa Fe, 25 de Mayo 358; Santiago del Estero, Florida 274; Tucumán, Mitre 836; Tierra del Fuego, Sarmiento 745, 8th floor; Ushuaia and Lago Argentino, Av. Santa Fe 790. Bariloche hotel, flat and bungalow service at Florida 520, enter *Galería* and walk up to room 116. Calafate bookings for *Motel La Loma* and *Refugio and Autocamping Lago Viedma*, excursions with Transporte Ruta 3 and lake excursions with Empresa Paraíso de Navegación booked from Turismo Argos, Maipú 812, 13th floor C, T 392-5460. Municipalidad de Buenos Aires, Sarmiento 1551, 4th floor, has an excellent free booklet about the city centre and maps. Further offices at Aeroparque (Aerolíneas Argentinas), Mon.-Fri., 0830-2000 and Sat. 0900-1900, and Ezeiza Airport, Mon.-Fri. 0830-2200; also Florida with Diagonal Norte and Florida with Córdoba, open at 0830-1930 Mon.-Fri. and 0900-1900 Sat. On Fri., the youth section of *Clarín*—Sí - lists free entertainments. *Where*, a tourist guide in English, published monthly, is available free in hotels, travel agencies, tourist kiosks on Florida, and in some newsstands at US$2.50. The *Buenos Aires Times* is a bilingual monthly newspaper covering tourist topics. A good guide is *Guía Peuser*, US$3, available from newsstands. Country-wide maps at Instituto Geográfico Militar, Cabildo 381, reached by 152 bus from Retiro station, open 0800-1300 Mon.-Fri. Federico B. Kirbus has written *Guía de Turismo y*

Aventuras, de la Argentina desconocida, arqueológica y misteriosa, obtainable at El Ateneo, or from the author at Casilla de Correo 5210, RA-1000. Bs. Aires. The Fundación Vida Silvestre (conservation organization and bookshop), Defensa 245/251, has information and books on Argentine flora and fauna. Field guide to Argentine birds: *Las aves argentinas*, by Claes Chr. Olrog, US$35, poor drawings but good range maps.

Tourist Agents Exprinter, Santa Fe, and San Martín 176, Galería Güemes; American Express, Av. Libertador 448; Thos. Cook & Son, Av. Córdoba 746; Fairways, Viamonte 640, 3° piso (392-1716). City Service Travel Agency, Florida 890, 4th floor (32-8416), with British staff to advise people travelling to the UK; Sol-Jet, Cerrito 1328, warmly rec.; ATI, Esmeralda 516, very efficient and helpful, with branches in Brazil; Astra Travel, Tucumán 358, 5th floor, English spoken by director, efficient; Agencia Marítima Mundial, Av. Córdoba 653, helpful and efficient. Turismo Flyer, Reconquista 621, 8° piso, T 312-9164/313-8165, English, Dutch and German spoken, accepts credit cards, rec. Schenker Argentina, Lavalle 530, German (T 394-2074). Diners Travel, Avenida Sarmiento, takes Diners card, unlike most other travel agents. Germania, Lavalle 414, excellent service, (English not spoken) esp. for tours to the N, branch in Salta (T 393-1265/0035). Patagonia Turística, specialists on that region, Florida 755 (T 311-9216). English is widely spoken.

Tours A good way of seeing Buenos Aires and its surroundings is by Autobuses Sudamericanos, Pasaje Rubens 4876, T 311-0056 (with an information and booking office at Bernardo Irigoyen 1370, 1st floor, Offices 25 and 26, T 27-6591 or 631-1108). For reservations in advance for sightseeing or other tours, with a 20% courtesy discount to *South American Handbook* readers, write to Casilla de Correo No. 29, Sucursal 34, 1434 Buenos Aires. A 3-hour tour of Buenos Aires in English and Spanish is run by City Tours, Lavalle 1444 (T 40-2304/90), US$9, rec., as is Eurotur (T 312-6170), US$6.50, in English. Some tours (e.g. Buenos Aires Tur, Carlos Pellegrini 509) include dinner and a tango show, or a gaucho *fiesta* at a ranch.

Motoring Associations See page 166 for details of service. Parking, safely, at El Balneario within the old port, but ask the military post for permission first.

Passenger Boats The *Buenos Aires Herald* (English-language daily) notes all shipping movements. Flota Fluvial del Estado (Corrientes 489, T 311-0728) organizes cruises from Buenos Aires, Dársena Sud; up the Paraná river. South coast, down to Punta Arenas and intermediate Patagonian ports, served by the Imp. & Exp. de la Patagonia and Elma (state shipping line). Very irregular sailings. For connections with Uruguay, **see page 60**.

To Antarctica with the Jefatura de Servicio de Transportes Navales in February, one sailing a year, for 30 days on Transporte ARA, *Bahía Buen Suceso*, stopping 2-5 days at each port of call, including Puerto Belgrano, Antarctica (6 days), Ushuaia, Puerto Madryn, including side trips. 2-4 berth cabins US$1,350-1,950, includes meals. Information from: Jefatura del Servicio de Transportes Navales, Reconquista 385, 7° piso, T 45-0034 and 45-1116, 0900-1200 and 1300-1700.

Airports Ezeiza, 35 km. from the centre by a good divided lane highway, which links with the General Paz circular highway round the city. The airport is up-to-date, has a duty free shop, exchange facilities (beware short-changing), but its hotel, the *Internacional*, is closed for renovation. Airport information, T 620-0217. Airport tax US$13. Ezeiza is used by international services but Jorge Newbery airport (normally known as Aeroparque), on the N side river front at the end of the New Port, 4 km. from the centre, is used for internal services (airport tax US$1.50) and also flights to Punta del Este, Montevideo and Aerolíneas flights to Asunción, Santiago and Santa Cruz (Bolivia). (Airport tax US$3.) If stuck for cash because banks are closed you can try the Newbery airport exchange facilities (bills only), run by Banco de la Nación (close at 2100).

Buses from the Manuel Tienda León counter, in the airport, only, T 89-0661/6 to and from Ezeiza airport operate at a fixed price (US$4.50), to the centre (leave from near *Hotel Colón*, at Carlos Pellegrini 509, more-or-less hourly, every day). There is now also a reliable standard taxi service operating from Ezeiza, US$18. Do not take an unmarked car, however attractive the fare may sound; the drivers are adept at separating you from far more money than you can possibly owe them for the journey. When landing at Ezeiza, buy tickets for city centre at the kiosk in the terminal building, before boarding the bus. No. 86 bus can also be caught at corner of Perú and Av. de Mayo (500—starts at Irala 800 block in the Boca), US$0.50, but no good if you have much luggage, and takes 1½ hrs. for the journey. Make sure bus has sign "Aeropuerto" in the front window; many 86's stop short of the airport. Two or three stops in the Ezeiza airport area, *servicio diferencial* an shuttle bus comfort, every 20-30 mins. from Av. Colón y Estados Unidos, US$1. Other routes to the airport: train to Liniers, then bus 86, or train from Constitución to Ezeiza, then bus 138.

Journeys to and from Jorge Newbery (Aeroparque) by *remise* taxi, e.g. US$6.50 to Retiro, US$20 to Ezeiza. Taxis are charged according to meter (about US$3 from the centre, but up to US$5 to the centre), or you can catch the local No. 33 or 56 bus (US$0.25) from outside the airport to the Retiro railway station. You can also use your Pase Americano from De la Torre station (just past the race track) after having walked across the Palermo park or having taken a US$0.35 bus-ride to the station. Take train from there to Retiro. Manuel Tienda León operates buses between Ezeiza and Jorge Newbery airports, stopping in city centre, US$5.

Aerolíneas Argentinas and Austral offer daily flights to the main cities, for details see text under intended destination; **see also page 165** for the Visit Argentina fare. If travelling in the south, book ahead if possible with LADE, whose flights are cheaper than buses in most cases.

Local Airline Offices Aerolíneas Argentinas, Calle Perú 2, with a branch office at Santa Fe and Esmeralda; reservations and enquiries, T 393-5122. Austral Líneas Aéreas, Flórida 429, T 774-1076. Líneas Aéreas del Estado (LADE), Calle Perú 710, T 361-7071. Aerolínea Federal Argentina (ex Alfa), Perú 2, 30-8551.

Railways Terminals (good snacks available at Retiro and Constitución at all hours).
Retiro: Ferrocarril Nacional Mitre (Central)—312-6596; Ferrocarril Nacional San Martín (Pacific)—311-8054; Ferrocarril Nacional Belgrano (North-Western)—311-5287/8/9.
Constitución: Ferrocarril Nacional Roca (Southern)—23-0021.
Once: Ferrocarril Nacional Sarmiento (Western)—87-0041/2/3.
F. Lacroze: Ferrocarril Nacional Urquiza (North-Eastern)—55-5214.

Principal Trains (The following table is designed merely as an indication; further enquiries will be needed, and details will be found under the provincial cities listed. Prices approximate only.

Destination	Departure Station	Trains per Week	Journey Time (hrs.)	Tourist	First	Fares (US$) Pullman	Sleeper
Bahía Blanca	Constitución	17	10-12	11.00	15.40	25.45	33.60
Bariloche	Constitución	3	34	25.00	41.00	63.00	70.00
Concordia*	F. Lacroze	15	8½	8.75	12.50	19.15	29.45
Córdoba*	Retiro	9	12	14.55	24.50	33.25	43.15
Mendoza*	Retiro	13	13-16	21.70	24.75	38.00	46.65
Paraná	F. Lacroze	6	10½-12	10.85	15.00	—	33.00
Paso de los Libres*	F. Lacroze	7	12	12.70	18.15	27.75	37.30
Posadas*	F. Lacroze	8	20	18.35	26.20	40.00	48.85
Rosario	Retiro	64	4	6.20	8.10	12.60	—
San Antonio Oeste	Constitución	4	19-22	18.35	26.00	40.00	48.35
Santa Fe	Retiro	32	7-10	9.45	11.90	—	—
Tucumán*	Retiro	11	18½-25	21.00	30.00	45.50	63.35
Zapala	Constitución	7	26	22.65	32.50	49.60	57.90

* Some trains have car-transporters

NB The railways maintain an information centre and booking office beside the Galerías Pacífico, Florida 729 (311-6411/14), open 0700-2100 Mon.-Sat., Sun. 0700-1300. There is a good left-luggage facility at Retiro station. Book tickets well in advance wherever possible (especially in July and December), also for connecting services, especially those going south of Buenos Aires. Outward journeys may be booked 45 days in advance, return journeys 60 days, but not later than 7 days in advance. Telephone reservations for named trains: 312-5680, 312-5686/9, 312-3686/9, 311-6325/9, 312-8610 and 312-8616/9. Pullman services are usually air conditioned but a/c often does not work, resulting sometimes in very hot journeys as carriage windows do not open. Tourist fares are about 30% cheaper than buses, but much slower and less reliable, and there is no guarantee of being able to stretch out to sleep. Buffet cars usually offer coffee and drinks; sandwiches and refreshments are usually touted down the train during journeys.

Buses The long-distance bus station, Estación Terminal de Omnibus, is behind Retiro, on Av. Ramos Mejía and Antártida Argentina (Subte C) T for information 311-6073/6088. All long distance buses leave from here. Some bus companies charge extra for luggage. **Fares charged by the country-wide Chevallier company are:** Bariloche, US$62; Córdoba, US$17; Mar del Plata, US$9.50; Mendoza, US$39; Rosario, US$8.10; San Martín de los Andes, US$30; and Tucumán, US$20. Fares may vary according to time of year and advance booking is advisable Dec.-March. Some companies may give discounts, such as 20% to YHA or student-card holders. For further details of bus services, look under proposed destinations. No exchange shop at bus station: only bank, giving official rate. Tourist office open from 1000, makes hotel reservations.

Hitch-hiking Heading S, take bus 96 to Ruta 3 for Comodoro Rivadavia, etc., US$0.35. Best to hitch from a service station.

Travel into Neighbouring Countries

By Road
Four branches of the Inter-American Highway run from Buenos Aires to the borders of Chile, Bolivia, Paraguay and Brazil. The roads are paved except when otherwise stated.

To Chile via Río Cuarto, Mercedes, San Luis, and Mendoza: Total: 1,310 km. paved throughout. (Three direct buses a week to Santiago, US$40, 23 hrs. e.g. TAC or Chevallier, 1,459 km; same price to Valparaíso or Viña del Mar.) Car-transporter train to Mendoza on Fridays. There are also road connections between Bariloche and Osorno and Puerto Montt, and between Salta and Antofagasta.

To Bolivia via Rosario, Villa María, Córdoba, Santiago del Estero, Tucumán, and Jujuy. Total: 1,994 km. There is no direct bus service from Buenos Aires to La Paz but through connections can be booked, about US$80. Also a train/ bus combination, train to Tucumán and then bus to Jujuy, but no sleepers. Try travel agent in Bernardo de Yrigoyen 957 shopping arcade. Car-transporter train to Tucumán, Mon., Tue., Wed. and Fri.

To Paraguay via Rosario (as for Bolivia), Santa Fe, Resistencia, Clorinda and Asunción (via new toll bridge). Total: 1,370 km (all paved). Buses take 20-22 hours, with N.S. de la Asunción, Juan D. Perón (ex-Cangallo) 2760; or Chevallier, Empresa Godoy, La Internacional or Expreso Brújula (all next to each other at the Retiro bus terminal). You have choice between *diferencial* (with food, drinks, about US$42) and *común* (without food, about US$32.50) services. Tickets can be bought up to 30 days in advance.

Those who wish to drive to Misiones to visit San Ignacio Miní or the Iguazú Falls can cross the river by the bridge between Santa Fe and Paraná, or the one between Resistencia and Corrientes. From there Route 12 leads NE through Posadas to the Iguazú Falls. The direct road from Buenos Aires to Posadas via the Zárate-Brazo Largo bridges is fully paved. From Corrientes to Esperanza is paved, and from Posadas to Iguazú. (Singer and Tigre-Iguazú buses to Puerto Iguazú leave daily at 1130 and 1500 respectively, US$28.75, 22 hrs.) From Posadas you can cross the river to Encarnación by the ferry (bridge under construction) and take a good 370-km. road to Asunción (see Paraguayan chapter). Car-transporter train to Posadas, Tues. and Fri.

To Brazil To the Iguazú Falls, go by the bridge from Puerto Iguazú, reached via Posadas. Another road to the border with Brazil, at Paso de los Libres, goes to Rosario, Santa Fe, cross by bridge and tunnel to Paraná; Villa Federal, Curuzú Cuatiá, Paso de los Libres, opposite Uruguaiana (Brazil), across the Río Uruguay. Total: 960 km. Direct buses to Brazil via Paso de los Libres by Pluma: São Paulo, 40 hrs. US$63.25, Curitiba, US$51.75, 38 hrs; Florianópolis, US$46, 32 hrs; daily at 1000 to Porto Alegre, US$40.25, 26 hrs. (The route across the River Plate and through Uruguay is a bit cheaper, not as long and offers a variety of transport and journey breaks; see also Uruguay under next section). Tickets from Onda, Florida 502 y Lavalle (392-5011), for any information also to combine travel via Uruguay. Buen Viaje, Av. Córdoba 415 (31-2953) or Pluma, Av. Córdoba 461 (311-4871 or 311-5986) or office branches in Rosario, Santa Fe and Paraná. Journey to Rio takes about 50 hrs, US$60; at least one bus per day. Car-transporter train to Paso de los Libres, Tues. and Fri.

To Uruguay Direct road connections by means of two bridges over the River Uruguay between Puerto Colón and Paysandú and between Puerto Unzué and Fray Bentos. "*Bus de la carrera*" links Montevideo and Buenos Aires (8½ hrs.) Departure from each city at 1000, 2200 and 2300 via Zárate-Gualeguaychú-Puerto Unzué-Fray Bentos-Mercedes, US$14.75. Book at Onda.

Air, River and Railway Services

Brazil Daily air services to São Paulo, Rio de Janeiro and other Brazilian cities. Shipping service between Buenos Aires and Brazilian ports by various transatlantic lines. See *Buenos Aires Herald*, English-language daily.

Chile Information about travel to Chile is available from Av. Córdoba 879. The passenger-train service across the Andes between Mendoza and Santiago has been discontinued, but bus services are available. The train service to Antofagasta via Salta and Socompa has also been suspended, but there are buses between Salta and Antofagasta.

Foreign and national lines fly daily between Buenos Aires and Santiago, US$135. Time taken: 1½ to 2 hours. There are 2 flights weekly by Aerolíneas Argentinas to Punta Arenas on the S coast of Chile, via Comodoro Rivadavia, Río Gallegos and Río Grande. Aerolíneas Argentinas also flies to Antofagasta via Salta.

Bolivia It was reported that at end-1988, a deluxe service Buenos Aires-La Paz was in service. Also, the connecting service from Tucumán and Jujuy to La Quiaca has been restored: the *Panamericano* leaves Tucumán on Mon. and Fri. 1500, arriving La Quiaca next day at 0920. On arriving in La Quiaca one must cross on foot to the Bolivian side and purchase a train ticket for the remainder of the journey, Villazón-La Paz. *El Norteño* train has no sleepers, leaves Retiro Tues. and Fri. at 1000, via Tucumán to Jujuy, US$20 1st cl. US$16 *turista*. Bus Panamericano Jujuy to La Quiaca. Villalonga Furlong, Balcarce 473, 2nd floor, open Mon.-Fri. 0900-1700, has information about trains (not Retiro); it is also a freighting company and sells the tickets. See under Tucumán (**page 80**) for other train services. There are no sleepers beyond Tucumán. Sleeper tickets to Tucumán carry no seat entitlement elsewhere in the train. Sanitary facilities poor. Hot soup and local dishes brought round carriages. Bar and restaurant car with same food, adequate. Travel rug recommended on this part of the journey. Train Villazón-La Paz has sleepers, worthwhile but may need paying over the odds to secure. Carriages, old, noisy and crowded; bad sanitary facilities.

Local food available on train. Cold night. Free baggage allowance 30 kg., and excess is charged. A weekly train (no sleepers) to Santa Cruz de la Sierra from Retiro Station via Salta, Güemes, Pocitos and Yacuiba takes 3 days, US$67; leaves Buenos Aires Sun. at 1000, arrives Santa Cruz 1015 Wed. From Santa Cruz, dep. 1000 Thurs., arrival 2100 Sat. at Retiro. **See page 86.**

There are also regular air services 5 or 6 times a week to La Paz by Eastern, Aerolíneas and Lloyd Aéreo Boliviano.

Paraguay The direct train to Asunción was withdrawn in 1984, but trains run daily to Posadas, and twice weekly from Encarnación to Asunción. From Encarnación you can get a connecting train (if it waits) or bus (saving up to 16 hrs.) to Asunción. There is a daily air service to Asunción by various companies. Time taken: 2 to 6 hours. See also Posadas, **page 119.** Occasional river boats to Asunción in winter and spring, 6 days, cabins cost US$300-560 p.p., food and nightly entertainment reported good.

Uruguay Tickets heavily booked Dec.-March. **N.B:** No money changing facilities in Tigre, and poor elsewhere. For boat services, take the train to Tigre (Mitre suburban line), 50 mins. (US$0.25), leaves at 5 min. intervals from Retiro. (No good hotels in Tigre, but try *Astor*, reasonable-looking.) Two daily boats to **Carmelo** at 0800 and 0830, 3½ hrs., tickets at Movilan, Lavalle y Florida, Bs. As. (T 392-5011) or Estación Fluvial, *local* 13 (T 749-4119), Tigre. It is advisable to book in advance; connecting bus to Montevideo (Onda, Florida y Lavalle, book in advance), arriving at 1530 and 1600; Tigre-Montevideo US$7.55.

From Dársena Sud, the following services go to Colonia, where connecting Onda buses go to Montevideo (3 hrs., US$4.45). Night boat (*vapor carrera*) to Montevideo, Ferrytur (bus from their office at Florida and Av. Córdoba at 1920), leaves at 2100, board between 1930 and 2030 only, single fare, shared cabin and breakfast, US$16 for seat, 36 for sleeper for 2; cars charged by weight. Ferry services to Colonia 0730 and 0900, 3 hours, US$13, bus connection to Montevideo 2½ hrs, US$3.75, with Ferrytur, Florida 780, 2nd floor, bus leaves from Florida and Córdoba to ferry. Also Buquebus, Suipacha 776, T 392-0365, 3-5 sailings a day, depending on season, 3½ hrs. to Colonia, total of 6½ to Montevideo. Uruguayan immigration officer on ferry.

Atlantic car ferry, daily, at 0800 arr. Colonia 1100, Montevideo 1430, US$32.65-53.35 p.p. w/o car, US$90 upwards per car; food on the ferry is not good, so take your own. Tickets from Flota Fluvial, Corrientes 375 or Onda.

Puente Fluvial runs hydrofoils (*aliscafos*) to Colonia six times a day (winter) or five times a day (summer), 4½ hrs to Montevideo including Onda bus journey, US$23. All tickets from Onda, Florida 502, T 392-5011; reconfirm seat at Onda in Montevideo, Plaza Cagancha. Beware of overcharging by taxis from the harbour to the centre of Buenos Aires. Buquebus offers services similar to those of Onda, has built a new ferry station at Dársena Sud.

Air service from Jorge Newbery Airport (Aeroparque) to Colonia 15 mins., 3 times daily by Lapa; US$22 one way. Tickets at Onda. Air service to Montevideo: shuttle 10 daily, 0730 to 2200, known as Puente Aéreo and run by AA and Pluna. Book at Jorge Newbery Airport or T 361-5008. Fare US$41; flight takes 35 mins. Punta del Este, daily with AA and Pluna US$66, 40 mins.

Suburbs of Buenos Aires

Avellaneda, a separate municipality of over 650,000 people, is one of the most important industrial centres in the country; the handling of hides, wool and animal produce is concentrated here. It is 5 km. from Plaza Constitución station, on the other side of the Riachuelo river from Boca.

Olivos, on the River Plate coast, 20 minutes by the Bartolomé Mitre Railway, is a favourite residential district. The presidential residence is there, many foreign residents. Population, about 160,000. (A rec. restaurant here is *Grinzing*, Córdoba 2864, European specialities, about US$20 p.p. inc. wines, historical objects in house, garden with swimming pool.) Nearby, at La Lucila, there are many American families.

San Isidro, just beyond Olivos, a resort for golf, yachting, swimming, and athletics, is one of the most attractive suburbs on the coast. There is a magnificent turf racecourse, an attractive central plaza and fine colonial buildings. Pop.: 80,000.

Martínez, nearby is an attractive residential area overloooking the River Plate, with an interesting shopping area. Sailing and windsurfing are well represented and river launches and other craft may be hired.

Quilmes (Bs.As.), with one of the world's largest breweries, an important industrial centre, was given that name because the Quilmes Indians were forcibly moved there in 1665 from the famous Inca site in Tucumán Province (**see page 82**). Population about 150,000. St. George's College, an English boarding school, is here. Bathing is now both dangerous and prohibited; in one day 19 lives were lost. It is served by the Roca Railway and buses.

The naturalist and writer W. H. Hudson (1841-1922) was born at Florencio Varela, near Quilmes, about 32 km. from Buenos Aires. His birthplace is now a national monument.

Tigre, on Tigre Railway from Retiro, US$0.70, on the delta of the Paraná, is about 29 km. (50 minutes) from Buenos Aires. It can also be reached by bus 60, which takes a little longer. Regattas are held in November and March on the River Luján. There are numerous "recreos" and restaurants on the river front, but sleeping accommodation is not good. Inland from Tigre are innumerable canals and rivulets, holiday homes, clubs, a profitable fruit growing centre and an attraction for holiday makers. The fishing is excellent and there is peace on the waterways, apart from motor-boats at week-ends. Regular launch services, each company with its own routes, for all parts of the Delta, including taxi launches— watch prices for these!—leave from wharf opposite railway station. The wharf where these are moored can be quite smelly. Four-hour excursion costs about US$5. Be warned that if you leave just before lunch the launch crew may stop along the way for a 1-1½ hr. lunch break! Catamarans make tours of canals and river channels, lunch included: a pleasant and inexpensive way of spending a lazy Sunday. Population: 40,000. In delta is *El Tropezón,* an old inn on an island (the boat crews know it). Delta **Youth Hostel** at Río Luján y Abra Vieja, Canal de San Fernando (take bus 7 from train station, US$0.15) US$0.90 clean, hot showers; ask at Talcahuano 214, Buenos Aires. Good restaurant near Youth Hostel, around the corner. Direct ferry to Carmelo, Uruguay (**see page 61**) from opposite railway station. (If you miss the boat, Antonio J. Pissini has guest rooms for US$5 a night at Montes de Oca 142, Tigre, or try *Hotel Astor.*)

The Naval Museum is worth a visit. It contains models old and new, navigation instruments, flags and banners, and paintings of naval battles. There are also relics of the 1982 South Atlantic war on display outside. The Reconquista Museum celebrates the reconquest of Buenos Aires from the British in 1806-07.

Excursion to *Martín García* island (Juan Díaz de Solís' landfall in 1516) in the River Plate, 45 km. from Buenos Aires, with La Valette Turismo, through channels in The Delta (approx. 12 hours there and back with day on the island; T 921-2050/2055).

Other Towns in the Pampas

There is one town which belongs to Argentina as a whole rather than to any province or area, though it is actually in the Province of Buenos Aires and only 71 km. W of the capital by Sarmiento railway from Once station (change at Moreno, 2 hours, US$2.30) or by bus from Once station, 1 hr. This is

Luján, a place of pilgrimage for all devout Catholics in Argentina. An image of the Virgin was being taken from church to church in the area in 1630 by ox cart. At a certain spot the cart got stuck, in spite of strenuous efforts by men and oxen to move it. This was taken as a sign that the Virgin willed she should stay there. A chapel was built for the image, and around it grew Luján. The chapel has long since been superseded by an impressive neo-Gothic basilica and the Virgin now stands on the High Altar. May 8 is her day. Each arch of the church is dedicated to an Argentine province, and two of the transepts to Uruguay and Paraguay. Population: 30,000. Very heavy traffic at weekends.

Museo Colonial e Histórico (The Colonial and Historical Museum) is in the old Cabildo building. Exhibits illustrate the historical and political development of the country. One of the most interesting museums. Open daily, except Monday and Tuesday, 1200-1800. No cameras allowed, and nowhere to store them, stroppy caretaker. General Beresford, the leader of an attempt to capture Buenos Aires, was a prisoner here, and so, in later days, were Generals Mitre, Paz, and Belgrano. There are also museums devoted to transport and to religious ex-votos. The River Luján is picturesque at this point, a favourite spot for picnic parties.

Hotels *España, La Paz.* There are numerous **restaurants:** an excellent one is *L'Eau Vive* on the road to Buenos Aires at Constitución 2112; it is run by nuns, pleasant surroundings.

There are dozens of small, prosperous towns scattered throughout the vast area of the pampas. They serve as clearing centres for the cattle and grain and supply the rural population, which is much denser in the Humid Pampa than elsewhere in Argentina. Only the larger towns and resorts are dealt with here.

La Plata, capital of Buenos Aires Province, on the River Plate and only 56 km. SE of Buenos Aires, is reached by Roca railway and by many buses. This modern city, founded in 1882, has a population of about 406,000. Its port is accessible to ships of the largest tonnage. Its major industrial interest is the YPF petroleum refinery; a 72-km. pipeline runs to the South Dock at Buenos Aires. Its Museum of Natural History is one of the best in Argentina and has several unique exhibits (open 1300-1800). A motorway is being built to link La Plata with Buenos Aires, via Riachuelo, Avellaneda, Berazátegui, Gonnet and Tolosa.

Points of Interest The Museum at La Plata, famous for its collection of extinct animals, is open daily except in January and on public holidays (admission US$0.30, but free on Mon.). Its treasures are largely ethnological and include human skulls, mummies, and prehistoric implements. There are zoological, botanical, geological, mineralogical, palaeontological and archaeological sections. Well laid-out Zoological Gardens; fine racecourse and Observatory. The Museum, Zoological Gardens, and Observatory are all in the public park. The city has a Garden of Peace, each country in the world represented by one flower, with a plaque in front of it; on October 12 flags are put up there. The Town Hall and Cathedral are in the Plaza Moreno. Ten minutes in the train takes one to the Islas de Río Santiago and to the Yacht Club, Arsenal, and Naval Academy. Nearby is an interesting children's village with scaled-down public buildings, built under the first Perón administration.

Local Holiday Foundation of the City, November 19.

Hotels *Corregidor*, new, expensive, on plaza; *Roga*, Calle 54 No. 334, E, new, small. *Plaza*, Calle 44 y 3, E with bath; *Roca*, Calle 1 y 42, F with bath.

Restaurant *El Fogón*, rec., main course about US$4.

Tourist Office In the old white theatre on the main plaza.

Buses To Buenos Aires, 1½ hrs. Fare US$0.85, about every quarter hour, Río de la Plata company (from Retiro in Buenos Aires).

On the coast 400 km. S of Buenos Aires, lies Mar del Plata, the most celebrated Argentine seaside resort. The road and rail routes S to it are through Chascomús and Dolores.

Chascomús, 126 km. from Buenos Aires, is on a wide plain on the shores of Lake Chascomús, which covers 3,000 hectares and swells greatly in size during the rains. Its slightly brackish water is an important breeding place for *pejerrey* fish; up to 1,000 kg. have been caught in one day during the winter season, when amateur fishing competitions are held. There is a *gaucho* museum, and also a Regatta Club and bathing beaches and camping grounds at Monte Brown, on the far side of the lake. Chascomús is the birthplace of President Alfonsín.

Hotels *Del Lago; Riviera; Americano; Santa María.*

Camping Sites *Estancia El Carmen* (US$2.10 p.p) and *Casa Amarilla.*

Dolores, 204 km. (3½ hrs. by bus) from Buenos Aires, has a district population of 30,000; it was founded in 1818, destroyed by Indians three years later, and rebuilt. It is a grain and cattle farming centre which is said hardly to have changed in 50 years. The Museo y Parque Libres del Sur, commemorating the revolt of the district against Rosas in the early 19C., is interesting and well displayed.

Hotel *Plaza*, very pleasant.

About 130 km. N of Mar del Plata a new seaside resort, **Villa Gesell**, has sprung up, very popular with young people and families. The town offers dunes, pine forests and sandy beaches, over a dozen pleasant, intimate hotels (*Tejas Rojas, Aloha, Capri*, etc.), and villas to let. Direct bus service to Buenos Aires by Empresas Antón and Río de la Plata.

Youth Hostel *Albergue Camping El Coyote*, Calle 212 y 306, Barrio Norte.

Camping Sites *Del Sol, El Faro, California.* The first is open all year round.

Air Aerolíneas Argentinas flies to Villa Gesell several times daily in summer.

Pinamar, 22 km. N of Villa Gesell, is a rapidly growing resort, with a casino. It is now very much the "in" place, with good water-skiing. Fish, including conger eel (*congrio*) may be bought on the beach from local fishermen.

Hotels *Playa* and *Libertador*. All hotels fully booked throughout Jan.- March. **Youth Hostel**, Nuestras Malvinas y Sarmiento, and *Moby Dick* campsite at Ostende. Many other campsites close to town.

Mar del Plata is 400 km. from the capital. The normal population is 350,000, but during the summer about two million visitors stay there; there are all classes of apartment blocks, boarding houses and lodgings. It is necessary to book in advance between late December and mid- March (when the night-life continues all night). For the rest of the year the town is fairly quiet. The city is famous for its casino: the upper floor is open to the public, for a small admission charge (men must wear jackets and ties). Interesting municipal art museum at Villa Ortiz Basualdo, Av. Colón 1189.

There are fine squares, especially Plaza San Martín, and eight km. of beaches, including fashionable Playa Grande, with its private clubs and the summer estates of wealthy *porteños*; Bristol Beach, where the casino is; and Playa Perla, with moderately priced hotels. At Punta Iglesia there is a large rock carving of Florentino Ameghino, the palaeontologist who collected most of the fossils in the museum at La Plata. The wooded municipally owned Parque Camet is 8 km. to the N. It has polo grounds and playing fields. For those who do not care for surf bathing, there are salt-water pools. Fishing is good all along the coast and *pejerrey, corvina* and *merluza* (hake) abound; it is possible to charter a private launch for shark fishing. Football fans might enjoy seeing San Lorenzo play at their stadium—a very good atmosphere.

The port can be reached by bus, 15 mins. from bus terminal. There are a large fishing fleet, excursion boats, seafood restaurants.

Visits can be paid to the rocky promontory of Cabo Corrientes to watch the breakers; to Punta Mogotes lighthouse (open Thursdays 1330-1700); to the Gruta de Lourdes, and the Bosque Peralta Ramos.

Local Holidays   Feb. 10 (Foundation of City); Nov. 10 (Day of Tradition); Nov. 22 (St. Cecilia). Mar del Plata is known for its hand-finished sweaters.

Hotels   Four-star (category A) are the *Provincial*, 500 rooms, Boulevard Marítimo 2500; the *Dos Reyes*, Av. Colón 129; the *Hermitage*, Blvd. Peralta Ramos 2657, 150 rooms; and the *Sasso*, M. de Hoz 3545. Among the 3-star hotels (category B) are the *Astor*, Entre Ríos 1649; *Benedetti*, Av. Colón 2198, rec.; *Gran Continental*, Córdoba 1929; *Presidente*, Corrientes 1516; and *Gran Dora*, Buenos Aires 1841. 2-star hotels (category C) include the *Flamingo*, Moreno 2155, has seen better days, but comfortable; *Finisterre*, Garay 1786, without breakfast, clean, comfortable (near the bus station). There are scores of good hotels at reasonable rates e.g. *Boedo*, Almirante Brown 1771 (T 24695), E, with bath, hot water, clean, good value, near beaches; *Residencial San Mateo*, Arenales nr Alberdi, E with bath, friendly; *Peley*, on Alberdi near bus station, E, clean, comfortable, open all year, rec.; *Hospedaje Paraná*, Lamadrid 2749, near bus terminal, E, with bath; *Hospedaje Misiones*, nr railway station, at Calle Misiones and Pedro Luro, F, clean; *Niza*, Santiago del Estero 1843, E (F out of season), bath, clean, safe, friendly, restaurant; *Little Hotel*, Lamadrid 2461, near bus station, nice and cheap; *Monterrey*, Lamadrid 2627, F, clean, good; *Don Quijote*, Sarmiento 2478 near bus station, F, quite clean; *Hospedaje Alfa*, Garay 1731, close to bus station, cramped but very friendly. During summer months it is essential to book in advance. In the off-season, bargain everywhere. *Youth Hostel*, Tucumán 2728. Many hotels and restaurants close when the summer is over; worth looking round the bus-station area out of season.

Camping   *Pinar de la Serena* and other sites, reasonable prices. Several on the road S out of town; *Los Horneros* has been rec.

Restaurants   *Taverna Vaska*, 12 de Octubre 3301, very popular seafood. *Sorrento*, Av. H. Yrigoyen 1549, Italian family style, excellent and reasonable. *Hostería del Caballito Blanco*, Av. Rivadavia, excellent, German decor. *Cantina Capri*, Belgrano 2161 (near Casino), not cheap but excellent value; *Los Cercos*, Belgrano, between Entre Ríos and Corrientes, for meat; *La Paella*, Entre Ríos, between Bolívar and Moreno, good; *La Caracola*, Nuevo Complejo Comercial Puerto, seafood, good but dear; *Don Pepito*, opposite casino, big portions, reasonable prices, very popular, rec.; *Raviolandia*, Colón y Heras, good, cheap; *La Tablita*, Av. Rivadavia, excellent *asado*. *Montecatini*, Av. Colón, good and cheap; *Comedor Naturista*, vegetarian, Av. Salta 1571, cheap, highly rec. Also vegetarian: *El Jardín*, Plaza de San Martín, all you can eat for US$1.25, and *La Huerta*, close to pedestrian shopping street in centre. *Los Inmortales*, Corrientes 1662, good, moderately priced. Tea, coffee and spirits in port area at Cristóbal Colón.

Casino   Open December to end-April, 1600-0330; 1600-0400 on Sats. Winter opening, May-December, Mon.-Fri. 1500-0230; weekends 1500-0300. Entrance US$2.

Exchange   Lloyds Bank (BLSA) Ltd, Av. Luro 3201. Open 1000-1600. American Express, Av. Colón 2605. Exchange houses on San Martín and surroundings.

Sociedad de Cultura Inglesa, San Luís 2498.

Post Office   on Santiago del Estero, Pedro Luro.

Tourist Office   opp. Casino, near beach; free maps; also at bus terminal.

Trains (ten each day) leave Buenos Aires from Constitución, 10 minutes from the centre by any bus marked "Constitución". The best trains (a/c) take 5 hours (US$7 tourist, US$10 first, US$15 Pullman), 3 times a day (and others). Book very early for Dec.-March trips. 25% reduction for persons under 20 years of age. In Buenos Aires tickets from Galerías Pacífico, Florida 753.

Buses Bus station at corner of Alberti y Las Heras, convenient. Companies from Retiro terminal in Buenos Aires: El Cóndor, Micromar, Costera Criolla. Chevallier US$9.50, 5½ hrs. Bus to Miramar from Mar del Plata, US$2.80. El Cóndor and Rápido Argentino to La Plata, day and night, US$9. La Estrella goes to San Martín de los Andes, US$26, and Bariloche, US$32.50 (none direct; change at Bahía Blanca or Tres Arroyos). To Bahía Blanca, only Pampa, daily at 0800 and 1300, US$12.25, 9 hrs. For hitch-hiking S, take a colectivo to the monument to El Gaucho.

Air Services Camet airport, 10 km. from town. Many flights daily to and from Buenos Aires with Austral and Aerolíneas Argentinas. *Remise* taxi from airport to town, US$6.

Outside the city the country is undulating. To the N (34 km.) is a lagoon—the Mar Chiquita—joined to the sea by a narrow channel. There is good fishing, yachting, boating and bathing here. Picturesque spots reached from the road to Balcarce are (19 km.) Laguna de los Padres, and Sierra de los Padres and (32 km. beyond) the Laguna La Brava, at the foot of the Balcarce hills.

In these hills, 68 km. by paved road from Mar del Plata, is the town of *Balcarce*, a centre for hill visits to La Brava, above Ruca-Lauquén, and the Cinco Cerros, five hills most strangely shaped. Balcarce is the birthplace of the great racing driver Juan Fangio; it has a racing circuit.

Hotel *Balcarce*, good, D.

Beyond Balcarce a paved road runs 103 km. to Tandil, also reached from Mar del Plata (254 km.) by rail. Tandil is reached by road from Buenos Aires via Azul.

Tandil, at the northern end of the Sierra del Tandil, a ridge of hills which run W from the sea into the pampa for 250 km., is 390 km. by road from Buenos Aires. It is a resort with fine views of *sierra* scenery. The air is splendidly clear and refreshing, and the Holy Week festivities are outstanding. Excursions to the Sierra La Aurora. Population: 70,000.

A balancing stone, the Sentinel Stone, is on top of Cerro Américo Rossi nearby.

Hotels *Plaza*, General Pinto 438, E, very friendly, clean, comfortable and quiet. *Continental; Palace; Roma; Eden; California; Manantial.* Others near railway station.

By Air Lapa flight Buenos Aires-Tandil.

From Mar del Plata, along the rocky sea-front to the SW, there are a road (53 km.) and railway line to Miramar.

Miramar, like Mar del Plata, is a summer bathing resort, but the cliffs backing the beach are higher, the surrounding hills more picturesque, and it is a good deal cheaper to stay at. There is a fine golf course at *Hotel Golf Roca* and a casino. Fourteen km. by road or railway to the S, among dunes and black rocks, is Mar del Sur (*Atlantic Hotel*) with good fishing in a lagoon and bathing on the beach.

Hotels Dozens of hotels and apartments. *Atlántico*, somewhat run down; *Santa Eulalia*, Calle 26 No. 851, D, friendly but run down. *Normandie; Ideal; Putamar; Gran Rex; Royal; Palace; Villa Cruz*, friendly, clean, near the beach, D.

Camping *Escargot, El Fortín, Miramar.* Many sites, reasonably priced. *El Pescador Romano*, good seafood take-away.

Restaurant *El Aguila*, good value; *El Pescador Romano*, good seafood take-away.

Exchange None for travellers' cheques; must go to Mar del Plata. Money changers (cash) in front of Banco de la Provincia.

Railway *Cruz del Sur* daily train, via Mar del Plata, leaves Buenos Aires (Constitución) daily at 2345, arrives Miramar 0550; leaves Miramar 2205, arrives Buenos Aires 0500. Fares are US$16.45 Pullman, US$9.50 first and US$7.30 tourist class. *El Atlántico* train, daily at 1520 from Buenos Aires to Mar del Plata arriving at 2000, connects with a railcar service (*automotor*) to Miramar (US$6.15 extra), arriving 2140.

Bus Buenos Aires-Miramar with Cóndor, five daily, US$8, and Costera Criolla, four a day.

About 110 km. further by road along the coast to the SW is another famous seaside resort:

Necochea, 500 km. from Buenos Aires, is reached by Roca Railway in 10½ hours. It stands next to Mar del Plata in repute. The surroundings are picturesque. Visits can be paid to the Paseo del Puente, Punta Negra, the Cascada (or waterfalls) 16 km. up the Río Quequén Grande, Los Manantiales, and the Laguna de los Padres. Grain is exported from the port. Urban population: 50,000 including large Danish colony: there are a Danish club and consulate. About 100,000 tourists visit during the season, for the 24-km. long beach is one of the best in the country. There is a municipal recreation complex, boasting a large modern casino and various sports facilities; entry charge is nominal. The casino is open in summer. Airport.

Hotels *Royal; Atlántico; San Miguel; Trocadero; Marino; Moderno,* Av. 79, No. 311, D, close to beach, friendly, helpful, bath and breakfast. *Zure Echea,* Av. 79, E with bath, modern, clean, friendly, secure. **Camping** Beach sites reported expensive in summer.

Restaurants *Parrilla La Rueda,* excellent beef, cheap, rec.; *La Vieja Taberna,* Calle 85, reasonable, good chicken and beef dishes; *Caviar,* by fishing wharf, good steak, chicken, seafood. *Mi Cantina,* excellent family restaurant. *Parrilla El Palenque,* Av. 79 y 6; *Pizzería Kapotte,* Av. 79 next beach, both rec.

Railway Train No 117 (Mon.-Wed.-Fri.) leaves Buenos Aires (Constitución) at 1930, arrives Necochea 0645; leaves Necochea at 0025 Sun.-Wed.-Fri. arriving at 1150 at Buenos Aires. Fares are US$11.30 Pullman, US$7.30 first, US$6.00 tourist class.

Bus El Cóndor from Buenos Aires six times a day, Costera Criolla 5 times a day.

About 3½ km. across the mouth of the river from Necochea is

Quequén, with an excellent beach, good bathing, and pleasant scenery. The channel to the port has to be dredged daily.

Hotels *Quequén; Faro; Costa Azul.*

Camping *Monte Pasuvio* and *Doble J* (rec.) sites.

Over 320 km. westwards from Necochea by paved road through the coastal area is the port of Bahía Blanca, which can be reached by rail (900 km.), by air, or by a 688-km. paved road (Route 3) through Las Flores, Azul, Juárez and Tres Arroyos.

Azul, 264 km. from Buenos Aires, is a cattle centre with an attractive plaza. Population: about 45,000. A good stopping place if driving S from Buenos Aires. The river has been dammed to provide a water-sports centre.

Hotels *Gran Hotel Azul,* C, excellent cafetería; *Argentino; Roma; Torino.*

Restaurant *Mitre,* Av. Mitre, *Londres.*

Tres Arroyos, about 195 km. from Bahía Blanca, is a cattle and wheat growing centre of 70,000 people. Many inhabitants are of Dutch origin; there are a Dutch consulate and a primary school named Holanda, supported by funds of the Argentine Dutch. There is also an important Danish colony, with school, club and consulate. A 68-km. paved road runs S to the sea at the pleasant little resort of **Claromecó,** with a beautiful beach of dark sand backed by high dunes.

Hotels at Tres Arroyos *Alfil, Parque,* rec. (restaurant) and *Andrea* are best. *City, París, Plaza* and *Tres Arroyos* (friendly), all modest. **Restaurant** *Di Troppo,* near *Hotel* Parque, good.

Hotels at Claromecó *Claromecó* (only open in summer; restaurant); *Residencial La Perla.*

Camping at Claromecó Good campsite *Dunamar,* hot showers, fire pits and laundering basins, US$1 a day; also ACA campsite.

Bus Buenos Aires-Claromecó with El Cóndor, US$20. Tres Arroyos-Claromecó twice daily off season, extra buses from mid-December in season. Pampa bus to Mar del Plata 0650, 4½ hrs., US$5.50. Modern, efficient bus terminal a few blocks from centre of Tres Arroyos.

Bahía Blanca, population 300,000, the most important centre S of Mar del

Plata, stands at the head of a large bay where the river Naposta runs into it. The region has over a million people. Bahía Blanca consists of the city itself, built back from the river front, and five ports at various distances from the city strung along the N bank of the Naposta: Arroya Pareja and the naval base of Puerto Belgrano at the mouth of the estuary; Puerto Ingeniero White, 23 km. inland, Puerto Galván, 3½ km. beyond, and Cuatreros, 8 km. upstream. Bahía Blanca is also a rail, air and pipeline transport terminal for the rich Río Negro valley.

The city has some fine modern buildings and two parks. In the Parque de Mayo are lakes fed by the River Naposta and interesting statuary. There is a very poor Zoological Garden in Parque Independencia, on the outskirts.

To the E of Bahía Blanca is an enormous stretch of sandy beaches, scarcely developed for visitors (in the afternoon, however, it is usually windy). Pehuén-Có, 70 km. away, is an example of the beaches with camping places, well shaded by pine trees. Signs to it on the main road 24 km. from Bahía Blanca. Another fine beach, with hotels and camping places (*El Americano* and *Monte Mar*), is **Monte Hermoso,** 2 hours by bus at 0830 and 1830, US$2.50 (106 km.) from Bahía Blanca. Return daily at 0900 and 2100. Good cheap meals, several restaurants. (Its hotels are open only Jan.-March: *Isabel, Americano, Ameghino,* E, *América*).

Local Holidays Sept. 24 (Our Lady of Mercy); Nov. 10 (Day of Tradition).

Hotels *Austral*, C, and *Del Sur*, C, with restaurants (not good in the former), noisy with traffic; *City Hotel*, Chiclana 132, D. *Atlántico*, Chiclana 251, E; *Argentino* (restaurant), Chiclana 466, E. Opposite railway station: *Residencial Roma*, D with private bath, cheaper without. Cheap: *Hogar*, Rodríguez 64, F, clean, good, near Plaza; *Tizón*, Chiclana 422, E. *Victoria*, Gral. Paz 82, F, nice rooms, hot water; *Hospedaje Brandsen*, Brandsen 276, F with private bath, friendly, near railway station.

Camping Balneario Maldonado, 5 km. from centre, bus from Plaza every ½ hr. until 1930 (not very reliable in evening), US$1.60 per tent; salt water swimming pool, US$0.80. Many others.

Restaurants *La Cigala*, opp. railway station, very good; *Il Vesuvio*, Chiclana 231, cheap and good. *Gambrines*, Arribeños 174, central. Very good seafood and fish at Ingeniero White, e.g. *Michos* and *El Greco*; buses go there.

Exchange Lloyds Bank (BLSA), Calle Chiclana 102. Citibank. Open 0800-1400 on Nov. 15-March 31, 1000-1600 on April 1-Nov. 14. **Casa de Cambio** Pullman, Av. San Martín close to main plaza, will change US$ cheques into US$ notes; good rates.

Tourist Office In town hall, friendly and helpful.

Airport Comandante Espora, 15 km. from centre. Austral and Aerolíneas Argentinas flights to Buenos Aires daily. To Comodoro Rivadavia, Sun. at 0800 arrive 1005. To Neuquén daily at 1900, arrive at 1955. Flights to Río Gallegos and Trelew on Sun., at 0800 arrive at 1135 and 0905, respectively.

Trains Two trains daily from Buenos Aires, fairly comfortable, go via Olavarría from Constitución; *Estrella del Valle* daily at 1000, arrive at 2115, with dining car, return 0910 daily, arrive 2050; and at 0910 daily, arriving 0840, returning at same time, arriving Buenos Aires 0825. Five other trains on different days of the week. Sleeper US$33.60; Pullman US$25.45; 1st class US$15.40, tourist US$11. Daily train to Bariloche, 19 hrs., sleeper US$29, pullman US$24, first class US$17, tourist, US$12. To Zapala at 2150 (arrive 1000), same classes as Bariloche. Can be cold. There is no other link between the Bahía Blanca-Bariloche line and the more northerly Bahía Blanca-Zapala line.

Roads Well built paved highway (Route 3) S to Comodoro Rivadavia; major paved route W to Neuquén and the Lake District. Several routes go North.

Buses Terminal is 2½ km. from centre in old railway station; no hotels nearby. To Trelew, 3 per week, US$20, 734 km. Río Gallegos with Don Otto US$60; Mar del Plata bus, US$12.25 with Pampa, 7-8 hrs., 469 km. Bus Río Colorado US$5.20. Bus to Buenos Aires frequent US$17. To Neuquén, 6 a day, 9hrs, US$15.50, 580 km., one company only. To Zapala daily at 0630 and 1030. To Viedma daily at 0740, 1230, 1800, 4 hrs.

Hitch-hiking S or W from Bahía Blanca is possible but not too easy. N to Buenos Aires, take bus 10 to outskirts, or bus 510 from centre to Ruta 51 (10 km).

Some 100 km. to the N is the Sierra de la Ventana, a favourite area for excursions from Bahía Blanca. The small town of **Sierra de la Ventana** is a good centre for exploring the hills, with hotels (*Golf*, near station, is OK) and the excellent *Don Diego* campsite (hot water, open all year round); also municipal campsite, *Ventana Village*. (Four hours' round trip.) Tres Picos, rising bare and barren from the rich farmlands to 1,070 metres, is only 6¼ km. away. There is a 9-hole golf course, and good trout fishing in the Río Sauce Grande.

193 km. N of Bahía Blanca by road/rail through Saavedra is

Carhué, served by three railways, one of which, via Bolívar, runs to Buenos Aires (603 km.). Five km. away is a sheet of water, Lake Epecuén, which covers over 40,000 hectares and is over twenty times saltier than the sea. No fish can live in it. These waters are recommended for chronic rheumatism and skin diseases. There are many hotels and *residenciales* at the lake side. A fort used in the wars against the Indians is now a museum of those wars. Pop.: 18,000.

Hotels at Lake Epecuén With restaurant: *Gran Parque Patera, Plage, Elkie, Victoria, Rambla, Cuatro Hermanos, Villa Marta, Italia, Española, Las Familias, Gran Rose.* Also: *El Lago, Castello.*

Hotels at Carhué With restaurant: *Buenos Aires, Marconi.* Without: *Volpe, Bristol.*

About 38 km. by road NE of Carhué, on the Roca Railway, is **Guaminí** (Hotels: *La Aragonesa, Roma*), a pleasant summer hill resort of 3,500 inhabitants on the shore of Laguna del Monte, not as salty as Lake Epecuén; *pejerrey* fishing is one of the attractions.

Santa Rosa (Hotel: *Calfacura*, 4-star, no restaurant, B without breakfast, but excellent steak restaurant around the corner; *Motel Calden*, Route 35, km. 330, D, good restaurant attached), capital of the Province of La Pampa, is 332 km. NW of Bahía Blanca by road, and can be reached (619 km.) by Route 5, via Chivilcoy and Pehuajó, from Buenos Aires.

THE CORDOBA REGION (2)

The pattern of the land in Northern Argentina, from the crest of the Andes in the W to the river Paraguay in the E, consists of a high, dry Altiplano rising to a Puna cut into on its eastern face by rivers which flow into the Lowlands. This configuration of the land, similar to Bolivia, is carried southwards into all the north-western provinces of Argentina as far S as Tucumán, but the altitudes in Argentina are not so great as in Bolivia, and the whole area not so large. The E-running rivers born on the Puna flow into the Chaco; their broad valleys, or *quebradas*, make access to the heights comparatively easy. Between the base of the Puna and the Chaco lie a series of front range hogback hills running roughly from N to S; the lowlands between them are known in Argentina as the *valles*. Tucumán is the southern boundary of this kind of land. N of Tucumán crops can be grown without irrigation (though there is irrigation where the soil is absorbent) but S of Tucumán is droughty land, with long N-S ranges of low hills such as the Sierras de Córdoba, set in plains which have salt flats and swamps in the depressions.

Settlement and Economy The Puna is windswept, stony and treeless: the only growth is a low, blackish shrub (*tola*), and an occasional cactus. The first Spanish expedition from Bolivia came down the main Inca road (long since disappeared in Argentina) in 1542. A little later a better and lower route was discovered—the main route used today—descending from La Quiaca to Jujuy through the Quebrada de Humahuaca, with rugged and colourful mountain ranges closing in on both sides. Along this new route the Spaniards pressed S and founded a group of towns in the north-west: Santiago del Estero (the first) in 1551, Tucumán in 1565, Córdoba in 1573, Salta in 1582, La Rioja in 1591, and Jujuy in 1592. Mendoza (1561), San Juan (1562), and San Luis (1598) were all colonized by people who crossed the passes from Chile. All these colonies were hemmed in by the warlike tribes of the Pampas, and until the war of extermination in 1880 the route from Buenos Aires to Córdoba was often unsafe. The Indians raided frequently for cattle, which they drove S and over the Andes for sale in Chile.

During the whole of the colonial era the trade of the area, mostly in mules, was with Bolivia and Peru rather than with Buenos Aires, which was little more than a garrison and smuggling port. The mules were bred mainly in the plains between Rosario, Santa Fe, and Córdoba, and driven finally into Salta for the great fair in February and March.

Historically, Tucumán was always important, for the two river routes of the Salado and the Dulce across the dry belt forced the mule traffic to pass through Tucumán on the way to Salta. Tucumán still produces most of Argentina's sugar. Tobacco is becoming important in the area, and an important factor in the North West is the growth of tourism.

In nearly all the provincial towns everything shuts between 1200 and 1600 except restaurants, hotels and post offices. There is nothing to do or see, and we suggest that this is a good time for travelling; buses are generally preferable to trains, being faster (except to Córdoba). (Panamericano buses have been recommended in the NW as new, clean and with a good service.)

From Buenos Aires to Córdoba

If hitch-hiking, take the train from Retiro (San Martín line) to Pilar to reach main Córdoba highway via Rosario. There are two main road routes: the shorter (713 km.) via Rosario and the longer (835 km.) via Río Cuarto. The latter goes through **San Antonio de Areco**—also on the Mitre Railway— 113 km. NW of Buenos Aires (also Chevallier bus, 2hrs, US$3, every hour). Here is the Museo Gauchesco Ricardo Güiraldes, on Camino Güiraldes and Aureliano, a typical *estancia* of the late 19th century with manor house, mill, tavern, open Wed.-Sun., 1000-1200, 1500-1800 in summer; in winter 1000-1200 and 1400-1700. Check if it is open in Jan.-Feb. Souvenir shop opposite. Güiraldes was a writer who described *gaucho* life; his best-known book is *Don Segundo Sombra*. Visitors can also see over Cina-Cina, a working *estancia*, tour for US$20 includes visit, typical lunch and riding display. Día de la Tradición is a *gaucho* festival with traditional parades, games, events on horseback, music and dance, celebrated on Nov. 10, 11 and 12 each year.

Camping near the centre of town; 12 km. from centre, Auto-camping *La Porteña* on the Güiraldes *estancia*, good access roads. Six hotels. Many handicrafts, mainly *gaucho* objects, ceramics, silver, leather, colonial furniture. The Argentine artist Gasparini has a museum-school where he sells his drawings of *gauchos* to tourists; Calle de los Martínez, between Bolívar and Rivadavia. There is also a local natural history museum, Parque Metri, on Matheu and Hernández. For tourist information go to the Sub-Dirección de Turismo at Alsina and Lavalle. T 2101. *Hotel San Carlos*, opp. tourist office, E, clean and friendly, ask in advance for meals; *Residencial Areco*, Segundo Sombra y Rivadavia, T 2166, good, E, comfortable, clean. Opposite Museo Gauchesco is *Hostería del Palomar*, typical barbecue; *Restaurant La Porteña* on the riverside, typical, very good.

Beyond Pergamino, 146 km., is **Venado Tuerto,** a pleasant town of 58,000 people with a fine Country Club at which race meetings and tournaments are held twice a year. At **Río Cuarto,** 70,000 people, there is a golf club and a fine old municipal building with an outlook tower worth seeing.

Hotels *Gran,* on Plaza, D, new, 1st class; *City Hotel,* good, D. *Opera,* 25 de Mayo, C; *Victoria,* Buenos Aires 183, E, small beds; *Gran Hotel Mendoza,* Constitución 483; *Alihué,* Sarsfield 69, E, good value, very friendly, big rooms. Near bus station on Calle Sobremonte 100-200 block are 3 cheap *residenciales, El Ciervo, Hospedaje El Bambi, Residencial Monge,* all F.

Restaurants *Cantina Italiana Sorrento,* fair. Best exchange rate at Banco de la Nación; post office on plaza. *Pizzería Costa Azul,* Belgrano 67, sit in or out, pleasant.

Buses Buenos Aires, US$12. Bus to Mendoza, US$24; to Córdoba US$7.75; frequent departures to Santiago US$35, daily.

Córdoba is 225 km. N of Río Cuarto across flatlands and rolling hills. About half-way along the road runs on the retaining wall of the great Río Tercero dam; the artificial lake here is used for recreation. Río Tercero has gained in importance

NORTH-WEST ARGENTINA

with the development of groundnut plantations and a local military factory. *Hotel Argentino,* adequate, D, with a/c.

Villa María, on the Mitre Railway and at a vital crossroads on the main Buenos Aires-Córdoba road, where it meets the most convenient highway route linking central Chile with Paraguay, Uruguay and Brazil, is a prosperous agricultural town. Hotel: *City,* D. Restaurant: *La Churrasquita.*

Córdoba, capital of Córdoba Province and Argentina's second city, has about a million inhabitants; it stands at an altitude of 440 metres. The district is well known for its countryside and the city for its buildings; it was founded as early as 1573. Its university, founded in 1613, was the first in the country. The heart of the city is Plaza San Martín (the Liberator's statue is there). On the western side is the old Cabildo, now the police headquarters. Next to it stands the Cathedral, started in 1697 and finished 1787. The neo-gothic church of the Sacred Heart (Sagrado Corazón), built in 1933, at Buenos Aires e Yrigoyen, is worth a visit. Córdoba was once a very picturesque place, but modernization is catching up fast. Pedestrianization schemes have recently improved the centre.

On Calle Independencia, leading S from the Plaza San Martín, is the church and convent of Santa Teresa (beautiful doorway, 1770). An old colonial building, the Viceroy's House (Casa del Virrey), is on Calle Rosario, E of the central plaza; it houses the Historical and Colonial Museum, open Tues.-Fri. 0830-1300, 1530-1930, Sat.-Sun. 0900-1200. N of Plaza San Martín, on Calle Rivadavia, is the church of La Merced, whose old colonial pulpit is well worth seeing. The church of La Compañía, on Calles Trejo y Caseros, with a simple façade, dates from about 1650 and is a far better building than the Cathedral; its façade was rebuilt in the 20th century. The barrel vault and cupola of the Capilla Doméstica of this church, built entirely of Paraguayan cedar, are unique. There are some pleasant small 18th century churches with striking bell gables and undulating pediments. The C.16 Carmelite convent at Independencia 122 has a religious art museum, open Wed., Sat., 1000-1200. La Merced, on Rivas, has fine modern tile murals, showing angels wearing blue jeans. Natural History Museum, Av. Yrigoyen 115 (open Mon.-Fri. 0830-1230 and 1430-1830, Sat.-Sun. 0900-1200). There is a very interesting and well laid out Museum of Mineralogy; ask permission to visit from Dra. Hebe Gay at Universidad de Ciencias Exactas.

The Academy of Fine Arts, the theatre and the Olmos School are near the Plaza Vélez Sarsfield (there is a statue to this jurist, who gave Argentina its civil code). A diagonal, Avenida Yrigoyen, runs to the round Plaza España, where the Museum of Fine Arts (open Mon.-Fri., 0900-1300) is housed in a pillared building. E from this plaza is Parque Sarmiento, where there is a Zoological Garden with a serpentarium and a small waterfall. Argentina's main observatory is at the S end of Calle General Artigas. Córdoba is a good shopping city, but prices tend to be higher than in Buenos Aires. Pajas Blancas airport, 15 km. from the city, is modern and has a good restaurant. Taxi to airport, US$10. **N.B.:** Churches are open mornings and after 1600.

Local Holidays July 6 (Foundation of the City); September 30 (St. Jerome); October 7-10.

Industries Córdoba is the centre of Argentina's motor industry.

Hotels Best are: *Ritz,* San Jerónimo 495, B; *Mediterráneo,* Av. M.T. de Alvear 10, B; *Cañada,* Av. M.T. de Alvear 580, B, good, being extended; *Sussex,* Buenos Aires 59, B, comfortable, roomy, discounts for ACA members; *Palace,* Buenos Aires 101, C; *Royal,* Blvd. Reconquista 180, C; all these have garages. Also *Crillón,* Rivadavia 85, D, very friendly, comfortable. More economical: *Rivera,* Balcarce 74, near bus station, D, friendly, clean. *Grand Hotel Bristol,* Corrientes 64, F, bathroom, a/c, telephone. For economy: *Sportsman,* San Jerónimo 590, F, very good, near bus and railway station; *Residencial Plaza,* Balcarce 336, 150 metres from bus station, clean, friendly and quiet, E; *del Sol,* Balcarce 144, D with bath, clean, fan, close to stations, rec.; *Mallorca,* on Balcarce, E, quite clean and near bus and railway station. *Hospedaje El Progreso,* also on Balcarce, F, not too clean but pleasant. Plenty of hotels of all classes on San Jerónimo. *Hospedaje Suiza,* Corrientes 569, near bus terminal, very friendly but not too clean, F; *Hospedaje My House,* near *Suiza* on Corrientes, clean, quiet, very friendly, rec. *Entre Ríos,* close to bus terminal on Entre Ríos, F, reasonably clean, hot-pillow place, hot water. Small, clean and nice, family-run: *Residencial Mi Valle,* Corrientes 586, washing facilities, E; *Pasajeros,* Corrientes

TO SANTIAGO DEL ESTERO

RAMÍREZ VELAZCO

AV. LAS HERAS
PARQUE LAS HERAS

TO AIRPORT

12 DE OCT. RINCON
IGUALDAD LIBERTAD
LA TABLADA ONCATIVO
SARMIENTO
CATAMARCA
LIMA
25 DE MAYO
SALTA
SGO. DEL ESTERO

HUMBERTO 1°
LA RIOJA
TUCUMAN
SANTA ROSA
AV. COLON
SUCRE
JUJUY
9 DE JULIO
DEAN FUNES
27 DE ABRIL
CASEROS
D QUIROS
BV. SAN JUAN
TREJO
MONTEVIDEO
SAN LUIS
LAPRIDA
RODRIGUEZ
ACHAVAL
LARRAÑAGA
J.M. ESTRADA
PEREDO
BRASIL
PERU AV. AMBROSIO OLMOS
BOLIVIA
COLOMBIA
CRISOL
CHILE

FRAGUERO
ALTAGRACIA
LAVALLEJA
BOLIVAR
AYACUCHO
AV. MT. DE ALVEAR
AV. VELEZ SARSFIELD
H.Y. YRIGOYEN
TUZAINGO
OBISPO ORO
DERQUI
AV. LEOPOLDO LUGONES
SAN LORENZO

AV. GRL. PAZ
BELGRANO
SALTA BRIA
INDEPENDENCIA
BUENOS AIRES
SAN JERONIMO
SAN MARTIN
RIVERA INDARTE
PUE. RIO DE ISRAEL
AV. OLMOS
RIVADAVIA
ROSARIO DE SANTA FE
SAL BERTRAND
AV. CHACABUCO
ENTRE RIOS
CORRIENTES
A. ILLIA
BV. AV.
OBISPO
PARAN
RONDEAU
BALCARCE
ALBERDI

ALVEAR
MAIPU

AV. RECONQUISTA
MITRE RAILWAY
BV. GUZMAN

TO VILLA CARLOS PAZ

TO BUENOS AIRES

T
B

NOT TO SCALE

CÓRDOBA

1. Plaza San Martín	10. Casa del Virrey/Historical and Colonial Museum
2. Plaza España	11. Natural History Museum
3. Plaza General Paz	12. Museum of Minerology
4. Parque Sarmiento and Zoo	13. Museum of Fine Arts
5. Cathedral	14. Theatre
6. Santa Teresa	15. Post Office
7. La Merced	16. Tourist Office
8. La Compañía	
9. Old Cabildo	

564, F, pleasant; *Res. Corrientes*, Corrientes 540, F, good rooms; *Soledad* (not very clean), San Jerónimo, friendly, cheap. *Florida*, E, clean, Rosario de Santa Fe 459, friendly, rec., some rooms with a/c, D. Across the pedestrian bridge from the top of the bus station into a residential precinct are many low cost hotels and restaurants, around the precinct park or ½ block into bordering streets. No cheap hotels near Alta Córdoba railway station.

Camping Nearest site in Alta Gracia. Local bus takes 40 mins.

Restaurants Good but not cheap: *Hotel Crillón* (US$8 per head). Good food and moderate prices: *Florida Grill*, across from *Hotel Crillón*, good, informal meals. Next to *Crillón* is *Jerónimo*, simple, pleasant, US$7 per head; nearby is *Casino Español*, good. *El Recodo*, Rivadavia 0-100 block, very good and reasonable. There are also numerous grills of all categories on the outskirts of the city, especially in the Cerro de las Rosas district, for meals out-of-doors when the weather is suitable. Many cheap restaurants along San Jerónimo. Restaurant in *Hotel Familiar*, S. Jerónimo, near railway station, cheap and good, rec. *Restaurant Alborada*, nr bus station, good meals; *Romagnolo*, opposite the Mitre railway station, rec., and *Comedor Albéniz*, opposite Alto Córdoba station, a bit noisy. *Rigoletto*, Entre Ríos 73, cheap meals, *La Cabaña*, Maipú 230, cheap and good. *La Casona*, Rivera Indarte 337, O.K.; *Don Pipo*, Santa Rosa 212, good, cheap *parrilladas*. Excellent fruit juices (*licuados*) at *Kiosco* Americano, Tucumán 185.

Rent-a-Car Avis and AI International at airport and in the centre. Entre Ríos 70. T 42-036/38 central depôt.

Casino Nearby, at Alta Gracia.

Exchange Lloyds Bank (BLSA), Buenos Aires 23. Citibank. Oct.-March, 0730- 1330; April-Sept., 0800-1400. American Express, 25 de Mayo 125. Exchange at banks and following travel agencies: Exprinter, Rivadavia 39, opposite is Maguitur, Rivadavia 30, good rates, Viacor, Avincor, Epoca and Barujel, San Martín 37. Also Cambio Coín, Rivadavia y 25 de Mayo, best rate for US$ cash. Many *cambios* on Rivadavia just off Plaza.

Post Office Parcel Service on the ground floor of the Correo Central, Av. Colón 201, beside the customs office, up to 20 kg; wrapping service for small fee.
British Council Blvd. San Juan 137, has a good library.
Goethe Institut, Chacabuco 476, open Mon.-Fri., 1700-2100.
Laundry Laundromat (self-service) at Tucumán 135; also Chacabuco 32, and Av. Colón 300.
Tourist Office Dirección Provincial de Turismo. Information centres: Plaza San Martín on San Jerónimo and Obispo Mercadillo, Rosario de Santa Fe 39. Also at bus station. Tourist Office desk at airport often unmanned, but car-hire desks next to it are most helpful.
Club Andino, Duarte Quirós 1591.

Air Airport bus leaves terminal opposite railway station. Several flights to Buenos Aires daily, about 1 hr., US$56; to Mendoza daily at 1400 (55 mins.); to Tucumán at 1235 daily exc. Sun. arr. 1335. To Iguazú, AA, US$66. Night flights: Buenos Aires to Córdoba Thurs. at 2230. Córdoba-Mar del Plata Thurs. and Sat. at 2350, returns Tues. and Fri. at 2330. Aerolíneas Argentinas, Av. Colón 520. Austral, Av. Colón 678.

Buses Excellent bus station with Tourist Office, many public telephones, shops, bank, post office, restaurants, and showers in bathrooms (about 6 blocks from centre), crowded at weekends. Buenos Aires-Córdoba (US$17.50 with Costera Criolla or with Cacorba) by bus takes about 13 hours, and on from Córdoba to Salta (US$15) and Jujuy (US$20) with Panamericano, about 12 and 15 hours. Chevallier, Buenos Aires to Córdoba via Route 8, four services, at 0600, 1600, 2015 and 2345; via Route 9 at 0745, 2100, 2200, and 2340. Many buses on both routes, 10½ hrs, US$17. Bus to Mendoza (10 hours), 3 a day, book early, US$13. Bus to Tucumán, US$13, about 8 a day, Panamericano has more than other companies. To Posadas (Expreso Singer) Tues., Thurs., Sat., 1730 arrive at Posadas at 1335; Thurs. and Sat. bus continues to Iguazú arriving 1930 next day, no air-conditioning. Onda operates a service from Paraná via Santa Fe and Rosario to and from Córdoba. Bus Córdoba-Asunción (Paraguay) direct with Brújula, four times a week, also with Cacorba 19 hrs, US$25. Regular bus between Córdoba and Montevideo (Uruguay). In general, it is best to travel from Córdoba if you are going N, as at stations in between it may be hard to get a seat; a seat is only guaranteed if one pays US$1 extra. To Santiago del Estero, US$8. To La Rioja 3-4 a day with Cotil and Cotap; some go on to Catamarca. Córdoba-La Rioja-Aimogasta-Tinogasta-Fiambalá with El Cóndor, Tues., Thurs., Fri.; leaves Tinogasta 1140 arr. Fiambalá 1240, returns from Fiambalá same day 1445, from Tinogasta at 1600 **(see also page 106)**. La Calera bus leaves for Belén (Catamarca) on Mon., Wed., Fri., at 2100, arr. Belén 1030; return journey, also via Andalgalá, Wed., Fri., Sun., dep. 1600 arr. Andalgalá 1735, dep. 1750, arr. Córdoba 0055. Cacorba, efficient a/c buses, serve Villa Carlos Paz, Cosquín and La Falda in the Sierras de Córdoba.

Railways The Mitre Railway *Rayo de Sol* night train takes 11 hours to and from Buenos Aires. Tourist class US$14.55, 1st class US$24.50, Pullman US$33.25, Sleeper US$43.15, car transporter daily. *Rayo de Sol* leaves Buenos Aires (Retiro) 2100 daily and Córdoba 2030 daily.

The Belgrano Railway runs *El Norteño* train on Tues., and Fri., from Buenos Aires (Retiro) at 1000; from Córdoba, 0750, Wed., Sat. (12 hours), no sleepers. The Alta Córdoba railway station for long-distance journeys is a good 2 km. from the city centre. The No. 6 bus will transport you from the Mitre railway station to the Belgrano station. Three trains per week to Tucumán, Tues., Wed. and Sat., 1040. It is advisable to check all trains as services are sometimes suspended without notice. The *Rayo de Sol* trains connect with bus services to various resorts in the Sierras de Córdoba, and the *Norteño* to La Rioja and Catamarca.

The **Sierras of Córdoba**, rising in undulating hills from the pampas, their lower slopes often wooded, particularly in the S, attract each year a large number of visitors. The highest peak, Champaquí (2,975 metres) has a small lake about 2,550 metres up. The hills run, roughly, for 500 km. from N to S; west of Córdoba they are 150 km. wide. There are three ranges of them: the Sierra Grande, the longest, in the middle, with Sierra Chica to the E and Sierra de Guisapampa and its continuation, the Sierra de Pocho, to the W. A network of good roads gives pleasant contrasts of scenery, but there are few footpaths and trails for the walker. The region's climate is dry, sunny and exhilarating, especially in winter.

At the foot of the Sierra Chica are large dams to contain the waters of the Río Primero at Río Molinos (29 km. from Córdoba, Route 5, good *pejerrey* and trout-fishing; bus to Villa Carlos Paz, US$2), San Roque, and Río Tercero. There are two other large dams in the hills, at Cruz del Eje and La Viña. They provide power and irrigation, and the lakes are in themselves attractive. The Government keeps them stocked with fish. Sailing is popular.

Information can be obtained at travel agencies, at the Dirección Provincial de Turismo or at Casa de Córdoba at Callao 332, Buenos Aires.

Note There are innumerable good hotels and *pensiones* in the Córdoba mountain region; names are therefore not always given.

A road running NW from Córdoba through the Punilla valley leads to the following string of popular resorts shadowed by the Sierra Chica. Many of them have daily bus connection with trains between Buenos Aires and Córdoba.

Villa Carlos Paz (buses from Córdoba bus terminal every 15 mins., 36 km., US$ 1; Buenos Aires-Villa Carlos Paz with Costera Criolla, US$18—bus terminal on Calle Alvear), on man-made Lake San Roque, in the Punilla valley. It is the nearest resort to Córdoba and is therefore often crowded. Tours possible on amphibian buses which go as far as the two dams on the lake. Launch trips, US$2.40 for 2½ hours. Much frequented by the British community in Argentina. At the Casa de Gaspar, Miguel Cané and El Redentor, roller-skating and optical illusions, Fri.-Sun. 1400-1900 out of season. A chair-lift (US$2.10) runs up the slopes to a tearoom and night club overlooking the valley, between 0900 and 1900. Bus tours to areas such as Sierra Chica, for those who like snack bars, fun slides and gravity-defying houses. Plenty of hotels, big and small, e.g. *El Ciervo de Oro*, Hipólito Yrigoyen 995, on the lake, D, rec. *Las Junturas*, Florida 181, excellent, clean and friendly, hot shower, use of barbecue and fridge. *Mar del Plata*, E, friendly, rec.; *Riviera*, E with bath, clean, rec. Cheap *Recreo El Ancla* across the road. Cheapest and cleanest *Hostería Mil-Gui*, Irigoyen 615, with barbecue facilities. Camping at ACA campground, and associated sites at *Las Tolderías* and *El Mirador Lago San Roque*; there is a municipal campground with swimming at Bialet Massé, N of Carlos Paz. Best buys: leather mats, bags, pottery. Tourist office at bus station, very friendly. *Restaurant Carlos Paz* highly rec. for food and setting. *Restaurant Pamilla Mingo*, Av. Uruguay opp. *Hotel Uruguay*, not cheap but good. Post Office and telephone on Av. Gral. San Martín.

Cosquín, Bus Córdoba-Cosquín US$1.40. with La Capillense; 1½ hrs., via Carlos Paz or with La Calera via the San Roque dam. 63 km. by Route 38 from Córdoba, on the banks of a river. Altitude, 720 metres. Camping on south bank of river. Tourist office at San Martía 560, *Hotel La Serrana*, P. Ortiz 740, near bus station, F, friendly, good; likewise *Hotel Italia*, across from bus station, F, rec. Take a bus to the Pan de Azúcar hill from where there is a good view over the Punilla valley, at 0930 ret. 1630 or 2 hrs. walk. Chairlift to top (all year round). 19 km. on is **Valle Hermoso**, near La Falda (buses from Villa Carlos Paz). Altitude, 850 metres. Old restored chapel of San Antonio, a little gem. Riding, motoring. Youth hostel, address "Steinhaus", dirty, no heating, very cold, US$2 p.p., pay extra for gas. Camping near river, US$0.60 p.p., all facilities, but not too clean. A folklore festival is held in the last half of January at Cosquín, from 2200-0500, tickets from US$6 per night. (Recent reports suggest that the festival is becoming commercialized.)

La Falda, 82 km. from Córdoba. Bus 2 hrs., US$1.90. Altitude, 933 metres. Helpful tourist offices at bus station and in old railway station building. Model railway museum at Las Murallas zoo at the end of Av. 25 de Mayo. *Hotel Fénix*, 25 de Mayo 218, good, F. *Restaurant El Bochín*, Av. España 117, good, cheap. Students of all nations welcome at Córdoba University holiday centre at Vaquerías, 2 km. from La Falda. Camping near small river. (Bus from Buenos Aires, US$19.50)

Excursions to Quebrada Chica, Cascada del Molino. 3½ km. on by Route 38 is **Huerta Grande**, at 971 metres, a bathing resort with good fishing and medicinal waters.

Round trip excursion to **Cascadas de Olaén**. Take the road to Valle Hermoso back 10 km. towards Cosquín, then follow dirt road about 12½ km. to the crossing marked "Cascadas de Olaén"; from here walk 4½ km. to the falls: quite spectacular canyon—the water splashes into a small lake full of little fish. Return to the dirt road and 2½ km. to a monolith and another dirt road, which leads to La Falda. See the Pampa de Olaén, where there are many quartz mines.

Bus connections with Uruguay from La Falda on Mon., Fri., Sat. and Sun. at 1730, arriving at 1200 next day with CORA (of Uruguay). Connections to Rosario, Mendoza, Catamarca, Santiago del Estero, Tucumán, Salta and Jujuy. Route: La Falda-Córdoba-Santa Fe-Paraná-Colón-Paysandú-Montevideo. Expreso Encón operates a similar service with similar connections.

Candonga, altitude 810 metres, 11 km. from Huerta Grande, is in the Sierra Chica. The road from Córdoba (55 km.) goes through Argüello, Villa Allende, Río Ceballos (*Albergue La Gloria*, affiliated to IYHA, E, warmly rec., and campsites *Río Camping* and *La Quebrada*), and Salsipuedes (*AT Camping*) to El Manzano, where it branches off to the left leading to La Cumbre. The historic colonial church at Candonga, now a National Monument, was built in 1730 as an oratory of the Jesuit Estancia of Santa Gertrudis. The arch protrudes to form a porch which covers the entrance.

La Cumbre, 97 km. from Córdoba. Bus, US$3, 2½ hrs. Altitude, 1,141 metres. Trout streams with good fishing from November to April. Swimming, golf, tennis. Has an airport. *Hotel Lima*, swimming pool, D, quiet, clean. Charming small inn, *Victoria*; *La Cumbre Inn*, large and commercial, good views; *Residencial Peti*, good, friendly, D/E. Good restaurants. *El Toboso*.

Los Cocos, just N of Cruz Chica and 8 km. from La Cumbre, is a delightful, extremely popular mountain resort with 3 first rate hotels and many holiday houses. *Hostería Zanier*, E, full board C, rec. Hang-gliding nearby at Cuchi Corral.

Cruz Chica, altitude, 1,067 metres, has very English houses and gardens in pine woods. Most attractive. Good English boys' school.

Capilla del Monte, 106 km. from Córdoba, (bus US$4, *Hospedaje Italiano*, C, good and clean, showers, opposite bus station; municipal campsite on the way to Cerro Uritorco and also some 9½ km. from Capilla del Monte) in the heart of the Sierras. Altitude, 914 metres. Medicinal waters, rocks and waterfalls and wide views; see particularly El Zapato rock, despite its graffiti. Excursions in the hills, particularly to Cerro Uritorco (1,950 metres). Good trout fishing at Los Alazanes dam; and good path on Uritorco, walk takes 2½ hrs. Permission to walk obtainable from a house beyond the river crossing (US$0.60). You can walk on to the direct dirt road to San Marcos Sierra (22 km.); many parakeets and small farmhouses. Along the way you will also get views down to the **Cruz del Eje** dam and see one of the two villages with its own "micro-climate" (the other is Merlo in San Luis Province) and own honey production—try that made from carob (*algarrobo*) blossom (1 kg. about US$2). Excellent trout fishing at Tío Mayo, an hour from Capilla del Monte by car.

A road runs N from Córdoba to Ascochinga and Jesús María.

Ascochinga, 63 km. N of Córdoba by road via pleasant little townships such as Villa Allende, Unquillo, and La Granja. Altitude, 700 metres. Picturesque, dating from colonial days. Nearby is Santa Catalina, originally a Jesuit mission founded in 1622 and the most elaborate Jesuit establishment in the hills around Córdoba. (See the church begun in 1754, workshops and stone conduits; the families who now occupy the place as a summer home will show you round.)

Jesús María, 51 km. N of Córdoba. Altitude, 533 metres. Good 18th century Jesuit church and the remains of its once famous winery; in the cloister is an excellent Museo Jesuítico, said to be one of the best on the continent (open 1500-1900 Dec.-March, except Mons.). Good trout, *dorado*, and carp fishing in winter. Road to Córdoba paved but rough. Some 4 km. N of Jesús María is Sinsacate, with an interesting church. There is also a fine colonial posting inn, with long, deep verandah and chapel attached. Beyond Jesús María the paved road runs another 132 km. to **Villa de María**, the birthplace of Leopoldo Lugones, a poet of country life. His house is a museum. *Hotel City*, good, at Villa de María, D.

From Córdoba (1 bus a day at 1530, 4½ hrs., US$4), or Jesús María (daily, 1610) you can take a bus to **Cerro Colorado**, 160 km. N. of Córdoba and 14 km. W of Route 9 at Argañadas, near Santa Elena. There are more than 30,000 rock paintings by the Comechingones Indians in the Cerro Colorado archaeological park, where there is cheap accommodation (*e.g.* with Sosa family) and camping. You can stay with Don Elvio, who runs the *pulpería* near the archaeological station, but watch prices. The bus back to Córdoba leaves Cerro Colorado 0600 Mon.-Sat., 1800 Sun.

South-west of Córdoba a scenic road climbs through the Sierra Grande to another chain of resorts, Mina Clavero, Villa Dolores and Yacanto.

Mina Clavero, 140 km. from Córdoba by bus (US$9) through grand lake and hill scenery, and curious palm trees. A good centre for exploring the high *sierra*. No money exchange available. There is a nice church and a most interesting museum, dedicated by a French archaeologist, 13 km. from Mina Clavero and about 5 km. from the village of Nono, entrance US$0.60, called "Rocsen" open 0900 till sunset, with furniture, minerals, instruments, animals, etc. Altitude, 915 metres. (Restaurant: *Rincón Suizo*, Calle Champaquí, good pastries.) Road from Mina Clavero over the Sierra Grande to *Hotel El Cóndor*, goes to Carlos Paz—not yet paved. Views from El Cóndor over Lake San Roque. If hitching from Córdoba down this route to Mendoza, best starting point is Ycho Cruz, beyond Carlos Paz.

Villa Dolores, 187 km. from Córdoba (bus takes 5 hrs.), 48 km. from Mina Clavero. Altitude, 529 metres. Population: 10,000. The road from Córdoba crosses the two mountain ranges to reach finally the Pampa de Achala, a huge desert plateau of grey granite. (Camping: nearest site is Piedra Pintada, 15 min-bus-ride away, pleasant little village well situated for walks into mountains.) Bus to San Luis 5¼ hrs.

Rail Buenos Aires (Retiro)-Villa Dolores: *Sierras Grandes* train via Villa Mercedes, Mon., Wed., Fri. at 1615, arriving 0800; leaving V. Dolores 2240 Tues., Thurs., Sun, arriving Retiro 1350. Fares: Pullman US$23, first US$16.45, tourist US$12.75. Car transporter from Buenos Aires on Fri., from Villa Dolores on Sun.

From San Javier you can explore *Champaquí* (altitude 2,975 metres). For top, follow path to Capilla La Constancia, set in river valley with pine and nut trees, 2-3 hrs. Take water from here, then cross the river (path), keep left through a pinewood up to a mountain range and follow it up to the top of a huge plateau. Good path, about 4-5 hrs, and then you reach a square enclosure, whence you keep left. Follow stone mounds about 2 hrs. until you see the higher of two peaks, which is Champaquí. Lovely views, descent 4 hrs. to La Constancia. Not to be attempted in misty weather.

Yacanto, near Villa Dolores, at the foot of Champaquí, in a region of woods and waterfalls. Reached by road from Villa Dolores railway station. Curative waters.

A road S from Córdoba runs to Alta Gracia and to the Río Tercero dam.

Alta Gracia, altitude 580 metres, 48 km. SW of Córdoba. (Bus 1 hr., every 15 mins, US$0.75.) Interesting colonial church, finished c.1762, open a.m. and after 1700, and buildings housing Museo del Virrey Liniers, about the Estancia de Alta Gracia, founded in 1588 and taken over by the Jesuits in 1643, beside Lake Trajamar, open Tues.-Sun. 0900-1200 and 1500-1800 (all day in summer). There is also the Museo Manuel de Falla on Pellegrini Final, open Tues.-Fri. 0900-1900, entry US$0.30, where the Spanish composer spent his last years. Take the local bus to La Paysanita or La Serranita for a quiet environment (but no cheap accommodation). *Hostería Reina*, Urquiza 129, good. Two camping sites, one scruffy, the other better and free in winter, which is by golf course. A few reasonably priced restaurants in town centre. Tourist office inside clock tower by Lake Trajamar. New casino. To the Bosque Alegre and Observatory is 24 km., open Thurs. 1600-1800 Sun. 1000-1200 and 1600- 1800. Good views over Córdoba, Alta Gracia and the Sierra Grande. To the Río Tercero dam is 79 km.; on the lake is a workers' holiday colony and an ACA *Unidad Turística*. Gruta de la Virgen de Lourdes, 3 km. out of town, beautiful views from cross on top of hill.

Villa General Belgrano, 85 km. S of Córdoba on Route 36, is a completely German town founded by the surviving interned seamen from the *Graf Spee*, some of whom still live in the town. It is a pleasant resort and a good centre for excursions in the surrounding mountains. If walking between here and La Cumbrecita, lodge with Siegfried at *Alta Vista*, F, friendly. There are two *Youth Hostels*, one at Estancia Alta Vista, 14 km. from the town, and one, El Rincón, in the town.

La Cumbrecita, a German village reached from General Belgrano by daily bus at 1500 or by taxi (US$25-30, 1-1½ hrs.) along a dirt road, is another Sierra resort. Good walking and riding. Hotels: *Cascadas*, B, with pool, tennis etc.; *Panorama*, C, higher up hill; three others (C) and *Residencial Casa Rosita*, E. *Youth Hostel* at Villa Alpina, 17 km. from the town.

Some 200 km. NE of Córdoba the Río Dulce, flowing in places through salt flats, runs into the shallow Mar Chiquita on the southern margin of the Chaco. People who live in the valley of the Río Dulce are so used to the taste of its water that they often add a pinch of salt to the water they drink when away from home. Mar Chiquita, which is now growing rapidly, is naturally salty, and the water is warm. No river drains it, though two other rivers flow into it from the Sierras of Córdoba in the flood season. There are several islands in the lake. On its southern shore is the small town of *Miramar*, which is being gradually overwhelmed by the expanding Mar Chiquita. The area is a very popular resort during the summer months; its salt waters are used in the treatment of rheumatic ailments and skin diseases. It is best reached by a railway W from Santa Fe to Deán Funes, which runs within a few km. of the southern shore. The lake is about 320 km. SE of Santiago del Estero.

Hotels *Savoy*, cheap, very friendly

Camping Autocamping Lilly. Bahía de los Sanavirones.

(**Note** This Mar Chiquita and its town, Miramar, must not be confused with the other Mar Chiquita to the N of Mar del Plata and the seaside resort of Miramar, S of Mar del Plata.)

SANTIAGO DEL ESTERO, TUCUMAN, SALTA AND JUJUY (3)

The broad-gauge Mitre Railway and the metre-gauge Belgrano Railway (slower) both run N past Santiago del Estero to Tucumán, 522 km. away. From Recreo on the Belgrano a branch runs W to Chumbicha, where it connects with a line N to Catamarca and S to La Rioja; they will be described later.

Santiago del Estero, the oldest Argentine town, was founded in 1553 by settlers pushing S from Peru. It is about 360 km. N of Córdoba and 167 km. SE of Tucumán. A 1½-km. steel bridge across the Río Dulce carries the Mitre railway from La Banda (6½ km.) on the Buenos Aires-Rosario-Tucumán route. There is a branch line via Forres to Córdoba. Population, 92,000. The main square, Plaza Libertad, contains the Casa de Gobierno, and the Cathedral (the 5th on the site) stands next to it. Also on the plaza is the tourist office, open 0800 to 2000 daily, and very helpful. On Plaza Lugones is the pleasant old church of San Francisco, the city's first, which, was founded in 1590 by San Francisco Solano, patron saint of Tucumán. His cell is in the near-by convent; his festival, celebrated with folk-music (he himself played the viol), is on July 24. Beyond the church is the pleasant Parque Aguirre, with a good zoo. Airport (Aerolíneas Argentinas flights daily, except Thurs.).

In the convent of Santo Domingo is a "Holy Sheet", one of the three copies of the sheet that covered the body of Christ, given by Philip II to his "beloved colonies of America". The Provincial Museum of Archaeology (Calle Avellaneda) founded by Emil and Duncan Wagner, has over 10,000 samples of Indian pottery. There is also a provincial history museum, previously known as the Museo Gancedo.

Hotels *Savoy,* simple, well run, good and very ample food; *Bristol,* Moreno 67; *Gran Hotel,* Avellaneda and Independencia; *Residencial San Antonio,* Belgrano 485, E, very basic rooms but clean bathrooms. *Residencial Rodas,* Pedro L. Gallo 432, E, next to bus station, café attached, very friendly. *Hotel-Residencia Iovino I,* on Moreno y San Martín, D; *Residencial Iovino II,* Santa Fe 259, 2 blocks from bus station, E with bath, clean, fan, but doors and windows don't close properly; *Residencial Santa Fe,* F, next to *Iovino II. Embajador,* Buenos Aires 60, E, reductions for longer stays; unmarked *pensión,* Moreno 665, F, adequate.

Restaurant *La Rotonda,* at edge of town on road to Tucumán, reasonable *asado.* Easy to hitchhike N from here. *Mía Mamma,* on Plaza is good restaurant/salad bar.

Exchange Noroeste Cambio, 200 block of 24 de Septiembre, good rates.

Festival Carnival in February is to be avoided: virtually everything throwable gets thrown by everyone at everyone else.

Buses to Resistencia, 3 a day, US$12, 11 hrs., run by El Rayo company, via Quimili and Roque Sáenz Peña (US$9, 8 hrs.); also to Córdoba, 12 a day, US$8; to Tucumán (via Río Hondo) US$3. To Buenos Aires, 3 a day, 12 hrs., US$20. Three a day to Salta, 5½ hrs., and to Jujuy, 6¼ hrs. Tourist Office extremely helpful.

The *Termas de Río Hondo* are 65 km. from Santiago del Estero along the road to Tucumán, at 264 metres. Their water is recommended for blood pressure and rheumatism; good to drink, too, and used for the local soda water. Swimming in public baths. Bus US$1.50 from Santiago del Estero, 1 hr. Aerolíneas Argentinas have combined flight and bus excursion from Buenos Aires, via Santiago del Estero, to the Termas, daily 1030, return 1245 from Santiago. The huge Río Hondo dam on the Río Dulce is close by; it forms a lake of 33,000 hectares, used for sailing and fishing. Very popular in August, so book accommodation well in advance.

Hotels *Grand Hotel Río Hondo; Los Pinos,* the most pleasant; *Panamericano; Palace; Ambassador; Aranjuez,* C, newest. Three campsites by river.

Food In the main street is a corner shop where you can watch *alfajores,* the local sweet (**see page 169**) being made. Around the corner from there is a small restaurant with excellent home-made pasta. There are two restaurants on the plaza: *Sabot* is quite good.

N.B. In Tucumán, Salta and Jujuy the only fuel one can get at the service station is *alconafta* (85% gasoline, 15% ethanol) which is a harmless substitute for gasoline.

Tucumán (properly San Miguel de Tucumán), capital of its province and with a population of almost a million, is the busiest and the most populous city in the N. Its natural beauties are great: it stands on a plain, at 450 metres, but to the W towers the Sierra de Aconquija. The city was founded by Spaniards coming S from Peru in 1565. There are still many colonial buildings left, and among rows of elaborately stuccoed, spacious, one-storey houses (many of them sadly dilapidated) rise three or four handsome churches with blue, yellow and white tiled domes. Summer weather can be very hot and sticky.

Tucumán's main square is Plaza Independencia. On its W side is the ornate Government Palace, next is the church of San Francisco, with a picturesque façade. On the S side is the Cathedral, with an old rustic cross, kept near the baptismal font, used when founding the city.

To the S, on Calle Congreso, is the Casa Histórica where, in 1816, the Congress of the United Provinces of Río de la Plata met to draft and proclaim Argentina's Declaration of Independence. The simple room in which it was proclaimed survived the destruction of the original house in 1908 and has now been enclosed in a modern museum. A bas-relief on the museum walls shows the delegates proclaiming independence. Some distance to the W is Plaza Belgrano, with a statue to General Belgrano, who won a decisive battle against the royalists here in 1812. Two blocks E is the University, with a grand view from the *vivero*. Nightly, at 2030, *son et lumière* programme at **Casa Histórica**, US$0.70, no seats, in garden.

In the large Nueve de Julio park (avoid at night) is the house of Bishop Colombres, who introduced sugar cane to Tucumán in the early 19th century. In the house is his first milling machine.

Local Holiday Sept. 24 (Battle of Tucumán). Independence celebrations include music and speeches at the Casa de Independencia on July 8, followed by *gauchos* bringing in the National Flag at midnight. Next day there are many folklore markets and music. Also Día de la Tradición, Nov. 10.

Hotels *Grand Hotel del Tucumán*, Av. de los Próceres 380, B, large, new five-star hotel opposite the Parque Centenario 9 de Julio, efficient, outstanding food and service, swimming pool, tennis courts, discotheque; *Metropol*, 24 de Septiembre 524, expensive, B, but good service, worth it; *Premier*, with a/c, good, friendly, accepts Visa credit card, C. Alvarez 510, D. Also good: *Viena*, Santiago del Estero 1054, E; *Corona*, on main square next to Tourist Office; *Plaza*, D, San Martín 435. In summer, best to stay at *Hotel St. James*, on top of Sierra de Aconquija, expensive, comfortable, good food, swimming pool, good views, and fine walking; *Los Arrieros*, on the Metán road, rec.; *Congreso*, Congreso 74, clean but old, rec., friendly, E, with bath, extra charge for fan. There are other cheap hotels near the bus station, e.g. *Boston*, F, on Sáenz Peña, nice courtyards, restaurant, but some are very dirty. *Palace*, 24 de Septiembre 233, E, friendly, clean, rec.; *Colonial*, San Martín 35, E, 5 mins. from bus station, very clean, private bath, fan; *Estrella*, just outside bus station, 24 de Septiembre, clean, cheap and basic, a bit noisy, open 24 hrs. Nameless hotel opp. bus terminal, F with bath, radio and heating; *Florida*, 24 de Septiembre and 9 de Julio, E, very good value; *Italia*, Catamarca and Corrientes, F, by Mitre station, friendly, hot water, reasonably clean, hot-pillow place; *Petit*, C. Alvarez 765, a bit noisy, spacious, friendly, clean, E with bath, highly rec. Many cheap hotels in streets around General Belgrano station. *El Parque* or *El Bosque* (both names used), across from bus station, F, fan, clean (though used as a brothel), friendly, safe. Marta Ruiz offers accommodation in her house at Rondeau 1824, F, not including food, very comfortable. If they arrange beforehand, students can stay in the University residence of Horco Molle.

Camping Parque Nueve de Julio, one site for locals, one for tourists (US$0.25 per tent, US$0.25 p.p.): reported to be dirty. Two roadside camp sites 3 km. E and NE of city centre.

Restaurants *El Duque*, San Lorenzo 440, very large, popular, excellent, and *La Chacha*, Córdoba 476, good value. Good meat in open air at *La Rural*, Parque 9 de Julio, reasonable prices; *Isoscelles*, Junín 583, original dishes, good service, US$6 for 2 with wine; both warmly rec. *El Rincón de Cholo*, Chacabuco 31, Arab and other food, esp. lunches, very friendly, good, cheap. *La Leñita*, 25 de Mayo, inexpensive, good meat. *Bar Risco*, B. Araoz and Avellaneda, nr. bus station, good cheap sandwiches. *Rocca Bianca*, next to *Hotel Congreso* on Calle Congreso 32, good all round, very popular; *La Cantina*, San Martín 750, good; also good, cheap meals at *Champaquí*, Av. Sarmiento, corner with Catamarca, opp. Mitre station, and at *Las Brasas*, Maipú 700 block. Good fast food at *Palacio de las Empanadas*, Maipú 900 block; and at *Pic Nic*, San Juan 600 block and Ayacucho 500 block, meal US$1.50. *Sorrento*, C. Alvarez near 9 de Julio, cheap, all-you-can-eat, average food; *Comilandia*, cheap set meals, San Martín 181. *Café and*

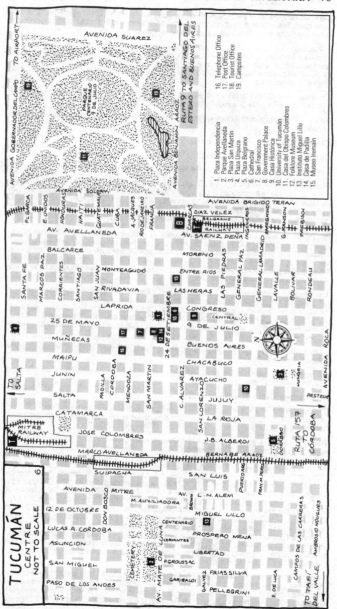

TUCUMÁN
CENTRE
NOT TO SCALE

1. Plaza Independencia
2. Parque Avellaneda
3. Plaza San Martín
4. Plaza Urquiza
5. Plaza Belgrano
6. Cathedral
7. San Francisco
8. Government Palace
9. Casa Histórica
10. University of Tucumán
11. Casa del Obispo Colombres
12. Folklore Museum
13. Instituto Miguel Lillo
14. Casa de Padilla
15. Museo Iramain
16. Telephone Office
17. Post Office
18. Tourist Office
19. Campsites

Sandwichería, corner of 24 de Septiembre and Buenos Aires, good. Set lunches near bus station good value. The local beer is very good (Cervecería del Norte), and in this part of Argentina "black beer" (e.g. Salta Negra) is available; also in Salta and Cafayate.

Shopping An active centre, cheaper than Buenos Aires. *Valles Colchaquíes*, Congreso 178, opp. Casa Histórica, good handicrafts, others adjacent. *Discoteque*, Galería at San Martín 675, good selection of records, English-speaking owner. *Libreria Sarmiento*, San Martín 600 block, for maps. All shops close 1200-1630. Good 2nd-hand book shop in centre, *Los Primos*, with English, French, German books.

Casinos The Winter Casino is in an elegant 19th century building on the outskirts. It is open all year except January. The Summer Casino at the top of Aconquija is now closed.

Taxis Many unscrupulous drivers, who "rig" their meters. Better to arrange price in advance if possible.

Car Hire Al International and Avis; airport and in centre.

Car Repairs Rubén Boss, Av. Aconquija 947, rec. esp. for Volkswagen.

Laundry Lavarap (self-service), Las Piedras y 9 de Julio; also one at Santiago and Laprida.

Museums Casa Histórica, Calle Congreso, open Tue.-Sun. 0830-1200 and 1730-2000, US$0.20, but you're encouraged to buy a guide, see previous page; Anthropological Museum, 25 de Mayo y Mendoza in University building, not well staffed, good exhibits; Folklore Museum, open Wed. and Sun. 0800-1230 and 1730- 2030; the Instituto Miguel Lillo, associated with the natural history department of the University, has a large collection of animals, insects, and a herbarium, with the display greatly improved. One of the library's treasures is one of eight copies of the original edition of von Humboldt's travels in Spanish America; another is a sixteenth-century Pliny. Open Mon.-Fri. 1500-1800. All these four museums have been described as "quite exceptional". Casa de Padilla, next to government palace, houses a collection of international art and antiques in the home of a prominent Tucumán family. Next to *Hotel Colonia* on Av. Entre Ríos is Museo Iremaín, a very interesting memorial to the sculptor, open 0830-1200 and 1500-1800, Mon.-Fri. All museums now make a small charge.

Exchange Lloyds Bank (BLSA), San Martín 622. Open 0700-1300; charges high commission on traveller's cheques. American Express, San Martín 845. Noroeste Cambios, 24 de Septiembre 549 (3% commission on cheques, open Sat. a.m.) Dinartur, San Martín 678, cheques and cash, and Maguitur, San Martín 765, near main square, good rates for cash; also Imperio de Oro, *local* 3, Galería Pezza, San Martín 650, good rates for cash. (See note on provincial bonds used as currency, **169**.)

Immigration Office Buenos Aires 2719, take bus No 6. Will only extend stay on the last day of the original permit.

Library North American Centre, Junín 565, open 1700-2100. Alliance Française, Mendoza 255, free events in French.

International Calls Entel, Muñecas 226.

Tourist Office In Plaza Independencia, 24 de Septiembre 484, 1st floor, open 0800-1300 and in summer 1600-2000; helpful in finding accommodation in private houses (about US$3 with cooking facilities); English spoken. Has details on Tafí **(see page 81)**.

Rail 1st class and Pullman often booked up 2 weeks in advance. The daily *Estrella del Norte* train leaves Retiro station, Buenos Aires, at 1800, returns daily from the Mitre station in Tucumán at 1845, costs US$63.35 sleeper, US$45.50 Pullman, US$30 first, US$21 tourist class; takes 18½ hours. The Belgrano train, the *Norteño*, leaves Buenos Aires 1000, Tues. and Fri.; and Tucumán (Belgrano station opp. bus station) 1845, Tues., Fri., taking 25 hours, no sleeper. *Independencia* train leaves Buenos Aires Tues. and Fri. at 1600, returns Sun. and Wed. at 1715 (Mitre station) sleeper, car transporter, can combine with bus La Veloz del Norte (5½ hrs.) to Salta, for about US$7 more, also to Jujuy (US$10, 5 hours) as can *Estrella del Norte* (bus quality, daily at 1300). *Panamericano* train leaves Mitre station, Tucumán, Mon., Fri. 1500, arrives La Quiaca 0920 next day, fare US$13.50 1st class; at Villazón there is a connecting train on Saturday to La Paz. Three trains a week to Córdoba, 1745, 14 hrs., 1st US$23, 2nd US$17.

Beyond Tucumán the Belgrano line runs N via Rosario de la Frontera to Jujuy, and La Quiaca, on the Bolivian border, 644 km. from Tucumán. There are also buses to all these places and their use seems preferable; the trains N of Tucumán, though comfortable (with a dining car and crowded only when there are *fiestas*), are slow.

Road For travellers to Salta from Tucumán the road via Santa María and Cafayate (a very interesting journey through many microclimates, **see page 81**) is longer but more interesting than the direct road. Aconquija bus Tucumán to Cafayate (8 hrs.) via Tafí and Santa María (6 hrs.) leaves at 0600. Direct bus in summer from Tucumán to Cafayate Tues., Thurs., Sat., 6½ hrs., at

1000 (0600/0700 in winter). Direct Tucumán bus to Salta (but not via Cafayate), 4 hours, several daily, US$8. (slow bus 5½ hrs). Hitch-hiking from Tucumán to Salta is difficult beyond Tafí del Valle. Plenty of buses to Jujuy, e.g. Veloz del Norte, leaves at 0900, 6 hrs. (US$7).

For those who wish to travel direct from N Argentina to Central Chile, there are daily La Estrella buses (US$20) from Tucumán to Mendoza, leaving 1300, 1400 and 2000 (19 hours), via Catamarca, La Rioja, and San Juan. Bus to Córdoba 480 km, US$14, 8 hours, many companies (incl. El Tucumano Panamericano). *La Veloz de Norte* serves free coffee, cake and soda. To La Paz, take train or bus to the frontier, then at Villazón, connect with train to Oruro at 1330, reach Oruro at 0450 and arrive at La Paz at 1045. Bus to La Rioja, 7 hours, US$10. To Catamarca, 7 a day with Bosio, about US$5.50. Buses also to Santiago del Estero (US$3), Paraná, Termas de Río Hondo, Orán (US$12), Resistencia and Tinogasta. Bus to Buenos Aires, Chevallier at 1250 and 2100, 19 hours, US$20; El Trébol at 1600, 16 hrs., US$20.

Air Airport: Benjamín Matienzo, 9 km. from town. Bus for each flight, US$0.60, starts from *Hotel Mayoral*, 24 de Septiembre 364. Day flights to Buenos Aires (US$95) with Aerolíneas Argentinas and Austral; discounts on night flights. Austral Tucumán-Mar del Plata at 0240 on Mon., Mar del Plata-Tucumán Tue. and Sat. at 0150; Tucumán-Córdoba with Austral daily exc. Sun. at 1355. Alfa to Iguazú, Thurs. 1710.

Excursions Simoca, 50 km. S of Tucumán on Route 157, has authentic Saturday morning market, handicrafts and produce; essential to get there early. 36 km. to Villa Nougués, an hour up the mountain side (one of the most interesting tours), the summer residence of the well-to-do Tucumanos; it has an excellent private hotel; Aconquija park, with glorious trees, is at the foot of the mountains. Bus at 1130 (the only one; returns immediately); tours from Terra, 9 de Julio 80, US$5.25. El Cadillal dam, in the gorge of the Río Sali, 26 km. N of Tucumán, supplies electricity and water for the city and permanent irrigation for 80,000 hectares of parched land. There are restaurants, a good ACA campsite, good swimming, and a small museum at the dam. Reached by frequent bus from the depot near the railway station, US$1. Another possible excursion is to San Javier (hotel), plenty of buses to foot of hill, 20 km., beautiful views. To Salta via Cafayate, take the Ruta Nacional 38 SW, passing the Quebrada de Lules (20 km.), which is worth visiting.

At Km. 46, Route 307 branches NW to *Tafí del Valle* (97 km. from Tucumán, not to be confused with Tafí Viejo which is 10 km. N of the city) known to archaeologists as a holy valley of the precolumbian Indian tribes, where there is a dam (*Hostería ACA*, C; *Hotel Nuñorco*, D; *Colonial*, nr. bus station, no singles, friendly, clean, F. *Pensión La Cumbre*, F, hot water, basic; better one opposite *Colonial*, in billiard hall). Hotels and bungalows (D) at El Pinar del Ciervo. Camping, *Los Sauzales*, very clean, hot showers, rec. Tafí del Valle, which is becoming touristy, is often shrouded in fog because of the dam. Try local cheese. Ten mins. from Tafí is Museo La Banda in the old chapel of San Lorenzo.

Bus, Tucumán-Tafí, with Aconquija, sit on left-hand side, travels through luxuriant gorge with subtropical vegetation, 0700 and 1600, 3½ hrs, US$3.25.

Just before Tafí del Valle are Dique El Mollar, formerly La Angostura dam, and nearby the menhir park of *El Mollar*, with 129 standing stones and good views (closed in winter). *Hosterías* and small Ambrosetti museum nearby. Paved road between Tafí and El Mollar. Tours to El Mollar and Tafí from the agency next door to the tourist office, US$11.50 each for 4 people minimum. Local buses from Tafí, several a day, US$0.05, and the Tucumán-Tafí bus stops nearby. Entrance to the park is 10 km. S of Tafí del Valle; you can drive around it by car, or walk.

NW of Tafí is *Amaicha del Valle* (bus from Tucumán, US$5, 0600) with 360 sunny days a year, free municipal campsite, *Juan Bautista Alberdi*, 10 min. out of town (blue gate) (ACA hostel, rec., *Pensión Albarracín*, F). La Pachamama festival at end of pre-Lent Carnival; also see Sr. Cruz' craft workshop.

Over the 3,040 metre Infiernillo pass 21 km. from Tafí and 15 km. from Amaicha the road is paved and again after Amaicha to the junction with the Ruta Nacional 40 (15 km.) which leads N to Cafayate (55 km.- **see page 87**) and S, 24 km. to *Santa María*, population 18,000.

Hotels *Plaza*, on plaza, clean, modern, rec., D; *Provincial de Turismo*, San Martín, friendly, rec., dining room, D, with bath; *Residencial Palacios*, Mitre 592, F, basic, hot water, clean, reasonable and friendly; *Residencial Reinoso*, Av. 1° de Mayo 649, G, good, 2 blocks from plaza, hot showers, clean, friendly. Municipal **campsite** at end of Sarmiento.

Restaurants *El Cardón*, Abel Acosta 158, cheap and good, regional dishes.

Buses   To Tucumán 6 hrs., 0220, 0800 (US$6). To Cafayate daily at 0700 exc. Thurs. at 1030. Empresa Bosio goes to Catamarca, Sat.; via Tucumán Sun. at 1230, 9 hrs. Most start from Belgrano 271 on main Plaza; Empresa San Cayetano (600 block of Esquiú) goes to Belén (see page 107) 4 hrs., Mon., Wed., Fri. at 0500.

Excursions   to Fuerte Quemado (Indian ruins) 15 km. away, not as impressive as Quilmes (see below); Cerro Pintado, 8 km., coloured sandstone mountains; important ruins of Loma Rica, 18 km. away; Ampajango, 20 km. away, important indigenous finds.
   Quilmes (Tucumán), 37 km. away, with splendid views from the fortifications and interesting cacti, has the most southerly Inca ruins (dam, village and posting house—*tambo*), an *hostería* (summer only), camping facilities and a guide at the site from 0700 to 1730. It is 5 km. from the main Santa María-Cafayate road. There is also a provincial archaeological museum. Bus from Santa María at 0655, 1½ hrs., US$1.50, returns about 1030.

A railway and road run N from Tucumán to (145 km.) **Rosario de la Frontera,** a popular resort from June to September. Altitude: 769 metres. Eight km. away there are sulphur springs. Casino. From Buenos Aires, by Belgrano Railway: 1,296 km.

Hotels   *Termas,* rambling place, being remodelled, but beware of loose accounting, good food but many rooms without private bath (6 km. from bus station, taxi US$5), room with bath and 3 meals, C. Baths US$1.50. About 1 km from *Hotel Termas* is ACA motel. Across the road is man-made lake owned by Caza y Pesca Club—ask in your hotel for permission to fish. *Real*, E, basic, clean, not all doors close.

Bus   Rosario de la Frontera-Tucumán, Veloz del Norte, with stewardess, coffee and biscuits.

Excursions   To **El Naranjo** (19 km.) a Jesuit colonial town; a church contains images and carvings made by Indians.
   About 80 km. N of Rosario de la Frontera, at Lumbreras, a road branches off the Inter-American Highway and runs 80 km. NE to the Parque Nacional **Finca El Rey**, a 44,160- hectare tropical forest and wildlife preserve set among 900-1,500 metre hills with clear streams (good fishing). It can also be reached from Salta, 196 km., US$20 p.p. round-trip excursions of at least 6 with agencies. Public transport: take Benjamín Araoz bus at 0700 to Lumbreras, 2 hrs., US$2.50; there catch same line bus at 0915 to Paso de la Cruz, 45 min., US$1.30. From Paso de la Cruz it is 35 km. N to the park entrance and 10 km. from the entrance to the park hotel and administration. Only local farm and roadbuilding traffic, which may give a ride. A *National Tourist Hotel*, C, usually but not always closed at the height of the rainy season, Jan.-March (check at Terra Tours, Tucumán, T 214333, ask for Eduardo Cendoyo). It is clean and comfortable, has a large enclosed veranda overlooking the park. Also bungalows, and basic student accommodation. Mosquitoes, ticks and chiggers thrive; bring lotion. Camping allowed. Horseback riding. Landing strip for small planes. The access road is still poor and fords the river 9 times; passable for ordinary cars only in the driest of years.

From Güemes, 148 km. N of Rosario de la Frontera, a branch line and road run W through the mountains for 43 km. to

Salta, at 1,190 metres, 294,000 people, on the Río Arias, in the Lerma valley, in a mountainous and strikingly beautiful district. Salta, capital of its province, is a handsome city founded in 1582, with fine colonial buildings. Follow the ceramic pavement plaques, or get map from Tourist Office, for an interesting pedestrian tour. The Cathedral (open mornings and evenings), on the N side of the central Plaza 9 de Julio, was built 1858-1878; it contains the much venerated images of the Cristo del Milagro and of the Virgin Mary, the first sent from Spain in 1592, and has a rich interior mainly in red and gold, as well as a huge late baroque altar. The miracle was the sudden cessation of a terrifying earthquake when the images were paraded through the streets on September 13, 1692. They still are, each September, when 80,000 people visit the town. The Cabildo, on Calle Caseros, was built 1783. The Convent of San Bernardo, at Caseros and Santa Fe, was built in colonial style in the mid-19th century; it has a famous wooden portal of 1762. San Francisco church, at Caseros and Córdoba, built around 1880, is said to have the tallest church tower in South America. The Museo Arqueológico (US$1) on Av. Antártida Argentina has many objects from Tastil (see page 89) reached by a 3-hr. bus ride. Salta, 1,600 km. from Buenos Aires by rail or paved road, is now a great tourist and handicraft centre (visit the craft market at La Casa el Alto Molino and shops—open 0800-2000 weekdays, 0800-1300 Sat. and the onyx factory; prices are lower than in Tucumán or Buenos Aires) and the best starting place for tours of the NW.

1. Plaza 9 de Julio, 2. Post Office, 3. Telephone Office, 4. Tourist Office, 5. Municipality, 6. Casa de Gobierno, 7. Cabildo Museum, 8. Museo de Bellas Artes, 9. Museo Arqueológico, 10. Museo de Ciencias Naturales, 11. Casa Uriburu, 12. Cathedral, 13. San Francisco, 14. Convento de San Bernardo, 15. Aerolíneas Argentinas, 16. Market, 17. Banco de la Nación.

In Salta, visit the Cerro San Bernardo (1,458 metres), now accessible by cable car, US$1 return, from Parque San Martín. Very beautifully set at the foot of the hill is an impressive statue by Víctor Cariño, 1931, to General Güemes, whose *gaucho* troops repelled seven powerful attacks by the Spaniards between 1814 and 1821. A steep path behind the Archaeological Museum with Stations of the Cross leads to the top of the hill, where there is an old wooden cross, together with restaurant and artificial waterfalls. The guards at the provincial government palace on the Plaza 9 de Julio (changing of the guard at 1200) wear red ponchos with black stripes to commemorate the death of General Güemes; extended ceremony on Sats,—but not always.

Festivals Sept. 24, commemorating the battles of Tucumán and Salta. On June 16-17, folk music by youngsters in the evening and *gaucho* parade in the morning around the Güemes statue at the foot of the San Bernardo hill. Salta celebrates Carnival with processions on the four weekends before Ash Wednesday at 2200 in Av. Belgrano (seats optional at US$2-4); lots of shaving foam (*nieve*) in the early morning; also Mardi Gras (Shrove Tuesday) with a procession of decorated floats and of dancers with intricate masks of feathers and mirrors. It is the custom to squirt water at passers-by and *bombas de agua* (small balloons to be filled with water) are on sale for dropping from balconies on to unwary pedestrians below. Wear a light waterproof!

Hotels Salta is a favourite convention town. Many hotels are closed for a vacation during the Christmas season until January 10, so check. The last two weeks in July are often fully booked because of holidays. *Victoria Plaza*, B, Zuviría 16, excellent restaurant, the foyer overlooking the plaza is one of the centres of *salteño* life; *Salta*, Buenos Aires 1 (B), in main plaza, first class, refurbished, swimming pool, restaurant from 2100 only, and *California*, Alvarado 646 (C), 1st class, one block from main plaza, singles are small, rec. Also on main plaza is *Cabildo*, Caseros 527, D, pleasant. *Regidor*, Buenos Aires 9, opp. the *Salta*, English-speaking owner, avoid 1st floor, D, lunch US$5. *Colonial*, D, with bath, Zuviría 6, a/c. 24-hr. cafeteria; *Colón*, J. B. Alberdi 165, old fashioned, central, opposite railway station, no hot shower, F; *Plaza*, España 508, E, old, fair; *Portezuelo*, very good hotel at foot of Cerro San Bernardo, D with breakfast, some rooms a/c, swimming pool, clean, helpful, better and cheaper than the ACA's *Motel Huaico*, Av. Bolivia, Campo Castanares; *Crillón* (near main plaza, Ituzaingó 30), good; *Italia*, Alberdi 210, E, next to jazz club/casino, very clean and friendly, rec.; *Residencial Güemes*, on Necochea (600 block) near railway station F, basic, clean, private bath, laundry service. *Savoy* (near railway station), E, or F without bath, basic, clean, with cheap restaurant; *Residencial Elena*, E, clean, friendly and quiet, "charming", Buenos Aires 254; *Residencial San Jorge*, Esteco 244 y Ruiz de los Llanos 1164, rec., E with bath, parking, safe deposit, garden, washing and cooking facilities, horse-trekking advice by friendly proprietor, Sr. Dejean; *Hospedaje Doll*, Pasaje Ruiz de los Llanos 1360 (7 blocks from centre), F with bath, friendly, safe; *Residencial Viena*, Florida 184, D with bath, clean, a/c; *Florida*, E (no singles), hot showers, F without bath, very friendly, clean, will store luggage, Calle Florida y Urquiza 722. *Residencial Italia*, Alberdi 210, modern, good value, E, with bath; *Residencial Cepmer*, Yrigoyen 1195, E, good. *Residencial Cayetano*, Balcarce 747, E, clean, hot water; *Residencial Balcarce*, Balcarce 460, friendly, clean. *Residencial Centro*, Belgrano 657, friendly, F. *Casa Familiar*, San Martín 540, 1st floor, Apt. 2, run by Sra María Florencia Zavalia de Márquez Valladares, E, hot showers, cooking facilities, very friendly but near bus station, so noisy. Very cheap fruit and veg. market in same street. *Petit*, H. Yrigoyen 225, D, some rooms shared, swimming pool, nice; *Nápoli*, Mitre 1021, F, fairly near railway, laundry, friendly, quiet; *Candilejas*, Balcarce 980, F, without bath, erratic water supply, clean, comfortable, close to railway station. Many other cheap hotels near railway station (e.g. *Internacional*, F, opp. station, hot water, basic, with good cheap restaurant), but few near new bus station.

Camping Casino Provincial municipal grounds, by river, swimming pool available, 3 km. from centre. Bus 13 to grounds. There is no signposting. In front of the Casino turn left, go to the *balneario* administration office, US$2.15 each, car US$3. Free hot showers available if there is gas, safe and excellent facilities. At *Motel Huaico*, Campo Castanares, and *Residencial Hispano*, San Juan 619.

Restaurants *Hotel Victoria Plaza* restaurant warmly rec. *El Rey de Bife*, rec., near bus station, with excellent cold buffet and bife; *Balcarce*, near railway on Balcarce 934, delicious and reasonable. *El Monumento*, Gurrachaga 300 (opp. Güemes monument), good food, slow service, good atmosphere, reasonably priced; *Jockey Club*, reopened at Güemes 452; *La Castiza*, Alberdi 134, huge, little atmosphere, reasonable; *Italiano*, Buenos Aires y Urquiza, 1st floor, highly rec. and reasonable, good *pizzería* opposite. *Don José*, Urquiza 484, good, cheap, popular on Sun., asado de tira and grilled kid warmly rec. *La Madrileña*, España 421, quite good; *La Posta*, España 476, food and atmosphere both excellent, highly rec.; *La Casona*, Caseros 511, good, reasonable; *9 de Julio*, Urquiza 1020, rec.; *El Mesón de Pepe*, Rivadavia 714, fish specialities. Pleasant outdoor restaurants in Parque San Martín, at foot of Cerro San Bernardo. Good pizza at *La Selecta*, Belgrano 511. *El Quebracho*, near bus station, has peña show, at 2030. *El Antigal*, Balcarce, ½ block from railway station, cheap and good. Good set menu at *El Sorpaso* on Balcarce, cheap; *Miguel's Rotisería y Pizzería*, Balcarce nr. Belgrano, cheap, popular. Many good cheap restaurants on and near San Martín, by market. *Rotisería Pizzería Roque*, Alberdi y San Martín, cheap; *J.A.*, H. Yrigoyen y San Martín, excellent kid; *Boliche Balderrama*, San Martín 1126, has folk music, US$5 entrance for the show, also US$1 for good 4-course lunch. *Gauchos de Güemes*, for hearty late dinner and music, US$10, Uruguay 750. *El Rincón del Artista*, in 1200 block of San Martín, also rec. *Alvarez*, Buenos Aires y San Martín, cafeteria style, cheap and good. *Rubero 88*, Buenos Aires 88, good pizza/pasta. *Café del Paseo* at *Hotel Colonial*, Zuviría 6, open 24 hrs. *Confitería Milk 1000*, 20 de Febrero y España, good ice cream. *Heladería Gianni*, España 486, ask for copa del amor; excellent coffee served. *Heladería Cercena*, Pasaje Continental 7, Mitre 55 by Plaza 9 Julio, excellent natural ice-cream. Cheap restaurants near the railway and bus stations, many lunch-only restaurants (closed Suns.) with meals at US$1-2. *Unión Sirio Libanesa*, San Martín 677, has a good restaurant open to the public.

Try local Cafayate wines, such as Michel Torino and Echart Privado, and typical Torrontés-grape wine. Also, the good local water makes excellent beer.

Shopping Mercado Municipal, corner of San Martín and Florida, for meat, fish, vegetables and other produce and handicrafts, closed 1200-1700 and Sun. Mercado Artesanal is interesting (closed early Jan.); excellent quality goods, much better and cheaper than the tourist shops opposite, or in town. It is just out of town (San Martín 2555, T 219195), 0800-1930, take bus 2 or 3 from the centre. Woodcarvings of birds etc. from RUD, Santiago del Estero 202. Tiwanaku handicrafts store, museum upstairs, Caseros 472. Centro de Comercialización de Artesanías, Catamarca 84, cheaper handicrafts than in tourist shops. High quality, hand-made *salteño* boots from Calle Vicente López 1046. Shoemakers on Calle Urquiza make boots to order in 48 hours. Fair selection of books in English at Feria del Libro, Buenos Aires 69.

Rent-a-Car   Avis, airport and Alvarado 537; AI International in centre; several local companies.

Bathing   Balneario Municipal on outskirts, reached by bus No. 13 from Calle Ituzaingó, entry US$1.00. Bus fare US$1.20.

Laundry   Lavarap, self-service, Virrey Toledo y Alvarado. Also Santiago del Estero 221 (open Sun. a.m.) Speed Queen (cheap) Juramento 315.

Museums   Cabildo Histórico, Caseros 549, fascinating colonial and historical museum, open Wed.-Sun., 1500-2100, US$0.20. Museo de Bellas Artes, Florida 51, open every day 1600-1900 and Wed.-Sun. 0900-1200. Casa Uriburu, Caseros 421, has relics of a distinguished *salteño* family. Museo Foldórico Pajarito Velarde, Pueyrredón 106. Museo Arqueológico, interesting, moved to Av. Antártida Argentina. Museo de Ciencias Naturales, Mendoza 2, has a full display of stuffed birds. In the Casa el Alto Molino (Av. San Martín 2555), much rawhide work is on display. Centro Cultural, on Calle Caseros, has slide shows on Fridays about the local countryside, free.

Exchange   Banco de la Nación on Mitre and Belgrano, open 0730 until 1330, better overall rate (pays 5% more on cheques than on notes, but doesn't change money after 1000); Banco Provincial de Salta, España 526 on main square, closes at 1200 but changes travellers' cheques. Amex representative, Chicoana Turismo, Caseros 665, Galeria Margolet, *local* 20. Many *cambios* on España: Cambio Dinar at 609 changes cheques (3% commission) and cash; Saltur on the main square. Maguitur, España 678, only cash. (see note on provincial bonds used as currency, **page 169**).

Post Office   Deán Funes 140, corner of España; also in shopping arcade at corner of Florida and Gral. San Martín. **Telephone** office at Av. Belgrano 824, 24 hrs., also at Av. Vicente López 118, 0800-1930.

Consulates   Bolivia, Santiago del Estero 179; open Mon.-Fri., 0900-1300. Chile, Ejército del Norte 312; Spain, Las Heras 1229; Italy, Zuviría 380; France, Santa Fe 20; West Germany, España 671.

Tourist Office   Buenos Aires 93 (one block from main square). Open every day, inc Sun., till 2100. Very helpful, gives free maps and offers slide shows some evenings, also a self-guiding tour, Circuito Peatonal, to see important landmarks on foot. This office will also arrange accommodation in private houses. Ask for the Tourist Market here, excellent leather goods.

Travel Agencies   Saltur, Caseros 525, T 212012, very efficient. *Continente Viajes*, Zuviría 60 (on main plaza), has a wide variety of tours, rec. Chicoana Turismo, Caseros 565 (Local 20), T 218134, very helpful, rec.

Bus Services   There is no direct bus from Salta to Asunción, but Salta provides the most reliable cheap land connection between Bolivia and Paraguay. Buses daily, US$18 (with La Veloz del Norte), 14-16 hrs. to Resistencia, 1700 and 2200 for crossing into Paraguay (an arduous journey, but a/c, many stops in the night; for description of road, **see page 117**). Salta-Formosa with Atahualpa, which would provide the shortest route to Asunción, operates only twice weekly because of the state of the road. Bus to Córdoba, 8 a day, 14 hrs, US$15. Bus to Cafayate, US$4, 3½ hrs., several daily. To Cachi (5 hrs.) and Molinos (7 hrs.) with Marcos Rueda daily at 0700 (or 0630 from Marcos Rueda office at Olavarría 658). Marcos Rueda also has a service from Salta (Sat., 1300) to **La Poma**, arriving 1945 (via Cachi at 1750). The bus returns from La Poma next day at 1320. La Poma is reportedly a beautiful hamlet, and there is a *hostería*. Trout fishing is currently forbidden while stocks recover.
   The road (no buses) between La Poma and San Antonio de los Cobres (**see page 89**) crosses the highest pass in South America negotiable by car, the Paso Abra del Acay (4,900 metres).
   To Santa María, El Indio, 6½ hrs., 0700, US$10. To Mendoza via Tucumán, US$20, twice weekly. Bus to Tucumán, 4½ hrs, several firms, US$8. Bus to Embarcación daily at 0700. Bus to Jujuy, Atahualpa 16 a day between 0600 and 2300, "directo", US$2.40, 2¾ hours; to La Rioja, US$13.30; to La Quiaca, 11 hours, US$7 (see below).
   Bus to Calama and Antofagasta (Chile) leaves Wed. at 1600, US$26 (20-hour journey at least, very cold), run by Balturis, Urquiza 272. Take own food. Gemini bus to Antofagasta on Sat. at 1600 (said to be better than Atahualpa); reservations are hard to get on either service, have your name added to the list of reservations and try again on the evening before departure. The route is suspended in winter, and also in summer if there is heavy rain. Bus to Rosario de la Frontera, US$3.50, 2½ hrs, stewardess service, very pleasant trip. The new bus station is eight blocks from the main square. Taxi from bus station into Salta US$2.

Airport　Bus connection from town on corner of the main Plaza to El Aybal airport. From London, cheapest to fly standby to Miami, connect with LAB flight via Santa Cruz once a week to Salta. Two AA flights a week to Santa Cruz (Bolivia), Wed. and Sun. at 1145, arr. 1215 Bolivian time, and also Lloyd Aéreo Boliviano (LAB office on Caseros 376). To Orán and Tartagal (Bolivia) with SEAL. One flight a week to Asunción. AA flies Antofagasta (Chile) on Wed. and Sat. (US$72). AA flies to Bs. Aires (2 hrs., US$103) Tucumán, Córdoba (US$70) and Rosario. There are flights across the N of Argentina, e.g. Salta to Resistencia by Alfa (office in same building as tourist office), US$60 via Formosa, Sat. and Mon. (tickets and reservations only in these towns, propjets). There is a flight to Iguazú on Tues., return Sun. Special bus service between airport and Plaza 9 de Julio, US$1.50. Taxi from airport to bus station US$9.

Railways　Ticket office open weekdays 0900-1100, 1700-1900. (Salta is not on a direct line, it is connected with Güemes by local trains and by bus). Services to Buenos Aires also serve Tucumán (6 hrs.). Also bus/train combination with La Veloz del Norte (1) daily at 1230, arr. Tucumán 1700; see Tucumán section for details to Buenos Aires. **N.B.** If buying ticket from Buenos Aires to Salta via Tucumán, purchase train ticket to Tucumán and bus ticket to Salta at the same time so that you can transfer directly to the bus which meets the train, otherwise you must take local bus to bus terminal and wait (fare Buenos Aires-Salta US$48.40 and US$33.55). Ordinary train to Tucumán (continues to Córdoba), Tues., and Fri., 0835, 11½ hours (very slow). Train to Córdoba, leaves Tues. and Fri. at 1430, 20 hrs, no sleepers. From Salta to Mendoza, one takes a train to Villa María, near Córdoba, and after a 3-hr. wait gets another to Mendoza, takes about 40 hours. Slow but pleasant. Avoid during rainy periods as the track can get washed out; in summer can be hot and dusty. The Salta-Resistencia passenger service has been abolished, but for the hardy there is a regular freight service that leaves Metán (150 km. SE of Salta and a steam locomotive graveyard) after 1000 daily. The journey takes about 3 days, is very uncomfortable and involves frequent changes. It is best to buy all food before starting and to take plenty of drinking water with you. No direct train to Formosa. No direct trains between Salta and Jujuy, but connections are possible; buses much quicker.

　　In October 1980 Chile suspended its rail service from Socompa to Antofagasta, so it is not now possible to travel from Salta to Antofagasta direct except by air (see above) or by Atahualpa or Gemini bus. Argentine railways still maintain a train service from Salta to Socompa, where tourist cards are available (**see page 89** for description of line, tourist train to San Antonio de los Cobres, and goods train, and also for road taking similar route.)

Routes to Bolivia　To La Quiaca, on Bolivian frontier, 4 buses daily, Atahualpa (US$13), 11 hrs., at 0630 (direct), 1000 and 2130 (via Jujuy, prolonged stop), can be very cold, dusty. Buses also NE to Orán, six hours, for connection with Tarija, Bolivia (can involve taking overnight bus (Atahualpa, 7-10 hrs.) to Aguas Blancas at 2200 (road now paved), arriving before dawn—cold—then crossing river in motor boats to Bermejo, Bolivia and the next bus out is often full. Spectacular 8 hr. mountain ride alternative to the latter in open-air pick-up: hair-raising!); and to Yacuiba, via Pocitos (Bolivian frontier), for Santa Cruz, Bolivia. US$10 with Atahualpa to Pocitos, 7-10 hrs, very full, with passengers standing, can be uncomfortable, road now paved. Customs at Pocitos not to be trusted—beware of theft; and overcharging for "excess baggage" (on bus), for which there is no official limit written up anywhere. (Hotel at Pocitos, *Buen Gusto*, F, just tolerable.)

　　Trains to La Quiaca run via Jujuy, but not direct from Salta. The other route is served by train: Salta to Pocitos, Wed. 2000, arrive 0715 if you are lucky; go through Argentine exit formalities, **cross the bridge into Bolivia** then take a taxi to Yacuiba (US$0.25), whence the train leaves at 0815 to Santa Cruz (if you miss it, other trains to Santa Cruz on Wed. and Sat. at 1230—*rápido*, or Mon. and Fri. at 1900 - *mixto*). **See also page 95** on the route via Orán.

Excursions　Just S of Salta you pass Coronel Moldes: 26 km. from there is the dam of Cabra Corral, one of the largest artificial lakes in Argentina; water skiing, fishing, hotels. Paved road ends at the Presa General M. Belgrano, impressive views of the bridge across the lake. 11 km. NW of Salta, along a steep wooded valley (*quebrada*), is the picturesque village of San Lorenzo (new restaurant in high tower, *El Castillo*, owned by John Johnston (US), good food and music, no accommodation yet; otherwise camping and picnicking beside rocky stream—meals also at hillside lodge) and 2 km. further the Lomas de San Lorenzo with a little river and subtropical vegetation (a popular Sunday picnic spot). Can be reached by hourly bus from Salta, ½ hr. journey. To Jujuy and Humahuaca, day trip through many agencies, about US$15 p.p. To Cuesta del Obispo and the Forgotten Valley, on return, with Saltur day trip, superb. In summer, guided tours are few and far between because of a lack of tourists. Saltur also does US$8 guided trip to Cafayate, with stops at major rock formations along road. The El Rey National Park (**see page 82**) is about 200 km. E of Salta, at junction of Chaco and pre-Andean regions. Much wildlife and varied scenery. *Hostería*, D p.p. full board, and campsite next to it. Horses can be hired. Best time to visit is winter (drier). Tours arranged from Salta, e.g. by Mallorca on España 400 block.

A magnificent round trip of about 520 km. can be taken going SW from Salta to Cafayate (well paved, through a splendid canyon), then N through the Valles Calchaquíes and Cachi, and back E to Salta. The first part of this trip, S from

Salta, goes through El Carril (30 km.) where a road from Cachi intersects; continuing S for 25 km. Coronel Moldes is reached. Here, a side road to the left goes to Embalse Cabra Corral (see above). After Coronel Moldes goes through the Quebrada del Río de las Conchas with fascinating rock formations, all signposted: Anfiteatro (a gorge), El Sapo, El Fraile, El Obelisco, Los Castillos. The road goes through wild and semi-arid landscapes with many wild birds, including ñandúes (rheas).

Cafayate (altitude 1,660 metres) A quiet, clean, little town, with low rainfall, lying between two ranges of Andean foothills and surrounded by vineyards. Its church is narrow but has 5 arches. About 18 km. S. is Tolombón, where there are reported Indian ruins among giant cacti and other scrub plants. (The ruins are vestigial; the cacti are far more interesting.) Cafayate is much frequented by Argentine tourists. A walk to La Cruz (3 hrs.) takes you to a view of the Aconquija chain in the S to Nevado de Cachi in the N.

See Sr. Rodolfo Bravo's private museum of Calchaquí archaeology on Calle Colón, full of Indian artefacts dug up nearby, interesting slide show (US$0.50). Excursions to *bodegas* and vineyards possible, e.g. La Rosa owned by Michel Torino, open Mon.-Fri., 0800-1200 and 1600-1900, weekends a.m. only, no need to book, 30 min. tours and tasting; also Etchart, 2 km. on road to Tucumán, now has tours: the Etchart Cabernet Privado, red, has been recommended. La Banda, a small vineyard near La Rosa, is interesting because it is more primitive. Near Bodega La Rosa a local kiln makes enormous pots. The Museo de Vitivinicultura is in an old cellar on Av. Güemes, 2 blocks from main square, US$0.40, very well laid out. Locally woven tapestries are interesting, and very expensive; see them at workshops of Ricardo Miranda, Av. Güemes 330. Also Platería of Jorge Barraco, Colón 147, for silver craft work. Handicrafts in wood and silver by Oscar Hipaucha on main plaza.

Hotels *Hostería Cafayate* (ACA), modern, quiet (but cold), colonial-style, D, good food; *Gran Real*, Güemes 128, *Asturias*, Güemes 158, *Melchor*, Güemes y Almagro, all C; *Pensión Arroyo*, Camila Q. de Niño 160, rec., friendly, clean, F; *Colonial*, Almagro 134, E, charming patio; *Parador*, colonial style; *Güemes*, Salta 13, one block off main square, E; *Briones*, on main square, clean and comfortable, E with bath and hot water, accepts Amex card; *La Posta del Rey*, Güemes, E, clean; *Savoy*, off main square, with nice restaurant, D; *Confort*, on main street, E with bath, clean, comfortable. Accommodation in private houses is available. Municipal **campsite** Lorohuasi at S access to town, hot water, swimming pool, well maintained, bungalows for rent.

Restaurants *Miguelito*, simple, on plaza, good regional dishes and nice atmosphere, but lots of flies; *Bárbara*, also on plaza, good food, expensive; *Café La Barra*, also on plaza, rec. *La Carreta de Don Olegario*, also on plaza, good, pleasant, and spotless but rather expensive; *La López Pereyra*, Av. Güemes between La Banda and Lamadrid, well rec. *El Criollo*, Güemes 254, tourist menu US$1.25, clean, fan, rec. *El Rancho*, for parrilla. Another *parrillada* is *La Tinaja* on the corner of the main square. Good cheap wine at café opposite El Indio bus station in street off plaza, provide own container. Try excellent pan casero (local bread).

Pancho Silva and his family have a workshop selling and displaying their own and locals' handicrafts. A very informative family.

Tourist Office Av. Güemes 101 (in art shop), 3 blocks from main square.

Bus Service (Aconquija) to Tucumán (US$5) on Wed., Fri. and Sun at 0600 via Santa María, 8 hrs., Mon. Thurs., and Sat. at 1000, 6½ hrs. Alternatively go to Santa María with 1100 El Indio bus (2 hrs.) over good dirt road and take bus to Tucumán, Empresa Aconquija, leaving at 0200 and 0600, daily, taking 5-6 hrs. Colectivo leaves at 0400, taking 3½-4 hrs. (minimum 4 or 5 passengers). Bus to Salta several times a day, 3½ hrs, US$4.

Taxi owner, Millán, can usually be found in *La Tinaja*, Cafayate, but he is expensive.

Reinhard Böhm-Raffay writes: "On entering Cafayate from Tucumán there is a municipal campsite (US$2). If you follow the Río Colorado on foot just before this campsite, you can cross and follow the road towards the mountains. (An alternative is to take Calle 25 de Mayo (a dirt road), 4 blocks from the main plaza; carry on along this road, including a sharp left turn, and you reach the start of the road to the ridge.) Adobe houses with orange trees and chickens, dogs and horses along the riverbank. The road becomes a path, leading past Indian village up 3,500 metres to a mountain ridge. Spectacular view down the river valley and towards Cafayate and its vast, flat valley. From the last hut in the valley is where the path leads up for about 3-5 hrs." Alternatively, hitch-hike, or take the El Indio bus to Salta as far as Km. 30, then walk the Quebrada de Cafayate; best done in the afternoon, take fruit and/or water.

Horses can be hired for US$1 for 1½ hrs. from La Florida, Bodega Etchart Privado (2 km. from Cafayate on road to Tucumán).

Continuing S from Cafayate, the road goes to Santa María (see page 81), and SE to Tafí del Valle and Tucumán.

About a day is needed for the 160 km. trip from Cafayate to Cachi (Route 40). The road is mainly gravel and can be very difficult after rain, but the views of the Andean-foothill desert country are fascinating for those to whom strange rock formations and unexpected colours have an appeal. The population is largely Indian, and regional costumes abound. Salta and the Valles Calchaquíes are the centre for US archaeologist John Hyslo's study of Inca roads in the Andes. Between Cafayate and San Carlos is Aninominá, with municipal campsite.

About 24 km. N of Cafayate is **San Carlos** (altitude 1,660 m), a small settlement destroyed four times by Indians. It has a pleasant white church completed 1854, and another ACA *hostería*, as well as a municipal campsite. The Quebrada de Flechas, N of Cafayate on the road to Angastaco, is beautiful and desolate.

Bus   The El Indio bus on the Salta-Cafayate-Angastaco run arrives in San Carlos by noon and on the return journey at 0745. Cafayate to San Carlos daily at 1535 and 2205, 45 mins., US$0.60; returns at 0500 and 1655.

Entering the Calchaquí valley, one comes N into a hillier region centred on **Angastaco,** 2 km. off the main road, another small town, expanding rapidly, surrounded again by vineyards. You can sample the local Vino Patero, red or sweet white, in a house close to the river bridge; apparently *bodegas* can be visited, *vino patero* is supposed to be made by treading the grapes in the traditional manner. (*Hostería* with pool, run by municipality, F, good; also a small *residencial* off the main plaza, G, clean, comfortable. Electricity is cut off at 2230 and remains off until at least 0630.) Weekly bus Angastaco-Molinos, leaves Molinos Thurs. 1400, returns from Angastaco Fri. 0500. Ask in the main square for transport to Molinos, Cachi or Cafayate. Also ask for Sr. Gutiérrez in the shop by the bus stop, or for Yapura in the shop on the side of the same block; it's 1-1½ hrs. to Molinos, locals charge US$10-15. From the Angastaco turn-off it is 40 km. on a winding road through beautiful and desolate rock formations to **Molinos** (*Hostería Provincial*, recommended, D with breakfast, meals, in Isasmendi house with small museum, manager, Jorge Staude, speaks English, French and some German, and sells good local *artesanía*). Its church (a national monument, built c. 1720, now covered in a yellowish paste to preserve it), contains the mummified body of the last governor appointed by Spain, Colonel Severo Siqueira de Isasmendi y Echalar, who died in 1837. This relic can be seen by arrangement with the priest. A pleasant walk is down from the church, crossing a creek and then climbing a gentle hill, from which there are good views of Molinos and surrounding country. Sra. de Guaymas, who runs a store, serves meals, and rents beds (3 to a room) in accommodation opposite the diesel electricity plant very noisy and basic. On the left bank of the river, ask at the village of Seclantás for the authentic *ponchos de Güemes* (red with the black mourning stripe for General Güemes). Daily bus to Salta.

We are informed that *ponchos de Güemes* are made in most of the villages in the Valles Calchaquíes.

From Molinos it is 46 km. to **Cachi** (Quechua for "salt"), a beautiful little town renowned for its weaving and other crafts; the natives claim people die only of old age, because the climate is very invigorating; height above sea level, 2,280 metres. The church's floor, roof and confessional are made from the wood of the *cardón* cactus. The local archaeological museum is described by Federico Kirbus as the best such in Argentina. It is in the "Land of the Pimentón", the pepper-growing area. *Hotel Nevado de Cachi*, F, near bus station, basic but good restaurant, also a good one opposite; good *ACA Hostería Cachi*, E; good municipal campsite with swimming pool, on hill at S end of town. From Cachi, you follow Route 40 for 11 km. N, then turn right to Route 33. This road climbs continuously to the Cuesta del Obispo passing a dead-straight stretch of 14 km. known as Recta Tin-Tin with magnificent views of the Los Cardones national park with the huge candelabra cacti, which grow up to 6 metres in height, reaching the summit (3,620 metres) after 43 km. Then it plunges down through a luxuriously-wooded steep valley populated by Indians in local costumes. The road rejoins Route 68 at El Carril, from where it is 37 km. back to Salta.

If you wish to make a round trip just to Cachi, take a bus at 0630 from Salta (5 hrs.) stay the night and return the next morning at 0900. Take the bus from Marcos Rueda, Olavarría 658, *not* at bus station, where it arrives full (buy bus ticket the day before, from Islas Malvinas 339); sit on left-hand side, to see remarkable Quebrada de Escoipe. The bus goes on to Molinos. One-day excursions to Cachi from Salta (US$10) give insufficient time.

Ask also at tour agencies about excursions to Quebrada del Toro, rugged and striking countryside (see below).

There is a metre-gauge railway from Salta through the little town of **San Antonio de los Cobres** to Antofagasta, in north Chile (trains only as far as Socompa, on the Chilean frontier). It is 900 km. long and reaches an altitude of 4,453 metres as it passes over the Chorrillos pass. Do not eat, drink, smoke in excess on the way up; resident doctor on board for altitude problems. Take plenty of film, but do not take pictures in San Antonio: it is a military zone. From Salta to San Antonio de los Cobres (a squat, ugly mining town on a bleak, high desert at 3,750 metres, pop.: 2,200 only of interest if you want to visit the copper, zinc, lead and silver mines with shuttle bus from La Concordia company office, about 20 km, from the mine you can walk to La Polvorilla viaduct, 20 mins., vicuñas and condors en route; *Hospedaje Belgrano*, painted blue, G, no heat, basic, use of kitchen and restaurant; *Pensión Los Andes*, G with restaurant; both on main street) it passes through the Quebrada del Toro, even more picturesque and impressive than the Humahuaca valley. Muñano, on a desert plateau after one goes over the mountains at Abra Muñano (4,165 metres), is the highest railway station in Argentina, 3,936 metres. The gorge is peculiar in that there is no pass over the mountains. The line is hewn out of the wall closing the end of the valley, zig-zags up and then across the top of the ridge at both El Alisal and Chorrillos. The Argentine side is a barren, rocky plateau 2,150-3,350 metres above sea level and inhabited by Coya Indians who bear a far closer resemblance to their cousins in Bolivia than to the Salteño lowlander. The train turns E at Puerto Tastil to climb to Muñano and misses the archaeological areas, which can however be reached by bus or car. The vertiginous, many-forded road from Salta to San Antonio de los Cobres (6 hours, bus four times a week, US$2.30; Empresa Quebradeño, unreliable timetable, serves Muñano 3 times a week, better to hire a car in San Antonio, US$10 return, to make the journey—take your own water if hiking; there is none in mountains) follows much the same route as the railway but is at a much lower level, which makes it prone to flooding, and the view from the train is much more impressive. The vegetation is low scrub and cactus. Day trip from Salta by minibus US$6, stop at Santa Rosa de **Tastil** to see Indian ruins. The roofs of the houses are said to have been made of cactus. Try the *quesillo de cabra* (goat's cheese) from Estancia Las Cuevas. No through trains to Chile.

From Salta the main connection with San Antonio is now the train to **Socompa on the Chilean frontier** (570 km.). Train to Socompa leaves Salta Weds. 1640 (sometimes runs Sat. instead, check, tickets available 1½ hrs. before departure, arr. 1215 Thur.), first class US$10.60, tourist US$7.90; returns Thurs. at 1400, arriving in Salta 1005 Fri. Wait in Socompa for the freight train which runs to and from Calama and ask officials if you can take this, a long, hard, cold ride, but cheap (total cost Salta-Baquedano, Chile, US$18).

In April 1982, the *Tren a las Nubes* (Train to the Clouds) was reinstated, running the 218 km. between Salta and La Polvorilla viaduct. The service (1st class) operates on Sat. from April to November (July and August Thur., Fri. and Sun. as well), leaving at 0645 and arriving back at 2205, US$11, US$2 for lunch. Book up to 45 days in advance at station; or in railway office, Florida 753 Buenos Aires. Be warned, though, that its departure and arrival points are at 1,200 metres while it climbs to and descends from 3,960 metres in 15 hours—you will need a remedy for *soroche*.

A goods train goes on Weds. from Salta at 1910 (arrive 0820) to Pocitos, beyond San Antonio. It serves the British-built borate plant at Campo Quijano. It is a single track line so you can change to come down at e.g. Diego de Almagro at dusk. Obtain authorization for travel by this train at the "Movimientos" bureau, 1st floor Office No. 110, change voucher for ticket at the downstairs counter. The train leaves from the goods depôt, a few metres from the Belgrano Railway station. Show up ½ hour early, on the platform where the big bell hangs and where the conductors (guards) meet; there is now one passenger coach (first class US$7.90, tourist US$5.90).

There is a road from San Antonio de los Cobres over the pass of Huaytiquina (4,200 metres) to San Pedro de Atacama. At its highest, the road is 4,560 metres. It is a very beautiful trip: you cross salt lakes with flamingoes and impressive desert around. The road on the Argentine side is very good, but on the Chilean side there are very steep gradients. Gasoline is available in San Pedro and Calama. Because of snow, this route is available only part of the year. A car must be in very good condition to cope with the heights.

The direct road from Salta to Jujuy is picturesque with its winding 92-km. stretch through the mountains, now paved, known as *la cornisa*. The longer road, via Güemes, is the better road for hitch-hiking.

Jujuy (pronounced Hoo-hooey) properly San Salvador de Jujuy, the capital of Jujuy province, 66 km. by rail N of the Güemes junction on the Belgrano railway, was founded first in 1565 and then in 1575, when it was destroyed by the Indians, and finally established in 1593. The Government House is in a fine square lined with orange trees, Plaza Belgrano, in the eastern part of the city. On the western side of this plaza is a colonial Cathedral (often shut) with very fine 18th century images, pulpits, walls and paintings finished about 1746. It has been heavily restored, but in the nave is a superb wooden pulpit, carved by Indians and gilded, a colonial treasure without its equal in Argentina. You can see the doorway on Calle Lavalle through which General Lavalle, the enemy of Rosas, was killed by a bullet in 1848, but the door is a copy; the original was taken to Buenos Aires. On Alvear, between Senador Pérez and Lamadrid, are the Teatro Mitre (worth a visit) and the Mercado Artesanal. In the western part of the city are the Parque San Martín and an open space, La Tablada, where horses, mules and donkeys used to be assembled in caravans to be driven to the mines in Bolivia and Peru. See the Palacio de Tribunales near the river, one of the best modern buildings in Argentina. Jujuy stands at 1,260 metres, completely surrounded by wooded mountains. Streets are lined with bitter-orange trees. Pop.: 120,000. The scenery is varied and splendid.

Public Holidays   August 6, and 23-24. Festival on Nov. 6.

Hotels   Best is *Fenicia*, B, on riverside at 19 de Abril 427. Second best is *Internacional*, Belgrano 501 (main square), B. *Alto la Viña*, attractive, on hill 5 km. away, C, swimming pool. *Augustus*, Belgrano 715, D, modern, comfortable but noisy. *Sumay*, Otero 232, C, central, clean; *Avenida*, 19 de Abril 469, on riverside, with fair restaurant, D (F off season, cafeteria only); *Residencial Los Andes*, Rep. de Siria 456, 3 blocks from bus station, clean, hot water, E. Across the street is *Residencial San Carlos*, Siria 459, E, friendly, clean, some rooms a/c; *Motel Huaico* (good), just outside on road to Humahuaca. *Residencial Lavalle*, Lavalle 272, near station, rec., E (dog bites if touched). *Del Norte*, Alvear 444, F, clean and friendly, near railway station, with good cheap restaurant; next door is *Carlitos*, also F, very friendly. *Chung King*, Alvear 627, friendly, very noisy, E, good restaurant. *Savoy*, F, basic and very clean, but damp.

Camping   *Autocamping Municipal*, US$2.40 per tent, ask for a cheaper rate for one person. 14 km. N of Jujuy on Humahuaca road, also *Autocamping*, 3 km. N outside city at Huaico Chico, US$1.50 per tent, motel opposite. Buses frequent. Hot showers, clothes washing facilities, very friendly.

Restaurants   *Casa del Médico*, Alto La Viña, French cooking, expensive and excellent; *Chung-King*, very good, Alvear 627; *Conrad*, Belgrano 952, good; *La Royal*, on Belgrano, good food and atmosphere. *Bar-Restaurant Sociedad Obrera* for cheap food, General Balcarce 357, but not attractive, cheap bar opposite. *Restaurant Sirio Libanesa*, Lamadrid 568 (don't be put off by the uninviting entrance). Very good ice cream around the corner of the Cathedral, made by Greek owner.

Museums   Histórico Provincial, Lavalle 266; Museo de Paleontología y Mineralogía, Independencia and Lavalle. Museo de Bellas Artes, Güemes 956, open Mon.-Fri., 0800-1300, 1600-2100, Sat. 0900-1200.

Exchange   at travel agencies on Calle Belgrano change cash and dollar travellers' cheques (e.g. Noroeste Cambio, No. 592; Dina Tour, No 931). Cheques can also be changed at Horus, about 50 metres from the Tourist Office, on Güemes. (see note on provincial bonds used as currency, **page 169**)

Consulates   Migración is on Belgrano 499. Bolivia, Av. Mitre 32, Barrio V. San Martín; Spain, R. de Velasco 362; Italy, Av. Fascio 660.

Post Office   Otero 262; Independencia y Lamadrid; bus terminal. *Intel*, Senador Pérez 141.

Shopping   Camera Repairs Sr Calve, Siria 345. Backpack repairs, San Martín y Gorriti. Good cheap ponchos at cooperative on Necochea, near Belgrano.

Tourist Office   on corner of Belgrano 690 and Lavalle, very helpful.
For information on bird watching, contact Mario Daniel Cheronaza, Pratonal 38, No. 848-830, Viviendos "El Arenal", Jujuy. La Estación Biológica de Fauna Silvestre, Av. Bolivia 2335, Jujuy, is open to the public on Sundays (for private tours on other days, contact Dr. Arturo A.Canedi, T 25617-25845), very interesting.

Travel Agencies   Many along Belgrano. Turismo Lavalle, Belgrano 636, does car tours through the Quebrada de Humahuaca, US$10 to see the villages.

Train No direct services to Salta. Train to Buenos Aires only Tues. and Fri. at 1240, very crowded and can be endlessly delayed. There is also a bus/train combination via Tucumán with La Veloz del Norte (US$10) Sun. and Wed. at 1100 arr. Tucumán 1600; Independencia train leaves at 1715, Bs. As. to Jujuy, Tues. and Fri. with *El Norteño* at 1000; Sun. and Thurs. at 1800. No sleepers. Train services to La Quiaca, for Bolivia, have been restored; there are two trains a week to La Quiaca, leaving 0900 Tues. and Thurs., arriving 1900.

Airport 40 km. out of town or 45 mins. by bus. Service to Buenos Aires by Aerolíneas Argentinas, two flights a day via Salta, Tucumán, Córdoba, US$87; Sun. 0315 flight US$52. Check for weather conditions in connecting airports before you fly or you may find yourself stranded elsewhere.

Buses via Tucumán to Córdoba, at 1400, 1845, 2130 (Panamericano), at 1100, with La Veloz, daily, Tucumán 5 hrs., US$7, and Córdoba, 14 hrs. US$20 with Atahualpa. To Salta, from 0700 to 0930, 2¾ hours, US$2.40. To La Quiaca, leaves 0745, 1100, 1800, 2315, 6½ hrs., Panamericano, US$6.50. Road paved only as far as Humahuaca, reasonably comfortable, but cold. To Orán daily at 1700; to Humahuaca, US$3, 3 hrs., sit on left side. To Embarcación, US$5.25 with Agencia Balut, via San Pedro and Libertador San Martín. Jujuy-Purmamarca-Susques, leaves Purmamarca at 1330 on Wed. and Sat., returning Thurs. and Sun., crossing the Abra Potrerillos (4,164 m.) and the Salinas Grandes of Jujuy. Jujuy-Tilcara 1½ hrs., US$2.50.

Some 19 km. from Jujuy is *Termas de Reyes,* where there are hot springs. This resort, with the *Gran Hotel Termas de Reyes,* (C, run down but friendly, good meals), is set among magnificent mountains 45 mins. by bus from Jujuy (No. 14 from corner of plaza, 6 times a day). US$2 to swim in the thermal pool at the hotel; municipal baths free but closed Weds. It is possible to camp below the hotel free of charge.

East from Jujuy The Loving Team of London write: **San Pedro de Jujuy** is a sugar town of 60,000; interesting factory area with houses, hospital, Anglican church, recreation centre built by the English Leach family who owned the sugar mill; now all falling to rack and ruin. *Hotel Alex*, opp. bus station, E, clean; *Residencial Gorritti*, on Gorritti, F. Bus to Jujuy, US$2, 1½ hrs.; Atahualpa to Embarcación, US$3.50, 2½ hrs.

North from Jujuy Lovers of old churches will find Salta and Jujuy excellent centres. Franciscan and Dominican friars arrived in the area from Bolivia as early as 1550. The Jesuits followed about 1585. Along both the old Camino de los Incas and the new route through the Quebrada de Humahuaca the padres, in the course of two centuries, built simple but beautiful churches, of which about 20 still exist. They are marked by crosses on the map. All of them can be visited by car from Salta or Jujuy, though some of the roads are very rough. A spare fuel can should be carried because service stations are far apart. (There are ACA stations at Jujuy, Humahuaca and La Quiaca, and YPF stations at Tilcara and Abra Pampa.)

One group, in the Puna de Atacama, on the old Camino de los Incas (which has completely disappeared), can be reached by the road which runs W from Salta through the picturesque Quebrada del Toro to San Antonio de los Cobres (**see page 89**). The road S from San Antonio to Antofagasta de la Sierra is pretty severe going. The road N to Susques (105 km.), is comparatively comfortable, but runs through utter desert. There is lodging at Susques and an interesting 16th century chapel. Close to the Bolivian and Chilean frontier is El Toro, lovely ride through *altiplano*, past Laguna Turilari, mining territory, bizarre rock formations. Lodgings may be available in first-aid room, ask male nurse, Don Juan Puca. From El Toro on to Coranzulí is very rough.

The second group can be reached from the road N from Jujuy to La Quiaca through the Quebrada de Humahuaca, which is itself extremely beautiful, with spectacular and dramatic rock colours and giant cacti in the higher, drier parts; the Inter-American Highway through it has been paved as far as Humahuaca.

Beyond Tumbaya, where there is a church originally built in 1796 and rebuilt in 1873, a road runs 5 km. to **Purmamarca**, a very poor but picturesque village; there is a *hospedaje*, or lodging can be obtained by asking at the ceramic shop opposite the church (mid-17th century) or at the police station, and there is a campsite (no facilities). At the entrance to Purmamarca a right turn leads to a new gravel road, which leads through another *quebrada* over a 4,170-metre pass to the Salinas Grandes salt flats at about 3,500 metres on the Altiplano. The road continues on to Susques (see above).

Not far N of the turn, on the main road, is Maimará (*Albergue Maimará,* also camping, 5 km. from Maimará, US$1.20 a day). Between the turning to Purmamarca and Maimará is a new folk museum called Posta de Hornillos, a

ANDEAN CHURCHES
IN ARGENTINA
CROQUIS.

recently restored old colonial posting house, of which there used to be a chain from Buenos Aires to the Bolivian border. Highly recommended. *Tilcara*, a short distance N in the *quebrada*, has a folk museum run by Buenos Aires University (closed in June), the Ernesto Soto Avendaño museum where a scaled-down model of the independence monument at Humahuaca can be seen, the regional museum José A. Terry with paintings, and the *Hotel Tilcara* (D, closed in winter, swimming pool—usually dry); *Hotel Edén*, Av. Rivadavia, one block from plaza, clean, friendly, F; *El Antigal*, on same street, E. *Restaurante Pucará*, on main square, rec. Within walking distance is a *pucará*, or Inca fort, entry US$0.40, incorrectly reconstructed but with good views of the valley, closed in June. Botanic garden at the foot of the *pucará* and museum at the main square with excellent display of Andean items.

The churches of Huacalera, Uquía, and Humahuaca are on the main road. At Huacalera is the *Hotel Monterrey*, D, friendly but run down. Two km. S of Huacalera, a small obelisk 20 metres W of the road gives the exact latitude of the Tropic of Capricorn. At Uquía (church built 1691, with *cuzqueño* paintings) and Casabindo, the walls of the naves are hung with 17th century paintings of winged angels in military dress: the so-called *ángeles caballeros*. Cactus-wood decoration is found in many local churches.

Both in Tilcara and Humahuaca there are displays of pictures of the Passion made entirely of flowers, leaves, grasses and seeds at Easter and a traditional procession on Holy Thursday at night joined by thousands. No beef is sold during Holy Week in shops or restaurants. All along the Quebrada de Humahuaca the pre-Lent carnival celebrations are picturesque and colourful.

Humahuaca (alt. 2,940 metres), 126 km. from Jujuy (3 hrs., US$3, by bus), is a small traditional town with an attractive church (originally begun 1631, but totally reconstructed in 1873-80), a mechanical figure of San Francisco Solano which blesses the town from the town hall at 1200, and a large independence monument flanked by huge cacti. See the Estudio Museo Ramoneda, combined studio and museum, entrance US$0.50. Museo Folklórico Regional, Buenos Aires 435, open daily 0800-2000, US$0.80, privately owned (run by Sr Sixto Vázquez Zuleta, an authority on the area's folklore), well worth seeing. Market near Humahuaca railway station, where *colla* women sell everything from homeopathic herbs to fresh bread. Folklore festival at Rodero, close to Humahuaca, around January 13-15, with local groups and dancing. Humahuaca's main festival is Candelaria, February 2, with a procession after 1400 with traditional dress and music. Near Humahuaca, 9 km. NE, is Cotaca, a large unexplained archaeological site with an Indian village nearby, a nice walk; you can also see Indian artistic remains nearby at Hornaditas (18 km. on La Quiaca road) and Incacueva, and an Indian mine at Rinconada.

The Instituto de Cultura Indígena offers guided tours of Indian communities, information, Quechua classes, exhibitions, concerts, lectures and a public library specializing in anthropology, folklore, history and archaeology, on Buenos Aires 740.

Hotels *Provincial de Turismo*, Buenos Aires 650, D, swimming pool dry even in summer; *Hotel Humahuaca*, Córdoba y Corrientes, E, basic, run down, with hot water, food is not rec.; *Residencial Humahuaca*, E, some a/c, traditional, clean, friendly. *Residencial Colonial*, F, excellent and clean, on Entre Ríos, one block from bus station. Several *residenciales* (F). Youth Hostel, *Albergue Humahuaca*, Buenos Aires 447, F.

Camping Across bridge by railway station, small charge includes use of facilities.

Restaurants *El Cardón*, at foot of large independence monument, good (try cabrito al horno with queso de cabra); *La Cacharpaya*, near church, good food and music, but avoid middle of the day when bus tours invade. Good place at bus station.

North of Humahuaca, at Iturbe (one bus a day), a road leads right to La Cueva (6 km.) and on 70 km. over the 4,000-metre Abra del Cóndor to *Iruya*, a beautiful village with a fine 17th-century church and Rosario festival on first Sunday in October; no bus from Humahuaca, but you may get a seat on a truck. Roads to Cochinoca (25 km.) and Casabindo (62 km.) branch off left at a point 4 km. N of Abra Pampa, where mining is important. (*Residencial* nr. plaza in Abra Pampa on

Senador Pérez, clean, hot water, F.) About 60 km away is Laguna Pozuelos, a natural monument and flamingo reserve. Truck transport daily exc. Sun. 15 km. from Abra Pampa is the vicuña farm at Miraflores, the largest in Argentina. Information offered, photography permitted; colectivos go a.m. Mon.-Sat. from Abra Pampa to the vicuña farm.

Yavi, with the fine church of San Francisco, which has magnificent gold decoration and windows of onyx, is reached by a good, paved road (16 km.) from La Quiaca; taxi available. (Find the caretaker at her house and she will show you round the church, open Tues.-Sun. 0900-1200 and Tues.-Fri. 1500-1800.) Opposite this church is the house of the Marqués Campero y Tojo. Three-room *hostería* at Yavi. Only a mule track leads on to the two churches of Santa Victoria (a forlorn Indian village in a rain forest valley) and Acoyte.

Beyond Humahuaca the *puna* is bleak and barren all the way, and the road unpaved, for the 167 km. to **La Quiaca,** on the Bolivian border and 292 km. from Jujuy. There is a market across the footbridge over the railway tracks, then one block on. La Quiaca is joined to its Bolivian neighbour, Villazón, by a concrete bridge. Altitude, 3,442 metres. On the third Sunday in October the Manca Fiesta, or the festival of the pots, is held here, and the Colla Indians from Jujuy and the Bolivian *altiplano* come, carrying all sorts of pots; local food is eaten. The climate calls for warm clothing the year round. If going on into Bolivia, buy your basic rations, medicaments etc. in La Quiaca. (Border on Argentine side closed 1200-1500.) If it rains heavily when you are travelling by car between Jujuy and La Quiaca, wait, or you may find yourself on flooded roads.

Hotels *Turismo,* D, rec., clean, modern, comfortable, two blocks S and one W of bus station; *Cristal,* best, four blocks from railway station, E, clean and comfortable, with café and bus office adjacent. *Residencia Argentina,* clean; *Grand,* opp. railway station, clean, good hot showers, F; *Residencial El Turista,* very good, but expensive, has garages and swimming pool; *Alojamiento Cruz del Sur,* cheap; cheap alojamiento, *Pequeño,* Av. Bolívar 236, friendly and clean. *Residencial Victoria,* near railway station and church, F, hot water. *La Frontera* hotel and restaurant, uphill from Atahualpa bus stop, good and cheap.

Camping is possible near the control post on the outskirts of town.

Restaurant *Cristal,* opposite the Atahualpa bus office in small shopping arcade on the main shopping street, good, cheap; *Café Victoria* and *Panamericano* in same building as *Grand Hotel.*

Exchange Travel agency around corner from *Hotel Cristal* gives good rates for cheques.

Transport Difficult to obtain information in La Quiaca about buses leaving Villazón for points in Bolivia (see page 214 for Villazón), though Bolivian buses tend to be more reliable than Bolivian trains. 4 Atahualpa (next to *Hotel Cristal*) buses a day to Salta (US$13) via Jujuy, 1100, 1300, 1800, 2130 (5-8 hrs. to Jujuy, 9-11 hrs. to Salta), also several to Jujuy. Panamericano (next to *Hotel Grand*) bus company has 5 buses a day to Jujuy, US$6.50, 6½ hrs. Some meal breaks, but take own food, as sometimes long delays. Buses may be stopped and searched for coca leaves. *Común* bus at 2130, 12 hours. The railway line between Jujuy and La Quiaca has been restored following storm damage in February 1984; train leaves for Jujuy and Tucumán Tues. and Sat. The railway goes up to 3,692 metres at Tres Cruces. Take warm sweaters, as temperature drops sharply after sunset.

To Bolivia Take a taxi or hire a porter with a luggage barrow to take you through the immigration office opposite the Automóvil Club, and customs and final control on the frontier.There are few exchange facilities on the Argentine side (only until 1300 at Banco de la Nación in La Quiaca). Travellers' cheques can no longer be cashed at the Turismo building; only dollar notes are accepted there (good rates) and at the exchange shops. In La Quiaca some of the large supermarkets give good rates for the Argentine austral. You can also buy australes in Villazón for US funds, but not for travellers' cheques. *Cambios* are open on Sundays at Villazón but give a very poor rate. Food is good and cheap. Tip conductor at start and end of trip for service. Motorists should visit the Argentine Automóvil Club just off the international bridge for maps, gasoline, etc., and information; and in Villazón, the Servicio Nacional de Turismo to obtain the Hoja de Ruta, which all motorists must have. It is not restrictive in any practical sense; just a nuisance! If the Bolivian Immigration Officer at Villazón is not in his office, you can ask for him at *Hotel Panamericano,* just up from the Post Office. Taxis are available from the Argentine station, or the frontier, to the Bolivian station.

Warning Those travellers who need a visa to enter Bolivia are advised to get it before arriving in

La Quiaca because the consular staff there try to charge US$15 per visa; pleading may reduce the charge.

Medical   There are a good hospital in La Quiaca and a doctor in Villazón. Farmacia Nueva, ½ block from Church, has remedies for *soroche* (mountain sickness).

Entering Argentina from Bolivia, Argentine immigration and customs are open 0730-1200, 1500-1800; Sats., Suns., and holidays pay special fee of US$3 after 1100. Buses arriving outside these hours will have to wait, so check before travelling. Porters US$1 from Villazón bus station to border; another US$1 from border to Argentine station. You can cross the border at night, without luggage, and your passport will not be stamped. Very thorough customs searches are made some 20 km. after the border in Argentina. Border crossing into Argentina may take up to 1½ hours: formalities are very thorough.

N.B.   Bolivian time is one hour earlier than Argentine. Lunch Bolivian side is 1200-1400 (Bol. time) and Argentine side 1200-1500 (Arg. time) so customs reopen at same time.
Make sure you book a seat when buying a railway ticket; it is also essential to arrive well in advance of advertised time of departure to get your seat.

Bolivia can also be reached by road from *Orán,* an uninteresting place (*Hotel Centro,* E; dirty room at *Hotel Crillón,* E; *Residencial Crisol,* General San Martín, near bus stations, F, without bath, hot water, friendly, rec.; several hotels near bus station) where there are bus services to Agua Blanca (1½ hrs., US$1.30, luggage checks on bus), on the frontier. There is nowhere to stay at Agua Blanca nor anywhere to change money, but there are restaurants (*El Rinconcito de los Amigos*) and shops; spend your remaining Bolivian money here, not accepted in Orán; buses to Orán every 2-3 hrs., e.g. 1615, 1830, 2100. The passport office at Agua Blanca is open from 0700 to 1200 and 1500 to 1900 hrs. There is no exit tax. There is a through bus service from Agua Blanca to Salta at 1100 daily. Buses run twice daily from Bermejo, across the river (ferry US$0.10), to Tarija (6 hours, US$2). There is also a direct bus (Sat., US$15, 16 hrs journey) from Orán to Asunción, Paraguay.
Buses, five daily from Orán to Salta, last at 2100, 8½ hrs.; direct bus to Tucumán at 2130, connecting for Mendoza bus which leaves at 1300. Bus to Tartagal daily at 0630 and 1800; to Jujuy at 1200 daily; to Formosa, US$22, 14 hrs., leaving Tues., Thurs., Sat. at 0930; Orán to Embarcación, US$1.30.
Embarcación has several hotels (*Punta Norte,* on España, D, new, clean, a/c, friendly; Sr. Sarmiento's Hotel; *Universal,* hot water), of which the cheaper are near the railway station. Restaurant of *Sociedad Sirio Libanesa,* H. Irigoyen and 9 de Julio, cheap and good. 2 km. from Embarcación you can walk to the Loma Protestant mission for Matacs and Toba Indians, who sell unpainted pottery there. These Indians lead a fairly miserable existence. Buses go to Orán, 1 hour, US$1.30 on a paved road, from whence there are frequent buses to Agua Blanca (1 hour, US$1). Buses Embarcación-Pocitos. Bus Embarcación-Salta US$10. Embarcación-Formosa railway (dusty in summer) has *coche-motor* link leaving Embarcación 1325 Mon. and Fri., 20 hours, US$18 1st class, US$15.50 tourist, plenty of wildlife to see, but check details as this service is sometimes replaced by a bus when there is weather damage to the line. (Regular bus runs Tues. 1445.)

THE CUYO REGION: OVER THE ANDES TO CHILE (4)

In the Cuyo region, in the W, there is little rain and nothing can be grown except under irrigation. On the irrigated lands grapes and fruit are possible, and alfalfa takes the place of the maize grown in the N. Three of the more important oases in this area of slight rainfall are Mendoza itself, San Rafael, 160 km. to the S, and San Juan 177 km. to the N.

Of the 15 million hectares in Mendoza Province, only 2% are cultivated. Of the cultivated area 40% is given over to vines, 25% is under alfalfa grown for cattle, and the rest under olive groves and fruit trees. Petroleum is produced in the Province, and there are important uranium deposits.

The Transandine Route   Travelling by rail or road from Buenos Aires westward across the pampa, one comes first to:

Mercedes, in Buenos Aires Province, a pleasant city with a population of 40,000. It has many fine buildings, and is a railway junction of some importance. Travellers have been told here that it is against the law to take one's shoes off in the station! (Not to be confused with Villa Mercedes in San Luis Province—see below.) Tourist Office on plaza, very friendly.

Hotels *Aragón,* ½ block from Plaza, friendly, F, hot water. *Libertador,* E, opp. bus station, good.

The workshops of the San Martín railway are at *Junín,* 256 km. from Buenos Aires. (Eva Perón was born near here.) Also served by Mitre railway, the town is close to lagoons from which fish are taken to the capital. Population, about 60,000.

Hotels *Junín; Central. La Piemontesa,* E, reasonable.

Camping Chimihuin municipal campsite, US$1.50.

At Rufino, on Route 7, 452 km. from Buenos Aires, is the very reasonable, rec. *Hotel Astur* (Córdoba 81), D with ACA discount; also at La Boulaye, on Route 7, 517 km. from Buenos Aires, there are several good and cheap hotels, e.g. *Victoria.*

At **Villa Mercedes** (San Luis Province), 693 km. from Buenos Aires (where the old municipal market is now an arts and community centre), a line runs NE to (122 km.) Río Cuarto. About 65 km. beyond Villa Mercedes we begin to run into the rolling hills of San Luis; beyond there are stretches of woodland. (ACA hotel *San Martín,* Lavalle 435, D, restaurant, garages, clean, friendly; the ACA restaurant at the service station on Route 7, outside town, is very good value; *Hostal del Sol,* on main highway; *Avenida,* in centre, E.)

Bus Villa Mercedes—Buenos Aires US$20.

Train Buenos Aires-Villa Mercedes, *El Aconcagua* daily at 2115, arrives 0730; returns 2206, arrives 0830; sleeper US$35.50, Pullman US$25.60; 1st Class US$16.85, tourist US$11.75.

Air Airport: Villa Reynolds, 10 km. from Villa Mercedes. Austral to Buenos Aires and to San Juan on Mon., Tues, Wed. at 1225, Fri., at 2000.

San Luis, 98 km. from Villa Mercedes, is the capital of the Province of San Luis. It stands at 765 metres at the southern end of the Punta de los Venados hills. It was founded by Martín de Loyola, the governor of Chile, in 1596, and is still faintly colonial. The area is rich in minerals and an onyx quarry is worked. Visit the Centro Artesanal San Martín de Porras, run by the Dominican fathers, on 25 de Mayo, opp. Govt. Palace, where rugs are woven. Open 0700-1300 exc. Sat. and Sun. Population: 85,000. San Luis to Mendoza is 264 km.

A "Via Crucis" sculptured in white marble skirts the mountainside. Beyond Salto Grande, Salto Colorado and the Gruta de la Virgen de las Flores is El Volcán, in whose neighbourhood is Cruz de Piedra dam (drives, fishing), and Cañada Honda (placer gold mining, riding and fishing). Hotels and inns along the road.

Hotels *Dos Venados,* Junín and Sucre; *Gran Palace,* Rivadavia 657; *Aiello,* Av. Quintana 431, a/c, priv. bath, garages. *Gran San Luis,* Av. Quintana 470, pool, 50 metres from ACA; *Regidor,* San Martín 804; *Gran Hotel España,* Av. Quintana 300; and *Novel,* Junín 748, all category C. *Castelmonte,* Chacabuco 769; *Grisel,* Bolívar 321; and *Miramar,* Maipú 874, all category D. *Mitre,* Mitre 1043; *Rivadavia,* Rivadavia 1470; *Casino,* Uruguay 804; *Los Andes,* Los Andes 1582; *Royal,* Colón 878; and *Buenos Aires,* Buenos Aires 834; all category E. *Hotel Residencial 17,* hot water, friendly, opp. bus station, basic, F. *Hotel San Antonio,* with restaurant; many others opposite bus and railway station; these are category F.

Camping No site but plenty of waste ground between bus and railway stations.

Restaurants *Suany,* Bolívar 991, rec.; *Los Venados,* Colón and Bolívar. *Michel,* rec. (address please?).

Exchange House *Alituris,* Pringles 983, opp. Plaza, no commission.

Tourist Office San Martín 741, excellent.

Train Buenos Aires-San Luis leaves at 2115, *El Aconcagua,* costs US$13.30 tourist, US$19 first, US$29 Pullman, and Sleeper US$38.50. Can continue on train to Mendoza, 4 hrs. Return daily at 2006, arrives 0830 next day.

29 km NE of San Luis is **La Toma** (*Hotel Gran Italia,* F, hot showers; *Residencial Days,* P. Graciarena 158, private bath) the cheapest place to buy green onyx—about 20 shops. From here you can make an excursion to Cerros Rosario, interesting hills and rock scenery, 10 km. NW; and San José del Morro, a group of mountains which were originally volcanoes (there is a model in the Museo de Ciencias in Buenos Aires). You will find a lot of rose-quartz.

Beyond San Luis (27 km.) the line climbs to a height of 460 metres and descends again along the valley of the Río Desaguadero. From the small junction of Las Catitas, 92 km. from Mendoza, a branch line runs S to (183 km.) San Rafael, through country typical of this region: sometimes arid, sometimes marshy, and sometimes cultivated. At **San Rafael** itself, at the foot of the Andes, irrigation makes it possible to grow fruit in large quantities. The town—there are some oil wells near—has a population of 46,000. There is a small but interesting natural history museum. A road runs W over El Pehuenche pass to Talca (Chile). Bus to Mendoza, frequent, US$4. Bus to Neuquén, US$15.

Hotels *Rex; España,* corner of San Martín and España, D with bath, clean but shabby, no restaurant. *Luis 1,* España 23, E with bath, a/c, clean; *Hospedaje Residencial Comercio,* F, opp. station on Rivadavia.

Campsite at Tunuyán, 77 km. S of Mendoza on road to San Rafael; there are three more campsites on the road from Luján outside Mendoza to Potrerillos (52 km.).

Above the town, up the Río Atuel valley, there is beautiful scenery in the Valle Hermoso up to the dams of El Nihuil which provide irrigation water and hydroelectric power to Mendoza. There is fishing in the reservoir above the highest dam. Good skiing at **Las Leñas,** 2,250 metres up in Valle Hermoso, a new resort with 15 ski-courses, three T-bars, three ski-lifts. It claims to be the foremost ski resort in the southern hemisphere and hopes to host the World Ski Championships in 1991 or 1993. Three stonebuilt hotels: *Escorpio, Acuario* and *Gemini* and a disco, shop renting equipment and expensive restaurant. All the hotels are L; for cheaper accommodation you have to stay in Los Molles (bus from San Rafael US$3.80; from Las Leñas US$0.50) where is *Hotel La Huenca,* B, a/c, clean. There is an airport in **Malargüe** (*Hotel del Turismo, Restaurant El Cisne,* both rec.), 70 km. from Las Leñas, with flights to Buenos Aires.

Mendoza, at the foot of the Andes, 1,060 km. from Buenos Aires, is linked to it by air, the San Martín railway and a paved road, which continues across the Andes to Chile. (No rail service now between Mendoza and Chile.)

Mendoza (756 metres) is an expanding and very pleasant city. Rainfall is slight, but irrigation has turned the area into a green oasis of fruit trees and vineyards. The city was colonized from Chile in 1561 and named in honour of the then governor of Chile. It was from here that the Liberator José de San Martín set out to cross the Andes, to help in the liberation of Chile. Mendoza was completely destroyed by fire and earthquake in 1861, so today it is essentially a modern city of low dwellings (as a precaution against earthquakes), thickly planted with trees and gardens. There was a serious earthquake, which made 40,000 homeless, in January 1985. The main street is Calle San Martín, which runs S to N parallel to the San Martín railway line. Population of city and suburbs: 600,000.

See the Cerro de la Gloria, a hill above the great Parque San Martín on the W side of the city, crowned by an astonishing monument to San Martín. There is a great rectangular stone block with bas-reliefs depicting various episodes in the equipping of the Army of the Andes and the actual crossing. In front of the block, San Martín bestrides his charger. In the park at the foot of Cerro de la Gloria steep and twisting paths run to the Zoological Gardens. There are watercourses and an artificial 1 km-long lake in the park too, where regattas are held, and views of the Andes (when the amount of floating dust will allow) rising in a blue-black perpendicular wall, topped off in winter with dazzling snow, into a china-blue sky. The entrance to the Parque San Martín is ten blocks W of the Plaza Independencia and is reached by bus 3 from the centre; bus 11 takes you up to the top of the hill. There is an hourly open-topped bus ("Oro Negro") that will take you to the top of the Cerro de la Gloria, which runs from the eastern end of the park, on Av. Libertad, to the monument— it's a long walk (45 mins.). You can wait for the bus **half-way up the hill,** at the entrance to the zoo.

The San Martín Museum (US$0.15) is at Av. General San Martín 1851, some 8 blocks N of the city centre (closed weekends). The Historical Museum, on Calle Montevideo near Calle Chile, beautifully furnished, has a collection on San Martín and history of Mendoza. The Museum of Natural History is on Plaza Independencia, lodged underground; this, too, has some colonial exhibits but is best known for its collection of Argentine plants and animals (open Tues.-Fri. 0900-1300, Sat.-Sun. 1500-1900). Museum of Modern Art, San Martín 1143. The Palacio Municipal has a rooftop observation platform, no charge. The Municipal Aquarium is underground at Calle Buenos Aires and Ituzaingó, very

MENDOZA
NOT TO SCALE

1. Cerro de la Gloria
2. Parque San Martín
3. Plaza Independencia
4. Plaza España
5. Plaza San Martín
6. Plaza Chile
7. Plaza Italia
8. San Francisco
9. San Martín Museum
10. Museum of Natural History
11. Municipal Aquarium
12. Historical Museum
13. Tourist Office
14. Post Office
15. Telephone Office
16. *Hotel Alcor*

☐ Detail of centre

interesting, admission US$0.50, open Mon.-Fri. 1000-1200 and 1530-2100, Sat. and Sun. same times a.m. but open an hour longer in the evening, until 2200. Worth seeing, also, are the ruins of the San Francisco church near Plaza Pedro de Castillo.

The best shopping centre is Avenida Las Heras, where there are good souvenir and handicraft shops; leather goods are cheaper here than in Buenos Aires. The municipal market is clean and well-stocked; worth a visit. The vintage festival, Fiesta de la Vendimia, is held in the amphitheatre of the Parque San Martín in the first week of March. There is a wine museum (at the Giol *bodega*), with good guides and wine tasting, just behind the Palacio de Gobierno, opening hours from the tourist office. Outside Mendoza, about 40 km. due E, there is a satellite town, very modern, called San Martín. N.B. Official tours of the city are a waste of time and money.

Wine   Wine *bodegas* (wine-making season March/April) and fruit preserving; visiting times available from Tourist Office. Giol winery, take 15 bus marked "Maipú" (every hour), visits possible weekdays, tours every hour, including a tasting, Spanish only, one of the world's biggest now. Also Maipú district is Peñaflor, ½ hr. by taxi SW of city, good visit and tasting. Bodega de Arizú is open to inspection any time, bus No 7 from city centre; so are many of the others, and they offer you a glass after the visit. Try Bodega Escorihuela (bus 15 from centre) if you are more interested in the information than the wine-tasting. The Toso bodega is close to the city centre and has excellent wines. San Felipe winery visit rec., with museum, bus 17 from terminal, tours 0900-1400, 1600-1800, tasting. Prices at the bodegas have roughly a 40% mark-up from supermarket prices. Recommended: Cruz del Sur from Bodega Arizú, Cuesta del Parsal, Valroy-Borgoña, Valroy-Cabernet Sauvignon, Viejo Toro, Trapiche from Bodega Peñaflor, and Vino de Mesa Arizú Tinto Seco. Many tourist agencies include the bodegas in their half-day or day-long tours (but these visits are too short, with too few guides and little tasting—only of the cheaper wines).

Local Holidays   January 18 (Crossing of the Andes); July 25 (St. James); September 8 (Virgin of Carmen de Cuyo). Annual wine festival at the beginning of March, when hotels fill up fast; book ahead!

Hotels   *Aconcagua*, C, comfortable, San Lorenzo 545, good restaurant, tourist advice and bookings available; *Plaza*, Chile 1124 on main plaza, B, not too clean, but obliging; *Alcor*, Gral. Paz 86, E, central, good, accepts Amex; *Royal*, old part, Las Heras 145, adequate value; *Nutibara*, Bartolomé Mitre 867, D, central, modern swimming pool, rec.; *Crillón*, Perú 1065, D, small, clean. *San Martín*, on Espeje at Plaza, E, rec.; *El Libertador*, Av. España 3-7, E without breakfast, D with bath, clean, free taxi service to bus terminal; *City*, Gen. Paz 95, D, clean, helpful; *Escorial*, San Luis 263, E, with bath, clean, central; *Messidor*, Alberdi 690, D, reasonable, friendly, clean, comfortable, arranges tours; *Santa Clara*, 9 de Julio, central, clean, hot water, own bath. Lower ratings: *Mayo* 25 de Mayo 1265, E incl. breakfast, warmly rec.; *Imperial*, Las Heras 88, E, washing facilities, friendly, rec.; *El Descanso*, Gen. Paz 463, F, without bath, clean, quiet, friendly, highly rec.; *República*, Necochea 541, E, pleasant, cheerful, English spoken; *Líbano*, Gen. Paz 227, excellent, clean, from E; *Petit*, Perú 1459, D with breakfast, 1½ blocks from railway station, clean, friendly, rec.; *Escorial*, San Luis 263, E, very friendly and clean, rec.; Residencial D'Amore, Perú 1346, E, clean, use of kitchen, used as brothel. *El Rosario*, Chile 1579, between Las Heras and Paz, E, good, clean, hot water, heating, rec.; *Margal*, Juan B. Justo 75, clean, F; *Ideal*, Juan B. Justo 270, E, transport to bus station; *Premier*, Juan B. Justo 700 block, E, private parking, clean, good value; *Zamora*, Perú 1156, reasonable and friendly, converted house, E; *Vigo*, Necochea 749 (T 250208), D, good value, good *comedor*; *Galicia*, Av. San Juan 881 (near Av. L. M. Alem), F, very clean, hot water; *Quijote*, San Juan 1407, E, clean, friendly, restaurant; Residencial Unión, Patricias Mendocinas, nr. Plaza España, E, without bath, breakfast, clean, hot water; many cheap *alojamientos* near railway station; *Gran Marta*, Gen. Paz 460, clean, but only cold showers, rec.; Residencial Miami, Necochea 278, E, very clean; *Savoy*, Belgrano 1377, F, good, clean, some rooms without window, tours offered at 20% discount. Several cheap *residenciales* in Alberdi, Güemes and Bandera de los Andes, near bus station. *Nevada*, Av. Perú, near railway station, F with bath, hot water, clean, cheap meals. Unnamed *pensión* at Montecaseros 1682, F, basic, hot water, cooking facilities; another at Catamarca 264, F, cheapest, crowded. *El Piño Azul* apartments, San Martín 2872 (T 304593), D per day. Hotels also at Challao. Lodgings (F) in private houses: ask at Escuela de Hotelería, Paso de los Andes 1249, near entrance to Parque San Martín. Sra. Ada Zárate, San Juan 564, 1°, Dept. 5-6, close to bus station, E in dormitory, has been rec. Small *Youth Hostel* at Paso de los Andes 1249.

Camping   In Parque General San Martín permitted, free, in cars, but not in tents. Three campsites at Challao, about 14 km. from the city centre, reached by colectivo No. 11 leaving every hour. *Camping Suizo* best value, has shop, US$1.50 p.p. and US$1.50 for tent, safest of all sites, friendly but loud music at night from nearby amusement arcade. About 13 km. from Mendoza, two sites near the turn-off for Barballón. *El Salto*, 50 km. W of Mendoza, near mountains, well situated.

Restaurants *Trevi*, Las Heras 68, good. Good ones are the *Automobile Club*, Italian restaurants *Montecatini*, Gral. Paz 370, *Mi Piace*, on Sarmiento, and *Marchigiana*, Patricias Mendocinas 1550; *San Marco*, on Las Heras, and the *Mendoza Regatta Club*, Av. de las Palmeras, Parque San Martín. *Bárbaro*, San Martín 914, English spoken, US$6.25 for main course (speciality is roast kid) plus wine for 2. *Tristán Barraza*, 658 Av. Sarmiento (parrilla), good. *Trattoria Aveni*, 25 de Mayo 1162, crowded, good, meal US$6.50. *Vecchia Roma*, Av. España 1619, rec. for good food, atmosphere and service. *Parrillada Arturito*, Chile y Las Heras, good cheap steak; *La Rueda*, Mitre 1468, good grill. *Don Angelo*, Lavalle 148, cheap; *Club Alemán*, Necochea 2261, Godoy Cruz, rec. Good value is *Petit Progreso*, Córdoba with San Juan; *San Boccadoro*, Mitre 1976; *La Nevada*, Chile 1495, 3-course meal for US$2, excellent value; *San Agustín*, Av. L. M. Alem 477 opposite hospital, big meals at reasonable prices. *Chino*, 25 de Mayo 1553 (near Las Heras), very good; *La Tapita*, 25 de Mayo, 1½ blocks from *Hotel El Descanso*, serves 4 course set meal at low price. Good cheap menu at *Hotel Francia*, Las Heras. *Pizzería Pic-Nic*, Las Heras 475, good, cheap pizzas. Also on Las Heras is *Cervecería Zurich*, good food and service, cheap, rec. Ice cream at *Soppelso*, Las Heras 409, rec. *São Paulo*, San Martín 1214, very popular standup coffee bar. *El Gran Lomo*, Rivadavia and San Martín, cheap filling sandwiches, open 24 hrs. Good snacks at *Cerrito Bar*, L.M. Alem 41. Vegetarian: Mitre 523, US$2 for all you can eat. Cheap and good eating places near San Martín railway station. In bars 20% extra is charged if you sit at a table rather than at the counter. Out of town, *Lomo Loco*, a few km. S on Luján road, locals' favourite *parrilla* but not cheap. *Chopería Bull and Bush*, José Zapata, large sandwiches and good draught lager.

Nightclubs in the suburb of Chacras de Coria. Discothèques: *Blow Up*, Mitre 1520; *Kangaroo*, Rivadavia 430; *La Cueva*, Chile 1285; *El Grillo*, Chile 1243; *Casino*, 25 de Mayo 1123; *Al Diablo*, Ruta Internacional Vistalba Luján.

Casino 25 de Mayo 1123, daily 2100-0300.

Car Hire Avis, Espejo 228; Lis Car, San Lorenzo 110, T 291416; A.S. Rent-a-Car, Garibaldi 186, T 248317.

Mountain Climbing Information from Tourist Office. There is a three-day (Thurs.-Sat.) climbing and trekking expedition via Godoy Cruz and Cacheuta to Cerro Penitentes (4,351 metres), sleeping in mountain refuge, food included. See also page 103.

Exchange Lloyds Bank (BLSA), Av. San Martín 1498. Banco de Credito Argentino, España 1168, gives cash advance on Visa card. Good rates at Bank of America (not travellers' cheques though). Citibank (which does not give dollars for US travellers' cheques). Open 0715-1315. Currency changed between 0715 and 1030 only. **N.B.** No travellers' cheques changed at weekends, except at the *cambio* at Galería Tonsa, 1100 block of Av. San Martín, open till 2000 on Sat. Best rate for Chilean currency at the bus terminal (open from 0715). Many *cambios* at Espejo y Catamarca and along San Martín. Good exchange house opposite LAN-Chile office in San Martín. Exprinter, San Martín 1198, and Santiago *cambio* opposite, well rec. Also rec.: Maguitur, Av. San Martín 1203. Another at 9 de Julio, by Av. Las Heras. No exchange facilities Sun.

Consulates Bolivia, 9 de Julio 1357, 2nd floor; Peru, Av. España 533, T 241462; Chile, Av. Emilio Civit, esq. Rodríguez.

Goethe Institut Morón 265, Mon.-Fri. 0800-1200, 1600-2230. German films.

Shopping Leather goods good and cheap; try Jorge Ruben Pacheco, 9 de Julio 1455, subsuelo Loc. 1. Books (English and German selection) from Historias on Av. San Martín. English language magazines and *Buenos Aires Herald* usually available at kiosk at corner of San Martín and Alem. Free film shows at Salón Cultural Rivadavia, José V. Zapata 349.

Coin-operated **laundromat**, Colón 543, also on Garibaldi near La Rioja, and on Salta near San Luis.

There is a **gynaecological clinic** about three doors away from *El Descanso* hotel; helpful and relatively inexpensive.

Tourist Offices at airport, T 306484, helpful (frequently closed), also at the bus terminal, T 259709, at Av. San Martín 1143, T 242800, which is also the Museum of Modern Art. They have a list of reasonable private lodgings, but not much other literature apart from lists of *bodegas*. Good town map available at most kiosks.

Travel Agencies Lots in Las Heras, between Perú and San Martín. Turismo Jocolí, Las Heras y 25 de Mayo, T 230466, rec. for tours in and around the city, and to El Cristo Redentor statue. Turismo Sepeán, San Juan 1070, friendly and helpful, have branch in Santiago. Ibiza, Espejo 217, T 258141, helpful and efficient. Hunuc Huar Expediciones, Av. España 1340, 8° piso, oficina 7, specializes in assistance to climbers, especially on Aconcagua.

Post Office   Av. San Martín and Av. Zapata.

Airport   Plumerillo, 8 km. from centre; *remise* taxis (US$2-3) and buses (infrequent) run. Bus No. 6 stops at corner of San Juan and Alem and takes you close to the terminal; make sure there is an "Aeropuerto" sign on the driver's window. Flying time from Buenos Aires: 1¾ hours. Aerolíneas flies three times a day (US$63), and has Tuesday night flight (US$38); Austral twice a day. 40% discount on night flight from Buenos Aires (night flight to Buenos Aires, Sat. 2315). AA to Santiago, US$70, daily except Sun., fare must be paid in US$. AA to and from Bariloche, 3 times a week. Several flights to Córdoba with AA and Austral (1515). Neuquén 3 weekly with TAN.

Trains   to Buenos Aires: *El Libertador*, leaves Mendoza Mon. and Fri. at 2015, arrives at 0930; car transporters, luxurious bar, film show and airconditioning, steward service, good dining cars, meal US$4, good value; take drinks with you. *El Aconcagua* leaves Mendoza daily at 1545, arrives Bs. As. at 0830; *El Sanjuanino* at 2015, arrives at 0930 (Tues., Wed., Thurs.). Trains from Buenos Aires to Mendoza: *Libertador*, leaves at 2015, Sun. and Thurs., arrives 1000. *El Aconcagua* leaves at 2115, arrives at 1400 the next day, *El Sanjuanino* at 2015 Mon., Tues., Wed. Fares: Sleeper US$46.65, pullman US$38, first, US$24.75, tourist US$21.70. There are no trains to Chile but local buses meet train to take you to bus station, to catch buses for Chile. Train from Mendoza to San Luis 4 hrs.; to San Juan, 1420 daily, 1020 four a week, 2½ hrs. daily. Book pullmans well ahead in winter; they're heated. Bus from railway to bus terminal, No. 5, US$0.15.

Buses   (all from smart new bus station) to Santiago, **see page 103**. Buses run to Bariloche, leave 1300 Sun., Tues., US$25, on a mostly paved road, about 22 hours, book well ahead; to Córdoba, TAC daily at 1000 and 2300, 9 hrs., US$13; to San Rafael, US$4; to San Juan every 2 hours, US$3.75, 2 hrs. (2 companies, TAC and Villa del Sur y Media Agua). To La Rioja US$11 (US$15 luxury), 10 hrs., leaves 1430, 1930 or 2130. Catamarca overnight only, 12 hrs., daily, US$15. Daily at 1730 to Tucumán, US$17.25. Comodoro Rivadavia Tue., Thurs., Sat., 36 hrs., at 2000, US$80 incl. meal stops. Bus to Mar del Plata US$32; to Puerto Iguazú at 0700, Tues. and Sun. US$40, 38 hrs., Chevallier. To Buenos Aires via Route 8, 2nd class daily at 1315, arrives 0550, US$28, 1st class daily at 1630, arrives 0700, US$32; luxury service daily at 2100 (Chevallier), US$39 including meals; via Route 7 (Junín-Mercedes) at 2020, arrive 1205, US$26. Dull scenery, and very cold across the Pampas at night. Hitch-hiking between Mendoza and Buenos Aires is quite easy. If hitching to San Juan, take bus No. 6 to the airport near the highway. Hitching from Mendoza to Los Andes (Chile) is easy; go to the service station in Godoy Cruz suburb, from where all trucks to Chile, Peru and elsewhere leave.

Excursions   If driving in mountains remember to advance the spark by adjusting the distributor, or weaken the mixture in the carburettor, to avoid the car seizing up in the rarified air. Buses run to the hot springs at **Cacheuta**, US$2.40 round trip, US$5 entry (thermal baths for those with doctors' certificates only, can be arranged at travel agents for US$4), 45 km. to the SW (hotels not rec.). The charming resort of **Potrerillos** is 13 km. from Cacheuta, with ski slopes not far away and excellent birdwatching in summer. *Gran Hotel; Hotel de Turismo*, B, with meals; ACA campsite (US$2 for members) *Restaurant Armando* rec.; the skiing at Vallecito (reached by tour bus or car only), however, is reported less good than at Portillo, on the Chilean side of the Andes. In summer, you can hike 20 km. from the resort of Potrerillos to Vallecito, taking two days. On the first you will see desert scenery, blooming cactus flowers, birds and an occasional goat or cow. The second you walk surrounded by peaks, a steep but not difficult climb to the San Antonio refuge, usually open with beds and meals. Two other popular resorts within a few km. of the city are Barballón, to the NE, and Challao, to the NW. An excursion is also available from the Mendoza bus station to the small ski resort of Los Penitentes, 170 km. away; equipment hire US$5 a day, lift ticket for a day US$9. The best skiing is at (2,250 metres) Valle de las Leñas, S of Mendoza in the Valle Hermoso (**see page 97**). Excursions also to the dam at El Nihuil, with artificial lake, and to the Río Atuel canyon. On the road to Luján de Cuyo (buses go every 15 mins. from near bus terminal) is a fine arts museum dedicated to Argentine artists, surrounded by sculpture in gardens, admission free (Museo Provincial de Bellas Artes Emiliano Guiñazu, Casa de Fader). Day-trips can also be made to Puente del Inca with Turismo Vitar for about US$10 (**see page 102**). Turismo La Cumbre, Necochea 541, also includes it on its 19-hour circular tour, as does Cata Turismo, Las Heras 426, 13 hours. Local bus (Expreso Uspallata) for Uspallata and Puente del Inca 4 hrs., 0600 and 1000, returning from Puente del Inca 1300 and 1615; local buses also go on from Puente del Inca to Las Cuevas, Expreso Uspallata, US$4.

Hotel Termas   at Villavicencio is closed. Many tourists come to visit the springs, which are all set in concrete. Pleasant walks round the area.

N.B.   It is no longer possible to go from Mendoza to Santiago via the statue of Christ the Redeemer at 3,854 metres. To see the statue you must go on a 12 hr. excursion from Mendoza (US$15 return, weekends early a.m., all travel agencies) since the Chilean side of the frontier at the statue is closed. The excursion also includes Puente del Inca (see next page). All buses and cars go through the tunnel to Chile, leaving the statue unseen above.

Over the Andes to Chile

N.B. No visas into Chile are available at the border, so if you need one and haven't got it, you will be turned back. There is a time change: travelling from Argentina into Chile remember to move your watch back 1 hr. between mid-March and mid-October.

There are 2 alternates of Route 7, which meet at **Uspallata,** the only settlement of any size between Mendoza and the Chilean frontier. Near Uspallata are the ruins of Las Bóvedas, built by the Huarpe Indians under the Jesuits, and an Inca *tambería.* They are just off the road which leads to Barreal and Calingasta (**see page 104**), unpaved for its first part and tricky when the snow melts and floods it in summer. (Prices are usually much higher at frontier, temperatures much lower. Frontier closes early.) The fully-paved southern branch, via Cacheuta and Potrerillos, is wider and better than the northern branch, which goes via Villavicencio with a stretch of one-way traffic just beyond the resort, where the road leads up spectacularly to the 3,050 metres high Cruz del Paramillo. (The return loop, a little longer and less steep, is through the picturesque Quebrada del Toro.) This northern branch is still unpaved.

Hotels *Hotel Uspallata,* C, dinner at 2100; payment for meals and drinks in cash, bowling alley, nice location, but hotel run down, service friendly, but vast herds of people get driven through it. *Hostería Los Cóndores,* clean, friendly, cheap.

Camping There is a pleasant ACA site at Uspallata, US$3 per head, full washing facilities, hot water.

People travelling by car over the Andes in winter are advised to enquire about road conditions from ACA in Mendoza (San Martín y Amigorena).

The crossing of the Andes, taken by San Martín, is the old mountain trail the Spaniards named the Camino de los Andes. Beyond Uspallata is a vast, open, undulating plain, wild and bare. On all sides stand the grey, gaunt mountains. On the far side of this plain the valley narrows till Río Blanco is reached, and there the mountain torrents rush and froth into the river. At Punta de Vacas we look left up the Tupungato Valley at the majestic cone of Tupungato, one of the giants of the Andes, rising 6,550 metres. An equally majestic mass of pinnacled rocks, Los Penitentes, is passed on the left; they are about 7 km. away. The climber to their base (an easy task from Puente del Inca with a guide) sees a remarkable sight. The higher rocks look like a church and the smaller, sharper rocks below give the impression of a number of cowled monks climbing upwards.

In a short time we are at **_Puente del Inca,_** 2,718 metres above sea level, 160 km. from Mendoza, a sports resort set among mountains of great grandeur. (*Hostería Puente del Inca,* C for room, less off-season, very pleasant, about US$40 extra for full board, also bookable from *Plaza Hotel* in Mendoza it.) Camping possible next to the church, if your equipment can withstand the winds. 5 km. from Puente del Inca on the road to Mendoza is a ski club, *Cruz de Caña,* with comfortable dormitories, E, and a good restaurant. The owner organizes trekking expeditions; prices: US$50 a day full board during expedition, and US$20 per mule.

The natural bridge after which Puente del Inca is named is one of the wonders of South America; it crosses the river Mendoza at a height of 19 metres, has a span of 21 metres, and is 27 metres wide, and seems to have been formed by sulphur-bearing hot springs. Puente del Inca is the best point for excursions into the higher Andean valleys or for a visit to the base of Aconcagua, which was first climbed by Zurbriggen of the Fitzgerald Expedition in 1897. Visits can be paid on horseback from Puente del Inca to Los Penitentes (*La Taberna del Gringo*, Km. 151, Villa Los Penitentes, E, rec.); or on foot to the green lake of Laguna de los Horcones; or by car (only with a well regulated engine) or bus or on horseback to the statue of Christ the Redeemer set above La Cumbre (or Uspallata) pass on the frontier at an altitude of 3,800 metres. It was erected jointly by Chile and Argentina in 1904 to celebrate King Edward VII's decision in the boundary dispute of 1902. It is, unfortunately, somewhat disappointing from the road, for it is completely dwarfed by the landscape. (The road from the tunnel to the statue is closed for the season after the first snowfall in April.)

After Puente del Inca, on the right, we get a good view of Aconcagua (6,960 metres), sharply silhouetted against the blue sky. In 1985, a complete Inca mummy was discovered at 5,300 metres on the mountain.

Best time for climbing **Aconcagua** (the highest peak in the Americas) is from mid-January to mid-February. Rob Rachowiecki writes: it is first necessary to obtain a permit from the Dirección de Deportes, Recreación y Turismo Social (offices at the Mendoza football stadium). The Club Andinista Mendoza will help you with the paperwork; Sr. Parra is particularly helpful. Allow a couple of days for this. From Mendoza take a bus or colectivo to Puente del Inca. From here mules are available but cost US$20 per mule per day; you have to pay for 3 days there and back (1 day rest) and for the muleteer and his wages. This only takes you to the base camp at Plaza de Mulas (4,200 m). Of the huts above this point only La Libertad (Berlín) hut at about 6,000 m is in serviceable condition. Both huts are small with no facilities. Bring a tent able to withstand 100 mph + winds, and clothing and sleeping gear for temperatures below -20°C. Allow at least one week for acclimatization at lower altitudes before attempting summit (4 days from Plaza de Mulas). Treks and climbs organized by Sr Fernando Grajales, the famous climber, in *Hostería Puente del Inca*, or at J.F.Moreno 898, 5500 Mendoza, Telex 55-154.

The frontier railway tunnel is no longer used by road traffic, which now takes the new 4-km. El Libertador-Las Cuevas toll road tunnel (US$2 toll). The Chilean frontier is beyond **Las Cuevas,** a neat, modern settlement being developed as a ski-ing resort (though there is no ski-lift as yet), but recently damaged by landslides and a fire. It is wise to take snow chains from June to October. Officially, driving without chains and a shovel is prohibited between Uspallata and the border, but this can be resolved in a friendly way with border policemen. Both ACA and Chilean Automobile Club sell, but do not rent, chains.

Hotel *Hostería Las Cuevas*, only one, poor food, no heating in annex. Food available at kiosk at Expreso Uspallata bus terminal point.

Beyond Las Cuevas, the road, now completely paved, goes through the new road tunnel (charge for car, US$2, for a VW bus, US$3). The old road over La Cumbre pass is now closed to through traffic; the famous statue of Christ can be visited only by excursion from Mendoza (see above).

Transport to Chile Turismo cars (Chi-Ar—some adverse reports—and Nevada) carrying 4 to 5 passengers (US$15, 5 hrs) and minibuses (5½-6 hrs) do the trip to Santiago daily. If travelling by bus from Mendoza to Santiago take a direct bus as it is not possible to walk across the border. Buses Mendoza to Santiago daily at 0600-1200; several companies, TAC-Choapa at 0830 (meals included) recommended for cheapness (US$10) and service; adverse reports on Chile Bus. Most buses are comfortable and fast (6½-8 hrs.), air-conditioned and hostess service (including breakfast), worth it when crossing the border as waiting time can be a matter of several hours. All companies in same part of Mendoza bus station: you can easily shop around. Passengers are normally collected from their hotels, fare US$13, those with hostess service US$17 (to Viña del Mar and Valparaíso US$15), children under 8 pay 60% of adult fare, but no seat; book two days ahead. Passport required. The ride is spectacular. Information at main bus station. If you want to return, buy an undated return ticket Santiago-Mendoza; it is cheaper. A taxi Mendoza-Santiago costs about US$70 for 4-5 people. Empresa Andesmar runs direct service to La Serena, Chile.

All Argentine entry and exit formalities are now dealt with at Punta de Vacas, 30 km. from Las Cuevas. One can hitch-hike, or possibly bargain with bus drivers for a seat, from Punta de Vacas to Santiago, but if one is dropped at the entrance to the tunnel in winter, one cannot walk through. Travellers however report that customs men often help by asking passing motorists to take hitch-hikers through the tunnel to Chile. Chilean migration and customs check is after the tunnel—searches for fruit, meat, vegetables, which may not be imported into Chile, in a new building with the bus parked inside. Customs at the frontier are closed 1200-1400. Members of ACA need only the *Libreta de Pasos por Aduana*, otherwise you need the *Documento de Exportación* to enter Chile. Good food at frontier hotel, and there is an excellent motel on the Chilean side about an hour down.

NORTH OF MENDOZA (5)

There are three other oases standing between the plains and the mountains to the N of Mendoza, in much the same way as San Rafael to the S. San Juan is prosperous, La Rioja does fairly well with its wines and olive oil, but Catamarca has always lived on the brink of economic disaster. The first oasis, 177 km. from Mendoza by paved road or railway, is

San Juan, 400,000 people, the capital of the Province of San Juan, founded in

1562 by Don Juan Jufré de Loaysa y Montese, at 650 metres. An earthquake in 1944 practically destroyed the place but the centre, including the Cathedral, has been rebuilt. Domingo Sarmiento, the historian and educationist, and President from 1868 to 1874, was born here; his house contains the Sarmiento Museum, with a signed portrait of Lincoln. There is an Archaeological Museum 10 km. E of town, with a number of mummies. Also a Natural Sciences museum, open 0830-1230 and 1530-1930, US$0.15. The ruins of the Santo Domingo Convent are worth seeing. The surrounding country is picturesque. About 60 km. from San Juan is the famous religious site of **Difunta Correa** at **Vallecito**; the shrine in the desert commemorates a woman who died of thirst there, but whose milk kept her baby alive for 3 days until it was found. There is an interesting collection of items left for blessing.

Hotels *Nogaró*, Ignacio de La Roza 132, T 227501/5, the best, pool, B (15% discount to ACA members); *Jardín Petit Hotel*, 25 de Mayo 345, B (10% discount to ACA members), bath-water sometimes cold, guarded car-park next door; *Selby*, Av. Rioja 183, C, poor value; *La Toja*, Rivadavia 494, C; *Argentino*, Estados Unidos 381, E; *Plaza*, Sarmiento 344, D, friendly; *Bristol*, Entre Ríos 368, D, a/c, hot water, clean, rec.; *Brescia*, Av. España 336, opp. railway station, D; *Austria*, Sarmiento 246, E, warmly rec. Others are less good, including *Lido*, 9 de Julio 429; *Lara*, Rivadavia 213; *Hispano Argentino*, and *San Francisco*, on España, 410 and 284; *Tajamar*, Jujuy 45, pleasant, reasonable; *Rex*, Gral. Acha 187; *Central*, Mitre 131; *Roy*, Entre Ríos 180; *Marsella*, Sarmiento 8, F, over pizzería, small rooms, clean.

Camping "Camping permitted" signs along road from Mendoza to San Juan. Campsite in olive grove, 7 km. S of San José de Jachal on the road to San Juan, and 23 km. after Jachal, on Villa Unión road.

Restaurants Not many in centre. *Hostal de Palito*, Circunvalación Sur 271 (between San Martín and 1. de la Roza, open Sundays only), excellent; *La Cabaña*, Salta y Circunvalación, on edge of town, *parrillada*; many good grillrooms. *Club Español*, good, try Maravilla wine here, well-priced, on Rivadavia 32 Este. *Pizzería Cuyo*, Mitre 644 Oeste, near railway station, small, excellent food; *Un Rincón de Nápoli*, Rivadavia 175 Oeste, good, with large glasses of fresh orange juice, good delicatessen next door. *Las Leñas*, *parrillada* on Av. San Martín, good, some way from the centre, eat under thatched shelters (quinchos); opposite is *Parrilla El Fierro II*. *Confitería City*, Rivadavia between Entre Ríos and Mendoza, good meals for US$1.

Car Hire Parque Automotor, España y Libertador, T 226018, cash discount if you ask.

Tourist Office, at San Martín and Sarmiento, large and well organized, arranges tours, has good leaflets on the province. Large maps of the province available from bookshops, US$5.

Travel Agent Yafar Turismo, Laprida y Aberastaín, rec.

Exchange Good rates at Cambio Santiago, Gral. Acha 52, open weekdays until 2000, and Sat. a.m.

By Air Airport: Chacritas, 14 km. from town. Daily flights to Buenos Aires stopping at Córdoba or Villa Mercedes.

Bus to Catamarca, 660 km., US$17.50 over secondary roads in arid country. To La Rioja, 550 km., US$10, 6½ hrs. Only connexion with Santiago (Chile) is via Mendoza. To La Serena, Tas-Choapa Thurs. at midnight (but check that the Agua Negra pass is open); to Salta (US$22) via Catamarca (US$13), 2 a day; to La Rioja daily; to Chilecito, Mon., Fri., Sun. 2130, Tues., Sat. 0900, 9 hrs., US$13.

Rail The two named trains (see page 101) that ply between Mendoza and Buenos Aires (*El Sanjuanino* and *Aconcagua*) also serve San Juan. They reach San Juan 2½ hours after Mendoza, and leave for Buenos Aires 2½ hours before Mendoza departure times. Fares Buenos Aires-San Juan: sleeper (to and from Mendoza only on *Aconcagua*) US$51.55; pullman US$43.30, 1st class US$28.45; tourist US$19.90.

Travel from San Juan If hitchhiking to La Rioja, take route 141 to Chepes (ACA Hostería), then N to Patquía, because the road is paved and there is more traffic; to start with, take bus 39 to airport, out of town (this route is, however, less interesting than going via San Agustín or San José de Jachal, see below).

Along Route 20, heading West, one reaches *Calingasta* (135 km. from San Juan, *Hotel La Capilla*) in the valley of the same name. A spectacular drive: the road is open for traffic towards Calingasta in the morning, towards San Juan in the afternoon (but it is poor condition). South of Calingasta is Barreal on road to Uspallata (*Hotel Barreal*, recently improved, good value in restaurant; also *Hotel Jorge*, F, clean, very simple. *Hostería San Eduardo*, small, quaint, few rooms with bath, open in summer only; *Restaurant Isidoro*, owned by local baker and sandyacht champion, food very reasonable).

Sr Ramón Luis Ossa, the physical-education teacher at Barreal's high school, runs 15/21 day mule treks in the summer in the Andean foothills; he can be reached at 5405 Barreal, Pcia. San Juan, T (0648) 41024. We are grateful to Herbert Levi for a detailed account of Sr. Ossa's treks. In addition to the organizer's list of essential items, Sr. Levi recommends taking the following on any trip into the Andes: metal drinking mugs, metal containers to stop tubes of tooth paste etc. emptying themselves in mule packs, long underpants to stop chafing of skin, woollen cap, insect repellent, sunburn cream, laxative pills, soap, nylon sheeting for under or over sleeping bag (depending on weather), foldable tent if you want privacy, and, for those who want to/approve of, catching their own meals, fishing gear (No. 3 spoons best for Andean streams—permit required).

Route 40, the principal tourist route on the eastern slope of the Andes, heads northwards towards Cafayate and Salta, via San José de Jachal. After 55 km. is Talacasto, where the road to the Chilean frontier branches off to the left (Route 436). This road crosses the Puerta del Colorado pass (2,759 metres) with an extensive view to the north and reaches Las Flores after 125 km. Las Flores is on Route 150 from San José de Jachal to the Chilean frontier (road very bad—frontier reported closed in 1988) at the Agua Negra pass (4,765 metres), carrying on down the Elqui valley to La Serena. Turning left at Las Flores, you reach the customs post after about 45 km. in a river valley; off the road is another glacial formation known as Los Penitentes. The road may be closed from May onwards for the winter.

Turning right at Las Flores you reach the *Hotel Termas de Pismanta* (5 km.), D without, B with full board (good, but dining room not too clean), individual thermal bath and large swimming pool with thermal water under an orange tent. Camping seems possible. The hotel is in a pleasant spot, with trees, in the desert. There is also a casino. Many people from Mendoza flock here in the summer; there is a bus service. Nearby, in Rodeo, Ing. Megliolo raises guanaco and vicuña, and sells local produce and handicrafts. From Termas de Pismanta it is 61 km., partly on a very winding road high above the Río Jachal, to **San José de Jachal** (hotel, C; *Plaza*, E, basic but clean; good *El Chato Flores* restaurant; bus San Juan-San José, Expreso Argentino at 0730, arr. 0940).

From San José de Jachal, Route 40 continues to Villa Unión (see below). If you have your own car, you can take the old road (Route 491) for the first part, which offers good views from a pass and goes through a tunnel. Buses take the new road via Huaco. The road is paved to the border between San Juan and La Rioja provinces, but it is constantly up and down, passing dozens of dry watercourses.

Another interesting road from San Juan to Villa Unión goes via San Agustín del Valle Fértil through coloured desert hills, making it possible to do a round trip. Take Route 141 east towards Chepes; after 133 km. at Marayes, a paved road goes north for 114 km. to **San Agustín del Valle Fértil**. On a hill in town is the good ACA *Hostería*, with a wide view of the desert; at the foot of the hill is the ACA campsite, the municipal swimming pool, and on the other side of the hill a lake (fishing possible). Also *Pensión Andacollo*, E, and *Pensión Los Olivos*, similar prices. There are service stations. (Bus: Valle Fértil bus leaves San Juan at 2000, arr. 2300; a bus from San Juan to La Rioja passes San Agustín about midnight, if you wish to journey on; book in San Juan to get a seat).

From San Agustín the paved road runs north; after 56 km., a left turn at a police checkpoint goes 17 km. to the entrance of the interesting **Valle de la Luna (Ischigualasto)** park. Fossils found are exhibited in the Museo Bernardino Rivadavia in Buenos Aires. You may see around the park's coloured and strange rock formations only in a private car, and a guide will have to go with you. The circular tour, on a well-maintained, but unpaved road, lasts 2-3 hrs., entrance fee including guide US$1.25 p.p., children free. Local bus from San Juan, Sat. p.m., if there are enough passengers.

4 km. beyond the police checkpoint, a junction to the right goes 51 km. over a lonely but paved road to Patquía and on to La Rioja or Chilecito. The left turn (Route 26) is the excellent road to Villa Unión. After 58 km. a paved road branches off to the right to the **Puerta de Talampaya** national park. The park entrance is at the turnoff, where guides wait with a pickup. Entrance fee including pickup for the tour and guide is US$3 p.p. for up to 8 people. After 14 km. the paved access road ends at the park centre (under construction). From here the actual visit starts, following the river bed of the Río Talampaya in a canyon. Herbert Levi writes: "There are 6,000 year old petroglyphs with pictures depicting animals. The whole area is said to have been covered with water long ago; now there are two visible strata, the *tarjado* and the *talampaya*. After that one enters a canyon with 'balconies', sheer overhanging walls. Across these is a small wood with many wild plants which are used for curative purposes. Coming out of the canyon there are rocks shaped like a cathedral, a bird, a castle, a chessboard, a monk and three kings on a camel." Finally, before returning the same way, you may go to the top of a little hill with a good view. The tour lasts about 2 hours. Buses from Chilecito to San Juan pass Talampaya.

From the park entrance it is 58 km. on the excellent Route 26 to **Villa Unión** (Hostería Provincial, simple, E, highly rec.; Sr. Werner Lorenz, the owner, who also owns vineyards, is very knowledgeable on the area and gives detailed plans for, and runs, excursions, including to Valle de la Luna and Talampaya). Excursions can also be made by jeep to Laguna Verde and Laguna Veladero. Bus station behind the plaza.

From Villa Unión to Chilecito, the road is only partly paved and goes over the Cuesta de Miranda, continuing down as a corniche through a deep, narrow canyon in a series of hairpin bends. After 92 km., it joins the paved Route 74 Patquía-Chilecito road, where you turn left for 18 km. to

Chilecito, the second town in La Rioja province and a pleasant place, with good views of Sierra de Famatima. At Sra. Pizetti's souvenir shop, you can see her unique ceramic statuettes.

Hotels *ACA* on T. Gordillo and 9 de Julio, good, D; *Belsavac*, 9 de Julio y Dávila, good, paperthin walls; *Ferrito*, Pelagio Luna 661; *El Cordobés*, Dávila y Libertad; *Los Cerros*, Caminito 270; *Riviera*, Castro Barros 133, E-F, highly rec., clean, hot showers; *Americano*, Libertad 68; *Bellia*, El Maestro and A. Marasso, and *Mis Montañas*, J. V. González 27.

Camping Club Atlético Chilecito has site near ACA hotel; unofficial sites at 15 km. from Chilecito on the road to Guauchía, near a Jesuit *estancia* established in 1652; also 6 km. along Calle de La Plata, at Santa Florentina; and 2 km. further at Los Tabas.

Restaurants *Yayo y Silvia*, Independencia and 9 de Julio, good *chivito*; *Capri*, on main square, very good; *Comedor Club Atlético Newells Old Boys*, La Plata, opp. bus station, good.

Tourist Office on 19 de Febrero and La Plata, very helpful; post office on J. V. González and Mitre. For treks, and trips to see gold washers at Famatima or to Talampaya, ask Carlos de Caro, at tourist office close to bus terminal.

Transport Líneas Aéreas Riojanas fly La Rioja-Chilecito, US$10 including transport to airport, 20-minute flight.
Bus to San Juan, Tues., Thurs., Sat. at 2200 (arrive 0705). Bus, Chilecito-Tinogasta (see below), Mon. and Fri., direct route at 0700, via Famatima, Angulas, Campanas, Santa Cruz, Costa de Reyes, returning from Tinogasta same day at 1600, same route. Tues. at 0700 and Sat. at 1330, same route to Campanas, then Pituile, San Blas, Cerro Negro junction, Salado, Carnival, Copacabana, Tinogasta. Return trip, Wed. at 0600, Sun. at 1400. Belén-Londres: No service Sun.; weekdays 0930 and 1215, Sat. 0900 and 1200. Reverse journey weekdays at 1630 and 1900, Sat. 1630 and 1930, about 20 mins. Connections with Catamarca and Córdoba (see relevant sections).

Excursions To La Mejicana mine at Santa Florentina (6 km). Impressive cable car systems along which ore could be conveyed to the railway station at Chilecito, now disused. To **Samay Huasi**, the house of Joaquín V. González, founder of La Plata University, open 0800-1200 and 1500-1800, pretty garden (the view from the hill above the statue in the gardens is splendid, over Chilecito, the Famatima ridge and connecting valley; from the hill you can walk directly back to Chilecito); not far is the house of Sra. Inocente de Pizetti, who sculpts religious motifs. In Chilecito is a museum, at Jardín de Ocampo 63, corner of Famatima, open 0900-1300, 1800-2000. Half a block from the museum is the 17th-century flour mill of San Francisco. For the Valle de la Luna and Parque Nacional Talampaya, see above.

With the construction of an excellent new road, almost complete except in the area of Salicas, the numbering of the roads has been changed. Route 40 no longer goes north via Tinogasta but via Salicas (because the Cuesta de Zapata, N of Tinogasta, has been closed since the road was washed away in 1981). From Chilecito it is 21 km. to the junction of the old and new roads: to the left the old road goes via Famatima (ACA *Hostería*) to

Tinogasta, a half-Indian copper-mining township, which lies cradled, by virtue of rare water, in a deep green valley lush with vineyards, olive groves and rows of poplar trees.

Hotels *Provincial de Turismo; Hostería Novel*, near airport.

Restaurants *Persegoni*, Tristán Villafane 375; *Rancho Huairipaca*, on Moreno.

Transport Bus Tinogasta-Tucumán, Empresa Gutiérrez, Tues., Fri., Sun. at 1700, Mon. at 0615, Fri. also at 0845. Return Tues., Fri. and Sun., arrives at Tinogasta at 0715, Thurs. at 1545. Tinogasta-Chubut, Empresa Ortiz; also Tinogasta-Comodoro Rivadavia, Caleta Olivia. For air services, see under Catamarca.

Fiambalá is reached from Tinogasta with El Cóndor on the Córdoba-Fiambalá route. Interesting mountain landscape. There is a *Hospedaje* at the end of the route (serves excellent *locro*). Drive from here (US$10 in a pick-up, asphalted road) to the *aguaditas*, hot water springs (bathing possible). Fiambalá-Tinogasta-Cerro Negro (junction)-Catamarca with Empresa Gutiérrez daily, depart Fiambalá 1345, depart Tinogasta 1500. Cerro Negro 1610, connects with Coop.

Catamarca bus to Belén coming from Catamarca about 25 mins later; 85 km. trip Cerro Negro-Belén, bad road, about 2 hrs. Also departures from Fiambalá at 0530, dep. Tinogasta 0650, Cerro Negro 0810. 36 km. beyond Fiambalá is Palo Blanco, a township of the "pre-puna".

Turning right at the junction you follow the new Route 40 to Pituil, where the pavement ends at present, and on to Salicas (ACA Hostería), thence to the Cerro Negro intersection (59 km.) with Route 60, the Tinogasta (69 km. W of Cerro Negro)—Aimogasta road. Turning left at Cerro Negro for 2 km. you rejoin Route 40 heading north (right), well-paved, to **Londres**. This is the second oldest town in Argentina, founded in 1558 and named in honour of the marriage of Mary Tudor and Philip II in 1554. At the town hall one can see a glass coat of arms of the City of London and a copy of the marriage proposal.

15 km. further (paved) is **Belén** (Hotel Samai, Urquiza 349, D, new, Hotel Provincial, run down; Hotel Doña Pilar, forlorn-looking. Cheap breakfast at bus terminal; Restaurant Dalesio, near YPF service station, excellent and cheap). Hot, but rewarding view after walking up a path where Calle General Roca (unnumbered) starts, about ½ hr., to a new statue (1982) of Virgin of Belén. Interesting archaeological museum, Lavalle y Rivadavia, close to bus station. Belén is hemmed in by mountains, except towards the SE, lush vegetation along river. The Huaco district is famous for weaving: ponchos, saddlebags, rugs. Then 177 km. to Santa María (only 16 km. paved), 22 km. (partly paved) beyond Santa María (see page 81) is Amaich del Valle on 14 km. (paved) to Río Santa María and then 52 km. unpaved to Cafayate (see page 87).

Transport   Villavil (springs), including side trip to Corral Quemado and end of line at Barranca Larga, 19 km. N of Villavil, Tues., Thurs. and Sun. from Belén at 0800, returns from Villavil 1830. (Sit on right-hand side for best views of impressive quebrada and artificial lake.) To Santa María, leaves Tues., 1330, Fri. and Sun. at 2020. Returns Belén Tues. and Thurs. at 0930, Sun., 1945. Belén-Salta, via Hualfín (curative waters), Santa María, Cafayate on Thurs. at 0600. To Catamarca, 1600, 5 hrs.

From Cerro Negro it is 38 km. east to Aimogasta and another 30 km. to the turn off to the Termas de Santa Teresita (7 km.), an ACA Hostería, with thermal bath in each room, and thermal swimming pool; excellent food at reasonable prices. From the turn off near Santa Teresita it is 15 km. east on Route 60 to where a good new road branches off north to Saujil (60 km.) and **Andalgalá** (130 km.); Hostería Provincial. This town, famous for strong alcoholic drinks, can also be reached by Bus 129 from Belén. The road passes, on the left, the long Salar de Pipanaco, and on the right, the Sierras de Ambato and Manchao.

Beyond Andalgalá, the road over the Cuesta de Capillatas in the direction of Santa María is very beautiful, but extremely difficult after the pass where you have to cross a river bed 15 km. wide. No public transport, only trucks to the mines at Capillatas, just beyond the pass, on weekdays.

(We are most grateful to Volker Filss of Oberhausen, W. Germany, for detailed information on the roads N of San Juan.)

For an alternative route to Salta, turn off the Route 40 52 km. after Belén on to Route 53 to Antofagasta de la Sierra and then on to 78 for San Antonio de los Cobres (see page 89). This route is possible in ordinary cars, but you must carry enough fuel for 600 km. at high altitudes on unmade roads (fill up at Hualfín, 10 km. beyond turn off to Antofagasta de la Sierra, where there is a municipal campsite). Also, the stretch beyond the right turn at Puerto de Corral Quemado is very difficult (37 km. of fords) and should not be attempted in the rainy season. At Km. 87 is Cerro Compo (3,125 metres); magnificent descent; at Km. 99 the road turns left to Laguna Blanca (don't go straight on at the junction). **Antofagasta de la Sierra** (260 km.) can be reached on the ground only by hiring a pick-up or by hitch-hiking, or by plane; enquire at Dirección de Aeronaútica, Aeródromo de Choya, T 24750. Bus L 22 goes from town centre to airfield. Pensión Darín; no petrol station, fuel may be obtained from the intendencia (fill up here). This is the main township of the NW of Catamarca, together with El Peñón and Laguna Blanca in the puna, and with Villavil and La Hoyada in the "pre-puna". La Hoyada can be reached from Sta. María in the NE via Provincial Route 118. There are lunar-like landscapes, with salt lakes, around Antofagasta, and several peaks of over 5,000 metres; Dos Conos, Bertrán, Sierra de Laguna Blanca. Deposits of marble, onyx, sulphur, mica, salts, borates and gold. There is a varied fauna including vicuña, guanaco, suri, chinchilla, pink flamingo and fox. The region is sparsely populated.

La Rioja, at 500 metres, 85,000 people, is the capital of La Rioja province. It has some colonial buildings and a folk museum, Instituto del Folklore Riojano at

Pelagio B. Luna 811 (Tues.-Sat. 0900-1300 and 1600-2030, Sun. open 0900-1300, donation US$0.25) a fine traditional house, in which local crafts are carried out. Regional costumes are sometimes seen, and its peculiarly flavoured dry wine is interesting. Worth a visit are the cell (*celda*) in which St. Francisco Solano lived, with the orange tree (now dead) that he planted in 1592, and the solid adobe ruin of the Jesuit church at Las Padercitas, 7 km. outside town (now enclosed by protective walls) in which he baptized the local Indians. A remarkable image of the Child Jesus, known as the Niño Alcalde, can be seen in the church of San Francisco; ring the bell at 25 de Mayo 218 to see it. Santo Domingo church at Pelagio B.Luna and Lamadrid (1623) is said to be oldest surviving church in Argentina. Inca Huasi museum (at Alberdi 650, Mon.-Fri. 0900-1300 and 1600-1900, Sun. open at 0900-1300) has Indian skulls, a fine collection of funerary urns, and "pregnant pots" or jars thought to belong to the Florescent Era around the time of Christ. Replicas sold in entrance hall. Casa de Joaquín V. González, a castle-like building, can be visited free at Rivadavia 952. There is a Museo Histórico at Adolfo E. Dávila 79, free, open Sat. at 1430-2000 and Sun., 0900-1230. Museo de Bellas Artes is at Copiapó 245, Mon.-Fri. 0700-1400 and 1430-2130, Sat.-Sun. 0900-1200. The Mercado Artesanal, Pelagio B. Luna 790, is interesting. There is a famous casino at Avenida Sarmiento (now renamed Juan D. Perón) and Quiroga.

In the town are many examples of the strange *palo borracho* tree, with a bottle-shaped thorn-studded trunk at a drunken angle hung with pods like avocado pears which, when ripe, open to disclose large brown seeds in a kapok-like substance. The tree is also found in several parks and gardens in Buenos Aires.

Hotels *Internacional Sussex*, Ortiz de Ocampo 1551, adverse report; *King's*, Av. Quiroga 1070; *Luxor*, Av. Quiroga 25; *Provincial Casino*, J.D.Perón 1235; *Libertador*, Buenos Aires 223. *Talampaya*, J.D.Perón 951; *Provincial de Turismo*, Santa Fe 950, well set up but poorly run; *Emperador*, San Martín 258; *Centro*, Rivadavia 499; *Plaza*, Bartolomé Mitre and 9 de Julio, rec., but noisy street; all C. *Parlamento*, Rivadavia 549; *Savoy*, Roque A. Luna 14 and Bartolomé Mitre, excellent value, E, hot shower. *Ritz*, 25 de Mayo 195. *El Gringo*, Cnel. Lagos 427; *Aparicia*, Copiapó 119, all D, rec. Good value from *La Rioja*, *Libertador* and *Central*. *Residenciales*: best is *Sumaj Kanki*, Castro Barros 1199 y Cnel. Lagos, F, friendly, pleasant, a bit run down but you can't leave before 0730. At Aniliaco, on Highway 75, between La Rioja and Aimogata, there is a *Hostería ACA*. The Tourist Office has a list of private lodgings; try Familia Lazzarotto, San Martín 156, friendly, hot showers, cooking facilities.

Restaurants *La Cantina de Juan*, H. Yrigoyen 190, excellent empanadas, local white wine, local cheese with nuts; *La Posta* and *Don Facundo*, both on J.D.Perón. Good take-away food at *Très Bien* on 9 de Julio near cathedral.

Tourist Office One of the most helpful in Argentina, at Av. J.D.Perón 401 y Urquiza, and near Plaza, maps, information, bus timetables for routes off the main road.

Exchange Banco de la Provincia, behind main office on Plaza. (See note on provincial bonds used as currency, page 169.)

Transport From Buenos Aires, 2,092 km., by train, 39 hours. *El Norteño* train goes via Córdoba Tues., and Fri. at 1000 and links with buses to La Rioja and Catamarca and tickets can be bought at Retiro. Return journeys (*automotor* returns from Córdoba Wed., and Sat. at 0751) can be booked from La Rioja and Catamarca bus offices. Tickets may be booked up to 90 days in advance. Villa Unión-La Rioja bus daily at 1440, reverse journey at 1330.

Daily AA flights from Buenos Aires. Twice daily service, Mon.-Fri., at 0800 and 1330, La Rioja to Catamarca with Líneas Aéreas Riojanas, about 20 mins. Passengers have to go to Oficina Aeronáutica, Rivadavia 461 (T 28887); transport provided free.

By road from Mendoza (see above). Bus to Mendoza and San Juan only by night, two companies: Bosio, 11 hrs, US$11, very comfortable, four per night. If you want to travel to San Juan by day (good scenery) take 0715 Cotil bus to Chepes (new bus station and ACA motel) and take Cotil next day from Chepes to San Juan at 0900 (or 20 de Junio bus at 1000 for San Juan or 1230 for San Luis). Bus terminal is about 5 blocks from the centre. Bus to Salta, US$13.30; bus to Tucumán, at least once a day, 7 hrs, at 0300 or 1200, US$10. To Catamarca, Cotil, daily at 0615 and 1545, Bosio at 0515, 1645, 2200, about 2½ hrs, US$2.60. La Estrella and Libertador on the Mendoza-Tucumán run follow same routes, but arrival times are unreliable.

Excursions To Valle de la Luna and Talampaya (via Nonogasta, Cuesta de Miranda and Villa Unión), US$12 including transport and guide, and to Samay Huasi (see page 106). Good fishing at El Portezuelo dam (see below). Swimming and fishing at Los Sauces dam, 15 km. away; beyond

Los Sauces is Villa Sanagasta, nice run, daily El Cóndor buses at 1200 and 1500 (US$0.60), returning at 1400 and 1700, 45 mins. Very good view of La Rioja from Cerro de la Cruz (1,680 metres). There is a bad 12 km. road from the dam to the top, which is now a centre for hang-gliding. Condors and falcons can be sighted.

A paved road runs NE to the third oasis, Catamarca.

Catamarca, capital of its province, lies on a river at 490 metres between two of the southern slopes of the Sierra de Aconquija, about 240 km. S of Tucumán. Cotton growing is added here to the cattle, fruit and grapes of the oasis. It is also famous for the hand-weaving of ponchos and for its preserves; an especially excellent one is from the fruit of a cactus (try Casa Valdés, Sarmiento 586). Pilgrimages to the church of the Virgen del Valle. A regional mountain wind, the Zonda, strong and dry, which can sometimes raise temperatures to 50°C (122°F) afflicts this area, together with San Juan, La Rioja and Mendoza. There is a *feria* in July, at which handicrafts are sold, the Festival del Poncho. Four nights of music, mostly folklore of the NW. Population about 79,000.

Hotels *Provincial de Turismo* (much as at La Rioja), República 108 y Caseros; *Ancasti,* Sarmiento 520, E, has first class expensive restaurant; *Inti Huasi,* República 297, D. *Pucará,* Av. Esquiú, 1 block from ACA station, D, clean, a/c, friendly; *Suma Huasi,* Sarmiento 547, E, ask for room *not* above TV lounge. *Centro,* Juan M. de Rosas, esq. 9 de Julio, basic. *Residenciales*: *Venecia,* Tucumán 115, *Plaza,* Rivadavia 278, *Sirio,* Salta 1184, E, reasonably clean, small rooms, *Familiar,* Güemes 841, F (opp. bus station), friendly and clean; *Esquiú,* Esquiú 365, *Avenida,* Av. Güemes 754 (E with bath, F without), *Menen,* Av. Güemes 793, *Comodoro,* República 851, *Yunka Suma,* V. Segura 1255, *Valle Viejo,* Ruta Nac. 38, all F. The *Ancasti, Inti Huasi* and *Suma Huasi* grant a 10% discount to members of ACA (Argentine Automobile Club). Very cheap pensión, clean, unnamed, on Tucumán 1294, no shower or hot water, treble rooms, friendly.

Restaurants *Club Español; El Encuentro; La Cabaña,* on Esquiú; (and *Carlos I* at weekends) has folklore dancing. *La Tinaja,* excellent and cheap with live music, warmly rec.; *Pizzería Maryeli,* Esquiú 473, basic (but good empanadas). Roofgarden of *Hotel Ancasti* has restaurant. In this area soup is eaten after the meal, said to be a Chinese custom. Many cheap restaurants along Av. Güemes; bars and cafés along Rivadavia (pedestrian street).

Shopping *Regionales Sevita,* next to Aerolíneas Argentinas office, Catamarca specialities. Artisan exhibition hall, *Casa del Poncho,* on General Urquiza, corner with Mota Botello, very worthwhile; handwoven articles. Open 0700-1330. The value of these depends on the number of knots used. Reached by infrequent colectivo 23 from centre.

Museum The Instituto Cultural Esquiú, Sarmiento 450 (archaeology, colonial history, iconography, mineralogy). Museo Arqueológico Adán Quiroga, interesting, opens daily at 0800-1200 and 1600-2100, Sat.-Sun. 0800-1200. Well worth a visit. There are traces of the Belén civilization elsewhere in the province, at Hualfín and Punta de Balasto.

Post Office San Martín 753, slow, closes at noon. Telephones at Rivadavia 758.

Tourist Office very helpful but not too reliable, in Plaza (500 block of San Martín). Also at Manzana del Turismo at Urquiza 951. Try Yokavil agency, on Güemes.

Exchange No *casa de cambio*; try Turi Tat travel agency, 800 block of República, or tourist shops.

Buses Road to Tucumán is paved and in good condition except for the two *cuestas* (Cuesta del Tortoral) at the border between Catamarca and Tucumán provinces (steep gradients, hairpin bends, many potholes for 25 km.), bus US$5.50, 5 hrs., 238 km., 5 a day with Bosio. To Buenos Aires, 2nd class at 2200, US$30; 1st class at 1900, US$37, daily. To Belén, via Cerro Negro, with Coop. Catamarca, returns daily from Belén at 1300 (**see page 107**). Also to Catamarca via Andalgalá; Coop. Catamarca via Saujil, Poman, Chumbicha, Tues. and Thurs. at 1000, Fri. and Sun., 1300, about 8 hrs. To El Rodeo-Las Juntas, daily from platform 9 of the Catamarca bus terminal (800 block of Güemes) at 1300, arrive at Las Juntas 1500, returns at 1700. Buses to and from Córdoba, twice a week, connect there with *Norteño* train for Buenos Aires; about 5 buses a day to Córdoba in all. To Santiago del Estero, 1630, US$6.

Air Cooperativa de Transportes Catamarca, not as reliable as Aerolíneas Riojanas; service twice a week from Tinogasta to Belén, Tues. and Thurs. Officially departs Tinogasta at 0810, but one is told to show up at the municipal building at 0815 to be at the plane at 0830. Route is circular: Catamarca-Tinogasta-Belén-Andalgalá-Catamarca, in 6-seater Cessna or Piper. Aerolíneas Argentinas offices on Sarmiento, near *Hotel Suma Huasi.*

Excursion to the Dique Las Pirquitas, 3 hrs with local bus 1A every 90 mins. from bus station, with terminus at Isla Larga, pleasant hills and woods. Bus stops at *Hostería de Turismo* at Villa Pirquitas, about 45 min. walk. Opening hours, Mon.-Fri., 1000-1900, Sat., Sun. and holidays, 0830-1900.

A road runs NE to Lavalle (on the way to Santiago del Estero). This 116-km. run over the **Cuesta del Portezuelo** pass (1,980 metres), with its 20 km. of steep gradients and numerous hairpin bends—small hairpins—is one of the toughest in the country (superb views of Catamarca). No bus service over Portezuelo to Lavalle, but a service to Frías, E and also in Santiago del Estero province—No. 9 and *not* No. 18 (which runs over the Tortoral) run by the Coop. de Transportes de Catamarca. Leaves at 0500, Tues., Thurs., Fri., Sat., arrives at Frías at 1000, returns from Frías on same days at 1400, arr. Catamarca at 1900. From Frías travel to Lavalle.

Catamarca to Frías via Tortoral: Bus 18, Mon., Wed., Fri., Sat., leaves at 0500, arrives at Frías 1030, returns 1330, back at Catamarca at 1900. Mon. and Fri., Bus 14 goes via El Alto, longer journey, at 0430, arrives at Frías at 1045. Catamarca-Lavalle via Tortoral, same Bus 18, leaves Tues., Thurs., Sun., at 1100, arrives Lavalle 1510.

THE CHACO (6)

Between the north-western highlands already described and the Río Paraná to the E lies the Argentine Chaco, containing the provinces of Formosa and Chaco, part of Santiago del Estero, and northern Santa Fe. Its southern limit is the Río Dulce valley. This great lowland is covered with thorn scrub and grassy savanna, the thorn bushes sometimes impenetrable and sometimes set widely apart on grassland. The highest summer temperatures in all South America have been recorded in the Argentine Chaco; the winters are mild with an occasional touch of frost in the S. Rain falls in the winter according to location: the further W, the less the rain.

Communications Before the recent building of highways, the only all-weather routes were provided by the Belgrano Railway. There are two main north/south lines from Buenos Aires: the international route to La Paz and the line through Rosario and Santa Fe to Resistencia. There are two east/west rail connections, Resistencia-Metán and Formosa-Embarcación; only the latter carries passengers regularly (see page 119). A third line runs SW from Roque Sáenz Peña to Anatuya in the province of Santiago del Estero. (It is advisable to check all rail services, since many were suspended years ago without being formally abolished.) Roads are given in the text and air services link the major towns.

Tannin and cotton are the two great industries of the Chaco. The iron-hard *quebracho* (axe-breaker) tree grows only in the Chaco of northern Argentina and Paraguay; it is the purest known source of tannin. The industry is struggling against competition from synthetic tannin and the huge mimosa plantations in South Africa. The most accessible forest is worked out; most of the cutting is now in the N and W of the province.

Cotton growers, centred on Roque Sáenz Peña in Chaco Province, have had difficulty in maintaining production in the face of soil exhaustion. Sunflower is the chief crop replacing cotton, and there is also some maize and sorghum.

Roque Sáenz Peña can be reached by an excellent road from Puerto Pilcomayo. Hot springs have been found here and a modern hotel has been built to develop the city as a spa. Other hotels are: *Residencial Sáenz Peña*, near bus station, cheap, clean and friendly; *Residencia Asturias*, D, fair. Daily bus, La Internacional, to Buenos Aires, 2000, 19 hrs. From Buenos Aires, also 2000. Bus from Salta at 1700, 10 hrs., US$12.50; bus to Resistencia, US$3. North of Roque Sáenz Peña is the village of Castelli, which has a large Tobas Indian community and an *artesanía* shop. *Hotel Guc*, F, basic. 23 km. SE of R.S.Peña, on Route 16, is Quitilipi, with municipal campsite.

The rest of the Chaco is cattle country but there are few animals to the square km. Large *estancias* are the rule, some growing cotton, linseed and other crops by irrigation. The bird life of the area—flamingoes, black-necked swans, heron egrets, storks and various birds of prey—is most interesting.

Towns of the Chaco The most important ones—Resistencia and Formosa—are on the W bank of the Paraná and Paraguay and will be described, for convenience's sake, under Argentine Mesopotamia. Apart from Roque Sáenz Peña, the only other town of any importance is Santiago del Estero, on the western boundary of the Chaco (see page 77).

Federico Kirbus tells us that on the border of Chaco and Santiago del Estero provinces is Campo de

Cielo, a meteorite impact field about 15 km. by 4 km. where about 5,000 years ago a planetoid landed and broke into 30 main pieces. Some of the meteorites are on display in Buenos Aires (the Rivadavia museum and the Planetarium), but the largest, "El Chaco", (33.4 tonnes), is on display at the Campo. Access from Route 89 (between Resistencia and Santiago del Estero) at Gancedo, where you travel 15 km. S to Las Víboras (many buses).

MESOPOTAMIA (7)

Between the rivers Paraná and Uruguay lies Argentine Mesopotamia: the provinces of Entre Ríos, Corrientes, and Misiones. The distance between the rivers is 390 km. in northern Corrientes, but narrows to about 210 km. in the latitude of Santa Fe. Mesopotamia was first colonized by Spaniards pushing S from Asunción to reoccupy Buenos Aires; both Corrientes and Paraná were founded as early as 1588. Alison Brysk and Mark Freeman (San Francisco) tell us that there was Jewish agricultural settlement in Entre Ríos at the beginning of C.20 ("Los gauchos judíos"). Vestiges of these settlements remain at Domínguez (museum) and Basavilbaso, and across the river in Moisesville (Santa Fe).

Much of Entre Ríos and Corrientes is still pastoral, a land of large *estancias* raising cattle and sheep. Maize (a gamble in the N) is largely grown in southern Entre Ríos, which is also the most important producer of linseed, citrus fruit and poultry in Argentina. In Corrientes, along the banks of the Paraná between the cities of Corrientes and Posadas, rice and oranges are grown.

The province of Corrientes, in the N, is marshy and deeply-wooded, with low grass-covered hills rising from the marshes. The normal rainfall is about 2,000 mm, but the rains are not spread uniformly and drain off quickly through the sandy soil. Entre Ríos, to the S, has plains of rich pasture land not unlike those of Uruguay. Winters in Mesopotamia are mild; the summers are hot and much rain falls in short, sharp storms, though both Entre Ríos and Corrientes often suffer from summer drought.

Misiones Province, in the far NE, was first occupied by the Jesuit Fathers fleeing from the Brazilian Alto-Paraná region with their devoted Indian followers before the slave-hunting Bandeirantes. These missions and their history are described under Posadas (**see page 119**). Misiones is a hilly strip of land between the Alto Paraná and the Uruguay rivers, 80-100 km. wide and about 400 km. long; its capital is the river port of Posadas. Its boundary to the N is the river Iguazú, which here tumbles over the great Iguazú Falls. Misiones is on the Paraná Plateau; much of it is covered with forests of pine and cedar and broad-leaved trees, and the look of the land, with its red soil, reminds one strongly of Brazil. Here too the rainfall is heavy: twice as heavy as in Entre Ríos. The days are hot, and the nights cool.

It was the Jesuits who first grew *yerba mate* in plantations; Misiones has always been a large producer of this leaf, and also of citrus, tobacco, timber and tung oil. The province has of late years attracted immigrants from Eastern Europe, from Paraguay and from the rest of Mesopotamia. There is good fishing in many of the small river-towns. In NE Corrientes and in Misiones more Indian tea is now grown than can be absorbed by the internal market.

The Indian-tea industry was started by Sir Herbert Gibson, who sent for seed from Assam in 1929; it was sown in Playadito, Corrientes province. Six seeds developed into sturdy bushes. Year after year their seed was given to anyone interested. All Argentina's tea plantations today have their origin in Sir Herbert Gibson's enterprise.

Communications in the area are by road (now greatly improved), by railway, and by the two rivers the Paraná and the Uruguay, which bound it to E and W. Neither river is very good for navigation. Bridges between Fray Bentos (Uruguay) and Puerto Unzué, near Gualeguaychú, and between Paysandú (Uruguay) and Colón were opened in 1976, and there are a road and railway over the Salto Grande dam, near Concordia.

The area is served by the Urquiza railway, the only standard-gauge line in the country; the most

NORTH-EAST ARGENTINA

10

important line runs from Buenos Aires to Posadas with connection over the river to Asunción, the capital of Paraguay, and a branch at Monte Caseros for Corrientes.

Most of the important towns of Mesopotamia lie on the E bank of the Paraná or the S bank of the Alto Paraná. A journey up these rivers is given here; the towns on both banks are described.

Up the Paraná River

Navigation River boats carry passengers along various stretches of the river, but there are no long-distance passenger services up the river from Buenos Aires, except those to Asunción, Paraguay. According to the tide, boats enter the Paraná river by either the Las Palmas reach of the delta, on which is Zárate, or the Paraná-Guazú reach, on which is Ibicuy.

Zárate, with 52,000 inhabitants, is industrially important, with large *frigorificos* and paper works (*Hotel San Martín,* Ameghino 773, D, clean; *Restaurant La Posta de Correa,* cheap, good service). It is served from Buenos Aires (90 km.) by bus (US$2) and two railways: the Mitre and the Urquiza. Urquiza trains used to be ferried 84 km. across the river, but a link including two large and beautiful bridges has been built between Zárate and Brazo Largo, accelerating both rail and road journeys alike (the bridge toll is US$6). The picturesque Ibicuy Islands can be visited by boat. Near Zárate is San Pedro, where fine riverfront camping can be had at either the *Centro Turístico, Club Pescadores* or *Camping Municipal.*

On the way upstream to Rosario, on the western bank, are two ports which export grain: San Nicolás (55,000 people), 80 km. below Rosario, and Villa Constitución, 37 km. below Rosario. Both are served by a railway from the capital. At San Nicolás is the General Savio steel plant. Pergamino, an important road/rail junction in the pampas, is 72 km. S by road or rail.

About 108 km. N of Ibicuy is *Gualeguay,* with a population of 26,000. It is the centre of one of the richest cattle and sheep ranching regions in Entre Ríos. The house in which Garibaldi was tortured by the local chief of police in 1837, in the time of Rosas, still exists. Eight km. S is its river port, Puerto Ruiz. The road from Gualeguay northwards along the E bank of the Paraná is paved most of the way to Posadas.

Hotels *Gran Hotel Gualeguay,* Monte Caseros 217, C; *Italia,* E. There is a municipal **campsite**. In the centre there are practically no **restaurants**, but the *Jockey Club* and the *Club Social,* both on the main square close to the *Gran Hotel Gualeguay,* cater also for non-members. The *Club Social* has a very nice atmosphere, good food, and you might be invited to see films on certain nights.

Rosario, chief city of the province of Santa Fe, 320 km. N of Buenos Aires, is the third city of the republic, with a population of well over a million. It is a great industrial and export centre. The streets are wider than those of Buenos Aires, and there are fine boulevards and handsome open spaces. From October to early March it is warm, and from December to the end of February uncomfortably hot. Changes of temperature are sudden.

Points of Interest Monument of the Flag, a memorial on the river bank in honour of General Belgrano, designer of the Argentine flag, who raised it on this spot for the first time; Parque Independencia (Rose Garden): Boulevard Oroño; Cathedral in Calle 25 de Mayo; St. Bartholomew's Church (Anglican), Calle Paraguay; racecourse, the Alberdi and Arroyito boat clubs, and Saladillo Golf Club, with its own Links station on the Mitre line. The Aero Club is at the fashionable suburb of Fisherton, headquarters of the British community. The Juan B. Castagnino Municipal Museum and the provincial Historical Museum (open Thurs. and Sat. 1500-1800, and Sun. 1000-1200, 1500-1800) are in Parque Independencia. Swimming at sandy Florida beach, about 8 km. N of Rosario. The boat *Ciudad de Rosario* does a short trip round the nearby river islands Sat. 1730, Sun. 1600 and 1830, US$1; leaving from the Estación Fluvial near the Monument of the Flag.

Local Holiday October 7 (Foundation of the City).

Hotels *Riviera,* San Lorenzo 1460, air conditioned, B; *Plaza,* Barón de Mauá, C; *La Paz,* next door at No. 36, E, clean, quiet, friendly, rec.; *Presidente,* Av. Corrientes 919, C, good; *Micro,*

Santa Fe 3650, D; *Onix*, Vera Mujica 757, D; *Río*, opp. railway station, E, clean, friendly; *Moderno*, by Norte railway station, F with bath, OK; *Oviedo*, near railway station, F, with bath.

Restaurants *Don Rodrigo*, Sante Fe 968, and *Fenix*, Santa Fe next to Citibank, are both very good. *Doña María*, also on Santa Fe, does good Italian food; *Catay*, off Plaza Murillo, rec. for Chinese food; *Scaramouche*, just off Prado, on Loaysa, excellent US$4 menú del oficinista; *Casa Uruguaya*, Alvear 1125 (T 69320), away from centre, good.

Markets Mercado Central, Calle San Martín; also Mercados Norte, Sud, and Abasto. Best time, 0600-0800.

Exchange Lloyds Bank (BLSA), Calle La Rioja 1205; Citibank, Santa Fe 1101; First National Bank of Boston, Córdoba esq. Mitre. Open 1000-1600.

Tourist Office At Monument of the Flag, helpful but information inadequate.

Airport at Fisherton, 8 km. from centre. Taxi charges vary. Several flights daily to Buenos Aires. Austral to Corrientes once a week, to Posadas, three times and to Resistencia twice a week.

Rail Rosario is 4 hours from Buenos Aires (320 km.) on the Mitre Railway by express train, Pullman US$12.60, 1st class US$8.10, tourist US$6.20. It is served also by the Belgrano (metre gauge—5 hours). All trains heading N stop at Rosario.

Road Transport There are regular bus services to Arroyo Seco, Casilda, Cañada de Gómez, San Lorenzo and other important centres up to 80 km. from the city. Also from Buenos Aires, by paved roads via San Nicolás and General Pacheco on Route 9 (3¾-4 hrs) or via Pergamino, 309 km. less frequent on Route 8 (Chevallier bus, US$8.10), and from Rosario via Bell Ville NW to Córdoba (bus, US$8) and Tucumán. To Santa Fe, US$3.25. Local bus fare, US$0.50.
　　Rosario can be reached from Buenos Aires by Route 8 (marked Córdoba) to Pergamino, and then, following signs, by Route 188, and then 178 to Rosario. This is a better way than lorry-packed Route 9. Hitching to Salta along Route 34 is possible.

Ferries to Victoria, in Entre Ríos, which has a municipal **campsite**.

Above Rosario the river is very braided and islanded. Boat trips to river islands can be made at weekends. Canoes can be hired. Some 23 km. N of Rosario is **San Lorenzo,** where an associate company of ICI has one of the largest chemical works in Argentina. See the restored San Carlos monastery on the river bank, where in 1813 San Martín won his first battle in the War of Independence. Visitors are shown a pine tree grown from a cutting of the tree under which the Liberator rested after the battle. Some 180 km. above Rosario, on the E bank, is

Paraná, capital of Entre Ríos (pop., 200,000), founded in 1588. From 1853 to 1862 the city was the capital of the Republic; it is a handsome place, with a fine centre, the Plaza San Martín, where there are fountains and a statue of the Liberator. The Cathedral, E of the plaza, is notable for its portico and its interior; opposite it is the tourist information office. A modern building on Plaza Alvear houses the Bazán Museum of Fine Arts (good) and the local history museum, open 0900-1200 and 1500-1800 except Mon. The Government Palace (Casa de Gobierno), in another plaza, has a grand façade. But the city's glory is the Parque Urquiza, to the NW. It has an enormous statue to General Urquiza, and a bas-relief showing the battle of Caseros, at which he finally defeated Rosas; also an open-air theatre. There are excellent views of the country and of Santa Fe on the other side of the river (launch trips). There is a paved road to Paso de los Libres, 483 km., on the Brazilian frontier (**see page 127**).

Hotels *Mayorazgo*, on Costanera Alta, with fine view of park and river, has casino and swimming pool, B; *Super Luxe*, Villaguay 162, C; *Gran Hotel Paraná*, Urquiza 976, D; *Almafuerte*, Av. Almafuerte 1295, D; *Las Colonias*, Cervantes 89, E. Cheap hotels near railway station, and *Plaza* and *Bristol* close to the bus terminal. The *Centro Autoturismo* motel on the road to the Hernandarias tunnel, C.

Restaurants *Musmón*, Urquiza 843, rec.; *La Posta del Olivo*, just off Plaza San Martín; good. *Los Guinchos*, Corrientes 149, excellent fish.

Santa Fe and Paraná do not face one another. It takes 20 mins. to get from one to the other by car, and 1 hour by bus, US$1, every half-hour. You cross a bridge close to Santa Fe, an uninhabited island, another bridge, and another uninhabited island to dive into the 2-km. Hernandarias tunnel, which leads up to Paraná city (toll US$1.90).

Air Service Airport: General Urquiza, 12 km. from town; two flights to Buenos Aires daily with Austral. To Goya and Reconquista at 0820 thrice weekly.

Train *Río Paraná* train to Buenos Aires daily except Sat. at 2020, arrives 0710. From Buenos Aires (F. Lacroze) 2215, arrives 0857.

Bus E across Entre Ríos to Concordia on Río Uruguay, 5 a day, 5 hours.

Santa Fe, a larger city of some 300,000 inhabitants, is the capital of its Province and the centre of a very fertile region. It was founded by settlers from Asunción in 1573, though its present site was not occupied until 1651. It was in its Cabildo (town hall) that the Constitution of 1853 was adopted. The oath of allegiance was taken before the crucifix in the sacristy of the church of San Francisco, built in 1680 from materials floated down the river from Paraguay; this old colonial church has been tampered with but is still fine, especially the carved wooden ceilings, which were fitted without nails.

Most of the best buildings are grouped round Plaza Mayo and Plaza San Martín in the eastern part of the city. Plaza Mayo, on Calle General López, has the small Jesuit church of La Merced (1660-1754), next to the majestic Casa de Gobierno, and (on the N side) a church begun in 1741 (see an old painting from Cuzco and the interesting archives). A block SE of the Plaza has the famous church of San Francisco (see above). Opposite it is the Museo Histórico Provincial. In Calle General López is the Rosa Galisteo de Rodríguez Museum of Fine Arts, where local painters hold their exhibitions. The church of Nuestra Señora de Guadalupe has beautifully painted glass windows and may be reached by bus 8 or 14 from the centre. Twice weekly boats from Buenos Aires, 483 km. to the south; regular only in winter.

Local holidays Sept. 30 (St. Jerome); Nov. 15 (Foundation of City).

Hotels *Hostal de Santa Fe de la Vera Cruz,* best, genial management, well-kept and run, San Martín 2954, B; *Río Grande,* San Gerónimo 2586, B, modern, rec.; *El Conquistador,* 25 de Mayo 2676, C; *Corrientes,* Corrientes 2520, C; *Colón,* San Luis 2862, D; *Pacífico,* Obispo Gelabert 2950, D; *Hospedaje Nueva Tripolitania,* Vera 2230, F, friendly, good restaurant; *Royal,* clean, modern, private bath, opposite bus station, D; *Niza,* Rivadavia 2755, T 22047, D, very clean, friendly; *Brigadier,* San Luis 3148, E, two blocks from bus station, good, clean, friendly, 50 rooms, a/c extra, but rec. if the river is in flood and there are lots of mosquitoes, some English spoken; *Bristol,* Belgrano 2859 by bus terminal, E; next door to it is *Gran Hotel Terminal,* Belgrano 2839, opposite bus terminal, E/F, basic, clean, water shortage; *Astur,* near the bus station, F (cheaper than most).

Camping Possible in municipal site near town centre, Parque Azul, bus No. 5. Site at Guadalupe beach by the lake.

Restaurants Many good ones, offering excellent meals with good wine for US$5. *El Quincho de Chiquito,* Obispo Príncipe y Almte. Brown, excellent and cheap, huge helpings. Excellent grills including *surubí* (local fish) at *Gran Parrillada Rivadavia,* Rivadavia 3299. Surubí also at *Aston,* San Jerónimo 2619, said to be best in town, and *España,* cheaper, San Martín 2644. *Apolo,* opposite bus terminal, good, cheap. Also good and cheap, *Comedor Tío Carlos,* Rivadavia y Suipacha, US$2 for unlimited antipasto and pasta or meat; and *Nochera Española,* next to railway station.

Exchange Lloyds Bank (BLSA), Calle 25 de Mayo 2501, open 0715-1315. Amex representative, Vacaciones Felices, San Martín 2347. Tourfé, San Martín 2901, changes travellers' cheques.

Swimming On river at Guadalupe beach; local bus.

Tourist Office at the conveniently situated bus terminal: maps, friendly.

Railways The quickest link from Buenos Aires is by Mitre railway to Rosario, and connecting bus (7 hours). Belgrano railway to Buenos Aires, 483 km., 8-10 hours (US$9.45 tourist, US$11.90 first class), also N to Resistencia.

Roads Fully paved to Rosario, 160 km. (3 hours by bus); to Formosa, 894 km.; to Roque Sáenz Peña, with spurs S to Villa Angela and General Pinedo and N to San Martín. Large and modern bus terminal. Bus for Asunción (Paraguay) leaves daily at 2125, US$28, 17 hrs. Bus to Córdoba, US$7, 5 hrs. Many buses to Buenos Aires, Paraná and Rosario; daily to Mendoza (2100) and Santiago del Estero/Tucumán (2010).

Airport   At Sauce Viejo, 17 km. from the city. Three daily flights (2 on Sun.) to and from Buenos Aires.

Upstream from Santa Fe the Paraná rapidly loses depth and is navigable only by river boats and small coastal vessels.

Between Paraná and Goya, on the left bank, is *La Paz (Entre Ríos)*, a small port with regional museum, riverside park and golf club. Buses to Buenos Aires, Rosario and Concordia. Small restaurants in port and near bus station.

Between Santa Fe and Corrientes the boat calls at several river ports, including La Paz, Goya and Empedrado. *Goya* (airport 7 km. from centre), on the E bank, the second town of the Province of Corrientes, is near the junction of the Paraná with the Santa Lucía river. It is a large tobacco centre on the Urquiza railway, with a population of 40,000. There is a vehicle-ferry service across the river to *Reconquista*. Both towns are served by Austral (which flies from the military base at Reconquista, between the airport and town, 10 km. from town). Austral, Bs. As.— Reconquista, stopping at Paraná on Tues., Thurs. and Sat. at 0955. The road N from Goya to Empedrado and Corrientes is paved; many buses.

Empedrado, further up the river on the E bank, has a population of 21,000. It is on the railway line between Buenos Aires (1,014 km.) and Corrientes. Oranges and rice are grown in the neighbourhood.

Hotels at La Paz   *Milton*, San Martín e Italia, modern; *Plaza*, main square; *Rivera*, San Martín 376; *San Martín*, San Martín 551, E, clean.

Hotels at Goya   *Hotel de Turismo*, modern, rec. *Cervantes*, J. E. Gómez 723; *Goya*, Colón 929; *España*, España 345, F, clean, hot water, friendly, near bus station. *Hoguimarsa*, B. Mitre 880/90 (the last-named also has establishments at Curuzú Cuatiá, Esquina, Empedrado and Mercedes in Corrientes province). *Restaurant El Colonial* said to be the best, US$4 for full meal, near bus station at Loza 415.

Hotels at Reconquista   *Magni*, D, on main street, adequate, excellent restaurant. *Olessio*, opposite bus terminal, F. *Residencial San Martín*, F, with bath, on B. Mitre and Bolívar. *Motel Hostal del Rey*, located on the edge of town, clean, new, D, with bath. Many around bus station, e.g. *Ideal*, E, good.

Hotel at Empedrado   *Turismo*, with swimming pool and fine views. **Campsite.**

About 600 km. upstream from Santa Fe, on the W bank, is the little port of Barranqueras, served also from Santa Fe by railway (17 hours). It is on a steep bluff overlooking the Paraná. A paved road connects it with

Resistencia, the bustling, hot and energetic capital of the Province of Chaco, a galaxy of neon after dark, 6½ km. up the Barranqueras stream. Pop.: 94,000. The road N from Resistencia to Formosa (200 km.) and on to Puerto Pilcomayo (137 km.) is paved. There are many modern statues, mostly female nudes, promoted by the *Fogón de los Arrieros* (see below), along the streets and a museum, the Museo Histórico Ichoalay, at Donovan 425, in the Catholic girls' school, which traces the development of the city. International airport.

Area Products   Cotton, *quebracho*, cattle. Sculptured Chaco woods from Domingo Arenas, cubist-type wood-statues. Tradicional Pampeya, on Güemes 154, sells local handicrafts and has an Indian handicraft display. Handicrafts also sold by Toba Indians in the Toba district.

Hotels   Many accept Visa cards. *Covadonga*, Güemes 200, C, a/c, *Tabaré* snack bar; *Lemirson*, Rawson 167, C; *Colón*, Sta. María de Oro 139, C, friendly, clean, rec.; *Sahara*, Güemes 169, D, Telex 71104. *Esmirna*, H. Irigoyen 83 on corner of Plaza, D with bath, good. *Residencial*, Av. Alberdi 317, F; *Las Torres*, Güemes 757, D; *Residencia Monaco*, Tucumán 350, E, OK. Several cheap ones near bus station, e.g. *Alfi*, E; *Aragón*, Santiago del Estero, F; *Comedor El Oriente*, Av. 25 de Mayo 554, E, with bath.

Camping   *Parque Dos de Febrero*, very pretty, near artificial lake, tent US$2; adequate free site nearby. *Parque Mitre*, showers and toilets. There is another site, shady but no facilities, NW of Resistencia on Route 16.

Restaurants   *Círculo Residentes Santafecinos*, tasty meals at family style restaurant, US$6 for large meal, on Vedia 152. Try chupín de surubí, a sort of bouillabaisse, delightful. Nearby is *Cirilo*, Vedia 164, lunch for US$1.35, good. *Parrillada Clemente*, Santa María de Oro 399 near bus station. *Parrillada Las Brasas*, Brown 71, less good. Meat also at *Kebon*, on 200 block of Brown. Good pizzas at *San José* in main square. *Antiguo Farol* and *La Recova* both on Güemes and Don Bosco.

Fogón de los Arrieros, Brown 350, between López and French, a famous house-and-club full of local art and "objets" from abroad. No fee. Anyone can drink at the bar, open to the public from 2100 to 2300, Tues.-Thurs. Good place to meet local people.

Car Hire   Avis, French 701 and at airport.

Exchange   Banco del Chaco, Güemes on main plaza, high commission on travellers' cheques, good for buying guaraníes. Cambio Espinoza, Güemes 160 and at Santa María del Oro 136, good rates.

Tourist Office   In municipal building, one block N of main square, Vedia and Tucumán, maps, very helpful; open 0800-2000.

Air   Airport 8 km. from town. Austral weekend night flights to and from Buenos Aires with 40% discount. Two flights a day to Buenos Aires, some stopping at Rosario. Alfa flies to Salta Sat. 0800, US$60.

Rail   S to Santa Fe, leaves on Tues. and Sat. at 1830 (0600 in winter), 15½ hrs, nothing to eat or drink on train (Belgrano Railway). No regular passenger service to Formosa, Metán or Salta.

Buses   Buses leave every 15 mins. to Corrientes over the Paraná River bridge, 40 mins., US$0.40, the Resistencia terminal is on Sta. Maria del Oro, 3 blocks from main plaza. 3 *especiales* a day to Buenos Aires (US$23) 14 hrs., 3 *comunes* a day (US$19), 17 hrs.; bus to Santa Fe (US$11.50). 8 a day to Formosa (2½ hrs.) and Puerto Pilcomayo, 6-7 hours, US$6.50. To Posadas, 6-7 hours, 4 a day, US$9, dull, hot journey. Two Veloz del Norte buses direct to Salta (US$18) at 1630 and 2300, 14-16 hours, bus may get bogged down on dirt roads; can be crowded. Few stops and no toilet on bus; El Rayo to Tucumán at 1930 and 2200, 15 hrs., US$14.50. Bus to Rosario, daily, 2015, US$17.25. Bus to Paraguayan border US$2, 5 hours. Many searches, watch your belongings and make sure everything is there afterwards. Also to Asunción daily, via Formosa, with Godoy and Brújula, US$7.50, 6½ hrs.

Roads   between Resistencia and Salta: Most of Route 16, through Roque Sáenz Peña (**see page 110**), Avia Teray, Pampa del Infierno (good ACA *Hostería*), Río Muerto, Monte Quemado, El Quebrachal, Joaquín V. González (good municipal campsite at YPF service station), then on Route 30 to Las Lajitas and Lumbrera, is paved, but there are two bad stretches of 30 km. each before Pampa del Infierno and J.V.González. No service stations along most of the route. It is 830 km. and can be done in one day by car, but it may be hot and there are several police check points; beware of cattle crossing the road. A south-western route (No. 94), from Avia Teray to Quimili, thence to Santiago del Estero, is very bad.

On the other side of the river from Resistencia (25 km.) is Corrientes. The 2¾-km. General Belgrano bridge crosses the river (toll free); the best view of it is from the Corrientes side.

Corrientes, the site of Graham Greene's *The Honorary Consul,* is the capital of Corrientes Province. The river can make the air heavy, moist and oppressive, but in winter the climate is pleasant. Population, 200,000. The city was founded in 1588. The church of La Cruz (1808) houses a miraculous cross placed there by the founder of the city, Alonzo de Vera—Indians who tried to burn it were killed by lightning from a cloudless sky. The Cathedral is in the renaissance style. Plaza Sargento Cabral has a statue to the sergeant who saved San Martín's life at the battle of San Lorenzo. A beautiful walk along the Paraná river leads to Parque Mitre, from where there are good views of sunsets over the river. On the Costanera, above the bridge to Resistencia, is a zoo with animals of the region. There is a Colonial, Historical and Fine Arts Museum. The pre-Lenten carnival is said to be interesting; reserve hotel in advance; otherwise stay in Resistencia, which is cheaper. Calle Junín is pedestrianized, with restaurants and shops, crowded at night. Road to Posadas, 320 kms., now paved.

Hotels   *Corrientes,* Junín 1559; and *Gran Hotel Guaraní,* Mendoza 970, B; *Turismo Provincial,* Entre Ríos 650; *Cadena de Oro,* Ruta Nacional 12; *Orly,* San Juan 861, C; *Waikiki,* Gobernador A. Ruiz 2260, D; *Sosa,* España 1050, D, a little overpriced; *Pavón,* Av. Maipú, km 3. Residenciales *Aialay,* Córdoba 314; *Avenida,* Av. 3 de Abril.

Camping   Near bus terminal and railway station is *Camping-club Teléfono,* US$1 p.p., hot showers or bath, friendly.

Restaurants   *Maximiliano,* H. Irigoyen 1331, open until 0300; *Yapeyú,* Av. Vera 1352; *Michelangelo,* C. Pellegrini y Catamarca; *Raviolandia,* Nueve de Julio 652; *Che Camba,* Av. Independencia 4175; *El Mangrullo,* Junín y Don Bosco. *La Rueda,* Av. 3 de Abril. *La Reforma,* Rioja and Julio. Ice creams at *Italia,* Nueve de Julio 1301 and *Verona,* Av. Ferré 1750. Tea rooms:

Confitería Viki, San Juan 721 y Maipú 1198. *Café Mecca*, Junín 1264/66; *Gualeyán*, Junín 1426. Several on San Juan. *Pizzerías: Gaselli*, Av. Tres de Abril 686, *San Jorge*, Irigoyen 2265; *Los Pinos*, Catamarca and Bolívar; *Gandolfo*, Av. Tres de Abril 563.

Nightclubs Several on or near Mendoza, and on or near Pellegrini.

Car Hire Avis at *Gran Hotel Guaraní* and airport; only credit cards accepted from foreigners.

Exchange Virtually unobtainable. Aerolíneas or travel agents may help unofficially.

Tourist Office La Rioja 149.

Travel Agencies Quo Vadis, Pellegrini 1140; El Cabure, San Juan 671; Viamir, Junín 1459; Viajes Atlas, Mendoza 1073.

Airport Camba Punta, 10 km. from city. Aerolíneas Argentinas office Junín 1301, T 23850; Austral, Córdoba 935, T 25278. Daily AA and Austral flights to and from Buenos Aires. Austral to Rosario twice a week.

Rail Office on Córdoba 990, T 22009. Daily train leaves Lacroze station, Buenos Aires at 1230 or 1500 daily, arriving at Corrientes (1,046 km.) at 0900 or 1230 next day; it leaves Corrientes at 1825 daily, reaching Buenos Aires at 1545 next day. Fares: sleeper US$47.85, first US$24.75, tourist US$17.80.

Bus New terminal 5 km. from centre; bus No. 6 from terminal to town centre (US$0.15). Corrientes-Posadas US$7.50, 4½ hrs. Buses to Resistencia US$0.40, Cota, every 15 mins., 40 mins. journey, labelled "Chaco", leave from harbour; Buenos Aires-Corrientes, US$21.50; there are many more buses to Buenos Aires, Rosario and Santa Fe from Resistencia than from Corrientes.

At 20 km. along Route 12 from Corrientes is Santa Ana de los Guacaras, a 17th-century settlement with attractive colonial architecture. To the N of Corrientes is the small town of *Paso de la Patria* (38 km., Route 12), a paradise for *dorado* fishing, with plenty of bungalows to stay. (Hotels: *Hostería Oficial*, C; *Cabaña Don Julián*, C, full board.)

A tiny port on the Alto Paraná—*Itatí* (pop. 5,700)—is reached by bus (73 km. on Route 12). Here, on July 16, is held a gala festival which celebrates jointly the crowning of the Virgin of Itatí (housed in a sanctuary built 1638), and St. Louis of France. Thousands of pilgrims arrive on the 16th (when the religious ceremonies begin) from San Luis del Palmar (pop. 15,000) in picturesque procession. Also on Route 12 (250 km. from Corrientes) are the Saltos de Apipé, where one can fish or swim.

210 km. SE of Corrientes, on the edge of the Iberá marshes, is the Estancia of San Juan Poriahú (16,500 hectares), a wildlife reserve with a superb array of animals and birds. Among the species are the endangered aguará-guazú (a large, red fox), deer, otters, the Juan Grande stork, kingfishers, snakes, etc. Visitors can explore the estancia on horseback, or in pick-ups or tractors. Iberá itself is a nature reserve containing more species, it is claimed, than the Pantanal in Mato Grosso, Brazil.

Corrientes is 40 km. below the confluence of the Paraguay and Alto Paraná rivers. Up the former are Formosa and Asunción; up the latter are Posadas and Iguazú.

The only Argentine port of any note on the Paraguay river is **Formosa,** 240 km. bove Corrientes. It is the capital of Formosa Province, and has a population of 40,000. There is an interesting colonial museum in the town centre. There are many Indians in the area (bus from Rivadavia y San Martín, No. 1 ("Lote 68"), 15 mins., to the Barrio de los Indios.) At the Casa de Artesanía ask about the ACA in Ingeniero Juárez, from where excursions to see Chaco Indian settlements may be made. The surroundings are flat and swampy, the climate and vegetation tropical. From the port a trip can be made to Isla Alberdi, a Paraguayan duty-free spot; no possibility of continuing into Paraguay, and can only be done if you have a multiple entry visa. By road from Buenos Aires; 1,365 km. Airport (at least one Aerolíneas Argentinas flight per day).

Hotels *Turismo*, best; *Residencial City*, near railway station, D. Several others on San Martín, E, e.g. *Residencial Italia*, nr. station, E, clean, hot showers. *Residencial Rivas*, ½ block from bus station, F, clean, friendly. *Hotel Royal*, E. Many along Belgrano.

Camping Possible on the river about 2 km. from the centre along a dirt road, upstream and over the railway lines.

Restaurant *Ser Bran*, near bus terminal, cheap and good. *El Ciervo*, Av. 25 de Mayo 65, excellent fish (surubí) and empanadas.

Tourist Office On San Martín, near the port, helpful.

Exchange Banks close at about noon and there are no exchange shops; buy australes in Asunción or Clorinda if en route when they're closed. Banco de la Provincia de Formosa changes travellers' cheques.

Shipping Bolivian vessels (cargo and passenger) to Puerto Suárez (Bolivia), with call at Asunción. Irregular.

Roads S to Resistencia (200 km.); N to Clorinda and Asunción, paved, 150 km., via new toll bridge. Direct road to Salta very bad: the bus service appears to run only rarely.

Bus Formosa-Puente Loyola US$4.25. Formosa-Asunción US$4, 0800 and 1630, Expreso Brújula and other companies on main street. Empresa Godoy to border. Six a day to Resistencia.

Railway across the Chaco to Embarcación, N of Jujuy and Salta. *Cochemotor* passenger service, dusty in summer, Sun. and Thurs. 1200, 1st class US$18.15, tourist class US$12.40, buy ticket at 1000 and get on train as soon as you can; 20 hrs., noisy, uncomfortable but worth it for the birdlife.

Excursion Nature reserve (flora and fauna) at Guaycotea, 6 buses a day from Formosa, ½ hr.

About 137 km. N of Formosa, almost opposite Asunción (Paraguay), is *Clorinda*, whence the new Loyola bridge crosses to Puerto Falcón, Paraguay. Border crossing is easy. Many buses from Argentine to end of bridge: to Formosa (10 a day), Resistencia (4) and Santa Fe/Rosario/Buenos Aires (3). Clorinda has a well-known banana festival in early October. Street money changer at Clorinda bus station, gives good rates austral/guaraní. From Puerto Pilcomayo, close to Clorinda (bus US$0.30) one can catch a ferry to Itá Enramada (Paraguay), a US$0.50 five-minute journey every 20 minutes. Argentine migration office at Puerto Pilcomayo does not operate at weekends.

At the confluence of the two rivers above Corrientes the Paraguay river comes in from the N, the Alto Paraná from the E. The Alto Paraná is difficult to navigate; it is, in parts, shallow; there are several rapids, and sometimes the stream is braided, its various channels embracing mid-stream islands. Much rice is grown on its banks.

The main Argentine port, on the S bank, is *Posadas,* capital of the province of Misiones, 377 km. above Corrientes, and very hot in summer. Many street numberings have been changed: beware! A bridge has been built across the 2½ km. of river between Posadas and the Paraguayan town of Encarnación opposite, to link the road systems of the two countries. A motor launch and car ferry link Posadas and Encarnación; the former runs 6 times a day Sat. and Sun., 7 daily in the week (US$1 plus US$0.10 for baggage), the car ferry runs 4 times a day. Thorough baggage and body searches when entering Argentina. Population, 130,000. *Yerba mate*, tea and tobacco are grown in the area. There is a Museo Regional near the amphitheatre on J. B. Alberdi, open daily 0800-1000, US$0.15. (not rec., dilapidated). Better is the Museo Arqueológico e Histórico Andrés Guacurarí (on Gen. Paz, near municipal market), which has Jesuit remains and archaeological pieces from the areas to be flooded by the Yacyretá hydroelectric project. There is a relatively expensive Mercado Artesanal (craft market). The Montoya Natural History Museum in the centre of Posadas, with live birds and snakes, well-kept, extensive range. The roads to Corrientes and Iguazú are paved.

Route 12 along the Río Uruguay from Zárate north (now fully paved) is the shortest and least crowded route from Buenos Aires to Posadas and Iguazú and avoids the major population centres. On this route, S of Posadas, is San Miguel Apóstoles, where a *mate* festival is held at the beginning of Nov.

Hotels Prices in the Province of Misiones are on the whole significantly higher than elsewhere, and double if you want a private bathroom. Best is *Libertador*, San Lorenzo 2208, C; *Continental*, Bolívar 314, D, comfortable, but noisy, reasonable breakfast; *City*, Colón 280, D, clean and reasonable, good restaurant; *Residencial Colón*, also on Colón, E, good and clean; *Posadas*, Bolívar 272, C, good; *Grand Hotel*, Ayacucho 272, reasonable, central, reasonable, and *Río de Oro*, Colón 433 (ground floor, S side rooms coolest), both E; *Turismo*, Bolívar 171, D, modern but poor maintenance; *Savoy*, Sarmiento 296, clean and pleasant, good restaurant next door, D/E; *Residencial Nagel*, Pedro de Mendoza 211, near bus station, noisy, basic, F; *Eldorado*, near bus station, Av. Mitre 84, basic, E, dirty, friendly; *Argentina,* corner of Colón and Sarmiento, basic, with fan; *Gran Hotel Misiones,* E, on Líbano, a/c, good restaurant, one block from bus terminal; next door to it at Líbano 2655 is *Horianski,* E with bath, garage for cars, family atmosphere but many mosquitoes in season. *Gato Negro,* Mitre 58 near railway station, E. Many adequate *residenciales* in the centre, F.

Camping Municipal camping ground on the river, off the road to San Ignacio Miní, hot showers and shop, good.

Restaurants *El Tropezón,* San Martín 185, good, inexpensive; *Jockey Club,* San Martín 159; *El Encuentro,* also on San Martín, one block from plaza; *Los Troncos,* Colón y San Martín, excellent food and service; *Pescadería Bárbara,* corner of Junín and Entre Ríos, good, wide selection; excellent US$3 buffet on ground floor of *Hotel Savoy.* There is an excellent restaurant *La Querencia,* at Bolívar 322; *Bar Itá* for good coffee and sandwiches, on San Martín. *Pizzería Los Pinos,* San Lorenzo 286, excellent and cheap; *Pizzería La Grata Alegría,* Bolívar y Junín, good. Breakfast at ACA.

Exchange Banco de La Nación changes travellers' cheques. Opens very early, 0615-1215. *Caneva,* Bolívar 609, changes Amex cheques; *Cambio Mazza,* Bolívar 443, near main square, changes travellers' cheques. If stuck when banks and *cambios* are closed, cross the river to Encarnación and use the street changers.

Tourist Office Colón 1985, corner Rioja, on central plaza, T 24360, helpful, open late at weekends, maps and brochures in English of Posadas, Formosa and Iguazú Falls. Hotel listings for Misiones province.

Paraguayan Consulate San Lorenzo 179.

Buses from Buenos Aires, US$24.50, 16½ hrs; Expreso Singer, 1030, 1500 and 1600. Tigre-Iguazú at 1500; some go via Resistencia, some via Concordia. Expreso Singer and Tigre bus terminal is 5 mins. walk from the main bus terminal. Express bus to Puerto Iguazú leaves at 0900 and 0500, 4½ hrs., US$6.50, daily; stops at San Ignacio Miní. Another service to San Ignacio and Puerto Iguazú is by A. Martignoni. Bus to Córdoba with Singer, Tues., Thurs., Sat. at 1730, arrive at 1335 next day. Bus to Corrientes US$7.50; to Formosa US$6.50; to Santa Fe US$11.50. Bus to Rosario US$14; to Paso de los Libres (7 hrs.) US$7.75, interesting, 60 km. not paved. To Resistencia, 6-7 hrs., dull trip, US$9. To Concordia (Expreso Singer) US$11.50, 2100 daily, 8¾ hrs. Singertur, Av. Mitre 54 (T 4771, 4772) in Posadas. **N.B.** The bus station, at junction of Av. Uruguay and Av. Bartolomé Mitre, is on the upper level of the town, some distance from the ferry terminal.

International To Asunción (Expreso Singer), US$10. To Montevideo, a roundabout journey because the main Asunción-Montevideo route passes through Corrientes. One can take Expreso Singer bus to the junction for Colón, at Villa San José (ACA hostel), D, (US$15), local bus to Colón; two local buses over the bridge to Paysandú (US$1.50), then plenty of buses to Montevideo (US$8). For those continuing to Brazil (Uruguaiana) have the bus drop you off about 3 km. before Paso de los Libres at Puente Internacional—Argentine customs—the bus from here to the Brazilian border on the other side of the Río Uruguay costs US$0.25. Expreso Singer bus to Porto Alegre (via Oberá, Alba Posse and Porto Mauá) Mon., Wed., Fri. at 1500, arriving 0600 next day, US$18. If the bus is full it is possible to buy a ticket (without a seat) in Oberá. The bus usually empties before long and you can get a seat.

Train from Buenos Aires (Lacroze Station). Information available in Galerías Pacífico, Florida 729, T 31-6411/5. *El Gran Capitán,* which leaves at 1200 daily, arrives at 0830. From Posadas *El Gran Capitán* leaves at 1745 daily, arrives in Buenos Aires about 1545 next day, sleeper US$48.85; pullman US$40; 1st class US$26.20; tourist US$18.35, not crowded. There is a car transporter on the Mon. and Fri. trains, returning to Buenos Aires on Thurs. and Sun. *Cataratas,* leaves Lacroze 1800 Fri., arrives 1123 Sat., returns 2300 Sat., arriving Buenos Aires 1617 Sun., cinema, a/c sleepers, pullman, car transporter. One advantage over the buses is that the wild life in woods and swamps may be seen more easily (because it is less often disturbed) from the railway than from the road. Meals on board, US$4.45. Train to Asunción leaves Encarnación 1100 Wed., arrives 0600 next day. Returns Tues. at 2000. There is a 4 hr. layover between Bs.As. and Asunción at Posadas. Tourist US$8, 1st US$12.

Airport General San Martín (12 km.), reached from Posadas by Bus No. 8 from opp. bus terminal in 20 mins., US$0.30. Daily flights to Buenos Aires with Austral (with one connection a week to Rosario), and Aerolíneas Argentinas; one night flight a week to Buenos Aires with each company: 40% discount.

From Posadas a visit should be paid to the impressive ruins of Jesuit settlements and to the magnificent Falls of Iguazú. The express bus takes 4½ hours (US$6.50) from Posadas to Puerto Iguazú, but may not stop at San Ignacio Miní (see below); the ordinary buses, which will, take 11-12 hours for the journey and there are hourly departures from Posadas; these buses make 35 stops in all.

Not far from Posadas are the ruins of thirty old Jesuit missions among the Guaraní Indians, from which the province of Misiones derives its name. Tourists should see those at San Ignacio Miní (very well maintained), reached by paved road in 1¼ hours (bus, US$1.45, every 1-1½ hours, from terminal, Nuestra Señora, check return time with office). You need about 1½ hrs. for a leisurely look; the ruins begin 3 blocks from the road where the bus stops. There are heavy rains at San Ignacio in February. 16 km. before San Ignacio are the ruins of Santa Ana, only partially cleared but very impressive.

At **San Ignacio Miní**, founded on its present site in 1696, the grass-covered plaza, a hundred metres square, is flanked north, east and west by 30 parallel blocks of stone buildings with ten small, one-room dwellings to the block. The roofs have gone, but the massive metre-thick walls are still standing except where they have been torn down by the *ibapoi* trees; it looks as if there was an arcade in front of each block. The public buildings, some of them still 10 metres high, are on the south side. In the centre are the ruins of a large church finished about 1724. To the right is the cemetery, to the left the school and the cloisters of the priests. Beyond are other buildings which were no doubt the workshops, refectory and storerooms. The masonry, a red or yellow sandstone from the Paraná River, was held together by a sandy mud. There is much bas-relief sculpture, mostly of floral designs. Now maintained as a National Monument (open 0800-1800, entry free, but tip appreciated if the guards look after your luggage). Mosquitoes can be a problem. A new museum was opened in 1987 at the entrance.

The Jesuits set up their first missions among the Guaraní Indians about 1609, in the region of Guaíra, now in Brazil. The missions flourished: cotton was introduced, the Indians wove their own clothes, dressed like Europeans, raised cattle, and built and sculpted and painted their own churches. But in 1627 they were violently attacked by the slave-hunting Bandeirantes from São Paulo, and by 1632 the position of the mission had become impossible: 12,000 converts, led by the priests, floated on 700 rafts down the Paranapanema into the Paraná, only to find their route made impassable by the Guaíra Falls. They pushed for eight days through dense virgin forests on both sides of the river, then built new boats and continued their journey; 725 km. from their old homes they founded new missions in what is now Paraguay, Argentine Misiones, and Brazilian Rio Grande do Sul. By the early 18th century there were, on both sides of the river, 30 mission villages with a combined population of over 100,000 souls. Only four of these show any signs of their former splendour: San Ignacio Miní, São Miguel (Brazil), and Jesús and Trinidad (Paraguay). At the height of its prosperity in 1731 San Ignacio contained 4,356 people. In 1767, Charles III of Spain expelled the Jesuits from Spanish territory; the Franciscans and Dominicans then took over. After the Jesuits had gone, there was a rapid decline in prosperity. By 1784 there were only 176 Indians at San Ignacio Miní; by 1810, there was none. By order of the Paraguayan dictator Francia, all the settlements were evacuated in 1817, and San Ignacio was set on fire. The village was lost in the jungle until it was discovered again in 1897. In 1943 an agency of the Argentine Government took control. Some of the craft work produced at the settlement can be seen at two museums in Buenos Aires: the Museo Colonial Isaac Fernández Blanco and the municipal Museo de Arte Colonial. Museo Jesuítico on site, close to ruins on main avenue. The caretaker, Sr Miguel Nadasdy, will show you a 350-mm. statue of Moses, said to be by Michelangelo, kept in the museum, and tell you of other worthwhile sites. Also Museo Provincial in main street. Interesting local crafts sold opposite ruins. Wooden carvings are especially worthwhile. *Son-et-lumière* show after dark (1930) at the ruins, Spanish only, tickets from museum.

Accommodation   There are ACA hostels (E; lunches at US$5 each) both at San Ignacio Miní and at Monte Carlo, half-way between San Ignacio and Iguazú. Also at San Ignacio is *Hotel San Ignacio*, friendly, good, clean, restaurant with light meals (closed in August), E. **San Martín** church in main street close to Museo Provincial has hostel, E; ask the padre. *Hospedaje Alemán*, Quiroga 870 near bus station. Clemens speaks German and English. There are *Restaurant Artemio I*, good and cheap, open till midnight, and two *comedores* (lunch only) opposite the entrance to the ruins. Festival July 30-31. The ACA *hostería* at Monte Carlo is warmly rec.; take town bus from centre.

Camping   outside the ruins in municipal site; cold showers and toilets. Two pleasant sites by small lake about 5 km S of San Ignacio, on Route 12.

At Jardín América, 48 km N of San Ignacio, there is an excellent municipal campsite 2 km. off Route 12. At Puerto Rico, 21 km N of Jardín América, there is a good hotel, *Suizo*, D; campsite at Club de Pesca; rec. restaurants are *Don Luis* and *Churrascaría Flach*, both on main street.

The most successful colonization in Argentina of late years has been at *Eldorado,* on this route. This prosperous small town is surrounded by flourishing *mate,* tung, citrus, eucalyptus and tobacco plantations. There are tung oil factories, sawmills, plywood factories, *mate* drying installations and a citrus packing plant. The ACA office is very helpful and has a large illuminated map of Eldorado and its surroundings.

Hotels at Eldorado   *Alpa,* D; *Hostería ACA* and *Atlántida,* both E; *Castellar,* D with bath. *Ideal,* F, clean, opp. bus station. Restaurant: *Copetín al Paso,* excellent, reasonable for price, but doesn't cook every day.

Camping   Camping site with showers and toilets; take the road toward the river from the main highway, for 2 km.

To see something of the Province of Misiones, the following way to return from Puerto Iguazú to Posadas is suggested by Reinhard Böhm-Raffay. If you are interested in flora and fauna, travel from Puerto Iguazú on Route 12 to Wanda; nearby are two amethyst and quartz mines which sell gems; there are guided tours. Carry on to Eldorado, then follow Route 17 (buses 0800 and 1530), paved to Bernardo Yrigoyen, a nice village, lovely vegetation en route. The direct (dirt) road from Puerto Iguazú to Bernardo Yrigoyen crosses the National Park of Iguazú, passing Andrecito, Cabuneí and San Antonio. Local buses ply the route if the weather is dry. From B. Yrigoyen follow Route 14 to Tobuna, where you will see the Alegría falls. On to the small village of Paraíso, see Moconá falls 82 km. from there, then Dos de Mayo (*Hotel Alex*). Pass through Oberá (*Hotel Quatro Pinos,* Av. Sarmiento 853, good value) and follow Route 105 W to Santa Ana, with Jesuit ruins of Loreto, not restored. From here you can return via San Ignacio to Puerto Iguazú or turn 16 km. in opposite direction to Posadas.

THE IGUAZU FALLS (8)

For specific references to the Brazilian side of the Falls, with accommodation and transport links, see Brazilian section page 338. For a general description, local transport arrangements, and specific Argentine references, see below.

The **Iguazú Falls** are the most overwhelming falls in South America. They lie about 350 km. upstream from Posadas where, 19 km. above the confluence of the Iguazú with the Alto Paraná, the waters fall thunderously in virgin forest bright with orchids and serpentine creepers festooning the branches. Above the impact of water on basalt rock hovers a perpetual 30-metre high cloud of mist in which the sun creates blazing rainbows. The Iguazú (Guaraní for great waters) rises in the Brazilian hills near Curitiba and receives some 30 streams on its course across the plateau. Above the main falls the river, sown with wooded islets, opens out to a width of 4 km. There are rapids for 3½ km. above the 60-metre precipice over which the water plunges in 275 falls over a frontage of 2,470 metres, at a rate of 1,750 cubic metres a second. Their height is greater than Niagara's by 20 metres or so and their width by one half, but most of the falls are broken midway by ledges of rock. The tumbling water in its setting of begonias, orchids, fern and palms with toucans, flocks of parrots and cacique birds, swifts (*vencejos*) dodging in and out of the very falls, and myriads of butterflies (at least 500 different species), is majestically beautiful, especially outside the cool season (when the water is much diminished, as are the birds and insects). One cannot cross the river at the Falls themselves; this can only be done by bridge between Porto Meira and Puerto Iguazú.

Visitors to the Falls should note that the Brazilian side (best visited in the morning because the light then is better for photography) shows the best panorama of the whole falls and should therefore be preferred if your visit is limited to, say, half a day, but the Argentine side (which needs most of a day to explore properly: the area is much greater) shows more close detail of the individual falls and is much more interesting from the point of view of seeing the forest with its wildlife and butterflies. There are a bird hide overlooking a marsh (Bañado), an interpreted (Spanish) nature trail (Macuco) in the jungle, a self-guided trail around the *Circuito Inferior,* all of which are very lovely. (An advantage in visiting the Argentine side first is that the information provided at the Visitors' Centre is far superior to anything offered in Brazil.)

The Devil's Throat, the most spectacular fall (for which you need waterproof clothing or swimming gear), is best seen from Puerto Canoas, to which buses run (see below), or you can drive (parking US$1). On the Argentine side the upper series of catwalks on the river, *Circuito Superior*, were largely destroyed by floods in 1983. The 1 km. catwalk from the river bank to the Devil's Throat has been replaced. There is also a short boat trip from Puerto Canoas to join the catwalk. Recommended in the evening when the light is best and the swifts are returning to roost on the walls, some behind the water. Below the falls the Iguazú runs swiftly for 19 km. through a deep canyon before it joins the Alto Paraná.

To walk along the lower series of catwalks, at the level of the midway ledge, waterproof coats or swimming costumes are advisable but not absolutely necessary. Wear good shoes when walking around, e.g. sneakers, as the rocks are very slippery in places. Put your camera in a plastic bag. At the base of Dos Hermanas fall is a natural, idyllic swimming pool, so take bathing gear in summer to cool off.

The Argentine Iguazú National Park embraces a large area. The fauna are rich and various but hunting is not allowed. Fishing is no longer permitted. The months to avoid are July (holidays) and December-March (hot). Information and permits can be got from the Visitors Centre information desk, open daily 0800-1800 in the old Cataratas Hotel, now converted. The Visitors' Centre organizes a 4-hour walk (8 km.) through the jungle, beginning at 0900 daily; fixed price US$25 to share among the party. Catch 0825 bus from Puerto Iguazú. It also runs night-time walks between *Hotel Cataratas* and the falls when the moon is full. Helicopter rides over the Falls, about 15 mins. for US$30, start from the airport. There is a museum of local fauna and an auditorium for periodic slide shows (on request for 8 or more people), no commentary, just music. A good guide book on Argentine birds is for sale. Administration for the park's headquarters is in a colonial-style building at Puerto Iguazú.

There is a US$0.60 charge which allows one-day entry to the Argentine Park, free information leaflet provided with ticket (guests at *Hotel Internacional* do not have to pay).

Getting to the Falls Transportes Cataratas buses run hourly from the Puerto Iguazú bus station to the Falls, stopping in town outside the Aerolíneas Argentinas office, taking about 30 minutes for the 22½ km. These buses are sometimes erratic, even though the times are clearly indicated, especially when it is wet. They stop at the National Park entrance for the purchase of entrance tickets. Fare to the Falls, US$0.50; first bus at 0700, last at 1700; first back at 0815, last at 1900. Inclusive fare, including ride to Puerto Canoas and boat to San Martín island (US$1 return), is US$2.50. The bus continues from the Park Adminstration to Puerto Canoas (for Devil's Throat), hourly on the half-hour, US$0.20; returning hourly at quarter-to-the-hour. There are fixed rates for taxis, US$10, up to 5 people. A tour from the bus terminal, taking in both sides of the Falls, costs US$11. Hitch-hiking to the Falls is difficult, but you can hitch up to the Posadas intersection at Km. 11, then it is only 7 km. walk.

Frontier crossing to see both sides is easy. If you are coming from one side and you just want to see the other, returning on the same day to the side you came from, tell the officials, and they won't stamp your passport. However, we have been advised that this may be difficult for British visitors (if you haven't a visa, you will not be allowed into Argentina unless very lucky). Similarly, US, Australian, New Zealand and French citizens must have all necessary visas. Some say that, for fear of being stranded in no-man's-land, it is best to insist on having one's papers stamped at all posts.

Travel between Argentina and Brazil has been greatly improved by the opening of the 480 metre Puente de Fraternidad/Ponte Presidente Tancredo Neves, which joins Puerto Iguazú (Route 12) and Porto Meira (BR-469). Six buses run each hour (US$0.70) from the Puerto Iguazú bus terminal on Av. Córdoba to the Terminal Urbana in Foz do Iguaçu, pausing at the border but not stopping long enough for passport controls (US$0.60); you have to wait for the next one if you need a stamp (keep the ticket so as not to pay twice); on the other hand if you are simply crossing to see the other side of the Falls, you can stay on the same bus. The passenger and car ferries between Puerto Iguazú and Porto Meira no longer run a regular schedule, and there are no immigration offices on either side.

Change some money into new cruzados before going into Brazil: they try to charge you triple the

TO ASUNCIÓN 325 KM.
HOTEL ACARAÍ & CASINO
FRIENDSHIP BRIDGE
Cd. Pte. Stroessner
IGUAZÚ FALLS
B R A Z I L
TO CURITIBA
PTO. PTE. FRANCO
Foz do Iguaçu
PTO. MEIRA
Ponte Presidente Tancredo Neves
Pto. Iguazú
3.2 KM
2.8 KM
HOTEL INTERNACIONAL IGUAZÚ
HOTEL DAS CATARATAS
RÍO IGUAZÚ
PUERTO CANOAS
TO POSADAS 373 KM.
P A R A G U A Y
RÍO ALTO PARANÁ
A R G E N T I N A

true cost if you use Argentine money. The new cruzado exchange rate is better in the town of Puerto Iguazú than in Brazil itself. Foz do Iguaçu being much the larger town, tends to be cheaper, with more choice than Puerto Iguazú for hotels and food.

There is a Brazilian immigration office on the road between Foz do Iguaçu and the bridge. Customs on Brazil-Argentina border do not now close until 0200; they can be very thorough with their luggage checks.

It is not possible to go direct by road to Puerto Franco (Paraguay) from Puerto Iguazú; one must go through Brazil. If passing through Foz do Iguaçu en route from Puerto Iguazú to Paraguay, make sure that Brazilian officials stamp your passport. "Ponte-Ponte" buses ply (US$0.20) between the Brazilian ends of the bridges into Argentina and into Paraguay, via Foz do Iguaçu. However, there are launches plying on the rivers Paraná and Iguazú between Puerto Franco and Puerto Iguazú: every 2 hours or so, US$0.50.

On the Argentine side is **Puerto Iguazú**, a small modern town above the river. There is a helpful tourist office (but no English) at Av. Victoria Aguirre and Brasil, open 0800-1200, 1500-2000 Mon.-Fri., 0800-1200, 1630-2000 Sat. and Sun.

Museum Imágenes de la Selva, housed in a shop on Av. Victoria Aguirre, open daily, free, has wood sculptures by Rodolfo Allou who uses natural shapes of roots and branches.

Hotels Crowded during summer (Jan.-Feb.), Easter and July holiday periods. *Internacional Iguazú*, L, five-star, pool, casino, good restaurant, business facilities, overlooking the falls. Reservations at Av. Eduardo Madero 1020 (T 3114259, or 3136292), Buenos Aires. *Iguazú*, on Paraguay, in the town (no swimming pool), is being used to offer rest accommodation to the elderly, but transients are still welcome, D. The *Paraná*, E, is clean and friendly, Brasil 367. *La Cabaña*, Av. Tres Fronteras 434 (D, with shower and breakfast, a/c, good, clean and friendly) is nice, with an older part and a new annexe, and has communal washing facilities and swimming pool; opp. is *Residencial Tres Fronteras*; in same street (No. 341) is *Residencial Tucán. Tierra Colorada*, Av. Córdoba and El Urú 265, very good, E with fan and bath, nice restaurant, trips arranged. *Esturión*, L, Av. Tres Fronteras 650, clean, arbitrary pricing, comfortable, swimming pool, good restaurant, reservations at Belgrano 265, 10th floor, Buenos Aires. *Las Orquídeas*, Ruta 12, Km. 5 (T 2472), very comfortable, clean, set right in the jungle outside Puerto Iguazú, restaurant, C. *Alexander*, Córdoba 685, opp. bus station, C incl. meagre breakfast, swimming pool; *El Yaguaraté*, Av. Victoria Aguirre (entrance to town), bungalows, D, with kitchen, excellent value; *Residencial San Fernando*, Av. Córdoba 693, close to bus station, E, with bath, clean, quiet, restaurant, highly rec. *Residencial Paquita*, Av. Córdoba 731, E, clean, and friendly, nice setting, 14 rooms, opposite bus station, rec. *Turismo*, D with bath, hot water, charmingly old fashioned, spectacularly set above river. *Saint George*, Av. Córdoba 745, opp. bus station, C, with breakfast, comfortable, has good, expensive restaurant. Behind this hotel is *Residencial Los Helechos*, E, with bath, owner speaks German, clean, new, motel-style accommodation. *Residencial Gloria*, Av. Uruguay, E with bath (electric showers) and fridge, clean, quiet, friendly. *Residencial Los Naranjos*, E, clean, mosquito-free, private bath. *Residencial Arco Iris* (with private shower), basic, cooking facilities available, E. Cheapest hotel is *Misiones*, E, opp. Tourist Office, but there are some *hosterías* in the F range.

Camping   Free site 600 metres past parking area at Puerto Canoas. Tables, but no other facilities. Camping sometimes permitted at the school just inside the Park entrance. Municipal campsite in Puerto Iguazú reported "grim". Camping Pindó at the edge of town, charges US$0.60 p.p., US$6 per tent and US$1.00 for use of pool, friendly, but for US$1.20 p.p., US$1.20 per tent, there are better ones at Camping América (T 2820/2788), incl. swimming pool.

Restaurants   Restaurant (nameless), ½ block from *Hotel Sol de Iguazú*, Brazilian food, all you can eat for US$5. *La Rueda*, Av. Córdoba, good; *El Tío Querido*, Perito Moreno 345, friendly service, excellent cooking, guitarist at night; *Casa de Comercio*, Aguirre 327 through arch, on square opp. church, good food, moderate prices; *Ser Barbas* and *Trébol*, rec. Good meals in the bus terminal.

Money Exchange   three *casas de cambio* opposite the tourist office, change cash and travellers' cheques at good rates. Good rates for buying cruzados.

Car Hire   Al International at airport and in town; *Hotel Internacional*; Avis plan to open an agency. Cars may be taken to the Brazilian side for an extra US$5.

Brazilian Consulate   U.S. citizens continuing to Paraguay from Foz do Iguaçu must obtain visas here (2 passport photos required); takes a day.

Travel Agent   Turismo Dick, Av. Victoria Aguirre 425, also in Foz do Iguaçu, good rates of exchange; does not close at lunchtime. Reports vary. Reinhard Foerster, Privat Servis, Av. Tres Fronteras 335, T 2774, offers naturalists' and birdwatchers' programmes. Turismo Caracol, Moreno 357, Tel.:2124, does good all-day tour of both sides of falls, US$10 including meal in Brazil. Agency at bus terminal does tour of Argentine side of falls for US$2.50.

Airports   There is an Argentine domestic airport near the Falls, and a Brazilian international airport about half-way between Foz do Iguaçu and the Falls. Taxi between the two airports over the new bridge costs US$20. Aerolíneas Argentinas office in centre of Puerto Iguazú (bus from here to airport about 2 hours before plane's departure, 1445 and 2145); US$60 one way to Buenos Aires.

Air Transport   By Boeing 737 (Aerolíneas Argentinas and Austral) from Buenos Aires, via Rosario, Corrientes or Posadas, or direct to improved Iguazú airport (1 hr. 40 mins.) several daily. Direct flights (AA) from Córdoba, US$66. For best view on landing, sit on left side of aircraft. Flights back to Buenos Aires are very crowded. The Argentine side can be seen in one day from Buenos Aires: there is a flight between 0730 and 0830 with either Aerolíneas Argentinas or Austral on most days of the week from BA domestic airport, flight time 1 hr. 40 mins; bus to falls takes ½ hr., leaving according to plane arrivals. Bus from *Hotel Internacional* to airport leaves according to flight departure times.

Rail Transport   from Buenos Aires is comfortable and cheap. There are sleeping and restaurant cars, good meals and wines. Passengers take a train from **Lacroze Station** in Buenos Aires to Posadas (for details, see under Posadas, **page 119**). There is a road, now paved, from Posadas to Puerto Iguazú; express bus to Iguazú meets train, 4½ hrs.

Road Transport   From Buenos Aires N to Clorinda, then by new toll bridge to Asunción. Or crossing the Paraná at Santa Fe or Resistencia, taking the paved road to Posadas, and on to the falls. The more direct run via Zárate and Concordia is now completely paved. Direct buses take some 21 hours, leaving at 1130 (returns at 1200), with Singer, no a/c, and Buenos Aires-Posadas-Iguazú (returns at 1600 to Buenos Aires) Expreso Tigre-Iguazú, daily at 1500, offices at Plaza Once, Buenos Aires leaving from Retiro terminal (US$28.75). Expreso Iguazú said to offer discounts to students. To Córdoba, daily except Tues. and Sat. at 1130, via Posadas 26 hrs, US$34.50, with Singer or El Litoral. To Rosario daily except Thurs., 24 hrs. Expres Iguazú to Posadas, 5 hrs., US$6.50 (310 km.) e.g. with Transportes Iguazú at 0930 and 1530; ordinary bus takes 8 hrs., every 1½ hrs. All go by the Falls and stop at San Ignacio Miní (US$8). To Resistencia daily 0900 and 2000, 12 hrs., US$13.50. Alternative to direct bus to Buenos Aires (**see above**), take bus to Posadas and take train from there; slower, but more comfortable. Puerto Iguazú to Eldorado, 2 hrs., US$3.50 with Cotal.

Up the River Uruguay

The Río Uruguay is the eastern boundary of Mesopotamia and forms the western border of the Republic of Uruguay. There are no regular passenger shipping services.

Boats leaving Buenos Aires go past Martín García island, and enter the wide estuary. At 193 km. from Buenos Aires, the Uruguayan town of Fray Bentos is to the right; there is a bridge between Fray Bentos and the Argentine town of Puerto Unzué, near Gualeguaychú, but pedestrians and cyclists cannot cross it other than on motor vehicles; officials will give lifts on either side. The river now becomes braided into channels and islands. Opposite Fray Bentos, on the left, is the mouth of the Río Gualeguay; 19 km. up is **Gualeguaychú**, which can be reached by rail and good road from Buenos Aires (370 km.) and Concordia. It is a very pleasant town with a river promenade, a country club (free for tourists), street entertainment and a camping site (La Delfina, US$3.50 p.p., good; also possible in Parque Saturnino Unzué). Lively Carnival at beginning of March. Population, 60,000, with quite a large German contingent. Airport. Customs formalities at Puerto Unzué take 10 minutes.

Hotels *Embajador*, C; *Posada del Charrúa*, D; *El Faro*, E; *París*, E; *Yapo*, E; *Entre Ríos*, F; *Mayo*, F; *Alemán*, F, friendly, German-speaking, rec.

Exchange There are banks on either side of the bridge, but in Uruguay you can obtain only Uruguayan pesos and the Argentine-side bank is almost always closed. Next bank at Gualeguaychú has very good rates. There is also a service station a few km. beyond the border in Argentina, where you can sell Uruguayan pesos.

Transport Buses to Fray Bentos, Uruguay, 0845, 1230, 1800.

Concepción del Uruguay, the first Argentine port of any size on the river, was founded in 1778. There are train services to all parts of Mesopotamia. Population, 40,000. Paved roads to Paraná and Colón.

Hotels *Virrey*, Aceso Ruta 131, D; *Gran Hotel*, Colón 134, D; *General Ramírez*, Galarza y Blvd. Ramírez, E; *Residencial 3 de Febrero*, E; *Residencial La Posada*, E; *Centro Hotel*, E. Many hotels of all classes by the bus station, none near the railway station.

Local Boats Daily to Paysandú (Uruguay).

Colón, 350 km. from Buenos Aires, is 37 km. above Concepción del Uruguay. The river is more picturesque here with sandy beaches, and cliffs visible from a considerable distance; a road bridge now links Colón and Paysandú. (Toll for cars US$1.40. All border formalities, including stamping of vehicle carnets, are conducted at both ends of the bridge, easy crossing.) The town is known for *artesanía* shops down San Martín, the main street, and there is a large handicrafts fair at Carnival time (Feb.). Tourist office by river not very helpful. It is possible to get a bus from Colón to Paysandú, US$1.50, but there are none between 1145 and 1645, and none on Sundays. There are 2 buses a day to Buenos Aires, US$8, 5 hrs., daily buses to Concordia (2½ hrs., US$2.65), Paraná and four a week to Córdoba.

Hotels *Quirinale*, Av. Quirós s/n, 5-star, A (with casino), *Nuevo Hotel Plaza*, D, 12 de Abril y Belgrano; *Palmar*, E, Blvd. Ferrari 295, good; *Vieja Calera*, E, Bolívar y Maipú; *Holimazu*, E, Belgrano 28; *Ver-Wei*, F, 25 de Mayo 10; *Residencial JR*, Chacabuco 185. **Restaurant** *Marito*, good and cheap. Several **campsites** along river bank.

Parque Nacional El Palmar lies between Colón and Concordia, has both free and paying camping facilities, a small hotel 8 km. N of the Park, with restaurant opposite, and a small shop. The Park contains varied scenery with a mature palm forest, Indian tombs and other remains, and many rheas and other birds. Buses from Colón, 40 mins., US$1.75.

Concordia, about 105 km. above Colón, a little downriver from Salto, Uruguay, is a prosperous city, with a population of 56,000, which has some fine public buildings, a racecourse, rowing clubs, and a 9-hole golf club. Five km. out is Parque Rivadavia, with a circular road used occasionally as a motor-racing track;

there are pleasant views here of the river and a ruined French-style palace. Paved roads to Buenos Aires, Paraná and Posadas.

The river is impassable for large vessels beyond the rapids of Salto Chico near the town, and Salto Grande 32 km. up-river, where there is a large international hydro-electric dam, providing a route for an international road and railway. Take No. 2 bus from bus terminal marked "Puerto", for ferry crossing to Salto from Concordia US$1 (tickets obtainable at a small kiosk outside customs) departures 5 times a day on weekdays, twice Sat. but none Sun.; takes 15 mins. Few cars, but people willing to give rides. Above Salto Grande the river is generally known as the Alto Uruguay.

Hotels *San Carlos,* Parque Rivadavia, C; *Salto Grande,* Urquiza 575, C; *Palmar,* Urquiza 511, D; *Imperial Argentino,* E, very friendly; *Central,* 1° de Mayo 185, E; *Gran Hotel Colón,* E, highly rec., simple, clean and charming, highly rec.; *Embajador,* San Lorenzo 75, F, nr. bus station, good value, neat and clean. *Terminal* above bus station, surprisingly quiet, good value, F.

Camping *La Tortuga Alegre. La Posada de Suárez—Club Viajantes* on Av. Costanera near the park, warmly rec., with good *parrillada* alongside.

Restaurants *Lion d'Or; Don Juan,* 1° de Mayo 21, near main plaza, excellent and cheap. *El Abrojito,* Pellegrini 1203, rec.

Tourist Office Plaza 25 de Mayo, helpful.

Rail *El Correntino* train has sleepers, pullman, 1st class (heating ineffective) and tourist class (US$29.45, US$19.15, US$12.50, US$8.75) and leaves Lacroze station at 1500, daily, arriving at 2314, returns daily at 0729, arr. 1545. *El Gran Capitán,* same prices, leaves at 1500 daily, arrives at 2314 daily. Returns daily at 0729, arrives 1545. This train also goes on at 2045 to Paso de los Libres and Posadas (sleeper US$35.50, pullman US$23.50, 1st US$16.50, tourist US$11.60 from Buenos Aires), arrives at 0230 and 0730, respectively.

Buses To Buenos Aires, 6 daily; to Paraná 5, to Posadas 3 (8½ hrs., US$11.50), to Iguazú one (1810, 13½ hrs). Bus to La Paz (Entre Ríos)—**see page 116,** 1100, US$7.70, 8 hrs. Possible to sleep overnight on benches in bus terminal.

About 153 km. upstream from Concordia lies the small port of *Monte Caseros,* with the Uruguayan town of Bella Unión, on the Brazilian border, almost opposite. Above Bella Unión, the **Alto Uruguay** is the boundary between Argentina and Brazil. Ninety-six km. above **Monte Caseros** is **Paso de los Libres,** with the Brazilian cattle town of **Uruguaiana** opposite: a bridge joins the two. From Uruguaiana into Brazil the buses are much quicker than trains, though there is a comfortable railway service to Porto Alegre. Paso de los Libres was founded in 1843 by General Madariaga; it was here that he crossed the river from Brazil with his hundred men and annexed Corrientes province for Argentina. Road (paved) to Paraná.

Hotel in Paso de los Libres, *Alejandro I,* Coronel López y Pago Largo, best in town.

Rail See above under Concordia. Fares a/c sleeper US$27.30, Pullman US$27.75, first US$18.15, tourist US$12.70 Buenos Aires-Paso de los Libres.

N of Paso de los Libres, on the road to Alvear, is *Yapeyú,* famous as the birthplace of the liberator, José de San Martín. There is a pleasant little museum and part of the house where he was born is well preserved, inside another building.

THE LAKE DISTRICT (9)

Northern Patagonia has two railway lines. The more northerly runs westwards from Bahía Blanca to Neuquén and Zapala; the southern line runs from Bahía Blanca southwards across the Colorado to Viedma and then westwards through San Antonio Oeste to Bariloche and the Lake District. The roads along which buses ply, and airlines are mentioned in the text. (For map, see the Chilean section, page 483.)

The **Lake District** contains a series of great lakes strung along the foot of the Andes from above 40° South to below 50° in the Los Glaciares National Park area. In the N the western ends of these lakes cut deeply into the mountains, their water lapping the forested skirts of some of the most spectacular snow-capped peaks in the world; their eastern ends are contained by the frontal moraines deposited there by the ancient glaciers which melted to form these huge fjord-like lakes. The water is a deep blue, sometimes lashed into white froth by the region's high winds.

On the far side of the Andes, in Chile, lies another system of lakes: these can be visited (unpaved roads) through various passes. The Puyehue route is given on **page 134**, with an alternative in the Chilean section.

National Park   Lake Nahuel Huapí with its surroundings, an area of 7,850 square km., was set aside in 1903 as a National Park. It contains the most diverse and spectacular natural phenomena: lakes, rivers, glaciers, waterfalls, torrents, rapids, valleys, forest, bare mountains and snow-clad peaks. Most of the area is covered with abundant vegetation, though it is notably more abundant on the Chilean side, which gets more rain. Many kinds of wild animals live in the region, but they are extremely shy and seldom glimpsed by the explorer. Bird life, on the other hand—particularly swans, geese and ducks—is seen at any time and everywhere in large flocks. In the far N of this region, near Zapala, these species and many others can be seen in their hundreds in the nature reserve of Laguna Blanca.

The outstanding feature of this National Park is the splendour of the lakes. The largest is *Lake Nahuel Huapí*, 531 square km. and 460 metres deep in places. It is 767 metres above sea level, in full view of the snow-covered peaks of the Cordillera and of the forests covering the lower slopes. Towering over the scene is Cerro Tronador. Some 96 km. long, and not more than 12 km. wide, the lake is very irregular in shape; long arms of water, or *brazos*, which look like fjords, stretch far into the land. There are many islands: the largest is **Isla Victoria**, on which stands the forest research station where new species of vegetation are acclimatized. The Zoological Board is adding to the indigenous fauna; the trout and salmon of the lakes, for instance, have been introduced from abroad. Lake Nahuel Huapí is drained eastwards by the Río Limay; below its junction with the Río Neuquén it becomes the Río Negro. The Limay has good trout fishing but the rivers farther N—the Quilquihue, Malleu, Chimehuín, Collón-Curá, Hermoso, Meliquina and Caleufú—are much less fished. They are all in the neighbourhood of San Martín de los Andes (**see page 139**). The season is from early November to the end of March. Do not take fishing equipment out-of-season; it will only cause suspicion. Also remember that fishing anywhere in Argentina requires a permit.

A mere sand bar in one of the northern *brazos* separates Lake Nahuel Huapí from Lake Correntoso, which is quite close to Lake Espejo. Lake Traful, a short distance to the NE, can be reached by a road which follows the River Limay through the Valle Encantado, with its fantastic rock formations. S of Nahuel Huapí there are other lakes: the three main ones are Mascardi, Guillelmo, and Gutiérrez. On the shore of Lake Gutiérrez, in a grotto, is the Virgen de las Nieves (Virgin of the Snows). There is a road to these lakes from Bariloche.

Fishing   The lakes are full of fish, and the best time for fishing is at the beginning of the season, that is, in November and December. Among the best are: Lakes Traful, Gutiérrez, Mascardi, Futalaufquen (in Los Alerces National Park), Meliquina, Falkner, Villarino, Nuevo, Lacar, Lolog, Curruhué, Chico, Huechulafquen, Paimún, Epulafquen, Tromen (all in Lanín National Park), and, in the far N, Quillén. In the far S, the fishing in Lake Argentino is also good.

Bariloche (San Carlos de), on the southern shore of Lake Nahuel Huapí, founded 1898, is the best centre for exploring the National Park. It is a Swiss-looking town of steep streets, its wooden chalets perched upon a glacial moraine at the foot of Cerro Otto. To the S lie the heights of the Ventana and the Cerro Colorado (2,135 metres). The place is full of hotels and cheap *hosterías*. The cathedral, built in 1946, dominates the town; interior unfinished. There is a belvedere at the top of Cerro Otto with wide views of lake and mountain. The main road into Bariloche from the E is paved and in good condition. Unhappily, because of its phenomenal growth, the town has become noisy and overcrowded, and the best time to visit it is out of season either in the spring or autumn. The 24 km. road to Llao-Llao (bus, ¾ hr., US$0.60) is ribbon-developed, except near Cerro Catedral. Population, over 70,000. Lido swimming pool on the lake shore is beautifully sited but somewhat run down.

BARILOCHE

LAKE NAHUEL HUAPI

1. Civic Centre, Tourist Office, Post Office and Museum. 2. Municipality. 3. National Park Office. 4. Banco de la Nación. 5. Banco de Rio Negro. 6. Hospital. 7. Cathedral. 8. Market. 9. Catedral Turismo. 10. Transporte Mercedes.

Hotels   The most complete listing with map is published by the Oficina Municipal de Turismo, which you are advised to consult if you arrive in the high season without a reservation. It also has booking service at Florida 520 (Galería), room 116, Buenos Aires. Out of season, prices are quite reasonable, in all ranges, but in season everything is very expensive. Most hotels outside the town include half-board, and those in the town include breakfast. Hotels with high-season lake views normally charge US$3-4 extra, per room per day, for the view; we give lake-view high-season prices where applicable. The best outside town are: *Huemul* (road to Llao-Llao, 1.5 km.); *El Casco* (Av. Bustillo, road to Llao-Llao 11 km.), German-run, excellent, luxurious, warmly rec.; *Apart-hotel Casablanca* (same road, 23.5 km.), good, on a peninsula between Lakes Nahuel Huapí and Moreno, all L, some offering half-board. Also at Llao-Llao, 24 km. from Bariloche, are *Tunquelén*, L, and *Hostería Aunancay*, L, including 2 meals, friendly and delightful setting. *Hostería Katy*, on Llao-Llao road Km. 24, warmly rec., reasonable, B. *Hotel Los Andes*, Moreno 594, affliated to youth hostel organization, good and cheap. Out of town (many birds to see) is *Hostería del Viejo Molino*, Av. Bustillo km 6.400, D, buses to town, T 22411, friendly, rec.

In the town are the following: *Edelweiss*, Av. San Martín 232, L, 5-star, modern, spotless, excellent food, enclosed pool, highly rec.; newest is *Panamericano*, San Martín 536, L, 5-star, heated swimming pool; *Bariloche Sky*, San Martín 352, L, 4-star, T 22913, Telex 18273, good; *Interlaken*, E. O'Connor 383, L, lake view, 4-star; *Tres Reyes*, 12 de Octubre 135, L, lake view, 4-star. First class: *Residencial Tirol*, Libertad 175, C, clean, friendly, good; *Casita Suiza*, Quaglia 342, very nice, 4-star. At Rolando 197 is *Val Gardena*, B with breakfast, excellent service, clean, no restaurant, 2-star; opp. is *Sunset*, B, 4-star. *Residencial El Ciervo Rojo*, Elflein 115, B, 2-star, very pleasant; *Austral*, San Martín 425, B, 2-star, restaurant, small rooms; *Hostería Madinette*, Morales 534, very well run, half-board; *Los Pinos*, 20 de Febrero 640, C, clean, spacious rooms, private bath, central heating, rec.; *King's Hotel*, Moreno 136, very nice, clean, warm, BC, with bath (D off-season); *La Pastorella*, Belgrano 127, C, with bath and breakfast, German-run, English and German spoken, central, rec.; *Residencial Portofino*, Morales 439, two blocks from plaza, C, small but spotless. *Venezia*, also on Morales, D, rec.; *Nevada*, Onelli y Moreno, C with shower, nice rooms; *Residencial Elisabeth*, J. J. Paso 117, D, cheaper rates for longer stays, German-run, clean, central, private bath, hot water, towels, good value; *Residencial Piuké*, Beschtedt 136, C inc. breakfast (A in skiing season), clean, friendly, rec.; opposite is *Residencial Sur*, Beschtedt 101, excellent value, C with bath and breakfast. *Residencial La Fontana*, Saavedra 689, Plaza Belgrano, clean, friendly, A; *Residencial Matterhorn*, Swiss-run, Pasaje Gutiérrez 1122, D, rec., good breakfast; *Ideal*, Libertad 121, behind police station, pleasant, clean, quiet, away from the commercial centre, C with private bath, cheaper without, restaurant, some doubles have lake view; *Hospedaje Nahuel*, Gallardo 454, C, warm and clean, hot showers; *Residencial Panorámico*, Moreno 646, A, private shower, rec.; *Hostal de Los Alpes*, Diagonal Capraro 1034, C, very modern, clean, friendly; *Victoria*, C-D, for a studio with bed, kitchen, bath with hot shower, Mitre 815, friendly but grubby. *Internacional*, also on Mitre, C, rec. Others: *El Mirador*, Moreno 652-76, E, hot water, eccentric owner speaks German, very pleasant, with lake views; *Residencial Premier*, Rolando 263, ½ block from main street, E, clean, hot showers, English and German spoken, rec.; *Angelina*, San Martín 66, E, clean, friendly, helpful; *Hostería El Radal*, 24 de Septiembre 46, E, clean, friendly; *Residencial Adquintue*, E. O'Connor 776, E, clean and comfortable; *Residencial El Ñire* (T 2-3041), E. O'Connor 710, corner J. O'Connor, hot showers, clean, very pleasant, E, prefers longer-stay visitors, highly rec. *Huecho Ruca*, Moreno 816, D with bath, hot shower, rec. *Residencial Rosán* (Sra Milena de Arko), E, strongly rec., Güemes 691, T 23109, English and German spoken, cooking facilities, four rooms, two showers. Also rec., *pensión* of Sra Carlota Baumann, Av. de los Pioneros 860 (T 24502), close to main square, F p.p., kitchen, bath, hot water, laundry service, friendly, Sra Baumann speaks English and German. *Residencial Alpina*, Discornia 90, D, clean, friendly, good value. *Residencial Millaray*, Libertad 195, F, good and cheap, shower; *Belgrano*, Güemes 648, E, friendly. Rec. family *pensión* at Salta

571, heated. Ask at tourist office, which has private homes listed. For longer stays try private house at Elflein 507 (Sra. Heidi Landolf), F, or Anasagasti 345, US$3; also at 12 de Octubre 2008 (road to airport), US$3. *Alojamiento Familiar Pire-Cuyen*, Anasagasti 840, E, clean, good, no single rooms. *Alojamiento Familial*, Frey 635, F, 6 rooms, clean, hot shower, reasonable, friendly, rec., has space for motorcycles.

Camping Several sites (Km. 2.7, 5.8, 13.2) on road to Llao-Llao: *Petunia* rec.; list from Tourist Office.

Restaurants *Casita Suiza*, Quaglia 342, excellent and rec. (US$45 p.p.); *Viejo Munich*, good, Mitre 102; *Sobremonte*, Mitre 420, good meat and wine; *La Marmita*, Mitre, small, cosy, excellent, mixed fondues particularly rec.; *La Costa*, Rosas 485, excellent fillet steak; *La Andina* on Elflein and Quaglia specializes in inexpensive but good "fast food", rec.; *Caza Mayor*, Quaglia and Elflein, game and fish, good; *Nikola*, Elflein 49, very good value; *Kandahar*, 20 de Febrero 698, T 24702, excellent, run by Argentine ski champion Marta Peirono de Barber; *Parrilla 1810*, Elflein 167, T 23922, good meat and reasonable, highly rec.; *El Barrilito*, Moreno 180, good and reasonable; *Asociación Española*, Rolando 142, fine paellas; *Mangiare*, pizzas and other Italian, Palacios 86. Good pastries and hot chocolate at *Hola Nicolás*, Moreno 66 and Urquiza. *Jauja*, Moreno (near Villegas), good typical dishes; *Canguros*, Palacios 181, no longer Australian run, try the hot wine, service slow. *La Andinita*, Mitre 56, rec., reasonable, trout a speciality, friendly; *Pizza Vía Roma*, Mitre 5, big choice of good pizzas; *Villegas*, Villegas 363, rec. for trout and friendly service. Vegetarian: *La Huerta*, Morales 362, good, cheap, pleasant. On Av. Bustillo (the road to Llao-Llao), Km. 10, is *La Posta del Río*, reasonable, *Dirty Dick's Pub*, Km. 5 and *La Glorieta*, Av. Bustillo, km. 3.8, good. Superb coffee and cakes at *Chocolate Casero del Turista* at Mitre 239, but nowhere to sit. *T-Bar Café*, Mitre 201, good hot chocolate. *La Mamadera*, Mitre 358, rec. *Saloom*, Mitre 208, restaurant with video films, open 24 hours, as are others on Mitre; *Panda*, just off Mitre, good Chinese. *Friends*, San Martín, good sandwiches, gateaux, quick meals. Many good delicatessens in the area with take-away food, including chicken pizzas and cheeses, for picnics.

Best Buys Woollen goods, e.g. at Arbol on Mitre, or Manos del Uruguay, Mitre 216. The products of the local chocolate industry are excellent: Fábrica de Chocolate Cerro León on Av. 12 de Octubre, near railway station. You can watch chocolates being made at Turista San Martín 220. Very good chocolate at Gallardo (be sure to get the 10% discount). Try "Papas de Bariloche", the local chocolate speciality. Also chocolates at *Benroth*, Beschtedt 569, above Gallardo. Handicraft shops all along San Martín; some will change money.

Museums The "Perito Francisco Moreno" Nahuel Huapí Museum in the Civic Centre, well worth seeing for collection of Indian artefacts, houses, open 1000-1200, 1400-1900 Mon.-Fri., 1000-1300 Sat. The Museo de la Patagonia has a nice collection of stuffed animals, US$0.50, heated, not to be missed. Open 0900-1400, and 1800-2100 in summer. Closed public holidays. The clock in the Civic Centre has four figures which rotate at noon; photos with St. Bernard dogs may be taken in the Civic Centre square.

Exchange There are several banks and official exchange shops, which buy and sell virtually all European and South American currencies, besides US dollars; Sat. is a bad day. Exchange houses cash cheques for 5-10% . Casa Piano, B. Mitre 131, T 23733, rec., open 0900-1300 and 1600-2000 (charges US$2 on all cheques below US$100, 2% over US$100). Kiosko Suyoi, Elflein 87, for newspaper-quoted rate, cash only. Austral, Quaglia 230, good both for cash and cheques. Kiosko Anri, Mitre 339 (rear of Galería Arrayanes), US$ cheques and Chilean pesos accepted, good rates, highly rec. Good exchange rates at *Kiwanis* (boot rental), Mitre 210. The American Express Co., B. Mitre 139, sends you across the street to the Banco Provincia to buy travellers' cheques. Beware forged Argentine banknotes.

Laundry *Express*, Villegas 258, English manager, friendly, opp. cathedral. Laundromats at Quaglia 427 (US$2 for 2 kg.), on Palacios, on San Martín, and on Villegas nr. Mitre.

Car Hire Hertz, Avis, and A1 International, at airport and in town (latter at Bartolomé Mitre 26, T 24869, 22038); no flat rates. Permission to enter Chile may be obtained.

Bicycles may be hired beside the lake in high season.

Tourist Office Oficina Municipal de Turismo in Centro Cívico, open Mon.-Sat., (ski season) 0800-2000, daily at those times in summer but check times out of season (March-April, October-November) when closed at weekends; very helpful. Has details of hikes and campsites in the area. Also has the address of a motorcycle hire company—a good way of getting around the National Park. National Park information (scanty) at San Martín 24, open 0800-2000. Information also from Sociedad Profesional de Guías de Turismo, Casilla de Correo 51, 8400 S.C. de Bariloche (President: Ama Petroff).

Tourist Agencies Tour buses pick you up from your hotel. *Patagonia Travel*, Mitre 150 (Telex 80746 Patra), efficient, rec., English spoken; their guide Daniel is a good naturalist. *Catedral Turismo*, Mitre 399, runs boats to Chile for Peulla-Puerto Montt trip; *Alunco Turismo*, groups first, friendly. *Transport Mercedes; Turisur*, Quaglia 227, T 26109, organizes US$10 trips on lake. *Lake Travel Service*, Moreno 126, 3rd floor, efficient, English spoken. *Polvani Tours*, Quaglia 268 (T 23286), see Hans Schulz (speaks Spanish, German and English) to arrange horse trekking at the Estancia Nahuel Huapí, run by Carol Jones (from US$24 for ½ day to US$75 overnight incl. meals and gear); both the agency and the treks rec. Arrange trekking with Sr Daniel José Gorgone, San Martín 127, DT 0706, T 26181.

Chilean Consulate Villegas, near Mitre, friendly, helpful.

Post Office Centro Cívico (same building as tourist office).

Immigration Office Next to *Hostería Tirol*, Libertad 175.

Clinic Cruz Azul, Capraro 1216.

Air Services Airport, 11 km. from town. Many flights to Buenos Aires. Aerolíneas Argentinas, 2 a day, US$84; no night flight. Also Austral, same fare. AA has a Mendoza-Bariloche flight via Neuquén and there is an Austral Neuquén flight daily, exc. Sun., from Bariloche at 1320, arrival 1405. LADE to Trelew, US$33, Mon. 1255, Fri. 1340. LADE flies to Comodoro Rivadavia Tues., Fri. and Sun., US$31; AA US$35. AA to Río Gallegos, US$62. LADE to Río Gallegos, 3 a week, US$36, usually booked 2 weeks in advance in season; continues to Calafate. Flights, 3-4 times a week, with Aerolíneas and LADE to Esquel. (It is reported that it is difficult to obtain LADE flights from Bariloche now, especially the cheaper night flights to Buenos Aires.) Small tax at airport on leaving. Taxi to or from airport, US$8-10; bus US$2 from Austral or Aerolíneas office. (Aerolíneas and LADE offices are, conveniently, in the same building.) Turismo Catedral, Mitre 399, have US$1 airport bus service into town.

Rail Services The railway station is 5 km. E of centre (booking office closed 1200-1500 weekdays, Sat. p.m. and all Sun.), reached by local bus 20 (US$0.20). Information from San Martín 127 in centre. *Expreso Lagos del Sur*, leaves Buenos Aires, Sun. (with car transporter), 0730, 34 hrs (not much heat); *Lagos del Sur* Tues., Fri. 40 hrs.; both at 2300. *Expreso* leaves Bariloche, 2135, Tues., *Lagos del Sur* 2030 Thurs. and Sun., all arrive at 0650 two days after, fares US$70 sleeper, US$63 Pullman, US$41 first, US$25 tourist class. Trip can be extremely dusty. Scenery only interesting between Bariloche and Jacobacci (4½ hrs.), where you catch the train to Esquel; food on board reasonable (US$4 for 3 courses).

Road Services Paved road from Buenos Aires via Neuquén, 1,600 km. Chevallier, Buenos Aires to Bariloche, daily at 1215, 22½ hrs., US$62. Also La Estrella daily at 1315 (US$56.50) and El Valle via Neuquén at 1300 (US$55). These three return daily between 1500 and 1600, respectively. For Mar del Plata, take Buenos Aires bus and change at Bahía Blanca or Tres Arroyos (e.g. La Estrella, 1500, arrive Tres Arroyos 0555, US$26). Bus to Mendoza, TAC, Tues., Thurs. and Sat., US$25, 22 hrs., on a paved road via Zapala, Buta Ranquil and San Rafael. Bus Córdoba-Bariloche, TUS, 25 hrs., US$46, Mon., Wed., Fri., and Sun. at 1000. Buses to El Bolsón (US$4, 3½ hrs.) and Esquel (US$9.50 with Don Otto or Mercedes) exc. Sun., with a 4 times weekly extension on paved road to Comodoro Rivadavia US$40 (Don Otto). To Puerto Madryn, 24 hrs. via Esquel and Trelew. To Jacobacci (for Esquel train) only one bus a day, arrives after train has left. To San Martín de los Andes, 0800, US$10, 4½ hrs. Buses also to Neuquén (550 km.) US$11.50 by Transportes Mercedes on Bartolomé Mitre or daily with La Estrella, Palacios 246 at 1415, 6½ hrs. (a dull journey). (No direct bus to Río Gallegos; you have to spend a night in Comodoro Rivadavia en route.) To Santiago (Chile), Tues., Fri. and Sun., 24 hours with tea and breakfast served en route. To Puerto Montt, see the route to Chile from Bariloche, **page 134**.

Activities Apart from sailing and boating, there are golf, mountaineering, walking, birdwatching, skiing, and fishing (for which you need a permit). Racquet Club, Ruta Llao-Llao, Km. 13.5, tennis and squash, snack bar. Before going hiking you are recommended to buy moisturizing creams for exposed skin areas and lips. Excellent trout fishing Nov.-March; boat hire arranged with tackle shops. Horseflies (*tábanos*) frequent the lake shores and lower ares in summer; lemon juice is good for keeping them away in summer. For horse riding, see above under Tourist Agencies.

Mountain Climbing In the area there is something for every kind of mountaineer. National Park mountain guides are available but can be expensive. Book: *Excursiones, Andinismo y Refugios de Montaña en Bariloche*, by Tonek Arko, available in local shops, US$2, or from the author at Güemes 691. In treks to *refugios* remember to add costs of ski lifts, buses, food at *refugio* and lodging (in Club Andino *refugios*: US$3 per night, plus US$1 for cooking, or US$1 for breakfast, US$2 for lunch, US$3 for dinner). Information from Club Andino Bariloche, 20 de Febrero 30, open 0900-1200 and 1500-2000 Mon.-Fri. and Sat. 0900-1200. The climbing may mean a ride on horseback or a skilled ascent of the slopes of Cerro Tronador (excursion by bus US$15, full day, including 1 hr. walk to black glacier, leaves at 0800, but too much time spent on the bus) which looms over the area. The Club Andino Bariloche arranges for guides; ask for Sr. Ricardo, the secretary, who organizes easy weekend climbs and walks with friendly visitors. It also provides maps and details of all campsites, hotels and mountain lodges. The Government has convenient rest lodges at from 1,000 to 2,000 metres on the mountains. Firing, light and food are provided at these points.

Swimming   in the larger lakes such as Nahuel Huapí and Huechulafquen is not recommended, for the water is cold. But swimming in smaller lakes such as Lolog, Lacar, Curruhué Chico, Hermoso, Meliquina, Espejo, Hess and Fonck is very pleasant and the water—especially where the bottom shelves to a shingly beach—can be positively warm.

Skiing   There is good skiing during the winter season (July to early October), supervised by the Club Andino at Bariloche. It is best organized with a tour company, through whom you can secure discounts as part of an inclusive deal. (Skiing is cheaper, however, at smaller resorts, such as Esquel, though more expensive at San Martín de los Andes.) The favourite skiing slopes are on Cerro Catedral, and a new ski-lift is to be built higher up, to permit a longer skiing season. (Regular bus service with seasonal timetable from Mercedes bus company on Mitre 161, US$3 return.) There are a cable car (US$6 single, 7.50 return) and a chair lift (US$22.50 full day, 17.50 afternoon only) from the foot of Cerro Catedral to points high on the ridge. Red and yellow markers painted on the rock mark a trail from the top, which leads to Refugio Frey (well equipped, blankets, meals, accommodation E) on the edge of a small mountain lake (allow 6 hours; one can return through the forest to the ski complex the next day and take a bus back to Bariloche). The seasonal cable car, with a chair lift from its upper terminus, takes one higher than the main (2-stage) chair lift. Bus tours from Bariloche to the foot of Cerro Catedral give time for less than 2 hours on top of the mountain. Entrance to the Cerro Catedral ski slopes, below the snowline, is US$0.40. The only disadvantage at Bariloche is that the snow is unreliable except at the top. There are other skiing slopes 5 km. out of Bariloche, on Cerro Otto (cable car, US$7 p.p.; open 0900-1900 Jan., Feb., July, August, and 1400-1800 rest of year; station at foot reached by bus No. 50 "Teleférico", 15 mins., US$0.30, entry to revolving restaurant at top, US$3.50), which can be reached in 2-3 hours' walk from the town; take the paved Av. de los Pioneros, then switch to the signed dirt track 1 km. out of Bariloche (splendid views), or in a minibus which goes every ½ hour from a car park near the National Park headquarters (closed public holidays), between 1400 and 1600, US$5 round trip (local bus US$1.50 return); at Piedras Blancas (bus US$5 return); also on López (try a car trip, rough road, US$10 for a tour, 1400-1830), Dormilón and La Ventana. Ski hire US$5-9 a day, depending on quality, dearer at Cerro Catedral than in town. Ski clothes can also be rented by the day, at US$1-2 per item, from Kiwanis sport stores in Bariloche or El Iglú, Galería Arrayanes II, Rolando 244. **N.B.** Summer skiing on grass has been organized 20 km. S of Bariloche, on Route 258 to El Bolsón.

Excursions   Whole-day trip to Lakes Gutiérrez, Mascardi, Hess, the Cascada Los Alerces and Cerro Tronador (3,554 metres) leaves at 0800, US$20. Turismo Llao-Llao organizes the following: 8-hour excursion to Río Limay, Valle Encantado, Lake Traful, Lake Correntoso, Villa La Angostura, returning via Paso Coihue. Catedral and Turisur have a 9-hour excursion, leaving at 1030 (afternoon dep. Dec.-March), to Puerto Pañuelo, sailing down to Puerto Blest and continuing by bus to Puerto Alegre and again by launch to Puerto Frías (US$14). A visit to the Cascada de los Cántaros is made. Several 12-hour excursions to San Martín de los Andes, US$25, through 2 national parks. Beautiful scenery at Llao-Llao for walking; one can walk the 15 km. Circuito Chico, or the 17 km. "motor tour" route back to Bariloche (take the 3 de Mayo bus there from Moreno and Rolando, and the ferry for Isla Victoria; there is a chairlift at km 17.7 on Llao-Llao road (Campanario) one can walk to km. 18.3 and take the road to the left to Colonia Suiza and Punto Panorámico, which winds around Lago Moreno, unspoiled surroundings, all in 16 km. to Puerto Pañuelo). The chairlift at Campanario offers fine views of Isla Victoria and Puerto Pañuelo, 0900-1200, 1400-1800 daily, US$1.60. Another excursion involves going to Pampa Linda, which is 8 km. from the road ending at Tronador and has the *guardaparque* station. From there you can ask the ranger to show you a path for a two-day walk over Paso de las Nubes to Laguna Fría, which is not always well marked, especially one place early on where the track branches after crossing a river by a series of temporary footbridges. The right hand track should *not* be attempted by inexperienced walkers. The left hand track, once a road, leads one west up a spur to the edge of the glacier with a well appointed hut (3-4 hours journey).

From Pampa Linda ranger post you can also walk past the glacier on Tronador to Peulla in Chile (2½ days); details in Bradt and Pilkington's backpacking book. Turismo Catedral has 11-12 hr. excursion, US$36, crossing Lake Todos los Santos into Chile taking in Peulla (lunch at hotel, US$6.50) and the Petrohué falls. Alun-Co Turismo, Mitre 22, 2nd floor, operates a rubber raft excursion mid-Nov. until mid-April to Confluencia, leaves Bariloche at 1000 up River Limay, stopping for lunch at Valle Encantado, returns to Bariloche at 1900, US$16. A half-day excursion is possible taking a bus to Virgen de las Nieves, walking 2 km. to arrive at beautiful Lake Gutiérrez; walk along lake shore to the road from El Bolsón and walk back to Bariloche (about 4 hrs.).

A recommended one-day trip by car is Bariloche-Llao Llao-Bahía-Colonia Suiza-Cerro Catedral-Bariloche; the reverse direction misses the sunsets and afternoon views from the higher roads, which are negotiable in winter (even snow-covered). If one is staying only 1-2 days in the area the best excursions are to Cerro Tronador the 1st day, and on the 2nd to Cerro Catedral in the morning and Isla Victoria in the afternoon (possible only Dec.-March when there are afternoon departures for the island). Camping facilities for firing, food and water are good. Good walks to Lake

Correntoso (4 km.) and Quetrihué Peninsula (15 km. to forest of Arrayanes). Also to the *refugio* at Laguna Negra (16 km. trail) and to Cerro López (3 hrs., with a *refugio* after 2); in both cases take Colonia Suiza bus and for the former alight at SAC, for the latter at Picada. Hitching to local sights is difficult.

A half-day excursion (1300-1830) may be taken from Bariloche to Puerto Pañuelo, then by boat to Isla Victoria. The full-day excursion (0900-1830, or 1300 till 2000 in season) at US$18-20 includes the Arrayanes forest on the Quetrihue peninsula and 3 hours on Isla Victoria, picnic lunch advised. Half-day excursions to Isla Victoria are available. Some boats going to Arrayanes call first at Isla Victoria, early enough to avoid boat-loads of tourists. These boats carry the names of Paraná river provinces—Corrientes, Misiones, Santa Fe—and they have no open deck. For open decks try the *Modesta Victoria* or the *Don Luis*. (Turisur have 3 catamarans with a bar and cafeteria.) For a cheaper excursion take Transporte 3 de Mayo bus marked Estación Llao-Llao from Moreno and Rolando at 0900 or 0930 (Rte 6091) for 1030 dep. from Puerto Pañuelo (1130 or 1200 for 1300 dep.) to go to Isla Victoria and Arrayanes by boat (US$7). From Puerto Pañuelo, opposite the *Hotel Llao-Llao*, boats also leave for Puerto Blest. All boats are very crowded in season, but operators have to provide seating for all passengers. The Arrayanes forest can also be visited by walking 12 km. from Villa la Angostura (**see next page**).

Roads   There are 500 km. of highways (mostly unpaved) running through the park. There are numerous excursions; prices vary very widely, and it is best to buy tours on the spot rather than in advance, although they get very booked up in season. The old road to El Bolsón and Esquel (a new, faster, but less interesting road has been built between Bariloche and Esquel) is paved for the first 30 km. and goes past the beautiful lakes of Gutiérrez, Mascardi and Guillelmo and over fine mountain passes.

The Route to Chile from Bariloche   The preferred route is over Puyehue pass, being 4-5 times cheaper than via the lakes, on a good broad highway which is paved on the Chilean side up to Termas de Puyehue, but not yet on the Argentine ("120 km of dirt road . . . tough on the car and the nerves" - David Mackintosh). Road from Bariloche goes around east end of Lake Nahuel Huapí, then follows north side of lake through resort town of Villa La Angostura to junction with "Ruta de Siete Lagos" for San Martín at Km. 94, Argentine customs at Km. 109 and pass at Km. 125 at elevation of 1,280 metres. (About 22 km. from the Argentine customs is Camping Correntoso; 4 km. further is Camping El Cruce, ACA, and another 2 km. brings you to Camping Osa Mayor, ACA.) Chilean customs at Km. 146 in middle of a forest. The frontier is closed at night. *Hotel Termas de Puyehue* is at Km. 168. Possible to camp nearby, but bring own food as restaurant is expensive. Very pleasant *Motel Ñilque* on Lake Puyehue (Chile) is at Km. 174. A six-hour drive.

N.B.   You are strongly advised to get some Chilean pesos before you cross into Chile from Bariloche, as the austral is not easily exchanged in Chile. The Argentine and Chilean border posts are open every day; the launches (and hence the connecting buses) on the lakes servicing the direct route via Puerto Blest to Puerto Montt generally do not operate at weekends; check. There is an absolute ban in Chile on importing any fresh food—meat, cheese, fruit—from Argentina. Bariloche Tourist Office may not be up to date on lake crossings to Puerto Montt, check details at travel agencies, particularly if travelling to meet connections.

Several bus companies run services from Bariloche to Puerto Montt, Osorno and Valdivia, there is at least one bus every day from Argentine side. Two go the all-road crossing via Osorno: Visión Turismo and Bus Norte, Mitre 10, daily exc. Mon. and Wed. Perimel and T. Lanin (not rec.), Moreno 138, daily exc. Fri. and Sun.; all at 0800, 8 hrs., US$ 17.50 (although it is cheaper to go to Osorno and buy a separate ticket on to Puerto Montt). Mercedes offers a Bariloche-Puerto Montt road trip for US$17. Sit on left side for best views. Turismo Catedral operates a 12-hour crossing to Puerto Montt, via the lake with lunch at Peulla, about US$35. Alternatively you can buy a ticket to the Chilean border (US$10.50), then another to Puerto Montt (US$32), or pay in stages once in Chile. The route is Bariloche to Llao-Llao by road, Llao-Llao to Puerto Blest by boat (2½ hrs.), Puerto Blest to Puerto Frías (20 mins. by boat), then 1½ hrs. by road to Peulla. (A Bariloche-Peulla day excursion costs about US$25 p.p.) Leave for Petrohué in the afternoon by boat (2½ hrs.), cross Lake Todos Los Santos, passing the Osorno volcano, then by bus to Puerto Montt. All other agencies sell excursions to Puerto Frías using a Mercedes bus to Puerto Pañuelo, a Turisur boat to Puerto Blest and share a bus and boat to Puerto Frías with excursion groups going on to Chile. Request information at Turismo Catedral which owns the exclusive rights to the excursion via the lakes, using their own boats and bus from Puerto Pañuelo to Puerto Frías (Andina del Sud operates with them on the Chilean side). You can do the trip by paying as you go along but there is now little advantage in doing so. The most satisfactory way of doing the trip full-circle is by car from Bariloche, going first via Puyehue to Puerto Montt, returning via Tromen Pass (see the Villarrica volcano, good road), then Junín and San Martín de los Andes. It is reported that Peulla suffers from swarms of biting flies in summer and that the shorelines there are receding. No cars taken on ferry on Lake Todos Los Santos. There are daily boats from Puerto Pañuelo to Puerto Blest, with daily through connections by boat and bus to Puerto Montt.

Further information on border crossings in the Lake District, and details of accommodation in

Peulla will be found in the Chilean section, **page 493**. Older travellers are advised not to attempt the Bariloche-Puerto Montt trip all in one day; about 70 km. of road on the Argentine side of the Puyehue route are being reconstructed, and the lake route is long and tiring.

N.B.   At the Futaleufú and Palena border crossings, Argentine border officials only give transit visas: legalize your stay within 10 days either by leaving the country or by renewing entry stamp at an immigration office.

N.B.   Obtain maps and information about the district in Buenos Aires at the National Park Tourist Office at Santa Fe 690, or at the provincial offices (addresses given on **page 57**); it is hard to obtain these in the provinces themselves. Park wardens are also useful sources of information.

Río Villegas, about 80 km. S of Bariloche on the road to El Bolsón, is very beautiful. Cheap but pleasant *hostería* just outside the gates of the National Park, by the river.

Villa La Angostura on Lake Correntoso is picturesque, 90 km. W of Bariloche on the way to Chile, by excursion bus (day trip; try Turismo Llao-Llao, 8 hrs.) or local bus (at 1900 daily, returning 0730, Transporte Mercedes, US$5) which requires staying overnight; hotels a little dearer than Bariloche. The port, 3 km. from town, is spectacular in summer. It is best to return to Bariloche if going on to Osorno (Chile): otherwise you have to pay twice the fare to Osorno from Bariloche and arrange for the bus company to pick you up at La Angostura. Daily bus at 1700 to San Martín de los Andes.

Hotels   *Correntoso, A.* Cheaper are *La Cabañita* (Belvedere s/n)and *Don Pedro* (El Cruce), both E. Ask in the tourist office, opposite ACA, for lodgings in private houses, cheaper than hotels. *Hotel Ruca Malen,* warmly rec., 24 km. away on lake shore.

Camping   *El Cruce, ACA Osa Mayor* (2 km. along Bariloche road, pleasant, US$1.35 p.p., open late Dec. to mid-May), *Autocamping San Martín, Municipal Lago Correntoso.*

Restaurants   *Guatraché,* grills; *Cuernavaca; Parrilla Gallegos, Confitería de los Amigos* (also lets rooms, E, no bath).

Excellent *Hostería Los Peraltoches* on Lake Gutiérrez, 116 km. from Bariloche, A with meals; magnificent views, English spoken, very homelike, open Nov.-March and June-Aug.

El Bolsón is 130 km. to the S, on the old road to Esquel. It is a most attractive small town (pop. 8,000) in beautiful country, with many mountain walks and waterfalls nearby, though as it lies in a hollow at about 200 metres, it can be very hot in summer. Good fishing. Within half an hour's drive are Lakes Puelo and Epuyén (shops and petrol available). The farms and the orchards sell their produce at Bariloche. Famous local fruit preserves can be bought at the factories in town. The Balneario Municipal is 300 metres from the town centre, pleasant river swimming. There is a full-day tour from Bariloche, about US$9, at 0800 (stops at Lake Puelo) Empresa Don Otto (very crowded and difficult to get on in high season) Mercedes or Turismo Llao-Llao, 11 hrs. Mercedes bus from Bariloche US$4, 3¼ hrs.

Accommodation   *Hostería Steiner,* clean and pleasant, on the Lake Puelo route, F; *Motel La Posta,* smart and new (Route 258). *Residencial* at Playa Onelli 3076, clean, friendly, E. *Piltriquitrón,* E, large, clean rooms. *Rhona-Hué,* Villa Turismo, E, T 0944-92416, run by John and Rhona Gough, who speak English and Welsh, friendly and hospitable, rec. Up to 2 days' stay possible at the Franciscan school, but get recommendation from tourist agent. *Hotel Salinas,* Rocas 641 in private house, E, friendly, clean, rec. Several *residencias* and camping sites nearby. The campsite (US$1) at Lake Puelo has beautiful views across the lake to Tres Picos, but the walking is limited. Frequent public transport from El Bolsón. Very difficult to find accommodation in the high season.

Restaurants   *Don Diego,* good; *Parrilla Achachay,* where the buses stop (anti-British and anti-US sentiments reported); *Munich,* ½ block from tourist office; four or five others. *Ricardo,* on Rocas, good coffee. Welsh tea room, *Casa del Té Galés.*

Tourist Office   The agent, Sr. Sigfrido Janett, is most helpful, and a great authority on the area. Ask for sketch maps of the beautiful walks in the neighbourhood including up Cerro Piltriquitrón. Office open 0900-2000, on main plaza.

On the way from Epuyén to Esquel is *Cholila*, with superb views of Lake Cholila, crowned by the Matterhorn-like mountains of Cerros Dos and Tres Picos. There are bus services between Bariloche, El Bolsón, and Esquel, and between Comodoro Rivadavia and Esquel. A recommended journey for motorists is to spend the night at El Bolsón, enter the Los Alerces park via Cholila and drive right through it to Esquel, travelling the whole length of Lakes Rivadavia and Futalaufquen.

Hotel *El Trébol,* E with bath, US$1.50 farm breakfast. **Restaurant** *Hue Telén,* open 24 hrs., near ACA.

Camping Parque Nacional camping ground at Lake Puelo, with hot showers (cold in winter) and small store on lake-shore, US$2; or free inside National Park.

Esquel, about 260 km. S of Bariloche, was originally an offshoot of the Welsh colony at Chubut, nearly 650 km. to the E. It is now a modern town with reasonable amenities (population 17,000). Major skiing location at La Hoya, 7 ski-lifts, 15 km. north of Esquel (skiing much cheaper than at Bariloche). Restaurant. For skiing information ask at Club Andino Esquel; bus to La Hoya from Esquel, 3 a day, US$3, lift tickets US$7 a day, gear hire US$6 a day. Esquel is known for its tulips, chocolate, jellies and jams (also for the mazard berry liquor made by the Braese family, interesting, but expensive). There is a museum on Belgrano and Ameghino, very varied exhibits, including stuffed local animals. Free, open Mon.-Fri., 0900-1200 and 1800-2100. Sat. at 1900-2100; 15 min. tour.

Hotels *Tehuelche,* 9 de Julio 961 y Belgrano, D, good; *Residencial Gingin,* Rivadavia 1243, E, friendly, grubby; *Hostería los Tulipanes,* Fontana 365, D, good rooms and service; *Residencial Angelina,* Av. Alvear 18 (Luis Scaglioni), D, very friendly and clean; *Residencial Huemul,* Alvear 1015, D; *Hostería,* at Italian consulate, Ameghino 505, F, nice, friendly, clean, quiet, meals; *Hotel-Restaurant Vascongada,* Mitre y 9 de Julio, E with shower, friendly, good cheap food. *Hospedaje* at Roca 839, good, E with bath. *Motel La Hoya,* Ameghino 2296, D, on road to airport, 1 km. Also *Hostería La Hoya* at the Centro Deportivo de Ski at La Hoya itself, E. *Hosksia Huentru Niyeu,* Chacabuco 606, F, clean, quiet, friendly. Mrs Megan Rowlands' guesthouse at Rivadavia 330, F, meals available, Welsh and English spoken, rec. *Hospedaje Beirut,* 25 de Mayo 200, Ameghino, F, shared room, not very clean but friendly. Many others. Ask at tourist office for lodgings in private houses.

Camping Municipal site 3 km. from centre on Trevelin road, near gravel-crushing plant, hot showers, US$1.50 p.p. Parque Nacional camping ground in the Park, by Lake Futalaufquen, 6 km.; hot showers and small store. Permit needed from Intendencia, who also provide fishing permits (US$51.35 for a whole season, with reductions for shorter periods). Camping facilities closed in winter; also on the way to El Bolsón. Free campsite at Laguna Z, 5 km. along Calle Fontana. Camping at *Cabañas Tejas Negras* (C), good facilities for US$3.50, by *Pucón Pai Motel,* which has its own campsite. Those with sleeping bags can go to the Salesian school and sleep in the school classrooms, Dec. to March; get recommendation from tourist office. On the road from Esquel to Trevelin, signposted on the righthand side, is *La Granja Trevelin,* owned by Domingo Giacci, macrobiotic meals, sells milk, cheese and onions; camping US$0.90, hot water and w.c., bungalows US$15 a day.

Restaurants *Jockey Club,* Alvear 947, excellent, reasonably priced; *El Cóndor, rotisería,* near bus station, Alvear 1250, good for packed lunches; also for snacks. *Rotisería Las Brasas,* clean, friendly, cheap. *Ahla Wasahla,* San Martín 1100, opposite Tour d'Argent, good cheap, friendly, TV, closed Sun.; *Red Fox,* Sarmiento 795 and Alvear, a British-style pub with light, but expensive meals, open from 2200, closed Tues. *Parrilla La Estancia,* 25 de Mayo 541, quite good; *Pizzería Don Pipo,* Rivadavia 820, good pizzas and empanadas. *Casa Suiza,* good confitería.

Bank and Post Office Banco de la Nación on Güemes and San Martín (official rate, Amex only), very high commission on cheques, but none on cash; open Mon.-Fri., 1000-1300. Post Office at Roca 445. Opposite the bus terminal on Fontana and Alvear (open 0800-2000) is a new post and telecommunications office. **Exchange** travellers' cheques very difficult to change in Esquel, apart from Amex or Banco de la Nación.

Tourist Office Operates from the bus terminal, very friendly, and good. Closed Sat. p.m. and Sun. off-season.

Tourist Agencies Mencué (for complete tours only), Lago Verde, Via Sur, all near Sarmiento. Esquel Tours, Fontana 754, T 2704, run a service to and from the airport (US$0.70) where they also have an office.

Airport 20 km. E of Esquel, by paved road, US$10 by taxi. US$1.60 by bus. One flight daily to Buenos Aires; 3 a week via Bariloche; 4 a week via Trelew. LADE flight to Ushuaia; also to Trelew and to Bariloche.

Rail From Buenos Aires, *Lagos del Sur* train arrives in Jacobacci (E of Bariloche) after 27½ hrs., returns at 1820 Wed. A steam-operated, narrow-gauge train (described by Paul Theroux in *The*

Old Patagonian Express) waits for the train from Buenos Aires, and normally leaves Jacobacci Thurs. and Sat., at 1500, for Esquel (arrives 0500), which is the most southerly point in the connected South American railway system. It returns Mon., and Thurs., at 2200, arriving at Jacobacci at 1210. Fares from Bs.As. to Esquel: tourist US$29.35, 1st class US$43, pullman and sleeper, available only as far as Jacobacci, US$52 and US$70. Tourist train to Nahuel Pan leaves Mon. at 1500, returns same day, US$7.75. Tickets from Tehuelche Viajes, Fontana 574, or Esquel Tours, Fontana 754. There are only two engines at Esquel, so go to El Maitén (train from Esquel, Sun. and Thurs. 2200, arrives 0300, cold), where there are about 12, arriving at 0830. From El Maitén it is possible to hitch to Bariloche or take the Esquel-Bariloche bus.

Buses None direct from Buenos Aires to Esquel so travel via Bariloche. To Comodoro Rivadavia, Giobbi, US$10, 6 buses a week, Transportes Patagónicos (Don Otto) leaves Comodoro Rivadavia on Tues., Thurs., Fri., and Sun., passing through Esquel at midnight. This bus runs slowly to El Bolsón, where it stays over one hour before leaving for Bariloche. Empresa Mercedes goes daily (9 hrs.) to Bariloche at 0800 (also at 2200), US$9.50. To El Bolsón, 5 hrs., US$8, rough road, goes alternate days via El Maitén (for train buffs) and via Cholila (for views). To Trelew, US$12, 10½ hrs., leaves 0900 Tues., Thurs., Sat., and 1900 Mon., Wed., Fri.; other bus companies on Av. Fontana and Alvear (bus terminal) are Empresa Don Otto, Chubut, Denis. Bus terminal T 2233, also for taxis.

Los Alerces National Park Sixty km. W of Esquel, which can also be reached by road from Rawson, is the Los Alerces National Park, with centuries-old larch trees. An interesting part of the park can be reached from a separate entrance through Trevelin (see below) following the Río Futaleufú. Because the Futaleufú hydroelectric dam has been built there, one can only go a short distance into the park this way, and entry to Lake Situación is forbidden. Entrance by car to see Futaleufú dam is only allowed at 1500, under police supervision; photography not permitted, except on top of the dam itself. There is no public transport, but Mencué in Esquel go there. (Hotels on Route 258, on E side of Lake Futalaufquen are, *Quime Quipán* and *Cume-Hué*, both closed in winter). The eastern side of Los Alerces has much the same natural attractions as the Nahuel Huapí and Lanín parks, but is much less developed for tourism. Esquel to Los Alerces, Mon. and Sat. at 0630, returns at 1800, US$4 round trip—check schedule as it varies. Its great Lake Futalaufquen has some of the best fishing in this huge area, begins Nov. 15. Bus to Lake Futalaufquen US$8.50, on Thurs., Sat. and Sun. at 0830 and 1730 (it passes 3 hotels and drives into 2 camp sites). Off-season, the bus only goes to the southern tip of the lake (the administration building, or Intendencia), US$5.15. Taxi, US$72. There are food shops in the area, near camping ground. The 0830 bus connects with the Trelew bus. The *Hostería Los Tepúes*, on the E side, is simple, rustic, and frequented by teenagers, A, open all year round, also has a family bungalow for rent. Recommended for fishermen are the *Quime Quipán* and *Pucón Pai* motels. (The *Pucón Pai* holds a fishing festival to open the season, A, friendly, open all year; reservations: Casilla 150, Esquel. It has a good restaurant.) On the W side, which is untouched by tourism (by law), is *Hotel Futalaufquen* just N of Puerto Limonao, rec., especially rooms 2/3 and 4/5 which have balconies overlooking the lake, L, open all year (no heating in rooms); good walking around the hotel, e.g. to Cinco Saltos, and El Dedal. Regular full day launch trip from Puerto Limonao (reached by early morning minibus) on Lake Futalaufquen (a sheer delight) through Arrayanes river to windless Lake Verde (camping ground). From there one can walk out to Lakes Rivadavia and Cholila (*Hostería El Trébol* on Lake Mosquito), and to the end of Lake Menéndez, famous for its giant larch trees (US$15 incl. launch trip on Lake Menéndez, with Tehuelche Viajes y Turismo, Av. Fontana 574, from Esquel); the boat leaves at 1000 but book the day before, as it will not leave if there are not enough passengers. There are local guides with outboard motor boats for fishermen. From Lake Menéndez one can also take a launch to see the beautiful Cerro Torrecilla. Lovely view of Lago Cisne (Swan Lake) to the NW end of Lake Menéndez. One then walks a 3 km. nature trail looking across the Andes to Chile before returning. Tours arranged at Esquel. Other excursion tours offered are less interesting because they only involve short stops in front of points of interest. A road connects all the lakes.

From Esquel one can also drive to Perito Moreno (**see page 150**) via Teckia (95 km. paved), Gobernador Costa (84 km. unpaved), La Laurita (last 61 km. paved, ACA service station, breakdown truck and snack bar), 65 paved km. to join route 22 (60 km.) which is being paved, and on to Río Mayo, with 121 km. unpaved road to Perito Moreno.

Crossing into Chile Colectivos leave Esquel Mon., Wed. and Fri. for Futaleufú (Chile) and there are more that just go to the frontier at La Balsa. Campsite (Camping Río Grande) on Argentine side of river. Cross the frontier river by barge (*balsa*) after passing Argentine customs; Chilean customs is 1 km. on the other side of river. Colectivo from Chilean customs to Futaleufú (8 km.) is US$1.50. Very little traffic for hitching. The colectivos from Esquel pass through Trevelin on the way.

Trevelin (pop. 5,000), 23 km. SW of Esquel (local bus, US$0.60, every ½ hour, 0700-1900; *Hostería Estefania*), is also an offshoot of the Welsh Chubut colony (**see page 143**). There is a modern Anglican church beside the Catholic church.

has a historical museum (entrance US$0.30) in the old mill. Grills at *Che Ferrada*, good mixed *parrillada* at *El Quincho*, and tea rooms offering *té galés* and *torta negra* (e.g. *El Adobe* on Av. Patagonia). La Cabaña, 7 km. out on the road from Trevelin to Lake Futalaufquen, serves Welsh teas. There is a custom of giving a newly-married couple a "black cake" on their wedding day, to be eaten on their first anniversary.

Neuquén, capital of Neuquén Province, is near the confluence of the Limay and Neuquén rivers. It is a pleasant, clean industrial city of nearly 60,000 people, serving the rich oilfields to the W with heavy equipment and construction materials, and the irrigated fruit-producing valley to the E. There are also many wine *bodegas* nearby. Much farm machinery is sold to the orchards where apples, pears, grapes, hops and plums are grown. At the Parque Centenario is a *mirador* with good views of the city and the confluence of the Rivers Neuquén and Limay (be sure *not* to take the bus to Centenario industrial suburb). There is a jet airport (7 km. from centre) and Neuquén is the transport centre for Mendoza (N), Bahía Blanca and Buenos Aires (E), Zapala and Chile (W), and Bariloche (S).

Hotels   *Apollo*, D-C, Av. Olascoaga 361, very good; *Cristal*, D-C, Av. Olascoaga 268, adequate; *Comaline*, 4-star, new, very good; *ACA Cipolletti*, just outside Neuquén; other *Hospedajes* on San Martín, all E; 13 km. S on Zapala road is *Hostal del Caminante*, T 33118, with pool and garden, popular. *Residencial Libeam*, M.Alcorta 41, E with bath, fairly clean, near bus station. Some 50 km. W of Neuquén there is a motel at Arroyitos. Municipal camping site at Neuquén and various camping sites, mostly by the river.

Restaurants   *Las Tres Marías*, Alberdi 126, excellent; *Bariloche*, good food but poor service. Pleasant bars on Av. Argentina.

Exchange   *Casa de cambio* at Ministro Alcorta 144.

Museums   Museo Histórico Provincial, Santa Fe 163; Museo de Ciencias Naturales, at entrance to airport (as is the Casino).

Tourist Office   Félix San Martín y Río Negro.

Transport   El Cóndor (La Estrella), El Valle and Chevallier bus Buenos Aires-Neuquén, daily US$24, 18½ hours; paved road throughout. Connections with Copahué and Córdoba; also with San Rafael (US$15) and San Martín de los Andes (US$12.25). Bus to Zapala daily, 7 hours. To Bariloche, take La Estrella or Chevallier (not El Valle as it stops too often), and sit on left. Bus La Unión del Sud to Temuco (Chile) all year Mon., Tues., Thurs. and Sat. 0200, 16 hrs., US$23, returns on alternate days at 0430.
    Daily train, *Estrella del Valle*, leaves Constitución station, Buenos Aires, at 1000, arriving Neuquén 0745; sleeper US$51, pullman US$40, first class US$28, tourist US$19.65; goes on to Zapala, 4 hours. Leaves Neuquén 2330, arrives Buenos Aires 2050. Takes car transporter Buenos Aires-Neuquén Thurs.; returns Fri.

If driving from Neuquén to Buenos Aires on Routes 151 and 21, via Catriel, fill up with fuel here because there is no other fuel for 323 km. of desert before General Achá. Driving from Neuquén to Bariloche, go via El Chocón hydroelectric lake, Junín and San Martín (both "de los Andes"), taking Routes 237, 40 and 234; route more attractive than that via Zapala.

Air   Daily flights to and from Buenos Aires with AA and Austral (one night flight each). Connecting flights to San Martín de los Andes with TAN, who also fly to Mendoza three times a week.

A road and railway go W from Neuquén to **Zapala** (247 km.) through the oil zone at Challacó and Plaza Huincul. There is an excellent geology museum in Zapala, visited by specialist groups from all over the world. Among the collections of minerals, fossils, shells and rocks, is a complete crocodile jaw, believed to be 80 million years old.

Hotels   *Huincul*, Roca 313, F; *Coliqueo*, Etcheluz 159, E; *Petuién*, Vidal y Etcheluz, E, rec. *Odetto's Grill*, Ejército Argentino 455, moderate prices, 2 mins. from bus terminal. There is a municipal camping site.

Transport   A Pullman bus, with hostess service, plies twice daily between Bahía Blanca and Zapala (15 hrs.). El Petróleo bus leaves Zapala 0230 and 1630 for San Martín de los Andes (5½ hrs.) via Junín de los Andes. In winter the direct route from San Martín de los Andes via the lakes may be impassable, so a bus must be taken back from San Martín to La Rinconada and then round to Bariloche (4 hrs.). There is also an overnight (at 2200) Neuquén-Zapala-San Martín bus that comes through Zapala at 0230; same service at 0915 (US$23). From Zapala to Bariloche by bus, one must change at La Rinconada. Zapala-Temuco (Chile) all year with La Unión del Sud at 0500, US$20, 13 hrs., as under Neuquén (see above). Also with Igi-Llaimi Wed. and Fri. at 0530, return 0330, twice weekly. Buy Chilean currency before leaving.

Train from Buenos Aires to Zapala, *Estrella del Valle*, 1,367 km., 26 hrs.; daily via Bahía Blanca at 1000 from Constitución station, arr. 1140. Zapala-Buenos Aires at 1925, arrives 2050 next day. On Sundays tickets go on sale at 1500, buffet car on train, scenery largely uninteresting. Fares: sleeper US$57.90, pullman US$49.60, first US$32.50, tourist US$22. The line follows the Río Colorado for some distance, then crosses it into the valley of the Río Negro where large fruit growing areas at (343 km.)

Choele-Choel (ACA motel on edge of town, D, with bath, good restaurant at bus station and fine modern *Hotel Choele-Choel*) and at (472 km.) Villa Regina are irrigated from the Río Negro dam. Two low-priced clean places: motel and *residencial* at edge of town near the main road. Cheap food at one of the service stations. There is an excellent free municipal campsite at Choele-Choel; shady, beside the Río Negro; no showers. Many local buses ply from Choele-Choel to El Chocón (large hydroelectric plant) and Zapala.

North of Zapala on the Chilean border is the Copahué National Reservation, best-known for its thermal baths and volcano of the same name. At 1,980 metres above sea-level in a volcanic region, **Copahué Termas** is enclosed in a gigantic amphitheatre formed by mountain walls, with an opening to the E. There are bus services from Neuquén and Zapala to Copahué, which may also be reached by road from Mendoza. The Laguna Blanca National Park to the W of Zapala is famous for its animal and bird life, but has not yet become a tourist centre.

Hotels N of Zapala include those at Churriaca (131 km.), Chos Malal (202 km.) and Río Barrancas (at 340 km.). Road mostly unpaved.

Bariloche is 418 km. S of Zapala by a road through Junín de los Andes and San Martín de los Andes. A short detour from Junín leads to the very beautiful lake of Huechulafquen; from Junín, too, a road runs W over the Tromen Pass through glorious scenery to Pucón (135 km.) on Lake Villarrica, in Chile (easy to hitchhike to Villarrica from the Argentine border post); on the way there are splendid views of Lanín volcano, extinct and 3,747 metres high, one of the world's most beautiful mountains. At *Junín de los Andes*——a famous spot for salmon and rainbow trout, known as the trout capital of Argentina——is the *Chimehuín*, a very small fishing hostelry (C); *Restaurant Ruca Hueney* is the town's social centre. Some 30 km. N of Junín are the *ACA Las Rinconadas* facilities; paved road. There is an airport between Junín and San Martín, but it is mainly used by the military.

The Tromen (Chileans call it Mamuil Malal) pass route between Argentina and Chile is much less developed than the Puyehue route, and definitely not usable during heavy rain or snow. Parts are narrow and steep. Argentine customs are at the pass. The Chilean *aduana* is at Puesco, 58 km. SE of Pucón and 16 km. from Tromen. Ferry at Lake Quilleihue, which is halfway between the posts, has been eliminated by road blasted across cliffs. It is possible to camp in the area (though very windy), but take food as there are no shops at the pass. From the border, it is 24 km. to Curarrehue, from where several buses a day go (either at 0600 or at the latest at 1400) to Pucón. The international bus will officially only pick up people at Tromen but at the discretion of the driver can pick up passengers at Puesco (customs, but no hotel) at 0900 and Currarehue stops. Hitch-hiking over to the Tromen Pass is difficult.

San Martín de los Andes, 40 km. S. of Junín (paved road), and 196 km. from Zapala, is a lovely but expensive little town at the eastern end of Lake Lacar; it is the best centre for exploring Lanín National Park, with its sparkling lakes, wooded mountain valleys and the snow-capped Lanín Volcano. The numerous deer in the park are the red deer of temperate Europe and Asia. There is excellent ski-ing on Cerro Chapelco, to which there is a road. Tourist Office at Rosas 790, on main square, corner of San Martín, open 0800-2400, very helpful. Police station at Belgrano 611. Chapelco airport: AA direct flights Mon., Wed., Sat., Sun. from Buenos Aires; also LADE and TAN flights from Neuquén.

Lanín Volcano A 4-hour hike from the Argentine customs post at Tromen pass (speak to the *guardaparque* at the border) to *refugio* at 2,400 metres. Climb from *refugio* to summit is easy but crampons and ice-axe are needed. Permission for the climb must be obtained from the army post in Junín de los Andes.

Hotels Motel, *El Sol de los Andes*, very expensive and nice, set above the town (Cerro Cnl. Díaz), A-L, closed end-1988 for refurbishing; *La Cheminée*, Roca y Moreno, B, very good, breakfast included, but no restaurant; *Hostería Villa Lagos*, Av. Villa Lagos, E, good, ski hire. *Posta del Cazador*, very highly rec. *Hostería Arrayán*, one of 2 English-run guest lodges in the Lake District, is 3 km. from San Martín. (Self-contained cabins for 14 guests; superb view over Lake Lacar; US$25 a day, all in.) At San Martín is *Los Pinos*, D with breakfast, Almte. Brown 420, German-run, with a/c and heating, clean, friendly; also *Residencial Pinos*, E, pleasant, nice garden. *Turismo* is rec., Mascardi and R. Roca, D-C, shared bathroom; *Hostería Anay*, Cap. Drury 841, E, central, good value, rec. Also good, *Casa Alta*, Gabriel Obeid 659 E; *Residencial Peumayen*, Av. San Martín 851, very clean, C-D, with bath and breakfast. Private home, *Casa Ravelo*, Av. San Martín 413, E, excellent; *Casa del Amigo*, Obeid y Cnel. Pérez, E, very friendly. Consult very good tourist office for other private addresses, but these are not available in winter. *Residencial Villa Bibi*, E, with private bath, breakfast extra, clean, family-run, near lake, Cnl. Díaz 1186, rec. At 24 km. from Villa La Angostura (see page 135) is *Hotel Ruca Malen* on Lake Correntoso, warmly rec.; at 53 km. *Hotel Pichi Traful*, and at 75 km. *Hostería Lago Hermoso*.

Camping ACA Camping and Autocamping San Martín de los Andes, both with hot water and laundering facilities US$2.20 p.p. Municipal, with shop and showers, US$2.50 p.p. Cabins on the camp site are US$5 p.p. Not open all year round. Pleasant site by the lake at Quilaquina, 27 km. from San Martín, with beaches, and another on the lake at Catritre, just 6 km. from town. Hitchhiking to Bariloche and San Juan is slow.

Restaurants Try smoked venison, wild boar or trout, at *El Ciervo* restaurant. *Parrilla La Tranquera*, good value; and *Parrilla del Esquiador* on Belgrano 885, reasonable home-cooked food. *El Jockey*, *La Raclette* and *Pisces* also good. It is difficult to get dinner before 2200, but there are various good restaurants in the area. *Pizzería La Strada*, San Martín 721, excellent; *Fanfani*, on Rodhel, has good pasta.

Exchange Banco de la Nación on San Martín exchanges cash and Amex cheques only; also at camera shop on main square.

Buses Station at Gral. Villegas 251, good toilet facilities. Bus Buenos Aires-San Martín, US$30, three a week, Chevallier goes Mon. and Fri. at 1430, arrives 1520 next day.

Excursions The most popular trips by car are to Lakes Lolog, Alumine, Huechulafquen and Paimún, to a campsite in the shadow of Lanín Volcano. Shorter excursions can be made on horseback or by launch; recommended day excursion by El Valle at 0930, return 1700 on Lake Lacar for US$10. The road goes on via Lake Hermoso and Villa La Angostura to Bariloche, a beautiful drive of 220 km., 10 hours (US$7) by bus, which stops for views and an hour for lunch at La Angostura—an excellent, well organized bus route, but not in winter. (Beware bad connections at La Angostura if you change buses there.) Many buses, however, use a rather less scenic route following Río Traful, then Lake Lanín and joining the paved Bariloche highway at Confluencia (ACA station and a hotel, also motel *El Rancho* just before Confluencia).

Villa Traful, beside Lake Traful about half-way between San Martín and Bariloche on a side road, is described as a "camper's paradise". Marvellous views, fishing (licence needed) excellent. All roads are dirt; drive carefully, avoiding wild cattle! *Hotel Pichi Traful* and *Hostería Traful* provide accommodation.

Camping along this "Seven Lake Drive" route is freely allowed to National Park permit-holders. No buses from Seven Lakes to San Martín de los Andes. If however you want to travel from **Bariloche to San Martín via Junín and the Seven Lakes**, you must buy a round trip excursion from one of the tour companies (e.g. Velox in Bariloche) for US$17.75, leaving at 0800, and not return with them. This is actually cheaper than a one-way ticket with the El Valle company who go there direct, via the less scenic route (US$20, at 1430). It is difficult to hitch-hike along this route as there is little traffic. When there is sufficient demand, there are two buses a day San Martín-Bariloche, 5 hours, making tourist day trips via the Seven Lakes, US$10.35. There are also daily buses San Martín-Bariloche via a paved route (least scenic) leaving San Martín at different times through four days in the morning and three days in early afternoon.

Skiing There are a chair-lift on Cerro Chapelco and a ski-tow higher up. Bus from San Martín to slopes, US$5 return. Very good slopes and snow conditions. As yet uncrowded. Lift pass US$23, ski hire US$5 a day from *Hostería Villa Lagos*. Atmosphere friendly.

To Chile Excursion San Martín de los Andes-Panguipulli (Chile): boat leaves San Martín daily to Hua-Hum at the end of Lake Lacar, except Thurs., at 0900, US$4.25. Camping with shop at Hua-Hum. Excursion buses run to Hua-Hum when the launch arrives across the border to Pirehueico, US$2.35. There is now a road between San Martín and Puerto Pirehueico (Chile). Buses daily at 1000 (US$3), 2 hr. journey through Lanín National Park. The ferry across Lake Pirehueico (Tues., Thurs., Sat. 1730; at 0830 in other direction) takes 2 hours (US$2) to Puerto Fuy; beautiful scenery. Daily bus 0600, US$1.50, 3 hrs., Puerto Fuy-Panguipulli; or ask for lift among vehicles on ferry (friendly boat crew may help). Boats also leave Puerto Fuy Mon., Tues. and Thurs. to Pirehueico for a day trip, US$3.45, and there is a daily ferry at 0600. Buses leave Puerto Fuy at

0600 to meet the boat from Choshuenco-Panguipulli on Mon., Tues., Thurs. and Sat. This route is open all year round and is an alternative service from Temuco to San Martín when the Tromen Pass is blocked by snow (usually June-mid-Nov.). When the pass is closed, the buses drive right on to the boat to cross between Puerto Fuy and Puerto Pirehueico. Check with customs at Hua-Hum about arrangements.

Bus San Martín de los Andes to Pucón (US$12) and to Temuco US$15.75; mid-Nov.-May Empresa San Martín Mon., Wed. and Fri., at 0700, returns from Temuco the following day at 0500, Igi-Llaimi Tues., Thurs. and Sat. at 0700, ret. next day at 0630, US$16 for Pucón, Villarrica and Temuco. When the pass is closed Empresa San Martín switches its return and forward journey days but not the times. Igi-Llaimi goes Wed. and Fri. only at 0500, returning from Temuco Tues. and Thurs. at 0330. This route passes through Panguipulli, Villarica and Temuco only. For Pucón change to JAC bus in Villarrica. The companies will not give information about each other, and do not run buses in winter when the pass is blocked.

PATAGONIA (10)

South of the Río Colorado is the vast plateau known generally as Patagonia. The area is sub-divided into the provinces of Neuquén, Río Negro, Chubut, Santa Cruz and the Territory of Tierra del Fuego. The area covers 780,000 square km.: 28% of the national territory, but has a population of only 600,000, little over 2.7% of the total population; and 57% of it is urban. Wide areas have less than one person to the square km., and there are virtually no trees except in the north and the Andean foothills.

Over the whole land there blows a boisterous, cloud-laden strong wind which raises a haze of dust in summer, but in winter the dust can turn into thick mud. Temperatures are moderated by the proximity of the sea and are singularly mild, neither rising high during the summer nor falling low during the winter. Even in Tierra del Fuego, where the warmest summer months average 10½°C, the winter days' average can reach a high of about 2°C. Make sure you have plenty of warm clothing, and anti-freeze in your car, available locally. Rain falls mostly in the winter, but not more than 200-250 mm. a year. The whole eastern part of the area suffers from a lack of rainfall and the land is more or less desert. Deep crevices or canyons intersect the land from E to W. Few of them contain permanent water, but ground water is easily pumped to the surface. The great sheep *estancias* are along these canyons, sheltered from the wind, and in the depression running N from the Strait of Magellan to Lakes Argentino and Buenos Aires and beyond. During a brief period in spring, after the melting of the snows, there is grass on the plateau. Most of the land is devoted to sheep raising. The wool, which is shipped N to Buenos Aires, is mostly the fine and finecrossbred wool used by the Argentine mills, and is often heavy with sand. Over-grazing leads to much erosion. Wild dogs and the red fox are the sole enemies of the sheep.

Because of the high winds and insufficient rainfall there is little agriculture except in the N, in the valleys of the Colorado and Negro rivers. Some cattle are raised in both valleys where irrigation permits the growing of alfalfa. A large area has been irrigated from the Río Negro dam near Neuquén and here, as a supplement to cattle raising, fruit growing has been highly successful: apples and pears are the chief crops, and many are exported.

Patagonia is rich in extractive resources: the oil of Comodoro Rivadavia and Tierra del Fuego, the little exploited iron ore of Sierra Grande, the coal of Río Turbio, the hydro-electric capacity of El Chocón, plentiful deposits of minerals (particularly bauxite) and marine resources, but their exploitation has been slow. Tourism is opening up too. The wildlife is attractive. *Guanacos* and rheas are a common sight: there are also *maras*, Patagonian hares. On and off parts of the coast, particularly the Valdés peninsula, seals, sea-elephants, right whales and other aquatic mammals may be seen, as well as penguins, especially between October and April. Further S, particularly in Tierra del Fuego, the antarctic wild goose (*quequén*) is the most commonly seen of the 152 species of birds. Patagonia Turística, Florida 755, Buenos Aires (Tel.:311-9216) are very helpful on travel to the region.

N.B. We are informed that in summer hotel prices are grossly inflated (by as much as 100% in

PATAGONIA

Ushuaia, 75 % in Calafate); also that in some places there may not be enough hotel beds to meet the demand. Camping is increasingly popular, and *estancias* seem hospitable to travellers who are stuck for a bed. During Argentine summer holidays (Jan., Feb., March) getting a hotel room in Ushuaia, Río Grande, Río Gallegos and Calafate is practically impossible. In this connection, remember that ACA establishments, which charge the same prices all over Argentina, are a bargain in Patagonia and Tierra del Fuego, where all other accommodation is expensive.

Discovery and Colonization   The coast of Patagonia was first visited by a European late in 1519, when the Portuguese Fernão Magalhães (Magellan), then in the service of Spain, was on his voyage round the world. Early in 1520 he turned W into the strait which now bears his name and there struggled with fierce headwinds until he reached that Sea of Peace he named the Pacific. Later European expeditions that attempted to land on the coast were repulsed by the dour and obdurate local Indians, but these were almost entirely wiped out in the wars of 1879-1883, generally known as the "Campaign of the Desert". Before this there had been a long established colony at Carmen de Patagones; it shipped salt to Buenos Aires during the colonial period. There had also been a settlement of Welsh people in the Chubut Valley since 1865 (see below). After the Indian wars colonization was rapid, the Welsh, Scots and English taking a great part. Chilean sheep farmers from Punta Arenas moved northwards along the depression at the foot of the Andes, eastwards into Tierra del Fuego, and northwards to Santa Cruz.

The Welsh settlement   On July 28, 1865, 150 Welsh immigrants landed at Puerto Madryn, then a deserted beach deep in Indian country. After three weeks they pushed, on foot, across the parched pampa and into the Chubut river valley, where there is flat cultivable land along the riverside for a distance of 80 km. upstream. Here, maintained in part by the Argentine Government, they settled, but it was three years before they realized the land was barren unless watered. They drew water from the river, which is higher than the surrounding flats, and later built a fine system of irrigation canals. The colony, reinforced later by immigrants from Wales and from the United States, prospered, but in 1899 a great flood drowned the valley and some of the immigrants left for Canada. The last Welsh contingent arrived in 1911. The object of the colony had been to create a "Little Wales beyond Wales", and for four generations they kept the Welsh language alive. The language is, however, dying out in the fifth generation. There is an offshoot of the colony of Chubut at Trevelin, at the foot of the Andes about 650 km. to the west, settled in 1888 (**see page 137**). It is interesting that this distant land gave to the Welsh language one of its most endearing classics: *Dringo´r Andes* (Climbing the Andes), written by one of the early women settlers.

Gary Luton, of the Welsh Patagonia Expedition 1980, writes: "To me Chubut will always foster memories of horses on an open wind-swept plain, or tethered, with brown sheepskin saddles, outside a *pueblo* inn. It is shuttered houses with poplar windbreaks. Chubut is relative prosperity surrounded by shanties of mud brick and tin; it is Coca-Cola and tea houses, sea lions and right whales sounding a short distance from shore; and *asados* washed down with red wine and *mate*. Chubut is a moonscape of neutral colours where sheep lose themselves in the grey-green saltpans of thornscrub, and dust and wind blow across scattered pockets of civilization. And it is the Eisteddfod at Gaiman, a Welsh festival of the arts in a chapel nestled among the poplars, on a cloudless night, where boys in white shirts recite poetry and choirs sing as a culture fights a subsiding battle to maintain itself."

Recommended Reading   *In Patagonia* by Bruce Chatwin, a good introduction to the area and its people.

In all Patagonia there is only one town—Comodoro Rivadavia—with a population over 100,000. Most of the towns are small ports, which used only to work during the wool-shipping season but have livened up since the local economy began to diversify. The high tidal range makes it impossible in most of them for ships to tie up at the docks (except at Madryn and Punta Arenas, Chile). The short railways inland from the ports have little traffic except during the sheep-shearing season.

Communications   Calls at the chief ports by passenger/cargo ships of the Flota Carbonera del Estado. Navy transport ships go as far as Ushuaia (Tierra del Fuego) once a month and carry 60 passengers for a nine-day trip.

Air Services   Aerolíneas Argentinas from Buenos Aires either direct to Río Gallegos or calling at Bahía Blanca, Trelew and Comodoro Rivadavia on the way. Austral from Buenos Aires to Río Gallegos via Bahía Blanca, Trelew and Comodoro Rivadavia daily (night flight Mon. via Bahía Blanca). Cía. Argentina de Transportes Aéreos (CATA) from Buenos Aires to Bahía Blanca, Trelew, Comodoro Rivadavia and Río Gallegos. Beware delays for bad weather.

Many air force LADE flights in the region S of Bariloche—Río Gallegos to Bariloche, to Ushuaia, to Calafate—must be booked in advance from departure point of flight. The planes are small and fly low; passengers miss little of what there is to be seen. The baggage allowance is 15 kg. Travellers are warned that the flights are often heavily booked ahead, but always check again on the day of the flight if you are told beforehand that it is sold out. Sometimes, individual passengers are allowed to fly on air force carriers if planes are full or inopportune, through LADE. Also, LADE tickets are much cheaper for a long flight with stops than buying separate segments. LADE's computer reservation system is linked to Aerolíneas Argentinas, so flight connections are possible between these airlines. Also LADE's flights synchronize with both AA and Austral flights.

Roads The main road, Route 3, which runs near the coast, is paved from Buenos Aires to Fitz Roy, near Comodoro Rivadavia. From Comodoro Rivadavia to Piedra Buena the road has a very well maintained all-weather surface. The last 230 km. to Río Gallegos are paved. S of this town to Ushuaia is a combination of fair all-weather road and pavement in a bad state of repair. Sometimes passengers going South have to pay for baggage by weight.

The principal roads in Patagonia roughly form an inverted triangle. Route 3, which has regular traffic (hitch-hiking good in spring and summer) and adequate services, it has little to interest the tourist. At the southern end, this route enters Chile and crosses the Magellan Straits to Tierra del Fuego by the car ferry at Primera Angostura. The western route (Route 40) zigzags across the moors and is lonely and largely unpaved (advised speed 30 kph); there is hardly any traffic except in December, January and February, the tourist season. However, it is by far the more interesting road, with fine views of the Andes and plenty of wild life as well as the Alerces and Glaciares National Parks. Camping is no problem, and there are good hotels at Esquel, Perito Moreno, Piedra Buena, Calafate and (in Chile) Puerto Natales. Third class accommodation also at Gobernador Gregores, Río Mayo and Esperanza, and also in Coyhaique, Chile. The northern part of the triangle is formed by the paved highway running from Bariloche through Neuquén to San Antonio Oeste.

Many of the roads in Southern Argentina are gravelled. A good windscreen protector costs US$50 in Buenos Aires, but more primitive versions can be bought for much less—e.g. US$5 in San Julián, and probably elsewhere. The best types to buy are the grid-type, or inflatable plastic ones which are made for some standard-type vehicles, the only disadvantage being some loss of visibility.

N.B. Keep passport handy as examination is required when passing from one province to another. Also, be prepared for roadblocks at which one has to declare one's destination, nationality, vehicle particulars, etc.

The upper course of the Río Colorado is the northern limit of Patagonia. 160 km. S of where it reaches the sea (250 km. S of Bahía Blanca), about 27 km. from the mouth of the Río Negro, is

Carmen de Patagones (20,000 people), standing on high ground on the northern bank, with **Viedma** (30,000 people) the capital of Río Negro Province, across the river, which is spanned by a connecting rail and road bridge. There is also a frequent ferry service for pedestrians. On a hill behind Patagones a monument commemorates an attack on the twin towns by a Brazilian squadron in 1827. (Beware of pleasant-looking campsites near this monument; there is an artillery range nearby.) There are four museums, open 1000-1200 only: the one in the Viedma Municipalidad is good, with interesting sections on Indian tribes. There are air services to Viedma, 966 km. from Buenos Aires daily except Thursday (continuing either to Bariloche or General Roca). The swimming is recommended on the Viedma side of the river, where there is a nice shady shore. A law has been passed nominating Viedma as the site of the new federal capital, but building has not yet begun.

Hotels at Carmen de Patagones: *Percaz; Gran Argentino.* At Viedma: *Peumayen*, Buenos Aires 334, D; *Viedma; Austral*, rec., modern. *Hotel Roma* has good restaurant. *Restaurant Munich*, Buenos Aires 161, open late.

Tourist Office Belgrano 544, 9th floor, Viedma.

Camping Further camping sites on the Río Negro where the main route into Patagonia meets the river (some 170 km. from Viedma due NW) with all facilities including a small shop. Additional shops at General Conesa, 2 km. away. Mosquito repellant needed. There is another campsite N of General Conesa (about 140 km.) at Río Colorado again alongside the Patagonian road. All facilities.

Excursion Beautiful beach, El Cóndor, 30 km. S of Viedma, 3 buses a day, hotel open Jan.-Feb., restaurants and shops, free camping on beach 2 km. S. 30 km. from El Cóndor is a sealion colony (*lobería*); no public transport, but hitching easy in summer.

Almost due W and 180 km. along the coast, on the Gulf of San Matías, is **San Antonio Oeste** (10,000 people). 17 km. S is a seaside resort, **Las Grutas**, developed in the 1960s with good safe beach; the caves are not really worth visiting, but there is a good seafood restaurant, *Parrilla Bariloche*. ACA has a

Unidad Turística, with 6-bed rooms, no restaurant. *Tour du Golfe,* friendly, 3-bed rooms, E, provide cooking facilities. There is also a camping ground. *Restaurant Rambla* recommended. The whole of Las Grutas closes down in mid-March and retires to Buenos Aires. Between San Antonio and Puerto Madryn is Sierra Grande, where iron-ore deposits are being rapidly developed. The ore is piped in solution to an ocean terminal 32 km. E.

Hotels at San Antonio *Iberia,* Sarmiento 241, E with bath; *Kandava,* 2 blocks from bus and railway station, E with bath, hot water, clean, good; *Vasquito,* just acceptable, F; *Americana,* F, cheap and pleasant. Good beach 7 km. away.

Railway   via Viedma to Bahía Blanca and Buenos Aires and westwards to Bariloche. Trains from Buenos Aires (Constitución) (19 hours) 0820 Wed. and Sat. (*Lagos del Sur*). Leaves San Antonio Oeste 2225 Tues., Wed., Fri. and Sat. Fares: sleeper US$48.85, pullman US$40, first US$26, tourist US$18.35.

Buses   From San Antonio N to Bahía Blanca and S to Río Gallegos and Punta Arenas by Transportes Patagónicos. To Viedma 0700 daily. To Puerto Madryn and Trelew, Don Otto, 0430 and 1400, 4 hrs., US$6.50, leaving 45 mins. after arrival of trains from Buenos Aires. To Buenos Aires, US$23 via Bahía Blanca, frequent.

Route to Bariloche: paved. Continue 201 km. through bush country providing fodder for a few cattle, with a view to the S of the salt flats called Salina del Gualicho. The road then meets the Zapala-Buenos Aires highway at Choele Choel. Then 223 km. to Neuquén through an unbroken series of groves of tall trees sheltering vineyards and orchards. On (424 km.) to Bariloche along fast road, skirting the entire length of the reservoir formed by the Ezequiel Ramos Mejía dam. Then it drops over an escarpment to cross the Collón Curá river. Continue through the valley of the river Limay to Confluencia and the Valle Encantado. The journey can be completed in 11 hours.

About 250 km. to the S, in Chubut, is

Puerto Madryn, a port on the Golfo Nuevo. It was founded by the Welsh colonist, Parry Madryn, in 1865. Population, 40,000. A large aluminium plant is now operating (ask at tourist office for details of visits), and the town is becoming a popular tourist centre, with a casino, skin-diving and nature reserves, both near the town and on the nearby Valdés peninsula. Museo de Ciencias Naturales y Oceanografía on Domecq García and J. Menéndez, US$0.60, open 1700-2030 Suns. Airport. No Youth Hostel.

Hotels   (Very full in summer, make bookings early.) *Gran Madryn I,* L. Lugones 40, C, 2-star, friendly but rooms just acceptable; *Hostal del Rey,* Blvd. Brown 681, on beach, rec., C, 2-star, with radio and television, breakfast included; *Motel ACA,* Ribera Marítima Norte, D; *Gran Palace,* 28 de Julio 390, C, some E rooms without bath; *Yanco,* Av. Roca 627, on beach, C; *Península Valdés,* J.A.Roca 165, B, 4-star, sea view, suites available, comfortable, rec.; *Suyay,* 9 de Julio 57, E with bath, friendly, TV in lounge; *Argentino,* 25 de Mayo 275, E, clean, quiet, friendly, hot water, with shared bath; *Atalaya,* Domecq García 149, D, with bath, clean; *París,* Roque Sáenz Peña and 25 de Mayo, E, very friendly, rec.; *Tolosa,* R. Sáenz Peña 250, B, 3-star, friendly; *Vaskonia,* 25 de Mayo 43, F, hot water sometimes; *Apart-Motel Palma,* Av. Roca 7, new, E, heated, showers, no food but clean; *El Dorado,* San Martín 545, E, clean, shower, patio, but landlady not keen on backpackers; *Residencial La Posta,* J.A.Roca 33, E with bath (cheaper without), cooking facilities, clean, good. British not welcome; *Residencial Paula,* Albarracín 249, E, good.

Camping   At far end of bay, 6 km. S of town, is ACA site with hot showers and shady trees (Punta Cuevas) but many people camp on beach. There is a swimming pool in the rocks near the ACA camp site, which gets its water at high tide, very pleasant, and free. Also ACA and municipal at Ribera Sur, 2 km. S of town along beach. All facilities, very crowded. Camping out can be interesting as one can watch foxes, armadillos, skunks and rheas roaming around in the evening. Charges about US$2.50 a night p.p. and per car; discounts at ACA sites for automobile club members and holders of International Driving Licence.

Restaurants   *Aguila,* M.A.Zar and R.S.Peña, highly rec., good for seafood; *La Caleta,* San Martín 156, excellent; *Cantina El Náutico,* Julio Roca and Lugones, good food, especially fish; *Comedor ACA,* Costanera Norte; *París,* R.S.Peña 112, excellent and reasonable; *Parrilla Mayoral,* R.S. Peña 12; *Pizzería Quine,* Roca y R.S.Peña, good and not only for pizzas; *Parrilla El Soledad,* R.S.Peña 214, good salads; *Pleno Centro Confitería,* 28 de Julio y 25 de Mayo, good.

Tea Rooms   *Panadería La Proveedura,* good pastries; *Centenario,* on Belgrano and Paraguay. For excellent Welsh afternoon teas, *La Goleta,* Roca 87, 1700-1900 (poor sign).

Exchange   Banco de la Nacíon. There are no *cambios* as such, apart from Turismo Pu-Ma, 28 de Julio 46, but fair rates from travel agents. Some shops will change US$ cash.

Tourist Agencies   Tur-Mar, 25 de Mayo 157; Pu-Ma, 28 de Julio 40; Mar y Valle, Roca 39, does day trips to Valdés peninsula, 8 hrs., US$15; Receptivo, Roca 141 and Roca 303 y Belgrano, T 71910 or 71291, does tours at weekends to Valdés peninsula in off-season, US$7.50 p.p. The local tourist office, at Julio Roca 444, is open until after midnight in the tourist season, but only 0700-1300 Mon.-Fri. in winter. Recommended guide: Dr Pedro Fuentes Galliardo.

Car Hire   On Roca next to *Hotel Peninsula Valdés*, US$12 a day for small Peugeot.

Laundromat Lavarap, 25 de Mayo near Sarmiento.

Sport   Puerto Madryn is being promoted as a diving centre. Tours for those who have never dived before are organized by Safari Submarino, Mitre 80; Turismo Submarino, Av. Roca 743; Pimino in the harbour, all about US$11 per excursion. Swim in the so-called *parque submarino* amid sunken cars and a few fish! Trained divers seriously interested in marine life who have at least a week's stay should contact the Centro Nacional Patagónico at Av. Roca.

Transport   Buses from Buenos Aires, 2 a day with La Puntual, 21 hrs., comfortable, US$34; Sun., Mon., Thurs. and Fri., at 2030, with El Cóndor, daily with Costa Criolla at 2130, via San Antonio Oeste, change at Bahía Blanca, (US$ 29), 22-24 hrs. To Río Gallegos, also 24 hrs., four times a week. Bus to Bahía Blanca 0800 and 1000 daily, 12 hrs. (US$8 with Don Otto); 10½ hrs., US$18, with La Puntual to Mar del Plata, changing at Bahía Blanca. Patagónicos to San Antonio Oeste at 0800 and 2230, US$6.50. Same times to Buenos Aires, US$29 (cheaper to go to San Antonio Oeste and change to the train, but 9 hr. wait). Bus to Trelew with 28 de Julio company (every hour, 8 on Sun. US$1.60). Don Otto to Comodoro Rivadavia, Wed., Thurs., Fri., Sun. 0915 and daily at 1600, US$15.50. No direct bus to Bariloche, change at Trelew and Esquel (Aerolíneas Argentinas flight to Esquel Mon. and Tues. 1215). Taxi rank on the plaza. Bicycles rented at Roca and Yrigoyen on harbour, US$1.75 for 2 hrs.

Excursions   There are nature reserves nearby at Punta Loma on Golfo Nuevo (sea-lions), only 15 km. from Puerto Madryn (sea-lions, whales, penguins and flamingoes also frequent the Puerto Madryn area itself, sea-lions even invading the harbour); Punta Pirámides (sea-lions) and Isla de los Pájaros (sea birds) Golfo San José and Punta Norte (killer whales), on the Valdés Peninsula (see below). (Check opening times of reserves in Puerto Madryn; they vary.) The natural history of the region is most interesting, with other seal and penguin colonies, breeding ground at Golfo Nuevo for right whales, fossils in the cliffs, and *guanacos*, rheas and armadillos in the countryside. Most animals (except the whale) can be seen in the warm seasons, from October to April. See whales at Puerto Madryn in Sept.-Oct. Past the lighthouse and Naval Zone at Punta Delgada on the other side of the Valdés peninsula is Salina Grande, Argentina's lowest point, 35 metres below sea level.
    Take bus or hitch-hike (28 de Julio bus 0900, Sun., Tues., Thurs., Sat.-Sun. only in winter at 1000, US$3, return 1925) to **Puerto Pirámides**, with a population of 70 (ACA motel, C, also ACA campsite, and small friendly *hostería*, open Sept.-March, the *Posada del Mar*, 10 minutes from the sea, D. Also *Cantina El Salmón*, on the beach, good seafood. There is a shop that sells original Patagonian Indian work). Hydro Sports rents scuba equipment and boats, has a small restaurant, and organizes land and sea wildlife tours (ask for Mariano), boat trips US$10 for 1 hour. About 79 km. from Puerto Madryn is Isla de los Pájaros, on a good road. No one is now allowed to visit the island without special permission (only granted to recognized ornithologists), but free powerful telescopes are available on the opposite bank. At Punta Norte (176 km.) on the Valdés Peninsula, there are sea-elephants (breeding time in first fortnight in August, best seen at low tide), late spring and summer (Nov.-March), take own food, since the restaurant is expensive. At Caleta Valdés, you can see penguins and sea elephants at close quarters, but not at any specific point. Camping at hangar nearby, but bring fresh water with you as supplies are unreliable. At Punta Delgada (at the S of the Peninsula) most wildlife can be seen except the penguins, which have moved away. The peninsula is private property. One third belongs to one man, who grazes 40,000 sheep.
    Tourist excursions are organized by Tur-Mar, Receptivo and Coyun-Co Turismo, Av. Roca 37, Puerto Madryn. The usual tour takes in Puerto Pirámides, Caleta Valdés (or Punta Norte) and Isla de los Pájaros; the costs are US$20 p.p. on a bus tour, US$13 on a minibus (minimum 6 persons, e.g. Tur-Mar), US$ 90 for a car with guide, US$80 in a taxi for 4-5 people, US$80 in a taxi for 4 (will stay as long as you like and may also go to Riacho San José to see flamingoes); tours including a boat trip to see whales charge up to US$12 extra. Trips last about 9 hours, starting at 0800. On all excursions take drink with you (binoculars are also a good idea). Most tour companies stay 50-60 minutes on location, not considered sufficient by some. The excursion buses run in Jan.-March, but the peninsula is easily reached if one has one's own car in fact, the best way to see the wildlife is by car. Peninsular roads are excellent and there is a permanently-stationed Conservation Officer at the entrance to the Peninsula (he is very helpful). Tour to Punta Tombo **(see page 148)** including a little sight-seeing tour of Rawson, Trelew and Gaiman, US$7.50. Turismo Receptivo runs full-day excursions to Punta Tombo, Gaiman, Rawson and Trelew (US$20). Taxis to Punta Loma for sealions charge official price, US$12; Tur-Mar does 12-hour US$20 p.p. trip to Punta Loma and

the Ameghino dam (see below). The Punta Loma sealion reserve is open 0900-1200, 1430-1730 (easy hitch-hike from Madryn), Sept. and Oct. are best months. Tursur is the only agency that will arrange a minibus out of season, if you can gather eight people, to go to Punta Norte, Punta Pirámides and the shore opposite Isla de los Pájaros. You will not see whales between Dec. and June and there will only be young sealions as the older ones will have gone south.

N.B. If possible check all excursion dates in advance; it is very disappointing to arrive in Puerto Madryn only to find that one cannot reach the wildlife reserves. From March to September (when there is less wildlife to be seen) it has been necessary to take a taxi but we are now informed that the tours run all year, depending on numbers. Tours seem cheaper from Madryn than from Trelew, probably because Trelew has the airport.

The roads between Puerto Madryn and Puerto Pirámides (94 km.) and between **Puerto Pirámides** and San Antonio Oeste (328 km.) are now paved.

The Florentino Ameghino dam, 110 km. inland on the River Chubut, covers 7,000 hectares with water and irrigates 28,000 hectares in the lower Chubut valley, as well as producing electric power.

Along the Río Chubut are several towns. ***Rawson***, the capital of Chubut Province, 7 km. from the sea (*Hotel Provincial*, Mitre, C, good restaurant, hotel clean, but seems to be falling down), has law courts, a museum in the Colegio Don Bosco, a fishing port, and a riverside Tourist Office, 9 de Julio 64, T 213. Puerto Rawson is about 5 km. down river; you can camp on the beach, and *Cantina el Marinero* serves good seafood.

Some 20 km. up the Río Chubut is ***Trelew*** (90,000 people), a prosperous town which has lost its Welsh look. There is a pretty red-brick chapel in the centre, and a small museum in the old railway station, open 0900-1300, 1500-2045. A paved road runs from Rawson through Trelew, Gaiman (see page 148) and Dolavon, all on the river, to Las Plumas (mind the bridge if driving) and the upper Chubut Valley, all the way to Esquel (see page 136) and Trevelin.

Local Holidays   July 28 (Founding of Chubut); Dec. 13 (Petroleum Day).

Hotels   *Centenario,* San Martín 150, C, good and cheap restaurant, best to stick to simpler dishes; *Libertador,* Rivadavia 73, D, without breakfast 4 blocks from Plaza, service good, quiet, *Plaza,* F, on main square, clean, friendly, helpful; *Parque,* Irigoyen and Cangallo, D, good; *Residencial Rivadavia,* Rivadavia 55, F with bath, clean, rec.; *Touring Club,* Av. Fontana 240, excellent, E (with bath), the social hub of Trelew, chess is played here, colour TV, breakfast rec., coffee the best in town; *Galicia,* 9 de Julio and Rivadavia, very warm, E; without bath, clean. Cheapest are *Residencial San Carlos,* F, with private bath, Sarmiento 758, and *Provinciano,* Yrigoyen 525, F, poor and noisy. *Argentino,* Abraham Matthews and Moreno, E, clean, quiet, near bus station. *Hostal Residencial Plaza,* F in triple, clean, friendly, rec. *Hostal Avenida,* E, friendly, quiet, "rec., cheapest in town, nice rooms". Camping possible south of the town on the road to Rawson and Comodoro Rivadavia, on right about 200 metres beyond the bridge over River Chubut; turn off at the sign *Frasers Tea Room;* one can camp by the river, but beware of mosquitoes.

Restaurants   *Martín Fierro,* very good; *Luque,* H. Yrigoyen and Chile; *Parrilla Don Pedro,* intersection of Routes 3 and 25; *El Quijote,* 25 de Mayo 86, rec.; *El Mesón,* Rivadavia 540; *El Progreso,* San Martín 140; *Galicia,* Rivadavia and 9 de Julio; *Cantina Acapulco,* Belgrano and San Martín. *Pizzería Rosselli,* 25 de Mayo on Plaza, good and cheap.

Shopping   Mr Sturdee Rogers, *Rogers Shop,* Moreno 463, T 20696, serves Welsh afternoon teas, US$2, and sells traditional regional articles; also gives information on the Welsh of Patagonia. Welsh and English spoken.

Car Hire   Information at the airport; fixed rate plus charge per km. Also Alquilauto Fiorasi, España 344, T 31160.

Exchange   Lloyds Bank (BLSA), Av. 9 de Julio esq. Belgrano. Banco de Italia. Open 0700-1300 Oct.-March, 1200-1800 April-Sept. (1% commission). Turisur, Belgrano 320, accepts travellers' cheques at poor rate.

Post Office and Entel   25 de Mayo and Mitre.

Tourist Office, room 20 on 1st floor of Terminal Terrestre, additionally opens briefly at 0515 for travellers arriving from Esquel, also at airport. Free maps.

Tourist Agencies   Sur Turismo (exchanges cash and travellers' cheques), Belgrano 320, organize a few excursions to Punta Tombo US$15, to Punta Norte US$20; Punta Tombo Turismo, in *Hotel Centenario.* Recommended tours by taxi to the Valdés Peninsula (see above) cost US$75 for 4 for a whole day.

By Air   Airport 5 km. from centre; taxis cost about US$4. Buses from Puerto Madryn do stop at the airport, however. LADE flies, Trelew-Río Gallegos, 1-3 flights daily US$40, US$50 with Aerolíneas. Daily to Buenos Aires, AA and Austral, US$75. To Ushuaia, US$116 with Aerolíneas. Buenos Aires-Trelew night flights once a week in each direction with AA and Austral. LADE Buenos Aires-Trelew US$67. Río Grande (via Río Gallegos), 2 flights a week, US$113, with Aerolíneas or Austral, stopping at Comodoro Rivadavia, and Río Gallegos; to Comodoro Rivadavia- Esquel-Bariloche with LADE, Trelew-Bariloche US$28; crowded, book preferably in Buenos Aires in advance; 4 times a week, to Esquel with Aerolíneas.

Buses   from Buenos Aires to Trelew daily at 2100, 21½ hrs, US$25 (return 0700 and 2130 daily, 1705 Tues., Thurs., Fri. and Sat.). Bus to Bahía Blanca, 734 km., US$20 daily with Don Otto, 0600, few a week with La Puntual, 0600; to Mar del Plata, changing at Bahía Blanca, US$17.25 with La Puntual; to Esquel, US$12, 2130, 9¾ hrs.) with Empresa Chubut. Buses to Rawson every 20 min.; every 90 mins. to Gaiman, US$0.60; every hour to Puerto Madryn (last at 2200), US$1.60 with 28 de Julio; to Comodoro Rivadavia daily at 2000, and Sun., Wed., Thurs. and Fri. at 1035, US$9.20, 6 hrs; to Río Gallegos, Sun., Tues., Thurs. 2005, via Puerto Deseado. Rent-a-Car (Godfrey Davis) at Citrelew, 25 de Mayo and Entre Ríos. If hitching from Trelew, take the Rawson bus to the flyover 5 km. out of town.

Gaiman, 18 km. from Trelew, a pretty place with well-built brick houses, is now the most Welsh of the Chubut valley towns, and has a museum of the colony, US$0.30, in the old railway station (open in winter, Tues., Thurs. and Sat., 1500-1800; in summer, Tues.-Sat. 1000-1130 and 1600-2000). The only restaurant seems often to be closed, but tea rooms such as *Casa de Té Gaiman,* Yrigoyen 738 (US$3 with lots of cakes) and those opposite the square, *Plas y Coed* and *Ti Gwyn,* *Ty Nain,* and *Elma,* Tello 571, are open from 1500. Small municipal campground by river. Interesting local agriculture. Welsh-speakers will be interested in the cemetery above town. The Eisteddfodd, Welsh festival of arts, is held in early August each year.
     Wildlife may be seen at *Punta Tombo* and Camarones. Punta Tombo is 120 km. S of Trelew, on a dirt road branching off 5 km. SE of Trelew on the road to Rawson, driving time 1¾ hrs. There the wildlife is very varied: penguins, *guanacos,* etc. Season for penguins, Sept.-March (Dec.-Jan. is the time when the young are taking to the water). Check with the Tourist Office that it is all right to visit the penguins as from late March they are "off limits" as they prepare to migrate. You can share a taxi from Trelew; US$70 for one, US$90 for up to 4 passengers. Taxis available from J. A. Roca 200, Moreno 291, Av. Fontana y L. Jones, San Martín 470 and 751. Sur Turismo takes you there and back in a morning (0800-1300) for US$10. About mid-way between Rawson and Punta Tombo, a road leads off Ruta 1 to Isla Escondida (9 km., signed), no facilities, but lovely rock and sand beach with bird and wildlife; secluded camping. Good place to camp if you are visiting the wildlife at Punta Tombo early a.m. (the best time).
     Camarones, 275 km. from both Trelew and Comodoro Rivadavia, is less crowded. There is a large **penguin colony** 35 km. away at Cabo Dos Bahías along a dirt road (open in season only); free camping is possible there and in the town itself. Local buses very scarce; two a week, US$8, on Mon. and Fri. from Trelew (Don Otto), book at Uruguay 590, Trelew; bus leaves 0800 from San Martín and Belgrano, arrives 1130, returns to Trelew same day 1600 (reports disagree on whether Don Otto bus continues from Camarones to Comodoro Rivadavia). In Camarones take a taxi (if you can find one) to the penguin colony (US$15 return) and return to Trelew Tues. Hotel and restaurant at Camarones, *Kau-i-Keuken,* E, clean, friendly, good food, highly rec.

Comodoro Rivadavia, the largest city in the province of Chubut, is 396 km. S of Trelew. Petroleum was discovered here in 1907 and about 30% of all Argentina's oil production comes from wells to the S and W. A 1,770-km. pipeline carries the natural gas to Buenos Aires, and a petrochemical plant has been built. Renewed interest in the local oil industry is making the town boom. There is a regional Patagonian Museum at the ex-Hotel de Turismo, on the 2nd floor, worth visiting. Population: 120,000. From here southward, prices begin to rise very rapidly, so stock up before reaching Río Gallegos. Good beach at Rada Tilly, 5 km. south; walk along beach at low tide to see sealions (information from El Recreo campsite).

Local Holidays   July 28 (Founding of Chubut); Dec. 13 (Petroleum Day).

Hotels   *Austral,* Rivadavia 190, D, noise from street traffic but otherwise comfortable; *Colón,* on San Martín, E, run down, but quiet, safe and cheap; *Hospedaje Praga,* España y Sarmiento, E, shower, clean; *Residencial Azul,* C, good service, Sarmiento 724; *Comercio,* Rivadavia 341, friendly, near bus station, hot showers, F (may be bargained lower), good meals, US$3.80; *Pensión Boedo,* Rivadavia 453, cheap restaurant, mediocre food; *Hospedaje Belgrano,* Belgrano 546, D, with bath, clean, hot water; *Cari-Hué,* Belgrano 363, clean, quiet, cheap, F; *Rada Tilly,* E, modern, clean, 5 km. S. *España*, 9 de Julio 935, F, basic. *Hosp. Nanet*, España 1095, T 28867, F, clean, friendly. *El Patagón Motel*, access (S) of Route 3.

Camping ACA, 5 km. S at Rada Tilly, may be reached by hourly Expreso Rada Tilly bus from town, at N end of beach, cold water only; El Recreo, Rada Tilly, US$0.50 p.p., friendly, informative; and at 20 km. N signposted "Bar y Camping"; less inviting.

Restaurants No one eats at night until 2200. *Austral*, fair; *La Rastra*, Rivadavia 384, very good; *El Ancla de Oro*, Caleta Córdoba (18 km. from Comodoro); *Mar del Plata*, San Martín 371, good sea food, reasonable prices. *Los Troncos*, Av. Costanera and Rada Tilly; *Cocorico* (better) and *El Náutico*, Playa Costanera. Several *rotiserías*, much cheaper, on 400 block of Rivadavia, in municipal market.

Exchange Lloyds Bank (BLSA), Av. Rivadavia 264. Oct.-March 0700-1300; April-Sept. 1200-1800; no exchange transactions after 1000 in summer, 6 % commission on travellers' cheques; the Banco de la Nación, San Martín 108, has the best official rates on US$ but does not change travellers' cheques. *Hotel Comodoro* changes US$ at poor parallel rate. Roqueta Travel, Rivadavia y Pellegrini, and Ceferino, 9 de Julio 852, will change money. Video shop Ostoich, 25 de Mayo 957, will change at free rate, at back counter.

Post Office San Martín y Moreno. Branch in central bus station (beware of overcharging) closed Jan.-Feb.

Consulates Belgian Vice-Consul, Rivadavia 283; Chilean Consul, Sarmiento 936; Italian Vice-Consul, Belgrano 1053.

Tourist Office In the bus terminal. Travel agencies: Puelche EVT, Rivadavia 527; Richard Pentreath, Mitre 952; San Gabriel, Atlas, Monitur and Ceferino, at San Martín 488, 263, 811 and 372, respectively.

Buses Bus service to Buenos Aires daily at 1530 (Don Otto), 32 hrs., US$39 (also daily with La Puntual/Cóndor at 1300 and Sat. 2400). Angel Giobbi buses to Coyhaique (Chile), US$20, 13 hrs., twice a week (Tues. and Fri.), 0100, June-Sept. and 3 a week (Mon., Wed., Fri.) Oct.-May (weather permitting). Three buses a week to Bariloche, US$40, (Don Otto leaves 1400, Sun., Tues., Thurs., stops at Esquel midnight (US$30), arrives 0600 at Bariloche). Three a week to Río Gallegos (Patagónica), US$35). To Puerto Madryn US$15.50 (Don Otto at 1600). To Sarmiento, US$5, 2½ hrs. at 0700, 1300, 1900. To Mendoza, daily at 0130, 20 hrs.; to Córdoba, Tues., Fri., Sun., 1200, 33 hrs.

Air Services Airport, 9 km. Bus to airport from downtown terminal or opp. Aerolíneas Argentinas in main street hourly (45 mins), US$0.30; take bus No.6. 4-7 flights to Buenos Aires a day with Aerolíneas or Austral, stopping at Trelew, Bahía Blanca or both; offices on San Martín 421 and 291; Aerolíneas and Austral flight daily to Río Gallegos. Aerolíneas fly to Ushuaia; LADE flies twice a week Comodoro Rivadavia-Perito Moreno-Gobernador Gregores-Calafate-Río Gallegos-Río Grande-Ushuaia, with detour over Calafate glacier, weather permitting (fare to Calafate, US$38). Also to Río Gallegos via Puerto Deseado, San Julián, Santa Cruz. Taxi to airport, US$6.

Hitch-Hiking There is a truck stop outside Comodoro Rivadavia on the road to Bahía Blanca, where you can contact drivers if hitching. Take the bus leaving at 1200 from the bus station marked "Astra Km 20'. Expensive truckdrivers' restaurants along the road; buy food in supermarkets.

The road to Chile runs inland from Comodoro Rivadavia, amid oil wells, to (156 km.) Colonia Sarmiento (commonly known just as **Sarmiento**), population: 12,000 (archaeological museum next to cathedral, check opening times, may be closed at weekends), on Lake Musters, near the large Lake Colhué Huapí. 30 km. by dirt road S of Sarmiento there is a large petrified forest (Ormachea), well worth a visit (see next page). Taxis, US$17.50, leave from opposite *Hotel Lago Musters*, there are not many so book early. Sr. Gómez is reputed to do the cheapest tour, ask at bus station. The taxi allows only one hour to see the forest; bargain for longer, or hitch; in summer it's not too difficult. However, the warden, Juan José Valera, lives at Uruguay 43, Sarmiento, and is willing to give lifts to those in need when he makes his frequent journeys to the park. No bus station; all buses stop and start at a little office beside *Hotel Lago Musters*.

Hotels *Lago Musters*, P. Moreno and Ing. Coronel, run down; *Hostería Los Lagos*, Roca and Alberdi, D, good, friendly, heating, has restaurant. Food at *Colón*, P. Moreno 645, F, clean and friendly, and *El Gaucho*, Route 20, access Sarmiento. *Ismar*, 200 block of Patagonia; *Oroz*, 200 block of Uruguay. In Dec.-March you may be permitted to sleep in the Agricultural School (bring sleeping bag) on the road opp. the petrol pump.

Travel Agency   Julio Lew, Roca and Alberdi.

Bus   Overnight buses to Esquel on Sun. Tues. and Thurs. 3 buses a day to Comodoro Rivadavia, 0700, 1300, 1900 and Giobbi buses to Chile leave at 0200.

The road runs West from Sarmiento via **Río Mayo** (which has three hotels, the *Covadonga*, E, very good, *La Ruta* and *San Martín*), to Puerto Aysén in Chile. The Giobbi buses from Comodoro Rivadavia to Coyhaique, Chile, leave Río Mayo at 0600. A branch from this road goes 130 km. S to Perito Moreno, by Lake Buenos Aires. Another branch on the Río Mayo-Perito Moreno road turns W at 31 km. to Lago Blanco, where there is a small *estancia* community, 30 km. from the border with Chile (about 150 km. from Río Mayo). No hotel, but police are friendly and may permit camping at the police post. No public transport to Chile; wild but beautiful place. From Sarmiento you can reach Esquel (448 km.), at the southern edge of the Lake District (**see page 136**). The first 210 km. from Sarmiento are paved, then it is mostly a dirt or all-weather road, though short stretches have been paved.

Perito Moreno (population 1,700), at 400 metres, with an airport (flights to Río Gallegos Tues., Thurs. at 1100, US$18), is close to Lake Buenos Aires, which extends into Chile as Lake General Carrera. Also nearby are Lakes Belgrano and Burmeister, and the source of the River Deseado. Daily buses (US$2, 1½ hrs.) to Los Antiguos (*Hotel Argentino*, E, restaurant; service station) on Lake Buenos Aires (67 km. along Route 520), surrounded by orchards, where *pejerrey* can be caught. Halfway is Las Chilcas where Indian remains are found. The famous Cuevas de las Manos, a series of galleries with 10,000-years-old paintings of human hands and of animals, are interesting for those interested in rock art; they are beyond the "sprayed-on" version in the cave— red, orange, black, white and green colours. (The canyon on the way there is, however, very beautiful.) 118 km. S of Perito Moreno on Route 40, a marked road goes directly to the caves (68 km.) No buses, but the tourist office at Perito Moreno can supply names of drivers who can take you there, US$55, to be split among a party of visitors. On leaving Perito Moreno on the way to the caves you will pass Cerro de El Volcán, its crater is accessible; after pasing the Gendarmería on your right, take the first left (dirt road) at the 3-road junction with Route 40. It is 12 km. to the path to the crater—ask permission at the Estancia to continue. LADE flies from Perito Moreno to Calafate (Tues.) and Río Gallegos and Ushuaia (Thur.). Hitch-hikers to the S are warned that, outside the tourist season (Jan.-mid-Feb.), it is usually quicker to head for the coast at Caleta Olivia and go S from there than to take the road via Gobernador Gregores and Piedra Buena. There is a weekly LADE flight to Calafate, Tues.

Hotels   *Belgrano*, D with shower, clean, no heating, with good restaurant; *Austral*, D, modern, clean, open Dec. to Feb., both on San Martín; *Fénix*, E; *Argentino*, E; *Santa Cruz*, on Belgrano, E. Food is very expensive in Perito Moreno. **Restaurant**   *Americano*, opp. *Hotel Fénix*, good and cheap.

Camping   Parque Laguna in town, good hot showers, well shielded, US$2.50 p.p., (slide shows at the tourist office there) Municipal camping at Laguna Cisnes, with showers, toilets, shade, US$1 for tent, US$0.50 p.p., cars extra.

Exchange   US dollars can be exchanged at Banco del Sud, *Hotel Austral* and *Hotel Belgrano*, former gives better rates. Difficult to exchange travellers cheques.

There are 3 routes from Perito Moreno to Coyhaique in Chile: Perito Moreno to Chile Chico, then by twice-weekly ferry boat across Lake Buenos Aires, and then on by road to Coyhaique (very little public transport); Perito Moreno to Río Gueuguel, Paso Huemules, Coyhaique; Perito Moreno to Río Mayo, Coyhaique Alto, Coyhaique. There is a bus connection from Caleta Olivia (see below) through to Los Antiguos (border with Chile) every Mon. and Thurs., at 1500 (from Perito Moreno) and back to Caleta Olivia every Tues. and Fri. at 0800 (1000 from Perito Moreno), with Empresa Comi. Los Antiguos has *Hotel Argentino*, E, comfortable, with restaurant. Chile Chico is 8 km. from Los Antiguos; several jeeps a day cross border; ask in *Hotel Argentino*.

The road to Fitz Roy, 110 km. S of Comodoro Rivadavia, is paved, and a major short-cut now bypasses Puerto Deseado. Fitz Roy to Piedra Buena (2,600 inhabitants, **see page 152**) is unpaved, but paving is complete (although in very bad condition) from Piedra Buena to Río Gallegos (231 km.). Fitz Roy (named for the captain of Darwin's *Beagle*) is a tiny town, only two small *hosterías*, very primitive, not rec. Better stay 22 km. N at **Caleta Olivia** on Route 3 (13,400 inhabitants); hotels *Residencial Robert*, *Grand* and one other, all D; and camping at Yacht Club. Caleta Olivia, a good start-point for hitching S, is the urban centre for important oilfields, and is near Pico Truncado, the gas field which feeds the pipeline to Buenos Aires.

This is the area of the **petrified forests**, 70,000 years old, of fallen araucaria trees, nearly 3 metres round and 15-20 metres long: a remarkable sight. Taxi, Sarmiento to forests, US$15. It is best to do the trip by taxi or in groups, as tyre punctures are a menace. There are three sites you can visit: the Bosque Petrificado José Ormachea, due W of Comodoro Rivadavia, about 140 km. by road (116 km. paved—the unpaved part is practically impassable in the wet season), 32 km. S of Sarmiento, in Chubut; the Víctor Szlapelis, some 40 km. further SW along the same road; and Monumento Natural Bosques Petrificados, W of Puerto Deseado in Santa Cruz, surrounding the Laguna Grande on a road SW from Fitz Roy, 113 km. away. A new road has been built from Route 3 about 65 km. S of Fitz Roy to the Bosques Petrificados, which reduces the journey by several km.

South of Comodoro Rivadavia (254 km.), at Tres Cerros, is a new ACA hotel, C, quite attractive. At Piedra Negra, the previous turn-off for Puerto Deseado, there is a cheap hotel, *Florida Negra*. The only other building is a police post.

About 300 km. S of Comodoro Rivadavia is **Puerto Deseado,** with a population of 3,750 (airport), at the mouth of a river which drains Lake Buenos Aires, far to the W. (Hotels: *Los Acantilados*, C, and *Colón*, D.) The town was founded on July 15, 1884; its harbour takes large ships. A local tourist attraction is the Cañadón de las Bandurrias, sometimes known as the Grotto of Lourdes, 40 metres high. Nearby are islands with penguins and other birds, including the unique grey cormorant; local launches available. Lake Buenos Aires is reached by road in 7 hours; 280 km. to Las Heras, on to Perito Moreno, on the lake, 177 km., and a further 72 km. to the Chilean border at Chile Chico. This can only be crossed by walking across the river (you will wade waist-deep) or by going in a 4-wheel drive car.

It was at Puerto Deseado that a Welshman in Cavendish's expedition of 1586 gave the name of *pengwyn* (white head) to a certain strange-looking bird. It is only fair to mention the opposing theory that the name is derived from a Spanish word, *pingüe*, meaning fat.

Local holidays Jan 31 (St. John Bosco); Oct. 9 (Coat of Arms day).

From Puerto Deseado to Santa Cruz by the old road is about 470 km. Some 156 km. short of Santa Cruz and 4 km. off Route 3, it reaches **San Julián** (founded 1901, population of 4,480), the best place for breaking the 925 km. run from Comodoro Rivadavia to Río Gallegos. There is much wildlife in the area: red and grey foxes, *guanacos*, wildcats in the mountains, rheas, etc. The main activities are sheep raising for export, fish canning, and production of kaolin and clay. Clay grinding can be seen at Molienda Santa Cruz and ceramics made at the Escuela Provincial No.4. There is a regional museum. The ruins of Florida Blanca, a colony founded in 1870 by Antonio Viedma, can be visited. The cascade of San Julián is formed by two different tides. Punta Caldera is a popular summer beach. The first mass in Argentina was held here after Magellan had executed a member of his crew. Francis Drake also put in here to hang Thomas Doughty, after amiably taking breakfast with him. Near San Julián (15 km.) is Cabo Curioso beach, with an attractive natural cave.

Hotels *Municipal,* Av. Costanera and 25 de Mayo, very nice, well-run, good value, D, but no restaurant. *Residencial Sada*, on San Martín, E, nice, clean, hot water, own bathroom. Also older *Colón,* D, Av. San Martin 301 and Águila, F, friendly, clean. Good municipal campsite at town entrance, all facilities, but not suitable for tents, Av. Costanera betweeen Rivadavia and Roca.

Restaurants *Sportsman*, Mitre and 25 de Mayo; *Dos Anclas*, Berutti 1080; *Mi Refugio*, Mitre and Vélez Sársfield, *Soc. Chilena de Socorros Mutuos*, Ameghino 961; *Astra* on Route 3. Restaurant at San Martín 1375. Bars and tearooms: *Nos Amis*, Ameghino 1091; *Sweet Helen*, San Martín 485, *Aero Bar*, J. B. Alberdi and Pellegrini. Dancing at *Franoi*, 25 de Mayo 1198.

Post Office At Belgrano and Av. San Martín; telephone exchange also.

Banks Banco de la Nación on Mitre and Belgrano, and Banco de la Provincia de Santa Cruz on San Martín and Moreno.

Pharmacy *Del Pueblo* on San Martín 570. Hospital on Av. Costanera between Roca and Magallanes. Good wire car-windscreen protectors for US$5.

Air Weekly services to Río Gallegos, other routes end in Buenos Aires; many connect with flights from Comodoro Rivadavia by Austral and Aerolíneas.

Bus Transportadora Patagónica comes from Río Gallegos en route to Buenos Aires; Transportes Staller goes weekly to Lago Posadas stopping in Gobernador Gregores, Hotel Riera, Las Horquetas, Caracoles and Río Blanco. Transportes El Cordillerano cover the previous route but also stop at Olivia.

Santa Cruz, one of the best of the coastal harbours (airport) is near the mouth of the Santa Cruz river which drains Lake Argentino. Founded on December 1, 1878 and capital of Santa Cruz province until 1904. A deep-water port is being built 22 km. outside Santa Cruz at Punta Quilla. Population 3,000 (ACA *Hostería*, D; *Hotel Anel Aike*, D). Isla Monte León, 66 km. away (Route 1601, then Route 3 and dirt track) has walruses, penguins, beaches, fishing and camping facilities.

An unpaved road (Route 521) runs NW from San Julián to Route 40 along the foothills of the Andes. About halfway is **Gobernador Gregores** (Hotel San Francisco, acceptable, similarly Adelino, C).

At **Piedra Buena**, 35 km. W of Santa Cruz (10 km. N of Piedra Buena unpaved, but paved road to Río Gallegos and to Comodoro Rivadavia) is ACA motel, simple, functional but good, warm and nice food (E), also campsites N of town on Route 3. ACA breakdown station at Km. 247 on Route 3. The *Select* restaurant is very dear for what it offers. Route 1603 (unpaved, no petrol) from Piedra Buena to Calafate runs along the edge of a plateau with occasional panoramic views across the valley of the River Santa Cruz below. Then at about 170 km. it drops down into the valley itself to follow the river into the hills and to Lake Argentino. A pleasant run, without being spectacular.

Río Gallegos, at the mouth of the Río Gallegos, the capital of Santa Cruz Province, is 265 km. S of Santa Cruz; it has a deep-water port with a dry-dock. The tidal range here during spring tides may be as high as 16 metres. There is a large trade in wool and sheepskins. The town has recently improved greatly, and has a good shopping centre. (The cave paintings at Laguna Azul, 60 km. from Río Gallegos, are now reported not available for visiting.) Population: 42,000. Foundation Day: Dec. 9, 1885. Museum at Perito Moreno 35. The Regional Provincial Museum has collections of local flora, fauna, rock samples. ACA service centre. Cheap sheepskins (tanned) and very warm leather coats (*gamulanes*) at Puerto Aymond factory of Mr. Szasack (half the Buenos Aires price). Handicraft market at Roca 658, open 1300-2000.

Hotels Strongly recommended: *Alonso*, Corrientes 33, C, simple, very clean and comfortable. *Covadonga*, Roca 1214, C, fairly good; *Comercio*, Roca 1302, C, reported not too clean, overpriced, very busy; *Residencial Sachas*, Rivadavia 122, E, clean; *Río Turbio*, Zapiola 486 (opp. bus station for Punta Arenas), D, shared bath, English spoken, good. *Central*, Av. Roca 1127, E, central, quiet, cold shower, no heating; *Pensión Belgrano*, Calle Belgrano 119, very cheap, has good restaurant; *Florida*, first block of Vélez Sarsfield, E, hot water; private house at Vélez Sársfield 505; *Residencial Internacional*, at Roca and Sphur 78, E, with heating, friendly; *Colonial*, Urquiza y Rivadavia, E, shower, friendly, clean, can be noisy; *Entre Ríos*, Entre Ríos, E, fairly good; *Viejo La Fuente*, E, basic, dinner for US$3 incl. wine; *Aparthotel Niza*, quiet, good breakfast included, clean, rec.; *Tehuelche*, 16 km. from ferry at Primera Angostura on junction of Punta Arenas-Río Gallegos route, F, old fashioned bar.

N.B. Accommodation is hard to find in Río Gallegos because of the number of transient workers in town. Apparently no camping is allowed around Río Gallegos because it is a military zone apart from authorized municipal site on Route 3, S of town (US$1.30 p.p.). One is not allowed to take photographs either, for the same reason.

Restaurants Plenty and good, some specializing in sea food. *La Casa de Miguel*, Roca 1284, good. *Restaurant Díaz*, Roca 1157, good and cheap, rec. *Montecarlo*, Zapiola 558, good seafood, not the cheapest; opp. is good *heladería*. *El Palenque*, Corrientes 73, rec. *Café Carrera* has good but expensive breakfast, on Fagnano and Pres. Roca. *Pizzería Don Pizza*, excellent.

Car Hire Andrés Etura, Sarmiento 204.

Motorcycle Mechanic Juan Carlos Topcic, Costa Rica 25, friendly and helpful.

Exchange Lloyds Bank (BLSA), Sarmiento 47. Open 1000-1600. Banco de Santa Cruz; *Sur Cambio*, San Martín y Roca (no travellers' cheques); *Casas de cambio*, best rates. Change travellers' cheques in Río Gallegos if going to Calafate, where it is more difficult; good rates at Cambio El Pingüino (Zapiola 469); may also change European and South American currencies.

Chilean Consulate Mariano Moreno 144, Mon.-Fri., 0900-1400.

Post Office Roca 893. Telephones, Entel, Roca 613.

Tourist Office Roca 1551, friendly, helpful. (Also Alberdi 154.) They will phone round hotels for you.

Road Travel Poor road to turn-off to Puerto Natales, then good road to Punta Arenas, 303 km. (one lane only); taxi US$50-70; Punta Arenas via Puerto Williams will cost some US$140, with boat trip, one night at the port and a flight to Punta Arenas; buses (US$10.35) daily at 1300 (1200 Mon., 1230 Sat., with additional buses at 0900 on Tues., Thurs., Fri. and 1000 on Mon.) by Expreso Pingüino (booking office Zapiola 455, 0800-1250 and 1500-1930 Mon.-Fri. 0800-1230 and 1530-1900 on Sat.), take 6 hours including border-crossing process, now greatly simplified following the settlement of the Beagle Channel dispute.

Daily to Río Turbio: Expreso Pingüino goes at 1200 plus 1600 Mon., Wed., Fri., 6 hrs., US$15; San Ceferino (Entre Ríos 371) Mon., Thurs. at 1130, US$12.30; one bus on Sat. at 0830, US$11.50, to Puerto Natales. Make sure your car papers are in order if driving to Puerto Natales, Chile (go first to Tourist Office for necessary documents, then to the customs office at the port, at the end of San Martín, very uncomplicated); a weekly boat, but no air service. Pingüino daily at 2100 to Caleta Olivia, 11 hrs. Bus to Puerto Madryn 28 hrs. Route 40, which goes to Calafate (312 km.) is paved for about 220 km., with an ACA station and motel (under reconstruction in 1988) at La Esperanza (146 km.). A provincial road that goes west from Route 3 to Calafate is rough. A better alternative is Route 1603, which branches off Route 3 some 43 km. from Piedra Buena.

Occasional ships and buses (48 hrs.), to Buenos Aires, 2,575 km. Buses (Transportadora Patagónica, Gobernador Lista 330, T 2330) Tues., Thurs., Sat. at 2330, 14 hrs., to Comodoro Rivadavia, 808 km., stops at Fitz Roy daily at 2200, arr. 1000 next day, US$28; Calafate (Interlagos and Pingüino in summer, in winter pooled service, 1130, 6 hrs., US$9, very crowded; turn up with ticket 30 mins. before departure) Bus (Interlagos), Río Gallegos-Calafate, daily (Tues., Thurs., Sat. in winter) 1545, 5½ hrs.; Pingüino in summer Sun. 1300, Mon., Wed., Fri., 0930 and Tues., Thurs., Sat. 1600. No direct bus to Bariloche; you have to spend a night in Comodoro Rivadavia. Hitchhiking to Buenos Aires is possible in about 3½ days; appearance important. Car parts and repairs at Repuestos Sarmiento, on Sarmiento, owner very friendly and helpful.

Air Travel Seats on flights out can be difficult, especially in summer; make sure of your booking as far ahead as possible. AA and Austral fly daily to Buenos Aires, fare US$100 (day) and US$60 (night). LADE flies to Mar del Plata. AA cheap night flights are booked up several days in advance. AA's Buenos Aires-Auckland-Sydney flight (twice a week) stops at Río Gallegos, but the return journey does not. Numerous flights to Ushuaia (Tierra del Fuego), direct or via Río Grande (AA and LADE, US$22, cheaper than by bus, always booked, try waiting list). To Río Grande, 40 mins, LADE, or Aerolíneas Argentinas. Aerolíneas also has two flights a week between Río Gallegos and Punta Arenas (Chile). LADE flights to Calafate US$14, 2 a day in summer (about 3 a week out of season—also local airline Aeroposta, daily); to Río Turbio (2 per week). LADE flights also to Bariloche via Santa Cruz, San Julián, Puerto Deseado, Comodoro Rivadavia (3 a week, US$53), Trelew (twice a week) and Esquel, twice a week, US$40. To Comodoro Rivadavia with Aerolíneas Argentinas, daily, 1 hr; LADE to Perito Moreno, Tues. and Fri. Personal controls and luggage search at Río Gallegos, delays of 30 min. to 2 hrs. Book seats in Buenos Aires to avoid difficulties with departures. Taxi (*remise*) to town, US$3, no bus, hitching from car park is easy. **N.B.** Flights may leave early, sometimes up to 40 mins. LADE flights should be booked as far in advance as possible.

Excursion 134 km S, there is a penguin colony at Cabo Vírgenes; follow Route 526 (unpaved). (On the way is El Cóndor ranch, where the manager, Mr Blake, is reported to welcome visitors.) The Navy allows visitors to climb up Cabo Vírgenes lighthouse for a superb view.

From Río Gallegos a railway runs 260 km. to **Río Turbio** (6,000 people) where is found Argentina's largest coalfield; reserves are estimated at 450m tons and the state coal company YCF is building a deep-water port at Punta Loyola to service it. There is a director of tourism, Prof. César Cetta, in the municipality on San Martín. Hotels, always almost full: *Hostería Capipe*, Dufour (9 km. from town), C; *Gato Negro*, expensive (D) and poor; *Azteca* (ex-*Victoria*), E; *Hostería Municipal*, by ski-run in hills, 6 km. from town. Visitors can see Mina 1, where the first mine was opened in the hills; area good for trekking and horseback riding. The present mining and industrial area, with the school museum, can also be visited. Ask at YCF office in Río Gallegos for possibility of taking the coal train to Río Turbio (steam locomotives, 10-12 hrs.); it usually leaves at 0900, passengers free, lots of wild life to be seen. Train stops 3 km. from town, hitch or walk. Río Turbio is reported to have better travel connections than Puerto Natales and once in Río Turbio it is easy to catch a local bus into Chile. (Río Turbio to Argentine border post: 3 km.,—bus, US$0.30, last at 2230, some reports suggest that there are no buses either side of the border, though—a further 4 km. to Chilean post and then 14 km. to paved section of road connecting Puerto Natales with Punta Arenas.) The bus from Río Turbio to Puerto Natales (31 km.) connects with the bus arriving from Río Gallegos. No direct bus to Calafate. There is a LADE office and Expreso Pingüino runs daily at 0600 (plus 1300 Tues., Thurs., Sat., 6 hrs.) in summer or 1300 Wed., Thurs., Sat. in winter to Río Gallegos, but flights are cheaper and avoid the numerous passport checks as well as the essentially uninteresting ride. *Restaurant El Ringo*, near bus station, will shelter you from the wind.

Calafate (properly El Calafate), on Lake Argentino, 320 km. NW of Río Gallegos, pop. 3,000, is an expensive and developing tourist centre. There is a chapel dedicated to Santa Teresa in the centre; behind it Calle Perito Moreno gently climbs the large hill S of the town, from which one can see the silhouette of the S end of the Andes, the Laguna Redonda and Isla de la Soledad on Lake Argentino. It is the southern gateway to the Parque Nacional de los Glaciares, which is 50 km. away (the northern end is at Lake Viedma). On the alluvial plain by the lake there are many interesting birds, and in the other direction there is scope for good hill-walking. Colourful cave paintings (now closed except with special permission at Punta Gualichú) some 8 km. from Calafate, walking through the fields bordering the lake, or 12 km. by road. The Lake Argentino area is very popular; booking all transport in advance is a *must*. The store *Las Plantas* in Calafate is helpful with travel arrangements and exchange. The tourist office has a list of taxis but undertakes no arrangements; it is helpful but some information may be incorrect, so check. Small museum at airport. Note that credit cards are not popular, apart from hotels.

Camping and fishing permits, limited to official sites, from the Parque Nacional rangers in Calafate. Although the mountains are snow capped, you can camp out in the pleasant woods around the lake in summer and even swim in it on warm days. (Campsite details below.) ACA bungalows at glacier's edge (10 blocks from it) charge US$30 without breakfast a day; sleep 4 (staple foods for sale); there are 10 bungalows, 4 beds each, bath and wood-burning stove, restaurant (good) and *confitería* (poor). In summer, they are very popular and difficult to book; there is often no food available (especially out of season), so, as cooking is not permitted in the cabins, take food to eat cold. There is utter stillness apart from squawking flocks of parakeets and an occasional roar as ice falls off the glacier and thunders into the lake. People flock to the rural show on February 15 (Lago Argentino Day) and camp out with much revelry; dances and *asados* (barbecued sides of sheep). There are also barbecues and rodeo etc. on Día de la Tradición, November 10.

Hotels *Los Alamos*, A, comfortable, good food and service, has a mixed-media show, with dinner afterwards, rec.; *La Loma*, B in season (Oct.-April), E in low season, Roca and 15 de Febrero (can be booked in Buenos Aires at Av. Callao 433, 4° H, T 40-7476/40-9123), with bath, breakfast included, excellent view, modern, multilingual, restaurant, tea room, also has 14 cheaper rooms (also with bath), C, with special rate for International Youth Hostel members and owners of *South American Handbook*, also has two kombis for excursions for guests (run on most days); *ACA Motel Calafate*, Av. Libertador 1153, C for non-members, much less for members (can be booked at ACA, Buenos Aires), extremely popular, capacity 27 rooms, washing facilities, bungalows with good restaurant; next to this is ACA *Hostería El Calafate*, on Manzana 36, D, modern, good view, 26 rooms; *El Quijote*, D, friendly, comfortable, good restaurant; *Carlitos*, Comandante Espora, C, modern, clean and very friendly; *Tehuel Aike*, Av. Libertador 992, C, good meals, clean and modern; *Michelangelo*, Espora, C, modern, clean, excellent, reasonable, good restaurant, will accept travellers' cheques in payment (at a poor rate, though); *Cabañas El Sol*, Av. Libertador 1956, friendly, clean, D, good meals, rec.; *Hostería Kau-Yatún*, A, with bath, many facilities, 25 de Mayo (10 blocks from town centre), old *estancia* house, comfortable, barbecues, horses for hire; *Upsala*, Comandante Espora 139, C, with bath, good and clean; *Hospedaje Belén*, E, clean, warm, hot water, cooking facilities. Several slightly cheaper hotels but none less than E, e.g. *Hospedaje Jorgito*, Gob. Moyano 934, E, clean, hot water, heating, breakfast extra, always full; *Hospedaje del Norte*, Los Gauchos 813, E open all year, comfortable, a similar house across the street; *Hospedaje Echevarría*, Libertador 989, E, quiet, very clean, highly rec.; *Residencia Los Lagos*, 25 de Mayo, bakery pizzeria on ground floor, E, very comfortable and clean; *Residencia Bórquez*, also on 25 de Mayo, E, friendly. Rec. bed and breakfast at Espora 60, E p.p.; *Hospedaje El Arroyo*, 25 de Mayo 345, E, clean, use of kitchen. *Youth Hostel* at Roca y 15 de Febrero. Calafate has a tourist office from which caravans, tents (US$2 each, sleep 4) and 4-berth *cabañas* (US$3 p.p.) may be hired, showers extra. Note that all hotels except ACA are open only from October to April. Some private houses offer accommodation such as Enrique Barragán, Barrio Bahía Redonda, Casa 10, E, rec. Ask at tourist office if in difficulty.

Camping The nearest camping sites with sanitary facilities (2) are 10 km. from the glacier. Sites include a municipal camp site, dusty, crowded, run down, behind YPF service station, US$0.50, and US$2.50 for warm showers, no tents for rent; but beds in trailers, US$3.75, near airport. Park *refugio* is free, with firing for cooking and heating supplied free, suitable for 3. Permission obtainable from the Intendencia in Calafate, some 77 km. away. There is no water at the *refugio*. Take enough food and drink with you. Key from warden at the site. Also two free camp sites by lake—the lower one sometimes floods (no facilities). Autocamping Lago Roca (S area of the Glaciares National Park, 50 km. from Calafate), good restaurant, fishing, boating, horse-riding, beautiful scenery, cave paintings nearby. Hostería and Autocamping at Fitzroy village, 90 km. off road to Lake Viedma (Route 40), at the base of Cerro Fitzroy (or Chaltén). Horses for hire.

Restaurants *ACA Grill; Onelli*, Libertador 1197, excellent lamb, stays open out of season; *Michelangelo*, Tomás Espora, good food and atmosphere, rec.; *La Tablita*, used by locals, barbecues; *El Mirador del Lago*, excellent food, beautiful views; *Kauyatun*, for barbecues; *Tehuel Aike*, Av. Libertador 992, central, good food; *La Loma*, friendly, home food, picnic lunches supplied, good cakes and chocolates, beautiful view. Tea rooms: *Maktub*, excellent pastries, *Mirador del Lago*, *Kasbah*. *Bar Don Diego de la Noche*, at end of main road in direction of the glacier, good atmosphere. *ACA Unidad Turística*, near Moreno glacier, has a restaurant and a bar, expensive.

Exchange Travellers' cheques and cash may be changed at the Banco de la Provincia de Santa Cruz (Av. del Libertador) which charges US$15 on top of the usual commission. Advances (costly) on some credit cards given. Tourist office reported to change money. Avoid changing US$ at the administration of the ACA motel, which charges 30% commission. Travel agencies such as Interlagos and Lake Travel may be able to help. YPF garage and Chocolate El Calafate and some other shops give good rates for cash; also at reception of *Hotel La Loma* for travellers' cheques and cash.

Tourist Information In new building by bridge over Río Calafate. Tourist office friendly (has no 'phone, so you must walk to the hotel of your choice to check on vacancies); the area's infrastructure still requires development, especially accommodation. Tour to Moreno glacier information available here, US$10. Good map available from National Park office. Hotel prices detailed on poster at the airport and on large chart at tourist office. Sr. Jorge Antolín Solache owner of *Hotel La Loma*, Casilla de Correo 36, 9405 Calafate (T 0902-91016, Dec.-May), rest of the year Callao 433-4°H, 1022 Buenos Aires (T 40-7476), to whom we are very grateful for updating the Calafate section, has kindly offered to provide any information to travellers in the region. He speaks English, French, Italian and Portuguese.

Travel Agents Interlagos, Libertador 1175; Lake Travel Tours, Libertador 932; and Gador Viajes, on Libertador. To Moreno glacier at 0930 return 1700, without lunch US$14; Lake Roca, at 0930 return 1700, US$14; Fitz Roy, at 0700 return 1900, US$30, Gualichu caves, 2 hrs., US$4; Upsala and Onelli glaciers (boat trip and bus to Punta Bandera), US$42. Also try at *Hotel La Loma*, with *kombis*, where prices are usually lower. Aeroposta at Calafate airport flies over Moreno glacier in Aero Commander twin-engined planes, 5 passengers.

Film and slide show about Calafate, the Moreno glacier and climbing the Cerro Torres at *Tío Cacho* discothèque, every night, 1930 and 2230, US$1.50, also good audiovisual at *La Posta* restaurant every day in summer, US$4.

Transport By air from Río Gallegos (US$14, LADE, 2 a day in summer, out of season 3 per week) and Comodoro Rivadavia (often fully booked), US$38, Tues. only, also Río Grande (US$38, LADE), Ushuaia (US$28, AA or LADE), daily in summer and Perito Moreno, US$15 with LADE. Aeroposta also flies daily to Río Gallegos and back. To Esquel weekly on Tues., US$45. In winter there are often no flights for weeks if the weather is bad. The airport is about a ten-minute walk from the centre of town.

Bus Calafate to Ushuaia requires four changes, and ferry; total cost of journey US$43. By a rough but interesting road from Santa Cruz, Route 1603 (Route 288 is 100 km. longer with two bridges replacing old ferry crossings), 5 or 6 hrs. by car, but not always possible after rain. From Esquel go via Perito Moreno, good accommodation; then via Gobernador Gregores (**see page 152**), or better via Piedra Buena and stay at ACA motel, making journey only 50 km. longer. Very lonely road, occasional *guanacos*, flamingoes and armadillos, but mostly sheep. Few shrubs or trees. Sparse population. Interlagos Turismo bus runs daily at 0630 (summer) or 0915 (winter) to Río Gallegos; in addition El Pingüino runs daily at 0700 (1000 Tues., Thurs., Sat. in season, 6 hrs. US$9. Taxi to Río Gallegos, 4 hours, US$185 irrespective of number of passengers, up to 5 people. The Río Gallegos-Calafate road (323 km., of which about 220 km. paved) trip is worth while for the number of animals and birds one sees. No direct bus Calafate-Río Turbio.

There are no direct buses to Chile, apart from Lake Travel Tours' 3 services a week to Puerto Natales (US$40) via La Esperanza. The road trip from Calafate to Punta Arenas is very interesting for animal and bird watchers: from Calafate take Route 40 and "Complementaria O" to La Esperanza (150 km.), where there is a petrol pump and ACA hotel; thence to Cancha Carrera (border post Dec.-April), 63 km. to La Laurita, pay US$0.50 at control, then 4 km. to border, then paved road (14 km.) to Puerto Natales and 245 km. to Punta Arenas, 42 km. paved. Virtually impossible to travel between Calafate and Puerto Natales via Torres del Paine National Park because of the state of the road on the Argentine side. The easiest way to Río Turbio for Puerto Natales is to fly to Río Gallegos then take the daily bus; this avoids a long wait to change buses at La Esperanza. A cheaper, but laborious, way to Chile is to take a bus from Calafate to the checkpoint outside Río Gallegos, there catch the 1200 Pingüino bus to Río Turbio, there take a local bus to the frontier where the Chilean bus to Puerto Natales will be waiting.

N.B. The road between Calafate and Torres del Paine National Park requires 4-wheel drive as it is incomplete, and several large rivers have to be forded. It is nearly impossible to hitchhike from Calafate to Perito Moreno.

Excursions At the far end of Lake Argentino (80 km.) the Ventisquero Moreno, one of the few glaciers in the world that is growing larger, descends to the surface of the water over a five-km. frontage and a height of about 60 metres. In a cycle of roughly three years it advances across the lake, cutting the Brazo Rico off from the Canal de los Témpanos; then the pressure of water in the Brazo Rico breaks up the ice and reopens the channel. Pieces break off and float away as icebergs. When visiting the glacier, do not go down too close to the lake as these icebergs can cause great waves when breaking off, and wash people off rocks. From Calafate there are daily trips by Patagonia and Interlagos bus trips Nov.-April only, to the glacier's edge (return, US$10 from 9 de Julio at 0930 returning 1530, giving 3½ hrs. at glacier); you can negotiate to use the return fare if you come back next day. Taxis, US$60 for 4 passengers round trip. Lake Tourist agency does cheap trips to the glacier in summer, at US$9. The Parque Nacional truck leaves Calafate most mornings at 0800 and may give lifts (but arrive at 0500!); ACA Unidad Turística provides basic accommodation and cafeteria (in season, poor) about 1 hr's walk from the glacier. Out of season, trips to the glacier are difficult to arrange, but one can gather a party and hire a taxi, about US$43 for 1 hr. 20 mins. one way; take warm clothes, and food and drink; try asking at *Hotel La Loma* (where they have 2 station wagons/kombis) or taxis at cooperative, T 91044 (for 4 people).

Travel by road to the most interesting spots is limited and may require expensive taxis; the best connections are to Perito Moreno. Tours can be arranged at travel agencies, *Hotel La Loma* or with taxi drivers at the airport who await arrivals. Two recommended walks: (1) From the Centro Cívico in Calafate, visit Capilla Santa Teresita in Plaza San Martín; behind it is Calle Perito Moreno; walk to the top of the hill for a view of Calafate. Then go S to the Río Calafate, then to the new section of the town, where the ACA grill is. (2) From the Intendencia del Parque, follow the new road among cultivated fields and orchards to Laguna de Los Cisnes, a bird reserve, with flamingoes, ducks, etc. Walk down to Lake Argentino; 8 km. along the lakeside are the painted caves at Punta Gualichú. Unfortunately the paintings have greatly deteriorated but there are fascinating geological formations caused by erosion, on the edge of Lake Argentino, 12 km. from Calafate on the road to Río Gallegos: Excursion to Lake Roca, 50 km. S from Calafate. Trout and salmon fishing, climbing, walking, camping and branding of cattle in summer.

A worthwhile trip is by motor-boat (120-150 passengers, take your own food) from Punta Bandera, 50 km. from Calafate, to the Upsala glacier at the end of Lake Argentino, Lake Onelli and glacier (restaurant) and Spegazzini glacier, leaves 0800 daily in summer from Punta Bandera, returns 1600. Cia. Paraíso de Navegación (9 de Julio y Gregores) runs the lake excursions, tickets US$38 including transport to the port. Nova Terra does similar trip, same price lunch US$6.50 extra. leaves 0645. The boat passes by the 30-metre high glacier; it is reported however that the master often decides the weather is too rough and does not go to Upsala. Tourist Office is not always helpful about complaints. Put inshore and cross a little forest to reach the small Lake Onelli, quiet and very beautiful, beech trees on one side, and ice-covered mountains on the other. Small icebergs in the lake. Out of season it is extremely difficult to get to the glacier. Smaller boats (39 passengers) may run in winter; sometimes they don't run because of the danger of the glaciers "calving". Book tickets at Empresa Nova Terra, and at least two days in advance; take a taxi (US$35 round trip for up to 5 people); bus Calafate-Punta Bandera US$6, at 0700. On the road from Calafate to Punta Bandera, at the foot of Cerro Comisión, is a rock formation that looks like a herd of elephants facing you.

Another worthwhile excursion is to the N end of the Glaciares National Park to Cerro Fitzroy and Cerro Torres, 230 km. from Calafate; organized trip US$42 p.p. return. Interlagos and Chaltén now run a daily bus at 0700 from Calafate to Cerro Fitzroy, about US$5, 4½ hrs., returns 1530, allowing 2-3 hrs. at site. A new highway has been built from Calafate to Lake Viedma, journey is about 4 hours. There is a very friendly hostel there, *Lago Viedma*, providing also a restaurant, shop, horse-hire and guide service. The Fitzroy massif can be seen from the hostel, and one can walk for 3 hours (stupendous views: "anyone within 500 miles would be a fool to miss them" - Gordelia Thomas) to see Cerro Torres, where there is a *refugio*. There is a base camp at Cerro Fitzroy, good day's hike from Chaltén; Chaltén Patagonia Tours offers day trips Mon., Wed., Fri. To reach the base camp here, and at Cerro Torres, one must cross the Río Fitzroy; there is now a bridge. Ask at the *gendarmería* (border-police) in Calafate if you can join their truck which goes once or twice a week. On the way to Cerro Fitzroy (often bad weather) on Route 40, is the Southern Astronomical Observatory, managed by the Observatory of La Plata.

There is a *hostería* at Fitzroy and a camping site nearby, US$2.50 no matter how many days (food very expensive). A certificate is required from the National Park Office in Calafate to camp elsewhere.

Organized trips to the Glaciares National Park are too short to appreciate it fully; either go on a tour bus, then camp (good gear essential) or hire a taxi/minibus. The travel agencies charge US$200 for up to 8 people, US$300 to take you and return later to collect you; private drivers (e.g. Martín Drake, Bo. Plan Alborada 390—speaks English) charge US$300 for up to 8 to take you and collect later (also does similar arrangements for the Moreno glacier).

TIERRA DEL FUEGO (11)

Tierra del Fuego is the island at the extreme south of South America. It is bounded by the Magellan Strait to the north, the Atlantic Ocean to the east, the Beagle Channel to the south—which separates it from the southern islands—and by the Whiteside, Gabriel, Magdalena and Cockburn Channels etc, which divide it from the islands to the west. The western side belongs to Chile and the eastern to Argentina. The local Ona Indians are now extinct. Throughout Tierra del Fuego the main roads are narrow and gravelled. The exception is the road for about 50 km. out of Porvenir (Chile), which is being widened. The south has beautiful lakes, woods and mountain scenery. Part of this country is a National Parks Reserve: trout and salmon in nearly all the lakes and rivers, and in summer wild geese, ducks, 152 other species of birds, and imported musk rats and beaver. Local tax exemptions apply throughout Tierra del Fuego. **Note** that accommodation is sparse and the island is becoming popular among Argentines in summer. Hotel beds and seats on aircraft may begin to run short as early as November.

N.B.   Argentine time is normally one hour ahead of Chilean time.

Books   *Tierra del Fuego* (3rd edition), in English, by Rae Natalie Prosser de Goodall, US$10 (obtainable in Ushuaia and Buenos Aires), colourful maps by the same author. Also *Tierra del Fuego: The Fatal Lodestone*, by Eric Shipton, and *Uttermost Part of the Earth*, by E. Lucas Bridges. Available in U.S.A.: *Birds of Isla Grande (Tierra del Fuego)* by Philip S.Humphrey, and *A Guide to the Birds of South America*, by Rodolphe Meyer de Schauensee.

March-April is a good time to visit because of the beautiful autumn colours.

Camping   is very easy in Tierra del Fuego. You can, if so inclined, camp at most service stations. Many towns have municipal campsites which are either free or cost up to US$1. Private campsites can be very expensive.

There are two ways of crossing the Straits of Magellan to Tierra del Fuego. Coming S from Río Gallegos, an unpaved road turns left for Punta Delgada (1 hotel, 2 *hosterías*). (On the road Río Gallegos-Punta Delgada is Laguna Azul—3 km. off main road in an old crater; an ibis breeding ground, beautiful colours). A 30-minute crossing can be made by fast modern ferry from Punta Delgada to Punta Espora (no hotel—if desperate, ask the lighthouse keeper). The boats, which take 4 lorries and 2 cars, run every hour, with schedule determined by tides and a 1200-1400 lunch hour rest. Under normal conditions they run from 0800 to 2100 daily, with tidal breaks lasting 4 hours (autumn and winter timetable). Ferry-operators accept US dollars or Argentine or Chilean currencies. If going by car, do not go before 1000, as first crossings are taken by buses, etc. However, there is no bus service from Punta Espora (or Punta Delgada); buses to and from the island only through Punta Arenas. From Punta Espora (Bahía Aril is ferry terminal) a road runs through Chilean territory to San Sebastián (Chile) and 14 km. further to San Sebastián (Argentina) (usually 15 min. delay in crossing borders), Río Grande and Ushuaia. There is an Esso service station 38 km. from Punta Espora. Accommodation is scarce in the Chilean part (except for Porvenir—**see page 511**), and it is not always possible to cross it in one day because of the irregularity of the ferry. It is sometimes possible, coming and going, to spend the night at the guest house of ENAP at Cerro Sombrero (petrol there for employees only, but if you are running out, they may help), but do not count on it. Try *Hostería Karu-Kinka*.

The road from Río Gallegos goes on to Punta Arenas, from where (dock at Tres Puentes 5 km. E of town) there are is a daily crossing to Porvenir (passenger US$2, motor car US$33, 2½-3 hours; there is a passenger saloon with small cafeteria; get on first and you are invited on the bridge, get on last and you stand outside in the cold), from Porvenir at 1400 (Sun. 1700). If you want to continue, Senkovic buses to Río Grande leave at 1400 on Sat. and Wed. A 225-km. road runs from Porvenir E to Río Grande (6 hours) via San Sebastián; or by alternative route through Cerro Sombrero (see previous paragraph). On Chilean side of Tierra del Fuego, petrol available only at Porvenir. Reservations must be made at the hi-fi shop at Bulnes 637, Punta Arenas. The Argentine Consul in Punta Arenas is at Calle Valdivia 961 (T 22887). Border police at San Sebastián (ACA motel) will sometimes arrange lifts to Ushuaia or Río Grande. Hitching after San Sebastián is easy. Distances are roughly as follows in this area: Border with Chile at Monte Aymont; to Río Gallegos 73 km.; road to Río Grande via Kimiri-Aike (114 km. from Río Gallegos)—no buses; from here to Punta Delgada 30 km.; Punta Delgada-Punta Espora (ferry, free for pedestrians) 20 km.; on to Punta Sombrero (60 km.) and San Sebastián (60 km.) reaching Río Grande 80 km. on. The best way to hitch from Río Gallegos to Punta Arenas is to take any lorry as far as the turn-off for Punta Delgada ferry. Then there is plenty of Chilean traffic from Punta Delgada to Punta Arenas. *Hotel San Gregorio* will put you up if you get stuck near the turn-off.

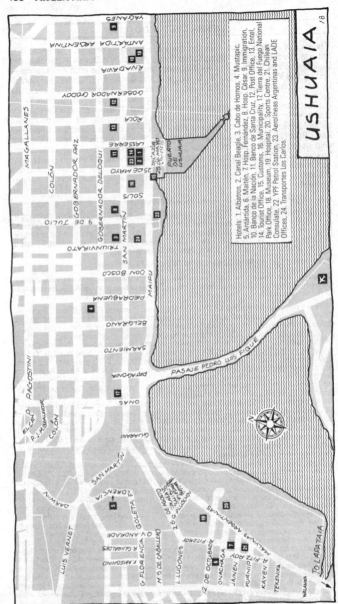

USHUAIA /8

Hotels: 1. Albatros; 2. Canal Beagle; 3. Cabo de Hornos; 4. Mustapic; 5. Antártida; 6. Mantén; 7. Hosp. Fernández; 8. Hosp. César; 9. Immigration; 10. Banco de la Nación; 11. Banco de Santa Cruz; 12. Post Office; 13. Entel; 14. Tourist Office; 15. Customs; 16. Municipality; 17. Tierra del Fuego National Park Office; 18. Museum; 19. Hospital; 20. Sports Centre; 21. Chilean Consulate; 22. YPF Petrol Station; 23. Aerolíneas Argentinas and LADE Offices; 24. Transportes Los Carlos.

Entering Argentina from Chile, be firm about getting an entry stamp for as long as you require.

The largest town in the Argentine part, with a population of 25,000 and growing, is **Ushuaia,** the most southerly town in Argentina, and probably the most expensive. Its steep streets (there are mountains, the Cerro Martial, at the back of the town) overlook the green waters of the Beagle Channel, named after the ship in which Darwin sailed the Channel in 1832. It is reached from Buenos Aires by plane (5 hours). There are impressive views of the snow-clad peaks, rivers, waterfalls and dense woods. There is a naval station at Isla de los Lobos. The people are engaged in sheep raising for the Río Grande *frigorífico*, timber cutting, fishing, and trapping, and Ushuaia's main street is lined with tax-free shops. A new road has been built between Ushuaia and Río Grande via Paso Garibaldi. Some skiing is done in the area. Ushuaia and its environs are worth a 2-3 day visit. Those arriving from Chile by road should report to Investigaciones on Kuanip 787. See Documents, **page 165**. **Warning** There have been complaints about the tap water in Ushuaia.

Hotels *Cabo de Hornos*, San Martín and Triunvirato, B, comfortable, TV, spotless, good value (but surcharge on credit cards); restaurant no longer open to non-residents; *Las Lengas*, Goleta Florencia s/n, C, cold, no English spoken, breakfast only meal; *Maitén*, 12 de Octubre 138, D-C, good value, clean, English spoken by manager Herbert Locker, who is very helpful; *Canal Beagle*, Maipú 599, B (reductions for members of the ACA), good restaurant (catering usually for tour groups); *Albatros*, Maipú 505 and Lasserre, clean, modern, good service, B including large breakfast, but lighting poor; *Malvinas*, Deloqui 609, C, with bath, breakfast included, pleasant, helpful, central heating; *Antártida*, San Martín 1600, C, friendly, restaurant with fine views, rec.; *Capri*, San Martín 720, D, clean, friendly, permanent residents; *César*, San Martín 752, D, with bath, comfortable, friendly, clean, no breakfast, rec.; *Mustapic*, Piedrabuena and Deloqui, friendly multi-lingual owner (Sr Miro, from Yugoslavia), C/D (may bargain lower), no singles, highly rec., good breakfast, exceptionally clean, can leave luggage; *Hospedaje Ona*, 9 de Julio 27, on waterfront, noisy, E (without breakfast), heater in room, used by lorry drivers, difficult to get into, but rec. *Las Goletas* (no sign) Maipú 857 on waterfront, D, some rooms shared (3-6), in bunk beds, TV room (where they will allow sleepers if there is scarce accommodation), hot showers, heating. *Fernández*, Onachaga 68, very friendly, hot water, good but expensive meals, D. *Ushuaia Apartment Hotel* for self-catering visitors, very friendly. *Club Naval*, on hill 3 km. out of town, has begun taking visitors, D, restaurant. *Casa de Sra Hilda Sánchez*, Deloqui 786 (corner 9 de Julio, T 92438), E, crowded and noisy but rec., clean, students and backpackers catered for; camping at the back, with use of facilities; cheap meals available. Sra Sánchez is reported to be building a new hotel at the site of her old house, Deloqui 395. Rooms, D, at home of Ismael Vargas (some way from centre), Kayen 394 (T 91125) Sra Vargas speaks English; *Kau Pen*, Piedrabuena 118 y San Martín, E, clean, warm, hot water, kitchen, but little privacy. Youth hostel in the Sports Complex; also at Piedrabuena 180, E. *Cabaña* at Colón 631, sleeps up to 4, E p.p., modern, comfortable. Lodging in Ushuaia has recently become rather a problem esp. Jan.-Feb., but even in winter hotels are very expensive. Enquire at Tourist Office for accommodation in private homes (they are said to have a list of 200), and for campsites, some of which are free.

Camping Camping Lago Roca, at Lapataia, by forested shore of Lake Roca in Parque Nacional, with facilities for car and tent, US$1 p.p., caters for travellers without car, hires horses, Dec.-March, including gas (18 km. from Ushuaia; weather can be bad). Can be reached by bus Jan.-Feb. Hot showers evenings, small shop, cafeteria. There is a free site by restaurant, with no facilities, on road to Parque Nacional about 4 km. from Ushuaia at Cascadas de Río Pipo, and another, 2 km. from the Lake Roca campsite close to a beaver dam. Camping at Monte Susana, 10 km. W, Ensenada, 14 km. W, and Río Olivia, 12 km. E of Ushuaia. Tents for hire at Parque Nacional Tierra del Fuego, US$3 per night. Hot showers at Sports Centre on Malvinas Argentinas.

Restaurants *Los Canelos*, Maipú y 9 de Julio, reasonable, rec.; *Tío Rico* on San Martín is good. *Tante Elvira*, Av. San Martín 238 near Rumbo Sur, good seafood. *Los Amigos*, San Martín, cheap; *Moustacchio*, San Martín y Godoy, sea food, good value, warmly rec.; *Los Gringos*, Triunvirato between San Martín and Maipú, pleasant, reasonable, open 1200-1500, 2030-2300. *Los Inmortales*, on San Martín, good, cheap; *ACA Grill*, good value and food. *Cafetería Acuario*, San Martín 124, pleasant. Best place to eat lamb is at *Tolkeyen*, Estancia Río Pipo, 5 km. from town. Cheap and good food at restaurant above the sports gymnasium at Maipú and 12 de Octubre. *Blanco y Negro Importaciones*, delicatessen; *Tío Carlos*, Colón 756, good *parrillada*; Ideal, San Martín 700 block, good food (especially seafood stew and empanadas) and cheaper than those listed above, but watch the bill, rec. Also cheaper and well rec. is *La Pasiva*, San Martín 1275, very good for pasta. *Der Garten*, Swiss *confitería*, San Martín 620, in Galería shopping arcade, rec. Excellent homemade chocolate sold at a shop at San Martín 785. *Panadería Primavera*, San Martín, good. The coffee bar at the airport is very expensive. Ask around for currently available centolla (king crab) and cholga (giant mussels). Food and drink (apart from the duty-free items) in Ushuaia are very expensive. Supermarkets: Surty Sur (with clean toilets, San Martín y Onas) and Sucoop, Paz 1600. Popular spots at night include *Magnum* on San Martín, *Yoppen* at Rivadavia 200 and the disco *Alexander* at 9 de Julio y Maipú.

N.B. Restaurants here and elsewhere on Tierra del Fuego do not begin to serve until 2100-2130 in summer; it is advisable to book in advance in the high season.

Shopping Many duty-free shops along main shopping street. Cheap cigarettes, perfume, clothing, drink and chocolates available. Prices said to be lower, and stocks better, than in Punta Arenas or Ciudad Stroessner/del Este (Paraguay). Good boots at Stella Maris, San Martín 443. Bookshop at San Martín y Sarmiento.

Car Hire Rentacar, San Martín 330, T 92185; Remise, San Martín 987, T 92222, Rent Austral, Antártida Argentina 75, T 92620; Aukiler, T 93350 code 360; AutoSar, T 93350 code 223.

Museum Museo Territorial, Maipú 173, open Mon.-Sat. 1600-2000, US$0.60, small but interesting display of early photos and artefacts of the local Indian tribes; relics from the missionaries and first settlers, etc. Also known as the "museum at the end of the world". Highly recommended. Good bookshop in building. Also Post office in building, open afternoons when the main one is closed.

Exchange Banks are open mornings only in Ushuaia. Travellers' cheques can be changed at Banco del Sud (Roca 30). No cash advance on Visa card available. Parallel rates available with difficulty; tourist agencies give poor ones. Said to be better at Monsieur Charles' shop, Av. San Martín; try also *El Globo Naranjo* (same street), or *La Ponderosa* shop at Antártida Argentina 209, or other duty-free shops, or *Hotel Cabo de Hornos*.

Laundromat on Triunvirato, between San Martín and Deloqui, open weekdays 0900-2100.

Chilean Consulate on Maipú and Kuanip.

Tourist Office Av. San Martín 512 office 2 (T 91423), friendly and helpful (will look after luggage while you trek). Large chart of hotels and prices and information on staying at Estancia Harberton, off road to Río Grande. Tourist Office at airport has information on hotels. *Magnum Restaurant* on Av. San Martín has an audio-visual show (slides and music) most evenings at 2230, US$6 including first drink.

Travel Agents Rumbo Sur, San Martín 342, does US$12 short tour every morning, and a medium (US$20) and longer (US$28) tour alternate afternoons, and organizes bus to ski slope; Antartur, in *Hotel Cabo de Hornos*. Onas Tours, 25 de Mayo 50, just off main street, very friendly. Tiempo Libre, San Martín 154, T 91296, recommended. Recommended guides: Domingo Galussio, Intervú 15, Casa 211, 9410 Ushuaia, bilingual, not cheap; and Karl Renoth, Don Bosco 321, 9410 Ushuaia, T 92723, speaks English and German.

Buses run daily between Ushuaia and Río Grande (4 hrs.) at 1930 and also at 2400 on Sat. and Sun., US$10, Transporte Los Carlos, Triunvirato 57. Taxi to Río Grande about US$75. There are bus services between Río Grande (**see page 161**) and Porvenir in the Chilean part of the island (242 km., 6-8 hrs.) but no air connection.

Airport Aerolíneas Argentinas flights daily (twice, except Tues,. and Sat.) from Buenos Aires all year round (change at Río Gallegos). (LADE office on Av. San Martín, Aerolíneas at Maipú y Lasserre, open Mon.-Fri. 0900-1200, 1500-1800). To Río Grande US$10 (LADE and AA), daily at 0900 and several afternoons at 1300-1400; to Calafate via Río Grande and Río Gallegos (book early) US$28, 4 a week at 0900; to Trelew, US$125; to Comodoro Rivadavia, via Río Gallegos, US$84; to Río Gallegos, US$18, heavily booked (daily). To Bariloche, US$60, Tues. and Sun. at 0800, stops at Río Grande, Río Gallegos, Santa Cruz, San Julián, Puerto Deseado, Comodoro Rivadavia, Trelew and Esquel. To Buenos Aires, day flight US$90, night flight US$50 (booked up at least 5 days ahead). LADE flies every day: Ushuaia, Río Grande, Río Gallegos, Calafate (US$28), Gobernador Gregores, Perito Moreno, Comodoro Rivadavia; with small detour over complete glacier, weather permitting. Get window seat on left side.

Weather often impedes flights in winter, and in the summer tourist season it is sometimes difficult to get a flight out. At the airport ask around for a pilot willing to take you on a ½ hr. flight around Ushuaia; US$16 for 2 people. Alternatively ask about flights at the tourist office. Taxi to airport, US$1, or 20 mins. walk (no bus).

New airport being built: stopovers for flights between Buenos Aires and New Zealand are being planned.

Sport Sports Centre on Malvinas Argentinas on W side of town (close to seafront). Ice skating rink at Ushuaia gymnasium. Diving: write to Club de Actividades Subacuáticas for information about scuba diving in the Beagle Channel. The Austral marine biology station has a display on Calle Roca of marine life. Director: Dr. C. Kuhnermann, Casilla 157, Buenos Aires. Beachcombing can produce whale bones. Fishing: trout, contact Asociación de Caza y Pesca at Maipú and 9 de Julio, with small museum. Fishermen may be interested in visiting the fish hatchery 7 km. E of Ushuaia, visiting hours daily 1400-1700. There are brook, rainbow and brown trout and land-locked salmon. Take No. 1 bus E-bound on Maipú to the end of the line and continue 2½ km. on foot to the hatchery. Birdwatchers will also find this ride rewarding. Skiing, hiking, climbing: contact Club Andino, Solís 50. Skiing: A downhill ski run (beginner standard) with chairlift (US$3), equipment rental (US$5.70), lessons and cafeteria is found on Cerro Martial. It is open June-July, has lights for night-skiing and is run by Club Andino; bus leaves Rumbo Sur, San Martín 342, each hour for ski slope, US$1.50 return. 20 km. E of Ushuaia is Valle Tierra Mayoria, a large flat valley with facilities for cross country skiing, snow shoeing and snowmobiling; rentals (US$7 the day) and a cafeteria; bus a.m. and 1400 from *Hotel Las Lengas*, US$3 return.

Excursions   For *Lapataia* bay, take van from Solís 50, 4-6 times a day, about US$4 p.p. plus US$1.50 National Park fee; also good catamaran trips. Lake Escondido US$8, 50 km., 3-4 hrs, to *Petrel Inn*. There is a minibus (US$2) into the National Park, from San Martín 56, at 0900, 1100, 1500, 1900, returning from National Park *confitería* an hour later. There are excursions to the Martial glacier (itself unspectacular but fine scenery) about 7 km. behind the town; take road behind *Hotel Antártida*, 2 km. to small dam, then 3-4 hour walk along trail. There is a chairlift to the glacier (operating schedule unclear), US$1.50 round trip. (In winter the glacier is inaccessible, even on foot.) Also to the so-called Indian Cemetery, 5 km. W of town (archaeologists on site pleased to tell of Indian history), to Lendegaia and Lapataia bays, the falls of the Olivia river. In winter the temperature drops to as low as -12°C, in summer it goes up to 25°C. Beaver inhabit the Parque Nacional near the Chilean border; one may see beaver dams and with much luck and patience the beavers themselves after dark, stand still and down-wind of them: their sense of smell and hearing are good, but not their eyesight.

Hosterías at Lapataia: *Alakush*, L, 20 km. W of Ushuaia, on Route 3, in the Parque Nacional Tierra del Fuego, open for summer season from Dec. 1 to March, minibus service to Ushuaia, friendly and helpful, rec. At Lake Fagnano: *Hostería El Kaiken*, also bungalows, nice site, well-run facilities, cheap drinks, on a promontory 93 km. from Ushuaia, C including real bath. At Lake Escondido *El Petrel Inn*, 54 km. from Ushuaia, D (after a spectacular climb through Garibaldi Pass, on the road to Río Grande). Facilities at *Kaiken* are open all year round, but at *Petrel* only from Dec. to March. All are run by the ACA and offer reductions to its members; these inns are rec. for peace and quiet.

Road-wise, the old Route 3 circles close to the lake while the newer Route 3 bypasses most of it. Even in the summer the climate can often be cold, damp and unpredictable. It is possible to hitch-hike, though with difficulty, as far as Lapataia; only tour buses go there. Rangers in the park are friendly and will sometimes put people up for a couple of days (as will police) and help with places to visit. A ranger truck leaves Ushuaia every weekday at 1300 and picks up hitch-hikers along the road. Park entrance US$1.

Rumbo Sur runs good excursions: 3 hour trip to Tierra del Fuego Parque Nacional, US$5. Taxi to Park, US$9-12, shop around. Los Carlos bus to Lake Fagnano, 2½ hrs., US$4.70, then from Lake to Río Grande 2 hrs., US$5. Tours also arranged to Lake Fagnano and aerial excursions over the Beagle Channel (with local flying club, hangar at airport, 3-5 seater planes, 30 mins. US$19), Lake Fagnano, Lapataia and Ushuaia Bay. To Lake Escondido/Fagnano US$11.15; bus to Puerto Almanza (on Beagle Channel), 75 km., 4-5 hrs, US$9. Rumbo Sur does a whole-day, US$35 (or half-day US$20) trip by catamaran down the Beagle Channel to see wildlife, with return by bus, highly rec.

Off the road to Río Grande from Ushuaia is the Estancia Harberton, the oldest on the island, which now offers tours and tea, and where you can camp.

Sea Trips   Boat and bus 7 hr. tour to the Isla de los Lobos y Pájaros along the Beagle Channel, US$36. Take food, on board overpriced. Antartur, *Hotel Cabo de Hornos*, organizes 2-3 weekly tours to Antarctica by boat, 11 days, visit military base, in Jan. and Feb., US$1,250 and more. Similar trips are organized on the ship *Mediterranean Sky*, price range US$580-3,300, by Cruzadas Argentinas; can be arranged with Calafate Travel, Zapjola 130, Río Gallegos. No ferry service to Puerto Williams, Chile; only accessible by private launch (from US$90 p.p.) or via Punta Arenas. The ship *Ethel B*, captain Pedro Esteban Buchet (of Kilak Expeditions) does trips up the Beagle Channel to the Chilean border (he is also planning trips to Cape Horn, using the shelter of islands en route, weather permitting). In summer, 3 hr. boat trips may be taken to see sealions at the Isla de los Lobos (US$14), also Les Eclaireurs lighthouse (US$13, 4 hrs, in the *Angel B*), the Bridges islands and Isla Redonda, where the Government is breeding *guanacos*. Ask at Rumbo Sur, leaves at 1500 daily. Interesting boat trips of 3 weeks' duration on the 2,346-ton *Lindblad Explorer* cost from US$4,600.

Río Grande (20,000 people) 236 km. from Ushuaia, is a port in windy, dust-laden sheep-grazing and oil-bearing plains; the oil is refined at San Sebastián (with ACA motel, D) in the smallest and most southerly refinery in the world (service station open 0700-2300). The *frigorífico* plant in Río Grande is one of the largest in South America; so is the sheep-shearing shed. Accommodation is very difficult (especially if arriving at night); we hear that one can sleep in the hospital's emergency room, if it's not in use. ACA garage on sea-front has free hot showers for men, as has the gymnasium. Fill up with gasoline here.

Local Festivals *Trout Festival*, 3rd Sunday in February; *Snow Festival*, 3rd Sunday in July; *Woodsman Festival*, 1st week of December.

Hotels *Federico Ibarra*, Rosales and Fagnano, rec., good restaurant, B; *Villa*, San Martín 277, C, very warm; *Hospedaje Noal*, Rafael Obligado 557, D, clean, cosy, friendly, rec.; *Arboleas*, E, Rivadavia 637, excellent value, rec.; *Atlántida*, Av. Belgrano and Rosales, said to be best, always full; *Yaganes ACA*, Av. Belgrano 319, A, clean, comfortable, has a restaurant; *ACA Albergue*, on Luis Piedrabuena near Gymnasium, B, 4-bed rooms, very comfortable, central heating, hot showers, restaurant, US$10 a meal; *Miramar*, Belgrano and Mackinlay, E-D without bath, no breakfast, heated, hot water ("a plywood palace"); *Hospedaje Dany*, Moreno 781, E, heated, hot shower, clean; *Residencial Arboles*, Rivadavia 649, E, clean, heated, hot showers; *Motel Sur*, on beach, truckers' place, clean and cheap, being enlarged. *Residencial Las Lenguitas*, Piedrabuena 436, E, bathroom shared between 2 rooms, good value; *Hospedaje Irmary*, Estrada 743, clean and pleasant, E (being enlarged); *Residencial Rawson*, Estrada 750, E with bath, clean, rec.; *Pensión La Cabaña*, 9 de Julio 1025, E; *Tierra del Fuego*, Perito Moreno 98, F, basic, clean. *Pensión Río Bueno*, J. B. Alberdi 616, E, simple, clean and friendly, men only.

Youth Hostel, for males only, but apparently always filled by local workers.

Restaurants *Las Malvinas*, reasonable; *Yaganes* (good for centolla); *Rotisería El Trébol*, Calle Belgrano, counter snacks; *Don Rico*, in ultra-modern building in centre, interesting; *Confitería Roca*, Roca 629, open all hours, reasonably priced food and bar; likewise *A Todas Horas* in same street. Good workmen's café, *Mary's*, Moyano 373. *Supermarket Sados* on San Martín, near 25 de Mayo. Smart place for a drink, *Paris*, Rosales 448.

Exchange Parallel rate in import shops, e.g. Yehuín, San Martín y Rivadavia. Try *Confitería Roca*, Roca 629. Tends to be difficult: if coming from Chile, buy australes there.

Car Hire Rent-a-Car, Belgrano y Ameghino, T 22657.

Tourist Information at the Municipalidad, Mon.-Fri., on Calle Sebastián El Cano.

Airport 4 km. W of town. Río Grande-Buenos Aires flight (Aerolíneas Argentinas, several daily, 3 night flights weekly), 5 hours, stops at Río Gallegos and Comodoro Rivadavia (some also at Bahía Blanca). LADE to Buenos Aires, Wed. and Fri., many stops, always full; to Bariloche, 8 hrs., US$45. LADE flight Río Grande to Ushuaia, US$15.50 return, heavily booked (also Aerolíneas, US$10 one way). A bus Río Grande-Ushuaia also connects with the Aerolíneas night flight from Buenos Aires. To Río Gallegos, US$40 (book early in summer). To Calafate, stopping at Río Gallegos, US$38; to Comodoro Rivadavia, US$67. Telephone LADE office (behind *Hotel Yaganes*) open Mon.-Fri., 0900-1200 and 1530-1900, 0700-1200 on Sat., T 308. Conversely, travel with Aeronaval (if you're lucky), mostly Hercules transports, for half the price—enquire at airport. "Rent-a-plane" at airport, US$25 an hour. No flights to Chile.

Buses leave at 0600 Tues. and Sat. US$10 (Senkovic, San Martín 959, T 22345), for Porvenir, Chile (about 230 km.), no food or drink provided, no toilets, nor stops, for 6 hrs., meticulous passport and luggage control at San Sebastián (ACA motel, 144 km. before Porvenir). Ferry journey from Porvenir to Punta Arenas (2 hrs.) can be very rough and cold, US$2 p.p., US$33 per car. Bus from landing stage, Tres Puentes, into Punta Arenas (5 km.) necessary (US$0.85). Flight across Strait, US$20 each. Transportes Turicisne go to Porvenir, very crowded and filthy, avoid at all costs. Daily bus service at 1230 and 1900 except Mon. and Fri., and at 1400 and 1900 on Mon. and Fri., with Los Carlos, Estrada 568 to Ushuaia, 234 km., on an unpaved road, US$10, 4 hours, stopping at *Hostería El Kaikén*, Lake Fagnano, for a drink. Book tickets to Ushuaia at the *Hotel Antártida*, as far ahead as possible. The bus leaves one block away from *Hotel Miramar*. In winter the bus leaves on Mon., Wed. and Fri. only (1830).

Excursion 11 km. N lies the Salesian mission and the regional museum housed in the original chapel and first parish church of Río Grande. Although the exhibits are not at all organized or classified, there is a great deal to see. There are Ona Indian materials, Salesian mission works, fossils, handicrafts and flora, fauna and mineral exhibits of the area. Just past the mission, on the right side of the road, is the old cemetery.

Isla de los Estados Robert T. Cook writes: "This long (75 km.) and guarded island lies east of Tierra del Fuego. Except for the caretakers of the lighthouse and an occasional scientist few people ever set foot on this cloud-shrouded reserve of Fuegian flora and fauna that no longer exist on the main island. During the 18th and 19th centuries hundreds of ships were wrecked or lost in the treacherous waters surrounding this island. Much gold, silver and relics await salvage." Information and tours from Rumbo Sur, San Martín 342, Ushuaia.

Argentina apparently has plans for tourist developments in **Antarctica** (accommodation at

Marambio and Esperanza stations) and Argentina and Chile are planning a mountaineering camp about 600 km. from the South Pole.

THE ECONOMY

Argentina is one of the more highly developed countries of the region and is potentially one of the richest farming countries in the world. The importance of agriculture and livestock production is shown by the fact that this sector still provides about 70 % of export earnings with sales of cereals, oilseeds, meat and processed foodstuffs. Although Argentina has lost its dominant position as an exporter of cereals and beef, it has great resources in relation to its population, which increases at a rate of only 1.6 % a year. Per capita income is therefore relatively high, at about US$2,740. Agriculture, livestock, forestry and fishing account for about 16 % of gdp. There has been a shift from livestock to crop production since the 1960s in line with changes in relative prices and the introduction of new technology which has sharply increased crop yields. Cereals account for a substantial proportion of crop production, with over 15m hectares under cultivation in the mid-1980s, of which nearly 6m were sown to wheat and produced about 12m tonnes a year. The area sown to oilseeds has risen steeply, now just exceeding that of wheat, and producing about 12m tonnes of soyabeans and sunflower seed a year. Livestock, faced with stiff competition abroad from other exporting countries, has declined in importance. The cattle stock fell from around 57m head in the late 1970s to less than 54m in the mid-1980s. Exports declined but annual domestic consumption stayed high at about 80 kg per person.

The manufacturing sector has developed behind high import protection barriers; it accounts for a quarter of gdp and benefits from increased agricultural activity, so that natural resource-based and labour-intensive industries such as food processing, textiles and clothing are reasonably dynamic. Food processing and beverages account for a quarter of manufacturing output and a fifth of industrial employment, while they are the second largest foreign exchange earners after farming. Metal working, engineering and the steel industry were depressed in the 1980s as inflation surged, dampening domestic demand and creating investment uncertainties. In the construction industry, output plummeted by 53 % in 1981-85.

Energy development has been a priority with emphasis on hydro and nuclear power sources to reduce dependence upon thermal power. In the mid-1980s, liquid fuels supplied 48 % and natural gas 25 % of energy consumption, while hydroelectricity was only 11 %. By the end of the century it is planned to reduce liquid fuels' share to 37 % and raise natural gas to 35 %. Argentina is virtually self-sufficient in oil and there is an exportable surplus of natural gas and petroleum derivatives. Hydroelectricity generating plants provided 50 % of total electricity generation in the mid-1980s, thermal plants 36 % and nuclear plants 14 %. The country's hydroelectric potential lies on the rivers Paraná and Uruguay in the north and on the network of rivers in Río Negro and Neuquén provinces.

Extremely high rates of inflation were recorded in the 1980s through a combination of large fiscal deficits, monetary expansion and a high velocity of circulation. These were difficult to contain because of structural imbalances in the economy arising from supply shortages caused by inadequate levels of investment and inefficiencies in both the public and private sectors. As the economy reached hyperinflation at a rate of 1,129 % in the twelve months to June 1985, the government introduced a stabilization programme known as the Austral Plan. This included a price and wage freeze, a new currency, the Austral, and attempted to cut the fiscal deficit by raising tax revenues and suspending financing of the deficit by the central bank. The initial positive results were weakened by the failure to cut the fiscal deficit and within 18 months 3-digit inflation had returned.

The Government also tackled the problem of servicing the external debt, which had risen sharply by an annual average of 35 % in 1978-82 to over

US$50bn in the mid-1980s, making Argentina the third largest debtor in the region. Several debt rescheduling agreements were negotiated with commercial bank creditors together with new loans and IMF financing facilities. Several World Bank loans were granted for restructuring a number of economic sectors, such as agriculture and foreign trade, but agreements with all creditors repeatedly collapsed as the Government failed to implement fully its policy commitments. By the end of the 1980s, Argentina was seriously in arrears and the newly elected Government inherited an unsustainable debt burden.

	1961-70 (av)	1971-80 (av)	1981-85 (av)	1986-88 (av)
Gdp growth (1980 prices)	3.0%	2.3%	-2.2%	2.5%
Inflation	21.3%	119.4%	322.6%	169.1%
Exports (fob) US$m	1,426	4,564	8,222	7,304
Meat	342	665	610	555
Maize	168	465	842	535
Wheat	178	361	1,003	520
Imports (fob) US$m	1,127	3,693	5,024	5,066
Current account balance US$m (cumulative)	-423	-2,729	-12,950	-9,300

INFORMATION FOR VISITORS

How to reach Argentina

By Air   Aerolíneas Argentinas (AA) and the relevant national airlines fly from São Paulo (US$280), Rio de Janeiro, Caracas, Madrid, Lisbon, Rome, Lima (US$385), Mexico City, Los Angeles, Sydney, Auckland, Paris, Amsterdam, Frankfurt, Miami, New York, Montreal, Quito (US$527), Guayaquil (US$501), Bogotá, Panama City, Zurich, Geneva, Tel-Aviv, Santiago de Chile (US$185), Antofagasta, La Paz (US$291), Santa Cruz (US$219), Asunción (US$199), Montevideo (US$40).

From New York there are non-stop services by Pan Am and Aerolíneas Argentinas, and Eastern flies 5 times a week from New York and Miami, and once from Los Angeles and Miami. Two direct flights a week Jujuy-Miami. From Canada, Canadian Air International fly to Buenos Aires from Toronto via Lima and Santiago. Other airlines include: Líneas Aéreas Paraguayas; Capetown by South African Airways; Viasa to Caracas; Bogotá, Lima, Santiago with Eastern and Avianca; Aeroflot (via Dakar); Ecuatoriana, which flies to Santiago, Quito, Guayaquil, Mexico, Miami, Los Angeles. AA flies twice weekly via Río Gallegos (difficult to board there in high season) to Auckland and Sydney; return flight Sydney-Auckland-Buenos Aires direct.

By Sea from Europe   Linea Costa "C" goes Genoa-Barcelona-Lisbon-Rio-Santos to Buenos Aires, but now only once a year, in November. Cars are cheaper to freight on the passenger ship than on the cargo boats which charge by the cubic metre bracket; the Johnson Line from Swedish and Baltic ports. Continental Shipping and Travel, 179 Piccadilly, London WIV 9DB, T 01-491 4968, offers a comprehensive service from France at reasonable prices. A similar service is offered by Calmedia SpA di Navigazione, PO Box 349, 16123 Genoa.

By Sea from the USA   There are sailings from New York to Buenos Aires by the American Republics Line, operated by Moore-McCormack Lines; sailings from San Francisco and Los Angeles by Pacific Republics Line, by the same operators; and from New Orleans by the Delta Line. Buenos Aires is 19 days by ship from New York or New Orleans.

Internal Air Services   are run by Aerolíneas Argentinas, Austral, Lapa, Alfa and the army airline LADE (in Patagonia, highly rec.). There are frequent flights to all neighbouring republics. LADE flights are cheaper than the others, and there is a good extended schedule with new Fokker F-28 jets. **N.B.** LADE will not accept IATA MCOs. (Even though sometimes offices in various towns may tell you the flights are full, it is usually worth a try out at the airport.) The naval air passenger service, Aeronaval, carries paying civilian passengers, 1/3 cheaper than LADE. No firm schedule though; 2 flights a week between Ushuaia, Río Grande and Río Gallegos; once a week between Ushuaia and Buenos Aires. Aerolíneas and

Austral have introduced a service of night flights, at fares 40-50% lower than the normal day tariff. If travelling by AA or Austral a long linear distance, e.g. Río Gallegos-Buenos Aires, but wishing to stop en route, cheaper to buy the long flight and pay extra (about US$2) for stopovers. **N.B.** All local flights are fully booked way in advance for travel in December. Don't lose your baggage ticket; you won't be able to collect your bags without it.

Visit Argentina Fare   For US$336 one can buy from Aerolíneas Argentinas or Austral a voucher available to non-Argentines not resident in Argentina which permits travel anywhere on the domestic network of Aerolíneas or Austral for a period of 30 days, provided that no point is visited twice except to make an immediate or first available connection. The voucher is surrendered for a complete set of tickets which are not refundable (i.e. the whole tour must be planned before it is begun). There is also a US$224 ticket, for 14 days. We are told that the 14-day ticket must be bought outside Argentina; the 30-day one can be bought inside or outside the country. Domestic timetables are given in *Guía Argentina de Tráfico Aéreo* and *Guía Internacional de Tráfico*. It is unwise to set up too tight a schedule because of delays which may be caused by bad weather; however, if your itinerary changes, it may be possible to trade off unused sections for others (there is a lot of confusion about this in local AA offices). Flights between Buenos Aires and Río Gallegos are often fully booked 2 to 3 weeks ahead, and there may be similar difficulties on the routes to Bariloche and Iguazú. Visit Argentina fare does not include Río Gallegos-Calafate or Río Gallegos-Ushuaia (only LADE flies this route). It is advisable to have an "OK" status put on your flight coupons even if you are "wait-listed", to be sure of your seat. Reconfirmation at least 24 hours ahead of a flight is important and it is essential to make it at the point of departure. Extra charges are made for reconfirming LADE flights (useful in Santa Cruz and Tierra del Fuego) but they are not high.

Airport Tax   US$13 for international flights, US$3 for flights to Uruguay, Chile, Brazil and Bolivia, and US$1.50 for internal flights. When in transit from one international flight to another, you may be obliged to pass through immigration and customs, have your passport stamped and be made to pay an airport tax on departure. A 3% tax on the purchase of air tickets has been reported.

N.B.   Do not send unaccompanied luggage to Argentina; it can take up to 3 days of form-filling to retrieve it from the airport. Paying overweight, though expensive, saves time.

Documents   Check visa requirements as they change frequently. In 1986 visa restrictions on British tourists were relaxed: visas (US$15) are now normally granted immediately on application. Passports are not required by citizens of neighbouring countries who hold identity cards issued by their own Governments. A visa is necessary for US citizens (not available at borders), but not for nationals of other Western Hemisphere countries (excluding Cuba), Western European countries (excluding UK and Portugal), and Japan, who may stay for 3 months, a period which can be renewed for another 3 months at the National Directorate of Migration. For all others there are three forms of visa: a business "temporary" visa, a tourist visa, and a transit visa. Australians, New Zealanders and South Africans need visas. Tourist visas are usually valid for three months in Argentina and for any number of exits and entrances during that period. Visitors should carry passports at all times; backpackers are particular targets for thorough searches—just stay calm; it is illegal not to have identification handy. When crossing land frontiers, remember that though the migration and customs officials are generally friendly, helpful and efficient, the police at the control posts a little further into Argentina tend to be extremely bureaucratic in their approach.

Railways   A permit (Argenpass) to travel anywhere by the Argentine railways costs US$95 a month, and US$150 for two months. There is no connected railway system south of Bariloche and Esquel. A "Pase Americano" (Amerailpass—check if still available) which enables you to travel on Pullman coaches through Uruguay, Argentina, Brazil, Chile, Bolivia, Paraguay, without mileage limit is US$120 for 16 days, US$140 for 23 days, US$175 for 30 days, US$260 for 60 days, also available for 90 days (payable in US$ only) free carriage, 30 kg. (children ½ price) and obtainable at the Centro de Información de Ferrocarriles Argentinos (CIFA) in Galerías Pacífico, Florida 729, Buenos Aires, open Mon.-Sat. 0700-2100, Sun. 0700-1300; also available in Mar del Plata, Bariloche, Mendoza, Córdoba, Tucumán and Posadas. There is no great difference between 1st and tourist class in trains, but if uncrowded, you can sleep across 5 seats in the latter (3 + 2), seats and only 4 in 1st class. As a rule, tourist class is 20% cheaper than 1st class, Pullman 50% more than 1st. Note, when travelling in winter, that heating may be available only in sleepers and pullmans, not 1st or 2nd.

N.B. Once out of Buenos Aires, train information is hard to come by, although we are informed that the CIFA has 328 agencies to book facilities for the named-train principal services from Buenos Aires. Stations have wall time-tables of complete schedules for their own line but no information for other systems. To avoid disappointments, make long-distance call to nearest station on the line you require—although this requires fluency in Spanish. The only general time-tables in circulation at present are those for named trains on the main lines to Mendoza, San Juan, Tucumán, Posadas, Córdoba, Mar del Plata, Bariloche, Zapala and Corrientes, which are available from the information centre at Galerías Pacífico; some of this information is summarized on **page 59**. The main services have been accelerated in recent years, but others remain slow and infrequent.

Motoring For entering Argentina by automobile the *Carnet de passages en douanes* (*Libreta de aduana*), issued by a recognized automobile club, is required. Tourists can now bring their cars into Argentina temporarily under international documentation. No specific papers are usually required to bring a Brazilian registered car into Argentina. A British international driving licence is valid only if it is endorsed by the Automóvil Club Argentino (ACA), and if the holder has a visa. Most main roads are paved, if rather narrow (road maps are a good indication of quality), and roadside services are good. Road surface conditions vary once one leaves main towns: high speeds are quite possible on the dirt and gravel roads, as long as you have the essential guard for the windscreen. All motorists are required to carry a warning triangle and a fire-extinguisher, and the handbrake must be fully operative. You may not export fuel from Argentina, so use up fuel in spare jerry cans while you are in the country. Always fill up when you can in less developed areas like Chaco and Formosa as filling stations are infrequent. Diesel fuel "gas-oil" prices are about 60% of those for gasoline ("*nafta*"). Octane rating is as follows: regular gasoline 83 (US$0.35 per litre); super 93 (US$0.50).

To obtain documents for a resident (holder of resident visa, staying at least 6 months in the country) to take a car out of Argentina, you can go to ACA in Buenos Aires, which may take up to 4 working days, or you can ask for a list of other ACA offices that can undertake the work; take forms with you from Buenos Aires, and papers may be ready in 24 hours. You will need at least 1 passport-size photo, which you can have taken at ACA at a fair cost. If the car is not your own, you require a special form signed by the owner and witnessed by a notary public. **NB** Non-residents may buy a car in Argentina but are in no circumstances allowed to take it out of the country; it must be resold in Argentina, preferably in the province where it was purchased.

Sometimes one may not be allowed to reach a border if one does not intend to cross it, stopping e.g. 20 km. from the border.

Automóvil Club Argentino (ACA), Av. Libertador General San Martín 1850, 1st floor, 1425 Buenos Aires, T 802-6061, has a travel document service, complete car service facilities, insurance facilities, road information, road charts (*hojas de ruta*-about US$1 each to members, if available) and maps (dated with the code letters in the bottom corner—road map of whole country, with service stations and *hosterías* shown, US$3.20 to non-members, and of each province), a hotel list, camping information, and a tourist guide book sold at a discount to its members and members of other recognized automobile clubs upon presentation of a membership card. (YPF, the state oil agency, also produces good maps for sale.) Members of other recognized automobile clubs can also, on presentation of membership cards, benefit from lower prices for their rooms and meals at ACA *hosterías*. The Club has service stations, some with parking garages, all over the country. The organization is efficient. Travellers do report, however, that if you are not a member of ACA you will not get any help when in trouble. ACA membership for 3 months costs US$40, which permits you to pay with Eurocard (Argencard) for fuel at their Service stations, gives 20% discount on hotel rooms and maps, and discounts at associated hotels, and 10% discount on meals.

ACA accommodation comes in 4 basic types: *Motel, Hostería, Hotel,* and *Unidades Turísticas,* and they also organize campsites (see below). A *motel* may have as few as 3 rooms, and only one night's stay is permitted. *Hosterías* have very attractive buildings and are very friendly. *Hotels* are smarter and more impersonal. All have meal facilities of some kind. Anyone can get in touch with the organization to find out about accommodation or road conditions.

Hitch-hikers, as well as motorists, are recommended to contact the ACA for its wealth of information.

Touring Club Argentino, Esmeralda 605 and Tucumán 781 3rd floor, T 392-6742 has similar travel services but no service stations.

Maps The best road maps are those of the ACA (see above). Topographical maps are issued by the Instituto Geográfico Militar, Cabildo 381, Casilla 1426, Buenos Aires (reached by Subte D to Palermo, then train to Carranza, where IGM is one block from station).

Car Hire Avis offers a good and efficient service with the possibility of complete insurance and unlimited mileage for rentals of 7 days or more. No one-way fee if returned to another Avis office, but the car may not be taken out of the country. Other companies are given in the text.

Camping is now very popular in Argentina (except in Buenos Aires) and sites with services are being installed, as well as good free municipal and paying private campsites in most tourist centres. Many are closed off-season. Camping is now allowed at the side of major highways and in all national parks (except at Iguazú Falls), at no cost. Many ACA service stations have a site where one can camp, and in general service station owners are very friendly to campers. A list of camping sites is available from ACA (labelled for members, but should be easily available and from the main tourist office in Av. Santa Fe, Bs. As.); see Autoclub magazine. References to sites will be found in the text. ACA campsites offer discounts to members, and to holders of the International Driving Licence. There are few Youth Hostels (many open only February to March), but some towns offer free accommodation to young travellers in the holiday season, on floors of schools or church halls; some fire stations will let you sleep on the floor for free (sometimes men only). Many garages have showers that you can use. Good lightweight tents now available, e.g. Cacique. Regular (blue bottle) Camping Gaz International is available in Buenos Aires, at an electrical goods store on Av. 9 de Julio, near Teatro Colón, and Suntime, Lima 225, Guatemala 5908 (Palermo), Juramento 2452 (Belgrano) at América Pesca, Alfredo Pollini Alvear 1461.

Motorhomes   US Motorhomes "Winnebago" is represented at Todotur, Av. de Mayo 1370-5th Floor, Room 92 (T 371552 or 380406) Buenos Aires. "Coachmen" Motorhome and "Pick-up" camper dealer at Av. Debenedetti 1285, (1871) Dock Sud, Avellaneda, Buenos Aires also represents Jensen, Wemac, Monogram, Peterson, Winegard, Monarch and Coleman (T 201-5289/6379). The best dealer for Motorhome equipment and repairs is Merello Hermanos S.R.L., Maipú 742, Vicente López, Prov. of Bs. As (T 795-3503/4335). Porta-Potti toilets are widely sold in Argentina, sometimes under a different name.

Hitch-hiking   Argentina is on the whole a good country for this (especially in Dec.-March), though recent problems with robberies have made drivers cautious. Carry little foreign cash on you, because of frequent stoppages along the road. Don't rely on hitching absolutely, though; traffic can be sparse, especially at distances from the main towns, and in Patagonia out of season. It may be useful to carry a letter from your Consulate. Though they tend to be more reserved in manner than most Latin Americans, Argentines are generally friendly and helpful. Sirikit Bhagwanani, of Walchuil, Switzerland, says there are no problems at all for a reasonably careful woman on her own in Argentina.

Walking   Information on trails in NW Argentina, the Lake District, Patagonia and Tierra del Fuego is given in *Backpacking in Chile and Argentina*, by Hilary Bradt and John Pilkington.

Buses   The price of bus journeys is approximately US$2.50 per 100 km. Most bus companies give a 20% student discount, but persistence is required to prevail with an international student card; a YHA card is useful. Express buses between cities are dearer than the *comunes*, but well worth the extra money for the fewer stops. When buying tickets at a bus office, don't assume you've been automatically alloted a seat: make sure you have one.

British Business Travellers   are strongly advised to read "Hints to Exporters: Argentina", obtainable from Department of Trade, Export Services Division, Sanctuary Bldgs, 16-20 Great Smith Street, London SW1P 3DB. Similar information is provided for US citizens by the US Department of Commerce.

Customs   No duties are charged on clothing, personal effects, toilet necessities, etc. Cameras, typewriters, binoculars, radios and other things which a tourist normally carries are duty-free if they have been used and only one of each article is carried. This is also true of scientific and professional instruments for the personal use of the traveller. Travellers may only bring in new personal goods up to a value of US$150 (up to US$50 for tourists entering from neighbouring countries); the amount of duty varies per item and according to exchange rates. However, the Argentine authorities allow goods to the value of US$500 to be introduced duty-free by travellers arriving in Tierra del Fuego. There are red and green divisions at airport customs, but officials make no difference between them. All incoming baggage is normally inspected.

Two litres of alcoholic drinks, 400 cigarettes, 50 cigars and 5 kg. of foodstuffs are also allowed in duty-free; for tourists originating from neighbouring countries the respective quantities allowed are 1 litre, 200, 20 and 2 kg. You can buy duty-free goods *on arrival* at Ezeiza airport.

If having packages sent to Argentina, do not use the green customs label unless the contents are of real value and you expect to pay duty. For such things as books or samples use the white label if available.

N.B.   Never carry weapons, or drugs without prescriptions. The open season for fishing is between November and February or March. Enquire as to dates, so as to avoid carrying equipment unnecessarily, and remember that fishing anywhere requires a permit.

Health   Argentina is in general a healthy country to visit, with good sanitary services. Smallpox vaccination no longer required to enter Argentina. If intending to visit the low-lying tropical areas, it is advisable to take precautions against malaria. **See page 57**. Chagas' disease (**see page 33**) is found in NW Argentina.

Climate   ranges from sub-tropical in the N to cold temperate in Tierra del

Fuego, but is temperate and quite healthy in the densely populated central zone. From mid-December to the end of February Buenos Aires can be oppressively hot and humid, with temperatures ranging from 27°C (80°F) to 35°C (95°F) and an average humidity of 70%. Beware of the high pollen count in the pollinating season if you have allergy problems. The winter months of June, July and August are best for a business visit, though spring weather in Buenos Aires is often very pleasant indeed. The skiing season in Bariloche ends by August 30. Corrientes and Misiones provinces are wet in August and especially September.

Clothing   Shorts are not worn in city centres, though their use has become more common in residential suburbs in spring, summer and autumn, and in Buenos Aires in the hottest months. In general, dress tends to be formal (unless casual wear is specified on an invitation) in Buenos Aires and for evening outings to shows, etc. The general standard of dress among Argentines is very high: collar and tie, with jacket, are very much the standard for men, and women "should always err on the side of elegance" - David Mackintosh.

Hours of Business   Banks, government offices, insurance offices and business houses are not open on Saturdays. *Government Offices:* 1230-1930 in the winter and 0730-1300 in summer. *Banks:* generally 1000-1600 but time varies according to the city, and sometimes according to the season. (See under names of cities in text.) *Post Offices:* 0800 to midnight for telegrams. Stamps on sale during working days 0800-2000 but 0800-1400 on Saturdays. *Shops* are open from about 0900 to 1900, though many close at midday on Saturdays. Outside the main cities many close for the daily afternoon siesta, reopening at about 1700. 24-hour opening is allowed except on Mondays; this applies mainly to restaurants, foodshops, barbers, newspaper shops, art, book and record stores.

Language   Spanish, with variant words and pronunciation. English comes second; French and Italian may be useful.
   The chief variant pronunciations are the replacement of the "ll" and "y" sounds by a soft "j" sound, as in "azure" (though note that this is not done in Mendoza), the omission of the "d" sound in words ending in "-ado", the omission of final "s" sounds, the pronunciation of "s" before a consonant as a Scottish or German "ch", and the substitution in the north and west of the normal rolled "r" sound by a hybrid "rj". In grammar the Spanish "tú" is replaced by "vos" and the second person singular conjugation of verbs has the accent on the last syllable e.g. *vos tenés, podés*, etc.

Photography   We are told that slide film is quite difficult to find outside Buenos Aires, apart from tourist spots such as Iguazú and Calafate.

Standard Time   is 3 hours behind GMT.

Holidays   The main holiday period, generally to be avoided by business visitors, is January-March, though some areas, such as Tierra del Fuego, begin to fill up in November/December. Winter school holidays, in which travelling and hotels may be difficult, are the middle two weeks of July. No work may be done on the national holidays (May 1, May 25, June 20, July 9, August 17, October 12 and December 25) with the exceptions specifically established by the legislation in force. There are no bus services on May 1. On the non-working days (January 1, Holy Thursday and Good Friday, and December 8) employers are left free to decide whether their employees should work, but banks and public offices are closed. Banks are also closed on December 31. There are gaucho parades throughout Argentina, with traditional music, on the days leading up to the Día de la Tradición, November 10. On December 30 (not 31 because so many offices in centre are closed) there is a ticker-tape tradition in downtown Buenos Aires: it snows paper and the crowds stuff passing cars and buses with long streamers.

Food   National dishes are based in the main upon plentiful supplies of beef. Many dishes are distinctive and excellent; the *asado,* a roast cooked on an open fire or grill; *puchero,* a stew, very good indeed; *bife a caballo,* steak topped with a fried egg; the *carbonada* (onions, tomatoes, minced beef), particularly good in Buenos Aires; *churrasco,* a thick grilled steak; *parrillada,* a mixed grill, mainly roast meat, sausages (including *morcilla,* black pudding to the British, or blood sausage) and offal; and *humitas,* made with sweet corn, tasty but not strictly national. *Arroz con pollo* is a delicious combination of rice, chicken, eggs, vegetables and strong sauce. *Puchero de gallina* is chicken, sausage, maize, potatoes and squash cooked together. *Empanada* is a tasty meat pie, and *chorizo* a highly spiced sausage, though do not confuse this with *bife de chorizo,* which is a rump steak (*bife de lomo* is fillet steak). *Ñoquis* (gnocchi), potato dumplings normally served with meat and tomato sauce, are tasty and often the cheapest item on the menu. *Locro* is a thick stew made of maize, white beans, beef, sausages, pumpkin and herbs. Pizzas come in all sorts of exotic flavours, both savoury and sweet. Almost uniquely in Latin America, salads are quite safe. A popular sweet is *dulce de leche* (especially from Chascomús), milk and sugar evaporated to a pale, soft fudge. Other popular desserts are *almendrado* (ice-cream rolled in crushed almonds), *dulce de batata* (sweet potato preserve), *dulce de membrillo* (quince preserve), *dulce de zapallo* (pumpkin in syrup); these *dulces* are often eaten with cheese. *Postre Balcarce*, a cream and meringue cake and *alfajores*, maize-flour biscuits filled with *dulce de leche* or apricot jam, are also very popular. Sweets: the Havana brands have been particularly recommended. Excellent Italian-style ice-cream with exotic flavours. For local recipes (in Spanish) *Las Comidas de Mi Pueblo,* by Margarita Palacios, recommended.

Offices close for 2 to 2½ hours for lunch between 1200 and 1500. Around 1700, many people go to a *confitería* for tea, sandwiches and cakes. Dinner often begins at 2200 or 2230; it is, in the main, a repetition of lunch.

Drink Argentine wines are sound throughout the price range. The ordinary *vinos corrientes* are wholesome and extremely cheap cost about US$3.50 a bottle in shops (US$8 in a restaurant—US$15-20 for a good wine); reds better than the whites. The local beers, mainly lager-type, are quite acceptable and cost about US$0.50 a litre in supermarkets. Hard liquor is relatively cheap, except for imported whisky, at about US$3 in shops for gin and vodka. Local liqueurs may be as cheap as US$0.70 a litre. *Clérico* is a white-wine *sangría* drunk in summer. Tap water in the main cities is safe, but often heavily chlorinated. It is usual to drink soda or mineral water at restaurants, and many Argentines mix it with their cheper wine, with ice, as a refreshing drink in summer. *Yerba mate*, or Paraguayan tea, is widely drunk, especially in the interior, continuing the old *gaucho* custom.

Best Buys Local leather goods in Buenos Aires, men's leather coats, US$200; suede, US$200-250 three-quarter-length coats are about US$130 and suede blousons about US$80; handbags and shoes (leather is much cheaper in Uruguay). *Ciudad del Cuero*, Florida 940, has clothing, footwear and luggage from 40 manufacturers. A gourd for drinking *yerba mate* and the silver *bombilla* which goes with it, perhaps a pair of *gaucho* trousers, the *bombachas*. Ponchos (red and black for men, all colours for women). *El Guasquero* in Calle Anasagasti specializes in old *gaucho* objects, saddlery, *bolas*, horn items, all genuine and reconditioned by Sr Flores, the owner. The shop is N of Av. Santa Fe, near Calle Bulnes, Buenos Aires (postcode 2028). Articles of onyx, specially in Salta. Silver handicrafts. In Buenos Aires, there is a good, reasonable and helpful souvenir shop on Av. de Mayo near Chacabuco. Knitted woollens, especially in Bariloche and Mar del Plata. If you like honey, the Casa de Miel has different honeys from every province. Try Mendoza or Tucumán varieties.

Value-Added Tax VAT is not levied on most medicines and foodstuffs but on all other products and services up to 20%.

Currency In mid-1985, a new currency was introduced, the *austral*, divided into 100 centavos, worth 1,000 of the existing pesos argentinos (themselves introduced as recently as mid-1983). Austral notes are being issued, but peso argentino notes not overprinted with austral denominations went out of circulation at end-March 1988. Notes in circulation: A100, A50 (beware forgeries of these two from street money-changers), A 10, A 5, A 1, 50, 10, 5, 1 and ½ centavos. 5, 1 and ½-centavo coins have been introduced to co-exist with 50, 10 and 5-peso argentino coins, and coins for up to 50 centavos bearing the austral sign (A with an extra crossbar) are being struck. There is an acute shortage of small change, and the different series of coins in circulation are very confusing. It is usually difficult to change travellers' cheques in the smaller towns. Commissions can be as high as 6% and in general it takes a long time and many forms to transact these cheques. Other travellers have warned not to engage in unsolicited currency transactions in the streets, etc. as you may be tricked or land in prison. Some of the major towns have exchange shops *(casas de cambio)* and these are given in the text. There is a 3% tax on cheques and an extra commission which can be avoided if you go to a branch of the issuing bank, especially if changing small amounts. Market rates, as opposed to official rates, are quoted in major newspapers daily, and available at some cambios (but not usually posted in the windows); there is at the moment a premium of about 30% over the official rate. Money remitted to Argentina from abroad is normally paid out in australes. It is possible to obtain money from Europe through an express transfer, which takes 2-3 days, and the currency will be subject to tax.
Various Argentine provinces (Tucumán, Salta, Jujuy, La Rioja are examples) have issued *bonos*

(bonds) which circulate at face value alongside the national currency. Two warnings: they are not accepted outside the province of issue; and they bear redemption dates, after which they are valueless. Beware!

When crossing a land frontier into Argentina, make sure you have some Argentine currency as there are normally no facilities at the border.

Credit Cards It is reported that American Express, Diners Club, Visa and Mastercard cards are all useful. All shops, hotels and places showing Argencard (head office, H.Yrigoyen, Buenos Aires) signs will accept Eurocard and Access, but you must state that these cards are affiliated to Mastercard. Argencard will not permit cash advances on these cards in outlying regions, and is itself very slow in advancing cash. The use of Mastercard/Access and Eurocard is very limited in the south.

Weights and Measures The metric system is used.

Postage and Telephone Rates The minimum rate for airmail is about US$0.30. Letters from Argentina take up to a week to get to the UK, and about 5 days to the USA. The local telephone system is hopelessly overloaded. On weekdays, 1800-2200, and on Sat. and Sun., 0700-2200, Christmas to New Year and Easter Week, international calls are half-price. The normal rate for international calls is from US$2 to US$3.50 a minute, and for telex about US$1.00-1.75. Direct international telephone dialling is almost unknown in hotels and private homes. No reverse-charge calls to Australia or South Africa.

Small parcels only of 1 kg. at post offices; larger parcels from Encomiendes Internacionales, Centro Postal Internacional, Av. Antártida Argentina, near Retiro Station, Buenos Aires, and in main provincial cities, about US$16 for 5 kg. Larger parcels must first be examined, before final packing, by Customs, then wrapped (up to 2 kg.) in brown paper; over 2 kg. must be sewn in linen cloth), then sealed by Customs, then taken to Encomiendas Internacionales for posting. Cheap packing service available (US$3.50). Open between 1100 and 1700 on weekdays. Used clothes have to be fumigated before they will be accepted.

Press Buenos Aires dailies: *La Nación, La Prensa*. Tabloids: *Clarín, La Razón, Tiempo Argentino* Evening papers: *Crónica*. English language daily: *Buenos Aires Herald*. Magazines: *Siete Días, Gente, La Semana, Redacción, Mercado, El Gráfico* (sports). New daily, *Página Doce*, very popular among students and intellectuals. English language magazines: *The Review of the River Plate* (commercial, agricultural, political and economic comment), and *The Southern Cross* (Irish community).

Radio English language radio broadcasts can be heard daily on short wave: 0100-0130 on 6060 KHz 49m, 0230-0300 on 11710 KHz 25m, 0430-0500 and 2230-2300 on 15345 KHz 19m; Radiodifusión Argentina al Exterior, Casilla de Correo 555, Arg 1000, Beunos Aires. This is a government station and broadcasts also in Japanese, Arabic, German, French, Italian and Portuguese. Broadcasts by foreign radio stations (including the BBC) are receivable on short wave.

We wish to offer our profound thanks to Tom Brandt (Amsterdam, resident in Bs. As.), Julian Anderson (Bs. As.), Prof. César José Cetta (Director of Sports, Recreation and Tourism, Río Turbio), Jorge Carlos Dejean (Salta), Martin R Eayrs (Bs As), Federico B Kirbus (Bs. As.), Herbert Levi (Buenos Aires) for further important details, Manuel Pestalozzi (Swedish Embassy, Bs. As.), Cristina Ravaglia (Italian Consul General, Bs. As.), Janet J Russell (Bs. As.), Christian Scherlenzky (Villa Ballester, Buenos Aires), and Kathy Smith (Bs. As.). We also wish to thank the following travellers: Tom Aabo and Karin Henningsen (Aarhus, Dmk), Dr J.R.J Van Asperen de Boer (Amsterdam), Tim Austin (Shere, Sy.), Thomas Axthammer (München 90), Lee Azus (San Francisco), Alison Ballance and friends (Wellington), Dexter Ball (Chicago), Carolyn Bargman (El Paso, Tx.) Bruce Barnes (Gloucester, NSW), Urs Baumann (Wildberg, Switz), Eric Beauchemin (Hilversum), Dale Bedford (Auckland 9), Pierre-Y Berney (Geneva), Claire Best (Sevenoaks), Gordon Bethell (St Leonards, Sx.), Robin Biellik and Pegi Henderson (Brasília), Gregory and Shelley Blake (Hounslow, Mx.), Lennart Blomberg (Göteborg), Tad Bonlecki (Woollahra, NSW) R.J. Brown (London SW4), Alison Brysk and Mark Freeman (San Francisco, Ca.), Dan Buck and Anne Meadows (Wash. DC.), John Burke (Bristol 7), Michelle Burrows (Brisbane), Chris Burton (Norwood, S. Aust.), Pamela Caunt and Bob Brass (London N1), Helen and Gilles Cormerais (Plymouth), Paulo Couto (São Paulo), John Crane (Sunbury), Dale and Anne Dickinson (Menlo Park, Ca.), Fabienne Dufayet (Petit Lancy, Switz.), Paul Eaton (Victoria, BC), Simon Ellis (San José, CR), Fred and Marianne Emery (London SE26), Josef Engert (Schlieren, Switz.), Andreas Erne (Zürich 8055), Margaret and Martin Evans (Brighton), Per Einar Evensen (Bergen), Or Ezer (Kibbutz Gonen, Israel), Ulla Faarup (Arslev, Dmk), Didier Faget and Sabine Fleury (Vernon, Fr.), Karsten Feucht (Berlin 61), Ed Forszt (Seaside Pk, NJ), Bernd Fremgen (Freiberg, W.Ger.), Volker Fritsch and Iris Köhler (Berlin 41), Anna Frostenson (Hagersten, Swe.), Bjørn Gabrielsen (Oslo 11), Margaret and Stuart Goodchild, Christina Gräwe (Tautkirchen) and Joachim Hoell (Wernstadt, W.Ger.), Jan Jacob de Groot (Vroomshoop, Neth.), Jon and Julia Gruffydd (Lima), Rupert Hafner (Wien 1238), Knut Per Hasund (Stockholm), Alan Hausrath (Boise, Id.), Henri and Nicki Hendriksen (North Ryde,

NSW), Dave Henson (San Francisco, Ca.), Flavio Heubeck (Winterthur), Deborah J Hoover (San Antonio, Tx.), Jane Horton (Montevideo), Martin Hostettler (Spiegel, Switz.), Don Hoyle (London EC2), David Hutchinson and Susie Maddox (London W8), Ingrid Iversen (Streatham), Gretke Moen Johansen (Kolbotn, Norway), Mariann Johnsen (Brandbu, Norway), Ruth Kamm (München 19), Omer Karchi (Tivon, Israel), Simon Kennedy and Sally Constable (Melbourne), Susanna Kent (Auckland 3), Ronen Khayat (Jerusalem), Peter Kocan (Summit, NJ), Thomas and Bettina Kräuchi (Kloten, Switz.), Robert and Daisy Kunstaetter (Richmond Hill, Ont.), Dr Ramona Lages (Galesburg, IL), Esther Lange and Peter Dellenbach (Untersiggenthal, Switz.), Darquise and Paul Lapointe (Cornwall, Ont.), Dean Lasko (Seattle), Joseph Laure (Guatemala City), Kenneth and Nancy Leighton (Vancouver), Christian Levin (Kiel, W.Ger.), Margy Levine and Jordan Young (Lexington, MA), John Lewis (London NW3), Manoel A Lima (Northwood, Mx.), Paul Living (Reading) for a most useful contribution, Peter S Lobin (Chicago), Dr John Maddock (Rio), Christine Marthaler and Jürg Briner (Zürich 8038), James Mathias (Minneapolis), Elaine and George McClellan (Danville, Ca.), Anita McConnell (London EC2), Stryker McGuire and Julie Jedamus (Ashfield, Mass.), Carla McLean (San Francisco), Amanda Meads and Mark Barton (London W14), Andrea Meier (Volkach, W.Ger.), Claudia Meyer and Angelika and Wolfgang Schwab (Berlin 41), Nichola Morgan (Swanage, Dorset), Beri and Mary Morris (Raleigh NC), Michael Mortensen (Oelstykke, Dmk.), Christoph Müller (Zürich 8004), Hallam Murray (London SW11), John and Christine Myerscough (Glossop, Derbys), Diane O'Brien (Tilburon, Ca.), Charles O'Hern (Mesa, Ariz.), Bertil Olin (Johanneshov, Swed.), Graham J. O'Neil (London SW7), William Parton (London SW11), John M. Raspey (Dolores Hidalgo), Chris Robertson (Stockholm) and Patricia Galvin (Galway), John Roberts (Dunedin, NZ), Gisele Rochat and Jean-Paul Corboz (Neuchâtel, Switz.), Andreas Ruck (Berlin 46), Dr Wolfgang and Karin Sass (Kiel), R van der Schaaf (Amsterdam), Dr. Marcus Schiltenwolf (Mainz 2), H Schouwenburg (London SW18), Leon van der Schoor (Neth.), Markus Schulz (Gambach, W.Ger.), Ingo Sdorra and Arne Ackermann (Flensburg, W.Ger.), Elizabeth and Virginia Segal (London N2), Prof Arthur M Shapiro (Univ of California, Davis), James Sharp (Boulder, Co), Antony Sherlock (Edinburgh 12), Sverker Skoglund (Göteborg), David Smitham (Christchurch, NZ), Lynn Sowell (Clarksville, TN), Armin Straub (Bovenden, W.Ger.), Anna Syriänen and Marko Sorvaniemi (Tampere, Fin.), Simon Tanner (Groningen), Lisa Tenuta (Kenosha, Wisconsin), Erik Thier and Patricia Wessels (Amsterdam), Julian and Cordelia Thomas (London), Barry Tiffen and Lucy Stephens (Torksey, Lincoln), Pernille Tranberg (Copenhagen), Douglas B Trent (Focus Tours, Belo Horizonte), Anthony and Kathalijn Verhulst (Registro, SP), Angus Walker (Edinburgh EH9), David H Watson, Roland Wiemer and Karla Menner (Hamburg 50), Gordon Williams (London W12), Ray Williams (Pwllheli), Alida and Gordon Wilson (San Rafael, CA.), Wytske Winter and Hans Haringa (Aberdeen), Eran Zelikovitch (Israel), and Helmut Zettl (Ebergassing, Aust.).

BOLIVIA

BOLIVIA, straddling the Andes, is a land of gaunt mountains, cold desolate plateaux and developing semi-tropical and fertile lowlands. Its area of about 1,098,580 square kilometres makes it twice the size of Spain. It is land-locked, with Chile and Peru to the W, Brazil to N and E, and Argentina and Paraguay to the S. Of the population of some 6.73m people some 70% are Indians, 25% *mestizo* and 5% European.

The Andean range is at its widest—some 650 km.—in Bolivia. The Western Cordillera, which separates Bolivia from Chile, has high peaks of between 5,800 and 6,500 metres and a number of active volcanoes along its crest. The passes across it are above 4,000 metres. To the E of this range lies the bleak, treeless, windswept Altiplano, much of it 4,000 metres above sea-level. It has an average width of 140 km., is 840 km. long, and covers an area (in Bolivia) of 102,300 square km., or nearly 10% of the country. Its surface is by no means flat, for the Western Cordillera sends spurs into it which tend to divide it into basins. The more fertile northern part is the more inhabited; the southern part is parched desert and almost unoccupied, save for a mining town here and there. Nearly 70% of the population lives on it, for it contains most of the major cities; almost half of the people are urban dwellers.

Lake Titicaca, at the northern end of the Altiplano, is an inland sea of 8,965 square km. at 3,810 metres: the highest navigable water in the world. Its maximum length and breadth are 171 and 64 km., and the greatest known depth is 280 metres. There are large annual variations between high and low water levels; 95% of the water flowing into it is lost by evaporation, making it more salty than most freshwater lakes. The immense depth of the water keeps the lake at an even all-the-year-around temperature of 10°C, and modifies the extremes of winter and night temperatures on the surrounding land. There is therefore a large farming population of Indians in this basin, tilling the fields and the hill terraces and tending their sheep and llamas.

The Altiplano is a harsh, strange land, a dreary grey solitude except for the bursts of green after rain. The air is unbelievably clear—the whole plateau is a bowl of luminous light. A cold wind blows frequently in the afternoons, causing dust storms. During the winter temperatures fall below freezing point; there is frost every night in July and August, but during the day the tropical sun raises temperatures over 20°C.

The animals of the Altiplano are fascinating. Llamas serve as pack animals—they carry up to 22 kg. loads up to 20 km. a day and yield about 2½ kg. of wool when sheared at intervals of from two to five years. The alpaca, bred not for work but for wool, belongs to the same group; the two may be distinguished by

Legend:

1. La Paz, Titicaca and the Peruvian Frontier.
2. The Yungas.
3. South from La Paz.
4. Eastern Bolivia.
5. The Northern Lowlands.

BOLIVIA

differences in the texture of their coats and shape of their tails. The vicuña, chinchilla and red fox are the main wild animals. The vicuña, an untamed smaller member of the family to which the llama and the alpaca belong, is found, though in diminishing numbers, on the bleak pampas. It may not be hunted, but its fine silky, tawny coloured wool may be sold.

Agriculture in the Altiplano is also interesting: the potato and the *oca* (another tuber), eaten in the dehydrated form of *chuño* and *tunta,* are the main crops. *Quinoa,* a kind of millet, and *cañava,* a smaller and darker grain, are the main cereals; both are extremely nutritious. *Chicha,* the national intoxicant, is brewed from maize (corn). Edible fish (small *boga,* large white-fleshed *pejerrey* and rainbow and salmon trout—Lake Titicaca has been stocked with the last two) are widely sold in the towns of the Altiplano.

Far more important to the economy of the Altiplano than agriculture is mining.

210 km. S of La Paz along the passageway at the base of the Eastern Cordillera is Oruro, where a low belt of hills supplies tin, copper, silver and tungsten. The Spaniards of Peru discovered the Cerro Rico in 1545. It is a mountain rising out of the Puna to a height of 4,780 metres, and was almost a solid mass of ore containing tin, silver, bismuth and tungsten. The Spaniards, interested only in silver, built Potosí at its base, 4,065 metres above sea level. The city grew till it had a population of 150,000, but rapidly dwindled after the richest deposits had been worked out. It remained a dead town till demand for tin rose early this century.

The presence of tin also accounts for the mining communities in the Cordillera to the SE of Oruro: the ex-Patiño mines at Catavi, to which there is a branch railway from Oruro, produce nearly half the tin of Bolivia. The high cost of producing Bolivian tin was a major contributor to the industry's decline in 1986, when the world tin market collapsed. Silver is still mined or extracted from the tailings left by past generations, and variable amounts of lead, bismuth, antimony, tungsten and zinc from pockets in the Cordillera are exported. Large deposits of silver have been found south of the Altiplano, near Lípez, and mines are being reopened, and their tailings reprocessed, two centuries after the Spaniards abandoned them.

Recommended reading: *We Eat the Mines and the Mines Eat Us* by June Nash, New York, 1979, and *The Potosí Mita 1573-1700* by Jeffery Cole, Stanford University Press, 1985.

From the Altiplano rises, to the E, the sharp façade of the Eastern Cordillera. As luck would have it there is a gently graded passageway along the plateau at the foot of the Eastern Cordillera from Lake Titicaca, in the N, to the Argentine frontier, in the S. From Viacha, near La Paz, the main line of the Bolivian railways runs along this passageway to Villazón, with connections to Chile (from Uyuni) and Buenos Aires. The giant masses of the northern parts of the Eastern Cordillera rise to very great heights in the Cordillera Real to the east of Lake Titicaca: four peaks soar to above 6,000 metres. This magnificent sight can be seen on a clear day from the top of a ridge on the Titicaca-La Paz highway. Their far sides fall away to the NE, very sharply, towards the Amazon basin.

These heavily forested north-eastern slopes are deeply indented by the fertile valleys of the Nor Yungas and Sud Yungas, drained by the Río Beni and its tributaries, where cacao, coffee, sugar, coca and tropical fruits are grown. The problem of transport to the consuming centre of La Paz is formidable: the connecting all-weather road, hair-raising in places, climbs 3,430 metres in 80 km. to surmount La Cumbre pass, at 4,725 metres within 24 km. of La Paz.

From a point just N of Cochabamba to the S the Eastern Cordillera is tilted, not to the NE, but to the E. This part of the Eastern Cordillera rises abruptly in sharp escarpments from the Altiplano, and then flattens out to an easy slope eastwards to the plains: an area known as the Puna. The streams which flow across the Puna are tributaries of the Río Grande flowing NE to the basin of the Amazon, and of the Pilcomayo flowing SE through the Chaco to the River Plate system. They cut increasingly deep incisions as they gather volume until, to the E, the Puna is eroded to little more than a high remnant between the river valleys. These valleys deeply incising the surface of the eastern-sloping Puna are densely inhabited; a variety of grain crops and fruits is grown. All these semi-tropical mountain valleys are known as Yungas: the generic name is not confined to the valleys of the Provinces of Nor and Sud Yungas to the E of La Paz. Rainfall in the Yungas is from 700 to 800 mm. a year, as opposed to the 400 to 700 mm. of the northern Altiplano and much less further S. The heaviest rain is during December, January and February. The mean average temperature is between 16° and 18°C, but in spite of a high humidity the Yungas are not unhealthy. Chulumani in the Sud Yungas and Coroico in the Nor Yungas are popular resorts.

Typical valleys are the very fertile basins in which Cochabamba, Sucre, and Tarija lie. These send food and cattle to the towns of the Altiplano, but other valleys have no way of doing so. The basins and long ribbons of valley farmland are isolated, and transport to the areas where they might sell their produce is only now being developed.

The lowland tropics, stretching from the foothills of the Eastern Cordillera to the frontiers with Brazil to the NE and E and with Paraguay and Argentina to the SE and S, take up 70% of the total area of Bolivia, but contain only about 20% of its population. Rainfall is high but seasonal, and large stretches suffer from alternate flooding and drought. The climate is hot, ranging from 23° to 25°C in the S and to 27°C in the N. Occasional cold dust-laden winds from the S—the *surazos*—lower the temperature considerably. In the N and E the Oriente has dense tropical forest. Open plains covered with rough pasture, swamp and scrub occupy the centre. Towards the end of the 18th century this was a populous land of plenty; for 150 years Jesuit missionaries had controlled the area and guided it into a prosperous security. A symbol of their great effort is the cathedral at San José de Chiquitos: a gem of elegance and dignity. But the Jesuits were expelled in 1767; years of maladministration, spoliation and corruption reduced the area to lethargy.

This once rich land, drained by the Madre de Dios, Beni and Mamoré rivers into the Madeira, a tributary of the Amazon, has been isolated from the rest of the country. It is as difficult to get at from the E as from the W, for there are rapids and falls in the Madeira which limit navigation. In its heart lie the seasonally inundated tropical Llanos de Mojos, ringed in by rain forest or semi-deciduous tropical forest—230,000 square km. with only 120,000 people. Roads and river connections are still being improved; there are roads between Cochabamba and Todos Santos and between La Paz and Trinidad. Meat is already brought in from Trinidad, capital of Beni Department, and from airstrips in the area, to the urban centres of La Paz, Oruro, and Cochabamba.

The forests and plains beyond the Eastern Cordillera sweep S towards the Pilcomayo River, getting progressively less rain and merging into a comparatively dry southern land of scrub and arid savanna. The main city of this area is Santa Cruz de la Sierra, founded in the 16th century, now the second city of Bolivia and a large agricultural centre. Here conditions favour the growing of sugar-cane, rice, oil plants and citrus fruit. The plains to the E are mainly used as grazing lands with small areas under cultivation, but in this area are extensive oil, gas, and iron-ore deposits, possibly Bolivia's greatest asset when developed.

Communications After centuries of isolation new roads are now integrating the food-producing eastern zones with the bulk of the population living in the towns of the Altiplano or the westward-facing slopes of the Eastern Cordillera. Under Spanish rule there were four great trails in use within the country: three of them led through passes in the Western Cordillera to the Pacific; the fourth led from La Paz southwards into Argentina. At the turn of the century, railways replaced the llamas and mules. By far the shortest line is the one from La Paz to Arica (Chile), completed in 1913. Arica ships a large part of the exports together with Antofagasta (Chile) and Matarani (Peru).

Bolivia has 3,774 km. of railway. There are two private railways: Machacamarca-Uncia, owned by the Corporación Minera de Bolivia (108 km.) and Uyuni-Pulacayo (52 km.) owned by the Empresa Minera Pulacayo. Plans to construct a railway to link Cochabamba and Santa Cruz, with Brazilian assistance, have often been studied. Bolivia has over 14,000 km. of navigable rivers, which connect most of the country with the Amazon basin. The national highway system at the end of 1985 totalled 40,987 km., of which only 3.75% were paved and 22.6% gravel-surfaced.

The People The racial composition varies from place to place: pure Indian around Lake Titicaca; more than half Indian in La Paz; three-quarters *mestizo* or European in the Yungas, Cochabamba, Santa Cruz and Tarija, the most European of all. During the 1980s, regional tensions between the "collas" (*altiplano* dwellers) and the "cambas" (lowlanders) have become more marked. Under 40% of children of school age are attending school even though it is theoretically compulsory between 7 and 14.

About two-thirds of the population lives in adobe huts, and medical services are sketchy outside the towns and mining camps; birth rate, 44.0, general death rate, 15.8 per 1,000, but infantile mortality is 124 per 1,000 during the first year. Epidemics are comparatively rare on the Altiplano, but malaria and yellow fever are still problems in the Oriente and Santa Cruz, and hepatitis and Chagas disease (**see page** 33) are endemic in the warmer parts of the country. About 49.6% is urban. Annual population growth: 2.7%; urban growth: 4.3%. Life expectancy at birth: 51 years; unemployment in 1986 was estimated at 22% of the work-force.

The Indians are mainly composed of two groups: those in the north of the Altiplano who speak the guttural Aymará, and those elsewhere, who speak Quechua, the Inca tongue. Outside the big cities many of them speak no Spanish, but knowledge of Spanish is increasing.

The most obdurate of Bolivian problems has always been that the main mass of population is, from a strictly economic viewpoint, in the wrong place, the poor Altiplano and not the potentially rich Oriente; and that the Indians lived largely outside the monetary system on a self-sufficient basis. Since the land reform of 1952 isolated communities continue the old life but in the agricultural area around Lake Titicaca, the valleys of Cochabamba, the Yungas and the irrigated areas of the south, most peasants now own their own land, however small the plot may be. There has also been appreciable migration to the warmer and more fertile lands of the eastern region, encouraged by the Government.

The Indian women retain their traditional costume, with bright petticoats, and in the highlands wear, apparently from birth, a flattish brown or grey bowler. In Cochabamba they wear a white top hat of ripolined straw. However, traditional headgear is being replaced by the baseball cap which sells for US$2.50 against US$7 for a bowler. Indians traditionally chew the coca leaf, which deadens hunger pains and gives a measure of oblivion. On feast days they drink with considerable application, wear the most sensational masks and dance till they drop.

N.B. Remember to refer to rural Indians not as "indios" (an insult) but as "campesinos" (peasants).

History

At Tiahuanaco (Tiwanaku), near Lake Titicaca, stand the impressive remains of a pre-Inca civilization. The Aymará-speaking Indians in this area emerged around 1000 BC into a civilization characterized by massive stone buildings and monuments, exquisite textiles, pottery and metalwork. This phase seems to have been ended abruptly by some unexplained calamity, which greatly reduced the size of Lake Titicaca, around AD 900. When the Quechua-speaking Incas of Cuzco conquered the area around AD 1200, they found the Aymarás at Tiahuanaco living among ruins they could no longer explain. The Aymarás resisted obstinately and were not finally conquered until the latter part of the 15th century under the reign of Inca Túpac Yupangi (1471-93). Even so, they kept their traditional social structures and language, and fought for the Incas under their own leaders. Only religion was formally imposed by the Incas.

Francisco Pizarro landed in Peru in 1532. Six years later Spain conquered Bolivia, and the next year Sucre (then Charcas), still the official capital, was founded. By 1559 Bolivia had become the *audiencia* of Charcas, in the Viceroyalty of Peru, for it had become extremely important for the Spaniards after the discovery of the silver mountain at Potosí in 1545.

The excellent Inca communications and economic organization fell into ruin. Revolutionary movements against the colonial rule of the Spaniards began early; there were revolts at La Paz in 1661, at Cochabamba in 1730 and at Sucre, Cochabamba, Oruro and La Paz from 1776 to 1780. In 1809 the University of San Francisco Xavier, at Sucre, called for the independence of all Spain's American colonies. Finally, on December 9, 1824, Bolívar's general, Sucre, won the decisive battle of Ayacucho in Peru and invaded what is now Bolivia, defeating the Spaniards finally at the battle of Tumusla on April 2, 1825.

On February 9, 1825, when he first entered La Paz, Sucre had already promulgated the decree of independence, but his second in command, Santa Cruz, was for retaining links with Peru; Bolívar was in two minds. Sucre had his way and Bolivia was declared independent. On August 25, 1825, Bolívar named the new country after himself. In 1828, when Sucre left the country, Santa Cruz became President; pursuing his dream of amalgamation he proclaimed a Peruvian-Bolivian confederation in 1836, but Chile and Argentina intervened, and in 1839 Santa Cruz was overthrown and the confederation dissolved.

Since its independence, Bolivia has suffered a grievous contraction of its territory. In the War of the Pacific (1879-1883) Bolivia in alliance with Peru fought the Chileans for the right to retain the nitrate-rich Atacama desert. After a year the Bolivians withdrew and Chile took over the desert and the port of Antofagasta, though it later compensated by building Bolivia the railway between Arica and La Paz. Railways traded for valuable territory has been Bolivia's fate. A railway to Yacuiba was Argentina's return for annexing some of the Chaco. When Brazil annexed the rich Acre Territory in 1903, Bolivia was compensated by yet another railway, but this Madeira-Mamoré line never reached its destination, Riberalta, and proved of little use; it was closed in 1972. A fourth railway, completed in the 1950s, connects Santa Cruz in East-Central Bolivia with Corumbá in Brazil.

There was not even an unbuilt railway to compensate Bolivia for its next loss. Constant disputes between Bolivia and Paraguay over the Chaco led to open warfare between 1928 and 1930, and again between 1933 and 1935. In 1938, by arbitration, Bolivia ceded to Paraguay three-quarters of the Chaco, but obtained a doubtfully valuable outlet to the Río Paraguay. Bolivia's failure to occupy its empty spaces is partly the explanation for these losses.

The moral results of this last defeat had revolutionary consequences. After over fifteen years of disorder, Víctor Paz Estenssoro was elected to the presidency in 1951 on a left-nationalist ticket. A military junta intervened, but in April 1952 a popular revolution overthrew it: Paz Estenssoro returned as president. His government committed itself to a profound social revolution, introducing the expropriation and the nationalization of the tin mines; universal suffrage without literacy or income qualifications; and a policy of land reform and redistribution of the large estates. Hernán Siles Zuazo, a revolutionary leader and vice president under Paz from 1952-56, was president from 1956-60. During his term the economy was stabilized. Paz Estenssoro was again elected president from 1960-64, but shortly after beginning a third term was overthrown in 1964 by General Barrientos, killed in an air crash in 1969. After three ephemeral governments, power was taken in August 1971 by a right-wing general, Hugo Banzer Suárez, who after seven years' rule called for elections in July 1978. Then came another sequence of short-lived military governments, despite disallowed elections which gave victories to ex-President Hernán Siles Zuazo. In August 1982 the military returned to barracks and Dr. Siles Zuazo assumed the Presidency in a leftist coalition government with support from the communists and trade unions. Under this regime inflation spiralled out of control. The elections of July 14, 1985 were won again by Víctor Paz Estenssoro, who imposed a most rigorous programme to stabilize the economy. In the elections of May 7, 1989, Gonzalo Sánchez de Losada of the Movimiento Nacionalista Revolucionario (chief architect of the stabilization programme) was given the presidency by the narrowest of margins; but at the time of going to press, the final result was still in some doubt.

The Constitution of 1967 vests executive power in the President, elected by popular vote for a term of 4 years; he cannot be immediately re-elected. There are nine departments; each is controlled by a Delegate appointed by the President.

Bolivia has, in effect, two capitals. Although Sucre is the legal capital, La Paz is in almost all respects the actual capital, being the seat of the Government and of Congress. On the other hand, the Supreme Court still holds its sessions in Sucre.

Recommended reading: Herbert S.Klein, *Bolivia: The Evolution of a Multi-Ethnic Society* (Oxford University Press).

LA PAZ (1)

La Paz, the highest capital in the world, lies at 3,636 metres in a natural basin or canyon; it is sunk about 370 metres below the level of the Altiplano in its north-eastern corner. Mount Illimani, with its snow-covered peaks (6,402 metres), towers over the city. The Spaniards chose this odd place for a city on October 20, 1548, to avoid the chill winds of the plateau, and because they had found gold in the River Choqueyapu, which runs through the canyon. The mean average temperature is 10°C, but it varies greatly during each day, and the nights are cold. It rains almost every day from December to February, but the sun usually shines for several hours. The rest of the year the weather is mostly clear and sunny. Snow is rare. At first the visitor will probably feel some discomfort, known as *soroche* (altitude sickness), from the rarified air; a few hours resting when you arrive will put that right, though visitors with heart problems should consult a physician. Oxygen is available at the better hotels. In 1986, the population of La Paz was 1.1 million, over half of it Indian.

Most of the Indians live in the higher terraces. Below are the business quarter, the government offices, the main hotels and restaurants and the university. The wealthier residential district is lower still: strung from Sopocachi to the bed of the valley at Obrajes, 5 km. from the centre and 500 metres lower than Plaza Murillo. Beyond Obrajes are the upper-class districts of Calacoto and La Florida. The main sports and social clubs have moved to these districts.

There is some colonial building left; probably the best examples are in the Calle Jaén, but much of La Paz is modern. Plaza Murillo, on the north-eastern side of the river, is the traditional centre. Facing its formal gardens are the huge Cathedral (modern but very graceful); the Presidential Palace in Italian renaissance style, usually known as the Palacio Quemado (burnt palace) twice gutted by fire in its stormy 130-year history; and on the E side the National Congress. Across from the Cathedral on Calle Socabaya is the Palace of the Condes de Arana, now the Museo Nacional del Arte. Calle Comercio, running

Key to map of La Paz
1.Plaza Murillo; 2. Congreso Nacional; 3. Museo Nacional de Arte; 4. Cathedral; 5. Government Palace (Palacio Quemado); 6. General Post Office; 7. Iglesia La Merced; 8. Museo de Costumbres; 9. Museo y Casa de Murillo; 10. Iglesia Santo Domingo; 11. Museo Nacional de Etnografía y Folklore; 12. Villaverde Palace; 13. Casa de la Cultura; 14. Basílica de San Francisco; 15. Witchcraft Market (Mercado de Hechicería); 16. Parque Prehistórico Tiahuanaco (Museo Semisubterráneo); 17. Alcaldía; 18. U.S. Embassy and Citibank; 19. Banco Central; 20. Tourist Office; 21. TAM; 22. Museo Arqueológico de Tiahuanaco; 23. Lloyd Aéreo Boliviano; 24. Mercado Camacho; 25. Biblioteca Municipal. Hotels: 26. La Paz; 27. Sucre Palace; 28. Gloria; 29. Libertador; 30. Plaza; 31. El Dorado; 32. Panamericano; 33. Res. Rosario; 34. Milton; 35. La Paz.

cross-wise past the Plaza, has most of the stores and shops. On Av. Bolívar (to which Mount Illimani provides a backdrop), continuing the Av. Camacho, is the Central Market (called "Mercado Camacho"), a picturesque medley of Indian victuals and vendors presiding raucously over stalls, their black braids topped by hard-brimmed bowler hats. Av. Camacho leads to the residential district of Miraflores.

From the Plaza Venezuela, Avenida Mariscal Santa Cruz leads to the Plaza San Francisco and to the church and monastery of San Francisco, well worth seeing; the church is colonial, richly decorated on native religious themes, and Indian weddings can be seen on Sats. 1000-1200. SW from Plaza San Francisco runs Calle Sagárnaga, with rows of handicraft shops. Going higher still up Sagárnaga is a local market, and turning right on Max Paredes, heading west, one reaches Avenida Buenos Aires, one of the liveliest streets in the Indian quarter. A worthwhile walk is to Mirador Laicacota on Avenida del Ejército.

Other churches of more than passing interest are Santo Domingo (originally the cathedral) on Calles Ingavi and Yanacocha; La Merced, with its decorative 18th-century façade, on Calles Colón and Comercio; and San Sebastián, the first church to be built in La Paz, in Plaza Alonso de Mendoza (named after the church's builder).

Hotels Prices are inclusive of tax and service charge (20% in all).

Hotel	Address	Telephone	Single US$	Double US$
Hotel La Paz	Av. Arce	356950	86-88	117-147
Plaza	Av. 16 de Julio	378311	80	93
Sucre Palace	Av. 16 de Julio 1636	355080	60	63
Crillón	Plaza Isabel La Católica	352121	24	30
Eldorado	Av. Villazón	363355	19	24
Gloria	Calle Potosí esq. Sanjinés	370010	29	42
Libertador	Calle Obispo Cárdenas 1421	343360	27	33
Emperador	Plaza del Stadium 90	367327	18	24

Try to arrive in La Paz as early in the day as possible, as accommodation, especially at the cheaper end of the market, can be hard to find.

The *Plaza* is excellent, and its restaurant is open to the public; peña show on Fridays. The *Libertador* is very good value (although continental breakfast is reported to be poor) and nearest the business section, helpful (baggage stored). The *Eldorado* has been highly rec., secure parking nearby. The *Sucre* gives good value, but hot water a problem, restaurant. For people staying several weeks, often looking for permanent residences, boarding houses (*pensiones*) are popular. For those wanting to stay in the suburbs at a lower altitude there is the *Calacoto*, Calle 13 No. 8009 on the corner of Bustamente, in Calacoto, D, with bath. The following medium-priced hotels have been rec.: *Panamericano*, Manco Kapac 454, clean, E with hot electric showers; *Avenida*, Av. Montes 690 y Bozo (Casilla No. 48), D with bath, clean, central, near market; *Residencial Rosario*, Illampu 704, travel agency downstairs, organizes trips to Puno and Tiahuanaco, D with bath (electric showers), F without, popular with foreigners, laundry expensive, recently modernized and extended (Tel.:325348); *Residencial Copacabana*, Illampu 734, T 367896, 3-star, E, hot water, safe; *Hostería Florida*, on Viacha off Av. Muñecas, E with bath, clean, good views, cheap breakfast, rec.; *Continental*, E, Illampu 626, T 378226, new, clean, friendly; *Milton*,

Illampu and Calderón, D with bath (hot water, friendly, helpful, will store luggage, local market outside).

Cheaper: *Neuman*, Loayza 442, E with bath, recommeded; *Florida* (also *Hostería Florida* above), Ingavi 727, F, good, warm water for shower; *Yanacocha*, Yanacocha 540, E, expensive for what is offered (no breakfast) with bath, clean, but has seen better days (check bill carefully); *Austria*, Yanacocha 531, E with bath, F without, rec.; *Hostal República*, Comercio 1455 (T 357966), remodelled, clean, hot water, E with bath (will store luggage), warmly rec.; *Residencial Independencia*, Comercio y Bueno, moderate prices, rec.; *Torino*, Socabaya 457, safe, clean, central, noisy, hot water on request, E with bath (F without), clothes-washing not permitted, stores luggage, bar, generally popular with young travellers, beware of drug-raids by police; *Sucre*, Plaza San Pedro 340, good. *Sagárnaga*, Sagárnaga 326, D with bath, E without, friendly, helpful, good location and value; next door and slightly cheaper, is *Alem*, No. 334, hot water but inadequate plumbing. *Alojamiento Illampu*, Illampu 635, F, clean, hot water all day. Hotels located in the Indian quarter include: *Andes*, Av. Manco Kapac 364, E with shared bath, clean, hot water, good value (one of the few that offers single rooms). *Pullman*, Av. Montes 665, F, likely to be "full", spartan, good cheap restaurant. *Bolivia*, opp. railway station, F, clean, shared hot showers. *Max Paredes*, on street of same name No. 660, modern, clean, F; *Residencial La Estancia*, México 1559, rec., helpful; *Residencial Don Guillermo*, Colombia 222, E, good value, clean, hot water, rec.; *Urkupiña*, Max Paredes 527, hot shower, good, clean, F; *Residencial Imperial*, Av. General Pando 130, F without bath, E with, clean; *Residencial Illimani*, Av. Illimani 1817, F, highly rec., often full. *Alojamiento Universo*, Inca 175, T 340431, F, good value, hot water, a/c, clean, friendly, safe to leave luggage; *Viena*, Loayza 420, E with bath, F without, beautiful old building, friendly staff, arrive early often full; *Hostal Residencial*, Sucre 949, F, clean, hot showers, friendly; *Plaza* on Plaza Pérez Velasco 785, clean and hot water, F, without bath, E with. Two cheap ones, between the Prado and the University, on Av. Villazón, are *Claudia* and *Posada*, both F. Cheapest possibly is *El Carretero*, Catacora 1056, G p.p., 5 beds to a room, helpful, pleasant, hot shower extra.

Motels *Kori-Tambo*, Achocalla, outside the city, Tel.:327078. *San Bartolomé* rec., own bus service to and from La Paz.

Camping No organized site, but Mallasa (Municipal Park, unmarked, turn left at Alders Infantiles S.O.S.), Valencia and Palca below the suburb of La Florida have been rec. Club Andino Boliviano (T 794016) rents equipment. Kerosene for pressure stoves is available from a pump in Plaza Alexander. Public showers at Duchas La Paz, 20 de Octubre 1677.

Restaurants in La Paz can be roughly divided into two categories: either they serve international cuisine and are expensive or they serve local dishes and are fairly cheap. The restaurants with international cuisine are to be found mainly on three streets, Av. 16 de Julio (the Prado), Av. 6 de Agosto and Av. 20 de Octubre. Service charges and tax of up to 23 % are usually included on the bill but it is customary to leave a tip anyway of a few bolivianos. Always check prices before ordering, and then your bill and change.

Av. 16 de Julio: (street numbers given in brackets.)As well as the hotel restaurants, there is, in the expensive range: *New China* (1577), good international cooking. Slightly cheaper restaurants include the *China* (1549), good Chinese food; *Picol*, corner of Prado and Bueno, good value. *Bistro Paragayo*, nr. *Hotel Plaza*, German food, cheap. There are many snack bars, including *Confitería Elis* (1497), with good plate lunches, excellent soups, breakfasts and pastries, English and German spoken. *Capri* (1605) English spoken, rec. The *Tokio* (1832) next door to the *Hotel Copacabana* has been rec.

Off the Prado, on Calle Campero, one can recommend the *Club de la Prensa*, set in a pleasant garden, the limited menu is typical Bolivian and the company is lively. *Club de La Paz*, Camacho

203, is a good tea room. The *Club Alemán*, off Calle Reyes Ortiz, is expensive but good; may need a member to introduce you. The *Carreta*, an Argentine-type restaurant at Batallón Colorados 32, serves a rec. mixed grill and very good steaks, a favourite of businessmen for lunch. *Panchos*, Landaeta 402, T 342518, steakhouse, Chilean wine, English spoken, rec.

On the continuation of the Prado going west, in Av. Mariscal Santa Cruz, is *Los Escudos* (Edif. Club de La Paz, T 322028/350586), Munich-type bierkeller with fixed 4-course lunch for US$2, food and shows (rec.) Friday and Saturday nights (2000-2400, US$10-12 p.p.). *Lido Grill* (restaurant and confectionery), at No.815, popular meeting place, good food, reasonably-priced. *Parrillada Las Tablitas,* at Mariscal Santa Cruz 1283, excellent steaks, US$6; on the corner of Colón with Santa Cruz is *Restaurant Verona* for economical plato del día. At Av. Ayacucho 206 is the *Internacional,* a lunch-time favourite of local businessmen and has good shows Friday and Saturday nights. *Naira,* Sagárnaga, moderate price, rec. At the other end of the Prado, at Edificio Villazón, Av. Villazón, is *Monaco* (T 365014), good, reasonably-priced international and Bolivian dishes. *Pizzeria Morello,* Av. Arce very good. Further E still, opp the *La Paz* is *Maison Suisse,* Av. Arce, good steaks and raclette, closed Sat. and Sun., gourmet restaurant on first floor. *Viva La Pizza*, J. José Pérez 322, rec., expensive.

Among those on Av. 6 de Agosto: *Hoyo 19* (T 322320), international and local dishes, and *Casa del Corregidor,* Calle Murillo 1040, a colonial mansion, attractive, rec. (see *Entertainments* below). *Helados Kivon,* Plaza Murillo 542, snack bar open Sunday morning.

Av. 20 de Octubre: there is *Max Bieber's Restaurant and Tea-Room,* ice-cream, cakes and other dishes (2080); next door is *Stefano's,* art gallery by day, good Italian restaurant at night; *Churrasquería La Maison* (2344), good steaks. *Patito Pekin* (2463), very good Chinese, about US$5 p.p.

In the shopping and business district: there are numerous snack bars and cheap restaurants. One can recommend: *Marilyn,* corner of Potosí and Socabaya, salteñas, 3-course lunches for US$1.50; *Paulo,* on Potosí between Colón and Ayacucho for confectionery and coffee, offers excellent, cheap family lunches; *Lasky,* on Plaza Venezuela, offers huge helpings and varied meals for less than US$4. *Huari,* corner of Manco Kapac and Tumusla, offers good value; *El Lobo,* Illampu y Santa Cruz, good, clean, rec. Good food can be had at *Ballivián.* Rec. Mexican place: *Tacos Teru K,* Ignacio Cordero 1294, San Miguel (behind Loreto College) T 794513. There are many other snack bars and Chinese restaurants on Calles Sagárnaga, Comercio and Colón.

Cheap vegetarian restaurants to recommend are the *Gran Fraternidad,* Calle México 1790 and *Aquarius* at 1844; *Man Jari,* Potosí 1315, Mon.-Sat. 0900-2100, Sun. 0900-1200, good value vegetarian meals (US$2), bread, muesli; *Nutricentro*, Comercio 1013, 2nd floor, rec. Other recommendations include *Chingo's Hamburgers*, Av. Saavedra, clean; *Arabesque*, corner Loayza and Juan de la Riva. There is a *MacDonalds* on Plaza del Estudiante. *Le Grand Chevalier*, Belisario Salinas 530, charming bar serving crêpes. *El Refugio*, Plaza Avaroa, not cheap, but best meat in La Paz; *Arte y Cocina*, Aspiazu 637, restaurant and bar at night, good, small selection.

Comedor Popular, often referred to as *Comedor Familiar*, for the strictly limited budgets, cheap but filling local meals around US$1, available at Camacho and Loayza markets. The foodstalls at the top of Jiménez sell good T-bone steak cheaply. Bread from street vendors. Fresh dairy produce at *Pil* on Bueno y Cárdenas. *Salteñería Comercio*, Comercio 1439, excellent salteñas and Bolivian food, outdoor seating, inexpensive.

Books Foreign language books at *Los Amigos del Libro*, Mercado 1315, and El Alto airport; they also sell tourist maps of the region from Puno to the Yungas, and walking-tour guides. Treat the details with caution. Gisbert on Calle Comercio 1270 (corner Plaza Murillo), and Juventud on Mercado and Yanacocha have good stocks (Gisbert also stocks maps). Amigos del Libro and Gisbert will ship books. There are 2nd-hand stalls on Av. Ismael Montes. Centro Boliviano Americano (CBA), Parque Zenón Iturralde (near Av. Arce), has public library and recent US papers (Mon.-Fri. 0900-1200, 1430-1920). USIS has lending library and 2nd-hand paperbacks. Alliance Française, Calle Ingavi (open Mon.-Fri. 1600-2000), has an old library. Goethe-Institut, Av. 6 de Agosto 2118 (Mon.-Thurs., 1600-1900), good library, recent papers in German, videos in German and Spanish.

Films For Kodak, Casa Kavlin, Calle Potosí 1130; Laboratorio Fuji Color, Potosí 1316; Foto Linares, Mercado y Loayza, will develop both Ansco and Agfa colour film 1-day service on black-and-white, but only repairs Minolta cameras. Repairs also at Av. Sánchez Lima 2178 by Rolando Calla C, just ring bell (1000-1200), there is no bell; also at Potosí 1316, between 1400—1900, T 373621, very helpful, professional, fair prices. Film is available at black market prices around Av. Buenos Aires and Pasaje Ortega, Calle Granerdo, but otherwise it is expensive, as is developing. Fuji transparency film available at half shop price in market. In all cases check dates on film.

Shopping Look around and bargain first. There is inexpensive silver and jewellery in the little cabinets outside Lanza market on Av. Santa Cruz. Up Sagárnaga, by the side of San Francisco church (Mercado Artesanal), are booths and small stores with interesting local items of all sorts. There are good jewellery stores throughout the city but visit the gold factories for lower prices and special orders. At Sagárnaga 177 is *Artesanía Nacional Tiwanaku*, for paintings, silver jewellery and woven goods. Although there have been complaints about quality and price, a visit is a must. Pacha-Marka, Sagárnaga 272, good selection of antiques, knowledgeable owner. Many Indian objects are sold near Av. Buenos Aires, and Indian musical instruments on Calle Granier, near the General Cemetery. *Puma Punku*, Av. 16 de Julio, for weaving. *Artesanías Titicaca*, Av. Sánchez Lima 2320, and Marka Tambo, Jaén 710, retail and wholesale weaving. *Millma*, Sagárnaga 225, and in *Hotel Plaza*, for alpaca sweaters (made in their own factory) and antique and rare textiles. *Wari* on Sagárnaga will make to measure very quickly, prices reasonable. *Suri*, Av. Juan de la Riva 1431. *Curerex* has four shops in La Paz, rec. for leather goods. Good value is to be had at the *Hotel La Paz* shops. *Artículos Regionales* in Plaza de los Estudiantes is rec. *Suma Ampara*, Av. Villazón 1958, wide variety of woven goods, but prices not as low as in street markets. Along Murillo and between Sagárnaga and Santa Cruz are various little shops selling old ponchos and rugs. *Artesanía Sorata*, off Sagárnaga, specializes in dolls made by a women's cooperative. The market between sells alpaca articles and other textiles—but bargain hard. Generally, the higher up one goes along Calle Santa Cruz, the cheaper woollen goods seem to become. Also weavers' co-operative in central plaza. Alpaca goods are more varied than in Peru. Try *Inti Art* on the Prado (expensive modern designs), which is next to an antique store, in turn next to the *Restaurant China* and another on Calle Goitia. *Algo Más* on the Prado has an unusual selection of handicrafts. *Punchay Artesanías y Folklore*, Calle Santa Cruz 156 (T 362253), has been highly rec.—worth a visit; also *Rumillajta*, one of the Galería shops adjacent to the San Francisco church entrance. *Schohaus* at Calle Colón 260 has good pewter. Many shops closed Saturday afternoon and Sunday.

The Indian market is a good place for ponchos and local handicrafts. See also the "witchcraft market" on Melchor Jiménez, 3rd street on left walking up Calle Santa Cruz from Av. Mariscal Santa Cruz, fascinating items for sale. Food market is the Mercado Camacho (Camacho y Bolívar). The Tourist Office has a full list of all markets.

Taxis US$0.25 p.p., for short trips within city limits. Between city and airport, US$10, can be shared, more at night including luggage. Current prices (incl. luggage) should be on display at the Airport exit. If not, enquire at the Airport Tourist Office (not too reliable, or their office in town). Moon Valley plus cactarium, US$20 for about two hours. Taxi drivers are not tipped; tip for porters—US$0.20 for each large piece of luggage. Sharing of taxis is common. Taxi to Tiahuanaco, US$20 return for 2; no time limit on stay at site. Radio taxis, T 371111 or 322424.

Taxi-like vehicles flying various coloured flags are *Trufis*, following fixed routes on a standard charge.

Car Hire Cars may be hired direct from Imbex, Av. Arce 2303, T 379884, Suzuki jeep US$25 per day plus US$0.25 per km.; Rent-a-Car International, F. Suazo 1942, T 357061; Kolla Motors,

Rosendo Gutiérrez 502, T 341660/351701; Bolivia Rent-a-Car, Cap. Ravelo 2445, US$25, or through a travel agent. Kolla have well-maintained four-wheel drive Toyota jeeps (which seat 6) at US$198 per week, plus US$0.50 per km., plus insurance and gasoline (very expensive). Oscar Crespo, Av. Bolívar, rents Brazilian-made VWs; Ruben Hidalgo Nogales of Domicilio Graneros 304, Zona Rosario, hires out Dodge Darts. One can also hire experienced drivers for US$25 a day plus accommodation and meals. You must have an international driving permit to drive in Bolivia, and outside the city you need an Hoja de Ruta (**see page 226**). Long queues for fuel, few stations.

Garage for VW and other makes: Ernesto Hug, Av. Jaime Freyre 2326, T 342279.

Local Buses Fares: US$0.10 in town; US$0.15 to Obrajes and US$0.20 to Calacoto. Minibuses (*Micros*) are dearer than buses, but much less crowded.

Festivals Particularly impressive is the Alacitas Fair held from Jan. 24 to Feb. 15, on the upper part of Plaza Villarroel, mostly on Calle Tejada Sorzano (take *micro* B, K, H, 131 or X). "It is dedicated to Ekeko, an Indian household god. You can buy plaster images of him at many of the booths. He is a red-nosed cheerfully-grinning little personage laden with an assortment of miniature cooking utensils, coins, balls of wool, tiny sacks of sugar, coffee, salt, rice and flour; a kind of Bolivian Santa Claus. Ekeko is said to bring prosperity and to grant wishes. If you buy a toy house, or a cow, or a sheep at the Alacitas, you will get a real one before the year is out. There are also model motor-cars and planes, for the extreme optimists." (Christopher Isherwood, "The Condor and the Cows.") End May, early June, Festividad del Señor de Gran Poder, huge procession of costumed and masked dancers. December 8, festival around Plaza España, not very large, but colourful and noisy. On New Year's Eve fireworks are let off and make a spectacular sight, and a din, view from higher up. **See also page 227** for festivals outside La Paz.

Entertainment Best entertainment for visitors are the folk shows (*peñas*), though they are reported as packed with tourists and increasingly commercialized. Outstanding (up to 7-group) folk show at *Peña Naira* (US$5, includes first drink), Sagárnaga 161, next to pizzeria, every night about 2215. Various restaurants have shows worth seeing. At these folk shows, visitors will be able to listen to the wide variety of local musical instruments, the different types of flutes, including the *queña*, and the *charango*, a small guitar with five strings, the back often made from the hide of an armadillo. Enquire at the *Rumillajta* shop (in the *galería* close to San Francisco church) about future performances by the famous folk group of that name. Good *peña* at *Casa del Corregidor*, Calle Murillo 1040, US$5 good food, exc., Fri. and Sat. p.m. only; similarly *Marko Tambo* on Calle Jaén, US$7 (all incl.) repeatedly rec. Indian dance halls, for example on Max Paredes, should only be visited in the company of Bolivians. There are a few discotheques of which the best are *Alambra, Onix, Michelangelo's*, Av. 20 de Octubre 1832, and the *Viejoteca*, in Obrajes, which also has shows at week-ends, or the *Baccara* in Calle 25 de Agosto. For drinks, there is *Giorgissimo* on Loayza, which is very popular (but not cheap by Bolivian standards) and also serves good meals, *Charlie's Bar* on Plaza Isabel La Católica, and *St. George's Pub* at Av. 20 de Octubre 2019 (both expensive lounge bars). The *Sky Room* in the *Hotel Gloria* has been rec. La Paz has a resident ballet and symphony orchestra (*Teatro Municipal* on Sanjinés and Indabura) but no theatre company. There are some good cinemas, films being mainly in English. For film buffs there is the excellent Cinemateca Boliviana, corner of Pichincha and Indabura, La Paz's art film centre with festivals, courses, etc. (entry US$0.75 for students). The Casa de Cultura (almost opposite Plaza San Francisco) sometimes has exhibitions, concerts or film festivals, most of which are free.

Spanish Courses Centro Boliviano Americano (address under **Books** above), US$140 for 2 months, 1½ hrs. tuition each afternoon; Centro de Estudios Brasileños, Av. Sánchez Lima 2226, T 3-22110, 2 hrs. tuition each morning, US$125 for 6 weeks.

Sport There are two golf clubs (Malasilla, the world's highest, and Pinos. Non-members can play at Malasilla on weekdays subject to the usual payments, but it may be difficult to hire clubs); two tennis clubs (La Paz Tennis and Sucre Tennis); and two riding clubs. Football is popular and played on Thursday and Sunday at the Siles Stadium in Miraflores, two clubs (Micro A); there are reserved seats. Basketball is played in Plaza del Estudiante on Mon., Wed. and Fri. in season. Fishing and duck-shooting on Lake Titicaca and other lakes and rivers. There is a yacht club at Huatajata on Lake Titicaca (**see page 195**); sail and motor boats can be hired there and at Chúa. YMCA sportsground and gymnasium, opposite the side of the University of San Andrés, Av. Villazón, and clubhouse open to the public, Av. 20 de Octubre 1839 (table tennis, billiards, etc.), regular meetings Tues. and Thurs. 1930 of a mountaineering group which runs weekend excursions.

Mountaineering See page 191

Museums
Museo Nacional de Arte, across from the Cathedral at Calle Socabaya 432, housed in the 18th century baroque palace of the Condes de Arana, with beautiful exterior and patio. It has a fine collection of colonial paintings and also exhibits the works of contemporary local artists.

Admission US$0.25; open Mon. Thurs. 1000-1200, 1500-1730. There are other exhibits at the Galería Municipal, on Colón, and at Galería Naira, on Sagárnaga.

Museo Tiahuanaco (Tiwanaku), or National Museum of Archaeology, easily reached by the flight of stairs by María Auxili church on the Prado. This modern building, simulating the Tiahuanaco style, contains good collections of the arts and crafts of ancient Tiahuanaco and items from the eastern jungles. Admission US$0.50; Tues.-Fri. 0900-1200, 1500-1800 (summer 1530-1700).

Museo Semisubterráneo, in front of National Stadium, with restored statues and other artefacts from Tiahuanaco. It's in a sunken garden out of doors, and much can be seen from street level.

Museo Nacional de Etnografía y Folklore, on Calle Ingavi 916, is housed in the palace of the Marqueses de Villaverde, worth seeing (especially the exhibit on the Chipaya Indians), small contribution requested. Mon.-Fri. 0830-1130, 1430-1700.

The following four museums, all on Calle Jaén, are included on a single ticket, which costs US$2, from Museo Costumbrista. All are open Tues.-Fri. 0900-1200, 1430-1830, Sat. and Sun. 0900-1200. Calle Jaén, a picturesque colonial street with many craft shops, is well worth seeing for itself.

Museo Costumbrista, Plaza Riosinio, at top of Jaén. Miniature displays depict incidents in the history of La Paz and well-known Paceños. T 378478.

Museo Murillo, on Jaén, T 375273 (closed in 1987 for renovating) was originally the home of Pedro Domingo Murillo, one of the martyrs of the abortive La Paz independence movement of July 16, 1809. This colonial house has been carefully restored and has a good collection of paintings, furniture and national costumes of the period; there is also a special room dedicated to herbal medicine and magic. Warmly rec.

Museo de Metales Preciosos, Jaén 777, well set out and warmly rec., T:371470.

Museo de Litoral, Jaén 789, with artefacts of the War of the Pacific.

Mineral Museum, Banco Minero, Comercio 1290, 3rd floor. Open Mon.-Fri. 1000-1200, 1500-1700. Good gold and silver exhibits; free.

Núñez del Prado, Ecuador 2034, Mon.-Fri., 0900-1200, 1400-1800, excellent sculpture.

Zoo at the upper end of Av. Bolivia, small, US$0.20.

Banks Citibank, on the Prado (cashes its own travellers' cheques, 1% commission and will receive money sent from any US bank); other banks; American Express agent: Magri Turismo, Av. 16 de Julio 1490, 5th Floor (doesn't change Amex travellers' cheques). Open 0900-1200, 1400-1630. Closed Saturday. Cash advance on Visa card at Bano de La Paz on Prado. Money is changed in hotels or *casas de cambio* rather than in banks.

Exchange Houses Sudamer, Colón 256, good rates also for currencies other than US$; Titikaka Tours, Loayza 203; Tony Tours, Yanacocha y Asbún. Farmacia Hispania, Yanacocha, has been specially noted (cash US$ from travellers' cheques, 1% commission), also the Shampoo Shop *perfumería* at Yanacocha 319, where you ask for Sr. Koli. Airport exchange booth will only change up to US$50 (commission) in travellers' cheques. Casas de cambio and street changers can be found on Camacho, Colón and Prado. It is not worth dealing on the black market since there is virtually no difference between black and official rates. It is very difficult to change money off the beaten track. You are advised to stock up in La Paz, or even before entering Bolivia. If you leave Bolivia with bolivianos you may not be able to change them in neighbouring countries. Watch out for forged currency, especially dollars and Chilean pesos.

Addresses
Instituto Nacional de Arqueología de Bolivia, Calle Tiwanaku 93.
Immigration, Calle Landaeta 220, near Plaza del Estudiante.
French Consulate, Av. Hernando Siles 5390, esq. Calle 08, Obrajes, T 782849.
British Embassy and Consulate, Av. Arce 2732-2754. T 351400. Closed 1200-1300 and Wed. p.m.
United States Embassy, Calle Colón and Mercado (has a good reading room), Consulate on Av. Potosí—(T 350251).
West German Embassy, Av. Arce 2395. T 352072 or 352389.
Canadian Consulate, Av. Arce 2342 (1000-1400), T 375224.
Austrian Consulate, Edif. Petrolero, 7th floor, Oficina 1, Av. 16 de Julio 1616, T 326601, 1600-1800.
Danish Consulate, Calle Layanza 250, Edif. Casilla, 5th floor, No. 509, T 322601/325589.
Netherlands Consulate, Av. Arce 2031, Edif. Victorio, 2nd floor.
Norwegian Consulate, Av. Mscal. Santa Cruz, Edif. Esperanza, 11th floor, T 322528.
Spanish Consulate, Calle Cordero T 343518.
Swedish Consulate, Av. Arce 2856, Casilla de Correo 852, T 327535.
Swiss Embassy, Av. 16 de Julio 1616, 6th floor. T 353091. Open 0900-1200, 1300-1400.
Argentine Consulate, Av. 16 de Julio 1480, over Aerolíneas Argentinas T 353233/353234.
Brazilian Consulate, Fernando Guachalla 494, T 350718. Visa office is round corner at Sánchez Lima 2199, 0900-1300, Mon.-Fri.

Paraguayan Consulate, 7th floor Edificio Montevideo, Av. Arce, just below Calle Montevideo.
Peruvian Consulate and Embassy, 6 de Agosto 2190 y Calle F.Guachalla (a visa costs US$5 in US$ bills).
Venezuelan Embassy and Consulate, Av. Arce 2678, Ed. Illimani, 4th floor (consulate open Mon., Wed., Fri. 0900-1200).
YMCA, 20 de Octubre 1839, Casilla 963.
Asociación Boliviana de Agencias de Viajes y Turismo, Edif. Litoral, Mariscal Santa Cruz 1351, Casilla 3967.

Doctor   Dr René Coloma Rector, Edificio Cosmos, 11th floor, Office 1, Av. 16 de Julio (El Prado) T 377914 (private surgery, Mon.-Fri. from 1500), or 355456 (home—any time). Rec., speaks good English. Also Dr. César Moreno, Calle Pinilla 274, T 792665/328805 (trained in Spain and Germany) **Dentists**   Dr Rigoberto Mena Morales, Rm. 705, Edif. Libertad (T 327636). Also Dr and Dra Osorio at *Hostal Austria*, Yanacocha 531. Tourist Office has a list of doctors and dentists who speak foreign languages.

Hospital   Clínica del Accidentado, Plaza Uyuni 1351, T 328632/321888 offers first aid. Efficient and well run nursing homes such as Clínica Americana, Clínica Alemana, Clínica Rengel (T 390792/8), Clínica Santa María etc. Red Cross opposite Mercado Camacho will give inoculations if required. The Methodist Hospital (12th block of Obrajes, take "A" *micro* from the Prado) runs clinic at US$5, telephone for appointment.

Hygiene Tampons may be bought at the *farmacia* next to the *Hotel La Paz*, otherwise hard to find.

Church   Protestant Community Church (inter-denominational), in English, American Co-operative School, Calle 10 Calacoto (T 795639 or 792052). The former pastor and his wife (The Rev. & Mrs. Charles F. King) have written an excellent duplicated guide to "Life in La Paz" which can be got on Sunday at the Community Church. Sunday service at 1045, but there are "lots of activities during the week". Anglican-Episcopalian services are held at the Community Church on the third Sunday of each month.

Synagogues   Calle Landaeta 330 (Sat. a.m. services only); Colegio Boliviano Israélito, Canada 1846 for Friday service—it looks like a private house.

N.B. In the San Pedro Prison (nr. Plaza Sucre) there are some Commonwealth, US, and European citizens. Enquire at your consulate to see if one of your countrymen is "inside". A name of a prisoner helps to get a visitor in. Visiting hours, through the bars, are 0900-1730 each day and prison visits on Thursday and Sunday at the same time. These people appreciate visits and old clothes (warm), books, food (milk, cheese), and company. You will be searched and have to leave all items of value with the guards. It may be better to leave these locked up somewhere securely. Passports also have to be shown, and these may be held by the guards during a visit.

Cables   Public Telex booths at Entel, Ayacucho 267 y Mercado.

Telephone   service to the USA is fairly good, though less so to the UK (now via satellite). Passports are kept to ensure prompt payment! Tolls are lower on Sundays. Entel office in Edif. Libertad, Calle Potosí, English spoken, and in Calle Ayacucho (see above).

Post Office   on Ayacucho, just above Potosí (open Mon.-Sat. 0800-2000, and until 1200 on Sun. and holidays). Poste Restante keeps letters for 3 months. Procedure for sending parcels: customs (upstairs) must check contents first; then go to stamp counter to fill in customs declaration and purchase stamps; next have value of stamps checked and stamps franked, at a separate counter; finally, go to opposite window for *certificado* ticket. (Don't forget sack, needle and string for sewing up, and moth balls for textile items).

Electric Current   Varies considerably. Generally 110 volts, 50 cycles A.C. in La Paz, 220 volts 50 cycles A.C. elsewhere, but check before using any appliance. (You may even find 110 and 220 in the same room). US-type plugs can be used in most hotels.

Laundromat   Wash and dry, US$2 per 4-kilo load, 6-hour service, at Gelmi-Lava-Sec, 20 de Octubre 2019, suite 9, US$1.35 for 1 kg.; Lavandería Select, Av. Arce, down from *Hotel La Paz*; 3-hour service, rec. Lavandería Cinco Estrellas, 20 de Octubre 1714. Finesse Limpieza, Illampu 863; laundry service at Oficina Gregoria Apazá, Colombia y Almirante Grau, T 369607, phone first. Dry cleaning, Calle Murillo 1366, US$1 per kg., La Esmeralda, Colon 558.

Tourist Office   Instituto Boliviano de Turismo (IBT) Plaza Estudiante, corner of México y 16 de Julio. Very helpful. English spoken. Maps and leaflets are available, but are not always up-to-date or accurate.

Maps   Instituto Geográfico Militar, Av. 16 de Julio 1471, (take Micro C or N), head office open 1500-1700 only, collect maps next day, delivery to your hotel not reliable. Passport is needed to get in, but worth it as they have the only railway map available in La Paz and a wide selection of others invaluable for the traveller. Topographic maps cost US$12 per sheet (scale 1:100 000 and 50,000) and about US$8 for standard tourist maps. Departmental road maps are meant to be

available in the tourist offices in the capitals of each department but often they are out of stock. Maps are sold at Ichthus bookshop on the Prado; also at Librería La Paz, Amigos del Libro and Gisbert (See page 183).

Guides   *La Paz Insólita* (7 maps) US$3 and *Guía de La Paz* by Jorge Siles Salinas (historical) US$5. *Guía Central de Bolivia*, US$2, information on transport, statistical and geographical data. In particular it contains the La Paz minibus schedules, which are unobtainable elsewhere.

Travel Agents   Crillon Tours, Av. Camacho 1223, Casilla 4785 (T 374566), expensive, rec.; they run a hydrofoil-bus service to Puno, US$160, via Copacabana and Isla del Sol, incl. lunch and breakfast; they also have a sunset to sunrise programme, based at the *Inca Utama Hotel* at Huatajata, involving trips on the lake, meals and lodging. Transturin, Camacho 1321 (T 328560/363654, Telex 2301 TRTURIN BV). La Paz-Puno, inc. boat crossing on Lake Titicaca, US$80, rec. Diana Tours, Sagárnaga 328, T 358757, very good value. Turismo Balsa, Av. 16 de Julio 1650 (T 356566 and 355817), has reservation service for air tickets; Turisbus (Illampu 704, Casilla 442, T 325348/326531), helpful, again mixed reports on its services (to Puno and Cuzco— US$29), and Marka Tambo, Calle Mercado 1328 (Ed. Mscal. Ballivián, Local 24) for local tours. Tourismo Tours, Bueno, rec.; Vicuna Tours, *Hotel Copacabana*, rec. Exprinter, Loayza 107, has tickets to Tumbes and Guayaquil (also operates exchange facilities) to Cuzco via Copacabana, US$30. Tawa Tours, Sagárnaga 161, run jungle tours with own camp as well as the Salt Lake areas, and the Amazon, friendly, good guides (also charter flights to Europe and USA); Profian Tours, Sra. Perales, Fernando Guachalla 319, rec. for local bus tours. Magriturismo, Av. 16 de Julio 1490, very helpful. Diplomatic Tours, managed by Rosario Zambrana, located at 2nd floor of Plaza Venezuela 1920, has been rec. (T 372611); will provide airport transfer (US$8). Leslie Iruzoque organizes "alternative" trips while her mother can provide accommodation near Moon Valley (T 360777 or 791767). Paititi S.R.L., Av. Arce 2630, and Calle Juan de la Riva, Ed. Alborada (oficinas 106-107, Casilla 106, T 329625), organizes adventure tours, rec., Javier Prudencio is helpful and speaks several languages. Bolivian Adventure Tours in hall of *Hotel Sucre* has tents for hire. Also Carmoar Tours, Calle Bueno 159, which is headed by Günther Ruttger, (T 340633), rec. as among the best and the cheapest. Many agencies arrange excursions or travel to Peru (Puno, Cuzco, Arequipa), as well as local tours. See also names and addresses under "Exchange Houses", page 185.

Airport   El Alto, on plain above La Paz, the highest commercial airport in the world (4,018 metres), about ¼ hour by taxi (US$5, colectivo US$2.50) from centre (Cotranstur bus leaves Plaza Obelisco half-hourly until 2000 US$0.50, recommended). A motorway links city and airport. International airport tax US$10 in bolivianos or dollars, internal US$1 in bolivianos. There is a duty-free shop but it can sometimes forget to open. No exchange facilities. The small tourist office at the Airport should know the price of a taxi to town, some maps available, English spoken, helpful. The coffee shop is slow but inexpensive.

Air Taxis   US$250 per hour, contact Major Pericón of Taxi Aéreo Urkupiña, T 350580, 812099. Aero Inca, T 361018. Alas Doradas T 354070.

Air Services   Lloyd Aéreo Boliviano (LAB), Camacho y Loayza, T 351163, and TAM, Av. Montes near Plaza Velasco (the air force and not recommended) fly to the main cities and towns, and also to Lima and Arica daily. Fares are comparatively low for internal flights. (For details of internal flights, see under proposed destinations.)

Bus Services   (for information, T 366783); to Copacabana (see page 195), Oruro (3 hours, US$5), Potosí (14 hours, US$9.50, very cold, all at night—1800-1830), Sucre (18 hours, US$11.50), Cochabamba (12 hours, US$ 5.50—obtain free ticket for luggage to be stored in compartment), Santa Cruz (23 hours, US$14), Tarija (26 hours, 1450, US$16), Coroico (0900,

Tues., Thurs., Fri., Sat. 5 hours, US$4) for views sit on the left hand side. However, after the rainy season the road is described as "a treacherous goat track, treacherous for goats too". Villazón, 26 hrs. (US$15), Tiahuanaco (US$1). There are also services to towns in the Yungas with Flota Yungueña, Av. de las Américas 354; take Micro K, U or V to Villa Fátima, get off at the big service station—the booking office is 20 metres in front. Buses to Sorata, Copacabana (except for Flota Copacabana, expensive, which does) and Tiahuanaco do not leave from the bus station but from the Cementerio district (Micro M goes there). Companies located in the Cementerio district include Manco Kapac, 2 de Febrero, Ingavi, Morales. As so few roads are well paved, train is usually preferable to bus when there is a *ferrobus* service (see below). The services of Cóndor are best avoided.

International Buses To Buenos Aires, daily at 1800, Expresos Panamericanos. Bus to Arica at 0530 Tues. and Fri, in each direction, US$28, Litoral (office at back of bus terminal), 20-22 hrs. (It is reported that Litoral buses are in poor condition and are liable to break down). Martínez, US$20, 22 hrs. (either service can take 40 hours), or (cheaper) El Cariñoso to Charaña on the frontier then Sanga from Visviri (Chile) to Arica, US$17, a very hard trip on a dirt road in the Bolivian section to Tambo Quemado, subject to cancellation in the wet, no food but beautiful. A fourth route to Arica is with Panamericana via Peru, Mon., 0730, 24 hrs., US$27.50. Colectivos to Puno daily with different companies most easily booked through travel agencies, US$11, 10 hrs. **N.B.** Of the various La Paz-Puno services, only Turisbus (Illampu 704) does not make you change to a Peruvian bus once over the border. For luxury and other services to Peru see **Travel Agents** above.

Trains There are acceptable *ferrobus* (railcar) services (with food and drink served) between La Paz and Cochabamba (8 hours, Mon., 0900, Wed. 0800, Fri. 2100, US$15 Pullman, US$10 special; and to Potosí (11½ hours), Mon., 0830, US$16.90 Pullman, US$11.20 special; train Wed. 1720, US$11 Pullman, US$8 special; goes to Sucre, US$15 Pullman, US$10 special. You may only buy tickets the day before you travel: office opens 0700, but get there beforehand. To Villazón (24 hrs.) for Argentina, Mondays, Wednesdays and Fridays, departs 1640; no food or drink is served (very dusty journey, arr. 1230 next day); *tren mixto* leaves Wed. and Sun. at 1915, fares for both, US$19 Pullman, US$13 special. Book ahead at central station; queue for booking at 0600 on previous day (queuing numbers are given out), take passport. All trains South (to Oruro and Villazón) are sold out by 0700 on Monday, so 1) go to station 2 hrs. before departure for returned tickets, 2) bus to Oruro then catch train, 3) try Exprinter travel agency, 4) try and board train anyway and pay the guard, 5) fly to Tarija and then go by road to Villazón. Phone to check times etc.: 352510. It is always advisable to check times before travelling as there are often changes.

Railways from the Coast (1) By the Southern Railway of Peru from Arequipa to Puno, on Lake Titicaca. Getting to La Paz from Puno: by road (several lines, 10-hour journey); Crillon Tours run a daily hydrofoil service (0600 from Puno; 0830 bus departure from La Paz).

From Guaqui to El Alto, above La Paz, a railway follows the broad plateau on an almost level gradient, rising only about 300 metres to El Alto. The journey is done once a week in about 2 hours by modern diesel railcar. It stops for 20-40 minutes at Tiahuanaco to give passengers a quick look at the ruins. Not everyone can get onto the railcar; some have to go on by bus every hour on the hour, 3½ hours, or colectivo (2 hours), or by the ordinary train (4 hours). Travelling from Bolivia to Peru, the train leaves La Paz on Fridays at 1400.

Of the ordinary Guaqui-La Paz train, Nicholas Humphrey writes: "It drooled down to La Paz so slowly that the fireman on our train stepped off at one point, walked into a field, picked up a lamb from a flock, and trotted back to catch the train, which had not decelerated to help him in his larceny."

(2) **Arica-La Paz International Railway**, 447 km.: either take a *ferrobus* straight through to Arica, every other Mon. and Fri. 0730, 12 hrs., US$50 incl. meals, book ticket one-two weeks in advance (many are taken up by travel agencies: ask around, e.g. Exprinter, if none on sale at station), or take a train to Charaña, then change to a bus to Arica. Fares: La Paz-Charaña: Pullman slow train US$23; special US$15; train leaves La Paz every Tues. at 2300, arriving Charaña at 0530.

The line from Arica skirts the coast for 10 km. and passes into the Lluta Valley, whose vegetation is in striking contrast with the barrenness of the surrounding hills. From Kilometre 70 there is a sharp rise of 2,241 metres, in 42 km. The line is racked for 48 km., but the rack is no longer used. At Puquíos station, Kilometre 112, the plateau is reached. The altitude here is 4,168 metres. In the distance can be seen the snowcapped heights of Tacora, Putre, Sajama, and their fellows. The greatest altitude is reached at General Lagos (4,247 metres). The frontier station of Visviri is at Kilometre 205, with a custom house. Beyond, the train enters Bolivia and the station of Charaña.

In the Bolivian section the line runs via Corocoro, the copper mining town, to Viacha, the junction of the several railways running to Antofagasta, Guaqui, and Buenos Aires. The mountain peaks visible include Illimani, Sorata, Huayna-Potosí, Muruata, and many others.

(3) Antofagasta-La Paz, by Antofagasta and Bolivia Railway, 1,173 km., now definitely a trip for the adventurous who are impervious to cold, is by train as far as Calama in Chile, then by bus (240 km.) to Antofagasta; the bus ticket (US$3) is given when entering Chile. This, the most southerly of the three railway routes connecting La Paz with the Pacific coast, passes through magnificent

scenery but the timetable has been described as "pure fantasy". There is one train a week (with restaurant car only on Bolivian side), leaving La Paz on Friday at 1150 (latest reports are that it leaves from Oruro, about 1700), arriving Calama Saturday 1700; arrive by bus in Antofagasta 2100 Sunday. Fare: US$30; bookable the day before. Be at La Paz station by 1200 Thursday (tickets are on sale to 1400) to be certain of a seat (all reserved). There are no sleeping cars and it can be very cold. Money changers not allowed on the train, but still manage to operate. Watch out for forged Chilean notes especially if the light is bad. It is advisable to buy Chilean currency and sell bolivianos before journey. All passports are collected and stamped in the rear carriage, they should be ready for collection after 1-2 hours (beware, as the train goes down to Chile, carriages are added; the reverse happens in the other direction).

Going from Chile to Bolivia, Calama, 2,255 metres above the sea, is a useful point at which to stay for a day or two to get used to the altitude before going higher. The summit is reached at Ascotán (3,960 metres), and the line descends to 3,735 metres at Cebollar, where it skirts a great borax lake, 39 km long. The Bolivian frontier is crossed a short distance beyond (444 km.) Ollagüe station (a change of trains—very cold—be quick to get your seat), from which there is a 77 km. spur to the copper mines of Collahuasi. For the next 174 km. to Uyuni the line maintains an almost uniform level of 3,660 metres. The timetable is (approximately): leave Calama 1300, arrive Ollagüe 2300 (1-2 hr. stop, though you can spend as much as 10 hrs. in the bitter cold waiting for the Bolivian train, and up to 3 hours for Customs searches), arrive Uyuni 0500; the down train should leave Uyuni for Calama at 0500, may not leave till 1400. The train is full of smugglers who will throw others' bags out to get their gear on.

Uyuni, the junction with the branch line of 90 km. to Atocha, gives rail access, via Villazón on the Argentine border, to Buenos Aires, a route which is not interrupted by snowstorms. Change at Uyuni or Río Mulato for *tren mixto* from Villazón, or better at Oruro (which you can visit) and then *ferrobus* or express from Uyuni or Río Mulato to Potosí or La Paz reserving your seats the day before. After crossing the Bolivian border you need bolivianos to buy food on the train, so if you have no bolivianos make sure you have some small dollar notes for changing into bolivianos at the first stop in Bolivia. Money can be changed at Ollagüe (Chilean Customs) and Oruro. **Watch baggage** at Oruro; the thieves are notorious.

(4) Buenos Aires-La Paz: This railway journey of about 2,400 km. takes 71 hours. There is no through train service. Take Monday, Wednesday or Friday La Paz train (1640) to Villazón (arrives 1230), then cross frontier to La Quiaca to catch train or bus to Jujuy or Tucumán (for trains) to Buenos Aires (Retiro) The railway line from La Quiaca to Jujuy in northern Argentina has been repaired, and two trains are running per week **(see page 94)**.

Note that many travellers from La Paz on the Buenos Aires and Antofagasta lines take a bus to Oruro (more comfortable and quicker than the train) and board the train there. Again, you may have trouble getting a sleeper if you do this. Remember that in northern Argentina buses tend to be much quicker than trains.

Excursions from La Paz   There is trout fishing in the many glacier lakes and streams near La Paz.

The best near-by excursion is to Río Abajo and Malasilla golf course: through suburbs of Calacoto and La Florida follow the river road past lovely picnic spots and through some weird rock formations, known as the "Moon Valley". About 3 km. from bridge at Calacoto the road forks; sharp right leads to the Caza y Pesca Club and Malasilla golf course. Moon Valley can also be reached by Micro 11 ("Aranjuez") from Plaza San Francisco, which runs along the Prado and goes as far as Aranjuez Forest (US$1); cross the bridge on your right then walk 2 km. uphill past the cactus garden to Moon Valley. Most of the local travel agents organize tours to Moon Valley, but taxis are not dear (US$12), especially if shared; make sure the price is per car and not per person. Near the Arcillo Arce cactus gardens (dilapidated) is the *Balneario Los Lobos*, popular for lunch at weekends. To Zongo Valley: a steep but scenic ride down past several of La Paz's electric power plants. In 32 km. the altitude drops from 4,265 to 1,830 metres. A beautiful ice cave under the Chacaltaya glacier may be visited. Take taxi for a day US$30. Drive, 2 hours, to Laguna Zongo. Walk 2 km. along right bank of aqueduct, cross bridge, then uphill 500 metres.

To Ashumani (past Valley of the Moon) for good views of the valley and houses of the wealthy (no buses). Walk back along the valley and catch frequent buses into town.

To El Organo del Diablo—a gigantic, tooth-shaped rock, take Micro "Ñ" (last stop Cota Cota) or 21 from Calle México to the end of the route, then continue for 1 km. more and you will see the rock on the left—"more impressive especially if the wind is blowing than Moon Valley". A further 4 km. on is the top of the mountain with a superb view of Illimani. The road continues to Ventilla, the start of the Inca trail.

For the Takesi (Inca) road hike, take an Emta bus at 0900, Mon. Wed. or Sat. from the bus terminal, or from a street on the right below Plaza Belsu (which is below the Mercado Rodríguez) take a colectivo or truck to Ventilla on Palca road (alternatively take a Cota Cota bus to the end of the line or a taxi to Ovejura vehicle checkpoint above Cota Cota, US$6.35, then truck to Ventilla). Take the track to the left, parallel to the Río Palca for 10 km. track to San Francisco mine. At Choquecota, before San Francisco, there are shops, and you can stay at the mine if necessary. The "camino de Takesi" goes over the pass (4,650 metres), passes the Laguito Loro Keri and then follows the valley which ends at Chojlla and on 5 km. to Yanacachi, some meals available in private homes—colectivo to La Paz at 0800. (If you miss that, it's a 45-min. walk down to Santa Rosa, which is on the main La Paz-Chulumani road.) One powerful river can be crossed by applying to houses on the bank, where they will rig up a pulley for you for US$1-2. The Bradts' book *Backpacking in Peru and Bolivia*, and the La Paz tourist office leaflet with sketch map both describe this 3-5 day walk, which shows exceptionally fine Inca paving in the first part. Please take care not to litter the route. The highest point is 4,650 metres and the lowest 2,100. The trail can also be used as a starting point for reaching Chulumani or Coroico. The scenery changes dramatically from the bitterly cold pass down to the humid Yungas. At Chojlla one can sleep at the school house for a fee.

Another trail is the Choro hike from La Cumbre pass to Coroico, descending from the snow-covered heights to tropical vegetation. Take a bus to Villa Fátima, then a truck or pick-up to the statue of Christ at La Cumbre where the trail starts. The hike takes at least 4 or 5 days; you pass Choro, the first village, on the second day. (The tourist office has a map of the trail.) There are reports of thieves at night. Try to camp away from villages with other walkers and set a guard if possible. From Chairo (accommodation—US$2.50—and food with Família Paredes de la Tienda, very friendly, swimming pool), trucks go to the main road, but there is a stiff climb remaining up to Coroico.

A third hike is Yunga Cruz, from Chuñaví to Chulumani in the Sud Yungas (sketch map available from La Paz tourist office).

For the acclimatized only: A climb to Corazón de Jesús, the statue at the top of the hill reached via the steps at the north end of Calle Washington, then left and right and follow the stations of the cross. Worth the climb for the views over the city and the Altiplano, but watch out where you put your feet.

To see Puya Raimondii flowers, go to the village of Comanche, 2½ hrs. from La Paz (micros from railway station to Viacha—1 hr.—then truck to Comanche—rough, dusty and cold); some travel agencies arrange tours.

The route to **Huayna Potosí**, an attractive peak (2 days) starts from Zongo lake. Micro G to Alto Lima, then truck at about 1300 to Milluni. Alternatively taxi to Zongo from about US$7 (buses return at about 1500). On Friday about midday the electriciy company's truck leaves its office near La Paz bus station for Zonga lake: negotiate! Huayna Potosí (about 6,000 metres) requires mountaineering experience with ice and crevasses on the way to the top; however bad weather, apart from mist, is rare. Alternatively Condoriri or Pequeño Alpamayo are reached in one or two days from Tuni at Km. 21 on the La Paz-Tiquina road.

Mountaineering Increasing numbers are visiting the Cordillera Real, to the east of La Paz. The range has the marked advantages over many high massifs of settled weather from May-Sept., easy access via numerous mine tracks, and favourable starting altitudes (4,200-4,700 m.). The Cordillera Real is 150 km. long with six peaks over 6,000 m. (20,000 ft.)—Illampu 6,380 m., Ancohuma 6,420 m., Chearoco 6,100 m., Chachacomani 6,100 m., Huayna Potosí 6,090 m., Illimani 6,460 m. All can be climbed relatively easily from La Paz, the latter two within a few hours' driving. There are also a large number of impressive 5,000 m.-plus peaks. Normal alpine experience and equipment will enable most peaks to be ascended, and many new routes remain to be explored. Several peaks can be climbed in a day, but the 6,000 m. mountains usually require 2-4 days. There are no huts (except Chacaltaya ski-lodge). Do not underestimate altitude problems: at least 1-2 weeks' acclimatization is usually necessary before exceeding 5,500 m. (A visit to Chacaltaya and its ski-slopes is an easy way of judging one's reaction to altitude). Also rescue services are virtually non-existent; prudence and proper gear (incl. crevasse rescue abilities) are indispensable. Note that mountaineering gear and high altitude camping equipment cannot be bought in Bolivia.

A good guidebook is *The Southern Cordillera Real*, R.Pecher & W.Schmiemann, Plata Publishing Ltd (1977), possibly obtainable in La Paz; distributor: Los Amigos del Libro (W.Guttentag), Casilla 450, Cochabamba. Also numerous expedition reports. The Club Andino Boliviano, Calle México 1638, PO Box 1346, will help with advice on routes and has maps on access, etc. Excellent maps covering most of the range are the photo-surveyed 1:50,000 IGM Series, US$5 each. Club Andino Boliviano will be very pleased to accept "surplus" gear after climbing is finished. Access routes from La Paz: Illimani, 4-5 hours via Calacoto and Huancapampa; Huayna Potosí, 2 hours via El Apto and Milluni tin mine to Zongo Lake beyond pass.

Other ranges: Western Cordillera including Sajama (6,530 m.)—mainly extinct volcano ice cones. Also Cordillera Apolobamba, northern extension of Cordillera Real extending into Peru with many 5,000 m.-plus peaks. (Joyce, Tony and Mark Harrison).

Alfredo Martínez at the Club Andino is the country's foremost guide, or contact the well-regarded and friendly Bernardo Guarachi, Plaza Alonso de Mendoza, Edif. Santa Anita, oficina 314, T 320901, Casilla 20886, La Paz (he has equipment for hire) or Norbert Kloiber, Herrenstrasse 16, 8940 Memmingen, West Germany (T 08331-5258). Iván Blanco Alba, Asociación de Guías de Montaña y Trekking, Calle Chaco 1063, Casilla 1579, La Paz, T 350334, has been recommended (the association has about 10 guides in all and arranges climbing and hiking expeditions). Also recommended, José Camarlinghi (licensed by the German Alpine Club), Casilla 3772, Pedro Kramer 924, La Paz (T 352266).

Skiing Ninety minutes by car from La Paz (36 km.) is Chacaltaya, the highest ski run in the world. Season: November to March, sometimes longer. Skiing equipment may be hired, and a rope-tow reaches 5,221 metres, facilities basic. Taxi US$30 (whole car) for a half-day trip, or similar to the top by rented car costs about US$60, and really only at weekends; no visitor should miss the experience and the views. However the trip can be hair raising, buses carry no chains and the drivers have little experience on snow. Occasionally the buses only go half way. The Club Andino, México 1638 y Otero de la Vega, runs its own Saturday and Sunday buses; the day trip, beginning at 0830 and returning at 1730, comes to about US$24 for bus ticket and ski pass for the day; your bus ticket (US$10) gives free access to the ski station restaurant, otherwise US$2 entrance, hot drinks only. Equipment for hire is available (US$10 skis and boots from the Ski School—in the same building as the Ski Club, limited equipment for hire, queue at once) or Ricardo Ramos, 6 de Agosto 2730, about US$ 10 per day (T 343441 or 372920). A good tip is to share equipment since, at that altitude, you will need a long break between activities. The lift pass costs US$4—out of season the lift only goes if there are 5 or more people (N.B. Club Andino's oxygen bottle at the Chacaltaya station is reported to be empty). Crillon also does a day trip, at US$15. Club Andino also occasionally arrange trips to Mount Illimani. One can walk to the summit of Chacaltaya for a view of Titicaca on one side and La Paz on the other. Tiring, as it is over 5,000 metres, but one has most of the day to do the climb. Take plenty of mineral water when going to the mountains as it's thirsty work in the rarefied air. Laguna de Milluni, near Chacaltaya, is a beautiful lake to visit, but do not drink its water; it is dangerously contaminated by acid residues from mining.

Urmiri Take road S towards Oruro, turn left at Urmiri sign at Km. 75. To get this far take Flota Bolívar or Flota Copacabana bus; lifts from the crossroads are few and far between. A steep scenic descent leads to pool filled by mineral springs and a pleasant primitive inn. Worth visiting. A 2½ hour trip one way. The La Paz Prefectura runs buses to Urmiri, where they have a hotel (D), price includes food.

Sorata is 105 km. from La Paz at 2,695 metres, giving appreciable relief, and is very beautiful. A 4-6 hour trip each way, bus every day with Transportes Flores, Calle Eyzaguirre (near Cemetery), 0645, or La Perla del Illampu, Calle Miguel Angel Bahía 1556 at 0700, US$2.50 (arrive in good time for either service). Plenty of trucks to Sorata from by cemetery, US$2. It is in a valley at the foot of Illampu. Area has lovely views, mountain climbing, cave exploring. Climbers of *Illampu* (experience and full equipment necessary) start here: hire horses at Candelaria mine and on to Coóco where llamas are hired to reach the base camp at 4,500 metres. Swimming pool 2 km. along road to river. Sunday market. Also Sunday market festival, including bull market, at village of *Achacachi* (*Pensión*, F, tiny) on the road. Not far from Sorata, along E shore of Lake Titicaca, is a tremendous marsh giving the best duck shooting in Bolivia. Typical *fiestas*, both at Sorata and Achacachi, on Sept. 14. Pleasant walks: splendid one to San Pedro village and cave with ice-cold swimming in underground lake, 75 metres below surface (take torch). Ulla Ulla vicuña reserve off the Achacachi-Puerto Acosta road around the northeast corner of Lake Titicaca, about 200 km. from La Paz.

Sorata Hotels *Prefectural*, rec., good value, C, with meals, hot water. *Residencia Sorata* above Casa Gunther, C (rec.) with good meals. *Perlandina*, F, friendly, basic. *Alojamiento Central*, main plaza, No. 127, F, basic. *San Cristóbal*, near market, F, bargain. *Copacabana*, F, basic, clean and cheap.

Sorata is the starting place for the "Camino del Oro" or "Gold-digger's Trail", a strenuous 7-8 day hike to Guanay (**see page 198**), via La Cumbre, Ancoma, Wainapata, Chusi, Llipi, and Unutulumi (from where lifts can be taken to Guanay past all the present gold mines). After Ancoma it is very hot; in the dry season take water. There is a shop in Chusi. (Details in the Bradts' book—see above).

Tiahuanaco (Tiwanaku) The ruins of Tiahuanaco (admission US$2.20 including museum—beware of overcharging, open 0900-1700) are near the southern end of Lake Titicaca, by partly paved road through the village of Laja (solid silver altar in church, but church closed to visitors), the first site of La Paz. Simple meals at US$0.80 available in village. There is a restaurant near the ruins, for those on booked tours (drinks are expensive, but it does good sandwiches). The village church is in striking contrast with the pre-Incaic statuary in front of it. The ruins, which are being reconstructed, comprise four main structures: the Kalasasaya compound, the Acapana pyramid, the underground temple, and the Gate of the Sun, with carved stone blocks weighing many tons; this is reported in a bad state as the locals used it for shooting practice. Many archaeologists believe that Tiahuanaco existed as early as 1600 BC; the reason for the demise of the Tiahuanaco civilization is not entirely clear. Ticket to Tiahuanaco also gives entrance to Puma Punku (down the road 1 km.), which contains a pair of andesite gates (among the finest examples of stone cutting in South America) while its sandstone platforms are made up of cut slabs weighing 13 tonnes each. There is a museum near the ruins: entrance free to those with admission tickets for the site; however most of the best statues are in the Museo Tiahuanaco or the Museo Semisubterráneo in La Paz. Indians trade arrowheads and bronze figures (almost all fakes). There is a very basic *alojamiento* on Calle Bolívar, cheap but good views.

Guidebook in English   *Tiwanaku*, by Mariano Baptista, Plata Publishing Ltd., Chur, Switzerland, or *Discovering Tiwanaku* by Hugo Boero Rojo. They are obtainable from Los Amigos del Libro (or 2nd-hand from stalls in Av. Ismael Montes). *Guía Especial de Arqueología Tiwanaku*, by Edgar Hernández Leonardini, a guide on the site, recommended. Written guide material is very difficult to come by, so if you can hire a good guide take him with good grace (US$10).

Buses for Tiahuanaco (72 km.) can be caught opposite the Cemetery off Plaza Garita de Lima but may be full already! Taxi for 2 costs about US$20 (can be shared), return, with unlimited time at site. Transportes Ingavi, Av. Manco Kapac 445 (take any Micro marked 'Cementerio') US$1 (2½ hrs.), every 15 mins. or so, arrive at terminal by 0600. (Tourist buses cost US$15 return; some tours include Moon Valley.) Some buses go on from Tiahuanaco to Desaguadero; virtually all Desaguadero buses stop at Tiahuanaco, US$0.50. Return buses (last one back at about 1700) can be caught at the crossroads in the village at the "Tránsito" sign; cannot be booked in advance (return is often difficult).

Lake Titicaca

The road and railway go to **Guaqui,** the port for the Titicaca passenger boats (service suspended in 1985/86; in 1989 the ferry and railway were carrying only freight. *Hotel Guaqui*, G, good value; tiny restaurant on the Plaza de Armas has been rec.). The road crosses the border at Desaguadero into Peru and runs along the western shore to the Peruvian port of Puno, at the northern end. Desaguadero is noted for its lack of accommodation. At Yunguyo a side road to the right re-enters Bolivian territory and leads to Copacabana. (Hourly buses, taking 45 minutes, US$0.40.)

Copacabana, 158 km. from La Paz, is an attractive little town on Lake Titicaca. It has a heavily restored cathedral containing a famous 16th century miracle-working Dark Virgin of the Lake, also known as the Virgin of Candelaria, the patron saint of Bolivia. Candlelight procession on Good Friday. The cathedral itself is notable for its spacious atrium with four small chapels; the main chapel has one of the finest altars in Bolivia. An *hospicio* (serving now as an almshouse) with its two arcaded patios is worth a visit; ask permission before entering. There are 17th and 18th century paintings and statues in the sanctuary and monastery. Good food and drink at the hotels and in the market. Bank only opens Wednesday-Sunday (does not change travellers' cheques); a few restaurants and shops give poor rates, so buy Bolivian money in Yunguyo (beware, much counterfeit money here) before crossing frontier, if coming from Peru. Major festival on August 5-8 makes town full, and dangerous. There are good walks beside the lake for those unwilling to do penance on the hill, or to an Inca site, Horca del Inca, on the hill behind the town overlooking the lake (rec. sunset walk). On the other side of the lake is El Baño del Inca, about 2 km. Ask for directions on reaching the woods. Copacabana's water supply can be intermittent. **NB** The local police need watching: they have been known to accuse travellers of "photographing secret buildings" and "fine" them US$10.

Hotels   *Playa Azul*, B, full board (rooms fair, half-board a possibility), hot showers, water supply poor, some adverse reports, T 320068. *Ambassador*, E (bookings through the Copacabana bus company in Av. Montes, La Paz); *Patria*, in main square, E, dirty, cold water, good food;

LA PAZ Rough sketch

LAKE TITICACA
La Paz, Lake Titicaca and
the Peruvian Frontier.

Prefectural, E without food, hot water, some rooms have lake view; *Alojamiento Imperio,* Calle Visconde de Lemos, F, clean, new, some hot water (shower US$0.50 extra), repeatedly rec., will change money; *Kota Kahuaña,* Av. Busch 15, pink house, F, hot showers, cheap, clean, some rooms with lake view, rec. *Emperador,* behind the Cathedral, F, clean, rec., washing done, communal baths, hot showers 0600-1300; *El Turista,* 13 de Mayo and Jaure, F, rec., cheap and clean; *Residencial Porteñila,* F, clean, safe, rec. Many basic, but cheap and clean, *pensiones,* F.

Restaurants *Aransay,* Av. 6 de Agosto 130 friendly, good food. Watch out for gringo pricing of food and in restaurants. *Peña Clima* has music on Saturdays, behind the market; *Turistas* is rec., as is *La Patria* on Plaza Principal, left-hand corner of the Cathedral. Many other restaurants offer acceptable US$2 meals; trout rec..

Transport By car from La Paz to Copacabana (direct), 4 hours. Bus: either take an agency bus for US$6 (pick up at your hotel; US$0.40 ferry fare at Tiquina not normally included); or public bus: 2 de Febrero, José María Aliaga 687, T 377181, US$2.50, 0800, 1500 each direction; Manko Kapac, José María Aliaga, T 350033, US$2, 0700 and 1315 each way; book one day in advance. Bus, Copacabana-Yunguyo (for Peruvian frontier), hourly, US$0.40, from plaza below *Hotel Playa Azul.* Minibuses to Puno leave 1200-1400, US$4.50 from *Hotel Litoral* on Plaza, or *Hotel Patria,* or *Playa Azul* (Colectur); they leave same time same place for La Paz. To reach Copacabana (or Tiquina) you cross the lovely straits of Tiquina (coming from Peru, the ferry fare has to be paid in Peruvian currency). On the La Paz side of the Strait, there is a clean blue restaurant with excellent toilets. Vehicles are loaded on to a barge equipped with outboard motors. The official charge for a car is US$2, though they ask for more and there is a US$0.50 municipal car toll to enter Copacabana. Delays on the lake crossing during rough weather, when it can get very cold. Even when one has a bus ticket passengers pay US$0.25 each to cross and passports are checked. **N.B.** It is impossible to travel from Copacabana to Guaqui direct, because of border crossings.

Visiting the Lake Avoid Sundays. Sailing boats and motor-boats can be hired in Copacabana to visit the **Island of the Sun**. It contains a sacred rock at its NW end, worshipped as the site of the Inca's creation legend. In the middle of the E shore are Inca steps down to the water. A 2-km. walk from the landing stage to the SE takes one to the main ruins of Pilko Caima—a Sun Gate (not as impressive as at Tiahuanaco), a two-storey building with false domes and superb views. The Island of the Moon (or Coati) may be visited—the best ruins are an Inca temple and nunnery. A cheap way to visit the Island of the Sun is to catch the public ferry from the Bolivian naval station (passport required); it leaves 1300 on Weds., Sats., Sundays. Worth taking camping equipment and food as there is no boat back on the same day nor any accommodation. Ask permission at the *hacienda,* good spring water available opposite hydrofoil landing. Beware of thieves. Boats (not tackle) are hired at reasonable rates for fishing. Dawns and sunsets are spectacular. At *Chúa,* on the lake, there is duck shooting, fishing, sailing and at ***Huatajata*** a yacht club—restaurant open to public, serves reasonable trout, and Crillon Tours International Hydroharbour and *Inca Utama Hotel* (*Hotel Chúa,* situated on lake between Huatajata and Tiquina, rec.). From Huatajata boats may be taken to Suriqui, where the reed boats are made (US$20 return—share the cost). Thor Heyerdahl's *Ra II* and *Tigris* reed boats were constructed by craftsmen from Suriqui, and so was the balloon gondola for the Nazca (Peru) flight experiment (**see page 777**).

Boats on Lake 6 hours to Island of Sun and back, about US$50 for boat taking 12 (you can bargain) or US$40 for a 6 seater, best ruins on S, good scenery on N side, but difficult to persuade boatmen to go there. There is accommodation, bed and blankets, near the Inca steps and at Challa on the other side of the island and some basic supplies from villagers. Ask for Juan Mamani Ramos in Challa. Similar rates for Island of the Moon. Motor boat trips from Copacabana to Suriqui may be arranged for US$16. (Sailing boats, which take five and cost less, often suffer from lack of wind in the morning.) Rowing boat, US$6.50 an hour. Cheaper boats can be found by walking 15 km. along the lakeside outside Copacabana to Yampupata where fishermen cross in ½ hour, US$1-2. Danger of sunburn on lake even if it does not feel hot.

Crillon Tours, Avenida Camacho 1223, run a hydrofoil service on Lake Titicaca with a bilingual guide. Leaving La Paz at 0600 (except Saturday), you get to Huatajata on Lake Titicaca for breakfast by 0800. The hydrofoil sets off at 0830, moves past groups of reed fishing boats, and stops in the Straits of Tiquina for a few minutes to watch the wooden ferry boats crossing. Only the Island of the Sun is visited to see the ruins. You arrive at Copacabana for sightseeing and a trout lunch, with local folk music. The short tour returns to La Paz from Copacabana; the longer one continues to Puno (Peru). Charge: US$160 from La Paz to Puno. Expensive but fascinating, not least for the magnificent views of the Cordillera on a clear day. Turismo Balsa's tour of the

Lake, including Isla de Suriqui, has been recommended, except for the fact that the motor boat has no liferafts.

Tristan Jones, who crossed South America in his sailing cutter *Sea Dart* (see his book *The Incredible Voyage*, Futura Publications) wrote to us as follows: "During my crossing I spent over eight months cruising Lake Titicaca and probably know it (as a whole) better than anyone, including the Indians. On the Bolivian side, in Lake Huanamarca, i.e. from Straits of Tiquina south, the best way to visit the Lake from La Paz is to take a bus from Avenida Buenos Aires to Huatajata and there ask for Nicolás Catari. He is a great boatbuilder and knows the Lake well. Avoid Suriqui Island, which has become very commercialized. The best islands to visit are *Pariti,* where the weaving is very good indeed and, only a mile or so away, *Quebraya*, where there are pre-Inca *chulpas*, or tombs, stretching along the shore. This was the ancient port for Tiahuanaco, when the lake fell back from that city. No-one lives there, and it is best always to go with an Aymará guide, for the locals are very jealous of the place.

"The only hotel on Lake Huanamarca, at Chúa, is now expensive, but the trout is good. Nicolás Catari will also, if he likes you, arrange sleeping accommodation but it is very rough and you would have to take your own sleeping gear.

"Note The Titicaca Indians' most interesting music, and quite rare, is at masses held for the dead."

Crossing the Peruvian Frontier

We give below the journey by road (see Peruvian section, **page 796** for other routes). A visa to Peru will cost US$5 in US currency (if you need one). Also, the Bolivian navy (assorted hovercraft and motor boats) may be seen at Tiquina. The road between La Paz and Tiquina is now motorway to El Alto, then surfaced.

No hotel at Tiquina, but ask for the Casa Verde, where you can stay for US$0.50 p.p. Two cheap eating places at Yunguyo.

Just as interesting as the water route is the bus journey from Puno along the western side of the lake via Juli, Pomata, Yunguyo (from there to Copacabana is 13 km. so take taxi or bus), then back almost to Pomata to take the main road on to Desaguadero at the border. Puno-Desaguadero takes 5 hours by taxi and 6 hours by bus. La Paz is reached any time between 1800 and 2100. This is a colourful trip, with wonderful views of the lake against the snow-capped Cordillera. The road on the Peruvian side is nearly all paved, and you really see the Indian life of the Altiplano. The Desaguadero-La Paz road is mostly good gravel with some fords (treacherous in the dark) and railway level crossings. There are many checkpoints for motorists.

A colectivo from Puno to La Paz costs US$11 p.p. (8 hours). A bus can be caught at Desaguadero for La Paz, 114 km., US$5, but there is sometimes a shortage of buses. Another problem with the Desaguadero route is that on Tuesday and Friday it is reported that cars are not allowed to cross because these days are set aside for "interchange of national produce". At the risk of another change it may be better (and certainly more scenic) to catch buses Puno-Yunguyo (get exit stamp) Yunguyo-Copacabana (frequent buses) and Copacabana-La Paz, via Tiquina (**see page 195**). This is possible in one day in the reverse direction.

If you are leaving Copacabana for Peru, get exit stamp at Bolivian immigration office (open 0800-1900) on Yunguyo road, or you can get exit/entrance stamp at Immigration Office on Copacabana near the edge of the town, if border post is closed. Be careful that dates stamped are correct on all documents. Generally, though, this is now a very straightforward border crossing, with customs and immigration posts at either side of the border; the buses stop at each one, 4 in all (or you can walk, but it is over 1 km.). Make sure, however, if arranging a through ticket La Paz-Puno, that you get all the necessary stamps en route, and ascertain whether your journey involves a change of bus.

It is also possible to enter/leave Bolivia via the east side of the lake. However, the Peruvians do not officially recognize the road as being a border crossing. (Officially, you must get your entry stamp in the Department of Puno, but as this is next to impossible on this route, you will run into difficulties later on.) The Bolivian frontier is at *Puerto Acosta* (there is an immigration office, but it is advisable to get an exit stamp in La Paz first, especially if you have not been staying at a recognized hotel (**see page 227**). One *alojamiento* (G) and one restaurant (*pensión*) on the main plaza (2 smaller *pensiones*/kitchens on the smaller plaza).The road to La Paz (fine during the dry season only) passes through splendid scenery while the area around Puerto Acosta is good walking country and the locals are friendly. Ask for directions to the thermal water swimming pool. The Acosta road northwards to Peru rapidly deteriorates and is only recommended in the dry season (approximately May to October). The only transport beyond Acosta is early on Saturday mornings when a couple of trucks go to the markets, some 25 km. from Puerto Acosta on the border (no formalities); the Peruvian and Bolivian markets are completely different.

N.B. Remember that if you wish to enter Peru from Bolivia you must have an onward ticket (or return ticket) out of Peru. A ticket outward from Peru can be purchased at Exprinter in La Paz, but you will have to pay in foreign currency rather than bolivianos.

THE YUNGAS (2)

NE of La Paz a road runs to the Yungas. It circles cloudwards over La Cumbre pass at 4,725 metres; the highest point is reached in an hour; all around stand titanic snowcapped peaks and snowfields glinting in the sun. Then at Unduavi the paving ends; the road becomes "all-weather" (dangerous, especially in the rainy season) and drops over 3,400 metres to the luxuriant green Alto Beni in 80 km. The little town of **Coroico** is perched on a hill at 1,525 metres; the scenery is beautiful (a walk to the river for a swim is a must). A visit to the old cemetery is recommended especially for camera buffs.

The roads to Coroico and to Coripata and Chulumani divide at Unduavi at a height of about 3,000 metres on the E side of La Cumbre. Here the well-surfaced road ends; the only petrol station is at Unduavi. There is no good place to eat at Unduavi, nor at Santa Rosa on the road to Coripata. From Coroico one can go by road and boat to Puerto Linares and Santa Ana, starting points for trips on the Río Beni.

Hotels *Prefectural,* C, up the hill, biggest in town with full board (F without food) but very run down, water 0700-1030 and 1400-1700, and food poor. *Bel Jardin en los Pinos,* F, uphill past cemetery, ½-hr. walk from town (ask for La Alemana, Victoria), cooking facilities, swimming pool, garden, rec. *La Casa de Sigrid,* F, German-run, out of town, pool, clean, friendly, helpful, meals. *Lluvia de Oro* (good value, food rec., billiards downstairs, cheap), swimming pool, F, top floor rooms are best. *Alojamiento Pijoán* is very basic, F, cold water. *Hostal Kori,* swimming pool (open to all), good value, F, top floors rec., clean. The hotel near the junction of the La Paz-Chulumani and Coripata-Chulumani roads has been rec.; C. A camping site will be found by the small church on the hill overlooking the town—a stiff climb though; at the church take the left-hand path for another stiff climb to a waterfall (only worth it in the wet season). Coroico is an attractive place to wander around, especially towards evening. Hotels can be difficult at holiday weekends.

Restaurants *La Tasca,* only one menu and under new ownership, not as good as before; *La Casa* is German-run, good food and setting, excellent fondue for dinner, wonderful views, rec.; *Don Pepe,* good food. *Kory,* good breakfast; *El Rodeo,* Caranavi road, brilliant view. The convent has been rec. for its chocolate biscuits, peanut butter and coffee liqueurs, and interesting cheap wine.

Festivals There is a colourful four-day festival on October 19-22. On November 2, All Souls' Day, the local cemetery is festooned with black ribbons.

Buses from La Paz to Coroico (US$4) leave at 0900 on Tues., Thurs., Fri., and Sat., returning from Coroico on Wed., Fri., Sat. at 0700 and Sun. at 1300 and take 5 hours each way; sit left hand side (book return to La Paz well in advance). Flota Yungueña (Villa Fátima, La Paz—beyond petrol station). Trucks to and from La Paz are more frequent (daily) and cheaper, US$2.10. Take Micro B, 25 minutes from or to the suburb of Villa Fátima in La Paz, from where trucks leave, one block above the bus company. Transport can be a problem at holidays. Reconfirm onward bookings from and to Coroico as it is possible to get stuck for days at a time. In Coroico, trucks leave from the market.

Chulumani, the capital of Sud Yungas, is the main regional centre. Citrus fruits are the main products from this area as well as some coffee. Along the road from Puente Villa to Coripata you enter the main coca growing area of northern Bolivia and the countryside is quite different from that near Coroico, where coffee, as well as coca and fruits, is the main crop.

Hotels *Hotel Prefectural,* D; *Motel San Bartolomé* (T 358386), B, pleasant and *Motel San Antonio,* C, with pleasant cabins and swimming pools. *Hotel Bolívar,* cheap, clean and friendly.

Bus La Paz-Chulumani, Flota Yungueña, 120 km., 6 hours, US$3.30.

From below Coroico the road forks, the lower fork following the river NE to **Caranavi,** 164 km. from La Paz, at times along a picturesque gorge, towards the settled area of the Alto Beni, and Santa Ana. Truck from Coroico, US$1.65. Market day is Saturday; lots of transport in late afternoon.

Hotels *Esplendido, Universo* and *Alojamiento Buen Amigo,* E; *Caravani,* F, clean and friendly. *Prefectural,* F, not rec., but has a swimming pool. *Avenida,* F, very basic; *Residencial Rosedal,* clean, friendly, cheap.

Bus Yungueña buses leave La Paz for Caranavi at 0900 each day, US$5.20; the 164-km. journey takes 6-7 hours and trucks 12½ hours. Direct bus Coroico-Caranavi on Sundays, or you can take the La Paz bus to Yolosa, where a *camioneta* can be taken to Coroico (US$0.60). For the route from Caranavi to the Beni Lowlands, **see page 223**.

Some 70 km. from Caranavi lies the gold mining town of **Guanay,** an expensive but interesting place. To stay, *Hotel Panamericano,* Av. Sorata, F, seems the best, though there are no locks on the doors; *Hotel Minero,* F. Permission to stay for only 48 hours is granted by the police. Electricity is rationed—every 10 mins. or so. Other gold mining sites are Tipuani and Mapiri. Buses direct from La Paz (Yungueña, Trans. 16 de Noviembre on main square).

N.B. The Yungas are a coca-growing region, so it is advisable not to wander too far off the beaten track.

SOUTH FROM LA PAZ (3)

Oruro is built on the slopes of a hill at an altitude of 3,704 metres. The population, mostly Indian, is 178,393. It is about 190 km. from La Paz, and is important as a railway centre and for its tin, silver, and tungsten. A 20,000 tons-a-year tin smelter has been built nearby at Vinto; reported no longer open to visitors, following an accident. There is good *pejerrey* fishing on a large nearby lake. Excellent daily market, near railway station. The zoo is not really worth a special visit. Rail travellers from Antofagasta or Buenos Aires can alight at Oruro and continue to La Paz by bus (quicker). Hotel prices at least double at Carnival time and a severe water shortage puts showers at a premium. We are informed that in hotels water is only available in the mornings, owing to city ordinances.

La Diablada At carnival on the Saturday before Ash Wednesday, Oruro stages the Diablada ceremony in gratitude to Pachamama, the Earth Mother. Two figures, a bear and a condor, clear the way for a procession of masked dancers, led by two luxuriously costumed masqueraders representing Satan and Lucifer. Alternating with them in the lead are St. Michael the Archangel and China Supay, the Devil's wife, who plays the role of carnal temptress. Behind them come hundreds of dancers in ferocious diabolical costumes, leaping, shouting, and pirouetting. The parade ends in the crowded football stadium, where the masqueraders perform various mass and solo dances. These are followed by two masques: the first is a tragic re-enactment of the Conquest, in the second the golden-haired Archangel conquers the forces of evil in battle.

In the contest between good and evil, the result in favour of the good is pronounced by the Virgen del Socavón, the patroness of miners, and after the performance the dancers all enter her chapel, chant a hymn in Quechua and pray for pardon. The Diablada was traditionally performed by Indian miners, but three other guilds have taken up the custom.

The costume always features the heavy, gruesome mask modelled in plaster, with a toad or snake on top; huge glass eyes; triangular glass teeth; a horsehair wig; and pointed, vibrating ears. Tied around the neck is a large silk shawl embroidered with dragons or other figures, and the dancer also has a jewelled, fringed breastplate. Over his white shirt and tights he wears a sash trimmed with coins, and from it hang the four flaps of the native skirt, embroidered in gold and silver thread and loaded with precious stones. Special boots equipped with spurs complete the elaborate outfit. Satan and Lucifer wear scarlet cloaks, and carry a serpent twisted around one arm and a trident. The working-class Oruro district known as La Ranchería is particularly famous for the excellence of the costumes and masks made there. One of the most famous folklore groups is the stately Morenada. Carnival lasts 8 days with displays of dancing by day and night often superior to those given on the opening Saturday. It is compulsory to sit to watch the Diablada processions; benches line the streets and a seat costs from US$1 to US$4, although on the main square they are reserved for tourists and cost US$10. Seats can be booked at the town hall. Take raincoats as protection against water pistols and *bombas de agua* (water-filled balloons). Latest reports suggest that the processions on Saturday before Ash Wednesday are fine, but degenerate thereafter as all the participants are drunk; also participants now have to be wealthy to afford to take part, so *campesinos* have been forced to the periphery (selling food, etc.). Beware of sharp practices and prices for gringos during the period of carnival.

Guide *Carnival de Oruro.* Dance costumes and masks, Calle La Paz, 400 block.

Hotels *Repostero,* Sucre 370, good by local standards but unfriendly, C with bath, hot water unreliable on upper floors; *Prefectural-Oruro,* Pagador y Galvarro, C, near station, improved, good restaurant; *Lipton,* Av. 6 de Agosto 225, E, with bath, TV and hot water (cheaper without bath and TV), breakfast; *Residencial Ideal,* Bolívar 386, F, clean but no hot water. *Alojamiento Bolívar,* Bolívar y Sargento Tejerina, F, poor, but restaurant is good and cheap. *Terminal,* above bus depot, D, modern, good, hot water, night club, expensive restaurant. *Residencial Familiar* annex, F, 25 de Mayo, is clean. *Hispanoamericano,* Galvarro y Aldana, opposite station, F, no hot water and no running water after 2200. *Alojamiento Central Oruro,* Potosí 5917, F, clean, warm showers; *Alojamiento Ferrocarril,* Galvarro 6278, F, basic, no hot water, opp. railway station, nearby is *Alojamiento San Juan de Dios,* Galvarro 6338.

Restaurants *Fuente Suiza,* 6 de Octubre y Bolívar, very good but not cheap; *La Prensa,* Murguía (500 block, Press Club restaurant), quite good; *Pigalle,* Plaza 1° de Febrero, is well regarded but not cheap; *El Chef,* 6 de Octubre 6056, T 50712, good, not cheap; *Don Pepe,* Pagador y 1° de Noviembre, above Ciné Elisa, good; *Prague,* 6 de Octubre, near centre, good bakery, cheap food at *Pensión 10 de Febrero,* at bottom end of Octubre. Vegetarian: *El Huerto,* Bolívar 359. *Pastelería La Polar,* C. Presidente Montes 5985, is good place to get warm; *Pastelería Suiza,* Bolívar, near 6 de Octubre, clean and excellent tea and pastries. *Donut Shop,* 6 de Octubre y Mier, for the obvious, and good hamburgers and beer; rec. nameless restaurant at 6 de Agosto 1166, huge portions.

Sauna Ayacucho y Galvarro, wet or dry, showers US$0.75. Duchas Oruro, 500 block of Av. 6 de Agosto (near bus terminal); Santa Bárbara, Pagador 6801.

Shopping *Infol,* Ayacucho 426 for alpaca, high quality but not cheap nor a large selection and *Reguerín* on the junction with Mier; also sell devil masks. Handicraft market at bus station, cheap souvenirs. Items are generally cheaper in Cochabamba. **Laundry**: Alemania, Aldana 280.

Museums Worth a visit are Patiño legacies, e.g. the Sala de Conciertos (now a cinema). Museo Arqueológico Vivero Municipal, near the zoo on Calle Lizarraga (reached on foot, or Micro 'A Sud') has unique collections of stone llama heads and carnival masks. Guide available, US$0.75. Geology Museum at the university. Ask the tourist office whether they are open.

Exchange Banks not helpful. It is quite easy to change dollars (cash) on the street, specifically 1 block E of main plaza, or at Ferretería Findel, Calle Pagador 1491, near the market (large hardware store; owner, Don Ernesto, speaks English and is helpful and friendly). Cheques can be changed at pharmacy close to Ferretería Findel.

German Consulate at Adolfo Mier.

Post Office Presidente Montes 1456.

Tourist Office, Edificio Prefectural, Plaza 10 de Febrero (T 51764), open Mon.-Fri., 0900-1200, 1400-1800, has map of city, helpful. Also on Bolívar and Galvarro, Mon.-Fri., 0900-1200, 1400-1800, Sat. 0900-1200.

Cables Cables can be filed at the Empresa Nacional Office (Entel) with the routing via: Cable West Coast.

Trains About 5 hours to La Paz (daily 0600, US$5.50 Pullman, US$3.50 special) and 7 to Cochabamba (daily 0820) Ferrobus US$5.50, Pullman US$1.60 special; to Potosí, Ferrobus Mon., Thurs., Sat., 2200, express Sun., Wed., 2020, US$7.75 Pullman, US$4.65 special; to Sucre, same timetable, US$14 Pullman, US$10.75 special. To Villazón, *mixto,* coming from La Paz, Mon. and Thurs., 0100, 18 hours, exhausting but exhilarating to hardy traveller, Express, Mon., Wed., Fri. about 2200, US$13 Pullman, US$9 special. Ticket office opens at 0700, best to be there early. Calama, for Antofagasta (Chile), 29½ hours, train from La Paz calls here (Fri., 1800), very crowded and dusty for first few stops.

Buses To La Paz, 3 hours, seven bus lines work the route, US$5; to Potosí, 10 cold and rough hours, US$6.85, two companies, both at 1900 daily; to Llallagua, Bustillo, 7 a day, US$1.65, Enta 0900 and 1700 daily US$1.45; to Cochabamba, 4½ hours, US$5, six lines, most leave 0800-1000 (one night bus 2000). To Sucre, best to go via Cochabamba if wet as the road to Potosí is so bad. Roads to Río Mulato and Uyuni are very bad, but some trucks work the route; train (8 hours) recommended. Bus agencies are all at the new terminal near the railway station in the centre. Trucks to Potosí and Sucre leave from Av. Cochabamba near the Mercado Bolívar.

Excursions From Machacamarca, 24 km. S of Oruro, a branch line runs to Uncia (108 km.) and the ex-Patiño tin mines.
   A taxi to Lake Uru Uru costs US$5-7.50 (agree price and waiting time in advance); or take Micro A to its terminus and then walk 1 hour along road, take Micro B for return trip, US$0.15 each way; flamingoes and other water-birds, highly recommended, but not at the height of the dry season (October) when wild life moves elsewhere. Boats may be hired only out of the rainy season.
   There are hot springs at Obrajes, where there is the choice of private baths or swimming pool,

both hot. Wait at the bus stop at 6 de Octubre 1420 for the (intermittent) bus. Taxis sometimes make the run. Take picnic lunch.

Visitors with a Land Rover might explore the country W of Oruro towards the Chilean frontier. It's a day's drive to the western mountains following tracks rather than roads. There are no hotels in any of the towns, such as Escara or Sabaya, but lodging could be found by asking a school-teacher or local mayor. From Escara it is only 25 km. S to *Chipaya,* the main settlement of the most interesting Indians of the Altiplano. They speak a language closely related to the almost extinct Uru, their dress is distinctive and their conical houses unique. This is a very difficult trip without your own transport. Sometimes trucks leave from Plaza Walter Khon in Oruro for Chipaya; or the village may be reached by taking a bus to Sabaya or Turco, then a truck. Bring your own food; shelter for US$0.25 per head in adobe *alojamiento*. Bicycles may be hired in Chipaya to visit lake 2 hours away with great variety of bird life.

A one-day drive to the west is the Parque Nacional Sajama, the world's highest forest. The road is reported to be very bad. To climb *Sajama*, Bolivia's highest mountain (6,530 metres) take the Litoral La Paz-Arica bus and pay the full fare. Ask for the Sajama stop, 20 minutes past the village of that name, before Lagunas, and about 11 hrs. from La Paz. A cheaper way is to take a La Paz-Oruro bus as far as Patacamayo (1½ hrs. from La Paz), then take a truck to Estación Tomarapi (dusty, but very interesting, US$2). Tomarapi is in the Parque Nacional Sajama; no fresh food is available in the Park, so take plenty from La Paz. If continuing into Chile (by truck—possible but hard) remember that no meat, dairy products, fruit or vegetables may be taken across the border. To return to La Paz, walk to Lagunas and take a truck or the Litoral bus (twice weekly). Crampons, ice axe and rope are needed for the climb, which is not technically difficult; the routes to base camp and beyond are fairly obvious. Water is available, but beware of sulphurous streams. It can be very windy.

About 100 km. S of Oruro is **Llallagua** (*Hotel Bustillo*, F; *Santa María, Hotel Llallagua*, F, the best). Nearby is the famous Siglo Veinte, the largest tin mine (ex-Patiño) in the country (trucks up from town). Tourist visits start at 0700. Prior permission to visit must be obtained from Comibol in La Paz. There is an acute water shortage. Llallagua can be reached by bus from Oruro, but only trucks make the journey to Sucre (without going via Potosí), beautiful but uncomfortable. Also buses 1900 from La Paz.

On the road to La Paz is Patacamaya which has a Sunday market (no tourist items); *Alojamiento 18 de Julio*, F (no w/c). A recommended driver is Freddy Barron M., Casilla 23, Oruro, T 55270, for excursions.

From Oruro a railway runs eastwards to Cochabamba (204 km.). It reaches a height of 4,140 metres at Cuesta Colorada before it begins to descend to the fertile basin in which Cochabamba lies. It is 394 km. from La Paz to Cochabamba by road, now paved to Oruro and from there paved except for 50 km. midway, where the going is very rough; about 8 hours by private car. A new highway is being built to Cochabamba, via Quillacollo. On the present road, a short cut from Caracollo to Colhuasi avoids Oruro and saves 65 km.

Cochabamba, Bolivia's third-largest city, founded in 1542, is set in a bowl of rolling hills and is an important agricultural centre. Population: 954,790; altitude 2,570 metres; excellent climate with average temperature of 18°C. It has fine buildings (though much of the modern building looks seedy), a University, an excellent archaeological museum, 25 de Mayo Norte 145, with a small but interesting collection of prehistoric pieces and Indian hieroglyphic scripts, and little-known collection of pre-Inca textiles (Mon.-Fri. only, 0830-1200, 1400-1800, US$1.50 with guide). Many Spanish houses with overhanging eaves, and much for the tourist: a grand view from San Sebastián, a hill on the edge of the city; the Golf Club on Lake Alalay (you need a member to introduce you); and Los Portales, the Patiño mansion in the northern part of the city (take Micro G), set in beautiful grounds, completed after 10 years' effort in 1927 but never occupied (check times with tourist office). The Cathedral in the main plaza is pleasantly decorated; panels painted to look like marble. Just off the plaza is La Compañía, whose whitewashed interior is completely innocent of the usual riot of late Baroque decoration. The municipal market and the Cancha, a retail market (Wednesday and Saturday), are also full of local colour. Beware: street numbering can be chaotic.

Fiestas are frequent and fascinating. Carnival is celebrated 15 days before Lent. Rival groups (*cumparsas*) compete in music, dancing, and fancy dress, culminating in El Corso on the last Saturday of the Carnival. Beware the rains around and after Carnival, and water-throwing the day after, when you are likely to get drenched. *Mascaritas* balls also take place in the carnival season, when the young women wear long hooded satin masks.

To the N, in a high fault-block range of mountains, is Cerro Tunari, 5,180 metres. A road runs to within 300 metres of the top, usually sprinkled with a little snow. There are beautiful views of the Cochabamba valley from the mountain road which goes into the Parque Tunari from Cala Cala, ending at the lake which supplies drinking water; best in the afternoon, but no public transport.

An imposing monument overlooks the town from La Coronilla, part of the same hill as San Sebastián. It commemorates the heroic defence of Cochabamba by its womenfolk during the War of Independence. It has fine views and just below it is a charming little old bull ring, little used. There are thermal baths near the city. The Palacio de Cultura, Av. Heroínas y 25 de Mayo, has a group of local museums under one roof (entrance free, but exhibits usually locked). Churches worth a visit include Santo Domingo (Santiváñez and Ayacucho) and Santa Teresa (Baptista and Ecuador). Cochabamba is an expensive city, only surpassed by Santa Cruz. The water is notoriously bad, especially in the rainy season.

Hotels   *Gran Hotel Cochabamba*, Plaza Ubaldo Arze, T 43524, beautifully set in the northern part of the city (2 blocks from Los Portales at La Recoleta), with garden, swimming pool (guests only) and tennis courts, good food, the most expensive, A. In the city: motel-type *Berkeley* (French run, solarium with each room, swimming pool); *Ambassador*, Calle España 349 (T 48777), private bath, hot water, telephone, modern, central and reasonable, C, good restaurant. *Capitol*, near museum, C, private bath, TV, clean and friendly. *Colón*, in Plaza Colón, E, hot water, breakfast included. *City Hotel*, Calle Jordán 341, near centre, F with shower but without breakfast, cheaper rooms on upper floors, clean, noisy but modern. Both *Alojamiento Oruro*, F, and *Residencial Agustín López*, near bus station, E, clean, comfortable, hot water. *Residencial Pullman*, Av. Aroma 370, very clean, F, hot showers. *Las Palmas*, Av. Salamanca 5536, D, spotless. *Residencial*, Calle Uruguay 213, F, good; *Gran Hotel Las Vegas*, E, bath, rec., Esteban Arce 352. *El Dorado*, D, rec., clean, hot water, is in 25 de Mayo; *Alojamiento Cochabamba*, F, clean, rec., Calle Nataniel Aguirre; *Florida*, 25 de Mayo 583, clean and friendly, E (hot showers); *Residencial San Severino*, 25 de Mayo 621, hot showers and clothes washing facilities; *Residencial Escobar*, Uruguay y Nataniel Aguirre 159, E, hot shower, modern; *Hostal Doria*, Junín 765, D with bath, good, clean; *La Coruña*, Junín 5961 (garden), rec., D; *Ideal*, Calle España 329, E, with breakfast, Italian management, noisy, but repeatedly rec.; *Residencial Lanza*, Lanza 929, T 2-4494, E with bath (F without), friendly, by market, rec. *Residencial Urkupiña*, Esteban Arce 750, F, clean, hot water, near bus station, highly rec. *Residencial Elisa*, C. Agustín López, D with bath, E without, breakfast and water for clothes washing extra, modern, clean, garden, 2 blocks from bus station, friendly, rec. *Residencial Palace*, Av. San Martín 1023, E, hot shower. Outside town (15 mins., bus 1) *Hostal Inca*, pool, tennis court, US$10 (E) per cottage, T 42732.

Restaurants   *Guadalquivir* (N of town); good Spanish-type food out of doors (wine garden), and *Victor* (on Prado), same ownership and quality (rec. for duck, a local speciality). *Pasatiempo* on Plaza Colón serves very large steaks. Behind *Doña Lucha's* store, Av. Simón López, *Cala Cala* (1st corner past 1st bridge), is a good bar and restaurant, inexpensive. *Don Gerardo*, 7 km. out of town, good and cheap, traditional Bolivian food. *La Taquiña*, 500 metres down from brewery 12 km. from city, roast duck lunches Friday, Saturday and Sunday (US$5), superb views, take bus No.3 to Cruce La Taquiña, then walk 30 mins. uphill, or take taxi from Cala Cala, reached by Micro A from plaza. Oriental: medium-price *Shangai*, good food although like the *China* nearby, on Av. San Martín, overpriced. *El Dragón de Oro* on main plaza (mixed reports) also *La Puerta del Dragón* on corner of Avenida Arce and Ravelo, 2nd floor. International menu available at *Don Quixote*, Plaza Colón, and *La Costilla de Adán*, Aniceto Padilla 120, good value. *Karpels* on Calle Achá serves Black Forest cake. Rec. is *La Estancia*, in a side street off Plaza Recoleta; just beyond are *Casa del Campo* (Bolivian dishes), *Black Angus* (Argentine style) and *Lai Lai* (good, but slow service). Good Bolivian food at *El Paraje*, Av. Salamanca, half way between Plaza Colón and the bridge to Plaza Recoleta; *El Sauce* on Quijarro 70 serves local specialities, not too cheap but worth it; *Gallo de Oro*, Calle Lanza Sur 0567, rec. Also worth trying is *El Mesón*, Colombia Este 379 and 25 de Mayo—Argentine style. Vegetarian restaurant opposite Jasmín on M. Rocha and Ayacucho, lunch US$1, rec. On Av. España are *Don Corleone* (pizzas, opp. *Hotel Ambassador*), *España* (No. 272), *Heladería España* and many *confiterías*; many cheap places on 25 de Mayo (incl. *California Donuts*, *Dallas*) and Bolívar. *Burger House* and *Kentucky Chicken* on main square. *Heladería Imperial* (off Plaza de Armas) for good ice cream; also *H. Sabor* at Esq. Colón and Prado, nice surroundings; Good food at *Restaurant-Confitería Continental*, on main plaza; excellent pastries and ice cream at the *Zurich Tea Room*, Av. San Martín Norte 143, closes 2000, and *Café Berneck* on Colombia and San Martín, both expensive; *Salón Berna*, Av. San Martín Norte 209 y Colombia, Swiss pastry, ice creams inexpensive. Rec. salteñas at *Confitería*

Caravelle on Calle Sucre, as well as *Confitería Maggy*, Sucre and 25 de Mayo, for breakfast and ice cream. The local place for cakes is *Dulce Ilusión* on Calle España.

Shopping Main market is called San Antonio. Large market (La Cancha) near railway station (for tourist items). *Fotrama* for alpaca sweaters, stoles, rugs, etc. (expensive); there is also a branch at Av. de Heroínas, or Madame Eleska's *Adam* shop, now run by her son (expensive), or *Amerindia*, Calle San Martín, for good rugs and lengths of alpaca material, as well as ponchos and jumpers; or picturesque Indian market and nearby shops. For leather try *Confecciones Gamucuer*, Destacamento 317. Market fruit and vegetables excellent and very cheap, but on more expensive articles do not expect prices to drop very much when bargaining. Try local hot drink, *api*, made from maize. Main markets Wed. and Sat.; beware pickpockets and thieves. Camera repairs recommended at shop on General Achá, next door to *Cromos*. Cycle repairs: parts in market at Lanza 700 Sur. *Foto Broadway*, España y Colombia, for developing at reasonable prices. A very good bookshop is *Los Amigos del Libro*, Av. de Heroínas 311 y España, and Gral. Achá 110. Books cheaper than in La Paz.

Local Transport Micros and colectivos, US$0.10; *trufis* (vans), US$0.12; anything marked "San Antonio" goes to the market. Taxis: agree fare before getting in; about US$0.50 from anywhere to the Plaza; double after dark.

Entertainment *Camel* (discotheque), *Colonial* (discotheque), *El Trocador* (peña), *Alexander* (restaurant/*peña*), all near intersection of Heroínas and Oquendo (all start around 2300); *Pier Seven* (disco) Heroínas 464.

Exchange Houses Exprinter, Plaza 14 de Septiembre 252 (will change travellers' cheques into dollars at 2% commission); American Ltda., Plaza 14 de Septiembre. Universo, on España, 1 block from plaza. Money changers congregate in Plaza Colón. Try also Los Amigos del Libro and Librería Juventud in main plaza.

Consulates W. Germany, España 149; US, Av. de Heroínas 464, office 115, T 25896; Brazil, Potosí 1455 (opp. Patiño Museum), open 1400-1800; Argentina, Av. Pando 1329, visa applications 0900-1300; Perú, Av. Pando 1143.

Addresses At 25 de Mayo 25698, Telephone 21288; is the Centro Boliviano Norteamericano with a library of English-language books, open 0900-1200 and 1500-1900. Goethe-Institut, Plaza 14 de Septiembre, beside Cathedral behind a *farmacia*; Alliance Française, Santiváñez 187.

Language Classes Sra. Blanca de La Rosa Villareal, Av. Villazón 5218 (T 44298) charges US$3 for a 45 minute lesson. Instituto de Lenguaje (Idelco), Plaza Busch, Bolívar 826, T 44868.

Festivals Fiesta de la Virgen de Urkupiña, Quillacollo, mid-August, see below; and September 14, dancing.

Swimming *El Paraíso*, halfway to Quillacollo, sauna and pool, US$0.50 entrance, accessible by bus or train. Pool at Club Social, Calle Méjico (US$1.20), is open to the public as well as La Rivera on Simón López (Micro A) or Los Chorrillos, both US$1, crowded on Sunday (Micro G), or outside town there is *Posada de Los Cisnes* at Quillacollo, at Km. 13 on Cochabamba road (entrance US$1.60). Also at *Don Gerardo* at Km. 7. Pool, sauna, restaurant at Estancia El Rosedal at Tiquipaya, take bus number 12 from Antezana y Cabrera to end of line.

Tennis Club de Ténis de Cochabamba admits non-members for US$5 per day.

Fishing Excellent trout fishing in lake formed by the Corani dam, 48 km. N of Cochabamba.

Post Office Av. Heroínas, next to TAM office; Mon.-Sat. 0800-1900, Sun. 0800-1200.

Cables can be filed at Empresa Nacional Office.

Tourist Office Calle General Achá, and Plaza 14 de Septiembre (helpful). Kiosks at Jorge Wilstermann airport and near Entel building. A useful photocopy map of the city can be obtained from Los Amigos del Libro, who also publish a guide book. Recommended travel agency, Gitano Tours.

Railway Tickets available on day before travel (office opens 0600-1000, be there early). There are *ferrobuses* leaving for La Paz Tues., Thurs., Sat. (0800) 8 hours; fares US$15 Pullman, US$10 special. Express train to Oruro 0830, Tues., Fri., Sun.; *ferrobus* daily at 0725, US$5.50 1st, US$1.60 2nd. Sit on left side for the best views. Train to Sucre on Mon. and Thurs. at 0700.

Air Service Jorge Wilstermann airport. Airport bus is Micro B from Plaza 14 de Septiembre, taxis about US$2 (no set rates, so bargain). Daily by LAB to and from La Paz (½ hour), US$23 one way (15 kg. baggage allowance), book early for morning flights, and to Santa Cruz, (½ hour, US$30). Three flights a week to Sucre and Tarija (US$32), also to Trinidad (connects with Riberalta flight). LAB in town at Ayacucho and Heroínas, open 0800; at airport LAB office opens 0500. TAM (Hamiraya 122, nr. Av. Heroínas) to La Paz, US$16; flights to Riberalta US$100, but infrequent; best to fly from La Paz or Santa Cruz, via Trinidad.

Bus Services Buses (overnight) and colectivos (day and night) to Santa Cruz, taking 12 to 16 hours (US$14), a beautiful trip. To La Paz via Oruro (0800, 1000 and 1300 with Nobleza), US$5.50, 8 hrs., over a terrifying road (but good surface for all but 1½ hours), you have to change buses in Oruro and get a new ticket at the same time on a different floor, luggage is automatically transferred to the new bus; or via Caracollo, by night or by day, 10-12 hours (US$9.50). Bus to Oruro, US$5, 6½ hrs. Epizana (US$3.35). Daily to Sucre, by Flota Minera, Aroma 120, or Flota Unificada, between 1800 and 1830, 12 hours, US$7, all but the first 2 hours are very bad. There are 3 bus stations: Av. Aroma, near Plaza San Sebastián, for long-distance buses; the Avenida at the foot of La Coronilla for local buses to Tarata, Punata and Clisa; Av. Oquendo (at the edge of Lake Alalay) to Villa Tunari, US$3.50; Chimoré, US$4.50; Eterazama, US$4.50; Puerto Villarroel, US$6; Puerto San Francisco, US$5; and other destinations—all leave 0800-1000 if sufficient passengers. Trucks to Oruro leave from Plaza San Sebastián. Trucks to Sucre leave from end of Av. San Martín (US$3.30). Trucks to Puerto Villarroel from Av. República, US$3.30.

The Cochabamba basin, dotted with several small townships, is the largest grain and fruit producing area in Bolivia. **Quillacollo** (20,000 people), a 20 minute bus ride from Av. Ayacucho y Av. Aroma, just beyond the markets in Cochabamba (good Sunday market but no tourist items; the *campesinos* do not like being photographed). Fiesta de la Virgen de Urkupiña in mid-August lasts 4 days with much dancing and religious ceremony (designed to make you rich); very interesting, plenty of transport from Cochabamba. 2-3 km. beyond Quillacollo is a road to the beautiful Pairumani *hacienda*, centre of the Patiño agricultural foundation. The house may be visited (T 60082 to arrange visit, or check times at Los Portales in Cochabamba); the Patiño mausoleum may be visited if one is accompanied by a member of the family. Don't miss Tarata, a sleepy old village with beautiful Plaza, nearby, market day Thursday (bus also from Av. Ayacucho, US$0.50). Punata, an hour's bus ride from Cochabamba, has an interesting, lively market on Tuesday. Behind the main church, new vehicles are lined up to be blessed by the priest. The local speciality is *garapiña*, a mixture of *chicha* and icecream. Beyond Punata, at Villa Rivera, woven wall hangings are produced. A railway line runs from Cochabamba through the Punata valley as far as Arani, the population of which consists almost entirely of potters, who produce good ceramics. Another runs to Vila-Vila (132 km.). There is a large Sunday market at **Clisa**, accessible by bus from Av. Ayacucho. For those interested in *charangos* (of wood) a visit to Aiquile (6 hrs.) is recommended (by train, or bus US$3.50; *Hotel Escudo*, F, basic). To the north is the Parque Tunari, which is partly forested, and Laguna Wara Wara at 4,000 metres surrounded by 4,500 metre mountains.

Three seldom visited Inca ruins might be of interest: Inka-Rakay, a small outpost about 45 minutes' drive from Cochabamba and a 2-hour hike up a mountain; and Inkallajta and Samaipata (see below).

The Inka-Rakay ruins are near the village of Sipe-Sipe; the main attraction is the view from the site over the Cochabamba valley, as well as the mountains ringing the ruins. Take a bus to Quillacollo where the bus for Sipe-Sipe waits until there are enough passengers. From Sipe-Sipe to the ruins there is either a 4 km. footpath, or a 12 km. road with almost no traffic, which, to walk, takes three hours. Either hitch or hire guides and Land Rover in Cochabamba. Several letters indicate that it might be less terrifying to walk but all admit that this is a beautiful trip. Start early for it is a full day. Leave the Square at Sipe Sipe going up the street past the church, then left at the top and then right when you come to the wider road. Follow this road to the ridge ahead. Just below the ridge, the road loses a little height to take a bend. There is an outcrop of rock and here look for a track leading away downhill. The Inka-Rakay ruins are about 200 metres below. **N.B.** Carry plenty of water as there is none available.

The 500-km. road to Santa Cruz (**page 215**) is paved, but the surface has greatly deteriorated. Before the Siberia pass, 5 km. beyond Montepunco at Pocona (Km. 119), the 23-km. road to Inkallajta (unpaved and very bad) turns off. The ruins, on a flat spur of land at the mouth of a steep valley, are extensive and the temple is said to have been the largest roofed Inca building. To get there without your own transport a reader advises: "Take a micro to the checkpoint 10 km. from Cochabamba, take a truck to Km. 122, walk on towards Pocona or take a truck for 12 km. A large yellow sign indicates the trail. After approx. 10 km. the trail divides, take the downhill path and the ruins are a further 2 km. Take food and camping gear". At Km. 386 are the ruins of Samaipata, worth a stop. At

Epizana, a lovely dilapidated colonial village, 13 km. beyond Montepunco (Km. 128), with poor hotels and service stations, a branch road, right—dusty, stony, and narrow in parts, but very scenic—goes 233 km. to Sucre, 7-8 hours drive. Totora, described as one of the loveliest sleepy, friendly colonial villages, is said to be better to stay in than Epizana. Another road has been built to link Cochabamba with the Beni area (**see page 221**).

S of Oruro the railway from La Paz skirts Lake Poopó, over 90 km. long and 32 km. wide. From Río Mulato a branch line runs eastwards to Potosí (174 km.) and Sucre. The track reaches the height of 4,786 metres at Cóndor: one of the highest points on the world's railway lines.

Potosí, with a population of 103,183, stands at 4,070 metres, the highest city of its size in the world. The climate is often bitterly cold and fireplaces are few;

Key: 1. Plaza 10 de Noviembre, 2. Plaza 6 de Agosto, 3. Plazuela Daniel Campos, 4. Cathedral, 5. Jerusalén, 6. San Lorenzo, 7. San Agustín, 8. La Compañía, 9. San Martín, 10. Convent of Santa Teresa, 11. Convent of San Francisco, 12. Casa Real de Móneda, 13. University Museum, 14. Alcaldía, 15. Central Market, 16. Handicrafts Market, 17. Tourist Office, 18. Post Office warm clothes essential. It was founded by the Spaniards on April 10, 1545, after they had discovered Indian mine workings at Cerro Rico, the hill at whose foot it stands.

Immense amounts of silver were once extracted from this hill. In Spain "éste es un Potosí" (it's a Potosí) is still used for anything superlatively rich. Early in the 17th century Potosí had a population of 113,380, but two centuries later, as its lodes began to deteriorate and silver had been found in Peru and Mexico, Potosí became little more than a ghost town. It was the demand for tin—a metal the Spaniards ignored—that lifted the city to comparative prosperity again. Silver, copper and lead are also mined. A new seam of silver has been discovered recently.

Large parts of Potosí are colonial, with twisting, narrow streets and an occasional great mansion with its coat of arms over the doorway. UNESCO has declared the city to be "Patrimonio de la Humanidad." Some of the best buildings are grouped round the Plaza 10 de Noviembre, the main square. The Convent of Santa Teresa (entry US$1.50, opening times vary, check at Tourist Office) has an interesting collection of colonial and religious art. The old Cabildo and the Royal Treasury—Las Cajas Reales—are both here, converted to other uses. The Cathedral (open only between 0900 and 1000 on Sundays) faces the square, and near-by is the Mint—the Casa Real de Moneda (founded 1572, rebuilt 1759)—one of the chief monuments of civil building in Hispanic America. The Moneda (entrance US$1, tours at 1000 and 1430) has a museum in many sections. The main art gallery is in a splendid salon on the first floor: the salon better than the paintings. Elsewhere are coin dies and huge wooden presses which made the silver strip from which coins were cut. You are advised to wear warm clothes, as it is cold inside; a guided tour (essential) starts at 0900 and 1400. The smelting houses have carved altar pieces from Potosí's ruined churches. Open Mon.-Sat. 0900-1200 and 1400-1700. Among Potosí's baroque churches, typical of the Andean or "mestizo" architecture of the 18th century, are the Compañía (Jesuit) church, with an impressive bell-gable (1700), San Francisco (monastery closed to visitors, church can be visited in morning and evening, museum of ecclesiastical art, open 1400-1600, Mon.-Fri.) with a fine organ, and San Lorenzo, with a rich portal (1728-1744); fine views from the tower. San Martín, with an uninviting exterior, is beautiful inside, but normally closed for fear of theft. Ask the German Redemptorist Fathers to show you around; their office is just to the left of their church. Other churches to visit include Jerusalén, close to the *Hotel Centenario*, and San Agustín (only by prior arrangement with tourist office) on Bolívar, with crypts and catacombs. Tour starts at 1700, US$0.10 admission. From San Cristóbal, at Pacheco with Cañete, one gets a fine view over the whole city. The University has a museum (Mon.-Fri., 1000-1200, 1500-1700, entrance US$1).

Festival San Barolomé, 24th August, costumes for hire in artesanía market on Calle Suere.

Hotels Best hotel is *Hostal Colonial*, Hoyos 8, C, a pretty colonial house (T 24265) near the main plaza. *Turista*, Lanza 19 (T 22492), E, helpful, now remodelled, but no heating, hot shower, breakfast (US$1 only) highly rec. *Casa de Huéspedes Hispano*, Matos 62, clean rooms with or without bath, F; *Res. San Antonio*, Oruro 140, F, hot shower, clean; *Residencial Sumaj*, Gumiel 10, F, friendly, good breakfast. *Hotel IV Centenario*, D, hot water, but no heating, has seen better days but friendly, central; *Santa María*, Av. Serrudo 166, E, clean, hot water; *Alojamiento Ferrocarril*, Av. E. Villazón 159, F, basic, uncomfortable beds but clean (no hot water but clean showers available for US$0.55), friendly, close to the railway station. The best cheap lodgings (for which Potosí has a bad reputation) between Av. Oruro and Av. Serrudo, clean, but rarely with hot water; *Alojamiento Tumusla* (avoid ground floor—cold), near the bus station, F, good; *Hostal Oruro*, Oruro 292, F, shared shower, clean and basic; *Residencial Copacabana*, Av. Serrudo, F, shared room, restaurant, safe car park; *Villa Imperial*, dirty, noisy, same prices, good motorcycle parking, US$0.20 for hot shower. *Alojamiento San Lorenzo*, Bustillos 967, G, close to market, very basic, no shower or hot water. In times of drought there may be rationing of water for showers etc.

Restaurants *Sumac Orko*, 25 de Mayo, near Bolívar, reasonable, friendly; *Confitería Royal*, just off main plaza, small selection of good cakes and coffee; *El Aldabón*, Plaza 10 de Noviembre 35, good set meal, US$1; *Scaramuch*, Bolívar 843 and *La Tranquita* at Bolívar 957, good and cheap. Reasonable priced restaurant (salteñas, soft drinks or beer) is *Imasumac*, Bustillos 987.

Siete Vueltas, Bolívar 816, serves a decent almuerzo. *Bolívar*, Sucre y Bolívar, 4 course lunch US$1.25, rec.; *Colonial*, US$1 for 4 courses, food clean and fresh. Cakes and ice creams along Linares and in Plaza 25 de Mayo. *Don Lucho*, Bolívar 765, good cheap food, *peñas* at weekends, check entrance fee for show before eating. *The Sky Room* at Bolívar 701 has interesting views of the town and the Cerro, unfriendly. Breakfast can be a difficult meal to find, but it is available in the Mercado Central, Calle Bolívar: worthwhile to see if the hotel serves it as most restaurants seem to be closed at this time. *Alemania Confitería*, Hoyo y Sucre (opp. tourism kiosk), very good (but check bill); *Coffee Shop*, Boulevard 20, good coffee and cakes. To get fresh bread you have to be up at 0630-0700 and go to Bustillos between Ingavi and Oniste and up a passage on the upper side of the street.

Shopping Silver (sometimes containing nickel) and native cloth; there are stalls in Calle Bustillos. Silver coins, jewellery and coca leaves in market between Av. Camacho and H. del Chaco. Artesanías Pachamama, Hoyos 10, is recommended for textiles. There is also an interesting gift shop in the post office. Silver is sold in the main market near the Calle Oruro entrance. There is an informal swap market every Friday night at the Plaza, at Bolívar and Quijarro. There is a handicraft market at the junction of Calle Sucre and Plaza Saavedra. Some Fridays the merchants organize music, food and drink (*ponche*), not to be missed. The best bookshop is at the University, open Mon.-Fri., 1000-1200, 1500-1700.

Local Transport Taxi within city limits US$1.20; approx US$0.50/km. for longer journeys. Buses US$0.10.

Exchange Ask at Tourist Office. Street changers around Oruro 430; also shops and restaurants around main plaza. Amex cheques may be changed at Hidalgo Tours, Junín y Bolívar.

Clinic Clínica Británica, on Oruro near *Alojamiento La Paz*, clinics a.m. and p.m. English spoken, US$6.

Tourist Agents Potosí Tours, on the Plaza, good city tours; Candería Tours, Bolívar 634, T 22458 and Tursul Ltda, Calle San Alberto, 24, T 21360.

Tourist Office On 2nd Floor, Cámara de Minería, Calle Quijarro (T 25288). ½ block from main plaza, and booth on main plaza (both closed Sat. and Sun.); sells good town maps (US$0.25), information booklet (US$2.50), helpful.

Post Office, Lanza and Chuquisaca; unreliable for overseas mail.

Police station On Plaza 10 de Noviembre. Beware so-called "plain-clothes police"; they are not authentic.

Sauna Bath and showers in Calle Nogales. Sauna Florida, Plaza Chuquimina, near bus station, open Thurs. and Fri., US$1.50.

Trains To La Paz, *ferrobus*: book previous day only: Tues., 1100, 10½ hrs., US$16.90 Pullman, US$11.20 special; express: Thurs., US$11.90 Pullman, US$8 special. To Sucre, *ferrobus* Thurs. Sat. at 0700, US$9 Pullman, US$6 special. To Oruro *ferrobus* and express US$7.75 Pullman, US$4.65 special; connection to Cochabamba leaves 1800. To Calama for Antofagasta, either take train to Uyuni, Sat. 0730 or Sun. 0200, or take the bus to Uyuni on Tues., Wed. and Thurs. between 1200 and 1500 from Villa Imperial, Toledo 216, off Av. Antofagasta where it crosses the railway, US$5 (buy ticket night before or early same day) and connect with the La Paz-Antofagasta train/bus route on Fri. night. Alternatively, take the Tues. *ferrobus* to Oruro and then book Pullman on Fri. train to Calama; fares can be paid in bolivianos. To Villazón, go to Uyuni and connect with La Paz-Villazón train there.

Buses Bus station out of town, below railway station and 20 minute walk (or *micros* C, I or L) from main Plaza; through buses from La Paz call here at the toll gate, as they are not allowed to enter city limits. To Tarija, 10 de Noviembre, Thurs., Fri. and Sun. 0800, very poor buses; Tarija is reached by car or lorry leaving Plaza Minero (Bus "A"), full range of scenery. To Sucre, Soltrans, US$6, several daily, 4½ hrs., US$5, first at 0700; also Hidalgo (minibus), Bolívar y Junín, 0700, 1830, 4 hrs., US$7.50 incl. snack. La Paz (12 hrs., overnight only, US$9.50) leaves 1800 daily. Oruro, US$6.85. Trucks for Tarabuco leave from Plaza San Francisco. Heavy overbooking reported on buses, also, timetables change frequently; the trucks from the plaza are an alternative if you are in a hurry.

Warning It has been reported that men with false police I.D. cards meet trains and buses. They demand to see passports and currency and confiscate dollars. Insist on going to the police station, if possible with a witness.

Car Spares VW spares are obtainable at Hauwa Ltd, but it takes several days to get parts from La Paz.

A suggested tour round the town is to walk down Quijarro from San Agustín on Bolívar as far as Oniste then return by Junín, looking at "the passage of the seven turns" on the way. There is a fine stone doorway (house of the Marqués de Otavi) in Junín between Matos and Bolívar. Calle Lanza 8 was the house of José de Quiroz and of Antonio López de Quiroga. Along Millares between Chuquisaca and Nogales one sees on the right a sculpted stone doorway and on the left a doorway with two rampant lions in low relief on the lintel. Turning left up Nogales one comes to an old mansion in a little square. Turn left along La Paz and three blocks along there is another stone doorway with suns in relief. At the corner with Bolívar is the Casa del Balcón de la Horca. Turn left and one comes to the Casa de las Tres Portadas.

Excursions A recommended guide to the cooperative mines and ore-processing plant is Eduardo Garnica Fajardo, Hernández 1035, Casilla 33, T 2-3138 (or via *Hotel Ferrocarril*, or in main plaza 0800-0830); he speaks English, French and some Hebrew. He charges about US$3 for a 4½ hr. morning tour, which involves meeting miners and seeing them at work in conditions described as "like stepping back into the nineteenth century"; a contribution to the miners' cooperative is appreciated, take cigarettes and coca leaves as presents. If visiting the mines, wear old clothes and take a good torch and a handkerchief to filter the dusty air, visitors need to be reasonably fit. Another guide is Salustio Gallardo, Calle Betanzos 231, near Plaza Minero, price negotiable; also Braulio Mamani (T 223002, he operates from Plaza 10 de Noviembre, 0800-0830), about US$2.50 p.p., Spanish only. Visitors can approach Padre Gustavo, a Belgian priest at the Concepción church who occasionally organizes visits to the cooperative mines. More interesting than a visit to the State mine, which is now automated. Bus Emta 100 from main plaza goes to the state mine.

A recommended Sunday trip is to Manquiri, a sanctuary in the mountains. Wait from 0730 at Garita de San Roque for a truck. Another trip is to Caiza on the fork off the Tarija road at Ingeniero Cucho; for this you will need a tent, etc., as there is no hotel. Only one bus a day from Potosí: it should leave from Plaza del Minero at 1330 but is often late. Caiza is where cooperatives produce handicrafts in tin. Their Caiza outlet is the Belgian Catholic Agricultural School in the main square. Cheap *mantas* and other hand woven goods can be purchased at villages betweeen Challatapa and Potosí, on the road from Oruro along Lake Poopó. At Betanzos (1 hour on the Sucre road), the Feria de Papas is held on May 14-15: folk dances, music and costumes, especially on the 15th (buses from Plaza Uyuni, Potosí).

Thermal Baths at lake below city. Laguna de Tarapaya, Miraflores truck or van from Plaza Chuquimina to 25 Km. post, just before crossing the bridge. Above Tarapaya is the crater, which is reached by a track from 23 Km. point. When bathing take great care as the current is very strong; whirlpools can develop, which have claimed many lives. There are buses back from Tarapaya at 1400 and 1600. A good place to spend a lazy day resting. Also Chaqui (by truck or bus from Plaza Uyuni, tiring journey, but clean, pleasant baths), Tora and San Diego (on the main road to Sucre, it also has a restaurant). Alternatively there is a thermal pool 1 km. before the village on the other side of the river. It is best to get off bus at the bridge 400 metres on the Potosí side of the river and pool.

Hallam Murray writes: One of the most interesting and varied mountain walks I have experienced in Bolivia can be made from Potosí. It takes 8 hours at a gentle pace and covers about 24 km. (map Hoja 6435, serie H631, from Instituto Geográfico Militar is helpful but not essential). Take Av. Hoyos east out of Plaza Alonso Ibáñez and continue beyond the Iglesia San Martín. Follow the road or path south east and climb the hill above the city, aiming for Laguna San Ildefonso. Ask directions if in doubt. This lake was built in 1767 to provide water for the city and is in a wonderful position. It has duck, and fish deep down in the clear water. Beyond, to the east, are some very inviting-looking, lumpy hills and mountains. Follow up the valley, passing herds of llama and old mine openings. It is probably best to start on the path to the south east of the lake (to right). This valley is full of fascinating plants, animals, and rock formations.

Continue beyond a second unnamed, and possibly dried-up lake and turn south to climb steeply to the adjoining valley, just beyond the peak of Cerro Masoni. The time from Plaza Alonso Ibáñez to the highest point between the two valleys is 4 hours. The views from this point are spectacular, with mountain peaks to the south towards Argentina. Closer at hand is moon-like scenery. This is an excellent spot for a picnic. Continue down and back to Potosí via the small lake which can be seen from the high point. Probably best to keep high to the left (south) of Lagunas San Sebastián and to approach Cerro Rico on its eastern flank. The walk back into Potosí is depressing and bleak, passing miners' houses, close to a heavily polluted stream and with the most extensively worked face of Cerro Rico to your left, but this is a side of Bolivia which should also be seen.

Sucre, (pop. 86,609) the official capital of Bolivia, is reached from Potosí (175 km.) by daily train (a grand trip) or by road (the best *dirt* road in Bolivia). A branch road runs to it from the Cochabamba-Santa Cruz highway. The altitude is 2,790 metres, and the climate is mild (mean temperature 12°C, but sometimes 24°C in November-December and 7°C in June).

Key: Public Buildings: 1. Casa de la Libertad, 2. Palace of Justice/Santo Domingo. Churches: 3. Cathedral, 4. San Miguel, 5. San Lázaro, 6. Santa Mónica, 7. San Francisco, 8. San Felipe Neri, 9. Santa Rita, 10. San Sebastián, 11. Santa Bárbara, 12. Santo Domingo, 13. Santa Clara, 14. Museums: Charcas, Anthropology & Modern Art, 15. Teatro Mariscal. Services: 16. Post Office, 17. Entel – communications, 18. Tourist Office, 19. LAB, 20. *Hostal Sucre*.

Sucre (originally Charcas) was founded in 1538. Long isolation has helped it to preserve its courtly charm; local law now requires all buildings to be painted original colonial white. Public buildings are impressive. Opening times are as reported but seem to be variable. Be prepared to get frustrated. Among these are the Casa de la Libertad (open 0900-1200 and 1400-1700, Sats., 0900-1200, US$0.50, US$1 to take photographs), where the country's Declaration of Independence was signed; the modern Santo Domingo (Palace of Justice), the seat of Bolivia's judiciary, R. Moreno y Ravelo (entry free but must leave passport with guard, no photographs allowed); the modern Government Palace; the beautiful 17th century Cathedral, open 0730-0915, and museum (US$0.25), open 1000-1200 and 1500-1700 (1000-1200, Sat.) (worth seeing are the Chapel of the famous jewel-encrusted Virgin of Guadalupe—1601, most easily seen just before or after mass (*fiesta* September 8), and the monstrance and other church jewels by appointment with the Padre Tesorero); the Consistorial building; the Teatro Gran Mariscal Sucre, and Junín College. Sucre University was founded in 1624. Early 17th century wooden ceilings (*alfarjes*) with intricate patterns of Moorish origin are found in San Miguel (see below) and San Francisco (0700-0930 and 1600-1930).

Behind the town a road flanked by Stations of the Cross ascends an attractive hill, Cerro Churuquella, with large eucalyptus trees on its flank, to a statue of Christ at the top. There is also a *mirador* in the square opposite La Recoleta, at the end of Calle Dalence. The cemetery is reported interesting

Churches San Miguel is being restored and is very beautiful with carved and painted ceilings, pure-white walls and gold and silver altar. In the Baptistery there is a painting by Viti, the first great painter of the New World, who studied under Raphael. In the Sacristy are another of his paintings and some early sculpture. It was from San Miguel that Jesuit missionaries went south to convert Argentina, Uruguay and Paraguay. San Felipe Neri, church and monastery, attractive courtyard with cloisters. Roof gives view of city; open 1630-1700, US$0.50 entrance. Entrance requires a guide from Universidad de Turismo office, opposite the convent, at N. Ortiz 182. Santa Mónica (Arenales with Junín) is perhaps one of the finest gems of Spanish architecture in the Americas, note the main altar and pulpit in filigree (closed in 1987, but the ex-convent—now a school—can be visited). San Francisco in Calle Ravelo has altars coated in gold leaf; the bell is the one that summoned the people of Sucre to struggle for independence. Capilla de la Rotonda (Av. L. Cabrera, near the station), Santa Rita, San Sebastián and Sta. Bárbara (Plaza Pizarro). Santo Domingo, corner of Calvo and Bolívar (1545), open only Fridays and Sunday night. Next door at Calvo 212 is the Santa Clara museum with art gallery and silver collection (see below), and Church of San Lázaro, built in 1538 and regarded as the first cathedral of La Plata (Sucre). On the nave walls are six paintings attributed to Zurbarán; it has fine silverwork and alabaster in the Baptistery, open 0700-0745 Sat., and Sun. after church service at 1900. La Merced (Azurduy and Pérez) has gilded altar pieces.

Festival Independence celebrations, May 24-26, most services, museums and restaurants closed.

Hotels Best hotel is *Hostal Cruz de Popayán*, Calle Loa, C, rec., a beautiful colonial house with interior courtyard, no heating, good breakfast served in rooms; *Hostal Sucre*, 3 stars, Bustillos 113, D, good, clean, rec.; *Hostal los Pinos*, Colón 502, clean, comfortable, hot showers, D. *Londres*, Av. Hernando Siles, 3 blocks uphill from station, F, breakfast, good; *Residencial Bolivia*, near plaza in Calle San Alberto, E, with dangerous electric showers, hot water, noisy, breakfast included (clothes washing, cooking not allowed); *Residencial Oriental*, Calle San Alberto, E, clean, friendly but basic, hot water; *Alojamiento El Turista*, Ravelo 118, F, clean, showers, friendly, good. *Alojamiento San Francisco*, esq. Av. Acre and Camargo, bath or shower, F has seen better days, but pleasant, meals available; also near station, *Municipal*, Av. Venezuela, E (T 21074), rec., restaurant; *Residencial Bustillo*, Calle Ravelo 158, E, clean and modern, hot water, shared showers, will store luggage at a price; *Alojamiento Austria*, Av. Ostria Gutiérrez 33, E, hot showers, good value, near bus station as well as *Alojamiento Central*, E, rec. (beware the buses which stop at 2000).

Restaurants Best restaurant is *La Recoleta*, or *Aranjuez*, Calvo 16 (closed Tues.), expensive. *Las Vegas* on east side of Plaza (icecream, no breakfast, at lunchtime no drink without food); *Pizzería Napoletana*, on Plaza, excellent pizzas and good home-made ice cream; *China*, Ravelo y Arce, 1st floor, not cheap but good. The *Alliance Française*, Aniceto Arce 35, serves crêpes, Mon. and Thur. 1100-1300, 1600-2000, soft music etc. *Pizzería Love*, Aniceto Arce 369, T 22742, good, English manager, reasonably-priced; good breakfast at *Leblon*, Aniceto Arce 99, opp. San Francisco church. *Medeval*, Plaza San Francisco 105, international food (reports vary). Good almuerzo at Hernando Siles 953. *Los Laureles*, Ortiz, is rec. for good cheap food; other places along Ortiz, near Plaza 25 de Mayo, are *Snack Paulista* (no. 14) and *Bibliocafé Sureña* (No. 30), good coffee, "bohemian", with English and German magazines. The *Plaza* restaurant, Plaza 25 de Mayo 34 (1st floor), rec.; *Palace*, Plaza 25 de Mayo 38, good, reasonably priced. *El Fogón*, Junín y Colón, cheap, home cooking. *Los Bajos*, Loa 761, serves special sausages. *Doña Máxima*, Junín 411, good, attached to hotel, near bus station. Good value is given at *El Solar*, Bolívar 800 (Sun. closed); *Snack Anni*, Avarea y Bolivia, for the best empanadas; *La Casona*, Av. Ostria Gutiérrez 401, local food. Foodstores in the new market, highly rec., serve clean cheap meals for US$1 until 1400. *Bar El Tío*, Calle España, is pleasant as is *Pip* (breakfast especially), esq. Ravelo and Lourdes, Loa 581. *Ghandi*, Arenales 15, excellent curry, US$1.50. *Sagitario*, Arenales 17, good cakes and pastries. The local brewery produces an interesting sweetish porter or stout. *Café Hacheh*, Pastor Sainz 241, coffee bar and art gallery near university, interesting to visit. Hallam Murray, cycling round the continent, strongly recommends the local chocolate.

Shopping Antique woven items must be sought. Permanent market along Av. Jaime Mendoza, for food and household goods. There is a wide selection in Calle Argentina, opposite Post Office, and Coinca, Loa 616, and Candelaria at Bolívar 634 (expensive). Artesanías Calcha, Calle Hernando Siles 713, rec., very knowledgeable proprietor. Good selection in arcade at Junín 403. Doña Máxima sells woven goods from the basement of *Alojamiento Guadalupe*, Junín 411, opp. Central Market: best to know what you're looking for, not especially cheap. *Charangos* from Tarabuco are obtainable in the main plaza. Prices for souvenir items tend to be much higher than in La Paz.

Night Clubs   Night Club Municipal, Av. Venezuela; *El Sótano* at the Parque Bolívar, acceptable; El Cuerno Colonial, España 162. Disco-Viva María, US$2.80, entrance includes a beer, San Alberto 6. Charleston Piano Bar, cover charge US$1.50. *peña* Fri. and Sat.

Folklore   Centro Cultural Masi aims to promote traditional culture. It offers instruction in Quechua, traditional Bolivian music making and handicrafts. The director, Roberto Sahonero, who will give further details, is to be found at Colón 138 (T 23403).

Museums   These include the University's anthropological, folkloric, and colonial collections at the Charcas Museum (Bolívar 700), and its presidential and modern-art galleries. There are also the Museo de Santa Clara (Calle Calvo 212), paintings, and the Museo de la Recoleta (Calle Pedro de Anzúrez), open 0930-1130 and 1500-1700 US$0.50 for entrance to all collections. The Recoleta monastery on a hill above the town is notable for the beauty of its cloisters and gardens; the carved wooden choirstalls in the chapel (upstairs) are especially fine (0930-1130 and 1400-1730). The Glorieta mansion (now very neglected), with the Princesa collection (leaflet available from tourist office), 5 km. outside the city bus E on the road to Potosí, has beautiful painted ceilings and Arabian gardens; worth a visit: "a delightful mixture of many styles", open Mon.-Fri. 0900-1200 and 1400-1800. It is in the military compound, passports must be surrendered at the gate, do not cross the river. At the back of the Grand Marshal's theatre, the faculty of medical sciences recently opened a museum of human anatomy and pathology—open 0830-1200 and 1400-1800 Mon.-Fri.

Post Office   Argentina 50, between Estudiantes and Olañeta. **Telephone** Entel, España 271.

Exchange   Banco del Estado, no exchange facilities; Banco Nacional, cash only at a poor rate. Banco Santa Cruz, Calle España will change cash and travellers' cheques. Travel agencies' rates are good. Most shops and hotels will change money. Street changers on Hernando Siles/Camargo between España and Junín. For travellers' cheques, try at Bolívar 342.

Consulates   West German, Arenales 215 (T 21862). The Goethe Institute shows films and has German newspapers and books to lend (1030-1230 and 1700-2000). Spain, Pasaje Argandoña (T 21435); Italy, Defensa 33 (T 22650).

Motor-cycle Mechanic   Sr Jaime Medina, Motorservi Honda, Calle René Calvo Arana, T 5484. Will service all makes of machine.

Laundry   Lavandería Copacabana, Dalence 187, T 23588. Lavandería Cristal, España 214 y Camargo.

Hospital   Recommended, staffed by Japanese and locals. Doctor Roger Mortojo Panoso, Av. Hernando Siles 911, or Dr. Gastón Delgadillo Lona at Colón 33 (T 21692/ 21187), speaks English, French and German.

Tourist Office   Calle Potosí 102 esq. San Alberto, T 25983, helpful map US$0.25. Check church and museum opening hours. Sub-office at airport, helpful. Tourist information office opp. San Felipe Neri, at Nicolás Ortiz 182, is run by students studying tourism, who will show you around tourist sites for free (see above under **Churches**). All offices closed Sat. and Sun.

Travel Agencies   Candelaria Tours, Bolívar 634; Teresita's Tours, Bustillos 146; Solarsa Tours, Arenales 212; Hidalgo Tours, Bustillos 105; Sucre Tours, Bustillos 107. Soltours, N.Ortiz 6, next to Cathedral, T 30500.

Train Service   to Potosí, Oruro and La Paz Sun. and Thurs. 1450 (book seats as far in advance as possible: from 0800-1000 and then 1400-1700, Sats. 0800-1000, holidays 0800-0930), to Potosí, US$9 Pullman, US$6 special—often no connection in the rainy season; to Oruro, US$14 first, US$10.75 second class, *ferrobus* 3 times weekly; to La Paz 20 hours (take food), US$15 Pullman, US$10 special, Station, behind Parque Bolívar, T 21114-21115.

Air Service   By LAB there is a Mon., Wed., Fri. La Paz-Sucre direct (US$35) air service, to La Paz via Cochabamba (US$20) on Tuesdays, Thursdays and Saturdays (US$40) and Santa Cruz (US$25) daily. Puerto Suárez, 0900 Mondays, TAM. There are also LAB flights to Tarija (Mon., Wed. and Fri., US$24) and Yacuiba, and F27 flights to Camiri (Tues., Thurs., Sat.). TAM fly on Wed. to La Paz, Santa Cruz and Puerto Suárez, and on Sundays to Santa Cruz. All flights heavily booked but some "stand by" available. Your best chance is to lie in wait at the airport; they know nothing in town. Airport 5 km. from town. (T 24445). LAB office is at Bustillos 121-127 (T 21140), from where free bus for passengers leaves 1½ hrs. before flight. Taxi US$5; buses from main road (difficult to get on with luggage). Beware of pickpockets at airport. Local airport taxes total US$2 (3 in all), pay before checking in.

Bus   daily to La Paz via Cochabamba (18 hrs., US$11.50), very rough and roads liable to flooding during the rainy season, but worthwhile; via Potosí, US$17 (18 hrs.); to Cochabamba daily, 1800, 12½ hrs., US$7; (also by truck for slightly less, night trip caught at cement works 1½ km. off Cochabamba road—Micro A goes as far as turning), also daily buses and *micros* to Potosí (0700, 1700 with Hidalgo, US$7.50 incl. snacks; 4½ hrs., US$5 with Soltrans). Bus to Santa Cruz, via Cochabamba, Flota Unificada, Mon. and Thurs., 1700, 18 hrs, US$16. Once a week to Tarija at 1030, Saturday, US$16, 18 hrs. To Monteagudo, Thurs. and Sun., 1500, US$5.30. Oruro, via Potosí or Cochabamba, none direct. To Llallagua, Wed. and Sat., 0700, US$8.20, 10 hours. (Take Micro A to bus station 3 km. from centre, taxi US$0.80, T 22029.)

Warning   Police all wear uniform and carry I.D. cards with photographs. Insist on going to the police station, if possible with a witness, before showing passport or money to anyone without these credentials.

Excursion   *Tarabuco*, 3,295 metres, 64 km. by road and 78 km. by rail from Sucre, has a most colourful Indian market on Sundays, starting about 0930. Buses and trucks leave from 0700 from top of Calle Calvo, Sucre, 2 ½ hr. journey, US$1.50 (or taxi, US$40). Train (*ferrobus*) from Sucre, Fri. and Sun. 0700, Mon. 0600, 2½ hrs., US$1.50, returning 1600 (check in advance, train may only go on Sun., and track is liable to mudslides in rainy weather).

There is a direct bus to Cochabamba, US$9.50, 11 hrs. There is a basic hotel, *Residencial Florida*, no water, no toilet, G (*Bar California*, basic). Festival with fair: Virgen de Rosario, 1st Sunday in October and March 12. If you are hardy take a sleeping-bag and sleep in the only restaurant.

"Surely this is one of the most colourful Indian markets in S America. The costume of these Indians is unique and fantastic, and the men wander around playing the *charango*. Women do most of the work. The woven skirts and belts of the women are some of the finest to be found in Bolivia, and good weaving may be bought." - Hilary Bradt. Although the market is popular with tourists, it is still worth a visit. Best bargains are to be had on weekdays, or before the bulk of tourists arrive, or late in the day. Our latest reports indicate that prices at the market are high, but that the real appeal is the Indians in their authentic dress. To see the weaving in progress, visits to Candelaria (two hours truck from Tarabuco) or Macha (8 hours from Sucre), Pocata (one hour from Macha), or Ravelo will save you from hordes of other tourists (travel to Ravelo: by lorry or *micro*, mostly in the morning from departure point near airport, 3 hrs. one way; *micro*, US$1.30, check at shop at Hernando Siles 843 if it's running, it's supposed to leave at 0900, return 1600— lorries back to Sucre invariably full). Specially recommended is a trip to Potolo, where they weave red animals on a black or brown background. Trucks (Thurs. and Fri. in the dry season) go direct from near Sucre airport; in the wet, you can only get to Challanaca and you walk for 3 hours to get there—the prices will probably be lower in the wet season. It has even been suggested that it is cheaper to buy in Peru or from street vendors in Sucre—so check and compare. Swimming in the rainy season only at Cachimayo, Yotala and Nujchu on the road to Potosí.

A main road runs SE from Sucre through Tarabuco and *Monteagudo* (*Hotel Salamanca*, F) for 216 km. to *Villa Serrano*, where the musician Mauro Núñez lived. A music festival is held on December 28-29. (The journey is beautiful through wild mountains.) 460 km. from Sucre is *Camiri* (20,000 people), growing rapidly because of nearby oilfields—the oil refinery may be visited. Flota El Chaqueño runs from Sucre to Camiri on Fri., theoretically at 0700, at least 20 hrs., US$16, returns, again in theory, on Tues. From Camiri there is a bus to Santa Cruz which should be booked up well in advance as it is always crowded (terrifying road), office on Av. Busch next to *Gran Hotel Londres*, goes 4 times a week if enough passengers, 8 hrs., US$11; *camioneta* leaves from in front of the market when there are enough passengers, US$7.80, 7 hrs. (boring journey, dusty). As a garrison town it has some hotels (*Hotel Ortuño*, Calle Comercio, E; *Residencial Marieta*, Av. Petrolera 15, E; *Residencial Premier*, Av. Busch 60, E; *Residencial Familiar*, Calle Comercio, F; *Gran Hotel Londres*, Av. Busch 36, F), restaurants, bars (nothing is cheap) and also flights to La Paz and Santa Cruz, 180 km. If you arrive by car: at Tránsito checkpoint pick up a slip of paper with instructions on how to reach Guardia where you collect permits to stay overnight. Next visit army post on Plaza de Armas to be checked there. Before leaving town visit Guardia again to collect a permit to proceed—all permits cost about US$0.50 each. Hotels will *not* accept car passengers without permit. S along a very bad road is *Villa Montes*, more easily reached from Tarija (260 km., bus leaves Tues., Fri. and Sat. at 0700, US$11), famous for the highest temperatures in Bolivia; take mosquito repellant. Opposite the railway station 2 km. out of town is *Hotel El Rancho*, F, with bungalow-type accommodation; the food is expensive so eat in town. It is on the edge of the Gran Chaco and has a road and railway S to Yacuiba and Argentina and another dry-season road E to Paraguay which is O.K. for high clearance vehicles. *Hotel Pilcomayo*, F, dirty, communal bath, and *Hotel Demia*, F, clean and friendly. The bus trip via Tarabuco and Camiri to Argentina is very rough; poor road and little comfort. Two buses a week (Wed. and Sat. 0730) to Llallagua (**see page 200**).

It is possible to drive from Camiri into Paraguay direct in a truck or 4-wheel-drive vehicle, carrying food and water for a week. No help can be relied on in case of a breakdown. At Camiri, obtain a US$3 permit from the Guardia to go 64 km. (1½ hours) over a rough road to **Boyuibe**, the last town in Bolivia (*Hotel Guadalquivir*, or *Hotel Chaqueño* next door, both F, both serve meals); once there pay US$2 at Customs for an exit stamp. Passports must be stamped by commander of the army post south of the town. There are some rivers to ford and although they are dry in the dry season they can be impassable if there is rain in the area. Some road junctions are unmarked; get accurate directions from the army before leaving Boyuibe. At Boyuibe gas and water are available, and it is on the Yacuiba railway. A new line is being built West out of Boyuibe, then North, to Tarabuco, to link up with Cochabamba (it has reached Monteagudo).

Tom Courtenay-Clack tells us: "¾ km. after the military checkpoint turn left past a large water tower. From then on just follow the most used road. The road is much better now than it used to be, owing to black market fuel truck traffic. It's still quite difficult though and four wheel drive and high clearance is essential. A winch is also advisable especially if there's been rain. The insects are appalling.

"The road turns disconcertingly South for several km. at one point but it's O.K. We saw a tapir and a puma on this road. It is 134 km. from Boyuibe to the Bolivian border post at Villazón (not to be confused with the other Villazón on the frontier with Argentina—Ed.). It took us 6 hours. (It is reported that this trip can take up to 3 days if there are unseasonable storms—Ed.) The officer at Villazón will give you your exit stamp. The nine soldiers at each of the fly-infested lonely posts on either side of the border will vie for your company if you arrive at nightfall. Enormously appreciated by these poor fellows are small gifts of soft drinks, beer, cigarettes or canned fruit. They do six month stints here.

"The Paraguayan post is 3 km. from the Bolivian post. Just a passport check here. Camping is better here than at the Bolivian post because they have a shower and will let you use their kitchen. 13 km. from the Paraguayan border post is Fortín Garay. Here the commanding officer will give you entry stamps. The road is somewhat better from here on, sandy and bumpy but straight.

"There is a police check point later at Mister Long, and still one more at an airforce base. All these take time. It took us nearly nine hours to get to Mariscal Estigarribia. Here there's a large military base and passports are cleared by the commandant. He is unavailable from 1300 to 1600, so be prepared for a wait. If you have to wait, there's a nice German-run pension 100 yards away where you can get excellent ice-cream, a meal and a room. They have a pet rhea (ostrich) if you want to see one close up.

"One and a half hours from Mariscal is Filadelfia (340 km. from Fortín Garay). About 20 km. South of Filadelfia the road is newly and beautifully asphalted all the way to Asunción. The birds along this road are incredible."

There are no buses beyond Camiri on this road. Fuel tankers and other trucks go through to Paraguay (about one a week on average); they will sometimes take one passenger, as regulations forbid more, from Camiri to Filadelfia for US$5—possibly less. The army goes to Villazón once or twice a month; you can camp at Villazón, but no food is available, nor is there much water. Not much food on the Paraguayan side until Mariscal Estigarribia.

The railway line S from Río Mulato goes through **Uyuni** (3,660 metres), the junction for the line to Chile. Warning: do not take photos between Uyuni and the border. Trains to La Paz (US$11.20 Pullman, US$7.50 special) and Oruro (5 a week: 3 express, 2 *trenes mixtos*). The road down from Oruro is sandy, and after rain very bad. Buses to Potosí, 1300, 12-18 hrs. Uyuni lies bitterly cold and unprotected on the plain at the edge of a vast salt lake, the Salar of Uyuni. Julián Quispe charges US$25 for 3 hour trip to the Salar. His green jeep holds 8 and is in front of the cathedral around 1000-1100.

"When it still has water in it (up to 4 or possibly 6 inches), being in the middle of the Salar de Uyuni is like being an ant on a gigantic mirror. The blue sky merges into the blue water, the islands are perfectly reflected and since there is no horizon they appear suspended in space. Some areas may be dry, in which case the salt crust is as blinding-white and featureless as the most perfect snowfield (sunglasses essential)." - Stephen Saker, who endorses our warning on the **Ollagüe-Uyuni track (see below)**.

Uyuni's 20,000 inhabitants are mostly Indian. Its market is the only point of interest best on Thurs. and Fri. (public showers). There is also supposed to be gasoline available at YPFB near cemetery.

Hotel *Avenida*, basic, fairly clean, F, US$1, hot shower in mornings, only breakfast and bar. The *patrón*, Don Jesús Rosas, runs jeep excursions to the Salar (US$35). *Residencial Uyuni*, F, *Residencial Copacabana*, F, *Residencial Urkipiña*, F, all three on Av. Acre, basic and quite clean. *Restaurant Ferrocaril* cooks very good llama meat in the traditional manner, order several hours before. Banco del Estado will not change money. The pharmacy on the main street will change money, but it is very difficult to find out the current rate of exchange.

Motorists must be warned against a road from Río Mulato into Chile by way of Ollagüe. "Between Río Mulato and Uyuni it is deep soft sand and possible only for 4-wheel drive vehicles and trucks. Beyond there is the danger of getting lost on the many tracks leading over the deserted salt lakes, no gasoline between Uyuni and San Pedro de Conchi (Chile), and little hope of help with a breakdown on the Bolivian side unless you don't mind waiting for perhaps a week. After rain the route is impassable. Where the road has been built up, *never* forsake it for the appealing soft salt beside it. The salt takes a man's weight but a vehicle breaks through the crust into unfathomable depths of plasticine mud below." - Andrew Parkin.

Excursions Dan Buck and Anne Meadows write: "*Laguna Colorada,* about 350-400 km. SW of Uyuni, 12 hours' straight driving over unmarked, rugged truck tracks, is featured in Tony Morrison's two books, *Land Above the Clouds* and *The Andes.* It is one of Bolivia's most spectacular and most isolated marvels. The rare James flamingoes, along with the more common Chilean and Andean flamingoes, breed and live in its red algae-coloured waters. The shores and shallows of the lake are crusted with gypsum and salt, a bizarre arctic-white counterpoint to the flaming red waters.

"The standard rate for hiring a truck or jeep, Uyuni-Laguna Colorada 3 day round trip, is US$300-400, negotiate. The Uyuni *Hotel Avenida* is a good contact for making arrangements. There is a welter of tracks, and even locals easily get lost. Truck rides can be arranged at the Sindicato de Chóferes in town, behind the church. A map, compass, and a guide are all useful, plus asking directions of every person one meets along the way— which won't be many. In our round trip we met no vehicles, only 4 *campesinos* on bicycles and a handful on foot. Going out we went Uyuni-Corpina-Quetena Chica-east side Laguna Colorada; on the return we travelled west side Laguna Colorada-Alota-Uyuni. Beware: if approaching the lake from the east side, take the south shore of the lake to the *campamento,* it is longer but better than the north shore which is deep, treacherous volcanic ash and sand. A map of Laguna Colorada may be obtained from Instituto Geográfico Militar in Uyuni. Sr. Erasmo Ansa, Calle Loa between Uruguay and Mexico, drives a truck to Laguna Colorada twice a week. He will leave you there and pick up after 2 or 3 days on his way back, US$25-50 depending on his load.

"There is no dependable transport linking any of the towns and mining camps in the Uyuni-Laguna Colorada area. No one should travel in the area without cold-weather camping gear, sufficient food, etc." At Laguna Colorada, you must camp out of doors, no alternative. A map of Laguna Colorada may be obtained from the Instituto Geográfico Militar in Uyuni. Sr. Erasmo Ansa, Calle Loa between Uruguay and México, drives a truck to Laguna Colorada twice a week. He will leave you there and pick up after 2 or 3 days on his way back, US$25-50 depending on his load.

There is a truck on Saturdays which leaves Chiguana, a town on the Uyuni-Antofagasta railway, once the La Paz train arrives, going to Laguna Verde, 3 hrs., south of Laguna Colorada. There are also trucks which go to the Laguna Colorada and the Susana sulphur mine. A lorry back sometimes leaves on Friday afternoon, but this is by no means certain. There is transport from Uyuni with people taking petrol to the *campamento* at Laguna Colorada—ask at the mining offices at Uyuni. At Chiguana and Laguna Verde the army will normally provide a place to sleep (no bedding). You may also be able to sleep on a floor at the sulphur mine at Laguna Verde, or at the workers' quarters for the Sol de Mañana geothermal project, 45 km. from Laguna Colorada. Hot food can also be purchased although there is none at Laguna Colorada. Travel in this region is possible anytime between May and October, but there is no petrol, mechanical assistance or supplies S of Salinas de Garci Mendoza (270 km. from Oruro) or Uyuni (petrol in Salinas de Garci Mendoza is twice as expensive as in Uyuni). The army can be helpful for transport in the area if you persist.

The scenery between Laguna Colorada and Laguna Verde is spectacular (geysers, boiling mud pools, steaming streams, lakes with flamingoes, wind-eroded rocks). Just past Laguna Verde is a deserted Bolivian border sign, from where it is possible to walk 40 km. to a small Chilean border town, with regular transport to Calama.

One can visit *Llica,* the capital of Daniel Campos Province, in 5 hours over the Salar by truck, or about 12 hours by boat, if there is enough water in the lake. There is a new, basic *Alojamiento Municipal* in town, F. Also Angel Quispe in the plaza has 3 beds. Food is "difficult". There is a teachers' training college but not much special to see. Two fiestas: July 26 and August 15. Good for llama and other wool handicrafts.

SW of Uyuni, 2 hours by irregular bus or truck is San Vicente where Butch Cassidy and the Sundance Kid are said to be buried in an unmarked grave, following a gun battle with the police in 1908.

S of Uyuni, 200 km., is *Tupiza* (2,990 metres, 11,000 people), a centre of the silver, tin, lead, and bismuth mining industries (*Hotel Mitru,* F, private shower and bath; next to it is *Residencial Crillón,* F, with good motorcycle parking; also *Hotel Americano,* G, opposite railway station). Chajri Huasi, a palazzo-style, abandoned Indian home, may be visited, across Río Tupiza. Interesting statue in main square. IGM office, for maps, is in the Municipal building. Three trains to border every week. Bad road from Potosí which goes on S to Villazón; often closed in rainy season because there is no bridge over the Río Suipacha. Bus to Villazón US$1.25 (many daily).

From **Villazón** (13,000 people, good local market), on the border with Argentina, there is an improved road to Tarija, 965 km. by road from La Paz. The road linking Potosí with Villazón via Camargo is in poor condition and about 100 km. longer than the better road via Tupiza. For information on border crossing with Argentina **see page 94**; US$1 usually charged for crossing; remember Argentina is 1 hour ahead if making a connection. Little to see in Villazón (has two cinemas) and not at all welcoming; border area must not be photographed.

Hotels at Villazón *Panamericano*, F, breakfast and lunch (showers extra); *Residencia Martínez*, ½ block from bus station, well signed, F, hot water when town's supply is on; *Residencial El Cortijo*, clean, E, good value, hot water, restaurant; *Residencial Avenida*, F, but try bargaining. *Grand Palace*, clean, E. Restaurants opposite bus station and on first floor of covered market.

Argentine Consulate in main plaza, open 1400-1700, Mon.-Fri.; not very helpful.

Exchange Money-changing at Cambio Porvenir or other cambios on main street, rates said to be good (cash only); Banco del Estado changes travellers' cheques. Out of hours try the Ciné Rex. Warning: do not show passport or money to men claiming to be plainclothes police.

Buses from Villazón To Potosí at 1600 and 1700, 13-15 hrs., US$7.50 (terrible in the wet); to Tupiza, 0700 and 1500; to Tarija, Mon., Tues., Thur., Sun. at 1100, Wed. and Sat. at 0900 (US$6.50-7), 7 hours; trucks for Tarija from beside bus station. Bus passengers for La Paz must cross from Argentina the previous day. Watch out for overcharging by Panamericano bus company— the "direct" La Paz bus sometimes goes only as far as Potosí. Bus station is near the main square, behind Ciné Teatro Libertador Bolívar; it is about 6 blocks from the border. Taxi to border, US$0.20 or hire porter, US$1, and walk across.

Trains from Villazón To La Paz (very dusty and cold journey), Tues., Fri., Sat. at 1450, arr. La Paz 1110 next day (US$19 Pullman, US$13 special). Journey very crowded, especially 2nd class. Train stops at Tupiza (US$9.50) for evening meal at 1900 (no cutlery or napkins provided), Atocha (US$12.50), Uyuni (US$14.25) and Oruro, US$13 Pullman, US$9 special; *tren mixto* twice a week to Oruro, Mon. and Thur. at 1340 (cold journey). The express from La Paz/Oruro connects with a bus to Tarija (in theory), tickets from railway station, about 1 km. out of town on main road.

At *Camargo*, on road from Potosí to Tarija, is an excellent restaurant, *Media Luz*. Guest rooms have been built for overnight stop.

Tarija, at 1,956 metres (population, 60,621) was founded July 4, 1574, in the rich valley of the Guadalquivir river. The road from Villazón, 183 km., is the shortest route from Argentina; there is also a road to Potosí via Camargo. The alternative route from Argentina via Bermejo (13,000 people, no exchange facilities, get australes in Tarija, thorough customs searches), 216 km., is at a fairly low altitude and in a mild climate, but the views are rewarding; not recommended in the rainy season or a month or so after. The road is in an appalling condition apart from 50 km. which are paved. Daily buses take 5 or 6 hours. Do not try to cycle. There is no railway. Tarija had a tumultuous struggle against Spain, declaring itself independent in 1807, and has a strong cultural heritage. Its own university was founded in 1946. There is a large archaeological collection; the entrance is at the corner of the building. Maize, vegetables, wheat, potatoes and splendid grapes thrive in the basin. Bolivia's best wines are produced here (no organized tours to *bodegas*, phone for appointment). Its people are markedly religious and strongly individualistic, and the Indian strain is less marked here than elsewhere in Bolivia. The modern Avenida Costanera gracefully flanks the curves of the river. The Casa Dorada is being reconstructed with a view to becoming the Casa de Cultura (interested visitors may be shown round by the restorer), note the figures in the roof. A good view can be had from Cerro San Juan; follow Calle D.Paz to the top of the rise where the buses gather, turn right on the cobbled street, then right through the gate and follow the Stations of the Cross to the top (it's about 4 blocks up from zoo).

The city is famous for its *niño* (child) processions: colourful and charming. During processions of San Roque in a 3-day festival from the first Sunday in September the richly dressed saint's statue is paraded through the streets; wearing lively colours, cloth turbans and cloth veils, the people dance before it as it goes, and women throw flowers from the balconies. Dogs are decorated with ribbons for the day. On the second Sunday in October the flower festival commemorates the Virgen del Rosario, and another in Easter week.

Hotels *Prefectural*, D with bath and pool, shabby, poor service (2 km. from city centre, upstream on road); *Hostal Carmen*, Ingavi 0-0784, T 3372/4342, E, shower, clean, good value; *Hostal Costanera*, Av. Las Américas, rec., reasonably-priced, modern facilities; *América*, Bolívar 257, hot showers, good, F, restaurant attached (good); opp. is *Residencial Bolívar*, E with bath, rec., clean, comfortable, hot water, breakfast US$1; *Residencial Miraflores*, Calle Sucre, F, clean and rec. *Terminal*, behind bus station, family-run, good lunches, suitable for a night's stop-over; *Residencial Familiar*, F, hot shower, friendly, good food; *Residencial Ocho Hermanos*, near main plaza, F, clean, collective rooms only.

Restaurants *Chapaco*, on main plaza, expensive. *Guacho*, Av. Costanera, is rec. *Arlequín*, Gral. B.Trigo, just off plaza, nice but expensive bar; *La Cabaña de Don Pepe*, Campos 138, has excellent steaks at reasonable prices; *El Rinconcito Andaluz* on the Plaza is cheap and the food reasonable. On La Madrid, *La Princesa* (excellent keperi—meat that is first boiled, then fried); for pizza and icecream on same street, unnamed parlour at the Agencia Kohlberg sign near Suipacha (opp. No. 268); ice cream also at *Gloria*, Ingavi y Gral. B. Trigo; *Snack Te Ve*, Sucre 622, just off plaza, popular. Excellent food, cheap breakfast, in market, but get there before 1300. After, go to Calle Carrero. Try the local wines, e.g. the white Aranjuez, Arce, Colonial or Kohlberg, also local beer.

N.B. Restaurants (and everything else in town) close in the middle of the day.

Shopping Craft goods in market and in co-operative shop in plaza; some cheap stuff, shoddy. Ceramics at Frial Susy, Sucre 776. Felt for hats at La Nueva Italia, Ingavi y Sucre; they will show you where to have your hat made up for US$3.50.

Tourist Office J.M.Saracho 685, just off Calle Bolívar, very helpful, free map.

Zoo Out on Av. Costanera ("a tatty children's park, but worth the US$0.15 to see the condors", Michael J.Finnerty).

Exchange Banco del Estado will change money. Try Comercial Salinas at Mcal. Sucre 758. Money changers on Bolívar at Daniel Campos, also at shops in the vicinity, between Colón and Suipacha. Better rates for australes than in Villazón.

West German Consulate Sucre 665, helpful.

Argentine Consulate Corner of Ballivián and Bolívar, Mon.-Fri., 0800-1300.

Travel Agents Internacional Tarija, Sucre 721, Tel.:4446/7, helpful.

Air Service TAM and LAB to Cochabamba, La Paz (Mon., Wed., Fri., US$39), Santa Cruz, Trinidad, Yacuiba, and Sucre (Tues). Flights are frequently cancelled and/or strike-bound. LAB office, Ingavi 244; TAM office between Sucre and Bolívar. Free LAB bus to airport. Taxi to airport, US$1 p.p., or *micro* drops you 2 blocks away.

Buses Mon., Wed., Thurs. and Sat. on 935-km. route Potosí-Oruro-La Paz, leaving 1700 (26 hrs., US$16; check which company operates the best buses). To Potosí (386 km.), with 10 de Noviembre, takes 13 hrs. (US$12.50), cold. For Sucre, you must change buses in Potosí. To Villazón: EMTV, Tues., Thur., Sat., 0830, US$6.50, Veloz del Sud, Mon., Wed., Sat. 0900, US$7, taking 6½ hrs.; otherwise you need to take a local truck (US$5). On Tues. and Fri. there is a combined bus/train service to Villazón and La Paz, US$22.75, leaves Tarija 0630, seat guaranteed on both services. Daily buses to Bermejo (1900-1930, 9 hrs., US$5.75, truck US$3.50) not recommended in rainy season; at Bermejo cross river by ferry to Agua Blanca, Argentina. To Villa Montes (see page 211), 12 hrs., Wed., 0730, US$11. Also to Yacuiba, daily by Flota Tarija. The new bus station is in the outskirts on Avenida de Las Américas (30 mins. walk from centre, 7-8 mins. from airport). Cía. El Chapaco uses poor quality vehicles. Trucks to all destinations leave from Loma, near the market.

Swimming Municipal swimming bath down the hill from the Mercado Negro. Tomatito, bus from San Juan at 0800, a trip of 5 km., popular picnic area. For those with their own transport El Rincón de la Victoria, 18 km., or Tolomosita, 7 km., sandy beach on river bank, and Los Churros de Jurina with natural rock pools, 22 km., or the Ancón gorge. Sauna at Acuario, 15 de Abril 679. Also interesting walking tours.

EASTERN BOLIVIA (4)

Santa Cruz de la Sierra (437 metres) is the only other city of note, capital of the Department of Santa Cruz, Bolivia's largest and richest in natural resources, lying in the vast and now rapidly developing plains to the E of the Eastern

SANTA CRUZ 26

To VIRU
VIRU AIRPORT
AND THE NORTH

SEGUNDO ANILLO

AV. CRISTÓBAL
DE MENDOZA

SANTA FE

CAÑADA STRONGEST

RIVERO

FORTÍN TOLEDO

BAPTANILLOS

P. RICO

FORTÍN CORRALES

ASUNCIÓN

D'ORBIGNY

J.R. COIMBRA

M.J. JUSTINIANO

QUIJARRO

CAMPERO

C. LLANOS

ACRE

BAURES

MOXAS

MAMORE

ABUNA

ITENES

AV. BUSCH

CENTRO
CÍVICO

MONS.

RIBERALTA

PERU

AV. CAÑOTO

AV. URUGUAY

ANDRES IBÁÑEZ CELSO CASTEDO

RAFAEL PEÑA VACA DIEZ

PARQUE
DEL
ARENAL

6 DE AGOSTO

6 DE AGOSTO

OBISPO AGUIRRE

PRIMER ANILLO

HOSPITAL
SANTA
CRUZ

HOSPITAL
S.J. DE
DIOS

CUELLAR

SEOANE

CABALLERO

SUÁREZ ARANA

CHARCAS

N

SANTA BÁRBARA

BUENOS AIRES

FLORIDA

8 24 DE SEPTIEMBRE

CHARCAS

CHARCAS

ARENALES

ARENALES

JOSE CALLALI

CORDILLERA SARAH

VALLE GRANDE

COLÓN ESPAÑA

VELASCO 21 DE MAYO

INDEPENDENCIA LIBERTAD

JUNÍN

BOLÍVAR

BOLÍVAR

CAMIRI

ISABELA CATÓLICA

EYACUCHO

PLAZA
24 DE
SPTBRE

B. BENEMORENO

CHUQUISACA BENI

LA PAZ MURILLO

COCHABAMBA AROMA

POTOSÍ GUIJARRO

TARIJA CAMPERO

SUCRE

SUCRE

INGAVI

INGAVI

BALLIVIÁN

BALLIVIÁN

AV. CAÑOTO

SUÁREZ DE FIGUEROA ÑUELO DE CHÁVEZ

WARNES

PARI

WARNES

REPUBLIQUETAS

MERCADO

MONS. SALVATIERRA
ASILO
DE
HUERFANOS

MOLDES

LEMOINE

SAAVEDRA

PARADETI

LA RIVA

AV. IRALA

B

AV. IRALA

PRIMER ANILLO

DIEGO DE MENDOZA

SOLOD

To
COCHABAMBA

PICADA

CAÑADA

SENDA

H. DE ZALAZAR

PLAZA
HEROES
DEL
CHACO

AV. ARGENTINA

TTE. A PEÑA

T

SOLÍS DE OLGUIN

To EL TROMPILLO
AIRPORT

Cordillera, 552 km. by air from La Paz. This hot, windswept (May-August) boom town, whose population is now 600,000, making it Bolivia's second city, was founded in 1561 by Spaniards who had come from Paraguay.

Santa Cruz is usually hot and dusty, although when the cold *surazo* blows from the Argentine pampas the temperature drops sharply (May-August); the rainy season is December-February. The Plaza 24 de Septiembre is the city's main square with the Cathedral (interesting hand-wrought colonial silver), the University and prefecture set around it. The Cathedral museum is open on Tuesdays and Thursdays (1000-1200, 1600-1800), and Sunday (1000-1200, 1800-2000). Worth seeing if only to wonder how such an isolated community maintained such high artistic standards (but entry is expensive). Pleasant residential areas are being developed on the outskirts of town. The water supply is quite good, though typhoid and hepatitis are endemic in the area.

Cruceños are famous for their gaiety—their music, the *carnavalitos*, can be heard all over South America. Of the various festivals, the brightest is Carnival, celebrated for the 15 days before Lent: music in the streets, dancing, fancy dress and the coronation of a queen. Beware the following day when youths run wild with buckets and balloons filled with water—no one is exempt. The *mascaritas* balls also take place during the pre-Lent season at *Caballito Blanco*: girls wear satin masks covering their heads completely, thus ensuring anonymity!

Until recently Santa Cruz was fairly isolated, but new rail and road links in the 1950s ended this isolation and now there is an ever-increasing flow of immigrants from the highlands as well as Mennonites mostly from USA and Canada and Japanese settlers, such as the Okinawan colony 50 km. from Montero, to grow cotton, sugar, rice, coffee and other crops, which yield profusely. Cattle breeding and timber projects are also becoming important. A trip out of Santa Cruz to see these newly-settled areas is interesting, especially towards the Río Grande or Yapacaní (beautiful birds and butterflies; the fish are highly recommended). About 7 km. E. of town new Botanical Gardens are being developed. At the N edge of town (Barrio Equipetrol, towards airport) is a good, small zoo, take bus 8 or 16.

The exploitation of oil and gas in the Department of Santa Cruz has greatly contributed to the city's rapid development. There are several oil fields: at Caranda, 50 km. to the NW, at Colpa, 32 km. to the N and a large gas field at Río Grande, 40 km. to the SE. YPFB has an oil refinery at Santa Cruz.

Warning The influence of drug-trafficking has made Santa Cruz into an expensive and, according to most travellers, unpleasant place. Always carry your passport with you as there are constant checks by Immigration. Failure to do so will result in extra hours at the police station. There seems to be no escape from plainclothes policemen "fining" foreigners for some misdemeanor or other: "having an invalid visa"; at the airport "failing to pay the airport tax"; needing "safe conduct" to travel to Brazil. Bribes are charged arbitrarily at the bus station and, especially, at the railway station en route to Brazil. Watch out also for the "planting" of drugs. If possible never be without a witness, always ask for the policeman's identity card (green, embossed with a coat of arms), take his name and number, and say you will take the matter to his superior. Try also to enlist the help of the military police. There may be no alternative but to pay up: complaints, or even requests for a receipt, have often led to jail.

Hotels *Los Tajibos*, the biggest and most expensive, A, Av. San Martín in Barrio Equipetrol out of town, restaurant good but overpriced, swimming pool for residents only; *Cortez*, Av. Cristóbal de Mendoza 280, also out of town, on 2nd Anillo near the Cristo, also has pool and good reputation, C, rec. for medium or long stays; *Las Palmas*, Av. Trompillo, near airport, new, friendly, rec.; in the centre of town is the *Gran Hotel* with pool and laundry service, English spoken; good value, C. *Santa Cruz*, central, Pari 59, good with pool, B, much used by British visitors (with English managers), not really rec. for families; *Asturias*, Moldes 154 with 2 pools, rec. for families C; all those mentioned above are air-conditioned. *Brasil*, Santa Bárbara 242, T 23530, E, breakfast, bath and friendly; *Roma*, 24 de Septiembre 530, D, pleasant, no restaurant; *Cataluña*, 10 km. N on Montero road, pool, basketball, grounds, D, very popular at weekends with cruceños; *Residencial Bolívar*, Sucre 131, E, (hot showers), some rooms with bath, nice courtyard with hammocks; *Hotel Copacabana*, Junín 129, D, with bath (E without), laundry facilities, rec.; *Residencial Copacabana*, Junín 217, near centre, F, acceptable; *Bibosi*, Junín 218 (T

SANTA CRUZ: Map Key.
1. Plaza 24 de Septiembre; 2. Plaza Ñuflo de Chávez; 3. Parque Arenal; 4. Plaza Héroes del Chaco;
5. Cathedral; 6. Bus Terminal; 7. Railway Station; 8. Post Office; 9. Tourist Office.

48887/51791), D, hot showers, breakfast extra, good; *Colonial*, Buenos Aires 57, comfortable, rec., C; *Hostalería Rojas*, Cuéllar 257, F, central, cold showers, safe, adequate; *Residencial Los Pozos*, opp. Mercado Los Pozos, E, hot shower, clean, safe. The better hotels have some air-conditioned rooms but there is usually an extra charge. For those taking buses, *Residencial Arze* at the back of the terminal, F, or *Querencia*, F, is about half a block north of the bus terminal and *Alojamiento San José*, Canadá 136, hot showers, clean, F, about 1½ blocks. *La Quinta*, Barrio Urbari, has individual chalets, good for families but out of town. For all hotels there is 3-tier pricing: locals, South Americans and others. All prices include taxes.

Restaurants The best restaurants are the *Floresca*, Av. Velarde 136, which has a good discotheque upstairs; the *"85"* at Bolívar 85 (very dear); *La Fonda de Ariel* (chicharrón on Sundays and pork), Av. Irala, and the *Ambassador*, Av. San Martín (all air-conditioned). *La Empalizada*, Barrio Cooper 3, has very good parrilladas (grills) in a very pleasant outdoor setting with discotheque. *El Tropero*, Av. Cañoto 310, is rec. for its churrasquería and parrillada, and *Candilejas*, next to *Hotel Cortez*. *Don Miguel*, on Av. Uruguay, has good parrilladas (repeatedly rec.). *El Fogón*, Av. Viedma 436 and *La Buena Mesa*, 2nd Anillo near Cristo, both excellent for parrillada and churrasquería; *Amadeus Pizzería*, Tercer Anillo 761, Barrio Equipetrol, T 45319, good; *El Mauricio Rancho*, Av. Ejército Nacional for excellent steaks. Two quite good duck restaurants are located on Km. 2 (*Los Patos*) and Km. 8 on the road to Cochabamba. *London Grill* in Bolívar is run by British ex-airman and his Bolivian wife. *El Surubí*, Av. Irala, serves only surubí (fish); *El Boliche*, Bení 222, serves good crêpes. Chinese restaurants include *China*, Sucre 209; *China Law*, Castedo Barba 127; *China Town*, Velasco 58; *Patito*, 24 de Septiembre 301; *Shanghai*, Av. 27 de Febrero 33, *Nueva China* on 24 de Septiembre or the expensive *New Hong Kong* on Ballivián 137. *El Mandarín*, Av. Irala 673, excellent. Japanese *Kiku*, near Los Pozos market. *El Deportista* a few doors down (Independencia 42) serves good cheap meals. Also good value is the *Bonanza*, Junín 177, across from the Post Office, clean; next door is *Gandhis*, opinions divided on the curries (ask if you want a hot one), English-speaking, helpful Indian owner. *El Dorado*, Libertad y Junín (main square), good; *Cochero's Bar*, Bolívar 165, good lunches; *Monterrey*, René Moreno, good value with cheap meals and snacks. *Hannes*, Calle Campero, serves continental food, both English and German spoken. Outside the centre, *Chopp Rudi*, Av. Paraguay 739, before that on same road, *La Corona Krone*, German and English is spoken in both and they serve good continental food. Many cheap restaurants near the bus terminal on the main avenida. Also on the extension of Calle 6 de Agosto behind Los Pozos market (daytime). The bakeries on Junín, Los Manzanos and España look scruffy but sell the local specialities: empanadas de queso (cheese pies), cuñapés (yuca buns), rice bread and humitas (maize pies); try the *Panadería Trieste*, 21 de Mayo 369, not the cheapest, but good breakfasts as well. *El Patio* and the *Palace* on the main square sell good cakes. *La Pascana* on the Plaza is a favourite of tourists and locals alike for ice-cream and snacks, though service is slow. Ice-cream specialities at *Ca-Ri-Na*, Ingavi 213 and at *Kívón*, Ayacucho 267, highly rec.

Clubs Tennis Club; Club Las Palmas, 2½ km. on road to Cochabamba, has 9-hole golf course and pool; Club Hípico, riding club, nearby.

Books Los Amigos del Libro, René Moreno 26, sells foreign language books (expensive) and *Newsweek*, and a useful guide *Con Usted La Señorial Santa Cruz de la Sierra* for US$0.25 (list of cheap boarding houses); Cruz del Sur, 21 de Mayo 62, sells *Time*.

Shopping Leather goods (Dorian, Florida 39, esq. Libertad, honest), baskets, hammocks. Carvings and other objects made from beautiful guayacán and jacarandá wood (though reported these crack in drier climates). The market Los Pozos is new, clean, good for mid-day meals and worth going to in summer for its exotic fruits: ambaiba (looks like a glove and the fruit is sucked out of the "fingers"), *guapurú* (like a cherry), *ocoro* (like a prickly mandarin), *achachayrú* (mandarin-like with hard skin), *pitón* (like sour grapes) as well as better-known tropical fruits. There are plenty of smuggled Brazilian goods on sale, exchanged for Bolivian coca (made into cocaine). Beware of bag-snatching in the market. Another market (nothing for tourists, but also has a wide variety of fruit) is *Bazar Siete Calles*: walk down Vallegrande, past Ingavi.

Taxis about US$0.75, fix fare in advance. Luggage extra.

Entertainment Discotheques: El Mau-Mau, open only during Carnival (a vast auditorium), The Viva María is the largest night club. Another recommended night club is El Cuerno Colonial at España 162; on El Paso, Tramps Bar and The New Orleans Bar (both expensive). Also Caaly and Mermelade (Av. Uruguay 30). Tijuana Piano Bar Saloon has offered a courtesy drink to bearers of the *South American Handbook* at Av. Velarde 230. They also co-own Number One Disco, Calle Boquerón 83. The bar at *Hotel Los Tajibos* usually has live music. There are numerous cinemas in town; see local press for details.

Museum Casa de la Cultura, on the plaza, with occasional exhibitions and also an archaeological display; has plays, recitals, concerts and folk dancing.

Exchange Bank of America, Velasco 19; Banco do Brasil, Ayacucho 168; Banco Popular del Perú, 24 de Septiembre 156; Banco de la Nación Argentina, Sucre 31; also local banks. Open 0730 to 1300. Use Casas de Cambio for money exchange, on 24 de Septiembre for example. Magri Turismo, Edificio Oriente, Of. 215, T 45663, 2 blocks from main plaza, the American Express agent, changes American Express travellers' cheques. Money changers on Av. Libertad, and Plaza de Armas.

Consulates Brazil, Florida 25, one block north of the main plaza. Argentina, Banco de la Nación Argentina building, Sucre 31. Uruguay, Colón 58, Mon.-Fri. 0900-1100; Paraguay, Bolivia 568; Peru, La Paz 726.

Health Clínica Lourdes, René Moreno 362, T 25518. Dr. Pepe Arzabe, Quiroga Felix Romero 65, is reported to have specialised knowledge of regional illnesses.

Post Office Calle Junín 146.

Cables can be sent from Entel just off the Plaza at Warnes 83.

Tourist Agents Santa Cruz Tur and Orientur are on the Plaza; Exprinter is at Libertad 149; Magri Turismo, address under **Exchange**, helpful, rec.; Chovy Tours, 21 de Mayo 309/317, T 24445, recommended; Camba Tur, Sucre 8; and Turismo Balas, Bolívar 16, recommended. Many agencies (there are over 100) are to be treated with caution since travel is not their primary business.

Tourist Office Chuquisaca and Ñuflo de Chávez (T 48644). Open Monday-Friday, business hours only, no city maps. Also kiosk at bus station.

Air Service LAB flies daily to La Paz and Cochabamba (US$39). LAB (twice a week) and Líneas Aéreas Paraguayas (LAP—rec., once a week) fly Asunción-Santa Cruz. It is reported that up to US$40 can be saved by breaking your flight at Santa Cruz from Asunción and buying a La Paz ticket, rather than flying direct. Cruzeiro do Sul has 5 flights a week and LAB has 4 a week to São Paulo and Rio de Janeiro. LAB and Aerolíneas Argentinas also fly to Salta (3 flights in all, US$79) and Buenos Aires (5 in all, US$214), and AA fly to Tucumán once a week. There are also flights by LAB to Manaus, Caracas and Miami. LAB flies to some of the outlying towns in the Dept. of Santa Cruz and to Trinidad, Camiri, Sucre (US$25), San Ignacio de Velasco (Mon., Wed., Sat. but check with LAB), Tarija and Yacuiba (US$35.90). There is a weekly flight to Roboré and San Matías every Tues.—one can then enter Brazil via Cáceres, taxi US$2.40.

The international airport is at Viru-Viru, about 16 km. from the town. T 44411 or 33473 (has luggage lockers, duty free shop, and restaurant; no exchange facilities). The bus every 20 minutes to Viru-Viru leaves from the old Trompillo airport, or the bus terminal (US$1). Viru-Viru taxi, US$9 (beware of overcharging). TAM, office at Aeropuerto Trompillo, flies to Puerto Suárez (US$16.50 Tues., Fri., Sun.) fills up quickly, book well in advance, and Yacuiba (US$12, daily). LAB office is at Chuquisaca y Suárez de Figueroa. On LAB internal services baggage allowance is 15 kg. (excess US$0.35 per kg.). Tax: internal US$1, international US$10. Often it is worth going out to the airport as neither LAB or TAM seems to be very aware of empty seats.

Buses Bus terminal on corner of Av. Cañuto and Av. Irala. Most buses seem to run at night. Daily buses to Cochabamba (US$14, 15 hrs.) 0700 by Bolívar (sit on left for best views) or 1700 with connections to Sucre (US$16). Some afternoon buses direct to Sucre (US$12). Oruro and La Paz (US$14, 23 hrs.). For Sucre it is sometimes quicker and cheaper to fly, avoiding changing buses at Cochabamba, i.e. an extra 300 km. The only day time possibility for travel is by colectivo or truck to Cochabamba: either take Micro 17 to Km. 12 where there is a police checkpoint at which all the trucks stop, or go to the office of Transportes Peco in Av. Landívar, half a block west from the Cañuto statue, on Calle Ayacucho. The fare after negotiation will only be marginally less than that for the bus, but at least you will get good views. Flota Chiquitana leaves for San Ignacio Mon., Wed. and Fri. (US$12), 18 hrs., more if raining. To Camiri, bus US$11, 8 hrs., *camioneta*, 7 hrs., US$7.80. Minibuses and colectivos run to Trinidad; the office is below the *Alojamiento Cañuto* in Av. Cañuto, just south of the statue. Trinidad US$25, Samaipata buses leave at 0430; Yapacaní at 0725; and to Abapó and Puerto Banegas for river journey to Guayaramerín. Lorries also leave for Trinidad from the Plaza behind the statue.

Excursions   The country surrounding the city is flat and scenically uninteresting—except to the agriculturist. The sand-dunes (Las Lomas de Arena) 20 km. to the south are worth a visit but impossible to get to without private transport. There is a fresh-water lake in the dunes, but a 4-wheel drive vehicle is required. Los Espejillos, where a mountain stream plunges over a waterfall and carves its way through limestone rocks down a beautiful green and forested valley is well worth the effort to get to—4-wheel drive, only in the dry season. Turn right at Km. 26 on Cochabamba road, cross the Piray river and drive some 12 km. up a forested valley. At a green field on the left (football goal posts) stop and walk a few hundred metres up to the stream. A favourite day trip is to the Yapacaní bridge where *surubí* from the river or *jochi* and *tatú* (armadillo) from the forest may be eaten in one of the riverside eating houses. The drive up to Samaipata, 120 km. along the Cochabamba road, takes a full day—visit the Inca site near the town, an exhausting walk, but the drive up the Piray gorge and "over the top" makes a splendid trip. Take daily bus to Vallegrande which passes the site (2½-3 hrs.)

A recommended round trip taking about a week starts by arriving by train at San José de Chiquitos (with beautiful church that looks like a candle. From there by truck to San Rafael (134 km.), San Miguel (169 km.) and then San Ignacio, and Concepción, all with interesting old churches. From *Concepción* there are daily tours to San Javier or Santa Cruz. Accommodation is limited, but best at *San Ignacio* (*Hotel Santa Cruz*; also luxury bungalows, US$55d, or US$150 weekly for groups of over 6, contact Lucy Hartmann, Cochabamba, T 24258). Concepción is roughly 300 km. NE of Santa Cruz. Still reasonably wild though being opened up. Accommodation at *Grand Hotel Guarayas*, F; *Residencial 6 de Agosto*, shower, clean.

A good road has been driven into fertile lowland to the NW of Santa Cruz. It goes 37 km. N to *Montero* (30,000 people), where sugar and cotton are grown and processed, and on to Puerto Grether, high on the River Ichilo, a tributary of the Mamoré. It will later connect at Todos Santos with the 200-km. road to Cochabamba. A non-stop shuttle minibus service leaves from Santa Cruz bus station for Montero when full. From Montero a minibus connects to Buena Vista (*pensión*); from there trucks run to El Terminal after which one can walk to the Surutú river, the eastern boundry of Amboró National Park (180,000 hectares)—walk to Cerro Amboró (guide required) recommended. The park is home to butterflies, humming birds, macaws, and other native fauna (many of them endangered species). Beware of the insects—do not wear shorts or short-sleeved shirts; much wading is required to get around the park.

Travel to Brazil   The Santa Cruz-Corumbá railway (take bus 4 from the centre to the station) is still rather primitive (and the time-table has been described as flexible, or pure fantasy) but has recently been improved; toilets are still dirty but there is an adequate dining car. Trains stop at Quijarro near the frontier. From there travellers must go by taxi to Corumbá in Brazil; these meet the trains as they arrive and try to overcharge (fare should be about US$0.50 per seat). The *ferrobus* train service is much faster and better, but also ends at Quijarro; it leaves Santa Cruz at 1800 Mon., Wed., Fri. 12-hr trip, returning from Quijarro the following day at 0800 (meals served at seats). *Ferrobus* tickets are only available at the station (T 48488), ticket office opens 0800-0830, but queuing starts at 0500; don't buy tickets for seats 2c and 2d, they don't exist. There is also a "fast" train (*rápido*) that leaves Santa Cruz Sun., Tues. and Thurs., but maybe daily, at 1210; returns following day at 1800. Stopping trains leave Thurs. and Sun. at 1404 and goods trains (mixed) Mon. and Fri. at 2115. Slow trains from Quijarro leave Mon. and Fri. at 1150 or goods (mixed) train at 1500 on Wed. or Sun. Fares: for ordinary trains Pullman, US$12, (comfortable, but sways a lot) first class US$10, second class US$6; *ferrobus*, Pullman, US$20, special, US$15. Check *all* times before setting out. Take a torch, whichever class you are travelling. It is a monotonous journey through jungle except for the frequent stops at trackside towns, where the train's arrival is the chief event in life. A rail flat-car can be hired to transport cars, US$185; you may have to wait several days for a flat-car, however. Food is available on the train or at frequent stops. There is now an unpaved road between Santa Cruz and the Brazilian border, but not recommended, especially in the rainy season, take water, map, food and compass.

The ticket office at the station is not open before 0800 to Corumbá and Yacuiba; purchase only the day before. The customs and emigration post at Quijarro closes very soon after the arrival of the *ferrobus*. You are advised to book as early as possible on all services to Corumbá, which are reported to be getting very crowded. Failing that you can try to buy a ticket on the platform ½ hr. before train departure. Before buying a railway ticket, you must obtain a free safe-conduct pass from the police at Santa Cruz station. Travel agent Orientur sells tickets for the *rápido* (but not *ferrobus*). Foreign exchange generally little problem, but you are likely to be sold cruzados in largish denominations; also you will probably only be able to sell bolivianos in Bolivia, while a few dollars in cash have been known to make irritating border formalities less troublesome. However do beware of showing large quantities of money around. If there are heavy rains check that the line has not been washed out.

Travellers who need a visa for Brazil are advised to obtain a visa before arriving in Santa Cruz. The Brazilian consulate in Santa Cruz can take up to 2 weeks to process applications. Such travellers will be refused entry to Brazil unless they have a visa. Yellow-fever certificates are often asked for (failure to produce one is another "fineable" offence—**see warning on page 217**). All travellers, except Brazilian citizens, have to pay US$2.50 to the Bolivian Ministry of the Interior at the border; an official receipt is given.

On the railway, half way between Santa Cruz and Corumbá, is *San José de Chiquitos*, with huge Jesuit church. (*Hotel San Sebastián Silvestre*, F, basic, clean, good food, near railway station.)

Puerto Suárez Beware thieves. *Hotel Sucre* on main plaza, F, barely adequate; *Hotel Banidi* (more comfortable and the most obvious), and *Residencial Puerto Suárez*, E, clean, fans and showers. *Hotel Bolivia*, D; *Hotel Domingo*, near railway station, dirty, unsafe. Beware the water, it is straight from the river. Most people prefer to go on to Corumbá where hotels are better.

The simplest way to Brazil is to fly La Paz-Puerto Suárez, US$85, then share a taxi to the border, US$7.30-US$10.90 (per car).

A tip if travelling from Brazil to Bolivia is to arrive a week in advance, take a day trip from Corumbá to Puerto Suárez to purchase a train ticket at a travel agency (or book a flight), return to Brazil (to the Pantanal, say) and prepare yourself for the journey.

Travel to Argentina To Buenos Aires by train via *Yacuiba* (11,000 people; many cheap hotels in town centre) takes 3 days and is a long and tiring trip. First class and second class passengers must disembark at Yacuiba, taking taxi (US$0.25) to Pocitos on the border and walking across to Argentine side before boarding train for Buenos Aires. Tickets should be purchased from Incatur travel agents in Santa Cruz. A more comfortable alternative is to take the *ferrobus* from Santa Cruz to Yacuiba (9-10 hour journey) and then to take a bus from Pocitos on the Argentine side of the border to Güemes (2 buses daily with connections to Salta and Buenos Aires). Trains Yacuiba-Santa Cruz: Mon. and Fri., *mixto*, at 1900, 24 hrs., US$3.10; Wed. and Sat., *rápido*, at 1230, Pullman, US$12, 1st class US$6.20, 2nd US$3.80, 10 hrs.; or Thursday at 0815; *ferrobus*, 2100, US$20. Trucks for Santa Cruz leave from Lourdes market, not advisable after rain. Be warned that the immigration police have been shaking tourists down for "smuggling dollars" and will offer you the option of jail or a fine. Contact a superior officer and/or Consulate to help stop this banditry. LAB flies to Santa Cruz and La Paz (US$60) on Tues. and Sun., 1500 (supposedly); TAM also flies from here but has a much more flexible timetable.

THE NORTHERN LOWLANDS (5)

A road to open up the underinhabited Beni Department runs from Cochabamba NE for 200 km. to Todos Santos, on the Chaparé river, a tributary of the Mamoré (the previous narrow road has now been much improved and paved). To *Villa Tunari* by bus between 0800 and 1000 (no standing allowed, won't go if not enough passengers) from Av. Oquendo 985, Cochabamba, US$3.50, 3-6 hrs. *Hotel San Antonio*, E, water intermittent, *Hotel Las Vegas*, basic but clean; *Pilundiy*, F; *Las Rosas*, not clean but friendly, full board available. Especially good is *Cabañas Sumuque*, D, pool and good view. Sr. Carlos at the *Hotel Rosas* does jungle trips to see birds and crocodiles. Ask for the Piscinas Naturales for beautiful swimming. Bus or pick-up to Guayaramerín, 2½ hours.

A road goes through from Villa Tunari to *Puerto Villarroel* (*Hotels Rivera*, *Hannover*, best, E, and some cheap *alojamientos*) from where cargo boats ply irregularly to Trinidad in about 4-10 days (US$10, meals included). You can get information from the Capitanía del Puerto notice board. Take a hammock, mosquito net, plenty of reading matter, water-sterilizing tablets and any interesting food you can find beforehand (rain water available from pharmacy - on the boat one can only get river water tasting of mud). (There are very few stores in Villarroel. Sr. Arturo Linares at the Cede office organizes boat trips to the jungle—not cheap.) You get to Guayaramerín in 10-15 days (fare US$10), depending on the depth of the river (may be best in August/September when the water is lower but cleaner, and there are more animals around on the shore). The Cochabamba-Villa Tunari run is highly recommended for scenery, and fishing at San Fernando. However, the river boat people seldom fish although you might be offered turtle eggs, a local delicacy.

From Cochabamba you can get a bus to Puerto San Francisco (US$5), Todos Santos or Puerto Villarroel (US$6), and thence by boat down the Securé, Chaparé or Mamoré rivers to

Guayaramerín, then by road to Riberalta and back up river to Santa Ana on the River Santa Elena, or Puerto Linares, thence by road to Coroico and back to La Paz.

Ulricke Ramcke-Mensing writes:

Boat trip from Puerto Villarroel to Trinidad   There are now daily except Sunday (US$6) buses from Cochabamba to Puerto Villarroel, taking about 6 hours. (Police checkpoints may ask for bribes from *all* bus passengers on the Cochabamba-Puerto Villarroel route; similarly at the Capitanía del Puerto office in Puerto Villarroel where you are supposed to register. Either do not register, or demand a receipt and say you will check the facts with a superior—Ed.) Puerto Villarroel is the main port for the river transport to the north of Bolivia. As the road running from Santa Cruz to Trinidad can only be used in the dry season, river transport is still the most important means of communication. There are boats running between Puerto Villarroel, Trinidad and Guayaramerín on the Brazilian border, taking passengers. This trip is only for the hardy traveller. In the rainy season when the river is high it takes about 4 to 5 days to go from Puerto Villarroel to Trinidad, but in the dry season, i.e. between May or June and September or October, it may last 8 to 10 days. The launches do not provide berths; you just have to sleep on the cargo which, if you are lucky, may be sugar bags and the like. We paid US$15 for the trip including food. The food is native, that is to say all kinds of fish, dishes like *massaca* (stewed yuca with cooking bananas, *charque* or dried meat, oil and salt) and turtle eggs (rather delicious!). If you are fussy about food, don't make the trip because the kitchen is beyond description and the toilet facilities, too. Take your own drinking water, as the water served is taken from the river. The food served is very starchy and heavy because it is nearly always fried in oil. The trip is not as exciting as those in the real jungle; the countryside between Puerto Villarroel and Trinidad is more or less cultivated, with plantations of bananas and cattle ranches, some with 20-30,000 head. There is no jungle with orchids, crocodiles, etc., but one can see *petas*—small turtles basking in the sun, river dolphins, jumping fish, now and then monkeys playing on the beach, and many types of birds. At night, there are never-ending frog concerts. This trip could be described as quite relaxing if it was not for the poor food and the spartan accommodation.

Bathing in the river can be done without any harm. One night we caught quite a few *pirañas* but we were told that they do not usually attack men. (The Editor advises care, all the same!)

If one does not know how to enjoy the "green symphony" as it is passing by, one should take a good book, as the trip might otherwise get very long!

A mosquito net is a "must".

Trinidad, the capital of the lowland Beni Department (237 metres), founded 1686, population 40,288, is reached by air from La Paz, Cochabamba, Riberalta or Santa Cruz, or by river from Puerto Villarroel. Sleeping-bag and mosquito-net essential on boats; passengers sleep on the deck. The port is on a mud bank 8 km. out of town. Dry season, Oct.-Dec., boats do not reach Villarroel from the north. Food value varied. The main mode of transport (even for taxis) is the motorbike. Excursions interesting for wildlife, as is the river trip (hire a motorbike or jeep to go to the river; good swimming on the opposite bank; boat hire US$5). A road has been built to link La Paz with Trinidad (via San Ignacio, San Borja and Puerto Linares), and occasional colectivos and trucks use it (but don't depend on it); the road is of typical "penetration" standard, not for use during the rainy season, and gasoline is very difficult to come by. Take water, and a compass. A railway from Santa Cruz to Trinidad, via Montero and Colonia San Juan, has reached the confluence of the Ichilo and Grande rivers, 105 km. from Trinidad. The flight to La Paz is cheaper by TAM than by LAB (book early in either case). Bus service to Cochabamba leaves 0700; poor service to Santa Cruz, 18 hrs. A fleet of over 20 air taxis also provides local transport. LAB tend to cancel flights, especially during rainy season. Ask around at airport for private-hire air fare prices. Exchange cash dollars at Farmacia de Tarno, Santa Cruz 470.

Hotels   *Ganadero*, B, rec., friendly, roof top pool. *El Bajío*, Av. Nicolás Suárez 622, T 21344/20203, C with bath and fan, breakfast extra, modern, swimming pool; *Mi Residencia*, near plaza, D, friendly, clean; *Residencial Loreto*, Calle La Paz, E, clean. Some cheaper alternatives on Calle 18 de Octubre. *Residencial Palermo*, E, Av. 6 de Agosto, clean with hot water. Slightly out of town (no transport) is *Hostelería*, D, swimming pool, air-conditioned, friendly.

Restaurants   Loreto, rec., between Plaza and Calle La Paz. Also *Churrasquería El Cachón de Mamita*, Av. Sucre 737, expensive; *Dragón China*, Calama 700, good Chinese food; and *Chifa Hong Kong* on the Plaza. *Pacumutu*, Nicolás Suárez, for plato común; *El Dorado*, Santa Cruz 522, cheap; *Snack Brasilia*, La Paz 662, serves a good dinner. *Carlitos*, on main square, rec.

Guayaramerín   A primitive small town (12,500 people) and centre for gold prospectors, is on the bank of the Mamoré river, N of Trinidad, opposite the

Brazilian town of Guajará-Mirim. Passage between the two towns is unrestricted, but if going from Brazil into Bolivia you need your passport stamped by the Bolivian consul in Guajará-Mirim before leaving Brazil, and by the Bolivian immigration office. Similarly, if you are travelling on into Brazil and not just visiting Guajará-Mirim, get your passport stamped when leaving Bolivia and entering Brazil (US citizens need visas to enter Brazil). Exchange money in Bolivia, as this is very difficult in the State of Rondônia in Brazil. Boat trip, US$0.20, speed boat US$ 0.50 during day, US$2.50 at night. If you don't want to stay, check the notice of boats leaving port on the Port Captain's board, prominently displayed near the immigration post on the river's bank. Boats up the Mamoré are fairly frequent—a three-day wait at the most.

Hotels   *Santa Ana*, E, rec. *Playa*, F. *Litoral*, F, cold water only, friendly. *Central*, F, just off the Plaza, and *Mexo Plaza*, E, on the main Plaza.

Restaurants   *La Querencia*. Best is *La Puerta del Sol* for US$4-6 evening meals, or the old municipal market, two blocks west of the main square. *Snack Gino* at Av. 25 de Mayo 511 is also a possibility. At mid-day try the port area, where rapid short-order meals can be had for US$1-1.50.

Buses to Riberalta 3 hrs., US$4.75, 0930 and 1600 daily (first return bus at 0700). Also trucks available from the 1100 block of Gral. Federico Román.

Air Transport   Daily flights to Trinidad and to La Paz (0930), and others to San Joaquín and Santa Ana. LAB and TAM offices at airport, 10 minute walk from town.

Riberalta   Only 175 metres above sea level, another expanding town (40,000 people), which with the whole region attained temporary importance during the natural-rubber boom of the late 19th century; the cattle industry is providing a new boost for the town. It is at the confluence of the Madre de Dios and Beni rivers, which together flow into the Mamoré a few km. N of Guayaramerín.

Hotels   *Noreste*, clean, friendly, *Cochabamba, Residencia, Santa Rita*, all F (without breakfast). *Residencias Julita*, F, good, clean; *Comercial Lazo*, Calle N.G. Salvatierra (F, not too clean but comfortable), and *Colonial*, Plácido Méndez 1, are worth a try, E; *Residencial Los Reyes*, near airport, D, with fan, clean.

Restaurants   *Club Social Progresso*, US$1 a meal; *Club Social Riberalta*, better, on Maldonado; *Restaurant Popular Cochabamba*, US$0.50. Restaurants on main square are mediocre; good breakfast in market; food stalls outside *Comercial Lazo*, tasty meals.

Transport   Flight, Riberalta-Cochabamba (US$100 TAM, US$105 LAB). LAB to La Paz, via Santa Cruz and Tarija. Expect delays in the wet season. LAB office Linares 31, TAM office is opposite LAB. A motorcycle can be hired for US$2 an hour (no licence or deposit required) for visits to jungle; taxi drivers can give you the address.
   Boat trip from Riberalta to Puerto Rico via River Aruña, from there to Conquista by road (US$4.10) and thence by River Madre de Dios to Riberalta (US$5.25). There are long gaps between boats from Riberalta.

Exchange   Bazar La Paz on main Plaza buys dollars cash and travellers' cheques.

N.B.   Food in the Beni tends to be expensive, but the steaks are good. Electricity is turned off between 2300-0600: do not rely on the fan to keep the insects off.

Cobija, capital of the lowland Department of Pando, N of La Paz, population, 4,989 (252 metres), only connections by air (e.g. TAM to Puerto Rico, Trinidad and LAB to Guayaramerín and Riberalta) and river transport. It is close to the Brazilian and Peruvian frontiers and the area has many Brazilian residents. It is difficult to get more than a month-long entry stamp in your passport here; if needing longer, press for it. Cobija hotels are expensive.

From Caranavi to the Beni Lowlands Grace Osakoda writes: On Friday or before leave La Paz for Caranavi, from where trucks go on Sunday to the market at Bellavista (the restaurant will provide a mat for sleeping on the floor if stuck). Between 1200-1300, Sun., trucks go on to Puerto Linares (*Alojamiento Don Pancho*, best beds, shared showers, no doors, friendly; *alojamiento*, opposite is dirty, sleep on mats, no locks on doors). Across the river is Santa Ana, originally an Indian village, more interesting than Puerto Linares. In the dry season you can go by road from Puerto Linares to Rurrenabaque; in the wet, when the road is impassable, small boats take a day (at least) to Rurrenabaque. The road route to Rurrenabaque is, by truck, via Palos Blancos (market day, Saturday; *Hotel Magdalena*, G p.p., no running water; *Doña Luisa's* restaurant, good non-alcoholic *chicha*). The road from Palos Blancos to Rurrenabaque is very bad, requiring several days; take food, water sterilizers and insect repellent.

Rurrenabaque is a small, picturesque jungle town, with San Buenaventura on its opposite bank. Hotels: *Santa Ana*, E with bath, less without; *Porteño*, similar prices, better; *Safari*, on outskirts, for tours, all rooms with bath, not open all year round; an unnamed place by the river, cheapest, dirty, rooms with or without bath. Best meals at *Club Social Rurrenabaque*, US$1.25; *Snack Horeb*, no sign, run by Jorge Pacheco, friendly, helpful, a good meeting place. LAB and TAM fly to Rurrenabaque if the runway is dry (the wet periods are long); better services go to Reyes, from where trucks go to Rurrenabaque for US$2.50. Boats to Riberalta are infrequent; the fastest and largest is the *Don Carlos* (Captain Fong), US$30 incl. meals, 5 days to Riberalta (take a hammock). In the rubber season, the *Don Carlos* stops at the *estancia* of the Fong Rocas family, where you can see the rubber process and the conditions of the indebted workers. There may also be boats to Santa Cruz (try radioing in advance to the Capitanía del Puerto at Rurrenabaque to find out about boats).

THE ECONOMY

Bolivia is the poorest country on the South American mainland, with annual income per head estimated at about US$600. Its backwardness is partly attributable to its rugged terrain, which makes communications between the various parts of the country extremely difficult, and to its landlocked position.

The agricultural sector employs over 56% of the working population and contributes about 23% to gdp, but less than 2% of export earnings. Employment in agriculture has fallen since the mid-1960s because of increasing urbanization. Production of crops for food takes place primarily in the Altiplano, mainly by subsistence farmers, while crops for industrial use (cotton, sugar and soya) are concentrated around Santa Cruz. Croplands cover about 5% of total land area. Most commercial agriculture is in the east, where there are a number of food-processing plants: vegetable oils, a maize mill and sugar refineries. One of the major growth areas in agriculture is the cultivation of the coca leaf, used for chewing by the Indians and to make the drug cocaine. The extreme economic depression and rising unemployment has driven increasing numbers in search of the lucrative cocaine trade. Coca is easy to grow, up to four crops a year can be harvested, and Bolivia's production is believed to be worth about US$2bn a year, although less than a quarter of that actually returns to the country.

In contrast to agriculture, mining, including oil, employs only 2-5% of the labour force and contributes less than 7% of gdp, yet 95% of export earnings. Bolivia is a major producer of tin, antimony, wolfram and bismuth. Silver, lead and zinc are also produced and there are large unexploited reserves of lithium and potassium. Tin is the major mineral export, but because of the collapse of the world tin market, it has lost its first position in overall exports to natural gas. The mining sector is in decline and many mines are being closed.

Estimated reserves of natural gas are sufficient to meet domestic demand and export commitments for 30 years, but oil reserves, at 155m barrels in the mid-1980s, were being exploited faster than the rate of discovery. Production of around 20,000 b/d was just sufficient to meet domestic demand, but would be insufficient were there to be a general economic recovery.

The recession which afflicted most Latin American countries from 1980 hit Bolivia with six consecutive years of contraction of gdp, accompanied by accelerating inflation, massive and frequent devaluations of the currency and social unrest. Government spending to support key export sectors was hampered by widespread inefficiency, corruption and strikes in state enterprises, which led to massive public sector deficits and external indebtedness. Economic problems were compounded in 1983 by a severe drought in the Altiplano and floods in the eastern lowlands, which devasted farming. The resulting food shortages exacerbated existing inflationary pressures and led to hyperinflation with annual rates reaching over 20,000%.

In the mid-1980s the government of President Paz Estenssoro introduced severe austerity measures to stabilize the economy, in which price controls were lifted, subsidies removed, public sector wages frozen and the currency linked to the US dollar in a controlled float. Tax reform was passed, a new currency, the boliviano, was created, worth 1 million pesos, the IMF agreed to disburse a standby credit, bilateral and multilateral lending began to flow again and steps were taken to reschedule the external commercial bank debt. Inflation came down to 10% a year, although unemployment continued to rise and living standards to fall. Nevertheless, there were encouraging signs that growth could be renewed towards the end of the decade and structural adjustment would put Bolivia on a firmer footing for the 1990s.

	1961-70 (av)	1971-80 (av)	1981-85 (av)	1986-88 (av)
Gdp growth (1980 prices)	6.0%	4.5%	-2.4%	0.0%
Inflation	6.1%	18.7%	610.6%	35.5%
Exports (fob) US$m	122	517	779	509
Natural gas	—	70	369	300
Tin	82	245	253	80
Zinc	5	33	36	30
Imports (fob) US$m	126	460	536	731
Current account balance US$m (cumulative)	-222	-965	-1,243	-829

INFORMATION FOR VISITORS

To Bolivia by Air

(1) *From Europe:* Either fly to Lima by Air France, etc., whence 12 flights a week to La Paz (Lufthansa's Frankfurt, San Juan, Lima flight connects directly with LAB for La Paz); or via Rio de Janeiro, São Paulo or Buenos Aires. Tawa Tours, Sagárnaga 161, La Paz, T 329814, sells and confirms Aeroflot flights to Europe. Cheapest route is with Líneas Aéreas Paraguayas: Frankfurt-Brussels-(Madrid)-Recife-Asunción-Santa Cruz; on the outward journey you will have to stay for 1,2 or 6 nights in Asunción (first night may be paid for by LAP), but the return connection is immediate.

(2) *From North America:* Eastern, 3 flights weekly from Miami to La Paz. Lloyd Aéreo Boliviano (LAB, timekeeping poor), daily from Miami via Caracas, Manaus and Santa Cruz, or Panama to La Paz. Otherwise, connections via Lima.

(3) *Within South America:* From Caracas twice weekly by LAB. From Lima, several a week by Aero Perú, LAB or Aerolíneas Argentinas. From Arica, twice weekly by LAB and LAN-Chile. From Santiago, 4/5 a week, 2 by LAN-Chile (via Arica and Iquique), and 2 by LAB. From Buenos Aires (US$291), 5 flights by LAB and Aerolíneas Argentinas. From Asunción, three a week by LAB, one by Líneas Aéreas Paraguayas, one by Eastern (US$50 more). From Rio and São Paulo (US$277), five a week by Cruzeiro do Sul and 4 a week by LAB. *Note:* LAB international flights to and from points E of La Paz tend also to call at Santa Cruz or Cochabamba, or both. TAM services are one third cheaper than LAB.

Tax on airline tickets 12.3%.

Airport tax of US$10 (only US$0.75-3 on internal flights, payable in bolivianos) is levied on leaving. No tax if leaving overland, or if you stay in Bolivia less than 24 hours, although there have been reports of US$10 being charged overland.

By Sea   To Arica or Antofagasta, then by rail or road.

By Rail   From Argentina and Chile (**see page 189**). For freight from Europe to South/East Bolivia, Paraguay Linie provides a sea-rail or road service via Buenos Aires; agents' details in Paraguay section.

By Road   From Cuzco or Puno, several services. Peruvian and Bolivian roads partly paved. Also links with Argentina and Chile (see below).

Motoring (1) From Puno (Peru) via border stations at Desaguadero (for Guaqui and La Paz) or Yunguyo (for Copacabana, the straits of Tiquina, and La Paz). Peruvian customs at Desaguadero do not work after 1730 unless you are prepared to seek out the officials and pay them "overtime" (US$3 at weekends). Bolivian customs now operate to 1900 but immigration formalities can be completed at Copacabana if the border post is closed. Peruvian time is an hour behind Bolivian time.

(2) From Salta-Jujuy-La Quiaca (Argentina) to Potosí or Tarija. Roads ford many rivers in Bolivia and are impassable in wet weather (Argentine section, despite much work, is reported still to be bad). Bolivian border controls work mornings and 1400-1800 only.

(3) Alternative routes lead from the Argentine province of Salta via Bermejo or Yacuiba into Tarija. Dry weather only.

(4) From Ollagüe (Chile) to Uyuni, very bad. A new dirt road has been built from Arica (Chile) via Tambo Quemado.

Internal Air Services are run by Lloyd Aéreo Boliviano (LAB) and TAM, the army airline, between the main towns. LAB offers a 28-day unlimited domestic flight ticket for US$99 for international travellers using LAB, which must be bought outside Bolivia (one is not allowed to leave from the same airport twice, which may cause problems as so many flights radiate from La Paz or Cochabamba). To avoid paying the 12.3% tax on the air-pass, purchase it as an MCO outside the country, then exchange this for flight tickets later. You must enter Bolivia using LAB or under the pooling arrangement LAB has with Lufthansa or Aeroperú at the moment. Also LAB is promoting limited stay tickets as well as the normal Apex type fares. Spouse fares (i.e. one goes free with one paying full fare) available on certain international flights. There are also reductions for special excursion flights. LAB will be glad to supply current information on request. In out-of-the-way places TAM is more reliable than LAB, which will not go if there are insufficient passengers. Your seat priority on TAM is low, though. Insure your bags heavily as they tend to get left around.

NB If your internal flight is delayed keep your baggage with you and do not check it in until the flight is definitely announced. There have been robberies of prematurely checked-in baggage.

Motorists (including motor-cyclists) must buy an **Hoja de Ruta (driving permit)** from local offices of the Servicio Nacional de Tránsito for every road journey, specifying final destination and date. If hiring a car, the company can arrange a "blanket" driving permit for tourist purposes which is valid for several days and destinations. Tolls vary from US$0.50 to US$2.50 for journeys up to 100 km. You also need an International Driving Permit (and, since a driving licence number is requested, also your national driving licence, or some ingenuity). For hints on high-altitude motoring, see **Introduction and Hints** at front of book.

Petrol (gasoline) is bad; only one grade—less than 2-star. Gas oil is slightly cheaper. Costs are higher in Guayaramerín, Riberalta and Puerto Suárez.

Buses (interurban ones are called *flotas*, urban ones *micros*) ply on most of the roads. Reporting time is half an hour before the bus leaves, but you should always try to reserve a seat as far as possible in advance. In the wet season, bus travel is subject to long delays and detours at extra cost. On all journeys, take food and toilet wipes.

Trucks congregate at all town markets, with destinations chalked on the sides, they are not much less comfortable than buses or ordinary trains and are normally about half the cost when there is competition. Otherwise they charge what they judge the market will bear and can therefore seem expensive.

Internal Roads La Paz-Oruro, completely paved; Oruro-Challapata, paved first 30 km., then dirt (or mud in the wet season); La Paz-Tiquina: *autopista* to El Alto (toll US$0.25), then surfaced to Tiquina; La Paz-Cochabamba paved; Oruro-Cochabamba, all-weather; Cochabamba-Santa Cruz, paved, but in a very bad state; Cochabamba-Sucre and on to Potosí, S of paved road, paved for 127 km. to Totora, then dirt (bad in rainy season). Oruro-Potosí, dirt, very bad in rainy season. La Paz-Yungas, well-engineered and surfaced to Unduavi, but most roads in the Yungas offer "hair-raising driving". La Paz-Beni-Trinidad, mixed reports. Puerto Suárez-Arroyo Concepción open. Nearly all Bolivian road surfaces, even the paved sections, are bad, and after flooding or rough weather they are even worse. Even main roads may be closed in the rainy season.

Travel to Paraguay Apart from the adventurous journey described on page 211, a cheap way of getting to Paraguay is to travel by bus to Salta or Orán (Argentina), then on to Asunción via Resistencia (Argentina). Alternatively LAB have been tipped as a potentially cheap way to travel across South America.

Travel by Train The "Pullman" services are reported to be improving the general slow train service. The railways have recently renewed their rolling stock with Fiat railway coaches from

Argentina. "Slow" trains have speeded up but they cannot take the curves and gradients at the same rate as the *ferrobuses*. Always check departure times in advance.

Documents   A passport only is needed for citizens of the Western European countries, USA, Canada, New Zealand and Israel; all others need visas unless they have tourist cards, which can be obtained free from Consuls and travel agencies; they are good for 30 days and can be renewed twice, at the Ministry of Immigration in La Paz, Calle Landaeta 220, by Plaza de Estudiantes, lower end of Prado, Mon.-Fri. 0900-1830, Sat. 0900-1200. Extending tourist visas is time-consuming, and costs US$25; ensure that visas and passports are stamped with the same, correct date of entry or this can lead to "fines" later. Business visitors (unless passing through as tourists) are required to obtain a Determined Object Visa quoting reference Tasa-03.03. D from a Bolivian consulate. This costs US$60. Hotels automatically register their guests with the immigration authorities but visitors staying as private guests should present their passports at the nearest immigration office.

We have repeatedly been asked to warn against people impersonating Interpol men who want to see all your money—ask (politely) to see identification first and then only in front of friendly witnesses. This warning applies especially to Santa Cruz and the rail link to Brazil, also the La Paz-Arica railway (point to the "Gratis" on the stamp, and stand your ground). Now reports state that this happens in La Paz, Sucre and Potosí also. Do not show money or passport to anyone not in police uniform. Genuine police and immigration staff are not above pretending that your documents are not in order, and demanding US$10 or so p.p. to "rectify" them. In such cases it is probably best to pay up with good grace.

Duty-free Imports   200 cigarettes, 50 cigars and 1 lb. tobacco; one opened bottle of alcoholic drink.

Walking   *Backpacking and Trekking in Peru and Bolivia*, by Hilary and George Bradt, describes 3-9 day hikes in the Cordillera Real within easy reach of La Paz. The local tourist office also produces a leaflet with sketch maps on walks available from La Paz. There are also some excellent guides available through local clubs.

Camping   Chet and Jeri Wade, of Sacramento, California, tell us that one can camp almost anywhere in safety. Warm sleeping gear essential, even in the lowlands in the winter. Sleeping bags are also useful for getting some sleep on the buses or long distance trains, especially those crossing the Andes. Mosquito nets can be purchased in La Paz, but they are not cheap. Beware sandstorms S of Oruro. No camping gas is available in Bolivia.

British Business Visitors   are strongly advised to consult "Hints to Exporters: Bolivia", which can be obtained from Dept. of Trade, Export Services Division, Sanctuary Blgs, 16-20 Great Smith Street, London SW1P 3DB. Similar publications for U.S. business visitors may be obtained from the Department of Commerce.

The best time for a visit   is May to November, the dry season. May, June, and July are the coldest months.

Festivals   January (last week), La Paz, "Alacitas", on Av. Montes. Feb. 2, Aug. 25: Virgin Copacabana. May 3: Fiesta de la Invención de la Santa Cruz, various parts. In La Paz El Gran Poder, end May/early June, at the "Calvario". June 23: San Juan, all Bolivia. June 29: San Pedro y San Pablo, at Tiquina. July 28: Fiesta de Santiago (St. James), Altiplano and lake region; Achocalla a convenient place to go to. Nov. 1 and 2: All Saints and All Souls, any local cemetery. For other festivals on the Altiplano enquire at hotels or tourist office in La Paz. Remember that the cities are very quiet on national holidays, but colourful celebrations will be going on in the villages.

Climate   There are four distinct climatic zones: (1) The tropical departments of Santa Cruz and Beni, drained by the Amazon; altitude between 150 and 750 metres; average temperature, 29°C. (2) The Yungas, or low valleys, north of La Paz and Cochabamba, among the spurs of the Cordillera; altitude, 750-1,500 metres; average temperature, 24°C. (3) The Valles, or high valleys and basins gouged out by the rivers of the Puna; average temperature, 19°C. (4) The Puna and Altiplano; average temperature, 10°C, but above 4,000 metres may get down to -25°C at night in June-August (don't forget antifreeze). Little rain falls upon the western plateaux between May and November, but the rest of the year is wet. There is rain at all seasons in the eastern part of the country, and heavy rain from November to March.

Clothing suitable for Great Britain, with a raincoat or light overcoat, should be worn by visitors to the Altiplano and the Puna, where it is particularly cold at night. The climate in the Eastern Lowlands is tropical. Oruro and Potosí are colder than La Paz; Cochabamba can be very warm. There is a prejudice against the wearing of shorts in town centres.

Health Whatever their ages, travellers arriving in La Paz by air (too quickly, that is, for a progressive adaptation to the altitude) should rest for half a day, taking very little food and drink. They will be up and doing the next morning. In Bolivia, do as the Bolivians do: above 3,000 metres, walk slowly, very slowly uphill. Never go out for the whole day without taking an outer garment: the temperature drops sharply at sunset. Inoculate against typhoid and paratyphoid (also have yellow fever inoculation and anti-malaria tablets if visiting the lowlands) and stock up on necessary medicines; they are dear in Bolivia. Visitors are being asked for yellow-fever vaccination certificates when visiting Santa Cruz or the Oriente. We have also been asked to mention that hepatitis is very common. Chagas disease is endemic in the Yungas and other warmer parts of Bolivia. There is no known cure, so that adobe huts with thatched, or leaf-protected, roofs should be avoided as sleeping places because they play host to the *vinchuca* beetle which is the vector; half Bolivia's population has the disease, which leads to heart failure but shows few other immediate symptoms (see **Health Hints**, page 33).

Hotels Throughout Bolivia the cheaper hotels impose their own curfews. In La Paz it tends to be midnight (check) but it can be as early as 2130 in Copacabana. These locking up times are strictly adhered to by hotel keepers.

Cost of Living Rents, appliances, and some clothing, and especially toilet goods and medicines, are high priced. With inflation now under control, Bolivia has become much more expensive for the traveller. Basic hotels in the larger cities cost about US$5 double, while *almuerzos* cost from US$1-2; all other meals are dear.

Best Buys Llama-and alpaca-wool knitted and woven items are at least as good as those from Peru. La Cancha market in Cochabamba is highly recommended but you *must* bargain. Ponchos, *mantas*, bags, *chullos* (bonnets). Gold and silverware. Musical instruments such as the *charango* (mandolin with armadillo-shell sound-box) and the *queña* (Inca flute), and other assorted wooden items.

Food and Drink The normal international cuisine is found at most good hotels and restaurants. Some local dishes are interesting (see below). The 3 makes of local beer (Pilsener), lager-type, are recommendable; the local hot maize drink, *api* (with cloves, cinnamon, lemon and sugar), should be tried (usually US$0.12), as well as *singani*, distilled from grapes, good, cheap and bracing. *Chicha* is a fermented maize drink, popular around Cochabamba. Bottled water cannot always be found (rain water is sometimes offered as alternative); the local tap water should not be drunk without first being sterilized. We do not recommend Bolivian market food except to the desperate and, of course, to those accustomed to South American food, but buy it only if it is cooked in front of you. Be very careful of salads; they may carry a multitude of amoebic life as well as vile green bacteria.

In the *pensiones* and cheaper restaurants a basic lunch (*almuerzo*—usually finished by 1300) and dinner (*cena*) are normally available. Lunch can also be obtained in many of the modern market buildings in the main towns.

Salteñas are meat stew pies, eaten regularly by Bolivians, mostly in the morning. Some are *muy picante* (very hot) with red chili peppers, but *medio picante* and *poco picante* ones can normally be obtained. For milk, try sachets of Leche Pil (plain, chocolate or strawberry-flavoured), at US$0.25 each.

N.B. Bolivian highland cooking is usually very tasty and often *picante*, which means highly spiced with chili peppers. Local specialities, which visitors should try, include *empanadas* (cheese pies) and *humitas* (maize pies); *pukacapas* are *picante* cheese pies. Recommended main dishes include *sajta de pollo*, hot spicy chicken with onion, fresh potatoes and *chuño* (dehydrated potatoes), *parrillada* (a Bolivian kind of mixed grill), *fricase* (juicy pork dish served with *chuño*), *silpancho* (fried breaded meat with eggs, rice and bananas), and *ají de lengua*, ox-tongue with chilis, potatoes and *chuño* or *tunta* (another kind of dehydrated potato). The soups are also good, especially a *chairo* soup made of meat, vegetables, *chuño* and *ají* (hot pepper) to which the locals like to add *llajua* or *halpahuayca* (hot sauces always set on restaurant tables) to make it even more *picante*.

Currency The unit of currency is the boliviano (Bs.), divided into 100 centavos. There are notes for 200, 100, 50, 20, 10, 5 and 2 bolivianos, and coins of 1 boliviano and 50, 20, 10, 5 and 2 centavos. The boliviano replaced the peso boliviano in 1986 at the rate of 1:1,000,000; bank notes and other paper denominated in pesos are legal tender until December 31, 1989. Change is often given in forms other than money: e.g. cigarette, sweet, or razor blade. It is almost impossible to buy dollars at points of exit when leaving or to change bolivianos in other countries. Inflation is low; there is no need to buy bolivianos in small amounts to avoid depreciation. The official rate of exchange in May 1989 was 2.58 bolivianos per US$. The black market is more-or-less dead, since rates are no different on the street and in *casas de cambio*.

Credit cards are accepted hardly anywhere; it is impossible to get cash on them. Only American Express and Visa are of any use, mainly in La Paz. Many shops displaying credit card signs do not, in fact, accept them. Although acceptable, travellers' cheques are difficult to change outside La Paz.

Post, Telegraph, and Telephone Post offices use the post box (*casilla*) system. Items sent by post should therefore bear, not the street address, but the *casilla* number and town. Hours are Mon.-Sat. 0800-2000, Sun. 0800-1200.

Air-mail letters to and from Britain take between 5 and 10 days. Radio telephone services run by the Serval Company serve Cochabamba and other parts of the interior. There is now direct satellite communication with Bolivia. Direct calls possible from major cities to Europe (station to station, US$7.20/3 mins.), no collect calls can be made.

Hours of Business are normally 0900-1200, and 1400-1800. Saturday is a half day. Opening and closing in the afternoon are several hours later in the provinces. Government offices are closed on Saturday. Banks 0900-1200, 1400-1630, but closed on Saturday. Local time is 4 hours behind GMT.

The Press In La Paz: morning papers—*Presencia*, daily (available in other main cities), about 75,000, the largest circulation, largely Catholic, with good coverage of world events; *Hoy* and *El Diario*. *Meridiano* (midday): *Ultima Hora*, and *Jornada* (evenings). In Cochabamba—*Los Tiempos*, *Extra*. In Oruro—*La Patria*, mornings (except Mondays). *El Mundo* and *Crónica Deber* are the Santa Cruz daily papers; *Deber* also appears in Trinidad. La Paz papers are on sale in other cities. The *Miami Herald* is sometimes available in La Paz. Also, there are about 85 radio stations, a commercial government T.V. station as well as a university T.V. service.

Public Holidays

January 1—New Year's Day	Corpus Christi (moveable)
Carnival Week—Monday, Shrove Tuesday, Ash Wednesday.	July 16—La Paz Municipal Holiday.
Holy Week—Thursday, Friday and Saturday.	August 5,7—Independence
	Oct. 12—Columbus Day.
May 1—Labour Day.	November 2—Day of the Dead.
	Christmas Day.

There are local holidays at Tarija, on April 15; at Sucre on May 25; at Cochabamba, Sept. 14; at Santa Cruz and Cobija Sept. 24; at Potosí, Nov. 10; at Beni, Nov. 18, and at Oruro, Feb. 22.

We are deeply grateful to Sylvia Brooks for doing the updating of this chapter, also to Andrea Bodekull (La Paz), Eduardo Garnica Fajardo (Potosí), Dr Cesar H. Moreno (La Paz) and Turismo Balsa Ltda (La Paz) and to the following travellers: Tom Aabo and Karin Henningsen (Aarhus, Dmk), Julian Anderson (Buenos Aires), Dr J.R.J Van Asperen de Boer (Amsterdam), Ian Atkinson (Hanley Castle, Worcs), Thomas Axthammer (München 90), Baker (Cropredy, Oxon), Josep Barba (Barcelona), Carolyn Bargman (El Paso, Tx.) Cliff and Martin Barker (High Wycombe), Jane Barlow (London NW6), Bruce Barnes (Gloucester, NSW), Urs Baumann (Wildberg, Switz), Dale Bedford (Auckland 9), Hans and Lena Bengtsson (Gothenburg,

Swe), Pierre-Y Berney (Geneva), Christine Blenntoft (Santiago 9), Lennart Blomberg (Göteborg), Frank Böhme (Frankfurt 71), Karen Brooks (London N19), Alison Brysk and Mark Freeman (San Francisco, Ca.), Dan Buck and Anne Meadows (Washington DC.), John Burke (Bristol 7), Michelle Burrows (Brisbane), Chris Burton (Norwood, S. Aust.), John J. Chesarek (Billings, Montana), Peter and Alison Clarke (Leicester), Marion Clemens (Bonn 3), Jane Coburn and Philip Barnes (Thirroul, NSW), Beat Denzler and Nicole Livet (Zürich), Jeroen Dijkgraaf (Eindhoven), Paul Eaton (Victoria, BC), Dieter Eigenstetter and Yesim Yazicioglu (München 80), Fred and Marianne Emery (London SE26), Josef Engert (Schlieren, Switz.), Or Ezer (Kibbutz Gonen, Israel), Didier Faget and Sabine Fleury (Vernon, Fr.), Thomas Fedrizzi (Horgen, Switz.), Karsten Feucht (Berlin 61), Erik Friis-Pedersen (Copenhagen), Felicity Gallagher (Saxon, Switz), Anita Gee and Ian Boonin (Ilford), Theodor A. Gevert (Barueri, S.P. Brazil), Dan Golopentia (Seattle), Martin Gorst (London W13), Christina Gräwe (Tautkirchen) and Joachim Hoell (Wernstadt, W.Ger.), Jan Jacob de Groot (Vroomshoop, Neth.), Jon and Julia Gruffydd (Lima), Monika Gwerder (Muotathal, Switz.), Knut Per Hasund (Stockholm), Robert Hauer (Bonn 1), B Hemmerich (Zürich), Henri and Nicki Hendriksen (North Ryde, NSW), Dave Henson (San Francisco, Ca.), Christian and Nickolaj Hoff (Holte, Copenhagen), Don Hoyle (London EC2), Gretke Moen Johansen (Kolbotn, Norway), Mariann Johnsen (Brandbu, Norway), Simon Kahn (Los Angeles), Chris Kapolka (London N3), Omer Karchi (Tivon, Israel), Simon Kennedy and Sally Constable (Melbourne), Martin Ketels (Hamburg 50), Ronen Khayat (Jerusalem), Agnes Kranz (USA), Thomas and Bettina Kräuchi (Kloten, Switz.), Harald Kremer (Stuttgart 40), Rudolf Kühne (Berne), Darquise and Paul Lapointe (Cornwall, Ont.), Christian Levin (Kiel, W.Ger.), John Lewis (London NW3), Paul Living (Reading), Mika Määttänen (Tampere, Finland), Susan MacCallum and Peter Hedvlin (Sydney, Aust.), Dr John Maddock (Rio), Carla McLean (San Francisco), Cindy McNamara (Bath), Kelvin Moody (Stratford, NZ), Melanie Morningstar and Peter Charley (New York 10002), Beri and Mary Morris (Raleigh NC), Michael Mortensen (Oelstykke, Dmk.), Christoph Müller (Zürich 8004), Hallam Murray (London SW11), John and Christine Myerscough (Glossop, Derbys), Melanie Newman (with John Pritchard, Ros Harris, Danial Taylor, Carol Finn and Finn Bangshaad Jensen—London W9), Winfried Overbeek and Hennie van Vree (Wageningen, Neth.), Mark Pangbourne (Hastings), Devendra Rana (London NW1), Chris Robertson (Stockholm) and Patricia Galvin (Galway), Gisele Rochat and Jean-Paul Corboz (Neuchâtel, Switz.), R van der Schaaf (Amsterdam), Christian Scherlenzky (Villa Ballester, Buenos Aires), Arno Schmid (Hamburg 71), Rolf Schneider (Effretikon, Switz.), Leon van der Schoor (Neth.), Markus Schulz (Gambach, W.Ger.), Antony Sherlock (Edinburgh 12), Ian Skeet (Winchester), Karl Stanley (Cheam, Sy.), Armin Straub (Bovenden, W.Ger.), Thomas N Taylor (Houston), Barry Tiffen and Lucy Stephens (Torksey, Lincoln), Nicholas Tongue and Uta Rössler (Brussels), M.B. Vallance (Harrogate), John Walker, Conrad Wiesendanger (Münchenstein, Switz.), Gordon Williams (London W12), Ray Williams (Pwllheli), Rosemary Williamson (Auckland), Alida and Gordon Wilson (San Rafael, CA.), Wytske Winter and Hans Haringa (Aberdeen), Anna Wrench (Haywards Heath, Sx.), Donald Wurm (W.Ger.), Cecilia Ydell and Jonas Martensen and Helmut Zettl (Ebergassing, Aust.).

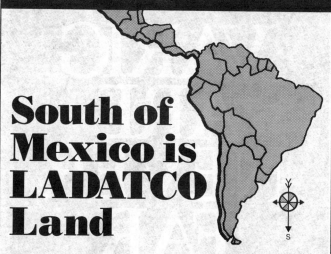

VARIG ARE NEVER FAR FROM BRAZIL.

Brazil is a country at the forefront of technological achievement. But it is also much more. There's a spirit about Brazil. A spirit of warmth and vitality. A spirit that's perfectly reflected in the friendly efficiency of its national airline.

VARIG is Brazil.

VARIG

Brazilian Airlines

BRAZIL

BRAZIL, the fifth largest country in the world, has the eighth largest population. It is almost as large as the United States of America. Its 8,511,965 square km. is nearly half that of South America. For neighbours it has all the South American countries save Chile and Ecuador. Distances are enormous: 4,320 km. from north to south, 4,328 km. from east to west, a land frontier of 15,719 km. and an Atlantic coast line of 7,408 km. Its population of 141 million (1987) is half that of all South America, and one in every two is under 25 years of age.

Brazil's topography may be divided roughly into five main zones: the Amazon Basin; the River Plate Basin; the Guiana Highlands north of the Amazon; the Brazilian Highlands south of the Amazon; and the coastal strip. The two great river basins account for about three-fifths of Brazil's area.

The Amazon Basin, in northern and western Brazil, takes up more than a third of the whole country. This basin is plain, broadly based on the Andes and funnelling narrowly to the sea; most of the drained area has an elevation of less than 250 metres. The rainfall is heavy, for the winds from the north-east and south-east lose their moisture as they approach the Andes. Some few places receive from 3,750 to 5,000 mm. a year, though over most of the area it is no more than from 1,500 to 2,500 mm. Much of the basin suffers from annual floods. The region was covered by tropical forest, with little undergrowth except along the watercourses; it is now being rapidly cut down. The climate is hot and the humidity high throughout the year.

The River Plate Basin, in the southern part of Brazil, has a more varied surface and is less heavily forested than the Amazon Basin. The land is higher and the climate cooler.

Most of the remainder of Brazil's territory is highland. The Guiana Highlands, north of the Amazon, are partly forested, partly hot stony desert. Those that face the north-west winds get heavy rainfall, but the southern slopes are arid. The rainfall, which comes during the hot season, is about 1,250 mm. a year. The summers are hot and the winters cool.

The Brazilian Highlands lying SE of the Amazon and NE of the River Plate Basin form a tableland of from 300 to 900 metres high, but here and there, mostly in South-Eastern Brazil, mountain ranges rise from it. The highest peak in southern

Brazil, the Pico da Bandeira, north-east of Rio de Janeiro, is 2,898 metres; the highest peak in all Brazil, the Pico da Neblina on the Venezuelan border, is 3,014 metres.

For the most part the Highlands cascade sharply to the sea. South of Salvador as far as Porto Alegre the coast rises steeply to a protective barrier, the Great Escarpment. In only two places is this Escarpment breached by deeply cut river beds—those of the Rio Doce and the Rio Paraíba; and only in a few places does the land rise in a single slope making for comparatively easy communication with the interior. Along most of its course, the Great Escarpment falls to the sea in parallel steps, each step separated by the trough of a valley.

The few rivers rising on the Escarpment which flow direct into the Atlantic do so precipitously and are not navigable. Most of the rivers flow deep into the interior. Those in southern Brazil rise almost within sight of the sea, but run westward through the vast interior to join the Paraná. In the central area the Escarpment rivers run away from the sea to join the São Francisco river, which flows northwards parallel to the coast for 2,900 km., to tumble over the Paulo Afonso Falls on its eastward course to the Atlantic.

The Great Escarpment denies to most of Brazil the natural valley outflows and lines of travel from the interior to the sea. Of its rivers the Amazon alone is directly navigable for a great distance inland.

Climate The average annual temperature increases steadily from south to north, but even on the Equator, in the Amazon Basin, the average temperature is not more than 27°C, and the highest recorded has been only 36°C. Six degrees more have been recorded in the dry north-eastern states. From the latitude of Recife south to Rio de Janeiro, the mean temperature is from 23° to 27°C along the coast, and from 18° to 21°C in the Highlands. From a few degrees south of Rio de Janeiro to the boundary with Uruguay the mean temperature is from 17° to 19°C. Humidity is relatively high in Brazil, particularly along the coast.

It is only in rare cases that the rainfall can be described as either excessive or deficient: few places get more than 2,000 mm.—the coast north of Belém, some of the Amazon Basin, and a small area of the Serra do Mar between Santos and São Paulo, where the downpour has been harnessed to generate electricity. The north-eastern droughts are caused not by lack of rainfall, but by irregular rainfall; the area is also subject to floods.

The rainy season in the South is from December to March; as this is also the holiday season in Brazil when hotels and flights tend to be booked solid, it seems a good time for tourists to stay away—unless, of course, they want to see the famous Carnival seven weeks before Easter.

Distribution of the Population By 1987 the population of Brazil had reached 141 millions, but this population is heavily concentrated in a comparatively small area—chiefly along the coastal strip where the original Portuguese settlers exploited the agricultural wealth, and further inland in the states of Minas Gerais and São Paulo where more recent development has been centred. Much of the interior of Pará, Amazonas, Goiás and the Mato Grossos has densities of one person per sq. km. or less. Brazil's attention is officially focused on these relatively underpopulated regions as a means of syphoning off some of the population excess in the urban centres—the industrialized South-East contains more than 50% of the total urban population and its two largest cities, São Paulo and Rio de Janeiro, both have over ten million people in their metropolitan and surrounding areas.

The urban population of Brazil has been increasing at rates more than double the overall average rate, and much of this growth is concentrated in the larger cities—those over 100,000, which numbered 95 in 1980. Internal migration is the major cause of these phenomenal growth rates, bringing to the cities problems of unemployment, housing shortage, and pressure on services which are already stretched to breaking point; shanty towns—or *favelas, mocambos, alagados*, according to the region—are an integral part of the urban landscape and a constant reminder of the poverty of some of the rural areas from which these people come.

The deep interior (Sertão) has been relatively unaffected by European and Far Eastern immigration, which has gone to the big cities and the more intensely cultivated lands of the South-East and the South. Its inhabitants are people of mixed Portuguese and Indian origin (*mestiço*); most live off a primitive but ecologically effective method of cultivation known as "slash and burn", which involves cutting down and burning the forest for a small patch of ground which is cultivated for a few years and then allowed to return to forest.

The decision to found a new federal capital, Brasília, deep in the interior, was a symbolic act of faith in the future of the Sertão: a bold attempt to deflect population from the coastal regions to the under-developed central and western plateaux of the country.

Political and Social History The first system of government adopted by the Portuguese was a Capitânia, a kind of feudal principality—there were thirteen of them, but these were replaced in 1572 by a Viceroyalty. In the same year it was decided to divide the colony into two, north and south, with capitals at Salvador and Rio de Janeiro; it was not until 1763 that Rio became the sole capital.

The economic structure was, in the main, that of huge estates run by slave labour brought over from Africa, with an aristocratic white element that played the absentee landlord and did no manual (but much procreative) work. The Portuguese crown expected both a personal and a state revenue from its colony. This was raised partly by payment of a tenth of the produce from grants of land made to colonists, a fifth from mining production, and about forty other taxes.

The bulk of the colonists, right up to the early 19th century, lived along the coastal belt. The main exceptions were the settlers in the states of São Paulo and Minas Gerais, the Paulistas and Mineiros, who had thrust far into the interior in search of gold, precious stones, and slaves.

Three hundred years under the paternal eye of Portugal had ill-prepared the colonists for independent existence, except for the experience of Dutch invasion

N.W. BRAZIL 0 KM 500
Not to same scale

1 Brasília.
2 The state of Rio de Janeiro.
3 Espírito Santo.
4 Minas Gerais.
5 The state of São Paulo.
6 Southern Brazil.
7 The North East.
8 Northern Brazil.
9 Southern Amazonia.
10 The centre West.

BRAZIL

State boundaries

0   500   1000
Km

(1624 in Salvador, and 1630-1654 in Recife). The colonists ejected the Dutch from Brazil with little help from Portugal, and Brazilians date the birth of their national sentiment from these events. In 1789 infiltration of European thought led to the first unsuccessful revolution against Portuguese rule, the Inconfidência in Minas Gerais, led by Tiradentes. When the troops of Napoleon caused the Portuguese Royal Family to sail in British ships to Brazil in 1808, the fate of the colony was decided: Brazil became the senior partner, as it were, in the Portuguese empire. King João VI returned to the mother country in 1821, leaving his son, the handsome young Pedro, as Regent. The Portuguese Parliament (the Cortes) mistrusted this arrangement, and called on Pedro to return, but the Brazilians asked him to stay. On May 13, 1822, he agreed to stay, and assumed the title of "Perpetual Defender and Protector of Brazil". On September 7 he declared Brazil's independence with the cry "Independence or Death" by the Ipiranga River; on October 12 he was proclaimed constitutional emperor of Brazil, and on December 1 he was crowned in Rio de Janeiro.

Dom Pedro the First had the misfortune to be faced by a secession movement in the north, to lose the Banda Oriental (today Uruguay) and to get somewhat involved in his marital relations. Finally, he abdicated as the result of a military revolt in 1831, leaving his five-year-old son, Dom Pedro the Second, in the hands of a regent, as ruler. On July 23, 1840, the lad, though only 15, was proclaimed of age and the regency discontinued. Dom Pedro the Second, a strong liberal at heart, promoted education, increased communications, developed agriculture, stamped on corruption and encouraged immigration from Europe. Under his rule the war with the dictator López of Paraguay ended in Brazilian victory. Finally, he declared that he would rather lose his crown than allow slavery to continue, and on May 13, 1888, it was finally abolished by his daughter, Princess Isabel, who was acting as Regent during his temporary absence.

There is little doubt that it was this measure that cost him his throne. Many plantation owners, who had been given no compensation, turned against the Emperor; they were supported by elements in the army and navy, who felt that the Emperor had not given due heed to their interests since the Paraguayan War. On November 15, 1889, the Republic was proclaimed and the Emperor sailed for Europe. Two years later he died in a second-rate hotel in Paris, after steadfastly refusing a pension from the conscience-stricken revolutionaries. At the time of the first centenary of independence in 1922 the imperial family was allowed to return to Brazil, and the body of Dom Pedro was brought back and buried in the cathedral at Petrópolis.

The history of the "Old Republic" (1889-1930), apart from the first ten years which saw several monarchist rebellions, was comparatively eventless, a time of expansion and increasing prosperity. Brazil declared war on Germany during both wars and Brazilian troops fought in the Italian campaign in 1944-45. In 1930 a revolution headed by Getúlio Vargas, Governor of Rio Grande do Sul, who was to become known as "the Father of the Poor" for the social measures he introduced, deposed President Wáshington Luís and Vargas assumed executive power first as provisional president and then as dictator. He was forced to resign in October 1945. In 1946 a liberal republic was restored and the following 18 years saw considerable economic development and social advance. There was, however, increasing government instability and corruption leading to growing military intervention in civil affairs; this culminated in the military movement of March 1964, which ruled until March 1985 with increasing liberalization and great economic success (up to 1980). In January 1985 a civilian, Tancredo Neves, representing a broad opposition to the military regime, was elected President by the electoral college introduced under the military's 1967 constitution. He was unable, because of illness, to take office: the vice-president elect, Sr. José Sarney, was sworn in as acting President in March 1985, and became President on Sr. Neves' death in April. A Constituent Assembly completely revised Brazil's constitution in 1987-88. A new constitution was approved in 1988 which opened the way for direct presidential elections to be held in November 1989, with a new president taking office in March 1990.

Settlement and Economic History Brazil was discovered by the Portuguese, Pedro Alvares Cabral, in 1500. The first settlement was at Salvador da Bahia, and the settlers came mainly from southern Portugal, with its feudal tradition of great estates. For the first few years Portugal, then much concerned with the Orient, paid little attention to Brazil. But about 1507 a second colony was settled at São Vicente, near Santos, and in 1537 a third at Olinda, near Recife. The settlers at São Vicente, who founded the first settlement in the highlands at São Paulo in 1534, were unlike those at Salvador and Recife: they came from the poorer and more energetic north of Portugal. All of them were attracted less by the prospect of earning their living by self-supporting labour than by opportunities of speculative profit. To do the work they impressed the primitive Tupi-Guarani Indians, many of whom died from European diseases (see *Red Gold*, by John Hemming). They cohabited freely with the Indians and, later, with slaves imported from Africa.

Sugar cane had been introduced at São Vicente in 1532, but it was the wealthy settlers of the north-east who had the necessary capital to establish the crop and to buy African slaves to work it; the Indian, with his hunting-and-gathering culture, was a disappointment as a labourer. In the matter of sugar, Salvador and Recife had the advantages over São Vicente of being very much nearer home, and of having better ports and easier access to the interior. During the latter half of the 16th and the whole of the 17th centuries, the provinces of Bahia, Pernambuco, and Paraíba were the world's prime source of sugar.

The settlers at São Paulo, envious of the more fortunate north-east, sent out expeditions to explore the interior for gold, which had already been found in small quantities in their own streams. These hardy Bandeirantes pushed as far south as Colonia, opposite Buenos Aires, as far west as the River Paraguay, and north into the area west of the sugar plantations of the north-east. In 1698 they struck gold in central Minas Gerais. More was found soon after in central Mato Grosso, and in 1725 in Goiás. Diamonds were discovered in 1729 north of the goldfields of Minas Gerais.

There was a great gold and diamond rush in which the sugar planters took part. Sugar by that time was on the decline: there was competition from the Caribbean; profits had fallen, and the Brazilians had made no attempt to lower costs by ploughing back profits: that was not in their tradition. The gold boom started early in the 18th century, lasted a hundred years, and then petered out. Minas Gerais was transformed from a wilderness into a well populated agricultural, pastoral, and mining region. It was as an outlet for this area that Rio de Janeiro was developed. Some of the wealth went to create the extraordinarily beautiful city of Ouro Preto, to-day a national monument of superb building, painting and sculpture, and the similarly attractive cities of São João del Rei, Mariana, Congonhas do Campo, Diamantina and others.

Brazil was ready for the next speculation, coffee, introduced about 1720 from French Guyane. Coffee planting began near Rio de Janeiro and at many places round the coast as far as the Amazon, but by 1825 it had mainly been concentrated in the Paraíba valley, west of the capital. From there it spread into São Paulo, where its cultivation attracted a large number of immigrants after 1850. About a third of the total production normally still comes from São Paulo state.

There have been many other typical Brazilian booms and recessions. The best known is the famous rubber boom in the Amazon valley; competition from SE Asia wiped it out after 1912. Sugar, coffee, and cocoa were alike the subject of booms. In each case Brazil was challenged by other sources of supply, where more intensive methods of production were applied. The result in Brazil has been a lack of stability of settlement.

This boom tradition still holds, but it is shifting from agriculture to industry. Agricultural products accounted for the bulk of Brazil's exports until recently and some 40% of the people are still rural, but Brazilians today prefer to think of themselves as a rising industrial nation. Industrial production has increased greatly and now two thirds of total exports are defined as "of manufactures". Nevertheless, Brazil still remains a country where oases of prosperity are edged by deserts of poverty and wilderness.

One interesting aspect of the various booms is the large internal migration which has accompanied them: each product, as its popularity grows, has proved a magnet for people from the rest of Brazil. Because of its poverty, the North-East has lost many workers to the industries of the South-East; on the other hand many rural workers from southern Brazil have moved north, drawn by the rapid development of Amazonia.

The People At first the new colony grew slowly. From 1580 to 1640 the population was only about 50,000 apart from the million or so indigenous Indians. In 1700 there were some 750,000 civilized people in Brazil. Early in the 19th century Humboldt computed there were about 920,000 whites, 1,960,000 Africans, and 1,120,000 Indians and *mestiços*: after three centuries of occupation a total of only four millions, and over twice as many blacks as there were whites.

Modern immigration did not begin effectively until after 1850. Of the 4.6 million immigrants from Europe between 1884 and 1954, 32% were Italians, 30% Portuguese, 14% Spanish, 4% German, and the rest of various nationalities. Since 1954 immigrants have averaged 50,000 a year. There are some 1 million Japanese-descended Brazilians; they grow a fifth of the coffee, 30% of the cotton, all the tea, and are very active in market gardening.

Most of the German immigrants settled in the three southern states: Santa Catarina, Rio Grande do Sul, and Paraná. The Germans (and the Italians and Poles and other Slavs who followed them) did not in the main go as wage earners on the big estates, but as cultivators of their own small farms. Here there is a settled agricultural population cultivating the soil intensively. It is only by such methods and by such an expansion that the wastes of the Sertão, given sufficient water, can be put to effective use.

Today the whites and near-whites are about 53% of the population, people of mixed race about 34%, and blacks 11%; the rest are either aboriginal Indians or Asians. There are large regional variations in the distribution of the races: the whites predominate greatly in the south, which received the largest flood of European immigrants, and decrease more or less progressively towards the north.

The seven censuses of the present century show the growth of the population, from 17.3 million in 1900 to 119.0 million in 1980. In 1970, 56% of the population was urban; by 1980 this proportion had risen to 71%. Of the total labour force in 1980, 30% was occupied in agriculture and fishing, compared with 44% in 1970, 24% worked in industry (18% in 1970), 9% in commerce (8% in 1970) and 36% in government and services, compared with only 19% in 1970. The average life span has increased from 39 years in 1939 to 58 years today. The population grew 2.5% between 1970 and 1980. By region, population growth 1970-80 was: N, 5.0%; NE, 2.2%; S, 1.4%; and SE, 2.7%.

Though there is no legal discrimination against black people, the economic and educational disparity—by default rather than intent of the Government—is such that successful Afro Brazilians are active almost exclusively in the worlds of sport, entertainment and the arts. By the way, don't refer to black people as "pretos" or "negros": describe them as "oscuros" or "gente de cor "—more acceptable terms.

The following table gives the census returns by states for 1960 to 1980. The capital of each state is given in brackets.

		Population (thousands)		
	States	1960	1970	1980
North:	Acre (Rio Branco)	160	218	302
	Amazonas (Manaus)	721	961	1,406
	Pará (Belém)	1,551	2,197	3,411
North-east:	Maranhão (São Luís)	2,492	3,037	4,002
	Piauí (Teresina)	1,263	1,735	2,140
	Ceará (Fortaleza)	3,338	4,492	5,294
	Rio Grande do Norte (Natal)	1,157	1,612	1,900
	Paraíba (João Pessoa)	2,018	2,445	2,772
	Pernambuco (Recife)	4,137	5,253	6,145
	Alagoas (Maceió)	1,271	1,606	1,988
	Sergipe (Aracaju)	760	911	1,142
	Bahia (Salvador)	5,991	7,583	9,470
South-east:	Minas Gerais (Belo Horizonte)	9,799	11,645	13,382
	Espírito Santo (Vitória)	1,189	1,618	2,024
	*Rio de Janeiro (Niterói)	3,403	4,795	11,298
	*Guanabara (Rio de Janeiro)	3,307	4,316	—
	São Paulo (São Paulo)	12,975	17,959	25,023
South:	Paraná (Curitiba)	4,278	6,998	7,617
	Santa Catarina (Florianópolis)	2,147	2,930	3,628
	Rio Grande do Sul (Porto Alegre)	5,449	6,755	7,776
Centre-west:	†Mato Grosso (Cuiabá)	910	1,624	1,141
	†Mato Grosso do Sul (Campo Grande)	—	—	1,368
	Goiás (Goiânia)	1,955	2,998	3,864
	Federal District	142	546	1,176
Territories (4)	Amapá, Roraima, ‡Rondônia, Fernando de Noronha	177	275	753
	Total	70,976	93,244	119,024

*In 1975, the State of Guanabara was incorporated into the State of Rio de Janeiro, with the city of Rio de Janeiro as the capital.

†In 1977 Mato Grosso was divided in two, the southern portion forming the new state of Mato Grosso do Sul, with its capital at Campo Grande.

‡In 1981, the Territory of Rondônia became a State, with its capital at Porto Velho.

The most recent official surveys indicate that 31% of the population is illiterate. Of the 13 million children between 7 and 14, 2 million have no school to go to. Of those who go to school, not all stay long enough to learn how to read and write. Adult literacy campaigns have, however, recently improved the picture. Gdp per capita is US$2,230.

Railways, of which there are about 30,500 km., were originally built to supply export markets and did not combine into a unified system. To join them effectively, however, would mean—besides 3,200 km. of new construction—the unifying of Brazil's five existing gauges. About 2,450 km. have now been electrified. Many lines have been closed in recent years.

Roads Though the best paved highways are still heavily concentrated in the South-East, those serving the interior are now being improved to all-weather status and many are paved. Brazil has over one million kilometres of highways, of which in 1985 about 120,000 km. were paved, and the recent road-building programmes have emphasized inter-regional connections and the opening up of the Centre, North and West of the country. Interurban bus services are frequent and good.

Air Services The first commercial flight in Brazil was in 1927. Because of the great distances and the comparative paucity of good highways and railways, aircraft have eased the traveller's lot more spectacularly in Brazil than in any other country. The larger cities are now linked with each other several times a day by air, and even the more remote points in the country can now be reached by light aircraft.

Government The 1988 constitution provides for an executive president elected by direct popular vote, balance by a bicameral legislature (72 seats in the Federal Senate, 487 seats in the Chamber of Deputies) and an independent judiciary. The vote has been extended to 16-year olds and illiterates. Presidential elections were to be held on November 15, 1989, with perhaps a second round in December, and the new President would take office in March 1990. Congressional elections are due in November 1990. Municipal elections were held in November 1988. Deputies wil be elected by proportional representation for a four-year term, the President and Vice President for a five-year term.

Local Administration Each State has a popularly-elected Governor who exercises the executive power, and a Legislative Assembly which legislates on all matters affecting provincial administration and provides for State expenses and needs by levying taxes. Each municipality has a similar structure, with a mayor (*prefeito*), also popularly elected, and a local council (*câmara de vereadores*).

BRASILIA (1)

Brasília On April 21, 1960, Rio de Janeiro ceased to be the Federal Capital of Brazil; as required by the Constitution, it was replaced by Brasília, 960 km. away in the unpopulated uplands of Goiás, in the heart of the undeveloped Sertão. The population of the Plano Piloto (the official name for central Brasília) is 411,000 (1980 census—the Federal District as a whole, with an area of 5,814 square km., has nearly 1.2 million inhabitants).

The new capital lies 1,150 metres above sea-level on undulating ground. The climate, unlike that of the old capital, is mild and the humidity refreshingly low, but trying in dry weather. The noonday sun beats hard, but summer brings heavy rains and the air is usually cool by night.

The creation of an inland capital had been urged since the beginning of the last century, but it was finally brought into being after President Kubitschek came to power in 1956, when a competition for the best general plan was won by Professor Lúcio Costa, who laid out the city in the shape of a bent bow and arrow.

Along the curve of the bow are the residential areas made up of large six-storey apartment blocks, the "Super-Quadras". They lie on either side (E and W) of the "bow" (the Eixo Rodoviário) and are numbered according to their relation to the Eixo and their distance from the centre. Thus the 100s and 300s lie west of the Eixo and the 200s and 400s to the east; Quadras 302, 102, 202 and 402 are nearest the centre and 316, 116, 216 and 416 mark the end of the Plano Piloto. The numbering applies equally on either side of the centre, the two halves of the city being referred to as Asa Sul and Asa Norte (the north and south wings). Thus, for example, 116 Sul and 116 Norte are at the extreme opposite ends of the city. All Quadras are separated by feeder roads, along which are the local shops. There are also a number of schools, parks and cinemas in the spaces between the Quadras (especially in Asa Sul), though not as systematically as was originally envisaged. On the outer side of the 300s and extending the length of the city is the Avenida W3 and on the outer side of the 400s is the Avenida L2, both of these being similarly divided into north and south according to the part of the city they are in.

Asa Sul is almost complete and Asa Norte (which for years was looked down on) is growing very fast, with standards of architecture and urbanization that promise to make it more attractive than Asa Sul in the near future. The main shopping areas—with more cinemas, restaurants and so on, are situated on either side of the old bus station. Several parks—or at least green areas—are now in being. The private residential areas are W of the Super-Quadras, and on the other side of the lake.

BRASÍLIA
28

To Taguatinga

To Taguatinga

N

To Núcleo Bandeirante
Goiânia
São Paulo
Belo Horizonte

To Salvador

Campo da
Esperança
Cemetery

North
Cemetery

915

Parque
Rogério
P Faria

Camp Site

912

Asa
Sul 711
311

Autó-
drome

712
Asa
Norte 312

To Airport

EIXO   V·3

EIXO   SUL

208
408

111

Sports
Centre

S. Hotel
Sector 901

703

906

N. Hotel
Sector

703

111

210

410

102
302

302

102

Eixo Norte

202
402

202
402

University

S. Embassy
Sector

N. Embassy
Sector

AVENIDA DAS NAÇÕES

EIXO MONUMENTAL

Parque dos
Três Poderes

LAGO DO
PARANOA

Golf
Course

To Salvador

At right angles to these residential areas is the "arrow", the 8-km. long, 250-metre wide Eixo Monumental. At the tip of the arrow, as it were, is the Praça dos Tres Poderes, with the Congress buildings, the Palácio do Planalto (the President's office), the Palácio da Justiça (Supreme Court) and the Panteão Tancredo Neves (a memorial to the president-elect who died in 1985 before taking office). The Cathedral and the Ministry buildings line the Esplanada dos Ministérios, W of the Praça. Where the bow and arrow intersect is the old bus station (Rodoviária), with the cultural and recreational centres and commercial and financial areas on either side. There is a sequence of zones westward along the shaft of the arrow; a hotel centre, a radio city, an area for fairs and circuses, a centre for sports, the Praça Municipal (with the municipal offices in the Palácio do Buriti and a great cross marking the spot on which the first mass was said in Brasília, on May 3, 1957), and, lastly (where the nock of the arrow would be) the combined new bus and railway station (Rodoferroviária) with the industrial area nearby. The most impressive buildings are all by Oscar Niemeyer, Brazil's leading architect.

The main north-south road (Eixo Rodoviário), in which fast-moving traffic is segregated, follows the curve of the bow; the radial road is along the line of the arrow—intersections are avoided by means of underpasses and cloverleaves. Motor and pedestrian traffic is segregated in the residential areas.

The Palácio da Alvorada, the President's residence, which is not open to visitors, is close to the lake. The 80-km. drive along the road round the lake to the dam is attractive. There are spectacular falls below the dam in the rainy season. Between the Praça dos Tres Poderes and the lake are sites for various recreations, including golf, fishing and yacht clubs, and an acoustic shell for shows in the open air. The airport is on the far side of the lake. Some 250 hectares between the lake and the northern residential area (Asa Norte) are reserved for the University of Brasília, founded in 1962. South of the university area, the Avenida das Nações runs from the Palácio da Alvorada along the lake to join the road from the airport to the centre. Along it are found all the principal embassies. Also in this area is the attractive vice-presidential residence, the Palácio do Jaburu, again not open to visitors. This area is almost completed and very scenic.

Sightseeing   A fine initial view of the city may be had from the television tower, which has a free observation platform at 75 metres up (lift will not ascend with less than 5 people; also bar and souvenir shop; open 0800-2000, long queues Sat. and Sun.; the TV tower sways quite a bit), or from the old Rodoviária tower. A general impression can be gained in a day by bus or taxi tour—don't try walking much unless fit and fairly impervious to heat (and even so not recommended for single females). This impression is best gained at weekends when the city is quieter, though then there are fewer buses to move you around (some say the city is "totally dead" at weekends). The city can also be seen at night by taking the Alvorada circular bus from the old Rodoviária. Congress is open to visitors Mon.-Fri. 0800-1200 and 1400-1700, guides free of charge (in English 1400-1600), and visitors may attend debates when Congress is in session. The Planalto may be visited; admission restricted to men in long-sleeved shirts and trousers and women in skirts, Fri., 0900-1100 and 1500-1700. The marvellous building of the Ministry of Foreign Affairs, the Itamarati, has modern paintings and furniture, beautiful water gardens and offers one of the most rewarding visits (guided visits at 1000 and 1600, free). Opposite the Itamarati is the Palácio de Justiça, the Supreme Court building, with artificial cascades

Key to Map of Brasília
1. Congress; 2. Palácio de Planalto; 3. Palácio da Justiça; 4. Itamarati; 5. Buriti; 6. Palácio da Alvorada; 7. Palácio do Jaburu; 8. Ministries; 9. Army Ministry; 10. Observatory; 11. TV Tower; 12. J.K. Monument; 13. National Theatre; 14. Cathedral; 15. Dom Bosco; 16. Igrejinha/Fátima; 17. Post Office, Telegraph and Postal Museum; 18. S. Banking Sector and Gold Museum; 19 Rodoferroviária; 20. Old Rodoviária; 21. Convention Centre and Tourist Office; 22. *Hotel Brasília Palace*; 23. Hospital.

between its concrete columns. Visiting (dress as for the Planalto, Mon., Wed., Fri), 1400-1900; Tues. and Thurs. 0800-1030. The Cathedral, on the Esplanada dos Ministérios, a most spectacular circular building in the shape of the crown of thorns (still under construction), is open 0900-1100, 1400-1700; see also the Ceschiatti statues of the evangelists and the baptistery in the shape of a large pebble. The outdoor carrillon was a gift from the King of Spain. W of the TV tower on Avenida W3 Sul, at Quadra 702, is the Sanctuary of Dom Bosco, a square building constructed largely of blue glass. Other religious buildings worth seeing are the Fátima church (the Igrejinha) in the Asa Sul at Quadras 307-308, the Sanctuary of Our Lady of Fátima, the "orange caterpillar" on Av. W5 a little S of the Dom Bosco sanctuary, and the chapel (Ermida) of Dom Bosco, on the other side of the lake opposite the Alvorada, though the site is not well maintained. Some 15 km. out along the Belo Horizonte road is the small wooden house, known as "O Catetinho", in which President Kubitschek stayed in the late 1950s during his visits to the city when it was under construction; it is open to visitors and most interesting. A permanent memorial to Juscelino Kubitschek, the "Memorial JK", containing his tomb together with a lecture hall and exhibits, is worth visiting (open Mon.-Fri. 0900-1200, 1300-1800, Sat.-Sun. 0900-1900, entry US$0.50). The Brazilian Army headquarters, designed by Oscar Niemeyer, is interesting; The Monumental Parade Stand has unique and mysterious acoustic characteristics (the complex is north of the Eixo Monumental, between the "Memorial JK" and the Rodoferroviária).

Light industry alone is allowed in the city and its population is limited to 500,000; it is now about 411,000 and about 250,000 more live in a number of shanty towns, with minimal services, located well away from the main city.

Entertainment Social amenities are greatly improved, with more cinemas and night clubs opening. The three auditoria of the Teatro Nacional, the Sala Villa-Lobos (1,300 seats), the Sala Martins Pena (450), and the Sala Padre José Maurício (120) are now open; the building is in the shape of an Aztec pyramid.

The Federal District authorities have opened two theatres, the Galpão and Galpãozinho, between Quadra 308 Sul and Av. W3 Sul. Concerts are given at the Escola Parque (Quadras 507-508 Sul), the Ginásio Presidente Médici (Eixo Monumental, near TV tower), the Escola de Música (Av. L2 Sul, Quadra 602) and the outdoor Concha Acústica (edge of lake near Brasília Palace Hotel). The Planetarium, on the Eixo next to the TV tower, gives shows Sat. and Sun. at 1600 and 1700.

There are 15 cinemas in the Plano Piloto; programmes are available daily by dialling 139 on the telephone.

Information about entertainment etc. is available in two daily papers *Jornal de Brasília* and *Correio Brasiliense*. Any student card (provided it has a photograph) will get you into the cinema/theatre/concert hall for half price. Ask for "uma meia" at the box office.

Ceremonies The guard is changed ceremonially at the Palácio do Planalto on Tues., 0830 and 1730. The President attends if he is present.

Sculptures Brasília is famous for its wealth of modern sculpture. Examples are: "Culture" (on the University campus), "The Meteorite" (above the Itamarati water-mirror), and "The Warriors" (in front of the Planalto)—all by Bruno Giorgi; "Justice" (in front of Supreme Court building), the four evangelists in front of the Cathedral and "The Water-Nymphs" (above the Alvorada water-mirror)—all by Alfredo Ceschiatti; "The Rite of Rhythms" (Alvorada gardens), by Maria Martins; and the beautiful "Mermaid" in front of the Navy Ministry on the Esplanada dos Ministérios. A statue of Juscelino Kubitschek is adjacent to the "Memorial JK".

Hotels	Single US$	Double US$	Pool	Stars	Telex No. (061)
Nacional, Southern Hotel Sector	53	58	Yes	4	1062
Carlton, Southern Hotel Sector	50	60	Yes	4	1981*
Eron Brasília, Northern Hotel Sector	62	67	No	4	1422
Torre Palace, Northern Hotel Sector	44	48	Yes	4	1902
Américas, Southern Hotel Sector	36	44	No	3	1484*
Aracoara, Northern Hotel Sector	42	50	No	4	1589
Bristol, Southern Hotel Sector	44	52	Yes	3	1981*
Brasília Palace, Lake Sector	under renovation				
Alvorada, Southern Hotel Sector	30	33	No	3	1484*
Nações, Southern Hotel Sector	34	40	No	3	1484*

*Shared telex

Another good hotel is the *Casablanca,* Northern Hotel Sector, A; *Riviera,* B, 3-star, in the Southern Hotel Sector. Other central hotels, all B, are the *Brasília Imperial* (2-star, deposit for room requested, good breakfast, motel-style), *Itamaraty Parque, Planalto* (Sector Hoteleiro Sul, Quadra 3, Bloco A, T 225-6860, comfortable, reasonably-priced, city tours); and the *Aristus, Byblos* (C), *Diplomat* (B-good), *El Pilar* (B, friendly) and *Mirage* (C, Q2N, T 225-7150, fan, good, clean) in the Northern Hotel Sector. Prices include breakfast but 10% tax must be added. Moderately-priced hotels can be found in the Northern Hotel Sector only. The *Petrobrás Motel* at the Saída Sul is far from the centre but clean and cheaper (D) for motorists. Also at Saída Sul: Shell's *Motel Sabataia,* D, no breakfast; *Paranoá,* E, basic. Cheaper pensions available; enquire at airport information desk, which also has the phone number of the Youth hostel, Albergue Projeto Rondon, Av. W Sul, Superquadra 712, Bloco O, Casa 44.

However, the hotels outside the city in Taguatinga and Núcleo Bandeirante, though fairly basic, tend to be recommended for cheapness. Núcleo Bandeirante: *Jurema,* at Av. Central 1390, D; *Valadares,* E with bath but no breakfast; *São Judas Tadeu,* E, noisy, clean but cockroaches, poor breakfast; *Ypacaraí,* round corner from *Hotel Rio de Janeiro,* E, O.K. for "young and hearty" but many mosquitoes; *Buriti,* 2° Avenida 1415, E, with bath; has cheaper single rooms. Taguatinga is pleasanter than the Núcleo, which is full of shanties; there are many cheap hotels and restaurants of a reasonable standard, for example, *Solar,* near Jumbo Supermarket, E, basic and clean. *Colorado,* Setor Hoteleira, Projeção B, T 561-3500, D, with bath, fridge, TV, good, in the centre; *Pousada Brasília,* next door, E with bath and breakfast; *Globo,* CNB4, Lote 1, T 561-1716, E, without breakfast, friendly, basic. *Rodoviária,* E, without bath, more with, including breakfast, clean and friendly. Bus "Estrutural" from Brasília Rodoferroviária to Taguatinga Rodoviária where you change, without extra charge to 700 bus which passes, in order: *Rio Verde,* Bloco Norte QNE 26, E; *Camará,* QNE 16, F (hourly rentals also); *Palace,* CNB 11, E, clean, basic, hot water, communal shower; *Taguatinga,* by roundabout near clocktower, about 10 mins. from Rodoviária, E with breakfast, hot showers, TV, clean, back rooms are quieter, clothes-washing facilities, used by prostitutes. Bus 700 or 800 (marked "Eixo") goes from opp. Jumbo Supermarket in Taguatinga to old Rodoviária in Brasília.

Camping The city's main site is 2 km. out, by the Centro Esportivo, near the motor-racing track, with room for 3,100 campers. US$0.50 p.p., average charge, though apparently some travellers have stayed free. Take bus 109 (infrequent) from old Rodoviária. Agua Mineral Parque, 6 km. NW of city, direct buses only at weekend: US$1 p.p., mineral pool, showers. One site a few km. S on Belo Horizonte road, another out in the country about 70 km. E. Associação Brasileira de Camping (Edif. Márcia, 12th floor, Setor Comercial Sul, T 225-8768) has two sites: one at Km. 19 on the Belo Horizonte road and one 25 km. NE of Brasília at Sobradinho. Camping Clube do Brasil has site at Itiquira waterfall, 100 km. NE of the city, near Formosa; information from Edif. Maristela, room 1214, Setor Comercial Sul, T 223-6561. There is a Forestry Commission site 10 km. out of Brasília on the BR-041. There are signs to the sites. "Wild" camping is possible.

Restaurants There are new restaurants opening in Brasília every week. (The Southern Hotel Sector tends to have more; there are many cheap places on Av. W3 Sul. e.g. at Blocos 502 and 506.) At weekends few restaurants in central Brasília are open. The following are classified by their speciality:

International Cuisine: *Aeroporto,* terrace of international airport, very pleasant, food reported very good. Most of the big hotels' restaurants. *Restaurant Gaff,* Centro Gilberto Salomão, South Lake (very good, especially meat, but expensive).

Churrascarias (barbecues): *Brasas,* first floor of Conjunto Nacional; *Boi na Brasa,* Km. 15 on Brasília-Belo Horizonte road; *Galetão,* Galeria dos Estados; *Júlio,* on road to Taguatinga; *Churrascaria do Lago,* beside *Brasília Palace Hotel; Pampa,* beside Carrefour hypermarket, *Tordilho,* on edge of lake near *Brasília Palace Hotel; Muken,* in Taguatinga; *Toys,* a rancho among the trees below the Avenida das Nações; *Churrascaria do Paranoá,* beside the dam.

Brazilian food: Cantina Caipira, 104 Sul; *Fogão de Lenha,* 402 Sul; *Maloca Querida,* 107 Sul.

Northern Brazilian/Amazonian: *Pororoca,* 411 Sul; *Marajoara,* 113 Sul.

Seafood/Fish: *Panela de Barro,* Galeria Nova Ouvidor, Setor Comercial Sul; *Chorão,* 302 Norte; *Jangadeiro,* 213 Sul; *Sereia,* 212 Sul (open until the early hours); *Kastelinho,* 411 Sul.

Portuguese: *Cachopa,* Galeria Nova Ouvidor; *Ginga,* 104 Sul.

Spanish: *O Espanhol,* Avenida W3 Sul, quadra 506; *Salamanca,* 113 Sul.

French: *Français,* 404 Sul; *Forty Five,* 203 Sul (overpriced); *Le Coq,* Galeria Karim, 110/111 Sul; *La Chaumière,* 408 Sul.

Chinese: *China,* 203 Sul; *New China,* 209 Sul (the best according to Chinese diplomats); *Fon Min,* 405 Sul; *Fon Pin,* 403 Sul; *Fon Shian,* 201 Sul; *Pequim,* 212 Sul; *Ran Gon,* Praça dos Tres Poderes.

Japanese: *Nipon,* 314 Sul and 112 Sul.

Lebanese/Middle Eastern: *Alef,* 302 Sul; *Arabeske,* 109 Sul; *Beirute,* 109 Sul; *Beduino,* 102 Sul; *Almenara,* 204 Sul. *Chez Karam,* Centro Gilberto Salomão; *El Hadji;* Hotel Torre, N. Hotel Sector (self-service, very good).

German: *Tirol* and *Bierfass,* both in Centro Gilberto Salomão, South Lake.

Italian/Pizzerias: *Kazebre 13,* Avenida W3 Sul, quadra 504; *La Grotta Azzurra,* 208 Sul; *Roma,* Avenida W3 Sul, quadras 501 and 511, good, quite cheap; *La Romanina,* 303 Sul;

Tarantela, 202 Sul; *Pizzaiola*, 310 Sul; *Prima*, 106 Sul; *Roma*, 311 Sul; *Romassas*, Avenida W3 Sul, quadra 505.

Macrobiotic/Vegetarian: *Coisas da Terra*, Avenida W3 Norte, quadra 703; *Vegetariano*, Avenida W3 Sul, quadra 505; *Portal*, 209 Sul, one at front of Setor Comercial Sul, close to Rodoviária, lunch only, set-price meal; *Ken's Kitchen*, Quadra 302 Norte (English spoken).

Local: *Bom Demais*, Av. W3 Norte, Quadra 706, comfortable, inexpensive, serving fish, beef and rice, etc., live music at weekends (cover charge US$0.50).

Pubs   There are two "English style" bars: *Gates Pub*, 403 Sul and *London Tavern*, 409 Sul. The *Grenada* bar near the *Hotel Nacional* (pedestrian area across road, 250 metres away) has good pavement atmosphere in early evening.

Snack Bars   (i.e. those serving *prato feito* or *comercial*, cheap set meals) can be found all over the city, especially on Avenida W3 and in the Setor Comercial Sul. (e.g. *Max Burger*) Other good bets are the Conjunto Nacional and the Conjunto Venâncio, two shopping/office complexes on either side of the old bus station (Rodoviária), which itself provides the best coffee and *pásteis* in town (bottom departure level). For ice creams (especially tropical fruit flavours) try the two ice-cream parlours in 302 Norte or the *Marajoara* restaurant. Freshly made fruit juices in all bars; for Amazonian fruits try the bar at the eastern (i.e. Setor Bancário) end of the Galeria dos Estados.

Nightclubs   *Aquarius* (gay), *Bataklan*, *Le Bateau*, all in Conjunto Venâncio; *Kako*, *Senzala*, in Centro Gilberto Salomão; *Tendinha*, *Odara*, 405 Sul; *Xadrezinha*, Avenida das Nações. Also in the main hotels.

Local Holidays   Ash Wednesday; Maundy Thursday, half-day; Dec. 8 (Immaculate Conception); Christmas Eve.

Shopping   There are eight big shopping complexes, including the Conjunto Nacional on the north side of the Rodoviária (supposedly the biggest complex in South America), the Conjunto Venâncio on the south side, the Centro Venâncio 2000 at the beginning of Avenida W3 Sul and Park Shopping and the Carrefour hypermarket just off the exit to Guará, 12 km. from centre. For fine jewellery, H. Stern has branches in the *Nacional* and *Carlton* Hotels and at the Conjunto Nacional and Park Shopping (with *McDonald's* and other restaurants). The embassy sector is good for low-priced, high quality men's wear. For handicrafts try *Galeria dos Estados* (which runs underneath the *eixo* from Setor Comercial Sul to Setor Bancário Sul, 10 mins. walk from old Rodoviária, south along Eixo Rodoviário Sul) with shops selling handicrafts from all the Brazilian states; *Lampião*, 208 Sul; *Di Barro*, 302 Norte; *Zé Artesanato*, 215 Sul. For Amerindian handicrafts, *Artindia* in the bus station and at the airport. Also at the bus station is a Funai shop. Dried flowers (typical of the region) outside the Cathedral. There is a *feira hippy* at the base of the TV tower every Saturday, Sunday and holiday: leather goods, wood carvings, jewellery, bronzes. English books (good selection) at Livraria Sodler in Conjunto Nacional and at the airport.

Historical Museum   Praça dos Tres Poderes, really a hollow monument, with tablets inside; open Tues.-Fri. 0800-1200, 1300-1800.

Museum of Gold   at the Banco Central exhibits old and new notes and coins and gold prospecting in Brazil; open Mon.-Fri. 1000-1600, Sat. 1400-1800.

Museo Postal y Telegráfico da ECT, Setor Comercial Sul, Ed. Apolo, Quadra 13, Block A. Very interesting, stamps, telegraphic equipment, etc. Entry, US$ 0.30. Closed Sun.-Mon.

Museo da Imprensa Nacional, Setor de Indústrias Gráficas, Quadra 6; bus 152 from old Rodoviária: admission free. Old printing and embossing equipment, etc.

Banks   Lloyds Bank (ex. BOLSA), Avenida W3 Sul, quadra 506; First National Bank of Boston, Avenida W3 Sul, quadra 501; Citibank, Edifício Citibank, Setor Comercial Sul; Banco Francês e Brasileiro, Avenida W3 Sul, quadra 506; local banks. Open 0930-1630. Foreign currency (but not always Amex cheques) can be exchanged at these banks and at the branches of: Caixa Econômica Federal at the airport; Banco Regional de Brasília and Banco do Brasil, Setor Bancário Sul. American Express, Kontik-Franstur, Setor Comercial Sul, Edifício Central, S/1007. Diners Club office, Av. W3 Norte 502. Use of international credit cards in Brasília tends to be difficult, though it should not be. Good exchange rates from hotels with "exchange-turismo" sign (e.g. *Nacional*).

British Commonwealth Chamber of Commerce, at the British Embassy.

Addresses   British Embassy: SES, Avenida das Nações 8, Caixa Postal 070586, T 225-2710. US Embassy: SES, Avenida das Nações 3, T 223-0120. Australian: Caixa Postal 11-1256, SHIS QL-09, Conj 16, Casa 1, T 248-5569 (in residential district, S of the lake). Canadian: SES, Avenida das Nações 16, T 223-7515. West German: SES, Avenida das Nações 25, T 243-7466. Netherlands: SES, Av. das Nações 5, T 223-2025. Swiss: SES, Av. das Nações 41, T 244-5500; Austrian: SES, Av. das Nações 40, T 243-3111; Swedish: Av. des Nações 29, T 243-1444 (postal address: Caixa Postal 07-0419, 70.000 Brasília, D.F.). British Council: CRN 708/709 Bloco 3 Lotes 1 e 3, T 272-3060. Cultura Inglesa, SEPS 709/908 Conj. B. American Library: Casa Thomas

Jefferson, Avenida W4 Sul, quadra 706, T 243-6588 and 243-6625. Institut-Cultural Goethe, Edifício Dom Bosco, Setor Comercial Sul, Bloco A, 114-118, Mon.-Fri., 0800-1700, 1600-2000. Immigration Office, at end of W3 Norte.

Poste Restante   Central Correio, 70001; SBN-Cj 03, BL-A, ED. SEDE DA ECT.

Electric Current   220 volts, 60 cycles.

Tourist Offices   at the Centro de Convenções (Detur); small stand at Rodoferroviária, not very helpful (open 24 hours, every day). Tourist office at the Air Terminal is on the international arrival side only, will book hotels, generally helpful; French and English spoken. Tours by bus (US$12-20), may be booked at the airport or *Hotel Nacional*; check that you will be taken back to the airport if you have a flight to catch. Touring Club do Brasil, on Eixo, has maps (members only).

Tours   A good and cheap way of seeing Brasília is by taking bus rides from the old Rodoviária at the centre: the destinations are clearly marked. The circular bus route 106 goes right round the city's perimeter (you can also take buses 108 or 131). If you go around the lake by bus, you must change at the Paranoá dam; from Paranoá Norte take bus 100, "Rodoviária", back to centre, bypassing the airport. A one-day visit by air from Rio gives 4 hours in Brasília for a minibus tour, starting and ending at airport (but the city is worth much more of anyone's time than this). Cheaper tours, from 1300-1700, from US$7 up, start from the downtown hotel area and old Rodoviária. All tour operators have their offices in the shopping arcade of the *Hotel Nacional*; Toscana has been recommended as cheap and good. Presmic Turismo, *Galeria do Hotel Nacional*, lojas 33/34, T 225-5515, offers full-, half-day and nighttime tours (0845, 1400 and 1930 respectively), from US$11.45 p.p. Some tours have been criticised as too short, others that the guides speak poor English. Tour guides meet arriving air passengers at the airport, offering city tours, ending at a destination of your choice (3-4 hrs., English commentary, inexpensive but bargain)—a convenient way of getting to your hotel if you have heavy baggage.

Roads   From Saída Sul (the southern end of the Eixo) the BR-040/050 goes to Cristalina where it divides; the BR-040 continues to Belo Horizonte and Rio de Janeiro, the BR-050 to Uberlândia and São Paulo (both paved).

Also from Saída Sul, the BR-060 to Anápolis, Goiânia and Cuiabá; from Anápolis the BR-153 (Belém-Brasília) heads north to Belém (paved—for a description of this road, **see page 406**) and from Goiânia the BR-153 goes south through the interior of the states of São Paulo and Paraná (also paved).

From Saída Norte (the northern end of the Eixo) the BR-020 goes north to Formosa, Barreiras, and after Barreiras on the BR-242 (all paved) to Salvador and Fortaleza; in wet weather the Rio São Francisco is liable to flooding with consequent long delays on the ferry service (though smaller vehicles are used to complete the load after trucks and buses are loaded).

Road distances, in km.: Belém, 2,110; Campo Grande, 1,405; Corumbá, 1,834; Cuiabá, 1,127; Foz do Iguaçu, 1,415; Goiânia, 202; Manaus, 3,421; Porto Alegre, 2,021; Recife, 2,303; Rio, 1,204; Salvador, 1,520; São Paulo, 1,015.

Buses   To Rio: 20 hours, 6 *comuns* (US$20) and 3 *leitos* (about US$40) daily. To São Paulo: 16 hours, 7 *comuns* (about US$14) and 2 *leitos* (about US$28) daily (Rápido Federal rec.). To Belo Horizonte: 12 hours, 9 *comuns* (US$12) and 2 *leitos* (US$24) daily (alight at Curvelo, 8½ hrs., US$7 for Diamantina. To Belém: 36 hours, at 0715, 1200, 1915, 2400 (US$36, Trans Brasília, buses poorly-maintained, but no alternative), *leito* (US$68) Tues., Wed. and Sat. To Goiânia: 2½ hours, every hour from 0600 to 2000 and at 2200 and 2400 (US$3). To Cuiabá, twice daily 1200 and 1945 (São Luiz), US$22, 20-24 hours, book journey in advance. To Curitiba, US$25, Tues., Thurs. and Sat. To Porto Alegre: 35 hours, every evening at 2100 (US$35). To Natal: every evening at 2000. To Campo Grande, US$23, 23 hours. To Fortaleza: 40 hours, every day at 0800 (US$40). To Recife: 40 hours, daily at 1100 and Mon., Wed. and Fri. at 1830. To Salvador: 23 hours, daily at 1200 and 2000 (US$28). To Barreiras, 9 hrs. To Teresina: daily at 0900 and 2130. To São Luís: daily at 1400. To Anápolis, 2½ hours, US$2.50 Manaus via Porto Velho and Cuiabá involves several changes, taking up to 6 days (road is good as far as Porto Velho). Bus tickets for major companies are sold in a subsidiary office in Taguatinga, Centro Oeste, C8, Lotes 1 and 2, Loja 1; and in centre of the city on a side street opposite the Pão de Açúcar store. Left luggage, post office, telephone and telegram facilities available at new bus terminal (Rodoferroviária) beside the railway station, from which long-distance buses leave; bus 131 between Rodoviária and Rodoferroviária, US$0.25. The waiting room at the Rodoferroviária is very comfortable, but one is not permitted to sleep stretched out. There are showers (US$0.50). Both bus stations have large luggage lockers.

Car Hire   Critical reports on Hertz cars hired at airport.

Rail   In 1981 a metre-gauge rail link from Brasília to Campinas was opened; at Campinas one changes train for São Paulo. The train "O Bandeirante" leaves Brasília on weekdays only at 2050, arriving at São Paulo Terminal da Luz at 1920 next day; US$13.50 sleeper, US$8.50 first class. A cheap and interesting way to the South; very slow, but it passes through some interesting country. Cheap meals are served. The station is at the far end of the Eixo Monumental, past the TV tower.

Air Services Varig to Caracas and Miami on Tue.; to Rio and São Paulo regular shuttle service (2½ hours in both cases); daily flights to other main cities; regional services to the interior of Goiás, São Paulo, Pará, etc. Vasp to Corumbá via Goiânia and Cuiabá, daily. Transbrasil offers reduced-fare night flights to Manaus at 0145 twice weekly. Bus 102 or 118 to airport, regular, US$0.35, ½ hour. Taxi is US$4.50, worth it. Left luggage facilities at airport (tokens for lockers, US$0.50). Airport tax US$1.25.

Of the seven *cidades satélites* that contain between them over half the Federal District's population, five are new and two (Brazlândia and Planaltina) are based on pre-existing settlements.

Planaltina, 40 km. N of the Plano Piloto via Saída Norte, was originally a settlement on the colonial pack route from the mines of Goiás and Cuiabá to the coast. The old part of the town (50,000 inhabitants) still contains many colonial buildings. There are two good *churrascarias* on the main street and it is a good place for a rural Sunday lunch. 5 km. outside Planaltina is the Pedra Fundamental, the foundation stone laid by President Epitácio Pessoa in 1922 to mark the site originally chosen for the new capital.

Just before Planaltina, at Km. 30 on the road from Brasília, lies the point known as Águas Emendadas: from the same point spring two streams that flow in opposite directions to form part of the two great river systems—the Amazon and the Plate. Permission from the biological institute in Brasília is now required, to visit the site. Continuing along the same road (BR-020), at Km. 70 is the town of Formosa (*Hotel Mineiro*, E). Some 20 km. north of the town is the Itiquira waterfall (158 metres high). From the top are spectacular views and the pools at the bottom offer good bathing. It is crowded at weekends. There are four smaller falls in the area. Camping is possible. To get there take the road into the centre of Formosa and follow the signs or ask. It is not possible to get by bus to the Itiquira falls from Brasília in one day; the only bus from Formosa to Itiquira leaves at 1500 and returns the next morning.

In the other direction (S) is the Cristalina waterfall; take the BR-040 (Belo Horizonte road) and at Km. 104 take a left turn along a dirt road just after the highway police post. The waterfall is 11 km. along this road. The town of *Cristalina* is famous for its semi-precious stones, which can be bought cheaply in local shops.

Nearer Brasília, good bathing can be had at Água Mineral, two mineral pools 10 km. from the centre of the city. The newer pool is the better; turn right immediately after entering the main gate. North West of Brasília, but only 15 minutes by car from the centre is the **Parque Nacional de Brasília** (about 28,000 hectares), founded in 1961 to conserve the flora and fauna of the Federal Capital. For information, contact Delegacia Estadual do IBDF, Av. W-3 N, 0513, Edif. Imperador, rooms 301-320.

For information on the State of Goiás, which surrounds the Federal District, **see page 405**.

STATE OF RIO DE JANEIRO (2)

The State of Rio de Janeiro covers 43,305 sq. km. (the size of Denmark) and in 1980 had a population of 11.3 m., 88% of whom lived in metropolitan areas. The working population of 3.5 m. is about 15% of Brazil's total labour force, and the State is Brazil's second-largest industrial producer.

Rio de Janeiro, for 125 years the national capital, is on the south-western shore of Guanabara Bay, 24 km. long and from 3 to 16 km. wide. The setting is magnificent. The city sweeps twenty kilometres along a narrow alluvial strip between the mountains and the sea. The combination of a dark blue sea, studded with rocky islands, with the tumbling wooded mountains and expanses of bare grey rock which surround the city is very impressive. Brazilians say: God made the world in six days; the seventh he devoted to Rio. Man is now attempting to undo God's work, by putting up far too many high-rise buildings.

The best known of these rocky masses are the Pão de Açúcar (Sugar Loaf, 396 metres), the highest peak of a low chain of mountains on the fringe of the harbour, and the Corcovado (Hunchback), a jagged peak rising 710 metres behind the city. There are other peaks, including Tijuca (1,012 metres), the tallest point in the foreground, and 50 km. away rise the strangely shaped Organ Mountains with the "Finger of God".

Rio has one of the healthiest climates in the tropics. Trade winds cool the air.

RIO DE JANEIRO
ORIENTATION MAP 29

1 Pico da Tijuca.
2 Corcovado and Statue of Christ.
3 Station for Corcovado.
4 Vista Chinesa.
5 Parque da Cidade.
6 Jardim Botánico.
7 Jockey Club.
8 Logoa Rodrigo de Freitas.
9 Largo do Boticário.
10 Pão de Açúcar (Sugar Loaf).
11 Station for Pão de Açúcar.
12 Botafogo (end of Metro Line 1).
13 Largo do Machado.
14 Catete (cheap hotel area).
15 Glória.
16 Parque do Flamengo.
17 Santa Teresa.
18 New cathedral.
19 Business centre.
20 Sambódromo.
21 Maracaná Stadium.
22 Quinta de Boa Vista.
23 Santos Dumont Airport.
24 Galeão International Airport.
25 Rodoviária Novo Rio.
26 Pedro II Railway Station.
27 Ferries to Paquetá and Niterói.

June, July and August are the coolest months with temperatures ranging from 22°C (18° in a cold spell) to 32°C on a sunny day at noon. From December to March temperatures are high, from 32°C to 42°C. Sunstroke is uncommon, but humidity is high. It is important, especially for children, to guard against dehydration in summer by drinking as much liquid as possible. October to March is the rainy season, and the annual rainfall is about 1,120 mm. The population in 1980 was 5,093,000, while that of the Metropolitan Region was 9,019,000.

History The Portuguese navigator, Gonçalo Coelho, discovered Rio de Janeiro on January 1, 1502, but it was first settled by the French, who, under the Huguenot Admiral Villegaignon, occupied Lage Island on November 10, 1555, but later transferred to Sergipe Island (now Villegaignon), where they built the fort of Colligny. The fort has been demolished to make way for the Naval College (Escola Naval), and the island itself, since the narrow channel was filled up, has become a part of the mainland. In January 1567, Mem de Sá, third governor of Brazil, defeated the French in a sea battle and transferred the Portuguese settlement to the São Januário hill—the Esplanada do Castelo covers the site today. Though constantly attacked by Indians, the new city grew rapidly, and when King Sebastião divided Brazil into two provinces, Rio was chosen capital of the southern captaincies. Salvador became sole capital again in 1576, but Rio again became the southern capital in 1608 and the seat of a bishopric. There was a further French incursion in 1710-11.

Rio de Janeiro was by now becoming the leading city in Brazil. On January 27, 1763, it became the seat of the Viceroy. After independence, in 1834, it was declared capital of the Empire, and remained the capital for 125 years.

Points of Interest Two of the main streets are particularly impressive. The Avenida Rio Branco, nearly 2 km. long and 33 metres wide, is intersected by the city's main artery, the Avenida Presidente Vargas, 4½ km. long and over 90 metres wide, which starts at the waterfront, divides to embrace the famous Candelária church, then crosses the Avenida Rio Branco in a magnificent straight stretch past the Central do Brasil railway station, with its imposing clock tower, until finally it incorporates the palm-lined canal-divided avenue formerly known as the Avenida Mangue. The Avenida Rio Branco is lined with ornate buildings, including the Brazilian Academy, National Art Museum, National Library, Municipal Council Chamber, and Municipal Theatre. The Rua Ouvidor, crossing the Avenida Rio Branco half way along its length, contains the centre's principal shops. Other shopping streets are the Ruas Gonçalves Dias, Sete de Setembro, Uruguaiana, Assembléia, and also the arcade running from Av. Rio Branco to the Rua Gonçalves Dias. The most stylish shops, however, are to be found in Copacabana and in the various large shopping centres in the city (see under **Shopping** below). (The quality of souvenirs is higher in Copacabana than in the centre, and higher still in São Paulo.) The Av. Beira Mar, with its royal palms, bougainvilleas and handsome buildings, coasting the Botafogo and Flamengo beaches (too polluted for bathing), makes a splendid drive; its scenery is shared by the urban motorway along the beach over reclaimed land (the Aterro), which leads to Botafogo and through two tunnels to Copacabana, described on **page 268**. Some of the finest modern architecture is to be found along the Avenida Chile, such as the Petrobrás and National Housing Bank buildings, and the new Cathedral, dedicated in November 1976.

Sightseeing   See, within the city, Candelária church, the monastery of São Bento, the convent of Santo Antônio, the Glória church (see under Churches), the Museum of National History, the National Museum of Fine Arts, the Municipal Theatre, the National Library, the Ruy Barbosa Museum (see under Public Buildings). Outside the centre you should see Copacabana, Ipanema, Leblon and Barra da Tijuca beaches, the Sugar Loaf, Corcovado, Tijuca Forest, Botanical Gardens, Quinta da Boa Vista and Zoological Gardens, the Maracanã Stadium, Santa Teresa and, if there is time, Niterói and Icaraí, Paquetá Island and Petrópolis.

Carnival   Carnival in Rio is spectacular. On Shrove Tuesday and the three preceding days, the main avenues are colourfully lit, and many young people and children wear fancy dress. Special bandstands throughout the city are manned for public street-dancing (see *Daily Post/Brazil Herald* for where and when) and organized carnival groups, the *blocos carnavalescos*, are everywhere, dancing, drumming and singing. There are numerous samba schools in Rio. They are divided into four leagues, the first and second of which are allowed to parade in the Sambódromo. The second league (10 schools) parades on Saturday, the first league (16 schools) on Sunday and Monday. The order of appearance of the first league is determined by lottery, so there is no better day. Each school parades with 3,000-5,000 participants, divided into 40 groups and as many as 30 floats. Each school has 90 minutes to parade, and will lose points if it takes longer. The third and fourth leagues parade on Av. Rio Branco (less spectacular -has been described as a "mass of people walking up and down with three or four music groups"- but free).

Each school chooses a theme, then composes a samba, and designs costumes and floats to fit it. All the schools are judged on each element, the best ones being promoted to a higher league, those with fewest points being relegated, as in a football league. Competition is intense. For the winners there is a monetary prize, funded by the entrance fees.

To understand the traditions of the schools, the meanings of the different parts of the parade, and carnival as a whole, visit the carnival museum in the Sambódromo; although small, it has lots of photographs and the English-speaking staff are very informative (entrance free).

The Sambódromo parades start at 2030 and last about 12 hours. Gates (which are not clearly marked) open at 1800. The best places are those reserved for tourists, and sectors 4 and 11 (sectors 6 and 13 are not recommended). Seats are closer to the parade, but because they are not elevated you see mostly the people in front of you. Tickets are sold through Banco do Brasil, and start at about US$40; tickets are also sold at the Maracanã Stadium box office, but touts outside will try to sell you places at double the price. Tourist tickets range from US$138-240 to US$1,000 for the most expensive cabin and are available through Riotur or travel agencies. On Tuesday there is an amalgam of events including a huge float parade by the *grandes clubes carnavalescos*, and exhibitions by the previous year's champion samba groups, *blocos carnavalescos* and *frevo* and *rancho* groups. On the Saturday after carnival, the samba schools voted best on Sun. and Mon. parade in the Sambódromo (admission from US$20).

The **Sambódromo**, a permanent site at Rua Marquês de Sapucaí, Cidade Nova, not far from the centre, has a length of 600 metres, with seats for 60,000 people.

There are also innumerable fancy-dress balls (highly recommended); the main public one is at the Canecão (Sat. night) but there are scores more in hotels and clubs. Two that have been recommended are those at Clube Monte Líbano in Ipanema which have a different theme each night (you don't have to go in fancy dress), very crowded after midnight, and the Grande Gala Gay on Tues. (entry US$10). The Tourist Office has a list of all balls.

Carnival takes place at a time when Rio is packed with summer visitors enjoying the beaches. So visitors wishing to attend the Carnival are earnestly advised to make sure of their accommodation well in advance. Virtually all hotels raise their prices during Carnival.

Pickpockets and thieves are very active during Carnival (but the Sambódromo itself is quite safe—it's getting in that's the problem). Don't wander into dark corners on your own, don't brandish your camera, and take with you only as much money as you need for fares and refreshments (food and drink is expensive in the Sambódromo). It gets hot! Wear as little as possible (shorts or Bermudas and a T-shirt).

If you can't be there at Carnival time, rehearsals are held at various places from November onwards; e.g. the Portela *escola* at Rua Arruda Câmara 81, Madureira, late Sat. nights. Samba shows are given at the Teatro Tereza Rachel, Rua Siqueira Campos 143, Copacabana, on Mon. nights (not December), T 235-2119 (see also page 261); rec. Also, Beija Flor, one of the best samba schools, performs on Mon. nights at Urca (half-way up to Sugar Loaf Mountain), dinner available at 2000, reservations required (on Fri. and Sat. at this venue is the "Noite Carioca" show, or a disco).

Other Festivals Less hectic than Carnival, but very atmospheric, is the festival of Iemanjá on the night of December 31, when devotees of the spirit cults brought from Africa gather on **Copacabana, Ipanema and Leblon beaches**, singing and dancing around open fires and making offerings, and the elected Queen of the Sea is rowed along the seashore. There is a firework display on Copacabana beach at midnight, so the crowds tend to concentrate there, in front of the Copacabana Palace and Meridien hotels. At midnight small boats are launched as sacrifices to Iemanjá. Again, if you go, beware thieves.

The festival of São Sebastião, patron saint of Rio, is celebrated by an evening procession on Jan. 20, leaving Capuchinhos Church, Tijuca, and arriving at the cathedral of São Sebastião. The same evening an *umbanda* festival is celebrated at the Caboclo Monument in Santa Teresa.

Museums and other Public Buildings

All museums and the Jardim Botânico are closed over Carnival.

The **National Museum** in the Quinta da Boa Vista is said to be one of the most important museums in South America but is dsiappointing, and the park surrounding it is dangerous (take a taxi or tour bus to the door). The building was the principal palace of the Emperors of Brazil, but only the unfurnished Throne Room and ambassadorial reception room on the 2nd floor reflect past glories. In the entrance hall is the famous Bêndego meteorite, found in the State of Bahia in 1888; its original weight, before some of it was chipped, was 5,360 kg. Besides several foreign collections of note, the Museum contains collections of Brazilian Indian weapons, dresses, utensils, etc., and of minerals and of historical documents. There are also collections of birds, beasts, fishes, and butterflies. Open 1000-1645, closed Mon.; entrance US$0.10 (free Thursday). Buses: 472, 474, 475 from centre, Flamengo and Copacabana, 583 from Largo do Machado. Nearest metro São Cristóvão. Some of the collections are open to qualified research students, but not to the general public.

Museu de Fauna also at Quinta da Boa Vista, contains a most interesting collection of Brazilian fauna. Open Tues.-Sun. 1200-1700.

The **National Library** (Biblioteca Nacional), at Avenida Rio Branco 219, was founded in 1810. Its first collection came from the Ajuda Palace in Lisbon, and to-day it houses over 2 million volumes and many rare manuscripts. The library is open Mon.-Fri. 1030-1830, and Sat. 1200-1800.

National Museum of Fine Art (Museu Nacional de Belas Artes), at Avenida Rio Branco 199. There are about 800 original paintings and sculptures and some thousand direct reproductions. Exhibitions of works by contemporary Brazilian artists are often held here. Open Tues.-Fri. 1230-1800; Sat., Sun. and holidays 1500-1800; free.

Those interested in contemporary art will also visit the former Ministry of Education, designed by Le Corbusier, to see the great murals of Cândido Portinári, whose canvas, "Café", is in the Museum of Fine Art.

Opposite the Art Museum is the **Municipal Theatre**. Opera and orchestral performances are given here; the small museum that used to be below the theatre is now at Rua São João Batista 103/105, Botafogo, normally open 1100-1700 Tues.-Sun, but reported closed since 1987.

The **Paço Imperial** (former Royal Palace on Praça Quinze de Novembro), a beautiful colonial building begun in 1743, has been restored. It has a gallery for tempory exhibitions and the occasional free concert.

The **Museum of Modern Art** (Museu de Arte Moderna), is a spectacular building at Avenida Infante D. Henrique 85, near the National War Memorial (see page 255). It suffered a disastrous fire in 1978; the collection is now being rebuilt, and several countries have donated works of art. There is also a non-commercial cinema. Entrance US$0.85, Tues.-Sat. 1200-1900 (open till 2200 on Thurs.), Sun., 1400-1900. Closed for repairs 1989, except for special exhibits.

The **National Historical Museum** on Praça Rui Barbosa (formerly Praça Marechal Âncora) contains a most interesting collection of historical treasures, colonial sculpture and furniture, maps, paintings, arms and armour, silver, and porcelain. The building was once the old War Arsenal of the Empire, part of which was built in 1762. Open Tues. to Fri., 1100-1700; Sat., Sun. and holidays 1400-1700; admission US$0.40. The building also houses the **Military Museum**.

Naval and Oceanographic Museum, Rua D. Manoel 15, daily 1200-1645. There is a particularly large collection of paintings and prints, besides the more usual display of weapons and figureheads.

The warship *Bauru* (*ex-USS McCann*) has been made into a floating museum, in the Glória Marina, opposite the war memorial on the Praia do Flamengo.

Museum of Image and Sound, also on Praça Rui Barbosa, has many photographs of Brazil and modern Brazilian paintings, open Mon.-Fri., 1200-1800; also collections and recordings of Brazilian classical and popular music and a non-commercial cinema open Fri.-Sun. Closed for repairs 1987.

The **Museum of the Indian** (Museu do índio) is at Rua das Palmeiras 55, Botafogo, T 286 0845, open Tues.-Sun., 1000-1800. Highly rec.; has handicrafts shop, which closes for lunch 1200-1400. It contains 12,000 objects from many Brazilian Indian groups.

The **Museum of the City** (Museu da Cidade) at Estrada Santa Marinha, Gávea, in the delightful Parque da Cidade (see page 256), contains a collection of Rio's historical objects. Open Mon.-Fri., 1300-1700; Sat.-Sun., 1100-1700. Buses from centre, 176, 178; from Copacabana, 591, 593 and 594.

The **Fundação Raymundo Ottoni de Castro Maia,** generally known as **Chácara do Céu,** Rua Murtinho Nobre 93, has a wide range of art objects and particularly works of modern Brazilian painters. Take Santa Teresa tram to Rua Dias de Barros, then follow signposts. (Open Tues.-Sat. 1400-1700, Sun. 1300-1700, US$0.30.) Castro Maia's former residence on the Estrada do Açude in the Tijuca Forest bears the same name and is also a museum, currently under restoration.

Museo do Instituto Histórico e Geográfico, Av. Augusto Severo 8 (10th floor), just off Av. Beira Mar, has a very interesting collection of Brazil's products and the artefacts of its peoples. Open Mon.-Fri. 1300-1700.

The **São Cristóvão Pavilion,** designed by Sérgio Bernardes, has the world's largest open floor space without columns or transverse walls, but is now closed to the public. It is in very poor condition. Sunday market is worth visiting for North Eastern food and hammocks. Bus 472 or 474 from Copacabana or centre.

The **National Observatory** (founded 1827) is on São Januário hill, Rua Gen. Bruce 586, São Cristóvão. Visitors advised to call 248-1182 after 1700 to arrange a night viewing.

The **House of Rui Barbosa,** Rua São Clemente 134, Botafogo, former home of the Brazilian jurist and statesman, containing his library and other possessions, is open Tue.-Fri. 1000-1615, Sats., Suns. and holidays 1400-1700. The large garden is also open to the public. Buses 106, 176, 178 from centre; 571 from Flamengo; 591 from Copacabana.

Itamarati Palace, the former Foreign Ministry, at Avenida Marechal Floriano 196, contains much interesting old furniture, tapestry and other objects of art. Now called Museu Histórico e Diplomático, open Tues.-Fri., 1200-1615 (doors close at 1700); admission free on Thurs.

Museum of the Republic, in Catete Palace (Rua do Catete 179), entrance in Rua Silveira Martins, was the official residence of the President for 63 years when Rio was the Federal Capital. Under renovation in 1988, but good Folklore Museum in same building was open. Bus 571 from Copacabana, and close to Catete metro station.

Guanabara Palace, once the residence of the Princess Isabel, daughter of Dom Pedro II, is now the office of the Governor of the State of Rio de Janeiro.

Carmen Miranda Museum, Tues.-Sun. 1100-1700, Flamengo park area in front of Rui Barbosa 560 (small display of the famous singer's gowns etc). **Museum of Fringes of the Unconscious,** Ramiro Magalhães 521, Engenho de Dentro, Mon-Fri. 0800-1600. Closed for repairs 1987. **Villa-Lobos Museum,** Rua da Imprensa 16, Tues.-Sat. 1000-1600, with instruments, scores, books, recordings. **Capão do Bispo Estate,** Av. Suburbana 4616, Del Castilho, Mon.-Fri. 1400-1700 with archaeological exhibition.

Planetarium, Padre Leonel Franco 240, Gávea, Sat. and Sun. at 1600, 1700, 1830: inaugurated in 1970, sculpture of Earth and Moon by Mario Agostinelli. Free *choro* concert Fri. at 2100. Buses 176 and 178 from centre and Flamengo; 591 and 592 from Copacabana.

Aerospace Museum, Av. Marechal Fontenelle 2000, Campo dos Afonsos, Tues.-Fri. 0900-1600, early Brazilian civil and military aircraft.

Carnival Museum. Av. dos Desfiles, entrance by Rua Frei Caneca, Tues.-Sun. 1000-1600.

Antônio Lago Museum, R. Andradas 96, centre, Mon.-Fri. 1400-1700. Reproduction of historical apothecary's shop.

Churches and Religious Foundations

Check opening hours before attempting to visit.

The oldest foundation is the **Convent of Carmo,** built early in the 17th century on Rua Primeiro de Março close to Praça 15 de Novembro, now used as a school. Its present church, the Carmo Church in Rua Primeiro de Março, next to the old cathedral, was built in the 1770s and rebuilt between 1797 and 1826. It has strikingly beautiful portals by Mestre Valentim, the son of a Portuguese nobleman and a slave girl. He also created the main altar of fine moulded silver, the throne and its chair, and much else.

The second oldest convent is the seventeenth-century **Convent of Santo Antônio,** on a hill off the Largo da Carioca, built between 1608 and 1615. Its church has a marvellous sacristy adorned with blue tiles. St. Anthony is a particular object of devotion for women who want to find husbands, and many will be seen in the precincts.

The crypt contains the tomb of a Scottish soldier of fortune known as "Wild Jock of Skelater". He was in the service of the Portuguese Government during the Napoleonic War, and had the distinction of being appointed the first Commander-in-Chief of the Army in Brazil. The statue of St. Anthony was made a captain in the Portuguese army after his help had been sought to drive out the French in 1710, and his salary paid to the monastery. In 1810 he became a major, in 1814 a lieutenant-colonel, and he was granted the Grand Cross of the Order of Christ. He was retired without pay in 1914.

Separated from this church only by some iron railings is the charming church of **São Francisco da Penitência,** built in 1773. The carving and gilding of walls and altar are superb. In the ceiling over the nave is a fine panel painted by José de Oliveira. There is a museum attached to the church, open first and third Sun. of the month, 0700-1000.

The **Monastery of São Bento** (1641); entrance at Rua Dom Gerardo 68, contains much of what is best in the 17th and 18th century art of Brazil. "O Salvador", the masterpiece of Brazil's first painter, Frei Ricardo do Pilar, hangs in the sacristy. The carving in the church is particularly good. The Chapels of the Immaculate Conception and of the Most Holy Sacrament are masterpieces of colonial art. The organ is very interesting. The monastery is a few minutes' walk from Praça Mauá, turning left off Av. Rio Branco just before the Rua São Bento. The intimate view of the harbour and its shipping from the grounds of the monastery (behind the church) is in itself worth climbing the hill on which it stands. (Male visitors must wear long trousers.)

The **Old Cathedral** of São Sebastião, in the Rua Primeiro de Março, was built between 1749 and 1770. In the crypt are the alleged remains of Pedro Alvares Cabral, the discoverer of Brazil (though it is only fair to note that Santarém, Portugal, also claims to be his last resting-place).

The **New Cathedral,** on Avenida República de Chile not far from the Largo da Carioca, dedicated in 1976, is a very exciting cone-shaped building. Its internal height is 68 metres, diameter 104 metres, external height 83 metres; capacity 5,000 seated, 20,000 standing. The most striking feature is four enormous stained-glass windows (60 metres high). It is still incomplete.

The Church of **São Francisco de Paula,** at the upper end of the Rua do Ouvidor, was built in 1759. It contains some of Mestre Valentim's work—the carvings in the main chapel and the lovely Chapel of Our Lady of Victory. Some of the paintings, and probably the ceiling, are by Manuel da Cunha. The beautiful fountain at the back plays only at night.

The Church of **Nossa Senhora da Candelária** (1775-1810), on Praça Pio Dez, at the city end of Avenida Presidente Vargas, is well worth a visit to see its beautiful interior decorations and paintings. It is on the site of a chapel founded in 1610 by Antônio da Palma after he had survived a shipwreck, an event depicted by paintings inside the present dome.

In the Rua de Santa Luzia, overwhelmed by tall office buildings, is the attractive little church of **Santa Luzia.** When built in 1752 it had only one tower; the other was added late in the 19th century. Feast day: December 13, when devotees bathe their eyes with holy water, considered miraculous.

In the Rua Primeiro de Março, at the corner of Ouvidor (near the Old Cathedral), is the church of **Santa Cruz dos Militares,** built 1780-1811. It is large, stately and beautiful.

The beautiful little church on the Glória hill, overlooking the Parque do Flamengo, is **Nossa**

Senhora da Glória. It was the favourite church of the imperial family; Dom Pedro II was baptized here. Built in 1791, it contains some excellent examples of blue-faced Brazilian tiling. Its main altar, of wood, was carved by Mestre Valentim. The church, open 0900-1200 (only Sat.-Sun.) and 1300-1700 weekdays, is reached by bus 119 from the centre and 571 from Copacabana. The adjacent museum of religious art is open on application to the priest.

The church of **Nossa Senhora da Penha**, in the N suburb of Penha (early 20th century), is on a bare rock in which 365 steps are cut. This staircase is ascended by pilgrims on their knees during the festival month of October; there is a funicular for those unable to do this. Bus 497 from Copacabana, 340 and 346 from centre.

When the Morro do Castelo was levelled to build the Esplanada do Castelo, the old church of São Sebastião had to be demolished. Its successor, the Capuchin church of São Sebastião in the Rua Haddock Lobo, Tijuca, built in 1936, contains the tomb of Estácio de Sá, founder and first Governor of Rio de Janeiro.

Churches where worship is conducted in English:

Christ Church, Rua Real Grandeza 99, Botafogo (Church of England/American Episcopalian). The British School, for children of 5-16, is nearby.
Chapel of Our Lady of Mercy, Rua Visconde de Caravelas 48, Botafogo. (Roman Catholic, with primary school.)
Union Church (Protestant undenominational) Services held at Rua Parque da Lagoa de Marapendi, C.P.37154-CEP 22609 Barra da Tijuca.
International Baptist Church, Rua Desembargador Alfredo Russel 146, Leblon.
First Church of Christ Scientist, Av. Marechal Câmara 271, room 301.
Masonic Temple, in the British School at Rua da Matriz 76, Botafogo.
Synagogues, General Severiano 170, Botafogo; Rua Barata Ribeiro, Copacabana.
Swedish Church, Igreja Escandinava, Av. Rui Barbosa 170, Bloco B 1, 5 And.
British Cemetery, Rua da Gamboa 181, granted to the British community by Dom João, Regent of Portugal, in 1810. It is the oldest cemetery in Rio.

Parks, Squares and Monuments

The city abounds in open spaces and squares, many of which have ornamental gardens and statuary.

On the Glória and Flamengo waterfront, with a view of the Sugar Loaf and Corcovado, is the **Parque do Flamengo,** designed by Burle Marx, opened in 1965 during the 400th anniversary of the city's founding, and landscaped on 100 hectares reclaimed from the Bay. Behind the War Memorial (see below) is the public yacht marina.

In the park are many sports fields and a botanical garden; for children, there are a sailboat basin, a marionette theatre, a miniature village and a staffed nursery. There are night amusements, such as bandstands and areas set apart for dancing.

The National War Memorial to Brazil's dead in World War II and the Modern Art Museum (see page 252) are at the city end of the park, opposite Praça Paris. The Memorial takes the form of two slender columns supporting a slightly curved slab, representing two palms uplifted to heaven. In the crypt are the remains of the Brazilian soldiers killed in Italy in 1944-45. It is well worth a visit, but beach clothes and rubber-thonged sandals will get you ejected—and don't sit on the wall. The crypt and museum are open Tues.-Sun. 1000-1700.

Those who want to see what Rio was like early in the 19th century should go by bus to the **Largo do Boticário,** Rua Cosme Velho 822, a charming small square in pure colonial style. Buses to Cosme Velho from all parts of the city. The square is close to the terminus for the Corcovado rack railway (see page 270).

Botanical Gardens (Jardim Botânico) founded 1808, open daily, 0800-1800 in summer and 0830-1730 in winter (US$0.30); well worth a visit. The most striking features are the transverse avenues of 30-metre royal palms. There are over 7,000 varieties of plants, herbarium, aquarium, and library (some labels are unclear). The Gardens are 8 km. from the centre, 140 hectares in area; take any bus from the centre, e.g. 104, to Leblon, Gávea or São Conrado marked "via Jóquei". From Copacabana any bus whose number begins with 5 and ends with an even number, except 592.

Bird-watchers should visit the Botanical Gardens, preferably early in the morning. 140 species of birds have been recorded there. Flycatchers are very prominent (the social flycatcher, great and boat-billed kiskadees, cattle tyrant); also tanagers (the sayaca and palm tanagers, and the colourful green-headed tanager), and over 20 different kinds of hummingbird. Birds of prey include the roadside hawk, the laughing falcon and the American kestrel, and there are doves, cuckoos, parakeets, thrushes and woodpeckers, and occasional flocks of toucans. (John and George Newmark, Eastbourne.)

Parque Laje, near the Jardim Botânico at Rua Jardim Botânico 414, almost jungle-like, has small grottoes, an old tower and lakes. (The Institute of Fine Arts is housed in the mansion.) Open daily, 0730-1730, admittance free.

Quinta da Boa Vista, formerly the Emperor's private park, contains the zoo (see below) and many specimen trees. The Palace now houses the National Museum (**see page 252**). The park is very run down, with many abandoned children living in it and armed gangs who have been undeterred by greater police presence.

Zoological Gardens, which contain Brazilian and imported wild animals, and a fine collection of birds (as well as many "visitors" - also good for bird-watchers), are in the Quinta de Boa Vista (admission US$0.05). Open 0800-1800 daily, except Mon. The gateway is a replica of Robert Adam's famous gateway to Syon House, near London. Near the Zoological Gardens is the Museum of Natural History which is small but excellent. Take bus 474 or 472 from Copacabana or Flamengo; bus 262 from Praça Mauá.

Parque da Cidade A pleasant park a short walk beyond the Gávea bus terminus. It was previously the grounds of the home of the Guinle family, by whom it was presented to the City; the house itself is now the Museu da Cidade (**see page 253**). Admission to the park is free; open Tues.-Fri. 0730-1730, Sat., Sun. and holidays 1100-1700. The proximity of the Rocinha favela means that the park is not very safe. It is advisable to carry your passport (or copy) here because of frequent police checks.

Jockey Club Racecourse, at Praça Santos Dumont, Gávea, meetings on Mon. and Thurs. evenings and Sat. and Sun. 1400, entrance US$0.30. Take any bus marked "via Jóquei". Betting is by totalizator only.

Praça da República and **Campo de Santana** is an extensive and picturesque public garden close to the Central Railway station. At Praça da República 197 lived Marshal Deodoro da Fonseca, who proclaimed Brazil a republic in 1889 (plaque). The Parque Júlio Furtado in the middle of the square is populated by playful agoutis (or gophers), best seen at dusk; there is also a little artificial grotto, with swans.

Passeio Público (turn right at S end of Avenida Rio Branco) is a garden planted by the artist Mestre Valentim, whose bust is near the old former gateway. Coin and stamp market on Sun., a.m.

Praça Quinze de Novembro contains the original royal palace (**see page 253**). Every Sat. 0900-1900, handicraft fair and flea market; nearby on waterfront is Sun. antiques market, 1000-1800.

Praça Tiradentes, old and shady, has a statue to D. Pedro I, first Emperor of Brazil. Shops in nearby streets specialize in selling goods for *umbanda* and *macumba* - African-type religion and magic respectively. Several theatres nearby.

Praça Mahatma Gandhi, at the end of Avenida Rio Branco, is flanked on one side by the cinema and amusement centre of the city, known as Cinelândia. The fountain (1789) by Mestre Valentim in the ornamental garden was moved here from Praça Quinze de Novembro in 1979.

Parque do Catete is a charming small park between the Catete Palace (Museum of the Republic) and Praia do Flamengo; it has many birds and playful monkeys.

Praça Paris, built on reclaimed ground near the Largo da Glória, is much admired for the beauty of its formal gardens and illuminated fountains.

Fountains The oldest, the Fonte da Glória (1789), has eight bronze spouts. Possibly the finest is at the back of the church of S. Francisco de Paula, at the inland end of the Rua do Ouvidor. These, and nine other old fountains, are illuminated by night.

Hotels All hotels in the following list are air-conditioned. A 10% service charge is usually added to the bill. Note that not all higher-class hotels include breakfast in their room rates.

	Single US$	Double US$	Stars	Telex

Centre   (Well placed for transport, 30 min. from the beaches. Most offices and commerce are located here, but no night life)

	Single US$	Double US$	Stars	Telex
Ambassador, Senador Dantas, 25	46	50	3	21796*
Ambassador Santos Dumont, Sta. Luzia 651	52	58	3	32540
Granada, Gomes Freire, 530	45	49	3	
Grande Hotel OK, Senador Dantas, 24	46	51	3	30366
Othon Aeroporto, Av. Beira Mar, 280	50	56	3	22655*
Presidente, Pedro I, 19	44	48	3	21244*
São Francisco, Visc. de Inhaúma, 95	44	47	3	21244*

Flamengo (Residential area midway between centre and Copacabana.)

Flamengo Palace, Praia Flamengo, 6	47	49	3	
Glória, Rua do Russel, 632	136	156	4	21683
Novo Mundo, Praia Flamengo, 20 (well rec.)	52	55	3	33282

Copacabana (Seaside residential and commercial area.)

Apa, República do Peru, 305	54	56	3	30394
†*Astoria*, República do Peru, 345	46	51	3	
Bandeirante Othon, Barata Ribeiro, 548	52	55	3	22655*
Castro Alves, Av. Copacabana, 552	52	55	3	
†*Copacabana Palace*, Av. Atlântica, 1702	125	145	5	22248
Califórnia Othon, Av. Atlântica, 2616	73	79	4	22655*
Debret, Av. Atlântica, 3564	50	54	3	
Lancaster Othon, Av. Atlântica, 1470	60	70	4	23265*
Leme Palace, Av. Atlântica, 656	67	73	4	23265*
Luxor Continental, Gustavo Sampaio, 320	70	85	4	21469
Luxor Copacabana, Av. Atlântica, 2554	93	101	4	23971
Luxor Regente, Av. Atlântica, 3716	90	95	4	23887
†*Meridien*, Av. Atlântica, 1020	160	170	5	23183*
Miramar Palace, Sá Ferreira, 9	72	77	4	21508
Olinda Othon, Av. Atlântica, 2230	72	78	4	23265*
Ouro Verde, Av. Atlântica, 1456	90	100	4	23848
Rio Copa, Av. Princesa Isabel, 370	45	48	3	23988
†*Rio Othon Palace*, Av. Atlântica, 3264	104	114	5	23265*
†*Rio Palace*, Av. Atlântica, 4240	160	190	5	21803*
Savoy Othon, Av. Copacabana, 995	75	80	4	
Trocadero, Av. Atlântica, 2064	55	60	3	23265*

Ipanema/Leblon (Outer seaside residential and commercial area.)

Arpoador Inn, Francisco Otaviano, 177	43	48	3	22833*
†*Caesar Park*, Av. Vieira Souto 640	140	160	5	21204
†*Everest*, Prudente de Morais, 1117	102	110	5	22254
Marina Rio, Av. Delfim Moreira, 696	75	80	4	30224*
Marina Palace, Av. Delfim Moreira 630	96	107	5	30224*
†*Praia Ipanema*, Av. Vieira Souto, 706	75	80	4	31280*
Sol Ipanema, Av. Vieira Souto, 320	72	77	4	21979*

São Conrado and further out (Spectacular settings, but isolated and far from centre.)

†*Sheraton*, Av. Niemeyer, 121	125-185	145-205	5	21206

†*Nacional*, Av. Niemeyer, 769	110	118	5	21238
†*Intercontinental*, Av. Litorânea, 222	170	180	5	21790
Atlântico Sul, Recreio dos Bandeirantes	39	45	3	

Airport, Galeão

Luxor Hotel do Aeroporto	104	114	3

*Shared telex.   †Swimming pool.

Other Hotels in Copacabana (all air-conditioned; number of stars in brackets) Our categories A-B: *Royalty Copacabana*, Toneleros 154, 4 blocks from beach (4), a/c, swimming pool on 13th floor with view; *Praia Leme*, Av. Atlântica 866, pleasant, Austrian run, overlooking beach, English and German spoken (2); *Riviera*, Av. Atlântica 4122, very good, excellent breakfast but other meals disappinting, well placed, (3). *Atlantis Copacabana*, Av. Bulhões de Carvalho 61, a/c, TV, very good, close to Ipanema and Copacabana beaches (2). *Ipanema Inn*, Maria Quitéria 27 (Ipanema) T 287-6092, good, swimming pool.
Our category C, unless stated E: *Biarritz*, Rua Aires Saldanha 54 (2), good, accepts American Express; *Angarense* (2), Trav. Angarense 25, clean, friendly, C-D with shower, a/c, breakfast in room; *Toledo* (2), Rua Domingos Ferreira 71, T 521-4443 or 257-1990, friendly, good breakfast, safe, luggage stored, warmly rec. (except for single rooms which are gloomy); *Santa Clara* (2), Rua Décio Vilares 316, T 256-2650, rec., quiet; *Copa Linda*, Av. Copacabana 956, incl. breakfast, friendly and clean, funky décor reported, D (2); *Plaza Copacabana*, Av. Princesa Isabel 263 (3), highly rec. as most hospitable.

Economy Hotels   are found mainly in three districts of Rio: Flamengo/Botafogo (best), Lapa/Fátima and Saúde/Mauá. Rates are for doubles, and include continental breakfast.
   Flamengo/Botafogo (Residential area between centre and Copacabana, with good bus and metro connexions.) Walking from the centre, you will come across the hotels in this order: Rua Cândido Mendes, off Rua da Glória: *Alameda*, No. 112/118, D with bath, TV, radio, phone, good value, near Glória metro and Copacabana buses; *Monte Castelo*, No. 201 (T 222-1733), E (with bathroom), clean, central, safe deposit (but get a receipt for your valuables), rec. *Benjamin Constant*, Rua Benjamin Constant 10, nr. Glória metro, F, men only; *Bahia*, Santo Amaro 42, F (without bath), clean; on same street, No. 75, *Opera*, E (a/c extra, cheaper without bath), also good, safe, near Glória metro (T 221-8759/242-3583). Across from here, on the hillside is Ladeira da Glória: *Turístico*, Ladeira da Glória 30, sold out Dec.-March, E, with bath, including breakfast, money and valuables can be left safely, Spanish spoken, tourist information provided, rec. but popularity does not always guarantee. *Victória*, Rua do Catete 172, E, with breakfast, bath and hot water, a/c, clean and friendly, also on Rua do Catete: No. 233, *Rio Claro*, E, recently renovated, breakfast, shower, a/c, safe, rec.; No. 160, *Monte Blanco*, E, breakfast, bath, a/c, radio, refurbished, clean, friendly, safe, very popular (try for a room about 1200), rec. To the left is Rua Silveira Martins: No. 20, *Inglés*, D, reasonable breakfast; at No. 135, *Hispano Brasileiro*, E, a/c, with bath, friendly owner speaks Spanish, but little else to recommend it. Walking down Praia de Flamengo you will come across the next streets: Ferreira Viana: No. 20, *Mayflower*, E with bath, no breakfast, simple; *Regina*, No. 29, 2-star, C-D, a/c, bath, fridge, TV, poor service; No. 58, *Ferreira Viana*, (E, with bath and breakfast, always heavily booked, valuables may be left safely); No. 69-81, *Florida*, private shower and breakfast, good souvenir shop, highly rec., safe-deposit, D and up. Correia Dutra: *Mengo*, E (not very clean, friendly), No. 31 (T 225-5911); No. 141, *Leão*, E, clean, bath, a/c, unfriendly staff; *Caxambu*, E with breakfast and radio, good. *Monterrey*, Rua Artur Bernardes 39, D with bath, very good; at No. 29, *Rio Lisboa*, D with bath, a/c, cheaper rooms without bath, clean, safe, rec.—both hotels in this quiet street are family hotels. Rua Paissandu: No. 34, *Venezuela*, E, with bathroom, very clean, but rooms small and breakfast poor. Beyond Largo de Machado: Rua Gago Coutinho: No. 22, *Serrano*, D, pleasant; and *Argentina*, Cruz Lima 30, C, rec.
   Lapa/Fátima   (Area between Lapa and Praça Tiradentes, inner residential area, less desirable than Flamengo.) *Hospedaria Sul América*, Rua da Lapa, E, without breakfast, rec. *Universo*, Visconde do Rio Branco 61, E, good, but area deserted from 2200 on. Near Cinelândia metro station are *Itajubá*, Rua Alvaro Alvim 15, E, good, and *Nelba*, Senador Dantas 46, E, with shower, friendly, also good. There are a lot of cheap hotels in this area, but many are hot-pillow establishments. In Lapa itself, near the Arches just beyond Passeio Público, is Rua Joaquim Silva: No. 87, *Ipiranga*, E, old but clean; and No. 99, *Marajó*, D, with breakfast, varied rooms, clean; also *Love's House*, Rua Joaquim Silva, E, ask for room with window, safe, respectable, good value. Passing under the Arches you come to Av. Mem de Sá (bus 127 from bus terminal): No. 85, *Mundo Novo*, E, clean, air-conditioned. Turning towards Praça Tiradentes is Rua Resende, No. 31, *Estadual*, D, good; No. 35, *Pouso Real*, D, good, but the area is dubious. *Marialva*, Gomes Freire 430 (nr. New Cathedral, convenient for Av. Rio Branco, buses etc.), 2 star, D with bath, a/c, breakfast in room, rec. Praça Tiradentes, *Rio Hotel*, clean, noisy rooms on Praça, quieter overlooking São Sebastião cathedral, D with breakfast (only served in rooms). Beyond Praça Tiradentes is Rua dos Andradas (towards centre): No. 19, *Globo*, D a/c, shower, TV, very good (beware the sharp lift doors).
   Saúde/Mauá   (Area between the railway station and the docks, a dubious part of town.) *Rio*

Grande, Rua Senador Pompeu 220, E, rec.; *Internacional,* Rua Senador Pompeu 82, E, clean and friendly. The very cheapest hotels in town are in this area, but it is not too safe at night.

Near the Rodoviária *Conceição,* Rua Garibáldi 165, good and cheap; *Rodoviária,* adequate, cheap, E without breakfast, fan, clean, hot water.

In the traditional **Santa Teresa** district, Rua Almirante Alexandrino 660, is the *Santa Teresa Hotel,* C, with swimming pool and full board. Also Dona Ana's hostel on the same street at No. 501, C, T 232-9603. Take the "Dois Irmãos" tram from Largo da Carioca.

The Federal University puts up men during vacations. *Pousada Estácio,* Rua do Bispo 83, F in 4-bedded apartments with breakfast, rec. (in campus of Faculdades Integradas Estácio de Sá). There is a **Youth Hostel** on the tenth and eleventh floors of the *Casa do Estudante,* at Praça Ana Amélia 9 (Rua Sta. Luzia), near Santa Luzia church, open all year, F—student card required—international youth hostel card is best, you can check in at any time of day, and can come in at any time of night, but after 0100 you must pay the lift man US$0.10. (Adverse opinion from some travellers—uncomfortable, showers not working.) Adverse reports of *Casa do Estudante Universitário,* Av. Rui Barbosa 762; said to be unsafe for property. Cheap food at canteens for those with international student cards. Other Youth Hostels at Rua Almte. Alexandrino 2840, Santa Teresa (*Pousada do Garuda,* T 225-0393/326-1419), Santa Amaro 162, Glória, T 222-8576; and Rua Emílio Burla 41, Copacabana (T 236-6472), good, YHA card not necessary, but you pay a bit more without it, cleaner than the one at Sta. Luzia. Youth hostels are fully booked between Christmas and Carnival; if intending to stay at this time reserve well in advance. Remember that the "motels" in the suburbs and along the main highways are mainly for the use of very-short-stay couples.

The city is extremely noisy. An inside room is cheaper and much quieter. (If you are desperate and it is late, some smaller hotels and hostelries may let you sleep on the floor.)

Apartments If they prefer, tourists can look after themselves in flatlets (small apartments) in Copacabana, Ipanema, Leblon, or, more cheaply, in the centre or more northerly areas (for example, furnished apartments, accommodating up to 6, cost US$200 per month in Maracanã, about US$300 per month in Saúde, Cinelândia, Flamengo). Bookings for Copacabana at Rua Barata Ribeiro 90, room 205, Copacabana, Av. N.S. da Copacabana 583, room 1007, T 235-3748, and at Rua Barata Ribeiro 87/ 202, T 255-2016 or 237-1133. Also Rent Fiat Imobiliária Ltda, Rua Barata Ribeiro 207 s/101—CEP: 22011, T 256-9986. The *Praia Leme Hotel,* Av. Atlântica 866, has apartments, with maid and laundry service at Av. Princesa Isabel 7, close to the beach; US$27d in low season, US$30 in high season (when reservation is necessary). José Silva da Ferreira, Rua Pompeu Loureiro 56A, Apto. 401, Copacabana (T 256-9957) lets good apartments (US$30/day); Hans Peter Corr, Rua Belfort Roxo 158, Apto. 701, Copacabana (T 541-0615), several apartments from US$50 upwards, 30% reduction for people staying 4 weeks or more (U.K. representative Mrs M.A.Barker, 20 Farrer Rd, London N8 8LB, T 01-340 4163). Yvonne Reimann, Av. Atlântica 4.066, Apto. 605, T 227-0281, rents apartments with phone, a/c, maid service, starting from US$25; also Ruth Haeberlin, Rua Hilario Gouveia 88, Apt. 702, T 236-4496, from US$30 per day (1-3 people). *Rio Hotel Residencia,* Av. Sernambetiba 6250, Barra da Tijuca, offers one-bedroom suites (for 2) with sitting-room and kitchen for US$50 a day, two-bedroom suites (for 4) for US$70. *Rio Flat Service,* Almirante Guilhém 322, Leblon, reservations through SASS Ltda, Ataulfo de Paiva 566/305, T 274-9546, Telex: 30245. Estate agents dealing in more expensive apartments include Tower Real Estate, Rua Aníbal de Mendonça 157, Ipanema; Coroa Real, Rua Buenos Aires 4 and Av. Copacabana 647, Loja 205/206; Lowndes and Sons S.A., Av. Presidente Vargas 290, 2° andar, T 253-5622. For cheaper apartments, and rooms in private homes, try classified ads, e.g. *Balcão* (like *Exchange and Mart*), twice weekly, look for word "proprietário", or *Jornal do Brasil,* under section 100, subsection 101—Temporada. The word "conjugado" abbreviated to "conj" means bedsitter, "vaga" a bed in a private home or a shared apartment and "quarto" a room in a private house. Do check security arrangements in apartment buildings since robbery is common.

Camping Camping Clube do Brasil has beach site at Av. Sernambetiba 3200 (bus 233 from centre or 554 from Leblon, US$1.20—a long way from the centre), Barra da Tijuca, costing US$6 p.p. per night (half price for members). During January and February this site is often full and sometimes restricted to members of the Camping Clube do Brasil. Also at Recreio dos Bandeirantes, Estrada do Pontal 5900, and *Ostral,* Av. Sernambetiba 18790, US$2 p.p. and *Novo Rio,* at 17.5 km. on Rio-Santos road, US$2.50 p.p. "Wild" camping possible on beaches further out; if trying it nearer centre, risk of thieves. If travelling by trailer, you can park at the Marina Glória car park, where there are showers and toilets, a small shop and snack bar. Pay the guards to look after your vehicle. Camping gear for sale at Montcamp, Teixeira de Melo 21, Ipanema, T 287-1143.

Electric Current 110-220 volts, 60 cycles, A.C.

Restaurants: In Rio, avoid mussels! **Centre:** *La Tour,* revolving restaurant, Clube Aeronáutica building, Rua Santa Luzia 651, 45th floor. Marvellous views, but food said to be poor and expensive. (Reservations, T 224-2221 for French meals, 242-3221 for international and 252-8234 for fish). *Alba Mar* (fish, very good and reasonable, Praça 15 de Novembro overlooking ferry station): *Academia*, Av. Pres. Wilson, not expensive; *A Cabaça Grande* (Casa das Peixadas, Rua do Ouvidor 12, best for fish, closed Sun./holidays); *Spaghetti*, Av. Rio Branco 25, Italian, self-service, good salads, cheap; *Miura*, Av. Rio Branco 156, 2nd mezzanine, No. 324/325 (Japanese); *Rio Minho*, Rua do Ouvidor 10, for seafood, expensive, old-fashioned, very good. Vegetarian: *Naranda*, Rua da Alfândega 112—1st floor, good value; *Health's*, Rua Benedito 18, Mon.-Fri. lunch only, *Zan*, Travessa do Ouvidor 25, *Lida* and *Saúde*, Rua Rosário 142, 2nd floor. There are several Arab restaurants on Av. Senhor dos Passos, also open Sat. and Sun. *Buksky* (*Paulista*), Rua do Rosário 133 (German), rec. for wholesome food and speedy service: on same street, *N.S. de Guia*, good, lunch only; and *La Table*, pancakes, good and cheap; *Oxalá*, Rua Álvaro Alvim 36, good Bahian food, quick service, reasonable; *Churrascolandia*, Rua Senador Dantas, quick and simple, "but with character"; *Pensão Guanabara*, Rua Buenos Aires by flower market, meal for US$1. *Kit-Kat*, Primeiro de Março, near Post Office, Chinese, self-service, good selection. *Café Nice*, Av. Rio Branco 277, beside main Varig-Cruzeiro do Sul office, interesting, old-fashioned, not cheap. *Bar Americano Antártica*, Rua Evaristo da Veiga, near Opera House, cheap 2-course meals with drink; *Taverna do Galeto*, near Cinelândia metro station, good. *Navona*, Rua da Carioca, very good Italian food; *Lanchonette N.S. da Mo*, Rua São Bento 22, rec.; *Lanchonete Brasilândia*, Rua das Marrecas, and in same street, No. 44, *Luciano*, all you can eat at buffet, and *Portuense*, rec. Many lanchonetes for good, cheap meals in the business sector. Cheap eating places on Praça Tiradentes. *Bar dos Estudantes*, opp. Casa dos Estudantes, prato comercial is cheap, filling and balanced, friendly staff. *Nova Carioca*, Rua Carioca 21, good snack bar. **Santa Teresa**: *Maçã d'Ouro*, Largo das Neves opposite church at end of Paula Mattos tram line, excellent, American-run, will change money. **Lapa**: *Mario*, Rua Joaquim Silva 130, and *Semente*, same street No. 138, both vegetarian. **Glória**: *Braseiro Galeto*, R. Cândido Mendes 116-C, good, cheap barbecued chicken, meats; *Vila Rica*, Rua Cândido Mendes, corner with Rua da Glória, good selection, inexpensive; *St. Moritz*, in same building as Swiss Consulate, Rua Cândido Mendes 157, bar/restaurant, good atmosphere; *Hobby Lanches*, R. da Glória, near Metro, good, cheap. **Flamengo and Catete:** *Planalto do Flamengo*, churrascaria, Rua Barão do Flamengo 35-S (Praça José de Alencar), rec. *Bar KTT*, Rua do Catete, US$2 for 2-course meal, excellent; same road, No. 212, *Catetelândia*, reasonable meals at the bar; No. 239, *Pastelaria Wong*, very cheap, good and, No. 234B, *Amazônia*, downstairs, one-price counter service, upstairs for good, reasonably-priced evening meals, over-zealous service, rec. *Restaurante e Pizzaria Guanabara*, Rua do Catete 150, excellent value and selection; *Rio Galicia*, Rua do Catete 265, near *Hotel Vitória*, very good pizza, good service; *Machado*, Rua do Catete 286, good Italian food at reasonable prices; *Rio's*, Parque de Flamengo, opp. Morro da Viúva, T 551-1131, French, expensive, good service, piano bar; *Restaurante Praia Bar*, Praia do Flamengo 144, elegant Italian, reasonable; *Galeto, Restaurante e Bar Cabanas*, Praia do Flamengo 122A, bar meals, reasonable; *Lamas*, Marquês de Abrantes 18-A, excellent value, good food; *Gaúcha*, Rua Senador Vergueiro 114, good and cheap. *Cozinha Arabe Brasileira*, Severo 176, cheap, small Arab dishes; *Pensão*, Rua Arturo Bernardes 9, cheap meals, good. **Largo do Machado:** *Adega Real*, Rua Gago Coutinho, very good. Plenty of pizza places. **Botafogo:** *Aurora*, Capitão Salomão 43 (Mon.-Sat. till 2330) good food, excellent value; *La Mole*, Praia de Botafogo 228, good, cheap Italian food (other locations in Rio); *Churrascaria Galeto na Brasa*, Praia de Botafogo 358-60, cheap and good; *Churrascaria Estrela do Sul*, Av. Repórter Néstor Moreira, s/n, excellent *rodizio*. *Neal's*, Rua Sorocaba, US-style, burgers, chili, steaks, good value; *Café Pacífico*. Rua Visconde Silva 14, good, cheap, Mexican; *Restaurante Natural*, Rua 19 de Fevereiro 118. **Copacabana and Leme:** The main hotels, including particularly *Rio Palace* and *Ouro Verde* (international food, highly rec.); *Churrascaria Marius*, at Leme end of Av. Atlântica, excellent but not cheap; *Príncipe Legítimo das Peixadas*, Av. Atlântica 974B, good but expensive; *Churrascaria do Jardim*, R. República do Peru, rec.; *Churrascaria Palace*, Rua Rodolfo Dantas 16-B, 22 different kinds of meat, very good value; *Baalbeck*, Rodolfo Dantas 225, Arab food and pastries, reasonable; also Arabic is *Novo Stambul*, Rua Domingos Ferreira 221-B, good; same street, No. 242-A, *Nino*, good but not cheap; *El Pote Galetos*, Rua República do Peru 143B, good chicken; *Moenda*, Av. Atlântica 2064, live music but formal, good food; *La Mole*, Av. N.S. de Copacabana, good service; *Beliscão*, Rua Siqueira Campos 23A e B, good beef stroganoff; nearby is *Cantina Veneziana*, good and cheap. *Aux Tropiques* (French), corner of Rua Siqueira Campos and Rua Barata Ribeiro, 3rd floor, very good; *Akasaka* (Japanese) Av. Copacabana and Rua Joaquim Nabuco, rec.; *Zingaro's* (Italian) Rua Figueiredo Magalhães, reasonable. *Bip-Bip*, R. Almirante Gonçalves 50 D, for batidas; *Ariston*, Santa Clara 18A and B, good; *Rian*, Santa Clara 8 (international), excellent and reasonable, especially seafood. *Le Streghe*, Rua Prudente Morais 129, *Barone Fasoli*, Rua Jangadeiros 14-D, and *Enotria*, R. Constante Ramos 115, all Italian and 4 star. Cheap and good inclusive meal at *Frango na Brasa*, Rua Constante Ramos 35; and also at *Cervantes* and *El Cid*. Cabral 1500, Rua Bolívar 8, good; *Maxim*, Av. Atlântica 1850, good and reasonable, pleasant place and atmosphere; *La Tratoria*, Av. Atlântica (opp. *Hotel Excelsior*), Italian, good food and service. **Ipanema:** *Lagoa Charlies*, Rua Maria Quitéria 136, supposedly Mexican, not cheap (margaritas are prohibitively expensive). For a meal with a view, try the restaurant and nightclub at the *Panorama Palace Hotel*, Rua Alberto de Campos 12. *Hotel Caesar Park*, rec. for Saturday feijoada, all you can eat; *Bardo Beto*, Rua Farme de Amoedo 51 (T 267-4443) excellent food, big servings, good value; *Lord Jim Pub*, Paul Redfern 63, does English food including tea, great atmosphere, not cheap, closed Mon. Ipanema is quieter than

Copacabana, many nice places round main square, Praça General Osório, such as *Romanos*. At corner of Prudente de Morais and Vicícius de Morais there are 4 restaurants: *Del Mare* particularly rec. *Porcão*, churrascaria, rec.; branches everywhere. Health food at *Restaurante Natural*, Rua Barão de Torre 171. **Jardim Botânico** *O Philippe*, R.Jardim Botânico 617, very good and reasonable, close to the Garden. **Lagoa:** *Castelo da Lagoa*, on Av Epitácio Pessoa: on same road. *Rive Gauche*, No. 1484 (T 247-9993), French, excellent; **Gávea:** *Schwarze Katz*, Estrada do Vidigal 471, German and international. **Leblon:** *Un, Deux, Trois*, Rua Bartolomeu Mitre 123, very fashionable; restaurant and night club; *Antiquarius*, Rua Aristides Espínola 19, restaurant-cum-antique shop, seafood and international cuisine. *Sabor Saúde*, Av. Ataulfo de Paiva 624, very nice. *Mediterráneo*, Rua Prudente de Morais 1810, excellent fish, reasonable prices; *Celeiro*, vegetarian and health food, on Dias Ferreira between Aristides Espínola and Rainha Guilhermina, rec. (good bookshop 3 doors away). *Bar Degrau*, Av. Ataulfo de Paiva 517b, good atmosphere. In **São Conrado**, *El Pescador*, Praça São Conrado 20, Spanish-style fish restaurant, excellent value and variety of paellas. The *Sheraton* coffee shop has good feijoada on Sat. p.m.

Grill or barbecue houses (churrascarias) are relatively cheap, especially by European standards. There are many at São Conrado and Joá, on the road out to Barra da Tijuca (**see page 271**). Look for the "Churrascaria Rodízio", where you are served as much as you can eat. There are plentiful hamburger stands (literally "stands" as you stand and eat the hamburger) and lunch counters all over the city. *McDonalds* and *Big Bob's* (similar) can be found at about 20 locations each. *Galetos* are lunch counters specializing in chicken and grilled meat, very reasonable. In the "shopping centres" there is usually a variety of restaurants and snack bars grouped around a central plaza where you can shop around for a good meal. Most less-expensive restaurants in Rio have basically the same type of food (based on steak, fried potatoes and rice) and serve large portions; those with small appetites, and especially families with children, can ask for a spare plate, and split helpings. There are many juice bars in Rio with a wide selection. Most restaurants are closed on 24 and 25 December.

Tea Rooms For those who like their teas served English style, the sedate Belle Epoque 80-year-old *Confeiteria Colombo*, Rua Gonçalves Dias 32, is highly rec. for atmosphere, being the only one of its kind in Rio, with the original décor, open 0900-1800. It has also a most attractive branch at Av. Copacabana 890. More modern but similar establishments in some of the main hotels, and at *Casarão*, Souza Lima 37A, Copacabana; *La Bonne Table*, Visc. de Pirajá 580 sala 407, Ipanema; and *Ponto de Encontro*, Barata Ribeiro 750B, Copacabana. *Café de la Paix*, Av. Atlântica, 1020; *Chá e Simpatia*, Av. Atlântica 4240; *Um Chorinho chamado Odeon*, Gávea Shopping Centre; *Bolo Inglês*, Cassino Atlântico Shopping Centre; *Concorde*, Av. Prudente de Morais 129. These establishments have become very fashionable.

Night Clubs Note that respectable night clubs permit entrance only to couples. Of most interest to the visitor will be shows featuring samba dancing. *Hotel Nacional* at São Conrado has the most lavish show in town, price for entrance and one drink is US$20. Other good samba shows at: *Solaris*, Rua Humaitá 110; *Oba-Oba*, Visconde de Pirajá 499 e.g. US$32 for two dinners and show considered one of the best in Rio. For the best Brazilian shows try *Canecão*, Rua Venceslau Bras 215, where the best-known Carnival ball is now held. *Plataforma I*, Rua Adalberto Ferreira 32, Leblon, receives mixed opinions. Rio has its share of lively discotheques; among the best are; *New Jirau*, Rua Siqueira Campos 12-A, Copacabana; *Ye Bateau*, Praça Serzedelo Correia 15-A, Copacabana; *Crocodilus*, Rua Xavier da Silveira 7, Copacabana; *Privé*, Praça General Osório, Rua Jangadeiros 28-A; *Papagaio Disco Club*, Av. Borges de Medeiros 1426, Lagoa (Fri. and Sat. only); *Zoom* at São Conrado is very good. For something quieter and more intimate, look in at any of the following piano bars: *Balaio* (Hotel Leme Palace), Av. Atlântica 656. *Crazy Rabbit* on Av. Princesa Isabel. 3 rec. bars in Flamengo area: *Tronbada*, Rua M. de Abrantes 64, Spanish-style tapas, very popular; *Planalto Flamengo*, Largo de Machado end of Rua do Catete, very friendly and crowded and, nearby, a bar at the corner of Paiçandu and Senador Vergueiro. Two good (and expensive) restaurants with live shows are *Fossa*, Rua Ronaldo de Carvalho 55, Copacabana, and *Carinhoso*, Rua Visconde de Pirajá 22, Ipanema. On the beach, not far away, is *Albericos*, Av. Vieira Souto 240. *Scala*, Av. Afranio de Mello Franco, Leblon, large, 1¾ hr. show at 2300, lavish and loud, reasonably-priced drinks, entry US$11. Also in Ipanema on Rua Vinicius de Morais 49-A, *Garota de Ipanema*, where the song "Girl from Ipanema" was written, excellent atmosphere, food reasonable. *Help*, Av. Atlântica 3432, is also very popular with young people, but dangerous for drinkers. *Forró de Copacabana*, Av. N.S. de Copacabana 435, forró music upstairs on first floor, disco on second floor, very popular, cheap, safe for single women. On Fri., Sat. and Sun. nights, 2100-0200, there is dancing to live bands at *Circo Voador* beneath Arcos da Lapa, in a circus tent, popular (other events during the week).

One of the centres of gay life is Cinelândia, in the centre (another is Galeria Alaska); in this area extending up to the Viaduto is found the whole gamut of human life. The essentially local character of night life in this area seems to make it relatively safe. Other gay places are *Papagaio* (see above);

RIO DE JANEIRO CENTRE 30

Cochrane, Rua das Palmeiras 66, Botafogo, done out like a traditional English pub; *Tamino*, Rua Arnaldo Quintela 30, near Rua da Passagem, Botafogo.

Another good place to see Brazilians at play, and at the same time for the English to feel some *saudades* (homesickness), is *Lord Jim Pub*, Paul Redfern 63 (Ipanema). Authentic pub atmosphere, afternoon tea, English food upstairs—steak-and-kidney pie, fish and chips. Phone in advance to check opening hours.

There are also gafieras, restaurants or night clubs with live Brazilian music for dancing. The best (and most expensive) is *Carinhoso*, Rua Visconde de Pirajá 22, Ipanema. Others, *Elite Club*, Rua Frei Caneca 4, 1st floor, in the centre. *Asa Branca*, Av. Mem de Sá 17, Lapa, high class, expensive, live music daily. *Roda Viva*, beside the Sugar Loaf cable car station, and *Cordão da Bola Preta* (pretty rough, but typical, only on Friday evening), Av. Treze de Maio 13, 3rd. floor, beside the Municipal Theatre, centre; *Gafiera Estudiantina*, Praça Tiradentes and one, enthusiastically rec., at Botafogo under the beach highway. Other bars which have music *shows* include: *Chucrute*, Largo de São Conrado; *Barbas*, Álvaro Ramos 408, Botafogo; *Equinox*, restaurant/bar, Rua Prudente de Morais 729 (piano music); *Jazzmania*, Av. Rainha Elisabeth 769, T 227-2447, show at 2200; *Western Club*, Rua Humaitá 380; *Gente da Noite*, Rua Voluntários da Pátria 466, both in Botafogo; *Klaus Bar*, Rua Dias Ferreira 410, Leblon (live music irregularly on Fri. and Sat.); *Existe um Lugar*, Estrada das Furnas 3001; *Four Seasons*, Paul Redfern 44, Ipanema, for jazz; *Vogue*, Rua Cupertino Durão 173, Leblon; *People*, Av. Bartolomeu Mitre 370, Leblon. In Barra de Tijuca there are a multitude of small night clubs, discotheques and gafieras, as well as some very luxurious motels for very-short-stay couples.

Many people look for Macumba religious ceremonies. Those offered on the night tours sold at hotels are not genuine, and a disappointment. You need a local contact to see the real ones, which are usually held in *favelas* and are none too safe for unaccompanied tourists.

Theatres There are about 20 theatres in Rio. The best known are: *Teatro Municipal*, Av. Rio Branco, for concerts, opera and ballet; *Tereza Rachel*, R. Siqueira Campos 143, Copacabana (has samba shows, much cheaper than night clubs); *Sala Cecília Meireles*, Largo da Lapa (often free classical concerts); *Teatro Villa-Lobos*, Av. Princesa Isabel, Copacabana; *Senac*, Rua Pompeu Loureiro 45, Copacabana. Good value entertainment at "Seis e Meia" (1830) shows at various downtown theatres (e.g. *João Caetano* on Praça Tiradentes): 1½ hr. musical shows with top-name Brazilian artists—check local papers.

Cinemas A very few give cheaper tickets to students, but not at weekends. Listings in *Jornal do Brasil* newspaper (best) and *O Globo*.

Shopping A good jewellery shop is Badofsky Brothers, Av. Copacabana 680, Room 315, 3rd floor; English, German, French spoken. Maximino Jeweler, Av. Rio Branco 25, 11th floor, and other branches. H. Stern, jewellers, Rua Garcia D'Avila 113, Ipanema; they also offer a tour, with head-phone commentary, of their lapidary and designing workshops, arranged through representatives at better hotels. Gregory & Sheehan, jewellers, Rua da Alfândega 65, 1st & 2nd floors; Corcovado Jóias, Av. N.S. de Copacabana 209, Loja F; Roditi and Amsterdam Sauer offer free taxi rides to their workshops. For mineral specimens as against cut stones, try Mineraux, Av. Copacabana 195, Belgian owner. Saara is a multitude of little shops along Rua Alfândega and Rua Sen. dos Passos (between city centre and Campo Sant'ana) where clothes bargains can be found (especially jeans and bikinis). Good "hippy fair" at Ipanema (Praça General Osório on Suns.). Sunday market in Glória district (Rua da Glória), colourful, cheap fruit, vegetable and flowers. "Shopping centres:" Rio Sul, at Botafogo end of Túnel Novo, Copacabana, Cassino (Copacabana), Norte Shopping (Meier), Plaza Shopping (Niteroi), Barra on Barra de Tijuca (**see page 271**). The Funai shop (Government Indian Agency) is very disappointing.

Cameras and Film Processing Dino's, Rua Buenos Aires 241; others in same street. Camera repair, Av. Rio Branco 151, 2nd floor, room 204. Kodachrome slide film difficult to get in Rio. For processing, One Hour Foto, in the Rio Sul and Barra shopping centres, is rec.; also a laboratory at Rua do Russel 344, Glória (1 hour for transparencies).

Key to Rio de Janeiro Map
1. Praça Mauá; 2. Praça da República and Campo de Santana; 3. Praça Duque de Caxias; 4. Praça Tiradentes; 5. Largo da Carioca; 6. Praça 15 de Novembro; 7. Passeio Público; 8. Parque do Flamengo; 9. Praça Mahatma Gandhi; 10. Praça do Expedicionário; 11. Aqueduto da Carioca (Arches, or *arcos*); 12. New Cathedral; 13. Monastery and church of São Bento; 14. Church of Candelária; 15. Church of Santa Cruz dos Militares; 16. Old Cathedral and Church of Carmo; 17. Monastery of Santo Antônio and Church of São Francisco da Penitência; 18. Church of Santa Luzia; 19. Church of São Francisco de Paula; 20. Itamarati Palace; 21. Viceroys' Palace (Paço Imperial); 22. National Archive; 23. National Museum of Belas Artes; 24. Museu da Imagem e do Som; 25. Museu Histórico Nacional; 26. Instituto Histórico e Geográfico; 27 Museu de Arte Moderno; 28. Second World War Memorial; 29. National Library; 30. Tram terminus; 31. Ferry dock; 32. Riotur and Flumitur offices; 33. Central Post Office; 34. Teatro João Caetano; 35. Teatro Municipal; 36. Flower Market; 37. Mariano Procópio bus terminal (for greater Rio de Janeiro); 38. Menezes Cortes bus terminal (Castelo—a/c buses to Zona sul).

Electronics repair (radio, walkman, etc.), Eletrônika Tekron, Rua Figueiredo Magalhes 870, Copacabana, T 235-4096, efficient, friendly.

Bookshops For international stock, Livraria Kosmos, Rua do Rosário 155, good shop (in the centre and Av. Atlântica 1702, loja 5) and there are many others, e.g. Livros Técnicos, Rua Miguel Couto 35, wide selection; Nova Livraria Da Vinci, Av. Rio Branco 185 loja 2/3, all types of foreign books; Livrarias Siciliano, Av. Rio Branco 156, loja 26, English, French and German books, also at N.S. de Copacabana 830 and other branches. Unilivros, Largo do Machado 29C, French and English bestsellers; Livraria Nova Galeria de Arte, Av. Copacabana 291D, international stock. El Dorado, Av. das Américas 4666, loja 207. Second-hand books also at Livraria São José, Rua Carmo 61 (only a few in English); Livraria Brasileira, Av. Rio Branco 156, S/Loja 229 (some in English); under *Rio Hotel*, corner of Rua da Carioca and Praça Tiradentes; Livraria Antiquário, Sete de Setembro 207 and in Rua Pedro I, all in centre. Also on Av. Marechal Floriano, near Av. Rio Branco, especially at No. 63. On S side of Praça Tiradentes, Casa dos Artistas trades in second-hand paperbacks. Second-hand English books at the Anglican church, Rua Real Grandeza 99, Botafogo.

Markets North-eastern market at Campo de São Cristóvão, with music and magic, on Sun. mornings. Flower market at Praça Olavo Bilac, off Rua Buenos Aires, in centre. Saturday antiques market on waterfront, near Praça 15 de Novembro (1000-1800) and handicraft and flea market Sat. (0900-1900) in Praça 15. Sunday stamp and coin market in Passeio Público, a.m. Sunday open-air handicrafts market at Praça General Osório, Ipanema. Excellent food and household-goods markets at various places in the city and suburbs (see newspapers for times and places).

Buses Good services to all parts, very crowded, not for the aged and infirm during rush hours. Hang on tight, drivers try to emulate Nelson Picquet and Ayrton Senna. Fare normally about US$0.10, watch your change! Bus stops are often not marked. Four private companies operate air-conditioned buses which can be flagged down practically anywhere: Real, Pegaso, Anatur and Carioca. They run from all points in Rio Sul (Barra, São Conrado, Leblon/Ipanema, Copacabana) to the city centre, Rodoviária and the airports. Fares about US$1 (US$2 to international airport).

Trams Try the remaining tram service from Largo da Carioca (where there is a museum, open only Fri. 0830-1700) across the old aqueduct (Arcos) to Dois Irmãos or Santa Teresa— historical and most interesting, and now refurbished, US$0.05. **Warning:** Beware of theft in trams even despite the increased police presence; in this connection it is best to avoid rush hours.

Car Hire For self-drive, try Avis, Rio International airport, less helpful than office at Praia do Flamengo 224 (205-5796); Hertz, Av. Oswaldo Cruz 67 (245-0678) US$30 all-in for 24 hrs. in a VW Beetle. Hertz, US$40 for a VW Kombi, US$60 for a/c Ford Galaxie. Nobre, Gustavo Sampaio 826 (275-5297) and Av. Princesa Isabel 350 (T 541-4646) Copacabana, has special deal for 7 hrs. Telecar, Rua Figueiredo Magalhães 701 (257-2620). Many agencies on Av. Princesa Isabel, Copacabana. Remember service stations are closed in many places on Saturdays and Sundays; some agencies will supply gas to customers at the weekend.

Taxis start at US$0.60 and are quite reasonable. There is a 40% surcharge between 2300 and 0600 and on Suns. and holidays. Taxis have red number plates with white digits (yellow for private cars, with black digits) and have meters. Smaller ones (mostly Volkswagen) are marked TAXI on windscreen or roof. Meters are often out-of-date because of inflation and drivers will consult updating sheets (make sure the updating sheet is an original in black and red, and not a photocopy—this is a well-known fiddle!); all the same, beware of overcharging, which is rife (**See also page 268** in Rodoviária section). Make sure meters are cleared. If there is no meter, you *must* fix the fare before entering. Radio Taxis (white with red and yellow stripe) are safer and not much more expensive, e.g. Cootramo, 270-1442, Coopertramo, 260-2022. Luxury cabs are allowed to charge higher rates.

Underground Railway Line 1 operates between Tijuca and Botafogo, via the railway station and Glória, with 19 km. in operation; it is being extended 1 km. at the Tijuca end and 7 km. at the other. It will go from Botafogo via Copacabana and on to Ipanema and Leblon (Jardim de Allah). Line 2, running past the Maracanã stadium northward to Irajá, will eventually run from Praça 15 de Novembro (Estação das barcas Rio-Niteroi), through the city centre, to Estácio. Line 1 operates 0600-2300, Line 2 0600-2000, both closed Sun and holidays. Fare US$0.15; integrated bus/metro tickets available (cheaper if bought in bulk). Substantial changes in bus operations are taking place because of the extended metro system; buses connecting with the metro have a blue-and-white symbol in the windscreen. The metro system is due for completion in 1990. If you speak Portuguese, apply to the Municipality and allow 10 days for arranging a sightseeing tour.

Public Conveniences There are very few in Rio de Janeiro, but many bars and restaurants (e.g. Macdonalds) offer facilities; just ask for the "banheiro" (banyairoo). Try the Castelo bus terminal in city centre. Also Praça Tiradentes, and 5th floor of Rua da Assembleia 10 (same building as Riotur). Best conveniences are to be found in the Shopping Centres.

Crime Rio has been getting worse, both for assaults and for pickpocketing, but the number of patrolling police has been steadily expanded in recent years. Precautions are advisable, especially on the famous beaches, where small boys work in gangs, some distracting your attention while others go through pockets and bags. It is best not to take any belongings to the beach. It is suggested to women that they do not visit the cinema alone. Venturing out alone at night is not advisable for anyone. Always carry some money (but never large amounts): robbers may be incensed and very aggressive if their victims have nothing at all. Do not wear jewellery or carry openly tourist goods such as a camera, maps or guide books to make yourself an obvious target. Carry your belongings in a "day-pack", as the locals do (can be bought at any street corner—joggers' arm-bands have also been suggested). Pickpockets and purse-snatchers operate at bus stops, bus turnstiles and among passengers while the bus is passing through a tunnel; also at street-corner newsagent stands. The centre of Rio can be dangerous at weekends, when most of the police force is patrolling the beaches. Among the more problematic areas at any time are Dois Irmãos, Santa Teresa, on Copacabana's Av. Atlântica and Rua Belfort Roxo, on the train between the zoo and Maracaña stadium, Pão de Açúcar, Corcovado, Quinta da Boa Vista, Jardim Botânico/Jóquei Clube racecourse area, and beyond Leblon out to Barra da Tijuca. To avoid swindling in bars, especially if sitting outside, pay as soon as you receive your order (although contrary to custom) and always ask for an itemized bill and check your change; alternatively, pay at the cash desk. Be especially careful after changing money in a public place; thieves often wait outside *câmbios*. Drivers, watch out for live snakes being thrown through open car windows: you jump out, the thief jumps in. The Tourist Police (Poltur) office is at Rua Humberto de Campos 319, Leblon, but, if robbed, you must report the incident at the station in the district where the incident occured.

It should be added that Rio remains a beautiful and fascinating city. Whilst warnings should not be ignored, using your common sense should help towards a trouble-free visit.

Addresses

British Consulate, Praia do Flamengo 284, T 552-1422 (UK citizens can use telephone to phone UK at normal rates).
Irish Consulate, Rua Fonseca Teles 18, CEP 20940, T 254-0960.
Swiss Consulate, Rua Cândido Mendes 157, 11° andar, Cx. Postal 744-7c-00, T 222-1896 (open 0900-1200, Mon.-Fri.).
West German Consulate-General, Rua Presidente Carlos de Campos 417, T 285-2333.
French Consulate, Av. Pres. Antônio Carlos, 58, T 220-6022.
Austrian Consulate, Av. Atlântica 3804, CEP 22070, T 227-0040/048/049.
Netherlands Consulate, Rua Sorocaba 570. T 246-4050. (Dutch newspapers here; also at KLM office on Av. Rio Branco.)
Swedish Consulate-General, Praia do Flamengo 344, 9° andar, 22210, Rio de Janeiro, T 552-2422.
Danish Consulate, Praia do Flamengo 284, Apt. 101, T 552-6149.
U.S. Consulate General, Avenida Presidente Wilson, 147, T 252-8055.
USICA Reference Library, U.S. Consulate General, Av. Presidente Wilson 147.
Argentine Embassy, Praia de Botafogo 242; Consul, Praia de Botafogo 228, T 551-5198, very helpful over visas, 1130-1600.
Uruguayan Embassy, Rua Artur Bernardes 30.
Paraguayan Embassy, Av. N.S. de Copacabana 427, room 303, 0900-1300, visas US$5.
Venezuelan Consulate, Praia de Botafogo 242, 5th floor, open 0830-1300.
Australian Trade Commission, Rua Voluntários da Pátria 45, 5°, Botafogo, T 286-7922; for visas etc. you must go to Brasília.
Y.M.C.A., Rua da Lapa, 40.
The British Council, Rua Elmano Cardim 10 (formerly Rua Iguatu), Urca. T 295-7782.
The British School of Rio de Janeiro, Rua da Matriz 76.
The American School of Rio de Janeiro, Estrada da Gávea 132.
Sociedade Brasileira de Cultura Inglesa, Av. Graça Aranha 327, and in Copacabana. T 227-0147.
American Chamber of Commerce for Brazil, Praça Pio Dez 15, 5th floor.
American Society and American Club, Avenida Rio Branco 123, 21st floor.
German Cultur-Institut (Goethe), Av. Graça Aranha 419, 9th floor; open Mon., Wed., Thurs., 1000-1400, 1500-1930, Fri., 1000-1300.
S. Africa Consulate, Rua Voluntários da Pátria 45, 9th floor, Botafogo, T 266-6246.
Policia Federal, Av. Venezuela 2 (near Praça Mauá), for renewal of 90-day visa, US$4.
Poltur, Tourist Police, Rua Humberto de Campos 319, Leblon (unmarked door beside main police station, helpful, English spoken, will type report for insurance).

Sports Paissandu Athletic Club, Av. Afrânio de Melo Franco 330, Leblon—Tennis, bowls, swimming. Leme Tennis Club, Rua Gustavo Sampaio 74—Tennis. Rio de Janeiro Country Club, Rua Prudente de Morais 1597, Ipanema—Tennis and swimming. Gávea Golf and Country Club, Estrada da Barra da Tijuca 2005—Golf and polo. Itanhangá Golf Club, Jacarepaguá, visiting cards from Avenida Rio Branco 26, 16th floor. Clube Hípico Brasileiro, Av. Borges de Medeiros 2448, Jardim Botânico—Riding. Iate Clube do Rio de Janeiro, Av. Pasteur, Botafogo—Yachting.

Squash at Rua Cândido Mendes 581, Glória, T 242-0642. Ice skating at Barra Shopping, Av. das Américas 466, Barra da Tijuca. Roller-skating at *Roxy-Roller*, opp. Clube de Regatas Flamengo on Av. Borges de Medeiros, Lagoa.

Travel Agents   Grand Tours, Av. Copacabana 166, T 237-0658; American Express Kontik Franstur, Av. Atlântica 2316A; Roxy, Av. Winston Churchill 60, helpful, rec. (ask for Michael Oeary who speaks English); Exprinter, Av. Rio Branco, 128 (said to be particularly good for money-changing); Itatiaia Turismo, Av. Rio Branco 120, helpful, will sometimes change money; Creditur, Av Almirante Barroso 63, suite 2508, for non IATA flights to N. America and Europe; for cheap flights to Europe, Líneas Aéreas Paraguayas, Rua Santa Luzia 827 and A.G.S. Viagem e Turismo Lda, same street No. 799, T 262-5867 (N.B. LAP will not accept American Express cards); Brazilian Holidays, Rua Visconde de Pirajá 414, Suite 819/820, T 267-5749, Ipanema, English and German spoken, helpful regarding tickets and information; Soletur, Visconde de Pirajá 550, sala 1708, rec. Victor Hummel, Av. Presidente Vargas 290/4, T 223-1262, Swiss-run, rec. T 231-1800. Also Swiss-run and highly rec., South American Turismo Ltda, Av. N. S. de Copacabana 788, 6th and 7th floors, T 255-2345. Americatur, Av. Rio Branco 156 (T 262-4293, 262-2659) runs tours on the Rio São Francisco, flying from Rio to Belo Horizonte (**see page 294**). Regular sightseeing tours operated by Gray Line (294-0393), American Sightseeing (236-3551), Sul América (257-4235), Canbitur (of Copacabana), Passamar Turismo, Av. Rio Branco 25 (233-8883, 233-4833, 253-1125; also at *Hotel Nacional*). Adrianotour, T 208-5103, for guided tours, reservations and commercial services (English, French, German and Spanish spoken). For a good, private tour, contact Prof. Roquette, a professor of history, who charges US$20 p.p., T 322-4872. Enasa, for Amazon river travel, Rua Uruguaiana 39 (Sala 1402); they try to sell tickets on first-class boats only.

Tourist Information   There are several excellent information centres. Embratur, Rua Mariz e Barros 13, near Praça da Bandeira, T 273-2212, gives information on the whole country. Touring Club do Brasil, Pres. Antônio Carlos 130 and Av. Brasil 4294 (out of town) no English spoken. Riotur (for the city of Rio), Rua da Assembléia 10, 8th floor (T 297-7117), sells a huge map of the city. Official Riotur information stands at Pão de Açúcar cablecar station (0800-2000); Marina da Glória, Flamengo; Rodoviária Novo Rio (the bus station—0600-2400; very friendly and helpful in finding accommodation). Riotur also has a multilingual telephone service operating 24 hours, T 580-8000. Flumitur (for the state of Rio de Janeiro) at Rio International Airport, helpful with hotel information and Rua da Assembléia 10, 8th floor, very helpful.

N.B. Tourist packs are sold for US$20 at the International Airport—these contain a map, restaurant list and a blank passport facsimile, which has no legal standing even though they may try to persuade you otherwise. Best guide to Rio, with excellent map, *Guia Quatro Rodas do Rio* in Portuguese and English, US$3. *Guia Rex* street guide, US$8. *Guia Schaeffer Rio de Janeiro* (US$3) is an excellent sheet. Also, *The Insider's Guide to Rio de Janeiro*, an annual guide book by Christopher Pickard, published by Streamline Ltda, Av. N.S. de Copacabana 605/1210 (distributed in UK and Europe by Roger Lascelles, 47 York Rd., Brentford, Middlesex, TW8 0OP, and in USA by Luso-Brazilian Books, 32 Nevins St., Brooklyn, New York 11217). Many hotels provide guests with the weekly *Itinerário* (*Rio This Month*).

Maps are available from Riotur information desks (US$1), Touring Clube do Brasil (US$0.40), newsstands (US$0.65), touring agencies and hotels; Geomapas tourist map is clear, US$1.20. Also maps free from H. Stern, the jeweller, at Rua Visconde do Pirajá 490, Ipanema. Also from Paulini, Rua Lélio Gama 75 (outside the entrance of the downtown tram station): topographical and other maps of Brazil and of South America. **Note** Tourist agencies do not normally provide lists of cheap accommodation for travellers; some initiative is required.

Laundromats   Lavandaria Automática, Rua Barão do Flamengo 42, and Rua Bambina 164 (Botafogo); Automática do Catete, Rua Andrade Pertence 42, Loja 6; Fénix, Rua do Catete 214, Loja 20; Rua Marques de Abrantes, about No. 80 (Flamengo); Laundromat at 1224 Av. N.S. de Copacabana. In Rio Sul are self-service laundrettes such as Lavlev, about US$3-4 for a machine, including detergent and drying, 1 hr.

Doctor   Rio Health Collective, Av. das Américas 4430, sala 303, Barra da Tijuca, C.E.P. 22600, T 325-9300, ext. 44, for medical referral service, Mon.-Fri., 0900-1400 (but 24-hr phone service for *emergencies only*), which will direct you to doctors of all specializations, in languages other than Portuguese, belonging to a non-profit organization designed for travellers' use (any contributions gratefully received). N.B. the doctors and clinics to which foreigners are directed are in the private sector and therefore usually expensive (i.e. make sure you have medical insurance). Vaccinations at Saude de Portos, Praça 15 de Novembro. Policlínica, Av. Nilo Peçanha 38, rec. for diagnosis and investigation. Hospital Miguel Couto, Mário Ribeiro 117, Gávea, has a casualty ward (free), but no eye doctors T 274-2121; these can be found at Hospital Souza Aguiar, Praça da República III (casuality ward also free), T 296-4114.

Dentist   English-speaking, Amílcar Werneck de Carvalho Vianna, Av. Pres. Wilson 165, suite 811.

Banks   Lloyds Bank (ex-BOLSA), Rua da Alfândega 33; Banco Internacional (Bank of America and Royal Bank of Canada), Rua do Ouvidor 90; Banco Holandês Unido, Rua do Ouvidor 101; Citibank, Rua Assembléia 100; The First National Bank of Boston, Av. Rio Branco 110; Banco de Crédito Real de Minas Gerais, S.A., Av. Rio Branco 116; Banco Lar Brasileiro, Rua do Ouvidor 98; Banco Econômico, Rua Miguel Couto 131, 2nd floor (accepts Master Charge); and many others. Banks are open 1000 to 1630. Closed on Sat. Banco do Brasil at the International Airport is open always. Banks use the legal tourist exchange rate.

Exchange Houses American Express, Av. Atlântica 2316, Copacabana; at Exprinter, Av. Rio Branco 57A, cash and cheques (good rates also at their Av. N.S. de Copacabana branch); Casa Piano, Rua Visconde de Pirajá 365, Ipanema (cash only), also Praça da Paz, Ipanema, and Av. Rio Branco 88 (cash only); Turismo Portuguesa, Av. Rio Branco 45; Cualitour, Av. Rio Branco 25B; Behar Turismo, Av. Rio Branco esq. Teófilo Ottoni/Visc. de Inhaúma, rec. for cheques; nearby Casa São Jorge changes Amex cheques at parallel rate; Kontik, Av. Presidente Vargas 309, Irmãos Capello, Av. Rio Branco 31A; Sultur, Av. Rio Branco 151C, Xanadu, Rua do Rosário 171. In Copacabana (where parallel market rates are generally worse than in centre): P. M. (no travellers' cheques), Av. Copacabana 391-B and Av. Rio Branco 124-A; Sala 309 (3rd floor), Ed. Monte Carmel, Av. N.S. de Copacabana 680, good rates; Paladium Travel, 3rd floor of Shopping Cassino Atlântico, Ipanema end of Av. Atlântica, Copacabana, Kraus, Praça Pio X 55, 2nd floor (German spoken), and Passamar, Rua Siqueira Campos 7. (Try Atlântica Joias, Rua Fernando Mendes 5). **N.B.** Many *câmbios* will give you the parallel rate for cash, but a worse rate for cheques; some will also change US$ cheques for US$ cash with a 4% commission. These transactions are not strictly legal, so you will have to look around for the *câmbios* that do them.

Cables Embratel, Av. President Vargas 1012. Telegrams may be sent through any post office. Larger offices have telex.

Telephones Buy *fichas* for calls from public phones (in acoustic shells) at chemists and news stands; they are hard to come by late at night. International calls at Av. Copacabana 462, 2nd floor, international airport, Praça Tiradentes (centre), Rodoviária, or Rua Dias da Cruz 182-4, 24 hrs, 7 days a week, or at Santos Dumont airport, 1st floor (0530-2300). Collect calls, national and international, dial 107 (no charge).

Post Office Central Post Office, Rua Primeiro de Março, at corner of Rua do Rosário. Overseas parcels may be sent from here. **Poste Restante** American Express, Av. Atlântica 2316, Copacabana (for customers), and all large post offices (letters held for a month, rec., US$0.10 per letter).

Portuguese Instituto Brasil-Estados Unidos, Av. Copacabana 690, 5° andar, only for those with student visas; tourists will be referred to private teachers. Good English library at same address. Curso Feedback, branches in Botafogo, Centre, Copacabana and Ipanema (addresses in yellow pages): individual tuition from girl students about US$10/hr., rec.

Rail Central do Brasil Railway to São Paulo and Belo Horizonte. To São Paulo there are only the "Santa Cruz" night trains with sleepers and lounge cars (from US$4 for a seat to US$15 for a double cabin, 9 hrs., leaving 2300— rec., book cabins 2 weeks ahead for weekend journeys, 3-5 days for weekdays in holiday times), provision of service is erratic, check! Thurs. and Sat. night service to Belo Horizonte (US$10 pullman, US$20 bunk, US$27 cabin for two, 11 hrs., leaves 2100). No service to Brasília. There are suburban trains to Nova Iguaçu, Nilópolis, Campo Grande and elsewhere. Buses marked "E. Ferro" go to the railway station. For guided excursions by rail, contact Platur.

Airports Rio has two airports. The Santos Dumont airport on Guanabara Bay, right in the city, is used exclusively for Rio-São Paulo shuttle flights (US$55), air taxis and private planes. The shuttle services operate every half hour throughout the day from 0630 to 2230. Sit on right-hand side for views to São Paulo, other side coming back. The main airport (Galeão), on Governador Island, some 16 km. from the centre of Rio, is in two sections, international and domestic (including Vasp and Transbrasil's jet shuttle from Rio to São Paulo). Duty-free shops are well-stocked, but not especially cheap. The Real company runs an air-conditioned bus (*frescão*) from Galeão to Santos Dumont Airport, via the city centre, every half-hour (for Flamengo/Catete hotel area, take this bus, then a taxi from Santos Dumont) and another goes to Copacabana at approx. half-past every hour, with space for baggage, US$2 (also stops at Rodoviária). Air-conditioned taxis (Cootramo and Transcopass) have fixed rates (US$6 downtown, US$8 Copacabana) and you buy a ticket at the counter near the arrivals gate before getting into the car. The hire is for taxi, irrespective of number of passengers, and therefore the possibility of sharing with other passengers arises. Ordinary taxis also operate with the normal meter reading—make sure you are given the card which gives the number to phone if you are overcharged (about US$8 downtown, US$10 Copacabana). A good policy is to check at the Riotur counter before leaving, for folders, maps and advice; watch out for pirate taxis, whose drivers will want to charge up to US$50! Town bus No. 322 goes to Rio International airport, first one with direction Bananal. No bank or *câmbio* in departure hall of airport, and the 24-hour banks before passport control give worse rates than the lift attendants, etc. (if you can wait, on arrival, till you get into town, so much the better). There is a wider choice of restaurants before passport control, but seats for flights are not allocated until after passport control. We have been told that X-ray machines at Galeão are not safe for film.

Buses Bus fares to the following cities, with approximate journey times (book ahead if you can), are as follows:

	distance km.	ordinary US$	executive US$	leito US$	hours
São Paulo	434	6.00	9.00	12.00	6
Brasília	1,134	20.00	31.00	40.00	20
Belo Horizonte	429	8.00	12.00	16.00	7
Curitiba	839	13.00	—	26.00	11
Florianópolis	1,154	16.00	—	32.00	20
Foz do Iguaçu	1,500	18.00	—	36.00	23
Porto Alegre	1,603	24.00	—	48.00	26
Juiz de Fora	177	3.00	4.50	—	4
Vitória	519	8.00	—	16.00	8
Salvador	1,690	25.00	—	50.00	28
Recife	2,309	34.00	—	68.00	38
Fortaleza	2,861	45.00	—	90.00	48
São Luís	3,093	49.00	—	—	50
Belém	3,187	52.00	—	—	52

To Campo Grande, 21 hrs. with Andorinha, US$32. To Santos, 6 a day with Normandy, US$6, 7½ hrs., but not along coast road—which can only be done by taking local buses (Atlântico to São Sebastião, US$6, 7 hrs., 1030 and 1800) and changing at Ubatuba, Caraguatatuba or São Sebastião. The trip to Santos along the coast road can be done in one day, in either direction, but it needs at least a 0600 start. To Ouro Preto, direct bus (Util) at 0830 and 2330 daily US$6.50, 7½ hrs.

International: Asunción, 1,511 km. via Foz do Iguaçu, 30 hrs., (Pluma) US$35, *leito* US$70; Buenos Aires (Pluma), via Porto Alegre and Santa Fe, 44 hrs., 1230, US$70, *leito* US$140 (book 2 days in advance); Montevideo, only from São Paulo; Santiago de Chile, US$100 with Pluma or Gral. Urquiza, about 70 hours. The Buenos Aires and Montevideo services are fully booked a week in advance.

You are allowed to sleep at the bus station, if you don't lie down. The main bus station (the Rodoviária, at Av. Rodrigues Alves, corner with Av. Francisco Bicalho, just past the docks, reached by buses 104 from the centre, 127 and 128 from Copacabana and 136, 456, 171 and 172 from Flamengo, or taxi about US$8), has a Riotur information centre. From Rodoviária, take bus 104 to Largo do Machado or to Catete for central location with buses and cheap hotels. The local bus teminal is just outside the Rodoviária: turn right as you leave and run the gauntlet of taxi drivers. **If you do need a taxi collect a ticket**, which ensures against overcharging, from the official at the head of the taxi queue. On no account give the ticket to the taxi driver.

Hitch Hiking To hitch to Belo Horizonte or Brasília, take a C-3 bus from Av. Presidente Antônio Carlos to the railway station, cross through the station to a bus station, and catch the Nova Iguaçu bus. Ask to be let off at the Belo Horizonte turn off. For the motorway entrance north and south take bus 392 or 393 from Praça São Francisco.

Ferry Service From the "barcas" at Praça 15 de Novembro, ferry boats and launches cross every 10 mins. to Niterói (20-30 mins., US$0.05); to Paquetá Island (70-90 mins., **see page 272** for fares). There are also hydrofoils ("aerobarcas") to Niterói every 10 mins. (about 10 mins., US$0.70). The Niterói ferry service is still being maintained, despite the competition from the 14 km. bridge linking the two sides of Guanabara Bay. (The approach to the bridge is on the elevated motorway from the centre, or via Av. Rio de Janeiro, in the Caju district; take the Av. Rodrigues Alves past the docks.) Bus 999 from the Passeio Público crosses the bridge.

The Suburbs of Rio de Janeiro

Copacabana, built on a narrow strip of land—only a little over 4 square kilometres—between mountain and sea, has one of the highest population densities in the world: 62,000 per square kilometre, or 250,000 in all. Its celebrated curved beach backed by skyscraper apartments is an unforgettable "must" for visitors. On all Rio's beaches you should take a towel or mat to protect you against sandflies; in the water stay near groups of other swimmers; bathing is generally dangerous.

Copacabana began to develop when the Old Tunnel was built in 1891 and an electric tram service reached it. Week-end villas and bungalows sprang up; all have now gone. In the 1930s the Copacabana Palace Hotel was the only tall building; it is now one of the lowest on the beach. The opening of the New Tunnel

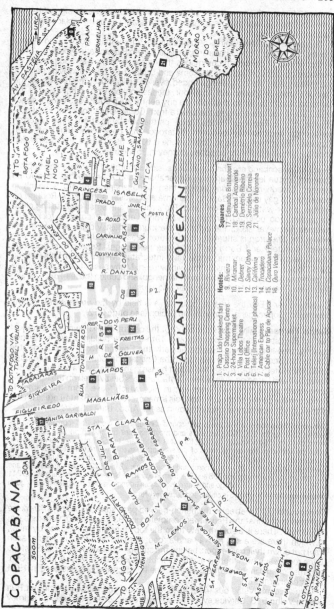

COPACABANA

500m

30A

ATLANTIC OCEAN

1. Praça Lido (weekend fair)
2. Cassino Shopping Centre
3. 24-hour Supermarket
4. Villa Lobos Theatre
5. Post Office
6. Teleri (International phones)
7. American Express
8. Cable car to Pão de Açúcar

Hotels:
9. Riviera
10. Miramar
11. Debret
12. Savoy Othon
13. Califórnia
14. Trocadero
15. Copacabana Palace
16. Ouro Verde

Squares
17. Edmundo Bittencourt
18. Cardeal Arcoverde
19. Demétrio Ribeiro
20. Serzidelo Correia
21. Julio de Noronha

in the 1940s led to an explosion of population which shows no sign of having spent its force. Buildings of less than 12 storeys are still being replaced by high flats and luxury hotels.

There is almost everything in this fabulous "city within a city". The shops, mostly in Avenida Copacabana and the Rua Barata Ribeiro, are excellent. A fort at the far end of the beach commands the entrance to Rio Bay and prevents a seashore connection with the Ipanema and Leblon beaches. However, parts of the military area are now being handed over to civilian use, the first being the Parque Garota de Ipanema at Arpoador, the fashionable Copacabana end of the Ipanema beach. Buses to and from the city centre are plentiful and cheap, about US$0.10. If you are going to the centre from Copacabana, look for "Castelo", "Praça 15", "E. Ferro" or "Praça Mauá" on the sign by the front door. "Aterro" means the expressway between Botafogo and downtown Rio (not open Sundays). From the centre to Copacabana is easier as all buses in that direction are clearly marked. Aterro bus does journey in 15 minutes.

Beyond Copacabana are the beautiful seaside suburbs of Ipanema and Leblon; they are a little less built-up than Copacabana, and their beaches tend to be cleaner, though no less dangerous, than Copacabana's. (Posto 9 beach in Ipanema is a gay beach.) Backing Ipanema and Leblon is the Lagoa Rodrigo de Freitas, a salt-water lagoon on which Rio's rowing and small-boat sailing clubs are active; too polluted for bathing. Beyond Leblon the coast is rocky; the Avenida Niemeyer skirts the cliffs on the journey past Vidigal, a small beach where the *Sheraton* is situated, to the outer seaside suburbs of São Conrado (beach polluted) and Barra da Tijuca (see next page). Buses from Botafogo Metro terminal to Ipanema: some take integrated Metro-Bus tickets, saving 25 % ; look for the blue signs on the windscreen. Many buses from Copacabana to Ipanema (buses 154 and 158 from Flamengo) and Leblon (buses 158, 434 and 488 from Flamengo, continuing to Barra da Tijuca).

On New Year's Eve the festival of Iemanjá is held by the *umbandistas* on the beaches of Copacabana, Ipanema and Leblon (**see page 252**).

Santa Teresa, a hilly inner suburb SW of the centre, well known as the coolest part of Rio, still has many colonial and 19th-century buildings, set in narrow, curving, tree-lined streets. See particularly the Convent (only the outside; the Carmelite nuns do not admit visitors), the Chácara do Céu Museum (**see page 253**), the Hotel Santa Teresa (the oldest house in the area), Vista Alegre, the Rua Aprazível, and Largo de Guimarães. Santa Teresa is best visited on the traditional open-sided trams, the only ones left in Rio, which leave from the Largo da Carioca in the centre of the city, for Dois Irmãos, crossing to Santa Teresa on top of the old 18th-century aqueduct known as the Arcos (fare US$0.05).

Maracanã Stadium is one of the largest sports centres in the world. The football ground has seating capacity for 200,000 spectators and most matches are played on Sun. about 1700 (entrance from US$0.50-*geral-*, to US$2 for a seat, good, safe, to US$8; matches are worth going to for the fireworks and samba bands of the spectators, even if you're not a football fan. N.B. agencies charge about US$20). Buses 433, 434 and 455 from Copacabana; 433 and 434 from Flamengo; from Leblon, 464 via Ipanema and Copacabana; 221 and 231 from Castelo; 249 and 269 from Praça Tiradentes; and 238 and 239 from Praça 15 de Novembro; from Praça Mauá, 241 or 262; also Metro from Botafogo and centre. Hotels can arrange visits to football matches: good idea Sundays when the metro is closed and buses very full.

Corcovado (710 metres) is the hunch-backed peak surmounted by a 40-metre high statue of Christ the Redeemer completed in 1931, weighing, with its base, 1,200 tons. There is a superb view from the top (sometimes obscured by mist), to which there are a cog railway and a road; both car and train (30 mins. each way) put down their passengers behind the statue—there is a climb of 220 steps to the top, near which there is a café for light refreshments. Mass is held on Sun. in a small chapel in the statue pedestal. The floodlighting was designed in 1931 by Marconi himself.

Take a Cosme Velho bus (422, 497, 498) to the **cog railway station at Rua Cosme Velho 513**. Service every 10-20 minutes according to demand, journey time 10 minutes (cost: US$3 return; single tickets available). Minibuses also operate from the station, return trip (1 hour stop) US$1.50, tickets obtained from office. Also, a 206 bus does the very attractive run from Praça Tiradentes (or a 407 from Largo do Machado) to Silvestre (the railway has no stop here now). An active walk of one hour will bring one to the top, and the road is shady. (Best done in company; robberies are very common in this neighbourhood.) Coach trips tend to be rather brief. N.B. There is too much interference around the statue for taking video pictures.

Pão de Açúcar (Sugar Loaf, 396 metres) is a massive granite cone at the entrance to Guanabara Bay. The bird's eye view of the city and beaches is very beautiful. There is a restaurant (excellent location, mixed reports on food, closes 1900) and a playground for children on the Morro da Urca, half way up, where there are also shows at night (weekends and Mon., 2200). You can get refreshments at the top. On the small path that leads down in the direction of Morro Cara de Cão there are toucans and macaws in cages. Buses 107 or 442 (from the centre or Flamengo) and 511 or 500 "jardinière" (from Copacabana) take you to the cable-car station, Av. Pasteur 520, at the foot.

The cable car timetable: Praia Vermelha to Urca: first car goes up at 0800, and the last comes down at 2215. From Urca to Sugar Loaf the first connecting cable car goes up at 0815 and the last leaves the summit at 2000; the return trip costs US$2.50 (US$1.25 to Morro da Urca, half-way up). The old cableway has been completely rebuilt. Termini are now ample and efficient and the present Italian cable cars carry 75 passengers. Even on the most crowded days there is little queuing. Beware of thieves at the cable car starting point. If you want to climb the Pão de Açúcar, contact the Clube Excursionista de Rio de Janeiro, or the rock-climbing club, Andre Illa and Xavier de Silvera, Copacabana, T 237-5229. There are 35 routes up the mountain, with various degrees of difficulty (best months for climbing: April to August).

Tijuca National Park, open 0600-2100, is for those interested in taking a forest walk through mountain scenery. An approximately 2-3 hr. walk will bring you to the summit of the Pico da Tijuca (1,012 metres), which gives a good idea of the tropical vegetation of the interior and a fine view of the bay and its shipping. On entering the park at Alto de Boa Vista, follow the sparse signposts to Bom Retiro, a good picnic place (1½ hrs walk), passing by the Cascatinha Taunay, Mayrink Chapel (built 1860) and the restaurant *A Floresta*. At Bom Retiro the road ends and there is another hour's walk up a fair footpath to the summit; take the path from the right of the Bom Retiro drinking fountain; not the more obvious steps from the left. The last part consists of steps carved out of the solid rock; take care of children at the summit as there are several sheer drops, invisible because of bushes. The route is shady for almost its entire length. The panels painted in the Mayrink Chapel by Cândido Portinari have been replaced by copies and the originals will probably be installed in the Museu de Arte Moderna. Maps of the Park are available.

Take a 221 from Praça 15 de Novembro, 233 or 234 bus from the Rodoviária, or 454 from Copacabana or from Praça Sáenz Pena, Tijuca (reached by metro) to Alto da Boa Vista, for the park entrance. Other places of interest not passed on the walk to the peak are the Paul and Virginia Grotto, the Vista do Almirante and the Mesa do Imperador (viewpoints). A good restaurant in Parque Floresta is *Os Esquilos*. Allow at least 5 to 6 hrs. for the excursion. Also, one of the Raymundo Castro Maia museums is nearby (see page 253).

Barra da Tijuca This new and very rapidly developing residential area can be reached from the Tijuca Forest by continuing on the 233 or 234 bus (from Praça Sáenz Pena, very good views of São Conrado and Barra), or from the city bus station at Rua São José, from Santos Dumont airport, and from Copacabana via Leblon beach (bus 553). From Botafogo metro terminus, take bus 524. Robberies on the buses have been reported.

Barra da Tijuca is also one of the principal recreation areas of Rio, the prime attraction being its 20-km. sandy beach, with good waves for surfing. Bus 700 from Praça São Conrado (terminal of bus 553 from Copacabana) goes the full length of the beach to Recreio dos Bandeirantes. Apart from this, there are innumerable bars and restaurants, campsites (**see page 259**), motels and hotels. The facilities include Riocenter, a 600,000 sq.m. convention complex and the huge Barra Shopping and Carrefour shopping centres. Watch the hang-gliders jumping from the hilltops at weekends. Live concerts on São Conrado beach during summer (Nov.-Feb.).

The Autódromo (motor racing track) is beyond Barra in the Jacarepaguá district. The Brazilian Grand Prix is held here or at Interlagos, São Paulo, alternately in January.

Viewpoints Apart from the Pico da Tijuca, Corcovado and Pão de Açúcar, splendid views of different parts of Rio can be seen from the Vista Chinesa (420 metres), where from a Chinese-style pavilion one can see the inland lake (the Lagoa), Ipanema and Leblon; the Mesa do Imperador (Emperor's Table) and Vista do Almirante (Admiral's View) in the Tijuca Forest; and the Mirante de Dona Marta (340 metres) off the Corcovado road, with the same direction of view as the Corcovado, but as it is lower the details can be seen more clearly. There is as yet no public transport to any of these places.

Paquetá Island in Guanabara Bay can be visited by more or less two-hourly ferry services from Praça Quinze de Novembro (fare US$0.15 by boat, 1 hr., US$1 by hydrofoil, every ½ hr., 20 mins. journey, which more than doubles its price Sats., Suns. and holidays). Horse-drawn carriages hire for US$6 per hr. (many have harnesses which cut into the horse's flesh). Tour by "trenzinho", a tractor pulling trailers, US$0.80. Bicycles for hire from US$1 per hr. (deposit US$2). Very crowded at weekends and public holidays, but usually very quiet during the week, though there can be aircraft noise. Reasonable food and drink prices.

Hotel Paquetá, E, *Flamboyant* and *Lido. Porto Fino Restaurant*, expensive and poor food.

Other boat trips, by *bateau mouche* (restaurant), around Guanabara Bay depart from Av. Néstor Moreira 11, Botafogo, first two trips at 0930, third at 1420, fares from US$25. Other companies: Aquatur (T 230-9273), Brazilian Marina Turismo, Camargo (T 275-0643), Passamar, Siqueira Campos 7 (T 236-4136), Greyline (T 274-7146), Soletur (Bay trips Sat. and Sun. only) and American Sightseeing, Av. N.S. Copacabana 605, Sala 1204 (T 236-3551). The last three offer a day cruise, including lunch, to Jaguanum Island (**see page 279**, under Itacuruçá) and a sundown cruise around Guanabara Bay, also deep-sea fishing expeditions and private charters.

Entering Rio from the W, an alternative to the BR-101 and Avenida Brasil, is to leave BR-101 on the road to Santa Cruz, continuing 6 km. to the fishing village of Sepetiba, quiet other than at weekends. Along the coast is Pedra de Guaratiba, from where you join Avenida das Américas, turning off right soon afterwards to Ponta do Picão and Guaratiba, a pretty seaside resort on a rocky, narrow, steep ledge between mountain and sea (good beaches and a playground for the rich). Another 2 km. along the main road is another (unmarked) right turn leading to a restaurant at the summit, with fantastic views, then down to Praia de Grumari, which is unspoilt except for 2 restaurants and a campsite (US$1 p.p.). It is then 30 km. to Copacabana, via Recreio dos Bandeirantes (Dieter Reinmuth).

The State of Rio de Janeiro: East from Rio

Niterói, founded in 1573, the ex-capital of the State of Rio de Janeiro, across the bay by bridge or ferries, is a city with 386,000 population.

Frequent ferry boat and hydrofoil service (**see page 268**) from Praça 15 de Novembro, Rio. There is a Flumitur tourist information booth to the right of the ferry-boat station. Nearby you can take the 33 bus (marked "via Froes") to the beaches of Icaraí, São Francisco and Jurujuba on the bay, a beautiful ride. Sit on the right-hand side. A few minutes' walk from where the bus route ends at Jurujuba are the attractive twin beaches of Adão and Eva, with lovely views of Rio across the bay. From Praça General Gomes Carneiro, near the ferry boats, take a 38 bus to Piratininga, Itaipu and Itacoatiara, fabulous ocean beaches and the best in the area, about 40 minutes' ride through picturesque countryside. The beaches inside the bay, though calm, are often overcrowded and polluted, but no more so than those opposite in Rio. The forts on this side of the bay include Santa Cruz (16th century, still a military establishment), Barão do Rio Branco (1633), Gragoatá and Nossa Senhora da Boa Viagem.

You should also visit the church of Boa Viagem (1633), built on an island connected to the mainland by a short causeway, a few minutes' walk from Icaraí beach. Nearby, on Rua Tiradentes, is the interesting Antônio Parreira Museum. The Museu de Arqueologia de Itaipu is in the ruins of the 18th century Santa Teresa Convent, and also covers the archaeological site of Duna Grande on Itaipu beach.

The Rio-Niterói bridge (Ponte Costa e Silva) has a length of 14 km. Toll for cars, US$0.30. Motorway connection to centre of Rio. Bus 999 from the corner of Senador Dantas and Av. Beira Mar, Rio, crosses the bridge to Niterói and Icaraí (US$0.30); also 996 and 998 from the Jardim Botânico (all three go to the Rodoviária in Rio).

Hotels *Novotel Rio-Niterói*, Praia de Gragoatá, Telex 021-7252, A; *Samanguaia*, D; *Niterói Palace*, Rua Andrade Neves 134, D-C; *Imperial*, D.

Clubs   Rio Cricket, bus 57 from ferry. Rio Sailing, bus 33 marked "via Froes".

Electric Current   110 volts, A.C., 60 cycles.

To the east of Niterói lie a series of salt-water lagoons, the Lagos Fluminenses. Two small lakes lie behind the beaches of Piratininga and Itaipu near Niterói, but they are polluted and ringed by mud. The next lakes are much larger, those of Maricá and Saquarema; though they are still muddy, the waters are relatively unpolluted, and wild life abounds in the scrub and bush around the lagoons. At the outlet to the lake of Saquarema (turn right off the main road at Bacaxá) is the holiday village of **Saquarema**. Of particular interest is the little white church of Nossa Senhora de Nazaré (1675) built atop a green promontory jutting into the ocean. Saquarema is the centre for surfing in Brazil, and the national championships are held here each year in May. Beware of strong currents, though.

The largest lake is that of **Araruama,** famous for its medicinal mud. It is so large that it seems more like a bay than a lagoon. The salinity is extremely high, the waters calm, and almost the entire lake is surrounded by sandy beaches, making it very popular with families looking for safe, unpolluted bathing. The major industry of the area is salt, and all around one can see the saltpans and the wind pumps used to carry the water into the pans. At the eastern end of the lake lies the village of **São Pedro de Aldeia,** which, in spite of intensive development, still retains much of its colonial charm, and has a lovely Jesuit church built in 1723.

Hotels in the lake district: Saquarema: *Sol e Mar*, B; *Katy Motel*, B; *Pousada do Holandés*, Av Vilamar 377, at Itaúna beach, D, highly rec., many languages spoken by Dutch owner and his Brazilian wife (who runs the local day-care centre), good meals—follow the signs, or take a taxi (US$0.50) from Saquarema. Restaurant in Saquarema, *Tem Uma Né Chama Teré*, very good, in main square. Araruama: *Senzala*, on Iguabinha beach, 10 km. from Araruama, A with meals; *La Gondola*, on the lake beach, C, overpriced; *Parque Hotel*, A; *Lakes Hotel*, over the bus station, A; *Chalés do Coqueiral*, chalets on lake beach, A. São Pedro de Aldeia: *Solar de Iguaba*, C; *Vilabranca Village*, over 100 chalets, A with meals, and *Costa do Sol*, A, on Iguaba Grande beach, 14 km. from São Pedro. At Ponta Negra is *Pousada Colonial*, suites and bungalows in B

The ocean beaches beside these lagoons, except for the sheltered coves of Ponta Negra and Saquarema, are rough and lonely. The whole area is perfect for camping; there are campsites (including Camping Clube do Brasil) at Araruama (close to the *Parque Hotel*) and São Pedro de Aldeia. A very steep road connects the beaches of Itaipu and Itacoatiara with BR-106 (and on to Araruama) via the village of Itaipu-Açu, with beach and good camping. Most maps do not show a road beyond Itaipu-Açu; it is certainly too steep for buses.

An alternative to the route from Niterói to Araruama through the lagoons is via Manilla, Itaboraí and Rio Bonito, on the BR-101 and RJ-124; this is a fruit-growing region.

Cabo Frio, 156 km. from Rio, is a popular holiday and week-end haunt of Cariocas because of its cool weather, beaches, scenery, sailing and good under-water swimming (but mosquitoes are a problem). The ocean beach is much less frequented than the bay beach. The São Mateus fort nearby was built by the French; it is in a state of disrepair. If in the area, take a look at the huge church under construction at Arraial do Cabo nearby; it totally dominates the town (bus every 20 mins. from Cabo Frio).

Hotels   *Marliru Acapulco*, A; *Cabo Frio Sol* (motel), C. 20 other hotels with descending prices down to *Caravela* and *Colonial*, both D. *Jangada*, Granaola 220, near canal, D, very friendly, good breakfast, rec. *Nanaque*, 2 blocks from bus station, follow signs, 3 blocks from sea, E with bath and breakfast, clean, highly rec.; two similar nearby. Youth Hostel, both sexes, open all year to IYHF members (F p.p., more for non-members), on Rua Kubitschek, 1 block from bus station, very friendly. 2 youth hostels in Arraial do Cabo, one at Escola Municipal Ione Nogueira (T 43-0369) and the other at Rua Gen. Bruno Martins 9881 (T 262-6360).

Camping Camping Clube do Brasil sites at Estrada dos Passageiros, near town; at Km. 135 on the Rio road, 4 km. outside town, in Palmeiras; and at Arraial do Cabo on Praia dos Anjos, crowded beach. 10 km. to S. Cambrás has a site at Estrada dos Passageiros. Also site at Cabo Yacht club.

Buses Rodoviária is 2 km. from centre. Bus from Rio every ½ hr., 2½ hrs., US$4. To Búzios, from local bus terminus in town centre, every hour, US$0.50.

Búzios, NE of Cabo Frio, is a resort built up in Portuguese colonial styles, with unmade roads so as to discourage fast drivers. It has 27 sandy coves, calm unpolluted waters (superb for windsurfing), beautiful scenery, plenty of good hotels and *pousadas* (mostly C upwards, e.g. *Casa D'elas Pousada,* and *Pousada do Sol,* Praia da Armaçaõ; *Pousada Casa de Pedra,* Trav. Lúcio A. Quintanilha 57, T (0246) 231499, D, TV, fridge, safe, in centre of town, rec.), but very expensive, as is everything else (except the vicious mosquitoes). Best route from Rio (2 hrs. by car) is the paved road towards Macaé, with a paved turnoff to Búzios. Direct road from Cabo Frio (bus 45 mins.) is unpaved. Camping is allowed but dangerous. Tourist information office near bus station. Very crowded during Brazilian holiday season and extremely difficult to get hotel booking. Good restaurants: *Frank's* in Ossos and *Natural* in Armação (try the camarão tropical). Popular bars are *Delikatessen* and *Tempero's.* Tartaruga beach is not marked and not developed (take dirt road up small hill opp. *Pousada Baer Búzios*); there is a restaurant and snack bar in season.

Continuing to the north, one comes to the seaside resorts of Barra de São João, *Rio das Ostras* (*Hotel Saint Tropez,* C; *Hotel Mirante do Poeta,* C) and *Macaé* (Hotels: *Colonial,* C, friendly, helpful, comfortable; *Turismo* and *Panorama,* C; *Central,* Rua Rui Barbosa, E, clean, nice, friendly, good breakfast, secure parking), all containing sheltered coves with good swimming and scuba diving. Macaé is also the supply centre for the offshore oil industry so there are usually several foreigners in town enjoying a beer.

From Rio and Niterói a first class highway, the BR-101, runs NE past Macaé to Campos (bus Rio-Macaé 2½-3 hrs., every ½ hr., Mil e Um or Rápido Macaense; bus Macaé-Campos, 1¾ hrs., US$1.50). At Km. 222 is the Biological Reserve of Poço das Antas (2 hrs. drive from Rio; it is not open to the general public, for details, Delegacia Estadual do IBDF, Av. Pres. Antônio Carlos 607-12°, CEP 20.000, Rio de Janeiro). Many animals (including the *mico-leão* marmoset—this is its only natural habitat) roam in the forest.

Campos is a busy industrial city, some 276 km. (4½ hrs. by Mil e Um bus, hourly) from Rio de Janeiro (70 km. from Macaé). It stands 56 km. from the mouth of the Rio Paraíba, up which coffee planting originally spread to São Paulo state. Coffee is still grown near Campos, though the region is now one of the largest sugar-producing zones in Brazil. Important offshore oil discoveries have been made nearby. Town is quite interesting. Population: 174,000.

Hotels *Terraza Tourist,* D, 2-star; *Planície,* Rua 13 de Maio 56, D; *Palace,* Av. 15 de Novembro 143, D. *Silva,* some way behind church on municipal square, E, breakfast, clean, safe parking.

Travelling N, as an alternative to BR-101 to Vitória, one can take a detour inland, going through São Fidélis, Cambiasca, Itoacara and on to *Santo Antônio de Pádua,* 130 km. from Campos, a pleasant town on the Rio Pomba (*Hotel das Aguas,* a short walk from the centre, D, a resort hotel in a park with pool, health centre and bottling plant for the local mineral water which is used for treating cardiovascular illness; *Braga,* in town, E, clean, friendly, good food.) Take road No. 393 to Itaperuna, Bom Jesus do Itabapoana and into Espírito Santo, then road No. 484 to Guaçuí (*Grande Hotel Minas,* F, friendly, clean; *Restaurant Kontiki,* very good), one of the starting points for the Parque Nacional do Caparaó (see page 295). Then take the road 482 to Cachoeira do Itapemirim and the BR-101 (see page 280).

Petrópolis (population: 149,000) is a summer hill resort and industrial city at 840 metres, 68 km. N of Rio. It is reached by bus along a steep, scenic mountain toll road (US$1 weekdays, US$1.50 weekends). Until 1962 Petrópolis was the "summer capital" of Brazil; it was founded in 1843 as a summer refuge by Dom

Pedro II. Now it combines manufacturing industry (particularly textiles, which may be bought cheaply) with floral beauty and hill scenery. The Imperial Palace (Museu Imperial), which seems to express very faithfully what we know of Dom Pedro II's character, is a modest but elegant building, fully furnished and equipped, containing the Crown Jewels and other imperial possessions. It is assiduously well-kept: one might think the imperial family had left the day before one's visit, rather than in 1889. Open Tues.-Sun., 1200-1730. Entry US$0.30. Well worth a visit is the Gothic-style Cathedral, completed in 1925, which contains the tombs of the Emperor and Empress (guide in English, US$0.20).

Hotels *Casa do Sol,* 4-star hotel out on road to Rio, B; *Margaridas,* Monsenhor Bacelar 126, chalet-type hotel set in lovely gardens with swimming pool, charming proprietors, C; *Auto-Tour (Fazenda Inglesa)* at km. 51 on the Petrópolis by-pass, very chic, A, with meals; *Riverside Parque,* Rua Hermogéneo Silva 522, C; *Casablanca Center,* General Osório 28, B; *Casablanca,* Sete de Setembro beside Imperial Palace, C, good atmosphere in older part, pool, very clean; *Casablanca Palace,* Primeiro de Março 123, C; *Gran Solar (Pousado do Carmo),* Benjamin Constant 288, C; *Dom Pedro,* D, on main square, pleasant; *Comércio,* opp. bus station, E, with breakfast; *Pensão Esther,* Rua do Imperador, E, incl. breakfast.

Camping Associação Brasileira de Camping and YMCA, Araras district. Can reserve space through Rio YMCA, T 231-9860.

Restaurants *Churrascaria Majórica,* Av. do Imperador (ex 15 de Novembro) 754; *Mirthes Paranhos,* Irmãos d'Angelo 99; *Cantina Italiana,* Paulo Barbosa 48, clean, pleasant; *Maloca,* Wáshington Luís 466; *Bauernstube,* João Pessoa 297. *Vegetariano,* Rua do Imperador 288, sobreloja 1, good and cheap.

Attractions and Excursions Museu Ferreira da Cunha, Fernandes Vieira 390 (old road to Rio) shows large collection of arms, open Sat. and Sun. (only to groups; need to arrange in advance) 0900-1700. Summer home of air pioneer Santos Dumont, showing early inventions. Crystal Palace in Praça da Confluência, former imperial ballroom and now exhibition centre. Orquidário Binot, Rua Fernandes Vieira 390 (take bus to Vila Isabel; open Mon.-Sat., 0800-1100, 1300-1700), a huge collection of orchids from all over Brazil (plants may be purchased).

Buses leave from Rio every 10 mins. throughout the day (US$1.00). Return tickets are not available, so passengers must buy tickets for the return bus as soon as they arrive in Petrópolis. Journey 75 mins. each way. The ordinary buses leave from the Rodoviária in Rio; there is a new service of air-conditioned buses, hourly from 1100, from Av. Nilo Peçanha, US$1.50. There is a direct overnight bus from São Paulo.

Teresópolis (population: 80,000; 910 metres), near the Serra dos Órgãos, is 124 km. NE of Rio. It was the favourite summer residence of the Empress Teresa Cristina. See the Colina dos Mirantes hill, the Sloper and Iaci lakes, the Imbui and Amores waterfalls, and the Fonte Judith. Tourist information office some way from bus station (not very helpful). São Pedro festival on June 29 is celebrated with fireworks.

About 30,000 hectares of the Serra dos Órgãos, so called because their strange shapes are said to recall organ-pipes, are now a National Park. The main attraction is the precipitous Dedo de Deus (God's Finger) Peak. There is also the rock formation Mulher de Pedra 12 km. out on the Nova Friburgo road, and the Von Martinó natural-history museum. The highest point is the Pedra Açu, 2,400 metres. A path leads up the 2,260-metre Pedra do Silo, 3-4 hours' climb. Entrance to park, US$0.25. IBDF (The National Forestry Institute, office in Teresópolis, Serra dos Órgãos, Casa 8, CEP 25.950) has some hostels, US$4.60 full board, or US$3.10 first night, US$1.50 thereafter, a bit rough. Camping, US$0.50. A good way to see the Park is to do the Rio-Teresópolis-Petrópolis-Rio circuit; a scenic day trip. The Rio-Teresópolis road, which passes right next to the Serra dos Orgãos, is now a toll road (cars US$1, US$1.50 at weekends) from Km. 10.6.

Martin Crossland writes: Leave the Rodoviária bus station in Rio on the 0800 bus or before (Viação Teresópolis) for the 1¾-hour ride and up into the mountains to Teresópolis (sit on right side of bus). Upon arrival at the bus station, buy another ticket right away for Petrópolis (Viação Teresópolis) for the 1200 bus in order to get a good seat, as the bus fills rapidly. This gives you 2¾ hours to wander around. If you feel up to a steep ½-hr. climb, try the Colina dos Mirantes for a sweeping view of the city and surroundings. For the less energetic, a taxi is not dear.

The 90-minute drive from Teresópolis to Petrópolis is beautiful. (Sit on left side.) The views on either side are spectacular. Again, upon arrival in Petrópolis at 1330, buy your ticket to Rio (Facil or Unica). Take the 1715 bus "via Quitandinha", and you might catch the sunset over the mountains (in May, June, July, take the 1615 bus). This gives you time to visit most of the attractions listed in the city description.

Hotels   *São Moritz,* Swiss-style, outside on the Nova Friburgo road, km. 36, lowest rates, B, with meals; *Clube Caxangá,* resort-type, B; *Philips,* Rua Duval Fonseca, B; *Alpina,* Parque Imbui, on Petrópolis road, B; *Higino Palace,* Av. Oliveira Botelho 328, C, *Vila Nova do Paquequer,* Av. Alberto Torres 1149 (by the Guarani waterfall), D; *Várzea Palace,* Rua Sebastião Teixeira 41, E. *Florida,* Av. Lúcio Meira 467, E, with bargaining. Youth hostel: Retiro da Inglesa, 20 km. on road to Friburgo, Fazenda Boa Esperança (reservations, Rua Papa Pio XII 50, Jardim Cascata 25963 Teresópolis).

Camping   National Park, entrance to Teresópolis from Rio, full facilities; Quinta de Barra, km. 3 on Petrópolis road; Vale das Choupanas, km. 30 on Rio road.

Restaurants   *Taberna Alpina,* Duque de Caxias 131; *Cantina Riviera,* Praça Baltazar de Silveira 112; *La Cremaille,* Av. Feliciano Sodré 1012; *De Stéfano,* Av. Lúcio Meira 695. *Bar Gota d'Água,* Praça Baltasar da Silveira 16 for trout or feijoada (small but rec.).

Bus, Rio-Teresópolis   Buses leave every half-hour from Rodoviária. As return tickets are not issued, passengers should book for the return journey as soon as they arrive at Teresópolis. Time, 1¾ hrs. each way; fare US$1.50. From Teresópolis to Petrópolis, every 2 hrs. from 0900-2100, US$1.75.

Nova Friburgo (850 metres above sea-level), is a popular resort (around 30 hotels) during summer months, in a beautiful valley with excellent walking and riding possibilities. Founded by Swiss settlers from Fribourg, it can be reached by bus (US$3) from Rio (every half hour) in 3 hrs. or by car in 1 hr. 45 min. Pop.: 80,000. Cable car from Praça dos Suspiros 650 metres up the Morro da Cruz, for view of rugged country. Road to Teresópolis paved.

Hotels   *Bucsky,* 5 km. out on Niterói road, B, with meals; *Everest,* behind Chess Club, E, comfortable, good breakfasts; *Sans-Souci,* 1 km. out, B, with meals, D without; *Garlipp,* German-run, in chalets, B, with meals, at Muri, km. 70.5 from Rio, 10 km. from Nova Friburgo, T 0245-421330. Under same ownership is *Fazenda São João,* C, T (0245) 42-1304, 11 km. from *Garlipp* up a side road (impassable in the wet), riding, swimming, sauna, tennis, hummingbirds and orchids. Also *Mury Garden,* with swimming pool, B, with meals, 10 km. away at Muri (km. 70 on Niterói road). 12 km. from Nova Friburgo at Amparo is *Jequitibá,* C, T 0245-221831, sports facilities, restaurant.

Camping   Camping Clube do Brasil has sites on Niterói road, at Cônego (7 km. out) and Muri (10 km. out). Cambrás site also at Cônego, and private site at Fazenda Sanandu, 20 km. out on same road.

Restaurants   *Majórica,* traditional churrascaria. *Natural,* Rua Farinha Filho 2515, in centre, vegetarian, good and cheap.

The State of Rio de Janeiro: West from Rio

Volta Redonda stands on a broad bend of the Rio Paraíba at an altitude of 565 metres, 113 km. W of Rio along the railway to São Paulo. In 1942 it was a little village; today it has one of the largest steel works in Latin America and a population of 178,000. The mills are on the river bank and the town spreads up the surrounding wooded and gardened slopes.

Hotels   *Sider Palace,* Rua 33 No. 10, C; *Embaixador,* 1-star, E; *Bela Vista,* Alto de Boa Vista, on a hill overlooking town, B.

Visitors who have a permit from the Companhia Siderúrgica Nacional, Av. Treze de Maio 13, Rio de Janeiro (apply ten days in advance), or locally from the *Bela Vista* hotel, are allowed to inspect the mills. Visits start at 0900, and last 2½-3 hrs. The town can be reached from Rio by buses or minibuses in 2½ hrs., US$1.50.

North of Volta Redonda is Miguel Pereira, set in the mountain region with an excellent climate; nearby is the Javari lake, a popular recreational spot. Two *Hotel-Fazendas* (both C) near Miguel Pereira are *Quindins* and *Javari,* both with restaurant, swimming pool, sports grounds, etc. In town is the *Rei dos Montanhas,* F, Swiss-chalet style, clean, chilly at night. A tourist steam train runs from Miguel Pereira to Conrado, very scenic. Further north, and still in the mountains are the university centres of Vassouras and Valença; both are

RIO DE JANEIRO,
EASTERN SÃO PAULO &
SOUTHERN MINAS GERAIS
NOT TO SCALE

historical monuments. 35 km. from Valença is Conservatória, another colonial town. This region can also be reached via the Japeri turn-off on the BR-116 (a beautiful mountain drive). Some 30 km. W of Volta Redonda, in the town of Resende, is the Military Academy of Agulhas Negras. Grounds, with captured German guns of World War II, are open to the public. *Resende* can be reached by bus from Aparecida do Norte (**see page 317**), several daily, US$1.25, or from Rio, frequent, 1¾ hrs., US$1.75, also from São Paulo and Volta Redonda.

Hotels *Leme*, Rua Dr. Cunha Ferreira, 100 m. from Rodoviária, clean, basic, F p.p.; *Dormitórios Amazônica*, Dr. Cunha Ferreira esq. Praça Oliveira Botelho. Shops across river before railway station.

In the same region, 175 km. from Rio, is the small town of *Penedo,* which in the 1930s attracted Finnish settlers who brought the first saunas to Brazil. This weekend resort, popular with the prosperous of São Paulo and Rio, hippies and naturalists, also provides horseback riding, and swimming in the Portinho river. Some 33 km. beyond Penedo (part of road unpaved) is the small village of *Visconde de Mauá*, which has cheap lodgings: enquire at *Vendinha da Serra* (run by John from Leeds), excellent natural food restaurant and store. Fine scenery and walks, lots of holidaymakers, pleasant atmosphere; roads to 3 other small hill towns, Maringá (several E hotels), Marumbá and Mirantão, at about 1,700 metres. 6 km. up river from Maringá are the well-known Santa Clara falls. Buses to Visconde de Mauá from Resende, 1500 and 1630, 1½ hrs., US$1.50 (you reach Maringá before Visconde de Mauá). Further along the Dutra Highway (186 km. from Rio) is the small town of *Engenheiro Passos*, from which a road (BR-354) leads to São Lourenço and Caxambu in Minas Gerais (**see page 295**), passing Agulhas Negras. One can climb Agulhas Negras from this side by taking the road from Registro pass (1,670 metres) to the Abrigo Rebouças refuge, which is manned all year round (take your own food, US$0.80 to stay), at 2,350 metres.

Hotels Penedo: *Bertell*, B, with meals; also *da Cachoeira, Moradas do Penedo*, 2 campsites. Restaurants *Viking, Mariska* (Hungarian), and *Baianinha*. Engenheiro Passos: *Villa Forte*, B, with meals; *Pensão das Flores*, Visconde de Mauá, D, with meals. Nine campsites in the area.

The *Itatiaia National Park* (founded 1937), on the Serra de Itatiaia in the Mantiqueira chain of mountains, is a few km. N of the Via Dutra (Rio-São Paulo highway). Road to it is paved. The town of Itatiaia is surrounded by picturesque mountain peaks and lovely waterfalls. It has good hotels, and plenty of camping sites: the Camping Clube do Brasil site is entered at Km. 148 on the Via Dutra. This is a good area for climbing (Pico das Agulhas Negras 2,787 metres, Pico da Prateleira 2,540 metres), trekking and birdwatching; information and maps can be obtained at the park office. Worth seeing are the curious rock formations of Pedra de Taruga and Pedra de Maçã, and the waterfall Véu de Noiva (many birds). Basic accommodation in cabins and dormitories is available in the park; you will need to book in season, say 30 days in advance, by writing to Administração do Parque Nacional de Itatiaia, Itatiaia 27540, RJ. The Administração operates a refuge in the park which acts as a starting point for climbs and treks: information on these from Club Excursionista Brasileira, Av. Almirante Barroso 2, 8th floor, T 220-3695, Rio. Tres Picos wildlife trail near *Hotel Simon*; ask at hotel desk for info. There is a Museum of Flora and Fauna, closed Mondays. Entrance to Park, US$0.35.

Hotels *Simon*, Km. 13 park road, A, with meals, lovely views; *Repouso Itatiaia*, Km. 10 park road, A, with meals; *Hotel do Ypé*, Km. 13 park road, B, with meals; *Fazenda da Serra*, Via Dutra Km. 151, B, with meals; *Tyll*, Via Dutra Km. 155, B, with meals. *Motel Jahu*, Via Dutra Km. 156, D, very friendly, clean, comfortable.

The **new Rio-Santos highway**, and even more the parallel road along the coast, are making the forested and hilly coastal region SW of Rio more accessible. It is now complete right through to Bertioga (**see page 311**), which has good links both with Santos and (avoiding Santos) to São Paulo. There are direct Rio-Santos buses, and direct services from Rio to Angra dos Reis, Parati, Ubatuba,

Caraguatatuba, and São Sebastião. Hotels and *pousadas* have sprung up all along the road.

Itacuruçá, 91 km. from Rio, is a delightful place to visit if you like fine scenery and peace and quiet, with islands off the coast.

Hotels On Ilha de Itacuruçá, is *Hotel Pierre*, reached by boat from Coroa Grande, north of Itacuruçá on the mainland, 5 mins. (boats also go from Itacuruçá); hotel has 27 rooms in price range L, restaurant, bars, sporting facilities. For bookings T Rio 521-1546 or 289-7546, or Saveiros Tours, 267-2792. At S end of the island is *Pousada do Artur*, A; T Rio 256-6227. The *Hotel Jaguanum*, Ilha de Jaguanum, Itacuruçá, has apartments and chalets with private bathrooms. There are beautiful walks around the island. Reservations for the hotel, which include the boat trip to and from the island (at 1000 and 1700), cost US$120-130 per day for two with all meals. The only extra is the bus, US$3 return, which picks you up at your hotel. Book by calling 235-2893 or 237-5119, in Rio, or enquire at Sepetiba Turismo, Av. N.S. de Copacabana 605, s. 202.

Ilha de Itacuruçá can also be reached from Muriqui, a popular beach resort at Km. 27; bathing also in the Véu de Noiva waterfall. The next beach along the coast is Praia Grande.

Mangaratiba, half-way from Rio to Angra dos Reis, has muddy beaches, but pleasant surroundings and better beaches outside the town, for example Ibicuí, São Brás, Praia Brava, Saco, Guiti and Cação.

Hotels *Moreira*, and *Mendoza* (both have same owner), E without breakfast (US$1.90 extra), without bath, good, clean; 2 others, more expensive. None is crowded because the town is not a tourist resort.

Daily ferry (Conerj) to Ilha Grande island (see below), at 0830 daily, 1½ hrs., highly rec.; return ferry Mon., Wed., Fri. at 1700, Wed. at 1600, other days at 1100. Fare US$0.45, US$0.90 weekends. Tues. and Thur. departures continue on to Angra dos Reis. Ferry departures and destinations can be checked at ferry station at Praça Quinze de Novembro, Rio. Buses from Rio Rodoviária 7 a day, US$1.50.

Angra dos Reis, said to have been founded in 1502, is 197 km. SW of Rio by road. A small port with an important fishing and shipbuilding industry, it has several small bays with good bathing within easy reach and is situated on an enormous bay full of islands. Boat trips around the bay are available, some with a stop for lunch on the island of Jipóia (5 hrs., US$7.50 p.p.); boats for hire US$10/hour). Of particular interest are the convent of Nossa Senhora do Carmo, built in 1593, the parish church (1626), the ruins of the Jacuecanga seminary (1797), and the Senhor do Bonfim church (1780).

Hotels *Frade* (A, the most expensive), *Da Praia* and *Pousada do Retiro*, small resort hotels, bookings Rio 267-7375, all B; *Palace*, C, and *Londres*, C; *Caribe*, central, and *Acrópolis* both C; *Porto Rico*, E without breakfast, clean, quiet; *Angra Turismo*, D; *Cherry*, D. At Km. 115 on BR-101 is *Hotel Porto Bracuhy*, B, with lots of facilities for watersports, nightly shows and dancing, restaurant, etc. (23 km. from Angra dos Reis). *Porto Atlântico*, A, also beyond Angra.

Restaurants *Costa Verde, Verde Mar,* both specializing in sea food. Also *Jaques*. For meat, *Adega dos Dragos*, good. *Chez Dominique.*

Bus Hourly from Rio's Rodoviária, Viação Eval, take the "via litoral" bus and sit on the left, US$3, 2½ hrs.

The Hotéis do Frade group (*Frade, do Retiro, Pousada Dom João* in Parati and *Hotel Portogalo*, 1½ hrs. from Rio on a cliff top) in conjunction with Aquatur owns a schooner, the *Frade-Mar*, which runs cruises off Angra dos Reis, exploring islands, snorkelling, diving, etc. Trips are Mon.-Wed., or Fri.-Sun.; bookings for cruises,and for Frade hotels: Rua Joaquim Nabuco 161, Copacabana, 22080 Rio de Janeiro, T 267-7375, Telex: 31034, or Portuguese Tours Inc., 321 Rahway Av., Elizabeth, N.J. 07202, T 352-6112, Telex 138-203 or 178-051.

A road runs inland (about 18 km. beyond Angra), through Getulândia, to join the BR-116 either just S of Pirai or near Volta Redonda, through nice mountain scenery.

Two hours by ferry boat (Mon., Wed., Fri. at 1530, return 1015—so you have to stay 2 nights; for day trips, go from Mangaratiba) takes you on a most attractive trip through the bay to *Ilha Grande,* once an infamous pirate lair, and now occupied principally by fishermen and one of Brazil's larger prisons, with two good hotels, *Paraiso do Sol* (A, inclusive of meals, reservations, Rio, T 252-9158) and *Mar da Tranqüilidade* (B, reservations Rio, T 288-4162). Hotel reservations are necessary; alternatively you can camp on beaches; ask in the port at Angra dos Reis for a fishing boat going to Proveta, where you can stay in boat sheds or, if lucky, with a fisherman. It is a beautiful village, from which you can walk through tropical forest on a mountain to Praia do Aventureiro (a day's leisurely walk each way). Take mosquito precautions and register with police post in village of Abraão.

Beyond Angra dos Reis, the road continues 100 km. along the coast (on the way is *Pousada do Bosque*, Mambucaba, B, rec.), past the nuclear-power plant at Itaorna, to **Parati,** a charming colonial town only accessible these last few years with the opening of the road. The centre has been declared a national historic monument in its entirety. It used to be a very important place, being the chief port for the export of gold in the 17th century. The churches were built separately for each race, Indian, black and white. There is a great deal of distinguished Portuguese colonial architecture in delightful settings. On the northern headland is a small fort, 15 mins.' walk, pleasant views. There is a festival of sacred music in September. The town centre is out of bounds for motor vehicles. It is now very popular with tourists, and an expensive place to visit. Local patchwork is for sale in the community centre on the waterfront. Boat trips round the bay daily at 1200, returning 1700, US$10.50 p.p., beautiful trip; alternatively you can hire small boats by the hour. Take mosquito repellent.

Hotels   *Pousada Pardieiro*, A, attractively housed in colonial building with lovely gardens, but always full at week-ends. Also *Pousada Dom João*, A, bookings Rio 267-7375; *Santa Rita*, Rua Santa Rita 2, D, good, with bath and breakfast; other central *pousadas*: *do Ouro*, A, *das Canoas* (rec., clean, swimming pool, a/c) and *Aconchego*, both C; *Hotels Pescador* and *Sila Coupê*, central, C; *Pouso Familiar*, Rua J.V.Ramos 262, E, run by Belgian (Joseph Yserbyt) and his Brazilian wife (Lucia), near bus station, laundry facilities, English spoken, T 0243-711475, rec.; *Hotel Solar dos Gerânios*, formerly *Johnny Gringo*, Praça da Matriz, D, clean, friendly, good breakfast; *Posada Patitiba*, E, without bath or breakfast, basic, hot.

Good **restaurants,**   *Vagalume*; *Paulinho*, a "sort of shed" on the waterside, good, cheap churrascaria; cheaper places away from older centre. e.g. *Ceu de Boca*, good; *Couto Marquese*, good, cheap, but small portions. Snack bars, *Maré Alta, Sem Nome* (expensive).

There is a small Camping Club site on the fine Pontal beach, very crowded in January and February, and also a private camping site and a site next to the police station after the bridge, US$2 p.p. Apart from camping, very little cheap accommodation.

Bus   7 a day to Rio (4 hrs., US$4.25) and to Angra dos Reis (1½ hrs., every 2 hrs., US$1.75); three a day to Ubatuba (70 km.), Taubaté (170 km.) and Guaratinguetá (210 km.); two a day to São Paulo (0930, 2230, 5½ hrs., US$5, booked up quickly) and São Sebastião.

The coast road continues from Parati into the State of São Paulo. Another road, rough but scenic, climbs the Serra do Mar to Cunha and Guaratinguetá, also in São Paulo.

ESPIRITO SANTO (3)

N of Campos (**see page 274**) is the State of Espírito Santo, with its capital at Vitória. The State has a mountainous interior and a hot, damp seaboard. It is an important grower of coffee. In the north there are large forests containing hardwoods. The people are known as Capixabas, after a former Indian tribe. Just across the frontier between the states is the resort town of **Marataizes,** with fair hotels and good beaches.

Hotels   *Praia*, Av. Atlântica 99, on beach, D; *Saveiros Palace,* Av. Miramar 119, on beach, D; *Dona Judith*, Av. Lacerda de Aguiar 353, D; *Jona Balbina*, same street, No. 397, similar prices.

Camping   Municipal site on Praia do Siri, 10 km. from centre; Xodó private site, Av. Atlântica, 2 km. from centre.

The main road N passes **Cachoeira do Itapemirim**, a busy city on both banks of the fast-flowing Rio Itapemirim; many hotels of all classes, a cheap one being *Planalto*, facing the river, E.

Further north, 58 km. south of Vitória, is **Guarapari,** whose beaches attract many people seeking cures for rheumatism, neuritis and other complaints, from the radioactive monazitic sands. Bus from Vitória, 1 hr., US$0.80. (Both Marataizes and Guarapari are very crowded mid-Dec. to end Feb.)

Hotels *Porto do Sol,* Mediterranean style village on rocky point overlooking a calm beach, pool, sauna, etc., A, rec., T 261-0011, Telex: 0272-488; *Coronado,* Av. Lourival de Almeida 312, B; *Hostess,* Rua Joaquim Silva Lima 701, B; *Thorium,* Praça Floriano Peixoto 17, C; *Atlântica,* Av. Edísio Cirne 332, on beach, rec., D; *Guará,* Rua Getúlio Vargas 179, D.

Camping Camping Clube do Brasil, Setiba beach, 9 km. from centre. Cambrás site off Vitória highway close to beach, 4 km. from centre. Private site near Cambrás site. Less crowded than Guarapari is Praia Iriri, 30 km. to the South, served by a regular bus; 2 beaches, beautiful setting, lodging in private houses is possible.

1 hour S of Guarapari, is Praia dos Castelhanos, near Anchieta (*Hotel Thanharu Praia,* good; *Restaurant Moacyr,* main courses US$2.75-4). Fishing/diving boat hire from Sr. Romildo, Peixaria do Onça (2 km. N of Anchieta) US$12 for 3 hrs., US$25 to Ilha dos Franceses.

There are coastal and inland road routes to **Vitória,** 509 km. from Rio de Janeiro, reached several times a day by plane (80 min.), and by bus (9 hrs.). Two bridges connect the island on which it stands with the mainland. The town is beautifully set, its entrance second only to Rio's, its beaches quite as attractive, but smaller, and the climate is less humid. On Avenida República is the huge Parque Moscoso, an oasis of quiet, with a lake, playground and tiny zoo. The Teatro Carlos Gomes, on Praça Costa Pereira, often presents plays, also jazz and folk festivals. The upper, older part of town, reached by steep streets and steps, is much less hectic than the lower harbour area which is beset by dreadful traffic problems. Vitória is a growing centre for the sport of sea fishing. Population, one million.

Its growing importance is due to its connection westwards with Minas Gerais by the Vitória-Minas railway, which transports for export millions of tons of iron ore and a large tonnage of coffee and timber. Ships drawing 11 metres and 240 metres in length can enter the port. A supplementary iron-ore port has been built at Ponta do Tubarão, near Vitória, to load ships up to 250,000 tons. These installations have led to some beach and air pollution at places near Vitória, such as Camburi (quite a pleasant beach, though, partly built up, palms, drink stands, fair surf).

See the fortified monastery of Nossa Senhora da Penha, on a high hill above the small settlement of Vila Velha. Most of the (unremarkable) structure, now in ruins, is of the 17th and 18th centuries; the views are superb. The Dutch attacked it in 1625 and 1640. Vila Velha has an excellent beach, but it is built up and noisy: take bus from Vitória marked Vilha Velha or Praia da Costa. A fine bridge has been built across the bay to Vila Velha. Pleasant excursions in ferry-boats to Vila Velha.

Warning Robberies on the street are common. If you are robbed, yell "thief" or "*ladrão*" and give chase (if you think it safe to do so); most likely most of the street will join you and if the thief is caught he will receive a severe beating.

Hotels *Senac Hotel* (Government-run hotel school), luxurious, swimming pool, restaurant, enthusiastic attention to guests by student staff, on the ocean at Rua Sete, 417 Ilha do Boi, B, T 227-3222; *Novotel,* Av. Adalberto Simão Nader 133, A. *Helal,* Jerônimo Monteiro 935, B; *Cannes Palace,* Jerônimo Monteiro 111, B; *Estoril,* Praça Pres. Roosevelt 532, D, some rooms overlook the port; *Vitória,* Cais de São Francisco 85, near Parque Moscoso, E with bath, excellent restaurant, changes money, good, clean; *Minister,* Av. Cleto Nunes, off Parque Moscoso, F; *Europa,* Sete de Setembro, corner of Praça Costa Pereira, F, clean, noisy but cheap, good value restaurant (nearby is a good value vegetarian restaurant and a money changer, ask at the hotel); *Catedral,* opp. Cathedral in upper part of city, E, clean; *Avenida,* Av. Florentino Avidos 350(ish) (T 223-4317/0770), E with breakfast, friendly, clean; *São José,* Av. Princesa Isabel 300, C. Hotels located in beach areas, Camburi to the N, Vila Velha to the S, both about 15 mins. from city centre. *Walter,* across from Rodoviária, adequate, but *Lisboa,* opp. Rodoviária, is not rec.

Camping Serra Verde and Dalla's, private sites with some facilities, about 30 km. N of the city on Manguinhos beach.

Restaurants *São Pedro* (fish a speciality). *Trattoria Toscana,* Av. República and Cleto Nunes, by Parque Moscoso, on first floor, good food and service. *Acácia,* Cleto Nunes 273, good.

Banks Local banks. *Casa de Câmbio* at Vitur, Av. Getúlio Vargas, big ESCAL sign, next to *Bar*

Scandinave (where moneychangers of a less trustworthy type can be found); Plumatur, Av. Governador Bley 465, Edif. Glória, Conj. 101, T 222-5955.

Cables Embratel, Palácio do Café, Praça Costa Pereira 52. Tel.:30914.

Tourist Information Emcatur, Av. Getúlio Vargas (corner of Av. Jerônimo Monteiro), and at Rodoviária (bus. station, friendly, good free map). Plumatur, Av. Governador Bley (first floor), tourist information, coffee and parallel exchange rate.

Roads (distances in km.): Belém, 3,075; Brasília, 1,238; Belo Horizonte, 541; Foz do Iguaçu, 2,002; Manaus, 4,489; Porto Alegre, 2,038; Recife, 1,948; Rio, 509; Salvador, 1,175; São Paulo, 932.

Buses Rodoviária is 15 mins.' walk from centre. Rio, 8 hrs., US$8. To hitch to Rio, take Itapemirim bus to Aracatiba (26 km). 5 buses a day to Campos, US$2.40 (Itapemirim), one to Macaé, 2330. Salvador, 18 hrs., US$16; Porto Seguro direct 11 hrs. with lots of stops (Agua Blanca, dep. 0900), US$8, alternatively, take bus to Eunápolis, then change buses which run every hour, US$1. To hitch to Salvador, take a bus to Sara, which is beyond Carapina; alight where the bus turns off to Sara. Diamantina, 5½ hrs., US$5. To Ouro Preto, 2215 only, Thurs., US$5.50; to Belo Horizonte, either by bus, 8 hrs., US$8, or take train at 0720 to Itabira, site of a large iron ore mine, where there is a connecting bus to Belo Horizonte at 2000, arrives 2200. Possible also to go by train to Ipatinga, site of the Usiminas steel mill (visits can be arranged); hourly buses Ipatinga-Belo Horizonte, 3 hrs. (no trains Vitória-Belo Horizonte).

Excursions Visit *Santa Leopoldina* or *Domingos Martins,* both around 45 km. from Vitória, less than an hour by bus (2 companies run to the former, approx. every 3 hrs.). Both villages preserve the architecture and customs of the first German and Swiss settlers who arrived in the 1840s. Domingos Martins (also known as Campinho) has a Casa de Cultura with some items of German settlement (Hotels *Campinho,* E, clean, breakfast, *Imperador,* 2 star, D). Santa Leopoldina has a most interesting museum (open Tues.-Sun., 0900-1100 and 1300-1800) covering the settlers' first years in the area, and a large number of fascinating constructions dating from the end of the last century showing Swiss and German influence.

To *Santa Teresa,* a charming hill town 2½ hours by bus from Vitória, US$1.75 (beautiful journey). There is a unique hummingbird sanctuary—difficult to visit because of illness of director, Dr Augusto Ruschi. Also the Nova Lombardia National Biological Reserve. Basic accommodation available. Previous permission must be obtained to visit from Instituto Brasileiro de Desenvolvimento Florestal, Av. Mal. Mascarenhas de Moraes 2487, CP 762, CEP 29.000, Bento Ferreira.

75 km. N of Vitória is the town of Aracruz. A whole new town is being built beside the impressive Scandinavian/Brazilian cellulose plant, surrounded by vast new eucalyptus forests.

136 km. N of Vitória is *Linhares,* on Rio Doce, with good hotels, for example *Linhares,* C, best in town; *Grande,* E, pleasant, and others; *Restaurant Mocambo,* good and cheap. Mid-way between Linhares and Vitória, 5 km. off BR-101 between Fundão and Ibiraçu, is a Zen Buddhist monastery. 84 km. N of Linhares is São Mateus, a pleasant town with no decent hotels (*Grande,* E, tiny, bad rooms), 13 km. from good beaches (buses). The Comboios Biological Reserve, just S of Linhares, is designed to protect the species of marine turtles which frequent this coast (for information, contact IBDF at address above). Similarly the Sooretama Biological Reserve, also in the vicinity of Linhares; this protects tropical Atlantic rain forest and its fauna and birds.

The most attractive beaches in the State are around *Conceição da Barra,* 242 km. N of Vitória. Basic hotels *Cricaré, Nanuque,* and *Rio Mar,* E. Camping Clube do Brasil site with full facilities. An interesting excursion is to Itaúnas, 21 km. up the coast; the small town has been swamped by sand dunes, so it has been moved to the opposite river bank. There is now a fantastic landscape of huge dunes and deserted beaches. A few pousadas and a small campsite can be found. Bus from the *padaria* in Conceição da Barra at 0700, returns 1700.

MINAS GERAIS (4)

The inland State of Minas Gerais, somewhat larger than France, is mountainous in the S, rising to the 2,787-metre peak of Agulhas Negras in the Mantiqueira range, and in the E, where there is the Caparaó National Park containing the Pico da Bandeira (2,890 metres). From Belo Horizonte north are undulating grazing lands, the richest of which are in the extreme W: a broad wedge of country between Goiás in the N and São Paulo in the S, known as the Triângulo Mineiro.

MINAS GERAIS & ESPÍRITU SANTO

NOT TO SCALE

Most of the upland is also good grazing country. Being frost-free, Minas Gerais is again becoming one of the main producers of coffee.

Minas Gerais was once described as having a heart of gold and a breast of iron. Half the mineral production of Brazil comes from the State, including most of the iron ore. Diamonds and gold are still found. Its exports move through Rio de Janeiro, Santos, Vitória and Angra dos Reis. The easy availability of power and the local agricultural and mineral production has created a large number of metal-working, textile, mineral water, food processing and timber industries.

There is much to interest the tourist: the old colonial cities built during the gold rush in the 18th century, some splendid caves, the Rio São Francisco in the N, and a number of fine spas and hill resorts. You can easily visit the colonial cities from Rio or Belo Horizonte; many companies, including Tropical Tours of Belo Horizonte, provide tours. The chief glory of the colonial cities is the architecture and, even more, the sculpture of one of the world's great creative artists, Antônio Francisco Lisboa (1738-1814), the son of a Portuguese architect and a black slave woman. He is known as "O Aleijadinho" (the little cripple) because in later life he developed a maiming disease (possibly leprosy) which compelled him to work in a kneeling (and ultimately a recumbent) position with his hammer and chisel strapped to his wrists. His finest work, which shows a strength not usually associated with the plastic arts in the 18th century, is probably the set of statues in the gardens and sanctuary of the great Bom Jesus church in Congonhas do Campo, but the main body of his work is in Ouro Preto, with some important pieces in Sabará, São João del Rei and Mariana (see following pages).

We survey first the places on, or easily reached from, the Rio de Janeiro-Belo Horizonte highway, then the colonial cities of central Minas, then the outlying parts of the State. 129 km. north of Rio by air and 155 km. by road is the pleasant city of *Juiz de Fora*. It lies on the Paraibuna river, in a deep valley between the Mar and Mantiqueira mountain chains, at 640 metres. Population: 299,000. The Museum of Mariano Procópio is well worth a visit.

Industries   Steel-making, textiles, brewing, timber sawing, sugar refining.

Hotels   *Ritz* (best), Barão do Rio Barras 2000, C; *Imperial*, Batista de Oliveira 605, D (simple, but well run). Many hotels on Rua Getúlio Vargas of (our) category E: declining street numbers for Hotels *Glória* (good), *Transmontana*, *Hilton* (no relation), *Brasília*, *Mauá* and *Big. Picache*, opp. Rodoviária. *Imperador*, Av. Rio Branco 25, E. Boarding houses (F) in side streets, e.g. Rua Marechal Deodoro, *Pensão Sulamericana* at No. 86, *Belo Horizonte* at No. 120.

Camping   Camping Clube do Brasil site at Represa Dr. João Penido.

Bus   Hourly from Rio 0600-2200, US$3, 3½ hrs. (spectacular trip), Belo Horizonte (many, US$5.50) and Petrópolis. Bus station outside town, Av. Brasil 3405.

From *Barbacena*, 103 km. on (with an important horse and cattle fair, and a rose festival in October), a paved road runs W to the colonial city of *São João del Rei* (population 50,000), at the foot of the Serra do Lenheiro, with a fine bridge and three splendid 18th century churches: Pilar, the earliest, with rich altars and bright ceiling, and good *azulejos* in choir, and a sacristy with portraits of the Evangelists, new sacred art museum next door, entry US$0.10; São Francisco de Assis (1764), with exterior and interior sculptures by Aleijadinho (recent restoration has removed the plaster from the altars, revealing fine carving in sucupira wood) and the Carmo, on the other side of the river, designed by him and with interior sculptures by him, recently very well restored, all in white. Near São Francisco is the tourist office in the house of Bárbara Heliodora (1759-1819), one of the Inconfidentes (**see page 290**), which also contains the municipal museum, whose chief treasure is a reputed portrait of Aleijadinho. The railway museum (see below) is well worth seeing. Museu da Arte Sacra, small but well recommended. There are also the Museu de Arte Regional do Patrimônio Histórico, in Praça Severiano (open Tues.-Sun., 1300-1600, US$0.25), and a pewter factory (with exhibition and shop) run by an Englishman, John Somers. Tourist office also in old bus station. A good view of the town and surroundings is from Alto da Boa Vista, where there is a Statue of Christ (Senhor dos Montes).

Festivals The morning masses on Sundays and religious festivals at São Francisco (0915) and Mercês (1030)—behind and above Pilar— are accompanied by choir and orchestra who maintain a tradition of over 200 years of local composition.

John Parsons writes: *Tiradentes* (originally São José del Rei). The centre of this charming little town, 15 km. from São João, with its nine streets and eight churches, at the foot of the green Serra São José, hardly belongs to this century. The Santo Antônio church, first built in 1710, contains some of the finest gilded wood carvings in the country and a small but fine organ brought from Oporto in the 1790s. The reconstructed façade is said to follow a design by Aleijadinho. There is also a sun-dial by him. Also of unusual interest and charm are the Rosário church, with fine statuary and ornate gilded altars; this and Nossa Senhora das Mercês have interesting painted ceilings and the latter a notable statue of the Virgin.

At the bottom of the stone paved road which descends from Santo Antônio is the fine fountain (*chafariz*), installed in 1749. The water is brought by a stone aqueduct from springs in the forest at the foot of Serra São José, which offers fine walks including the lane beside the aqueduct. The museum, housed where Padre ToLedo (another Inconfidente) once lived, is of particular interest and there are some good pieces of furniture exhibited. The simple pilgrimage church of Santíssima Trindade is also well worth seeing. Tourist Office in the Prefeitura, Rua Resende Costa 71. See the artists' lithographic printing shop of Largo do Ô. There are attractive walks in the neighbourhood, and a 1½-hr. walk to the natural pools of Águas Santas.

Barbacena Hotel *Grogotó*, excellent, C; operated by Senac.

São João del Rei Hotels *Novotel Porto Real*, Av. Eduardo Magalhães, comfortable, B; *Lenheiro Palace*, Av. Pres. Tancredo Neves 257, T 371-3914, B/C, good; *do Espanhol*, R. Marechal Deodoro, C; cheap *pousadas* in same street; *Pousada Casarão*, opp. São Francisco church, C, converted mansion. *Colonial*, opp. *Porto Real*, D, clean and comfortable. *Pensão N.S. de Lourdes*, near bus station, E, meals US$1.10, good; *Pousada Ramón*, opp. bus station, F, good; *Brasil*, opposite railway station so back rooms much quieter, clean, friendly, cheap, E, rec., no breakfast (*Cafeteria Globo* in the same street, 2 blocks away, is good, though). *Hotel Porto Real* restaurant and *Restaurant Quinta do Ouro*, also good vegetarian restaurant, all rec. Good *Churrascaria* next to railway station.

Buses Rodoviária is 2 km. W of centre of São João. Direct buses to Rio (5 hrs., US$4), São Paulo (8 hrs.) and Belo Horizonte (3½ hrs.)

Tiradentes Hotels *Solar da Ponte*, Praça das Mercês (prop. John and Anna Maria Parsons) T 032-355-1255, atmosphere of country house, A, including breakfast and tea, only 12 rooms. Fresh flowers in rooms, bar, sauna, garden, swimming pool, light meals for residents only, for larger meals, the hotel recommends five local restaurants listed below. Also *Pousada Maria Barbosa*, D, pool, very pleasant, *Hotel Wellerson*, *Pousada Tiradentes*, *Hotel Ponto do Morro*, *Pousada de Laurito*.

Restaurants Local food: *Quinta de Ouro*, rec.; *Estalagem*; *Padre Toledo*. Meat: *Thé*. Italian: *Donatelli*.

Martin Crossland and the Editor both recommend the train trip between São João del Rei and Tiradentes (13 km.). The train has been in continuous operation since 1881, using the same locomotives and rolling stock, running on 76 cm. gauge track, all now lovingly restored and cared for. Maximum speed is 20 km. per hour. Price: US$1.20, one class only. Fri., Sat., Sun. and holiday steam train service to Tiradentes, 1000 and 1400, returning 1300 and 1700. Railway museum at the railway station in São João del Rei; open daily 0900-1200, 1330-1730; there are also an engine shed and a steam-operated machine shop, still working.

From Belo Horizonte, the shortest road to São João del Rei is via Lagoa Dourada. Just past Lagoa Dourada is the turning (12 km. on dirt road) for *Prados*, a small town 15 km. from Tiradentes known for its musical and handicrafts traditions. Near the turn is Entre Rios de Minas (*Hotel Camapuã*).

Belo Horizonte, the capital of Minas Gerais, is the third largest city in Brazil. It is situated over 800 metres above sea-level, surrounded by mountains, and enjoys an excellent climate except for the rainy season. It was Brazil's first modern planned city. Sights to be seen are the Praça da Assembléia, with three fine modern buildings: Legislative Assembly, church and Banco do Brasil; the Palácio da Liberdade, in Praça da Liberdade amid other fine *fin-de-siècle*-style public buildings (every Sun. morning and Thurs. evening an open-air craft market operates here—very good, also a flower market each Fri. from 1800); the Palácio das Artes, Afonso Pena 1567, which is in the Parque Municipal and contains the Centro de Artesanato Mineiro (craft shop open 0900-1700, Tues.-Sun.); the Museu Mineiro, Av. João Pinheiro, in old Senate building near centre; the City Museum; the Museum of Mineralogy, Rua da Bahia 1149, a Gothic building near the park, with interesting exhibits (open Mon.-Sat., 0800-1800, entrance free); the Museu Histórico, in an old *fazenda* house which is the last reminder of Belo Horizonte's predecessor, the village of Arraial do Curral d'el Rey, with most interesting historical exhibits (open 1000-1700 Wed.-Mon.); the Museu do Telefone, Av. Afonso Pena 1180 (open Mon.-Fri., 0900-1800, Sun., 0900-1300); the railway station, with museum, and the railway headquarters in a mansion on the hill above the station, with locomotive and railway coach used by Dom Pedro II; the Municipal Park (an oasis of green, right in the centre of the city, small amusement park and playground, not too safe at night). Museo Histórico Natural, in the Instituto Agronómico, Rua Gustavo da Silveira 1035, T 461-7666, has a local geological and palaeontological display and good archaeological exhibits (take bus 3803A from Praça Rio Branco).

Eight km. from the centre is the picturesque suburb of Pampulha, famous for its modern buildings and the artificial lake (many infestations, do not swim in it), many buildings designed by the renowned Brazilian architect Oscar Niemeyer (who later designed much of Brasília); in Pampulha the glass and marble Museum of Modern Art may be visited (Av. Octacílio Negrão de Lima, open 0800-1800 daily, reported disappointing), as well as the Chapel of São Francisco (the interior of which was decorated by the Brazilian painter Cândido Portinári). There is a bus (not the 4403) from the city centre to the Jardim Zoológico (at the far end of the lake from the dam—small selection of birds with some rarities, animals well kept for the most part) that passes the chapel and also the Mineirão stadium (see below); bus 2004 goes from Av. Afonso Pena to the chapel.

In the southern zone of the city, on the Serra do Curral, the Parque de Mangabeiras has forest trails, sports facilities and snack bars. The natural amphitheatre where the Pope spoke in 1982 is nearby; there is an iron monument marking the occasion (take bus 2001 from Afonso Pena). In 1984, the Minascentro, a convention centre for exhibitions and congresses, was opened in the city centre. The huge Mineirão stadium is the second largest in Brazil after the Maracanã stadium in Rio. The population of Belo Horizonte in 1980 was 1,442,000 and it is one of the fastest growing of Brazil's main cities; atmospheric pollution has recently been reported.

The industrial area, about 10 km. from the centre, has now become the third largest industrial centre of Brazil, and apart from being the traditional centre of mining and agricultural industries (as well as diamond cutting and precious stones), it has steelworks and an automobile industry. The city has a good public transport system (red buses serve central and express routes, yellow are circular, and blue diagonal), and taxis are plentiful, although hard to find at peak hours.

Local Holidays Maundy Thursday; Corpus Christi; August 15 (Assumption); December 8 (Immaculate Conception).

Electric Current 120-220 A.C. 60 cycles.

Hotels (number of stars in brackets) *Othon Palace* (5), Av. Afonso Pena 1050, T 226-7844, L, deluxe, best, rec.; *Brasilton* (4), out of town at km. 3.65 on Rodovia Fernão Dias, Contagem, L, very good restaurant; *Real Palace* (4), R. Espírito Santo 904, T 224-2111, A; *Internacional Plaza Palace* (4), R. Rio de Janeiro 109, T 201-2300, A, good but seedy part of town; *Boulevard Plaza* (3), Av. Getúlio Vargas 1640, Savassi district (chic), A, T 223-9000, very nice; *Wembley Palace* (3), Rua Espírito Santo 201, T 201-6966, A, excellent, central, clean, but poor rate for travellers' cheques; *Del Rey* (4), Praça Afonso Arinos 60, A; *Normandie* (3), Rua Tamóios 212, B, excellent grill; *Serrana Palace* (3), Rua Goitacases 450, B, pleasant restaurant but hotel rather run down, seedy area; *Estoril*, Rua Carijós 454, C with bath, comfortable, pleasant; *Ambassy* (3), Rua Caetés 633, near bus station, D, helpful, English spoken, clean, a/c, noisy, good restaurant; *Itatiaia* (2), Praça Rui Barbosa 187, D, near railway station, central, clean, a/c, with bath and good breakfast; *Esplanada* (2), Av. Santos Dumont 304, D, (E without bath), clean, good restaurant, own garage; *Sul América Palace* (2), Av. Amazonas 50, D, clean, friendly, TV and fridge in rooms, warmly rec.; *Paraná*, Av. Paraná 437 (T 222-3472), D, with shower, clean, noisy at weekends from discothèque; *Casa dos Municípios*, Rua Rio Grande do Norte 1017, Funcionários (in Savassi, chic shopping area), T 226-5177, clean, inexpensive; *Continental* (2), Av. Paraná 241, D, central, clean, friendly; *Minas*, Rua São Paulo 331, D, friendly, rec.; *Dom Pedro II*, R. Curitiba 248, E, clean, rather faded; *Vitória*, same street, No. 224, E without bath, good. Cheaper places are: *Magnata*, Rua Guarani 124, F, with breakfast, near bus station, cheap and clean, bath, good hot shower, rec.; near bus station and in Rua Curitiba many hotels are for very-short-stay couples; *Pensão Rodoviária* and away from traffic, *Pensão Nova Rodoviária*, Rua 21 de Abril 89, E, a bit dubious, basic, and many others; *Pensão N.S. Aparecida*, Av. de Fátima 1320 (near Rodoviária), E, basic, friendly but noisy. Within 10 mins. walk of Rodoviária: Rua Espírito Santo, No. 284, *Majestic*, E; No. 227, *São Salvador*, E; No. 237, *Magalhães*, E, basic, clean, friendly, good restaurant over the road; *Lux*, No. 220; Rua dos Caetés, *Solar*, No. 265. You may spend the night in the bus station only if you have an onward ticket (police check at midnight); area round bus station said to be dangerous. *Dona Carolina*, Rua dos Timbiras 1969, unsigned, in centre, 20 mins. walk from Rodoviária F p.p. per day with full board, most residents are students, good atmosphere and food. Youth hostel, *Pousadinha Mineira*, Rua Araxá 514, Bairro Colégio Batista, 31.110 Belo Horizonte, T 442-2049/444-8205.

Camping Wild camping near Alto do Palácio, near river and waterfalls.

Restaurants *Tavares*, Rua Santa Catarina 64 (local dishes), excellent value. Chinese: *Yun Ton*, R. Santa Catarina 946, rec.; Churrascarias: *Carretão Guaiba*, Av. do Contorno 8412; *Rodeio*, Av. do Contorno 8222; *Farrounilha*, Afonso Pena 3300; *Picanha na Talha*, Rua Curitiba, unprepossessing but highly rec.; *Chico Mineiro*, Rua Alagoas, corner of Av. Brasil, local chicken specialities, good, closed Sun.; *Santa Felicidade*, Rua Dr. Morais, good; *Arroz com Feijão*, typical food, Av. Contorno 6510, Av. Contorno 7438 and R. Antônio de Albuquerque 440, all friendly, reasonably-priced; *Martini*, Rua Curitiba, and *Pizzaiolo*, Av. Contorno 8495, good for pizzas. *Tokyo* (Japanese), R. Guajajaras 909; *Ninho*, (Chinese), Rua São Paulo 1271, Centro, cheap, good; *Via Natural, No. 1*, Av. Afonso Pena 941, vegetarian, open till 2200 (except 2000 on Sun.), *No. 2*, Av. Andradas 367; *O Armazem*, Rua Alagoas 1468, also vegetarian, as is *Alquima Mercearia*, Rua Tomé de Souza 855, and *Folhas*, same street, No. 503; *Superbom* (vegetarian), R. São Paulo, 971, 1100-1500, Mon. to Fri. *Casa do Ouvidor*, near central square highly rec. but expensive. *Degrau*, Av. Afonso Pena 4221, excellent restaurant and bar, very pleasant; *Giovanni*, Av. Afonso Pena opposite park, good Italian; *Pinho's*, Rua Pouso Alto 740, set high above the city, tremendous views by day or night, can be very busy on Fri. and Sat.; *Mangueiras*, at Pampulha, next to Niemeyer chapel of São Francisco, very popular; *Dona Derna*, behind the Palácio de Liberdade, highly rec.; *Buona Távola*, R. Alagoas 777, Savassi, excellent Italian; *Cantina do Ângelo* (Italian), Rua Tupinambás 267, rec., and in same street, No.253, *Torino* (Italian excellent, huge and varied menu, also at Guajajaras 460), and *Alpino* (German), same street, No. 173, both good value and popular, corned beef and fresh boiled vegetables available, open-air; *Flor de Líbano*, opposite *Hotel Magalhães* at Espírito Santo 234, cheap and good; *Quibelândia*, Rua dos Caetés 188, good. *Mister Beef*, Rua Gonçalves Dias, American-style, rec. Good snack bar at corner of Av. Afonso Pena and Rua Bahia, *Doce D'ocê*, Av. Afonso Pena 2712, also *Formula 1*, Galeria Praça 7, Rua Rio de Janeiro. We are told that the splendid Minas typical dishes are more authentic— and more toothsome—outside Belo Horizonte.

Shopping Mercado Central, Av. Aug. de Lima 744, large and clean, open every day, Saturday social centre. Market for fruit, vegetables, meat and other items at corner of Rua Santa Catarina and Av. Amazonas (near Praça Raúl Soares). There are huge hypermarkets just outside the city on the highways to Rio and to São Paulo. Splendid delicatessen with foreign food and wines—and liquors—*Au Bon Gourmet*, Rua Tupinambás 187. For gemstones, try Manoel Bernardes, Rua Espírito Santo 835, very reasonable, ask for US saleswoman Manuela, who can arrange tours of workshops. "Hippie fair" Thurs. evenings and Sundays in Praça da Liberdade; other fairs on Fri. and Sat. Belo is said to be very good for slide film, cheese and chocolate.

Bookshop Daniel Vaitsman, Rua Espírito Santo 466, 17th floor, for English language books. Foreign language books at Livraria Van Damme, Rua das Guajajaras 505, also good local and Portuguese selection (and said to change travellers' cheques). Used foreign-language books at Livraria Alfarrábio, Rua Tamóios 320.

Exchange Lloyds Bank (ex-BOLSA), Av. João Pinheiro 580; Citibank, Rua Espírito Santo 871; Banco do Brasil, Rua Rio de Janeiro 750; Banco Econômico, Rua Bahia 360, 9th floor, and other local banks, 1000-1630. American Express, Rua Espírito Santo 1204, T 273-1288. Exchange: Sr Abdul, Rua Caetés 323; H. Pichiommi, Rua Espiritu Santo and Rua Guajajanas. Nascente Turismo, Rio de Janeiro 1101, T 224-3334, ask for Luiz Carlos de Oliveira, changes money at a good rate.

Addresses British Vice-Consulate: Av. Afonso Pena 952, s. 500. Caixa Postal 2755. Sociedade Brasileira de Cultura Inglesa: as British Vice-Consulate. W. German Consulate: R. Carijós 244. Austrian Consulate, Rua José Américo Cancado Bahia 199, T 33 33 622.

Hospital Mater Dei, Rua Gonçalves Dias 2700, T 335-2200, has been rec.

Post Office with poste restante, Av. Afonso Pena 1270.

Tourist Information Turminas, Av. do Contorno 8471; Praça Sete de Setembro; at Rodoviária (particularly polyglot, reasonable free map of centre), railway station, airport (very helpful). Touring Club do Brasil.

Travel Agent Focus Tours, R.Grão Mogol 502, in Sion district, T (031) 223-0358, telex (031) 3823 RAPT, run by Douglas Trent, offer specialized tours all over Brazil and have a special interest in ecology and tours to the Pantanal. Tours in Minas to see a great variety of wildlife. Reliable information and a portion of their profits is used for conservation project in Brazil. Mangabeira Turismo, R. Goitcazes 71-8° andar, and Unitour, Av. Tupis 141, organize river trips on the São Francisco (see page 294).

Roads (distances in km.): Belém, 2,827; Brasília, 747; Foz do Iguaçu, 1,663; Manaus, 3,948; Porto Alegre, 1,709; Recife, 2,137; Rio, 426; Salvador, 1,355; São Paulo, 588; Vitória, 541.

Buses Rodoviária is by Praça Rio Branco at end of Av. Afonso Pena (left-luggage lockers, attended service 0700-2200). To Rio, 7 hrs., US$8 (ordinary), *leito*, US$16; to Brasília, 12 hrs., 9 a day incl. 2 *leitos*, only one leaves in daylight (0800), US$12, *leito* US$24; to Ouro Preto, 2 hrs., US$2, several daily (buy ticket well in advance); to Mariana (via Ouro Preto), 2¼ hrs., US$2.25; to Congonhas do Campo, 1½ hrs., US$1.50. To Sabará, US$0.50, ½ hr., from separate part of Rodoviária from main departure hall. To São Paulo, 10 hrs., US$10; route passes the great Furnas reservoir. To Salvador US$29, 22 hrs., at 1800 and 1900 daily. **For Porto Seguro** take Gontijo bus to Nanuque, then Rio Doce bus to Eunápolis, then Espresso São Jorge to Porto Seguro, total time 22 hrs., US$18. To Recife, US$32; to Belém, US$48. To Cuiabá, Expresso São Luiz, 0800 and 2000 daily, 26 hrs., US$25; to Vitória, 8 hrs., US$8.

Train Railway station is at Praça Rui Barbosa. Trains leave Friday and Sunday at 1230 (the Vera Cruz) for Rio de Janeiro: cabin for two costs US$27 single fare. There are no trains to São Paulo or Brasília. No direct train to Vitória, but buses leave at 0530 for Itabira, where connecting train (dining cars) leaves 0800, arriving Vitória 1937.

Airport A new international airport near Lagoa Santa, at Confins, 39 km. from Belo Horizonte, has been opened. Taxi to centre, US$12; airport bus, either *executivo* from the exit, or comfortable normal bus from far end of car park every hour on the half-hour, US$1. From centre, catch bus at Terminal Turístico JK, R. Olegário Maciel and R. Guajajaras.

Hitch-hiking to Rio or Ouro Preto, take a bus marked "Shopping", to the shopping centre above Belo Horizonte on the Rio road.

Excursions Within easy motoring distance from Belo Horizonte are several of the 400 caves and grottoes for which Minas Gerais is famous. The best and most famous is the Gruta de Maquiné with 7 chambers, well lit, with guides, but hot—26°C, 126 km. NW of Belo (well signposted and with restaurants nearby, bus at 0915, return at 1500, 2¼ hrs., US$2; in the nearby town of Cordisburgo is a museum to the writer Guimarães Rosa). The Gruta de Lapinha, almost as good, is only 51 km. N of the city (entrance to caves and small museum, US$0.30; bus at 0930, 1130 and others, via Pampulha, return 1230, 1600, 1¼hr., US$0.75 one way—don't alight at Lapinha bus station, it's 6 km. before the cave). Lapinha cave is closed Mon.

10 km. before Lapinha is the town of *Lagoa Santa*, a weekend resort for Belo Horizonte. The sandy beach on the lake (close to the town centre and bus station) is used for fishing, sun-bathing and boating (do not swim, the water is infected with schistosomiasis). Along the beach are bars and restaurants, with more in the nearby main square which also has two small hotels and an interesting modernistic church. The road to Belo Horizonte (half-hourly bus service, US$0.75) passes Belo Horizonte's new international airport. Bus Lagoa Santa-Lapinha every half hour.

To the NE of the city, a few km. off the BR-262, is the Serra de Piedade, a high peak giving spectacular views over the surrounding countryside. A popular excursion point but only accessible by car or special bus service. There are a small chapel and a *churrascaria*. From the peak can be seen the small town of *Caeté*, which has one or two interesting churches and the remains of an old ironworks near the railway station. Take the Conceição do Mato Dentro bus to Alto do Palácio; near there are waterfalls and campsites. Further from Belo, turn off the BR-262 (towards Vitória) at km. 73 and go via Barão de Cocais and Brumal to Caraçá (120 km.), where the monastery has been converted into a hotel (C). Reservations through Instituto São Vicente in Belo, T 031-441-5399.

From Belo Horizonte, excursions can be made to Nova Lima and the picturesque colonial cities described in the following pages. The road follows the Rio das Velhas in which, at points, one can see the *garimpeiros* waist-deep washing for gold.

Nova Lima, about 27 km. SE of Belo by a good road, is set in eucalyptus forests. Its houses are grouped round the gold mine of Morro Velho, opened by a British firm in 1834 but sold to Brazilians in 1959, the deepest mine in the Americas. The shaft has followed a rich vein of gold down to 2,591 metres. There are interesting carvings by Aleijadinho, recovered from elsewhere, in the (modern) parish church. Population: 34,000.

A paved road branching off the Belo Horizonte-Brasília highway leads (30 km., ½-hr.) to the colonial gold-mining (and steel-making) town of Sabará. Return by the old road over the mountain range of Serra do Curral for fine views. There is also a railway: 3 trains a day between Belo and Sabará, taking one hour.

Sabará is strung along the narrow steep valleys of the Rio das Velhas and Rio Sabará. Its old churches and fountains, its rambling cobbled streets, its simple houses with their carved doors, and its museum of 18th century gold mining in the Intendência de Ouro (built 1732, open 1200-1700 Tues.-Fri.) are of great interest. The churches are so spread out that a taxi is advisable if you wish to see them all. Population, 42,000. Very few places to stay.

Passeio a Sabará, by Lúcia Machado de Almeida, with splendid illustrations by Guignard, is an excellent guide to the place. The main sights are the Prefeitura, in Rua Pedro II, an old mansion, with oratory and main reception room (*salão nobre*) to be seen; the Imperial Theatre (1770, restored 1960) in the same street, for its fine interior; the Casa Azul, in the same street, for its portal; the Churches of Nossa Senhora do Carmo (1774), with doorway, pulpits and choirloft by Aleijadinho and paintings by Athayde; Nossa Senhora do Rosário dos Pretos (left unfinished at the time of the slaves' emancipation); São Francisco; Nossa Senhora da Conceição (1720) with much gilding, and paintings by 23 Chinese artists brought from Macau; and, last of all, Nossa Senhora do O, built in 1698 and showing unmistakable Chinese influence (paintings much in need of restoration), 2 km. from the centre of the town (take local bus marked "Esplanada"). Also the fountains of Kaquende (1757), and Rosário.

Hotel: *Pensão Bobagato,* above an art gallery, E, or ask for Senhor Sérgio at the Sports Centre, he may have accommodation. **Restaurants:** *O Quinto do Ouro,* close to the bus station; *314,* Comendador Viana 314, near main praça; *Imperial Restaurant/Pizzaria,* in Rua Pedro II.

At 27 km. S along the Belo Horizonte-Rio de Janeiro highway a 68 km. road, the Rodovia dos Inconfidentes, branches off to Ouro Preto. On the way (48 km.) it passes Cachoeira do Campo, which was the centre of the regional mining administration in colonial times: now a sleepy, unspoilt village.

Ouro Preto, the famous former capital of the State, was founded in 1711. Population, 38,000. There is a famous School of Mining (Escola Minas), founded in 1876, in the fortress-like Governor's Palace (1742), facing the main square (Praça Tiradentes); it has the interesting Museo de Mineralogia e das Pedras, a must, US$0.35, the only one open on Mondays, but closed Sundays. Opposite the Palace, next to Carmo Church, is the Museu da Inconfidência, a fine historical and art museum which has some drawings by Aleijadinho; the building, begun in the eighteenth century, has been a prison and also the local chamber of commerce (entry, US$0.45). See the Casa das Contas, now also a museum (open 1230-1700). Another museum, the Casa Guignard, on Rua Conde de Bobadela, displays the paintings of Alberto da Veiga Guignard, free. Buy soapstone carvings at roadside stalls and bus stops rather than in the cities; they are much cheaper. (However, gems are not much cheaper from freelance sellers in the square than from the shops around the square, and in the shops themselves, the same quality of stone is offered at the same price—Brasil Gemas and De Bernard is recommended.)

The city, built on rocky ground 1,000 metres above sea-level, was declared a national monument in 1933. Its cobbled streets wind up and down steep hills crowned with 13 churches. Mansions, fountains, churches, vistas of terraced gardens, ruins, towers shining with coloured tiles, all blend together to maintain a delightful 18th century atmosphere.

Ouro Preto is famous for its Holy Week processions, which in fact begin on the Thursday before Palm Sunday and continue (but not every day) until Easter Sunday. The most famous is that commemorating Christ's removal from the Cross, late on Good Friday. This is very much a holiday period and many shops are shut—as indeed they are on winter weekends. Carnival is also memorable, with samba and happenings in the streets.

The topaz mine of Vermelho Topásios Mineração Saramenha can no longer be visited.

Ouro Preto displays many superb baroque carvings, in wood and in soapstone, of the sculptor Aleijadinho. The church of São Francisco de Assis and the façade of the Carmo church are his work, and so are the two pulpits in the church of São Francisco, and much else.

In the **Praça de Independência** there is a statue of José Joaquim da Silva Xavier, known as Tiradentes, leader of the **Inconfidentes** (unsuccessful revolutionaries of 1789), and regarded in Brazil as the precursor of independence. Another Inconfidente, the poet Tomás Antônio Gonzaga (whose house is close to São Francisco de Assis), was exiled to Africa. (Most Brazilians know his poem based on his forbidden love affair; visitors are shown the bridge and decorative fountain where the lovers held their trysts.) On June 24 of each year Ouro Preto again becomes, for that day only, the capital of the state of Minas Gerais.

Churches The following churches are all closed Mon., but are open at following times on other days: Santa Efigênia (1720, decorated with gold dust washed out of slaves' hair), Padre Faria, 0800-1200; Francisco de Assis, N.S. Conceição, 0800-1130, 1300-1700 (under restoration 1988/89); Senhor Bom Jesus, N.S. Carmo, 1300-1700 (being restored 1988/89); N.S. Pilar (1733, heavily gilded work of Aleijadinho's father, Manuel Lisboa), Rosário, 1200-1700; das Mercês e Perdões, are open in afternoons only. The Antônio Dias parish church (1722), heavily gilded, contains Aleijadinho's tomb, and a museum devoted to him. Of the **museums** only Aleijadinho Paróquia is open a.m. and p.m.; Escola Minas, Inconfidência and Prata da Matriz do Pilar are open from 1200 onwards only; all except Escola Minas are closed Mon. At least two days are needed to see them all; the tourist office on Praça Tiradentes (opens 0800, Portuguese only spoken) and the hotels offer a leaflet showing the opening times; also sells good map for US$0.80. Most of the churches now charge for admission, usually about US$0.45. Shorts may not be worn in churches.

The mid-18th century paintings by Mestre Athayde (1732-1827), to be seen in S. F. de Assis, Sta. Ifigênia and elsewhere, are of particular interest: the pigments were obtained from local iron ore and from forest fruits. They are also very fine artistically; he was a worthy colleague of Aleijadinho.

N.B. In most churches and museums, tourists' handbags and cameras are taken at the entrance and guarded in lockers.

Hotels *Grande,* Rua Sen. Rocha 164, largest hotel in town and the only modern structure, designed by Oscar Niemeyer, B, not well kept; *Pouso Chico Rei,* a fascinating old house with Portuguese colonial furnishings, very small and utterly delightful though extremely difficult to get a reservation, Rua Brig. Mosqueira 90, C, T 551-1274 (room No. 6 has been described as a "dream"); *Luxor Pousada,* Praça Antônio Dias 10, converted colonial mansion, no twin beds, friendly, clean, comfortable, T 551-2244, reservations in Rio, T 256-2680, B, food poor value; *Hospedária Antiga,* Rua Xavier da Veiga 1, T 551-2203, a restored colonial house, reasonable rates, friendly, rec.; *Estrada Real,* 8 km. outside city, good but often fully-booked. *Pousada e Galeria Panorama Barroco,* Rua Conselheiro Quintiliano 722, fine views, T (031)551-3366, E (F p.p. without bath), with good breakfast, restored house with antique furniture, art gallery, music, videos, bulletin board for local events, reservations made, excursions organized, run by David and Lucia Peterkin (US/Brazilian), helpful, rec.; *Solar das Lajes,* Rua Conselheiro Quintiliano 604 (T 551-2330), C with bath, a little way from centre, excellent view, being extended, friendly and well run; *Pilão,* Praça Tiradentes 57, on main square, D, noisy; *Colonial,* Rua Camilo Veloso 26, D; *Tófolo,* São José 76, near Contas fountain, D, cheaper rooms available, reasonable, sometimes overcharges, so pay in advance; *Pousada Ouro Preto,* Praça Tiradentes 70, T 551-2778, 4/5 rooms, E, clean, laundry facilities, hot showers, English spoken by owner, Gérson Luís Cotta (most helpful), rec.; *Pensão* at Rua Coronel Alves 2, T 551-2393, clean reasonable, friendly; *Conde,* Rua Direita, D, old furniture, clean, rec.; *Miranda,* same street, E, shared shower; *N. S. Aparecida,* Praça Cesário Alvim 21, E, better rooms good, cheaper rooms without bath, restaurant cheap. *Pousada dos Inconfidentes,* Felipe dos Santos 31, E; same street, No. 241, *Pousada Ciclo do Ouro,* (T 581-3201/2210), clean rooms available. Try *pensões* in Ruas Randolpho Bretas, Getúlio Vargas, Paraná, *(Pensão da Conceição,* E, Paraná 137, has been rec.), also *Vermelha Dormitório,* Praça São Francisco de Assis 30, T 551-1138, quiet, shared shower), E. *Residencia* *de Doña Iva*, simple and friendly but noisy, D. Also try *casas de família*, reasonably-priced, but more expensive if booked through tourist office. Difficult to get hotel rooms at weekends and holiday periods; a good idea to telephone ahead. A number of travellers have rec. staying in Mariana where hotels are cheaper; three buses an hour to Ouro Preto.

Students may be able to stay, during holidays and weekends, at the self-governing student hostels, known as *repúblicas*, for about US$2 a night. (e.g. *República Vaticana*, Rua das Mercês 198, or *Pif-Paf*, in front of the Pilar church, *Tabu*, on road with main Post Office, or *Serigy*). Many are closed between Christmas and Carnival. Enquire at the city's tourist office on the main square (Praça Tiradentes 41), for this type, and other forms of accommodation. It shows filmstrips at 0900, 1200 and 1600 on weekdays, 0900, 1030, 1300, 1500, 1600 at weekends and holidays.

Camping Camping Clube do Brasil, 2 km. N of city, is quite expensive but very nice. Do not camp beside the waterfall, Cachoeira dos Andorinhas, 1½ hrs. walk from city; there have been robberies there. Also a site reached by car up a very steep hill at the top end of town: about 5 km. Also at picnic site 4 km. west of Ouro Preto, and at Rio Acima nearby.

Restaurants *Calabouço*, good, Conde de Bobadela 132, with an antique shop; *Pilão*, in main square (local painters), and good rooms above; *Quinta do Ouro*, Rua Camilo de Brito 21, good, a bit pricey, avoid window seats, rec.; also *Pelique*, US$2 prato do dia rec., another branch at Rua São José 131, no sign; opposite *Pelique* is *Chalet*, warmly rec. *Chafariz*, Rua São José 167, good local food; *Casa Grande* (watch your belongings) and *Forno de Barro*, both on Praça Tiradentes, good local dishes; *Casa do Ouvidor*, Conde de Bobadela 42, above De Bernardis jewellery shop (good), near main square, good, but expensive. On same street, *Chicken Inn*, No. 40, *Taberna La Luna* (very friendly), No. 138, good and cheap. *Chelvo Verde*, Rua Getúlio Vargas 250 (nr. Rosário church), good vegetarian and other dishes, pleasant, quite cheap. Bar Tropical, near *Hotel N.S. Aparecida*, cheap. Cheap *lanchonetes* on opposite side of square to *Hotel Pilão*. Excellent sandwich bar, good breakfast at *lanchonete* on corner of São José and Getúlio Vargas. Tea shop. Students may be able to eat at the School of Mining on Praça Tiradentes.

Electric Current 110 volts A.C.

Exchange arranged through Amsterdam Sauer jewellers on main square.

Post Office on Rua Direita, opp. *Hotel Miranda*.

Guides Bandeira's *Guia de Ouro Preto* in Portuguese and English (US$3.50 with coloured map, US$1 with black and white one), normally available at Tourist Office (helpful). Also available is Lucia Machado de Almeida's *Passeio a Ouro Preto*, US$6 (in Portuguese, English and French). Tourist Office's map costs US$0.80. A local guide for a day costs about US$3 (US$10 if obtained through Tourist Office). Ourotur runs a tour of Ouro Preto in a vintage-style bus for US$5, 0900 and 1430, from the bus station (T 551-2764).

Transport An early plane from Rio to Belo Horizonte and a bus (15 a day) gets to Ouro Preto by lunch (2 hrs.); bus fare, each way, US$2. Day trips are run; alternatively take an overnight bus from Rio, for example Util at 0830 and 2330 (US$6.50, 9 hrs), return bus to Rio leaves at same times. There is a new bus station (Rodoviária) at Ouro Preto, above the town near the São Francisco de Paula church. Book your return journey to Belo Horizonte early if returning in the evening; buses get crowded. There are also buses to Conselheiro Lafaiete for connections to Belo Horizonte and Congonhas, or to Rio via Barbacena and Juiz de Fora (direct bus to Rio is often fully booked 2-3 days in advance). Direct bus Ouro Preto to Vitória at 2100, US$5.50, 5½ hrs., not daily. Direct bus to São Paulo, 1900, 11 hrs., US$10.50. Check that your bus ticket from Ouro Preto is in fact from Ouro Preto and not from Belo Horizonte. Two buses an hour to Mariana (20 mins.). A tourist train, the Trem dos Inconfidentes, leaves Ouro Preto for Mariana 0900 Sat. and Sun., returning at 1600, US$2.50.

Mariana (population 20,000, 697 metres above sea level), another old mining city, founded 1696, much less hilly than Ouro Preto, is 12 km. E of Ouro Preto on a road which goes on to join the Rio-Salvador highway. See the beautiful old prison (Cadeia, 1768, now the Prefeitura Municipal, closed for restoration in 1988), the Carmo church (1784, steatite carvings, Athayde paintings, chinoiserie panelling), next to it is the fine São Francisco church (1762, granite painted to look like marble, pulpits designed by Aleijadinho, Athayde paintings and tomb, fine sacristy, one side-altar by Aleijadinho, entry, US$0.15) and the old Palace of the Governors connected with it, the Museum (formerly the Bishop's Palace) for its church furniture, gold and silver collection, Aleijadinho statues and ivory cross (open 0900-1100 except Tues. and 1200-1700; entrance US$0.80, good guide book), the city hall and the former post office, once a mansion. The Cathedral has been reopened, after repairs (entry US$0.15). Between the old prison and São Francisco is a stone monument to

Justice, at which slaves used to be beaten. The house of the poet Afonso de Guimarães, Rua Direita 35, is open to visitors: photographs and letters (free). There are viewpoints at the churches of N.S. do Rosário and São Pedro dos Clérigos. Some people still pan for gold in the river running through the town. Between Ouro Preto and Mariana is the Minas de Passagem gold mine, dating from 1719.

Minas de Passagem A guided tour visits the old mine workings and the processing plant, entrance US$3 each, visiting hours 0900-1800, T Ouro Preto 551-1068, Mariana 557-1340/1255. Bus between Ouro Preto and Mariana, every 20 mins., all stop, US$0.15 to Ouro Preto, US$0.20 to Mariana. Taxi from Ouro Preto, US$4.

Hotels *Itacolomi*, 6 km. out on Ponte Nova road, C; *Silva*, Rua Getúlio Vargas, D; *Faisca*, Rua Antônio Olinto 48, T 557-1206, F includes breakfast, spotless, excellent, friendly; *Müller*, Av. G. Vargas 34, E, *Central*, Rua Frei Durão 8, E, on attractive square, pleasant, quiet, clean but poor breakfast; *Dormitório Bandeirante*, Direita 185, F, basic. *Providência*, Rua Dom Silverio 161, T 557-1147, run by nuns, small rooms, D (electric shower), clean, quite. The modern service station (posto) on the highway above the town offers good clean rooms at F, with hot showers.

Restaurants *Alvorada*, Praça Claudio Mansel 42, US$1-3; *Panetão*, Rua Dom Viçoso; *Taubaú*, Praça da Sé; *Papinha della Nonna*, Praça Gomes Freire 246, Italian, rec. *Fundão 17*, Rua Direita 17, good and cheap.

Tourist Office Praça Bandeirantes, helpful for a guide or pamphlet and good map. Get off bus at first stop in Mariana rather than continuing to Rodoviária.

Congonhas do Campo (altitude 866 metres) is a small hill town with a good road through pleasant farming country connecting with Ouro Preto, and a paved 3½-km. road link with the Rio-Belo Horizonte highway. It is also on the Central do Brasil railway between Rio and Belo Horizonte (but no through train to Rio). The town is dominated by the great pilgrimage church of Bom Jesus do Matozinho (1773), which opens at 0815; indeed there is little else of architectural interest. There is a wide view of the country from the church terrace, below which are six small chapels set in attractive sloping gardens, showing scenes with life-size Passion figures carved by Aleijadinho and his pupils in cedar wood. The church is mainly famous for its group of prophets sculpted by Aleijadinho, standing on the parapets of the terrace. These twelve great dramatic statues (thought of as Aleijadinho's masterpieces), carved in soapstone with dramatic sense of movement, constitute one of the finest works of art of their period in the world—not just in Latin America. Inside the church, as well as the Room of Miracles, there are paintings by Athayde and the heads of four sainted popes (Gregory, Jerome, Ambrose and Augustine) sculpted by Aleijadinho for the reliquaries on the high altar. (Buses run from opposite the Rodoviária to Bom Jesus, US$0.10.) Pleasant excursion to waterfall with park and swimming, at Cachoeira Santo Antônio.

Congonhas is also celebrated for its Holy Week processions, which centre on the Bom Jesus church. The most celebrated ceremonies are the meeting of Christ and the Virgin Mary on the Tuesday, and the dramatized Deposition from the Cross late on Good Friday. Pilgrimage season, first half of September, draws many thousands.

Hotels *Colonial*, opp. Bom Jesus, good and comfortable, breakfast extra, no showers/toilets in room, blankets only, E-D; *Santuário*, Praça da Basílica 76, with fascinating restaurant downstairs full of colonial handicrafts and good local food, right next to Bom Jesus, "a bit run down, but charming", friendly, E; *Freitas*, Rua Marechal Floriano 69, F, basic. There are handicraft shops selling soapstone artefacts.

Bus From Belo Horizonte, US$1.50, 6 times a day, best to buy a return ticket. None direct from Rio; you have to change buses at Conselheiro Lafaiete (*Rhud's Hotel and Restaurant*, D; *Hotel Cupim*, on main Rio road, also D). To Congonhas from São João del Rei, take a São João-Belo Horizonte bus (5 a day) and alight at Murtinho, the crossing with the main Rio-Belo Horizonte highway (US$2); from there (it's an official bus stop) take a local bus (every ½ hr., US$0.50). Bus to Ouro Preto: either go via Belo Horizonte (US$1 to Congonhas), or bus (every ½ hr.) to Murtinho or Conselheiro Lafaiete, US$0.30 (30 mins.), then 0745, 1200, 1500 or 1845 bus to Ouro Preto, US$1.40, via Itabirito. Rodoviária is 1½ km. outside town.

Diamantina, the most remote of these cities, is reached from Belo Horizonte by paved road (289 km., 6 daily buses via Pássaro Verde, US$5, 5½ hrs.) but there is no scheduled air service. Take the road to Brasília almost as far as the turnoff for Curvelo (a lively town, *Hotel Sagarana*—5-star, very good; *Restaurant Denise* with sleeping accommodation, on main highway, very clean), then through the impressive rocky country of the Serra do Espinhaço. The old railway service has been discontinued. 30 km. N of Belo Horizonte on this road, is the *Hotel Fazenda* at Ipê Amarelo—horses to ride, etc. Further on, between Paraopeba and Caetanópolis, is the *Flora Eunice* (*Leite ao Pé de Vaca*) snackbar (good toilets) with small private botanic garden and zoo with contented animals, recommended. About 120 km. N of Belo Horizonte, 33,400 square km. of the Serra do Espinaço has been named as the **National Park of Serra do Cipó**, in view of its scenic beauty and rich variety of plant and animal life (IBDF office: Av. do Contorno 8121, CP 1304, CEP 30.000, Belo Horizonte).

Diamantina, centre of a once active diamond industry founded in 1729, has excellent colonial buildings. Its churches (difficult to get into, except for the modern Cathedral) are not so grand as those of Ouro Preto, but it is possibly the least spoilt of all the colonial mining cities, with carved overhanging roofs and brackets; try walking through the lower part of the town. This very friendly town is in the deep interior, 1,120 metres up amid barren mountains, with about 25,000 people; it is the birthplace of the late President Juscelino Kubitschek, the founder of Brasília. His house has been converted into a museum.

After repeated thefts, the diamonds of the Diamond Museum, in the house of Padre Rolim, one of the Inconfidentes (see under Ouro Preto) have been removed to the Banco do Brasil. Diamonds are still sought; see traditional methods at Guinda, 7 km. away. *Passeio a Diamantina*, an excellent guide, is written by the author of *Passeio a Sabará*. The town's latest industry is the making of Portuguese Arraiolos-style tapestry carpets by hand, at a cooperative in the centre; it was started by a diplomat, Sr Flecha da Silva, who was perturbed by the amount of local unemployment, and it has become very successful. Also etchings on leather are made locally.

The house of Chica da Silva, an 18th-century slave who married a rich diamond contractor, is at Praça Lobo Mesquita 266 (not worth a visit, entry US$0.30); Chica has become a folk-heroine among Brazilian blacks.

Hotels *Tijuco,* Macau do Melo 211, C, best, good food; *Grande,* Rua da Quitanda 70, D, *Carvalho,* same street No. 12, and *Dália,* Praça JK (Jota-Ka) 13, fairly good, E. *Pensão Avenida,* Av. Francisco Sá 243. Unnamed *pensão* at Rua Direita 131 (Dona Tazinha), F; *Esplanada,* F; *Nosso,* opp. bus station, F without breakfast, good value; also opp. bus station, *J.K.* Other cheap hotels around the bus station. Wild camping near waterfall just outside town.

Restaurants *Bar-Restaurant Confiança,* Rua da Quitanda 39, good. *Capistrana,* R. Campos Carvalho 36, near Cathedral square, rec. *Serestas* (serenades) Fri. and Sat. nights.

Voltage 110 A.C.

Tourist Information Dept. de Turismo in Casa de Cultura in Praça Antônio Eulálio 53 (no sign), 3rd floor, pamphlets and a reliable map.

Buses 6 a day to Belo Horizonte, via Curvelo, for connections to Brasília, with Pássaro Verde: 2½ hrs. to Curvelo, US$1.70, to Belo Horizonte, US$4.

Excursion Walk along the Caminho dos Escravos, the old paved road built by slaves between the mining area on Rio Jequitinhonha and Diamantina. A guide is essential (ask at the Casa de Cultura—cheap), and beware of snakes. Along the river bank to (12 km.) Biribiri, a pretty village with an abandoned textile factory (its inhabitants are reported to be leaving the village in great numbers). About half-way, swimming pools in the river; opposite them, on cliff face, animal paintings in red, age and origin unknown. Interesting plant life along river, and beautiful mountain views.

Serro, 92 km. by paved road from Diamantina and reached by bus from there or from Belo Horizonte, is an unspoilt colonial town on the River Jequitinhonha (17,000 people) with six fine baroque churches, a museum and many beautiful squares. It makes *queijo serrano,* one of Brazil's best cheeses, being in the centre of a prosperous cattle region. The most conspicuous church is Santa Rita, on a hill in the centre of town, reached by steps. On the main square, by the bottom of the steps, is the Carmo, arcaded, with original paintings on ceiling and in choir.

The town has two large mansions: those of the Barão de Diamantina, now in ruins, and of the Barão do Serro across the river, beautifully restored and used as the town hall and Casa de Cultura; there are old mine entrances in the hillside behind the courtyard.

Hotels *Pousada Vila do Príncipe,* D, very clean, in old mansion on main street, contains own museum, the artist Mestre Valentim said to have been born in slave quarters; other cheap hotels (e.g. *Dormitório,* Rua Rio Branco, opp. Banco do Brasil, F). Restaurants: *Itacolomi,* Praça João Pinheiro 20, fair; good one on main square, also *Churrascaria Vila do Príncipe* nearby on main street.

Just by the Serro turnoff is the town of Datas, whose spacious church (1832) decorated in red and blue, contains striking wooden image of Christ with the crown of thorns.

Tres Marias Some 240 km. NW of Belo Horizonte is a lake five times as large as Rio de Janeiro bay, formed by the Tres Marias dam on the upper reaches of the São Francisco river. There is a motel, and **the power company, Cemig, runs a guest house** (book in advance through its head office at Belo Horizonte). At Barreiro Grande is the *Clube Náutico Tres Marias,* E, simple. There are plans to develop the Tres Marias area for tourism.

(Almost the same distance SW of Belo is the even larger lake formed by the Furnas dam. It can be seen from the BR-381 road to São Paulo.)

Also north of Belo Horizonte is ***Pirapora,*** terminus for boat journeys on the River São Francisco (**see also page 360**). The town itself is also a tourist attraction because of the falls in the river which make for excellent fishing: catches weighing 73 kg. (160lb) have been reported. The sandy river beaches are used for swimming. The grotesque figureheads of the riverboats, *carrancas,* are made in the workshops of Lourdes Barroso, Rua Abaeté 390. There are several hotels: *Canoeiras,* used by river-tour parties, *Pirapora Palace,* on Praça Melo Viana (7 blocks west and 1 block south of Rodoviária), E, ask for room on garden, clean, friendly, safe, and *Hotel Rex,* Rua Antônio Nascimento 357, F, small breakfast, not very good. Camping near the Praça on riverside. Restaurants: *Borretos* on the riverfront, and *Barrenko,* next door, better value. Watch the fishermen at work in their punt-like canoes.

The old river passenger service of the Companhia de Navegação do São Francisco (Franave) to Juazeiro has been discontinued, but it is still possible to arrange journeys down the river on cargo boats if you talk to the masters, in the port. The *Taina* has been rec.: a trip to Ibotirama costs about US$70. If you can get on a cargo boat, the regular stops are at Januária (famous for Brazil's reputed best *cachaça*) and Bom Jesus da Lapa (a pilgrimage centre with a church built in a grotto inside a mountain, but a very poor town). Between Pirapora and Januária is the colonial town of São Francisco, with many attractive houses and a good handicraft market in the town hall; the boats do not always stop there. If you want to see the real Sertão, get off at Xique-Xique and take a bus to Utinga, Rui Barbosa and Itaberaba, then on to Salvador. Of the two remaining wood-burning stern-wheel boats, allegedly built for Mississippi services in the 1860s and imported from the USA in 1922 to work on the Amazon, one, the *Gaiola,* has been restored for tourist-agency use. A weekly trip (starting Sunday) is made downriver visiting various ports as far as São Francisco, organised by **Unitour or Mangebeira Turismo,** of Belo Horizonte, for about US$200 including return bus journey Belo-Pirapora (reportedly a jaunt for the wealthy).

If you can't get a boat, an adventurous journey to the Bahia coast is as follows: bus 0730 Pirpora-Montes Claros (also reached by train once a week from Belo Horizonte, next morning bus Montes Claros— Almenara (12 hrs.) then bus Almenara-Salto da Divisa (2½ hrs.), then after night in Salto at hotel facing bus station, take 0600 bus to Porto Seguro.

Eastern Minas

Eastern Minas Gerais is not of great cultural or historical interest, but is a centre of semi-precious stone processing and crystal carving, and also contains the Serra do Caparaó, where are found several of Brazil's highest mountains. The two principal towns, Governador Valadares and Teófilo Otôni, are both on the BR-116 inland Rio-Salvador road, and both have good connections with Belo Horizonte. **Focus Tours (see Belo Horizonte, see page 288)** offers naturetours in this area to see four rare monkey species, including the muriqui, and a number of other animals including tree sloths, maned wolves, and an incredible array of birds.

Douglas Trent writes:

Governador Valadares, 324 km. from Belo Horizonte, 5½ hours by bus (US$5 normal, US$10 *leito*) and also by regional air service, is a modern planned city of 250,000. The altitude is 170 metres. It is a centre of semi-precious stone mines and lapidation, as well as for the cut-crystal animals one finds in tourist shops all around Brazil.

Hotels Governador Palace, Av. Minas Gerais 550, B; *Real Minas*, Praça Serra Lima 607, C; *Panorama*, C; *São Salvador*, Rua Prudente de Morais 915, D, new, clean.

Restaurants Main hotels; *JB*, Rua Bárbara Heliodora 384, rec., huge servings; *Joazeiro*, Rua Pessanha 639; *Tabu*, good fish dishes.

Airport is on the BR-381, 6 km. from the city centre with flights to Belo Horizonte and Ipatinga.

Excursion to the top of the Pico de Ibituruna, 960 metres.

Hospital São Lucas, Rua Barão do Rio Branco 662, T 70-0121.

Teôfilo Otôni, 335 metres, population 129,000, 138 km. from Governador Valadares, is a popular buying spot for dealers of crystals and semi-precious stones. The best prices in the state are found here (try K. Eluwar Ltda, Rua Epamin 458—change money also).

Hotels *Nobre Palace*, Av. Francisco Sá 43; *Teôfilo Otôni*, BR-116 Norte km. 275, 5 km. from centre; *Lancaster*, Rua Frei Gonzaga 142, D; *Metropole*, Av. Francisco Sá 14, D; *Beira-Rio*, Av. Israel Pinheiro 671, E; *São Francisco*, Rua Dr. João Antônio 287; *Presidente*, Av. Getúlio Vargas 183, F, clean, good breakfast, laundry facilities.

Restaurants *Amigo do Rei*, Rua Benedito Valadares 161, T 521-4927; *Rio Grande*, next to *Teôfilo Otôni Hotel*; *Intermezzo*, next to *Lancaster Hotel*.

Bus to Porto Seguro via Nanuque (*Hotel Minas*, at Rodoviária, F, adequate).

Caparaó National Park, 49 km. by dirt road from Manhuaçu on the Belo Horizonte-Vitória road (BR-262), has the Pico da Bandeira (2,890m), Pico do Cruzeiro (2,861m) and the Pico do Cristal (2,798m). You can reach the car park at the base of the waterfall by car (6 km. from park gate). From there it is a spectacular hike to the top of Pico da Bandeira (2-3 hours). The park features rare Atlantic rainforest in its lower altitudes and Brazilian alpine on top. It is best to visit during the dry season (April-October). Camping is permitted within the park and in two spots and it can be quite crowded in July and during Carnaval. (IBDF address under Serra do Cipó, **page 293** above).

Hotel *Caparaó Parque*, near park entrance 15 mins. walk from the town of Caparaó, nice, B, T (032) 741-2559.

How to get there There are buses from Belo Horizonte, Ouro Preto or Vitória to *Manhumirim* (*Hotel São Luiz*, E, meal $1.10, good value, but *Cids Bar*, next door, Travessa 16 do Março, has better food). From Manhumirim, take a bus direct to Caparaó, 0930, 1630 US$0.50, or to Presidente Soares (several, 7 km.), then hitch 11 km. to Caparaó. From there jeeps (US$12 per jeep) run to the car park at 1,970 metres (2½ hrs.' walk), then it's a 3-4 hour walk to the summit of the Pico da Bandeira, marked by yellow arrows; plenty pf camping possibilities all the way up, the highest being at Terrreirão (2,370 m.). It is very difficult to get to the Pico da Bandeira from Manhumirim and back in a day. This is good walking country. It may also be possible to visit local *fazendas*, for example Fazenda Modelo, 8 km. from Manhumirim.

Southern and Western Minas

The spas of southern Minas Gerais are easily reached by road and in some cases by air from Rio de Janeiro and São Paulo. They are also popular holiday places; the high season is from December through March.

São Lourenço, easily accessible from Rio de Janeiro or São Paulo, stands at 850 metres above sea-level. There is a splendid park, tennis, boating, swimming, a flying field, and fishing from the Ilha dos Amores in a lake ringed by gardens and forests. There is a grand ride through fine scenery to the Pico de Buqueré (1,500 metres). Population: 15,000.

Its rich mineral waters are used in the treatment of stomach, liver, kidney and intestinal complaints. There is an up-to-date hydro establishment for douches and for the famous carbogaseous baths, unique in South America.

Bus service from Rio de Janeiro, 277 km., 5-6 hrs.; from São Paulo, 338 km., 6-7 hrs.

Hotels *Brasil*, nice; *Sul Americano Grande; Ponto Chic*, etc.

Caxambu, N of São Lourenço, at 900 metres, is one of the more sophisticated of these resorts. Its waters are used for treating stomach, kidney and bladder diseases, and are said to restore fertility. (They seemed to work for Princess Isabel, daughter of Dom Pedro II, who produced three sons after a visit. The little church of Santa Isabel da Hungária stands on a hill as a thank-offering.) The mountains and forests around are very beautiful. View over the city from Morro Caxambu, 1,010 metres. Population: 12,000. Excellent hotels.

Hotels *Glória; Palace; Avenida; Caxambu; Bragança*, and 20 others.

Lambari, a lesser-known resort, is 56 km. W of Caxambu by road at 900 metres. Efforts are under way to reopen the casino, closed in 1945. Hotels are not luxurious but fairly comfortable. The Parque das Águas has seven springs and a swimming pool. There are boat trips on the Lago Guanabara.

Hotels *Itaicy*, largest, on lake near Casino. Many others.

Cambuquirá, a little N of Lambari by road at 946 metres, very popular, with friendly atmosphere and picnic sites close by.

Hotels *Grande Hotel Empresa*; also *Santos Dumont*, and many others.

Poços de Caldas, in western Minas, is reached by road or plane from São Paulo (272 km.), Rio (507 km.) or Belo Horizonte (510 km.). The city is sited on the crater of an extinct volcano in a mountainous area. Venetians from Murano settled here and established a crystal-glass industry. It is the best-known of the resorts, and is a traditional honeymoon centre. It has complete and up-to-date thermal establishments for the treatment of rheumatic, skin and intestinal diseases; you need a local doctor's certificate to use these facilities. Excursions include several lakes within a few km. of the city with boating and restaurants; the Véu das Noivas with its three waterfalls illuminated at night; the tall statue of Cristo Redentor at an altitude of 1,678 metres, which can be reached by cable car; nearby is an 80-metre granite rock, Pedra Batão. There are also the lovers' well, Fonte dos Amores, and the Japanese teahouse at the Recanto Japonês. Hippie fair every Sunday in Praça Pedro Sanches. Festivals include Carnival, São Benedito ending on May 13, and recently established Festival de Música Popular Brasileira. Excellent climate. There is now a small industrial estate. Altitude: 1,180 metres; pop.: 110,000.

Hotels Some 80 hotels and pensions. *Palace,* old fashioned but well run, with sulphur baths; *Continental*, Av. Francisco Salles 235; *Pousada Vale das Rosas*, Rodovia a Belo Horizonte Km. 5; *Minas Gerais*, Rua Pernambuco 615.

Restaurants *Castelões*, Praça Pedro Sanches 207; *Lareira*; *Sem-Sem*, Rua Assis Figueiredo 1080; *Cantina do Araújo*, Rua Assis Figueiredo 1705.

Buses Rio, 8 hrs., US$6; São Paulo, 4½ hrs., US$3.50; both by Viação Cometa.

Tres Corações, also in southern Minas but not a spa, is the birthplace of Pelé, the legendary football star (statue). Hotels: *Italian Palace*, E; *Capri*, F; good food at *Cantina Calabresa*. Reached by daily buses from Rio, São Paulo and Belo Horizonte. Daily bus to (32 km.) **São Tomé das Letras**, beautiful hilltop village with frescoed 17th-century church and many caves in surrounding hills.

Note that there are also mountain spa resorts (Serra Negra, Lindóia, Campos do Jordão) in São Paulo State (**see page 316**).

Araxá, in the Minas Triangle, about 193 km. before Uberaba at 970 metres, is a quiet little place with thorium and radio-active waters and sulphur and mud baths. It can be reached from Rio (848 km.) or São Paulo (549 km.) Belo Horizonte (374 km.), by bus. Pop.: 30,000, Airport.

Hotels   *Grande de Araxá,* luxury, 8 km. away; *Grande Hotel Pinto; Colombo.*

South of Araxá is the **Serra da Canastra National Park**, in which the Rio São Francisco rises. It is a cool region (temperatures in May and June average 18°C), best reached from Piumhi, on state road 050, 267 km. W of Belo Horizonte.

Uberaba, also in the Minas Triangle, is on the Rio da Prata, 718 km. from São Paulo. It is an important rail and road junction, being on the direct highway between São Paulo and Brasília, and serves a large cattle raising district. At the beginning of May each year the Rural Society of the Minas Triangle holds a famous cattle and agricultural exhibition at Uberaba. Altitude, 700 metres. Population, 180,000. Hotels: *Palácio; Grande.* Bus from Belo Horizonte, US$6 (*leito* US$12), 7 hrs.

To the N of Uberaba is *Uberlândia*, founded in 1888; good communications by air and road (buses to Brasília, 6 hrs., US$5; to Belo Horizonte, 9 hrs., US$7.50, to São Paulo, US$8). Population, 230,000. *Hotel Nacional*, opposite Rodoviária, F, with view (cheaper without), shower and breakfast, clean.

THE STATE OF SÃO PAULO (5)

The State of São Paulo, with an area of 247,898 square km. and a population of 25 million, is larger than the states of New York and Pennsylvania together and about the same size as Great Britain and Northern Ireland. A narrow zone of wet tropical lowland along the coast rises in an unbroken slope to the ridge of the Great Escarpment—the Serra do Mar—at from 800 to 900 metres above sea level. The upland beyond the Great Escarpment is drained westwards by the tributaries of the Rio Paraná. The broad valleys of the uplands are surmounted by ranges of low mountains; one such range lies between the São Paulo basin and the hinterland of the state. West of the low mountains between the basin and the rest of the state lie the uplands of the Paraná Plateau, at about 600 metres above the sea. One of the soils in this area is the *terra roxa*, the red earth in which coffee flourishes. When dry it gives off a red dust which colours everything; when wet it is sticky and slippery. There is ample rainfall in São Paulo State; indeed, the highest rainfall in Brazil (3,810 mm.) is over a small area between Santos and São Paulo; at São Paulo itself it is no more than 1,194 mm. Temperatures on the plateau are about 5°C lower than on the coast, but it is only south of the latitude of Sorocaba that frosts occur and then not frequently. Temperatures are too low for coffee in the São Paulo basin itself, but the State produces, on average, about 7 million bags a year.

Between 1885 and the end of the century a boom in coffee and the arrival of large numbers of Europeans transformed the State out of all recognition. By the end of the 1930s there had arrived in São Paulo State a million Italians, half a million each of Portuguese and immigrants from the rest of Brazil, nearly 400,000 Spaniards and nearly 200,000 Japanese. The population is now almost equal to that of Argentina or Colombia. Today the State produces 50% of the country's cotton, 62% of its sugar, a third of its coffee and over 50% of its fruit exports. It turns out 90% of Brazil's motor vehicles, 65% of its paper and cellulose, and 60% of its machinery and tools, being also responsible for 60% of the country's industrial consumption of electric energy. All this comes, in sum, to some 20% of Brazil's agricultural output and 65% (40% in São Paulo city alone) of its industrial production. São Paulo provides 33% of the total exports of Brazil and takes 40% of the total imports: nearly all pass through the port of Santos.

São Paulo is 429 km. from Rio de Janeiro, and is connected with it by air, the Via Dutra highway, and the Central do Brasil railway. It was founded in 1554 by two Jesuit priests from São Vicente, Blessed José Anchieta and Padre Manuel Nóbrega, as a mission station. The original settlement, not yet effectively preserved, was at the Pátio do Colégio in the centre of the city, where a copy of Anchieta's original church has been built (it is open Tues. to Sun., 1300-1700).

SÃO PAULO
ORIENTATION MAP

NOT TO SCALE

33A

1. Cathedral
2. São Paulo Museum of Art (MASP)
3. Butantã Snake Farm and Museum
4. University City
5. Ibirapuera Park
6. Parque da Independência and Museu Paulista
7. Parque do Estado, Botanical and Zoological Gardens
8. Pacaembu Stadium
9. Anhembi
10. Morumbi Stadium
11. Parque Agua Branca
12. Casa do Bandeirante
13. Museum of Lasar Segall
14. Casa do Sertanista
15. Casa Brasileira
16. Museum of Brasilian Art

São Paulo (altitude 730 metres) is one of the fastest growing cities in the world. It is already the most populous city in South America, and the continent's leading industrial centre. Until the 1870s it was a sleepy, shabby little town, but it now covers more than 1,500 square km.—three times the size of Paris. The citizens are intensely proud of its skyscrapers, of its well-lit streets, of its efficient water supply, and especially of its underground railway, the first in Brazil, which began operating in September 1975, linking Jabaquara in the south with Santana in the north. (A second line is now open.) The traffic pattern is extremely exasperating: you may have to drive around 10 blocks to reach a point half a block away. Also exasperating is the amount of air pollution: in dry weather eyes and nose are continually troubled. The city's population is now estimated at almost 9 million; in 1983 the metropolitan area population was estimated at 13 million, growing at about 150,000 a year, compared with 9.5 million for the metropolitan area population of Rio.

The two main reasons for the city's development lie in its position at the focus of so much agricultural wealth, and in its climate, which makes the Paulistanos the most hard working and energetic people in Brazil. Visitors, however, find the characteristic sharp changes of temperature troublesome and even Paulistanos seem to catch cold often. (Incidentally, one differentiates between Paulistas— inhabitants of the State—and Paulistanos— inhabitants of the city.) There is another and a most potent factor which explains its industrial growth: the availability of plentiful hydro-electric power.

The shopping, hotel and restaurant centre embraces the districts of Av. São Luís, the Praça da República, and Rua Barão de Itapetininga. The commercial quarter, containing banks, offices and shops, is contained within a central district known as the Triângulo, bounded by Rua Direita, Quinze de Novembro, São Bento and Praça Antônio Prado, but it is already rapidly spreading towards the apartment and shopping district of Praça da República. Rua Augusta, near Avenida Paulista, once the home of the wealthier citizens, is now full of boutiques and fashion shops. Avenida Paulista houses most consulates in skyscrapers, many banking head offices, and the Assis Chateaubriand Art Museum of São Paulo (MASP—opened by Queen Elizabeth in 1968). It is becoming a new downtown area, more dynamic than the old centre, and so is Av. Faria Lima, 8 km. from Praça da República. (Good view of the city from Conjunto Nacional, Horsa II, Av. Paulista, free on presentation of passport).

The park in Praça da República is worth going into between 0800 and 1400 on Sun.: birds, trees and Brazilians in all their variety, and a famous handicrafts fair. Near the Praça is the city's tallest building, the Edifício Itália on the corner of Av. Ipiranga and Av. São Luís. There is a restaurant on top (very reasonable), and a sightseeing balcony.

The Viaduto do Chá, which bridges the central avenue, Anhangabaú, leads to the opera house, one of the few distinguished 19th-century survivals that São Paulo can boast (closed for repair 1987/88). The Av. Paulista and the "jardins" América, Paulista and Paulistano still contain some mansions of beauty and interest and are on one of the routes to the Butantã Institute or "snake farm". About 10 minutes' walk from the centre of the city is the old Municipal Market, covering an area of 27,000 square metres; a new Municipal Market has been built in the outskirts. The Municipal Library, surrounded by a pleasant shady garden, is well worth visiting.

The Cathedral's foundations were laid over 40 years before its inauguration during the 1954 festivities commemorating the 4th centenary of the city. This massive building in neo-Gothic style, with a capacity for 8,000 worshippers, is in the heart of the city.

The large Municipal Stadium in the Pacaembu valley, a flourishing residential district, is well worth seeing. Built on Olympic lines in an area of 75,500 square metres, it holds nearly 70,000 spectators. Besides the flood-lit football ground and athletics field and basketball court, there are also a covered gymnasium, open-air and covered tennis courts, an illuminated 50-metre long swimming pool, a youth hostel, and a great hall for receptions and rallies. There is a larger stadium holding 100,000 people in Morumbi, one of the more elegant residential districts.

Typical of modern development are the huge Iguatemi, Ibirapuera and Morumbi shopping centres. They include luxurious cinemas, snack bars and most of the best shops in São Paulo. Parking in each for over 1,000 vehicles. On a rather humbler level are the big supermarkets of El Dorado (Av. Pamplona 1704) and Pão de Açúcar (Praça Roosevelt, near the *Hilton*); the latter is open 24 hrs. a day (except Sun.).

The palatial Jockey Club racecourse is in the Cidade Jardim district with easy access by bus. Race meetings are held on Sat., Sun., Mon. and Thurs. nights. The new town premises of the Jockey Club (Rua Boa Vista) are well worth a visit.

Ibirapuera   Take the Monções bus (675-C) from Ana Rosa metro station to Ibirapuera Park for the architecturally impressive new Legislative Assembly. There is also a planetarium equipped with the most up-to-date machinery (shows at 2000 Tues. and Thurs.; 1600, 1800 and 2000 weekends and holidays); a velodrome for cycle and motor-cycle racing; an all-aluminium covered stadium for indoor sports which seats 20,000 people. The Museum of Contemporary Art (of the Universidade de São Paulo), founded in 1963, has an important collection of Western and South American modern art. The collection is divided between the Bienal building in Parque Ibirapuera (entrance at back of building, open Tues.-Sun., 1300-1800, closed holidays, free) and a building at Rua da Reitoria, 109, Cidade Universitária, open Weds.-Sun. 1000-1700, closed holidays, students free (it is hoped to unite the collection at the Cidade Universitária). Buses to Ibirapuera, 6414 (Gatusa) from Praça da Bandeira; to Cidade Universitária 702U or 7181 from Praça da República.

In this park, too, are the Museums of Modern Art, Aviation (showing the Santos Dumont plane; US$0.40 entrance, open to 1600 only), Folklore (interesting) and Sciences. There is also a unique display of nativity scenes and scenes of the life of Christ. (Concerts held at Christmas-time). At the entrance is a majestic monument to the Bandeirantes, or pioneers. All the Ibirapuera museums (except Aviation) are open Tues.-Sun., 1400-1700. (For other museums **see page 305**.)

Anhembi (Av. Assis Chateaubriand, Santana) is the largest exhibition hall in the world. It was inaugurated in 1970 and all São Paulo's industrial fairs are held there. It has a meeting hall seating 3,500 people, three *auditórios*, 24 conference rooms (*salas de reunião*) and two restaurants. Parking space is provided for 3,500 cars. It may be reached by underground (short walk from Tietê station).

Local Holidays   Jan. 25 (Foundation of City).

Warning   Beware of assaults and pickpocketing in São Paulo.

Hotels   Among the most luxurious are the *Maksoud Plaza*, the *Caesar Park*, the *Grand Hotel Cà d'Oro* (superb restaurant), the *Brasilton*, the *Eldorado* (excellent), the *Della Volpe Garden*, and the *Hilton*, all with swimming pools, nightclubs and convention halls. The *Grand Corona*, *Monfarrej Sheraton*, and *Cambridge* have been rec. (although the last named's location is uninspiring). Here follows a selection in our categories L, A and B. Prices for the cheapest room in each category are as follows (incl. breakfast), in US dollars:

	Single	Double	Rooms	Class*
Maksoud Plaza, Alameda Campinas 150	195	215	420	L
Caesar Park, Rua Augusta 1508	192	215	200	L
Mofarrej Sheraton, Alameda Santos 1437	120-280	120-300		L
Della Volpe Garden, Frei Caneca 1199	170	223		L
Eldorado Boulevard, Av. São Luís 234	137	153	154	L
Hilton, Av. Ipiranga 165	115	130	391	L
Grand Hotel Cà d'Oro, Rua Augusta 129	120	140	400	1+
Brasilton, Rua Martins Fontes 330	115	130	111	1+
Bristol, Rua Martins Fontes 277	94	114		
São Paulo Center, Largo Santa Ifigênia 40	63	73	253	1+
Othon Palace, Rua Líbero Badaró 190	66	74		
Samambaia, Rua Sete de Abril 422	60	70	65	1+
Vila Rica, Av. Vieira de Carvalho 167	56	70	215	1+
San Raphael, Av. São João 1173	94	108	197	1+
Jaraguá, Rua Major Quedinho 44	50	62	197	1+
Grand Corona (ex-*Cà d'Oro*), Basílio da Gama 101	71	88	82	
Excelsior, Av. Ipiranga 770	37	42	180	T
Planalto, Cásper Líbero 117 (Varig-Tropical chain)	46	51	268	1
Terminus, Av. Ipiranga 741	31	38	67	T
Normandie, Av. Ipiranga 1187	74	88	200	S
Cambridge, Av. Nove de Julho 216	35	41	120	S
Solar Paulista, Rua Francisca Miquelina 343	40	48	60	S

*Class: L—de luxe; 1+—first class plus; 1—first class; S—standard; T—tourist.

There are scores of cheaper hotels, of which we append a selection: *Hores Belgrano*, Rua Marquês de Paranaguá, 88, D, central, English spoken, special rates for long stays, rooms with

1. Cathedral
2. Praça da República
3. Praça Roosevelt
4. Praça Princesa Isabel
5. Praça Alfredo Issa
6. Praça Júlio Prestes
7. Museum of Sacred Art
8. Luz Station
9. Sorocabana Station
10. Bus Station for Santos
11. Tiete Metro Station
12. Old Municipal Market
13. Anhembi Exhibition Centre
14. Military Hospital
15. Cheap Hotel Area

SÃO PAULO
CENTRE
MAIN STREETS ONLY 33

kitchenette. Another residential hotel, rec. for longer stays, is *Metropolitan Plaza*, Alameda Campinas 474, A. *Las Vegas*, Rua Vitória 390 (corner Av. Rio Branco), E, excellent; *Continental*, same street, No. 223, F, clean, safe, highly rec.; *Rio Branco*, Av. Rio Branco 234, near corner with Ipiranga, D, central, with bath, rec.; *Paris*, 7 de Abril (close to Anhangabaú metro station), D with shower, TV, clean, honest, highly rec.; *Marechal*, Av. Barão de Limeira 339, 67 rooms, D with bath and telephone, safe, excellent; *Kolins*, Alameda Gilete 1017 (off São João, nearest subway Praça República), D, clean, hot water, private toilet; *Metro*, Av. Paulista at Paraíso Metro station, E without breakfast, quiet, convenient. *Banri*, Rua Galvão Bueno 209, B, good; *Isei*, Rua da Glória 288, D, good value, simple, nice, both near metro station Liberdade (Japanese quarter). *Center Bela Vista*, 13 de Maio 198 (T 257-2658), near plenty of restaurants in an old Italian suburb (Rua Santo Antônio/Rua 13 de Maio, nr. Praça da Bandeira).

Also suggested: *S. Sebastião*, 7 de Abril 364 (T 257-4988/255-1594), E, rec., cheap and clean, and now has rooms with bath; *Cineasta*, Av. São João 613, 80 rooms, D; *Plaza*, Av. São João 407, 42 rooms, D; *Central*, Av. São João 288, E with shower, F without, clean, good if a little run down, central; many others in and around Av. São João. On Rua do Triúnfo: *Condeixa*, No. 145, F, showers; *Maringá*, F, friendly, basic; *Noroeste*, No. 285, F, basic, clean, hot showers; *Saturno*, F, hot water, soap and towel. Very many of the cheap hotels are hot-pillow establishments.

Take the metro to Luz station and in the block behind the old Rodoviária, off Av. Rio Branco, there are scores of cheap hotels with prices ranging from category F to category C; try: Rua Santa Ifigênia: *Trinidade*, No. 737, E, clean but noisy and shabby; *Lima*, E, friendly, rec.; *Luanda*, No. 348, F with breakfast, English-speaking owner, helpful, rec.; *Aliança*, No. 235 (corner Santa Ifigênia), E, nice; *Ouro Fino Hotel Familiar*, No. 388, E, friendly; *Uai*, No. 66, E, clean and pleasant, rooms on street are good, rec. Rua dos Gusmões: *Galeão*, No. 394, E, clean, safe, helpful, hot showers; *Hospedaria Apuliense Familiar*, No. 218, F, with shower; *Santa Ifigênia*, E, lunch available for US$1.70. Rua dos Andradas: *Itaipu*, No. 467, E, good, clean. Rua Barão de Piracicaba, *São José*, F without breakfast, basic, good value; *Osiris*, Cásper Líbero 591, E with bath and breakfast, clean, quite good, hot water, near Luz railway station; *Lisboa*, same street, E, basic, shared shower, safe; and *Lepanto*, No. 359, E, shower, TV, clean; *Tatuí*, Praça Princeza Isabel 171 (on corner of Av. Duque de Caxias, 2 blocks from old bus station), F, clean with bath. **N.B.** the redlight district is in the blocks bounded by Ruas Santa Ifigênia, dos Andradas, dos Gusmões and Av. Ipiranga, and is definitely not rec. for women travelling alone. *Casa do Politécnico*, Rua Afonso Pena 272, cheap accommodation. *Comendadore*, Largo Santa Cecília, E, safe, quiet. A rec. "Apart-hotel" for longer stays is *Residencial Alameda Nothman* (Santa Cecília), Al. Nothman 682. *Residence Saint Thomas*, Av. Joaquim Eugênio de Lima 1360, good value service apartments (B); in same chain *Residence Saint James* and 2 others. *Service-Flat Monterey*, Alameda Itu 265, Jardim Paulista, has been rec. for longer stays, at US$600/month; safe parking, comfortable accommodation. Accommodation of the youth-hostel type is available at the Pacaembu Stadium at a fee in (our) category E. A letter addressed to the Secretário de Esportes is required. The Youth Hostel (*Albergue da Juventude*) is in the Ibirapuera gymnasium, Nóbrega e Estados Unidos, very cheap but you must first join the Brazilian YHA (15 de Novembro e Av. São João—office in centre) for about US$5 a year. Also Magdalena Tagkiaferro, Estrada Turística do Jaguará 651, Km. 18, via Anhanguera, 05173 São Paulo (T 229-3787/3011).

Electric Current   110-220 volts A.C., 60 cycles.

Camping   Cemucam, at Cobia (Rodovia Raposo Tavares, km. 27). List of sites can be obtained from Camping Clube do Brasil, R. Minerva, 156—Perdizes (T 263-024).

Restaurants   Apart from the international cuisine in the first-class hotels listed above, here are only a few out of many:

Portuguese   *Abril em Portugal*, Rua Caio Prado 47; and others.
Italian   *Tibêrio*, Av. Paulista 392; *Famiglia Marcini*, Rua Avanhandava 81; *Trattoria do Piero*, Rua Caconde 323, popular and good; *Gigeto*, Avanhandava 63; *A Camorra*, R. de Consolação 3589; *Trattoria del Sargento*, Al. Campinas (3 establishments), popular; *Leonardo*, Al. Santos 1508 (opp. *Sheraton*), good; *Pastasciutta*, Rua Barão do Triúnfo 427 (Brooklin Paulista); *Cantina Roma*, Rua Maranhão 512 (Higienópolis); *Trastevere*, Al. Santos 1518; *Bongiovanni*, Av. 9 de Julho 5511; *Da Fierella*, R. Bernardino de Campos 294; *Don Ciccillo*, Praça Souza Aranha 185; *L'Osteria do Piero*, Alameda França 1509; *Via Veneto*, Al. Barros 909; *Giovanni Bruno*, Rua Martinho Prado 165; *Il Sogno di Anarello*, Rua José Maria Lisboa 661, Jardim Paulista; *Grupo*

Key to Map of São Paulo (Centre Detail)
1. Praça da Sé; 2. Praça da República; 3. Parque Dom Pedro II; 4. Pátio do Colégio and Museu Padre Anchieta; 5. Praça Dr. João Mendes; 6. Praça da Bandeira; 7. Praça Roosevelt and Church of Consolação; 8. Praça Dom José Gaspar and Municipal Library; 9. Praça Ramos Azevedo; 10. Largo do Arouche; 11. Largo Paiçandu; 12. Largo São Bento; 13. Praça Clovis Bevilagua; 14. Praça Antônio Prado; 15. Cathedral; 16 São Bento; 17. São Francisco do Assis; 18. São Gonçalo; 19. Old Municipal Market; 20. Teatro Municipal; 21. Edifício Itália; 22. Central Post Office; 23 Embratel; 24. State Tourist Offices (2 locations). **Hotels:** 25. Hilton; 26. Grand Cà d'Oro; 27. Cambridge; 28. Othon Palace; 29. Excelsior; 30. Samambaia.

SÃO PAULO
CENTRE DETAIL
33B

Sérgio, Post Office building in Av. São João near Rua Marconi (rec.); *Piemontese*, Al. França 1509, Jardim Paulista, popular, huge meals; and many others in Rua 13 de Maio (Bela Vista)— *Lazzarella, Roperto, La Fontana di Trevi, La Tavola*—and neighbourhood. *Casa de Pizza Rodízio*, Rua Augusta 1585, all you can eat for US$4. *La Farina*, Av. Ipiranga 924, for good cheap pasta, popular.

French *David's*, R. Oscar Freire 913; *La Cocagne*, Rua Amaral Gurgel 378; *La Casserole*, Largo do Arouche 346, US$25; *La Gratinée*, Rua Bento Freitas, 42; *La Maison Basque*, Av. João Dias 239; *Le Bistrot*, Av. Adolfo Pinheiro 510; *Freddy*, Praça Dom Gastão Liberal Pinto 11; *Marcel*, Rua Epitácio Pessoa 98.

German *Juca Alemão*, Av. Santo Amaro and Al. Lorena; *Bierhalle*, Av. Lavandisca 263; *Biergarten*, Av. Ibirapuera 3174; *Kobes*, Av. Santo Amaro 5394; *Zillertal*, Av. Brig. Luís Antônio 909.

Swiss *Chamonix*, Rua Pamplona 1446, very expensive; *Maison Suisse*, Rua Caio Prado 183.

Austrian *Kitzbühel*, R. Frei Gaspar.

Greek *Mikonos*, R. Henrique Monteiro 218.

Middle East *Almanara* (Arab), good and reasonable, Av. São João 1155, Oscar Freire 523, Av. Vieira de Carvalho 109 and 124; *Rubayat*, Av. Vieira de Carvalho 134, Al. Santos 86 and Av. Faria Lima 5332, excellent meat.

Oriental *Sino-Brasileiro*, Rua Alberto Torres 39 (Perdizes); *Gengis Khan*, Av. Rebouças 3241 (Chinese); *Golden Dragon*, Av. Rebouças 2371; *Yamanga*, R. Tomás Gonzaga 66; *Heike* and *Notre Dame*, both Av. Paulista 2064 (Center 3); *Akasaka*, Rua 13 de Maio 1639; *Shushi-Kiyo*, also 13 de Maio, rec. Many other Chinese and Japanese restaurants in Liberdade, the Japanese quarter, where there is a Japanese food market in the square by the metro station. *Kokeche*, Rua dos Estudantes 41 (Liberdade), good, reasonably-priced *sushi* bar; *Hare Krishna*, Rua Pandiá Calógeras 54, Liberdade, near São Joaquim metro station; *Korea House*, Galvão Bueno 43 (Liberdade).

Vegetarian *Superbom*, Viaduto 9 de Julho 180, Praça da Sé 62, Praça da República 128 (lunch only); *Salade e Chi*, Rua Aurora, US$2.50 for all you can eat; *Sattua*, Rua da Consolação 3140; same street, No. 2961, *Mãe Terra* (shop also); *O Arroz de Ouro*, Largo do Arouche 46 (shop as well); *Cheiro Verde*, Peixoto Gomide 1413; several off Av. Paulista, including *Boy Papi*, on Rua Augusta; *Nectar*, Alameda Gabriel Monteiro da Silva 1931 (open to midnight except Mon.); *Jasmin Casa de Chá*, vegetarian food and tea house, Rua Haddock Lobo 932; *Intergrão*, Av. Rebouças 2036; *Delícia Natural*, Av. Rio Branco 211 (4th floor), corner Av. Ipiranga, lunch only, good; *Herva*, Rua Pinheiros 541; good one next to Geomapas, 300 block of Libero Badaró, buffet lunch US$1.50. "Vida Integral" newspaper (US$0.35) gives details of all health food restaurants and stores in São Paulo.

General *Terraço Itália*, on top of Edifício Itália, 41 floors up, good fixed price lunch, dancing with excellent band and superb view (must consume to be allowed to see the view); *Mexilhão*, Rua 13 de Maio 62, Bela Vista, very good. *Buffalo Grill*, Rua Bela Cintra 2231, US$20, very good; *O Beco*, Rua Bela Cintra 306, dinner only; *Dinho's Place*, Largo do Arouche 246, Al. Santos 45 and Av. Morumbi 7976, US$25; *Rodeio*, Rua Haddock Lobo 1468, excellent meat dishes, US$25; *Paddock*, Av. São Luís 228 and Av. Faria Lima 1541 (genuine Brazilian, serves feijoada completa, very expensive); *Um, Dois, Feijão e Arroz*, Rua Ipiranga, modest (US$3 or 4) but excellent (4 other branches); *Cantina Amigo Piolin*, Rua Augusta 89, excellent and cheap; *Alvear*, Rua Seminario, near Central Post Office, cheap surtido; *Bolinha*, Av. Cidade Jardim 53 for feijoadas (on Wed. and Sat.); *Maria Fulô*, Av. 9 de Julho for Bahia and other regional dishes—fixed menu, fixed price, very expensive; *Oxalá*, Maria Antônia, just off Consolação, Bahian specialities at modest prices; *O Veleiro*, Santo Amaro 15 (Praça da Bandeira), Amazonian specialities; Airport Restaurant (very good); *Jack in the Box*, fast food, several locations. *Pizza d'Oro*, in Vila Mariana (local painters and sculptors); many snack-bars and pizzerias throughout the city. For fast food, there are now several McDonalds in São Paulo. There are plenty of atmospheric restaurants in the "artists' quarter" of Bexiga (Bela Vista), best Fri. and Sat. nights. Another atmospheric place is *Recanto Goiano*, just off Praça 14 bis (Av. 9 de Julho), typical dishes, caipira music.

Bars *Bar Brasil*, Bela Ciutra 1209, Jardins; *Spazio Pirandello*, Augusta 371, Zona Central (not expensive, a meeting place for intellectuals); *Scotch Bar*, Rua 24 de Maio 35, conjunto 411; *Pepe's Bar*, Edifício Metrópole; *Finnegan's*, Alameda Itú 1529 (esq. Consolação) and Cristiano Viana 358 (esq. Artur de Azevedo), rec., international clientéle; several outdoor bars in Largo do Arouche and in Moema; all major hotels. Many gay and lesbian bars.

Tea Rooms Chá Mon (Edifício Metropole); Chelsea Art Gallery, *Hotel Eldorado*. *Jasmin*, Rua Haddock Lobo 932.

Night Clubs There are several first-class night-clubs serving excellent meals; they prefer couples to single people. Besides very good dance-bands, the majority have floor-shows in which internationally-famed artists perform. *A Baiúca*, Praça Roosevelt 256; *Silvio's* and *Plano's*, Oscar Freire 913 and 811 respectively; *Stardust*, Largo do Arouche 336. *Catedral da Samba* (Rua Rui Barbosa 333); *Igrejinha* (Rua Santo Antônio 973) and *O Beco* (Rua Bela Cintra 306), rec. for samba. Also rec.: *O Jogral*, Rua Maceió 66, Higienópolis (reasonable). Several small clubs with live music in the Bela Vista area of Av. Santo Antônio and Rua 13 de Maio.

Discotheques   London Tavern (Hilton Hotel, subsolo); Ton Ton (Rua Néstor Pestana 115); Moustache (Rua Sergipe 160—gay), Madame Satã, Conselheiro Ramalho 873, Bela Vista, zona central (new-wave type), among others. Jazz at Opus 2004, Rua Consolação 2004.

Shopping   Rua Augusta for boutiques. All types of stores at Shopping Center Iguatemi, Av. Brig. Faria Lima, Shopping Centre Ibirapuera, Av. Ibirapuera (**see page 300**), and Shopping Centre Morumbi, also El Dorado Shopping Centre (corner of Av. Rebouças and Marginal Pinheiros). Souvenirs from Mimosa, Joaquim Nabuco 275, Brooklin Paulista; Indian handicraft, Artíndia, Rua Augusta 1371 (Galeria Ouro Velho), T 283-2102; Coisarada, Rua Tabapuã 390, Itaim Bibi (T 881-4810). Also good for souvenirs is the area between Rua 24 de Maio and bars and pizzerias Rua 7 de Abril (just off Praça da República); bargaining is rec.; plenty of jewellers here. H. Stern, jewellers, at Praça da República 242, Rua Augusta 2340 and at Iguatemi, Ibirapuera and Morumbi shopping centres and at main hotels. Open air markets: "Hippy" fair, Praça da República, Sun. 0800-1400, very varied, many tourists, good selection of inexpensive fossils, Bahian food, lots of artists; "Oriental" fair, Praça de Liberdade Metro, Sun. p.m., good for Japanese snacks but not much else; at Praça da Sé, Liberdade, Sun., very picturesque, with remedies on sale, tightrope walking, gypsy fortune tellers, etc. Below the Museu de Arte de São Paulo, a flea market takes place on Sun., 0800-1700; there is another flea market Suns. in the main square of the Bexiga district. São Paulo is cheap for film and clothes. The Ceasa flower market, Tues. and Fri. a.m., is supposedly one of the largest in the world; ask taxi drivers how to get there.

Bookshops   Livraria Cultura, Eva Herz e Cia., Av. Paulista 2073, loja 153. Livraria Triângulo, Alameda Tietê 46. Ilco, Barão do Triúnfo 371, Brooklin Paulista, books in English. Livraria Kosmos, Praça Dom José Caspar 134, loja 30, international stock. Livraria Alemã, Rua Laplace 159, Brooklin; Librairie Française, R. Barão de Itapetininga 275, wide selection. Book Centre, R. Gabus Mendes 29 (near Praça de República), books in English.

Local Transport   The metro is clean, cheap and efficient; book of ten tickets US$1.25. Combined bus and metro ticket are available, e.g. to Congonhas airport. The East-West line (2) is being extended 14 km. from Barra Funda (the interchange with Fepasa and RFFSA railways and site of a future, third Rodoviária) to Itaquera. Local buses are normally crowded and rather slow, but clean. Maps of the bus and metro system are available at depots, e.g. Anhangabaú. Taxis display cards of actual tariffs in the window. The municipal transport agency CMTC organizes tours of the city by metro and bus (US$1) or by metro only (US$0.50). Information and tickets at the Sé metro station. Sightseeing tours also leave on Sundays from Praça da República.

Golf Courses   About half an hour's drive from the centre there are two 18-hole golf courses, one at Santo Amaro, and another, the São Fernando Golf Club, in beautiful surroundings. There is a sporting 9-hole course at São Francisco club, beyond the Butantã Institute.

Sport   The most popular is association football. The most important matches are played at Morumbi and Pacaembu grounds. At Interlagos there is a first-class racing track (**see page 309**). There is yachting, sailing and rowing on the Santo Amaro reservoir. For nature trails, etc., Free Way, Rua Leôncio de Carvalho 267, Paraíso, CEP 04.003 São Paulo, T 285-4767/283-5983.

Entertainment   The Teatro Municipal is used by visiting theatrical and operatic groups but has no resident company. There are several first-class theatres: Aliança Francesa, Teatro Arena, Itália, Maria Della Costa, Paiol, Ruth Escobar among others. There are also ballet companies and the usual multitude of luxurious cinemas.

Culture and Education   There are three universities: the official university of São Paulo, the Pontifical Catholic University, and the Mackenzie University. The official University of São Paulo is now situated in the Cidade Universitária (buses from main bus station), outside the city beyond Pinheiros. There are a number of architecturally interesting buildings housing different faculties and the four museums of archaeology, ethnology, anthropology and mineralogy. (All keep different hours, but all are open Mon.-Thurs. 1400-1700.)

Galleries and Museums The Museu de Arte de São Paulo (founded by Assis Chateaubriand, Av. Paulista 1578, immediately above the 9 de Julho tunnel, nearest metro is Paraíso, or circular bus 805A from Praça da República) has a large group of French Impressionists, Florentine and Umbrian painters (including Botticelli and Raphael), several Hieronymus Bosch and Frans Post, sculptures by Rodin, some interesting work by Brazilian artists, including Portinári. Particularly interesting are the pictures of the North-East done by Dutch artists during the Dutch occupation (1630-54): the exotic tropical landscapes— even the Paulo Afonso falls!—have been made to look incredibly temperate. (Exhibitions vary, not all the artists above may be on view.) Temporary exhibitions are held in the basement. Entrance US$0.25, Tues.-Fri. 1300-1700, Sat.-Sun. 1400-1800. **The Museum of Brazilian Art** is at Rua Alagoas 903, Higienópolis, entrance free, Tues.-Fri. 1000-2200, Sat.-Sun. 1400-1800. Here there are copies of Brazilian sculptures, including those of Aleijadinho. **The Museum of Anthropology and Ethnology** is on the fourth and fifth floors of Bloco D in the main Arts Complex just opposite the entrance to the Butantã Institute (**see page 309**). Every odd-numbered year the **São Paulo Bienal** at Ibirapuera has the most important show of modern art in Latin America, open from beginning of Sept. till Nov. For the other museums at Ibirapuera (including the Museum of Contemporary Art), **see page 300**, and for the Museu Paulista and Casa do Grito at Ipiranga, **see page 309**. There is an interesting Museum of Japanese Immigration at Rua São Joaquim 381, Tues.-Sun. 1130-1730.

There are two museums on Av. Tiradentes, near the Luz Park; the **Museum of Sacred Art** in the Convento da Luz (open Tues.-Sun. 1300-1700, US$0.20) and the State Art Collection (**Pinacoteca do Estado**) at No. 141 (open Tues.-Sun. 1400-1800, free).

Not far from the Butantã Institute (**see page 309**) are the **Casa do Bandeirante** (being renovated) at Praça Monteiro Lobato, the reconstructed home of a pioneer of 400 years ago (Tues.-Sun. 1200-1730, free); and the **Casa do Sertanista**, a museum of Indian folklore and handicrafts mounted by the famous expert on the Indians, Orlando Villas Boas, at Av. Francisco Morato 2200, open Tues.-Sun., 1230-1730, entrance free.

The **Casa Brasileira**, Av. Faria Lima 774, has been established as a museum of Brazilian furniture. Open weekdays 0900-1200 and 1400-1700. **Museo Padre Anchieta**, Pátio do Colégio, is a restored mission house; inside are examples and relics of the Jesuit era, entrance US$0.05. The **Sound and Image Museum** is at Av. Europa 158. The **Museum of Lasar Segall**, at Rua Alfonso Celso 362, Vila Mariana (near Santa Cruz metro station), shows the works of a German expressionist painter who emigrated to Brazil. **Museum of Japanese Immigration**, Rua São Joaquim 381, Liberdade, excellent, nice roof garden, ask at desk for English translation of the exhibits. Museo da Fundação Maria Luisa e Oscar Americano, Av. Morumbi 3700, Morumbi, a private collection of Brazilian and Portuguese art and furniture, well-displayed; hours Weds.-Sun., 1000-1700. There is a Museo de Discoteca e Biblioteca da Música at Rua Catão 611, 5th and 6th floors, open Mon.-Fri., 0900-1300 (take bus 819 P from Praça Princesa Isabel to Lapa district). Museu do Telefone, Martiniano de Carvalho 851, Paraíso, Tues.-Fri., 0900-1730, Sat.-Sun., 1400-1800, quite good, but you're not allowed to operate anything.

The **Centro Cultural São Paulo**, Rua Vergueiro 1000 (metro Vergueiro) has art and photographic exhibitions, a library, music and dance shows (often regional) and films; open daily until 2200.

Addresses

British Consulate General, Av. Paulista 1938, 17th floor; Caixa Postal 846. T 287-7722.
American Consulate General, Rua Padre João Manuel 933, T 881-6511.
Irish Consulate, Av. Paulista 2006, 5th floor, 01310 São Paulo, T 287-6362.

British Chamber of Commerce of São Paulo, Rua Barão de Itapetininga 275, 7th floor; Caixa Postal 1621. T 255-0519.
American Chamber of Commerce for Brazil, Rua Formosa 367, 29th floor, T 222-6377.
Canadian Consulate General, Av. Paulista 854-5th floor. T 287-2122.
West German Consulate, Av. Brig Faria Lima 1383, 12th floor, T 814-6644.
Swiss Consulate-General, Av. Paulista 1754, 4th floor, Caixa Postal 30588. T 289-1033.
Austrian Consulate-General, Al Lorena 1271, 01424 São Paulo, T 282-6223.
Swedish Consulate-General, Rua Oscar Freire 379, 3rd floor. T 883-3322 (postal address: Caixa Postal 51626, 01499 São Paulo).
Dutch Consulate, Av. Brigadeiro Faria Lima 1698.
Argentine Consul, Rua Araújo 216, 8th floor (open 0830-1300, very easy to get visa here).
Bolivian Consul, Rua Quirino de Andrade 219, 3rd floor, (open 0900-1300), T 255-3555.
Paraguayan Consul, Av. São Luiz 112, 10th floor, T 259-3579.
Uruguayan Consul, Al. Campinas 433, 7th floor, T 284-5998.
Venezuelan Consul, Rua Jerônimo da Viega 164, 16th floor, T 883-3000.
Samaritans' Hospital, Rua Conselheiro Brotero 1486. T 51-2154.
Sociedade Brasileira de Cultura Inglesa, Avenida Higienópolis 449.
St. Paul's Anglican (Episcopal) Church, Rua Comendador Elias Zarzua 1231, Santo Amaro. T 246-0383.
American Library, União Cultural Brasil-Estados Unidos, Rua Coronel Oscar Porto 208, T 287-1022.
Goethe-Instituto, Rua Frei Caneca 1246 (open Mon.-Thurs. 1400-2030).
Instituto Hans Staden, Rua Cons. Crispiniano 53, 12th floor.
Lutheran church, Av. Rio Branco 34.
Swedish Church: Igreja Evangelica Luterana Escandinava, Rua Job Lane 1030, CEP 04639, T 011-247 88 29.
Police, T 228-2276; Radio Patrol, T 190.
Federal Police, Av. Prestes Maio 700, open 1000-1600 for visa extensions.

Emergency First Aid, T 71-8673, 71-0757.

Physicians (English-speaking) Edwin Castello, José Maria Lisboa 861, s/104, T 287-9071; Ruy Silva, Conselheiro Brotero 1505, No. 64, T 67-2470; Wilson Frey, Barão de Jacegua 1102, T 241-4474. Christel Schlünder, Rua Alvares de Azevedo 127, Sto. Amaro, T 247-5963, German speaking, and for children. Also Samaritans' Hospital (see above).

Banks Times when open vary from bank to bank. Lloyds Bank (ex-BOLSA), Rua Quinze de Novembro 143-165. (Open 1000-1630.) Banco Internacional, Rua Quinze de Novembro 240. Banco Holandês Unido, Rua Quinze de Novembro 150. Citibank, Av. Ipiranga 855, or Av. Paulista IIII (T 576-2211) will receive money from abroad (US$20 charge, takes 5 days). First National Bank of Boston, Rua Líbero Badaró 487. Banco Lar Brasileiro (Chase Manhattan owned), 131 Rua Alvares Penteado, and other national banks. Banco Mercantil de São Paulo, Av. Paulista 1450, for cash advances on Access/Master Charge, but slow.

Exchange Many *câmbios* near Praça da República. American Express (Kontik Franstur—address below) very helpful; Exprinter, Barão de Itapetininga 243, also deals in foreign currencies (cash only). Boreal Turismo, Rua Dom José de Barros 326. Tourist Cambio, Rua Badaró (turn left off Viaduto do Chá); Agency Faro, Av. São Luis 157, for travellers' cheques; Interpax, Praça da República 177, loja 13, changes cheques at good rates. For parallel rates ask at tourist kiosks for details.

Post Office Praça do Correio, corner Av. São João.

International Telephone Rua 7 de Abril 295, near Praça da República.

Cables Embratel, Av. São Luís 50, and Av. Ipiranga 344.

Tourist Offices Praça da República (very helpful), and Praça da Sé, Praça Dom José Gaspar and Liberdade metro stations (small red kiosks). Office at Guarulhos airport is not very helpful. Information on São Paulo State, Praça Antônio Prado 9, 6th floor, Av. São Luís 115. On Sundays a free cultural tour of the city starts at the Pátio do Colégio, near the cathedral (buses every 20 mins. from 0900 to 1600), to see Casa do Bandeirante, Casa do Sertanista, Capella do Morumbi, the old market, and Casa do Grito. For weekly information on cultural activities, addresses and recommended bars, see the supplement "Veja em São Paulo", of the magazine *Veja*. Tourist offices have free magazine, *Visão*. *Guia Turística Carto Plum* available from banks etc. around Praça da República. Also recommended is *Quatro Rodas* guide to the City.

Maps of São Paulo in train timetables at news-stands (US$2.50), and in the monthly tourist guide published by the Prefeitura. Also obtainable from the tourist offices, the Rodoviária (upstairs), the better hotels, American Express and H. Stern, the jeweller. 2 private map producers: Geo Mapas, Rua Libero Badaró 336, C.E.P. 01008, T 259-2166 (40% discount for volume purchases, excellent 1988 1:5,000,000 map of Brazil, town maps), and Editorial Abril, Rua Geraldo Flaufino Gomez 61, Barrio Brooklin, C.E.P. 04575, T 545-8122.

Travel Agents Wilson, Sons S.A., Av. São Luís 715; Exprinter, Rua Barão de Itapetininga 243; Receptur, same street, 221; Wagon-Lits Cook, Av. São Luís 285; Tunibra, Praça da Liberdade 63, T 36-0101, helpful; Itatiaia Publicidade e Turismo, Cons. Crispiniano 69 (for hotel reservations especially); Transatlântica Turismo, Rua Coronel Xavier de Toledo 98 (for local excursions); Kontik-Franstur (American Express representative), Rua Marconi 71. Royal Turismo, Manoel da Nóbrega off Av. Paulista, helpful to budget travellers. Visits to coffee *fazendas* (May-June) and round trips into the surrounding country are organized by the travel agencies.

Railways The Estrada de Ferro Santos a Jundiaí (ex São Paulo Railway) to Santos "down the hill" (passenger service suspended in 1985), also to Jundiaí and the interior; Companhia Paulista de Estradas de Ferro, into the coffee, fruit and cattle districts; Central do Brasil Railway to Rio de Janeiro, 9 hrs. journey, night sleeper train (the Santa Cruz) leaving São Paulo Luz Station at 2300; warmly rec., US$15 for a double cabin; Cia Mogiana to NE of state, from Campinas through Ribeirão Preto; Fepasa through Sorocaba to Bauru. No through tickets from São Paulo to Campo Grande or Corumbá are sold; you must go by bus or train (0830, 1925, 2225) from Luz station to Bauru (risking a day's wait there for train connections) from where Estrada de Ferro Noroeste do Brasil goes daily across Mato Grosso do Sul to Corumbá (34 hrs. from São Paulo), and on, after crossing frontier by road, from Quijarro (Bolivia) to Santa Cruz de la Sierra by the Estrada de Ferro Brasil-Bolívia (**see page 409**). There is a railway from São Paulo to Brasília, changing at Campinas; US$24.50 sleeper, US$ 14.50 1st class, leaves Luz station on Sun. at 1000, reaching Campinas at 1125, and Brasília 0830 on Mon. (through tickets available). The track is bad, but the journey interesting. There are several railway stations in São Paulo; Júlio Prestes for former Sorocobana services into the State; Luz for Bauru, Santos a Jundiaí commuters, night trains to Rio and former Paulista and Araquara Railways (metro links with Rodoviária at Tietê); Roosevelt for suburban trains.

RFFSA is planning to restore the uppermost stage of the São Paulo—Paranapiaçaba cog railway and the railway buildings; the line was the first to link São Paulo with the coast and Santos. Steam services were expected to recommence from São Paulo in 1988.

Roads Distances in km.: Belém, 2,917; Brasília, 1,100; Belo Horizonte, 586; Curitiba, 397; Florianópolis, 700; Fortaleza, 3,065; Foz do Iguaçu, 1,071; Manaus, 4,052 (last stretch not paved); Natal, 2,992; Porto Alegre, 1,143; Recife, 2,671; Rio, 429; Salvador, 1,944; Vitória, 932. To take the picturesque new coast road to Rio, take the Via Anchieta to the Guarujá turn, before Guarujá take Bertioga turn and you're on the Santos-Rio highway. To thoth to Rio, take the metro to Ponte Pequeno, then a bus to Guarulhos, alighting where the bus turns off the Rio road for Guarulhos.

Buses To get to the new Rodoviária, take the metro to Tietê, very convenient. Bus to centre, US$0.20. Bus to Rio, 6 hrs., frequent service, US$6 (*leito*, 12), special section for this route in the Rodoviária; to Curitiba, 6 hrs., US$6 (*leito*, 12); to Blumenau, 9½ hrs., US$10; to Porto Alegre, 18 hrs., US$16.75 (*leito*, 33.50); Rio Grande 25 hrs., US$25; to Belo Horizonte, 10 hrs., US$10 (*leito*, 20); to Salvador, 30 hrs., US$30 (*leito*, 60); to Recife, 40 hrs., US$42 (*leito*, 84); to Fortaleza, 48 hrs. US$46 (*leito* 92); to Natal, US$41, 55 hrs.; to Cuiabá, 24 hrs., US$18 (Andorinha at 1700, connects with Cuiabá-Porto Velho bus); to Campo Grande (Mato Grosso do Sul), 16 hrs., US$14.50; to Porto Velho, 60 hrs. (or more), US$50; to Brasília, 15 hrs., US$14 (*leito*, 28); to Foz do Iguaçu, 16 hrs., US$15 (*leito*, 30). To Santos, US$1.50 (there is a bus station for Santos and São Vicente at the southern end of the Metro line, at Jabaquara, buses from here leave every 5 minutes, taking about 50 minutes; São Sebastião, 4 hrs. US$4 (say "via Bertioga" if you want to go by the coast road); to Parati, Angra dos Reis and also to Ilhabela, 2 daily, 8 hrs., US$7.50.

To Montevideo, via Porto Alegre, with TTL, departs 2200, 31 hrs. US$40; to Buenos Aires 36 hrs., US$60 (*leito*, 120); to Santiago, Pluma or Gral. Urquiza (both start from Rio), 56 hrs., US$110; to Asunción (1,044 km.), 18 hours with Pluma or RYSA, US$28 (*leito* US$48).

Air Services There are air services to all parts of Brazil, Europe, North and South America from the new international airport at Guarulhos (30 km. from the city); the local airport of Congonhas, 14 km. from the city centre, is used for the Rio-São Paulo shuttle and private flights only. From Guarulhos there are airport taxis which charge US$15 on a ticket system. Metro bus service every 25 mins. to Guarulhos from Praça da República, US$3; metro bus trip (US$2.50) to the Rodoviária do Tietê and Congonhas airport, every 20-40 mins., approx. 1 hr. There are about four hundred flights per week to Rio de Janeiro (about US$55). All airline offices in triangle formed by Av. São Luís, Av. Ipiranga and Rua da Consolação. Amex provides free transport for cardholders from airports to city centre.

Air freight Pan Am, at Carga Aérea Terminal, T531-4366/4052/9602, has a small package "sprint" service to the USA, max 30 kg., US$4.46/kg., but not for business purchases (for these you need an export broker)—open Mon.-Fri. 0900-1800. Varig will send anything, anywhere, for US$6.65/kg. (cheaper if paid in new cruzados), but involves more red tape, office next to Pan Am.

The Butantã Snake Farm and Museum 10901015 (Instituto Seroterápico at the University), Av. Dr. Vital Brasil 1500, Pinheiros, is the most popular tourist attraction. The snakes are milked for their poison six times a day but you may not witness this; the antidotes made from the venom have greatly reduced deaths from snakebite in Brazil. Open daily from 0800-1700 (except 1300-1700 Mon.), entrance US$1.50. Informative museum; details in English and Portuguese. From Praça da República take bus marked "Butantã" along Av. Paulista, and ask to be let out at the right place.

Parque da Independência, in the suburb of Ipiranga, contains the famous Ipiranga Monument to commemorate the declaration of Brazilian independence; beneath the monument is the Imperial Chapel, with the tomb of the first emperor, Dom Pedro I, and Empress Leopoldina (open Tues.-Sun., 1300-1700). Take bus 4612 from Praça da República. The **Casa do Grito**, the little house in which Dom Pedro I spent the night before his famous cry of Ipiranga— "Independence or Death"—is preserved in the park (open Tues.-Sun. 1300-1730). The **Museu Paulista**, housed in a huge palace at the top of the park, has old maps, traditional furniture, collections of old coins and of religious art and rare documents, and a department of Indian ethnology. Behind the Museum is the Ipiranga Botanical Garden. Open Tues.-Sun. and holidays, 1300-1730. Take bus 478-P (Ipiranga-Pompéia for return) from Ana Rosa. There is a *son et lumière* show on Brazilian history in the park on Wed., Fri. and Sat. evenings at 2030.

Parque do Estado (Jardim Botânico), out at Água Funda (Av. Jabaquara), has a vast garden esplanade surrounded by magnificent stone porches, with lakes and trees and places for picnics, and a very fine orchid farm worth seeing during the flowering season, November-December. Over 32,000 different kinds of orchids are cultivated. Open Tue.-Sat., 0900-1700. The astronomical observatory nearby is open to the public Thurs. afternoons. Bus 475 from Brig. Luís Antônio or metro to Jaguaribe (2nd last stop), then a bus marked "Zoológico".

Zoological Gardens Near the Jardim Botânico, not more than half an hour's drive from the city centre. A very large variety of specimens can be seen in an almost natural setting of about 35 hectares of forest: a most interesting site. Open 0900-1800, admission US$0.45 (bus 4742, "Jardim Celeste", from São Judas Tadeu). There is a wild-life park, Simba Safari, nearby, admission US$0.80 per pedestrian, US$2 p.p. with a car, open Tues.-Sun. 0900-1800.

Aquarium The one formerly on Av. Pacaembu has closed, but the "Exotiquarium" on the bottom level of the Morumbi Shopping Centre claims to be the largest in South America, US$2; it has a pink river dolphin.

Parque Água Branca (Avenida Água Branca, 455) has beautiful gardens with specimens of tropical plants, Brazilian birds and wild life. Pavilions house a well stocked aquarium, a zoo, and exhibitions of food produce.

In Tremembé, a little beyond Cantareira, half an hour from the down-town area, is the **Horto Florestal**, containing examples of nearly every species of Brazilian woodland flora (admission daily, 0800-1800).

Santo Amaro Dam (Old Lake), is 3 km. from the centre of Santo Amaro suburb. This is a popular boating resort with several sailing clubs and many attractive cottages along the shore. There is a bus (30 min.) from São Paulo to Santo Amaro.

Interlagos, which has a motor-racing circuit with 18 km. of track, is São Paulo's lake resort on the Santo Amaro dam. It can be reached from Santo Amaro by bus. Close to the track, where the Brazilian Grand Prix takes place every second year, usually in February, is the 32-km. long Guarapiranga artificial lake with good restaurants and several luxurious sailing and sports clubs. Camping Clube do Brasil site. Guarapiranga is less polluted than the other artificial lake, Billings, which also has restaurants.

Pico de Jaraguá (1,135 metres) the highest peak in the neighbourhood, gives good views of Greater São Paulo on a fine day. This peak is reached from km. 18 on the Campinas highway (Via Anhanguera) by a good road through Taipas and Pirituba.

Embu, 28 km. from São Paulo, is a colonial town which has become a centre for artists and craftsmen. On Sunday afternoons there is a large and popular arts and crafts fair; not to be missed. Buses from close to the Largo de Pinheiros, São Paulo, or Santo Amaro bus.

The Coast of the State of São Paulo

Santos, 63 km SE of São Paulo and 5 km. from the open sea, is the most important Brazilian port. (Over 40 % by value of all Brazilian imports and about half the total exports pass through it.) It is reached from Rio by ship (320 km.) in 12-15 hrs., and a direct highway between the two cities has been completed (**see pages 278** and **312**). A railway (no passenger service) and the Anchieta and Imigrantes highways run to São Paulo. A free-port zone for Paraguay, 1,930 km. by rail or road, has been established. A few km. outside the city there is an important industrial area round the steelworks, oil refinery and hydroelectric plant at Cubatão (known locally as the Valley of Death because of the pollution from chemical factories, among the worst in the world).

The plain upon which Santos, a city of 411,000 people, stands is an island which can be circumnavigated by small boats. The city has impressive modern buildings, wide, tree-lined avenues, and wealthy suburbs. The streets around Praça Mauá are very busy in the daytime, with plenty of cheap shops. In the centre, an interesting building is the Bolsa Oficial de Café, in Rua 15 de Novembro. The night-life can best be seen in the Gonzaga area which has the large hotels. Although best known for its commerce, Santos is also a holiday resort, with magnificent beaches and views. The port is approached by the winding Santos Channel; at its mouth is an old fort (1709).

There are many monuments: one in Avenida Ana Costa to commemorate the brothers Andradas, who took a leading part in the movement for independence; one in the Praça Rui Barbosa to Bartolomeu de Gusmão, who has a claim to the world's first historically recorded airborne ascent in 1709; one in the Praça da República to Bras Cubas, who founded the city in 1534; and one in the Praça José Bonifácio to the soldiers of Santos who died in the Revolution of 1932. There are a disappointing municipal aquarium on Av. Bartolomeu de Gusmão (Ponta da Praia) and a Museu do Mar, Rua República do Equador 81.

Local Holidays   (in addition to national): Jan. 26 (Foundation of Santos); Good Friday; Corpus Christi.

Hotels   *Holiday Inn* complex at the centre of Gonzaga, Ana Costa 555, A, with shopping centre; *Atlântico,* Av. Pres. Wilson 1, C, good value; *Gonzaga,* Av. Pres. Wilson 36, D with bath; *Indaiá,* Av. Ana Costa 431, C; *Transmontana,* Rua Marechal Floriano Peixoto 202, rec.; *Maracanã Santos,* Pres. Wilson, beach front, C; *Avenida Palace,* Pres. Wilson 10, beach front, C; *Santos,* Bartolomeu de Gusmão 16, C with bath *Estoril,* Rua Bitencourt 55, E, with bath, cheap (has round beds, red lights and mirrored ceilings); small, family-style hotels can be found in this area; many cheap hotels near the Orquidário Municipal, 1-2 blocks from the beach. *Potiguar,* Rua Amador Bueno 116, 300 m. from bus station, E, breakfast, showers, clean, good.

Restaurants   *Cantina Dom Fabrízio,* Av. Ana Costa 482; *Jangadeiro,* Ponta da Praia; *Hong Kong Palace,* Av. Conselheiro Nébias 288 (Chinese food); *Rincón Argentino,* Av. Manuel da Nóbrega 666, at São Vicente (Gaucho food); *Ilha Porchat Grill,* on Ilha Porchat, off São Vicente, at edge of island, overlooking bays of São Vicente and Santos; first class *Pizzaria Zi Tereza,* Av. Ana Costa 451; also *Pizzaria Santa Izabel,* Av. Bartolomeu de Gusmão 165 (also serves seafood). *Chico's Bar,* Av. Floriano Peixoto (Boqueirão), good. *Fonte das Vitaminas,* Ana Costa 534, good for juices, lunches.

Electric Current   220 A.C. 60 cycles.

Tram   Restored service along the Praia from 0800 to 2200 daily, US$0.10.

Taxis   All taxis are supplied with meters. The fare is a fixed charge of US$0.25 plus US$0.10 per km. Taxi, Gonzaga to bus station, US$2.

Consulate   (British) Largo Senador Vergueiro 2, first floor. Caixa Postal 204. T 25733, 29608.

All Saints Church   Praça Washington 92, José Menino. Services in English held every Sun.

Cables   Embratel, Largo Senador Vergueiro 1 and 2.

Banks   Banco Internacional, Rua General Câmara 24; Banco Holandês Unido, Citibank, Banco do Brasil, all in the Rua 15 de Novembro. The First National Bank of Boston, Praça Visc. de Mauá 14. Banks open: 1000-1630.

Exchange Houses   Casa Faro, Rua 15 de Novembro, 80 & 260; Casa Bancaria Branco, Praça de República 29.

Tourist Information Praça dos Expedicionários 10, 10th floor; booths at Aquarium, Rodoviária, Casa do Café, Orquidário Municipal.

Coastal Shipping Irregular services to Brazilian ports by Companhia de Navegação Lóide Brasileiro. Consult their agents, Rua General Câmara 22, 2nd floor, conjunto 34.

Rail The British-built Santos a Jundiaí up the hill to São Paulo is one of the railway wonders of the world; it passes through Cubatão and then, running on toothed tracks up the escarpment, interesting hill scenery. Passenger services were suspended in 1985.

Air Services From São Paulo; Santos has no airport.

Bus Services Buses start for most suburbs from Praça Mauá, in the centre of the city. There are buses to São Paulo (50 mins., US$1.50) at intervals of approximately 15 mins., from the Rodoviária near city centre. Enquire about being picked up or put down outside usual terminal points. Express cars also run to São Paulo at regular intervals. Fare, US$2.75 each way, per passenger. (The two highways between São Paulo and Santos are sometimes seriously crowded, especially at rush hours and weekends.) Buses for Santos are caught in São Paulo in the Jabaquara bus station, not the new Rodoviária. There are direct buses to Rio but not along the coast road (Normandy company, 6 a day, 7½ hrs., US$7, *leito* at 2230, US$14); to get to Rio along the coast road, you must take an Atlântico bus to Ubatuba or Caraguatatuba, change there for Rio.

Excursions

To the coasts E of Santos (Guarujá, Bertioga, Ilhabela) and SW (Praia Grande, Itanhaém). Short excursion along the Guarujá road to José Menino for the orchid gardens in the Praça Washington (flowering Oct.-Feb.). There is an open-air cage containing humming-birds of 20 different species and the park is also a sanctuary for other birds.

The *Ilha Porchat,* a small island reached by a bridge at the far end of Santos/São Vicente bay, has beautiful views over rocky precipices, of the high seas on one side and of the city and bay on the other. At the summit is a splendid night club, the *Top House Restaurante e Discoteca.* No entrance fee but there is a minimum charge of US$8.

To **Alto da Serra,** the summit of the forest-clad mountain range; magnificent views. The return journey can be done in under 2 hrs. by road.

Monte Serrat A funicular railway to the summit (every ½ hr., US$1 return), where there is a semaphore station and look-out post which reports the arrival of all ships in Santos harbour. There is also a quaint old church, dedicated to Nossa Senhora da Monte Serrat, said to have performed many miracles. The top can be reached on foot. Seven shrines have been built on the way up; annual pilgrimages are made by the local people. Fine views.

Guarujá

The route from Santos to the resort of Guarujá is along Av. Conselheiro Nébias to the seafront, continuing along the beach to the Guarujá ferry (every 10 min., free for pedestrians) at Ponta da Praia. On the other side proceed as far as Turtle Bay. During the season and weekends there is a long delay at the Ponta da Praia vehicle ferry; to avoid this take the ferry on foot and get the bus on the Guarujá side; motor boats also cross for US$0.06. There is a strong undertow on nearly all the Guarujá beaches; the Jequiti-Mar beach (officially called Praia de Pernambuco) is the safest. Golf club at Guarujá; population, 94,000. (Trolleybus from Praça Mauá in Santos to the ferry, then buses.)

Turn left in centre of Guarujá and drive less than 1 km. to reach *Delfim Hotel* (A) and its restaurant *La Popote* at the beginning of the long beach of Praia da Enseada. Close by, at Av. Miguel Estefno 999, is *Casa Grande Hotel,* luxury, A, in colonial style, with clean beach. Facing sea is the luxurious *Ferraretto Hotel,* B (night club, swimming pool). Camping Clube do Brasil site at Praia do Perequé (where the best fish restaurants are), near municipal nursery.

The Jequiti-Mar holiday complex, 8 km. beyond Guarujá on the road to Bertioga, is extremely attractive. There are private beaches (excellent swimming and boating) and very fine fishing grounds, and chalet accommodation, A or B, according to size and situation. There is an excellent restaurant and two night clubs; they are open each weekend and every night from December to March, in the holiday season. 2 km. further north is a beach where fishing boats land their catch—a number of good seafood restaurants line the seafront.

There are good sea-food restaurants on the road to **Bertioga,** an attractive place, where the fort of São João houses the João Ramalho museum (bus Guarujá-Bertioga, 1 hr., US$0.30). (Hotels: *Marazul,* Av. Tomé de Souza 825; *Indaiá Praia,* same street, No. 1079, both C; restaurants *Zezé e Duarte* (2), *O*

Camarão de Bertioga.) The coastal road beyond Bertioga is paved, and the new Rio-Santos highway, 1-2 km. inland, is completed, and provides a good link to São Sebastião. Going NE, the beaches are Praia de Bertioga, Praia São Lourenço, Praia Guaratuba, Praia Boracéia (campsite, US$0.70 with meals), all are empty except for the light traffic. 30 km. beyond Boracéia is the beach resort of Maresia (hotels, campsite), from where it is 21 km. to **São Sebastião** (two buses a day from Rio, 1030 and 1830, to Rio 0600 and 2330 not along the coast, heavily booked in advance; 4 a day from Santos, 3½ hrs.; buses from São Paulo (US$4) run inland via São José dos Campos, unless you ask for the service via Bertioga, only 2 a day), and **(free ferry) to Ilhabela** (4 hrs. by bus from Santos, 3 a day, US$3). There is a Museu de Arte Sacra in the chapel of São Gonçalo in the town centre. Tourist Office; Av. Dr Altino Arantes 174, friendly and helpful except regarding Ilhabela. The São Sebastião beaches are polluted; foreigners can stay in the Camping Clube do Brasil grounds for US$3 a night. 6 km. S of São Sebastião is Camping do Barraquecaba Bar de Mar de Lucas, US$2 per night, rec. (*Hotel Roma*, on the main square, excellent, E and upwards, very well rec.; *Recanto dos Pássaros*, *Porto Grande*, both C; *Arrastão*, B with most facilities; *São Paulo*, E with breakfast, clean, friendly.) Ilhabela tends to be expensive in season, when it is cheaper to stay in São Sebastião.

Half-way between Bertioga and São Sebastião, on the Praia de Juqueí beach, is *Hotel Timão*, C, German-owned, with excellent fish meals.

Ilha de São Sebastião (Ilhabela). The island of São Sebastião, known popularly as Ilhabela, is now easily accessible by car or bus from Santos. A bus runs along the coastal strip facing the mainland. Cavendish, the English pirate, had his secret anchorage in one of the sheltered caves there. Last century it was used as a landing place for illegal slave-traffic.

The island is of volcanic origin, roughly about 390 sq. km. in area. Its highest peak, Morro do Papagaio, rises 1,300 metres above sea-level, with its bare peak often obscured by mist; the slopes are densely wooded. There are many beautiful waterfalls, easily accessible to the enterprising walker. Most of the flatter ground is given over to sugar-cane.

The only settled district lies on the coastal strip facing the mainland, the Atlantic side being practically uninhabited except by a few fisherfolk. The place abounds in tropical plants and flowers of the most extraordinary variety, and many fruits grow wild, whose juice mixed with *cachaça* and sugar makes as delicious a cocktail as can be imagined.

No alterations are allowed to the frontage of the main township, **Ilhabela**: There are several hotels, ranging through the whole price-range. Visitors abound during summer week-ends; motorists are warned to avoid those days as the car-carrying capacity of the ferry is very limited.

The energetic can climb over the hump of the island down towards the Atlantic, sometimes through dense tropical forest following the old slave trail, but for this 50-km. return journey a local guide is required. There is a rough road to the Atlantic side, but it is very difficult to drive. A visit to the terraced Toca waterfalls amid dense jungle close to the foot of the 970-metre Baepi peak will give you cool freshwater bathing (entry, US$0.50). In all shady places, especially away from the sea, there abounds a species of midge known locally as *borrachudos*. A locally sold repellant (Autum) keeps them off for some time, however. Those allergic to insect bites should remain on the inhabited coastal strip.

Hotels in Ilhabela: *Mercedes*, B, T 7-0071; *Siriuba*, C, T 7-0265; *Ilhabela*, A, T 7-0083. Next door is *Itapemar*, windsurfing equipment rented at US$3 an hour, A. Also in the C price range are *Bella Vista* (nice position), *Petit Village*, *Solar dos Bandeirantes*, *Ilhabela Praia*, *Colonial* and *Caiçara*. *Pousada dos Hibiscos*, C, good atmosphere, swimming pool, rec. There are several other less expensive pensions in D/E range, such as *Sul America*. *Camping Porto Seguro*, accessible by two-hourly bus from Ilhabela, US$8 p.p.

Restaurant *Les Boucaniers*, French-run, rec., US$3.50 per head. *Telma*, Perequê, reasonable.

Sightseeing Visit the old Feiticeira plantation, with underground dungeons. The road is along the coast, sometimes high above the sea, towards the south of the island. You can go by bus, taxi, or horse and buggy.

Pedras do Sino (Bell Rocks) These curious seashore boulders, when struck with a piece of iron or stone, emit a loud bell-like note. Another campsite nearby.

Bathing Bathing on the mainland side is not recommended because of oil, sandflies and jelly fish on the beaches and in the water. Praia dos Castelhanos, reached by a rough road over the island (no buses), is recommended.

Transport Passenger ferry every 2 hours; stops at Perequê and Ilhabela; separate car ferry runs through the night and serves Perequê only.

North of São Sebastião, on the Santos-Rio road, is São Francisco, a village with *Pontal Hotel* (not rec., expensive, noisy), and *Restaurant Flipper* (excellent); good beaches. Further on is **Caraguatatuba**, with 17 good beaches to the NE and SW (several hotels, popular at weekends, good restaurants: *Brisa*, Av. Artur Costa Filho 1821, *Xamagu*, near main square). Good camping site US$1.60 per night on beach and other sites. Direct buses to Caraguatatuba from Rio de Janeiro, São Paulo and Santos; direct buses from São Paulo do not use the coast road. Further E is **Lagoinha**, 34 km. W of Ubatuba, with chalets and sailing boats for hire. Exotic birdlife and virgin forest. Maier's Mar Virado is owned by Hans Maier, who speaks English and arranges hirings. Then we come to **Ubatuba**, with two Camping Clube do Brasil sites at Maranduba and Perequê-Açu beaches. In all, there are 72 beautiful beaches, quite spread out, most with campsites (Grande, just S, and one 6 km. N of Ubatuba, US$1 p.p., are rec.). There is also a yacht haven. The area gets very crowded at Carnival time as people from Rio come to escape the crowds in their city. Ubatuba has numerous hotels; rec. are *Tropicana*, Praia da Enseada, C; *Restaurante Beija Flor* with apartments, D; *Solar das Aguas Cantantes*, Praia do Lázaro (11680 S.P., T 0124-42-0178), reached by local bus, swimming pool, restaurant, B; *Saveiros*, Praia do Lázaro (T 0124-42-0172), pool, restaurant, C, run by a Rumanian, Lucian Strass, English spoken, who welcomes users of *South American Handbook*. Youth Hostel Cora Coralina, Rodovia Oswaldo Cruz, Km. 89, T 229-3787/229-3011, extension (ramal) 286 for details. Furnished flats and cottages may be rented from Lúcio Martins Rodrigues, Rua Amaral Gurgel 158, Apto. 121—CEP.01221, Vila Buarque, São Paulo; T 853-8101, 532-0496, 577-6482, 221-1357. The flats are in the town centre, 400 m from beach, the cottages 7½ km. from the centre with a natural swimming pool, each can sleep a maximum of 5 (bedroom for 2-3, 2 extra in living room), and has kitchen with cooker and fridge, bathroom and laundry facilities. Cost is US$5 a day, payable in US or Canadian dollars, or any Western European currency. The road from São Sebastião is paved, so a journey from São Paulo along the coast is possible, 5 buses daily. Ubatuba is 70 km. from Parati (**see page 280**), several buses daily, on the hour, from *Lanchonete Nice*, near Rodoviária. If driving from Ubatuba along the coast to Rio, one can stop for lunch at Porto Aquarius, where there is a cave and hotel in a beautiful setting (not cheap). Direct buses from Rio, São Paulo and Santos.

Straddling the border of São Paulo and Rio de Janeiro states is the **Parque Nacional Serra da Bocaina**, which rises from the coast to heights of over 1,900 metres, encompassing three strata of vegetation (IBDF office, Al. Tietê 637, Caixa Postal 7134, CEP 01.312, São Paulo).

In the opposite direction (SW) from Santos, it is 50 km. beside the Praia Grande to the town of **Itanhaém,** with its pretty colonial church and semi-ruined Convento da Conceição on a small hill. There are several good sea-food restaurants along the beach, and a Camping Clube do Brasil site nearby at Peruíbe beach, and many others which are cheaper. There are many attractive beaches here, and hot springs with medicinal mud (hotels *Maison Suisse, Príncipe, Glória*). The whole stretch of coast is completely built up with holiday developments. Frequent buses from Santos US$0.85, 1 hr.

Further south is the town of **Iguape** , founded in 1538. Typical Portuguese architecture, the small municipal museum is housed in a 16th century building. Buses from São Paulo, Santos, or Curitiba, changing at Registro (see below) It has a market, hotels and restaurants. Camping Clube do Brasil site on beach. Opposite Iguape is the northern end of the Ilha Comprida with beautiful beaches stretching SW for 86 km. A continuous ferry service runs from Iguape (passengers free; cars at a small charge); buses run until 1900 from the ferry stop to the beaches and campsite Britânia (clean, friendly, US$0.70 p.p., drinkable tap water, tastes bad). The island is being developed as a resort; good restaurants, hotels, supermarket—fresh fish is excellent. At the southern end **Cananéia** is more commercialized than Iguape; it has 3 or 4 hotels (mostly E).

From Iguape it is possible to take a boat trip down the coast to Cananéia and Ariri. Tickets and information from Dept. Hidroviário do Estado, Rua Major Moutinho 198, Iguape, T 41 1122. Boats leave Iguape on Mon. Thurs. (but check in advance), returning next day. It is a beautiful trip, passing between the island and the mainland. The boat has a toilet, fresh water, and meals. In wet weather, the cabin gets crowded and uncomfortable. Ariri has no road connections; there is a hostel, F, run by the shipping line.

Caves Inland, W of the BR-116 are the caverns of the Vale do Ribeira; among the best known is the 8-km. Gruta da Tapagem, known as Caverna do Diabo (Devil's Cave—as huge "as a cathedral" with well-lit formations), 45 km. from Eldorado Paulista. The caves are open 0800-1100 and 1200-1700; bar and toilets. *Hotel Eldorado*, friendly, clean, with breakfast, F. Bus to Eldorado Paulista from Santos or São Paulo, US$2.60, 4-5 hrs., then hitch-hike on banana trucks or tourist buses (which run from both cities); most traffic on Sats. and Suns. From Curitiba, change buses at Jacupiranga for Eldorado Paulista. A suitable stopping place for visiting the caves area is *Registro* on BR-116, in the heart of the tea-growing region, populated mainly by Japanese Brazilians. (*Lito Palace Hotel*, D; *Hotel Continental*, F; *Hotel Brasília*, Rua Brasília, round corner from Rodoviária, F, no breakfast, shower, clean, quiet; good churrascaria next to bus station, US$3 p.p.). 43 km. from Caverna do Diabo is Caverna de Santana, 10 km. from the town of Iporanga; it has 5.6 km. of subterranean passages and three levels of galleries. (Iporanga is the most convenient town for visiting both sets of caves; it is 42 km. from Apiaí, which is 257 km. SW of São Paulo.)

Towns in the State of São Paulo

About 13 % of Brazil's population lives within 200 km. of São Paulo city, a circle which includes 88 municipalities. Four of them—the big ABCD towns— sharing a population of over a million, are Santo André, São Bernardo, São Caetano and Diadema; they have many of the largest industrial plants. There are some 70 cities in the State with populations of over 50,000 and São Paulo is linked with all of them by road, and several of them by railway. One important line, the broad-gauge Santos a Jundiaí, runs from Santos to São Paulo (passenger services suspended on this stretch), and across the low mountains which separate São Paulo city from the interior to its terminus at

Jundiaí, 58 km. from São Paulo, which has textile factories and other industries. The district grows coffee and grain and there is an annual Grape Festival. Population, 210,000.

Hotel   *Grande Hotel,* Rua do Rosário 605, with good restaurant.

The Paulista Railway, with the same broad gauge, continues from Jundiaí through Campinas, Limeira, and São Carlos do Pinhal—the richest part of the state. A metre-gauge line now links Campinas and Brasília.

Campinas, 88 km. from São Paulo by the fine Via Anhanguera highway (many buses, US$1.60), is important as a clearing point for coffee, for its Agricultural Institute, and its rapidly growing industries. The Viracopos international airport is 11 km. from Campinas, which also has its own airport. Population, 567,000 (1980), believed in 1987 to be over 1 million.

See fine cathedral, old market, colonial buildings, 8 museums, arts centre (noted symphony orchestra; the city is the birthplace of the noted 19th century Brazilian composer Carlos Gomes), and the modern university outside the city. Visits can be made to the Agricultural Institute to see all the aspects of coffee growing. Ten trains a day to and from São Paulo; trains and buses also to Ribeirão Preto, Araguari, Brasília and Rio de Janeiro, 7 hrs., US$6.

Hotels   *Holiday Inn,* Praça Rotatória 88, A; *Vila Rica,* Rua Donato Paschoal 100, B; *Savoy,* Rua Regente Feijó 1064, B; *Terminus,* Av. Francisco Glicério 1075, B; *Opala Avenida,* Av. Campos Sales 161, central, C. *Solar das Andorinhas,* a health farm with pool, sauna, horses, sports, etc. 18 km. outside city on the Mogi-Mirim road, B, with meals. Many cheap hotels near Rodoviária.

Restaurants   *Bar Restaurante Barão,* Barão de Jaguará 1381 and *Churrascaria Gaúcha,* Av. Dr Campos Sales 515, excellent for Brazilian food. *Kirinu's Place,* Av. Moraes Salles 1102, all you can eat for US$4.50. *Papai Salim,* Benjamin Constant 1293, Arab food, good. *Natureza* (vegetarian) at Rua José Paulino 1248, 2nd floor and Av. Francisco Glicério 984; lunch only, closed Sat. *Vegetariano,* Rua Barão de Jaguara 1260, 2nd floor, closed Sat. (and Fri. for dinner).

Shopping   H. Stern jewellers at Shopping Centre Iguatemi.

Banks   Lloyds Bank (ex-BOLSA), Rua General Osório 859. The First National Bank of Boston, Av. Francisco Glicério 1275, and local banks. Open 1000-1630. Good rates at Valortec (Dona Daiuza), Av. Dr. Moraes Salles 1212, 6th floor.

Community Church   Services in English at School of Language and Orientation, Rua Eduardo Lane 270.

Americana (pop. 122,000), an interesting town, is 42 km. from Campinas. This area was settled by Confederate refugees from the south of the USA after the Civil War. Most of the original settlers soon returned to the States, but some stayed, and there still exist reminders of their occupation here. A visit to the cemetery reveals an unusual number of English surnames. (*Hotel Bradesco*, 12 km. away at km. 118 on the Anhanguera Highway, C; *Cacique,* Rua Wáshington Luís 143, E.)

The metre-gauge Mogiana line, connecting with the broad-gauge Paulista at Campinas, serves the north-eastern part of the state. It goes through Ribeirão Preto and into the Triângulo of Minas Gerais, a great area for fattening beasts which are trucked to the *frigoríficos* of São Paulo. No São Paulo-Ribeirão Preto tickets are sold, so you may have to wait a day at Campinas for a connection (or go by bus). From Araguari there is a line into the state of Goiás (train Araguari-Goiânia once a week) and to Brasília (train from Campinas daily except Sunday). 25 km. from Campinas, at Jaguariúna, is a railway preservation group with steam engines and wagons; hourly bus from Campinas US$0.50. The group meets at weekends, just outside the town centre.

Ribeirão Preto, the centre of a rich coffee-growing district, also has a steel industry. The town is 422 km. from São Paulo city by rail via Campinas or paved road (5 hrs. by bus); airport has TAM flights to São Paulo, Rio, Poços de Caldas. Population 301,000. Altitude, 420 metres. It is a distribution centre for the interior of São Paulo State and certain districts in Minas Gerais and Goiás. Products: coffee, cotton, sugar, grain and rice.

Hotels   *Black Stream,* Rua General Osório 830, B, with T.V.; *Umuarama Recreio,* Praça dos Cafeeiros 140, 6 km. from centre, very pleasant, pool, gardens, C; *Brasil,* Rua General Osório 20, E; *Holiday Inn,* Rua Alvares Cabral 1200.

All the southern part of the state and most of its western part are served by the metre-gauge Sorocabana railway. The main line runs from São Paulo through Sorocaba to Bauru, where it connects with the Noroeste, to Corumbá, 1,223 km. The line from a junction near Sorocaba extending (through connections with other lines) across the southern states to the border with Uruguay is for freight only.

Sorocaba, 110 km. west of São Paulo, is an important industrial centre. The altitude is 540 metres, and the climate temperate. The population is 255,000. It has textile mills; produces cement, fertilizers, footwear, hats, alcohol, wines; there are railway workshops, extensive orange groves and packing house installations. It is an important cotton centre. Other products are timber, sugar, cereals, coffee, and minerals. Communications with São Paulo are better by road than by rail; the Castello Branco highway passes nearby.

Hotels   *Terminus,* Av. General Carneiro 474, C; *Nova Sorocaba,* Rua Mons. João Soares 158, D. *Manchester,* Rua 15 de Novembro 21, E, basic, friendly, excellent breakfast.

There is a picturesque paved road along the Tietê valley from São Paulo to Bauru, via the colonial towns of Pirapora and Itu.

Pirapora de Bom Jesus is a popular place of pilgrimage, in a most attractive setting on both sides of the river. *Itu* was founded by the Bandeirantes in the 17th century. The beautiful falls of Salto de Itu, 8 km. N, are flanked by a park and a textile mill.

Itu Hotels   *International,* Rua Barão do Itaím 93, D; *Sabará,* Praça Padre Miguel 90, E.

Camping   *Casarão de Itu,* km. 95 on the Jundiaí road; *Itu,* at km. 89 on the Cabreúva road.

Bauru (population: 179,000) was founded at the end of the last century. Its points of interest include the Horto Florestal, an experimental forestry station opened in 1928, the Vitória Regia amphitheatre in the Parque das Nações and the Tenrikyo temple, Rua Newton Prado. It is used by Paulistanos as a weekend resort. Currency exchange is difficult.

Hotels   *Bekassin,* Av. Duque de Caxias 1717, swimming pool, C; *Colonial,* Praça Rui Barbosa 248, D; *Alvorada Palace,* Rua Primeiro de Agosto 619, D. Cheaper ones too, such as *Hotel Português* near bus station. Opp. railway station, *Lisboa,* E, clean, hot shower, restaurant, rec., very friendly; to right of railway station exit is *Cariani,* E, clean, good breakfast, rec. *Phenix,* near rly. stn., E.

Restaurant   *H 2 Churrascaria; Cantina Bello Nápoli,* cheap. Homemade ice-cream at sorveteria near *Hotel Lisboa.*

Rail   to São Paulo, US$2.50 1st class, US$2 2nd class, three a day (6½ to 7½ hrs., compared to 4½ hrs., US$4, by bus); one train from Corumbá arrives 1600 (take 1800 bus—Expresso da Prata—to São Paulo). One of 2 daily trains to Corumbá leaves 1300 (take 0700 bus from Tietê station in São Paulo). There are no reliable connections between São Paulo-Bauru and Bauru-Corumbá or Campo Grande trains in either direction.

Marília, W of Bauru, is a pleasant clean town with a good hotel, *Sun Valley Park Hotel* (ex-*Holiday Inn*), B, friendly. Texaco garage rec. for car repairs, top of hill, Japanese owner.

Presidente Prudente, in the West, is on the railway which runs to Presidente Epitácio (see page 340) on the Paraná river, and is a useful place to make bus connections for Campo Grande (US$9), Porto Alegre and São Paulo; also to Ribeirão Preto, US$8, 9 hrs. *Hotel Aruã*, B, single rooms poor but doubles said to be nice. *Hotel Alves* opp. bus station, E, clean, nice but noisy. Beware of assaults and pickpockets.

Serra Negra is a very pleasant spa town and summer holiday resort up in the mountains at 1,080 metres, 145 km. from São Paulo. Visitors tour the countryside in horse-drawn buggies. The population is about 5,000, and there are many first class hotels, a *balneário* and a small zoo.

Hotels   *Rádio Hotel* (B, very nice indeed), and several others.

Near Serra Negra is the even better-known spa town of Lindóia, whose still waters are bottled and sent all over Brazil.

Another weekend resort, 70 km. north of São Paulo on the Dom Pedro I highway, is **Atibaia**; nearby is the strangely-shaped Pedra Grande mountain summit. There are two campsites, Pedra Grande, and Taba, which is near the *Hotel Village Eldorado* (with sports facilities, American-plan accommodation).

Campos do Jordão, between Rio de Janeiro and São Paulo, is a mountain resort at 1,710 metres, in the Serra da Mantiqueira. It is prettily set in a long valley. The climate is cold and dry in winter and cool in summer, a great relief from the coastal heat and humidity. There are many hotels; but no airport, as yet. Population: 18,750.

The resort, about 190 km. from São Paulo, is reached by an 87 km. paved road from São José dos Campos, 100 km. from São Paulo, on the Presidente Dutra (BR-116) highway. By car it takes about 3 hrs. from São Paulo, 6 to 7 from Rio de Janeiro.

Places of Interest   Palace of Boa Vista, 4 km. from Abernessia Centre, Governor's residence and museum, open Wed., Sat., Sun., 1000-1200, 1400-1700; Pedra do Baú (1,950 metres), to get there take a bus to São Bento do Sapucaí at 0800 or 1500, then walk to Paiol Grande and then on an unmarked path to the Pedra. Return buses from São Bento at 0915 and 1615. Near Paiol Grande is the small waterfall of Cachoeira dos Amores. Pico do Itapeva (2,030 metres) and Imbiri (1,950 metres) command a beautiful view of the Paraíba valley; see also Morro do Elefante (chairlift available); Gruta dos Crioulos; nature reserve at Horto Florestal (20 km), signposted from chairlift station, very pretty - go in the morning to avoid crowds; lots of streams with bridges, waterfalls nearby. Campos do Jordão is a popular place for hikers; most of the roads leading off the main avenue lead to quiet areas with nice views, e.g. up Av. Dr. Antônio Nicola Padula, turn left 500 metres past *Refugio na Serra* for waterfalls and Pico do Itapeva. The villages of Emílio Ribas and São Cristóvão are connected by a railcar which runs frequently, US$0.10.

Hotels   *Toriba; Vila Inglesa; Refúgio Alpino*, at Capivari; and others. *Refugio na Serra*, Av. Dr. Antônio Nicola Padula 275, C, comfortable, good breakfast, very helpful owners (some English spoken), rec.; Youth Hostel, Rua Diogo de Carvalho 86, T 229-3787/3011, ramal 286; membership card and permission from Dr Fernando at Tourist Office in the bus terminal required. Camping Clube do Brasil site in the Descansópolis district. Book accommodation in advance if going June/July.

Restaurants   Sole Mio (on road to Horto Florestal), Italian, big portions; *Baden Baden*, German, good. Good cheese on sale at a shop just past sports centre on way out of town, also jams and chocolates; plenty of other chocolate shops. "Milbaho" mineral water is produced here.

Stalls on main square Thurs.-Sun. sell local produce. **Exchange** at Geneve Sweater shop, or Cadij Imóveis, "if they want to", check rates.

Transport   Bus from São Paulo, US$3, 3 hrs.; from Rio, changing at São José dos Campos,

US$5. No through rail service: railcars make round trips between Campos do Jordão and Santo Antônio do Pinhal, in season between 0800 and 0900 and at 1310, out of season (Oct.-Nov., March-April) at 1310 only, a bit bumpy, but beautiful views (sit on the right on the way there, left coming back): hills, valleys, tight corners. The train is very crowded even though you are assigned a seat; fare US$0.75 (buy ticket in advance, and get return immediately on arrival in San Antônio; watch your belongings on board). Whole trip takes about 3 hrs.: 1 hr. each way on train, 40 mins.-1 hr. in Santo Antônio (not much on offer there: a few snack bars, nice views, statue of Madonna and Child). There is a local railcar service within São José (very crowded but cheap). From Pindamonhangaba buses run to São Paulo and Taubaté; also to Aparecida do Norte, 1030, US$1.00. The short road down to "Pinda", starting from the paved road 24 km. SW of Campos do Jordão, is now paved. A new road branching off the BR-116 near Caçapava provides a quicker drive from Rio, or São Paulo, than the route via São José dos Campos.

Nearer to Rio than the Pindamonhangaba turn, just off the BR-116, is *Aparecida do Norte,* Brazil's chief place of pilgrimage and the seat of its patron saint, Nossa Senhora Aparecida. This small black image of the Virgin is said to have been taken by a fisherman from the nearby River Paraíba, and quickly acquired a miraculous reputation. It is now housed in a huge modern basilica in Romanesque style on top of a hill, with the clean white-walled, red-roofed town below.

For the route to the Paraná River, from São Paulo to Presidente Epitácio, see page 340.

SOUTHERN BRAZIL (6)

This consists, from S to N, of the three states of Rio Grande do Sul, Santa Catarina and Paraná. The conformation of the land is not unlike what it is further north; the Great Escarpment runs down the coastal area as far as Porto Alegre, receding from the coast in a wide curve between Paranaguá and Florianópolis. South of Tubarão to the borders of Uruguay the hills of southern Rio Grande do Sul, which never rise higher than 900 to 1,000 metres, are fringed along the coast by sand bars and lagoons.

Rio Grande do Sul

North of the Rio Uruguai the land is deeply forested, but the area of prairie, small in São Paulo, Paraná and Santa Catarina, grows more extensive than the forest in Rio Grande do Sul, south of the Uruguai valley. In southern Rio Grande do Sul, south and west of the Rio Jacuí (draining into the Lagoa dos Patos) there are great grasslands stretching as far as Uruguay to the south and Argentina to the west. This is the distinctive land of the *gaúcho*, or cowboy (pronounced ga-*oo*-shoo in Brazil), of *bombachas* (the baggy trousers worn by the *gaúcho*), of the poncho and *ximarão* (or *mate* without sugar) the indispensable drink of southern cattlemen. There are many millions of cattle, sheep and pigs, and some 75% of all Brazilian wine comes from the state. Its population (who all call themselves *gaúchos*) now number about 8 million. Rio Grande do Sul has the highest proportion of literate people in Brazil.

There are three sharply contrasted types of colonization and land owning in Rio Grande do Sul. During the colonial period, wars with the Spaniards of Uruguay were frequent, and the Portuguese government brought into the grasslands of the south a number of military settlers from the Azores; these soldiers inter-married with the Brazilian herdfolk in the area. In the colonial period, also, the Jesuits built several settlements to acculturate the local Indians; relics of this process include the impressive ruins of the **Sete Povos das Missões Orientais** (São Borja, São Nicolau, São Luiz, São Lourenço, São Miguel, São João, Santo Ângelo). West from Porto Alegre, in the floodlands of the Rio Jacuí and its tributary, the Rio Taquari, rice is cultivated in typical Brazilian fashion: large estates with tenant workers.

At São Leopoldo, north of Porto Alegre, a group of Germans were settled in 1824 on their own small farms, and during the next 25 years over 20,000 more were brought into the area by the Brazilian Government. The Germans concentrated on rye, maize, and pigs. Between 1870 and 1890, settlers from

SOUTHERN BRAZIL

34

northern Italy arrived, bringing viticulture with them, and settled north of the Germans at Alfredo Chaves and Caxias do Sul.

Porto Alegre, capital of Rio Grande do Sul, lies at the confluence of five rivers which flow into the Rio Guaíba and thence into the great fresh-water lagoon, the Lagoa dos Patos, which runs into the sea. It is the most important commercial centre south of São Paulo. Population, 1,109,000 (1980).

Standing on a series of hills and valleys on the banks of the Guaíba, with its business centre jutting out into the water on a promontory, Porto Alegre is one of the most up-to-date cities in Brazil. The older residential part of the town is on a promontory dominated previously by the Governor's Palace, the imposing modern cathedral, and the two high white towers of the old church of Nossa Senhora das Dores, but Governor and God have now been utterly dwarfed by the skyscraper of the Legislative Assembly. The streets in the centre are famous for their steep gradients. The climate is temperate through most of the year, though the temperature at the height of summer can often exceed 40°C. The surrounding suburbs are very pleasant. For instance, Ipanema, on the banks of the Guaíba, has a selection of bars and small restaurants; a popular rendezvous, with spectacular sunsets over the river.

Do not miss that section of the Rua dos Andradas (Rua da Praia) that is now permanently closed to traffic. It is the city's principal outdoor meeting place, and by around 1600 it is full of people; at the peak hour of 1900 the street is jammed for about 6 blocks.

Points of Interest The Jockey Club at which races are held on Saturdays and Sundays; the Country Club (picturesque 18-hole golf course); the Parque Farroupilha, a fine park near the city centre; the interesting cathedral of the Anglican-Episcopal church of Brazil; the Zoological Gardens near São Leopoldo (bus US$0.50; Hotel: *Rima*, D, standard), the Botanic Gardens (Bairro Jardim Botânico, bus 40 from Praça 15 de Novembro) and the Cidade Universitária are well worth a visit. The Mercado Público (said to be a replica of Lisbon's Mercado da Figueira) is next to the Prefeitura, in the centre of town. In the Cidade Baixa quarter are the colonial Travessa dos Venezianos (between Ruas Lopo Gonçalves and Joaquim Nabuco) and the house of Lopo Gonçalves, Rua João Alfredo 582, which houses the Museu do Porto Alegre, free, 0900-1700 Tues.-Sun. The 5-km. wide River Guaíba lends itself to every form of boating and there are several sailing clubs. Tourist boat trips (2 hrs.) leave from the Doca Turística near the Guaíba bridge, for a journey among the river islands. The Museu Júlio de Castilhos, Duque de Caxias 1231, has an interesting historical collection, and there is the Museu do Trem in the old railway station of São Leopoldo. Museo de Arte do Rio Grande do Sul, Praça Senador Florêncio (Praça da Alfândega), Tues.-Sun. 1000-1700, entry free, is interesting. Varig airline museum, open Wed. and Fri. 0900-1200. The old Hotel Majestic has become the Casa de Cultura Mário Quintana, at Rua dos Andradas 736: exhibitions, theatre etc. Plays by local and visiting companies at São Pedro (opposite Government Palace) and Leopoldina (Av. Independência), theatres. Modern cinemas. Centro de Tradição Gaúcha has *gaúcho* shows every Sat., starting at 2200. A good view of the city may be had from the Morro de Santa Teresa, approached from Av. Padre Cacique (take bus 95 from Rua Salgado Filho).

Porto Alegre is a fresh-water port for ocean-going vessels of up to 7,000 tons and 4.87 metres draught. Vessels must come up through Rio Grande and the Lagoa dos Patos, some 275 km. from the open sea. Large areas of reclaimed land have been used for residential building and to extend the port facilities and quays, now among the most up-to-date in Brazil.

Porto Alegre's most important industries are food and farm products, textiles, metal-processing, chemicals and leather products. Chief exports are pinewood, rice, wheat, soya, meat, hides, wool, animal hair, semi-precious stones, wine and tobacco. A visit to Varig's installations and workshops is well worth while.

Festivals February 2 (local holiday) is the festival of Nossa Senhora dos Navegantes, whose image is taken by boat from the central quay in the port to the industrial district of Navegantes. Semana Farroupilha, celebrating *gaúcho* traditions, main day September 20.

Warning The market area in Praça 15 de Novembro is dangerous at night.

Hotels *Plaza São Rafael*, Av. Alberto Bins 514, A; *Conceição-Center*, Av. Senador Salgado Filho 201 (T 26-0610), good; *Alfred Executivo*, Av. Otávio Rocha 270, B; *Plaza Porto Alegre*, Senhor dos Passos 154, B; *Embaixador*, Jerônimo Coelho 354, B; *Everest Palace*, Rua Duque de Caxias 1357, B; *Ritter*, A, opp. Rodoviária, good service, English spoken, conveniently located; *São Luiz*, Av. Farrapos 45, D, spotless, good service, but near Rodoviária and the freeway and so a bit noisy; *Conceição II*, Garibáldi 165, T 24 3987, near Rodoviária, a/c, TV, fridge, OK, D; *Terminaltur*, opp. Rodoviária, D with bath, a/c, TV, breakfast, heating, but small rooms and tiny bathrooms; *Vitória*, Voluntários da Pátria 459, F without breakfast, safe and cheap, very basic and dirty, laundry service; almost next door, *Coliseu*, E with shower, clean; *Porto Alegre*, Pinto Bandeirantes 339 (round corner from *Vitória*), good, clean, F; other hotels (in particular Rua Garibáldi) in this area are used for very short stays. *Minuano*, Farrapos 31, F without breakfast or bath (E with bath), noisy but otherwise good, and *Elevado*, Av. Farrapos 63, F with hot shower, clean, very friendly, rec., both near bus station. *Glória*, Travessa Eng. Acelino de Carvalho 67, E, with shower, central, quiet, clean; *Palácio*, Av. Vigário José Inácio 644, F, central, clean, friendly,

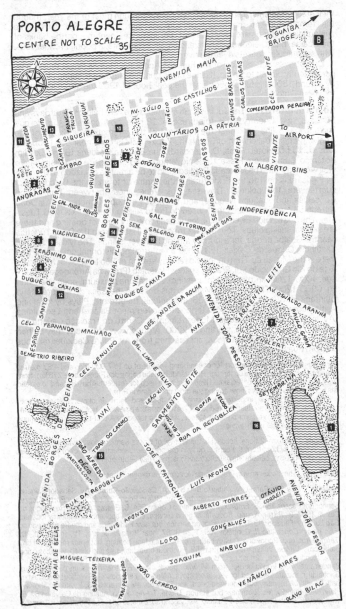

PORTO ALEGRE
CENTRE NOT TO SCALE

hot water, rec.; *Ritz*, André da Rocha 225, E, friendly, central, helpful, Spanish spoken; next door is *Finks*, same price range; *Uruguay*, Dr. Flores 371, F, good; *Marechal*, Rua Andrade Neves 123, F, basic, clean (not far from Mercado Municipal). Two *Casas dos Estudantes* (for those with student cards), at Av. João Pessoa 41, and Rua Riachuelo 1355 (both not far from bus station), night free, breakfast and evening meal US$0.40, lunch US$0.60, if there's room. **Youth hostel** *Laçador*, Rua Aurora Nunes Wagner 148, Morro Santa Tereza, T 287717.

Camping Do Cocão, 10 km. out on Viamão road; Praia do Guarujá, 16 km. out on Av. Guaíba.

Restaurants (except on the *Everest Roof* and at the *Korote* and *Panarea* (US$10-20), the normal cost of dinner is US$8-12). General: *Everest Roof*, Duque de Caxias 1357; *Mosqueteiro*, Estádio Olímpico; *Rodo Ferroviária*, Rua Voluntários da Pátria 1177, good; at No. 509 same street, *Panorama Lancheria*, always open, good large meals; *Rancho Alegre*, Cristóvão Colombo 2168, good "gaúcho" music; also with folklore shows, *Bon Ami*, Av. Salgado Filho 360, good and reasonable; *Gaúcho* at Rodoviária is good, with live entertainment nightly; *Fogão de Chão*, Cavalhada 5200, for churrascos; *Tutty's*, Centro Comercial, Loja 15, Av. da Independência, rec.; *Churrascaria Quero-Quero*, Praça Otávio Rocha 47; *Panorâmico*, Correia Lima 1949; *Grumete*, 24 de Outubro 905; *Umbu*, Av. Farrapos 292; *Ipanema*, Av. Coronel Marcos 1645; *Korote*, Silva Jardim 16; *Ratskeller*, Cristóvão Colombo 1654; *Panarea*, Eça de Queirós 819; *Scherazade*, Av. Protásio Alves 3284; *Barranco*, Av. Protásio Alves 1578.

Vegetarian: *Aroma*, Rua Lima e Silva 292, 2nd floor; *Macrobiótico*, Rua Marechal Floriano Peixoto 72; *Ilha Natural*, Rua Andrade Neves, lunches only.

Chinese: *Palácio do Dragão*, Luciana de Abreu 471; *Chinatown*, Rua Andrade Neves (nr. *Metrópole* hotel), Chinese and other food, good value; *Gold Dragon*, Rua Dr. Valle 479; *Tai Seng Nhe*, Andradas 1097.

German: *Printz*, Protásio Alves 3208; *Steinhaus*, Paulino Teixeira 415; *Floresta Negra*, 24 de Outubro 905; *Germânia*, 24 de Outubro 945; *Franz*, Av. Protásio Alves 3250.

Portuguese: *Casa de Portugal*, João Pessoa 579; *Galo*, João Alfredo 904.

Italian: *Copacabana*, Praça Garibaldi; *Cantina do Peppe*, Getúlio Vargas 273; *Jardim Itália*, Av. Protásio Alves 3580; *Cantina Vila Romana*, Av. Carlos Gomes 1385.

Night Bars (beer and sandwiches, etc.) *Tivoli*, Av. Protásio Alves 766; *Hubertus*, Rua Professor Annes Dias 116; *Xuvisko*, Cristóvão Colombo 927; *Julius*, José de Alencar 480; *Bartok*, José de Alencar 173; *Barril*, Estádio Internacional; *Bar Occidentes*, Av. Osvaldo Aranha and Gral. João Telles, popular; *Bologna*, Av. Coronel Marcos 2359; *Dom Jayme*, Mostardeiro 112.

Discotheques Água na Boca, Discoate, Looking Glass, Maria Fumaça. Av. Farrapos has an assortment of less reputable establishments.

Electric Current 110-120 A.C. 50 cycles.

Bookshops Livraria Kosmos, Rua dos Andradas 1644 (international stock); Livraria Lima, Borges de Medeiros 539; Livraria Globo, Andradas 1416; airport bookshop. Livres e Artes bookstall in book market, Praça Senador Florêncio, new English books with front covers missing!

Shopping H. Stern jewellers at Shopping Center Iguatemi and international airport. There is a street market (leather goods, basketware, etc.) in the streets around the central Post Office. Good leather goods sold on the streets. Sun. a.m. handicraft and bric-a-brac market (plus sideshows) Av. José Bonefacio (next to Parque Farroupilha). Very good food market.

Exchange on Av. Borges de Medeiros, good rate, cash only (e.g. Agência Platina, on corner with Andradas). Many *câmbios* in the centre will change travellers' cheques at parallel rates; e.g. Platino Turismo, Dos Andrades e Av. Borges de Medeira (only one to change travellers' cheques, Amex, but 6% less than cash), Exprinter, Sen. Salgado Filho 247 (best for cash); for other addresses consult tourist bureau brochure. Lloyds Bank (ex-BOLSA), Rua General Câmara 249 (open 1000-1630). Citibank, Rua 7 de Setembro (open 1300-1700).

Addresses U.S. Consulate, Rua Uruguai 155, 11th floor. Austrian Consulate, Rua 7 de Setembro 1069, conj. 1714, Caixa Postal 1771, T 2460 77/85. Argentine Consulate, Rua Prof. Annes Dias 112, 1° andar, T 24-6799/6810/6786. British Club, Av. Carlos Gomes 534 (Montserrat). Touring Clube do Brasil, Av. João Pessoa 623. Instituto Goethe, 24 de Outubro 122 (open Mon.-Fri., 0930-1230, 1430-2100). Instituto Cultural Americano Brasileiro, Mon.-Fri., 0800-2000 (Sats. 0800-1700).

Dentist Ursula Finkenwerder, R. Quintino Bocaiúva 655, Sala 301, Mon.-Fri. 0830-1130.

Key to Porto Alegre
1. Parque Farroupilha; 2. Praça Senador Florência; 3. Praça 15 de Novembro; 4. Praça Mal. Deodoro; 5. Cathedral; 6. Prefeitura; 7. University; 8. São Pedro Theatre; 9. Government Palace; 10. Mercado Público; 11. Alfândega; 12. Júlio de Castilhos Museum; 13. Post Office, Embratel; 14. Telephone Office; 15. Epatur Tourist Offices (x2); 16. Touring Club do Brasil; 17. Hotel São Luiz; 18. Hotel Vitória; 19. Hotel Palácio.

Cables Embratel, Rua Siqueira de Campos 1245. T 41233.

Post For sending parcels abroad: Rua Araújo Ribeiro 100; bring parcel unopened.

Tourist Information Epatur, Travessa do Carmo 84 (head office), helpful as is branch in Praça 15 de Novembro; Branch offices: Salgado Filho airport; interstate bus station, very helpful (free city maps); Rua General Câmara 368; Av. Salgado Filho 366. CRTur (Companhia Riograndense de Turismo), Rua dos Andradas 1137, 6th floor. Epatur maintains information booths at the frontier towns. A monthly booklet is available.

Swimming from the beaches near or in the city is forbidden because of pollution. See "Beaches", next page, for out-of-town beaches.

Rail The only long-distance passenger service from Porto Alegre is the line W to (386 km.) *Santa Maria* (pop. 151,000, *Hotel Itaimbé Palace*, B, useful road junction for connections N to São Miguel mission ruins and Iguaçu, and S direct to Pelotas) and on to Cacequi, where the line branches for Uruguaiana (**see page 326**), for connections to Argentina, and for Santana do Livramento, for connections to Uruguay (by bus only, there are no longer passenger rail services in Uruguay). 6 days a week a standard train (no sleepers) leaves Porto Alegre at 2050 to Santa Maria, continuing to Cacequi, thence 3 a week to Uruguaiana and 3 a week to Santana do Livramento. There is also a suburban service from Mercado station (Av. Mauá) north to Sapucaia do Sul, serving Esteio and Canoas. The suburban train service (faster than the bus) links the centre, Rodoviária and airport (10 mins.).

Buses Bus to Rio, US$24 (*leito* 48), 26 hrs.; São Paulo, US$16.75 (*leito* 33.50), 18 hrs.; Uruguaiana, US$9, 9 hrs.; Santa Maria, 4¾ hrs., frequent service with Planalto; Santana do Livramento, 1230 and 2300, 8½ hrs., *leito* at 2330; to Pelotas, 8 daily, US$4.60, 3-4 hrs.; to Gramado, 8 daily, 2hrs.; to Canela, 5 daily, 2½ hrs.; to Caxias do Sul, almost hourly, 2 hrs., US$2.65, *executivo* service also. Florianópolis, US$5.50, 7 hrs. with Viação São Cristóvão (beware of overbooking and of stopping buses—e.g. Santo Anjo—on this route); Curitiba, US$10.50, 11 hrs.; Blumenau, US$8.50, 9 hrs.; Rio Grande, US$6, 8 per day, 0600 to 2000, 4½ hrs. Foz do Iguaçu, US$15, 15 hrs.; Londrina, 22 hrs. To Cascavel (Paraná) for connections to Campo Grande, Cuiabá and Porto Velho: daily except Sat. with Aguia Branca, 21 hrs., or Unesul, 19 hrs. To Jaguarão on Uruguayan border at 2400, 6 hrs., US$5.50.

Bus to Montevideo, with international buses TTL (daily 1730 and 2000) or Onda (daily 2200, not rec. as a/c is too cold and window blinds inadequate), 12 hrs., US$19; alternatively take bus to border town of Chuí at 1200 or 2330 daily, 7½ hrs., US$8.75 (night bus more), then Onda or Rutas del Sol bus to Montevideo (US$8, cheaper bought in Porto Alegre or Chuí than in Uruguay). Ouro e Prata operates a 2-3 times weekly service to Salto and Paysandú (Uruguay), via Santana do Livramento/Rivera. To Asunción with Unesul at 1900 daily via Foz do Iguaçu. Expresso Singer bus Porto Alegre-Posadas (Argentina) via Oberá, Alba Posse, Porto Mauá, departs 2100 on Tues., Thurs., and Sun. arriving following day at 1135. There are bus services to Buenos Aires (US$35) 19 hrs. (depending on border) with Pluma, Mon., Fri., Sun., 2200, route is Uruguaiana, Paso de los Libres, Entre Ríos and Zárate, or 22 hrs. with General Urquiza company, Mon., Thurs. **N.B.** take your passport when purchasing international bus tickets. The new and excellent bus terminal on Av. Mauá with Garibáldi has good facilities, including a post office and long-distance telephone service until 2100. A regular bus runs from the Rodoviária to the airport, also the suburban train service (see above).

Roads Good roads radiate from Porto Alegre, and Highway BR-116 has a paved surface to Curitiba (746 km.). To the S it is paved to Pelotas (though this stretch is in poor condition), and on from there to Chuí on the Uruguayan frontier. The new paved coastal road to Curitiba via Itajaí (BR-101), of which the first 100 km. is a four-lane highway, is much better than the BR-116 via Caxias and Lajes. The road to Uruguaiana is now entirely paved but bumpy.

Air Services There is a large modern international airport, Salgado Filho, 8 km. from the city, connected to the centre by train (see above). There are daily flights to Rio, São Paulo, Curitiba, Buenos Aires and Montevideo, and many other Brazilian cities. Vasp flies to Iguaçu and Brasília on Mon., Wed., Fri., and Sun. The airport is served by all Brazilian airlines, Pluna and Aerolíneas Argentinas.

Excursion Cervejaria Brahma, Av. Cristovão Colombo 545, offers tours of its brewery (but not Dec.-March).

Beaches The best beach resorts of the area are to the north of the city. The towns of **Tramandaí** (126 km.) and **Torres** (209 km.) are the most popular, with lots of luxury (and more reasonable) hotels and motels, bars, restaurants, and other standard requisites associated with seaside resorts. Between the two towns are the small resorts of Arróio Teixeira (Camping Clube do Brasil site), Capão da Canoa (*Hotel Kolman*, R. Sepé 1718, youth hostel *Riveira di Fiori*, Av. Venâncio Aires 711, T 265944, swimming pool, rec., and others) and Atlântida.

There is no lack of cheap accommodation, but hotels tend to be very full during the summer season. There are fully equipped campsites at both towns, and camping is also allowed on some beaches.

Torres Hotels *A Furninha*, Rua Joaquim Porto 281, D, good service; *Farol*, Rua José A. Pirasol 240, D to B with full board; *Grande Hotel Torres*, Rua Júlio de Castilhos 124, D with bath, balcony and breakfast (off-season). On Av. General Osório, *Camping*, No. 450, E, clean, friendly, and *Mini-Torres*, E with breakfast and bath out of season; *Salth*, central, E with bath, friendly, clean. Other hotels, E, bath and breakfast are available. Rec. **restaurants**: *A Furninha* for fish, and *Bom Gosto*, churrascaria.

Tramandaí Hotels *Samburá*, Av. Beira Mar. *Motel Junges*, on main street, D with bath and breakfast, friendly, German spoken. Many more.

Another popular beach area is south of Porto Alegre, around Cassino, near Rio Grande (**see page 325**). 40 km. to the south (towards Rio Grande) begins the Costa Doce of the Lagoa dos Patos; noted bathing points are Tapes, Barra do Ribeiro, Arambaré, São Lourenço do Sul (rec. camping site 1 km. out of town on lake shore) and Laranjal.

At *São Lourenço do Sul* is *Hotel Vilela*, Rua Almirante Abreu 428, family hotel, clean, friendly. The town is a good place to stop to enjoy the lake, the beaches, fish restaurants and water sports.

Inland is the pleasant Serra Gaúcha, the most beautiful scenery being around the towns of *Gramado* and *Canela,* about 130 km. from Porto Alegre (chocolate factory between the two towns). There is a distinctly Bavarian flavour to many of the buildings. In spring and summer the flowers are a delight, and in winter there are frequently snow showers. This is excellent walking and climbing country among hills, woods, lakes and waterfalls. There are many excellent hotels at all prices in both towns, but it is difficult to get rooms in the summer. Local crafts include knitted woollens, leather, wickerwork, and chocolate. Gramado has two fine parks, Parque Knorr and Lago Negro, and Minimundo, a collection of miniature models.

Gramado Hotels *Hortensias*, Rua Bela Vista 83, C; *Serrano*, Costa e Silva 1112, C; *Serra Azul*, Rua Garibáldi 152, C; *Pequeno Bosque*, Rua Piratina 486, D with bath, fridge, TV, good breakfast, located in wood close to Véu da Noiva waterfall; *Parque*, bungalows, good breakfast, friendly, maid will do laundry reasonably, D; *Ritta Höppner*, Rua Pedro Candiago 305, T 054-286-1334, D in cabins, very good value, friendly, good breakfasts, German owners, cabins have TV, fridge, some have own swimming pool, pool and miniature trains in grounds. *Luiz*, Senador Salgado Filho 432, E, good breakfast, clean, good value; *Tia Hulda*, Av Borges de Medeiros 1817, friendly, E; *Dinda*, Rua Augusto Zatti 160, one of the cheapest, E; try in the private house opposite the tourist office, not very friendly but very clean and comfortable, (E).

Restaurants *Saint Hubertus*, Rua da Caixa d'Água; *Nápoli*, Av. Borges de Medeiros, good Italian. **Coffee shop,** *Tia Nilda*, Av. Pres. Costa e Silva. *Pyp* yoghurt factory, Av. S. Diniz 1030, has snack bar serving health food sandwiches and yoghurt. The local speciality is *café colonial*, a 5 o'clock meal of various dishes, including meats, rec. at *Café da Torre* (order one helping for 2 or more people, very filling). Visitors should also sample hot pinhões (pine nuts) and quentão (hot red wine, cachaça, ginger, cloves, sugar and cinnamon, often topped with gemada—beaten egg yolks and sugar).

Tourist Office Corner of Borges de Medeiros and Coronel Diniz, Gramado (½ block from Rodoviária, no English spoken).

Canela Hotels *Laje de Pedra*, new holiday hotel, all amenities. *Charrua*, Av. das Nações 351, D; *Bela Vista*, Rua Oswaldo Aranha 160, near Rodoviária, clean, good breakfasts, F (D with additional facilities). Cheap hotels: *Jubileu*, Oswaldo Aranha 223, F-G (acts as **Youth hostel**, T (054) 282-2133), and *Central*, Av. Júlio de Castilhos 146.

Camping Camping Clube do Brasil, 8 km. from Canela, near waterfall in Parque do Caracol; excellent honey and chocolate for sale here. Wine merchant in Canela, *Joliment*, Estrada de Morro, Calçado.

Electric Current 220 volts A.C.

Bus Several daily Canela-Caxias do Sul, 2 hrs., US$1.65. From Florianópolis, you have to go via Porto Alegre.

8 km. from Canela is the Parque Estadual do Caracol (bus marked "Caracol Circular" from corner R. Melvin Jones and Av. Oswaldo Aranha, adjacent to old steam engine, US$0.20, 20 mins. 4 a

day, return about ½ hour after departure time); a slippery path leads to the foot of the falls, which are 130 metres high. Good paths lead to smaller falls above Caracol; from the high point at Ferradura there is a good view into the canyon of the River Cai. 80 km. from São Francisco de Paula is the **Parque Nacional de Aparados da Serra,** where the major attraction is the 7.8-km. canyon, known locally as the Itaimbezinho. Here, two waterfalls cascade 350 metres into a stone circle at the bottom. Tourist excursions, mostly at weekends, from São Francisco de Paula. At other times, take a bus to Cambara, get off at the *cruce,* from where it is 15 km. to the park—walk or hitch hike if you're lucky. There is a free campsite and a restaurant, which has a few rooms, in the park. From the restaurant one can walk to the canyon of Malacara. For experienced hikers (and with a guide) there is a difficult path to the bottom of Itaimbezinho. One can then hike 20 km. to Praia Grande in Santa Catarina (**see page 327**).

24 km. W of Gramado (99 km. from Porto Alegre, 30 km. from Caxias do Sul) is **Nova Petrópolis** (bus US$0.40), another city with strong German roots; there is a Parque do Imigrante, an open-air museum of German settlement. (Hotels include *Veraneio dos Pinheiros, Recanto Suiço,* 3 star; *Petrópolis, Veraneio Schoeller,* one-star.) N of Nova Petrópolis is Jammerthal, a valley in the Serra Gaúcha with German farms, many of whose inhabitants still speak German (go to Joanette and walk from there).

Caxias do Sul, 122 km. from Porto Alegre, is the centre of the Brazilian wine industry. The population (199,000) is principally of Italian descent, and it is an expanding and modern town. One should not miss the opportunity to visit the many *adegas* (but do not always expect free tasting), and the neighbouring towns of Farroupilha (Hotels *Don Francesco,* Rua Dr. J. Rossler 88, 2 star; *Grande,* Júlio de Castilhos 1064), Bento Gonçalves (hotels *Dall'Onder,* C; *Vinocap,* D) and *Garibáldi* (hotels *Pietá,* D; *Estação de Esqui,* D in cabins without breakfast; there is a "wine supermarket" on the road between Bento Gonçalves and Caxias; a selection of 40 wines at low prices). A good *adega,* with free tasting, is Cooperativa Viti Vinícola Emboaba Ltda, in Nova Milano (bus to Farroupilha, then change—day trip). Good tour and tasting (6 wines) at Adega Granja União, Rua Os 18 de Forte 2346, US$0.25. That at Chateau La Cave (BR-116, Km. 143, Bairro São Ciro, bus from Sinimbu, US$0.15) is poor. Caxias do Sul's festival of grapes is held in February-March. The church of São Pelegrino has paintings by Aldo Locatelli and 5 metre-high bronze doors sculptured by Augusto Murer. Vines were first brought to the region in 1840 but not until the end of the century and Italian immigration did the industry develop. Good municipal museum at Rua Visconde de Pelotas 586 (open Tues.-Sat., 0800-1200, 1400-1800), with displays of artefacts of the Italian immigration. The best time to visit is Jan.-Feb. Garibáldi has the distinction of a dry ski slope and toboggan slope (equipment hire, US$2 per hour).

Caxias Hotels *Volpiano,* Ernesto Alves, 1462, C; *Cosmos,* 20 de Setembro 1563, D-C; *Alfred Palace,* Rua Sinimbu 2302, C; *Itália,* Av. Júlio de Castilhos 3076, D; *Real,* Rua Marquês de Herval 606, E; *Alfred,* Rua Sinimbu 2266, C; *Bandeira,* same street, No. 2435, E with T.V. and bath; *Santa Rita,* Os 18 do Forte 2149, E without breakfast, cheap; *Pérola,* corner Ernesto Alves and Marquês de Herval (No. 237), E, clean, good value; *Peccini,* Rua Pinheiro Machado 1939, E, shared bath, good breakfast. *Samuara,* 10 km. out on RS-25 road, D. Hotels fill up early p.m.

A good **restaurant** is *Angelo; Fogo de Chão,* Os 18 do Forte 16, reasonably priced, live music (not touristy), "gaúcho"-style; also *Cantina Pão e Vino,* Rua Ludovico Cavinato 1757, Bairro Santa Catarina, Caxias, good value.

Camping Municipal campsite, 4 km. out on Rua Cons. Dantas; *Palermo,* 5 km. out on BR-116 at km. 118; *Belvedere Nova Sonda,* 38 km. out in the district of Nova Pádua. At Garibáldi, near the dry ski slope.

Tourist Office Praça do Centro Administrativo; kiosk in Praça Rui Barbosa, also in Ed. Bonifa, Júlio de Castilho 1634, 2nd floor.

On the road north, 112 km. from Porto Alegre, is *Osório,* a pleasant town near sea and lakes, with a good cheap hotel, *Big Hotel,* E.

Rio Grande, at the entrance to the Lagoa dos Patos, 274 km. S of Porto Alegre, was founded in 1737. The city lies on a low, sandy peninsula 16 km. from the Atlantic Ocean. To-day it is the distribution centre for the southern part of Rio Grande do Sul. Its cattle and meat industries are important. Population, 125,000.

During the latter half of the 19th century Rio Grande was an important centre, but today it is a rather poor town, notable for the charm of its old buildings. (Museu Oceanográfico, US$0.30, 0900, 1400-1700 daily, interesting, 2 km. from centre; bus 59 or walk along waterfront.) At Praça Tamandaré is a small zoo.

Hotels *Charrua,* Rua Duque de Caxias 55 (rec. for good value), D; *Paris,* Rua Marechal Floriano 112, D; *Europa,* Rua Gen. Neto 165, main square, D. Cheap hotels: *City, Iria,* both E (latter clean, friendly), on Rua Luís Loréa; *Ritter,* Silva Paes 373.

Restaurants *Haiti* (Italian); *Porcão,* Rua Dr. Nascimento 389, cheap churrascaria, good service; Chinese restaurant on Rua Luís Loréa, good but not cheap; *Pescal,* for fish, fairly expensive and a long taxi ride from the centre; *Angola,* Benjamin Constant 163 (corner of Luís Loréa), very good and reasonable.

Exchange *Hotel Charrua* for US$ notes.

Cables Embratel, Rua Andrade Neves 94.

British Vice-Consul.

Tourist Office Rua Gral. Bacelar, near Cathedral; good map.

Transport Frequent daily buses to and from Pelotas (56 km.), Bagé (280 km.), Santa Vitória (220 km.), and Porto Alegre (US$6, 4½ hrs.). To Itajaí, 14 hrs., US$13. Road to Uruguayan border at Chuí is paved, but the surface is poor (5 hrs. by bus, at 0700 and 1430, US$4.50).

Boat Trip By boat across mouth of Lagoa dos Patos, to pleasant village of São José do Norte, US$0.25. In this vicinity is the recently created **National Park Lagoa do Peixe** (details from Rua Miguel Teixeira 126, Praia de Belas, Cidade Baixa, CEP 90.000, Porto Alegre).

Excursions
To *Cassino,* a popular seaside resort on the Atlantic Ocean, 24 km., over a good road. The breakwater (the Barra), 5 km. north of town, through which all vessels entering and leaving Rio Grande must pass, is a major tourist attraction. Barra-Rio Grande buses pass the Superporto, very impressive. Very good fishing. The coastline is low and straight, lacking the bays to the N of Porto Alegre; unfortunately the beach is used as a roadway. The Cassino beaches are always populous (note the statue of Yemanjá); those further N are mainly used in summer. One attraction is railway flat-cars powered by sail; the railway was built for the construction of the breakwater.

Hotels *Atlântico,* Av. Rio Grande, 387, D, clean, refurbished, special rates for students; *Marysol,* Av. Atlântica 900, D, near beach, friendly. Private campsite on Avenida 33, on the way out to Rio Grande. Camping Clube do Brasil site near town.

Pelotas, on the BR-116, 56 km. N of Rio Grande, is the second largest city in the State of Rio Grande do Sul, on the left bank of the River São Gonçalo which connects the Lagoa dos Patos with the Lagoa Mirim. Its proximity to Rio Grande has hindered the development of its own port. **Pelotas** is prosperous, with an array of shops and pleasant parks. Like Rio Grande, it is rather damp. Population: 197,000.

Within a radius of 60 km., say an hour's drive, there are numerous excursions into the hilly countryside. Simple and clean accommodation and cheap, good and plentiful food can be found on the farms of settlers of German descent.

Hotels *Curi Palace,* Gen. Neto 1279, C; *Curi,* Gen. Osório 719, D; *Estoril,* Rua Gen. Osório 718, a/c, reasonable, D; *Tourist Parque,* motel-type, 7 km. south on the BR-116, D; *Rex,* Praça Pedro Osório 205, E, friendly, dowdy; *Grande,* Praça Pedro Osório 51, old, some rooms with electric shower, F; *Germano,* next bus station, owner speaks some German, E.

Camping 60 km. out at the Arco Iris waterfall, no facilities; *Cascata,* 25 km. out on the Cangussu road. Between Pelotas and Chuí, 1 km. S of junction with Rio Grande road, 1,200 metres from road at a working ranch, rec., clean, meals included.

Restaurant Tyrolean restaurant, opposite *Hotel Rex,* excellent, cheap. 29 km. out of town, on the road to Rio Grande, is an excellent restaurant owned by Tia Laura, who specializes in home cooking and café colonial.

Exchange Difficult to change travellers' cheques. Try Sr. Jesus Faria at 15 de Novembro 626 for good cash rate.

Communications Plane a day to Porto Alegre. Rodoviária is far out of town, with bus every 15 mins. to centre. Frequent daily buses to Porto Alegre, 244 km. (US$4.60, 3-4 hrs., paved road);

Rio Grande, 90 min. (paved but in poor condition); Jaguarão, on frontier with Río Branco, Uruguay (dirt); and inland to Bagé (*Hotel Medronha*, near bus station, E, without breakfast, clean) and other towns. The road to the Uruguayan frontier at Chuí (paved), has international bus service. Onda and TTL bus services (Montevideo-Porto Alegre) stop at the bus station for Montevideo (Ruas Chile and Venezuela); tickets must be purchased from agency during day. Bus to Buenos Aires (via Uruguaiana), US$28.75. From Bagé, the Uruguayan company Núñez runs buses 3 times a week to Melo, via Aceguá. Good direct road NW to Iguaçu via São Sepe (*Trevo Parque Hotel*, D, a/c, very friendly), Santa Maria (**see page 322**) and São Miguel mission ruins (see below).

The southern interior of the state is the region of the real *gaúcho*. Principal towns of this area include **Santana do Livramento** (population: 64,000, bus and train—3 a week—services to Porto Alegre) with its twin Uruguayan city of Rivera (**see page 871**)—a great attraction of the latter being its casino. Rivera is generally considered to have the better hotels and better exchange facilities. Duty free shopping.

Hotels: *Portal*, B, garage, clean, rec.; *Piranga*, cheap and clean, E; *Uruguaiana*, E, close to bus station.

In the extreme west are **Uruguaiana**, population 75,000, a cattle centre 772 km. from Porto Alegre (*Hotel Glória*, Rua Domingos de Almeida 1951, E, good; *Califôrnia* and *Pampa*, near the bus station, both D; *Moderno*, Rua Santana, E; *Palace*, Praça Rio Branco, E, without breakfast; *Fares Turis Hotel* may let you leave your bags while you look around town) and its twin Argentine town of Paso de los Libres, also with a casino (**see page 127**). A 1,400-metre bridge over the River Uruguai links the two cities; taxi or bus across about US$2. Buses connect the railway and bus stations, and centres of each city every half-hour; if you have to disembark for visa formalities, a following bus will pick you up without extra charge. There are train and bus services to Porto Alegre.

The west of Rio Grande do Sul also contains the Sete Povos das Missões Orientais (**see page 317**). The only considerable Jesuit remains in Brazilian territory (very dramatic) are at **São Miguel** (church, 1735-45, and small museum) some 50 km. from *Santo Ângelo*. (*Hotel Nova Esperança*, behind bus station, F, without breakfast; other cheap central hotels near old railway station). At São Miguel there is a *son et lumière* show, weekdays at 2000, weekends at 1930, but ends too late to return to Santo Ângelo; in São Miguel village is *Hotel-Churrascaria Brillante*, E. East of Santo Ângelo is Passo Fundo, "the most *gaúcho* city in Rio Grande do Sul", so much so that the town's square boasts a statue of a maté gourd and bombilla— otherwise not much of interest; *Hotel dos Viajantes* opposite bus station, F. Planalto buses run from Uruguaiana via Barra do Quaraí/Bella Unión to Salto and Paysandú in Uruguay.

Entering Uruguay   Those requiring a visa face problems: a medical exam is required before a visa can be issued, cost approximately US$20 and US$10 respectively. All buses, except those originating in Pelotas, stop at customs on both sides of the border; if coming from Pelotas, you must ask the bus to stop for exit formalities. You must have a Brazilian exit stamp to enter Uruguay. The Brazilian immigration office (and tourist caravan) is about 2½ km. from the border, on Av. Argentina; the bus from Porto Alegre stops here and the conductor hands over tourist cards to the officials. Make sure you get out to get your stamp, asking the driver to wait; or walk back from town at your leisure. The Brazilian border town, Chuí is much cheaper than its Uruguayan neighbour, so stock up with food and drink before crossing. At Santana do Livramento all one need do is cross the main street, but the Uruguayan immigration is hard to find, in a side street. No customs formalities, but luggage is inspected on boarding bus for Montevideo, and there are checkpoints on the roads out of town. Bus to Montevideo, US$7. For motorists there are 3 customs offices in Santana do Livramento, about ½ hr. needed for formalities.

Entering Brazil   from Uruguay, on the Uruguayan side, the bus will stop if asked, and wait while you get your exit stamp (with bus conductor's help); on the Brazilian side, the appropriate form is completed by the Rodoviária staff when you purchase your ticket into Brazil. The bus stops at Polícia Federal (Av. Argentina) and the conductor completes formalities while you sit on the bus. Buses run from Chuí to Pelotas (6-7 daily, US$4, 4 hours), Rio Grande (0700, 1400, 5 hrs., US$4.50) and Porto Alegre (1200, 2300, 7½ hrs., US$7); also from Chuí to Santa Vitória nearby, where there are a few hotels and rather quicker bus services to the main cities. **N.B.** Change all remaining Uruguayan pesos into new cruzados before leaving Uruguay since not even black marketeers in Brazil want them. Also, if entering by car, fill up with petrol in Brazil, where fuel is much cheaper.

Chuí hotels San Francisco, Av. Colombia e Rua Chile, E, shower, clean, restaurant; *Cairo*, Av. Uruguay (opp. Atlantic petrol station), D, shower, breakfast, clean, TV lounge; on Rua Chile, *Hospedagem Roberto* at No. 1631 and *Pensão* in private house at No. 767, F. In Chuy (Uruguay), there is a *hospedaje* on Av. Brasil, opp. the Atlantic petrol station.

Exchange Cambios on Uruguayan side of Av. Brasil/ Av. Uruguay, between Calles L. Olivera and Gen. Artigas; best rates fro AmEx travellers' cheques at Val de Marne.

Post Offices Av. Uruguay, between Colombia and Argentina (Chuí); Av. Brasil, 4 blocks from Gen. Artigas (Chuy).

Telephones in Brazil, corner of Rua Chile and Av. Argentina; in Uruguay one block behind plaza, between Calles L. Olivera and Gen. Artigas.

Tourist Information On Av. Argentina (Chuí), 2½ km. from border; Uruguayan office in middle of Av. Brasil/Uruguay, at Av. Argentina/Calle Gen. Artigas junction.

Santa Catarina

Further up the coast, in Santa Catarina, a group of Germans was settled at Lajes in 1822. In 1848 a new German-speaking settlement was founded at Blumenau. The Germans spread inland over the mountains from the port of São Francisco to Joinville. The Italians came later. Over northern Rio Grande do Sul and Santa Catarina the vast majority of people to-day can trace their origin to these immigrants.

In Santa Catarina, a state of small holdings, the farmer owns his land and cattle: the familiar European pattern of mixed farming worked by the family. Sixty per cent of the population is rural. There is coal in the S, and flourishing food processing and textile industries. Itajaí and São Francisco do Sul are the main ports, handling 90% of the trade. Except for the summer months of January and February, the beaches of Santa Catarina are pleasant and uncrowded.

386 km. NE of Porto Alegre is the small fishing port of **Laguna** (pop.: 50,000; *Hotel Laguna Tourist*, first class; *Hotel Itapirubá*, 4-star with beach and pool; *Turismar*, Av. Rio Grande do Sul 207, view over Mar Grosso beach, C, TV; several others, medium-priced, *Grande*, opp. post office, clean, E, without breakfast), in southern Santa Catarina. At Laguna is the Anita Garibaldi Museum, containing documents, furniture, and the personal effects of the Brazilian wife of the hero who fought in the 1840s for the independence of Rio Grande do Sul and later helped to unify Italy (US$0.05). Laguna's beach, 2 km. from the centre, is not very good, but 16 km. away (by ferry and road) are beaches and dunes at Cavo de Santa Marta. South of Laguna is **Praia Grande**, on the Ilha de São Francisco (cheap hotel at bus station, F). Buses from Praia Grande to Araranguá and Laguna. Also from Laguna, take a Lagunatur or Auto Viação São José bus to Farol (infrequent, US$0.70). You have to cross the mouth of the Lagoa Santo Antônio by ferry to get to Farol; look out for fishermen aided by dolphins (*botos*). Here is a fishing village with the alleged third oldest lighthouse in the world (Farol Santa Marta)—guided tours available (taxi, US$8.25, not including ferry toll). No hotels, but it is possible to bargain with fishermen for a bed. (Bus to/from Porto Alegre, 5½ hrs., with Santo Anjo Da Guarda; same company goes to Florianópolis, 2 hrs., but you can't buy a ticket before the bus arrives in Laguna—as soon as it comes in, follow the driver to ticket office.) Another 32 km. to the north of Laguna is the port of **Imbituba,** where there is a carbo-chemical plant, from which air pollution is very bad. Imbituba sends the coal mined in the area between Araranguá and Tubarão in coastal vessels to Rio de Janeiro, where it is railed to the steel mills at Volta Redonda for coking. The rail link between Imbituba and Tubarão is one of the busiest steam services in South America (freight only). There are good beaches (those near Garopaba and Araçatuba have been particularly recommended), and bus services to Porto Alegre.

The coalfield towns of **Tubarão** (*Hotel Mossi*, in centre, E, excellent), Criciúma and Içara are interesting, and the nearby beaches are good.

From Tubarão one can visit the Termas do Gravatal. (There is one first class hotel, and two others, good value, quiet, good food.) Also, buses go inland to Lauro Müller, then over the Serra do Rio do Rastro (beautiful views of the coast in clear weather). At Bom Jardim da Serra there is an apple festival every April. A dirt road continues to São Joaquim (**see page 330**), and over Pericõ to Urubici (*Pensão Anderman*, E, clean, friendly, big meals). A new paved road is being built, as far as Santo Amaro da Imperatriz. There are direct buses from São Joaquim to Florianópolis.

J. P. Monnickendam, of Elstree, writes: About 60 km. inland from Tubarão is Orleães. It has one of the most interesting and least known museums in the area, which has an original water-powered workshop and sawmill, complete with waterwheel. It dates from the original settlers (late 19th century), and is still in working order. To get there one must get off the bus at the junction about 3 km. from town.

The festival of São João in June can be seen best in Santa Catarina at Campo Alegre, the first town on the road inland to Mafra. There are bonfires, a lot of (German) folk dancing, and large quantities of *quentão* (a hot drink made of red wine, cinnamon, ginger and *cachaça*) and *pinhões* (the nuts of the Paraná pine tree). It is a beautiful climb on the road from the BR-101 to Campo Alegre. The road continues through São Bento and Rio Negrinho to Mafra, from where a good road (the BR-116) goes to Curitiba.

124 km. N of Laguna is **Florianópolis** (founded in 1726), capital of the State, on the Ilha de Santa Catarina joined to the mainland by two bridges, one of which is Ponte Hercílio Luz, the longest steel suspension bridge in Brazil (closed to all traffic in 1983). The newer Colombo Machado Salles bridge has a pedestrian and cycle way beneath the roadway. It is a port of call for coastal shipping, 725 km. from Rio de Janeiro and 420 from Santos. The natural beauty of the island, beaches and bays are making Florianópolis a popular tourist centre (only January and February are very crowded); it seems a pity that the waterfront, scene of a traditional market, has been filled in and reclaimed and that the city is not in general better maintained. The cathedral on Praça 15 de Novembro has a life-size sculpture in wood of the flight into Egypt, originally from the Austrian Tyrol. Forts include the Santana (which houses a Museum of Military Arms), São José da Ponta Grossa and Nossa Senhora da Conceição. There are three other museums, the Historical Museum in the old Palácio Cruz e Souza, on Praça 15 de Novembre (1000-1800, Tues.-Sun.), the Anthropological Museum at the Federal University and the Sambaqui Museum at the Colégio Catarinense, Rua Esteves Júnior 159 (last-named open 1330-1730 Mon.-Fri., others 0800-1200, 1400-1800, Mon.-Sat.). There is a look-out point at Morro da Cruz (take Empresa Trindadense bus). Carnival is recommended as beautiful. Urban population 170,000 (municipality, 220,000).

Hotels *Florianópolis Palace,* Rua Artista Bittencourt and Rua dos Ilhéus 26, new, best, B; *Royal,* Trav. João Pinto, B, good; *Oscar Palace,* Av. Hercílio Luz 90, C, watch the bill carefully; *Valeiro,* Rua Silva Jardim 234, E with a/c and TV, new, rec., take Cidade Universitária bus; *City Hotel,* Rua Emílio Blum 31, F, very basic, friendly. Within 10 minutes' walk of the Rodoviária: Rua Felipe Schmidt, *Faial Palace,* No. 87, C, good restaurant; *Valerim,* No. 74, central, D with bath, E without (cheaper off season), fridge, radio, T.V.; stove; *Sumaré,* No. 53, E, good, clean, good value but check rooms for ventilation; *Querência Palace,* Rua Jerônimo Coelho 1, B, clean, good. On Conselheiro Mafra: *Colonial,* No. 45, basic, hot water, fair, safe, pleasant, F; *Center Plaza,* D, No. 70; *Felippe,* one block from 15 de Novembro at Rua João Pinto 25, D, friendly, clean, small rooms, 10% off to Youth Hostel members. Dormitória Estrela, Rua Mafra, nr. Rua Bento Gonçalves, very basic but cheap.On the mainland: *Oasis,* Rua Gral. L. Bittencourt 201, E, with breakfast, clean, good (take bus 201 from here to bus terminal); *Bruggeman,* Rua Santos Saraiva 300 (bus 236 or 226 from Terminal Urbano do Aterro), E for motel-type rooms and 2-star accommodations. Cheap hotels around Rodoviária reckoned less good than those of similar price on the mainland, close to the bridge. To rent a room, contact Leny Saboia, Rua J. Colago 525, Jardím Santa Mônica, T 33-4684 (take a bus to Beira Mar Norte, alight at Santa Mônica supermarket).

Youth hostels on the island: *Ilha de Santa Catarina,* Rua Duarte Schutel 59 (T 22-3781); *Barra da Lagoa* (T 22-6746) and *Fortaleza da Barra* (T 32-0169), both on Estrada Geral da Barra da Lagoa; *Praia do Campeche* (T 22-6746) and *Praia dos Ingleses* (T 22-6746) also)

Camping Camping Clube do Brasil, São João do Rio Vermelho, near the lagoon, 21 km. out of town; also at Lagoa da Conceição, Praia da Armação, Praia dos Ingleses, Praia Canavieiras. "Wild" camping allowed at Ponta de Sambaqui. Beaches of Brava, Aranhas, Galheta, Mole, Campeche, Campanhas and Naufragados. 4 km. S of Florianópolis, camping site with bar at Praia do Sonho on the mainland, beautiful, deserted beach with an island fort nearby. Take bus to Laguna and walk or hitch to beach (5 km. from highway). "Camping Gaz" cartridges from Riachuelo Supermercado, on Rua Alvim with Rua São Jorge.

Restaurants *Braseiro*, R. Trajano 27 (behind Governor's Palace), crowded at lunch-time. *Dalton's*, Rua Trajano 29, first floor meals better than ground floor pizzas, etc.; *Galerie*, Trajano 41, very good and reasonable; *Manolo's*, Rua Felipe Schmidt 71, near centre, good, but not cheap. *Lindacap*, Rua Felipe Schmidt 178 on outskirts (closed Mon.), rec., good views. All the above give a good meal and beer for around US$7. *Dom Dom*, Praça Pereira Oliveira 6, cheap, good; *Rotisserie Acapulco*, Rua dos Ilhéus 20, central, cafeteria-style, popular. Shrimp dishes are good everywhere. *Polly's*, Praça 15 de Novembro, good food and service, reasonable prices; *Macarronada Italiana*, Av. Beira Mar Norte 196, good. *Churrascaria Ataliba*, Rúa Jaú Guedes da Fonseca s/n, 2 km. from centre at Coqueiros, excellent rodízio, US$3.75. Vegetarian: *Sol da Terra*, Rua N. Ramos 13, popular, *Vida*, Rua Visconde Ouro Preto 62, *Neu Sol*, Rua Vida Ramos 36 (all closed Sun.). *Padaria União*, R. Tenente Silveira, very good.

Electric Current 220 volts A.C.

Car Hire Auto Locadora Coelho, Felipe Schmidt 81, vehicles in good condition.

Exchange Banco do Brasil, Praça 15 de Novembro 20; Banco do Estado de São Paulo, Tenente Silveira 55; Banco Estado de Santa Catarina, Trajano 33. Turismo Holzmann, Rua Conselheiro Mafra 53, parallel exchange rate in adjoining room.

Post Office Praça 15 de Novembro 5, T 22-3188.

Cables Telesc, Praça Pereira Oliveira 20, T 23-3700 (interstate and international telephones).

Tourist Office Head office: Portal Turístico de Florianópolis (Setur), at the mainland end of the bridge, 0800-2000 (Sat., Sun. 0800-1800); Praça 15 de Novembro, 0800-1800 (2200 in high season); at bus terminal (0700-2200, 0800-1800 Sat., Sun.), and airport, 0700-1800, (0800 Sat., Sun.); maps available, free.

Communications Daily flights to Porto Alegre and São Paulo. There is a new bus terminal with helpful tourist information at the east (island) end of the Ponte Colombo Machado Salles; the Terminal Urbano do Aterro for the island nearby, between the Rodoviária and the Mercado Municipal, which serves the northern beach towns, the east coast and most of the southern ones, and a further terminal at the junction of Rua José da Costa and Av. Mauro Ramos which serves the other towns. All local bus destinations and schedules are clearly posted. Regular daily buses to Porto Alegre (US$5.50, 7 hrs.), São Paulo, US$11.65, Rio, US$16 ordinary, Brasília, 3 a week at 0300, US$23; Curitiba (US$5, 5 hrs.), Blumenau (US$3, 4 a day, 3 hrs.), Joinville (2½ hrs. direct, 3½ with stops) US$3 and other towns in the State. Also regular daily buses to Foz do Iguaçu (with Catarinense, US$10.50, continuing to Asunción), to Montevideo US$29 by TTL. The coastal highway (BR-101) is preferred as an alternative to the congested inland BR-116; it runs close to Florianópolis but it is bad in places and has many lorries.

Excursions The local buses (US$0.10) take you hourly to virtually every place on the island. To Lagoa da Conceição (Emflotur bus 403) for beaches, sand dunes, fishing, church of N.S. da Conceição (1730), boat rides on the lake (restaurants: *Oliveira*, excellent seafood dishes; *Miguelão*, Praça Pio XII 5, popular way; *Leca*, try *rodízio de camarão*, prawns cooked in a dozen ways; *Caminho das Índias*, Av. das Rendeiras 69, warmly rec.). Across the island at Barra da Lagoa is a pleasant fishing village and beach which can be reached by Emflotur bus 403 (US$0.10, every ½ hr.). Bus 401 goes to beach at Joaquina (surfing championships in January). At Barra da Lagoa, *Cabanas da Barra*, Rua Geral 23, D, good, German and English spoken. Hotel near Barra da Lagoa: *Gaivota* (Familia Coelho), Praia do Moçambique. Also visit the "city of honey bees" with a Museo da Apicultura, and the Church of Sto. Antônio Lisboa on the way to Sambaqui beach and fishing village. There is a pleasant fishing village at Ponta das Canas, and the beach at Canavieiras is good. In the north of the island, at Praia dos Ingleses (bus 602) is *Sol e Mar*, D, excellent, friendly, rec. In the S of the island are Praia da Armação with, just inland, Lagoa do Peri (a protected area), Praia dos Naufragados and Farol beaches: take bus to Caieira da Barra do Sul and take 1-hr. walk through fine forests. There are 42 beaches around the island almost all easily reached by public buses from the centre (buses of the Empresa Canavieras go from Rua José da Costa, corner Av. Mauro Ramos to the northern towns and beaches, Empresa Ribeironense from next to the Rodoviária to the south-eastern ones, schedules from Tourist Office). Excursions can be made on the mainland to the hot springs at Caldas da Imperatriz (41° C) and Águas Mornas (39° C); at the former are 2 spa hotels (*Caldas da Imperatriz*, C, meals and baths included, built in 1850 under the auspices of Empress Teresa Cristina, houses public baths; *Plaza Caldas da Imperatriz*, from B, with baths, swimming pools, very well appointed), at Águas Mornas, the *Palace Hotel* is on the site of the springs, A, baths open to public Mon.-Fri. a.m. only. Boat trips can be made from Florianópolis in the bay, T 22-1806, from US$4.50-6.80.

From Florianópolis a poor road runs SW inland via São Joaquim (see below) to **Lajes**, a convenient stopping place on BR-116 between Caxias do Sul and Curitiba. Despite the poor road, however, this journey is perhaps the most interesting in the State (2 buses a day do this journey, via Alfredo Wagner, otherwise go via Blumenau). (New *Grande Hotel*, good, but no heat; cheaper is *Presidente*, E; *Natal*, cheap, adequate; *Rodalar*, *Centauro*, both F, near bus station. Bus station is ½-hr. walk S.E. of centre. Voltage 220 A.C.) Population, 109,000.

On the coast N of Florianópolis there are many resorts. They include Porto Belo, a fishing village with a calm beach (and wilder beaches reached by rough roads nearby: bus Florianópolis—Porto Belo with Praiana or Biguaçu, 8 daily, 4 on Sat., 3 on Sun.); Itapema (66 km., many hotels); **Camboriú** (86 km., beautiful beach, hotels *Dinamarca*, *Paraná*, *Motel San Carlos*, all near bus station, D, *Balneario de Camboriú*, central, on beach, D, friendly, clean; camping *Mag-Mar* is good; buses from Florianópolis, Joinville and Blumenau); and Meia Praia, which is quieter and cleaner than Camboriú. Between Itajaí and Camboriú is the beautiful, deserted (and rough) beach of Praia Brava.

São Joaquim, at 1,360 metres, the highest town in Southern Brazil, regularly has snowfalls in winter; very pleasant town with an excellent climate (Camping Clube do Brasil site). To the East of the town, in the Serra Geral is the **São Joaquim National Park** (33,500 hectares), with canyons containing sub-tropical vegetation, and araucaria forest at higher levels. The local IBDF office is at Av. Moura Ramos 187, Florianópolis (Caixa Postal 660, CEP 89.000). Hotels: *Nevada* (expensive meals) and *Maristela*, E (good breakfast) both on Rua Manoel Joaquim Pinto, 213 and 220 respectively (5 mins'. walk from Rodoviária). Bus to Florianópolis 0830 and 2230, 7½ hrs., US$6. To Caxias do Sul, 4½ hrs., US$4.

One hundred km. up the coast N of Florianópolis by the BR-101 paved road or by sea is the most important port in Santa Catarina:

Itajaí, at the mouth of the Itajaí river. It is well served by vessels up to 5½ metres draught, and is the centre of a district largely colonized by Germans and Italians. Main exports: timber, starch, tapioca, sassafras oil, and tobacco. Population, 64,000. Airport. You can walk to Cabeçudas beach, which is quiet and small.

Hotels *Balneário Cabeçudas*, at Cabeçudas beach, best, 6 km. out of town, C; *Grande*, Rua Felipe Schmidt 44, good value, D; *Maringá*, N of town, friendly, cheap and clean, with Shell service station next door, providing good food, open all night. *Rex*, *Cacique*, both on R. Asseburg, cheap, near market. Rec. **Bar**, *Trud's*, on riverfront at end of main street.

Resorts north of Itajaí include Piçarras, with sandy beaches interspersed with rocky headlands (ideal for fishing), and Barra Velha (*Hotel Mirante*, E, good, cheap restaurant, and 2 dearer hotels).

There is a 61 km. paved road to **Blumenau** (population, 145,000), 47 km. up the Itajaí river. It is in a prosperous district settled mostly by Germans; see Museo da Família Colonial, German immigrant museum, Av. Duque de Caxias 78, open Mon.-Sat., 0830-1130, 1330-1730, US$0.05. German Evangelical Church. Places of interest include the houses, now museums (open 0800-1800) of Dr Bruno Otto Blumenau and of Fritz Müller (a collaborator of Darwin), who bought the Blumenau estate in 1897 and founded the town, which is a notable textile centre. A "traditional" Oktoberfest beer-festival was started in 1984 here, and was expected to attract a million visitors in 1987 and become the second largest in the world after Munich's. It is repeated, but called a "summer festival", in the 3 weeks preceding Carnival.

Hotels *Himmelbleu Palace*, Rua 7 de Setembro 1415, C; *Blumenau Tourist Hotel*, 200 m. from bus station, D, new, helpful; *Garden Terrace*, Rua Padre Jacobs 45, C; *Grande Hotel*, Alameda Rio Branco 21, D; *Glória*, Rua 7 de Setembro 954, D, German-run, excellent coffee shop (all aforementioned hotels have heating in room); *Plaza Hering*, 5-star, 7 de Setembro 818, B, heating and a/c; *Paraíso dos Poneis*, motel 9 km. out of town on the Itajaí road, C; *Central*, Rua 7 de Setembro 1036, basic, E with bath, F without, both without breakfast, clean, but not safe for luggage; *Herrmann* (formerly *Durma Bem*), central, Floriano Peixoto 213, rec., E, a/c, shower, clean. *City*, Rua Ângelo Dias 263, F. Many cheap hotels do not include breakfast. Most hotels and restaurants very clean. **Youth Hostel** at Rua Paraíba 66 (T 22-8420).

Camping Municipal campsite, 2 km. out on Rua Pastor Osvaldo Hesse; Paraíso dos Poneis, 9 km. out on the Itajaí road; Refúgio Alpino, 11 km. out on Rua da Glória.

Restaurants Good German food at *Frohsinn* (panoramic view) and *Cavalinho Branco*, Av. Rio Branco 165, huge meals, international eating at *Moinho do Vale*. *A Cantina de Mai*, Rua R.C.

Deeke 165, large helpings, good; *Blumental*, 15 de Novembro 962 and Av. Castelo Branco 671, good value; *Caféhaus Glória*, in *Hotel Glória*, excellent coffee shop; *Rancho Alegre*, 7 de Setembro 1335, good value; *Das Cafehaus*, serves huge, delicious cakes (tortas); *Gruta Azul*, Rodolfo Freygang, good, popular, not cheap.

Voltage   220 A.C.

Exchange   Cambios: Tilotur Turismo, next to President Turismo, 7 de Setembro, 2nd floor; Ilhatur Turismo, Rodolfo Freygang 5, 1st floor.

International Telephones   Corner of Av. Brasil and República Argentina.

Tourist Office   in town hall, Rua 15 de Novembro 420, corner of Rua Nereu Ramos; also kiosk on 15 de Novembro, and at bus station; helpful, but prices out of date; good town map. Only Portuguese spoken.

Amenities   Teatro Carlos Gomes is also exhibition centre; public library open 0800-1800; German bookshops, Librerias Alemãs, at bus station and Ruas 7 de Setembro and 15 de Novembro. Craft shop, Casa Meyer, 15 de Novembro 401.

Bus   The Rodoviária for interurban travel is in the village of Fortaleza, US$0.10 by Rodoviária-7 de Setembro bus from the old bus station at Av. 7 de Setembro and Padre Jacobs (US$2.50 by taxi). Good bus connections in all directions from Blumenau. Blumenau to Caxias do Sul at 1930 only, arrives 0400, US$8; to Curitiba, 4 hrs., US$4.

Excursions   By bus to Timbo and Pomerode (from riverside road opp. Prefeitura) past rice fields and wooden houses set in beautiful gardens. At *Pomerode*, 32 km., US$0.50 (*Hotel Central*, E, big lunches) there is an interesting zoo (US$0.60). Tourist office. The North German dialect of *Plattdeutsch* is still spoken here. Rex Bus goes to Iraguã from Pomerode; change for connection to Joinville, US$1.50. Boat trips down the River Itajaí, daily in season, Sat. and Sun. out of season, unspectacular. ½-day excursion to Gaspar to visit the cathedral set high above the river (Verdi Veli bus company from stop outside the huge supermarket on Rua 7 de Setembro in the centre).

To Iguaçu   We have received from Gerry Monahan and Gary Rubkin an interesting account of a bus journey from Blumenau to Iguaçu by mostly unpaved roads, through rich and interesting farming country (as an alternative to direct Catarinense bus, daily from Florianópolis and Itajaí to Iguaçu via Blumenau). They stopped at *Joaçaba,* a town of German immigrants (8 hrs. by bus; *Hotel Colonial*, at bus station, *Lotus*, across bridge, both F), Erechim (6 hrs. by bus, *Hotel Rex*, E, strong *gaúcho* influence), *Iraí* (6 hrs. by bus, Italian immigrant area, town with thermal springs, *Hotel São Luís*, E, with full board, town good for semi-precious stones), and Pato Branco (8 hrs. by bus, immediate connection to Cascavel for Foz do Iguaçu). The Tourist Office has details of combined ticket to Iguaçu—bus to Curitiba, then flight to Iguaçu—for US$ 62.

São Francisco do Sul, 80 km. up the coast (population 15,000), is the port for the town of Joinville, 45 km. inland at the head of the Cachoeira river. Most of the colonial architecture has been replaced by modern buildings. There are some excellent beaches nearby such as Ubatuba, Enseada (3 camp sites, Pascerella recommended) and Cápri. (At weekend trips to Ilha do Farol in port's supply boat.) Petrobrás oil refinery. *Hotel Avenida*, E with breakfast, clean, friendly; *Zibamba*, R. Fernandes Dias 27, central, C. The *Restaurante Franciscano*, on the Praia dos Coqueiros, is recommended, so are the *Metralhas* and *Flutuante* (good seafood.) Bus terminal is 1½ km. from centre. Direct bus (Penha) daily to Curitiba at 0730, US$3, 3½ hrs. Train from Joinville leaves daily at 0810 and frequent buses. Men are not allowed to wear shorts here.

Joinville, the state's second largest city (population, 217,000), lies 2 km. from the main coastal highway, BR-101, by which Curitiba and Florianópolis are less than two hours away. To Guaratuba (**see page 337**) by bus, 1¼ hrs., US$1 (connections to Paranaguá). To Blumenau, US$2, 2¼ hrs. The bus terminal is 2½ km. outside the town (regular bus service).

See the Museum of History in the Prince of Joinville's mansion, which has a collection of objects from the original German settlement. The interesting Museo de Arte is in the old residence of Ottokar Doerfeu, Rua 15 de Novembro 1400 (open Tues.-Sun., 0900-1800). The Archaeological Museum has a collection of the Sambaquis period dating back to 5000 BC (open Tues.-Fri., 0900-1800, Sat., Sun., and holidays, 0900-1200, 1400-1800; US$0.20). Other museums are Museum of Immigration and Colonization, R. Rio Branco 229 (closed Mon.) and the Museum of the sculptor Fritz Act, Rua Aubé (closed Mon.).

At Expoville, 4 km. from centre on BR-101 (continuation of 15 de Novembro) is an exhibition of Joinville's industry and an industrial museum. The industry does not, however, spoil the considerable charm of the city. There is an annual flower festival in the first fortnight of September.

Hotels *Tannehof*, Visconde de Taunay 340, 4 stars, restaurant on 14th floor; *Anthurium Parque*, São José 226, C, colonial style, good value, English spoken, friendly; *Ideal*, Jerônimo Coelho 98, D, with excellent breakfast, friendly, clean; *Novo Horizonte*, at bus station, basic, clean; *Konig*, 15 de Novembro 937, E; same street No. 811, *Matles*, E.

Camping Camping Clube do Brasil, Rua Saguaçu, Horto Florestal. Municipal site, same road, 1 km. from centre.

Restaurants *Petisqueira Pinheiro*, 7 de Setembro, is well worth a visit for excellent fish and shrimp dishes for about US$5. For meat or German specialities, *Churrascaria Rex, Churrascaria Ataliba*, near Expoville; *Bierkeller*, 15 de Novembro 497; *Dietrichs*, Rua Princesa Isabel, excellent beer and German food (especially cakes). *Pasteleria Japoneza*, R. Princesa Isabel, excellent pásteis; *Jerke*, a bar on Dr João Colin, has good empadas; *Padaria Brunkow*, 9 de Maio, good snacks. Vegetarian: *Cozinha Natural*, Rua Marinho Lobo 38. The cheapest place to eat is the *Sociedade Ginástica*, Rua Ginásticos—you don't have to be a member.

Banks Banco do Brasil. Open 1000-1630.

Tourist Office corner Praça Nereu Ramos with Rua Príncipe; no information on cheap hotels. Good exchange rates

Air Service Airport 5 km. from city. Daily flights to major cities.

Excursions Four daily buses go to Ubatuba beach, a week-end resort (see above under São Francisco do Sul). The Sambaqui site of Rio Comprido can be reached by Gideon Bus, but there is not much to see.

The State of Paraná

The Italians were first in Paraná, but apart from a few Germans most of the later settlers were of Slavonic origin—Poles, Russians, Ruthenians and Ukrainians. Paraná made astonishing progress until the past few years. It is now the leading producer of wheat, rye, potatoes and black beans, but its population, 7,630,200 at end-1982, no longer expands as quickly as it did, partly because of the displacement of rural workers following the uprooting of coffee plants in the more frost-prone areas and the turning of the land over to cattle. The recent boom crop, soya, also employs fewer workers throughout the year than coffee.

Curitiba, capital of Paraná state (pop. 1.5 million), is a modern city at 900 metres on the plateau of the Serra do Mar. The commercial centre is busy Rua 15 de Novembro (old name: Rua das Flores), which has a pedestrian area where there are Sat. morning painting sessions for children. Another pedestrian area is behind the cathedral, near Largo da Ordem, with sacred art museum, flower clock and old buildings. Art market Sat. morning in Praça Rui Barbosa, and on Sun. morning in Praça Garibáldi (rec.), beside attractive Rosário church. The Civic Centre is at the end of Avenida Dr. Cândido de Abreu, 2 km. from the city centre: a monumental group of five buildings dominated by the Palácio Iguaçu, headquarters of the state and municipal governments. In a patio behind it is a relief map to scale of Paraná. The Bosque de João Paulo II behind the Civic Centre contains the Polish immigrants' museum: both are worth a visit. In contrast to the Civic Centre is the old municipal government building in French Art Nouveau style, now housing the Museu Paranaense in Praça Generoso Marques. Nearby, on Praça Tiradentes, is the Cathedral (1894). The most popular public park is the Passeio Público, in the heart of the city (closed Mondays); it has a good little zoo, a network of canals with boats, and a small aquarium. On the north east edge of the city is Parque do Barigui, take bus 450 "São Braz" from Praça Tiradentes. Near the shores of Lake Bacacheri on the northern edge of the city (R. Nicarágua 2453) is an unexpected Egyptian temple (the Brazilian centre of the Rosicrucians—visits can be arranged)—take Santa Cândida bus to Estação Boa Vista, then walk). There are three modern theatres, the Guaíra for plays and revues (also has free events—get tickets early in the

CURITIBA 36
(Centre)
Not to Scale

1. Praça Tiradentes
2. Praça João Cândido
3. Praça Garibáldi and Flower Clock
4. Praça Generoso Marques and Museu Paranaense
5. Praça Santos Dumont
6. Praça Zacarias
7. Praça Carlos Gomes
8. Largo da Ordem
9. Cathedral
10. Rosário Church
11. Sacred Art Museum
12. Museum Guido Viário
13. Museum of Contemporary Art
14. Railway Museum
15. Post Office (× 2)
16. Telephone Office
17. Tourist Kiosk
18. Hotel Lancaster
19. Hotel Tourist Universo
20. Cheaper hotels and wholesale market area

day), one for concerts and ballet, and the Teatro Paiol in the old arsenal. Many of the main streets have been widened and the city is being rapidly transformed.

Local Holidays Ash Wednesday (half-day); Maundy Thursday (half-day); September 8 (Our Lady of Light).

Hotels The following, in our category A, are rec.: *Caravelle Palace*, Rua Cruz Machado 282, first class; *Lancaster*, R. Voluntários da Pátria 91, tourist class; *Ouro Verde*, R. Dr. Murici 419, standard class. *Mabu*, Praça Santos Andrade 830, L; *Deville Colonial*, R. Com. Araújo 99, A; *Guaía Palace*, Praça Rui Barbosa 537, A. *Iguaçu*, Cândido Lopes 102, first class, A, and *Del Rey*, Ermelino de Leão 18, A, both have good restaurants. *Tourist Universo*, Praça Gen. Osório 63, B, good restaurant, rec.; *Climax*, Rua Dr. Murici 411, good value, popular, C; *Palace*, Rua Barão do Rio Branco 62, E with bath, central, European atmosphere; *Regência*, Rua Alfredo Buffern 40, D, with breakfast, excellent; *San Rafael*, Av. 7 de Setembro 1948, near bus and railway station (Rodoferroviária), E with breakfast, bargain for cheaper rates without breakfast, clean. Lots of cheap hotels around Rodoferroviária; they are also close to wholesale market, which operates noisily through the night: *Itamarati*, Tibagi 950, 500 m. from Rodoferroviária, E, clean, with bath, fan, friendly; *Costa Brava Palace*, Rua Francisco Torres 386, D, well rec.; *Vitória*, Rua São Francisco, F, central, pleasant, clean, friendly, but security a problem. They include the *Império*, Av. Pres. Afonso Camargo 367, D with bath, E without, small and poor breakfast, quiet, (take insect repellent); next door, *Maia*, E with bath, incl. breakfast, clean and quiet; *Wang*, same street, No. 549, E, safe, clean, good value; *Jaguará*, opposite station, very clean, noisy, good breakfast, rec. (but not the buffet supper), D; *Doral*, TV, frigobar in room, good breakfast, D, clean, good breakfast, private bath, 4 blocks from station through market; *Nalini*, Pedro Ivo 713, 1 block from bus terminal, F, helpful owner speaks German, T 234-1449, hot shower; *Casa dos Estudantes*, Parque Passeio Público, F, with student card. Youth hostels in Paraná state: Asociação Paranaense de Albergues de Juventude, Av. Padre, Agostinho 645, Curitiba PR, CEP 80.410; in the city, *Hans Staden*, Rua Pe. Agostinho 645.

Camping Official site 7 km. N of city, on São Paulo road, US$1 a night. Camping Clube do Brasil, 14 km. out on same road.

Restaurants Ile de France (French), Praça 19 de Dezembro 538; *Schwartze Katz* (German and international), Rua Francisco Torres 18; *Schwarzwald*, Claudino dos Santos 63, beerhaus/restaurant, in centre (German); *Matterhorn*, Mateus Leme 575, centre. Lunch at *Nino's*, on 20th floor of a building near Praça Carlos Gomes, for grand views. *Golden Chopp*, Rua André de Barros (near corner with Rua Barão do Rio Branco), good value, rec.; *A Sacristia*, Rua João Manuel 197, restaurant, pizzeria, bar, very good; *Tempo*, Rua Marechal Deodoro, good. *Oriente*, Rua Ebano Pereira 26 (1st floor), excellent, huge Arab lunch. Good Arab food also at *Casa da Efina*, Cruz Machado 247, and *Cantina Árabe*, Al. Augusto Stellfeld 143. Local and Italian food and local red wine in nearby Santa Felicidade (10 km. out of town on road to Ponta Grossa), e.g. *Madalosso*, Av. Manoel Ribas 5875, Italian self-service, rec. Sukiyaki at *Vemura*, near Cine Arlequin, on the Rua Vicente Machado, and also at *Yuasa*, Av. Sete de Setembro, cheap and good, rec. Vegetarian: *Transformação* (macrobiotic, shop also), Al. Augusto Stellfeld 781; *Vegetariano*, Carlos de Carvalho 127, 13 de Maio 222; *Ao Natural*, Rua São Francisco 332 (lunch only, shop also); *Verde Jante*, Rua Pres. Faria 481, very good; *Super Vegetariano*, Rua Pres. Faria 121, Cruz Machado 217, Rua Dr. Murici 315, lunch and dinner Mon.-Fri., very good and cheap. At the corner of Rua 15 de Novembro and General Carneiro is a nameless restaurant, good value for lunches. *Palâchio*, Barão Rio Branco, is all-night restaurant, good food and cheap; cheap food also near old railway station. Close to the Rodoferroviária is the market, where there are a couple of *lanchonetes*. Students can eat at University canteen (student cards required). Hot sweet wine sold on the streets in winter helps keep out the cold. Rec. tea house: *Chez Arnold*, Av. Manoel Ribas 526, in the Mercês district.

Electric Current 110 v. 60 cycles.

Bookshop Livrarias Ghignone, Rua 15 de Novembro 409, has good selection of English books.

Shopping Curitiba is a good place to buy clothes and shoes. H. Stern jewellers at Mueller Shopping Centre.

Local Transport The city has a very efficient bus system; all bus stops have maps. Express buses on city routes are orange: for example, from centre (Praça Rui Barbosa) take Leste bus marked "Villa Oficinas" or "Centenário" for Rodoferroviária (combined bus and railway station).

Museums Museu Paranaense, Praça Generoso Marques, (open Tues.-Fri. 1000-1800, other days 1300-1800, closed first Mon. of each month). Museu David Carneiro, on Rua Comendador Araújo 531, Sat., 1400-1600. Museo Guido Viário, R. São Francisco 319, painter's house; Museum of Contemporary Arts, Rua D. Westphalen 16 (closed Sats., and Sun. morning), next door are historical and archaeological museums. Casa Andersen, R. Mateus Leme 336, house of painter, open Mon.-Fri. Railway Museum, Av. 7 de Setembro, in the old railway station, open Tues.-Fri., 1300-1900, Sat.-Sun., 0800-1300; Second World War Museum, Casa Expedicionário,

Praça do Expedicionário; Museo do Automóvel, Av Cândido Hartmann 2300 (Sat. 1400-1800, Sun. 0900-1200, 1330-1800), all worth a visit.

Addresses Centro Cultural Brasil-Estados Unidos (Mon.-Fri., 0800-1200, 1400-2100); Sociedade Brasileira de Cultura Inglesa (British Council), Rua General Carneiro 679 (Caixa Postal 505). Instituto Goethe, Duque de Caxias 4, open Mon., Wed., Thurs., Fri., 1500-1900. Austrian Consulate, Rua Marechal Floriano Peixoto 228, Edif. Banrisul, 17 andar, Caixa Postal 2473, T 22 46 795.

Banks Lloyds Bank (ex-BOLSA), Rua Quinze de Novembro 317, and national banks. Open 1000-1600. **Money Exchange**; Jade travel agency, Rua Quinze de Novembro 477 (cash only); Triangle Turismo Travel, Praça General Osório 213, cash and travellers' cheques; Diplomata, Rua Presidente Faria 145 in the arcade, cash and travellers' cheques.

Tourist Office Av. Sete de Setembro 2077, CEP 80.050, Curitiba, maps and information in English. *Guía Turística de Curitiba e Paraná*, annual, US$4, on sale at all kiosks, has been rec. Paranatur has booths at Rodoferroviária, in the old rail car at Rua 15 de Novembro 141 and Ebano Pereira, and at airport, helpful, English spoken, but no maps. Free weekly leaflet, *Bom Programa*, available shops, cinemas, paper stands etc.

Church services held in German at the Evangelical Church.

Post Office Main post office is at Marechal Deodoro 298; post offices also at Rua 15 de Novembro and Rua Pres. Faria. **Cables** Embratel, Galeria Minerva, Rua 15 de Novembro.

Transport Passenger trains to Paranaguá (book ahead). Frequent buses to São Paulo, including night bus at 2320 (6 hrs., US$6; *leito* 12) and Rio de Janeiro (11 hours, US$13, *leito* 26). To Santos, 3 a day (*leito* at 2300), 6½ hrs., US$7. Buses to Foz do Iguaçu, 10 buses a day, 10 hrs., US$6 (3 *leito* buses at night, US$12); to Porto Alegre, US$17, 18 hrs (*leito* US$34); to Londrina via Ponta Grossa, 8 hrs.; to Guaíra, 0700, 1915 and *leito* 1930 (12 hrs). Itajaí, 4 hrs., US$3.50; Blumenau, 4½ hrs., US$4. Florianópolis, US$5 (*leito* US$10); Rodoferroviária at end of Av. 7 de Setembro, very efficient (bus to centre US$0.10); short-distance bus services (up to 40 km.) begin at old bus station at Rua João Negrão 340. TTL runs to Montevideo, 26 hrs., US$25, 0300 departure (*leito*) US$46. If travelling by car to Porto Alegre or Montevideo, the coastal highway (BR-101) is preferable to the inland road (BR-116).

Excursions The beautiful Ouro Fino estate (34 km.) is open to the public every day except Mon., Dec.-March, and every second Sunday the rest of the year. The nearest bus stop is 16 km. away at Campo Largo, so car is the best way to get there. Advance permission needed, from Rua Silva Jardim 167, Curitiba, T 232-7411, or phone Ouro Fino (041) 292-1913. On the first and third Sunday of each month, a steam train runs from Curitiba to Lapa (about 80 km. SW), returning after a tour of the town.

20 km. from Curitiba (at Km. 119) on the road to Ponta Grossa on the Museu Histórico do Mate, an old water-driven mill where *mate* was prepared (free admission). On the same road is **Vila Velha**, now a national park, 97 km. from Curitiba: the sandstone rocks have been weathered into most fantastic shapes. There is a Camping Clube do Brasil site near Vila Velha, 85 km. from Curitiba. Alternatively, stay in Ponta Grossa (**see page 337**, from which buses leave for Vila Velha at 0900, 40 mins., last bus back at 1830). The park office is 300 metres from the highway and the park a further 1½ km. (entrance US$0.30—opens at 0800). If taking a bus from Curitiba, make sure it's going to the Parque Nacional and not to the town 20 km. away. Transport from the Park to a swimming pool (free—costumes can be rented for US$1.20), 2 km. away. Princesa dos Campos bus from Curitiba at 0730 and 0930, 1½ hrs., US$1 (return buses pass park entrance at 1500 and 1800). The Lagoa Dourada, surrounded by forests, is close by. Nearby are the Furnas, three water holes, the deepest of which has a lift (US$0.30—not always working) which descends almost to water level (the same level as Lagoa Dourada); entrance US$0.05. Bus from Vila Velha at 1310, 1610 and 1830, US$0.30, 4½ km. to turn-off for Furnas (another ¼-hr. walk) and Lagoa Dourada (it's not worth walking from Vila Velha to Furnas because it's mostly uphill along the main road). From the turn-off buses to Curitiba pass 10 minutes before they pass Vila Velha. Allow all day if visiting all 3 sites (unless you hitch, or can time the buses well, it's a lot of walking). Since the afternoon buses which pass en route to Curitiba are often full, it may be advisable to go to Ponta Grossa and return to Curitiba from there.

Popular expeditions during the summer are by paved road or rail (4½ hrs.) to Paranaguá. Two trains a day do the journey, the most spectacular railway trip in Brazil. Book well ahead. The ordinary train leaves Curitiba at 0700, Thur., Sat. and Sun. only, arriving in Paranaguá at 1030 (US$1.30 one class, tickets on sale at 0600, except for Sun. train where on sale on Fri., no seat reservations—ticket office is closed on Sun.; sandwiches, chocolate and drinks for sale on board). Avoid the front coach. A modern air-conditioned rail-car (the Litorina, called the *automotriz*) leaves at 0830, arriving at 1100 (US$5 each way, reserved seats bookable 2 days in advance; latest reports say it only runs Wed., Sat. and Sun.) with recorded commentary (in Portuguese, French, Spanish and English) and stops at the viewpoint at the Santuário da N.S. do Cadeado and at Morretes (only a few minutes). Sit on the left-hand side on journey from Curitiba (in the *automotriz*, the seats, not the car, are turned round, so you sit the same side in each direction). If Litorina is full, take bus to Paranaguá, US$1.30, then take Litorina back: return journeys start at 1530 (Litorína) and 1630 (ordinary train) so remember that in winter part of the ordinary train's journey is covered in the dark (also, in winter, on cloudy days there's little to see on the higher parts). The train is usually crowded on Saturdays and Sundays. Many travellers recommend returning by bus (1½ hrs., buy ticket immediately on arrival), if you do not want to stay 4½ hrs. A tour bus meets the train and offers a tour of town and return to Curitiba for US$3. **There are numerous tunnels**, with sudden views of deep gorges and high peaks and waterfalls as the train rumbles over dizzy bridges and viaducts. Near Banhado station (Km. 66) is the waterfall of Véu da Noiva; from the station at Km. 59, the mountain range of Marumbi National Park can be reached: good hiking.

You can also visit **Antonina** (not on main route) and **Morretes** (on main route), two sleepy colonial towns which can be reached by rail and also by bus on the old Graciosa road, which is almost as scenic as the railway. Bus Paranaguá to Morretes at 1830, US$0.60, to Antonina, stopping en route at Morretes, 6 a day, (US$1). 12 buses daily Morretes-Curitiba US$1; 20 buses a day Curitiba-Antonina. On Tues., 0700, a train runs from Curitiba to Morretes only (and does not take passengers on the return journey). Every fourth Sunday, a steam train runs from Antonina to Morretes to connect with the ordinary train from Curitiba.

Morretes hotel: *Nhundiaquara*, in town centre, beautifully located, E and up; good restaurants in town (try "barreado", beef cooked for 24 hrs.) and a river beach. Antonina hotels: *de Lazer*, B, 3-star; *Christine*, F and up, clean. Antonina is a port, but there are no beaches. 14 km. N of Morretes is the beautiful village of São João de Graciosa, 2 km. beyond which is the flower reserve of the Marumbi Park. The Graciosa road traverses the park for 12 km., with 6 rest stops with fire grills, shelters and camping. The park is very beautiful; you can also hike the original trail which follows the road and passes the rest-stops. Take food, water and plenty of insect repellent. The Marumbi Park can be entered at a gate 3-4 km. from the BR-116 Curitiba-São Paulo highway.

Paranaguá, and chief port of the state of Paraná and one of the main coffee-exporting ports, was founded in 1585, 268 km. south of Santos. It is on a lagoon 29 km. from the open sea and is approached via the Bay of Paranaguá, dotted with picturesque islands. The fort of Nossa Senhora dos Prazeres was built in 1767 on a nearby island; one hour's boat trip. The former Colêgio dos Jesuitas, a fine baroque building, has been converted into a Museum of Archaeology and Popular Art (Tues.-Fri., 1000-1700, Sat.-Mon., 1200-1700; entrance US$0.10). Other attractions are a 17th century fountain, the church of São Benedito, and the shrine of Nossa Senhora do Rocio, 2 km. from town. There is an interesting market near the waterfront. The part of town between the waterfront, railway station and new bus station has been declared a historic area. Population, 68,366. Paranaguá is a free port for Paraguay.

The paved 116-km. road to Curitiba is picturesque, but less so than the railway (see above), which offers one of the most beautiful trips in Brazil.

Hotels *Santa Mônica*, Praia de Leste, 30 km. from town, on fine beach, C; *Auana*, Rua Correia de Freitas 110, E-D, good value, rec. (but electric showers in the more expensive rooms). *Ribamar*, E, with breakfast; *Litoral*, Rua Correia de Freitas 66, F without breakfast, clean and comfortable; *Rio Mar* and *Mar de Rosas*, both on waterfront, E.

Camping Camping Clube do Brasil site at Praia de Leste, on the beach, 27 km. from Paranaguá.

Restaurants *Bobby's,* Faria Sobrinho 750, highly rec., esp. for seafood. *Danúbio Azul* 15 de Novembro 91, good, not cheap, view of river; *Bela Vila* on waterfront, good value. A very good T-bone steak (with good salads) at *Churrascaria Cacique,* Dr. Leocádio 290; another at *Churrascaria do Maneco,* Praça Eufrásio Correia 560, cheap. *Aquarius,* Av. Gabriel de Lara 40, good but not cheap seafood.

Tourist Information kiosk outside railway station.

Air Services Curitiba airport.

Bus Station At right-hand end of the waterfront (as you look at the water) corner João Esteban and João Regis, beyond Municipal Market. All buses operated by Graciosa. To Curitiba, US$1.30, many, 1½ hrs. (only the 0745 in either direction takes the old Graciosa road).

Excursions *Matinhos* is a Mediterranean-type resort, invaded by surfers in October for the Paraná surf competition; several cheap hotels, including *Bolamar,* (F, basic, cheapest) and *Beira Mar.* 3 camp sites, but the municipal site is closed until November. Cruises on Paranaguá Bay by launch, daily from Cais do Mercado. Bus from Paranaguá at 1000, 1400 and 1615, US$0.50. 6 buses a day to Guaratuba, US$0.60. *Guaratuba* (which is less built up than Caiobá) has *Pensão Antoinet,* E, clean, dangerous showers, and other hotels; campsite. All Guaratuba buses pass *Caiobá* (*Hotel Caiobá,* D, cheapest). Caiobá to Guaratuba by ferry, free for pedestrians, US$0.80 for cars, 10 minutes, frequent departures.

To *Ilha do Mel,* take bus to Pontal do Sul (many daily, 1hr., US$1); turn left out of the bus station and walk 25 metres to main road, turn right for 1½ km. and bear left along a sandy road for 2 km. to fishermen's houses from where a ferry runs (US$0.75). On the island, at Praia dos Encantados, one can camp or rent a fisherman's house—ask for *Valentim's Bar,* or for Luchiano. Dona Ana and Dona Maria sell bread and cakes, and meals if you ask in advance. There are two bars, fresh water, but no electricity. The beaches, caves, bays and hill walks are beautiful. 4 hrs.' walk from the village is an old Portuguese fort, possible to hitch a ride in a fishing boat back. If camping, watch out for the tide, watch possessions and beware of the *bicho de pé* which burrows into feet (remove with a needle and alcohol) and of the *borrachudos* (discourage with Autum repellent). In summer and at holiday times the island is very crowded.

About 117 km. from Curitiba the road inland (which passes Vila Velha— **see page 335**) reaches *Ponta Grossa,* a town of 186,618, at 895 metres. It now calls itself the "World Capital of Soya" (as does Palmeira das Missões, in Rio Grande do Sul). Roads run north through Apucarana (Camping Clube site) and Londrina to São Paulo, and south to Rio Grande do Sul and the Uruguayan border.

Hotels *Vila Velha Palace,* Rua Balduino Taques 123, C; *Planalto Palace,* Rua 7 de Setembro 652, plain and clean, E; *Gravina,* Rua Cnel. Bittencourt 92, E. *Scha Fransky,* Rua Francisco Ribas, 104, D, very good breakfast; almost next door, same street No. 162, is *Central,* E, with fan and basin, good breakfast; *Luz,* bargain, near railway station. *Cristina,* F without breakfast, OK. *Esplanada,* in bus station (quiet, however), E with bath and breakfast, clean, safe. Try area around Praça Barão de Garaúna.

Camping Camping Clube do Brasil, 26 km. out at the entrance to Vila Velha.

Restaurants *Chopin,* for excellent churrascos. *Shanadu,* on main square, good value.

Buses Princesa dos Campos to Curitiba, 6 a day, 2 hrs., US$2; same company to Iguaçu, 4 daily, 11 hrs., US$7.50.

In Alto Paraná in the extreme NW of the State, connections have traditionally been with São Paulo rather than with Curitiba. Large new centres of population have risen in a short time. In 1930 four Japanese and two Germans arrived in **Londrina** (developed by a British company). Today it is a city with skyscrapers, modern steel and glass cathedral, wide streets and 309,420 people. (*Hotel Coroados,* Sen. Souza Naves 814, D, standard; *Hotel Aliança,* nr. bus station, E, very clean, good breakfast; Youth Hostel, Rua Gomes Carneiro 315, centro Esportivo Moringão). **Maringá,** 80 km. W of Londrina, founded in 1947, has 168,619 people, about a third of them Japanese. There is a small conical cathedral; Parque Ingá is shady, with a Japanese garden. (*Hotel Santos,* nr bus station, F, basic, clean; others in this area. São Carlos, Joules de Carvalho 422, E, rec.) Londrina and Maringá are good points for connections between the south (Porto Alegre), Foz do Iguaçu and Mato Grosso do Sul (Campo Grande). Bus from Londrina to Porto Alegre takes 22 hours; to Campo Grande 11 hours, via Presidente Prudente (**see page 316**). A number of bus services from Paraná state to Porto Alegre (Aguia Branca, Unesul) and to Campo Grande, Cuiabá and Porto Velho (Eucatur) commence at Cascavel, further S on the Curitiba-Iguaçu road.

The Paraná River

In the extreme SW of the State, on the Argentine frontier, are the *Iguaçu Falls*, approached by a good paved road from Curitiba, through Guarapuava and Cascavel, with frequent bus services. There is an international airport about 14 km. from the Falls, and 32 km. from the Falls is the city of Foz do Iguaçu, with excellent road connections with Argentina and Paraguay.

For a detailed description of the Falls as a whole, and the Argentine side in particular, together with an account of road links between the Argentine and Brazilian sides, **see the Argentine section, page 122**.

Ideally, one should first visit the Brazilian side to get some idea of the size and magnificence of the whole, and to take one's introductory photographs in the morning, and then cross to the Argentine side to see the details; this can all be done in a day, starting at about 0700, but the brisk pace needed for a quick tour is very exhausting for the non-athletic in that heat. If one's time is very limited, then the Brazilian side, with its marvellous distant views, is the one to visit.

A 1½ km paved walk runs part of the way down the cliff near the rim of the Falls, giving a stupendous view of the whole Argentine side (the greater part) of the falls. It ends up almost under the powerful Floriano Falls, where a new catwalk was brought into use at the end of 1984. Waterproof clothing can be hired although it is not absolutely necessary. An elevator (from 0800) hoists the visitor to the top of the Floriano Falls and to a path leading to Porto Canoa. Helicopter flight over Falls—US$30 per head—lasts 4 minutes. (The helicopter rides may be stopped: the noise is seriously disturbing the wildlife, especially the birds.) There is a small but worthwhile museum 5 km. from the Falls (1 km. from park entrance is side road to museum, look for sign) and opposite it are some steps that lead down the steep slope to the river bank. Beautiful walk. It can be misty early in the morning at the Falls. Entry to the Brazilian side of the Falls is about US$0.70, included in the bus fare out, or payable at the National Park entrance.

From Foz do Iguaçu, Dois Irmãos buses (from local bus station—*Terminal Urbana*—on Av. Juscelino Kubitschek, opp. Infantry Barracks, 1½ blocks from *Rodoviária*— interstate bus station) marked Cataratas run the 32 km. to the falls every hour from 0700 to 1700, then less frequently to 2200, past airport to *Hotel das Cataratas*, takes 40 mins. Buses return 0700-1900, about US$0.80 one way. (The taxi fare is US$4.50, plus US$2 for each hour of waiting.) The tours of the Falls organized by the various hotels have been recommended in preference to taxi rides. At least 4 buses an hour (Tres Fronteiras company) ply over the bridge between the *Terminal Urbana* and the bus station in Puerto Iguazú.

Be sure to get a stamp on your passport if intending to stay in Brazil. There is an entry tax on the Brazilian side for car passengers only, not for bus passengers. If driving into Brazil insist on visiting customs. You *must* get entry papers for your car here or you'll have serious problems later.

There are Brazilian immigration offices on the Brazilian sides of the bridges into Paraguay and Argentina; if you are just visiting Ciudad Stroessner or Puerto Iguazú and the Argentine side of the Falls and returning to Brazil the same day, no need to have your passport stamped. There are Brazilian customs patrols looking for undeclared goods on the roads past the frontier.

Foz do Iguaçu is a rapidly developing and improving town of about 200,000 people, with a wide range of accommodation and good communications by air and road with the main cities of southern Brazil, and with Asunción, Paraguay.

Hotels On a height directly overlooking the Falls, 32 km. from Foz, is the *Hotel Tropical* (ex-*das Cataratas*), an attractive colonial-style building with nice gardens and a swimming pool not without insects. Much wildlife can be seen in the grounds at night and early a.m. Rates: L (but 30 % discount for holders of the Brazil Air Pass). Non-residents can have US$8 lunch here (midday and evening buffets—good value, or else wait 45 minutes for *à-la-carte* dishes).

Many out-of-town hotels on the Falls road state their address as km. from Foz. *Salvatti*, Rua Rio Branco 577, B, all a/c (with restaurant and cinema); *Internacional*, L, good; *Rafahin Palace*, Br 277-Km. 727. *Rafahin*, Mal. Deodoro 909, B, good restaurant, pool, well spoken of. Rec.: *Foz*

Presidente, Rua Xavier da Silva near *Internacional*, superb value, E in winter D in summer, luxury room, shower, a/c, good restaurant, swimming pool, trips arranged to Falls, English spoken. On road to Falls (Rodovia das Cataratas) are the *Bourbon*, all facilities, (Km. 2.5), *Carimã*, B, (Km. 16), *Dom Pedro I*, B, (Km. 3), *Panorama*, B, (Km. 10), *Belvedere*, C, (km. 6). *Colonial*, A, near airport, swimming pool, fine location. On Av. Brasil: *Diplomata*, No. 678, some a/c, D with shower, value for money; *City*, No. 938, F, own bathroom, fan, hot water, clean; *Americano*, 3 blocks from bus station, run by Paraguayan couple, very noisy, hot showers, rec.; *Foz do Iguaçu*, No. 97, B, good laundry and breakfast, will look after luggage, fair; *Syaden*, No. 16, opp. Rodoviária, F, hot water, clean, comfortable, friendly. *Bogari Palace*, No. 106, D, excellent restaurant, swimming pool; *Cisne*, No. 144A, D-E, good breakfast, clean, friendly, English spoken, fridge; *Imperial*, No. 168, E with bath, clean; *Ortega*, No. 1140. *Espanhol*, Kubitschek e Tiradentes, E; *Turis*, Rua Xavier da Silva 699, 2 blocks from bus station, E, fans, bathroom, noisy, excellent breakfast, comfortable, organizes tours; *Hospedaria Antunes*, Taroba e Av. República Argentina, F with coffee, fans, friendly; *Taroba*, Taroba 878, quiet, clean, E with bath; *Riviera*, Mal. Deodoro 559 with Bartolomeu de Gusmão, E, clean, friendly. *Pousada Vale Verde*, Eng. Rebouças 335, F, T 74-2925, simple, comfortable, clean, helpful, near bus station; *Trento*, Rebouças 665, E, shared bath, clean, rec.; *Teresópolis*, F, near bus station, basic, fans, friendly. *Dormitório Apolo*, Almte. Barroza, one block from Rodoviária, F, clean. *Hospedaria*, Floriano Peixoto 263, E with bath, F without, fridge, fan, clean, German spoken. Rec. accommodation: house of Laura Coivo, Rua Naipi 629, 4 rooms with bath, D, friendly, helpful; also house of Gertrudis Roth, Rebouças 907, pleasant, 3 rooms, deals fixed up with restaurants, exchange dealers etc. Be sure to leave hotels punctually, or you will be charged an extra day. Many hotels have a minibus service to the airport for guests for a small fee and also offer excursions to Falls. Sra Murro, at Estrada Velha das Cataratas, T 72-1808, rents rooms at her house, D, with fine breakfast, lovely atmosphere. Leave town on road to falls, drive 1 km. then on to road to Porto Meira for 1 km., then turn left for 3.4 km. at School of Agriculture; house is on left, painted red.

Camping   (pretty cold and humid in winter) 8 km. from Foz, on road to Falls is the *Cataratas*, quite clean; 1 km. from Churrascarias Boina Brasa and (best) *Rafahin* on Route 277 (Paraguayan music) next to *Rafahin Palace Hotel*. By National Park entrance Camping Club do Brasil, 17 km. from Foz, US$3 p.p. a night (half with International Camping Card), swimming pool, clean; park vehicle or put tent away from trees in winter in case of heavy rain storms, no restaurants, food there not very good, closes at 2300, there are cheaper sites nearer the town on the same road. Not permitted by hotel and Falls. Sleeping in car inside the park also prohibited. Avoid *Camping Internacional*, where several assaults have been reported, 5 km. from Foz centre.

Electric Current   110 volts a/c.

Restaurants   Many open till midnight. *Rafahin* before the policia rodoviária post at Km. 533, with Paraguayan harp trio, good alcatra (meat), excellent buffet, next to *Rafahin Palace Hotel* on Route 277, km. 727. There are two other establishments called *Rafahin:* one, *Rafahin Center*, at Av. Brasil 157 in Foz, good value, fast food, and a third at Av. das Cataratas Km. 7, between Foz and the airport, is a *churrascaria*. *Las Tres Fronteras*, Av. J. Kubitschek 393, Argentine owner, cheap and friendly; *Arandela*, Brasil 1179, Italian style, full meal, US$3.30, rec. The pizzas at Av. Brasil 1283, have been rec. *Churrascaria Cabeça de Boi*, Av. Brasil 1325, large, live music, dinner US$5, also for coffee and pastries. *Cataratas late Club* serves feijoada (bean stew) Sat. and Sun., fish and other specialities, Av. Gen. Meira, opp. agricultural college. *Karvés*, Av. Kubitschek e Xavier de Silva, good food, large helpings, US$4. *Casa do Frango*, chicken specialities, also take-away, on Almte. Barroso, opp. *Hotel Basso*. *Akitem*, vegetarian, Av. Brazil 531, rec. A fruit shop and restaurant are next to the Atlantic gasoline station, 2 blocks from the bus station, and one block behind the bus station is an excellent *churrascaria*, *Espetão. Italia*, behind bus station, cheap and popular, huge quantities; *Amigo John*, behind the bus station, cheapest in town, excellent value.

Beware of overcharging at *lanches* (small restaurants)—sometimes three times the posted price; have the right change available.

N.B.   There are increased reports of night-time assaults at Foz, with thieves carrying knives or guns.

Entertainment   Discotheque *Whiskadão* with three different dance halls, Alm. Barroso 763, reasonable, lively at weekends. Fun fair, Centro de Diversões Imperial, on Av. Juscelino Kubitschek.

Consulates   Argentina, Rua Don Pedro II, close to Paranatur, open 0800-1300; Paraguay, Bartolomeu de Gusmão 777.

Post Office Praça Getúlio Vargas 72, next to Tourist Office.

Tourist Office   Paranatur, very helpful, Praça Getúlio Vargas 56. No English spoken at small office (Almte. Barroso y Ruy Barbosa) with list of accommodation; also kiosks on Av. Brasil, by Ponte de Amizade (helpful) and at airport, will book hotels.

Travel Agents and Currency Exchange   Transatlântica Turismo, Av. Brasil 99, and others. Dicks Tours has been rec. for its all-day tour to the Brazilian side of the Falls, to Paraguay (Ciudad Stroessner) and to the Itaipú dam, US$12 with good lunch included. Very difficult to exchange on Sunday, but quite possible in Paraguay. *Turismo Ortega*, Av. Brasil 1140, also handles exchange; Cambio Iguaçu, Av. Brasil 268; Casa Jerusalém, Av. Brasil 1055, for new cruzados, australes, guaraníes, good rates. Frontur on Av. Brasil accepts travellers' cheques, so does Venson Turismo, next to *Hotel Foz do Iguaçu*; many street changers nearby.

Excursions   From Foz, you can make an excursion to the 12,600-megawatt **Itaipú dam** (see below), which Brazil and Paraguay have built nearby. The Sete Quedas Falls were flooded in 1982-83 under the project. Bus marked Canteira da Obra from Terminal Urbana goes every 35 minutes to the Public Relations office at the main entrance, visits free (but in groups only)—film in German, English or Portuguese and then the dam (only one stop for taking photos). Tours (US$0.30) start at 0800, 0900, 1000, 1400, 1500, 1600; and 0730, 0800, 0830, 0930, 1030 on Suns. There are also an "executive" bus and agency tours but these are an unnecessary expense as the visit itself is free. If it's sunny, go in the morning as the sun is behind the dam in the afternoon and you will get poor photographs. You cannot go alone to the site as it is fenced in and guarded by its own security force. You can also visit the Paraguayan side, **see page 701**.

It is also possible to stay in Ciudad Stroessner (Paraguay) visiting both sides of the falls without immigration stamps (unless you are British); documents must be carried at all times, however. Take the Foz do Iguaçu bus or walk over the Ponte de Amizade (Friendship Bridge, Brazilian post open until 0200, pay US$2 in dollars, guaraníes or new cruzados at the Paraguayan end) past Brazilian Customs and take Ponte-Cidade bus (US$0.05) to local bus station (10 mins. from *Rodoviária*) where buses go to the Falls or to Argentina.

Airport   The Iguaçu international airport has daily flights from Río, São Paulo, Curitiba and Asunción, Paraguay, and good connections from other Brazilian cities. Taxis to town from the Brazilian airport 18 km from Foz, or about half-way between Foz and the Falls, are expensive (*comum*, US$5; *especial*, US$7); Dois Irmãos town bus for US$0.35, first at 0515, does not permit large amounts of luggage. Varig/Cruzeiro office in Foz: Av. Brasil 821, T 74-3344; staff speak foreign languages.

Buses   Foz do Iguaçu can be reached by paved road from São Paulo or Curitiba (buses return to both at 2130). Rodoviária, Av. Brasil 99, T 73-1525; has trustworthy baggage store. Foz is reached by many buses from Curitiba (9-11 hours, US$7, *leito* US$14 Sul America), from Guaíra via Cascavel only (5 hrs., US$4.25), and from São Paulo (18 hours, about US$15 with Pluma). Foz-Florianópolis, daily, 1900, US$10.50, 16 hrs., with Catarinense or Pluma. Porto Alegre-Foz US$15, direct bus daily at 1900, 14 hrs. with Unisul. To Campo Grande, 22 hrs. by Maringá company (9 hrs. to Paranaí and 13 from there to Campo Grande); Nacional Expresso to Brasília direct, 26 hrs. There are direct buses from Rio (US$18 one way pullman bus), 22 hours (return to Rio daily at 0900 with Pluma direct, or 1400 with Maringá, US$14; for a *leito* to Rio, you must change in Curitiba).

Travel From Paraguay   By daily plane from Asunción to Foz do Iguaçu, or by paved road from Asunción (book in advance to take the 0730 bus from Asunción, arriving at 1300 at the Brazilian border and at the bus terminal at 1500) about US$4. (If you wish to return to Asunción the same day, get a small bus to the falls and return at 1730 to the bus station, to be back at 2400.) Several bus companies ply the route: Nuestra Señora, Rysa, Pluma etc., fare US$4-6 according to quality, about 5 hrs.

In the far NW of the state, also on the River Paraná, were the tremendous waterfalls known in Brazil as Sete Quedas (the Seven Falls), and in Spanish Latin America as the Guaíra Falls; they were drowned by the filling of the lake behind the Itaipu dam in 1982. Guaíra (about 130 km. N of Iguaçu by air or road) will not be flooded, but much of its agricultural land and its clay beds will be. A train for **Presidente Epitácio** on the Paraná leaves São Paulo (Júlio Prestes station) daily at 1600 (900 km.), reaching the port at 1020 the next morning and leaving at 1530. It has sleepers and a restaurant car. Price for a double sleeper, US$35. Normal 1st class fare US$8.50 (this service is under threat of closure—check). An alternative to the 17½ hour train ride is a bus journey. Andorinha several daily, US$15. A luxury passenger vessel, the *Epitácio Pessoa*, sails twice monthly (weekly during holiday periods) on Wed. at 1700 downstream to *Guaíra*, 400 km. S, getting there at 1900 Thurs. evening. Return trips on Sat. at 1100, arrive at Pres. Epitácio at 2200 Sun., US$100. (Note: These schedules appear to be variable.) Prices per person using double cabin, including meals, US$170. Cheaper accommodation available on lower decks. Bookings should be made in advance with: Comércio e Navegação Alto Paraná Ltda., Praça da República 177, Loja 15, São Paulo, T 259-8255, Telex: 011-32400. Passages can also be purchased (subject to space available) at the office by the port in Presidente Epitácio, and in Guaíra from Ernst Mann, Americatur, Rua Alvorada 253. Alternatively it may be possible to obtain passage on a cargo boat.

The 4 km. from Guaíra to the lake can be walked or done by car (US$1.50 one way, return taxi up to US$10). Entrance to park US$0.30; small museum three blocks from Guaíra bus terminal, 0800-1100 and 1400-1700.

Presidente Epitácio Hotels *Primavera*, E, including breakfast, good value, near station.

Guaíra Hotels *Guarujá Motel*, Rua Alvorada 400, D. Near the bus station: *Palace Hotel*, D; *Majestic*, opposite bus station, E with or without bath, with breakfast, good; also *Hotel Itaipu*, E with bath, hot showers, good food (restaurant closed Sun.); *Sete Quedas*, Otávio Tosta 385, E, with breakfast and sandwich lunch, not too clean; *Ichapena*, E, not very clean but very friendly; and others.

Camping Municipal site at Bosque do Kartódromo, 2 km. out of town on the road from the bus station; ask at the Prefeitura for details. Basic facilities at each.

Restaurants *Recanto da Costela*, churrascaria, all you can eat for US$4. *O Chopão*, pleasant. Cheap snacks at *Bar São José*. *Restaurant Otto* for fish dishes.

Buses Guaíra-Campo Grande: buy a ticket (US$18) at the Guaíra bus terminal, take ferry to Ponta Porã, then bus to Mondo Novo, change bus there for Campo Grande; morning and night bus, 12 hrs. in all. There is a bus service between Curitiba and Guaíra, US$12, 10 hrs.; bus to São Paulo, US$15, 16 hrs.; Guaíra to Presidente Epitácio, US$1.80. The road is surfaced throughout. Also a bus from Londrina (US$7.20, 7½ hrs.) and Cascavel (connecting with bus from Iguaçu). The direct route Iguaçu-Guaíra is very bumpy, but interesting, takes 5 hrs. in the dry, but buses may be cancelled in the wet, US$5, or US$6 via Cascavel. There are also flights.

Note If entering Brazil from Paraguay in the Guaíra region, make sure to get passport stamped at the nearest available location (probably Foz do Iguaçu)—there is no passport control when coming off the boat from Salto Guaíra, Paraguay. There is an hourly passenger ferry service from Porto de Lanchas and Porto Guaíra to Paraguayan side, US$0.50, and hourly car ferry from Porto Guaíra. There is a time change when you cross the Paraná.

THE NORTH-EAST (7)

The nine states of the north-eastern bulge of Brazil are best considered as one entity. They cover 2.6 million square km. and contain a third of Brazil's people. The birthrate is the highest in Brazil, but so is the infant mortality rate. The average annual income from subsistence farming is deplorably low. Despite the misery, both regional and state loyalty remain ineradicable.

There was a brief period of colonization from northern Europe in the NE, when the Dutch West India Company, based at Recife, controlled some seven captaincies along the coast. They gained control in 1630, when Portugal was subject to Spain. After 1640, when Portugal freed itself, the colonists fought the Dutch and finally expelled them in 1654.

The nine states are Bahia, Sergipe, Alagoas, Pernambuco, Paraíba, Rio Grande do Norte, Ceará, Piauí, and Maranhão. They by no means form a homogeneous unity, but may be roughly divided into three contrasting parts. One is the sugar lands of the Zona da Mata along the coast between Salvador (Bahia) and Natal, where the rainfall can be depended upon. This was the first part of Brazil to be intensively colonized; hence the number of 16th century buildings and the density of old settlements are way above the national average. Inland from the Zona da Mata is the Zona do Agreste, with less rainfall, but generally enough for cattle raising. Inland again is the true interior, the Sertão, where rainfall cannot be depended upon; there is a little agriculture where water allows it but the herding of goats, and occasionally cattle, is more important. There are few blacks in the interior; the inhabitants are mostly of Portuguese-Indian stock, one of the most distinctive in Brazil. They are known as the *flagelados*, the scourged ones.

When there is rain, food in the zone is plentiful and varied. Manioc is a basic food; in addition, there are goat's milk and cheese, beef, beans, and sweet potatoes. But in the years of drought, when the hot dry winds from Africa scorch the earth, the effects can be tragic. Migration towards the coast and the southern towns begins, and the people are exposed to castigation of yet another sort: exploitation by grasping labour contractors. But at the first news that there is rain, the *flagelado* heads for home.

The main export crops of the north-east are sugar, cotton and cacao. Sugar and cotton have long been in decline, and now the southern states grow more than half of the Brazilian total. But cacao is grown almost entirely in southern Bahia, inland from the port of Ilhéus.

Brazil's main oilfields are in the State of Bahia; there are also offshore wells in the coastal waters of Alagoas, Sergipe and Rio Grande do Norte.

South of Cape São Roque there is abundant rainfall, but in Pernambuco the zone of ample rain stretches only 80 km. inland, though it deepens southwards. São Luís in Maranhão also gets plenty of rain, but between eastern Maranhão and Pernambuco lies a triangle, with its apex deep inland, where the rainfall is sporadic, and occasionally non-existent for a year. Here the tropical forest gives way to the *caatinga*, or scrub forest bushes which shed their leaves during drought. In this area grow the palms that produce carnauba wax and babaçu nuts, and the tree that produces oiticica oil.

Cities of the North-East

Salvador (often known as Bahia) is the capital of Bahia state and the fifth city of Brazil; Brasillia is 1,529 km. away. São Paulo 1,972 km. and Rio 1,702 km. The BR-116 inland road to Rio and the shorter coastal road, the BR-101, are both paved throughout. From the city you can visit some of the bay's 34 islands. It rains somewhat all the year, but the main rainy season is between April or May and September. In general the climate is pleasant, and the sun never far away. Temperatures range from 25°C to 32°C, never falling below 19°C.

Salvador's population is 1,496,000. It was founded in 1549, and was till 1763 the capital of Brazil. Most of its 135 churches, the fortifications, and some other buildings date from the 17th and 18th centuries. The centre of the city is divided into two, the Baixa (or lower part, known as Comércio), and the Alta (or higher part, known as Centro) on a small plateau some 70-odd metres above the lower city and overlooking the sparkling bay. The commercial quarter, the picturesque market near Praça Cairu, and the old port are in the lower city. The older parts of the upper city, from the Praça Terreiro de Jesus to beyond the Carmo church, are now a National Monument and extensive restoration work is being undertaken. A new administrative centre has been built near the airport.

Salvador is the main centre of the cigar-tobacco trade, and is famous for its excellent mild cigars. There is a small oil refinery at Mataripe, across the bay, serving the nearby oilfields of the Recôncavo area. The new industrial centre is at Aratu, and at Camaçari nearby there is a petrochemical centre.

The upper city is reached from the lower by steep slanting streets (*ladeiras*), and various public lifts and funiculars. The Lacerda lift raises passengers 71 metres from Praça Cairu in the lower city to Praça Tomé de Sousa (Municipal) in the upper, where are the old Government Palace (Palácio Rio Branco, now the Tourist Office) and the Biblioteca Municipal (1811); a steep road runs from the Customs House to Largo dos Aflitos, just behind the Governor's Palace; it has been continued under a viaduct at Campo Grande and on to the Canela valley, where the University is. The Gonçalves funicular railway runs from near the Praça da Sé down to the lower city. From Praça Municipal runs Rua Chile, with the best shops; several hotels are in its further extension, Rua 7 de Setembro, which continues along the Atlantic coast as Av. Presidente Vargas. New roads have been built inland: the Periférico Vale dos Barris, a divided-lane highway, runs from close to the centre, behind the Atlantic coast suburbs, to the administrative centre and the airport.

In the upper city interesting walks and drives can be taken across Praça Castro Alves, past the São Bento church (rebuilt after 1624 but with fine 17th century furniture), the Instituto Geográfico e Histórico, São Pedro fort (1646-1877), and the fine Praça 2 de Julio (also known as Campo Grande), with its column. At Campo Grande (magnificently lit at night) is the Castro Alves theatre. The route can be continued past the British Club (the sea side of Campo Grande, at Rua Banco dos Ingleses 20), the old Legislative Assembly, the Vitória and the Graça church (rebuilt 1770), down the Barra hill, past forts and the lighthouse at the bar, to Avenida Pres. Vargas and along the sea front to Rio Vermelho and beyond. On Av. Pres. Vargas, half-way to Rio Vermelho, there is a Zoo (daily

1. Lacerda Lift, 2. Gonçalves Funicular, 3. Cathedral, 4. Church of the Ordem Terceira de São Francisco, 5. Church of the Ordem Terceira de São Domingos, 6. Santa Casa da Misericórdia, 7. Conceição de Praia, 8. Monastery of São Francisco de Assis, 9. Church of São Bento, 10. Church of São Pedro dos Clérigos, 11. Church of Palma, 12. Church of Sant'Ana, 13. Nossa Senhora da Ajuda, 14. Convent of Lapa, 15. Convent of Santa Teresa/Museum of Sacred Art, 16. Afro-Brazilian Museum, 17. Museum of the City, 18. Museum of the Santa Casa, 19. House of Rui Barbosa, 20. House of the Sete Mortos, 21. Archbishop's Palace, 22. Palace of Saldanha, 23. Town Hall, 24. Berquió Mansion, 25. Fort of São Marcelo, 26. Customs House (Alfândega), 27. Government Palace (Rio Branco) and Bahiatursa Tourist Office, 29. Central Post Office, 30. Post Office, 31. Mercado Modelo.

0800-1700, entrance free) in the Botanical Gardens at Ondina, and a restaurant at the top of Ondina hill, overlooking the sea. A road between Rio Vermelho and the airport, 32 km. from the city, runs picturesquely beside the sea for 13 km. before turning inland to the airport. Some of the best hotels are on the sea front at Ondina and Rio Vermelho, and beyond at Pituba, Placafor and Itapoan. By all accounts all the local beaches are dirty, although Piatã beach is less polluted than most. Bathing inside the bay, for instance at Itapagipe, near the Bomfim church (Ribeira bus, from Elevador, lower station) is not recommended because of pollution.

Near the turning to the airport is the palm-fringed beach of Itapoan (primitive eating stands, with good sea food), where the traditional fishing rafts (*jangadas*) may occasionally be seen. There are two campsites on the beach, past the lighthouse. Quite near is the dark-green freshwater lake of Abaeté, circled by brilliant white sand dunes, now becoming built-up (bus direct from Praça da Sé and Campo Grande, marked "Aeroporto" or "Itapoan", 1 hr. US$0.10).

Many of the old forts are worth looking at, though most are closed to the public. The oldest, Santo Antônio da Barra (1598), is by the beach at Barra, where you can choose between bay and ocean bathing. One of the forts normally open to the public is that of São Marcelo in front of the Mercado Modelo.

Near the old churches in the upper city are untouched colonial mansions and dwellings (especially in the Rua Gregório Mattos), some with heavily carved doors. See particularly the church of the monastery of São Francisco de Assis for its sculptures in wood, and the cloisters of the monastery itself for its excellent tiles and paintings (open 0700-1100, 1400-1700, Frei Salvador Macedo de Oliveira is not an official guide, but he is extremely helpful, and you should seek him out even when the monastery is closed, a guide is compulsory, US$1.50, guides usually ask for a US$0.50 donation on top of the entrance fee); the church (1701) of the Ordem Terceira (the Franciscan Third Order), next door to São Francisco, for its rich façade and, within, a quite remarkable Chapter House (0830-1130 and 1400-1700) with striking images of the Order's most celebrated saints; the Cathedral (Terreiro de Jesus, upper city), formerly the Jesuit church, for its general design, the tomb of Mem de Sá, coloured marble and inlaid furniture (0700-1100 and 1400-1800); Santa Casa de Misericórdia (late 17th century), for its high altar and painted tiles; the convent of Santa Teresa, for the gate and the tiles in the floor of the kitchen; the 18th century church and monastery of Nossa Senhora do Carmo, for its altar and stalls, and statues in the sacristy; the church of Rosário dos Pretos, next to the Senac restaurant, Largo do Pelourinho, for its *azulejos* in the nave and its fine painted ceiling.

See also the famous church of Nosso Senhor do Bomfim on the Itapagipe peninsula in the suburbs, whose construction began in 1745; it draws endless suppliants (particularly on Fri. and Sun.) offering favours to the image of the Crucified Lord set over the high altar; the number and variety of ex-voto offerings—often of parts of the body deemed to have been cured by divine intervention—is extraordinary. The processions over the water to the church on the third Sun. in January are particularly interesting.

Also on the Itapagipe peninsula is a colonial fort on Mont Serrat point, and at Ribeira the church of Nossa Senhora da Penha (1743). The beach here has many restaurants (bus from Praça da Sé or Av. França).

Local Holidays Jan. 6 (Epiphany); Ash Wed. and Maundy Thurs., half-days; July 2 (Independence of Bahia); Oct. 30; Christmas Eve, half-day. An important local holiday is the Festa do Nosso Senhor do Bomfim, on the first Sun. in Feb., but the colourful washing or *lavagem* of the Bomfim church takes place on the preceding Thurs. The Festa da Ribeira is on the following Mon. The most colourful festival of all is that of the fishermen of the Rio Vermelho district on Feb. 2; gifts for Yemanjá, Goddess of the Sea, are taken out to sea in a procession of sailing boats to an accompaniment of *candomblé* instruments. The Holy Week processions among the old churches of the upper city are very colourful.

The **pre-Carnival festive season** begins towards the end of Nov. with São Nicodemo de Cachimbo (penultimate Sun. of Nov.), then comes Santa Bárbara (Dec. 4), then the Festa da

Conceição da Praia, centred on the church of that name (open 0700-1130 normally) at the base of the Lacerda lift. (Dec. 8 is the last night—not for those who don't like crowds!) The last week of Dec. is the Festa da Boa Viagem in the lower city; the beach will be packed all night on the 31st. On January 1 is the beautiful boat procession of Nosso Senhor dos Navegantes from Conceição da Praia to the church of Boa Viagem, on the beach of that name in the lower city. The leading boat, which carries the image of Christ and the archbishop, was built in 1892. You can follow in a sailing boat for about US$1; go early (0900) to dock by Mercado Modelo. A later festival is São Lázaro on the last Sun. in January.

Folklore Carnival in Salvador is particularly lively, with nearly everyone in fancy dress and dancing in the streets; parades are centred on Campo Grande (grandstand seats cost about US$5). Visitors find it exciting and entertaining, but look out for the more violent elements and don't carry any valuables. The *blocos* (samba groups) can be seen practising at any time from end- November; ask locals, Bene at *Zanzi-bar* or Bahiatursa for details. Many clubs have pre-carnival and Carnival dances; Baile das Atrizes has been recommended (always book tickets early). To make the most of carnival, arrive a week or two in advance and enjoy the festivities of the preceding week. Some have expressed disappointment at the preponderance of *trios elétricos* over samba during Carnival.

The Bahianas—black women who dress in traditional 18th century costumes—are street vendors who sit behind their trays of delicacies, savoury and seasoned, made from the great variety of local fish, vegetables and fruits.

See *capoeira*, a sport developed from the traditional foot-fighting technique introduced from Angola by African slaves. The music is by drum, tambourine and *berimbau*; there are several different kinds of the sport. If you want to attempt *capoeira*, the best school is Mestre Bimba in Terreiro de Jesus, at Rua Francisco Muniz Barreto 1. Classes are held in evenings (if you want to get the most out of it, knowledge of Portuguese is essential). There are two more schools in Forte de Santo Antônio behind Pelourinho, but check addresses at tourist office. Exhibitions take place in the Largo do Pelourinho, very picturesque, in the upper city (cost: US$2). You can also see the experts practising outside the Mercado Modelo on most days and at Campo Grande and Forte de Santo Antônio on Sunday afternoons; they often expect a contribution. At the Casa da Cultura at Forte de Santo Antônio there is also free live music on Saturday night.

Candomblé, the local Africa-derived magico-religious ceremonies (counterpart of Rio's *macumba*) may be seen by tourists—but not photographed—on Sundays and religious holidays. Contact the tourist office, Bahiatursa, or see their twice monthly calendar of events.

One of the best ways to get the "feel" of Salvador before visiting it is to read the works of the great Brazilian regional novelist Jorge Amado, most of which are set in and around the city. Several are in English translation. The **Casa da Cultura Jorge Amado** is now established in a colonial building at the top of the Largo do Pelourinho (a must for his fans).

Warning Salvador has a crime problem, ranging from armed robbery to pickpocketing and bagsnatching. Be very careful of your money and valuables at all times and in all districts. Avoid the more distant beaches out of season, when they are empty (e.g. Itapoan, Piatã, Placafor); on Sundays they are more crowded and safer. Conversely, the old city on Sundays is deserted and should therefore be avoided. At night, the historical centre (especially the Largo do Pelourinho), around the lifts, and buses are unsafe. On no account change money on the streets; this is a guaranteed way to be robbed. Leave valuables securely in your hotel (inc. cameras if possible), particularly at night. Parts of the centre to the NE of the Praça da Sé are run down and rather dubious, and one is warned not to walk down the Ladeíra de Misericôrdia, which links the Belvedere, near the Lacerda lifts, with the lower city. The civil police are reported to be very sympathetic and helpful.

Hotels Most of those away from the centre have swimming pools. Prices are lowest available. Those listed below are in our categories L and A.

Name	Address	Single (US$)	Double (US$)
Quatro Rodas	Rua da Passárgada, Farol de Itapoan (recommended)	95	110
Meridien	Rua Fonte do Boi 216, Rio Vermelho	77	89
Bahia Othon Palace	Av. Pres. Vargas 2456, Ondina	78	86
Salvador Praia	Av. Pres. Vargas 2338, Ondina	75	80

Farol	Av. Presidente Vargas 68	48	64
Grande da Barra	Av. Sete de Setembro 3564	55	64
Marazul	Av. Sete de Setembro 3937	64	72
Paulus	Av. Otávio Mangabeira, Pituba	40	46
Ondina Praia	Av. Pres. Vargas 2275, Ondina (*recommended*)	50	58
Luxor Convento do Carmo	Largo do Carmo 1	58	70
Praiamar	Av. Sete de Setembro 3577, Vitória	60	66
Vilha Velha	Av. Sete de Setembro 1791	45	49
Pelourinho	Rua Alfredo Brito 20 (*recommended*)	30	34
Vela Branca	Av. Antônio Carlos Magalhães, Pituba	46	50
Itapuã Praia	Jardim Itapuã, Placafor	45	58
Armação	Av. Otávio Mangabeira, Armação	38	45
Ondimar	Av. Presidente Vargas (*recommended*)	35	42
Bahia Praia	Av.Presidente Vargas 2483, Ondina	47	54
Bahia de Todos os Santos	Av. Sete de Setembro 106 (Ladeira de São Bento)	40	45
Villa Romana	Rua Lemos Brito 14 (*recommended*)	34	39
Bahia do Sol	Av. Sete de Setembro 2009, Ondina	50	55
Praia do Sol	Praia de Piatã	38	46

For people who like something out of the ordinary the *Luxor Convento do Carmo*, in a converted monastery dating from 1580 with colonial-type furniture and decoration, swimming pool, is rec., sometimes cheaper in mid-year. *Quatro Rodas* is a complete vacation hotel, extensive grounds, peaceful but plenty of activities available. *Chalé Enseada das Lajes*, Av. Presidente Vargas 511 (Morro da Paciência), A-L, 9 rooms in what used to be a private house, good service, good but expensive meals, ocean views, 2 mins. from beach. *Da Bahia*, Praça 2 de Julho 2 (Campo Grande), new, deluxe, very expensive, rec. (owned by Varig, so 15% discount if using Airpass). *Pituba Praia*, Av. Manoel Dias da Silva 2581, Pituba, T 248-6822, D with fan, rec.; *Solar da Barra*, Ladeira da Barra 433, C, good breakfast.

Palace, Rue Chile 20, C-D, rec., much better value than *Chile* opp., which is also unsafe. *Joana Angélica*, in street of same name, cheap, friendly, no breakfast; *Santiago*, Rua Visconde de São Lourenço 52 (near Praça Campo Grande), F with shower, breakfast, friendly, good; *Mater Café Teatro Hotel*, Rua M. Floriano 5 (also near Campo Grande), E, clean (but poor locks on doors), breakfast, with good café, *dos Artistas*, next door (Spanish spoken); *Caramuru*, Av. 7 de Setembro 2125, very clean, friendly, safe parking, E with bath. *Estrela Dalva*, 7 de Setembro 1013, cheap and clean. Nearby, on Largo São Bento, is *São Bento*, E, friendly, good cheap restaurant. *Anglo Americano*, Av. 7 de Setembro 1838 (near Campo Grande) T 247-7681, D with breakfast and bath, E without bath, safe, pay in advance, good gringo hotel, pleasant district, clean. *Granada*, Av. 7 de Setembro 512, F, good value, good breakfast; *Pousada Cosme e Damião*, Av. 7 de Setembro 76, 2nd floor, F, clean; *Meridiana*, Av. 7 de Setembro (Ladeira de São Bento) 29, 1st floor, E, clean, friendly, rec. *Amaralina*, Av. Amaralina 790, F, clean but a bit out of the way; *Calor Baiano*, Marques de Caravelas 136, Porto de Barra, E p.p., a/c and bath, quiet, clean, friendly, in converted mansion, rec.; *Barra Praia*, Av. Almirante Marques de Leão 172, Barra (one street from beach) E, clean, rec.; *Porto da Barra*, Av. 7 de Setembro 3783, small, rec.; *Enseada Praia de Barra*, Barão de Sergy 49, C, clean, safe, money exchanged, laundry bills high otherwise good value. *Paris*, E (a/c rooms more expensive), breakfast, shared showers, restaurant in same building, Rua Rui Barbosa, rec.; also *Pousada da Praça*, at No. 5, E, without bath, clean, friendly, rec., bar and sandwiches, safe. *Nova Esperança*, Ladeira das Hortas, friendly, F. *Internacional*, Rua Senador Costa Pinto 88, T 243-6151, clean, convenient, good value at E-D; *Meridional*, Rua do Paraíso 330, friendly and clean, F. *Solar São Francisco*, Praça Anchieta 16A, F, noisy but rec., friendly, good breakfast. *América*, Rua Monte Alverne, F, laundry service, clean, safe, quiet, friendly.

It is not recommended that you stay in hotels near the Praça da Sé as this is a dangerous area at night. There are, however, plenty of hotels in this area; the following have been rec.: *Jequié* off Praça da Sé at Ciné Liceu, clean, F without breakfast, some rooms preferable; *Solara*, Rua José Alencar 25, Largo do Pelourinho, central, E with shower, toilet, breakfast, clean, facilities for laundry, Spanish spoken by manager, safe; *Vigo*, Rua 13 de Maio 18, 2 blocks from Praça da Sé, F with bath and breakfast, fairly clean, safe, owner is Spanish (also owns *Hotel Center*, Rua Monte Alverne, F).

Pensionatos are cheap places to stay in shared rooms (up to four persons per room); e.g. *Pensionato No. 20*, Av. Cerqueira Lima; part or full board available. A huge Hilton hotel complex is being built 16 km. from the city, along the road to the airport. Youth Hostels: *2 de Julho*, Rua Areial de Cima 44, Dois de Julho, T 254-7038, and *Senzala*, Rua Florianópolis 134, Jardim Brasil, Barra, T 247-5678. Houses or rooms can be rented for US$5-35 a day from Pierre Marbarcher, Rua K (Rua Carlos Coqueijo 68a), Itapoan, T 249-5754 (PO Box 7458, 41600 Salvador); he is Swiss, owns a beach bar, and speaks English, French and German. At carnival it's a good idea to rent a flat; the tourist office has a list of real estate agents (e.g. José Mendez, T 237-1394/6).

Camping Near the lighthouse at Itapoan, take bus from Praça da Sé direct to Itapoan, or to

Campo Grande or Barra, change there for Itapoan, about 1 hr., then ½ hr. walk; two campsites, one Camping Clube do Brasil, at US$6 p.p. per night (members half price), and a cheaper one opposite. Camping de Pituaçu, Av. Prof. Pinto de Aguiar, Jardim Pituaçu. Sea bathing is dangerous off shore near campsites.

Restaurants Upper City: *Palace Hotel,* Rua Chile, serves a different traditional Portuguese entrée each lunchtime, except Sunday; *Mini Cacique,* Rua Rui Barbosa 29, behind *Palace Hotel,* good Bahian cooking, lunch only, very popular; *Ibiza,* Largo do Pelourinho, good fish and fruit; *Hotel Pelourinho,* indoor and outdoor, good views, good food, US$5; *Quindins de Iaiá,* Rua Direita de Santo Antônio 376, good, cheap (north of Pelourinho); *Kentefrio,* Av. 7 de Setembro 379, excellent clean snack bar, counter service only, closed Sunday; in same street, No. 1755, *Xangai,* Chinese restaurant opp. *Hotel Anglo Americano,* fair but cheaper than Chinese restaurants in Barra; *Pérgola,* next to *Anglo Americano,* at No. 1838, 6% discount to hotel guests, good value; *La Portuguesa,* Av. 7 de Setembro 600 block, good, cheap; *Casa d'Itália,* corner of 7 de Setembro and Visconde de São Lourenço, good, reasonable prices, good service; opposite *Bela Nápoli,* Av. Joana Angélica, Italian and fairly good. *Génova,* Rua da Força, excellent Italian, large portions, reasonable. *Mão de Vaca,* Rua Monte Alverne 10, downtown. *Frutas do Mar,* Rua Marqués de Leão, good seafood. *Tong-Fong,* Av. Joana Angélica 101, Chinese, highly rec.; *Hong Fong,* Rua Chile, good value; *Sushi House,* Rua Teixeira Leal 4, Graça, good, not cheap. *D. Velázquez,* Rua Direita da Piedade, good; opposite is *Baita-Kão* which serves good, cheap sandwiches. *Kowloon,* off Politeama do Baisco, next to Cinema Bristol, you can eat for US$2.50; *Teng Teng,* snackbar, Rua Carlos Gomes; same street, *Lanchonete O Camarade,* good and cheap. Good breakfast at *Café Brasil,* Praça da Sé.

Lotus, Rua do Paraíso 34, macrobiotic, good, excellent value. *Grão de Bico,* 7 de Setembro 737, very good vegetarian; *Fruta de Terra,* Rua Carlos Gomes 21, vegetarian, good food, fine views of city and the bay; *Tao Chi,* Rua General Labatut 23 and *Nectar,* Rua A. França 16, also vegetarian; *Nutre Ben,* Av. Joana Angélica 148 and *Trigal,* Rua Prof. Américo Simas 48, vegetarian, both open Mon.-Fri. for lunch only. Reported best vegetarian restaurant is *Grão de Arroz,* Coqueiros da Piedade 83, Barra. Huge variety of salads in Barra at *Alface e Companhia,* Barão de Sergy 67. Also in Barra, *Perini,* Miguel Bournier 22, for excellent icecream.

Solar do Unhão, in modernized sugar-estate house off Av. do Contorno, right on the side of the bay, is beautiful and expensive (US$20; folk dancing and son et lumière; closed Sundays). *Don Quichoppe,* Av. Carlos Gomes, US$1.50-3, good variety. *Casa de Gamboa,* Rua Newton Prado 51, old colonial house, reported best place for Bahia's regional food; *Lanches Apolo,* R. Portugal and Miguel Calmon 3, clean, daily specials about US$2. There is a good hamburger stand near Igreja N.S. da Piedade, good value, real orange juice; *Perini Sorveteria,* R. Miguel Bournier 22, superb ice cream, cakes, savouries, chocolates, branches also at Iguatemi shopping centre, Pituba, and Rua Portugal, in Cidade Baixa. *Salada de Frutas,* on A. Brito, is a good fruit salad bar. Opposite the fire station, a Chinese *lanchonete* serves good fruit juices. *Baby Beef,* Hipermercado Paes Mendonça, Pituba (Av. Antônio Carlos Magalhães s/n), very good food and service; *Juarez,* Mercado de Ouro, Av. Federico Pontes s/n, Cidade Baixa, good, cheap food. Opposite the Mercado Modelo, you can eat cheaply at the self-service counter of Paes Mendonça supermarket. At foot of Elevador Lacerda is *Cinqüenta Saladas,* not only salads, very reasonable. *Cantina Lua,* Praça 15 de Novembro, wholesome meal for under US$2, good atmosphere, live samba shows outside on Sats. 1900-2100; nearby is *Bar Ibiza,* rec.

Senac runs a restaurant school at Largo do Pelourinho 19, serving 40 dishes including regional ones, US$2.50 for Bahian supper, US$4.25 for all you can eat, open Mon.-Sat., 1130-1530, 1830-2230; at 2000 Thur., Fri., Sat. there is a folklore show, US$1.50 entrance fee (rec. for an introduction to Bahian culture, but not always for the food).

Famous atmosphere and local food at *Maria de São Pedro* and *Camafeu de Oxóssi* (extra charge for the show), on the second floor of the Mercado Modelo, overlooking the port. Excellent French cuisine, though more expensive than average, at *Le Privé,* Av. 7 de Setembro 554, and *Le Bistroquet,* Rua Santos Dumont 9. Another rec. French restaurant is *La Grille,* near Teatro Castro Alves, very popular, especially with artists and actors. Good churrascaria: *Las Palmas,* Rua Manuel Dias da Silva.

Restaurants and bars in the Atlantic coast suburbs: *Churrascaria Moenda* and *Bargaço* (Rua P, Quadra 43, Jardim Armação, T 231-5141, Bahian seafood dishes, reasonable) at Praia da Armação; *Popular* (bar), *Rodaviva Churrascaria,* Av. Octávio Mangabeira (on the beach, good value), *Iemanjá,* Av. Otávio Mangabeira (Armação/Boca do Rio, T 231-5069) and *Agdá,* Rua Orlando Moscoso I and Av. Otávio Mangabeira (Boca do Rio, T 231-2851), both excellent (Aeroporto bus passes in front of them); *Gererê* (typical food) at Largo de Amaralina; *Oxalá, Clave do Sol,* and *O Marisco* (for good seafood, very popular, rec.) at Rio Vermelho, also *Cheiro de Mar,* Rua Borges dos Reis 14, typical food, live music, T 247-1106, English spoken; *Vagão,* Rua Almirante Barroso 315, Rio Vermelho, bar with drinks (but little food) and live music, open air among trees and flowers, worth visiting. Another good restaurant serving Bahian food is *O Jangadeiro,* Av. Otávio Mangabeira (at Pituba beach). *Manga Rosa,* Rua César Zama 1, Porto da Barra, health food and fish, good; several good pizzerias on Rua Afonso Celso in Barra; *Fino Real,* Rua Barão de Sergy, Barra, good steaks, good sandwich bar. *Restaurant-bar Berro d'Agua,* Rua Barão de Sergy, Barra, good steaks, pleasant.

Bahian food is spiced and peppery. Typical dishes are those which feature oysters, shrimps and crabs, as well as *vatapá*, made from fish, rice, cashew-nuts, ginger, mint and parsley cooked in an earthenware dish and garnished with—and this is most important— *dendê* (palm) oil. *Muqueca* is fish or shrimp in spicy stews, and *xin-xin* is chicken stewed with fish or shrimp, onion and squash. Good food on the streets from the Bahianas: delicious *acarajés* (deep-fried bean cake stuffed with *vatapá*, green salad and usually shrimp, with optional hot sauce) are sold in the streets.

Nightlife Most of the modern night clubs are between Barra and Itapoan: *Lingua de Prata* at Praça Dorival Caymmi (small); *Close-up Drinks*, Rua Fernando Luz 12, Barra; *Casa Verde*, Av. Otávio Mangabeira 1230, Boca do Rio, and *Zum Zum* next door at No. 1240; *Bual Amour*, same street, further out in Corsário; *Pá de Baleia*, even further out on same street, in Piatã; and *Charles Night* at *Itapuã Praia Hotel*, Placafor. *Hippopotamus*, Othon Palace Hotel (both latter require membership or invitation). Typical show after dinner (at 2300) at *Tenda dos Milagres*, Amaralina and *Ondina*—Teatro de Arena (see under **Theatres** below). **Bars** *Banzo Bar*, Praça José de Alencar 6, Pelourinho, pleasant, cheap food, popular with travellers. *Ibiza* and *Bauru*, both on Rua Alfredo Brito, and *Cantina da Lua*, Terreiro de Jesus, all friendly.

Cinema Maria Bethania film theatre, Rio Vermelho, art and foreign films.

Markets The Mercado Modelo, at Praça Cairu, lower city, offers many tourist items such as wood carvings, silver-plated fruit, leather goods, local musical instruments. Lace items for sale are often not handmade (despite labels), are heavily marked up, and are much better bought at their place of origin (e.g. Ilha de Maré, Pontal da Barra and Marechal Deodoro, **see page 359**). Cosme e Damião, musical instrument sellers on 1st floor, has been rec., especially if you want to play the instruments. Bands and dancing, especially Sat. (but very much for money from tourists taking photographs), closed at 1200 Sun.; two restaurants on top floor, large balcony provides good view over harbour; restaurants on ground floor are cheaper. Photograph exhibition of the old market in basement. (Many items are often cheaper on the Praça da Sé in the nearby Cidade Alta.) Largest and most authentic market is the Feira de São Joaquim, 5 km. from Mercado Modelo along sea front: barkers, trucks, *burros*, horses, boats, people, mud, all very smelly, every day (Sun. till 1200 only), busiest on Sat. morning; interesting African-style pottery and basketwork; very cheap. (Car ferry terminal for Itaparica is nearby.) Instituto Mauá, Av. 7 de Setembro 261, and at Barra, and the Iguatemi Shopping Centre sells good handicraft items, but prices are fixed. There is also a good gift shop at the Convento do Carmo museum. Centro Artesanal do Maciel, Largo do Pelourinho 12, good for handicrafts. Mosquito nets can only be bought in O Mosquiteiro, in Calçados, or sometimes in the market area. Beware money-changers in street outside market, and at foot of Lacerda lift: many are thieves.

Bookshops Livraria Selso, Rua Barbosa 4-B, T 243-5383, secondhand and English books. Livraria Brandão, Rui Barbosa 46 (opp. *Hotel Paris*), secondhand books in English, French, Spanish, German. Currupio, Dra. Dragner Froes, Barra, is bookshop selling posters of old Salvador, and high quality books.

Shopping H. Stern, jewellers, at Hotels Meridien and Othon, Iguatemi Shopping Centre, and at the airport. Another jeweller is João Teobaldo Silva, Praça Anchieta 19, 1st floor. Also Frank Ribeiro da Silva, Praça do Alencar, precious stones and handicrafts. Jewellers along Rua do Carmo (e.g. Gérson Joalheiros, Largo do Carmo 26), and in the Convento do Carmo. **Camera repair**: Pepe, Rua da Ajuda, ed. Triunfo, first floor.

Hairdresser Edmea Penteados, Praça da Sé, Edificio Themis, 3rd floor, rec.

Laundry Lavanderia Lavalimpo, Rua do Pilar 31, Comércio, Mon.-Sat. 0800-1800.

Local Transport Taxi meters start at US$0.25 for the "flagdown" and US$0.10 per 100 metres. They charge US$5 per hour within city limits, and "agreed" rates outside. Taxi-drivers tend to overcharge, especially at night; the night-time charge should be 30% higher than daytime charges. Teletaxi (24-hr. service), 243-4333. Local buses US$0.20, air-conditioned *frescões* US$0.50. On buses and at the ticket-sellers' booths, watch your change and beware pickpockets. To get from the old city to the ocean beaches, take a "Barra" bus from Praça da Sé to the Barra point and walk to the nearer ones; the Aeroporto *frescão* (last 2130) leaves Praça da Sé, passing Barra, Ondina, Rio Vermelho, Amaralina, Pituba, Costa Azul, Armação and Boca do Rio, before turning inland to the airport.

Hitching out of Salvador, take a "Cidade Industrial" bus from the bus station at the port; it goes on to the highway.

Theatres Castro Alves, at Campo Grande (Largo Dois de Julho), daily concerts; Teatro da Gamboa; Teatro Vila Velha; Senac; Instituto Cultural Brasil-Alemanha (ICBA); Teatro Santo António, part of the Escola de Teatro da Universidade Federal da Bahia; Teatro de Arena, Alto de Ondina, Ondina (good folklore show, 2 hrs., US$4); and the Tenda dos Milagres in Amaralina.

Museums The city has 27 museums. **The Museum of Contemporary Art,** converted from an old estate house and outbuildings of Av. Contorno, is only open for special exhibitions. The good restaurant (*Solar do Unhão*) is still there, and the buildings are worth seeing for themselves (*son et lumière* most evenings).

There is a remarkable **Museum of Sacred Art** in the 17th century monastery and church of Santa Teresa, at the bottom of the steep Ladeira de Santa Teresa, at Rua do Sodré 276. Many of the 400 carvings are from the Old World, but a number are local. Among the reliquaries of silver and gold is one of gilded wood by the great Brazilian sculptor Aleijadinho. Open Tues.-Sat. 1300-1700, US$0.40. Many of the treasures which used to be in an old mansion, the Casa de Calmon, Av. Joana Angélica 198, are here now. This important collection is well worth a visit.

The **Carmo Church** has a museum with a collection of icons and colonial furniture, including carvings by Francisco Manuel das Chagas, known as "O Cabra"; see particularly his statue of Christ bound to the pillar (open daily, 0800-1200, 1400-1800, US$0.35). Next door is a State museum which is architecturally notable and has period furnishings. **Museu Abelardo Rodrigues**, in the Solar Ferrão, Pelourinho (Rua Gregório de Mattos 45, open Mon.-Fri. 1000-1200, 1400-1700, closed Tues., Sat.-Sun. 1100-1700), is another religious art museum, with objects from the 17th, 18th, and 19th centuries, mainly from Bahia, Pernambuco and Maranhão.

Museu Costa Pinto, Av. 7 de Setembro 2490, US$0.35 (1500-1900 except Tues.) is a modern house with collections of crystal, porcelain, silver, furniture etc.

Museu de Arte da Bahia, Av. 7 de Setembro 2340, Vitória, Tues.-Sun. 1400-1800, poor.

Afro-Brazilian Museum, in former Faculty of Medicine building, Terreiro de Jesus, open Tues.-Sat., 0930-1130, 1400-1730, comparing African and Bahian Orixás (deities) celebrations, beautiful murals and carvings, highly rec. Medical and ethnographic museums in same complex.

City Museum, Largo do Pelourinho (centre of old upper city), arts and crafts, old photographs, entrance free, Mon.-Sat. 0800-1200, 1330-1800. **Hydrographical Museum**, Forte de Santo António, free (Tues.-Sun. 1100-1700).

Thirty-six km. from the city is the **Museu do Recôncavo** (Museu do Wanderley Pinho, 0900-1200, 1400-1700) in the old Freguesia mill (1552), (closed for refurbishing) in which one can find artefacts and pictures of three centuries of the economic and social life of this region. The Casa Grande e Senzala (the home of the landowner and the combined dwelling and working area of the slaves) is still intact. It is a peaceful way to spend an afternoon, but difficult to get to by public transport, the museum is 7 km. from main highway. The **State Geological Museum** is at Av. 7 de Setembro 2195, Vitória, open Mon.-Fri. 1000-1200, 1400-1800 and Sat. and Sun. 1400-1800. Opposite the Museum of Sacred Art is Temposta, a private museum of postcards, open Tues.-Sat., 1000-1130, 1400-1730, at Rua do Sodré 276 (proprietor, Antônio Marcelino do Nascimento). Convention Centre at Praia Armação in operation.

N.B. Many guides offer their services in museums, but their English is poor and their expectations of a tip high.

Tourist Office (with lists of hotels and pension stays in private homes) Bahiatursa, Palácio Rio Branco (former government palace, which may be viewed), Rua Chile on Praça Municipal, open 0800-1830. Visitors can obtain weekly list of events and itineraries (on foot or by car) planned by the city, well worth doing, but be warned that the itinerary goes through some very run down areas of the city. Map, US$1.25, good; offices have noticeboard for messages. Also at bus station (good, English spoken); airport and other offices at Porto da Barra. Also details of travel throughout State of Bahia. Phone 133 any time for tourist information in English. Maps from Departmento de Geografia e Estatística, Av. Estados Unidos (opp. Banco do Brasil, lower city); also from newsstands; maps of Brazil US$ 1.50.

A multilingual tour guide is Manfred von Büttner (Manfredo), to be found at *Hotel Colón*, Praça Anchieta, T 241-1531. Tours in English, French, German, Italian and Spanish. Helpful with exchange.

The tours of L.R. Turismo have been rec.: Bahia á Noite includes transport from hotel to *Ondina* in Alta da Ondina, for meal and folklore show (US$8.50 p.p.); L.R. and Alameda Turismo run an all-day boat trip to the Bahia de Todos Os Santos, from 0800-1700, including visit to Ilha Frades, lunch on Itaparica (US$5 extra), and drinks (US$14.50 p.p.).

Electric Current 110-220 A.C., 60 cycles.

Exchange Do not be tempted to change money on the street (see above), especially in the Upper City (where rates are usually better). Lloyds Bank (ex-BOLSA), Rua Miguel Calmon 22; Citibank, Av. Estados Unidos; Banco Holandês Unido, Praça da Inglaterra; and national banks.

Banco Econômico, Av. 7 de Setembro 302, 5th floor. Banco do Brasil, Rua Rio de Janeiro 750 (4th floor). Banco Mercantil de São Paulo, Rua M. Calmon, near Mercado Modelo, and Banco Nordeste, close by, accept Master Charge cards, Banco Real, Rua Ourivés (Visa). Banco Mercantil do Brasil, Rua Portugal; open 1000-1630. Also exchange shops, e.g. Watt Representações, Rua Miguel Calmon 63, room 601; American Express, Kontik-Franstur, Praça da Inglaterra 2, 1st floor (Lower City); travel agency at Estados Unidos 4 (in the arcade of Edifício Visconde de Cayru) changes travellers' cheques; López e López, Rua Conselheiro Dantas 57, Edifício Paraguassu, Room 101. Catedral Corretora de Câmbio, Rua Miguel Calmon 382-5°, in the Banco Francês e Brasileiro building; funeral parlours on Praça da Sé and Praça Anchieta give good rates. Carlos, Av. 7 de Setembro 1451, loja F, Campo Grande Sul, next to *Hotel Bahia*, T 245-3012/237-5331; Asta, Rua Dantas 22/24, edifício Pradesco. Good rates for cash (in small amounts) from manager of *Hotel Modelo*, at foot of Lacerda lift. Good rates also at Marquisa S.A. (Sr. Nelson), Rua Visconde do Rosário 04, Edifício Senador Dantas, Conjunto 101-106 (corner Rua Portugal).

Consulates British Vice-Consulate, Av. Estados Unidos 4, Edifício Visconde de Cayru, Salas 1109/1133, CEP 40000, Caixa Postal 38, T 241-3120/241-3222. Austrian, Av. Almirante Marqués Leão 46, apt.33, Caixa Postal 4032, T (071)24 76 013; Dutch, Rua da Bélgica 10, sala 604, T 242-1749/1756; Danish, Av. Sete de Setembro 3959, T 247-9667.

Post Office Main post office and poste restante is in Praça Inglaterra, in the Lower City.

Immigration (for extensions of entry permits), corner of Ruas Polonia and Santos Dumont, Lower City.

Communications Embratel, Av. Estados Unidos, near Mercado Modelo. Cia. Rádio Internacional do Brasil, Rua Miguel Calmon 41. Tebehahia has offices at Campo da Pôlvora, on Rua Hugo Baltazar Silveira (open always), Porto da Barra, airport, Rodoviária and Mercado Modelo.

British Club, Inglesa 20B, just off Campo Grande. **Associação Cultural Brasil-Estados Unidos**, Av. 7 de Setembro 1883, opp. *Hotel Anglo Americano*, has a library and reading room with recent U.S. magazines, open to anyone, and at No. 1809 on the same avenue is the German **Goethe Institut**, also with library and reading room with recent papers.

Clinic Barão de Loreto 21, Graça. Dr Argemiro Júnior speaks English and Spanish. First consultation US$24, second free. Dr Manoel Nogueira, (from 1000-1200), Av. Joana Angélica 6, T 241-2377, English-speaking. Yellow fever vaccinations free at Delegação Federal de Saúde, Rua Padre Feijó, Canela. Israeli travellers needing medical (or other) advice should contact Sr. Marcus (T 247-5769), who speaks Hebrew and is glad to help.

Buses Bus station 5 km. from city but regular services to centre (bus RI or RII, "Centro-Rodoviária-Circular"; in centre, get on in lower city at foot of Lacerda lift; buses also to Campo Grande; journey can take up to 1 hr. especially in peak periods. Executive bus from Praça da Sé runs to Iguatemi Shopping Centre from where there is a walkway to the bus station. To Recife, US$12 (*leito*, 24), 13 hrs., 3 a day; plenty to Rio (28 hrs., US$25, *leito* 50, buy ticket 5 days in advance, 27 hrs. leaves at 1300); São Paulo (30 hrs.), US$30, *leito* US$60, Belo Horizonte 22 hrs, 2 normal (US$29), 2 *leito* buses (US$58); to Fortaleza, 19 hrs., US$18 at 0900 and 2100 with Viação Brasilia; Ilhéus, 7 hrs., US$6, several (e.g. Sulba at 2210 daily); Valença, 5 a day, 5 hrs., US$4; Porto Seguro, 2000, 2100, 12 hrs., US$10.50; Maceió, US$8.50, 4 a day, 9-10 hrs, book early (only service, Empresa Bomfim at 2000). Belém US$36, 37 hrs. There are daily bus services to Brasília along the new (fully paved) road, BR-242, via Barreiras; buses leave at 1200 and 2000, 23 hrs. (US$28). To Paulo Afonso, US$8, 10 hrs., leaving 0430, 2000, and 1910 on Sun., Wed. and Fri, partly paved road. (Travel agency Remundi, Rua da Grécia 8, 1° andar, Cidade Baixa, T 242-5286, sells bus tickets.)

Motorists to Rio can do the trip on the BR-116 highway in 3 days, stopping at **Vitória da Conquista** (524 km. from Salvador), *Hotel Bahia*, D, with huge meals; *Hotel Alianca*, D and *Hotel Livramento*, E, with restaurant; also Camping Clube do Brasil site at Km. 1,076; Teófilo Otôni, 946 km. **see page** 4015; or Governador Valadares, 1,055 km. **(see page 295)**, and Leopoldina (1,402 km.). There are also various motels; two in the State of Bahia are at Vitória da Conquista; and at Feira de Santana; also between Feira and Salvador. Fairly good hotels are also available in Jequié (*Itajubá, Rex*, and motels), and basic ones in Milagres. Stopovers on the BR-101 coastal road can be made at Vitória and Itabuna (or Ilhéus), and there are many other towns on or near the coast.

Motorists to Brasília can save 3 hours (we are told) by taking the ferry to Itaparica and then going across country to Itaberaba for the BR-242 highway. The journey can be broken at Itaberaba (*pousada*), Lençóis **(see page 353)**, at Ibotirama on the River São Francisco; at Barreiras on the River Negro, where buses stop for 2-3 hrs. (*Hotel Vandelena*, D, full board); or at Alvorada do Norte (several poor-looking places), Sobradinho (*Hotel Alvimar*, D) or at Posse (Goiás).

Rail From Salvador there are only local train services, though the tracks are continuous to Rio.

Air To Brasília, daily, 2 hrs; to Rio, about 2 hrs. Dois de Julho airport is 32 km. from the city.

Buses go between airport and city centre, bus "Aeroporto-Politeama" goes to Av. 7 de Setembro, US$0.10, 1 hr., or special taxi (buy ticket at airport desk) US$10. Bus service from Praça da Sé to Pituba and airport US$1.50.

Shipping National coastal vessels.

Excursions From the lower city the train (Trem do Leste) leaves Calçada for a 40 min. journey through the bayside suburbs of Salvador—Lobato, Plataforma (canoes and motor boats for Ribeira on the Itapagipe peninsula), Escada (17th century church), Praia Grande, Periperi and Paripe (take bus for 17th century church at São Tomé de Paripe). The same trip can be made by bus, less picturesquely. From Ribeira a small boat goes 25 km. to **Ilha da Maré** between 0900 and 1100, connecting the island's villages of Itamoaba, Praia Grande and Santana (US$0.70); boat returns next day from Santana at 0400-0500. Santana is a centre for lace making, Praia Grande for basket-weaving. None of the villages has a hotel, but there are restaurants and bars and camping is possible.

There are ferries every half-hour (50-min. journey) from next to the Mercado Modelo (US$0.20, more on Sundays, good juices at the landing stage) to Vera Cruz on the island of **Itaparica**, on the other side of the bay from the city; the car ferry leaves hourly from São Joaquim (bus from in front of Lacerda lift to São Joaquim) to Bom Despacho, 45 mins. journey. At Vera Cruz there are good beaches, swimming, horses and bikes for hire, but to other parts of the island one has to take a taxi. From Bom Despacho buses go to other parts of the island. The island has beaches (most of which are dirty, but good one at Ponta de Areia (1 hr. walk from Itaparica town), and at Club Méditerranée), adequate hotels (*Grande Hotel de Itaparica*, near sea, *Icaraí*, Itaparica, D, fair food, run by Fernando Mesquita, very friendly and obliging, and one at Gameleira); *Club Méditerranée*, of which some very poor reports. Restaurants are expensive (although *Santa Bárbara* on the main square is good and inexpensive), but there are food shops and a self-service restaurant at the Paes Mendonça shopping centre in Gameleira. Camping is worthwhile. The church and fortress of São Lourenço are in Itaparica town. **Mar Grande,** which can be reached direct by ferry from Mercado Modelo (first one at 0630, last back at 1700, every half-hour, but hourly after 1600, 45 mins.), US$0.50, or by VW *Kombi* or launch from Itaparica (0630, 0900, 1400, 1700— may not leave until full), is very unspoilt, but beach very dirty. To rent houses costs up to US$55 for one month. (*Hotel Galeão Sacramento*, suites in four separate buildings, swimming pool and other sports facilities; *Arco Iris Pousada*, C, magnificent building and setting in mango orchard, overpriced hotel, good restaurant; next door is a campsite, same owners, filthy but shady, 1 block from beach and town centre. Another *pousada*, C, 4-star.) Eat at *Philippe's Bar and Restaurant*, Largo de São Bento, good French and local food, local information in French and English, or at *O Pacífico*, Praça da Gamboa, local cuisine, rec., friendly and peaceful. There is a minibus service between Mar Grande and Itaparica. Bicycles for hire. At the southern tip of the island is Cacha Pregos (VW bus from Mar Grande, US$6.70); *Pousada Cacha Pregos*, next to supermarket, T 839-1594, E-D (bargain) with bath, fan, clean, no breakfast. Nice beaches across the bay, but you have to pay US$6.50 to get a boat across. From Bom Despacho on the island, trips can be made to the picturesque small colonial port of **Jaguaribe** and to Nazaré (see below), with its market (both on the mainland). Jaguaribe can be reached by boat from the Mercado Modelo, leaving Thursday and Saturday and returning Friday and Monday.

The Companhia de Navegação Bahiana provides excursions in the ship *Bahia de Todos os Santos*, from near the Mercado Modelo. An excursion along the city front (Tues., Thurs., Sat.), taking 3 hours, costs US$6; an all-day trip around the bay's islands, including a 3-hour stay at Itaparica, costs US$10 (Wed., Fri., Sun.). Small boats for trips round the bay may be hired privately at the fishing port (Porto dos Saveiros) at the W side of the Mercado Modelo. There is also an excursion to all parts of the city accessible by boat. For other excursions by boat contact agencies such as L. R. Turismo, Av. Sete de Setembro 3959; Grey Line, Av. Presidente Vargas 2456; Remundi, Rua da Grécia, 8 (1st floor); Kontik, Praça da Inglaterra, 2. For cheaper excursions to the bay's islands, watch for notices in lunch bars and in bank windows in the lower city bank district, put up by employees looking for people to go on trips (US$2.50-3.75, including a beer and sandwich).

Nazaré das Farinhas, 60 km. inland from Itaparica, and reached over a bridge by bus from **Bom Despacho**, is an 18th-century town celebrated for its market, which specializes in the local ceramic figures, or *caxixis*. There is an especially large market in Holy Week, particularly on the Thursday and Good Friday. 12 km. from Nazaré (taxi US$3, also buses) is the village of Maragojipinha, which specializes in making the ceramic figures. Bus from Salvador, 1530, takes 5 hours.

Feira de Santana (225,000 people), 112 km. NW of Salvador on both the coastal BR-101 and the inland BR-116 roads to Rio, the centre of a great cattle breeding and trading area; its Monday market, known as Feira do Couro (leather fair), said to be the largest in Brazil, attracts great crowds to its colourful display of local products. The permanent Artesanato market in the centre has a bigger selection, including leather, than the Monday market. Bus every half hour from Salvador, 2 hrs., US$1.60. (Bus station has a wall of painted tiles made by Udo-Ceramista, whose workshop is Brotas, Av. Dom João VI 411, Salvador.)

Hotels Half-way to Feira from Salvador is the turn off to the *Hotel Fazenda*, Alto da Ipê. At Feira: *Luxor Pousada da Feira*, Km. 1,470 on BR-116, B; *Vips Hotel Restaurante*, Rua Visconde do Rio Branco 367; *Flecha Motel Feira*, E, about 20 km. away at Km. 1,067 BR-101; *Hotel da Bahia*, Rua Visconde do Rio Branco 562; *Vitória*, Rua Marechal Deodoro, E, with breakfast; several cheap ones in Praça da Matriz and near the bus station, which is quite near the centre.

Bar Restaurant *A Kaskata*, Rua Presidente Dutra, good food, open terrace.

The Recôncavo The area around Salvador, known as the Recôncavo Baiano, was one of the chief centres of sugar and tobacco cultivation in the 16th century.

Leaving Salvador on the Feira road, at km. 33 one forks left on to the BR-324 to the **Museu do Recôncavo Wanderley de Pinho (see page 349)**. Further W, round the bay, is São Francisco do Conde, 54 km. from Salvador, with a church and convent of 1636 and the ruins of Don Pedro II's agricultural school, said to be the first in Latin America.

At 60 km. from Salvador the BA-026 road branches off the BR-324 to Santo Amaro, Cachoeira and São Félix. Seventy-three km. from Salvador is **Santo Amaro da Purificação,** an old sugar centre now with a population of 20,000 noted for its churches (often closed because of robberies), municipal palace (1769), fine main square, house of the poet and singer Caetano Veloso (his wife, the singer Maria Bethânia, is also from here), and ruined mansions including Araújo Pinto, former residence of the Barão de Cotegipe. Other attractions include the splendid beaches of the bay, the falls of Vitória and the grotto of Bom Jesus dos Pobres. Festivals in January and February (Santo Amaro and N.S. da Purificação) are interesting. Craftwork is sold on the town's main bridge. No good hotels or restaurants.

At 54 km. from Santo Amaro, and only 4 km. from the BR-101 coastal road, are the twin towns of **Cachoeira** (Bahia's "Ouro Preto"), and **São Félix,** on either side of the Rio Paraguassu below the Cachoeira dam. Cachoeira, recently declared a national monument, was twice capital of Bahia: once in 1624-5 during the Dutch invasion, and once in 1822-3 while Salvador was still held by the Portuguese. It was the birthplace of Ana Néri, known as "Mother of the Brazilians", who organized nursing services during the Paraguayan War (1865-70). There are beautiful views from above São Félix. Cachoeira's main buildings are the Casa da Câmara e Cadeia (1698-1712), the Santa Casa de Misericórdia (1734—the hospital, someone may let you see the church), and the 16th-century Ajuda chapel (now containing a fine collection of vestments), and the Monastery of the Carmelites' Third Order, whose church has a heavily gilded interior. Other churches: Carmo (1548) and its Third Order (fine *azulejos* and gilding), the Matriz with 5-metres-high *azulejos*, and Nossa Senhora da Conceição da Monte. Beautiful lace cloths on church altars. All churches either restored or in the process of restoration. Ruined Jesuit seminary. Tourist office in the Casa de Ana Néri. In the same building is the Hansen-Bahia collection of wood-engravings (see also the Hansen house on the hill above São Félix, where the engravers Karl and Ilse Hansen lived; it is to be opened as a museum). Festivals: São João (June 24) "Carnival of the Interior" celebrations, well-attended by tourists, Boa Morte (early August), and a famous *candomblé* ceremony at the Fonte de Santa Bárbara on December 4. Try the local dish, *maniçoba* (meat, manioc and peppers). Craftwork in ceramics and wood readily available. Buses from Salvador (Carnurujipe) every hour or so.

Hotels Cachoeira: *Pousada do Convento de Cachoeira* (run by Bahiatursa), in newly restored 16th-century convent, C, good restaurant, *Pousada do Guerreiro*, 13 de Maio 40, no restaurant; *Pousada do Convento*, rec., swimming pool, reasonable. **Restaurants:** *Cabana do Pai Thomaz*, excellent Bahian food, good value; *Recanto de Oxum*, nearby, *Gruta Azul*, lunch only. São Félix: *Xang-hai*, F.

Excursion 6 km. from Cachoeira, on the higher ground of the Planalto Baiano, is the small town of Belém (turning 2½ km. on road to Santo Amaro). Church and seminary of Carmo. Healthy spot:

people from Salvador have summer homes. We are told there is an 8 km. secret passage between the Carmo churches here and in Cachoeira, but have not seen it—reports welcome.

The tobacco centre of Cruz das Almas can also be visited, although transport is poor. The São João celebrations here (June 24) are not rec.: very dangerous games with fireworks are involved.

Maragogipe, a tobacco exporting port 22 km. SE of Cachoeira along a dirt road (BA-123), can also be reached by boat from Salvador. See the old houses and the church of São Bartolomeu, with its museum. The main festival is São Bartolomeu, in August. Good ceramic craftwork.

Inland from Salvador 400 km. W of Salvador on the BR-242 to Brasília is **Lençóis,** a town which is a historical monument, founded in 1844 because of diamonds in the region (there are still some *garimpeiros*, pop. 2,000. It is the headquarters of the new (1985) **Parque Nacional da Chapada Diamantina,** of which the director is Roy Funch, who used to be a tour guide in the area. *Pousada de Lençóis,* B, with breakfast, swimming pool; *Colonial,* D; *Tradição,* E with bath, breakfast, fridge, mosquito net, pleasant; *Pous Alegre,* Praça Aureliano Sá, T 334-1124, E with good regional breakfast, friendly, hot showers, good restaurant; *Canto de Águas,* D, comfortable; *Pensão Diamantina,* Rua Miguel Calmon, E, not rec.; *Casa dos Nomadies,* simple and reasonable (F p.p.); 2 campsites, one 2 km. before Lençóis, one in the town centre (friendly, rec.). Restaurant: *Dom Ratão,* sometimes has armadillo, snake, toad, piranha and alligator included on the menu; *Laredo,* good food. The Parque Nacional contains 1,500 square km. of mountainous country, with waterfalls (including the Cachoeira de Glass, 400 metres, the highest in Brazil), large caves, rivers with natural swimming pools and good walking tours. Ask for English-speaking guide Luís Krug near the central campsite. There is also a Casa do Artesão, where children learn to fill bottles with patterns of coloured sand, a local speciality. There is a local liquor factory. 30 km. away is Morro de Pai Inácio with good views from the left-hand hill as you come up the gravel road, hard work scrambling down (bus from Lençóis at 0815, 30 mins., US$.60); good prato comercial at the *churrascaria.* Paraíso bus from Salvador 0915 and 2030 (0900 and 2100 Sat.), US$6.30, Feira de Santana, Ibotirama, Barreiras or Brasília stops at Lençóis.

South from Salvador 271 km. from Salvador, on an asphalted road, is **Valença** (5 buses a day to Salvador, 5 hrs., US$4, and to Itabuna (Expresso São Jorge), 5 hrs., US$4, very slow, and Ilhéus), a small, attractive and bustling town at the mouth of the River Una (the quickest, cheapest way to get there is to take a ferry to Bom Despacho/Itaparica, from where it's 3 hrs. to Valença.) So. Two old churches stand on rising ground above the town; the views from Nossa Senhora do Amparo are recommended. The town is in the middle of an area producing black pepper, cloves and *piaçava* (used in making brushes and mats). Other industries include the building and repair of fishing boats (*saveiros*). Tourist office opposite Rodoviária on other side of river, friendly. The River Una enters an enormous region of mangrove swamps. The main attraction of Valença is the beaches on the mainland (Guabim, 14 km. N) and on the island of Tinharé.

Hotels *Tourist Hotel,* Marechal Floriano 167, D, good; *Rio Una,* fairly chic, expensive, swimming pool; *Guabim,* Praça da Independência, modest, E; good *Akuarius* restaurant; *Universal,* E, Marquês de Herval 98, clean, helpful, good breakfast, restaurant.

Tinharé is a large island (with good walking, beaches and camping, but no banks or exchange) separated from the mainland by the estuary of the River Una and mangrove swamps, so that it is hard to tell which is land and which is water. Boats (US$0.75) leave every day from Valença for Galeão (1½ hrs.) and also for Gamboa (1½ hrs.) and Morro de São Paulo (2 hrs.). The boat for the two last named leaves at 0600, 0930 and 1500 on weekdays, first on Sun. at 0700, first returning from Morro de São Paulo at 0600 (fishing boats will go to Morro de São Paulo for US$2 p.p.). May be fewer boats in winter. Boats can be arranged in p.m., but not after dark. **Morro de São Paulo** is very popular in summer, situated on the headland at the northernmost tip of the island, lush with ferns, palms and birds of paradise, dominated by the lighthouse and the ruins of a Dutch colonial fort (1630). The village has a landing place on the sheltered landward side, dominated by the old gateway of the fortress. From the lighthouse a path leads to a ruined lookout with cannon, which has panoramic views. *Pousada do Campo,* C, on top of the hill, individual chalets, swimming pool, run by Stefano and Linda Starita; *Pousada Cio do Mar,* E with bath (D in season), fan, simple breakfast, lots of steps up to rooms; *Pousada Bora Bora,* F p.p., shared bath, OK; *Pousada Casa Rolã,* F with shared bath, has rooms for up to 4, near first beach; plenty of restaurants (*Gaúcho* good food, cheap; *Canto da Sereia*, excellent value, friendly; *Ilha de Saúde*, very good, esp. breakfast), bars, and small hotels and *albergues*, F (just ask by the fountain). Camping is possible, but not too safe on the beach to the S of the village; fresh water from springs in the village, washing at the public fountain. Fish can be bought from the fishermen in summer, or borrow a pole and catch your own at sunset. Secondhand books (English, German, and others) sold almost opp. *Pousada Bora Bora* nightly (when not raining), will trade 2 for 1 if he's in the mood. The place is expensive December-March, crowded at holiday times, but cheaper during the rest of the year. All roads are unmade, but beaches are good.

Galeão is another village in the island, but has no beach, only mangrove swamps. The church of São Francisco Xavier looks imposing on its hill. (Another island worth visiting is Boipeba.) It is sometimes possible to get a direct boat from Salvador, 2-3 times a week in summer, 6-7 hrs, ask for Sr. Cacu and the *Natureza* at the fishing port next to the Mercado Modelo.

On the coast, south toward Ilhéus, is the picturesque fishing village of **Itacaré**. It is a beautiful area with a protected beach with crystal-clear water to the right of town; across the river there are beaches with good surfing. It is becoming a popular weekend spot, especially for surfers.

Hotels Bom Jesus, at bus station; *Sta. Bárbara*, Praça Izaac Soares 4, clean, good food. *Bela's Casa de Família*, nice rooms, F (next to *Hotel Santa Bárbara*); *Pousada Iemanjá*, near praça; *San Miguel*, 1 street from waterfront, nr. the cannon at N end of town, F, basic, uncomfortable; *Pousada da Paz*, nr. waterfront, S end of town. Camping site.

Restaurant Marconi, bar also, good, cheap, friendly.

Buses To Ilhéus (70 km.), 3-4 hrs., US$1.50; to Salvador, change at Ubaituba (3 hrs., US$1, several daily), 6 hrs. Ubaituba-Salvador, US$5, several daily.

Ilhéus, near the mouth of the Rio Cachoeira, 380 km. south of Salvador, serves a district which produces 65% of all Brazilian cocoa. Shipping lines call regularly. A bridge links the Pontal district (airport) to the mainland. Population, 108,000. The town is the scene of the famous novel by Jorge Amado, "Gabriela, Clove and Cinnamon". The local beaches are splendid (except those in the bay and close to town—polluted, and being dug up) and the place is highly recommended for a short stay. Among the churches to visit: Nossa Senhora da Vitória, in Alto da Vitória, built in 17th century to celebrate a victory over the Dutch; São Jorge, in city centre; and the cathedral of São Sebastião on sea shore. Tourist office on Av. Soares Lopes, near cathedral.

Hotels Hotel Barravento on Malhado beach, Rua N.S. das Graças, ask for the penthouse—usually no extra charge, C, including bath, breakfast and refrigerator; next door is *Motel Barravento*, D. *Britânia*, D, Rua 28 de Junho 16, and at 29 the *San Marino*, E, friendly, clean. *Lucas*, Rua 7 de Setembro 17, D, central, O.K.; *Central*, Araújo Pinho 115, E with bath no breakfast, adequate; *Vitória*, Rua Bento Berilo 95, T 231-4105, E without breakfast, poor value; *Pontal Praia*, Praia do Pontal, B, swimming pool; *Florida*, Rua General Câmara, E without bath; *Ilhéus Praia*, Praça D. Eduardo (on beach), B, pool, helpful, rec.; *Litorânea*, Rua Antônio Lavigne de Lemos 42; *Motel Cana Brava*, Km. 6 on Ilhéus-Olivença road; *Real*, Rua General Câmara 102, E with breakfast, near beach, friendly. *Rio Cachoeira*, road to Itabuna, Km. 7, pool, also good churrascaria. *Pousada G.G.*, Praça Cairu 18, E without breakfast (restaurant next door), clean, near beach. In Rua Carneiro da Rocha are *Tropical*, No. 129 and *Bahiano*, No. 94 (helpful, clean, friendly), each E, and two *dormitórios*. Plenty of cheap hotels near municipal bus station in centre.

Restaurants Luanda Beira Bahia, Av. Soares Lopes s/n, *Moqueca de Ouro. Cabana do Mirante*, Alto do Ceará, E, with good views. *Tokyo*, 2 de Julho, Japanese, very good, not cheap. At Pontal, *Cabana Cinco Estrellas*, excellent, cheap Bahian food. *Vesúvio*, Praça D. Eduardo, next to Cathedral, made famous by Amado's novel (see above), now Swiss-owned, very good but pricey. Local drink, coquinho, coconut filled with cachaça, only for the strongest heads! Also try suco de cacau at juice stands.

Local Festivals include Festa de São Sebastião (January 17-20), Carnival, Festa de São Jorge (April 23), Foundation day, June 28, and Festa do Cacau (October).

Buses Station is some way from centre, but Itabuna-Olivença bus goes through centre of Ilhéus. Several daily to Salvador, 7 hrs., US$6 (*leito* US$12, Expresso São Jorge); 0620 bus goes via Itaparica, leaving passengers at Bom Despacho ferry station on the island—thence 50-minute ferry to Salvador. To Itacaré, early a.m. and 1530, 4 hrs., US$2.50; to Eunápolis, 7 hrs., US$3.

Buses run every 30 mins. to **Itabuna** (32 km.; 130,000 people), the trading centre of the rich cocoa zone. (Ceplac runs tours to its model cocoa plantation between Itabuna and Ilhéus; it is possible to visit *fazendas*.) Bus from Salvador, 6½ hrs., US$4.50. Of the hotels, the *Príncipe, Lord* and *Itabuna Palace* (Av. Cinquentenário 1061, B, restaurant) are probably the best (*Rincão Gaúcho*, E, small, friendly, overlooking river; opposite Rodoviária is *Dormitório Rodoviária*, F, basic; several motels on the outskirts). The paved BA-415 links Itabuna to Vitória da Conquista (275 km.) on the BR-116. Ceplac installations at Km. 8 on the Itabuna-Ilhéus road show the whole processing of cocoa. Tours of cocoa plantations can be arranged through the *Ilhéus Praia* hotel; Jorge Amado's novel "The Violent Lands" deals with life on the cocoa plantations.

The beaches between Ilhéus and Olivença are good, e.g. Cururupe, and frequent buses run to Olivença. For the good beaches at Pontal, take "Barreira" bus and get off just past *Hotel Jardim Atlântico*.

About 400 km. south of Ilhéus on the coast is the old town of **Porto Seguro**, now developed for tourism (the airport has been enlarged to take jets). Direct buses from Rio, São Paulo and Salvador. (For the routes from Vitória **see page 281** and from Belo Horizonte **page 288**.) At Brazilian holiday times, all transport north or south should be booked well in advance.

It was N of the site of Porto Seguro that Cabral first landed in 1500; a cross marks the supposed site of the first mass in Brazil on road between Porto Seguro and Santa Cruz Cabrália. 23 km. to the N of Porto Seguro is Santa Cruz Cabrália (simple accommodation, good restaurant *Coqueiro Verde*—try *pitu*, a kind of crayfish); dugout ferry crosses the river, then a short walk to the beach at Santo André. Trips on the river can be made. Bicycles for hire at hardware shop, Dois de Julho 242, US$2 a day. In this area there are *borrachudos*, little flies that bite feet and ankles in the heat of the day; coconut oil keeps them off; at night mosquitoes can be a problem.

Across the Rio Buranhém (10 minutes, US$0.25, ferries take cars, every ½-hr. day and night), and a further 5 km. (US$0.30 in bus), is the village of Arraial da **Ajuda**; about 15 mins. walk from the beach (better for camping than Porto Seguro). Pilgrimage in August to the shrine of Nossa Senhora da Ajuda (interesting room in church, full of ex-voto offerings). Ajuda has become very popular with tourists and there are many *pousadas*, a good Japanese restaurant at Pasaje (just across the ferry), bars and small shops. Beach protected by coral reef. At Brazilian holiday times it is very crowded, and with the coastline up for sale, it may become overdeveloped in a few years. The beaches in this neighbourhood are splendid, for instance Pitinga, also protected by coral reef.

25 km. to the S of Porto Seguro and 15 km. from Ajuda is **Trancoso**, reached by bus from the other side of the Rio Buranhém, 3 a day, (US$0.80, 50 mins., last returns at 1530, more buses and colectivos in summer), by colectivo, hitch-hiking or by walking along the beach; the village is simple but also popular with tourists and many Europeans have built or bought houses there. There are good restaurants around the main square. Trancoso has a historic church. Colectivos run from Trancoso to Ajuda (US$1.20). Between Ajuda and Trancoso is the village of Rio da Barra.

Porto Seguro Hotels *Porto Seguro Praia*, 3 km. N of city on coast road, B; *Cabanas do Tio João*, BR-367, Km. 64, 2 km. N of Porto Seguro, a/c, pool, retaurant, English and French spoken, rec.; *Vela Branca*, Cidade Histórica, C, top of cliff, good; *Pousada Casa Azul*, 15 de Novembro, D with bath, swimming pool; *Pousada Coroa Vermelha*, Getúlio Vargas 12, E, with bath, clean and good, no breakfast, run by Dutchman; a number of cheap *pousadas* on Av. Getúlio Vargas, most without breakfast; *Mar Azul* at No. 109, E with bath, clean, friendly; *Pousada São Luiz*, E, rec. *Pousada do Cais*, Portugal 382, T 228-2121, C with bath, colonial house on sea-front, good; several others on same street; *Pousada Rio do Prado* (No. 236), rec., E with big breakfast; *Porto Brasília*, Praça Antonio Carlos Magalhães 234, E with breakfast, F without, clean, friendly; *Pousada Vera Cruz*, Av. 22 de Abril 100, E with bath, good breakfast, clean. *Pousada Navegante*, near port, rec. *Pensões* and *dormitorios* near the port are cheap; those near the bus station are dearer.

Ajuda Hotels *Pousada Le Cottage* (across ferry from Porto Seguro, but before Ajuda), French owner, Sr. Georges, D with bath, C in chalet; also here *Pousada Ivonnet*, by landing stage, E, good, clean, safe, use of kitchen; *Pousada Canto d'Alvorada*, on road to Ajuda, C in season, D out of season, Swiss run, 7 cabins, restaurant, washing facilities; *Thaina Plage*, D, reserved in São Paulo, T 011-533-5898, or in Paris T 43-26-31-41, and *Pousada Tororão*, D, rec.); *São João*, good set lunch, bungalows for rent, hot shower. *Pousada dos Guaiamuns*, on the road to Ajuda, E, very good, French owner is very knowledgeable; *Jardim Tropical*, hot showers, clean, good breakfast, E, rec.; also rec., *Flamboyant* and *Broadway*, E with bath, mosquito nets, breakfast, clean (on road to beach), and *Marimar*, F, garden, no breakfast, near church. Many rooms for rent (for days, weeks or months); best accommodation in private houses behind the church (F). Camping rec. at Arraial de Ajuda Praia, on beach, US$1 p.p.; also at Da Gringa, BR-367 (beach), and Mucugê, Ajuda.

Trancoso Hotels French-owned *Pousada do Gilberto*, E; *Pousada Miramar*, next to church (good view, hammock space); several other *pousadas*, mostly in E/F range (of which Henry Giese's *Pousada do Bosque*, Rua de Cuba, and Bianca and Jurgen's oriental bungalow (E) and dinner (US$2) are rec.); private houses, also houses for rent. *Pousada do Brasil* may allow free camping if you use its restaurant, its rooms in D range (on beach).

Porto Seguro Restaurants *Cruz de Malta*, Av. Getúlio Vargas 358, good seafood; *Preto Velho*, Praça da Bandeira, 30 (small helpings); *Arrecife*, good and cheap, near harbour. *Calda de Pau*, Av. Getúlio Vargas, rec.; *Umbertina*, same street, lunch only, good; *Anti-Caro*, Rua Assis Chateaubriand 26, restaurant (cheap and good) and antique shop; *Casa da Esquina*, very good, moderately priced. *Sambuca*, opp. bus station, good for pizza; *Travessia*, near ferry and bus station; Bahian food, OK, takes credit cards; bar opp. bus station very expensive; *O Circo*, good sandwiches.

Tourist Office Rua Dois de Julho 172, Porto Seguro, open daily 0800-2200. Public telephone, same street, No.71.

Buses from Porto Seguro: Salvador, daily, 12 hrs., US$10.50; Vitória, daily, 11 hrs.; Ilhéus daily 0730, 5½ hrs., US$4; Eunápolis, many, 1½ hrs., US$1. For Rio direct buses (São Geraldo), leaving at 1745, US$17, 18 hrs. For Minas Gerais, take a bus to Nanuque on the Bahia MG border, then change to Teôfilo Otôni. To São Paulo direct, 1045, 25 hrs. US$24; other services via Eunápolis or Itabuna (5 hrs., US$4). All now leave from terminal by boat dock.

Air Rio Sul and Nordeste from Rio (Santos Dumont), one stop, 3 hrs., daily, about US$70.

North from Salvador

The paved BA-099 coast road from near the airport is known as the Estrada do Coco (coconut road) and for 50 km. passes some beautiful beaches. The best known from south to north are Ipitanga (with its reefs), Buraquinho, Jauá, Arembepe, Guarajuba, Itacimirim, Castelo Garcia D'Avila (with its 16th century fort) and Forte. Buses serve most of these destinations.

Some 50 km. to the north of Salvador is the former fishing village of **Arembepe**, now a quiet resort. *Pousada da Fazenda* on the beach, thatched huts, good seafood, not cheap. *Privê* seafood restaurant, very good. Best beaches 2 km. N of town. Bus from Terminal Francês, Salvador, every 2 hours, 1½ hrs., US$0.60, last one back at 1700; or from Itapoan. Buses from Salvador run to Praia do Forte (75 km.), where there are Hotels *Club Maritime* (5-star, L, sports facilities, good meals), *Praia do Forte*, L, and a few *pousadas* (e.g. *Ouxi Mari*, clean, good breakfast, shower). There is also a fishing village, a ruin and turtles.

247 km. N of Salvador, on BR-101, is Estância, with pleasant hotels: *Turista*, E, and *Dom Bosco*, opposite, E, slightly cheaper, bath and breakfast, both pleasant.

Monte Santo About 270 km. N of Feira da Santana, via the direct BR-116 road to Fortaleza (partly paved but bad between Petrolina and Juazeiro del Norte), is the famous hill shrine of Monte Santo in the Sertão, reached by 3½ km. of steps cut into the rocks of the Serra do Picaraça (about 45 mins'. walk each way—set out early). This is the scene of pilgrimages and great religious devotion during Holy Week. The shrine was built by an Italian who had a vision of the cross on the mountain in 1765. One block north of the bottom of the stairs is the Museu do Sertão, with pictures from the 1897 Canudos rebellion. **Canudos** itself is 100 km. away; religious rebels led by the visionary Antônio Conselheiro defeated three expeditions sent against them in 1897 before being overwhelmed. These events are the theme of two great books: *Os Sertões* (Revolt in the Backlands) by Euclides da Cunha, and *La Guerra del Fin del Mundo* (The War of the End of the World) by the Peruvian writer Mario Vargas Llosa. The Rio Vaza Barris, which runs through Canudos has been dammed, and the town has been moved to Nova Camidos by the dam. Part of the old town is still located 10 km. West.

Hotels *Grapiuna*, Praça Monsenhor Berenguer 401 (T 275-1157), E-D, with bath (cheaper without downstairs), rec.; *Santa Cruz*, opp. Banco do Brasil, E, shared bath, basic but clean; pleasant bars. At Euclides da Cunha, on the BR-116 and 39 km. from Monte Santo, are *Hotel Lua*, simple and *Hotel Conselheiro*.

Buses Direct from Salvador and São Paulo (since the paving of BR-324).

Aracaju, capital of Sergipe, 327 km. N of Salvador, founded 1855, clean and lively, has a population of 288,000. It stands on the right bank of the Rio Sergipe, about 10 km. from its mouth, and can be reached from Maceió or Salvador by road. The city—unusually for Brazil—is laid out in the grid pattern. It has a beautiful park, clean streets (some in centre reserved to pedestrians); there is a handicraft centre, the Centro do Turismo, open 0900-1300, 1500-1900, in a restored colonial building on Praça Olímpio Campos, the cathedral square. A 16-km. road leads to the fine Atalaia beach: oil-drilling rigs offshore. There is an even better beach, Nova Ataláia, on Ilha de Santa Luzia across the river, reached by boat from the ferry station. On December 8 there are both Catholic (Nossa Senhora da Conceição) and Umbanda religious festivals.

Hotels *Parque dos Coqueiros*, A, Ataláia beach, large pool, luxurious and attractive; *Praia Avenida*, very clean and friendly, B; *Brasília*, Rua Laranjeiras 580, T 222-5112, D, good value, good breakfasts; *Serigy*, Rua Santo Amaro 269 (T 222-1210), D, comfortable, no hot water in rooms; *Turista*, opp. Rodoviária in centre, E, friendly; *Oasis*, Rua São Cristóvão 466 in centre, E with good breakfast, rec.; *Guanabara*, noisy, cold water in rooms, Rua Florentino Menezes 161 (near market), E, good meals. Many cheap hotels in Rua Gen. Caru and Rua Santa Rosa.

Camping Camping Clube do Brasil site at Ataláia beach.

Restaurant Tropeiro, on boulevard, seafood and live music, highly rec.

Tourist Information Emsetur, Av. Barão de Maroim 593, near Praça Fausto Cardoso, maps of Aracaju, Laranjeiras, São Cristovão. *Artesanato* interesting: pottery figures and lace particularly. Fair in Praça Tobias Barreto every Sun.

15 km. from Aracaju is *Laranjeiras*, reached by São Pedro bus, from old Rodoviária in centre, 30 mins-1 hr. A small pleasant town, with a ruined church on a hill, it has two museums (Museu Afro-Brasileiro and Centro de Cultura João Ribeiro), and the Capela de Sant'Aninha with a wooden altar inlaid with gold.

São Cristóvão, SW of Aracaju on the road to Salvador, an unspoiled colonial town, was the old state capital of Sergipe, founded in 1590 by Cristóvão de Barros. Worth visiting are the Museu de Arte Sacra e Histórico de Sergipe, the Assembly building, the Provincial Palace and five churches including Misericórdia and Nossa Senhora da Vitória (all closed Mon.). Outdoor arts festival in 2nd half of October. Buses (São Pedro) from Aracaju, from old Rodoviária in centre, 30 mins.-1 hr. (No hotels, but families rent rooms near the bus station.)

Between Aracaju and the next port to the north—Maceió—is the mouth of the São Francisco river, whose great Paulo Afonso falls upstream (see page 360) can be visited from Maceió or (if travelling from Aracaju to Maceió by bus) from Penedo by river and bus. The BR-101 between Aracaju and Maceió is now paved, crossing the São Francisco by bridge between Propriá and Porto Real do Colégio.

Penedo, in Alagoas near the mouth of the River São Francisco, 451 km. from Salvador (US$9, 10 hrs., by daily bus at 0830; 115 km. from Maceió), is a charming town, with a nice waterfront park with stone walkways and walls. Long two-masted sailing vessels cruise on the river (they can be rented for US$2.40 per hour, regardless of the number of people, possibly stopping to swim or visit beaches on islands in the river). Frequent launches across the river to Neópolis, 25 mins., US$0.45. Also half-hourly car ferry (US$0.50; take care when driving on and off). Daily street market. Good hammocks. Buses from Maceió,US$2, 4 hrs. One bus to Aracaju daily, 0600.

Hotels *São Francisco*, Av. Floriano Peixoto, D, rec. except for poor restaurant; *Pousada Colonial*, Praça 12 de Abril 21, E with bath, clean, good cheap restaurant, most rooms with view of Rio São Francisco; *Turista*, Rua Siqueira Campos 148, E with bath, rec., close to bus station; in same street *Majestic* and *Victoria*, both E; *Imperio*, Av. Floriano Peixoto, E. Good **restaurant**, *Forte da Rocheira*, Rua da Rocheira, good food, especially ensopada de jacaré (alligator stew).

Tourist Office in Casa da Aposentadoria, Praça Barão de Penedo, helpful.

Maceió, capital of Alagoas state, is about 287 km. NE of Aracaju by road, and 244 km. S of Recife. It is mainly a sugar port, although there are tobacco exports handled also, with a lighthouse on an eminence built in a residential area of town (Farol), about one km. from the sea. Population of Maceió is 376,000.

Two of the city's old buildings, the Government Palace and the church of Bom Jesus dos Mártires (covered in tiles), are particularly interesting, as is the recently restored Cathedral. The Associação Comercial has a museum, near the beach, in a beautiful, though deteriorating building. There is an enjoyable lagoon (Lagoa do Mundaú), 2 km. S at **Pontal da Barra**: excellent shrimp and fish at its small restaurants and handicraft stalls. It is a ten-minute taxi ride (US$2.50) from the town centre (or take "Ponta da Terra" bus) to Pajuçara beach, where there are a nightly craft market and several good hotels and restaurants. The beaches, some of the finest and most popular in Brazil (such as Jatiúca, Cruz das Almas—both good for surfing, Jacarecica, Guaxuma, Mirante, Garça Torta, Riacho Doce, all within 30 mins. taxi ride from town; buses to the last two from terminal, US$0.65, or local "Fátima" bus, US$0.10), have in most cases a protecting coral reef a kilometre or so out, but it is said that underwater reef life is not plentiful, and visibility is poor. Beaches fronting the old city and between Salgema terminal and the modern port area (Trapiche, Subra) are too polluted for swimming.

Jangadas take passengers to a natural pool 2 km. off Pajuçara beach (Piscina Natural de Pajuçara), at low tide you can stand on the sand and rock reef (beware of sunburn). *Jangadas* cost US$2.15 per person per day (or about US$9.25 to have a jangada to yourself)—negotiable (at weekends lots of jangadas anchor at the reef selling food and drink). From Maceió, a ferry crosses the lagoon to Coqueira Seca (30 mins., US$0.20), a small pretty fishing village.

Local Holidays August 27 (Nossa Senhora dos Prazeres); Sept. 16 (Freedom of Alagoas); December 8 (Nossa Senhora da Conceição); Christmas Eve; New Year's Eve, half-day.

Hotels It is better to stay on Praia Pajuçara than on Praias Avenida or Sobral: many hotels on Av. Dr Antônio Gouveia and Rua Jangadeiros Alagoanos, Pajuçara. *Othon*, Av Antônio Gouveia 1113, Pajuçara, good cinema downstairs; *Verde Mar*, same street, No. 1, D with bath, a/c, hot water, TV, T 231-2669, very good. Good *pousadas* can be found in the Pajuçara beach district, not too expensive; *e.g. Buon Giorno*, Jangadeiros Alagoanos 1437, 1 block from beach, T 231-7577, D, a/c, fridge, clean, English-speaking owner, rec.; *Laguna Praia*, same street No. 1231, clean, highly rec.; *Pousada Rex*, E with bath, clean, friendly, honest, helpful, highly rec. (esp. the breakfast); also *Pousada Saveiro* and *Pousada Tropical*, both E, on beach; *Pousada Pajuçara*, F, Jangadeiros Alagoanos 1163, clean, friendly, rec.; *Pousada Sete Palmeiras Coqueteiras*, E, rec.; *Hotel do Mar*, Av. R. Kennedy 1447, D, good. *Sol de Verão*, Rua Eng. Mário do Gusmão, Ponta Verde, E with bath, F in small rooms without, clean, friendly. **Youth hostel** *Nossa Casa*, Rua Prefeito Abdon Arroxelas 177, Ponta Verde, T 231-2246. *Jatiúca*, Lagoa da Anta 220, L, a/c, on the beach, swimming pool, heavily booked, good breakfasts, but small rooms with thin walls; *Hospedaria de Turismo Costa Azul*, Av. João Darino and Manoel Gonçalves Filho 280, T 231-6281, E, clean, hot shower, fan, English spoken, discounts over a week.

Luxor, Av. Duque de Caxias 2076, first class, 4 star, L; behind is *Praia Avenida*, Artur Jucá 1250, 2 star, C, clean, comfortable; *Sorbal Praia*, Av. Assis Chateaubriand 8022 (Praia do Sorbal), C, shower, a/c, excellent restaurant, pool, reductions out of season; *Beiriz*, Rua João Pessoa 290, comfortable, E-C, good value (except for breakfast), pool; *Parque*, Praça Dom Pedro II 73, D, a/c, good, central, comfortable; *Golf*, Rua Prof. Domingos Moeda 38A (near Praça D. Pedro II), clean, F; *Pousada Sol e Mar*, Av. Rosa da Fonseca s/n, E with bath, helpful owners, safe, rec.; *Florida*, Rua Senador Luiz Torres 126, central, E with bath but without breakfast, noisy on street side, not safe, does not charge by the hour (unlike most other cheap hotels). Cheap hotels (mostly without windows) in Rua Barão de Ataláia, e.g. *Pajuçara*, F, clean, friendly; *Rodoviária* (friendly), F. *Sany*, next to bus station, F with shower and fan, clean; *Reencontro*, next door, F. Avoid both hotels *Maceió*.

Camping There is a Camping Clube do Brasil site on Jacarecica beach, a 15-min. taxi drive from the town centre. Camping also possible on the Avenida beach, near the *Hotel Atlântico*.

Electric Current 220 volts A.C., 60 cycles.

Restaurants *Bem*, Praia de Cruz das Almas, good seafood and service; *Ao Lagostão*, Av. Duque de Caxias 1348, seafood, fixed price (expensive) menu; *O Gaúcho*, Av. Duque de Caxias 1466, good Brazilian food from all regions; *Pizza Nostra*, Av. João Davino, nr. Praia de Jatiúca, excellent pasta; *Bar das Ostras*, Rua Cruzeiro do Sul 487, Vergel do Lago, expensive but good. *New Hakata*, Av. Assis Chateaubriand 3146, Praia do Sobral, Japanese, quite good; *Passaporte Santa Lucia*, Praia da Avenida, good cheap sandwiches, juices on beach. Vegetarian: *O Natural*, Rua Libertadora Alagoana (Rua da Praia) 112; *Nativa*, Osvaldo Sarmento 56; *Chegança*, Rua do Imperador 342A; *Calabar*, Antônio Gouveia 293, Pajuçara, live music nightly after 2100; *O Dragão*, Antônio Gouveia 21, Pajuçara; *Paraíso*, Av. Antônio Gouveia 631, Pajuçara. Italian and Arab cooking at *Comes e Bebes*, Antônio Gouveia 943; *Mello's Bar*, Rua Epaminondas Gracindo 194 (continuation of Jangadeiros Alagoanas, at Pajuçara), excellent food and value; many food stalls (barracas) on Praia Pajuçara, e.g. *Sete Coqueiros* and *Pedra Virada* for shrimp. At Ponto da Barra, on the lagoon side of the city, *Alipio*, and many others. Good eating places on the road to Marechal Deodoro and at Praia do Francés. Local specialities include oysters, pitu, a crayfish (now becoming scarce), and sururu, a kind of cockle. Local icecream, Shups, has been rec.

Entertainment Teatro Deodoro, Praça Marechal Deodoro, in centre; Cinema São Luiz, Rua do Comércio, in centre; the other cinemas tend to be fleapits. *Bar Chapéu de Couro*, José Carneiro 338, Ponto da Barra, is a popular music bar for young people. Many bars at end of Av. Roberto Kennedy by Parque de Sete Coqueiros, e.g. *Bar Lampião* (or *Tropical*), R. Kennedy 2585, food and *forró* every night.

Museums Instituto Histórico, Rua João Pessoa 382, good small collection of Indian artefacts and Lampião relics. Museu de Arte Sacra, same street (closed indefinitely). Museu Folclórico Theo Brandão, in the old University building, Mon.-Fri., 0800-1200, 1400-1700, Sat., 1400-1700, free, Av. Duque de Caxias 1490, interesting local artefacts.

Exchange Banco do Brasil, etc. Open 1000 to 1630. Aeroturismo, Rua Barão de Penedo 61 or Pajuçara Turismo on same road, which begins opposite Ferroviária at Praça Valente de Lima (but not named on all maps). Good rates at *Luxor Hotel*.

Cables Embratel, Rua João Pessoa 57, Praça Dom Pedro II 84. Telegráfico Nacional.

Tourist Information Ematur, Av. Siquera Campos (Estádio Rei Pelé), 2nd floor, T 223-6868; at Largo do Livramento, on Av. Senador Mendonça, and on ground floor of *Hotel Othon*. Also at airport and at Rodoviária. Helpful, has good maps.

Tourist Agencies Alatur, Duque de Caxias 1416; Dreamar Turismo, Av. Cons. Lourenço Albuquerque 261; Lysturismo, Duque de Caxias 1338.

Buses Rodoviária is 5 km. from centre; take bus marked "Ouro Preto p/centro" or "Serraria Mercado" which has a circular route from centre to suburbs and bus terminal (taxi quicker—all local buses are very crowded, taxi to Pajuçara, US$2.15). Bus to Recife, 20 a day (but buses full), 4 hrs., US$4; to Salvador, 9-10 hrs., 4 a day (3 at night), US$8.50. **N.B.** If travelling to Salvador, or if booking through Bom Fim, check all details on your ticket; they are not reliable. To Penedo, several, 4 hrs, US$3.

Airport 20 km. from centre, taxi about US$8.50. Buses to airport from near *Hotel Beiriz*, Rua João Pessoa 290, signed "Rio Largo"; alight at Tabuleiro dos Matrices, then 7-8 min. walk to airport, bus fare US$0.25. Tourist flights over the city.

Excursion By launch or bus (22 km. South) past Praia do Francés to the attractive colonial town and former capital of Alagoas, **Marechal Deodoro**, with the fine old churches of São Francisco, Terceira Ordem (being restored) and Rosário. There is also the State Museum of Sacred Art, open Tues.-Sun., 0900-1700. The town is the birthplace of Marshal Deodoro da Fonseca, founder of the Republic; the modest house where he was born is on the Rua Marechal Deodoro, close to the waterfront, open Tues.-Sun. The cleanliness of this little town is exemplary: on Mondays everyone is required by local law to sweep the streets. The trip by launch, leaving from Trapiche on the lagoon, is very pleasant indeed. Good local lacework. *Restaurant São Roque*, simple but good. A recommended excursion is to take Real Alagoas bus from Rodoviária to Marechal Deodoro (every 30 mins., US$ 0.45, 1 hr.) then after visiting the town spend some time (beware the *borrachudos* behind the beach) at beautiful **Praia do Francês**, the northern half of the beach is protected by a reef, the southern half is open to the surf (restaurant and guest house *Tortuga*, rooms E, on beach; recommended restaurants *Panela Mâgica* and *Chez Patrick*; try *agulhas fritas* on the beach), where Quatro Rodas is to build a new hotel; many existing ones including are *O Pescador* and *Pousada das Águas*, both D; *Agua Prai*, E, good, clean. Return to Maceió by bus (last one leaves 1800) or *kombi* van, 20 mins. Further out from Maceió is the beach of Barra de São Miguel, entirely protected by reef, with *Pousada da Barra*, good, new, and *Village Praia Hotel*, C-B, pool, restaurant, excursions to other beaches.

There are many interesting stopping points along the coast between Maceió and Recife, such as Barra de Santo Antônio, 45 km. N, a busy fishing village, with beach on a narrow peninsula, a canoe-ride away; *Hotel Peixada da Rita*, E, good food in the restaurant. Also Japaratinga (*Hotel Solmar*, F, 2 rooms, basic, good restaurant—bus from Maceió at 0515) and São José da Coroa Grande (*Hotel Lar Ana Luiza*, E (cheaper without breakfast); *Hotel do Francês*, D, further from beach; a few families rent rooms); at low tide watch colourful fish in the rock pools on the reef. Along this coast, the protecting reef offshore prevents garbage and silt from being taken out to sea at high tide, so water is muddy and polluted. At Paripueira, 40 mins. bus ride from Maceió (Rodoviária) is the *Paripueira Praia Hotel*, E, good value, very clean, friendly.

The Falls of **Paulo Afonso**, once one of the great falls of the world but now exploited for hydroelectric power, are 270 km. up the São Francisco river, which drains a valley 3 times the size of Great Britain. There are 2,575 km. of river above the Falls to its source in Minas Gerais. Below the Falls is a deep, rock gorge through which the water rushes. The lands around are a national park, an oasis of trees and the lake amid a desert of brown scrub and cactus. The best time to visit the Falls is in the rainy season (Jan.-Feb.); only then does much water pass over them, as almost all the flow now goes through the power plant. The best view is from the northern (Alagoas) bank. The Falls are in a security area; no admission for pedestrians, so need to visit by car or taxi (US$4.50 an hour). Admission is from 0800 onwards, but it depends on the availability of guides, without whom one cannot enter; go to the tourist information office in the centre of the town and sign up for a tour of the hydroelectric plant, 2 hrs., US$5.75 per car.

There are the *Hotel Casande* (B), *Grand Hotel de Paulo Afonso* (B, a/c, TV, pool) and a guest house (apply for room in advance) at the Falls. The town of Paulo Afonso (35,000 people) is some distance from the Falls, reached by paved road from Recife, bus, 7 hrs., US$5.50, from Salvador, bus (475 km., 160 paved, the rest bad), or from Maceió (306 km.) via Palmeira dos Índios, partially paved. Hotels *Guadalajara* and *Paulo Afonso*, friendly, cheap; *Belvedere*, D, a/c, swimming pool and *Palace*, D with bath, a/c, swimming pool, "best value in town", next door to each other on Rua André Falcão; *Hospedagem Lima*, very basic, F, near *Hotel Guadalajara*; *Hotel Dormitório*, F—all hotels within walking distance of bus terminal. Plenty of restaurants, e.g. *Kilanche*, next to Tourist Office. For information about Paulo Afonso and the *sertão*, ask the Italian fathers (Mario, Antonio and Riccardo) who are most helpful. Handicrafts (embroidery, fabrics) from Núcleo de Produção Artesanal, Av. Contorno s/n. It is possible, with plenty of time, to go upstream from Penedo (**see page 357**) to about Pão de Açúcar or Piranhas, but on to the Falls is complicated and involves non-connecting buses. **Piranhas**, 80 km. from Paulo Afonso (road almost completely paved, buses difficult), is a charming town with good beaches on the Rio São Francisco; it has picturesque houses and an old railway station which is now a *Pousada* (3-4 rooms, F, restaurant) with a small museum (photographs of the severed head of Lampião, the Brazilian "Robin Hood"). If you have a car, you can drive south from Paulo Afonso to Jeremoaba (76 km.), then west to Canudos (111 km.—**see page 356**).

Travel on the River São Francisco (see page 294). The river is navigable above the Falls from above the twin towns (linked by a bridge) of **Juazeiro** (62,000 people) in Bahia, and **Petrolina** (74,000), in Pernambuco (buses from Salvador, 6 hrs., also from Recife, Fortaleza, Teresina) to Pirapora in Minas Gerais, linked by road to the Belo Horizonte-Brasília highway. Like Pirapora, Petrolina is famous for the production of *carrancas* (boat figureheads, mostly grotesque) of wood or ceramic. River transport has changed rapidly in the past few years; for information telephone Juazeiro (075) 811-2465. On the road between Juazeiro and Feira de Santana (BR-407 and 324) is Senhor do Bonfim, a busy market town with lots of life (also banks and post office).

John Hale writes: Juazeiro and Petrolina are thriving towns compared with many others on the upper São Francisco. Petrolina has its own airport and close to this is the small Museu do Sertão—relics of rural life in the North-East and the age of the "coronéis" and the bandit Lampião. *Hotel Newman*, Av. Souza Filho 444, E; *Pousada da Carranca*, BR-122, km. 3, D; *Espacial*, EF Leste Brasileiro km. 2, E; *Grande Rio*, Rua Padre Praga, B; and *Restaurante Rancho Grande*. *Restaurante Panorâmico*, the only one on the river front, is good. Juazeiro is the poorer of the two cities. Hotels: *Grande Hotel*, Rua Pititinga, *Vitória*, and *União* (rec.) and *Oliveira*, the last two in Rua Conselheiro Saraiva. *Hotel Pousada de Juazeiro*, 6 km. S on BR-407, C with bath, a/c, pool, restaurant, bar, pleasant. Unique restaurant known as the *Vaporzinho* is high and dry on the river front, a side-wheel paddle steamer (poor food), the *Saldanha Marinho*, built at Sabará in 1852. Market on Fri. and Sat.

Margy Levine and Jordan Young (Lexington, MA) write:
There are three new wineries in the area: one in Casa Nova (Bahia); Ouro Verde in Lagoa Grande (Pernambuco); and Fazenda Milano in Santa Maria da Boa Vista (Pernambuco), on the north shore of the Rio São Francisco. Fazenda Milano (24 km. from Lagoa Grande, towards Santa Maria da Boa Vista) was the first winery in the north-east, and makes wine from European grapes, with 150 hectares of vines. Owned by Forestier, a winemaker from the south, they make red, white and rosé, blended and varietals. You can visit the winery on Thursdays, if you call in advance on (081) 961-4669 or, in Recife, (081) 251-2200. Wine can be bought at US$3 for 3 bottles. When you get to the Fazenda Milano sign on the Lagoa Grande-Santa Maria road, turn south towards the river, and drive 8 km. on a dirt road to the gate.

About 244 km. N of Maceió and 835 km. N of Salvador is

Recife (Pernambuco), founded on reclaimed land by the Dutch prince Maurice of Nassau in 1627 after his troops had burnt Olinda, the original capital, is the capital of Pernambuco state and the fourth largest city in Brazil, with about 1.8 million people. It consists of three portions, all on islands: Recife proper, Santo Antônio, and Boa Vista. The three districts are connected by bridges across the rivers Capibaribe and Beberibe. Olinda, the old capital, is only 6 km. to the North (see page 367).

Churches The best of them are the churches of São Francisco de Assis (1612), on Rua do Imperador; São Pedro dos Clérigos in São José district (1782, for its façade, its fine wood sculpture and a splendid *trompe l'oeil* ceiling, open Tues.-Fri. 0800-1130, 1400-1630, Sat. 0800-1200; Santo Antônio (1753), in Praça da Independência, rebuilt in 1864; Conceição dos Militares, in Rua Nova (1708), grand ceiling and a large 18th century primitive mural of the battle of Guararapes (museum next door), open Mon.-Fri., 0700-1100, 1300-1600, Sat. 0700-1200; Nossa Senhora do Carmo, Praça do Carmo, (1675), open Mon.-Fri. 0800-1200, 1400-1800; Madre de Deus (1706), in the district of Recife, with a splendid high altar, and sacristy; the Pilar church (1680), Rua do Pilar; the Espírito Santo (1642), the original church of the Jesuits, in Santo Antônio district; Santo Antônio do Convento de São Francisco (1606; beautiful Portuguese tiles), in the Rua do Imperador; the Capela Dourada (Golden Chapel, 1697), in Rua do Imperador (the finest sight of all, 0800-1130 and 1400-1700, Sat. 0800-1130: no flash photography; it is through the Museu Franciscano de Arte Sacra); S. José do Ribamar (19th century), in São José. There are many others. Most of them are closed to visitors on Sunday, because of services.

A few km. S of the city, a little beyond Boa Viagem and the airport, on Guararapes hill, is the historic church of Nossa Senhora das Prazeres, open daily 0800-1700. It was here, in 1648-9, that two Brazilian victories led to the end of the 30-year Dutch occupation of the North-East in 1654. The church was built by the Brazilian commander in 1656 to fulfil a vow. Boa Viagem's own fine church dates from 1707.

Other Attractions You may be able to visit Fort Brum (1626), which is an army museum. You can certainly visit the fort of Cinco Pontas (with Museu da Cidade do Recife—cartographic history of the settlement of Recife—open Mon.-Fri. 0900-1800, Sat.-Sun. 1400-1800, free), built by the Dutch in 1630 and altered by the Portuguese in 1677. Visit the city markets in the São José and

Santa Rita sections. Go fishing on log rafts—*jangadas*—at Boa Viagem with a fisherman who charges US$2. Visit sugar plantations in interior (though few tour agencies offer such trips), try Sevagtur, Tel. 341-3956, in Casa da Cultura.

Boa Viagem, now a southern suburb, is the finest residential and hotel quarter. The 8 km. promenade commands a striking view of the Atlantic, but the beach is crowded at weekends. The main square has a good market Sats., with *forró* being danced. Good restaurants along sea shore. Bus from centre, take any marked "Boa Viagem"; from Nossa Senhora do Carmo, take buses marked "Piedade", "Candeias" or "Aeronautica" - they go parallel to the beach all the way to Praça Boa Viagem (at Av. Boa Viagem 500). Back to centre take buses marked "CDU" from the main road one block from the beach.

The artists' and intellectuals' quarter is based on the Pátio de São Pedro, the square round São Pedro dos Clérigos (see under **Churches**). Folk music and poetry shows in the square on Fri., Sat. and Sun. evenings and there are pleasant little restaurants, with good atmosphere, at Nos. 44, 46 and 47, and No. 20 *Caldeira de Cana e Petisqueira Banguê*. The square is an excellent shopping centre for typical North-East craftware. Not far away is the Praça do Sebo, where the city's second-hand booksellers concentrate; this Mercado de Livros Usados is off the Rua da Roda, behind the Edifício Santo Albino, near the corner of Av. Guararapes and Rua Dantas Barreto.

The former municipal prison has now been made into a cultural centre, the Casa da Cultura, with many cells converted into art or souvenir shops and with areas for exhibitions and shows, and the Museu de Imagem e Som, open Tues.-Sun., 1300-1900, (also public conveniences). Local dances such as the *ciranda*, *forró* and *bumba-meu-boi* are held as tourist attractions on Mon., Wed. and Fri. at 1700 (but may not happen). Among other cultural centres are Recife's three traditional theatres, Santa Isabel (Praça da República, open to visitors 0800-1200, 1400-1700), Parque (Rua do Hospício 81, Boa Vista, newly restored and beautiful, open 0800-1200, 1400-1800) and Apolo (Rua do Apolo 121, open 0800-1200, 1400-1700).

The State Museum, Av. Rui Barbosa 960, Graças (closed Mon.), has excellent paintings by the 19th-century landscape painter, Teles Júnior. The Museu do Homen do Nordeste, Av. 17 de Agosto 2223, Casa Forte (open Tues., Wed., Fri. 1100-1700; Thurs. 0800-1700; Sat. Sun. and holidays 1300-1700) comprises the Popular Art Museum, containing ceramic figurines (including some by Mestre Vitalino and Zé Caboclo); the Museu do Açúcar, which contains models of colonial mills, collections of antique sugar bowls and much else; the Museum of Anthropology, the Nabuco Museum (at No. 1865) and the modern museum of popular remedies, Farmacopéia Popular. Take the "Dois Irmãos" bus (check that it's the correct one, with "Rui Barbosa" posted in window, as there are two—one for each brother, we suppose) from in front of the Banorte building near the Post Office on Guararapes, half-hour ride 10 km. outside the city to the zoo (US$0.20, not very good) and Botanical Gardens; it passes the museum complex, and together with the zoo they make a pleasant day's outing. Also the Museu do Trem, Praça Visconde de Mauá, small but interesting, especially the Garrett steam locomotive (open Tues.-Fri., 1000-1200, 1300-1700, Sat.-Sun., 1400-1800). The first Brazilian printing press was installed in 1706 and Recife claims to publish the oldest daily newspaper in South America, *Diário de Pernambuco*, founded 1825. Museu da Abolição (of Slavery), Rua Benfica 150, Madalena, is worth a visit, in an early 19th-century tiled house, once owned by the abolitionist João Alfredo, open Mon.-Fri., 1000-1200 and 1400-1700. You may like to visit Cerámica Brennand, a factory in the western suburbs at Várzea, 16 km. from the centre, on the Camaragibe road (take a taxi, or walk the 3 km. along Rua Gastão Vidigal—past hotels *Costa Azul* and *Tropical*—from the end of the bus line along Av. Caxangá). They make ceramic tiles, and one of the brothers is a sculptor of idiosyncratic works on display, for those interested in the wilder shores of artistic endeavour. Entry is free, and it is very friendly. They also have a shop at Av. Conselheiro Aguiar 2966, loja 4, convenient for Boa Viagem.

Local Holidays January 1 (Universal Brotherhood). June 24 (São João). July 16 (Nossa Senhora do Carmo, patron saint of the city). São João, though cancelled by the Pope, is still celebrated with bonfires and fireworks on June 24 all over the State of Pernambuco—and, indeed, throughout Brazil. December 8 (Nossa Senhora da Conceição).

Carnival The carnival groups dance at the doors of all the churches they pass; they usually go to the Church of Nossa Senhora do Rosário dos Pretos, patron saint of the slaves, before proceeding in procession into the down-town areas. A small car at the head bears the figure of some animal; it is followed by the king and queen under a large, showy umbrella. The *bahianas,* who wear snowy-white embroidered skirts, dance in single file on either side of the king and queen. Next comes the *dama do passo* carrying a small doll, or *calunga.* After the *dama* comes the *tirador de loas*: he chants to the group which replies in chorus, and last comes a band of local percussion instruments.

Still flourishing is the dance performance of the *caboclinhos.* The groups wear traditional Indian garb: bright feathers round their waists and ankles, colourful cockades, bead and animal-teeth necklaces, a dazzle of medals on their red tunics. The dancers beat out the rhythm with bows and arrows; others of the group play primitive musical instruments, but the dance is the thing: spinning, leaping, and stooping with almost mathematical precision.

There is a *pre-carnavalesca* week, followed by the main days Sunday to Tuesday; on the Saturday the *bloco* "Galo da Madrugada" officially opens Carnival (wild and lively), see local press for routes and times. The groups taking part are *maracatu, caboclinhos, trocas, blocos, ursos, caboclos de lança, escolas de samba* and *frevo* (the costumes are better than the music). Usually they start from Av. Conde da Boa Vista and progress along Rua do Hospício, Rua da Imperatriz, Ponte da Boa Vista, Praça da Independência, Rua 1° de Março and Rua do Imperador. During Carnival (and on a smaller scale throughout the year) the Casa de Cultura has *frevo* demonstrations where visitors can learn some steps of this unique dance of Pernambuco (check local press for details of "Frevioca" truck and *frevo* orchestras during Carnival in the Pátio de São Pedro). The best place to see the groups is from the balconies of *Hotel do Parque.*

In the "Festivais Juninos", the June *festas* of São João and São Pedro, the *forró* is danced. This dance, now popular throughout the North-East, is believed to have originated when the British builders of the local railways held parties that were "for all".

Hotels (for Olinda hotels **see page 368**)

		Price (US$)		
Name	Address	Single	Double	Stars
Recife Palace*	Av. Boa Viagem 4070	100	110	5
Quatro Rodas (Olinda)*	Av. José Augusto Moreira 2200 (Olinda)	78	87	5
Miramar‡	Rua dos Navegantes 363 (Boa Viagem)	83	92	5
Internacional Othon Palace*	Av. Boa Viagem 3722	59	66	4
Quatro de Outubro	Rua Floriano Peixoto 141	38	43	3
Mar‡	Rua Barão de Souza Leão 451 (Boa Viagem)	85	102	4
Vila Rica*	Av. Boa Viagem 4308	72	78	4
Jangadeiro*	Av. Boa Viagem 3114	50	56	4
Savaroni*	Av. Boa Viagem 3772	60	70	4
Pousada Casa Forte	Av. 17 de Agosto 735	28	32	3
Do Sol*	Av. Boa Viagem 987	64	69	3
Casa Grande e Senzala‡	Av. Conselheiro Aguiar 5000 (Boa Viagem)	43	47	3
Boa Viagem‡	Av. Boa Viagem 5000	55	60	4
Grande	Av. Martins de Barros 593	40	44	4
Canto do Mar‡	Av. Barão de Souza Leão 400 (Boa Viagem)	56	61	3
Park‡	Rua dos Navegantes 9 (Boa Viagem)	58	64	3

*On beach ‡Near beach

There are several other hotels and pensions. *Recife,* Rua do Imperador 310, T 2240799, E with bath (cheaper without), central, pleasant; *Treze de Maio,* Rua do Hospício 659, E with breakfast; next door (and better) is *Suiça,* at No. 687, E, and up, safe parking, clean, but a bit run-down, friendly; *Parque,* Rua do Hospício 51, good value, F with cooked breakfast, noisy, safe, rec., good bars and restaurants nearby; *Lido,* Rua do Riachuelo 547, E, good breakfast, hot water, friendly, rec.; *Pousada Paris*, Rua do Riachuelo 630, Boa Vista, T 231-4627, E, good breakfast, fan, basic but pleasant. *América*, Praça Maciel Pinheiro 48, Boa Vista, 2-star, D with a/c (cheaper without), clean, quiet; *Palácio*, Rua Henriques Dias 181, Boa Vista, D, T 221-0222, shower and breakfast, quiet, friendly, a/c, mangoes in the patio. *Nassau*, Largo do Rosário 253, E, clean, hot showers, but a bit noisy (breakfast only, served on 7th floor, with a balcony overlooking the city). *Sete de Setembro*, Matias de Albuquerque 318, E including breakfast, rec., but not very clean or quiet; *Central*, Av. Manoel Barba 209, D without bath, clean; *Hospedaria Ysa* (ex-*Rigor*), Praça 17, central, F, including breakfast, clean, fan, mosquito net. *Santini*, Rua Barão de Vitória 295, near railway station, E, with shower, reasonably quiet.

There are several hotels in Boa Viagem (check all prices carefully—beware of sudden price increases), e.g. *Marazul*, José Brandão 135, D, comfortable, clean, friendly, pleasant, care with electric shower; *Pousada das Flores*, Rua Padre Leandro Carmelo 57, D, German-owned, pleasant; *Pousada da Praia*, Alcides Carneiro Leal 66, Boa Viagem, D with bath, a/c (may be able to bargain lower rates for longer stays), mixed reports; *Veraneio*, Rua Conselheiro Sérgio Henrique Cardin 150, Boa Viagem, D, close to beach; *Solimar*, Rua Solidômo Leite 180, D, near beach, bath, warm water, a/c, good location, friendly but pricey for what's offered; *Saveiro*, R. Conselheiro Aguiar 4670 (T 326-6073), no pool, mosquitoes, but new and clean, a/c, D; *Pousada Aconchego*, Félix de Brito 382 (T 326-2989) D with bath, a/c, pleasant, swimming pool, good meals, English-speaking owner; *Beira Mar*, Av. Boa Viagem 5426, D, with breakfast, no bath, hot water, clean, friendly; *Praia e Sol*, Av. Boa Viagem 5476, T 341-0674, a/c, helpful, reasonable prices; *Albergue Mandacaru*, Rua Maria Carolina 75, E, stores luggage, English and German spoken, rec.; *Sea View*, Rua dos Navegantes 101, E, Dutch-owned (Dutch, English, French spoken), small, very friendly, rec.; *Guest House Pousada*, Luis Marques Teixeira 155, E, a/c, secure, proprietor Ricardo Teixeira is a Sevagtur guide, helpful, highly rec., English and German spoken; *Pousada Casuarinas*, just off R.Joaquim da Silva and Av. Domingos Ferreira, E, family-run, very clean, fine garden, English spoken, warmly rec.

Youth Hostel: *Albergue Arrecifes*, Padre Carapuceiro 132, Praia de Boa Vista, T 081-326-7549, friendly, clean, F, restaurant below rec.; also *Mandacaru*, Rua Dona Maria Carolina 75, T 326-1964, and *Maracatus do Recife*, same street No. 185, T 326-1221. For longer stays rooms may be rented in the centre for about US$20 a month, make inquiries on the streets. For example, contact Dr. Bezerra dos Santos, Rua Floriano Peixoto 85, Edif. Vieira da Cunha S/511, T 224-1098 (English-speaking dentist). Hotels near the bus station are not rec.; this area, especially Santa Rita, is dangerous at night.

During Carnival, private individuals rent rooms and houses in Recife and Olinda; Lins Turismo has listings as does the *Diário de Pernambuco*, or ask around the streets of Olinda. This accommodation is generally cheaper, safer and quieter than hotels, which inflate prices at Carnival.

Electric Current   220 volts A.C., 60 cycles.

Restaurants   There are many good restaurants, at all prices, in the city, and along beach at Boa Viagem.

City: *Adega da Mouraria*, R. Ulhoa Cintra 40; *Panorâmico AIP*, Av. Dantas Barreto 576 (12°); *Pierre* (French), R. Ulhoa Cintra 102; *Faia*, R. Ulhoa Cintra 122; *Buraco da Otília*, Rua da Aurora 1231 (lunch only). *Rex*, Rua do Hospício, and next door, *Viena*, better value; *Le Buffet*, Rua do Hospício, Japanese food and vegetables, helpful, friendly, English-speaking owner; *Fuji* (Japanese), R. do Hospício 354, economical, good tofu dishes; *Lisboa á Noite*, Hospício nr. Conde da Boa Vista, good, reasonable, open Sun. evenings (unlike many); *Leite* (lunches only), Praça Joaquim Nabuco 147/53 near Casa de Cultura, old and famous, good service, meal for US$4. *Galo de Ouro*, Gamboa do Carmo 83, rec., US$3 for main course; *Dom Pedro*, Rua do Imperador 376, specializes in fish dishes. *Bar Esquina 17, Grande Hotel*, rec. *O Pirata*, on Av. 17 de Agosto (Casa Forte) near Museu do Homem do Nordeste. *O Vegetal*, Rua Cleto Campelo (2nd floor) behind Central Post Office, lunch only, less than US$2, highly rec. *Rosa de Ouro*. Rua das Flores 59, delicious food and cheap. *Café do Joca*, Av. Rui Barbosa 1071, local specialities, cheap, good. *Casa dos Frios*, da Palma 57, loja 5, delicatessen/sandwich bar, salads, pastries etc., very good. Good baker *Nabuco* opposite park at Rua do Sol and Rua Concórdia.

Boa Viagem: Main hotels. *Canton* (Chinese), Rua Desembargador João Paes 123; *Golden Dragon* (Chinese), Rua Barão de Souza Leão 691; *Maurício de Nassau*, Av. Boa Viagem 908; *Lobster*, Av. Boa Viagem 2612 and *Churrasco*, Av. Boa Viagem 1700, both rec.; *Canto da Barra*, 20 km. from centre at the far end of candeias, the beach past the S end of Boa Viagem, very expensive, but excellent, live music (taxi from Boa Viagem US$4.30); *Ceia Regional*, Rua Prof. Andrade Bezerra 1462 (by Centro de Convenções) rec. for regional dishes. *Moenda*, Rua dos Navegantes 1417; *Baiúca*, Praça Boa Viagem 16; *Shangai* (Chinese), Av. Domingos Ferreira 4719, excellent, plenty of food; *Futuba*, on a tiny side street towards beach from Av. Conselheiro Aguiar 1313, Japanese, good; *Chinés*, Herculano Bandeiro (just after bridge, on Boa Viagem side), good value; *Prá Vocês*, Av. Herculano Bandeira 115, Pinas (town end of Boa Viagem beach), good but pricey seafood; *O Chocalho*, Av. Barão de Souza Leão 297, for local dishes; *Snack Bar Flamingo*, Av. Cons. Aguiar 542, good hamburgers and ice cream. *Bar Branco e Azul*, near bus station, good.

(For Olinda restaurants see under Olinda, **page 367**). Be careful of eating the local small crabs, known as guaiamum; they live in the mangrove swamps which take the drainage from Recife's shantytowns (mocambos).

Bars The following are suggested: *Lapinha,* Praça Boa Viagem; *O Veleiro,* Primeira Jardim. Also try *Café Passacole,* Av. Visconde de Suassuna 871, Boa Vista, *Depois do Escuro,* Rua da Amizade 178, Graças, and the cafe/ice cream parlours *Fri-Sabor* and *Eskimo,* both close to Praça Boa Viagem. *O Beliscão,* Av. Boa Viagem, by Sea View Hotel, rec.; *Mustang,* Av. Conde de Boa Vista, Boa Vista, also rec. for a beer and watching the "movimento".

Discotheques tend to be expensive and sophisticated: Esquina 90 Disco Club, corner Av. Conselheiro Aguiar and Wilfred Shorto (Boa Viagem); Misty, Riachuelo 309, Boa Vista; Caktos, Av Conselheiro Aguiar 2328, Boa Viagem; Disco 34, Av. Boa Viagem 3114 (*Hotel Jangadeiro*); Gaslight, Rua dos Navegantes 363 (*Hotel Miramar*), Boa Viagem; Skorpios, Rua Barão de Souza Leão (*Mar Hotel*), Boa Viagem; Aritana, Rua José de Alencar 44, Loja 4, Boa Vista; Leandro's, Av. Conselheiro Aguiar 5025, Sobreloja, Sala 116, Boa Viagem.

Also visit a typical North-Eastern *forró* where local couples dance to typical music, very lively especially on Fridays and Saturdays. Among the best are: Belo Mar, Av. Bernardo Vieira de Melo, Candeias; Casa de Festejo, Praça do Derby; Torre.

Markets Permanent craft market in Casa da Cultura (old prison). Mercado São José (1875) for local products and handicrafts. Casa Amarela for a truly typical market on Sats. Sun. evenings: "hippy fair" at Praça Boa Viagem, on the sea front, life-sized wooden statues of saints (a good meeting place is the *Bar Lapinha* in the middle of the square). New Sat. craft fair at Sítio Trindade, Casa Amarela: during the feast days of June 12-29, fireworks, music, dancing, local food. On April 23, here and in the Pátio de São Pedro, one can see the *xangô* dance.

Hairdresser Dellos Cabeleireiros, Av. Visconde de Jequitinhonha 106, Boa Viagem, T 326-4414.

Bookshops Livraria Brandão, Rua da Matriz 22 (used English books and some French and German) and bookstalls on the Rua do Infante Dom Henrique. Perhaps best bookshop is Livro 7, Rua Sete de Setembro 329 and Guararapes airport. Ao Livro Técnico, R. Princesa Isabel, has thrillers in English and beginners' readers. Also a great local character, Melquísidec Pastor de Nascimento, second-hand bookseller, at R. Bispo Cardoso Aires, 215; he also has a second-hand stall at Praça de Sebo (see page 362).

Exchange Lloyds Bank (ex-BOLSA), Rua do Fogo 22; Banco Internacional; Citibank. Open 1000-1600. For good advice on exchange, ask at one of the consulates. Lins Câmbio, Rua da Palma corner with Guararapes, better rate than banks (but not as good as some others), but dollars cash only. Money changer hangs out at *Casa dos Frios* deli. next door. Edifício Bancomérica, 7th floor, Rua Matias de Alberquerque 223, takes cash and travellers' cheques. *Restaurante Leite*, Praça Joaquim Nabuco 147/53, good rates for travellers' cheques and cash. Good rates from Sr Manuel E. Cal Muinôs, Rua Santa Rita 290.

Consulates British, Av. Marquês de Olinda 200. Caixa Postal 184. T 224-0650. Swedish, Rua do Moeda 63, 1st floor, 50.000 Recife, T 224-1622/1329/1772. West German, Dantas Barreto 191, Edif. Santo Antônio, 4th floor. U.S., Gonçalves Maia 163. T 221-1412.

Post Office including poste restante, Central Correios, 50001, Av. Guararapes 250 (or American Express, Rua da Concórdia 278 for poste restante).

Church Episcopalian, Rua Carneiro Vilela 569.

Cables Embratel, Av. Agamenon Magalhães, 1114, Parque Amorim district, T 221-4149; also Praça da Independência. Telex, public booth, Av. Guararapes 250.

International Telephones Rua Diário de Pernambuco, 38; also at airport (first floor).

Tourist Offices Empetur (for the State of Pernambuco). Main office, Av. Cruz Cabugá 553, near corner of Coutinho; Casa da Cultura, Rua Floriano Peixoto (old prison), unhelpful, Mon.-Sat., 0900-2000, Sun. 1400-2000. Emetur (for Recife), Pátio de São Pedro, loja 10. At Carnival-time they have a full programme. Maps available: Empetur, US$0.33, who also publish walking tour schedules for Recife (one leaves Sun. 1500 from Santo Antônio church on Av. Dantas Barreto) and Olinda in several languages; also central map in monthly guide *Itinerário Pernambuco*. Offices at airport—24 hrs. (will book hotels, helpful, English spoken). Information trailer parked corner Av. Dantas Barreto and Av. Guararapes, 0800-1900.

Hours of opening of museums, art galleries, churches etc. are published in the daily newspaper *Diário de Pernambuco*.

Rail Recife is the centre of the Rede Ferroviária do Nordeste, with lines from the Cinco Pontas station south to Maceió, north to Paraíba and Natal (no passenger services), and a western route to Salgueiro (train Sat. 0700, with de luxe car to Caruaru, returns from Caruaru Sun. 1700). Commuter services, known as the **Metrô** but not underground, leave from the Central station; they have been extended to serve the new Rodoviária at São Lourenço da Mata (frequent trains,

RECIFE 39

0600-2300, US$0.10). If going to Boa Viagem from the Rodoviária, get off the Metrô at Joanna Bezerra and take a bus from there.

Buses To Salvador, 13 hours, 3 a day (all at night) US$12 (*leito*, 24), 12 hrs. to Fortaleza, US$11, and 5 hrs. to Natal US$3.50. To Goiana, every ½ hr., US$0.90. To Rio, 38 hrs., US$34 (*leito* 68); to São Paulo, 40 hrs., US$42 (*leito*, 84); to Belo Horizonte, 36 hrs., US$32. To Teresina (Piauí), 19 hrs. (US$17), and further to São Luís, 26 hrs., US$24; to Belém, 34 hrs., US$30 (Boa Esperança bus rec.). To Paulo Afonso, US$5, 7 hrs. on completely paved road. Good roads N to João Pessoa, Natal and Fortaleza, W to Arcoverde and Caruaru (and ultimately Belém), SW to Garanhuns and S to Maceió, US$4, 4 hrs. (Maceió can be reached either by the main road or by the coast road "via Litoral"); in all 20 buses daily. A new Rodoviária, mainly for long-distance buses, with 30-minute rail connection to the central railway station, entrance through Museu do Trem (opp. Casa da Cultura) (US$0.10), has been built 12 km. outside the city at São Lourenço da Mata (it is called Terminal Integrado dos Passageiros, or TIP, pronounced "chippy"); from Boa Viagem taxi US$12, bus US$0.25, 1 hr., from centre. The train to the centre is much quicker than the bus.
Local Buses The Prefeitura issues a guide to routes. Buses to the nearby destinations of Igaraçu and Itamaracá leave from Avenida Martins de Barros; those to beaches beyond Olinda from Av. Dantas behind the post office.

Coastal Shipping Lóide Brasileiro ships run frequently between Brazilian coastal ports. They have several up-to-date vessels, some de luxe.

Air Services The principal international and national airlines fly to Guararapes airport, 12 km. from the city. Three direct flights a week from London to Recife via Lisbon by Varig and by TAP. Direct flights from Paris with Air France. Bus to airport, No. 52, US$0.25, 30 minutes from N.S. do Carmo. Tourist taxis at the airport are twice as expensive as ordinary red taxis picked up on the main road.

Olinda, the old capital, founded in 1537 and named a "Patrimônio de Humandade" by Unesco in 1982, 6 km. to the north, is served by buses and taxis (US$3). This city, which has recently become very commercialized, contains many fine old colonial churches, monasteries and convents; tourist handout gives schedule of opening times (available in Casa da Cultura in Recife). Particularly interesting are the Prefeitura, once the palace of the viceroys; the monastery of São Bento, founded 1582, restored 1761, the site of Brazil's first law school and the first abolition of slavery, by the Benedictine monks (paintings, sculpture, furniture, open 0800-1100 and 1300-1700 daily) and the beautifully restored Rua São Bento; the convent of Santa Tereza (1687), the monastery of São Francisco, 1585 (splendid woodcarving and paintings, superb gilded stucco, and azulejos, in Capela de São Roque, open daily 0800-1130, 1400-1630); the Igreja da Misericórdia, built 1540, open daily 0700-1700, fine tiling and gold work, and Academia Santa Gertrudes; the Cathedral (1537), the first church to be built in the city, of simple and severe construction; São João Batista dos Militares (1581), the only church not burnt by the Dutch; the Graças church (seminary) built 1582, no fixed visiting times; Nossa Senhora do Monte, built early 16C., likewise; the Carmo church (1588—under restoration), likewise, and the colonial public fountain, the Bica de São Pedro. There are some houses of the 17th century with latticed balconies, heavy doors and pink stucco walls, including a house in Moorish style at Praça João Alfredo 7, housing the *Mourisco* restaurant. There is a large colony of artists (as the superb grafitti at election times testify), and excellent examples of regional art, mainly woodcarving and terra-cotta figurines, may be bought in the Alto da Sé, the fine square on top of the hill by the Cathedral, or in the handicraft shops at the Mercado da Ribeira, Rua Bernardo Vieira de Melo (Vieira de Melo gave the first recorded call for independence from Portugal, in Olinda in 1710.) There is a Museum of Sacred

---

Key to Map of Recife
1. Praça da República; 2. Praça da Independência; 3.Praça do Sebo; 4. Pátio de São Pedro and São Pedro dos Clérigos; 5. Capela Dourada; 6. Church of Santo Antônio; 7. Conceicão dos Militares; 8. Nossa Senhora do Carmo; 9. Church of Madre de Deus; 10. Church of Pilar; 11. Church of Espíritu Santo; Santo Antônio do Convento de São Francisco; 13. São José do Ribamar; 14. Nossa Senhora do Rosário dos Pretos; 15. Matriz de Boa Vista; 16. Nossa Senhora do Livramento; 17. Fort Brum; 18. Fort of Cinco Pontas/Museu da Cidade de Recife; 19. Teatro de Santa Isabel; 20. Teatro do Parque; 21. Teatro Apolo; 22. Governor's Palace; 23. New Municipality; 24. Casa da Cultura; 25. Diário de Pernambuco; 26. Museu do Trem and Central Metrô Station; 27. Banco do Brasil; 28. São José Market; 29. Empetur Tourist Office; 30. Post Office; 31. Telephone Office.

Art in the beautiful Bishop's Palace (1696) at Alto da Sé 7, open Tues.-Fri., 0800-1200 and 1400-1800, Sat.-Sun. 1400-1800. At Rua 13 de Maio, in the old jail of the Inquisition, is the Museum of Contemporary Art; also the old slave market. A programme of restoration, partly financed by the Netherlands Government, has been undertaken in order to comply with the recently-conferred title of National Monument. The Regional Museum, Rua do Amparo 128, is excellent. There is a contemporary art museum in the 18C. prison on Rua 13 de Maio. The Tourist Office, helpful and friendly (Rua de São Bento 225), has a map with a recommended walking tour of the sights, opening times, as well as churches, museums and other places of interest, and houses to stay during Carnival, when hotel prices rise vertiginously. Taxis between Olinda and Recife put their meters on to higher rates at the new Convention Centre (between the two cities), best to start a journey either way there. Population: 360,000.

Buses From Recife, take any bus marked "Rio Doce", No. 981 which has a circular route around the city and beaches, or No. 33 from Av. N.S. do Carmo, US$0.25; from Boa Viagem, take bus marked "Rio Doce/Piedade" or "Casa Caiada/Piedade". From airport to Olinda by bus, take airport bus to Holliday (a Y-shaped building on Av. Conselheiro Aguiar, Boa Viagem), ask to be let off, and catch a "Rio Doce" or "Bairra de Jangada/Casa Caiada" bus to Praça do Carno, Olinda. In all cases, alight in Praça do Carmo.

Hotels At Casa Caiada, Av. José Augusto Moreira 2200 (T 431-2955), is *Quatro Rodas* (L), with swimming pool, excellent restaurant, tennis courts, gardens, very good. *Quatorze Bis*, Av. Beira Mar 1414, C, friendly, helpful, clean, run by Dutchman. *Pousada dos Quatro Cantos*, Rua Prudente de Morais 441, D-C (E without bath), in a converted mansion, very good, highly rec. apart from alleged overcharging during Carnival, T 429-0220/1845; *Pousada São Francisco*, Rua do Sol 127, T 429-2109/0386/1469, up to B, clean, comfortable, pool, rec.; *Albergue da Olinda*, Rua do Sol 237, E, new, reasonable, clean, friendly, popular with gringos; *Pousadas do Mar* and *da Praia*, E-F, Av. Beira Mar 497 and 633, Bairro Novo, T 429-2883 for either, each has 16 rooms with bath, some a/c, cheaper for stay longer than 3 days. Also on Av. Beira Mar, *Portolinda*, No. 295, T 429-3198, opened 1987, E, warmly rec.; *Hospedaria do Turista*, No. 989, E, excellent, T 429-1847; *Coqueiro Verde*, No. 1173, F, family atmosphere, excellent breakfast; *Marolinda* (No. 1615), 2 star, D, rec., rooms at front very noisy at weekends; *Pensionato Beira Mar* (No. 1103, E) and *Hospedaria Olinda Beira Mar* (No. 1473, E). Several **youth hostels**: *Portalinda*, Av. Beira Mar 295, Bairro Novo, T 429-3198; *Da Praia*, same avenue, No. 633; *Bomfim*, Rua do Bomfim 115, Carmo, T 429-1674; *Palanquim*, Prof. Cândido Pessoa 1833, Bairro Novo, T 222-1084. At Carnival, houses or rooms may be rented for 5-10 days (up to US$800 for a house, US$230 for a room, often without bed); try Maria da Silva, Rua Epitácio Pessoa Sobrinho, Bairro Umuaramê, T 429-0320, 2 rooms to let (US$50 a week each).

At Carnival, the price of accommodation rises. Ask at the AmEx office in Recife about lodging in Olinda at this time.

Camping Olinda Camping, Rua Bom Sucesso 262, Amparo, T 429-1365, US$3 p.p., space for 30 tents, 5 trailers, small huts for rent, quiet, well-shaded, town buses pass outside, rec.

Restaurants *L'Atelier*, Rua Bernardo Vieira de Melo 91, Ribeira, small converted workshop with beautiful view, run by Swiss tapestry artists, excellent international food, local dishes with reservation (necessary) T 081-429-3099, open Wed.-Sun. *Mourisco*, Rua João Alfredo 7, calm and pleasant, discotheque attached; *Las Vegas*, Av. Beira Mar 1571, food good (watch the bill) but sanitary facilities not reliable; *Zé Pequeno* and *Samburá*, Av. Beira Mar (no number—both with terrace) rec. to try caldeirada, agulhas fritas (at former) and pitu (crayfish), also lobster in coconut sauce or daily fish dishes at latter, very good; *Churrascaria La Cabaña*, on beach, good, medium-priced; *Lanchonete Coqueiro Verde*, Av. Beira Mar 1173, good; *Las Vegas*, Av. Beira Mar 2619; same street, *Ouriço*, local food good; *Cantinho da Sé 305*, lively, good view of Recife; *Chin Lee*, Av. Beira Mar, excellent Chinese food; many others, mostly for fish, along Av. Beira Mar; *Saúde*, Av. Prudente de Morais 411, serves vegetarian meals. *O Cachorrão* (lunch stand), Praia do Quartel, good cheap sandwiches. The traditional Olinda drinks, Pau do Índio (which contains 32 herbs) and Retetel, are both manufactured on the Rua do Amparo.

Discotheques *Menphis*, Av Beira Mar 1051, Bairro Novo; *Restaurant Mourisco*.

Entertainment At Janga beach on Fri. and Sat., you can join in a *ciranda* at the bar-restaurant *Ciranda de Dona Duda*. For the less active, there is the *Casa da Seresta*, also in Janga on the beach side of the main road. On Praça do Carmo is *Cheiro do Povo*, a *forró* dance hall.

Beginning at dusk, but best after 2100, the Alto da Sé becomes the scene of a lively street fair, with arts, crafts, makeshift bars and barbeque stands, and impromptu traditional music. Street urchins try to tell you the history of Olinda (for a price). The fair becomes even more animated at Carnival.

At Olinda's carnival thousands of people dance through the narrow streets of the old city to the sound of the *frevo*, the brash energetic music which normally accompanies a lively dance performed with umbrellas. The local people decorate them with streamers and straw dolls, and form themselves into costumed groups to parade down the Rua do Amparo; Pitombeira and Elefantes are the best known of these groups.

Beaches North from Olinda, there are beautiful, usually deserted, palm-fringed beaches beyond Casa Caiada, at Rio Doce, Janga, and Pau Amarelo (though they are said to be dirtier than Boa Viagem, S of Recife). At many simple cafés you can eat *sururu* (clam stew in coconut sauce), *agulha frita* (fried needle-fish), *miúdo de galinha* (chicken giblets in gravy) and *casquinha de carangueijo* (seasoned crabmeat and *farinha de dendê* served in crabshells). Visit the Dutch fort on Pau Amarelo beach; small craft fair here on Sat. nights. A beautiful beach, reached by direct bus from Recife at weekends, US$0.75, otherwise via the town of Nossa Senhora do Ó, 2 hrs., is Porto de Galinhas. It has cool, clean water, and waves. *Solar Porto de Galinhas*, on beach, D, good food, many facilities, beautiful place, warmly rec.; *pensão* of Dona Benedita in the street where the bus stops, very basic, clean; food at *Rang Bem* in same street.

Excursions About 30 km. S of Recife, beyond Cabo, is the beautiful Gaibu beach, reached by bus from Cabo. **Cabo** itself, Pernambuco's main industrial city (135,000 people), has interesting churches and forts and a Museu da Abolição, and at nearby Suape are many 17C. buildings and a Biological Reserve.

Biological Reserves For information on Pernambuco's two reserves, contact IBDF, Av. 17 de Agosto 1057, Casa Forte, CEP 50.000, Recife. They are **Saltinho**, which preserves some of the last vestiges of Atlantic Forest in the North East, and **Serra Negra**, which has some of the last remaining forest at higher altitude in the interior.

Igaraçu, 32 km. N of Recife on the road to João Pessoa, has the first church built in Brazil (SS Cosme e Damião), the Livramento church nearby, and the convent of Santo Antônio with a small museum next door. The church of Sagrada Coração is said to have housed Brazil's first orphanage. Much of the town (founded in 1535) has been declared a National Monument; it is an attractive place, with a number of colonial houses and Brazil's first Masonic hall. (Pop.: 55,000.) Hotel: *Fazenda Praia da Gavoa*, Estrada do Ramalho, A; Camping Clube do Brasil has site nearby at Engenho Monjope, an old sugar estate, now a historical monument and interesting (it is 3 km. before Igaraçu coming from Recife—bus US$0.30—; alight at the "Camping" sign and walk 5-10 mins.). Igaraçu buses leave from Av. Martins de Barro, Recife, 45 mins., US$0.35. N of Igaraçu you pass through coconut plantations to Itapissuma, where there is a bridge to **Itamaracá** island, where, the locals say, Adam and Eve spent their holidays. It has the old Dutch Forte Orange; an interesting penal settlement with gift shops, built round the 1747 sugar estate buildings of Engenho São João, which still have much of the old machinery; charming villages and colonial churches, and fine, wide, clean beaches. Buses from Recife (Av. Martins de Barros opp. *Grand Hotel*) and Igaraçu. (*Hotel Caravela*, C with shower, good restaurant, on beach; *Hotel Pousada*, C, pool etc., some minutes from beach; *Pousada Teihadão*, Av. Beira Mar 3, Quatro Cantos, D, clean, excellent restaurant, swimming pool, garden, warmly recommended; *Itamaracá Parque*, C.)

Goiana, on the Recife-João Pessoa road, founded 1570, is one of the most important towns for ceramics. Carmelite church and monastery, founded 1719, impressive but poorly restored; San Benedito, needs restoring; Matriz do Rosário, only open for 1800 mass, Soledade convent (1755); Amparo church with Sacred Art museum; Misericórdia church (1723). The uniformity of many of the dwellings is due to their construction, for his workforce, by the owner of a now-defunct textile factory. Hospedaria Durma Bem, open weekends only; ask at Prefeitura at other times. Visit the workshop of Zé do Carmo, opposite the *Buraco da Giá* restaurant (excellent seafood; owner has tame crab which will offer you a drink), R. Padre Batalha 100. Just north of Goiana is a sugar-mill, Usina Nossa Senhora das Maravilhas, which can be visited during the week; ask for Dr Jairo.

At the Pernambuco-Paraíba border, a 27 km. dirt road to the fishing village of Pitimbu, with *jangadas*, lobster fishing, surf fishing, lobster-pot making. No tourist facilities but camping is possible; food from *Bar do Jangadeiro*. Bus from Goiana, US$0.50.

Another possible excursion is by a slow railway or a good roads via Caruaru or Palmares to the city of **Garanhuns,** 243 km. SW of Recife. It claims to be the best holiday resort in the North-East, partly because of its cool climate—it stands at 890 metres, and has an average temperature of 21°C—and partly because of its mineral waters and beautiful landscapes and parks. Population: 100,000.

Hotels *Familiar,* Av. Santo Antônio 12. *Grande Hotel Petrópolis,* Praça da Bandeira 129. *Tavares Correia,* B, Av. Rui Barbosa 296. *Monte Sinai,* Av. Rui Barbosa 1122, B. **Camping** *Camping Treze,* BR-432, km. 105.

Tracunhaém, 30 km. from Recife, is a peaceful town (12,000 people) where fine ceramics are made; there are two interesting early 19C. churches. To get there, turn off the Limoeiro road at Carpina, on to the road to Nasaré da Mata. Even the children are adept in working in clay.

Carpina, 54 km. from Recife, 65,000 people, is well-known for its Carnival and for the traditional Epiphany festival early in January, and also for the carpets made in nearby village of Lagoa do Carro. There is a historical museum. Hotels (*Pousada das Acácias,* BR-408, B; *São João da Escócia,* Av. João Alfredo 136, D) and restaurants.

Caruaru (pop. 138,000), 130 km. W of Recife by paved road (many buses, 2 hrs., US$3) and rail, has a big Fri. to Sun. market with a separate site across the river for leather goods, pottery and articles of straw, although it is disappointingly tourist-oriented now (smaller market on other days of the week). See the hand-painted textiles of Sr Valério Cristóvão, Rua 13 de Maio 94, 1st floor; he is very helpful and his work depicts local history. The little clay figures (*figurinhas de barro*) originated by Mestre Vitalino, and very typical of the North-East, are a local speciality; many local potters live at Alto da Moura 6 km. away, where a house once owned by Vitalino is open, but has no examples of his work. Bus, ½ hour, bumpy, US$0.30. Rodoviária is 4 km. from town. Bus to Maceió, 0700, 5 hrs., US$3.50. Bus to Fazenda Nova 1030, 1 hr., returns for Caruaru 1330. Train to Recife, de luxe car, 1700 Sunday.

Hotels *Do Sol,* A (4-star) on hill outside town, good restaurant; pool; *Centenário,* 7 de Setembro 84, E, clean, friendly, restaurant. Cheap *hospedarias* around central square, Praça Getúlio Vargas.

Restaurants *Mãe Amara,* R. São Paulo, for regional food. *Guanabara,* clean, cool, not too expensive. *Churrascaria São Luís,* Rua dos Guararapes 15, near Praça Getúlio Vargas, good and cheap; *Churrascaria Trêvi,* said to be good.

On the way to Caruaru is Gravatá, 60,000 people (*Hotel Fazenda Portal,* L, BR-232; *Grande da Serra,* BR-232, D; *Central,* Av. C.B. de Oliveira 301 (BR-232), D), known as the Switzerland of Pernambuco for its scenery and good hill climate.

During Easter Week each year various agencies run package tours to the little country town of **Fazenda Nova,** a few km. from Caruaru. Just outside the town is **Nova Jerusalém,** where from the Tuesday before to Easter Sunday, an annual passion play, suggested by Oberammergau's, is enacted. The site is one-third the size of the historic quarter of Jerusalem, with 12 permanent stages on which scenes of the Passion are presented; the audience moves from one to another as the story unfolds.

Hotels in Fazenda Nova *Grande,* best; *Mansão Verde; Fazenda Nova.*

Camping Close to site.

Arcoverde, about 126 km. W of Caruaru, is a market town in the Sertão, market every Saturday, cool at night. Hotel: *Grande Majestic* (fair), E, with breakfast.

Triúnfo, about 200 km. W of Arcoverde via Serra Talhada, delightful small town in Serra de Borborema, good climate, with great variety of crops, flowers and fruits. There are also a sugar mill that can be visited (Engenho Boa Esperança), waterfalls, sounding rocks, the convent of São Boaventura, and the Museu do Cangaça, showing the lives and relics of the traditional bandits of the Nordeste. Stay at *Hotel-Orphanage Lar St. Elizabeth,* run by German religious sisters, D, with private apartment and 3 excellent meals. Two buses daily to and from Recife (6½ hrs.); trains run from Recife to Serra Talhada, *Hotel Municipal* on main square, F with breakfast.

Fernando de Noronha is a small archipelago 345 km. off the NE coast, under military control and declared a Marine National Park in 1989: only one island is inhabited. Total population about 1,340, of whom many are fishermen or civilians working for military. Only hotel, *Pousada Esmeralda*, A full board, runs a tour boat for guests. Most food is brought from mainland but prices are reasonable. The islands were discovered 1503, and were for a time a pirate lair. In 1738 the Portuguese built the Forte dos Remédios, of which remains exist as well as a deserted town nearby, and a prison. Sea landing is difficult, but an airstrip has been built; from Recife, daily flight with Nordeste, US$1.30 return (all flights and hotel bookings operated by Toulemonde, Av. Ipiranga 313, 4th floor, São Paulo, T 231-1329, bookable through any travel agency; 8-day package from Recife, leaving Saturday, costs US$850 p.p.). The island, which is dominated by a 321-metre peak, has interesting wildlife; fishing is very good, and so is scuba-diving. Take sufficient new cruzados: travellers' cheques and dollars are heavily discounted. **NB** The time is one hour later than Brazilian Standard Time.

It is a bus ride of 2 hours through sugar plantations over a good road from Recife (126 km.) to

João Pessoa, capital of the State of Paraíba, on the Paraíba River, with 290,000 inhabitants, a port for coastal traffic. Ocean-going ships load and unload at Cabedelo (6,872 population), 18 km. by road or rail. The old monasteries are worth seeing, and the 18th century church of São Francisco is a beauty (currently under restoration). Other tourist points include the Casa da Pólvora, an old gunpowder store which has become the city museum, the Cabo Branco lighthouse at Ponta do Seixas, the most easterly point of continental Brazil, with palm-lined but oil-polluted beaches (½-hr. trip); the city parks; and trips on the River Paraíba. Airport for internal services. See the booklet *Relíquias da Paraíba*, by Padre Antônio Barbosa.

Hotels *Tropical* (ex-*Tambaú*), A, comfortable, good service, rec., though sometimes they pretend no standard rooms are available when they are; *Gameleira*, Av. João Maurício 157, opposite *Tropical*, D, good breakfast, rec.; *Aurora*, Praça João Pessoa 51, E with a/c and bath, clean, friendly; *Tropicana*, Praia de Tambaú; *Pedro Américo*, Praça Pedro Américo, E (no breakfast on Sun.); *Motel Veraneio*, on BR-230; *Motel Fogeama*, Rua das Trincheiras (with restaurant); *Pousada do Conde*, BR-101 Sul (with churrascaria); cheap hotels near the old bus station, e.g. *São Pedro*, Rua Irineu Pinto 231, clean, basic, friendly, E. **Youth hostels**, on Av. das Trincheiras, at Palácio dos Esportes, T 221-7220/1, and *Cabo Branco*, Av. Pe-José Trigueiro 104, Praia de Cabo Branco, T 221-2903/226-6171.

Electric Current 220 volts A.C, 60 cycles.

Restaurants *Cabo Branco Clube* has two restaurants, one in Rua Peregrino de Cavalho and the other in the Miramar district. Two good restaurants on Tambaú beach are *Adega do Alfredo* (Portuguese) and *Wan Li* (Chinese); *A Caravela*, Quadra 3, Jardim Beiramar; *Badionaldo*, Praia do Poço (20 km. from centre) and also *Bardilucena*. *Itacoatiara*, near *Hotel Tropical*; *Pescador*, near Cabo Branco lighthouse; *O Luzeirinho*, Av. Vasco da Gama, Jaguaribe; *O Boiadeiro*, Av. Coração de Jesus; *A Gameleira*, Av. João Maurício, Tambaú. *Pavilhão do Chá*, pleasant, drinks, sandwiches, TV, open air, in centre.

Tourist Information PB Tur, Av. Getúlio Vargas 301, Centro João Pessoa; also bus terminal (helpful). Crafts at Casa do Artesão, R. Maciel Pinheiro near city bus station.

Tourist Agencies Planetur, Av. Miguel Couto 5, Loja 12, and *Hotel Tropical*. Agência de Viagens e Turismo Arnaldo von Sohsten, Rua Gama e Melo 100.

Cables Embratel, Rua das Trincheiras 398.

Bus Station is 10 mins. from centre. To Recife, every 60 mins., US$1.50, 2 hrs. To Natal, every 2 hrs., US$2.50, 3 hrs.; to Fortaleza, 2000 only, 10 hrs., US$8. Warning: you will be refused permission to travel from João Pessoa Rodoviária wearing shorts, whether or not you arrived in shorts (Bermuda shorts are acceptable).

Excursions Twenty minutes by car or taxi, or 30 by bus, to Tambaú, fishing village and seaside resort with lovely beach and excellent bathing. Halfway along is Cabo Branco club, open to visitors: good food, beautiful views; hotels (none less than US$10, fully-booked in season) and restaurants also at Tambaú. At

Cabedelo are the impressive walls of the 17th-century fortress of Santa Catarina.

Campina Grande, the "Porta do Sertão", is 120 km. from João Pessoa (bus 2 hours), a rapidly growing centre for light industry and an outlet for goods from most of the North-East. There is a museum of modern art, and another of the cotton industry. Most genial climate. Population: 222,000. Near Campina Grande is Lagoa Seca, where the local craft is the making of figures in wood and sacking.

Hotels *Rique Palace Hotel* (excellent) is on the top floors of the tallest building in town: the restaurant is on the 11th floor. Other hotels: *Ouro Branco*, E; *Barborema*, near old bus station, E, friendly. *Dormitório São Paulo*, also near bus station, F, cheap, clean. Many others near old bus station. **Restaurant** *Miura*, Rua Major Juvino 262, good steaks, and in old bus station.

W of Campina Grande on the main highway, still paved, leads on through **Patos** (*Hotel JK*, E) to Ipaumirim (Ceará). Here a left turn leads to the twin towns of **Crato** (*Hotel Crato*, E) and **Juazeiro do Norte** (Ceará), oases of green in the dry Sertão. Mosquitoes can be a problem at night.

Juazeiro do Norte is a small pilgrimage town; it was the home of Padre Cícero, one of the unofficial saints of the North-East. A statue to him stands in the Logradouro do Horto, a park overlooking the town; either take the pilgrim trail up the hill or go by bus. **Hotels**: *Panorama*, D, good value; *Vieira*, corner of Rua São Pedro and Rua Santo Antônio, E; private bathroom and breakfast; and *Municipal*, E, rec.

Many beautiful fishing villages along the coast, often difficult to reach; one of the most popular is Baía Formosa in Rio Grande do Norte (daily bus from Natal, 2½ hrs.). No hotel; ask in town for accommodation in fishermen's houses, infinitely preferable to the overpriced accommodation at the *Miramar* bar.

Natal, 377,000 people, capital of Rio Grande do Norte, a friendly town on the estuary of the Rio Potengi, is about 180 km. to the north of João Pessoa. It is served by weekly coastal vessels and there is a railway S through the State of Paraíba to Recife and Maceió (only suburban passenger services). There is a large airport 13 km. from the city (taxi US$6.50). The old part of the city is called Cidade Alta. The main square, the Praça João Maria, oblong in shape, has a traditional cathedral at one end and a fine modern bank building at the other. The city is centred on the Av. Rio Branco. The church of Santo Antônio, Rua Santo Antônio in the centre, dates from 1766, and has a fine, carved wooden altar. The Museu Câmara Cascudo, Av. Hermes de Fonseca 1398 (T 222-0923), has exhibits on archaeological digs, Umbanda rituals and the petroleum industry (open Tues.-Fri., 0800-1100, 1400-1600, US$1.40). The Forte dos Reis Magos (16th-century) on the coast at Rocas is open Tues.-Sun. 0800-1700; between it and the city is a military installation, and the walk along the beach road is not very safe. Best to go in a tour, or by taxi; it is worth it for the views (entry US$1.40). The Casa da Música Popular Brasileira has dancing on Friday and Saturday night and Sunday afternoon, very popular. The Marine Research Institute at the Praia da Areia Preta can be visited; bus marked "Areia Preta" from Av. Rio Branco. Good local craftware Sats. at Mercado do Alecrim, along Rua Quaresma near Rua Gonçalves. At Mãe Luiza is a lighthouse with beautiful views of Natal and surrounding beaches (take city bus marked Mãe Luiza; get key from the furthest of the three cottages at the base). Some 20 km. from Natal is the rocket base of Barreira do Inferno, near Eduardo Gomes, which can no longer be visited by foreigners.

Hotels *Reis Magos*, Av. Café Filho, Praia do Meio, facing sea, obligatory full board in high season, food not rec., B; *Marsol Natal*, Via Costeira 1567, km. 7, Parque das Dunas, 3-star, new; Via Costeira is a good place to stay, but hotels mostly in A-B range; e.g. *Barreira Roxa Praia*, clean, helpful, good. *Santo Antônio*, R. Santo Antônio 724, E, with breakfast, very clean and helpful; *Natal*, Av. Rio Branco 740, E with breakfast and bath, but said to be less good than *Fenícia*, Av. Rio Branco 586, E (more with a/c), with breakfast and shower, friendly; *Casa Grande*, Rua Princesa Isabel 529, E with a/c, F without bath, good breakfast, pleasant, excellent value; *Casa da Maçã*, near *Casa Grande*, good value, friendly; *Pousada Meu Canto*, Manoel Dantas 424, Petrópolis, E incl. good breakfast, clean, friendly, nice garden, trips organized; *Pousada O Caipira*, Manuel Maschado, F without bath, clean, friendly, between beach and centre; *Samburá*, Rua Prof. Zuza 263, C, rec.; *Majestic*, Rua Dom Pedro I 20, clean, friendly, E; *Beira Mar*, Av. Pres. Café Filho, Praia dos Artistas, on the beach front, D, with breakfast, but no a/c, small, good value, popular; a few doors away (Av. Beira Mar 680) next door is *Praia do Meio*, D, a/c, clean, friendly, good value; *Farol*, Av. Gouv. Silvio Pedrosa 174 (on beach), T 222-4661, E with a/c; *Tirol*, Av. Alexandrino de Alencar 1330 D, good but noisy. *Pousadas* at Ponta Negra and Genipabu beaches, e.g. *Caminho do Mar*, nr. Ponta Negra beach, clean, very friendly. Cheap accommodation at *Casa de Estudantes*, near the Tourist Centre (separate facilities for men and women), "Via Tirol" bus from Rodoviária to centre passes here. **Youth hostel**, *Meu Canto*, Rua Dr. Manoel Dantas 424, Petrópolis, T 222-8351, highly rec.

Camping on the Praia do Forte beach, near the Forte dos Reis Magos, not rec. because unsafe. Camping Clube do Brasil site at Sítio do Jiqui.

Electric Current 220 volts A.C., 60 cycles.

Restaurants *Casa de Mãe*, Rua Pedro Afonso 230, up hill from *Hotel Reis Magos*, regional food, rec.; Rua Princesa Isabel No. 717-C has *Bom Demais*, cheap, good; same street, *Casa Grande*, good value; *Casa da Macã*, Av. Marechal Deodoro, central, beer and good, cheap dishes; *Pietro's*, same avenue, opp. cathedral, cheap, good; *Marinho*, Rua do Areial 265, 15 mins. walk from centre, clean, friendly, inexpensive; *Raizes*, Av. Campos Sales, with C. Mossoró, good regional dishes; *Tirraguso*, Av. Café Filho 27, good; *Rampa*, Rio Potengi, good for grilled fish but not service; *Café de Paris*, south end of Praia de Meio, very good and cheap. *Thin-San*, Mipibu 710, Petrópolis, Chinese, quite good, not expensive. Vegetarian (with shops): *Amai*, General Varela 624, and *A Microbiótica*, Princesa Isabel 524. Good, inexpensive lanchonets on Rua Judas Tadéu, just off Rio Branco. For snacks try the stalls outside the *Hotel Reis Magos*; there are also various restaurants along the beach road nearby, where itinerant musicians play. Try the restaurants on the point that separates Praias dos Artistas and da Areia Preta (e.g. *Calamar*), for seafood.

Cables Embratel, Av. Duque de Caxias 99. T 1230. International phone calls, Telern, 2 blocks behind cathedral.

Exchange Cash advances against Visa card at Banco do Brasil only. *Hotel Luxor Natal* will change dollars cash and AmEx cheques, but not Thomas Cook.

Tourist Information Centro de Turismo (a converted prison with handicraft shops) Rua Aderbal de Figueiredo s/n, off Rua General Cordeiro, Petrópolis; Rodoviária (helpful) and Aeroporto Augusto Severo. Natal is a very poor place to change money.

Tourist Agencies Aertur, Rua João Pessoa 219; Bradesco, Av. Rio Branco 692, 1° andar; Aparecida Turismo, Av. Rio Branco, Ed. Barão do Rio Branco.

Airport Augusto Severo, 15 km. from centre; flights to Belém, Belo Horizonte, Fortaleza, Manaus, Rio, Salvador, São Paulo. Bus every half-hour from old bus station near centre US$0.35, taxi US$9.50.

Bus (terminal is about 6 km. out of town, bus "Cidade de Esperança Av. 9", "Areia Preta via Petrópolis" or "Via Tirol" to centre); to Recife, 5 hrs., US$3.50; to Fortaleza, 8 hrs., US$6 (*leito*—freezing—US$12); to Maceio, buses of Real Alagoas go either direct, or via Recifé, 4-6 hrs.; to João Pessoa, US$2.50, 3 hrs.

At Pirangi, 25 km. S, or 30 mins. by bus from new Rodoviária, is the world's largest cashew-nut tree (*cajueiro*); branches springing from a single trunk cover an area of some 7,300 square metres. Opposite is a good beach. From Natal (Viação Campos), 5 times a day from 0630 to 1815, 3 on Sun., 0730, 0930, 1645; the snack bar by the tree has schedules of buses back to Natal.

Beaches Natal has excellent beaches (for example Ponta Negra, with many new hotels and restaurants, 20 mins. by bus from centre), some on the far side of the Potengi river, for example Redinha and Genipabu—where you can toboggan down the sand-dunes—reached by direct bus from old Rodoviária—N.B. muggings have been reported in Genipabu. You can hire buggies to get to the beaches for US$20-30 a day.

The state of Rio Grande do Norte (whose people are called "Potiguares" after a former Indian tribe) has three main paved roads radiating from Natal: S to João Pessoa and Recife, SW to Caicó and W to Mossoró (pop. 118,000) and Fortaleza. Between *Caicó* (Hotel Guanabara, rec., F) and **Mossoró** (Hotel Termas, C, comfortable, with a hot, mineral water pool system, each pool on a terrace, with temperatures ranging from 54°C at the top to 30°C at the bottom; Hotel Grand, F, Hotel Pax next to market; Hotel Zenilândia, F, highly rec.) there is a turning to **Patu** with its huge basilica on a hillside, with passable "hotels", rather primitive. Trains run twice a week S from Mossoró to Sousa, via Patu. From Mossoró you can visit the salt pans at Grossos on the coast, but get written permission from the administrative offices in Mossoró. Bus Mossoró-Aracati at 0800 with Emp. Nordeste, 2 hrs., US$1.15.

Fortaleza, capital of the State of Ceará, with a population of 1,308,000, is about 520 km. from Natal, NW along the coast. It is 1,600 km. by road from Belém and 885 km. from Recife. There are fair dirt roads throughout the State, and paved roads W to São Luís and SE to Recife; the federal highway S to Salvador (BR-116) is now largely paved but much is in poor condition. A fine tourist centre in the old prison on the waterfront (Av. Senador Pompeu 350) includes the Museu de Arte e Cultura Popular (open Mon.-Fri., 0800-1200, 1400-1800, Sat. 0800-1200, most interesting), shops and restaurants. Other museums: Museu Histórico e Antropológico do Ceará, Av. Barão de Studart 410 (open Tues.-Fri., 0730-1230, 1430-1730, Sat.-Sun., 0800-1200, 1400-1800); take bus marked "Dom Luís"); in the next street, the Museum of Ceará's Minerals, Rua José Vilar 196 (open Mon.-Fri., 0700-1300), bus to centre, "Praia do Futuro" or "Serviluz". Museu das Secas, Pedro Pereira 683, 0800-1100, 1400-1700, collections of photographs and anti-drought equipment. Also visit Forte Nossa Senhora da Assunção, originally built by the Dutch. The mausoleum of President Castello Branco (1964-67), next to the state government building, may be visited. The new cathedral, in gothic style but built in concrete, stands opposite the Mercado Central; it has beautiful stained glass windows. At night the centre of town is dead, but by day it is very busy with vendors and crowds. Still, it is not over-agitated or dirty.

Beaches are fine (take bus marked "P. Futuro" from Praça Castro Carreira, "Praia Circular" bus which does a circular route to Praia Futuro, or bus marked "Caça e Pesca", which passes all SE beaches on its route), and you can watch the boats coming in before sundown with their catch. The majority of high class hotels are on the beach from Praia de Iracema (which is the most popular beach, though rather polluted eastwards; in the evenings everyone promenades along this beach and on Sunday a huge TV screen is erected on the beach close to *Hotel Beira Mar*—see and be seen!). Another near town is Barra do Ceará, where the Rio Ceará flows into the sea. Praia do Futuro is 8 km. to the SE, Praia de Icaraí 22 km. to the NW (it is under development); also Cumbuco where one can swim safely and there are palm trees (bus from Av. Tristão Gonçalves to Caucaia, then another bus). Iguape beach is recommended, but is at end of 90 min. bus ride—São Benedito bus marked "Iguape" from Praça F. de Melo (trips on *jangadas* for US$7). The Serra de Maranguape with tropical growth and distant views back to the city is 30 km. inland. The local dance, *forró,* can be experienced at the *Clube dos Vaqueiros* out on the BR-116 road South, Wed. 2230; or at *Viva Maria,* Vieira e Estados Unidos, Sat. at 2200 (check by phone first).

Local Holidays Jan. 6 (Epiphany); Ash Wed.; March 19 (São José); Christmas Eve; New Year's Eve, half-day.

A festival takes place on the last Sunday in July, during which the traditional *jangada* (raft) races take place. On August 15, the local Umbanda *terreiros* (churches) celebrate the Festival of Iemanjá on Praia do Futuro, taking over the entire beach from noon till dusk, when offerings are cast into the surf. Well worth attending (members of the public may "pegar um passo" - enter into an inspired religious trance—at the hands of a *pai-de-santo*). Beware of pick-pockets and purse-snatchers.

Hotels *Beira Mar,* on beach, swimming pool, A; *Novotel,* Av. Pres. Kennedy 2380, A; *Othon Palace,* 5-star, beach front location; *Esplanada Praia,* Av. Presidente Kennedy 2000, A; *Colonial,* 4-star, pleasant, with best grounds and biggest pool, laundry service (10 mins. walk from Av. Kennedy). *Nordeste Palace,* Rua Assunção 99 in centre, large rooms, friendly, good value; *Samburá Praia,* Av. Beira Mar 4530, B, cheaper than most beach hotels; *Pousada Jardim,* run by Sr. Abelardo Bezerra at Ildefonso Albano 950 (T 231-7991) in Aldeota district, by Iracema beach, B, very clean, friendly, nice garden, excursions arranged, many languages spoken, warmly rec.; another on same street, No. 644, E, clean and friendly (T 226-9206); *Ondas Verdes,* Av. Pres. Kennedy 934, T 226-0871, D, fan, TV, shower, clean, rec.; *Cabana Praia,* at Rua João Lourenço 441 (224-2557) and at Av. Rui Barbosa 555, both D, small, friendly; *Excelsior,* Guilherme Rocha 172, D, with good breakfast, no bath; *Premier,* Rua Barão do Rio Branco 829, D, good. *San Campio,* Guilherme Rocha 1156, a/c, D, quiet, friendly. *Chevalier,* Av. Duque de Caxias 465, E with bath and fan, pleasant; *Blumenau,* Rua 25 de Março 705, E, noisy, a/c, TV, friendly, helpful;

Minas Gerais, Av. Duque de Caxias, E, friendly. *Lord*, Praça José de Alencar, F and up, private bath, hot water, fan, large and clean (restaurant not rec.). *Pousada da Praia*, Av. Mons. Tabosa 1315, Iracema, 2 blocks from beach, E, fan, valuables may be left in safe of English-speaking owner, rec., buses to centre stop at door; *Pousada do Mar*, behind *Esplanada*, near Av. Mons. Tabosa, F, clean and friendly; *Pousada d'Antonietta*, Carlos Vasconcelos 660, T 224-3454, good breakfast, clean, quiet, 5 mins. from beach, buses to centre and other beaches nearby, E with bath; *Paraíso da Praia*, R. dos Pacajus 109, Iracema, small, on beach, helpful and friendly, good *trattoria* next door; *Apart-hotel*, at beginning of Praia Iracema, 20 mins.' walk from centre, F and up, with bath, pool and bar, clean, quiet, but dishonest staff; *Nossa Pousada*, Rua Ana Bilhar 123, Meireles, E without bath, near beach, friendly, helpful; *Temporada Atlântica*, Praia do Futuro, F, clean, friendly, good. Inexpensive hotels along Rua Senador Pompeu, e.g. No. 492, *Savoy*, E with breakfast (cheaper rooms without bath), basic, grubby but friendly; *Moreira*, No. 562, F with fan, central, good, clean, laundry; *Universo*, at No. 1152, F with breakfast, clean, friendly, may rent by the bed (i.e. single sex clients 3 to a room) some rooms have mosquito nets; No.725, *Tio Patinho 2*, F, less good than *Tio Patinho 3*. *Jacanã*, Rua 24 de Maio 845, E with breakfast, safe; across street are *Tio Patinho 3* and *Dormitório Belo Horizonte*, both F. *Passeio*, Rua Dr. João Moreira 221, E with bath, fan, good breakfast, good value. *Caxambu*, General Bezerril 22 (T 231-0339), a/c, D with breakfast, and bath, clean, good value, but poor food, central (opposite Cathedral, in market area). Note that the central area is deserted at night. *Arautuma*, D, pool, sauna, by Rodoviária (6 km. from centre), entrance by service station. Try student houses on Av. Universitários, cheap or even free. **Youth Hostel**: Rua Frei Mansueta 370, T 244-1254, IYHA card with photo necessary.

Camping Official site about 5 km south of city, but expensive, messy and hard to find.

Electric Current 220 volts A.C., 60 cycles.

Restaurants Several good fish restaurants at far end of Av. Presidente Kennedy, where the boats come ashore between 1300 and 1500, for example, *Trapiche*, No. 3950 (expensive, but excellent except for wine list). At Praia de Iracema (Av. Kennedy 4544) are *Alfredo* (good fish) and, next door, *Peixada do Meio* (better). Also Italian are *La Trattoria*, Praia de Iracema between Tabajaras and Av. Kennedy, and *La Távola*, Aquidabã 393, good pizzas. *Sandras*, Av. Perimetral, Praia do Futuro, lobster from US$7 upwards, has been specially rec. *Rancho Gaúcho*, Praia Náutica (between *Novotel* and *Othon Palace*), good. *Churrascaria Tourão*, Av. Mons. Tabosa, all you can eat for US$4.50; *Opção*, Mons. Tabosa with Albano, good, inexpensive. Good restaurant in Clube Náutico. A short taxi ride from Clube Náutico is *O Ozias*, Rua Canuto de Aguiar 1449 (T 224-9067), good for seafood, but hard to find. Good Chinese: *HongKong*, Av. Pres. Kennedy 4544, Mucuripe, and *Tung Hua*, Av. Visconde de Mauá 81, Meireles. Vegetarian: *Caminho á Saúde*, lunch only, US$1.50, very good value, Barão do Rio Branco 1468; next door is *Alivita*, Barão do Rio Branco 1486, good, lunch only, US$1, Mon.-Fri.; *Céu da Boca*, Rua Franklin Távora 136, lunch and 1800-2000 Mon.-Fri., good and inexpensive. *Rio Lanches*, Almirante Barroso 1003, good sandwiches and fruit juice; *Caminho á Saúde* also has lanchonete and store at Mons. Tabosa 1326. *Kury*, Rua Senador Pompeu 959, good food at reasonable prices. Another good place in centre is *Belas Artes*, Major Facundo 82, just up from Passeio Público. Cheap meals at railway station. Emcetur restaurant, in old prison, good atmosphere. Good view of Fortaleza from *Restaurant Panorâmico*, Rua Mirante, in Mucuripe district, near the lighthouse.

Shopping Fortaleza has an excellent selection of textiles at reasonable prices (among the cheapest in Brazil) and some handicrafts. Also good for clothes. The local specialities are lace (some hand-made) and embroidered textile goods; also hammocks (US$8-10—try Gerardo, Loja Cifa, Travessa Crato 28/32, in mall opp. Mercado central), fine alto-relievo wood carvings of North-East scenes, basket ware and clay figures (*bonecas de barro*). Bargaining is O.K. at the Mercado Central in the Praça da Sé, and the Emcetur tourist market in the old prison (more expensive). Every night (1800-2300), there are stalls along Av. Pres. Kennedy (the beach), lively but more expensive than the Mercado Central, where some stallholders will accept a better price if you're paying in dollars. The Centro de Artesanato Lucila Távora is decaying. Boutiques along Monsenhor Tabosa between Senador Almino and João Cordeiro. Cashew nuts at the Mercado Central are excellent.

Theatre Teatro José de Alencar, near railway station in centre, built 1810, building contains also newer theatre built 1910.

Exchange Lloyds Bank (ex-BOLSA), Rua Barão do Rio Branco 862; and national banks. Open 0900-1630. Exchange at travel agent for cash and cheques or at Ari, Sapataria Brasileira, Rua Gen. Bezerril 142, or at the Zely shop in the old prison. *Hotel Oberon Palace* on Av. Kennedy for cash and travellers' cheques.

Post Office in centre. Parcels must be taken to Receita Federal office at Barão de Aracati 909, Aldeota (take "Dom Luiz" bus).

Telephone International calls from Emcetur hut on Iracema beach and from Teleceará offices (Rua João Moreira esq. Rua Floriano Peixoto).

Cables Embratel, Rua Castro e Silva 286/290.

Tourist Information Emcetur, in ex-municipal prison, helpful, has maps. Open 0700-1800, Sun. 0700-1200. Also on Iracema beach.

Tourist Agencies Mundiatur (helpful, English spoken), Turismo Viagens, Itala Viagens Turismo and Intertur. Advised that it is best to book beach trips through Emcetur.

Car Hire Beach buggies rentable for US$30 a day plus small km. charge, from Junna's Buggy, Av. Abolição 2480, T 244-7872.

Rail South to Baturité (tourist train round trip Sun.), Iguatu and Crato (once a week) and to Crateus once a week.

Air Service Direct flights to Belém, Recife, Rio and other cities in Brazil. Bus from airport to Praça José de Alencar.

Bus Service New bus station 6 km. from centre, bus to Praça José de Alencar marked Aguanambi 1 or 2 (and others). The Expresso de Luxo runs daily to Recife (12 hrs., US$11, leave at night), also Rio de Janeiro, 48 hrs., US$45 (*leito* 90), São Paulo, 48 hrs., US$46 (*leito* 92), Crato, Parnaíba, and many other cities. To Brasília, Expresso Ipu-Brasília, same company to Belo Horizonte, 42 hrs. Salvador, 19 hrs., US$18; Natal, US$6, 8 hrs. (Nordeste has *leito* US$14, an *executivo* at noon, and 5 *semi-leitos* which make only 3 stops); Teresina, US$7, 9 hrs. (at least); São Luís, US$16, 18 hrs., 4 a day; Belém US$21, 5 buses a day, 23 hrs., (2 companies, Exp. Timbira good). To Piripiri, for Parque Nacional de Sete Cidades, US$5, 9 hrs.

Excursions *Caponga* beach, to the SE, is reached by direct bus from Fortaleza (2 a day) or by taking a bus from Fortaleza to Cascavel (80 mins., US$0.75) then a bus from Cascavel (20 mins., US$0.25); accommodation at *Caponga Praia*, on the beach front, simple cheap rooms and good meals, and at *Pousada Sereia*, very friendly, good, E. A ½-hour walk S along the deserted white-sand beach leads to a river mouth, offering a combination of fresh-and salt-water bathing. Jangadas set sail in the early morning (arrangements can be made to accompany fishermen on overnight trips); there is a fish market on the beach. 174 km. SE of Fortaleza is *Aracati* (bus every 2 hrs., US$1.70; bus to Natal, via Mossoró, 6 hrs., US$5). From this town take a VW Combi-Bus to *Canoa Quebrada* (US$0.50, ask locals for bus stop—taxi US$3.50), a fishing village on a sand dune, 10 km. from Aracati. There are now many *pousadas* (*Pousada Cultural*, F, basic, clean, friendly; 2 rooms behind *Sol de Manhã* café on mainstreet, clean, with shower, F, good breakfast in the café; *Tenda do Cumbe*, at end of road on cliff, thatched huts E, restaurant, warmly rec.; also on cliff above beach, *Pousada Ao Nascer do Sol*, F, clean, shower, friendly, hammocks for rent) and villagers will let you sling your hammock or put you up for about US$1.50 (Brendan is rec., but his food is expensive, European books exchanged; Sr Miguel rents good clean houses for US$7.50 a day); bars and restaurants for food, vegetarian food in *Espácio Cultural*, cheap seafood (don't drink the water); only a few places have running water. The village is famous for its *labirinto* lacework and coloured sand sculpture, for sand-skiing on the dunes, for the sunsets, and for the beaches, though beware of jiggers (*bicho de pé*) there, best to wear shoes. Canoa Quebrada has been "discovered" and is becoming a major tourist attraction; basic tours (no food) from Fortaleza, 12 hrs., US$10.

40 km. from Fortaleza, along the coast, is *Prainha*, a fishing village and weekend resort (bus terminal in Fortaleza opp. Escola Normal at 1430 and 1700, return 1530 and 1800). You can see jangadas coming in daily in the late afternoon. The beaches are clean and largely empty. *Prainha Solex Hotel*, Rua Pericich Ribeiro 5, T 361-1000/01/02, ramal 156.7, D, pool, comfortable. Good fish restaurant, *O Leonção*, on same street. There are several small, cheap and good restaurants, where it is possible to see displays of the *carimbó*, the main local dance of Ceará. 87 km. from Fortaleza (too far for a day trip) is *Morro Branco* (4 km. from Beberibe, bus), with spectacular beach, craggy cliffs and beautiful views. Jangadas leave the beach at 0500, returning at 1400-1500; hotel-restaurants, E; *Cabana do Morro*, *Pousada do Morro*, E, clean, but mosquitoes, fan and shower, *Novo*, E, clean, noisy at weekends and *Recanto Praia*, F, clean, good breakfast, rec. (first two have swimming pool); or you can rent fishermen's houses; meals can also be arranged at beach-front bars (try *O Jangadeiro*). Double room for rent at *Bar São Francisco*, F, or 7-room house for rent. São Benedito bus from Fortaleza, US$1; 2½ hrs., 4 a day. To get to Natal, take 0600 bus to Beberibe, then 0800 bus (only one) to Aracati, US$0.50, then on to Natal. Town is very crowded at holiday time. No money exchange available.

Two hours NW of Fortaleza by bus is *Paracuru*, a small fishing port (fish readily available), which is being developed as Ceará's carnival city (*Teto da Praia*, E, cooking facilities, close to beach; restaurant *Ronco do Mar*, good fish dishes also *Balança do Mar* and a pizzaria; breakfast at Dona Luci's *sitio*, No. 25 in the market; *Boca do Poço* bar is scene of *forró* at weekends). It has some lovely deserted white sand beaches with good bathing, and the people are very friendly. Some 7 hours from Fortaleza is the sleepy fishing village of *Almofala*, served by many buses. There is electricity, but no hotels or restaurants, although locals rent hammock space and cook meals (usually US$2 p.p., food and lodging). Bathing is better elsewhere, but the area is surrounded by dunes and is excellent for hiking along the beach to nearby lobster-fishing communities. In Almofala, the church with much of the town was covered by shifting sands and remained covered for 50 years, reappearing in the 1940s.

Nestled in the dunes near the border with the state of Piauí is the tiny fishing community of *Jericuacuara* (known as Serrote by locals). Described as one of Brazil's most secluded primitive beaches, it is becoming increasingly popular with travellers and Brazilians, despite the difficulty of getting there. There is no real road, so the trip is part of the adventure: the least difficult route is to take the bus from Fortaleza to Gijoca at 0800 or 2000 (8 hrs., US$4), then a jeep meets the bus: Jericuacuara from Gijoca costs about US$2 per person for the hour-and-a-half journey. (A direct journey from Fortaleza on a 3-day tour is possible in a VW Kombi.) You can also get there by boat from Camocim (a little further west), "seasickness guaranteed". Once there, the visitor is rewarded with towering sand dunes, deserted beaches with little shade, cactus-covered cliffs rising from the sea, and a chance to savour life in a sleepy, primitive fishing community. Pigs, chickens and donkeys roam the streets at will; there is no electricity and no running water (take your showers at the town pump). Fortunately, ice-cold beer is available in several tiny lantern-lit bars and there is *forró* on Fri. and Sat. nights. Many locals rent hammock space (US$0.50), hammocks, and cook food (about US$2 per day, room and board), and there is one *pousada* (E) and restaurant belonging to a very helpful German. There are several restaurants serving vegetarian and fish dishes (*Restaurante Central*, rec.). Fresh banana tart available most days at about 1300. Sevral shops sell basic provisions, so camping is possible. Returning, the bus leaves Gijoca for Fortaleza at midnight and 0630.

The pilgrimage centre of Canindé may be visited, 3-hour bus ride from Box 21 of the Rodoviária (Viação Nova Esperança). Large modern church on hill with carved baptistery doors, many ex-votos, interesting dry-land vegetation along route. (Hotels: *Plaza*, by basilica, food OK; *Santo Antônio*). Another inland town, Baturité, can be seen, 3 hrs. from Rodoviária (Box 45) by Redenção bus, mornings only, also a tourist train round trip Sundays.

The Ubajara cave in the **Ubajara National Park** is worth seeing; it is 18 km. off the road to Teresina, on a good paved road, 3 km. from Ubajara town. A cablecar used to descend the cliff to the cave entrance but has not been repaired since it broke down in 1985. Ask for a guide at the park entrance (they leave at 0800 for the 6 km. round trip); a torch is necessary for the cave, which is an hour's walk down a rocky, wooded path (also take drinking water). The views of the *sertão* from the upper cablecar platform are superb. Here is the *Pousada Neblina*, E, near caves, with swimming pool, with breakfast and private shower, meals rec.; opposite is an unnamed hostel, G with bath, clean, friendly, rustic, restaurant, rec. In *Ubajara* town are *Hotel Gruta*, Rua 31 de Dezembro 74, F, basic, good breakfast, helpful owner, and *Hotel Churrascaría Ubajara*, Rua Juvêncio Pereira 370, E, clean and friendly, hot water, good breakfast, restaurant. Interesting Sunday morning market. Several buses a day to Fortaleza.

The road to Sobral and Teresina is paved, but in poor condition. To hitch-hike to Teresina, take a bus W to the BR-222, the Teresina road.

Sobral, the principal town in western Ceará and well-known for straw hats, has *Hotel Municipal*, E, meals available. South of Sobral is the remote town of *Crateús* (rail link, but no paved roads there), with the *Crateús Palace Hotel*, very reasonable and clean, F, with breakfast. Good restaurant, *Churrascaria Pequena Cabana*, at back of hotel. Bus service from Crateús over very bad road to Teresina, every two days. At Tianguá, 311 km. from Fortaleza on the Teresina road, is *Serra Grande* hotel, built 1980, all amenities, D, good.

Between the states of Maranhão and Piauí, which has a coastline of only 27 km., runs the river Parnaíba. Near its mouth is the anchorage of Luís Correia, where ships unload for final delivery by tugs and lighters at **Parnaíba**, 15 km. up river, the collecting and distributing centre for the trade of Piauí: tropical products and cattle. Population, 79,000.

Hotels *Parnaíba Palace; Rio Parnaíba. Cívico*, E with bath and a/c, good breakfast, friendly, rec.; *Rodoviária*, F and other basic hotels in the centre.

Beaches at Luís Correia, which with Parnaíba has radioactive sands (good hotel at Luís Correia, F). Some 15 km. from Parnaíba is Pedra do Sal: dark blue lagoons and palm trees.

Teresina, about 435 km. up the Parnaíba river, is the capital of the State of Piauí, reputed to be the poorest in Brazil. There are paved road and rail connections with the neighbouring state capitals. The city itself is reputed to be the hottest after Manaus (temperatures rise to 42°C). Population is 339,000 The Palácio de Karnak (the old governor's palace), just South of Praça Frei Serafim, can be visited, Mon.-Fri., 1530-1730; it contains lithographs of the Middle East in 1839 by David Roberts R.A. There is an interesting open market by the Praça Marechal Deodoro and the river is picturesque, with washing laid out to dry along its banks. The market is a good place to buy hammocks, but bargain hard.

Every morning along the river bank there is the *troca-troca* where people buy, sell and swap, but it is no longer spontaneous; an under-cover complex (Mercado Central do Artesanato) has been built at Rua Paissandu 1276 (Praça Dom Pedro II), open daily 0800-2200 (not weekends). Most of the year the river is low, leaving sandbanks known as *coroas* (crowns).

Hotels   *Luxor Hotel do Piauí*, A, and *Teresina Palace*, luxury class; *Grande*, Firmino Pires 73, E, very friendly and clean; *Sambaíba*, Rua Gabriel Ferreira 230-N, 2-star, C, central, good; *Victoria*, Senador T. Pacheco 1199, F, friendly, basic, clean; *São João e São Pedro*, F, rec.; *São José*, João Cabral 340, E, reasonable restaurant; *Fortaleza*, Felix Pacheco 1101, Prça. Saraiva, T 222-2984, F, fan, basic, rec.; many cheap hotels and *dormitórios* around Praça Saraiva. *Rex*, Rui Barbosa 36, E, central, clean, a/c, good breakfast; *Gurgueia*, Rui Barbosa 519, D, a/c; *Viana*, R. Senador T. Pacheco 899, F, cheap. Many cheap ones in Rua São Pedro: *Bom Clima*, No.890, E; *São Pedro*, No. 905, E; *Globo*, No. 861, E; and in Rua Alvaro Mendes, *Glória*, at 823 (clean, best), and at 860, 906, all E. No hotels at new Rodoviária as yet.

Restaurants   *Churrascaria Gaúcha*, 12 km. W of newer river bridge, with all the meat you can eat for US$3.50. For fish dishes, *Pesqueirinho*, near the confluence of the rivers in Poti Velho district. Many eating places for all pockets in Praça Dom Pedro II. (*Típico do Piauí, good value*).

Exchange   For parallel market try Banorte Turismo, Av. Pacheco and Barbosa. Larger hotels may be helpful (e.g. *Luxor do Piauí*).

Laundry   Tintoraria São Paulo, Rui Barbosa 431, nr. *Luxor Hotel do Piauí*.

Shopping   Supermarket on Praça Marechal Deodoro 937, clean, good, fresh food. Local handicrafts include leather and clothes.

Tourist Information   Piemtur, Rua Alvaro Mendes 2003, Caixa Postal 36, information office at Rua Magalhães Filho s/n (next to 55 N -English spoken); kiosks at Rodoviária and airport.

Buses   The bus trip from Fortaleza is scenic and takes 9 hrs. (US$7, *leito* at 2100, arr. 0600, US$14). Another road, very bad, leads inland to Porto Franco and Imperatriz (Restaurant: *Bar Central*, OK) on the Belém-Brasília highway; daily bus takes 26-40 hrs. for the trip to Imperatriz (US$9), depending on the state of the road; these buses are very crowded. There are direct buses to Belém, but avoid the non-express (*parador*) service. The road to São Luís is quite good, bar a few potholes. Another main road, also very bad, runs SE to Picos (*Hotel Picos*, E, basic, but a/c); from there a good road runs via Salgueiro (many *pousadas*) to Recife (800 km.) and a bad one to Petrolina, on the River São Francisco opposite the Bahian town of Juazeiro. Bus, one or two a day, 15 hrs., US$10. Buses from Petrolina/Juazeiro (**see page 360**) SE to Salvador. Bus to Belém, about 16 hrs., US$12. To São Luís, bus takes 7 hrs., US$5.

Rail   Trains to Fortaleza, Mon. 1050, 17½ hrs, and São Luís, 453 km., Thurs. 0400, 16½ hrs (for the stout-hearted only). Teresina-Parnaíba, mixed train, once a week but often cancelled

Excursion   Some 190 km. NE of Teresina and 12 km. from Piracuruca is the interesting 20-sq. km. Parque Nacional de *Sete Cidades* with its strange eroded rock formations, just off the Fortaleza-Teresina road. From the ground it looks like a medley of weird monuments. The inscriptions on some of the rocks have never been deciphered; one Austrian researcher in the 1920s suggested links with the Phoenicians. There is plenty of birdlife. If hiking in the park, beware of rattlesnakes. IBDF guides drive round the park (2½ hrs.), you may be able to get around on their tractor, or else walk (takes all day, very hot). Small booklet with sketch map (not really good enough for walking), US$0.20; entrance US$0.30. There are camping facilities (US$0.60) and two natural swimming pools, although several years of drought have lowered their water level drastically. Local food is limited and monotonous: bring a few delicacies, and especially fruit.

6 km. from the park entrance is the hotel *Fazenda Sete Cidades*, C, with private bathroom, swimming pool, good restaurant and free bicycle or horse transport (it is at Km. 63 on BR-222, T (086) 261-3642); also has a free pick-up to the park (and a most unpleasant zoo). In the park is a IBDF (Forestry Institute) hostel, G p.p., rooms with bath, pleasant, good restaurant, natural pool nearby—closed for repairs in 1988. Ask the park administration (Sr Joaquim Menor) if there is room to sleep in the workers' house.

A free bus service leaves the Praça in **Piripiri** (in front of Telpisa office), 26 km. away, at 0700, passing *Hotel Fazenda Sete Cidades* at 0800, reaching the park 10 mins. later; return at 1630, or hitch-hike. Taxi from Piripiri, US$8, or from Piracuruca, US$10. Bus Teresina-Piripiri and return, throughout the day 2½ hrs. US$2.10. Bus São Luis-Piripiri, 1200, 1630, 2130, 10 hrs., US$6.50. Several daily buses Piripiri-Fortaleza, 9 hrs. US$5. Bus Piripiri-Ubajara (see previous page), marked "São Benedito", with Itapemirim, 2½ hrs.; US$2, first at 0700 (a beautiful trip, although one dirt stretch will get your belongings dusty unless protected by plastic). Hotels in Piripiri: *Dos Viajantes*, G, basic and clean; *Piripiri*, both near bus offices and behind the church. Exchange at the bank only.

In the south of the state is *Oeiras*, old capital of Piauí, where the state government is restoring some of the old buildings, such as the bishop's palace and the church of Nossa Senhora da Vitória.

Maranhão state is about the size of Italy; its land is flat and low-lying, with highlands to the S. The Atlantic coastline—a mass of sandbanks and creeks and sandy islands on one of which stands São Luís—is 480 km. long. A quarter of Maranhão is covered with *babaçu* palms, and by far the most important products are *babaçu* nuts and oil. Rice often takes second place, but well behind *babaçu*. There are salt pans along the coast. The huge Boa Esperança hydroelectric plant on the Parnaíba river now floods the State with energy, and some petroleum has been discovered. The main road from Teresina passes through the Maranhense town of Caxias, which has a good churrascaria, *Selva do Braz* (Av. Central 601), live music in the evening.

São Luís, the capital and port of Maranhão state, founded in 1612 by the French and named for St. Louis of France, is about 560 km. west of Fortaleza (1,080km. by road) and 400 km. SE of Belém (830 km. by road) in a region of heavy tropical rains, but the surrounding deep forest has been cut down to be replaced by babaçu palms. The city stands upon São Luis island between the bays of São Marcos and São José. The urban area extends to São Francisco island, connected with São Luís by three bridges. The old part, on very hilly ground with many steep streets, is still almost pure colonial: the damp climate stimulated the use of ceramic tiles for exterior walls, and São Luís shows a greater variety of such tiles than anywhere else in Brazil, in Portuguese, French and Dutch styles. See the Governor's Palace (state rooms open Mon., Wed., Fri. 1500-1800, take passport, beautiful floors of dark wood (*jacarandá*) and light (*cerejeira*), marvellous views from terrace) and the old slave market. The best colonial churches to see—some of them rebuilt and not improved by it—are the Cathedral and the churches of Carmo, São João, Rosário, and Santana. On Largo do Desterro is the church of São José do Desterro, finished in 1863, but with some much older parts. The restored Fortaleza de Santo Antônio, built originally by the French in 1614, is on the bank of the River Anil at Ponta d'Areia. The Fonte do Ribeirão, Largo do Ribeirão, was begun in 1796. The Museu do Estado, in a fine early 19th century mansion (complete with slave quarters) at Rua do Sol 302, US$0.35, is open Tues.-Fri., 1400-1800, Sat.-Sun., and holidays, 1500-1800. Also on the Rua do Sol is the Teatro Artur Azevedo (1816). The commercial quarter is still much as it was in the 17th century; best shopping area is Rua de Santana near Praça João Lisboa. Population: 560,000. Much renovation is in progress (President José Sarney is a Maranhense).

Festivals On June 24 (São João), the "Bumba-Meu-Boi", a fantastic bull dance and masque with traditional words. For several days before the festival street bands parade, particularly in front of the São João and São Benedito churches. The São Benedito, at the Rosário church in August. Festival in October, with dancing, at Vila Palmeira suburb (take bus of same name).

Hotels Good accommodation is in short supply, and the situation will worsen when Texaco begins oil exploration off-shore. *Quatro Rodas*, 8 km. from centre on Calhau beach, A, excellent, with all facilities; *Vila Rica*, 5-star, Praça D. Pedro II, A, central, many amenities; *Lord*, D, Rua Joaquim Távora 258, facing Praça Benedito Leite, comfortable, clean, rec., good breakfast; nearby is *Central*, Av. D. Pedro II 258, more expensive, but noisy at night with TV, D. *São Marcos*, D, Saúde 178, restored colonial house, a/c, family-run, rec. More basic, but with excellent food, *Pousada Solar do Carmo*, Praça João Lisboa 400, D-E, pleasant, friendly, light and airy. Many cheap hotels in Rua das Palmas, very central and Rua Formosa; *Klauss*, opposite *São Marcos* in side street off Rua Formosa, F, friendly, dirty; *Nazaré*, Rua de Nazaré (extension of Rua do Sol), F, central, fair facilities and breakfast, reckoned the best of the cheap hotels by one who has tried them all; *Globo*, E, with bath (F without) and breakfast, friendly, quite clean; *Casa do Estudante*, Rua do Passeio, 2 km. from centre. At Ponta d'Areia: *Ponta d'Areia*, Av. dos Holandeses, Quadra 13 (T 227-2737), about 3 km. from centre, C, a/c, bath, hot water, TV, fridge, restaurant, pool; *Praia Mar*, on the beach, A, 5-star, all amenities, opp. *São Francisco*. **Youth hostel**: *O Cortiço*, Rua 14 de Julho 93, central.

Restaurants *Solar do Riberão*, Rua Isaac Martins 141, T 222-3068, good buffet lunch and seafood, good value but not cheap, regional cuisine, closed Sat. p.m. and Sun.; *Hibiscus* and *Tia*

Maria, rec.; *Base do Germano*, Av. Wenceslau Bras in Canto da Fabril district, excellent *caldeirada de camarão* (shrimp stew), about US$4 per head. *Panorama*, Av. Dom Pedro II, 206, good, nice views; *Atenas*, Humberto de Campos 175, good stew for US$2; *Aliança*, Praça Benedito Leite, good regional food. *Egito*, friendly, good food and atmosphere. *Naturaleza*, Rua da Formosa, vegetarian, good, lunch only, Mon.-Fri.; *Naturalista Alimentos*, Rua do Sol 517, very good, open till 1900. *Marjuce* in Rua das Palmas, good value. Said to be more choice in new São Francisco district, just across bridge, e.g. *Oriental*, Av. Pres. Castelo Branco, good Chinese, and *Pizzaria Internacional*.

Exchange Travellers' cheques only at Banco do Brasil; Agetur, Rua do Sol 33.

Cables Embratel, Avenida Dom Pedro II 190. T 2500.

Tourist Offices Av. dos Franceses and Av. Pedro II; good information on walks in city. Recent travellers report Maratur offices of little use. Taguatur, in *Hotel Central* building, good. Town maps from agencies. Funai shop at Rua do Sol 371. Centro do Artesanato in main street of São Francisco suburb, over bridge from the city.

Airport Internal flights only. 15 km. from centre; buses ("São Cristovão") to city until midnight, US$0.20. Flight to Belém, US$46 (US$32 at night).

Railway 453 km. S to Teresina, through the Maranhense town of Caxias. Train leaves 0400, Mon., 20 hrs. US$2 1st class, US$1.90, 2nd class. A delightful if hard and dusty trip (no lights on train); frequent stops at country halts to buy coffee, cakes, fruit (but take food and water). Three trains a week on Carajás railway to Paraupebas, 16 hrs., 890 km., leave São Luís 0800, Mon. Wed., Fri., return 0300, Tues., Thur., Sat. (crowded, take own food); for station take "Vila Nova" or "Anjo da Guarda" bus.

Road Bus station 5 km. from centre, "Alemanha" bus to centre. The Teresina-São Luís road is paved ("just about OK"), bus service, US$5, 7 hrs. Bus to Piripiri, US$6.50, 10 hrs.; Expresso de Luxo continues to Fortaleza. Bus to Fortaleza, US$16, four a day, 18 hrs. (road also paved). Also to Recife, US$24, 25 hrs.

To Belém Direct road via Santa Inês and Alto Bonito paved, in reasonable condition, with petrol stations not far apart (about 9 hrs. driving with stop for lunch). There is a bus service 12 hrs., US$11, three daily (no *leito*). There are occasional coastal ships of the Costeira line.

Excursions Calhau is a huge beach, 10 km. away; Ponta D'Areia is nearer to São Luís but more crowded. An hour's bus ride from São Luís is Raposa, a fishing village built on stilts; another fishing village is Ribamar, a half hour's bus ride from São Luís, from in front of the market.

To the East of the city, on the Atlantic Coast is the **Parque Nacional Lençóis Maranhenses**, 155,000 hectares of beaches, lakes and dunes, with very little vegetation and largely unstudied wildlife. For information, the IBDF office is at Av. Jaime Tavares 25, São Luis (Caixa Postal 276, CEP 65.000).

Some 22 km. away by boat is *Alcântara*, the former state capital, on the mainland bay of São Marcos. Construction of the city began at the beginning of the seventeenth century and it is now a historical monument. There are many old churches (e.g. the ruined Matriz de São Matias) and colonial mansions (see the Casa, and Segunda Casa, do Imperador), the traditional pillory, the Pelourinho, in the Praça Gomes de Castro, also a small museum in the square (US$0.20) and the Forte de São Sebastião (1653) now in ruins. See also the Fonte de Miritituva. The city has a population of 2,000. Good beaches, good walking around the coast, but mosquitoes after dark. A rocket-launching site is being built nearby. Principal festival: Festa do Divino, at Pentecost (Whitsun).

Transport A boat service leaves São Luís daily at 0800, 80 minutes, from close to the Governor's palace, for Alcântara, returning between 1200 and 1300, but check return time, US$1.50 plus US$0.25 each for boat to take you from ferry to Alcântara dock; sea can be rough.

Hotels *Picandinho*, Praça Gomes de Castro, D, converted 17th-century house; *Pousada do Pelourinho*, Praça Gomes de Castro, D, clean, friendly, good restaurant, communal bathroom; one can also stay cheaply in houses (e.g. Dona Maria, 3rd house on left on Rua Neto Guterres, near harbour, US$1.50 for hammock space and 2 meals), or in restaurants, *Dois Amigos*, Rua da Miritituva, US$3 for hammock space and a meal. Try bargaining for hammock space in private houses. Children who offer themselves as guides can help arrange accommodation in private houses, friendly but no great comfort; provide your own mineral water.

On the Eastern bank of the Rio Tocantins, at Maranhão's western border with Goiás, is *Imperatriz*, a city serving a large cattle region. Go down Av. Getúlio Vargas and see the range of goods on offer. It is also in an area of violence over landholding; in 1986, a priest was shot in his church. To get to the ferry across the river, go along Rua Luis Domingues, which runs parallel to Av. Getúlio Vargas. **Hotels**: *Poseidon*, Rua Paraíba 740, T 721-4466, central, best, D, a/c, TV, swimming pool, rec.; *Anápolis*, BR-010, Km. 1345, T 721-2255, opp. Rodoviária, E, a/c, fridge, swimming pool, friendly; a lot of cheap hotels near Rodoviária. There is a good, expensive discotheque at Beira Rio, north of the ferry crossing, *Fly Back Disco Club*; it has two dance floors, one fast, one slow (for couples only). Telephone office on Rua Rio Grande do Norte, a side street off Av. Getúlio Vargas, near *Hotel Poseidon*. Lying on the Belém-Brasília highway, Imperatriz has bus connections with both cities; there is a slow, crowded bus service to Teresina. To get to Marabá on the Transamazônica, you can either take a Transbrasiliana bus direct, 7-10 hrs (starting on the Belém highway, the bus then turns west along a poorer road, passing finally through destroyed forest, new fazendas and unplanned cities), or, a faster route, involving taking a ferry across the river in the early morning (0600-0700) to catch a pick-up on the other side, takes about 5 hours, but is more expensive.

NORTHERN BRAZIL (8)

Northern Brazil consists of the states of Pará, Amazonas, Rondônia and Acre, and the territories of Amapá and Roraima.

The area is drained by the Amazon, which in size, volume of water—12 times that of the Mississippi—and number of tributaries has no equal in the world. At the base of the Andes, far to the west, the Amazonian plain is 1,300 km. in width, but east of the confluences of the Madeira and Negro rivers with the Amazon, the highlands close in upon it until there is no more than 80 km. of floodplain between them. Towards the river's mouth—about 320 km. wide—the plain widens once more and extends along the coast south-eastwards into the state of Maranhão and northwards into the Guianas.

Amazonia, much of it still covered with tropical forest, is 56% of the national area, equivalent to two-thirds of Canada. Its jungle is the world's largest and densest rain forest, with more diverse plants and animals than any other jungle in the world. It has only 8% of Brazil's population, and most of this is concentrated around Belém (in Pará), and in Manaus, 1,600 km. up the river. The population is sparse because other areas are easier to develop; the rainfall is heavy, the humidity high and the climate hot; and the soil, as in all tropical forest, is poor.

The Government is now making strenuous efforts to develop Amazonia. Roads have been built parallel to the Amazon to the south (the Transamazônica), from Cuiabá (Mato Grosso) northwards to Santarém (Pará), and NE from Porto Velho through Humaitá to the river bank opposite Manaus. Agricultural settlements are being established along these roads, and great concern has been expressed at the wholesale destruction of the forest. The area is changing rapidly, especially under the impetus of major energy and mining projects for bauxite and iron ore now in progress. This is reflected in the burgeoning cities. Manaus now suffers from air pollution.

Anyone interested in the Amazonian development programme and its ecological, social, economic and political effects should read Richard Bourne's masterly "Assault on the Amazon" (London, Gollancz, 1978), "Dreams of Amazonia", by Roger D.Stone (Penguin, 1986), or "Amazon" by Brian Kelly and Mark London (Harcourt Brace Jovanovich, New York, 1983).

Along the Transamazônica

The Transamazônica, about 5,000 km. in length, represents the greater part of a direct road connection between Brazil's furthest E and furthest W points. It skirts the southern edge of the Amazonian plain, linking the following places: Estreito (junction with the Belém-Brasília highway, N of Araguaína, **see page407**), Marabá (on the Tocantins river), Altamira (on the Xingu), São Luís do Tapajós, near Itaituba (on the Tapajós), Jacarèacanga, Humaitá (on the Madeira), Rio Branco, and Japim, in the far W of the State of Acre. The road was officially opened in December 1973; parts are paved and buses are running along virtually the whole length; they are operating between Marabá and Humaitá and there are also services from Santarém to the Belém-Brasília road and to Cuiabá along a very bad road, can take a week in the rainy season (October onwards) and it is dangerous to stay in small villages en route.

From **Marabá**, pop. 14,776 (*Plaza*, Nova Marabá, by rodoviária, T 321-1661, E with fan, pleasant, helpful, some English spoken; *Hotel São Félix, Hotel Hilda Palace*, E; *Norte-Sur*, F; *Pensão Nossa Senhora do Nazaré*, F, clean, near bus terminal; *Avenida*, F; *Churrascaria Beira Rio*; *Restaurant O Calmon* for fish) buses leave daily at 0430, 1200 and 1500 for Belém, for Santarém (34 hrs.) at 1730 and many daily for Imperatriz (7-10 hrs., US$5, there is also a pick-up to the bank of the Tocantins opp. Imperatriz, 5 hrs., but more expensive, US$6-8); buses can be caught going south at Toncantinópolis, opposite Porto Franco on the Belém-Brasília road. Also a bus can be taken to Araguaína, 12½ hrs., US$10; bus Marabá-Goiânia (change at Araguaína), US$25. Bus to Santa Inês (Maranhão, on Belém-Terisina road), 1700, 19 hrs., US$12. On these bus trips take plenty of food and drink—local supplies are expensive. With the filling of the Tucuruí dam the town has been moved; even so it suffers from flooding. A new city of 200,000 is planned. The bridge across the Toncantins at Marabá is now open. Banco do Brasil will not cash travellers' cheques; parallel market in larger stores.

To visit the **Serra Pelada** gold mines, take Marabá city bus at 0600 to the village of "Kilo Seis" (bus marked "KM06" or "Beira Rio", cheap hotels at "Kilo Seis"), where a bus leaves for Serra Pelada (3 hours—first half good, second half on dirt road). 11 km. before the town is a police post: search for weapons and alcohol (forbidden); second search at airport 2 km. from the mine. Return buses leave from airport throughout the day. *Hotel Serra de Ouro*, E, all of wood, shower; good *Churrascaria* in main square near public TV set; juice bars and *DiscoTony* discotheque. No prior permission needed to visit mines, which are still being worked by individuals. They are usually friendly and like being photographed, but enquire about the conditions before going there.

From Marabá, or from São Luis or Belém, one can reach the Carajás iron mine (the largest mineral development in Brazil) by road—quite an adventure—or train (see under São Luis above, train can be caught at station 12 km. from Marabá, Mon. Wed., Sat. 0500). Plenty of Transbrasiliana buses daily Marabá-Carajás, 4-5 hrs, US$3; Military Police check for weapons and drugs at Curianópolis. Many unplanned towns along the road. To get into Cerajás (checkpoint 35 km. from the project), you must have a permit, available from Companhia Vale Rio Doce (CVRD) in Marabá, São Luis, São Paulo or Rio (hotel bookings handled here too); apply in advance and have a good reason. Between Marabá and Belém, on the Tocantins river, is the Tucuruí hydroelectric scheme (which is causing much ecological damage), reached either by bus or by day and night riverboat from Belém. *Hotel Transamérica* best in Tucuruí; *Marajoara*, Rua Lauro Sodré 685, T 787-1776, E, simple but OK. Floating bar (light meals), *Fluente*, 1½ km. N, take a taxi or motorboat, or walk, popular. To go to the dam, take bus "V Temp. I II" or "Vila Temporávia". From Marabá to Tucurui, take Transbrasiliano bus, 3 a day, 8 hrs., US$5, road good to Itupiranga, deteriorates thereafter; also boat from Belém (32 hrs.).

The Transamazônica crosses the river Xingu at Altamira (pop. 47,000); the crossing is by ferry. The town is served by jets and boats from Belém. *Garimpeiros* sift the waters of the river bend to the east.

Rurópolis (Presidente Medici) lies at the junction of the Transamazônica and the Santarém highway. **Hotel** run by Incra, "by all accounts, like the rest of the place: cracked, empty, dreaming of a future that never came" (Kevin Healey).

At **Itaituba**, (the jumping-off place for the **Amazonia national park**; see Father Paul Zoderer, who may help to arrange a visit, at church on waterfront—nearest IBDF office, Av. Cons. Furtado 1303, Belém, CEP 66.000) the Transbrasiliana company has a bus station on the river Tapajós, near the ferry docks. Bus fare Itaituba-Marabá, US$17. At Marabá, a new bridge has been built over the river Itacaiunas. The ferry service no longer runs.

In **Humaitá** there are several basic hotels on the eastern edge of town; *Hotel Humaitá*, F, basic but friendly; *Aquarius Palace*, E with breakfast, is also the Expresos Humaitá bus stop; a similar hotel is the Andorinha bus stop. The Soltur bus station is in the centre. Lots of military activity in Humaitá.

There is very little traffic on the Transamazônica between Itaituba and Humaitá; local drivers may give lifts. The road is very good for about 350 km. from Humaitá, then it deteriorates badly. It is hilly, narrow, and the jungle usually grows over the side of the road. Expresos Humaitá depart at 1500 daily. It takes 24 hours from Humaitá to Jacarèacanga (which is 8 km. off the highway). One must stay overnight and catch the Transbrasiliana bus to Itaituba (24 hours, schedule erratic; the bus is replaced occasionally by a truck). There are two insanitary and expensive hotels in Jacarèacanga (try the gas station on the Transamazônica near the Jacarèacanga turn-off, they may have hammock space). Bus fare Humaitá-Jacarèacanga, US$15.60; Jacarèacanga-Itaituba, US$8; travel time depends on the weather conditions, the condition of the bus, and whether the driver decides to stop somewhere for the night.

Up the Amazon River

The Amazon system is 6,577 km., long, of which 3,165 km. are in Brazilian territory. Ships of up to 4/5,000 tons regularly negotiate the Amazon for a distance of about 3,200 km. up to Iquitos, Peru. Regular passenger services as far as Manaus are operated by the State shipping line Enasa. Distances upstream from the river mouth to Manaus in nautical miles are:

Belém	80	Santarém	538
Narrows (entrance)	225	Óbidos	605
Narrows (exit)	330	Parintins	694
Garupa	334	Itacoatiara	824
Prainha	452	Manaus	930

What to wear Remember that some Enasa boats' restaurants do not permit shorts. At night put on a sweater or coat, for it gets quite cold. From April to October, when the river is high, the mosquitoes at night can be repelled by Super Repelex spray or K13; protective clothing is advisable. Leather sandals fall apart in the wet, rubber ones are better, but proper shoes or boots are best for going ashore: there are many foot-attacking parasites in the jungle. A hammock is essential on all but the most expensive boats; often too hot to lie down in cabin during day.

Health There is a danger of malaria in Amazonia. On the smaller boats sanitary standards are low and one is very likely to contract intestinal infections; take plenty of tablets (Colestase are the locally available brand), toilet paper, soap, water sterilization tablets (none available in Belém) and some plain biscuits. A good idea also to take oranges, mineral water, tea bags, seasonings, sauces and jam. A yellow-fever inoculation is strongly advised; it is compulsory in some areas.

N.B. If going in the smaller boats, be prepared for mechanical breakdowns that prolong the journey. If you have the choice, remember that the small boats often keep close to the banks; the patient watcher can see plenty of wildlife.

There has recently been much criticism of food and sanitary conditions on the Enasa boats, and travellers have recommended the smaller boats, despite their well-known disadvantages.

Joanna Burrill and Henry Perks (of Hornsea, E. Yorkshire) have sent us the following information on river travel: Most boats have two decks and are divided into three classes: 1st class cabins (upper deck), which can be very hot and cramped; 1st class hammock space on upper deck, seems best as this is pleasanter during daytime; 2nd class hammock space on the lower deck, can be cramped because of cargo, and hot and noisy from the engine. Food is ample but monotonous. Fresh fruit is a welcome addition. Fresh coffee available; most boats have a bar of sorts. Plates and cutlery may not be provided. A strong fishing line and a variety of hooks can be an asset for supplementing one's diet; with some meat for bait, *piranhas* are the easiest fish to catch. Negotiate with the cook over cooking your fish. "The sight of you fishing will bring a small crowd of new friends, assistants, and lots of advice—some of it useful.º

Light cotton hammocks seem to be the best solution. Buy a wide one on which you can lie diagonally; lying straight along it leaves you hump-backed. Mosquito nets are not required when in motion as boats travel away from the banks and too fast for mosquitoes to settle, though repellant is a boon for night stops. Most boats begin their journeys in the evening, but stops en route come at any hour. If making connections en route it is easy to miss a boat in the night. On arrival at the final destination it is usually possible to negotiate with the captain to stay an extra night on the boat (perhaps more) for no extra charge. This can be useful if arriving in a town late.

Exchange facilities are sparse in Amazonia, outside Belém and Manaus. Bargaining with the masters of small boats may be greatly helped if one has some low-value dollar bills.

Food in Amazonia Inevitably fish dishes are very common, including many fish with Indian names, e.g. *pirarucu*, *tucunaré*, and *tambaqui*, which are worth trying. Also shrimp and crab dishes (more expensive). Specialities of Pará include duck, often served in a yellow soup made from the juice of the root of the manioc with a green vegetable (*jambo*); this dish is the famous *pato no tucupi*, highly rec. Also *tacaca* (shrimps served in *tucupi*), *vatapá* (shrimps served in a thick sauce, highly filling, simpler than the variety found in Salvador), *maniçoba* (a green vegetable mixed with cheaper cuts of meat). Avoid food from street vendors.

Belém (do Pará), founded in 1616, 145 km. from the open sea and slightly S of the equator, is the great port of the Amazon. It is hot (mean temperature, 26°C), but frequent showers freshen the streets. There are some good squares and fine buildings. The largest square is the Praça da República; the main business and shopping area is along the wide Avenida Presidente Vargas leading to the river and the narrow streets which parallel it. The Teatro da Paz, one of the largest theatres in the country, is of neo-classical splendour, worth visiting (recently restored, tours cost US$0.40). There was much renovation of public places in 1985-87, but just as many old buildings are being replaced with ugly new ones. Population 934,330.

Places to visit are the Bosque (0900-1200, 1400-1700 closed Mon., Fri p.m., Sun. open 0800-1745), a public garden (which is really a preserved area of original flora, renovated to include a good collection of archaeological items of Amazonian Indians) with a small animal collection (admission free, yellow bus marked "Souza" or "Cidade Nova" - any number—30 mins. from "Ver-o-Peso" market), and the Goeldi Museum. Both can be reached by bus from the Cathedral. The Goeldi Museum, Av. Magalhães Barata, takes up a city block and consists of the Museum proper (with a fine collection of Marajó Indian pottery, an excellent exhibition of Mebengokre Indian lifestyle), a zoological garden (including manatees), and botanical exhibits including Victoria Régia lilies; open Tues. to Sun, 0900-1730 (Fri. and Sat. afternoon, garden and zoo only). Entry US$0.50, now renovated.

In the Belém market, known as "Ver-o-Peso" (see the weight) after the large scales on which the fish landed nearby were weighed, now has lots of gift shops with the charms on sale for the local African-derived religion, *umbanda*; the medicinal herb stalls are also interesting. In the old town, too, is the fort, which you can enter on request; the site also contains the *Círculo Militar* restaurant (entry US$0.75; drinks and *salgadinhos* served on the ramparts from 1800 to watch the sunset, restaurant is good). At the square on the waterfront below the fort the *açaí* berries are landed nightly at 2300, after picking in the jungle (*açaí* berries ground up with sugar and mixed with manioc are supposed to provide a balanced diet)—Mary Beath, NY. Visit the Cathedral (1748) with several remarkable paintings, and directly opposite the 18th-century Santo Aleixandre church (now being restored) noted for its wood carving. The 17th-century Mercês church, near the market, is the oldest church in Belém; it forms part of an architectural group known as the Mercedário, the rest of which was heavily damaged by fire in 1978 and is being restored. The Basílica of Nossa Senhora de Nazaré (1909), built from rubber wealth, is an absolute must for its beautiful marble work and stained glass windows.

Local Holidays Maundy Thurs., half-day; June 9, Corpus Christi; August 15, accession of Pará to independent Brazil; Our Lady of Nazaré, second Sun. and fourth Mon. in October, known as Cirio. Oct. 30, half-day; Nov. 2, All Souls Day; December 8, Immaculate Conception; Christmas Eve, half-day.

Cirio, the Festival of Candles in October, is a remarkable festival based on the legend of the Virgin of Nazaré, whose image is kept in her Basílica; it apparently was found on that site around 1700. To celebrate, on the second Sun., a procession carries a copy of the Virgin's image from the Basílica to the cathedral. On the Mon., two weeks later, a further procession takes place, to return the image to its usual resting-place. There is a Cirio museum in the crypt of the Basílica, enter at the right side of the church; free. Exhibits from the celebrations of the past 100 years; enthusiastic guide. (All hotels are fully booked during Cirio.)

Hotels Expensive: *Hilton*, Av. Pres. Vargas 882, L, swimming pool, sauna, restaurants; *Seltom*, 2 km. from airport, A, swimming pool; *Novotel*, Av. Bernardo Sayão 4808, L, with bath, a/c, TV, swimming pool, unprepossessing neighbourhood, far from centre (take Universidade bus); *Excelsior Grão Pará*, Av. Presidente Vargas 718, B, fair breakfast, noisy a/c and internal rooms, reports vary, but good food; *Vitória Régia* restaurant, bars, swimming pool, sauna, Lusotur travel agency. Less expensive: *Sagres*, Av. Gov. José Malcher 2927, opp. bus station, T 228-3999, air conditioning, good meals, swimming pool, English-speaking manager, rec., C; *Verde Oliva*, Boaventura da Silva 1179 (T 224-7682), 10 mins. from centre, D, a/c, TV, good value, rec.; *Cambará*, 16 de Novembro 300, esq. Tamandaré, T 224-2422, D, a/c, good, mosquitoes; *Executivo*, Av. Alcindo Cacela 866, 20 mins. walk or US$1 taxi ride from centre, D, good. *Ver-o-Peso*, Castilhos Franco, opposite Ver-o-Peso market, E, rooftop restaurant, TV and fridge in room, rec. *Central*, Av. Presidente Vargas 290 (T 222-3011), E without bath (D with bath and a/c), noisy, but friendly, clean, comfortable, good breakfast; *Vidonho*, same ownership, good, E-C with abundant breakfast, Rua O. de Almeida, 476, T 225-1444, in a side street opp. *Novo Avenida*, Av. Presidente Vargas 404, C/D, central, some rooms better than others, no backpackers, recently upgraded, good breakfast; *Plaza*, Praça da Bandeira, 2-star, E-D, a/c, bath, fridge, restaurant good value; across square is *Lis*, Rua João Diogo 504 (old city), 1 star, E, with bath, a/c, fridge, gloomy, short-stays accommodated, has good cheap restaurant; *Vitória Régia*, Frutuoso Guimarães 260, F, with breakfast, good, clean, friendly, convenient for Enasa boats, owner changes money and cheques at good rates; next door but not so good is *Fortaleza*, Frutuoso Guimarães 276, E, with fan, safe. *Transamazônico*, Travessa Indústria 17, waterfront by docks, F, with breakfast, clean, will store luggage for short periods. Many cheap hotels close to waterfront, in old part of town, for example dormitory bed in *Pensão Canto do Rio* opposite the dock, a "classic and unspoilt waterfront dive", F; try bargaining for cheaper rate if you have hammock; next door is *Grajaú*, F with or without breakfast, reasonable.

Camping nearest at Mosqueiro, 86 km. away.

Restaurants All the major hotels have good but expensive restaurants. *Hotel Internacional*, Av. Lobo nr. Presidente Vargas, prato do dia US$2, rec. *Círculo Militar* rec. for Belém's best Brazilian food and situation in the grounds of the fort with view over river (good choice, expensive). *Churrascaria Sanambaia*, Quai Kennedy. Also rec.: *Inter*, turn off Av. Pres. Vargas at *Hotel Central*, good and reasonable; also *Trevu*, Pres. Vargas 396, good value, tasty meals; *Regatão*, Av. Senador Lemos 3273; *Marisqueira do Luiz*, Av. Senador Lemos 1063; *Marcilias*, Frutuoso Guimarães 329, good for fish; *Capitol*, Av. Presidente Vargas near docks; *Casa Portuguesa*, Rua Manoel Barata 897, good, inexpensive; *Miako*, Travessa 1 de Março 766, behind Praça de República (menu includes very good medium-priced oriental food); *Kyoto 294*, Av. Dr. Morais, good Chinese; *Livorno*, Dr. Morais 314, good, mid-price; *Avenida*, Praça Justo Chermont 1294 (opp. Basilica), very friendly; *La Romana*, Av. Gentil Bittencourt 574 and *Pizzaria Napolitano*, Praça Justo Chermont 12 (in particular pizzas and Italian dishes); *Pato de Ouro*, Rua Diogo Móia 633 (next to *Sorveteria Santa Martha* ice-cream parlour); *Renasci*, Travessa José Pio 322 (in particular for regional dishes); *Paraense*, US$2, rec.; *Churrascarias Linda Cap* and *Tucuravi*, both on the highway leading out of Belém. Vegetarian: *Nutribem*, Rua Santo Antônio (off Av. Pres. Vargas) US$2 for as much as you can eat, lunch only.

Specially rec. for tourists are also some very good snack-bars (mostly outdoors in Belém) where you can buy anything up to a full meal, much cheaper than restaurants: *Pappus*, Av. Conselheiro Furtado 637 (nr. Padre Eutíquio); *Garrafão*, Av. Serzedelo Correa (below Ed. Manuel Pinto); *Café do Parque*, Praça da República, popular with young people, a good meeting place; *Charlotte*, Av. Gentil Bittencourt 730, at Travessa Quintino Bocaiuva, for best salgadinhos in the city, also good desserts, very popular. *Bos's*, Av. Gentil Bittencourt/Travessa Quintino Bocaiúva (snacks, standing only); *Milano*, Av. Presidente Vargas, next to *Hotel Grão Pará* (especially for espresso, desserts, cakes); also a good bar next to *Hotel Central* on same street. *Só Delicias*, Nazaré 251, rec. for pastries, sweets, soft drinks. *La Crème*, snack bar on Praça Nazaré, sells exotic fruit ice creams, view of Basilica; *Sorveteria Cairu* in Umarizal has excellent ice creams, including 30 fruit flavours. *Casa dos Sucos*, Av. Presidente Vargas, Praça da República, serves 41 types of juice (including Amazonian fruits) and delicious chocolate cake (disappointing vegetarian restaurant upstairs). *Tip-Top*, Trav. Pedro Catiquio and Rua Pariquis (40 mins'. walk from harbour), excellent ice cream. *Bar do Parque*, next to Municipal Theatre, excellent place for meeting local people. There are also many street and market vendors, who, although they should be viewed with care, often sell delicious local food.

Shops in Av. Presidente Vargas; also try the Indian handicrafts shop at Praça Kennedy, set in a garden with Amazonian plants and animals. Funai (Indian agency) shop, Av. Presidente Vargas 762, loja 2, near Casa dos Sucos, is highly recommended. We have been told that Belém is an even better place than Fortaleza to buy hammocks.

Camera Repairs Henri van Ligten, Conjunto Parklandia, Quadra B, Casa 9, T 231-5839 (take Nova Marambaia-Telégrafo bus from Praça Dom Pedro, ½ hr.). Recommended: a Dutchman who speaks English and German.

Exchange Lloyds Bank (ex-BOLSA), Rua Quinze de Novembro 275, and Brazilian banks (open 0900-1630, but foreign exchange only until 1300). Dias Lopes e Cia, 5th floor Rua Santo Antônio 316, also photo shop, 15 de Agosto on Av. Presidente Vargas, Orion Perfume Factory, Trav. Frutuoso Guimarães, Sr. Milo, Travessa Campos Sales 28. *Central* (cash only) and *Victória Rêgia Hotels*.

Electric Current 110 A.C., 60 cycles.

Post Office Av. Presidente Vargas.

Cables Embratel, Travessa Quintino Bocaiúva 1186 (T 22-9099) or at the Post Office, Av. Presidente Vargas. For phone calls: Telepará, Av. Presidente Vargas.

Consuls British, Rua Gaspar Viana 490, Caixa Postal 98. T 224-4822. Swedish, Rua Santo Antônio 316, mailing address Caixa Postal 111, 66.000 Belém, T 222-4788, open 1600-1800; Danish (Consul Arne Hvidbo), Rua Senador Barata 704, sala 1503, T 223-5888, (P.O. Box 826); U.S. Av. Oswaldo Cruz 165. T 23-0800. **Venezuelan:** Trav. Benjamín Constant 1303 (Venezuelan visa takes 3 hrs., must have yellow fever vaccination certificate, free for Danes, US$0.70 for Swedish, Swiss, W. German and Canadian citizens, US$2 for US citizens, all others US$10).

Health Clinic Clínica de Medicina Preventativa, Av. Bras de Aguiar 410 (T 222-1434), will give injections, English spoken, open 0730-1200, 1430-1900 (Sat. 0800-1100).

Tourist Office Municipal office, Detur, Av. Nazaré 231 (no sign), 2 blocks SE of Praça da República, near Edifício Manuel Pinto, friendly and helpful (as are offices in airport and Rodoviária), good free map. Paratur, Praça Kennedy on the waterfront, inside the handicraft shop; has a good map of Belém in many languages (but some references are incorrect). Town guidebook, US$2.75.

Travel Agent Ciatur, Av. Presidente Vargas 645, T 224-1993, good half-day tour on water and in forest (US$13) and 32-hour trip to Marajó (US$200).

Roads A good asphalted road leads E out of the city to the coast town of Salinópolis, some 228 km., at the extreme end of the eastern part of the Amazon Delta. Various paved roads branch off: 118 km. out of Belém one turns right on to the paved highway S to Brasília (2,100 km.). Straight on, the road leads to Bragança, the centre of an early, unsuccessful, attempt in the 1900s to transfer population to Amazonia. At Capanema (Hotel São Luís, F, good), on the road to Bragança, the road for São Luís, Teresina, Fortaleza and Recife branches right.

Bus Services The Rodoviária is located at the end of Av. Gov. José Malcher 5 km. from centre, take Aeroclube, No. 20 bus, or Arsenal or Canudos buses. It has a good snack bar and showers (US$0.10). There are four buses a day to Brasília (US$36), modern and comfortable, and also a leito bus— US$72, 36 hours. Belém-Imperatriz bus takes 10-12 hrs. (US$9). There are also direct buses from Belém to Marabá (16 hrs.), on the Transamazônica, via Porto Franco and Toncantinópolis, and then change to Santarém (Marabá-Santarém 34 hrs.). One direct bus Belém-Santarém once a week (US$36, more expensive than by boat and can take longer). To Salvador (US$36) and also to Recife (US$34), 1 daily, to each, 2000, 34 hrs. The trip to Recife can be broken at Teresina, Picos (Picos Hotel, F, with meals) and Ouricuri (Hotel Independência, E, with bath). To São Luís, 3 a day, 12 hrs., US$11; to Teresina, US$12, frequent (but avoid Transbrasileira unless you want to stop everywhere); to Fortaleza, 1,595 km. 23 hrs., US$21, 3 daily; to Rio, US$52; to Belo Horizonte, US$48.

Hitch-hiking Going south, take bus to Capanema, 3½ hrs., US$2, walk ½ km. from Rodoviária to BR-316 where trucks stop at the gas station.

Shipping Services Regular coastal services to Southern Brazil. Agency for international services, Agências Mundiais Ltda, Av. Pres. Vargas 121, T 224 4078.

Services to Manaus and Porto Velho by the Government's Enasa boats (office: Av. Presidente Vargas 41, T 223-3011 or 223-3572, Telex 2064, or Rua Uruguaiana 39, sala 1402, T 229-9149 or 224-7267, Rio de Janeiro) whose schedules are published the 20th for the next month: they leave for Manaus at 2200 on the same day of the week in each month, normally Wed., but the day may change monthly, taking 5 days; they take cars and motorcycles (Sonave and Jonasa are reportedly cheaper than Enasa). You must show your passport when buying an Enasa ticket, at boat dock on Av. Castillo França (10-minute walk from centre). Fare to Manaus, US$29, hammock space only, terribly crowded (least crowded are the couples' and single women's sections). Sanitary conditions are appalling, but the 3 meals a day now not too bad (take your own cutlery to speed up the queuing). A hammock and rope are essential (easily bought for between US$5 and US$25, buy cotton ones); also useful is a light blanket. Arrive early (some say 8 hrs.) to ensure a good hammock space, chain belongings to a post in the hammock area (thieves abound) and don't drink from the drinking fountains on board: the small canteen sells mineral water, beer and soft drinks. Some advise sleeping outside, as it's cooler if the boat stops. For an inducement of say US$100, the captain may let you have a cabin. Enasa has a 12-day tourist service Belém-Santarém-Manaus-Santarém-Belém in new boats (Pará, Amazonas), leaving Belém every other Wed., Manaus every other Thurs., at 2000 with air-conditioned cabins, restaurant, swimming pool, bar, night club, with fares from US$370 per person in a 4-berth cabin, to US$430 internal double, US$520 external double cabin, US$1,300 special cabin. Also bookable through Soletur, Rua Visconde de Pirajá 550, Suite 1708, 22410 Rio de Janeiro (T 239-7145, Telex 212 3858, 213 0237 SOLE BR); can include at extra cost a night in Manaus or Belém, or a week in Rio. Belém-Manaus (about US$70 less to Santarem in 4-berth and double cabins); foreigners allowed only to travel 1st class.

Non-Enasa fare to Manaus US$50 in covered hammock space (cabins US$100)—take food and water; look after your equipment, especially at night and in port. Ask guards at the dock gate for permission to look for a boat. Two companies that are recommended are Rodomar for destinations close to Belém (office near cathedral) and Fe em Deus, Av. Bernardo Sayão 3590 (take bus to Cremacão), recommended to Santarém (US$20 in Fe em Deus IV, 1st class hammock space, basic, crowded, take fruit, mineral water, books, 3 days, 4 nights). Also recommended to Santarém, Santo Agostinho company, and Terra Santa I, also from Doca 15, Av. Bernardo Sayão, US$22.25 hammock space, US$26.70 cabin space, 3 meals included. Also from Franz Rossy, every second Thursday at 1800, 3 days, US$23 hammock space, US$26 cabin, from Armazem 09, Portão 15, Cais do Porto, but this service not rec. Take a bus 514 from the city centre to the intersection 10 mins. beyond the Cata textile factory, and ask directions from there to the posto comercial area.

There is an **Enasa ferry to Macapá**; check at docks; the Sonave vessel, Idalino Oliveira, sails approximately once a month, departs Belém 0300 Weds., arrives Macapá 1000 Thurs., crowded, US$16 1st class, US$8 2nd, free chilled drinking water, good food and bar on board, passengers may embark at 2000 on night prior to sailing (tickets from Av. Castilhos 234), boat goes through the channels of Marajó Island; Representação do Governo do Território de Macapá ferry Belém-Macapá every 4 days or so, tickets from Av. Castillo França 234 (opp. Ver-o-peso), US$8 for hammock space, US$12 for cabin, 28 hrs. Other non-regular sailings, *Príncipe do Mar* and *Príncipe do Mar II*, US$16 upper deck, US$14 lower, with food, 2 days. Also *Barco Souza*, every Friday, return Tuesday, US$12 for hammock space, US$13.50 for cabin (only 2), wait on board while cargo is loaded at Porto Santana; *São Francisco de Paula*, US$15, friendly, clean, food not too good, best to take some of your own. Weekly Enasa boat to Tucuruí on the Tocantins River at 1730 or later (with 5 stops, 32 hrs.; there are other boats to/from Tucuruí).

Warning Boat passengers arriving from Manaus (a free trade zone) may experience long delays at customs. Note that dress in Amazonia is often more conservative than further south.

Air Services Regular flights N to Miami and New York and S to Brazilian cities, Montevideo and Buenos Aires; to Brasília and to Santarém and Manaus, the latter with connection for Leticia, Colombia, with Saturday flight giving connection for Bogotá. Nightly flight to Manaus costs only US$75; to Fortaleza US$80. To Iquitos; weekly to Paramaribo and Cayenne; Barbados (with stopovers). Bus "Perpétuo Socorro-Telégrafo" or "Icoaraci", every 15 mins. from Prefeitura to airport, US$0.10. Taxi to airport, US$6 (ordinary taxis cheaper than Coop. taxis, buy ticket in advance in Departures side of airport). Airport has a hotel booking service but operated by, and exclusive to, 5 of the more expensive hotels, discounts offered. There are now no flights between Belém and Trinidad and Guyana. To Oiapoque on French Guyane frontier by Taba (Rua O. de Almeida 408, T 223-8811). Travellers entering Brazil from Guyane may find it necessary to obtain a 60-day visa (takes two days) before airlines will confirm their tickets. Check, as there is only one flight a week (Sunday). Daily service (except Sun.) to Macapá at 0400 (40 mins.).

Tour Volker Filss, a German traveller, has sent us the following suggestion for a one-day sightseeing tour, subsequently revised by Philip A. Smith, recently of BOLSA, Belém: "Go to the Ver-o-Peso market early in the morning when the boats are coming in and watch the unloading of the fish and the vendors in the market. Take a bus marked Souza at the market and ask the driver to drop you at the Bosque (open 0800-1100 and 1400-1700). Take the same bus back and get off at the Museu Paraense (Goeldi) in Av. Magalhães Barata (formerly Independência). After visiting museum and gardens, walk down avenue to the Basílica (Nossa Senhora de Nazaré) and then on to the Praça da República (on the way the Tourist Office will be passed on the right). From the Edifício Manuel Pinto de Silva at this end of the Praça, you walk to the Teatro da Paz and along Av. Presidente Vargas. Before reaching the docks, turn left along, say, Av. Santo Antônio and Av. João Alfredo, through the shopping and commercial area (interesting narrow streets and open-fronted shops) to reach the harbour with its fishing boats and to the left the Prefeitura Municipal and Palácio do Governo. Beyond stand the Cathedral and the old fort (entry US$0.10) and *Círculo Militar* restaurant. Depending on your progress, lunch can be taken by the Basílica (e.g. *Avenida* restaurant directly opposite), or on the terrace of Edifício Manuel Pinto, or, say, at *Hotel Central* on Av. Presidente Vargas".

Excursions Travel agents offer short and longer visits to the rivers and jungle. The nearest beach is at **Outeiro** (35 km.) on an island near Icoaraci, about an hour by bus and ferry (the bus may be caught near the Maloca, an Indian-style hut near the docks which serves as a night-club). Further north is the island of **Mosqueiro** (86 km.) now accessible by toll bridge (US$0.20) and an excellent highway, with many beautiful sandy beaches and jungle inland.

Many hotels and weekend villas at the villages of Mosqueiro and Vila; rec. *Hotel Farol*, on Praia Farol, D, 1920s architecture in good repair, small restaurant, good views; *Hotel Murumbira*, on Praia Murumbira, C, pool, restaurant. Restaurants at Mosqueiro: *Ilha Bela*, Av. 16 de Novembro 460, rec. for fish, at Praia Chapeu Virado; under same management is *Marésia*; *Pizzeria Napolitana*; *Sorveteria Delícia*, Av. 16 de Novembro, good local fruit ice creams, owner buys dollars. At Praia do Farol (Mosqueiro) is *Bar-restaurant O'Stop* which has a shower and will let you leave luggage and hang your hammock. The traffic is heavy in July and at weekends, and hotels are full. Food at hotels US$3.50, but same quality costs US$2 at stalls along beach. Camping is easy. Buses Belém-Mosqueiro every hour from Rodoviária, US$0.75, 80 minutes.

Marajó Island is worth visiting for a weekend's buffalo hunting (use a camera, not a gun, or the buffalo won't last long). Boats to Marajó leave every Wed. and Fri. at 2000, Sat. 1400, return Thurs. 1700 and Sun. 1700 and Mon. a.m., 6 hrs., US$3 for a seat, US$20 for cabin for two (buy return ticket in Belém to ensure passage). Trips to the island are arranged by the *Grão Pará Hotel* and travel agents in Belém. Alternatively, a light aircraft may be hired to see Marajó from the air (with pilot, about US$80 for 2 hours) e.g. from Kovacs, Av. Dr. Freitas, opposite the airfield of the Aero Clube do Pará. (Cheap weekend flights are easier to find than boats.) The island was the site of the precolumbian Marajoaras culture.

At Soure, on the island, are Hotel Soure, (walk straight on from Enasa dock, then take 3rd street on left), E p.p. full board, good; Pousada Marajoara, and Pousada Parque Floresta, nearby, E, friendly and clean, good meals. Changing money is only possible at very poor rates. Take plenty of insect repellent. There are fine beaches, Araruna (2 km.), do Pesqueiro (bus 1030, returns 1600, from near market place—big, deserted beach, 13 km. away) and Caju-Una (15 km.).

Salinópolis (228 km.) about 4 hrs. by bus (US$3) on excellent highway, also worth a visit. Seaside resort with many small places where you can eat and drink at night by the waterfront, and fine sandy beach nearby (buses and cars drive on to the beach). Best during holiday month of July. Atalaya, opposite Salinópolis, is pleasant, reached by taxi (US$5) or with a fisherman.

Hotels   Solar, Av. Beira Mar s/n, D with bath, best in town, good restaurant; Salinas, on beach, E; Jeanne d'Arc, E with breakfast.

There are ferries (check departures at Porto São Benedito, Av. Bernardo Sayão 868, T 222-6025, **see page 386**) two 45-minute flights daily (Cruzeiro do Sul, Varig, at 2200 and 0500, taxi airport—town US$2.25, about 4 km.), US$20.50, from Belém to **Macapá,** a town on the northern channel of the Amazon Delta, which used to be decrepit but is now improving, particularly along the riverfront. (The ferries often go to Porto Santana, 30 km. from Macapá, to which there are frequent buses, US$ 0.30, and shared taxis US$2 pp., boats readily hired to visit river communities). Macapá is the capital of the Territory of Amapá (agriculture, gold, manganese, coal, timber), one-quarter the size of France but with only 180,000 inhabitants, of whom 95,000 live in Macapá. Each brick of the Fortaleza de São José do Macapá, built 1764, was brought from Portugal as ballast. Interesting market behind the Fortaleza. A handicraft complex has been built next to the Novotel. The riverfront has been pleasantly developed. There is a monument marking the equator halfway between Porto Santana and Macapá, known as Marco Zero, with nightclub underneath and more nearby. Gold is sought by washing sand in the river, using a gallon kerosene can: if you find less than 5 grams of gold in a canful of sand you move on.

The popular local beach is at Fazendinha (take bus of same name), extremely lively on Sundays.

Hotels   Novotel (formerly Macapá), French-owned, on waterfront, small, 4-star, A, all rooms a/c, swimming pool, service and cleanliness strongly criticized as being far below acceptable standard; Tropical, Av. Antônio Coelho de Carvalho 1399, 20 mins. from centre, one star, T 231-3739, E with a/c (cheaper without), rec.; Glória, Leopoldo Machado 2085 (just round corner from Tropical, 20 mins. walk from centre), T 222-0984; Excelso, E, has been rec. Santo Antônio, Av. Coriolano Jucá 485, T 222-0226, near main square, F, very clean, fan, shower, good breakfast. Amapaense Palace, Rua Tiradentes 109, E-D, 2 star, a/c, cold showers, comfortable, clean (lanchonete in same building, poor). The following are 10-mins. walk from port and from Praça São José (where bus from Porto Santana stops): Palace, Rua Cora de Carvalho 144, F with breakfast; Mata, Rua São José 2390, F with fan; Mercúrio, Rua Cândido Mendes, 1300 block (no sign), F.

Restaurants   O Boscão, Hamilton Silva 997, no sign, quite good; Portenho, Hamilton Silva 1390; O Paulistano, Av. Henrique Galúcio 412, a/c, good; Pizza San Carlos, Cândido Mendes 1199, good for lunch; Lennon, good pavement café, no meals, at Rua Gen. Rondón esq. I.C.Nunes; Lanchonete Zero Grau, in city centre, rec. for food. Excellent ice cream sold in Macapá.

Exchange   Banco do Brasil, near Novotel, or in Novotel itself. Better rates with gold merchants around Canal da Fortaleza.

Rubber was almost the only product of the Territory until the 1950s, when manganese was discovered 150 km. NW of Macapá. A standard-gauge railway, 196 km. long, the only one in Brazil, has been built from the mining camp to Porto Santana, from which there is an excellent road. Malaria is rampant in Amapá; the illiteracy rate is 85%; smuggling goes on in a big way. But the mining area—Icomiland; pop. 4,000—is a startling exception: swimming pools, football fields, bowling alleys, supermarkets, dance halls, movies, a healthy oasis in the wilderness.

IBDF office, Rua Hamilton Silva 1570, Santa Rita, CEP 68.900, Macapá, has details on the **Cabo Orange National Park** in the extreme north of the Territory, and the **Lago Piratuba Biological Reserve**, neither accessible by road.

Sr João Batista de Oliveira Costa in Macapá is a good pilot who flies around the delta, particularly to the mouth of the Araquari river to see the *pororoca*, a tidal wave that travels upriver in the high tides of spring and autumn.

An unpaved road has been built from Macapá northward to the small town of **Oiapoque** (one hotel), on the coast near the French Guyane border; road completed halfway to Calçoene (government-owned hotel by bus stop E, expensive food in adjoining canteen; sleeping space advertised in a café on Oiapoque road, very cheap), via Amapá (*Tourist Hotel* and one other, E, clean, comfortable—one block from square towards docks, turn right, 2nd house on left). Amapá is better than Calçoene for travelling on. Macapá-Amapá bus, US$6.50, 6 hrs.; daily Estrela de Ouro bus Macapá-Calçoene from Praça Veiga Cabral (timetable varies), US$8, 7 hrs. (minimum), many delays, book at least 2 days in advance. 80 km. from Calçoene is Lourenço, the centre of the local gold rush. For the 216 km. from Calçoene to Oiapoque there is a bus scheduled for 0700, Mon., Wed., Fri. (US$5), but it often does not run (also an unscheduled government lorry, which does not run in the rainy season, Jan.-Apr.); you can hitch from Macapá, take a private lorry (little traffic), costing US$7 to 15, or hire a vehicle—for all means you will be overcharged. From Oiapoque a ferry goes to St. Georges (Fr. Guyane), US$2—a bridge is being built; be sure to get exit and entry stamps on either side of the border: in Oiapoque the Federal Police station is past the church on the road to Calçoene, and in St. Georges visit the Gendarmerie Nationale (no customs). Accommodation in Oiapoque for US$2 p.p. near ferries, basic. It is impossible to get francs anywhere in St. Georges (try in Brazil). **Warning** Everyone must have a visa for entering French Guyane here, obtainable in Belém, but not Manaus. This is a most difficult border crossing for tourists: the authorities seem to believe that no-one other than Brazilians or Guyanais will want to make the attempt.

A government boat makes the trip from Macapá to Oiapoque once or twice a month, US$10. The boat service on its journey south stops at Calçoene (24 hrs., US$8.50, including food) and from there a trip can be made by lorry (US$5) to Macapá. There are Taba flights from Macapá to Oiapoque on Tues., Fri., Sat. (return Tues., Wed., Sat., continuing to Belém), US$52 (US$107 to Belém), unreliable service; Taba office in Oiapoque on the quay by the ferry, rarely open (flights usually booked up). It is possible, but hard, to fly Amapá-Oiapoque. (Taxi into Oiapoque US$4, bus US$1.25.) If using Paris-Cayenne route as a cheap way to South America, it is recommended to fly Cayenne-Belém, US$135, compared with five days of discomfort and delays overland from Cayenne to Macapá (you have to fly Cayenne-St. Georges anyway; the boat, *São Pedro*, from S.T.M.G., 136 Monnerville (opp. Market), Cayenne, T 311388, apparently does not run any more).

Belém to Manaus

A few hours up the broad river the region of the thousand islands is entered. The passage through this maze of islets is known as "The Narrows". The ship winds through 150 km. of lanes of yellow flood with equatorial forest within 20 or 30 metres on both sides. In the Furo Grande the vessel rounds a hairpin bend almost touching the trees, bow and stern.

After the Narrows, the first point of special interest is formed by the curious flat-topped hills, on one of which stands the little stucco town of Monte Alegre (airport), an oasis in mid-forest.

Santarém, 2-3 days upstream on the southern bank, stands at the confluence of the Tapajós River with the Amazon, just half-way between Belém and Manaus. It was founded in 1661, and is the third largest town on the Brazilian Amazon, with 150,000 people. The yellow Amazon water is mottled with greenish patches from the Tapajós; the meeting of the waters is said by some to be nearly as impressive as that of the Negro and Solimões near Manaus. There is now a road southwards to Cuiabá (Mato Grosso), meeting the Transamazônica at Rurópolis (**see page 382**). (The southward leg from the Transamazônica to Cuiabá begins about 90 km. W of this point, or 20 km. from Itaituba.) Timber, bauxite and gold discoveries have promoted very rapid growth of the city, which has become very expensive. It is the jumping off point for gold prospectors in the Mato Grosso territories to the South. It is reported that prospectors are exploited by high prices, and that lawlessness abounds in the goldfields. The unloading of the fish catch between 0500 and 0700 on the waterfront is an interesting scene. There are good beaches nearby on the river Tapajós.

N.B. Santarém is one hour behind Brazilian Standard time.

Hotels *Novotel*, at edge of town by the water, by the university, A with a/c, TV, bath, fridge, hot water; *Santarém Palace*, close to city centre, Rui Barbosa 726, good, C with bath and TV;

Tropical, Av. Mendonça Furtado 4120, B, de luxe, swimming pool seems to be unrestricted, friendly staff, good chef (but not "de luxe" cooking), meals for around US$5, excellent value; *San Rafael*, Rua dos Bares 222 (T 232-8335/8488), B, pleasant, rec., English and German spoken; *City*, Trav. Francisco Correia 200, D with bath, a/c, TV, radio, frigobar, good; *Uirapura*, Av. Adriano Pimentel 140, D, for a/c with breakfast and bath, with fan, E, good breakfast, run down but clean, view of "meeting of the waters" from front porch and some rooms. *Central Plaza*, Praça Rodrigues dos Santos 877, E, with bath and fan, run-down, friendly, *São Luís*, near market, E, good value, meals; *Brasil*, E, including breakfast, clean, basic; *Horizonte*, Travessa Lemos 737 (across from *São Luís*), E, clean; *Drink Hotel*, on waterfront, safe and friendly but rooms hot, E. *Equatorial*, F, good value, friendly.

Restaurants   *Mascotinho* bar/pizzeria, on beach in front of *Hotel Uirapuru*, popular, good view, US$5 for pizza for 2; *Storil*, Travessa Turiano Meira, 2 blocks from Rui Barbosa, good fish (dinner about US$4.25), live music, takes credit cards; *Ritz*, Praça do Pescador, good, US$3 lunch; *Lanchonete Luci*, Praça do Pescador, good juices and pastries; *Pirâmides*, good local fish dishes; good value restaurant beneath *Equatorial Hotel*. Good ice-cream at *Sorveteria Go-Go*, Siqueira Campos 431.

Banks   Banco do Brasil changes foreign currency and travellers' cheques.

Airport   15 km. from town. Internal flights only. No buses to centre or waterfront, only taxis (US$10 to waterfront); *Hotel Tropical* has a free bus for residents; you may be able to take this.

River Services   Small launches leave for Manaus 2-5 days, most days, e.g. Luciatur, US$20 including food, 3rd class. Other examples of fares to Manaus: US$37.50 1st class (upper deck cabin), US$20, 2nd class (upper deck hammock), US$18.50, 3rd class (lower deck). You may sleep on board (in hammock) days before departure. Enquire at the waterfront. Enasa, Trav. Agripina Matos 1089; T 522-1138. For Manaus, *Moreira da Sibra III*, US$12 with good meals for 1st class hammock space; *Rio Nilo*, US$16 for hammock space, also rec.; and *Onze de Maio*, has bar. For Belém, *Franz Rossy*, every second Thursday at 1200, 2-3 days, US$23 hammock space, US$26 cabin (not rec.); *Cidade de Teresina*, Wed. 1800, US$22 hammock space, cabin US$28, 2 nights, adequate. For Macapá (Porto Santana), 36-48 hrs., US$18, e.g. *São Francisco de Paula*, clean, efficient, friendly, good food, leaves Mons. at 1830. Boats, to Manaus or Belém, including Enasa, may leave from the waterfront in town, as well as from the "Cais do Porto" dock (where all boats arrive), about 4 km. from the centre; take bus marked "Circular" or "Circular Externo" (US$0.10), both of which go to Cais do Porto, and pass Rodoviária. Guards will allow you to enter the dock and look for boats, but you may have to wait several days for a cargo/passenger boat going in either direction. Along the river, closer to the centre, are numerous boats, usually leaving daily, for Itaituba (daily, 1800, arr. late next morning), Óbidos, Oriximiná, Alenquer or Monte Alegre.

Travel Agents   Amazon Tours, Trav. Turiano Meira 1084, T 091-522-2620, run by Steve Alexander (from Alaska), highly reasonable and recommended, has produced useful guidebook on Santarém. He also has a property in the jungle for overnight tours, also highly recommended.

Buses   Rodoviária is on the outskirts, take "Rodagem" bus from the waterfront near the market, US$0.12. Santarém to Itaituba, 8 hrs. US$5.40; there connecting service east to **Marabá on the River Tocantins**, 28 hrs. (if lucky, can be 60 hours, or even 6 days), US$ 25, 1830 with Trans Brasiliana. Also to Imperatriz, 46 hrs., US$30, office on Av. Getúlio Vargas and at Rodoviária. (Beware of vehicles that offer a lift, which frequently turn out to be taxis.)

Excursion   to Altar do Chão, a village set amid Amazonian vegetation on the river Tapajós, at the outlet of Lago Verde; hotel (D), comfortable; luxury hotel to be built shortly; *Restaurant Mongote*, Praça 7 de Setembro, good fresh fish, huge portions; good swimming in the Tapajós from the beautiful, clean beach; bus from Mercado Municipal, Santarém, leaves 0500, 1100, 1600, 1½ hrs., returns 0630, 1230 and 1730 approx. (rugged, but fun). Also by 1000 bus to Porto Novo, 3 hrs. into jungle by a lake, bus returns 0330 next morning (you can sleep in it). Interesting wildlife on lake; canoe can be hired.

37 km. S from Santarém on a dirt road is **Belterra** (pop. about 8,000), where Henry Ford established one of his rubber plantations, in the highlands overlooking the Tapajós River. Ford built a well laid-out new town; the houses resemble the cottages of Michigan summer resorts. Many of the newer houses follow the white paint with green trim style. The town centre has a large central plaza that includes a band stand, the church of Santo Antônio (circa 1951), a Baptist church and a large educational and sports complex. There is a major hospital which at one time was staffed by physicians from North America and attracted people from Manaus and Belém. There has been little replacement of old trees: extraction has been the only activity. As a result, the rubber forest is in bad condition since the late 1940s. (*Hotel Seringueira*, F, with about 8 rooms and pleasant restaurant.)

Fordlândia was the Ford Motor Company's first rubber plantation, founded in 1926, but it was never profitable; it is a friendly town since there are few visitors. *Hotel Zebu*, in old Vila Americana (turn right from dock, then left up the hill); one restaurant, two bars and three shops on town square. There is a little pebble beach north of the town.

Bus from Santarém to Belterra (from unmarked *Café Amazonas*, Travessa Moraes Sarmento between Rui Barbosa and São Sebastião), 1000 and 1230, Mon.-Sat., return 1300 and 1530, US$1, about 2 hrs.—note: one hour time difference between Santarém and Belterra so if you take the 1230 bus you'll miss the 1530 return bus). If driving, take Av. Santarém-Cuiabá out of town, which is paved for 8 km. At Km. 37 is a small Shell station; fork right and stop at the guardhouse; it's 15 km. into town, following the electricity cables. Boats from Santarém to Itaituba may stop at Fordlândia if you ask (leave Santarém 1800, arrive 0500-0600, US$5 for 1st class hammock space); ask the captain to stop for you on return journey, about 2300. Boats may stop for Belterra, but it's a walk of several km. from the river to town.

110 km. up-river from Santarém is Óbidos, with a population of 27,000. There the river is comparatively narrow, and for many kilometres little is seen except the wall of the great Amazonian forest. Small airport.

Manaus, the next city upstream, was until recently an isolated urban island in the jungle. This remote "free port" is, in fact, the collecting-point for the produce of a vast area which includes parts of Peru, Bolivia and Colombia. There is superb swimming in the natural pools and under falls of clear water in the little streams which rush through the woods, but take locals' advice on swimming in the river; electric eels and various other kinds of unpleasant fish, apart from the notorious *piranhas*, abound and industrial pollution of the river is growing.

Until recently Manaus' only communications were by river and air, but now a road SW to Porto Velho, which is already connected with the main Brazilian road system, has been completed and partly paved. Another, not yet fully paved, has been built due N to Boa Vista, from where other roads already reach the Venezuelan and Guyanese frontiers.

Manaus (613,000 people) is the capital of the State of Amazonas, the largest in Brazil, with a population of almost 1.2m. Though 1,600 km. from the sea, it is only 32 metres above sea-level. The average temperature is 27°C. The city sprawls over a series of eroded and gently sloping hills divided by numerous creeks (*igarapés*). Dominating the centre is a Cathedral built in simple Jesuit style on a hillock; nothing distinguished inside or out. Nearby is the main shopping and business area, the tree-lined Avenida Eduardo Ribeiro; crossing it is Av. Sete de Setembro, bordered by ficus trees. The main shopping area between Av. Sete de Setembro and the rear of *Hotel Amazonas* is now reserved to pedestrians. There is a modern air-conditioned theatre. Manaus is building fast; 20-storey modern buildings are rising above the traditional flat, red-tiled roofs. It was the first city in South America to instal trams, but they have now been replaced by buses.

The main attractions are the Botanic Gardens (to enter you must have the mayor's permission), the military zoo, the well stocked public library, and the legendary Opera House, the Teatro Amazonas, completed in 1896 during the great rubber boom and rebuilt in 1929. It seats over a thousand people and was restored in 1974; it was restored again in 1987/89. When functioning, it is used about once a month for plays; entry to view, US$0.10, open Sun.-Fri. 0900-1700. See the two markets near the docks; best early in morning. There is a curious little church, the Igreja do Pobre Diabo, at corner of Avs. Borba and Ipixuna in the suburb of Cachoeirinha; it is only 4 metres wide by 5 metres long, and was built by a worker (the "poor devil" of the name); take Circular 7 Cachoeirinha bus from cathedral to Hospital Militar.

The Rio Negro has an average annual rise and fall of 14 metres. The remarkable harbour installations have a floating ramp about 150 metres in length leading from street level to the passenger-ship floating dock. When the water is high, the roadway floats on a series of large iron tanks measuring 2½ metres in diameter. The material to build the large yellow Customs building near the harbour was brought block by block from Scotland as ballast. Tourists can visit the docks on Sun., 0600-1000.

Manaus has been a free trade zone, since 1967. All travellers are required to fill out a customs declaration on all articles bought there, which you are requested to pack in your hold luggage; in fact it is a good idea to declare goods of non-Brazilian origin such as cameras, radios, tape-recorders etc. on arrival in order to avoid any problems. It is only necessary to give information to

Key: 1. Government Palace, 2. Cathedral, 3. Floating Harbour, 4. Customs House, 5. Municipal Market, 6. Opera House/Teatro Amazonas, 7. Museu do Indio, 8. Museu do Porto, 9. Museu do Homem do Norte, 10. Instituto Geográfico Histórico (off map), 11. Rubber factory, 12.Tourist Office, 13. Post Office, 14. *Hotel Amazonas*, 15. Cheap hotel area.

Customs on goods already possessed if one is travelling into Brazil. You have to go through customs when leaving the Rodoviária. If flying from Manaus to a destination outside Brazil, no such documentation is required. Nor is it required of boat travellers.

Duty-Free Imports   Travellers entering Brazil through Manaus may import from the zone, duty-free, foreign electrical or electronic goods and food products, up to maximum values that are often changed.

Local Holidays   Jan. 6 (Epiphany); Ash Wed., half-day; Maundy Thurs.; June 24 (St. John); July 14; Sept. 5; Oct. 30; Nov. 1, All Saints Day, half-day; Christmas Eve; New Year's Eve, half-day.
   The annual Folklore Festival (dates vary, but about end of June) is well worth seeing for its colour, noise, and pleasure. On Sept. 5 there is a celebration march-past between 0800 and 1100, with bands of marchers from all the local schools, clubs, associations, etc.

N.B. Manaus time is one hour behind Brazilian standard time.

Museums   The Museu do Índio (formerly the Museu Indígena Salesiano), in

Catholic school at end of Av. Sete de Setembro, corner of Rua Duque de Caxias, has most interesting exhibits of Indian culture in Amazonas (entry 0800-1100 and 1400-1700, Mon.-Sat., US$0.30). In the next block, on Rua Duque de Caxias, is a rubber factory that may be visited free. The coin museum, Museu Numismático, is at Rua Henrique Martins 458, free. Indian artefacts and documents can also be seen at the Instituto Geográfico Histórico, Rua Bernardo Ramos 117 (Tues.-Sat., 0900-1700; entry US$ 0.20). Museu Tiradentes, Praça Heliodoro Balbi, run by the military police, Mon. 1400-1800, Tues.-Fri. 0800-1200, 1400-1800; Minerals and Rocks museum, Estrade do Aleixo 2150, Mon.-Fri. 0800-1200, 1400-1800. Museu de Ciencias Naturais da Amazônia, Colonia Cachoeira Grande, Conjunto Petro-Aleixo, open Tues.-Sun. 0900-1700. Museu do Porto de Manaus, a small museum of memorabilia, Vivaldo Lima 61, near port (Mon.-Fri., 0800-1100, 1400-1700, Sat., 0800-1100); Museu do Homem do Norte, Av. Sete de Setembro 1385, showing the way of life of the local population and their products (Mon. 0800-1200, Tues.-Fri. 0800-1200, 1400-1800).

Zoo Run by the military; known as CIGS. Bus 205 or 217 (marked "Ponta Negra"), US$0.10, every ½ hr from Rua Tamandaré, opp. cathedral in centre, alight 400 metres past the 1st Jungle Infantry Barracks (a big white building). The zoo is in the Headquarters of the Jungle Training Centre (CIGS); entrance for foreigners, US$0.75. Small zoo also at *Hotel Tropical*, see below. Instituto Nacional de Pesquisas Amazonas (INPA), Estrada de Aleixo, at km. 3 (any bus to Aleixo), has named trees and manatees (best seen Wed. and Fri. at 0830 when water is changed), caimans and giant otters; good for birdwatchers.

Hotels Extremely crowded, especially in Jan.-Feb., when hotels often raise their prices steeply (prices are high generally, though, we give high season prices, so reductions may be available at other times). *Tropical*, Praia de Ponta Negra, T (92)234-1165, a lavish, 5 star Varig hotel 20 km. outside the city, in a superb setting by the river, L, *Restaurant Tarumã* open for dinner only, *churrascaria* by pool, open to non-residents on weekdays only (well-dressed non-residents may use pool on weekdays, take free bus from Rua José Paranaguá in front of Petrobras building esq. Dr. Moreira 0830, 0930, 1130 to *Hotel*, 1200, 1400, 1500, 1800 to town). Reserve as far ahead as possible through Varig, though it is reported reservations are sometimes lost, but found if inducement is offered. Park, pools, small zoo with healthy animals ("more wildlife than you're likely to see in 3 days on the river"), river boats, tennis. *Novotel*, Av. Mandu 4 in the Industrial Area, L, 4 star, luxurious, pool, US$1.75 taxi ride from centre, reported markedly less good than *Tropical*; at Av. Getúlio Vargas 215 is *Plaza*, new, A; next door to it is *Imperial*, A but neither rec. *Amazonas*, Praça Adalberto Vale, 4 star, A-L, very poor reports recently; opp. *Amazonas* is *Ana Cassia Palace*, expensive, Rua dos Andradas 14, A; *Premier*, Marcílio Dias 217/225, A-L, some rooms a/c, expensive for what they offer, with good breakfast, good service; has a cheaper annex. *Da Vinci*, Rua Belo Horizonte, about 2 km. from centre (convenient bus route), A, swimming pool, all facilities, poor value, poor restaurant; *Janelas Verdes*, Leovegildo Coelho 216, C, a/c, shower, TV, small, quiet (except Sun.), safe, T 233-1222; *Manaus*, Rua Lobo D'Almada 48, D, a/c, clean, friendly, poor value, poor restaurant; *Flamboyant*, Av. Eduardo Ribeiro 926, C, good. *Floriano*, on pedestrian street near *Amazonas*, D with a/c, rec.; *Premier*, Av. Eduardo Ribeiro 124, D some rooms with TV and fridge, friendly, good value; *São Rafael*, Rua dos Barés 222, C, clean, safe, helpful, tours arranged, close to waterfront and market. In Av. 7 de Setembro; *Palace* (593), old building, now refurbished with a/c but cramped, C; *Topaz* (711), C, incl. breakfast, central, rooms have fans, new but scruffy, still rec.; *Martins* (1429), D, with breakfast, stores luggage, friendly; *Modelo*, near Av. 7 de Setembro, E, clean, friendly, rec. *Monaco*, Rua Silva Ramos 20, 3 star, A, luxury rooms have good view, pleasant, good rooftop restaurant/bar; *Nova Avenida*, Av. Pres. Vargas, D, helpful, rec.; *Fortaleza*, Rua dos Bares, E with fan, reasonable, rec. In Rua Dr Moreira: *Rio Mar*, (325), incl. breakfast and bath C, dear, clean, central; *Central* (202), T 234-7374, D, some a/c, quiet; *Internacional* (168), B-C (2-stars), T 234-1315, a/c, clean, friendly, central, coffee most of the day, good exchange rates; *Hospedagem Familiar Garrido* (148), D, as much as you can eat for US$2, dirty, friendly, showers; *Nacional* (59), C with bath, fridge, a/c. In Av. Joaquim Nabuco: *Hospedaria Manaus* (703), E, clean, spacious, washing facilities; *Doral* (687), E/C, T 232-4102, a/c, friendly, excellent breakfast, rec.; *Hostal Rondônia* (565), E, noisy, cold water, fan, friendly, will change money; *Vidal* (681), E, no breakfast, pleasant rooms at rear, cheap; *Pensão Sulista* (347), T 234-5814, E with fan, no breakfast, laundry facilities; *Alugam* (154), rented apartments, E full board; *Aurora* (130), D with bath, a/c, friendly, clean, noisy TV; *Artêrio*, near corner with R. Lima Bacuri, D with a/c, E with fan, without breakfast, clean, large rooms with bath; *Bela Vista*, F without bath or breakfast; *Karam*, waterfront end, E with bath, a/c, fridge, coffee all day, friendly, has TV; *Hospedaria Paulista*, E with breakfast, fan, popular; next door is *Astoria*, E with breakfast, a bit run down; *Luz* and *Iguaçu* are better than most on this street: the former is singles only above a gym, clean, breakfast included at *Iguaçu*, both F. *Rio*

Branco, Rua dos Andradas 484, E, a great many mixed reports about this place, popular, clothes-washing facilities; other cheaper places in same area. *Nadie*, opp. Rodoviária, F. *O Explorador Youth Hostel*, Rua Silva Ramos 685 (central, T 234-6796, P.O. Box 2890), F p.p. not inc. bedding or beakfast, non-IYHA members welcome, tours arranged; *Cetur* (Amazon Safari Club) doubles as youth hostel, at Km. 13. Rodovia Tarumã, 10 km. from airport (T 233-8658/1573), at Ponta Negra, described as a ripoff, D without breakfast, sheets extra, extra charge to use pool, US$1 pick up from airport, no bus service nearby. **N.B.** Lori Kornblum suggests keeping your room key, in view of reports of staff allowing bogus police officers into guests' rooms. **N.B.** also, when taking a taxi from the airport, insist on being taken to the hotel of your choice, and not to the one which pays the driver commission.

Camping   There are no campsites in or near Manaus; it is difficult to find a good, safe place to camp wild. It is possible to camp "wild" on the bank of the Rio Negro near the *Hotel Tropical*; through outskirts of city via Tarumã bathing waterfalls to Ponta Negra bathing beaches, 20 km. Good swimming. Bus daily (US$0.15). Camping Praia Dourada, showers, toilets, restaurant, boat hire, good swimming, busy at weekends.

Electric Current 110 volts A.C.; some hotels 220 volts A.C., 60 cycles.

Restaurants   *Fiorentina*, Rua José Paranaguá 44 (opposite Praça da Polícia), Italian, reasonably priced, good salad, pizza (government rating A); *São Francisco*, Blvd. Rio Negro 195, ½ hr. walk from centre (or bus 705), in Educandos suburb, good fish, huge portion, US$ 5.50, highly rec.; *Panorama* next door, No. 199 (also good for fish, but service indifferent); *Caçarola*, Rua Maués 188, Cachoerinha, T 233-3021, very good local fish dishes (take a taxi); *Casarão*, Joaquim Nabuco 497, good fish dishes. Good cheap Chinese at *Mandarim*, Av. Eduardo Ribeiro 650, has buffet lunch, US$2 all you can eat (not on Sun. though); also *China*, Av. Getúlio Vargas 1127, warmly rec.; Japanese at *Miako*, Rua São Luís 230, also *Suzuran*, Blvd. Álvaro Maia 1683, Adrianópolis, good, closed Tues., taxi US$2; and at *Tokyo*, Rua Silva Ramos 456, good; *O Gauchão*, Av. Castelo Branco 2009, fixed price of about US$5 for as much as you can eat, rec. Another churrascaria is *Rodaviva*, Av. Ajuricaba 1005, open air, all you can eat for US$4, also *Churrascaria Rodízio*, Joaquim Nabuco 628, all you can eat (of high quality) for US$8, and *Churrascão*, Av. Castello Branco, Cachoeirinha. *O Vegetariano*, Rua Rui Barbosa 128, good, also take-away, open 1100-1430 Mon.-Fri.; another at Saldanho Marinho 429B. *Sorveteria Pingüim*, Av. Eduardo Ribeiro, good, medium-priced; *Cantinha Carioca*, Rua Dr. Moreira, 2nd floor of Edifício Moreira, excellent food, good value; *Sirva-Se*, Rua Dr. Moreira 124, plenty of choice, rec., good value; *175*, Rua Dr Moreira 175, menu in Portuguese and English; *Forasteiro*, same street, No. 178; *Mister Pizza*, R. José Paranaguá 104 (Praça da Polícia), good pizza and sandwiches, a/c, upstairs; *Central*, Rua José Clemente, US$1.50; *Jangada Bar*, opp. *Hotel Amazonas*, good for snacks; *Alemã*, cafeteria, Rua José Paranaguá/Praça da Polícia, good for juices, sandwiches, cakes; good *pratos* at Brasileiros department store, Av. 7 de Setembro; *Lanchonete Bali*, Rua Marechal Deodoro 172, US$1.50 for prato comercial. *Arigato*, R. Guilherme Moreira and Av. 7 de Setembro, for American food. On river front at end of Av. Joaquim Nabuco are several floating restaurants serving fish very cheaply, less than US$1. Reasonable, but probably not completely hygienic. The floating restaurant in the harbour below the market building is rec. for best tucunaré fish. Many restaurants close on Sunday nights and Mondays. City authorities grade restaurants for cleanliness: look for A and B. Good juice bars along Av. Joaquim Nabuco: *Lanchonete Pigalle* particularly rec.

The fishing catch is brought to the waterfront between 2300-0100, including the giant pirarucu. Good fruit and vegetable market by the port.

Cinema   on R. J. Clemente, opp. Teatro Amazonas.

Bookshop   Livraria Nacional, Rua 10 de Julho 613 opp. Teatro Amazonas, stocks some French books, the Livraria Brasília next door has some English books.

Souvenirs   Indian handicrafts in the Museu do Índio, Sete de Setembro 217. Central do Artesanato, Rua Recife, run by Amazonas State Social Welfare Dept., Mon.-Sat. 0900-1900. Funai shop on main market street, near *Hotel Amazonas*. H.Stern, jewellers, at *Hotel Tropical* and international airport. The Humming Bird, Rua Quintino Bocaiúva, 224, good. Hammocks from Redes Sta Luzia, Miranda Leão 46 (centre); also good in the old market area. There is an art fair every Sun. from 1700 in Praça da Saudade.

Clubs   Ideal; Athletic Club of Rio Negro; Bosque (bathing pool, tennis courts). For evening entertainment (including gambling): Vogue Club (jacket and tie obligatory), Boite Inglês, The In Crowd, Danielo's.

Hospital of tropical medicine, treatment free, some doctors speak a little English: take "Dom Pedro" bus from main terminal, about 20 min. ride.

Car repairs Mavel VW, highly recommended, English spoken.

Tourist Information   Emantur, Praça 24 de Outubro, Rua Tarumã 379 (not very good), airport and floating harbour. Town map from *Hotel Amazonas* or from Amazon Explorers, *Hotel Lord*. *Guide Book of Manaus*, US$3, available from *Hotel Amazonas* and other places, in English, useful.

Exchange Lloyds Bank (ex-BOLSA), Rua Guilherme Moreira 147; Banco do Brasil, Rua Marechal Deodoro; many local banks. Open 0900-1600. Most offices shut afternoons. Foreign exchange operations 0900-1200 only, or close even as early as 1100. Reported that only Banco do Brasil and Lloyds will change US$ notes. It is possible to change US$ at the airport; open 24 hrs. per day. Exchange at the main hotels (poor rates at *Tropical*, through), at Souvenirs de Manaus shop and at Luciatur, Rua Eduardo Ribeiro 365, Minitur and Selvatur (good rates); try also bakery opp. *Hotel Rio Branco* for cheques, Francisco or Agostinho at 1st floor, Dr Moreira 105, in pedestrian shopping centre, and Sr. Ayoub, Av. 7 de Setembro 711. Canto Turismo, Rua Rui Barbosa, good rates.

Post Office Main office including poste restante in Marechal Deodoro (for American Express, Rua Saldanho Marinho 530). For airfreight and shipping, Alfândega, Av. Marones Santa Cruz (corner of M. Deodoro), Sala 106.

Telephone TeleAmazonas on Rui Barbosa, opp. Banco do Brasil (most central); Av. Getúlio Vargas, about 7 blocks N of 7 de Setembro, or Rua Guilherme Moreira.

Consulates British, Eduardo Ribeiro 520, 12th floor, T 234-1018. United States, Rua Maceió 62, Adrianópolis, opens 1000, T 234 4546 (office hours) and 232 1611 (outside office hours), Mr. James R. Fish. Will supply letters of introduction for US citizens. W. Germany, Rua Barbosa 355, 1st floor, T 232-0890; Spain, Instalação 100, T 234-0842; Dutch, Rua M.Leão 41, T 234-8719/223-6874; Italy, R. Belo Horizonte 240, T 234-8059; Japanese, Av. 7 de Setembro 1251, T 232-3694; Danish and Norwegian, Rua M.Leão 45, T 234-5769; Peruvian, Conjunto Aristocratais, Chapada, Rua A, Casa 19 (T 236-3666, open 0800-1400). Colombian, please note that apparently the Colombian consul (Rua Dona Libânia 62, near opera house) has been advising travellers from Manaus to Leticia that if they are only visiting Leticia they do not require a tourist card. Either get your Colombian tourist card before reaching Manaus or tell the consul you are travelling further into Colombia, which will probably then require proof of money and return ticket. Venezuelan, Rua Recife 1620 (bus Cachoeirinha Chapada, alight near Detran), 0800-1500; the Consul will give you a visa only if you have an air ticket into and out of Venezuela.

Tours There are 3 kinds of tours: "luxurious", which are comfortable but "set up" for tourists; "exotic", involving about 8 days travelling away from the city, seeing lots of animals; and "real-life", seeing how the people in the jungle live, but not many animals. Many people have expressed disappointment with the shorter tours. The problem is that authentic jungle life, whether human or animal, does not easily co-exist with a large city. Be sure to ascertain in advance the exact itinerary of the tour, that the price includes everything (even drink and tips), that the guide is knowledgeable and he himself will accompany you, and that you do not want to kill anything rare. **N.B.** Guides must be officially registered with Embratur and must carry an identity card.

Amazon Explorers Tour Service, run by Manoel (Bebê) Barros, Rua Quintino Bocaiúva 189; his day's tour including "meeting of the waters", Parque Januário and rubber collecting, US$20 including lunch, has been highly recommended by most users; 32-hour trips, require a minimum of 4 people; other tours available. Boat *Amazon Explorer* available for hire at about US$230 per day. Kurt Glück, Quintino Bocaiúva 224, Caixa Postal 361, offers a more personal service at US$100 day plus food and fuel; his shortest boat trips, which need to be booked as far in advance as possible, last five days in an open 5.5 metre canoe, and he explores many of the tributary rivers of the Amazon; maximum two persons. Transamazonas Turismo, Leonardo Malcher 734, T 232-1454/232-4326 (reservations through South American Turismo, Av. N.S. de Copacabana 788, T 255-2345, 22050 Rio de Janeiro), for parties of 10 or less offers a 3-days-plus stay at Amazon Lodge, a floating lodge on Lake Periquitão, 80 km. from Manaus (US$260 p.p. with extras for 3 days), recommended, book well in advance. The better hotels also arrange tours (ask for Joe Sears in *Hotel Tropical*), and so do Selvatur (office in *Hotel Amazonas*), Rio Negro trip per person, US$10, 0800-1300, with lunch at *Janaurylândia* floating hotel, returning at 1500, US$30 or 2-day trip for US$200 p.p. Luciatur, Av. Eduardo Ribeiro 355, 0800-1500, US$35; Amazon Explorer 0730-1500 with lunch US$27; Jungle Trips, R.Guilherme Moreira 281, 3-day jungle trip, all included, irrespective of numbers, for US$130; Amazon Odyssey, Rua Guilherme Moreira 286-A (T 234-2348/1147), run by Englishman, Richard Bryan, 2-3 day jungle trips (*Janauaca Jungle Lodge*—US$170), good value; and Mundial (Av. Pres. Vargas) agencies. Safari Ecológico, Av. Marechal Câmara 160, Sala 621, Caixa Postal 3321, CEP 20.010, Rio de Janeiro, T (021) 240-6785, has been recommended for its 3-day/3-night ecological tours on the Amazon (Manaus address: Amazon Treasure Tours, Av. Floriano Peixto 259, Sala 109, T 232-9654).

There appears to be an endless supply of guides: those listed below have been positively recommended by travellers: for trips by canoe on the Amazon and Rio Negro, Moacir Fortes, R. Miguel Ribas 1339, Santo Antônio, Manaus, T 232-7492 (has his own 19-metre boat *Amazonia Expedition*), he speaks English and German (US$100 per day, plus fuel and food). Ernesto Carvalho, Cx. Postal 2890, Manaus, contactable through *Hotel Rio Mar*, does a 3-day, 3 night trip for US$100 per couple 80 km. up the Solimões to the Lagoa do Janauaca, using local boats. Also Arlendo da Vicente Silva (Rua Vista Alegre, Educandos, T 624-3550, or seek him out at the waterfront), for 3 day tours on tributaries of the Solimões and into the jungle—only speaks Portuguese, maximum 8 people, about US$65 p.p. inclusive. Other guides: Margareth Rose Fernandes, Jungle World Turismo, Guilherme Moreira 297 (3 Andar, Sala 21), rec.; Amazon Indian Turismo (Soares), Av. 7 de Setembro 1643 (T 234-2924); Elmo de Morais López and Cássio Serra Vieira, Rua Henrique Martins 369, Centro, for 2-5 day tours, 2-4 people, sleeping in hammocks, US$100 a day per couple; Gentil Metelo, P.O. Box 2792, Manaus, T 236-5894/232-4876, has his own agency, 10-metre covered canoe, access to 14-metre, diesel-powered boat with crew, will arrange tours from 1 hour to 1 month, very knowledgeable, speaks Portuguese, English, French, Spanish and Italian; Marco Valério Teixeira, P.O. Box 2968, Manaus, offers a 3-day tour for US$80 p.p., involving a one-day canoe journey beyond the Lago do Janauaca, one day in a camp, then the final day returning by bus (along BR-319) and ferry. José Nunes is a guide who speaks fluent English and has a combi for general transport (T 233-5102); Gustavo, a Peruvian, 3-day tours for US$110 p.p. for 2 (less for more people), he speaks several languages, T 233-0958; Cristóvão Amazonas Turismo, Marechal Deodoro 89, Salas 605/1203, T 233-3231, experienced jungle guides, reasonably-priced tours for 1, 2 or more days, German, English, French, Italian, Spanish spoken. Miguel M. Barbará (El Barón), Caixa Postal 1227, Manaus 69.000, operates the *Xarrua* for tours on the Rio Negro, US$100-120 for 4; Francisco Almeida, Aventura Turismo, Rua 10 de Julho 130, loja 2, P.O. Box 949, T 234-0197, also arranges tours on the Rio Negro; Rubens Silva, Eduardo Ribeiro 420, has been recommended for his 3-day trip up the Rio Branco for 2-5 people, US$110 p.p.; Carlos Francisco Viana, Av. Epaminondas 751-9, US$60 p.p. for 3 days, all inclusive; Francisco da Silva Karaja, Rua Dapaz 189A, T 238-5592, speaks English and French; Luis Alberto Motta, Rua Carla Tupinambá Nobre, Quadra 22, Casa 30, Conjunto Belvedere (take bus "Alvorada 2", alight at Panificadora Belvedere). Motorized canoes can be hired from behind Mercado Municipal, US$50 for 6-hr. trip, takes 8, with navigator/guide, goes to inaccessible places.

For those prepared to spend around 10 days in the interior on a real expedition, contact Carlos Colares, Av. Atlântica 91, Raiz, 69.000 Manaus, T 092-237-1961, Telex 092-165 XPMNA, or P.O.Box 360, who conducts private excursions, with fishing, hunting and exploring in the more remote regions of the Rio Negro (max. 4 people—US$200). Carlos Colares has been highly recommended by readers as an excellent, well-informed guide and biologist (British-educated). He and his Indian guide provide well-planned, informative trips which do not follow the usual tourist routes (make sure Sr. Colares is leading the tour).

Generally, between April and September excursions are only by boat; in the period October-March the Victoria Regia lilies virtually disappear. Fishing is best between September and March (no flooding).

Bird-watchers can see many kinds of birds in and around the grounds of the *Hotel Tropical* (for instance: fly catchers—kingbirds and kiskadees—, swallows, yellow-browed sparrows, aracaris—member of the toucan family—, woodpeckers, woodcreepers, thrushes, anis, three species of tanager, two of parrots—the dusky and blue-headed). Sloths and monkeys may also be seen. Bird-lovers anxious to pursue their hobby on the Amazon River and its backwaters should contact Moacir Forbes, see above for address and further details (we are grateful to John and George Newmark of Eastbourne for this information).

The enterprising go to the Capitânia do Porto and find out what boats are making short trips; e.g., Manaus-Itacoatiara, US$6 first-class. For swimming, it is possible to travel to Ponta Negra beach (no shade) by Soltur buses for US$0.25, though beach virtually disappears beneath the water in April-August and is now polluted. Good swimming is at Bolívar Falls and in the river Tarumã, lunch available, shade, crowded at weekends, but still nice; take Tarumã bus from Rua Tamandaré or Rua Frei J. dos Inocentes, ½ hr., US$0.15 (very few on weekdays), getting off at the police checkpoint on the road to Itacoatiara.

About 15 km. from Manaus is the confluence of the Solimões (Amazon) and the Rio Negro, which is itself some 8 km. wide. Here you can see the meeting of the blue-black water of the Rio Negro with the yellow-brown Solimões flood; the two rivers run side by side for about 6 km. without their waters mingling. Tourist agencies run boat trips to this spot, or if travelling on a tight budget you can get up about 0330 in Manaus, take a "milk boat" such as the *Capitão Braga* (try to arrange the day before) at about 0400. It returns about 1300, passing through the confluence. Also the *Joanne d'Arc* leaves the dock area around 0730 and returns late afternoon, and the *Castelo*, 0800 to 1500 to the confluence, US$2. Alternatively hire a motorized canoe from near the market for about US$10 per hr. (you'll need 3 or 4 hrs. to take in the experience properly). The simplest way is to take a taxi or "Vila Buriti" bus to the Careiro ferry dock, and take the car ferry across. The ferry goes at 0700, returning 0900, 1100, returning 1400, and 1500, returning 2000 (approx.). You can also take small private launches across, 40 mins. journey, about US$10 per seat. A 2-km. walk along the Porto Velho road from the Careiro ferry terminal will lead to a point from which Victoria Regia water lilies can be seen in April-September in ponds, some way from the road. If you continue over the Capitari bridge, you reach unspoilt jungle. There are several small restaurants on the S bank in Careiro, where the road SW to Porto Velho and the South begins.

Urs Bucher, of Zug, Switzerland, recommends a trip to Manacapuru, by bus 304 (30 mins.) at 0800, ferry from São Raimundo (30 mins.) and 2-hr. bus ride (bus every hour), to see a typical Amazon town (buy bus ticket before you get on the ferry: don't wait till you arrive at the other side). A small market town on the Solimões W of Manaus, with three basic hotels and *Il Maccarone* pizzeria, Av. Eduardo Ribeiro 1000, with its friendly Italian owner Mário. Another village one can visit is Araçá, a 3-hr bus ride from Rodoviária in the direction of Castanho; the journey includes a ferry crossing at the confluence of the Negro and Solimões (fare to Araçá US$0.70). The village is on the banks of the River Mamori; canoes can be hired for US$3-5 for a day (night trips also possible) and you may be able to sling your hammock in a private house. Plenty of wildlife close at hand. 3 buses a day return to Manaus.

Roads To *Itacoatiara*, 285 km. E on the Amazon, with Brazil-nut and jute processing plants (bus service); now paved.

A mostly unpaved road runs N (759 km.—see below) from Manaus to Boa Vista (daily by Eucatur, 20 hrs., US$18, book at least 4 days in advance, 1800 and 1900, often extra buses put on, continuing to Santa Elena on Venezuelan border, insect repellant advisable for ferry crossings, also a good idea to take food and water).

The Catire Highway from Manaus to Porto Velho, which is supposedly paved with work continuing (in poor shape nonetheless throughout), sometimes closed March-May during the rainy season (877 km.). Bus, Manaus-Porto Velho, 1330 and 1500 with Eucatur, 25 hrs., best to book in advance. Bus to Humaitá; 670 km., where the Catire Highway crosses the Transamazônica, more than one a day, 17 hrs. (including 4 ferry crossings), US$6; three buses a day from Humaitá to Porto Velho (3 hrs. with one ferry crossing, paved stretch), 257 km., US$3. If driving this highway, the following information may be useful (but note that conditions change greatly according to season): the first ferry (Careiro) is pretty disorganized; at Km. 40 there is a bridge and a floating grocery store; at the town of Careiro (second place of this name), about Km. 80, there is a service station where you can camp, and the US priest here (Father Jim) welcomes English speakers at his church on the square. At Km. 245 there is petrol and camping; between the third ferry and Km. 325 (service station) the road deteriorates, but improves a little to Km. 500, where there is a clean restaurant with showers and toilets (service station also at Km. 370). If there is no petrol at Km. 500, there is another station at Km. 570. As the road approaches the turnoff to Humaitá (Km. 610), it improves. Between Humaitá and Port Velho there is a service station at Km. 700.

Bus station is 5 km. out of town at the intersection of Av. Constantino Nery and Rua Recife; take local bus from centre, US$0.30, marked "Aeroporto Internacional" or "Cidade Nova" (or taxi, US$4). Local buses to Praça 14 or airport leave from opposite *Hotel Amazonas* (take airport bus and alight just after Antártica factory) or take local bus to Ajuricaba. Hitch-hiking from Manaus can be very difficult. For Boa Vista, take the Tarumã bus to the customs building and hitch from there, or try at "posta 5", 2 km. beyond Rodoviária.

Air Services direct from Miami, Bogotá, La Paz, Santa Cruz, Caracas (LAB, twice weekly), Panama (Varig, twice weekly) and from most Brazilian cities. To Bogotá, Varig on Fri. Manaus-Iquitos, Cruzeiro do Sul, Sat. and Wed. at 1015, US$270 one way, stopping at Tefé and Tabatinga for Leticia (separate Manaus-Tabatinga—US$90, Tabatinga-Iquitos—US$80 available and cheaper). Flights to Benjamin Constant, opposite Leticia, 3 times a week. There are also flights to Boa Vista (US$60), Cruzeiro do Sul, daily at 2100, 55 mins., return flights 1 hr. after arrival, Porto Velho, Corumbá, Santarém, Teresina. About 17 flights a week to Belém. The taxi fare to or from the airport is US$5, but settle price before journey or obtain a ticket that fixes flat-rate fares, or take bus 608 or hourly bus 201 marked Aeroporto Internacional from Rua Tamandaré near cathedral, US$0.20. Last bus at night to airport from R. Tamandaré at 2345; last from airport is 2330. (Taxi drivers often tell arrivals that no bus to town is available, be warned!) Check all connections on arrival. N.B. Check in time is 2 hours in advance. Allow plenty of time at Manaus airport, formalities are very slow, and there are queues for everything (try asking an official if you can queue-jump if you are a foeigner with no duty-free items to declare). Local flights, such as Taba to Tabatinga, leave from airport terminal 2: make sure in advance of your terminal.

Shipping For details of Enasa services, **see page 386**. We are advised that it is better to travel Manaus-Santarém and Santarém-Belém in local boats than to use the normal Enasa service, though to Belém the direct trip by M.V. *Benjamín* is acceptable. Enasa to Belém once a week at 1800, the day is normally Thur., but may change every month, but in any one month it's the same day of the week (buy ticket in advance, Enasa office closes 1130 on Sat. very crowded, board early); 4 days, one class, hammock space only, US$29; bar on board (foreigners 1st class only fare comparable with night flight). The address of the Enasa line is Av. Eduardo Ribeiro 58. Taxi from centre to docks, US$1.20. Occasional German vessels.

Fairly frequent (irregular) river boats to Tefé (3 days, US$20, including food), and Benjamin Constant (see below). Boa Vista (not good), and Porto Velho (US$70 in 2-berth cabin, US$30 2nd class, 7 days, 3 days downstream at high water, rec. boat, *Clívia*). Buy a hammock (*rede*—pronounced "hedgie") if travelling 2nd or 3rd class, plenty of drinking water and plenty of books to read; often the boats only stop at night. Boats to Santarém almost every evening except Sun. (about 1800), from E end of dock, journey can be as little as 33 hrs.; prices vary, roughly US$14 lower deck, US$15 upper deck, US$37.50 cabin (Navio Motor Emerson); *Dejard Viera*, leaves Wed., 1800 37 hrs., US$16 lower deck, US$20 upper, US$28 cabin, US$12 by *Cidade de Natal*, well rec.; also rec. *Miranda Dias*, small, family-run, reasonable food and sanitary conditions, US$30 for hammock space and food; *Ayapua*, US$28 d, a/c cabin (cold at night) including meals, leaves Manaus every Fri. 1830 (no guaranteed connexion to Belém). Also rec. to Santarém, *Rio Nilo*, leaves Wed. 1800, clean, good food, US$16 for hammock space, US$28 cabin, 2 nights; also M.V. *Onze de Maio*, leaving each Tues. evening, its sister ship doing return at same time, good meals, top deck with chairs, tables. Shipping a car: either with Enasa (fortnightly), Elvira, or Sonave Cia, Entrada do Bombeamento 20, Compensa, Manaus, T 234-4803/4302, telex 092-2463 SOCN, rec., driver free, one passenger and car US$250 (weekly) to Belém, inc. meals (no variety), sleep in car or hammock; cheaper if you load the car on to an empty truck (trucks are shipped on pontoons, so you may get your car on one of these). Another company, Jonasa, which also leaves from Compensa, is somewhat cheaper than Enasa and Sonave for shipping cars to Belém. The Capitânia do Porto, Av. Santa Cruz 265, Manaus, has a list of all shipping (you won't be allowed in wearing shorts). All boats, when berthed, display destination and time of sailing so you can check facilities and costs. Boats for Belém and international shipping leave from west end of the docks (entrance at Capitânia do Porto), all others from east end, where a new pier is being built.

N.B. Be careful of food on the boats; may be cooked in river-water. You may need a visa to travel to Peru; consulate at Rua Tapajós 536 (T 234-7900). Those arriving from Leticia should go to the police for their immigration entrance stamp, but you should get this in Tabatinga. Departures to the less important destinations are not always known at the Capitânia do Porto. Be careful of people who wander around boats after they've arrived at a port: they are almost certainly looking for something to steal.

Passports For those arriving by boat who have not already had their passports stamped, the immigration office is on the first of the floating docks next to the tourist office. Take the dock entrance opposite the cathedral, bear right, after 50 metres left, pass through a warehouse to a group of buildings on a T section.

Tefé lies approximately halfway between Manaus and the Colombian border. A small town of some 22,000; the waterfront consists of a light sand beach; waterfront market Mon. a.m.; the nuns at the Franciscan convent sell handicrafts and embroidery; there are three small hotels and five pensions (*Anilce*, Praça Santa Teresa 294, E, clean, a/c, do not leave valuables in your room), the restaurant *Au Bec d'Or* by the port, French/Amazonian cuisine, and an airport with connection to Manaus. Recommended boat, *Captain Noonan* (safe food, plenty of space, drinks on sale). Also *Jean Filho*, leaves Manaus 1800 Sat. (arrives Mon. p.m.), leaves Tefé Tues. 1900 (arrives Wed. p.m. or Thurs. a.m.). US$10.50 first class with food bottled water, 2nd class and small cabins available.

For jungle tours, contact Joaquim de Jesus López, Rua Hermes Tupina No. 740, Barro Holaria, Tefé, not a professional guide, but he has been recommended for self-organized trips (cost for 4 for 1 week, US$200). No English spoken.

Benjamin Constant A small river-town on the frontier with Peru, with Colombian territory on the opposite bank of the river. Several hotels, including, *Benjamin Constant*, beside ferry, C, all a/c, some with hot water and TV, good restaurant, arranges tours, postal address Apartado Aéreo 219, Leticia, Colombia; store opposite exchanges cheques and cash at good rates. Hotel *São Jorge*, E, meal US$2, try bargaining, recommended; *Araponga*, C, run down; *Hotel Lanchonete Peruana*, F, good food; *Márcia Maria*, E with bath, a/c, fridge, clean, friendly, rec. Eat at *Pensão Cecília*, meals US$ 1.80 each; *Bar-21 de Abril* for less than US$1. Clothes shop on road reaching to port (left hand side) changes US$ cash. Boat services from Manaus, 7 days, or more, US$40, to Manaus, 4 days, or more, cabin (Wed. and Sat. evenings) US$50. Boats from Manaus to Benjamin Constant normally go on to Tabatinga, and start from there when going to Manaus. Prices do vary, try bargaining. Recommended vessels are *Almirante Monteiro*, US$24 with hammock space, US$28 in cabin; *Dominique* and *Cidade de Teresina*, cleaner than most, cabin US$33 p.p., hammock space US$28; *Clívia*, from Manaus every 2nd Sat., 6½ days, returns Wed., 3 days, cabins US$100 for 2 with fan, hammock space US$40 each, good food, clean; *Itaúna* leaves Wed. or Sat. at 1900, 72 hrs. to Manaus, US$33.30 inc. 3 meals, take fresh water; hammock space on the *Comandante Soares* costs US$35, but food is poor. The frigorífico *Conte Maciel* returns empty to Manaus every 10 days, comfortable, clean, good food, 3 days, US$22.50. It is wise to bring food to supplement the rice, beans, chicken and salt fish, and sterilized water (some boats sell chilled beer or Coca Cola); mosquito spray is a must when you are in port, all year round. Ferry (Recreio) to Leticia (Colombia) twice daily, US$1.30, 1½ hrs., ferry calls at **Tabatinga** (Hotel *Miraflores*, expensive; *Halley*, F, clean, safe, rec.; *Residencial Aluguel Paji*, F with bath, fan, clean, unfriendly; *Solimões*, run by the military—in army camp 10-15 mins. walk from airport—E with breakfast, other meals available if ordered in advance, excellent value, clean—some taxi drivers are unaware that this hotel accepts non-military guests, but there is a VW colectivo minibus from the barracks to town centre, harbour and Leticia; excellent *Tres Fronteiras* restaurant), only 4 km. from Leticia, hitch or get a ride for US$0.20, or a taxi. Cruzeiro flies Wed. and Sat. Manaus-Tabatinga-Iquitos (Manaus-Tabatinga US$90, best with Cruzeiro; Tabatinga-Iquitos US$80) and return. (Flights may be booked up 10 days in advance from Manaus.) Hammock (good) will cost US$12 in Tabatinga (try Rei de Redes on main road) or Benjamin Constant, much more in Leticia. It is difficult to change travellers' cheques in Tabatinga (try Casa Branca, Casa Verde or Casa Amarela on main road, or general manager of the main shopping centre), and far harder to purchase Peruvian intis than in Leticia. Airport to Tabatinga by minibus, US$0.40. The Port Captain in Tabatinga is reported as very helpful and speaking good English. N.B. The port area of Tabatinga is called Marco. Mosquito net for hammock essential if sailing upstream from Tabatinga; much less so downstream.

Entering Brazil from Colombia Cross frontier between Leticia and Tabatinga. Boats to Manaus depart from Benjamin Constant (see preceding paragraph). Brazilian exit/entry formalities at Marco (Tabatinga) are essential: walk through docks and follow road to its end, turn right at this T-junction for one block, white immigration building is opp. *Café dos Navegantes*, ten minutes' walk from docks, Mon.-Fri., 0800-1200, 1400-1800 (airport immigration only works Wed. and Sat.), proof of US$500 or exit ticket may be required. This is a frontier area: carry your passport at all times, but travel between Leticia and Tabatinga is very informal. Taxi to Leticia, US$4, colectivo US$0.25. Brazilian Consulate in Leticia, Calle 8, No. 8-71, Mon.-Fri., 1000-1600, requires two black-and-white passport photos and 36 hrs. for visa (best to get your visa beforehand); go there if you have entry problems coming from Peru into Brazil.

Entering Brazil from Peru Boats from Iquitos to the Brazilian border stop at Ramón Castilla, or at an anchorage off this town, or at Islandia, a mud-bank anchorage off Benjamin Constant (passengers are ferried by canoe between the two: Peruvian boats are not allowed to stop at Benjamin Constant); catch boats from Benjamin Constant to Manaus. You must have a Peruvian exit stamp (obtained on the boat, or at Peruvian consulate in Leticia, or at Puerto Alegría or Ramón Castilla, practice seems to vary so check first in Iquitos), and you must get an entry stamp in Tabatinga (yellow fever certificate needed); without either you will be sent back to Peru. Don't wear shorts in the Brazilian immigration office. Leave boat at Ramón Castilla for Tabatinga. Alternatively, take one of the ferries from Benjamin Constant to Tabatinga (1½-2 hrs., US$0.80, or hire a canoe, US$3), get off at first stop, walk 1 km. to the main road, police offices are on the right. Tans flies Islandia to Iquitos (US$12.75), but there are no guarantees of flights.

To Peru and Colombia N.B. Exit stamps in Tabatinga are given at the airport, whether you are leaving by air or by boat; you are permitted one week in transit; Tabatinga-Iquitos flights available on Wed. and Sun (US$80); get your Brazilian exit stamp at the airport. Entering Colombia from Brazil, you must have a tourist card to obtain a stamp to go beyond Leticia, but there appears to be no problem in staying in Leticia without a stamp (but you cannot change travellers' cheques without a stamp); check these details on arrival. Colombian consulate on unnamed street opp. Restaurant *El Canto de las Peixadas*, open 0800-1400. The best places for boats to Manaus or Iquitos are Benjamin Constant and Ramón Castilla (or Islandia) respectively, customs point in Ramón Castilla gives good boat information. Frequent sailings from Peruvian border jetties (Ramón Castilla/Islandia) to Iquitos, US$15, 3 days. Peruvian tourist cards obtained from Puerto Alegría, 2 hours up river where boats stop for police checks (these formalities may change).

It is possible to get a launch up the Rio Negro, but there are hardly any villages of more than a few houses; these places are important in terms of communications and food resources. It is vital to be self-sufficient in food and to be able to speak Portuguese or have a Brazilian guide who can negotiate with the locals. Nova Airão, on the west bank of the Negro, is about two days upstream from Manaus. It has a large boat-building centre at the south end, and a fish and vegetable market at the north end. Ice and bread can also be purchased here. The town has many similar houses of wood and corrugated-iron construction. It has a telephone (from which calls to Europe can be made—after a fashion). Airão is the starting point for the **Parque Nacional Jaú** (IBDF office in Manaus, BR-319, Km. 01, Distrito Industrial, Caixa Postal 185, CEP 69.000). Moura is about 5 days upstream from Manaus; it has about 120 people based around the military-run granite quarry. There are basic medical facilities and the military base has an airstrip (only usable September to December) and telecommunications. About a day further upstream is Carvoeira, almost opposite the mouth of the Rio Branco; although small, it has a vibrant festival in the first week of August. A great distance further upstream is São Gabriel da Cachoeira, from where you can continue to Venezuela (see Venezuela section). São Gabriel is near the **Pico de Neblina National Park** (Pico de Neblina is the highest mountain in Brazil, 3,014 metres, IBDF office in Manaus, see above); in São Gabriel, Tom Hanly, an Irish Salesian brother, is helpful, friendly and informative. The town has one hotel, cheap, clean, good food (ask for it), shops and, in the river, rapids for 112 km.

About two days up the Rio Branco is Santa Maria de Boiaçu, a village of about 30 families. There is a military airstrip which is in use in July and August, very basic medical facilities and an indirect radio link with Manaus. There are three small shops selling basic necessities (but they aren't often open), and several tiny, but lively churches. The Rio Branco is yellowish in colour, and less acidic than the Negro. Therefore, biting insects and their associated diseases are more prevalent outside the wet season. The river is better for fishing, though, and there is more wildlife to see. (We are grateful to Marianne Evans of Northampton, for much of this information).

River traffic on the Rio Branco connects Manaus with *Carcaraí*, a busy river port with modern installations. When the Manaus-Boa Vista road is washed out, this is the only route through to Venezuela. There is a passenger boat once a fortnight, or you can ride on the barges which take trucks and their drivers (not recommended for single women). In the rainy season, transport is quite easy to arrange (bargain for your fare, and sling your hammock under a truck); it's a nice journey, 96 hours upstream, 48 down. Bus on from Caracaraí to Boa Vista costs US$3, 3 hrs.

Hotels   Márcia, F, next to bus stop, a/c, breakfast, clean; *Roraima*, F, cold shower, basic. *Pizzeria Delícia*, good, English spoken. N.B. The Perimetral Norte road marked on some maps from Caracaraí E to Macapá and W to the Colombian frontier does not yet exist; it runs only about 240 km. W and 125 km. E from Caracaraí, acting at present as a penetration road.

The road which connects Manaus and Boa Vista (BR-174 to Novo Paraíso, then the Perimetral, BR-210) is of rough dirt, except for the last 60 km. to Boa Vista, which are paved. For drivers on this route, some advise being defensive with regard to lorry drivers (who drive for too long, haul too much and drink); others say they are very helpful to anyone in difficulties. There are service stations with toilets, camping, etc., every 150-180 km, but all petrol is low octane. At Km. 100 is Presidente Figueiredo, with shops and a restaurant. About 100 km. further on is a service station at the entrance to the Uaimiri Atroari Indian Reserve, which straddles the road for about 120 km. Traffic may not stop in daytime except for emergencies or fuel; this part of the road is hilly, with virgin forest and real jungle sounds. There is a police checkpoint and service station at the other end (Km. 325). At Km. 434 is the clean and pleasant *Restaurant Goaio*. The road junction 65 km. further on is a popular stopping place, with petrol, restaurant and showers. Beyond here, large tracts of forest have been destroyed for settlement, but already many homes have been abandoned. The road, built up with poor bridges, then enters a region of dense vegetation. 12 km. before Carcaraí, there is a ferry across the Rio Branco; continue then to Boa Vista. (If you do not want to go through the hassle of driving this route, you can try to have your vehicle taken by truck.)

Boa Vista has road connections with the Venezuelan frontier at Santa Elena de Uairen (237 km., a rough road, very slippery when wet) and Bomfim for the Guyanese border at Lethem.

Boa Vista (population 69,000), capital of the extreme northern Territory of Roraima, is 759 km. N of Manaus. Mount Roraima, after which the Territory is named, is possibly the original of Sir Arthur Conan Doyle's "Lost World". There is swimming in the Rio Branco, 15 mins., from the town centre (too polluted in Boa Vista) reachable by bus only when river is low. This town has a modern functional plan, which often necessitates long hot treks by the traveller from one function to another. Because of nearby goldmining, the town is expensive. Industrial estate S of town. New government district is being built on the NW edge of town. Interesting modern cathedral; also a museum of local Indian culture (poorly kept). Taxi from airport should cost no more than US$3.50 (45 min. walk) and will assume you want *Hotel Tropical* unless you indicate otherwise.

Hotels Generally expensive and heavily booked. *Praia Palace*, A, on river, with beach, hard beds but service friendly, T (095) 224-4147 (good food in restaurant next door); *Tropical* (Varig), C, on main square, security recently improved but accommodation poor value, however, good pool, friendly, manager speaks English, good food; *Eusébio's*, C-D, always full, book ahead, demand single if on your own, very good restaurant, swimming pool, free transport to bus station or airport, recommended; *Paraíso*, Getúlio Vargas e Araújo Filho, D with bath, popular with Guyanese shoppers (reportedly a centre for narcotics trading, "arrogant and overpriced"); *Roraima*, Av. Cecília Brasil e Benjamin Constant, E-D with bath, not very good value; *Colonial*, Ajuricaba 532, near Consolação church, E, a/c with bath and breakfast, clean; *Brasil* in Rua Benjamin Constant 331 W near Drogafarma, E (do not confuse with sleazy *Hotel Brasa* in same street), also *Lua Nova*, F without, E with a/c, English spoken, often full. *Casa Nova*, Av. Sebastião Diniz, D with a/c, E with fan; *Ideal*, E, mixed reports. *Rodoviária*, at bus station about 1½ km. from town centre, F, communal rooms, clean, shower, clean, friendly, rec.; *Pensão* at grocery at Rua

Benito Brasil 566, F. *Tres Nações*, Av. Ville Roy 1885, also close to bus station, E, some rooms a/c, others more basic. There are also two missions who offer hospitality to those in need. If all else fails, sling your hammock in the trees around the Rodoviária.

Camping Rio Caviné, 3 km. N of town.

Restaurants *Hotel Tropical* and *Eusebio's Hotel*, both very good; *Senzala*, Av. Castelo Branco 1115, where the town's high society eats; *Casa Grande*, Av. Villa Royo, good; *Churrascaria Venezuela*, bus station; *Bigode*, on waterfront, fish, music at weekends; *Café Pigalle*, just off central square, next to *Eusébio's*, good food, drinks and atmosphere, open till all hours; *Góndola*, Benjamin Constant and Av. Amazonas, good; restaurant and bar in Parque Anana, near airport. Snacks at *Top Set*, Av. Jaime Brasil, *Catequeiro*, Araújo Filho with Benjamín Contant, rec. prato feito. Good prato feito at the restaurant by the petrol station opp. *Hotel Brasil*.

Exchange US$ and Guyanese notes can be changed in Boa Vista; try Ramiro Silva, Rimpex, Av. Jaime Brasil. Travellers' cheques in Banco do Brasil. There is no official exchange agency and the local rates for bolívares are low: the Banco do Brasil will not change bolívares. Try *Hotel Tropical* where manager is helpful, speaks English, some German and French. Best rate for dollars, Casa Pedro José, Rua Araújo Filho 287, T 224 4277 (in the street behind *Hotel Tropical*); try the chemist/drugstore opp. *Hotel Tropical* for dollar exchange or the Compra e Vende Ouro shop on Av. Araújo Filho, or the gold dealers in front of *Hotel Paraíso*.

Bus (See also Border Crossings below). To Manaus, by Eucatur, 2300, and 0600, US$18, 15-25 hrs., advisable to book because sometimes buses are fully booked days in advance, check times. Breakdowns are frequent. Buses often run late, and the night bus has to wait up to 4 hrs. for the Rio Branco ferry. Boa Vista-Caracaraí US$3, 3 hrs. To border, see below. Rodoviária is on town outskirts, 3 km.; taxi to centre, US$2.30, bus US$0.30 (marked "13 de Setembro" to centre). Local bus terminal is on Av. Amazonas, just off central praça. Note that it is difficult to get taxi or bus to Rodoviária in time for early morning departures; as it's a 25 minute walk, book a taxi the previous evening.

Hitch-hiking from Boa Vista to Manaus is fairly easy on the many trucks travelling to Manaus; try from the service station near the Rodoviária. You may have to change trucks at Caracaraí. At the ferry crossing over the Rio Branco there is usually a long queue of waiting hikers; try to arrange a lift on the ferry. Hitching to Santa Elena, Venezuela, is not easy; either wait at the bridge and police checkpoint on the road to the border, or try to find a Venezuelan driver passing the *Hotel Tropical*. Drivers often charge for hitches—maybe as much as a bus fare.

Air Travel To Manaus (US$60, night flights available at 20% less); to Georgetown, Guyana twice a week, with Guyana Airlines; tickets sold at Varig/Cruzeiro office in town. Aircraft maintenance, baggage checking and handling are unreliable; Guyanese come to Boa Vista to buy goods unavailable in Guyana—make sure your luggage is not among the excess that has to be taken off the plane. Also to Lethem. No left luggage facilities at airport, and no public transport other than taxis.

Border Crossing, Guyana Get exit stamp at police station in Lethem, Guyana, then take rowing-boat over border river Tacutu. No car ferry, but river can be forded in dry season. Once in Brazil, register at military camp at Bomfim (hotels: *Blessing*, F, and *Bomfim*) and get entry stamp (closed for lunch). Phone Boa Vista 2290 (for one G$) for car to take you to Boa Vista (US$45), or if lucky, take a colectivo (US$15, 3 hrs.) or daily bus at 1500. The bus leaves Boa Vista for Bomfim at 1300 only, US$6, 3 hrs.; luggage is checked at the Ministério da Fazenda checkpoint, before Bomfim, from where a jeep takes travellers to the Brazilian immigration post (US$1) and then walk the short distance to the river, 5 km. in all. To cross the river, yell "Boat" and a motor boat will come. It is very difficult to hitch between Boa Vista and Bomfim. From Bomfim to Boa Vista the road is acceptable (2 buses daily), but subject to washouts; bridge over Rio Branco. There is another border crossing at Iaramonta from where it is a hard, but rewarding walk to the Guyanese town of Orinduik. A weekly jeep connects Iaramonta with Boa Vista (US$25), also flights once a week, US$84 to Georgetown, often fully booked. A good rate for new cruzados is reported in the Guyana border area. New cruzados can be changed into G$ in the shop at Brazilian immigration post, better rates in Guyana at Lethem; Bomfim is a much better place for exchange, but Boa Vista is best. If you need visa to enter Guyana, you must get it in Brasília; no consulate in Boa Vista.

Border Crossing, Venezuela Everyone who crosses the border from Boa Vista, regardless of nationality, requires a visa (passport must be valid for 1 year). These can be obtained (allow 2-3 days) from the Venezuelan Consulate in Boa Vista, Av. Benjamín Constant 525E (T 095-224-2182, (open Mon.-Fri. 0830-1300 but may close earlier—no shorts allowed); requirements are a malaria test certificate (test at the Socorro hospital, takes about a day and costs US$10) yellow-fever vaccination certificate (obtainable at the airport—at Km. 350, Department of Health officials inoculate anyone arriving in Boa Vista who cannot produce a yellow fever vaccination certificate), certificate of medical checkup, done by doctor appointed by consulate (US$7.50), an onward ticket (an MCO will not suffice, according to latest reports) and 2 passport photographs. It is much simpler to get a visa for Venezuela in Manaus, Belém (see page 385), or maybe even Rio (check in advance); if you have no alternative but the consulate in Boa Vista, you can ask for Embassy in Caracas to telex Boa Vista to prove that you are a bona fide tourist. Border officials may also insist on a ticket out of Venezuela and US$20 a day—however, regulations state that a visa is sufficient. Trucks leave for Venezuela from Rua Benjamin Constant, drivers are not officially supposed to take passengers. Andorinha runs a daily bus between Santa Elena and Manaus, via Boa Vista, US$26. Buses leave Boa Vista for Santa Elena at 0600 (direct) and 0800, US$8 (stopping at all check points), in front of *Hotel Fronteras*, rough and dusty, take water, journey 6-8 hrs. Border search is thorough and you may be asked to show US$300 (there are also road checks in Venezuela). Entry stamp can be obtained only in Santa Elena; border closes at 1700. There are a bank and a basic hotel, *Pacaraima Palace*, on Brazilian side and you can camp. The road from the frontier is well-maintained and is being paved; it passes through some very scenic countryside.

SOUTHERN AMAZONIA (9)

Porto Velho (300,000 and growing at an estimated 20,000 a month), capital of the State of Rondônia with a population of 1.2 million, stands on a high bluff overlooking a curve of the River Madeira; at the top of the hill is the cathedral, built in 1950. The principal commercial street is Av. Sete de Setembro, which runs from the railway station and market hall to the upper level of the city, past the Rodoviária. Parks are under construction. Rondônia is the focus of experimental development in agriculture, with concomitant colonization of the area. At the same time, much of the state is being reserved for Indians and national forests. Porto Velho is expensive because of the local gold rush. About 20 km. from Porto Velho, the Samuel hydroelectric scheme is under construction, with a new town to house the workers. The first phase was due to enter in operation in 1987, but it had not started up in 1989. When it does come on stream in the 1990s, it will be insufficient to provide power for the states of Rondônia and Acre as was originally intended. The population has grown too rapidly. Malaria is common. With the growth in population, crime has increased in the city and outside.

The Madeira is one of the major tributaries of the Amazon. The four main rivers which form it are the Madre de Dios, rising a short distance from Cuzco (Peru); the Beni, coming from the southern Cordillera bordering Lake Titicaca; the Mamoré, rising near Sucre, Bolivia; and the Guaporé, coming out of Mato Grosso, in Brazil.

Hotels *Rondón Palace*, B, Av. Jorge Teixeira with Jacy Paraná, about 4 blocks to the left of bus station, T 221-3166, a/c, hot water, rec.; *Samaúma Palace*, Rua Dom Pedro II, 1038, B, nice rooms but said not too friendly (221-3159); *Vila Rica*, L, tower block, "flashy, flamboyant and mechanically efficient"; *Floresta*, C, a/c, good breakfast, swimming pool, which non-residents may use for the price of a drink or two; *Vitória*, D, plus private bath, quiet, good food. Hotels within sight of the Rodoviária: *Libra*, *Avenida Palace*, 2-star, *Porto Velho Palace*, 2-star, *Príncipe da Beira*, Rua Getúlio Vargas 2287, D (221-6135). From Rodoviária, take bus No. 301 "Presidente Roosevelt" (outside *Hotel Pontes*), which goes to railway station at riverside, then along Av. 7 de Setembro, passing: *Yara*, Gral. Osório 255, E; *Guaporé Palace*, 7 de Setembro 927, E, a/c, restaurant; *Nunes*, 7 de Setembro 1087, F, probably best value among cheapest hotels; *Sonora*, 7 de Setembro 1103, E, clean, fan, clothes washing facilities; *Rio*, Av. Joaquim Nabuco 2110, F, basic, good breakfast, friendly, fairly good cheap meals; *Laira*, Joaquim Nabuco 2005, F with fan; *Brasil*, Av. Pres. Kennedy, 15 mins. from Rodoviária, clean, cheap, breakfast; *Tres Irmãos*, Av. Nações Unidas 30. Hotels often full.

Electric Current 110 volts A.C., elsewhere in Rondônia 220 volts.

Restaurants At hotels: *Tarantella*, Av. Joaquim Nabuco with 7 de Setembro, fairly good pizza; *Juazeiro*, *Carreteiro*, *Dejoca*, *Tóquio* (cheap).

Shopping Bookshop off Av. 7 de Setembro, near the port, a few English paperbacks; manageress speaks English. Indian handicrafts at Casa do Índio, Rua Rui Barbosa 1407.

Car hire Silva Car, Rua Almirante Barroso 1528, CEP 78.900, Porto Velho, T (069) 221-1423/6040, Telex (069) 1129 SLVL. US$30/day.

Travel Agent Rotur, near *Hotel Floresta*. Guaporetur, Av 7 de Setembro 925, Helga speaks English and German.

Exchange Banks; try *Hotel Vila Rica* (Carlos, the doorman, for cash), *Hotel Floresta* (cash), *Hotel Río*, Varig/Cruzeiro office. Local radio news and papers publish exchange rates; try local businesses too. Difficult elsewhere in Rondônia.

Air Services   Airport 8 km. W of town. Daily flights to Manaus, Brasília, Cuiabá, Rio Branco, Corumbá, Cruzeiro do Sul, via Rio Branco, Mon.

River Services   Manaus, 1st class, with passable food; 2nd class very crowded US$30. Journey takes 3-4 days when river high; as much as 7 days when low. The boat leaves on Sat. at 1800. 1st class means upper deck, with more hammock-hanging room, or, if lucky, one of two 2-person cabins (US$70). Advantages to 1st class: more room, better view, coffee with milk, meals served first. Food is safe to eat, though monotonous; water-purifying tablets or bottles of sterilized water strongly recommended. Wait at the Capitânia do Porto in the centre of town for a possible passage on a cargo boat; these boats leave from Porto Bras, down river from Porto Velho. Porto Velho-Humaitá US$6.66 (boat *Dois de Junho*).

Six days a week a boat leaves at 1800 for Manaus from Manicoré, at the confluence of the Rivers Madeira and Manicoré, US$32 for two nights, and one day's journey, including food; boats from Porto Velho to Manicoré on Mon., Wed. and Sat. (1800, arr. 0200, but you can sleep on the boat), connecting with Manicoré-Manaus boats. **Manicoré** (about 10,000 people) is a pleasant town; the Praça de Bandeira is at the corner of Av. Getúlio Vargas and Av. Pedro Tinoco (one block to left of road that goes up from the dock). *Hotel Manicoré*, 4 blocks left from Praça on Av. Vargas, just before the big church; *Restaurant Tapuia*, 1 block from Praça in opp. direction to river on Av. Tinoco; slow but good restaurant at floating dock. Fruit market on Av. Vargas.

Buses   New Rodoviária on outskirts of town, Av. Pres. Kennedy. Bus to Manaus, 1600, and 2000 normal (US$15), 1700 and 1800 (*leito* US$30), 24-26 hrs. (up to 4 days in the rainy season); to Humaitá, US$2; to São Paulo, sixty-plus hrs., US$42; to Cuiabá, 23 hrs. US$17, take plenty of food and drink. To Guajará-Mirim, see below. To Rio Branco, twice daily, 18 hrs. (but can take 3-5 days), US$15. Daily bus with Eucatur from Cascavel (Paraná) via Maringá, Presidente Prudente, Campo Grande and Cuiabá to Porto Velho. To Cáceres for the Pantanal, Colibri, 18 hrs., US$12. Hitching difficult, try at the *posto* 2 km. out of town. For Manaus try at the ferry crossing just outside town (may be impossible in the rainy season).

Roads   to Cuiabá (BR-364—Marechal Rondon Highway, 1,450 km., fully paved; **see page 413**); Rio Branco, 490 km., following Madeira-Mamoré railway, due to be fully paved by 1988; to Humaitá (205 km.) on the Madeira river (fully paved), connecting with the Transamazônica Highway, and on to Manaus (877 km.), not completely paved and in poor condition. Road journeys are best done in the dry season, the second half of the year; the Manaus road (Catire Highway) is sometimes closed in the rainy season.

A result of the paving of BR-364 is the development of towns along it: Ariquemes (159 km. from Porto Velho, pop. 200,000, buses hourly from 0600, 3-4 hrs., Banco do Brasil, some hotels, *Valerius Palace*, E); Nova Vida (200 km.), Jaru (257 km.), Ouro Preto d'Oeste (297 km.), **Ji Paraná** (337 km., pop. 200,000—bus to Porto Velho, US$7, 14 hrs.; to Cuiabá, 15 hrs., US$11, 22 *leito*; hotels *Horizonte*, E, rec. with reasonable restaurants, *Sol Nascente*, F with churrascaria, *Hotel Transcontinental*, B, rec.; trips to frontier towns possible, e.g. Nova Colina), Presidente Médici (373 km., 50,000 people), Cacoal (404 km., 200,000 people, Hotels *Cacoal Palace* (D) and *Amazonis*), Pimenta Bueno (440 km., pop. 50,000) and Vilhena on the Rondônia-Mato Grosso border (658 km. from Porto Velho, 710 km. from Cuiabá; *Diplomata Hotel*, D, near bus station; *Rodoviária*, F, rec.; *Gastão*, F). At Vilhena proof of yellow-fever inoculation required: if no proof, new shot. Two cities have grown without prior planning: Rolim de Mouro, W of Pimenta Bueno, with a population of over 60,000 and a *Transcontinental Hotel*, and Itarua do Oeste, 91 km. S of Porto Velho, at what used to be a bus waiting station (population about 5,000).

The **Pacaás Novos National Park**, 765,800 hectares, lies west of the BR-364; it is a transitional zone between open plain and Amazonian forest. Details from IBDF, Av. Gov. Jorge Teixeira, CEP 78.900, Porto Velho; also enquire here about the Jaru and Guaporé Biological Reserves in the State.

Porto Velho was the terminus of the Madeira-Mamoré railway of 367 km. (closed 1971), Brazil's price to Bolivia for annexing the Acre territory during the rubber boom. It cost a life for every hundred sleepers, 6,208 in all, during construction. The line, built 1907-12, by-passed the 19 rapids of the Madeira and Mamoré rivers, and gave Bolivia an outlet of sorts to the Atlantic. It was supposed to go as far as Riberalta, on the Rio Beni, above that river's rapids, but stopped short at **Guajará Mirim** (12,000 people). 3 locomotives operate out of Porto Velho. The railway expert will enjoy the ancient steam locomotives in the railway station and on a siding 2 km. away. There are still two engines in working order, which run Sunday excursion trains as far as Santo Antônio, 7 km. away (US$0.10). Small railway museum at station has been moved so that the station can accommodate passengers on the newly restored line. (The conductor on the Saturday train, Silas Shockness, who also runs the shop where the locomotives are being repaired, is from Grenada; his brother Denis runs the museum.) The railway is now replaced by a fair road, which uses its bridges (in poor condition); the 370-km. bus ride (3 buses a day, US$7, takes 14 hrs. or more depending on season—road often closed March-May) is far faster than the train was. The Bolivian town of Guayaramerín is across the Mamoré river (expensive speedboat service or ferry, which is free for foot passengers); it is connected by road to Riberalta, and there are air services to other Bolivian cities. An ancient stern wheeler plies on the Guaporé; 26-day, 1,250 km. trips (return) can be made on the Guaporé from Guajará Mirim to Vila Bela in Mato Grosso, fare including food, is US$5. 170 km. from Guajará Mirim, on the Guaporé river, is the Forte Príncipe da Beira, begun in 1777 as a defence of the border with Bolivia. The fort, which is being restored, can be reached from Costa Marques (20 km. by road), which can only be reached by air or by river.

If travelling by road between Porto Velho and Guajará Mirim, two possible stops are at Maluca dos Índios, from where you can visit villages of gold prospectors by the Madeira river; the other is from the railway bridge just before Vila Murtinho where you can see gold panners, and, walking a few hundred metres, the rapids on the Mamoré river.

Guajará Mirim Hotels *Comercial*, E; *Mini-Estrela*, Av. 15 de Novembro 460, E; *Fénix Palace*, Av. 15 de Novembro 459, E; *Hudson*, Av. Marechal Deodoro s/n, E, rec. *Camponés*, F.

Restaurant Best is *Oasis*, at Posto Nogueira service station, Av. 15 de Novembro 837, US$5 with drinks.

Museum Museu Municipal at the old railway station beside the ferry landing—small, with railway memorabilia and a few stuffed birds.

Exchange Banco do Brasil (foreign exchange a.m. only). Loja Nogueira, Av. Pres. Dutra, esq. Leopold de Matos (cash only). There is no market in Brazil for bolivianos.

Note If you need a visa to enter Brazil, apply to the Brazilian Consul at Guayaramerín (Bolivia), open 1100-1300, before crossing the Rio Mamoré into Brazil. If the Policia Federal are not on duty at the waterfront, you must get passport stamped at their office in town, address below. Similarly, before crossing into Bolivia you may need a visa (free) from the Bolivian consul in Guajará Mirim (2 photos needed) in 600's block of Av. 15 de Novembro. Western Europeans can cross river and visit the Immigration Office; which closes at 1100 on Sat. You will need a Brazilian exit stamp from Policia Federal, Av. Antônio Correia da Costa 842.

From Abunã, 220 km. from Porto Velho (*Hotel Ferroviário*, E, including meals, however town is best avoided if at all possible) the road from Porto Velho continues W to **Rio Branco**, the capital of the State of Acre, 90,000 people. Hotels always crowded: *Inacio's*, C, overpriced, dirty, fair restaurant; *Rio Branco*, C, on park, nice but simple; *Amazonas*, *Fontes* (best of a bad bunch of budget hotels, F, not clean), *Fortaleza*, all on left bank. On right bank, *Sucessor*, F, showers, fan, clean, comfortable, friendly. Cheap meals at *Dos Colonos* near market. *Marayina*, for pizzas, sandwiches, cakes, ice cream, popular at night; *Casarão*, also popular; *Churrascaria Triângulo*, near airport, as much charcoal-grilled meat as you can eat, rec.; *Churrascaria Modelo*, Rua Marechal Deodoro 360, less good. There is a park with a military post on one side; beyond is the Governor's palace and another park leading to the market on the bank of the Acre river. There is a bridge across the river, which is only navigable to Manaus in the wet season. The city has a cathedral, an airport and an agricultural research centre.

Warning The road from Porto Velho to Rio Branco should be travelled with much caution; not only can the journey take as much as 3 to 5 days, but the area is seriously affected by malaria. We have also received reports of lawlessness on the BR-364 after dark; to be safe, be in a city before nightfall.

At Rio Branco the Transamazônica Highway meets the road from Brasília and goes on to Cruzeiro do Sul and Japim; it is expected to reach the Peruvian frontier further N when completed; it is hoped that it will be continued by the Peruvians to the river port of Iquitos. It is very difficult to get from Rio Branco to Cruzeiro do Sul by road because there is no bus service, and the occasional lorry goes mainly in the dry season. There is a plane (Varig) every Monday at 1130 to Cruzeiro do Sul (originating in Porto Velho).

Cruzeiro do Sul, an isolated Amazonian town of 10,000 people, is situated on the river Juruá; cheap excursions can be made on the river, for example to the village of Rodrigues Alves (2-3 hrs., return by boat or by road, 15 km.). In the jungle one can see rubber-tapping, and collecting the latex into "borrachas" which weigh up to 45 kg. Hotels: *Sandra's*, D; *Novo do Acre*, F, rec., a/c, clean; *Hospedaria Janecir*, F; *dos Viajantes*, F, facing river, clean, showers, full board available. Restaurant *O Laçador*, good food. Money changing is very difficult; none of the banks will change dollars. Try the airline staff (poor rates). From Cruzeiro do Sul to Pucallpa one can go either by air: Sasa, US$37.50, 50 mins.,—details from Blvd. Taumaturgo 25 (no phone), flies only when plane is full, it seats 5; undertake all formalities at Policia Federal before leaving. Alternatively one can go by boat when river is high (Nov.-Feb.): only for the hardy and well-equipped; journey takes about 10 days: 4 by boat to Tamburiaco, on rivers Juruá and Juruá-Mirim, then 2 days' walk through the jungle to the Peruvian border at Canta Gallo, then 3-4 more days by boat on the rivers Amonia and Abojao to Pucallpa. The regional airline Taba have a permit to fly to Eirunepé on the Juruá river from Manaus and Tabatinga; Eirunepé is a small town near Carauari, where Dutch missionaries live.

A road from Rio Branco (the BR-317), paved as far as Xapuri, goes to Brasiléia (bus daily, 6 hrs., US$4, basic hotel, Federal Police give exit stamps), opposite the Bolivian town of Cobija on the Acre River, and finally to Assis Brasil where the Peruvian, Bolivian and Brazilian frontiers meet; across the Acre River are Iñapari (Peru) and Bolpebra (Bolivia). There is no public transport, and little else, beyond Brasiléia to Iñapari. In Assis Brasil, there is one small hotel (a dormitory, basic but clean, friendly), one snack bar, a bank which does not change US dollars (the hotel owner may be persuaded to oblige) and river transport only, which is dependent on the seasons.

N.B. Rio Branco time is one hour behind Manaus time; this means two hours behind Brazilian Standard Time.

THE CENTRE-WEST (10)

The so-called centre-west of Brazil is occupied by the states of Goiás, Mato Grosso and Mato Grosso do Sul. Goiás is one of Brazil's most rapidly developing agricultural areas, producing cattle, coffee, soya and rice. The Federal District of Brasília (**see page 241**) was subtracted in 1960 from the territory of Goiás.

Goiânia, 202 km. SW of Brasília, the second (after Belo Horizonte) of Brazil's planned state capitals, was founded in 1933 and succeeded Goiás Velho as capital of the State of Goiás in 1937. It now has a population of 703,000. Goiânia is a spacious city, with its main avenues excellently lit and ornamented with plants; tourists can enjoy the Parque Mutirama with its planetarium on the city's eastern side and the Horto Florestal, with good zoo and anthropological museum in the west; there are a racecourse and a motor racetrack. The Jaó Club on the edge of a reservoir provides for sun bathing and water skiing. Every Sunday morning there is a handicrafts fair in the city's central square, the Praça Cívica, where there is a small museum of local handicrafts, animals and Indian artefacts.

Warning Tourists are advised to check the safety of Goiânia in advance following the radiation accident here in 1987.

Hotels   *Castro Park,* A, new, warmly rec.; *Samambaia,* Av. Anhanguera 1157; *Bandeirantes,* same street, No. 3278; *Umuarama,* Rua 4, No. 492; *São Conrado,* Rua 3, No. 652; *Augustus,* Praça Antônio Lizita 702 (all good D-C). Many cheap hotels e.g. *J. Alves,* opp. Rodoviária; *Santo Antônio,* Av. Anhanguera 6296, F.

Restaurants   *Jaó Club; Long Feung.* Goiânia is much cheaper for eating and sleeping than Brasília. Restaurant at the Rodoviária for good food at very low prices, and plenty more eating places nearby.

Bookshop on Rua 4 has some secondhand English books; will exchange.

Banks   National banks.

Tourist Office Goiastur, in the football stadium (Estádio Serra Dourada), very friendly: it's rather remote!

Travel Agents Cardealtur, Av. Goiás 382; Incatur, Av. Goiás 151; Transworld, Rua 3, 560, in Galeria Central. All good for exchange.

Airport   Nearby, with daily flights to main cities.

Roads and Buses To Cuiabá (Mato Grosso) paved, 4 buses a day, US$12, 13 hrs.; continues to Porto Velho (Rondônia) and Rio Branco (Acre). To Brasília (about 17 a day, 2½ hrs., US$3) and São Paulo (bus services, US$19, 14 hrs.); Campo Grande 18 hrs. US$15. To Goiás Velho, 136 km. Distances by road (km.): Belém, 2,017; Brasília, 202; Campo Grande, 1,212; Corumbá, 1,641; Cuiabá, 934; Foz do Iguaçu, 1,232; Manaus, 3,222; Porto Alegre, 2,025; Recife, 2,505; Rio, 1,354; Salvador, 2,301; São Paulo, 918.

Anápolis, 61 km. nearer Brasília, with a population of 161,000, is an important trading centre.

Hotels   *Itamarati; Príncipe; Central Palace; Anápolis.* Many cheap ones around bus station, e.g. *Serra Dourada,* Av. Brasil 375, E, good value.

Goiás Velho (25,000 population), a picturesque old gold-mining town founded in 1727, was capital of the State of Goiás until 1937. There is a regular bus service between Goiânia and Goiás Velho. The city has seven baroque churches, the oldest being São Francisco de Paula (1761).

Museums The Museu da Boa Morte in the colonial church of the same name has a small but interesting collection of old images, paintings, etc. The Museu das Bandeiras is in the old town hall and prison (Casa da Câmara e Cadeia), by the colonial fountain. The old Government Palace, with fine rooms, is now open to the public, next to the red-brick Cathedral in the main square. A local tradition is the Fogaréu procession in Holy Week.

José Joaquim da Veiga Valle, who was born in Pirenópolis in 1806, was the "Aleijadinho" of Goiás. Many of his works are in the Boa Morte museum. British artist Robin Macgregor, whose paintings are widely collected throughout Brazil, is a resident of Goiás Velho.

Hotels *Vila Boa*, large, C, pool, views; *Municipal*, simple, F; *Minas Goiás*, F incl. small breakfast, clean, in Rua Dr Americano do Brasil.

Restaurants *Pito Aceso*, grills; *Hotel Vila Boa*; *Pedro's Bar*, good cold beef. Try the local meat pie, empadão goiano.

Shopping Centro de Tradições Goianas, in *Hotel Vila Boa*.

Excursion Centro de Gemologia de Goiás, Quadra 2, Módulo 13, Daia, about 10 km. by bus from Anápolis, will show visitors how real and synthetic gem stones are distinguished; you can also buy stones. Cachoeira Grande, 7 km. from Goiás Velho on the Juçara road, has bathing place and snack bar.

Pirenópolis, another colonial town, is 128 km. from Goiânia, 220 km. from Brasília. There is a regular bus service between Anápolis and Pirenópolis (66 km.). **Hotels**: *Rex*, E, *Central*, F (for the desperate).

Chapada dos Veadeiros This national park is about 200 km. N of Brasília, reached by paved road to Alto Paraíso de Goiás (buses from Brasília 1000 and 2200, US$3) and gravel road from there W towards Colinas. The park entrance is on a side turning from the Colinas road, just before the village of São Jorge. The park's main attraction is a series of waterfalls on the Rio Negro, 7 km. from São Jorge by rough track; there are other falls about 2 km. from the park entrance. Rough camping is permitted. There is a hotel, F, by the bus station in Alto Paraíso and *residencias* in São Jorge.

Caldas Novas, 187 km. SE of Goiânia (many buses; best reached via Morrinhos on the BR-153 Goiânia-São Paulo highway, population 10,000) is a newly-developed thermal resort with good hotels and camp sites with hot swimming pools. Daily bus from Morrinhos, US$0.50, 1½ hrs. There are three groups of springs within this area: Caldas Novas, Fontes de Pirapetinga (7 km. from the town) and Rio Quente (25 km. from the town, bus from Caldas Novas; the *Pousada Hotel* (5 star) has lots of pools, entry US$20); water temperatures are 37-51°C.

Hotels 48 in all. *Tamburi*, R. Eça de Queirós. Very fashionable is *Hotel Turismo* (5-star, L, full board, a/c) at Rio Quente, and, sharing some of its facilities, *Pousada do Rio Quente*, 3-star, A, full board, but not a/c. (The *Turismo* has a private airstrip; flights from Rio and São Paulo with agencies.) *Parque das Primaveras*, R. do Balneário, A, rec. by locals, cheaper than the Rio Quente places. Also *Motel Aguas Calientes* and *Cabanas do Rio Quente. Serra Dourada*, Av. Correia Neto 574, D, rec. *Goiás*, E with breakfast, rec. Camping at Esplanada, and Camping Clube do Brasil site on the Ipameri road, 1 km. from the centre. Many other "Clubes e Campings°: *Tropical*, US$1 p.p., 2 sites in town, can use both in 1 day, others mostly US$1.30 a day, all have snack bars; *Berro d'Água* in Bairro do Turista rec.

Two other natural attractions in Goiás are the Cachoeira do Salto (160 km. from Brasília) and the thermal waters of the Lagoa de Aporé on the border with Mato Grosso. At Cristalina (120 km. from Brasília) there is a waterfall; also semi-precious stones for sale (**see page 248**). The River Araguaia, forming the border between Goiás and the two Mato Grosso states, provides many sandy beaches and good fishing: 1,600 km. of the river are navigable by boat.

A dirt road connects Goiás Velho with Aragarças (on the Goiás side) and *Barra do Garças* (on the Mato Grosso side) on the River Araguaia (Barra can also be reached by a more southerly route from Goiânia). Barra has various hotels on Av. João Alberto, e.g. *Avenida*, clean, E; *churrascarias* near main bridge and on Av. João Alberto; pleasant river beach with bars and snacks; campsite on island in river; night-time entertainment by the port. A road to the north of Barra extends as far as São João do Araguaia; where this road crosses the Rio das Mortes is the town of *Xavantina* (*Hotel Xavantina*, F, basic; *Churrascaria Arca de Noé*, highly rec.). The road is paved as far as Serra Dourada (160 km. N of Barra). Anti-malaria precautions are recommended for the Rio Araguaia region. June-Oct. is said to be the best time to visit the region; low water allows camping on beaches and islands. Avoid July, when the fishermen and their families all come. Boats and guides can be hired in Aruanã, Britânia or Barra do Garças.

The BR-153, Brasília-Belém road, runs north through the heart of Goiás state. At Guaraí the road forks, one branch continuing west into Pará, then turning north to Marabá on the Transamazônica and onto Belém. The other branch goes to Araguaína, whereafter the BR-226 goes to Estreito in Maranhão, from where the BR-010 runs north through Imperatriz to Belém.

Araguaína is a small settlement of some 3,000 on the Brasília-Belém road (Brasília, 1,102 km.; Belém 842 km.; Imperatriz, 174 km.). Several hotels near Rodoviária including *Esplanada*, F p.p., may have to share a room, friendly, clean, fan, no breakfast, good; *Líder*, *São Jorge*, *do Norte* and *Goiás* (all F). Bus leaves Araguaína for Marabá 0700 and 1400. Ordinary bus to Goiânia takes 24 hours: try to get an express. If travelling to Belém or Brasília by bus, reservations are not normally accepted: be at the terminal 2 hrs. before scheduled departure as buses tend to leave early; as soon as bus pulls in, follow the driver to the ticket counter and ask if there are seats. Buses also to Santarém.

Off the Brasília-Belém road are fast-developing frontier regions between the lower Araguaia and Xingu rivers. Kevin Healey writes: There is now a soaring concrete bridge spanning the Araguaia just south of Conceição do Araguaia, although the road connection to the Belém highway at Guaraí is still gravel and nasty in the wet. (This is the only bridge across the Araguaia between Barra dos Garças and Marabá.)

   North and west of Conceição are many new townships and ranches. Places like Redencão and Xinguara are raw, dusty and not very salubrious for tourists. At Xinguara (pop. 20,000 already) is the *Hotel Rio Vermelho*, F, pretty grotty, pigsty outside windows, orange water in taps, bed legs in cans of paraffin to discourage ants and termites. To the west, Cumaru is a *garimpeiro* settlement, from where the local military governor keeps "law and order" over the gold mining centres near the Rio Fresco. Here, the miners and prospectors are already on the edge of the Gorotiré Indian Reserve and a road is poised to enter the Indian land. To the south is Campo Alegre (pop. 6,000), the centre of cow country, with a huge new slaughterhouse serving the corporate ranches around the region (e.g. the experimental ranch of Cristalino, owned by VW Brasil). This is a perfect place to see the destruction of the rainforest and the changing climate pattern.

   At *Conceição do Araguaia* the best hotel is the *Taruma Tropical* (E), each room a concrete cell, soft and squishy beds, ant parades along the walls, but clean and functioning bathrooms; a/c—when it works; the hotel is well-patronised by ranchers and absentee landowners from Brasília. The town has a frontier atmosphere, although mudhuts are being replaced by brick: cowboy hats, battered Chevrolet pick-ups, skinny mules and a red light district. Airport 17 km. SW. Conceição would be a useful base for visiting the Ilha do Bananal.

Douglas Trent, of Tropical Tours, Belo Horizonte (**see page 288**), writes: *Bananal* is the world's largest river island, located in the state of Goiás on the northeastern border of Mato Grosso. The island is formed by a division in the south of the Araguaia River and is approximately 320 km. long. The entire island was originally a national park (called **Parque Nacional Araguaia**), which was then cut in half and later further reduced to its current size of 562,312 ha (of an original 2 million). The island and park are subject to seasonal flooding and contain several permanent lakes. The island, and especially the park, form one of the more spectacular wildlife areas on the continent, in many ways similar to the Pantanal. The vegetation is a transition zone between the *cerrado* (woody savanna) and Amazon forests, with gallery forests along the many waterways. There are several marshlands throughout the island.

   The fauna is also transitional. More than 300 bird species are found here, including the hoatzin, hyacinthine macaw, harpy eagle and black-fronted piping guan. The giant anteater, maned wolf, bush dog, giant otter, jaguar, puma, marsh deer, pampas deer, American tapir, yellow anaconda and South American river turtle also occur here. The island is flooded most of the year, with the prime visiting (dry) season being from June to early October, when the beaches are exposed. Unfortunately, the infrastructure for tourism aside from fishing expeditions (the island is a premier spot for big fish!) is very limited. Access to the park is through the small but pleasant town of **Santa Teresinha** (6,000 people), which is north of São Felix (see below), and is the gateway to the park. A charming hotel is the *Bananal*, Pça Tarcila Braga 106, CEP 78395 (Mato Grosso), B with full board. There is room only for 10; make your reservations well in advance. Reservations can be made by mail, allowing several months for the mail to get through, or through Tropical Tours, T (031) 223-3811 Tlx. (031) 3823 RAPT BR.

   Permission to visit the park should be obtained in advance from Sr. Levi Vargas, Director of the Park, IBDF, Rua 229, No. 95, Setor Universitário, 74.000 Goiânia. There is some simple accommodation for scientists at the park, which can sometimes be reserved at the address above or from IBDF, the National Parks department in Brasília. Bring your own food, and the severely underpaid but dedicated staff would appreciate any extra food or financial help, although it will not be solicited. A boat to the park can be lined up at the *Hotel Bananal*.

São Félix do Araguaia is a larger town with more infrastructure for fishing. A very simple hotel with the best view in town is the *Mini Hotel Araguaia*, Av. Araguaia 344, T (065) 522-1154, E with breakfast. They have a/c rooms, not rec., electricity is turned off at night and the closed-in room gets very hot. Another hotel, *Xavante*, is in the city centre. A good restaurant is the *Pizzaria Cantinho da Peixada* on Av. Araguaia, next to the Texaco station, overlooking the river. *Bar Paralelos* has live music. Many Carajás indians are found in town; a depot of their handicrafts is between the *Pizzaria* and *Mini Hotel* on Av. Araguaia.

   Bananal can be visited from São Félix (with permission from Funai in the town) by crossing the river to the Carajá village of Santa Isabela de Morra and asking to see the chief, Aruiana, who can tell you the history of the tribe. The island can be crossed from São Félix to São Miguel de Araguaia by taking an 8-hour trip (departures twice a week) with Zico in his van (contact him at the *Bar Beira*), US$8 p.p. From São Miguel a 5-hour bus trip brings you to Porangatu (*Hotel Mauriti*, F, shower, restaurant) on the Belém-Brasília highway.

Access to both Santa Teresinha and São Félix is by Brasil Central/TAM flights, and to São Félix by bus from Barra do Garças, 17 hours, and from Marabá. The service is unreliable and, as the planes hold just 15 passengers, it is common to get held over for a day or two. In Sta. Tersinha look out for a man in a yellowish taxi who kindly offers a free ride and then tries to collect outrageous sums from foreigners. There are legitimate taxis available—use them. Mosquito nets are highly recommended: high incidence of malaria.

In the far SW of Goiás is the **Emas National Park**, about 130 km. from Mineiros, a town just off the Brasília-Cuiabá road. Father Herbert Hermes (US) at the São José convent, Mineiros, can arrange permission to visit (necessary, or from IBDF address above), also Sr. José Roberto Carvalho at Prefeitura. A 3-day, 4-night visit to the Park costs about US$50. The park, of 1,300 sq. km., contains rolling prairies with numerous termite mounds, savanna-type woodland and forested rivers. Among the mammals encountered are armadillos, giant anteaters, marsh and pampas deer, the maned wolf and the rare giant otter. Birds include rheas, king vulture and crested screamers (seriema).

To the west of Goiás are the states of Mato Grosso and Mato Grosso do Sul, with a combined area of 1,231,549 sq. km. and a population of only about 2.5 million, or just over two persons to the square km. The two states are half covered with forest, with a large swampy area (220,000 sq. km) called the Pantanal (roughly west of a line between Campo Grande and Cuiabá, between which there is a direct road), partly flooded in the rainy season **(see page 411)**. East of this line the pasture plains begin to appear. The Noroeste Railway and a road run across Mato Grosso do Sul through Campo Grande to Porto Esperança and Corumbá, both on the River Paraguay; much of the journey is across swamps, offering many sights of birds and other wildlife.

Campo Grande, the capital of the State of Mato Grosso do Sul (pop. 283,000), is a pleasant modern town. In the centre is a shady park and nearby the Casa do Artesanato (Av. Calógeras and Afonso Pena) has a good collection of Indian jewellery and arrows on sale. Mato Grosso do Sul is a good region for buying cheap, good leather shoes.

Regional Indian Museum (Museu Regional Dom Bosco), Rua Barão do Rio Branco 1843 (open daily 0700-1100, 1300-1700), has interesting exhibits and handicrafts of the Pantanal and Mato Grosso Indians. There is also a collection of animals and birds (particularly good and well-preserved, if not well labelled) from the Pantanal, and a fossil collection.

Hotels *Jandaia*, Rua Barão do Rio Branco 1271, well located, best, A. *Campo Grande*, Rua 13 de Maio 2825, a/c, luxury, B. *Concord*, Av. Calógeras 1624, very good, swimming pool, a/c, B. *Fenícia*, Av. Calógeras 2262, a/c, D. *Iguaçu*, opposite bus station but quiet, modern, clean, pleasant, D; *Gaspar*, Av. Mato Grosso 2, opp. railway station, E with bath, ask for quiet room, good breakfast, clean. *Rio*, Marechal Rondón 1499, in city centre, E, with bath, breakfast, a/c, good value in rooms with bath (communal baths serve too many rooms), friendly, good restaurant; many cheap and shabby *pensões* on Avs. Calógeras and Mato Grosso within a few blocks of railway station. *União*, E, Calógeras 2828, near the station, good breakfast, clean, but noisy, friendly; *Continental*, Rua Maracaju 229, 2 blocks from railway, 5 from bus terminal, F, clean, comfortable; *Plaza*, same street, F, clean, unfriendly; *Paulista*, António Maria Coelho 1085, F, basic but adequate facilities, cheap café (on the street behind *Gaspar*); *Tupi*, between bus and railway stations, cheap, basic; *Cosmos*, at bus station, E, reasonable (*Califórnia* at Rodoviária is F, but very basic and dirty); *Nacional*, Rua Dom Aquino 610, near bus station, E, basic, shabby but friendly, clean; *Rocha*, Barão do Rio Branco 343, 1 block from Rodoviária, E without breakfast, fan, clean, T 383-6874; *Turis Rodoviária*, Av. Barão do Rio Branco 342, close to bus station, E, good, friendly. *União*, Av. Calógeras, E with bath, F without, clean, ask for quiet room, 1½ blocks from railway station; *Caçula*, Av. Calógeras, F, cheap, safe, clean, washing facilities, 300 m. from railway station, 700 m. from Rodoviária. Some hotels near bus station both seedy and dear, best go into town (*Presidente*, opp. Rodoviária, is F, OK; *Dormitório*, F, is basic).

Restaurants *Cabana Gaúcha*, Av. Afonso Pena, 1919, rec., live music evenings; *Vitório*, next door, slightly cheaper, also live music evenings; *Churrascaria do Papai*, at bus station, huge meal; *Carinca*, SE corner of main *praça*, modern, clean, good plain food. *Shanghai*, Rio Branco 1037, rec.; *Hong Kong*, Rua Maracaju 131, centre, good Chinese food; *Lanchonete Arabe* rec. *Cafeteria Lojas Americanas*, Marechal Rondón 1336, in a supermarket; *El Café*, R. Dom Aquino 1248, both good. *Nutre Bem*, vegetarian, Pedro Celestino 1696, good. Plenty of good, cheap places in Rua Barão de Rio Branco, e.g. *Sabor e Artes*, No. 1016.

Exchange   Banco do Brasil changes travellers' cheques. Parallel rate hard to find, try at Rodoviária, *Hotel Caranda*, 1 block from Rodoviária; Sr. Abdala in the clothes shop at 14 de Julho 2581; or try in Las Vegas billiard hall, Barao Rio Branco 1130.

Post Office   on corner of R. Dom Aquino and Calógeras.

Health   Yellow and Dengue fevers are both present in Campo Grande. There is a clinic for both at the railway station, but it's not very hygienic (take precautions in advance).

Tourist Information, maps, etc. at MSTur, Rua Antônio Maria Coelho 2802, T 384 3095. Extremely helpful.

Tourist Agency   Tainá Turismo, Rua Bahia 22, Jardim dos Estados, T 384-6544; Dallas, Rio Branco 1454.

Roads   Distances in km. from Campo Grande: Belém, 3,299; Brasília, 1,405; Corumbá, 429; Cuiabá, 712; Foz do Iguaçu, 1,141; Goiânia, 1,212; Manaus, 3,006; Porto Alegre, 1,786; Recife, 3,708; Rio, 1,475; Salvador, 2,935; São Paulo, 1,046.

Buses   (Taxi to Rodoviária, US$1.75.) São Paulo, paved road, US$14.50, 16 hrs. 6 buses daily, 1st at 0800, last at 2100, *leito* buses at 1600 and 2000. Cuiabá, US$9, 10 hrs., 12 buses daily, *leito* at 2100 and 2200. To Brasília, US$23 (Motta rec.), 23 hrs. at 0900. Rio de Janeiro, US$32, 21 hrs., 4 buses daily, *leito* at 1745. Corumbá, with Andorinha 1000, 1100, 1300 and a relief bus at 0800, US$8, 6 hrs., on paved road. Campo Grande-Corumbá buses connect with those from Rio and São Paulo, similarly those from Corumbá through to Rio and São Paulo. Ponta Porã, 5½ hrs., Expresso Queiroz, US$5, 5 ordinary buses a day, 2 executive buses, US$7.50, 8 buses daily, 1st at 0630, last at 2130. Dourados, same schedule as Ponta Porã, 4 hrs., US$3. Beyond Dourados is Mundo Novo, from where buses go to Punta Porã (0530) and to Porto Frajelli (many between 0420 and 1900, ½ hr.); from Mundo Novo ferries for cars and passengers go to Guaíra for US$0.20. Buses Campo Grande-Mundo Novo, 0900, 10 hrs. in dry weather, US$4.20, return 0730 and 1800; buses Dourados-Mundo Novo, unpaved road, four a day. No direct service to Foz do Iguaçu, though you can buy a through ticket; journey takes 17 hrs. with Maringá company via Cascavel, with good connections, US$15.50 (the reverse direction is via Maringá and is quicker).

Air   Daily flights to São Paulo, Rio, Corumbá, Cuiabá, Brasília, Manaus, Porto Velho. To Foz do Iguaçu, 4 a week, 1 hr. flight with VASP. Reduction of 12% on VASP night flights to Rio and São Paulo. City bus stops outside airport. Taxi to airport, US$3.

Trains   The railway station is 5 blocks from the bus terminal. Ponta Porã, slow train (8¾ hrs.) daily at 1000 (not Sun.; lone females are advised to sit on left-hand side since, 1 hour before Ponta Porã, is a predominantly male factory town where you may get some unwanted attention). Ponta Porã to Campo Grande at 0845, US$4 1st class, US$2.25 2nd class on the train (this service is under threat—check). To Corumbá: twice daily. Fast night train at 2010, arriving 0640, US$15 double sleeper (rec.), US$5.50 pullman, no 2nd class. Day train leaves at 0845, arriving 1945, meals served at seats, US$3. Fares US$3 1st class, US$2 2nd class (no advance ticket sales, office open 0640-0815), a very tiring journey. Thefts and drugged food reported on this journey. Latest reports indicate that the only **trains to Bauru** are those which originate in Corumbá (i.e. no local Campo Grande-Bauru train); best to check in advance if possible. First class fare to Bauru is US$5.70.

The Campo Grande—São Paulo journey can be broken at *Tres Lagoas* near the Paraná river and on the railway, and 10 hours by road to São Paulo (bus Campo Grande—Tres Lagoas, 8 hrs., US$8, dep. 1100, a bumpy, interesting journey). *Novo Hotel* near bus station, F. friendly.

The road from Campo Grande to the Paraguayan border passes through *Dourados* (*Hotel Alphonsus*, C, Av. Pres. Vargas 603). Good bus connections to Campo Grande, Ponta Porã and Mundo Novo (see under Campo Grande, Buses, above).

A road (being paved) and railway run SW from Campo Grande to **Ponta Porã** (14,500 people), on the Paraguayan border opposite the town of Pedro Juan Caballero.

Hotels   *Pousada do Bosque,* very nice motel type with a/c, restaurant and swimming pool, Av. Pres. Vargas, out of town, C. *Barcelona,* Rua Guia Lopes, maze-like building, pool, restaurant, a/c, D-E. *Internacional,* Rua Internacional 1267, E with a/c, F with bath or without, hot showers, clean, good breakfasts, rec.; *Francia,* E, opposite *Barcelona,* bath, clean, friendly, restaurant, US$3 for big meal. *Grande,* Av. Brasil 1181, E. *Alvorada,* F, clean and pleasant. *Dos Viajantes,* across park opp. railway station, F, very basic, clean.

Restaurants   *Top Lanches,* beside *Hotel Barcelona,* cheap and friendly. *Chapão,* good food at reasonable prices. *Pepe's Lunch e Pizzeria,* good, fairly cheap; *Karina Lanches,* near Federal Police office, good, cheap; *Santa Antônia,* rec.

Electric Current   220 volts A.C.

Exchange Banco do Brasil changes travellers' cheques. Several *cambios* on the Paraguayan side, but none deal in cheques. Many in the centre of town (but on Sun. change money in hotels or the gambling hall beneath Livraria Sulamérica).

The border post at Ponta Porã normally closes at 1700 (it is also closed on national holidays). The Federal Police office is in a new white building shared with an engineering supply company in the same block as the Expresso Queiroz Rodoviária; open 0800. To reach Paraguayan control, follow the Rua Guia Lopes 4 blocks into Paraguay. If crossing into Paraguay some nationalities require visa from Paraguayan consulate next door to *Hotel Internacional*, Rua Internacional (check requirements carefully).

A new area of tourist interest in Mato Grosso do Sul is being established in the municipalities of Bonito (hotels: *Bonanza, Alvorado, Florestal*, all F; campsite at Ilha do Padre, 10 km. N of Bonito, very pleasant, no regular transport; restaurant, *Tapera*) and Aquidauana (several hotels around railway station, including *Fluminense*, F with fan and breakfast, a/c more expensive), where cave formations comparable to those found in the Lagoa Santa region of Minas Gerais are encountered. Two of the first to be opened are the **Lago Azul and N.S. Aparecida** (Sérgio Gonzales in Prefeitura of Bonito controls entry), both 26 km. from Bonito (no buses) and 320 km. from Campo Grande. Lago Azul has a lake 150 metres long and 70 metres wide. It is best visited in Jan.-Feb., 0700-0900 for the light, but there are no organized visits as yet, so Brazilian holiday times are best. Bus Bonito-Campo Grande, US$4, 3 hrs, 0545 and 1600. Also possible by changing at Jardim. Daily bus between Bonito and Aquidauana, about 3 hrs. on dirt road.

Corumbá, on the River Paraguay, with Bolivia on the opposite bank and beautiful views of the river, has a population of 180,000 people and millions of mosquitoes, but is a pleasant place nevertheless. River boats ply occasionally between it and Buenos Aires. The Forte de Coimbra, the city's most historic building, which may be visited, was built in 1775. In the hills to the south is the world's greatest reserve of manganese, now beginning to be worked. From the Bolivian border town of Quijarro a 650-km. railway is open westwards to Santa Cruz de la Sierra, and there is a road of sorts. The Campo Grande-Corumbá road, via Aquidauana, crosses the Paraguay by ferry (now mostly paved, often flooded, no gasoline between Miranda and Corumbá). The scenery between Campo Grande and Corumbá is most interesting, the road and railway follow different routes, but the train is more reliable and cheaper than the bus (though slower).

Warning Police have very strict controls on drug-trafficking in Corumbá; there are many drug-runners, searches are very thorough.

Hotels *Santa Mônica*, R. Antônio Maria Coelho, 369, a/c, D, good restaurant; *Alphahotel*, next door, D, clean; *Nacional*, R. América 934, C, good pool, river trips arranged; *Santa Rita*, Dom Aquino 860 (unsigned), E, with bath, F without, bathrooms dirty otherwise clean but basic, noisy, good meals in restaurant, reported not safe for luggage; *Paris*, R. Antônio Maria Coelho, E, with fan, quiet, many very short-stay couples. *Salette*, Rua Delamaré 893, F, rec.; *Santa Cruz*, No. 909, E, restaurant, improved; *Schabib*, Rua Frei Mariano 1153, F, basic but clean, owner friendly, multilingual and helpful, rec. *Residencila*, opposite railway station, F, basic, adequate, friendly, meals available; *Milka*, F, on steep street down to port, friendly and clean. *Esplanada*, opp. railway station, F, clean, cold shower, basic; *Espanha*, Rua 13 de Junho 776, F, meals for US$2.

Restaurants *Churrascaria Gaúcha*, R. Frei Mariano; *Tarantella* (Italian), R. Frei Mariano and América, large helpings, not cheap, but rec. *Peixaria de Lulu*, nr. centre, good; *El Dorado*, on waterfront, good for fish; *Churrascaria Rodeio*, very good; another good, cheap *churrascaria* in Rua Antônio Maria Coelho. *São Paulo*, Rua Delamaré, in centre, good juices and sandwiches, cheap. Good beer at *Bar Zico*, Rua Frei Mariano. *El Pacu*, on the waterfront, run by a German, Hermann, and his Brazilian wife, good source of information on river travel and Pantanal excursions.

Museum Museu Regional do Pantanal, Rua Delamaré 939, 0800-1100, 1400-1800; Sat. 0800-1200; closed Sun. Arts and Crafts Centre, Rua Dom Aquino Correa, in a converted prison.

Exchange Banco do Brasil changes travellers' cheques (open a.m. only). Try at the border— cash only (it is impossible to change bolivianos into new cruzados in town). Street traders in shopping street between Rua Delamaré and Post Office.

Tourist Office Rua Delamaré 1557, T 231-6030, Portuguese only spoken, not very helpful.

Travel Agents Turismo Pantanal, R.Manoel Cavassa 219, good one-day river tour with

Lancha Pêrola. Turismo Sandino, Frei Mariano 1163, C.E.P. 79300, T 231-3345, US$50 for a 3-day Pantanal tour, recommended.

Shipping Paraguayan FME to Asunción: the *Presidente Stroessner* leaves every second Monday at 1100 (be on board 0730), tourist class US$30 with bed, US$20 hammock space, meals extra, beautiful trip. When you enter Corumbá by boat, officials board vessel to stamp passports. No regular passenger service. Seek information at *El Pacu* restaurant, or from small cargo boats at the waterfront. (**See page 413**, under Cáceres.)

Air To Cuiabá, Manaus, Porto Velho. VASP daily to Campo Grande at 1110, and on to São Paulo. VASP also daily to Rio. Daily private flights to Santa Cruz, Bolivia, especially in rainy season, US$100 per person—cheaper to travel overland to Asunción and fly from there.

Trains and Buses The day train from Corumbá to Bauru, via Campo Grande and with very poor connections to São Paulo, leaves at 0900, arriving in Campo Grande at 2030 (US$6 in 1st class, US$4 in 2nd), and Bauru the next afternoon US$17.25, (very crowded and tiring). Tickets can only be booked as far as Bauru (tickets can be bought from 1300 on previous day). Buses from Campo Grande to São Paulo are quicker, but dearer. Fare Corumbá to Campo Grande US$3 1st., US$2 2nd; ordinary train takes 11 hours. A second train (express) leaves Corumbá for Campo Grande at 2055, arriving 0700 (US$15 double sleeper—good, US$5.50 pullman, no 2nd class). Trains pretty comfortable, but dusty; good food on board. Thefts and drugged food reported. The Corumbá-São Paulo bus journey takes 24-30 hrs. (US$18). Bus, Corumbá-Brasília, 24 hrs., US$17, not many; better to go Corumbá-Campo Grande, 6 hrs., US$8, leaves at 2100, then Campo Grande-Brasília. Two buses (Andorinha) to Rio daily 0800 and 2300, US$22, 27 hrs., with change Campo Grande, US$21. Bus station is on R. Antônio Maria Coelho, 8 blocks from railway station (where passport control is done) and 1 block from town centre (also for Andorinha buses; Viação Motta bus terminal is nearby). Taxis from railway station to centre are extortionate. Don't rely on getting a supply of new cruzados in Bauru; exchange is difficult there. Stock up in Corumbá.
   There are four train services to Santa Cruz in Bolivia, the *ferrobus*, *rápido*, *omnibus* and *mixto*; all leave from Quijarro, the Bolivian frontier station, not from Corumbá. The schedule of each appears to change frequently so check on arrival in Corumbá; also check when the ticket office is open for the train you wish to take, to purchase tickets as early as possible. Quijarro-Santa Cruz *ferrobus*, Tues., Thurs., Sat., 0800 (Santa Cruz-Quijarro, Mon., Weds., Fri., 1700) Pullman US$14.50, special US$13.50; *rápido* Quijarro-Santa Cruz, Mon., Weds., Fri. (perhaps daily), 1500 (Santa Cruz-Quijarro Tues., Thurs., Sun., 1210); *omnibus* (stopping train), Quijarro-Santa Cruz, Mon., Fri., 1150 (Santa Cruz-Quijarro, Thurs., Sun., 1404); *mixto* Quijarro-Santa Cruz Weds., Sun., 1500 (Santa Cruz-Quijarro, Mon., Fri., 2115), fares on last 3, Pullman US$12, first US$10, second US$6 (all converted from bolivianos). If immigration is closed, buy your train ticket before going there. It is worth buying a 1st class seat, which is much more comfortable on night trips than the 2nd class, but these are often mysteriously "sold out". 2nd class is on the baggage van floor, is crowded and there are no toilet or water facilities. Stops at stations are brief; take your own water; journey time 19½ hrs (not rec.). Colectivo Corumbá-Quijarro, US$1.50, from in front of Dona Aparecida's store, *A Favorita*, R. Antônio Maria Coelho (Dona Aparecida changes money outside banking hours; bargaining recommended). Also taxis, US$12 per taxi; colectivo border—Quijarro US$1. The railway to Santa Cruz is liable to flood damage.

Going to Bolivia Immigration and emigration formalities are constantly changing so check procedure in advance. Have passport stamped by Brazilian Policia Federal at Corumbá train station (published opening hours, 0600-1130, 1300-1600, 1915-2100, Sat. and Sun. 0600-0730, 1030-1130, 1900-2100). Take taxi, or walk, to Rodoviária, then bus to Bolivian border post (15 mins.), go through formalities, then take colectivo to Quijarro for train. Best to get some bolivianos in Corumbá. Bolivian Consulate in Corumbá: Rua Antônio Maria Coelho 825 (colectivos may be caught nearby for frontier), Mon.-Fri., 0700-1100, 1500-1730, Sat. and Sun. closed. They tell everyone a visa is necessary, but this may not be true: check Bolivian section "Information for Visitors". Public transport to Quijarro and Puerto Suárez is spasmodic. Alternative to train: Bolivian TAM flight, from border to Santa Cruz, daily between 1100 and 1300, US$27.

Coming from Bolivia If you arrive at the border when the Bolivian offices are closed (e.g. at night) and you therefore have no exit stamp, be prepared to be sent back for an exit stamp by Brazilian officials in Corumbá (the Bolivian border post opens at 0700). If you arrive in Brazil without a yellow fever vaccination certificate, you must go to Rua 7 de Setembro, Corumbá, for an inoculation. When travelling from Quijarro, take a taxi (bargain fare) or walk to the Bolivian border, go through formalities (US$0.15), outside office take bus to Corumbá Rodoviária (US$0.10). Taxi or walk to railway station for Brazilian formalities (some buses go direct to the station): be quick to catch the office open.

Pantanal This vast swampy area, located between Cuiabá, Campo Grande and the Bolivian frontier, is one of the world's great wildlife preserves, slowly being opened up to tourism. The flora and fauna are similar in many ways to those of the Amazon basin, though because of the more veldt-like open land, the wildlife can be viewed more easily than in the dense jungle growth. Principal life seen in this area are over 600 species of birds, in the main, waders and water fowl, storks (the *tuiuíu* is almost two metres tall), herons, coots, ducks, as well as pheasants, quails and parrots. There are some 350 varieties of fish, from the giant *pintado*, weighing up to 80 kilos, to the voracious *piranha*. Fishing here is exceptionally good, especially during the season, December through March. Animal life is represented by deer, ocelot, puma, boar, anteaters, *pacu*, tapir, rhea and the ubiquitous *capivara*, a species of giant aquatic guinea-pig. Probably the most impressive sight is the *jacaré* (Brazilian alligator). The extraordinary thing is that man and his domesticated cattle thrive together with the wildlife with seemingly little friction. Local farmers and the National Parks Authority protect the area jealously. (Only one area is officially national park, the Biological Reserve of Cará-Cará in the municipality of Cáceres, 80,000 hectares of land and water, only accessible by air or river. Permission to visit at Delegacia Estadual do IBDF, Av. A, esquina Rua O, CPA de Cuiabá, CEP 78.000, Cuiabá.) Hunting in any form is strictly forbidden. Fishing is allowed throughout the year, but not encouraged in the breeding season (August to beginning of the rains). The International Union for the Conservation of Nature is concerned at the amount of poaching, particularly of *jacaré* skins and *capivaras*, so further restrictions on visiting may be introduced.

There are two distinct seasons. In the rainy season (wettest in February), most of the area floods, and animals crowd on to the few islands remaining above water. It is extraordinary to see ocelots and pumas living side by side with deer and *capivara*. During the dry season (June to beginning of September), is the nesting and breeding season. At this time the birds form vast nesting areas, with hundreds and thousands crowding the trees creating an almost unsupportable cacophony of sounds. At this time the white sand river beaches are exposed, where *jacarés* bask in the sun.

The Pantanal is not easy to visit. One finds public transport all around the perimeter, but none at all within. Hitching is easier at weekends, when local sport fishermen drive into the Pantanal. Litter is becoming a problem, don't contribute to it. Wild camping is possible if you have your own transport.

There are several lodges with fair to good accommodation, some only approachable by air or river; most are expensive. Advance booking may be necessary, but note that travel agents charge a fee. The best plan is to hire a car and check accommodation for yourself. Following is a list of those presently operating:

From Cuiabá: Focus Tours of Belo Horizonte (**see page 288**) is specializing in tours in this part of the Pantanal. Cuiabá Tours offers 11-hour excursion (US$75 per car) along Transpantaneira to Fazenda Pixaim. *Santa Rosa Pantanal Hotel*, reservations at the Santa Rosa Hotels or Selva Turismo in Cuiabá, 250 km. from Cuiabá near Porto Jofre. A, with full board, an old *fazenda*, latest reports very critical ("unfriendly", too far from Pantanal, "a centre for drug dealing"). Buses run from Cuiabá to **Poconé** (a large town, 100 km., US$1.50) from where one can hire a taxi (US$9) from *Hotel Skala*, E, in the main square or hitch to Porto Jofre (just a gas station), or hire a vehicle to get there, around US$150 (see under Cuiabá). Poconé also has *Pousada Pantaneira*, F, good restaurant, European-run, clean and simple, on Porto Jofre road, T 721-1220. At Km. 30 on the Transpantaneira is *Hotel das Araras*, 10 rooms with bath, good food, home-made *cachaça* (hotel itself has no phone, but T 065-321 6754), rates L with full board. Where the road crosses the river Pixaim is *Hotel Beira Rio*, 3 rooms with several beds in each, no electricity, good home-grown food (expansion is planned). *Fazenda Pixaim*, D, 170 km. from Cuiaba, halfway between Poconé and Porto Jofre; direct TUT bus from Cuiabá via Poconé. *Hotel-Fazenda Cabanas do Pantanal*, A, 142 km. from Cuiabá, 50 km. from Poconé by the rivers Pixaim and Cuiabá, on the northern edge of the Pantanal, 10 chalet bedrooms with bath, restaurant, boat trips (few in dry season), horse-riding, fishing, helpful proprietor and staff, everything except boat trips and bar drinks included in price (booking: Praça da República 108, Cuiabá, T 065-322-1353). *Jauru-Taiamã* camp, 140 km. south of Cáceres, bus to Cáceres (**see page 413**) then by boat, or air taxi from Cuiabá; reservations at T 321-6808, or Toulemonde Turismo, Av. Ipiranga 313, office 42, São Paulo, no rates available. Fishermen will not give lifts on the Pantanal since some have been murdered. Boats ply between Porto Cercado (near *Cabanas do Pantanal*) via Porto Jofre to Corumbá (48 hrs.) about once a week, e.g. *San Antônio* and *Elza*.

From Corumbá: *Pousada do Pantanal*, 125 km. from Corumbá near the Campo Grande road at Fazenda Santa Clara (still a working cattle ranch), easy access by bus, reservations from Pantanal Empreendimento Turísticas Ltda, Rua Antônio Maria 320, CEP 79300, Corumbá, T 231-5797 or São Paulo, Dallas Viagens e Turismo, Alameda Santos 1432, Parque Trianon, T 284-4877; US$50 p.p. for groups of 4-6 for 3 days/2 nights, good food, with horseback, car and boat excursions, guides included, canoes, simple fishing gear, motor boats for rent, (try bargaining in the off-season for reduced rates). *Fazenda Santa Blanca*, on the Rio Paraguai, 15 mins. by boat S of Porto Esperanza, C, full board, very clean and friendly, good kayak excursions, horseriding, (US$5), information from Rua 15 de Novembro 659, 79300 Corumbá, T 067-231-1460, or Flins Travel (Walter Zoss), Rua do Acre 92, 6th floor, 602, CEP 20.081, Rio de Janeiro, T (021) 253-8588/0195, Telex 021 32971 ATDA. *Fazenda Morrinhos* (*Motel do Severino*), 67 km. from Corumbá on the Campo Grande road, easy access by bus, reservations in Corumbá, T 231-4460, A with full board. Highly recommended is *Fazenda Leque*, Roberto Kassan (contact through Rua América 262, Corumbá, T 231-1598): US$65 p.p. for 3 days, 6 per group, US$5-10 p.p. per day if you want to stay longer; take mosquito coils; unlimited use of horses and boats, on small lake behind the farm, good food; plenty of wildlife to be seen. *Rancho Kué*, 120 km. by air from

Corumbá, or 210 km. by river, on the junction of the São Lourenço and Paraguai rivers; located in the centre of the Pantanal, probably the best location of all, and the most difficult to reach; at present in refurbishment; reservations in Aquidauana, T 2-1875, or São Paulo, T 228-8015, Rua Beneficência Portuguesa 24, 3rd floor, room 317, Ms. Cristina Schmitt. or Sr. Macedo, Rua 13 de Junho 1044, Suite 44, T 231-1460. In Corumbá, you can purchase a cheap tour (e.g. US$45 p.p. for 3 days/2 nights with Joaquin, Katu or Rodríguez), but you may sleep in the open with no protection from rain or mosquitoes, and no boats or horses will be provided. Camping out is preferable to staying in *fazendas* because less driving (which scares animals) is involved, and you can see the wildlife at its greatest period of activity—dawn and dusk (protection against mosquitoes essential). In the wet season, access to the Pantanal from Corumbá is only by boat. Tues. boat Corumbá-Poconé, 36 hrs., US$12. Boats can be hired for US$25 a day through the Varig/VASP tourist agency. Cattle boats will take passengers on their round trips to farms in the Pantanal, 3 days, US$6.50 but take your own food—it is not possible to disembark. Ask at Bacia da Prata, 10 mins. out of Corumbá on the Ladário bus (the gatekeeper is unhelpful). Road trips from Corumbá into the Pantanal US$35 for 6 hours per vehicle.

From Campo Grande: *Hotel dos Camalotes*, Porto Murtinho, 440 km. from Campo Grande; access by bus long, tedious, bumpy and dusty; best access by air taxi. 4-star luxury hotel on the shores of the Paraguai river, favoured by wealthy Paulistas, A, with full board. *Cabana do Pescador*, 50 km. from Aquidauana on the Miranda river, access by bus to Aquidauana, and local bus to Bonito, possible to visit the impressive Bonito Caves, A, includes breakfast. *Pesqueiro do Lontra*, 180 km. from Aquidauana on the Corumbá road, access by bus, same rates as *Cabana do Pescador*. Both the latter lodges can be reserved at the same place as *Rancho Kué*. *Fazenda Solabra*, 6 km. from Miranda, which is 209 km. from Corumbá, 198 from Campo Grande, is rec., C; it is by the Rio Salobra (clear water) and Rio Miranda, with birds and animals easily seen. Take bus from Campo Grande to Miranda, and alight 50 m. from the bridge over Rio Miranda, turn left for 1,200 m to the *Fazenda*; by train, coming from Campo Grande, get out one stop after Miranda, 250 m. to the *Fazenda*. Alternatively, hire a car in Corumbá and drive to Miranda, but note that the road is in bad condition (consequently not much traffic and more wildlife can be seen). Car with driver can be hired at Salobra for US$25.

A suggestion from Stephen L. Meredith, London SW19, is to take the 0715 train from Corumbá to Agente Inocêncio, where you change for the local train to Porto Esperança, a 10-minute journey. There you may be able to hire a boat for a 2-3 hr. trip on the River Paraguai (about US$15, but bargain). The return train connects with the main line train at 1718. You can walk back along the track, but this is dangerous on the bridges, which have gaps between the sleepers.

It seems that wildlife has already disappeared from the River Paraguai, so it is now necessary to make trips on the smaller rivers to see it.

Tours to N or S Pantanal arranged in Rio de Janeiro by Pelajo Turismo, Av. Rio Branco 52, 16th floor, T 296-4466 or 233-5085: from 4 to 8 days; also Excursões Soletur, and many others. Most tours last 4 to 15 days, and are based at Corumbá. 20% discounts are offered in December, but this is the wet, and mosquito, season.

River trips from Cuiabá to Corumbá are very difficult since boats on the Cuiabá river are few and irregular. You can get to Corumbá by river from *Cáceres*, a riverside town (pop. 60,000), 250 km. west of Cuiabá, very hot but clean and hospitable. There is a yacht club, with swimming pool, volley ball and children's playground. Annual cattle fair at the airport. *Hotel Fênix*, C-D, fridge, a/c, TV; *Santa Terezinha*, Rua Tiradentes 485, F with fan, breakfast, not clean, friendly. Many other cheap hotels, e.g. *Hispano*, F, clean. Good restaurants: *Jeripieca*, on stilts in the river (boat service if needed), excellent fish; *Paraná*, on 7 de Setembro. Change money elsewhere: travellers' cheques take 10 days to change at the banks, Soteco by the main square changes cash at the official rate. From Cáceres the *28 de Setembro* sails to Corumbá; it is a cattle boat run by Serviço de Navegação da Bacia da Prata, leaving Cáceres at most twice a month, around the 15th and 30th. The 2-3 day journey covers 482 km., US$16 with meals (excellent food—rec.) or US$4 with no food. The Serviço de Navegação has no office in Cáceres: you must wait until the boat arrives to see it if you can get on. For information on boat sailings, ask at the Capitânia dos Portos, on the corner of the main square at the waterfront. If possible phone in advance to Cáceres, Posto Arrunda, 221-1707 to find out which boats are going. Also Portobrás on the outskirts of the waterfront (T 221-1728), helpful, but ultimately it is up to the boat's captain. If you ask at Portobrás you may (with a lot of luck) be able to get passage on a cement boat; they run about twice a month, US$5, food extra, 3 days to Corumbá (8 the other way). These boats are officially not allowed to take passengers. You may have a better chance of getting a boat in Corumbá since there are more head offices and river traffic. Bus Cuiabá-Cáceres, US$5, 10 a day (book in advance, very crowded), 3½ hrs. now that the road is paved, one stop in the jungle at a restaurant.

From Cáceres to the Bolivian border: Get passport stamped by the Federal Police then take the 1600 bus to San Matías, Bolivia, where you must have your passport stamped (*Residencial Génova*, F, rec.; military flights on Fri. and Sun. to Santa Cruz via Roboré—book in advance).

Cuiabá, the capital of Mato Grosso state, on the Rio Cuiabá, an upper tributary of the River Paraguai, has an imposing government palace and other fine buildings round a green main square. Alt.: 165 metres; pop.: 168,000 (350,000 including the suburb of Várzea Grande). There is a paved road to Campo Grande (712 km.), on the Noroeste railway to São Paulo, and the 2,400 km. BR-364 road from Brasília to Porto Velho and Rio Branco passes through Cuiabá; it is paved all the way between Brasília, Cuiabá and Porto Velho. The more direct road to Brasília through Barra do Garças and Goiás Velho (the BR-070) is being paved, not directly to Cuiabá, but to São Vicente, 80 km. E on the Rondonópolis road (BR-364). Several paved feeder roads connect the BR-070 and BR-364. A road to connect Cuiabá with Corumbá (which can be reached by water in the rainy season), across the Pantanal, has reached Porto Jofre on the Cuiabá River. Work has been suspended indefinitely because of difficulties, costs and ecological considerations. It is very hot; coolest months for a visit are June, July, and August, in the dry season. Good fishing in the Cuiabá and smaller Coxipo rivers (fish and vegetable market, picturesque, at the riverside); wildlife for photography, and the Aguas Quentes hot springs, 90 km. (*Hotel Aguas Quentes*) can be visited. The University of Mato Grosso has an attractive museum of Indian objects (closed Sat. and Sun.), and the military post near the University has a small zoo.

Hotels *Santa Rosa Palace*, Av. Getúlio Vargas 600, A, overpriced; *Colorado Palace*, Jules Rimet 22, opp. bus station, a/c, good range of room prices. *Mato Grosso Palace*, Joaquim Murtinho 170 (T 322-9254), 4-star, A with bath and breakfast; *Aurea Palace*, Gen. Melo 63, B, pleasant rooms, restaurant, swimming pool, good; *Fenícia*, Av. Getúlio Vargas 296, D, with a/c, breakfast, shower, clean, central, good. *Real Palace*, Praça Ipiranga 103, D with shower, a/c, TV, good breakfast, helpful, good value; *Abudi Palace*, Coronel Escolástico 259, good; *Bandeirantes*, Av. Coronel Escolástico 425, D, a/c, out of centre; *Almanara*, Av. Coronel Escolástico 510, D, opposite *Bandeirantes* and better. *Mato Grosso*, Rua Comandante Costa 2522 (T 321-9121), 2-star, almost opposite the *Fenícia* and down a side street, small, clean, restaurant, good value, D-E. *Capri*, F, Rua Papa João (off Av. General Valle), friendly, clean, safe, good food. *Santiago*, Av. General Mello 115 (Centro), F, very friendly, clean, laundry, meals. *Samara*, Rua Joaquim Murtinho 150, central, E, breakfast, cold shower, fan, basic but good, clean, friendly; *Presidente*, Av. Getúlio Vargas 119, central, fans in rooms, F p.p. Cheap clean hotel near old bus station, *Cidade Verde*, F. *Dormitório Cézar*, near bus terminal, F p.p.; others in same area.

Youth hostel association, contact Amilton Martins da Silva, Praça de República s/n, C.E.P. 78015, T 322-5363, or Rua Duque de Caxias 19, Barrio Alvorada, C.E.P. 78070, T 319-1231, he also runs reasonably-priced tours to the Pantanal (only speaks Portuguese and a little Spanish, contact him through Turimat).

Restaurants *Karlitus Pizzaria*, Praça Porto at Ponte Julio Muller, good for fish and pizzas, on riverside; try *Novo Mato Grosso*, next *Sayonara Club* on Coxipo river (club is a good place for children). Try also *Tip-Top;* or at Várzea Grande, nearby, there is a floating fish-restaurant on the river. *Churrascaria Majestic*, Av. Coronel Escolástico 585, very good; *Bierhaus*, Isaac Póvoas 1200; *Cristóvão*, Av. Isaac Póvoas 1200, good churrascaria. *Fuji*, Comandante Costa 745 (T 321-1875), Japanese and Chinese cooking, good, rec.; *Peixaria do Queiroz*, Praça Jaime Figueiredo, good but difficult to find; *Beija Flor*, Rua Galdino Pimentel, good and cheap.

Electric Current 110 volts A.C., 60 cycles.

Entertainment Cuiabá is quite lively at night; *Pino's Ball* bowling alley, on Av. C.P.A.

Souvenirs Handicrafts in wood, straw, netting, leather, skins, Pequi liquor, crystallized *caju* fruit, compressed *guaraná* fruit (for making the drink), Indian objects on sale at airport, bus station, and craft shops in centre, interesting; Funai (Indian Foundation) shop, poor stock, Rua Barão de Melgaço 3900, opposite Shopping Cuiabá.

Money Exchange Best at *Abudi Palace Hotel*; very difficult to find parallel rates.

Car Hire At airport; National; Locadora de Veículos Trescino, Rua Comandante Castro with Av. Dom Bosco; a VW Beetle costs about US$30 a day. (Beyond Poconé on the Transpantaneira, diesel and gasoline available in Porto Jofre, alcohol available in Pixaim.) Can be arranged through Turimat.

Tourist Information Turimat, state tourist authority (T 322-5363), Praça República, next to Post Office building. Good maps, friendly, quite helpful regarding hotels and car hire, but double-check information. Maintains a counter at the airport, frequently unstaffed. Santa Rosa Hotels also has a counter there. Ramis Bucair, Rua Pedro Celestino 280, is good for detailed maps of the region.

Travel Agents Confiança, Mariano 434, T 321-4142, very helpful travel agency, but tours to

Pantanal are expensive. Also recommended is Cuiabá Tour, Rua Barão de Melgaço 3508 (Edif. Irene), Sala 4, only Portuguese and Spanish spoken, and Ametur, Rua Joaquim Murtinho 242 (esq. Trav. João Dias), very helpful, advice on Pantanal tours (also run their own tours, from 12 hours—US$30—to 5 days, not cheap). Another agency offering tours is Onlitur, Rua das Bandeirantes 79, e.g. US$55 for 1 day to Chapada dos Guimarães, or to Pantanal, US$118 for 2 days to Pantanal (see below for private guides). Selva Turismo (T 32-2007) can take bookings for Pantanal hotels.

Excursions To *Chapada dos Guimarães*, 68 km. from Cuiabá, a pleasant ride into the mountains (bus from Cuiabá US$0.80—8 a day). See the 70-metre Véu de Noiva waterfall (12 km. from Chapada, get bus to drop you off after Buruti; there is a short route, or a longer route through forest to the falls, recommended, small restaurant), strange rock formations, canyons, and the beauty spots of Mutuca, Salgadeira (camp and waterfall), Rio Claro, Portão do Inferno viewpoint, and the falls of Cachoeirinhas (small restaurant)—all unspoilt. Salgadeira, Portão do Inferno, rock formations, and the Véu da Noiva and Cachoeirinhas falls can easily be reached from the Rubi bus between Cuiabá and Chapada. Chapada itself is a small village with the oldest church in the Mato Grosso, Our Lady of Santana (1779), a huge spring-water public swimming pool, a good *churrascaria*, and restaurant (*Nivio's*, opp. church); it is still inhabited mainly by *garimpeiros* (diamond-seekers), but a craft community is being established, complete with health food shops. Just outside the town is the official Geodesic Centre of South America, marked by a plaque on a plateau which offers panoramic views of the surrounding plains.

To the Pantanal by the Transpantaneira Highway to Porto Jofre. Guides available at Cuiabá airport; Carlos Wolff de Arruja and Vinícius de Albuquerque Maranhão (through Wildlife Tours/Geotur, Rua Cel. Benedito Leite 55-Porto Cuiabá, T (065) 321-2639) both rec. A 2½-day tour with Vinicius Maranhão costs US$300 for everything except drinks; he has his own jeep, speaks excellent English and is very knowledgeable. Also recommended is Joel Souza, whose tours are good value and informative; he speaks fluent German and English. Another guide is Amilton Martins da Silva (see above under **Youth Hostel**). Excursions (very expensive) can be arranged by Selva Turismo, or by Santa Rosa hotels to the *Santa Rosa Pantanal Hotel*, or by bus to Poconé, and hitch-hike to Porto Jofre (see section on Pantanal, **page 411**). Very little traffic on this road, except at weekends. Watch out for park rangers, who can be very helpful and friendly, after you have persuaded them you are not poachers or hunters. The research station 40 km. from the end of the Transpantaneira is for Brazilian scientists only. There are buses (TUT) from Cuiabá to *Hotel Pixaim* via Poconé, and via Mimosa to Barão de Melgaço.

Transport By air to Corumbá (US$30), São Paulo, Manaus, Campo Grande, Goiânia, Brasília, Rio de Janeiro (US$120), Belo Horizonte (US$95), and Porto Velho. Comfortable buses (toilets) to Campo Grande, 719 km., 10 hrs., US$9, 12 buses daily, *leito* at 2000 and 2100. To São Paulo, 24 hours, US$18, Rio de Janeiro, 32 hrs., US$28. Goiânia, 14 hrs., US$12; direct to Brasília, São Luiz company, 24 hours, US$22. Direct São Luiz bus to Belo Horizonte, 2000, 26 hrs., US$25; from Belo Horizonte bus passes through Ituiutaba (*Hotel São Luiz*, E, rec.), Nova São Simão (a new dam nearby), and Jataí. Now 4 buses daily (including one *leito*) to Manaus, via Porto Velho, around 80 hrs. To Porto Velho, 10 buses a day, US$17 (Colibri said to be better than São Luiz). Spectacular scenery between Cuiabá and Porto Velho, road newly paved, 1,450 km., bus journey takes 21 hrs., (Andorinha 1700 bus São Paulo-Cuiabá connects with Porto Velho service). (Eventually a paved road from Brasília to Caracas is envisaged). Hitch-hiking from Cuiabá to Manaus is possible—ask truck drivers for lifts at the roadside eating places. The road due N to Santarém has been completed and is paved to Colíder, where the paving diverts to Alta Floresta: daily bus at 2000. Yellow fever inoculations insisted on when travelling this route. Rodoviária at Cuiabá is now on outskirts: bus link (No. 117) with centre costs US$0.15.

Road Distances (km.): Belém, 2,955; Brasília, 1,127; Campo Grande, 712; Corumbá, 1,141; Foz do Iguaçu, 1,849; Goiânia, 934; Manaus, 2,294; Santarém, 1,777 km.; Porto Alegre, 2,356; Recife, 3,430; Rio, 2,118; Salvador, 3,226; São Paulo, 1,758.

From *Rondonópolis*, population 60,000 (many cheap hotels, such as *Dormitório Beija Flor*, near bus station, or *Sumaré*, clean but unfriendly, both E) about 215 km. SE of Cuiabá on the road to Goiânia, a paved road branches southwards to Campo Grande and thence to the western parts of the State of São Paulo.

Buses from Rondonópolis Brasília, US$12, 14½ hrs.; Goiânia, US$10, 11 hrs.; Campo Grande, US$5, 6½ hrs.; Presidente Epitácio, US$4; Presidente Prudente, US$6. Beware of overbooking on Viação Motta buses.

Airport, for internal flights.

Indians The Bororo tribe, on a reservation three hours by truck from Rondonópolis, have long been "civilized". It may be possible to visit the Xavantes at one of the Reservas Indígenas along the BR-158, N of Barra do Garças (**see page 406**). Funai is reluctant to permit travellers to visit Indian reservations on their own.

A journey along the Porto Velho road from Cuiabá (BR-364) demonstrates the amount of development along Brazil's "Far West" frontier, **see page 403**. A side road off the BR-364 goes to Vila Bela on the Guaporé River, which used to be the capital of Mato Grosso. It has a ruined church, cannon balls lying around, and is very interesting.

N.B. When travelling N of Cuiabá, yellow fever vaccination is obligatory; if you do not have a certificate, you will be (re)vaccinated.

THE ECONOMY

Brazil is the world's tenth largest economy and eighth largest market economy. It has abundant and varied natural resources and a long-standing development record, obtaining a positive growth rate every year since 1931 apart from 1963 and 1981-83 and 1988. The most striking features of economic development since 1945 have been state intervention and control, and industrialization, particularly in the areas of energy, heavy industry, transport equipment and capital goods. The vast majority of consumer goods are now manufactured locally, as well as a wide range of capital goods. Since the 1970s there has been a rapid expansion of technology-based industries. Manufactures now account for 70% of total exports. Industry accounts for 35% of gdp and 25% of total employment.

Brazil remains a large farming country and is generally self-sufficient in food production. It is the world's largest producer and exporter of coffee and sugar cane. Since the mid-1970s soya and orange juice production have been developed, so that dominant positions in international markets in these products have been secured. Agriculture customarily produces about two-fifths of exports, 9% of gdp and 30% of total employment. However, the sector is backward in its use of techniques and yields are comparatively low. Mechanization is largely limited to southern areas. A concentrated land holding structure and a preference for export cash crops have generated structural problems which have prevented satisfaction of domestic demand for food.

The country is richly endowed with metals and other minerals. Their exploitation has only recently begun, since low demand and high transport costs have previously rendered them uneconomic. Brazil has up to a third of the world's total iron ore reserves, found mainly in Minas Gerais and certain parts of the Amazon basin, especially the Serra dos Carajás region (Pará). Brazil is also a significant exporter of manganese and gold and produces increasing amounts of tin and copper.

Energy sector development has aimed at substituting local for imported energy. Oil reserves are estimated at 2.1 bn barrels with substantial additions in recent years from the Campos basin off the coast of Rio de Janeiro state. Oil production has steadily risen to 0.6 m barrels a day, and this satisfies two-thirds of local requirements. Large investments have been made in hydroelectricity, alcohol and nuclear power. Hydroelectric plants produce 90% of electricity and several major schemes are in preparation, including Itaipú on the River Paraná, a joint project with Paraguay and reportedly the world's largest. The Proálcool programme begun in 1974 aims to substitute alcohol derived mainly from sugar cane for oil products, and 90% of the country's vehicles are powered by alcohol. A 620-Mw nuclear reactor at Angra dos Reis (Rio de Janeiro) came on stream in 1985, but financial restrictions have slowed nuclear power development.

High rates of inflation have been recorded particularly in the 1980s because of domestic and external factors. These included urbanization and food supply bottlenecks, energy consumption patterns heavily dependent on oil imports, public accounts disequilibrium, and generalized indexation covering wages, prices and financial instruments. A stabilization programme, known as the Cruzado plan, was introduced in February 1986, including a price freeze, introduction of a new currency, the cruzado, and partial dismantling of indexation. Inflation was sharply cut, but the generation of excess demand caused the plan to collapse by the end of the year and inflation soon rose again to over 200% a year. In 1989 a new stabilization plan, dubbed the summer plan, was introduced when inflation rose to 1,000%. The new cruzado was created, worth 1,000 cruzados, but failure was inevitable considering the lack of political will to tackle the structural causes of inflation.

During the 1970s large-scale, high cost projects and current account deficits were financed by foreign borrowing, and Brazil accumulated the region's largest external debt, estimated at US$113 bn at end-1988. From 1982 annual rescheduling agreements were concluded with creditors, with new money and, in 1983-85, IMF standby facilities. The World Bank and Inter-American Development Bank granted large loans for sectoral development. These arrangements did not, however, help to reduce the burden of interest payments and in February 1987 Brazil declared a moratorium on interest in order to preserve foreign exchange reserves and halt the net transfer of resources to creditors. The plan did not prosper and a year later reserves were even lower as lenders declined to extend credit and favourable terms were being awarded to other borrowers. In 1988 Brazil returned to the international financial community and negotiated a financing package from all creditors aimed at restoring its creditworthiness.

	1961-70 (av)	1971-80 (av)	1981-85 (av)	1986-88 (av)
Gdp growth (1970 prices)	6.0%	6.7%	1.7%	3.5%
Inflation	48.0%	36.8%	148.9%	280.5%
Exports (fob) US$m	1,829	9,994	23,600	21,497
Coffee	779	1,552	2,087	2,000
Soya	38	1,291	2,595	2,390
Iron ore	104	654	1,674	1,740
Imports (fob) US$m	1,462	13,007	18,301	14,632
Current account balance US$m (cum)	-2,515	-62,142	-34,100	-1,101

INFORMATION FOR VISITORS

How to Get to Brazil: By Air Brazil is connected with the principal cities of Europe by Air France, KLM, Scandinavian Airways, Lufthansa, Alitalia, Iberia, Swissair, Aerolíneas Argentinas, Varig and TAP. Varig flights from London to Rio (three times a week) take only 11½ hrs. British Airways flies thrice weekly, non-stop London to Rio and on to São Paulo. Cheap carriers to Europe are Pluna and LAP (non-IATA) from Rio to Madrid (latter also from Recife).

Brazil is connected to the USA direct by Varig, Pan American, Aerolíneas Argentinas and Japan Airlines (Varig—4 times—and Japan Airlines twice a week, fly Tokyo-Los Angeles-Rio, and Pan Am, LA-Rio). The cheapest route is probably from Miami. Non-stop New York-Rio by Pan-Am or Varig is 9 hrs. 20 min. Lloyd Aéreo Boliviano (non-IATA) flies twice weekly between Miami and Manaus/Rio; book through Monark Turismo, Visconde de Pirajá 207, Ipanema, Rio (T 287-9746).

All South American capitals are connected by air services to Rio. Caracas, 4 weekly (Varig, Viasa); Bogotá, 5 weekly (Varig, Avianca); Lima, 7 weekly (AeroPerú, Varig); La Paz, 3 weekly (Cruzeiro; also LAB to São Paulo); Quito/Guayaquil, once a week with Varig; Asunción, 11 weekly (Varig, LAP, Iberia); Santiago, 19 weekly (LAN-Chile—also daily from São Paulo, Ladeco, Varig and others); Montevideo, 22 weekly (inc. Varig, Cruzeiro, Pluna); Buenos Aires, several daily; Paramaribo, twice a week by Cruzeiro do Sul and Suriname Airways to Belém; Cayenne-Belém by Cruzeiro do Sul (once a week), Suriname Airways, SLM (once a week) both heavily booked. Iquitos, Peru, via Tabatinga (on the Brazilian border with Colombia, a few km. from Leticia) to Manaus by Cruzeiro on Wed. and Sun. La Paz and Santa Cruz twice weekly to São Paulo.

For many travellers flying to Rio de Janeiro from Europe via South Africa, there is little difference in air fares compared to the direct route. Varig and SAA have two flights each per week between Rio and Johannesburg, and SAA has a weekly flight Rio-Capetown. Varig has a weekly flight from Rio to Luanda and Maputo, and to Lagos. Varig and Japan Airlines each fly twice a week Tokyo-Los

Angeles-Rio. Airline tickets (international and internal) are expensive in Brazil, so buy them with new cruzados.

N.B. Regulations state that you cannot buy an air ticket in Brazil for use abroad unless you first have a ticket out of Brazil.

Airport Tax   US$10 is charged for international flights and US$1 (or US$0.50 for 2nd-class airports) for local ones. Tax is waived if you stay in Brazil less than 24 hrs.

By Sea   Cargo ships carrying up to 12 passengers are run by several European shipping lines. The voyage takes about 14 days. The Booth Line serves North Brazil, from Liverpool and New York. Continental Shipping and Travel of London have sailings to Santos, and Nedlloyd of Rotterdam to Rio. Cargo ships, taking a few passengers, ply between Recife and African ports. Cars can be shipped from Genoa, Barcelona and Lisbon to Rio, Santos and Buenos Aires by Linea C.C. Costa, now the only regular passenger line from Europe. It charges on a 1,000 kg basis and is cheaper than other cargo lines which transport cars, and charge on a cubic metre basis usually quoted in Deutsche marks (leaves Europe in Nov.)

Regular services from the United States are: from New York by Moore-McCormack Lines, Booth Line, and Lamport & Holt Line; from New Orleans by Delta Line; from San Francisco and Los Angeles (via Panama Canal) by Moore-McCormack Line, returning by the Straits of Magellan; from Los Angeles to Rio de Janeiro and Santos and vice-versa by Mitsui O. S. K. Lines. **N.B.** There is an 8% tax on international shipping-line tickets bought in Brazil.

By Car   To drive in Brazil you need either a translation of your home driving licence, or an international licence. There are agreements between Brazil and border countries (Uruguay, Paraguay, Argentina and Bolivia, and probably now Venezuela) whereby a car can be taken into Brazil (or a Brazilian car out of Brazil) for a period of 60 days; an extension of up to 60 days is granted by the customs authorities on presentation of the paper received at the border; some reports suggest this may be done at most customs posts.

This now applies to cars registered in other countries; the requirements are proof of ownership and/or registration in the home country and valid driving licence (international or from home country). It is better to cross the border into Brazil when it is officially open (from 1300 to 1800 Mon. to Fri.) because an official who knows all about the entry of cars is then present. The motorist should in any case insist on getting the correct paper "in accordance with Decree No. 53.313/63", or he might find it impossible to get the 60-day extension. You must specify which border station you intend to leave by, but application can be made to the Customs to change this. If you want to leave by ship the Touring Club in Rio (possibly also elsewhere, but this is less definite) will arrange it for about US$60; you can also arrange the paper yourself by taking your car away by ship, but it takes about two days and costs about US$15 in port and police charges; the Touring Club provides information on how to go about it. (Klaus Elgner, of Hannover, reports this can be done with a letter in Portuguese saying you wish to leave by ship plus passport number, vehicle number, entry forms data plus an *ordem de embarque* supplied and stamped by the shipping agent. These should be presented to the Customs.) Crossing by a land border is, in any case, easier and probably cheaper. The law allowing for free entry of tourist vehicles applies only to vehicles entering from Argentina, Uruguay, Paraguay and Bolivia; a large deposit is still required if shipped from other countries.

Any foreigner with a passport can purchase a Brazilian car and travel outside Brazil if it is fully paid for or if permission is obtained from the financing body in Brazil. Foreigners do not need the CPF tax document (needed by Brazilians—you only have to say you are a tourist) to purchase a car, and the official purchase receipt is accepted as proof of ownership. There are second-hand car markets on Sun. mornings in most cities—but don't buy an alcohol-driven car if you propose to drive outside Brazil. Brazilian cars may not meet safety regulations in N. America and Europe, but they can be easily resold in Brazil.

Most main roads between principal cities are now paved. Some are narrow and therefore dangerous. Service stations are rare on some roads, e.g. Belo Horizonte-Brasília. There is a 80 km. per hr. speed limit, to save gasoline, and there are frequent radar checks. Penalties for speeding (which can be negotiated with difficulty) vary from US$40 to US$160.

Warnings   Motorists are warned that it is virtually impossible to buy premium grades of gasoline anywhere. Gasoline in Brazil is expensive; about US$2 a US gallon. It is only 85 octane (owing to high methanol content), so be prepared for bad consumption and poor performance and starting difficulties in non-Brazilian cars in winter. However, diesel fuel is cheaper and a diesel engine may provide fewer maintenance problems for the motoring tourist. Service stations are free to open when they like, but have mandatory opening hours of Mon.-Sat. 0600-2000.

Motor Spares   Volkswagen spares in Brazil are not always interchangeable with German VW spares, but in the main there should be no problems with large components (e.g. gears).

Young tourists crossing the frontier may get "shaken down" by police on both sides for alleged infringements; one way of overcoming this is to refuse to pay and wait to be released—generally an hour or so. (Advisable only for the strong-minded with plenty of time!)

Passports   Consular visas are not required for stays of up to 90 days by tourists from Western European (except for French nationals) or Latin American countries, Morocco and the Philippines. For them, only the following documents are required at the port of disembarkation: valid passport (or *cédula de identidad* for nationals of Argentina, Chile, Paraguay and Uruguay); and adequate proof that you can pay your way and your return fare, subject to no remuneration being received in Brazil and no legally binding or contractual documents being signed. (Some consulates, e.g. Santiago, ask to see an onward ticket). 90-day renewals are easily obtainable, but only within 15 days of the expiry of your 90-day permit, from Policia Federal, open till 1600: the procedure is, buy 3 DARF forms from a *papeleria* and take them back to a bank; pay US$2 tax; then go to Policia Federal who will stamp the extension in your passport after they have seen onward flight tickets, receipt from the bank for the tax, and proof of sufficient funds for your continued stay. For longer stays you must leave the country and return (immediately if you wish) to get a new 90-day permit. US, Canadian and French citizens and people of other nationalities, and those who cannot meet the requirements above, *must* get a visa before arrival, which may, if you ask, be granted for multiple entry. Do not lose the emigration permit they give you when you enter Brazil. Leaving the country without it, you may have to pay up to US$100 per person.

Officially, if you leave Brazil within the 90-day permission to stay and then re-enter the country, you should only be allowed to stay until the 90-day expires. Usual practice, though, is to give another 90-day permit, which may lead to charges of overstaying if you apply for an extension.

You must always carry identification when in Brazil; it is a good idea to take a photocopy of the first 5 pages of your passport, plus that with your Brazilian immigration stamp, and leave your passport in the hotel safe deposit. Always keep an independent record of your passport details. In Rio it is a good idea to register with your consulate to expedite document replacement if yours gets lost/stolen.

Clothing and personal articles are free of import duty. Such articles as cameras, movie cameras, portable radios, tape-recorders, typewriters and binoculars are also admitted free if there is not more than one of each. Tourists may also bring in, duty-free, 2 litres of spirits, 2 litres of champagne, 3 litres of wine, 600 cigarettes, 25 cigars, 280 grams of perfume, and 700 grams of toilet water. Duty free goods may only be purchased in foreign currency.

British Visitors   are referred to "Hints to Exporters: Brazil", obtainable from Dept. of Trade, Export Services Division, Sanctuary Bldgs, 16-20 Great Smith Street, London SW1P 3DB.

Road Transport   There is no lack of transport between the principal cities of Brazil; few are connected by railway, but almost all are by road. Ask for window seats (*janela*), or odd numbers if you want the view. Brazilian bus services have a top speed limit of 80 kph (buses are supposed to have governors fitted). They are extremely comfortable (many have reclining seats and toilets), stopping fairly frequently (every 4-5 hrs.) for snacks; the cleanliness of these *postos* has greatly improved, though generally less good in the poorer regions. Buses only stop at official stops. Take something to drink on buses in the North. The bus terminals are usually outside the city centres and offer fair facilities in the way of snack bars, lavatories, left-luggage stores, local bus services and information centres. *Leito* buses ply at night between the main centres, offering reclining seats with foot and leg rests, toilets, and sometimes in-board refreshments, at double the normal fare. For journeys over 100 km., most buses have chemical toilets. Air conditioning can make *leito* buses cold at night, so take a blanket or sweater (and plenty of toilet paper); on some services blankets are supplied; others have hostess service. Bus stations for interstate services and other long-distance routes are usually called *rodoviárias*. It is not easy to sell back unused bus tickets. Some bus companies have introduced a telex system enabling passengers to purchase return tickets at point of departure, rather than individual tickets for each leg. Buses usually arrive and depart in very good time; you cannot assume departure will be delayed. In the South East and South a *Horário de Ônibus* is available at *rodoviárias* (not available for North or North East). Many town buses have turnstiles which can be inconvenient if you are carrying a large pack. Urban buses normally serve local airports.

Hitch-hiking   Information on hitch-hiking (*carona* in Portuguese) suggests that it is difficult everywhere. Try at the highway-police check points on the main roads (but make sure your documents are in order) or at the service stations, or *postos*. Large increases in the price of gasoline and restrictions on its sale have diminished the amount of road traffic, especially pleasure traffic at weekends.

Rail   Trains are appreciably slower than buses. The sleeper services between Rio and São Paulo, and Rio and Belo Horizonte, can be recommended. There are services in the state of São Paulo and between Campinas and Brasília. There is a service between Porto Alegre and the Argentine and Uruguayan frontiers at Uruguaiana and Santana do Livramento. More and more services are being withdrawn; travellers are normally advised to go by air or road. Timekeeping is good on the whole. To obtain the Amerailpass (see Introduction) one is theoretically required to purchase the ticket in new cruzados equivalent to US$120 (16 days), US$140 (23 days), US$175 (30 days), US$260 (60 days), exchanged at the official rate. The Ministry of Transport, Esplanada dos Ministerios, Bloco 9, DF 70 062 Brasília, or Praça Mauá 10, Rio, insist on seeing the exchange receipt; Fepasa, Praça Júlio Prestes 148, São Paulo (T 011-233-7211) do not insist on the receipt. However, a number of travellers have suggested that, as rail travel in Brazil is so cheap, the Amerailpass is not good value for money.

Air   Internal air services are highly developed. A monthly magazine, *Guia Aeronáutico*, gives all the timetables and fares. All four national airlines—Varig, Vasp, Cruzeiro and Transbrasil (said to be rather cheaper)—offer excellent service on their internal flights (although Varig has been criticised recently for giving poor information to passengers). Between 2400 and 0600, internal flights cost 30% less than daytime flights. On some flights couples can fly for the price of one-and-a-half.

Varig, Vasp and Transbrasil each offer a 21-day, unlimited travel, round-trip Airpass, which costs US$330. The Airpass must be purchased outside Brazil by holders of an international flight ticket to Brazil, routes must start in either Rio or São Paulo, no journey may be repeated, it is not transferable between airlines and may not be used on the Rio-São Paulo shuttle, but unlimited stop-overs are allowed. Excellent value. Varig also has a Brazil Airpass II, valid for 14 days, and four sectors, for US$250, purchasable outside Brazil. Make sure you have two copies of the Airpass invoice when you arrive in Brazil; otherwise you will have to select all your flights when you book the first one. Hotels in the Tropical and Othon chains, and others, offer discounts of 15-20% to Airpass travellers; check with Varig, who have good hotel reservation service. We have been told that it is advisable for users of the Airpasses to book all their intended flights on arrival in Brazil, as so many internal flights are full these days, especially around summer holiday and Carnival time. Remember that you can transfer your Airpass between airlines, as long as you have not committed yourself to an actual itinerary and booked the flights. Another cheap alternative is to buy an internal flight ticket which includes several stops.

The small feeder airlines have been formed into scheduled domestic airlines, and now operate Brazilian-built *Bandeirante* 16-seater prop-jets into virtually every city and town with any semblance of an airstrip. It has been reported that Cruzeiro do Sul and Varig may combine their flights, with consequent last minute changes in flight time and/or number. **N.B.** Internal flights often have many stops and are therefore quite slow. Foreigners are not allowed to travel on Brazilian air force flights. Most airports have left-luggage lockers (US$0.30 for 24 hours).

Information All Brazil's States, and most cities and towns have their own tourist information bureaux. They are not usually too helpful regarding information on very cheap hotels, tending to imagine that no foreign tourist should consider staying in anything of that kind. It is also difficult to get information on neighbouring states. *Quatro Rodas*, a motoring magazine, publishes an excellent series of guides in Portuguese and English at about US$5 each. Its *Guia do Brasil* is a type of Michelin Guide to hotels, restaurants, sights, facilities and general information on hundreds of cities and towns in the country. The same company also publishes a camping guide and more specialized guides to Rio, São Paulo, Salvador and the South, with other cities and areas in preparation. These guides can be purchased at street newspaper vendors throughout the country. Quatro Rodas Guides may be bought in Europe from Distribuidora Jarim, Quinta Tau Varais, Azinhaga de Fetais, Camarate 2685, Lisbon, Portugal, T Lisbon 257-2542. There is also the "Transbrasil Guide to Attractions and Services" with maps, in Portuguese, English and French.

Many of the more expensive hotels provide locally-produced tourist information magazines for their guests. Travel information can be very unreliable and it is wise to recheck details thoroughly.

Climate and Clothing Conditions during the winter (May to September) are like those of a north European summer in Rio de Janeiro (including periods of rain and overcast skies), but more like a north European autumn in São Paulo and the southern states. Summer-weight woollens can be worn without discomfort in winter in Rio de Janeiro (temperatures vary at this season from 14°C to the high 20s), but further south something heavier is often required. It can get very cold in the far South. In São Paulo, which is in the Highlands, light-weight clothing is only required in the summer; the climate can be treacherous, however, with large temperature changes in a brief space of time. It can get surprisingly cold S and W of Rio, and on high ground anywhere in Brazil, at night; warm clothes are needed. The season of heavy rains is from November to March in Rio and São Paulo, January to April in the north, and from April to August around Recife.

Summer conditions all over the country are tropical, but temperatures of 40°C are comparatively rare. On the coast there is a high degree of humidity. The luminosity is also very high; sunglasses are advisable.

Casual clothing is quite cheap to buy; indeed we are advised that even fashionable clothing is cheap by London and Paris standards. In general, clothing requirements in Brazil are less formal than in the Hispanic countries. It is, however, advisable for men visiting restaurants to wear long trousers in Rio and Manaus (women in shorts are also likely to be refused entry), trousers and jackets or pullovers in São Paulo (also for cinemas). As a general rule, it is better not to wear shorts in official buildings, cinemas and inter-state buses. Trousers and long-sleeved shirts are advisable for visits to government offices.

Security As pointed out in the chapters on Rio de Janeiro and Salvador, personal safety in Brazil has deteriorated of recent years, largely because of the economic recession of the early 1980s. The situation is now improving, with a larger police presence in tourist areas.

Apart from the obvious precautions of not wearing jewellery, do not travel alone (this applies especially to women), do not camp or sleep out in isolated places and if you are hitch-hiking, never accept a lift in a car with two people in it. Money belts are safer than bags for your valuables. If you are held up and robbed, it is worth asking for the fare back to where you are staying. It is not uncommon for thieves to oblige. Do not leave valuables in hotel rooms.

Warning Most houses and hotels outside the large cities have electric showers operated by water pressure, delivering a supply of tepid to warm water. Despite electrical earthing, these showers are potentially dangerous. Care must be exercised in their use.

Best Time for a visit is from April to June, and August to October, inclusive. Businessmen should avoid from mid-December to the end of February, when it is hot and people are on holiday. These are not good months for tourism either, because hotels, beaches and means of transport tend to be crowded. July should also be avoided: it is a school holiday month.

Health Vaccination against smallpox is no longer required for visitors, but vaccination is necessary against yellow fever if you are visiting Amazonia, or are coming from countries with Amazonian territories, e.g. Bolivia, Colombia, Ecuador and poliomyelitis for children from 3 months to 6 years. It is strongly recommended to have a yellow fever inoculation before visiting northern Brazil since those without a certificate will be inoculated on entering any of the northern and centre-western states, probably in unsanitary conditions. If you are going to Amazonia, or to other low-lying forested areas, malaria prophylaxis is advised and water purification tablets are essential. Dengue fever is now endemic in Brazil, and Rio is one of the worst places: protect yourself against mosquitoes. Also, in the Amazon basin, sandflies abound; take a good repellent and get inoculations against hepatitis and typhoid. Be very careful about bathing in lakes or slow rivers anywhere in Brazil: harmful parasites abound (including the snails that carry schistosomiasis—this disease is rampant in Minas Gerais and most of central Brazil). South of the Amazon beware of *borrachudos*, small flies with a sharp bite that attack ankles and calves; coconut oil deters them. Water should not be drunk from taps unless there is a porcelain filter attached or unless you have water sterilizing tablets ("Hydrosteril" is a popular local brand); there is mineral water in plenty and excellent light beer, known as "chopp" (pronounced "shoppi"), and soft drinks. For those who have been in Brazil for a while, *água gelada* (chilled water) is usually safe to drink, being filtered water kept in a refrigerator in most hotels, restaurants and stores. Avoid ice in cheap hotels and restaurants; it is likely to be made from unfiltered water.

Yellow fever (**see page 416**) and some other vaccinations can be obtained from the Ministério da Saúde, Rua Cais de Pharoux, Rio de Janeiro. Less common vaccinations can be obtained at Sande de Portos, Praça 15 de Novembro, Rio de Janeiro.

An excellent hospital, supported by the American and British colonies in São Paulo, is Hospital Samaritano, Rua Conselheiro Brotero 1486, São Paulo (T 51-2154). Good Brazilian medical service is dear. If staying in Brazil for any length of time, it is recommended to take out Brazilian health insurance; Banco Econômico and Citibank are reported to provide good advice on this matter.

Hotels The best guide to hotels in Brazil is the *Guia do Brasil Quatro Rodas* (although it does not list the cheapest places), with good maps of regions and towns. Motels on the outskirts of cities are primarily used by very short-stay couples. The type known as *hotel familiar*, to be found in the interior—large meals, communal washing, hammocks for children—is much cheaper, but only for the enterprising. Usually hotel prices include breakfast; there is no reduction if you don't eat it. In the better hotels (our category D and upwards) the breakfast is well worth eating: rolls, ham, eggs, cheese, cakes, fruit. Normally the *apartamento* is a room with a bath; a *quarto* is a room without bath. The service stations (*postos*) and hostels (*dormitórios*) along the main roads provide excellent value in room and food, akin to truck-driver type accommodation in Europe, for those on a tight budget. The star rating system for hotels (five-star hotels are not price controlled) is not the standard used in North America or Europe. Low-budget travellers with student cards (photograph needed) can use the Casa dos Estudantes network. **Warning** Hotel safe-deposits are not always secure: take a substantial part of your funds in travellers' cheques.

Business visitors are strongly recommended to book accommodation in advance, and this can be easily done for Rio or São Paulo hotels with representation abroad. Varig has a good hotel reservation service, with discounts for its customers.

N.B. Taxi drivers will try to take you to the expensive hotels, who pay them commission for bringing in custom. Beware!

Camping   Members of the Camping Clube do Brasil or those with an international campers' card pay only half the rate of a non-member, which is US$8 p.p. (US$6 for meals). The Club has 43 sites in 13 states and 80,000 members. For enquiries, Camping Clube do Brasil, Divisão de Campings, Rua Senador Dantas 75—29° andar (T 262-7172), Rio de Janeiro. For those on a very low budget, service stations can be used as camping sites; they have shower facilities and food; some have dormitories. There are also various municipal sites; both types are mentioned in the text. Campsites often tend to be some distance from public transport routes and are better suited to those with their own transport.

Good camping equipment may be purchased in Brazil and there are several rental companies: Rentalcenter, Av. Brig. Luís Antônio 5088, São Paulo (T 852 0081 and 853 5147) and Av. Bernardino de Campos 661, Santos (T (0132) 41489); Camping Service, Rua Tibiriçá 115, Brooklyn, São Paulo. For special jungle equipment, Selva SA, Rua do Carmo 65-3° andar, Rio de Janeiro (T 242 9695); for equipping camping vans, Camp Car, Rua Piauí 375, Todos os Santos, Rio de Janeiro. It may be difficult to get into some Camping Clube campsites during the high season (Jan.-Feb.). *Guia de Camping* is produced by Artpress, Rua Araçatuba 487, São Paulo 05058; it lists most sites and is available in bookshops in most cities. Quatro Rodas publishes a *Guia de A°reas de Camping* annually.

Tipping   is usual, but less costly than in most other countries, except for porters. Hotels and restaurants, 10% off bill if no service charge but small tip if there is; taxi drivers, none; cloakroom attendants, small tip; cinema usherettes, none; hairdressers, 10-15%; porters, fixed charges but tips as well; airport porters, about US$0.50 per item.

Cost of Living   There has been heavy inflation in Brazil for some years. Good rates of exchange on the parallel market, especially in Rio, have made Brazil inexpensive for travellers, except for high-class hotels and restaurants, but the parallel market is illegal. Taxi meters are out of date. Drivers have a list of price alterations which should be consulted: make sure it's not a photocopy as that is a well-known minor swindle! Taxis have a 40% surcharge on Sundays.

Currency   The currency unit is the new cruzado (NCz), which in January 1989 replaced the cruzado, itself introduced in February 1986 to replace the cruzeiro, both at a rate of 1:1,000. At the time of going to press there were in circulation cruzeiro and cruzado notes, both of identical design, some cruzado notes overstamped as new cruzados, and new cruzado notes (smaller than old cruzado ones), up to a value denomination of 50 new cruzados. In April/May 1989 the mint was on strike and chaos reigned. Any amount of foreign currency and "a reasonable sum" in new cruzados can be taken in; residents may only take out the equivalent of US$1,000.

Money sent to Brazil is normally paid out only in Brazilian currency at the official exchange rate, so do not have more money sent to Brazil than you need for your stay in the country itself. Tourists cannot change US$ travellers' cheques into US$ notes, nor can they obtain US$ travellers cheques on an American Express card.

In the summer plan of 1989, banks were permitted to exchange foreign currency at a new, official tourist rate, which was set close to the black, or parallel rate (which is illegal). In May 1989, the tourist rate stood at NCz 2.78, the parallel rate at NCz 3.1, compared with an official rate of NCz 1.11 to the US dollar. It is therefore no longer too disadvantageous to change money in banks, but we have no indication that the parallel market has disappeared. The Banco do Brasil in most major cities will change cash and travellers' cheques; also Lloyds Bank (ex-BOLSA) branches. For the latest rate, see "Inflation and Exchange Rates" near end of book. If you keep the exchange slips, you may convert back into foreign currency one-third of what you changed into new cruzados. This applies to the official markets only; there is no right of reconversion unless you have an official exchange slip. The parallel market "mercado paralelo" is so common that travellers use it without problems (as far as we have been told). It is to be found in travel agencies, exchange houses and among hotel staff. Loiterers outside hotels will direct you to money changers—they will expect a tip. It is also possible to change money on the street, but this is very dangerous, especially in the Upper City in Salvador, where conmen abound. Finding the parallel market where there are no exchange houses may involve a lot of walking; ask around in imported goods shops, chemists, souvenir shops or big hotels. The best rates are to be found in the tourist centres. If you want to use the parallel market, take plenty of US dollars in cash, and be prepared to haggle (note, however, that travellers' cheques are a safer way to carry your money, but also that rates for cheques are usually lower than for cash). Wherever possible in the text, we quote prices converted from new cruzados to dollars at the parallel rate; travellers should bear this, and subsequent fluctuations in both the exchange and inflation rates, in mind when working out budgets. Black market and official rates are quoted in the papers and on TV news programmes. While inflation is high, change only what you need for a few days at a time, except when travelling in remote areas. Look in the daily press for advance warning of hikes in transport or other prices as a result of inflation. New cruzados can also be bought more cheaply outside Brazil, for instance in Asunción, Lima, La Paz, Montevideo, or Puerto Iguazú (Argentina).

Credit cards are widely used; Diners Club, Master Card and American Express are useful. Visa-Elo is the Brazilian Visa but many places will not take overseas Visa. Master Charge/Access is accepted by Banco Econômico and Banco Real and some airline offices, but hardly at all outside Rio. Banco do Brasil handles money forwarded on Visa card. Credit card transactions are charged at the official rate, so are expensive. Cash advances on credit cards will only be paid in new cruzados and incur a high commission. Automatic cash dispensers are becoming common in Brazil: you need only a passport and address to open an account with a large Brazilian bank, and you can then draw cash from a machine as required.

Working in Brazil Work-permit restrictions are making it harder to find work as an English language teacher than it used to be, though many people do it unofficially and leave Brazil every 90 days in order to re-enter as tourists. One's best bet would be in a small language school. Charges: private, US$5 per hr.; school, US$2 per hr. Or advertise in the Press.

Weights and Measures   The metric system is used by all.

Cables Cables are listed under cities. Cable facilities are available at all post offices, and the main ones have public telex booths. Post offices are recognizable by the ECT (Empresa de Correios e Telégrafos) signs outside. There is a 40% tax added to the cost of all telegraphic and telephonic communications, which makes international service extremely dear. Local phone calls and telegrams, though, are quite cheap. Make sure that hotels equipped with telex facilities can send outgoing telexes; some are unable to do so, or only at certain times of day.

Telephone The system has been greatly improved. There is a trunk-dialling system linking all parts: for the codes look up DDD in the telephone directory. There are telephone boxes at airports, post offices, railway stations, hotels, most bars, restaurants and cafés, and in the main cities there are telephone kiosks *for local calls only* in the shape of large orange shells, for which *fichas* can be bought from bars, cafés and newsvendors; in Rio they are called *orelhões* (big ears). Phone calls are half-price after 2000. Phone calls abroad are US$4 for first 3 mins. to Europe. Note that Brazil is now linked to North America, Japan and most of Europe by trunk dialling (DDI). Codes are listed in the telephone directories. For collect calls from phone boxes (in Portuguese: "a cobrar"), dial 107 and ask for someone who speaks English or French. No collect calls available to New Zealand, though to Australia is OK. It is useless trying to dial long-distance from hotels or orange *orelhões*, as a blocking device is installed on those lines. There are special blue *orelhões* for long-distance DDD calls; for these you need to buy *fichas interurbanas* from telephone company offices. Making phone calls abroad from hotels is very expensive.

Postal charges are high (we do not publish rates owing to the rapid changes caused by inflation). Air mail takes 4 to 6 days to or from Britain or the U.S.; surface mail takes some 4 weeks. "Caixa Postal" addresses should be used when possible. Leaflets on postal rates are not issued; ask at the post office. Some post offices will not accept picture postcards unless enclosed in an envelope. Postes restantes usually only hold letters for 30 days. Letters from abroad may be subject to random checks by Brazilian officials. The Post Office sells cardboard boxes for sending packages internally and abroad (they must be submitted open); pay by the kilo; you must fill in a list of contents; string, but not tape, provided. Postal services are reported to have deteriorated because of the theft of stamps for resale (franked and registered letters are more secure). Poste Restante for AmEx customers efficiently dealt with by the AmEx agents, Kontik-Franstur, with offices in most large towns.

National Holidays   are January 1 (New Year); 3 days up to and including Ash Wed. (Carnival); April 21 (Tiradentes); May 1 (Labour Day); Corpus Christi (June); September 7 (Independence Day); October 12, Nossa Senhora Aparecida; November 2 (All Souls' Day); November 15 (Day of the Republic); and December 25 (Christmas). The local holidays in the main cities are given in the text. Four religious or traditional holidays (Good Fri. must be one; other usual days: November 1, All Saints Day; December 24, Christmas Eve) may be fixed by the municipalities.

Working hours are 0900-1800 Mon. to Fri. for most businesses, which close for lunch some time between 1130 and 1400. Shops are open on Sat. till 1230 or 1300. Government departments are open from 1100-1800 Mon. to Fri. Banks 1000-1500, but closed on Sat. The British and American embassies' hrs. are 0830-1245 and 1415-1700 Mon. to Fri. The consular section's hrs. are 0830-1230; 1330-1630 Mon. to Fri.

Language The language is Portuguese. Efforts to speak it are greatly appreciated and for the low-budget traveller, Portuguese is essential. If you cannot lay your tongue to "the language of the angels", apologize for not being able to speak Portuguese and try Spanish, but note that in remoter parts you may well not be understood, and you will certainly have difficulty in understanding the answers.

One important point of spelling is that words ending in "i" and "u" are accented on the last syllable, though (unlike Spanish) no accent is used there. This is especially important in place names: Parati, Iguaçu. Audioforum, 31 Kensington Church Street, London W8 4LL, T 937-1647 does cassette course on Brazilian Portuguese.

Time Brazilian Standard Time is 3 hrs. behind GMT; of the major cities, only Manaus, Cuiabá, Campo Grande and Corumbá are different, with time 4 hrs. behind GMT. Clocks move forward one hour in summer for approximatley 5 months, but times of change vary.

Press: Rio *Daily Post/Brasil Herald,* the only English-language daily in Brazil, Rua do Resende 65, Rio de Janeiro 20231, T 221 2772. Not published Mons. The main papers are *Jornal do Brasil, O Globo,* and *Jornal do Commércio.* **São Paulo** Morning: *O Estado de São Paulo, Folha de São Paulo, Gazeta Mercantil* and *Diário de São Paulo. Daily Post/Brasil Herald* (except Mons.) Evening: *A Gazeta, Diário do Noite, Ultima Hora.* A monthly publication, *Jornal de Turismo* (Largo do Machado 29, Rio), gives notes on tourism, hotel prices, timetables, etc. There is a similar monthly magazine in English, *Rio Visitor* (Rua Marquês de São Vicente 52, Loja 318, Gávea, Rio).

English-language radio broadcasts daily at 15290 kHz, 19m Short Wave (Rádio Bras, Caixa Postal 04/0340, DF-70 323 Brasília).

Food The food can be very good indeed. The most common dish is *bife* (*ou frango*) *com arroz e feijão,* steak (or chicken) with rice and the excellent Brazilian black beans. The most famous dish with beans is the *feijoada completa:* several meat ingredients (jerked beef, smoked sausage, smoked tongue, salt pork, along with spices, herbs and vegetables) are cooked with the beans. Manioc flour is sprinkled over it, and it is eaten with kale (*couve*) and slices of orange, and accompanied by glasses of *aguardente* (unmatured rum), usually known as *cachaça* (booze), though *pinga* (drop) is a politer term. Almost all restaurants serve the *feijoada completa* for Saturday lunch (that means up to about 1630). Bahia has some excellent fish dishes (**see note on page 348**); some restaurants in most of the big cities specialize in them. *Vatapá* is a good dish in the north; it contains shrimp or fish sauced with palm oil, or coconut milk. *Empadinhas de camarão* are worth trying; they are shrimp patties, with olives and heart of palm. A mixed grill, including excellent steak, served with roasted manioc flour (*farofa;* raw manioc flour is known as *farinha*) goes under the name of *churrasco* (it came originally from the cattlemen of Rio Grande do Sul), normally served in specialized restaurants known as *churrascarias* or *rodízios;* good places for large appetites. Minas Gerais has two splendid special dishes involving pork, black beans, *farofa* and kale; they are *tutu á mineira* and *feijão tropeiro.* A white hard cheese (*queijo prata*) or a slightly softer one (*queijo Minas*) is often served for dessert with bananas, or guava or quince paste. Meals are extremely large by European standards; if your appetites are small, you can order, say, one portion and one empty plate, and divide the portion. Unless you specify to the contrary many restaurants will lay a *coberto opcional,* olives, carrots, etc., costing US$0.50-0.75. **NB** The main meal is usually taken in the middle of the day; cheap restaurants tend not to be open in the evening. **Warning** Avoid mussels, marsh crabs and other shellfish caught near large cities: they are likely to have lived in a highly polluted environment.

For vegetarians, there is a growing network of restaurants in the main cities, where a main meal is unlikely to cost more than US$2. We list several. Most also serve fish. Alternatives in smaller towns are the Arab and Chinese restaurants.

There is fruit all the year round, ranging from banana and orange to strawberries (*morango*), pineapple (*abacaxi*) and avocado pear (*abacate*). More specialized fruits include mango (*manga*), pawpaw (*mamão*), custard-apple (*fruta do conde*) and guava (*goiaba*). One is especially recommended to try the *manga de Uba,* a non-fibrous small mango. Also good are *mora* (a raspberry that looks like a strawberry), *jaboticaba,* a small black damson-like fruit, and *jaca* (jackfruit), a large yellow/green fruit.

The exotic flavours of Brazilian ice-creams should be experienced. Martin Crossland recommends readers to try *açaí, bacuri, biribá, buruti, cupuaçu* (not eveyone's favourite!), *mari-mari, mucajá, murici, pajurá, pariri, patuá, piquiá, pupunha, sorva, tucumá, uxi* and others mentioned below under "drinks".

If travelling on a tight budget, remember to ask in restaurants for the *prato feito* or *sortido,* a money-saving, excellent value *table-d'hôte* meal for US$2.50

or less. The *prato comercial* is similar but rather better, costing up to US$3. *Lanchonetes* are cheap eating places where you must pay before eating. *Salgados* (savoury pastries), *coxinha* (a pyramid of manioc filled with meat or fish and deep fried), *esfilha* (spicey hamburger inside an onion-bread envelope), *empadão* (a filling—e.g. chicken—in sauce in a pastry case), *empadas* and *empadinhas* (smaller fritters of the same type), are the usual fare. Hamburgers are referred to as "X" (pronounced "shees" - often spelt on menu-boards "cheese"), e.g. *X-Salada*. In Minas Gerais, *pão de queijo* is a hot roll made with cheese. A *bauru* is a toasted sandwich which, in Porto Alegre, is filled with steak, while further north has tomato, ham and cheese filling. *Cocada* is a coconut and sugar biscuit.

Drinks Imported drinks are expensive, but there are some fair local wines. Chilean and Portuguese wines are sometimes available at little more than the cost of local wines. The beers are good and there are plenty of local soft drinks. *Guaraná* is a very popular carbonated fruit drink. There is an excellent range of non-alcoholic fruit juices, known as *sucos*: *caju* (cashew), *pitanga, goiaba* (guava), *genipapo, graviola* (= *chirimoya*), *maracujá* (passion-fruit), *sapoti* and *tamarindo* are recommended by the Editor personally. *Vitaminas* are thick, mixed fruit or vegetable drinks, often with milk. *Caldo de cana* is sugar-cane juice, sometimes mixed with ice. Remember that *água mineral*, available in many varieties at bars and restaurants is a cheap, safe thirst-quencher (cheaper still in supermarkets). Apart from the ubiquitous coffee, good tea is grown and sold. N.B. If you don't want sugar in your coffee or *suco*, you must ask when you order it.

Among the better wines are Château d'Argent, Château Duvalier, Almadén, Dreher, Preciosa and Bernard Taillan. The red Marjolet from Cabernet grapes, and the Moselle-type white Zahringer have been well spoken of. It has often been noticed that a new *adega* starts off well, but the quality gradually deteriorates with time. Greville Brut champagne-type is inexpensive and very drinkable. A white-wine *Sangria*, containing tropical fruits such as pineapple and papaya, is worth looking out for. The Brahma and Antárctica beers are really excellent, of the strong lager type, and are cheaper by the bottle than on draught. Buying bottled drinks in supermarkets, you may be asked for empties in return.

Some genuine Scotch whisky brands are bottled in Brazil; they are very popular because of the high price of Scotch imported in bottle; Teacher's is the most highly regarded brand. Locally made gin, vermouth and campari are very good. The local firewater, *aguardente* (known as *cachaça* or *pinga*), made from sugar-cane, is cheap and wholesome, but visitors should seek local advice on the best brands; Martin Crossland recommends São Francisco and the Editor Praianinha; Maria Fulô, "51" and Pitu are other recommended makes. Mixed with fruit juices of various sorts, sugar and crushed ice, *cachaça* becomes the principal element in a *batida*, a delicious and powerful drink; the commonest is a lime batida or *batida de limão*; a variant of this is the *caipirinha*, a *cachaça* with several slices of lime in it. *Cachaça* with Coca-Cola is a *cuba*, while rum with Coca-Cola is a *cuba libre*.

Best Buys Jewellery (especially in Minas Gerais), costume jewellery, and articles made of gemstones, such as lamps; ornamented articles of jacaranda and other tropical hardwoods; clay figurines from the North-East; lace from Ceará; leatherwork; strange pottery from Amazonia; carvings in soapstone and in bone; tiles and other ceramic work, African-type pottery and basketwork from Bahia. Good general shops for those with little time to search are "Folclore" shops in Copacabana next to *Rio Othon Palace* and also in Ipanema. Brazilian cigars are excellent for those who like the mild flavours popular in Germany, the Netherlands and Switzerland; in the Editor's opinion, those manufactured by Suerdieck of Bahia are the best of the easily available brands, but C. Loughnane recommends trying the unbranded ones when you go to Salvador.

Indian artefacts are perhaps best obtained from the Funai shops: *Brasília*, bus station and airport; *Rio de Janeiro*, airport and Museu do Indio; *São Paulo*, Galeria Ouro Velho, Rua Augusta 1371; *Cuiabá*, Rua Pedro Celestino 305; *Manaus*, Praça da Matriz; *Belém*, Galeria do Edifício Assembléia Paraense, Avenida Presidente Vargas. Also recommended purchases are musical instruments, e.g. guitars made of fine, exotic woods, other stringed, and percussion instruments. A shop worth visiting is Pro-Musica, Av. Copacabana 435, Lojas M e N, Posto 2, T 237-2688, Rio de Janeiro.

We wish to offer our grateful thanks for help in revising the Braizilian chapter to Paulo Couto (São Paulo), Karin Kubitsch and Ricardo Heyenn (temporarily of Rio) for a most useful contribution including a new map of Copacabana, Debbie Macklin (São Paulo), Dr Sidney A Schwartz (Rio), Michael R Scott (São Paulo) and Douglas B Trent (Focus Tours, Belo Horizonte). Also to the following travellers: Tim Austin (Shere, Sy.), Lee Azus (San Francisco), Cliff and Martin Barker (High Wycombe), Bruce Barnes (Gloucester, NSW), Dale Bedford (Auckland 9), Erika Berger (Moosseedorf, Switz.), Christophe Beusch (Geneva), Gregory and Shelley Blake (Hounslow, Mx.), Lennart Blomberg (Göteborg), Tad Bonlecki (Woollahra, NSW) Ingelise Brønbech and Hans Zørben (Balborg, Dmk.), Karen Brooks (London N19), Alison Brysk and Mark Freeman (San Francisco, Ca.), Michelle Burrows (Brisbane), Chris Burton (Norwood, S. Aust.), Leigh Butler and Trish White (Warrambool, Vict.), Pamela Caunt and Bob Brass (London N1), John J. Chesarek (Billings, Montana), Peter and Alison Clarke (Leicester), Marion Clemens (Bonn 3), Margaret Coates and William Thomson (Edmonton, Alb), Helen and Gilles Cormerais (Plymouth), John Crane (Sunbury), Jeroen Dijkgraaf (Eindhoven), A.J. Dolphin (Welwyn Garden City), Bernd Dralle (Hannover), Fabienne Dufayet (Petit Lancy, Switz.), Paul Eaton (Victoria, BC), Dieter Eigenstetter and Yesim Yazicioglu (München 80), Eva Ekelund and Jim Lindsay (Stockholm), Henry Elwell, Andreas Erne (Zürich 8055), Fred and Marianne Emery (London SE26), Marianne J Evans (Operation Rainforest, Northampton), Ulla Faarup (Arslev, Dmk), Didier Faget and Sabine Fleury (Vernon, Fr.), Karsten Feucht (Berlin 61), Mark Field (New Barnet, Herts), Donald L Fischer (Decatur, Ga), John Fitzpatrick (Bern), Helen Fossmo and Arne Herløv Petersen (Humble, Dmk.), Ari Franklinos, Margarete Friedhuber (Berlin 65), Erik Friis-Pedersen (Copenhagen), Anna Frostenson (Hagersten, Swe.), Bjørn Gabrielsen (Oslo 11), Margaret and Stuart Goodchild, C Goosen (Leiden, Neth.), Christina Gräwe (Tautkirchen) and Joachim Hoell (Wernstadt, W.Ger.), Jan Jocob de Groot (Vroomshoop, Neth.), Jon and Julia Gruffydd (Lima), Rupert Hafner (Wien 1238), Prof. Eylard V Van Hall (Univ of Leiden), Peter Hartmann (Bad Vilbel, W.Ger.), Knut Per Hasund (Stockholm), Charles Havekost (Greenbelt, Md.) and Eva Lindholm (Zug, Switz.), Dave Henson (San Francisco, Ca.), Flavio Heubeck (Winterthur), David K Howe (Short Hills, NJ), V G Ilic (New York 10017), Mariolina Inaudi (Morbio Inferiore, Switz.), Floris Italianer and Erik Wilbers (Amsterdam), Ingrid Iversen (Streatham), Gretke Moen Johansen (Kolbotn, Norway), Mariann Johnsen (Brandbu, Norway), Dave Jones (Taunton), Kim Kelly (Amex, Calgary, Alb.), Simon Kennedy and Sally Constable (Melbourne), Susanna Kent (Auckland 3), Thomas and Bettina Kräuchi (Kloten, Switz.), Valerie and Verlen Kruger (2-Continent Canoe Expedition), Robert and Daisy Kunstaetter (Richmond Hill, Ont.), Darquise and Paul Lapointe (Cornwall, Ont.), Dean Lasko (Seattle), Moshé Leshem and Naomi Loeb (Jerusalem), Christian Levin (Kiel, W.Ger.), Herbert Levi (Buenos Aires), Margy Levine and Jordan Young (Lexington, MA) for a particularly helpful contribution, John Lewis (London NW3), Manoel A Lima (Northwood, Mx.), Paul Living (Reading), Ariel Lofsky (D.N. Habikaa, Israel), Loving Team (London), Richard Malengreau (London W13), Robert E Manley (Cincinnati) for a most useful piece on Rondonia, James Mathias (Minneapolis), Elaine and George McClellan (Danville, Ca.), Anita McConnell (London EC2), Dr Bruce Means (Tallahassee), Andrea Meier (Volkach, W.Ger.), Frédéric Meinders (Den Haag), B.E.Miles (N Baddesley, Southampton), Kelvin Moody (Stratford, NZ), Nichola Morgan (Swanage, Dorset), Michael Mortensen (Oelstykke, Dmk.), Nicole Mouzon (Tangissant,Belg.), Christoph Müller (Zürich 8004), Apostolos Natsiopoulos (London W7), Walter Ogden (Heywood, Lancs), John O'Flynn (Salvador), Charles O'Hern (Mesa, Ariz.), Bertil Olin (Johanneshov, Swed.), Winfried Overbeek and Hennie van Vree (Wageningen, Neth.), Timothy and Anna Oxton (Colchester), Pia Parolin (Milano), William Parton (London SW11), Isafrir Rabinovitz (Israel), Pierre Rambaud (Echirolles, Fr.), Peter A Riding (London W1), Michael Ridley (S. Croydon), Chris Robertson (Stockholm) and Patricia Galvin (Galway), John Roberts (Dunedin, NZ), Gisele Rochat and Jean-Paul Corboz (Neuchâtel, Switz.), John Rothschild (Seattle), Andreas Ruck (Berlin 46), Y Ruggins (London SW19), Sheila and Roman Russek (Scarboro, Ont.), R van der Schaaf (Amsterdam), Dr. Marcus Schiltenwolf (Mainz 2), Arno Schmid (Hamburg 71), H Schouwenburg (London SW18), Leon van der Schoor (Neth.), Markus Schulz (Gambach, W.Ger.), Elizabeth and Virginia Segal (London N2), Antony Sherlock (Edinburgh 12), David Smitham (Christchurch, NZ), Lynn Sowell (Clarksville, TN), Wiepke Staal and Frits Hoekstra (Zwolle, Neth.), Mr and Mrs Ernest Stead (Pudsey, W Yorks), Dolf Straub (Berlin 12), Anna Syriänen and Marko Sorvaniemi (Tampere, Fin.), Lisa Tenuta (Kenosha, Wisconsin), Erik Thier and Patricia Wessels (Amsterdam), James S Todd (Walla Walla, Wash.), Roderick Tye (Beckenham, Kt.), Anthony and Kathalijn Verhulst (Registro, SP), Ronald van Vliet (Haarlem), K.J. Vollers (Amsterdam), Angus Walker (Edinburgh EH9), Jürg Weber (Hasle-Rüesgsan, Switz.), Andrew R Welch (Chipstead, Sy.), Maks Westerman (New York), Roland Wiemer and Karla Menner (Hamburg 50), Gordon Williams (London W12), Ray Williams (Pwllheli), Jonathon Winckworth (Farnborough, Berks.), Wytske Winter and Hans Haringa (Aberdeen), Martin Wisckol (San Diego, Ca.), Lucinda Wright (Australian Embassy, Mexico), Herbert Wüstermann (Salzgitter, W.Ger.) and Cecilia Ydell and Jonas Martensen.

CHILE

CHILE, with an area of 756,626 square km., is smaller than all other South American republics save Ecuador, Paraguay and Uruguay, but is nonetheless larger than France. Its territory is a ribbon of land lying between the Andes and the Pacific, 4,329 km. long and, on average, no more than 180 km. wide. Of this width the Andes and a coastal range of highland take up from a third to a half. Chile contains within itself wide variations of soil and vast differences of climate; these are reflected, from area to area, in the density of population and the occupations of its 12,536,000 people.

In the extreme north Chile has a frontier with Peru running ten km. north of the railway from the port of Arica to the Bolivian capital of La Paz. Its eastern frontier—with Bolivia in the far north and with Argentina for the rest of its length—is along the crest of the Andes, gradually diminishing in height from Santiago southwards to the southern seas, where the Strait of Magellan lies, giving access to the Atlantic. Chile's western and southern coastline is 4,500 km. long.

Down the whole length, between the Andes and the coastal range, there runs a valley depression, though it is less well defined in the north. North of Santiago transverse ranges join the two massifs and impede transport, but for 1,044 km. south of the capital the great longitudinal valley stretches as far as Puerto Montt. South of Puerto Montt the sea has broken through the coastal range and drowned the valley, and there is a bewildering assortment of archipelagos and channels.

From north to south the country falls into five sharply contrasted zones:

1. The first 1,250 km. from the Peruvian frontier to Copiapó is a rainless hot desert of brown hills and plains devoid of vegetation, with a few oases. Here lie the nitrate deposits and several copper mines.

2. From Copiapó to Illapel (600 km.) is semi-desert; there is a slight winter rainfall, but great tracts of land are without vegetation most of the year. Valley bottoms are here cultivated under irrigation.

3. From Illapel to Concepción is Chile's heartland, where the vast majority of its people live. Here there is abundant rainfall in the winter, but the summers are perfectly dry. Great farms and vineyards cover the country, which is exceptionally beautiful.

4. The fourth zone—Forest Chile—between Concepción and Puerto Montt, is a

country of lakes and rivers, with heavy rainfall through much of the year. Cleared and cultivated land alternates with mountains and primeval forests.

5. The fifth zone, from Puerto Montt to Cape Horn, stretches for 1,600 km. This is archipelagic Chile, a sparsely populated region of wild forests and mountains, glaciers, fjords, islands and channels. Rainfall is torrential, and the climate cold and stormy. There are no rail links S of Puerto Montt, but the Carretera Austral Presidente Pinochet now provides road access for more than 1,000 kilometres S of that city. Chilean Patagonia is in the extreme south of this zone. To make the most of this trip, read Darwin's *Voyage of the Beagle* beforehand.

A subdivision of the fifth zone is Atlantic Chile—that part which lies along the Magellan Strait to the east of the Andes, including the Chilean part of Tierra del Fuego island. There is a cluster of population here raising sheep and mining coal. Large offshore oilfields have now been discovered in the far South, and the area is developing rapidly.

History A century before the Spanish conquest the Incas moved south into Chile from Peru, moving across the desert from oasis to oasis at the foot of the Andes. They reached the heartland and conquered it, but were unable to take the forest south of the Río Maule; there the fierce Mapuches (Araucanians) held them. In 1537 Diego de Almagro, at the head of a hundred Spaniards and some thousands of Indians, took the Inca road from Peru south to Salta and across the Andes. Many of the Indians perished, but the heartland was reached; bitterly disappointed at not finding gold they returned to Peru. The next *conquistador*, who took the desert road, was Pedro de Valdivia; he reached the heartland in 1541 and founded Santiago on February 12. Reinforced by fresh colonists from Peru and Spain, Valdivia widened his conquest and pushed S into Mapuche land, but was able to hold only the settlement to which he had given his name. The Mapuches fought desperately—they soon mastered the use of the horse—and in 1554 they captured Valdivia himself and killed him. Fighting continued for three centuries, and it was not until 1881 that peace was made, and immigrants were able to settle in the Mapuche lands.

The colonial period was greatly troubled by constant wars against the Mapuches and by internal dissensions, particularly between the landowners and the priests, who strongly objected to a system of Indian serfdom—the Indians were constantly in revolt. There have been, too, natural disasters in the form of earthquakes and tidal waves which have wiped out the cities again and again. From the end of the 16th century British and French pirates frequented the coasts. From the first, Chile formed part of the Viceroyalty of Peru; it was controlled from Lima, and trade was allowed only with Peru. This led to uncontrolled smuggling and by 1715 there were 40 French vessels trading illegally along the coast. It was not till 1778 that trading was allowed between Chile and Spain.

In 1810 a group of Chilean patriots, including Bernardo O'Higgins— the illegitimate son of a Sligo-born Viceroy of Peru, Ambrosio O'Higgins, and a Chilean mother—revolted against Spain. This revolt led to seven years of war against the occupying troops of Spain—Lord Cochrane was in charge of the insurrectionist navy—and in 1817 General José de San Martín crossed the Andes with an army from Argentina and helped to gain a decisive victory. O'Higgins became the first head of state: under him the first constitution of 1818 was drafted. But there was one thing which was dangerous to touch in Chile: the interests of the dominant landed aristocracy, and O'Higgins's liberal policies offended them, leading to his downfall in 1823. A period of anarchy followed, but in 1830 conservative forces led by Diego Portales restored order and introduced the authoritarian constitution of 1833. Under this charter, for almost a century, the country was ruled by a small oligarchy of landowners. It was during this period, from 1879 to 1883, that the War of the Pacific was fought against Peru and Bolivia; all three contestants were claiming the new nitrate wealth of the desert in the north. Chile emerged victorious—even Lima was occupied—and for 40 years thereafter it drew great wealth from the nitrate fields. One unexpected result of the war was that the Chilean land workers or

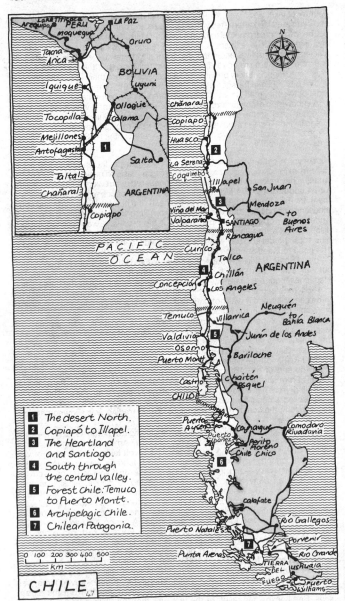

N

Arequipa
LAKE TITICACA
LA PAZ
PERU
moquegua
Tacna
Arica
Oruro
BOLIVIA
Iquique
Uyuni
Ollogue
Tocopilla
Calama
Mejillones
Antofagasta
Salta
Taltal
ARGENTINA
Chañaral
Copiapó

1

Chañaral
Copiapó
Huasco
La Serena
Coquimbo
Illapel
San Juan

2

3

Mendoza
Viña del Mar
Valparaíso
SANTIAGO
to Buenos Aires
Rancagua

PACIFIC OCEAN
Curicó
Talca
Chillán
Los Angeles
ARGENTINA

4

Concepción
Temuco
Villarrica
Neuquén
to Bahía Blanca

5

Valdivia
Osorno
Puerto Montt
Junín de los Andes
Bariloche
Castro
CHILOE
Chaitén
Esquel

Puerto Aysén
Puerto Ibáñez
Coyhaique
Comodoro Rivadana
Perito Moreno
Chile Chico

6

Calafate
Puerto Natales
Río Gallegos
Punta Arenas
Porvenir
Río Grande

7

TIERRA DEL FUEGO
Ushuaia
Puerto Williams

1 The desert North.
2 Copiapó to Illapel.
3 The Heartland and Santiago.
4 South through the central valley.
5 Forest Chile: Temuco to Puerto Montt.
6 Archipelagic Chile.
7 Chilean Patagonia.

0 100 200 300 400 500
—— km ——

CHILE 47

inquilinos, after a taste of liberty, were unwilling to return to the bondage of the big estates; the demobilized soldiers migrated to the cities, and later pushed south into the new lands beyond the Bío-Bío recently opened by pressure on the Mapuches. The free labourer had made his appearance.

The rule of the Right was challenged by the liberal regime of President Alessandri in 1920. Acute economic distress in 1924, linked to the replacement of Chile's natural nitrates with artificial fertilizers more cheaply produced in Europe, led to army intervention and some reforms were achieved. The inequalities in Chilean society grew ever sharper, despite the maintenance of political democracy, and gave rise to powerful socialist and communist parties. President Eduardo Frei's policy of "revolution in freedom" (1964-70) was the first concerted attempt at overall radical reform, but it raised hopes it could not satisfy. In 1970 a marxist coalition assumed office under Dr. Salvador Allende; the frantic pace of change under his regime polarized the country into Left-and Right-wing camps. Gradually increasing social and economic chaos formed the background for Allende's deposition by the army and his death in September 1973. A military regime, led by Gen. Augusto Pinochet Ugarte, succeeded him. In its early years particularly, it suppressed internal opposition by methods which were widely condemned. Despite efforts to make the regime more popular and economic prosperity, President Pinochet's bid to be chosen for a further eight years in office after 1989 was rejected by the electorate in 1988.

The People There is less racial diversity in Chile than in most Latin American countries. There are about 150,000 pure blooded Mapuche Indians, 95 % of whom live in the forest land around Temuco, between the Bío-Bío and Toltén rivers. A fifth is European; the rest is *mestizo*, a compound of bloods. The stock has been much less modified by immigration than in Argentina and Brazil. The German, French, Italian and Swiss immigrants came mostly between 1846 and 1864 as small farmers in the forest zone S of the Bío-Bío. Between 1880 and 1900 gold-seeking Serbs and Croats settled in the far S, and the British took up sheep farming and commerce in the same region. The influence throughout Chile of the immigrants is out of proportion to their numbers: their signature on the land is seen, for instance, in the German appearance of Valdivia, Puerto Montt, Puerto Varas and Osorno.

The population is far from evenly distributed: Middle Chile (from Copiapó to Concepción), 18 % of the country's area, contains 77 % of the total population. The Metropolitan Region of Santiago contains, on its own, about 39 % of the whole population. The rate of population growth per annum—1.7 % — is slightly under the average for Latin America. Gdp per capita is US$1,613.

The birth rate is highest in the cities, particularly in the forest zone. The death rate, 6.7 %, is highest in the cities. Infant mortality is 23.7 per thousand live births; it is highest in the rural areas. There are 300 hospital beds per 100,000 population and 1,038 inhabitants per doctor. Life expectancy is 71. Of the total population, only 8.3 % are illiterate.

Today, there is in process an intense urbanization of the populace. The cities are expanding, partly because so many people have left the land, and some 83% now live in the towns. Housing in the cities has not kept pace with the increased population; many Chileans live in slum areas called *callampas* (mushrooms) in the outskirts of Santiago and around the factories.

Chile grows only about half of the food it needs; about 20% by value of the total imports are food. An inheritance from colonial days of huge estates (1.1% of the owners held 63.7% of the land) coupled with wretched farming methods was largely reponsible for this. Agricultural production has improved greatly in the past fifteen years, and there has been a great expansion of exportable crops, particularly fruit.

Communications   Chile's difficult topography—archipelagos, forests, mountains, deserts—makes communications a formidable problem. It would be much more serious if 90% of the Chilean population did not live in the compact central rectangle, with good roads and adequate railways, between La Serena and Puerto Montt. Only a short distance along one river—the estuary of the Bío-Bío—is navigable.

Railways   There are 10,100 km. of line, of which most are state owned. Most of the privately owned 2,130 km. of line are in the desert north, where the northern terminal is Iquique. From the longitudinal Iquique-Puerto Montt trunk line branches run westwards to the ports and seaside resorts, and eastwards to mines and mountain resorts. The main gauge on the Valparaíso and southern lines is 5 ft. 6 in. (1.676 metres). Passenger services on N of Santiago have virtually ceased except for the international routes to La Paz.

Five international railways link Chile with its neighbours. There is a local line between Arica and Tacna, linking Chile with Peru. There are two railways to Bolivia: between Arica and La Paz (448 km.), and from Antofagasta via Calama to La Paz. Between Chile and Argentina there are two lines: one between Antofagasta and Salta, in the Argentine north-west, and the Transandine Railway linking Santiago with Buenos Aires. International services on both these lines to Argentina have now ended. The Ferrocarriles del Estado publish an annual *Guía Turística*, available in various languages from the larger stations.

Roads   About one-half of the 88,000 km. of roads can be used the year round, though a large proportion of them are unimproved and only about 9,700 km. are first class. The region round the capital and the Central Valley are the best served.

The Pan-American (Longitudinal) Highway runs from Arica through Santiago to Puerto Montt and recently extended by the Carretera Austral to Cochrane; from Llay-Llay a branch goes to Los Andes and over La Cumbre (Uspallata) pass to Argentina. Another main international road in the Lake District goes from Osorno across the Puyehue pass to Argentina. The Longitudinal Highway, vital to the Chilean economy, is paved throughout, but many sections are in a bad state.

Constitution and Government   After the deposition and death of President Salvador Allende on September 11, 1973, Chile was ruled by a military president, Gen. Augusto Pinochet Ugarte, and a 4-man-junta with absolute powers. The pre-1973 constitution was replaced by a new one, which was approved in a plebiscite held on September 11, 1980 and put into effect on March 11, 1981. Under this Constitution, President Pinochet was to remain in office until the end of the decade. In 1988 a plebiscite was held to determine whether he should remain in office for a further 8 years. A large 'no' vote resulted in direct presidential and congressional elections being called in 1989, with a new president to take office in 1990. The Constitution provides for an eight-year non-renewable term for the President of the Republic, a bicameral Congress and an independent judiciary and central bank.

N.B. In 1974 Chile established thirteen regions to replace the old system of 25 provinces. The regions (now named) are subdivided into 51 new provinces.

THE DESERT NORTH (1)

Regions	Provinces	Population ('000) 1975	1982
I (Tarapacá)	Arica, Parinacota, Iquique	210	273
II (Antofagasta)	Tocopilla, El Loa, Antofagasta	287	341
III (Atacama)	Chañaral, Copiapó, Huasco	179	183

The 1,250 km. between Arica and Copiapó are desert without vegetation, with little or no rain. The inhospitable shore is a pink cliff face rising to a height of from 600 to 900 metres. At the bottom of the cliff are built the towns, some of considerable size. The far from pacific Pacific often makes it difficult to load and unload ships. The nitrate fields exploited in this area lie in the depression between Pisagua and Taltal. Copper, too, is mined in the Cordillera; there are two large mines, at Chuquicamata, near Calama, and at El Salvador, inland from Chañaral.

Life in the area is artificial. Water has to be piped for hundreds of km. to the cities and the nitrate fields from the Cordillera; all food and even all building materials have to be brought in from elsewhere. Only the small populations of the oases, such as Calama, are self-supporting.

There is some difference of climate between the coast and the interior. The coast is humid and cloudy; in the interior the skies are clear. The temperatures on the coast are fairly uniform; in the interior there is often a great difference in the temperature between day and night; the winter nights are often as cold as -10°C, with a cruel wind. Drivers must beware of high winds and blowing sand N of Copiapó.

Chile's most northerly city, 19 km. S of the Peruvian border, is

Arica, with a population of 145,415, built at the foot of the Morro headland and

CHILE
RAILWAYS
MAIN ROADS ┼┼┼┼┼
48

fringed by sand dunes. The Andes can be clearly seen from the anchorage. The Morro, with a good view from the look-out park on top (an hour's walk along the road from town, ½ hr. by footpath from the south end of Colón, or 10 mins. by taxi), was the scene of a great victory by Chile over Peru on June 7, 1880.

There is no rain, winter or summer. The average, daytime winter temperature is 19°C, and the average summer temperature 24°C. It is frequented for sea-bathing by Bolivians as well as the locals. The attractive cathedral church, San Marcos, built in iron by Eiffel and fitted with bright coloured windows, is in the Plaza de Armas. It was brought to Arica from Ilo (Peru) in the 19th century, before Peru lost Arica to Chile, as an emergency measure after a tidal wave swept over Arica and destroyed all its churches. Eiffel also designed the customs house. A 63-km. railway connects the town with Tacna, in Peru, and another (448 km.) with La Paz, the capital of Bolivia; the old steam locomotive (made in Germany in 1924) once used on this line can be seen outside Arica station. In the station is a memorial to John Roberts Jones, builder of the Arica portion of the railway. It is this railway, over which today flow about half the imports and exports of Bolivia, that makes Arica important; it will become more important now that the international highway to Tambo Quemado, Bolivia, is completed for normal traffic. An oil pipeline runs from Bolivia. There are large fishmeal plants.

The Free Zone   in the First Region now imposes customs duties on many articles, but vessels, aircraft and other transport still enter the Zone without payment of customs dues and other charges. Articles such as calculators are cheaper here for Peruvians and Chileans, but not for Europeans. Spirits are slightly more expensive than in Santiago, cigarettes marginally cheaper.

Local Festival   Fiestas for the Virgen de las Peñas at the Santuario de Livircar in the Azapa Valley (see below) are held on the first Sunday in October and a lesser festival on December 7-9 (on Dec. 8 the festival moves to Arica). Take a bus from Av. Chacabuco y Vicuña Mackenna, then walk 12 km. from where it stops to the sanctuary. The December festival is not particularly outstanding but it takes place in a part of the valley not normally accessible.

Hotels   *Hostería Arica* Av. Cdte. San Martín 599 (T 31201), best, B (no breakfast, but set lunch for US$6) about 2 km. along shore, reached by frequent bus service along front (Nos. 7, 8), outstanding beaches with clean water and sand; *El Paso*, bungalow style, pleasant gardens, Av. Gral. Velásquez, 1109, T 31965-32288, B; *Central*, 21 de Mayo 425 (T 252575/231116), new, central, nicely decorated, C; *King*, Colón 376 (T 32094), D, with bath, overpriced; *Motel Azapa*, attractive grounds but several km. from beaches and centre: G. Sánchez, Azapa, T 42612-42613, A, but cheaper cabins available, fair restaurant ½ km. away; nearby is *Motel Rucal*, C (*Motel Status* is very-short-stay only); *Savona*, Yungay 380, C (T 32319); *Residencial Lynch*, Lynch 657 (T 231581), D with bath, clean, quiet and pleasant; *Residencial Puerta del Sol*, 21 de Mayo 480, E, 12 rooms, shared bath, meals available, clean, quiet, excellent service; *Residencial Blanquita*, Maipú 472, good, clean, hot water, F; *San Marcos*, Sotomayor 367 (T 232149/232970), clean, helpful, D; *Residencial Madrid*, Calle Baquedano 685 (T 31479), clean, good value, F, communal toilets and showers (only one hot), theft from washing line reported; *Residencial Valencia*, also on Baquedano, similar facilities, but tiny rooms; *Residencial Patricia*, Maipú 269, F, basic, safe, friendly, but tiny rooms and poor beds, no hot water; *Residencial Núñez*, Maipú 516, F, basic but friendly. *Residencial Leiva*, Av. Colón 347, F, incl. breakfast, shared bath, hot water a.m. only; *Residencial Universo*, Colón 662, F, inexpensive and clean. *Residencial Velásquez*, Velásquez 669 (T 31989), good, clean, hot water, laundry available. Private house, at Av. D.Portales 885 (Barbino Guajardo C.), room for rent in F range (opp. bus station, friendly); also Velázquez 721, F, rec., safe, good breakfast. Youth Hostel, Av. 18 de Septiembre 2221.

Camping   On beach at S end of town, past fishmeal factories. Interesting shoreline; caves, waves, blow-holes and birdlife.

Restaurants   *Acuario*, Máximo Lira, Terminal Pesquero; *El Rey de Mariscos*, corner Colón and Maipú, 2nd floor, cheaper. *890*, pizzeria, 21 de Mayo; also at Blanco Encalada 402; *El Padrino*, 18 de Septiembre 332, rec. pizzeria; *Bavaria*, Colón 611, good, cheap; *Centro Español*, Bolognesi 311, good and cheap. *Govinda Vegetarian Restaurant*, Bolognesi y 21 de Mayo; *El Sitio*, Centro Comercial Parque Colón, Chacobuco y Colón 2nd floor. Good eating at fire station, *Casino de Bomberos*, on Colón; good ceviche and juices in market. Bread from Maipú 510. **N.B.** In this area, pensión means restaurant, not hostel.

Cafés   *La Tranquera*, 21 de Mayo 431; *Café Americano*, 21 de Mayo 249, good. *Café Scala*, Pasaje Bolognesi y 21 de Mayo, good juices, sandwiches and fruit salads; *Shop 18*, 18 de Septiembre, good, cheap sandwiches; *Café Suceso Inn*, 18 de Septiembre 250.

Night-Clubs   Casino, Gral. Velásquez 955, open all year.

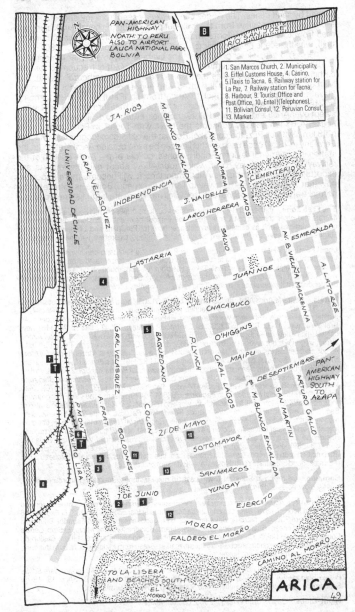

PAN-AMERICAN HIGHWAY

NOATH: TO PERU ALSO TO AIRPORT LAUCA NATIONAL PARK BOLIVIA

RIO SAN JOSE

B

1. San Marcos Church, 2. Municipality, 3. Eiffel Customs House, 4. Casino, 5.)Taxis to Tacna, 6. Railway station for La Paz, 7. Railway station for Tacna, 8. Harbour, 9. Tourist Office and Post Office, 10. Entel)(Telephones), 11. Bolivian Consul, 12. Peruvian Consul, 13. Market.

J.A. RIOS

M. BLANCO ENCALADA

AV. SANTA MARIA

CEMENTERIO

UNIVERSIDAD DE CHILE

GRAL. VELASQUEZ

INDEPENDENCIA

J. WAIDELLE

ANGAMOS

LARCO HERRERA

SALVO

AV. B. ESMERALDA

LASTARRIA

JUAN NOE

AV. B. VICUÑA MACKENNA

A. LATORRE

4

CHACABUCO

O'HIGGINS

5

BAQUEDANO

P. LYNCH

MAIPU

GRAL. VELASQUEZ

GRAL. LAGOS

18 DESEPTIEMBRE

PAN-AMERICAN HIGHWAY SOUTH TO AZAPA

A. PRAT

COLON

M. BLANCO ENCALADA

SAN MARTIN

ARTURO GALLO

7

T

P. MONTT

MAXIMO LIRA

6

T

BOLOGNESI

21 DE MAYO

10

SOTOMAYOR

9

11

3

13

SAN MARCOS

8

7 DE JUNIO

2

1

YUNGAY

EJERCITO

12

MORRO

FALDEOS EL MORRO

CAMINO AL MORRO

TO LA LISERA AND BEACHES SOUTH EL MORRO

ARICA

49

Cinemas   Colón, 7 de Junio 190; Rex, 21 de Mayo 570.

Shopping   Handicrafts: Pueblo Artesanal Arica, Rotonda Libertador Bernardo O'Higgins; Cema-Chile, Baquedano 311; Hugali, Pasaje 10, No. 932; Casa Martínez, 21 de Mayo 423; Feria Sangra, Sangra 350; Feria Dominical, Av. Costanera, Sun. a.m. only; Mercado Central, Sotomayor, 0800-1500 daily. Fruit, vegetable and old clothes market at Terminal Agropecuario at edge of town; take bus marked "Terminal Agro".

Laundry   Lavandería Americana, Patricio Lynch 651, reasonable.

Shoe Repairs   and leather goods, Calzado El Eléctrico, Maipú y Baquedano.

Car Hire   Alen Rent a Car, 21 de Mayo 821, T 51121.

Automóvil Club de Chile   Chacabuco 460, T 32780.

Car Service   Shell, Panamericana Norte 3456; Esso, Av. Diego Portales 2462; Shell Cánepa, Chacabuco, San Martín. Volkswagen/Michelin, very helpful for repairs and assistance.

Museums   At San Miguel, 12 km. along road towards Azapa Valley, small but good for pathological analysis of mummies, including one dating from 5000 BC if you are feeling strong. Open Tues.-Fri., 1100-1800, Sat., Sun. and holidays 1300-1800; much of the information is in English. Colectivo with "Azapa" sign, from Calles Lynch y O'Higgins, passes museum (US$0.40 one way). Anthropological Museum, University of Tarapacá Saucache Campus, Av. 18 de Septiembre (just beyond stadium), Tues.-Fri. 0900-1230, 1500-1900; Museo Histórico Salitre, Calle Sotomayor 415, voluntary contributions expected; free Pacific War Museum on the Morro.

Exchange   Many banks and money changers on 21 de Mayo and its junction with Colón. Also at tourist office on main square. When banks closed money can be changed at *Hotel International*, *Hotel King*, or at the exchange houses (Tacora. 21 de Mayo 171, good rates; Yanulaque, Colón 380 or 21 de Mayo 175; Marta Daguer, 18 de Septiembre 330), which stay open until 2000.

Consulates   Honorary British Consul (the only one in Chile north of Valparaíso) and Instituto Británico reading room, opposite *Restaurant Aduana*, both on Baquedano, between 21 de Mayo and Sotomayor. Argentina, M.Rodríguez 954, Depto. 41, T 31322; Belgium, Sotomayor 504; Bolivia, Bolognesi 344; Costa Rica, Sotomayor 802; Denmark, 21 de Mayo 399; Peru, Yungay and Colón; Holland, 18 de Septiembre; Italy, Chacabuco with San Martín; France, Santa María 2860; Spain, Santa María 2660; Instituto Cultural Chileno Norteamericano, San Marcos 581.

Telephones   21 de Mayo and Baquedano, open 0900-2200.

Tourist Office   National office: Calle Arturo Prat 375, 2nd floor; post-office complex. T 32101. Very helpful, but not all information is accurate. Also kiosk in main square (Nuestra Sra. del Carmen) part way up to Cerro Moro. Closed weekends.

Travel Agencies   Turismo Payachatas, Bolognesi 332, T 51514, rec.; Jurasi, Bolognesi 360 A., T 32635, will hold mail, helpful; Kijo Tour, Bolognesi 359, T 232245; and many others.

Bathing   Olympic pool at one end of Parque Brasil, Tues.-Sat. 0900-1800, US$0.30. Take No. 2 bus to beaches south of town, or walk along seaside promenade. For swimming, better La Lisera than El Laucho (very rocky); Playa Chinchorro receives mostly good reports; Playa Brava (surf beach) to south with fine, white sands; Playa Arenillas Negras, 3 km. to south; Playa Corazones, 15 km. to south (no buses, take taxi or hitch), rec. not for swimming but picnics and fishing.

Airport   Chaculluta, to town costs US$6.50 for taxi. Lan-Chile run a free bus service to and from their office in Plaza de Armas. Flights to La Paz (Mon. and Fri., also with LAB), Iquique, and Santiago. Ladeco, 18 de Septiembre 370, fly to Santiago direct once a week, or via Iquique and Antofagasta or El Salvador.

Rail   To La Paz by Arica-La Paz Railway (see page 189 for description of the line): either direct by *ferrobus*, Tues. 0900, 11 hrs., US$50 one way, or by Martínez bus from Arica (P. Montt 620) to the border, then train Charaña-La Paz; very cold change over, waiting on the track for tickets. Change money in the market or on the train. To Tacna, Peru, by rail costs US$1.20, daily except Sun. at 1200 and 1800, 1 hr. (exit stamp obtainable at station, but allow ½ hour for this—it is preferable to relying on the Town Hall); it is best to avoid Sats. because of crowds and delays at the border.

Road Services   Terminal at corner of Av. Portales and Santa María, T 41390, bus or colectivo No. 8 (US$0.10, or US$0.20), 10 mins. from Maipú y Baquedano (US$0.50 to use terminal). The Longitudinal (Pan-American) Highway S is mostly good, fast, 2-lane, concrete with hard shoulders and well signposted and served. All buses are modern, clean and air-conditioned, but ask carefully what meals are included. To Antofagasta, Flecha Norte, US$10, 10-11 hrs., via Tocopilla, not a comfortable trip. To Calama and Chuquicamata, 6 a day all between 0800-1000, 10 hrs., US$10. To Iquique, daily, US$5, 4½ hrs. To Viña del Mar, US$30. To Santiago, 28 hrs., Chile Bus (1030 and 1530, 28-30 hrs.), with meals, US$30; Fenix Pullman Norte (0800, 0830 and 1430) with meals, good, US$30. Several other companies, some more luxurious (Pullman Fichtur, 29-31 hrs., all meals inc. for US$56), student discounts available. To La Serena, daily at 1400, 18 hrs.

To Arequipa, Peru, with Ormeño, 3 a day, US$12.50, supposedly 6 hrs. To La Paz, Bolivia, via Tambo Quemado: Litoral bus, Chacabuco 454, journey to La Paz via Chungará takes at the very least 20 hrs. (involving very cold change at border—take blanket/sleeping bag, food and sense of humour), leaves on Tues. and Fri. at 0530, US$28. US$ cash only can be exchanged with the Bolivian Immigration Officer at Tambo Quemado.

Colectivo taxis run to and from Tacna for about US$2.50-3 p.p. (telephone Arica 31376 or Tacna 2288) one way and take about an hour for the trip (drivers take care of all the paperwork). Colectivos leave from Chacabuco and Vicuña Mackenna. Bus costs US$1.75 and leaves from the bus station, as does Taxibus, 2 hourly, US$2. Money-changing at frontier, but reported better rates in Tacna.

Drivers are required at the Chile-Peru frontier to file a form, *Relaciones de Pasajeros* (7 copies, no carbons), giving details of passengers, obtained from a stationery store in Tacna, or at the border in a booth near Customs. You must also present the original registration document for your car from its country of registration. The first checkpoints outside Arica on the road to Santiago also require the *Relaciones de Pasajeros* from drivers. If you can't buy the form details on a piece of paper will suffice or you can get them at service stations. The form is *not* required when travelling south of Antofagasta.

N.B. Remember that between October and March, Chilean time is 1 hr. later than Bolivian, 2 hrs. later than Peruvian time (1 hr. vis-à-vis Peru the rest of the year).

Several checkpoints on the Longitudinal south from Arica. It is illegal to take fruit S from Arica; there is a checkpoint for fruit at Cuya (Km. 105); 20 km. further on are petroglyphs to the right (signposted), a checkpoint for buses and lorries at Huara (Km. 234, hotel), and customs and fruit control at Quillagua on Río Loa (Km. 430, where there is a museum of local Indian artefacts—key held by lady in telephone exchange). Also customs check at Arica bus terminal before departure south (painfully slow). **N.B.** If driving S, en route to Quillagua there are some steep ascents and descents best tackled in daylight (at night, sea mist, *camanchaca*, can reduce visibility).

Service stations between the Peruvian border and Santiago can be found at: Arica, Mapocho, Iquique, Pozo Almonte (also hotel), Oficina Vitoria, Region I and II border, Oficina María Elena, intersection of Pan-American Highway and road to Calama, Antofagasta, La Negra, Agua Verde, Taltal, Chañaral, Caldera, Copiapó, Vallenar, La Serena, Termas de Soco, Los Vilos, and then every 30 km. to capital.

Excursions   To the fruitful Azapa valley by colectivo (US$1), from Patricio Lynch and Maipú, or taxi, US$13; book through tourist agency. To the Lluta valley, 10 km. to north, figures built with stones on sandy hills, and to the wild desert and mountain scenery at the foot of the Andes.

Lauca National Park   A visit to the Parque Nacional Lauca, some 120 km. E of Arica, is highly recommended. It is in the Altiplano (so beware of *soroche*, if you are not coming from Bolivia); the scenery shows snowy volcanoes reaching to 6,300 metres, blue cold lakes swarming with waterfowl, and much mammalian life including vicuñas, pumas and vizcachas. The Park is maintained by the Corporación Nacional Forestal (Conaf), Sotomayor 216, 3rd and 4th floors, Arica (T 31559, closed weekends), and it is advisable to obtain their advice before making the visit; they may also give you a lift. There are 4 refuges in the Park, but only those at Parinacota and Lake Chungará allow sleeping: at Putre (a scenic village at the Park entrance); at Las Cuevas (good for seeing wildlife, 20 km., inside the Park); at **Parinacota** (need sleeping bags, plenty of space, only 4 beds though, US$1, fully equipped kitchen—there is supposed to be oxygen for those suffering from *soroche*, but it is often not available, beware) 4,392 metres up, at the foot of the Payachatas volcano (interesting 17th-cent. church with wall paintings and churchyard statuary; local resident Lorenza de Calle will knit alpaca sweaters for US$18-20; weavings of wildlife scenes also available), and at Lake Chungará (2 beds and floor space, cooking facilities) one of the highest lakes, a must (4,600 metres above sea-level). Limited possibilities of purchasing food at Chucuyo, a village just beyond the police control 30 km. from Putre, better to take your own (enough for yourself and the Park guards). Trips can be arranged with Turismo Payachatas, or Jurasi (addresses above, US$20 p.p.).

Public transport to Lauca: The Arica-Bolivia road passes through the Park. Lorries leaving port of Arica early in the morning will often give lifts to the Park on their way to La Paz. Best place to wait is at the Pocón Chile control point on the road through the Valle de Lluta, about an hour out of Arica on the Putre road. From Parinacota you can hitch to Visviri on Tues. with lorries going to meet the train; catch the train to La Paz at Charaña. Hitching is good every second Sunday when trucks go to the international market at Visviri. Buses leave from Germán Riesco 2071, Arica, for Putre on Tues., Thurs., Sat. at 0630 (returning Tues., Thurs., Sun. at 1200), US$2.50, then take daily "Vialidad" truck at 0700 into the Park. On Tues. and Fri. at 1030 Sanga buses leave Arica for Visviri on the Bolivian border (to connect with the La Paz train, see above, and arriving at 1900 Wed. and Sat. for international market); they pass Parinacota after 6-7 hrs., US$7. Lake Chungará is on the road route to La Paz, it is a 1 hr. walk to the border (Tambo Quemado), which opens at 0800; trucks pass infrequently, or you may be lucky and get on the Litoral bus which will charge full Arica-La Paz fare. The road into Bolivia is terrible, especially in the wet.

Dr. Klaus Busch, of Osnabrück, describes driving in the Park (he used a Toyota Landcruiser): "The road can be managed with a city car. Leave Arica via Panamericano North/Aeropuerto. After 9 km. turn off right; at 39 km. you will reach Pocón Chile, the control point for cars, and at 62 km. Molinos. Zapahuira, at 3,270 metres, marks the end of the paved road, with a marvellous view over the mountains. Later, at 152 km., at the turn off to Putre, you can see the Nevado de Putre (5,825m.) The track to Chucuyo and back to Zapahuira is not even suitable for 4-wheel cars, or at least must be taken very slowly."

Humberstone, at the junction of the Pan-American Highway and the road to Iquique, is a large nitrate ghost town; ancient Indian drawings are to be seen and there is an interesting British cemetery 10 km. to the north. 2 km. beyond the junction to Humberstone is the Oficina Santa Laura, an impressive early nitrate plant, through which you can walk.

Iquique, the capital of the First (Tarapacá) Region and one of the main northern ports, is 304 km. by road south of Arica. The name of the town is derived from the Aymará word *ique-ique,* meaning place of "rest and tranquillity". It was founded in the 16th century on a rocky peninsula sheltered by the headlands of Punta Gruesa and Cavancha. The city was partly destroyed by earthquake in 1877. It has some old wooden houses, gaily painted, in a Victorian style, an outstanding square, Plaza Prat, with a clock tower and bell, and wide avenues bordered by trees. One, Av. Balmaceda, runs along the coast. The Museo Regional, Sotomayor 726, open Mon.-Fri. 0800-1300, 1500-1900 and Sat., 1000-1300, small but well displayed, includes a section on minerals and a shop selling goods made by Chilean Aymarás (entry US$0.25, Thurs. free). At the back of the Customs House is a Naval Museum (entry US$0.15). The Palacio Astoreca on Calle O'Higgins esq. Lynch, built in 1903, formerly the Intendencia and now a cultural centre, has fine pinewood architecture and exhibitions of shells and on the history of the nitrate industry (open Tues.-Fri. 1000-1300, 1600-2000, Sat. and Sun. 1000-1300 US$0.25). Population: 111,000. There are checkpoints on the road N to Arica, on the road S at Quillagua, and on the road inland (to Mamiña).

The harbour is well protected and ships tie up to load at modern docks. Sealions and pelicans can be seen from the harbour. It was at Iquique that the *Esmeralda* and another wooden ship, under Captain Arturo Prat, resisted the attack of the Peruvian ironclad ship *Huáscar* on May 21, 1879, during the War of the Pacific (**see page 478**). The main exports are fishmeal, fish oil, canned fish and salt.

Iquique has a Free Zone, at the north of town: it is worth a visit, goods from Hong Kong and Taiwan, reasonably priced cameras, electronics and cheap Ektachrome films are sold.

Local holiday During the ten days before July 16 there is a religious festival, "La fiesta de Tirana", at a village 70 km. E of Iquique (near Pica, see next page). Over 100 groups dance night and day, before making their pilgrimage to the church of the Virgen del Carmen.

Hotels *Hostería Cavancha,* A, south of city, on water's edge; *Primeras Piedras,* 3 km. from city, B-C, good food, friendly; *Tamarugal,* Tarapacá 369, central, clean and modern, C, good restaurant. *Arturo Prat,* in Av. Aníbal Pinto, facing Plaza Prat; *Barros Arana,* Barros Arana 1330 (T 24420), clean, modern, good value, D; *Inti-Llanka,* Obispo Labbe (T 26383), good, D; *Durana,* San Martín 294 (T 28055), good, D; *Phoenix,* Aníbal Pinto 451 (T 21315) room with bathroom, breakfast, old but nice, E; *España,* Tarapacá 465, near Plaza Prat, F, shared bath, friendly, moderately clean. *Res. Li Ming,* B. Arana 705, near Thompson, and *Res. Nan-King,* Thompson 752, both F; *Res. Danny,* Vivar 1266, F, not central but may have room when others are full. Reasonably priced pensiones include *Residencial Catedral,* Obispo Labbe 252, F, clean, friendly, but breakfast expensive; *Residencial Marclaud,* Juan Martínez 753, F, rec., quiet, clean, motorcycle parking (good cheap restaurant at the corner); *Condel,* Thompson 684 esq. Vivar, nice, clean, quiet, F; *Alvimar,* San Martín, F, cheap, pleasant. *Casa de familia,* Bulnes 1110, F with breakfast, clean, friendly. Youth Hostel, Av. Pedro Gamboni 2828.

Restaurants Las Urracas, Avenida Balmaceda 551, on seafront regarded as best place for fish; *Don Lolo,* Thompson 930, good, cheap, tasty food. *Club de la Unión,* reasonable lunch. Also, the *Sociedad Protectora de los Empleados de Tarapacá* (Plaza Prat) is open to tourists and has reasonable prices. *Casino Español,* excellent meals well served in cool, Moorish decorated 100-year-old rooms; attractive. Several good, inexpensive seafood restaurants can be found on the second floor of the central market, Barros Arana with Latorre. *Portofino*, Thompson 650, 3 courses for US$2. Yacht Club serves inexpensive lunch. *El Pescado Frito*, Bulnes y Juan Martínez, very nice local place with good and cheap seafood dishes.

Cafés *Salón de Té Chantilly*, Tarapacá 520 and Barros Arana 716; *Café Diana*, Vivar 836, speciality mango ice cream; *El Mastique*, Thompson 728; *La Tentazione*, Sargento Aldea 749; *Ciocolatta*, Aníbal Pinto 487.

Theatre Teatro del Norte at Sotomayor 728.

Cables Post and Telegraph Office, Calle Bolívar y P.Lynch; telex available.

Exchange National banks; black market in the Free Zone (Zofri).

Tourist Information Aníbal Pinto 436. T 21499; another office on Plaza Prat, corner Thompson, open when other office is closed.

Fishing Broadbill swordfish, striped marlin, yellowfin tuna, oceanic bonito, March till end of August. In the harbour there are hundreds of sea lions (for a closer look you can hire a boat for a few dollars).

Bathing Balneario Cavancha and Huaiquique, reasonable, November-March. Restaurants at Cavancha. Piscina Godoy, fresh water swimming pool on Av. Costanera at Aníbal Pinto and Riquelme, open p.m., US$1.

Buses To Arica, 6 daily, US$5, 4½ hrs., comfortable in spite of various checkpoints. To Antofagasta, daily 2000, US$10, a dusty, hot 8-hr. drive through the desert, relieved by the occasional oasis. To Calama and Chuquicamata, daily at 2100, 2130 and 2200, 8 hrs. to Calama (US$7). To Santiago, 28 hrs. Ramos Cholele and Tarapacá are the cheapest, about US$25 incl. meals. All buses leave from terminal at N end of Obispo Labbe, except Tramaca, which has own terminal on B. O'Higgins; bus offices are at corner of Sargento Aldea and B.Arana.

Airlines Diego Aracena international airport, 35 km. S at Chucumata. Free airport bus to city centre. Lan-Chile, Av. Aníbal Pinto, next to *Hotel Prat*; Ladeco, San Martín 191 (Santiago-Iquique daily). To Antofagasta, Arica and Santiago daily by Lan-Chile.

Excursions   Good roads run to the nitrate fields, which are 900 metres above sea level. A road runs NE to the hot mineral springs in the mountains at Termas de *Mamiña* (2,700 metres), where there is good accommodation for tourists (*Hotel Termas de Salitre*, D, full board, thermal pool in each room, electricity till midnight; *Residencial Ipla*, D, cheapest). The rainy season in Mamiña is mainly in January and is called *Invierno Boliviano* (Bolivian winter). Near Mamiña, 5 km. SW, is an Inca village with lots of pottery lying around.

The Iquique-Mamiña bus trip (130 km.) takes 2½ hrs.; Iquique-Mamiña, Mon.-Fri. 1600, from Mamiña same days, 0900, US$2. (The police control point just outside Iquique requires registration by foreigners, but the bus waits.) The road is well paved for the first 50 km., but from Pozo Almonte onwards is unpaved and very bad. There is a large ravine, Quebrada Duplisa, where no vehicle can pass another, but as it is located slightly on a bend it is easy to avoid trouble.

The Pan-American Highway continues South: 13 km. after the turn-off to Iquique is a detour to Tirana (10 km.—see above) and the fertile oasis of *Pica* (2,750 metres), famous for its citrus groves and two natural springs. Hotels: *O'Higgins*, D; *San Andrés*, E. Campsite US$0.80 p.p. Carmelita/Julita bus leaves Iquique from near market, Mon.-Fri. 1700, from Pica at 0700, 2 hrs., US$1.75; Flonatur leaves 0900, returns 1800, US$3 one way (also near market, check if running at weekends). Beyond Pica is the oasis of Matilla, whence a road in poor condition returns to the Pan-American Highway. There are well-preserved petroglyphs 2-4 km. W of Pintados, which is 43 km. S of Pozo Almonte.

Tocopilla, 195 km. S of Iquique, exports nitrate and iodine from two famous nitrate fields—María Elena (68 km.), and Pedro de Valdivia (85 km.). Population: 22,600. There are two sports stadiums and two good beaches: Punta Blanca and Caleta. In the centre is the copper concentrate plant of Cía. Minera de Tocopilla. There is a sporting 18-hole golf course and fine deep sea fishing if you can find a boat and a guide. There are two paved roads out: a 193-km. coast road S to Antofagasta via Mejillones (see below) and the other E up the narrow valley 72 km. to the Pan-American Highway (with a short spur to María Elena and Pedro de Valdivia nitrate mines) and on to Chuquicamata. From Tocopilla to Chuquicamata is poor, particularly the eastern half which is eroded by the heavy lorries which use it (requires careful driving). A new coastal road runs N to Iquique.

THE DESERT NORTH 441

Hotel *América* (middling). *Hostal Bolívar*, Bolívar 1332, F, clean, friendly.

Cables All America Cables & Radio, Inc., Calle Serrano 1180.

Bus To Santiago, Tues. and Sat. To Antofagasta daily, 0730 and 1730, US$6.

Mejillones, 64 km. N of Antofagasta (130 km. S of Tocopilla), has a good natural harbour protected from westerly gales by high hills. Since the export of tin and other metals from Bolivia ceased, Mejillones lives solely by fishing. The town comes alive after 1700 when the fishermen prepare to set sail. There is a Museo del Mar in the old customs building (1866) on Aníbal Pinto. The sea is very cold because of the Humboldt current. Population: 6,000.

Hotels *Posada San Juan*, A.Goñigg, with restaurant; *Residencial Elisabeth*, Alto Latorre 440, F, friendly, restaurant. *Juanito Restaurant*, Las Heras 24.

Antofagasta is 1,373 km. N of Santiago and 700 km. S of Arica. It is the capital of the Second (Antofagasta) Region, and its population of 190,000 makes it the largest city in northern Chile. It exports the nitrates of the area and the copper of Chuquicamata. A huge anchor stands high in the mountains, and was used as a navigational aid by ships. The main historical interest lies in some ruins at the edge of town, and a Bolivian silver refinery dating from 1868 (Huanchaca, now a military zone—you may visit, but not take photos), but it is lively and attractive, with a university of high standing, quite good parks and public gardens, an interesting waterfront, a clock tower on the main plaza donated by the British community, and very expensive shops. There is a small museum near the university, which has an interesting handicraft shop; museum opens Tues.-Fri., 0900-1200; 1500-1900; Sat. 0900-1200; Sun. 1100-1300. There is also an archaeological museum on Pasaje López (Prat 482 y Latorre), Mon.-Fri. 1530-1900, Sun. 1030-1300; Museo Regional (formerly Universidad del Norte museum in Iquique) on Balmaceda y Bolívar is also interesting. The modern sports stadium is close to the most popular beach (S end of city) where there is also a restaurant-pool-discotheque complex. The climate is delightful (apart from the lack of rain); the temperature varies from 16°C in June/July to 24°C January/February, never falling below 10°C at night. The tap water is not potable.

Local Holiday June 29, San Pedro, patron saint of the fishermen: the saint's image is taken out by launch to the breakwater to bless the first catch of the day.

Festivals On the last weekend of October, the foreign communities put on a joint festival on the seafront, with national foods, dancing and music.

Hotels *Antofagasta*, Balmaceda 2575, run-down, garage, swimming pool, lovely view of port and city, B with breakfast (discount for Automóvil Club members, but still not very good value), beach; *Diego de Almagro*, Condell 2624, very good; *San Martín*, Calle San Martín 2781, ½ block from main plaza, D, poor value; *San Antonio*, Condell 2235, E, clean, good but noisy from bus station; *Residencial La Riojanita*, Baquedano 464, F, good, use of kitchen permitted, washing facilities; *Rawaye*, Sucre 762, shared bathroom, clean, friendly, F; *Residencial Paola*, Prat 766, good value, friendly, F; *Residencial Familiar*, 500 block of Balmaceda, F, dark rooms; *Res. Cobre*, Prat 749, F, shared bath (more with bath), clean, good, 2 blocks from bus station; *Plaza*, Baquedano 461, D, modern, clean, comfortable; *Residencial Vargas*, Condell 2342, F without bath or windows, but clean and friendly. *Tatio*, Av. Grecia 1000, D, out of old town on the beach, has buses converted into caravans, friendly, beautiful views. Youth hostels: men: Matias Rojas 522; women: Díaz Gana y Eduardo Lefort.

Camping Las Garumas, 16 km. on route to Coloso, US$10 for tent, US$15 for cabins; hot water, showers and beach. Official campsite at S end of beach beyond university.

Restaurants *Apoquindo*, Prat 616, reasonable, good, as is *Club Náutico*, Pinto 3051; *Centro Español*, Prat 430; *Grill Bar Americano*, Malta 621; *Tío Jacinto*, Calle Uribe, by Tramaca terminal, friendly, good seafood; *El Arriero*, good grills, Spanish-style, Condell 2632; *Chifa Wai Lin*, Sucre 721, average Chinese food. The al fresco luncheons at the *Auto Club* are fashionable both in summer and winter. *Club de la Unión*, Calle Prat 470 (quite good). *Societá Italiana*, next to *Residencial Paola* on Prat, rec. *Café Express* and *Café Haiti*, next to each other on Prat, good coffee; *Café Roma*, Sucre 717, good breakfasts and lunches; *Chico Jaime* above the market, seafood, US$3 p.p. incl. wine. Many eating places in the market.

442 **CHILE**

Clubs Club de Tenis Antofagasta, Av. Angamos 906, connected with Av. Brasil, and the Automobile Club, 6½ km. from Antofagasta; Yachting Club, Calle Balmaceda.

Market Municipal market, corner of Matta and Uribe.

Car Rental Rent-a-Car, Prat 810, T 225200; Avis in *Hotel Antofagasta*; Hertz, Balmaceda 2646, offer city cars and jeeps (group D, Toyota Landcruiser) and do a special flat rate, with unlimited mileage, if you hire the car for over a week.

Discotheques *Eden* is popular.

Bookshop Multilibro, Baquedano 522.

Cinemas Gran Vía, Av. Angamos; Nacional, Sucre 735; Arte, Copiapó 1125; Colón, San Martín 2755 (2 for the price of 1 on Thursdays); Teatro de la Barra, Baquedano y Condell (cine and live theatre).

Exchange in main square will not buy or sell Argentine or Bolivian money, and only change dollars at poor rates and 5% commission. Good rates at Farmacia Rimassa, Prat 656, for cash and cheques; also in travel agency at Latorre 2563, Olivetti shop on Latorre, and San Marcos at Latorre y Baquedano. N.B. There is practically no official opportunity to change currency S of Antofagasta until you reach La Serena.

Swimming Olympic pool at Condell y 21 de Mayo, US$1.20, open till 1800, best to go in a.m.

Post Office Washington 2623; Telephones, Uribe 746.

Travel Agent Tatio Travel, Latorre 2579, highly rec. Turismo Cristóbal in *Hotel Antofagasta*, helpful.

Tourist Office at Baquedano 360 (one block from sea front); also Prat y Matta, T 224834, and Airport.

Shipping PSNC, O'Higgins 1906, freight direct to Liverpool. **Customs Agent** Luis Piquimil Bravo, Prat 272, oficina 202, excellent, fast service, efficient.

Roads To Tocopilla, 187 km.; to Mejillones, 62 km.; to Pedro de Valdivia, 168 km.; to María Elena, 193 km.; to Taltal, 307 km.; to Calama, 196 km.; to Chuquicamata, 206 km. **N.B.** the Pan-American Highway between the N and S exits to Antofagasta is not paved (20 km.).

Buses To Santiago, 20 hrs., (luxury double decker/sleeper coach, Flota Barrios, US$43 including drinks and meals; 30% reduction on Inca and Gemini buses for students; many cheaper, about US$20, book 2 days in advance). Bus station at S end of town (Av. Argentina, Díaz Gana) often has seats left when buses from N terminal (at Uribe) are booked. Alternatively, catch a bus to La Serena (US$14 or 25 with lunch and supper) or Ovalle and travel to Santiago from there. To Valparaíso, US$17.50. To Arica, US$10 (Flecha Norte), 13½ hrs. (It is forbidden to take fruit south from Antofagasta because of fruit-fly control.) To Chuquicamata, Flecha del Norte leaves at 0700, returns at 1900, as well as many others. To Calama, several companies, US$2.50-3 (3 hrs.). Direct to Copiapó on Thurs. and Sat. at 2230, US$10.50. Frequent buses to Iquique; US$10, 8 hrs., checkpoints near Iquique for foreigners. To Mejillones, twice a day from Latorre 2700. Bus station has a left luggage office.

Empresa de Transportes Atahualpa (Uribe 936) runs a Sat. bus service to Argentina, as does Geminis (Díaz Gana 1074, T 225494—better), Wed., both US$30; via Calama, immigration check at San Pedro de Atacama, then on to high Cordillera (very cold) and to San Antonio de los Cobres; change bus at Salta. There is nowhere to change Chilean pesos en route. (No service July-September.)

If hitching to Arica or Iquique try at the beer factory a few blocks N of the fish market on Av. Pinto, or the lorry park a few blocks further N.

N.B. There are no more railway passenger services from Antofagasta. The famous journey to Bolivia now starts from Calama (see below), and the line into Argentina has been closed to passengers for some years.

Air To Santiago, Lan-Chile (US$103) and Ladeco fly daily. To Salta, Aerolíneas Argentinas twice weekly, US$75; official agents Viajes Pieper, Latorre y Sucre. They arrange colectivo for trip to airport (US$2). Airport tax US$5. Taxi to airport US$7, but cheaper if ordered from hotel.

Excursions to derelict nitrate *oficinas*, over good roads (140 km.). The most interesting are Rica Adventura, Buenaventura, Puelma and Ibérica. There are two favourite spots for picnics: near the town of La Chimba, and the fantastic rock scenery at La Portada (16 km.) taxi fare, US$1.50 (if you have a bike, go at dusk). Alternatively, ask the driver of the airport bus, which leaves every 2 hrs. from *Hotel Turismo*, to drop you at the junction for La Portada—only 1 km. walk to beach. Last bus back leaves at 1830. A number of bathing beaches are within easy reach, including La Portada. Oficina Chacabuco is a military camp and "off limits"; in 1938 it was a town with 7,000 inhabitants (at junction of Antofagasta-Calama and María Elena roads). 50 km. from Antofagasta at Juan López is a windsurfers' paradise. Buses leave from Latorre 2723 (Sat. and Sun. only).

215 km. NE of Antofagasta is the oasis town of **Calama**, population 100,365, at an altitude of 2,265 metres. The Cía. Sud Americana de Explosivos manufactures high explosives. The town is modern and has a developed commercial centre. Travellers by car coming from the N can drive via Chuquicamata, although the road is quite poor on either side of that town, or, from the S, by a paved road (94 km.) leaving the Pan-American Highway 98 km. N of Antofagasta. 2 km. from the centre on Av. B.O'Higgins is Parque Loa, with an exhibition of pre-cordillera life, 2 museums, a zoo and a copy of Chiu Chiu church; open Tues.-Sun. 0930-1230, 1430-1700, US$0.40.

Hotels *Hostería Calama*, Latorre 1521, A, good food, slow service; *Atenas*, Ramírez 1961, new, clean, shared baths, E; *Quitor*, Ramírez 2116, C. Casablanca on Plaza, D; *Prat*, Vivar 1957, E, friendly; *Residencial Internacional*, hot water, E, friendly but noisy; *Residencial Casa de Huéspedes*, Sotomayor 2073, clean, noisy, shared hot shower, E; *Res. Tacora*, Sotomayor 1992, friendly, clean, hot water, rec., E; *Residencial King's*, Balmaceda 2040 (only one room with bath), E; *Res. Toño*, Vivar 1970, next to Kenny bus, E, shower (extra); *Capri*, Vivar, E, friendly but dirty, hot water; *Residencial El Tatio*, P.L. Gallo, E, clean, reasonable.

Restaurants *La Nueva Florida*, Calle Vargas 1974, good and cheap, *Ollantay*, on Vivar, set lunch for US$1.75, good. *Bavaria*, Sotomayor 2095, modern, clean, good coffee; *Fuente de Soda Moltis*, Ramírez 2120, good bar with cakes; good eating at fire station (*Casino de Bomberos*). Yugoslav club serves good lunches, but not very cheap.

Car Hire Comercial Maipo S.A., Barrio Industrial, sitio 14, T 211965, take taxi—½ hr. out of town, cheapest, US$28/day for car, US$37/day for pickup. Hertz, Latorre 1510; Comercial Automotriz Miranda, Granaderos 2625, T 211175, helpful.

Exchange La Media Luna dry goods store, Ramírez 1992, Casatel (electricity shop), Ramírez 1831, *Hotel Los Andes* and Farmacia Frankfurt will change travellers' cheques and cash at a good rate, also try other *farmacias* (who are less fussy about their clients); Banco de Crédito e Inversiones will only change cash (but not dollars). Money changers selling Bolivian money for Chilean can be found outside the railway station (last chance before Oruro or La Paz). If arriving from La Paz by train on Sat. p.m. without pesos, you may find nowhere to obtain them; try to get some before leaving Bolivia.

Consul The Bolivian Consulate (Vicuña Mackenna 1896) is open 0900-1230 and 1530-1830, Mon.-Fri., friendly, helpful.

Laundry Ramírez 1867, English spoken; Sotomayor 1984, both expensive.

Tourist Office José La Torre and Mackenna, T 211314. Map of town, arranges car hire. Open Mon.-Fri. 0900-2000, Sat.-Sun. 0900-1400.

Buses Daily bus services to Santiago (22 hrs., US$20), Arica (Geminis, 2130 and Tramaca, at 2100 daily, except 2230 on Sunday, US$10), Iquique (US$7) and Ovalle. Student reduction on Tramaca Bus. Also to San Pedro daily (US$3, US$4.50 return) with Tramaca on Félix Hoyos and Morales Moralitos, Av. Balmaceda y Ramírez (see below for schedules), Morales bus continues to Toconao Tues., Thurs., Sat.; to Chuquicamata (see below). Antofagasta, 3 hrs., several companies, e.g. Tramaca, US$3 and Libac, US$2.50 (cheapest). Bus to Salta, Argentina, Wed., a.m. and Sat. p.m. (2), 17 hrs., US$27. 2 companies: Geminis (Av. Granaderos) and Atahualpa.

Air Ladeco flights to Antofagasta and Santiago leave daily—except Sat.

Rail Antofagasta (Chile) and Bolivia Railway to Oruro and La Paz starts at Calama now. Ferrobus to La Paz, Fri., 1200, US$66 inc. food and drinks, 19 hrs. Bus leaves Antofagasta (Uribe 936) Wed. a.m. to connect with train leaving Calama at 1245 (check in advance), via Ollagüe and Uyuni, arriving in La Paz a.m. on Thurs. p.m. (all times are "pure fantasy"). No sleeping cars available from Calama to La Paz so take blankets or sleeping bag. The frontier is the scene of considerable palaver. There is a change of trains at the border (just after Ollagüe); your ticket is supposedly valid for both, but ensure that it is stamped with a reservation for the second, and be quick at the changeover. One class only to La Paz is US$25.10; to Oruro US$19; to Uyuni US$11.60; scenery beautiful but journey crowded (especially with smugglers), very slow and uncomfortable. Bus Calama-Ollagüe, Morales Moralitos Wed. 1100, US$7.50 or Trans. Abaroa, Vivar 1962, same price, leaves Tues. night, both heavily booked in advance. Many passengers leave train at Oruro, and go on by bus to La Paz (3¾ hrs.). For Potosí and Cochabamba change trains at Río Mulato and

Oruro respectively; note that the connection is not always assured. There is a freight-train to Potosí (free) some hours later, a bus one day later and a train on Sat. Note that before leaving you must visit (a) the Bolivian consulate for visa if needed, and (b) the railway station. It is advisable, but not necessary, to visit the railway office at Bolívar 255, Antofagasta (open Tues. 0900-1300 and 1500-1630, and Wed. 0900-1230) to make sure if there is a seat, but they can be purchased (with luck) at Calama (office opens Tues. 1500 and Wed. a.m.). You must have your passport with you when buying ticket. It can be very cold at night (-15°C) and into the day. Meals available at Ollagüe and Río Mulato (only for the conditioned).

N.B. Remember, if arriving from La Paz between October and March, then Chile is 1 hr. later than Bolivia.

Excursion Just E of Calama is the village of Chiu Chiu, with a very interesting old church and nearby a unique, perfectly circular, very deep lake. An ancient fortress and rock carvings are to be found in the Río Loa valley. This excursion is only possible by private or hired car.

At **Chuquicamata,** 16 km. from Calama at 2,800 metres, is the world's largest open-cast mine, a state-owned copper mine that used to belong to a U.S. firm. It is an astoundingly large hole. All the processes can be seen; there are guided tours with a film show three times a week on Mon., Wed. and Fri. at 1300 (daily in January and February only) from the Public Relations Office, near Puerta Una, taking 2 hrs. (very interesting but only given in Spanish). Register at Gate No. 1 beforehand; passport essential. You must wear a long-sleeved garment (shorts and skirts not allowed) if you wish to see the industrial plants.

Travellers can eat inexpensively beforehand at the Lions' Club, 200 metres diagonally uphill from the tourist-reception office. The clean, modern and pleasing town has about 30,000 people. (Guest house at east end of Plaza, nice, but book at Santiago or Antofagasta; overnight accommodation may be difficult.) There is a country club with a golf course at Río Loa. Within 30 km. of Chuquicamata there are several small towns and villages nestling in remote oases in the Andean massif. Due E of Chuquicamata, 37 km. on the way to Ayquina (see page 445), are the pre-Incaic ruins of Lasana, a national monument, with explanatory tablets. They are arguably the most impressive in Chile; the road from Calama through the *quebrada* is more scenic than that via Ollagüe.

Bus marked "Chuqui" from main plaza in Calama to Chuquicamata, US$0.50, ½ hr., frequent, then colectivo (marked "Local Chuqui") to mine, US$0.25. To Arica at 2200 (weekends at 2300), US$9, 9 hrs. To Antofagasta, ten a day, US$6 single. To Iquique at 2300. To Santiago at 1400, US$25, 24 hrs.

419 km. from Antofagasta, at 3,690 metres, on the dry floor of the Salar de Ollagüe near the Bolivian border, is **Ollagüe,** surrounded by a dozen volcanic peaks of over 5,000 metres. Population: 500; one service station (with unusual opening hrs.). A 77-km. spur railroad of metre gauge runs to the copper mines of Collahuasi, and from there a 13-km. aerial tram to the highest mine in the world: the Aucanquilcha, at 6,100 metres. Its sulphur is taken to Aruncha, a town at the foot of the volcano, to be refined. The highest passenger station in this spur is Yuma, at 4,400 metres. A train can be taken from Calama on Wed. at 1255, US$3.30 to Ollagüe, but if you stop off, you will have to hitch back, the daily freight trains are not allowed to take passengers. Bad unmade road from Ollagüe into Bolivia (see page 212).

At this altitude nights are cold, the days warm and sunny. Minimum temperature at Ollagüe is -20°C, and at the mine, -37°C. There are only 50 mm. of rain a year, and water is very scarce.

The main stock animals are llamas and alpacas, whose principal forage is the *ichu* bunch-grass covering the lower slopes. There is no timber. *Taqui*—dried llama dung— and *tola* scrub are used for cooking fires, but the main fuel is *yaretal*, a resinous moss growing in pillow-like masses in rocky outcrops from 3,500 to 5,000 metres high. Its calorific value is half that of bituminous coal. It apparently is an Ice Age relic, growing very slowly but now worked out in this area. Across the border in Bolivia there is plenty, which is used as fuel for the Laguna Verde sulphur mine. It is claimed, like mineral land, and broken up with dynamite into chunks for transport.

103 km. SE of Calama is **San Pedro de Atacama,** (2,436 metres, pop. 1,600), a small town more Spanish-Indian looking than is usual in Chile, well worth a visit. Both Diego de Almagro and Pedro de Valdivia stopped in this oasis (Valdivia's house on the main square may be visited by knocking at the green door next to it and asking for the key). A most impressive archaeological museum now under the care of the Universidad del Norte (Mon.-Fri., 0900-1300, 1500-1900; Sat., and Sun., 1000-1200, 1500-1900, entry US$0.30) is stocked with Indian skulls and artefacts, as well as the contents of the study of the late Father Le Paige, who used to run the museum. The Director's Brazilian wife gives an excellent guided tour in Spanish. Labels on displays are good (English pamphlet soon to be

available). Graham Greene tells us that "the striking feature of the museum is . . . the mummies of Indian women with their hair and dresses intact dating from before the Conquest, and a collection of paleolithic tools which puts the British Museum in the shade". Along the road are mounds of lava ash and dried-up geysers, making the landscape look rather lunar (see also below) as well as various archaeological remains. There are Tramaca buses daily at 0900, 1000 on Sun. and Morales Moralitos Mon.-Sat. 1700 (1600 in winter), 2 hrs., US$3 from Calama to San Pedro de Atacama, returning from the plaza at 1800 (Tramaca) and 0830 (Morales Moralitos, Tues.-Sat.). Extraordinary sunsets.

The Valle de la Luna, with fantastic landscapes caused by the erosion of salt mountains, is traversed by a road 13 km. before reaching San Pedro; the San Pedro-Calama bus does not pass through the valley but passes the old road which used to cross it (most bus drivers know where it is and will let you out—the sign is not visible if coming from Calama). From here it is a 3-hr. walk back to San Pedro (best done at sunset, take torch and food). Alternatively, a trip can be arranged through *Residencial Chiloé*, or Tourist Office on main plaza. A recommended guide is Robert Sánchez (he speaks German). To hire a 4-wheel-drive vehicle with driver costs US$25. Driving through the Valle de la Luna at sunset, with the Licancábur volcano, 5,916 metres, in the background, is a superb experience. If you are in your own car, make the detour on your way south (i.e. from Calama), as from N drifting sand makes uphill driving difficult. There are also some pre-Conquest, Indian ruins about 3 km. from San Pedro at Pucará, and a fine sandstone cave nearby. Pucará can be reached on foot by following the river bed (or crossing it, 3-5 times going upstream, if there is water in it), or US$1.20 for pick-up truck, seats 6.

Hotels *Hostería San Pedro*, recently refurbished, D, rec., Australian joint proprietors Luis Hernández and Mrs. Bobbee Andrews have prepared a short guide to the area in English, German, French, Spanish and Japanese; the *hostería* has a swimming pool, shop and a Copec petrol station, tents for hire, US$3 for 2 people, camping in grounds, US$0.75 p.p., 2 cabins with 6 and 3 beds, hot water, electricity 1800-2300, restaurant and bar, T 21-1511. *Residencial Chiloé*, F, good, hot water, friendly (if possible the Sra. will cook for vegetarians), trips for up to 4 people to Valle de la Luna arranged; next door is *Residencial Solcor*, G p.p., friendly, good meals; *Pukará*, F, good value; *Pensión Florida*, good, F, hot water; *Pensión y Restaurant Porvenir*, good value and excellent food (only one self-contained room with toilet), rec.; *Hostal-camping Takha-Takha*, F p.p., cold showers, hard beds, but friendly, restaurant (owner Sr. Q. López).

Restaurants *Juanita's*, reasonably priced; *Cobreloa.*

Swimming Pool Pozo Tres, 3 km. outside village, was drilled in the late 1950s by Unesco as part of a mineral exploration project, US$0.25 to swim, sometimes empty. Worth asking around before walking there. Camping.

Travel Agent Nada organizes local tours, to Valle de la Luna and villages on the Salar. Copper Tour Agency, at lobby of *Hotel Alfa*, Telex 325710, offers trips by estate car to the geysers (mornings), Valle de la Luna (afternoons), bargain for prices. Atacama Desert Tours on plaza, good, not cheapest, ask for Juan here or at *Takha-Takha.*

An interesting route from San Pedro de Atacama to Calama is to go north on a maintained road which passes the Baños de Puritama (27 km., truck drivers leaving from behind the police station for the sulphur mine at 0500 may give you a lift and collect you on return), then to the geysers at El Tatio. The geysers, at an altitude of 4,500 metres, are at their best 0630-0830. There is no public transport, so if going in a hired car, make sure the engine is suitable for very high altitudes and is protected with antifreeze; 4-wheel drive is preferable. It is easy to get lost if driving in the dark. Tour arranged by the Tourist Office, leaving 0430 for the thermal baths at 4,500 and 3,500 metres, costs US$20 p.p. Also ask the army outside San Pedro, who may give groups of 10-12 people a lift in a truck (US$3 p.p.); beware, it gets very cold in the truck. Taxi drivers Héctor Ochoa and Segundo Ugalde (contact through *Hostería San Pedro*) are rec. for this trip. From Calama, trips for El Tatio leave at 0300, continuing to San Pedro and the Valle de la Luna, arriving back at 2000 (US$15.50-20 p.p.). Villages between El Tatio and Calama include Caspana, beautifully set among hills, with an interesting museum, and **Ayquina**, in whose ancient church is enshrined the statue of the Virgin of Guadalupe. Her feast-day is September 8, when pilgrims come from far and wide. There is day-long group dancing to Indian rhythms on flute and drum. Towards sunset the Virgin is carried up a steep trail to a small thatched shrine, where the image and the people are blessed before the dancing is renewed at the shrine and all the way back to the village. The poor people of the hills gather stones and make toy houses all along the route: miniatures of the homes they hope to have some day. With a detour, the thermal waters and ruins of Baños de Turi may be visited and, 35 km. north, Copo, on a scenic road with herds of llama and alpaca, giant cacti and flamingos on the mudflats. The route to Calama continues via Lasana, Chiu Chiu or Chuquicamata.

SE of San Pedro, 39 km. on a reasonable unpaved road, is the lush oasis of **Toconao**, with some 500 inhabitants on the eastern shore of the lithium-salt lake Salar de Atacama. All houses are built of bricks of volcanic stone, which gives to the village a very characteristic appearance totally different from San Pedro. Its colonial clock tower is modelled in the same volcanic stone by the local craftsman and it has an attractive oasis called Quebrada de Jérez. (Worth visiting are the intricate irrigation systems on both sides of the canyon.) Morales Moralitos buses to Toconao from San Pedro Tues., Thurs., Sat. 1800, returning Wed., Fri., Sun. 0630, US$1. An alternative is to hitch from San Pedro (most traffic at weekends). Tour arranged by Tourist Office, US$13. Camping possible along river bank of Quebrada de Jérez.

Ask the *jefe de carabineros* in San Pedro or Toconao for a chance to go with police patrols to the Bolivian or Argentine border areas (paying your share of fuel).

From San Pedro de Atacama one can cross into Argentina over the pass of Huaytiquina to San Antonio de los Cobres. Travellers by car should make careful enquiries into road conditions (often impassible in rainy season, Jan.1 to mid-March, and blocked by snow in winter); gasoline may be bought in Calama or at *Hostería San Pedro*. Passport control and customs clearance must be undertaken in San Pedro.

The first village reached is Toconao (see above; cars registered at the entrance to the village); the Atacama desert can be seen in the distance. A detour can be made to the scenic villages of Camar (where handicrafts from cactus may be bought), Socaire (which has domesticated llamas, knitwear for sale) and Peine (woollen goods and knitwear); good views of the Quebrada de Jérez and Lascar Volcano. After a steep climb, you reach the Laguna Lejía (4,190 metres), where flamingoes abound. You then pass through the high plains of Huaytiquina (4,275 metres), where only a few herdsmen are found. Before reaching Catua, the first Argentine settlement, you cross the *salares* (salt lakes) and the road winds its way through the pass (3,880-4,200 metres). The highest altitude reached during the trip is at Chorrillos (4,560 metres). The road crosses the railway, descends into the ghost-like town of Agua Castilla, and after 8 km. reaches San Antonio de los Cobres. It is a further 3½ hours by car to Salta.

The next important port to the south is

Taltal, 309 km. S of Antofagasta, connected with it by the Pan-American Highway and a poor but scenic road along the coast. It is a nitrate and copper ore centre with 8,275 people. There is an airport, but few flights.

Hotels   *Hostería Taltal,* Esmeralda 671, T 101; *Casa Verde* (no sign), near central plaza, F with shared bath, clean, restaurant, rec. Several boarding houses; one, *La Goyesca,* Martínez 279, has a pleasant cheap restaurant. "The water supply is random, and the Salón de Te has no tea" (J. D. H. Smith).

Buses   Three a week to Santiago; several to Antofagasta.

Chañaral, a neglected looking port and town with wooden houses perched on the hillside and beset by water shortages, is 100 km. S of Taltal and 400 km. S of Antofagasta by sea or Pan-American Highway. Population, including Potrerillos and Caleta Barquito: 39,225. Anchorage is very near jagged rocks which rear out of the sea all round.

Hotels   *Hostería El Sarao; Jiménez; Mini; La Marina,* Merino Jarpa 562, F without bath, clean; *Hostería Chañaral,* D, with evening meal.

Buses   All companies on Merino Jarpa; 3 a day to Santiago; to Antofagasta at 0930 and 2100.

Copiapó, 240 km. S of Chañaral, capital of the Third (Atacama) Region, is an inland town in a ribbon of farms and orchards about 150 km. long on the river Copiapó, the river generally regarded as the southern limit of the Atacama desert. It is an attractive mining centre with an important mining school, and a population of 72,165. There is a monument to Juan Godoy, a pioneer of the mining industry. The plaza is interesting, with an unusual church and piped music on Sundays. The best mineralogical museum in Chile is at Colipí y Rodríguez, 1 block from Plaza de Armas (east), no fee; Tues.-Sat. 1000-1300, 1830-2200, Sun. 1000-1300. Many ores shown are found only in the Atacama desert. Also Museo Regional Atacama Copiapó; entrance US$0.35, interesting. Open Tues.-Sat. 0930-1300, 1600-1900, Sun. 1000-1300. The museum at the railway station is dull, but an early steam locomotive can be seen at the university on the northern highway. Airport.

Hotels   *Inglés,* Atacama 357, F; *Residencial Rodríguez,* Rodríguez 508; *Carrera* (small rooms round courtyard); *Los Carrera*, between Maipú and Chacabuco, F, reasonable value, good dining room; *Derby*, Yerba Buena 39, E, clean; *Maipú*, between *Los Carrera* and *Rodríguez*, F, rec. *Willy Beer* restaurant, Maipú 386, has fancy hot-dogs, hamburgers and entertainment. *El Corsario*, Atacama 245, good restaurant; *La Chispa*, Chacabuco 157, opp. bus station, good, cheap; *Bavaria Restaurant*, on main square, excellent but not cheap.

Tourist Office   Los Carrera 691, T 2838.

About 70 km. W of Copiapó is the port of *Caldera,* which has a pier of 230 metres; 1½ km. to the S there is a terminal for the loading of iron ore.

Hotels   *Costanera*, Wheelwright 543, C inc. tax, takes credit cards, unwelcoming; *Hostería Parque del Sol*, Wheelwright 750, D inc. tax, cabins with bath and kitchen, view over bay; *Portal del Inca*, Carvalho 945, C inc. tax, cabins with bath and kitchen, English spoken, restaurant not bad, order breakfast on previous night; *Pucará*, Ossa Cerda 460, E; *Los Andes*, Edwards 360, F.

Camping   Bahía Inglesa, 6 km. W of Highway, 3 km. S of Caldera. Swimming in the Pacific.

A road runs NE through the pass of San Francisco in the Andes to Tinogasta, in Argentina (suitable only for 4 wheel-drive vehicles, often closed by landslides). South of the pass rises the Ojos del Salado mountain, believed to be the second highest peak in the Americas; its height is now thought to be in the range of 6,875-6,887 metres. There is fumarolic activity 300 metres below the summit of Ojos del Salado, which makes it a contender with Cotopaxi in Ecuador for the title of the world's highest active volcano.

COPIAPO TO ILLAPEL (2)

The second geographic zone, lying between the valleys of the Copiapó and the Aconcagua, contains the southern half of the Third (Atacama) Region and the whole of the Fourth (Coquimbo) (population at 1982 census, 419,956). The zone is about 600 km. long.

This is a transitional zone between the northern desert and the fruitful heartland. S of Copiapó the central valley is cut across by transverse spurs of mountain which link the Andes and the coastal *cordillera*. Between these spurs several rivers flow westwards. Southwards the desert gives way slowly to dry scrub and bush interspersed with sand dunes. Winter rainfall (there is no rain in summer) is still light and lasts only a short time: it is about 115 mm. at Copiapó and 500 mm. at Illapel. In the river valleys under irrigation, fruit, vines, and barley are grown, and some alfalfa for cattle. There are many goats.

Vallenar (airport), inland up the Huasco valley, is 144 km. S of Copiapó; it is the second city of the Third (Atacama) Region, with a population of 42,000. Good wines are produced in the Huasco valley, in particular a sweet wine known as Pajarete. A road runs down the valley to *Huasco* (Hotel Miramar), an interesting port. 1½ km. S of Huasco is a terminal for loading iron ore from the deposits at Algarrobal, inland 35 km. N of Vallenar. Population: 7,065.

Vallenar Hotels   *Hostería Vallenar* (good); *Cecil*, Calle Prat, E with bath and hot water, clean, rec.

La Serena, on the coast 187 km. S of Vallenar, 480 km. N of Santiago (95,400 people), is the capital of the Fourth (Coquimbo) Region, an attractive town built on a hillside, which has become a tourist resort. It was remodelled in the 1950s and is now one of the pleasantest towns in Chile, with many colonial-style buildings, pretty gardens and a lot of *azulejos*, or coloured tiles. It has a Cathedral, 29 churches and several old convents. Many rodeos are held, and Chilean independence is celebrated on September 20 with a huge open-air picnic on the sands at nearby Coquimbo. The most popular nearby beaches are Peñuelas, half way to Coquimbo, and La Herradura. A road (about one-third paved) runs 500 km. E over the pass of Agua Negra (4,775 metres) to San Juan in northern Argentina (closed in winter). The climate is often damp and rarely hot. Market on Sun. New market (La Recova) on Cienfuegos, cheap food and souvenirs.

History   La Serena was founded by Juan de Bohón, aide to Pedro de Valdivia, in 1544, destroyed by Diaguita Indians in 1546, rebuilt by Francisco de Aguirre in 1552, and sacked by the

English pirate Sharpe in 1680. Legends of buried treasure at Guayacán Bay, frequented by Drake, persist.

The Archaeological Museum, in a colonial-style building, has an interesting collection of Diaguita and Molle Indian exhibits, especially of most attractively decorated pottery, at corner of Calles Córdovez and Cienfuegos. It is open Tues.-Sat. 0900-1300, 1600-1900, Sun. 1000-1300, entrance, US$0.35. There is a mineralogical museum in the Technical University, Calle A. Muñoz between Benavente and Infante (for geologists, open Mon.-Fri. 0930-1230, free).

Hotels *Mediterráneo,* Córdovez y Cienfuegos, Casilla 212, T 215233, A, rec.; *Francisco de Aguirre,* Córdovez 210, B inc. tax and breakfast, shower, good rooms, reasonable restaurant; *Londres,* Córdovez 566, D, fair restaurant; *Pucará,* Balmaceda 319, T 211966, C with bath and breakfast, good; *Alameda,* D (less without bath), Av. de Aguirre 450, clean and comfortable, towels supplied; opp. is private *hospedaje* at No. 481, E, clean, friendly; *Residencial Brasilia,* Brasil 555, E, good, friendly; *Res. La Florida,* Brasil 700 block, F good value, friendly; *Res. Chile,* Matta 561, basic, clean, E, hot shower, breakfast, rec. *Residencial El Loa,* Bernardo O'Higgins 362, E with shower, good inexpensive home cooking (US$2.50-3 per main meal), friendly; *Residencial Petit,* Edo de la Barra 586, F, basic; *Residencial Americanas,* Calle Andrés Bello 800 block, E, without bath, grubby; *Residencial Carreras,* Los Carrera 682, T 51-213646, E, clean, comfortable, cheapest; unnamed *residencial* at Los Carrera 880, F, OK. Family pensión of Isabel Ahumada, Eduardo de la Barra 315, D. *Casa del Turista,* Colón 318, E, clean, hot water, friendly. *Youth hostel,* Av. Francisco de Aguirre 424. **Motel** *Les Movettes,* Av. de Mar, good.

Campsite Maki Payi, 153 Vegas Norte, about 5 km. N of La Serena, near sea, friendly, rec., self-contained cabins available; US$3.10 per tent and US$9.50 p.p. for chalet. Also on the beach near the Drive-In *Donde ya Sabemos* (expensive snacks).

Restaurants *Club Social,* Córdovez 516, unpretentious but excellent. *Restaurant Galeón,* Brasilia, good seafood; *La Barca,* Av. del Mar, good seafood; *Mi Casa,* Av. Aguirre 596, 2nd floor, cheap *almuerzos*; *Café Milan,* Balmaceda 655, good pastries. *Rapsodia,* Arturo Prat 470, tea house with good cakes; *Torreón,* Prat 545, good coffee. Good selection of cheap meals on 1st floor of market hall. Copec gas station on S-bound side of Pan-American Highway, excellent food. N.B. All restaurants are closed on Sundays.

Discotheques Oriente, Balmaceda 677.

Italian Vice-Consulate Plaza de Armas, Los Carrera 446, also Alitalia representative.

Post Office Plaza de Armas.

Tourist Office Prat y Malta, 1st floor, T 213134 (open Mon.-Fri. 0830-1300, 1430-1800); kiosk in market area (Cienfuegos y Prat) and in bus terminal.

Transport Bus terminal, El Santo y Amunátegui, in Coquimbo direction. Buses daily to La Calera and Santiago at 0800 and evening, 8 hrs, US$6-8.50; to Arica, US$20; to Calama, US$17, 16 hrs. To Valparaíso, 7 hrs., Pullman at 1300 and 2315, Incabus at 1300, US$8. By bus to Antofagasta takes 13 hrs., US$10-14 and to Iquique 20 hrs, US$21. Bus to Vicuña, Transportes Via Elqui, Calle Peni y Benavente, 9 daily; to Coquimbo, from Av. Aguirre, US$0.25. Bus to San Juan, Argentina, US$26, on Tues. (before attempting this route, check that the Agua Negra pass is open).

Excursion La Serena is at the mouth of the Elqui river valley, where the Nobel Prize-winning poet Gabriela Mistral was born. She described the valley as "confined yet lofty, many-sided yet simple, rustic yet a mining area". The road up the valley has been rebuilt and paved as far as Vicuña; "its branches all lead to fertile nooks, to shady vegetation, to dense groves, to gardens fed by the very sap of the hills". Except for Vicuña, most of the tiny towns have but a single street. Of the *elquinos*, the people of the valley, she says that "even the most taciturn of them come out with witty and charming remarks". There are still a few descendants of the Diaguitas, the tribe that inhabited the valley at one time.

Vicuña (66 km.) capital of the valley, is on the way to Rivadavia at an altitude of 600 metres and has a population of 19,395. Beautiful hand-woven rugs may be purchased at the village of Chapilca (25 km. from Vicuña). There are mines, vineyards and orchards in the district, which produces pisco and dried fruits. Vicuña is picturesque, fairly clean and friendly; it is within reach by car (120 km.) of Termas del Toro in the mountains. A small Gabriela Mistral Museum has been opened. Her grave is at Monte Grande, 20 km. S of Rivadavia. Good cinema, on plaza on San Martín, open on Fri., Sat. and Sun. Post office in public services building on same plaza. Tourist Office kiosk on Av. de las Delicias will also arrange a visit to the Pisco distillery, Capel, between 0800-1200 and 1400-1800. Alternatively, you can walk there; walking in farmland around Vicuña, for instance to Peralillo (7 km. along Route 41), is delightful. Good views from Cerro La Virgen, N of town. Last bus Vicuña-La Serena at 1815, others in day, US$1.25, colectivo US$1.60; 2 buses a day to Santiago, US$8.

Hotels *Hostería,* swimming pool; *Gran Hotel Jasna,* Gabriela Mistral 542, F with bath (cheaper without), hot water, charming, clean, safe restaurant; *Residencial Moderna*, at No. 718 same street, F, full board available, no hot water; camping at airstrip a few km. from town (ask police).

Restaurants *Halley*, Gabriela Mistral 404, not cheap but good; *Club Social* on same street; *Café Cecilia* (opens 1800); 2 or 3 good bakers and *Frutería Guayaquil* on Gabriela Mistral.

The road to Rivadavia continues up the valley, in which there are orchards and orange groves. Beyond Rivadavia the road runs to the small towns of Paihuano and Pisco Elqui (*Hotel Plaza*, F) (34 km.), where you can visit old-fashioned pisco distilleries. Table wine is made at Pisco Elqui.

Up the Elqui valley, beyond Monte Grande, on the road to El Colorado, are several Ashram places, some of which welcome visitors (e.g. Rama Mission, 12 km. from Monte Grande); one can camp ("a firm belief in UFOs is a help" - Quentin Crewe).

The La Serena district is one of the astronomical centres of the world. On a peak about 35 km. S of Vicuña is the new Cerro Tololo Inter-American Observatory, which has a 400-cm. (the largest in the Southern Hemisphere), a 150-cm., a 100-cm., a 90-cm. and two 40-cm. reflecting telescopes. Visits only on Saturdays and Sundays at 0900 and 1300 and permission must first be obtained from the AURA office in La Serena (near new University) or write to Observatorio, Cerro Tololo, Casilla 603, La Serena in English or Spanish. In peak season book a week in advance. No transport provided, takes 1½ hrs. by car from La Serena, or take taxi from Vicuña, hitch, or Vicuña bus from La Serena to AURA sign (about 1 hr.), walk 3 km. to entrance, then wait for other visitors. On Cerro La Silla, 100 km. NE, is the European Southern Observatory, with 13 more large telescopes, the largest of which is 360 cm. Visiting with permission from ESO, Av. Alonso de Córdoba 3107, Las Condes, Santiago, or AURA in La Serena; free excursion every Sun.

Only open on first Saturday of the month, 54 km. from La Silla, are three large telescopes, a 250 cm., and a 100 cm. run by the Carnegie Institution of Washington, and a 61-cm. telescope owned by University of Toronto. Permission to visit must be obtained from office at Colina El Pino, La Serena.

Coquimbo, 11 km. S of La Serena and on the same bay, is a port of considerable importance and with several industries. The city has one of the best harbours on the coast. A pleasant walk is along Aldunate, past the port and fishmeal factory to view a guano covered rock, 50 metres offshore, with many seabirds, penguins and an occasional sealion (binoculars a help). Population: 92,105.

Hotels (generally cheaper and less full than La Serena) *El Bucanero* at La Herradura, on Guayacán Bay, 1½ km. from Coquimbo port, listed "de luxe" but is not; *La Valle*, F, in front of bus station. Cheap hotels near bus terminal at south end of Aldunate, e.g. *Castex*, No. 459, a rambling barn with large rooms, F.

Campsites Guanaqueros, at km. 430 on the Pan-American Highway, 30 km. S of Coquimbo. Camping also available at Morrillos (several sites), km. 442 on the Pan-American Highway. Both are beside clean beaches. There are also several campsites between Coquimbo and Los Vilos.

Restaurants *La Barca; Mai Lan Fan* (excellent Chinese cuisine), *Don Pepe* (seafood).

Museum In 1981 heavy rain uncovered 39 ancient burials of humans and llamas which had been sacrificed. A small museum has been built behind the Post Office to exhibit these.

Excursions Good beaches to the S at Totoralillo (good swimming), Guanaqueros (30 km.) and Tongoy (56 km.). If motoring, watch the fuel gauge; the nearest service station is at Coquimbo. In the suburb of Guayacán there is one of Eiffel's steel churches.

From here to Santiago, the Pan-American Highway mainly follows the coastline, passing many beautiful coves, alternatively rocky and sandy, with good surf, but the water is very cold, as is the air. The last stretch before Santiago is through green valleys with rich blue clover and wild artichokes. Beware, the green caterpillars crossing the road in November sting!

From La Serena or Coquimbo, 51 km. SE by road, is the little town of **Andacollo.** (colectivo, US$2.40; bus, US$1.70—last 20 km. of road very bad). Here, on December 24 to 28, is held a most picturesque religious ceremony. The pilgrimage to the shrine of the miraculous Virgen del Rosario de Andacollo is the occasion for ritual dances dating from a pre-Spanish past. The church is huge. Alluvial gold washing and manganese and copper mining in the area. No hotel, but some *pensiones*; during the festival private houses rent beds and some let you pay for a shower. Colectivos run to the festival from Calle Benavente, near Colocolo, in La Serena, but "purists" walk (torch and good walking shoes essential). 2 villages are passed on the route, which starts on the paved highway, then goes along a railway track and lastly up a steep, dusty hill.

Ovalle is S of Coquimbo in the valley of the Limarí river, inland from the sea. There are bus services from Coquimbo and La Serena (US$2.25 return). It is the centre of a fruit, sheep-rearing, and mining district. Population: 72,765. 115 km. S by gravel road is the town of Combarbalá, where there is a TB sanatorium. Campsite. A 30 km. road runs NW to the small port of Tongoy, which has become quite popular among the locals for their summer break. The Paloma dam, at the confluence of the Grande and Huatulame rivers, SE of Ovalle, is one of the largest in Chile.

Hotels *Hotel de Turismo; Quisco; American Hotel; Residencial Lolita*, F, friendly, clean; *Residencial Londres*, F. *Residencial Atenas*, Socos, F. Youth Hostel, Vicuña Mackenna 783. **Restaurant** *El Bosco*, Benavente 88, good, cheap.

Museum Museo Regional, Calle Vicuña Mackenna 521, open Tues.-Sat. 0900-1300, 1500-1900, Sun. 1000-1300, has 3 rooms, information on petroglyphs.

Excursions The Parque Nacional Valle del Encanto, about 22 km. from Ovalle, has Indian petroglyphs as well as dramatic boulders, its own microclimate, cacti and lizards. No local bus service; you must take long distance bus and ask to be dropped off; may be necessary to hitch back. Camping facilities are being upgraded. The Parque Nacional Fray Jorge (40 km.) has interesting forest land, which contrasts with the otherwise barren surroundings. Round trip in taxi, US$30. 2 km. N of Ovalle along Monte Patria road is Balnearia Los Peñones, on a clean shallow river.

Termas de Socos, 35 km. S of Ovalle, has fine thermal springs (entrance US$1.30), a good hotel (C) and a campsite (about US$1.50 p.p.) nearby. Bus US$2.

About 165 km. S of Ovalle by road, and 59 km. by new paved road from Los Vilos, is *Illapel,* in the basin of the river Choapa (Hotel). Population: 25,600. Fruit, grains and cattle are raised in the valley.

Los Vilos, 280 km. S of Coquimbo, is a small seaside resort with frequent launches to the off-shore Isla de La Reina and a beautiful nearby beach (26 km. S) at *Pichidangui.*

Hotels in Los Vilos *Cabañas Antulanquen*, B (negotiable during off season), good service, own porch, kitchenette, rec.; *Hostería Puquey*, good restaurant, clean, honest, D, good restaurant; *Hostería Arrayán*, clean, E. *Bellavista*, F, shared bath, hot water, clean. Campsite on Av. El Bosque. **In Pichidangui** *Hotel Kon-Tiki*, owned by the army—sometimes not open to the public. The *Panamerican Motel* is right on the highway, and is a convenient stopping place between La Serena and Viña del Mar or Santiago; it claims to be American style, which will surprise Americans, but is quite good.

Just south of Pichidangui is Los Molles, a small town where many wealthy residents of Santiago have their summer homes. There are two small hotels, one down at the beach and the other on the cliff overlooking the beach. *Restaurant La Pirata Suiza*, excellent European-style cooking, run by a Swiss couple.

See page 438 for list of service stations between Santiago and the Peruvian border.

SANTIAGO AND THE HEARTLAND (3)

(From the River Aconcagua to the River Bío-Bío)

Nearly 70% of the people of Chile live in the comparatively small heartland. The capital, Santiago, is here, and so is the largest port: Valparaíso. The rural density of population in the area is exceptional for Latin America: it is as high as 48 to the square km. in the Central Valley running S from Santiago to Concepción.

		Population ('000)	
Region	Provinces	1975	1982
V (Valparaíso)	Petorca, Los Andes, San Felipe de Aconcagua, Quillota, Valparaíso, San Antonio, Isla de Pascua	1,124	1,205
Metropolitan	Santiago, Chacabuco, Cordillera, Maipo, Melipilla, Talagante	3,806	4,295
VI (O'Higgins)	Cachapoal, Colchagua, Cardenal Caro	529	585
VII (Maule)	Curicó, Talca, Linares, Maule	685	723
VIII (Bío Bío)	Ñuble, Concepción, Arauco, Bío-Bío	1,406	1,517

CHILEAN HEARTLAND AND SANTIAGO

From a third to half of the width of the area is taken up by the Andes, which are formidably high in the northern sector; at the head of the river Aconcagua the peak of Aconcagua, the highest in the Americas, rises to 6,964 metres. S of Talca, and to the W of the main range, there is a series of active volcanoes; the region suffers from earthquakes. There is a mantle of snow on the mountains: at Aconcagua it begins at 4,300 metres; at Curicó at 3,350; at Bío-Bío at 1,980. The lower slopes are covered with dense forests. Between the forest and the snowline there are alpine pastures which narrow towards the S; during the summer cattle are driven up to these pastures to graze.

The coastal range takes up another third of the width. It is lower here than in the northern desert, but the shoreline is still unbroken; it is only at Valparaíso, San Antonio and Talcahuano (the port for Concepción) that good harbourage is to be found. The coastal range is over 2,130 metres high in the N, but it falls gradually to about 600 metres near Concepción.

Between the coastal range and the Andes lies the Central Valley; most rivers cross it at right angles and cut their way to the sea through narrow canyons in the coastal range, but the Maule and the Bío-Bío have broad valleys along the whole of their courses. The valley of the Aconcagua is separated by a mountainous spur from the valley of the Mapocho, in which Santiago lies, but from Santiago to Concepción the Central Valley is continuous. The land here is extremely fruitful.

There is rain during the winter in the heartland, but the summers are dry. The rain increases to the S. On the coast at Viña del Mar it is 483 mm. a year; at Talcahuano it is 1,168 mm., but is somewhat less inland. Temperatures, on the other hand, are higher inland than on the coast. There is frost now and then in the Central Valley, but very little snow falls.

Santiago, founded by Pedro de Valdivia in 1541, is the fifth largest city in South America, with 4m people, and one of the most beautifully set of any, standing in a wide plain, 600 metres above the sea. The city is crossed from E to W by the Mapocho River, which passes through an artificial stone channel, 40 metres wide, spanned by several bridges. Public gardens, laid out with admirable taste, are filled with flowers and kept in good order. The magnificent chain of the Andes, with its snow-capped heights, is in full view, rain and smog permitting, for much of the year: there are peaks of 6,000 metres about 100 km. away. More than half the country's manufacturing is done here; it is essentially a modern capital, full of bustle, noise, traffic, smog (tables for which are published in the daily papers) and skyscrapers.

The centre of the city lies between the Mapocho and the Avenida O'Higgins. From the Plaza Baquedano (Plaza Italia), in the E of the city, the Mapocho flows to the NW and the Avenida O'Higgins runs to the SW. From Plaza Baquedano the Calle Merced runs due W of the Plaza de Armas, the heart of the city; it lies 4 blocks S of Mapocho station on Avenida Presidente Balmaceda, on the southern bank of the Mapocho. On the eastern and southern sides of Plaza de Armas there are arcades with shops; on the northern side the Post Office and the City Hall; and on the western side the Cathedral and the archbishop's palace. The Cathedral, much rebuilt, contains a recumbent statue in wood of St. Francis Xavier, and the chandelier which lit the first meetings of Congress after the liberation; it also houses an interesting museum of religious art and historical pieces. In the Palacio de la Real Audiencia on the Plaza de Armas is the Museo Histórico Nacional, which covers the period from the Conquest until 1925 (well worthwhile). A block W of the Cathedral is the Congress building; the Congress has held no sittings since 1973. Nearby are the law courts. At Calle Merced 864, close to the Plaza de Armas, is the Casa Colorada, built in 1769, the home of the Governor in colonial days and then of Mateo de Toro, first President of Chile. It is now the Museum of the History of Santiago, opened in 1981.

The Avenida O'Higgins (usually known as the Alameda) runs through the heart of the city for over 3 km. It is 100 metres wide, and ornamented with gardens and statuary: the most notable are the equestrian statues of Generals O'Higgins and San Martín; the statue of the Chilean historian Benjamín Vicuña Mackenna who, as mayor of Santiago, beautified Santa Lucía hill; and the great monument in honour of the battle of Concepción in 1879.

From the Plaza Baquedano, where there is a statue of General Baquedano and the Tomb of the Unknown Soldier, the Alameda skirts, on the right, Santa Lucía hill, and on the left, the Catholic University. Santa Lucía hill, a cone of rock rising steeply to a height of 70 metres, can be scaled from the Caupolicán esplanade, on which, high on a rock, stands a statue of that Mapuche leader, but the ascent from the northern side of the hill, where there is an equestrian statue of Diego de Almagro, is easier. There are striking views of the city from the top (reached by a series of stairs), where there is a fortress, the Hidalgo Castle (the platform of which is its only colonial survival): each day the report from its mid-day gun reverberates down the city streets. In the basement is an Indian historical museum, often closed. It is best to descend the eastern side, to see the small Plaza Pedro Valdivia with its waterfalls and statue of Valdivia. The area is famous, at night, for its gay community.

Beyond the Hill the Alameda goes past the neo-classical National Library on the right, which also contains the national archives. Beyond, on the left, between Calle San Francisco and Calle Londres, is the oldest church in Santiago: the red-walled church and monastery of San Francisco. Inside is the small statue of the Virgin which Valdivia carried on his saddlebow when he rode from Peru to Chile. Beside the church is the Museum of Colonial Art, well worth seeing (Av. Bernardo O'Higgins 834). On the left, a little further along, is the University of Chile; the Club de la Unión is almost opposite. N of Plaza de la Libertad, hemmed in by the skyscrapers of the Civic Centre, is the **Palacio de la Moneda** (1805), containing historic relics, paintings and sculpture, and the elaborate "Salón Rojo" used for official receptions. With some persistence, you can see some of the rooms by applying at about 1400 to the building's secretariat. The Moneda was damaged by air attacks during the military coup of September 11, 1973; repairs are now completed and the presidential offices have been restored.

In front of the Palace is the statue of Arturo Alessandri Palma, who was President of the Republic for two terms. The Municipal Theatre is on Calle Agustinas with Calle San Antonio 149, and nearby on Calle Nueva York is the Bolsa de Comercio. Further along, any of the streets on the left leads to the great Parque O'Higgins (Parque O'Higgins subway station on Line 2), with a small lake, playing fields, tennis courts, swimming pool, an open-air stage for local songs and dances, a discothèque, the racecourse of the Club Hípico, an amusement park, Fantasilandia, admission US$2, and a group of about twenty good "typical" restaurants, some craft shops, the Museo del Huaso and a small insect and shellfish museum at El Pueblito (local 12). Cars are not allowed in the Parque. The Alameda runs westwards to Plaza Ercilla, on the southern side of which is the Alameda (Central) railway station for the S. On Avenida Matucana, running N from Plaza Ercilla, is the very popular Parque Quinta Normal park. The Natural History Museum, in the Parque, has an excellent exhibition of Chilean landscapes. A railway museum has recently opened in the Quinta Normal; it has 13 steam engines built between 1884 and 1953 (open Tues.-Sun. 1100-1300, 1400-1900, on Thurs. till 2000). The Museo de Aviación by the Parque Quinta Normal (Av. Portales 3530) is also worth a visit; T 90 888. There is a Museo de la Escuela Militar, Los Militares 4800, Las Condes, with displays on O'Higgins, the Conquest and the Pacific War. Also interesting are the Museo Chileno de Arte Precolombino, Bandera 361, recommended, open Tues.-Sat. 1000-1800, Sun. (free) 1000-1400 and the Museo de la Merced, MacIver 341 (colonial art). The Centro Cultural Mapuche, José Victorino Lastarria, near the Alameda, has art galleries and a good café. The Alhambra Palace, Compañía 1340 (with Amunátegui) is a national monument sponsored by the Society of Arts; it stages exhibitions of paintings (open Mon.-Fri., T 80875).

On Calle Dieciocho, some 5 blocks S of the Alameda, is the Palacio Cousiño, a large elaborate mansion amongst crumbling buildings and shanties; it contains some good oriental rugs and second-rate European furniture. It is run by the Municipality as a museum and official guest house. Can be seen by written permission from the Municipalidad. Open Tues.-Sun. 1000-1300.

There are several other parks in Santiago, but perhaps the most notable is the

Parque Forestal, due N of Santa Lucía hill and immediately S of the Mapocho. The National Museum of Fine Arts is in the wooded grounds and is an extraordinary example of neo-Moorish architecture; it has a large display of Chilean and foreign painting and sculpture, and art exhibitions are held several times a year (closed for repair in 1987/88), the Art School is in the building. Also in the Parque Forestal is the Museo de Arte Contemporáneo, containing Chilean art (also closed in 1987/88). The Parque Balmaceda, E of Plaza Baquedano, is perhaps the most beautiful in Santiago (the Museo de los Tajamares is here), but the sharp, conical hill of San Cristóbal, to the NE of the city, is the largest and most interesting. A funicular railway goes up the 300-metre-high hill every few minutes from 1000-1830 Mon.-Fri., 0900-2000 Sat. and Sun., for US$2 return. There is also a chairlift (same price) from Av. Pedro de Valdivia Norte (only taxis go there), and an orange bus and colectivos run up for US$0.75. The hill has several summits: on one stands a colossal statue of the Virgin, which is floodlit at night; on another is the astronomical observatory of the Catholic University; and on a third a solar observatory (Victoria Castle). The hill is very well laid out with terraces, gardens, and paths; there are good restaurants with splendid views from the terrace, especially at night, and an Enacoteca, or exhibition of Chilean wines, with restaurant and tastery. (You can taste one of the three "wines of the day", US$0.30, and buy if you like.) If you alight at the intermediate stop on the funicular railway, there is a cultural centre in a small castle, where free concerts are held on Sundays. There are two good swimming pools. The Zoological Gardens are near the foot of the hill (interesting exhibits—entrance US$0.75). The interesting Central Market is at Puente 21 de Mayo.

Ballet is popular. During the summer, free performances are given in the city parks, but seats are usually hard to get. The theatre (there are 12 houses) is more active than in most Latin American capitals. The Lastarria neighbourhood (Universidad Católica metro, Plaza Mulato Gil de Castro) is worth a visit for those interested in antique shops (for instance Mulato Gil de Castro, on Alameda and Av. José V. Lastarria, an old estate with crafts, antiques, etc.), art studios and theatres.

Things to do   Daily list of events in *El Mercurio* should be consulted. During November there is a free art fair on the banks of the Mapocho River flowing through Parque Forestal, lasting a fortnight.

In October or November there are a sumptuous flower show and an annual agricultural and industrial show (known as Fisa) in Parque Cerrillos. Religious festivals and ceremonies continue throughout Holy Week, when a priest ritually washes the feet of 12 men. The image of the Virgen del Carmen (patron of the Armed Forces) is carried through the streets by cadets on July 16.

Climate   In the central region (including Santiago and Valparaíso) the climate is Mediterranean: temperatures can reach 29°C in January, but fall to 13°C (3°C at night) in July. Days are usually hot, the nights cool.

Hotels (Lowest prices, do not include 16% tax)

		Our Price Range	1989 Price Single	Double
San Cristóbal Sheraton	Av. Santa María 1742	L	125	135
Galerías	San Antonio 65	L	80	90
Carrera *	Teatinos 180	L	90	100
El Conquistador *	Miguel Cruchaga 920	A	60	75
Santa María *	S. María 2050	A	52	64
Tupahue *	San Antonio 477	A	61	69
El Hotel de Don Tito *	Huérfanos 578	A	29	46
Los Españoles	Los Españoles 2539	B	26	44
Orly	Pedro de Valdivia 27	A	40	52
Las Acacias de Vitacura	El Manantial 1782	B	20	32
Santa Lucía (garage 2 blocks away)	Huérfanos 779	B	28	38
Panamericano *	Teatinos 320 y Huérfanos	B	27	35
Metrópoli (ex-Miami)	Dr. Sótero del Río 465	C	15	20

* Breakfast included.

Key to Santiago Map 1 Quinta Normal, 2 *Hotel Panamericano*, 3 US Consulate,
4 SAS (Scandinavian), 5 *Hotel Carrera*, 6 Ministry of Finance, 7 Alameda Station, 8 La Moneda,
10 Argentine Air lines, 11 Transradio, 12 City Museum, Casa Colorada, 14 Pre-Colombian Museum,
16 Palace of Justice, 17 Congress, 18 Mapocho Station, 19 The Cathedral, 20 *Hotel
City*, 21 Air France, 22 Lastarria neighbourhood, 23 Exprinter SA, 24 PSNC (B. Cal.), 25 Lufthansa,
26 University of Chile, 31 *Chez Henry*, 32 Post and Telegraph Office, 33 Santo Domingo (burnt
out), 34 Entel, telephone company for long distance calls, 36 *El Pollo Dorado*, 37 San Francisco
Church, 38 Teatro Municipal, 39 KLM, 40 *Restaurant Nuria*, 41 *Hotel Santa Lucia*, 43 Merced
Church, 44 National Library, 46 Museum of Fine Arts, 47 Catholic University,

Hostal del Parque, Merced 294, A, excellent, central; *Monte Carlo*, Subercaseaux 209, bottom of Santa Lucía, rec., modern, restaurant, with heating, B; *City*, Compañía, between Puente and Bandera, central, clean, hot water, reasonably priced, rec.; *Gran Palace*, Huérfanos 1178, B, with shower, clean, noisy rooms facing street (others quiet), good restaurant; *Apart-Hotel* (ex-*Agustinas*), Agustinas 1990, clean, quiet at back, C, rec. *São Paulo*, San Antonio 357, T 398031/2/3, D with bath, clean, good value; *Residencial Mery*, Pasaje República 36 (T 696-8883), big green building down an alley, E, hot showers, quiet, rec.; *Res. Alemania*, República 220, T 712388, E, hot water, nice house. *Du Maurier*, Moneda 1512, E, handy for catching early (0630) Aerobus Tour Express; *Residencia Alicia Adasme*, Moneda 2055, T 6960787, hot water, friendly, with breakfast, C; *Residencial Tabita* (Tabita Gutiérrez), Príncipe de Gales 81 (cul-de-sac off Moneda between Amunátegui and Teatinos, T 715700), E p.p., clean, safe, central, temperamental hot showers upstairs, popular; *Residencial Londres*, Londres 54 (T 382215), near San Francisco Church, with breakfast, former mansion, Victorian furniture, some gloomy rooms, otherwise rec. repeatedly, E, more with bath (often full after 1000—don't confuse with *Hotel Londres* opp., which is not rec.). *París*, Calle París, central, E with bath, quiet, clean, also short-stay; *Libertador*, Av. O'Higgins 853, E-D with bath, helpful, rec., will store luggage, good restaurant, bar, roof top pool; *Imperio*, O'Higgins 2879, near central station, E with bath, good restaurant; *Antiguo Palace*, San Alfonso 24, 2 blocks E of Central Station, 1 metro stop from southern bus station, F, good value, clean. *Caribe*, E, San Martín 851, clean, basic, hot showers, convenient to centre and bus station, safe to leave luggage but mainly short-stay; *Res. Santo Domingo*, Santo Domingo 735, near Maclver, central, E with full board, good cheap lunches Mon.-Fri.; *Indiana*, Rosas 1339, convenient for buses to centre, only front rooms with bath, hot water, back rooms poor, basic but OK, E; *España*, Morandé 510, D/E without bath, hot water, clean, friendly; *Cervantes*, Morandé 631, D, T 696-7966, good value but noisy; *Nuevo Valparaíso*, Morandé 791 (T 715698), F, hot shower, shared showers, basic but clean; *Gran*, Morandé y San Pablo, F-E (with bath), simple but OK, short and long stay. **N.B.** Many hotels on Morandé, Gen. Mackenna, San Martín and San Pablo are convenient for northern bus terminal, but are in the red light district and are therefore cheap in both senses of the word.

Sra Marta, Amengual 035, Alameda Alt. 4.400 T 797592 lado Norte (metro Ecuador), F p.p., good family accommodation. *Residencial O'Higgins*, San Ignacio 882, friendly, cold water only, no kitchen, US$46 s, US$62 d, per month. Sra. Marianne Corvely's *pensión*, Los Jardines 462 B, rec.; the owner is a professional translator and works as a tourist guide. Sra. Maria Aguilera, Av. Eliadoro Yáñez 809, apt. 93, (metro, Salvador) also rents rooms, very friendly. *Hospedaje* at Amunátegui 712, F, hot shower, friendly, incl. breakfast. *Hospedaje* (unnamed) at Almirante Latorre 617, T 696-8700 (nearest metro Toesca—20 min. walk from centre), F p.p., clean, hot water, rec.; private house/*residencia* at Los Algarrobos 2135, E incl. 3 large meals, friendly, helpful landlady. *Casa del Estudiante Americano*, Huérfanos 1891, G p.p., good dormitory accommodation—acts as youth hostel out of season, must be in bed by 2200 and out by 1000 (Metro Los Héroes—7 blocks from centre over motorway). *YMCA* rooms, at Marco Antonio Reyes 84, Moneda, San Martín, with card only, D, hot water and heating. YH information available from Holanda 268, Providencia (nearest metro Tobalaba), T 231-5649 (worth getting list of YH addresses around country as these change year by year—even in Santiago).

Accommodation in Providencia (E of centre) is generally good, but more expensive than central hotels. Not all *residenciales* are rec.

Camping The campsite on San Cristóbal hill has been closed because of muggings. Alternatives are the Farellones road near the river; or S of Santiago near Puente Alto (take Av. J. Pedro Alessandri S to Las Vizcachas and La Obra where there is a small park on left side of road). At Km. 25 S of city on Panamericana, Esso garage offers only a vacant lot near highway. Club

Camping Maki, and Casino Camping, both 70 km. from Santiago, **see page 462**. Rec. camping at Tenis Centrum Alemán, Parcela 68, Santa Ana de Chena, Camino Lonquén, run by Dieter and Myriam Mittelstaedt (take Panamericana Sur for 9 km., turn right at blue and white water tower, then 4.5 km. on road to Los Espejo, look for sign, then 4 km. on right); 5 good courts, hot showers, small restaurant, US$1.50 p.p. per day. Standard camping gas cartridges can be bought at Unisport, Providencia 2503, or Santo Domingo 1079. Other equipment for camper-vans from Bertonati Hnos, Manuel Montt 2385. Caravans (US model Tioga) can be rented from Castanera Turismo, Av. Providencia 1072, local 14 D. Tent repairs: Juan Soto, Silva Vildosola 890, Paradero 1, Gran Avenida, San Miguel, Santiago, T 555-8329. Reinaldo Lippi, Toesca 2171, makes tents, sleeping bags, back packs, etc., and does repairs, most helpful. Camping goods from Club Andino and Federación de Andinismo (**see page 463 below**): expensive because these articles are imported. Cheaper boots from Edvobal, Paseo Las Palmas 2242, metro Los Leones, T 251 5488.

Electric Current   220 volts A.C., 50 cycles.

Restaurants   In addition to those at the main hotels and those in Parque O'Higgins there are, in the centre of the city; *Pinpilinpausha*, Matías Cousiño 62, good, cheap; *Da Carla*, MacIver, Italian food, very good; *Monjitas*, Monjitas 753, old-fashioned, good, reasonably-priced local food; *Goyescas*, Morandé 526, good food, good source of information, English-speaking owner; *Savoy*, Morandé 526, good and cheap; *El Rey del Pescado*, Banderas, good seafood; *Atelier*, Tenderini 171, rec., good expensive seafood. *El 27 de Nueva York*, Nueva York 27, central, good seafood; *Chez Henry*, on Plaza de Armas, excellent empanadas, parrillada de mariscos a speciality, reckoned best in Santiago, dining room at back of shop has live music and dancing (also does take away meals); *Marco Polo* in Plaza de Armas, local dishes, clean; *El Pollo Dorado*, Agustinas 881 (closed Sun.); *Moulin Rouge*, Estado between Huérfanos and Agustinas, rec. for complete meal (US$10); *Mermoz*, Huérfanos 1048, good; *Gui-Ma*, Huérfanos y Teatinos, good, reasonable prices; *Las Alemanas*, Huérfanos 837, good value; *Café Dante*, Merced 801, for pastel de choclo; *La Danze*, San Antonio, cheap, open till 0100. *Savory Tres*, Ahumada 327, good and reasonable, particularly seafood; *Internacional*, Victoria Subercaseaux 15 (near Sta. Lucía), good, cheap almuerzos; *Les Assessins*, Merced 297, French, rec.; *Sing Hwa*, Merced 627, Chinese, good and cheap; *Pekín*, Agustinos 656, Chinese, resaonable; *Los Rubíes*, Lira 75, Chinese; *Pei Fu*, Santa Rosa y París, good, Chinese; *Japón*, Marcoleta 39, off Vicuña Mackenna, good but not cheap; *Los Adobes de Argomedo*, Argomedo 411, Chilean food and spectacular floor show including cueca dancing. *Eladio*, Pío Nono, nr. foot of San Cristóbal funicular, good steaks; *Karim*, Av. Pío Nono (Arabian), good; *Calloa*, Corrientes y Bellavista, good food and pleasant atmosphere; *El Mar de Bellavista*, Ernesto Pinto Lazarrigue 62-A, excellent seafood.

Vegetarian restaurants: *La Huerta*, Orrego Luco 54 (Providencia), metro Pedro de Valdivia, rec., open daily, live music Fri. and Sat. evenings; *Alternativa Macrobiótica*, Santa Beatriz 84, *El Naturista*, Moneda 846, rec.; *El Vegetariano*, Huérfanos 827, Galería Victoria, mixed reports.

For snacks and excellent ice cream, try *Coppelia*. Excellent ice cream and good hamburgers can be found in many places on Ahumada. Airport meals and snacks are good. There are many cheap restaurants around the Municipal Market and fish stalls serving lunch (e.g. *La Playa Chonchi*, and in the market areas across the river from the Municipal Market). Good, cheap snacks can be had from stalls in the arcade of the Plaza de Armas.

Outside centre, the Providencia district is preferable to the more fast-food oriented downtown area: *La Pizza Nostra*, Providencia and Pedro de Valdivia, sells good Italian food; *El Parrón*, Providencia 1188; *Lomitos*, Av. Providencia, very good; *Tung Kung*, Providencia 1091, Chinese; *La Concepción*, La Concepción 155 (next to British Embassy, Providencia), good seafood, also *Aquí está Cocó*, La Concepción 236; *Catalán*, Av. Suecia near Lota, good, reasonably-priced; *Da Vinci*, Suecia 113, Italian, also *Domencio*, Suecia 0133. *München*, El Bosque Norte 204, Providencia. Typical Chilean dishes at *El Pollo Al Coñac*, Lo Barnechea 127, good, (local delicacy of sea-urchins, *erizos*, may not always please the visitor). *Danubio Azul* (Chinese), Reyes Lavalle 3240 (near Metro El Golf). *Las Consentidas*, Alvaro Casanova 260-C, La Reina Alta, T 273-2221, reasonable.

Many first-class restaurants out of the centre can be found in the Las Condes district, including grills, Chilean cuisine (often with music), French cuisine and Chinese. They tend to be more expensive than central restaurants. Good examples are *Balthazar*, Av. Las Condes, Estoril, open all night at weekends, dancing, lively, excellent food, particularly salads; *El Alero de Los de Ramón*, Av. Las Condes 9889 (Chilean cuisine and music, expensive but really excellent in both departments); *Canta Gallo*, Av. Las Condes 12345 (ditto); *La Querencia*, Av. Las Condes 14980, not dear for the quality; *Los Gordos*, Camino El Bajo, El Arrayán (perhaps the best food of all).

Cafés and Bars   Many bars (some serve snacks) on Pedro Valdivia, very popular. *Huichipirichi*, San Martín 85, cheap meals, and sandwiches next door at *Cafetería Gilda*. *Izakaya Yoko*, Japanese Café, Merced 456, good, cheap, friendly. *Full Bar Ltda.*, Alameda 833, good and cheap; *El Lugar de Don Quijote*, good, corner Morandé and Catedral; *Café Paula*, Estado and Pasaje España, excellent coffee and cake, good breakfast. *Bar-Restaurant Casa Suiza*, Huérfanos 640 local 5 (Metro Sta. Lucía), good Swiss and Chilean food. *Café del Cerro*, Ernesto Pinto Lazarrigue

192 (at foot of San Cristóbal) has different concert or cabaret each evening, highly rec. *Bar-Restaurant Nacional No. 1*, Huérfanos 1087, good; *Cosnes Bar* on Moneda, good soups. Try *Café Haití* and *Café Caribe*, both on Paseo Ahumada for delicious coffee. *Tiptop Cookies* rec. for freshly baked biscuits. *Geo Pub*, Encomenderos 138, T 231-3060, owner Francisco Valle speaks English, pub and restaurant with travel films once a week in winter, music occasionally, popular with travellers, rec.; *Phone Box Pub*, Providencia 1670, T 496627, slightly more expensive; *Violin Pub*, Providencia 1684, good lunch. Note that almost all hotel bars are closed Sun.

Tea Rooms   *Carrera*, Teatinos 180; *Villa Real*, Compañía 1068; *Nuria*, Agustinas 715; *Oriente*, Plaza Italia; *Paula*, San Antonio 218.

Clubs   Ñuñoa (T 223 7846), with swimming pool, tennis courts and school; Polo y Equitación San Cristóbal; Chess Club, Alameda O'Higgins 898, Mon.-Sat. 1800, lively.

Shopping   There is a fairly good shopping area on Paseo Ahumada and Paseo Huérfanos, two intersecting streets now reserved to pedestrians, in the centre of the city. About 3 km. from the centre there is a very contemporary shopping centre full of boutiques in Providencia (Metro stop, Los Leones, *dirección* Las Condes). Best bargains are handicraft articles, black pottery (best bought in Pomaire, 50 km. away, **see page 462**) and beautiful wrought copper and bronze. The best place for handmade tapestries is Talleres Artesanales, Lyon 100, in a subway near Los Leones metro, Providencia. Good shops for local copper work are Bozzo, at Ahumada 12 in the centre, and at Av. Providencia 2125. Near the Iglesia de los Dominicos, on Av. Apoquindo, is Los Graneros del Alba, or El Pueblo de Artesanía, open daily except Mon.; all types of ware on sale, classes given in some shops. The gemstone lapis lazuli (only found in Chile and Afghanistan) is best bought in the numerous workshops on Bellavista, but is cheaper around the market. H. Stern jewellery shops are located at the San Cristóbal Sheraton and Carrera hotels, and at the International Airport. Cema-Chile (Centro de Madres), Portugal 351 and at Universidad de Chile metro stop, Artesanía Popular Chilena, Av. Providencia 2322 (near Los Leones metro), and Artesanía Chilena, Estado 337, have a good selection of handicrafts, and so do Cema-Chile branches in the provinces. Talleres Solidarios, 1st floor Vicaría de la Solidaridad, on Plaza de Armas (next door to the Cathedral). *Pel y Pel*, Pedro de Valdivia 20, fur and leather articles, good. The shopping arcade at the Central Station is good value, likewise the street market outside. There is a good outside fruit market at Puente 815, by Frutería Martínez. There is an antique fair on Sun. (1000-1400) in the summer and a Fiesta de Quasimodo on the first Sunday after Easter at Lo Barnechea, 30 min. by bus from Santiago, other antique stores near Merced and Lastarria (Santiago).

Bookshops   Librería Kuatro sell the *South American Handbook*. Librería Albers, Merced 820, local 7 and Av. Tobalaba 032 (Spanish, English and German—good selection, prices about twice as high as in Europe); Librería Altamira, Huérfanos 669; Feria Chilena del Libro, Huérfanos nr. McIver; Librería Ivens, Moneda 730 (international magazines, expensive); Andrés de Fuenzalida 36 and Tenderini, for books in English. Librería Inglesa, Pedro de Valdivia 47, classical and pre-C19 books, sells *South American Handbook*. Second-hand English books from arcade at San Diego 121, 1½ blocks south of Alameda and *Librería El Patio*, Providencia 1652, nearest Metro stop Pedro de Valdivia; exchange for best deal. Also, from Henry at Metro station, Los Leones. Reading rooms at British and U.S. cultural associations (see **Addresses**). German books at Humboldt, 645, 2216 Providencia. Librairie Française, books and newspapers, Calle del Estado 337. Newspapers also at Staud, Ahumada y Huérfanos (*New York Times*, *Herald*, *Le Monde* etc. often one or two days old); English newspapers at the news kiosk opp. *Hotel Carrera* on Plaza de la Constitución.

Camera Repairs   Harry Müller, Ahumada 312, oficina 402, rec.; speaks German and English. For Minolta and Canon repairs, Nueva York 52, Of.302, rec. Developing (Fuji), Reifschneider Laboratory, Carmen 1313, 1 day service. Full color, on Ahumada, is to be avoided.

Buses and Taxis   There are three kinds of buses: the small fast kind called *liebres* (hares) which cost US$0.25-0.35 a ride; the regular buses at US$0.25, and the large buses marked Expreso. At present charges are slightly higher at night and on Sun. Taxis are now abundant (black with yellow roofs), and not expensive, with a minimum charge of US$0.40 (50% surcharge on basic rate after 2230). At bus terminals, drivers will try to charge more (illegally)—best to walk a block and flag one. Large blue taxis do not have meters. There are also colectivo taxis to the suburbs. Visitors going outside the city should arrange the charge beforehand. The private taxi service which operates from the bottom level of *Hotel Carrera* has been rec. (same rates as city taxis).

Underground Railway   The first line of the underground railway system (Metro) runs between San Pablo and Escuela Militar, under the Alameda, and the second line runs from Los Héroes to Callejón Ovalle. Line 3 is to be constructed between Buen Pastor and Vivaceta. The ticket for Line 1 costs US$0.20; save queuing by buying a ten-ticket booklet. Fares on Line 2 are half this price. The trains are fast, quiet, and full. The first train is at 0600 (Mon.-Sat.), 0800 (Sun. and holidays), the last about 2245.

Car Hire Hertz, Avis and Budget available from airport. Hertz (Av. Costanera 1469, T 225-9328, and airport) appears to have the best network in Chile and cars are in good condition.

Theatres Plays in Spanish at Petit Rex, L'Atelier, Antonio Varas, Camilo Henríquez; Maru, Moneda, Talia, La Comedia and Municipal, where the Chilean ballet company performs (US$11 for tcikets) and concerts are given. Lunchtime concerts on Tues. at 1315, for US$1.25. Baquedano, just off Plaza Baquedano, shows same companies but is cheaper than Municipal. Three others, the Opera (Huérfanos), Humoresque, and Picaresque, show mostly Folies Bergères-type revues. Outdoor rock concerts from March onwards at the National Stadium Velodrome.

Cinemas Films of famous operas shown on Mon., 1900, at Salón Claudio Arrau, Teatro Municipal building, free. Most other cinemas cost about US$1 p.p., films start at 1100. Poor accoustics in many but good in Lido, Cervantes, Gran Palace. Several cinemas along Huérfanos.

Night Clubs *El Pollo Doro* and *La Casa de San Isidro* (near Estación República), both folklore; *Dancing Brazil* on Plaza Brasil, cheap; *Gato Viudo*, on Vitacura, very popular, live music, cheap, fun; *Gato Hydráulico*, in big shopping centre E of Santiago, also popular, but slightly older clientèle than *Gato Viudo*; *Red Pub*, Av. Suecia at Providencia, very international, American-style. *La Candela*, Purísima 129, good entertainment. Folk club at San Isidro 51, Nanno Parro, 2400-0600, cheap drinks, lots of fun, relaxed atmosphere.

Discotheques *Gente*, Av. Apoquindo 4900; *Las Brujas*, Av. Príncipe de Gales, Parcela 158, Las Condes; *Caledonia*, Av. Larraín Parcela; *Eve*, Av. Vitacura 3418; *La Scala*, Av. Américo Vespucio Norte s/n. *Kasbba*, Calle Suecia 081 (Metro Los Leones), entry US$5 with drink.

Swimming Pool Antilen (closed Tues.) and Tupahue, better, open daily 1000-1500 (Mon.-Fri., US$2, Sat.-Sun. US$3), bus 27 from San Francisco Church to the park entrance marked Zoológico, at Cerro San Cristóbal. In Parque O'Higgins, same prices. Take colectivo "Plaza Caupolicán", Calle Pío Nono. Olympic pool in Parque Araucano (nr. Arauco Shopping Centre, closest Metro E.Militar), open Tues.-Sat. 0900-1900 November-March.

Tennis Santiago Tennis Club; also, Club de Tenís Jaime Fillol, Rancho Melnichi. Par.4. See also Tenís Centrum Alemán, under **Camping** above.

Bowling Bowling Center, Av. Apoquindo 5012.

Racecourses Club Hípico, racing every Sun. and every other Wed. afternoon (at Viña del Mar, January-March); Hipódromo Chile every Sat. afternoon; pari-mutuel betting.

Exchange Banco Central de Chile, one block from Plaza Constitución, demands the minimum of formalities, although there is usually a commission charge for most transactions. Banco O'Higgins, Av. Agustinas, will change travellers' cheques into dollars with no commission. American Express, Citbank, Ahumada 40 and Afex, Agustinas 1360, will change travellers' cheques into US dollars for up to US$300 a day without commission. Banks, open from 0900 to 1400, but closed on Sat.

Official daily exchange rates are published in *El Mercurio*. Parallel market rate can be obtained at corner of Agustinas and Ahumada and around the Moneda; agents on the street take you to exchange offices (bargain with them before going to the office, but it is better to go to the office direct). Financiera Ciga, Agustinas 1287, Casa de Cambio Blancas, opp. *Hotel Orly* on Pedro de Valdivia, and Exprinter are rec. for good rates, low commission, also Inter, Moneda 940, upstairs office at Ahumada 131 (oficina 103) and Teletour, Bandera 191. Most exchange houses are on Agustinas (American Express is at No. 1360 for Exchange and No. 1173 for travel information and collection of mail) and Huérfanos and some, such as Huso, Providencia 1990 (Metro Pedro de Valdivia), are open on Sat. mornings. Sr. Fernando Sáez (travel agent), M. Cousiño 150, Oficina 322, T 382885, for good exchange rates (and australes). Casa de Cambio, Calle Bombero A. Ossa 1010, Of. 214 (near Ahumada/Agustinas), open 0900-2200 (Mon.-Sat.), 1000-1600 (Sun.) MasterCard, at its office at Morandé 315, offers its full range of services (even lost or stolen cards are replaced in a couple of days); open Mon.-Fri. 0900-1730.

British Community maintains the British Commonwealth Society (old people's home etc.), the interdenominational Santiago Community Church, at Av. Holanda 151 (Metro Tobalada), Providencia, which holds services every Sunday at 1045. Schools (The Grange and Redlands—coeducational, and Craighouse and Braemar—girls).

Addresses *British Embassy and Consulate*, La Concepción 177, 4th floor, Providencia 1800, Casilla 72-D; *British Chamber of Commerce*, Bandera 227, Casilla 536, T 698-5266; *British Council*, Av. Eliodoro Yáñez 832, nr. Providencia, T 694-6005; *Chilean-British Institute*, Santa Lucía 124 (has English papers in library, open 1000-1200, 1600-1900 except Mon.); also at Dario Urzúa 1933 (Providencia) and Renato Sánchez 4369 (Las Condes). *U.S. Embassy*, Agustinas 1343; *U.S. Consulate*, T 710133, Merced 230 (visa obtainable here); *Chilean-North American Cultural Institute*, Moneda 1467, good for US periodicals, cheap films on Fri.; *Canadian Embassy*, Ahumada 11 (prints a good information book). *Australian Embassy*, Gertrudis Echeñique 420, Las Condes. *New Zealand Embassy*, Av. Isadora Goyenechea 3516, Las Condes

(T 487071). *West German Embassy*, Agustinas 785 (T 693-5031/ 693-5035); *German Chamber of Commerce*, Ahumada 131. *Goethe Institut*, Esmeralda 650. *Austrian Embassy*, Av. Pedro de Valdivia 300, Barros Errázuriz, 3rd floor. *Italian Embassy*, Triana 843. *Spanish Consulate*, Av. Providencia 329, 4th floor; *Swedish Embassy*, Dario Urzúa 2165, Casilla 55-D, T 495052; *Swiss Embassy*, Av. Providencia 2653, 16th floor, T 232-2693, open 1000-1200 (metro Tobalaba); *Belgian and Japanese embassies* in same building. *Argentine Embassy*, Vicuña Mackenna 41 (T 226947), Australians need letter from their embassy to get visa here, open 0900-1400 (visa US$15); *Brazilian Embassy*, McIver 255, 15th floor; *Bolivian Embassy*, Av. Santa María 2796 (T 232-8180, Metro Los Leones); *Panamanian Embassy*, Bustos 2199 (open 1000-1330); *Paraguayan Consulate*, Burbos 245, Las Condes (metro Alcántara); *Peruvian Embassy*, Andrés Bello 1751 (T 490045). *Academia Chilena de la Historia*, Clasificador 1349, Correo Central, for information and help on archaeology.

Language Courses Spanish at Chilean-British Institute and Chilean-North American Cultural Institute (addresses above).

Laundry Dry cleaning, Merced 494. **Laundromat** Dr. Luis Middleton 1738, nr. Providencia 1777 (nearest metro Pedro de Valdivia). US$3 for 5 kg., US$4 for 8 kg. Also at Diagonal Paraguay 361, about US$0.50/kg., quick; Voronof, Bandera 818, charges per item, will return clothes to hotel; Providencia 1033, and Merced y McIver (dry cleaning only). Wet wash laundry service at Miraflores 331, about US$3 per kg.

Health Emergency hospital at Marcoleta 377 costs US$12. For a yellow fever vaccination Hospital San Salvador, Salvador 420, T 2256441. Arrive at correct time, Tues. 0900-1000, or you have to pay for a whole capsule (enough for 20!) Also Vaccinatoria Internacional, Hospital Luis Calvo, Mackenna, Antonio Varas 360. **Emergency Pharmacy**, Portugal 155 (T 382439).

Post Office Agustinas 1137, Plaza de Armas, poste restante well organized (though only kept for 30 days), list of letters received in the hall of central Post Office; also has philatelic section, for stamp collectors. Go to Moneda 1155, round corner, for mailing postcards and letters. If sending a parcel, the contents must be checked at Post Office; parcel is then sealed for US$0.75. If receiving a parcel, you must collect it from international branch at Marsella, near Parque O'Higgins.

Cables and Telephones Compañía de Teléfonos de Chile, Moneda 1145. International phone calls: Entel, Huérfanos 1132, Mon.-Fri. 0830-2200, Sat. 0900-2030, Sun. 0900-1400, calls cheaper 1400-2200. International telex service, Bandera 168.

The National Tourist Board Servicio Nacional de Turismo (Sernatur), Catedral 1159 (Casilla 3927, Correo Plaza de Armas), T 698-2151/696-0474, opposite the Congreso Nacional, open Mon.-Fri. 0900-1700, Sats. 1030-1230. Closed all week-end in winter. English is spoken and maps (road map US$1.50), brochures and posters are available. Off-season discount booklets available. They also sell *Qué Hacemos*, which is a monthly magazine about events in Chile. Information Office at Antofagasta-La Paz railway, Agustinas 972, oficina 904, and at airport (open daily 0900-2100). N.B. Many tourist offices outside Santiago are closed in winter, so stock up on information here. A recommended guide book is *Turistel*, published annually, with information and maps covering the whole country, in Spanish only. Excellent road maps may also be obtained from the **Automóvil Club de Chile**, Pedro de Valdivia 195. Shell also produce a good map, as do Rutas Camineras. Geophysical and topographical maps are available from **Instituto Geográfico Militar**, at their sales office, Alameda 240 (Universidad Católica metro) or main office Dieciocho 407 (opposite Palacio Cousiño, Toesca metro) (closed in holiday season) and from **Conaf** (Corporación Nacional Forestal), General Bulnes, 285 (T 696-0783/3801). Walkers' maps are not available outside Santiago. The Chilean Telephone Company also publishes a tourist guide of most of the country and the phone book has a detailed street map of the city.

Tourist Agencies Wagons-Lits Cook (Calle Agustinas 1058, Casilla 1534), Turismo Cocha (American Express representatives), Agustinas 1173. Agency Pudahuel, Paseo Ahumada 312, oficina 1024, highly rec. For local tours: Tour Service, Teatinos 333, 10th floor, T 6960415/727166, and at same address Sportstours, German-run, are helpful (offices also at Hotels *Carrera*, and *San Cristóbal*). Altue Expediciones, Encomenderos 138, T 2313060, for wilderness trips, rec. (above *Geo Pub*). Turismo Cabo de Hornos, Agustinas 814, Of. 706, T 338480/1, for DAP flights (Punta Arenas-Puerto Williams) and Tierra del Fuego/Antártica tours. Ugarte International, Huérfanos 1178, Loc.A, very helpful. Blanco, Pedro Valdivia near Providencia, good for flight information and exchange. Rapa-Nui, Huérfanos 1160, specializes in trips to Easter Island. Turismo Grace, Victoria Subercaseaux 381, T 693-3740, good service.

Airport Arturo Merino Benítez (at Pudahuel), 26 km. from Santiago with a speed limit. Airport taxi, US$15-18. Fixed taxi fares on board by cab rank. Pullman service by Aerobuses Tour Express to and from city centre, Moneda 1523, T 717380 (US$0.75) buses every ½hr., 0630-2315, ½-¾ hr. journey; plenty of luggage space; Flota LAC from Calle Manuel Rodríguez, Metro Los Héroes, and others, also run a bus service, US$0.80. Internal flights by Lan-Chile and Ladeco operate from the International Airport. For schedules, see under individual towns. Airport tax US$12.50 if leaving country, not included in ticket price. Bank and *cambio* (better rates) outside customs hall; tourist office in same area will book accommodation. No duty free shop, so buy your wine etc. in town.

For information on flights with the Air Force, Relaciones Públicas Fuerza Aérea, Alameda O'Higgins 1170, first floor.

Rail   International service to Buenos Aires suspended. No passenger trains to northern Chile nor to Valparaíso and Viña del Mar. Mapocho station is being renovated (1989), so all trains leave from Estación Central at Alameda O'Higgins 3300. To Concepción, 5 daily, Temuco, 2 daily; Valdivia ("Rápido del Calle Calle" 2030 daily) and Puerto Montt, one Rápido a day at 1830 with sleepers, about 18 hrs., reservations necessary (at O'Higgins 853, or at station). Train built in Germany in 1926, bunks lie parallel to rails so comfortable despite poor track; an attendant for each car; bar car shows 3 films—no cost so you must purchase a drink ticket in advance. Expreso, 2100, about 23 hrs., no reservations (get your ticket the morning of the day the train leaves and sit on the train as soon as you can get on; otherwise you'll stand for the whole journey; check on discounts for IYHA members). Free hot water supplied, so take own mug and coffee. To Osorno, Rápido at 2000, 14½ hrs. Also a car-transporter service to Temuco, Osorno and Puerto Montt. Also trains to Rancagua, Curicó, Talca, Chillán and Pichilemu (direct Fri.-Sun., otherwise via Chillán). Trains are still fairly cheap (though none too reliable), meals are good though expensive. For a family it may be cheaper to buy one ticket for an *apartamento*, rather than separate seats. Booking offices: for State Railways, Alameda O'Higgins 853 in Galeria; T 301818/330746, 331814 for "autotrén"; or Metro Esc. Militar, Galería Sur L-3, T 228-2983; central station, T 699-2157/699-1682; for Antofagasta-La Paz, Ahumada 11, Of. 602, T 698-5536. Left luggage office at Estación Central.

Buses   There are frequent, and good, interurban buses to all parts of Chile. The longest journey within the country, N to Arica (2,113 km.), costs about US$30, and takes 29 hrs., check if student rates available (even for non-students), or reductions for travelling same day as purchase of ticket. Worth bargaining over prices. Also take a look at the buses before buying the tickets (big differences in quality among bus companies; ask about the on-board services). Fichtur and Chile-Bus rec. for Arica, fully reclining seats with footrests on each bus. Antofagasta, 20 hrs., US$20 ordinary, US$30 with Flota Barrios, with sleeper, meals, hostess, 1500, an interesting trip to see the changes in landscape, but cold at night. To Viña del Mar/Valparaíso, 2 hrs., US$2-3 (Pullman, Tur-Bus have their own terminal on Al. B. O'Higgins 3712, metro Universidad de Santiago, Línea 1); Los Andes, US$2; to La Serena, US$6-8.50, 8 hrs.(sit on left); San Felipe, US$2. Bus to Valdivia, US$13.75-US$8. To Puerto Montt (1,060 km.), US$15, first class, US$10, second, 16 hrs.; to Concepción, 8½ hrs., US$7; to Chillán, US$7.50, to Temuco, 10 hrs., US$9. Varmontt buses (own terminal at San Francisco depot, but best to board bus at Tobalaba) to Puerto Montt, 17 hrs., US$25, including reclining seats, meals and wine, colour TV, stereo headphones, highly rec. In winter most fares on this route are reduced. Igi-Llaima (near La Moneda bus station) runs a comfortable service to Temuco and points south, at 1700, arrives 0600. Bus offices all along Morandé. You can bargain for lower fares. Buses to Valparaíso, Viña del Mar, Osorno, S and coast leave from Terminal de Buses Santiago, Al. B. O'Higgins 3878, T 791385, 796452 for Valparaíso and Viña del Mar (Metro, Universidad de Santiago/Universidad Técnica/Terminal de Santiago— all same place). In general, buses N leave from Terminal del Norte, Gral. Mackenna and Amunátegui (T 712141). Beware: Buses very punctual, so do not be late for departure!

International Buses   Long distance: to Buenos Aires, leaves from Santiago terminal, Alameda O'Higgins 3878, take Metro to Universidad de Santiago, US$37-45, 22 hrs.; also to Montevideo; Caracas (Tues. and Fri. 0900); Lima 51 hrs., it is cheaper to take a bus to Arica (US$30), another to Tacna (US$1.75), thence bus to Lima. Bogotá (7 days); São Paulo and Rio de Janeiro (US$76 and 80 respectively); Asunción (US$80); Guayaquil; and Quito. Short distance: there are frequent minibus services from the Terminal del Norte over the Andes to Mendoza, about US$15 (Cata bus), 10 hrs., other companies, 7 hrs., book as far ahead as possible; they do not run in winter. Transportes Caracoles sell a combination ticket but there are many changes. All buses now go through the Cristo Redentor tunnel, and it is no longer possible to go to the Cristo Redentor statue from the Chilean side. Chi-Ar taxi company, Morandé 890, rec., leaves at 0800 and charges US$22 for Santiago-Mendoza (although more expensive than buses, the advantage is shorter waiting time at customs).

Bus companies: Tepsa, Amunátegui 324 (not rec., no food on bus in Peru); Pul-Bus-Norte (not rec.); Flota Barrios, Morandé 766; Igi-Llaima. Fenix Pullman Norte, good. Try to change money before entering Chile, as Santiago bus station lies far outside the city (beware taxi drivers overcharging).

Shipping   M/n *Tierra del Fuego*: Puerto Montt to Puerto Natales and return, reservations accepted for all classes, and M/n *Evangelistas*: Puerto Montt-Puerto Chacabuco 1st class, Navimag, Miraflores 178, piso 12, T 696-3211, Telex 341234 NISA CK (or contact Turismo Cocha, Agustinas 1173, T 6983341; also Transcontainer, see below). M/n *Skorpios*: luxury cruise out of Puerto Montt to Laguna San Rafael, Constantino Kochifas C., MacIver 484, 2° piso, Oficina 5, Santiago T 336-187, Telex 240764 NATUK CL. M/n *Quellón*: cruise out of Puerto Montt to Laguna San Rafael, early December to late March, Transcontainer S.A., Estado 360, Oficina 502-c, Santiago, T 337-118, Telex 340002 TCSA CK VTR. Enquire at Transcontainer for trips to

Antarctica. PSNC, Agustinas 1066-70, Casilla 4087; Empresa Marítima del Estado, Estado 359, 5th floor.

Hitch-hiking to Valparaíso, take Metro to Pajaritos and walk 5 minutes to W—no difficulty. Or, take bus "Renca Panamericana" from MacIver and Monjitas. To hitch south, take Metro to Estación Central, then Buses del Paine at Calle Borja as far as possible on the highway to the toll area, about US$1, 75 mins.

Excursions from Santiago   Several small resort towns are easily reached by car from the capital. Peñalolén, 16 km., with a lovely park and a beautiful view of the city (bus in front of Mapocho station at Av. Independencia and Balmaceda, take your bathing gear); Colina (915 metres), an attractive, popular spa in the mountains 32 km. to the N (bus from Av. La Paz and Juárez, US$0.50 one way), thermal baths, US$3.70, swimming pool, US$2.70, last return bus at 1900; San José de Maipo, some 80 km. to the SE (return journey by car: 3 hrs., buses every 15 mins. from N end of Parque O'Higgins, return fare US$1.75), particularly beautiful in spring; just beyond is the mountain town of Melocotón (*Millahue Hotel*). Just past Melocotón between San José de Maipo and El Volcán is San Alfonso, in the Callejón del Maipo (*Hostería Café Cordillera*, D, full board, warmly rec., ring 72-4082 in Santiago, also others). Buses at hourly or 2-hour intervals from Parque O'Higgins, Santiago. Beautiful mountain-river area, with vineyards. Three buses a day (US$2) run from Parque O'Higgins (same metro) to El Volcán in the Andes, 77 km. to the SE (1,400 metres); there are astounding views, but little else (the village was wiped away in a landslide). (Bus, 0800 Sat. and Sun., to Puente Alto.) From El Volcán the road runs 12 km. E and then N to the skiing slopes of *Hotel Lo Valdés*, C. A splendid region which deserves the journey required to get there. *Refugio Alemán*, D, with full board, rec. 12 km. away are hot natural baths, Baños Morales; the water temperature is 27°C (bus leaves daily from Parque O'Higgins at 0730, arriving at Baños Morales 1100, US$2 each way; returns at 1800). By Baños Morales is a National Park with a glacier. Several *residenciales* incl. *Hostería Inesita*, F. Drinks can be obtained from Negro José nearby. The Lo Valdés area is popular at weekends and holiday times, but is otherwise deserted. The small towns in the Aconcagua Valley to the N—San Felipe, Jahuel and Los Andes—are described in the section "To Buenos Aires across the Andes", page 470.

The National Votive Temple of Maipú, of fine modern architecture and stained glass, 30 min. by car (or about 45 mins. by bus from corner of Calle Teatinos and Av. Bernardo O'Higgins) from Santiago, commemorates O'Higgins' battle; interesting, and so is the attached museum of carriages, furniture, clothing and other colonial and later items, Sun. only, 1000-1200, 1600-2000.

Campsites   Excellent facilities about 70 km. from Santiago at Laguna de Aculeo, called **Club Camping Maki**. Facilities include electricity, cold water, swimming pool, boat mooring, restaurant, US$2 p.p. daily, but only available to members of certain organizations. An alternative site is Casino Camping, 1 km. away, on edge of lake, US$2 for family per night. Very friendly, café sells fruit, eggs, milk, bread and kerosene. Good fishing. No showers, water from handpump.

Pottery   is best bought in **Pomaire**, a little town about 50 km. from Santiago towards the coast, where the artists can be observed at work. The area is rich in clay and the town is famous for its cider (*chicha de manzana*, 3 strengths: *dulce, medio* and *fuerte*) and Chilean dishes. Pomaire may be reached by Mellipilla bus from San Borja 60 (behind supermarket on O'Higgins 3390) leaving daily at 1130, Sat.-Sun. at 0800 also, US$1.35, 1 hrs. (alight at side road to Pomaire, 2-3 km. from town, colectivos every 10-15 mins.); en route, delicious *pastel de choclo* can be obtained at Restaurant *Mi Ranchito*.

Vineyards   Another agreeable excursion is to the vineyard of Concha y Toro at Puente Alto, 40 km. south of Santiago. Tours of the *bodega*, and wine can be bought direct from vineyard. Pirque vineyard of Concha y Toro, entry free, bus from San Francisco and Tarapacá, ¾ hour, US$0.50. The Undurraga vineyard at Santa Ana, north-west of Santiago, also permits visits on weekdays (tours given by the owner-manager, Pedro Undurraga).

Horse-Breeding   A specially rec. excursion is to Los Lingues, a private *hacienda* 120 km. S of Santiago, where it is said the best horses in Chile are bred. Rosie Swale was lent two of them for her epic ride from Antofagasta to Cape Horn, described in *Back to Cape Horn* (Collins, London, 1986). Visits can be arranged to the C.17 house, a gift of the King of Spain, at Hacienda Los Lingues, Torre C. de Tajamar, Of. 205, Santiago, T 223-3518, Telex 340200 STORE CK. To 6060

LINGUE. A one-day tour costs US$35 p.p. including transport, rodeo and lunch; vacations (all inclusive) cost US$125 per day p.p. (the Hacienda is a member of the French Hotels et Relais de la Campagne).

Skiing   There is an excellent ski centre at *Farellones,* 51 km. E of Santiago at 2,470 metres, and reached by car, bus, or truck in under 90 min.: *Motel Tupungato,* one third-class *pensión* and annex. Most skiers stay in the two *refugios* belonging to Santiago's universities (full board US$10 p.p.). High season: June to September/October, weather depending. An excellent network of five ski-lifts. There are excursions for a day from Santiago at US$15, including ski-lifts ticket; enquire Ski Club Chile, Goyenechea Candelaria 4750, Vitacura (north of Los Leones Golf Club), T 211-7341. In season, small buses leave from Av. Apoquindo (El Faro shopping centre), Sat. and Sun. between 0800 and 0900, but it is easy to hitch from the junction of Av. Las Condes/El Camino Farellones (petrol station in the middle): take a Las Condes bus from Calle Merced almost to the end of the line. Alternatively, go by ordinary bus which leaves at 0800, weekdays, from front of Omnium building, Av. Apoquindo (Escuela Militar metro), US$5 return (buy ticket day before, office open until 2000). Beautiful views for 30 km. across ten Andean peaks. Incredible sunsets. Large restaurants. No telephone, only communication is by radio. Five min. away by car (6 km.) is the village of La Parva with eight lifts (good hotel and restaurant), where the runs are a little easier. In summer, this is a good walking area. Lift ticket, US$12, and equipment rental, US$7-10 depending on quality. Another skiing area close by is El Colorado. Sunglasses are a must for skiers.

Other skiing and mountaineering clubs: **Club Andino de Chile,** Enrique Foster, 29, ski club (open 1900-2100 on Mon. and Fri.). **Federación de Andinismo de Chile,** Almirante Simpson 77 (T 232 4338), open daily, sells guides and equipment. Club Alemán Andino, Arrayán 2735, open Tues. and Fri., 1800-2000. For information write to Federación de Ski de Chile, Vicuña MacKenna 40, Casilla 9902, or phone 222-8733. Also try Skitotal, Apoquindo 4900, Oficina 32,33,43, T 246-0156, for one-day excursions.

Portillo, 145 km. from Santiago and 62 from Los Andes, is the greatest centre for skiing and winter sports in Chile. The weather is ideal, the snow conditions excellent, the runs many and varied; four lifts carry skiers up the slopes. The season is from June to September/October, weather depending. Cheap package can be arranged at the beginning and out of the season. On three sides the mountains soften into snow-clad fields and finally slope gently into the Laguna de Inca, 5½ km. long and 1½ km. wide; this lake, at an altitude of 2,835 metres, has no outlet, is frozen over in winter, and its depth is not known. Out of season this is another good area for walking, but get detailed maps before setting out.

Portillo is easily reached from Santiago by daily bus services (except in bad weather). In summer, ask the bus driver to stop, as it is not a routine call and on the way down you may have to hitch to the customs station with your baggage. In summer take a bus to Los Andes (US$2.25), then to Río Blanco (US$0.70), then hitch (**see page 472**). The train service from Santiago no longer operates.

Hotels   *Hotel Portillo* (L), including a cinema, night club, swimming pool, sauna baths and medical service, on the shore of Laguna de Inca. Rates, meals, tax and service included, in US dollars: 180 to 200 a day for lake front suites; single room and bath, 60 to 75; double room and bath, 100 to 110; family apts. for 4, 75; bunk room, community bath, 17 up; bunk room and private bath, 25 up. A fabulous view, and parking charges even if you go for a meal; jacket and tie must be worn in the dining room. Self-service lunch, US$12 p.p. Lift charges are US$12 per day. Open all year. Reservations, Roger de Flor 2911, T 231-2412, Telex 440372 PORTICZ, Santiago. Cheaper food available at **Restaurant Yuly** across the road, and **Restaurant Los Libertadores** at the customs station 1 km. away. *Hostería Alborada,* A, including all meals, tax and service. During Ski Week (last in Sept.), about double normal rate, all included. Reservations, Agencia Tour Avión, Agustinas 1062, Santiago, T 72-6184, or Calle Navarro 264, San Felipe, T 101-R.

There are boats for fishing in the lake; but beware the afternoon winds, which often make the homeward pull 3 or 4 times as long as the outward pull. There are some gentle ski slopes for beginners near the hotel. The major skiing events are in August and September. Mules for stupendous expeditions to the Cristo, to the glacier at the head of the valley or of the Cerro Juncal, to the pass in the west side of the valley.

Lagunillas is a favourite ski-resort only 50 km. from Santiago, 2 hours by gravel road along the beautiful Maipo valley road to the Ojo de Agua area. Accommodation in the lodges of the Club Andino de Chile (bookings may be made at Ahumada 47, Santiago).Tow fee US$12; long T-bar and poma lifts; easy field.

Valparaíso, the principal port of Chile and capital of the Fifth (Valparaíso) Region, is built on the shores of a sweeping bay and on a crescent of hills around it. Seen from the ocean, the city presents a majestic panorama: a great circle of hills is backed by the snow-capped peaks of the distant Cordillera. Population, 277,220.

There are two completely different cities. The lower part is the business centre, with fine office buildings on narrow, clean, winding streets. Above, in the hills, is a fantastic agglomeration of tattered houses and shacks, scrambled in oriental confusion along the littered back streets. *Ascensores,* or funicular railways, and winding roads connect the lower and the upper cities.

The climate is good, for the summer heat is tempered by fresh breezes and sunshine mitigates the unkindness of a short winter. (The mean annual temperature is 15°C, with -1°C and 31°C as the extremes.) The city was founded in 1536, but not many antiquities have survived the sequence of pirates, tempests, fires and earthquakes. A remnant of the old colonial city remains in the hollow known as El Puerto, grouped round the low-built stucco church of La Matriz. The last devastating earthquake was in 1906, and most of the principal buildings date from that time. Until recently, all buildings were low, as a precaution against earthquakes, but during the last few years modern multi-storey blocks have appeared. There was another serious earthquake in July 1971 and, most recently, in March 1985.

The main business quarter stands on land reclaimed from the sea. A further large tract has been regained for the port works, which are partially protected by a sheltering mole; but there is always a high swell, particularly when a north wind blows. Mail and passenger vessels moor alongside.

The Plaza Sotomayor is opposite the passenger landing pier (handicraft shops on pier). It has a fine statue to the "Heroes de Iquique"; the Palacio del Intendencia (Government House) is across the way. Near the landing pier is the railway station for Santiago; passenger services discontinued in 1987. The streets of El Puerto run N and S from Plaza Sotomayor. To the N Calle Cochrane runs for 7 blocks to the Plaza Echaurren, on which stands the old church of La Matriz. A block beyond rises the bold hill of Cerro Artillería, crowned by the huge Naval Academy and a park. To the W of the Cerro the Avenida Playa Ancha runs to a stadium, seating 20,000 people, and to Playa Ancha park. From the western base of the hill the Avenida Altamirano runs by the sea to Las Torpederas, a picturesque bathing beach.

Leaving Plaza Sotomayor by the Calle Serrano and Plaza Echaurren, the Plaza Aduana is reached, where there is a public lift for the Paseo Veintiuno de Mayo, a terrace on Cerro Artillería giving views of the bay and the hills. The New Year is celebrated by a firework display on the bay, which can be seen from this and the many other terraces on the surrounding hills (arrive early for a good place).

Hotels *Prat,* Calle Condell 1443, T 7634, 220 beds, restaurant; *Residencial Dinamarca,* Dinamarca 539 (take Subida Bellavista), E, excellent value; *Res. Florencia,* Victoria, E, friendly; *Residencial Maureen,* Edwards 700, F, hot water, comfortable. Many cheap hotels on Cochrane and Blanco Encalada, S of Plaza Sotomayor; for example, *Zurich,* Blanco Encalada 328, F; and *Residencial Lily,* Blanco Encalada 866, 2 blocks from Plaza Sotomayor, F, clean, safe (despite no locks on doors), but not always hot water. *Residencial Gemini,* Pedro Montt 2062, F, good, clean, and *Gemini II,* Condell 1386; *Mackenna,* Av. Mackenna, near north bus terminal, clean, good, F. *Residencial* at Calle Valparaíso 618, F, good. *Reina Victoria,* Plaza Sotomayor, F, with small breakfast, hot shower, clean and central. *Copihues,* Chacabuco 2883, behind bus terminal, friendly, F. Many of the "cheap" hotels in the Chacabuco area are for short-term occupation only. Youth hostel office at Edwards 695, 3rd floor, will extend membership; nearest hostel in Viña del Mar.

Restaurants *El Castillo* Av. Altamirano (on the sea front), also in the same street *El Membrillo,* good seafood, nice place. *Marisquería La Sureña,* Valdivia 169, near market, lunch only, very good; in market, good stalls on second floor. *Hamburg,* O'Higgins 1274, German management,

German beer, and reasonably-priced food. *Café Express Delmónico*, Av. Prat (near Plaza Sotomayor), good, cheap lunches, popular; *El Faro*, same street, good; *Natur-in*, Francia 549, 2nd floor, vegetarian; fresh juices at *Salud*, Condell 1678; *Bernal Fuente de Soda*, Esmeralda 1140. *Casino Social de Pescadores*, 1 km. N of university in Valparaíso, good, cheap fish meals; the "casino" of the Asociación de Clubs de Regata, on the waterfront, is rec. for good seafood. *La Tentazione*, Av. Pedro Montt 2484, good, cheap; *Café Apollo*, Av. Argentina 179, cheap and sustaining. Chocolate from the factory and retail store, Hucke on Gral. Cruz 824, rec.

Discotheques   *Topsi-Topsi* and *La Nouvelle Epoque. Bar Roland* and *Yako Bar* on Cochrane are "classic sailors' dives".

Transport   Cars for hire by the hr. or day. Taxis; more expensive than Santiago: a short run under 1 km. costs US$0.50. Public transport good. Fares within city limits US$0.20.

Museums   Museum of Fine Arts, Museo Baburiza, Paseo Yugoeslavo, in fine old house overlooking harbour (closed for restoration), take *Ascensor El Peral* from Plaza Sotomayor opposite Law Courts. Severin Library; Museo del Mar Almirante Cochrane, in Lord Cochrane's house overlooking city, take *ascensor* from Plaza Sotomayor to Cordillera (closed temporarily for restoration).

Exchange   Centrobanco will change travellers cheques. National banks. Open 0900 to 1400, but closed on Sat. Rate of exchange at Banco de Santiago (Prat 816) and Banco de Crédito e Inversiones (Cochrane 820) good. Parallel market outside Exprinter, Prat 895, good rates, no commission on travellers' cheques (open 0930-1400, 1600-1900); Cambinter (good) exchange house, close to railway station, on corner of Errazúriz 627.

Addresses   British Consulate, Blanco 737, T 56117; YMCA, Blanco 1113; YWCA, Melgarejo 45; Chilean-British Cultural Institute, Blanco 725, T 2828; Valparaíso Seamen's Institute, Blanco 394, T 2717; PSNC, Calle Almirante Señoret 48; Instituto Chileno-Norteamericano, Esmeralda 1061.

Cables   Transradio Chilena, Esmeralda 932.

Tourist Office   at bus terminal (good map available). For day trips around Valparaíso and Viña del Mar, Turismo Continental T 6992807.

Shipping Services Transcontainer S.A., Prat 772, 5th floor, for information on M/n *Tierra del Fuego*.

Buses   Excellent and frequent bus service runs between Valparaíso (Av. Brasil)/Viña del Mar (25 min.) and Chorrillos; fare US$0.25. No. 9 company "Central Placeres" bus gives fine scenic drive over hills to fishing port; also bus "Mar Verde" (O or N) from Av. Argentina. To Santiago, 2 hrs., US$2 (returns to the capital heavily booked on Sun. p.m.); to Concepción, 11 hrs., US$10. La Serena, 7 hrs., 1000. Terminal Rodoviario is on Pedro Montt 2800 block, corner of Rawson, 1 block from Av. Argentina.

If driving from Santiago there are two tunnels, toll of US$2.25 paid at the first.

Hitch-hiking   to Santiago is easy from service station on Av. Argentina.

Lighthouse   The Faro de Punta Angeles, on a promontory just beyond the Playa Ancha, was the first on the West Coast; you can get a permit to go up. On another high point on the other side of the city is the Mirador de O'Higgins, the spot where the Supreme Dictator exclaimed, on seeing Cochrane's liberating squadron: "On those four craft depends the destiny of America".

Pleasure Resorts near Valparaíso

Laguna Verde, a couple of hours' dusty walk over the hills (or a short road journey, buses from Calle Buenos Aires) to the W of Valparaíso, is a picturesque bay for picnics. Camping site *Los Olivos*, good facilities, well run and friendly (US$3.50 for two). Wayside restaurant.

Viña del Mar, one of the foremost South American seaside resorts, is 9 km. from Valparaíso by one of the innumerable express buses, which run along a narrow belt between the shore and precipitous cliffs. Halfway, on the hill of Los Placeres, is the Universidad Técnica. The popular bathing resort of El Recreo is passed, then Caleta Abarca with its crowded beaches, floral clock and big *Hotel Miramar*. Beaches are often closed because of pollution.

At the entrance to Viña del Mar there is a steep bluff, worth climbing for the views over Viña from its *paseos*. Here also is Cerro Castillo, the summer palace of the Presidents of the Republic. Below, to the left, is the lagoon of the Marga

Marga, crossed by a bridge which leads direct to the Casino, built in the 1930s and set in beautiful gardens, US$2.40 to enter, jacket and tie for men required (open all year). Population: 259,300 (1982).

One of the sights is the municipally owned Quinta Vergara, set in superb gardens with a double avenue of palms; it houses a collection of pictures and an art school. Take bus to El Salto. Part of the grounds is a children's playground, and there is an outdoor auditorium where concerts and ballet are performed in the summer months, and an international song contest is held every February.

"The Song Festival is recommended as a fascinating experience not to be missed, but make sure you have a place to stay before going to Viña! It may be better to watch for the first 3 nights on the television (to familiarize yourself with the songs and performances), and then to attend in person the last two nights. Pay the extra money and sit down near the Quinta Vergara stage (reserved seats and much better views). Otherwise, for the economy seats, you will have to arrive several hours in advance. Doors open at 1700 (except for the last night, when they open at 1500)—show doesn't start until 2130, so bring a hat for sun protection, snacks and something to read!" (Richard Crowe, Univ. of Toronto).

The Teatro Municipal is on Plaza Vergara. Near the Valparaíso Sporting Club with its racecourse and playing fields are the Granadilla Golf Club and a large stadium. In the hills behind a large artificial lake, the Tranque Sausalito, is frequented by picnic parties, and popular with waterskiers; not far away is the Salinas golf course.

Festival El Roto, Jan. 20, in homage to the working men and peasants of Chile.

Hotels Many in A-B range, some with beach. *San Martín*, Av. San Martín 304, T 975440, D with breakfast; *José Francisco Vergara*, Calle Dr. von Schroeders, has garden houses for up to 5; *Iberia*, same street, E with breakfast; *Alejandra*, 2 Poniente 440, T 974404, with shower and breakfast, C (D in low season, breakfast included); *El Escorial*, two places: one at 5 Poniente 114, the other at Poniente 441 (T 975266), D with breakfast, shared bath, clean, central. *Blanchait*, Valparaíso 82A, clean, E with breakfast, hot water, clean, good service; *Residencial Sandy*, Quillota near Valparaíso, near bus and railway stations, E. *Magallanes*, Arlegui 555, T 685-101, with breakfast, clean, friendly, run by a family, good meals, D.

Motels Several at Reñaca (5 km. from Viña del Mar).

N.B. It is cheaper to stay in Valparaíso and commute to the Viña beaches.

Youth Hostel Alberto Blest 384, US$0.80 p.p. a night for YHA card holders. Open Jan.-Feb.

Camping At the *Aku-Aku* at Reñaca, US$1.50 p.p.; *Doña Panchita* and *Internacional,* also at Reñaca; *Marbella* and *Quintay* on Playa Grande, Quintay, 42 km. from Viña del Mar. At Sausalito. Unofficial site in woods behind Quinta Vergara park. Camping gas and similar articles for sale at Valparaíso 464.

Restaurants At hotels; *Chez Jaques*, on beach. *Cap Ducal*, also on beach near Naval Museum, expensive, highly rec. *Casino Chico*, Valparaíso 99, Chilean and international dishes; *Salòn de China*, 5 Poniente y 4 Norte; *Han's Dragón*, Libertad y 8 Norte; *Sen San*, opp. Ciné Rex on Valparaíso, Chinese, good. *El Rincón de Carlos*, in family house, 1 Poniente 714, good cheap menu. *Mapuche*, San Martín 529, excellent. *Airport,* Valparaíso 503, reasonable. Many restaurants on Av. Valparaíso, try in the Galerías (arcades, e.g. *Café Big Ben*). Many smaller ones along the sea front. *Terminal Pesquero*, 1st floor, interesting. *El Pancho* at Reñaca, good seafood and service. Discotheque *Topsy Topsy*, with fantastic views.

Market At intersection of Av. Sporting and river, open Wed. and Sat.

Museums The Museum of Naval History, in the Castle, good, next door is a small Aquarium. Institute of Oceanography, in Montemar, worth seeing; Palacio Rioja, built at turn of century by a prominent local family and now used for official municipal receptions, main floor open to visitors during season, Archaeological Museum on a lower floor. On the coast road between the Naval Museum and the *Hotel Miramar* there is an Easter Island statue (easy to miss as it is on a small traffic island, opposite side of street from beach).

Cultural Associations North American Institute, in fort off Avenida Alvarez; British, Calle 3 Norte. Goethe Institut, in plaza opposite station.

British Community The community here maintains two schools: St. Margaret's and Mackay. There is also an Anglican church, with a resident English chaplain, postal address Casilla 561.

Exchange Agencia de Viajes Star, Valparaíso 328, Exitour, Ecuador 140, La Araucana, Valparaíso 322.

Tourist Office Av. Valparaíso 507, 3rd floor, T 684117. Arrangements may be made at the Tourist Office for renting private homes in the summer season.

Bus to Santiago, US$2-3; to La Serena, 6 daily, 7 hrs., US$8; to Antofagasta, 20 hrs., US$20. Terminal at Av. Valparaíso and Quillota.

Excursions Beyond Reñaca beach is Cochoa with its large sealion colony, 100 metres offshore.

Resorts N of Valparaíso There is a very fine drive N of Viña del Mar along the coast (many motels being built) through Las Salinas to Concón, then inland to Quintero. Las Salinas, beach between two towering crags, is very popular. *Concón*, on the NE point of Valparaíso Bay, is 16 km. further (take bus 9 from Av. Libertad between 2 and 3 Norte). Main attractions: tennis, bathing, fishing, and riding. Main eyesore: an oil refinery (not visible from beach). Near the Concón beach there is a very interesting pelican colony. There is also a new inland road, much faster than the coast road, between Viña del Mar and Concón.

Concón Hotels *Playa Amarilla, Inter Motel, Motel Bosquemar, Motel Embassy*, B. Good seafood empanadas at bars.

Campsite Las Gaviotas. Camping Mantagua Playa, new sites at US$6 each.

Horse riding Horses for hire from Ernesto Farias Usario, Las Encinas 55, Las Romeras, Concón Alto (last bus stop on route 9 or 10 from Viña del Mar or Valparaíso), US$2/hour. Rides in forest or along sand dunes.

Another 16 km. to the N of Concón over the new bridge is the resort of *Quintero,* the naval aviation centre. **Hotels** *Isla de Capri; Hotel Yachting Club.*

Horcón, set back in a cove surrounded by cliffs, is a pleasant small village, mainly of wooden houses. Vegetation is tropical with many cacti on the cliff tops. Seafood lunches with the catch of the day rec. **Hotels** *Horcón, Aranciba* and *El Faro*, all E and on beach. Restaurant *El Ancla* rec.
From Las Ventanas the road continues N to the fashionable resort of *Zapallar* and the once fashionable *Papudo.* Excellent bathing, but water is cold. Hotels are 3rd class. **Hotels** at Zapallar: *Motel Aguas Claras; César.* At Papudo: *Moderno; Di Peppino.*

Excursions There is a fascinating drive to Cachagua, where a colony of penguins may be viewed from the northern end of the public beach.
Several excellent sea beaches are frequented by people from Santiago: some lie N of Valparaíso (already described), and some at the mouth of the Río Maipo. The railway runs to the port of *San Antonio*, 113 km. from Santiago and 112 km. south of Valparaíso. Its shipping shows a considerable growth, mostly at the expense of Valparaíso. The port exports copper brought by railway from the large mine at El Teniente, near Rancagua. Population: 60,826. Itself a popular resort (although the sea is polluted), it is also the centre for other resorts to the N and S: *Cartagena*, the terminus of the railway 8 km. to the N (occasional passenger trains in summer), an old town, is a great playground for Santiago residents. N of Cartagena there are several small resorts—Las Cruces, *Residencial La Posada,* E, good birdwatching; El Tabo, *El Quisco* with a beautiful white sand beach, and particularly *Algarrobo* with its yacht club, marina and penguin colony, access to colony by fishing boat—landing not permitted. On the road between El Quisco and Algarrobo is the town of Isla Negra where the house of the Chilean poet Pablo Neruda is located. *Llolleo* (a famous resort for those who suffer from heart diseases, 4 km. S of San Antonio), and *Maipo,* at the mouth of the Río Maipo, are other resorts. Near Llolleo are many beautiful places, including La Boca. *Santo Domingo,* with a good hotel, is about 10 mins. by road S of San Antonio. It has a golf course, and is by far the most attractive place on this coast.

Hotels At San Antonio: *Jockey Club.* At Cartagena: *Biarritz; La Bahía; Prince.* At Llolleo: *Oriente; Allhambra.* At Santo Domingo: *Rocas de Santo Domingo.* At El Tabo: *Hotel El Tabo,* quite nice, and *Motel El Tabo,* next door. At Algarrobo: nice *residencial* next to roller skating rink, E. At El Quisco, *Hotel El Quisco,* F p.p. with breakfast, clean; *Motel Barlovento* and *Motel Los Acantilados; residenciales* 100-200 m. from beach in E range. Excellent seafood restaurant *La Galleta* on beach. At Algarrobo, there are restaurants and *residenciales* on beach (e.g. *Vera*, E with breakfast, good).

N.B. This entire coastal area, and especially San Antonio, was damaged in the severe earthquake of March 3, 1985.

THE CHILEAN PACIFIC ISLANDS (4)

Juan Fernández Islands, some 650 km. W of Valparaíso, were discovered by Fernández in 1574. One of them was the home (1704-09) of Alexander Selkirk (the original of Defoe's *Robinson Crusoe*), whose cave on the beach of Robinson Crusoe island is shown to visitors. The main island has 550 people housed in log huts, who fish for crayfish which they send to the mainland. The village of San Juan Bautista has a church, schools, post office, and wireless station.

The climate is mild, the vegetation rich, and there are plenty of wild goats—and some tourists, for the islands are now easily reached by air. The boat service, about every three weeks from Valparaíso, is for cargo only; Empremar, Almirante Gómez Carreño 49, Valparaíso (T 258061) or Estado 359 (4th floor), Santiago. There is an air taxi daily in summer (subject to demand) from Santiago (Los Cerrillos airport, US$370 round trip), by Taxpa, Nueva York 53; also from Valparaíso. The plane lands on an airstrip in the W of the island; passengers are taken by boat to San Juan Bautista (1½ hrs., US$2 one way).

The anvil-shaped peak, El Yunque, is the highest peak on Robinson Crusoe and it was upon this hill that Selkirk lit his signal fires. A tablet was set in the rock at the look-out point by British naval officers in 1858, to commemorate Selkirk's solitary stay on the island for 4 years and 4 months. This look-out (Mirador de Selkirk) is the only easy pass between the north and south sides of the island. The official names of the three islands are: Robinson Crusoe (previously Más a Tierra), Alejandro Selkirk (previously Más Afuera) and Santa Clara (the smallest island). In summer, a boat goes once a month between Robinson Crusoe and Alejandro Selkirk if the crayfish catch warrants it, so you can visit either for a few hours or a whole month.

Hotels *Hostería Robinson Crusoe,* L (US$30-35 d, full board, plus 20% tax), about 20 minutes' walk from the village. *Daniel Defoe Hotel, El Pangal Hotel, Renaldo Green Pensión,* good, all slightly cheaper, but not as good as *Robinson Crusoe.* Lodging with villagers is difficult. T Valparaíso 81573.

Easter Island (Isla de Pascua) is just S of the Tropic of Capricorn and 3,790 km. W of Chile; its nearest neighbour is Pitcairn Island. It is triangular in shape, 24 km. across, with an extinct volcano at each corner. The population was stable at 4,000 until the 1850s, when Peruvian slavers, smallpox and emigration (encouraged by plantation-owners) to Tahiti reduced the numbers. Now it is about 2,500, of whom about a quarter are from the mainland, mostly living in the village of Hanga Roa. Just north of Hanga Roa, there is a reconstructed site with a temple, houses and a ramp leading into the sea. Further along, there is a mediocre museum (Mon. to Sat., 0900-1200, 1400-1700, Sun. 0900-1500). About half the island, of low round hills with groves of eucalyptus, is used for sheep and cattle, and nearly one-third constitutes a National Park. The islanders, of Polynesian origin, have preserved their indigenous songs and dances, and are extremely hospitable. Tourism has grown rapidly since the air service began in 1967. Paid work is now more common, but much carving is still done; the better items are no longer cheap (about US$30), but are readily bartered for clothing. Airport shop is expensive; there are cheaper stalls in the Mercado Municipal, east of Tahai, and Cema store. You may find cheaper carvings still in Santiago. The islanders have profited much from the visits of North Americans: a Canadian medical expedition left a mobile hospital on the island in 1966, and when a US missile-tracking station was abandoned in 1971, vehicles, mobile housing and an electricity generator were left behind. The unique features of the island are the 600 (or so) *moai,* huge stone figures up to 9 metres in height and broad in proportion. One of them, on Anakena beach, was restored to its (probably) original state with a plaque commemorating Thor Heyerdahl's visit in 1955. Heyerdahl's theories, as expressed in *Aku-Aku, The Art of Easter Island* (New York: Doubleday, 1975), are not as widely accepted as they used to be, and South American influence is now largely discounted (see below). Other *moai,* at Ahu Tepeu and Ahu Tahai, have since been re-erected. The rainy season is from February to the end of August. Useful information is contained in David Stanley's *South Pacific Handbook,* and there is a very thorough illustrated book by J. Douglas Porteous (a frequent, and valued, correspondent of ours), *The Modernization of Easter Island* (1981), available from Department of Geography, University of Victoria, BC, Canada, US$6.

David Bulbeck, an anthropologist from Adelaide, writes: Far from being the passive recipient of external influences, Easter Island shows the extent of unique development possible for a people left wholly in isolation. It is believed to have been colonized from Polynesia about AD 800: its older altars (*ahu*) are similar to those of (French) Polynesia, and its older statues (*moai*) similar to those of the Marquesas Islands. The very precise stone fitting of some of the *ahu*, and the tall gaunt *moai* with elongated faces and ears for which Easter Island is best known were later developments whose local evolution can be traced through a comparison of the remains. Indigenous Polynesian society, for all its romantic idylls, was competitive, and it seems that the five clans which originally had their own lands demonstrated their strength by erecting these complex monuments. The *moai* were sculpted at the Rano Raraku quarry and transported on wooden rollers over more or less flat paths to their final locations; their red topknots were sculpted at and brought from the inland quarry of Puna Pau; and the rounded pebbles laid out checkerboard fashion at the *ahu* all came from the same beach at Vinapu. The sculptors and engineers were paid out of the surplus food produced by the sponsoring family: Rano Raraku's unfinished *moai* mark the end of the families ability to pay. Over several centuries from about AD 1400 this stone work slowed down and stopped, owing to the deforestation of the island caused by roller production, and damage to the soils through deforestation and heavy cropping. The birdman cult represented at Orongo is a later development after the islanders had lost their clan territoriality and were concentrated at Hanga Roa, but still needed a non-territorial way to simulate inter-clan rivalry.

Things to See   The visitor should see the crater of the volcano Rano Kau with its reed-covered lakes; best for photographs in the afternoon. The adjacent ceremonial city of Orongo with its petroglyphs (entrance US$1.50, pamphlet in Spanish extra) is famous for the birdman cult and gives good views of Motu Nui, Motu Iti and Motu Kaokao, the so-called bird islets. The volcano Rano Raraku; the statues at Ahu Tahai; the beaches of Ovahe and Anakena (Thor Heyerdahl's landing place, also restored *moai*); and the *ahu* and *moai* at Vinapu, Akivi/Siete Moai, Pitikura, Vaihu and Tahai. Ahu Tongariki, once the largest platform, was badly damaged by a tidal wave in 1960. Cave paintings at Ana Kai Targata. Music at the 0830 Sun. mass is "enchanting". Museum near Tahai. If you are hiring a car, you should do the sites from south to north since travel agencies tend to start their tours in the north (also a high-clearance vehicle is better-suited to the roads than a normal vehicle).

Accommodation and Food   A comprehensive list of all accommodation available is displayed at the airport information desk. *Hotel Hanga Roa* (L) including all meals (120 beds), does not take credit cards, breakfast included; *Hostal Nanatura*, A, excellent food; *Hotel Otai*, comfortable, friendly, run by a family, rec.; *Hotel Victoria*, Av. Pont, T 272, L, friendly, helpful owner Jorge Edmunds arranges tours; *Iorana Hotel*, on Ana Magara promontory (5 mins. from airport), 14 rooms, friendly, excellent food, T 345; convenient for visiting Ana Kai Targata caves; *Residencial Evert House*, Arapiku-Nui-on-Hill, comfortable and homely; *Easter Island Hotel*, on main street of Hanga Roa, A with breakfast and dinner (excellent restaurant), good service, nice garden (T 294); *Toro Nui* on main street, B, full board with private bathroom, will provide packed lunch. *Hostería Robinson Crusoe* at Pangal, B, but far from village; *Hostería Green* opposite landing stage, B, full board. Homes offering accommodation and tours (rates ranging from US$15 to US$35, including meals): Yolanda Ika's (*Residencial Tiare Naoho*), Rosita Cardinale's, B with breakfast, rec., modern, will arrange Land Rover at US$100 per day; Krenia Tucki's *Residencial Kai Poo*, B, small, clean, friendly with hot water; Maná Reina Paoa and Juan Edmunds, A; *Residencia Hanga Roa Reka* (Sra. Milarosa Rirokakot), B full board, good, friendly; Gonzalo and Elsa Nahoe, B; María Georgina Hucke, of Tiki Tours, C with half board, rec.; *Residencial Pedro Atán* (A, full board); Sophia Gomero and María Luisa Pakarati. *Residencial Tehai*, next to airport, B with breakfast and dinner, very good; Emilio and Milagrosa Paoa, B with full board, rec. accommodation and tours. Some families (such as Anakena and Raraku) and *Residencial Pedro Atán* will rent their gardens to travellers with a tent, US$7, with meal; the lack of natural water makes this uncomfortable. On arrival at the airport, visitors are met in force by guest-house keepers, drivers, horse-hirers, etc.

Kopa Kabana restaurant, quite good; another opp. municipal market (which does not sell food). There are a couple of expensive supermarkets, cheapest is ECA on main street. Local produce which can be found free (but ask) includes wild guava fruit, fish, "hierba Luisa" tea, and wild chicken. Food, wine and beer expensive because of freight charges. Bring all you can from the mainland (and remember that wine, whisky, watches, clothing—especially army surplus gear and tennis shoes—are good items for barter). There are two discotheques in Hanga Roa. Both are popular, but drinks are expensive: a bottle of wine costs US$4, canned beer US$1.50. Beware of extras such as US$3 charge for hot water.

Camping   Free in eucalyptus groves near the Ranger's house at Rano Raraku, and at Anakena. Officially, camping is not allowed anywhere else, but this is not apparently strictly enforced. Several habitable caves around the coast: e.g. between Anakena beach and Ovahe.

Warning   The water on the island is not safe to drink; its high magnesium content may make you sick: drink only boiled or iodized water. Also, although the islanders are very nice about getting you a horse—they will get you *any* horse, so beware.

Bank   at Tahai, open 0900-1400 daily. Bank charges 10% commission per cheque. AmEx credit cards are accepted on the island, and while most places accept travellers' cheques, cash dollars are expected. **Post Office** 0900-1700.

Tourist Office Kia-Koe, at *Hanga Roa Hotel*, excellent range of excursions which include all the island's sites in 2½ days (to see it all you must start with the 1530/1600 tour on the day you arrive).

Travel Agency Mahinatur Ltda, will make your car reservations in advance.

Medical There are a 20-bed hospital, 2 resident doctors and 2 dentists on the island.

How to Get There Lan-Chile fly three times a week Dec.-Feb. (Sun., Tues., Fri.), 5 hrs (rest of year twice a week). Return to Santiago is Mon., Wed., Sat. (Mon. and Sat. out of season). Lan-Chile's *insular* tour-ticket, which includes length of Chile and Easter Island, is US$520 but must be purchased outside Chile. Lan-Chile fare in Feb. 1989 was US$367 each way business class, US$167 tourist; confirm and reconfirm all bookings as flights are heavily oversubscribed. Students studying in Chile eligible for 30% discount. The flight to Tahiti stops at Easter Island for ¾hr. going east, but 1½ hrs. in the other direction; a taxi may be hired during the stopover. Leaves Tahiti for Easter Island once a week, on Fri., from April to November and twice a week, Fri. and Sun., between December-March. Coming from Tahiti, you can stay for 2 days on Easter Island, Lan-Chile flight arriving Sat. 0600, leaving Mon. 0630 for Santiago (enough time to see all the important sites, but not to take it all in properly). (From Tahiti, connections can be made *direct* to Santiago, Lima, USA, Japan, Australia/New Zealand, S. Pacific in general.) The airport runway has been improved. There is strict plant quarantine on the island. A US project to extend the airfield, to provide an emergency landing for space shuttles, has been completed.

Transport on Easter Island Lan-Chile office in *Hotel Hanga Roa* provides tours of the island. Hitch-hiking up main road is possible. Jeep tours of archaeological sights cost US$60 per day (lunch included). It is possible to split the cost between up to 6 people. (Jeep hire without driver US$60/day). A horse can be hired for US$10 a day or less, and is the best way to see the island. Motorbikes may be rented for about US$20-30 a day including gasoline (Suzuki 125 rec. because of rough roads; for an extra US$5 you can get a driver), or truck US$15 p.p./day. Aku-Aku Tours arrange accommodation with islanders and excursions around the island, US$25 per person for full day, US$13-14 for half-day. Krenia Tucki of *Residencial Kai Poo* will also organize jeep tours, US$25 per day, as will Michel Fage. Some islanders, including Fernando and Marcelo León (Pai Tepano Rano, rec.) and Hugo Teave (good English, well-informed, polite) also provide tours. Charles Wilkins, Agencia de Viajes Mahinatur Ltda, T 20, English-born guide, rec., as is Victoriano Giralde, Kia-Koe Tours: provides transport for groups, arranges various activities and owns a local supermarket. Others may provide internal transport at a discount but be discreet, as an islander so doing is subjecting himself to social disapproval. The English of other tour guides is often poor. No good maps available on the island: best to get one in Santiago.

Dr. R. H. Webber writes: "It is possible to walk around the main part of the island in two days, either camping at Anakena or returning to Hanga Roa and setting out again the next day (but most correspondents agree that this is far too quick). From Hanga Roa, take the road going past the airport and continue northeast until you come to a right turn at a wireless station. Continue along the south coast, past many *ahus* to Rano Raraku (20 km.). The statues have been pushed over in some places, exposing the hollow chambers where human bones are still to be found.

"There are also many temple sites in the Hanga Nui area nearby; the road goes past "the trench of the long-ears" and an excursion can be made to Poike to see the open-mouthed statue that is particularly popular with local carvers. The jeep-track continues to Ovahe, passing many temple sites and conical houses. At Ovahe, there is a very attractive beach with pink sand and some rather recently carved faces and a cave.

"From Ovahe, one can return direct to Hanga Roa or continue to Anakena, site of King Hotu Matua's village. From Anakena the coastal path is variable in quality, but there are interesting remains and beautiful cliff scenery. At Hanga o Teo, there appears to be a large village complex, with several round houses, and further on there is a burial place, built like a long ramp with several ditches containing bones.

"From Hanga o Teo, one can venture inland to Aku Akivi, where there are several other sites and a cave at Tepahu. Near here there is a trail to Puna Pau; a track near the church leads to the top of the volcano.

"Rano Kau, south of Hanga Roa, is another important site to visit; one finds the curious Orongo ruins here. One final place not to be missed is Vinapu, where the *ahu* masonry work rivals that of the Incas."

A shorter walk is from Hanga Roa to Ahu Akivi, down to the South West coast, and back to Hanga Roa (8 km. one way).

To Buenos Aires across the Andes The Pan-American Highway runs north from Santiago to the rich Aconcagua Valley, the so-called Vale of Chile. The transandine route to Argentina branches east just after Llay-Llay.

RAPA NUI
EASTER ISLAND

55

If driving from Valparaíso, Route 62 runs through Viña del Mar, climbs out of the bay and goes through (16 km.) *Quilpue,* 1½ km. from El Retiro, a popular inland resort with medicinal springs. It crosses a range of hills and reaches the Aconcagua Valley at *Limache* (40 km. from Valparaíso); population 22,511 (*Hotel Colegio Alemán*). Between Quilpue and Limache is Peñablanca, the town of the white windmills. It then runs NE to *Quillota,* an orchard centre (Balneario El Edén, 5 km out of town, good swimming), and La Calera (88 km. from Valparaíso), where it joins the Pan-American Highway; turn SE and E for Llay-Llay, San Felipe, Los Andes and the pass over the mountains to Mendoza.

San Felipe, the capital of Aconcagua Province, is 96 km. from Santiago and 128 km. from Valparaíso; it is an agricultural and mining centre with 42,000 inhabitants, 635 metres above sea level, with an agreeable climate. Part of the Inca highway has recently been discovered in the city; previously, no traces had been found further south than La Serena. A paved highway (13 km.) runs N from San Felipe to the old town of Putaendo.

Hotel *Hostería Pedro Aguirre Cerda,* Merced 204, D.

Termas de Jahuel (hotel), is high in the Cordillera (1,190 metres) 18 km. by road from San Felipe. The hill scenery includes a distant view of Aconcagua. Good roads in the neighbourhood.

Curimón, between San Felipe and Los Andes, has a historic church, with a small museum attached.

Sixteen km. SE of San Felipe is *Los Andes,* in a wealthy agricultural, fruit-farming and wine-producing area. There are monuments to José de San Martín and Bernardo O'Higgins in the Plaza de Armas, and a monument to the Clark brothers, who built the Transandine Railway (much of which is now either disused or pulled up). Good views from El Cerro de la Virgen. Trail starts at the municipal picnic ground on Independencia (easy to climb taking approx. 1 hr.). It is 77 km. to Santiago by road. Population: 30,500. Altitude: 730 metres.

Hotels *Continental*, D; *Balneario El Corazón, Hostería La Ribera*, E; *Plaza*, E, good but restaurant expensive. *Baños El Corazón*, with full board, A, use of swimming pool but thermal baths extra; take bus San Esteban/El Cariño (US$0.50). *Central*, Esmeralda 278 (1 block from bus station) T 421275, F, reasonable and very friendly (excellent bakery opposite, try the empanadas). *Restaurante Círculo Italiáno*, near bus station, rec.

Beyond Los Andes the Pan-American Highway passes into the Cordillera and winds along the Río Aconcagua for 34 km. until it reaches the village of **Río Blanco** (1,370 metres), set at the confluence of two rivers which go to form the Río Aconcagua: the Blanco and the Juncal. There is a fish hatchery with small botanical garden at the entrance of the Andina copper mine. *Hostería Luna*, 8 km before Río Blanco on road from Los Andes, good value, clean, helpful, but poor food. *Hostería Guardia Vieja*, expensive but untidy. Possible to camp. Buses run daily from Los Andes; from Santiago, Bus Ahumada, at 1930 daily, direct, 2 hrs., US$2.

(Do not wait around at Los Andes for bus transport to Argentina as the local buses only go as far as Río Blanco; much better from Santiago. Hitch-hiking over Andes possible on trucks from Aduana building in Los Andes).

Beyond Caracoles (Customs post; long delays; no fruit can be taken across) the highway over La Cumbre (Uspallata) pass rises by steep grades to the Redentor tunnel: the road over the pass is more scenic, but is often closed. The tunnel is open from 0800 to 1800, Chilean time. Toll US$0.50. The top, at an altitude of 3,856 metres, is 8 km. beyond the tunnel and can be reached only on foot. The frontier is crossed at the foot of the statue of Christ the Redeemer, dwarfed by the scenery. The mountain views (including Aconcagua) are stupendous; as are the wild flowers in late January and early February. On the far side of the Andes the road descends 203 km. to Mendoza, where there are road and rail connections for Buenos Aires. The road from the tunnel to Mendoza is in fair condition, all of it paved.

SANTIAGO S TO TEMUCO (5)

Road and railway run S through the Central Valley, one of the world's most fruitful and beautiful countrysides, with the snowclad peaks of the Andes delimiting it to the E. Most of Chile's population lives in this valley.

The railway has been electrified from Santiago to S of Chillán. Along the road

SOUTH THROUGH THE CENTRAL VALLEY 56A

from Santiago to Temuco there are several modern motels. From Santiago to San Fernando, the highway is dual carriageway, with two tolls of US$2 to pay.

Rancagua, the capital of the Sixth (Libertador General Bernardo O'Higgins) Region, 82 km. S of Santiago (1½ hrs. by train, less by bus, US$2.10), is an agricultural centre with a population of 140,000, where a battle was fought in 1814 by O'Higgins against the Royalists. Its Merced church is a national monument; it also has a historical museum. El Teniente, the largest underground copper mine in the world, is 67 km. to the E, at 2,750 metres; a permit to visit may be obtained in Santiago only (Huérfanos 1270). On this line, 37 km. from Rancagua by rail or road, are the thermal springs of Cauquenes, and nearby is the hydroelectric plant of Rapel, with large lake.

Festivals at Rancagua The national rodeo championship is held there at the end of March. Festival del Poroto (Bean Festival), Feb. 1-5.

Hotels *Central; Turismo; Santiago; Ducal,* all D. *España,* San Martín near Brasil, F (without bath, more with), central, hot water, pleasant, clean. *Termas de Cauquenes,* D, quiet, clean, expensive but excellent food (colectivo from Rancagua market, US$1.10). Many hotels do not accept guests before 2000 hrs., or may charge you double if you arrive in the afternoon. Some 50 km. south is *Hacienda Los Lingues,* **see page 462.**

Tourist Office Germán Riesco 277, T 225777.

San Fernando (*Hotel Imperio*), founded in 1742, capital of Colchagua Province, with 44,500 inhabitants, is 51 km. S of Rancagua. It stands in a broad and fertile valley at a height of 340 metres. A branch railway and road (buses) run W to the seaside resort of Pichelemu (train daily at 1815, 3¼ hrs., returns 0730, US$1.75). A road runs E towards the Cordillera and bifurcates: the northern branch runs to the Termas del Flaco, near the Argentine frontier; the southern branch goes to the resort of Sierra Bella Vista, a private *fundo* where many Santiago businessmen have holiday houses, but there is also a *hostería* which caters for about 20 to 25 guests. Cowboy rodeos in October and November.

Curicó, 60 km. S of San Fernando and 192 km. from Santiago, is in the heart of the wine country; population: 74,000. The surroundings are picturesque and the town's main Plaza de Armas is one of the finest in the country. A branch railway runs W to Licantén, 26 km. from the popular sea beaches of Iloca and Retén Llico (*Pensión Chile,* F, no hot water, basic). There is a toll (US$2) on the Longitudinal Highway south of Curicó.

Hotels *Luis Cruz Marines; Comercio* (rec.); *Curicó; Prat,* near Plaza de Armas, cheap and good value.

Camping Elfenwald, on Lake Vichuquén, near Llico.

Buses To Santiago, US$3.

From Curicó you can visit the Siete Tazas National Park, where a river flows through seven rock bowls, each with a pool emptying into the next by a small waterfall. The river then passes through a canyon, 15 metres deep but only 1½ metres wide, which ends abruptly in a cliff and a beautiful waterfall. Go to Molina from where buses run to the Park, daily in Jan. and Feb., twice weekly in March, and Oct.-Dec. Camping may be permitted at the park or at Parque Inglés 5 km. away.

Talca, 56 km. S of Curicó (258 km. from Santiago) is the most important city between Santiago and Concepción and an important maufacturing centre; it is the capital of the Seventh (Maule) Region, and has a population of 300,000. It was founded in 1692, and destroyed by earthquake in 1742 and 1928; it has been completely rebuilt since 1928. Chilean independence was declared in Talca on January 1, 1818. The market is near the bus station, where there are also stalls selling cheap food. A 175 km. road runs E through the pass of Pehuenche (2,490 metres) to San Rafael (Argentina). Near the border is Lake Maule (2,130 metres). The road passes through some of the finest mountain scenery in Chile, but permission to visit this area must be obtained from the Vice Comandancia del Regimiento de Infantería No. 16, Calle 3 Oriente, Talca (T 38159). There is no transport, accommodation or food there. A visit to an old estate at Villa Cultural Huilquileru is rec., 10 km. away.

Hotels *Plaza,* good commercial standard, and *Claridge,* both D; *Alcázar,* 2 Sur 1359 and 7 Oriente, F, breakfast and meals available, rec. as reasonable and clean. Also, *Cordillera Residencial,* 2 Sur 1360, near new bus terminal. Youth Hostel: Ciudad de Constitución, Desembocadura del Río Maule. *Café-bar El Gobelino,* on Plaza de Armas, English-style pub.

Museum Museo O'Higgins, 1 Norte 875, entrance US$0.35, open Tues.-Fri. 0930-1300, 1500-1900, Sat. till 1830, Sun. 1000-1300; interesting.

Tourist Office Edificio Intendencia (at the town hall), T 33669.

Bus Terminal, corner 12 Oriente and 2 Sur. To Chillán, frequent service, US$2; also frequent to Constitución, 2 hrs., US$1.20.

Excursion To *Vilches,* the starting point for the climb to the volcanoes Quizapu and Descabezado (3,850 metres) 2 buses a day, US$1.50, 2-2½ hrs., leave Talca 1300 and late p.m., leave Vilches 0700 and 1730. *Hostería Rancho Los Canales* has log cabins, D bed and breakfast, use of kitchen, hospitable, knowledgeable family (postal address: Clasificador 28, Correo de Talca). 2 km beyond Vilches is a national park, with beautiful walks; visit the lakes Los Patos, La Encantada and El Toro, and the Piedras Tacitas, a stone construction supposedly made by the aboriginal inhabitants of the region.

Constitución, 105 km. from Talca by rail, and also reached by paved road from San Javier, is the centre of a prosperous district producing grain and timber, but its main attraction is as a seaside resort. The beach, an easy walk from the town, is surrounded by very picturesque rocks. The nearby scenery is attractive, despite nearby factory. There are plenty of hotels and *pensiones,* but accommodation is difficult from January to March, and bookings must be made well in advance.

Hotels *Hostería Constitución,* best; *Residencial Mistral,* D, very friendly; *Residencial Bulnes,* Bulnes 673, F with breakfast, hot water, clean.

Restaurants *Colonial,* good but expensive; *Portales,* good, cheaper; both on Portales.

About half-way between Talca and Chillán is the road and rail junction of Parral, 342 km. S of Santiago, celebrated as the birthplace of the Nobel Prize-winning poet Pablo Neruda.

Chillán, 105 km. S of the road junction of Linares (youth hostel, Av. Valentín Letelier 1162), was the birthplace of Bernardo O'Higgins. In Chillán Viejo there is a monument and park in his honour; it has a mural depicting his life, and a Centro Histórico y Cultural (park closes at 1800). (Chile's naval hero, Captain Arturo Prat, was born 50 km. from Chillán, at Ninhue.) It is an important agricultural centre with a population of 121,000. When the city was destroyed by earthquake in 1833, the new city was built slightly to the N; that, too, was destroyed by earthquake in 1939 and there was a further earthquake in 1960. It is a pleasant city with a modern cathedral (containing a famous mural). The outdoor Municipal Market has tourist items and good restaurant; open daily, Sun. until 1300. Murals by David Alfaro Siqueiros, the great Mexican artist, in library of Escuela México.

Hotels *Gran Hotel Isabel Riquelme,* Arauco 600, T 223664, A; *Rucamanqui,* Herminda Martín 590 (off Plaza de Armas), T 222927, D, clean, spartan; *Chillán,* D, good service though dirty, full board only; *Real,* 18 de Septiembre 357, E; *Hostería Sur,* O'Higgins 770, E; *Claris,* Libertad 219, 2 blocks from plaza, friendly, F, hot water; *Bahai,* opp. railway station, basic, F. Youth hostel, Herminda Martín 579.

Restaurants 3-course meal in *Hotel Chillán* for US$2. *O'Higgins,* Constitución 199, good almuerzo; *Español,* good food and snacks throughout the day. *Fuente Alemán* for churrasco; opposite is *Café París,* expresso coffee.

Exchange Both Banco de Concepción and Banco Sudamericano give poor rates.

Tourist Office Centro Histórico Cultural de Chillán Viejo, T 23272; try also public relations office, 2nd floor of Municipal building, corner of Libertad y 18 de Septiembre.

Train To Concepción daily at 1345 and 1710, 2 hrs., US$2.20. To Santiago, 4 daily, 6 hrs., saloon US$8.25, *económico* (one train only) US$5.65, 1st US$4.90, 2nd US$4.60. Check times in advance.

Bus   Terminal at Maipon and Sgto. Aldea for local buses (4 blocks from centre). For Santiago, 7 hrs, US$7.50, buses leave from the interprovincial terminal at Constitución 10 y Brasil (opp. railway station). Tegualda 860 and Barrios Arana 90, bus to Concepción, every ½ hr.

Excursions   27 km. SW of Chillán is **Quinchamalí**, a village famous for the originality of its craftsmen in textiles, basketwork, black ceramics, guitars and primitive paintings (all on sale in Chillán market). Its ferry, at Confluencia, 5 km. away, powered by the flowing river and manned during daylight hours, except 1200 to 1400, is a must for enthusiasts of alternative technology; in summer, when the current is weak, it runs on human power. To the thermal baths, Termas de Chillán, 82 km. E, 1,850 metres up in the Cordillera, reached by a good road all the way. Season: middle December to the end of March (no public transport at other times, except from *Hotel Isabel Riquelme* at weekends). Here the Ski Club de Chile has a tourist centre with hotel (L, full board) and ski-lifts. There is excellent ski-ing on the slopes and views of the Chillán volcano, E of the Termas. Cheaper than centres nearer Santiago; packages available.

From Chillán there are various road routes to Concepción: (1) SW to Penco and S along the coast—there is a scenic railway; (2) along the Longitudinal Highway to Bulnes, where a branch road goes SW to Concepción; or (3) along the Highway past the Salto del Laja to Los Ángeles, from which a main road and a railway run NW to Concepción.

Concepción, the capital of the Eighth (Bío-Bío) Region, 15 km. up the Bío-Bío river and 515 km. from Santiago, is the most important city in southern Chile and the third city of the Republic. Its port, Talcahuano, is 15 km. away. Population: 240,000 (with Talcahuano: 468,000).

The climate is very agreeable in summer, but from April to September the rains are heavy; the annual average rainfall, nearly all of which falls in those six months, is from 1,250 to 1,500 mm. Concepción has been outstandingly unfortunate in the matter of earthquakes; it was founded in 1550, but its site has had to be moved more than once during its history.

In the attractive Plaza de Armas at the centre are the Intendencia, the city hall and court house and the Cathedral. The old arcades have given way to a new shopping area. In the Parque Ecuador, there is a craft fair every February.

Cerro Caracol can easily be reached on foot starting from the statue of Don Juan Martínez de Rozas in the Parque Ecuador, arriving at the Mirador Chileno after 15 minutes (necessary to obtain permission first from Entel office). Chile's largest river, the Bío-Bío, and its valley running down to the sea lie below. On the far side of the river you see lagoons, the largest of which, San Pedro, is a water-sport centre. On the city side, among cypress trees, is the modern Barrio Universitario. A stroll through the grounds, which are beautifully kept with geese, ducks, swans, hummingbirds and a small enclosure with *pudu-pudu* (miniature deer) is rec.; the Casa del Arte here contains a fine allegorical mural, 35 by 6 metres, the *Presencia de América Latina*, by Jorge González Camerena. There is a golf club on the road to Coronel, La Posada, by the side of a picturesque lake.

There are striking massive rock formations along the banks of the Bío-Bío estuary. Concepción is linked with Talcahuano, on the bay, by railway and 2 good roads, half-way along one of which is the Club Hípico's racetrack. Races are held on Sun. and holidays. A branch road leads to good beaches, including Penco with two good seafood restaurants. It passes through the Parque de Hualpén, which can be reached by bus in summer (US$1) and taxi all the year (US$10). In it, on a farm, is a small museum containing curious local and Mapuche Indian items. Nearby is the strikingly set beach of Desembocadura del Río. Two other beaches are Las Escaleras (a private club)—a flight of natural stairs down a sheer 53-metre sea cliff leads to it—and Ramuntcho, named after a novel by a visitor in 1875: Pierre Loti.

Concepción is one of Chile's industrial centres. It has plenty of the most important industrial raw material, water, and good port facilities at Talcahuano and other places in the bay. It is near the

SOUTH-
CENTRAL CHILE

56B

coalfields, has ample sources of hydroelectric power, good rail and road communications with the consuming centres further N, and plenty of room to expand.

Hotels *El Araucano*, Caupolicán 521, *City*, Castellón 510; *Cruz del Sur*, Freire 889 (not very friendly), all three C; *Bío Bío*, better, but smaller, near main square, B, with private bath; *Ritz*, Barros Arana 721, D, reasonable: *El Dorado*, Barros Arana 348, T 229400, Telex 260031 DORAL Cl; *Alborada*, Barros Arana 457, Casilla 176, T 228226, C; *Tabancura*, Barros Arana 790, C, clean; *Res. Turismo*, Calle Caupolicán 67, E with breakfast (optional, fortunately), hot water a.m. only, clean, fireplace, nice, doors close at 0030; *Res. Metro*, Barros Arana 464, F, hot shower, friendly; *Res. Concepción*, Freire 552, across from the market; *Res. O'Higgins*, Av. O'Higgins 457, central, E, pricey, grubby, good value; *Youth Hostel*, Colo Colo 354, draughty but O.K.

Campsite Fundo Santa Sara, at Yumbel (1½ hrs. drive from city).

Restaurants *Le Château* (French), Colo Colo 340, excellent seafood and meat; *Casino Español*, Plaza de Armas, good; *El Parque*, in Parque Ecuador (Víctor Lamas y Colo Colo), good, open Sun.; only other places open on Sun. are *Chung Hwa*, Barros Arana 270; *Da Salvatore* (Italian), Av. O'Higgins 448; *Carnoteca*, Bulnes; *Fortín Bulnes*, same street; *La Estancia* (Arab), Ejército 452. Arab specialities at *Veteranos del 79* by Víctor Lamas (Parque Ecuador), good, cheap; *El Rodizio*, Castellón 366, good, interesting fixed menu; good sandwiches at *Entrepanes*, Caupolicán, between B.Arana and Freire. "Acceptable with moderate prices" is the *Concepción* grill room at Barros Arana 101; *Ciro's*, Barros Arana 887, excellent food and service. Many *fuentes de soda* in centre; *Fuente Alemana*, Av. O'Higgins, rec. Also, *El Estribo*, one block from main plaza. *Nuria Café Bar*, Barros Arana, serves excellent "lomo a lo pobre", steak with 2 eggs, chips, bread and brown ale. The market place has excellent seafood and the best pastel de choclo.

Clubs Concepción at Los Copihues; Alemán; Círculo Francés; Chilean-British Institute, San Martín 573 (British newspapers, library); Chilean-North American Institute, Caupolicán 301; Chileno-Italiano, Barros Arana. Country Club, Pedro de Valdivia, outside swimming pool, tennis.

Museum Museo de Concepción, near Barrio Universitario, Tues.-Sat. 1000-1300, 1400-1700, Sun. 1430-1730. Entrance US$0.30. Interesting on history of Mapuche Indians.

Exchange For travellers' cheques, best rates at Travel Agent opposite *Hotel El Araucano*; also Banco Concepción.

Laundry O'Higgins 900 esq. Castellón.

Tourist Office Aníbal Pinto 460, T 223272. Will advise on the more expensive hotels.

Air In the summer, flights daily to and from Santiago (in winter, only four a week) and connections to Temuco, Puerto Montt and Punta Arenas. The new jet airport is by the fast road from Talcahuano and Concepción.

Rail Daily to Temuco at 0800 and 1220, US$3.25, 5 hrs.; to Puerto Montt three times weekly, 18 hrs., change at Temuco; to Santiago daily and in the summer special fast diesel trains three times weekly, 10 hrs., saloon US$9.20, *económico* (one train daily) US$4.75, 1st US$5.85, sleeper US$15.10/22.

Buses Long distance terminal on outskirts, on Av. Gen. Bonilla, next to athletics stadium; buses from Av. Maipú in centre. To and from Santiago, 8½ hrs., US$7; to Loncoche, 7 hrs., US$6.50; to Puerto Montt US$8.50, leaves Concepción 0745, arrives Puerto Montt 2000, only one ½ hour stop so take food and drink with you; to Pucón, 8 hrs., US$7.35. Igi-Llaima, to Temuco, 5 hrs., US$4.25, at 0800 and 1130. To Los Angeles, US$1.50. Best direct bus line to Chillán is Línea Azul, 2 hrs., US$2, at 0700, connects with 0900 train to Santiago. For a longer and more scenic route, take Costa Azul bus which follows old railway line, through Torné, Coelemu and Nipas on to Chillán (part dirt-track, takes 5½ hrs.). Frequent service to Coronel (US$0.45). For Arauco and Bío-Bío line, buses leave from railway station on Av. Prat. To Lota, from Carrera y Prat, every 15 mins. (ask tourist office for details of all services).

Excursion to Lirquén, a small, old, pretty town of wooden houses with a good beach (walk along railway to reach it). Recommended. Plentiful cheap seafood for sale (try *Casa Blanca*, on Calle Manuel Rodríguez). At Penco, near the beach, is *Casinoriente*, another good seafood place, and *Hotel La Terraza*, E. Local buses from Av. Prat 484 take 20-30 mins., US$0.40. 16 km. further along is Tomé, 1½ hrs., US$0.70, another picturesque village; *Restaurante Piña*, main Plaza (owner speaks English); *Hotel Roxy*, and *Residencial Linares*, both F. An interesting cemetery, Miguel Gulán Muñoz, is set on a cliff overlooking the ocean. **Dichato**, a 1-hr. bus ride away, is also worth visiting: it is a beautiful fishing village and has the oceanographic centre of the University of Concepción. In summer it is a holiday resort. *Hotel Chicki*, E; *Montecarlo*, F; *Residencial Santa Elena*, on beach, G, clean, cold water; *Restaurant Monte Carlo*, on beach, good. Private Museo del Mar, by Benjamín Ortega, interesting, free. Take a local bus to the tiny village of Cocholgüe.

Between Concepción and Lota (see below) are the Lagunas Chica (swimming) and Grande (water sports), just across the Bío-Bío river. Nearer Lota are Playa Negra (small, few people, black sand) and Playa Blanca (bigger, bars, cafés, crowded, white sand).

Talcahuano, on a peninsula jutting out to sea, has the best harbour in Chile. It is Chile's main naval station; its dry docks accommodate vessels of 30,000 tons. PSNC ships call on both their northward and southward voyages. Population: 228,000. 1½ km. away the steel plant at Huachipato has its own wharf to unload the iron ore shipped from the N. "Base Naval" bus from main plaza in Concepción, going W on O'Higgins.

Hotel Res. San Pedro, E. **Restaurants** *El Alero de los Salvo,* Colón 3396; *La Aguada,* shellfish dishes; *Domingo Lara Lara,* Aníbal Pinto 450, seafood specialities, excellent.

The *Huáscar,* a relic of the War of the Pacific, is in the naval base. On May 21, 1879, at the beginning of the war, the Peruvian Navy's huge ironclad, the *Huáscar,* and a small one arrived at Iquique. Chile sent two small wooden ships under Captain Arturo Prat to challenge them. Prat fought with ferocity. When his broken vessel, the *Esmeralda,* was rammed by the *Huáscar* Prat called upon his men to follow him, boarded the enemy and continued fighting until he was killed. Chile later captured the *Huáscar* at the battle of Angamos, Mejillones, on October 8, 1879. The ship is open 1000-1200, 1400-1600, Tues.-Sun., but it seems admittance is sometimes not granted. Photography is not permitted and cameras must be handed in at main gate.

The railway to Curanilahue links the coal-producing districts near Concepción. It crosses the Bío-Bío by a 1,885-metre bridge, the longest of its kind in Chile. A new road bridge has been built. The town of *Coronel,* in the heart of the coal area, is 27 km. on. Coronel was the scene of a British naval defeat in 1914, which was later avenged at the Falklands with the destruction of the German squadron. The coast is very picturesque, the country wooded.

Buses Buses to Concepción every hour. Bus to Lota US$0.25.

Lota, 8 km. S of Coronel, is a coal-mining centre with 52,000 inhabitants. In the neighbourhood is the famous Parque Cousiño Isidora, laid out with views of the sea by an English landscape architect in the last century. It contains many flower gardens, romantic paths, and peafowl and pheasants roaming freely. (Admission US$0.60, no picnicking; open 1000-1800 daily, till 2000 in summer.) The Cousiño mining company runs an excellent ceramic factory. The road is paved beyond Lota as far as the seaside resort of Laraquete (an hour's run by car from Concepción), where there are miles of golden sands, and on to Arauco (*Hotel Plaza; Hostería Celulosa Arauco*), past the Celulosa Arauco wood-pulp plant.

Hotel Third house (blue, no numbers) in Calle Condell rec., F. Bus drivers from Agencia Miramar stay there. *Residencial Central,* Cousiño 656, F. Campsite at Playa Blanca, free.

Buses to Coronel (20 min.), and Concepción (1½ hrs., US$0.50). No rail services.

From Curanilahue, 96 km. from Concepción, a 32 km. road runs to Los Alamos, where a bus (26 km.) can be taken W to *Lebu,* a coal port with a population of 17,000 (*Hoteles Central*—F, and *Rocha*—G, on Pérez; *Res. Alcázar,* Alcázar 144, G with breakfast, cold water, friendly). It lies at the mouth of the Río Lebu, and is the capital of Arauco province (buses S leave from Los Alces, next to train station). The lower river reach and the beach are popular with tourists in summer.

13 Km. S of Los Alamos, is *Cañete,* a small town on the site of Fort Tucapel where Pedro de Valdivia and 52 of his men were killed by Mapuche warriors in 1554. Museo Mapuche de Cañete, half-hour walk from town in direction of Contulmo. Open, Tues.-Sun. 1000-1230, 1400-1800. Entrance US$ 0.60. Interesting for its architecture, landscape, gardens with flowers cultivated by the Mapuches. Ask for Sr. Mauricio Rivera Osorio.

Accommodation Some shops rent rooms, F. Mormons in Calle Condell offer accommodation, free and friendly.

Buses Buses to Purén, US$1.50; sit on right-hand side to get good views of Lake Lanalhue. To Concepción, 3 hrs., US$2.75.

From Lebu or Los Alamos you can go to Puerto Peleco on the highly picturesque Lake Lanalhue, 63 km. S of Lebu (buses S leave Los Alces, next to train station). 3½ km. S of Peleco, the road forks, the west branch running parallel to the coast (from this road, a dirt road goes along the south side of the lake to *Hostería Lanalhue*—16 km. from Peleco, adequate, nice location—and continuing to Contulmo bus terminal, taxi US$14, negotiable). By taking the west branch of the road for about 25 km. and then asking the way to Contulmo, you can reach the south-eastern end of the lake after crossing a high ridge from which you can see both the ocean in the W and the snow-capped Andes to the E. In **Contulmo** *Hotel Contulmo* is highly recommended, F with full board (Eduardo Videla and family love to break out the wine and guitar with visitors). Taxi from Contulmo to lake beach US$2; good swimming, but fishing not so. Bus Contulmo-Temuco 0800 and 1715 (0800 only Sun.), more frequent to Concepción (check times in advance).

Travelling on the Longitudinal Railway S from San Rosendo, the junction for Concepción, we come (24 km.) to Santa Fe, from which there is a branch line E to (21 km.) **Los Angeles,** a town of 106,000 inhabitants in a wine, fruit and timber district. It is a pleasant city, with a large Plaza de Armas; Colón is the main shopping street. There is a good daily market.

Hotels   *Gran Hotel Musa*, B, Valdivia 222 (Plaza de Armas), T 323163, good restaurant open to non-residents; *Mariscal Alcázar*, Lautaro 385 (Plaza de Armas), D; *London Bar*, Lautaro 281, E; *Central*, Almagro 377, E. On Caupolicán, *El Fogón Criollo*, No. 639, F; *Los Angeles*, No. 656, T 22551, with restaurant, E; *Residencial Capri*, No. 659, F; *Santa María*, Caupolicán 504 and Valdivia (Plaza de Armas), very clean, E, hot showers a.m., breakfast dreadful; will fetch your bags from bus terminal. Private house at Caupolicán 651, F, basic but OK. *Familia González*, Camilo Enríquez 156, E inc. breakfast, highly rec. Campsite: *Las Cabañas*, US$0.25 per tent.

Restaurants   *Centro Español* (top floor), *Fogón Gaucho*. *El Arriero*, Colo Colo 235, T 322899, good parrillas and international dishes; *Julio's Pizzas*, Colón 452 and *Rancho de Julio*, Colón 720, excellent parrilla; *Brasilia*, Colón 431. *Brisa Mamina*, Mercado Central Local 22, Villaquán 599, good, check bill.

British Cultural Institute   Vicuña 648.

Post Office on Plaza de Armas.

Tourist Office   Av. Caupolicán and Villagrán; also kiosk on Plaza de Armas.

Bus   to Santiago, 9 hrs., US$7.50. To Viña del Mar and Valparaíso 10 hrs., US$8.25, 4 daily to Concepción, US$1.50, 2¼ hrs. Hourly buses to Temuco. To Curacautín, daily at 0600, 3 hrs., US$2.25.

Excursion The *Salto del Laja* is a spectacular waterfall in which the Laja plunges 47 metres over the rocks. It costs a few pesos to enter the "parque" and walk up to the falls, or to walk on the hotel side. There is a good motel (the *Motel Salto del Laja*, C, address: Casilla 562, Los Angeles) with fine restaurant, 2 swimming pools and chalet-type rooms on an island overlooking the falls. Campsite, Los Coyuches (US$3.50 per tent). Also campsite at Salto Chico, overlooking falls, very good facilities (signs on the roads South of the falls). It is 6 hrs. drive from Santiago (by bus, US$7.25). To see the falls, buy bus ticket (Bus Sur or Bio Tal) from Los Angeles (32 km., US$0.60, ½ hr.—fairly frequent buses back to Los Angeles) or Chillán (US$2).

A road runs to the Parque Nacional Laguna de Laja past the impressive rapids of the Laja river. A car can take about 3 hours to get to the lake, where there is stark volcanic scenery of scrub and lava, dominated by the Antuco volcano and the glacier-covered Sierra Velluda. Take a bus to Abanico, 20 km. past Antuco (US$1.35, 2 hrs., 5 a day but only 0845 in a.m., return 0715), then 4 km. to park entrance, passport retained by guards till you leave (details from Conaf in Los Angeles, José de Manzo 275, 0800-1300, 1430-1800 Mon.-Fri.). Small hotel close to lake charges F p.p. in bunks; camping not permitted on lake shore. 7 km. further on from the lake there is the *Hotel Los Canelos*, F, while 14 km. on is the *Refugio Chacay* offering food, drink and bed (B). Following the road one reaches the Club de Esquí de los Andes with two ski-lifts, giving a combined run of 4 km. on the Antuco volcano (season, May-August). There is swimming in the Río Duqueco, ten minutes away by bus, US$0.80.

The road continues from Los Angeles to Santa Bárbara on the Bío-Bío river, and then via Collipulli (campsite), Victoria, Púa and Lautaro to Temuco.

From Collipulli and Los Angeles paved roads run W to **Angol** (25,000 people), capital of the Province of Malleco (Ninth Region), founded by Valdivia in 1552, seven times destroyed by the Indians and rebuilt. Bus from Los Angeles, US$1.20. Worth seeing are the Vergel experimental fruit-growing station, the Dillman S. Bullock regional museum with stone-age Indian artefacts (open Mon.-Sat. 1000-1230, 1500-1800, Sun. 1500-1800; free, a 5 km. bus-ride from town) and the San Francisco church. 22 km. W is the Parque Nacional Nahuelbuta, in the coastal mountain range, reached by bus to Vegas Blancas, 0700 and 1600 Mon., Wed., Fri., 1½ hrs., US$1, 27 km. from Ayol, then walk (or possibly hitch) 7 km. to park gate, and a further 7 km. to the campsite (US$0.70 to enter park, US$0.70 to camp). The park has many araucaria trees (monkey-puzzles) and viewpoints over both the sea and the Andean volcanoes. Roads run W to Los Sauces and Purén. Bus to Temuco, US$2.15.

Hotels   *Residencia Angol*, F; cheaper, unmarked *residenciales* on Prat.

Restaurant   *Angol*, Lautaro 194.

Mulchén, a small, old-fashioned town, 32 km. to the south of Los Angeles, has few cars, no concrete and is a glimpse of a world gone-by.

A small town which has hot springs nearby, *Curacautín*, is some 25 km. E of Púa, 111 km. S of San Rosendo and can be reached by paved road from Victoria; bus from Los Angeles or Temuco. The beautiful pine-surrounded Termas de Tolhuaca, with hot springs, are 37 km. to the NE of Curacautín by road. (*Hotel Termas de Tolhuaca*, B with full board, use of baths, and horse riding included, good; camping near the river, good.) It is a short walk from the hotel to the waterfalls of Malleco and Culiebra, and to Lake Malleco; superb scenery. SE of Curacautín (32 km. by road) are the hot springs and mud baths of Río Blanco (hotel), at 1,046 metres on the slopes of the Sierra Nevada and near Lake Conguillo (bus to Conguillo National Park only at 1800). 18 km. from Curacautín (direction Lonquimay) are the Termas de Manzanar, reached by bus from Temuco and Victoria (*Hotel Termas*, luxury, but also has cheaper rooms which are poor value; *Hostería Abarzua*, simple, friendly). The nearby Lonquimay volcano has the Puelche ski-run, open June-Oct. (Lonquimay last erupted in December 1988).

Curacautín Hotels   *Turismo; Internacional; Plaza.*

THE LAKE DISTRICT (6)

		Population ('000)	
Region	Provinces	1975	1982
IX (Araucanía)	Malleco, Cautín	649	698
X (Los Lagos)	Valdivia, Osorno, Llanquihue, Chiloé	693	848

South from the Bío-Bío river to the Gulf of Reloncaví the same land formation holds as for the rest of Chile to the N: the Andes to the E, the coastal range to the W, and in between the central valley. The Andes and the passes over them are less high here, and the snowline lower; the coastal range also loses altitude, and the central valley is not as continuous as from Santiago to Concepción. The climate is cooler; the summer is no longer dry, for rain falls during all the seasons, and more heavily than further N. The rain decreases as you go inland: some 2,500 mm. on the coast and 1,350 mm. inland. This is enough to maintain heavy forests, mostly beech, but there are large clearings and an active agriculture; irrigation is not necessary. The farms are mostly medium sized, and no longer the huge *haciendas* of the N. The characteristic thatched or red tiled houses of the rural N disappear; they are replaced by the shingle-roofed frame houses typical of a frontier land rich in timber. The farms raise livestock, fruit and food crops, and the timber industry is being encouraged.

About 20,000 pure blooded Mapuche Indians live in the area, more particularly around Temuco. There are possibly 150,000 more of mixed blood who speak the Indian tongue, though most of them are bilingual.

A Mapuche music festival (plus market) is normally held mid-February in Villarrica. Enquire at the Santiago or Temuco tourist office.

Between parallels 39° and 42° S is found one of the most picturesque lake regions in the world. There are some 12 great lakes of varying sizes, some set high on the Cordillera slopes, others in the central valley southwards from Temuco to Puerto Montt. Here, too, are imposing waterfalls and snowcapped volcanoes. Anglers revel in the abundance of fish, the equable climate, and the absence of troublesome insects (except for enormous horseflies between mid-December and mid-January). The season in the lake district is from mid-December to mid-March, when prices are higher and it is best to book well in advance. It is a peaceful area, with fewer tourists than across the border in the Argentine lake district.

The Lake District proper does not begin until we reach Chile's newest city, Temuco, founded 1881 after the final treaty with the Mapuches.

Temuco, 676 km. S of Santiago, has 220,000 inhabitants. It is the capital of the Ninth (Araucanía) Region, and one of the most active centres in the S. Wheat, barley, oats, timber and apples are the principal products of the area. The cattle auctions in the stockyards behind the railway on A. Malvoa, Mon. and Thurs. are interesting; you can see the *huasos*, or Chilean cowboys, at work. Also, cattle sales at Feria Agroaustral, just outside Temuco on road to Nuevo Imperial, on Fri. (take bus 4 from Calle Rodríguez), auction starts at 1400, and at Nuevo Imperial, 35 km. away, on Mon. and Tues. Temuco is the Mapuches' market town and you may see some, particularly women, in their typical costumes in the market next to the railway station. The best places to look for Indian textiles, pottery, woodcarving, jewellery etc. are the indoor market in centre of town (corner of Aldunate and Diego Portales); or, for textiles, early in the morning, near the bus station. There is a grand view of Temuco from Cerro Ñielol (closed Mon.), where there is a fine array of native plants in the natural state, including the national flower, the *copihue rojo*. There are also a casino (restaurant) and a bathing pool (US$0.40). On Cerro Ñielol is also La Patagua, the tree under which the final peace was signed with the Mapuches in 1881.

Hotels   *Turismo*, slightly run-down restaurant, good value, E (C with bath), Claro Solar 636, near main square; *Nuevo Hotel de la Frontera*, A, opposite, excellent; *Nicolás*, Mackenna 420, D with shower and heating, restaurant; *Espelette*, Claro Solar 492, E, clean, friendly; *Casa de huéspedes Centenario*, Aldunate 864, E, with breakfast, hot water, clean; *Terraz*, Av. Prat 520, F, not always hot water, restaurant, fair; *Residencial Méndez*, Matta 382, F, hot water. Many cheap *residenciales* and *pensiones* near railway station in market area. Also *Rupangue*, nr. Igi-Llaima terminal, 2 blocks from Terminal Rural, E, hot shower, clean, helpful, good value; *Omega*, opp. bus terminal, overlooking market, F p.p., hot shower, friendly but thefts reported. Unnamed *hospedaje* at Pedro Lagos 576, F p.p., meals, good, friendly. Sra. Veronica Kiekebusch, Av. Alemania 0649 (T 32079), E with breakfast, good transport connections; Casa familiar Mirtha Lagos de Concha, Zentano 525, E with breakfast, nice, clean. Private house, Blancolat 959, corner of San Martín, F p.p., use of kitchen, rec.; also G. Cruz 212, 2nd floor, E, breakfast, clean, friendly, good value; Bulnes 995, E; Claro Solar 151, E with breakfast; Bello 886, E. Youth Hostel, Av. Prieto Norte 280, basic.

Restaurants   *Hostería Allen Cley*, Bulnes 902 at bus station, excellent; *Kim Long*, Portales 1192, Chinese, excellent; *Fuente de Soda Ñam-Ñam*, Diego Portales 802, good hamburgers; *Centro Español*, Bulnes 483. Several in indoor market in centre, quite good; also *Restaurante Capri*, cheap, clean. Outside town: *Hostería La Estancia* (dancing), highly rec.; *Hostería Yacará*, *Frontera Country Club* (dancing), all on Longitudinal Norte; *Casino Ñielol* (dancing), on top of Cerro Ñielol.

Museum   Museo Araucano de Temuco, Alemania 084, a well-arranged Indian collection. Open Mon.-Sat. 0900-1300, 1500-1830; Sun. 1000-1300, US$0.50.

Car Hire   Hertz, Bulnes 726-733, T 36190/31226. Puig, on Portales, near Prat, cheap.

Exchange   Frontera Tours, Bulnes 750 and Turismo Narquimalmal, Bulnes 460, local 2, for parallel market; exchange also at Turismo Money Exchange, Pratt 656, and Huguette S. Larrere R., Bulnes 443, local 2, Caracol.

Tourist Office   on main square, at Calle Bulnes 586, esquina Clara Solar, T 34293. Open 0830-2030, all week in summer, Mon.-Fri. in winter. Has full list of places to stay. Also at Balmaceda and Av. Prat. Automóvil Club de Chile, Bulnes 763. **Conaf**, Bilbao y Caupolicán, T 34420.

Rail   Station at B. Arana and Lautaro. Twice daily to Talcahuano; daily to Puerto Montt, at 0520 (US$5 economy) and 1115 (US$3.25-4.25) and to Concepción at 1300 and 1315 (but not all year). To Valdivia: once a day in winter (0710), twice a day in summer. To Carahue: daily. To Santiago: twice a day (1930 and 2150, both with sleeper) saloon US$12.50, *económico* US$7.20, 1st US$6.85, 2nd US$6, sleeper US$19.20/27.35. Ticket office at Bulnes 582, open Mon.-Fri. 0900-1300, 1430-1800, Sun. 0900-1300 as well as at station.

Air   Ladeco has several flights a week to Valdivia, Osorno and Santiago; also one to Concepción.

Bus to neighbouring towns from Terminal Rural at Pinto and Balmaceda, near Mercado Municipal. To Curacautín, US$1.40, Flota Erbuc, 6 daily, 2¾ hrs. Frequent buses to Villarrica (US$1.60, 1½ hrs.) and Púcon (US$2.50, 2 hrs.); Buses JAC from Terminal Rural and V.Mackenna 798 y Bello, every hour. Long-distance buses leave from individual company terminals. To Valdivia, Osorno, Puerto Montt, Ancud and Castro, Buses Cruz del Sur from V.Mackenna 671, 3 a day to Castro, 5 a day to Puerto Montt (US$4.50). To Junín de los Andes (Argentina) Mon.-Sat. To Valdivia US$2; to Osorno US$3. Night buses to Santiago (Igi-Llaima, V. MacKenna 448), 11 hrs., US$9. Bío Bío bus to Concepción (US$4.25), six daily.

Excursions A road and railway run W to (55 km.) Carahue (*Hotel El Sol*). About 30 km. further, at the mouth of the navigable River Imperial, is **Puerto Saavedra**, where there is a stretch of beach with black volcanic sand. It comprises 3 distinct towns: the first administrative; the second, 2 km. away, the fishing port with one poor *residencial*; the third, a further 2 km., the tourist area with many *hosterías* in E-F category. It is reached from Carahue by car (1 hr.), or by bus.

From Puerto Saavedra there are interesting excursions to Nehuentue, on the other side of the river, or to Lakes Budi and Trovolhue, both well worth seeing. Trovolhue is reached by a specially chartered launch which takes 4 hrs. to go up the Moncul River. Puerto Domínguez, on Lake Budi, a picturesque little place famous for its good fishing, is reached by dirt road from Carahue (40 km.). From Puerto Saavedra beach or fishing port, walk 1 hr. to Balsa Budi from where a raft goes to Isla Huapi. A further 3 hrs.' walking leads to a ferry for Puerto Domínguez.

"Another pleasant trip through Mapuche country is to take a minibus from the Central Market to the country town of Chol-Chol, 30 km. to the north-west. There are 2 buses per day (Lar at 1100 and JAC at 1000), laden with corn, vegetables, charcoal, animals, as well as the locals. The trip traverses rolling countryside with panoramic views. On a clear day it is possible to see five volcanoes. Nearer Chol-Chol, the traditional round houses made of thatch (*rucas*) can be seen. There is not much to see in Chol-Chol itself, but it does have a delicious wild west flavour somehow." (Ian H. Dally, Iglesia Anglicana de Chile). For an overnight stay and information, contact Sra. Lauriza Norváez, Calle Luzcano (s/n), who prepares meals, and is very helpful. You can continue from Chol-Chol to Imperial and Puerto Saavedra, but bus connections few and slow (stay overnight in Puerto Saavedra).

The smoking 3,050-metre Llaima volcano has at its foot one of the prettiest skiing resorts in Chile: **Llaima**, at 1,500 metres, 80 km. E of Temuco. It stands in the middle of two large national parks, Los Paraguas (named for the umbrella-like araucaria pine trees) and Conguillio (open 20 Nov.-13 March). The latter, too, is full of araucaria forests and contains the Laguna Conguillio and the snow-covered Sierra Nevada. It is one of Chile's most popular parks, but is deserted outside the Jan./Feb. season. Take a bus from Temuco to Curacautín (**see page 480**) then a bus at 1830, Mon., Thurs., and Fri. towards the park, 1 hr., US$1, or hitch, to Conaf hut (you can camp nearby). It is then 10 km. to Laguna Captren situated in araucaria forest, where you pay a park entrance fee of US$0.50; campsite (US$4 including firewood but no other facilities), good hiking. 6 km. further on is Laguna Conguillio (take the Sendero de los Carpinteros), with a visitor's centre, campsites (US$6 per site, hot water, showers, firewood; *cabañas*, summer only, US$20, sleep 6, no sheets or blankets, gas stove) and café/shop, from where you can hike into the Sierra Nevada. At Laguna Verde in the Park is a free campsite without facilities. 15 km. beyond Laguna Conguillio, mostly across deserted lava fields, is the other entrance to the park, and then it is 13 km. though farmland to the village of Melipeuco (*Hotel Central*, F, good; *Hosteria Hue-Telén*, E, good; buses to Temuco, US$1.75, several daily, last at 1630). Transport can be arranged from Melipeuco into the park, but in summer buses from Temuco go, via Melipeuco, right through the park (3 a week).

For details of these excursions visit the Corporación Nacional Forestal, IX Región, Caupolicán y Bulnes, Temuco. Tours are arranged to lakes, sea beaches, Indian settlements, and salmon and trout streams. For best touring, hire a 4-wheel drive vehicle in Temuco.

The way from Temuco to Villarrica follows the paved Longitudinal Highway as far as Freire (24 km.), then (also paved) runs 63 km. SE. A road to Villarrica from the S runs substantially parallel with the old railway line from Loncoche. Wooded

THE LAKE DISTRICT

Lake Villarrica, 21 km. long and about 7 km. wide, is the most beautiful in the region, with snow-capped Villarrica volcano (2,840 metres) in the background.

Villarrica, pleasantly set at the extreme SW corner of the lake, was founded in 1552 but destroyed by the Indians; the present town (24,000 population) dates from the 1890s.

Hotels   *Yachting Club,* pleasant atmosphere, terraced gardens, swimming pool, restaurant, boating and fishing, rec., C, but cheaper rooms in motel annex; *Hostería Riñimapu,* outstanding, B; *Hotel El Ciervo,* German-run, also rec., C; *Parque Unión,* E; all one block from lakefront. *Residencial Royale,* near bus station, E, no private bathroom or hot water; *Residencial Pachi,* Valdivia 678, F, hot water, good restaurant; *Fuentes,* Reyes 665 (T 195), hot water, cheap, clean, F, reasonable restaurant; *Residencial Victoria,* Anfión Muñoz 530, hot water, clean, F; *Casa San Jorge,* Calle Catedral, F, is a Scouts' hostel, good value dormitory accommodation. Also, rooms in private homes, e.g. Calle Francisco Bilbao 969, run by Tom Funk, F; at No. 827 and also V. Letelier 702 (open throughout the year).

Camping   See under Pucón (below). Also 25 km. south of Villarrica (1 hour, US$1 bus), at Lican-Ray on Lake Calafquén (see below). Bus leaves from near tourist office. Summer houses available in Dec.-Feb. Also nearby *Acapulco* campsite.

Restaurant   *Club Social,* on main street, good, Henríquez 379, for snacks and ice-cream dishes. Also *Yandally,* Camilo Henríquez 401. *Café 2001,* Camilo; *Panaderías,* at Gral. de Aldunate 632 and 6003.

Exchange   Banco de Osorno will change travellers' cheques; also Carlos Huerta, Anfión Muñoz 417, for cheques and cash (dollars and australes—rec. that only men deal with him). Grocery shop opp. *Residencial* on Valdivia changes australes.

Post Office Anfión Muñoz esq. General Basilia Urrutia, open 0830-1230, 1400-1800 (Mon.-Fri.), 0830-1230 (Sat.). Telex service also available.

Tourist Office   Next to museum at Valdivia and Acevedo, will give information and maps (open all day all week in summer).

Buses   To Santiago, US$13.50. To Pucón, ½ hr., US$0.60; 3 a day to Valdivia (JAC, Reyes 621), US$2, 3-5 hrs.; daily service to Panguipulli at 0700, US$2, scenic ride. To Coñaripe and Liquiñe at 1600 Mon.-Sat., 1000 Sun. Temuco, US$1.60. To Loncoche (road and railway junction), US$1.15. N.B. JAC has 2 terminals: long distance at Montt y Reyes, local on Reyes between Henríquez y Muñoz. To Argentina at 0615 on Tues., Thurs. and Sat. with Empresa San Martín (Av. A. Muñoz 417) and at 0730 on Mon., Wed. and Fri. with Igi-Llaima, US$12, but passes can be blocked for four months by snow. If Tromen Pass is closed, buses go via Panguipulli instead of Pucón.

About 25 km. S of Villarrica and 125 km SE of Temuco is **Lican-Ray**, with 2 good beaches, on Lake Calafquén, full of islands and good for fishing. Boats can be hired from the beach. Sevral buses daily from Villarrica (JAC and García, Reyes y Henríquez). 4 km. away to the E is the river of lava formed when the Villarrica volcano erupted in 1971. Buses Mon.-Sat. at 0730 from Lican-Ray to Panguipulli.

Hotels (all closed out of season) *Anakena, Bellavista; Refugio,* B, Mr and Mrs Jack Douglas Feka, Canadian couple, with North American standards, on Playa Grande, has a Travellers' Exchange Library for English-language books, all donations of paperbacks (in reasonable condition) welcome (please send to Jack D. Feka, Casilla 299, Temuco—for information contact the hotel or office at Antonio Varas 976, Temuco, T 236-228). *Cabinas Los Pinos,* 3 blocks from lake, F, nice; *Rio Negro,* Gerónimo 776, F; several motels (e.g. at Huenuman 105, D for a chalet for 6 with hot water), *hosterías,* and camping sites *Café Ñaños,* Gral. Urrutia 105, very good, reasonable prices, helpful owner.

Pucón, a most attractive little town on the south-eastern shore of Lake Villarrica, can be reached by bus from Villarrica (26 km.) or Temuco (US$1.75), not by water. Pucón has a good climate and first-class accommodation. Queen Elizabeth II stayed there during her visit in 1968. The season is from December 15 to March 15, when the town is extremely crowded and very expensive. There is a pleasant walk to a convent above the town, also to La Peninsula for fine views of the lake and volcano, pony rides, golf, etc. (private land, you must get permission first). Launch excursion from the landing stage at end of O'Higgins at 1500 and 1900, US$4 for 2 hours. There is a large handicraft centre where you can see spinning and weaving in progress.

Pucón Hotels State owned *Grand Pucón* (9-hole golf course), open mid December to April, L (US$100 full board), C room only, disappointing, accessible in off season for entrance fee; *Interlaken,* A-B, on lakeside 10 minutes from town, Swiss run, chalets, rec., will exchange travellers' cheques (only open December to February); *Antumalal,* luxury class, 30 metres above the shore, 3½ km. from Pucón, very small (18 rooms), picturesque chalet-type, with magnificent views of the lake (take lunch on terrace), expensive and excellent (the Queen stayed there), L, with meals (open year round). Good beach, and good fishing up the river. *Hostería Suiza,* O'Higgins 135, D, clean, has a small café which is cheap and serves excellent empanadas; *Vista Hermosa,* a comfortable residencial; *Gudenschwager,* Pedro de Valdivia 12, classic Bavarian type, D, views over lake, specializes in natural food. *Los Castaños,* in centre, rec.; *Residencial Araucarias,* Caupolicán 243, C, clean, comfortable but not luxurious; *Residencial Lincoyán,* Av. Lincoyán, clean and comfortable; *Hostería Viena,* clean and pleasant, E, being extended; *Hostería El Principito,* Av. Gral. Urrutia and Fresia, E, with bath, very friendly but expensive; *Salzburg,* E, breakfast extra, rec., German spoken, some rooms with view over volcano (possible to borrow crampons). Familia Acuña, Palguín 233 (ask at *peluquería* next door), good, inexpensive, use of kitchen and washing facilities. Juan Torres, Lincoyán 445, good, clean, cooking facilities, (log fires in winter), very friendly, F; Lincoyán 485 (Sonya), F, friendly, rec.; *Casa de Familia,* Don Juan, Lincoyán 815, cooking facilities (information on climbing Villarrica); *El Refugio,* Lincoyán 348, vegetarian menu, limited but good; *Residencial Mónica,* Lincoyán y O'Higgins, F, friendly, cooking facilities; Sra. Lucía Sandoval, Lincoyán 565, F p.p., good; Lucila Oliva y familia, nr. petrol station, rec., kind, use of kitchen. Also ask in bars/restaurants, e.g. next to garage opp. *Gran Hotel Pucón.*

Camping Next to lake, 20 mins. walk from town, US$1.50 for two. There are several campsites between Villarrica and Pucón: *Huimpalay,* 12 km. from Villarrica; *Lorena,* 10 km. from Villarrica; *Acapulco, Playa Linda* (Villarrica), *Suyay, Honsa, Millaray,* 7 km. S of Pucón; *Trancura* and *Saltos del Molco; Albergue Juvenil,* US$1 p.p./night, tent provided, sleeping bags required, 2 km. out of town. Other sites between US$12-20, regardless of number of people. Cheaper sites en route to Caburga.

Travel Agents On O'Higgins: Nieve y Sol, another in the same block and Expediciones Chones. The last two arrange trips to thermal baths, trekking to volcanoes, whitewater rafting, etc. and are exceedingly good value.

Tourist Office Av. Caupolicán and Av. Brasil; Cama-Chile shop at same location. If closed, Municipal at O'Higgins and Palguin will provide information and sells fishing licences.

Telephone International service at O'Higgins 170.

Bus JAC terminal: O'Higgins 478. Cordillera, Av. Miguel Anselmo (nr. O'Higgins) for Apallaco and Lake Caburga—see below.

Pucón and Villarrica are celebrated fishing centres, for the lake and the very beautiful Lincura, Trancura and Toltén rivers. The fishing is now reported to be even better further S, in Lake Ranco (**see page 489**) for example. Local tourist office may supply details on licences and open seasons etc. Windsurfers and laser dinghies can be hired by lakeside (US$3.50).

Excursions from Pucón may be made to Rinconada; to the active Villarrica volcano in a National Park 8 km. S of the town for the grand view (no bus from Pucón, either hitch, or take a taxi to national park entrance, US$4.30, to volcano, US$16.50; national park entry US$0.75, or US$1.50 to camp). There is a refuge without beds 4 km. inside the Park, insecure and in desperate need of renovation (which is due to start soon). Campsite with drinking water, toilets, below refuge. The volcano can be climbed up and down in 8 hrs., good boots, iceaxe and crampons, and sun block essential—beware of sulphur fumes at the top; taking a guide is highly rec., it is not an easy hike, ask the park guards about conditions before attempting the climb. If you don't go with a guide, go in a group of at least 3. Guides: Alvaro Martínez, Cristóbal Colón 430 (US$14 for 7 hrs.), also Juan Carlos, at Lucila's *pensión,* or his pool room on main street. Crampons, ice axe, sunglasses can be rented for US$3.60/day from the Taller de Pollo bicycle shop on Calle Palguin, Pucón, near fire station—a cloth mask moistened with lemon juice helps to filter the sulphur fumes at the summit.

To Lake Colico to the N and Lake Caburga, very pretty, to the NE, both in wild settings (rowboats may be hired, US$1.50 per hour). Two buses a day. Lake Caburga is unusual for its beautiful white sand beach whereas other beaches are black sand of volcanic origin (campsite expensive in season, US$2.50 car, US$6.50 tent, but cheap out of season, US$2.50 for tent). Bus departs 1230, returns 1400, 2nd bus leaves in the afternoon and returns next morning (US$1 single). No shops, so take own food. Three more beautiful lakes are Verde, Chico and Toro in the Huerquehue National Park, W of Lake Caburga; there is a well-signed track to them from the car park at Lake Tinquilco (it is more-or-less straight uphill, 2 hrs.—sign says 5 km., but worth it). In the Huerquehue Park are the Huife thermal baths, US$2.50, "very upmarket, but pleasant". For Huerquehue, take Cordillera bus to Apallaco, 1½ hrs., US$1, from where it's 7 km. (3 uphill, 3 down, 1 along Lake Tinquilco) to park entrance, where there is a campsite. Park open officially only Jan.-March, but you can get in at other times. Warden very helpful; people in park rent horses and boats. To protect against horse flies, do not wear dark clothes. Termas de Quimayco can be reached from the road to Huife: new, less ostentatious than Huife, camping allowed, 2 cabins and *hostería*. To the thermal baths of Menetue, N of the road to Argentina, Palguin, S of the same road (*Hotel*—address, Casilla 1D, Pucón—D full board, baths US$1.50, lots of hikeable waterfalls in the area) and Liquiñe, 52 km. E of Lican-Ray. To Panguipulli (**see page 489**), on the lake of the same name.

There is a road from Pucón to the Argentine town of Junín de los Andes. The route is past the volcanoes of Villarrica and Quetropillán and round Lake Quilleihue, a gem set between mountains at 1,196 metres above sea level. On the border, to the S, is the graceful cone of Lanín volcano (3,747 metres), and beyond the border is Lake Tromen, much visited by Argentine tourists. The Argentine road from the border to Junín de los Andes goes on to San Martín de los Andes, and via Lago Hermoso and Villa Angostura (a beautiful drive) to Bariloche. There is a more direct road from San Martín de los Andes to Bariloche but it is not so interesting (see under Argentina, **page 140**).

The Longitudinal Highway runs from Loncoche (good place for hitchings) through Lanco to Valdivia, then cuts SE to Paillaco and S to Osorno. It by-passes all towns except Chillán and Valdivia.

From Antilhue, 148 km. S of Temuco, a road runs 40 km. W to Valdivia.

Valdivia, a city standing where two rivers join to form the Río Valdivia, is 18 km. from the port of Corral and the Pacific Ocean. It is the capital of Valdivia Province and has a population of 140,000. It is 820 km. by rail or road (about 16 hrs.) from Santiago.

The city is set in a rich agricultural area receiving some 2,300 mm. of rain a year; it was founded by Pedro de Valdivia in 1552. Lord Cochrane's greatest victory for Chilean independence was at Valdivia, when he took the forts at Corral, Amargos and San Carlos (the Niebla fort surrendered—see below). From 1850 to 1860 a comparatively small number of German colonists settled in the area; their imprint in terms of architecture and agricultural methods, order, education, social life and custom is still strong. In particular they created numerous industries, most of them on Teja Island (5 by 2 km.) facing the city. The Universidad Austral de Chile was founded in Valdivia in 1954. The riverside market is fascinating.

Hotels   *Pedro de Valdivia*, Carampangue 190, B with bath, good; *Naguilán*, Gen. Lagos 1927, T 2851/52/53, B, clean, quiet; *Raitúe*, Gral. Lagos 1382, E with bath; *Villa del Río*, B with bath, Av. España 1025, restaurant expensive (try salmon in almond sauce), rents apartments with kitchen for US$20 a day; *Las Encinas*, same street No. 181 (E) and *Tejas* (C), same street; *Melillanca*, rec. but pricey, C. Several medium-priced hotels on Calle Chacabuco. *Villa Paulina*, Yerbas Buenas 389, T 216372/212445, D, hot showers, clean, pool, parking, highly rec. On Picarte, *Hostal Montserrat* (No. 849), E with breakfast, clean, comfortable; the Salvation Army (US$1.50); *Residencial Anilebu*, No. 875, (nr. bus station) and *Residencial Germania*, No. 871, clean but no heat in rooms, both E with breakfast; cheaper hotels in same street include Nos. 979 and 1005 (no hot water); hospedaje (no name—one of 2 white *hospedajes* opp. bus terminal) at No. 1953, F with breakfast, good value, clean, heated lounge; the other white hospedaje, No. 1151, is also good. *Schuster*, Calle Maipú, is an old Victorian-type German hotel, a godsend to those who dislike modern ones, deteriorating, noisy, D with bath—F without, hot water; *Hospedaje* at Arauco 905, F, clean, friendly. Student *pensiones* include *Juan XXIII*, Lagos, and Arauco 852. The house at Aníbal Pinto 1335 (T 3880) is friendly and cheap; *pensión* of Sra. Armida Navarrete Uribe, Calle A.R. Phillippi 878, E/F, full board if desired, hot water, good value; Sra. Segovia, A. Muñoz 353, opp. bus station, E, breakfast, hot water, rec.; and Sra. Paredes, García Reyes 244, E without breakfast (more with), hot water, rec. For houses offering lodgings in E-F range in summer, leave bus station and turn right into Calle Anwandter (e.g. No. 246, nice), or left into Av. Picarte. Youth Hostel at Escuela España, Beauchef 975.

Campsite   Quillín, between Ranco and Valdivia. Also in Parque Saval, Valdivia and at Av. Picarte 1160, US$1.80 per tent. White gas impossible to find, other than in pharmacies/chemists.

Restaurants   *Centro Español*, Calle Henríquez, good; *Club de la Unión*, on Plaza, serves a large lunch US$2 p.p.; *Sociedad Protectora E.E. de Comercio*, Independencia near Plaza, good and cheap; *Delicias*, Camila Henríquez 372, T 213566, rec. for meals and cakes; *Selecta*, Av. Ramón Picarte 1093, clean, good fish and meat; *Café Haussmann*, O'Higgins 394 (good tea and cakes); *Bomba Bar*, Saval on Teja Island; *Hostería Costanera*, beside town's boat dock, has good food and good atmosphere. *Pizza Trattoria la Nonna*, Chacabuco 325, good. *Restaurant y Bar*

VALDIVIA 58

Legend:
1. Plaza de la República
2. Municipality
3. Museum
4. Botanical Gardens
5. Universidad Austral
6. Muelle Fluvial (dock)
7. Tourist Office
8. Post Office
9. Market
10. Hotel Pedro de Valdivia
11. Hotel Schuster

La Posada del Turista, Puerto 13, does cheap, seafood lunches. *Café Colonia*, Maclver 161, good meals, good value; *Café Paula*, Pérez Rosales 633-45, good lunch; *Entrelagos*, Pérez Rosales 622, ice cream and chocolates. Bakery: *La Baguette*, Libertad 110, French-style cakes, brown bread.

Clubs   Chilean-North American Institute, Calle Beauchef; Santa Elvira Golf Club (9 holes); tennis, sailing, motor, and rowing clubs like Phoenix on Teja Island; also Club Español.

Museum   run by University on Teja Island, free in off-season, US$0.25 in summer, closed Sun. afternoons, cartography, archaeology, history of German settlement (including cemetery), local Indian crafts, etc. Open Tues.-Fri., 1000-1300, 1500-1800. Also on the island, a botanic garden and arboretum with trees from all over the world. "Lago de Lotos" on the island—has beautiful November blooms.

Festival   Semana Valdiviana, Feb. 12-18.

Exchange   Bank at Arauca y Henríquez. Turismo Cochrane, Caupolicán 500 block, rec. for changing pesos to australes. Also *Café Palace*.

Tourist Office   Calle Arturo Prat 555, by dock. Good map of region and local rivers. Kiosk in bus station. Regional office, 2 km. from market. **Conaf** Ismael Váldez 431.

Rail   Station at Ecuador 2000, off Av. Picarte; information and booking office at Arauco 220. Daily to Santiago; 3 times a week the Pullman Express to Santiago leaves 1830, Saloon US$14.50, *económico* US$8.50, 1st 7.85, 2nd US$6.85, sleeper US$22/30. Daily at 0700 (summer only) and 1305 to Osorno and on to Puerto Montt, US$3 and US$4. To Trumao (for launch to La Barra) daily at 1115, 40 mins., US$0.65 (**see page 491**). No train services to Pucón.

Bus   Terminal is at Muñoz and Arturo Prat, by the river. To Santiago: Pullman daily, leaving 2100, arriving next morning at 0830, about US$8-13.75. Pullman daily to and from central and southern towns. ½ hourly buses to Osorno, 1½ hrs., US$1.50 (cheapest). To Lanco, US$2. Thrice daily to Llifén, US$2.50. 15 buses daily to Panguipulli, US$2. Many daily to Puerto Montt, US$2.50, 3 hrs. To Puerto Varas, ETC bus, 3 hrs., US$2.35. To Frutillar, on Pullman Sur Temuco-Puerto Montt bus, US$2.75, 3 hrs. To Villarrica, by Bus JAC, 3-5 hrs., US$2, daily at 0700, 1100 and 1600. For Pucón change at Villarrica, to Bus JAC, Vicente Reyes 621. The road is paved from Loncoche to the Argentine border (via Osorno). To Bariloche via Osorno (10 hrs.) with Bus Norte and Tas Choapa, 5 a week. Twice daily to Riñihue, Mon.-Sat., 1630 and 1830, Sun. 1945 and 2015.

Air   Ladeco to Santiago via Temuco 3 times a week.

Excursions   The district has a lovely countryside of woods, beaches, lakes and rivers. The various rivers are navigable and there are pleasant journeys to Futa, Putabla, and San Antonio, behind Teja Island and through the Tornagaleanes, the Isla del Rey. Among the waterways are countless little islands, cool and green. Ferryboats (almost every hour in summer) leave from dock, Muelle Fluvial, behind tourist office on Av. Prat 555, making the beautiful trip down the river to Corral in about 1¼ hours (US$1.50 one way; occasional buses are cheaper) where there is *Residencial Maviel*, F, on Calle Arica, and *Santa Clara*, E (*El Popular* restaurant, good for seafood). The boats call at the seaside resorts of Niebla, 10 mins. away, US$0.80 extra (less hectic than Corral, with good Youth Hostel on top of the hill; *Hosterías Rucantu*, E, and *Santa Clara*, F; can also be reached by bus, every 1½ hrs. from Valdivia bus terminal to Los Molinos), and Mancera. 4 km. along the coast from Corral is San Carlos, with its *Hostería los Alamos* (F), a delightful hideout for those seeking a quiet life.

The tourist boats (*Neptuno* or *Calle-Calle*) to Isla Mancera (no restaurants) and Corral, including a guided half-day tour (US$12 with meals—cheaper without) leave at 1330 and return at 1830. A cheaper boat to Corral leaves 5 times a day, from 0800, from Valdivia and returns between 0800 and 1900(if you want to stop en route, you must first pay full fare, US$1, then US$0.70 for each "leg"). In Corral is the Castillo, a national monument with a battery of 24 guns, and opposite it, on a promontory W of Niebla is the Fuerte San Luis de Alba, a substantial earthwork fort. In the Niebla-Corral area there are ruins of 17 forts in all; roads have been built to some of them. The coastal walks are splendid. A cruise boat, *Capri*, run by *Hotel Pedro de Valdivia*, can be hired to take you to Fuerte San Luis de Alba.

A road runs from Valdivia along the River Calle Calle to Los Lagos (61 km.), and on to the beautiful Lake Riñihue (39 km.). The road around the southern edge of the Lake from Riñihue to Enco is now closed, so Choshuenco can only be reached by road from Panguipulli or Puerto Fuy. To avoid an overnight stay in Los Lagos, catch the bus from Riñihue to Los Lagos, departing 1530 Sun., US$0.50, train north from Los Lagos at 1620 to Lanco, US$1.30, and bus in evening (1920) on to Panguipulli. Riñihue, a beautiful but very small and isolated village, is worth a visit. Campsite by the lake; *Restaurant del Lago* has rooms, E (no meals). The road to Coñaripe, a small village on the east side of Lake Calafquén, offers superb views of the lake, and of Villarrica volcano. Afternoon bus goes on to Lican-Ray (**see page 484**), a particularly beautiful spot and a good start for hiking expeditions. Bus north, five times a day to Villarrica, US$1.

Panguipulli, on the W bank of the lake of the same name, is in a beautiful setting, with roses planted in all the streets (the name is Mapuche for "town of roses"). Excursions can be made to Lakes Panguipulli, Calafquén, Neltume and Pirehueico, and south to the northern tip of Lake Riñihue at El Desagüe (*Hostería Riñimapu*, B, excellent). There is a new 30-km. road around the lake to Choshuenco, a beautiful coastline, wooded, with cliffs and sandy beaches. Buses leave daily at 1530 and 1600 along the North bank of the lake, but it is not possible to return from Choshuenco on same day. (Bus returns from Choshuenco at 0630 and 0645.) Choshuenco volcano is at the SE end. For fishermen, daily excursions on Lake Panguipulli are recommended. The waterfalls of Huilo-Huilo are most impressive and reached by the Choshuenco bus, get off beyond Choshuenco at *Alojamiento Huilo Huilo*, where the road crosses the Huilo Huilo river. From here it is a 1½ hr. walk the following day to the falls. Alternatively, walk from Choshuenco along Puerto Fuy road for 3½ hrs. and turn right at sign to the falls. A scenic road runs through rainforest around the Choshuenco volcano from Puerto Fuy to the river Pillanleufú, Los Llolles and Puerto Llifén on Lake Ranco (see below); only possible by car or on foot, and permission must be obtained from the lumber mill at Neltume (Sr. Thomas Morefield), 5 km. from Neltume, 3 km. from Puerto Fuy.

A boat crosses Lake Pirehueico Tues., Thurs., Sat. at 1400, US$2, 2-3 hrs. from the Argentine side to Puerto Fuy; bus daily to Panguipulli at 0600, 3 hrs., US$1.50. Ferry returns to Pirehueico at 0600.

Hotels At **Panguipulli:** *Central*, clean, hot water, E; *Hostería Panguipulli*, F; *Hostería Quetropillán*, Etchegaray 381, E, comfortable, food; also, private house opposite; Sra. Pozas, Pedro de Valdivia 251 (E, clean, clothes washing extra); *Residencial Riquelme*, good value. *Las Brisas* restaurant, has rooms to let, E; *Restaurante Valparaíso*, rec.; *Café Central*, Martínez de Rosas 880. At **Liquiñe:** *Hostería Termas de Liquiñe*, D; private houses, F. At **Choshuenco:** *Hotel Choshuenco*, F; various *hosterías*, including *Los Notros*, F, *Hostería Rayen Trai* (former yacht club), María Alvarado—s/n, good food, rec.; *Hostería Pulmachue*, E, and *Club Andino*, on Independencia 625; Sra. Elena Arrigada, Padre Vernave 198, F, rec.; free camping. At **Pirehueico:** *Hostería Pirehueico* occupied by military, but beds available for US$1 or so in private houses. You can stay in white house by the ferry dock. At **Río Bueno:** *Plaza*; *Río Bueno*, Casilla 157, A. At **Carboneros:** *Villa Lucía*. At **La Unión:** Hotels *Turismo* and *La Unión*.

Campsite Imahuito, on Lake Ranco, 8 km. from Futrono. Free camping on lakeside at Panguipulli possible. Also, at Los Molinos.

Tourist Office in plaza next to police station.

NB No foreign exchange facilities.

Bus to Santiago daily at 1845, US$9; 14 daily (Sun. only 4) buses to Valdivia, 2 hrs., US$1.50 and 9 daily to Temuco, 3 hrs., US$2.25. To Calafquen, 3 daily at 1200, 1545 and 1600. To Lican Ray and on to Villarrica at 1530, 2 hrs., US$2. Bus to Villarrica leaves from depot in Calle Etchegaray, 100 yards uphill from *Hostería Quetropillán*.

Rail To Puerto Montt at 0730, change at Antilhue, arrive 8 hrs. later; a long, slow trip but worthwhile for the scenery around the lake.

Sports The Club Andino Valdivia has ski-slopes on the Mocho and Choshuenco volcanoes. The southern shore of **Lake Ranco** offers excellent fishing.

Mehuin, 2 hrs. bus ride from Valdivia; post office, good sea bathing and several hotels: *Hostería Pichicuyín* (E), 1 km. away, highly rec. Don Kurt who lives in Ing. Haverbeck may be able to put up guests. He is also planning to build a youth hostel on the peninsula of Chanchán, 13 km. S. Quelle,

6 km. from Mehuin, has two simple *residenciales*. Good beach but bathing dangerous at high tide because of undercurrents; safer to bathe in the river near ferry.

The 76-km. road from Valdivia to La Unión and Río Bueno on the Longitudinal Highway goes on to Puerto Nuevo (Hotel, A, very good) on lovely, island-starred Lake Ranco and to **Lake Maihue**. A branch of this road curves round the north of Lake Ranco to **Llifén**, a picturesque place on the eastern shore. From Llifén, visits can be paid to Lakes Maihue and Verde.

Hotels   *Llifén*, B and *Hostería Cholinco*, 3 km. out of town on the road towards Lake Maihue, B, poor food, limited electricity, and also the *Calcarrupe Lodge*, run by *La Cascada*, on Correo Llifén, A; *Huequecura*, Casa 4, *Cumilahue Fishing Lodge*, A, including meals and fishing services.

On the south side of Lake Ranco is Lago Ranco, an ugly town (one *residencial*) and Riñinahue; the road is terrible (lots of mud and animals, including oxcarts), but is worth taking to see an older lifestyle, the beautiful lake, waterfalls and sunsets on the distant volcanoes (if walking, beware the numerous guard dogs in the area).

Some 42 km. S of Río Bueno is Osorno, another centre for exploring the Lakes.

Osorno, 900 km. from Santiago and 105 km. N of Puerto Montt (103,000 people) was founded in 1558. It was destroyed shortly after its foundation, and was later settled by German immigrants, whose descendants are still of great importance in the area. The Argentine town of Bariloche is reached by a road E through Puyehue pass (bus 2-3 times a week, daily in summer, US$17.50) or via the lakes of Todos los Santos and Laguna Verde, both crossed by ferries. The trip via the lakes takes at least a whole day; maybe 2-3 in winter (April-Nov.). The road via Puyehue (120 km.) is more reliable, and still a very beautiful trip.

Hotels   *Waeger*, Cochrane and Bilbao, B; *Del Prado*, Cochrane 1162, T 5020, swimming pool, B; *Villa Eduviges*, Eduviges 856, T 5023, D; *Inter-Lagos*, Cochrane 515, T 4695, C; *Gran* (good restaurant), main square, C, with bath; *Tirol*, Bulnes 630, D, with bath; *San Fernando*, Bulnes 836, F, good supper for US$2; *Residencial Riga*, Antahuer 1058, D, highly rec. but heavily booked in season. *Hospedaje Eliana del Río Cortés*, Bulnes 876, F and *Alcázar*, F, next door; *Residencial* at Amunátegui 520, run by Sra. Gallardo, near Provincial bus terminal, good, D; *Residencial Schulz*, Freire 530, E. *Residencial Ortega* (strongly rec.) Colón 602, nr. Errazúriz, 1 block from bus terminal, toilet facilities limited, F; *Germania*, Rodríguez 741, F p.p., no hot water, cooking facilities. For youth hostels, contact Secretaria Provincial de la Juventud, Bilbao 850. Private houses at Germán Hube, pasaje 1, casa 22, población Villa Dama, E, hot water, clean, use of kitchen, rec.; Lynch 1306 (1 block from bus station, use of kitchen), and Los Carrera 1154, E, reasonable.

Restaurants   *German Club*, O'Higgins 563; *Bahía*, Ramírez 1076, rec. for quality and economy; good ice cream at Ramírez 939. The *Club de Campo* is open to non-members for meals. *Peter's Kneipe*, M.Rodríguez 1030, excellent German restaurant; *La Casona*, Juan MacKenna 945, service and cuisine excellent, price moderate. *Café Dino*, expensive, on the plaza. Good restaurant in the bus station. *Hostería Socavi*, 25 km. S on the Longitudinal Highway, excellent roast chicken. Try chicha (cider) or local pisco sour.

Shop   Reinares and Thone, Ramírez 1100, for good fishing gear.

Museum   Museo Histórico Municipal, Matta and Bilbao.

Garage   Good Volkswagen garage in Calle Los Carrera—owner speaks German. **Car Hire**, Hertz, Bilbao 857, T 5401/2.

Laundry   Av. Arturo Prat 678 (allow at least a day).

Exchange   Banco Osorno y La Unión, on Plaza is the only official place; poor rate and minimum commission of US$5. For parallel rates try Globus Viaje, Cochrane 646; Fronter Ltda., Ramírez 951, local 6 (in arcade—in alley behind Freire 630); Café Waldis, O'Higgins 611.

Tourist Office   Provincial government office, 1st floor, T 4104. Has details of accommodation. Closed at weekends. Instituto Chileno-Norteamericano, Los Carrera 770, offers advice to tourists (open 0830-1300, 1400-1730). Also, office in upstairs of 1st class bus terminal, Errázuriz 1400 (summer only).

Buses   Most leave 1 block from municipal market at Errázuriz 1400. Varmontt buses every ½ hr. (from 0700 to 2200) to Puerto Varas and Puerto Montt (to former, 1½ hrs., US$2). To Puerto Octay, from market on Mon.-Fri. 6 buses, Sat. 5; Sun. 4. Frequent buses to Santiago, US$11, 16 hrs. Buses to Valdivia, every half hour, 1½ hr. journey, US$1.50 and up, Entre Lagos, US$2. Local bus to Anticura (Chilean customs post) leaves at 1620, 3 hrs., 22 km. from border. Left luggage at terminal, open 0730-2030. Local bus fare, US$ 0.30.

Rail Station at Juan Mackenna 600. To Santiago one Rápido daily (1630 winter, 1830 summer), 14 hrs., Saloon US$15.10, *económico* US$9.90, sleeper US$23.90/32.75. Rail services S may be suspended in winter; buses connect with Santiago trains.

Air Ladeco operates flights 3 times a week to Santiago, via Temuco.

Excursions Drive 48 km. SE to *Puerto Octay*, on northern shore of Lake Llanquihue, a small town in a lovely setting (buses daily). Follow the road along the lakeside, with the Osorno volcano on your left, to Ensenada for lunch, a short distance up the road (20 mins.) is Petrohué with its beautiful falls, and the Osorno volcano again in the background, and Lake Todos los Santos; continue to Puerto Varas for tea, then along the W side of the lake to Octay and back. *Café Kali* on main square at Octay, Amunátegui, recommended. Playa Maitén, 5 km. from Puerto Octay; "highly recommended, nice beach, marvellous view to the Volcán Osorno, no tourists"; campsite.

Hotels Puerto Octay, *Haase*, very pleasant, D (rooms with and without bath), US$70 for rooms, breakfast and supper for family of 6; *Posada Gubernatis*, Calle Santiago, lakeside, motorboat, excellent food, clean, comfortable, D; *Hostería y Cabañas Villa Veneto*, Gral. Lagos 591, E; *Hostería La Baja*, Casa 116. *Centinela* (3 km. S; *Hotel Centinela*, Casa 114, D (rooms with or without bath). Centinela is beautiful, with a headland and good views of Volcán Osorno. Camping allowed. Very popular in good weather.

E to the Pilmaiquen waterfall, and on to Lake Puyehue and the thermal waters at *Termas de Puyehue* (US$1.50 p.p. for bathing); 2 hrs. by car, 2½ by bus; Empresa Buses Puyehue depart 0915 and 1615 from outside Osorno municipal market; tickets can be bought from booth 2 in shop parade, return US$3. Bus does not stop at Lake (unless you want to get off at *Gran Hotel Termas de Puyehue* and clamber down), but goes to Aguas Calientes (later one goes to Anticura and Argentine border). Aguas Calientes has National Park headquarters, an open air swimming pool with hot thermal water, US$0.80 p.p. (free after 1900), a Conaf campsite, at entrance to park (US$3), private sites (US$6.85) and a café. Campsite also at Anticura, beside Río Gol-Gol; also restaurant and cabañas in summer. In the Puyehue National Park is surviving temperate rain-forest. Continue 18 km. to Volcán Antillanca (good *hostería*, C, developed as a ski resort with two ski lifts) through a lovely region of small lakes and fairytale forests. The views from Antillanca are breathtaking, with the snow-clad cones of Osorno, Puntiagudo, and Puyehue forming a semicircle. The tree-line on Antillanca is one of the few in the world made up of deciduous trees (southern beech). Bus continues from Aguas Calientes to Antillanca in winter only (otherwise, hitchhike—always difficult).

Hotels at Puyehue *Gran Hotel Termas de Puyehue* has a hot-springs swimming pool, large and well kept, B, main meals US$8 each, breakfast US$3, in beautiful scenery, heavily booked Jan.-Feb. (Telex 273146, SOTERCL); also near Lake Puyehue, about 4 km. from Termas is *Aguas Calientes*, cheaper and less commercial (take food if you want to cook) than the *Termas*, cabin-type accommodation C per cabin, or good camping, meals available. In *Entre Lagos*, at E end of Lake Puyehue, *Pub del Campo*, highly rec. restaurant, reasonable prices, owner is of Swiss descent; 7 km. E. of Entre Lagos is the *Hostería Tramahuel*, Casa 16 (six rooms and two family cabins), C; *Motel Ñilque*, cabins, A-L, half-price April to November, by Osorno-Bariloche road on S shore of Lake Puyehue; *Hostería Muller*, Casa 147, D; *Hostería Entre Lagos*, Ramírez 65, E; *Hostería Isla Fresia*, located on own island, transport provided.

Drive or take bus N to Río Bueno, celebrated for its scenery, to La Unión, and to Trumao, a river port on the Río Bueno, whence a launch may be taken to La Barra on the coast; leaves Wed. and Sat. only at 0900, 5 hrs., US$6; returns Sun. at 0900.

Bus to Las Cascadas (Mon.-Fri. at 1700, Sat. 1400, Sun. 1900), next day to La Picada (24 km.), stay at *Refugio La Picada*, then on to Lake Todos los Santos and Petrohué (14 km.). From Petrohué (see page 493) go to Saltos de Petrohué or by bus to Ensenada and Puerto Varas.

A further excursion can be made to the S shore of Lake Rupanco (65 km.) taking the road to Puerto Octay and turning E after 33 km.

The sea beaches at Maicolpue (60 km. from Osorno—*Hostería Millor*, on the beach, E, clean, good service, rec.) and Pucatrihue (*Hostería Incalcar*, summer only) are worth a visit in the summer (daily bus service).

Two hours' walk to top of Volcán Casabla, though no path; excellent views over Osorno, Puntiagudo, Puyehue, Cerro Tronador.

The Club Andino Osorno has three shelters (US$3 p.p.) at La Picada (84 km. from Osorno), on the ski slopes on the Osorno volcano at 950 metres and on a road off the main road between Octay and Ensenada; *Las Pumas* on the Volcán Osorno at 900 m., with plenty of beds at about US$1.75 p.p. and cooking facilities. Apply at the Oficina de Turismo de Osorno. At 1,200 metres is **Refugio Teski Club**; not open all year (usual ski season is June to September). If you wish to climb Volcán Osorno, ask first at Las Pumas or Refugio Teski for advice (**see page 494**). To reach Volcán Osorno, take bus to Ensenada from Puerto Varas (US$1) then walk 12 km. to Las Pumas. A ski resort is under construction on Volcán Osorno.

Campsites   Lake Puyehue, Camping Municipal. Entre Lagos, Camping Muelle de Piedra (7 km. E of Entre Lagos); Camping Los Copihues (9 km. E of Entre Lagos), hot showers, good; and a site at Anticura (see above). Wild camping allowed at Aguas Calientes; ask the rangers.

From Osorno it is 117 km. S to Puerto Montt, including 25 km. along the shore of Lake Llanquihue. Across the great blue sheet of water can be seen two snowcapped volcanoes: the perfect cone of Osorno (2,680 metres) and the shattered cone of Calbuco (2,554 metres) and, when the air is clear, the distant Tronador (3,554 metres). Lake Llanquihue covers over 540 square km. and is the third largest natural lake in South America. There is a road, 187 km. long, around it.

Puerto Varas, a beauty spot of about 23,300 inhabitants, is on the shore of Lake Llanquihue, with standard roses grown along the streets. Parque Philippi, on top of hill, recommended for good views and an interesting craft centre. It is 1,046 km. from Santiago and only 26 by rail or 24 by paved road from Puerto Montt. Casino charges US$2.65 entry, including first drink.

Hotels   *Puerto Varas,* Klenner 351 (*Gran Hotel Turismo*), B, luxury class with casino; *Cabañas del Lago,* Klenner, cabins, B; *Hospedaje Loreley,* Maipo 911, D, rec., homely, quiet, good restaurant; *Playa,* lakeside position, Salvador 24, clean, but spartan, C, restaurant is good, though comparatively expensive; *Licarayén,* small, B with bath, highly rec., book in season; *Residencial Hellwig,* F, San Pedro 210; *Grand Hotel Heim,* San Pedro and San José, basic, but good food, E. Student hostel, *Centro Juvenil,* Colón 251, US$1.50 p.p., including bathing and cooking facilities, TV, games room; *Hotel Atalaya,* Santa Rosa 710, D, incl. breakfast, comfortable, English spoken. Also cheap *residenciales* opposite bus station and in Plaza de Armas. *Motel Altué,* Av. V. Pérez Rosales, C, incl. breakfast; *Motel Sacho,* San José 581, E. *Residencial Unión,* Calle San Francisco 669 (opp. bus station), clean, basic, hot water, F, with restaurant, good cheap food. Residencial at Salvador 423, D, run by a German lady, rec., as is María Schilling Rosas' *hospedaje* at La Quebrada 752; Sra. Elly. A. Prat 151, F p.p. with breakfast. Familia Niklitschek-Pozas, Calle Imperial 8 (opp. *Motel Trauco*), highly rec.

Campsite   Playa Venado, apply to Playa Venado Municipal Office. Camping Municipal Puerto Varas (4 km. E), good beach; Camping Playa Niklitschek (8 km. E), full facilities, US$5 per night.

Restaurants   *Club Alemán,* best, dinner, expensive; *Mercado,* next to market, good and reasonable, about US$4 for lunch; *Café Asturias,* San Francisco 316, good empanadas; restaurant on shore road to Puerto Chico. *El Molino,* an excellent coffee house in an old mill, on road to Ensenada; also about 40 km. from Ensenada *Fogón y Hostería Pucará,* good steaks.

Exchange   Better rate of exchange for travellers' cheques obtained in Puerto Montt.

Tourist Agent   Graytur; Andina del Sur (beside Igi-Llaima bus office) offer trips for US$42 to Lake Todos los Santos, Peulla, Cerro Tronador and return.

Buses   To Santiago: Igi-Llaima leaves from Salvador at 1830, arrives 1130 (US$11.50). To Puerto Montt every ½ hr. from Varmontt station, 30 mins., US$0.65

To Bariloche, daily at 0900, arrives 2130 (by boat and bus), US$36. It is not possible to go by private car from Puerto Varas direct to Bariloche, as the ferry on the Argentine side does not take cars; one must go via Osorno.

Excursions   Buses run on the southern side of the lake between Puerto Varas and (50 km.) Ensenada (Transporte Esmeralda, Del Salvador 57, see below), in the south-eastern corner of the lake, and on to Petrohué for lunch: (bus from San Pedro 210—see below). In summer, Varmontt excursion on Sat. and Sun. to Ensenada, Petrohué, Laguna Verde and Osorno Volcano, US$3.50, good value. The drive around the lake is very picturesque. On the northern road are Puerto Octay and Centinela (**see page 491**).

Puerto Varas is within easy reach of many famous beauty spots—Desagüe,

Totoral, Frutillar, Los Bajos, Puerto Octay (direct bus only from Osorno), Puerto Chico, Puerto Fonck, La Poza, the Loreley island, the Calbuco volcano, La Fábrica, Puerto Rosales, Playa Venado, Ralún and Río Pescado. The Falls (Salto) of Petrohué should not be missed. The whole countryside with its primeval forest, deep blue rivers and snowcapped volcanoes is very beautiful; interest is added by the timber-frame buildings with shingle roofs—even the churches.

Bus every half hr. from Varmontt terminal on San Francisco, Puerto Varas to "Welcome to Frutillar" sign on Ruta 5; cross railway down the only side road into Alto *Frutillar* (where windsurf boards can be hired), US$0.75. It's 5 mins. by half-hourly colectivo to Bajo Frutillar, 4 km. away and possibly the most attractive town on the lake. Frutillar, a beautifully kept town, offers a classical music festival in late January to early February. Museo Colonial Alemán, including watermill, and a German colonial house are open to the public. *Hotel Frutillar*, on stilts above lake, B, best, good restaurant and bar, Andina del Sud travel agency in reception; *Hostería Alemán* by lakeside, very clean, excellent food, C, including breakfast. Also, *Casona del 32*, C with bath and breakfast, comfortable old house, central heating, English and German spoken, T 323, P.O.Box 101; and *Posada Campesino Frutillar*, German-run, good food. *El Retiro*, run by Betty Heim, friendly, E; *Hospedaje Costa Azul*, Philippi 1175, T 388, mainly for families, good breakfasts, E; *Frutillar Alto*, Calle Principal 168, F, clean. Many German-style cafés and tea- rooms on Calle Philippi (the lakefront). *Café Hermosa*, good breakfast (view of lake and Volcán Osorno). Tourist Office on lakeside, helpful; Viajes Frutillar in Alto Frutillar (Richter y Alissandre) run tours. Buses back to Puerto Varas from Av. Philippi (between O'Higgins and Montt) in Bajo Frutillar every ½ hr.; also to Puerto Montt.

La Poza is a little lake to the S of the main lake and reached through narrow channels overhung with vegetation; a concealed channel leads to yet another lake, the Laguna Encantada. The motorboats that tour Lake Llanquihue stop at Loreley Island, very beautiful and well worth a visit.

East of Lake Llanquihue is the most beautiful of all the lakes in southern Chile: Lake Todos los Santos, a long irregularly shaped sheet of water with the ports of **Petrohué** at its western and **Peulla** at its eastern ends; a boat trip costing US$4.50 can be taken between the two, leaves Petrohué at 1030, Peulla at 1500 (2½ hrs.). If you prefer to go walking, ask for the park guard, Hernán, who organizes expeditions from Petrohué in the summer months. Peulla is a good starting point for hikes in the mountains. Trout and salmon fishing at Petrohué are excellent. The waters are emerald green. It is only 18 km. by a scenic paved road from **Ensenada**, a lovely spot on Lake Llanquihue (3 buses a day from Varas, 1½hrs., 50 km., US$1.50, first at 0945, may continue to Petrohué; also to Petrohué, Tues., Thurs., and Sat., US$1.75; schedules vary). There are shops in Petrohué, but bread is sometimes short. There is also a post office. The Salto de Petrohué (entrance, US$0.75) is 6 km. from Petrohué on the Ensenada road (only worth a visit in summer).

Petrohué is infested by *tavanos* (local horseflies) in Jan. and Feb. Cover up as much as possible with light-coloured clothes.

Hotels   At **Ensenada**: *Hotel Ensenada*, B with bath, olde-worlde (closed in winter) good view of lake and Osorno Volcano; *Millantu*, reminiscent of cheap hotels in the Alps, used by climbers, E; *Hostería Los Pumas*, 3 hrs. up the hill also highly rec., in season only, D; *Ruedas Viejas*, E, has popular restaurant (another restaurant opposite).*Pucará*, D; opp. is *Hospedaje Opazo*, F with breakfast, no hot water, friendly; *Refugio Teski*, 4 hrs. walk up the volcano from *Hotel Ensenada* (where you should call to check if refugio has food), bleak site above tree line (**see page 492**). Youth Hostel, *Centro Juvenil*, US$2, rather noisy as shared with an orphanage. *Bellavista*, D, rec., a few km. N, serves excellent meals. At **Petrohué**: *Hostería Petrohué*, C, with bath, E p.p. b and b (reports vary), built for Queen Elizabeth; *Familia Küscher* on other side of river, F, meals available, rec., camping possible; Refugio above being repaired. At **Peulla**, on the opposite shore: *Hotel Peulla*, B, beautiful setting by the lake and mountains, good restaurant and bar, but cold in winter, often full of tour groups (tiny shop at back of hotel); a private house offers half board, E p.p. Homemade marmalade, dulce de leche available from Mrs. Gisela Schwitzgaeble, Ruiz Moreno 938. Otherwise food hard to find in Peulla, so take your own.

Bus   To Puerto Montt via Puerto Varas on Tues., Thurs. and Sat. (2 hrs.) leaves 1820 (US$1.50); stops at Salto de Petrohué for 15 minutes. To Lake Frías (1½ hrs.), US$13. There are day return bus and boat tours to Peulla from Puerto Montt, with possibility of continuing to Bariloche.

Market   On Tues. and Thurs. mornings; a number of lorries sell food, wine and clothes.

Campsites   on Llanquihue: Alcalde Manuel Droquett, Chinquahue, Playa Maki, and at Petrohué, a National Parks Environment Centre with display and slide show (camping US$4.50), near *Hotel Petrohué*; an unofficial one by lake shore 1 km. beyond *Hotel Ensenada* at Playa Larga, basic.

A dirt road runs 31 km. SE from Ensenada along the wooded lower Petrohué valley to *Ralún*, on the salt-water Estuario de Reloncaví. Here is the *Hotel Ralún*, at S end of the village, a magnificent timber building to a fine modern design by Cristián de Groote, with a choice of rooms or cabins, warmly rec., A (25 % more in summer than rest of year) plus US$35 p.p. full board (cabins rented at US$80 a night). Telex 40048 Santiago or 70071 Puerto Montt; address Casilla 1044, Puerto Montt. *Restaurant El Refugio*, 1 km. N of *Ralún*, rents rooms, F; also *Navarrito*, restaurant and lodging, F; *Posada Campesino*, F for simple room; *El Encuentro*, village shop and post office, with telex, F. Bus from Ensenada, US$0.70, daily 1015; more easily reached by twice daily bus from Puerto Montt, also from Puerto Varas, 3 times a week.

Lake Todos los Santos has no roads round it, but from Petrohué a rather poor road (rec. only for jeeps) runs N through mountain land to the ski-ing hut on La Picada; the hut is more usually reached from Ensenada or Osorno.

As for the lake itself, its shores are deeply wooded and several small islands rise from its surface; in its waters are reflected the slopes of **Osorno volcano**. Only experienced climbers should attempt to climb right to the top, ice climbing equipment required: there are many deep crevasses, the weather can change suddenly, never go alone, and set off early in the morning; there is a shelter for hikers. The dangers involved in climbing Osorno are illustrated by the disappearance on its slopes in 1987 of one of our valued correspondents and an experienced hiker, Brian Spearing. Antu Tours organize a one-day hike to the summit for a reasonable fee (rec.). They can be contacted through their postal address: Casilla 24, 29 Santiago 29; T 2712767, Telex 440019 RECAL CZ, or during Dec.-Feb. through the Tourist Office in Puerto Montt. Beyond the hilly shores to the E are several graceful snow-capped mountains, with the mighty Tronador in the distance. To the N is the sharp point of Cerro Puntiagudo (2,278 metres), and at the north-eastern end Cerro Techado (1,720 metres) rises cliff-like out of the water. Visitors stay at the *Hotel Peulla* for the night when going into or coming out of Argentina. For those who stay longer there are motor launches for excursions on the lake; two good day trips are to Cayutué and Río Blanco. The only way to reach **Petrohué from Cayutué** is by boat, US$28, and you may have to wait several days. The *Esmeralda* (or *Don Ricardo*) crosses Lake Todos los Santos in 2 hrs.

Puerto Montt, capital of the Tenth (Los Lagos) Region, 1,080 km. from Santiago, is the terminus of the railway. The first German colonists arrived in 1852; they have remained to this day a small but influential percentage of the 106,000 inhabitants. The houses are mostly faced with unpainted shingles; here and there stand structures in the Alpine manner, all high pitched roofs and quaint balconies. The handicrafts market by the port merits a visit. See the little fishing port of Angelmó and sample its shellfish or fresh cooked crab; Angelmó is 2 km. from the centre of town and is also noted for its handicrafts. It has become a tourist centre.

The port is much used by fishing boats and coasting vessels, and it is here that passengers embark for the island of Chiloé, for Aysén, and for the long haul S to Punta Arenas. A paved road runs 55 km. SW to Pargua, where there is a ferry service to Chiloé.

Hotels   Check Tourist Office. *Vicente Pérez Rosales,* Antonio Varas 447, T 252470, Telex 270056, A, with bath and breakfast, excellent restaurant, seafood and tourist information, rec.; *Montt,* Av. Varas and Quillota, T 253651-2, C, with bath, D without, poor water supply but clean, friendly, good value (good restaurant); *Residencial Panorama,* San Felipe 192, T 254094, F, some rooms with bath, crowded meeting place for Europeans and Americans, watch belongings (good restaurant), great view; *Millahue,* D, Copiapó 64, good food; *Residencial Urmeneta,* Urmeneta 290, D, with bath, clean, comfortable, good breakfast, rec.; *Burg,* Pedro Montt and Portales, modern, central heating, centrally located, good, D; *Royal,* Quillota 136, E, near railway station, very nice, good meals. *Reloncaví,* G. Gallardo 228, E with bath and hot water (F shared bath), clean, central, rec., breakfast extra; *Petorca,* San Martín 233, good, residential, E, with breakfast; *Residencial Embassy,* Calle Valdivia 130, E, clean, quiet; *Residencial Talquino,* Pérez Rosales 114-116, near bus terminal, F, hot water, clean; *Residencial Calypso,* Urmeneta 127, T 254554, F, with breakfast, shared bath, hot water, clean and friendly; *Residencial El Turista,* Varas esq. Ancud 91, F with breakfast, friendly; *Residencial Sur,* San Felipe 183, F (poor breakfast

PUERTO MONTT

1. Plaza de Armas
2. Cathedral
3. Museum
4. Tourist Office
5. Post Office
6. Hospital

extra), basic, clean. Many private homes give you a bed for US$4, look for signs in windows, particularly rec. is *Casa Haraldo Steffen*, Serrano 286 (T 253823), F, with breakfast, excellent, homemade bread and jam, free transport to/from bus station; *Uncle Renato*, Guillermo Gallardo 621, US$1 with own sleeping bag, popular, packed in summer, boiled water for coffee available; *Hospedaje*, Balmaceda 300, E, with breakfast, friendly; at Gmo. Gallardo 415, Sra Luciana Lazo, E. Student hostel at Guillermo Gallardo 632, G, hot water, kitchen facilities; there are also several inexpensive hostels in Calle Huasco, e.g. at No. 16, F, with breakfast (hot water), and private house at No. 131, with large garden, E, as well as in Calle V. Pérez Rosales, near bus station. Also J. J. Mira 1002, F, excellent, breakfast included; Aníbal Pinto 328, E with breakfast, friendly, popular, can do laundry, rec.; Ancud 117, F, bed and breakfast, hot water, good; Sr. Raúl Arroyo at Concepción 136, F with breakfast, often packed (rec.—discount for Israelis); also Concepción 120, F, good; Sra. Olivia, A. Prat 412, F p.p. bed and breakfast; Familia Turra, Calle Regimiento 842, Población Lintz, F with breakfast, excellent but for nearby noisy disco; and Calle Vial 750, Ida Soto de Arras, F, very friendly, good breakfast, safe. Near Puerto Montt *Cabiñas Los Abedules*, Calle Pto Montt 55, Pelluco (see under **Excursions**), T 254231, D, comfortable, completely furnished incl. cooking facilities (sleep 2-6 people): Mailing address—Casilla 338, Pelluco, Puerto Montt.

Youth Hostels　Information is available from Albergues Juveniles de la X Región, Urmeneta 183, Puerto Montt, T 2384, open only in summer.

Camping　At Chinquihue, 10 km. W of Puerto Montt (bus service), about US$1.50 p.p. Open October-April US$8 per site, for any size of tent. Each site has table, two benches, barbecue and plenty of shade. Toilets and showers. Small shop, no kerosene. Good camping shop, "Winkler", on Calle Varas, will buy used gear. "Wild" camping possible along the front. 4 km. E of Puerto Montt, Copec have a network of 18 "Rutacentas" between Quillagua and Puerto Montt, which, apart from selling petrol and oil, have good shower (US$0.25) and toilet facilities and restaurants. At Los Alamos on the road to Panitao and Calbuco.

Restaurants　*Embassy*, Ancud 104 and Pelluco, is rec. for reasonably priced seafood; *Club de Yates*, good, Av. J.S. Manfredini, on waterfront beyond railway station; *Super Yoco*, Urmeneta 478, good, but poor service; *Nettuno*, Illapel 129, cheap Italian food, good atmosphere; *Rapanui*, Benavente 550, good, reasonable prices; *El Bodegón*, popular, cheap but basic, Mexican as well as local music; *Café-Restaurant Kiel*, Capilla 298, Chinquihue, 9 km. from centre, owner Helga Birker de Bauer speaks excellent German, Danish and English, lovely view over bay. *Café Real*, Rancagua 137, near main plaza, good for empanadas, hot dogs, coffee and cakes; *Café Central*, Rancagua 117 and A. Varas, good atmosphere, food and pastries. *Restaurant Café Dino*, Calle Varas, excellent restaurant upstairs, snacks and delicious pastas downstairs (try the lemon juice). *La Llave*, by the sea, in railway station. On road to Chinquihue, *Restaurant Stop* rec. *Café Amsel*, Pedro Montt y Portales, good variety and quality; fish restaurants in market and along wharves, rec. Also excellent and cheap food at the central bus depot (all credit cards accepted). Restaurants in market at Angelmó, and on the road there, highly rec. for fish (not so good for hygiene but food can be trusted), as is the "restaurant-ship" at the ro/ro terminal with its congrio frito and erizos (ask prices first as there is no menu). *Patache* in Angelmó, try picoroco al vapor, a giant barnacle whose flesh looks and tastes like crab; curanto, a regional dish (seafood, chicken, sausages and potatoes), at the "restaurant-ship" *Catepumontt*, highly rec. Bakery: *La Estrella*, Gallardo 174, self-service, good.

Shopping　Woollen goods and Mapuche-designed rugs. Cheaper at roadside stalls between port and market, or in Castro (Chiloé), than at tourist shops in town. Secondhand clothes stalls behind the food market on Presidente Ibáñez.

Museum　at Avenida Diego Portales, interesting. Open Mon.-Fri. 0915-1245, 1415-1740; Sat., Sun. 1000-1300, 1500-1900. See also private collection at Museo Chiloye, Calle M. Rodríguez. Museo Juan Pablo II, on seafront, opp. Av. Valdivia.

Car Hire　Hertz, Urmeneta 1036; Automóvil Club de Chile, Cauquenes 75 and airport.

Exchange　You are advised to change money here if visiting Chiloé as reports indicate that it is difficult on the island. Banco del Estado and Banco Chile (cash only) and Turismo Latinoamericano, Urmeneta 351, offer good rates. *Hotel Pérez Rosales* will change money at parallel market rate. Varas Tours change travellers' cheques at a good rate without commission (they also run good excursions). Vasatur, A.Varas 445, will change travellers' cheques as well as cash. Also Turismo Los Lagos, Varas 595, local 3, and El Libertador, Urmeneta 529-A, local 3. Try also *Café Real*, Calle Rancagua 137,or the Korean at Varas 805.

Consulates　Argentine, Cauquenes 94, 2nd floor; Dutch, Talca 119; German, O'Higgins 114, and Spanish, Rancagua 113.

Laundry　Opposite Banco O'Higgins on Pedro Montt; Rex at Varas 621; another next to *Hotel Reloncaví*.

Books　Useful pamphlet, in Spanish, published monthly "Bienvenidos a Puerto Montt" - NSD

Publications, Calle Quillota 232 (also secondhand bookshop with French and English books) or free from certain hotels.

Post Office Rancagua 12, open 0830-1900 (Mon.-Fri.), 0830-1200 (Sat.-Sun.).

Tourist Office Edif. Intendencia Regional, Av. Décima Región 480, T 254580, Telex 270008. Open 1000-1300, 1500-2000 Mon.-Fri. Also at annex in railway station. Town maps available. Best map for the region is the blue "Atlas Caminero de Chile".

Rail Station at San Felipe 50. Daily to Santiago, via Osorno and Temuco. Daily *expreso* to Santiago leaves at 0930, 23 hrs. (US$8.50 and US$10). Rápido at 1345, 16-19 hrs., US$65 for sleeper compartment; *salón* US$15.50, *ecónomico* US$11.50. Ticket office opens 0830-1130, 1300-1700.

Bus Service Bus station on sea front, at Av. Diego Portales and Av. Lota. To Puerto Varas (US$0.65) and Osorno every 30 min., US$1.70, 1½ hrs.; to Santiago, express 15 hrs., US$15 first class, 10 second; Varmontt are the most expensive, double-decker bus (US$25 including cocktails, cold dinner, breakfast). Bus service to Punta Arenas, Bus Norte, Turibus and Ghisoni, each twice a week in summer, once in low season, about US$60, 38 hrs. Many buses daily to Temuco US$5, to Valdivia, US$2.50. To Bariloche, US$21 with Bus Norte (daily 0830), Tas-Choapa (thrice weekly) and Rápido Argentino Lanín (4 times), or with Andina del Sud, Mon.-Sat. 0900, US$36 inclusive (see also routes to Argentina given on **page 501, 502** and **503**). Quellón, US$5.25. Ferry-buses to Chiloé (several), to Ancud, US$2.25, Castro US$3. Empresa Andina del Sud, very close to central tourist office, Varas 437 (Casilla 15-D, T 3253) sells tour to Puerto Varas, Parque Nacional V.Pérez Rosales, Petrohué, Lake Todos los Santos, Peulla and back.

Hitch-hiking is difficult and may take as long as four days between Puerto Montt and Bariloche.

Air Service Ladeco run 3-5 flights a week to Coyhaique/Balmaceda, and daily flights to Santiago, US$74, and Punta Arenas, US$100. In January, February and March you may well be told that the plane to Punta Arenas is booked up; however, cancellations may be available from the airport. There are air force flights to Punta Arenas about once every two weeks (ask at Tourist Office for telephone number); seat availability is only known when plane arrives from Santiago, price about US$35 compared with US$80 Lan-Chile, which has daily flights to Santiago. TAC, Fokker 27, run twice daily service to Chaitén and Coyhaique (will stop at Puerto Aguirre if 6 or more passengers want to get off there). El Tepual airport is 16 km. from town, bus from ETC Terminal, Pedro Montt. Bus to centre of town, US$1. Lan-Chile and Ladeco offices at Benevente 305 and 350, TAC, Gmo. Gallardo 167.

Shipping Service The roll-on/roll-off vehicle ferry m/n *Tierra del Fuego* of Navimag (Naviera Magallanes S.A.) runs about every nine days or so (double check times) throughout the year to Puerto Natales, taking 3 days and 2 nights. First class accommodation ("gran turismo") comprises 6 cabins (all double with bath); tourist class 34 bunks; and third class ("pioner") 120 reclining seats. The first class fare is US$450; third class fare is about US$65. All fares include 3 meals; all drinks cost extra. Book in advance. Reservations handled in Santiago (**see page 461**). Priority is given to lorry drivers for tourist class tickets which go on sale at the last minute (4 hrs. before departure, perhaps earlier). The dramatic 1,460 km. journey first goes through Seno Reloncaví and Canal Moraleda. From Bahía Anna Pink along the coast and then across the Golfo de Peñas to Bahía Tarn it is a 12-17 hrs. sea crossing, usually rough. The journey continues through Canal Messier, Angostura Inglesa, Paso del Indio and Canal Kirke (one of the narrowest routes for large shipping). The only regular stop is made off Puerto Edén (1 hr. south of the Angostura Inglesa), where the local Alacalufe Indians come out to sell their shellfish.

The roll on/roll off vehicle ferry m/n *Evangelistas*, also of Navimag, runs twice weekly to Puerto Chacabuco (80 km. to the east of Coyhaique). The cruise lasts about 24 hrs. First class accommodation include 2 cabins with bath; tourist class, 14 bunks; and third class, 400 reclining seats. First class reservations must be made in advance at the Santiago offices. There are canteens and bars on board.

The m/n *Calbuco* of Empremar (Empresa Marítima del Estado) leaves Puerto Montt every Tuesday at 1900 for Puerto Chacabuco. Arrives on Fridays at 0800, and returns to Puerto Montt on Sundays at 0900. From late December through early March she sails from Puerto Chacabuco on Fridays at 1800, stays Saturdays 0900 to 1900 at Laguna San Rafael, calls again at Puerto Chacabuco on Sundays at 0800 and returns to Puerto Montt on Tuesdays at 0800. She is a simple ship with only 4 berths in 2 cabins plus 36 seats in tourist class and 53 seats in 3rd class. The fare from Puerto Montt to Puerto Aysén is US$30 first class, US$19 tourist class; to Laguna San Rafael US$100 first class, US$70 tourist class (food on board poor, advisable to supplement with own provisions). Sailing dates are published in *El Mercurio* newspaper.

Between early December and late March, the m/n *Quellón* of Empremar leaves Puerto Montt on Saturdays at 1400, calling at Melinka, Pto. Aysén (with a shore excursion to Coyhaique), Laguna San Rafael, Castro and returns to Puerto Montt on Fridays at 0800. This journey is sold on a round-trip basis only by Transcontainer S.A. in Santiago and Puerto Montt. Fares range from US$435 to 600; excellent food, good accommodation, rec.

The m/n *Skorpios* of Constantino Kochifas C. leaves Pto. Montt on Saturdays at 1100 for a luxury cruise with stops at Puerto Aguirre, Quitralco, Laguna San Rafael, Melinka, Castro and returns to Puerto Montt on Fridays at 0800. The fare is about US$700. It has been reported that there is little room to sit indoors if it is raining, and that conditions are generally not up to standard.

Transmarchilay Ltda. run the ferry *Pincoya* from Pargua or Conchi to Chaitén and back and the ferry *El Colono* between Quellón and Puerto Chacabuco. For sailing dates, their timetable should be consulted. Ticket availability better at the ports than at head office.

Shipping Offices in Puerto Montt: Navimag, Terminal Transbordadores Angelmó, T 253754/253204, Telex 370055 NAMAG CK. Empremar/Transcontainer, Av. Diego Portales 1450, Tel. 2548, Telex 370001 EMAR CK. Constantino Kochifas C., Angelmó 1660 (Castilla 588), T 2952, Telex 270028 NATUK CL. Transmarchilay Ltda., Angelmó 1668, T 4654, telex 270031.

Excursions   The wooded island of Tenglo, close to Puerto Montt and reached by launch, is a favourite place for picnics. Magnificent view from the summit. The island is famous for its *curantos*, a local dish. (*Hostería Miramar*, F, with breakfast, basic, but a nice view overlooking the port of Angelmó; *Hoffmann*.) Chamiza, up the River Coihuin, has fine fishing. There is a bathing beach (polluted) at Pelluco (*Gran Papa*, opposite ETC bus terminal, good chicken; *Fogón Criolla*—meat, *Jahuel*, and *Pazo*—curantos, all rec.; *Restaurant Juan Pazos*, rec.), a fair walk from Puerto Montt. The (cargo) launch trip from Angelmó jetty up the Reloncaví estuary (8 hrs.) is very beautiful, fjords, sealions, local colour, and rec. The estuary is the northernmost of Chile's glacial inlets. At **Cochamó**, at the end of the estuary, there is the *Hotel Cochamó*, basic but clean, F, good meals, rec., and a large number of *pensiones* (just ask), e.g. *Mercado Particular Sabin*, F p.p., Calle Catedral 20 (Sra. Suni, next to *Hotel*), Sra. Flora Barrientos offers floorspace in her bar/restaurant/drugstore, same street No. 16, F; also *Restaurant Copihue* and *Residencial Gato Blanco*, both F; cheapest accommodation in same street, No. 2, by the pier (floor space only). Cochamó itself is pretty but limited; a side trip is to the Termas de Sotomó, but this requires an affinity for mud. Boats to Cochamó from Angelmó jetty leave Tues., Thur., Fri., and Sun. at 0830, US$4, taking up to nine hours (tip the locals who row you to the launch), returning to Puerto Montt next day. Advisable to take warm clothes and plenty of food, check at Angelmó port for details. An alternative by land is by bus to the head of the estuary, near Ralún (**see page 494**) then cross the Petrohué river by small boat, 3 times daily, US$0.80, then by bus to Cochamó (2 buses a day to Cochamó from Puerto Montt). The road will soon be completed to Puelo, and thence it is intended to continue it to Río Negro and the Carretera Austral (**see page 501**). There is a beautiful 2-day hike from Cochamó through forests to Cayutúe, a quiet, peaceful village (see the Bradts' book, *Backpacking in Chile and Argentina*, for route); the settlement is on Lake Todos los Santos and occasional boats go to Petrohué—US$15 to hire one (**see page 494**); you can camp by the lake. The Maullin River, which rises in Lake Llanquihue, has some interesting waterfalls and good fishing (salmon). The little old town of **Maullin** (*Motel El Pangal*, A), at the mouth of the Maullin River, is worth a visit. **Calbuco** (*Hostería Huito*), centre of the fishing industry, with good scenery, can be visited direct by boat or by road. Puerto Montt is a good centre for excursions to the lakes via Puerto Varas. From Puerto Montt to Puerto Varas by the old (dirt) road is a short but beautiful journey.

Isla Huar may be visited by boat from Angelmó harbour (1600, 2 hrs.); boat returns from other end of island at 0730. The north shore is rocky. Accommodation, if lucky, at the church; best to camp.

Chiloé island is 250 km. long, 50 km. wide, 9,613 sq. km., and has a population of 116,000. There are two main towns, Ancud and Castro (airport), and many fishing villages. Seaweed is harvested for export to Japan. Typical of the island are substantial wooden houses (*palafitos*) built on stilts over the water. The hillsides in summer are a patchwork quilt of wheat fields and dark green plots of potatoes. Inland are impenetrable forests. There has recently been appreciable development, and power and water shortages and poor sanitation are now things of the past. Though the weather is often cold and foggy, the island is extremely beautiful when the sun is out. Sweaters and woollen caps are good purchases. Music is popular, with many players in the waterfront cafés in Castro.

The local sailing sloops, *lanchas*, are fast being replaced by diesels, in fact more can be seen in Puerto Montt now.

From Puerto Montt buses run 15 times a day (US$1.50) to Pargua (55 km.) on the Straits of Chacao. (At Chacao, *Pensión Chiloé*, F; *Hospedaje Angelino*, F.) The harbour water is beautifully clear. Buses drive on to ferry across the Chacao Strait to Chiloé, then to Ancud and Castro. The ferry passes through beautiful scenery with a great variety of wildlife: pelicans, seals, penguins and albatross. There are 12 trips a day to Chiloé by the ferry (US$0.50); cars US$4.50 (½-hr. journey). The Tourist Office brochure, *Conozca a Chiloé*, free, is rec.

Ancud   Beautiful views, Spanish fort (Fuerte San Antonio) and powder magazine restored, a good regional museum on the Plaza de Armas open 0900-1230, 1430-1830 (Mon.-Fri.), 0930-1230, 1430-1800 (Sat.), 1000-1200, 1430-1730 (Sun.) (entry, US$0.25), the tourist office, Libertad 699 (T 387), and craft shops (speciality is basketwork). Oyster beds interesting. Buses every day to Mar Brava and Playa de Pumillahue, 20 km. east of Ancud.

Hotels   *Hostería A. de Ercilla*, Libertad 669, C, chilly showers, reasonable restaurant; *General Quintanilla*, Libertad 751, rec., C, with bathroom and breakfast, good but expensive restaurant; *Hostería Ancud*, friendly and helpful, but meals overpriced; *Residencial El Tráfico*, Libertad 569, G in shared rooms, serves good meals at weekends; *Residencial Montenegro*, Río Blanco 451 and Dieciocho, F, fair, no hot water; *Residencial* on Aníbal Pinto 515, good, F. *Hospedaje Miranda*, Mocopulli 753, cheap, friendly, hot water; *Residencial Wescheler*, D, clean, unfriendly; private house at Bellavista 449, E, with sleeping bag on floor much cheaper, no hot water; Edmundo Haase Pérez, Ramírez 299, F, breakfast, clean, basic, good value; also Ramírez 396, T 489, Sra. Edith Hualibota, E, nice; Elena Bergmann at Aníbal Pinto 382 (5 rooms in private house), clean, friendly, E f p.p.; Sra. Lucía, San Martín 705, G. In summer, the school on Calle Chacabuco is open for lodging, US$1.30 p.p.

Campsite   5 km. W of town.

Restaurants   Excellent. Seafoods, especially king crabs (very cheap), almejos and cheese in market area. *Polo Sur*, on seafront, good but not cheap; *Coral*, Pudeto 346, good, cheap; *Jardín*, same street No.263; *Macaval*, Chacabuco 691; *Pica del Loco*, A.Prat, excellent; *El Tirol*, Maipú 746; *El Cangrejo*, Dieciocho 155, seafood highly rec.

Bus   Ancud-Castro, US$2.25; frequent buses daily on both routes, 1½ hrs. No direct Sunday bus from Ancud to Dalcahue, need to stay in Castro. To Puerto Montt, US$3. Local buses leave from terminal at Pto. Montt 538.

Shipping   Transmarchilay has offices in Ancud, Libertad 669 (T 317-279, Telex 270071); office in Santiago, Agustinas 715, Of. 403, T 335959.

Castro   Capital of the Province and a very friendly town, 88 km. from Ancud. Tremendous variety of styles in housing. Waterfront market (Thurs.). Cheap woollen articles available at Mercado Municipal de Artesanía on Lillo. Large cathedral (1906) with excellent wooden interior on the Plaza de Armas, built by Italian architect, Eduardo Provosoli; the outside of the cathedral is an unusual shade of orange. One-room museum (Blanco Encalada 261) contains history, folklore, handicrafts and mythology of Chiloé. Very good views of the city from Millantuy hill above the cemetery, which is legendary. Helpful tourist office in main square; Conaf at Gobernación, 3rd floor, Plaza de Armas.

Hotels   *Hostería Castro*, Chacabuco 202, T 301, D with bath and breakfast, but 16% VAT on top, hot water, good restaurant, interesting building (in summer coach and boat trips are organized to other places on the island); *Residencial Mirasol*, San Martín 815, good, F; *La Bomba*, Esmeralda 270, T 300, F, without bath, decent, hot water (showers may be rented for US$1), 3 course menu (US$4). *Quinta Niklitschek*, Panamericana Norte 331, better inside than out, D; *Unicornio Azul*, Pedro Montt 22-8, C, good; *Residencial Lydia*, Blanco Encalada 276, F, clean, cold shower, good; *Res. Inés de Banen*, Blanco Encalada 266, F, OK, breakfast US$1; *Costa Azul*, F, Lillo 67, friendly, hot water but restaurant poor value; also on Lillo, *Res. El Gringo*, G, O.K.; *Plaza*, Blanco 366, D, rec. on 3rd floor, breakfast included, good restaurant; *Moteles Auquilda*, on way to Aeropuerto Gamboa, D. *Hospedaje* at Las Delicias 287, E, hot shower, nice family and place; Adriana Gutiérrez, Freire 758-9, E, breakfast, clean, good value; Maruja Vera, O'Higgins 841, O'Higgins 446 (hot water, clean), Chacabuco 449 (no hot water), and *El Rusgo*, San Martín 700, all E. Private house at Luis Espinoza 380, G p.p. with sleeping bag, friendly, washing and cooking facilities; also San Martín 879 (Sra. Judith Mancia), F, quite good.

Restaurants   *Café Plaza*, Blanco 366; *Krill Café* and *La Amistad* (seafood); *Sampayes*, Calle Thompson 243, good food; *Chilo*, San Martín 419, pleasant; *Lidia*, Av. Prat Blanco, good, friendly; *El Sacho*, Balmaceda 286, just off main plaza towards post office, good food, not too dear, clean; *Brisas del Mar No. 1*, very good; and others, like *Palafito*, on the waterfront and *Vista Hermosa*, south end of Calle Esmeralda, clean, wonderful views. *Don Octavio*, Lillo 67, T 440, seafood incl. curantos. *Confitería Haití*, Blanco Encalada 60, good pies. In the market, try "milcaos", fried potato cakes with meat stuffing; also "licor de oro", like Galliano.

Camping with permission from controllers at airfield; some water available. Motel opposite will change money. Banco del Estado de Chile on main square accepts travellers' cheques (at a poor rate). The Punta Arenas-Puerto Montt cargo boats call at Castro occasionally; US$3 to Puerto Montt (3¼ hrs.), last bus to ferry each day at 1715. Bus to Quellón (2 hrs.), US$2; to Ancud (1½ hrs.) US$2.25.

Doctor Muñoz de Las Carreras, near police station, surgery 1700-2000 on weekdays, rec.

Tours Trans Chiloé, San Martín 359, T 497, day trips around the island, US$3 without food.

Dalcahue 21 km. N of Castro, the wooden church dates from 1858, on older foundations. Market on Sundays, open 0700 to 1300 at this picturesque village. Good choice early on, but better bargains in late morning. Tourist kiosk in season. Bus from Castro, 40 mins., US$0.75. Colectivos also available. (*Pensión Montaña*, G, basic; *Pensión San Martín*, F, better; many private houses offer accommodation).

From Castro, buses every day in summer, 3 a day (but none Tues. and Thurs.) otherwise, 2 hrs. US$2 (via Dalcahue and Curaco de Vélez de Achao and a ferry (US$3 return) takes one to *Achao*, 39 km. away on the Isla de Quinchao (*Hotel Splendid*, F, hot water; *Hotel Sao Paulo*, reasonable, hot water, F; *Hotel Delicia*, Serrano y Ochoa, F, clean, friendly, small restaurant; *Restaurant Octavio*, at waterfront, cheap and good; *Restaurant La Nave*, Prat y Sargento Aldea, good salmon; *Cocinería Insular*, F, friendly, rec. excellent breakfast; *Restaurante Cristina*, excellent seafood), a quiet, pretty fishing village with a lovely old wooden church, built in 1730, which inspired most other churches in the area (2-roomed museum close to church). It is possible to return to Castro same day. Many excursions S and W are available (best to take sleeping bags if visiting remote islands). Tourist office on the Plaza de Armas, highly rec., provides excellent literature and good advice on accommodation. Good place to buy woollen goods. Camping possible on the shore: ask. Tenaún, 56 km. NE of Castro, is an interesting fishing village with a good 18th-century church, as has Vilpulli, 20 km. S of Castro. Quilquico, between Castro and Rilán, has a wooden church dating from 1767.

Chonchi, 25 km. S of Castro (bus US$0.75, paved road), is a picturesque fishing village with rambling shingled houses painted in many colours and a lively wharf for fishing (neo-classical wooden church, 1850). *Hotel Antiguo Chalet*, Irarrazaval, T 221, winter D, summer B, charming, very good, restaurant rec. (try 'licor de oro'); *Hospedaje Chonchi*, O'Higgins 379, G p.p., F with full board, very nice; *Hotel El Sacho*, Centenario 102 (main street), F with breakfast and bath, rec., and *Pensión Turismo*, also F. Rooms available in *Hostería* next to *Provisiones Magallanes*, G p.p. in shared room, or floor space, use of kitchen; at *Almacén la Patagonia* and with Sra. Gamín Chacón, Calle Andrade, corner Alvarez and Manuel Gómez, baker at P.J. Andrade 184, G with breakfast.

Visits to Queilen beach, the island of Lemuy and the village of Cucao are rec. Lemuy Island, 90 sq. km., is quiet, with good walking through undulating pastures and woodland. Daily ferry service from Chonchi. The main town is Puqueldón which offers basic accommodation, clean, F, good food, in Calle J. M. Carrera. *Restaurant Lemuy* is next to the municipal offices and *Café Amancay* opposite. Good walks to Lincay, 5 kms., or Lincura, one-day expedition.

Cucao, a village 40 km. west of Chonchi and the only settlement on the West coast of Chiloé, can now be reached by road. There is an immense 15 km. beach with thundering Pacific surf. Nearby is the Chiloé National Park (opened in 1984), with reception centre, small museum, helpful staff, guest bungalow available for visiting scientists (apply to Conaf, through your Embassy, stating environmental interests). The forests in the park are vast and impenetrable; ask at Conaf for directions or guides. Many house rent horses for US$1/hour, US$5/day. Camping, US$2 (beware of theft in Jan./Feb. season). Accommodation, F, with full board or *demi-pension* at *Provisiones Pacífico* (friendly), Sra. Boreuel or with Sra Luz Vera, next to school (rec.). Buses from Castro daily except Sat. in summer at 0700, and at 1130 and 1630 on Mon., Wed., and Fri., returning immediately, and Sun. 0900, 2½ hr. journey; hitching is very difficult. Half way between Castro and Cucao is Huilinco, a little town on a large lake, a charming place to stop on the way to the ocean (one *hostal*, G p.p. with good food, or stay at the Post Office).

Quellón Southernmost port on Chiloé; 92 km. from Castro, fishing boats built at wharf, pleasant beaches (*Hotel Playa*, P. Montt 255, F, good, clean, hot water, restaurant; same street, *Hostería Quellón*, E, basic; *Pensión Vera*, A. Gómez García, casi P.Montt, F, good, clean; *Hostería La Pincoya*, La Paz 64, F; *Restaurant Las Brisas* on seafront, good). Daily service from Castro to Quellón, US$2, 2 hrs. Transmarchilay ferry *Colono* leaves 1500 for Puerto Chacabuco, Aysén, Tues., Thurs. and Sun., returning from Chacabuco Mon., Wed. and Fri. (more sailings in summer), 18-hr. trip, tickets US$10.50, US$14.50 and US$17.50), all luggage has to be stowed (tickets must be bought on morning of departure, do not book bunk, benches in dining area more comfortable; Transmarchilay office in Quellón, Pedro Montt 265, T 290) takes vehicles. A cargo boat, *Marítimo*, also does this route, but takes longer. Timetable should be obtained from tourist office and foot passengers should note that priority is given to those travelling in vehicles. Lovely trip (forested islands, snow-capped peaks in background) dolphins and small penguins may be seen en route.

The islanders of Chiloé were the last supporters of the Spanish Crown. When Chile rebelled the last of the Spanish Governors fled to the island and, in despair, offered it to Britain. Canning turned the offer down. The island finally surrendered to the patriots in 1826, the last remaining Spanish possession in South America.

Exchange If going on south, stock up well with pesos. It is difficult to change money at the weekend.

With the opening of the **Carretera Austral Presidente Pinochet** (Southern Highway) in 1988, the Pan-American Highway has been extended a further 1,013 km. through southern Chile to Cochrane. The highway is divided into three major sections: Puerto Montt-Chaitén (242 km.) and three ferry crossings; Chaitén-Coyhaique (435 km.), and Coyhaique-Cochrane (336 km.). The Puerto Montt-Chaitén route includes three access roads in the Reloncaví, Compu and Peñihue fjords. By 1990, a further 125-km. stretch, linking Cochrane with Puerto Yungay is expected to be completed.

The port of **Chaitén** on the mainland has grown in importance because of the military camp and the new road. *Hotel Continental*, D, no heating nor private bath, but good meals, very helpful and friendly, rec.; *Restaurant/Hotel Mi Casa*—on a hill—, E with bath, negotiable; large youth hostel, F, sleep on floor; also, *Hostería Schilling*, D, on waterfront, with bath and heating, no restaurant; *Pensión* at Juan Todesco 205, F (G for floor space), hot water and meals extra, free use of kitchen; free campsite 4 km. N, with hot showers and close to sea; shopping and most facilities. Ferry from Pargua, Sun. 2000, returning Mon. 2200 (Transmarchilay). Check in advance for ferries to Chiloé; office is next to *Hostería Schilling* on Av. O'Higgins, T Chaitén 272. Flights to Puerto Montt, US$37.50; Fierro bus twice a week from Puerto Montt. At least 4 microbuses a week run between Chaitén and Coyhaique (and the number is increasing all the time), e.g. Aerobus, Artetur, US$24, 12-14 hrs., with ½-hour stops at Puyuguapi and La Junta. Other stops on request, but it is easier to get through than pick up a bus en route. Hitching the whole route takes about a week, but you must be prepared for a day's wait if you find yourself out of luck.

A road runs to Puerto Cárdenas (good *hostal*) on Lake Yelcho (public bus service), 46 km. 26 km. from Chaitén on this road are thermal springs, free bathing in mud bath or covered pools, camping, refreshments available. At the other end of the lake, around which a road runs, and across which 3 ferry companies operate, is Puerto Ramírez (*Hostería Río Malito*—Sr. Soto—nearby, rooms, camping, fishing), whence there are two roads to the Argentine border at Futaleufú (*Hotel Carahue*, F; *Hotel Continental*, Balmaceda 595, F, basic, hot water, clean; and others) and **Palena**.

It is possible to travel from Chaitén, via border towns of Futaleufú and Palena, to Esquel in Argentina, the starting point for several Argentine national parks. Coming from Argentina, it is 2 km. from the free, hand-winched ferry across the Río Grande to the border (allow 1½ hrs. for formalities); continue from Futaleufú to Puerto Ramírez, but don't go into Ramírez, take the unsigned right turn to Chaitén (left goes to Palena). A bumpy, single track leads to Villa Santa Lucía military camp; keep right to Chaitén, crossing en route the free ferry at Puerto Cárdenas. **N.B.** Only transit visas are issued at border points, so you must either leave within 10 days or renew your entry stamp at an immigration office.

There is superb salmon fishing in the rivers, and the local people are very friendly. 25 km. from Chaitén is Amarillo (accommodation in village bar, F, breakfast US$1); 5 km. from the village are thermal baths (2 wooden sheds with very hot pool inside), camping possible. From the thermal baths it is possible to hike along the old trail to Futaleufú, 4-7 days, not for the inexperienced, be prepared for wet feet all the way. The trail follows the River Michinmawida (passing the volcano of the same name) to Lake Espolón. Ferry across early Mon. and Thurs., US$1, then 8 km. to Futaleufú. Campsite at this end of the lake also has bungalows. At Puerto Cárdenas there are 2 places to stay (out of 10 houses and a police post), full board available; beautiful setting. At Costa Brava/Santa Lucía (one shop, bread from a private house) there is a military camp; accommodation at No. 13 on main street, F, breakfast US$1. La Junta, at the confluence of Río Rosselot and Río Palena, Km. 270 from Coyhaique, is a drab, expensive village, but the fishing is good; 3 *hosteriás*, one at Antonio Varas 33, F, breakfast US$1.50, use of kitchen; walks to Lake Rosselot beautiful.

Puerto Puyuguapi, about half way, at the end of the Puyuguapi Canal, is an intriguing town built by Germans fifty years ago. There are several springs with 50°C water filling two pools near the beach (take a boat 18 km. S of the village, or rent a boat for a group, for US$30, baths cost US$6 p.p.). Accommodation is available in a large wooden house on the right-hand side of the road which leads from the quayside through the village, 150 metres before the police post, owned by Sra. Ursula Flack Kronscheky, very good board and lodging; alternatively, 300 metres south at Sur Rolando, stay at Sra. Sophía's house; *pensión* at Tureo 18, F. There are 2 bars and a general store behind the petrol station. Transport out of Puyuguapi is very scare.

At Puerto Cisnes along the Seno Ventisquero (33 km. from the main road), you can buy food and find accommodation (*Posada del Graal*, E, rec., as is *Posada Gaucho*, F with breakfast, dinner available, *pensión* at Carlos Condell 195, F, occasional hot water, also a youth hostel and campsite). Parque Nacional Queulat (Km. 160 on Carretera Austral) nearby, is, according to legend, the place where the rich town of Césares once was. The Colgado glacier can be seen from the park, very beautiful, camping possible. The Río Cisnes is rec. for rafting or canoeing; 160 km. of grand scenery, with modest rapids except for the horrendous drop at Piedra del Gato; there is a 150 metre cliff at Torre Bright Bank. Good camping in the forest. At Cisne Medio (no hotel, restaurant or telephone, there is **a road to La Tapera** and to the Argentine border. Villa Mañihuales, 20 km. S of El Tocqui copper mine, is connected by bus with Coyhaique and Puerto Aysén; there are at least 3 *pensiones*; restaurant *Villa Mañihuales* (right-hand side of road going S at south end), F, friendly, breakfast US$0.75. At Villa Ortega, the *Restaurant Farolito* takes guests, F, rec.

ARCHIPELAGIC CHILE From Puerto Montt and Chiloé to Cape Horn.(7)

		Population ('000)	
Region	Provinces	1975	1982
XI (Aysén)	Aysén	57	67
XII (Magallanes)	Magallanes and Antarctic Territory	101	131

South of Puerto Montt lies a third of Chile, but its land and its climate are such that it has been put to little human use: less than 3 % of the country's population lives here. There is no real dry season. On the offshore islands and the western side of the Andes it is frequently wet and windy, particularly south of the Río Baker. North of that river, the summers are drier than the winters, but to the south, summers are windier and marginally wetter. Impenetrable forest covers most of the land. It is only the northern part, as far south as Coyhaique—and the far S that are inhabited. S of Chiloé, for 1,100 km., there is a maze of islands—the tops of submerged mountains—separated by tortuous fjord-like channels, a veritable topographical hysteria. It is fortunate for shipping that this maze has a more or less connected route through it: down the channel between Chiloé and the mainland, about 290 km. of open sea beyond the southern tip of Chiloé and then down the Moraleda, Mesier, Inocentes and Smyth channels into the Straits of Magellan. In some places along this route the tide levels change by 12 metres. In one particular place two sharp-cut walls, 900 metres high, enclose the constricted channel which leads to Puerto Natales; here the waters are deeper than the cliffs are high and slack water lasts for 30 mins. only. The Smyth Channel enters the Straits of Magellan at Cape Thamar. January and February are probably the best months for a trip to this region.

Lan-Chile has excellent air services to Balmaceda (for Puerto Aysén), Coyhaique and Magallanes from Puerto Montt. Air force flights half-price.

The Eleventh (Aysén) Region lies between Chiloé and Magallanes. The main port of Aysén, **Puerto Chacabuco** (with *Parque Turístico Loberías de Aysén*, B, *Hotel Moraleda*, *Res. Chacabuco* and *Res. El Puerto*, all F; most taken up by fishing companies), is 15 km. from Puerto Aysén. There is a bus service (daily except Sun.), US$0.40, but make sure to reserve seats.

Puerto Aysén, no longer a port, population 20,000, has good connections with Argentina and daily bus service at 1000 to Coyhaique, 67 km. away. The road from Puerto Aysén to Coyhaique passes through the Parque Nacional Río Simpson, with beautiful waterfalls. Folklore festival in 2nd week of November. Walk to Laguna los Palos, 2 hrs., rec.

Accommodation hard to find, for same reason as at Puerto Chacabuco. *Residencia El Aramei*, Av. Montaner, E, clean, full board available; *Roxy*, Aldea 960, F. *Residencial Marina*, Aldea 382, F, clean, only cold water; unnamed *pensión* at Aldea 1026, G p.p. with sleeping bag; *Posada*, last house on right on Coyhaique road, F, hot water. *Café-Restaurant Yaney Ruca*, Aldea 369, clean, friendly; *Café-Restaurant El Fogón*, nearby, same street, both E. No campsite but free camping easy.

Exchange on Plaza de Armas will only change cash, not travellers' cheques

Post Office on other side of bridge from Plaza de Armas.

Tourist Office in Municipalidad, Arturo Prat y Sgto. Aldea, Dec. 1 to end-Feb. only; helpful.

Bus to Puerto Chacabuco, US$0.60, colectivo US$6.

Shipping   Empremar office at Teniente Marinero 778; cruise line, Constantino Kochifas Carclamo, Teniente Marinero 868; T 342. The owner of a 65 ft. sailing yacht, who organizes 4 day cruises to Laguna San Rafael (US$700), lives on the plaza opposite Ladeco office. (Out of season, trips to Laguna San Rafael are impossible to arrange).

A ferry service (the *Colono*) runs from Puerto Chacabuco (Aysén) via the Canal Moraleda to Quellón on Chiloé on Mon., Wed. and Fri. at 1500 and takes 19 hours (seats US$14.50 and US$17.50); meals are available. Beware of fleas. Information from Transportes Marítimos Chiloé-Aysén (Transmarchilay), Ancud, Puerto Montt (addresses under towns), or Av. O'Higgins s/n, Pto. Chacabuco. Navimag agent (for *Evangelistas*), Agemar, near Plaza de Armas.

Coyhaique (population, 40,000), the administrative and commercial centre of the region, is located in a large green valley surrounded by mountains. The town provides a good base for hiking and skiing excursions in the area and has a good Museo Regional de la Patagonia Central in the college on the square. Excellent views of the Río Simpson valley from the hill, 4 hrs. walk north of town, at Reserva Forestal.

Hotels   at Coyhaique (rooms in very short supply): *Chible*, José de Moraleda 440, C; *Residencial Puerto Varas*, Serrano 168, E, hot water, rec.; *Hostería Coyhaique*, on La Onza, B, poor beds, unreliable hot water, good restaurant *Los Nires*, Baquedano 315, T 22261, D; *Pensión América*, 21 de Mayo 233, E, basic and cheap. *Motel Hostal del Rey*, near buses, D with kitchen, bath and heater; *Residencial Tejas Verdes*, Baquedano 198, E; Subteniente Cruz 57, F, off Plaza de Armas, basic. *Residencial* at Cochrane 532 (no sign), F, quite nice except for bathroom; *Res. La Pastora*, Pratt 553, E, no hot water, meals available. *Hospedajes* at Barroso y 21 de Mayo, E (white house); Colón 203, E (owner arranges tours); Colón 495, F p.p. without breakfast (more with), hot water, clean; Ignacio Serrano 391, T 21408, E with breakfast, not as good. Youth hostel in summer at the school, G p.p. with sleeping bag.

Camping   6 km. north at Laguna Verde in Reserva Forestal is free.

Restaurants   *Loberías de Chacabuco*, Barroso 553, good seafood; many others. *Parador Munich*, Prat y Dussen, pizzas and sandwiches; *Estancia*, José Carrera y Moraleda, also rents rooms (G p.p., hot water) and allows use of kitchen; *Café Oriente*, Calle 21 de Mayo y Condell, good bakery, tea; *Café Kalu*, A. Prat 402, serves good hamburgers. *Café Ricer*, Calle Horn, cheap.

Shopping   Three large well stocked supermarkets; dehydrated camping food available. Food, especially fruit and vegetables, is much more expensive than in Santiago.

Car Hire   Automóvil Club de Chile, Prat 348, rents Suzuki jeeps. About US$20/day, plus US$0.15/km., plus fuel.

Post Office Cochrane 202.

Exchange   will change travellers' cheques. For australes, dollars and cheques go to Lavaseco on Gral. Parra.

Tourist Office   At Horn, on Plaza. Conaf office, Ogana 1060. Maps (photocopies of 1:50,000 IGM maps) from Dirección de Vialidad on the plaza.

Shipping Empremar, telephone Puerto Aysén 332716/26 to reserve *Calbuco*. Transmarchilay, 21 de Mayo 417, T 21971, Telex 281057.

Buses   Terminal at Lautaro y Magallanes. Comodoro Rivadavia (Argentina), Giobbi, T 22067, Tues., Thurs., Sat. 0800, US$20, 12 hrs.; Puerto Aysén-Coyhaique, several daily, US$1.75, Puerto Chacabuco, US$2, 3 a day, 2 companies, but only if there's a boat in; otherwise to Aysén. Puerto Cisnes on Wed., 1300, Tues. and Sat. at 1100, US$8; La Junta, Fri. at 1000, US$11. There are now daily buses to Mañihuales and Balmaceda and to Chile Chico; to Chaitén about 4 a week, US$24, 12-14 hrs., ½-hr. stops in La Junta and Puyuguapi; Mon., Wed., Fri. and Sun. to Puerto Ibáñez on Lake Carrera, the Chilean section of Lake Buenos Aires (US$4.50), connects with *El Pilchero* ferry, see below; ask at *Residencial Tejas Verdes*, Baquedano 198. 3 buses a week to Cochrane, US$18.

Travel to Argentina   Either via Coyhaique Alto or Balmaceda. Transport to Los Antiguos in Argentina by colectivo from Chile Chico, US$2 (17 rivers have to be crossed). From border either hitch or take bus (Tues. or Thurs. 0800) to Perito Moreno. Beware, many border posts closed at weekends.

Air   Ladeco (office at Gral. Parra 210, T 21188) to Puerto Montt (US$31), Punta Arenas (US$75), March-Dec. only and Santiago. To Comodoro Rivadavia (Arg.), departs Tues. 0700. Air taxi to visit glaciers, US$400 (five passengers), also to southern archipelagic region. Charter flights: TAC, Lillo 315, T 21889, to Puerto Montt. Transporte Aéreo "Don Carlos", Subteniente Cruz 65, T 21981 to Chile Chico and Cochrane.

Excursions   Several reserves: Reserva Forestal Mañihuales, 76 km. from Coyhaique, has largely been destroyed by forest fires, but Reserva Forestal Lago Las Torres, 126 km., is worth a visit. There is a free camping place and the lake is full of fish. Good walking for the experienced in the Divisadero range.

The Carretera Austral continues south of Coyhaique to Puerto Ibáñez and Cochrane. 35 km. S of Coyhaique is El Blanco, a hamlet with *pensión* at *Restaurant El Blanco* (or *El Nuevo*—G, breakfast US$0.75). At **Puerto Ibáñez**, on Lake Carrera, there are three *residenciales*: *Ibáñez*, Buenos Aires 201 (warm, hot water) and, next door, *Mónica*, good meals (both F), and *Hostería Batada Río Ibáñez*, E, and *pensión* at B. Dickson 165, F, use of kitchen extra, breakfast US$1.25 or US$1.75 with fried eggs.

To reach **Chile Chico** (population of town 800, of region 2,400), on the southern shore of Lake Carrera, one can either go by boat from Puerto Ibáñez or go through Argentina. The region prides itself in having the best climate in Southern Chile with some 300 days of sunshine; much fruit is grown as a result. Rainfall is very low but strong winds are common. The lake itself covers 2,240 sq. km.; the Chilean end is predominantly Alpine and the Argentine end (Lake Buenos Aires, 881 sq. km.) dry pampa.

Hotels   at Chile Chico: *Aguas Azules*, Rodríguez 252, E full board (F without), rec. *Residenciales Frontera*, O'Higgins 41 and *Nacional*, Freire, same rates. Private house, Blest Gana 240, basic but nice, F. Youth hostel at Blest Gana 320, from Jan. to end Feb. *Casa Quinta/No me Olvides* (María Sánchez de Campaña), F p.p. just by Puerto Márquez on road to Argentine border, clean, cooking facilities, warm, no hot water, honey, eggs, fruit for sale, rec. **Restaurants** *Cafetería Elizabeth y Loly* on Plaza serves coffee and delicious homemade cakes; will prepare meals if asked; *La Cabañita*, typical, cheap; *Rapa Nui*, cheap and good. It is very difficult to change dollars; change australes in shops and cafés on main street. Ask at the Municipalidad for help in arranging tours.

Regular service by Transmarchilay car ferry, *El Pilchero*, across the lake, leaves Puerto Ibáñez for Chile Chico 0800 Tues. and Thurs., 1000 Sat., and 1600 Sun.(2½ hrs, each way: US$2.25 p.p., US$26 for car; offices in Ancud or Coyhaique). The Sun. boat from Puerto Ibáñez goes only to Chile Chico; other services continue to Fachinal, and other ports, to Murta on Lago Gen. Carrera. Number of passengers limited to 70; locals given preference, no reservations possible. Chile Chico is connected by road S only as far as Fachinal (50 km.); from where there is a trail to Mallín Grande (a ferry jetty and little else) and Puerto Guadal (shops, post office, rooms at Quemel "Sade" Guerrero— 1st shop you see from jetty, No. 382 on corner of Los Pinos—*Restaurant La Frontera*, Los Lirios y Los Pinos). A road from Guadal leads to Puerto Bertrán and on to Cochrane on Lake Cochrane. Trails through the valley of Río Baker to Puerto Yungay are rec. for serious walkers, and horses can be hired to go up into the mountains. There are bus services to Coyhaique.

The Carretera Austral branches off the Coyhaique-Pto. Ibáñez road 97 km. S of Coyhaique. It goes through Villa Castillo (small supermarket), Murta (on the northern tip of the central "arm" of Lago General Carrera, *Res. Patagonia*; *Res. y restaurante Lago Gen. Carrera*, welcoming; free camping by lake, good view of Cerro Castillo), Tranquilo, and on to Cochrane via El Maitén junction with the Pto. Guadal road. Splendid scenery.

The country to the S and W of Chile Chico provides good walking for the mountaineer. The weird rock formations and dry brush-scrub give a "wild west" feel to the country. The northern and higher peak of Cerro Pico del Sur (2,168 m.) can be climbed by the agile from Los Cipres (beware of dogs in farmyard). You will need a long summer's day and the 1:50,000 map. Follow the horse trail until it peters out, then navigate by compass or sense of direction until the volcano-like summit appears. After breaching the cliff ramparts at an obvious point, there is some scrambling and a 10-foot pitch to the summit: indescribable views of the Lake and Andes. (Brian Spearing)

Some 150 nautical miles south of Puerto Aysén is the Laguna San Rafael glacier, 30 metres above sea level, and 45 km. in length. It calves small icebergs, carried out to sea by wind and tide. The thick vegetation on the shores, with snowy peaks above, is typical of Aysén. The glacier is one of a group of four that flow in all directions from Monte San Valentín. This icefield is part of the Parque Nacional Laguna San Rafael (1.35m. hectares), one of Aysén's 12 national parks, all set up in 1967 and now regulated by the National Forestry Council (Conaf). The only way there is by plane or by boat: Air Taxi from Coyhaique (C. Fischer, Bilbao 563, T 21712), US$160, or US$100 each if party of 12; some pilots in Puerto Aysén will fly to the glacier for about US$85, but many are unwilling to land on the rough airstrip. The glacier is best seen from the sea: there are expensive cruises (for instance those of Empremar, or Kochifas, with offices in Santiago and Puerto Aysén); Mar del Sur, 21 de Mayo 417, 2nd floor, has a boat, *Ana Pink*, which goes to Laguna San Rafael, US$168 for 3-day trip; local fishing boats from Chacabuco/Puerto Aysén take about 18-20 hrs. each way, charging the same as the tourist boats. Ask for Jorge Prado at the port (he takes a minimum of 7, more expensive than others); Andino Royas, Cochrane 129; Justiniano Aravena, Dr. Steffen 703; Rodrigo Azúcar, Agemar office, T 716; or Sr. Ocuña, ask at the port.

The *Calbuco* of Empremar, a government supply ship, leaves Chacabuco on Fri. at 1800, returning from the Laguna on Sat. at 1800, arriving Chacabuco on Sun. at 0800, two lifeboats make the trip to the glacier (bring food as you may be left at the glacier for 3 hours). Operates to San Rafael only between December and March, book in advance in Aysén in Jan./Feb. season (all year round the *Calbuco* runs from Puerto Montt to Puerto Chacabuco). Cost Chacabuco-San Rafael and back is US$65 in pullman chair, US$105 for a bed (all fares include food). (On the return journey you can continue to any of stops back to, and including Puerto Montt, 48 hrs.) Rooms can be hired for US$1.50 p.p. at the old hotel administered by Conaf (bring a week's supply of food: unless lucky enough to hitch back on another boat, you'll have to wait for the *Calbuco*; also bring anti-mosquito cream and candles—no electricity. Water can be scarce and the hot shower only works when water is plentiful, 2 very cold waterfalls nearby if necessary—take biodegradable soap). At the glacier there is a small ranger station. The rangers are willing to row you out to the glacier in calm weather, a 3-hr. trip. Robert af Sandeberg (Lidingö, Sweden) describes this journey as follows:

"The trip in the rowboat is an awesome venture. At first it is fairly warm and easy to row. Gradually it gets colder when the wind sweeps over the icy glacier (be sure to bring warm clothes). It gets harder to row as small icebergs hinder the boat. Frequently somebody has to jump onto an icefloe and push the boat through. The glacier itself has a deep blue colour, shimmering and reflecting the light; the same goes for the icebergs, which are an unreal, translucent blue. The glacier is very noisy; there are frequent cracking and banging sounds, resembling a mixture of gun shots and thunder. When a hunk of ice breaks loose, a huge swell is created and the icebergs start rocking in the water. Then great care and effort has to be taken to avoid the boat being crushed by the shifting icebergs; this is a very real danger."

In the national park are puma, pudu pudu (miniature deer), foxes, dolphins, occasional sealions and sea otters, and many species of bird. Walking trails are limited (about 10 km. in all) but a lookout platform has been constructed, with fine views of the glacier.

N.B. If you plan to go to Laguna San Rafael by boat, check first with the Gobernación Marítima in Puerto Aysén that the boat is licensed for the trip.

CHILEAN PATAGONIA (8)

The Twelfth Region (Magallanes), which includes the Chilean part of Tierra del Fuego, has 17.5% of Chile's total area, but it is inhabited by under 1% of Chile's population. In summer rains are frequent. In winter snow covers the country, except those parts near the sea. The country is then more or less impassable, except on horseback. Strong, cold, piercing winds blow, particularly during the spring, when they reach a velocity of 70 to 80 km. an hour. During the winter they do not blow all that hard, and from May to August a strong wind is almost exceptional. The dry winds parch the ground and prevent the growth of crops, which can only be cultivated in sheltered spots.

Until the discovery of oil—Tierra del Fuego and N of Magellan Strait produce all Chilean oil—the most important industry was the breeding of sheep. At one time there was a large British colony there; it has been diminishing steadily of late. Coal has been discovered on the Chilean side of the frontier, at Pecket, but the mine is considered uneconomic; miners still cross into Argentina to work at Río Turbio.

Punta Arenas, the most southerly city in Chile, and capital of the Twelfth Region, 2,140 km. S of Santiago, is on the Straits of Magellan at almost equal distance from the Pacific and Atlantic oceans, 1,432 nautical miles from Valparaíso, and 1,394 from Buenos Aires. The population is about 102,000. Most of the smaller and older buildings are of wood, but the city has expanded rapidly, and practically all new building is of brick or concrete. All the main roads are paved and the country roads are of gravel; when driving in Patagonia, some form of windscreen protection is absolutely essential. Punta Arenas is a busy little city somewhat neater looking than the average Chilean town. The cemetery, at Av. Bulnes 929, is even more fantastic than the one at Castro (Chiloé), with a statue of Indiecito, the little Indian, and many memorials to pioneer families and victims of shipping disasters (open 0800-2000 daily).

Punta Arenas is the centre of the sheep farming industry in that part of the world and exports wool, skins, and frozen meat. Besides the export of oil and gas, there is the regular carriage of crude between the Strait oil terminals and the refineries in central Chile. Good roads connect the city with (240 km.) Puerto Natales in Ultima Esperanza and Río Gallegos in Argentina. There are no railways. Punta Arenas has certain free-port facilities; the Zona Franca is 3½ km. N of the centre (open 1030-2000 Mon.-Sat.), but shops close 1230 to 1500 for lunch. (The restaurant is open at lunch time on Sundays.)

PUNTA ARENAS

1. Plaza de Armas
2. Cathedral
3. Cemetery
4. Museo Braun – Menéndez
5. Bus Sur
6. Bus Fernández
7. Lan-Chile
8. Ladeco
9. Tourist Office
10. *Hotel Cabo de Hornos*
11. *Hotel Los Navegantes*

There is a modern museum in the Colegio Salesiano, "Mayorino Borgatello" dealing with the Indians, animal and bird life of the region, and other interesting aspects of life in Patagonia and Tierra del Fuego, at Av. Bulnes 374, entrance next to church. Open Tues., to Sun. 1600-1800 (entry US$0.25). Museum of regional history, Braun Menéndez, Calle Magallanes 949, off Plaza de Armas, located in a mansion built by one of the early millionaires, is well worth visiting. Part is set out as room-by-room regional history, the rest of the house is furnished and visitors are taken round in groups by a guide. Closed Mon., otherwise open 1100-1300 (entry US$0.50). The British School on Waldo Seguel, and St. James' Church next door, are wooden, in colonial style.

Hotels *Cabo de Hornos,* Plaza Muñoz Gamero 1025, T 222134, A, excellent, rec.; *Los Navegantes,* José Menéndez 647 (Casilla 230, T 224667), A, excellent restaurant, slightly cheaper than *Cabo de Hornos; Savoy,* same street, No. 1073, T 225851, C, good place to eat; *Hostal de la Patagonia,* O'Higgins 478, T 223521, C with bath, excellent; *Turismo Plaza,* José Nogueira 1116 2nd floor, T 221300, C (cheaper without bath), pleasant; *Monte Carlo,* Av. Colón 605, E, with breakfast, clean; *Residencial Villegas,* Boliviana 238, E with meals; *Residencial París,* J. Nogueira 1116, T 223112, 3rd floor, D, rec., though some rooms are without windows. *Residencial Central,* Balmaceda 545, D, with breakfast; *Residencial* at Armando Sanhuesa 965, F, hot shower, run-down, but pleasant atmosphere, meals available; *Residencial Roca,* Calle Roca 1038, T 223803, clean and pleasant, E; *Casa Deportista,* O'Higgins y Errazúriz, F with breakfast, several bunks to a room, noisy. Private house, Sra. Carolina Ramírez, at Paraguaya 150, F, nice and friendly, no heating, breakfast included; Sra. Angela Hernández, Rómulo Correa 0370, Barrio Prat, G, with or without breakfast; Nena's, Boliviana 366, friendly, F with breakfast. Cheap floor space for the hardy at the *Salvation Army building,* Calle Bella Vista 577, US$0.50 per head, or ask for private house accommodation at tourist office. **Camping** is possible near the warden's house in Parque María Behety, 2 km. south of centre. Also in Reserva Forestal Magallanes, 8 km. from Punta Arenas (check with Tourist Office for directions).

Restaurants Main hotels. *El Mercado,* Mejicana 617, reasonably-priced lunch, expensive dinner; *Union Club,* Plaza Muñoz Gamero 716, accepts non-members for meals, and is reported to be very good. *Centro Español* is excellent, above Teatro Cervantes on Plaza de Armas; *Iberia,* Av. O'Higgins 974, highly rec., try steak au poivre. Seafood at *Sotitos,* O'Higgins 1138, good service and cuisine, expensive. American Service restaurant good. *El Infante,* Magallanes 875 (accepts Visa). Local specialities at *Moreau,* Chiloé 1132 and *El Lloco II,* Covadonga 227, peña Fri. and Sat. US$1. *Café Garogha,* Bories 817, open Sun. p.m., pleasant but busy at night. *Don Quixote,* Navarro 1087, good café; *Café Monaco,* Bories y Menéndez, cheap snacks and drinks. *Sayonara,* Errázuriz, good value bar. Restaurant above fish market offers centolla and oysters, but slow service and expensive. Cheap fish meals available at stalls near the fishing cooperative near the docks. The bakeries on Calle O'Higgins are well worth a visit, with excellent rye bread sold on Mons. and Thurs. Also, *Pancal,* 21 de Mayo 1547, good bread and cakes. Try Polar beer. Lobster has become more expensive because of a law banning fishing them with nets, allowing only lobster pots.

Night Club *Normita* discotheque, Balmaceda, downmarket, all night, free on Fri. and Sat. Peñas El Fogón and El Trovador.

Car Hire Hertz, Lautaro Navarro 1064, T 222013. Autómovil Club, O'Higgins 931, T 221888; Turismo Pehoé, 21 de Mayo 1464, T 224223/224506; Turismo Cabo de Hornos, Plaza Muñoz Gamero 1039, T 222599.

Exchange National banks. Open 0900 to 1400 but closed on Sat.; but the Casa de Cambio Andino, Roca 886, Office 25 is open until 1900 on Fri. Banco O'Higgins good for exchange. If buying Argentine australes with dollars it is advantageous to do so at a bank, if with Chilean pesos as *casa de cambio.* Good rates at Cambio Gasic, Lautaro Navarro 549, T 222396, La Hermandad, same street No. 1099, T 223991, Cambio Taurus, 21 de Mayo 1502, and at Bus Sur office on Menéndez 565, T 224864 and Lautaro Navarro 1001, T 225656 (accepts travellers' cheques). Kiosco Redondito, Mejicano 613, T 227369. If banks and *cambios* are closed, exchange is available at *Hotel Los Navegantes,* José Menéndez 647, or *Hotel Cabo de Hornos.*

British Vice-Consul Mr Roderick Matheson at 21 de Mayo 1243, T 228001, Casilla (P.O. Box) 327, helpful and friendly. Hours 1000-1300, 1500-1700. **Argentine Consulate** Av. 21 de Mayo 1878, open 1000-1400. Visas take 24 hrs., US$15. Other consulates: W. German, Independencia 865 (T 223781), Danish, Bories 911 (T 221850), Dutch, 21 de Mayo 1243 (T 224275), Swedish, Errazúriz 891 (T 224107), French, Colón 399 (T 224482), Italian, Balmaceda 357 (T 223518), Norwegian, Mejicana 916 (T 222156).

Laundry Self-service, O'Higgins 969; Lavaseco Josseau, Pinto 766.

Dentist Dr. Hugo Vera Carcamo, España 1518, T 227510, rec.

Post Office Carlos Bories y J.Menéndez, open 0830-1230, 1400-1830 (Mon.-Fri.), 0830-1230 (Sat.), closed on Sundays.

Cables Calle Pedro Montt 841. **Telephones** Nogueira y Roca, Plaza de Armas, 0800-2200, international and local.

Tourist Office Sernatur, Waldo Seguel 689, Casilla 106-D, T 224435, at the corner with Plaza Muñoz Gamero, 0830-1230, 1430-1830. English spoken. Kiosk on Colón between Bories and Magallanes. **Conaf**, J.Menédez, between Montt and Quilota.

Travel Agents Skartour and Cabo de Hornos Tur, Plaza Muñoz Gamero 1013 and 1039. Ventistur in lobby of *Hotel Las Navegantes*, T 224677, competent, run by Sr. Ernesto Fernández de Cabo, helpful and excellent for arranging tours to Patagonia. Turismo Aventour, J. Nogueira 1255, T 224926, English spoken, helpful, organizes trips from Punta Arenas to Puerto Williams by plane, with 2-3 days visiting glaciers around Tierra del Fuego by boat (US$500-600). Austral Adventure Services (Lautaro Navarro 975, T 228159, Telex 380090 AASPA CK) arranges tours and adventure expeditions in the region (they also provide information on boat trips to glaciers and the southern Patagonian icecaps). And others.

Shipping Navimag, office at Independencia 830, T 226600 and 222593, but buy tickets at Comapa, Magallanes 970. Tourist tickets are not sold in the off-season, so try truck companies, or truck drivers at the dock (male passengers only should try this). Government supply ships are recommended for the young and hardy, but take sleeping bag and extra food, and travel pills. Empremar's *El Navarino* to Puerto Edén, Chacabuco and Valparaíso sometimes sells passenger tickets. Ask at Tourist Office for details or enquire at Empresa Marítima del Estado (Empremar), Lautaro Navarro 1338, T 221608. For transport on navy supply ships to Puerto Williams, enquire at Tercera Zona Naval, Calle Lautaro Navarro 1150, or ask the captain direct.

Ferries Regular services between Punta Arenas and Puerto Porvenir (Tierra del Fuego) in *Melinka*, leaving Tres Puentes (5 km. from Punta Arenas) at 0900 daily (1000 on Sun.), depending on tides, US$2 p.p., US$2 per bike, US$25 per vehicle. Buy tickets on board, or at Agencia Broom, Roca 924. It returns from Porvenir (Sampaio 302) at 1400 (1500 Sat.), 2¾ hrs. each way. Bus to ferry at either end is US$0.25, take "Tres Puentes" bus to within 250 m. of ferry at Punta Arenas, or take colectivo No. 14 or 15 (US$1.50) all the way.

Air Services Lan-Chile and Ladeco run daily flights to Puerto Montt and Santiago. With Lan-Chile flights there is a free bus service to Ancud and Castro on Chiloé. Aerovías DAP, Carrero Pinto 1022, T 223958, fly to Porvenir daily (US$15), and to Puerto Williams Tues. (US$110 return), plus other irregular flights, with a Twin-Otter aircraft. (Heavily booked so make sure you have your return reservation confirmed.) Flights to Tierra del Fuego, **see page 511**. Also, military (FACh) flights US$27, approx. twice a month to Puerto Montt. Information and tickets from airforce base at the airport; need to book well in advance. Reserve passages in advance in January and February. Bus from airport, US$0.75; colectivos run from Colón y Magallanes. DAP and Ladeco have their own services from town. The airport restaurant is good.

Bus Service To Río Gallegos, daily, 4 companies (at least 2 a day except 1 on Sun. and Mon.— e.g. El Pingüino, Roca 915, and Viajes Vera, 21 de Mayo, English spoken, helpful; all leave before 1200), US$12.50, 7 hrs., including ½ hr. lunch at km. 160. All customs formalities now undertaken at the border, but ask before departure if this has changed. Puerto Natales, 4 hrs. with Fernández, Chiloé 930 and Buses Sur, José Menéndez 556, each twice a day. To Puerto Montt (via Argentina) and Santiago twice a week in summer (once in low season) with Bus Norte, Ghisoni and Turisbus; the last two also go on to Castro, Chiloé. Fares approx. US$60. Private cars can be hired.

Skiing Cerro Mirador, only 9 km. from Punta Arenas, one of the few places in the world where one can ski with a sea view. Transtur buses 0900 and 1400 from in front of *Hotel Cabo de Hornos*, US$3, return. Daily lift-ticket, US$4.50; equipment rental, US$6 per adult. Mid-way lodge with food, drink and equipment. Season June to September/ November, weather depending. Contact the Club Andino (on the hill, not far from Las Minas Reserve) about crosscountry skiing facilities. Also skiing at Tres Morros.

Excursions Within easy reach are Puerto Hambre and Fuerte Bulnes (reconstructed, old fort, a 56-km. trip). At Río Penitente is Morro Negro, a large rock outcrop. The trip can be done in a day. To the west of town is the Las Minas Nature Reserve (follow Independencia right through town and up the hill). There is a botanical trail (US$0.30); there are sandcliffs which one can descend with care to the Río Las Minas valley, but beware of boggy ground, and thence back to Punta Arenas. The most interesting excursions are to the Ultima Esperanza region (see below under Puerto Natales) and so to the Torres del Paine National Park. Ventistur offer excursions from Fri. night to Sat. night; Turismo Pehoé, 21 de Mayo 1464, goes to Paine for US$200; Cabo de Hornos Tur organize tours with station wagons. Sr. Mateo Quesada, Chiloé 1375, T 222662, offers local tours in his car, up to 4 passengers.

The fjords and glaciers of Tierra del Fuego (70 km. by schooner) are exceptionally beautiful. Once a fortnight there is a 22-hr. 320-km. round trip to the fjord d'Agostino, 30 km. long, where many glaciers come down to the sea. A three-day tour to Puerto Natales, the glacier, Balmaceda and Torres del Paine can be arranged from Punta Arenas for US$150, inclusive of meals and accommodation. Empresa Buses Fernández, Calle Chiloé 930, runs this excursion and also afternoon excursions to Club Andino and the Fuerte Bulnes (US$15), and to the penguin hatchery and fine scenery on Otway Sound (US$15). **Buses Sur** also run the 3-day, Puerto Natales/Paine trip for US$50, transport only, or US$135 with food and lodging. Aiketour, Menéndez 750, Oficina 6 (T 226916), also goes to the penguin colonies.

Antarctica Punta Arenas has become the number one starting point for visits to Antarctica. The following possibilities exist: Turismo Cabo de Hornos, Plaza Muñoz Gamero (Casilla 62-D), Punta Arenas, T 222599, Telex 280342 HORNO CL, now offers in March and October six-day packages, which include three nights accommodation at the *Hotel Estrella Polar* at the Teniente Rodolfo Marsh base on King George Island in the South Shetlands. Air transport is by Chilean Air Force (FACh) C-130 Hercules aircraft. Cost US$2,500. Lindblad Travel, P.O. Box 912, Westport CT 06881, USA, T (203) 226-8531, has made cruises to Antarctica with the luxury chartered Chinese ship m/v *Yao Hua* of 10,151 grt . Fare range US$2,490-15,325 for land/cruise arrangement. Telex 643443 LIND UR.

Society Expeditions Cruises, 723 Broadway East, Seattle WA 98102, T (206) 324-9400, (800) 426-7794, Telex (910) 444-1381, using the luxury small cruise ships *World Discoverer* of 3,153 grt and *Society Explorer* of 2,367 grt (formerly *Lindblad Explorer*), have made cruises to Antarctica, fare range US$4,750-17,775. In addition, the *World Discoverer* has made an Antarctica Circumnavigation from Ushuaia, Argentina to Wellington, New Zealand. Fare range US$8,900-23,900.

Adventure Network International, 200-1676 Duranleu St., Vancouver, BC, Canada V6H 3SS, T (604) 683-8033, Telex 0636-700-749 MBX CA. Local contacts: Hugh Macleary, Casilla 0124, Punta Arenas, T 224484, Telex 380076 LANAS CK; Javier Lopetegui, Portales 780, San Bernardo, Santiago, T 028593081. *Hotel Cabo de Hornos* arranges trips to Antarctica in October. Depending on the number of travellers, the price ranges from US$800 to US$2,200 for a 2-day visit.

Joe and Cristina Kessler of New York write: "From Punta Arenas we went with the Chilean Navy to Antarctica. To say it was an exceptional trip is a vast understatement. We went from Punta Arenas through the southern canals to Puerto Williams, then S past Cape Horn, across the Drake Passage to the Antarctic Peninsula. We traversed back and forth between 5 Chilean bases including Deception Is. The furthest south we went was the American Palmer station at 65° S." Going rate is US$40 per day; but to secure a place on board ask the ship's captain direct. The Antarctica flotilla consists of two ships: the *Piloto Parto* which sails from Valparaíso and the *Yelcho* from Punto Arenas. The trips take place at the beginning of the year, but space is limited. Information, in person only, from Tercera Zona Naval, Calle Lautaro Navarro 1150, Punta Arenas.

Puerto Natales (17,000 people) is 247 km. N of Punta Arenas and close to the Argentine border at Río Turbio. It stands on the Ultima Esperanza gulf amid spectacular scenery, and is the jumping-off place for the magnificent Balmaceda and Paine national parks.

Hotels *Eberhard*, Pedro Montt 25, T 411208, A, excellent views, good; *Natalino*, Eberhard 371, T 411968, clean and very friendly, E, breakfast included, rec. (tours to Milodón Cave arranged); *Palace*, D, Ladrilleros 105, T 411134, good food; *Austral*, Valdivia 949, T 411193, clean, friendly, good food, run by Eduardo Scott, E, without bath, D with bath and breakfast. *Residencial Temuco*, Ramírez 202, T 411120, friendly, reasonable, good food, E; opp., at *zapatería* at Bulnes 810, is Elba Edita Solo Pérez, T 411026, F p.p. with breakfast, clean, hot water, heated rooms, will store luggage; *Residencial La Busca*, Valdivia 845 (no sign outside), F, rec., good and cheap food available; *Res. Termas de Puyehue*, O'Higgins (nr. hospital), F, clean, friendly, dinner extra; *Pensión Magallanes* on Calle Magallanes (no sign), F, hot water; many mountaineering parties stay here, the owner's son runs day excursions to Lake Grey. *Pensión Bahía*, Teniente Serrano 346, excellent food, especially king crabs. *Residencial Grey*, Bulnes 90, F incl. breakfast, hot water, some rooms with heating, very friendly; *Residencial Bulnes*, Calle Bulnes 407, T 411307 (no sign), beside police station, good, F, stores luggage; *Casa de Familia Dickson*, Bulnes 307, T 411218, F p.p., good breakfast, other meals available to order, clean, rec. *Pensión* at Baquedano 1038 (Iris and Sergio), F, highly rec. for lodging and baking; and O'Higgins 431 and Perito 443; *Casa de familia* at Galvarino 846, F with breakfast, rec.; also O'Higgins 70, same terms; Sra. Nelly, Uvaldo Segero (opp. hospital), F, friendly, clean, use of kitchen. Sra. Elsa, A. Prat 15, with breakfast, cooking facilities, G. The youth hostel at Sec. Nac. de la Juventud, Ramírez 856, accepts IYHF cards, US$2.50 (open summer only). If locked contact Srta. Nancy Segura at Domeyco 621 or secretary of YH at Ramírez 857.

Hotels in the countryside and around include: *Hostería Llanura de Diana*, Km. 220 Road 9

Sector Río Tranquilo, T 222350, on road to Punta Arenas (hidden from the road), highly rec.; *Posada de Cisne de Cuello Negro*, a former guest house for meat buyers at the *frigorífico*, D, friendly, clean, reasonable, all rooms with bath, excellent cooking, new owners, 5 km. from Puerto Natales at Km. 257 Road 9 Sector Puerto Bories; *Patagonia Inn*, D, Km. 257 Road 9 Sector Dos Lagunas, T 222134, 23 km. from Puerto Natales, open only in summer, from November to March.

Restaurants *Nikol's*, Barros Arana 160, seafood and salmon very good; *Socorro* is also rec. as is *Don Alvarito*, Blanco Encalada 915; *La Ultima Esperanza*, M.Rodríguez 216, also has rooms, F with bath and breakfast, and *Midas*, Rogers 169, both good, clean. *Café Tranquera*, Bulnes 579, good coffee, meals, snacks. *Centro Español*, Magallanes 247, reasonable restaurant. Cheap meals at *Club Deportivo Natales*, Eberhard 332.

Tourist Office in kiosk on waterfront, Av. Pedro Montt y Phillipi. **Conaf**, opp. hospital, Av. Carrera.

Exchange *Casas de cambio* on Blanco Encalada 226 and 266 where australes (and sometimes US$) can be changed. Cambio Stop, Baquedano 380, good for cash. Another two at Bulnes 683 and 1087 (good rates). Australes are accepted everywhere.

Travel Agents Turismo Paine, Calle Eberhard. Urbina Tours, Eberhard 554 (contact either here or at Tourist Office in Punta Arenas, Telex 282009 CL), tours to Paine National Park, Milodón Cave, etc. in 11-seater Toyota; also tours tailored to individual requirements.

Museum Museo De Agostini, Tierra del Fuego fauna.

Laundry at *Tienda Milodón*, on Bulnes.

Buses to Punta Arenas, 4 times daily, 4 hrs. US$7. Thrice weekly to Río Gallegos (Argentina), hourly to Río Turbio (Argentina), US$1.50, 2 hrs. (depending on Customs—change bus at border). 1000 bus to Río Turbio arrives in time for 1300 El Pingüino bus to Río Gallegos or Calafate (summer only). Bus Fernández, Eberhard 555 and Bus Sur, Baquedano 224. Empresa Gómez runs a minibus direct to Calafate, Argentina, for US$32, Mon., Wed. and Fri. (Nov.-March). Scott Turs, at *Hotel Austral*, goes to Calafate for US$20, but no regular schedule.

Shipping The m/n *Tierra del Fuego* of Navimag runs the 1,460 km. between Puerto Natales and Puerto Montt and carries passengers (**see page 497**). Navimag offices: Independencia 840 Punta Arenas, T 222593, 226600, Telex 380060 NAVIN CK, and Pedro Montt 380, Terminal Marítimo, T 411287, Puerto Natales (direct telex with Punta Arenas office, which is better). Tourist tickets only available in off-season if not enough truck drivers turn up.

Excursions A recommended walk is up to Cerro Dorotea which dominates the town, with superb views of the whole Ultima Esperanza Sound. Take Río Turbio bus and alight at jeep track for summit. 25 km. NW of Puerto Natales the Cueva Milodón can be visited. It now contains a plastic model of the prehistoric ground-sloth whose bones were found there in 1895. Fernández bus is cheapest, going on Fri. and returning Sun., mid-Nov. to mid-March only; at other times, take a taxi (US$15 return). A launch sails from the pier to Balmaceda National Park on Wed. and Sun. at 0900 if enough passengers book. An interesting trip, viewing glaciers and the rugged mountains at the S end of the Patagonian ice cap. On the trip one usually sees dolphins, sea-lions, black-neck swans, penguins and the quaint steamer ducks.

Some 150 km. NW of Puerto Natales is the ***Torres del Paine*** National Park, covering 1,630 sq. km., a "must" for its wildlife and spectacular scenery. Along the (gravel) road it is common to spot the Andean condor and herds of *guanaco*. The Torres and Cuernos del Paine are oddly shaped peaks, surrounded by glaciers, which fall straight down to the valleys, now covered with beautiful lakes at 50 to 200 metres above sea level. The glaciers Grey, Dickson and Zapata are three of the main ones branching off the huge mass forming the Patagonian icecap.

There are about 250 km. of well marked hiking trails and nine National Park shelters; bring food, a tent, sleeping bag and cooking gear. The area is very popular in summer and the shelters often crowded, and in poor condition.

The park is administered by the forestry department (Conaf) with a centre at the southern tip of Lake Pehoé and seven guardhouses located throughout the park. There the friendly wardens (*guardaparques*) give advice and one should register with them before setting out for a hike.

Refugios cost US$0.15, and an entrance fee to the Park (US$1) is charged. Most of the *refugios* have good areas, so take your own food (beware of mice!) as it is expensive to buy and limited in the Park. In most cases a tent is preferable to the *refugios*. Maps (US$0.50, obtainable at Conaf offices in Punta Arenas or Puerto Natales, but beware inaccuracies: some of the trails marked peter out and bridges get washed away) and protective clothing are essential. Eduardo Scott, who speaks English, can be contacted at his hotel, *Austral*, Valdivia 955, Puerto Natales (T 411593), he runs tours of the Park in a 8-seater bus (US$72). Also José Torres of Sastrería Arbiter in Calle Bulnes. The Visitor Information Centre, an old *estancia*, has a good slide show on Sat. and Sun. at 1900; guards will store luggage and arrange transport back to Puerto Natales. Horses may be rented from Brigitta Buhofer for US$18 a day with guide (US$10, ½day); horses for beginners and experienced riders available.

Accommodation   *Posada Río Serrano*, C, shared facilities, 2 km. from park administration, with expensive restaurant and a shop. (Reservations: Serco Ltda., Casilla 19-D, Punta Arenas, T 223395). *Hostería Pehoé*, A, 60 rooms, private facilities, 5 km. S of Pehoé guardhouse, 11 km. N of park administration, on an island with spectacular view across the Lake to Paine Grande and Cuernos del Paine, runs a boat up to Grey Glacier (Reservations: Turismo Pehoé, 21 de Mayo 1464, T 224223 in Punta Arenas or Nataniel 31, office 68, T 718709, Telex 240875 PEHOE CL in Santiago).

Camping   Pehoé (32 lots, hot shower US$2.15 p.p.) and Camping Río Serrano (25 lots) are operated by Serco Ltda., Camping Laguna Azul (10 lots) and Laguna Amarga (15 lots) by Conaf. Camping and lighting fires are permitted outside official campsites, but only where indicated by park wardens.

Buses Fernández and Sur (addresses above) run a daily service to Paine National Park between November and March (Fernández at 0800, returning 1700, US$6 one way). Out of season they go twice weekly if there are 5 or more passengers (US$13.50); Sur buses leave Puerto Natales on Mon., Wed., and Fri. at 1900 (1500 from Punta Arenas), returning from the Park headquarters Tues. Thurs., and Sat. at 0830. For these 2 companies' 3-day, all-in trip from Punta Arenas, twice a week in summer, **see page 509**. Enap weekend tours in summer cost US$45 including accommodation and meals. Taxi costs US$80 per day, run by Sergio Zaley (Arturo Prat 260), but may be cheaper if you catch him when he's going to the Park anyway. A minibus can be hired for about US$20 at Puerto Natales, to take a party of up to 8, or drivers for about US$33 return, to a *refugio* in the Paine National Park. After mid-March there is no public transport and trucks are irregular.

The most popular hike starts from either the administration building at the south end of Lake Pehoé or the Park entrance, and takes seven days going from *refugio* to *refugio* past the spectacular Grey Glacier and round the back of the Cuernos and Torres del Paine. It is tough, the longest lap being 30 km., but not too steep. (Note that the main footbridge to Grey Glacier was washed away by floods in 1983.) To walk from the administration just to Grey Glacier takes at least 3 hours to the *refugio* at the N end of Lake Pehoé (no firewood nearby), then 6-10 hours there and back to Grey Glacier (where the *refugio* has been burnt down).
   The scenery in the Park is spectacular. Walking along the trails one is constantly rewarded by changing views of fantastic peaks, ice-fields, vividly coloured lakes of turquoise, ultramarine and grey and quiet green valleys. Wild life abounds: one can expect to see *guanaco*, hares, foxes, condors, black-neck swans and many other birds. Apparently the park has a micro-climate especially favourable to plants and wild life. The Park is open all year round, although snow may prevent access in the winter: best time is January-April.
   Another recommended walk is to Ventisquero (glacier) del Francés, 2 hrs. from Pehoé to the Río Francés, 5 hrs. on to Campamento Británico. Also recommended is the walk to Lake Pingo, with *refugios* half way and at the Lake.
   Descriptions of several walks in the Torres del Paine area are found in *Backpacking in Chile and Argentina*, by Hilary Bradt and John Pilkington.

Tierra del Fuego is the island off the extreme south of South America. It is surrounded by the Magellan Strait to the north, the Atlantic Ocean to the east, the Beagle Channel to the south—which separates it from the southern islands—and by the Whiteside, Gabriel, Magdalena and Cockburn channels etc. which divide it from the islands situated to the west. The western side belongs to Chile and the eastern to Argentina. It produces most of Chile's oil.
   In Chilean Tierra del Fuego the only town is **Porvenir**, with a population of 4,500, several hundred from Yugoslavia. There is a small museum, the Fernando Cordero Rusque, Samuel Valdirieso 402, mainly Indian culture.

Porvenir Hotels   *Los Flamencos*, Teniente Merino, T 580049, best, A; *Turismo*, Soto Salas 698, E, good value; *Residencial Cameron* (ask at bar called *Somos o no Somos*), F, for shared room, "friendly folk", good meals, sleep on dining-room floor for US$1; *Central*, Phillippi 298, T 580077, D, hot water; *Residencial* at Santos Mardones 366, F (E with full board), clean, friendly, heaters in rooms, hot water, good; *Res. Cabo de Hornos*, Damián Riobó 198; many good *pensiones*, E, with full board. **Yugoslav Club** does wholesome and reasonable lunch (about US$5), also **Restaurante Puerto Montt** for seafood. Many lobster fishing camps where fishermen will prepare lobster on the spot.

Exchange at *Estrella del Sur* shop, Calle Santos Mardones.

Buses on Tierra del Fuego Two a week between Porvenir and Río Grande (Argentina), US$16. Bus from Río Grande arrives 1300, ferry to Punta Arenas leaves 1400; from terminal to ferry, taxi US$2.75, bus (if running) US$1, ferry US$2; trip takes 7-8 hrs. depending on border crossing. Beware: taxis are not allowed to cross the border. If you go to the police station and ask for a ride to the border on a truck, you can save the fare to Río Grande. Hitch-hiking elsewhere is difficult as there is so little traffic. Argentine time one hour ahead of Chilean time.

Bus from Calle Manuel Señor, Porvenir, Mon. and Fri., 1700, US$10, to Cameron, from where a road runs SE to Estancia Vicuña. Before Vicuña is a scenic fishing-ground; beyond Vicuña a horse trail leads across the Darwin Range to Yendegaia. From there you can either retrace your steps, or cross the unmanned border to Ushuaia (get permission from the Argentine consul in Punta Arenas first).

Puerto Williams is a Chilean naval base on Isla Navarino, S of the Beagle Channel, the most southerly place in the world with a permanent population (about 1,500-1,800. Position 54° 55′ 41″ South, 67° 37′ 58″ West). The island is totally unspoilt and beautiful, with a chain of rugged snowy peaks, magnificent woods and many animals, including beaver. The *Hostería Wala*, on the edge of Lauta bay, T 223571, with attractive locally-made furniture and soft furnishings, roaring log fire in lounge, is now owned by the Navy (but run by civilian management), B in summer, D in winter (monthly rates available); 2 km. out of town, splendid walks. Hotel can arrange car trips to the beaver dams, cascades, and other sights (the Ubika Village, 2 km. east of town, the place where the last descendants of the Yamana people live; the local *media luna* where rodeos are held). *Residencial Onashaga* (run by Señor Ortiz—everyone knows him), C (poor value), full board available; bakery next to *Café Beagle*, E, full board; you can also stay at private houses. Ask where you can eat king crab (*centolla*) pizza. *Restaurant Beagle* on coast, excellent. There is a supermarket. You can camp near the *Hostería*: collect drinking water from the kitchen, bring food from Punta Arenas as it is expensive on the island, but you can buy gasoline for stoves at the *Hostería*. Aeropetrel will charter a plane, if a sufficiently numerous party is raised, to Cape Horn. Near Puerto Williams there is a *centolla* canning factory which is well worth a visit (closed Feb.-March).

Museum Excellent museum in Puerto Williams, full of information about vanished Indian tribes, local wildlife, and voyages including Charles Darwin and Fitzroy of the *Beagle*. Open 1000-1300, 1500-1800 (Tues.-Fri.); 1500-1800 (Sat.-Sun.), Monday closed. Admission free.

Offices Post Office, telephone, telex, Aerovías DAP, Lan-Chile, Ladeco in the centre of town. Tourist Office (closed in winter) near the museum.

Transport to Tierra del Fuego For ferry services from Punta Arenas, **see page 508**. There are two ferries running across the Primera Angostura (First Narrows) between Delgada (*Hostería Tehuelche*, D with restaurant) and Espora points, 170 km. NE from Punta Arenas, schedule varying with the tide. Reservations at the ferry. Price US$1 p.p. and US$12 per car, one way. There is no ferry between Ushuaia and Puerto Williams. By air from Punta Arenas—weather and bookings permitting, Aerovías DAP (Ignacio Carrera Pinto 1022, T 223958 Punta Arenas and Oficina Foretic, T 80089, Porvenir) cover the same routes twice daily, but not Sat., US$15 to Porvenir, and Tues., to Puerto Williams, US$100 return; cheaper are Cabo de Hornos (TACH), Montt 687, T 223335 (Señoret 408, Porvenir), also twice daily to Porvenir, Mon. and Fri. to Puerto Williams, US$80 return. Heavily booked so make sure you have your return reservation confirmed. The flight to Puerto Williams is beautiful, with superb views of Tierra del Fuego, the Cordillera Darwin, the Beagle Channel, and the islands stretching S to Cape Horn. Also army flights available (they are cheaper).

THE ECONOMY

Chile is endowed with a diversified environment, allowing the production of all temperate and Mediterranean products. Agriculture, however, supplies only about 10% of gdp, employs 20% of the labour force and contributes about 16% of merchandise exports. Given the country's topography, only 7% of the land is devoted to crop production, while 14% is used for pasture. Traditional crops, such as cereals, pulse, potatoes and industrial crops (sugarbeet, sunflowerseed and rapeseed) account for about 37% of the value added of agriculture, and vegetables for about 25%. The area showing fastest growth is fresh fruit. Another area of expansion is forestry. Chile has over 9 m hectares of natural forest of which planted forests cover 1 m hectares, with more than 90%

planted with insignis radiata pine, a species which in Chile grows faster than in other countries. Chile is the most important fishing nation in Latin America and the largest producer of fishmeal in the world. Industrial consumption absorbs about 93 % of the fish catch; fresh fish and fish products contribute about 11 % of merchandise exports.

The dominant sector of the economy is mining. Chile has been the world's largest producer of copper since 1982 and also produces molybdenum, iron ore, manganese, lead, gold, silver, zinc, sulphur and nitrates. Chile has a quarter of the world's known molybdenum ore reserves (3m tonnes), and is believed to have around 40 % of the world's lithium reserves. The fall in world prices for metals in the 1980s put pressure on the country's external accounts. In real terms, the copper average price contracted by 23 % in 1982-85. Mineral ores, most of which is copper, account for over 50 % of total export revenue.

Chile is fortunate in possessing reserves of oil, natural gas and coal, and abundant hydroelectricity potential. About 60 % of its energy requirements are met by oil and gas, 15 % by coal, 24 % by hydroelectricity and the balance by biomass. Almost all the country's hydrocarbon reserves are in the extreme south, on Tierra del Fuego, in the Strait of Magellan and the province of Magallanes. Oil reserves are estimated at 736 m barrels, 188 m of which are offshore.

Manufacturing has been particularly vulnerable to changes in economic policy: nationalization during the Allende administration in the early 1970s; recession brought about by anti-inflationary policies in the mid-1970s; increased foreign competition resulting from trade liberalization in the early 1980s, and greater exports together with import substitution in the mid-1980s. The contribution of manufacturing to total gdp fell from 25 % in 1970 to 22 % in 1987 although its share of exports rose. Activity is mostly food processing, metalworking, textiles and fish processing.

High rates of inflation were recorded in the first half of the 1970s, but were brought down from over 500 % at the end of 1973 to less than 10 % by end-1981, largely because of fiscal balance and an overvalued currency. Following the freeing of the exchange rate in 1982 inflation accelerated somewhat, but was successfully moderated by tight monetary control and a lower public sector borrowing requirement. Monetary policy was formulated to cope with high domestic indebtedness in the light of restrictive IMF programmes. IMF involvement was sought following a sharp fall in international commercial lending in 1982 and a decline in Chile's terms of trade. The average annual rate of growth of external debt fell from 32 % in 1978-81 to 6 % in 1982-84. Chile has successfully negotiated several debt refinancing packages with commercial banks and with the Paris Club of creditor governments. In the second half of the 1980s, Chile's foreign debt stopped growing as the government introduced schemes whereby debt could be converted into equity in Chilean companies.

	1961-70 (av)	1971-80 (av)	1981-85 (av)	1986-88 (av)
Gdp growth (1980 prices)	4.2 %	2.5 %	-0.4 %	6.0 %
Inflation	21.2 %	120.4 %	20.4 %	18.0 %
Exports (fob) US$m	674	2,120	3,753	5,490
Copper	581	1,266	1,726	2,343
Imports (fob) US$m	628	2,286	3,862	3,975
Current account balance US$m (cum)	-1,162	-6,381	-11,521	-1,718

INFORMATION FOR VISITORS

How to get there by Air

From Europe: Air France (3 per week), Iberia (4), KLM (2), Lufthansa (2), Sabena, SAS, Swissair (1) and Alitalia (1) fly to Santiago. Some flights go via Rio/São Paulo, Montevideo and Buenos Aires; others via New York, Lima and/or other points in northern S. America. Also, Varig, Aerolíneas Argentinas, Viasa and Avianca offer services between Europe and Santiago, with connections via Rio, Buenos Aires, Caracas and Bogotá respectively.

From North America: Eastern has flights from Miami, New York and/or Washington, and Los Angeles; one service is non-stop from Miami, taking 8 hrs.—others stop at Panama City, Lima or Quito. Lan-Chile has 5 flights per week from New York and Miami. Also from Miami, Ladeco flies either via Bogotá and Guayaquil or Bogotá and Arica; Aeroperú has 7 flights and Aerolíneas Argentinas 2 per week; Pan Am 3 per week. Also to Miami fly Avianca, Ecuatoriana, LAB and Líneas Aéreas Paraguayas (LAP); change at Asunción for Miami. There are good connections via Bogotá (by Avianca) or Lima (by several other carriers). CP Air have one flight per week from Montreal and Toronto, and 2 from Vancouver—all via Lima. Lan-Chile flies once or twice a week, depending on season, between Tahiti (making connections from Japan, Australia and New Zealand) and Santiago; they stop over at Easter Island. For excursion fares between Australia/New Zealand and Chile, the stopovers at Easter Island now carry a surcharge of about US$125.

Within South America: from Buenos Aires (over 30 per week) by Lan-Chile, Aerolíneas Argentinas, Varig, Aeroperú, Avianca, CP Air, Air France, Iberia, KLM or Lufthansa; from Rosario, Córdoba or Mendoza (5 per week) by Aerolíneas Argentinas; Ladeco flies twice a week to Mendoza. From Montevideo (5 per week) by Lan-Chile, Iberia, KLM; from Asunción (five times a week) by Ladeco or LAP; from Rio/São Paulo, non-stop by Lan-Chile, Ladeco, Varig, Swissair or by several other airlines via Buenos Aires; from La Paz (4/5 per week) by Lloyd Aéreo Boliviano (LAB), Lan-Chile; from Caracas via Lima 2 a week; from Lima (up to 30 per week) by Aeroperú, Lan-Chile, and others; from Bogotá (6 per week) by Avianca.

To Arica, from Cochabamba and La Paz (4 per week) by LAB and Lan-Chile.

Airport Taxes US$12 for international flights; US$1 for domestic flights. There is a tourist tax on single air fares of 2%, and 1% on return fares beginning or ending in Chile; also a sales tax of 5% on all transport within Chile.

From the U.S.A. by Sea: By Lykes Line from New Orleans via Panama Canal, time taken: 20 days, 2 departures monthly.

From Europe by Sea: By Compagnie Générale Maritime from La Pallice, France, via Panama Canal; time taken: 28 days, every 6 weeks.

From Neighbouring Countries by land. There are railways from La Paz (Bolivia) to Calama for Antofagasta, and to Arica (see Bolivia section). All passenger services have been suspended on the lines between Chile and Argentina. Roads connect Santiago with Mendoza, and Osorno and Puerto Montt with Bariloche, in Argentina. Less good road connections N of Santiago are described in the main text. The roads connecting N Chile with Bolivia are poor.

Internal Air Services Lan-Chile serves Santiago, Antofagasta, Iquique, Arica, Puerto Montt and Punta Arenas. The private airline Ladeco flies between Santiago and El Salvador, Antofagasta, Calama, Iquique, Arica to the north and between Santiago and Balmaceda, Puerto Montt, Punta Arenas in the south. Both Lan-Chile and Ladeco now offer a 21-day "Visit Chile" ticket (five prices: US$269 takes you to Santiago, Antofagasta, Iquique, Arica, Pto. Montt and Pta. Arenas; US$310 takes you to Coyhaique also; there are three island prices, of which the highest, US$520, takes you to Easter Island) which enables you to visit the length of country both ways. It must be purchased abroad and reservations made well ahead since many flights are fully booked in advance.

N.B. The ticket cannot be changed, though reservations can, so it is worth including as many destinations as possible. It is also possible for the route Santiago-Antofagasta-Arica-Santiago to take a coupon ticket which allows greater flexibility.

Surface Transport Reservations are sometimes problematic. Buses are frequent and on the whole good. As a general rule long-distance buses cost about US$1.25 per 100 km., but in the south twice that, depending on services. Prices are highest between Dec.-March. Since there is lots of competition between bus companies, fares may be bargained lower. Students generally get discounts. Trains in Chile, which now run only on the lines S of Santiago, are moderately priced, and not as slow as in other Andean countries, but dining car food is expensive. There is a railway information office at O'Higgins 853 (at end of arcade), Santiago, for all lines except the Antofagasta-Bolivia (Ahumada 11, Oficina 602, T 698-5536). English spoken. Shipping information at Empresa Marítima del Estado (Empremar), Estado 359, 5th floor, and Kochifas, Av. Maciver 484, 2nd floor, Room 5. Transcontainer, Estado 360, Of. 502-C and Navimag, Miraflors 178, piso 12, T 696-3211. Local newspapers are useful for all transport schedules.

Motoring in Chile Car drivers require a *Relaciones de pasajeros* document, available at borders, and must present the original registration document of their vehicle, as must most cyclists. The Carta Caminera from the Dirección de Vialidad is the most detailed road map (series of twenty-six) but is only available at Vialidad, Marsende and Alameda, Santiago. Reasonable road maps may also be obtained from the Automóvil Club de Chile, Pedro de Valdivia 195, Santiago; or other regional offices. Town maps from the Automóvil Club and Copec service stations. Hydrographic maps from Instituto Hidrográfico, Malgarejo 59, Valparaíso. Members of foreign motoring organizations may join the Chilean Touring Club, and obtain discounts at hotels. Gasoline costs US$1.80 a gallon; it becomes more expensive the further north you go. Spare car parts available from many shops on Calle Diez de Julio, Santiago. Diesel fuel is only available along Longitudinal Highway.

Walking Serious walkers are advised to get *Backpacking in Chile and Argentina*, by Hilary Bradt and John Pilkington, published in 1980. Also recommended: *Chile and Easter Island: A Travel Survival Kit*, by Alan Samagalski (Lonely Planet).

Travel Documents Passport and tourist card only are required for entry by all foreigners except citizens of France, Mexico, Guyana, Haiti, Suriname, Kuwait, African countries and the Communist countries, who require visas. National identity cards are sufficient for entry by citizens of Argentina, Brazil, Paraguay, and Uruguay. The tourist card is valid for 90 days and is renewable for 90 more; it is available from Chilean consulates, immigration office at the Ollagüe land frontier, as well as at Arica, airline offices and most aircraft bound for Chile; it will be surrendered on departure. If you wish to stay longer than 180 days (as a tourist), it is easier to make a day-trip to Argentina and return with a new tourist card, rather than to apply for a visa, which involves a great deal of paperwork. Visa is required for French passport holders, US$5.25; valid for no more than 90 days, strictly one entry only. This can create problems if you wish to travel overland to or from Tierra del Fuego since the Argentine-Chilean border is crossed more than once, requiring multiple entry.

All foreigners who wish to work in Chile must obtain visas. Smallpox vaccination and health certificates no longer required.

Customs Allowed in free of duty: 500 cigarettes, 100 cigars, 500 grams of tobacco, 3 bottles of liquor, camera, and all articles of personal use. Fruit, vegetables, flowers and milk products may not be imported.

Time GMT minus 4 hrs.; minus 3 hrs. in summer. Clocks change on second Sat. in March and October.

Seasons The best time for a visit to Santiago is between October and April when fine weather is almost assured, but business visits can be made any time during the year. During the holiday season, between January and March, it is sometimes difficult to make appointments.

Clothing Warm sunny days and cool nights are usual during most of the year except in the far S where the climate is like that of Scotland. Ordinary European medium-weight clothing can be worn during the winter (June to mid-September). Light clothing is best for summer (December to March), but men do not wear white tropical suits.

Health Tap water is fairly safe to drink in the main cities but bottled water is safer on trains and away from the larger centres. Hotels and restaurants are usually clean. Inoculation against hepatitis and typhoid is a wise precaution. Travellers should not eat salads, strawberries or ground-growing food; hepatitis and typhoid are all too common as the result of the use of untreated sewage for fertilizer (Check extra precautions against typhoid are necessary e.g. 3-pill preventative treatment, available locally.)

Hours of Business Banks: 0900-1400, but closed on Sat. Government offices: 1000-1230 (the public is admitted for a few hrs. only). Business houses: 0830-1230, 1400-1800 (Mon. to Fri.). Shops (Santiago): 1030-1930, but 0930-1330 Sat. British business visitors are advised to obtain "Hints for Exporters: Chile" from the Department of Trade, Sanctuary Bldgs, 16-20 Great Smith Street, London SW1P 3DB.

Taxis have meters, but agree beforehand on fare for long journey out of centre or special excursions. A 50 % surcharge is applied after 2100 and Sun. Taxi drivers rarely know the location of any streets away from the centre. There is no need to tip unless some extra service, like the carrying of luggage, is given.

Language The local pronunciation of Spanish, very quick and lilting, with final syllables cut off, can present difficulties to the foreigner. See also Argentine section, page 168.

Telephones　　Local telephones use two 10 peso coins.

Living Conditions and Cost　　Shops throughout Chile are well stocked and there is a seasonal supply of all the usual fruits and vegetables. Milk in pasteurized, evaporated, or dried form is obtainable. Chilean tinned food is dear. Food is reasonable, but food prices vary tremendously. Santiago tends to be more expensive for food and accommodation than other parts of Chile. Southern Chile can be expensive between December 15 and March 15.

Shopping　　There is an excellent variety of handicrafts: woodwork, pottery, copperware, leatherwork, Indian woven goods including rugs and ponchos in the South. Good quality at the Cema-Chile shops (Av. Portugal 351, Santiago, and main provincial cities).

Hotels　　On hotel bills service charges are usually 10%, and taxes on bills are 16%. Whether or not the 16% is added to bills in hotel restaurants that are signed and charged to the hotel bill depends on the policy of the establishment. When booking in make certain whether meals are included in the price or only breakfast or nothing at all, and don't rely on the posted sheet in the bedroom for any prices. Small *residenciales* are often good value.

Youth Hostels　　There are youth hostels throughout Chile; average cost about US$1 p.p. Hostels are open only from Jan. to the end of February and a Chilean membership card is necessary (US$3.50). They are usually crowded and noisy, with only floor space available. An additional stamp costing US$4 enables one to use the card in Argentina, Uruguay and Brazil. This can be obtained from the Asociación Chilena de Albergues Turísticos Juveniles, Holanda 286, Providencia, Santiago, T 231-5649; together with a useful guidebook of all Youth Hostels in Chile, *Guía Turística de los Albergues Juveniles*. If you carry an IYHF card you can stay in summer in makeshift hostels in many Chilean towns, usually in the main schools.

In almost every town, private houses offer *alojamiento* (bed, breakfast and often use of kitchen) for about US$2 p.p. (bargaining may be possible).

Camping　　is easy but no longer cheap at official sites. A common practice is to charge US$10 for up to 5 people, with no reductions for less than 5. "Camping Gaz International" stoves are recommended, since green replaceable cylinders are available in Santiago.

Tipping　　Standard is 10% in hotels and restaurants and 20% in bars and soda fountains. Railway and airport porters: US$0.10 a piece of luggage. Make a deal with dock porters. Cloakroom attendants and cinema usherettes: US$0.05. Hairdressers: 10% of bill. Taxi-drivers are not tipped.

Currency and Exchange　　The unit is the peso, its sign is $. Notes are for 500, 1,000 and 5,000 pesos and coins for 1, 5, 10, 50 and 100 pesos.

Travellers' cheques must be changed before 1200 except in exchange shops (*cambios*) and hotels, which give better rates than banks. Changing travellers' cheques can be time-consuming and has become difficult in most towns apart from Arica, Antofagasta, Santiago and Puerto Montt. Traveller's cheques can be changed into dollars, but check if a commission is charged as this practice seems to vary. Foreigners may no longer exchange pesos for dollars when leaving the country. Visa and Mastercharge are common in Chile (Bancard, the local card, is affliated to both), but American Express is less useful (use in American Express banks does not incur commission). Try and change as much as you can in Santiago.

N.B.　　Prices in dollars in this chapter are converted at the official exchange rate. Travellers can buy pesos on the parallel (black) market, which is tolerated, at slightly better rates. *El Economista* quotes rates, and you can get fairly close to the *paralelo* nowadays in *cambios* and hotels.

The **metric** system is obligatory but the quintal of 46 kilos (101.4 lb) is used.

Posts and Telegraphs　　Airmail takes 3-4 days from the UK. Seamail takes 8-12 weeks. There is a daily airmail service to Europe with connections to the UK. Poste restante only holds mail for 30 days; then returns to sender. Lista de Correo in Santiago, Central Post Office, is good and efficiently organized. Telegrams to Britain: ordinary rate, US$3.40 (minimum 7 words); L.T. rate: US$5.60 (minimum 21 words). A 3-min. telex call to Britain costs US$5.65.

International telephone and telegraph communications are operated by the Entel; by Transradio Chilena (2 offices); and by the Cía. Internacional de Radio (2 offices). Calls may be made collect. International calls cost US$11 for first 3 mins. to North America and Europe (US$9 between 2000 and 2200); US$2.25 for each subsequent min.

Astonishing how throughout Chile one post office official will charge rates different from the next, and they are all "right". Public telex booths are available at the offices of Transradio Chilena in Santiago and Valparaíso. Amex Card holders can often use telex facilities at Amex offices free of charge.

Public Holidays

Jan. 1—New Year's Day.	Sept. 18, 19—Independence Days.
Holy Week (2 days).	Oct. 12—Discovery of America.
May 1—Labour Day.	Nov. 1—All Saints Day.
May 21—Navy Day.	Dec. 8—Immaculate Conception.
Aug. 15—Assumption	Dec. 25—Christmas Day

Santiago daily papers *El Mercurio, La Nación, La Epoca* (liberal/left), *La Segunda* and *La Tercera. Las Ultimas Noticias, El Cóndor,* weekly in German.

Weekly magazines; *Hoy, Qué Pasa; Análisis, Ercilla* and *Panorama Económico* are best economic journals. Monthly: *Rutas* (official organ, Automobile Association).

Local Dishes   A very typical Chilean dish is *cazuela de ave,* a nutritious stew containing large pieces of chicken, potatoes, rice, and maybe onions, and green peppers; best if served on the second day. Another popular Chilean dish is *empanadas de horno,* which are turnovers filled with a mixture of raisins, olives, meat, onions and peppers chopped up together. *Pastel de choclo* is a casserole of meat and onions with olives, topped with a maize-meal mash, baked in an earthenware bowl. *Prieta* is a blood sausage stuffed with cabbage leaves. The popular *empanada frita,* a fried meat pasty, is delicious. A normal *parrillada* is a giant mixed grill served from a charcoal brazier. The *pichanga* is similar but smaller and without the brazier. Goat cheese is a delicacy of the Fourth Region, but can be a source of food poisoning.

What gives Chilean food its personality is the seafood. The delicious conger eel is a national dish, and *caldillo de congrio* (a soup served with a massive piece of conger, onions and potato balls) is excellent. *Paila Chonchi* is a kind of bouillabaisse, but has more flavour, more body, more ingredients. *Parrillada de mariscos* is a dish of grilled mixed seafood, brought to the table piping hot on a charcoal brazier. Other excellent local fish are the *cojinoa,* the *albacora* (swordfish) and the *corvina.* An appetizing starter is the shellfish *loco* (known to Australians as abalone), and in the S one should try the *centolla* (king crab). *Cochayuyo* is seaweed, bound into bundles, described as "hard, leathery thongs". Avocado pears, or *paltas,* are excellent, and play an important role in recipes. The *erizo,* or sea-urchin, is also commonly eaten. Make sure whether vegetables are included in the price for the main dish; menus often don't make this clear. Always best, if being economical, to stick to fixed-price *table d'hôte* meals or try the local markets. *Luche* is a black cake, like "flakey bread pudding". Ice cream is very good; *lúcuma* and *chirimoya* are highly recommended flavours.

Lunch is about 1300 and dinner not before 2030. *Onces* (Elevenses) is tea taken at 1700 often accompanied by a couple of fried eggs. The cocktail hour starts at 1900. Waiters are known as *garzón*—never as *mozo.* Good, cheap meals can usually be found in Centros Españoles or Casinos de Bomberos.

It seems impossible to get real coffee unless you go to expresso bars and specify *café-café, expresso.* If you ask just for *café,* you get soluble coffee. The soluble tea should be avoided. If you order *"café,* or *té, con leche°,* it will come with all milk; to have just a little milk in either, you must specify that. After a meal, instead of coffee, try an *agüita*—hot water in which herbs such as mint, or aromatics such as lemon peel, have been steeped. Very refreshing.

Drinks   Imported whisky and other spirits are still cheap, but are increasing relatively in price. The local wines are very good; the best are from the central areas. Among the good *bodegas* are Cousiño Macul, Santa Carolina, Undurraga, Concha y Toro, Tocornal, San Pedro and Santa Helena. Santa Elena (no H) is less good. The bottled wines are graded, in increasing precedence, as *gran vino, vino especial* and *vino reservado.* Champagne-style wines are also cheap and acceptable. A small deposit, US$0.30, is charged on most wine bottles. Beer is quite good and cheap; the draught lager known as Schop is good; also try Cristal

Pilsener or Royal Guard. Malta, a brown ale, is recommended for those wanting a British-type beer.

Good gin is made in Chile. Reasonably good brandy, *anís* and crème de menthe are all bottled in Chile. *Vaina* is worth trying, and so is the traditional Christmas drink, *cola de mono*, a mixture of *aguardiente*, coffee, milk and vanilla served very cold. *Pisco* is worth sampling, especially as a "Pisco Sour" or with grapefruit or lemon juice. *Manzanilla* is a local liqueur, made from *licor de oro* (like Galliano); *crema de cacao*, especially Mitjans, has been recommended. *Chicha* is any form of alcoholic drink made from fruit; *chicha cocida* is 3-day-old fermented grape juice boiled to reduce its volume and then bottled with a tablespoonful of honey. Cider (*chicha de manzana*) is popular in the South. *Chicha fresca* is plain apple juice.

Sports   The Chilean State Railways and the tourist agencies will give all the necessary information about sport. **Skiing**   Season from June to September/October, weather depending. For information write to: La Federación de Ski de Chile, Casilla 9902, Santiago. Horse racing is also popular and meetings are held every Sunday and on certain feast days at Viña del Mar, Santiago and Concepción throughout the year; horseback riding is also popular. Santiago and Valparaíso residents fish at the mountain resort of Río Blanco, and some of the world's best fishing is in the Lake District. The licence required can be got from the local police or such angling associations as the Asociación de Pesca y Caza, which gives information on local conditions. Other popular sports are football and basket ball. Viña del Mar has a cricket ground; on Saturdays there are polo matches at Santiago.

We are deeply grateful to Sandy and María Luisa Campbell who did the updating of this chapter at very short notice, and Edgardo Bennett (Santiago 10), Christine Blenntoft (Santiago 9), Julie Eisenberg and Andy Daitsman (Santiago), Jack D. Feka (Temuco), Sonia Marcela Janez Alvarado (Tourist Office, Punta Arenas) for a most valuable contribution and Ignacio Tapia (Concepción). Also to the following travellers: Tom Aabo and Karin Henningsen (Aarhus, Dmk), F.R.Allemann and Xenia von Bahder (Kleinrinderfeld, W.Ger.), Julian Anderson (Buenos Aires), George Arnon (Israel), Ian Atkinson (Hanley Castle, Worcs), Tim Austin (Shere, Sy), Thomas Axthammer (München 90), Lee Azus (San Francisco), Dexter Ball (Chicago), Carolyn Bargman (El Paso, Tx.) Jane Barlow (London NW6), Bruce Barnes (Gloucester, NSW), Urs Baumann (Wildberg, Switz), Eric Beauchemin (Hilversum), Hans and Lena Bengtsson (Gothenburg, Swe), Gordon Bethell (St Leonards, Sx.), Lennart Blomberg (Göteborg), Frank Böhme (Frankfurt 71), Jens Borchers (Herzberg/Harz, W.Ger.) and Michael Frantz (Sieber, W.Ger.), Alison Brysk and Mark Freeman (San Francisco, Ca.), Dan Buck and Anne Meadows (Washington DC.), John Burke (Bristol 7), Michelle Burrows (Brisbane), Teresa H. Castro (San Francisco, Ca.), Pamela Caunt and Bob Brass (London N1), Bain Chadsey (Corrales, NM), John J. Chesarek (Billings, Montana), Sandra L. Cohen and Richard Struve (Seattle, Washington), Paulo Couto (São Paulo), John Crane (Sunbury), Mark Crathorne (Woking), Beat Denzler and Nicole Livet (Zürich), Dale and Anne Dickinson (Menlo Park, Ca.), Rolf Ditsch (Steinbach, W.Ger.), James W Dow (Muncy, Pa.), Fabienne Dufayet (Petit Lancy, Switz.), Paul Eaton (Victoria, BC), Hanna Elvrum (Cochabamba), Fred and Marianne Emery (London SE26), Josef Engert (Schlieren, Switz.), Andreas Erne (Zürich 8055), Margaret and Martin Evans (Brighton), Per Einar Evensen (Bergen), Didier Faget and Sabine Fleury (Vernon, Fr.), Dr. R.A. Felton (Hamburg 50), Paul Forte (London NW1), Anna Frostenson (Hagersten, Swe.), Björn Gabrielsen (Oslo 11), Felicity Gallagher (Saxon, Switz), Anita Gee and Ian Boonin (Ilford), Theodor A. Gevert (Barueri, S.P. Brazil), Dan Golopentia (Seattle), Margaret and Stuart Goodchild, Christina Gräwe (Tautkirchen) and Joachim Hoell (Wernstadt, W.Ger.), Jan Jacob de Groot (Vroomshoop, Neth.), Jon and Julia Gruffydd (Lima), Christian E. Gurney (Thornhill, Ont.) for many important updatings, Monika Gwerder (Muotathal, Switz.), Alan Hausrath (Boise, Id.), Alison Henry, Jane Horton (Montevideo) for a very useful piece, Torfinn Horte (Birkeland, Norway), Martin Hostettler (Spiegel, Switz.), David K Howe (Short Hills, NJ), Don Hoyle (London EC2), David Hutchinson and Susie Maddox (London W8), Ingrid Iversen (Streatham), Gretke Moen Johansen (Kolborn, Norway), Ruth Kamm (München 19), Prof Alexander Kennaway (Ashtead, Sy.), Ronen Khayat (Jerusalem), Peter Kocan (Summit, NJ), Esther Lange and Peter Dellenbach (Untersiggenthal, Switz.), Stuart Lee (Auckland), Kenneth and Nancy Leighton (Vancouver), Christian Levin (Kiel, W.Ger.), Herbert Levi (Buenos Aires), John Lewis (London NW3), Manoel A. Lima (Northwood, Mx.), Frans Lindenkamp (Vlissingen, Neth.) and Todd McLeod (Calgary), Paul Living (Reading), Peter S. Lobin (Chicago), Charles Locher (San Francisco) and Nancy Blackstock (Berkeley, Ca.), Loving Team (London), Susan MacCallum and Peter Hedvlin (Sydney, Aust.), Dr John Maddock (Rio), Christine Marthaler and Jürg Briner (Zürich 8038), James Mathias (Minneapolis), Elaine and George McClellan (Danville, Ca.), Stryker McGuire and Julie Jedamus (Ashfield, Mass.), Carla McLean (San Francisco), Amanda Meads and Mark Barton (London W14), Andrea Meier (Volkach, W.Ger.), F.P. Mom (Amsterdam), Kelvin Moody (Stratford, NZ), Beri and Mary Morris (Raleigh, NC), Dimitri Moursellas (Manhattan Beach, Ca.), Christoph Müller (Zürich 8004), Richard Müller (Gümligen), Hallam Murray (London SW11), John and Christine Myerscough (Glossop, Derbys) for a most useful contribution, Claus Nørgaard and Bitten

Pedersen (Silkeborg, Dmk.), Bertil Olin (Johanneshov, Swed.), Graham J. O'Neil (London SW7), William Parton (London SW11), Wulf Peters (Querenhurst, W.Ger.), Michelle Portman (Haifa, Israel), Chris Robertson (Stockholm) and Patricia Galvin (Galway), Miranda Roberts (London SE3), Yaniv Sagee (Kibbutz Ein-Hashofet), Christian Scherlenzky (Villa Ballester, Buenos Aires), Rolf Schneider (Effretikon, Switz.), H Schouwenburg (London SW18), Leon van der Schoor (Neth.), Markus Schulz (Gambach, W.Ger.), Colin Sears and Caroline Richard, Elizabeth and Virginia Segal (London N2), James Sharp (Boulder, Co), Antony Sherlock (Edinburgh 12), Sverker Skoglund (Göteborg), David Smitham (Christchurch, NZ), Kathy Smith (Buenos Aires) for a particularly helpful contribution, Lynn Sowell (Clarksville, TN), Martin Squirrell and Huw Williams (St Albans and Sutton Abinger, Sy.), Armin Straub (Bovenden, W.Ger.), Hal Stufft and Dorothy Young (Imler, PA/Evesham), Lisa Tenuta (Kenosha, Wisconsin), Barry Tiffen and Lucy Stephens (Torksey, Lincoln), Nicholas Tongue and Uta Rössler (Brussels), Douglas B. Trent (Focus Tours, Belo Horizonte), Adrian Wainer (Dublin 16), John Walker, Martin Walker (London EC4), Ignaz Wanders (Haarlem), David H Watson, A.G. Marschall Wesselingh (Calgary), Roland Wiemer and Karla Menner (Hamburg 50), Conrad Wiesendanger (Münchenstein, Switz.), Ray Williams (Pwllheli), Alida and Gordon Wilson (San Rafael, CA.), Mrs N.L. Windsor (Harrow), Eran Zelikovitch (Israel) and Helmut Zettl (Ebergassing, Austria).

WILL YOU HELP US?

We do all we can to get our facts right in *The South American Handbook*. Each chapter is thoroughly revised each year, but Latin America and the Caribbean cover a vast area, and our eyes cannot be everywhere. A new highway or airport is built; a hotel, a restaurant, a cabaret dies; another, a good one is born; a building we describe is pulled down, a street re-named. Names and addresses of good hotels and restaurants for "budget-minded" travellers are always very welcome. We would especially like to receive diagrams of walks, national parks and other interesting areas to use as source material for the Handbook and other forthcoming titles.

Your information may be far more up-to-date than ours. If your letter reaches us early enough in the year it will be used in the next edition, but write whenever you want to, for all your letters are used sooner or later.

Thank you very much indeed for your help.

 Trade & Travel Publications Limited
5 Prince's Buildings, George Street,
Bath BA1 2ED. England

COLOMBIA

COLOMBIA, with 1,138,618 square km., is the fourth largest country in South America and has the third largest population (29.9 millions). It has coast lines upon both the Caribbean (1,600 km.) and the Pacific (1,306 km.). Nearly 55 % of the area is almost uninhabited lowland with only 4 % of the population; the other 96 % are concentrated in the remaining 45 %, living for the most part in narrow valleys or isolated intermont basins, or in the broad Caribbean lowlands. The population is infinitely varied, ranging from white, Indian, and black to mixtures of all three.

The 620,000 square km. of almost uninhabited land in Colombia lie E of the Eastern Cordillera. Near the foot of the Cordillera the plains are used for cattle ranching, but beyond is jungle. Islands of settlement in it are connected with the rest of the country by air and river, for there are no railways and very few roads: communication is by launch and canoe on the rivers.

In the populous western 45 % of the country four ranges of the Andes run from S to N. Between the ranges run deep longitudinal valleys. Of the 14 main groups of population in the country, no less than 11 are in the mountain basins or in the longitudinal valleys; the other three are in the lowlands of the Caribbean.

The first 320 km. along the Pacific coast N from the frontier with Ecuador to the port of Buenaventura is a wide, marshy, and sparsely inhabited coastal lowland. Along the coast N of Buenaventura runs the Serranía de Baudó. E of this range the forested lowlands narrow into a low trough of land; E of the trough again rise the slopes of the Western Cordillera. The trough—the Department of the Chocó—is drained southwards into the Pacific by the Río San Juan, navigable for 200 km., and northwards into the Caribbean by the Río Atrato, navigable for 550 km.; there are vague plans to link the two rivers by canal. The climate is hot and torrential rain falls daily. The inhabitants are mostly black.

From the borders of Ecuador two ranges of mountain, the Western Cordillera and the Central Cordillera, run N for 800 km. to the Caribbean lowlands. Five peaks in the Western Cordillera are over 4,000 metres but none reaches the snowline. The Central Cordillera, 50-65 km. wide, is much higher; six of its peaks, snow clad, rise above 5,000 metres and its highest, the volcano cone of Huila, is 5,439 metres. There is hardly any level land, but there are narrow ribbons of soil along some of the rivers.

Between the two ranges, as they emerge from Ecuador, lies a valley filled in the S to a height of 2,500 metres by ash from the volcanoes. Not far from the frontier there is a cluster of self-subsisting Indians around Pasto. Further N between these two ranges lies the Cauca valley; in its northern 190 km., roughly

COLOMBIA
65

1 Bogotá.
2 Bogotá to Cúcuta.
3 The Llanos and Leticia.
4 The North coast and Islands.
5 Up the Magdalena River.
6 The central Cordillera : Medellín and Manizales.
7 The Cauca valley.
8 Southern Colombia

CARIBBEAN SEA

Barranquilla
Riohacha
Santa Marta
Maicao
Maracaibo
Cartagena
Valledupar
PANAMA
4
Sincelejo
Montería
TO Caracas
VENEZUELA
Turbo
Cúcuta San Cristóbal
Barrancabermeja
Bucaramanga
Arauca
6
5
2
Rio Cauca
Medellín
Quibdó
Villa de Leiva
Tunja
Puerto Carreño
Puerto Ayacucho
Río Orinoco
Manizales
Pereira
Cartago
Armenia
1
BOGOTÁ
Río Meta
PACIFIC OCEAN
7
Ibagué
Villavicencio
Cali
Buenaventura
Neiva
3
Popayán
La Plata
5
Puerto Inírida
Garzón
Río Guaviare
San Agustín
Tumaco
Florencia
Túlcan
Pasto
Mocoa
Mibú
Ipiales
8
Río Apaporis
To Quito
Río Caquetá
ECUADOR

PERU

Río Putumayo
BRAZIL
0 100 200 300 400
km
Río Amazonas
Leticia
To Manaus
Benjamin Constant

from Popayán N past Cali to Cartago, there is an important agricultural region based on a deep bed of black alluvial soil which yields as many as five crops a year. This valley, which is at a height of about 1,000 metres and up to 50 km. wide, is drained northwards by the Cauca river. Cali is the business centre of the valley, and a road and railway run from Cali over a low pass of less than 1,500 metres in the Western Cordillera to Buenaventura. Sugar cane was the great crop of this valley in colonial times, but has now been varied with tobacco, soya, cotton, pineapple, and every other kind of tropical fruit. There is still some cattle raising. Coffee is grown on the Cordillera slopes above 600 metres. A "Tennessee Valley" scheme of development to drain the swamps, control floods, irrigate parched areas, improve farming, and produce electric power has been applied in the Cauca Valley since 1956.

At Cartago the two Cordilleras close in and the Cauca valley becomes a deep gorge which runs all the way to the Caribbean flatlands. In the Cordillera Central, at an altitude of 1,540 metres, is the second largest city and industrial centre in Colombia: Medellín. Much of the coffee and 75 % of the gold comes from this area. N of Medellín the Cordillera Central splits into three ranges, separated by streams flowing into the Caribbean.

Near Latitude 2°N, or about 320 km. N of the Ecuadorean border, the Eastern Cordillera, the longest of all, rises and swings N and then NE towards Venezuela. About Latitude 7°N it bifurcates; one branch becomes the western rim of the Maracaibo basin and the other runs E into Venezuela, to the S of the Maracaibo basin.

Between this Eastern Cordillera and the Central Cordillera runs the 1,600 km. long Magdalena river, with the Caribbean port of Barranquilla at its mouth. There are more intermont basins in the Eastern Cordillera than in the others. Some of its peaks rise above the snow line. In the Sierra Nevada del Cocuy (just before the Cordillera bifurcates) there is a group of snowy peaks, all over 5,200 metres; the highest, Ritacuba Blanca, reaches 5,493 metres. The basins are mostly high, at an altitude of from 2,500 to 2,750 metres. In the Lower Magdalena region the river banks are comparatively deserted, though there are a few clearings made by the descendants of black slaves who settled along the Magdalena after their emancipation. There are oilfields in the valley, particularly at Barrancabermeja.

In a high basin of the Eastern Cordillera, 160 km. E of the Magdalena river, the Spaniards in 1538 founded the city of Bogotá, now the national capital. The great rural activity of this group is the growing of food: cattle, wheat, barley, maize and potatoes.

Roads run N from Bogotá to the basins of Chiquinquirá and Sogamoso, over 160 km. away. Both are in the Department of Boyacá, with Tunja, on a mountain between the two, as capital. Both basins, like that of Bogotá, produce food, and there are emerald mines at Muzo, near Chiquinquirá.

There are other basins in the N of the Eastern Cordillera: in the Departments of Santander and Norte de Santander at Bucaramanga and Cúcuta, and a small one at Ocaña. Movement into these basins by Europeans and *mestizos* did not take place until the 19th century, when chinchona bark (for quinine) rose into high demand. By 1885 this trade was dead, but by that time coffee was beginning to be planted. In Bucaramanga coffee is now the main crop, but it has been diversified by cacao, cotton and tobacco, all grown below the altitude suitable for coffee.

There is one more mountain group in Colombia, the Sierra Nevada de Santa Marta, standing isolated from the other ranges on the shores of the Caribbean. This is the highest range of all: its snow-capped peaks rise to 5,800 metres within 50 km. of the coast.

To the W of this Sierra, and N of where the Central and Western Cordilleras come to an end, lies a great lowland which has three groups of population on its Caribbean shores; at Cartagena, Barranquilla and Santa Marta. The rivers draining this lowland (the Magdalena, Sinú, Cauca, San Jorge and César) run so slowly that much of the area is a tissue of swamps and lagoons with very little land that can be cultivated. Indeed the whole area E of the channel of the Magdalena is under water at most times of the year. When the floods come, large areas of the land W of the Magdalena—the plains of Bolívar—are covered too, but during the dry season from October to March great herds of cattle are grazed there.

Communications A major problem still facing the country is that of surface transport. Its three Cordilleras, separated by valleys often no more than 1,500 metres above sea-level, make internal communications extremely difficult. The 3,700 km. of narrow-gauge railways and the 38,200 km. of roads have eastern and western systems, with inter-communicating laterals (see maps and text). Only about 10% of the road system is paved. Given these difficulties it is natural that Colombia, which ran the first airline in South America, has taken ardently to the air.

History Before the coming of the Spaniards the country was occupied by Indians, most of whom were primitive hunters or nomad agriculturists, but one part of the country, the high basins of the Eastern Cordillera, was densely occupied by Chibcha Indians who had become sedentary farmers. Their staple foods were maize and the potato, and they had no domestic animal save the dog; the use they could make of the land was therefore limited. Other cultures present in Colombia in the precolumbian era were the Tairona, Quimbaya, Sinú and Calima. Exhibits of their and the Chibcha (Muisca) Indians' gold-work can be seen at the Gold Museum in Bogotá, the one total "must" for all visitors to the city (see page 533).

The Spaniards sailed along the northern coast as far as Panama as early as 1500. The first permanent settlement was by Rodrigo de Bastidas at Santa Marta in 1525. Cartagena was founded in 1533. In 1536, Gonzalo Jiménez de Quesada (who wrote a full account of his adventures) pushed up the Magdalena river to discover its source; mounting the Eastern Cordillera in 1536, he discovered the Chibchas, conquered them, and founded Santa Fe de Bogotá in 1538. In the meantime other Spanish forces were approaching the same region: Pizarro's lieutenant, Sebastián de Benalcázar, had pushed down the Cauca valley from Ecuador and founded Pasto, Popayán and Cali in 1536. Nicolás de Federmann, acting on behalf of the Welser financiers of Germany, who had been granted a colonial concession by Charles V, approached from Venezuela. Benalcázar reached Bogotá in 1538 and Federmann got there in 1539. As in Peru, the initial period of settlement was one of strife between contending *conquistadores*. The royal Audiencia de Santa Fe set up in 1550 gave the area a legislative, judicial and administrative entity. In 1564 this was followed by a **presidency of the kingdom of Nueva Granada** controlling the whole country and Panama, except Benalcázar's province of Popayán. The Presidency was replaced in 1718 by a viceroyalty at Bogotá which controlled the provinces now known as Venezuela as well; it was independent of the Viceroyalty of Peru, to which this vast area had previously been subject.

The movement towards independence from Spain was set going in 1794 by a translation into Spanish by the *criollo* Antonio Nariño of the French Declaration of the Rights of Man. The movement was given point and force when, in 1808, Napoleon replaced Ferdinand VII of Spain with his own brother Joseph. The New World refused to recognize this: there were several revolts in Nueva Granada, culminating in a revolt at Bogotá and the setting up of a *junta* on July 20, 1810. Other local juntas were established: Cartagena bound itself to a *junta* set up at Tunja. Late in 1812 the young Bolívar, driven out of Venezuela, landed at Cartagena. In a brilliant campaign in 1813 he pushed up the Magdalena to Ocaña, and from there to Cúcuta, and obtained permission from the *junta* at Tunja to advance into Venezuela. In 90 days he marched the 1,200 km. to Caracas over mountain country, fighting six battles, but he was unable to hold Caracas and withdrew to Cartagena in 1814.

Napoleon fell in 1815, and the Spanish Government immediately set about reconquering, with some success, Venezuela and New Granada. General Pablo Morillo took Cartagena after a bitter siege of 106 days—Bolívar had withdrawn to Jamaica—and was later "pacifying" Bogotá with a "Reign of Terror" by May 1816.

Bolívar had by now assembled an army of Llaneros, fortified by a British legion recruited from ex-servicemen of the Peninsular wars, in Venezuela at Angostura, or Ciudad Bolívar as it is called today. In the face of incredible difficulties he made a forced march across the Andes in 1819. After joining up with Santander's Nueva Granada army, he defeated the royalists at the battle of the Swamps of Vargas in July and again at Boyacá on August 7. He entered Bogotá three days later.

Bolívar reported his success to the revolutionary congress sitting at Angostura, and that body, on December 17, 1819, proclaimed the Republic of Gran Colombia, embracing in one the present republics of Venezuela, Colombia, and Ecuador. A general congress was held at Cúcuta on January 1, 1821, and here it was that two opposing views which were to sow such dissension in Colombia first became apparent. Bolívar and Nariño for centralization; Santander, a realist, for a federation of sovereign states. Bolívar succeeded in enforcing his view for the time being, but Gran Colombia was not to last long; Venezuela broke away in 1829 and Ecuador in 1830. The remaining provinces were named Nueva Granada; it was not till 1863 that the name Colombia was restored.

Almost from its inception the new country became the scene of strife between the centralizing pro-clerical Conservatives and the federalizing anti-clerical Liberals. The Conservative president Tomás Cipriano de Mosquera (1845) encouraged education, began building roads, adopted the metric system, and put steamers on the Magdalena. The Liberals were dominant from 1849 for the next 30 years of insurrections and civil wars. In 1885 the Conservatives imposed a highly centralized constitution which has not been modified in this respect to this day. A Liberal revolt in 1899 turned into a civil war, "the War of the Thousand Days". The Liberals were finally defeated in 1902 after 100,000 people had died. It was in 1903 that Panama declared its independence from Colombia, following U.S. pressure.

After 40 years of comparative peace, the strife between Conservatives and Liberals was re-ignited in a little-publicised but dreadfully bloody civil war known as *La Violencia* from 1948 to 1957 (some 300,000 people were killed); but this was ended by a unique political truce. It was decided by plebiscite in 1957 that the two political parties would support a single presidential candidate, divide all political offices equally between them, and thus maintain political stability for sixteen years. In 1978 the agreement was ended, though some elements of the coalition— representation of the main opposition party in the Cabinet, for instance— were allowed to continue until 1986. Sr. Belisario Betancur, the Conservative president from 1982-86, offered a general amnesty to guerrilla movements in an attempt to end violence in the country. Following an initial general acceptance of the offer, only one of the four main guerrilla groups, the FARC, upheld the truce in 1985-7. In May 1986, when the Liberal candidate, Sr. Virgilio Barco, won the presidential elections, FARC's newly-formed political party, the Unión Patriótica, won 10 seats in congress; the Liberal party took the majority. Right-wing groups, unwilling to accept the Unión Patriótica, began a campaign of murder against UP's elected representatives. This, together with continuing left-wing, and drugs-related, violence, provoked civil instability through 1988 and 1989.

The People of Colombia The regions vary greatly in their racial make-up: Antioquia and Caldas are largely of European blood, Pasto is Indian, the Cauca Valley and the rural area near the Caribbean are African or *mulatto*. No colour bar is legally recognized but it does exist in certain centres. Colombia has 19 cities with over 100,000 people.

Over two thirds live in the cities, with about 30 % engaged in agriculture, pastoral and forest pursuits, hunting and fishing. Gdp per capita is US$1,220. The birth and death rates vary greatly from one area to the other, but in general infant mortality is very high. Hospitals and clinics are few in relation to the population. About 66 % of the doctors are in the departmental capitals, which contain 12 % of the population, though all doctors now have to spend a year in the country before they can get their final diploma. Deplorable *barrios clandestinos* (shanty-towns) have sprung up around Cali, Barranquilla, Cartagena and Buenaventura.

Education The literacy rate is 82 %. Education is free, and since 1927 theoretically compulsory, but many children, especially in rural areas, do not attend. There are high standards of secondary and university education, when it is available.

Constitution and Government Senators and Representatives are elected by popular vote. The Senate has 112 members, and the Chamber of Representatives has 199. The President, who appoints his 13 ministers, is elected by direct vote for a term of four years, but cannot succeed himself in the next term. Every citizen over 18 can vote.

Administratively the country is divided into 22 Departments, 5 Intendencias, 5 Comisarias, and the Special District of Bogotá.

Liberty of speech and the freedom of the press are in theory absolute but in practice more limited. The language of the country is Spanish. Its religion is Roman Catholicism. There is complete freedom for all other creeds which do not contravene Christian morals or the law.

President, 1986-90: Sr. Virgilio Barco Vargas (Liberal).

BOGOTA (1)

Bogotá, capital of the Republic and a city of 5.3 million people, is on a plateau at 2,650 metres. The average temperature is 14°C (58°F). It is built on sloping land, and covers 210 square km. The central part of the city is full of character and contrasts: colonial buildings stand side-by-side with the most modern architecture. For the most part the houses are low, with eaves projecting over the streets; they are rarely brightly painted. The traffic is very heavy.

Visitors should not be too active for the first 24 hrs. Some people get dizzy at Bogotá's altitude. Be careful with food and alcoholic drinks for the first day also.

There is a very good view of the city from the top of Monserrate, the lower of the two peaks rising sharply to the E. It is reached by a funicular railway and a cable car. The new convent at the top is a popular shrine. At the summit, near the church, a chairlift (US$0.20) and a platform give a bird's-eye view of the red-roofed city and of the plains beyond stretching to the rim of the Sabana. Also at the top are a Wild West-style train for children, a restaurant and snack bar (good *tamales*, US$1), and the Calle del Candelero, a reconstruction of a Bogotá street of 1887. Behind the church are popular picnic grounds. The fare up to Monserrate is US$0.75 return (US$0.40 children); four trips per hour. The funicular works only on Sun. and holidays (expect to have to queue for an hour if you want to go up before about 1400, and for coming down); the cable car operates 0900-1800 weekdays, 0600-1800 on Sun.

The neighbourhood can be dangerous; at weekends there is so much traffic (cars and pedestrians) that it is usually safe to walk there, and there is a police station nearby, but during the week muggings are frequent even in daylight. Take a bus or taxi to the foot of the hill Mon.-Fri., and never be tempted to walk down from the top. (This warning cannot be overemphasized.) Taxi to foot, allowing 1 hour at the top, US$5.30.

At the foot of Monserrate is the Quinta de Bolívar, a fine colonial mansion, with splendid gardens and lawns. There are several cannons captured at the battle of Boyacá. The house, once Bolívar's home, is now a museum showing some of his personal possessions and paintings of events in his career. (Open 1000-1700, Tues.-Sun.; its address is Calle 20, No. 3-23 Este; charge US$0.50.)

The Plaza Bolívar, with a statue of the Liberator at its centre, is at the heart of the city; around the Plaza are the narrow streets and massive mansions of the old quarter (known as the Barrio La Candelaria), with their barred windows, carved doorways, brown-tiled roofs and sheltering eaves. The district is becoming popular as a residential area and has a growing artists' community. Most of the mansions and best colonial buildings are in this district: the Palace of San Carlos, the house of the Marqués de San Jorge (housing an archaeological museum), the Municipal Palace, the Capitol, and the churches of San Ignacio, Santa Clara, San Agustín, and the Cathedral.

The Calles (abbreviated "Cll.", or "C") run at right angles across the Carreras ("Cra." or "K"). It is easy enough to find a place once the address system, which is used throughout Colombia, is understood. The address Calle 13, No. 12-45 would be the building on Calle 13 between Carreras 12 and 13 at 45 paces from Carrera 12; however transversals and diagonals (numbers with letters appended) can complicate the system. The Avenidas, broad and important streets, may be either Calles (like 19) or Carreras (like 14). Av. Jiménez de Quesada, one of Bogotá's most important streets, owes its lack of straightness to having been built over a river-bed. Carrera 7, one of the main shopping streets, is now closed to motor traffic on Sundays.

The street map of Bogotá on **page 527** is marked with numerals showing the places of most interest for visitors. Each place will be described under the numeral for it in the map.

1. The Plaza Bolívar, heart of the city, coeval with the city's foundation. On the eastern side is the Archbishop's Palace, with splendid bronze doors. To one side of it is the colonial Plazuela de Rufino Cuervo. Here is the house of Manuela Sáenz, the mistress of Bolívar. On the other side is the house in which Antonio Nariño printed in 1794 his translation of "The Rights of Man" which triggered off the movement for independence.

See the Casa del Florero or 20 de Julio museum in a colonial house on the corner of Plaza Bolívar with Calle 11. It houses the famous flower vase that featured in the 1810 revolution and shows collections of the Independence War period, including documents and engravings. Entry fee US$0.40, open Tues.-Sat., 0915-1830. On the northern side of the Plaza is the spectacular Palace of Justice, wrecked in a guerrilla attack in 1985.

2. The Cathedral, rebuilt in 1807 in classical style. Notable choir loft of carved walnut and wrought silver on altar of Chapel of El Topo. Several treasures and relics; small paintings attributed to Ribera; banner brought by Jiménez de Quesada to Bogotá, in sacristy, which has also portraits of past Archbishops. There is a monument to Jiménez inside the Cathedral. In one of the chapels is buried Gregorio Vásquez Arce y Ceballos (1638-1711), by far the best painter in colonial Colombia. Many of his paintings are in the Cathedral.

3. The beautiful Chapel of El Sagrario, built end of the 17th century. Several paintings by Gregorio Vásquez Arce.

4. The Municipal Palace.

5. The Capitol, an imposing building with fine colonnades (1847-1925). Congress sits here.

9. The church of Santa Clara, another colonial church, is now a religious museum and concert hall.

10. San Ignacio, Jesuit church built in 1605. Emeralds from the Muzo mines in Boyacá were used in the monstrance. Paintings by Gregorio Vásquez Arce.

11. The Palace of San Carlos, where Bolívar lived. He is said to have planted the huge walnut tree in the courtyard. On September 25, 1828, there was an attempt on his life. His mistress, Manuela, thrust him out of the window and he was able to hide for two hours under the stone arches of the bridge across the Río San Agustín. Santander, suspected of complicity, was arrested and banished. Now the Presidential Palace, with a huge banquet hall used for state affairs. The guard is changed—full-dress uniform—every day at 1700.

The Museum of Colonial Art, across from the Palace of San Carlos (Carrera 6, No. 9-77) is one of the finest colonial buildings in Colombia. It belonged originally to the Society of Jesus, and was once the seat of the oldest University in Colombia and of the National Library. It has a splendid

collection of colonial art and paintings by Gregorio Vásquez Arce, all kinds of utensils, and 2 charming patios. Open Tues. to Sat. 0930-1830; Sun. and holidays, 1000-1700. Entry fee US$0.40 for adults; students US$0.20.

12. Colón Theatre, Calle 10, No. 5-32 (operas, lectures, ballets, plays, concerts, etc.), late 19th century with lavish decorations. Seating for 1,200, and very ornate.

13. The Mint (Casa de la Moneda), built in 1720, is at Calle 11, No. 4-93; contains a museum of religious paintings and numismatics. Open Mon.-Sat. 0900-2100, Sun. and holidays, 0900-1800. In the same street, No. 4-16, is the Banco de la República's Luis Angel Arango library, one of the best endowed and arranged in South America, with 3 reading rooms, research rooms, an art gallery and a splendid concert hall. There are free concerts and exhibitions. The architecture is impressive and the lavatories are recommended.

14. Palacio de Nariño (1906), the presidential palace. Spectacular interior, fine collection of modern Colombian paintings. Free tours every Sat. morning with guide, 0930 in Spanish, 1000 in English, but not open to the public any other time.

15. Church of San Agustín, strongly ornamented (1637). Fine paintings by Gregorio Vásquez Arce and the Image of Jesus which was proclaimed Generalísimo of the army in 1812.

16. Santa Bárbara church (mid-16th century), one of the most interesting colonial churches. Paintings by Gregorio Vásquez Arce.

17. Church of San Juan de Dios, well worth a visit.

18. Palace of Communications (postal and telegraph), built on the site of the old colonial church of Santo Domingo.

19. Government Palace of Cundinamarca Department, almost as imposing as the Capitol. Corinthian style.

20. San Francisco church (mid-16th century), with notable paintings of famous Franciscans, choir stalls, and a famous high altar (1622). Remarkable ceiling is in Spanish-Moorish (*mudéjar*) style.

21. Church of La Veracruz, first built five years after the founding of Bogotá, rebuilt in 1731, and again in 1904. In 1910 it became the National Pantheon and Church of the Republic. José de Caldas, the famous scientist, was buried along with many other victims of the "Reign of Terror" under the church. Fashionable weddings.

22. La Tercera Orden, an old colonial church famous for its carved woodwork, altars, and confessionals.

23. The Banco de la República, next to Parque Santander. Next to the Bank is the wonderful Gold Museum (see page 533). In Parque Santander there is a bronze statue of Santander, who helped Bolívar to free Colombia and was later its President.

24. Las Nieves, old colonial church, has been demolished and replaced by an ugly modern church.

26. Planetarium, Natural History Museum and Museum of Modern Art, in Parque de la Independencia. Two daily showings of best foreign modern painters, US$0.30. (see also page 532)

27. *Tequendama Hotel*. Nearby (on Carrera 7 and Calle 26) are the church and monastery of San Diego, a picturesque old building recently restored. The Franciscan monastery with fine Mudéjar ceiling was built in 1560 and the church in 1607 as its chapel. It is now used as a crafts shop by Artesanías de Colombia. SE of the *Tequendama Hotel* is the National Library, with entrance on Calle 24.

28. Parque Mártires (Park of the Martyrs) with monument, on the site of the Plaza in which the Spanish shot many patriots during the struggle for independence.

29. Church of María del Carmen, with excellent stained glass and walls in bands of red and white.

Warning The old part around Plaza Bolívar and from Calle 28, extending to the centre and South (i.e. declining Calle numbers) is less dangerous than it was, with increased police patrolling. The central area is less safe at weekends after 1900. Mugging, however, may occur in other parts of the city.

Under state-of-siege legislation police may shoot and kill a suspect during any narcotics operation and it will be automatically classified as self-defence. A large number of would-be drug traffickers have been killed in this way.

The Judicial Unit for Tourism (Tourist police) offers 24-hour service for tourists at Carrera 7, No. 27-42, T 283-4930. If you are robbed of documents, contact police at Calle 46 y Carrera 14, of valuables, police at Calle 40, No. 8-09.

Hotels

Name	Address	Single (US$)	Double (US$)	No. of Stars	Category
Bogotá Royal	Av. 100, No. 8A-01	82	101	5	L
Hilton	Cra. 7, No. 32-16	119	136	5	L
Tequendama*	Cra. 10, No. 26-21	68	85	5	L
La Fontana	Diagonal 127A, No. 21-10	94	111	5	L
Charleston*	Cra. 13, No. 85-62	90	100	4	L
Bogotá Plaza	Calle 100, No. 18A-30	85	102	4	L
El Belvedere*	Tr. 18, No. 100-16	38	50	4	A
Cosmos Cien	Av. 100 No. 21A-41	49	57	4	A
Bacatá	Calle 19, No. 5-20	42	55	4	A

*Continental**	Av. Jiménez, No. 4-16	22	29	4	C
Dann	Calle 19, No. 5-72	37	48	3	A
*Nueva Granada**	Av. Jiménez, No. 4-77	32	40	4	B
El Presidente	Calle 23, No. 9-45	25	33	3	B

* = recommended. Whenever possible, book hotel reservations in advance.

Aparta-Hotel América, Carrera 8, No. 65-89 (Aptdo Aéreo 59859, T 212-81-10, 212-44-90, 212-42-09), A for apartment for one to four persons, clean, comfortable, quiet; *Country*, Calle 85 with Carrera 15, apartments with kitchen, very clean, close to a good supermarket, reservation necessary; *Nuechatel*, Calle 90, No. 7A-66, A, old-fashioned, safe district, good restaurant but poor plumbing; *Las Terrazas*, Calle 54, No. 3-12, C, 2-star, "rustic charm", nice view of city; *Monserrat*, Av. Caracas, 18-08, D, rec., clean, impeccable service; *Cristal*, Calle 17, No. 7-92, C, similar quality; *Regina*, Carrera 5, No. 15-16, D, with private bath, TV, phone, friendly, good; *Bogotá Internacional*, Carrera 7A, No. 21-20, T 343898, D, very central, comfortable, clean, restaurant and bar, highly rec.; *La Hostería de la Candelaria*, Calle 9, No. 3-11, T 283-5258/242-1727, Aptdo. Aéreo 15978, D, highly rec. for comfort, atmosphere and service (good for longer stays). On Calle 14 near Carrera 4 are: *Dann Colonial*, No. 4-21, C; opposite is *Santa Fe*, No. 4-48, hot shower, good service, E, quiet, clean, friendly, safe, warmly rec.; *Residencias Florián*, Calle 14, No. 4-67, F; also rec., *Residencia Aragón*, Carrera 3, No. 14-13, clean and safe, F, run down, but friendly and honest, no hot water, warmly rec. (cheap taxi to airport can be arranged); *Residencias Las Vegas*, Calle 13, No. 3-81, F, clean, central. *De Lujo*, Carrera 13, No. 22-46, T 242-8849, D, with bath, clean, safe, friendly, recommended; *San Diego*, Carrera 13 y Calle 24, D, good value; *Centro International*, 3-star, Carrera 13, No. 38-97, friendly, small rooms, D; *Avenida 19*, Avenida (Calle) 19, No. 5-92, D, with shower, good price considering its central location, clean, very helpful service; *Pensión Alemana*, Carrera 14, No. 25-15, E, safe, rec.; *Pensión Halifax*, Calle 93, No. 15-93, English spoken, friendly, B with all meals included in daily rate; *Regis*, Calle 18, No. 6-09 (also known as *Residencias María*), E (C with shower), sometimes hot water, old-fashioned, run down but safe, clean; *Ile de France*, Calle 18, No. 14-56, C, hot water, good food, either breakfast or dinner; *Hollywood*, Calle 18, No. 8-68, E, clean but small rooms with bath; *Hostal Alexander*, Calle 23, No. 5-23, D, safe, clean, friendly, hot water; *El Buen Amigo*, Carrera 16, No. 14-45, E, friendly, cheap, noisy at night; *Hostal Residencias Moreno*, Transversal 33 No. 95-28, T 257-9127, D inc two meals, two house taxi drivers, nearby frequent bus service to town centre, very friendly, safe for left luggage, quiet, comfortable, hot water, highly rec.; *Los Cerros*, Avenida 19, No. 9-18, D, clean, friendly, restaurant, rec., TV in rooms; *El Turista*, Av. Jiménez, between Cras. 4 and 5, E with bath, hot water, safe, small establishment, rec.; opp is *Zaratoga*, E with bath, quite noisy; *Internacional*, Av. Jiménez, nr. *Nueva Granada*, E, hot water, safe, friendly; *Vas*, Calle 15, No. 12-30, E, with bath, safe, clean and friendly; *Residencias Schlief*, Calle 33A, No. 14-38, E, with breakfast, no twin beds, pleasant; *María Luisa*, Carrera 14, between Calles 15 and 16, hot water, very reasonable and food is good; *Geber*, Carrera 10, No. 22-45, D, good, but water supply can be faulty; under same management, *Quindio*, Calle 17, No. 16-94, F; *Residencia Dorantes*, Calle 13, No. 5-07, very clean, E (cheaper without bath), hot water, reasonable, safe, rec.; *Residencias R-B*, Av. Jiménez with Carrera 4, central, clean, E; *Residencias Real No. 1*, Carrera 15, No. 17-71, E, safe, dubious water supply, good value, as is *Residencias La Villa*, E, which is opposite; *Residencias Elis*, Calle 14, between Carreras 14 and 15, good and cheap; *Residencias Ya*, Calle 24 y Carrera 14, E, clean, secure garage; *Residencias Ambala*, Carrera 5, No. 13-46, E, cheap, clean, friendly and central. *España*, Carrera 7, Calle 23, D, clean, safe; *Regio*, next to Gold Museum, E, clean, noisy. *Residencias Panamá No. 2*, Carrera 16, No. 16-88, T 241-04-05, F, friendly, clean, safe, hot shower (unsafe area). *Alcron*, Calle 20 y Carrera 5, F, simple, safe; *Residencias Españolas*, Calle 13 and Carrera 16, clean, F; *Residencias El Hogar*, Calle 16, No. 15-87, clean, small rooms, warm water, F (gringos pay a US$1 surcharge). *Camelia*, Calle 16, No. 15-20, F, clean, safe, hot water, good value, T 243-4131; *Asturias*, next door (No. 15-36), T 242-0931, F, same standard but no hot water; *Residencia Bucamaranga*, Calle 15, No. 16-68, G with bath, cold water, basic; many other cheap hotels in this area, which is dangerous especially for women alone. We are informed that from Calle 12 southwards, Carrera 13 westwards is not salubrious: visitors are therefore advised to pick hotels in streets NE of Calle 12, with higher numbers. There are certainly many hotels between Calles 13 and 17 and Carreras 15 and 17, many of which are cheap, some of which are clean. Private vehicles should be parked in lockable, guarded parqueaderos.

Restaurants 10% value-added tax is now charged. *Refugio Alpino*, Calle 23, No. 7-49, is an excellent Swiss restaurant; *Casa San Isidro*, on Monserrate, good, not cheap; *Tramonti*, Vía La Calera Km. 1½ (Cra. 1, No. 93-80, approached via Carrera 7 and Calle 84), in hills to NE of city, beautiful views, open fires, parking, luxurious, open daily 1200-2400; *Eduardo*, Carrera 11, No. 90-43, international and expensive; *Las Acacias*, Carrera 11, No. 65-46, for typical Colombian food; *Verners*, Calle 25, No. 12-23 (very good German food); *Casa Vieja del Claustro*, Carrera 3, No. 18-60, typical food; *El Café de Rosita*, Carrera 3, No. 8-65, connected with *Hostería de la Candelaria*, breakfast, lunch, bar and tapas, concerts Thurs. and Fri., rec.; *Casa Vieja*, Av. Jiménez 3-73, traditional Bogotá food in traditional atmosphere, live music; close by on Av. Jiménez is *La Guayacana*, Colombian food, reasonably priced lunches; *El Zaguán de Las Aguas*,

Calle 19, No. 5-62, local dishes, atmosphere and national dancing in evening, but expensive and poor cooking and drinks (beer and soft drinks not available) very expensive; good cheap local food at *Doña Lilia*, Calle 17 No. 14-33; also *Regia*, Calle Pallau (next to Gold Museum); *Los Sauces*, Carrera 11, Calle 69, also has traditional music and dancing, expensive with cover charge; *Chalet Suizo*, Av. 21, No. 39A-48, Swiss and international food; similar is *Club Suizo*, excellent and reasonable, Calle 18, No. 4-48; *Donde Canta la Rana*, Carrera 24-C, No. 20-10 Sur, a few km. from centre, is refreshingly local and unspoilt, open 1400-1900. *Doña Bárbara*, Calle 82, corner of Carrera 11, dinner costs US$4-7, excellent latino jazz played; *La Piragua*, corner of Av. Jiménez and Carrera 5, cheap and good; *Temel*, Carrera 19 at Calle 118, good steaks, expensive; *Giuseppe Verdi*, Calle 58, No. 5-85, excellent pasta; *Petit Paris*, Carrera 4 and Calle 74, expensive French food; *Jeno's*, Carrera 15, near Calle 85, serves good, though not cheap, pizzas, another outlet at Calle 19, near Cra. 6; *Berlín*, Carrera 15 and Calle 74, German food; *Chalet Europa*, Carrera 9, No. 16-91, 4-course meals for US$5; *Cafetería Romano*, Av. Jiménez, between Carrera 6 and 7, all meals, very clean and reasonable, well rec., as is its sister restaurant *Salerno*, Carrera 7, No. 19-43; *Punta Roja*, Carrera 7 y Calle 24, good 3-course meal for US$2; *Brisas del Valle*, Carrera 7, Calle 22, good, reasonably priced; *Barra Llanera*, Carrera 9, No. 21-45, open weekends and rec. for cheap fish. *Robin Hood*, near *Hotel Nueva Granada*, very good, three-course weekday lunch for US$4, there are other branches. Also on Avenida Jiménez, *Balmoral*, No. 4-92, good food, reasonable prices, open Sun. and holidays, and *Restaurante Briceño*, 5-19, large portions, cheap. *Tierra Colombiana*, Carrera 10, No. 27-27, good, expensive food, evening floor show. There are two restaurants called *Sandricks*, one on Carrera 16, No. 91-25, the other on Carrera 15, No. 79-92; they are run by two brothers and are highly rec., though not cheap (US$6-9 for a main dish). There is a small chain of restaurants called *La Sultana:* the best is at Carrera 7, No. 20-86; *Doña Hertha*, Calle 19, No. 8-61, 3-course meal US$3, specialty is goulash; *Ranch Burger*, Centro El Lago, on Carrera 15, serves hamburgers; *Burger King*, Cra. 7 with Calle 34 next to *Hilton*, also *Centro Granahorrar*, Av. Chile with Cra. 9, in Chapinero at Carrera 13 with Calle 64, and more; several *Wimpy Bars* on Cra. 7, good burgers and grills but not cheap; *Dominó*, a chain of good, fairly cheap, typical food restaurants, at Calle 19 with Cra. 3, Cra. 11 with Calle 71; another chain is *Crepes y Waffles*, good value; *La Gran Barilla*, Carrera 4, with Calle 13, cheap, rich meals; *Parrilla de Oro*, Carrera 4, No. 17-94, excellent inexpensive typical food; *Delphi*, opposite Teatro Gaitán, Carrera 7 No. 22-66, rec. for cheap meals; *Trattoria Bistro*, Calle 59, No. 8-50, with branch at Unicentro (Local 2-45), not cheap, but good food, must book at weekends; for US$1.20 a two-course meal can be had in the cafeteria of the Ley and Tía supermarkets; also Cafam, Calle 17 y Carrera 9 (Centro Colseguros).

El Vegetariano, Calle 22, No. 8-89, set meals for US$1, rec. (the restaurant on 3rd floor with only a small sign); there is another branch at Calle 8, No. 5-74; *El Trópico*, Carrera 8, No. 17-72, vegetarian restaurant, good food (especially the fruit cake) and whole wheat loaves for US$1.20 (4-course meal, US$3); *El Vegetariano Fleber*, Calle 17, No. 10-49, good; *Vegetariano de Sol*, Calle 63, No. 10-62 with Yoga Institute in Plaza de Lordes. *Jugos Cali*, Carrera 11, No. 64-60, mostly juices, with pastries. 4 rec. vegetarian restaurants, all with the same owner, are: *El Champiñón*, Transversal 20, No. 122-05 (T 213-2278), near Unicentro; *Samovares*, Carrera 11, No. 69-89 (T 249-4549—lunch only, fixed menu, US$6, nice atmosphere), Carrera 11, No. 67-63 (T 249-6515) and Av. Caracas No. 32-64 (T 285-6095). *El Integral Natural*, Carrera 11, No. 95-10, health food shop with a few tables at street level, restaurant downstairs, fixed menu US$1.50; *Los Vegetarianos*, Calle 41, No. 8-65 (good) and another location with courtyard, very good; *Acuarius*, Carrera 16, No. 43-30 and also at Calle 18, good vegetarian food, rec.; *Gran Fraternidad*, Carrera 8, No. 21-39, also rec. Vegetarian food, excellent, at Calle 74, No. 12-30.

El Dorado, Carrera 15, No. 16-39, good meal for US$2.60; *Freddy*, Carrera 15, No. 16-55, good, budget, popular. *Monte Blanco*, Carrera 7a, No. 17-31, and other branches, very good. *Diana*, Calle 8 with Carrera 6. Good pizzas are served at branches of *Little John's*; *Tío Tim's*, Carrera 13, Calle 67, for pizza, beer and mechanical bull (owned by a Welshman); *Pizzería*, Calle 33, No. 15 (opp. *Hotel María Isabel*), excellent food, atmosphere and music; *La Candelaria*, Calle 11, No. 3-89, 3-course meal for US$2; *Residencias Lido*, Calle 11, No. 8-79 (just off Plaza Bolívar) serves good, cheap, complete meals; *La Fregata*, Calle 15, No. 9-30 and Calle 77, No. 15-36, expensive but excellent for sea food. Spanish food at *El Mesón de la Paella*, Calle 39, No. 12-14. French food at *La Reserva*, Calle 39 and Carrera 15, expensive (dinner for 2, US$30), good food and service in an old house with open fire. For Italian food, *Il Piccolo Café*, Carrera 15, No. 96-55, very good. *Longaniza*, Carrera 15, No. 92-73, very good for meat, with salad bar. For Chinese food, *Nanking*, Calle 23, between Carreras 6 and 7; and *Pagoda China* on Calle 69, Cra. 6. Japanese and Korean dishes at *Restaurant Arirang*. For excellent inexpensive Arab food, *Ramses*, Carrera 7, No. 18-64. For the traveller on a budget, *bandeja* (the local *plato del día*) can cost US$1.50- 2 for a 2-course meal at the right places. *Mi Ranchito*, Calle 21, No. 5-77, good cheap bar, drinks only. Good ice cream at *Yeti Helados*, Carrera 11 with Av. Chile. *El Fogón de la 5a*, Carrera 5 No. 14-24, rec. for good cheap fruit salad. On Sunday nights it is difficult to find anywhere open; try Calle 22 (the entertainment district).

All along Carrera 15 in El Chicó are shops, bars and restaurants, many of which have tables out on the pavement. *Pimm's*, Carrera 15, Calle 83; *Tony Roma's*, Carrera 15 esq. Calle 77 and Calle 93, No. 13-85, good quality food and excellent service. Also on Carrera 15, 85-42, interior 7, is *Academia de Golf* which has a good beef/fish and salad restaurant, as well as golf driving and putting ranges, and equipment for sale. *Quiebracanto*, 2 locations, Carrera 5 near Calle 16, and next to University of Los Andes, Calle 18 and Carrera 2, student places with recorded music, occasional films, talks, etc.; *Café Libre*, Carrera 15, near Universidad Católica, bar with live music, also serves lunches; *Café Oma*, Carrera 15, Calle 89/90, good food and coffee, nice atmosphere, open till 0100; *Café Omo Lago*, Carrera 15, No. 82-60. *Chicanos*, Carrera 11, No. 78-70, good value and quality (about US$15-20 for 2), excellent juices and cocktails; *Shamua*, Calle 85, No. 11-69, good cocktails, small selection of well prepared food, US style. Many small, popular bars and cafés around Calle 82, Carreras 12, 13, 14, frequented by young people, not cheap. For those visiting the Centro Administrativo Nacional (CAN, on Av. El Dorado near airport), a good restaurant nearby is *La Casa de Fernando*, Transversal 42, Diag. 40, No. 43-22; others nearby.

Tea Rooms   *Benalcázar*, near Plaza de las Nieves on Carrera 8, No. 20-25, excellent pastries and quite all right for women alone; *La Suiza*, Calle 25, No. 9-41, excellent pastries; as good, but cheaper, is *Pastelería Castilla*, Calle 19 and Carrera 10 and 12; *William Tell*, Carrera 13, Calle 23. *Fábrica del Pan*, Av. Jiménez at Carrera 8, good for breakfasts, teas, snacks, reasonably priced. A chain of *Cyranos* throughout the city offers good pastries.

Clubs   Anglo-American Club, Country Club (golf, polo, swimming), Magdalena Sports Club (tennis), San Andrés Golf Club, Club de Los Lagartos (social; with a pool heated by hot springs, water-skiing, a golf course and tennis courts), Club Campestre Fontanar (tennis), America Tennis Club, Lions' Club, Bogotá Sports Club (cricket, football, tennis, squash, rugby and hockey). Both the Lagartos and the Country Club have beautiful gardens designed by Enrique Acosta.

Shopping   10% value-added tax on all purchases. *Artesanías de Colombia* (state-owned), Almacén San Diego, in the old San Diego church, Cra. 10, No. 26-50, Almacén Las Aguas, next to the Iglesia de las Aguas, Carrera 3A, No. 18-60, Almacén del Norte, Cra. 15, No. 95-74, has best selection of folk art and crafts, at fair prices. A good place for handicrafts is *El Lago*, Carrera 7, No. 16-81. Another good place is *El Balay* on Carrera 15, No. 75-63, rather expensive, and, of course, there is the shop in the Museo de Artes y Tradiciones Populares, which is recommended. *Artesanía* shop at Carrera 15, No. 83-30 often has cheap objects. *Lana Lana Cuero Cuero*, Cra. 15, No. 74-47, moderate prices. See H. Stern's jewellery stores at the International Airport, *Hilton Hotel* and *Tequendama Hotel*. A street market on Avenida Jiménez and Carrera 14 (Avenida Caracas) sells cheaper *ruanas*, blankets, leatherware, etc. Good ruanas can be bought at *Tipicentro*, Calle 17, No. 5-46 and No. 5-37, with better prices at the smaller shop although bargaining can bring them down a bit further. Shopping centre at Chapinero, Carrera 13, Calles 55-60, specializes in men's shoes and leather. Women's shoes are found on Calle 18 between Carrera 7 and 9. Boutiques are to be found in El Chicó on Carrera 15, Calles 76-100. Permanent crafts markets at Calle 100, Carrera 15 and Carrera 7 opp. *Hotel Tequendama*. There is another market, at Christmastime only, which is good for handicrafts, at Carrera 10, Calle 10. Another seasonal market is held at Carrera 7 and Calle 72. High-quality leather goods on Calle 18, between Carreras 4 and 7, also at *Todo en Cuero*, Calle 19, No. 6-56; and Carrera 10, between Calles 13 and 19. Also the *Boots and Bags* and *Pecarí* chains for high-quality leather. *Galería Cano*, Edificio Bavaria, Carrera 7, Bogotá Hilton, Unicentro, Loc. 218, Airport, sells gold and gold-plated replicas of some of the jewellery on display in the Gold Museum. *Mitus* (in *Hotel Tequendama*) also sells reproduction jewellery from its own workshop, and Indian pottery. *Galería 70*, Avenida 13, No. 70-14, exhibition of and shop selling hand-woven textiles and rugs. Primitive paintings are often on show in the *Galería El Callejón*, Calle 16, No. 6-34, as well as old maps and prints. Banco de Fotografías Movifoto, Calle 15, No. 4-66, has a very large selection of postcards from all over Colombia. There are several antique shops around Calle 66 and Carrera 11; check yellow pages for precise addresses. Antiques also at *Hijos de Antonio Cancino* on Plaza Bolívar.

The pavements and cafés along Av. Jiménez, below Carrera 7, Parque de los Periodistas, and Calle 16 and Carrera 3, are used on weekdays by emerald dealers. Great care is needed in buying: bargains are to be had, but synthetics and forgeries abound. (Beware of stones that seem too perfect or have a bluish colouring.) Three shops selling good emeralds at reasonable prices are: *Joyería Frida*, Carrera 7, No. 18-31; *Willis F. Bronkie*, Carrera 9, No. 74-08, oficina 801; *Jewelry Prado*, Carrera 7, No. 16-50. Also *El Palacio de la Esmeralda*, Carrera 10, No. 26-7, Int. 126, reasonable prices, certificates given. Also jewellery shops in the basement of *Hotel Tequendama*, and on Calles 12 and 13, between Carreras 7 and 9. Modern textiles and knitwear can be bought at low prices at *Unicentro*, a large shopping centre on Carrera 15 at Calle 127A (take "Unicentro" bus from centre, going N on Cra. 10—takes about 1 hr.). *Cafam*, Av. 68 with Calle 72, is said to be cheaper than Unicentro; *Centro Granahorrar*, Av. Chile (Calle 72) between Carreras 10 and 11 is another good shopping centre; also *Metropolis*, Calle 68 y Carrera 68 (with *Exito* supermarket opposite), and *Boulevard Niza*, Av. Suba, Calle 11-127. *Técnica*, Carrera 7A, No. 16-13 (first floor) will put gold lettering on leather goods quickly and cheaply.

Bookshops   *Librería Buchholz*, Carrera 7, No. 27-68 (opp. *Hotel Tequendama*), also at Calle 59, No. 13-13 (Chapinero); useful advice in a number of languages, low prices. *Librería Aldina*, Carrera 7, Calle 70-80, most helpful on books and Bogotá alike, excellent stock of English-language books, open 0930-1930, Sat. 0930-1700. *Librería Nacional*, Carrera 7, No. 17-51 (has small selection of English bestsellers). *Librería Francesa*, Calle 65, No. 9-07. *Librería Lerner*, Av. Jiménez, No. 4-35 (no English books). *Ateneo*, Calle 82, No. 13-19, in the north of the city, good selection of

Colombian titles, knowledgeable staff; *Librería Tercer Mundo*, Carrera 7, No. 16-91, knowledgeable; *Librería Culutural Colombiana*, Calle 72, No. 16-15; *Casa de Libro*, Calle 18 between Cras. 7 and 6. Books in Colombia are generally expensive. Book Exchange Stalls, Calle 19, between Carreras 7 and 10. English novels secondhand at Carrera 10 y Calle 21.

Photograph Cheap film for sale, e.g. Fuji 135-36 for US$2, and good quick developing at Foto Rapid, Calle 14 No. 6-05 (Plazoleta de Rosana).

Taxis have meters (although newer ones are reported not to have them); insist that they are used. Starting charge, US$0.35, plus US$0.07 for every 90 metres, minimum charge US$0.85. Additional charge of US$0.35 after 2000 and on public holidays and Sun. (a list of legal charges should be posted in the taxi).

Tan and green tourist taxis can be rented by the hour or the day through the *Tequendama Hotel*, most of the drivers speak English and are very helpful. Taxis are relatively cheap, so it is worthwhile taking one if you are carrying valuables, or at night. Taxi tours with Jaime Carvajal (Spanish spoken only), T 203-1063.

Travel in Bogotá Bus stops in centre by red and yellow "Paradero" boards; otherwise flag buses down. Bus fares are US$0.10, *busetas* charge US$0.15. Green buses with letters TSS (i.e. unsubsidized) cost US$0.12. There are some "super-executive" routes with plush seats and videos, at US$0.30-0.50 (if traffic is heavy you might see the whole film). Urban buses are not good for sightseeing because you will be standing as likely as not. A metro is planned.

Car Rental Dollar Rent-a-Car, airport and Cra. 13, 82-28; Hertz, at airport, and at Carrera 10, No. 26-35; National, Carrera 7, No. 33-27; Hernando Zuluaga & Cía, Carrera 7, No. 20-80; Aquilautos Ltda., Carrera 7, No. 34-81. Avis, Calle 79, 53-70, Cra 10, 27-79 and at airport.

Night Life Monserrate Room at the *Tequendama*. Unicorn, Calle 94, No. 7-75, expensive and spectacular; El Padrino, very good. Noches de Colombia, show 2100-0030, typical dances and songs from various parts of the country, not dear. Son de Grillos, near bullring, intellectual salsa place; La Teja Corrida, also next to bullring, need to reserve table at weekends, good lively salsa; Ramón Antigua, rather quieter than Teja Corrida, but they dance on the tables at weekends; San Líbero bar, in Candelaria district, open till 0400, highly recommended; opposite San Líbero is Goce Pagano, also good. (Information from Angela.) Many popular bars and dancing places on Carrera 5 with Calle 25, entrance between US$2-3, relatively safe area.

Theatre Many of the theatres are in the Candelaria area. Colón Theatre details on **page 528**. The following are the equivalent of the British fringe theatre: La Candelaria, Calle 12, No. 2-59; Sala Seki Sano, Calle 12, No. 2-65; Teatro Libre de Bogotá, Calle 13, No. 2-44.

Cinema Cinemateca Distrital, Carrera 7 No. 22-79. Good films, US$0.85. Also on Carrera 7: Teatro Municipal, No. 22-53, Metro, No. 21-78, Tisquesa, No. 27-29. Av. Chile shopping centre cinema, Calle 71, between Carreras 11 and 13 (usually prize-winning films). Consult *El Tiempo* for what is on; frequent programme changes. Admission, US$0.70.

Sauna Los Andes, Carrera 4, No. 16-29, good service, US$3.20, open daily 1000-2200.

Sports Bull fighting on Sats. and Suns. during the season at the municipally owned Plaza de Santamaría, near Parque Independencia. (Local bullfight museum at bullring, door No. 6.) Boxing matches are held here too. Horse races at Hipódromo los Andes, on Autopista Norte, races at 1400 (entrance US$1 and US$0.35), and at the Hipódromo del Techo, in the SW, on Sats., Suns. and public holidays. Nearby is the Municipal Stadium, which can hold 50,000 spectators. Football matches are played here. See also under **Clubs** above.

Football Tickets for matches at El Camplin stadium can be bought in advance at *Cigarrería Bucana*, Calle 18, No. 5-92. But not normally necessary to book in advance, except for local Santa Fe-Millionarios derby. Take a cushion; matches Sun. at 1545, Weds. at 2000.

Museums (all closed on Mondays) The National Museum, on Carrera 7, No. 28-66, the Panóptico, an old prison converted into a Museum (to the NE of the map), founded by Santander in 1823. Its top floor houses a fine art section, comprising national paintings and sculptures. Open Tues.-Sat. 0930-1830, Sun. 1000-1700, US$0.25. Many of its pre-conquest exhibits have been transferred to the Archaeological Museum at Carrera 6, No. 7-43, open Tues.-Sat. 1000-1700, Sun. 1000-1300, US$0.15. See map: 11 for Museum of Colonial Art, under 1 for Museo 20 de Julio and under 13 for the Banco de la República's Luis Angel Arango library.

The **Museum of Modern Art**, Calle 24, No. 6-55, entry US$0.15 (open Tues.-Sun. 0900-1900). It has a programme of films. The Planetarium and Natural History Museum, Calle 26 with Carrera 7, open Tues.-Fri. 0900-1800, Sat., Sun., and holidays, 1000-1800 (see map, no. 26). The Museo de Arte Colonial, Calle 6, No. 9-77, in an old convent with a garden.

The Museo Mercedes de Pérez, formerly the Hacienda de El Chicó, a fine example of colonial architecture, is at Carrera 7, No. 94-17. It contains a world-wide collection of mostly 18th century porcelain, furniture, paintings, etc. Open Tues-Sun., 0930-1230, 1430-1700.

The Museum of Popular Art and Tradition is at Carrera 8, No. 7-21 in an old monastery and exhibits local arts and crafts. It has a shop, selling handicrafts at higher prices than Artesanías de Colombia, and a reasonably-priced bar and restaurant (dishes typical of different regions of Colombia served in colonial setting, usually with regional traditional music). Open 0900-1730, Tues.-Sat., Sun. and holidays 1000-1400. The shop is not open on Sun. and holidays. Entry fee US$0.25.

Museo Siglo XIX, Carrera 8, No. 7-91, founded by the Banco Cafetero, has a collection of 19th-century painting, clothes and furniture. Open Mon.-Fri., 0900-1800, Sat., 1300-1700.

The Museo Arqueológico (belonging to the Banco Popular) is a fine and extensive collection of precolumbian pottery, assembled in the restored mansion of the Marqués de San Jorge, Carrera 6, No. 7-43. The house itself is a beautiful example of 17th century Spanish colonial architecture. US$0.30 entry. Open: 1000-1700, Tues. to Fri.; 1000-1300, Sat.-Sun. There is a restaurant.

Museum of Urban Development, Calle 10 No. 4-21 (open Tues.-Sat., 0900-1800, Sun. and holidays, 1000-1800), interesting maps and photos of the development of Bogotá in an attractive colonial house near the Palacio San Carlos.

Museo de los Niños, Carrera 48, No. 63-97, natural sciences explained for children, created by Sra. Ximena Rosas with funding from industry.

Museo del Oro (the Gold Museum), is in splendid premises at the Parque de Santander (corner of Calle 16 and Carrera 6-A). This collection is a "must", for it is unique. No less than 30,000 pieces of precolumbian gold work are shown. Open: Tues. to Sat., 0900-1600; Sun. and holidays, 0900-1200. (People in shorts not allowed). Charge, US$0.75 (US$0.35 for children). Do not miss seeing the collections kept in a huge strong-room on the top floor. Several film shows a day; at 1200 and 1530 they are in English.

The ancient gold objects discovered in Colombia were not made by the primitive technique of simple hammering alone, but show the use of virtually every technique known to modern goldsmiths.

The **Universidad Nacional** (about 13,000 students) is off our map, to the NW. The fine buildings are coated with political graffiti, and foreigners are not usually welcome on the campus. The oldest centres of learning are in the old centre: oldest of all is the Colegio Nacional de San Bartolomé (C 10, No. 6-57), in the same block as the Chapel of El Sagrario (3), founded 1573. The second oldest, founded on December 18, 1653, is the Colegio Mayor de Nuestra Señora del Rosario (C 14, No. 6-25); its beautiful colonial building is well worth a look.

Banks Banco de la República, the only bank permitted to exchange travellers' cheques in denominations of less than US$50 (up to 1500 Mon.-Thurs., to 1630 Fri., no commission charged), will give cash on American Express card, but not Visa, which is accepted at most other banks; Banco Anglo Colombiano, Carrera 8, No. 15-60, and eleven local agencies. Banco Royal de Colombia, Av. Jiménez with Carrera 8, will change cheques for US$50 but charges commission; Banco Internacional de Colombia; Banco Francés e Italiano de Colombia; Banco Franco Colombiano, and other Colombian banks. Open 0900-1500 Mon. to Thurs. and 0900-1530 on Fri. Closed on Sat.; also closed at 1200 on last working day of month.

Exchange American Express, Tierra Mar Aire Ltda, edif. Bavaria Torre B, Local 126, Carrera 10, No. 27-91, T 283-2955, Telex 41424 BOGCL. International Money Exchange, Carrera 7, No. 32-29, open till 1600 on Sats., check all transactions carefully; exchange at Av. 19, No. 15-35. Exprinter on Av. Jiménez and Carrera 6. Inside you can only get pesos and no travellers' cheques are exchanged, but the black market operates on the pavement outside, Peruvian and Ecuadorean currencies available (rates generally little different from official rates). Check the rate first, though, and if using it, be extremely careful.

Addresses
British Embassy, Calle 98, No. 9-03, 4th floor. T 218-5111. Postal Address: Apartado Aéreo 4508.
U.S. Embassy, Calle 38, No. 8-61 (Mailing address: Apartado Aéreo 3831, Bogotá 1, D.E.). T 285-1300/1688.
W. German Embassy, Carrera 4, No. 72-36, 6th floor, T 212-0511.
Canadian Embassy, Calle 76, No. 11-52; T 217-5555, open 0800-1630. (Mailing address: Apartado Aéreo 53531, Bogotá 2, D.E.)
Norwegian Consulate, Carrera 13, No. 50-78, Oficina 506, T 235-5419.
French Embassy, Carrera 7, No. 38-91, T 285-4311.
Finnish Embassy, Calle 72 No 8-56, 7th floor, T 212-6111.
Swedish Embassy, Calle 72 No. 5-83, T 255-3777.
Danish Embassy, Calle 37, No. 7-43, 9°, Bogotá 2, T 232-6753/93.
Swiss Embassy, Carrera 9, No. 74-08, oficina 1101, T 255-5280, open Mon.-Fri. 0900-1200.
Venezuelan Consulate, Avenida 13, No. 103-16, T 256-3015, hrs. of business 0900-1230, 1300-1500, visa free, but allow 3 days (if they don't merely send you to Cúcuta for all paperwork).
Panamanian Consulate, Calle 87, No. 11A-64, T 236-7531; Mon.-Fri., 0900-1300 (take "Usaquén" bus going north from centre, US$0.15).
Mexican Consulate, Calle 99, No. 12-08, Mon.-Fri., 0900-1300.

Costa Rican Consulate, Carrera 15, No. 80-87, Mon.-Fri. 0900-1300.

Guatemalan Consulate, Carrera 15, No. 83-43, Ap. 301, Mon.-Fri., 0900-1200, visa takes 48 hrs., US$10, one photo, one airline ticket (does not have to be return), tourist visa free for Canadians.

DAS Immigration office, Carrera 28, No. 17A-00, open 0730-1530, T 277-9211.

British Council, Calle 87, No. 12-79, T 236-25-42/257-96-32. Has a good library and British newspapers.

Anglo-Colombian School, Transversal 30, No. 152-38. Postal address: Apartado Aéreo 52969, Bogotá 2.

English School, Calle 170, No. 31-98 (T 254-1318 or 254-8874), Apartado Aéreo 51284, Bogotá.

American School, Colegio Nueva Granada, Carrera 2E, No. 70-20, T 212-35-11.

Postal Services   Main airmail office and foreign *poste restante* in basement of Edificio Avianca, Carrera 7, No. 16-36, open 0700-2200 Mon. to Sat. closed Sun., and holidays (0830-1200, 1530-1700, Mon. to Fri. for *poste restante*, letters kept for only a month). At weekend the Post Office only franks letters; stamps for postcards are not sold. Pharmacies and newsagents in Bogotá have an airmail collection. Parcel post, Calle 13 and Carrera 8, US$1.50 per kilo (3 months.)

International telephone calls made from several Telecom offices in centre of Bogotá (e.g. Calle 23, No. 13-49); all close 2000.

Laundry   La Solución No. 2, Carrera 5, 21-84, 0800-1200, 1400-1900, US$0.75 for 1 kg. Piccadilly, Calle 63, No. 7-10; Auto Servicio Burbujas, Edificio Procoil, Avenida 19, No. 3A-37, open Mon.-Sat. 0730-1930. Panorama, Carrera 7, Calle 67. Drycleaners: *Lavaseco*, Av. Jiménez, No. 4-30.

Health   Cruz Roja Nacional, Avenida 68, No. 66-31, T 250-661/231-9027/231-9008, open 0830-1800. Centro Médico La Salud, Carrera 10, No. 21-36, 2nd floor, T 243-13-81/282-40-21. Clínica Bogotá, Carrera 17, No. 12-65 (not a safe area to walk in), discourages travellers from having gamma-globulin shots for hepatitis. Walter Röthlisberger y Cía Ltda. imports medicines, including Vivotif for typhoid and gamma globulin, and stores them correctly; trade prices. The US Embassy will advise on doctors, dentists, etc. Profamilia, Calle 34, No. 14-46, for contraceptives. For health information, T 15; emergency medical service (TAS), T 277-6666.

Tourist Office   Calle 28, No. 13A-15, T 283-9466, Edificio Centro de Comercio Internacional (the name at the top of the building is Banco Cafetero), T 283-9466 (Mon.-Fri., 0900-1300, 1400-1700, and Sat. 0900-1200); they will tell you which parts of the country are unsafe; at Eldorado Airport and new bus terminal (both helpful, will book hotel rooms). Municipal tourist office, *Alcaldía* offices on Plaza Bolívar, and Carrera 35, No. 26-18 (Edif. Lotería de Bogotá). The Coordinadora de Turismo de Bogotá (Carrera 13, No. 27-95) has daily tours of the city with interpreters. For information on 24-hr. chemists (pharmacies), events, attractions, etc., T 282-0000.

Inderena, the National Parks Office, is on Diagonal 34, No. 5-84, for information and permission to visit the parks (very helpful). Good maps of Bogotá and road maps of Colombia can be purchased in the drugstore nearest the main road in the *Hotel Tequendama* arcade. Hiking maps from Instituto Geográfico, Agustín Codazzi, Carrera 30 y Calle 45, US$0.75 each (topographical details are generally accurate, but trails and minor roads less so). Esso road maps from service stations, US$0.40.

Travel Agents   recommended: Lands of Colombia, Carrera 16, No. 72A-16, friendly (helpful, English-spoken). Tierra Mar Aire, Cra. 10, No. 27-91, is Amex agent; does city tours from *Hotel Tequendama* (T 286-1111). Similar tours of the City (4 hrs.) can be arranged from *Hotel Nueva Granada*, much better value than tours to Zipaquirá (each costs about US$14). Viajes Don Quijote, Carrera 10 No. 27-51, also organizes tours of the city, 3½ hrs. by day, and 4 hours by night in a country-type bus (*chiva*) with musicians on the back seat. Expedición Colombia, Edificio KLM, piso 9, Calle 26, No. 4A-45, T 284-8284/8456, runs tours to the Llanos by private, chartered plane.

Thefts   Most hotels charge US$0.10 a night for insurance against theft. If you have something stolen go to the Corporación Nacional del Turismo for help and collect the insurance; this will probably take a few days of strenuous effort, but it has been known to work.

Airport   The airport at El Dorado has the world's second largest landing field. "Tourist Guide" policemen have white armbands. The taxi fare from airport to city is usually about US$4 (30% more at night and early a.m.). There are colectivos (US$0.30 plus luggage p.p.) from airport to centre; also buses, US$0.10. In the city centre buses and colectivos leave from Calle 19, going W between Carreras 10 and 14, to airport; buses marked "Aeropuerto" or "Universitaria Dorado"; colectivos marked "Aeropuerto". Make sure you get a registered taxi, where a policeman notes the numbers and gives you a paper stating fares, found at left (from inside) side of main terminal or Avianca terminal (drivers try to overcharge all the same). Unofficial taxis not advisable. Watch belongings outside airport, especially at night. Airport shops are beautiful, and there is a restaurant. Free Colombian coffee inside the customs area, between gates 2 and 3. Many snack bars and restaurants on first floor. There are luggage lockers at the airport. Hotel reservations can be made at the airport but their hotel rates are often out of date. The cheapest is in our Category D. Exchange rates are marginally lower than in the city, but pesos cannot be changed back into dollars at the airport without receipts. N.B. If flying from Colombia to Mexico and you do not need an exit ticket from Mexico, you may have difficulty persuading Avianca staff otherwise.

For internal flights, which serve all parts of the country, **see page 602**. For domestic shuttle flights to Medellín/Montería, Cali/Pasto, and Barranquilla, go to Puente Aéreo terminal, 1 km. before main terminal on Av. El Dorado. To Leticia, 1¾ hrs.; to Medellín, 45 mins.; to Cali, 40 mins. Avianca international flights also use this terminal (usually Miami and New York). It is more comfortable but there is not as much duty-free shopping. You have to cross eight busy lanes of traffic to get a bus into town, and negotiate two drainage ditches. As a rule, all flights are overbooked, so book well in advance. The Avianca office is at Carrera 7, No. 16-36, T 266-97-00. Satena, Avenida 19, 13A-18, T 283-55-57/282-55-57, military airline, not best for comfort and delays. SAM office is on Av. Jiménez, 5-14 (closed 1200-1400, then open till 1830). Many international airline offices are closed on Sat. and Sun. **See page 602** for procedure to obtain refunds on unused tickets.

Rail Although there are 3,700 km. of railways (metre gauge) in Colombia, the only long-distance route carrying passengers from Bogotá is to Santa Marta, called the Tayrona, which runs once a week, only between December and March. For the rest of the year you must go to La Dorada to take the Expreso del Sol train to Santa Marta, and that only goes twice a week. Luggage is checked into locked compartments, so you need to have light clothing available before journey starts. Sit on right to avoid afternoon sun. Station is at Calle 13 and Carrera 20. "Germania" bus goes from railway station to the city centre. Special excursions on steam trains go to Zipaquirá and Nemocón, Sat. and Sun., 0900, returning 1800, US$6 return; to Facatativá each Sun. and holiday, US$2.50 return; to Parque Duque, a pleasure park on the road to Tunja, Sun. and holidays, US$3 return, leave 1000, return 1830.

Buses There is a long-distance bus terminal on Av. Boyacá between El Dorado (Av. 26) and Av. Centenario (Calle 13). There is also access from Carrera 68. To get to the terminal take bus marked "Terminal" from "Terminal Transportes" bus stop at corner of Av. Jiménez de Quesada and Cra. 15; to get into town take Route No. 1 or No. 3 at the terminal and get off at Carrera 13 esq. Calle 13, closest to the centre (from this junction "Germania" bus goes to the centre). A *buseta* (US$0.05) runs from Carrera 68 to the terminal and back. Taxi US$2.50 (plus US$0.15 at night—police give price slip; avoid the unofficial taxis, normally touting for particular hotels), or take colectivo from beside Ruta 3 bus stop, US$0.30. The terminal is well-organized, comfortable and safe; free self-service luggage trolleys are provided. There are shops and restaurants. There are showers at the terminal (between Nos. 3 and 4), US$0.40, soap and towel provided. Companies are grouped according to routes. Buses to: Cali, 12 hrs., about US$10; Medellín, 12 hrs., on new autopista (often washed out), US$13; Manizales, 8-9 hrs., US$7-8.50; Honda, 4 hrs., US$3; Tunja, 2½ hrs., US$3; Villa de Leiva, US$3.50; La Dorada, 5 hrs., US$4; Popayán, 16 hrs., US$15; Florencia, US$19.50; Neiva, 5 hrs., US$5.50; Girardot, US$2.70; to Sogamoso, US$4, 4 hrs. (US$5 by executive minibus, 3 hrs.); Bucaramanga, 10-11 hrs., US$9; Cúcuta, 18 hrs., US$15 (the daily service by Berlinas del Fonce, 2 stops, 1600, rec., US$2 extra for *cochecama*); Cartagena, 23-28 hrs., US$23; Santa Marta US$20, 4 a day, 22 hrs., check if bus is going to Santa Marta, those continuing to Barranquilla may drop you short of town; direct bus to Barranquilla US$20 also; Pereira, 9-10 hrs., US$6.50, via Girardot, Espinal, Ibagué, Cajamarca, Armenia (fly if you wish to avoid the Quindío pass, 25 mins.); San Agustín, 12 hrs., US$10, only Coomotor, 4 daily, not a good service; Villavicencio, 4 hrs., US$2.75; Ipiales, 24 hrs., US$20, only gets crowded at Cali (the bus stops for an hour in Cali; it leaves from a different level of the terminal from that on which it arrived—don't lose your bus!); Pasto, 23 hrs., US$19.50. Velotax busetas are slightly quicker and more expensive, as are colectivos, which go to several long-distance destinations. For early morning start to Neiva (approx. hourly), Pitalito (0730 and 1030) and San Agustín take Taxis Verdes who will pick you up at your hotel. Buses can be caught along Av. Caracas, north of Calle 10, and can be stopped at street corners for: Zipaquirá, 1¼ hrs., US$0.45; Guatavita, 2-3 hrs., US$ 1.25; Chía, US$0.30.

Bus to Venezuela It is better not to buy a through ticket to Caracas with Exp. Berlinas as this does not guarantee a seat and is only valid for 2 Venezuelan companies; moreover no refunds are given in Cúcuta. Sometimes the border with Venezuela is closed because of illegal immigration; in this case, tickets can be refunded in Bogotá. Ideally, if you have time make the journey to Cúcuta in two stages to enjoy the scenery to the full. Bus connections from San Antonio de Táchira in Venezuela to Caracas are good.

Excursions from Bogotá

If you have a car, drive round the Av. Circunvalación for splendid views. The salt mines of Zipaquirá are described on **page 537**. Other excursions are to the beautiful artificial lake of Muña, formed by a dam; to *Sopó,* in the Sabana (63 km.), where they venerate an image of the Saviour which has appeared in an eroded stone; the paintings of angels in the church are very strange and worth seeing (ask at the Casa Cural for entry to church—give a tip); in Sopó a restaurant (previously *Nicolás*) serves good local dishes. Nearby are the Alpina yoghurt factory (no free samples) with another restaurant, *La Embarrada*, opposite, which specializes in cooking meat in clay dishes on coals; Parque Puerto de Sopó (with artificial lake) at km. 32.5 on Autopista Norte, and an amusement park a few km. N. For the Falls of Tequendama, **see below**. For Tunja (2 hrs. over first-class road), and Guatavita Nueva, **see page 539**. Bogotanos like to warm up at weekends: popular destinations are Melgar (**see below**) and Girardot (**Page 570**). About half-way to Girardot, near Fusagasugá (**see below**) is *Hotel Miramonti*, C, Italian-run family place, very quiet. To the east of Bogotá is **Choachí,** an attractive village set in a valley, where there are hot springs (good food at *El Colonial*, 1½ blocks from main square). Flota Macarena bus, Av. 17, No. 23-96, T 277-3900, several a day. A turnoff from the Choachi road brings one to the Santuario de San Francisco, with better views of Bogotá than one can get from Monserrate.

Hiking "Salsipuedes" is a hiking group based in Bogotá, hiking 15-25 km. every Saturday on trails in Cundinamarca; a very friendly group which welcomes visitors. Contact Alfonso Gamboa, Diagonal 123, No. 50-30, Bogotá.

Longer excursions are taken in four main directions, which are dealt with in the following pages. They are to the south-west (Fusagasugá, Melgar), the north-west (Facatativá, Guaduas, Villeta), the north (Chía, Zipaquirá) and the north-east (along the Cúcuta road). A fifth direction, east to the Llanos, will be dealt with separately.

South-West: The Simón Bolívar Highway runs from Bogotá to Girardot (**see page 570**); this 132-km. stretch is extremely picturesque, running down the mountains within 5 km. of the Salto de Tequendama.

At the **Salto de Tequendama,** the water of the Río Bogotá or Funza falls 132 metres over the lip of the Sabana; the water is dirty with sewage but the falls are still a spectacular sight though the smell can be most unpleasant. The site is 31 km. from Bogotá in an amphitheatre of forest-clad hill sloping to the edge of a rock-walled gorge. There is a good bus service from Bogotá.

After the Tequendama Falls turning is **Fusagasugá** which lies in a rich wooded valley famous for its fruits. A few kilometres beyond is the *Hotel Catama*. Fusagasugá is noted for its good climate and Sunday market. Population: 22,460, with an admixture of the wealthier families from Bogotá during the summer. A visit should be paid to the Jardín Luxemburgo for its splendid orchids, best flowering Nov.-Feb. but it is a long walk out of town; the Jardín Clarisa for orchids, and that at the Casa de la Cultura are pleasant. There are bathing spots on the Sumapaz river. Altitude: 1,740 metres. From Bogotá, Autos Fusa (Carrera 22, No. 14-27) and Cootransfusa (Carrera 14, Calle 10), US$1.

Hotels *La Scala*, F, rec.; *Castillo*, E, rec. There are many luxury hotels on the road to Melgar.

From Boquerón, beyond Fusagasugá, a side road goes about 10 km. to **Pandi** where there is a park with ancient stones. Nearby, on the road to Incononzu, is a famous natural bridge in a spectacular and very deep gorge through which runs the Sumapaz river.

Melgar, near Girardot, is a popular weekending place for Bogotanos who like a little warmth. There are lots of hotels in the area most of which have swimming pools; it is best to try whichever you like the look of and move on to another if it is full; the *Esmeralda*, *Plaza Crillón* (D) and *Nuevo Guadaira* have been recommended; there are also camping sites and the state-subsidized Cafam vacation centre, best visited in mid-week. Toll at 14 km. S of Fusagasugá, US$0.50, and 20 km. S of Bogotá, US$0.40.

North-West: The Sabana of Bogotá is dotted with white farms and groves of eucalyptus. The road passes through two small towns, Fontibón and Madrid. **Fontibón,** 10 km. from Bogotá, has a good colonial church, and about 3 km. outside the town are stones with Indian pictographs; nearby, on the road from the old Techo airport to Bogotá, there are replicas of San Agustín statues.

Facatativá, a town of 22,460 people, is 40 km. from Bogotá. Some 3 km. from Facatativá, on the road to the W, is the Piedras de Tunja, a natural rock amphitheatre of enormous stones; it has numerous Indian pictographs and has now been established as a park with an artificial lake. A road goes SW from Facatativá through Tocaima to Girardot. From **Tocaima**, a small, attractive holiday town (several hotels; *Bella Vista*, D, clean, friendly, good simple food, swimming pool, no hot water), a road runs through beautiful mountain country, via La Mesa, to Mosquera on the road between Madrid and Fontibón. This is a good alternative to the Simón Bolívar highway from Girardot to Bogotá.

71 km. from Facatativá is **Villeta** (9,700 inhabitants), which has become a popular weekend resort for the Bogotanos. Not far away are the waterfalls of Quebrada Cune. Hotels: *Pacífico* and *Mediterráneo* (both have swimming pools and are expensive); less expensive is the *Colonial Plaza*, Carrera 4, No. 6-07 (corner of main square), good restaurant, with swimmimg pool, pleasant. Nearby is *Llamarade* restaurant, good value; many good ice cream parlours around the square. The road continues to Honda (**see page 569**).

Midway between Villeta and Honda is **Guaduas;** in the main square is a statue of the liberator Policarpa Sala Varrieta. Also in the main square is a delightful colonial hotel. Public swimming pool in town. There is a Sunday market. Best local dish is *quesillos*. Bus to Honda, US$1.20, 1 hr. The surrounding countryside is beautiful, including waterfalls at Versalles (10 km.). Hotel: *Tacuara*, swimming pool, riding, *cabañas*, B; *Cacique*, 1 km. outside village, and *Real Agrada*, in resort area.

North: An interesting trip from Bogotá can be made to the salt mine of Zipaquirá and to the large centre of population around Chiquinquirá. Bogotá is left by an *autopista*, a northern extension of Avenida Caracas and Carrera 13. The *autopista* ends after 24 km. at an intersection where a road leads off left at a right-angle for Chía and Zipaquirá. Taking this road you soon come to a fork which takes you left to Chía and right to Zipaquirá. At the beginning of the road to Zipaquirá is the *Restaurant Arrieros*, where *antioqueño* food is served by waiters in the appropriate dress and *antioqueño* music is sometimes played.

Chía has a graceful colonial bridge and a typical Sunday market. Near Chía is Terijo, whose metalworks is famous. On the way there you pass through Fonqueta, where tapestries are made. Walk, or take a bus to La Barbanera church on a hill overlooking the *sabana* of Bogotá. Good restaurant just outside Chía, *Andrés Carne de Res*.

From Chía (via Cájica, 22,000 pop., pleasant town with good shopping) to **Zipaquirá** (40,850 people), centre of a rich cattle farming district, and famous for its rock salt mine, which has enough salt to last the world 100 years, though it has been exploited for centuries. The church in the central Plaza is also worth a visit for its stonework (despite its external appearance, it has a modern interior).

The immense black galleries of salt gleaming under electric lights are most impressive and a little eerie. A road has been opened into the galleries but because of damage cars are no longer allowed to drive in. You can walk its whole length in 15 mins. An underground cathedral dedicated in 1954 to Our Lady of the Rosary (patron saint of miners) is about 4 mins. on foot from the entrance and very impressive. The roof is 23 metres above the floor and the main altar table is a block of salt weighing 18 tons. It took ten years to complete. To photograph the interior you need a strong flash *and* a fast film. Entry (adults US$0.75, children US$0.37, open Tues.-Fri. 1100-1615, Sat. 0930-1200, 1300-1615, Sun. and holidays 1030-1614) is on a hill, which is a 20 mins. walk from the Plaza. Many buses from Avenida Caracas, Bogotá, US$0.45 each way, 1¼ hours. The Zipaquirá bus station is 15 minutes' walk from the mines and cathedral. Tours are also arranged by some of the Bogotá hotels and cost about US$15. Zipaquirá can also be reached from Tunja (**see page 539**), by taking a Bogotá-bound bus and getting off at Alcaro for connection to Zipaquirá, US$2. Leave plenty of time for the return journey as it can be difficult to stop Bogotá-Tunja buses at Alcaro. Minibus Zipaquirá- Chiquinquirá, US$2.75, 2 hrs.

The *Hostería del Libertador*, near the mine, good food, but no longer a hotel. *Hotel Colonial*, E, without bath, clean and friendly. Restaurants on main square, *El Mesón del Zipa*, good, cheap food, US$1.50-2.00; *Los Pijaos*, pleasant.

Not far from Zipaquirá, at **Nemocón**, there are salt mines and a church, but the mines have been closed to visitors, following accidents. A side (dirt) road connects with the Bogotá-Cúcuta highway.

A steam-hauled *tren turístico* runs on Saturday and Sunday at 0900 from the main station in Bogotá, calling at a halt at Calle 100 and Carrera 15 at 0927, going to Zipaquirá and Nemocón: 2 hrs. 20 mins. to Zipaquirá, 2 hrs. 45 mins. to Nemocón, where the train is met by the town band. At Nemocón there is time to have lunch and look around before train returns at 1800. Tickets in Bogotá from Tierra Mar Aire travel agency.

Ubaté is 48 km. by road to the N. On Sunday, the market in the big plaza has nothing of interest for the tourist. It is the cheese-making centre of the Sabana; the church is being refurbished. Here a branch road runs E to Lenguazaque (6,125 people). Close by, at Chirbaneque, is a worked-out emerald mine in lovely scenery. A spur from this road branches left to Guachetá, 21 km. from Ubaté, and slightly larger than Lenguazaque. Nearby is the Laguna de Fúquene (Devil's Lake, hotel), about 4,850 hectares of water with four cultivated islands.

Chiquinquirá, 50,000 people, 134 km. by road from Bogotá, is on the W bank of the Suárez river at 2,550 metres. It is a busy commercial centre and the focus of a large coffee and cattle region. In December thousands of pilgrims honour a painting of the Virgin whose fading colours were restored by the prayers of a woman. In 1816, when the town had enjoyed six years of independence and was besieged by the Royalists, this painting was carried through the streets by Dominican priests from the famous monastery, to rally the people. The town fell, all the same.

Hotels   *Moyba*, Carrera 9, No. 17-53, facing square, F, with bath (cheaper without); *Residencias San Martín*, Carrera 9, No. 19-84, F, basic; *Residencias Viajero*, G, opposite Banco de Colombia, good, cheap meals. Many others.

Restaurant   *El Escorial*, good but expensive.

In the shops of Chiquinquirá are displayed the toys made by local Indians: some ceramics painted in gay colours and others white and porous as they come from the kiln; tops and teetotums and other little things carved from tagua nuts; orange-wood balls to catch on a stick; the most durable tambourines in the world; shining, brightly coloured gourds; diminutive nine-stringed guitars on which children try the first measures of the *bambuca*; many scapularies; but better than anything else, the little pottery horses from Ráquira, or, by the same Indian craftsmen, little birds that whistle, hens with their chicks, and enchanting little couples dancing to an orchestra of guitars and mandolins.

Chiquinquirá has a new bus station. Bus from Chiquinquirá to Villa de Leiva takes 1¾ hr., US$1.70 (see page 540). Bus to Tunja, 3 hrs., US$3.25; to Zipaquirá, US$2.75; to Bogotá, 2½ hrs., US$3 (last returns at 1730).

Excursion   A road runs 105 km. SW to *Muzo*, on the banks of the Río Carare, 600 metres above sea-level. Population: 5,000. Sixteen km. away a famous open-cast emerald mine has been worked since 1567, and long before that by the Muzo tribe of Indians.

There are roads from Chiquinquirá to Tunja, the capital of the Department, and to Barbosa. Both are on the Bogotá-Cúcuta highway and are described below. On the Tunja road a short branch right at Tinjacá leads to **Ráquira**, where Indians make the pottery described above (sold in about 10 shops on the main street, including branch of Artesanías de Colombia). There's nowhere to stay, not much to eat. Market day Sunday. 30 minutes' walk along a very rough road is a beautiful 16th-century monastery, the Convento de la Candelaria, with anonymous 17th-century paintings of the life of St. Francis; they sell honey to finance the monastery. Also nearby are some waterfalls. The old colonial town of Villa de Leiva is also on this road. Ráquira is best reached from Tunja although there are direct buses from Bogotá (Rápido El Carmen, 0545, 0715, US$2.50, 6 hrs., returning 1300) on an appalling road. Last bus to Tunja 1330. If stuck after 1330, walk 5 km. to Tres Esquinas on Villa de Leiva-Chiquinquirá road (70 km.), where buses pass between 1530-1630, mostly going E.

BOGOTA TO CUCUTA (2)

A 618-km. road runs NE from Bogotá to Cúcuta, near the Venezuelan border, through Tunja, Barbosa, Monquirá, Socorro, San Gil, Bucaramanga and Pamplona. It runs through some beautiful scenery, and is good most of the way. Toll points 10 km. N of Bogotá, US$0.40, and at La Cara, S of Tunja, US$0.40. The railway via Tunja to Duitama and Sogamoso is now for freight only. The road out of Bogotá is the *autopista* to near Chía (**see page 537**), then follow Tunja signs.

At Sesquilé you can take a minor road to the right, to Guatavita Nueva.

Guatavita Nueva This modern town, 75 km. from Bogotá, was built in colonial style when the old town of Guatavita was submerged by a hydroelectric reservoir. Although the blend of old and new is fascinating, Guatavita Nueva has failed as a social experiment. All the country folk have left and it is now a weekend haunt for Bogotanos and tourists. (During the week the town is empty.) Cathedral, artisan workshops, museum, and small bull-ring for apprentices to practise Sun. afternoons. Sun. market best in morning, before Bogotanos get there. Bus from Bogotá (Flota Valle de Tenza, Carrera 25, No. 15-72, recommended; Flota Aguila, Carrera 15 No. 14-59), US$1.25, 2-3 hrs., departures 0730, 0800 and 0930; last return bus at 1730. You can walk (or ride, US$7 per horse) from the town to the Laguna de Guatavita (also called Lago de Amor by locals), where the legend of El Dorado originated, but it is a long (2-3 hr.) walk. It is easier to approach the lake from a point on the Sesquilé-Guatavita Nueva road (the bus driver will let you off at the right place) where there is a sign offering "Alpina Yoghurt" and a kiosk. It is a 2 hr. walk along a dirt track from the main road to the lakeside. This track can be driven to the lakeside (in the dry season, in a good car); turn right near the barn with the red door, and right again opposite small lake. Beside the lake are houses of rich Bogotanos.

There are no hotels in Guatavita Nueva, although rooms are sometimes to be found.

The basis of the El Dorado (Gilded Man) story is established fact. It was the custom of the Chibcha king to be coated annually with resin, on which gold dust was stuck, and then to be taken out on the lake on a ceremonial raft. He then plunged into the lake and emerged with the resin and gold dust washed off. The lake was also the repository (as with the *cenotes* in Yucatán, Mexico) of precious objects thrown in as offerings; there have been several attempts to drain it (the first, by the Spaniards in colonial times, was the origin of the sharp cut in the surrounding hills) and many items have been recovered over the years. The factual basis of the El Dorado story was confirmed by the discovery a few years ago of a miniature raft with ceremonial figures on it, made from gold wire, which is now one of the most prized treasures of the Museo de Oro in Bogotá. Part of the raft is missing; the story is that the gold from it is now reposing in one of the finder's teeth! (Read John Hemming's *The Search for El Dorado* on the subject.)

Beyond Chocontá (15,300 inhabitants), 88 km. from Bogotá, the route is across the western slopes of the Eastern Cordillera to Tunja, 137 km. from Bogotá.

Tunja, 180,000 inhabitants, capital of Boyacá Department, stands at 2,820 metres in an arid mountainous area. The climate is cold; mean temperature, 12°C. One of the oldest cities in Colombia, it was refounded as a Spanish city by Gonzalo Suárez Rendón in 1539. It was then the seat of the Zipa, one of the two Chibcha kings. The old city has been compared with Toledo, but the modern city is far less attractive. Of the many colonial buildings the most remarkable is the church of Santo Domingo, a masterpiece begun in 1594; the interior is covered with wood most richly carved. Another is the Santa Clara chapel (1580), now the hospital of San Rafael, with some fine wood carving. In Parque Bosque de la República is the adobe wall against which three martyrs of the Independence were shot in 1816. The Tourist Office in the Casa del Fundador (see below), on the main square, Plaza Bolívar, is helpful. Market open every day (good for *ruanas* and blankets). Bus from Bogotá, 2½-4½ hrs., US$3 (Duitama, Cotrans, and others). The bus station is a steep 500 metres from the city centre. Friday is market day.

The house of Don Juan de Vargas has been restored as a museum of colonial Tunja (0800-1200, 1300-1800). The Casa del Fundador Suárez Rendón, Plaza Bolívar, dates from 1540-43 and is one of the few extant mansions of a Spanish *conquistador* in Colombia; open as a museum (except Mon. and Tues.); see the unique series of plateresque paintings on the ceilings. The church of Santa Bárbara is full of colonial woodwork, and in the nearby parish house are some notable religious objects, including silk embroidery from the 18th century. Some houses still have colonial portals. There are some fine colonial buildings on Plaza Bolívar opposite the Cathedral. Also impressive is the church of San Ignacio.

The city formed an independent Junta in 1811, and Bolívar fought under its aegis during the campaign of the Magdalena in 1812. Six years later he fought the decisive battle of Boyacá, nearby (see below). For the Piedras de Tunja see under Facatativá (page 0).

Hotels　*Hostería San Carlos*, colonial style, good restaurant, highly rec.; *Pensión Suárez Rendón*, Plaza Bolívar (good food, D, friendly but basic); *Centenario*, hot water, good restaurant, D; *Res. Lord*, Calle 19, No. 10-64, F, small rooms but hot water, clean, friendly; *San Francisco*, Carrera 9, No. 18-90, on Plaza Bolívar, near cathedral, E, clean, check bill; also *Residencias Continental*, opposite cathedral, F, clean, meals US$1.25, but poor; *Príncipe*, F with hot water, small rooms but clean, near bus station, 5 mins. from Plaza Bolívar. Fairly cheap is *Dux*, off the plaza, F, quaint, basic; *Residencias Fundador* on the corner of Plaza Bolívar, F, has hot water, is safe and clean. Area around bus station said not to be safe at night.

Restaurants　Good cheap meal at *Bolo Club* and at a restaurant through an archway leading off the Plaza opposite the cathedral; *La Fonda*, US$1.50 for a big meal; *Estar de Hunzahúa*, Calle 20 No. 11-20 (2nd floor), good food and value, rec.; *Bodegón de los Frayles*, beside the church of San Ignacio, one block from the Plaza Bolívar, rec. as friendly with good food. On Carrera 10, there is a restaurant in a converted Jesuit church.

Bank　Banco de la República, Carrera 11, No. 18-12.

Excursions from Tunja　The battle of Boyacá was fought about 16 km. south of Tunja, on the road to Bogotá. On the bridge at Boyacá is a large monument to Bolívar. Bolívar took Tunja on August 6, 1819, and next day his troops, fortified by a British Legion, the only professional soldiers among them, fought the Spaniards on the banks of the swollen Río Boyacá. With the loss of only 13 killed and 53 wounded they captured 1,600 men and 39 officers. Only 50 men escaped, and when these told their tale in Bogotá the Viceroy Samao fled in such haste that he left behind him half a million pesos of the royal funds. There is now a huge modern restaurant overlooking the site.

On a hillside outside Tunja is the carved rock throne of the Chibcha king, the Zipa; ask for directions from the Tourist Office.

At *Paipa* there are municipal thermal baths, US$0.75, 30 mins. bus ride from Tunja, US$1. *Hotel Sochagota*, overlooking the lake, has a swimming pool fed by hot springs, C, cabins for hire, with 2 bedrooms, bathroom, log fires and private hot spring pools. Other places to stay include *Casona El Salitre* and *Panorama* (C, meals US$2.50, huge swimming pool, Turkish bath, sauna), *Cabañas El Portón*, Hotels *Victoria* and *La Posada*, *Posadero La Casona*, *Las Palmeras*, *Residencias Daza*, and *Minihotel Familiar* (all F p.p.). There are 7 restaurants: it's a popular centre for Colombians.

Villa de Leiva, an extremely pretty place, is reached by a branch road, left, at Arcabuco. (Toll at Arcabuco, US$0.40.) The drive affords some beautiful views and passes the Iguaque National Park which is the site of interesting oak woods and a lake, 2½ hrs. walk from the administration centre. (Camping is allowed and safe.) The town dates back, like Tunja, to the early days of Spanish rule, but unlike Tunja, it has been declared a national monument so will not be modernised. The first president of Nueva Granada (see page 523), Miguel Venero de Leiva, lived in the town. There are two colonial houses which are worth a visit: the house in which Antonio Nariño lived (Carrera 9, No. 10-39, open Tues.-Sun. 0900-1230, 1400-1800)—he translated the *Rights of Man* into Spanish—and the building in which the first Convention of the United Provinces of New Granada was held. Also worth a visit is the restored birthplace of the independence hero Antonio Ricuarte. A palaeontological museum has been opened 15 mins. walk N of the town on Carrera 9. The shops in the plaza have an excellent selection of Colombian handicrafts, while the Saturday market, not yet geared to the tourist trade, still offers many bargains. On the Plaza Mayor is the Casa-Museo Luis Alberto Acuña, housing fascinating examples of Acuña's work (recommended, entry US$0.40, US$0.35 extra to take photographs). The Monasterio de las Carmelitas has one of the best museums of religious art in Colombia, open Sat. and Sun. 1400-1700.

The mountains around Villa de Leiva abound in fossils. 5 km. along the road to Chiquinquirá can be seen the complete fossil of a dinosaur; there are road signs to it, ask for *El Fósil* (open 0800-1200, 1300-1500); the children sell fossils and rough emeralds. 2 km. from El Fósil along this road is the turning for (1 km.) the archaeological site known as El Infiernito, where there are several huge carved stones believed to be giant phalli and a solar calendar. 3 km. after the Infiernito turning, and one hour by bus (one per day) from Villa de Leiva is the Monastery of Ecce-Homo (founded 1620), which is worth a visit. The road goes through the desert of La Candelaria, a beautiful, highly-eroded countryside. Note the rectangular cromlech with 24 menhirs. Tourist Office just N of main square (Carrera 9, No. 13-01) most helpful. The town tends to be full of visitors at weekends and bank holidays.

Hotels *El Molino la Mesopotamia,* Calle del Silencio, which used to be a colonial mill, very good, C, meals US$4, breakfast US$3, including all meals (US$12.50), 10% rebate for booking 10 days ahead (closed during the first weeks of January), home cooking, excellent food, beautiful gardens. *Mesón de la Plaza Mayor,* Calle 79, No. 10-11, C (B full board), beautifully restored *hospedaría,* owner, Mauricio Ordóñez, speaks English, helpful; *El Marqués de San Jorge,* D, pleasant, on Calle 14, No. 9-20; *Hospedaje El Mesón de Los Virreyes,* Carrera 9, No. 14-51, D, with bath, good restaurant; *Cabaña Jequeneque,* opposite *la Mesopotamia,* D, with breakfast, open only at week-ends but rec. Unnamed *residencia* on Plaza Bolívar (the only one), F, hot water, pretty. *Hospedería Convento de San Francisco,* E, one of the cheaper hotels, quiet, spartan rooms, helpful staff, swimming pool not always filled; *Hospedería Duruelo,* C, above the town, magnificent view, good cooking, horse riding, rec., high standards. Accommodation with Señora Carmen Castaneda, Calle 14, No. 7-51, 4 rooms, all giving onto a flower-filled patio, E, clean, friendly; also Familia Fitortá, Calle 12, No. 7-55, E (F in week), breakfast extra, friendly, clean, safe. The telephone connection from Bogotá is poor and most hotels have reservation numbers in Bogotá. Information from the Tourist Office. Booking essential during holidays, and advisable at weekends (try bargaining Mon.-Thurs.). Accommodation also in *Hostería La Roca,* Calle 13, No. 9-54, F, hot water, very clean and pleasant, with rooms overlooking main square and reasonable breakfast, noisy at night because of bar music; cheap rooms available in bar-cum-bus-agency at entrance to town, also at restaurant/ *hospedaje* on the corner of the plaza near the Caja Agraria on the road out to Chiquinquirá, but some beds only have blankets, not mattresses over the springs. **Camping** at Los Olivares near village of Sáchica, 4 km. from Villa de Leiva (no services).

There are reasonable **restaurants** on the main square (try *Pueblito Viejo, Lino's Pizzeria,* very good, but expensive), and in and opposite the bus station. *La Parrilla,* Carrera 9, No. 9-17 and *Los Kioskos,* Carrera 9, No. 11-52; *Nueva Granada,* Carrera 9, No. 13-69, good value; *Los Balcones,* just off plaza, cheap, early breakfasts; *El Parrilón de los Caciques,* W side of town on Carrera 9, No. 9-05, warmly rec., good value. Visit the shop of Marcos A.Buitrago set in tropical gardens on El Paraíso de los Sachos, near the main square—he likes to talk to visitors.

Post Office in Telecom building, Calle 13, No. 8-26.

Another way of getting to Villa de Leiva is via Sáchica, either directly from Tunja or, coming from Bogotá, turning left (W) at the Boyacá monument, via Samacá. The houses are closed Monday-Friday out of season, but the trip is worth while just for the views. In any event, the town and surrounding hills are excellent for long, peaceful walks. Buses to Leiva from Tunja, 1 hr. 5 mins., US$1 with Flota Reina or Valle de Tenza company. (From Bogotá to Villa de Leiva, via Tunja, takes 4 hrs.) Colectivo taxis leave the bus station in Tunja for Villa de Leiva every hour and return from the main square. Leiva bus station in 8th block of Carrera 9. It is recommended to book the return journey on arrival. If driving from Tunja, watch out for rockfalls.

N.B. It is better not to visit Villa de Leiva on Mondays or Tuesdays as almost everything is closed.

From Tunja there are two possible routes to Cúcuta; the main road, almost entirely paved, goes via Bucaramanga, but the other via Duitama and Málaga, rejoining the main road at Pamplona, is also interesting, though there are few filling stations N of Sogamoso. In **Duitama** there is the interesting tourist complex Punta Larga, close to a furniture manufacturer. (*Hospedería D'la 18,* Carrera 18, No. 18-60, clean, quiet, F; many others nearby). About 3 km. from Duitama, on the road to Belencito, there is another hotel, also in an old *hacienda,* the *Hostería San Luis de Ucuenga.* Bus Duitama to Bucaramanga at 0900, 9 hrs., US$9. At Duitama turn right for **Sogamoso,** where a good museum of archaeology has been opened on the site of the centre of the precolumbian city. It is possible to camp in the museum grounds if you ask permission. A museum of religious art is open on the road from Duitama to Sogamoso (its most valuable exhibits were stolen in 1981). Hotel Hacienda Suescún, E, nearby in old *hacienda,* excellent service (but food not too good); Hotel Santa Marta, near bus station, F, clean, friendly (many others near Sogamoso bus terminal). E of Sogamoso the churches of Mongua (a pleasant colonial town, 20 km.) and Topaga are worth a visit, and so is the mountain-ringed **Lago de Tota** (3,015 metres above sea level). The *Refugio el Pozo Azul,* on the lakeside, is a private club run by Gary Clements and his Colombian wife, who will extend membership to readers of *The South American Handbook;* an excellent place to stay, in D price range, also has cabins for up to 7 people, US$40. Good food, fresh trout caught in the lake, suitable for children, very friendly atmosphere. Boats and fishing tackle for hire; good walking, and bird-watching country; recommended to book in advance, postal address: Apartado Aéreo 032, Sogamoso, Boyacá (or through Gladys García, Representative, Calle 80, No. 12-37, Bogotá, T 255-8682). Also on the lake is Las Rocas Lindas, D with bath and hot water, US$2.50 for each extra person, 2 cabins for 7 (US$30) one for 8 at Playa Blanca across the lake (US$40), boats for hire, dining room, bar, fireplaces, recommended. The owner, Sr. Mauricio Moreno Arenas, is very friendly. Aquitania is a cold, expensive town on the lake, reached by bus from Sogamoso, US$0.75, 1 hr.; bus from Bogotá (Rápido Duitama), via

Tunja and Sogamoso, goes round the lake to Aquitania, passing Cuitiva, Tota and the *Rocas Lindas* and *Pozo Azul* hotels (3 hr. wait in Aquitania). In Aquitania, *Residencia Venecia*, Calle 8, No. 144, F, with restaurant *Lucho* below, reasonable.

Just before the descent to the Lago de Tota, a road branches left, leading in 4 hours to **Yopal,** capital of the Intendencia of Casanare in the Llanos. (Pop. 10,000.) The road passes through *páramo* and virgin cloud forest. A fine waterfall can be reached in one hour's walk from the DAS checkpoint just above Pajarito. The best *residencias* in Yopal are usually full; direct buses from Sogamoso. **N.B.** Casanare and Arauca beyond are centres of guerrilla activity.

NE of Duitama, on the road to Málaga, is the turning at Belén for Paz de Río, where Colombia's national steelworks is sited; visitors can see over it. The road goes N to Soatá (*Residencias Colonial,* excellent, good restaurant; *Hotel Turístico,* E, swimming pool) and then descends to the very dry, spectacular valley of the Río Chicomocha.

By the bridge over the river at Capitanejo is the turning to the very attractive **Sierra Nevada del Cocuy** in the Eastern Cordillera. The Sierra extends in a half circle for 30 km., offering peaks of rare beauty, lakes and waterfalls. The area is good for trekking and probably the best range in Colombia for rock climbers. The most beautiful peaks are Cocuy (5,100 m.), Ritacuba Negra (5,200 m.), Ritacuba Blanca (5,200 m.) and El Castillo (5,400 m.). The area is good for climbing—details can be found in *Backpacking in Venezuela and Colombia* by George and Hilary Bradt. The main towns are **Cocuy,** on one side of the sierra, reached by Paz de Río bus from Bogotá, Av. 6, Carrera 15 (13 hrs., US$10), tourist office on Carrera 3, No. 8-06, *Residencia Cocuy,* F, cold water, laundry; and **Guicán,** on the other side, one hotel, F, good meals (extra), cold water. Both towns are 1-1½ hrs. drive by jeep from the mountains, so it is recommended to stay higher up. Above Guicán, you can stay at some farms or, at 3,600 metres, 3 tourist cabins have been built (each with 9 beds, well-furnished, open fires, electrically-heated showers, good meals included in room price, horses for hire), from which it is 3 strenuous hours' walk to the snowline on Ritacuba Blanca. This would also be the best base for the 2-3 day walk (described in the Bradts' book) round the N end of the Sierra and into Ratoncito valley, which is surrounded by snow-capped mountains. At Panquera is *Hospedaría El Portón de la Sierra,* owned by Jorge Ibáñez, who runs tours and has horses for hire, nice meals. Above Cocuy, accommodation is available at Estadero Don Pastor and, probably, Hacienda La Esperanza. Horses can be hired at both places. La Esperanza is the base for climbing to the Laguna Grande de la Sierra (3-4 hours), a large sheet of glacier-fed water surrounded by 5 snow-capped peaks, and also for the 2-day walk to the Laguna de la Plaza on the E side of the Sierra, reached through awesome, rugged scenery. Permission to camp can easily be obtained from the friendly people. It takes 1 to 2 days to walk between the two towns; maps available in Cocuy and La Esperanza. It takes 8-10 days to trek from one end to the other through a central rift, but equipment (crampons, ice pick, rope etc.) is necessary. The perpendicular rock mountains overlooking the Llanos are for professionals only. The area can also be reached by bus from Pamplona and Bucaramanga. The best weather is from December to April.

The area around **Málaga** is very picturesque: pretty red-tiled villages, horsemen in ponchos and cowboy hats, and mountains (some covered in flowering trees). The roads are twisty but spectacular. In Málaga there are several hotels (including *Príncipe,* near main square, F, shared bathroom, clean, friendly, good meals) and restaurants. Good bus services to Duitama (6 hrs.), Bucaramanga and Pamplona.

The main road goes on to **Barbosa** (*Hotel Príncipe,* clean rooms with private bath; *El Palacio del Pollo,* good, simple roadside restaurant), 64 km. NW in the Department of Santander. Eleven km. from Barbosa, at Puente Nacional, is *Agua Blanca,* a splendid hotel with a swimming pool.

A road runs NW to the Magdalena at Puerto Olaya, opposite Puerto Berrío. Eighteen km. from Barbosa is **Vélez,** a charming little town where horses and mules are raised. (*Hotel Galés,* G.)

The road (toll at Santana, US$0.40) goes NE for 84 km. to

Socorro (23,500 people), with steep streets and single storey houses set among graceful palms. It has a singularly large and odd stone church. The local museum, La Casa de la Cultura, is worth seeing, as is the market which is open every day.

At Socorro, in 1781, began the revolt of the peasant *comuneros:* not a movement for independence but a protest against poverty. It was led at first by a woman, Manuela Beltrán, and then, when other towns joined, by Juan Francisco Berbeo. They marched as far as the salt town of Zipaquirá, N of Bogotá; rebel terms were accepted by the Spaniards, and sworn to by the Bishop of Bogotá, but when they had returned home troops were sent from Cartagena and there were savage reprisals. Another woman from Socorro, Antonia Santos, led guerrillas fighting for independence and was captured and executed by the Spaniards in 1819; her statue is in the main square. The Casa de Cultura museum (opening hours vary according to season) has disappointingly little information on these local heroines, but is still worth a visit.

Hotels *Tamacara*, swimming pool, new, B-C; *Venezia*, F, with shower, has dining room, nice old rooms, good value (single women beware peeping toms); *Sucre*. **Restaurant** *Chanchón*; *Panadería Imperial*, Calle 14 y Cra. 13, very good, simple; avoid the local hamburger joint.

About 21 km. beyond Socorro is *San Gil*, an unspoilt and friendly colonial town with a good climate, which has the tourist attraction of El Gallineral, a riverside spot whose beautiful trees are covered with moss-like tillandsia. Bus to Bogotá, US$6; to Bucaramanga, US$1.90.

Hotels *Bella Isla* (swimming pool), C, a good stopover on the Bogotá-Cúcuta run (locked parking); *San Gil*, F, showers, clean, friendly; *Alcantuz*, Carrera 11, No. 10-15, E, clean, good location, pleasant but noisy facing street; *Residencias Royal*, Calle 10 y Carrera 10, F with bath but no a/c; *Residencias Guananta*, Calle 11 (same block as *Hotel Bogotá* and *Colombia*), F, small, clean, hard beds, noisy in daytime; *Pensión Victoria*, E, motorcycle parking, clean and friendly.

Restaurants Just outside Pinchote on the road from Socorro to San Gil is the *Mesón del Cuchicote*, which specializes in dishes from the Santander region. A good restaurant in San Gil is *Herberduc*, US$2-5; also good and cheap is *Santandereano*; *El Turista* is adequate; *Dusi's King*, on plaza, fast food.

A road runs E from San Gil to Onzaga (bus), through Mogotes and San Joaquín, dropping from high mountain ridges to tropical valleys. From Onzaga it is 20 km. to Soatá (see previous page); no public transport, if walking make sure you take the right road.

21 km. from San Gil is *Barichara*, a beautiful colonial town at 1,830 metres, founded in 1714 and designated as a national monument to preserve its character. There are many places of historical interest, the most important being the house of the former president Aquiles Parra (the woman next door has the key).

Hotel La Notoria, F, clean, comfortable, showers in rooms, no meals, you can make your own coffee, "elegant, friendly, talkative" landlady. 3 rooms for visitors available in the restaurant (not museum) *Casa de la Cultura* (F, and excellent meals for US$2). Buses from San Gil, from main plaza, US$0.75, 1 hr. An interesting excursion is to Guane, a town 9 km. away by road, or 1½ hrs. walk by trail, where there is an interesting archaeological museum in the priest's house, large collection of coins and a mummified woman (admission, US$0.25).

About 24 km. beyond San Gil, a little off the road, is the picturesque village of Aratoca, with a colonial church. Ten km. further on, the descent from the heights along the side of a steep cliff into the dry canyon, with spectacular rock colours, of the Río Chicamocha is one of the most dramatic experiences of the trip to Cúcuta, but, if driving, this is a demanding and dangerous stretch.

Bucaramanga, 420 km. from Bogotá, is the capital of Santander Department. It stands at 1,018 metres on an uneven plateau sharply delimited by eroded slopes to the N and W, hills to the east and a ravine to the S. The city was founded in 1622 but was little more than a village until the latter half of the 19th century. The metropolitan area has a population of 700,000, which has expanded rapidly because of the success of coffee, tobacco and staple crops. The Parque Santander is the heart of the modern city, while the Parque García Rovira is the centre of the colonial area. Just off Parque García Rovira is the Casa de Bolívar, Calle 37, No. 12-15, an interesting museum (0900-1200, 1400-1700, free, closed Sat. and Sun.). Opposite is the Casa de Cultura. Casa Perú de la Croix, Calle 37, No. 11-18, is a beautiful colonial mansion (closed, temporarily it is hoped, in 1989). There is a pleasant park where the market next to the bus station used to be. The city's great problem is space for expansion. Erosion in the lower, western side topples buildings over the edge after heavy rain. The fingers of erosion, deeply ravined between, are spectacular. The Club Campestre is one of the most beautifully set in Latin America. There is an amusement park, Parque El Lago, in the suburb of Lagos I, SW of the city on the way to Floridablanca.

Average maximum temperature is 30°C; average minimum, 19.4°C. Rainfall is about 760 mm., and humidity is high (68% to 90%).

Hotels *Chicamocha*, luxury, Calle 34, No. 31-24, A, a/c, clean; *Bucarica*, spacious, on main plaza, C, private bathroom, telephone, exceptionally good value, good restaurant and snack bar; *Andino*, Calle 34, No. 18-44, D, private bath; *Ruitoque*, nr. plaza, D, nice, colour TV; *Carolina*, near bus terminals, E, private bathroom, no hot water, some air-conditioned rooms; *Zulima*, Calle 36, Carrera 22, E, with bath, no hot water, also has an annex on Calle 31; *Balmoral*, uphill from centre, Calle 35, Carrera 21, E, with bath; *El Pilar,* Calle 34, Carrera 25, E (bargain), clean, hot water, rec., good service and food; *El Edén,* Calle 31, No. 19-25, one block from bus station, E, clean, safe; *Tamana,* Carrera 18, No. 30-31, E with bath, F without, clean, friendly, rec. A few blocks uphill from the bus terminal are several *residencias;* one is *Residencias Colonial,* rec., D, with hot shower and w.c., T.V., bar, expensive; another is *San Pablo,* G, clean and good; *Hospedaje y Lanchería La 55,* one block uphill from the Copetran terminal, F, good lodgings and restaurant. *Amparo,* Calle 31, Carrera 20, E, with bathroom, good; *Pasajeros,* F with bath, clean, comfortable, near bus station. *Morgan,* Calle 35 y Carrera 19, E-F, 2 blocks from bus station, central, old and new wings, O.K. Wide variety of hotels on Calle 31, between Carreras 18-21. *Residencias Real,* Calle 33 y Carrera 19, clean, friendly but noisy early a.m. Accommodation at the *Club Campestre,* E, is good, but you must have an introduction; try the mayor's office or Chamber of Commerce. **Note:** Since Bucaramanga is the site for numerous national conventions, it is sometimes hard to find a room.

Camping Half-an-hour drive S of Bucaramanga, on left of dual carriageway, with swimming pool and waterside restaurant.

Restaurants *La Carreta,* Calle 27, No. 42-27, excellent, not cheap, delightful surroundings, music at times; *Mi Bodequín,* Carrera 17, No. 31-77, also good; good food at *Club del Comercio* (by invitation or introduction). *Di Marco,* Calle 48, Carrera 29 esquina, excellent meat; *La Brasa,* Carrera 33, No. 34, good typical meals; *La Tranquera,* Carrera 33, Calle 40, good Baby Beef, US$6; *Corcobado,* on hill overlooking town Km. 4 road to Pamplona (another branch in Cabecera), slow service, but good, expensive; *La Puerta del Sol,* Carrera 30, No. 62-304 and *La Fonda,* Vía Girón Km. 4, serve typical dishes; *El Maizal,* Calle 31, No. 20-74, and *Consulado Antioqueño,* Carrera 19, No. 33-81, both serve Antioquian food; *Portofino,* Calle 37, No. 13-13, good; *Fujiyama,* Calle 38, No. 33-34, Chinese; *Oriental* and *Tokio,* both on Carrera 18, between Calles 35 and 34; in same area, *Aldana,* good grills; *Pesquera,* Carrera 33, for seafood; *Krakus,* Carrera 33, No. 38-02, Colombia's only Polish restaurant, good; pizzas at: *Piz Pan Pum,* Carrera 33, No. 31-107 (next to Cinema Rivera), *Oskar's* and *Alero del Castillo* in Centro Comercial Cabecera, also *Super Pizza,* Centro Comercial Cabecera (pizza by the slice, hamburgers, etc.). *Lonchería La 36,* Calle 36, No. 13-02, very good savoury pasties and snacks; *Desayunadero La 18,* opposite the Copetran terminal, cheap, friendly, English spoken, open every day till late; good snack bars including *Mucho Pin...chos* (Calle 54, No. 31-07); *Mar Villa* (in the centre and at Centro Comercial Cabecera); *Almuerzo Colonial,* Carrera 33, No. 38-33, good fixed price lunch only; *Los Arrayanes,* Calle 32, No.29, good value, especially lunchtime; *El Tony,* Carrera 33, No. 33, very popular, live music late at night; *Gran Gastby* (correct spelling! Carrera 33, No. 30-30).

Vegetarian: *Genesis,* Calle 35 y Carrera 25, good; *El Toronjil,* vegetarian at Carrera 33, No. 52-123, a bit dear; *Berna,* Calle 35, No. 18-30, best pastries in town. Try the *hormigas* (large black ants), a local delicacy mainly eaten during Holy Week. Service in Bucaramanga's many restaurants is slow, so be warned.

Discotheques On road to Girón are *El Pulpo* and *Capricornio; Ulisses 2000,* Av. Quebrada Seca y Carrera 28, gay. Many on Carrera 33, try *Silver Rose.*

Shopping Camping equipment, *Acampemos,* Calle 48, No. 26-30, last place in Colombia to get camping gas cartridges before Venezuela. Handicrafts in Girón (expensive—see below) and typical clothing upstairs in the food market, Calle 34 y Carreras 15-16. Similar articles (*ruanas,* hats) in San Andresito. *Fería de artesanías* in first 2 weeks of September, usually near the Puerta del Sol.

Banks Banco Anglo Colombiano, Calle 36, No. 20-04, and agency on Carrera 15. Banco de la República, Carrera 19, No. 34-93, is the only bank authorized to cash travellers' cheques. Long queues (cheques and passports have to be photocopied). Many other banks. Open Mon.-Fri. 0800-1130, 1400-1600, and last working day of month, 0800-1030. Closed Sats.

Tourist Office Carrera 19, Calle 35, friendly and knowledgeable.

Transport Taxis do not have meters but the fare within the city is US$0.70 (US$0.75 at night). Buses charge US$0.10.

Airport Palonegro, on three flattened hilltops on other side of ravine S of city. Spectacular views on take-off and landing. 3 Avianca flights to Bogotá, US$40, regularly overbooked; US$19 to Cúcuta. Flights to Medellín, at US$36, are better value and less hassle than going by bus. Taxi, US$3-4; colectivo, US$1. Buses are scarce despite the fact that some bus boards say "Aeropuerto" (direction "Girón/Lebrija" from Diagonal 15).

Roads To the Magdalena at Barrancabermeja, 174 km.; to Cúcuta, 198 km.; to Bogotá, 420 km.; to Medellín, 1,010 km.; to Santa Marta, 550 km., all paved.

Buses Bus terminals are mostly around Diagonal 15, S of the centre, until the new terminal on the Girón road has been completed. To Bogotá, 8-11 hrs.; US$9 (Pullman) with Berlinas del Fonce, Carrera 18, No. 31-06 (this journey is uncomfortable, there are no relief stops, and it starts off hot and ends cold in the mountains, come prepared), Copetran, Calle 55, No. 17B-57, has 3 classes of bus to Bogotá including Pullman, 10 hrs, US$10; Tunja, 9 hrs., US$5.10; Barranquilla, 9 hrs. (US$13.50 first class with Copetran); Cúcuta, 6 hrs., US$4.25 (Pullman), Berlinas buses often arrive full from Bogotá, Cotran also to Cúcuta; colectivo to Cúcuta, US$6; Santa Marta, 9 hrs., maybe more according to season, US$15 with Copetran; Barrancabermeja, 3 hrs., US$1.90, a scenic ride with one rest stop permitted; this road is now paved. Hourly buses to San Gil, US$1.90. To Berlín, US$1.

Excursions   The suburb of *Floridablanca*, 8 km. SW, has the famous El Paragüitas gardens, belonging to the national tobacco agency, reputed locally as "a replica of the Garden of Eden" - and known particularly for its pineapples; you can get a free pass (two needed if you want to visit both a.m. and p.m.) to the gardens from the Tourist Office in town. The gardens are now under development and open at weekends (1000-1130 and 1500-1630 only). It's a 2-hour walk from Bucaramanga to Floridablanca, but not very interesting; there are plenty of buses. Take the Cotandra bus (US$0.25) from Carrera 22, Bucaramanga, either Florida Villabel which goes by El Paragüitas, or Florida Autopista (continuation of Carrera 33) which goes direct to the square in Florida and you have to walk about a km. Toll on road to Floridablanca, US$0.20. *Rincón Santanera* restaurant, Cra. 8, No.4-41, good local food.

Lebrija (20,400 people), 17 km. to the W, is in an attractive plain. Rionegro (36,750 people) is a coffee town 20 km. to the N with, close by, the Laguna de Gálago and waterfalls. *Girón* (27,500 people) a tobacco centre 9 km. SW of Bucaramanga on the Río de Oro, is a quiet and attractive colonial town, filled with Bumangueses at weekends, with a beautiful church. The buildings are well preserved and the town unspoilt by modernization. By the river are *tejo* courts and popular open air restaurants with *cumbia* and *salsa* bands; in the square at weekends, sweets and *raspados* (crushed ice delights) are sold. (Hotels: *San Juan de Girón*, B, outside town on road from Bucaramanga, swimming pool; *Río de Oro*, in centre. Restaurant: *Mansión del Fraile* on the square, in a beautiful colonial house, good food—Bolívar slept here on one occasion, ask to see the bed.) Take the bus from Carrera 15 or 22 in Bucaramanga, US$1.45. In *Piedecuesta*, 18 km. SE of Bucaramanga (bus from Carrera 22, US$0.35, 45 mins.), you can see cigars being hand-made, furniture carving and jute weaving—cheap, hand-decorated *fique* rugs can be bought. There are frequent buses to all these places; a taxi costs US$5. Corpus Christi processions in these towns in June are interesting. They are all dormitory towns for the city, so there is plenty of public transport.

Another excursion is to *California*, about 30 km. NE of Bucaramanga, where there are gold mines that tourists can visit.

The road (bad and narrow) runs E to Berlín, and then NE (a very scenic run over the Eastern Cordillera) to Pamplona, about 130 km. from Bucaramanga.

Berlín has been recommended to the hardy camper as challenging and rewarding. The village lies in a valley at 3,100 metres, the peaks surrounding it rise to 4,350 metres and the temperature is constantly around 10°C, although on the infrequent sunny days it may seem much warmer. The scenery is awesome. The inhabitants are tolerant of visitors; ask a farmer for permission to camp in his field. There are no hotels, but there are several basic eating places. It has been recommended as an ideal place to appreciate the grandeur of the Eastern Cordillera and the hardiness of the people who live on the *páramo*.

Pamplona, Department of Santander del Norte, lies amid mountains at 2,200 metres. Population, 23,200. The climate is cold and uninviting, but the town is definitely worth seeing. Founded in 1548, it became important as a mining town but is now better known as a university city. Few modern buildings have as yet broken its colonial harmony. Cathedral in the spacious central plaza. The earthquake of 1875 played havoc with the monasteries and some of the churches: there is now a hotel on the site of the former San Agustín monastery, but it may still be possible to visit the ex-monasteries of San Francisco and Santo Domingo. The Iglesia del Humilladero, adjoining the cemetery, is very picturesque and allows a fine view of the city. Museum of religious art at Calle 5 y Carrera 5. See the Casa Colonial archaeological museum, Calle 6, No. 2-56, open Tues-Sat., 0900-1200, 1400-1800; Sun., 0900-1200. The town's easter celebrations are famous throughout Colombia.

Hotels   *Cariongo*, Carrera 5, Calle 9, D, very good, excellent restaurant (locked parking available); *Montaña*, Carrera 6, No. 8-02, E; *Residencias Doran*, Carrera 6, No. 7-21, E with bath (F without), large rooms, good meals, US$1.50; *Anzoátegui*, F with bargaining, for dinner, bed and breakfast. *Orsua*, on main square, F, clean, friendly, cheap, good food also available; *Llanos*, Calle 9 y Carrera 7, F, motorcycle parking, rec. Hotel accommodation may be hard to find at weekends, when Venezuelans visit the town.

Restaurant   *El Doran*, meals for US$1.60. *La Casona*, Calle 6, No. 6-57, limited but good menu; *El Gran Duque*, on main square, student-run, good music. *Los Bucaros*, close to main square, good value set meal US$2.

Shopping   Pamplona is a good place to buy *ruanas*. Good indoor market.

Banks   do not change dollars or travellers' cheques in Pamplona.

Tourist Office   Calle 5 y Carrera 6, on main plaza.

Buses   To Bogotá, US$11.50, 13-16 hrs.; to Cúcuta, US$1.65; to Bucaramanga, US$2.75, 4 hrs.; to Málaga, 0930 8 hrs. in dry weather, beautiful but very hard journey; to Tunja, US$9, 12 hours (leaving at 0600). To Berlín, US$1.75.

It is a run of 72 km. from Pamplona through sparsely populated country, descending to an altitude of only 215 metres, to Cúcuta.

Cúcuta, capital of the Department of Santander del Norte, and only 16 km. from the Venezuelan frontier, was founded 1734, destroyed by earthquake 1875, and then rebuilt, elegantly, with the streets shaded by trees, and they are needed for it is hot: the mean temperature is 29°C. Population: 600,000. Coffee is the great crop in the area, followed by tobacco. There are also large herds of cattle.

Cúcuta, because it is the gateway of entry from Venezuela, was a focal point in the history of Colombia during the wars for independence. Bolívar captured it after his lightning Magdalena campaign in 1813. The Bolívar Column stands where he addressed his troops on February 28, 1813. At El Rosario de Cúcuta, a small town of 8,000 inhabitants 14½ km. from Cúcuta on the road to the frontier, the First Congress of Gran Colombia opened on May 6, 1821. It was at this Congress that the plan to unite Venezuela, Ecuador, and Colombia was ratified; Bolívar was made President, and Santander (who was against the plan) Vice-President. (Santander was born at a *hacienda* near El Rosario which is now being developed as a tourist centre.) The international bridge between Colombia and Venezuela is a few km. from El Rosario; just beyond it is San Antonio del Táchira, the first Venezuelan town, and 55 km. on is San Cristóbal.

Hotels   *Tonchalá*, Calle 10, Av. 0, B, good restaurant, swimming pool, air conditioning, airline booking office in hall; *Tundaya*, Calle 10, No. 6-21, E, comfortable; *Victoria Plaza*, Calle 8, No. 2-98, D; also D are *Frontera*, Calle 12, No. 7-36 and *Sol*, Calle 10, No. 7-51; *Casa Blanca* (swimming pool), D, good, reasonable meals, rec.; *Nohra*, on main square, E, friendly; *Aurora*, Calle 11 No. 3-52, F, central, friendly, good cheap restaurant; *Residencias Los Rosales*, near bus station, Calle 2, 8-39, fan and private bath, good, F; *Imperial*, Av. 7, No. 6-28, F with bath, clean, secure, highly rec.; *Residencia Mary* at bus station, E, with bath (cheaper per person in triple room), good. Also near the bus station are *Zulia*, F, with bath, clean; and *Residencias Catacumba*, F, good value. *Residencias Los Dos Santanderes*, Calle 1 between Av. 9 and 10, F; *Amaruc*, Av. 5, No. 9-37, E, with fan, private bath, no hot water.

Restaurants   *"M"*, also called *Chez Esteban*, on road to Venezuela, very good; *Bahía*, just off main square, pleasant; other good restaurants at reasonable prices are *El Pollo Especial*, *El Jarrón de Baviera*, *Cantón* (Chinese).

Shopping   A good range of leather goods at possibly the best prices anywhere in Colombia. Cuchitril, Av. 3 No. 9-89, has a selection of the better Colombian craft work.

Exchange   A good rate of exchange for pesos is to be had in Cúcuta, at the airport, or on the border. There are money changers on the street all round the main square and many shops advertise the purchase and sale of bolívares. The price is usually better than at the Banco de la República, Diagonal Santander, Avs. 3E y 4E. Change pesos into bolívares in Cúcuta or San Antonio—difficult to change them further into Venezuela. AmEx and Citicorp travellers' cheques can be exchanged only in Banco de la República.

Tourist Office   Calle 10, No. 0-30, helpful, has maps, etc. At airport. Other maps obtainable from Instituto Geográfico, Banco de la República building; in the main plaza.

Airports   At Cúcuta for Colombian services (to Bogotá, at least twice a day, US$40 if paid in pesos, with Avianca; less with Satena, and with Aerotal), and at San Antonio, Venezuela (30 minutes) for Venezuelan domestic lines. At latter, be sure all baggage is sealed after customs inspection and the paper seals signed and stamped.

Note   Cúcuta is a great centre for smuggling. Be careful.

Transport   To San Cristóbal colectivo, US$2; bus, US$1 (Bolivariano); to San Antonio taxi US$6; bus US$0.30. Bus to Bogotá, hourly, 17-24 hrs., US$15, Berlinas del Fonce 1400, 2 stops, including 15 mins. with free refreshments in Bucaramanga, or Bolivariano, 20 hrs., often delayed at check points. There are frequent buses, even during the night. To Bucaramanga, US$4.25, 6 hrs, with Berlinas del Fonce Pullman, several departures daily; from there a connection to

Barranquilla can be made. To Tunja, US$9. The road is bad for the first part of the journey. Bus station: Avenida 7 and Calle O (a really rough area). Taxi from bus station to town centre, US$2.

Warning All sorts of odd practices at the bus station have been reported: watch out for dubious money changers, ticket sellers and security officers claiming to be from the tourist office (who tell you to put all your money in your socks—this is a ruse to rob you, we've received many reports). Don't put your valuables in bus company "safety boxes"; you'll get out half what you put in (Berlinas del Fonce is the most trustworthy company). Make sure tickets are for buses that exist; tickets do not need to be "stamped for validity". For San Cristóbal, only pay the driver of the vehicle, not at the offices upstairs in the bus station.

There are good roads to Caracas (933 km. direct or 1,046 km. via Mérida), and to Maracaibo (571 km.). Bus to Caracas, 14 hrs., Expreso Occidente, two daily, US$13; taxi colectivo US$15.75.

If travelling from **Venezuela to Colombia**, it is cheaper to fly Caracas-San Antonio (US$30 approx.), take a taxi to Cúcuta (US$6), then take an internal Colombian flight, than to fly direct from Caracas to Colombia. It will, of course, take longer. The airport transfer at San Antonio is well organized, with taxi drivers calling at necessary immigration offices, and at exchange places, the trip taking 25 mins. You do not have to buy your Colombian ticket in Cúcuta, you can make a reservation and purchase a ticket in a travel agency in Venezuela some days in advance (check exchange rates to see whether it is better to pay in Venezuela or Colombia). With a computer (*localizador*) reference number, you can avoid queues.

N.B. All visitors need a visa and tourist card to enter Venezuela. There is a Venezuelan Consulate at Cúcuta (Av. O, Calle 8—open 0800-1300, Mon.-Fri.) which supplies these—same applies at Venezuelan Embassy in Bogotá (may send you to Cúcuta for visas, etc.). You must also provide one photograph for a visa; evidence of onward transportation out of Venezuela, often with a date, is officially required, and proof of funds is sometimes requested. You are strongly advised to obtain visa and card from the Venezuelan embassy in your own country, if you know in advance when you will be arriving at the frontier. (Just to visit San Antonio de Táchira in Venezuela, no documents are required.) As there are no Colombian exit/entrance formalities at the international border bridge, it is necessary to obtain a DAS exit stamp before leaving the country from the offices in Cúcuta (open 0800-1200, 1400-1800, Mon.-Fri.; Avenida Primera, No. 28-57, 2 km. from centre); at weekends and holidays you must go to the DAS office at the airport. If you do not, you will be turned back by Venezuelan customs officials, and the next time you enter Colombia, you will be subject to a fine of US$7.50. Similarly, if arriving from Caracas, make sure bus stops at border for Venezuelan exit formalities. Obtain Colombian tourist card at the border, and entrance stamp from the DAS in Cúcuta because your passport will not be checked again until Pamplona. Border checks in Cúcuta are very strict. Air travellers can undertake all Colombian formalities at Cúcuta airport. Entering or leaving Colombia by car, you must have your passport stamped at the DAS in town and the car papers stamped at the Customs (Aduana) office on the road to the airport—watch hard for the small sign. At the Customs Office is a restaurant serving excellent, large meals for US$2. Venezuelan car documentation is checked at the border post in San Antonio.

7 km. from Cúcuta is Zulia (Petróleo *buseta*), worth a visit if waiting for a Venezuelan tourist card.

The Andes chain N of Cúcuta is the branch which sweeps north to the Guajira Peninsula after the bifurcation of the Eastern Cordillera near Cúcuta: the other branch crosses into Venezuela. This western branch is the Sierra de Perijá y Motilones, in which live the Motilones Indians, the only Indians in Colombia who have refused to accept absorption into the larger nation. Little is known of them; they have killed many of the missionaries sent to convert them, and the anthropologists sent to study them.

THE LLANOS AND LETICIA (3)

A spectacular 110-km. road (due for improvement) runs from Bogotá to **Villavicencio,** capital of Meta Department in the Llanos at the foot of the eastern slopes of the Eastern Cordillera. Population: 300,000. Rice is now grown near Villavicencio and milled there for transport to Bogotá. Altitude: 498 metres. The town fills up at weekends. It is also full of military police owing to guerrilla activity to the SE.

Hotels *Villavicencio*, in town, D, suites available, a/c, hot water, very comfortable, good restaurant, tell them if you don't want extras—TV, telephone, newspaper—and you won't be charged; *Centauros*, in centre, E, reasonably clean and quiet, small rooms; *Inambú*, E plus extras, Calle 37A, No. 29-49, central; *Savoy*, Carrera 31, No. 41-01, E, with shower and air conditioning, clean and friendly; *Carimagua*, F, shower, rec. *Residencias Don Juan*, Carrera 28, No. 37-21 (Mercado de San Isidro), attractive family house, E, with bath and fan, sauna, safe, rec. *El Nogal*, F, clean, comfortable, good value. *Residencias Myriam* (off main square), F, fairly clean, check roof for leaks.

Restaurants On main square: *Palace*, rec.; *La Brasa*. One Chinese; others, some with swimming pools, on the road to Puerto López.

Tourist Office on main square (Plaza Santander), helpful.

Airport Flights to Miraflores and Mitú for those who want to see "uncommercialized" jungle. To Puerto Carreño: Urraca, a freight service with some seats, 0630, Mon., Wed., Fri., arrive early to get a seat, 1½ hrs. Taxi to town, US$2; bus US$0.30.

Buses La Macarena and Bolivariano run from Bogotá about every half-hour, US$2.75, 4 hrs.; alternatively there are colectivos (e.g. Velotax, US$3.50, or Autollanos who run every hour, US$5.25). Be prepared to queue for tickets back to Bogotá.

Villavicencio is a good centre for visiting the Llanos and jungles stretching 800 km. E as far as Puerto Carreño, on the Orinoco, with Venezuela across the river. Cattle raising is the great industry on the plains, sparsely inhabited by mestizos, not Indians. The cattle town of San Martín may be visited by bus from Villavicencio, 1½ hrs., US$1.20 each way.

A good asphalt road has been built E from Villavicencio to *Puerto López* on the Meta river, a port of call for large river boats. Hotels: *Tío Pepe*, D, with swimming pool; *Marichal*, E, fans but no a/c, swimming pool; two good *residencias*: *Doña Empera*, F, and *Popular*, F, cheaper, friendly, every bed with mosquito net, good meals. Good food also at *Restaurante Yamiba*. Armando Mildenberg, at *Res. Popular*, speaks German, some English and French, is helpful; he may be able to arrange tours in the *llanos*, or trip to Puerto Carreño. The road E (unpaved and poor, but reported to be about to be improved) continues for another 150 km. through Puerto Gaitán, where there are hotels and restaurants, and San Pedro to Arimena. Here the road branches: one road goes N to the Río Meta at El Porvenir, where a ferry (dry season only) takes you across the river to the Orocue tourist centre, E, swimming pool, excursions. The main road, now degenerated to a rough track impassable in the wet season, continues E through Vichada to Puerto Carreño.

Puerto Carreño (population about 5,000) has two banks (one of which changes travellers' cheques); shopkeepers will exchange Venezuelan bolívares. The DAS office and Venezuelan Consulate are on the Plaza Bolívar. Passports are checked at the waterfront, then you must go to the DAS office and insist on having your passport stamped on entry. You may encounter problems over documents; the military are active in the area and frequently demand permits and proof of how much money you have, and carry out spot checks. There is a Satena office; next to it is *Residencias Mami*, F; *Hotel Samanave*, F (more expensive) with fan, clean, but breakfast is poor value; *Residencias La Vorágine*, F, friendly, clean, safe, good; the *residencia* on the waterfront doubles as a brothel.

For boats to Puerto López, be prepared to wait 4-5 days; check with Ulises, a bar owner on the river front by the moorings (he gives free coffee to those prepared to help with his son's English lessons). Between December and May, a bus runs on Thursday between Puerto López and Puerto Carreño at 0500, taking 2 days, night spent at La Primavera, US$25 (Flota La Macarena).

Air Services To Villavicencio and Bogotá with Satena on Tues., Thurs., and Sat., about US$50 to Bogotá; to Villavicencio, 4 hrs., following the Orinoco south as far as San Fernando de Atabapo, stopping at Inírida, not far from the confluence of the river of the same name with the Orinoco (*Hotel Orinoco* and *Refugio Safari*).

To Venezuela Launches take about 25 minutes to cross to Burro, stopping at Puerto Páez, from which Caracas can be reached by road. *Por puesto* service is available to Puerto Ayacucho.

The road S from Villavicencio is surfaced as far as San Martín. It runs on to *Granada* (*Hotel Yali*; *Tío Pepe Motel*, very clean) and from there deteriorates rapidly. *Vistahermosa* (Macarena bus from Bogotá, 0845, US$5, 9 hrs.), situated near the break-point between the Llanos and the jungle, lies further S along this road (*Residencias Royal* is cheap and comfortable; *Lilian's* restaurant). It is normally a good place from which to visit the Sierra de la Macarena, a Tertiary outcrop 150 km. long by 35 km. broad. Its vegetation is so remarkable that the Sierra has been designated a national park exclusively for scientific study, although latest reports suggest that the flora are rapidly being destroyed by colonization, with much marijuana and coca being planted, and the area has in any case been occupied by guerrillas since about 1982. The road from Vistahermosa to the Sierra de la Macarena is very muddy in the wet season (March-Nov.). For the energetic, a worthwhile trip is to the Sardinata or Cañones falls. Both can be reached from Maracaibo, which is a day's walk from Vistahermosa. In present conditions, as will appear from these lines, a visit to the Sierra de la Macarena is not recommended.

To the SE of Villavicencio, along the river Vaupés, and near the border with Brazil, is *Mitú*, which can be reached by air from Villavicencio and Bogotá. On arrival in the town you must fill in an entry card at the police station. Several anthropological studies are being carried out in the Mitú area and trips can be made from the town to Indian villages. The cost of a trip down river to visit an Indian village where you stay overnight is approximately US$10, plus the cost of the fuel used by the boat. Take your own food. The proprietor of Señor León's hotel (E) in Mitú will help you arrange such a trip. The hotel has the only restaurant in town, meals about US$2 each. Good local buys are baskets and bark paintings.

You can get a good away-from-it-all holiday in the Llanos. Plenty of reserve gasoline should be carried when travelling by car, as there are few service stations. Take food with you, unless you can live by gun and rod. Everybody lets you hang up your hammock or pitch your tent, but mosquito nets are a must. "Roads" are only tracks left by previous vehicles but easy from late December till early April and the very devil during the rest of the year. More information on the Llanos can be obtained from the office of the Gobernación del Departamento de Meta, Calle 34 and Carrera 14, Bogotá.

Leticia, 3,200 km. up the Amazon on the frontiers with Peru and Brazil, a fast-growing community of 15,000, is now becoming a clean modern town. It is rapidly merging into one town with neighbouring Marco in Brazil. There is a modern, well equipped hospital. The best time to visit the area is in July or August, the early months of the dry season. Tourist services are better than in Tabatinga or Benjamin Constant (Brazil). Small Amazonian zoo (huge anacondas) and botanical garden on road to airport.

Hotels *Parador Ticuna*, B, has 19 apartments (all with bathrooms which have hot and cold running water, but no lights or water between 2300 and 0600) which can each sleep up to 6. The hotel has a swimming pool (uncleaned), bar and restaurant, and is a little run down. The owners of the *Ticuna* also operate the *Parador Yaguas* in Leticia and the *Jungle Lodge*, on Monkey Island, an hour's boat ride from Leticia. *Colonial*, 16 double rooms and one triple, all with airconditioning or fans, power and water unpredictable, swimming pool, cafeteria, noisy, unhelpful staff, B, US$6 per additional person, not including tax and insurance. Cheaper accommodation: *Residencias La Manigua*, E, with bath, dirty. *Anaconda*, C, overpriced, no hot water; there is a restaurant (beware overcharging) which serves meals for about US$6, swimming pool; *Alemanas*, D, with bath, Romanian-run, clean; *Residencias Marina*, Carrera 9 No. 9-29 (T 7201/2), D/E, TV, some a/c, cold water, good breakfast and meals at attached restaurant, clean; *Residencias Ferrando*, Carrera 9 No. 8-80, E, well equipped but electricity only at night, clean, rec.; *Residencia Leticia*, Calle 8, No. 11-93, F, very friendly (not possible to sling hammock), good value, laundry facilities, clean, good cheap meals, use of kitchen, warmly rec.; *Residencia Familiar*, Calle 8, cheap, F, friendly, laundry facilities; *Primavera*, Calle 8 between Cras. 9 and 10, F with bath and fan; *Residencias Copacabana*, E, with bath, friendly, English spoken. (*Parador Ticuna* and *Hotel Colonial* boil water.)

Restaurant Several small sidewalk restaurants downtown with set meals at around US$1. *Café La Barra* serves beer, wine, and excellent fruit juices, serves sandwiches occasionally. Restaurant opposite *Residencia Leticia* serves good lunches and dinners, and *Señora Mercedes*, 3 doors from *Residencia Leticia*, serves good, cheap meals until 1930. *Restaurante Río Grande*, now a disco, serves excellent steaks. No meal with chicken or meat costs less than US$3-4. Cheap food (fried banana and meat, also fish and pineapples) is sold at the market near the harbour. Also cheap fruit for sale. The campsite also has a good restaurant.

Tourist Office Calle 10, No. 9-86. **DAS** office, Carrera 8 (between Calles 9 and 10), near Brazilian consulate. Make sure you get an entry stamp here before going to the airport for flights into Colombia. If you need a visa, but not a tourist card, to visit Colombia, don't be bullied into purchasing one of the latter.

Brazilian Consulate very efficient and helpful; 2 black and white photos needed for visa (photographer nearby).

Leticia is a good place to buy typical products of Amazon Indians, but the growth of Leticia, Tabatinga, Marco and Benjamin Constant has imposed an artificiality on the surrounding Amazon territory.

Exchange The *cambio* next to the *Anaconda Hotel* has good exchange rates for dollars, cruzados or intis. The street money changers and *cambios*, of which there are plenty, give a better rate of exchange than the banks, which charge a 15% levy on travellers' cheques, except Banco de la República on American Express. Travellers' cheques cannot be changed at weekends, and are hard to change at other times.

Excursions If you choose to go on an organized tour, do not accept the first price and check that the supplies and equipment are sufficient for the time you will be away. It is cheaper and better to find yourself a local guide. You can hire a dug-out for about US$3 a day. Motorboats cost much more (e.g. US$54, 8 hrs, for 10 people). Turamazonas, *Parador Ticuna*, Apto. Aereo 074, T 7241, offers a wide range of tours including day visit to Yagua and Ticuna Indians, jungle walk and stop at Monkey Island (rec.); provisions and bedding for overnight safaris are supplied by the agency, whose staff are all expert, especially Rolf Heumann, at Monkey Island. Not cheap but worth the extra money; Turamazonas has US representation at 855A, U.S. 19S, Tarpon Springs, FL 33581, T (813) 934-9713. Other reputable tour services are those of Amazonia (whose boatman, Hans, is recommended). The following tours are available: to Benjamin Constant to see a rubber plantation, 8 hrs.; to Monkey Island to see Ticuna and Yagua Indians, overnight trip, with full board. Turamazonas offers tours up the river to visit Indian communities, 3 days (price depends on number of people in group), recommended. Recommended tours from Leticia to Puerto Nariño are run by Punto Amazónico, Carrera 24, No. 53-18, 2° piso, Bogotá, T 249-3618 (guides Fernando and José), including fishing, visits to Indians, alligator watching for 4-5 days, about US$375 including flights and hotel accommodation. A cheaper guide is Guillermo Bueno, T 72-91. Many independent guides can be found on the river front; for example Bautista offers one day excursions to Yagua Indians (gifts of food and provisions much appreciated), Victoria Regia waterlilies, Monkey Island and more. A recommended guide is Luis Daniel González, Carrera 8, No. 9-93 (he can either be found at the airport, or contacted through *Hotel Anaconda*; he runs a variety of tours, is knowledgeable and speaks Spanish, Portuguese and English; a one-day tour, inc. meal and fuel costs US$110). Make sure the guides bring rubber boots as it can be quite muddy. Cheap guides do not have the experience or first aid equipment of the main tour companies. A small airline, ATA, offers flights in a Cessna plane at reasonable rates. An interesting walk is along the river bank to Marco and Tabatinga, in Brazil. (The bars in Marco, sometimes spelt Marcos, are friendlier and serve better (local) beer, than in Leticia.)

When going upstream remember that the slower and dirtier the boat, the more mosquitoes you will meet. (You can swim in the Amazon and its tributaries, but do not dive; this disturbs the fish. Also do not swim at sunrise or sunset when the fish are more active, nor when the water is shallow in the dry season, nor if you have a wound, however slight, which might open up and bleed.) We have been warned that most of the monkeys have disappeared from Monkey Island.

Transport Avianca flies to Leticia (Tabatinga airport if Leticia's is closed) from Bogotá, daily except Fri. and Sun. for US$60; Leticia to Bogotá, departs 1420, arrives 1605; to Cali (via Bogotá), US$62; Satena has flights on Thurs. afternoon, US$50; it is possible to return to Bogotá by freight plane, but you have to sit with the cargo, often fish. Check with Satena crew, who stay in the *Hotel Colonial*, if there is a seat available, or at the airport. (From Bogotá by freight plane, you have to be at the halls of the cargo companies—all at the same place—at 0400, and ask which company is flying.) Líneas Aero Caribe cargo flights twice a week; flight time 3½-4 hrs. Cruzeiro do Sul flies Manaus-Tabatinga (for Leticia)-Iquitos and back on Wed. and Sat. (there is a connection on Wed. for Pucallpa from Iquitos); fare from Tabatinga (for Leticia) to Iquitos US$49 + US$3 tax; Taba operates three flights weekly Manaus-Tabatinga-Manaus. TANS, the Peruvian military jungle airline, usually offers flights between Iquitos and Ramón Castilla nearby, in Peru, for about US$20, but you must book well in advance and make sure of getting to the airport well ahead of the flight time. These flights are on Fridays and Sundays. It is also possible to get a seat on a Petrobrás plane to Manaus. This leaves every Friday, and can be arranged with the crew, who stay at the *Anaconda Hotel*. A letter of recommendation helps. Taxi to airport, US$1.90. Expect to be searched before leaving Leticia airport, and on arrival in Bogotá from Leticia. If arriving in Leticia by plane with a view to leaving for Brazil or Peru, get your exit stamp at the airport while you are there.

The cheapest way to get to Leticia is by bus to Puerto Asís, and then by boat (**see page 598**). There are twice-daily ferries between Leticia, Tabatinga and Benjamin Constant, Brazil (US$5, 1½-2 hrs., US$15 in private launch); if leaving Brazil by this route, disembark at Tabatinga and obtain exit stamp from office which is 1 km. from dock: turn right one block at main street, office is on the left. There is a Colombian Consular Office near the border on the road from Tabatinga, where Colombian tourist visas are issued on presentation of 2 passport photographs. Most boats down to Manaus take passengers—all leave from Benjamin Constant, Ramón Castilla, perhaps Tabatinga—none from Leticia. The *Ayapua* has a comfortable passenger capacity of about 70, takes 5 days and costs US$40 for a basic cabin or US$50 for first class passage on the top deck. Second class is below decks with the cargo and not recommended. Most passengers sling a hammock on deck, which is much cooler. Departure times are uncertain, and the boats tend to be overcrowded. Recommended is the *Marcia Maria*, about US$37 for hammock space, US$45 p.p. in 2-person cabin. The *Cidade de Teresina*, a cargo vessel, has four cabins with four berths in each, and a top deck for slinging hammocks, US$28; passage in a cabin US$33, to be arranged with the captain. The trip takes at least 4½ days; there is a better selection of provisions in Leticia, but purchases are much cheaper in Benjamin Constant. Boats to Peru from Tabatinga wharf La Ronda sail daily at 1800 and take passengers and cargo. Boats to Ramón Castilla cost US$6 each way. There are irregular sailings for Iquitos on the *Huallacha*, cost US$40 (at least 10 days between sailings, on this and other vessels). Food is provided but is not recommended. Remember to get your passport stamped by the DAS office near the church, just off main square in Leticia before you leave the area; (there are no customs formalities for everyday travel between Leticia and Tabatinga in Brazil, taxis cost US$5.65 from a rank (or US$7.55 if you want to stop to change money, immigration, etc. en route to harbour), or US$0.70 as colectivos (N.B. colectivos increase their charges after 1800); bus, US$0.20; 24-hour transit stamps can be obtained at the DAS office for one-night stays in Leticia, although it appears that these are not necessary if you are not going beyond Leticia—best to check, though; also see below). From Ramón Castilla to Iquitos or Pucallpa the *Oro Negro* is highly recommended. The captain and owner is a characterful elderly lady and her crew a family affair. Passage for the 5-day journey costs only US$20-25, food included but take your own water, unless you want to drink river water, and your own eating utensils. Passengers' aid is sometimes solicited to gather firewood or yuca on the river bank.

N.B. Robert Smith and Geoffrey Dempsey tell us that if entering Colombia at Leticia, from Brazil en route to Peru, you should try to get your tourist card before Manaus because the Colombian consul there will tell you that a card is not needed just for passing through Leticia. This is not true: you must have a card. If you do have to see the consul in Manaus tell him you are going further into Colombia—you may have to show an onward ticket, or money—this may get you a card.

It is reported that for travellers interested in Amazonian wild life the Putumayo is more accessible than Leticia; it is best reached from Pasto (**see page 597**).

THE NORTH COAST AND THE ISLANDS (4)

The climate is much the same for the whole area: the heat is great—ranging from 26° to 36°C, and there is a difference of only 2° between the hottest and coolest month. From November to March the heat is moderated by trade winds.

Character, like climate, seems to change in Colombia with the altitude. The *costeños* (the people of the coast) are gayer and more light-hearted than the more sober people of the highlands. (The contrast is sharply drawn in the great modern Colombian novel, *Cien Años de Soledad*, by Gabriel García Márquez.) The coastal people talk very fast, slurring their words and dropping the final s's.

N.B. In this region hotel prices are subject to high and low season variations: high season is December 15-April 30, and June 15-August 31.

Barranquilla, with almost 2 million people, is Colombia's fourth city. It lies on the western bank of the Magdalena river, about 18 km. from its mouth, which has been deepened and the silted sandbars cleared so that it is now a seaport (though less busy than Cartagena or Santa Marta) as well as a river port. Those who know the people say they are the most friendly in Colombia.

Barranquilla is a modern industrial city with a dirty central area near the river, and a good residential area in the north-west, beyond Calle 53. The principal boulevard is Paseo Bolívar; there is a handsome Cathedral in Plaza San Nicolás, the central square, and before it stands a small statue of Columbus. The commercial and shopping districts are round the Plaza Bolívar, a few blocks N of the Cathedral, and in Calle Murillo. The colourful and vivid market is between Paseo Bolívar and the river, the so-called Zona Negra on a side channel of the Magdalena. Good parks in the northern areas, the favourite one is Parque Tomás Suri Salcedo on Calle 72. Stretching back into the north-western heights overlooking the city are the modern suburbs of El Prado, Altos del Prado, Golf and Ciudad Jardín, with the German-run *El Prado Hotel.* Not far away is the Country Club. There are three stadiums in the city, a big covered coliseum for sports, a bull ring and the Amira de la Rosa theatre. The metropolitan stadium is on Av. Murillo, outside the city. There is also a zoo, well maintained, with many animals not often seen in zoos, but many are in small cages. Calle 74, Carrera 50 (bus "Boston/Boston" or "Caldes/Recreo"), entrance US$0.60, students US$0.30, 0830-1200, 1400-1800. All the trees are labelled.

Festivals Carnival, lasting four days, parades, floats, street dancing and beauty contests.

Hotels *El Prado,* the social centre, swimming pool and tennis courts, B, good restaurant, some distance from the centre (Carrera 54, No. 70-10); in same district, *Royal,* Carrera 54, No. 68-124, T 35-78-00, E, good service, with swimming pool, modern; *Davega,* Calle 72 y Carrera 44, T 359020, D (incl tax), good value, rec.; *Génova,* swimming pool, Calle 44, No. 44-66, 10 blocks from centre, C; *Arenosa,* Carrera 48, No. 70-136, C, with bath, TV, pleasant staff and surroundings; *Majestic,* Carrera 53, No. 54-41, out of city centre, C, very good; *Los Angeles,* Calle 41, E with bath, safe, clean, friendly; *Spanish-American,* Paseo Bolívar, D, with bath, clean, meals available at about US$2; *Zhivago,* Plaza Bolívar, very good, E, without bath; *Horizonte,* Calle 45 y Carrera 44, F with bath, clean, quiet, fan, rec.; *Apartotel Salerno,* Calle 45 down from

Brasilia bus station, cheap, good and safe. *Embajador*, Calle 34 (Paseo Bolívar), No. 40-66, F with bath and phone, very good; *Real*, Paseo Bolívar, next to Plaza, D, clean, friendly, English and German spoken. At Puerto Colombia (20 mins.), *Esperia*, and just outside, *Pradomar*. **Note:** hotel prices may be much higher during Carnival. Watch for thieves in downtown hotels.

Restaurants   In El Prado and Alto Prado, between Calles 72 and 84 and Carreras 40 and 60: *Petit Chalet* and *Chez Catherine*, French and expensive; *La Puerta de Oro*, Calle 35, No. 41-100, central, a/c, good for meals (inc. breakfast); *Fonda Antioqueña*, local dishes, friendly; *El Calderito*, also local, tropical garden atmosphere; *Gambrinus* and *Taverna Gunter*, German; *Los Techos Rojos*, steak-house; various Lebanese (*Baalbek, Biblios, Tripoli*) with belly-dancers; several Chinese and *pizzerias*. *El Mesón de Morgan*, excellent sea-food, good service, but very expensive; *El Famoso Chino*, Paseo Bolívar, good and cheap self-service, clean; *Don Brisi*, rec. Local dishes at *José Pazos*, Calle 69F, La Colonia.

Clubs   Country (golf, tennis, swimming pool); Barranquilla; Anglo-American; German; Italian; Centro Israelita. **Night Life** La Cabaña at *Hotel El Prado*. Famous disco Agua Sala at beach.

Market   San Andrecito, or "Tourist Market", Vía 40, is where smuggled goods are sold at very competitive prices; a good place to buy film. Picturesque and reasonably safe. Any taxi driver will take you there.

Bookshop   Librería Nacional, Carrera 53, English, French and German books and a café which serves excellent fruit juices. Maps from Instituto Agustín Codazzi, Calle 36, No. 45-101.

Exchange   Banco Royal de Colombia; Banco Anglo Colombiano, Calle 34, No. 44-43, with agency on Calle 72; Banco Internacional de Colombia. Open: Mon.-Thurs, 0800-1130, 1400-1600; Fri. 0900-1130, 1400-1630; last working day of month 0800-1130. *Casa de cambio* El Cacique, Calle 34, No. 43-108, T 326392, reliable.

Addresses   US Consulate, Centro Comercial Mayorista, Calle 77, No. 68-15, opposite zoo (Apartado Aéreo 51565). T 45-70-88 or 45-71-81 (visas obtainable only in Bogotá). W. German Consulate, Calle 80, near Vía 40 (ask for Herr Schnabel). Dutch Consulate, Carrera 42H, No. 85-33, T 341282; Spanish Consulate, Calle 51, No. 37-64, T 313694; Venezuelan Consulate, Calle 70, No. 53-74 (Centro Financiero El Prado, 4° piso), T 580048/582832, 0800-1500 (take "Caldas/Recreo" or "Boston/Boston" bus), visa issued same day, onward ticket may not be requested. American Express agency at Tierra Mar Aire, downtown. Police (for declarations of theft, etc.), Policia F2, Calle 47 y Carrera 43.

Tourist   information at main hotels and at Calle 72, No. 57-43, of. 401, T 45-44-58 or 33-66-58. CNT is at Carrera 54, No 75-45, T 454458. A recommended taxi-driver/guide to the city is Henry Robinson, T 35-37-14; he speaks English. Locals will show you beautiful beaches off road to Cartagena.

Museum   Small archaeological collection, Calle 68 No. 53-45 (Mon.-Fri. 0900-1200, 1400-1700), with big physical relief map on front lawn.

Airport   Ernesto Cortissoz airport is 10 km. from the city; there is plenty of transport of all types. City bus from airport to town, US$0.10 (US$0.15 on Sunday). Taxi to town, US$4.50 (taxis do not have meters, fix fare in advance). Special bus from outside the airport, US$2.50 (to town, take only buses marked "centro"); the bus to the airport (marked Malambo) leaves from Carrera 44 up Calle 32 to Carrera 38, then up Calle 30 to Airport. ALM to Aruba and Curaçao; Lacsa to Maracaibo and Caracas, and Mexico City. Taxi to Cartagena, US$40.

Buses   Most bus companies operate from Calle 34 and Carrera 45 (Brasilia at Calle 45 y Carrera 35). To Santa Marta, US$1.80, Pullman (or US$1.60 in non-a/c, Coolibertador), about 2 hrs., also direct to Santa Marta's famous Rodadero beach; to Montería, US$9.25, 8 hrs.; to Medellín by Pullman, US$16, 16hrs.; to Bucaramanga, US$13.50 with Copetran, air-conditioned, first class, departures at 1130 most days, arriving 2030; to Bogotá, 20 hrs., US$20 direct; to Caucasia, US$9, 11 hrs. To Maicao US$6.50, 5 hrs. (with Brasilia, every ½ hour from 0100-1200); to Cartagena, 3 grades of bus, 3 hrs. (US$2.25 with Transportes Cartagena, US$2.75 with Expreso Brasilia, by Brasilia Van Tours mini-bus, US$2, from their downtown offices as well as the bus terminals), 2 hrs. by colectivo, US$2.50.

Warnings   When leaving by air for the USA, you may be searched by drug squad police; they are very civil, but acquisitive—check your belongings afterwards. Tourist Police can be very rough when searching foreigners. Beware also of people claiming to be ships' officers who say they can arrange a passage if you pay in advance; buy a passage only in a recognized shipping office or agency. If shipping a car into Barranquilla allow 2 days to complete all paperwork to retrieve your car from the port.

Roads   Regular buses from Plaza Bolívar and the church at Calle 33 and Carrera 41 to the attractive bathing resort of *Puerto Colombia*, 19 km. (US$0.50, ½ hr.). Beach clean and sandy, water a bit muddy. S along the Magdalena to the little town of Palmar de Varela. On this road, 5 km. from the city, is the old colonial town of *Soledad,* with 16,000 inhabitants. The cathedral and the old narrow streets round it are worth seeing.

Barranquilla-Cartagena, a good paved road but driving is violent, and cyclists have reported muggings. From Baranoa a branch road runs to Usicurí (72 km. from Barranquilla), known for its medicinal waters and for the grave of the popular Colombian poet, Julio Flores. The main road goes on via Sabanalarga (50 km. from Barranquilla) to Cartagena. From Sabanalarga an all-weather road continues to Puerto Giraldo, a port on the Magdalena River linked by ferry with the small town of Salmina (ferry 0500 to 1800). A spectacular new bridge over the River Magdalena gives a fine view of Barranquilla and the river. An all-weather road leads to Fundación, on the Atlántico Railway, and a junction point with the road from Santa Marta to Bucaramanga and Bogotá, which is now paved throughout, though surface somewhat uneven.

Cartagena, old and steeped in history, is one of the most interesting towns in South America. Its population is 700,000. An arm of the river, 145 km. long, canalized in 1650 by Spain—the Canal del Dique—from Calamar to Cartagena allows free access for ships from the up-river ports.

What interests the visitor is a comparatively small part of Cartagena, the old walled city almost completely surrounded by the Caribbean sea on the W, the waters of the Bay of Cartagena on the S, and lakes and lagoons to the N and E. Cartagena was one of the storage points for merchandise sent out from Spain and for treasure collected from the Americas to be sent back to Spain. A series of forts protecting the approaches from the sea, and the formidable walls built around the city, made it almost impregnable.

Cartagena was founded by Pedro de Heredia on January 13, 1533. There were then two approaches to it, Bocagrande, at the northern end of Tierra Bomba Island—this was a direct entry from the Caribbean—and Boca Chica. Bocagrande was blocked after Admiral Vernon's attack in 1741, and thereafter the only approach was by the narrow channel of Boca Chica from the S. Boca Chica leads into the great bay of Cartagena, 15 km. long and 5 km. wide. The old walled city lies at the head of it.

Entering Boca Chica by sea, the island of Tierra Bomba is to the left. At the tip of a spit of land is the fortress of San Fernando (entrance fee, US$1; guide, US$1.50 for one to five people); boat trips to it (1 hr.) are worth while. Opposite it, right on the tip of Barú island, is the fortress of San José. The two forts were once linked by heavy chains to prevent surprise attacks by pirates. North of Barú island stretches Manga island, much larger and now an important suburb. At its northern end a bridge, Puente Román, connects it with the old city. This approach was defended by three forts: San Sebastián del Pastelillo built between 1558 and 1567 (the Club de Pesca has it now) at the north-western tip of Manga Island; the fortress of San Lorenzo near the city itself; and the very powerful fortress of San Felipe inland on a height to the E of the city. Yet another fort, La Tenaza, protected the walled city from a direct attack from the open sea. The huge encircling walls were started in 1634 and finished by 1735. They were on average 12 metres high and 17 metres thick, with 6 gates. They contained, besides barracks, a water reservoir.

In spite of its daunting outer forts and encircling walls Cartagena was challenged again and again by enemies. Sir Francis Drake, with 1,300 men, broke in successfully in 1586. The Frenchmen Baron de Pointis and Ducasse, with 10,000 men, beat down the defences and sacked the city in 1697. But the strongest attack of all, by Sir Edward Vernon with 27,000 men and 3,000 pieces of artillery, failed in 1741 after besieging the city for 56 days; it was defended by the one-eyed, one-armed and one-legged hero Blas de Lezo, whose statue is at the entrance to the San Felipe fortress.

Cartagena declared its independence from Spain in 1811. A year later Bolívar used the city as a jumping-off point for his Magdalena campaign. After a heroic resistance, Cartagena was retaken by the royalists under Pablo Morillo in 1815. The patriots finally freed it in 1821.

The old walled city was in two sections, inner and outer. Much of the wall between the two was razed a few years ago. Nearly all the houses are of one or two storeys. The houses in El Centro were occupied by the high officials and nobility. San Diego (the northern end of the inner town) was where the middle classes lived: the clerks, merchants, priests and military. The artisan classes lived in the one-storey houses of Getsemaní in the outer city.

The streets are narrow and rarely straight. Each block has a different name, a source of confusion,

but don't worry: the thing to do is to wander aimlessly, savouring the street scenes, and allow the great sights to catch you by surprise. Our map is marked with numerals for the places of outstanding interest. The most attractive streets have been given a star (*). Most of the "great houses" can be visited.

The numbers stand for the following places:

1. The Puente Román, the bridge which leads from the island of Manga into the Getsemaní district. Visitors should on no account miss seeing the *casas bajas* or low houses of Getsemaní, but be careful; it is not a very safe neighbourhood.

2. The Chapel of San Roque (early 17th century), near the Hospital of Espíritu Santo.

3. The Church of Santísima Trinidad, built 1643 but not consecrated till 1839. The plaza in which it stands is most interesting. North of the church, at number 10, lived Pedro Romero, the man who set the revolution of 1811 going by coming out into the street shouting "Long Live Liberty".

4. The Monastery and Church of San Francisco. The church was built in 1590 after the pirate Martin Côte had destroyed an earlier church built in 1559. The first Inquisitors lodged at the monastery. From its courtyard a crowd surged into the streets claiming independence from Spain on the morning of November 11, 1811. The Church of the Third Order is now the Colón Theatre.

Immediately to the N is Plaza de la Independencia, with the landscaped Parque del Centenario just off it. At right angles to the Plaza runs the Paseo de los Mártires, flanked by the busts of nine patriots executed in the square on February 24, 1816 by the royalist Morillo when he retook the city. At its western end is a tall clock tower. Passing through the tower's arches (the main entrance to the inner walled city) we get to

5. The Plaza de los Coches. Around almost all the plazas of Cartagena arcades offer refuge from the tropical sun. On the W side of this plaza is the famous Portal de los Dulces, a favourite meeting place.

6. Plaza de la Aduana, with a statue of Columbus and the City Hall.

7. Church of San Pedro Claver and Monastery, built by Jesuits in 1603 and later dedicated to San Pedro Claver, a monk in the monastery, was canonized 235 years after his death in 1654. He was called the Slave of the Slaves: he used to beg from door to door for money to give to the black slaves brought to the city. His body is in a glass coffin on the high altar, and his cell and the balcony from which he sighted slave ships are shown to visitors. Entry, US$0.50. Guides charge US$1.

8. Plaza de Bolívar (the old Plaza Inquisición), very pleasant, and with a statue of Bolívar. On its W side is

9. The Palace of the Inquisition, established in 1610, but the building dates from 1706. The stone entrance with its coats of arms and well preserved and ornate wooden door is very notable. Indeed the whole building, with its overhanging balconies, cloisters and patios, is a fine example of colonial baroque. There is a very pleasant historical museum at the Palace, and a library. Entry charge US$0.40; good historical books on sale. Open Mon.-Sat., 0900-1130, 1400-1730, Sun., 0900-1300.

On the opposite side of the Plaza to the Palace of the Inquisition, the Museo del Oro y Arqueológico has been installed in an old building. Gold and pottery, very well displayed. Entrance free.

In the NE corner of Plaza de Bolívar is

10. The Cathedral, begun in 1575 and partially destroyed by Francis Drake. Reconstruction was finished by 1612. Great alterations were made between 1912 and 1923. A severe exterior, with a fine doorway, and a simply decorated interior. See the guilded 18th century altar, the Carrara marble pulpit, and the elegant arcades which sustain the central nave.

11. **Church and Convent of Santa Teresa**, founded 1609, now occupied by the police.

12. The Church and Monastery of Santo Domingo, built 1570 to 1579 and now a seminary. The old monastery was replaced by the present one in the 17th century. Inside, a miracle-making image of Christ, carved towards the end of the 16th century, is set on a baroque 19th century altar. Most interesting neighbourhood, very little changed since the 16th century. In Calle Santo Domingo, No. 33-29, is one of the great patrician houses of Cartagena, the Casa de los Condes de Pestagua, now the Colegio del Sagrado Corazón de Jesús. North of Santo Domingo, at

13. Calle de la Factoría 36-57 is the magnificent Casa del Marqués de Valdehoyos, now owned by the tourist authority and containing a Tourist Office; open to visitors.

14. The Church and Convent of La Merced, founded 1618. The Convent—a prison during Morillo's reign of terror—is now occupied by the Law Courts and its church is the Municipal Theatre.

15. The Monastery of San Agustín (1580), now the University. From its chapel, now occupied by a printing press, the pirate Baron de Pointis stole a 500-pound silver sepulchre. It was returned by the King of France but the citizens melted it down to pay their troops during the siege by Morillo in 1815. Adjoining the University is the Edificio Ganem, which offers a good, free view of the city from the 9th floor.

16. The Church of Santo Toribio de Mongrovejo. Building began in 1729. In 1741, during Admiral Vernon's siege, a cannon ball fell into the church during Mass and lodged in one of the central columns; the ball is now in a recess in the W wall. The font of Carrara marble in the Sacristy is a masterpiece. There is a beautiful carved ceiling (*mudéjar* style) above the main altar. Opens for Mass at 0600 and 1800, closed at other times.

17. Casa del Consulado (Calle Sargento Mayor) was one of the great houses but has now become a teachers' college.

18. Church and Monastery of Santa Clara of Assisi, built 1617-21, now the Hospital of Santa Clara.

19. Plaza de las Bóvedas. The walls of Las Bóvedas, built 1799, are some 12 metres high and from 15 to 18 metres thick. Cars can drive along the rampart, from which there is a grand view of the harbour. At the base of the wall are 23 dungeons, now containing tourist shops. Both a lighted underground passage and a drawbridge lead from Las Bóvedas to the fortress of La Tenaza on the sea shore.

Also worth visiting is the Casa de Núñez, just outside the walls of La Tenaza in El Cabrero district opposite the Ermita de El Cabrero and 5 minutes from the bullring. Here lived Rafael Núñez, president (four times) and poet (he wrote Colombia's national anthem). His grandiose marble tomb is in the adjoining church.

Three of the sights of Cartagena are off our map. One of them is the Fortress of San Fernando, already mentioned.

The Fortress of San Felipe, across the Puente Heredia (21) from the outer walled city, stands on the hill of San Lázaro, 41 metres above sea-level. Building began in 1639 and it was finished by 1657. Under the huge structure are tunnels lined with living rooms and offices. Some are open and lighted; visitors pass through these and on to the top of the fortress. Baron de Pointis, the French pirate, stormed and took it in 1697, but Admiral Vernon failed to reach it in the abortive attack of 1741. Entrance fee US$0.85. Guide US$1.50 for one to five people.

A lovely road leads to the summit of La Popa hill, nearly 150 metres high, from which there is a fine view of the harbour and the city (entry US$0.85). Here are the church and monastery of Santa Cruz and restored ruins of convent dating from 1608. In the church is the beautiful little image of the Virgin of La Candelaria, reputed a deliverer from plague and a protector against pirates. Her day is February 2. For nine days before the feast thousands of people go up the hill by car, on foot, or on horseback. On the day itself people carry lighted candles as they go up the hill. The name was bestowed on the hill because of an imagined likeness to a ship's poop. It is dangerous to walk up on your own; either take a guided tour, or take a public bus to Teatro Miramar at the foot of the hill (US$0.50), then bargain for a taxi up, about US$2.50 (or US$5 from centre of town). The Tourist Office recommends a guided tour from an agency opposite the *Hotel Playa* in Bocagrande, for US$5.50, which also takes in San Felipe and San Pedro Claver.

Feasts The other great feast, apart from Candlemas, is on November 11-14 to celebrate the independence of Cartagena. Men and women in masks and fancy dress roam the streets, dancing to the sound of *maracas* and drums. There are beauty contests and battles of flowers and general gaiety. This festival tends to be wild and can be dangerous.

Caribbean Music Festival For 5 days in March, groups from all over the region perform salsa, reggae, etc., etc.; loud and fun.

Warnings Carry your passport (or, safer, a DAS-approved photocopy of it) at all times. Failure to present it on police request can result in imprisonment and fines. Regarding sea passages, see warning under Barranquilla (**page 552**). In addition, if offered a job on a ship to the Galápagos or to New York, insist on full documentation at the Seamen's Union office and do not make any arrangements on the street.

Beware also of self-appointed tourist guides who charge very highly for their services, and can turn nasty if thwarted. Bus travellers are met by people offering to recommend a hotel; their services are not necessary and may lead to "coincidental" theft later.

Hotels On Bocagrande beach, 10 mins by bus from city: *Cartagena-Hilton*, El Laguito, L, T 50666 (Apto. Aéreo 1774); *Capilla del Mar*, B, Calle 8, Carrera 1, excellent French restaurant, swimming pool on 4th floor, be careful of their travel desk and check any reservations they make for you, no connection with restaurant of same name ½ km. away; *Las Velas*, Calle Las Velas, No. 1-60, C, opposite *Caribe Casino*, warm water all day, showers, good restaurant; *Hotel del Caribe*, B, all rooms a/c, older half nicer, administration could be better, nice grounds, swimming pool in the (expensive) restaurant, pancakes rec.; *India Catalina*, Carrera 2, No. 7-115, C, very good, with a/c, safe, clean; *Residencias Internacional*, Av. San Martín 4110, T 50-675, C, with bath and a/c, clean, safe, friendly; opposite at No. 5-86 is *Flamingo*, C (D in low season—recently renovated), with bath and a/c, clean, helpful, pleasant, highly rec.; *Del Lago*, Calle 34, No. 11-15, D, no hot water, phone, no singles, reasonable; *Succar*, Carrera 2, No. 6-40, D, clean, helpful. *Playa*, on Av. San Martín, all rooms with private bathroom, open air bar, restaurant (breakfast, US$1), swimming pool, noisy disco next door, Av. 2a, No. 4-87; *Residencias Bocagrande*, D, with shower, no hot water, clean and friendly, but noisy, try to get a room with a balcony and a view over the sea, good restaurant; *Leonela*, Carrera 3a, 7-142, D, quiet, comfortable; *Residencias Astoria*, D, bath, fan (air conditioning 25% extra), friendly, breakfast US$1.50, good, not actually on beach, but nearby. On Carrera 3, there are plenty of small, pleasant *residencias*, for instance Carrera 3, No. 5-29, D in season, clean and friendly. Apartments may be rented from Apartments Intercontinental, Diagonal 1 y Calle 1, e.g. US$40 a day for 6, on Bocagrande next to *Hilton*.

In town: *Veracruz*, Calle San Agustín, opp. San Agustín church, E, clean, safe, with or without a/c, helpful but noisy from disco on ground floor; *Bucarica*, San Agustín 6-08, F, quite popular with travellers, but rooms vary a lot and acts as a brothel; *Residencial Pacoa*, Calle Pacoa, E, noisy, friendly; *Magdalena*, same street, F with bath, cold water, fan, clean but small rooms; *Real*, Calle Espíritu Santo 29-70, E with shower, basic, clean, not very safe; *Roma*, E, with bath, safe, basic, fan, no hot water, popular; cheaper places on San Andrés: *Res. Valle*, El Dorado, but not a safe area; *San Francisco*, Plaza Independencia opp. Parque Centenario, E, quiet; *Plaza Bolívar*, Plaza Bolívar No. 3-98 (under renovation in 1988), D, good, nice restaurant, accepts dollars cash and credit cards; *Carisma*, Cuartel y Soledad, F, clean, safe, noisy, fan, no bath; *Residencias Venezia*, Calle del Guerrero No. 29-108, F, friendly, rec. some rooms with fan, clean and secure, and many others; *Doral*, Media Luna, friendly, nice, fan, large rooms, rec., E, good cheap restaurant; *Media Luna*, Media Luna y Centenario, F without bath, clean, good value; *Cafetaría San Felipe*, Media Luna 943, with rooms in F range, and good cheap meals; many cheap hotels on Calle Media Luna are brothels; area not advisable for women on their own. On the road to the airport are several hotels and *pensiones*, particularly at Marbella beach (e.g. *Bellavista*, Av. Santander, D, clean, nice patio, English-speaking owner, Enrique Sedó, secure; *Playa Blanca*, Av. Santander, E, very nice; *Miramar*, D, with toilet and shower, clean, secure).

N.B. Hotel prices tend to go up by as much as 25 per cent in December each year (i.e. increase Bocagrande hotels by a letter in our range at this time; in town nothing is below E); hotels tend to be heavily booked right through to March. Either book well in advance yourself, or avoid the city at this time. For hotel insurance, add 5%, plus US$0.05 p.p. per day.

Camping In a secure walled garden at *Hotel Bellavista*, Av. Santander, on the beach, US$2.50 p.p.; camper vans also welcome (price in E range). People camp on the beach, but may be troubled by thieves—and the police.

Restaurants *Nautilus*, facing the statue of La India Catalina, seafood; another *Nautilus* (same menu and service) on road to airport in Marbella; and yet another *Nautilus*, Carrera 3, Bocagrande. *Capilla del Mar*, rec., sea food dinner for 2, US$20-30; all-you-can-eat buffet on Tues. (shrimp) and Fri. (seafood) for US$15. Also in Bocagrande, Av. San Martín, *Da Marisa*, pizzas; *Fontana di Trevi*, Italian, rec.; *Alexander*, German food; *El Arca de Noé*, very good steaks; *El Patio de la Atarraya*, good fish restaurant overlooking the sea; *Rincón Argentino* for good steaks (US$4); *La Olla Cartagenera* and *La Petite Sensation*, both on Carrera 2, very good, but not cheap; *La Piragua*, Carrera 2, an open-air bar with live music, pleasant; *La Heladería Arabe*, Carrera 3, good ice cream; *Little Chicken*, Americanized Colombian food, clean, good food and juices (US$4 for steaks), English spoken by Ivan, helpful manager; *La Hormiga*, Calle Bocagrande, good, cheap; *Kokoriko* is a chain of barbecued chicken restaurants, US$6 for a whole chicken. Many good juice bars in Bocagrande.

Away from Bocagrande: *Club de Pesca*, at the Fuerte del Pastelillo: you can dine in the open air in a lovely setting, expensive (taxi, US$3.50-4.50); *Màrcel Hostería Sevillana*, Malecón 70, near *Residencias Ligia*, El Candilejo, more expensive than it looks, but good food (in Candilejo). *Loon Foon*, Chinese, good, on first street into city from the statue of La India Catalina; *Kon-Nam*, Calle San Pedro Claver, good Chinese cuisine; good, cheap Chinese restaurant in C. Estanco de Tabaco; *Nuevo Oriente*, near Santo Domingo, Chinese, good; *El Ganadero*, Calle Media Luna, good food, friendly; *Paco's Restaurant* on Plaza Santo Domingo, pleasant atmosphere, excellent food, not cheap; *Bodegón de la Candelaria*, Calle de las Damas (T 47251), excellent food and service, but expensive; *El Rinconcito*, near Plaza Fernando de Madrid, good cheap meals; also *El Pollo Dorado* on Calle Ricuarte, opposite Banco de Bogotá. *La Langosta*, Av. Venezuela, just outside old city walls, good food, reasonable prices; *Americano*, near central post office, good meals for US$1.50; *Bar La Vitrola*, rec. for its atmosphere; *La Fragata*, in old town, two blocks behind *Hotel Bolívar*, French maître d'hôtel, German cook. Many restaurants around Plaza Independencia have meals for about US$2. Restaurants in Calle San Andrés cost about US$1.30, with plenty to eat; cheap meals at *San Martín*, Calle de las Damas, and in a restaurant on the corner of Plaza de los Coches; *Panificadora la Española*, Calle 8, No. 7-61, fresh bread and pastries; *Heladería Almirante Vernón*, a block from San Pedro Claver church towards Plaza Bolívar, has hearty, reasonable meals and good fruit juices; *Heladería Cecilia* for good ice-creams. *Juguería Dino* (near the clocktower at entrance on landward side to the city walls) for fruit juices, good. At cafés try the patacón, a biscuit made of green banana, mashed and baked; also in Parque del Centenario in early morning. *Stella Maris*, near the harbour in Barrio Manga, used mainly by seamen, is a bar and shop, selling stamps (0900-2300) and souvenirs, administered by the Salvation Army.

Market There is a new market out of town, which is disappointing; bus from Av. Urdaneta Arbeláez. The fish market is in the SE suburbs of the old city.

Shopping A good selection of *artesanías* on Plaza Bolívar, but in general (except for leather goods) shopping is much better in Bogotá. Woollen *blusas* are good value, US$8-12; try the *Tropicano* in Pierino Gallo building in Bocagrande. Also in this building are reputable jewellery shops. H. Stern has a jewellery shop in the Pierino Gallo shopping centre and at the Hilton Hotel. Suntan oils and lotions can vary in price as much as 100%—shop around. Comercial Centro

Getsemaní, Calle Larga between San Juan and Plaza de la Independencia, a large new shopping centre has many establishments.

Gambling Casino Turístico, Av. San Martín and Casino de Caribe at Pierino Gallo shopping centre, Bocagrande.

Taxis From Bocagrande to the centre should be less than US$1; to the airport US$2.20; centre to airport, US$2 (more at night). Try to fix price for journey before committing yourself. A horse-drawn carriage can be hired for US$9, opposite *Hotel El Dorado*, Av. San Martín, in Bocagrande, to ride into town at night (romantic but rather short ride).

Car Rental National and Hertz at airport; Avis at *Hilton Hotel*.

Buses Within the city large buses (with no glass in windows) cost US$0.05, short-wheelbase type (with glass windows), US$0.10.

Sport Fishing; yachting. Windsurf rental, Bocagrande, US$6.50 per hour. Also bullfights and cockfights. The former take place mainly in January and February, the latter throughout the year on Sat., Sun. and holidays. From about 1500 cockfighting takes place at the Gallerita Popular de la Quinta and on Sun. at 1600 at Club Gallístico Pedro Rhenals in El Bosque.

Beaches Take bus from Plaza de la Independencia to Bocagrande, which has good beaches (although dirty). The Boca Chica beach is also dirty, and the boat service there unreliable. Boats leave from Plaza de la Independencia; the round trip can take up to 2 hrs. each way. *Ferry Dancing*, US$2 about half the price of luxury boats, carries dancing passengers; the much faster launches cost US$3.50. For about US$1.50 you can take a tour round the fort of San Fernando in a dugout canoe. There are boats from the city; the last return trip is at 1230. Swimming is good. Boats taking in Boca Chica and San Fernando are US$5 return without lunch or US$10.50 with lunch (children under 12, half price). Alcatraz run a daily trip from the Muelle Turístico leaving at about 1000, returning at 1530. There is a daily cruise to Islas del Rosario, US$14.50 including lunch (possible to bargain in low season), with Alcatraz, leaving 0630, returning 1630. The boat stops first at Playa Blanca on the mainland for 1 hr. (bargain with boatman to leave you for a day, camp on the beach, and continue the cruise next day—Playa Blanca is crowded a.m., but peaceful after the tour boats have left). At the Islas del Rosario is an aquarium in the sea, worth visiting, US$0.60. There are cheaper boats to the islands, shop around. Marbella beach, just N of Las Bóvedas (the locals' beach, and therefore quieter than Bocagrande) is good for swimming.

Art Gallery Contemporary Latin American paintings, Banco Ganadero, Plaza de la Aduana. Nearby is the Museo de Arte Moderno (open Mon.-Fri., 0900-1200, 1500-1800, Sat., 1000-1200), opposite the San Pedro Claver church.

Exchange Banco Anglo Colombiano. Banco Royal changes American Express travellers' cheques up to a maximum of US$300, with US$10 commission. Banco de la República, on Plaza Bolívar, changes American Express cheques, with commission, fingerprints and photo taken. There are many *cambios*; none change travellers' cheques. Be sure to count the pesos yourself before handing over your dollars. Never change money on the street, they are nearly all crooks and will short-change you. American Express (Tierra Mar Aire), Bocagrande, Carrera 4, Calle 8, is a travel agency only. Travellers' cheques can be changed Sat. a.m. (arrive early) at Joyería Mora, Román 5-39, in the old city.

Anglican Church Calle Ricuarte, services in English can be arranged.

Post Office beside Avianca office between Avs. Venezuela and Urdaneta Arbeláez.

Venezuelan Consulate Castillogrande, no visa issued without onward ticket, minimum wait 24 hrs. Better try elsewhere. **DAS** just off Av. Crisanto Luque, near La Ermita at foot of La Popa, T 64649 (take "Socorro" bus), very helpful. **Canadian Honorary Consul** (for emergencies only), Calle de la Inquisición con Santo Domingo, esq., No. 33-08, Apto. 201.

Tourist Office Carrera 3, No. 36-57 (Plaza Bolívar, T 43400); also at Casa del Marqués de Valdehoyos, Calle de la Factoría (T 47015/9). Recommended guide, Fernando Vargas Osorio, Calle de Magdalena, No. 7-52.

Shipping There are modern wharves. It is possible to ship a car from Cartagena to Panama (see Panama section, **page 1330**). Interoceánica, Centro Carrera 4a, No. 31-14, T 45976/ 44047; cargo ships. Comar agency for Lykes Line, formalities take 3 days. Cargo ships are not allowed to take passengers to San Andrés; some may risk it, charging about US$25. You have to ask the captain; ships leave from Embarcadero San Andrés, opp. Plaza de la Aduana.

Airport Crespo, 1½ km. from the city, reached by local buses from Blas de Lezo, SW corner of inner wall. Bus from airport to Plaza San Francisco US$0.10. Taxi to Bocagrande US$2.20, to town US$2, less if you share. Flights to Maracaibo. Commuter flights to Barranquilla. Tourist information desk gives list of taxi prices. Good self-service restaurant. No exchange facilities. SAM and Avianca offices both near the post office. From December to March all flights are overbooked—even reconfirming and turning up 2 hours early doesn't guarantee a seat; don't book a seat on the last plane of the day.

Buses All long-distance buses leave from Calle 32, with Av. Pedro Heredia, near foot of San Felipe fortress (any bus marked "E-Villa" goes to the old city and Parque Centenario). Pullman bus from Cartagena to Medellín 665 km., US$14 (1st class). Several buses a day, but book early (2 days in advance at holiday times), takes 13-16 hrs. The road is now paved throughout, but in poor condition with 4-5 checkpoints. To Santa Marta, US$4.75 (with Brasilia, Calle 32, No. 20D-55), 4 hrs., also cheaper lines, US$3.50. To Barranquilla US$2.25 with Transportes Cartagena, 3 hrs., or US$2.75 with Expreso Brasilia pullman or La Costeña, US$2.60, 3 hrs. To Bogotá via Barranquilla and Bucaramanga with Expreso Brasilia pullman, four a day, US$23, may take 21-28 hrs., depending on number of check-points. To Valledupar with Expreso Brasilia, pullman US$8.50 (with a ½ hour stop in Barranquilla), for Sierra Nevada and Pueblo Bello. To Riohacha, US$7.50. Bus to Maicao on Venezuelan frontier US$4.75 (with Expreso Auto Pullman, Expreso Brasilia at 2000, or Unitrasco, Av. Pedro Heredia), 12 hrs.; the road is in good condition, except for 30 km.

Travel from Cartagena To the little fishing village of **La Boquilla**, E of Cartagena, about 20 mins. past the airport. One small hotel, *Los Morros* (E, clean, good food) and campsite. On Sat. and Sun. nights people dance the local dances. Go there by taxi, US$3 (there is a reasonable bus service, and Carlos drives a green Dodge regularly to the bus terminal, US$0.50); can be dangerous for pedestrians and cyclists. Visit the mangrove swamps nearby to see the birds. To **San Jacinto**, 1½ hrs. by road S of Cartagena, good place for local craft work. To **Turbaco**, 24 km. SE by road (Botanical Garden, 1½ km. before village on the left, student guides, worth a visit for ½-day excursion) and on S through Sincelejo (193 km., see below), **Planeta Rica** (320 km.) and Yarumal (*Restaurante La Nena*) to Medellín. 60 km. beyond Planeta Rica there is a camping site in the grounds of the *Parador Chaubacú* (US$4 per tent); next door is the *Mesón del Gitano*. Five km. further on is **Caucasia**, which makes a good stopping point if you want to break the journey from Cartagena to Medellín. *Auto Hotel*, new, best, quiet, heavily booked; *Hotel Playa Mar*, F, good food available, friendly, but noisy; *Residencias San Francisco*, Carrera 49 esq. Calle 45, E, with bath, good value. Chinese restaurant, 3 doors up, good cheap food. A nice place to visit, Jardín Botánico, entrance fee US$0.25.

Ninety-six km. S of Cartagena along the coast is **Coveñas,** the terminal of the 420-km. crude oil pipeline from the Barco oilfields to the N of Cúcuta, on the Venezuelan frontier (*Hotel y Motel Fragata*, on the beach, rec.). 20 mins away, E, is **Tolú** village (*Residencias Manuelito*, F, and *Residencias El Turista*, very friendly, has own generator, F; *Residencias La Cabaña*, at western end of beach road, F, no running water, friendly; many fish stalls along the beach) whose beaches are not as nice as those at Coveñas, which are unsigned—ask to be let off the bus. W. of Coveñas are beautiful beaches at Porvenir, no food available, afternoon buses infrequent. Coveñas is 40 minutes from

Sincelejo, capital of Sucre Department, a cattle centre 193 km. S of Cartagena on the main road to Medellín (population, 109,000). It is well known for the dangerous bull-ring game, likened to the San Fermín festivities in Pamplona, Spain, in which bulls and men chase each other. The town is hot and dusty and power cuts are a factor of life.

Hotels *Majestic*, Carrera 20, No. 21-25, E; same range are *Palace*, Calle 19, No. 21-39, and *Marcella*, Calle 21, 23-59; *Finzenu*, Carrera 20 and Calle 22, D, with a/c and some good basic eating; *Sincelejo*, Plaza Santander, F with shower, clean, friendly, fair restaurant.

Montería, capital of Córdoba Department, on the E bank of the river Sinú, can be reached from Cartagena by air, by river boat, or from the main highway to Medellín. (Bus from Cartagena—dual carriageway almost completed, US$5.25, 5 hrs., with Brasilia, has own terminal in Montería.) It is the centre of a cattle and agricultural area turning out tobacco, cacao, cotton and sugar. Present population is 144,000. Compared with other Caribbean cities there is little to attract the tourist except for the one fine church, picturesque street life and the extremely friendly people. Average temperature: 28°C. Road to Planeta Rica (airport).

Hotels *Sinú*, Carrera 3, Calle 32, C, a/c and swimming pool, watch out for short changing in the restaurant; *Alcázar*, Carrera 2, No. 32-17, F, comfortable and friendly, restaurant not always open; *Embajador*, F, fan, OK; lots of cheap dives in the neighbourhood; *Pensión Rincón*, F, reasonable, clean, meals, US$1; *Residencias Imperial*, Carrera 2, F; *Santa Rosa*, F, with water, good.

Warning There is a high risk of kidnapping in rural areas of Sucre and Córdoba departments; tourists are advised not to stray from the beaten track.

On the Gulf of Urabá is the port of **Turbo,** now a centre of banana cultivation, which is booming. It is a rough frontier community; not too law-abiding, tourists are advised to be very careful. Turbo may be reached from Cartagena and from Medellín (6 buses a day, a gruelling 13-16 hrs., US$7.50; 4-wheel drive to Montería, 5 hrs., US$6, rough road between Turbo and Valencia, several army checkpoints). Hotels: *Playa Mar*, D, the best; *Sausa*, D, running water in early morning only, helpful owners, pleasant dining room; *Residencia Sandra*, F, good; *Residencia*

Turbo, Residencia Marcela, both F and best value; good rooms are hard to find, most hotels are brothels; in Playa district: *Miramar, Rotitom,* both D. No banks are open for exchange of travellers' cheques on Monday or Tuesday, either don't arrive then, or have dollars in cash with you.

To visit the **Los Katíos National Park (see page 1328)**, go first to the Inderena office in Turbo, where all necessary information is available (recommended trip). A description of an overland journey from Panama to Colombia via Turbo will be found in the Panama section; note that if going from Colombia to Panama via Turbo you should get an exit stamp from a DAS office. The nearest we have heard of is at Apartado, 30 km. from Turbo (40 mins. in colectivo, US$0.80, closed Sat. and Sun.) but even this may now be closed. If leaving Colombia, check the facts in Cartagena (or any other place with a DAS office); if arriving from Panama, you can either go to the police in Turbo for a letter stating your arrival date, then go to DAS in Cartagena, or just go straight there and explain yourself in full. We have also been informed that the immigration office at the Panamanian port of Puerto Obaldía can be extremely obstructive. Think twice about taking a trip in a small boat between Panama and Colombia: the majority are contraband, even arms runners and if stopped, you will be in trouble. (Even if not stopped you will have difficulty obtaining a DAS entry stamp because the captain of the boat must state officially that he is carrying passengers into Colombia.) If taking a reputable cargo boat be sure to arrange with the captain the price and destination before departure. Boats may also be stopped outside Turbo for medical checks: yellow fever inoculations will be given (free) to all without a certificate.

186 km. S of Turbo, on the road to Antioquia **(see page 580),** is Dabeiba (*Residencia Diana,* on main street, F, simple, clean, very helpful, free morning coffee).

San Andrés and *Providencia,* two small and attractive, but very expensive, islands in the Caribbean Sea, have belonged to Colombia since 1822. They are 400 km. SW of Jamaica, 180 km. E of Nicaragua, and 480 km. N of the Colombian coast. Henry Morgan had his headquarters at San Andrés. A beautiful road circles the island, of coral, some 11 km. long rising to 104 metres. The original inhabitants, mostly black, speak some English, but the population has swollen with unrestricted immigration from Colombia. The population in 1988 was put at 35,000, but it could now be about 65,000. Main products: coconuts and vegetable oil. Main problem: deteriorating water and electricity supplies (in most hotels the water is salty—a desalination plant was installed in 1987). Places to see: the actual Keys, like Johnny Key with a white beach and parties all day Sunday (US$1.90 return, you can go in one boat and return in another), and the so-called Aquarium (US$2 return), off a Key where, using a mask and wearing sandals as protection against sea-urchins, you can see colourful fish. Boats to these places all leave a.m.; none p.m. Snorkelling equipment can be hired on San Andrés for US$4-5, but it is better and cheaper on the shore than on the island. The Hoyo Soplador is a geyser-like hole through which the sea spouts into the air most surprisingly when the wind is in the right direction. Less spoilt parts of the island are San Luis, Sound Bay and the west side (but no beaches this side). Buses (which circle the island all day) US$0.25. Bicycles are a popular way of getting around on the island and are easy to hire, e.g. opposite *El Dorado Hotel*—usually in poor condition, choose your own bike and check all parts thoroughly (US$1.10 per hour, US$6 per day); motorbikes also easy to hire, US$3.60 per hour. Cars can be hired for US$15 for 2 hours, with US$6 for every extra hour. Pedalos can be hired at US$4 per hour. Diving trips to reef cost US$50 with Pedro Montoya at Aquarium diving shop.

The islands are a customs-free zone; they are very crowded with Colombian shoppers looking for foreign-made bargains. Although alcoholic drinks are cheap, essential goods are extremely costly, and electronic goods are more expensive than in the UK. In July and August, it is very difficult to get on flights into and out of San Andrés; book in advance if possible. Checking in for flights can be difficult because of queues of shoppers with their goods. There is a customs tax of about US$2 (rarely enforced) on merchandise exported from the islands. Banco de la República (Mon.-Fri., 0800-1300) will exchange dollars and travellers' cheques; Banco Cafetero will advance pesos on a Visa card. Aerodisco shop at airport will change dollars cash anytime at rates slightly worse than banks, or try the Photo Shop on Av. Costa Rica. (Rates are lower than in Bogotá.) Many shops will change US$ cash; it is impossible to change travellers' cheques at weekends. (Airport employees will exchange US$ cash at a poor rate.)

Only cruise ships and tours go to San Andrés; there are no other passenger services by sea. To ship a vehicle costs US$900 with bargaining (officially US$1,300). To ship a vehicle to Panama costs US$400-450. Interoceánica cargo ships, T 6624-6625. Beware of offers of tickets on ships to/from San Andrés, or of a job on a ship, these are con tricks. Officially, ships may not carry passengers to the mainland; if you want to leave by sea, speak only to the ship's captain.

There are Panamanian and Costa Rican consulates on San Andrés.

Airport Flights to most major Colombian cities: to Bogotá with SAM (you can arrange a 72-hr. stop-over in Cartagena) and Avianca (dearer); to Cartagena, with SAM or Avianca, US$50; to Barranquilla (SAM, Eastern Airlines, from Miami). SAM also flies to Cali (US$85) and Pereira. Also to Belize, Guatemala City (5 a week), San José, Tegucigalpa, Panama. Note that Panama, Costa Rica and Honduras all require onward tickets which cannot be bought on San Andrés, can be in Cartagena. Sunday flights are always heavily booked. 15 mins. walk to town (taxi US$2.50 p.p.). All airline offices in town, except Satena at airport. Exit tax for flights abroad, US$7.

Carry your passport (or photocopy) at all times.

Hotels *Gran Internacional*, Av. Colón, No. 2-77, B, a/c, swimming pool, decrepit; also on Colón, *Galaxia*, C with breakfast, bath, fan, smelly; *Mediterráneo*, D, poor water supply; *Nueva Aurora*, Av. de las Américas, B, fan and private bath; *Bahía Marina*, B, swimming pool, the largest on San Andrés, and good restaurant; *El Dorado*, Av. Colombia, No. 1A-25 (casino, swimming pool), C; *Abacoa*, Av. Colombia, B, with bath and a/c; also *Royal Abacoa*, A, on same avenue at No. 2-41; *Bahía Sardina*, Av. Colombia, across the street from the beach, a/c, TV, fridge, good service, comfortable, clean, no swimming pool; *Europa*, Av. 20 de Julio, No. 1-101, C, with bath, clean; *Calypso Beach*, A; *Capri*, Av. Costa Rica, No. 1A-110, B, with bath and a/c, good value; *Cacique Toné*, Av. Colombia, Cra. 5, A, deluxe, a/c, pool, on sea-front; *Tiuna*, Av. Colombia, No. 3-59, A, a/c, swimming pool; *Las Antillas*, Av. 20 de Julio, No. 1A-81, D with bath and fan, clean, safe, good water (inc. for drinking), good value; *Turista Natania*, in front of Coliseo, B; nearby are *Coliseo*, friendly, noisy, good restaurant, C, and *Malibú*, restaurant, B. *Residencia Restrepo*, "gringo hotel", near airport—turn left to beach, then left, second left at fish restaurant and it's a hundred metres on left (no sign), noisy ("share a room with a Boeing 727" - till midnight), F or G for a hammock in the porch, clean, some rooms with bath, breakfast US$0.50, other meals US$1.50, good place for buying/selling unwanted return halves of air tickets to/from Central America or the Colombian mainland; *Astor*, D inc. 3 meals; *Residencias Hernando Henry*, E, restaurant, fan, clean, good value, on road from airport. Campsite at South End said to be dirty and mosquito-ridden.

Restaurants *Oasis* (good); *La Parrillada* (Argentine), good meals at US$4; *Mar del Caribe*, Av. de las Américas, good meals for US$2, try the Redondo (fish, yucca, plantain, rice and toast); *Popular*, on Av. Bogotá, good square meal for US$4; comida corriente at *Don Joaco's* for US$2, good fish. *Mercapollo*, good value; *San Andrés* and *High Seas* are also rec. for cheap, typical meals; *Fonda Antioqueña Nos. 1 and 2*, on Av. Colombia near the main beach, and Av. Colombia at Av. Nicaragua, best value for fish; *Miami*, special for US$3; excellent fruit juices at *Jugolandia*, Calle 20 de Julio; *Jugosito*, Av. Colombia, 1½ blocks from tourist office towards centre, cheap meals; *Mundo Acuático*, snacks of fresh fish and papaya for US$1, cheaper beer, soft drinks and mangoes. *Fisherman's Place*, in the fishing cooperative at N end of main beach, very good, simple. Good ice cream next to *Hotel Gran Internacional*. *The Barboat*, a floating bar, off the beach between the Centro Comercial Dann and Club Náutico, English and German spoken, waterskiing and windsurfing rental, also instruction available, water taxi to the Keys. Fish meals for US$2.50 can be bought at San Luis beach.

Taxis round the island, US$8; to airport, US$3; in town, US$0.60; *colectivo* to airport, US$0.50.

Tourist Information, Avenida Colombia No. 5-117, beneath *Hotel Isleño*, English spoken, maps, friendly, helpful.

Providencia, commonly called Old Providence, 80 km. back to the NNE from San Andrés, is 7 km. long and is more mountainous than San Andrés, rising to 610 metres. There are waterfalls, and the land drops steeply into the sea in places. It is also an expensive island. The 3 main beaches are Manchincal Bay, the largest, most attractive and least developed, Southwest Bay and Freshwater Bay, all in the South West. Most of the accommodation is at Freshwater: *Cabañas El Recreo* (Captain Brian's), E, p.p.; *Cabañas El Paraíso*, *Cabañas Aguadulce* and *Hotel Royal Queen*; *Ma Elma's* rec. for cheap food; at Santa Isabela on the N end of the island, *Flaming Trees Hotel*, N, clean, restaurant, good value, but a long way from the beach; at Smooth Water Bay, *Dutch Inn* (C full board) and several houses take in guests. Camping is possible at Freshwater Bay. Truck drivers who provide transport on the island may be able to advise on accommodation. The sea food is good, water and fresh milk are generally a problem. Horse riding is available, and boat trips can be made to neighbouring islands such as Santa Catalina (an old pirate lair), and to the NE, Crab Key (beautiful swimming). Superb views can be had by climbing from Bottom House or Smooth Water to the peak. Day tours are arranged by the Providencia office in San Andrés, costing US$30 inclusive. Satena fly from San Andrés, US$30, 30 mins., once a day, sometimes twice, never on Sun., bookable only in San Andrés. (Return flight has to be confirmed at airport. Tourist office at airport.) Boat trips from San Andrés take 8 hours, but are not regular.

Santa Marta, capital of Magdalena Department (pop.: 350,000), the third Caribbean port, is 96 km. E of Barranquilla, at the mouth of the Manzanares river. It is best reached from Barranquilla by the paved road along the coast, which passes salt pans and skirts an extensive and most interesting lagoon, the Ciénaga de Santa Marta, in which all types of water birds, plants and animals may be seen. (There has been an ecological disaster there, as a result of cutting off the egress to the sea to build the coast road.) There is a paved road S to Bucaramanga (see page 543) and Bogotá.

Santa Marta lies on a deep bay with high shelving cliffs. The climate ranges seasonally from hot and trying to hot but pleasant in February and March; occasionally one can see snow-clad peaks of the Sierra Nevada to the E, less than 50 km. away and 5,800 metres high.

Its sandy beaches stretch from the Simón Bolívar airport to Punta Aguja across the Rodadero de Gaira and the little fishing villages of Villa Concha, surrounded by meadows and shady trees, and Taganga (see below). A jutting rock—the Punta de Betín—rises from the sea in front of the city and is topped by a lighthouse. Rugged Moro Island, 3 km. off Santa Marta, completes the panorama. Rodadero Bay is the most fashionable and tourist-oriented part of Santa Marta, though it lies some distance W of the city (local bus service, taxi, US$4.50). It is extremely dangerous to wander off the beaten track at Rodadero: correspondents have been robbed at gunpoint. Many of the buses coming from Barranquilla and Cartagena stop at Rodadero on the way to Santa Marta. There is also a dirty, unsafe beach with a seaside promenade close to the centre of town.

Santa Marta was the first town founded (1525) by the *conquistadores* in Colombia. Founder: Rodrigo de Bastidas. Most of the famous sea-dogs—the brothers Côte, Drake and Hawkins—sacked the city in spite of the two forts built on a small island at the entrance to the bay. It was here that Simón Bolívar, his dream of a Great Colombia shattered, came to die. Almost penniless he was given hospitality at the *hacienda* of San Pedro Alejandrino, 5 km. to the SE. He died on December 17, 1830, at the age of 47, and was buried in the Cathedral, but his body was taken to the Pantheon at Caracas 12 years later. The simple room in which he died and his few belongings can be seen today (admission, US$0.10, open Tues.-Sat. 1330-2000): take the "Mamatoca" bus from the waterfront (Carrera 1C) to the *hacienda*, US$0.20.

Warning The north end of town, beyond the railway station, is very dangerous and travellers are advised not to go there alone.

Hotels In town: *Residencia Park Hotel,* Carrera 1C, No. 18-63, on sea front, D with shower, reasonable; *Tairona,* Carrera 1, No. 11-41, T 32408, D, with fan, bath, clean and safe; *Dos Virreyes,* Calle 12, No. 1-34, near waterfront, can be bargained for, E, only 5 rooms, with fan and shower, friendly, rec.; *Residencias Miramar,* Calle 10C, No. 1C-59, F with fan (cheaper rooms without), "gringo hotel", very friendly, safe, 2 blocks from railway station and beach (not to be confused with *Hotel Residencias Miramar,* Carrera 1C, No. 18-23); several others nearby, e.g. *Res. Marinas,* Calle 10, No. 1C-83, F, clean, friendly, fan, bath; *Hotel Residencias Yarimar,* Carrera 1A, No. 26-37, E, clean, fan, noisy; *Yuldama,* Cra. 1, No. 12-19, C, clean a/c, reasonable food; *Residencias Adelita,* Calle 24 and Carrera 8, D; many on Calle 22. *Andrea Doria,* 300 m. from seashore, E, friendly, clean. *Residencias Costa Azul,* E, with bath and shower, rec. as impeccably clean with good mattresses, fan and window on to courtyard, in town, very friendly.

At Rodadero Bay: *Tamacá* (best, Carrera 2, No. 11A-98, B); *Irotama,* L (km. 14, between airport and Rodadero Bay; has bungalows); *Residencias Edma,* Carrera 3, No. 5-188, Rodadero, D, a/c, new, clean, cafeteria, run by two ladies, welcoming; *La Sierra,* Carrera 1, No. 9-47, C, good and relatively inexpensive restaurant; *Valladolid,* E, Carrera 2, good value, large clean rooms, helpful, changes travellers' cheques, rec.; *Puerto Galleón,* L, at km. 18 (difficult to reach by taxi at night); *Santa Mar,* at Km. 8, D. Cheapest is *Toronto,* E, clean, friendly, 2 blocks from sea. In season, it is difficult to find a single room for less than US$4. Apartments: *Patuca,* on beach, US$40 for 8.

Motels *El Rodadero,* Calle 11, No. 1-29, D, swimming pool, English-speaking manageress (Marino Salcedo), very helpful; *Taboga;* and *Lilium,* secure parking.

Restaurants *Grill Venecia,* in roof garden of Posiheuica building, facing the bay; the *Pan*

American, on the beach walk, is pleasant; good food and service; *Yarimar,* Carrera 1A, No. 26-37, next to hotel of same name, good seafood; opp. is *La Terraza Marina,* also rec. for seafood. *Madrid,* Calle 11, 100 metres from seafront, cheap and good; *El Platanal,* Calle 13, No. 1-33, good cheap food, good service. *La Gran Muralla,* Carrera 5, No. 23-77 and *Oriental,* Calle 22, No. 3-43, both good Chinese. A good breakfast in *Colonial,* on corner of *Hotel Zulia. Bermuz,* Calle 14, No. 4-08, good, cheap.

At Rodadero: *La Bella Napolés,* first class; *Pacabuy,* on seafront, highly rec.; *Porto Fino,* three blocks from *Tamacá,* good food, not too expensive; *Restaurante Karey,* highly rec. *Pekin,* Calle 22, between Carreras 4 and 5, good value.

Museum Casa de la Aduana, Calle 14 y Carera 2, displays an excellent archaeological collection, including a large number of pre-Columbian gold artefacts. Open Tues.-Sat., 0800-1200, 1400-1800, Sun. 0800-1200, during the tourist season, Mon.-Fri., 0800-1200, 1400-1800, the rest of the year; entry US$0.15.

Exchange Change money at the Banco de la República, on Carrera 5, No. 17-04; open 0800-1100 and 1400-1530. *Casas de cambio* in 3rd block of Calle 14.

Tourist Office in the former Convent of Santo Domingo, Carrera 2, No. 16-44. There is also an office at Rodadero, Calle 10, No. 3-10. Inderena office, Carrera 1C, No. 22-77, and at the Quinta de San Pedro Alejandrino.

Train Expreso del Sol leaves on Mondays and Thursdays at 0700 for La Dorada; 24 hrs. (US$10), long delays possible. One class only; meals at US$1.50 each, quite good. From La Dorada, one can also take a bus to Bogotá (**see page 569**). The Tayrona runs to Bogotá once a week between December and March only. The Nutibara runs once a week from Santa Marta to Medellín during the same months; connects with the Tayrona at Grecia.

Buses Terminal is at Calle 24 and Carrera 8 (take a taxi or walk to Calle 22, then take "Playa" bus to centre, passing waterfront—Carrera 1C). The Copetran bus to Bucaramanga takes about 9 hrs. (US$15). Journey time will be affected by the number of police checks. There is a good meal stop at Los Límites. From Bucaramanga the buses take 8 hrs. to Bogotá (11 minimum by 2nd class). Buses to Barranquilla, 2 hrs. (US$1.60-1.80); to Cartagena, 4 hrs. (US$3.50, or US$4.75, Brasilia). To Riohacha US$1.75; Pullman to Maicao, US$5.75. The buses stop at the Venezuelan border on the way to Maracaibo for exit and entry stamps, usually better organized than at Cúcuta. There are three buses a day (Brasilia) direct to Rodadero Beach from Barranquilla, taking 2 hrs. and costing US$1.50. They return to Barranquilla at 1300, 1530 and 1730.

Airport Simón Bolívar, 20 km. from city; bus, US$0.20, taxi from Santa Marta, US$7, from Rodadero, US$2.40. During the tourist season, get to the airport early.

Port It can take up to 4 working days to get a car out of the port, but it is usually well guarded and it is unlikely that anything will be stolen.

Sightseeing Tours in air-conditioned jeeps run by Airline travel agency at centre. Launches leave Rodadero beach every hour for the Aquarium and the closest safe view you can get of hammerhead sharks, US$3 return (includes admission). From the Aquarium, one can walk over slippery rocks (1½-2 hrs.) to the Playa Blanca (White Beach) where one can swim in less crowded conditions than elsewhere—food available at the beach.

Excursions Close to Santa Marta (bus US$0.10, 30 mins. taxi US$2, 10 mins.) is the fishing village and beach of *Taganga,* with hotel *La Ballena Azul,* D, most attractive, friendly, comfortable, clean, restaurant, also run boat tours to secluded beaches, horses for hire (postal address: Aptdo Aéreo 799, Santa Marta, Telex 38886 CCSMT CO). One can stay with Joselito Guerra on the beach, G for hammock space, secure for luggage, or rent houses on beach (not secure). Restaurants expensive, but a good one is *Tibisay,* seafood. Swimming good, especially on Playa Grande, 25 mins'. walk round coast, but thieving is common there. Taganga is quiet during week, but trippers from Santa Marta pour in on Sun. On the E shore of the Ciénaga de Santa Marta, is *Ciénaga,* a town of 75,000 people. Cotton, bananas, tobacco and cacao are grown in the area. Hotels in Ciénaga: *Tobiexa; Naval.* (Granturismo tours to Ciénaga are not recommended; much too fast). South of Ciénaga, just before Fundación, is *Aracataca,* birthplace of Gabriel García Márquez, fictionalised as Macondo in some of his stories (notably *One Hundred Years of Solitude*). His home, called a museum, may be seen in the backyard of La Familia Iriarte Ahumada—just ask for directions. There are *residencias* (G), but it is better to stay in Fundación. Best hotel is *Caroli,* Carrera 8, No. 5-30, Fundación, F (E with a/c); others all in this price range. Do not walk between Aracataca and Fundación at night, otherwise it is safe. Bus Fundación-Aracataca, US$0.15; Fundación-Ciénaga, US$0.75; Fundación-Barranquilla, US$3.50. Banana growing in the area has now been replaced almost entirely by African palm plantations.

To go to the *Ciudad Perdida,* discovered in 1975, permission is required from Inderena, Carerra 1a, No. 22-77, Santa Marta, T 36355; it is not always given because the area is dangerous. The site covers 400 hectares, at 1,100 metres altitude, near the Río Buritaca; comparisons have been made with Machu Picchu.

Ettore Grugni, of Roddi, Italy, writes: Ciudad Pedida was founded between 500 and 700 A.D. and was surely the most important centre of the Tairona culture. It stands on the steep slopes of Cerro Corea, which lies in the northern part of the Sierra Nevada de Santa Marta. It consists of a complex system of buildings, paved footpaths, flights of steps and perimetrical walls, which link a series of terraces and platforms, on which were built cult centres, residences and warehouses.

You can reach Ciudad Perdida by helicopter from Santa Marta in about 20 minutes. Ask at Helicol, at the airport, or at Corporación Nacional de Turismo, Carrera 2a, No. 16-44 (T 35773). Price: about US$180.

More adventurous trekkers can reach Ciudad Perdida in a six/eight days' excursion, leaving about 0700 from Santa Marta market, at the corner of Carrera 11 and Calle 11.

Toyota jeeps go up to La Tagua (about 3 hours), where it is possible to rent mules and pay local guides or to go on alone. The first day's walking is about 7 hours, through fine wild scenery. The first night will be spent in a hammock in a typical farmhouse. They are very hospitable, but you need to take your own food. The second day will bring you up to the heights of Alto de Mira where, after 8 hours' walking, you will stay the night in a hammock in a typical "bohío", where a group of archaeologists is still working. With their permission, you may be able to stop for a day to visit the excavations. The third day will bring you down to the Buritaca river and then, through impressive scenery, up to the steps which bring you to the archaeological site of Ciudad Perdida. The visit to the town will take you the fourth day; there is nowhere to stay as yet. The return to Santa Marta will take you three days.

Archaeologists and army guards will ask you for your permit. Don't forget that Ciudad Perdida is a National Park: it is strictly forbidden to damage trees and collect flowers or insects.

One week trips organized by the tourist office in Santa Marta cost US$200, but can be bargained much lower: price includes mules, guide and food, 3 days' hike there, 1 day at site, 3 days back. Take hammock, protection against mosquitoes, sleeping bag, warm clothing for the nights, and strong shoes. Hotels in Santa Marta or Taganga may charge up to US$400 p.p. Recommended guides: Joselito (see above under Taganga) and his cousin Pacho.

Jim Lindsay of the Australian Embassy in Carcaras recommends a circuitous route to the site, which can be arranged through *Hotel La Ballena Azul* (above). It costs about US$250 p.p. for the 6-day round trip, all inclusive. Its advantage is that it avoids all settlements, especially in the drug-growing lower valleys and Kogui villages which may not welcome foreigners. He also recommends Juan Mayr's book, *The Sierra Nevada of Santa Marta*(Mayr y Cabal, Apartado Aéreo 5000, Bogotá) which deals beautifully with the Ciudad Perida.

The **Tairona** national park, 35 km. E of Santa Marta in the Riohacha direction, wild woodland on the coast, is beautiful and unspoilt. Take a Maicao or Riohacha bus to the park entrance (US$0.70), then walk or hitch 5 km. to beach at Cañaveral (a safe place to visit). Alternatively, there is a tour bus at 1000 from *Hotel Zulia* in Santa Marta, direct to Cañaveral, return at 1500, US$3 (not long enough). Bathing not recommended as there is heavy pounding surf and the tides are treacherous. The place is not without thieves, but a most attractive spot for camping; the beach is less crowded and cleaner than Rodadero. (There are splendid and deserted sandy beaches, to which you have to walk, about 5 km. E of Cañaveral.) Relics of ancient Tairona culture abound. A taxi to Cañaveral and back from Santa Marta costs US$14. A guided tour round the Pueblito archaeological site is free, every Sat. or as arranged, under escort of a park guard (a full tour from *Hotel Irotama*, including transport and guide, costs US$55). Camping in the Park at Cañaveral costs US$5 per site. Many camping and hammock places on the path from the Park to Pueblito. The camp at Cañaveral has facilities but there is only one restaurant (expensive) with a tiny store, so take all supplies. There are plenty of mosquitoes. Good camping at Arrecife (US$1.75 for tent, US$1.10 for hammock space, US$2 to hire hammock, US$2.85 for hut), fresh water shower and toilets at campsite, one good restaurant, soft drinks available (e.g. from Alberto), beautiful beach nearby (sea dangerous). Avoid, if possible, camping at Finca Martínez—dirty, narcotics centre; Finca Bermúdez (on the road to Pueblito) has better camping, for US$1 p.p. Walking in the park, it is 1 hour from the entrance to Cañaveral, then another hour to Arrecife; follow the beach for ¼ hour to Rancho Viejo from where a clear path leads S to Pueblito (1½ hrs.). At the site there are Indians; do not photograph them. From Pueblito you can either return to Cañaveral, or continue for 2 hours to Calabazo on the Santa Marta-Riohacha road. It is advisable to inform park guards when walking in the park as it is a marijuana-growing area; also wear hiking boots and beware of bloodsucking insects. In the wet, the paths are very slippery.

You need to obtain permission from Inderena to camp in the park if you are not staying in Cañaveral, but this is normally forthcoming if you specify where you intend to stay.

Riohacha, capital of Guajira Department, 160 km. E of Santa Marta, is a port of 75,000 people at the mouth of the Río César: low white houses, sandy streets, no trees or hills. It was founded in 1545 by Nicolás Federmann, and in early years its pearling industry was large enough to tempt Drake to sack it (1596). Pearling almost ceased during the 18th century and the town was all but abandoned. (It is best to travel from Riohacha in a luxury bus, early a.m. as these buses are less likely to be stopped and searched for contraband.)

Hotels *Campestre* (state-owned); *Gimaura*, (also state-owned), on beach, D, including breakfast, they allow camping (free) in their grounds, with outside shower; *Los Delfines*, E, clean, friendly, one block from sea and central plaza, two from Venezuelan consulate. *Hostal* opposite the bus station, E, fan, clean, friendly, expensive food; *Nelly*, F, basic but convenient for bus stations on the edge of town.

Many small restaurants along sea-front including *Europa*, German run. *Tizones*, opp. *Los Delfines*, Carrera 2 y Carrera 10, rec. for food and juices (takes Visa and Diners Club); *Golosinas*, café near the beach, good food, friendly service. All accommodation and food is expensive (no hotel or *pensión* costs less than US$5). You can sling your hammock for free at the police station. There are an airport, a cinema, a tourist office on the beach front and a bank, which changes dollars cash, but not if you're in your beachwear. The best place for buying mantas and other local items is La Casa de la Manta Guajira, Carrera 6, No. 9-35, be prepared to bargain. At the weekend, Riohacha fills up, and bars and music spring up all over the place. The sea is clean, despite the red silt stirred up by the waves.

Venezuelan Consulate Calle 7, No. 3-75 (hours 0900-1300, and closed from 1500 Fri. to 0900 Mon.). With two passport photographs and an exit ticket most can get a visa on the same day, but be prepared for an interview with the consul himself; visas cost US$10 for all but Danish citizens (free), US, West German and Swiss (US$0.70).

Tourist Office Carrera 7, No. 1-38. **DAS Office** (immigration) Calle 1 y Carrera 6, T 72407.

There is a road connection between Riohacha and Bucaramanga. At La Paz (Hotel: *Turismo*; Restaurant: *La Fogata*) you join the road that leads through **Valledupar,** capital of César Department, said to be an unfriendly town, population 202,000 to Barranquilla and Santa Marta via Fundación (see above); bus from Santa Marta, 8½ hrs., US$1.75; from Cartagena, US$8.50 with Expreso Brasilia).

Valledupar claims to be the home of the *vallenato* music, in which the accordion features prominently. Each year there is a *vallenato* festival from 29 April to 1 May in the town.

Hotels *Sicarare*, two-star, Carrera 9, No. 16-04, D; cheaper 2-star hotel is *Kurakata*, Calle 19C, No. 7-96; *Residencial El César 1*, Calle 18 No. 9-39, *El César 2*, Calle 18, No. 11-58, both F with bath, clean; another opp. *El César 1*; *Central*, basic, E. *Residencia El Triunfo*, Carrera 7, No. 19-31, F with bath, fan, clean, good, but slightly dubious part of town; next door is *Hotel/Restaurant Nutibara*, excellent cheap meals and breakfast, excellent fruit juices; several other hotels in this street.

The Sierra Nevada, covering a triangular area of 16,000 sq. km., rises abruptly from the sea, or from lowlands which nowhere reach over 300 metres above sea-level. "Indeed, the north slope is one of the most striking anywhere, lifting from the Caribbean to 5,800-metre snow peaks in about 45 km., a gradient comparable with the south face of the Himalaya, and unequalled along the world's coasts. The interior is made up of some eight E-W ranges with their intervening valleys. . . . The lower parts of these interior valleys are flanked by forests—the homes of primitive Indians as well as of pumas, jaguars, and a variety of snakes and birds—but for the most part the Sierra is almost lunar in its sterile grandeur, bleak *páramos* leading to naked crag and scree and glacier, where only an occasional questing condor moves. In the rocky heart of the area are a large number of small, beautiful lakes, many in cirques." - Frank F. Cunningham, in an excellent illustrated article on exploring the Sierra in *The Geographical Magazine*. The rainy season in these mountains ends November; January is best month for a visit.

It is necessary to obtain a safe-conduct pass from the Casa Indígena (45 minutes out of town) and the police in Valledupar before visiting the Sierra Nevada, if you are going further than San Sebastián. From Valledupar the best route is along the Guatepuri valley. Jeeps and buses run from Valledupar, Carrera 7A, Calle 18, Nos. 37-55, to Pueblo Bello, 2 hrs. US$1.50. In Pueblo Bello (Hotel *El Encanto*, F, good meals US$1, friendly; *El Hogar de Mamí*, E, very clean; *El Hogar de Mercedes*, F), enquire for jeeps to San Sebastián de Rábago, the central village of one of the four tribes of Indians living in the Sierra, the Arhuacos (jeep owners Quico and Gudar Neader are the only ones who go frequently, US$20 per vehicle, or US$3 per seat, 2-2½ hrs.). It is set in beautiful surroundings and is the epitome of an Indian village; the jeep driver may be able to arrange for you to stay on a farm; Doña Inés recommended, F, clean, friendly, good food. Also recommended is Noco, a mestizo who has lived in the valley for 30 years; he has floor space and rents mules for trips in the Sierra (US$7 per mule and per guide, per day). Noco himself may act as guide if he is free (he runs a grocery store); he is very knowledgeable. Camping is also permiited in the valley.

Before hiking in the Sierra, visitors must pay a "tourist tax" to the Arhuaco chief in San Sebastián (at the police HQ); this ranges from US$7 to US$15, depending on what you want to do. (Do not leave litter or disrespect the Indians' sacred grounds.) **The Indians of the Sierra** distrust strangers (stay on paths; do not stray on to private land) and do not take kindly to being photographed, especially without permission. However they like to be given sea-shells which can be ground into powder and mixed with coca leaves and such a gift may improve their reaction to strangers and cameras. Those interested in the Arhuaco culture should seek out Celso Domingo, a dentist in Pueblo Bello, himself an Arhuaco. **N.B.** The Sierra Nevada is a marijuana-growing area—take care.

A recommended guide to the Sierra Nevada is Mauricio Guevera (T Bogotá 213-7002), who organizes treks (but not all year). You need to be fit for his 12-day hikes through the villages, valleys alive with butterflies, flowers and waterfalls, and to the lakes and the snowfields and summit of Pico Colón at 5,750 metres (Jim Lindsay, Australian Embassy, Caracas). It is also possible to hike on the coastal side of the Sierra, but it is absolutely essential to take a guide through the marijuana districts. Recommended is Juancho, at Restaurant Pilón de Gaira, at Rodadero, Santa Marta, or at the village of Bonda, half an hour from Santa Marta by taxi. Juancho is an ethnologist (formerly of Medellín) who has lived with Kogui Indians for 13 years, owns a farm and speaks the different dialects. You need to be fit for his treks too. US$130 p.p. for a week, maximum 6 people, minimum 4.

From Valledupar on to Codazzi is asphalted, but not beyond until the road joins the paved Bucaramanga-Santa Marta highway. There is a possible overnight stay at Curumaní (Hotel Himalaya), or at Aguachica, just off the road.

Beyond Riohacha to the E is the arid and sparsely inhabited Guajira Peninsula. The Indians here live primitively, collecting dividivi, tending goats, and fishing. To visit a small part of the Peninsula you can take a pick-up truck from Riohacha (they leave twice a day from the Indian market) to Manaure for US$1.50, or a daily bus, 0830 from bus station, which may be safer. It is an uncomfortable 3-hr. drive through fields of cactus but offers glimpses of the Indians. Manaure, which is known for its salt flats, has a residencia—restaurant (G). From Manaure there are trucks to Uribia (one basic residencia, no running water, but fresh water is a problem throughout the Guajira) and thence to Maicao. In Uribia you can buy handicrafts intended for local, not tourist, use by asking around. Sometimes it is possible to get a lift to Cabo de la Vela, further round the coast, where the lagoons shelter vast flocks of flamingoes, herons and sandpipers. There are fine beaches and, in Cabo de Vela, a basic but friendly, Indian-run hotel (rooms, hammock veranda, showers, good meals—excellent fried fish). Sunsets in the Guajira are magnificent. There is a paved road from Riohacha to Maicao near the frontier. The Caribbean coastal highway, now paved, runs direct from Santa Marta along the coast to Riohacha, and the Riohacha-Maicao road (also paved) has been greatly improved.

A large coal-mine (one of the largest in the world) is situated at El Cerrejón, in the Guajira. A good dirt road and a railway have been built between the mine and the new Puerto Bolívar. Visitors are apparently welcome, but it would probably be best to make arrangements first at the El Cerrejón offices in Barranquilla.

Maicao is full of Venezuelan contraband, and is still at the centre of the narcotics trade. Its streets are unmade and it has a considerable reputation for lawlessness; most commercial premises close before 1600 and after 1700 the streets are highly unsafe. If at all possible travellers should avoid Maicao and the road services that go there, which are liable to ambush. Also, all isolated areas of César and Guajira Departments are unsafe for tourists.

Entering Venezuela, everyone needs a visa; a transit visa will only suffice if you have a confirmed ticket to a third country within 3 days. The Venezuelan Consul in Maicao is reluctant to grant visas, given the area's reputation: much better to get a visa in Barranquilla or Riohacha; with all the right papers, border crossing is easy. Entering Colombia, immigration is at the border.

Hotels in Maicao: Maicao Juan Hotel, C, the only safe one; Residencia Gallo, E, private bath and pool; Hotel Hilda, C, reasonable; El Parador.

If stuck in Maicao, seek out Francisco Agudelo at ARA, Carrera 9, No. 13-16, T 8133, who can make arrangements with Guajira Tours, Riohacha, and help with transport, money changing, etc.

Buses (basic): Maicao-Riohacha, US$2; Maicao-Santa Marta, US$5.75; Maicao-Maracaibo, US$3.25 (Expreso Maicao, 0400-1800); Maicao-Barranquilla, US$6.50. Maicao-Cartagena, US$4.75-7.50. There are bus services along the Caribbean coastal highway, and also flights Barranquilla-Maicao. Colectivo, Maicao-Maracaibo, US$15.

Air Services with Avianca, Satena.

UP THE MAGDALENA RIVER (5)

Passenger travel by the lofty paddle boats on the river has now come to an end,

CENTRAL COLOMBIA

though the adventurous traveller may still find an occasional passage by cargo paddle boat. But in general the only way of getting from one place to the other along the river is by motor launch (chalupa), and this is more expensive. Insect repellants should be taken, for mosquitoes are a nuisance. Guerilla activity has been reported in the Magdalena valley away from the river and the main roads.

The Magdalena is wide but shallow and difficult to navigate because of surface eddies, and there are little whirlpools over submerged rocks. Away to the NE, in the morning, one can see the high snow-capped peaks of the Sierra Nevada de Santa Marta.

At Tenerife Bolívar had his first victory in the Magdalena campaign. At Zambrano, a cattle centre 96 km. beyond Calamar, there are tobacco plantations. Population, 4,000. There is a road W to the N-S Cartagena-Medellín road, and a trail E to the oil fields at El Difícil. Near Pinto the river divides: the eastern branch, silted and difficult, leads to **Mompós,** an old town of 20,000 people: cattle farming and tobacco, and the scene of another victory for Bolívar: "At Mompós", he said, "my glory was born." Mompós was founded in 1537 and, thanks to its comparative isolation, preserves its colonial character more completely than any other town in Colombia. Old buildings are the Casa de Gobierno, once a home of the Jesuits, and the Colegio de Pinillos. There are 7 churches and the Easter celebrations are said to be among the best in Colombia. The town is well known in Colombia for handworked gold jewellery. Airport. Malaria is endemic in the surrounding countryside.

Mompós Hotels   *Residencias Unión*, Calle 18, No. 3-43, F, with bath and fan; *Hostal Doña Manuela*, Calle Real del Medío, 17-41, D, a converted colonial house, quiet and peaceful but run down; with cockroaches; also *Residencias Solmar*, Calle Carrera 18-22, near main square, F, clean, friendly, basic; *Tropicana*, *Núñez*.

Restaurant   *La Brasa*, facing river.

Bus   To Cartagena with Unitransco and Brasilia daily, 4 hrs., US$4, but you can only book as far as Magangué; you pay a second time from there. From Magangué you have to take a launch to an island in the Río Magdalena, and thence a jeep to Mompós. Connections can be unreliable if the incoming bus misses the ferry. It is cheaper and quicker to Cartagena by shared taxi to La Bodega, US$1, 1 hr., then motor boat to Magangué, US$0.85, 20 mins. From Magangué, buses also go to Barranquilla and Sincelejo.

Most vessels go by the western arm of the loop to **Magangué,** a town of 40,800, the port for the savannas of Bolívar. To El Banco the charge is US$3, by *chalupa* 2¼ hrs. A road runs W to join the N-S Cartagena-Medellín highway. Hotel: *Mardena*.

Beyond Magangué, the Río San Jorge, 379 km. long, 240 km. of it navigable, comes in from the Western Cordillera. Later the Río Cauca, 1,020 km. long, comes in from the far S. Its Caribbean end is navigable for 370 km., and it is navigable again for a distance of 245 km. in the Cauca Valley above the gorge.

At *El Banco* (*Residencias Las Delicias*, Calle 9 near jeep terminal, F, basic), 420 km. from Barranquilla (airport), the river loops join. This is an old, dirty and beautiful town of 10,250 people. Along the river front are massive stone stairways. The Cordilleras are in the distance, a blue range on either side of the valley. Pink herons and blue macaws much in evidence. There are many sandy islands in the river to complicate navigationA difficult trail leads N of El Banco to the small town of Chimichagua (5,000 inhabitants), on the shores of the large lake of Zapatosa. Beyond this are the small towns of Gamarra (3,700 inhabitants) and Puerto Wilches (5,600). Daily buses from El Banco to Bucaramanga, US$7, Cúcuta and Valledupar. *Chalupa* service El Banco-Barrancabermeja with Cootransfluviales, 0800, 7 hrs., US$10.

Some 30 km. above Puerto Wilches is **Barrancabermeja** (usually referred to as Barranca), so called because of the reddish-brown oil-stained cliffs on which it stands. With a population of 66,400, the town is an important oil centre; it is a warm, humid place with an interesting indoor market, but the oil refinery is prominent. *Chalupa* to Puerto Boyacá, 0845, 6 hrs., US$10. In 1989, this city was reported to be "incredibly violent", and best avoided by travellers.

Hotels   *Residencias Ferroviario*, F with bath, opp. railway station, friendly. *Iris*, just up road from port, F, clean, friendly.

Puerto Berrío (airport; 12,750 inhabitants) is on the W bank 100 km. above Barrancabermeja and 756 km. from Barranquilla. It is the river port for Medellín and the rich Antioquia Department. A railway from Medellín (freight only) runs down the slopes of the Cordillera Central and over a low pass to Puerto Berrío, where it connects with the Bogotá-Santa Marta line. Bus to Barbosa, 10 hrs., US$4.50.

Hotels at Puerto Berrío   *Hotel Magdalena*, pleasant, on a hilltop near river, E; *Residencias El Ganadero*, F, with bath, clean, modern, with ceiling fans. Many other hotels, *residencias* and *apartamentos*. **Restaurants:** *Tabrona*; *La Buena Mesa*, good big meals; *Heladeria Joi*, good ice cream and sundaes.

Rail   To Santa Marta: 4 a week. Check days and times at Grecia station, 4 km. from the town and hotels, taxi service only.
    Note: to get to El Banco or Mompós from a Santa Marta-bound train, get off at Palestinos, 8 hrs. north of Puerto Berrío, then a shared taxi to Tamalameque (US$1; *Residencia Tamalameque* and restaurant, F, basic), or Puerto Boca, 2 km. further on (no accommodation), then take a motor boat.

River Transport   From Puerto Boca, *chalupas* run from 0500 till dusk; Cootrafturmag has a service to Barrancabermeja, Gamarra, San Pablo, La Gloria, El Banco (US$2.25, 45 mins.),

Mompós (changing at El Banco). Don't be bullied into taking an *expreso* service, or you'll pay for all the empty seats.

5 hours by road from Puerto Berrío is **Puerto Boyacá**. The road is mostly unpaved, passing zebu *fincas*, swamps and oil fields. There are army checkpoints on the road, owing to guerrilla activity in the area. (Hotels: *Residencias Lusitania; Santa Fe; Hotel* and *Heladería Embajador*.) Rápido Tolima has regular buses to Honda (3 hrs., US$1.50) and a daily 1100 bus to Puerto Berrío, US$3.50.

It is 151 km. up river from Puerto Berrío to **La Dorada** (6,000 people) on the W bank, but only 134 km. by rail (7½ hrs.) along the W bank. (Hotels: *Rosita*, Calle 17, No. 3-28, T 72301, F, with bath, friendly, pleasant, rec.; *Departamental*; on highway to Honda, *Magdalena Motel*; others near railway station). This railway crosses the Magdalena by a bridge from La Dorada to **Puerto Salgar,** on the E bank, from which the Cundinamarca Railway (198 km.) goes up the slopes of the Eastern Cordillera to Bogotá. Bus La Dorada-Bogotá, US$4, La Dorada-Medellín, US$4.25. Train La Dorada-Santa Marta twice a week; to Bogotá, the Tayrona (from Santa Marta) passes once a week, Dec. to March only. Hotels: *Salgar; Residencia Antioquia*, G, with fan. The Lower Magdalena river navigation stops at La Dorada as there are rapids above, as far as Honda. Cargo is taken by railway to Honda, where it is re-embarked. The Upper Magdalena is navigable as far as Girardot.

Honda (airport) on the W bank of the river, is 32 km. upstream from La Dorada (149 km. from Bogotá). It is a pleasant old town with many colonial houses. The streets are narrow and picturesque, and the town is surrounded by hills. El Salto de Honda (the rapids which separate the Lower from the Upper Magdalena) are just below the town. Population: 31,600. Average temperature: 29°C. Altitude 230 metres. Several bridges span the Magdalena and the Guali rivers, at whose junction the town lies. In February the Magdalena rises and fishing is unusually good. People come from all over the region for the fishing and the festival of the Subienda, as the season is called.

Hotels *Ondama* (swimming pool), rec.; *América*, with pool, similar standard; *Río Ritz*, good restaurant; *Campestre El Molino*, 5 km. from Honda on Mariquita road, D, swimming pools, fans in rooms, friendly; *Residencias Las Mercedes*, E, with bath, clean and friendly; *La Piscina*, E, fan, swinmming pool, clean, friendly, arranges safe parking at reasonable rates with neighbours, rec.; *Las Villas*, F, clean, pleasant; *Residencias Katty*, F; *Los Puentes*, next to cinema, a bit run down, across river from *La Cascada*, F.

Restaurants *La Cascada*, overlooking river, a good meal for US$3. There is a good *panadería* at the entrance. Good ice cream (La Campiña brand) at *heladería* next to Teatro Unión; *Fuente Mar* for yoghurt and ice cream. There is a row of good cheap restaurants across the Magdalena River bridge in Puerto Bogotá.

Buses from Bogotá by Velotax US$4, and Rápido Tolima, US$3. Manizales, US$3. Rápido Tolima run half-hourly buses to La Dorada (1 hour), and beyond, to Puerto Boyacá (3 hrs.), US$2.25. To Puerto Berrío, 8 hrs., departures at 0300 and 0800 with San Vicente. The new Bogotá-Medellín highway passes round the town.

West from Honda a paved road goes 21 km. to **Mariquita** (13,000 people; *Hotel Bocaneme* and others; campsites), the centre of a fruit-growing country. Buses depart from Honda every half hour, US$0.30, ½ hr. with Rápido Tolima. On the way is the clean and pleasant bathing pool of El Diamante. On again is the Club Deportivo: private, but visitors are welcome to its swimming pool, a blessing in this climate. There is another, El Virrey, in Mariquita. The town has several old houses and buildings: a mint, the viceroy's house, the parish church. Here José Celestino Mutis lived for 8 years during his famous Botanic Expedition towards the end of the 18th century (when he and his helpers accumulated a herbarium of 20,000 plants, a vast library, and a rich collection of botanical plates and paintings of native fauna). The collection was sent to Madrid, where it remains. Mariquita was founded in 1551, and it was here that the founder of Bogotá, Jiménez de Quesada, died in 1579. From Mariquita a road runs W up the slopes of the Central Cordillera to Manizales.

Motel *Las Acacias*, outside Mariquita, on the Armero road.

Fresno, in the heart of a big coffee growing area, is 30 km. from Mariquita. The road to Honda is appalling. Bus to Manizales (83 km.) US$2.80 (Rápido Tolima).

From Mariquita the road turns S to (32 km.) Armero, which used to be a cotton growing centre. This town and surrounding villages were devastated by the eruption of the Nevado del Ruiz volcano (**see page 582**) in November 1985.

(Armero can be reached by colectivo from Honda; no lodging in Armero, nearest at Mariquita or possibly Guayabal; no drinks available in Armero, either, only icecream and flowers; there are lots of mosquitoes, though). A branch road runs 35 km. W to **Líbano,** 29,700 inhabitants. (Hotels: *Cumanday; Rex*.) Coffee is the great crop here, with potatoes in the uplands. Away to the W looms the peak of Nevado del Ruiz, which before its eruption was the second highest in the Cordillera Central. Bus from Líbano to Ibagué, US$2.25, 4 hrs.

From Armero a branch road runs down to the Magdalena past Gambao to **Ambalema** (Hotels: *Barcelona; Nariño*). (At Gambao the river is crossed for the road to Bogotá.) The main road from Armero goes direct for 88 km. to Ibagué.

Ibagué, capital of Tolima Department, is a large city (350,000 inhabitants), lying at the foot of the Quindío mountains at 1,250 metres. It is cooler here (22°C) than in the valley. Parts of the town are old: the Colegio de San Simón is worth seeing, and so is the market. The Parque Centenario is very pleasant. The city specializes in two things: hand-made leather goods (there are many good, cheap shoe shops) and a local drink called *mistela*. There is an excellent Conservatory of Music.

The National Folklore Festival is held during the third week of June. The Departments of Tolima and Huila commemorate St. John (June 24) and Sts. Peter and Paul (June 29) with bullfights, fireworks, and music.

Hotels   There are many hotels of reasonable quality which are quite comfortable. *Ambala*, Calle 11, No. 2-60, C, not good value, slow service, no hot water; *Suiza*, D, but not very clean; *Italia*, cheap, reasonable; *Athabasca*, D, with restaurant; *Bram*, E, Calle 17 and Carrera 4, convenient, clean, secure, and insect-free; *Acapulco*, near bus station, E, hot water, shower, clean and pleasant, but noisy; *Ambeima*, Carrera 3 No. 13-32, E; *Raad*, E, next door; both good. *San Luis*, near Expreso Bolivariano bus station, G, good but noisy. *Residencia Puracé* (opposite Tolima bus station), E.

Restaurants   *Parador Los Cristales*, S side of town, reasonable; *Casino Chamaco*, with excellent, typical tamales at weekend. *Toy Wan*, Carrera 4, Chinese. 24 hr. restaurants include *Punto Rojo*, in the shopping precinct on Carrera 3, and *Punto Fácil*, Calle 15 y Carrera 3.

Tourist Office   Carrera 3, between Calles 10 and 11; helpful.

Just outside, on the Armenia road, a dirt road leads to the slopes of the Nevado del Tolima. Gerhard Drekonja of Vienna writes: For climbing the Nevado del Tolima (5,200 metres) take in Ibagué at 0600 the *mixto* train to Juntas and El Silencio (2 hrs.). From there half-an-hour walk to the primitive but fabulous thermal waters (90°C) of El Rancho (simple sleeping accommodation and food available). The climb starts from El Rancho. It takes 8 to 10 hours to the top; equipment (crampons and pica) indispensable. The final climb has to be done at sunrise because clouds and mist invariably rise around 0800. From the top a breathtaking view across the other snowcapped mountains of the Cordillera Central.

There is a road to Girardot, 79 km. E on the Magdalena, going on to Bogotá which is 224 km. by road from Ibagué. On this road is the village of **Gualanday**, with *Hotel Rozal*, F, clean, friendly, safe for motorcyclists and 4 good roadside restaurants (*Dona Eva's* also has accommodation). **Espinal**, pop.: 80,000, is an important agro-industrial town, but of little interest to the tourist. A 2-star hotel is being built outside the town. Restaurant *Parador Rokoko*, on the main street is costly but has decent meals; *El Maestro*, behind Mobil station on W side of main street, cheap and good. Bus to Ibagué, 1 hr., US$0.75, just flag one down; bus to Neiva, US$2. Toll between Ibagué and Espinal, US$0.50; between Espinal and Girardot, US$0.40. W of Ibagué the road runs over the 3,350-metre high Quindío Pass to Armenia, 105 km. from Ibagué across the Cordillera Central. The bus trip to Pereira takes 4 hrs. and costs US$2.55. To Cali, on Flota Magdalena pullman, 7 hrs., US$5.75; ordinary buses US$4; Velotax US$5. To Bogotá, 4½ hrs., US$3.75 with Velotax, US$3.50 by bus. Bus to Popayán, US$6.75.

Between Ibagué and Armenia, on the E side of the Quindío Pass, is **Cajamarca,** a friendly town in a beautiful setting; *Residencia Central*, E; *Residencia Balmoral*, E; both on same street, friendly and clean.

Girardot (airport) is on the Upper Magdalena. Altitude, 326 metres; population, 70,000. The climate is hot and there are heavy rains. Here the navigation of the Upper Magdalena ends, although in dry weather boats cannot get this far; walk across the fine steel bridge to see merchandise being loaded and unloaded—coffee and hides are the main items, although shipments of the former have declined considerably. Launch rides on the river can be taken, starting from underneath the bridge. Large cattle fairs are held on June 5-10 and December 5-10. There is a two-storey market, at its best in early morning but nevertheless good all day, and another good market on Sun. mornings. Bogotanos come down here at weekends to warm up.

Hotels *El Peñón,* on site of former *hacienda* just outside town, fashionable bungalow complex, casino, huge pool, lake, B per bungalow. *Bachué,* Carrera 8, No. 18-04, C, modern large cooled pool, excellent, rooms a/c with bath and TV, meals US$2.50-3.50; *Los Angeles,* on main plaza, D, clean, friendly, rec.; *Canala,* comfortable and reasonable; *Waldorf,* on market square, F, clean, showers; *Residencias La Paz,* Carrera 1 E, No. 11-3. Opp. new bus terminal, *Maroti,* F, and *El Cid,* F with fan.

Restaurants *Laresa,* Carrera 8a, US$2-3 for a meal; *Club 60,* across the bridge, US$3-8. There is a good food market.

Banks Only the Banco de la República will change travellers' cheques in Girardot.

Roads To Bogotá, 132 km., bus costs US$3, about 3½ hrs.; bus to Neiva, US$2.55, 3½ hrs.; to Ibagué, 78 km. To Fusagasugá, US$1.65.

Another centre of population in the Magdalena Valley lies upstream from Girardot, with Neiva as its capital. Coffee and tobacco are grown on the slopes here, and cattle are raised in the valley.

The road, and its short branches E and W, runs through a number of small towns of under 25,000 people. One of these, 35 km. from Girardot, is *Guamo,* with 21,000 inhabitants. Just before Guamo is a marked turn off to La Chamba, where internationally famous pottery is made and sold. The pottery is fired in the afternoon; lots of mosquitoes here. Eight km. beyond Guamo is *Saldaña,* where there are irrigation works that have made 15,000 hectares available for rice, sesame and cotton.

Hotel at Guamo *Lemayá,* modern, swimming pool, best in region. At El Espinal, before the road to La Chamba is *Hotel Yuma,* new. At **Saldaña,** *Hotel Saldaña,* not too good.

A pretty spot is the reservoir located near **Prado,** Tolima. Turn off the Ibagué-Neiva road at Saldaña for 25 km.; it is well signposted. There is a dirt road for the last 12 km. past Purificación. Buses can be caught in Bogotá, Ibagué and all intermediate towns. A pleasant government hotel is at the lake (D, B for cabin for 6-10, free camping on the shoreline, water-skiing US$2.50, short trip with a boat). The pretty part of the lake is hidden from the end of the road and must be seen from a boat. Official boat trips to the islands are about 3 times cheaper than those of "sharks" operating here; the official mooring-point is down the slope at the end of the road. Swimming is good and the water is warm, but wading is not advisable because of the presence of the fresh-water stingray. Cheap hotels are available in Prado, 4 km. from the lake. There are restaurants of questionable quality in town. Excellent food can be obtained at the end of the road in the boat-dock area, but sanitation leaves something to be desired.

A little beyond the 50 kilometre stone from Neiva you can turn to the left, cross a fence, and see the Piedra Pintada de Aipe, a stone not in fact painted but carved by precolumbian Indians with designs akin to the shapes of some of the gold pieces in the Museo del Oro at Bogotá.

Neiva, capital of Huila Department, has a population of 150,000. It was first founded in 1539, when Benalcázar came across the Cordillera Central from Popayán in quest of El Dorado. It was soon after destroyed by the Indians and re-founded in 1612. It is now a pleasant, modern city. There are rich coffee plantations around Neiva, for here the valley bottom is high enough to be in the coffee zone. The cathedral was destroyed by earthquake in 1967. There is a large and colourful market every day. Tourist information is given at the cultural centre with museum and gallery on the main square. Altitude: 470 metres; very hot.

Hotels *Hostería Matamundo,* in old *hacienda* 3 km. from centre, on road to Garzón and San Agustín, C, a/c, swimming pool, good meals, US$2.50-7, but slow and poor service, disco (does not accept Visa card; will not put extra beds in room for children); *Tumbaragua,* Calle 5A, No. 5-40, C, no swimming pool or hot water but nevertheless rec.; *Americano,* Carrera 5, No. 8-65, D, clean, swimming pool; *Plaza,* Calle 7, No. 4-62, D, swimming pool, fan, pleasant but food expensive and not reliable; *Central,* Cra. 3, No. 7-82, E, meals US$1 each, near market, good value. *Cali,* F, basic, reasonable, next door is *San Jorge,* F, cheaper, clean, adequate. *Res. San Agustín,* near bus station, F, basic, clean; *Res. Nena,* across from back of Coomotor terminal, F, clean, quiet, friendly. Several cheap hotels are to be found off the square where the bus companies are centred. Many small boys meet the buses and suggest accommodation.

Restaurants *Hostería Los Cerros*, Calle 11, No. 32-39; *El Caimo*, Calle 8, No. 7A-22; *Los Gauchos*, Carrera 15, No. 5-12; *Neiva Viejo*, Calle 9, No. 6-49.

Fiesta from June 18 to 28, when the Bambuco Queen is elected, with folklore, dances and feasting.

Exchange Banco de La República, Carrera 5, No. 5-73, including AmEx cheques.

Airport La Marguita, 1½ km. from city. Aires and Satena fly from Bogotá (Aires to Bogota daily, US$30; to Cali, US$33; to Medellín, either direct or via Ibagué, US$34). Satena flies to Leguizamo, via Florencia daily. Taxi to bus terminal about US$0.85 (overcharging probable).

Bus No central bus station. To Bogotá (331 km., paved road), 5½ hrs., US$5. Regular bus service with Autobuses Unidos del Sur (Carrera 2, No. 5-32) and Coomotor to San Agustín, US$4, 5½ hrs. (US$4.50 by colectivo). To Garzón, US$3; to Pitalito, US$4.35. To La Plata, for Tierradentro. To Espinal, 3 hrs., US$2, good road except for stretch between Nataguima and Aipe. To Pasto, US$9; to Popayán, US$7.75, ordinary bus at 0330, 1000, 1930, to Florencia, US$6.50. Long-distance buses leave from Carrera 2, Calles 5 and 6.

Warning At the bus stations in Neiva, Garzón and especially Pitalito, theft is rife.

Excursions To Rivera, a ½ hr. drive S, with thermal springs and swimming pools to cool off; to the Tacacoa desert to the N, past Tello and Villavieja, where there is a museum showing prehistoric finds in the area; to the Betania dam project with boat trips on the lake formed by the dam, from the village of Yaguará.

Beyond Neiva lie the plains of Huila Department, arid, but still capable of supporting cattle, and dominated by the snow-capped Nevado del Huila to the NW. The road runs S from Neiva, past (92 km.) *Garzón*, a pleasant cathedral town set in mountains with roads W across the Cordillera to Popayán and SE to Florencia, capital of the Intendencia of Caquetá (**see page 576**), and is paved past Pitalito to San Agustín. *Pitalito* (72,000 people), has little to offer the tourist. See map of area, **page 594**.

Hotels at Garzón: *Damasco*, D, colonial building, rec., good meals for US$3; *Cecil*, near bus station, E, with private bath; *Miami*, E, good. The *Abeyma*, a state hotel, is rec., D; it is possible to camp in the grounds, US$1. *Residencias Pigoanza*, on main square, E, rec. 32 km. before Garzón, at El Gigante, is *Posada*, E, swimming pool, hot shower, restaurant (breakfast overpriced); good views between El Gigante and Garzón. At **Pitalito** there is a *Hotel de Turismo*. There are 2 hotels with swimming pools: the *Calamó*, C, hot water, and the *Timanco*, a 3-star hotel; *Residencia Pitalito*, F, without shower, reasonable, Calle 5 round corner from police station; *La Laroyano*, on main street, cheap, adequate; *Residencial El Globo*, main street, F, clean, basic. *Grand Hotel*, F, bath, good food. *Restaurant Cando* rec.; also *Napolitano*, good, cheap.

Transport If you hitch you'll find it fairly easy to Garzón; slower on to San Agustín, but plenty of buses and colectivos (US$1). Buses in Pitalito go from Calle 3a; Taxis Verdes from the main square (US$9 to Bogotá). Aires fly from Bogotá to Pitalito, via Neiva, on Fri. and Sun. at 1500, 1¾ hrs, US$50, returning to Bogotá at 1745 same days, but the plane only goes if there are enough passengers (confirm tickets 24 hrs. in advance).

South of Pitalito is the *Cueva de los Guácharos* National Park; take a bus to Palestrina, US$1, 1 hour, and then walk for 6 hours along an eroded, muddy path. Between December and June swarms of oilbirds (*guácharos*) may be seen; they are nocturnal, with a unique radar-location system. The reserve also contains many of the unusual and spectacular cocks-of-the-rock. The rangers are particularly friendly, providing tours and basic accommodation; permission to visit the park must be obtained from the Inderena offices in Pitalito, Neiva or Bogotá.

The way to the remarkable Tierradentro underground burials in man-made caves painted with geometrical patterns is given on **page 592**; they can be reached by Popayán bus from San Agustín, Pitalito or Garzón, with a change at La Plata, or at the Cruce San Andrés de Pisimbalá.

San Agustín (altitude 1,700 m.) is 27 km. from Pitalito (all paved). Here, in the Valley of the Statues, are some hundreds of large rough-hewn stone figures of men, animals and gods, dating from roughly 3300 B.C. to just before the Spanish conquest. Nothing is known of the culture which produced them, though traces of small circular bamboo straw-thatched houses have been found. Various sculptures found here are exhibited in the National Museum at Bogotá, and there are some life-sized copies of San Agustín originals along the highway from Bogotá to the superseded Techo airport, near Fontibón. There are about 20 sites; information can be obtained from the tourist office, Calle 5, No. 15-47, T 73019, open 0830-1230, 1330-1730, Mon.-Fri., 0900-1200, 1300-1700, Sat.

and Sun., Sr Joaquín Emilio García is most helpful in all matters. Free maps to the area can only be obtained here or in Bogotá. It is recommended that visitors arriving in San Agustín should go initially to the tourist office which has a list of all hotels, their prices and quality, and a price list for guides, taxi rides and horse hire.

The nearest sites are the Parque Arqueológico and the Bosque de las Estatuas (open 0800-1600 daily, entrance to both costs US$0.20), both about 2½ km. from San Agustín town, 1½ km. from the *Hotel Yalconia*, and less than 1 km. from the *Hotel Osoguaico*. The statues in the Parque are *in situ*, though some have been set up on end and fenced in with wire; those in the Bosque (a little wood) have been moved and rearranged, and linked by gravel footpaths. Of particular interest are the carved rocks in and around the stream at the Fuente de Lavapatas in the Parque, where the water runs through the carved channels (visitors should not miss the Cerro de Lavapatas, above the Fuente, which has an extensive view, closes at 1600); refreshment stands at "Fuente" and on the way up to Lavapatas. There is a museum in the Parque which contains pottery and Indian artefacts (entry included on Parque ticket, closes at 1700 and on Mondays). You can get a very good idea of the Parque, the Bosque and the museum in the course of three hours. The whole site leaves an unforgettable impression, from the strength and strangeness of the statues, and the great beauty of the rolling green landscape. The further sites are a very long walk away: use of a jeep or a horse appears advisable.

Rainy season April-June/July, but it rains somewhat during most of the year, hence the beautiful green landscape; the driest months are Nov.-March. The days are warm but sweaters are needed in the evenings; average temperature 18°C.

The *fiesta* of Santa María del Carmen is held in mid-July (not on a fixed date) in San Agustín. Two festivals in June are San Juan (24th) with horse races and dances, and San Pedro (29th) with horse races, dances, fancy dress, competitions and other events. In the last week of October, the Casa de Cultura celebrates La Semana Cultural Integrada, with many folklore events from all parts of the country. There are cockfights in San Agustín on Sundays at 2030.

Hotels   *Yalconia*, outside town, B full board, cold water, very pleasant, remodelled, swimming pool, T (980) 73001 (camping allowed next door, sheltered tents available). Between San Agustín and the Parque Arqueológico is the *Osoguaico*, recently rebuilt after fire, friendly, warm water, very clean, restaurant, E, laundry; swimming pool, camping site, US$1 p.p. *Central*, Calle 3, No. 10-32, near bus offices, E, with bath (F, in the 3 rooms without bath, or G if you want a room just to dump your luggage in during day's visit), good meals at US$1.50, it is possible to do laundry here (but keep an eye on your clothes), clean and friendly, secure motorcycle parking, will hire horses, English and French spoken. *Colonial*, Calle 3, No. 10-54, F, shower, clean, pleasant, good restaurant, rec.; *Residencias Náñez*, Calle 5a with Carrera 16, F, singles may have to share room, hot water, friendly and clean; guests may use the kitchen; also the owners have horses for rent (US$5 for 5 hrs., check them first) and will act as guides to the archaeological sites. *Cabañas Los Andes*, Calle 4 y Carrera 10, fine views, F with bath, kitchen, rec. *Mi Terruño*, Calle 4, No. 15-69, 5 rooms, F, colonial house, some rooms with bath, hot water, friendly, morning coffee, rec., owner Carlos Arturo Muñoz also has 3 cabins, *Los Andaqui*, for rent. *Residencias Luis Tello*, Calle 4a, No. 15-33, run by a teacher, hot water, pleasant and friendly, F; also *Residencias Cosmopólita*, Cra. 16, No. 4-91, clean, safe, friendly, E, rec. *Residencias Eduardo Motta*, Calle 4, No. 15-71, has five rooms, friendly, clean, hot water, F, hard beds, but with morning coffee; similar establishment run by Luis who runs the post office, F; *Residencia Familiar*, Calle 3, No. 11-14, one block down from Coomotor-Autobuses Unidos del Sur office, 7 rooms, hot water extra, laundry, friendly, G p.p., book meals in advance, horses for hire; *Residencias La Gaitana*, Calle 6A, No. 14-47, F with bath, warm water, clean, friendly management, rec. Small boys (and thieves **beware**) will meet you off the bus with offers of such accommodation; they are also remarkably competent guides in many languages. There is accommodation in private houses for about US$2 p.p., which is often preferable (ask, for example, for Sra. Elena Rojas de Llanos, "La Gorda", near the church, whose house is clean, safe, but no hot water). Ask at Tourist Office about cabins for rent for about US$4, with hot showers and cooking facilities. Accommodation at the farm of Constantino Ortiz is rec., 3½ km. from town, bordering on the Parque Arqueológico, 4 rooms, meals and horses available, peaceful, inexpensive, also has camping; reservations at Calle 5, 1113 in town.

Camping   *El Camping* and *Camping Ullumbe* both provide tents or charge per site, both good. Next to *Yalconia* is Rafael Gómez's campsite, clean, pleasant, toilets, lights, laundry service, horse hire (see below).

Restaurants *Brahama*, Calle 5, No. 11-15, vegetarian meals and comida including soup and drink (also meat dishes), good fruit salads, rec. but beware special prices for gringos (has horses for rent); *Superpollo*, Diagonal a la Iglesia, US$2 for half chicken, good; *Pandi's* does European-style food at reasonable prices. *La Martina/Las Negras*, good comida for food, only Sat. p.m., all day Sun. and Mon.; *Los Idolos*, good also; *La Negra*, Carrera 12, No. 3-40, good tamales; *Nayn*, Cra. 11 y Calle 3, across from bus offices, good comida; *Palacio de Jugos*, Carrera 13, No.3-32, excellent fruit juices; also at *Heladería de Turista*, on main street. *El Ullumbe*, opp. *Hotel Yalconia* pleasant, nice salads, friendly owner, not cheap, has rooms to let. Also opp. *Yalconia*, *Villadolly*, local and international food, rec. Further on, *Casa Blanca*, opp. *Hotel Osoguaico*, good cheap breakfast. Tap water is not safe to drink.

Shopping Bring lots of film (you can't buy it in the town). Leather goods are beautiful and priced reasonably. Many local shops make boots to your own design for about US$27.50 (double-check the price beforehand); *Calzado Líder* is highly recommended, or *Artesanías El Viajero*, Calle 3 no. 11-33, T 73 102. Recommended handicraft shops are *Intillay*, Calle 5, No. 14-28 (wood and stone sculptures, weavings, jewellery), and *Nevay*, Calle 5, No. 15-04, bronze, ceramic, basket and leather ware. Don't buy artefacts on the street; if they are not fakes, their sale is illegal. Market day in San Agustín is Mon.

Exchange Travellers are warned to change travellers' cheques before arriving in San Agustín; the Caja de Crédito Agrario and the Tourist Office will exchange cash only, at a poor rate; the Banco de Colombia will not change money but does give cash on Visa cards; 0800-1300 Mon. to Fri., 0800-1000 Sat.

Transport San Agustín may be reached directly from Bogotá by taxi (Taxis Verdes have one service a day, leaving at 0500, US$12, 10-12 hrs. will pick you up at your hotel in Bogotá—ticket must be bought one day in advance or by bus (Coomotor, from new bus terminal, 4 a day, US$10, 12 hours). Alternatively there are frequent services from Bogotá to Neiva (US$7, 6 hrs.) as well as some to Pitalito (Taxi Verde costs US$9, leaving Bogotá at 0730). From Neiva there are 6 buses a day to San Agustín, taking 6 hrs. and costing US$4. To Neiva with Autobusco, US$5, 6 a day (1000 bus arrives in time for 1630 flight to Bogotá). The journey from Pitalito takes 1½ hrs., costs US$1 by jeep. To Popayán and Cali, Coomotor daily at 0600, via Pitalito, Garzón and La Plata, US$9, to Popayán, US$14 to Cali. The bus stops at La Plata (for Tierradento), 5 hrs.; La Gaitana also leaves for Popayán at 0530 (tickets from *Res. Familiar* and La Plata at 1600 (5 hrs., US$4.50), same company continues to Tierradento at 0500, 2½ hrs. **See also page 590**

A new 135-km. direct route has been opened between **Popayán and San Agustín (via Isnos)**; it is unpaved, with one stretch of 20 km. single track, suitable only for jeeps and lorries. Jeeps leave daily from Popayán along the new road: Transtambo, Calle 3, No. 11-14 (*Residencia Familiar*) leaves daily at 0500 and 1700, 5½-6 hrs., US$6, heavily booked, expect delays in the rainy season; Cotranslaboyana, 0500, 6-8 hrs., US$5.10—check these services in advance. (For information ask in the tourist office.)

There is good riding in the neighbourhood. The rate for hiring horses works out at between US$1.50-2 per hour. (Check the horses carefully before you hire them—they do not all, for instance, have shoes.) You must pay for the guide's horse, plus usual tip equivalent to the cost of one horse for the trip you have made. Good horses are hired out by Sra. Luz Angélica de Martínez, Calle 7, No. 14-16. There are 3 types of guide: *Baquianos* (white identity cards), permitted only to accompany visitors to sites reached on horseback; *Alquiladores*, who own horses, but may not explain the statues or enter the Archaeological Park; and qualified, *Guiatur* guides (orange cards) who are fully trained, may explain all the sites, and charge US$6 to explain the Archaeological Park, US$12 for full day's guidance. Always ask to see a guide's identity badge; if you have any problems, ask at the Tourist Office or seek a tourist police officer. Recommended guide: Sra. Luz Omayra González, employee of the Corporación Nacional de Turismo. Rafael Gómez (next to *Hotel Yalconia*) hires good horses, and will act as a guide for a little extra. Jorge Palacios, who has handicrafts shop opposite *Hotel Yalconia*, has also been recommended as a horseback guide. Lucas Peña at *Hotel Central* will act as guide on treks in the area; he also provides information on money exchange, etc. "Jerry" Luis Alfredo, Cra. 12 No. 2-78, speaks English, French and a little German, good guide, but check horses carefully; Lucás Garzón, Calle 3, No. 11-55, has also been recommended for information, horses, etc. Another recommended guide for the longer excursions (4 days, Puerto Quinchana-Valencia and return) is Sr. Segundo Arsenio Guzmán (see below).

Alternatively, jeeps may be hired and about 8 people can fit in one! Prices vary according to the number of sites to be visited, for example: to Alto de los Idolos, Alto de las Piedras, and the Mortiño and Bordones waterfalls, costs about US$4-5 p.p. Be clear about what you are to be shown before setting out, don't be rushed, don't let the driver pick up people *en route*, and don't let the driver charge more than the tourist-office-approved rate. The tourist office itself runs tours by jeep (max. 7 people) to Alto de los Idolos, Alto de las Piedras, and Mortiño, for US$6 p.p.; trip lasts 5 hrs., departure at 0900, book the day before. The *Hotel Central* offers a one-day excursion by jeep to Alto de los Idolos, Alto de las Piedras, and the 2 waterfalls. The area offers excellent opportunities for hiking, although some trails to remote sites are not well marked. Two sites easily reached on foot are El Tablón (5 sculptures) and La Chaquira (figures carved on rocks and good view of Río Magdalena. At the site of El Purutal (previously called La Pelota), two painted statues were found in 1984 (well worth a visit). The latest archaeological discovery (1986) in the area is a series of at least 30 stones carved with animals and other designs in high relief; they are on the right bank of the Río Magdalena, near the Estrecho (narrows) to which jeeps run. The leaflets given out by the Tourist Office disagree about distances to the sites; check before starting out to walk. Probably best for several people to organize their trips together; prospective horseriders and jeep passengers tend to congregate at the health-food restaurant near the Tourist Office.

The best books on the subject are *Exploraciones Arqueológicas en San Agustín*, by Luis Duque Gómez (Bogotá, 1966, 500 pages) or *San Agustín, Reseña Arqueológica*, by the same author (1963, 112 pages); a leaflet in English is obtainable from tourist offices. The Colombian Institute of Archaeology has published a booklet (English/ Spanish), at US$1.80, on San Agustín and Tierradentro (see page 592), available at museums in San Agustín and San Andrés (also available at the Tourist Office, free).

The visitor with time to spare should visit Alto de los Idolos, or about 10 km. by horse or on foot, a lovely (if strenuous) walk via Puente de la Chaquira, but 27 km. by road via San José de **Isnos** village (which is 5 km. from Alto de los Idolos), and to which a bus can be taken, US$1, 0500 on Sat. return bus at 1100, 1300, or catch a bus from the *cruce* on the Pitalito road or hitch, well signposted (the site is open until 1600, entry US$0.20). Here on a hill overlooking San Agustín are more and different statues known as *vigilantes*, each guarding a burial mound (one is an unusual rat totem). The few excavated have disclosed large stone sarcophagi, some covered by stone slabs bearing a sculpted likeness of the inmate. Alto de las Piedras, 6 km. from Isnos, has a few interesting tombs and monoliths, including the famous "Doble Yo". The Director of the Parque (Don Hernán Cuéllar Muñoz) can arrange transport and guide to outlying sites. Only less remarkable than the statues are the orchids growing nearby. There is the *Parador de los Idolos* (3 rooms), ½ km. from Alto de los Idolos, new, D. From San Agustín the Bordones waterfalls can be visited; best with a car; there is a 13-room *Parador* right by the falls, E, clean and pleasant (reservations at San Agustín Tourist Office).

From Isnos many of the sites can be visited by road. As you come S into Isnos from Popayán, turn left just after the bridge (sign Salto de Bordones). 6 km. on right is Alto de las Piedras, and 8 km. further is Bordones village. Turn left at end of Bordones and there is (½ km.) parking for the falls. Coming S through Isnos, turn right off main street to Alto de los Idolos (5 km.). From Isnos it is about 20 km. to San Agustín; after 7 km. turn left (½ km.) to Salto del Mortiño, 300-metre falls.

Market day is Sat. in Isnos—bus at 0500 from San Agustín (Hotel in Isnos: *Hospedaje Nueva*, F).

It is possible to walk from San Agustín to the Lago Magdalena, involving a bus ride or 6-hour walk the first day, 7-hour walk the second, and 8-10 hours walking on the third, either to the lake and back to the second *refugio*, or on to Valencia. Good bases for this excursion are *Residencias El Paraíso*, at Puerto Quinchana, 30 km. away on the road to the source of the Río Magdalena, 2 km. from the Cementerio Indígena de Quinchana, owned by Sr. Arsenio Guzmán, F, friendly, peaceful, restaurant; *Residencias El Páramo* at Juntas on same road, beautiful countryside, owner Alvaro Palechor, F, clean, safe, friendly, restaurant.

Caquetá

Lying to the E of the Cordillera Oriental is the Intendencia of Caquetá, reached by air, or by road from Neiva or Garzón. This region, although still sparsely populated is an area of intensive settlement. The population has trebled since about 1965 ; people have been moving down from the highlands to turn the area into a productive livestock region. The natural forest cover around Florencia, the capital of the Intendencia, has been cleared and for a radius of 10-15 km. lie well-established, undulating pasturelands, dotted with tall palms—the fruits of which are a delicacy for grazing cattle. To the SE, beyond the cleared lands, lie little-touched expanses of tropical forest inhabited by indigenous tribes and wide varieties of Amazonian flora and fauna.

The road Neiva-Florencia is 260 km.: possible in one day, but it is recommended that travellers should try to complete the last 100 km. over the mountains into Florencia by daylight. From the Garzón-San Agustín road, the only route for vehicles into Caquetá branches off at Altamira. Here the surfaced road ends and becomes a single-track dirt road, originally engineered in 1932 during the Leticia dispute between Colombia and Peru. The climb up over the mountains passes through a region of small farms (some of their cultivated fields appear to be on almost vertical valley sides), through sugar-cane cultivation and up into cloud at the higher points of the route. Here there is rain-forest, sporadically cleared for farms. Soon after the summit, and on a clear day, there are extensive views out over Caquetá and then the road winds down through substantial forests—ablaze with the colours of tropical flowers in the dry season (Jan.-March) and into the lowlands. The lower section of the road into the lowlands is prone to frequent landslides (or *derrumbes*) because of weak geological structures.

The roads in Caquetá run from Florencia along the foothills of the Cordillera; eventually a road is planned to run from Puerto Asís through Florencia to Villavicencio, skirting the foothills of the eastern Andes. Other routes are difficult and seasonal (although tracks, or *trochas*, are laid out as part of the settlement scheme, financed by the World Bank) and the main lines of communication into the lowlands are by boat along the rivers Caquetá and Guayas and their tributaries.

Florencia (pop. 78,000) is the capital of the region and the centre for settlement in Caquetá, originally established in 1908. The square contains sculptures, fountains, a large forest tree (*saba*) and flower beds. When the road to Garzón is obstructed by landslides, petrol supplies are limited.

Hotels *Plaza*, Carrera 1, No. 30-70, C; *Apartamentos Capri*, E, with bath, clean and safe; those located around the central square are reputed to be more salubrious, and charge about US$3-4 per night. *Residencia Cordillera*, E.

Cafés, Restaurants Plenty, but prices tend to be high because much food is trucked in. For good value try *Tocarema*, 4-course meal US$2, large portions. Vegetarian restaurant on main street for good patacones.

Fiesta The local Saint's day is on July 16, when there is a candlelight procession in the evening around the town.

Bank Cash cheques at the Banco de la República.

Car parking Overnight, cars are best left in the care of the fire-station (US$0.20 a night).

Buses There are regular services from Neiva (US$6.50, 7 hrs.), Garzón and Altamira to Florencia (bus Altamira to Florencia, US$3.15) and frequent services as far as Puerto Rico and Belén. Bus to Bogotá costs US$19.50.

Air Services To Puerto Asís, with Satena, on Mon., Wed., Fri., daily to Neiva and to Leguizamo, with Satena.

Excursions From Florencia down the Orteguaza river: take a morning bus to Puerto Lara or a bus to San Antonio (US$3.25) where there is a cheap hotel; you can visit Indian villages.

From Florencia the road runs as far as Puerto Rico: it is paved for 34 km. to La Montañita and then unsurfaced, passing through El Paujil (2,750 pop.), where the *residencias* are unnamed and are situated alongside the road into the town. A dry-weather road runs from here for 21 km. towards Cartagena before giving way to a mule track. Then comes El Doncello (5,500) a very pleasant town, overlooked by the church which has a brightly painted steeple. The *Residencias Americanas* is highly recommended, F. Popular Sun. market. Next comes Esmeralda, a small settlement located on a ford that is too deep for cars, although trucks and buses may cross, and there is a wooden suspension bridge over the river for which the toll is US$0.20. The hotel there provides a very plain but excellently cooked breakfast.

Puerto Rico (4,950) is at the end of the road—which is interrupted by the River Guayas. It is possible to cross the river by ferry (US$0.08) and travel by bus as far as San Vicente where a mule-track goes over the Cordillera to Algeciras in Huila Department. Puerto Rico is a river port; ferries travel downstream to Río Negro (1½ hrs.) and Cartagena (4½ hrs.). Houses built down by the river are raised on stilts above possible flood levels. River boats are made and repaired by the riverside. **Hotels** and *residencias* are full on Sat. nights—book a room early in the day. *El Gran Hotel*, despite its name, provides basic amenities. *Hotel Almacén* is the only place in Puerto Rico serving fresh fruit juices.

The road from Florencia to San José is unsurfaced. At Morelia there is a poor branch road S to the River Pescado, where a ferry will take you across the river to the town of Valparaíso (1,175). *Hotel Ceilán* is cheap and friendly; there is also the *Hotel Turista*. From Valparaíso mule tracks go further into the lowlands. If travelling to Valparaíso by car, make sure it is left well away from the river when catching the ferry as, during times of flood, the river may rise rapidly overnight. Morelia to Belén de los Andes is an unsurfaced road, passing through some very interesting scenery, and crossing very clean, fast-flowing rivers by metal bridges. For some reason prices are higher in *Belén* (2,235) than in other towns in Caquetá. Hotels fill up very quickly, and mosquito nets are not always provided, although they are needed. In the area are a group of co-operative farms, and an oil palm plantation. From Belén an unsurfaced road runs to Albania (1,075) which is a small frontier settlement with only one hotel. A semi-surfaced road runs from here for 11 km. further towards the new areas of settlement.

Anyone wanting to look at wildlife in Caquetá must travel beyond the settlement area. Toucans, monkeys, macaws etc. are kept as pets, but there is little wild-life. Boats and canoes are easily hired, but horses and mules are more difficult, especially in the dry season when they are needed to transport the harvest.

THE CENTRAL CORDILLERA: MEDELLIN AND MANIZALES (6)

The Central Cordillera lies W of the Magdalena River. In it are two of the most important cities in Colombia: Medellín, the third largest city in the country, and

Manizales. Manizales can be reached by a road (309 km.) passing through Facatativá and Honda; or through Girardot to Ibagué, then over the high crest of the Quindío pass via Armenia. (For the road from Manizales to Medellín, **see, page 583**.) Medellín can be reached from Bogotá by road three ways: the highway opened in 1982 (**see page 580**); the old direct road (478 km.) with a 207-km. unpaved stretch from La Dorada to La Unión; and the third via Manizales.

The town of Antioquia was founded in 1541, but the Spaniards, eager for gold, were not interested in the hinterland, which was then very sparsely inhabited by nomadic Indians who made very poor agricultural labourers. But during the 17th century a new wave of settlers came to Colombia from Spain; many of them were Jewish refugees who were deliberately seeking isolation, and found it in the little valley of the Río Aburrá, where they founded the city of Medellín in 1616. They were farmers with their families rather than *conquistadores*: they had an extraordinarily high birth rate; they intermarried very little with either Indian or black; and they divided the land into small farms which they worked themselves. Their exports were small: a little gold and silver from their streams. They lived on the food they themselves produced: maize, beans, sugar-cane, bananas, fruit.

In the early 19th century the settlement began to expand and to push out in all directions, particularly to the S. The settlers followed the forested slopes on the western side of the Central Cordillera and occupied all the cultivable land. Manizales, 120 km. S, was founded in 1848. In the second half of the century new lands were occupied further S.

It was coffee that brought stability to this expansion, but they were slow to adopt it. Coffee appeared in the Magdalena Valley about 1865, but none was being exported from Antioquia before the end of the century. It was the 1914-18 war that suddenly gave a fillip to the industry: within 20 years the Departments of Antioquia and Caldas were producing half the coffee of Colombia, and they are by far the most important producers today. The industrialization of Medellín followed the coffee boom. There has been little immigration since the original settlement, but the natural growth in population has been extraordinary.

Medellín, capital of Antioquia Department, is a fast growing city of 2.5 million people, at an altitude of 1,487 metres. It could hardly be less advantageously placed, for it faces forbidding mountain barriers in nearly all directions. Its climate alone, that of an English summer day (21°C), is in its favour, despite a certain amount of smog. Yet Medellín is one of the main industrial cities of Colombia, and seethes with energy. The first looms arrived in 1902. Today the city produces more than 80% of the textile output of the country, and textiles account for only half its industrial activity. A metro is planned for the city. Excellent views from Cerro Salvador (statue on top), SE of city, and from Cerro Nutibara, S of city, where there are an outdoor stage for open air concerts, miniature village, souvenir shops and restaurants.

Medellín is a well-laid-out industrial city. There are four universities, together with other higher educational institutions. The old colonial buildings have nearly all disappeared, but there are still some 17th century churches left: the old Cathedral on Parque Berrío and the churches of San Benito, La Veracruz, and San José. The new Cathedral of Villanueva (Catedral Metropolitana), one of the largest brick buildings in the world, is on Parque Bolívar, an attractive place. Below the statue of Bolívar in the park are inscribed the words of the conquered Indian leader Choquehuanca to his visitors: "With the centuries, your glory will grow as the shadows grow when the sun sets". Three churches of the 18th century survive: San Ignacio, in Plaza San Ignacio, San Juan de Dios, and San Antonio. The city's commercial centre, Villanueva, is interesting for its blend of old and modern architecture, including many skyscrapers. There is a fine sculpture, Monumento a la Vida, next to the Edificio Seguros Suramericana on Calle 50, where exhibitions of work by leading South American artists are held on the ground floor. The cattle auctions on Tues. and Thurs., held in specially built cattle yards on the outskirts, are interesting. There is a zoo, *Zoológico Santa Fe*, in the southern section of the city, mainly of South American animals and birds; reached by the Guayabal bus (US$0.07; admission US$0.80). In the zoo grounds is a Historical Museum (closed Mon. and Tues.), costing an extra US$0.20 to enter. Christmas illuminations are very good, in Parque Bolívar and Cerro Nutibara.

Warning Medellín is not a safe city at night; be particularly wary of the prostitutes, of both sexes.

Hotels *Intercontinental*, the best, some distance from the centre, A, excellent; *Amaru*, Carrera 50A, No. 53-45, A, central, quiet, good, expensive restaurant with excellent service; *Ambassador*, Carrera 50, No. 54-50, C, in connection with *Veracruz*, Carrera 50, No. 54-18, B, with bath, swimming pool, very good, restaurant on 11th floor gives fine view over city; *El Balcón*, near *Intercontinental*, in Transversal Superior, A, beautiful view of the city, good meals, US$6 p.p.; *Nutibara* (casino and swimming pool), Calle 52A, No. 50-46, A; *Residencias Nutibara*, an annex facing hotel of same name, slightly cheaper with all the same facilities; *Europa Normandie*, Calle 53, No. 49-100 (T 41-99-20), C, restaurant, cafeteria, sauna, disco, central, fair; *Horizonte*, Carrera 47 No. 49A-24, C, good and popular restaurant; *La Montaña*, Calle 48, No. 53-69, E, with shower, good meals available, in the dangerous market area; *Eupacla*, Carrera 50, No. 53-16, C, central, noisy, mosquitoes, but helpful staff; *Comercial*, Calle 48, No. 53-94, E, friendly, clean, hot water available in some rooms, the best of which are on the top floor, doors barred to all but residents after 1800, meals US$2; *Holiday*, Carrera 45, No. 50-25, E, with bath, clean, 5 mins. walk from centre; *Residencias Hotel Gladys*, Carrera 48 and Calle 45, E, modern, clean, friendly and helpful, but rather noisy; all rooms face street; *Linton*, Cra. 45, No. 47-74, E with bath and hot water, very clean. *Príncipe*, Bolivar and Carrera 51, E, clean and friendly; *Nuevo*, Calle 48 and Carrera 53, E, with bathroom, noisy but clean, good meals for US$1; *San Francisco No. 2*, Carrera 54, No. 48-44, F, good and clean, friendly but noisy; *Samaritano*, Carrera 45, No. 45-25, E, clean and friendly, but noisy; *Doris*, Carrera 45, No. 46-25, F, clean and friendly, cold water; *Internacional*, La Playa No. 46-56, F, secure, clean, good value; *Gómez Córdoba*, Carrera 46, No. 50-41, F, basic, safe; *Romania*, Av. Echeverri, Calle 58, No. 50-46, F with bath, clean, a bit noisy. Many *residencias* on Carreras 54 and 55, but this is not a safe area; a safer area for accommodation is around Carrera 43. An excellent private house to stay in is on Carrera 58, No. 53A-36, 3rd floor, US$3 a night, very safe. Calle 45 is said to be an unsafe street.

Restaurants *Cacique Nutibara*, on Cerro Nutibara, offers excellent views of the city and good, reasonably-priced food; *Hato Viejo*, opp. *Intercontinental Hotel*, good local cuisine (another branch on Carrera Junín); *Aquarius*, on road past *Intercontinental Hotel*, first class; on same road, and good also, *Las Sombrillas*, *La Yerra*, *Los Cristales*. Roast chicken is provided at the four branches of *Kokoriko*, for US$3; good steaks at *Texas Steak House*, Calle 44 and Carrera 80; good arroz con pollo from *Los Alejos* in Centro Comercial Boyacá. *Finale*, Av. El Poblado with Calle 8, bar serving excellent food, art gallery upstairs, manager speaks English, very friendly; also in El Poblado, *Bar-Pizzería Julio's* (T 46-04-37) open till 0300. Other restaurants in El Poblado, all near Parque Poblado: *Arepizza* on Calle 10 (local food, juices, cheap); *Che's*, Calle 9, good steaks; on Av. 43B, one block from Parque, *Frutos del Mar*, good seafood; *La Crêperie*, opposite, French; *La Torre de Pizza*, good. On Av. Poblado (Av. 43A), *Presto* hamburgers and 2 good chicken restaurants. *Piemonte* and *La Bella Epoca*, very good and expensive, both on road to Envigado, as are *La Mesa* and *Isla Verde* (good, but expensive); *El Boquerón*, on the mountain top; *Aguacatala* and *La Posada de la Montaña*, both outside off road to Envigado, good, Colombian food, expensive; *Noche y Día*, Carrera Junín, between Maturín and Amador, good meals for US$0.80; in fact there are several of these round-the-clock cafés in the vicinity which serve cheap meals. *La Vida*, round corner from *Hotel San Francisco No. 2*, US$1.60 for comida, excellent fruit juices, friendly, also, 2 doors from this hotel, *Popular*, is good. Two good self-service restaurants are *La Estancia*, Carrera 49, No. 54-15, on Plaza Bolívar, and *Contenalco*, Calle la Playa, between Av. Oriental and El Palo, clean, cheap, very busy in rush hours. *Cirus*, Calle 53, meals for US$1, good value. *Palma Sola*, Carrera 51 and Calle 48, comidas for US$1.50. Many good, cheap restaurants on Carrera 49, e.g. *Versalles*, on pedestrian precinct between Av. La Playa and Plaza Bolívar. Good cheap meals at *Helados Sayonara*, opp. Parque Bolívar, and at *Refugio*, Cra. 45 y Calle 47, across from *Residencias Doris*. For hamburgers and sandwiches, *Mr Ham*, *Hardy's*, four of each in the city. Excellent pastries at *Salón de Té Astor*, Carrera 49, No. 53-39. Many cheap cafés near bus station.

Clubs Campestre (good food, rooms, golf, tennis, swimming pool); Ejecutivos (lunch club in centre).

Shopping Silver seems cheaper than in Bogotá. Poor selection of handicraft shops in the city, but there are *artesanía* shops on the top of Cerro Nutibara. Cercado San Alejo, Parque Bolívar, open on the first Saturday of every month (handicrafts on sale). Carrera 47 has 3 antique shops. Many of the textile mills have discount clothing departments attached where good bargains can be had; ask at your hotel. *La Piel*, at Calle 53, No. 49-131, has an excellent selection of leather goods at very reasonable prices (the selection and price of leather goods in Medellín is better than Bogotá). *Supermarket Exito* is reaonable for cheap leather bags. There are 2 new shopping centres, San Diego and Oviedo.

Bookshop   Librería Continental, Junín No. 52-11, sells foreign-language books.

Taxis   Pay what is on the meter plus US$0.90. From airport, about US$2.70.

Discotheque   Delfos (in *Hotel Europa Normandie*); others in central hotels, and in El Poblado district.

Music   Monthly concerts by the Antioquia Symphony Orchestra. Band concerts in the Parque Bolívar every Sun. at 1130. Open air concerts, on Sundays, of Colombian music on Cerro Nutibara.

Museums   Museo Etnográfico Miguel Angel Builes, Carrera 81, No. 52B-120, has an extensive collection of artefacts housed in beautiful new building. The Museum of the Missionary Sisters of Mother Laura has a good collection of indigenous costumes and crafts from Colombia, Ecuador and Guatemala. Museo El Castillo, Calle 9 Sur, No. 32-269, formerly a landowner's home, has interesting objects and beautiful grounds; entry US$1.20; take bus to Loma de los Balsos, El Poblado (US$0.07), then walk 1 km. up the hill until you see the road lined with pine trees to the right. Open 1300-1700, closed Sun. The Museo de Antioquia (Carrera Cundinamarca and Diagonal Carabobo, opp. main post office) shows contemporary pictures and sculptures, including works by Fernando Botero, Colombia's leading contemporary artist (now living in U.S.A.), US$0.50. Museum of Modern Art, Carrera 64B, No. 51-64, small collection, open Tues.-Fri., 0900-1300, 1500-1800. The Museum of the Chamber of Commerce, Carrera 46, No. 52-82, (exhibitions of modern art). Casa Museo Maestro Pedro Nel Gómez, Carrera 51B, No. 85-24, T 332633/440725, house of the contemporary painter and sculptor. Museo Antropológico at University of Antioquia (new campus). (In the old University of Antioquia building, beside San Ignacio church, is a Museo Histórico.) Philatelic Museum in Banco de la República building. Most museums are closed on Mondays.

Botanical Gardens   Joaquín Antonio Uribe gardens, near the new campus of the University of Antioquia, which include an aviary, are open daily, 0900-1730, US$0.40 entrance, well worth a visit (some of the plants are named); there is a restaurant, pleasant but not cheap. There is also a zoo (see page *0197*); take Marinilla bus from centre. Also visit El Ranchito, an orchid farm between the towns of Itagüí and La Estrella (entry US$0.50; April to June is the best time to visit).

Bullfights   at the bull-ring of La Macarena in February.

Exchange   Banco de la República, Calle 50 (opp. Parque Berrío), changes travellers' cheques, but your photo will be taken; has other branches; Banco Anglo Colombiano, Calle 50 (Bolívar), No. 51-06; agency on Calle 45, No. 55-65 and two others; Banco Internacional, Banco Royal, Banco Francés e Italiano de Colombia, and various other Colombian banks. Open: Mon.-Thurs. 0800-1130, 1400-1600; Fri. 0900-1130, 1400-1630; last working day of month 0830-1100. Main hotels will cash travellers' cheques for residents when banks are closed. (The owner of *Café Arturo* is reported to cash cheques.)

Post Office   Main airmail office in Avianca building, Carrera 52, Calle 51A, Mon.-Sat., 0700-2200.

Telecommunications   Pasaje Junín and on corner of Calle 49 and Carrera 50.

Travel Agents Tierra Mar Aire (American Express agents), Calle 52, No. 43-124, helpful. Viajes Marco Polo, Calle 48, No. 65-94, T 230-5145, recommended; also Terra Nova, Calle 5A, No. 39-114, T 266-5000, who run an excursion by train to Cisneros, 3 hrs. journey, with 3-4 hours for a picnic and swim (US$5.20). Viajes Turandina, Calle 53, No. 49-80, T 455815.

Tourist Office   Calle 57 No. 45-129, in bus station (some English spoken, helpful), and in airport (will book hotel rooms); and Turantioquia, Carrera 48, No. 58-11, T 254-3864, has good maps, good information on Antioquia and owns 5 good hotels in the Department. For a cheap tour of the city take any "Circular" bus, for US$0.06.

DAS   T 239-5076; **Tourist Police** at airport, T 260-1212, ext. 3052; police T 12; general information T 13.

Airport   A new airport, José María Córdoba, 38 km. from Medellín and 13 km. from Rionegro, has been opened; *Presto* restaurant. Taxi to town US$7, colectivo US$3, *buseta* to centre, via bus terminal, US$1.25, frequent service, about 1 hr. journey, sit on right going to town (catch bus in town by *Hotel Nutibara*). To Rionegro, bus US$0.15, taxi US$8.50. By air to Bogotá, 45 mins. with Avianca, on shuttle flight, every ½ hour between 0730 and 1630. Copa office, Carrera 45B, No. 33-24. Daily flight to Panama with SAM or Copa, US$101 (excluding taxes), but you will have to buy a return unless you have another exit ticket out of Panama. See page 602 regarding transport of motorcycles by air to Medellín.

Roads The new **Medellín-Bogotá highway** has been completed, but beware of landslides in wet weather (near the Magdalena Valley is the California wildlife park, well-signposted). The road is totally paved but there are potholes, waterfalls and detours between Medellín and Honda. There are many campgrounds along the route, for example 130 km. and 150 km. from Medellín. A paved road, 665 km. long, goes N to Cartagena, and another S to Manizales, which provides an alternative route to Bogotá. There are two other important roads: one, 383 km. NW through Antioquia to Turbo, on the Gulf of Urabá; and another, 478 km. SE from Medellín through Sonsón and La Dorada and on to Bogotá. The latter is paved as far as Rionegro, but from Rionegro to Sonsón is in a bad state of repair. The scenery compensates for this to some extent.

Buses The new bus terminal for all long-distance buses is about 3 km. NW of the town centre, with shops, cafeterias, left luggage (US$0.30 per day) and other facilities. Quite safe. Bus service to city centre, US$0.15, buses to station from Calle 50, marked: "Terminal de Transporte". To Bogotá, 9-12 hrs. US$13, every 40 minutes or so, with 5 companies, to La Dorada, US$4.25. Frequent buses for Cali, Flota Magdalena US$11, 10-13 hrs. Frequent buses to Manizales, 6 hrs. (US$6.50 1st class, 4.50 2nd, by Empresa Arauca). To Cartagena, Brasilia, 17-20 hrs., or 14 hrs., by Pullman bus, US$14; road paved throughout but poor. To Barranquilla, US$16 by Pullman, 16 hrs. To Cartago, 8 hrs., Flota Magdalena, US$5. To Pereira, 8 hrs., US$6.25 by Flota Occidental Pullman. To Sincelejo, 9½ hrs. To La Dorada, 9 hrs. To Popayán, US$13.25, 16 hrs. To Turbo, US$7.50.

Rail Apart from the Medellín-Santa Marta Nutibara train in December to March, there are no regular passenger services from or to Medellín. The Nutibara connects with the Bogotá-Santa Marta Tayrona at Grecia. For the tourist train from and to Cisneros, see above under Travel Agents.

Excursions A run N along the Cartagena road to (132 km.) **Yarumal** (with 61,250 people and many hosterías), or NW (many hotels and resort areas, crowded weekends) to (80 km.) **Antioquia** (13,275 people) will give a good idea of the very beautiful countryside. Antioquia lies just W of the Cauca river; it was founded as a gold mining town by the Spaniards in 1541, the first in the area, and still retains its colonial atmosphere, with interesting Christmas/New Year fiestas. Until 1826 it was the capital of the Department. The fine old Cathedral is worth seeing, as is the church of Santa Bárbara. There is an interesting wooden bridge, 300 metres long, 3 km. downstream from the steel bridge which the buses use—ask for directions or take a taxi. Hotels: *Mariscal Robledo*, D, 37 rooms, swimming pool, good; *Hostería Real*, 2 km. from town, C full board, good food, pool; *Del Río*, also outside, *San Pedro* in resort area. Bus from Medellín US$1.50 (Flota Urbara or Transporte Sierra), 2½ hrs. The road goes on to Turbo (daily bus at 0900), on the Gulf of Urabá (**see page 559**).

Another interesting excursion from Medellín is along the Sonsón road SE to (39 km.) the town of **Rionegro**, in a delightful valley of gardens and orchards. Here was born one of Bolívar's generals, José María Córdoba, the hero of the battle of Ayacucho. Medellín's new airport has been built 13 km. away. The Casa de Convención (where the 1863 Convention took place) is now an archive museum, entry US$0.20. The cathedral, with its gold and silver altar, deserves a visit. A museum of religious artefacts is behind the altar (entry US$0.20) and you can climb up behind the Virgin donated by Philip II to look down into the cathedral. There are processions in Easter Week. Many interesting pottery and ceramics factories in Rionegro area, hardly mechanized, as well as leather working; they welcome visitors and explain the processes. A day trip can cost US$15, but the Medellín-Rionegro *rápido* taxi service is very cheap. Bus to Rionegro, from Calle 44, No. 44-43, US$0.75, one hr.; bus back to Medellín from plaza every ½ hr. Prices of leather goods are high. 10 km. from Rionegro (15 minutes by colectivo, leave when full from plaza, US$0.50; buses every 2 hrs., US$0.15) is **Carmen de Viboral**, well-known for its pottery; there are several factories just N of the market place.

Rionegro Hotels *Aymará*, E, hot showers, meals available; *Rionegro*, E, friendly, dark rooms, cold water; *residencia* on main square; *Gutier*, central, D with restaurant; *Oasis*, Carrera 50, No. 46-23, D, with restaurant, bar, laundry, TV in rooms. *Residencias Onassis*, F with bath, good value; *Residencias David*, same price, both near market. **Restaurants** Pizza at *La Mansarola* and *Capuccino*; *Kokorico* on main square for chicken.

Beyond Rionegro is El Peñol, a precipitous, bullet-shaped rock which towers above the surrounding hills and lakes. It has been eroded smooth, but a spiral staircase has been built into a crack which extends from the base to the summit. Entrance to rock, US$0.30. A snack bar has been built at the summit, and the views are very fine (meals available only in holiday seasons). Cabins can be rented at the foot of the rock for about US$28 per day (sleep six, everything except food provided), T Medellín 234-6966, Santamaría y Cía; architects, Calle 81A, No.51-79. Bus to the rock and to the pretty town of Guatapé with Cía. Fco. López, US$1.20. Bus back to Medellín is harder to catch; best take a colectivo to town of Peñol and bus from there. From Rionegro, take a colectivo to Marinilla (US$0.25, leaves from near market), then wait for the San Rafael bus which passes El Peñol (US$1.20); from Marinilla you can also take a colectivo to the new town of Nuevo Peñol (US$0.70), then another to El Peñol (US$0.50)—in all about 2 hrs., either route.

On the road to El Retiro is Fizebad, an old estate house, restored with original furniture and artefacts, and a display of flowering orchids; entry, US$1.75. In El Retiro itself is a small colonial church and an even older chapel which is seldom open: ask for the caretaker. On the road to La Ceja, have lunch in *Parador Tequendamita*, in a beautiful setting by a waterfall. The route is through splendid scenery, and one can see typical Antioquian life and costume. (To Fizebad by bus, catch a La Ceja or El Retiro bus).

La Ceja, also on the Sonsón road, is well worth a visit. Transportes La Ceja cover the route; the journey takes 1¾ hrs. For the energetic, any one of the surrounding hills affords an excellent view of the area. *Hotel Primavera* and one other, both delightful, have rooms (F). At **Sonsón,** there are the *Tahami* (F, very good value) and *Imperio* (F) hotels.

At **Bello,** 6½km. N of Medellín (pop. 153,000), is the hut in which Marcos Fidel Suárez, President 1918-1922, was born. It is completely covered in with glass for its preservation.

A good trip is by car to **Hatillo,** 32 km. along a road which parallels the railway to Puerto Berrío, and then another 80 km. along a new road to Caldas. There are many restaurants along this road.

To the SW of Medellín, the towns in the coffee-growing district (Fredonia, Jericó, Jardín, Venecia) are worth visiting; all have basic inns. The scenery is beautiful.

At **Envigado,** 10 km. S of Medellín, craftsmen have for generations turned out the traditional *antioqueño* pouch called *carriel*, carried by the men. Now used for money, its original use was for coffee samples.

55 km. S of Medellín is **Santa Bárbara**, at 1,857 metres on a green hill top, with stunning views in every direction of coffee, banana and sugar plantations, orange-tiled roofs and folds of hills. *Hotel Palomares* on main square, F, clean, well-maintained; restaurants and cafés also on square, as is the large church. Bus to Medellín, US$1. 140 km. S of Medellín is **Supia**, a pleasant little town with new hotel, *Mis Ninietas*, near plaza, no sign, F with bath, clean and good. Supia is 13 km. N of Riosucio (see page 583).

Quibdó, the capital of the Chocó Department, is a small jungle town (41,000; *Hotel Citará*, D; *Dora Ley*, E with bath, F without, rooms vary greatly in quality, meals available; *Pacífico*, E, good, with bath, its restaurant, *Club Náutico*, on 2nd floor has good food and views; several *residencias* including *Del Río* and *Darién*; Restaurant *El Paisa* rec.; *Chopán* bakery, good pastries and coffee.). There is a good museum at the Normal School. Sunday market is attended by many Indians, some painted, who arrive by canoe. Boats can be hired for river trips; try Ruffo at the sawmill, US$20 an hour. Quibdó can be reached (1) by bus from Medellín; (2) from Buenaventura by boat up the Río San Juan to Istmina and on by road (see page 588); (3) by the Río Atrato: small speedboats go to and from Riosucio, US$40 p.p., large cargo boats go from Quibdó to Riosucio, Turbo and Cartagena (one week, US$28 p.p. inc. meals, warm clothes and blankets necessary at night, wash in river water, stops allow enough time to disembark and look around); (4) by plane from both Medellín and Cali. Chocó Department, thickly wooded and mountainous, is impressive; travel is rough but the rewards are high. A road is planned from Quibdó to the Pacific Coast at Bahía Solano (good for skin-diving; *Cabañas El Almendral*, 40 mins. by decrepit taxi from Bahía Solano, rec. for its setting on the Pacific, for river trips and accommodation, E p.p., book through ACES which runs the airlink; see page 1330 for boats from Panama).

Manizales is dominated by its enormous (still unfinished) concrete Cathedral and the Nevado El Ruiz volcano, which erupted so catastrophically in November 1985. The city was founded in 1848 by settlers from the Department of Antioquia; it has a population of 450,000 and is the capital of the small Department of Caldas, which originally (until 1965) contained what are now the new Departments of Quindío and Risaralda. The old Department, now known as Viejo Caldas, produces about 30% of all Colombian coffee and picturesque coffee farms abound.

Manizales, at 2,153 metres above sea level, rides its mountain saddle uncompromisingly, the houses falling away sharply from the centre of the city into the adjacent valleys. The climate is extremely humid—average temperature is 17°C, and the annual rainfall is 3,560 mm.—and frequently the city is covered in cloud. The best months of the year are from mid-December through to early March, and early in January the Fair and Coffee Festival is held, with bullfights, beauty parades and folk dancing. The city looks down on the small town of Villa María, "the village of flowers", although with the rapid expansion of Manizales, Villa María is now almost a suburb.

The architecture is predominantly modern with high-rise office and apartment blocks, although traditional architectural styles are still seen in the suburbs and the older sections of the city. The departmental government building, the

Gobernación, opposite the Cathedral in the Parque Bolívar, is an imposing example of neo-colonial architecture; the bull-ring built 25 years ago is an impressive copy of the traditional Moorish style. The suburbs stretch away North (with best shopping around Calle 59) and South of the city centre and are reached by a four-lane highway lined with flowers—marguerites—which grow to enormous proportions (as also the geraniums) because of the damp and the altitude. Chipre, a recreational park, provides a good view of the city (well-visited on Sundays); El Tanque, near Chipre, is another vantage point.

Hotels   N.B. in January, during the fiesta, hotel prices are grossly inflated. *Carretero*, B, good (T 33206); *Fundadores*, C, good (T 22333); *Las Colinas*, Carrera 22, Calle 20 (T 29400), three-star, two bars, good restaurant, very comfortable, C; *Bonaire*, above Ley supermarket, not too noisy, spacious, very clean, hot water, D, shared rooms cheaper, rec.; *Europa*, Av. Centenario, No. 25-98 (T 22253), near the bull-ring, restaurant for breakfast only, comfortable and clean, D; *Rokasol*, Calle 21, No. 19-16, near bus station so noisy, hot water, clean, all rooms have bathrooms, E, good restaurant, set meal US$2; *Villa Kempis*, on road to Pereira, about 2 km. past bull-ring, old religious retreat house, beautiful view over the valley, very quiet, hot water a.m. only, restaurant and bar, good food at moderate prices, T 32961/ 30187, D; *Tama Internacional*, Calle 23, No. 22-43, next to Cathedral, E, with bath, meals US$1, clean and cheap, but noisy. Cheaper: *Residencias Nueva York*, Calle 18 between Cras. 22 and 23, extremely clean, hot water, clothes-washing facilities, some bar noise in front but rec., F; *Residencias Monaco*, near bus station, F, adequate, English spoken; *Residencias*, Carrera 19, No. 22-45, near bus station, F, US$1 surcharge on holidays, hot water, quiet, good; *Cosmos*, opp. bus terminal, F, clean but overpriced, hot water with luck.

  La Rochela hotel in the "hot country" about 30 km. W from Manizales on the road to Arauca, large swimming pool for adults and smaller one for children, E, for a room for six; no smaller accommodation, family holiday atmosphere, good food at moderate prices; in process of building separate cabins. *Hotel Termales Arbeláez*, 25 km., from Manizales on the road to the Nevado El Ruiz, D, hot swimming pool, private bathrooms, restaurant.

Restaurants   Two well-known places in the Chipre area of town overlooking valleys: *Los Arrayanes* has plain food at moderate prices; *Las Torres*, local specialities, more expensive. *El Cable*, so-called because it stands beside the remaining tower of a disused cable-way for coffee, good food, two-course meal, US$5.50 *Las Redes*, Carrera 23, No. 75-97, predominantly sea food, good but about US$8-10 per head; *Vitiani*, Carrera 23, No. 25-32, Italian and European food, quite smart, food and wine fairly expensive, has good trout and excellent crab-claws (muellas de cangrejo); *El Dorado Español*, moderate prices, good food, carne a la parrilla highly rec., on road to Chinchiná; *Holandesa*, Carrera 19, good, plentiful meals, about US$3; *El Pilón*, moderate prices, plato montañero and sopa de mondongo rec.; *Hong Kong*, opp. *Hotel Carretero*, good Chinese; *Chung-Mi*, Chinese, does take-away meals; *La Suiza*, Carrera 23, No. 26-57, good fruit juices and cakes; *Caballo Loco*, Calle 21, No. 23-40, expensive pizzas; *Domo*, modern-type hamburger joint and pizzeria, moderate prices; *Picaflor*, very good food at moderate prices; *El Ruiz*, Carrera 19, No. 22-25, US$2 for filling 3-course meal.

Teatro de los Fundadores   is a modern cinema-theatre auditorium. Interesting wood-carved mural by local artist, Fernando Botero, who also has murals in the entrance hall of the Club Manizales and *Hotel Las Colinas*. Events held here and at other locations during Theatre Festival in first two weeks of September.

Museums   Bellas Artes, anthropology museum with interesting selection of findings from Indian tombs (and a marvellous view of the Nevado El Ruiz), open in the afternoon (erratically) after 1400. Banco de la República, Carrera 23, No. 23-06, gold and anthropology museum open during banking hours, classical music every afternoon in the Bank. Universidad de Caldas, natural history museum open every day from 0800 to 1200 and 1400 to 1800 (take a "Fátima" bus to the University). La Galería del Arte, Av. Santander at Calle 55, exhibitions of work by local artists, pictures can be bought.

Bank   Banco Anglo Colombiano, Carrera 22, No. 17-10, and other banks. Open 0800-1130, 1400-1600, Mon. to Thurs., 0900-1130, 1400-1630 Fri. only. Last working day of the month 0830-1130.

Tourist Office   Parque Bolívar, opposite Cathedral, well-organized.

Airport   Manizales has a small airport, La Nubia, and the regional airline ACES provides an efficient and punctual service to Bogotá, Medellín, and Cali.

Excursion   To see the full process of coffee growing, apply to the Comité Departamental de Cafeteros de Caldas, Carrera 22, No. 18-21, T 41706; recommended.

Parque de los Nevados   national park includes El Ruiz, Santa Isabel, El Cisne, El Nevado del Tolima—all snow-capped peaks. Contact Inderena (National Conservation Institute) for details.

Also La Laguna del Otún, where there is trout fishing by permission of Inderena. To reach park take Bogotá road, then branch road leads to (22 km.) viewpoint for Nevado del Ruiz.

Roads To Medellín direct, 265 km. via the winding mountain road through the picturesque towns of Salamina (*Residencia Puerto Nuevo*, F, opp. bus office, clean, good meals), Pácora and Aguadas, all perched on mountain ridges, to La Pintada (*Hostería Los Farallones*, C, nice pool, meals fair), but further if we go West across the Cauca river via Arauca, Anserma, *Riosucio* (a delightful old town with fine mountain views all round and a large colonial church next to the Arauca bus terminal; many restaurants, bars and shops; boats S to Quibdó and N to Turbo on the river) and then on to La Pintada. Manzales-Honda-Bogotá: all paved but in poor condition. The road climbs to 3,000 metres, with most superb scenery and little traffic. First accommodation is in Padua, then Fresno (cheap hotels), Mariquita and Honda. **(See page 569).**

Buses New terminal with good restaurant. Buses to Medellín: Autolegal via Neira and Aguadas, 6 hrs., US$4.50; Empresa Arauca via Anserma, 10 hrs., 1st class, US$6.50 ordinary, US$4.50; colectivo to Medellín, US$8.55. Both routes offer impressive scenery, but the shorter route is largely unpaved between Aranzazu and La Pintada. Bus to Bogotá, 8-10 hrs. by Expreso Bolivariano Pullman, US$7, 9 hrs.; 7½ hrs. by Flota El Ruiz *buseta*, US$8.50—beautiful scenery. To Honda, US$3 (Expreso Bolivariano). Cali by bus Expreso Palmira, 5½ hrs., US$4.50 ordinary; Pullman 6 hrs., US$6. To Cartago, 4 hrs., every 20 mins., US$1.25; Pereira, Expreso Palmira, Expreso Trejos, hourly, 1¼ hrs., excellent road, beautiful scenery, US$1 ordinary. Armenia, Expreso Palmira, 3 hrs., US$2. **N.B.** Unlike in other places, town buses stop only at bus stops.

THE CAUCA VALLEY (7)

From Manizales a road runs S to Pereira (fine scenery) and then to Cartago, at the northern end of the rich Cauca Valley, which stretches S for about 240 km. but is little more than 30 km. wide. The road goes S up this valley to Cali and Popayán, at the southern limit of the valley proper. There it mounts the high plateau between the Western and Central Cordilleras and goes through to Ecuador. From Cali a railway (no passengers) and a road run W to the Pacific port of Buenaventura. The Valley is one of the richest in Colombia. From Cartago S the river Cauca is navigable by barges up to Cali.

Pereira, capital of Risaralda Department, 56 km. SW of Manizales, stands overshadowed by green mountains, at an altitude of 1,476 metres, above the Cauca Valley. Population, 450,000; a centre for coffee and cattle. It is a pleasant modern city, founded in 1863, with an undistinguished cathedral and four parks: the best is the Parque del Lago, with an artificial lake; a fountain is illuminated several times a week. (Good Christmas illuminations, too.) There is a lively market. Matecaña airport is 5 km. to the S (bus, US$0.05). Outside it is a good zoo (bus from town centre to zoo, US$0.06.)

Hotels *Meliá Pereira*, Carrera 13, No. 15-73 (T 50-770/53-970, Apartado Aéreo 4050), 5-star, A (taxes not included), restaurant, bars, swimming pool; *Soratama*, main plaza, C; *Gran*, Calle 19, No. 9-19, C, restaurant, bar, travel agency, etc.; *Residencias Bolívar*, opp. Cathedral, F, friendly but plumbing suspect, meals available; *Res. Metropolitana*, Cra. 7 No. 17-21, E, hot water, TV, friendly, some noise; *Cataluña*, E, clean and friendly, good set meal in dining room; *Royal*, Calle 16, No. 7-56, F, with bath and hot water, clean, highly rec.; *Residencia Edén No. 1*, Calle 15, Carrera 10, near market, F, clean, friendly. Plenty of *residencias* in Calle 19, e.g. *Savoy*, F with bath.

Restaurants *El Pollo Campestre* (near airport), *La Ricura*, Carrera 8, No. 22-21, very good meal, US$1.50; *El Manolo*, Calle 20, No. 8-22, which has good meals for over US$4 near the market; good self-service restaurant on main square; vegetarian restaurant *Naturista No. 2*, Calle 19 No. 5-73, good. *El Mirador*, on a hill overlooking the town (ask Tourist Office for directions), good food and views.

Clubs *Club Rialto; Club Campestre*, 5 km. from town.

Banks Banco Anglo Colombiano, Carrera 9, No. 17-48. Banco Internacional. Open 0800-1130, 1400-1600, Mon.-Thurs., 0900-1130, 1400-1630, Fri. Last working day of month, 0800-1030.

Transport New bus terminal, clean, with shops, outside city centre. Bus to Armenia, 1 hr., US$1, a beautiful trip. SAM flights to and from Bogotá, Cartagena, Cúcuta, Medellín and San Andrés. Bus to Cali, US$3.50, 4½-5 hrs.; Manizales, US$1, 1½ hrs.; to Armenia, US$1; to Bogotá, US$6.50, 7 hrs., rough journey, not recommended for motorbikes.

Excursion 15 km. away, at Santa Rosa de Cabal, a poor 11-km. road branches off to Los

Termales, where waters from a hot spring cascade down a mountain into a swimming pool. There are also cold showers fed from a natural spring. The hotel (B) is overpriced and food in the restaurant is disappointing. Bus Pereira-Santa Rosa, US$0.20; then bargain for a jeep ride, US$4, to the springs. Package tours from Santa Rosa to Los Termales, including meals and one night's lodging, are available, but an afternoon excursion is the best value.

From Pereira, a 2-day excursion to the Ucumari Park is recommended. This is one of the few places where the Andean spectacled bear survives (but you won't see one). Above 4,000 metres in the park are spectacular *frailejón* plants. Hikes can be made to the Nevado de Ruiz. Park guards run an excellent *refugio* (La Pastora, US$2 in bunk bed, good meals, US$1.20, hot shower, very good). Take a bus from Pereira (Transportes Florida, Calle 12, No. 8-82) at 0900 and 1440, to El Cedral (1½ hrs.—return at 1130 and 1630), then walk 2 hours to the *refugio* through lush forest. Reservations for the *refugio* must be made in advance at El Lago, piso 12, Calle 25 between Carreras 7 and 8.

Armenia, capital of Quindío Department, is in the heart of the Quindío coffee district; population 350,000; altitude 1,838 metres; mean temperature 19°C. This modern city, founded in 1889, is the seat of Quindío University. The Bogotá-Armenia-Cali road is fully paved, but slow through the mountains; fog at night, reckless drivers and stray animals make the Quindío Pass (3,350 metres) a hazard at night. A newer, more direct road from Armenia to Cali, joining the Panamericana S of Zarzal, has heavier traffic than the old road.

Hotels *Palatino*, Calle 21 at Cra. 14, E-D, central, comfortable; *Izcay*, Calle 22 with Cra. 14, D; *Residencial El Viajero*, opp. bus station, E; *Pensión Nueva York*, basic but clean and cheap, G; *Moderno Aristi*, Calle 18, Carrera 20, E, with bath, hot water, clean; opposite is *Superstar*, F.

Restaurants *La Fogotá*, near university; *Frisby*, Carrera 16, No. 20-22, good pizza or fried chicken; *El Pollo Campestre*, near Country Club.

Archaeological Museum Calle 21, No. 16-37.

Airport El Edén, 13 km. from city. Fog often makes air services unreliable.

Bus New terminal. To Neiva, Flota Magdalena, 0100, 0400, 2230, US$4.75. To Ibagué, US$2. To Bogotá: Velotax bus, US$6, hourly, 9 hrs.; Velotax colectivo, US$8, 7 hrs.

Before the road drops into the Cauca Valley, between Armenia and Buga is *Sevilla*; Hotel Estelar Sevilla, good, B/C; Residencias Soratama, Cra. 49, No. 51-48, F, secure parking; others similar. Restaurant: Chicken Loco. 30 minutes' bus-ride from Armenia is Montenegro, a coffee centre (ask at FNC office on Plaza Bolívar about visits to *fincas* in the district); Plaza Bolívar is heavily wooded.

Cartago, 64,830 people, about 17 km. SW of Pereira, is on a small tributary of the Cauca river before it takes to the gorge separating the two *cordilleras*. Coffee, tobacco and cattle are the main products. Founded in 1540, it still has some colonial buildings, particularly the very fine Casa de los Virreyes. Visit the cathedral, with the cross apart from the main building.

Hotels Around Plaza Bolívar: *El Gregorio*, Carrera 5 y Calle 10, best, most expensive; *Central*, Carrera 6, No. 11-51, G, basic; *Residencias El Dorado*, Carrera 6, No. 11-16, G. *Villa del Río*, F, rec. *Residencial Paraíso*, Carrera 9, No. 8-99, F, cold showers only, clean, Sat. noisy at night. Many others in same area, i.e. around bus terminals (Carrera 9) and railway station (Carrera 9 y Calle 6); those in the same block as Flota Magdalena office are better value than the others.

Restaurants *Mullipán*, Carrera 6 y Calle 12, good cheap meriendas; *El Portal*, Carrera 6 y Calle 11, OK.

Post Office on Plaza Bolívar.

Cinema Roblero, Calle 11 between Carreras 5 and 6 (opp. Hotel El Gregorio).

Transport Local train service to Cali via Zarzal, Tuluá, Buga, Palmira; tren ordinario at 0450 and 1405, US$2; ferrobus at 0625 and 1635, US$3 (crowded); 4-6 hrs., occasional derailments; on weekends and holidays, El Expreso Caleño at 1245. Bus to Cali, US$3.50, 3½ hrs.

About 27 km. S of Cartago is *La Victoria* (the Pan-American Highway bypasses it to the east), a pleasant, small colonial town with a shady plaza. There is a Hotel Turista (F, family atmosphere, clean and friendly, will change US$ cash), one block from the plaza, and several restaurants. La Victoria is in the centre of a scenic area where cattle are raised, and cotton, sorghum, maize and soya are grown. You can cross the Cauca River by turning right off the road going to the south (good fishing Jan., Feb. and July) and 10 km. (paved road) further on is *La Unión* at the foot of the mountains on the west side of the valley. La Unión is a small agricultural town, a centre for grape production. *Residencia Los Arrizos*, and *Residencia El Cacique*. The countryside around offers good walks. Just south of La Unión is Rondanillo, a small town in the hot Cauca Valley, with a museum of paintings by the Colombian artist, Omar Rayo. A road runs E to the main highway at Zarzal.

About 50 km. S of Cartago is Zarzal, and 71 km. S again is **Buga,** an old colonial city of 75,220 people and a centre for cattle, rice, cotton, tobacco and sugar cane. Founded in 1650, and its modern Cathedral contains the image of the Miraculous Christ of Buga to which pilgrimages are made. N of Buga, at Uribe (50 km.), is the junction of the road S from Medellín with the one from Bogotá and Venezuela. Bus to Cali, US$1.50. Toll 22 km. S of Buga, US$0.40.

Hotels *Guadalajara* (swimming pool), D, rec., cabins for family groups, excellent restaurant and self-service cafeteria; *La Casona*, E, good; *Capacari*, E, with bath, clean (swimming pool), but overpriced, poor restaurant; *residencias* around Cathedral better value.

Excursion If you take the road from Buga to Buenaventura you come to the man-made Lake Calima. Taking the southern route round the lake, 42 km. from Buga is the *Hotel del Lago Calima* (D) set in very pleasant surroundings on the edge. There is no swimming pool, but some brave people swim in the lake, which is cold at about 16°C, and a kilometre deep. Closer to Buga on this road, before the Río Cauca, is the Laguna de Sonso Reserve, which is good for birdwatching.

47 km. from Buga is **Palmira,** in the Department of Valle; population, 163,000. Good tobacco, coffee, sugar, rice and grain are grown, and there is a College of Tropical Agriculture. The Pan-American Highway runs direct to Popayán via Pradera, but the road through Cali is preferable. The best road S is from Palmira through Candelaria and Puerto Tejada, avoiding Cali, to Popayán; paved, straight, not much traffic. (Taxi connection with Cali, 29 km. south, US$5.55; bus US$0.45, Transportes Palmira, terminal on Calle 30, near Cra. 33)

Hotels *Las Victorias*, C; *Palmira*, E; *El Dorado*, D without bath, clean; *Residencias Belalcázar*, F, with bath, G without, clean, friendly, good value. *Escorial*, F, and many other cheap places.

Restaurants *La Fonda*, good; *Grill Caña de Oro*, nice; *Paradero los Parrales*, good breakfast, good service, clean loos.

At La Manuelita, 5 km. N of Palmira, is a famous sugar estate. Beyond La Manuelita any of 3 roads running E will reach, in 12 km., the fine restored colonial *hacienda* of El Paraíso, where the poet Jorge Isaacs (author of *La María*, a Colombian classic) lived and wrote. Entry US$0.50; there is a café. To visit the *hacienda*, take a bus from Palmira, corner of Cra. 25 and Calle 26, at 1230 (another in a.m.), which passes the *hacienda* ½-an-hour later (US$0.55); returns about 1515. 9 km. from El Paraíso is a sugar cane museum in the Hacienda Piedechinche (open 0930-1600, closed Mon.; admission, US$0.20; 42 km. from Cali, take a bus from Palmira, then taxi, or take bus from Cali to Amaime, a small place on the road to Cartago, US$0.60, then wait for bus to Santa Elena, which passes the turn off to the Hacienda. You can walk from Amaime: take the turning marked "El Paraíso" and walk for one hour to the turn off to the Hacienda (marked "Museo de Caño"), then it's another ½ an hour. There is no public transport connection between the two *haciendas*). Tours of this and Hacienda El Paraíso arranged by Comercializadora Turística Ltda, Carrera 4, No. 8-39, local 101, Cali (US$10, including transport, entrance fee, guided tour and lunch).

Cali, capital of Valle Department (2 million people), is the third largest city in Colombia, set in an exceptionally rich agricultural area producing sugar, cotton, rice, coffee and cattle. Altitude: 1,030 metres; average temperature: 25°C, hot and humid at mid-day but a strong breeze which blows up about 1600 hrs. makes the evenings cool and pleasant. It was founded in 1536, and until 1900 was a leisurely colonial town. Then the railway came, and Cali is now a rapidly expanding industrial complex serving the whole of southern Colombia. South of Carrera 10 are many one- and a few two-storey houses, tiled and wide-eaved. Through the city runs the Cali river, a tributary of the Cauca; with grass and exotic trees on its banks. On one overlooking mountain, from which the best views are obtained, there is a statue of Christ visible for 50 km. and there are three large crosses on another mountain. The statue of Benalcázar, the city's founder, is worth a look, beautiful views of the city. It is also worth while going up the skyscraper Torre de Cali, for good strong coffee and a view of the city. Two nearby *haciendas*, El Paraíso (see above under Palmira) and Cañas Gordas, have important historical associations.

The church and monastery of San Francisco are Cali's best buildings. Inside, the church has been renovated, but the 18th century monastery has a splendidly proportioned domed belltower. The 18th century church of San Antonio on the Colina de San Antonio is worth seeing and there are fine views. Cali's oldest church, La Merced (Calle 7, between Carreras 3 and 4), has been well restored by the Banco Popular. The adjoining convent houses two museums: Museo de Arte Colonial (which includes the church) and the Museo Arqueológico with precolombian pottery (US$1, but well worth it). More Indian pottery can be seen in the Sociedad de Mejoras Públicas, across the street from La Merced; this collection belongs to the Universidad del Valle. Another church worth seeing is La Ermita, on the river between Calles 12 and 13. The orchid garden along the Río Aguacatal, near the centre, is well worth seeing.

The city's centre is the Plaza de Caicedo, with a statue of one of the independence leaders, Joaquín Caicedo y Cuero. Facing the square are the Cathedral, the Palacio Nacional and large office buildings. Across the river, which is 2 blocks from the Plaza de Caicedo, is the Centro Administrativo Municipal (CAM) and the main post office. Lovely walks and parklands stretch along both sides of the river here, with the *Intercontinental Hotel*, Museum of Modern Art, and zoo (some distance from the centre, entrance fee US$0.50) on its South bank. See also the Museum of Natural History, Carrera 2 Oeste, No. 7-18, which has some precolombian exhibits as well as biological specimens from the area (entrance fee US$0.13, open Mon.-Fri. 0900-1700).

The Museo de Arte Moderno La Tertulia, Av. Colombia, No. 5-105 Oeste (10 mins. from centre) has an exciting exhibition of South American art (open Tues.-Sat. 0900-1300, 1500-1900, Sun. and holidays 1500-1900; good films shown at 1900 in the *cinemateca*, admission US$1). Within its Villa Olímpica in San Fernando, Cali has three stadiums: the Pascual Guerrero Stadium, holding 50,000 people; the Olympic Gymnasium, holding 7,000 people; and the Piscinas Olímpicas, holding 3,000 people. Another stadium holding 18,000 spectators, the Monumental de Cali, is 10 mins. from the city on the road to Meléndez. Outside the city also is the new first-class bull-ring.

Warning Cali has recently become a centre of guerrilla and counter-insurgency activity. Nowhere is safe after midnight. Carry your passport (or photocopy—DAS approved) at all times and be prepared for frequent police checks.

Hotels A *Hilton* is under construction, on Av. Colombia, Carrera 10 Oeste. *Intercontinental,* Av. Colombia, No. 2-72, recently extended, tennis and pool, rec. despite mediocre service, A (weekend discounts); *Americana,* for businessmen, B, a/c, Carrera 4, No. 8-73; *Dann,* opposite *Intercontinental,* A, (with weekend discounts), service could be improved; but good; *Don Jaime,* Av. 6, No. 15N-25, B, good, restaurant rec.; *Menéndez,* Av. Colombia, No. 9-80, D, all rooms have own bath, good, reasonably priced meals available, nice old colonial building, popular with Colombians; *del Puente,* Calle 5, No. 4-36, D, with bath, clean, will store luggage, rec.; *Aristi,* Carrera 9, No. 10-04, 3-star, C, but weekend discounts, rec., large and old by Cali standards, turkish baths, rooftop pool, restaurant; *New York,* Calle 12, No. 3-62, D, clean, hot water, basic, near bus station and market; *Los Angeles,* Carrera 6, No. 13-109, E, good; *La Merced,* Calle 7, No. 1-65, D, swimming pool, pleasant young staff are very helpful, restaurant expensive, English spoken, rec.; *Hotel Residencias Stein,* Av. 4N, No. 3-33, B, full board, C, bed only, friendly, very good, quiet, excellent food, dinner for non-residents US$5, French, German and English spoken, Swiss-run, swimming pool; *Residencial Paseo Bolívar,* Av. 3 Norte, No. 13N-51 (T 68-50-67) and *Paseo Bolívar II,* Av. 3N, No. 13N-43 (T 68-28-63), both F, cold water, clean, safe (cheaper rates for long stay); *Mónaco,* Calle 14 No. 2-13, F, central and friendly but on edge of unsavoury area; *Bremen,* Carrera 6, No. 12-61, T 761998, without bath, F; *Amoblador Bolívar,* Calle 25, No. 2N-47, near bus terminal, F, basic, safe, highly rec. for friendly atmosphere (the owner collects foreign coins); *Amoblador las Américas,* Calle 25, 2N-31, E with bath, F without, cold water, clean, safe; *Amoblador Belmonte* in same block; *Casa del Viajero,* Calle 15 Norte, No. 4-44 (T 621477), F or E, two *amobladores* next to it; *Arca de Noé,* on road leading up to the Cristo Rey, D, fabulous views, marvellous gardens, good food in restaurant, poor service but worth the effort.

Restaurants Cali is a good place for eating, as the attached list attests (but restaurants close early, and many close on Sun.): *Don Carlos,* Carrera 1, No. 7-53, excellent seafood, elegant and expensive; *Hostería Madrid,* Calle 9, No. 4-50, European specialities, good service, above-average price; *Canarias,* Calle 8, between Carreras 3 and 4, rec. for cheap meals; *Restaurante Suizo,* Carrera 30 y Diagonal 29, Swiss, excellent fondue bourguignonne, pleasant atmosphere, reasonably priced; *Los Farallones,* at *Hotel Intercontinental* on 9th floor, is Cali's most atmospheric restaurant, with shows starting at about 2230-2300; try their Chateaubriand for two with drinks and desserts, less than US$25 including tips, a real buy; also their weekday noontime buffet at about US$6.50 a head is very reasonable, eat all you want; *El Quijote,* Carrera 4, No. 1-64, atmospheric, European dishes, expensive; *Simonetta,* Diagonal 27, No. 27-117, pleasant, reasonable, Italian dishes; *El Rancho,* S end of Av. 6, near municipal building, good local food, draught beer, pricey, closed Sun.; *Dominique,* Av. 6N, No. 15N-25, good Italian food and service, reasonable; *La Terraza,* Calle 16, No. 6N-14, elegant, music and dance, nice atmosphere; *El Cortijo Andaluz,* Carrera 38 and Calle 53, atmospheric (converted residence), Spanish food; *Los Girasoles,* Av. 6N, Calle 35, steaks, other meat grills, good atmosphere; *Los Gauchos del Sur,* Calle 5 about Carrera 60, Argentine-style grilled meat, dancing, excellent food, very reasonable; *China,* Av. 6N, No. 24-52, excellent food and service, pleasant atmosphere, large servings for reasonable price; *Shanghai,* Av. 8N, No. 17-33, Chinese, excellent food in utilitarian setting, takeaway, very reasonable; *Embajada Antioqueña,* Av. Roosevelt, Antioquian regional food, relatively cheap; *Cali Viejo,* in the Bosque Municipal, about US$10 p.p. for very good local food in pleasant surroundings; also good is *La Cazuela,* Avenida Roosevelt, 26-30; *Los Panchos,* Carretera a Meléndez with Autopista Sur, very good Colombian food, a favourite of Caleños; *Gloria,* Carrera 6, Calle 14, good and cheap; *Eduardo VIII,* piano bar, attempt at English pub atmosphere, good food, well-stocked bar; *Mauna Loa,* Centro Comercial del Norte, seafood a speciality, reasonably priced, Lebanese food too; *Mac Club,* Centro Comercial Imbanaco (Calle 5a and Carrera 39), hamburgers and hotdogs, excellent, cheap; *Sears Cafeteria,* open 0930-1930, excellent food, rather expensive but large servings. *Kokorico,* places all around town, spit-roasted chicken; *La Calima,* Carrera 3, No. 12-06, good meal US$1.30, always open; *El Galeón,* Calle 8a, No. 1-27, very good seafood and atmosphere, expensive; *Jino's Pizza,* held to be Cali's best pizzas, reasonably priced; *La Veda,* near bus station, good gaucho food. At least 10 eating places in the bus station, *Doble Vía* is the best.

Vegetarian restaurants at Calle 16N, No 5-42, and Calle 17N, No. 6-39. Names please.

You can find lots of European-style side-walk places along Av. 6 at good prices. Cheaper are the *fuentes de soda,* mostly with Colombian-style cooking, a decent meal for US$3-4. There are also *Masserna* on Carrera 7 between Calles 10 and 11 and *La Sultana,* Calle 10, on the corner with *Hotel Aristi.* Try their buñuelos (cheesy fritters) and the pandebono (cheesy buns) next door at *Montecarlo.* Cafés and ice-cream parlours abound near the university, across the river from the main part of town.

Clubs Club Colombia; Club de Tennis de Cali; Club San Fernando, modern and luxurious; Club Campestre, as good as any club anywhere, with a magnificent golf course, tennis courts and swimming pool; Club La Ribera y Náutico.

Shopping *Platería Ramírez,* Carrera 11b, No. 18-64, for gold, silver, brass, jewellery, table settings, etc. *Artesanías de Colombia,* Calle 12, No. 1-20 and for larger purchases Av. 6 N, No. 23-45. For leather goods and shoes, try *Boots and Bags, Carlo's* and *Clogs,* all in the same precinct. For boots and shoes *Chaparro* (*Botas Texanas*), Av. 6, No. 14N-14, T 651007, good, owner Edgar speaks a little English. Best shopping district: Av. 6N, from Río Cali to Calle 30 Norte.

Bookshop Librería Nacional, on main square, has a café.

Taxis Black taxis are the most reliable; ensure that meters are used. Prices, posted in the window, start at US$0.11. On holidays an extra charge is made.

Nightclubs Locally known as "Grills". The ones along the Av. Roosevelt and along Calle 5a are safest and best known. *Arca de Noé, Farallones* at the *Intercontinental* and *El Peñol* on the Buenaventura road are probably Cali's best (and most expensive).

Fair Held during December; bullfights, masquerade balls, sporting contests. National Art Festival in June (painting, sculpture, theatre, music, etc.). Also in June Feria Artesanal at Parque Panamericano, Calle 5, handicrafts and excellent leather goods.

Exchange Banco Anglo Colombiano, Calle 11, No. 4-48 (Plaza de Caicedo), and agencies on Avenida Roosevelt and Av. 6; Banco Internacional; Banco Royal de Colombia, Calle 3; Banco Francés e Italiano; Banco Colombo Americano and other national banks. Open: Mon.-Thurs., 0800-1130, 1400-1600; Fri., 0900-1130, 1400-1630. Last working day of month, 0800-1130. Closed Sats. Money can be changed at Almacén Stella, Carrera 8, No. 9-64 (by *Hotel Aristi*) open 0800-1200, 1400-1800, or at travel agents.

Consulates Swiss: Carrera 5, No. 8-50. US Consul from Bogotá visits monthly at the centro Colombo-Americano, Calle 13N, No. 8-45, T 67-35-39.

Post Office Adpostal for national service, Calle 10, No. 6-25; Avianca for international service, near CAM.

Tourist Office Corporación Nacional de Turismo, Calle 12N, No. 3N-28 (T 686972); regional office, Carrera 3, No. 8-39 (closed Sat. and Sun.). Maps, posters and general information. **DAS** office, Av. 3N, No. 50N-20 (T 643809). Also co-operative for shopping. There is a Thomas Cook office at Wagons-Lits, Cra. 4 No. 8-20. Good street map from municipal building just N of river at Calle 11.

Rail   No passenger service, except to Cartago (US$3, 4 hrs.).

Buses   New bus terminal (connected by tunnel to railway station) is at Calle 30N, No. 2A-29, 25 mins. walk from the centre (leave terminal by the taxi stands, take first right, go under railway and follow river to centre). Hotel information available. *Casa de cambio*, cash only. Showers on second level (US$0.40). There are plenty of local buses between the bus station and the centre, which charge US$0.06. Taxi from centre to bus station, US$2. Buses to Popayán, US$3, 2½-3 hrs., also colectivos. To Pasto, US$10, 9 hrs.; to Ipiales (direct), US$11, 12 hrs. or by Bolivariano Pullman, US$9, departures at 0400 and 0615 and 0800; Coomotor have a direct service to San Agustín via Popayán, US$12; to Cartago, 3½ hrs., US$3.50; to Ibagué, US$6, 7 hrs.; to Buenaventura, US$3.15, 4 hrs.; to Manizales, US$4.50, 5 hrs.; to Medellín, US$11, 11-15 hrs.; to Bogotá, 10-15 hrs., by Magdalena (rec.) and Palmira, US$10. *Busetas* (Velotax and others) charge about 50% over bus prices but save time; taxi-colectivos about 2½ times bus prices and save even more.

Airport   Palmaseca, 20 km. from city, has *casa de cambio*. International standard, with good *Hotel Aeropuerto Palmaseca*. Services to Bogotá, Medellín, Pereira, Cartagena, Barranquilla, San Andrés, Leticia (Mon., Wed., Fri.). Minibus from airport to bus terminal (2nd floor), every 10 minutes, approx. 30 mins., US$0.75. Colectivo to city about US$1; taxi, US$6. Two flights a week to Quito (Weds. and Sat.); direct flights (e.g. Avianca) to Panama; also to Miami.

145 km. by road from Cali (4 hrs.) over a pass in the Western Cordillera is **Buenaventura,** Colombia's only important port on the Pacific. It was founded in 1540, but not on its present site. It stands on the island of Cascajal, 16 km. inside the Bay of Buenaventura. Port works are in progress. Beaches such as La Bocana, Juanchaco and Ladrilleros (many small hostels and restaurants) may be reached by motor launch, but they are not very safe. Trips to beaches cost between US$10-40 for 10-person launch (rate per launch, not per person).

Buenaventura is 560 km. by sea from Panamá, 708 km. by road from Bogotá. Population, 122,500, mostly black. Mean temperature, 27° C. It rains nearly every day, particularly at night; the average annual rainfall is 7,400 mm. (relative humidity 88%). There are still problems with malaria. The port handles 80% of Colombia's coffee exports, and 60% of the nation's total exports, including sugar and frozen shrimp.

The toll road to Cali is fully paved; the toll is about US$0.40 for cars and US$0.10 for motorcycles. The ordinary road is not paved. (Both give beautiful views of mountains and jungle, and from the old road you can reach the Parque Nacional Farallones. To reach the park, take the dirt road S from the plaza in Queremal, at 1,460 metres, about 1 hr. from Cali, 1½ hrs. from Buenaventura.) There are plenty of buses to Cali, US$3.15 each way, 3 hrs. Colectivos run at half-hourly intervals to Cali, US$4.75 p.p.

The commercial centre is now entirely paved and has some impressive buildings, but the rest of the town is poor, with steep unpaved streets lined with wooden shacks. It is more expensive than Cali and it is difficult to eat cheaply or well. Festive atmosphere every night. S of the town a swampy coast stretches as far as Tumaco (**see page 597**); to the N lies the deeply jungled Chocó Department, where the most important gold and platinum mines are found.

Hotels   *Estación*, B, good restaurant; on Carrera 3 with Calle 3, *Del Mar*, C, restaurant, TV, phone in rooms, and *Balmoral*, E with bath. Several F and G hotels on Carrera 5, e.g. *Comfort*, a/c; *Colombia* (fan), *Felipe II* (a/c, D with bath, restaurant). *Bahía*, Calle 3, F, clean, friendly. *Gran*, E with bath; *Continental*, Carrera 5, No. 4-05, E with bath; opposite is *Europa*, F without bath.

Camping   With the permission of the commandant, it is safe to camp in the police compound at the docks while awaiting your ship.

Restaurants   *Los Balcones*, Calle 2 y Carrera 3, very good, but expensive. Self-service restaurant on main plaza, clean, modern, open 24 hrs. *La Sombrita de Miguel*, on road to El Piñal, good seafood, reasonable prices. Chinese restaurant in street leading NE from telephone building. Good seafood at Pueblo Nuevo market, but not very cheap.

Exchange   Do not change money in Buenaventura, but in Cali.

Tourist Office   Calle 1, No. 1-26, Mon.-Fri., 0800-1200, 1400-1800. Cámara de Comercio nearby is also helpful; has plan of city.

Air Services   Local airport only; flights to Cali.

Shipping Passenger service from France: arrange with Continental Shipping and Travel, 179 Piccadilly, London WIV 9DB, T 01-491 4968.

Grace Osakoda from Hawaii tells us that you can get from Buenaventura to Quibdó (**see page 581**) on the Río San Juan, but that boats are scarce out of Buenaventura (lumber boats from El Piñal only go about a day and a half upstream, and port authorities are strict about allowing passengers on cargo boats). One way is to take a bus from Pueblo Nuevo, Buenaventura, to San Isidro on the Río Calima (28 km., 6 hrs., terrible road), then a motorized dugout (*panga*) to Palestina on the Río San Juan. From there take a dugout going upstream; they rarely go as far as Istmina, which is connected by road and bus to Quibdó. Try to get as far as Dipurdú (no hotels, but friendly locals who offer sleeping space, shops with tinned goods), from where daily boats go to Istmina.

The paved Pan-American Highway (142 km.) runs S through the Cauca Valley from Cali to Popayán. (Toll, US$0.40.) It takes 2½-3 hrs. by bus through splendid scenery. At first we pass through a land of rich pastures interspersed with sugar-cane plantations. To left and right are the mountain walls of the two Cordilleras. The valley narrows and we begin to climb, with occasional glimpses E of the Nevado del Huila (5,750 metres).

Warning All of rural Valle Department off the main roads is unsafe because of guerrilla activity. Similarly, Cauca Department E of the Highway is not recommended for tourists.

Popayán is in the valley of the Pubenza, at 1,760 metres, in a peaceful landscape of palm, bamboo, and the sharp-leaved agave. (Pop. 250,000.) The early settlers after setting up their sugar estates in the hot, damp Cauca valley, retreated to Popayán to live, for the city is high enough to give it a delightful climate. To N, S, and E the broken green plain is bounded by mountains. To the SE rises the snowcapped cone of the volcano Puracé (3,960 metres).

Popayán was founded by Benalcázar, Francisco Pizarro's lieutenant, in 1536. After the conquest of the Pijao Indians, Popayán became the regional seat of government, subject until 1717 to the Audiencia of Quito, and later to the Audiencia of Bogotá. It is now the capital of the Department of Cauca. The equestrian statue of Benalcázar on the Morro de Tulcán overlooks the city; it is worth climbing this hill, or even better the one with the three crosses on top, for the views. The streets of two-storey buildings are in rococo Andalusian style, with beautiful old monasteries and cloisters of pure Spanish classic architecture.

In March 1983, an earthquake devastated the city. Following restoration work, Popayán has come fully back to life and has managed to retain its colonial character. The churches of San Agustín (Calle 7 y Cra. 6) and Santo Domingo (Calle 4 y Cra. 5, used by the Universidad del Cauca) are again open to the public, as are La Ermita (Calle 5 y Cras. 2-3) and La Encarnación; other churches remain closed. Walk to Belén chapel, which is also open (Calle 4 y Cra. 0), seeing the statues en route, and then continue to El Cerro de las Tres Cruces if you have the energy, but best not to go alone (there are plenty of guides offering their services). Popayán was the home of the poet Guillermo Valencia; it has given no fewer than eleven presidents to the Republic.

The scientist Francisco José de Caldas was born here in 1771; it was he who discovered how to determine altitude by variation in the boiling point of water, and it was to him that Mutis (of the famous *Expedición Botánica*) entrusted the directorship of the newly founded Observatory at Bogotá. He was a passionate partisan of independence, and was executed in 1815 during Morillo's "Reign of Terror".

Festivals Easter processions are spectacular; the city is very crowded. The childrens' processions in the following week are easier to see. As at Pasto (but less violent), there are the Día de los Negros on Jan. 5 and Día de los Blancos on Jan. 6; drenching with water is not very common, but don't walk under windows when you see people on the first floor.

Hotels *Monasterio*, Calle 4, No. 10-50, in what was the monastery of San Francisco, lovely grounds, swimming pool, C, very good, T (939) 221 91-6 with shower; *Los Balcones*, Calle 3, No. 6-80, D, hot water, Spanish-style restaurant for breakfast and lunch (often closed), good, will change travellers' cheques; *Veraneo El Bosque*, 5 km. N of city, 1 km. off Cali road (turn left opposite service station) C, very quiet, good restaurant; *Chayani*, Panamericana Calle 17 Norte, D, travellers' cheques accepted, and change given in US dollars; *Camino Real*, Calle 5, No. 5-59, T 21546/21254, P.O.Box 248, C, good service, excellent restaurant, friendly, rec.; *Viajero*, Calle 8, No. 4-45, F, with bath, hot water, quiet, helpful, rec.; *El Príncipe*, Calle 8, No. 4-35; *El Gran Hotel*, on Plaza, F, room for up to 5 persons; *Hostal Santo Domingo*, Calle 4, No. 5-14 (T 21676),

D, with bath, friendly, good value, in colonial building; *Residencia Comercio*, Calle 6, just off Carrera 17, clean, friendly; *Casa Grande*, Cra. 6, No. 7-11, T 22225, E, family run, hot water, convenient, will store luggage, highly rec.; *La Casona del Virrey*, Calle 4, No. 5-78, E, excellent; *El Viti*, F, clean, with bath, no hot water, near old bus station; *Casa Suiza*, Calle 4, No. 7-79, E, pleasant, hot water, clean, rec.; *Residencias El Castillo*, Carrera 4 esq. Calle 1, D, bath and hot water, clean, very friendly, cafeteria and bar; *Residencias Bolívar*, Carrera 5, No. 7-11, F, clean, pleasant, good restaurant, parking across street; nearby *Residencia Panamá*, G, good, hot water, doors close at 2200; *Residencias Cataluña*, Cra. 5, No. 8-27, F, clean, quiet, friendly; there are many others (E) on Carrera 5 e.g. *Venicia*, No. 7-45, *Manizales*, No. 7-55, *Viena*, No. 7-56, *Cecilia*, No. 7-60. *Residencias San Agustín*, Cra. 6, No. 1N-15, behind the old bridge, clean, good beds, washing facilities; *Residencia San Diego*, just around the corner (turn right off Carrera 6), F, no hot water, but clean and safe, noisy from disco next door; *Plaza Bolívar*, Carrera 6N-12, F with bath, hot water, clean, safe, good value; many others in this area (around Parque Bolívar and market).

Restaurants *La Castellana*, Carrera 6, No. 6-47 (meal and soft drinks for two, good and cheap at US$4.50); *El Mesón del Arriero*, Carrera 6, No. 7-37, good value but limited menu; *Taberna La Tolda*, next to *Hotel Los Balcones*, friendly student-type place; *El Danubio*, Carrera 8, No. 5-33, good, open till midnight; *Mei Chow*, Carrera 10A, No. 10-81, good but not cheap; *Café El Alamo*, Calle 3, No. 5-65, nice colonial atmosphere and good coffee; *El Pasaje*, Calle 3, Carrera 2, good, reasonably priced typical food; *Pizzería El Recuerdo*, Carrera 6 Vía Cauca, cheaper. For good lunches (US$1) *Los Olivares*, Carrera 4, No. 7-37; and *Punto Aparte*, Carrera 9, No. 6-09. *Astoria*, Calle 7, No. 4-33, good for breakfasts; cheap lunches at *Bogotá*, Carrera 5, No. 6-57; *La Oficina*, Calle 4, No. 8-01, friendly, good value; *Pollo Pío Pío*, Carrera 6, No. 8-11 open, till 0300, good. On the continuation of Cra. 6 across the bridge from centre there are many cafeterias, bars and discos (good café: *Pitufos*, cheap, large menu). *El Bambo*, restaurant with swimming pool, on outskirts on road from Cali, friendly, camping permitted (US$0.50 for 2). Also on road to Cali (5 km.) is *El Rancho*, excellent. Wholemeal bread, information and occasional accommodation from Heinz Rose, Calle 5, No. 2-28 (Aptdo. Aéreo 1851).

Museums Museo Negret, Calle 5, No. 10-23, US$0.40, with works, photographs and furniture of Negret. Museo Guillermo Valencia, Cra. 6 y Calle 3, birthplace of the poet; Casa Museo Martínez, Calle 3 out of town. Small collection in Banco de la República. All others damaged and closed.

Cinemas Teatro Popayán, Calle 4, Carrera 8/9, best; Teatro Anarkos, Carrera 5, Calles 6/7.

Exchange Banco de la República, Calle 6, No. 2-78, is the only one that changes foreign currency and travellers' cheques. (Open 0800-1130; 1400-1600, Mon.-Thur., until 1630 on Fri.) However, the *Hotel Monasterio* will accept travellers' cheques when you pay your bill and will give you change in pesos. There is also Salvador's exchange shop on the main plaza, between the Diana shop and the cathedral.

Post Office Carrera 7, No. 5-77. **Telephone Office** Telecom, Carrera 4 y Calle 3.

Tourist Office Carrera 6, No. 3-69, between Puente del Humilladero and Plaza Mayor (T 22251), has good maps of the city, prices of all hotels and pensions, and bus schedules and prices. Ask for Sra. Haydée Gasca de Varela about accommodation. They are very friendly and helpful, giving information on places of interest, will tell you where horses may be hired for exploring, and will store your luggage. In addition to normal hours, they are open Suns. until 1200. Ask at the Tourist Office about which areas of the city are unsafe. They also offer coffee, and sell local crafts; telephone and mail service. The Tourist Office and the Colegio Mayor de Cauca have details on art exhibitions and concerts.

Travel Agent Avialoi Ltda, Calle 4, No. 7-59, good prices for air tickets bought with cash dollars.

Buses Popayán has a new bus terminal, next to the airport, 15 mins. walk from the centre (Ruta 2-Centro bus, terminal to centre, US$0.10, or taxi, US$0.50). Luggage can be stored safely (receipt given); there is a charge to use the toilets, and a US$0.07 departure tax. From the bus station, turn left to statue of Bolívar, then take second right to Parque Bolívar; here are the market and cheap hotels. To Bogotá, US$15. To Cali, US$3, 2½-3 hrs., or Velotax microbus, US$4.25, colectivos leaves from the main plaza (US$3.50); to Pasto, with Coop de Nariño, Carrera 6, No. 2-16, 1130, Cootranar (best and cheapest), Flota Magdalena, Exp. Bolivariano and Supertaxis del Sur, US$5, 5-8 hrs., spectacular scenery (sit on right); to Medellín, US$13.25, 16 hrs.; to Ipiales, something runs every hour; Supertaxis at 1230, US$6, or bus, US$7 (Transportes Ipiales at 0700, Bolivariano at 0530 or 0900, the best), 7½-10 hrs. To San Agustín, La Gaitana, 11 hrs., at 0900 and 2000, Coomotor, 13 hrs., US$9 each once a day. Transtambo runs over the new road via Isnos to San Agustín from bus terminal at 0800 and 1200 (or when full), 6 hrs., US$6. Another service on new road has been reported, from *Res. Huila*, Carrera 6, No. 2N-45, at 0900, 1230, buy ticket day in advance, US$4.60; check details beforehand. To Tierradentro (Cruce de Pisimbalá), with Sotracauca, 5 a day between 0500 and 1500 (T 26-46), US$3, 4-6 hrs.; and goes to La Plata.

Best to take the 0500 or 1000 bus, as the 1300 and 1500 will land you at the Cruce when it's dark, leaving you with a long unlit walk. Flota Magdalena to La Plata, US$3.75, 5 hrs, also Unidos del Sur (not via Tierradentro). To Puracé, US$1, 2 hrs. (Pullman is slightly more, Sotracauca at 0600, La Gaitana 0700, Coomotor later in a.m.) To Silvia (see below), daily Coomotorista *buseta* at 0800 (US$1.30) or: take Expreso Palmira bus to Piendamó on Cali road, every ½ hour, US$0.60; from there, colectivo to Silvia, US$0.70. On market day (Tuesdays) buses leave directly to Silvia at 0600.

Taxis No meters; normal price within city is US$0.60.

Air Services Service to Bogotá with Intercontinental or Aires, every day except Weds., 1650, Mon.-Sat. at 0825. Avianca office for airmail, Carrera 7, No. 5-77.

Excursions A favourite is the drive to Silvia, at 2,521 metres, one way through Totoró (partly paved) and the other through Piendamó (paved) two beautiful routes. In Piendamó there is one, unnamed hotel, behind the former railway station (E, clean, quiet, but has seen better days).

Silvia lies in a high valley. It is no longer an Indian town; the Indian market on Tues. mornings seems to be full of Otavalo Indians from Ecuador and their goods—more expensive than in Otavalo. Guambiano Indian farms can be reached by local bus: ask for the "paradero de los Guambianos". A typical Indian settlement, La Campana, is ½hour on the bus; 1½ hours' walk downhill back to Silvia. The Indians wear their typical blue and fuchsia costumes, and are very friendly and communicative. It is not safe to park cars in the street at night in Silvia, and guerrilla activity has been reported in the area. Horse hire from Sr. Marco A. Mosquiro, under US$1 per hour. On market days you can take a bus to Totoró (on the Popayán-Tierradentro road), departs 1200, US$0.50, and then a bus from Totoró to Tierradentro, US$1.25.

Hotels *Casa Turística*, E, helpful, good food; *Cali*, an old house, with good craft shop, E, including food, a little primitive, but very pleasant. *Silvia*, F, simple; *Ambeina*, F (3 beds per room), clean, friendly, efficient, rec., good meals; *Residencias La Villa*, about 200 metres up main road past *Cali*, F, good meals but poor plumbing. *La Parrilla*, F, water supply erratic, basic, restaurant is good. *Taberna El Buho*, friendly, with live music Sats. p.m.

For those who like to go off the beaten track, Sr. Camilo Arroyo (address: Carrera 3, No. 4-65, Popayán) arranges trips towards the coast, W of Popayán, for birdwatching or gold-panning (his family has a *finca* on the coast). He charges about US$50 a day p.p., depending on the length of the trip, size of the party, etc. His trips into the mountains are reported as less interesting—obtain full details before embarking on one.

Road to Neiva (page 571) from Popayán across the Central Cordillera, which is paved from Puerto Seco to Neiva, has interesting sights off it (best seen from left-hand side of the bus). Drive 37 km. along it (or take 0400, 0900 or 1100 bus, US$1) to the small town of *Puracé*, which has several old buildings. *Residencias Cubina*, F, clean, safe, friendly, cold showers, secure parking, no restaurant in the town but two stores will prepare meals on request. Drive to the Escuela and walk 5 mins. to see Chorrera de las Monjas waterfalls. About 11 km. E of Puracé towards Neiva a road branches S from the main road; 1 km.along this road is another fork at El Cruce de la Mina (bus 0530, US$0.50), the right branch leads to the Puracé sulphur mines (3,000 metres) 5 km. away; 1 km. along this road is a left fork to Pilimbalá, signed "Piscinas" (1½ km.) where are the Puracé National Park office, 5 warm sulphur baths in stone pools (which can be smelt a km. away), and a path leading to Puracé volcano. The Park is open all the week, but reduced service on Mondays. The volcano is steep; loose ash makes footholds difficult. It takes up to 5 hours to get to the top. Close to the main road (which continues to La Plata), and more easily reached from El Cruce de la Mina are Laguna San Rafael (10 km. from Pilimbilá), the Cascada de Bedón (15 km), the Cueva de los Guácharos (26 km.), and the Termales de San Juan (17 km., but only 700 metres from the main road; cafeteria; entry US$0.10; 2 hrs. by bus from Popayán). 112 hot sulphur springs combine with icy mountain creeks to produce spectacular arrays of multi-coloured mosses, algae and lichens—a must if you are in the area. Buses on the Popayán-La Plata route go near Pilimbalá and will drop you near any of these places (fare from Popayán about US$1.50).

The Tourist Office in Popayán will supply full information. The Park's fauna include the spectacled bear and mountain tapir. The only accommodation in the Park is at the thermal baths of Pilimbalá—cabins with up to six beds, D per cabin, up to 4 persons E, make reservations at Popayán Tourist Office(very cold, blankets and wood for the fire provided—rooms for 2 in the cellar can be hired at F rates); power goes off at 2200, but candles are provided. Camping costs US$3 p.p. and there are an expensive, but good restaurant/bar and a picnic area.

N.B. There has been some guerrilla activity in the areas traversed by this road.

Take warm clothes (and a sleeping bag) if climbing the volcano or visiting the baths; the nights are cold and blankets in the mountain cabins are thin. The weather is best, especially for climbing the volcano, in July and August. The highest point on the road is Quebrada Honda, at 3,340 metres above sea level.

Ute Lindner (of Freiburg) tells us that one may stay at a *finca* called Merenberg, 5 km. from Santa Leticia, on the road between Popayán and La Plata; the owners speak English and German. Take your own food (Santa Leticia is the only town in the mountains with shops); a good centre for walking.

Coconuco, at 2,734 metres, has beautiful landscapes. Turn to the right off the Popayán-Neiva road after 21 km. (16 km. short of Puracé); then 7 km. along is Coconuco (*Hotel de Turismo; Casa Familiar,* G, basic). There are good thermal baths near the village (camping US$1.50). Drive on 12 km. to the impressive scenery of the Paletará highland, where you can traverse vast areas of primeval forest; a bus to the village of Paletará takes 1 hour and costs US$0.40. Bus to Popayán, US$ 1, 1 hr. The direct 130-km. road from Popayán to San Agustin (**see page 574**) through Coconuco was opened in March 1985.

The Tierradentro Archaeological Park can be reached from Popayán, or San Agustín via *La Plata* (20,000 people), 147 km. from Popayán, 210 km. from San Agustín. Direct bus service with Coomotor from La Plata to Bogotá, 10 hrs., at 0900 and 2100.

Hotels *Berlin,* by church on square, 4 blocks from the bus office, E with bath, F without, friendly; next door is *Residencias Tunubalá,* F, OK, friendly; *Brooklyn,* clean, F, and *Norteño,* in the same price range; *Pensión Murucuju,* basic place to sleep and eat; *Residencias Nariño,* F; *La Familia,* F, dirty, unfriendly.

Restaurants *Es Aquí,* good meals for US$2. There is a café in the house where Bolívar stayed in 1829. *Patolandia,* good, cheap fruit juices. There is a cinema (2030).

From La Plata drive 35 km. NW to Guadualejo where one road goes N to Belalcázar (12 km.—a dusty drive). Another road continues NW to

Inzá (17 km.); hotels *Inzá* and *Ambalá.* Nine km. before Inzá is the Cruce de Pisimbalá, sometimes known as the Cruce de San Andrés, where a road turns off to San Andrés de *Pisimbalá* (4 km.), the village at the far end of the Tierradentro Park.
At Pisimbalá there is a unique and beautiful colonial church with a thatched roof; for the key ask behind the church. Some few km. before reaching Pisimbalá you pass the Tierradentro Museum, hours: 0700-1100 and 1300-1700, entrance US$0.40, camping is not allowed.

At Pisimbalá hire horses (US$2 an hr.)—or you can walk—for visiting the **Tierradentro** man-made burial caves painted with geometric patterns. There are four cave sites—Segovia, El Duende, Alto de San Andrés and El Aguacate. The main caves are now lighted, but probably as well to have your own torch. The surrounding scenery is splendid. It is very crowded at Easter-time.

For people on a one-day visit: go to Segovia, which has over 20 tombs, 5 of which are lit (these 5 are not opened until 0800-0900). Nos. 9, 10 and 12 are best decorated; Nos 8 and 28 are also impressive. The site is a 20 min. walk uphill from the administration building. El Duende (two of the four tombs are very good), is 15 mins. beyond Segovia. El Aguacate is a 2 hrs. hike one way (reported in disrepair in 1989), and one can return via El Alto de San Andrés (Nos. 1 and 5 tombs the best—the guard at El Alto is very helpful).

At El Tablón in the Parque there are 8 stone statues. There are several more in the new plaza at Inzá. A beautiful area for walking. From behind El Tablón, you can walk back to the museum via El Duende and Segovia in 2½ hrs. The surroundings have spectacular natural beauty; see small Indian villages in the mountains, e.g. Santa Rosa, 2 hours' hard walk beyond El Duende (get exact directions before setting out).

The Páez Indians in the Tierradentro region can be seen on market days at Inzá (Sat.), Pisimbalá (Wed.), and Belalcázar (Sat.); all start at 0600. The second floor of the museum at Pisimbalá is dedicated to their work: not to be missed. Take bus (US$0.50) from Tierradentro to Inzá market, on Sat. (buses leave from 0200); best to go into Pisimbalá and out again to be sure of getting a seat. On Saturdays there is plenty of transport going to and from Inzá on the Tierradentro road.

Hotels at Tierradentro   A short way up from the museum, state-owned *Albergue de San Andrés*, E, good, restaurant and swimming pool (also available to non-residents, US$0.80). Houses on either side of the Albergue offer accommodation, F, meals for US$1.50; green house next to museum, 2 rooms available, G, clean, friendly, rec.; *Residencia Turista*, in the village, basic, clean, F p.p., insufficient bedding; *Hospedaje El Viajero*, Sra. Marta de Angel, F, friendly, meals US$1.20 excellent; between Pisimbalá and museum, *hospedaje* of Sra Pola Angel de Velasco, Carmelita's house (*Hospedaje Lucerna*) next to museum, clean and friendly, F, showers, quiet, highly rec. Other cheap accommodation on village: *Residencias El Viajero* (Marta Veláquez), F, meals US$1, clean, friendly, rec.; *Residencias Murujuy*, F (breakfast, US$0.65, lunch and dinner, US$1); *Dormidero La Gaitana*, F, with shower, clean, friendly, owner also has a restaurant where all meals cost US$0.70, horses (US$0.75 an hour) and guide (US$2.50 a day) available. *Residencias Las Veraneras*, F p.p. 2 houses, 300 metres from Archaeological Park, rent rooms for US$2 p.p., clean, no hot water, food available if requested in advance. *El Gauchito* in Pisimbalá village, F, clean, pleasant, family atmosphere, meals available, rec.; camping.

Restaurants   There is a restaurant, meals about US$1; good fruit juices at the *Fuente de Soda y Artesanía* store. The house of Nelli Parra de Jovar, opposite the museum with the long antenna, is rec. for abundance but not cheapness; you must book meals in advance. She can also give up to date information on accommodation. At Dalia's home, *Su Repuesto*, almost opp. *Hosp. Lucerna*, good meals for US$1.25, again best to arrange in advance.

Transport   The road from Popayán to Tierradentro is difficult and narrow, but this is compensated by the beautiful scenery. Sotracauca buses from Popayán, US$3, 4-6 hrs. to Cruce Pisimbalá; take one of two morning buses as the two afternoon ones land you at the Cruce after dark. Walk (about 2 km.) from there to the museum. The village is another 20 mins. walk from the museum. Bus Cruce Pisimbalá-Popayán, 0600 (unreliable), 0800 and 1300. If you want to go to Silvia, take this bus and change to a colectivo (US$1) at Totoró. There are buses on market day, or trucks (US$1). Buses from Tierradentro to La Plata leave at 0900 and 1500 (unreliable) from the Cruce, US$2, 3 hrs.; if you cannot get a direct Cruce-La Plata bus, take one going to Belalcázar (US$1), alight at Guadualejo from where there is a more frequent service to La Plata; or one can hitch. On Fri. only, a bus leaves from Pisimbalá village for La Plata at 0400. Similarly, on Fri. only, a bus from La Plata to Pisimbalá goes at 1200, otherwise the only La Plata-Tierradentro bus (La Gaitana) leaves daily at 0500 for Inzá; alight at Cruce (2½ hrs.). Private jeep hire La Plata-Tierradentro, US$18 after bargaining, or less if you agree to pick up other passengers. The road follows the spectacularly beautiful Páez valley. Buses from La Plata to Neiva and Bogotá.

From San Agustín, take Coomotor at 0600 to La Plata, 5 hrs., US$3.50, or La Gaitana at 0530 or 1600. Next morning, take the 0500 La Gaitana bus from La Plata to Cruce de Pisimbalá, arrives 0800 (continues to Inzá and Popayán). Alternatively, on arrival in La Plata, take a pick-up to Guadualejo (US$1), then hitch, or try to get a bus going past Tierradentro (about 3 per day). Buses from La Plata to San Agustín at 0700, 0900 and 1500.

Another site of archaeological interest is **La Argentina**, best reached from La Plata (some direct buses), 8 km. off the La Plata-Popayán road. Gillian Handyside writes; It is set in beautiful surroundings but is largely ignored by the archaeological authorities and the tourist board. The Museo Arqueológico de la Platavieja contains statues and ceramics as interesting as those found at San Agustín. Ask for Sr. Carlos Hernández, who runs the museum almost singlehanded and is extremely knowledgeable about the archaeological aspects of the area. (He also keeps bees, and sells honey.) The Universities of Los Andes, Cauca and Pittsburg run an archaeological project at La Argentina during the dry season: contact Carlos Hernández for details.

SOUTHERN COLOMBIA (8)

The Pan-American Highway continues S from Popayán to Pasto. The entire road is now paved. After El Bordo (*Residencias Confort*, on main road, F, simple but recommended) the road takes a new route and the 294-km. drive takes 5 hrs. The express bus takes 7 hrs. in ordinary conditions, though landslides often block

UPPER MAGDALENA

the road. 93 km. S of Popayán is a tourist complex including hotel, swimming pool and campsite.

If one has time, the old route via La Unión and Mercaderes can be done by bus; enquire at Popayán or Pasto bus terminals. There are three basic hotels at La Unión (beware of overcharging at the *Hotel Nevada*). In El Bordo, the *Aquí Jaramillo* restaurant serves good Colombian dishes (US$3 per head).

163 km. S of Popayán is **Mercaderes,** a small town with a pleasant climate. Hotels (F) are good and the *Restaurante Tropical* is recommended. 30 km. before Pasto is Chachagui, where the *Hotel Imperio de los Incas* is recommended, E with bath, friendly, swimming pool, 2 km. from Pasto airport. Toll N of Pasto US$0.30.

Pasto, capital of the Department of Nariño, stands upon a high plateau (2,534 metres) in the SW, 88 km. from Ecuador, with a population of 370,000. The city, which retains some of its colonial character, was founded in the early days of the conquest. Today it is a centre for the agricultural and cattle industries of the region, which exports little. Pasto varnish (*barniz*) is mixed locally, to embellish the strikingly colourful local wooden bowls. A visit to the church of Cristo Rey (Calle 20 y Carrera 24) near the centre is recommended. Also La Merced, Calle 18, is worth seeing for its rich decoration and gold ornaments. From the church of Santiago (Carrera 23 y Calle 13) there is a good view over the city to the mountains, San Felipe (Calle 12 y Carrera 27) has green tiled domes. The interior courtyard of the municipal building on the main square (corner of Calle 19 and Carrera 24) has 2 tiers of colonnaded balconies. Do not visit Pasto on a Sunday: nearly everything is closed.

During the new year's *fiesta* there is a Día de los Negros on Jan. 5 and a Día de los Blancos next day. On "black day" people dump their hands in black grease and smear each other's faces. On "white day" they throw talc or flour at each other. Local people wear their oldest clothes. Things can get quite violent. On December 28 and Feb. 5, there is also a Fiesta de las Aguas when anything that moves—only tourists because locals know better—gets drenched with water from balconies and even from fire engines' hoses. In Pasto and Ipiales (**see page 599**), on December 31, is the Concurso de Años Viejos, when huge dolls are burnt; they represent the old year and sometimes lampoon local people. On Suns. a game of paddle ball is played on the edge of the town (bus marked San Lorenzo) similar to that played in Ibarra, Ecuador.

During the wars of independence, Pasto was a stronghold of the Royalists and the last town to fall into the hands of the patriots after a long and bitter struggle. Then the people of Nariño Department wanted to join Ecuador when that country split off from Gran Colombia in 1830, but were prevented by Colombian troops.

Hotels *Morasurco*, Avenida de los Estudiantes, B, rec., reasonable restaurant; *Zorocán*, Calle 18, No. 22-33, C, bath, TV, a/c, indifferent restaurant; *Sindagua*, Calle 20, No. 21B-16, D, rec.; *Cuellar's*, Carrera 23, No. 15-50, D, roomy, well-furnished, new, some noise from bowling centre underneath, but rec.; *Res. Santa Ana*, Carrera 25, 16-45, E with bath, F without, top floor rooms are quiet; *Residencias El Carmen*, near bus station, clean and comfortable, E; *Mayasquer*, Av. de las Américas, 16-66, E, with bath, clean, friendly, restaurant; next door at No. 16-40 is *Juanambú*, E, friendly, clean, safe, F for rooms without bath, rec. *Hostería Imperio de los Incas*, at Chachagui near the airport, E with shower, dubious electrics, noisy (near Panamericana), beware overcharging in taxis to town. *Isa*, Calle 18, No. 22-33, E with bath, clean, helpful, safe, 100 metres from bus station; *Residencias Colón*, Carrera 22, No. 19-61, F, clean, friendly, hot water; *Mallorca*, Calle 18, 21a-45, F, pleasant, hot water a.m.; *Nueva York*, Carrera 19 bis, 18-20, F, clean rooms, dirty toilets, hot shower, friendly, near Magdalena bus company, the only place in the town where you can put a motorcycle inside; *María Belén*, Calle 13, No. 19-15, new, clean, safe, quiet, friendly, hot water; near bus station are *Líbano* (O.K., hot water), *Las Pensas* (quiet, no hot water), *Cartagena* (cheap, adequate), *Jordán*, and others, in F price range; *Manhattan*, Calle 18, 21B-14, F, clean, pleasant, hot water old-fashioned, big rooms, rec.; *Residencia Indi Chaya*, Calle 16, No. 18-23 (corner of Cra. 19 and Calle 16), T 4476, F, good value, clean, good beds, carpets, hot water, safe; *Residencias Galeras*, Calle 17, nr. bus station, F, hot water, communal bath, clean, safe; *Residencia Santa Isabel*, Calle 19, No. 20-39, F, clean, close to bus station. *Viena*, clean, Carrera 19B, No. 18-36, cheap and near bus station.

Restaurants *El Chalet Suizo*, Calle 20, 41-80 (T 4419), high class food; *La Esquina del Barril*, Calle 19, No. 28-12, good; *Viena*, opposite *Hotel Nueva York*, good, cheap; *Parma*, Carrera 25, good, large meals; *Pollorrico*, Carrera 25, 17-50, good. *Pollo Listo*, opp. *Agualonga Hotel*, cheap, good chicken dishes; *Mister Pollo*, Calle 17 y Cra. 26, central, good, clean fast food. *La Picantería*, Calle 19, cheap, good food; *Alberto's*, Calle 17, No. 27-26, friendly; *Bar Concorde*, Calle 17, Carreras 26 and 27, French and English music, pleasant. *El Encinar*, Calle 16, No. 13-48, US$0.80, good value, rec. A cheap but good place to eat is the self-service cafetería at the Amorel shopping centre. *Riko Riko*, near bus station, good fast food; similar *La Espiga* close by. Most restaurants on main street are OK. *Moreno's* on the Panamericana, local dishes, excellent, live music some evenings. In the nearby village of Catambuco (15 mins. drive), the restaurant *Catambuey* is rec. if you like guinea pig.

Shopping Artesanías de Colombia have a branch on Carrera 25. Casa del Barniz de Pasto, Calle 13, No. 24-9, Artesanías Nariño, Calle 26, No. 18-91; Artesanías Mopa-Mopa, Carrera 25, No. 13-14, for *barniz*. See Colegio Artesanías, run by a government institute (Sena), 5 km. N on road to Popayán. Visitors welcome. Leather goods are cheaper here than in Bogotá, Ecuador or Peru. Most of the shops are on Calles 17 and 18. Also try the municipal market for handicrafts. Supermercado Confamiliar de Nariño, Calle 16b, No. 30-53, recommended, and, more convenient, Ley on Calle 18, next to Avianca postal office. On main square (Calle 19 y Cra. 25) is a new shopping centre with many types of shops and restaurants.

Drycleaners Calle 18 y Carrera 27.

Cinema Carrera 25 and Calles 17 and 18, good.

Exchange For changing travellers' cheques, Banco de la República on the main square. Banco Anglo Colombiano, Calle 17, No. 21-32, and at Amorel, and other national banks. Open Mon.-Thur., 0800-1130, 1400-1600; Fri., 0900-1130, 1400-1630; closed Sat. Last working day of month, 0800-1100. If going to Tumaco, this is the last place where travellers' cheques can be cashed. A *cambio* off the main square will change sucres into pesos, but the Banco de la República will not, though it does change Amex cheques without charging commission. An optician/pharmacist on the main square changes sucres into pesos (good rates).

Airmail Carrera 23, 18-42 and Calle 18, 25-86.

Telephones Long distance calls from Telecom, Calle 17 y Carrera 23.

Ecuadorean Consulate Calle 17, No. 26-55, 2nd floor. Four photos needed if you require a visa (but this office is not very knowledgeable about requirements for visas).

Tourist Office Just off the main square, Calle 18, No. 25-25, friendly and helpful. It will advise on money changing. Maps of Colombia and cities from Instituto Geográfico Agustín Codazzi, Calle 18, No. 23-36, 1st floor (Banco del Occidente building).

Buses Most buses leave from Calle 18. To Bogotá, 23 hrs., US$19.50 (Bolivariano Pullman). To Ipiales, 2 hrs., US$2.45, Cooperativo Supertaxis del Sur; by bus, US$1.50. To Popayán, ordinary buses take 10-12 hrs.; expresses take 5-8 hrs., cost US$5. To Cali, US$10, expresses, 8½-10 hrs. To Tumaco, 11 hrs. by bus, 10 hrs. by minibus, US$6.50. To Puerto Asis, 11 hrs., US$4.75 with Trans Ipiales or Bolivariano (both Calle 18), 0500 and 1100.

Air Services Daily to Popayán, 20 mins., and Bogotá; to Cali with Avianca at 0800, and to Ipiales by Avianca on Fri. Aerotal, Pasto to Cali, daily at 0800; to Medellín. Avianca to Leticia via Cali, US$95. The airport is at Cano, 40 km. from Pasto; by colectivo (beautiful drive), 45 mins. US$1.90 or US$11.35 by taxi. There are no currency exchange facilities, but the shop will change US$ bills at a poor rate.

Excursions There are some gold mines in the area. The volcano, Galeras (4,069 metres), is to the W. The last eruption took place in 1934. A highway traversing all kinds of altitudes and climates has been built round it; the trip along it takes half a day. A rough road goes to the summit where there is an army post guarding a TV relay station; you can scramble down into the crater. A taxi (arrange previous day, if possible) will take you to about 200 metres from the top; there is a fine view and the soldiers are glad to see people. If you can't get a taxi, take a bus to the village of San Vicente, then hitch as far up as you can, which will probably leave a 3-hour, but pleasant walk to the top. On it lies the village of *Sandoná* where Panama hats are made; they can be seen lying in the streets in the process of being finished. Sandoná market day is Saturday. (It is a worthwhile trip to Sandoná, 4 buses daily, the last back to Pasto is at 1700.)

Tumaco Region

The 250-km. road W from Pasto to Tumaco is paved for 20 km. beyond Túquerres, but is then unsurfaced (it was under reconstruction in 1988/89). The region is very different from highland Colombia, with two-storey Caribbean-style wooden houses and a predominantly black population. Small farms are mixed with cattle ranches, rice farms and oil-palm plantations. Cocoa is grown. The coastal area around Tumaco is mangrove swamp, with many rivers and inlets on which lie hundreds of villages and settlements; negotiate with boatmen for a visit to the swamps or the beautiful, newly-developed island tourist resort of *Boca Grande* (US$7.50 minimum, the trip takes 30 mins.; ask for Señor Felipe

Bustamante, Calle Comercial, Apto. 224, T 465, who rents canoes and cabins, has a good seafood restaurant and owns *Hotel Los Manglares* on the island, where water and electricity supplies are irregular).

Tumaco has a population of about 100,000; the unemployment rate is very high, the living conditions are poor, and the services and roads in the town are not good. It is in one of the world's rainiest areas; the yearly average temperature is in the 25°-35°C range. The movement of the tides governs most of the activities in the area, especially transport. A natural arch on the main beach, N of the town and port, is reputed to be the hiding place of Henry Morgan's treasure. Swimming is not recommended from the town's beaches, which are polluted; stalls provide refreshment on the beach. Swimming is safe, however, at El Morro beach, north of the town, only on the incoming tide (the outgoing tide uncovers poisonous rays). Hotels are well subscribed and of varying quality: it is advisable to get a bed early in the day. The northern part of the town is built on stilts out over the sea. Visit it during the daylight as it is reported to be dangerous at night, and not just because you could fall through the holes in the wooden pavements into the sea. There is an airport, and the area is also noted archaeologically for the finds associated with the Tumaco culture. The town has problems with water and electricity supplies. There is one cinema. There are no money exchange facilities (except in some shops that will buy dollars and sucres at a poor rate; change money in Cali or Pasto).

Hotels *Villa del Mar*, D, Calle Sucre, modern, clean, with shower, toilet and fan, no hot water, good café below; *Claudia*, Calle Mosquera, E, with restaurant; *Residencias Don Pepe*, near water-front and *canoa* dock, friendly but basic; *Porvenir*, G, far from luxurious, most of the family friendly. Children meet arriving buses to offer accommodation; most cheap places are in Calle Comercial, many houses and restaurants without signs take guests—nearly all have mosquito nets. Try opp. Trans Ipiales, under Cootranor sign, or 2 doors from Trans Ipiales (Barbería Nueva), both F. **Food:** The main culinary attraction of the town is the fish, in the market and restaurants, fresh from the Pacific. A number of good restaurants on the main streets (Calles Mosquera and Comercial): *La Tropicana, La Tortula, La Brasa*. **N.B.** Be very careful of food and water because there are many parasites.

Transport Tumaco to Pasto, 11 hrs. (10 hrs. by minibus), US$6.50, with Supertaxis del Sur or Trans Ipiales (better), 4 a day, very rough but interesting ride. An alternative is to catch a bus from Ipiales to Espino (US$0.60, colectivo, US$0.90) and there change buses for Tumaco (US$4, 7½ hrs., rough ride). There are no hotels in Espino. There are daily flights to and from Cali with Aces (US$40 one way) and on Wed., Fri. and Sun. with Satena (US$35), 1 hr. Flights also to Pasto.

To Ecuador It is possible to travel to Ecuador by water, but only by motorized canoe. Part of the trip is by river, which is very beautiful, and part on the open sea, which can be very rough; a plastic sheet to cover your belongings is essential. Daily service at 0800 to San Lorenzo, 7 hrs. US$6.50, Coop. de Transportes, tickets from Calle Comercial (protective plastic sheeting provided). Señor Pepello, who lives in the centre of Tumaco, owns two canoes: he leaves on Wed. and Sat. at 0700 for San Lorenzo and Limones in Ecuador—book in advance. Also enquire for Señor Lucho, or ask around the water-front at 0600. DAS stamp for leaving Colombia and visa for Ecuador (if required) should be obtained in Cali or Pasto (although there is a DAS office in Tumaco, Calle Sucre, No. 6-13); offices are open on weekdays only. Entry stamps for Ecuador must be obtained in the coastal towns.

Barbacoas, 57 km. from Junín, is interesting—a former Spanish gold-producing centre which still retains the remains of an extensive water-front, a promenade and steps coming down through the town to the river. Gold is still panned from the rivers by part-time prospector-farmers. *Hotel Telembi*, F, basic, friendly; *Residencial*, F, poor, unfriendly. Restaurant *Telembi* on the river front, good food. Problems with water and electricity supplies. River trips on the supply boats are possible, about US$6.75 for 8 hrs. Bus to Pasto, US$6, rough trip. The road to Barbacoas is limited to one-way traffic in places— enquire at the chain barring the road at Junín and the operator will telephone down the line to see if the route is clear for you to pass.

The *Putumayo*

One hour E of Pasto, on the road to Mocoa (capital of the Intendencia of Putumayo) is **Laguna La Cocha,** the largest lake in S Colombia (sometimes called Lago Guámez). By the lake is the Swiss-run *Chalet Guámez*, D, well recommended, particularly for the cuisine, cabins sleeping up to six can be hired, US$23; free van-camping allowed. Rafael Narváez has cheap, basic rooms to let. The chalet will arrange a US$22 jeep trip to Sibundoy, further along the road. Boats may be hired for US$2.20 per hour. La Cocha may be reached by taking a bus to El Encano and walking the remaining 5 km. Or walk 20 mins. from the bus stop to the fishing village of El Encano, where you can enjoy trout at very low prices at one of the many small restaurants, and from here take a *lancha* to the chalet for US$2-3. There is also a government hotel nearby, *Sindamanoy*, C, chalet style, good views, inviting restaurant with good but expensive food, free van-, and tent camping allowed with manager's permission. From the hotel you can take a 10-minute boat trip to the Isla de la Chorota nature reserve; interesting trees, but little wildlife. Taxi from Pasto, US$11.

The road from Pasto to the Putumayo deteriorates rapidly after El Encano. It is dangerous between Sibundoy and El Pepino and care should be taken, but there is a magnificent view out over the Putumayo by a large statue of the Virgin, just before the final descent.

Sibundoy   There is a beautiful church on the main plaza, completed in 1968. About a quarter of the valley is now reserved for Sibundoy Indian occupation. Market Sunday. Best handicraft shop is Fudak, Calle 16 No. 16-73, a cooperative run by the Kamza Indians. Also Marcelino Chindoy, Carrera 18, 18-66, who travels a lot around Colombia and can normally be found at handicrafts fairs in Bogotá. Roasted guinea-pig (*cuy*) may be eaten in the restaurant here. Bus from Pasto (3 hrs., US$2.25), passing through Colón (*residencias*) and Santiago.

Hotels and Restaurants   *Hotel Turista*, F, clean; *Oriente*, F, pleasant, with restaurant, best value in town; better meals at *Hotel Sibundoy*, also F; *Restaurant Viajero*, just off main street. You can camp in the hills, where there are lovely walks and you can see all kinds of flora and fauna.

Mocoa, the administrative capital of the Intendencia of Putumayo, is small (21,000 people), with a number of hotels (*Viajero*, D; *Central*, off main plaza, F, very clean and friendly) and *residencias*. The town has a very modern square, new offices and modern developments. Sugar-cane is grown in the area. The road (buses) to Puerto Asís is good, passing through a recently cleared area supporting cattle ranching. 12 hrs. by bus to Pasto. Bus from Sibundoy, US$2, 5 a day, continuing to Puerto Asís; a few police checks, a bit hair-raising in places, but stunning scenery between Sibundoy and Mocoa ("some of the best in Colombia").

Puerto Asís is the main town and port of the Putumayo. River traffic is busy. All boats that leave for Leticia (with connections to Manaus) are cargo boats, and only sail when they have cargo. Those carrying gasoline (and most do) are forbidden to take passengers. Only one company, Navenal, normally take passengers, and it can be weeks between their sailings. One can also try the army for a passage. Fares are about US$100; at least 8-10 days; it is best to see the Jefe de la Marina, or the Oficina de Transporte Fluvial, about a passage. Another possibility is to take a *canoa* to Leguizamo (see below), and try for a passage there. By boat to Leguizamo takes 2-3 days, US$4.50, food US$2.50 per day. For those interested in flora and fauna it is necessary to travel down river, beyond new areas of settlement. Boats will not go unless the rivers are high; sometimes, they get stuck halfway.

There are regular flights to and from Puerto Asís three times a week by Satena to Bogotá, via Florencia. Flights to Florencia are on Mon., Wed. and Fri. at 1000 with Sarpa, who also fly to Leguizamo. Occasional flights to Leticia.

Hotels   *Residencias Nevado*, Carrera 20, close to the airport, well kept and comfortable, air-conditioning optional, F, without board. *Residencias Liz*, Calle 11, F, with bath, very friendly; *Residencias Patiño*, G, rec.; *Residencias Gigante*, Calle 10, 24-25, F, clean. There are plenty of cheap hotels in the port, but it is hard to find a room late in the day.

Buses   may be taken to Pasto (a 10 hr. journey, at 0500, 0600 and 0900 daily, on mostly mountainous roads, US$4.50, be prepared for military checks). Bus Sibundoy-Puerto Asís, US$3.25. Local bus to San Miguel near the Ecuadorean border where the Sun. market provides a meeting place, and where *canoas* may be hired to visit villages 2-4 hrs. away on the river.

San Miguel   Accommodation is very limited: *Residencias Olga* is the only place available and has only 6 single rooms. Accommodation beyond San Miguel is non-existent, except in Orita, W of Puerto Asís, a small town on the oilfield.

Leguizamo, upstream from Puerto Asís, can also be reached by air from Florencia, with Satena, daily, flight originates in Neiva. There are boats to Leticia and to Peru, but transport on all boats carrying gasoline is forbidden. For information go to Naval at the port, Transporte Fluvial Estrella del Sur (Carrera 27, off Calle 10) or Transporte Fluvial Amazonas (Carrera 20, 14-59—English spoken). Hotels: *Leguizamo* and *Putumayo*, both G, basic. Further upstream are El Encanto and the nearby village of **San Rafael**, which is a good place to see the Huitoto Indians, the most important of the many tribes which live along the Putumayo river. At San Rafael there is a mission at which it is possible to stay.

We are informed that travellers interested in Amazonian plants, birds and animals will find Putumayo more accessible, with more abundant wild life, than Leticia. Restaurant food in the Putumayo region is often uninspiring; take some canned goods for variety. There is a road of a sort from Mocoa to Puerto Limón, on the Río Caquetá (see Caquetá section, **page 575**).

South to Ecuador

Passing through deep valleys and a spectacular gorge, buses on the paved Pan-American Highway cover the 84 km. from Pasto to Ipiales in 1½-2 hours. (Toll US$0.40). The road crosses the spectacular gorge of the Guaitara River near El Pedregal, 40 km. from Pasto. A detour via Túquerres (part unpaved) and its plain takes over an hour more; it reaches 3,050 metres at Túquerres, dropping to 2,440 at Guachucal, and rising again to 2,740 metres at **Ipiales**, "the city of the three volcanoes", with about 30,000 people; famous for its colourful Sat. morning Indian market. The Catedral Bodas de Plata is worth visiting. San Luis airport is 6½ km. out of town. "Intercontinental" flights to/from Bogotá daily, US$50.

If you have time, a visit to the nearby Sanctuary of the Virgin of **Las Lajas** is definitely recommended. On days set apart for religion, dazzlingly clean Indians come down from the hills in their traditional bright colours. Seen from afar the Sanctuary is a magnificent architectural conception, set on a bridge over the canyon: close to, it is very heavily ornamented. The altar is set into the rock face of the canyon which forms one end of the sanctuary. There are great pilgrimages to it from Colombia and Ecuador and the Sanctuary must be second only to Lourdes in the number of miracles claimed for it. The Church recognizes one only. Colectivo from Carrera 6 y Calle 4, Ipiales, US$0.30 p.p., taxi, US$5 return (it's about a 1½-hour walk, 7 km.); 3 basic hotels and a small number of restaurants at Las Lajas.

Hotels *Mayasquer*, 3 km. on road to frontier, D, modern, nice restaurant, very good, swings for children, discothèque, T (9304) 2643; *Pasviveros*, bright and clean, E, with bath and hot water; *Central*, Carrera 6a, 14-48, E, pleasant, clean; *Las Lajas*, E, hot water in the morning, good restaurant; *Buchue*, F, clean, comfortable, very good; *New York*, near main square, G, run down, friendly; *Colombia*, Calle 13, No. 7-50, F, hot water, mice but otherwise quite clean; opp. at No. 7-59 is *Valparaíso*, F, hot water; *Korpawasi*, Carrera 6, No. 10-47, E, good food, plenty of blankets; *Oasis*, Cra. 6, No. 11-34, 1 block from main plaza, E, hot shower, clean, helpful; *Rumichaca Internacional*, E, clean and comfortable with good basic restaurant; *Residencias Victoria*, good; *Residencial Belmonte* (*Hotel B*), Carrera 4, No. 12-111 (near Transportes Ipiales), F, very clean, hot water, rec., but crowded; *Residencia Tequendama*, Carrera 5, No. 14-08, F, family atmosphere, very basic; *San Andrés*, Carrera 5, No. 14-75, F, clean, hot water; same street, No. 14-25, *Residencias Santa Fe*, F. Young travellers can expect to be questioned and searched by police soon after checking in to a hotel.

Camping Possible above the bus parking lot, or free behind last Esso station outside town on road north.

Restaurants *Valparaíso*, very good value; *Don Lucho*, Carrera 5, No. 14-13 (antioqueño); *Bar D'Albert*, small, quiet, on main road from Bolivariano bus station into centre; *Greenhouse*, Carrera 6, No. 16-73, good, reasonable prices. *Pizza Napoletana* just off main plaza, very good; *India Catalina*, 24-hour café in centre, useful for late-night arrivals and departures. Plenty of cheap restaurants. Meals in Almacenes Ley cost US$1. Many good bakeries on Carrera 6.

Cinemas 2 on Calle Principal on road to Las Lajas.

Exchange It is possible to cash travellers' cheques only at the Banco de la República, a few blocks from the main square (closed 1100-1400); you will have to show two different pieces of identification and may have to recite passport number from memory. Casa de Cambio at Carrera 6, No. 14-09. There are money changers in the street and on the border, but better rates are to be had in Quito. There is an agency of Banco Anglo Colombiano, Carrera 6, 3 blocks from main square.

Frontier Ipiales is 2 km. from the Rumichaca bridge across the Carchi river into Ecuador. The frontier post stands beside a natural bridge, on a new, concrete bridge, where the customs and passport examination takes place from 0800 to 1800.

You obtain your Colombian exit stamp from the DAS at the frontier post. You have to get your entry stamp and tourist card for Ecuador at the frontier; if the border office is closed, you must go to the police station just before Tulcán. This applies at weekends, closed 1200-1400; taxis on the fast road to the border do not pass the police station. There is an Ecuadorean consulate on Carrera 6, Ipiales, one block from the main square, above Banco Cafetero, open weekdays. Ecuadorean officials do not usually give more than 30 days for visiting the country, but extensions are easy to obtain, from Amazonas 2639, Quito and the Migración offices in provincial capitals. Motorists have their *carnets* stamped at the border (very efficient). You may be required by Ecuadorean customs to show that you have enough money for your stay in the country. There can be long queues crossing into Ecuador.

Colombian customs have the same basic requirement of US$20 a day (US$10 for students), though you are not always required to show that you have this amount. Entering Colombia, tourist cards are issued at the frontier, and there is no need, if driving your own vehicle, to go through Tulcán: take the road signed Rumichaca. If entering Colombia by car, the vehicle is supposed to be fumigated against diseases that affect coffee trees, at the ICA office at the border; the certificate must be presented in El Pedregal, a village 40 km. beyond Ipiales on the road to Pasto. (This fumigation process is not always carried out.) There is a duty-free shop about ½ km. from the border. There are frequent police checks on the buses going to Popayán and neighbouring areas.

Transport From Ipiales to Tulcán: seat in car (waits till all seats are full), US$0.30, to the frontier, and same again from there to Tulcán; bus US$0.30 to Tulcán, US$0.20 to the frontier. Colectivo from frontier to Tulcán will charge extra (US$0.40) to go to the bus terminal. Taxi to border, US$2 after bargaining; from border to Tulcán, US$2. From Tulcán's modern bus terminal buses go to Quito throughout the day; a beautiful five-hour Andean trip.

Bus to Popayán, Expreso Bolivariano, US$7, 7½ hrs., hourly departures, 0430-2030; Transportes de Ipiales, US$7 (neither on main square, best to take taxi from border), Super Taxis and Cootranar *busetas*, US$6, beautiful trip. Bus to Cali, US$11, 12 hrs. To Pasto with minibus from main square, US$2.45 (frequent police checks); Flota Bolivariano buses every hr., US$1.50, 1¼ hrs. Buses to Bogotá leave every other hour between 0500 and 0830, US$20.

TAME (of Ecuador) has flights to Quito from Tulcán.

THE ECONOMY

Agriculture is the most important sector of the economy, contributing about 22 % of gdp and employing 34 % of the labour force. It is also the largest earner of foreign exchange, with over 57 % of total legal exports. The traditional crops are coffee, sugar cane, bananas, rice, maize and cotton. Colombia is the leading producer of mild Arabica coffee and second to Brazil in world production. Output has declined since 1984 as the Government has encouraged diversification, but coffee remains the dominant export item with up to 50 % of total revenues.

Manufacturing contributes almost as much to gdp as agriculture, with agricultural-related activities such as food processing, drink and tobacco accounting for 35 % of the sector's value added. Textiles and clothing are also important, and provide an outlet for home-grown cotton. Heavy corporate indebtedness in the first half of the 1980s affected the growth of manufacturing and led to a decline in employment to only 15 % of the total labour force. In the second half of the decade, however, strong growth was shown by chemicals, textiles and clothing, transport equipment, cement, metalworking and paper and unemployment fell.

Although contributing only 2 % of gdp, mining, mainly oil and coal, was the most dynamic sector of the economy in the mid-1980s, with growth rates of over 20% a year. With the exception of a few major projects, mining is concentrated in the hands of small scale producers with little technology or organization. Much of their output remains outside the formal economy. Colombia is, however, the largest producer of gold and platinum in Latin America, and these two metals, together with emeralds, have traditionally dominated the mining sector. Mining of precious metals, including silver, is primarily in the Departments of Antioquia and El Chocó; huge gold deposits have also been discovered on the borders of the Departments of Cauca and Valle, while others have been found in the Guainía, Vaupés and Guaviare regions near the Brazilian border. In 1984, Colombia became self-sufficient in energy. Rising production of hydrocarbons moved the oil trade into surplus for the first time in ten years and by 1988 oil imports had virtually ceased. Development of energy sources has been given high priority to satisfy domestic requirements and to diversify exports. Most of the oil production comes from the Magdalena basin, but these are older fields which are running down. The discovery of the Caño Limón field near Arauca has raised output to around 450,000 barrels a day. As well as oil and gas, Colombia has the largest coal reserves in Latin America, which partial surveys have put at 16.5 bn tonnes. The largest deposits are in the Cerrejón region, where a huge project has been set up to mine and export steam coal from a new port at Bahía de Portete. Hydroelectricity now accounts for 70% of installed generating capacity. It has an advantage over thermal power because 75% of the nation's hydroelectric potential is in the central zone, where 80% of the population live. Total potential is said to be 100,000 MW, of which only about 5% is harnessed.

Current account surpluses in the late 1970s during the coffee price boom were turned into large deficits in the first half of the 1980s, reaching over US\$3bn in 1982 and 1983, because of lower export receipts and rapidly rising imports. However, Colombia was able to avoid having to reschedule its foreign debts, and took steps to adjust its external accounts. The devaluation of the peso was speeded up, reinforced by import restrictions and export incentives, until from 1986 current account surpluses were recorded. The fiscal accounts were also turned around and the public sector deficit was reduced from 7.5% of gdp in 1984 to 2.0% in 1986. The World Bank and the IMF endorsed the Colombian economic strategy and commercial banks continued to lend to the country to refinance loans falling due.

	1961-70 (av)	1971-80 (av)	1981-85 (av)	1986-88 (av)
Gdp growth (1980 prices)	5.5%	5.5%	2.1%	4.8%
Inflation	11.2%	21.1%	22.3%	23.0%
Exports (fob) US\$m	575	2,162	3,446	5,450
Coffee	350	1,162	1,631	2,140
Fuel oil	9	94	307	730
Imports (fob) US\$m	575	1,910	4,443	3,895
Current account balance US\$m (cum)	1,619	-195	-10,809	235

INFORMATION FOR VISITORS

Travel by Air British Airways has a weekly service from London to Bogotá, via Caracas. Airlines with services from continental Europe are Air France, Viasa, Iberia, and Lufthansa. Avianca, the Colombian national airline, flies from Frankfurt via Paris and Madrid.

Frequent services to and from the U.S. by Avianca and Eastern. Varig and Avianca fly from Bogotá to the U.S. West Coast. The cheapest flight from Miami to Bogotá is via Panama with a couple of hours' stopover with Air Panama. Another cheap route is Miami-San Andrés, then take a domestic flight to your Colombian destination. Other flights from Miami: to Bogotá, Cali and Barranquilla with Eastern; to Barranquilla with Aeroperú; Avianca to Medellín, Cali, and San Andrés. Aerotal also fly to Miami. Lacsa flies to Barranquilla from Mexico City, and from San José to San Andrés and Cartagena. To Mexico City with Aeroméxico from Bogotá, from Barranquilla with Lacsa. Sahsa flies to San Andrés from Honduras, 4 times a week, and from Guatemala, Costa Rica and Belize. SAM flies to San José, 3 times a week; to San Salvador, Thurs. and Sun.; to Guatemala (calling at Cartagena and San Andrés), daily; also Barranquilla and San Andrés to San José, San Salvador and Guatemala. Fares between Central

America and Colombia are cheaper with a change in San Andrés, rather than direct.

From Neighbouring Republics Avianca, Pan-American Airways, SAM and Eastern connect Colombia with republics to N and S. If flying from Guatemala to Colombia with SAM, via San José and San Andrés, you have to purchase a round-trip ticket, refundable only in Guatemala. To get around this (if you are not going back to Guatemala) you will have to try to arrange a ticket swap with a traveller going in the other direction on San Andrés. There is, however, no difficulty in exchanging a round-trip ticket for a San Andrés-Colombian ticket with the airline, but you have to pay extra. Turismo Aero flies from Panama to Colombia. Bogotá-Panamá, via Medellín—do not be persuaded by SAM desk at Panama airport to buy an onward ticket out of Colombia—this may not be needed—if you fail, SAM in Bogotá will give refunds: first you must go to the DAS, Extranjería section, show your passport and ticket and obtain a permit for a refund; then go to the SAM office. **Medellín-Panama** (US$109) with Copa: one may not enter, or obtain a visa for, Panama without a return or onward ticket, so you must buy a return ticket and then sell half in Panama once you have purchased a flight ticket out of Panama. **Motorcycles** may be taken as luggage with Aerolíneas Medellín or Copa; remove oil, petrol, battery and anything breakable. Insist on supervising loading and unloading. Medellín customs take more than a day and you have to go from the airport to the *aduana interior*, in town; six copies of relevant papers have to be completed and delays can be experienced in getting hold of your property at Medellín. Officials, however, are helpful and friendly, despite the bureaucratic nightmare. The cheapest way to fly to Quito is to fly to Ipiales (Intercontinental from Bogotá), cross the border by road and take another 'plane at Tulcán. Avianca, Lufthansa, Air France and Ecuatoriana go S from Colombia.

For a cheap means of flying from Venezuela to Colombia, **see page 547**.

For travel overland from Panama, see note at end of Panama section.

N.B. There is an airport exit tax of US$25 (US$7 from San Andrés for flights to Colombian cities), from which only travellers staying less than 24 hours are exempt. When you arrive, ensure that all necessary documentation bears a stamp for your date of arrival; without it you will have to pay double the exit tax on leaving (with the correct stamp, you will only be charged half the exit tax if you have been in the country less than 30 days). Visitors staying more than 30 days have to pay an extra US$15 tax, which can only be avoided by bona-fide tourists who can produce the card given them on entry. There is a 15% tax on all international air tickets bought in Colombia for flights out of the country (7% on international return flights). Unfortunately it is no longer possible to avoid the purchase tax by buying tickets outside the country, as the charge is included automatically. Do not buy tickets for domestic flights to or from San Andrés island outside Colombia; they are much more expensive. When getting an onward ticket from Avianca for entry into Colombia, reserve a seat only and ask for confirmation in writing, otherwise you will pay twice as much as if purchasing the ticket inside Colombia.

Internal Air Services are flown by Avianca, SAM and 15 smaller companies. Avianca offers a round ticket (*Conozca a Colombia*) giving unlimited domestic travel for 30 days; conditions are that it allows up to ten stops, it must be bought outside Colombia, one may not pass through each city more than once, and a proposed itinerary (not firm) must be submitted when buying the ticket. There are two prices: US$325 if your 10 stops include San Andrés and Leticia; US$224 if they don't. For single flights, however, the army airline Satena tends to be cheaper than Avianca. Avianca's domestic shuttle flights (*Puente Aéreo*) go from Bogotá to Medellín/Montería, Cali/Pasto and Barranquilla; for example to Medellín every ½ hour between 0730-1630. But it is best to book a ticket as for an ordinary flight: just turning up will involve a long wait. Stand-by tickets are available to Barranquilla, Cali, Medellín; known as PET, *pasajero en turno*. Domestic airports are good, though the tourist facilities tend to close early on weekdays, and all Sundays. In-flight service and airline services on the ground tend to be poor. There is an airport tax of US$7.

Travel (in General) If driving yourself, avoid night journeys; the roads are often in poor condition, lorry-and bus-drivers tend to be reckless, and stray animals are often encountered. Hitch-hiking (*autostop*) seems to be quite easy in Colombia, especially if you can enlist the co-operation of the highway police checkpoints outside each town. Truck-drivers are often very friendly, but be careful of private cars with more than one person inside, especially if you are travelling on your own; they may be unmarked taxis. There have been many reports of muggings of cyclists in the Caribbean coastal area.

Buses Travel in Colombia is far from dull. The buses are generally fairly comfortable. Air-conditioned buses are often very cold (so take a sweater), or very hot (because the a/c has broken down, and the windows cannot be opened). The curtains may be down to keep the bus cool and/or to allow passengers to watch the video (so not much good for sightseeing). The luggage compartment is normally locked, but it is wise to keep an eye on your bags. Breakdowns are many. In all parts, police checks on buses are frequent. Note that meal stops can be few and far between, and short; bring your own food. Be prepared for climatic changes on longer routes. A full colectivo, such as a "Taxi Verde", costs only twice as much per person as a bus seat. The excellent minibus (*buseta*) services of Velotax have been recommended. If you entrust your luggage to the bus companies' luggage rooms, remember to load it on to the bus yourself; it will not be done automatically. There are few interdepartmental bus services on holidays. Always take your passport (or DAS-approved photocopy) with you: identity checks on buses are frequent.

Taxis Whenever possible, take a taxi with a meter, and ensure that it is switched on, otherwise you will be overcharged. All taxis are obliged to display the additional legal tariffs that may be charged after 2000, on Sundays and fiestas. If a taxi has a meter, do not haggle the price; if it does not (and most taxis on the N coast do not), fix a price beforehand. Don't take a taxi which is old; look for "Servicio Público" on the side. Women do not travel alone in taxis at night. If the taxi "breaks down", take your luggage out if you are asked to push, or let the driver push; it may be a trick to separate you from your luggage.

Motoring Roads are given in the text. Motor fuel: "premium" 95 octane (only in large cities), about US$0.70 per US gallon; "corriente" 84 octane, US$0.55 per US gallon. Diesel prices are similar. Roads are not always signposted. If you are planning to sleep in your car, it is better to stop in a parking lot (*parqueadero*); you will be charged a little extra, but the lots are guarded. In many guarded carparks, only the driver is allowed in; passengers must get out at the entrance.

National driving licences may be used by foreigners in Colombia, but must be accompanied by an official translation if in a language other than Spanish. International drivers licences are also accepted. To bring a car into Colombia, you must also have a valid, third-party insurance policy, documents proving ownership of the vehicle, and a tourist card/transit visa. These are normally valid for 90 days and must be applied for at the Colombian consulate in the country which you will be leaving for Colombia. Details of length of stay and car specifications will be sent to Bogotá and customs at the border, where the document should await your arrival. Carry driving documents with you at all times. N.B. Car hire is very expensive in Colombia. Even if you are paying in cash, a credit card may be asked for as proof of identity (Visa, Mastercard, American Express), in addition to passport and driver's licence.

Walkers are advised to get *Backpacking in Venezuela, Colombia and Ecuador*, by Hilary and George Bradt, who consider that Colombia offers some of the best hiking in South America. They describe 3-8 day treks in the Sierra Nevada de Santa Marta, Sierra Nevada del Cocuy, Sierra Nevada de Huila, and the hike from San Agustín to Popayán.

Documents A passport and an onward ticket are always necessary. Nationals of the following countries do not need visas or tourist cards: Argentina, Austria, Barbados, Belgium, Brazil, Costa Rica, Denmark, Ecuador, West Germany, Finland, Holland, Ireland, Israel, Italy, Japan, Liechtenstein, Luxemburg, Netherlands Antilles, Norway, Peru, Portugal, St. Vincent and the Grenadines, South Korea, Spain, Sweden, Switzerland, Trinidad and Tobago, UK, Uruguay. All other countries need visas or tourist cards (free). Normal validity for either is 90 days; extensions for a further month can be obtained in Bogotá (DAS, Carrera 27, No. 17-00, or any other DAS office; cost US$10, can take up to 3 days). Whether you need a tourist card or visa depends on your nationality, so check at a Colombian consulate in advance. Tourist cards are issued by CNT offices (in New York, or Caracas, for instance), or by Colombian airlines or authorized foreign carriers. Visas are issued only by Colombian consulates. A visa is required by U.S. citizens (for example), who must be prepared to show 1 photograph, an onward or return ticket, as well as a passport (allow 48 hours). Alternatively, in the USA only, Avianca issues tourist cards (transit visas), valid for 15 days, costing US$10—these cards are renewable only by leaving the country. In Miami insist at the Consulate, as they will assume that you can work it all out through the airline. U.S. citizens who arrive in Colombia by air from a third country without a visa must get a tourist card on the plane, otherwise they will be fined. Citizens of Asian, African, Middle Eastern and socialist countries (including Cuba, Nicaragua and East Germany), must apply at least 4 weeks in advance for a visa. You may find that your onward ticket, which you must show before you can obtain a visa, is stamped "non-refundable". The DAS does not give any "certificado" for cancelling onward tickets; insist on cancelling them without it. If you do not receive an entry card when flying in, the information desk will issue one, and restamp your passport for free. Visitors are sometimes asked to prove that they have US$20 for each day of their stay (US$10 for students). Note that to leave Colombia you must normally get an exit stamp from the DAS (security police). They often do not have offices at the small frontier towns, so try to get your stamp in a main city, and save time.

N.B. It is highly recommended that you have your passport photocopied, and witnessed by the DAS (about US$0.20). This is a valid substitute, and your passport can then be put into safe-keeping. Also, photocopy your travellers' cheques and any other essential documents. For more information, check with DAS or your consulate.

Duty-free admission is granted for portable typewriters, radios, binoculars, personal and cine cameras, but all must show use; 200 cigarettes or 50 cigars or 250 grams of tobacco or up to 250 grams of manufactured tobacco in any form, 2 bottles of liquor or wine per person.

Tourist Information The Corporación Nacional de Turismo (CNT), with its headquarters at Bogotá, has branches in every departmental capital and other places of interest. They should be visited as early as possible not only for information on accommodation and transport, but also for details on areas which are dangerous to visit. CNT also has offices in New York: 140 East 57th St., T 688-0151; Caracas: P.B. 5 Av. Urdaneta Ibarras a Pelota, T 561-3592/5805; Madrid: Calle Princesa No. 17 Tercero Izquierda, T 248-5090/5690; and Paris: 9, Boulevard de la Madeleine, 75001 Paris, T 260-3565. For details on National Parks, go to the Inderena Office in Bogotá (address on **page 534**).

The Automobile Club in Bogotá has offices on Avenida Caracas, No. 46-64 (T 2451534 and 2452684). Branches are at Manizales, Medellín, Cali, Barranquilla and Cartagena. It supplies Esso, Texaco and Mobil maps: good, but not quite up-to-date; a full set of Hojas de Ruta costs US$2.50. The Texaco map has plans of the major cities. Even the Shell series lacks detail. Maps of Colombia are obtainable at the Instituto Geográfico Militar, Agustín Codazzi, Carrera 30 y Calle 45, open 0800-1530, Bogotá, or from their office in Pasto. Drivers' route maps are available from the CNT. Buchholz and Central bookshops have a few country and Bogotá maps. Editorial Colina publish a series of books with colour photographs on different parts of Colombia (Cartegena, Antioquia, San Agustín) which have been recommended. Some of the photographs can be obtained as postcards.

Security Most travellers confirm that the vast majority of Colombians are honest and very hospitable. Sadly, reports of crime, sometimes violent, are still received. In addition to the general advice given on page 17 of the **Introduction and Hints** section, the following local conditions should be noted. The warning against accepting cigarettes, chewing gum, sweets or any other type of food from fellow bus-passengers cannot be emphasized too strongly. This crime is particularly common between Popayán and San Agustín, and Bogotá and Ipiales. We have received a number of reports confirming this practice.

Generally, when travelling by bus, try to get a window seat on the side where your luggage is stowed, so you can check what luggage is taken from the bus. Many bus companies give luggage tags (like airlines). Try to avoid having your luggage put on top; you won't be allowed to jump out of the bus at every stop to check it's still there. In town buses, do not open windows so wide that belongings can be snatched; beware of pickpockets by the doors. Small *busetas* are marginally safer than buses because there is only one door for escape. Travelling by car, always keep an eye on your petrol cap, windscreen wipers and hub caps. Thieves tend to be particularly active in and around bus and railway stations. It is socially acceptable for women to keep banknotes in their bras.

Avoid money changers on the street who offer over-favourable rates of exchange. They often short-change you or run off with your money, pretending that the police are coming. Beware of counterfeit dollars and pesos.

Colombia is part of a major drug-smuggling route. Police and customs activities have greatly intensified and smugglers increasingly try to use innocent carriers. Travellers are warned against carrying packages for other people without checking the contents. Penalties run up to 12 years in none too comfortable jails, and the police sometimes behave very roughly towards those they choose for a spot check at airports; complaints have been made in this connection to the Colombian authorities. All young travellers are suspect, so be very polite if approached by policemen. If your hotel room is raided by police looking for drugs, try, if possible, to get a witness to prevent drugs being planted on you. Colombians who offer you drugs may well be setting you up for the police, who are very active on the north coast and San Andrés island, and other tourist resorts. Again, this warning cannot be stressed too emphatically.

If someone accosts you on the street, saying he's a plain-clothes policeman or drugs officer, and asks you to go to his office, offer to go with him to the nearest policeman (the tourist police where possible) or police station, or to your hotel if it's dark. He may well be a "confidence man" (if he doesn't ask to see your passport, he almost certainly is). These conmen usually work in pairs. The best advice at all times is to take care, and above all to use your common sense.

Also be prepared for frequent bus stopping and searches which are conducted in a rather haphazard and capricious manner. Travellers in private cars are also stopped often, but not necessarily searched. Some roads are more heavily policed than others, and you can expect to be stopped several times when travelling to or from the Caribbean coast and when coming from Ecuador into Colombia. There is some guerrilla activity in Colombia: the departments near Venezuela have been mentioned, also the Pasto, Tierradentro and San Agustín areas; the Magdalena Valley in Santander and the Turbo/Urabá region. Police and army checks are common in this respect also. All luggage is searched leaving Leticia airport and most tourists are checked arriving in Cartagena from the airport. It has been reported that the police charge 10% of the value of stolen articles for making out a declaration for insurance claims.

Working Hours   Mon. to Fri., commercial firms work from 0800 to mid-day and from 1400 to 1730 or 1800. Certain firms in the warmer towns such as Cali start at 0700 and finish earlier. Government offices follow the same hours on the whole as the commercial firms, but generally prefer to do business with the public in the afternoon only. Embassy hours for the public are from 0900 to noon and from 1400 to 1700 (Mon. to Fri.). Bank hours in Bogotá are 0900 to 1500 Mon. to Thurs., 0900 to 1530 on Fri. except the last Fri. in the month when they close at 1200; banks in Medellín, Cali, Barranquilla, Bucaramanga, Cartagena, Pasto, Pereira and Manizales open from 0800 to 1130 and 1400 to 1600 on Mon. to Thur.; on Fri. they are open until 1630 but shut at 1130 on the last Fri. in the month; banks in Popayán, Cúcuta, Neiva, Tunja, Ibagué and Santa Marta open from 0800 to 1130 and 1400 to 1530 on Mon. to Fri. and 0800 to 1100 on Sat. and the last day of the month. Shopping hours are 0900 to 1230 and 1430 to 1830, including Sat.

British Business Travellers   should consult "Hints to Exporters: Colombia", from Room CO7, Export Services Branch, Department of Trade, Sanctuary Bldgs, 16-20 Great Smith Street, London SW1P 3DB. Similar U.S. publications may be obtained from the Department of Commerce, Washington, D.C. Also, *Colombian News Letter*, published monthly by the Colombian American Association Inc., 150 Nassau Street, New York, N.Y. 10038.

Climate and Clothing   Climate is entirely a matter of altitude: there are no seasons to speak of, though some periods are wetter than others. Tropical clothing is necessary in the hot and humid climate of the coastal fringe and the eastern *llanos*. In Bogotá medium-weight clothing is needed for the cool evening and night. Medellín requires light clothing; Cali lighter still; Manizales very similar to Bogotá. A dual-purpose raincoat and overcoat is useful in the uplands. Higher up in the mountains it can be very cold; woollen clothing is necessary.

The **best time for a visit** is December, January and February: the driest months. But pleasure—it happens sometimes—is in conflict with duty, because most business people are then on holiday. There is heavy rain in many places from June to September.

Health   Emergency medical treatment is given in hospitals: if injured in a bus accident, for example, you will be covered by insurance and treatment will be free. Bogotá has well-organized sanitary services, and the water may be safely drunk. Take sterilizer with you, or boil the water, or use the excellent mineral waters, when travelling outside the capital. Choose your food and eating places with care everywhere. Fruit drinks made with milk should be avoided. Hepatitis is common; have a gamma-globulin injection before your trip. Mosquito nets are useful in the coastal swampy regions. There is some risk of malaria and yellow fever in the coastal areas and the eastern *llanos*/jungle regions; prophylaxis is advised. The local insect repellant, Black Flag, is not reliable.

Hotels   There is a tourist tax of 5% on rooms and an insurance charge, but no service charge, and tipping is at discretion: 10% is generous. The more expensive hotels and restaurants also add on 10% VAT (IVA). Food is not expensive. A good lunch costs about US$5-6. A restaurant meal that business people might give to prospective customers would cost from US$6 to US$12 p.p. In many hotels outside the main cities you can only stay (very cheaply) at *en pension* rates and no allowance is made for missing a meal. The Colombian tourist office has lists of authorized prices for all hotels which are usually at least a year out of date. If you are overcharged the tourist office will arrange a refund. Most hotels in Colombia charge US$1 to US$6 for extra beds for children, up to a maximum (usually) of 4 beds per room. On the Caribbean coast and San Andrés and Providencia, high season is 15 December-30 April, 15 June-31 August. Although most hotels, except the very cheapest, offer private WC and shower as a matter of course, hot water often comes only in the more expensive hotels or in colder zones. Wash basin plugs are universally in short supply.

Camping   Sites are given in the text. Colombian Tourist Office has a list of official sites. Permission to camp is readily granted by landowners in less populated areas. Those in camper vans may camp by the roadside, but it is not particularly safe.

Tipping   Hotels and restaurants 10%. Porters, cloakroom attendants, hairdressers and barbers, US$0.05-0.25. Taxi-drivers are not tipped.

Electric Current   120 volts AC., as is general for the rest of Colombia. Transformer must be 110-150 volt A.C., with flat-prong plugs (all of same size). Be careful with electrically heated showers.

Weights and Measures   are metric, and weights should always be quoted in kilograms. Litres are used for liquid measures but US gallons are standard for the petroleum industry. Linear measures are usually metric, but the inch is quite commonly used by engineers and the yard on golf courses. For land measurement the hectare and cubic metre are officially employed but the traditional measures *vara* (80 centimetres) and *fanegada* (1,000 square *varas*) are still in common use. As in many other countries food etc. is often sold in *libras* (pounds), which are equivalent to ½ kilo.

Mail   There are separate post offices for surface mail and airmail. Send all letters by airmail, for surface mail is very unreliable. Avianca controls all airmail services and has offices in provincial cities. Correspondence with U.K. is reported to be good. It costs US$0.25 to send a letter or postcard to the U.S., and US$0.27 to Europe; a 1 kg. package to Europe costs US$13 by air (Avianca). Note that the AmEx agent, Tierra Mar Aire, does not accept mail to be held for AmEx customers.

Telecommunications   Empresa Nacional de Telecomunicaciones has offices in all main cities.

Telephone   systems have been automated; the larger towns are interconnected. Inter-city calls must be made from Telecom offices unless you have access to a private phone. Long-distance pay 'phones are located outside most Telecom offices, also at bus stations and airports. They take 20 peso coins. 1 peso coins for ordinary 'phones may be bought in 20 peso packets from Banco de la República. From the larger towns it is possible to telephone to Canada, the U.S.A., the U.K., and to several of the Latin American republics. International phone charges: for 3 mins., to USA or Canada, US$8 (20% discount on Sun.), to UK, US$9; a deposit is required before the call is made which can vary between US$18 and US$36, US$1 is charged if no reply, for person-to-person add an extra minute's charge to Canada, 2 minutes' to UK; all extra minutes' conversation costs ⅓ more. Collect, or reversed-charge, telephone calls are only possible from private telephones; make sure the operator understands what is involved or you may be billed in any case.

Difference in Time   GMT minus 5 hours.

Currency   The monetary unit is the peso, divided into 100 centavos. There are coins of 50 centavos (rare) and of 1, 2, 5, 10, 20 and 50 pesos; there are notes of 50, 100, 200, 500, 1,000, 2,000 and 5,000 pesos. Large notes of over 1,000 pesos are often impossible to spend on small purchases as change is in short supply, especially in small cities, and in the morning. There is now a limit of 500 on both the import and export of pesos. To change pesos back into dollars on departure (to a maximum of US$100), you need to keep the exchange slips received from banks. Travellers' cheques are not easy to change in Colombia; the Banco de la República prefers to change those of no more than US$20. Owing to the quantity of counterfeit American Express travellers' cheques in circulation, travellers experience great difficulty in cashing these cheques except in main cities, where the procedure is often slow, involving finger printing and photographs. The best advice we can give is to take Thomas Cook's or a US bank's dollar traveller cheques. Sterling travellers' cheques are practically impossible to change in Colombia. The few, legitimate *casas de cambio* give rates slightly worse than the banks, but are much quicker. Also in circulation are counterfeit US dollar bills in denominations of US$50 and US$100; US$20 bills are therefore more readily accepted. As it is unwise to carry large quantities of cash, credit cards are widely used, especially Diners' Club and Visa; Master Charge is less common, while American Express is only accepted in high-priced establishments in Bogotá. Many banks (e.g. Banco Cafetero) advance pesos against Visa, but in early 1989, the government was considering imposing a surcharge on this service. It is generally dangerous to change money on the streets, and you are likely to be given counterfeit pesos. The safest way to obtain black market rates is at the border in a neighbouring country.

Public Holidays are on the following days:

January 1: Circumcision of our Lord.	June 29: SS. Peter and Paul.*
January 6: Epiphany*.	July 20: Independence Day.
March 19: St Joseph.*	August 7: Battle of Boyacá.
Maundy Thursday.	August 15: Assumption.*
Good Friday.	October 12: Discovery of America.*
May 1: Labour Day.	November 1: All Saints' day.*
Ascension Day.*	November 11: Independence of Cartagena.*
Corpus Christi.*	December 8: Immaculate Conception.
Sacred Heart.*	December 25: Christmas Day.

When those marked with an asterisk do not fall on a Monday, or when they fall on a Sunday, they will be moved to the following Monday.

Best Buys Emeralds in Bogotá; handworked silver (excellent); Indian pottery and textiles. The state-run Artesanías de Colombia for craft work (see under Bogotá). In Antioquia buy the handbag—*carriel antioqueño*— traditionally made from otter skin, but nowadays from calf skin and plastic trimmed at that. At Cartagena crude rubber is moulded into little dyed figurines: odd but attractive. Clothing and shoes are cheap in Medellín. The Colombian *ruana* (poncho) is attractive and warm in any cool climate, and comes in a wide variety of colours; it may, however, be cheaper in Ecuador. Silver and gold work is cheaper than in Peru. Good duty-free shop at Bogotá airport. Leatherwork is generally good and not expensive.

Other shopping tips Colombia is one of the few countries which sell "white gas" for camping stoves etc., so stock up here.

Food Colombia's food is very regional; it is quite difficult to buy in Medellín, say, a dish you particularly liked in Bogotá. Restaurants in smaller towns often close on Sundays, and early on weekday evenings: if stuck, you will probably find something to eat near the bus station.

Locro de choclos is a potato and maize soup so rich and nourishing that, with salad and coffee, it would make a meal in itself. Colombia has its own variant of the inevitable *arroz con pollo* (chicken and rice) which is excellent. For a change *pollo en salsa de mostaza* (chicken in mustard sauce) is recommended. *Ajiaco de pollo* is a delicious chicken, maize, manioc, cabbage and potato stew served with cream and capers, and lumps of avocado; it is a Bogotá speciality; another Bogotá speciality is *sobrebarriga* (belly of beef). *Bandeja antioqueña* costs US$3 in most places and consists of meat grilled and served with rice, beans, potato, manioc and a green salad; the simpler *carne asada* may be had for as little as US$2. *Mazamorra*, boiled maize in milk, is a typical *antioqueño* sweet, and so is *salpicón*, a tropical fruit salad. *Lechona* (sucking pig and herbs) is a speciality of Ibagué. Cartagena's rice with coconut can be compared with rice *a la valenciana*. In Nariño, guinea pig (*cuy, curí* or *conejillo de Indias*) is typical. *Tamales* are meat pies made by folding a maize dough round chopped pork mixed with potato, peas, onions, eggs and olives seasoned with garlic, cloves and paprika, and steaming the whole in banana leaves (which you don't eat); the best are from Tolima. A baked dish of squash, beaten eggs and seafood covered with sauce is known as the *souffle de calabaza*. *Magras* is a typical Colombian dish of eggs and chicken baked together and served with a tomato sauce. *Sancocho* is a filling combination of all the tuberous vegetables, including the tropical cassava and yam, with chopped fresh fish or any kind of meat, possibly chicken. From stalls in the capital and the countryside, try *mazorcas* (roast maize cobs) or *arepas* (fried maize cakes). On the Caribbean coast, eat an egg *empanada*, which consists of two layers of corn (maize) dough that open like an oyster-shell, fried with eggs in the middle, and try the *patacón*, a cake of mashed and baked plantain (green banana). *Huevos pericos,* eggs scrambled with onions and tomatoes, are a popular, cheap and nourishing snack for the impecunious— available almost anywhere. *Pandebono,* cheese-flavoured bread is delicious. A good local sweet is the *canastas de coco:* pastry containing coconut custard flavoured with wine and surmounted by meringue. *Arequipe* is very similar to fudge, and popular (it is called *manjarblanco* in other parts of South America). *Almojábanas,* a kind of sour-milk bread roll, are delicious if fresh: "one day old and they are a disaster". There is, indeed, quite an assortment of little fruit pasties and preserves. Then there are the usual fruits: bananas, oranges, mangoes, avocado pears, and (at least in the tropical zones) *chirimoyas, papayas,* and the delicious *pitahaya,* taken either as an appetizer or dessert and, for the wise, in moderation, because even a little of it has a laxative effect. Other fruits such as the *guayaba* (guava), *guanábana* (soursop), *maracuyá* (passion fruit), *lulo* (*naranjilla*), *mora* (blackberry) and *curuba* make delicious juices, sometimes with milk added to make a *sorbete*—but be careful of milk in Colombia. Fruit yoghurts are nourishing and cheap (try *Alpina* brand; *crema* style is best). *Tinto,* the national small cup of black coffee, is taken ritually at all hours. Colombian coffee is always mild. (Coffee with milk is called *café perico; café con leche* is a mug of milk with coffee added.) *Agua de panela* is a common beverage (hot water with unrefined sugar), also made with limes, milk, or cheese.

Drink   Many acceptable brands of beer are produced. The local rum is good and cheap; ask for *ron,* not *aguardiente,* because in Colombia the latter word is used for a popular drink containing aniseed (*aguardiente anisado*). Try *canelazo*—cold or hot rum with water, sugar, lime and cinnamon. Local table wines include Santo Tomás; none are very good. General food and wine tips: wine is normally about US$3.50-4.50 in restaurants for an acceptable bottle of Chilean or Argentine; European wines are very expensive.

Warning   Great care should be exercised when buying imported spirits in shops. It has been reported that bottles bearing well-known labels have often been "recycled" and contain a cheap and poor imitation of the original contents. This can be dangerous to the health, and travellers are warned to stick to beer and rum. Also note that ice is usually not made from potable water.

Press   Bogotá: *El Tiempo, El Espectador* (both Liberal); *La República* (Conservative), *El Siglo* (extreme Conservative). Medellín: *El Mundo;* Cali: *El País, Occidente, El Pueblo,* all major cities have daily papers. Magazines are partisan, best is probably *La Semana.* U.S. and European papers can be bought at a stall in Bogotá on Av. 19 between Carreras 7 and 8.

Sport   The game of *tejo* is still played in Cundinamarca, Boyacá and Tolima. In Pasto it is played under the name of *sapo* (toad). This is the Spanish *juego de la rana,* in which a small quoit has to be thrown from an improbable distance into a metal frog's mouth. There are bullrings at Bogotá, Cali, Manizales, Medellín, Sincelejo and Cerete. Polo is played at Medellín and Bogotá. Most of the larger towns have stadiums. Association football is the most popular game. American baseball is played at Cartagena and Barranquilla. Cockfights, cycling, boxing and basketball are also popular.

Fishing is particularly good at Girardot, Santa Marta, and Barranquilla; marlin is fished off Barranquilla. There is good trout fishing, in season, in the lakes in the Bogotá area, particularly at Lake Tota, in the mountains.

This section has been revised with the very welcome help of P Lancefield (Canadian Embassy, Bogotá) and Richard Stoller (Bogotá) and the following travellers: Ian Atkinson (Upton/Severn), Eberhard Baer (Koenigsbrunn, W.Ger.) for a particularly useful contribution, Dexter Ball (Chicago), Bruce Barnes (Gloucester, NSW), Pierre-Y Berney (Geneva), Rüdiger Bernhardt (Köln 41), Lennart Blomberg (Göteborg), Erik A. Bloom (New Haven, Ct.), Rop Bomer and Wilh. ter Haar (Mex. City), J.N. Bowden and K.E. Badgery (Plymouth), Lucy Broadbent and Rick Palmer (Kerikeri, NZ), Karen Brooks (London N19), Michelle Burrows (Brisbane), John Crane (Sunbury), Beat Denzler and Nicole Livet (Zürich), Jeroen Dijkgraaf (Eindhoven), Maxx and Carol Dilley (State College, Pa.) and Claudia Alfonso (Col.), Eva Ekelund and Jim Lindsay (Stockholm), Hanna Elvrum (Cochabamba), Didier Faget and Sabine Fleury (Vernon, Fr.), Harald Fischer (Linz, Austr.), Janet Fox (London), Sharon Franklet (Lima), Christina Gräwe (Tautkirchen) and Joachim Hoell (Wernstadt, W.Ger.), Jan Jacob de Groot (Vroomshoop, Neth.), Alison Henry, Rony Hermans (Deurne, Bel.), Flavio Heubeck (Winterthur), Christian and Nickolaj Hoff (Holte, Copenhagen), David K Howe (Short Hills, NJ), Don Hoyle (London EC2), Gretke Moen Johansen (Kolbotn, Norway), Peter Kocan (Summit, NJ), Dean Lasko (Seattle), Frans Lindenkamp (Vlissingen, Neth.) and Todd McLeod (Calgary), Charles Locher (San Francisco) and Nancy Blackstock (Berkeley, Ca.), Susan MacCallum and Peter Hedvlin (Sydney, Aust.), Robert E Manley (Cincinnati), Daniel Morgan (Wellington, NZ), Michael Mortensen (Oelstykke, Dmk.), Dimitri Moursellas (Manhattan Beach, Ca.), Gabi Münzel (Punta Arenas), Vera Naujak (Heidelberg), Karl Olson (New York), Pia Parolin (Milano), Jean François Pin (Paris), Geoff A Richardson (Barranquilla), Miranda Roberts (London

SE3), Florian Schulz (Berlin 27), J.J. Schuitemaker (Schin op Geul, Neth.), Markus Schulz (Gambach, W.Ger.), Antony Sherlock (Edinburgh 12), Nicola J Smith (Kirby Muxbe, Leics.) and Jean-François Morerod (Les Diablerets, Switz.), John M Stafford (Northolt, Mx.), Doris Stöckli and Christophe Racine (Fislisbach, Switz.), Peter van der Stoop and Karin Strooij (Haarlem, Neth.), Anna Syriänen and Marko Sorvaniemi (Tampere, Fin.), Vicki Thomas (Antigua, Guatemala), Thorsten Truijens (Haan, W.Ger.), Heather Varden (Fleet, Hants), Gerhard Wenz and Brigitte Klaus (Mainz), Conrad Wiesendanger (Münchenstein, Switz.), Harald Willenbrock (Achim, W.Ger.), Ray Williams (Pwllheli), Martin Wisckol (San Diego, Ca.), Anna Wrench (Haywards Heath, Sx.) and Marilyn Zecker and B.B. Riefner (Rockville, Md.).

ECUADOR

ECUADOR is bounded by Colombia to the north, Peru to the east and south and the Pacific Ocean to the west. Its area is about 283,520 square km., which makes it the second smallest republic in South America. About 40% of its 9,923,000 (1987) people are Indians, 40% *mestizo*, 10% European; the remainder are black or Asian.

The Andes, running from the Colombian border in the north to the borders of Peru in the south, form a mountainous backbone to the country. There are two main ranges, the Eastern Cordillera and the Western Cordillera, separated by a 400-km. long trough, the Central Valley, whose rims are from 40 to 65 km. apart. The rims are joined together, like the two sides of a ladder, by hilly rungs, and between each pair of rungs lies an intermont basin with a dense cluster of population. These basins, which vary in altitude between 1,800 and 3,000 metres, are drained by rivers which cut through the rims to run either west to the Pacific or east to join the Amazon. The whole mountain area is known as the Sierra.

Both rims of the Central Valley are lined with the cones of more than thirty volcanoes. Several of them have long been extinct, for example, Chimborazo, the highest (6,310 metres), Cayambe (5,790 metres), standing directly on the equator, Illiniza (5,263 metres) and Altar (5,319 metres). At least eight, however, are still active; Cotopaxi (5,897 metres), which had several violent eruptions in the nineteenth century; Tungurahua (5,016 metres), which had a major eruption early this century; Antisana (5,704 metres), which showed signs of activity in the 1960s; Pichincha (4,794 metres), which erupted in 1981, and Sangay (5,230 metres) one of the world's most active volcanoes, continuously emitting fumes and ash. Nowadays all the main peaks except for Altar and Sangay, which are less accessible, are climbed fairly regularly.

East of the Eastern Cordillera the forest-clad mountains fall sharply to the plains—the Oriente—through which meander the tributaries of the Amazon. This eastern lowland region makes up 36% of Ecuador's total territory, but is only sparsely populated by native Indians and agricultural colonists from the highlands. In total, the region has only 5% of the national population, but colonization is now proceeding rapidly in the wake of an oil boom. There are substantial oil reserves in the northern Oriente near the Colombian border, and exports began in 1972.

Between the Western Cordillera and the Pacific lies the Costa, 685 km. from north to south and some 100 km. wide. It is from this area that Ecuador draws the majority of its agricultural products for export. Guayaquil, the main city of

ECUADOR

0 50 100
km

To Cali

Tumaco

C O L O M B I A

San Lorenzo
Limones
Pasta

Esmeraldas
Tulcán Ipiales
Puerto Asis
Atacamés
Puerto
Colón
San
Muisné
Ibarra
Miguel
Cojimies
Otavalo
Lago o
Pedernales
Cayambe
Agrio
Equator
Santo Domingo
Jama
de los Colorados
QUITO
Baeza
Coca
Bahía de
Caráquez
Saquisilí
Manta
Latacunga
Portoviejo
Quevedo
Tena
Misahuallí
Jipijapa
Ambato
Baños
Puyo
Puerto López
Guaranda
Shell-Mera
Manglaralto
Babahoyo
Cajabamba
Riobamba
Guayaquil
Durán
Bucay
Salinas
Alausí
Sibambe
Macas
Playas
Ingapirca
Posorja
Cuenca
Sigsig
Machala
Gualaquiza
Santa Rosa
Saraguro
Tumbes
Huaquillas
Zaruma
To
Loja
Trujillo
and Lima
Zamora
Macará

Sullana

P   E   R   U

1 Quito.
2 North of Quito.
3 North and West
Lowlands.
4 Guayaquil.
5 The Southern
Lowlands.
6 Guayaquil to Quito.
7 Southern Sierra.
8 The Oriente.
9 (off map) The
Galápagos.

this region, is 464 km. from the capital, Quito, which lies high in a northern intermont basin.

The Sierra   There are altogether ten intermont basins strung along the Sierra from north to south. There is little variation by day or by season in the temperature in any particular basin: temperature depends on altitude. The basins lie at an elevation of between 2,100 and 2,750 metres, and the range of shade temperature is from 6°C to 10°C in the morning to 19°C to 23°C in the afternoon. Temperatures can get considerably higher in the lower basins. There is one rainy season, from November to May, when the average fall in Quito is 1,270 mm; the skies are mostly cloudy or overcast at this time and there are frequent rainfalls during the afternoons and nights. Over half the area is now grassy *páramo* on which cattle and sheep are raised and subsistence crops grown. What crops are grown is determined by altitude, but the hardiest of them, the potato, cannot thrive above 3,800 metres or so. The intermont basins produce livestock, poultry, wheat, barley, oats, maize, quinoa, fruit and vegetables, some of which find their way down to the coastal plain.

Some 47% of the people of Ecuador live in the central trough of the Andes, and the majority are pure Indians. Most of the land is held in large private estates worked by the Indians, but some of it is held by Indian communities. With the limited application of an agrarian-reform programme, the *huasipungo* system whereby Indians were virtual slaves on the big highland *haciendas* is now disappearing, and co-operatives are proliferating. Though many Indian communities live at subsistence level and remain isolated from national centres, others have developed good markets for products using traditional skills in embroidery, pottery, jewellery, knitting, weaving, and carving.

The Costa   Most of the Costa region is lowland at an altitude of less than 300 metres, apart from a belt of hilly land which runs west from Guayaquil to the coast and trends northwards. In the extreme north there are two rainy seasons, as in Colombia, and a typical tropical rain forest. But the two rainy seasons soon merge into one, running from December to June. The further south we go, the later the rains begin and the sooner they end: at Guayaquil the rains normally fall between January and April. The forests thin out too as we move south, and give way to thorn and savanna. The Santa Elena Peninsula and the south-western coast near Peru have little or no rainfall.

The main agricultural exports come from a small area of lowland to the SE and N of Guayaquil. It lies between the coastal hills and the Andes; rains are heavy, the temperature and the humidity high: ideal conditions for the growth of tropical crops. One part of this Guayas lowland is subject to floods from the four rivers which traverse it: bananas, normally accounting for half the exports of the lowland, are grown here, as well as rice. Cacao too is farmed on the natural levees of this flood plain, but the main crop comes from the alluvial fans at the foot of the mountains rising out of the plain. High on these same alluvial fans excellent coffee is also grown; cacao, bananas, coffee and sugar, whether processed or unprocessed, are about 30 % of the exports by value. Cotton is developing. Add to this that the Guayas lowland is a great cattle-fattening area in the dry season, and its importance in the national economy becomes obvious. A good network of paved roads now links Guayaquil with the major zones of agricultural production, and the once thriving river-ports have now declined. Along the northern coast, the main areas of population are at Esmeraldas, along the highways inland, in the irrigated lands of northern Manabí, and near Manta, Montecristi, and Jipijapa.

Two areas of the coastlands have experienced spectacular rises in population and agricultural production: El Oro Province in the extreme south, centred on the town of Machala, and the Quevedo-Santo Domingo zone along the Andean fringe to the north of Guayaquil. In both areas, highland settlers have mixed with coastal entrepreneurs to produce a particularly progressive agriculture. Irrigation in El Oro has produced a thriving zone of very intensive banana plantations. In the Quevedo-Santo Domingo area, large areas of forest have been cleared; bananas used to be the main crop, but are now being replaced by African palm. Further north, in Esmeraldas Province, there still remain large areas of land which could be cleared and developed for farming, although the fertility of this zone is reputedly much lower than that of the Quevedo, Guayaquil and Machala areas.

Population   About 48 % of Ecuador's inhabitants live in the Costa region west of the Andes, and 47 % in the Andean Sierra. Migration is occurring from the rural zones of both the coast and the highlands to the towns and cities, particularly Guayaquil and Quito, and agricultural colonization by highlanders is occurring in parts of the coastal lowlands and the Oriente. About 15 % of the inhabitants over 15 years of age are illiterate. 53 % of the population is urban (living in a cantonal or provincial capital), and 47 % is rural. National average population density is 30 per square kilometre, the highest in South America. Average income per head has risen fast in recent years like that of other oil-exporting countries, but the distribution has not improved and a few citizens are spectacularly wealthy.

History   The Incas of Peru, with their capital at Cuzco, began to conquer the Sierra of Ecuador, already densely populated, towards the middle of the 15th century. A road was built between Cuzco and Quito, and the empire was ruled after the death of the Inca Huayna Capac by his two sons, Huáscar at Cuzco and Atahualpa at Quito. Pizarro's main Peruvian expedition took place in 1532, when there was civil war between the two brothers. Atahualpa, who had won the war, was put to death by Pizarro in 1533, and the Inca empire was over.

Pizarro claimed the northern kingdom of Quito, and his lieutenants Sebastián de Benalcázar and Diego de Almagro took the city in 1534. Pizarro founded Lima in 1535 as capital of the whole region, and four years later replaced Benalcázar at Quito by Gonzalo, his brother. Gonzalo later set out on the exploration of the Oriente. He moved down the Napo river, and sent Francisco de Orellana to prospect. Orellana did not return: he drifted down the river finally to reach the mouth of the Amazon: the first white man to cross the continent in this way.

Quito became an *audiencia* under the Viceroy of Peru. For 280 years Ecuador more or less peacefully absorbed the new ways brought by the conqueror. Gonzalo had already introduced pigs and cattle; wheat was now added. The Indians were Christianized, colonial laws and customs and ideas introduced. The marriage of the arts of Spain to those of the Incas led to a remarkable efflorescence of painting, sculpting and building at Quito. In the 18th century black slave labour was brought in to work the plantations near the coast.

There was an abortive attempt at independence in the strongly garrisoned capital in 1809, but it was not until 1822 that Sucre, moving north from Guayaquil, defeated the Spanish at Pichincha and occupied Quito. Soon afterwards Bolívar arrived, and Ecuador was induced to join the Venezuelan and Colombian confederation, the Gran Colombia of Bolívar's dream. On July 26 and 27, 1822, Bolívar met San Martín, fresh from liberating Lima, at Guayaquil. What happened at that mysterious encounter is not known, but San Martín left it silently for a self-imposed exile in France. Venezuela separated itself from Gran Colombia in 1829, and Ecuador decided on complete independence in August, 1830, under the presidency of Juan Flores.

Ecuador's 19th century history was a continuous struggle between pro-Church conservatives and anti-Church (but none the less devotedly Catholic) liberals. There were also long periods of military rule from 1895, when the liberal General Eloy Alfaro took power. During the late 1940s and the 1950s there was a prolonged period of prosperity (through bananas, largely) and constitutional rule, but the more typical pattern of alternating civilian and military governments was resumed in the 1960s and 1970s. Apart from the liberal-conservative struggles, there has been long-lasting rivalry between Quito and the Sierra on one hand and Guayaquil and the Costa on the other.

The country's eastern jungle territory has been reduced from that of the old Audiencia of Quito by gradual Peruvian infiltration, which means that the country's official claim to be a "país amazónico" has little relation to present reality. This process reached an acute phase in 1941 when war broke out with Peru; the war was ended with the Rio de Janeiro Protocol of 1942 which allotted most of the disputed territory to Peru. Ecuador has denounced the Protocol, and the country's official policy remains the recovery of all the territories of the Audiencia of Quito. Border skirmishes occur at times although there has been no serious incident since 1981.

Government

There are 20 provinces, including the Galápagos Islands. Provinces are divided into cantons and parishes for administration.

Under the 1978 constitution, the vote was extended to include all literate citizens over the age of 18. The president and vice-president are elected for a five-year term. The president may not stand for re-election. The legislative branch consists of a single Chamber of Representatives of 69 members, which meets for two months of the year. The first presidential and congressional election under the new charter took place on April 29, 1979. Prior to then there had been military rule for seven years, attended by growing oil-based prosperity, until August 10, 1979 when President Jaime Roldós Aguilera was inaugurated for a five-year term. His policy was to follow a programme of gradual reform. In May 1981, President Roldós was killed in an air crash and was succeeded by the vice-president, Osvaldo Hurtado Larrea. In 1984 President Hurtado handed power over to his elected successor and political opponent, the conservative Sr. León Febres Cordero, the first time in 23 years that such a transfer of power had occurred. President Febres Cordero's free market orientation was rejected by voters in the 1988 presidential and congressional elections. Rodrigo Borja, leader of the centre left Izquierda Democrática, was inaugurated as president on August 10 1988.

QUITO (1)

Quito (2,850 metres), with a population of 1,200,000, is within 25 km. of the equator, but it stands high enough to make its climate much like that of spring in England, the days warm or hot and the nights cool. Because of the height, visitors may initially feel some discomfort and should slow their pace for the first 24 hours. Mean temperature, 13°C, rainfall, 1,473 mm.; rainy season: Sept. to May with the heaviest rainfall in April, though heavy storms in July are not unknown. The day length (sunrise to sunset) is constant throughout the year.

Few cities have a setting to match that of Quito, the second highest capital in Latin America. The city is set in a hollow at the foot of the volcano Pichincha (4,794 metres). It was an Inca city, refounded by Sebastián de Benalcázar, Pizarro's lieutenant, in 1534. The city's charm lies in its colonial centre, where cobbled streets are steep and narrow, dipping to deep ravines. Through this

QUITO
New City

HOTELS

A. Embassy B. Alameda Real
C. Res. Lutecia D. Waldorf
E. Res. Los Alpes F. Colón
Internacional G. Tambo Real
H. Inca Imperial J. Coral Inter.

KH 4/87

1. Iglesia Sta. Clara de San Millán; 2. Turismundial; 3. Libri Mundi; 4. Ministry of Public Works; 5. Iglesia El Girón; 6. Ministry of External Relations; 7. Bank of London & South America; 8. Iglesia Santa Teresa; 9. Casa de cambio 'Rodrigo Paz'; 10. Ecuadorian Tours (Amex); 11. DITURIS (Tourist Office); 12. Universidad Católica (museums); 13. Ministry of Finance; 14. Expresso Turismo (bus); 15. Casa de cambio 'Unicambios'; 16. United States Embassy; 17. Flota Imbabura (bus); 18. Immigration; Dept. of Social Security; 19.Cultural Library; 20. Casa de la Cultura; 21. Nuevo Hospital Militar; 22. Colegio Militar; 23. Banco Holandés Unido; 24. Alitalia; 25. Palacio de Justicia; 26. Palacio Legislativo; 27. Instituto Panamericano de Geografía y Historia; 28. Instituto Geográfico Militar (IGM); 29. Ministry of Public Health; 30. Iglesia El Belén; 31. Maternity Hospital; 32. Colegio Mejía (museum); 33. Consejo Provincial de Pichincha; 34. Banco Internacional; 35. First National City Bank; 36. Astronomical Observatory; 37. Ciné Capitol; 38. TAME; 39. Banco de los Andes; 40. SAETA and Red Cross; 41. Banco Central (museums).

QUITO
Old City

GUATEMALA
Plaza Matovaile

KH 4/87

Parque La Alameda

41 ▬ ▪ 40
Plaza Bolivar

BRICENO
CALDAS

0   200   400m

CARCHI

42 ┃

□ **HOTELS**

Plaza de Basílica

44 ▪ ▪ 45

K. Viena Inter L. Humboldt
Capitol M. Auca Continental
N. Sucre P. Benalcázar
Q. Monasterio R. Caspicara
S. Grand T. Guayaquil U. Gran
Casino ("Gran Gringo")

✚ 43

GALAPAGOS
GARCIA MORENO

Plaza de San Blás

VARGAS

✚ 46

ORIENTE

CUENCA

ESMERALDAS

MONTUFAR

BABAHOYO

IMBABURA

COTOPAXI

MANABI

47 ✚
Plaza del Teatro

Parque Hermano Miguel

Colegio Simón Bolivar

✚ 48

OLMEDO

50

● Coliseo

CEVALLOS

51 ▪ 52 ▪ 53

MEJIA

54 ✚ 55 ✚ 56

57 ✚
Plaza San Martin

MIDEROS

61 ✚

CHILE

58 ▪ 59 ▪

Plaza de la Independencia

60

ESPEJO

✚ 66

62
63

L □

JUNIN

QUIROGA

ALIANZA

69 ✚

✚ 71
M ▪ 64
72

✚ 65
SUCRE

67 ▪

68 ▪
PEREIRA

79
Plaza Lucinda Toledo

SIMÓN BOLIVAR

70 ✚
Plaza San Francisco

N ↗

SEBASTIAN DE BENALCÁZAR

□ P

VENEZUELA

Plaza Sto. Domingo (Sucre)

CHIMBORAZO

IMBABURA

ROCAFUERTE

✚ 73

✚ 75
Q ✚ 76

R □
78

S □
T □

Plaza Sta. Rosa

✚ 74

AV
25 DE MAYO

77 ✚
MORALES

LA RONDA

B ▪

LOJA

Plaza Victoria

BARAHONA

BAHIA DE CARAQUEZ

U □
AMBATO

Plaza M. Sáenz

MALDONADO

↓ N

AGOYAN

LOJA

81 ✱

80 ▪
Plaza San Diego

Cementario San Diego

Panecillo

▬ 82

Pl. La Recoleta

Railway Station

section hurries the Machángara river, nowadays too polluted to wash clothes in. Westwards the valley is closed by Cerro Panecillo; from its top, 183 metres above the city level, there is a good restaurant and a fine view of the city below and the encircling cones of volcanoes and other mountains. There is a new statue on the hill to the Virgen de las Américas; Mass is held in the base on Sundays. There is a good view from the observation platform up the statue.

Warning On no account should you walk up the series of steps and paths which begin on García Moreno (where it meets Ambato) as assaults are common: take a taxi up and leave your valuables behind.

The heart of the city is Plaza Independencia, dominated by a somewhat grim Cathedral (open 0600-1000, 1400-1600) with grey stone porticos and green tile cupolas. On its outer walls are plaques listing the names of the founding fathers of Quito, and inside are the tomb of Sucre (tucked away in a corner) and a famous Descent from the Cross by the Indian painter Caspicara. Beside the Cathedral, round the corner, is El Sagrario, being restored. Facing the Cathedral is the old Archbishop's Palace, which has been renovated and now houses shops. On the northeast side is the new concrete Municipal Palace which fits in quite well, despite its material. The low colonial Palacio de Gobierno, on the northwest side of the Plaza, is silhouetted against the great flank of Pichincha; on the first floor is a gigantic mosaic mural of Orellana discovering the Amazon, and the President's offices on the second floor.

The best way to see old Quito is to walk its narrow streets. Wander down the Calle Morales, main street of La Ronda district (traditionally called Calle Ronda), one of the oldest streets in the city, past Plaza Santo Domingo to Carrera Guayaquil, the main shopping street, and on to shady Parque Alameda, which has the oldest astronomical observatory in South America (open Sat. 0900-1200). There are also a splendid monument to Simón Bolívar, various lakes, and in the NW corner a spiral lookout tower with a good view. The traditional colonial area is being preserved, with the buildings painted white and blue, but other parts of the city are being radically altered as a result of road improvements.

From Plaza Independencia two main streets, Carrera Venezuela and Calle García Moreno, lead straight towards the Panecillo to the wide Av. 24 de Mayo, at the top of which is a new concrete building where the Indians are supposed to do their trading since the street markets were officially abolished in 1981. Street trading still takes place, however, and there are daily street markets from Sucre down to 24 de Mayo and from San Francisco church west up past Cuenca.

Plaza San Francisco (or Bolívar) is west of Plaza Independencia; on the north-western side of this plaza is the great church and monastery of the patron saint of Quito, San Francisco, the earliest religious foundation in South America (1535), see below. Plaza Santo Domingo (or Sucre), to the south-east of Plaza San Francisco, has to the SE the church and monastery of Santo Domingo, with

Key to Quito (Old City)
42. The Basílica; 43. Iglesia San Juan; 44. Ciné Alhambra; 45. Ministry of Agriculture; 46. Iglesia de San Blás; 47. Ciné Central; 48. Instituto Ecuatoriano de Cultura Hispánica (Casa de Benalcázar); 49. Iglesia de Carmen Bajo; 50. Teatro Sucre; 51. Academy of History; 52. Museum of Colonial Art; 53. National Art Museum; 54. Basílica de la Merced; 55. Iglesia de la Concepción; 56. Archbishop's Palace; 57. Iglesia de San Agustín (and museum); 58. General Post Office; 59. Government Palace; 60.Municipal Palace (inc. Tourist Office); 61. Templo Evangélico; 62. Municipal Museum of Art and History; 63. Cathedral; 64. El Sagrario chapel; 65. Casa de Sucre (museum); 66. Iglesia de Santa Catalina; 67. Ciné Rumiñahui; 68. Flota Imbabura (bus); 69. San Francisco church, monastry and museum; 70. Catuña chapel; 71. Iglesia de la Compañia; 72. National Library; 73. Iglesia San Roque; 74. El Robo chapel; 75. Convent of Carmen Alto; 76. Hospital Chapel of San Juan de Dios; 77. Transportes Esmeraldas (bus); 78. Ministry of Public Education; 79. Iglesia de Santo Domingo (museum); 80. Iglesia San Diego (convent and museum); 81. Iglesia San Sebastián; 82. Panecillo lookout and restaurant.

618   **ECUADOR**

its rich wood-carvings and a remarkable Chapel of the Rosary to the right of the main altar. In the centre of the square is a statue to Sucre, pointing to the slopes of Pichincha where he won his battle against the Royalists. The modern University City is on the NW side of the city, on the lower slopes of Pichincha by the Avenida de las Américas.

There are altogether 86 churches in Quito. The fine Jesuit church of La Compañía, in Calle García Moreno, one block from Plaza Independencia (open 1000-1100, 1300-1800) has the most ornate and richly sculptured façade and interior. See its coloured columns, its ten side altars and high altar plated with gold, and the gilded balconies. Several of its most precious treasures, including a painting of the Virgen Dolorosa framed in emeralds and gold, are kept in the vaults of the Banco Central del Ecuador and appear only at special festivals. Not far away to the north-east is the church of La Merced. In the monastery of La Merced is Quito's oldest clock, built in 1817 in London. Fine cloisters entered through door to left of altar. La Merced church contains many splendidly elaborate styles; note the statue of Neptune on the main patio fountain.

The church of San Francisco, (open 0600-1200, 1430-1930), Quito's largest, is rich in art treasures. The two towers were felled by an earthquake in 1868 and rebuilt. A modest statue of the founder, Fray Jodoco Ricke, the Flemish Franciscan who sowed the first wheat in Ecuador, stands at the foot of the stairs to the church portal. See the fine wood-carvings in the choir, a magnificent high altar of gold and an exquisite carved ceiling. There are some paintings in the aisles by Miguel de Santiago, the colonial *mestizo* painter. His paintings of the life of Saint Francis decorate the monastery of San Francisco close by. Adjoining San Francisco is the Cantuña Chapel with sculptures.

Many of the heroes of Ecuador's struggle for independence are buried in the monastery of San Agustín (Flores and Mejía), where the treaty of independence from Spain was signed. The church of El Carmen Moderno has a fine collection of Quito ceramics. In the recently restored monastery of San Diego are some unique paintings with figures dressed in fabrics sewn to the canvas -a curious instance of our present-day "collage". Ring the bell to the right of the church door to get in, entrance US$0.75, 0900-1200, 1500-1700, all visitors are shown around by a guide. Also La Concepción, Mejía and García Moreno; San Blas, Guayaquil and 10 de Agosto. The Basílica of Guápulo (1693), perched on the edge of a ravine SE of the city, is well worth seeing for its many paintings, gilded altars and the marvellously carved pulpit. Take bus 21 (Guápulo-Dos Puentes) from Plaza de Santo Domingo. Notice also the curious new "French Gothic" basilica under construction (since 1926) on a hill in the centre of the town. (You go up Carrera Venezuela to see it, puffing all the way, but it's worth while to see the local sculptors and stonecutters at work, if you can get friendly with the administrator.)

Note A number of churches were temporarily closed after the 1987 earthquake and were still being restored in 1989. However, there are fears for the survival of La Compañía, El Sagrario and El Carmen Bajo, where the threat of subsidence from long term structural faults was compounded by earthquake damage.

The house of Sucre is at Venezuela 573, a beautiful restored house, open daily, entry free. The house of Benalcázar is on Olmeda with Benalcázar, a fully-restored colonial house. The house of Camilo Egas, a recent Ecuadorean artist, on Venezuela, has been restored by the Banco Central; it has different exhibitions during the year, entrance US$0.75.

Modern Quito extends northwards into a wide plain; it has broad avenues, fine private residences, parks, embassies and villas. Av. Amazonas, from Av. Patria to about Av. Colón, and the adjoining streets comprise Quito's modern tourist and business area: travel agencies, airlines, hotels and *residenciales*, exchange houses, moderate to expensive restaurants—several with sidewalk cafés, arts and crafts stores and stalls, jewellery stores, book stores, car rental agencies, and pastry shops are all clustered in this neighbourhood. Av. Amazonas has British double-decker buses running along it and on to the airport. On Sun. La Alameda and El Ejido parks are filled with local families.

Museums Quito prides itself on its art. The **Casa de la Cultura Ecuatoriana**, a large circular building at the east side of Parque El Ejido, has good collection of Indian costumes, a picture gallery, the Natural History Museum previously in the Eloy Alfaro military college, an exhibition of Ecuadorean books, and a unique museum of musical instruments. An open-air amphitheatre is under construction (open 0900-1230, 1500-1815, Tues.-Fri., 0930-1600 Sat.). There is a good collection of Ecuadorean sculptures and painting at the **Museum of Colonial Art**, on the corner of Cuenca and Mejía. The **Museo de San Francisco** has a fine collection of religious art, open 0900-1130, 1500-1730, entrance US$0.35, while the **Museo de Santo Domingo** has a further collection open Mon.-Fri., 0800-1100, 1500-1700, but not of quite the same quality. Similar collection in **Museo de San Agustín**, Chile y Guayaquil, open Mon.-Sat. 0830-1230, 1430-1800, interesting exhibition of restoration work (closed for reconstruction). The **Museo Jijón y Caamaño**, now housed in the Catholic University library building, has a private collection of archaeological objects, historical documents, portraits, uniforms, etc., very well displayed. Open 0900-1200, 1500-1800. Admission: US$0.30. There is also a Shuar ethnographic museum at the university. There are two first class museums in the Banco Central (Av. 10 de Agosto), the **Archaeological Museum** on the fifth floor with beautiful precolumbian ceramics and gold and the **Museo Colonial y de Arte Religioso** on the 6th. Open Tues.-Fri. 0900-1700. There are guided tours in English, French and German—Entrance fee is US$0.75 for foreigners, US$0.35 for Ecuadoreans, US$0.20 for students, but free on Sunday. At the Banco Central library on Av. 10 de Agosto, between the Alameda and El Ejido parks, you can see video film of Ecuadorean culture and the different Indian tribes, and listen to cassettes of music. Admission free. Leave your passport at the entrance. Open Tues.-Sat., 1330-2000. In Eloy Alfaro military college, Av. Francisco Orellana y Amazonas, is a zoo of Ecuadorean animals, open daily, with several condors and a large group of Galápagos tortoises. Passports must be shown for entry. There is a fine museum in Bella Vista north east of Quito, **Museo Guayasamín**: as well as the eponymous artist's works there is a precolumbian and colonial collection; open Mon.-Sat. 0900-1230 and 1500-1830, free admission. Works of art may be purchased. The museum is near the Channel 8 TV station, take Batán-Colmena bus no. 3 marked Bella Vista. Other museums: **Municipal Museum of Art and History**, Espejo 1147, near main plaza, was the old municipal offices; underneath is the cell where the revolutionaries of 1809 were executed (waxwork), reported closed indefinitely in 1987; **Museum of Ethnology**, Departamento de Letras, Ciudad Universitaria, Tues. to Fri. 0900-1230, Wed. and Fri. 1500-1700, Tues. and Thurs. 1500-1830; **Museo Histórico Casa de Sucre**, the beautiful house of Sucre on the corner of Venezuela and Sucre, open 0900-1200, 1300-1600, Tues.-Sat.; closes 1500 Fri. The **Museo-Biblioteca Aureliano Polit** at the former Jesuit seminary beyond the airport has a unique collection of antique maps of Ecuador. Open Mon. to Fri. 0900-1200 and 1500-1800. Take the Condado minibus from the Plaza San Martín in Av. Pichincha. **Cima de los Libertadores**, museum at the site of the 1822 Battle of Pichincha, splendid view. The Tourist Office recommends taking a taxi there as the suburbs are dangerous, but you can take a bus to the south of the city and walk up.

Note It has been reported that theft is on the increase in Quito. **N.B.** also: throughout Ecuador, you must carry your passport (not a copy) at all times.

Hotels *Quito*, with casino and pool, A, meals dear, often room on weekdays as business travellers prefer the more central *Colón Internacional*, Amazonas y Patria, L, excellent food, good discotheque, shopping arcade, casino. The *Colón* is in the **New City**, others in this part of Quito are: *Alameda Real*, Amazonas y Roca, L, can be booked through KLM airline, all rooms are suites and many have kitchenettes, rec.; *Tambo Real*, 12 de Octubre y Patria opp. US Embassy, C, rec., restaurant slow and extras can mount up; *Chalet Suisse*, Calama 312 y Reina Victoria, B, good except for restaurant; *Residencia Los Alpes*, Tamayo 233 y Washington, B, behind US Embassy, popular with Americans, clean, friendly, comfortable, water pressure poor on third floor, rec.; *Hostería Los Andes*, Muros 146 behind British Embassy, D, new, spotlessly clean, hot water, cable TV, family run, all speak fluent English, rec.; *Dan*, Av. 10 de Agosto 2482, E, a/c, private bathrooms, noisy rooms on Avenida, good food, services and laundry, rec. *Residencial Italia*, Av. 9 de Octubre 237, clean, rather cold at night, family-run, rec.; *Embajador*, 9 de Octubre 1046 y Colón, F, full board available, clean, spacious, good service; *9 de Octubre*, 9 de Octubre 1047 y Colón, E, shower, warm water, quick laundry service, safe deposit; *Res. Dapsilia*, 9 de Octubre 650 nr. Dávalos, T 550-529, E, good, hot showers, clean, parking, meals. *Residencial Cumbres*, Baquedano 148 y Av. 6 de Diciembre, E, clean, helpful, large breakfast; *Royal Inn*, 6 de Diciembre 2751, E, comfortable, helpful owner; *Pickett*, Pres. Wilson near J.L. Mera, E, reliable hot water; *Embassy*, Pres. Wilson 441 y 6 de Diciembre, E, highly rec., clean, well furnished, showers, parking, good French restaurant; *6 de Diciembre*, Av. 6 de Diciembre 1230, E, private bath, quiet, comfortable. *Residencial Santa Clara*, Gustavo Darquea Terán 1578, F, just off 10 de Agosto, clean, laundry service, some English spoken; *Residencial Carrión*, Carrión 1250 y 6 de Diciembre, E, 20 rooms with bath, restaurant, bar, good value; *Majestic*, Mercadillo 366 y Versalles, E, little hot water but clean and friendly. Further north are *República*, Av. República y Azuay, D, clean, reasonable; *Zumay*, Av. 10 de Agosto y Mariana de Jesús, E, clean, hot showers, no water after midnight, laundry service; and *Res. Román*, Av. Tomás de Berlanga 531, near airport, T 248-289, parking.

In between the new and old cities are: *Residencial Florida*, Versalles 1075, E with full board, excellent; *Coral Internacional*, Manuel Larrea 164, E, spacious, popular with families, clean, cafetería open 0730-2200; *Inca Imperial*, Bogotá 219, D, with bath, hot water, Inca style with lavish decor, car park, restaurant, theft from rooms reported; *Hostal El Ejido*, Juan Larrea 535 y Riofrío, E, clean, hot water, a bit overpriced; *Residencial Portoviejo*, Portoviejo y Av. America, F, clean, rec.; *Res. Dorado*, 18 de Septiembre 805, F, intermittent water, basic, a higher standard, dearer wing across the street.

In the **Old City**: *Residencial Marsella*, Los Ríos 2035, G, noisy, clean, modern, washing facilities, hot showers 0600-1200, top floor rooms are rec., overlooks Parque La Alameda. *Real Audiencia*, Bolívar 220, C, spacious, lavishly furnished rooms, parking, front rooms a bit noisy, restaurant O.K., generally rec.; *Benalcázar*, Benalcázar 388 y Bolívar (Plaza San Francisco), friendly, safe, laundry facilities, rec.; *Quitumbe*, Espejo 815 y Flores, F, clean, secure, rec. but not enough bathrooms and street-facing rooms are noisy; *Gran Casino Internacional*, 24 de Mayo y Bahía, E, clean, restaurant, has own travel agency for trips to the Galápagos and the Oriente (very mixed reports received); round the corner is *Gran Casino*, García Moreno y Ambato, G and F (better rooms), hot water 0600-1500, good meals, popular meeting place, laundry service, book exchange, luggage store at US$0.25 per bag, dirty; *Viena Internacional*, Flores y Chile, E, English spoken, hot water in a.m., phone, laundry, good meals, secure; *Viena*, opposite, F, clean, hot water, friendly; *San Agustín*, Flores 626 y Chile, E, clean, with bath, hot water, rooms dear but restaurant cheap and good; *Canarias*, Flores 856, F, rec.; *Huasi Continental*, Flores y Sucre, F, clean, noisy rooms on street; *Hogar*, Montúfar 208, F, parking, luggage can be stored; *Rumiñahui*, Montúfar 449 y Junín, F, safe, washing facilities, excellent restaurant, good value.

In the vicinity of the Terminal Terrestre: *Grand*, Rocafuerte, very good, restaurant, rec.; *Caspicara*, Rocafuerte, corner of Plaza, G, clean, friendly, but watch your belongings; *Juana de Arco*, Rocafuerte 1311 y Maldonado, F, only back rooms with shower, front rooms cheaper but noisier, good restaurant next door. *Roma*, Plaza Santo Domingo, F with bath, G without, basic, safe. Many cheap hotels on Calle Morales, e.g. *Cumandá*, no.449, F, comfortable, showers, rec., clean, safe, noisy from proximity to bus station; *Syris*, G, hot water, safe, laundry; *Pensión Ramírez*, no. 781; *Colonial*, Maldonado 3035, F, G without shower, hot water (most of the time), clean, safe, quiet, laundry, cheaper annex; *Amazonas*, Maldonado 915, F, safe, cold water, restaurant (often closed); *Indoamericano*, Maldonado 3022, F, hot water, well furnished, clean, washing facilities; *Ingatur*, Maldonado 3226, F, hot water, clean, washing facilities, safe; opposite is *Capitalino*, G, pleasant, hot water; *Guayaquil No.1*, Maldonado 3248, F, hot water, will store luggage for small fee, safe, basic. Many on Loja in the red light district, e.g. *Pensión Minerva*, no.656, G, hot shower, clean.

If you prefer not to stay in a hotel, 'phone Rosa Jácome, José Bustamante 153 y Zaldumbide, T 451-590, who has several rooms for guests, near airport with direct bus to centre, you may cook for yourself if you want, about US$5 p.p. She is a taxi driver and can make arrangements for visits to the city for tourists. For longer stays with room, kitchen, TV, laundry service etc., the following have been recommended: *Suites Ejecutivos*, 10 de Agosto 4032 y Rumibamba, F, US$150 a month; *Apartamentos Colón*, Leonidas Plaza 326, Casilla Postal 2103, T 230360, US$320 a month for two people; *Apartamentos Calima*, Luis Cordero y 10 de Agosto, US$140 a month for two people. Rates depend on length of stay and number of people. *Aparthotel El Sol* has suites for two people, Av. Orellana 1757, between 10 de Agosto y 9 de Octubre, T 524150, also suites for between 1 and 5 people. A self-contained flat with 4 bedrooms, kitchen, bathroom, laundry service, is available for rent from Sra. Blanca Espinales T., Lugo 115 y Laobrón de Guevara T 560601.

Casa Paxi, F, Pasaje Navarro 364 y Av. La Gasca, T 542-663, complete with cooking facilities, telephone and roof terrace, owned by Dutch guide Pieter van Bunningen; *Denmark House*, Ulloa 1710 y Cuero y Caicedo, T237-195, F p.p., cooking facilities, good information.

Note Those travelling by car may have difficulty parking in the centre of Quito and are therefore advised to choose the less central hotels.

Restaurants in the Old City tend to be cheaper, with more local and fast food types, than in the New City, where more foreign styles can be found. The following list is by type; all restaurants are in the New City unless otherwise stated.

International Excellent food at *Hotel Colón Internacional* for non-residents, Sun. buffet rec., US$6; cheaper in snack bar, excellent pastry shop too in the *Hotel Quito*, *Techo del Mundo* restaurant and *Cayambe* coffee shop are good; ; *Excalibur*, Calama 380, expensive; in the north of the city is *La Vista Real*, Sun. buffet US$4 p.p.

Ecuadorean and General In the Old City: *Viena*, Chile y Flores; *Oasis*, Espejo 812, cheap; *El Criollo*, Flores 825, clean, big helpings, very cheap, no alcohol, specialities; *Inti*, Mariana de Jesus y Hungría, typical, good service; *Monaco*, García Moreno y 24 de Mayo, cheap; *Café Madrillón*, Chile 1270 y Benalcázar, rec.; *Cafetería Dominó*, Venezuela y Mejía, cheap lunches, snacks, juices especially naranjilla, good for breakfast and coffee; cheap meals in the market behind the shoe shops on Flores y Olmedo, 1130-1400. In the New City: *La Bella Epoca*, Whymper 925, excellent; *Mamá Clorinda*, Reina Victoria y Calama, Ecuadorean, cheap; *Limonar*, Rodríguez 228 y Reina Victoria, fish and typical food, excellent, reasonable prices; *Cafetería Matrioshka*, Pinto 376 y Juan León Mera, good food and value; *La Choza*, 12 de Octubre y Cordero, typical Ecuadorean food; *Taberna Quiteña*, Amazonas 1259 y Cordero, Patria y Gral. Páez, and Manabí y Luis Vargas (in Old City), Ecuadorean food, slow service, insist on a menu with prices before ordering or you could be grossly overcharged.

French *Rincón de Francia*, Roca 779 y 9 de Octubre; *La Maison Marabac*, Baron von Humboldt 209, good atmosphere, Indian curries on Wed., bar with darts and billiard table; *Le Bistrot*, González Suárez, good steak Chateaubriand, live music at 2100, closed Sun.; *Fondue Bar*, Juan Rodríguez 175, fondues and French, reasonable prices, closed Sun., Mon. **Swiss** *Chalet Suisse*, Calama 312 y Reina Victoria, dear, good steaks; *Rancho Suizo*, Juan León Mera y Sta. María, expensive, slow service, closed Sat. **German** *El Ciervo*, Dávalos 270 y Páez, highly rec.; *Taverna Bavaria*, Cordero y Juan León Mera, good, German, French and English spoken, tours to mountains, Oriente and Galápagos arranged.

European and middle-eastern *Chawarma*, Amazonas 1215, excellent.

Spanish *La Rana Verde*, Juan León Mera near Veintimilla, good tapas and more, reasonably priced; *Costa Vasca*, 18 de Septiembre 553, entre Páez y 9 de Octubre, good food and atmosphere; *Casa Española*, Calama entre J.L. Mera y Reina Victoria, similar, flamenco on occasions; *El Hobo*, Amazonas 3837, steaks and paella, English spoken. In the Old City, *Las Cuevas de Luis Candela*, Benálcazar y Chile and Orellana y Coruña, not cheap, closed Sun.

Italian *La Gritta*, Santa María 246, entre La Rábida y Reina Victoria, home made pasta, very good; *Trattoria del Veneziano*, Roca 562 y J.L. Mera, good, but wine expensive; *La Bettola*, Cordero 11-87 y J.L. Mera, rec.; *Taberna Piedmonte*, Av. Eloy Alfaro, above stadium, expensive; *La Trattoria de Renato*, San Javier y Orellana, nice atmosphere, expensive, *Vecchia Roma*, Roca 618, good food and atmosphere. **Pizza** *El Hornero*, Amazonas 853, excellent; *Roy's Cervecería y Pizzería*, Amazonas nr. Orellana, and in Centro Comercial Naciones Unidas, good; *Farina Pizzería*, Carrión, entre J.L. Mera y Av. Amazonas, very good; *Pizza Nostra*, Amazonas 252 y Washington, not cheap. In Old City, *Pizza Hut*, on Espejo down hill from Plaza Independencia, very friendly service but not cheap.

Latin American and US *Churrasquería El Rodizio*, Amazonas (stuffed bull on terrace), Brazilian style, steak and salad, excellent value; *Tex Mex*, Reina Victoria 225 y 18 de Septiembre, closed Sun., good food, lively; *La Guarida del Coyote*, Baquedano, good Mexican; *Rincón Cubano*, Amazonas 993 y Veintimilla, Cuban, rec. *Hyatt*, Juan León Mera y Bruna, southern US menu, very select; *Adam's Rib*, Juan León Mera, American ribs, good atmosphere.

Fast Food *Self-service Americano*, 10 de Agosto 666 y Chota, clean, pleasant setting; there is an imitation *MacDonalds* on Av. Amazonas y Cordero; *Dimpy* on Amazonas and in most shopping centres, quick service, hot dogs, sandwiches, etc.; *Manolo's Churrería*, Amazonas 420, reasonable hot snacks; *Mario's*, Amazonas 410 y Roca, good hamburgers and coffee, popular; *Tom Pollo*, 6 de Diciembre, good, inexpensive; *Super Papas*, 6 de Diciembre 1329 entre Carrión y Roca, delicious stuffed baked potatoes, some vegetarian, takeaway service, inexpensive, highly rec. In the Old City: *Kentucky Fried Chicken* opp. Post Office on Plaza Santo Domingo and on Benalcázar; *Pollo Gus*, 24 de Mayo 1246 y Moreno, self-service chicken and meat cooked on open fire, waitress service downstairs; *Pollo Broster*, Sucre 258 y Venezuela, good also for ice cream, bread and pastries. Other inexpensive spit-roasted chicken places throughout Old City, e.g. *Piko Riko*.

Steak *Casa de mi Abuela*, J.L. Mera 1649, steak and salad, rec.; *Columbus* steak house, Colón 1262 y Amazonas, popular. **Seafood** *Moby Dick*, Amazonas 272; *La Jaiba*, Reina Victoria y Colón; *Los Redes de Mariscos*, Amazonas 845 y Veintimilla, excellent (closed Sun. p.m.).

Oriental *Mandarín*, Suárez 162, reasonable Chinese; *Chifa Feliz*, Carrión 661 y Amazonas, specializes in vegetarian (tofu) dishes, excellent, friendly; *Nuevo Shanhay*, Carrión 742 y Amazonas, cheap, rec.; *Pekin*, Bello Horizonte 197; *Chifa Gran Pino*, Colón y Juan León Mera, good; and others.

Vegetarian *Salud y Vida*, Reina Victoria 1138, good; *La Cabaña*, Cordero 1489 y Amazonas, friendly, excellent food, but expensive; *Tierra Buena*, close to *Chalet Suisse*; *Govinda* (Hare Krishna), José Calama 339 y J.L. Mera, good. The British Council does a good vegetarian lunch.

Pastry Shops/Bakeries *El Túnel*, Amazonas 1036 y Pinto, excellent; *Panadería Sevilla*, Edificio Torre Reina, Luis Cordero, try the sweets; *Baguette*, Amazonas y Mariana de Jesús, sells good pasteurized cheeses; good cheeses and meats at Spanish delicatessen next to Libri Mundi, Juan León Mera y Veintimilla; *Pastelería Frederica*, 10 de Agosto 679, rec. for very fresh cachos.

Top Cream, Naciones Unidas, nr. Amazonas, for ice cream. In **Old City**, *El Torreón*, on Plaza del Teatro, good for cakes, juices, ice creams and sandwiches, though a little more expensive than usual.

N.B. Many of the restaurants in the Old City close at about 2200 every evening; many throughout the city are closed on Sun. Also, prices listed on menus may not be true prices; it is worth checking.

Bars In New City: *Rumors*, Juan León Mera at Veintimilla, popular with Peace Corps, good atmosphere, not cheap; *Caento*, J.L.Mera, jungle theme, English spoken, pool table, popular; *El Pub*, opp. *Hotel Quito*, English menu, including fish and chips. In Old City, Teatro Bolívar has a good wine bar.

Public Baths Montúfar 534 (Old City), no sign, 0730-1930, cheap, good.

Bookshops Libri Mundi, Juan León Mera 851 y Veintimilla and at the *Hotel Colón Internacional*, Spanish, English (some second-hand available), French, some German and Italian books, international magazines, records, Ecuadorean maps when in stock, has a notice-board of what's on in Quito; very highly recommended. Librería Universitaria, García Moreno 739; Su Librería, books in English and German, García Moreno 1172 y Mejía; Librería Científica, Av. Colón y Juan León Mera; Librería Cima, Av. 10 de Agosto 285 y Sta. Prisca, good selection in Spanish; Pomaire, Av. Amazonas 863 (Spanish mainly). The United States Information Service has an excellent library. Biblioteca Luz, Manabí 568, runs a book exchange. Foreign newspapers at newsstand in *Hotel Colón* which also has a comfortable reading room open to non-residents.

Shopping Articles typical of Ecuador can be bought in the main shopping districts centred on Avenidas Amazonas and Guayaquil or at the two main markets. One of these, Mercado Ipiales, on Chile from Imbabura uphill, is where you are most likely to find your stolen camera for sale. The other is on 24 de Mayo and Loja from Benalcázar onwards. There are carved figures, plates and other items of local woods, balsa wood boxes, silver of all types, Indian textiles, buttons, toys and other things fashioned from tagua nuts, hand-painted tiles, hand-woven rugs and a variety of antiques dating back to colonial days. Panama hats are a good buy; Eljuri, Chile 1062. Indian garments (for Indians rather than tourists) can be seen and bought on the north end of the Plaza Sucre and along the nearest stretch of the nearby Calle General Flores. Ocepa, at Carrión 1336 y Versalles, good selection, government-run, also Jorge Washington 252 y Amazonas, near *Hotel Colón*, Amazonas 2222 and La Granja, and in Old City on Espejo y Venezuela; branches also in Guayaquil and Cuenca. Near *Hotel Quito* at Av. Colón 260 is Folklore, the store of Olga Fisch, a most attractive array of handicrafts and rugs, but distinctly expensive, as accords with the designer's international reputation; also at *Hotel Colón* and *Hotel Quito*.

Productos Andinos, an artisans' co-operative, Urbina 111 y Cordero, good quality, reasonably priced, recommended; there is a smaller branch store at Robles 900 y 9 de Octubre. After it in quality is Artes, Av. 6 de Diciembre 1118 y Veintimilla. La Bodega Exportadora, Juan León Mera 614 y Carrión, is recommended for antiques and handicrafts, and so is Renacimiento, Carrión y Mera. Galería Latina, next to Libri Mundi at J.L.Mera 823 y Veintimilla, has fine selection of handicrafts from Ecuador, Peru and Bolivia; also Centro Artesanal, Juan León Mera 804. Coosas, Juan León Mera 838, the factory outlet for Peter Mussfeldt's attractive animal designs (bags, clothes etc.). Goldwork from Antigüedades el Chordeleg, 6 de Diciembre y Cordero. Artesanías El Jaguar, Juan León Mera 234 and 18 de Septiembre, behind *Hotel Colón*, souvenirs especially from the Oriente, the owner, Gladis Escobar, paints balsawood birds in colours of your choosing (not cheap). Handicrafts Otavalo, Calle Sucre 255 and García Moreno, good selection, but expensive.

On Av. Amazonas, NE of *Hotel Colón*, are a number of street stalls run by Otavalo Indians, who are tough but friendly bargainers. Bargaining is customary in small shops and at street stalls. Recommended shops include Hamiltons, for jewellery, and Bonita Fashions where you can have a leather jacket made to order in 48 hours. See H. Stern's jewellery stores at the airport, *Hotel Colón* and *Hotel Quito*. Recommended watchmaker, Sr. Torres, Relojería Patek Phillippe, Mejía 329. La Guaragua, Washington 614, sells *artesanías* and antiques, excellent selection, reasonable prices; Joe Brenner sells folk art and handicrafts at reasonable prices at Galería Sul, Pontevedra 698 y Salazar near *Hotel Quito*, recommended for quality and price. El Scarabejo Azul, Portugal 948 y Shyris, near southern end of La Carolina, Indian handicrafts and works by modern craftsmen using indigenous materials. Rainproof ponchos at shops along Flores between Espejo and Bolívar. Casa de los Regalos, Calle Mañosca 456, for souvenirs and antiquities. "Typical" articles tend to be cheaper outside Quito.

Food is cheap at Centro Comercial Iñaquito (CCI) supermarket if you have their credit card, but you pay 10% extra without. There is one in the Multicentro shopping complex on Av. 6 de Diciembre y La Niña, about two blocks N of Colón, open 0830-1230, 1530-1900. (Supermaxi supermarket at this address has been recommended, sells tampons cheaply.) Multicentro on Amazonas on the way to the airport; buy masks and snorkels for the Galápagos here. El Feria supermarket on Calle Bolívar between Venezuela and G.Morena sells good wines and Swiss, German and Dutch cheeses. Cheap food at Frigorífico Los Andes, Calle Guayaquil. Casa Americana, on Venezuela, inexpensive department store.

Camping gaz cartridges hard to find, buy in Peru if convenient; otherwise Importadora Vega, opp. Banco Central, or Deportes Cotopaxi, 6 de Diciembre y Baquedano, or Globo, 10 de Agosto, sometimes have it in stock but it's expensive. For primus stoves and parts, Almacenes Jácome, Chile 955 (nr. Guayaquil). For hiking boots, Calzado Beltrán, Cuenca 562. For mosquito nets, hunting and climbing gear: Capitán Peña, Flores 200 y Bolívar.

Camera Repairs and Equipment Foto Gómez, Olmedo 827; Gustavo Gómez, Asunción 130 y 10 de Agosto, Ed. Molina, 1st floor; Fujicolor, Roca y Gutiérrez; Kis Colour, Amazonas 1238 y Calama, will develop and print 36 exposure film for US$7. Interfoto, Juan León Mera 1567, for repairs and parts.

Night Clubs *Licorne*, at *Hotel Colón Internacional*; discos at *JK*, Amazonas 541, *Mamma Rosa*, Amazonas 553, *Tobujas*, Amazonas y María, *La Diligencia*, 9 de Octubre 158, *Luis XVI*, Cordero 994 y Foch, rec.; *Castaway*, mainly for couples, Colón y Amazonas; *Salsa Bar*, Carrión y Reina Victoria, salsa disco. Casinos at *Chalet Suisse* and *Quito* hotels. *Tulsa*, República 471 next to Ciné República, is a dance hall frequented by US expatriates.

Local folk music is popular and the entertainment is known as a *peña*. Places include *Lira Quiteña*, Amazonas y Orellana; *Rincón Sentimental* and *Pan y Canto*, both at Veintimilla y 6 de Diciembre; *Peña del Castillo*, Calama 270 y Reina Victoria; *Billy Cutter*, Cordero 1952; *PGuayusas Bar*, Juan León Mera 555, good music, reasonable prices, rec., but small, T 553-274; *Peña del Chino*, and *Ñucanchi Llacta*, both at Rodríguez y Almagro; *Las Jarras* and *Inti Illimani*, both at Baquedano y Reina Víctoria. Most places do not come alive until 2230.

Theatre Teatro Sucre, Calle Flores with Guayaquil, the most elegant (box office down side-street, Montúfar, and is unmarked—brown door). Weekly concerts during the rainy season, but buy tickets in advance. Symphony concerts are free. Teatro Prometeo adjoining the Casa de la Cultura Ecuatoriana, 6 de Diciembre y Tarqui. Agora, open-air theatre of Casa de la Cultura (12 de Octubre y Patria) stages many concerts. Also, plays at the Patio de Comedia, 18 de Septiembre, between Amazonas and 9 de Octubre. Good music at Teatro Equitorial Experimental; check posters in Plaza Teatro for details. Centro Cultural Afro-Ecuatorian (CCA), Calle José Luis Tamayo 985 y Lizardo Garúa, Casilla 352, Sucursal 12 de Octubre, T 522318, sometimes has cultural events and published material (useful contact for those interested in the black community). Many cultural events, usually free of charge; see daily press for details.

Cinema The Colón (10 de Agosto y Colón), República (Av. República) and Universitario (Av. América, Plaza Indoamérica, Universidad Central) usually have the best films, the former often has documentaries with Latin American themes. There are many others; seats US$1 or less.

Festivals A New Year *fiesta*, the Inocentes, from Dec. 28 to Jan. 6, fills the streets with people; much bitter satire on the politicians. Another festival, for week ending Dec. 5, celebrates foundation of city. Hotels allowed to charge extra. Bullfights, and music in streets. On Dec. 11, there is a children's day festival.

Carnival at Shrovetide is celebrated, as elsewhere in the Andes, by throwing plastic bags of water at passers-by (especially tourists), so you need a raincoat and umbrella at that season. The Good Friday processions are the most impressive. Fancy-dress parades for Hallowe'en, celebrated last Sat. in October, along Av. Amazonas.

Sport A local game, *pelota de guante* (stone ball), is played, Saturday afternoon and Sunday, at Estadio Mejía. Football is played Sat. afternoons (1200 or 1400) and Sun. mornings (maybe as early as 0800) at Estadio Atahualpa (6 de Diciembre y Naciones Unidas, any northbound bus on 6 de Diciembre marked "Estadio" goes there), and basketball in the Coliseo. The first week of December is the main bullfighting season. Tickets are on sale at 1500 the day before the bullfight; an above-average ticket costs US$2.70 but you may have to buy from touts. There is a cold spring-water swimming pool on Maldonado beyond the Ministry of Defence building (US$0.10), hot shower (US$0.10). Rugby is played at Colegio Militar on Sun. 1000. Inquire at *El Pub*.

Climbing Nuevos Horizontes Club, Venezuela 659, T 215135, on Pasaje Amador near Plaza Independencia, meets evenings (1900 or 2000 hrs.), will advise on climbing Chimborazo and Cotopaxi, including purchase or hire of crampons, ice axes etc., but does not hire them (best to have with you). Non-members may go on the club's trips if these are not fully-booked. Cóndores, Padre José Ribas of Colegio San Gabriel is helpful. **Sr. Enrique Veloz** of Riobamba arranges trips to Chimborazo (**see page 655**). Useful climbing equipment stores (and sources of information) are Equipo Cotopaxi, 6 de Diciembre 1557, and Campo Abierto, on same street. Other clubs for climbers: Sadday, Manabí 621, near Plaza Independencia; the International Hiking and Climbing Group, c/o *Restaurant La Maison Marabac*, Baron von Humboldt 209, Casilla 624, T 238-397/356-409, organizes some type of mountaineering activity most weekends, all interested persons welcome; equipment rented, call G. Rae on 230-070. The Club de Andinismo of the Universidad Católica in Quito meets every Tuesday at 1930 and welcomes visitors. Those clubs needing a professional climbing guide can try Alan Cathey (T 230-847) who is fluent in English, Spanish and German and can also arrange ice climbing trips. Marco Cruz, guide for Sierra and Selva, can be contacted through Metropolitan Touring. Freddy Ramírez G., is a member of the Inti-Nan Club, works at the Dituris office in the Palacio Municipal and can act as a mountain guide, not expensive, highly recommended. Freddy and his brother Milton speak English and French and also do jungle tours. He has a 4-wheel drive Toyota jeep for rent, and will also rent climbing equipment. A Dutch guide, Pieter van Bunningen, Andrés de Artieda 444 y Av. La Gasca, Quito, takes small parties on mountain and jungle treks at reasonable rates, he is an experienced walker and climber and speaks Spanish, English and German. Rolf Helbling, Gral. Veintimilla 531 y Av. 6 de Diciembre, Quito, T 233-013, for information on climbing, transport and accommodation at his house; he speaks German, Spanish and some English. Camilo Andrade, Pres. Wilson 643-apto. 135, Tel.: 520-263 (speaks 7 languages), recommended for climbing expeditions, trekking equipment rental; he has a Land Rover for transportation. Nelson de la Torre, La Cumbre 189, Sector 32, Quito, T 242704, is a climbing guide and can organize climbing and trekking tours; he is fluent in English. The agencies offer climbs up the Illinizas (2 days, US$125), Cotopaxi (3 days, US$230), Tungurahua (4 days, US$260). For climbing the volcanoes, proper equipment and good guidance are essential.

Exchange Bank of London and South America, Av. Carrión y Amazonas, with Torres de Colón, Jipijapa and San Agustín agencies, quick service, rec.; Citibank (own cheques only); Banco Holandés Unido, 10 de Agosto 911; Bank of America, Patria y Amazonas (will provide cash against a Visa Card, but minimum of US$100, only once a month; Filanbank provides cash against Visa at 15% commission); Banco Internacional, opposite Bank of America, notes only; Banco de Pichincha, Amazonas y Colon branch, good exchange rates for cash or cheques; Banco Guayaquil arranges cash advances on Visa without commission or limit. Banco Popular, Amazonas 648, good service. Good rates at Banco de la Producción, Amazonas, opp. Ecuadorian Tours. Open 0900-1330. Closed Sat. Master Card, Amazonas y Veintimilla, in Banco Pacífico building. Bank open all day Sat. and Sun. a.m. in departure lounge at airport. The American Express representative is Ecuadorian Tours, Amazonas 399, T 528-177. Ecuacambio, Av. de la República 192 y Almagro, Thomas Cook agents.

Exchange Houses: Rodrigo Paz, Venezuela 659, and Av. Amazonas 370, will change travellers' cheques into US$ cash up to US$200 for US$0.50 commission, plus all major currencies. Jaramillo Arteaga, Mejía 401 y Venezuela, and Colón y Amazonas, will change up to a maximum of US$100, passport copy required. The airport *cambio* and the *Hotel 9 de Octubre* are the only places you can change money on Saturdays and Sundays. If you have trouble cashing American Express or Thomas Cook's travellers' cheques, try the Banco Popular. You are advised only to buy a few Peruvian intis in Ecuador for getting into Peru; you will get a much better rate in Peru.

Post Office The main post office is at Edif. Munich, Toledo y Madrid (for *poste restante*). Post office in old city is at Benalcázar 769 y Chile, which accepts parcels up to 20 kg (**see page 684**). Post Office also at Reina Victoria y Av. Colón for parcels up to 2 kg. Ecuadorian Tours accepts air mail packages with a minimum charge. Transpak (also called STAIR), Av. Amazonas y Veintimilla, will ship out packages for a minimum charge of US$50. Philatelic service, 3 de Octubre 354 y Eloy Alfaro, 7th floor.

Telecommunications letel office at Av. Colón y 6 de Diciembre, open until 2200, in Hotel Colón and at the Terminal Terrestre.

Embassies U.K., Av. González Suárez 111 (opposite *Hotel Quito*), letters to Casilla 314, T 560-309/669/670/671. U.S.A., Av. Patria y 12 de Octubre, T 562-890. (The US embassy does not hold mail for US citizens.) West Germany, Av. Patria y 9 de Octubre, Edificio Eteco, 6th floor, T 232-660. Austria, Av. Patria y Amazonas, Edificio Cofiec, 11th floor, T 545-336. Denmark, Ed. Las Cámaras, Av. Amazonas y Av. de la República, No. 3, T 458585/786; Sweden, Ed. Las Cámeras, 2nd floor, Av. República y Amazonas, Apartado 420-A, T 454-872/452-010. Switzerland, Av. Amazonas, Edificio Xerox, 2nd floor. Canadian Honorary Consul, Ed. Josueth González, Av. 6 de Diciembre 2816 y James Orton, 4th floor, T 564795/543214. Belgium, Austria

219 y Irlanda, T 434-631. Honorary Dutch Consul, Av. Colón 1480, T 567606, letters to Casilla 6294 CC 1. Colombian Consulate, Av. Amazonas 353, insists on a ticket to leave Colombia before issuing a visa. Peruvian and Brazilian Consulates both in Edificio España, Av. Colón y Av. Amazonas.

British Council Amazonas 1615 y Orellana, T 236-144, postal address: Casilla 1197. There is a library, open Mon.-Fri., 0800-1245, 1500-1915, which stocks back copies of British newspapers and a good café with cheap bacon and eggs.

Language Courses at the Universidad Católica, Av. 12 de Octubre 1076 y Carrión, Instituto de Lenguas y Linguística, T 529-240: 6-week Spanish courses, US$100, large classes; courses in Quechua. They will provide student cards, valid for reductions in Peru. Academia de Español Quito, Marchena 130 y 10 de Agosto, T 553-647/525-785, Casilla 39-C, one-to-one teaching, 7 hours a day, 5 days a week, full board and lodging with Ecuadorean family, US$700-750 for 4 weeks. Instituto Infraital, Venezuela y Meya, has been recommended, US$2 per hr. The manager, Ernesto, speaks English, French, German and Italian. Two new Spanish language schools, both run by former teachers of the Academia de Español Quito, opened in 1988. We have received numerous favourable reports on both: Academia Español Los Andes offers individual tuition for US$2 per hr., or a 4 week, 7 hrs. a day course for US$260. The school can arrange for accommodation with Ecuadorean families, and also organizes cultural trips in and around Quito; contact at Versalles 1009 y Jerónimo de Carrión, 2° piso, Casilla 676A. The second is Academia de Español "One-to-One", Reina Victoria 100 y Av. Patria Edificio Reina Victoria, Casilla 209A, US$7 per day staying with a family, flexible teaching hours. Also recommended: Pichincha, Av. América 3384 y Mariano de Jesús, 2° piso, Casilla 936-A, Sucursal 3, T 523-447, US$2/hr.; Ecuatoriano de Español; Edinburgh Linguistic Center, Av. Shyris 18-64, Casilla 32-05, T 247-492.

Anglican Church Joint Anglican/Lutheran service is held (in English) at the Advent Lutheran Church, Isabel la Católica 1419, Sun., 0900.

Charity The Centro del Muchacho Trabajador, or Working Boys' Centre, run by the Christ of the Andes Mission, is a charitable organization which welcomes visitors who wish to see the progress it is making in improving the conditions of the shoe-shine boys. It is located on one side of the Plaza San Martín coming down the Calle Chile from the Plaza de la Independencia. Handicrafts made by the boys are on sale at Caperucita Roja in the Palacio Arzobispal, Calle Venezuela with Chile, shop 12 and at some *artesanías*.

Medical The British and other embassies have telephone numbers of good doctors. Hospital Voz Andes, next to Voz Andes radio station, Villalengua 263 (T 241-540), emergency room, fee US$4, some English spoken (American-run), has out-patient dept., reached by No. 1 bus to Iñaquito; Centro Médico Alemania (Dr Klier speaks German), Eloy Alfaro y Alemania. Clínica Pichincha, Veintimilla 1259, for serious cases; Clínica Americana Adventista (some English spoken) 10 de Agosto 3366, 24 hrs., US$5. For amoebic dysentery tests, Análisis Médicos Automatizados, Alpallana 477 y Whymper, Ramírez Dávalos 202, T 545-945; for gamma gobulin prescriptions and injections, Clínica Santa Cecilia, Veintimilla 1394 (nr. 10 de Agosto). Dr. Rosenthal, La Rábida 160, German spoken. **Dentist:** Dra. Rosa Oleas, Amazonas 258 y Washington (T 524-859); Dr. Fausto Vallejo, Madrid 744 (1 block from end of No. 2 Camal/Colón bus line), rec., very reasonable; Dr Roberto Mena, Tamayo 1255 y Colón, speaks English and German. All-night **chemist**, Farmacia Alaska, Venezuela 407 y Rocafuerte (T 210-973). For injections and prescriptions, Rumipampa 1744 y Vasco de Contreras, opp. Coliseo de Colegio San Gabriel (old city), T 457-772.

Immigration Office Independencia y Amazonas 877. For visa extensions, Av. Amazonas 2639, open 0800-1200 and 1500-1800; take bus 15, go early and be prepared to wait; service more reliable a.m. in Extranjería, Reina Victoria y Colón, Mon.-Thurs., 0830-1230, for visas other than tourist.

Police Criminal Investigations, Calle Montúfar.

Laundromat Lavanderías Modernas, can take 2 days, Av. 6 de Diciembre 24-00 y Orellana (US$0.37 per 450 grams). Lavanderías Populares on Riofrio y Uruguay, central. Ropa Limpia, J. L. Mera y Lizardo García, good service. Dry-cleaning, Martinizing, Av. Colón y Mera (same day).

South American Explorers Club has a new office in Quito. Write to Apartado 21-431, Eloy Alfaro, Quito.

Tourist Office Dirección Nacional de Turismo (Dituris) at Reina Victoria 514 y Roca (T 239-044), at airport, and the new Palacio Municipal, Plaza Independencia, open Mon. to Sat., 0800-1630 (T 514-044; Freddy Ramírez, the climbing expert, works here) provide maps and other information. Some staff speak English. Their information on bus departure times is reported as being extremely inaccurate, so check at bus stations.

Maps Instituto Geográfico Militar on top of the hill at the eastern end of El Ejido park, on corner of Patria. Opposite the entrance to the Casa de Cultura on 12 de Octubre, running SE up the hill is a small street, Jiménez, which becomes Paz y Miño, follow this up and round to the IGM on the right. You have to exchange your passport for a visitor's pass. Map and air photo indexes are all laid out for inspection. The map sales room (helpful and efficient) is open 0800-1500, Mon.-Fri.

Tourist Agencies Ecuadorian Tours (American Express agent), Av. Amazonas 399, T 528-177 (Poste Restante can be sent for clients, Aptdo. 2605, Quito); Metropolitan Touring, helpful for information for non-customers, Amazonas 235, T 524-400; also downtown and at *Hotel Quito*; general agents for Galapagos Cruises and Transturi; runs tours to the Galápagos, also arranges climbing, trekking expeditions led by world-known climbers, generally rec. Transturi, part of Metropolitan Touring, operate a cruise ship, the *Flotel Francisco de Orellana*, in 4-5 day trips from Coca along the jungle rivers. Turismundia, friendly, Av. Amazonas 657 (reservations to Galápagos). Seitur, for the Galápagos and elsewhere, Pinto 525 y Amazonas, helpful, fluent English. Yanasacha, Av. República 189 with Diego del Almagro, T 528-964, arranges trips to the Galápagos and Oriente as well as mountaineering expeditions. Viajes Americanos, Amazonas y 18 de Septiembre, highly rec., including to Galápagos. Alpa Tours, Amazonas 631 y Carrión, rec., very helpful. Etnotur, Juan Léon Mera y L. García, helpful, English and German spoken, jungle, mountain and Galápagos tours. Latin Tour, office at airport, organizes various trips around the country in a jeep, English speaking and very friendly staff, frequently rec.

Galasam Cía. Ltda., Pinto 523 y Av. Amazonas, operates Economic Galápagos Tours as well as Condor Tours, Uniclán, Yanasacha, Sol Mar Tours and their tours can be purchased in Switzerland: Artou, 8 rue de Rive 1204, Geneva; France: Delta Voyages, 11 Rue Edouard Jacques, Paris 75014; Italy: Nouvelles Frontières, Vicolo del Divino Amore 180, 00186 Rome; Peru: Top Tours, A. Miró Quesada 247, Of. 704, Lima and El Punto, Av. Nicolás de Piérola 742, Lima 1; USA, Latin American Student Travel, 43 Millstone Road, Randallstown, MD 21133, T (301) 922 2409; Canada, Galapagos Tour, 161 Dupont St., Toronto M5R 1VF (T (416) 968-3664, Telex 06-217682), exclusive representatives, prices are the same as in Ecuador. For other agencies organizing tours to the Galápagos, **see page 676**.

Airport Mariscal Sucre Airport. Taxi (yellow) to centre US$1.50-2 (beware of black taxis which charge at least double). From airport catch bus 16 to go to Plaza Santo Domingo. The No. 1 Iñaquito and Aeropuerto buses go to the airport, look for a sign "*Aeropuerto*" on the windscreen; also No. 43, Marím-Carcelén. British Leyland double decker buses run all the way along Av. Amazonas to the airport. There is a US$25 airport and police departure tax on international flights, payable in sucres or US$. Beware of self-defeating porters: men or boys who will grab your luggage in the hope of receiving a tip. There are no facilities for long-term left luggage at the airport, but there are at *Hotel Aeropuerto*, just outside the terminal, US$2 per day. Watch out for thefts by security officials when searching your bags; it has been reported that while you walk through the metal detector they remove money from your hand baggage. There are three duty-free shops in the international departure lounge; they sell few appliances and no film.

Internal Flights There are about 10 flights a day to and from Guayaquil, US$12 (Tame, Saeta, SAN) and 4 to Cuenca (US$18). There are daily flights to Esmeraldas (US$9), Manta, Tulcán, Loja (except Sun., US$20), Lago Agrio and Coca, and the Galápagos; 2-3 flights a week to Portoviejo and Macas; flights to Machala (US$8) Mon.-Fri. only. Tame, Reina Victoria y Colón (T 549-100, another Tame office is at Av. 10 de Agosto 239); Saeta, Av. Colombia y Elizalde (T 217-681).

The Icaro flying school will organize trips in a light plane along "Avenue of the Volcanos", 4-5 people, US$25 each. (US$30 an hour for lessons.)

Local Transport Standard fare on local buses and *busetas* is US$0.02. The British double-decker bus running along Av. Amazonas to the airport costs US$0.03 (buy ticket on the bus) and passengers may not stand, even when it´s raining. Other buses are allowed along Av. Amazonas only before 0830. For trips outside Quito taxi tariffs should be agreed beforehand: usually US$30-32 a day. Outside main hotels cooperative taxi drivers have a list of agreed excursion prices which compare favourably with tourist excursion prices; most drivers are knowledgeable and speak some English. Standard tariff in the city is US$0.60 to US$2 and not more than double by night; no increase for extra passengers; by the hour, US$4 up. Although the taxis now have meters, look for "Equipado con taximetro" on front window, drivers sometimes say they are out of order. Insist on the meter being used, it is always cheaper! If they have no meter, it is imperative to fix fare beforehand.

Car Rentals All the main car rental companies (Hertz, International Avis, Ecuacar, Budget, Dollar and Carros Inteligentes) are at the airport, with some having small offices in the city. It is best to ignore these and catch bus directly to the airport. Cars are available at US$33 per day, unlimited mileage, but there is a minimum three-day rental period. Insurance is US$5, and tax is 6 per cent on the total transaction. Some car hire firms do not have adequate insurance policies and you will have to pay heavily in the event of an accident. Also be sure to check the car´s condition, not forgetting things like wheelnuts. We have received bad reports of Budget and Inteligentes, whilst Ecuacar is rec. Land Rover specialists at Calle Inglaterra 533, Talleres Atlas. Also Luis Alfredo Palacios, Iturralde and Av. de la Prensa, T 234341 and Expo, Av.América 1116 y Bolivia. 24-hour filling station where Baeza road enters Quito.

Buses Most main roads are paved, so interurban buses are fast and tend to be reliable. The Terminal Terrestre in the southern Villa Flora district, at Maldonado and Cumandá (near Plaza Santo Domingo), enlarged in 1986, handles all long-distance bus services. From Terminal Terrestre to Av.Amazonas area take bus "Colón-2-Camal". Take No. 10 bus marked "*terminal terrestre*" from city, No. 1 Bartolo-Miraflores from Plaza Santo Domingo, or a taxi (US$1). Most buses marked "*terminal terrestre*" do not go right to the bus station but stop 300-500 metres away, which is awkward if you have luggage. There are company booking offices but staff shout destinations of buses leaving; you can pay them and get on board. To Santo Domingo de los Colorados, 2½ hrs., US$1; to Quevedo via Santo Domingo, US$2, 4 hrs.; Esmeraldas, US$2.50, 7 hrs., good buses, 19 daily, or by Aerotaxi minibus, 5½ hrs., 8 a day (for which you need a reservation), US$2.10, 12 passengers. Buses to Otavalo, 2 hrs., US$1, 9 a day (Transportes Otavalo goes into Otavalo; Tranportes Andina by-passes the centre). To Ibarra, 2½ hrs., US$1.25; to Tulcán, 4 hrs., US$2.25, about 30 a day. Buses to Guayaquil, 8½ hrs., about US$3 on an ordinary bus or US$4.50 on a pullman coach. Ambato, US$1, 3½ hrs.; Cuenca, 10 hrs. US$4 (minibus, 8 hrs, US$4.50); to Latacunga, 1½ hrs., US$0.75; to Riobamba, 4½ hrs., US$1.50. To

Baños 3 hrs., US$1.50. To Huaquillas, 12 hrs., US$4; to Machala, US$3.50 first class, 10½ hrs. (Also minibuses.) For buses out of Quito it is often advisable to reserve the day before as they may leave early if they are full. To Oriente: Lago Agrio, US$4, 9½ hrs.; Coca, US$5, 0700 and 1400 daily, 10 hrs. Puyo, US$2.50, 7 hrs. (US$2.50, 9 hrs. via Baeza); Tena, US$2.50, 6½ hrs. (US$3, 8 hrs. via Ambato). Panamericana, Maldonado 3077, runs an "international" bus to Bogotá, but this involves many changes and greater expense; it is better to take a bus to the border and change. There are now no direct through buses to Peru so take a bus to Huaquillas via Machala, cross the border and catch one of the Peruvian long-distance buses from Tumbes on to Piura, Trujillo and Lima. The alternative route for crossing the Peruvian border via Loja and Macará takes much longer than the Machala route. Tepsa has an office at Pinto 539 y Amazonas but avoid buying Peruvian bus tickets here as they will be half the price in Peru; tickets also sold for other S.American destinations.

Drivers should note that there is now a ring road around Quito, and a by-pass to the S, the Carretera de Amaguaña.

Railway station is two km. S of centre, along continuation of Calle Maldonado, reached by buses along that street (e.g. No. 1 or Colón-Camal, No. 2). The ticket office at the station is frequently closed. Severe rains and flooding destroyed much of the track in 1983. Daily train leaves for Riobamba 0830, US$1, 5 hrs.; *autoferro*, 1500, US$1, 4½ hrs. (tickets on sale from 0430 on day of departure). Metropolitan Touring does 2-day tour: down to Riobamba by train on Tues. or Sat., overnight Riobamba, back by bus, US$120.

Cruz Loma and Rucu Pichincha Cruz Loma is one of the two antenna-topped peaks overlooking Quito from the west (it has two antennae, its neighbour one). On a clear day you can see about 50 km. down the central valley and to the east. Hiking up from Calle 24 de Mayo in central Quito takes 3-4 hrs. and the descent about 2. (To save time and energy one can take a cab or bus, e.g., Toctiuco, No. 14, to the upper reaches of Quito and start from there.) There are roads up to both peaks, but traffic is sparse. Try hitching early in the morning, but remember that it is difficult to hitch back after about 1730 and you will have to walk in the dark. On no account go alone or in small groups; armed robbery has been reported. The road to the northern hill is better for hitching; it leads to the radio station at the top of the hill; take bus no. 5 from Calle Gabriel García Moreno. Take a stick to ward off dogs. **Rucu Pichincha** (4,700 metres) cannot be seen from Quito, but can be climbed either via Cruz Loma or via its neighbour. The path to its foot runs due west over and around hummocks on the rolling, grass-covered *páramo*. The climb up to the peak is not technical, but is rocky and requires a bit of endurance. About half an hour beyond Rucu Pichincha, is a second peak, Paso de Muerte. From Cruz Loma to Rucu Pichincha peak takes about 3 hrs. and the return about 1½ hrs. Take rainproof and cold-weather gear just in case. (*Note*: please pick up your flotsam; the area is rubbish-strewn enough as it is.)

Pichincha A recommended route for climbing Pichincha volcano is to take a bus to Lloa, from where a 4-wheel-drive track goes to a *refugio*, maintained by Defensa Civil, at the crater rim. The descent into the crater is scree and sand, and very steep; use of a rope is advised (not for the novice). There are fumaroles and thermal springs at the bottom, and the ground shakes under you.

Excursions 23 km. N of Quito is the Equatorial Line Monument at an altitude of 2,483 metres. The exact equatorial line here was determined by Charles de la Condamine and his French expedition in 1735. The monument forms the focal point of a park and leisure area with restaurants, gift shops, etc., and has a museum inside (open Tues.-Fri., 0900-1500, Sat.-Sun., 1000-1300). Admission to the monument and museum, US$0.10. The museum is run by the Central Bank; a lift takes you to the top, then you walk down with the museum laid out all around with different Indian cultures every few steps. A paved road runs from Quito to the Monument, which you can reach by a "Mitad del Mundo" bus (US$0.10) from the market place near La Merced church, corner of Mejía and Imbabura. Two minutes' walk before the Monument is the restaurant *Equinoccio*, good food, good service, live music. Available at the restaurant are "certificates" recording the traveller's visit to the Equator. Other restaurants are now being opened.

A few km. beyond the Monument is the Pululagua crater, well worth visiting, and there is now a paved road. Continue on the road past the Monument towards Calacalí. After a few km. (1 hr. walk) the road bears left and begins to climb steeply; the paved road to the right leads to the rim of the volcano and a view of the farms on the crater floor. Buses to Calacalí (infrequent) will drop you at the fork, from where it is a ½ hr. walk. Plenty of traffic at weekends for hitching a lift. There is a rough track down from the rim to the crater, to give an impression of the rich vegetation and warm micro-climate inside the crater. Also in the vicinity of the Monument, 3 km. from San Antonio beyond the Solar Museum, is the ruined Inca fortress of Rumicucho. Restoration poor, but situation magnificent (investigations under the auspices of the Museum of the Central Bank, entry US$0.15). Start early if you want to visit all these in one day.

The Equator line also crosses the Inter-American Highway 8 km. south of Cayambe, where there are a concrete globe beside the road and a mark on the road itself. Midday by the sun, incidentally, is between 1200 and 1230. Take Cayambe bus (2 hrs., US$0.80) and ask for Mitad del Mundo.

According to the vulcanologists, the best hot springs in Ecuador are the Baños de **Papallacta**, 80 km. E from Quito on the road to Lago Agrio. There are three swimming pools, open 0800-1800. You can camp in the pastures up towards the baths, or sleep in the shelter at the hot springs themselves (no extra charge after the US$0.25 admission fee). There are showers, toilets and changing rooms. The restaurant is open daily. The farm next door sells milk and cheese. Bus Quito-Papallacta US$1, 2½ hrs. In the valley of Chillos (SE, 1 hr. by car) are the thermal pools of Alangasí and El Tingo. A few km. from El Tingo is La Merced, which has thermal baths. Camping is allowed in the vicinity. Further on from La Merced is Ilaló, a semi-private swimming club, admission US$2 but clean, fewer mosquitoes and people.

Another interesting trip is to **Sangolquí** about 20 minutes away by bus. There is a colourful Sun. market (and a lesser one on Thurs.), with Indians in traditional costumes and few tourists, and there are thermal baths nearby (pop. 18,000).

Day tours via Cotopaxi to Indian fairs at Pujilí and at Saquisilí (**see page 659**), about 93 km. each way, or to Cotopaxi itself.

NORTH OF QUITO (2)

A railway (no passengers) and the Pan-American Highway run north-east from Quito to Otavalo (121 km.) and Ibarra (145 km.). At Ibarra, the railway and Highway separate. The railway goes north-west to the Pacific port of San Lorenzo, a very spectacular trip, passenger services only from Ibarra: the highway runs north for another 108 km. to Tulcán and on to Ipiales in Colombia. The Pan-American Highway is now paved for the whole stretch Quito-Tulcán.

Calderón, 30 km. N of Quito, is the place where miniature figurines are made of bread; you can see them being made, and prices are much lower than in Quito. Especially attractive is the Nativity collection. Prices range from about US$0.10 to US$4 (excellent value). See the Indian cemetery on November 1-2, when the graves are decorated with flowers, drinks and food for the dead. Corpus Christi processions are very colourful. Many buses from Quito (W end of Av. Colón).

The road for the north traverses the Indian area around Calderón, descends the spectacular Guayllabamba gorge and climbs out again to the fertile oasis of Guayllabamba village, noted for huge avocados and chirimoyas. Further north the road runs through dry, dusty land before irrigated land is reached again at **Cayambe** (pop. 14,168), dominated by the snow-capped volcano of the same name. This area of rich dairy farms produces a fine range of European-style cheeses. Cayambe is the Agrarian Reform Institute's showplace; its only major project. The monastery of the Salesian fathers in Cayambe has a superb library on indigenous cultures.

Between Guayllabamba and Cayambe, before entering Tabacundo, a narrow dirt road to the left leads to Tocachi and further on to the Estancia **Cochasquí** national archaeological site; the whole area is covered with hills of pyramid shapes and ramps built between 900 and 1500 AD by Indians of the Caras or Caranquis tribe. Festivals with dancing at the equinoxes and solstices. Note the spectacular wind-eroded rocks. Students offer free, 20-min. guided tours which are recommended. The only bus to pass the turn off to Cochasqui is Transportes Lagos' Quito-Otavalo route via Cayambe; ask driver to let you out at the sign; from there it's an 8 km. walk (if you arrive at the sign between 0900-0930, you should get a lift from the site workers).

Rob Rachowiecki writes that about 1 km. before Cayambe an unmarked cobbled road heading right for 26 km. to the Ruales-Oleas-Berge refuge at 4,400 metres, opened in 1981. It costs US$2.50 p.p. a night and provides beds (bring sleeping bag), food, water and a kitchen. It is named after three Ecuadorean climbers killed by an avalanche in 1974 while pioneering a new route up the Cayambe volcano from the west. This has now become the standard route, using the refuge as a base. The climb is heavily crevassed, especially near the summit, and is more difficult and dangerous than either Chimborazo or Cotopaxi. Cayambe (5,790 metres) is Ecuador's third highest peak and the highest point in the world which lies directly on the Equator.

The road forks north of Cayambe: to the right a cobbled road, the very scenic *carretera vieja*, runs through Olmedo (just outside Olmedo, *El Coche*

Rojo restaurant is reasonable and serves excellent seafood), Zuleta and Esperanza, to Ibarra; to the left, the main paved road crosses a *páramo* and suddenly we descend into the land of the Otavalo Indians, a lively and prosperous group who have been making commercial woollens for over fifty years. The men are recognizable by their white, bell-bottomed, mid-calf-length trousers (whitened by using a special reed in washing), long braided hair and blue ponchos. Although some work on *haciendas* between San Pablo and Ibarra, most of the scattered homes in the fields belong to Indians.

An alternative route from Quito to Otavalo is via San Antonio (Inca ruins of Rumicucho) and San José de Minas. The road curves through the dry but impressive landscape down to the Río Pita, then climbs again, passing some picturesque oasis villages. After Minas the road is in a very bad condition and a jeep is necessary for the next climb (beautiful views; at both junctions on this stretch, take the left fork) and then descent to join the Otavalo-Selva Alegre road about 15 km. from Otavalo. The journey takes about 3 hours altogether and is rough but magnificent.

Otavalo (2,530 metres, population 18,000) is notable for its colourful Indian fair on Sat. The fair is a "must" for tourists. There are 4 markets in different places: (a) woollen fabrics and shawls, 0500-1330, in Plaza de Ponchos; (b) animal auction, 0530-0830 (Barrio San Juan at Cotocachi turnoff); (c) produce, 0800-1300, in Plaza 23 de Mayo; (d) *artesanías* at Plaza Centenario, Salinas y Sucre, Sats. only. The market is rated highly for woollen goods, though it is now rather highly organized and touristy and prices are not low; very little of the traditional weaving is now to be seen and many of the ponchos are made of orlon (these are easily recognizable). The earlier you get there the better; prices tend to be higher after 1100 when the organized trips from the *Hotels Quito* and *Colón* arrive. Bargaining is essential, but difficult. All the same, Otavalo is the best place in Ecuador to buy a man's woollen poncho. Your chances of being allowed to photograph Indians will improve if you buy something first, then ask politely. Watch out for pickpockets and bag slashers in the market. (Goods sold in the market can also be bought in local shops, sometimes cheaper and with less bargaining.)

The Otavalo Indian weavers come from the villages of Peguche, Iluman and Quinchuqui, close to Otavalo. They are very friendly and will indicate where you can buy their products more cheaply than from the loom. For a tour contact Rafael Perugachi, Calle Sucre 12-16; or Zulaytour, Sucre y Colón. Otavalo textile shops include *Tejidos y Artesanías Atahualpa*, Bolívar 1015, and *Coop. Indígena de Tejidos Peguche*, Bolívar 910. **Note:** If planning a spending spree, bring plenty of cash; Otavalo can be as expensive as Quito, and the exchange rate is very unfavourable, even in the bank.

We have received many reports of stealing from Otavalo hotel rooms; you are advised to ensure that your door is always locked, even if your absence is very brief.

Hotels May be full on Fri. nights, before fair, when prices go up. *Yamor Continental,* at northeast end of town, E, comfortable, some small cabins, water intermittent and only occasionally warm, lovely building, saunas, swimming pool, restaurant expensive; *Otavalo*, D, hot water, cheaper rooms without bath, clean, fine old building with attractive patio, run down but rec., the new part across the street is clean but noisy, Indian music in nice restaurant, set menu (homemade ice cream in the *Golden Eagle* coffee shop); *Residencial El Rocío*, Morales, E, clean, safe, friendly; *Riviera y Sucre,* F, Moreno y Sucre, hot water, clean, safe, rec., table-tennis table downstairs, the owner, Sr. Antonio Andrade, is an expert on the area; *Residencial Sami Huasi,* near market, friendly, clean, rec.; *Residencial El Indio*, Sucre 12-14, F, also has suites with sitting room and balcony, E for 3 people, rec., hot water, clean; *Pensión Los Andes*, Roca y Montalvo, G, grimy (see under Museums below). *Residencial Centenario*, Pasaje Saona y Jaramillo, F, clean, good parking; *Isabelita*, Roca 1107 y Quiroga, F, quiet, spacious rooms, hot water, washing facilities, very clean, helpful, parking space, rec. *Pensión Otavalo*, G p.p., basic, noisy from disco behind, showers, laundry facilities, friendly; *Residencia Santa Marta*, G, on Calle Colón, pretty courtyard, large rooms, ask for hot water, clean, safe, popular.

Restaurants *Sumak Mikuy*, Jaramillo y Pasaje Saona, criollo food; *El Triunfo*, Moreno y Jaramillo, good breakfast early, English spoken. *Camba Huasi* (with enclosed parking), self-service, good coffee; *El Mesón del Arrayán*, reasonable prices (check bill); *Ajadero Crystal*, Bolívar, clean, noisy jukebox. *Ali Micuy*, Jaramillo y Quiroga, vegetarian food, juices, and cheeseburgers, also on Plaza de los Ponchos, cheap and good value (except the soy burgers). *Jatun Pacha*, Morales 410 y Sucre, vegetarian, open all day, good wholemeal bread and lovely jams, inexpensive; *Mama Rosita*, Sucre, 1 block from plaza, prepares vegetarian meals if you order them in a.m. *La Portada Vieja*, good 3-course meal for US$3; *Casa de Corea*, opposite *Hotel Otavalo*, Ecuadorean food, good and cheap; *Chifa Tien An Men*, near Moreno and Bolívar, generous portions, inexpensive; try pollo pilipina, chicken roasted in a thick, black hot sauce; *Copacabana*, Montalvo y Bolívar, basic, clean, reasonable, set meal about US$1, good for breakfast; *Cafetería Shanandoa*, Salinas y Jaramillo, good pies, milk shakes (expensive) and ice cream, rec. for breakfast; *Tapiz Café*, Sucre 12-03, good, friendly; *Centro Latino*, Sucre y Calderón, good fried chicken and grills; *Royal*, on main plaza, clean (even the toilets), meal with cola about US$1.40.

Entertainment   *Peña Amauta*, Modesto Jaramillo opp. *Hotel Samihuasi*, Fri. and Sat. from 2200, US$0.60 entrance fee; *Peña Folklórica*, Quiroga y Jaramillo, on Fri. and Sat. nights, from 2200. 2 cinemas: *Apolo*, on Bolivia. There is also a cockpit (*gallera*), near the market, fights Sat. and Sun. 1500-1900, US$0.50.

Swimming Pool   Neptuno, open air at end of Calle Morales, near the railway track, 3 blocks from station.

Games and Festivals   Near the market, a ball game is played in the afternoons. It is similar to the game in Ibarra described below except that the ball is about the size of a table-tennis ball, made of leather, and hit with the hands, not a bat. From June 24 to 29, at the Fiesta de San Juan, there are bullfights in the plaza and regattas on the beautiful Lago de San Pablo, 4 km. away (bus to Espejo, US$0.20) and there is the *Fiesta del Yamor* in early September.

Museums   Instituto Otavaleño de Antropología, exhibition, on Panamericana Norte; Museo Arqueológico César Vásquez Fuller, at *Pensión Los Andes*, Roca y Montalvo (free if staying there); Museo Jaramillo, Bolívar, off Parque Central.

Tourist Information   Municipal Tourist Office at City Hall, Moreno y Sucre, helpful. Zulaytour, English spoken, Sucre y Colón 1014, runs good tours to local artisans' homes, very informative, good value (US$4-6 p.p.), repeatedly recommended.

Transport   Bus to Ibarra, every 15 mins., US$0.15, ½ hr. From Quito by taxi takes 1½ hrs. (US$15); by minibus (Transportes Andinas) from 18 de Septiembre and Av. Guerrero, 1½ hrs., US$1.15; by bus (Cooperativa Otavalo, Coop Las Lagos) 1 hr., US$1, every ½ hr. The Tourist Office in Quito will help with reservations; the organized tour sold by hotels is expensive. Travelling on Friday is rec. as the best prices and best goods are found early on Saturday morning before the tourist bus arrives.

Excursions   At the Lago de San Pablo is the Club de Tiro, Caza y Pesca where one can rent canoes. It is worth walking either to or back from Lago de San Pablo for the views, the walk back via the outlet stream from the lake (staying on the right hand side of the gorge), taking 2-3 hrs., is particularly recommended. The new 13-roomed *Hotel Chicapán*, C, on the lakeshore is recommended; from the restaurant there is a fine view of the lake and Imbabura mountain. *Cabaña del Lago*, on the lakeside, E, has cabins with bunk beds, clean, good food. Boats and pedalos for hire, pony rides etc. Also in San Pablo del Lago (half-hourly buses from Otavalo) is *Hostería Cusín* in a converted *hacienda*, D, but often open only Fri.-Sun. (run by an Englishman, Mr Creighton, who grows roses). Pleasant setting but less pleasant food. There are also other restaurants. There are several lakes in the mountains around, such as Lake Cuicocha (**see below**), and the four very picturesque Lagunas Mojanda, (take food and tent, no accommodation).

There is a network of old roads and trails between Otavalo and the Lago San Pablo area, none of which takes more than an hour or two to explore. It is only half an hour's walk to the Cascadas de Peguche through woods. Four km. from Otavalo are cold ferrous baths at the Fuente de Salud, said to be very curative (John Streather). It is also possible to hike much further south to Lagunas Mojanda and on to Tocachi (turn left after second lake); on the way you can visit the pyramids of Cochasqui (see above). For maps and information contact García Mora in Ateneo Móvil, Bolívar y Roca, or his brother Rodrigo Mora in Zulaytour, Sucre y Colón, who arrange good guided tours (8 hours, US$5.50) for information on local history and Indian handicrafts (including visits to several homes).

Off the road between Otavalo and Ibarra is *Cotacachi*, where beautiful leather goods are made and sold; credit cards widely accepted. (Hotels: *El Mesón de las Flores*, E-D, converted ex-hacienda off main plaza, good meals; *La Mirage*, E-D, ex-hacienda ½ km. from town, beautiful garden, very good rooms and food, and others.) A few km. before Cotacachi (turn off at Quiroga), at an altitude of 3,070 metres lies Lake *Cuicocha*, which has been developed for tourism (entrance US$0.15 to the nature reserve). This is a crater lake with two islands, although these are closed to the public for biological studies. There is a path around the lake, which takes at least 5 hrs. (best to go anticlockwise), and provides spectacular views of Cotacachi, Imbabura and, occasionally, glacier-covered

Cayambe peaks (best views in early morning). The Ministry of Agriculture also maintains a research station/visitors' centre on the lake shore, open 0800-1600 every day. The restaurant on the lake shore, *Muelle*, has been renovated with a dining room overlooking the lake, rooms for rent, clean, moderate prices. Nearby is *El Mirador* with food, excellent view. Motor boats can be hired for groups of five or more. The slopes of Cerro Cotacachi, N from the lake, are a nature reserve. From Otavalo or Ibarra take Cotacachi bus (US$0.10), and try to get a truck or colectivo to Lake Cuicocha from Cotacachi, US$1.60, one way; they await the buses from Otavalo. The 3-hr. walk back to Cotacachi is beautiful; after 1 km. on the road from the park entrance, turn left (at the first bend) onto the old road. You can also walk from Otavalo (Instituto Geográfico 1:50,000 or 100,000 maps recommended).

Warning Many people have been badly poisoned by eating the blue berries which grow near the lake. They are *not* blueberries; they render the eater helpless within 2 hrs., requiring at least a stomach pump.

Also off the main road between Otavalo and Ibarra is **San Antonio de Ibarra,** well known for its wood carvings, most of which are now reported to be either "cheap and nasty or expensive and tasteless". For the exceptions, visit the workshop of Moreo Santacruz, and the exhibition of Osvaldo Garrido in the Palacio de Arte. Luís Potosí's gallery on the main square has some beautiful carvings. (Buses from Ibarra, 13 km., ten mins.)

John Streather recommends a visit to **Apuela**, in the lush tropical valley of the Zona del Inca (*Pensión Apuela*, G, grim; small restaurant) for the thermal baths of Nungulví nearby (1 hr. walk). Apuela buses from Otavalo on a good new road (6 a day) pass Nungulví, where the swimming pool is emptied for cleaning on Tues. and Fri. About 2 hrs. drive (bumpy track) from Ibarra are the clean, hot mineral swimming pools of Cachimbiro in the parish of Tumbariro. Buses there reportedly run only at weekends; enquire in Ibarra.

Ibarra, founded 1606, at 2,225 metres, population 80,000, is a pleasant colonial town with some good hotels. Local festival, Fiesta de los Lagos, last weekend of September, Thurs.-Sun.; also July 16, Virgen del Carmen. Some interesting paintings are to be seen in the church of Santo Domingo and its museum.

Hotels The better class hotels tend to be fully booked during Holy Week. S on Quito road; *Hostería San Agustín*, E, beautiful location, clean, friendly, hot water; *Hostería Chorlavi*, off highway 2 km. S of Ibarra, D, US$2.10 per extra bed, rec., swimming pool open to non-residents, US$0.30, elegant surroundings of converted *hacienda*, Sun. excellent buffet, folk music and crafts, discotheque at weekends; nearer town, *Ajavi*, D, very good restaurant; *Residencial Madrid*, E, Olmedo 857 near main plaza, clean, comfortable; *Imbabura*, Oviedo 9-33, G, pretty and pleasant; *Residencial Familiar*, Moncayo 726 y Olmedo, E, clean and good; *Los Alpes*, E, Velasco 732 y Bolívar, clean with private bath; *Pensión San Lorenzo*, Olmedo 1056, F, no hot water, clean; *Residencial Astoria*, G, Velasco 809, hot water, safe, can store luggage, friendly, basic, not very clean, upper rooms have beautiful view, large terrace, laundry facilities; *Residencial Colón*, G, Narváez 5257 y Velasco, F (more with bath), pleasant, clean, friendly, laundry facilities, will change money. *Residencial El Príncipe*, Sánchez y Cifuentes 882, G, basic but clean, restaurant. Several others, F and G, along Bolívar, Moncayo and Olmedo.

Restaurants *Hostería Chorlavi* restaurant rec. (but it is crowded with tour buses on Sat. lunchtime), likewise *Hotel Ajavi. El Chagra*, Olmedo 7-48, rec., reasonable prices; *Marisquería Las Redes*, Oviedo 572 y Sucre, seafood, clean, good, breakfast for US$1, accept US$ at top rate. Good breakfast and excellent bread at *Café Pushkin*, Olmedo 7-75 and at *Mejor Pan*, Olmedo 7-52. *El Caribe*, Flores 757, chicken and local food, excellent three-course set meal for US$0.60. *Chifa Muy Buena*, Olmedo 723, does a good Chaulafan; *El Dorado*, Oviedo y Sucre, seafood, good, expensive, snacks; *Portón de Sevilla*, Oviedo 764, seafood; *Caldera del Diablo*, G. Moreno 443, cafetería, snackbar, good; *Koco Rico*, Olmedo 724, and *Asadero a las Doradas*, Oviedo 720, both chicken; *La Estancia*, García Moreno 7-66, very good grill but not cheap. *Los Helados*, Calle 27, near main plaza, for good ice cream; also *Heladería La Nevada*, Velasco 837. *Pan Danés*, Carrera 9, 7-93 y Calle 28, real coffee. Local specialities are sweets made from walnuts, blackberries (arrope de mora) and other fruits, and nougat (nogada).

Exchange Banco Continental, Cifuentes y Moncayo, changes travellers' cheques. *Las Redes* restaurant and *Residencial Colón* will change US$ notes.

Immigration Olmedo y L.F.Villamar (T 951-712), very quick for extensions.

Tourist Office Dituris, Liborio Madero y Flores (Radio Punto building). Also, travel agency, Itipungo, Rocafuerte y García Moreno and Bolívar 4-43, friendly.

Things to Do Museo Fray Pedro (open 0900-1200, 1500-1800, US$0.15, closed Sun.), Santo Domingo church, religious art. Balneario Primavera, Sánchez y Cifuentes 323, pool, sauna, turkish bath. *Peña Folklórica* at Poncho Libre, Olmedo 935. Piano bar, *El Encuentro*, Olmedo 953. A unique form of paddle ball is played on Sat. and Sun. near the railway station, also on way from bus station to centre, on left, just before the built-up area. The players have huge spiked paddles for striking the 2 lb. ball. On weekdays they play a similar game with a lighter ball.

Bus to Quito 3 hrs., US$1.25, about 50 departures a day. Colectivo taxis for about double. To Yahuarcocha, US$1. To Tulcán, US$1, 2½ hrs. To Otavalo, ½ hr. Bus station is 1 km. S of town, reached by bus No. 2 from centre.

Excursions Alexander Tkany, of Karlsruhe, recommends a visit to Guachara, NW of Ibarra, reached by bus from Ibarra railway station (US$0.10), or by train from Ibarra to Carchi and then bus. Tourists unknown, people friendly, mountains beautiful and hitch-hiking very possible. A pretty village to visit close to Ibarra, 10 km. directly south on the road to Olmedo, is **La Esperanza**, in beautiful surroundings with an Inca road which goes to Cayambe. Accommodation: *Casa Aída*, F, basic, Aída speaks some English and cooks vegetarian food. (Bus from Ibarra passes *Aída*.) Eugenio makes leather clothes cheaply to measure; e.g. US$60 for trousers. One particular lady does extremely fine embroidery; ask in village for her house. You can climb Cuilche volcano in 2 hours from La Esperanza for beautiful views; from the top you can walk down to Laguna de San Pablo.

At edge of **Yahuarcocha Lake** are *Parador El Conquistador*, 8 rooms, D, large restaurant, rec., run by Dituris, and *Hotel del Lago*, no accommodation, only refreshments.

It is possible to walk to Lake Yahuarcocha (4 km.) in about 1½ hrs. Follow Calle 27 to the end of town, cross the river and walk to the right at the first junction. At the end of this road there is a small path going steeply uphill. There are beautiful views of Ibarra and then from the top of the hill over the Lake surrounded by mountains and the village of the same name. Yahuarcocha, "bloody lake" in Quechua, named because legend says that the water turned red when the Incas threw in the bodies of the defeated Otavalo Indians. There are frequent buses back to Ibarra from the village. The beauty of the lake has been disfigured by the building of a motor-racing circuit round its shores.

Laguna Puruanta, 45 km. SE of Ibarra on Río Pisque, can be visited by bus to Pinampiro (US$0.40, 1 hr.), then walk to San Francisco de Sigsipamba (15 km.) and on trails from there to the Laguna. Return to Ibarra via Mariano de Acosta to complete 2-day excursion.

A 193 km. railway runs from Ibarra to the port of San Lorenzo (**see page 642**), N of Esmeraldas. An *autoferro* runs at least once a day at 0700 (check the day before), taking from 9 to 12 hrs. (US$1.75). The train is very crowded. You need to queue up at 0600 for the tickets and push like mad. Sit on the right side of the train: the track is on the left side of the valley down to San Lorenzo. The track is in very poor condition and lengthy delays and derailments are common.

Leaving Ibarra, the train descends past Salinas into the narrow gorge of the Río Mira (called Chota upstream) inhabited by blacks growing fruit and sugar cane, who sell fruit at the station (the train stops for 5 mins. for breakfast). After three hours the valley widens near Collapi (730 metres) and the land becomes better watered and has been more recently colonized. Lita (460 metres) is reached after five hours and a stop is made for refreshment (train returns from here at 1300—all foreigners' passports are checked at Lita). Through the lowlands cultivated land becomes commoner until we reach San Lorenzo.

North of Ibarra the Pan-American Highway goes past Lake Yahuarcocha, and descends to cross the Chota valley. The Highway divides in the valley, and you can go to Tulcán either via El Angel over a long stretch of *páramo* or, like most of the heavy vehicles, further east over eroded hill sides via San Gabriel (see below). On the El Angel road at the village of Chota and on the San Gabriel road at El Juncal, the highway descends to a mere 1,520 metres; in the tropical Chota valley you can buy excellent fruit from the local blacks, descendants of slaves brought from Africa in the 17th century by Jesuits to farm their estates. The El Angel route is still heavy going; the San Gabriel route is a good paved road but is subject to landslides, when the traveller is taken over poorly marked or unmarked dirt roads.

About 20 mins. to the west, off the El Angel road, is the town of **Mira** (pop. 5,000; bus from Ibarra, US$0.55, 1 hour). Some of the finest quality woollens come from this part of the country; there are two women in Mira who produce them for export and a cooperative which sells in the town at export prices. There are two carnivals held each year, on February 2, and August 18, with fireworks and free flowing Tardón, the local *aguardiente*. There is a clean *residencia* (*Mira*, F), but very few restaurants; the best is the *Bar Latino*. Stretches of virgin rain and cloud forest along the River Mira are accessible to the adventurous.

John Streather writes: **San Gabriel** (pop. 13,000) is a good place from which to visit the **Gruta de la Paz**, about 10 km. to the south, on the way to Bolívar. (Buses from Ibarra, Mira—US$0.50, 1hr.— and Tulcán; *Hotel Inti Huasi* and *Restaurant Oasis* on opposite sides of main plaza). (If you are driving, the road branches off the Panamerican at the village of La Paz. The sign says 7 km. to "Grutas", but it is more like 4 km., on a cobblestone road which leads down into mosquito country, but with beautiful views and at least two thundering waterfalls.) There is a huge hotel, but it only opens sporadically and unpredictably—mainly for religious conferences. Buy tickets (US$0.20) for the hot showers and warm swimming pool from the convent before going down to the grotto, near which are the showers and the pool, which is only open from Thur. to Sun. inclusive. There is a restaurant of sorts on the bridge above the grotto. To get back to the main road, cadge a lift!— very long walk. There is a weekly excursion to the Gruta de la Paz from Tulcán.

Tulcán is a chilly town of 33,000 people at an altitude of 2,960 metres, the centre of a rich farming area. It is not particularly interesting for the tourist except for the famous cemetery, where the topiarist's art reaches its apogee; bushes are trimmed into fantastic figures of animals, plants, geometrical shapes etc. Camera essential (take bus from terminal). Ecuador's unique form of paddleball is played every afternoon by the south side of the cemetery.

The migration office is situated at the border at Rumichaca, so all exit formalities are carried out there. The office and the border are open 0900-1800 with skeleton staff at lunch-time (if not closed till 1400). US citizens, Australians and New Zealanders need a visa to enter both Ecuador and Colombia and most nationalities a tourist card to enter Colombia, which can be obtained at the Colombian Consulate, Bolívar 54-076 y Junín (closed 1230-1430). Two photos and an onward ticket or MCO are needed. Colombian entry stamp is given at the border. Because of the high volume of local traffic, border crossing is fairly relaxed. Coming from Colombia into Ecuador, entrance stamp is given at the border. If entering Ecuador by car, fumigation costs US$1.50 and *carnet* must be stamped at the border. When leaving Ecuador by car, some travellers have not needed to go into Tulcán, whereas others have had to return to the town for customs formalities. Immigration office is at the border. A new 4-km. highway leads from Tulcán to the border. The old road descends tortuously for 6½ km. through the mountains to the River Carchi, on the border, which is crossed by the natural bridge of Rumichaca (*Parador de Rumichaca*, D, pool, restaurant, casino, discotheque) and a new concrete bridge. Ipiales is 1½ km. beyond the bridge. Airport between Tulcán and border, Mon.-Fri. TAME flight to Quito at 1400, US$6; there is a TAME office in Tulcán in the basement of *Hotel Azteca*, Bolívar y García Morena.

Hotels Quito, Ayacucho 450, G, clean, central; *San Francisco*, F, Bolívar y Atahualpa, ask for a key, clean; *Al Paso*, in centre, E; **Pensión Minerva**, G, 10 de Agosto y Bolívar, clean but cold; annex in centre, F, overpriced; *Residencial Carchi*, G, Sucre 576 y Pichincha, friendly, no hot water; *Residencial Oasis*, F, 10 de Agosto 395 y Sucre, private showers; *El Paso*, F, Sucre y Pichincha, communal shower sometimes has hot water. **Res. Ecuador**, opp. bus station, F, hot water, clean but poor bathrooms; *Avenida*, also opp. bus station, G, no hot water, clean; *Mallorca*, F, two blocks north of main plaza, friendly, hot water, but thin walls. If all are full (which they tend to be at weekends), try police station.

Restaurants Avenida, Bolívar y Ecuador, opp. bus station; *Terminal*, in bus station, reasonable. Many along Sucre: *Restaurant El Paso*, Chinese, good; and other *chifas*. **Parrilladas**, Roberto Sierran y Bolívar, good typical food, near cemetery; **Max Pan** for good breakfasts. Good cheeseburgers at *Café de la Rueda* just off main square.

Camping Possible at the sports field next to the cemetery.

Transport Taxi to border, US$2; to Ipiales, US$4, however many people share it. Bus, if you can get one, is cheaper, US$0.15. Bus to Quito 5 hrs., US$2.25, about 100 a day; to Ibarra, 2½ hrs., US$1. Otavalo, US$1.40, 3 hrs. (make sure bus is going to Otavalo; if not get out on the Highway at the turn off). To Guayaquil, 20 a day, 11 hrs., US$5. Plenty of colectivos also. Bus terminal is long uphill walk from centre; best to take taxi or little blue bus.

Exchange Those travelling from Ecuador into Colombia should change all their sucres into dollars before they reach the frontier, making sure they bargain for a good rate; this is better at Tulcán than at Ipiales, where you can get only Colombian pesos. Bad rates at bus station. There are many money changers who will exchange cash on both sides of the border. Travellers' cheques are reportedly difficult to exchange, but try Rodríguez Paz Casa de Cambio, on Ayacucho in front of *Hotel Quito*, or Carlos Burbano, Bolívar y Junín. For those arriving in Ecuador, change only what you need to get to Quito, where the rate is better. Banco de los Andes, Sucre y Junín, is the only bank which will undertake foreign currency transactions (cash only).

Excursions Weekly minibus trips with Cooperativa 11 de Abril, US$2 return, from opp. *Hotel Carchi*, to Gruta de la Paz (see above) at 0800 on Sats., and to Aguas Hediondas at 0800 on Suns. (leaves only if enough passengers). There are 3 daily buses from opp. Colegio Tulcán, near the cemetery, 0600, 0630, 0900, to Maldonado, passing Tufiño, 1 hr. From Tufiño walk 2 km. to turnoff for Aguas Hediondas, then 6 km. to springs themselves. You can probably hitch back to Tufiño. (Taxi Tulcán-Aguas Hediondas, US$6, including one hour wait.) John Streather tells us that Aguas Hediondas (stinking waters) is a pool of boiling sulphurous mineral waters in a wild, impressive, lonely valley. An ice-cold stream of melted snow water passes nearby—one needs to direct it into the pool to make it cool enough to enter! These waters are said to cure spots, rheumatism, etc. If one takes one's passport one can walk from Tufiño over the border to the various hot, warm and cold mineral baths, with a restaurant (friendly and cheap) about 2 km. away in Colombia (the public baths are free but not very clean, the private ones are clean and cost only US$0.20). One can spend the morning at these baths and return to Ecuador for the 1400 bus back to Tulcán, so long as the passport is shown at the border (a rope over the village street). There are five pools at Tufiño—the top, hot, one is good for liver and kidneys, the one below the restaurant for the nerves and rheumatism. The cold pool is some distance from the four others which are all close together. The landscape and the plants on the way up to Aguas Hediondas are really marvellous.

Another, longer but rewarding, trip from Tulcán is to go down to the hot jungle riverside town of Maldonado—same bus as for Tufiño—small *pensiones*, good swimming. The road to Maldonado passes the foot of the trail to the Chiles volcano. On the way up you see many Frailejón plants (related to the Puya Raimondii of Peru and found also in Venezuela).

THE NORTHERN AND WESTERN LOWLANDS (3)

From Quito, a scenic bus trip can be taken to (129 km. US$1.05, 2½ hrs.) *Santo Domingo de los Colorados,* in the W lowlands (pop. 66,661). There is a small daily market and a large Sun. market, but very few Indians now come to the town so both it and the market itself are unexciting and scruffy. You would do better to hire a taxi and go to their villages to see the Colorados (about US$10 for 1½ hrs). Very few of them now wear the traditional hair dress. Santo Domingo, now the hub of roads radiating to Quito, Guayaquil (by bus 5 hrs.), Esmeraldas (bus, 4 hrs.—the road is very bad N of Rosa Zárate) and Manta, once had the boom town air of the American west a century ago, but is now dusty, noisy, and decaying. Shops in the town are open Tues.-Sun., and banks Tues.-Sat. There is a cinema.

Carnival water throwing is particularly vigorous in Santo Domingo.

Hotels *Zaracay,* C, 2 km. out of town on the road to Quito, restaurant (disappointing), casino, gardens and a swimming pool, good rooms and service, best available, advisable to book, especially at weekend. On the same road, 20 km. from Santo Domingo, is *Tinalandia*, pleasant and small, C, with its own golf course, and excellent food. Many species of birds, flowers and butterflies in the woods behind the *hostal.* Poorly signposted, take small road between Km. 16 and 17 from Santo Domingo on the right (for cheaper accommodation near *Tinalandia*, *Florida* in Alluriquín, 7 km. away on main road, F, with swimming pool). Nearer the town centre, still on the Quito road, is *Victoria,* F, basic, restaurant, rec.; *Caleta,* Ibarra 137, E, good restaurant, private bath, good; *Colorado,* 29 de Mayo y Quininde, F, a bit noisy; two *Hostales Turistas, No. 1* at 3 de Julio y Latacunga and *No. 2* at Ambato y 29 de Mayo, both F with bath (hot water); *Hostal San José,* G, clean, Latacunga y 3 de Julio; *Pensión Don Pepe,* Calle Quito, F, clean, friendly, quiet. *Residencial Madrid,* G, Av. 3 de Julio 438, good and clean but used as a brothel and many rooms without windows.

Restaurants *Parrilladas Argentinas*, Chilenas, on Quevedo road Km. 5, for good barbecues. *Mocambo*, Tulcán y Machala, good; *La Fuente*, Ibarra y 3 de Julio, good; *Rico Pollo*, Quito y Río Pove, for chicken; two *chifas*, *Nuevo Hongkong* and *Nueva China*, on the Parque Zaracay; *Corea*, 3 de Julio y San Miguel. Several snackbars and pizzerias.

Exchange Banco Internacional, Esmeraldas y Quito.

Immigration Camilo Ponce (police station), T 750-225.

A busy paved highway connects Santo Domingo de los Colorados with Esmeraldas to the North (**see page 640**), and *Quevedo* (78,000 people) to the South (1½ hrs. by bus). Set in fertile banana lands and often flooded in the rainy season, Quevedo is known as the Chinatown of Ecuador, with a fair-sized Chinese colony. It is a dusty, noisy, crowded town which has grown exceptionally rapidly over the last 25 years.

Hotels None offers a quiet night. *Olímpico*, Bolívar y 19a, D, good restaurant, near stadium; *Ejecutivo Internacional*, E, 7 de Octubre y Calle Cuarta, modern, large rooms, a/c, private bath, good value, clean, the least noisy; *Guayaquil* opposite is a brothel, basic, G. *El Cóndor*, E with a/c, F without; *El Turista*, F. All are on, or near Av. 7 de Octubre and the plaza.

Restaurants *Hotel Olímpico*, best. Most others along 7 de Octubre: *Rincón Caleño* (Colombian), 1103; *Chifa 51* (Chinese), 928; other *chifas* at 806, 809 and 707; *Tungurahua* (local food), 711. Snackbar, *Quevedo City*, Bolívar y 4a.

Roads and Buses Quevedo is an important route centre. The old paved highway from Latacunga in the highlands to Portoviejo and Manta in the lowlands carries very little traffic, but for a leisurely traveller it is the most beautiful of the routes connecting the highlands with the coast. (Bus, Quevedo-Latacunga, Cotopaxi line, 4 hrs., US$1.50. Bus (*chiva*), Quevedo-Portoviejo, from 7 de Octubre and Calle 8, 5 hrs., US$1.40, watch your possessions, uncomfortable.) On this road is the *Selva Negra* hotel, basic accommodation, but excellent food.

Quevedo is connected with Guayaquil by two paved highways (bus, 3 hrs., US$1.25), one through Balzar and Daule, one through Babahoyo (41,000 people). The roads give a good idea of tropical Ecuador, with its exotic birdlife and jungle and plantations of cacao, sugar, bananas, oranges, tropical fruits and rice. To Quito, 4 hrs., US$1.80.

Popular beach resorts of the Western lowlands can be reached along a paved highway (toll) from Guayaquil. The road divides at Progreso (63 km.). One branch leads to Villamil, normally known as *Playas,* the nearest seaside resort to Guayaquil (2 hrs. by frequent bus—US$1). Its old charm as a fishing village has gone, although every day single-sailed balsa rafts can still be seen among the motor launches returning laden with fish. These rafts are unique, highly ingenious and very simple. The beaches shelve gently, but have been destroyed by hotel construction. As an alternative to the main beach take the unsurfaced road going north which leads to a long sandy beach backed by salt flats and giant cactus. Ecuadoreans flock to the sea from January to April and traffic is very heavy along the coastal roads. Anyone who goes to the beach in May-December will have it largely to himself, except on Sundays.

Hotels *Residencial Cattan,* sea view, D with good food, E without; *Miraglia*, F, run down but clean, sea view, seawater showers, fresh drinking water; *Playas*, E, beach hotel with seawater showers and plain rooms without fans or a/c, good restaurant; also with sea view in E range, *Rey David* and *Acapulco;* *El Galeón*, E, beside the church, friendly, clean, mosquito nets, water all day, cheap restaurant with excellent seafood attached; *Turístico*, F, just off square, clean, mosquito nets; *Hostería La Gaviota*, 500 metres out on Posorja road, D, colour TV, a/c, but rooms shabby with cockroaches, friendly, good clean restaurant. *Residencial California*, and *Restaurant Jalisco* nearby, good cheap food. *Hostería Costa Verde*, cheap, clean, F. Camping at S end of beach. Casino.

There is a water shortage all along the coast; drinking water has to be brought by tanker from Guayaquil and no hotel can guarantee water in the rooms at all times. There are showers on the beach.

An interesting place to visit, a walk or short drive from Playas, is the little village of El Morro. There is a picturesque wooden church and a large rock formation known as El Muerto. Beyond Playas lies *Posorja*, at the mouth of the Guayas estuary, home to a large commercial fishing fleet and fish processing plants. The ocean front is rubbish-strewn and muddy. Posorja and other coastal towns are receiving a population influx because of the economic boom caused by shrimp farming. Local people catch young shrimp in the sea and estuaries and sell them to large commercial ponds where they are grown to market size. From Esmeraldas to Machala, the ocean front is being transformed by shrimp farming. Native mangrove swamps are being destroyed rapidly; heavy construction equipment can be seen everywhere.

West of Progreso the road to Salinas runs through a vast area of arid thorn-scrub land whose inhabitants look very Indian and produce little besides charcoal. At **Santa Elena** the road forks. To the left, south, we pass a petroleum refinery and enter the busy port and regional market centre of *La Libertad* (*Hotel Villa María*, G, very run down, on Malecón, as are *Lido* and *Seven Seas*, both G, mediocre;

Hostería Samarina, E, Dituris-run, some bungalows, swimming pool, restaurant, coffee shop, bar; *Hotel Turis Palm*, Av. 9 de Octubre, F, fan, bath—G without, older place and a bit run down, next door and similar is *Reina del Pacífico*). Buses every hour to Manglaralto, Puerto López and Jipijapa from near market.

A few km. further on is **Salinas,** the self-styled best resort in Ecuador (population, 21,000, buses from Guayaquil, US$1, at the new Terminal Terrestre about 2½ hrs.; return journey, go to La Libertad by bus or colectivo and take bus from terminal there). The beaches are not good and the town is becoming increasingly more developed; it is very quiet outside the holiday season. The flat-topped hill at Punta Santa Elena dominates the landscape. Good deep-sea fishing and water-skiing. Pesca Tours, on the seafront, rents boats for US$250; four lines from the boat, you may keep any dorado you catch but Pesca Tours keeps the marlin. Car racing at the Autódromo.

Hotels   *Salinas*, D, modern, off Malecón, restaurant reported good; *Miramar,* with casino, B, with bath and telephone. *Samarina*, C, or US$32 bungalow with 6 beds, acceptable; *Cantábrico*, D, lines of hammocks outside, 4-course set meal; *Yulee,* D, with own bath (but try bargaining), clean, excellent food, friendly, well placed for beaches; *Residencial Rachel*, 2 blocks from beach, E, mosquito nets inadequate; *Herminia*, very basic, G, close to beaches but no running water.

Restaurants   *Saavedra* rec. for large portions of well cooked fish for about US$1.50. *Mar y Tierra*, close to *Hotel Miramar*, expensive but excellent seafood, especially lobster; also near the *Miramar* is *Flipper*, cheap, simple, clean and friendly. Discothèque, *El Caracol*. Night club, *Che Papusa* (near town hall), normally known after its owner as *Donde el Roy*.

Exchange It is not possible to change travellers cheques' in Salinas. Not all banks change cash; you can change cash at the supermarket and the *Hotel Salinas* but the rate is bad.

Cables   Ietel public telex booth at Radio Internacional.

At Baños San Vicente, about 7 km. E. of La Libertad, just off the main road to Guayaquil, Dituris has opened a large tourist complex, where for US$0.30 admission you have use of the whole facility, including swimming pools, thermal baths and a mud hole to cure assorted ailments. There is still more construction work to be done; a hotel is planned when finance is available.

Punta Carnero is on the S shore of the Santa Elena peninsula. Magnificent 15-km. beach with wild surf and heavy undertow, virtually empty during the week. To the E of Punta Carnero, along the coast, lies Anconcito, a picturesque fishing port at the foot of steep cliffs, but nowhere at all to stay; further on is Ancón, centre of the declining local oilfield.

The northward fork of the road at Santa Elena leads us along the coast (past Ballenita, pleasant beach, surfing with two good *ceviche* restaurants, cottages can be rented) as far north as La Entrada. Manta can be reached by going inland from La Entrada via Jipijapa. Part of the road is along the beach and therefore fast, but care should be taken as the tide rises fast and suddenly. La Entrada can be reached in less than 5 hrs. from Guayaquil, and because of this a number of attractive fishing villages along this stretch of coast contain the modern bungalows of Guayaquileños. Almost all the villages have good beaches, and there is particularly good swimming near the attractive fishing villages of Palmar and Ayangue (latter crowded at week-ends). Many kinds of cactus are found in this area because of the dry climate (fewer than five days of rain a year). A typical dish from this region is *sopa de bola de verde*, made from several kinds of vegetable: green *plátano* is crushed, kneaded and formed into balls filled with green peas and diced carrots.

At Valdivia, a small port, is the site of the supposed Japanese-Jomón culture contact, via fishermen, about 3000 B.C. Little for the visitor to see; the little museum is closed; most artefacts discovered at the site are in museums in Quito and Guayaquil. A visit to the archaeological dig at Salango, 5 km. south of Puerto López, is recommended. Some beautiful artefacts have been found, all of which are housed in a museum around which the mainly English archaeologists (voluntary and qualified) are happy to show travellers. There are two new restaurants in the village, and a nearby complex of bamboo houses was under construction in 1988.

Manglaralto, the main centre of the region north of Santa Elena, is reached by bus from Guayaquil (change at La Libertad) as well as by numerous trucks. 3 km. N, at Montañita beach, reported best surfing in Ecuador, cottages to let (Gabriela rents tents), 2 hrs., US$0.70, by bus or truck from La Libertad or Santa Elena.

Hotels   *Alegre Calamar*, N end of town, F, good seafood restaurant; *Corona del Mar* restaurant has rooms, F, shared bath, and a bungalow for rent. Sra. de Arcos' house next to post office; also *Habitaciones* next to post office, F with bath, clean, friendly. It is a nice place to stay and bathe, with a good, quiet, clean beach, but little shelter. *Comedor Familiar* has meals weekends only; also *Comedor Florencia*, cheap and friendly.

North of Manglaralto the rainfall increases and at La Entrada the road peters out in the wet season (Dec.-Feb.; July-Sept.). A bumpy ride takes one from Manglaralto through lush tropical scenery to **Puerto López**, set in an impressive bay with hills on either side. Buses often cannot make it all the way, be prepared for a muddy walk to complete your journey. The main attraction is the arrival of the fishermen at 0800 and again at 1630. The whole town seems to assemble on the beach to greet the hordes of small boats and buy the fish. It seems to be easy to go out with the fishermen in their boats. Next to the sports field is a small museum with information on the nearby Parque Nacional Machalilla.

Lodging and food   *Residencial El Pacífico*, F, on sea front, clean, basic, but insecure; *Residencial Soroya*, one street W, G; *Restaurant Viña del Mar* rents rooms next door, F, good, cheap food. Restaurant on sea front, next to *Carmita* (now closed), serves good ceviche and cold beer; *Acapulco* restaurant on main street, video shows nightly at 1930.

Buses   1½ hrs., US$1, hourly to Jipijapa. To La Libertad, 2½ hrs., US$1; to Manglaralto, 2 hrs., US$1.

A new dirt road has been made from Manglaralto to the main Guayaquil-Manta road. This road climbs into the humid hills of S Manabí, then descends to the dry savanna scrub around **Jipijapa** (27,500 inhabitants), an important centre for the region's farmers, trading cotton, fruit and kapok (from the fat-trunked ceiba tree). (*Pensión Mejía*, F, 2 blocks from plaza, clean, basic, noisy. Bus from Manglaralto, 2½ hrs., US$1.75.) Thirty-two km. across dusty hills is **Montecristi** (8,190 people), below an imposing hill, high enough to be watered by low cloud which gives the region its only source of drinking water. The town is also famous for its Panama hats which, along with cane-work products, are much cheaper than in Quito.

Soon after, we reach **Manta** (100,000 people), the main commercial centre of western Ecuador, a noisy, busy, and dirty town with steep streets and a fine wooden church. With its twin town, Tarqui, it has the largest population W of Guayaquil. The Tarqui beaches are reported to be good for sunbathing and swimming, but watch your belongings. Fishing boats are built on the beach. The beach at the Manta end is smelly, but fairly quiet, with moderate surf. The Banco Central museum, Calle 9 y Av. 4, has interesting specimens of the Huancavilca-Manteña culture (AD 800-1550); open during banking hours, curator speaks English and French. Sites can be visited from Bahía de Caráquez. All streets have been given numbers; those above 100 are in Tarqui.

Hotels   *Las Gaviotas*, Malecón y Calle 106, E, on beach, a/c, restaurant, tennis; *Manta Imperial*, D, Calles Playa y Murciélago, on beach, a/c, disco and dancing; *Haddad Manabí*, Av. 105 y Calle 103, E, on the beach in Tarqui; *Panorama Inn*, Calle 103 y Av. 105, E, a/c, bath, TV, rec., swimming pool and restaurant; *Residencial Las Mantas*, G, Calle 12 y Av. 8, dirty, unfriendly. Also on Tarqui beach, *Residencial Eugenia*, Malecón y Calle 105, F, safe, comfortable, hot water, clean; *Miami*, Malecón y Calle 107, F, private bath, good; *Residencial Niza*, Malecón y Calle 103, G, restaurant, shared bath, clean, pleasant. *Residencial Capri*, near bus station, G, good value.

Restaurants   Cheap restaurants by Tarqui market, Av. 108 y Calle 102; and on the nearby beach. *El Ceibo*, in the centre, is rec. *El Boulevard* on Tarqui beach near the Plaza Tarqui, good fish and seafood, reasonably priced; *La Cascada*, Av. 105 y Calle 103, cafetería with swimming pool; *Georgie*, Calle 16 y Av. 7, good fish, cheap. *Pelícan*, Malecón y Calle 105; *El Shirley*, *Playero* and *Costa Mar* seafood places nearby. In centre, *Andes* Cafetería, Av. 1 y Calle 12, and *La Choza*, Calle 13 y Av. 7.

Post Office   above Banco de Pichincha; **Telephone** Ietel on road to the beach.

Tourist Office Dituris, Edificio Emapa. **Travel Agents** Ecuadorian Tours, at Av. 2 y Calle 13; Metropolitan Touring at Av. 3 y Calle 12.

Immigration Av. 4 de Noviembre y J-1 (police station).

Exchange *Casa de Cambio* Zanchi, Banco de Pichincha and Banco del Pacífico change travellers' cheques.

Air Service Eloy Alfaro airport nearby. Every day by Tame to Quito, US$12, every day except Sun. to Guayaquil, US$9.

Buses To Quito, 8 hrs., US$3; Guayaquil, 3½ hrs., US$2; Esmeraldas, 8 hrs., US$3; Santo Domingo, 6 hrs., US$2.10; Portoviejo, ½ hr., US$0.30; Jipijapa, 45 mins., US$0.45; Bahía de Caráquez, 3 hrs., US$1. All from bus station.

24 km. inland from Montecristi is **Portoviejo** (101,771 inhabitants), a major commercial centre with connections by road with Quito and Guayaquil.

Hotels *París,* off main plaza, E; *Residencial Maroles,* 2 Av./Calle 1, F, friendly, noisy. *Cristal,* Calle Ricaurte 106, F; *San Marcos,* Olmedo y 9 de Octubre; The restaurant *Chifa China* on the plaza has a clean, cheap hotel upstairs; good Chinese restaurant at bus terminal.

From Portoviejo a road goes E to Quevedo (147 km). At Calderón, branch NE for Calceta, Chone (36,000 people) and on to Santo Domingo de los Colorados. From Calceta and Chone paved roads run 50 km. to **Bahía de Caráquez** (13,000 people), a tranquil town in a pleasant setting on the seaward southern end of an inlet; the river front is attractively laid out, but there are water shortages except in the hotels with their own supply. Smart new homes fringe the seaward side. The town is a centre of banana and other agricultural exports. On Isla de los Pájaros in the bay are many seabirds; launches can be hired to visit mangrove islands.

Hotels *Herradura,* Bolívar y Malecón (beach), D, good restaurant; *Centro Vocacional "Life°,* Dávila y García Moreno, D, full board; *Americano,* Ascazubi y Morales, C with a/c and bath; *Manabí,* nearby, G, clean and friendly; *Residencial Vera,* Ante y Bolívar, F, with bath and mosquito net, noisy, own water; *Palma,* Bolívar y Arenas, G, clean; cheap but dirty restaurant next door.

Restaurants Brisas del Mar, good fish, cheap; *Los Helecheros,* cafetería, good and clean, Bolívar y Malecón; *Chifa China,* cheap, good, Bolívar y Ascazubi.

Tourist Office Centro Vocacional "Life", T 690-496: the local coordinator, Sr. Darío Proaño Leroux, is friendly and helpful.

Bus from Bahía de Caráquez to Quito, 8 hrs., US$3.20, Esmeraldas, 8 hrs., and Portoviejo, 2 hrs., with Reina del Camino. To Guayaquil, 5½ hrs., US$2.80; to Manta, 3 hrs., US$1.

Airport at San Vicente (see below): Air Transportes Bahía flies twice a day to Guayaquil, US$14, with connections to Pedernales (US$5.50).

Those interested in exploring the coast further north can take the ferry (every 15 mins., US$0.13, also car ferry) from Bahía de Caráquez to **San Vicente,** on the far side of the Río Chone, a thriving market (*Hotel Vacaciones,* E, restaurant, TV in rooms; about 3 km. from San Vicente are *Cabañas La Playa,* US$20 for beach chalet sleeping 5, good food in restaurant; other *cabañas* on beach), and on by bus, truck or car north along the beach to Canoa, thence inland, cutting across Cape Pasado through the more humid pasture-lands to the small market centre of **Jama** (small *pensión*).

From there the road runs parallel to the beach past coconut groves, inland across some low hills and across the Equator to **Pedernales,** another small market town on the coast, bus from San Vicente (4 daily), 7 hrs., US$3.50; several houses where you can stay, a friendly spot (*Hotel Turismo,* G, clean, helpful; *Cabañas Cañaverales,* F; *Playas,* friendly, clean; *Residencial Comedor El Gitano,* F, meals, friendly) and 2 or 3 eating places. A rough new road has been finished between Pedernales and El Carmen (thence to Sto. Domingo and Quito)—the two towns are expected to become booming tourist resorts—and on to Cojimíes (enquire if passable in rainy season).

Buses—one or two a day—use the beach at low tide, take 7 hrs. from San Vicente (US$3.50), 45 mins. from Pedernales (truck US$0.50) to **Cojimíes** (*Residenciales España,* G, shabby, no water; *Mi Descanso* and *Cojimíes*—all look the same; *Hotel Coco Solo* is 14 km. before Cojimíes, D, overpriced, nice but no services and no choice in restaurant. Flower-decorated house on same street will serve meals at any hour; other houses serve food; one restaurant. Cojimíes was a major pre-conquest centre; little of this is noticeable now, although many artefacts are still dug up, it is being continually eroded by the sea and has been moved about three times in as many decades. A boat leaves at high tide every Sat. for Esmeraldas, stopping at Chamanga (US$4, 7 hrs.) and one from Esmeraldas on Sat. as well. There is a boat to Manta on Wed. and a direct canoe to Muisné (US$4) at 0600, 2 hrs. The entry into Cojimíes and Muisné is treacherous and many boats have been thrown into the shallows by swell.

North of Cojimíes is a rich banana-growing region. **Muisné,** an island reached by road from

Esmeraldas (bus US$1, 3 hrs., and a canoe over to the island), is the centre and main outlet of this area; through it some 50,000 stems of bananas a month are exported via Esmeraldas. On the Río Sucio, inland from Muisné and Cojimíes, is an isolated group of Cayapa Indians, some of whom visit the towns on Sun. All hotels F, but women should avoid *Residencial Narcisita*; we have been warned of sexual attacks by the owner; *Sarita*, F, has been rec., clean, fan, mosquito nets, private bathroom; you can also rent small huts on the beach, F, electric light, some with water, beautiful setting, beaches nearby and simple seafood *comedores*. The beaches are large at low tide but practically disappear at high tide. There is a lot of litter and wood lying around and hordes of mosquitoes. In the wet season there are boats between Muisné and Cojimíes, mostly early a.m., US$2.25, 2 hrs. Cargo boats ply between Muisné and Manta. A new road has been built between Muisné and Bolívar inland, behind the beaches; easier but less scenic. Be careful on the beaches; we have received reports of rape and violent attacks.

Esmeraldas (117,000 people) is reported dirty and overpriced. The electricity and water supplies are still inadequate. The main street is closed to traffic from 1930 to 2130 nightly. Gold mines nearby, tobacco and cacao grown inland, cattle ranching along the coast, timber exported, and an oil pipeline from the Oriente to an ocean terminal at nearby Balao; an oil refinery has been built nearby. A new road bridge over the river at San Mateo upstream from Esmeraldas gives a direct road link to the General Rivadeneira airport. Daily TAME flight to Quito at 0800, US$9. (Taxi to centre, about US$1.60 to Esmeraldas, US$8 to Atacamés). Las Palmas, just N of Esmeraldas, is being developed as a resort: several hotels have been built and restaurants opened. There is a broad sandy beach but it is reported as unsafe (theft) and dirty. White people have been advised to avoid the shanty-town on the Malecón. Even the water is muddy as it is close to a naval harbour and people use the beach as a speedway. Buses to Las Palmas (US$0.05, taxi US$1) leave regularly from the main square in Esmeraldas.

Mosquitoes and malaria are a serious problem throughout the province of Esmeraldas. All the beaches have mosquitoes that come out in hordes at night and bite through clothing. Take plenty of insect repellant because the Detán sold locally does not work well. Most *residencias* provide mosquito nets (*toldos* or *mosquiteros*); don't stay anywhere that does not. Best to visit in dry season, June-December.

Hotels Best in Esmeraldas are *Apart Hotel*, Av. Libertad 407 y Ramón Tello, D, excellent, good restaurant, and *Roma*, E, Olmeda y Piedrahita, with its *Restaurant Tres Carabelas*; *La Pradera*, 7½ km. S on Atacamés road, D, a/c, swimming pool, tennis courts, restaurant, and *Europeo*, D, between Esmeraldas and Las Palmas, no a/c, but the restaurant is very good, German-owned but under Chilean management. *Corea*, Mañizares y Bolívar, F, rec., private shower, fan; *Americano*, Sucre y Piedrahita, F with fan and bath, good value; *Diana*, Mañizares y Sucre, good, private showers, F. *Hostal Domínguez*, G, on Sucre near Plaza Central, noisy, hot water, open all night; *Valparaíso I*, Libertad y Pichincha, G, very basic but good value, cheap restaurant. *Turismo*, Bolívar 843, F with bath and fan, clean and friendly. Other cheaper hotels include *Bolívar*, F and cheaper still, *Central*, F, and *Asia*, F, both are basic but clean. Generally, hotels in the town centre are not up to much and you are rec. to stay in the outskirts. Some hotels are not keen to take single travellers.

Las Palmas offers the best hotels along Av. Kennedy: *Cayapas*, D, a/c, showers and hot water in all rooms, good restaurant; *Hotel del Mar*, D, on sea front, modern. *Atahualpa*, E, 14 rooms, private bath, hot water, garage, garden, Swiss-run, rec.; *Colonial*, Platat y L. Tello, D; *Chimborazo*, G, cheap and noisy.

Restaurants In Esmeraldas: *Chifa Restaurante Asiático*, Mañizares y Bolívar, Chinese, rather expensive; *Tía Carmen*, Sucre y 9 de Octubre, rec. for good, cheap, fish soup and stew. *La Marimba Internacional*, Libertad y Lavallén, has been rec.; *Daruma*, Olmedo y Mejía, is Japanese and local. *Café Congenita*, near Hotel Americano, for iced tea, milk shakes; other soda fountains at Olmedo y Piedrahita. In Las Palmas, *Atenas Tiffani*, Kennedy 707, good food but expensive; *Bayardo*, on the Malecón, good food, lively host, cheaper than *Tiffani*. There are numerous typical restaurants and bars by the beach selling ceviches, fried fish and patacones, etc.

Throughout Esmeraldas province a cheap meal is the *comida típica*, fish, rice, boiled *plátano*, sometimes beans (*minestre*), called *tapao*. There is also *cocado*, fish, crabs or shrimp cooked in coconut cream served with rice and *plátano*. There is a soup made of shellfish and coconut milk which is very good. *Cocada* is a sweet made of brown sugar and grated coconut; *conserva* is a paste of guava, banana and brown sugar, wrapped in banana leaves.

Shopping There is a Cayapa basket market across from the Post Office, behind the vegetables.

Also three doors down, Tolita artefacts and basketry. Exchange at bank until 1200; at Botica Koch, Sucre y 9 de Octubre, good rates.

Entertainment In Esmeraldas, *El Portón* peña and discotheque, Colón y Piedrahita; *El Guadal de Ña Mencha*, 6 de Diciembre y Quito, peña upstairs, marimba school at weekends; good *Bar Asia* on Bolívar by main Parque. *Los Cuervos*, discotheque. In Las Palmas, *El Náutico* and *Déjà Vue* on the Malecón, a/c, discotheques. Cockfights, Eloy Alfaro y 9 de Octubre, weekends.

Music Esmeraldas has been called "the capital of rhythm". The people prefer the livelier sound of Caribbean *salsa* to the *cumbia* heard in the sierra, and have retained the African-influenced marimba, usually accompanied by a bomero, who plays a deep-pitched bass drum suspended from the ceiling, and a long conga drum. Where there is a marimba school you will also find dancers, and the women who are too old to dance play percussion and chant songs handed down the generations, many with Colombian references, but the best marimba can only be seen in the backwoods of the province on Sundays and holidays as that in Esmeraldas is only for tourists. Centro Cultural Afro-Ecuadoriano (CCA), Calle Sucre y Catedral, Casilla 65, T 710603.

Cinema Ciné Bolívar, Bolívar y 9 de Octubre, is the best, with a/c and upholstered seating. Three other cinemas offer more basic accommodation with bats and rats.

Immigration Av. Olmedo y Rocafuerte, T 720-256.

Tourist Information The tourist office (Dituris) is in the Edificio de la Alcaldía, Bolívar 517 y 9 de Octubre, 2nd floor, half a block from the main square, singularly unhelpful.

Transport No central terminal. Buses to Quito, US$2.50, 6 hrs., 30 a day, good paved road, Trans-Esmeraldas, Av. Piedrahita 200, rec., or by Occidental; by Aerotaxi (small bus), 5 hrs., 12 passengers, reserved seats, office on main square. To Santo Domingo, US$1.40, 4 hrs.; to Ambato, 5 times a day with Coop. Sudamericana, 8 hrs., US$2.50; to Guayaquil, hourly, US$5, 7 hrs.; to Portoviejo and Manta, US$2, to Quevedo, 6 hrs. To La Tola (road good to Río Verde), 2 daily, US$1.60, 5 hrs.; to Muisné, 28 daily with La Costeñita, US$1, 3½ hrs. to Súa (road reasonable) and Atacamés every half hour from 0630 to 2030, US$0.30, 1-1½ hrs. Boats to Limones and San Lorenzo: service irregular; ask at Port Captain's office at Las Palmas. Combined boat/bus service leaves for San Lorenzo at 1330.

Atacamés, a beach resort 25 km. S of Esmeraldas, is still attractive, and the palm trees on the beach (washed away in 1983) are growing again. Atacamés is famous for its black coral and the local people make handicrafts from it. Most accommodation has salt water in the bathrooms; fresh water is not always available and not very good. *Hotel Jennifer*, E, cold shower, fan, clean; *Hotel Tahiti*, with shower, F, dirty, serves breakfasts, full meals in holiday periods, good restaurant, try the prawns, but check your bill carefully, also has new bungalows, F; *Hostería Los Bohíos*, C, prices cheaper (F) in low season (June, July, August), for a bungalow, safe, clean; *Hostería Cayapas*, beach huts, F, cooking and barbecue; *Casa Blanca*, Urbanización Iñaquito, cabins for 6, with bathroom, kitchen, F p.p., on beach; *San Sebastián* and *Marbella*, beach huts for 5, both F; *Residencial Sol de Oriente*, F, clean, near beach. *Castel Nuovo*, 3 km. N on road to Esmeraldas, C with bath and fan, swimming pool, on beach, rec.; *Edén*, cabins in F range, good location on beach, rec. Tents or beach bungalows can be hired at under US$1 a night; no facilities but can arrange with hotels. *Lumbaye* bungalows are rec., cheaper off-season. Beach bungalows with showers at *Cabañas Costa del Sol*, D, good breakfast and seafood; *Cabañas Arco Iris*, D, rec., charming, N end of beach, T Quito 525544 for reservations; *Cabañas South Pacific*, F, clean, American owner, fresh water showers. Rats are common in all these beach huts, and insect repellant is essential.

Restaurants are numerous, mostly seafood, are reasonable; try *Comedor Pelícanos*, fresh fish, chicken, ceviche, occasionally music, rec.; also *Cafetería Pelícanos*, best, includes vegetarian dishes and salads; *Comedor Popular*, good Italian and criollo cooking, order special requests in advance. 2 discotheques on beach. *Cocada*, a sweet made from different nuts, brown sugar, cocoa, etc., is sold in the main plaza. **Warning:** It is reported that there have been many assaults on campers and late-night beach strollers. The sea can be very dangerous, there is a powerful undertow and many people have been drowned.

Súa, another beach resort a little S of Atacamés (20 min. walk at low tide), is quiet, friendly, with a beautiful bay with pelicans and frigate birds, but the sandy beach is very dirty. *Pensión Palmar*, G, cabins; *Residencial España*, F; *Residencial Quito*, G, *Mar y Sol*, G, washing facilities poor. The hotels along the seafront vary little in standard but quite significantly in price. *Motel Chagra Ramos*, on beach, F, with good restaurant. Insect repellant is essential along this coast. Beyond Súa is Playa de Same, quiet and nice; *Cabañas Isla del Sol*, E (bargain), with bath, comfortable, safe, good restaurant, rec. **Tonchigüe,** 1 hr. S from Esmeraldas beyond Súa, is also lovely during the rainy season (Dec.-May).

There are no good beaches for swimming north of Esmeraldas. Río Verde, where the paved road ends, has a dirty beach and one hotel, *Paz y Bueno*, F, basic (N side of river). It was the setting for Morriz Thompson's book on Peace Corps life, *Living Poor*. Beyond Río Verde is **Rocafuerte**, recommended as having the best seafood in the province, including oysters and lobsters. At **La Tola**, where one catches the boat for Limones and San Lorenzo, the shoreline changes from sandy beaches to mangrove swamp. The wildlife is varied and spectacular, especially the birds. La Tola is 3½ hrs. (US$1.50) from Esmeraldas, by bus, four daily a.m., dusty, uncomfortable, buses often get stuck. Four boats go daily from La Tola to San Lorenzo via Limones, 2 hrs., US$1.50; seem to connect with boats from Esmeraldas. Try to avoid staying overnight in La Tola; take a raincoat.

Mangrove coastlands stretch north into Colombia, and have only two towns of note in Ecuador: Limones and San Lorenzo.

Limones, the main commercial centre, largely a saw-mill town, is the focus of traffic down-river from much of northern Esmeraldas Province where bananas from the Río Santiago are sent to Esmeraldas for export. The Cayapa Indians live up the Río Cayapas and can sometimes be seen in Limones, especially during the crowded weekend market (uninteresting), but they are more frequently seen at Borbón.

Limones has two good shops selling the very attractive Cayapa basketry; selection includes some items from Colombia. The first is opposite *Restaurant El Bongó* and the second by the dock opposite Banco de Fomento.

Two hotels, both execrable. Limones is "the mosquito and rat capital of Ecuador". A hired launch (6 pers. US$ 1.40 p.p., 1½ hrs.) provides a fascinating trip through mangrove islands and passing hundreds of hunting pelicans. Information on boat journeys from the Capitanía del Puerto, Las Palmas, reached by bus No. 1 from the main square in Esmeraldas. From Limones you can also get a canoe or boat to Borbón. Better to stay at San Lorenzo.

Borbón (*Residencial Capri*, F, with marimba dance hall next door), with population almost entirely black, is on the Río Cayapas past mangrove swamps. Buses to Esmeraldas, US$1.40, 4 hrs. Upstream are Cayapa Indian villages. From Borbón hire a dugout to Boca de Onzole one hour upstream, which is the confluence of the Cayapas and Onzole rivers. There is a fine lodge built by a Hungarian (for advance bookings write to Stephan Tarjany, Casilla 187, Esmeraldas), E with full board, good value, clean, warm showers. Water skiing available on request. You can hire a dugout with him for US$50 to Santa María (board and lodging with Sra. Pastora at missionary station, F, mosquito nets) and on upstream to San Miguel. Alternatively, a supply boat goes several times a week between Borbón and Santa María, which sometimes takes passengers, US$4 p.p. return. You pass Zapallo Grande, a friendly village with many gardens, where the American missionary Dr Meisenheimer has established a hospital, pharmacy, church and school. You will see the Cayapa Indians passing in their canoes and in their open long houses on the shore. San Miguel is the last outpost of civilization with a church and a few houses, beautifully situated on a hill at the confluence of two rivers. From there you go back 5 hrs. downstream to La Tola where you can pick up the bus from Esmeraldas or go on to Limones and San Lorenzo.

San Lorenzo is relatively more attractive than Limones. There is a beach nearby at San Pedro, reached by boat; make enquiries in the village for transport. The best places to see *marimba* are two schools, one Esmeraldeña and one Colombiana. The latter practice on Calle 24 de Mayo between *Residencial Pailón* and *Residencial Ibarra*; you can't miss the sound. The former practice Wed. and Sat. nights, are more disciplined, better musicians and dance more. They have toured the continent and are led by a woman called Lydia who can make marimbas to order. *Marimba* can be seen during the local fiesta on Sept. 30. San Lorenzo is an expensive town.

Hotels *Wilma*, F, basic, ask for rooms 15 or 16, they are newer and bigger; *Residencial Margaritas*, F, friendly, clean, good showers, Imbabura y Ortiz; *Pailón*, Ayora y 24 de Mayo, satisfactory, G, *Restaurant Jhonny* upstairs; *Ecuador*, Alfaro y 10 de Agosto, F, restaurant OK, basic, laundry facilities, mosquito net provided; *Residencial Vilmar*, Imbabura y Mariano, G, near the station. *San Lorenzo*, Alfaro y 10 de Agosto, G, rec. for meals, but not so good to stay; *Residencial Turista*, next to post office, G, multilingual staff, rec.; *Residencial Ibarra*, Coronel y 24 de Mayo, possibly the best, F, clean, friendly. **Restaurants**: *Cabaña del Sol*, rec. for good, cheap fish, Ayora y Alfaro. *Jhonny* (sic), Ayora y 24 de Mayo, upstairs, best in town, large helpings for US$1. *Rumory's* marimba and discotheque at Imbabura y 10 de Agosto. Insect repellant is a "must" in San Lorenzo. Be sure to check your bedding for scorpions.

Train The *autocarro* (motor rail-coach) leaves daily from the station 10 mins. from town centre (usually overcrowded; reserve day before travelling). The train journey gives an excellent transect of Ecuador (**see page 633**). To Ibarra, US$1.75, up to 12 hrs., departing at 0700. Reserve tickets the night before departure and pick them up an hour before the train leaves; the train can get very crowded and angry passengers unable to board have been known to beat up the driver! Because of heavy rains, roadworks and landslides, delays are frequent.

Boats Dugouts, with motors, to La Tola (2 hrs., US$1.50) and Borbón (2½hrs, US$2), via Limones, US$1. Boats leave daily at 0730 and 1400 (stops at Tambilla and Limones en route), bus from there to Esmeraldas, through ticket US$2.75. Beautiful journey but dusty bus trip. Boat to Esmeraldas, infrequent.

From San Lorenzo there are occasional boats to Tumaco in Colombia, but gringos are not normally welcome as passengers because contraband is being carried. When arriving in San Lorenzo from Tumaco, the customs office run by navy personnel is in the harbour, but you have to get your passport stamped at the immigration office in Ibarra, because the immigration police in the *Hotel Imperial* office do not handle passports.

Nancy Alexander, of Chicago, writes that about 75% of the population of Limones, Borbón and San Lorenzo has come from Colombia in the last fifty years. The people are mostly black and many are illegal immigrants. Smuggling between Limones and Tumaco in Colombia is big business (hammocks, manufactured goods, drugs) and there are occasional drug searches along the N coastal road.

GUAYAQUIL (4)

Guayaquil, the chief seaport and commercial city, founded in 1537 by Francisco de Orellana, stands on the west bank of the Guayas river, some 56 km. from its outflow into the Gulf of Guayaquil. Its population of 1,600,000 makes it the largest city in the Republic. The climate is at its best from May to December with little or no rain and cool nights, though the sky is overcast more often than not. The heat and humidity during the rainy season, January to April, are oppressive. The Puerto Marítimo, opened in 1979, handles about 90% of the country's imports and 50% of its exports.

The city is dotted with small parks and pleasant gardens. A waterfront drive, known as the Malecón, runs along the shore of the Guayas river. Here are the splendid Palacio Municipal and the severe Government Palace. From the landing pier of the Yacht Club the drive is known as the Paseo de las Colonias. The main street, Avenida 9 de Octubre, runs due west from a central pier; there are 11 piers in all, 6 to the north of 9 de Octubre, 4 to the south. About half-way along it is the Plaza Centenario, the main square of the city, where stands the large liberation monument set up in 1920. On Calle Pedro Carbo, between Vélez and 9 de Octubre, the restored interior of the colonial church of San Francisco is beautiful. At La Rotonda, on the waterfront near the beginning of Av. 9 de Octubre, is a statue commemorating the famous and very mysterious meeting of Bolívar and San Martín in 1822. The dazzling white cemetery, north of the city at the foot of a hill, is worth seeing, but best to go on Sundays when there are plenty of people about. The snow-capped peak of Chimborazo can sometimes be glimpsed from Guayaquil.

The city is bustling and prosperous, and much cleaner than it used to be. The locals are much livelier and more open than the people of Quito. There are clubs for golf, tennis, yachting, and a race track set in delightful surroundings some 5 km. outside the city: there are a football stadium and an enclosed coliseum for boxing, basketball, etc. The pleasant suburb of Urdesa, NW of the city, contains some of the best restaurants and places of entertainment.

One of the oldest and most interesting districts is Las Peñas, at the foot of Cerro Santa Ana, by the river. Here is the city's first church, Santo Domingo (1548). Nearby is an open-air theatre, the Bogotá. Then, up the hill, there is a flat space where two cannon point riverward, a memento of the days when pirates sailed up the Guayas to attack the city. Here begins a curving, narrow colonial street, Numa Pompilio Llona. Paved with huge stone slabs, and lined with many fine houses which used to be an artist's colony, it is picturesque but somewhat neglected. To reach Las Peñas, turn left at end of Av. 9 de Octubre and carry on along the Malecón, to its end. It is a picturesque but still poor area; even the locals say it is unsafe and you are advised not to walk up the adjacent streets on Cerro Santa Ana.

The pride of Guayaquil is the enormous River Guayas bridge linking the city with Durán, the rail terminal on the east bank of the Guayas River. About half an hour is saved in comparison with the ferry journey, which costs US$0.06 and leaves every 15 min. from Muelle 5. From Durán, paved highways fan out to Babahoyo, Milagro, Riobamba (pass 4,120 metres high on the way), Cuenca and Machala.

Warnings Guayaquil has many thieves and pickpockets, especially outside the hotel entrances and on the waterfront, often working in pairs, and the area south of Calle Ayacucho is generally unsafe. Except in the best hotels, there is a chronic water shortage. Dengue fever has been reported.

Local Holidays October 9 and 12. July 24 and 25, Bolívar's birthday, and Foundation of the City; Carnival is in the days before Lent: watch out for malicious throwing of water balloons, mud, ink, paint etc.; women are prime targets. In contrast New Year's Eve is lots of fun, there is a large exhibition of tableaux, featuring *Años Viejos*, along the Malecón, children begging for alms for their life-size *viejos*, families with cars taking their *viejos* for rides through the centre of town, and a vast conflagration at midnight when all these figures are set on fire and explode.

Museums The Museo Municipal is housed in the Biblioteca Municipal, at Sucre with Pedro Carbo (near the *Hotel Continental*) where there are paintings, gold and archaeological collections and also a good newspaper library. The museum (which contains Shuar heads) is open Wed.-Fri. 0900-1500 and 1500-1800; Sat. 1000-1500, Sun. 1000-1300. Entrance US$0.15 for Ecuadoreans and US$0.40 for foreigners (free on Sat., but passport must be left at desk). The Central Bank's anthropological museum is at José de Anteparra 900 and 9 de Octubre, open Mon.-Fri. 1000-1800, Sat. and Sun. 1000-1300. There is an impressive collection of prehistoric gold items at the museum of the Casa de la Cultura, together with an archaeological museum, Av. 9 de Octubre 1200 and Moncayo, open Mon.-Fri. 0900-1200 and 1500-1830, Sat. 0900-1600. There is a small zoo, open Sun., at the Colegio Nacional.

Hotels Hotel prices in Guayaquil are set by the Tourist Board and should be posted inside hotel. Rooms are much in demand in better hotels, the cheap ones being pretty basic, and singles seem very hard to find. All tend to be heavily booked, particularly in the week before July 24, the *fiesta*.

The best hotel is probably *Oro Verde*, 9 de Octubre y García Moreno, A; also good are *Unihotel*, Clemente Ballén 406 y Chile, B, good restaurant; *Grand Hotel Guayaquil*, Boyacá 1600 y 10 de Agosto, B, restaurants, swimming pool, sauna, etc.; *Continental*, Chile y 10 de Agosto, L (a KLM Golden Tulip hotel), rec.; *Apartamentos Boulevard*, 9 de Octubre 432, A, rec.; *Ramada*, Malecón y Orellana, A, pool, sauna, fancy restaurant, rec. *Palace*, Chile 214 y Luque, C, restaurant not clean; *Plaza*, Chile 414 y Clemente Ballén, D, friendly, some cheaper rooms, excellent restaurant; *Doral*, Aguirre y Chile, D, a bit run down, good restaurant; *Italia*, 10 de Agosto 115 y Pichincha, D, reasonable, convenient, quiet, a/c, rooftop restaurant; *Alexanders*, Luque 1107 y Pedro Moncayo, D, very comfortable but noisy and restaurant poor; *María del Cisne*, Colón y Chile, E, clean, a/c, no hot water or breakfast; *Residencial Cervera*, E, Gral. Córdoba 1036, a/c, clean, some rooms with bath; *Residencial Metropolitana*, V.M. Rendón 120 y Panamá, E, hot water, a/c, clean, friendly, safe for luggage; *Los Andes*, Garaycoa y Aguirre, E, clean, friendly, rec.; *Residencial Embajador*, Chimborazo 1106, F, clean but shower rarely works; *Pensión Pauker*, Baquerizo Moreno 902, F, English spoken, rooms on street side noisy, safe for luggage, beware cockroaches; *San Juan*, Vélez y Boyacá, E, own bathroom, no a/c, acceptable but most rooms without windows; *Sanders*, Pedro Moncayo 1100 y Luque, F with bath, phone and fan (E a/c), central, good; *Victoria*, Moncayo y Colón, F, shower, clean but noisy; *Santa María*, E, Villamil 102, central, adequate, restaurant; *Orchidea Internacional*, Centro Comercial at Villamil 210, E, good, clean, TV, a/c, hot water; *El Inca*, 10 de Agosto beside market, F with bath; *Libertador*, Parque Centenario, G with bath, good value, friendly; *Ecuatoriana*, Sucre y Rumichaca, F, clean, but some rooms with no window; *Delicia*, Clemente Ballén 1105, G, clean, fair, try to get room away from street. Sra Greta Portugal at Imbabura 214 y Rocafuerte, Aptdo 4-2, lets rooms at price category D, above. Total tax of 15% on all hotel rates.

Restaurants Centre: *El Fortín* restaurant in the *Hotel Continental* won the Gran Collar Gastronómico Internacional competition worldwide and has excellent food (but poor service); the cheaper *La Canoa* has local food. *1822* restaurant at the *Grand Hotel Guayaquil*, expensive, but pleasant surroundings, high quality cuisine with good daily outdoor barbecue at pool-side. Good dining at *Le Gourmet* and *La Fondue* in *Hotel Oro Verde*, its coffee shop, *El Patio*, has nice and reasonably priced platos típicos. *The Steak House*, García Moreno 811, opposite *Hotel Oro Verde*, pleasant atmosphere, good food and service. Good food at other hotels. *El Parque*, top floor of Unicentro, highly rec. (US$10-12 p.p.), buffet lunch (US$3 for as much as you can eat), overlooks Parque Bolívar. Well-known and expensive *Caracol Azul*, 9 de Octubre 1918 y Los Ríos, wonderful seafood and meats (US$10-12 p.p.). For good ice cream, *Crema*, Chimborazo y 9 de Octubre.

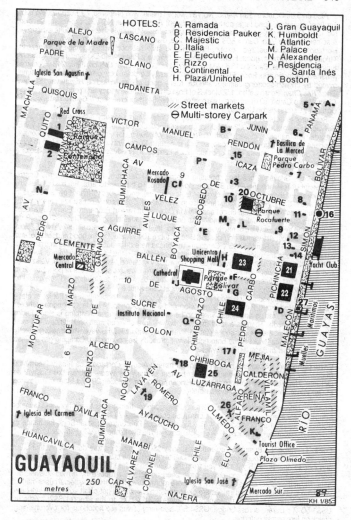

A. Ramada
B. Residencia Pauker
C. Majestic
D. Italia
E. El Ejecutivo
F. Rizzo
G. Continental
H. Plaza/Unihotel
J. Gran Guayaquil
K. Humboldt
L. Atlantic
M. Palace
N. Alexander
P. Residencia
   Santa Inés
Q. Boston

/// Street markets
⊖ Multi-storey Carpark

GUAYAQUIL

0   250
metres

KH 1/85

Key to Map of Guayaquil 1. Casa de la Cultura; 2. Supreme Court; 3. TAME; 5. Clínica Panamericana; 6. Banco Central; 7. Bank of London & South America; 8. Iberia Airlines; 9. Librería Científica; 10. Avianca; 11. Ecuatoriana de Aviación; 12. Bank of America; 13. Lufthansa; 14. Air France; 15. Servitours; 16. La Rotunda & Bolívar/San Martín monument; 17. Banco Continental; 18. Chamber of Commerce; 19. Medalla Milagrosa church; 20. San Francisco church; 21. Palacio de Gobernación, Immigration & Extranjería; 22. Palacio Municipal; 23. Main Post office; 24. Biblioteca Municipal/Museum; 25. University; 26. San Alejo church; 27. Clock tower.

Also on 9 de Octubre: *San Remo*, No.737, varied menu, well prepared; *La Rotonda*, No.432, 1st floor of casino, good large portions, not cheap; *Pizzería Italia*, No.706, expensive; *Bavaria*, No.1313, German run, good meat; also on this street, lots of US-style snack bars, quite expensive. Also central: *Don Vito*, Carchi 803 y 9 de Octubre, disco and bar, closed Sun.; *Tertulia de Hilda*, Hurtado y Tungurahua, rec., exotic, Esmeraldeño style seafood with vegetables; *Anderson*, Tulcán 810 y Hurtado, good, French, closed Sun.; *Pique y Pase*, Alejo Lascano 16-17 y Carchi, typical; *Pizzalandia*, Carchi y 1° de Mayo, good pizza. Local food at *Clérico*, Junín 213 y Panamá; *Muelle 5*, Malecón opp. Roca; *El Camino*, Pedro Ycaza y Córdova, economical, best at lunchtime, owned by English-speaking Jaime Mendoza. Many good *chifas*, including *Himalayas*, Sucre y Chile; *Res Chan*, Pedro Carbo, 1/2 block S of Post Office, Chinese and typical food, popular; *Gran Chifa*, Pedro Carbo 1018, ornate, reasonable prices. Best ice cream at *Il Gelato Italiano*, 9 de Octubre y Carchi, also in Urdesa.

Restaurants outside the centre are mostly in Urdesa and Kennedy suburbs. Urdesa: *Juan Salvador Gaviota*, Boloña 603 y Décima, good seafood, closed Sun.; *Il Fiorentino*, Datiles y V.E. Estrada, international, closed Mon. *Trattoria Da Migliorini*, La Primera 604 y Las Monjas, opposite Ietel, very good Italian food, service excellent; *Costa Brava*, Catalan food, Las Monjas 303 y Cuarta; many others of all kinds along V.E.Estrada. Kennedy: several on Francisco Boloña and Av. Kennedy.

Shopping Guayaquil has four shopping centres, the Policentro, the Unicentro, the Centro Comercial Urdesa and the Albán Borja shopping centre. To buy handicrafts, the best places are Madaleine Hollander's shop in the *Oro Verde*, (expensive), and *Manos* (offshoot of *La Bodega* in Quito) at the *Grand Hotel Guayaquil* and also in Urdesa, e.g. *Coosas* on V.E. Estrada, same quality as in Quito. *Lo Nuestro* (Olga Fisch) and *Galería Guayasamín* are at Policentro. Every day except Sun., Otavalan Indians sell their handicrafts under the arcades along Calle Chile between 9 de Octubre and Vélez. Beware of newly manufactured "Inca relics" and "Jívaro shrunken heads" sold in souvenir shops. *Artesanías del Ecuador*, 9 de Octubre 104 y Malecón, are good and reliable, and so are *Ocepa*, V.M.Rendón 405 y Córdova. The prices here differ little from those in the towns where the goods are made. Good shops include *Inca Folklore* in the Edificio Gran Pasaje, Av. 9 de Octubre 424, *Arte Folklore Otavalo*, 9 de Octubre 102 y Malecón; *Artesaniás Cuenca*, Vélez 110; and *Artesanías Mariel*, Vélez y Chile. There is an H. Stern jewellers shop at the airport. Stands in street near Post Office, and a small market in Calle Chile, between 9 de Octubre and Vélez, next to San Francisco church, open daily. Camera repairs at Calle Aguire 714, 2nd floor.

Everyone in Guayaquil, rich, poor and in-between, does their shopping in the Bahía, or black market, located along Pichincha, S of Colón and along Olmedo. A wide selection of shoes, appliances, TVs, radios and houseware can be found along Pichincha. Clothing is along Pedro Carbo and Olmedo. There is a food market ("*bahía*") in a covered area on Huancavelica near Pichincha, behind the Cepe gasoline station. Watch your valuables; however the area is generally safe, lots of police. Most name-brand goods will probably be counterfeit. Camping gas at Casa Maspons, corner of Ballén 517 y Boyacá.

Entertainment Discos and bars in the good hotels. Also *El Corsario*, Los Ríos y Piedrahita; *Buccaneer* and *Flashdance* in centre; *Cuartito Azul*, Luque y Garaycoa; *Zebras*, Los Ríos y 9 de Octubre. There is a peña (folklore show) at *Rincón Folklórico*, Malecón 208 y J.Montalvo. Casinos at *Oro Verde*, *Unihotel* and *Boulevard* hotels.

Books Librería Científica, Luque 223 y Chile, good for field guides to the flora and fauna of South America and the Galápagos. Librería Selecta, Aguirre 717. Librería Cervantes, Aguirre 606A. Su Librería at Chimborazo 416, Librerías ABC, Policentro Urdesa. Book Exchange at Nuevos Horizontes, 6 de Marzo 924. English books at The Bookshop, on V.E. Estrada (Urdesa).

Local Transport Buses and colectivos about US$0.06 (most visitors dare not try them, but they are not lethal although once on it is difficult to get off). The *busetas*, or minibuses, are cheap and safe to ride. Ruta 15 will take you from the centre to Urdesa, 13 to Policentro, 14 to Albán Borja. *Buseta* passengers and drivers have been occasionally robbed by armed thieves, but generally in the poorer areas of the city. For more roomy travel the *Servicio especial* buses marked with blue and white diagonal stripes are clean and convenient. To get off at your stop, yell *pare*. Taxis: short runs, US$0.50; to Policentro or Urdesa, US$0.08; to the airport US$2; by the hr. US$1.50. To Durán, across bridge, US$4.50; also ferry. Taxis are notorious for overcharging; check on fare before entering.

Car Hire Hertz, Avis, Budget, Dollar at airport, town centre offices and main hotels, prices around US$30 a day, inc. insurance and tax, for a small car. Dollar offers competitive prices but the cars are often reported in poor condition.

Horse-Racing Hipódromos Buijo and Río Verde in Salinas. Parimutuel betting. Amazingly low standard.

Exchange Bank of London and South America, Calle Pichincha 108-110 and Mercado Central and Urdesa agencies; Banco Holandés Unido, P. Ycaza 454 y Baquerizo Moreno, T 312900;

Citibank, Av. 9 de Octubre, Citicorp cheques only; Bank of America, Elizalde 100. Open 0900-1330. Closed Sat. Banco del Pacífico recommended, advances money on Master Card and changes Thomas Cook travellers cheques into dollars cash for small commission (San Francisco 300 building, 9th floor, next to Plaza San Francisco, enter either from Pedro Carbo or Gen. Córdova). Banco Popular, Pedro Carbo y 9 de Octubre, changes Amex travellers' cheques into cash dollars without commission.

There are several *Casas de Cambio* on Av. 9 de Octubre, also many on Av. Pichincha, between Aguirre and 9 de Octubre. All the *cambios* in the centre will exchange Amex travellers' cheques, though the banks generally offer better rates. Cambiosa, 9 de Octubre 113 y Malecón, rec.; also Cambitur, near *Pensión Pauker*. Most open 0900-1900, shut on Saturday. Wander Cambios at airport open 7 days a week (poorer rates than in town).

Consulates Austria, Av. 9 de Octubre 1310, T 392307. Peru, Av. 9 de Octubre 411, 6th floor, T 512-738. 0900-1330. Bolivia, P. Ycaza 302 of. 601, T 304260. Uruguay, V. M. Rendón 1006, T 513-461. Brazil, L.García 103, T 362-772. Argentina, Aguirre 104. USA, 9 de Octubre y García Moreno, T 323-570. Netherlands, Av. 9 de Octubre 2309, 5th floor. T 366410. Italy, 9 de Octubre y Baquerizo Moreno. W.Germany, 9 de Octubre 109; Canada, Ed. Torres de la Merced, 4th floor, office 11, Córdova 800 y Rendón (T 313747/303580); France, Boyacá 1215.

Telecommunications and post Instituto Ecuatoriano de Telecomunicaciones (Ietel). Telephone company and post office share same block, Pedro Carbo y Aguirre. Public telex booth. Many kiosks in arcades all round it, each with the flag and name of a different country, plenty of stationery.

Medical Dr. Angel Serrano Sáenz, Av. Boyacá 821, T 301-373, English speaking. Dr. Alfonso E. León Guin, Centro de Especialidades, Av. Boyacá 1320 y Luque, T 528-179/517-793; open 1100-1300 and 1400-1900 and Sat., also English speaking. The main hospital used by the foreign community is the Clínica Kennedy, T 396-963. It also contains the consulting rooms of almost every kind of doctor.

Churches Episcopalian Church of USA; Lutheran Church; Anglican Church, Luis Urdaneta y Malecón del Salado, Urdesa.

Schools US and German. School year, May -mid-January. The Inter-American Academy (US system), August-May.

Immigration Av. Pichincha y Aguirre (Gobernación), T 514-925/516-789, for visa extensions.

Tourist Bureau Dituris, Malecón 2321 y Av. Olmedo, first floor; T 518-926, 526-241. Helpful, English spoken by some staff, open 0900-1600, Mon.-Fri. Map of Ecuador. A Policía de Turismo man can be hired for a guided tour of Guayaquil. Cost will be about US$4 per hr. for taxi (2 hrs. will do) and US$3 to the Policía de Turismo.

Travel Agents Reportedly, none is open at weekends. Galasam Cía Ltda., Edificio Gran Pasaje, sala 1107, Av. 9 de Octubre 424, T 306-289; their Galápagos programme is called Economic Galápagos Tours; see Galápagos section (page 674) for details. Metropolitan Touring, Pichincha 415 y Aguirre. Machiavello Tours, 9 de Octubre y Anteparra (rec.). Galápagos Cruises, Los Ríos 0-80, T 390-893. Gordon Tours, 9 de Octubre 2009, rec. Ecuadorian Tours, 9 de Octubre 1900 at corner of Esmeraldas, is agent for American Express, T 397-111.

Rail Service to Quito suspended in 1983. Travellers arriving in Durán and ferrying to Guayaquil land on the Malecón Bolívar about 10 blocks N of the Palacio de Gobernación. The first ferry is at 0530, the last at 2130 but buses run later. From Durán to Alausí, the autoferro runs Mon., Wed., Fri. at 1800, 4 hrs., US$0.60; the ordinary train runs daily at 0620, 12 hrs., US$0.30.

Bus Services The new bus station (Terminal Terrestre) is near the airport, just off the road to the Guayas bridge (no left luggage depot). Several companies to Quito, US$3, 8½ hrs. To Cuenca, US$2.65, 7 hrs.; Riobamba 5 hrs., US$2.15. Santo Domingo de los Colorados, 4¾ hrs., US$2. Manta 3 hrs., US$2; Esmeraldas 7 hrs., US$5; to Portoviejo, 3½ hrs., US$2, and to Bahía de Caráquez, 5½ hrs., US$2.80. Machala (for Peru) 3½ hrs., US$2, frequent, or by minibus 2½ hrs., leave at 20 minute intervals between 0600 and 1900, 10 kg. baggage limit. For the Peruvian border, to Huaquillas, avoiding Machala, US$2.50, 5 hrs.; via Machala, 6 hrs. To Ambato, US$2.50, 6½ hrs. To Alausí, 4 hrs., US$2. Regular and frequent buses to Playas (2¼ hrs., US$0.90) and to Salinas (2½ hrs., US$1). Colectivos are not rec. for journeys to the Sierra, they drive too fast and are dangerous. Town buses 2, 66, 69, 70, 71 and 76 from new bus station to centre, US$0.06 (taxis very expensive, US$2). **Trucks** carry freight and passengers, slower, bumpy, cheaper than buses, and you see better. Inquire at Sucre 1104.

Simón Bolívar Airport, near the centre. US$0.12 for bus (won't allow backpacks on board), No. 2 from Malecón, No. 3 from Centro Cívico, No. 69 from Plaza Victoria, US$1.50 for taxi from centre, but if you are arriving in Guayaquil and need a taxi from the airport, walk ½ block from the terminal out to Av. Las Américas, where taxis and *camionetas* wait for passengers. The fare will be about half of what you will be charged for the same trip by one of the drivers who belong to the airport taxi cooperative. Dituris advises that visitors should not pay more than US$2.50 for taxis from the airport to town. There are several car hire firms at the airport; an information desk; Dituris office; a *cambio*.

Air Services About 12 flights daily to and from Quito, US$12 (TAME, Saeta, SAN; ensure seats are confirmed, not standby). Sit on the right side for the best views. Flights to Machala daily (except Sundays) with TAME or in light 5 or 7 seater planes with Cedta and Lansa, about six times a day from the Avioneta terminal on the city side of the international airport. There are flights to Cuenca (2 a day, US$14), Manta (1-2 a day, US$9), and Loja (1 a day, US$9). Daily to Galápagos **(see page 674)**. TAME, 9 de Octubre, Edif. Gran Pasaje (T 305-800); Saeta, Escobedo 1114 y 9 de Octubre (T 303-024). Flights to Lima: Aero Perú (9 de Octubre). Andes Airlines will ship vehicles to Panama.

Excursions To Playas, Salinas and the Santa Elena peninsula **(see page 636)**.

THE SOUTHERN LOWLANDS (5)

On the southern shore of the Gulf of Guayaquil is **Puerto Bolívar** (Hotels: *Pacífico* (restaurant) and *Jambelí*, both basic, G), built above a mangrove swamp and backed by jungle. Approximately one million tonnes a year of banana exports pass through this port. It serves (6½ km.) **Machala**, a growing agricultural town of 122,000 with an annual banana fair in September. The area is an unattractive (mosquitoes) but prosperous irrigated banana zone. It is also a centre for pond shrimp production. From Machala paved roads run inland to Pasaje (26 km.; *Hotel Pasaje*, F with bath), and Arenillas (76 km.), and NE from Puerto Bolívar via Pasaje and Girón to Cuenca. An all-weather road runs SE through Arenillas to Loja (161 km.).

Buses run every 10 min. from Puerto Bolívar to Machala (20 mins. journey), and taxis are available. There are TAME flights (Mon.-Fri.) from Guayaquil and Quito; alternatively, Cedta and Lansa have about 3 flights a day to Guayaquil by *avioneta*. The airport is about 1 km. from town centre, beside local prison.

Machala Hotels *Encalada*, Tarqui y 9 de Octubre, D, T 920681, restaurant, bar, cafeteria, disco; *Rizzo*, Guayas y Bolívar, D, T 921511, a/c, T.V., suites available, slightly worn luxury, pool, casino, cafeteria, restaurant, rec. for breakfast as well as dinner; *El Oro*, Sucre y Juan Montalvo, D, T 922408, refurbished, good, excellent restaurant; *Perla del Pacífico*, Sucre 603 y Páez, D, T 920915, T.V., a/c, no hot water; *Inés*, Montalvo y Pasaje, E, T 922301, good restaurant; *Residencial La Delicia*, Montalvo y Rocafuerte, clean, safe, electric fans, F; *Gran Hotel Machala*, Juan Montalvo y Rocafuerte, F, clean, T 920530; *Residencial El Oro*, 9 de Mayo y Bolívar, G, basic but OK; *Las Cuevas de los Tayos*, F, clean, parking, rec.; *Residencial Paula*, 9 de Octubre 912, F, with bath, a/c; *Hotel Ecuatoriano*, 9 de Octubre y Colón, F, bath, a/c. A mosquito net may be needed for sleeping.

Restaurants *Cafetería San Francisco*; Sucre block 6, good filling breakfast; *Pepe's Parrillada*, Av. 9 de Octubre y 9 de Mayo, food and service rec., but not cheap, specializes in kebabs and steaks, bife better than lomo; *Parrillada Sabor Latina*, Sucre y Guayas, steaks and grills; *Pío Pío Rico Pollo*, Av. Guayas, chicken; *Norberto's*, near town centre, very good; *Chifa China* and *La Peña*, both 9 de Octubre y Guayas; two branches of *Kingburger* offer good hamburgers, clean; *La Fogata*, near telephone office, for good chicken. In Puerto Bolívar, *El Acuario* offers excellent value in seafood dishes (on main street which runs back from the pier). A good spot for a beer and toasted sandwich or ceviche is the *Miramar* bar at the pierhead.

Tourist Office Dituris, Tarqui y Primera Constituyente; maps are in the basement.

Peruvian Consulate At the corner of Av. 3a Sur, on Pichincha y Guayas.

Post Office Bolívar y Montalvo; telephone and cable office, **Ietel**, 9 de Octubre near stadium.

Travel Agent Ecuadorian Tours, Bolívar y Guayas.

Exchange Banco del Pacífico, Rocafuerte y Tarqui, changes travellers' cheques and notes; the *casas de cambio* prefer notes.

Cinema There are several, of which *El Tauro* is the best, a/c, cushioned seats, good sound. The *Teatro Municipal* has wooden benches and rats, US$0.32 a seat.

Sport A development just outside Machala on the Pasaje road has two large outdoor swimming pools. The Machala tennis club has three clay and two concrete courts, a swimming pool and a club house. It is situated on the left-hand side of the Santa Rosa road just after the roundabout where the Pasaje road branches off, about 5 km. from Machala. Cockfighting takes place every Saturday afternoon at the cockpit on Calle 9 de Octubre.

Buses The bus companies Occidental, Panamericana, Ecuatoriano Pullman and Rutas Orenses (the best safety record) have depots in the town with direct services to Quito (10½ hrs., US$3.50), Guayaquil 3½ hrs., US$2), Esmeraldas, (11 hrs., US$3.70). Loja (7 hrs., US$2.75). Hourly (a.m.) service to Cuenca by Empresas Pullman Sucre, Sucre block 7, US$2.70, 5 hrs., "exciting ride guaranteed" along a winding road. Major construction work on roads in the area may cause delays.

Excursions From the old pier on the Puerto Bolívar waterfront motorized canoes go to the tourist beach at Jambelí, on the far side of the mangrove islands which shelter Puerto Bolívar from the Pacific. The beach is long and safe but there is no shade. Canoes cost US$12 return (arrange return time with boatman) or there is a regular boat service (US$1 p.p.), 1000 and 1300 returning 1500 and 1700 on weekdays, more frequent at weekends. A trip to the quieter beach at La Bravita can be arranged, but there are no facilities and again no shade, so take drinks, etc. If arranging a trip to the beach at Costa Rica (2 hrs.) be sure to carry passport as a military post has to be passed. This beach is pleasant but the waves and currents can be dangerous. The trip through mangrove channels is interesting, especially for bird watchers. All the above locations suffer from ferocious mosquitoes after about 1630 and it is better not to stray off the sand at any time as the driftwood is infested with biting insects. The gold mines at Zaruma can be visited. Frequent buses to Zaruma, Transportes TAC, Colón y Rocafuerte.

Crossing the Border into Peru
The normal route overland to Peru is via Machala. Buses run 8 times a day (US$0.50, 1¾ hrs.) to *Huaquillas,* the Ecuadorean border town, something of a shopping arcade for Peruvians (all shops close about 1730), described by one traveller as a "seedy one-horse banana town full of touts with black briefcases". Travellers who haven't obtained their Peruvian tourist cards in Guayaquil or Quito can get them at the border.

Hotels at Huaquillas *Parador Turístico Huaquillas*, E, at N of town, Dituris-operated, swimming pool, restaurant and bar; *Residencial Huaquillas*, Córdova y 9 de Octubre, G, basic, clean; *Residencial San Martín*, opp. Customs on main street, G, clean, noisy, mosquito nets, convenient; *Mini*, Av. República, G, mosquito net, adequate, reasonable restaurant downstairs.

Restaurants Best at *Parador Turístico*; also *Rapa Nui*, on ground floor of *Residencial Mini*, and *Sinqi*, Av. de la República, good. Expect bananas with everything here. There appear to be no set meals.

Complete Ecuadorean formalities at customs and immigration, Av. de la República y Portovelo, in Huaquillas, then walk along the main street and across the bridge. At the bridge, the police check passports. Then take a colectivo or bus to the new Peruvian customs and immigration office in Zarumilla (US$0.30, about 3km.); from here colectivos and buses run to Tumbes, US$0.70 (taxi to Tumbes, waiting at border for formalities, US$5). The border is officially open 0800-1800, but long lunches are common. It is often best to cross just after lunch when the officers are still sleepy and do not pay you much attention. Peruvian time is one hour earlier than Ecuadorean in Jan., Feb. and March. From Tumbes (or from the border), fast long-distance buses run to Lima.

Border practices tend to vary, so check to make sure what the authorities require. For example, Australians need a consular visa (US$2, available in Machala) from Peru's consular office near the main plaza, but much quicker in Quito.

Warning Officially, a ticket out of Peru is necessary for entry into the country. Although rarely asked for, some agencies reportedly still sell cheap tickets for non-existent runs out of Peru. (Tepsa sells tickets in Quito at twice the price they are in Peru.) If you are required to show a ticket, you can buy a Miscellaneous Charges Order, valid one year, minimum US$150, but remember there is a 10% tax on all tickets bought in Ecuador. (We have been told that one traveller's MCO was not accepted by Peruvian officials as an exit ticket.) Peruvian customs and police have asked for bribes at this crossing.

The Peruvian inti has been greatly devalued recently, so verify the rate with travellers leaving Peru. Exchange only what is needed immediately; a better rate is normally obtained in Peru. At the border, the best rate is for cash dollars. Be sure to count your change carefully; the money changers (recognizable by their black briefcases) are positively dishonest, and clever. Travellers leaving Peru should get rid of their intis inside Peru, and buy sucres on the Ecuadorean side. At Huaquillas, better rates are obtained in the town than in the vicinity of the border post when buying sucres, though it is difficult to change travellers' cheques.

Coming from Peru into Ecuador; take a bus to Tumbes or Santa Rosa and a colectivo from there. Some travellers crossing border from Peru to Ecuador at Huaquillas report being required by the Ecuadorean authorities to show an exit ticket (a bus ticket will do) but this is now less common.

Buses There are a few direct buses from Huaquillas to Quito each day, 14 hrs., US$4; most go via Quevedo, but if you get a slower one via Riobamba and Ambato you may see all the great volcanoes. To Guayaquil about 5 hrs., including several stops at military check points, US$2.50. If in a hurry to reach Quito or Guayaquil, it may be advisable to change buses in Machala. Ecuatoriano and Panamericana have a reciprocal arrangement regarding tickets across borders and onwards, but there are no through bus services between Ecuador and Peru. To Cuenca several daily, 7 hrs., US$3.10. The road is completely paved going up the coast towards Guayaquil and then turning inland at El Triunfo; a circuitous route but quicker than taking the more direct road (10 hrs.) via Girón which is still under reconstruction.

An alternative point for crossing the Peruvian border is Macará in Loja Province (see page 666).

FROM GUAYAQUIL TO QUITO (6)

Note to Motorists There is a 3¼-km. bridge from Guayaquil across the river to Durán. A good paved road from there (summit at 4,120 metres) connects with the Andean Highway at Cajabamba, near Riobamba (see page 651).

The floods in 1983 closed the Guayaquil-Quito railway for through traffic. Contracts for repair work were awarded in 1985 but it will be several years until normal service can be resumed. The Riobamba-Quito service (223 km.) is in operation. Service on the Alausí-Guayaquil (142 km.) section was resumed in 1987 (see page 647). The lowland section is in very poor condition. We have retained the description of the full journey in the hope that the complete service will be restored.

The 464-km. railway line (1.067 metre gauge) passes through 87 km. of delta lands and then, in 80 km., climbs to 3,238 metres. At the summit, at Urbina, 3,609 metres is reached; it then rises and falls before debouching on to the Quito plateau at 2,857 metres. The line is a most interesting piece of railway engineering, with a maximum gradient of 5.5 per cent. Its greatest achievements, the Alausí loop and the Devil's Nose double zigzag (including a V switchback), are between Sibambe and Alausí, on the reopened section.

Leaving the river the train strikes out across the broad, fertile Guayas valley. It rolls through fields of sugar cane, or rice, past split cane houses built on high stilts, past sugar mills with their owners' fine homes. Everywhere there are waterways, with thousands of water-birds.

The first station is **Yaguachi**. On August 15 and 16 more than 15,000 visitors pour into this little town to attend the feast day celebrations at the church of San Jacinto, who is honoured in the region for having put an end to many epidemics.

The first stop of importance is **Milagro**, a large but uninteresting town of 77,000 people (Hotel Viker, F, no food, communal washing facilities; Hotel Marta, F; Restaurant Topo-Gigio, nearby, good, cheap food). Women swarm about the train selling pineapples which are particularly sweet and juicy. About 87 km. from Durán the train stops at **Bucay,** at the base of the Andes (market Sunday). Buses run parallel to the train between Bucay and Guayaquil, but take only 2 as opposed to 4 hrs.

The landscape spreads before you in every shade of green; row on row of coffee and cacao trees, with occasional groves of mango and breadfruit trees, banana plantations, fields of sugar cane, tobacco, and pineapple. The train follows the gorge of the River Chanchán until it reaches **Huigra.** By road Bucay to Huigra is still rough going. After leaving Huigra the train crosses and recrosses the River Chanchán, and then creeps along a narrow ledge between the mountain and the canyon. Here begins the most exciting part of the trip. The first mountain town reached is Chanchán, where the gorge is so narrow that the train has to pass through a series of tunnels and bridges in its zigzag course. Next is **Sibambe,** the junction for trains to Cuenca. A train leaves Sibambe at 0500 for Cuenca (service resumed), arrives at 1100. Shortly after leaving Sibambe the Quito train starts climbing the famous Nariz del Diablo (Devil's Nose), a perpendicular ridge rising in the gorge of the Chanchán to a height of 305 metres. This almost insurmountable engineering obstacle was finally conquered when a series of switchbacks was built on a 5.5 per cent grade. The air is chilly and stimulating.

Next comes *Alausí*, an old and colourful village (Sunday market), in the mountains on the Pan-American Highway, popular with Guayaquileños (at present the end of the railway line from Durán: *autoferro* to Durán Mon., Wed., Fri. 0400, daily ordinary train at 0800). It is best reached by road from Riobamba (no train on this section): the Cuenca and Guayaquil road links are less good. Bus Alausí-Quito at 0400 and 0800, 5½ hrs., US$1.75, often have to change in Riobamba; to Ambato hourly, 3 hrs., US$1, from main street. *Residencia Tequendama*, F, clean, friendly, hot water, rec.; *Hotel Europa*, opposite, E, safe parking in courtyard. *Hotel Panamericano*, G, clean, but poor food; *Hotel Gampala*, E, basic but adequate, breakfast available, check restaurant bill carefully. Restaurants: *Paradero Chumpisti, Salón Oriental*. All buses stop in front of *Hotel Panamericano*. You can walk on the railway track to Chunchi, a friendly village with a Sunday market, 15 km. An Inca trail to Ingapirca (**see page 664**) can be followed: it starts at **Achupallas**, 25 km. from Alausí.

After crossing the 120 metre long Shucos bridge, the train pulls into Palmira, on the crest of the first range of the Andes crossed by the railway. The train has climbed nearly 3,350 metres in less than 160 km. Precipitous mountain slopes covered with temperate-climate crops such as wheat and alfalfa gradually change to a bleak, desolate *páramo* (moor) where nothing grows except stiff clumps of grass. Now and then the monotonous landscape is brightened by the red poncho of an Indian shepherd watching his sheep. One by one the great snow-capped volcanoes appear: Chimborazo, Carihuairazo, Altar, Tungurahua, and the burning head of Sangay. They all seem very close because of the clear air.

Guamote is another point on the Pan-American Highway, five hours by car from the capital. There is an interesting market on Thursdays and some good half day walks in the area. There is a *pensión*, F, near the railway station and also some places to eat nearby. There have been reports of finds of Inca pottery and gold in the area. The train skirts the shores of Lake La Colta, before reaching the fertile Cajabamba valley. A road is being built to Macas (**see page 673**).

Cajabamba is a small, rather poor town. In 1534 the original Riobamba was founded on this site, but in 1797 a disastrous earthquake caused a large section of the hill on the north side of the town to collapse in a great landslide, which can still be seen. It killed several thousand of the original inhabitants of Riobamba and the town was moved almost twenty kilometres north-east to its present site. The new Riobamba has prospered, but Cajabamba has stagnated. Indian market on Sun., small but uncommercialized and interesting. There are no hotels and few restaurants.

Cajabamba is connected to Riobamba and Quito by a good paved highway and there is another paved highway from Cajabamba to Bucay and Guayaquil. A fairly good dirt road leaves the Pan-American Highway soon after Cajabamba, to the west; it is one of the oldest of the coast-Sierra routes and links Cajabamba with Guaranda and Babahoyo.

Riobamba (2,750 metres) is the capital of Chimborazo Province. It has 148,000 inhabitants, is built on a large flat site and has broad streets and many ageing but impressive buildings. Altogether, it seems a quiet, dignified place, with the nickname "Sultan of the Andes". Riobamba has many good churches and public buildings, and magnificent views of three of the great volcanic peaks, Chimborazo, Altar and Tungurahua. Four blocks NE of the railway station, along Calle Juan de la Valle, the Parque 21 de Abril affords an unobstructed view of Riobamba and environs; the park also has a colourful tile tableau of the history of Ecuador and is especially fine at sunset. Another good viewpoint is La Loma de Quito.

Riobamba has a new market building, but only a small part of the activity at the Saturday market takes place there. Buying and selling go on all over town. The "tourist" market in the small plaza south of the Convento de la Concepción museum is particularly fascinating and a good place to buy local handicraft—*ikat* shawls (*macanas*), embroidered and finely woven belts (*fajas*), blankets, embroidered dresses and shirts, Otavalan weavings and sweaters, *shigras*. Indian women come to the plaza each week with sacks full of bead and coin necklaces, old belts and dresses, blanket pins (*tupus*), and much more. Since Indian-style clothing is also sold here, the plaza is full of colourful Indians from different parts of Chimborazo province, each group wearing its distinctive costume. Two blocks east, there is a huge produce market in another plaza, also pottery, baskets, hats. All the streets in this area are filled with traders. There are also 2 markets on Weds.: Mercado La Condamine and Mercado San Alfonso. A variety of *pelota* games can be seen on Sunday afternoons. On Saturdays at 1800 there are cockfights on the corner of Tarquí with Guayaquil, entrance US$0.25. Open-air restaurants do a flourishing business in that Andean delicacy, roast *cuy* (guinea-pig). Hotel prices rise during independence *fiestas* around April 20, and rooms are difficult to obtain during the November basketball tournament. There are three cinemas.

The Convento de la Concepción, Orozco y España, has been carefully restored by the Banco Central and now functions as a religious art museum, open Tues.-Sat. 0900-1230 and 1500-1830, Sun. 0900-1230. Admission: US$0.60 for Ecuadoreans, US$0.90 for others. The guides are friendly and knowledgeable (tip expected). The priceless Custodia de Riobamba Antigua is the museum's greatest treasure, one of the richest of its kind in South America. Well worth a visit.

Hotels *El Galpón*, A/B, Argentinos y Zambrano, pool, sauna, some very poor reports received (some way from centre); next to it is *Chimborazo Internacional*, D, spacious rooms, fully carpeted, noisy discotheque, restaurant with fair food at reasonable prices; *Hostería El Troje*, 4½ km. on road to Chambo, D, pleasant, tourist centre, restaurant; *Liribamba*, Pichincha y Primera Constituyente, E, only serves breakfast, rec.; *Humboldt*, Av. Daniel León Borja 3548, E without breakfast, clean, with bath; *Segovia*, F, Primera Constituyente 2228, friendly, safe, hot water, ask for front room, food rec., rooftop view of the volcanos. *Los Shiris*, 10 de Agosto y Rocafuerte, E, with private bathroom, clean, nicely furnished, friendly, restaurant good; *Imperial*, Rocafuerte 22-15 y 10 de Agosto, E, a good quality hotel, hot water, private or shared bathroom, laundry facilities, can store luggage, friendly and comfortable, but loud music from bar on Fri. and Sat. nights. *Whymper*, Av. Miguel Angel León 23-10 y Primera Constituyente, T 964575, F, private bath, cafeteria; *Zeus*, Borja 4139, E with bath, clean, friendly, good restaurant, English spoken; *El Altar*, Km. 2 on Ambato road, F, good; *Americano*, G, pleasant, above restaurant of same name on Borja near station; *Colonial*, G, clean, usually hot water, uncomfortable beds; *Venecia*, Dávalos 2221 y 10 de Agosto, G, hot water; *Metropolitano*, Borja y Lavalle, F with or without bath, a pleasant, central, traditional hotel; *Residencial Camba Huasi*, 10 de Agosto 2824, F, laundry facilities, clean, dormitory beds, hot water, spacious, friendly, owner is a mountaineer and organizes trips to Chimborazo, safe parking in courtyard; *Residencias Villa Ester*, Unidad Nacional y Lavalle, F, hot shower, basic; *Puruhua*, F, near bus station at Eplicachima 2076 y Borja, friendly, fairly clean, but noisy; nearby is *Monterrey*, Rey Cacha y Eplicachima, F with or without bath, clean, good.

Restaurants *Chuquiragua*, 2 km. out on Quito road, best typical restaurant; *El Mesón*, Veloz 4199 y Los Sauces, some way out, good, high-class; *Steak House*, Magdalena Dávalos y Veloz, good food, expensive; *El Rodeo*, 10 de Agosto y García Moreno, a bistro, not cheap but good; *Alexander*, Falconi y Brasil, bistro style, reasonable; *Cabaña Montecarlo*, García Moreno 2410, good food, friendly service, popular with tourists; *Chifa China*, León Borja opp. *Hotel Puruhua*, good, cheap; *Chifa Internacional*, Veloz y Dávalos, Chinese food, good; *Chifa Chung Wah*, 10 de Agosto 2558, good food; *La Biblia*, Primera Constituyente and Miguel León, piano bar, reports vary; *El Pailón*, Pichincha y 10 de Agosto, clean, good set meal; *Café Paola*, Calle Pichincha (between Guayaquil and 10 de Agosto), good breakfast, empanadas and hamburgers; *Latino*, 10 de Agosto, friendly, food OK; *El Molino*, 10 de Agosto, clean, friendly, cheap, good food; *Su Casa*, Primera Constituyente, between Pichincha and García Moreno, good food, nice serving; *Pato Juan*, España y 10 de Agosto, snack bar, pleasant. Many other snackbars along 10 de Agosto, of which *Pollo Gus*, simple chicken and chips, but cheap and tasty.

Entertainment Peña-restaurants *Media Estocada*, Borja y Duchicela, and *Parrillada Gaucha*, Unidad Nacional. *Peñas* at *Taquí Huasi*, Orozco y 4a Transversal, and *La Casa Vieja*, Orozco y Tarqui. Disco, Thurs.-Sun, at *Zero*, Km. 1½ on road to Cajabamba.

Note In Riobamba jail is a British citizen who welcomes visitors. You must hand in your passport at the gate and your bags will be searched.

Exchange Banco Internacional, 10 de Agosto y García Moreno.

Immigration Primera Constituyente y Tarqui, T 964-697.

Tourist Office Dituris, Calle Tarqui 2248 y Primera Constituyente. Open Tues.-Sat. 0800-1200, 1430-1700. Addresses for hirers of climbing equipment. Souvenir shops on 10 de Agosto between Carabobo and Rocafuerte.

Transport All trains to Guayaquil were suspended in 1983 after heavy rains destroyed much of the track. A daily *autoferro* runs to Quito, 0500, 5 hrs., US$1, buy tickets in advance. A tourist train runs to Quito on Sun. and Wed. a.m. (details from Metropolitan Tours or other travel agencies). Bus to Quito, US$1.50, 3½ hrs., about every 15 mins. Bus to Guaranda, US$0.80, 2 hrs., beautiful views. Bus to Cuenca, 6 a day via Alausí, 7 hrs., US$3.15. A more popular route to

Cuenca, entirely on paved roads, is via El Triunfo, on the Guayaquil bus US$2 to El Triunfo, where you change buses, then US$2.50 to Cuenca; mostly good roads and scenery. Bus to Santo Domingo, US$2, 5 hrs. Bus to Baños, US$0.50, 1 hr. Bus to Puyo, US$1.10, 3½ hrs. direct. There are 2 buses (US$3.50, 10 hrs.) to Huaquillas every evening (1915 and 2100), which avoid Guayaquil; book the day before, arrive early and be prepared to fight for your seat. Bus to Guayaquil, about 35 a day, US$2.15, 4½ hrs.; the trip is really spectacular for the first two hours. There are pirate buses which charge more than the regular lines and do not sell tickets in the bus station, first come first served, they can be useful when all the others are full up. There is a well-run *terminal terrestre* on Eplicachima y Av. D. L. Borja for buses to Quito, Guayaquil, Ambato, etc., but buses to Baños and the Oriente leave from the Terminal Oriental, 10 de Agosto y Puruhua.

Excursions Two are of great interest: the first, to **Guano**, an attractive hemp-working and carpet-making town of 6,000 inhabitants 10 km. to the north, with prehistoric monoliths nearby; there are frequent buses but nowhere to eat. You can have rugs made to your own design. After Guano you can take the bus on to Santa Teresita from where it is a 1 km. walk downhill to Balneario Las Elenas: 3 pools, 1 tepid, 2 cool. The second is to Baños, scenic route along Chambo River (**see page 656**).

Climbing To climb Chimborazo contact Enrique Veloz Coronado, mountain guide and technical adviser of the Asociación de Andinismo de Chimborazo, Chile 33-21 y Francia, Riobamba (T 960916). He will provide all the necessary equipment; you must agree on a fee with him for the trip you want to make (**see page 655**). He is best reached after 1500 and is very helpful even if you don't need his services as a guide. For Sangay, take a taxi to Alao and hire guides or carriers of food, tents, etc. there; remember you have to pay for and organize the food for your porters separately, otherwise you have to pay them a lot more. Make sure the fee covers the return journey as well. Also Expediciones Andinas (Marco Cruz), Argentinos 3860 y Zambrano, T 964-915 (office), 962-845 (house), recommended (he is a certified guide of the German Alpine Club).

To the crater of **Altar**: Travel to Penipe by bus (bargain for the price) from Baños or Riobamba/Ambato, then to Candelaria by truck, or bus which passes between 1200 and 1400. Walk out of the village, cross the bridge and go up to Hacienda Releche on your left (about 2 km.). There is a *refugio* (US$1.10) with beds, warm water, shower, cooking facilities and friendly keeper, about 1 km. from Candelaria, a light and dark green building at the turning for the Hacienda, marked by a Sangay National Park sign. It is not always open, ask in Riobamba beforehand at the Ministry of Tourism or the Sangay National Park office, Primera Constituyente y Pichincha, Ministry of Agriculture. In Penipe ask for Ernesto Haro, who will take you to the *refugio* in his jeep (US$3 one way) and pick you up from there at a pre-arranged time. The track to the Altares leads on past the Hacienda, but it is best to ask someone to point out the faint track which branches to the left about 30-40 minutes after the Hacienda and leads up a hill to a ridge where it joins a clear track. This goes south first and then turns east up the valley of the River Collanes. It is about 6 hrs. to the crater which is surrounded by magnificent snow-capped peaks. It is possible to camp in the crater, but better still, about 20 mins. before you turn into the broad U-shaped valley leading up to the crater there is a good-sized cave, the floor of which is lined with dry rushes; there is a fire ring at the entrance. Guides to Altar can be hired for about US$3.50 a day, and horses are US$3.50 each a day. Because of damage done to the track by mudslides the route is hazardous and you would be unwise to do it alone. Consult the National Park Office about conditions, they are in radio contact with the Guardería at Candelaria.

From Riobamba to Quito the road is paved. Between Riobamba and Cevallos the railway reaches its highest point at Urbina (3,609 metres). At the pass, there are fine views in the dry season (June is probably the first safe month) of Chimborazo and its smaller sister mountain, Carihuairazo. Then the railway and the Pan-American Highway wind down towards the Ambato basin. Between Riobamba and Ambato is Mocha, where guinea-pigs (*cuy*) are raised for the table; you can sample roast *cuy* at stalls by the roadside. The valley's patchwork of fields gives an impression of greater fertility and prosperity than the Riobamba zone. The houses seem larger and better built, and almost universally, a small crucifix crowns the roof, where figurines of domestic animals are also found. Large areas of apple orchards and onion fields are passed before Ambato is finally reached.

Ambato (population 140,000) was almost completely destroyed in the great 1949 earthquake. The modern cathedral faces the attractive Parque Montalvo, where there is a statue of the writer Juan Montalvo (1833-1889) who is buried in a memorial in a neighbouring street. His house (Bolívar y Montalvo) is open to the public; entrance free (T 821-024). In the Colegio Nacional Bolívar, at Sucre y Lalama, there is a museum of stuffed birds and other animals and items of local historical interest (US$0.05, closed Sat. and Sun.). The Quinta de Mera, an old mansion in gardens in Atocha suburb, open 0900-1200, 1400-1800, can be reached by bus from Espejo y 12 de Novembre. Out along the River Ambato (a pleasant walk) is the prosperous suburb of Miraflores. Ambato has a famous festival in February, the *Fiesta de frutas y flores*, during which it is impossible to get a hotel room unless you book ahead; similarly in Riobamba, Baños and Latacunga. The town has the unique distinction of prohibiting water-throwing at carnival, making it safe for tourists at this time! It is an important centre for the manufacture of rugs and has some excellent tourist shops in the centre, e.g. Artesanías Montalvo, Eguez y Cevallos: look for colourful and good-quality cloth shoulder bags. Leather clothes can be specially made quite cheaply. On a clear day Tungurahua and Chimborazo can be seen from the city.

The main market is held on Mon., and smaller markets on Wed. and Fri.; they are interesting, but have few items for the tourist.

Hotels *Ambato*, Guayaquil y Rocafuerte, C, best, clean, restaurant, casino, squash, highly rec.; *Florida*, Av. Miraflores 1131, D, pleasant, clean, set meal good at US$3; *Villa Hilda*, E, in Av. Miraflores, German spoken, rec., laundry, restaurant good, limited menu but lots to eat, big garden. Buses from the centre stop outside the *Florida*. *La Lira*, Montalvo y Cevallos, E, good, cheaper for long stay; *Cumandá*, F with bath, clean, safe, basic, water supply erratic in this area, 12 de Noviembre 2494; *Carrillo*, F, Av. de las Américas, clean, basic water supply, sometimes used as a brothel, near bus station, restaurant; *Residencial Americano*, Plaza 12 de Noviembre, G, basic, hot water; *Asia*, Espejo y 12 de Noviembre, F, hot water, central; *Executivo*, Espejo y 12 de Noviembre, F, large rooms, hot water; *Vivero*, Mera 504 y Cevallos, E, good. There are a lot of cheap *pensiones* and hotels on Calle Juan León Mera.

Restaurants *Cabaña del Negro*, Av. Miraflores 263, good seafood; *El Alamo*, Swiss-owned, excellent meals, now three restaurants, one at Sucre 660, *El Alamo Júnior*, self-service, for snacks, and the *Gran Alamo*, round the corner at Montalvo 520. *La Borgoña*, 13 de Abril y Mera, French; *Chambord*, Quito y Rocafuerte, international; *El Pollo Loco*, Lalama y Sucre, chicken, likewise *Pollo Rico*, Alfaro 521; local cooking at *Rincón Criollo*, Eguez y Bolívar. Seafood at *Monarca*, Bolívar y Eguez (best), *Los Sauces*, Mera y Bolívar, and *El Tiburón No. 2*, Primera Imprenta y 5 de Junio. Oriental at *Chifa Nueva Hongkong*, Bolívar y Martínez, and *Chifa Internacional*, 12 de Noviembre y Aillón; also along Cevallos (e.g. *Chifa Jao Fua* at No. 540, popular). Grills: *La Brasa*, Montalvo y Olmedo, *El Gaucho*, Bolívar y Castillo, and *El Faraón*, Bolívar y Lalama. Many good cafeterias and snackbars. *Mama Miche*, Centro Comercial, open 24 hrs. For rockbottom prices with rather dubious hygiene, try the markets. *Happy Chicken*, next to *Hotel Vivero* for clean, cheap, fast food.

Exchange Only Citibank travellers' cheques can be changed at Citibank, Calle Sucre; Banco del Pacífico changes notes only. Cambiaria Pichincha, Darquea y Sevilla, accepts travellers' cheques; Cambiato, Bolívar 686, changes Visa cheques; money exchange at *Café Español*, Montalvo 607, Mon.-Sat., 0900-1800.

Tourist Office Dituris is next to the *Hotel Ambato* on the 900 block of Calle Guayaquil. Open 0830-1230, 1430-1830, Mon.-Fri.

Travel Agents Metropolitan Touring, Bolívar 471; Coltur, Cevallos 536; Ecuadorian Tours (American Express) Bolívar 678. There is a *peña* on Fri. and Sat., *Peña del Tungurahua*, in block 2 of the Centro Comercial.

Immigration Av. Fermín Cevallos y Juan León Mera, T 820-000.

Buses To Quito, 3 hrs., US$1.25. To Guayaquil, 6½ hrs., US$2.50. To Cuenca, US$4, 7 hrs., to get to Cuenca in daylight take a morning Guayaquil bus to El Triunfo and pick up a Guayaquil—Cuenca bus, or take a bus to Biblián and change there. (There can be some discomfort from descent to under 200 metres and subsequent climb up to 2,600, and you may have a long wait at El Triunto; this route is 2 hrs. slower than the direct one.) To Baños, paved road, lovely scenery, 45 mins., US$0.40. To Latacunga, 30 mins. US$0.50. To Santo Domingo de los Colorados, 4 hrs., US$1.60; to Tena, US$2.20, 6 hrs. To Puyo, US$1.10, 3 hrs. To Esmeraldas, US$2.50, 8 hours. Main bus station is 2 km. N from centre, near the railway station; town buses go there from Plaza Cevallos in the city centre.

Ambato is connected by the excellent paved Pan-American Highway south to Riobamba and north to Latacunga and Quito. To the west, a narrow, winding road (now paved) leads up the valley of the Ambato river, over a high area of desert called the Grande Arenal, past Carihuairazo and Chimborazo, and down through the Chimbo valley to Guaranda. This spectacular journey takes about three hours.

Excursions To Salasaca (see below); to Picaihua by frequent bus to see the local work from *cabuya* fibre, and to Pinllo to see the leather work.

Chimborazo, 6,310 metres: there are two routes up the mountain:

1) The South West face: there are no direct buses so take a taxi (US$25 for one day, US$30 return next day or later, US$13 one way) from Riobamba to the Edward Whymper refuge, which takes 1 hr., 47 km., or a bus to San Juan village and hitch from there. The road ends at 4,800 metres, where there is a new refuge, or you can walk up to the Edward Whymper refuge at 5,000 metres which is at the foot of the Thielman glacier. There should be two keepers at this refuge, which provides water and a bed (US$1 p.p. a night, plus US$0.50 charge for gas in gas stove). Beware of thieves if you leave anything in the refuge or even in your car at 4,800 metres. From the refuge to the summit the climb is 8-9 hrs and the descent about 4 hrs. There are three routes depending on your experience and ability. Recommended to start at 2400 or 0100. There is a road from San Juan to Pogyos round Carihuairazo, making a round trip by jeep, Riobamba-Chimborazo-Ambato, possible.

2) The North West face, or Pogyos route: Take the Guaranda bus from Ambato along the new paved road or a truck along the spectacular old road (50 km.) to the valley of Pogyos. At Pogyos (4,000 metres) there is a house with a metal roof where you can hire mules for US$4 each to carry your luggage. (Beware of pilfering from your bags on ascent.) Walk about 3 hrs. to the Fabián Zurita refuge (4,900 metres); there are no facilities or furniture here, only the stone-floored building, which shelters about 20 people. Some climbers prefer to take their own tent. Take water up (obtainable at Pogyos, containers in Ambato). From the refuge to the summit is about an 8-hr. climb and 3-4 hr. descent. Advisable to start at 0100. (We are grateful to Enrique Veloz Coronado—**see page** 623—for much of this information.)

Dr Sverre Aarseth writes that in order to climb this mountain it is essential to have at least one week's acclimatization above 3,000 metres. The best season is December and June-September. Sr. Héctor Vásquez at Colegio National Bolívar, Ambato, has helped many expeditions with travel arrangements and information; he is a top-grade mountaineer. The original Whymper route is an attractive one, but is harder than the Pogyos route; especially the scree where rolling stones present a hazard during the afternoon descent (the upper part is quite straightforward with two or three on a rope). Previous parties will most likely have left marker flags; these are often needed for descent in a cloud. Very soft snow between first and second summit but usually there will be a good path from previous parties (otherwise snow shoes might be needed). The ascent to the summit is very steep and partly exposed (falling could be fatal). No one without mountaineering experience should attempt the climb, and rope, ice-axe and crampons must be used. Carihuairazo (5,020 metres) is a spur of Chimborazo.

Guaranda (14,000 inhabitants) is the capital of Bolívar Province. It is a quiet town which, because it is built on seven hills, proudly calls itself "the Rome of Ecuador". Carnival is very enjoyable. Market day is Sat. Guaranda is connected by a new paved road to Ambato (several buses) and Babahoyo, and a poor, narrow road to Riobamba. It is the main centre for the wheat and maize-growing Chimbo valley, but has long stagnated since newer, faster routes replaced the old Guayaquil-Quito road through Babahoyo and Guaranda.

Hotels *La Colina*, high up on Av. Guayaquil, D, well kept, good value; *Cochabamba*, García Moreno y 7 de Mayo, F with bath, best in town; *Pensión Ecuador*, opposite, F; *Residencial Bolívar*, Sucre y Rocafuerte, E, very good, hot showers; *Matiaví*, Av. Eliza Mariño, F, clean, next to bus station; *Residencial Acapulco*, 10 de Agosto y 9 de Abril, G, basic.

Restaurants Hotel Cochabamba, best; *Santa Fe*, opp. *Resid. Acapulco*, reasonable; *Guaranda* soda bar on G. Moreno y Pichincha.

Buses Bus station on road to Ambato. To Ambato, US$1.20, 3¼ hrs.; Riobamba, US$0.70, 2½ hrs.; Guayaquil, US$1.75, 3½ hrs. None direct to Quito.

To the east of Ambato, an important road leads to Salasaca, Pelileo, and Baños and then on along the Pastaza valley to Mera, Shell Mera, Puyo and Tena in the Oriente (**see page 671**). It is paved to Puyo.

Salasaca is a small modernized village 14 km. (½ hr.) from Ambato, at the centre of the Salasaca Indian zone. The Salasacas wear distinctive black ponchos with white shirts, trousers and broad white hats. Most of them are farmers, but they are best known for weaving *tapices*, strips of cloth with remarkable bird and animal shapes in the centre. A co-operative has fixed the prices on the *tapices* it sells in its store near the church. Throughout the village the prices are the same, and no cheaper than in Quito. If you have the time you can order one to be specially made; this takes four to six weeks, but is well worth the wait. You can watch the Indians weaving in the main workshop opposite the church.

Pelileo, 5 km. beyond Salasaca, is a lively little market town which has been almost completely rebuilt on a new site since the 1949 earthquake. In all Pelileo has been destroyed by four earthquakes during its 400-year history. The new town springs to life on Saturday, the main market day. The ruins of Pelileo Viejo can be seen about 2 km. east of the present site on the north side of the road to Baños. *Fiesta* on August 15.

From Pelileo, the road gradually descends to Las Juntas, the meeting point of the Patate and Chambo rivers to form the Pastaza river, and where the road from Riobamba comes in. It then continues along the lower slopes of the volcano Tungurahua to Baños (25 km. from Pelileo). The road gives good views of the Pastaza gorge and the volcano.

Baños (1,800 metres) is a holiday resort with a supposedly miraculous Virgin and hot springs; very busy at weekends and increasingly touristy. The central Basilica attracts many pilgrims; the paintings of miracles performed by Nuestra Señora de Santa Agua are worth seeing. There is a *fiesta* in her honour in October with processions, bands, fireworks, sporting events and a lot of general gaiety. The Basilica of Baños has a museum (stuffed birds, Nuestra Señora's clothing). There is another *fiesta* on December 15 to celebrate the town's anniversary when each *barrio* hires a *saka* band and there is much dancing in the streets. The following day there is a parade in which spectators are outnumbered by participants. There is a zoo off the road to Puyo on the left, about 1 km. from town, run by the Church authorities, US$0.20 entrance, cages far too small and excessive loudspeaker noise. The Pastaza river rushes past Baños to the Agoyán falls 10 km. further down the valley, marred by engineering works connected with the construction of a hydroelectric scheme. The whole area between Pelileo and Baños has a relaxing sub-tropical climate (the rainy season is usually from May to October, especially July and August). It is here that Ecuador's best *aguardiente* is made. Street vendors sell *canelazo*, a sweet drink of *aguardiente*, lime, water and cinnamon, also jawsticking toffee (*tafi*) made in ropes in shop doorways, and painted balsa-wood birds (see *El Chaguamango* shop by Basílica). Two sets of thermal baths are in the town: the main set is by the waterfall close to the *Hotel Sangay*; the Santa Clara baths are about ½ km. further W, up against the mountain, and the third, the Salado, which is pleasanter (entrance to each is US$0.20), is 1½ km. out of town on the Ambato road. There are regular buses every 30 mins. between the Salado baths and the Agoyán Falls, passing by the centre of town. All the baths can be very crowded and the water not very hot. **Interesting side trips** are possible from the main Pelileo-Baños highway across the main valley, north to Patate, or up the Chambo valley to Penipe and Riobamba, or take taxi to Puente Vendas, 2 hrs., US$2.20, beautiful ride.

Hotels *Sangay*, D, with bath, beautifully situated close to waterfall, restaurant (open to non-residents), tennis court, swimming pool, squash courts, accommodation in chalets reported better than in rooms (same price), rec. Information and some equipment for expeditions to the jungle and volcanoes may be provided by the hotel. *Villa Gertrudis*, Montalvo 2975, good situation on edge of town, with lovely garden, D, demi-pensión, reserve in advance, rec.; *Cabañas Bascún*, on edge of town (nr. El Salado hot springs), D, quite comfortable, pool, sauna, tennis, restaurant; *Paraíso (Humboldt)*, Ambato y Haflans, D with board or F without food, bath, clean, beautiful view from front rooms; *Palace*, opposite *Sangay* (even closer to waterfall) good facilities, D, restaurant, breakfast US$1, dinner US$3. *Residencial Magdalena*, Oriente y Alfaro, E with bath, clean, warm water, rec.; *Hostal Los Helechos*, F, on Parque Central, close to Post Office and Ietel, restaurant, noisy; *Timara*, near plaza (ask for *Tienda de Mariposas*—butterfly shop, serves good breakfast), F, hot showers, clean, laundry facilities, use of good kitchen, owner's son takes tours to Oriente (US$15/day); *Pensión Patty*, Eloy Alfaro 556, near market, F, G for stays of over one night, rec., clean, basement rooms poor, otherwise good facilities, use of kitchen, laundry, comfortable and quiet, family-run, the helpful owner is a mountaineer and can offer good, free advice, sell maps and hire equipment; *Residencial Los Pinos*, Rocafuerte y Maldonado, F, clean, friendly, ask for front room with view, preferably on second floor; *Residencial Baños*, F, Ambato y Alfaro, good, washing facilities; *Residencial Teresita*, on the

Parque de la Basílica, G, cooking facilities, hot water, prices vary; *Amborado*, on the plaza opposite *Teresita*, F with shower, modern, clean, friendly, rooms have balconies overlooking the square; *Americano*, G, 12 de Noviembre y Martínez, basic but friendly, cooking facilities available, thin walls. *Flor de Oriente*, Ambato y Maldonado, E, very good, lots of choice in restaurant, rec. There are two *Residenciales Las Delicias*, *1*, on the Parque Central, F, front rooms have lovely view, but are noisy, friendly; *Las Delicias 2*, Ambato y Haflans, is newer, both reported dirty; *Agoyán*, F, opposite Basilica, clean, good, ask for front room overlooking square; *Anita*, Rocafuerte y 16 de Diciembre, F, behind the market, clean, friendly, quiet, use of kitchen; *El Santuario* above Banco del Pacífico, F with bath, hot water on request, good value; *Chile*, in nearest square to bus station, clean, comfortable, private bath; *Santa Clara*, 12 de Noviembre y Montalvo, G, use of kitchen possible, washing facilities, noisy, nice garden, rec.; *Pensión Guayaquil*, on Parque de la Basílica, F, old and picturesque, good food, but no private baths. Several near corner Ambato with Alfaro. Houses for rent on a weekly basis: the owners of *El Paisano* restaurant have three houses, US$24 for the most expensive. *Casa Familiar*, 2 blocks behind clocktower, rooms, F, and vegetarian restaurant, use of kitchen, laundry facilities (Danish and Ecuadorean owners). Camping is not recommended on the mountainsides as several people have frozen to death.

Restaurants   *El Marqués No. 1*, on Montalvo, just beyond Hotels *Sangay* and *Palace*, in old house, closes early, good steaks for US$2, quiet and friendly. *El Marqués No. 2*, 16 de Diciembre y Rocafuerte, international food; *Monica's*, down the road from *Pensión Patty*, well-prepared and interesting menus, popular gringo meeting place, good, but be careful with overcharging, very slow service; *Pan-Tera*, Parque Central, good and cheap breakfast; *Donde Marcelo*, Ambato nr. 16 de Diciembre, good, inexpensive; *Le Petit Restaurant*, Eloy Alfaro 2-46 y Montalvo, excellent french cuisine; *Chifa Oriental*, Ambato y Alfaro, fair food, low prices, friendly; *El Paisano*, rec., Martínez y Santa Clara, on road to *Sangay* hotel, vegetarian, but meat also served, also good for breakfast, with yoghurt; *Rincón de Suecia*, opposite *Acapulco*, pizzas, good, evenings only, Swedish and English spoken; *Regines*, 12 de Noviembre y Montalvo, is a German café, popular with travellers, excellent Irish coffee; *La Fuente*, on main street, good set meal; *Lucerno*, also on main street, clean, friendly, good value set meal; good vegetarian restaurant next to *Pensión Guayaquil* on main square; *Country Kitchen*, Martínez 615 y Haflans, one block behind main square, mostly vegetarian, good value (American owned, Karen Rittenhouse). *Su Café*, next to the market, is rec. for breakfast; hot bread at 0600, also good butter and jam (sometimes only coffee available); *Edén*, nr. bus terminal, good food, slow service; *Hotel Humboldt* rec. for breakfast, in main street.

Entertainment   Cockfighting, Coliseo, Sun. 1400-1800. *Peñas La Burbuja* and *Agoyán* (near main baths), Fri. and Sat.

Bank   Banco del Pacífico, Carrera 3 y Calle 2, changes all travellers' cheques and foreign currency, but only from 1100-1330.

Spanish Classes given by Norwegian Jörgen Grönneberg, Corinca, 16 de Diciembre y Martínez, 5th floor, rec.

Book Exchange   J.Urquizo (local artist), 12 de Noviembre y Ambato.

Laundry   Clothes can be washed at the municipal washhouse next to the main baths for US$1.20 a bundle.

Warning Many people have been bitten by dogs in Baños, there are hundreds of strays. If you are bitten, report to the hospital where you will be treated, free of charge, and passed on to the public health inspector who will find out whether the dog concerned is rabid (**but see warning on page 682**).

Tourist Office   on Parque Central (Haflans y Ambato) open Tues.-Sat., 0800-1200, 1400-1800.

Buses   To Quito, via Ambato, US$1.50, 4½ hrs.; to Ambato, ¾ hr., US$0.40; to Riobamba, 1 hr., US$0.50; to Latacunga, 2½ hrs., US$0.60; to Puyo, 2 hrs., US$0.80 (road damaged by 1987 earthquake); for Macas, change at Puyo, 0830, US$1.30, 6 hrs., magnificent scenery; to Tena, 5½ hrs., US$1.80 by bus (more leg room) with Coop. Riobamba, or US$2 by *buseta*, only three direct buses Baños-Tena, but frequent passing buses from Riobamba and Ambato; seat reservations rec. (but buses don't always leave); to Misahuallí, change at Tena, buses leave every 20 mins., US$0.30, 1 hr.; or at the Río Napo crossing, **see page 671**. The bus station is on the Ambato-Puyo road a short way from the centre, and is the scene of vigorous volleyball games most afternoons.

From Baños it is possible to climb *Tungurahua* (5,016 metres—part of Sangay National Park); follow road opposite police control on Ambato side of town, then first mule track to right of store and follow the path to Pondoa; do not follow the road up to the baths. If you are driving to Pondoa, take the main Ambato road and turn off to the left about 1 km. from the town centre. The road runs parallel to the main road for several km. before turning east into the mountains. Park the car at the shop in Pondoa. The walk from the shop to the beginning of the trail takes 30 mins. *Pensión Patty* in Baños arranges equipment, guides (min. US$32 a day for two climbers and US$16 for each extra one), and jeeps to Pondoa Tues., Thurs., Sat. 0830, US$1 p.p. (return 1600-1700 next day); there is also an occasional bus from Baños to Pondoa, and a truck leaves at 0830, possibly daily (check at *Pensión Patty*). It takes 3-5 hrs. to reach the Santos Ocaña *refugio* (3,800 metres— US$1, purchase ticket at the shop in Pondoa, where sketch map of route can be obtained) situated 3-4 hrs. below the snowline, then about 4 hours from the *refugio* to the summit early next morning (about 0330). Leave summit about 0930 as clouds come down later in the day: allow 2 hours for descent to *refugio* and leave *refugio* by 1400 in order to get back to Baños on same day. Take a sleeping bag and food; there are cooking facilities at the *refugio*, but no eating utensils and rarely any lighting, no heating and it can be cold. For a guide and pack animals enquire at Baños tourist office or Pondoa shop; guide and mule for 1 pack US$5, for 2 packs, US$7. Horses can be hired for US$0.90 an hour (see Julio Albán, Segundo Sánchez or Víctor Barriga near the Plaza Central or through tourist office). A tiring but rewarding climb; requires experience and crampons for the summit. Best season is December to March.

There are many interesting walks in the Baños area. You can cross the Pastaza by a suspension bridge across the main road from the bus station. Short hikes include San Martín shrine, 3 hrs., which overlooks deep rocky canyon with the Pastaza River thundering below; along the old road to Ambato to Lligua, a flowery little village straddling the Lligua River at its junction with the Pastaza; to Runtún, a village of a dozen mud dwellings, two sporting a billiard table, from which there is a splendid view of Tungurahua (3½-4 hrs.). Cold drinks sold at the billiard hall, no food. There are two paths from Baños to Runtún, one from south end of Calle 9, the other from Calle 6.

20 km. from Baños on the Puyo road are the Río Verde falls; a bus goes from the Baños terminal, ¾ hr., US$0.12. Cross river and take path to right of last house on right, take immediate left fork, trail down to suspension bridge with view of falls.

Guides in Baños: apart from Patricio at *Pensión Patty*, whose trips cost US$14 a day, there is Sebastián Moya, who can be found either at *Country Kitchen* or Tsantse Tours (*Pensión Patty*—T 740202). He is a Shuar Indian who will lead tours anywhere for US$13 a day (careful planning needed to minimize travelling time), food not included. You may have to wait some weeks for him to be free. Also contactable through *Pensión Patty* is mountain guide Carlos Rodríguez, who takes climbs in both the Sangay and Cotopaxi National Parks. We have received some critical reports of tours out of Baños, especially of Siamgal Tours (also operate from Puyo and Misahuallí).
    Horses to hire on the square in front of the Post Office, US$0.75 per hour, without guide, for trekking in the mountains.

North from Ambato the railway and Pan-American Highway (many buses) pass through **Salcedo,** good Thurs. and Sun. markets (*Hostería Rumipamba de las Rosas,* D, restaurant, swimming pool, exchanges US$ notes; *Hostal Las Piedras*, G, on Parque; *Residencial Las Vegas*, Bolívar y Paredes, F, hot water, private showers; *Restaurant Ritz*, Bolívar y Sucre, chicken.) to Latacunga, the capital of Cotopaxi Province.

Latacunga, with 30,000 inhabitants, is a place where the abundance of light grey lava rock has been artfully employed. Cotopaxi is much in evidence, though it is 29 km. away. Provided they are not hidden in the clouds, which unfortunately is all too often (try the early morning), as many as nine volcanic cones can be seen from Latacunga. The central plaza, Parque Vicente León, is a colourful and beautifully maintained botanical garden, where the shrubs are sculpted into various shapes (e.g., fans, globes, wedding cakes). There are several other gardens in the town including Parque San Francisco and Lago Flores. The colonial character of the town has been well preserved.

Just off the Parque Vicente León is the Pasaje Catedral, a colonial building converted into an arcade of shops, offices, and a small art gallery that features a 17th-century aerial view painting of Latacunga (open Tues.-Sat. 0830 to 1800). Casa Cultural, the Museo Etnográfico (closed Sun. and Mon.). There is a Sat. (also, but smaller, on Tues.) market on the Plaza de San Sebastián; goods for sale include *chigras* (sweaters), and homespun wool and cotton yarn. Tourist Office at Quito 73-12.

Festival   The Fiesta de Nuestra Señora de la Merced (Sept. 22-24) is celebrated with dancing in the streets. Some of the masks and costumes used are on display in the Casa Cultural. Mama Negra festival, colourful costumes, headdresses and masks, in November.

Hotels   *Cotopaxi*, on main square, E, with bathroom, good, safe for luggage, clean, parking, hot water after 0700, rec., ask for view over plaza (these rooms noisy at weekends); *Estambul*, F, Belisario Quevedo 7340 y Salcedo, soap, toilet paper, rec., friendly. *Latacunga*, on main Quito road, E with bath, TV, friendly, restaurant rarely open at weekends. *Jacqueline* is G, but bad. Also

Costa Azul, G, unfriendly, good meals; this and the *Residencial Los Andes* (F) are along the Ambato road. Accommodation is not abundant.

Restaurants *Los Copihues*, on main square; *La Carreta*, Quito 150, good 4-course lunch; *Cyrano*, 2 de Mayo 7674, chicken; *Chifa Tokio*, Guayaquil 45-58, moderate prices, good value; *Chifa Yut Wah*, Quinchero y Ordóñez 6973, good, cheap; *Salón Coseñita*, Echeverría 1143, good cheap meals; *El Estudiante*, Antonio Vela 78, lunch US$0.50. *Pollo Dorado*, 5 de Junio y Vela, good value, US$ 1.30; milkshakes and real coffee recommended at *Pingüino*, Quito y Salcedo; *Los Alpes*, opposite the *Cotopaxi*, good, cheap. *Pollos Gus*, cheap roast chicken, on Ambato road. Ice cream store off main square, Salcedo y Quito. Superb bread at *Hector's*, opposite *Pingüino*. Difficult to eat after 2000.

Exchange Banco de Pichincha on Plaza, cash and travellers' cheques.

Buses to Quevedo, 6 hrs., US$1.60; to Quito, 2 hrs., US$0.75; to Ambato, ½ hr., US$0.40; to Guayaquil, US$2.50, 6 hrs. Day trips to Cotopaxi (**see page 660**) can be arranged with a taxi for about US$16.

A fine paved road leads west to *Pujilí* (good Sun. market; also, but smaller, on Wed.; beware local illicit liquor and pickpockets), 15 km. away (bus, US$0.18) and then on over the Western Cordillera to Zumbahua, Macuchi and Quevedo.

Zumbahua, a cluster of 40 houses by an old *hacienda*, 65 km. from Pujilí, has a fine Sat. morning market (a local market for produce and animals, not tourist items, but rated as one of the most interesting and colourful in Ecuador and not to be missed) with llamas on view. Buses US$0.60 from Latacunga throughout the day at 1½ hourly intervals—best for continuing to Quilotoa, 0630, leaves from corner of *Hotel Turismo*, 2 hrs., beautiful ride. Bus drivers on the Latacunga-Quevedo line often do not want to take tourists to Zumbahua as they want to fill up the bus with people going to Quevedo. Car hire has been rec. A taxi can cost the same as the bus. Many interesting crafts are practised by the Indians in the neighbouring valley of Tigua: skin paintings, hand-carved wooden masks, baskets.

Zumbahua is the point to turn off for a visit to *Quilotoa*, a volcanic crater filled by a beautiful emerald lake, to which there is a steep path from rim. From the rim of the crater several snowcapped volcanoes can be seen in the distance. It is reached by a dusty road which runs north from Zumbahua (turn right and over the bridge at the fork in the road, there are no road signs and the crater can only be recognized when you are on top of it) to Quilotoa and on to Chugchilán (this last stretch is the worst). At the crater itself, expect to be besieged by persistent beggars. It's wise to carry some food or small bills to buy them off, and take a stick against dogs on the road. Also be prepared for sudden changes in the weather. The walk to Quilotoa is 9-10 km., or about 2-3 hrs. hike from Zumbahua; take water as that from the lake is quite sulphurous and water is generally hard to find. Alternatively, you can get a bus on Saturdays, US$0.15, but it will only go part of the way, leaving you with a ½ hr. walk to the crater. Trucks go up after the Saquisilí market on Thurs. p.m. During the wet season, the best views are in the early morning so those with a tent may wish to camp. Alternatively, hitch a truck (which is easy on market day); you will be dropped close to the volcano; trucks back from Zumbahua leave about midday on market day, and a bus goes to Latacunga at 1300. Vehicles bound for Chugchilán drop the traveller 5 mins. from the lagoon, those for Ponce on the Ponce turnoff, still about a 40-min. walk north. Hitching a return trip should not be left till late in the afternoon.

The Sat. trip to Zumbahua market and the Quilotoa crater is one of the best excursions in Ecuador, but there are only two very small *pensiones* in Zumbahua, without plumbing; one has no beds and they do not like to rent rooms to foreigners, often claiming to be full. In Zumbahua, two houses sell cooked food. Macuchi, on the main road to Quevedo some way beyond Zumbahua, is a mining centre for gold and various non-ferrous metals. The mines were developed in the 1930s by an American company, and now they are almost abandoned.

It is 20 km. from Quilotoa crater to *Chugchilán*, a beautiful but tiring walk along the edge of a canyon. Water is available from small streams, but take a purifier. One bus leaves Zumbahua for Chugchilán at 1400; return buses (3) between 0300 and 0330 (also at this time on Thurs. to Saquisilí). In Chugchilán, a very poor village in one of the most scenic areas of Ecuador, you can buy an evening meal in a private house, and sleep on the bus till it leaves. It is an interesting journey back as local people board with their animals and produce for market.

About 30 min. by bus north-west of Latacunga is the small but very important market town of *Saquisilí*. Its Thurs. (0700-1100) market is famous throughout Ecuador for the way in which all eight of its plazas and most of its streets become jam-packed with people, the great majority of them local Indians with red ponchos and narrow-brimmed felt hats. The best time to visit the market is between 0900 and 1000; be sure to bargain, prices may be inflated. Rated the best market in Ecuador by a traveller who has visited them all, but less good for textiles than Otavalo. Saquisilí has colourful Corpus Christi processions.

Dan Buck and Anne Meadows write: Tightly woven decorated baskets plentiful but expensive, though somewhat cheaper than in Quito. Bargain hard, there is a lot of competition for your custom. Livestock market hectic and worth a visit. Some animal buyers set up small corrals in which they collect their purchases. Trucks brimming with oranges and yellow and red bananas; reed mats, fans, and baskets; beef, pork and mutton parts piled on tables; Indian women hunkered down beside bundles of onions, radishes, and herbs, and little pyramids of tomatoes, mandarin oranges, potatoes, okra, and avocados; *cabuya* and *maguey* ropes and cords laid out like dead snakes; and a food kiosk every five feet offering everything from full *almuerzos* to *tortillas de papa*.

Accommodation *Pensión Chavela*, main plaza, G, billiards and gambling hall downstairs, noisy; *Salón Pichincha*, Bolívar y Pichincha, G, good restaurant-bar below, friendly, not very clean, secure motor cycle parking. Some basic restaurants can be found in the same district (at the entrance to the village).

Transport The Saquisilí and Cotopaxi bus companies have frequent services between Latacunga and Saquisilí (US$0.10, ½ hr.) and several buses a day run to Saquisilí from Quito (catch them in Quito bus terminal, US$0.65, 1½-2 hrs.). Alternatively you can catch an Ambato bus from Latacunga, ask the driver to let you off at the junction for Saquisilí and get a passing pick-up truck (US$0.25) from there. The *Hotel Quito* and the *Hotel Colón* in Quito both organize efficient but expensive taxis for a 2-hr. visit to Saquisilí market on Thurs. Bus tours cost about US$17.50 p.p., taxis can be found for US$25, with 2 hr. wait at market.

North of Latacunga, the railway and the Pan-American Highway cross one another at Lasso, a small village with a milk bottling plant and two recommended cafés serving dairy products. Just north of Lasso, east of the highway, is the San Agustín hill, thought to be a prehistoric pyramid.

The area around San Agustín is owned by the Plaza family, which has two large *haciendas* and breeds bulls for the bull-fights in Quito in December. One of the two *haciendas* is actually at the base of the San Agustín hill and includes some converted Inca buildings.
About 2 km. off the road from Latacunga to Quito, near Lasso, is the *Hostería La Ciénega*, a good restaurant also operating as a small hotel (C) in an old *hacienda* with outstanding gardens and a small private chapel (reserve accommodation in advance at weekends). It used to belong to the Lasso family when their land spread from Quito to Ambato (T Quito 541-337).

A little beyond San Agustín, a poor road leads off towards the Cotopaxi volcano, at Parque Nacional de Cotopaxi sign. National Park authorities are breeding a fine llama herd on the lower slopes. Just north of Cotopaxi are the peaks of Sincholahua (4,893 metres), Rumiñahui (4,712 metres) and Pasochoa (4,225 metres).

Cotopaxi (6,005 metres). Rob Rachowiecki writes: There are two entrances to the Cotopaxi National Park: the first is near a sign for the NASA satellite tracking station, from where one can walk (or hitch hike on weekends and holidays) the 3 km. to the NASA station (army-run now, can be visited with preauthorization from Instituto Geográfico Militar, 4th floor, oficina Clirsen, in Quito) and then continue for over 30 km. more along a signposted dirt road, past two campsites, through the National Park gates, past Lake Limpio Pungo, past the old Armada Nacional refuge and on to the parking lot (4,600 metres) where the road ends. From here it is 30 mins. to 1 hr. to the José Ribas refuge (4,800 metres). The second entrance, about 6 km. further south, is marked by a small Parque Nacional de Cotopaxi sign. It is about 28 km. from here to the refuge. Nearly 1 km. from the highway, turn right at a T junction and a few hundred metres later turn sharp left. Beyond this the road is either signed or you take the main fork; it is shorter and easier to follow than the first route which you join just before the Park gates.
The ascent from the refuge takes 6-11 hrs. Equipment and experience are required. Climb the sandy slope above the hut and head up leftwards on to the glacier. Getting on to the glacier is the steepest and technically hardest part of the climb. The route then goes roughly to the right of Yanasacha and on to the summit. Allow 2-4 hrs. for the descent.
Dr. Sverre Aarseth writes that the best season is December-April; strong winds and clouds in August-December but still possible for experienced mountaineers. The route is more difficult to find on Cotopaxi than on Chimborazo (**see page 655**); it is advisable to seek information from Quito climbing clubs (Nuevos Horizontes is the best). The snow and ice section is more heavily crevassed than Chimborazo and is also steeper; however it is less climbing time.
Visitors to the Parque Nacional de Cotopaxi must register when entering and leaving the park. The park gates are open 0700-1800 with lunch 1200-1400. The refuge (US$0.85 p.p. a night) has a kitchen (you may use the stove for a small charge), water, many beds (bring sleeping bag) and lock-up facilities for your excess luggage when you climb. There are many campsites in the Park. If you have no car, the best bus to take from Quito is the Latacunga bus. Do not take an express bus as you have to get off before Latacunga.

At Cotopaxi the road and railway begin to dip into the Quito basin. In a valley below the bleak *páramo* lies the town of **Machachi**, famous for its mineral water springs and very cold swimming pool (US$0.35). The water, "Agua Güitig", is bottled in a plant 4 km. from the town and sold throughout the country. Machachi produces a very good cheese. Cockfights on Sun. *Pensión El Tiempo*, F, clean; *Restaurante Moderno*, round corner, very good. Bus to Quito US$0.35. Taxi to Cotopaxi, US$16 per car.

Machachi is a good base for climbing *Illiniza*. Illiniza Sur is very difficult and dangerous, but Illiniza Norte can be climbed without technical equipment. The rock is very crumbly, so caution is advised. There is a *refugio* on the saddle between the two.

THE SOUTHERN SIERRA (7)

The Pan-American Highway and railway S of Sibambe to Cuenca run through mountainous country and high above the valleys of the west-bound rivers. The countryside is poor, dry, chilly and wind-swept, and the Indians small, withdrawn and wrapped-up. Near Gun and Cañar, more Indians, dressed in black, are seen. At Gun an all-weather road runs to Cochancay in the coastal lowlands, from where there are paved roads to Guayaquil and Machala. Towards Cuenca the road loses height and the land is more intensively farmed. There are excellent roads linking Quito-Guayaquil and Guayaquil-Cuenca, which meet at El Triunfo on the coastal plain. Some transport goes this way rather than using the direct road, although there the scenery is magnificent; there are often detours which lead to deep ravines and precipitous peaks. The main road south divides at Cajabamba into two equally respectable-looking paved roads to Cuenca and Guayaquil; the paving of the Cuenca road is complete except for 12 km. around Alausí which are still terrible (**see page 651**). On this route, near Alausí, is Chunchi, a small, welcoming village with a Sunday market.

Cañar, 65 km. N of Cuenca (36 km. N of Azogues), is famous for its double weaving and is a good area for walking; it is close to the Inca ruin of Ingapirca (**see page 664**). Market on Sun. (*Residencia Patricia*, F, overpriced, insist on hot shower; *Pensión Guayaquil*, G, Guayaquil 76, OK; unmarked *pensión*, Av. 24 de Mayo 235, green house, on a corner on left side going towards Cuenca; restaurants close early in the evening about 1830, *El Rondador*, good set meal, one good one on corner of same street as *Res. Patricia*). Bus every 30 mins. to the *terminal terrestre* in Cuenca, US$0.60.

Azogues (14,452) is 31 km. N of Cuenca (1 hr. by bus) and a centre of the panama hat industry, though good quality hats for sale only at the large Sat. market (*Hotel Charles*, F, in centre, friendly; *Residencial Tropical*, G, showers sometimes electrocute guests). Both Azogues and nearby Biblián have attractive churches overlooking the towns from neighbouring hillsides.

Cuenca (2,595 metres), with 201,500 people, was founded by the Spaniards in 1557 on the site of the indigenous settlement of Tomebamba. The climate is spring-like, but the nights are chilly. The city has preserved its colonial air, with many of its old buildings constructed of the marble quarried nearby. A fine new cathedral (1885), which contains a famous crowned image of the Virgin, has been built in the central square, Parque Calderón, where the old cathedral still stands. The University is now on the other side of the Tomebamba river. Part of the Padre Crespi collection can be seen at the Banco Central "Pumapungo" museum (open Tue.-Fri. 0930-1630 and Sat. 0900-1230, free), Calle Larga y Huayna Capac, on the edge of town at the Tomebamba site (excavation continuing). (It is often shut if the exhibition is being changed; museum apparently moved, address not know.) Padre Crespi (died June 1982) used these artefacts to support his theory that the Phoenicians reached Cuenca via the Amazon. The Instituto Azuayo de Folklore, Sucre 176, San Blas district (open Mon. to Fri., 0800-1200, 1400-1800) has an excellent exhibition of popular art, with a few items on sale. The old Casa de Gobierno (now demolished) where Humboldt was a guest in 1802 formerly stood on this site and there is a plaque over the doorway. There is a municipal museum at Calles Sucre y Talbot (modern art and Indian artefacts, closed for renovation in 1988/89). A pleasant walk is upstream along the river.

The churches which deserve a visit are the old Cathedral, which has a fine organ (under restoration in 1988/89); La Concepción (convent founded 1599, religious art museum, San Blas, San Francisco, Santo Cenáculo, and Santo Domingo. Inca ruins have been found on the banks of the river: about 300 metres from the Pumapungo site, at Larga 287, there are excavations at the Todos Los Santos site (open Mon.-Fri., 0800-1600).

The main market is on Thursday when pottery, clothes, guinea pigs and local produce, especially baskets, are sold in the Plaza Rotary. There is also a colourful daily market. Be careful of pickpockets in the market. If you are robbed, however, contact the police, their efficiency has been praised by one traveller who had most of his money returned to him after paying them a small fee.

Cuenca has been criticized as not well organized for tourism; many places of interest are closed at weekends. Police searches of tourists' luggage at their hotels are not unknown.

Festivals On Christmas Eve there is a parade; children and adults from all the *barrios* and surrounding villages decorate donkeys, horses, cars and trucks with symbols of abundance: strings of dollar bills, bottles of Cinzano, strings of lemons and peppers, bunches of bananas, whole roasted chickens with banknotes in their beaks, toys etc. Little children in colourful Indian costumes or dressed up as Biblical figures ride through the streets accompanied by Indian musicians. The parade ends in the Plaza de Armas, which is a good place to watch it. Travellers in Cuenca over New Year's Eve report that the festivities include the parading and burning of effigies (some political, some fictional) which symbolize the old year; there is also much water throwing and tourists are a prime target. The festivities seem to go on all through January. The burning of straw puppets (*el hombre viejo*) takes place at the moment of the New Year throughout Ecuador. There are also festivals on April 10-13 (Foundation of Cuenca) and November 3 (Independence). There are also festivities involving the throwing of buckets of water at Carnival time before Lent and around Easter, and tourists in Cuenca and throughout southern Ecuador can expect to be thoroughly soaked. Visitors are welcome at the water plant, with its gardens.

Warning There is a short, dark, pudgy man who asks lone female travellers to write letters for him to non-existent friends, and then invites them out. He is a known rapist and dangerous, but seems to have close relations with the police. Avoid him. Also (and this may be the same man), a man, who claims to be a businessman travelling abroad, who asks women to answer questions and then go with him to meet his "sister", or a "woman friend", by way of thanks.

Hotels *El Dorado,* Gran Colombia y Luis Cordero, B, night club, the best in town, good restaurant, good view; *La Laguna,* Swiss-run, on lake in outskirts of town, A, the best available, lovely rooms, quick laundry, restaurant "pretentious and expensive"; *Hostería El Molino,* D, Km. 8.5 on road Azogues-Cuenca, pleasant position between road and river, Spanish run, typical Ecuadorean dishes, pool, rustic style, rec., advisable to book; *Crespo,* Calle Larga 793, D, with restaurant overlooking river, very clean, a lovely building, rec.; *Crespo Annex,* comfortable, nice, Cordero 422 y Larga, E; *Alli-Tiana,* Córdova y Aguirre, E, clean, hot water unreliable; *El Fuente,* F, Av. 12 de Abril, nr. Teatro Carlos Cueva, nice, hot shower, garden, good value; *Hurtado de Mendoza,* Sangurima y Huayna Capac, E, good, restaurant; *Las Américas,* Mariano Cueva 13-59 y Vega Muñoz, E, good value, carpets, hot water, telephone, friendly, helpful, good cheap restaurant next door; *El Conquistador,* Gran Colombia 665, E, without breakfast, sauna, good, friendly; *Tours Cuenca,* Borrero 1069, large rooms, TV, central, D with bath, clean; *Catedral,* Padre Aguirre 8-17 y Sucre, T 823204, E, overpriced but cheaper rates for Peace Corps and other service organizations, spacious, modern, English-speaking manager, safe, laundry service, good food; *Tomebamba,* E, quiet, clean, hot water, good breakfast. *Internacional,* Benigno Malo 1015, F, cheerful, good value for set meal; *Pichincha,* Gral. Torres y Bolívar, F, clean; *Milán,* Pres. Córdova 989 y Aguirre, F, friendly, helpful, reliable for storing luggage, good breakfast, warmly rec.; *Residencial Niza,* Mariscal Lamar 4/51, F, clean, water not too hot; *Residencial Atenas,* Cordero 1189, F, clean, comfortable, but not safe for left-luggage; *Pensión El Inca,* Gral. Torres 842, G, hot showers, friendly, irregular water supply, breakfast, popular, noisy; *Residencial Sánchez,* G, Muñoz 428 y Mariano Cueva, set meal rec.; *Emperador,* G, Gran Colombia 1077, clean, front rooms noisy; *Siberia,* G, Gran Colombia 531, hot water, bargain for room rates, laundry facilities, central and convenient; *Residencial Colombia,* Mariano Cueva 1161, G, clean but noisy, overlooking market, hot showers, thieving staff. In the vicinity of the bus terminal are: *Residencial Tito,* Sangurima 149, F, safe but rooms are very dark; *Residencial España,* Sangurima 117, G with bath and TV, friendly, laundry facilities, hot water, good restaurant, safe parking for motor cycles; *Alborada,* F, good, clean; *La Ramada,* Sangurima 551, F, friendly, clean and pleasant but noisy; *El Galeón*, Sangurima 240, F, large, modern rooms, own bathroom, hot water, parking; *Los Alamos*, F, modern, communal hot shower, clean, rec., Av. España, opposite main bus terminal.

Furnished two-bedroom apartments are available; *El Jardín*, Av. Pumapungo y Viracochabamba, US$5 per day p.p., cooking facilities and parking. T 830- 330, or write to address above, Casilla 298.

Restaurants Foreign styles *El Jardín*, Presidente Córdova 7-23, lovely, superb food, nouvelle cuisine (closed Sun.), allow US$5 p.p.; *El Fogón*, España 2472, Argentine, superb steaks. *Rancho Chileno*, España y Elia Liut, good steak and seafood; *Los Copihues*, Bolívar 6-31, Chilean empanadas, juices, coffee; *Tupahue*, 12 de Abril 1107 (near Vergel church), also Chilean. **Italian** *La Tuna*, on Gran Colombia, good pizzas, popular; *Pizzería*, Calle Colombia 8-80. **Criollo** El Escorpión, Malo y Largo, rec.; *Balcón Quiteño (Nos 1 and 2)*, Sangurima 649 near market, popular, quick service; *Nutibara*, Sangurima y Luis Cordero, inexpensive, limited menu; *El Bucanero*, Sangurima 617, set meals, clean, small helpings; *El Túnel*, Gral. Torres, next to *Pensión El Inca*, good; *La Cantina*, Borrero y Córdova, refurbished mansion, good. **Vegetarian** El Paraíso, Ordóñez 1023, 3rd floor; *El María*, Mariscal Lamar 1269 y Tarqui; *Primavera*, Borrero 5-29, whole food shop; good one at Gran Colombia y Tomás Ordena. **Seafood** El Cangrejo, Av. 12 de Abril (just beyond El Vergel church, near hospital), for lunch; *El Acuario*, Huayna Capac 138; *El Calamar*, Pizarro 148 y España. **Snackbars, bakeries, etc.** Los Pibes, Gran Colombia y Cordero, good; *Trattoría Césare*, Cordero y Larga, clean; *Pity's*, Gran Colombia 2087, hamburgers, rec.; almost next door, *Pollos Gus*, Gran Colombia y Unidad. *Picadilly*, bar with snacks, Pres. Borrero entre Sucre y Córdoba, nice. *Heladería*, at Larga 8-89 with Benigno Malo, ice cream, sandwiches, sweets, etc.; *Helados Honey*, Mariscal Lamar 4-15, clean, cheap, rec. milkshakes; *Capucuho*, Bolívar y Aguirre, good real coffee; *Mi Pan*, Pres. Córdova 842 and General Torres y Gran Colombia, cakes, tarts, doughnuts, good breakfast; *El Trigal*, Cordero 9-38, good fresh bread.

Shopping Many craftware shops along Gran Colombia, near *El Dorado* hotel, and on Benigno Malo. These include Ocepa, Productos Andinos, Artesanías Atahualpa, Arte Artesanías, Arte del Pacífico and Artesanías Paucartambo. Bazaar Susanita, Benigno Malo 1092, for good woollen sweaters at reasonable prices. Good souvenirs are carvings, leather, basketwork, painted wood, onyx, woven stuffs (cheapest in Ecuador), embroidered shirts, etc. On Bolívar, between Mariano Cueva and A. Miguel, are two shops side-by-side which sell excellent sweaters. Artesa, Presidente Córdova 6-96 y Borrero, sells modern Ecuadorean ceramics at good prices. Expensive shops on Borrero, behind old cathedral. Joyería Turismo, owned by Leonardo Crespo, at Gran Colombia 9-31, has been recommended; he will let wholesale buyers tour his factory. Jewellery prices are reported as high: shop around. High quality Panama hats are made by Homero Ortega, Vega Muñoz 9-33, T 823-429, who exports all over the world; panama hats also at Tarqui 6-93 y Córdova. Interesting market behind new cathedral. A Centro Comercial has opened in the industrial park, with interesting shops.

Entertainment Discos at Hotels *Conquistador* and *Alli-Tiana*, and *Las Galaxias*, Núñez de Bonilla 239. *Peñas* at *Hotel la Laguna*, outside town, and *La Pantera Rosa*, España 1080. 4 cinemas.

Taxis US$0.32 for short journey; US$0.40 to airport; US$1 per hr. Local buses US$0.05.

Exchange Citibank, Gran Colombia 749 (charges commission, even on its own cheques), and local banks. Filanbanco reportedly won't change Visa cheques despite being Visa agents. Cambidex on Luis Cordero are helpful. Cambistral in City Hall on Sucre 664 y Malo; Cambiosur, Borrero 8-20 y Sucre; another at Sucre y Pres. Borrero. Generally, the rates are quite good.

British Honary Consul Sr. Teodoro Jerves, Av. España y Chapetones, T 831996.

Post Office and **Ietel** on corner of Calles Gran Colombia and Borrero.

Immigration Bolívar y Luis Cordero (Gobernación), T 824-020.

Tourist Office Dituris, Pres. Córdova y Pres. Borrero. Very helpful. Maps of Cuenca US$0.20. They have little information on Ingapirca but a little booklet *Ingapirca, guía para visitantes* can be bought for about US$0.40 in bookshops. Yroo Tours, Larga y Malo, English spoken, recommended. Also Metropolitan Touring and Ecuadorian Tours, both at Sucre y Malo. A recommended guide for the Cuenca area is Vicente López Cárdenas, T 823-790, well-informed on local flora and culture, Spanish speaking only.

Buses The *Terminal Terrestre* is on Av. España, a 20-min. walk northwest of the city centre, or take a minibus, US$0.05. To Riobamba 5½ hrs., US$3.15, scenic. Ambato, US$4, 7½ hrs. (travel during day because scenery is magnificent, the road, not all paved, goes from 2,600 metres to under 200 and up again); Baños, from 12 de Noviembre, Turismo Baños; Quito, 10½ hrs., US$4.10. To Loja, 8 hrs., US$2.65, major construction work on this road, long delays; Machala, 5 hrs., US$2.70; to Guayaquil, 4½ hrs., US$2.65 (road now entirely paved). To Huaquillas, 6 hrs., US$3.10, at 2100—sit on left (the bus sometimes stops for 2 hrs. in Machala, it is often better to get a local bus from there to Huaquillas). The evening bus arrives in Huaquillas at 0300, but passengers sleep on the bus till daylight. Be prepared for frequent police checks on the way. To Azogues, US$0.25, leaves when full. To Saraguro, US$2, 6 hrs. To Macas, 11 hrs., US$1.80.

Trains The train service to Sibambe, leaving daily at 1500, has been restored. A pleasant round trip by train and bus can be made to El Tambo and back, to see Ingapirca (see next page).

Air Service Daily connections with Quito (US$18) and Guayaquil (US$14) with TAME (office at airport) and SAN.

Excursions There are sulphur baths at Baños, with a beautiful church in a delightful landscape, 5 km. S of Cuenca. Two separate warm baths, of which the lower one is better (US$0.80 for private bathroom, US$0.40 for swimming pool), the upper one is rather dirty (US$0.40). There are *Residenciales Baños* and *Rincón de Baños*, both F with bath, on the main road, and the *Hostería Durán*, D, rec., with restaurant, pool and amenities, at the baths. Buses from Cuenca (Calle Larga), US$0.05, taxis US$1.80.

About 40 km. NE of Cuenca in the beautiful Paute Valley is the *Hostería Uzhupud*, C, deluxe, swimming pool, very good food, excellent value, highly rec., Casilla 1268, Uzhupud, Paute, T Cuenca 821-853; also *Residencial Cutilcay*, G.

E to **Gualaceo** (Sun. market), 25 mins. by bus every ½ hr., on a recently-paved road, US$0.25 (leave from corner of *terminal terrestre*) pretty town in beautiful landscape, with charming plaza and fine new church with splendid modern glass; embroidered goods sold from private home above general store on main square; hotels: *Hostería Rivera*, E; *Gran Hotel Gualaceo*, F; *Residencial Gualaceo*, F; and *Español*, basic, G; restaurant *Manabí* on main road to Cuenca. Good shoes made locally; splendid bargains. To **Chordeleg** by colectivo (plenty), or by local bus, US$0.10 from Gualaceo market square (every ½ hr.; direct bus—1 hr.—from Cuenca, US$0.30), a village famous for its crafts in wood, silver and gold filigree and pottery, also panama hats, although it is very touristy nowadays. Watch out for fake jewellery. Joyería El Brillante has been found to sell gold-plated silver for solid gold. Joyería Puerto del Sol, on Juan B. Cobos y Eloy Alfaro, has been recommended. The church is interesting. Try *Restaurante El Turista*. Gualaceo is a very pleasant hour's walk downhill from Chordeleg. Chordeleg has a small Museo de Comunidad of fascinating local textiles, ceramics and straw work. With your own vehicle (4WD advisable), you can drive back to Cuenca through San Juan and San Bartolomé (2 small mines after this village welcome visitors).

Ingemar Tholin of Västerås, Sweden, recommends taking a bus (US$0.50, 1½ hrs.) from Cuenca to Sígsig (S of Gualaceo, 83 km. from Cuenca, *residencial*, G), and from there another to Chiqüinda (stay overnight with Sr. Fausto, the teacher). A trail from Chiqüinda goes to Aguacate (4-5 hrs. walking), a village of 70 people. Sr. Jorge Guillermo Vásquez has a *hospedaje*, horses can be hired for trekking to caves. There are shops, electricity at night only, and good *fiestas* at Christmas and New Year, and carnival in February (very popular). From Aguacate either walk or hire a horse to continue SE to Río Negro, a friendly village, from where daily buses at 1300 and 1600 go to Gualaquiza (1 hr., US$0.35—**see page 674**). A road is being built between Sígsig and Gualaquiza, along a beautiful and unspoilt route; the trail can be hiked by the intrepid but is not yet passable by wheeled vehicles.

NW of Cuenca, **El Cajas** is a national park with about 60 lakes, 2 hr. bus trip (one daily except Thurs. between 0600 and 0630, bus back between 1400 and 1600, US$0.50, arrive early as the bus can get very full, hitchhiking impossible, no traffic). Ideal but strenuous walking, 4,200 metres altitude. It is best to arrive in the early morning since it can get very cloudy after about 1300. Obtain a permit for entry to the park from the Cuenca office of the Ministry of Agriculture above the Banco Azuay, Bolívar 6-22, US$0.35, or pay US$2 at park entrance. They are supposed to provide maps but these are often unavailable. There is a refuge with four bunks in the park which you can book at the Ministry. The park is easy to miss; avoid being carried 8 km. further to the village itself. Camping possible but you need good equipment, warm clothing and waterproofs as it can get very wet; it is not possible to hire equipment in Cuenca. There are organized tours to the lakes from Cuenca, but these tend to be expensive, up to US$34. Alternatively, hire a private truck, US$16 with driver.

To the **Laguna de Surucucho:** catch the bus at the Plaza Santo Domingo to Sayausi (US$0.05) and walk from there; about 2 hrs. from Sayausi take a dirt road to the left and walk a further 20 minutes. There is good trout fishing in the lake and the river.

A beautiful hour-long bus trip on the Machala road from Cuenca takes one to the town of Girón, whose beauty is spoiled only by a modern concrete church. From there trucks take passengers up a winding road to the hamlets of San Gregorio and Chumblín. Friendly inhabitants will act as guides to three lakes high in the *páramo* where excellent trout-fishing is to be had. Take camping gear.

Ecuador's most important Inca ruin, **Ingapirca,** can be visited from Cuenca. You can take a taxi for the 5-hr. round trip from Cuenca bus terminal (US$35), or take any Guayaquil, Quito or Cañar bus. On the first two, ask to be let out at Tambo, 2 km. past Cañar (and 7 km., 2½ hrs. walk from the site), thence take a bus, colectivo, or truck to Ingapirca (US$0.20 maximum). From Cañar to Tambo a bus costs US$0.10. There is also a route from 2 km. before Cañar at a very bad side road to the right, 14 km. from Ingapirca. There is a basic *hospedaje* at El Tambo. A third possibility is to go to San Pedro, where there is a municipal *hospedería* where travellers can stay free of charge (although difficulties have been reported in obtaining the key); a 3 km. dirt road leads to the ruins. On Fri. there is an Indian market at Ingapirca. There is a good co-operative craft shop next to the church. Camping at the site is possible. There is no hotel at Ingapirca, but there is a basic restaurant, *Inti Huasi*, in the village; the (free) *refugio* has benches, table and fireplace but no beds. It is not available at night, cannot be locked during the day, and to use it at all you must surrender your passport.

Ingapirca is commonly known as a fortress complex although this is contradicted by archaeologists. The central structure is an *usnu* platform probably used as a solar observatory. It is faced in fine Inca masonry, and it is interesting to note that the length is exactly three times the diameter of the semicircular ends. This may have been connected with worship of the sun in its morning, midday and afternoon positions. (John Hemming) There is a good museum (closed Sun., Mon.), which sells a good guide book (US$0.80), and will look after belongings.

Warning   Be careful of overcharging by truck drivers.

There is a 3-4 day hike to Ingapirca from Achupallas (**see page 651**—take Coop. Chunchi or Coop. Patria bus from Riobamba to La Moya, then truck to Achupallas). It is a spectacular walk through valleys and on vestiges of an Inca trail; the locals are very friendly; take a fishing rod if you have one—the route is described in Rob Rachowiecki's *Climbing and Hiking in Ecuador*.

From Cuenca, the Pan-American Highway runs S to La Y, about 20 km. away near the village of Cumbe. Here the road divides into two all-weather gravel roads: one continuing the Pan-American to Loja (beautiful views on both sides) and the other, which is faster (or less slow), running to Pasaje and Machala. (One traveller reports that on a night trip on this route, the bus driver stopped before beginning the descent, made a collection from the passengers and having made the sign of the Cross, apparently tossed the money over the edge of the cliff.) Santa Isabella and Pasaje (pop. 27,000), the main towns along the route, have little to recommend them. Most buses travel NW to El Troncal and then S down the coast road to reach Machala and Huaquillas for the Peruvian border (**see page 649**).

The Pan-American Highway climbs S from La Y and rises eventually to the 3,500 metre Tinajillas pass. The road descends sharply into the warm upper Jubones valley past cane fields and rises again near the small town of Oña. From there it weaves through highland *páramo* pastures and then descends towards Saraguro. Here we meet Indians once more, the most southerly Andean group in Ecuador, dressed all in black. They wear very broad flat-brimmed hard felt hats: the men are notable for their black shorts (sometimes covered by a whitish kind of divided apron) and a particular kind of double bag, the *alforja*, and the women for their pleated black skirts, necklaces of coloured beads and silver *topos*, ornate pins fastening their shawls. They have entered the money economy with vigour: many now take cattle across the mountains east to the tropical pastures above the Amazonian jungle.

The road runs through **Saraguro** (picturesque Sun. Indian market—the Indians wear black, the men with a long plait of hair), over the mountain and then makes a long, very tortuous, descent towards Loja. The direct Cuenca-Loja road is under reconstruction and when the widening is completed it will be one of the most beautiful and breathtaking in Ecuador without the discomfort offered by the longer, alternative route via Arenillas.

In Saraguro, two pensions, one over the *farmacía*, F, friendly, family-run, freezing shower. Restaurant: *Salón Cristal*, behind the church. The restaurants are poor and the shops sell little. It is a very cold town.

Loja (2,225 metres, 71,130 inhabitants), lies near the Oriente. There are crude but original paintings on the patio walls of many of the old houses. There are two universities, with a well-known law school. Some of the Universidad Nacional buildings have good murals. The cathedral and San Martín church have painted interiors. Muesum on main square, by bank, 0800-1300, 1400-1530. The town, encircled by hills and pleasant countryside, can be reached by air from Quito or

Guayaquil to La Toma and then 35 km. by paved road. There is a market on Sat. and Sun. Travellers' cheques cannot be changed in the banks; good rate for US$ in gift shop in front of *Hotel Acapulco*, but there are no *casas de cambio* (El Iniverso agent will change money at weekends at a poor rate). Souvenir and craft shops on 10 de Agosto between Kennedy and 18 de Noviembre. Dituris is on the main square, 2nd floor of Post Office.

Hotels   *Residencial La Rivera*, Universitaria y 10 de Agosto, E, good; *Hostal Quinara*, opp. *La Rivera*, E, also good; *Saraguro Internacional*, Universitaria 724, E, hot water, TV, restaurant open Mon.-Fri.; *Ejecutivo Sudamérica*, Universitaria 1076, F, good, also "video club"; *Metropolitano*, 18 de Noviembre y Colón, F with bath and TV, hot water, clean; *París*, 10 de Agosto 1637,clean with electric hot showers, F, bargain for good rate, near food market, rec.; *Hostal Carrión*, Colón 1630, G, basic, clean, safe; *Miraflores*, 10 de Agosto 1656, G, can bargain, clean; *Londres*, Sucre y 10 de Agosto, F, constant hot water, clean; *Acapulco*, Sucre 743, F, clean, pleasant, private bathroom with copious hot water, safe for leaving luggage, rec. Basic *residenciales* in G range for instance on Rocafuerte; also *Alborada*, Sucre 1279 y Lourdes, F with shower, clean.

Restaurants   Mesón Andaluz, Bolívar y Eguiguren, best in town; *Suizo Lojano*, Guerrero y Eguiguren, international; *Palace*, Eguiguren y Sucre, local food; *Trece*, Universitaria y Colón, also Eguiguren 1468, good. Other criollo places are *Ocaso*, 10 de Agosto 1639; *Cordillera*, 10 de Agosto 1419; *La Choza*, Sucre y Riofrío. *La Casona*, 18 de Noviembre near Imbabura (the better of 2 branches), near Cuenca bus terminal, good, rec. Chicken at *Rico Pico*, 18 de Noviembre y Colón. Seafood at *Pescadería Pacífica*, Bolívar 931; and *Doscientas Millas*, Bolívar y Eguiguren (evenings only). *Chifa 85* on main plaza, clean, good quality food, including Chinese dishes. Chinese also at *Chifa Feliz*, Eguiguren y 18 de Noviembre. Good *Unicornio* piano bar on main square. Good snacks, pastries and yoghurt at *Pastelería Persa* (2 locations—one at Rocafuerte 14-58). *Helados de Paila*, Av. Kennedy, near market, good icecream and snacks.

Buses   To Cuenca, 7 hrs., 7 a day, US$2.65 with Viajeros (18 de Noviembre e Imbabura), the only company which leaves at 0500; Machala, 10 a day, 7 hrs., US$2.75. Cooperativa Loja (10 de Agosto y Cuarto Centenario) runs many buses in all directions, including Quito, 4 a day, 18 hrs., US$5, and Guayaquil, 5 a day, 11 hrs., US$4.40, and two nightly buses to Huaquillas at 2030 and 2230; Macará, 3 a day, US$2, 6½3 hrs., 2 checkpoints.

Excursions   A 1½-hr. bus ride, Sur Oriente, Calle Azuay and Av. Kennedy, hourly (US$ 0.50) from Loja is *Vilcabamba*, where people were reputed to live to over 100 as often as not; recent research has eroded this belief, but it's still a very pleasant and healthy valley, with an agreeable climate, 17°C min., 26°C max. There is the attractive *Parador Turístico*, E, with restaurant and bar; *Hotel Valle Sagrado*, G, on main plaza, basic but clean, friendly, hot showers rarely work; there are 4 restaurants on the plaza, including *Cabañita*. *Madre Tierra*, cabins, E p.p. full board, reductions for a long stay, health food (home made, home grown), horses to rent (about US$14 per day), mud treatment, private sun bathing, beautiful setting about 2 km. before village, English and French spoken; the Mendoza family make travellers very welcome. A small and peaceful farmhouse, owned by Sra. Leticia Jiménez de Macanchi, may be rented; very pleasant for a long stay. About 40 minutes from Vilcabamba, in the Capamaco valley at Yamburara Alto, is the ranch of René and Sabina Sangolqui, where you can camp, rent a cabin (US$30 irrespective of number of guests) and hire horses for excellent expeditions (prices from US$30 for 1 day to US$110 for 4 days, min. 2 people): recommended (Spanish, English and French spoken). With advance notice, they will meet you at Loja airport. Postal address: Casilla 812, Loja; in UK, contact David Hickmet, Southways, Lowfield Heath, Nr. Crawley, Sussex, RH10 2TQ, T (0293) 552743, Telex 878447.

The scenic road to Zamora (40 km.) is narrow but in good condition. You can carry on from there into the Oriente.

Most road travellers enter and leave Loja via Machala **(see page 648)**. There are two routes from Loja to Machala, one of which goes through Piñas and is rather bumpy with hairpin bends but has the better views, the other is paved and generally quicker (depending on the driver). Machala can be avoided, however, if you take a Machala bus to the Huaquillas crossroads, called La Avanzada, and there catch another one straight to Huaquillas, the border town. There is also a road into the Oriente, at Zaruma (on this road), where there are interesting carved wooden houses. The old Portovelo gold mines at Zaruma are worth a visit.

An alternative, more scenic route to Peru is, however, available from Loja via *Macará,* a dusty town on the border, in a rice-growing area, with road connections to Sullana near the Peruvian coast. (Population 8,000; altitude 600 metres.)

Hotels Paradero Turístico, E, pool, restaurant may not be open, not far from centre; *Residencial*

Paraíso, F, Veintimilla 553, new and clean, laundry facilities; *Guayaquil*, F, with shower, not rec., fleas, large cell-like rooms; *Internacional*, G, by Loja bus office and *Amazonas*, F, friendly, clean, basic, on same street. Restaurants *Colonial Macará*, Rengel y Bolívar (helpful, but food not too good), and *Macará*, opposite, a cafetería.

Leaving Loja on the main paved highway going westward, the airport at La Toma is reached after 35 km. (If flying to or from La Toma, stay at Catamayo, nearby, *Hotel El Turista*, Av. Isidro Ayora, F, shared bath; *Hotel San Marcos*, on plaza; taxi to airport US$0.50). At La Toma (where you can catch the Loja-Macará bus), the Pan-American Highway divides into two branches, one, the faster, via Catacocha, and the other going to Macará via Cariamanga. The road is unpaved but fair, offering lovely views. The bank at Macará does not change money, so change sucres through the *ambulantes* to give you enough intis to last you until you can find an open Peruvian *casa de cambio* or bank. A Peruvian tourist card can be obtained at the border if not already obtained in Quito or Guayaquil. There is a 2½ km. walk or taxi ride (US$1, US$0.55 in a pick-up from Macará market—less if more passengers) to the international bridge over the Río Macará. Border crossing formalities (0800-1800) can last about 1 hr. Peruvian officials may ask to see an onward ticket out of Peru. A colectivo (US$2.20, 3-4 hrs.) is then taken from La Tina on the Peruvian side to Sullana from where it is ½ hr. to Piura, a better place to spend the night. No hotels, and only food stalls, in La Tina. Buses leave Sullana from Av. Buenos Aires in early a.m.; if none running, there are plenty of *camionetas* to the border. There are many military checkpoints along the route but these are not usually a problem. Coop Loja runs four buses a day from Macará to Loja (6 to 8 hrs., US$2), at 0700, 1000, 1300, and 1800, so the whole journey can be done in a day if you arrive at the border at noon. The Loja-border journey takes only 3½ hrs. by car. There is less likelihood of bureaucratic hassle or of drug-pushing at Macará than at Huaquillas, but since not many travellers go by this route, be prepared for extensive, but generally good-natured searches by bored officials. Also, officials are not above acquiring things, or asking for a bribe if you do something unusual, such as crossing the border after 1800 hrs. and returning the next day to get your passport stamped.

THE ORIENTE (8)

Ecuador's eastern tropical lowlands can now be reached by four different road routes, from Quito, Ambato, Cuenca or Loja, all described below. These roads are narrow and tortuous, but all have regular bus services and all can be attempted in a jeep or in an ordinary car with good ground clearance. Their construction has led to considerable colonization by highlanders in the lowland areas. Several of the towns and villages on the roads can be reached by air services from Quito, Cuenca and Guayaquil, and places further into the immense Amazonian forests are generally accessible by river canoe or small aircraft. The country is particularly beautiful, and some of the disadvantages of other parts of Amazonia, such as the inadvisability of swimming in the rivers, are here absent. Anti-malaria tablets are recommended, however, and be sure to take a mosquito net. A yellow fever vaccination is recommended for travel into the Oriente.

Most visitors to the Oriente make a circular route Quito-Baeza-Tena-Puyo-Baños-Ambato-Quito. Another popular route is Quito-Baños-Puyo-Tena-Misahuallí-Coca-Lago Agrio-Baeza-Quito, using both bus and boat. Allow at least a week. Metropolitan Tours of Quito do trips to the Oriente for about US$600; and a Napo River tour, US$250, meals, flights, lectures included. Transturi of Quito (Orellana 1810 y 10 de Agosto, T 544963) do trips from Coca into the jungle on a floating hotel, *Flotel Orellana*, US$200 (3 days) per person in double cabin, US$375 (4 days) or US$465 (5 days) including Quito-Coca air fare and all meals, guides, etc. and visits to Limón Cocha, Monkey Island, *Hacienda Primavera*, and Pompeya Catholic mission. Going by bus etc. you can do a round trip much more cheaply. The Oriente also has an unpredictable air service provided by army planes; passengers pay insurance, US$1-2; apart from that, fares are low. Frequent military checks; always have your passport handy. You may be required to register at Shell-Mera, Coca, Misahualli, Puerto Napo and Lago Agrio.

From Quito to Coca or Misahuallí   From Quito as far as Pifo the road is paved and in excellent condition, but then it gradually worsens until it becomes a narrow, muddy, gravel-covered track, often impassable in the rainy season. A new road was built in 1987, following the earthquake which destroyed the old road to Coca. It crosses the Eastern Cordillera at an altitude of 4,064 metres at a pass just north of the extinct volcano **Antisana** (5,704 metres, which, according to Cliff Cordy, gets vast quantities of snow, has huge glaciers and is the hardest peak in Ecuador to climb), and then descends via the small villages of Papallacta (**see page 629**), and Cuyuja to the old mission settlements of Baeza and Borja. The trip between the pass and Baeza has beautiful views of Antisana, high waterfalls, tropical mountain jungle, *páramo* and a lake contained by a glacial moraine almost on the equator.

Baeza is a small town in the beautiful setting of the Quijos pass, recommended for long scenic walks (beware trucks passing) with many waterfalls (the town is about 2 km. off the main road—get off Lago Agrio bus at the police checkpoint and walk up the hill; Tena bus goes through the town). The old Spanish cobblestone trail can be found if you go past the *Hotel Samay*, hospital and cemetery; the path goes up over the hill (a beautiful walk). Because of the climate, *ceja de montaña*, orchids and bromeliads abound. Trout in the rivers. (See the books of Padre Porras Garcés, Centro de Investigaciones Arqueológicas, Pontífica Universidad Católica del Ecuador, Quito on archaeological remains in the area).

Hotels *Samay*, G, clean, cold shower, and *Nogal de Jumandy*, G, English spoken, parking, friendly; both have laundry facilities and are within a block of each other on main Tena road. *Oro Negro*, residencial and restaurant, at Tena/Lago Agrio junction, rooms with bath and cold water.

Restaurants *Gina*, and *Lupita*, good, opposite each other on Calle Chimborazo. Everything closed by 2030.

At Baeza the road divides, one branch heading S to Tena, the other NE, following the Quijos river past the villages of Borja, a few km. from Baeza (small hotel on roadside; *residencial* on corner of plaza, clean, cold shower, meals provided; basic restaurant *Costa Azul*) and El Chaco (hotel and eating places all reported as dirty) to the slopes of the still active volcano Reventador, 3,485 metres. (At the village of Reventador there is a *pensión, Las Orquídeas,* F, and a restaurant.) The road winds along the north side of the river, past the impressive 145-metre San Rafael falls (to see them, get off bus at Inecel sign, walk down side road, and then down a steep path, about 1 hr.), until it crosses the watershed between the Coca and Aguarico rivers. A ferry operates 0600-1800 across the Aguarico river until the bridge is rebuilt. The road runs along the north bank of the river to the developing oil towns of Santa Cecilia and Lago Agrio.

Lago Agrio is growing rapidly: it is still a rough place but the infrastructure is improving; excursions into the jungle can be made. Virtually everything in the town is along the main road, Av. Quito.

Hotels El Gofán, E, a/c, best, good restaurant; *La Mexicana*, F, reasonable, mosquito nets; *Willigram*, F with own bath, clean, rec.; *Putumayo*, F, shared bathroom; *Hilton, Oro Negro, Chifa China* (restaurant) and *Chimborazo*, all G with shared bathrooms.

Exchange Several *casas de cambio* on Av. Quito, good rates for notes.

Transport Several daily TAME flights to Quito at 1200, US$9. Buses to Quito (US$4, 9½ hrs.), Baeza (US$2.10, 6 hrs.), Coca (US$1.10, 3 hrs.) and Tena (US$3.20, 9 hrs.).

From Lago Agrio it is possible to take a bus to Chiritza and then a 2 hour boat ride to San Pablo de Kantesiya, a small village on stilts with one hut where visitors can stay. There are buses north to La Punta (US$0.40, 1¼ hrs., visit Migración in Lago Agrio, Quito 111—police station, T 125), where you get a boat across the Río San Miguel to Puerto Colón, in Colombia. There are canoes along the river to the village of San Miguel in Colombia and from there you can catch a bus (5 hrs.) to Puerto Asís (border formalities).

At Lago Agrio, a temporary ferry crosses the Aguarico River (bridge washed away), then the road heads south to **Coca** (officially named Puerto Francisco de Orellana—pop. 16,000), a river port at the junction of the Coca and Napo rivers; described as a typical oil town, dirty, noisy, with heavy drinking. All foreigners have to register with the police. The bank will not change travellers' cheques, but Sr. Londoño (at Almacén Londoño) may change them at a fair rate. At Carnival, water and petroleum throwing is the sport.

Hotels *Auca*, G, clean, electricity in p.m., big garden with monkeys roaming free, reasonable food but crowded, manager speaks English; *Florida*, on main road from airport, F with fan, good; *Residencial Rosita*, G, noisy, cold water; *Tungurahua*, F, favourite with oil workers; and 3 basic *residenciales*: *Turingia*, *Lojalita* (F) and *Camba Huasi*.

Restaurant *Doña Erma's* set meal is cheap and filling; *Venecia*, good food, away from main market area; *Cubayne*, delicious barbecues; *Mama Carmen*, good for early breakfast.

Canoes (irregular service, best to hire your own) pass Coca carrying passengers and cargo down-river to Limón Cocha (where *Flotel Orellana* has a lodge, closed to guests other than their own tour parties), the Capuchin mission at Pompeya with a school and museum of Napo culture, and Nueva Rocafuerte. Local tours can be hired from Limón Cocha and also canoes to return to Coca. In Nueva Rocafuerte, the missionaries and Sra. Jesús let rooms; there are no restaurants. There is a Monday boat from Coca to Nueva Rocafuerte but you must get a military permit to enter the area. The officer has to write exactly the area you wish to visit (e.g. Yasumi river, 2 Auca villages). The boat takes 24 hrs. at least (hammocks provided) US$5.50. You can stay overnight at the mission in N. Rocafuerte. There you can hire boat and guide for US$15 a week. Take plenty of food, tinned meat, ammunition, salt and lighters as presents for the Aucas. There is a boat back on Mon. but it doesn't always run and you may have to wait until Fri. To Coca it is a 2-day ferry ride (US$9) with an overnight stop at Sinchichieta and a meal stop at Pañacocha. From Coca there are also boats (daily) going upstream to Misahuallí (**see page 671**), from which a bus can be caught to Puerto Napo (officially known as Puerto Nuevo), and then another to Puyo (Coca to Misahuallí via motorized canoe, US$5 for gringos leaving at 0830, 9 hours in average conditions. Take a cushion and waterproofs for self and luggage). The canoe trip upstream to Misahuallí takes about 14 hrs.; if it is not reached before nightfall, the party will camp beside the river. For the less hardy the return trip downstream is advised, 6 hrs. For a price, of course, the willing traveller can hire his own canoe with owner and outboard motor to take him anywhere along the Napo. (To Misahuallí the charge is about US$120.)

Tours Canoes and guides for jungle trips can be hired from Fernando Silva, who lives at the end of the riverside lane next to the bridge. Large canoe for 6 people, 6 days, about US$250, exclusive of food and equipment. Kevin Johnsrude warns "Insist that there be no hunting or dynamite fishing or the only animals you will see will be in your soup!" This price is about half that charged by Misahuallí guides. More expensive is Fluvial Tours, US$15 p.p., per day (minimum 4 people). Since few other trips originate from Coca, you may have to arrange boat trips along the River Napo from Misahuallí. Pedro Grefa offers 5-day jungle tours on the Río Tiputini for US$10, all inclusive, or US$15 if only 2 people going. Take the 1200 Ranchero bus of Coop. de Coca from Coca to the bridge over the Río Tiputini (2½ hrs., US$0.50); his is the small, wooden house at left side of bridge. (Shell has a camp here, drinks only available.) Allow a day for the trip to be organized, ask for fruit and vegetables to be included in the provisions, take a torch and insect repellent, and ask Pedro (or his nephew Carlos—also rec. as leader) not to throw litter away in the jungle.

Two hours downstream from Coca is the *Hacienda Primavera* owned by Transturi of Quito, who own the *Flotel Orellana*. There are clean rooms available (E p.p.), or you can camp (US$0.50). Meals cost US$2.50, bring bread. There is a generator but candles are used for after-generator hours. Excursions are not cheap, but it is supposed to be possible to hire canoes from the *hacienda* to visit other places along the Napo. The *Flotel Orellana* also stops here for a visit. It has been reported that independent travellers to *Primavera* have experienced overcharging on transport back to Quito and difficulties in arranging independent activities.

La Selva, a hotel 3 hrs. down the Napo from Coca, has been recommended for the quality of its accommodation and food, and its interesting excursions into the jungle; not cheap, but worth it, will arrange transport if required. Book at *La Selva*, 6 de Diciembre 2816 y James Orton, P.O. Box 635/Suc. 12 de Octubre, Quito, T 550995/554686, Telex 2-2653 JOLEZ ED, Fax 563814.

Transport Bus to Quito (twice daily), 10 hrs., US$5; to Lago Agrio, 3 hrs., US$1.10; to Tena, 10 hrs., US$4.20; to Baeza, 9 hrs., US$3.25. We are told that TAME no longer flies to Coca, but there are military flights to Tena and Shell-Mera from Coca on Mon., Wed. and Fri. Cepe and Texaco oil companies also fly Quito-Coca and sometimes take travellers on board their small planes.

From Ambato Beyond Baños (**see page 656**), the road eastward winds along the north side of the Pastaza river until eventually, after a long descent, the broad extent of the Amazonian plains becomes visible. The road between Ambato and Baños is paved, and from Baños to Puyo it has been reconstructed. It is a dramatic and journey with superb views and a plethora of waterfalls. **Shell-Mera** (50 km. from Baños, 1½ hrs, *Hotel Esmeraldita, Residencial Azuay*) is the first major stop. Here there are an army checkpoint where foreigners must register (passports are stamped), and an airfield. Shell-Mera can also be reached by military flight from Quito, ½ hr.; also flights to Macas. Military flights from Shell-Mera to Montalvo and Tiputini. A few km. on is the larger and busier town of **Puyo,** the most important centre in the whole Oriente. The pioneer fringe has now left Puyo far behind, and its wooden buildings are giving way to concrete and cement. The electricity supply is turned off promptly at midnight. There is a cinema, Coliseo, and the Ñucaloma discotheque, and a cock-pit (cockfights Sun. 1400). Immigration office in Gobernación handles visa extensions.

Hotels *Hostería Turingia,* Orellana y Villamil, E, small huts with bath, in tropical garden, comfortable but noisy, restaurant quite expensive but good; *Europa,* F, with bath, good value and good restaurant, also newer *Europa Internacional,* E, and *California,* F, slightly cheaper, noisy, all on Calle 9 de Octubre; *Grenada,* Calle 27 de Febrero y Orellana, G, clean, rec.; *Pensión Susanita,* 9 de Octubre y Orellana, E, cafetería, rec. Some other *pensiones* F or G.

Restaurants Hostería Turingia, best; *California,* 9 de Octubre y Marín, good; *Rincón Ambateño,* Atahualpa y 24 de Mayo, local food, *Delicia* (local), *Viña del Mar* and *El Delfin* (both seafood), all on Marín; *Chifa China,* 9 de Octubre y 24 de Mayo, clean.

Buses to Baños, US$0.80, 2 hrs.; Ambato, US$1.10, 3 hrs.; Quito, US$2, 7 hrs.; Tena, US$1, 3 hrs. Riobamba, US$1.10, 3½ hrs.

From Puyo, a short road goes east to Vera Cruz, but the main highway (unpaved) runs northward to Puerto Napo and Tena. The whole area is a large-scale producer of sugar cane, yuca and *naranjillas* (an orange fruit related to the tomato, used for making a delightfully refreshing fruit drink), and tea has been introduced around Shell-Mera by two foreign companies. Puerto Napo, 72 km. north of Puyo (bus US$1), has a bridge across the Napo river.

On the north bank, a road leads eastwards to **Misahuallí**, about 17 km. downstream, a small port at the junction of the Napo and Misahuallí rivers. From the **Napo bridge** you can get a ride in a truck, US$0.50, or colectivos, thus avoiding going into Tena. At the *Hacienda Popoyal,* half way between Puerto Napo and Misahuallí, the owners, Frank and Ramón, welcome travellers. There are downriver canoe services with anything from 10 to 25 people in the vessel. Misahuallí provides one of the best opportunities to visit the jungle and is one of the easiest places to get to, as it is only 7-8 hrs from Quito and 5 hrs. from Baños; it is also one of the cheapest, since other jungle centres such as Iquitos, Manaus, and Leticia are more remote and more developed. However, there is not a great deal of wildlife around Misahuallí, although butterflies are plentiful, and for animals and birds you are advised to go further into the jungle to Coca or to take an excursion lasting several days; the 1-and 2-day trips have been described as disappointing. Oil exploration in the area is also diminishing chances of seeing wildlife. There is a fine, sandy beach on the Río Misahuallí, but don't camp on it; the river can rise suddenly and unexpectedly.

Hotels *Anaconda,* B, on Anaconda Island in the Río Napo, about 1 hr. by canoe downstream from Puerto Misahuallí; consists of three bungalows of bamboo and thatch, with space for about 32 guests, no electric lights, but flush toilets and cold showers, with water available most of the time (reported run down in 1988). Watch out for thieving monkeys. The meals are good. Canoe and hiking trips to see Indians arranged. Expensive. Opposite, on the river bank at Ahuano, is *Casa del Suizo* (Swiss, Ecuadorean-owned), F, or E full board, highly rec. for hospitality, food and location (for further information contact Gulliano Bonello, Koescherruetistr. 143, 8052 Zuerich, Switzerland, T 01-302-37-27). *Hotel Jaguar,* 1½ hrs. downstream from Misahuallí, congenial atmosphere, D p.p., with full board, good value, reservations from Quito, Ramírez Dávalos 653, T 239400, a full tour (3 days) including transport from Quito, all meals and good excursions into the jungle costs US$170 p.p. (US$70 from Baños) with an extra charge of US$32 for each additional day. Avoid paying in US$ as they give you a very bad rate (independent canoe journey there costs US$28, except by public canoe at 1100). In the village are *Cabañas Aliñahui,* D with full board p.p., new, good, private bath, good views, German and Cuban owners both speak English. Also, in the F price range (or G where stated): *El Paisano*, clean, washing facilities, hammocks, nice garden, rec., eight rooms behind restaurant; *Fifty-Five (55)*, on main square, G p.p., communal baths, good, clean, friendly, vegetarian restaurant; *Sacha*, owned by Héctor Fiallos, basic, bamboo walls, noisy, at point where rivers meet, dirty, apes in the garden, path to hotel floods when rains heavy, buy souvenirs of the Oriente here, cheaper than in Baños or Quito; *Balcón del Napo*, basic, central, meals available, clean, friendly; *Amazonas*, on riverbank nr. square, basic, 2 rooms with bath, reasonable; *Etsa*, F with or without bath, owner is guide Carlos Cordero. Douglas Clarke now provides basic accommodation in bamboo huts with bunk beds behind the restaurant, showers available. Beware of thieves poking hooks through the floor.

Restaurants Douglas Clarke's *Restaurant Dayuna* is reasonably good and cheap, as is *El Paisano*, mostly good vegetarian food (but meat should be treated with caution), and popular meeting place for gringos, hence its nickname *Restaurant Paleface*.

There are many guides available to take parties into the jungle for trips of 1 to 10 days, seeing river and jungle flora and fauna, visiting Indian villages, the Cuyabeno National Park and other jungle locations, all involving canoeing and varying amounts of hiking. The going rate is between US$15 and US$21 p.p. per day, depending on season and length of trip. This should include food and rubber boots, which are absolutely essential. Overnight tours are recommended only for the hardy. Héctor Fiallos, of Fluvial River Tours (information in Quito T 239044), arranges one-day outings, and it is possible to make 3- and 4-day tours. A 6-day tour takes in the Cuyabeno National Park (special permit needed and may be difficult to get), the Shushufindi tribe and the Aguarico River. A 10-day tour goes down the Napo to Nuevo Rocafuerte, up the Aguarico to the Cuyabeno National Park and various Indian tribes. Reports have reached us, however, that Héctor is less conscientious than he used to be and does not accompany his parties, leaving them in the care of less experienced guides: Domingo, Enrique and Bolívar have been recommended but not others. The longer tours cost between US$14 and US$25 p.p. a day. Julio Los Angeles is very knowledgeable on the flora and fauna. His two-day trip includes one day of fairly rigorous hiking and one day of light hiking and canoeing down river, but he will arrange anything you wish to do; his 4-day tour on Río Tiputini to see animals is the minimum time, US$14 a day (you can see very little in a shorter time); his cooking is good; a 6-day tour includes floating downriver on balsa rafts made by Julio, highly recommended by those who like peace and quiet and offering the opportunity of sighting wildlife undisturbed by motor launches. Adonis Muñoz of Caiman Tours has also been warmly recommended as good English-speaking guide (and cook). He was born in Limón Cocha and studied biology in the U.S.A. Douglas Clarke (speaks English), who runs the *Restaurant Dayuna*, and his sister, Billy, arrange trips. Their one-and two-day walks are recommended, but expensive. Also trips to Coca, to smaller rivers and lagoons, Limón Cocha, and longer ones into the jungle of up to ten days, similar to those organized by Héctor Fiallos but reportedly slightly more expensive. A short canoe trip to El Ahuano gives a good idea of the jungle river life. Carlos Lastra is recommended as knowledgeable, cheerful and a good cook. He offers much the same programmes of short or long trips, to various Indian villages. At *Hotel Balcón del Napo* contact Galo, who does 7-day jungle tours, or Carlos Sevilla, whose tours are 1-2 days; both charge US$11 p.p. per day, both are well recommended. Another tour operator is Walter Vasco, of Experiencia en Selva y Río, who has 2 or 3 canoes for fairly inexpensive trips. Luis Duarte (US$20 a day) has been recommended as very knowledgeable with close contacts among Indian families, but unless you insist otherwise, you will dine on products of his hunting: cayman, monkey, piranha fish and turtle eggs! He too can be contacted at the *Balcón del Napo*. Other good guides: Wilson Vasco, 6-10 day jungle tours US$15 a day, no English spoken; Elías Arteaga, office on main square, 3-day tours US$40 if 5 people, good meal at his house afterwards; Fernando Alomia, 4-day tours US$60 p.p. maximum 4 people, lives at *Residencial La Posada* on corner of square by road leading to the river.

Some tours have been criticized for too much walking for too few rewards, so make sure your guide knows enough to make your effort worthwhile; an inexperienced guide can mean a boring, or even distressing, walk. Remember that, however good your guide is, organization may be bad, resulting in delays. If short of time, think twice about taking a tour. Travellers into the Oriente must have their passports stamped at the naval office, which is clearly marked at the canoe embarkation point. Fees for chartering a canoe are open to bargaining; fares on excursions are fixed. Every canoe pilot is supposed to have his passenger list checked before going downstream but this is not always done. For your own safety ensure that the authorities have a record. Essential items for a trip of any length are rubber boots, sleeping bags, rain jackets, binoculars, insect repellant, sun tan lotions, mosquito net, water-purifying tablets, sticking plasters. The cautious might also take a tent, stove, extra food and playing cards.

Transport Direct bus to Quito, daily (2) in p.m., 10 hrs.; none direct Misahuallí-Baños. Buses to Puerto Napo and Tena. From Misahuallí, canoe services to the downriver ports of Coca, Limón Cocha and Nueva Rocafuerte. By motorized canoe to Coca, 1030, foreigners are charged US$4.50 p.p. for the 5½ hour trip (boats often crowded, best to be early, tickets sold early in the morning from the hut next to the police station, on the other hand, if not enough passengers, the canoe won't go; take waterproofs); there is also a mail boat in both directions twice a month.

During and after heavy rainfall there are obviously no services, nor are there any services during a long dry period.

The main road from Puerto Napo runs 10 km. north to **Tena,** the capital of Napo Province, and then on to Archidona, a small mission settlement about 10 km. further on. Archidona is a village (*Residencial Carolina*, F; *Residencial Regina*, pleasant and friendly) centred around its mission and an extraordinary church and luxuriant square. Both settlements have good views of Sumaco, an extinct volcano to the north (3,807 metres), and both have a large lowland Quechua Indian population living in the vicinity, many of whom are panning for gold in the rivers. These Indians are unlike the Indian groups further into the Oriente forests. "They are Quijos, of Chibcha stock, and their old territory extended in pre-conquest times from Puerto Napo up the Quijos pass to Papallacta and from there down to Coca. Their forthright character, bravery and their inherent honesty have not changed since the days when they held the Spaniards back from their efforts to find "El Dorado'." (Jay Louthian, Florida). From Tena or Archidona (bus from Archidona, ½ hr.), a visit can be made to the famous Jumandí caves by the Río Latas, 10 km. N. of Archidona (bus from Archidona, ½ hr.). It is necessary to go with a guide; take good boots and a strong torch. It is very muddy so it can be useful to take spare clothes. The side ducts of the caves are extremely narrow and claustrophobic. There are several colonies of the vampire bat (*Desmodus rotundus*) in the caves. Before going, make full enquiries about routes and conditions.

Hotels *Mol*, E, with bath, clean, restaurant, garage, rec.; *Tena*, G, noisy at night, due to restaurant below; *Amazonas*, G, clean, near main square; *Jumandy*, G, clean, friendly, breakfast from 0600; *Enmita*, G, near bus station, reasonable restaurant; *Res. Hilton*, G, good and clean; *Res. Alemania*, F, good and clean, own bath. *Hostal Baños*, near bus station, G, very basic, clean; *Res. Alexander*, F, 2 rooms with bathroom, near bus station, clean. A modern resort-style hotel is *Auca*, E, on the river out of town, 1½ km. on road to Archidona, Dituris-run, restaurant and bar, nice grounds, discotheque, casino, swimming in river, electricity and water unreliable.

Restaurants In Tena, *Don Quiño*, good, reasonable; *Niagara*, *Oriental*, *Tena*. Throughout the Oriente there are small, set-menu restaurants, about US$1. It is difficult to find a meal if you arrive on a late bus and you may prefer to go hungry rather than eat what is on offer.

Buses Quito (via Baeza), 5 daily (Coop. Baños, and 1 each Amazonas and Peliteo), US$2.50, 6½ hrs.; Baeza, US$1, 3 hrs.; Ambato (via Baños), 10 a day (several companies), US$2.20, 6¼ hrs.; Riobamba (via Puyo and Baños), 5 daily. Archidona every 20 mins., US$0.08, 15 mins.; Misahualli every 20 mins., US$0.35, 1 hr. (via Puerto Napo, US$0.08, 15 mins.) to Coca, 6 a day, 2 companies; Jumandy at 1800 to Lago Agrio; Puyo, US$1, 3 hrs.

From Cuenca The journey into the Oriente via El Descanso, Gualaceo, Limón (*Res. Limón*, clean, modern), Méndez, Sucúa and Macas is longer than and as spectacular as from Quito or Ambato; there are several beautiful stretches. **Sucúa** (9-hr. bus trip from Cuenca US$2.05) is of particular interest as the centre of the now-civilized branch of the ex-head-hunting Shuar (Jívaro) Indians; their crafts can be seen and bought but it is tactless to ask them about head-hunting and shrinking. You can visit the Shuar Federation and enquire about visits to Indian villages.

Hotel Oriente, clean, friendly, restaurant; *Hotel Cuhanda*, *Colón*, *Rincón Oriental*—friendly, good set meals— Cuenca, all F; Bar/restaurant *Sangay*, opp. *Rincón Oriental*. There are an interesting bookshop and (ten minutes walk from the town centre) a small museum in the Centro de Formación.

Macas (11 hrs., US$1.80 bus trip from Cuenca, hourly buses from Sucúa, 1 hr.; no regular service on Thurs.), the capital of Santiago-Morona province, is developing rapidly thanks to nearby oil deposits. Its environs are very beautiful and the surrounding hills give excellent views of the volcano **Sangay**, 5,230 metres, within the Sangay National Park, entrance US$10, reached by bus to village of 9 de Octubre, Wed. and Sun. 1600, then walk. You can cross the River Upano (footbridge) and take bus (½ hr.) to the Salesian Sevilla-Don Bosco mission (most welcoming), and various Indian villages. Good swimming. José Arcos of the Salesian Mission Flying Service may take pasengers to distant Shuar villages, ½ flight costs US$12 p.p. return. The whole settlement area has been developed for beef production. Malaria precautions essential. Flight to Quito, TAME, Mon. and Fri. 1500, US$12.

Macas Hotels *Orquídea*, best, roof restaurant, 9 de Octubre y Sucre, F, with bath, cold water;

Peñón del Oriente, Domingo y Amazonas, F p.p., clean, good, firm beds, electric showers; *Hostería del Valle*, 5 km. out on Sucúa road, self-contained cabins, F. Others are all G: *Residencial Macas*, clean and friendly; *Hotels Encalada, Amazonas, Residenciales Emperatriz* and *Elvira* (over liquid gas store); *Pensión Turismo*, basic.

Restaurants Hotels *Orquídea* and *Encalada, Fredy*, below *Resid. Macas. Chifa Perla Oriental, Mesón Dorado* and bus station restaurant, all on 10 de Agosto.

A round trip Cuenca—Gualaceo—Limón—Sucúa—Macas—Mera and onwards to Quito will be possible on completion of the road between Macas and Mera and construction of the bridge on the Pastaza river. This road is now completed from Macas to the Pastaza river (hourly bus Macas-La Punta, US$1, 2 hrs., then 4-hr hike to Pitirico) and from Mera S to Pitirico. A road is virtually completed between Macas and Guamote, S of Riobamba (see page 651), which will give quicker access to Quito. It is not possible to drive a passenger car from Cuenca to Macas because of river crossings.

From Loja The road to the Oriente (see page 665) crosses a low pass and descends rapidly to *Zamora*, an old mission settlement about 2 hours' drive away. From Zamora, the road follows the Zamora river to *Gualaquiza* (also bus from Cuenca, 2 a day, 8 hrs., US$2.80; *Hotel Turismo*, with restaurant). The valley produces large quantities of *naranjillas* and some sugar cane, maize, bananas and yuca. Regular bus services from Loja to Zamora and Gualaquiza (0400, 2200) and beyond with Cenepa-Pacífico and other companies. Cheap, basic hotels are available in Zamora and Gualaquiza.ffi

---

GALAPAGOS ISLANDS (9)

Lying on the Equator, 970 km. west of the Ecuadorean coast, the Galápagos consist of 6 main islands (San Cristóbal, Santa Cruz, Isabela, Floreana, Santiago and Fernandina—the last two uninhabited); 12 smaller islands (Baltra, with an airport, and the uninhabited islands of Santa Fe, Pinzón, Española, Rábida, Daphne, Seymour, Genovesa, Marchena, Pinta, Darwin and Wolf) and over 40 small islets. The islands have a total population of just over 6,000. The largest island, Isabela (formerly Albemarle), is 120 km. long and forms half the total land area of the archipelago. Its notorious convict colony was closed in 1958; some 650 people live there now, mostly in and around Puerto Villamil, on the S coast. San Cristóbal (Chatham) has a population of 2,321 with the capital of the archipelago, Puerto Baquerizo Moreno. Santa Cruz (Indefatigable) has 3,154, with Puerto Ayora, the main tourist centre; and Floreana (Charles) fewer than 50. The group is quite widely scattered; by boat, Puerto Baquerizo Moreno and Puerto Ayora are 6 hours apart.

The islands are the peaks of gigantic volcanoes, composed almost exclusively of basalt. Most of them rise from 2,000 to 3,000 metres above the seabed. Eruptions have taken place in historical times on Fernandina, Isabela, Pinta, Marchena, Santiago and Floreana. The most active today are Fernandina, Isabela, Pinta and Marchena, and fumarolic activity may be seen intermittently on each of these islands. There have been recent eruptions on Volcán, Sierra Negra, Isabela and Fernandina.

The Galápagos have almost certainly never been connected with the continent. Gradually, over many hundreds of thousands of years, animals and plants from over the sea developed there and as time went by they adapted themselves to Galápagos conditions and came to differ more and more from their continental ancestors. Thus many of them are unique: a quarter of the species of shore fish, half of the plants and almost all the reptiles are found nowhere else. In many cases different forms have evolved on the different islands. Charles Darwin recognized this speciation within the archipelago when he visited the Galápagos on the *Beagle* in 1835 and his observations played a substantial part in his formulation of the theory of evolution. Since no large land mammals reached the islands, reptiles were dominant just as they had been all over the world in very distant past. Another of the extraordinary features of the islands is the tameness of the animals. The islands were uninhabited when they were discovered in 1535 and the animals still have little instinctive fear of man.

The most spectacular species to be seen by the visitor are the giant tortoise (species still survive in 6 or 7 of the islands, but mostly on Isabela); marine iguana (the only seagoing lizard in the world and found throughout most of the archipelago; it eats seaweed); land iguana (on Fernandina, Santa Cruz, Santa Fe, Isabela, Seymour and Plaza); Galápagos albatross (which nests only on the island of Española, it leaves in December and returns in late March-early April); Galápagos hawk, red-footed, blue-footed and masked boobies, red-billed tropic-bird, frigate birds, dusky lava gulls, mockingbirds, 13 species of Darwin's finches (all endemic and the classic examples of speciation quoted by Darwin); Galápagos sea-lion (common in many areas) and the Galápagos fur-seal (on the more remote and rocky coasts). Santiago and Plaza islands are particularly interesting for students of these species.

There is a National Park Tax which every visitor has to pay; in January 1989 it was US$40, payable only in sucres, US$ cash or travellers cheques.

Alban Johnson and Luci Montesinos Aguilar write: The most-visited islands (and main attractions) are Plaza Sur (many birds flying close to the cliff top), Santa Fe (land and sea iguanas, sea-lions), Seymour Norte (magnificent frigate birds, blue-footed boobies), Rábida (sea-lions, flamingoes, pelican rookery), and Santiago (James Bay for fur seals; Sullivan Bay and Bartolomé Island for fantastic lava fields and maybe a few penguins). On a tour of these islands it may be possible to go also to Punto García on Isabela to see flightless cormorants (it takes at least a full day to climb up one of the volcanoes to see the tortoises). Daphne Island with very rich birdlife may be visited by each boat only once a month (a permit is required).

More distant islands are Española (blue-footed boobies, masked boobies, waved albatross, brightly-coloured marine iguanas), Genovesa (red-footed boobies, frigate birds and many others) and Fernandina (penguins and many other birds). Floreana, San Cristóbal and Baltra have little wildlife, and on Santa Cruz it is worth visiting the Darwin Station, Tortoise Reserve and Tortuga Bay. All the other islands are closed to tourists.

Tours generally leave from Puerto Ayora, but can finish at Baltra for the airport. Take some chocolate and biscuits with you; you will certainly miss them if you don't. Boat operators tend to underestimate the amount of drinking (mineral) water and overestimate the amount of Coca Cola that foreigners drink. Food can be good if they catch fish, poor if not.

In 1959, the centenary of the publication of Darwin's *Origin of Species*, the Government of Ecuador and the International Charles Darwin Foundation established, with the support of Unesco, the Charles Darwin Research Station at Academy Bay 1½ km. from Puerto Ayora, Santa Cruz, the most central of the Galápagos islands, open daily 0700-1300, 1400-1800. Collections of several of the rare races of giant tortoise are maintained on the station as breeding nuclei, together with a tortoise-rearing house incorporating incubators and pens for the young. The Darwin Foundation staff will help bona fide students of the fauna to plan an itinerary, if they stay some time and hire a boat. Avoid visiting in July and especially August (high season).

Travel to the Islands There are flights with SAN to the new airport at Puerto Baquerizo Moreno (San Cristóbal) from Guayaquil and connecting flights from Quito (on Mon., Wed. and Sat.). The round trip in 1988 cost US$324 from Guayaquil, and US$365 from Quito. One-way tickets are available and it is now possible to buy an open-ended ticket (valid one year—e.g. from Manatours, Av. Amazonas, Quito). SAN will change dates for return to mainland. TAME flies daily, except Sunday, to Baltra, across a narrow strait from Santa Cruz (reconfirming return flights is essential). Tour operators still buy up blocks of seats in advance and they always try to sell you one of their excursions. For this reason, if time is limited, it is probably advisable to go for a package tour. If you cannot get a flight within a week, try going to the airport to get a seat on stand-by.

The Air Force flights, known as *logísticos*, are apparently available on Fridays to foreign students, who must go to the Departamento de Operaciones of the Air Force at the Ministry of Defence, Av. Maldonado y la Exposición, Quito. Get your name on the list in advance, and pay the Friday before departure; to enter the office, leave identification, but not your passport which is needed for booking the ticket. Alban Johnson and Luci Montesinos Aguilar write: "The Air Force *logísticos* are cheap but unreliable (more so for the special midweek flights). To catch one, foreigners need the special authorization of the general commander of the Air Force, which can only be obtained with the support of their embassy and letters of introduction from a recognized educational/research institution where they work or study. There are Ecuadoreans who sell *logístico* tickets with a large mark-up, but these are not recommended—chances are that it will be a special (cancelled) flight and you lose a large part of your money." The student organization, Oetej, 6 de Diciembre 159 y Paz Miño, Quito, can get 30% discounts for students: ask for Martha Jiménez. Don't confuse Oetej with Ceptej, another student organization, which can't help in this way.

There are now many travel agencies operating tours of the Galápagos Islands. Their quality and price varies considerably so shop around. Prices are no longer significantly cheaper in the low season (Feb.-May, Sept.-Nov.) but ask if an agency has 1-3 spaces to fill on a cruise; you can sometimes get them at 20% discount.

We have received persistent reports that tour operators, whether contacted on the mainland or the Galápagos, are unreliable in sticking to their agreed programme, and that some of the guides deviate from the scheduled route, wasting time in port and leaving out some islands. Insist on a written itinerary or contract prior to departure as any effort not to provide this probably indicates problems later (written contracts seem to be ignored, none-the-less). The South American Explorers Club (Apartado 21-431, Eloy Alfaro post office, Quito, Av. Portugal 146, Casilla 3714, Lima, Peru, and 1510 York Street, Denver, CO 80206) has produced a useful, brief guide to the Galápagos which includes a specimen contract for itinerary and living conditions. Ensure that not more than a half-day is spent on either Santa Cruz or San Cristóbal for restocking of provisions. Count your money regularly and don't leave your beach gear unattended if other boats are in the vicinity when you are ashore. If you have problems afterwards, take your contract to the Capitanía (port captain).

In Guayaquil, **Galasam** (Economic Galapagos Tours), Av. 9 de Octubre 424, Edificio Gran Pasaje, 11° piso (T 306 289/ 313 724, Telex 42680 GALASA ED) sell flights as well as their own tours and can sell air tickets for their tours at a discount by using the free market. If you buy your air ticket from their office they throw in one night and lunch at a hotel in Puerto Ayora even if you do not purchase their tour. If you book the SAN flight to San Cristóbal with them, they throw in the Ingala boat trip to Santa Cruz free. In Quito, Galasam is at Pinto 523 y Av. Amazonas. The Galasam 8-day tours, Wed. or Sat. departure, normally cost about US$500, on 5 small boats each taking 8 people, on which conditions are fairly spartan; however their two 12 passenger boats are more comfortable (US$700 for an 8-day tour), and have specially trained bilingual guides; their newest boat, *Dorado*, is more luxurious still. Galasam say the guides on the smaller boats are English-speaking, but their knowledge of English may be very limited. It has also been alleged that their boats sometimes travel in convoy and that prices on board are exorbitant. Metropolitan Touring, Av. Amazonas 239, Casilla 2542, Quito (represented in the USA by Adventure Associates, 5925 Maple, Suite 116, Dallas, Texas 75235), T 524-400 offers 7-night cruises on the M.V. *Santa Cruz* (90 passengers), about US$120 a day, said to be the best boat, very professional service, with multilingual guides. They also have five yachts for private charters. Macchiavello Tours of Guayaquil (Anteparra 809 y 9 de Octubre, T 392-892) is ordering two new boats from Italy.

Other recommended agencies with tours to/in the Galápagos are: Galápagos Cruises, Los Ríos 0-80, Guayaquil, T 390-893, Telex 3610 ETICAG; Coltur, Robles y Páez 370, Quito, T 545-777, Telex 2302, with an office in Puerto Ayora; Nuevo Mundo, Av. Amazonas 2468, Quito T 552-617, Telex 2484; Castro Turismo, Vélez 205, Guayaquil, T 512-174; Viajes Wang, 10 de Agosto y Bolivia, Quito, T 551-946. Famitur, Veintimilla 928 y Amazonas, Quito, T 529-742. The *Hotel Gran Casino* in Quito, Av. 24 de Mayo y Bahía, arranges 8-day tours for US$350; reports on their reliability have not always been favourable. Kayaking trips in the Islands are organized by Northern Lights Expeditions, 5220 NE 180th, Seattle, WA 98155, USA.

There are cargo ships making the trip, but dates are irregular, the chances of a passage remote and some interesting but remote ports are missed. Check with the naval port authorities on the Malecón in Guayaquil, or with the boats themselves several days prior to departure. *Iguana* leaves on the 7th of each month, *Congal* on the 17th and *Piquero* on the 27th. None is reported to be reliable.

From Britain, inclusive tours can be booked through Twickers World, 22 Church Street, Twickenham, TW13NW, or through the Coltur representative in London, Cecilia Irivalo, T 01-221 0968. David Horwell, naturalist and author of *Galápagos, the Enchanted Isles*, London, Dryad Press, 1988 (£7.95), arranges tailor-made tours to Ecuador and the Galápagos islands. For further details write to him at 29 Palace View, Bromley, Kent, BR1 3EJ, England.

From the airport on Baltra, one takes a combination of bus (US$1), ferry (US$0.20) and bus (US$1.50) to Puerto Ayora, Santa Cruz. The whole process takes at least 3 hours. Airport buses leave Puerto Ayora (Pyky supermarket) at 0800 and 0830 for Baltra (best buy ticket night before—not possible for Sat. bus though). Tame office in P. Ayora closes Sat p.m. and Sun. Hotel may make prior arrangements.

Travel between the Islands There are official (Ingala) sailings on Tues. and Sat. from Santa Cruz at 1200 to San Cristóbal (US$10.50), returning at 1200 on Mon. and Wed. On Thurs. the Ingala boat leaves Santa Cruz at 0800 for Isabela; on Fri. it leaves Isabela at 0800 for Floreana, sailing from there to Santa Cruz at 1200. The Ingala office in Puerto Ayora is next to the hospital on the road inland from the waterfront. Get your name on the list here as early as possible on the day before sailing, buy ticket for San Cristóbal on day of departure between 0800 and 1000 and be at the quay at 1100. The Ingala office in Puerto Baquerizo Moreno is up the hill on the road leading inland, on the edge of town.

The best centre from which to visit the Islands is **Puerto Ayora**, Santa Cruz. Here you can hire boats (lists available from National Park Service) and a two-week sojourn will allow you to see most of the Islands. If you only have a short time, the northern islands are the more scenic with the more interesting wildlife. Reservations are strongly recommended for June-August and December-April. The Capitanía del Puerto will give information on fishing boats' movements. For cheaper tours it is generally recommended that you form a group of six to ten people once you reach the Islands, talk to people about the boats they may have used and then talk to the boat owners (known as *dueño*), not the captains, about what you wish to do. Bargain over the route and the price, and get a firm commitment from the owner on dates and itinerary, leave a deposit "to buy food" and get a receipt; however, prices have risen sharply and boat owners have reportedly formed a union so that it is now difficult to find a small boat taking six to eight people for less than US$50 p.p. per day for a full load (small boats are essentially for travellers who do not mind a lack of privacy and facilities). Larger, more comfortable boats can cost twice as much, especially if they have bilingual guides. Each boat has to be accompanied by a Park-trained guide, either a naturalist (who will be English-speaking, more knowledgeable and therefore more expensive), or an auxiliary; this is arranged by the boat owner. Most boats operate 4-8 day cruises, it appears that only the 50-berth *Isabela*, owned by Etica, can be booked for longer—up to 3 weeks. The *San Juan* is recommended for its friendly crew and its speed, which allows you to see as much in 7 days as some do in 10; it is also one of the cheaper boats. Also recommended is the *Golondrina*; friendly crew, knowledgeable guide and excellent food. Gil and Anita De Roy have been highly recommended for tours on their yacht *Inti*, which accommodates 4 to 5 passengers besides two crew; they speak French, German, English and Spanish, are experienced naturalists and guides and serve excellent food. Eduardo García has been recommended as one of the best guides. Coltur (see above) has been recommended for visits to North Seymour and Caleta Tortuga Negra on the north coast of Santa Cruz. Their representatives can arrange tours on the *Pirata* (Augusto and Georgina Cruz), which has been recommended for its friendly and helpful staff and good cooking; Georgina Cruz is English. The *Angelito* has been highly recommended, partly because the captain navigates by night so that you have more time on the islands by day; this makes it slightly more expensive. Others recommended in this category are *Española* (10 passengers, good crew and cooking, fast, US$25 p.p.—high season), *Cachalote* and *Sulidae*, also 10 passengers, *Daphne* and *San Antonio* (one of the cheapest, US$170 a day for a party of 8). The trimaran *Wind Shadow* (slow if there´s no wind), owned and sailed by Richard Núñez, costs US$180 per day (maximum capacity 4); Sr. Núñez is knowledgeable and speaks English. It must be stressed, however, that a boat is only as good as its crew and when the staff change, so will these recommendations. Check that the small boats can carry enough food and supplies for the length of journey so you do not waste a day restocking. **Warning**: it can take several days to arrange a tour, so allow yourself plenty of time (up to a week in high season). If you do get stuck, the Tourist Office in Puerto Ayora offers one-day tours (US$36 p.p. with lunch) to Floreana, Seymour Norte, Plaza Sur or Santa Fe. These smaller islands have a good sample of animal species (although fewer in numbers) and, together with sightseeing on Santa Cruz, can be a worthwhile experience for the tourist with only limited time. Never miss the chance to do a bit of snorkelling (for instance at the Corona del Diablo rocks, off Floreana), but enquire carefully about the likelihood of sharks (*tiburones*—not all are dangerous).

Byron Rueda offers day trips for 10 in his dinghy *Santa Fe* to Santa Fe and to the Plaza islands (US$18). His office is on the Ninfa dock and he also represents other boats (open 0800-1800).

The Cost of Living in the Galápagos is high. Most food has to be imported although certain meats, fish, vegetables and fruit are available locally in the Puerto Ayora market.

Hotels at Puerto Ayora   Hotel space is limited (more are being built) and reservations are strongly rec. in high season. *Galápagos*, B (local class 1), bungalows with private bathroom, hot water, ocean-view, laundry service, generator, restaurant with fixed menu, price and time, fruit and meat from hotel farm, near Darwin Research centre, reservations can be made through Ecuadorean travel agencies, day excursions can be made from hotel in Pedro and Sally García's own dinghy for 10, the *Fernandina*. *Delfín*, on far side of Academy Bay, with lovely beach, D (1), well rec., accessible only by boat, write to Rolf Sievers. *Residencial Angermeyer*: about 20 beds, F, described as very simple, and idiosyncratic; Mrs Angermeyer keeps the place spotlessly clean and is a mine of information, for guests, on good and bad boats. There is a peña next door. *Sol y Mar*: 20 beds (double, triples and quadruples) in cabins; E (1), without meals; B, with 3 meals; 10% discount for stays of 2 weeks or more; reservations can be made by writing to the owner (Sr. Jimmy Pérez), or Macchiavello Tours, Casilla 318, Guayaquil. *Castro*, F (2), with private bath, owned by Sr. Miguel Castro, he arranges Friday TAME flight, rec. He is an authority on wildlife and his tour includes one or two nights away visiting the islands of Plazas and Santiago, and a day-trip to Santa Fe, with visits to the tortoise reserve and the Darwin Institute. *Colón*: 22 beds (doubles) in third class rooms; F (3), without food; D, including 3 meals. Write to Sra. Piedad Moya. *Elizabeth*, F with bath (3), reasonable, now remodelled, has running water; *Ninfa*, E (2), has its own boat at reasonable price for day trips and Fernando Jiménez is helpful with arrangements; *Lobo de Mar*, E (2), 30 beds; *Gloria*, G (3), 12 beds, simple, Sr. Bolívar very friendly, clean, you can cook your own food over a wood fire, mosquito repellant needed; *Darwin*, F, with bath, clean, restaurant (order meals in advance), rec. but don't leave valuables in your room; *Las Palmeras*, F (2), private bath, cafeteria, laundry facilities, pleasant, clean; *Salinas*, opposite, also F, 20 beds. *Santa Cruz*, F (3).

Restaurants at Puerto Ayora Good food served at *El Túnel* (US$0.80 for breakfast) on main road; *Don Enriques*, same road, local dishes; *Los Gemelos*, near the school, good value; *La Garrapata*, open air, on road to research station, popular meeting place for travellers, pizzas, hamburgers, cakes, morning and evening but not Sun.; *Fausto's*, between Gloria and Angermeyer hotels, good pizzas, friendly owner speaks English; *Four Lanterns*, facing Pelican Bay, good, reasonable (dinner US$1.50); *Pastry Shop* (in front of hospital) for snacks and drinks; *Ninfa Dock Bar/Restaurant*, on dock, excellent grilled lobster, changes money, meeting place; nearby is *Pasty Pan* for bread and cakes (not open Sun.). *Bambú*, good light food, Spanish specialities, pleasant atmosphere; *Viña del Mar*, on main street, basic, O.K.; *Carmen's* pastry shop rec., good coffee and sweets; *Bibu*, yoghurt and good breakfasts; *Fragata Bar*, good, on road to research station, as is *Galaps Pizzería*. *Pelikano* and *Pastik-Shock* cafeterias. *Banana Bar*, near Angermeyer hotel, serves delicious banana flambée. Restaurants serve lobster dinners at US$5; *merienda* costs between US$1.50-2.

Entertainment Three discos (*La Terraza, Five Fingers* and *Disco Light*) and one *peña-disco* (*Peter Cheese*) in Puerto Ayora.

Hints For boat charters and camping trips most basic foodstuffs generally can be purchased in the islands (e.g. Pyky supermarket in Puerto Ayora), although occasionally there are shortages. However, no special items (dehydrated or freezedried foods) are available other than a few common ones such as oatmeal and dried soups. Fresh milk available in Puerto Ayora from Christine Aldaze, 0930, next to *Túnel* restaurant (24 hrs. notice appreciated).

Medicines, sun lotions (only up to factor 4 available in Ecuador), mosquito coils, film, and other useful items are either not available or cost a lot more than on the mainland. Take plenty of film with you; the birds are so tame that you will use far more than you expected; a telephoto lens is not essential. There is a souvenir shop next to Angermeyer's hotel, Galápagos Souvenirs, and a camera repair place next to the cemetery near the Darwin Station. Artesanías Bambú, near *Hotel Galápagos*, sells local handicrafts, printed T-shirts, etc.

Warning: Valuables should be watched.

Some of the prices charged are exorbitant. There is a cinema at Puerto Ayora—each evening at 2015. Information and retrieval of lost property from Radio Santa Cruz, next to Catholic Church. Short-stay camping permitted at the Caseta in the highlands and at Tortuga Bay.

There is a hospital in Puerto Ayora; consultations are free, medicines reasonably-priced.

Exchange It is advisable to take plenty of cash; there are few facilities for cashing cheques in Puerto Ayora, and rates are about 5 % less than for cash. The *Hotel Sol y Mar* and *Ninfa* restaurant will change notes and cheques, but at a poor rate. There is a bank at Puerto Ayora but it gives a poor rate of exchange and will not accept credit cards. Several shops change US$ notes.

Immigration The police will extend visas with a little persuasion for those who overstay their visa or tourist card; but such extensions are reportedly not valid.

British Consul David Balfour, C/o Etica, Barrio Estrada, Puerto Ayora.

Tourist Office Dituris, near the pier, open Mon.-Fri. 0800-1200, 1500-1800. Information also available at the boat owners' cooperative office nearby.

Excursions on Santa Cruz Walk to Tortuga Bay. A new, shorter track, 2 km. long (1½ hours) has been opened: turn at *Hotel Elizabeth* off main road, then left at *Hotel Santa Cruz*. Take drinking water.

Hike to the higher parts of the island called Media Luna, Puntudo and Mt. Crocker. Trail starts at Bellavista (which can be reached on foot, or by car, or 3 buses a day US$0.20, or hitch), 7 km. from Puerto Ayora. Round trip from Bellavista is 4 to 8 hrs., depending upon distance hiked, 10-18 km. (permit and guide not required).

There are two natural tunnels (lava tubes) 1 km. from Bellavista (on private land, US$0.70 to enter, torch provided—it takes about ½ hr. to walk through the tunnels). There is a barbecue each Sun. at La Choza, Bellavista; information in *El Túnel* restaurant, Puerto Ayora.

Hike to the Chato Tortoise Reserve; trail starts at Santa Rosa, 22 km. from Puerto Ayora; 3 buses a day, or hitch. Horses can be hired at Santa Rosa, US$5 each, guide optional US$6.50 extra. Round trip takes one day. Again, the Puerto Ayora-Bellavista bus stops at the turnoff for the track for the reserve (US$0.50). It's a hot walk; take food and drink. From Santa Rosa, distance to different sites within the reserve is 6-8 km. (permit and guide not required).

Two sinkholes, Los Gemelos, straddle the road to Baltra, beyond Santa Rosa; if you are lucky, take a *camioneta* all the way, otherwise to Santa Rosa, then walk. A good place to see the Galápagos hawk and barn owl.

Visit the giant Galápagos tortoises in pens at the Darwin Station, a short distance from Puerto Ayora. Small tortoises in rearing pens may be observed. The Station has a museum (explaining the geology and natural history of the islands) and a library. There are also public lectures (details from Dituris office near the pier).

Puerto Baquerizo Moreno, on San Cristóbal island to the E, is the capital of the archipelago, with a new airport with flights Mon., Wed. and Sat. by SAN. The island is being developed as a second tourist centre and, to encourage tourists, in late 1988 SAN was offering two free nights at the *Grand Hotel* included in the price of a Monday flight from Quito or Guayaquil. Three Ingala buses a week to Puerto Ayora (US$10.50); fishing boats also take passengers (US$7 to Puerto Ayora). Be warned that it can take several days to find room on a boat to Puerto Ayora or Santa Cruz.

Hotels *Grand Hotel Cristóbal*, owned by SAN, opp. a white beach to E of town, D with bath (not inc. tax), good restaurant; *Mar Azul*, on road from airport, D with bath, restaurant; *Residencial Northia*, E with bath; *Cabanas Don Jorge*, close to beach, F p.p., clean, friendly, "not luxurious"; *Res. Miramar*, F, good value, clean restaurant, good; *Pensión Gloria*, pleasant family, but leaky roofs, new rooms are being added; *Res. Flamingo*, F, basic; *Hotel San Francisco*, F, good, clean, friendly.

Restaurants Rosita, best in town; *Chatham*, good; *Laurita*, fair; *La Terraza*, on beach; *Fragata*, on road to airport.

Excursions Bus (shuttle) to El Progreso, then short walk to El Junco lake, tortoises may be seen on the way. From El Progreso (eating places), a trail crosses the high lands to Cerro Brujo and Hobbs Bay; also to Stephens Bay, past lakes. 2 buses go to the crater lake in the middle of the island, and may continue to the other side. SAN organizes a day trip (ask at *Grand Hotel*) to Point Lobo, reported as disappointing, and another to Española; the latter is often cancelled because the sea is too rough for their small boats.

The Galápagos Climate   can be divided into a hot season (January to April), when there is a possibility of heavy showers, and the cool or *garúa* season (May to December), when the days generally are more cloudy. Daytime clothing should be lightweight. (Clothing generally, even on "luxury cruises" should be casual and comfortable.) At night, however, particularly at sea and at higher altitudes, temperatures fall below 15°C and warm clothing is required. Boots and shoes soon wear out on the lava terrain and there is need for protection against rain. A good supply of sun block and skin cream to prevent windburn and chapped lips is essential. A hat is also recommended. Apart from Tortuga Bay, there are no beaches on Santa Cruz, but several on San Cristóbal.

Information   The *Galápagos Guide* by Alan White and Bruce White Epler, with photographs by Charles Gilbert, is published in several languages; it can be bought in Guayaquil in Librería Científica and the airport, Libri Mundi (US$5) in Quito, or at the Charles Darwin station. *Galápagos, the Enchanted Isles*, by David Horwell **(see page 677).** Also rec. is *Galápagos: a Natural History Guide* by Michael H. Jackson (US$20 from Libri Mundi, Quito). A must for birdwatchers is *Field Guide to the Birds of the Galápagos* (US$20). A map of the Galápagos, drawn by Kevin Healey and illustrated by Hilary Bradt, is published by Bradt Enterprises. The National Park now publishes a good guide in English and Spanish, with plans of all the places where visitors are allowed to land: *Guide to the Visitor Sites of Parque Nacional Galápagos*, by Alan and Tui Moore, US$3.30. National Park Office, Puerto Ayora, Santa Cruz, Mon.-Fri. 0800-1200, 1400-1800, Sat. 0800-1000. For more information write to the Director of the Charles Darwin Research Station or the Superintendent of the Galápagos National Park Service, Isla Santa Cruz, Galápagos (correspondence in English.)

THE ECONOMY

In the early 1970s, Ecuador underwent a transformation from an essentially agricultural economy to a predominantly petroleum economy. From 1972 when substantial domestic oil output began, economic growth has largely followed the fortunes of the oil market, except in 1983, when freak weather conditions resulted in large crop losses. Agriculture's contribution (including fishing) to gdp has dwindled from over 22% in 1972 to less than 14% by the mid-1980s although it still employs a third of the labour force. The major export crops of bananas, coffee and cocoa are grown on the coast. Ecuador is the world's largest exporter of bananas, although it is not a member of the Union of Banana Exporting Countries (Upeb). Production is being promoted with increased plantings of high-yielding varieties and provision of technical assistance and quality control. Coffee is the most extensive of Ecuador's cash crops, accounting for over 20% of total agricultural land, but it is also the lowest yielding crop. Cocoa production has been increased by a rehabilitation programme after the 1983 floods, but although yields have trebled, output of 498 kg per hectare is still well below Brazil's 914 kg/ha.

Fishing is a growing industry, offering lucrative export potential. As well as tuna, sardines and white fish, shrimp is being caught in increasing amounts and is the most valuable catch. Shrimp farming is booming along the coast and has provided much-needed jobs for agricultural workers. Mining has been relatively unimportant historically, but the discovery of about 700 tonnes of gold reserves around Nambija (Zamora) in the southeast created intense interest in precious metals and over 12,000 independent miners rushed to prospect there.

Although Ecuador's share of total world oil production is small (0.65% in 1985), foreign exchange earnings from oil exports are crucial to the economy. The main producing area is in the northern Oriente, and a 495-km. trans-Andean pipeline carries the oil to Esmeraldas on the coast, where it is refined and/or exported. There are also reserves of natural gas, mainly in the Gulf of Guayaquil, but these have not yet been fully developed. Hydroelectric potential is estimated at 90,000 MW, but generating capacity in the mid-1980s was only 2,000 MW. New projects on the Paute, Pastaza and Coca rivers could raise capacity to 12,000 MW by the end of the century.

Ecuador's foreign debt rose sharply in the 1970s when oil exports began and in the 1980s it joined other debtor nations in refinancing its external obligations. Adherence to free market economic policies in IMF programmes brought international approval and by 1985 Ecuador was widely acclaimed as a model debtor with sufficient creditworthiness to return to the voluntary market for loans. However, in 1986 oil prices crashed, cutting Ecuador's oil receipts by half, followed in 1987 by an earthquake which destroyed part of the trans-Andean pipeline and damaged other oil installations, causing a cessation of oil exports. It was clear that huge amounts of finance would be necessary for reconstruction of economic infrastructure and villages which had been destroyed. The effects on public finances were considerable, resulting in a higher rate of inflation. Subsequent loss of confidence in the Government's economic management resulted in a massive demand for dollars and a heavy devaluation of the sucre. Arrears on debt payments to all creditors built up in 1987 and 1988, and it was only in 1989 that the Government felt able to regularize some payments and begin negotiations.

	1961-70 (av)	1971-80 (av)	1981-85 (av)	1986-88 (av)
Gdp growth (1980 prices)	5.2%	8.9%	2.0%	1.1%
Inflation	4.5%	12.6%	27.5%	36.1%
Exports (fob) US$m	195	1,232	2,545	2,137
Crude oil	1	555	1,618	843
Bananas	93	158	186	275
Coffee	30	132	152	217
Imports (fob) US$m	169	1,132	1,826	1,766
Current account balance US$m (cum)	-440	-2,725	-2,445	-2,305

INFORMATION FOR VISITORS

By Air Air France and Avianca between them fly 3 times a week from Paris to Quito. Iberia flies from Madrid to Quito and Guayaquil and KLM weekly from Amsterdam to Guayaquil (Tues.). KLM also flies to Caracas, Aruba and on to Quito (Thurs.). Lufthansa has connections with Frankfurt and La Paz, Bolivia. Loftleidir (cheaper) flies from Luxembourg to Nassau where you can make a connection with Ecuatoriana. There are flights from New York via Miami by Eastern Airlines, which also flies to Panama, as does Air Panamá. Ecuatoriana, the national company, has international runs to Mexico City (three weekly), Lima, Caracas, Nassau, Miami and Los Angeles. Saeta also flies to Miami. Avianca flies to Mexico City via Bogotá. Varig/Ecuatoriana/Lasca (using Varig aircraft) fly to San José, Costa Rica. AeroPerú has an overnight flight from Miami to Guayaquil; the plane goes on to Buenos Aires via Lima and Santiago. Direct flights from other South American countries to Ecuador: from Chile (Ecuatoriana, 2 a week), Argentina (Ecuatoriana, 2 a week, Aerolíneas Argentinas weekly to Guayaquil), Brazil (weekly Varig flights); Paraguay and Bolivia (three a week by Eastern); there are none from Uruguay. There is a 10% tax on international air tickets for flights originating in Ecuador, regardless of where bought, and 12% on domestic tickets, and a tax of US$25, payable in sucres, on all passengers departing on international flights.

By Sea The only passenger service to Guayaquil is offered by Continental Shipping and Travel, 179 Piccadilly, London W1V 9DB, T 01-491 4968, with departures from France.

Warning Always carry your passport with you (a notarized photocopy will *not* do); if it is not in your possession you will be taken to prison.

Documents Passport (valid for at least six months required on arrival at Quito airport), and a tourist card valid for 90 days (tourists are now allowed only 90 days in any one calendar year) obtainable on arrival. You are required to say how many days you intend to stay and the card will be stamped accordingly; most travellers are given 15 or 30-day stamps irrespective of their requests (at Huaquillas, Macará and Tulcán), and travellers arriving by air may be given a stamp valid for only 10 days (transit pass) unless they request otherwise. It is therefore better to overestimate as you can be fined on leaving the country for staying too long. An extension can be routinely obtained at the Department of Immigration in Quito or Guayaquil, or at the Gobernación offices of several provincial capitals (addresses in the text); evidence of sufficient funds (see below) is sometimes required. A visa is required for French nationals (US$10), New Zealanders (US$7) and Australians (free) and for business people and students who stay longer than 90 days, application to be made in home country, and they must get an exit permit with both tax and police clearance.

The procedure for obtaining a student visa involves taking a letter from the school at which you will be studying to the Ecuadorean consulate, a letter from your bank and a ticket out of Ecuador (or South America), plus a fee of US$30 in cash (only dollars, wherever paid). There are many other essential procedures, for which at least 6 passport photos will be required (4 face, 2 profile). Holders of student visas do not have to pay the Cuoto de Compensación Militar on leaving, although business visa holders do. Verify all details at the Consulate before departure.

Tourists crossing from Colombia or Peru may be asked for evidence that they possess US$20 p.p. for each day they propose to spend in Ecuador. Theoretically you must have an onward ticket out of Ecuador, but this is almost never enforced if you are travelling overland. However, travellers arriving from Miami with Ecuatoriana have been refused entry without a ticket and an MCO may not be sufficient. For a car a *carnet de passage* is required; failing that a bond equal to the value of the car will be demanded.

Personal effects, a litre of spirits and a reasonable amount of perfume are admitted free of duty. No foreign cigarettes are allowed to be brought into Ecuador.

The **best time for a visit** is from June to October, during the dry season, though September can sometimes be wet. The coastal area is extremely hot and wet from December to May.

Clothing Spring clothing for Quito (mornings and evenings are cold). In Guayaquil tropical or light-weight clothes. Laundering is excellent, but dry-cleaning is expensive.

Local Time is 5 hrs. behind GMT (Galápagos, 6 hrs. behind.)

Health Amoebic dysentery is a danger. Visitors should drink mineral water (Güitig or Manantial), avoid uncooked vegetables or salads, and be inoculated against typhoid. Hepatitis (jaundice) is a very real risk and should be inoculated against with gamma globulin; see "Health Information" in front of book. Travellers in the Oriente and the Costa are advised to take anti-malaria tablets; mosquito netting is also useful. Yellow-fever vaccination is recommended for travel into the Oriente. There are excellent hospitals both in Quito and Guayaquil. Climbers are warned to undergo a period of acclimatization before attempting to scale the volcanoes.

It has been reported that the free rabies vaccine given out in Ecuador is made from mouse brain and is said to be dangerous, if not fatal. Human diploid vaccine (the correct type) is available from Hospital Voz Andes, Quito; the complete series costs US$700, so be sure to have adequate medical insurance (or be vaccinated before leaving home).

Food Well worth trying are *humitas* (*tamales* made of sweet maize), *llapingachos* (fried mashed potatoes with cheese), and *locro* (a soup of stewed potatoes and cheese topped with an avocado), served, with a beer, at bars. Local food is highly spiced only when *ají* (red pepper) sauce is added, and then it is very hot, but the food is often unspiced. *Tamales de moracho* (not unlike Venezuelan *hallaca*) and *empanadas de moracho* are delicious (same insides, breadcrust outside); *fanesca*, a kind of fish soup with beans, meat, and more, sold in Easter Week, is filling and rich. A typical meal (but a matter of taste) is roast *cuy* (guinea pig). *Cacho*, a croissant-like pastry, is cheap and filling. If economizing ask for the set meal in restaurants, *merienda*—very cheap; it costs between US$1 and US$2. There are interesting *encocada* (coconut) dishes on the coast. The fruits are magnificent: try *mamei colorado*, a fruit of the avocado family. A good sweet is *quimbolito*, a sweet sponge pudding made with maize flour.

Drink The local wines, often made from bananas, are safe but sickly, and cannot be recommended. Argentine and Chilean wines are cheaper than

European or US ones. The best fruit drinks are *naranjilla, taxo* and *mora* (blackberries). Beers available are Pilsener, Club, Malta (dark) and Löwenbräu. International drinks, when they can be had, are costly. Good *pisco, aguardiente* (Cristal is recommended), *paico* and *trago de caña*. The usual soft drinks, known as *colas*, are available. Instant coffee or liquid concentrate is common, so ask for *café puro* if you want real coffee.

Accommodation   outside the main towns; almost standard prices are charged of US$1.50-2 p.p. (without bath) in a *pensión, residencial*, or hotel (where this is the minimum charge). One can bargain at cheaper *pensiones* and *residenciales*. Outside the provincial capitals and the resorts of Salinas and Playas, there are few higher-class hotels. Service of 10% and tax of 10% are added to 1st and 2nd class hotel and restaurant bills. The cheaper hotels charge at most 5%, generally. Hotel owners tend to try and let their less attractive rooms first, but they are not insulted if you ask for a bigger room, better beds or a quieter area. The difference is often marked.

Camping For stoves, kerosene is known as "kerex" and is available where gasoline is sold (e.g. CEPE stations). Pure alcohol fuel is sold in hardware stores. **See also page 622.**

Tipping Hotels and restaurants, 10% usually in the bill (in cheaper restaurants, tipping is uncommon—but obviously welcome!). Taxi, nil. Airport and railway porters, US$0.08-0.20, according to number of suitcases; cloakroom attendants, US$0.04, hairdressers, 20%.

Electric Current 110 volts, 60 cycles, A.C. throughout Ecuador.

Internal Air Travel   The local airlines Saeta, SAN and TAME operate internal flights between the main cities. TAME and SAN fly to the Galápagos. Also local airlines Lansa and Cedta operating Machala-Guayaquil. Ecuavia operates charter flights. There are air taxis (Cessnas or Bonanzas) to anywhere you want to go to, also helicopters. On internal flights passengers may have to disembark at intermediate stops and check in, even though they have booked all the way to the final destination of the plane. Seats are not assigned on internal flights.

Railway Travel   The railways are not too comfortable or reliable. The total track length is 1,043 km., but the system is not yet completely restored following the 1983 floods. The Quito-Riobamba, Guayaquil-Alausí, Sibambe-Cuenca and Ibarra-San Lorenzo stretches are in operation for passengers.

Road Travel   Bus travel has improved greatly and is generally more convenient than in other Andean countries: since most buses are small they fill up and leave at frequent intervals. Half the 17,700 km. of road are open the year round. The length of paved highway is developing rapidly, including Quito-Guayaquil, Quito-Riobamba, Quito-Tulcán, Guayaquil-Cuenca, Guayaquil-Riobamba, Riobamba-Baños, Ambato-Puyo and the lowland (Costa) road Huaquillas-Machala-Guayaquil-Babahoyo-Santo Domingo-Esmeraldas. When touring by car, beware the bus drivers, who often drive very fast and rather recklessly. The lack of road signs can be a nuisance. Hitch-hiking on the main roads is reported to be easy in the north, but nearly impossible south of Riobamba, and it can be very cold in the mountains in the back of a truck. In the arid S the unpaved roads are dusty; use a wet cotton handkerchief to filter the air you breathe. Whether hitching or driving always take plenty of drinking water. In 1983 many coastal roads were washed out. Many are still in a bad state and will take time to repair, so if you are hiring a car make sure it has good ground clearance. Beware of large potholes and crevices in any road. Always carry your passport and driving licence; there are police checks on all the roads leading out of main towns and you can be in serious trouble if you are unable to present your documents. Car hire charges are about US$33 a day, unlimited mileage. Gasoline costs US$0.36 per US gallon for 80 octane and US$0.51 for 92 octane (only in the main cities). Gasoline shortages are common, so fill up where you can. Diesel costs US$0.22 per gallon.

The Instituto Geográfico Militar, on top of the hill at the E end of El Ejido Park, Quito (**see page 626**), produces a large detailed map of Ecuador on four pages which is among the best available for any South American country. A comprehensive road map is also available as well as various other maps, US$0.50-0.80 apiece. Maps of the Oriente take a day to be photocopied. There are also road maps issued as a small booklet (US$2) with 26 partial maps published by Nelson Gómez, Editorial Camino.

Walking   Walkers are advised to get *Backpacking in Venezuela, Colombia and Ecuador*, by Hilary and George Bradt, and Rob Rachowiecki's book (see next para.).

Climbing can be arranged through climbing clubs in Quito and other cities, or those associated with universities. Recommended guides to climbing: *Climbing and Hiking in Ecuador*, by Rob Rachowiecki (published by Bradt Enterprises) and *The Fool's Mountaineering for Ecuador and Peru* (from the South American Explorers' Club in Lima, US$3.50, which may only be available in Peru). The quality of hired equipment needs scrutiny.

Sport   The Sierra country is excellent for riding, and good horses can be hired. Quito, Guayaquil and Riobamba have polo clubs. There are golf clubs at Guayaquil and Quito and on the Santa Elena

Peninsula. There is excellent big-game fishing for bonito and marlin off Playas, Salinas and Manta. Bull fighting is rarely seen at Guayaquil, but there is a well-known bullfight festival on Dec. 6 at Quito. A favourite sport is cock fighting; every town has its pits, but association football is fast taking over as the national sport. Baseball, volleyball and basket-ball are also popular. There is Sunday horse-racing at Guayaquil.

Wild Life   includes the jaguar, puma, tapir, several kinds of monkey, the armadillo, ant-bear, squirrel, porcupine, peccary, various kinds of deer, and many rodents, including the guinea pig. There are also tortoises, lizards and iguanas. Among the birds are condors, falcons, kites, macaws, owls, flamingoes, parrots, ibises, cranes, and storks. Unhappily, every type of insect is found in the coastal towns and the Oriente. The Galápagos Islands have their own selection of nearly tame wildlife.

National Parks   All foreigners are charged US$10 for entry into each national park, except for the Galápagos which now costs US$40.

Public Holidays   New Year's Day; January 6; Monday and Tuesday before Lent (Carnival); Holy Thursday; Good Friday; Holy Saturday; May 1-Labour Day; May 24-Battle of Pichincha; July 24-Birthday of Bolívar; August 10-Independence of Quito, Opening of Congress, October 9-Independence of Guayaquil, October 12-Discovery of America; November 1-All Saints' Day; November 2-All Souls' Day; November 3-Independence of Cuenca; December 6-Foundation of Quito; Christmas Day.

Telecommunications   All the principal towns have long-distance telephone facilities.
Telephone call to Europe is US$17 for first 3 min. and US$5 per min. thereafter. For international operator dial 116, normally only 5-20 minute wait for call to UK. You can call collect to the USA and to Canada but not to Australasia or Northern Europe. A charge is made for person-to-person calls even when the person is not there. Telegrams, ordinary US$4.30 first 7 words and US$0.57 per word thereafter, nightletter US$0.20 per word. There are public telex booths in the best hotels in Quito and Guayaquil (US$13.50 for 3 mins.), and at Cuenca.

Posts   Many post offices away from Quito may not know the foreign rates (10g air-mail to the Americas US$0.20, Europe about US$0.35) and give incorrect ones. Postal service is extremely unreliable, with frequent thefts and losses. For a small extra charge you can certify your letters and parcels; ask for "*con certificado*" when you buy stamps, so that they are stamped separately (US$0.12 extra). The only post office (probably in all Ecuador) which deals in International Reply Coupons is in Quito, at Madrid y Toledo (new city). **For sending parcels:** maximum dimensions permitted is 70 X 30 X 30 cms. Contents and packaging (unpacked) must be taken to post office at Benalcázar 688 y Chile, Quito, for customs inspection. After this, go to "Recepción-Paquetes Internacionales" at the back of the building, where staff will help with packing and documentation. Allow 45 minutes; rates vary according to weight and destination.

Currency   The sucre, divided into 100 centavos, is the unit of currency. Bank notes of the Banco Central de Ecuador are for 5, 10, 20, 50, 100, 500, and 1,000 sucres; there are nickel coins of one sucre, 50, 20 and 10 centavos. The one sucre coin is also sometimes called an *ayora*.

There is no restriction on the amount of foreign money or sucres you can take into or out of Ecuador. It is said to be easier to cash Bank Americard cheques than American Express cheques. It is very easy to change US$ cheques into US$ notes at the *cambios*; the commission varies but is worth shopping around and *cambios* sometimes run out of US$ notes. Rodrigo Paz *cambios* are recommended as reliable, with only 0.5% commission, but may offer a slightly lower rate than banks. M. M. Jaramillo is also recommended and you can try to bargain for a better rate than shown on the blackboard. Many *cambios* ask to see the receipt for travellers' cheques purchased abroad. Ecuador is the best place in South America to have money sent to. All major credit cards are widely accepted. It is quite difficult to change US$, whether cheques or bills, outside the main towns, especially in the Oriente.

Weights and Measures   The metric system is generally used in foreign trade and must be used in legal documents. English measures are understood in the hardware and textile trades. Spanish measures are often used in the retail trade.

Newspapers   The main newspapers are *El Comercio, Hoy, Tiempo,* and *Ultimas Noticias,* in Quito; *Expreso, El Telégrafo, El Universo, La Prensa, La Razón* and *Extra* (an afternoon paper), in Guayaquil; *El Mercurio,* in Cuenca; *La Opinión del Sur,* in Loja; and *El Espectador,* in Riobamba. Newspapers cost more outside their town of publication, up to double the price in the Oriente.

Information for business travellers is given (1) in "Hints to Exporters: Ecuador", available from Department of Trade, Sanctuary Buildings, 16-20 Gt. Smith Street, London SW1P 3DB; (2) the Ecuadorean-American Association, Inc. (55 Liberty St., New York, NY 10005) issues monthly bulletins and a free sample copy may be requested. Telephone directories in Ecuador have "green pages" giving useful tourist information, sometimes in English.

We are most grateful to Janet Krengel of Lloyds Bank Economics Department for doing the updating of this chapter. We should also like to thank David and Lynda Gayton (Puerto Ayora), Mrs F.L. Gristock (British Vice-Consul, Quito), Bill McQuinn (Quito) and Ann K. Rodzai (Quito); also the following travellers: Renate Alversammer and Josef Wormsdobler (Altheim, Aust), Lucia L Armstrong (Ithaca, NY), Ian Atkinson (Upton/Severn), Lee Azus (San Francisco), Rupert Baker (Cropredy, Oxon), Susan Bald (Marco Island, Fl.), Jane Barlow (London NW6), Bruce Barnes (Gloucester, NSW), Rob and Marijke Barrois (Leidschendam, Neth.), Urs Baumann (Wildberg, Switz), Renate Becker (Heidelberg), Pierre-Y Berney (Geneva), Lennart Blomberg (Göteborg), Rop Bomer and Wilh. ter Haar (Mexico City) for a most useful contribution, Guiliano Bonello (Zuerich, Switz.), J.N. Bowden and K.E. Badgery (Plymouth), Lone Bregninge (Rødovre, Dmk.), Geri Brief (Chicago 60613), Alison Brysk and Mark Freeman (San Francisco, Ca.), John Burke (Bristol 7) for some particularly helpful updatings, Michelle Burrows (Brisbane), P. Christmas (Newcastle upon Tyne), Peter and Alison Clarke (Leicester), Jane Coburn and Philip Barnes (Thirroul, NSW), Gary R.Cox (Arlington Hts, Ill.), John Crane (Sunbury), Beat Denzler and Nicole Livet (Zürich), Gill Desborough and David James (London SW18), Jeroen Dijkgraaf (Eindhoven), Simon Van Dijk (Nussbaumen), Bernd Dralle (Hannover), Dieter Eigenstetter and Yesim Yazicioglu (München 80), Hanna Elvrum (Cochabamba), Margaret and Martin Evans (Brighton), Didier Faget and Sabine Fleury (Vernon, Fr.), Bernard Faure (Banff, Alberta), Thomas Fedrizzi (Horgen, Switz.) for most useful information, Karsten Feucht (Berlin 61), Harald Fischer (Linz, Austr.), Sharon Franklet (Lima), Felicity Gallagher (Saxon, Switz), Martin Gorst (London W13), Christina Gräwe (Tautkirchen) and Joachim Hoell (Wernstadt, W.Ger.), Thomas Gray (Houston, Tex), Jan Jacob de Groot (Vroomshoop, Neth.), Robert Hauer (Bonn 1), Charles Havekost (Greenbelt, Md.) and Eva Lindholm (Zug, Switz.), Verena Henauer (Olten, Switz.), Alison Henry, Dave Henson (San Francisco, Ca.), Rony Hermans (Deurne, Bel.), David K Howe (Short Hills, NJ), Don Hoyle (London EC2), Olli Inhelder (Basle), Gretke Moen Johansen (Kolbotn, Norway), Alan Jones (Santa Cruz de Tenerife), Martina Jost and Heinz Eisenhauer (Darmstadt), Anne Junk, Simon Kahn (Los Angeles), Omer Karchi (Tivon, Israel), Kim Kelly (Amex, Calgary, Alb.), Philipp and Sabine Keller (Dillingen, W.Ger.), Simon Kennedy and Sally Constable (Melbourne), Martin Ketels (Hamburg 50), Ronen Khayat (Jerusalem), Peter Kocan (Summit, NJ), Thomas and Bettina Kräuchi (Kloten, Switz.), Harald Kremer (Stuttgart 40), François Laffely (Montreux), P. Lancefield (Canadian Embassy, Bogotá), Tim Landeck (Santa Cruz, Ca.), Rachel Le Vay (London E5), John Lewis (London NW3), Charles Locher (San Francisco) and Nancy Blackstock (Berkeley, Ca.), Susan MacCallum and Peter Hedvlin (Sydney, Aust.), Bjarne Madsen and Gitte B. Andersen (Odense), Bernard Magier (Palo Alto, Ca.), Ian and Carol Martin (Falmouth), Carla McLean (San Francisco), Albert Meier and Evelyne Ott (Freudwil, Switz.), Lucy Meikle (Pershore) and Stuart Duncan (Scotland), Wolfgang Meusburger (Dornbirn, Aust.), Nichola Morgan (Swanage, Dorset), Michael Mortensen (Oelstykke, Dmk.), Dimitri Moursellas (Manhattan Beach, Ca.), Christoph Müller (Zürich 8004), Richard Müller (Bern), Vera Naujak (Heidelberg), Melanie Newman (with John Pritchard, Ros Harris, Danial Taylor, Carol Finn and Finn Bangshaad Jensen—London W9), Frank O'Connor (London W3), Esther Oester (Oberdiessbach, Switz.), Bertil Olin (Johanneshov, Swed.), Karl Olson (New York), Johan Olsson (Osby, Swe.), Graham J. O'Neil (London SW7), Susan B. Phillips (Lake Oswego, OR), Barbara Psotka (Rockville, Md.), Ulrike Ramcke-Mensing (Bogotá), Geoff A. Richardson (Barranquilla), Miranda Roberts (London SE3), Gisele Rochat and Jean-Paul Corboz (Neuchâtel, Switz.), Carlos A. Rodríguez (Mérida), Dr Teresa Rössler (Wien 1140), Susan Sawyer (Palo Alto, Ca.), Susan Scher (London NW8), Leon van der Schoor (Neth.), Florian Schulz (Berlin 27), Colin Sears and Caroline Richard, Elizabeth and Virginia Segal (London N2), Antony Sherlock (Edinburgh 12), Ian Skeet (Winchester), Nicola J. Smith (Kirby Muxbe, Leics.) and Jean-François Morerod (Les Diablerets, Switz.), Stanis Smith (Burnaby, B.C.), Karl Stanley (Cheam, Sy.), Doris Stöckli and Christophe Racine (Fislisbach, Switz.), Peter van der Stoop and Karin Strooij (Haarlem, Neth.), Traudi Sträussl and friends (Regensburg), Joseph Swillen (Tielt-Winge, Belg.), James Tansley (British Embassy Riyadh), Astrid and Jürg Thierstein (Winterthur, Switz.), Barry Tiffen and Lucy Stephens (Torksey, Lincoln), Nicholas Tongue and Uta Rössler (Brussels), Richard Tucker (Salvador), Heather Varden (Fleet, Hants), Avv. Giovanni Verusio (Rome), Ronald van Vliet (Haarlem), Fortunat Walther (Lima), Gerhard Wenz and Brigitte Klaus (Mainz), Joachim Weyrauch (Lippstadt, W.Ger.), Roland Wiemer and Karla Menner (Hamburg 50), Conrad Wiesendanger (Münchenstein, Switz.), Sarah Wilkins (Potton, Beds.), Ray Williams (Pwllheli), Martin Wisckol (San Diego, Ca.), Anna Wrench (Haywards Heath, Sx.), Cecilia Ydell and Jonas Martensen, Peter Zankl (Biel, Switz.), Stefani Zapf and Wolfgang Gross (Frising, W. Ger.), Marilyn Zecker and B.B.Riefner (Rockville, Md.), Helmut Zettl (Ebergassing, Aust.) and Mark Zimmermann (Zürich).

PARAGUAY

PARAGUAY is entirely landlocked, encircled by Argentina, Bolivia and Brazil. Its total land area is put at 406,752 square km., cleft into two quite distinct parts by the great river Paraguay. It has over 3.9 million people (roughly 41% living in towns). It has not as yet fully developed its potential, partly because it was deeply involved in two out of the three major wars staged in Latin America since independence.

To the W of the Paraguay river is the Chaco (246,950 square km., nearly 61% of the country's area), a sparsely inhabited tract of flat and infertile country. E of the river is Paraguay proper (159,800 square km.), a rich land in which almost all the population is concentrated. Paraguay proper is itself divided into two contrasting areas by a high cliffed formation which runs almost due N from the Alto Paraná river, W of Encarnación, to the Brazilian border. E of this cliff lies the Paraná plateau; W of it, as far as the Paraguay river, lie gently rolling hills and flat plains.

Paraguay's southern boundary with Argentina from the confluence of the Río Paraguay to that of the Río Iguazú is the Alto Paraná river. From the Iguazú Falls and the Itaipú Lake and the Alto Paraná form the eastern border with Brazil; from Guaíra Falls (now flooded) the northern boundary with Brazil runs north-westwards across the land mass to the confluence of the Apa and Paraguay rivers. From Resistencia far N as Asunción the Río Paraguay is the western boundary with Argentina. From Asunción as far N as the confluence with the Apa, the river divides Paraguay into two. For some distance N of the entry of the Apa, the Paraguay river is the Chaco's eastern boundary with Brazil. The S border of the Chaco with Argentina is along the Río Pilcomayo; its W and N borders are with Bolivia.

The Paraná Plateau, ranging from 300 to 600 metres in height, has comparatively heavy falls of rain and was originally forest. Across the plateau, much of which is in Argentina and Brazil, runs the Paraná river. West of the high cliff which forms the western edge of the plateau lies a fertile plain stretching to the Paraguay river. This plain is diversified by rolling, wooded hills. Most of Paraguay's population is concentrated in these hilly lands, stretching SE from Asunción to Encarnación.

Much of the flat plain is flooded once a year; it is wet savanna, treeless, but covered with coarse grasses. On this plain, rice, sugar, tobacco, grains, soya and cotton are grown. Several heavily forested rivers drain the plain and hill lands into the Paraguay.

The Chaco, lying W of the Paraguay river, is mostly cattle country or scrub forest. Along the river there are grassy plains and clumps of palms, but westwards the land grows drier and more bleak. Much of the north-western area is almost desert. The marshy, unnavigable Pilcomayo river forms the boundary with Argentina. Apart from Mennonite colonies, small settlements on the river banks, and a number of *estancias* in the SW, only a few nomadic Indian tribes live

PARAGUAY 92

in the vast region. (The average density is less than 1 person to the square km.) The *quebracho* (axe-breaker) tree, the world's principal source (with mimosa) of tannin, comes from the scrub forests of the Chaco and of the Paraná river.

Some 54% of the country is covered with forest, 40% is pastoral, 4% is agricultural but only 1% is intensively cultivated. In eastern Paraguay the land supports only 11 people to the square km.

Communications The only practicable water route is by the Paraná to the Plate estuary, and Buenos Aires is 1,450 km. from Asunción. So difficult is the river that communication with Buenos Aires was mainly by road before the railway to Asunción was opened in 1913. Most freight is now moved to Buenos Aires, or to Santos or Paranaguá in Brazil, by good paved roads, though river barges still ply along the Paraná.

History The original inhabitants of the area of Paraguay were the semi-nomadic Guaraní Indians; they had spread by the 16th century to the foothills of the Andes, along the coast of Brazil, and even into the basin of the Amazon. They did not contest the coming of the Spaniards, the first of whom, under the navigator Diego de Solís, arrived at the River Paraguay in 1524. A member of Solís's expedition, Alejo García, the discoverer of the Iguazú falls, was the first European actually to enter Paraguay; he was also the first European to fight against the Incas, as his career included an attack on them with a Guaraní army of 2,000. He set out through the Chaco in search of El Dorado in 1525. The main expedition, led by Juan de Ayolas, came from Buenos Aires, where the earliest Spanish settlement was planted in 1536. Finding no gold, and harassed by the hostile Indians of the Pampa, they pushed north along the river, seeking a short route to the gold and silver of Peru. They reached the friendly Guaraníes in 1537 and a member of the party, Juan de Salazar de Espinosa, is generally credited with founding Asunción on August 15.

Asunción became the nucleus of Spanish settlement in southeastern South America. Spaniards pushed NW across the Chaco to found Santa Cruz, in Bolivia, eastwards to occupy the rest of Paraguay, and southwards down the river to re-found Buenos Aires in 1580, 43 years after they had abandoned it.

During the colonial era one of the world's most interesting experiments in dealing with a native population was carried out, not by the conquerors, but by their missionaries, over whom the civil power had at first little control. In 1609 the Society of Jesus sent missionaries to Paraguay to civilize the Indians. During the 158 years until they were expelled in 1767, the Jesuits formed 30 "reductions", or settlements, run along theocratic-socialist lines. They induced the Indians to leave the forests and settle in townships, where they helped build magnificent churches, employing unsuspected native skills in masonry, sculpture, and painting. Selected natives were even given a sound classical education. The first reductions were further north, but they were forced to abandon these because of attacks by the *bandeirantes* of São Paulo, Brazil. They settled finally in Misiones; parts of the area of settlement are now in Argentina and southern Brazil. After the expulsion of the Jesuits, the reductions fell to pieces: the Indians left, and were reduced to peonage under other masters. Most of the great churches have fallen into ruin, or been destroyed; the few that remain are dealt with in the text.

Paraguay got its independence from Spain, without bloodshed, on May 14, 1811. Gaspar Rodríguez de Francia, known as "El Supremo", took power in 1814 and held it until 1840. His policy of complete isolation was a response to the landlocking of Paraguay by the *porteños* of Buenos Aires who wished to annex it: no one might leave the country, no one might enter it, and external trade was not permitted, but Paraguay achieved a high level of self-sufficiency. Francia was followed as president by Carlos Antonio López, who ruled until his death in 1862. He reversed Francia's policy of isolation and in 1854 began the building of the Central Paraguayan Railway from Asunción to Encarnación. He was followed by his son, Marshal Francisco Solano López, who saw himself as the Napoleon of South America and is today the most venerated of Paraguay's heroes. His Irish mistress Madame Eliza Lynch, who encouraged him in his ambitions, is also held in high esteem. In 1865 he became involved in the war of the Triple Alliance against Brazil, Argentina and Uruguay. His motive was that Uruguay, with whom Paraguay had a treaty of reciprocal help, had been occupied by Brazil and Argentina and forced to oppose Paraguay. The war was disastrous for the Paraguayans, who held out against overwhelming odds until Marshal López was killed at Cerro Corá in 1870, when the war ended. Out of a population of 800,000, only 194,000 were left alive after the war, and of these only 14,000 were male (only 2,100 of whom were over 20); out of 400,000 females at the beginning of the war, 180,000 survived. Paraguay was occupied for eight years during which time it was deprived of all its gold reserves, many national treasures and 156,415 square km. of territory. (Brazil took 62,325 square km., Argentina 94,090 square km.; previously Paraguayan were the Iguazú Falls and the town of Posadas, once called San José del Paraguay.) (For further reading on the origin and aftermath of the War of the Triple Alliance, see *Paraguay: un destino geopolítico*, by Dra. Julia Velilla Laconich de Aréllaga; *Genocídio Americano: a Guerra do Paraguai*, by Júlio José Chiavenalto; *Women on Horseback*, by William E. Barrett.) After 1870 a certain number of European immigrants arrived; their descendants are still influential in the social life of Paraguay. Various religious communities were among them; the Mennonites, mostly of German descent, who are largely responsible for the development of the Chaco, are the most notable.

The country's history since the "National Epic" of 1865-1870 has been the story of a recovery from disaster, but this process received a severe setback in the wars with Bolivia which broke out intermittently between 1929 and 1935 over the Chaco. The Paraguayans, fighting with their customary courage and tenacity, triumphed, and were given a large area of the Chaco in the final settlement. Bolivia was given an outlet, of little use, to the Paraguay river. Paraguay is still in the process of opening up and settling the Chaco.

After the Chaco War, Paraguay endured several years of political dictatorship, followed by disorder. This period was ended by the seizure of power in 1954 by General Alfredo Stroessner, soon appointed President. Thereafter he gained the support of the Colorado Party (founded in 1888), which has been an integral part of his regime ever since. He held power through repeated reelection until he was deposed in 1989 (surpassing El Supremo's 26-year tenure by 9 years) by General Andrés Rodríguez. On May 1, 1989, Gen. Rodríguez, also of the Colorado Party, won a presidential election unopposed, and he promised to hand over the presidency to an elected successor in 1993. The apparent committment to greater democracy permitted opponents, who had previously boycotted, or been banned from elections, to gain an unprecedented number of seats in the legislative elections of the same date.

The People of Paraguay Because the proportion of Spanish blood is smaller than elsewhere, the people of Paraguay today are bilingual, speaking both

Spanish and Guaraní. Outside Asunción, most people speak Guaraní by preference. There is a Guaraní theatre, and books and periodicals are published in that tongue, which has official status as the second national language. There are about 39,000 pure-bred Indians left: two-thirds of them are in the Chaco, and one-third in the southern part of Paraguay proper.

Population: 3.92 m. (1987 estimate). Urban growth: 3.2%; annual growth: 3.2%. Life expectancy at birth: 66 years. Infant mortality: 53 per thousand. Some 41% live in towns. Over 47% work on the land, nearly 14% in industry. Per capita income US$1,402 (1987). 25% of all Paraguayans live abroad.

Government There was a new Constitution in 1967. Executive power rests with the President, elected for five years. There is a two-chamber Congress. Voting is secret and obligatory for all citizens over 18. Uniquely in Latin America, the Constitution permits the immediate reelection of the President.

N.B. After the fall of President Stroessner, it was understood that all references to his name throughout the country would be removed. At the time of going to press, Ciudad Presidente Stroessner was reported to have been renamed Ciudad del Este; the airport, too, was to have been given a new title. Until such changes have been officially approved, we retain the old names.

ASUNCION (1)

Asunción, the capital and largest city in Paraguay, is built on the shores of a bay cutting into the eastern bank of the Paraguay river, almost opposite its confluence with the Pilcomayo. Its population is 600,000 (excluding suburbs). The city, built on a low hill crowned by the large modern church of La Encarnación, is laid out in the colonial Spanish rectangular manner; many avenues are lined with beautiful trees, including orange, rubber and jacaranda. The central plazas of the city are drenched in colour during July-August with the prolific pink bloom of the *lapacho* trees, which grow everywhere. The oldest part is down by the water's edge, but none of the public buildings is earlier than the last half of the 19th century. Dwelling houses are in a variety of styles; new villas in every kind of taste have replaced the traditional one-storey Spanish-Moorish type of house, except in the poorer quarters.

You see most public buildings by following Calle El Paraguayo Independiente from the Customs House. The first is the Government Palace, built during the Triple Alliance War in the style of the Louvre. In Plaza Constitución stands the Congressional Palace (debates can be attended during the session from April to December, on Thursdays and Fridays), with the Cathedral at the corner of the square. Two blocks SW, along Calle Chile, is Plaza de los Héroes, with the Pantheon of Heroes, based on the Invalides in Paris, begun during the Triple Alliance War and finished in 1937. It now contains the tombs of Carlos Antonio López, Marshal Francisco Solano López, two unknown Paraguayan soldiers, and Marshal Estigarribia, the victor of the Chaco War in the 1930s. The national cemetery, which resembles a miniature city, with tombs in various architectural styles, is on Av. Mariscal López, 3 km. from the centre.

The best of several parks are Parque Carlos Antonio López, set high and with a grand view (doctor and sports supervisor in attendance); Parque Caballero; and Parque Gaspar Rodríguez de Francia. The Botanical Gardens are 6½ km. out, on Av. Artigas with Primer Presidente at Trinidad, quickly reached by bus (Nos. 2, 6, 23, and 40, US$0.15, about 35 mins.; outward they can be caught on Luis A. Herrera, or Nos. 35 or 44B from Oliva or Cerro Corá). They lie along the Paraguay river, on the former estate of the López family, and have an enormous range of plants (poorly maintained), an eighteen-hole golf course, and a little zoo (animals kept in appalling conditions). Entrance fee US$0.10, or US$0.60 for 2 persons and a car. The Gardens temporarily housed the Maca Indians when they were moved from their reservation across the river; they were moved again in 1985 to very poor conditions (if you wish to photograph the Indians, bargain with them first). The López residence is in the Gardens; a typical Paraguayan country house with verandahs, which has become a natural history museum and library. The beautiful white church of Santísima Trinidad (on Santísimo Sacramento, parallel to Av. Artigas), where Carlos Antonio López was originally buried, dating from 1856 with paintings inside, is well worth a visit.

N.B. Av. España originally extended as far out as Av. San Martín, but the section between Av. Kubitschek and Av. Santísimo Sacramento was renamed Av. Generalísimo Franco (not to be confused with Presidente Franco) and the remaining section between Av. SS. Sacramento and Av. San Martín was renamed Av. General Genes. Many people still use the name Av. España for the whole of its original length, ignoring the renamings.

Hotels Hotel prices are given at the financial exchange rate at the time of going to press. Outside Asunción: 12 km. from town, at Itá Enramada, on its own beach on the River Paraguay is *Hotel del Yacht y Golf Club Paraguay*, L, 3 restaurants, super luxury, with pool, gym, golf, tennis, airport transfers, etc.; many extras free. The *Hotel y Casino Itá Enramada*, 7 km. S of Asunción, A/B, with breakfast (rec.), free bus link with town, 7-hectare park, swimming pools, sauna, tennis, mini-golf, water-skiing on river, reservations through KLM, or Hugen Int., Fort Lauderdale, Fla. (T 1-800-327-8571) or London (01-629-6611), fishing nearby, "Honeymooners get 20% off", T 33041/9.

In Asunción: *Excelsior*, L/A, Chile 980 between Manduvirá and Piribebuy, telex 5192, T 95632/5, best, new 175-room tower, another under construction, conference facilities, etc.; *Chaco*, Caballero y Mariscal Estigarribia, A, parking one block away (but no garden), rooftop swimming pool, good restaurant, T 92066/9; *Cecilia*, rec., Estados Unidos 341, T 91271/3, A/B, very smart, good restaurant; *Guaraní* on Plaza Independencia under new management, efficient, courteous, clean, A, good value, reasonable restaurant with good buffet; *Internacional*, Ayolas 520, T 94113, A, new, rec.; *Husa* (a Brazilian chain hotel), 15 de Agosto 420 y Estrella, B, 1st class, all rooms a/c, TV, swimming pool, restaurant, rec. cafeteria, bars, laundry service; *Presidente*, Azara 128, B, with breakfast and a/c, restaurant, has seen better days; *Gran del Paraguay*, C, Residente y Padre Pucheu, out of town, in a park, with swimming pool and a night club on Fridays, was the palace in which López lived; the rec. restaurant with floral murals, was the private theatre of Eliza Lynch; an air-conditioned annex has been built in the gardens, breakfast. *Touring 25*, 25 de Mayo 1091, D, small, modern, includes breakfast. *Amalfi*, D, Caballero 877, comfortable, modern; *Paraná*, Caballero, D with breakfast, central, secure, discounts negotiable, short-stays catered for too; *Córdoba*, Oliva 1275, D with bath, friendly, clean, 1 km. from centre (take taxi); *Sahara*, Oliva 920 nr. Montevideo, C with breakfast, a/c, good, small pool; *Gran Renacimento*, Chile 388 y Estrella, central, D, a/c, with poor breakfast in room, good service; *Señorial*, colonial style (Mcal. López 475 y Perú), D, with breakfast, a/c, swimming pool, parking, strongly rec.; *Azara*, Azara 850 (T 49754), E with bath, also F, rec. by Auto Club and travellers but rather run down, most rooms face a shady patio and pool, restaurant.

Residencial Ideal, Azara with Perú, F with breakfast, clean, quiet, very friendly; opposite is *Daniel*, F with bath and fan; *Española*, Herrera y Yegros, F, laundry, with meals, friendly; *Ambassador*, Montevideo 111, F, with bath, very old (rooms overlooking the Palacio del Gobierno must close their windows during working hours—fear of snipers—makes rooms very hot); *Lord*, Tacuary 576, E with bath (electric showers), breakfast, English spoken by Korean owner, Mr Lee, noisy; *Hispania*, Cerro Corá, F, Korean-run, watch bill carefully, friendly, recently refurbished, front rooms noisy; *Stella d'Italia*, Cerro Corá 945, F without bath (popular with Peace Corps volunteers), parking; *Lago Ypoa*, Azara 1161, small, new and rec., F, used by Peace Corps volunteers, as is *El Lapacho*, Kubitschek, near Mcal. López; *Ñandutí*, Presidente Franco 551, D with bath and breakfast, clean, comfortable, friendly; *Residencia* (also Restaurant) *Japón de Kikoyo Uchiyamada*, Constitución 763 (T 22038), E, management prefers Orientals, good meals; *Cardel*, Ygurey 1145 esq. Av. Dr. Eusebio Ayala, modern, clean, quiet, D, near Pettirossi market, excellent breakfast; *Casa Menonita*, República de Colombia 1050, E, friendly, German spoken, plain food (bus stop here for Filadelfia); *Gasthof Munich*, E, Ayala 163, pleasant; specially for German-speaking travellers: *Pensión Alemana Castillo*, Cruz del Chaco 925-959, E, German-owned, clean and friendly, T 650356); *Ayuda Social Germano-Paraguaya* (hospice attached), Av. España 202, near railway station, E, including breakfast, central, clean, most rooms a/c, nearly always full, friendly, T 49485; also *Deutsche Pensión*, E, Milano 222, T 43217, clean, friendly, owner's name Federau. *Hospedaje El Viajero*, Antequera 451, noisy, clean and friendly, F. *América*, Montevideo 160, F, clean, fans, mosquito nets, rec.; *Ipiranga*, Av. México 489 with Cerro Corá, F, with bath and breakfast, friendly, clean; *Miami*, México 449, T 444950, E, clean; *Residencial Rufi*, Cerro Corá, near Antequera, F, no breakfast, friendly, clean, helpful; *Rosa*, 25 de Mayo 350, F with bath, not too clean, rec. although used for short stay, good book exchange; *Hosp. Hollywood*, Azara 722, F, central, clean, very friendly, good basic restaurant; *Margarita*, Paraguarí y Azara, F without bath and breakfast, more with bath, clean, good, basic. Unnamed *pensión* at Tacuary 348, near Plaza Uruguaya, cheap, washing facilities, use of kitchen. *Residencial Nuevo Horizonte*, Calle Eligio Ayala, F with breakfast, clean, comfortable; *Hotel Residencial Cadi*, Piribebuy 150 (T 96901), also F, rec.; *Residencial Itapúa*, E, Calle Fulgencio R. Moreno 643, decent breakfasts, lunch available. Two hotels at the railway station, one is *Plaza*, simple but acceptable, E, the other is not good. *Residencial Familiar*, Eligio Ayala 843 near railway station, F, without breakfast, friendly, clean, will do washing. *Hospedaje El Sol*, Lapacho 185 (2 mins. from bus station), Korean-run, F with bath, clean, good value; *Hospedaje San Pablo*, nr. bus

ASUNCIÓN

terminal, F with bath, noisy rooms on courtyard. There are two motels, *San Martín*, Av. San Martín 889, F, and *La Cuesta*, Bogado y Cacique Lambaré, E. Family *pensiones* are expensive, in the D range.

The hotel bill does not usually contain a service charge. It pays to tip when you arrive as well as when you go, say US$1 to the table waiter at both ends of a week's visit. A tip of 10% is enough for non-residents, at hotels and in restaurants. Many hotels have electric showers.

Camping   The pleasant site at the Botanical Gardens now charges a fee, US$1.20 per car plus US$0.30 per person, US$0.60 p.p. plus tent, cold showers and 220v electricity. If camping, take plenty of insect repellant and beware large (but harmless) toads. You can camp at rear of *Restaurant Westfalia*, 5 km. out on Itá Enramada road, US$1 per night for car, cold showers, noisy, animals.

Restaurants   *La Preferida*, Estados Unidos and 25 de Mayo 1005 T 91126, rec. (part of *Hotel Cecilia*); *Talleyrand*, French, reported best in town, Estigarribia 932, T 41163; *La Pergola del Bolsi*, Estrella 389, good, wide choice of wines; under same ownership, *La Pergola Jardín*, Perú 240, good food and service. *Le Grand Café*, Oliva 476, French-owned, good value set lunch. You can get a fantastic view of the city from the *Zodiac*, 14 de Mayo 150, 13th floor, expensive, but good; *Hermitage*, 15 de Agosto 1360, food is good, mostly international, as is the music, moderately expensive, cover charge; *Munich*, Eligio Ayala 163, good German food, excellent value; *Hostería del Caballito Blanco*, Alberti 631, Austrian-run, good food and service; *Trevi*, on Palma, excellent; *Deutscher Ecte*, near the university, good value, German food; *San Roque*, Eligio Ayala esq. Tacuary, traditional and German. *Germania* in Cerro Corá, rec., reasonable prices; *Bayern-Stube*, authentic German.

La Taberna, Franco, excellent, Spanish; *Chalet Suizo*, Av. Kubitschek 975 (Ethiopian Goulash rec.). *Mastropiero* has 130 types of pizza at Av. España 1372 (T 60160); another Italian restaurant is *La Bettola*, rec. at C. del Maestro 1698, off the Av. San Martín; *La Piccola Góndola* is very good for Italian (and other) food, so is *Buon Appetito*, 25 de Mayo near Av. Mariscal López y Juan Motta. Good cheap lunches (try puchero) at *Copetín El Oro*, Benjamín Constant 473, behind central post office.

Da Vinci, Estrella 695, disco upstairs, rec.; *Asunción*, Estrella y 14 de Mayo (opp. Deutsche Bank), bar and restaurant very good, service a bit slow; *Pizzería Cábala* Estrella 602 y 15 de Agosto, good cakes too. Plenty of good, cheap places on Colón, south of Estrella. *Castel Blanc*, on Pacheco, T 66079, very good; *Bistro*, part of *Hotel Husa* at 15 de Agosto y Estrella, good and reasonable; *Lucho*, Estados Unidos y Cerro Corá, good local food, cheap. *Rincón Chileno*, Estados Unidos 314, friendly, excellent empanadas; *Bar de la Estacíon*, at railway station, Eligio Ayala 587, cheap, friendly, popular locally; *Tío Toms*, quiche and pizza, Av. Perú y Estigarribia; *El Molino*, Calle España near Brasil, good service and food (particularly steaks); nearby is *Casa Nostra*, good pizza. *American FC*, previously *Kentucky Fried Chicken*, on Plaza de los Héroes. *Subito*, 500 block of Palma, a/c, rec. for empanadas. For good roast chicken try *Nick's Restaurant*, on Azara near Iturbe. *Don Vitos* is well known for empanadas, San José 585.

There are many good oriental restaurants including: *Green*, Dr Franco 150 e Yegros, very good Chinese; *Gran Oriente*, Brasil nr. Luis Herrera; *Celestial* (ex *Taiwan*), Herrera 919, highly rec.; *Sinorama*, Av. Próceres 265; *Chino Embajador*, Ed. V. Haedo 668; *Hoy*, Azara 830; *Noodle House Pynong-Ynong*, Perú y Francia, excellent; *Suki Yaki*, Constitución 763 y Pettirossi, authentic Japanese; *Hiroshima*, also authentic, on Chóferes del Chaco; and others.

Vegetarian restaurant on Díaz, nr. Montevideo. *Superpán*, 25 de Mayo 845, "pan integral" and good sweets. *Wagner*, Presidente Franco 828 y Ayolas, excellent bread and sweet shop; good icecreams next door. Excellent fast food at *Bar Lido*, Plaza de los Héroes, corner Palma y Chile. Various ice cream parlours and fast food outlets are to be found in Av. Brasilia, near Av. España e.g. *Heladería París*, Brasilia y Siria, is very popular. The *Liverpool Bar*, Pte. Franco 590, and the *Taurina*, at No. 583 are reasonable bars; *Bar Victoria*, corner of Chile and main Plaza, has good food; English breakfast and bed from *Dispensia Chaco Boreal*, Loma Pyta (T 290-797, take bus 44 or 23).

Paraguayan harp music, good food and service at *Jardín de la Cerveza*, Av. República Argentina y Castillo, US$10, strongly rec. (but sometimes they ask extra money for the music), and *Yguazú*, Chóferes del Chaco 1334 (San Lorenzo) US$30 for two, both some distance from centre. About 20 mins. out of town on bus route 26 or 27 is the *Ñandutí Parrillada* (T 24643), an open-air restaurant with good atmosphere, highly rec., on Av. Eusebio Ayala y Bartolomé de las

---

Asunción: Key to Map
1. Government Palace; 2. Congressional Palace; 3. Customs; 4. Cathedral; 5. Encarnación Church; 6. San Roque Church; 7. Pantheon of the Heroes; 8. Casa de la Independencia Museum; 9. Nacional Archive and Museum of Fine Arts; 10. Railway station; 11. Tourist Office; 12. Post Office; 13. Centro Paraguayo del Diagnóstico; 14. British Embassy; 15. Lloyds Bank; 16. Citibank; 17. Finamérica; 18. American Express; 19. Deutsche Bank; 20. Casas de cambio; 21. Compañía Marítima; 22. Police Station; 23. Hotel Chaco; 24. Hotel Guaraní 25. Hotel Husa; 26. Hotel Plaza; 27. Hotel Presidente; 289. Hotel Ipiranga; 29. Hotel Lord.

Casas. Good Paraguayan harp/guitar group at *Churrasquería Sajón,* Av. Carlos A. López, bus 26 from centre. A rec. typical restaurant is *La Paraguayita,* Brasília y Siria.

Shopping Calle Colón, starting at the port, is lined with good tourist shops, and so are Calles Pettirossi, Palma and Estrella. Casa Arnoldo, Calle Palma 640, is worth a try for hand-embroidered blouse lengths. Catedral, at Eligio Ayala e Yegros, manufactures shirts or dresses in 3 days. La Asunceña, Palma 766, leatherware; Galería Colón, good for leather, near port; Boutique Yrene, Montevideo and Oliva, also rec. for leather goods. Calle Franco for handmade furniture. For wooden articles and carvings go to Artes de Madera at Ayolas (222), Palma y Pte. Franco. Also Artesanía Raity at Pai Pérez 778, woodcraft, prints and paintings, rec.; Arte Popular, 25 de Mayo 1138 and Casa Vera at Estigarribia 470 for Paraguayan leatherwork, cheap and very good. Other rec. shops, Artesanía Kuarajhy, Pte Franco 663; *Casa Overall,* Mcal. Estigarribia, nr. Plaza Uruguaya, good selection. On Rioja near the main park for all local handicrafts and imported items (4 floors). Pistilli has a fine selection of canework and furniture, Estados Unidos esq. Azara. Check the quality of all handicrafts carefully, lower prices usually mean lower quality. A small but excellent fruit and vegetable market is to be found at San José behind the España supermarket. The markets are worth a visit, especially the Pettirossi (food and ordinary clothes). There is a daily market on Av. Dr. G.R. de Francia, and a Saturday one on Plaza de la Independencia, where the nuns from Villeta sell their hand-made clothing for children. Supermarkets are usually well stocked, especially with imported liquor. Outside Asunción, visit Luque (musical instruments and jewellery—**see page 697**) and Itauguá (lace)—**see page 699**. Cameras can be bought cheaply in Paraguay; the selection of all types of consumer goods is better in Ciudad Stroessner.

Bookshops Librería Internacional, Oliva y Alberdi, Estrella 723 y Juan O'Leary and Palma 595 y 15 de Agosto, good for maps; also "Books" at Mcal. López 3971, at Villa Morra shopping centre, also carries English stock (at 3-4 times UK prices); the Cultural Centre (ex-Librería Francesa) at Alberdi 439 and magazine/newspaper kiosk El Lector on Plaza Uruguaya and 25 de Mayo have a full selection of foreign material. Librería Alemana, Av. Luis A. de Herrera 292, warmly rec.

Taxis Minimum fare in Asunción is US$0.40 plus US$0.10 for every 100 metres. The average journey costs about US$2. (Check if there is an extra charge for luggage, and that the meter has not been speeded up). Hire by the hour; about US$4. Tip 10%.

Trams (Streetcars) One line, the No. 5, still runs through the centre, along Calles Palma (one way) and Estrella (the other).

City Buses The system is extensive, running from 0600-2400; buses stop at signs before every street corner. Journeys within city, US$0.14, including from the centre to the new bus terminal.

Night Clubs and Discotheques Kaktus, Teniente Vera y San Martín; Musak, Bertoni y José Ocampos; J y C, Boggiani y O'Higgins; Fantasio, Av. Bogado and Felicidad, in front of Radio Primero de Marzo; Piper's, in the centre, good disco, drinks not expensive, popular; Torremolinos, Costa Azul Urbanización, 2001; and one in the *Hotel Casino Itá Enramada* (open every day in summer, Saturdays in winter).

Municipal Theatre, Pte. Franco, nr. Alberdi, has an extensive winter programme of concerts and ballets (entry US$4). Cinema programmes are given in the press; some offer 3 films at one price (US$1). Art gallery and dance studio (Taller de Movimiento Creativo), 15 de Agosto 530, English-speaking owner.

Exchange Lloyds Bank (ex-BOLSA), Palma y O'Leary (and six agencies in Greater Asunción - will give US dollars); Finamérica (ex-Bank of America), Oliva esq. Chile; Citibank, Estrella y Chile (will change Citibank travellers' cheques into dollars cash for a small commission); Banco Corporación (ex-Chase), V.E. Haedo e Independencia Nacional; Banco General (ex-Boston), Chile y Haedo (will give US dollars); Bank of Commerce and Industry, Caballero esq. Eligio Ayala, also gives dollars; Interbank, 14 de Mayo 339; Deutsche Bank, Estrella y 14 de Mayo (charges 2% commission on money sent from W Germany—very fast service, 2 days—paid by cheque which can be cashed into dollars at Cambio Guaraní for small commission); Banco Sudameris (ex-Francés e Italiano), Oliva e Independencia Nacional. Banco Holandés Unido, Independencia Nacional y V.E. Haedo. Also Argentine, Brazilian and local banks. Banco Unión branch at Alberdi will give quick cash advances in guaraníes on Visa or Mastercard in about 15 minutes, English spoken, friendly, only between 0730-0900.

Several *casas de cambio* on Palma (open Mon.-Fri. 0730-1200, 1500-1830, Sat., 0730-1200; rates for neighbouring countries' currencies usually good, except bolivianos). Deutsche Marks can be changed at good rates, and all rates are better than at the various frontiers. Be careful to count money received from street exchange-sellers (Palma and surrounding area—their rates are less good when banks and *cambios* are closed). *Casas de cambio* do not like changing sterling travellers' cheques, the only one that will do it is Cambio Paraná on Palma. Some only change one type of dollar travellers' cheque. Cambio Guaraní, Palma 449, between 14 de Mayo and Alberdi, T 90032/6, is good, will change dollar cheques into dollars cash, but charges 1% commission for this. German spoken at Cambios Menno Tour, Azara 532. Cambios Yguazú (Palma) is OK.

(Thomas Cook, but can't deal with stolen cheques). See **Currency** section in Information for Visitors.

General Post Office Alberdi, Benjamín Constant y El Paraguayo Independiente. T 48891, 0700-2000, but closed for lunch. Also philatelic museum, open 0700-1800, Mon.-Fri.; 0700-1200, Sat. Post boxes throughout the city carry address of the nearest place one can purchase stamps. Register all important mail; you must go to main P.O. for this. *Poste Restante* charges about US$0.25 per item collected. There are sub-offices at the railway station and at the docks.

Museums National Museum of Fine Arts (closed in November 1986), and the Asunción Seminary Museum, both showing some "mission" art. At the Museum of Fine Arts (in Archivo Nacional building, Calle Palma W of PLaza Uruguaya), the paintings are very badly displayed; it has a Murillo and a Tintoretto and collections of Acevedo (about 1910) caricatures. In the Botanical Gardens are the Museo de Historia Natural and the Museo Etnográfico, both open Mon.-Sat. 0730-1130, 1300-1700, Sun. 0600-1200, 1300-1700, neither in good condition. In the Casa de la Independencia (14 de Mayo y Presidente Franco) is an interesting historical collection; entry free. Pantéon Nacional de los Héroes, esq. Palma y Chile, open every day. Historical and military museum at Ministry of Defence, Mariscal López esq. Gen. Santos. Museo Dr. Andrés Barbero, 200 block of España (near Estados Unidos), open Mon.-Fri, 0800-1100, free, good. Most museums are small and basic.

Laundry Lavamático, Yegros 808 y Fulgencio Moreno. Lava Pronto, Azara 850, T 45147, good, quick service. Lavafácil, México y Moreno, good, cheap, fast.

Addresses British Embassy (Presidente Franco 706, esquina O'Leary, 4th floor (Casilla 404), T 49146; U.S. Embassy and Consulate: Av. Mcal. López esq. Kubitschek, T 201041; Swiss Embassy: O'Leary 409 esq. Estrella, T 48022; Spanish Embassy: Calle 25 de Mayo 175, esq. Yegros; Swedish Consulate, Bogado 1039-47, T 205561/9; Dutch Consulate, Franco y 15 de Agosto; Austrian Consulate, Nuestra Señora de la Asunción 764, T 25567. W. German Embassy: José Bergés 1003-1007. France, Av. España 676, T 23111; Israel, Ed. Líder, piso 3°, O'Leary y Gen. Díaz; South African Embassy, Banco Sudameris, piso 4°, esq. Cerro Corá e Independencia Nacional; Brazilian Consulate, in Banco do Brasil building on main square (open 0800-1200, Mon.-Fri.), Nuestra Señora de la Asunción y Oliva (may charge US$10 for visa); Argentine Consulate, in Banco de la Nación building, also on main square, open 0700-1100, visas processed in 1-2 hours, photograph needed (will only give transit visas unless you can prove, with a letter from your consulate, that you are a bona fide tourist). Chilean Embassy, Guido Spano 1740, T 660344; Bolivian Consulate, Eligio Ayala 2002, T 22662; Peruvian Consulate, Estrella 451, piso 3°, T 41741; Uruguay, Av. Brasil y Siria, T 44242 (visas processed immediately if exit ticket from Uruguay, overland travel to Uruguay and onward country visas can be shown); Mexico Edif. Ytá Ybate, esq. Cerro Corá y Juan O'Leary.

The US-Paraguay cultural centre has a good library at España 352 (open Mon.-Fr. 0900-2000, Sat. 0900-1200, also has snack bar); Instituto Anglo-Paraguayo, España 457, where you can acquire much useful information and read English newspapers. Goethe Institut behind Goethe school, small library with a few newspapers, open 1600-2000. Compañía Marítima Paraguaya S.A., Presidente Franco 199 esq. 15 de Agosto, for all shipping enquiries. Anglican Church: St. Andrew, on España with Uruguay; Synagogue at Gen. Díaz 657. Peace Corps has moved, get address from US embassy. Police, T 46105.

Camera Repair Panatronic, Benjamín Constant 516. Rodolfo Loewen, Camera Service, Blas Garay y Morelo, T 23807.

Tourist Office Alberdi y Oliva. Open 0700-1200, 1500-1800. T 45306, 49521, 47865. Helpful, free map, also one available for sale in bookshops. There is a display of lace and handicrafts.

Tourist Agencies (all very helpful) Inter-Express (Amex), Yegros 690, Maral on 25 de Julio and Caballero are helpful; Continental, Benjamín Constant 777. American Tours, Independencia Nacional, under *Hotel Guaraní*, both German and English spoken. Grupo Cataldi, Estrella 876, T 90458, can occasionally pick up at airport; real estate agents (German run) with good contact in hotels and apartment accommodation. Menno Tour, Azara 532, is also staffed by Germans and will book buses to Foz etc.

Airport Presidente Gral. Stroessner (new name?), 15 km. NE of centre. There is a desk where you can book a taxi to your hotel, US$5. Bus 30A to the centre (Calle Oliva-Cerro Corá) (US$1.14) stops every 15 minutes just outside the airport perimeter at the road fork, 300 metres from the main entrance. Ask to be set down at road fork. (Do not walk on the grass outside the airport or the police will fine you). Buses 30 and 18 to the bus terminal. Buses only rec. outside rush-hours, with light luggage. The *Asunción Palace Hotel* runs a colectivo service from the airport to hotels, and in the other direction, US$2 p.p. (don't pay more than the fixed tariff). Líneas Aéreas Paraguayas (LAP) has its own colectivo, which collects from hotels, US$3.10 p.p., as does TAM. Enquire at airline offices. LAP office at Oliva 467; Eastern at Independencia Nacional y Azara.

A new airport terminal has been built (duty free facilities, small *casa de cambio*—turn left as you leave customs and immigration, but rates poor—handicraft shop and restaurant), 1 km. from the old building. There is a helpful tourist office on the ground floor at the airport; they will book for the Varig flights to Foz do Iguaçu, as well as arranging transport into town (minibus arrives and leaves from Iberia Office), finding accommodation and changing money at poor rates.

Rail Presidente Carlos Antonio López Railway to Encarnación and Buenos Aires (1,510 km.) journey of 44 hours, Tues. (better to take bus to Encarnación and catch train in Posadas). To Encarnación: with wood-burning steam locomotive, Tues. and Fri. 1800, at least 14 hrs. (first 12 hrs. in the dark), US$3, 1st class (rec.), US$1.90 2nd class; tickets on sale 2 hrs. before departure. Good hot food can be ordered for US$1.50, drinks US$0.30. In dry weather dust, and in wet weather rain, gets into 2nd-class carriages. Track liable to flooding. (Trains may be cancelled on public holidays, such as Christmas.) See under Excursions for a trip to see the wood-burning locomotives. At the station is a steam engine called *Sapucai*, built in 1861. The platform is too short for trains, which block Calle Bogado when loading.

River Boats To Concepción (24 hrs.) with Flota Mercantil del Estado (FME), Estrella 672-682 (tickets from here only). Weekly (every Tues., 0800 hrs.—returns on Sun. 1200), US$7.50 1st class, US$5.50 2nd class (4 beds to a cabin, men and women segregated, comfortable, but 2nd class food is bad and service worse—take food with you), US$4.50 3rd class (wooden benches on upper deck, bring hammock and mosquito repellant). Restaurant on board; said to be good. Boats are modern, elegant and comfortable. Other boat lines work this route, but they are less comfortable, although cheaper, with no regular sailings; enquire at the small boat dock to the right of the main dock; you will have to take your own food. Ferries sail thrice weekly to Balletín one day's journey N of Concepción, 2 day's journey in all (seats and cabins).

On the 2nd and 4th Tuesday of each month FME sails to **Corumbá, Brazil**, leaving at 0700, arriving Friday a.m., leaving Corumbá Monday 1100; tourist class US$30 for bed, no meals (men and women segregated), hammock space US$20; 1st (OK) and 2nd (dire) classes much more expensive; to Bahía Negra, close to the frontier, US$20 first, US$15 second, and US$10 hammock space. All 1st class cabins on the upper deck to Corumbá are taken in advance by an Argentine tour company for the whole 12 day round trip (and if there are not enough Argentine tourists the boat does not leave), including excursions into the Pantanal, bookable in Asunción from Chacotur, Montevideo 1447, T 80318, US$210 in all (exit stamps not needed for the round trip, official on board takes charge of passports). If the river is flooded (a common occurrence in mid-year), the boats go only to Bahía Negra (3 days), (see also page 698), because in those conditions they cannot sail under the bridge S of Corumbá. Bird life along the river banks is well worth watching.

You can enter Brazil, as long as you have a Paraguayan exit stamp, by taking a boat from Asunción to Isla Margarita, where you can get a ferry to Porto Murtinho, Brazil. (You cannot get a Brazilian entry stamp there: for that you must go to Cáceres, Corumbá or Campo Grande.)

Ferry to Puerto Pilcomayo (Argentina) about every 20 minutes (US$0.50, 5 mins.) from Itá Enramada (Paraguayan immigration), take bus 9 from Asunción (Argentine immigration closed at weekends for tourists).

Roads There is a 10 km. road N from Asunción (passing the Botanical Gardens on Primer Presidente) to a concrete arch span bridge (Puente Remanso—US$1 toll) which leads to the border at Puerto Falcón and then to Clorinda in Argentina. The border is open 24 hours a day; last bus from Falcón to the centre of Asunción at 1830. The bus fare from Asunción to the border (at Falcón) is US$0.60; from Falcón to Clorinda costs US$0.25. Taxi from border to centre, US$15, shared. There is a good bus service to Resistencia and Buenos Aires from the Argentine side, by Empresa Godoy. There is a 32 km. road NW to Villa Hayes (bridge) and on through the Chaco (Route 9) to Filadelfia (paved to here) and Bolivia, 805 km. (an account of a direct journey from Bolivia by this road will be found on **page 211**). Route 8 is now paved N from Coronel Oviedo, 100 km. to San Estanislao (see also under Coronel Oviedo, **page 700**), where it becomes successively Routes 3 and 5 (being paved for about 100 km.) and runs 305 km. N and then NE, to Pedro Juan Caballero on the Brazilian frontier. Also paved are the long-distance Route 1 to Encarnación (372 km.), and Route 2 to Coronel Oviedo, which leads to Route 7 to Ciudad Presidente Stroessner and the Iguazú falls (362 km.). A round trip Asunción-Ciudad Stroessner-Encarnación-Asunción is easily done. The roads are described in the text.

Buses To Ciudad Stroessner, about 20 buses a day, 3-7 hrs., most with toilet, with the following companies: Sirena del Paraná, Rápido Caaguazú, Nuestra Señora de la Asunción and Rysa (Rápido Yguazú), US$4 (last 2 the best). Nuestra Señora and Rysa, with the Brazilian companies Pluma and Unesul, continue to Foz do Iguaçu; all luxury bus fares to Foz are US$5, 5-7 hrs., six direct buses a day in all. Seat reservations rec.; take the 0100 bus (easy to sleep), which arrives at Foz at 0700 if you want to visit the Brazilian side of the Iguaçu Falls in one day; take 1200 bus from Falls to bus station, then 1430 bus back to Asunción—remember to buy new cruzados in Asunción.

Bus to Encarnación (for Posadas in Argentina), many, 5½ hrs., Alborada SRL, Rápido Yguazú, Flecha del Oro (7 a day); Nuestra Señora de la Asunción, and La Encarnaceña, rec., US$3.50. To Villarrica, La Guaireña, US$2, La Yuteña, US$0.85. To Concepción, US$4.50, 10 hrs., La Encarnaceña (0100), San Jorge (1950, 2400),US$5; San Jorge runs to Guaira for US$3.70, and to Pedro Juan Caballero—dry season only—for US$4 (Amambaya also to P.J. Caballero). Bus to Filadelfia, Nasa, daily, at 1430, 8-10 hrs., US$5. San Bernardino, US$ 0.45; Itaguá, US$0.30; Yaguarón US$0.45; Caapucú (on Encarnación road), US$0.50.

COT runs to Montevideo, 0800, Sat. and Wed., 20 hrs., US$28 Brújula runs other days (the route is Clorinda, Resistencia, Reconquista, Santa Fe, Paraná, Colón, Paysandú). To Curitiba, US$24 with Pluma, buses daily, 17 hrs.; to São Paulo, Rápido Yguazú, Pluma and Brújula, US$24 (leito, US$48). Pluma to Rio de Janeiro, US$30. Unesul run to Porto Alegre on Thurs. and Sun., Nacional Expresso to Brasília 3 times a week.

Asunción-Buenos Aires (20 hrs.) daily with La Encarnaceña (0800), Nuestra Señora de la Asunción (1000), US$22.50, via Rosario and Santa Fe, also with Godoy, Brújula and La Internacional, each 6 times a week. To Resistencia (US$6.85) and Formosa (US$4), 3 a day, Brújula and Godoy; Brújula and Cacorba to Córdoba, each twice weekly.

All buses now leave from the new bus terminal, out of town at República Argentina esq. Fernando de la Mora. Take local bus numbers 8, 10, 25, 31, 38, either on Haedo, or Cerro Corá in the centre for Terminal Nuevo; from the terminal to the city, get off the bus at the corner of General Díaz and Chile. The terminal has tourist information desk (reported unfriendly), restaurant (quite good), café, shops, and lots of noisy televisions. Hotels nearby: turn left from front of terminal, 2 mins'. walk. Taxi from down town, rec. if you have luggage, US$2 p.p. or US$4 per taxi. Many bus companies still maintain ticket offices around Plaza Uruguaya.

Excursions At Barrio San José de Olera (follow the river bank north) is the local brick works with about 20 kilns. Everything is still done by man and horse power. To **Villeta** (27 km., 5,232 people), on the E bank, which has undergone a rapid economic expansion; it is well known for good river-fish restaurants and for the fine children's clothing hand-made by nuns at a local convent. A little North is a park at Ytororó where trenches used in the war of the Triple Alliance can still be seen. The town of **Luque** (population, 24,917), close to Asunción, is famous for the making of Paraguayan harps, difficult to find though (Guitares Sanabria is one of the best-known firms), and for fine filigree work in silver and gold (ask around for Alberto Núñez). There are also many fine musical instrument shops on the road to Luque; get off the bus—No. 30—from Asunción just before the major roundabout. Marshal López' house may be visited. 8 km. from Luque is Balneario Yukyry, with an artesian well, springs, swimming pools, football pitches and a snackbar; for details and reservations, T 23731 (closed in winter, but pleasant trip anyway).

Parque Nacional **Ybicuy** is reached by bus two to three times daily US$1.85, 4 hours. Good walks, a beautiful camp site (hardly used in the week, no lighting, some facilities may not be available) and lots of waterfalls; it is one of the few areas of protected forest in the country. At the entrance is a well-set out park and museum as well as the reconstructed remains of the country's first iron foundry (La Rosada). The only shops are at Ybicuy, 30 km. away (Hotel Pytu'u Renda, E/F, good food, clean, cooking facilities, friendly; Pensión Santa Rosa and San Juan, both F). Bus from Ybicuy at 0430 and 1120, returning 0700 and 1345, goes as far as camp site, 2 km. beyond the museum. Crowded on Sundays but deserted the rest of the week.

The most popular trip is east to Itauguá, and San Bernardino and Aregua on Lake Ypacaraí (**see page 699**).

A short steam train trip to Aregua leaving Asunción station at 1200 daily, takes 1½ hrs., US$0.15, to the shores of Lake Ypacaraí. Engine burns exotic tropical hardwoods; Ian and Carol Martin of Falmouth, tell us that this is the only train they know of where passengers lower the windows, to sample the aromatic smoke. Bus for return trip via Itauguá: a good outing. For a longer look at the countryside, hire a car with driver for US$12 from any travel agent (pick-up at your hotel—cheaper with private drivers) to drive the "Circuito Central" also called "Circuito de Oro": Asunción-San   Lorenzo-San   Lorenzo-Itá-Yaguarón-Paraguarí-Chololó-Piraretá-Piribebuy-Caacupé-San Bernardino-Ypacaraí-Itauguá-Aregua-Capiatá-Asunción. Some 200 km. on paved roads, 7 hrs. Lions, at Alberdi 454, 1°, T 90.278, run a full service of trips. Beware of the Argentine Hugo, otherwise O.K. Alternatively, from San Lorenzo, take Route 1 towards Encarnación and at Km 28 (L.P. Petrol station) turn right to Guarambaré, a sleepy town in the sugar area with many Peace

Corps trainees. From May to November bullock carts and trucks take the cane to the factory, 1 km. past the electricity sub-station. After your visit continue to Guaramabaré (bus Asunción-Guaramabaré, 45 mins., US$0.15, every 10 mins. from terminal). Take the second dirt road on the right after the Plaza and for about 10 km. continue through typical farmlands and citrus orchards. The road then continues through Ypané, Nemby and back to Asunción via Lambaré. In Lambaré, near the *Itá Enramada Hotel*, is Lambaré hill with very good views.

A 3-hour colectivo ride from Asunción is Sapucay, 88 km. away, where the main workshops for the wood-burning steam locomotives are located. There are cheap *hospedajes* in Sapucay; either stay there, or take the Asunción-Encarnación train which passes through Tues. and Fri. at 2130.

NORTH FROM ASUNCION (2)

A boat trip up the Paraguay to Concepción, about 312 km. N of Asunción, is one of the easiest ways of seeing more of the country. The winding river is 400 metres wide, with a lot of traffic, for in the absence of a direct road between Concepción and Asunción (though there are roads via the Chaco and by Coronel Oviedo) this is the main trade route for the products of northern Paraguay: cattle, hides, *yerba mate*, tobacco, timber and *quebracho*. Nevertheless, for passengers there are only two weekly boats. Every second Tuesday and Friday in the month there is normally a boat as far as Corumbá (See **page 696**).

Concepción (22,866 inhabitants), a free port for Brazil, lies on the E bank. This pleasant, friendly, quiet and picturesque town is the trade centre of the N, doing a considerable business with Brazil. There is an interesting market. A bridge is being built across the river; the regular ferry operates in the dry season; motor boats cross in the rainy season.

Hotels *Victoria*, Franco y Caballero, F without breakfast, cheap and clean, private bath with hot water, rec., has new annex; on same street, *Center*, F with breakfast, and *Concepción*, F with bath and breakfast. *Francés*, Presidente Franco 1016, E with bath and a/c, F bath and fan, cheaper without bath, no breakfast, restaurant, has character (run down). *Paraguay*, F, restaurant excellent, good food at low prices. Also F, *Boquerón*, dirty, noisy, mean. *Cosmos* (clean, fan, breakfast included) and *Bar Estrella del Norte* (near port), both F, basic but possible.

Restaurants Copetín Chino, A. F. de Pinedo 1188, fair. *Bar Victoria* under *Hotel Victoria* serves excellent empanadas. Bread shop at Mcal. Estigarribia 229. Prices may rise rapidly during Brazilian tourist seasons, but at other times can be negotiated downwards.

Exchange Bancopar, Garay y Franco, open a.m.

Consulate Brazilian, Presidente Franco 945, open Mon.-Fri. 0800-1200.

Communications The bus station is on the outskirts: from Pte. Franco, with your back to the port, it's 8 blocks up Gral. E. A. Garay (to the left). Arriving in town by bus, get out in town centre, don't wait for bus station. There is a bus from Concepción to Horqueta, 56 km. to the E (1½ hrs., US$0.55), a cattle and lumbering town of 10,000 people. There is a dry-season road—frequently closed—from Concepción (ferry) W across the Chaco, to Pozo Colorado on the Trans-Chaco highway. The Concepción-Pozo Colorado bus takes 2 hours, US$2.75, but it is difficult to get onward connections. Once a week the "Camioneta Cristo Rey", a jeep belonging to the Anglican Church, goes across to the Trans-Chaco highway. Concepción-Asunción via Chaco takes 7 hours (departure 0700, 0730, 1300), road impassable with heavy rains; to Coronel Oviedo, bus departs at 0700, 1800 and 1900, bad road, rains often delay departures. Bus to Pedro Juan Caballero, 4 hrs., several, US$2.50.

Air Service Asunción-Concepción flights are operated by LATN, Aeronorte and TAM (which tends to be cheapest). TAM to Asunción daily at 0800, US$10, book as early as possible (only 25 seats), free colectivo from TAM office on main street to airport. On Fridays TAM flies from Asunción and Concepción to Vallemí, Fuerte Olimpo and *Bahía Negra*, all three villages to N of Concepción on the Río Paraguay. Air services to these places are irregular because runways are sometimes flooded or muddy. From Puerto Casado, 210 km. N of Concepción, a 200 km. railway runs W into the heart of the Chaco (used mainly by Mennonite settlers, and soldiers). There is no direct air connection between Concepción and Pedro Juan Caballero.

NB Unless you already have an exit stamp (obtainable in Asunción or Concepción), you cannot go upriver to Bolivia or Brazil by small boat from Bahía Negra; no-one there is authorized to give you an exit stamp. In any case, very few boats pass these frontiers.

Shipping To Asunción, Weds. 1400, US$7.50 1st class, US$5.50 2nd class, US$4.50 3rd class, 19 hrs., also Sun. 0900 (*Cacique II*) To Balletín, once a week, 24 hrs. To Fuerte Olimpo, Mon. only; contact Agencia Marítima Ramón Velázquez, Presidente Franco 2, near dock.

There is a 260 km. road (Route 5—first 160 km. unpaved but moderate, last 100 km. very good) to the Brazilian border. The road is very scenic, passing through the Cordillera de Amambay. About half way between **Yby Yaú** (junction with road to Coronel Oviedo) and Pedro Juan Caballero is a short road to the National Park of Cerro Corá, which is the site of Marshal Francisco Solano López' death, with a monument to him and other national heroes; the site is constantly guarded. The border town of **Pedro Juan Caballero** (pop.: 37,331), opposite Ponta Porã, Brazil, which has a road and railway to São Paulo and the Atlantic coast. The two towns are divided only by a road (Rua Internacional) and the locals come and go as they please. To cross into Brazil officially, first obtain a Paraguayan exit stamp (ask around: the office is in a private house in Calle General Brughez), then report to Brazilian federal police in Ponta Porã. If you need a Brazilian visa go first to the Brazilian consul (closed 1200-1400) in the *Hotel La Siesta* in P. J. Caballero. From P. J. Caballero there are daily flights to Asunción (they may be suspended after heavy rain, at which time buses may not run to Asunción either, though colectivos, which cost about 25% more than buses, may run when buses do not). Much cheaper here than Asunción for most purchases.

Hotels *Peralta* (F) and *Holiday* (E) are on the same street as the TAM offices. *Eiruzú*, D, with breakfast, modern, rec., swimming pool; *La Siesta*, modern, luxury, good restaurant, close to border with Ponta Porã; *Paraguay*, D, with breakfast, good, friendly. *Corina*, very clean with breakfast, F, rec..

Buses Several to Concepción US$2.50, 4 hrs. To Asunción at 0900, 1700 and 1900 (direct), US$4, 11-12 hrs.

Exchange There are two *casas de cambio* on the corner of Dr. Francia and Mcal. Estigarribia, 3 blocks on the left opposite the Brazilian Consulate. For travellers' cheques you can go to the *casas de cambio*, or to *Hotel Eiruzú*, one block behind the *casas de cambio* (also deal in the European currencies). Reports vary as to which gives the better rates; some say neither changes travellers' cheques. There are illegal exchanges.

EAST FROM ASUNCION (3)

Route Two The Mariscal Estigarribia Highway leaves Asunción past typical markets, reached by 26 bus from Asunción. At km. 12 is **San Lorenzo** (pop.: 74,359), an industrial town with the National School of Agriculture (Universidad de Agronomía—it has an extensive insect collection; also excellent Museo de las Indígenas, by the Cathedral, handicrafts for sale at reasonable prices, non-profit-making organization run by Catholic Relief Services). Here is the Balneario El Tigre, with swimming pool and shady trees. (*Hotel San Lorenzo*, Gral. Caballero y Cerro Corá, T 2261, F with breakfast, excellent). At km. 20 is **Capiatá**, founded in 1640, where there is a fine cathedral with remarkable 17th century sculpture made by Indians under the tutelage of the Jesuit Fathers. Here there is a left turn sign-posted to Lake Ypacaraí via an inexpensive toll road, 7 km. to the lake, worth a visit.

Km. 30, **Itauguá** (5,369 inhabitants), founded in 1728, is where the famous ñandutí, or spiderweb lace, is made. The blocks of uniform dwellings in the broad plaza, with their reddish tile roofs projecting over the sidewalk and their lines of pillars, are very close to the descriptions we have of Guaraní Jesuit settlements. The church and the market are worth seeing, and the town looks most attractive with the ñandutí work spread or hanging outside the houses; you can buy the most beautiful hammocks, tablecloths, shirts, hats and dresses locally made. There is a 3-day festival in mid-July, including processions and the crowning of Señorita Ñandutí. Accommodation poor (there is only one *pensión*, F), but Itauguá is only 45 mins. by bus from Asunción, US$0.30.

At km. 40 a branch road, 5 km. long, leads off to **San Bernardino**, on Lake Ypacaraí, by bus from Asunción (Route 2, 56 km. 1½ hrs., US$0.45) or partly by rail. The lake is 24 km. by 5. Crowded from December through February.

Facilities for swimming and water sports, with sandy beach, but water is a bit dirty (*Hotel Casino San Bernardino*, with swimming pool and restaurant, a/c, T (0512) 391; *Restaurant Siddartha* is good).

Aregua, a pretty town on the far shore (church and convent across from railway station), is also a resort, with interesting ceramics cooperative. An increasing number of houses are being built around the lake. Riding is possible. (It is possible to camp right on the lake but there are many mosquitoes, inadequate sanitary facilities and not much safety for your personal belongings; also possible to camp in disused walled sports ground.)

Hotels *del Lago*; *Acuario*, new; IPS (the Medical Social Service of Paraguay) has a first-class hotel, open for tourists. *Santa Rita*, E, bed and breakfast, friendly (good German food, and Paraguayan folk music at weekends). It is possible to find rooms in private houses.

Camping At km. 43 is Casa Grande Camping Club with all facilities. For information, Corfín Paraguaya, Ayolas 437 y Estrella, T 92360/1, Asunción, or direct, T (0511) 649.

At km. 54 is *Caacupé*, a popular resort and religious centre with 9,105 inhabitants. Its sights include the beautiful Basilica of Our Lady of the Miracles. Her day is December 8, when pilgrims come to the town from far and wide. The old church is being demolished, but the very beautiful new basilica, with copper roof, stained glass and polychrome stone esplanade, was consecrated by the Pope in 1988. There is an interesting market next to it, where one can buy pottery, etc., and swimming pools in the streams nearby. Parque Anka, outside town on the Asunción road, has a swimming pool, tennis courts, ponies, a Disneyland, camp site and good restaurants.

Thousands of people from Paraguay, Brazil and Argentina flock to the shrine. Besides fireworks and candle-lit processions, pilgrims watch the agile gyrations of Paraguayan bottle-dancers; they weave in intricate measures whilst balancing bottles pyramided on their heads. The top bottle carries a spray of flowers and the more expert dancers never let drop a single petal.

Hotels *Gran Hotel Victoria*; *El Uruguayo*, F, with good restaurant, friendly service.

Camping Club de Camping Melli, all facilities, Km. 53, close to Caacupé, T (0511) 313.

Excursions Poor roads lead to several interesting churches. One is at Tobati, a tobacco centre 16 km. to the N. At km. 64 beyond Caacupé a paved road runs 13 km. SE to *Piribebuy* (pop.: 5,902, *Pensión Santa Rosa*, F, basic; *Restaurant Rincón Viejo*, reasonable), founded in 1640 and noted for its strong local drink, *caña*. In the central plaza is the church (1640), with fine sculptures, high altar and pulpit. Near the town are the attractive small falls of Piraretá. The road goes on to Chololó, with good views from a hill, and you can visit the Chololó falls (motel); it reaches Route 1 at Paraguarí, 22 km. from Piribebuy.

At km. 132, but off the main road (buses drop passengers at La Cruz), is *Coronel Oviedo*, an important road junction (21,782 people; *Hospedaje Juancito*, 1° de Marzo y Carmelo Peralta, F with bath, mosquito net, nice garden, rec.; *El Rey*, E, clean, modern, breakfast included; *Pensión Nanda Roga*, F, without breakfast, basic but friendly; on main road to the West, *Hotel Alemán*, rec., or in centre, *El Sueño Feliz*, F, clean and friendly). Here the road branches: one branch, Route 8, is paved for 42 km. S to Villarrica and continues S (unpaved) through Caazapá to Boquerón.

Villarrica, 173 km. by road or rail from Asunción and 219 from Encarnación, with 21,203 people, is delightfully set on a hill rich with orange trees. It has a fine cathedral, and a public, open-air swimming pool. Products of the region are tobacco, cotton, sugar, *yerba mate*, hides, meat and wine produced by German settlers.

Hotels *El Mesón III*, F, pleasant; *Guaíra*, E, near bus terminal, shower, fan, a/c, friendly. Also various F places: *Hospedaje Restaurant San Miguel*, Natalicio Talavera, and *Pensión el Toro*. Eating places are hard to find (except plenty of ice cream parlours): *La Casa Vieja*, good, simple, some distance from main road (ask); poor café at bus terminal (closes 1800).

Bus to Coronel Oviedo US$1.50; to Asunción, US$2; also direct service (Empresa Guaireña) to Ciudad Presidente Stroessner, US$2.30. By train from Asunción, Tues. and Fri. 1800, US$1, arrive Villarrica at midnight.

Excursions About 30 km. from Villarrica there are some petroglyphs worth visiting. The taxi drivers know the way (US$12 return including an hour at the site) and a nearby farmer's children will guide you to them.

There are three German colonies near Villarrica. At Colonia Independencia, *Hotel Tilinski*, E, full board, peaceful, good German food, German spoken, swimming pool (filled with river water), and Señora Bürg has two rooms for about US$6, full board; very good food, fresh milk, lemon juice. Makes a good stop, especially for German-speaking travellers, who can also visit the German cooperative farms. Direct bus to Asunción, three daily (US$1.60, 4 hrs.), as well as to Villarrica.

The other branch, the paved Route 7, runs 195 km. from Coronel Oviedo through cultivated areas and woods and across the Caaguazú mountain to the spectacular 500-metre single span "Friendship Bridge" across the Paraná (to Brazil) at *Ciudad Presidente Stroessner* (possibly renamed Ciudad del Este), where there is a grass-strip airport. This was the fastest growing city in the country (83,000 inhabitants) until the completion of the civil works of the Itaipú hydroelectric project, for which it is the centre of operations. Ciudad Presidente Stroessner has been described as the biggest late-night shopping centre in Latin America, with little to excite the tourist (except the prices for electrical goods, watches, perfumes, etc.)—but watch the exchange rates if you're a short-term visitor from Argentina or Brazil; hotels and restaurants tend to be dearer than elsewhere in Paraguay. The leather market is well worth a visit, be sure to bargain. The nearby towns of Hernandarias (pop.: 32,000; *Hotel El León*, E, clean, quiet) and Puerto Presidente Franco (pop.: about 24,000) have also had a tremendous increase in population and activity.

Hotels (incl. breakfast) *Acaraí Casino*, B, a/c; with swimming pool and casino, quiet; *Catedral*, C, a/c, with swimming pool, restaurant; *Mi Abuelo*, highly rec., E, including breakfast, shower and fan, on Adrián Jara; *Tres Monedas*, D, on the main street, decent breakfast. *Puerto del Sol*, D with bath, a/c, clean, just off main street. *Tripolis*, E, a/c, friendly, clean; *Munich*, rec. Other cheap ones near market. *Executive*, Av. Adrián Jara y Curupayty, T 8981/8982, B (incl. breakfast—restaurant rec.); also in this class are *Floresta*, Av. Teniente Cabello y C.A. López, T 8255/8197, and *Santo Domingo*, Emiliano R. Fernández y Alejo García, T 2505, superb.

Restaurants *Mburucuyá*, with music, at Alejo García y A. Jara; *Hostería del Lago* at the same address; *Cary-Bar* at Nanawa y Monseñor Rodríguez; *Tripolis* for good moderately-priced meal. *Tai Fu*, Chinese, very good value, on 8th floor above *Casa Mona Lisa*, good views. *New Tokio*, Jara 202, very good, authentic Japanese meal for US$3; opposite is *Mi Rancho*, quite good. *Dolíbar*, clean and fair value. Cheaper ones in market.

Exchange Banco Holandés Unido; Lloyds Bank (ex-BOLSA) agency; local banks (open Mon.-Fri. 0730-1100). Good rates for changing dollars into new cruzados available in town. Recent travellers say that exchange is better and easier in Foz do Iguaçu.

Communications The road links with the Brazilian road system at Foz do Iguaçu across the bridge (no money changers reported to be available on Brazilian side), from where another 32-km. road leads to the Iguaçu Falls. Passengers disembark on each side of the bridge. The international bus then goes to the inter-city depot, behind Av. Brasil, at the edge of Foz do Iguaçu. Crossing from Paraguay to Brazil other than on the international bus, you just pass through Paraguayan customs etc., walk across, visit Brazilian immigration, then take a bus to the city terminal (*terminal urbana*), US$0.05, just outside Foz, opposite a military training camp. There is a local bus from the Stroessner bus terminal to Foz, which drops you off at Brazilian immigration; keep your ticket and continue to Foz free on the next bus. Remember to put your watch forward 1 hr. From the *terminal urbana*, buses run to the Falls; if only visiting the Brazilian side of the Falls, immigration procedure on the Paraguayan and Brazilian sides of the Friendship Bridge is minimal, even for those normally requiring a visa to visit Brazil. If entering Paraguay, sit next to the bus exit so you can alight to visit Brazilian immigration for your exit stamp.

Direct journeys to Argentina may be made by launch from Puerto Presidente Franco to Puerto Iguazú, US$0.50, about every 2 hours.

Many buses (US$4) and colectivos (up to US$5) run to Asunción, 3-7 hrs. Nuestra Señora and Rysa reported to run the best buses. Bus to Encarnación, along fully paved road, 4½ hrs., US$3.50.

The *Monday* falls, 10 km. from Ciudad Stroessner, are worth visiting by taxi. There is good fishing below the falls.

The huge *Itaipú* hydroelectric project is close to Ciudad Presidente Stroessner, and well worth a visit. Take a bus from Terminal Urbano to the Visitors' Centre, open 0730-1200, 1330-1700, Sun. and holidays 0800-1200,

1330-1630. Free conducted tours of the project, including film and bus tour, start from here at 0830, 1000, 1400 and 1500 Mon.-Sat.; on Sundays and holidays they are at 0800, 0900, 1000, 1100, 1330 and 1430 (check times in advance). Take passport. If you don't like guided trips but still wish to visit the project, apply to head office in Asunción.

Another paved road from Coronel Oviedo runs N to San Estanislao (5,538 people, small historical museum), then (Route 10) NE for 323 km. to the Itaipú dam area, past numerous "colonies" where the jungle is being cleared at an alarming rate. At Mbutuy, S of San Estanislao, a dry-weather road branches eastwards through Curuguaty to where the Salto del Guaira waterfalls used to be (now under Itaipú lake). There is now a ferry from Puerto Guaira to Brazil. There are daily buses from Asunción (14 hrs.). A wide, dry-weather road runs N from Hernandarias, via Itaquyry to the Coronel Oviedo—Salto del Guaira road at Cruce Guaraní.

A rough road runs N from San Estanislao to Yby Yaú (see page 0), via Lima (*Hospedaje Mburucuya*, G, basic; *Restaurant La Delicia*). 40 km. N of Lima, a road suitable for 4-wheel-drive vehicles only goes east, through patches of beautiful jungle, to Capitán Badó.

SOUTHERN PARAGUAY (4)

South from Asunción

A trip down river can be made to *Pilar* (13,135 inhabitants), 306 km. S of Asunción, opposite the confluence of the Paraguay and the Bermejo, coming in from the Argentine Chaco. A road (Route 4) is open E to San Ignacio Guazú, on the Asunción-Encarnación highway; in the other direction, it continues to the extreme SW tip of Paraguay, near Humaitá, the site of a heroic siege during the War of the Triple Alliance. Flights from Pilar to Asunción and Resistencia, Argentina, on Mon. and Thurs. by LAP.

Hotels   *Gardel; Prinquelli.*

South-East from Asunción

Route One   runs through some of the old mission towns to Encarnación, 370 km. away, on the Alto Paraná.

Km. 37, *Itá* (9,308 inhabitants), an old town turning out rustic pottery. At Carapeguá there is a turn off Route 1 to Ybycuy; 18 km. away is one of the more accessible National Parks (see page 697). Km. 48, *Yaguarón*, founded in 1539, was the centre of the Franciscan missions in colonial times. It is set on a river at the foot of a hill in an orange-growing district, and has a famous church, begun by the Franciscans in 1640 and finished in 1720, and reconstructed in 1885. (Open 0700-1100, 1400-1900.) The tints, made by the Indians from local plants, are still bright on the woodcarvings. Most of Paraguay's petit-grain comes from the area. (For the by-road to Caacupé see page 700.) Buses every 15 mins. or so from Asunción (US$0.45). (*Hotel Silva*, *Bar Elsi*, both F.)

"The corridor, or outside walk under a projecting roof supported by pillars, is a typical feature of Paraguayan churches. Generally it runs all the way round the church, forming an entrance portico in front. An excellent example is the church at Yaguarón. It is the prototype of the mission sanctuaries of the early 18th century, when the structure was built with a sturdy wooden skeleton and the walls—simple screens of adobe or brick— had no function of support. The belfry is a modest little wooden tower somewhat apart from the church; in the missions it also served as a *mangrullo*, or watch tower." - Paul Dony.

Museum   Museo Doctor Francia, 700 metres from church, with relics of Paraguay's first dictator, "El Supremo". Open Tues., Thurs., Sat. 1500-1700; Sun. and holidays 0930-1130; 1500-1700.

Km. 63, *Paraguarí,* founded 1775, the N entrance to the mission area, is on the railway (5,724 people), set among hills with many streams. Its church, though cruder, is reminiscent of the famous church at Yaguarón. It has a curious bell tower.

Hotels *Paraguarí; Domínguez. Pensión San Luis*, F, cheapest, on edge of town.

24 km. north of Route 1 from Eusebio Ayala (pop.: 5,316) is the Vapor Cué National Park, with peaceful swimming and fishing in the river in the middle of fertile cattle country. It contains the remains of seven steamships sunk during the War of the Triple Alliance. Several boilers and one ship have been reconstructed. Camping is permitted, public transport runs to within 4 km. of the site. Transport can be hired in the village.

Just before Km. 141 where the Tebicuary river is crossed by bridge (toll) is Caapucú (*Hotel Misiones*, F). At Km. 161 is **Villa Florida**, an ideal holiday resort for sailing, fishing and relaxing, with first-class hotel, 2 *paradores*, camping near the river (good fishing); also at **Centú Cué,** 5 km. away, on the banks of the Tebicuary river, there are hotels (*Parador Centú Cué*, D full board, pleasant, peaceful) and camping facilities, for reservations at either, T Asunción 206570 or directly to Centú Cué 083219. At San Miguel (km. 178), all types of woollen articles are on sale (blankets, shawls, ponchos, hammocks, etc.). The delightful Jesuit town of **San Juan Bautista,** about half-way between Asunción and Encarnación, is worth a stop (population 6,872, *Waldorf Hotel*).

Km. 226, San Ignacio Guazú; there is a superb museum of Guaraní carvings in the old Jesuits' house. 12 km. to the NE (up a muddy side road) is the new church of Santa María de Fe, with some 60 to 70 Guaraní sculptures in the chapel. From San Ignacio Guazú a road, 156 km., runs W to Pilar (**see page 702**). At Santa Rosa (km. 248), the Casa de Loreto has a beautiful Annunciation group and the remains of frescoes of the flight of the Holy Family's house from Nazareth to Loreto in Italy (poorly restored; ask for the priest from Louisiana to open it up). A road at km. 262 leads 52 km. SW to Ayolas, associated with the Yacyretá hydroelectric scheme (*Hotel Nacional de Turismo*, D with shower, poor breakfast, otherwise OK; *El Dorado*, E, with good restaurant). Coronel Bogado (5,180 people), km. 319, is the southern limit of the mission area. Turn off Route 1 just before Coronel Bogado to reach the Jesuit ruins of **San Cosme y Damián** (343 km. from Asunción)—church, refectory, etc. (A great variety of birds can be seen from this road.) Route One reaches the Alto Paraná at Carmen del Paraná, km. 331, 40 km. W of Encarnación, the terminus of the railway from Asunción.

Encarnación (pop. 27,632), a busy port on the Alto Paraná, is connected by ferry to the Argentine town of Posadas; the bridge between the two was due to be opened in August 1988. The town is the centre for the construction of the Yacyretá-Apipé dam to be shared by Paraguay and Argentina. Encarnación exports the products of a rich area: timber, soya, *mate*, tobacco, cotton, and hides; it is fast losing its traditional and very rural appearance. (Travellers should be prepared for cold weather, despite the latitude). The upper part of the town is not especially interesting, although prices here are lower than downtown near the river. The lower, older part of the colonial town will be flooded when the Yacyretá dam is completed. The cost of living is higher in Encarnación than in most other parts of Paraguay, and souvenir prices are much the same as in Posadas. The road along the Alto Paraná to Puerto Presidente Stroessner is now paved.

Hotels *Novohotel Encarnación*, A, first class, Route 1, km. 2, T 071-5120/24; *Repka,* Arquitecto Pereira 43, a small grey house in pretty garden, private baths, very good home cooking, E, bed and breakfast; *Viena*, Caballero 568 (T 071-3486), F with bath and breakfast, German-run, friendly, good food, garage; *Paraná*, E without breakfast, satisfactory; *Central*, Mcal. López 542, includes private bath and meals; *Viera*, a/c, good location, E (F with fan), Estigarribia and 25 de Mayo, gambling, private bath; *Hospedaje Liz*, Estigarribia 1767, F with shower, fan, hot water, clean, good patio; *Hospedaje San Cayetano*, F, near station, clean, fan, hot shower, good restaurant downstairs; *Rueda*, F, near bus station, hot water, clean, fan, mosquito repellant required. *Suizo*, Mcal. Estigarribia 562, just below bus terminal, F without bath, E with, breakfast, clean; others near railway station, all F (basic). *Pensión Vila Alegre*, Antequera 951, F, very basic but the people are pleasant and the food excellent.

Restaurant *Ara-Mi*, centrally located in the upper town, good food, pleasant. *Rubi*, Chinese, Mcal. Estigarribia 519, near railway, excellent but pricey; and *Restaurant Paraná*, international cuisine, on Mcal. Estigarribia (main street) and Memmel. *Bar-Restaurant Imperial*, Iturbe, corner Estigarribia, good and cheap; *Rosita*, Mcal. Estigarribia 1109, good meal, US$3.50; *Karanday*, Gral. Caballero, good grill but poor wines; *Confitería Tokio*, Estigarribia 484, good. Two good cheap ones on square by bus station.

Taxis Horsedrawn (about US$0.25), but prices tend to be high if drivers suspect you don't know the distance you want to travel. Some motor driven ones for those in a hurry. Horse-drawn taxi from railway station US$1.25 (compared to US$3.75 by car).

Exchange Lloyds Bank (ex-BOLSA), agency at Villarrica y Mariscal Estigarribia, open Mon.-Fri. 0730-1100. Many money-changers at the Paraguayan side but will only change notes—better rates for australes here than in Argentina. *Casas de cambio* for travellers' cheques on Mariscal Estagarribia: Guaraní at No. 301, and Comercio at No. 1404 (Thomas Cook cheques preferred); it is difficult to change money at weekends.

Tourist Office Kiosk on the ferry pier.

Consulate Argentine, at Cabañas y Mallorquín.

Transport Bus to Asunción, about 6 hours, US$3.50 with Rysa, colectivo with Halcones. (Bus terminal is above the town, up the main street; good cheap snacks at the terminal.) Train to Asunción, 18 (can take 24) hours, US$3, 1st class, US$1.90, 2nd class, Sun. at 0500, Wed. at 1130. Bus to Trinidad, US$0.40, 30 mins., every hour. Bus to Puerto Stroessner US$3.50, several daily, 3 hrs. Buses also to Villarrica. Boats to Asunción leave Wed. 1600.
   Passenger ferry to Posadas, 6 a day (last at 1720), 3 on Sat. and 2 on Sun., less than US$1, baggage extra; car ferry 4 times a day. Taxi from dock to bus terminal, about US$0.75. The bridge linking Encarnación with Posadas will be open for cars and trains.

Warning On arrival, foreign travellers are searched at the ferry terminal (principally for "communist" literature). Entry card costs US$3, payable in dollars, australes or guaraníes.

Beyond Encarnación, the road goes on 28 km. to Trinidad, and then to the thriving German settlements of Obligado and Bella Vista (another, Colonia Hohenau—reported dirty—is due E of Trinidad on the Alto Paraná); this road continues N, fully paved, as Route 6, paralleling the Alto Paraná, to meet Route 7 near Ciudad Presidente Stroessner (long stretches without petrol). About half way, at the village of Santa María Auxiliadora, is *Hospedaje La Norma*, G, basic. 71 km. from Encarnación is the Japanese Colonia Pirapó.
   At **Trinidad** there is a great Jesuit church, once utterly in ruins but restoration should be finished soon and a museum set up. The church was founded in 1706 by Padre Juan de Anaya; the architect was Juan Batista Primol. For information, or tours of the ruins, contact Sr. Augusto Serván Goana, Ruinas Trinidad, Itapúa, Encarnación; a US$3 booklet by Clement MacWaspy is available at the site. A visit is recommended (hours of opening 0730-1130, 1330-1730), also for the surrounding countryside. Next to the ruined church at Trinidad is a small modern church; it contains a large carved wooden statue of the Deity, so hollowed at the back that a priest in hiding could simulate the resounding voice of the Eternal Father to impress the Indians of the mission. Bus Encarnación-Trinidad 0600, 0800 and 0830.
   Ten km. N of Trinidad, at Jesús, there is another ruined church, which is also being restored (frequent but irregular minibuses between Trinidad and Jesús, same opening hours in theory, man who has the key lives 2 km. from the ruins, ask at the village square). Bus service to Encarnación hourly from 0630 (US$0.25, ¾-hr. journey).

Twenty km. before Encarnación on the highway from Trinidad is *Hotel Tirol del Paraguay* (Capitán Miranda, Ruta 6, km. 20), with 3 swimming pools, chalets with private terrace, bath, TV, a/c for 40 people and a landing strip; recently reported to have deteriorated.

THE PARAGUAYAN CHACO (5)

Michael Wigan writes:
   The Paraguayan Chaco covers 24 million hectares, but under 100,000 people live there. A single road, the Transchaco Highway, runs in a straight line north-west to the Bolivian border 20 km. beyond Nueva Asunción. It begins as an excellent asphalt top turning (N of the Mennonite colonies) into a levelled earthen road of average quality. It seldom rains but if it does all vehicles slither about hopelessly: you cannot move till it dries. The elevation rises very gradually from 50 metres opposite Asunción to 450 metres on the Bolivian border.
   The Chaco is divisible into 3 terrains. The first, the Low Chaco, leaving Asunción, is open palm forest and marshes, much of which is permanently beneath shallow water. The lack of slope and the impermeable clay hardpan mean the water hardly moves. The palm forest is used for cattle ranching of the most extensive type, some *estancias* lying several hundred km. down tracks off the highway. The cattle are very mixed—English Herefords, Indian Brahmins, and Brazilian. Most

estancias are chronically overstocked and overgrazed; calving rates are very low. Remote *estancias* have their own airfields, and all are equipped with 2-way radios.

The Middle Chaco, around the capital, Filadelfia, has been settled by Mennonites, latterday Baptists chiefly of German extraction who arrived in Paraguay from 1930 onwards. They set up three distinct colonies: Menno (from Canada and Mexico, but originally from Russia); Fernheim (the first group directly from Russia) and Neuland (the last group to arrive, also from Russia, after 1945). The Mennonites speak "plattdeutsch" - a cross between Dutch and German, and normal "hochdeutsch"; very few speak Spanish. Altogether there are 118 villages with a population of about 10,000 Mennonites, 10,000 Indians and a very small number of other immigrants. The natural cover is scrubland with a mixture of hardwoods, and more cactus further north. The bottle-tree with a pear-shaped, water-conserving, trunk, and the *quebracho* (axe-breaker), used for tannin, are native.

The Mennonites, who run their own banks, schools, hospitals and a cooperative agricultural system, are the only organized community in the Chaco. They are mainly crop-farmers (though they also run dairy cattle and make cheese and butter) and grow grapefruit, lemons, groundnuts, sorghum and cotton.

From Filadelfia an alternative route goes north and into the north-west Chaco where most of the remaining jaguars are found. This road is very rough, but the main highway remains negotiable by car although it narrows. In the western sector scattered military outposts are the only human presence. The whole area is under military jurisdiction; the visitor may find a letter of authorization or military introduction useful.

The north-western part, the High Chaco, is a low thorn forest, an impenetrable barricade of hard spikes and spiny branches resistant to fire, heat and drought. Occasional tracks lead off the highway for a short distance. Towards Bolivia cactus becomes more concentrated. In this remote and extremely inhospitable region the Government has deliberately discouraged mining and oil companies, and is restricting land sales. However, there are a few *estancias* further south, where the brush is bulldozed into hedges and the trees left for shade. In summer it is very hot. The animal life—wild hog, puma, jaguar, tapir—congregates around the water-holes at night. The whole area is a national park.

The primeval character of the Chaco is reflected in the 1975 discovery of a kind of wild hog, formerly thought extinct since the Pleistocene era, now listed as Wagner's peccary. When camping out fires should be kept up to deter the local fauna; the greatest danger is from several species of poisonous snakes. Grass round the tent should be cut. The highway is a smuggling route from Bolivia, so it is unwise to stop for anyone in the night. In the High Chaco there is almost no traffic.

The Chaco's Indian population is nomadic and Guaraní-speaking, and sets up little brushwood and mud villages wherever there is a plentiful food-supply. The Indians eat everything, bird and mammal, and even the poisonous snakes. The great delicacy is armadillo. Anthropologists have found the Indians' social structures, marriage and death rites as inscrutable as the surrounding countryside. They are friendly and peaceful, and periodically work on the *estancias*.

No expedition should be without supplies of water, food and fuel. Although there are service stations in the Middle and Low Chaco self-sufficiency is advised. Ill-equipped expeditions have had to be rescued by the army or have come to grief. In winter temperatures are warm and comfortable by day, cooler by night. In summer heat and mosquitoes make it very unpleasant. The Low Chaco is one of the foremost bird habitats in the world, and although bird-life may be enjoyed from the road it is still comparatively unknown and rarely visited. Tourists are unheard-of. Until recently entry into the Chaco was by plane only. The rapid development of the Highway will surely open it up before long; land purchases, especially by foreigners, and oil exploration are on the increase.

A bus ride to **Filadelfia** (472 km.), in the Chaco, from Asunción, costs US$5 with Nasa (daily at 1430). After about 350 km., one starts seeing the Mennonites' neat little homes with painted wooden shutters, surrounded by flowering plants and orchards. Buses often get stuck on the unpaved part of the road, in the rainy season. The centres are Filadelfia and Loma Plata, clean modern agricultural communities with wide dusty streets. The Unger Museum at Filadelfia gives a good idea what this industrious people had to go through to make this rich area what it is today (open Tues. and Fri. 1100-1730; at other times ask at the Information Office, two doors left of *Hotel Florida*). Some Indian tribes live nearby, but have been "civilized", seemingly to their disadvantage.

The Mennonite bus company, Chaco Boreal, leaves from the colonies for Asunción daily, US$5; leaves Asunción at 1600 from the Comité Central Menonita, Colombia 1050 with Estados Unidos T 26059, make reservations early; the bus stops at all 3 communities and ends at Neuland (US$6). There is a travel agency, the Reiseburo, close to *Hotel Florida*.

Hotel *Florida*, in Filadelfia, new wing with a/c and private bath, E, old section, fans and shared bath, F (uncomfortable, beetles), breakfast extra, sells excellent German cakes. **Restaurants:** *La Estrella* rec. for good ice cream and *asados*; another good restaurant opposite; *Remi*, on same street, pizzas and good ice cream. Plenty of good ice cream parlours (you need them in the heat), but no bars. 2 km south-east is the Parque Trébol, a charming public park, with facilities where one can camp. Lots of frog noise at night, however.

Nearby is **Loma Plata** (*Hotel Loma Plata*, E/F, with restaurant, can be booked from the Mennonite centre in Asunción). Good hotel in the village of Neu Hallestadt, Neuland, is *Boquerón*, E with breakfast. Ask around in Filadelfia for people to drive you round the Mennonite communities (US$0.15 per km.). See also notes on travel into the Chaco under Concepción, **page 698**.

To Bolivia From Filadelfia to the Bolivian border at General Eugenio A Garay is 304 km. Best to fill up with fuel at Filadelfia. There are sparse facilities (cafés, fuel) until Mariscal Estigarribia (*Hotel Alemán*, F with breakfast, friendly). Thereafter only military outposts or *estancias* may offer food, fuel and perhaps a bed for the night. At km. 662 a Centro Urbano Rural is under construction, with motel and service station, at Estancia La Patria. Trucks travel all the way to Bolivia. You can try to hitch. Frequent Army identity checks are inevitable. It is important to have photographs on documents which are a good likeness to the bearer. Backpackers need expect no special difficulties. Take plenty of food and water since even the smallest amount of rain can cause delays.

THE ECONOMY

Paraguay is essentially an agricultural country; farming employs 50% of the labour force, and accounts for 27% of gdp. Agricultural exports earn over 93% of Paraguay's foreign exchange with normally about 80% coming from cotton and soya. Cattle raising and meat exports used to be the principal agricultural activities, but their importance has declined as a result of uncompetitive pricing policies and import restrictions in potential markets. Fluctuations in the value of exports characterize the performance of Paraguay's main commodities, since they are so subject to the weather and world prices. Other major products are timber, tobacco, tung and other industrial oilseeds, essential oils (mainly petit grain) and *quebracho*. Self-sufficiency in wheat has been achieved since 1985, and the country now grows most of its basic food requirements.

Industry has traditionally been dependent upon agriculture: for instance, cotton ginning, sugar milling, textiles, meat packing, timber processing and extraction of *quebracho*, industrial and essential oils. The country industrialized fast in the 1970s and early 1980s, and manufacturing now accounts for 17% of gdp. As a result of economic recession since 1983, between 40% and 50% of industrial capacity is unused. On the back of hydroelectric development, Paraguay has its own cement industry and a steel plant opened in 1986. Both these, shipbuilding and the distillation of alcohol for fuel and other purposes, are state-owned. 14% of the workforce are employed in manufacturing, 8% in construction.

The massive hydroelectric scheme undertaken by Brazil and Paraguay at Itaipú on the river Paraná is reported to be the largest of its kind in the world. Both the total cost, of about US$15.3bn, and the final capacity, of 12.6m kilowatts, are to be shared equally between the two countries. Paraguay's share already exceeds domestic requirements and the surplus energy is being sold to Brazil now that a high-tension line to São Paulo is in place. Paraguay is cooperating with Argentina on the construction of the Yacyretá-Apipé plant, also on the river Paraná, with capacity of 2.7m kilowatts. A third Argentine-Paraguayan hydroelectric project, Corpus, has been postponed until the turn of the century at the earliest. Paraguay has its own hydroelectric facility at Acaray.

Until 1983, Paraguay managed to offset its current account and trade deficits with capital inflows for Itaipú. Since the completion of civil works, the overall balance of payments has fallen into deficit, with a consequent drain on international reserves. In 1986, the situation was exacerbated by the World Bank and the Inter-American Development Bank refusing to disburse loans until a more realistic exchange rate was adopted. This was eventually done at the year's end, but too late to eliminate the effects of a long-overvalued guaraní on trade and industry. It is estimated that unrealistic exchange rates encourage about half of Paraguay's exports to leave the country illegally, while contraband imports have adversely affected industry's sales on the home market.

When General Straoessner was ousted at the beginning of 1989, the new administration moved quickly to introduce economic reforms, including freeing the exchange rate and lifting many controls. Dwindling reserves led to restructuring of Paraguay's debt to Brazil, its major creditor, and bilateral deals were expected with others, to spread out maturities on the estimated US$2.6 bn foreign debt. Ongoing talks with the IMF led to revisions in trade statistics, and methodological changes to include some trade previously reported under services inflows account for the sudden rise in export and import figures below.

	1961-70 (av)	1971-80 (av)	1981-85 (av)	1986-88 (av)
Gdp growth (1980 prices)	4.3%	8.6%	2.3%	3.4%
Inflation	3.3%	13.1%	15.8%	23.3%
Exports (fob) US$m	50	231	361	928
Cotton	3	46	151	110
Soyabeans	—	29	101	265
Imports (fob) US$m	59	300	640	1,062
Current account balance US$m (cum)	-158	-897	-1,539	-654

INFORMATION FOR VISITORS

Flights from Europe   Iberia has one weekly flight to Asunción from Madrid, via Rio and São Paulo. Líneas Aéreas Paraguayas (LAP—now a member of IATA) has a twice-weekly service from Frankfurt, via Brussels, Madrid (once a week) and Recife (cheaper than most). From other points in Europe, slow connections can be made via Rio or São Paulo (Varig or LAP).

From North America   Eastern operates twice a week to Asunción from Washington and/or New York, and three times a week Miami-Panamá-Lima-La Paz-Asunción. LAP also operates flights (four weekly) from Miami to Asunción. Alternatively from New York, connections every day via Rio, but Varig's connecting flights are slow. From California, connections most days via Lima; cheapest, Lloyd Aéreo Boliviano (LAB), Fridays.

Within South America   From Montevideo (5 flights a week) by Líneas Aéreas Paraguayas (LAP) or Pluna; from Buenos Aires (15 a week) by Aerolíneas Argentinas (via Resistencia or Corrientes), LAP or Iberia; from Santiago (5 a week) by Ladeco (Chile) and LAP; from Lima (4 a week) by LAP or Eastern; from Guayaquil (twice a week) by Eastern; from La Paz (twice a week) by Eastern, or via Santa Cruz (2 a week) by LAP or LAB; from Rio, São Paulo and Iguazú Falls (daily) by Varig; from São Paulo (daily) and thrice weekly from Rio de Janeiro by LAP; from Río and São Paulo, without stop at Iguazú, two Ladeco (Chile) and one Iberia flight per week.

Airport Tax   is US$5, payable in US$ or guaraníes (tends to be cheaper).

By Sea from Europe   for freight and occasional passengers, the only regular all-water direct service is Europe-Paraguay Line from Grangemouth, Rotterdam, Bremen, Hamburg, Antwerp and Bilbao, owned by Hamburg Süd Eggert & Amsinck, Ost-Weststrasse 59, Hamburg 11, and van Nievelt, Goudriaan & Co., B.V., Veerhaven 2, 3016 CJ Rotterdam. Agent: Scottish Express International, Glasgow (T 041-221 7552) and Belserve/Belgian Maritime Services, Antwerp (T 03-232 25 44).

From the USA   The Holland Pan-American Line, New York office: 233 Broadway, New York 10004. T 791-8450 (bookings also through van Nievelt, Goudriaan & Co.), has a direct service between New York and Asunción.

By Land/River from Argentina   The international rail route from Buenos Aires to Posadas is given on page 120. There is a paved road from Buenos Aires via Santa Fe to Clorinda and then on new paved roads via the borders at Puerto Pilcomayo and the new Remanso Castillo suspension bridge to Asunción: 1,370 km., about 23 hrs.; also via Posadas to Encarnación. Good bus services on these routes. After the border at Puerto Falcón, before the Remanso Castillo bridge, a road forks to the Paraguayan Chaco (paved part of the way) and on to Bolivia. Boat services on the River Paraná between Buenos Aires and Asunción are irregular, depending on the level of the river.

From Brazil   The headwaters of both the Paraguay and the Alto Paraná are in Brazil. There are unscheduled boat services from Asunción northward along the Paraguay river to Porto Esperança, Brazil (from which there is a railway to São Paulo), and scheduled services to Corumbá (1,220 km.—**see page 696**), which is connected by road, rail and air with Bolivian and Brazilian cities. The normal means of surface communications are by road between Foz do Iguaçu and Puerto Stroessner, and between Pedro Juan Caballero and Ponta Porã. Frontier with Brazil is officially closed at weekends but it is worth checking as sometimes passports will be stamped on Sunday.

International Bus Services   See under Asunción, page 696.

Travel in Paraguay: By Rail   There are more than 600 km. of public railways, and 732 km. of private industrial lines, mostly forest lines of metre gauge or narrower. The standard-gauge railways are the 370 km. from Asunción to Encarnación, the 200 km. from Puerto La Victoria into the Chaco, and 64 km. from Borja (on Asunción-Encarnación line) to Abaí. Passenger services are very slow. There are police on all passenger trains; make sure you are carrying your documents.

By Air   There are scheduled services to most parts of the country by Líneas Aéreas de Transporte Nacional (LATN) and to Concepción, Vallemí, Bahía Negra and Fuerte Olimpo by Transportes Aéreos Militares (TAM). Planes can be chartered.

By Road   Buses ply on the main roads. For motorists, there are sufficient service stations in Paraguay, except in the Chaco area. Motorists should beware stray cattle on the road at night. Diesel fuel is US$0.25 per litre in Paraguay; gasoline users should use only *super* (Shell Spark Aider Super is recommended), US$0.45 per litre (which is 93 octane; regular gas, *alconafta*, contains 10-15% alcohol at US$0.40 per litre). It is highly recommended that drivers in Paraguay (and neighbouring countries) use diesel-powered vehicles as almost all the locals do: not only is diesel usually cheaper than gasoline, but a diesel engine will not stop in water, has no ignition/carburettor problems, and will not encounter the corrosive effects of alcohol in the fuel. Gasoline in Paraguay is the most expensive on the South American continent. Motor fuel and oil are sold in Paraguay by the litre. The documents needed in Paraguay for private cars are *carnet de passages en douanes*, international car registration and driver's licence. Border police charge US$11 to stamp *carnet* on entry and exit. **Warning**: beware of traffic police claiming that an International Driving Licence is not valid, or some other vague charge, and then demanding an "on-the-spot fine" of US$5 (at the very least). For entry into Brazil the only document necessary is the title to the car (or other proof of ownership). Touring y Automóvil Club Paraguayo has a good map. It is essential to drive at walking pace through military areas and stop completely if a flag ceremony is in progress.

Motor Repairs   A recommended mechanic is Lauro C. Noldin, near corner of 14 de Mayo and Bolívar, T Asunción 33933; he repairs Land Rover, Range Rover, Jaguar and all makes of British, European, American and Japanese cars, diesel and petrol engines. Motorcycles, power generators for motor homes. Bosch Garage Office, Chispa S.A., Carios y José Rivera, Asunción, T 27290/1. Recommended garage, especially for Volkswagen repairs: Rodolfo Stecher, Av. Fernando de la Mora 920, Asunción. Caravan and camper repairs at *Rodantes Ypacaraí Metalint*, Av. Benjamín Aceval y Ruta Mariscal Estigarribia km. 36, Ruta 2, T (0513) 290. For diesel service, MBT service garage at Av. Eusebio Ayala y Lapacho km. 4, T Asunción 27350. Land Rover body repairs at Taller San José of José Escobar at Battilana, casi Santo Domingo; T 203311. A recommended Land Rover parts source is Repuestos Agromotor at Herrera 604, Asunción. Good mechanics at Premetal Alemán, near crossing Eusebio Ayala with Rep. Argentina (T 64131). Spares are available in Paraguay for all makes of car (European, North American, Asian); also available are most makes of tyre.

Tourist Information   The Dirección Nacional de Turismo has an office at the corner of Alberdi and Oliva, Asunción. Information about weather and roads from Touring y Automóvil Club Paraguayo (TYACP) at 25 de Mayo y Brasil (who also produce an excellent road map), and the office of the traffic police in Asunción. The best map is available from Instituto Geográfico Militar, Av. Artigas (on the way to the zoo), price US$4.50, take passport. Small national maps, made by Army, can be bought from shop across street from Tourist Office. The USAID office has a good booklet on Paraguay. Other books: *Así es el Paraguay* (with maps and very useful information) and *Paraguay, Land of Lace and Legend* (reprinted 1983, available from bookshops and Anglo-Paraguayan and US-Paraguay cultural institutes in Asunción); also *Green Hill, Far Away*, by Peter Upton.

Entry Requirements   Passport. Visitors are registered on arrival by the immigration authorities and get their documents back immediately. Visas are normally not required for a stay of up to 90 days, by visitors who hold tourist cards, which are issued to non-visa holders on arrival by air or land; they cost US$3 (payable in dollars or guaraníes—cheaper). If you do not complete formalities you can be turned back at the border, or have trouble when leaving Paraguay. This concession does not apply to citizens of France and the communist countries, who need visas (US$8); Canadians also need visas (US$5), and it appears from mid-1988 reports that US citizens need them also. Visitors from those countries who do not have visas, or with Soviet, Cuban and Nicaraguan entry stamps in their passports may have to surrender their passports and undergo interrogation by the police in Asunción before getting them back; there appears to be no hard and fast rule so a lot depends on the official's mood or even your appearance. (Restrictions on Asians are being applied for immigration purposes.)

Customs "Reasonable quantities" of tobacco products, alcoholic drinks and perfume are admitted free of duty. Travellers' books are vetted, in case they're subversive.

Warnings The prejudice against "hippie-looking" people carrying rucksacks seems to have diminished. The proverbial "official-looking" letter is, however, still useful. Searches for "communist" literature are made at land borders. Any public criticism of the Government is unwise and can result in a stay in prison; as can taking pictures of "military" installations, for instance, Itaipú. Backpackers entering via Clorinda may have problems crossing the International Bridge; it is therefore recommended that they enter Paraguay via Puerto Pilcomayo or Ciudad Presidente Stroessner. Apparently, hitch-hiking is still illegal, although possible in rural areas.

Currency The Guaraní (plural Guaraníes) is the unit of currency, symbolized by the letter G (crossed). There are bank notes for 100, 500, 1,000, 5,000 and 10,000 guaraníes and coins for 1, 5, 10 and 50 guaraníes. It is possible to buy US dollar bills in Asunción (**see page 694**), and rates for all foreign currencies, except bolivianos, are reasonable. Get rid of all your guaraníes before leaving Paraguay; there is no market for them elsewhere (except in some *cambios* in Buenos Aires or Montevideo). *Casas de cambio* will cash travellers' cheques for U.S. dollars in Asunción for a 1% commission; they sometimes want to see customers' records of purchase before accepting travellers' cheques. **N.B.** In 1989 reports suggested that it was increasingly difficult to change travellers' cheques; visitors are advised to check on the situation in advance. Visa and Mastercharge cash advances are a possibility in Asunción. Street dealers operate from early in the morning until late at night, even at weekends or public holidays. In Asunción their rates are marginally better than the *casas de cambio* during business hours only, but they are not recommended at Ciudad Presidente Stroessner. Many cheap hotels will neither accept nor change travellers' cheques although they may accept credit cards.

Visa and Mastercharge credit cards are widely accepted even for small purchases. Foreign-issued Visa cards may not always be accepted though a phone call will often resolve the problem; Visa is displayed as Unioncard. Credit card transactions are subject to a 10% tax.

Sports Football is very popular. Tennis and horse-racing are popular. There are two rowing and swimming clubs of some 2,000 members, and a motor-boat club with 150 members, in Asunción. Golf is played in the Botanical Garden, and there is a Paraguayan Aviation Club. There are two boxing rings. Fishing, basketball and rugby football are popular.

Business Visitors Foreign business is transacted in Asunción, Ciudad Presidente Stroessner and Pedro Juan Caballero (with retail outlets particularly in the last two). From May to October is the best time for a visit. British business travellers are advised to get a copy of "Hints to Exporters: Paraguay", obtainable from the Department of Trade, Sanctuary Buildings, 16-20 Gt. Smith Street, London SW1P 3DB.

Business Hours Paraguayans are up early and many shops, offices and businesses open between 0630 and 0700. *Siesta* (generally observed during the hot season) is from 1200 to 1500. Commercial office hours are from 0730 to 1100 or 1130, and 1430 or 1500 to 1730 or 1900. Banks: from 0700 to 1030 in summer and 0700 to 1130 in winter, closed on Sat. Government offices are open 0630 to 1130 in summer, 0730 to noon, in winter, open on Sat.

Weights and Measures The metric system is used except by carpenters, who use inches.

Electricity Nominally 220 volts AC and 50 cycles, but power surges and voltage drops are frequent.

Postal and Telegraph Services The telephone service (few telephone boxes) links the main towns, and there is a telephone service with most countries. Collect calls are difficult. Time is 3-4 hrs. behind GMT (clocks go on one hour in the local summer). A phone call to Europe, Australia, and South Africa costs US$2.50 a minute; U.S.A., Canada, US$2 a minute; Spain, US$1.50 a minute. A telex message to Britain is US$5 (1 minute). There is a US$2.50 tax charged by the Post Office for all telexes sent or received in Paraguay.

Postal services are cheap and efficient. A normal airmail letter to Europe costs US$0.25 and a registered air letter US$0.35. Register important mail if you want it delivered. Parcels may be sent from main post office on El Paraguayo Independiente, Asunción. Rates: up to 5 kg., US$4 by surface, US$10 by air; 15-20 kg., US$10 by surface, US$35 by air. Packages under 2 kg. should be handed in at the small packages window, not "encomiendas". Customs inspection of open parcel required.

Climate and What to Wear The climate is sub-tropical, with a marked difference between summer and winter and often between one day and the next throughout the year. Summer (Jan.-March) is hot (and humid in Asunción). Temperatures range from 25 to 43°C: tropical clothing; sunglasses and an umbrella are needed. The autumn (April-June) is mild, but nights are cold. During winter (July-Sept.) the temperature can be as low as 5°C, though it can equally well be much higher. Temperatures below freezing are rare, and it never snows. The best time for a visit is from May to September; at other times the heat is often oppressive. The heaviest rains are from October to April, but some rain falls each month.

Cost of Living is generally cheap. Hotels in our G range are hard to find although there are many good ones in our F-E ranges, with breakfast, private shower and toilet. Hotels near the hydroelectric construction sites are often more expensive and require booking.

Tipping Hotels, restaurants, 10%. Railway and airport porters US$0.15 a suitcase. Porters at docks US$0.40 a suitcase. Cinema usherettes are not tipped.

Car Hire Hertz offers unlimited mileage for reasonable rates, free delivery to airport, minimum rental 3 days, but no insurance whatsoever. You will be responsible for any accident, damage or theft.

What to Buy The famous *ñandutí* lace, made exclusively by the women of Itauguá (**see page 699**). The local jewellery is also attractive. Handmade *ahopoi* (fine cloth) is suitable for shirts and blouses, and there are cotton thread belts in all colours. The best place to buy these items is Villarrica. Tourists are often attracted by the leather articles, the pottery and small wooden articles made from Paraguayan woods. Some of these are exhibited, and sold, at the Inter-Express Travel Agency's shop, Galería del Turista. See also "Shopping", under Asunción (**see page** [4053]). Imported goods, especially cameras and film, are cheaper in Paraguay than in most other Latin American countries (although prices in the UK, for instance, are cheaper).

Health Tuberculosis, typhoid, dysentery, and hepatitis are endemic. Hookworm is the most common disease in the country, and there is much venereal disease, goitre and leprosy. Visitors should be inoculated against tetanus, typhoid, and paratyphoid. Be very careful over salad and tap water. Local mosquito repellant, *Repel*, is effective. Medical fees and medicine costs are high. The Centro Paraguayo del Diagnóstico, Gral. Díaz 975 y Colón, Asunción, is recommended as inexpensive, foreign languages spoken. Clínica Integral de Mujer, Mcal. Estigarribia 1085 y Brasil, Asunción, T 94722, has been recommended as a good gynaecological clinic. Dentists can be found either at the centre, or at Odontología 3, Mcal. Estigarribia 1414 y Pai Pérez, T 200175, Asunción.

Newspapers *El Diario; Hoy, La Tarde, Ultima Hora, El Diario Noticias* and *El Pueblo* are published daily in Asunción. English-language papers from Argentina and Brazil are available the following day at corner of Estrella and Chile.

Official Holidays Jan. 1, Feb. 3, March 1, Maundy Thursday, Good Friday, May 1, 14, 15, Corpus Christi, June 12, Aug. 15, 25, Sep. 29, Oct. 12, Nov. 1, Dec. 8, 25.

Food and Drink Typical local foods include *chipas* (yuca bread flavoured with egg and cheese), *chipa soo* (maize bread with meat filling) and *sopa paraguaya* (a kind of dumpling of ground maize and cheese). *Soyo* is a soup of different meats and vegetables, delicious; *albóndiga* a soup of meat balls; *bori bori* another type of soup with diced meat, vegetables, and small balls of maize mixed with cheese. *Palmitos* (palm hearts) should not be missed; the beef is excellent in better class restaurants (best cuts are *lomo* and *lomito*). Paraguayan *chorizos* (sausages) are good. *Parrillada completa* is recommended. *Surubí*, a Paraná river fish, is prepared in many different ways, and is delicious. Sugar-cane juice, greatly beloved, is known as *mosto*. Fruit is magnificent. Very typical of Paraguay is *tereré* (cold *mate* with digestive herbs) for warm days and hot *mate* to warm you up on cold days. The national wine is not recommended (better is imported from Chile), but the local lager beer is acceptable and the cane-sugar spirit, *caña* is good (the best is "Aristocrat"; ask for "Ari").

We are most grateful to Patricio van Nievelt and Clifford Percival (Asunción) and also to the following travellers: Jens Borchers (Herzberg/Harz) and Michael Frantz (Sieber, W.Ger.), Peter and Alison Clarke (Leicester), Theodor A. Gevert (Barueri, SP, Brazil), Martin Gorst (London W13), Knut Per Hasund (Stockholm), John Lewis (London NW3), A. McKenzie Brockman (Deux-Montagnes, Quebec), Dimitri Moursellas (Manhattan Beach, CA.), Mark Pangbourne (Hastings), Barry M. Pell and Judith L. Katz (Brookline, MA), Wulf Peters (Querenhurst, W. Ger.), Arno Schmid (Hamburg 71), M.B. Vallance (Harrogate) and T.C. Walker (Chobham, Sy.).

PERU

PERU, the third largest South American country, with an area of 1,285,216 sq. kms (over twice the size of France) presents formidable difficulties to human habitation. The whole of its western seaboard with the Pacific is desert on which rain seldom falls. From this coastal shelf the Andes rise steeply to a high Sierra which is studded with massive groups of soaring mountains and gouged with deep canyons. The highland slopes more gradually eastwards; the mountains in its eastern zone are deeply forested and ravined. Eastward from these mountains lie the vast jungle lands of the Amazon basin.

The coastal region, a narrow ribbon of desert 2,250 km. long, takes up 11% of the country and holds 44% of the population. When irrigated, the river valleys are extremely fertile. Almost 600,000 hectares are watered today, creating 40 oases which grow cotton throughout the country, sugar-cane and rice in the N, and grapes, fruit and olives in the S. Petroleum comes from the N and Amazonia. The coastal zone is the economic heart of Peru; it consumes most of the imports and supplies half of the exports. Climate is determined by cold sea-water adjoining deserts: prevailing inshore winds pick up so little moisture over the cold Peruvian current that only for five months, from June to October, does it condense. The resultant blanket of cloud and sea-mist extends from the S to about 200 km. N of Lima. This *garúa* dampens isolated coastal zones of vegetation (called *lomas*) and they are grazed by livestock driven down from the mountains. The Peruvian coastal current teems with fish, and Peru has had the largest catch in the world; however, in recent years, the *anchoveta* shoals have moved southward into Chilean waters. At intervals during December-April a current of warm water, known as "El Niño", is blown S from the equator over the cold offshore waters and the surface temperature rises, the fish migrate, and evaporation is so great that the desert is deluged with rain which creates havoc (most recently in 1983).

In the Sierra, at an average altitude of 3,000 metres, which covers 26% of the country, live about 50% of the people, an excessive density on such poor land. This high-level land of gentle slopes is surrounded by towering groups and ranges of high peaks. Ten are over 6,000 metres; the highest, Huascarán, is 6,768 metres. There are many volcanoes in the S. The continental divide is the western rim of mountains looking down on the Pacific. Rivers which rise in these mountains and flow towards the Amazon cut through the cold surface of the

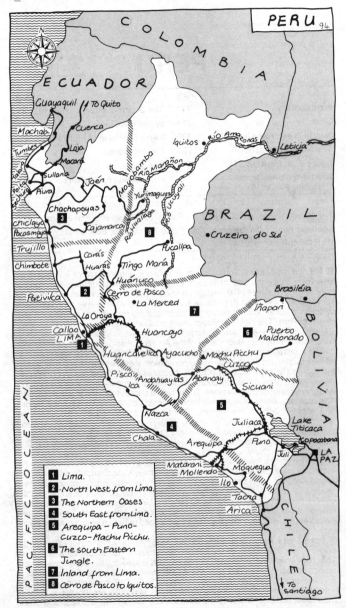

PERU 94

1 Lima.
2 North West from Lima.
3 The Northern Oases
4 South East from Lima.
5 Arequipa – Puno-
   Cuzco – Machu Picchu.
6 The South Eastern
   Jungle.
7 Inland from Lima.
8 Cerro de Pasco to Iquitos.

plateau in canyons, sometimes 1,500 metres deep, in which the climate is tropical. Pastoral farming is possible on about 13 million hectares of the plateau; the deep valley basins contain the best land for arable farming.

The plateau, mountains and canyons are inhabited mostly by Indians. There are 5,000 Indian communities but few densely populated settlements. Their literacy rate is the lowest of any comparable group in S. America and their diet is 40% below acceptable levels. Nearly 99% of the rural population and 60% of the town dwellers have no running water or drainage. About two million Indians speak no Spanish, their main tongue being Quechua, the language of the Incas; they are largely outside the money economy.

A mostly Indian labour force of over 80,000 is engaged in mining, and mineral exports from the Sierra represent half of total exports. Minerals are extracted as far up as 5,200 metres. Some of the sheep-farming areas are at altitudes ranging up to 4,250 metres.

The wide areas of high and wind-swept Altiplano in S Peru are near the limit of agriculture—though some potatoes and cereals (*quinoa* and *cañihua*) are grown—but the Indians use it for grazing llamas, alpacas and sheep; it cannot support cattle. The pastoral Indians of the area live off their flocks; they weave their clothes from the wools, eat the meat, use the dried dung for fuel and the llamas for transport. They are, in short, almost entirely self-supporting.

The **Montaña,** or **Selva,** the forested eastern half of the Andes and the land beyond covered with tropical forest and jungle, is 62% of the country's area but holds only about 5% of the population. Its inhabitants are crowded on the river banks in the cultivable land—a tiny part of the area. The few roads (given in the text) have to cope with dense forest, deep valleys, and sharp eastern slopes ranging from 2,150 metres in the N to 5,800 metres E of Lake Titicaca. Rivers are the main highways, though navigation is hazardous and the draught of the vessels shallow. The area's potential is enormous: immense reserves of timber, excellent land for the production of rubber, jute, rice, tropical fruits and coffee and the breeding of cattle. Few of these products come out by road to the W; most of them converge by river on Iquitos, which is 11,250 km. from Callao via the Panama Canal and the Amazon but only 1,010 km. as the condor flies.

Oilfields have been discovered southwards from the Ecuadorean border and estimates indicate that about 80% of Peru's oil reserves are in the jungle area. The Nor Peruano oil pipeline linking the Amazon area with the coast is in operation.

Climate The climate of the highlands is varied: the W side is dry, but the northern and eastern parts get very heavy rains from October to April, and are heavily forested up to a limit of 3,350 metres: the grasslands are between the forest line and the snowline, which rises from 5,000 metres in the latitude of Lima to 5,800 metres in the S. Most of the Sierra is covered with grasses and shrubs, with Puna vegetation (bunch grass mixed with low, hairy-leaved plants) from N of Huarás to the S.

Communications Several roads and two railways run up the slopes of the Andes to reach the Sierra. These railways, once British owned, run from Lima in the centre and the ports of Matarani and Mollendo in the S. There are in all 2,740 km. of railway. There are three main paved roads: the Inter-American Highway runs N-S through the coastal desert and sends a spur NE into the Sierra to Arequipa, with a partially paved continuation to Puno on Lake Titicaca which then skirts the lake to Desaguadero, on the Bolivian frontier, a total of 3,418 km.; the Central Highway from Lima to Huancayo, which continues (mostly paved) to Pucallpa in the Amazon basin; and the direct road from Lima N to Huarás. Both roads and railways are given in the text and shown on sketch maps.

Pre-History Two Harvard archaeologists, Michael Moseley and Robert Feldman, concluded, following excavations at coastal sites at Ancón, Supe, etc., that an early civilization sprang up on the coast on the basis of a fishing economy and was well developed by 2100 BC. (This is in complete contradiction of one of archaeology's basic tenets that development of agriculture must invariably precede civilization.) The key site is Aspero near Supe, where low mounds facing the shore revealed stone walls, plaster clap-board shaped friezes, wall niches, a trapezoidal doorway (predating the Incas by 3,500 years) and unbaked clay figurines. One of the mounds is bisected by a gigantic looters' pit which gives an interesting cross-section across the mound, showing at least fifteen different occupation levels defined by floors and bands of ash and burnt rocks (heated and dropped into gourds or tightly-woven baskets to cook fish before the days of cooking pots). The hypothesis of Moseley and Feldman has, however, been seriously questioned by further study such as that of David J. Wilson of the University of Michigan. He argues that a mixed agricultural-maritime economy based primarily on plant cultivation is evident at coastal sites such as El Paraíso and Aspero, and that El Niño conditions must be taken into account as a recurring and biologically devastating phenomenon creating critical lean periods in the diet of maritime-oriented coastal populations at all levels in the food chain.

This early start on the coast developed into a *huaca* (mound)-building culture of whose works the easiest to visit is Garagay, within sight of Lima airport and identified easily by an electricity pylon built on top. It is a U-shaped complex of three mounds with magnificent adobe friezes (not open to the public as there is no way of preserving them) half way up the main mound, dated by Dr. Roger Ravines to 1000 BC. In the huge plaza enclosed by the mounds a circular subterranean plaza has been found with symmetrical staircases. This is an important find, as a similar circular plaza was found recently at Chavín. The Chavín culture flourished mainly in the highlands near the coast from Piura S to Pisco, from about 800 to 200 BC. Whether it had origins on the coast or in the highlands is a matter for debate because it is unknown where the fusion of styles which characterized the Chavín cult took place. Its centre was Chavín de Huantar, which was a cross-roads of trade between coast, Sierra and jungle; the University of San Marcos has an interesting museum including a collection of Chavín pottery. It influenced heavily the Paracas culture of the S at about 200 BC to AD 200 (see under Nazca), the high Nazca culture (AD 400-800) the more primitive culture around Lima in the centre, and the Mochica culture in the N which had its beginnings just before the Christian era—some say as early as 300 BC—and lasted until the sixth century AD, characterized by realistic moulded pottery, sculptured wood and worked metals and by the huge adobe pyramids of the Moche valley (see under Trujillo). About AD 600, the Huari empire, based at Huari near Ayacucho, came to prominence; at its greatest its influence spread from Cajamarca and the Chicama valley in the North to almost the Titicaca basin and the Ocaña valley on the South coast. It overlapped with the Tiahuanaco culture, which was possibly an indigenous development, even if complementary to Huari and the Nazca culture. The classical Tiahuanaco culture, whose great monument is the ruins of Tiahuanaco, E of Lake Titicaca in Bolivia, dominated the coast until the 9th century. Possibly towards the end of the 11th century, the Incas had begun to rise in the Cuzco basin; their conquest of Peru and Ecuador was only completed around 1450. (Their civilization is briefly described under Cuzco, page 798.)

History A short time before the Spaniards arrived Peru was being ruled from Cuzco by the Inca Huáscar and from Quito by his half-brother Atahualpa, who was victorious in the civil war between the two. When Francisco Pizarro and

Diego de Almagro landed a tiny force in Peru in 1532, Atahualpa, no doubt anxious for allies, allowed them to reach the Sierra. Pizarro's only chance against the formidable imperial army he encountered at Cajamarca was a bold stroke. He drew Atahualpa into an ambush, slaughtered his guards, promised him liberty if a certain room were filled with treasure, and finally killed him after receiving news that another Inca army was on its way to free him. Pushing on to Cuzco, he was at first hailed as the executioner of a traitor: Atahualpa had killed Huáscar after the battle of Huancavelica two years previously. Panic followed when the *conquistadores* set about sacking the city, and they fought off with difficulty an attempt by Manco Inca to recapture Cuzco in 1538. (For the whole period of the Conquest John Hemming's *The Conquest of the Incas* is invaluable; he himself refers us to Ann Kendall's *Everyday Life of the Incas*, Batsford, London, 1978.)

In 1535, wishing to secure his communications with Spain, Pizarro founded Lima, near the ocean, as his capital. The same year Almagro set out to conquer Chile. Unsuccessful, he returned to Peru, quarrelled with Pizarro, and in 1538 fought a pitched battle with Pizarro's men at the Salt Pits, near Cuzco. He was defeated and put to death. Pizarro, who had not been at the battle, was assassinated in his palace in Lima by Almagro's son three years later. For the next 27 years each succeeding representative of the Kingdom of Spain sought to subdue the Inca successor state of Vilcabamba, N of Cuzco, and to unify the fierce Spanish factions. Francisco de Toledo (appointed 1568) solved both problems during his 14 years in office: Vilcabamba was crushed in 1572 and the last reigning Inca, Túpac Amaru, put to death. For the next 200 years the Viceroys closely followed Toledo's system, if not his methods. The Major Government—the Viceroy, the High Court (*Audiencia*), and *corregidores* (administrators)—ruled through the Minor Government— Indian chiefs put in charge of large groups of natives: a rough approximation to the original Inca system.

The Indians rose in 1780, under the leadership of an Inca noble who called himself Túpac Amaru II. He and many of his lieutenants were captured and put to death under torture at Cuzco. Another Indian leader in revolt suffered the same fate in 1814, but this last flare-up had the sympathy of many of the locally-born Spanish, who resented their status, inferior to the Spaniards born in Spain, the refusal to give them any but the lowest offices, the high taxation imposed by the home government, and the severe restrictions upon trade with any country but Spain. Help came to them from the outside world: José de San Martín's Argentine troops, convoyed from Chile under the protection of Lord Cochrane's squadron, landed in southern Peru on September 7, 1820. San Martín proclaimed Peruvian independence at Lima on July 28, 1821, though most of the country was still in the hands of the Viceroy, La Serna. Bolívar, who had already freed Venezuela and Colombia, sent Sucre to Ecuador where, on May 24, 1822, he gained a victory over La Serna at Pichincha. San Martín, after a meeting with Bolívar at Guayaquil, left for Argentina and a self-imposed exile in France, while Bolívar and Sucre completed the conquest of Peru by defeating La Serna at the battle of Junín (August 6, 1824) and the decisive battle of Ayacucho (December 9, 1824). For over a year there was a last stand in the Real Felipe fortress at Callao by the Spanish troops under General Rodil before they capitulated on January 22, 1826. Bolívar was invited to stay in Peru, but left for Colombia in 1826.

Important events were a temporary confederation between Peru and Bolivia in the 1830s; the Peruvian-Spanish War (1866); and the War of the Pacific (1879-1883), in which Peru and Bolivia were defeated by Chile and Peru lost its southernmost territory. A long-standing legacy of this was the Tacna-Arica dispute, which was not settled until 1929 (see under Tacna).

Population   20.7m. (1987 estimate), growing at an annual rate of 2.6%. Birth rate, 36.7 per 1,000 (1987); death rate 10.7 per 1,000 (1987).

Constitution   Legislation is vested in a Congress composed of a Senate and a Chamber of Deputies. Men and women over 18 are eligible to vote; registration and voting is compulsory until the age of 60. The President, to whom is entrusted the Executive Power, is elected for five years and may not be re-elected until after one presidential term has passed. He exercises his functions through a Cabinet of 12 members. A new Constitution was approved in July 1979. Peru's 25 Departments are divided into 150 Provinces, and the Provinces into 1,321 districts.

Government A reformist military Junta took over control of the country in October 1968. Under its first leader, Gen. Juan Velasco Alvarado, the Junta instituted a series of measures to raise the personal status and standard of living of the workers and the rural Indians, by land reform, worker participation in industrial management and ownership, and nationalization of basic industries, exhibiting an ideology perhaps best described as "military socialism". In view of his failing health Gen. Velasco was replaced in 1975 by Gen. Francisco Morales Bermúdez and policy (because of a mounting economic crisis and the consequent need to seek financial aid from abroad) swung to the Right. Presidential and congressional (60 senators, 180 deputies) elections were held on May 18, 1980, and Sr. Fernando Belaúnde Terry was elected President for the second time. His term was marked by growing economic problems and the growth of the Maoist guerrilla movement Sendero Luminoso (Shining Path). The April 1985 elections were won by the APRA party leader Alán García Pérez, who took office as President on July 28, 1985. Elections are due in 1990. The Sendero Luminoso and another guerrilla movement Túpac Amaru are still active, disrupting transport and electricity supplies particularly.

Education is free and compulsory for both sexes between 6 and 14. There are public and private secondary schools and private elementary schools. There are 32 State and private universities, and two Catholic universities. A new educational system is being implemented as too many children cannot complete secondary school.

Language Spanish. Quechua, the language of the Inca empire, has been given some official status; it is spoken by millions of Sierra Indians who have little or no knowledge of Spanish. Another important Indian language is Aymará, used in the area around Lake Titicaca.

LIMA (1)

Lima, capital of Peru, was the chief city of Spanish South America from its founding in 1535 until the independence of the South American republics in the early 19th century. It is built on both sides of the Río Rímac, lying at the foot of the Cerro San Cristóbal. From among the traditional buildings which still survive soar many tall skyscrapers which have changed the old skyline out of recognition. The city, which is now very dirty and seriously affected by smog for much of the year, is surrounded by "Pueblos Jóvenes," or shanty settlements of squatters who have migrated from the Sierra; much self-help building is in progress. There are still signs of damage after the disastrous 1970 earthquakes nearby, especially in the Rímac section of the city. Many of the hotels and larger business houses have moved to the plush seaside suburbs of Miraflores and San Isidro.

N.B. In 1989 there was a curfew between 0100 and 0500 because of guerrilla activity. If you arrive at the airport between these hours you are given a pass. If you find yourself in the street during curfew, walk in the middle of the road waving a white object above your head, until you can report to a policeman or soldier.

Half of the town-dwellers of Peru now live in Lima and Callao. The metropolitan area contains five million people, nearly 30% of the country's total population, and two-thirds of its industries.

In the older part the way the streets are named may confuse the visitor. Several blocks, with their own names, make up a long street, a *jirón* (often abbreviated to Jr.). The visitor is greatly helped by the corner signs which bear both the name of the *jirón* and the name of the block. The new and old names of streets are used interchangeably: remember that Colmena is also Nicolás de Piérola, and Carabaya is also Augusto N. Wiese. The city's urban motorway is often called "El Zanjón" (the ditch).

Only 12° S of the equator, one would expect a tropical climate, but from June to at least October the skies are grey; it feels chilly, clothes take ages to dry, and a damp *garúa*, or Scotch mist, is common. The rest of the year is mild and pleasant with temperatures ranging from 10° to 27°C.

History The University of San Marcos was founded in 1551, and a printing press in 1595: among the earliest of their kind in S. America. Lima's first theatre opened in 1563. The Inquisition was introduced in 1569 and was not abolished until 1820. For some time the Viceroyalty of Peru embraced Colombia, Ecuador, Bolivia, Chile and Argentina. The city's wealth attracted many freebooters and in 1670 a protecting wall 11 km. long, which was demolished in 1869, was built round it. Lima's power was at its height during the 17th century and the early 18th, until the earthquake of 1746 destroyed all but 20 houses and killed 4,000 inhabitants. There were few cities in the Old World that could rival its wealth and luxury. It was only comparatively recently, with the coming of industry, that Lima began to change into what it is today.

Sightseeing The heart of the city, at least in plan, is still what it was in colonial days. A single block S of the Río Rímac lies the Plaza de Armas; the Desamparados Station of the Central Railway is quite near. Most of what the tourist wants to see is in this area. The newer parts of the city are based on Plaza San Martín, S of Jirón de la Unión, with a statue of San Martín in the centre. One and a quarter km. W is the Plaza Dos de Mayo. About 1 km. due S of this again is the circular Plaza Bolognesi, from which many great *avenidas* radiate.

The Jirón de La Unión, the main shopping street, runs to the Plaza de Armas; it has been converted into a pedestrian precinct (street theatre, street vendors, etc., in the evening). Later the pedestrian area will be extended to cover the southern half of Jirón de la Unión, from Plaza San Martín to Plaza Grau. In the two northernmost blocks of Jr. Unión, known as Calle Belén, several shops sell souvenirs and curios: the nearer the shops are to the best hotels the dearer the souvenirs are. Around the great Plaza de Armas stand the Government Palace, the Cathedral (**see page 719**), the Archbishop's Palace, the City Hall and the Unión Club. The Central Post Office is opposite the visitors' entrance to Government Palace. Running along two sides are arcades with shops: Portal de Escribanos and Portal de Botoneros. In the centre is a bronze fountain dating from 1650.

The **Palacio de Gobierno** (Government Palace) was built from 1921 to 1938, on the site of and with some of the characteristics of Pizarro's palace. Visitors' entrance is on Jirón de la Unión. Guided tours at 1230, but you must present your documentation on previous day (Mon.-Thur. only). Under state-of-siege regulations it is difficult to get in at other times. The ceremonial changing of the guard behind the gates of the palace is worth watching, most days 0800 and 1245-1300 (check with the Tourist Office).

The **Municipalidad de Lima,** built 1945, has a picture gallery (open 0800-1500 Mon.,-Fri., free).

Near San Pedro, at Jirón Ucayali 363, is **Torre Tagle Palace,** the city's best surviving specimen of secular colonial architecture: a Sevillian mansion built in 1735. Now occupied by the Foreign Ministry, but visitors are allowed to enter courtyards to inspect fine wood-carving in balconies, wrought iron work, and a 16th-century coach complete with commode. During working hours Mon.-Fri,. visitors may enter the patio only.

A short taxi ride across the Río Rímac takes you to the Convent of Los Descalzos (**see page 720**) and the Quinta de Presa (incorrectly reputed to be the house of La Perricholi), now the Viceregal Museum (Museo Virreynal— **see page 721**), closed at present for repairs.

La Perricholi—real name Micaela Villegas—was a beauty, wit, actress, and mistress of Viceroy Amat (1761-1776). Legend says he installed her in this mansion, but the house the Viceroy built for her was torn down last century. She has inspired plays, an opera (by Offenbach) and many books, the best known of which is Thornton Wilder's *The Bridge of San Luis Rey.*

The Puente de Piedra, behind the Presidential Palace, is a Roman-style stone bridge built 1610. Hundreds of thousands of egg whites were used to strengthen its mortar.

Other important mansions worth visiting are the **Casa Pilatos,** opposite the San Francisco church

Key to Map.
1. Plaza de Armas. 2. Palacio de Gobierno. 3. Cathedral. 4. Union Club. 5. Plaza San Martín. 6. Torre Tagle Palace. 7. Plaza 2 de Mayo. 8. Plaza Bolognesi. 9. Plaza Grau. 10. Palacio de Justicia. 11. National Museum of Art. 12. Museum of Italian Art. 13. Panteón de los Próceres. 14. Museum of Peruvian Culture. 15. Las Nazarenas Church. 16. National Library. 17. *Hotel Bolívar.* 18. *Hotel Crillón.* 19. *Hotel Riviera.* 20. *Hotel Savoy.* 21. *Hotel Maury.* 22. Municipal Theatre. 23. Teatro Segura. 24. *Hotel Continental.* 25. *Hotel Sheraton.* 26. Civic Centre. 27. City Hall. 28. Parque Universitario.

N.B. A good map of Greater Lima may be bought at the Jorge Chávez airport and in the main shopping streets; it has street references and the main bus routes on the back (US$2).

at Jirón Ancash 390, now the Casa de Cultura, open 0830-1645, Mon.-Fri.; **Casa de la Riva** at Jirón Ica 426, now the German Institute; **Casa de Oquendo** at Conde de Superunda 298 has been reopened after restoration, and stages art exhibitions; **Casa Negreiros** (a restaurant), at Jirón Azángaro 532; and **Casa de las Trece Monedas** (also a restaurant), at Jirón Ancash 536. The **Casa Aliaga,** at Unión 224, is still occupied by the Aliaga family and has recently been opened to the public; Vista Tours has exclusive rights to include the house in its tours (T 27-6624, or any travel agent). The house contains what is said to be the oldest ceiling in Lima and is furnished entirely in the colonial style. Don Jerónimo de Aliaga was one of the 13 commanders to arrive with Francisco Pizarro, and all 13 were given land around the main square to build their own houses when Lima was founded in 1535. The house of the author Ricardo Palma is open to the public, Mon.Fri. 1000-1230, 1600-1900 (a.m. only Sat.), small entrance fee, Gral. Suárez 189, Miraflores—a 19th-century middle-class residence.

Other old mansions worth seeing: **Museo Berckemeyer** (art and bullfighting), Jr. Lima 341, a typical 17th-century *limeño* house—one of the few left; T 270025 for an appointment to visit, Mon.-Fri., 0830-1300. **Casa Barbieri**, Jr. Callao, near Jr. Rufino Torrico—a fine old 18th-century town house in the Sevillian style; ring bell in entrance hall for permission to look at the patios. **Casa Museo Prado,** Jr. Cuzco 448, visitable when Sr. Prado is in residence, a beautifully maintained house with early 19th-century front and, apparently, a 17th-century patio. **AAA Theatre,** Jr. Ica 323, is in a lovely 18th-century house. **Casa de la Rada,** Jr. Ucayali, opposite Palacio Torre Tagle—an extremely fine mid-18th-century town house in the French manner; patio and first reception room open occasionally to the public (now belongs to a bank).

Churches

The Cathedral   (open to visitors 0930-1200, 1400-1700 every day) is on the Plaza de Armas. See the splendidly carved stalls (mid-17th century); the silver-covered altars surrounded by fine woodwork; mosaic-covered walls bearing the coats of arms of Lima and Pizarro and an allegory of Pizarro's commanders, the "Thirteen Men of Isla del Gallo"; in a small chapel, the first on the right of the entrance, are remains in a glass coffin originally said to be those of Pizarro, but later research indicates that his remains lie in the crypt. Museum of Religious Art in the cathedral, guided visits, ask to see picture restoration room, all-inclusive entrance ticket, US$0.40. The Archbishop's Palace was rebuilt in 1924, with a superb wooden balcony.

Four notable churches are quite near the Plaza de Armas: **La Merced** (open 0700-1230, 1600-2000 every day) and its monastery (open 0800-1200 and 1500-1730 daily) are in Plazuela de la Merced, Jirón de la Unión, two blocks from the Plaza de Armas. The first mass in Lima was said on this site. Very fine restored colonial façade, and attractive cloister. See the choir stalls and the vestry's panelled ceiling. At independence the Virgin of La Merced was made a Marshal of the Peruvian army. **Santo Domingo,** built 1549, is in Jirón Camaná (first block). In an urn in one of the altars are the remains of Santa Rosa de Lima (1586-1617), the first saint of the New World: August 30 is her day. Pope Clement presented, 1669, the alabaster statue of the Saint in front of the altar (entrance, US$0.30, open 0700-1300, 1600-2000 daily; monastery and tombs open 0930-1230, 1530-1730 Mon.-Sat.; Sun. and holidays a.m. only). The main hall has some interesting relics. **San Francisco,** open 1000-1300 and 1500-1730, in first block of Jirón Lampa, corner of Ancash, is a baroque church with Arabic influences, finished 1674, under reconstruction. See carved "Sillería Coral" (1622), gold monstrance set with jewels made in Cuzco (1671), and José de Rivera's paintings (1672). The monastery is famous for Sevillian tilework and panelled ceilings in the cloisters (1620). Catacombs under church and part of monastery, well worth seeing; entry charge is US$0.50, by guided tour only, Spanish and English, last groups start at 1245 and 1745 daily. **San Pedro** (open 0700-1300, 1740-2030 every day), 3rd block of Jirón Ucayali, finished by Jesuits in 1638, has marvellous altars with Moorish-style balconies, rich gilded wood carvings in choir and vestry, and tiled throughout. Several Viceroys buried here; the bell called La Abuelita, first rung in 1590, sounded the Declaration of Independence in 1821.

Santuario de Santa Rosa (Av. Tacna, 1st block), small but graceful church. A pilgrimage centre; here are preserved the hermitage built by Santa Rosa herself, the house in which she was born, a section of the house in which she attended to the sick, her well, and other relics. Open 0930-1245 and 1530-1830 daily; entrance to grounds free.

Las Nazarenas Church (Av. Tacna, 4th block, open 0700-1130 and 1630-2000 daily), built around an image of Christ Crucified painted by a liberated slave in 1655. This, the most venerated image in Lima, and an oil copy of El Señor de los Milagros (Lord of Miracles), encased in a gold frame, are carried on a silver litter—the whole weighing nearly a ton—through the streets on October 18, 19, and 28 and again on November 1 (All Saints' Day).

San Agustín (Jirón Ica, 251), W of the Plaza de Armas, is a much changed old church, but its façade (1720) is a splendid example of churrigueresque architecture. There are carved choir stalls and effigies, and a sculpture of Death, said to have frightened its maker into an early grave. Open 0830-1200, 1530-1730 daily, ring for entry. Since being damaged in the last earthquake the church has been sensitively restored, but the sculpture of Death is in storage.

Fine 18th century carving also in gilt altars of **Jesús María** (Jirón Moquegua, 1st block), and in **Magdalena Vieja** (1557, but reconstructed in 1931), with altar pieces, of gilded and carved wood, particularly fine; it should be seen during visit to the Museum of Archaeology, Plaza Bolívar (in Pueblo Libre). Another church worth seeing for its two beautiful colonial doors is **San Marcelo**, at Av. de la Emancipación, 4th block.

The **Convent of Los Descalzos** on the Alameda de Los Descalzos in Rímac contains over 300 paintings of the Cuzco, Quito and Lima schools which line the four main cloisters and two ornate chapels. The chapel of El Carmen was constructed in 1730 and is notable for its baroque gold leaf altar. The museum shows the life of the Franciscan friars during colonial and early republican periods; the cellar, infirmary, pharmacy and a typical cell have all been restored. The library has not yet been incorporated into the tour. The convent is open Mon.-Sat. 0930-1300, 1400-1730, entrance US$1. Guided tour only, 45 mins. in Spanish, but worth it.

The church of **Santo Tomás** is now a school (Gran Unidad Escolar "Mercedes Cabello de Carbonera", on corner of Junín and Andahuaylas); it is said to have the only circular cloister in the world apart from St. Peter's in Rome, and a fine 17th-century Italian-designed baroque library. The headmistress is glad to show people round.
Note: Churches are open between 1830 and 2100 unless otherwise stated.

Museums

N.B. Foreigners visiting museums seem often to be charged more than Peruvians.

Museum of National History, Plaza Bolívar, Pueblo Libre, in a mansion built by Viceroy Pezuela and occupied by San Martín (1821-1822) and Bolívar (1823-1826). Exhibits: colonial and early republican paintings, manuscripts, portraits, uniforms, etc. Paintings mainly of historical episodes. 0900-1730, except Sat. Admission US$0.20. Bus 12 from corner of Tacna and Emancipación, minibus 2 from Rufino Torrico, bus 21, 42, 48 from Parque Universitario.

The Gold Museum (Museo Miguel Mujica Gallo), is in 7th block of Prolongación Av. Primavera (Av. de Molina 1110), Monterrico, several km. from centre (T 352919); bus 76 from Av. Alfonso Ugarte, or bus 2 from Plaza San Martín to Miraflores (corner of Avenida Arequipa and Angamos), then change to colectivo 112 which passes the door (call out "bajo en el museo"); alternatively, take any of the buses (such as 55) going up Angamos, they go past the side road to the museum—bus 59b goes from Parque Unversitario to Angamos (get out after the bridge under Panamericana Sur); by taxi, with 2½ hrs. at the museum, US$10 (US$3 without wait). It is still privately owned. An underground museum contains items which have been exhibited in the world's leading museums. The collection includes precolumbian metals (99 % pre-Inca), weavings, mummies and a remarkable arms collection. Well worth seeing. Open daily (incl. Sun. and holidays) 1200-1900. Admission: US$4, students (with card) half price. No photography allowed. Good copies of ancient pottery are on sale and there are high quality craft shops in the garden.

National Museum of Art, Paseo Colón 125, in the Palacio de la Exposición, built in 1868 in Parque de la Exposición. More than 7,000 exhibits, giving a chronological history of Peruvian cultures and art from the 2,000-year-old Paracas civilization up to today. Excellent examples of 17th and 18th century Cuzco paintings, a beautiful display of carved furniture, heavy silver and jewelled stirrups, also precolumbian pottery. During the autumn and winter seasons, starting in April, there are guided tours, lectures and films every Friday evening (see also under **Cinemas** below). Several good, English-speaking guides. Several times a day there is a multi-screen slide show called "Afirmación del Perú", covering all aspects of Peruvian life. 0900-1900 Tues.-Sun. Admission US$2. Recommended guide: José Luis Vilches, who speaks English and French, and is most helpful and informative.

Museum of the Inquisition, Plaza Bolívar, Calle Junín 548, near corner of Av. Abancay. The main hall, with splendidly carved mahogany ceiling, remains untouched. Court of Inquisition held here 1569-1820; until 1930 used by the Senate. In the basement there is an accurate re-creation *in situ* of the tortures. A description in English is available at the desk. Students offer to show you round for a tip; good explanations in English. Open 0900-1930 Mon.-Fri., 0900-1630, Sat.; entrance free.

DON'T LEAVE THE COUNTRY WITHOUT ONE!

The Bartholomew World travel Series is an invaluable set of maps to help you find your way around unknown territory

The following titles are available for the South American Traveller

South America 1:10 000 000

Argentina, Chile, Paraguay, Uruguay 1:5 000 000

Brazil & Bolivia 1:5 000 000

Peru, Colombia & Venezuela 1:5 000 000

Mexico 1 :3 000 000

West Indies & the Caribbean 1:3 250 000

© John Bartholomew & Son Ltd., 1983

**KEY TO
MAP SECTIONS**

These maps are for interest only
and are not of political significance

⑪

ON THE SAME SCALE

1:16M

miles 0   100   200   300   400
km. 0   200   400   600

South Georgia

Shag Rocks
C. Alexandra   ○Grytviken
C. Disappointment

A T L A N T I C

O C E A N

45°

50°

55°

**FALKLAND ISLANDS
ISLAS MALVINAS**

Jason Is

West Falkland   Stanley
C. Dolphin
Falkland Sd   East Falkland

Weddell   Beauchene Is

Golfo
San Matías
Pto Piramides
○Punta Delgada
Pto Madryn
Trelew
Gaimán   Rawson
Las Plumas

Camarones
C. Dos Bahías

Golfo
Comodoro Rivadavia
Caleta
Olivia   ○San Jorge
○Colonia Las Heras
Deseado
C. Tres Puntas
Pta Médanosa

C h u b u t

Osorno
Pto Varas
Puerto Montt   C. Carlos de
Ancud   **Bariloche**
Castro   El Bolsón
I. de Chiloé   Achao   Ñorquinco
Gastre

Maquinchao
Vienna

Archipiélago
de las
Chones   Melimoyu
2400   Musters
L.C. Huapi
Sarmiento
Esquel
Coihaique
Pto Aisén   Balmaceda
Buenos Aires
Perito

G. de Penas   Pen.
de
Taitao   L. San Valentín   L. Grl Carrera Moreno
4058

Gobernador Gregores
S. Julián

S a n t a   C r u z

Campana   L. Cochrane
Esmeralda   Madre de Dios   L. O'Higgins   Lautaro
L. San Martín   3600
Murallón▲
L. Viedma   Río
Turbio
Hanover   L. Argentino
Arch. de la   Calafate
Reina Adelaida   Pto Natales
Santa Inés

Bahía Grande
Río Gallegos

Est. de Magallanes
Punta Arenas
Porvenir
Pto
Río Grande
Pto Riesco   Peninsula
Brunswick   Isla Grande **Tierra del
de Tierra   Fuego**
Est. de Magallanes   del Fuego   ○Ushuaia
C. San Diego
Desolación   I. de los Estados

Londonderry   Navarino
Hoste   Is Wollaston
C. de Hornos

45°

50°

55°

60°

65°

50°

55°

60°

45°

50°

⑫

TRINIDAD 1:4M

Toco
Arima
Princes Town
Guayaguayare
Port of Spain
Gulf of Paria
San Fernando
Bonasse

TOBAGO 1:4M

Charlotteville
Plymouth
Scarborough
Port Antonio
Port Morant

JAMAICA 1:4M

Montego Bay
Falmouth
St. Ann's Bay
Brown's Town
Annotto Bay
Kingston
Spanish Town
May Pen
Mandeville
Blue Mtn. Pk. 2256m
Mt. Denham 986m
Savanna la Mar
Black River
Portland Point

ATLANTIC OCEAN

BARBADOS
Bridgetown
Tobago
Windward Islands
Leeward Islands
ANTIGUA
Point-à-Pitre
Barbuda
Guadeloupe
Montserrat
DOMINICA
Roseau
Virgin Is.
Anguilla
St. Martin
St. Kitts
Nevis
St. Croix
Martinique
Fort-de-France
ST. LUCIA
Castries
ST. VINCENT
Kingstown
GRENADA
St.Georges
LESSER
ANTILLES
Port of Spain
Asunción
I. Margarita
La Asunción
TRINIDAD
AND TOBAGO

CARIBBEAN SEA

San Juan
Ponce
PUERTO RICO
Mayagüez
Mona Passage
La Romana
Santo Domingo
DOMINICAN REPUBLIC
Santiago
Azua
Hispaniola
Cap-Haïtien
Gonaïves
HAITI
Port au Prince
Les Cayes
Windward Passage
Turks Is.
Caicos Is.

NETHERLAND ANTILLES
Aruba
Curaçao
Bonaire
Willemstad
Pto. Fijo
G. de Venezuela
Coro
La Tortuga
La Guaira
Uribia
Pta. Gallinas
Riohacha
Santa Marta
Barranquilla

THE BAHAMAS
Nassau
Eleuthera I.
Cat I.
Long I.
Andros Is.
Acklins I.
Gt. Inagua I.
Straits of Florida

CUBA
La Habana
Pinar del Rio
Matanzas
Santa Clara
Cienfuegos
Sagua la Grande
Sancti Spíritus
Camagüey
Holguin
Bayamo
Turquino 2005m
C. Cruz
Santiago de Cuba
Guantánamo
I. de la Juventud (I. de Pinos)
Cayman Is.

GREATER ANTILLES

JAMAICA
Montego Bay
Spanish Town
Kingston
Savanna la Mar

1:16M

0   100   200   300   400 miles
0   200   400   600 km.

L. de Caratasca
C. Gracias a Dios
Puerto Cabezas
Prinzapolca
Bluefields
HONDURAS
NICARAGUA

Museum of Anthropology and Archaeology, Plaza Bolívar (San Martín with Antonio Pola), Pueblo Libre (T 611312—not Av. José de la Riva as shown on Cartografía Nacional map), a museum for exhibition and study of art and history of aboriginal races of Peru. Most interesting textiles from Paracas and ceramics of Chimú, Nazca, Mochica and Pachacámac cultures, and various Inca curiosities and works of art. See the Raimondi stella and the Tello obelisk from Chavín, and the marvellous Mochica pottery, and a reconstruction of one of the galleries at Chavín. An impressive model of Machu-Picchu in the Sala Inca. Easily the most interesting museum in Peru. Open Mon.-Sun., 1000-1830. Admission US$0.50, plus US$1 to take photographs with flash. Guide book in English US$4.50. Bus 12 from corner of Tacna and Emancipación, Bus 41M from Cuzco and Emancipacíon, Minibus 2 from Rufino Torrico, also bus 21, 24, 41 or 42 from Parque Universitario. Direction "Avenida Brasil", alight at General Vivanco.

There is also an archaeological museum at Puruchuco (**see page 738**), and at the excavated mound of Santa Catalina, Parque Fernando Carozi in La Victoria (an insalubrious district); minibus 1 or 46 from Plaza 2 de Mayo.

Museo Banco Central de Reserva, Av. Ucayali and Lampa (one block from San Pedro Church, on same side as Torre Tagle Palace). Large collection of pottery from Vicus or Piura culture (AD 500-600) and gold objects from Lambayeque, as well as 19th and 20th century paintings. Both modern and ancient exhibitions highly recommended. (Don't be put off by the sombre bank exterior!) Admission US$0.05, Tues.-Fri. 1000-1700. Photography prohibited.

Museo Etnográfico de la Selva, Av. Tacna 120 (4 blocks NW of Plaza de Armas), houses cultural and household objects from Madre de Dios; run by Dominicans, open every day (except Mon.) until 1900, US$0.10.

Museum of Peruvian Culture, Av. Alfonso Ugarte 650, showing pots and popular art, and costumes worn by Indians in various parts of Peru, includes exhibition of *mate burilado* (carved gourds); open 1000-1700, Mon.-Fri., 0900-1700, Sat. Admission US$0.10; US$0.70 to take photographs.

Rafael Larco Herrera Museum, Av. Bolívar 1515, Pueblo Libre, is the Chiclín pottery museum brought from Trujillo. The greatest number of exhibits stem from the Mochica period (AD 400-800). The Cupisnique period, dating back to 1000 BC, and the Nazca, Chimú, and Inca periods are also well represented. There is an erotica section in a separate building. This is a museum for the pottery specialist; it is more like a warehouse than a museum, but the general visitor will enjoy the excellent collection of precolumbian weaving, including a sample of two-ply yarns with 398 threads to the inch. Also several mummified weavers buried with their looms and a small display of gold pieces. Admission US$3 (US$1.50 student-card holders), open Mon.-Sat., 0900-1300, 1500-1800, Sun. and holidays, 0900-1300. Photography not permitted. Bus 23 from Avenida Abancay, or minibus 37 from Av. Nicolás de Piérola (Colmena) or taxi (US$2).

Museum of the Viceroyalty (Quinta de Presa), is a fine 18th century mansion. Exhibits: colonial portraits, furniture, dresses, candelabra, and so on; one of the Viceroy's carriages is shown. Closed since 1986 for repairs.

Museo Histórico Militar (Real Felipe Fortress, Callao), has interesting military relics: a cannon brought by Pizarro, a cannon used in the War of Independence, the flag that flew during the last Spanish stand in the fortress, portraits of General Rodil and of Lord Cochrane, and the remains of the small Bleriot plane in which the Peruvian pilot, Jorge Chávez, made the first crossing of the Alps from Switzerland to Italy: he was killed when the plane crashed at Domodossola on Sept. 23, 1910. Open 0900-1200 and 1500-1700, Tues., Wed., Thurs.; 1400-1730, Sat., Sun. Entrance free. Closed April-August. Bus No. 63 from Post Office in Jirón Lima. The **Museo Miguel Grau,** Calle Lezcano 170 (near Basílica La Merced, just off Jr. Unión), is the house of Admiral Grau and has mementoes of the War of the Pacific. **Museo Morro de Arica,** Cailloma 125, Tues.-Fri., 1130-1900, gives the Peruvian view of the famous battle. **Museo Naval** (Av. Jorge Chávez, off Plaza Grau, Callao), open 0900-1230, 1500-1730 on Mon., Wed., Fri. and Sat. Admission free. Bus 63 from Post Office in Jirón Lima.

Museo Hospital Dos de Mayo open 0900-1800 daily, admission US$1.25.

Museo Peruano de Ciencias de la Salud, Jr. Junín 270 (just off Plaza de Armas), houses a collection of ceramics and mummies, showing precolumbian lifestyle; divided into five sections: *micuy* (Quechua for food), *hampi* (medicine), *onccoy* (disease), *hampini* (healing) and *causay* (life). Minibus Nos. 35 or 42 from Miró Quesada. Open: Mon.-Sat., 0900-1700, very interesting indeed. Admission, US$1. A guide is available in Spanish; signs in English and Spanish.

Pinacoteca Municipal (Municipal Building, Plaza de Armas), contains a large collection of paintings by Peruvian artists. The best of the painters is Ignacio Merino (1817-1876). Rooms and furnishings very ornate. Open: Mon.-Fri., 0900-1300.

Museum of Italian Art (Paseo de la República, 2nd block), is in a building, Italian renaissance style, given by the Italian colony to Peru on the centenary of its independence. Open Tues.-Sun., 0900-1900, but 0900-2000 on Fri., US$0.50. Large collection of Italian works of art, but most of the paintings are reproductions, including lithographs and etchings. Now also houses Institute of Contemporary Art, which has many exhibitions.

Museum of Natural History (Av. Arenales 1250) belongs to University of San Marcos. Exhibits: Peruvian flora, birds, mammals, butterflies, insects, minerals and shells. Prize exhibit is a sun fish (more plaster than fish)—only two other examples known, one in Japan and another in New Zealand. Open Mon.-Fri. 0830-1530, Sat. 0830-1200, 0900-1300; admission US$0.12. Bus No. 54A or minibuses 13 and 73 from Av. Tacna.

Philatelic Museum (Central Post Office, off Plaza de Armas). Open 0800-1330, 1400-1600, Mon.-Fri., 0800-1330, Sat., 0900-1200, Sun. Incomplete collection of Peruvian stamps and information on the Inca postal system. There is a stamp exchange in front of the museum every Sat. and Sun., 0900-1300. You can buy stamps here as well (shop hours: Mon.-Fri., 0800-1200, 1400-1500).

Bullfight Museum (Hualgayoc 332, Plaza de Acho, Rímac). Apart from matadors' relics, contains good collections of paintings and engravings— some of the latter by Goya. Open 0900-1300, 1500-1800. Closed Sat., Sun. and holidays in the afternoons. Admission US$0.20.

Contemporary Folk Art Museum, Saco Olivero 163, between Arenales and 3rd block of Arequipa, recommended. Shop in museum grounds. Open Tues.-Fri., 1430-1900; Sat. 0830-1200.

Amano Museum (Calle Retiro 160, Miraflores). A very fine private collection of artefacts from the Chancay, Chimú and Nazca periods owned by Mr. Yoshitaro Amano—one of the most complete exhibits of Chancay weaving. Particularly interesting for pottery and precolumbian textiles, all superbly displayed and lit. Open Mon.-Fri. Guided tours 1400, 1500, 1600, 1700. T 412909, at least one day in advance, for an appointment; try to get a small group (under 10) first. Admission free (photography prohibited). Bus No. 73 or Santa Cruz minibus (no. 13) from Av. Tacna, get out at Av. Angamos. Calle Retiro is unmarked: it is the street on your right as you stand with your back to the Pacific on the 11th block of Angamos.

Pedro de Osma Museum (Av. Pedro de Osma 421, Barranco). A private collection of colonial art of the Cuzco, Ayacucho and Arequipa schools. T 670019 for an appointment. No. 54A bus from Av. Tacna. (Apparently this museum is now closed.)

Numismatic Museum, Banco Wiese, 2nd floor, Cuezo 245, T 275060 ext. 553, open Mon.-Fri., 0900-1300, free admission. Peruvian coins from the colonial era to the present day.

Museum of Mineral Specimens at Krystal S.A., León Velarde 537, Lince, Lima 14 (T 710713, 711379).

Museo Miniatura de la Plaza de Armas del Siglo XIX in the house of Dr. César Revoredo, Salaverry 3052, is a private small scale reproduction of the Plaza de Armas in the last century. Dr. Revoredo also has a fine collection of prints by Rancho Fierro, the 19th century *costumbrista* watercolour artist.

Casa Galería de Esculturas de Sra. Marina Núñez del Prado, Antero Aspillaga 300, Olivar de San Isidro, another private collection, of fine sculpture; phone for an appointment on Weds., or Sats. Two more private collections that are occasionally open to visitors on application by telephone are: the collection of precolumbian artefacts belonging to Sra. Elsa Cohen, Esquina Larraburre Unánue 392 (Bus 54A, or minibus 13 from Tacna), and, at Parque Hernán Velarde 199, the collection of rural handicrafts (pottery, engraved gourds, etc.) belonging to Sra. E. Luza (bus 13, Tacna with Emancipación, or bus 2 from corner of Plaza San Martín).

Galería Wari 69, Cailloma 630, exhibits the tapestries of the Sulca family of Ayacucho; traditional designs and techniques are used in their beautiful work.

For those interested in modern Peruvian art, a gallery has been opened at Independencia 812, Miraflores, T 451058, by Gaston Garreaud, who speaks English and French and will kindly guide you if you make an appointment. Admission free.

Note Some museums are only open between 0900 and 1300 from Jan. to March, and some close altogether in January. Many are closed at weekends and on Monday.

Parks and Gardens

Lima and its suburbs have many parks and gardens. **Alameda de los Descalzos**, at the foot of the Cerro San Cristóbal, was laid out as early as 1610; it is a walk shaded by ancient trees and fenced by a wrought-iron grille. It was once a haunt of Lima's aristocracy. The marble statues, each representing a month of the year, and the marble seats date from 1856. Nearby is another walk, the **Paseo de Aguas,** created by the Viceroy Amat in the 18th century to please his mistress, La Perricholi. The great arch with cascades was rebuilt in 1938. This walk is in extremely poor condition.

Campo de Marte (Plaza Jorge Chávez and Av. Salaverry), a large open park, reportedly full of thieves and drug-pushers now. In the centre is a huge monument to the Peruvian soldier. The National Symphony Orchestra plays in the auditorium on the W side during the summer.

Parque Universitario, where the old San Carlos Jesuit church was turned into a **Pantheon of the Heroes** (Panteón de los Próceres) on the 100th anniversary of the Battle of Ayacucho. A graceful 18th century church with a circle of famous tombs under the rotunda. General Miller, the Englishman who fought in the wars of independence, and whose memoirs contain an excellent picture of the time, is buried here, and so is Admiral Guise, of Gloucestershire, who was killed at Guayaquil. Also the poet and composer who wrote the Peruvian national anthem. Next to the church is the former building of San Marcos University, which has now been restored and is used for meetings and conferences. Worthy of a visit are the beautiful patio and the small archaeological museum. In the centre is the clock tower presented by the German colony on the centenary of Peruvian independence. On the far corner of the park is the tall Ministry of Education building.

Between Paseo Colón and Av. 28 de Julio is **Parque de La Exposición**, a quiet place shaded by trees; several of the main avenues border it. It was opened for the 1868 International Exhibition. The great Palace of the Exhibition, facing Paseo Colón, is now the Museum of Art. South of the Parque de La Exposición is the **Parque Japonés**, which has a small admission fee.

Parque de la Reserva (Av. Arequipa, 6th block). In the middle is a statue of Sucre; of the other two statues, one is of Tangüis, who selected the famous cotton. By the park is the Edificio El Pacífico-Washington (British and Israeli embassies).

Parque las Leyendas, between Lima and Callao, is arranged to represent the three regions of Peru: the coast, the mountainous Sierra, and the tropical jungles of the Montaña, with appropriate houses, animals and plants, children's playground. Elephants and lions have been introduced so the zoo is no longer purely Peruvian (not recommended at weekends, too crowded). The Park is open 0900-1700 (closed Mon.), entrance US$0.35. There is a handicrafts fair (Feria Artesanal) at the entrance to the park; particularly good insect specimens can be bought here. Buses 2 from Av. Tacna, 23 and 57 from Plaza Dos de Mayo; also minibus 75 from Jirón Azángaro goes direct to the park.

Warning With the deterioration of the economy in the late 1980s, the centre of Lima has become run down, generally unsafe and, apparently with little of interest to visitors in the shops. Until conditions improve visitors are recommended to base themselves in San Isidro, Miraflores or Barranco (see **suburbs** below), and use caution when sightseeing in the historic centre. There have been reports of theft from hotel rooms left briefly unattended; also, small, sparsely-populated hotel lobbies are popular targets. Be especially careful in or near bus stations and on Miraflores beach. Never carry unnecessary money or valuables, and don't wear jewellery. It may be wise to take a taxi if carrying a backpack; slashing is very common.

Festivals January 18, Founding of Lima; July 28, Independence, with music and fireworks in Plaza de Armas on evening before; last week of August, Cañete; October, month of Our Lord of the Miracles with impressive processions (see *El Comercio* for dates and routes); November (every other year), Pacific International Fair.

Hotels Prices very negotiable outside peak July-August holiday season. There is a 12% tax on hotel rooms, and a service charge of 13% is usually added (neither is included in prices below). In cheaper hotels water may be scarce in the middle of the day. The more expensive hotels charge in dollars according to the parallel rate of exchange at midnight.

Name	Address	Beds	Single (US$)	Double (US$)	Price Range
Miraflores César	La Paz y Diez Canseco, Miraflores		78	89	L
Lima Sheraton	Paseo de la República 170	650	100-110	100-110	L
Gran Bolívar	Unión 958, Plaza San Martín (Tel.: 276400 Telex: 25201 PECP)	440	75	90	L
Crillón	Colmena 589 (Tel.: 283290, Telex: 25274PE)	700	60	80	L
Country Club	Los Eucaliptos, San Isidro	150	45	55	A
Plaza*	Nicolás de Piérola 850	56	36	43	B
Continental	Puno 196	150	20	28	C
Gran Maury	Ucayali 201	140	30	40	B
Savoy	Cailloma 224	400	23	33	B
Ariosto*	Av. La Paz, Miraflores (Tel.: 441414, Telex: 21195)	230	31	41	B
Riviera	Inca Garcilaso de la Vega 981	300	36	46	A
Columbus*	Av. Arequipa 1421	150	14	23	C

La Granja Azul *Country Inn*	16 km. out, off Central Highway	30	43	B
El Pardo	Av. Pardo 420, Miraflores (Tel.: 470283)	70	80	L
*María Angola**	Av. La Paz 610, Miraflores	60	70	A

* Recommended.

Accommodation in Miraflores: *El Condado* (close to *César*), L, deluxe. *José Antonio*, 28 de Julio 398, A, clean, friendly, good restaurant, rec.; *Residencial 28 de Julio*, 28 de Julio 531, T 470636/473891, C, with breakfast, parking, café and bar, phone and bathroom with each room, lax security, otherwise rec.; *Hostal El Ejecutivo*, Av. 28 de Julio 245, T 476310, D, with each bath and breakfast, clean, tariff negotiable for long stay, safe, luggage can be left; *Hostal La Alameda*, Av. José Pardo 930, D with limited breakfast, friendly, quiet, safe, clean, rec.; *Hostal Residencial Torreblanca*, Av. José Pardo 1453, C, including breakfast and tax, quiet, friendly, clean, helpful, rec.; *Ovalo*, Av. José Pardo, Plaza Morales Barros, C, quiet, good, breakfast served; *Colonial Inn*, Cmdte. Espinar 310, T 466666, C, room service, TV, parking; *Hostal El Patio*, Diez Canseco 341 (next to *Miraflores César*), C with reductions for long stays, clean, comfortable, friendly, English and French spoken; *Hostal La Castellana*, Grimaldo del Solar 222 (3 blocks E of Larco, between Schell and Benavides), T 443530, 444662, C (D off season), with bath, pleasant, good value, nice garden, safe, cafeteria, laundry, English spoken; *Hostal Señorial*, José González 567 (T 459724/457306), C, 60 rooms all with bath, including tax and breakfast, rec., clean, friendly, well-appointed, garden; *Hostal Palace*, Av. Miraflores 1088, C, very clean, comfortable, friendly; *Pensión San Antonio*, Paseo de la República 5809, T 475830, E, shared bathroom, clean, comfortable, friendly, helpful, ask for hot water; *Hostal Huaychulo*, Av. Dos de Mayo 494, excellent (German owner-manager); *Hostal Benavides*, Av. Benavides, block 22 (out of centre of Miraflores), D, good for longer stays; *Hostal Residencial Kimari*, Pasaje Los Pinos 156, piso C, Edificio El Comodoro, T 422266/422177, D for stays of more than week, clean, modern, safe, friendly; *Pensión Lucerna*, Calle Las Dalias 276 (corner Av. Larco), C with breakfast, friendly, clean, T 457321, rec.; *Pensión Hernández Romano*, Ugarriza 727, San Antonio district, D, use of kitchen, very friendly English-speaking owner; *Hostal Catalina*, Toribio Polo 248 (½ block W of Av. Ejercito blocks 7/8), D negotiable, friendly, English spoken, bath, good transport connexions, T 410192/424037; *Concorde*, Av. Ricardo Palma, D, modern and clean; *Hostal Miraflores*, Av. Petit Thouars 5444, D, leave valuables at desk, English and German spoken; *Bailiwick's Lodge*, Colón 577-79, T 471749 (no sign), E, English spoken, clean; Sra Greti Jordan, Porta 724, T 459840, E with breakfast, friendly, German lady, who speaks English. *Winnie's Bed and Breakfast*, La Calera de Monterrico, M-13, Lima 34 (close to Miraflores), T 455864, C, run by Winnie Reyes de Espinosa of VIP Travel Service, warmly rec. *Imperial Inn*, Av. Bolognesi, E, clean, but noisy and run-down; *Hostal José Luis*, Paula de Ugarriza 727, T 441015, F, pleasant, friendly, use of kitchen, rec. Visitors with vehicles are recommended to stay in Miraflores, since parking is difficult in the centre.

Accommodation at San Isidro, *Hostal San Isidro Inn*, Av. Pezet 1761, just off Salaverry; *Hostal Limatambo*, Av. Aramburú 1025, B, T 419615, 24-hour snack bar, won the "América-86" award for good service and quality; *Residencial Beech*, Los Libertadores 165, T 40-5595, C, with bath, including breakfast, rec.; *Garden*, rec., A, good, large beds, shower, small restaurant; *Hostal Santa Mónica*, Av. Pezet 1419, D, T 419280, rec.; *Residencial Los Petirrojos*, Petirrojos 230, Corpac (Sra. Miri), D, T 416044, clean, spacious, breakfast included; *Hostal Callacocha*, Coronel Andrés Reyes 100, C, very good; *Hostal El Olivar*, Raymundo Morales de la Torre 385, T 417745, C with bath, friendly, garden, nice restaurant; *Hostal Firenze*, Chinchón (2 blocks from Las Camelias), T 227382, D, clean, family-run, hot water, English and Italian spoken, highly rec.; *Pensión Doratina*, Los Cedros 285, D, excluding food (which is pricey), very good; *Sans Souci*, Av. Arequipa 2670, towards Miraflores, B with bath, clean, gloomy, noisy; *Residencial Javier

Prado, Av. Javier Prado Este 461, C with bath, toilet and breakfast (front rooms noisy), good, 4 blocks from colectivo to centre, transport to airport US$8; *Hostal Antarki*, Chacarilla 250, clean, quiet, helpful, E.

In Barranco, *Barranco*, D, Malecón Osma 104, converted mansion above the cliffs, swimming pool, access to beach, good views of sunset from the garden; *Armendariz*, Av. Armendariz (between Miraflores and Barranco), E, on convenient 2 bus line, cable TV, rec. In Magdalena del Mar, *Hostal Magdalena del Mar*, Jirón Miraflores (off Av. Brasil), T 611336, E (triples available), all rooms with bath and hot water, good restaurant (also hourly rates); *Los Cóndores*, Domingo Ponte 874, Magdalena Mar, C with bath, cheaper rooms available, safe, warm water, clean, free transport from airport, tour guide (Alfredo) operates from here. In Lince is *Hostal Ambassador*, Julio C. Tello 650, clean, safe, hot water, E, highly rec.

In central Lima: *Pensión Astoria*, Camino Real 155, C, with bath and breakfast; also has small apartments with kitchenette and maid service, US$22 per night. *Hostal Los Virreyes*, Jirón Cañete 826, C, comfortable, clean, hot water, central position, a bit noisy, rec.; *Hostal Renacimiento*, Parque Hernán Velarde 52, D, cheaper at the back, in a quiet cul-de-sac 2 blocks from central bus station, 10 mins walk from centre, not all rooms with bath but clean, helpful, T 318461/ 324821; *Pensión* at Hernán Velarde 72, run by Pablo W.See, C, very good, 5 mins. by bus from centre. *Hostal del Sol*, Rufino Torrico 773, C, with shower, helpful, fairly quiet, clean, safe, rec.; *Claridge*, Cailloma 437, D, with bath, friendly, good, hot water, takes most credit cards; *Hostal San Martín*, Av. Nicolás de Piérola 882, 2nd floor, Plaza San Martín, T 285377, rec., good value, C inc. taxes, a/c, with bath, breakfast served in room, helpful, money changing facilities, Japanese run, good restaurant, good service; *Granada*, on Huancavelica 323, T 279033, D without breakfast, clean, safe, hot water, English spoken, friendly; *Grand Castle*, Av. Carlos Zavala Loayza 218, opp. Ormeño bus station, D, including breakfast (poor), hot water, comfortable, good service, Japanese restaurant, rec.; *Residencial Santa Rosa*, Camaná 218, D, with bath, quiet, some hot water, laundry service. *Hostal La Bayamesa*, Angamos 8100, corner of Colmena, D, including continental breakfast, good, clean, English spoken. *Casa Vasca*, Carabaya 1033, good full board, D; *Hostal Belén*, Belén 1049, just off San Martín, Italian spoken, F, very popular, basic breakfast extra, hot water, friendly, music groups practising; *Asociación de Amistad Peruano Europea*, Jirón Camaná 280, 7th floor, F, dormitory (16 beds), one shower, clean, friendly, laundry facilities, will store luggage. Cheaper accommodation includes *Damasco*, Jirón Ucayali 199, a block from Plaza de Armas, F, shower, hot water, drab, friendly, stores luggage, rec. *El Dorado*, N. de Piérola, E with bath, clean and friendly, some rooms rented by the hour; *Hostal Niza*, N. de Piérola 206, F (triples available), breakfast, friendly, central, clean but not so the toilets, basic, noisy; *Europa*, Jirón Ancash 376, near Plaza San Francisco, G (s, or shared rooms, F for d.), no hot water, safe, will store luggage, some rooms without windows, mixed reports, three cafés in same block; *Pacífico*, Carabaya 113, near presidential palace and station, F, only front rooms have windows, basic, hippy, convenient; *Hostal San Sebastián*, Ica 712, T 23-2740, run by Nellie de Viana, F, clean, friendly, English spoken, popular, rec. gringo place, safe to leave luggage, bit noisy on street corner, restaurant and laundry facilities (runs taxi service to airport); *Hostal España*, Jr. Azángaro 105, F, in a restored house in old Lima, hot water, secure, rec.; *Residencial Roma*, Ica 326, T 277576, E, hot water, safe to leave luggage, quiet, basic but clean, rec., often full (good pastry shop below); *Gran*, Av. Abancay 546, F, spacious rooms, old, eccentric, safe, private bath; *Pensión Ibarra*, Av. Tacna 359, Apt. 162, 15th and 16th floors, no sign, E, including breakfast (less if staying several days), clean, friendly, very helpful owner, full board available; *Hostal Eiffel*, Jr. Washington 949, very clean, hot water, cheaper taxis to airport; *Hostal El Paraíso*, Jirón Unión 428, down a passageway, past bookshop, F, hot water all day, but erratic water supply, safe, dormitory and communal bathroom; *Hostal El Tambo*, Av. Bolognesi 373, D, including breakfast, laundry, dry cleaners and supermarket all nearby. *Pensión Alemana*, Av. Arequipa 4704 T 456999, C, comfortable, clean, excellent breakfast (triple-rooms available) book in advance, laundry service extra; *Hostal Colombia*, Av. Colombia 137 (with Av. Brasil), D, beware overcharging, with breakfast, clean, friendly, good; *Hostal Samaniego*, Av. Emancipación 184, Apto. 801, near Plaza San Martín, G, rec., 15 spaces available, hot water, friendly, safe; *Casa de Hospedaje*, Pasaje Acisclo Villarán 365, no sign, central, E, F without breakfast, clean, homely, good; *Pensión Sra. Bertha Bonilla de Barboza*, Montero Rosas 1379, E, including 3 meals; *Familia Rodríguez*, Av. N. de Piérola 730, 2nd floor, T 236465, F with breakfast, clean, friendly, will store luggage, dormitory accommodation with only one bathroom; *Residencial Francia*, Samuel Velarde 185, Av. Ejército, T 617054, D including taxes and breakfast, bath, hot water, laundry facilities, swimming pool, gardens, very friendly and helpful, 20 min. bus ride from centre; *Pensión Flory*, E, Urb. Sta. Florencia, Calle Guido 182, San Miguel, clean, hot water, popular with Germans; Sra. López, Jr. Carlos Baca Flor 421 in Urb. Ingeniería, near Avenida Eduardo Habich, also good, F. Spanish-speaking travellers who prefer family accommodation can contact Yolanda Cueva, T 363277. If arriving by air, especially at night, a visit to the tourist office at the airport (beyond passport control) is helpful if you want to arrange a hotel room. **Hotel reservations** for Lima and elsewhere in Peru can be made through Centro de Reservaciones, Av. Panamericana 6251, San Antonio/Miraflores, T 466-895.

Youth Hostel   *Albergue Juvenil Internacional*, Av. Casimiro Ulloa 324, Miraflores, T 465-488, F, basic cafeteria, travel information, laundry facilities, double rooms and dormitories, swimming pool often empty, "spacious, clean and safe". Open to non-members of the Youth Hostel Association, ten minutes walk from the beach. (Transhotel bus between airport and Plaza San Martín passes, so does Ikaros bus (Av. Benavides stop), so does bus No. 2 from Av. Tacna to Miraflores, 30 mins. to centre; taxi to centre, US$6.)

Camping   Under no circumstances camp on or near beach at Miraflores, theft and worse is rife in these areas. Propane gas in heavy iron gas bottles available from Delta-Gas, Av. Benavides (former Colonial) 5425, Lima. Camping gas (in small blue bottles) available from Técnica Import, Dávalos Lisson 323, nr. Washington, 0900-1300 and 1400-1700. Oechsle sell butane gas cartridges. N.B. Airlines do not allow the carriage of gas bottles.

Baths   Baños Pizarro, Unión 284, steam rooms, US$3, cold showers only, café and swimming pool.

Restaurants   In central Lima *Skyroom, Hotel Crillón*, good food and service, about US$25 p.p.; *Gran Hotel Bolívar* offers a quick lunch for US$3 and a 3-course executive lunch for US$6. *L'Eau Vive*, Ucayali 370, across from the Torre Tagle Palace, run by nuns, open Mon.-Sat., 1245-1430, 2030-2230, fixed-price US$4 lunch menu, Peruvian-style in interior dining room, or à la carte in either of dining rooms that open on to patio, excellent, profits go to the poor. *Las Trece Monedas*, in an old colonial mansion off Av. Abancay (Ancash 536), excellent, local food, insist on an itemized bill; *Domino*, in an arcade off Unión, near San Martín, good, Swiss-owned, expensive, rec. *Goyescas*, Plaza S. Martín, good food (full meal including drinks, US$6.20 p.p.); *Parrilladas San Martín*, Plaza San Martín (opposite *Bolívar*), rec. (especially the anticuchos and sauces), US$5-8; *1900*, Belén 1030, very good, US$15 for dinner, drinks and salads in patio, live music from 1930. *La Reserva*, Emilio Fernández 330 (near Parque de la Reserva), very good, expensive. *Balcón Colonial*, intersection of Jr. Cuzco and Camaná, open 1130-1530, good lunches. *Las Papas Fritas*, Av. Colmena, good meals for US$10; *Lukyi*, Callao 300, good Chinese, reasonable; another *chifa* in 6th block of Jirón Ica, friendly, food highly rec.; *Chifa Santos*, N. de Piérola, opp. *Hotel Colmena*, rec. *Café de París*, reasonable, N. de Piérola; *Giannino*, Rufino Torrico 899 (good Italian food); *La Granja Azul* (also hotel—see list above), Carretera Central (turn off between Km. 13 and 14 of Carretera Central, buses from Parque Universitario every 15 minutes; last bus back leaves 2000 but a minibus leaves the hotel for Lima at 2200), specializing in exotic cocktails and chicken dishes, dancing every night, rec.; *Rincón del Pescador,* opposite *Hotel Crillón*, excellent but expensive, US$20 per head; *Rico's Pizzería Americana*, Nicolás de Piérola 514, good, friendly service; *Chalet Suisse*, Av. Nicolás de Piérola 560, rec., international and Peruvian cuisine. *Rosita Ríos*, Av. El Altillo 100, Rímac, for highly seasoned Peruvian food at reasonable prices, to and from centre by bus No. 10; *Mesón La Ronda*, in the bullring, has an excellent bullfight museum. *Raimondi*, Miró Quesada 110, excellent, not too expensive. Cheaper restaurants include: *Alberto*, Carabaya 322, good food, plenty of it, reasonably priced, friendly; *Jerry's Restaurant and Coffee Bar*, Carabaya 336, simple, clean, cheap, open Sun. p.m.; *Rincón Toni*, Nicolás de Piérola, friendly service, rec., main dishes US$3 (German and Swiss food, good); *El Torreón*, Jirón Camaná 571, good, US$1.50 p.p.; *Ciervo de Oro*, Jr. Ica 322, good empanadas and cakes; *El Barroco*, Jr. Cañete 349, good and reasonable; *Don Juan* (off Plaza de Armas), good and cheap, open from about 1000, but not open late or on Sundays. Rec. is *Casa Camaná* on Camaná, south of N. de Piérola. Also try Rímac district, over Puente de Piedra, for cheaper food, e.g. the chicken restaurants on Av. Trujillo. There are several inexpensive restaurants on Av. Venezuela, and good snack-bars on Unión, particularly *Las Vegas*, western-style, good, cheap. On Jirón Ancash and Av. Abancay (near Buena Muerte church) there are restaurants serving good lunches. *Machu Picchu*, Azángaro 142, good, cheap, popular, also Jr. Ancash, next to *Hostal San Francisco*.

There is a reasonable vegetarian restaurant at Carabaya 744, where a meal costs US$1.05; also *Asociación Naturista Peruana*, Jirón Ucayali 133; *Natur*, Moquegua 132, rec., some English spoken; *Cooperativa de la Naturaleza*, less good, Moquegua 305 and Camaná 489; *Gran Fraternidad Universal*, Garcilaso de la Vega 911, 11th floor, lunch only US$1, another branch in Lince, César Vallejo y Arequipa.

For students, *Comedor Universitario Congallo*, filling meal for US$0.20. *Soda Bar La Esquina del Sabor*, Junín 500 and Moreno, rec.; decor basic but typical food good. A good coffee bar for snacks and sandwiches is *Googies* in Plaza San Martín; also *Tivoli* bar, Nicolás de Piérola 820; *Sandwich Tacna*, Tacna 327, popular and crowded at lunchtime. *Balkan*, Av. Tacna 555, good food (German spoken). There are good cheap fish restaurants near Parque Universitario. *El Rinascate*, NW corner of Parque Universitario, good and cheap. *Colonial* on Emancipación by Cailloma; *La Buena Muerte*, Jr. Paruro 394, corner Ancash, seafood, popular, open Mon.-Sat. 1200-1400. *El Abuelo*, Jr Camaná, spit-roast chicken, moderately clean; *Pizzería Romana*, Av. Sucre near hospital, good Italian food and pizzas, near Pueblo Libre museums; *Snack-bar Koala*, Camaná, Italian and Peruvian food, good, friendly, clean. *Alemania* pastry shop (near *Pensión Ibarra*, Swiss-run) is good, as is *Munich Cakehouse*, Cailloma 329 and Ica. Good bread rolls at

Hostal **Barranco** Lima 4 Peru
Tel. 671753 Fax 671719

Only ten minutes (10 km) from the noisy and congested center of Lima (23 km from the airport) located above the cliffs, overlooking the ocean. A converted mansion with a quiet, relaxing and homely atmosphere. At your feet Lima's most popular beaches (private access – beach Las Sombrillas). Swimming pool, sauna, dining room (also vegetarian food) piano bar, fitness room, billiards, ping-pong, front and inner gardens. Spacious double rooms, some with private bath, balcony, fireplace, bar-refrigerator, television and telephone. English, German, French spoken. Great security against robberies, etc. Double $ US 8 to $ 30 (depending on room).

MALECON OSMA 104, Barranco. Tel. 671753 (Priv. 671738 Fax. 671719)

corner of Moquegua and Unión. *Pastelería Lobatón*, Jr. Unión 672, good churros; *El Pan Nuestro*, Jr. Ica 265.

In San Isidro these restaurants are rec.: *Aquarium* (at the *Country Club Hotel*); the restaurant formerly called *La Barca*, Av. del Ejército 2195, excellent but expensive sea food; *Los Condes de San Isidro* (Av. Paz Soldán 290—an 18th-century mansion—T 222557) excellent; *Génova*, Av. Petit Thouars 3865, good, reasonable; *Valentino's*, Calle M. Bañón (near Camino Real and Av. Javier Prado), excellent food and service; *Don Adolfo*, Manuel Bañon 295, excellent food, helpful, friendly; *Los Cántaros de Darío*, Guillermo Prescott 337, excellent seafood in colonial-style setting, reasonable. *Chifa Mandarín*, rec., cheap and excellent; *Micasa* (Japanese); *Fredo*, very busy and good, on Conquistadores. *Blue Room* at Las Begonias 379; *Steak House*, Las Camelias 870, open 1200-2400, serves Argentine steak (about US$20 for 3 courses).

In Miraflores we recommend the following: *Miraflores César Hotel*; *Dom Beta*, José Gálvez 667, excellent seafood, moderate prices; *Rosa Náutica*, built on old British-type pier (Espignon No. 4) in Lima bay, near Miraflores, not to be missed, delightful opulence, finest cuisine (US$30 p.p.), sunset rec.; *Vivaldi*, Ricardo Palma 258, US$5-7 p.p., also for drinks and snacks, nice atmosphere; Italian restaurant at Benavides 346, good; *Café Restaurant Strauss*, Benavides 400, rec. for Peruvian and seafood dishes in German style at moderate prices; *El Faisán*, Diez Canseco 10, for traditional food; *Las Tejas*, Diez Canseco 340, good anticuchos and seafood at reasonable prices; *Parrillada en la Parque*, Av. Petit Thouars (N end), good steaks, expensive; huge steaks at *La Tranquera*, Av. Pardo 285; *Casiopeia Bar* at Centro Comercial Aurora, Swiss and Peruvian dishes, Swiss-owned; *El Dorado* (Chinese), Av. Arequipa, good food, expensive; *Kuo Wha*, Paseo de la República 5046; *Ajinomen*, Calle Los Pinos (between Benavides and Schell), Chinese, good; *Lau's Chifa*, Ricardo Palma 322, good and cheap Chinese food; *La Costa Verde* (on Barranquito beach, excellent food and wine, but expensive). *Rincón Gaucho* on Malecón at Av. Larco end and *El Gaucho*, not far away on Av. Larco, two of the best steak-houses in Peru, both serve superb steaks imported from Argentina; *Café Lusitania*, Av. Larco, good international cooking; *Haiti*, Av. Benavides, good food, cheap, rec. *La Colina*, Schell 727, cheap and good; *Kentucky Fried Chicken*, also Av. Schell. *Salad House*, Av. Grau 164, 42 different salads, very good, open (except Mon.), 1230-1530, 1930-2300. Typical Peruvian restaurants can be found at the end of Avenida Brasil, including *Gran Chifa Brasil*, opposite Av. Javier Prado.

Vegetarian restaurants are *Bircher Berner*, Av. Schell 598, good value, *Govinda*, Schell 630, and *Koricancha*, Petit Thouars 2686, 3rd floor. Try also *Carlín*, Av. La Paz 644, excellent, expensive, seafood specialities, good coffee; *Le Bistro*, in El Suche pedestrian mall, small, French, expensive; also in El Suche, *El Condado*, rec., and among other restaurants (and good shopping) in same area is *La Crêperie*, delicious filled pancakes; *Manolo*, Larco 608, good food, meals US$2, popular, rec.; *The Brenchley Arms*, Atahualpa 174, T 459680, English pub serving English food, English speaking, informal and relaxed, tourist information. *Friday's Pub*, on Benavides just S off Av. Larco, rec.; *Café Suisse*, main square, for cakes, coffee, European-style food and delicatessen. *La Tiendecita Blanca*, opp. *El Pacífico*, tea rooms/delicatessen, good cakes, sandwiches, coffee. Good ice cream at *Lamborghini*, Av. Larco, *Helados Sabores*, Av. Larco, *Heladería Italiana*, Angamos Oeste 408 (really excellent); *Pastelería Sueca*, Av. Larco 759, good hamburgers, pastries and salads. Good pisco sours at *El Estribo*, Av. Larco; just off Av. Larco are *Vivaldi*, Ricardo Palma 258, T 471636, expensive but good and *Liverpool*, good food, Beatles music and décor.

In Barranco, *El Otre Sitio*, Sucre 317, excellent Creole Buffet US$4-5, live music; *El Buen Gusto*, Av. Grau 323, good atmosphere and service; *El Puente*, below Puente de los Suspiros; *Karamaduke*; *La Casa de Florentino*.

In Magdalena, *José Antonio* (Peruvian food, music after 2200), Monteagudo 210 B, strongly rec.

In Monterrico, near the Gold Museum, *Pabellón de la Caza*, expensive, but very good food and service, "sumptuous gastronomic treat". Also *Puerto Fiel*, Av. Primavera 1666, 3 blocks from Gold Museum, rec., seafood.

N.B. Most restaurants now have 20% added to the bill: 15% for tip and 5% for taxes (although this can vary according to the restaurant; some show no extra charges at all).

Electric Current 220 volts A.C., 60 cycles throughout the country, except Arequipa (50 cycles).

Clubs Phoenix Club, Av. Nicolás de Piérola 1014, 3rd floor (Plaza San Martín). Lima Cricket and Football Club, Justo Vigil 200, Magdalena del Mar, T 610080/ 614030; anyone with a Commonwealth passport can become a temporary member (for a small fee)—ask the staff to phone a committee member. The club has extensive sports facilities, as well as football, rugby (training at 1700 on Thurs., May-October) and cricket, squash, swimming, snooker, etc. (Rugby players and cricketers are always welcome). Also cheap restaurant, pub and friendly place to meet people.

Chinatown Lima's Chinese district is centred on Jirón Paruro and Calle Ucayali, south of Av. Abancay. Chinese clothing, food and souvenirs. Watch out for pickpockets and thieves.

Shopping Silver and gold handicrafts of all kinds; Indian hand-spun and hand-woven textiles;

manufactured textiles in Indian designs; llama and alpaca wool products such as ponchos, rugs, hats, blankets, slippers, coats, sweaters, etc.; *arpilleras*, appliqué pictures of Peruvian life (originated in Chile with political designs), made with great skill and originality by women in the shanty towns; fine leather products mostly hand made. The *mate burilado*, or engraved gourd found in every tourist shop, is cheap and a genuine expression of folk art (cheaper in villages near Huancayo). *Silvania Prints*, Colmena 714 (near *Hotel Bolívar*), Conquistadores 905 (San Isidro) and in lobby of *Miraflores César Hotel*, sell modern silk-screen prints on Pima cotton with precolumbian designs. *Plaza México*, jewellery in precolumbian designs. On Av. Nicolás de Piérola vendors sell oil paintings of Andean scenes, bargains abound. One of the best selections of folk art, but not the cheapest, will be found at the *Artesanías del Perú* shops in Lima. *Cerámica Los Reyes*, Av. Nicolás de Piérola. Ground floor of *Hotel Bolívar* for all metal, pottery, woollen and handicraft items, reasonably priced, credit cards accepted. *Artesanía Huamanqaqa*, Belén 1041 between Hotels *Sheraton* and *Bolívar*, the best store for high-quality weaving (but very expensive), specializes in Indian weaving from San Pedro de Cajas. Next door is a permanent exhibition with a century-old loom. Also try the 24 stores in *Restaurant 1900*, Belén 1030, very good arpilleras. *EPPA (Empresa Peruana de Promoción Artesana)* government store for Peruvian handicrafts in San Isidro (Av. Orrantia 610). *Antisuyo*, Jr. Tacna 460, Miraflores, an Indian cooperative run by an Englishwoman, sells high-quality handicrafts from all regions, reasonable prices, T 472557. *Art-Andina*, Belén 1045, good selection of Indian weaving and rugs at very reasonable prices. Precolumbian textiles can be bought from the *Casa de Antigüedades*, Av. de Emancipación 253. On Unión is *Casa Mas*, with a wonderful display of gold and silver handicrafts, and antiques. In Miraflores, lovely shopping arcade *El Suche*, at La Paz 646, but high prices in the woollen goods, ceramics and leather shops. Antiques available in Miraflores on Calle La Paz. *Vicuña* is unobtainable for the time being in Peru and Bolivia alike. See H. Stern's jewellery stores at Hotels *Miraflores César*, *Bolívar* and *Sheraton*, and at the International Airport. (Note: It is better to buy pullovers in the Sierra. However, although Lima is more expensive, it is often impossible to find the same quality of goods elsewhere.) Alpaca cloth for suits, coats, etc. (mixed with 40% sheep's wool) can be bought cheaply from factories: Cirsa, Av. Argentina 2400, microbus 93, 70 or 84 from Plaza Castilla; Lanificio, Alberto del Campo 285, bus 59 from Av. Abancay (gives 10% discount to foreigners attached to their embassies). Alpaca wool for knitting or weaving from Alpaca III, Av. Larco 859, Miraflores. Made-to-measure cotton shirts in 24 hrs. from Sr. Hurtado, "Sir", Jr. Carabaya 1108. A good tailor is Navarro Hermanos, in Belén, below the Tourist Office. There are bargains in clothing made from high quality Pima cotton. Good Indian market on Avenida de la Marina, San Miguel, bus No. 10 from Miraflores. Records: Discos del Mundo, Unión 779, allows you to listen, in sound-proof booth, before you buy.

Markets   Parque Diagonal/Kennedy, Miraflores (by *Restaurant Haiti*): jewellery, sandals made to measure, paintings and other handicrafts, Dec.-June, Wed. to Mon., in winter Sat. and Sun. only; Feria Artesanal, Av. de la Marina 790 and Av. Sucre westwards, in Pueblo Libre (take bus 2, 7, 10, or 48 on Av. Abancay, but watch your possessions, as thieves are numerous): extensive market selling woollen goods, leatherwork, bric-a-brac and Peruvian goods and souvenirs; sidestreets off Lampa: hardware; sidestreets off Av. Colmena: books; Parque Universitario: bargains; Plaza San Martín, behind *Hotel Bolívar*: ambulantes (money-changers). There is an interesting flower market with enormous arrangements near Plaza George Washington, on the way to the Gold Museum.

Bookshops   Fair selection of foreign-language books at *Librería Delta*, N. de Piérola 689, Todos shopping area, Galax commercial centre (Todos and Galax are the largest stores), Miraflores and Jorge Chávez airport. *ABC Bookstores* also sell foreign-language books (including *South American Handbook*). *Librería Studium*, Plaza Francia 1164 (also on N. de Piérola), sells history/travel books in English. *Studium* and *Librería de la Universidad de San Marcos* give student discounts. Tourist books in English, French and German also available from *Librería Ayra*, Jirón Unión 560, rec., will supply works in Quechua. *Delta*, Av. N. de Piérola near Plaza San Martín. *Librería Internacional*, Jirón Unión (corner of Plaza San Martín) has a wide selection of books on South America in all languages. The *Book Exchange* at Ocoña 211a (near Plaza San Martín), open 1400-1900, is best place in centre for foreign-language books; will exchange them (mainly science-fiction, detective and porn) if you bought there; another shop is on Benavides 286 in Miraflores. *Librería El Pacífico* in Miraflores has the best selection of English books in Lima. Rare books, many shops on Av. Azángaro. French bookshop, *Plaisir de France*, Colmena 958. International newspapers, from newstands, Block 6, Av. N de Piérola.

Film The Agfa distributor, at Av. Tomás Marsano 390, sells film at reduced prices. Foto Mare, Belén 1047. Many developers using Kodak equipment offer same-day service; all at similar prices. Many on Jr. Unión and Plaza San Martín; also Av. Larco, Miraflores. Fujicolor offer a free film with developing. Quality tends to be poor. **Camera Repairs** Casa Hindú, Jr. Unión, repairs Olympus cameras.

Pharmacy Botica Inglés, Jirón Cailloma 336, sells Dr. Scholl foot supplies for those contemplating or recovering from the Inca Trail. Tampons reported only available in Miraflores.

Local Buses Standard fares in Lima: buses and minibuses, US$0.10, sometimes half price with student card, not very reliable. The main routes, such as from Plaza San Martín down Av. Arequipa to Miraflores and on to San Isidro, are also served by colectivos, US$0.25, which continue late at night after many buses stop.

Taxis No taxis use meters, you must bargain the price beforehand and don't give in to demands for payment in dollars, unless you get a bargain! Also, insist on being taken to the destination of your choice, not the drivers', about US$0.50 for short journeys and US$2.50 from the centre to the suburbs. After 2400 and on holidays, 35 % -50 % surcharge. Be careful of black "pirate" taxis; they usually charge 50 % more. Paco, T 616394, is dependable for phone hiring.

Drivers don't expect tips; give them small change from the fare. If hiring a taxi for over 1 hour agree on price per hour beforehand. To Callao, La Punta, San Miguel, Magdalena, Miraflores (should be US$1.50), Barranco, Chorrillos, by agreement, basis US$5 per hour. Colectivos are fine, with legally fixed prices, e.g. US$0.25 from Miraflores to Lima centre.

Car Hire Cars can be hired from Hertz Rent-a-Car, Ocoña 262 (beside *Hotel Bolívar*), T 289477; Budget Rent A Car, Airport, T 528706 and Miraflores; Graf Automóviles Seleccionados, S.A. (Avis), Av. Petit Thouars 915, Miraflores, T 233486; Turamérica, Ocoña 164 (beside *Hotel Bolívar*), T 276413, or Nicolás de Piérola 590 (opp. *Hotel Crillón*), T 278970. The condition of vehicles is usually very poor. Beware of deep street potholes. The standard of driving in Lima is very low. Make sure that your car is in a locked garage at night. Russian-made four-wheel drive Niva vehicles are often rented; they are up to the conditions of Andean driving, but the ordinary Lada saloon cars are not.

Motor Parts International Motors S.A. in Lima is the only Land Rover agent in Peru. Some BMW parts seem to arrive in Lima.

Night Clubs International cabaret—*Sky Room* at the *Crillón Hotel* (folk shows—disappointing, US$7), *Embassy* in the Plaza San Martín and *Yorkas* on Av. Nicolás de Piérola.

Folklore Every Sunday at the Coliseo Cerrado, Av. Alfonso Ugarte. AAA Theatre, Ica 323, has folklore evening every Tues., 2015, admission US$3. Also at the Teatro Municipal, Jirón Ica (tickets US$0.60-3.60), Tues. 2000 and at the Teatro La Cabaña. Cooperativa Santa Elisa, Cailloma 824 (3rd floor) has a folk group every Wed., 2000. The Museo de Arte has seasons of Peruvian folklore on Weds., at 2000, US$1.20 entrance. Many *peñas* have opened in recent years; these are generally cheap, tavern-like places with Peruvian music, much dancing and audience participation, *Hatuchay Peña*, Trujillo 228 (across the bridge past the Post Office), Fri., Sat., 2100, entrance US$2.20, inexpensive, crowded, good, but best to phone for taxi late at night; *La Peña de Pocho Ugarte* in Miraflores; *Las Brisas de Lago Titicaca*, just off Plaza Bolognesi, US$0.30, rec.; *Peña El Ayllu*, Jr. Moquegua 247, open every night, entrance free, rec.. *La Palizada*, Av. del Ejército 800, Miraflores; *Las Guitarras*, in Miraflores and *Wifala* on Calle Cailloma have been rec. Many others in Barranco around Plaza Grau and Puente de los Suspiros, e.g. *1900* above a bookshop on Plaza Grau; *La Estación de Barranco*, at Pedro de Osma 112.

Bars (with music) *Charlie's Peppermint Bar*, Av. Corpac, *Percy's Candlelight Room*, Todos shopping centre, San Isidro. *Satchmo Jazz Bar*, Av. La Paz 538, Miraflores, good.

Discotheques Ebony 56 in San Isidro. Las Rocas in San Isidro is good and not expensive. Recommended in Miraflores, Video Club, just off Av. Diagonal; La Miel, min. consumption US$5.50 (pay as you go, don't wait for a big bill), and Arizona, US$4. Unicorno del Mar at Herradura beach in summer. La Caverna, Aviación 2514, San Borja.

Theatre Most professional plays are put on at the Teatro Segura, Teatro Municipal (Jirón Ica, 300 block—also orchestral and ballet performances); Teatro Arequipa and Sala Alzedo; Teatro

Marsano, Av. Petit Thouars, Miraflores. Others are produced by amateur and university groups. See the newspapers for announcements. Teatro Cabaña in the Parque de la Exposición puts on a strong programme of progressive theatre. Theatre Workshop, Jirón Ica 323.

Cinemas Tickets cost about US$0.65 in Lima. Good films can be seen cheaply at the Cooperativa Santa Elisa, Cailloma 824, Thurs., Fri., Sat., and Sun. each week, Tel: 322641. Museo de Arte, Paseo Colón 125, has good international films, ask for monthly programme; Alianza Francesa (every Tues.), Av. Garcilaso 1550, as well as at the British and North American-Peruvian Culture Associations (usually Thurs.) Ciné Pacífico Miraflores, in central Miraflores, most films in English with Spanish subtitles.

Sports There are two bullfight seasons, one in October-November and a short one in March. They are held in the afternoons on Sun. and holidays. Tickets at 2nd block of Calle Huancavelica, or at the Plaza de Acho bullring early on the day of the *corrida*. Famous *toreros* practise in the Lima ring, the oldest in the Americas, and fighting bulls are of Spanish stock. Cockfights are frequently organized and advertised: the Plaza de Gallos at Calle Sandía 150, near Parque Universitario, is recommended, US$6 for best seats. Horse racing, Hipódromo Monterrico, on Tues. and Thurs. evenings (1900) and Sat. and Sun. (1300) in summer, and in winter on Tues. evening and Sat. and Sun. afternoons. Colectivos on race days leave from the Plaza San Martín, fare US$0.10. The popular stand is not recommended. Pelouse and Primera stands US$0.60. Tourists may enter the members' stand on production of their passports. For Paso horses, which move in four-step amble, extravagantly paddling their forelegs, National Paso Association, Miraflores, T 476331. The Lima, Inca, Granja Azul and La Planicie golf clubs and the Country Club de Villa all have 18-hole courses. The Santa Rosa, Cruz de Hueso and Huampani golf clubs have 9-hole courses. (Contact Gerard Astruck of Sudex S.A., T 28-6054, for particulars.) Polo and tennis are also played. Boxing or all-in wrestling (Sat. night) at the Coliseo Nacional.

Association football matches and various athletic events take place at the National Stadium, seating 45,000, in the centre of the city on ground given by the British community on the 100th anniversary of Peru's Declaration of Independence.

Exchange Banco de la Nación (e.g. Av. Abancay 491). Citibank, Las Begonias 580, San Isidro, charges 3% on its own travellers cheques, open 0830-1245 in summer. Bank of America, Augusto Tamayo 120, San Isidro; will change Bank of America travellers' cheques into intis, 1.5% commission. Interbanc on Unión changes cash and travellers' cheques. Peruvian banks. Open: Jan. 1 to March 31—0830 to 1130; April 1 to Dec.31—0915 to 1200. Closed Sat. except Banco de la Nación at Rufino Torrico 830 (opposite *Hotel Crillón*), which is open Sat. 0900-1200 (for changing dollar bills only—poor rate) and also open in the afternoons 1600-1830; small and crowded, it can be quicker elsewhere. Visa (Banco de Crédito, charges 2% on changing travellers cheques into US$), Jr. Lampa 499. Always check your money in the presence of the cashier, particularly bundles of pre-counted notes. Brazilian cruzados can be changed at good rates. The gold dealers near the *Hostal Kimari* on Pasaje Los Pinos, Miraflores, give good street rates. Many money changers at corner of Plaza San Martín and Jirón Unión, and in the streets behind *Hotel Bolívar*, identified by their calculator and hiss of "dollars", change money at the very profitable (for you) parallel rate; some change other South American currencies (beware, many forgeries in circulation). Best not to change money at your hotel: rates are usually better on the street. The optician opposite the *César* hotel gives a good rate. *Casas de cambio* were closed by order in July 1987.

British Schools Markham College, for boys, is one of only four Headmasters' Conference Schools outside the Commonwealth. Colegio San Andrés, for boys, run by the Free Church of Scotland. Colegio San Silvestre, a school for girls at Miraflores, is represented in the Association of Headmistresses. Colegio Peruano-Británico, San Isidro, co-educational. In La Molina, Colegio Newton offers the international baccalaureate.

American Schools Colegio Franklin Roosevelt, the American School of Lima, Monterrico, co-educational: Villa María, La Planicie (for girls); María Alvarado, Lima (girls).

Addresses

British Embassy and Consulate: Edificio Pacífico-Washington, Plaza Washington, corner of Av. Arequipa (5th block) and Natalio Sánchez 125 (Casilla de Correo 854). T 334738. (Yellow bus No. 2 passes the Embassy.)
U.S. Embassy and Consulate: Grimaldo del Solar 346, Miraflores, T 443621/443921.
Canadian Embassy: Av. Libertad 132, Miraflores, T 444015.
Irish Consulate, Carlos Povias Osores 410, San Isidro, T 230808.
Australian Trade Commission: Natalio Sánchez 220, T 288315.
New Zealand Embassy: Av. Salaverry 3006, San Isidro. (Casilla 5587.) T 621890.
South African Embassy and Consulate: Natalio Sánchez 125. T 247948.
Austrian Embassy, Av. Central 643, 5th floor, San Isidro. T 220467.
West German Embassy: Av. Arequipa 4210, Miraflores. T 459997.

French Consulate, Arequipa 3415, San Isidro, T 704968.
Belgian Consulate, Angamos 380, Miraflores, T 463335.
Swiss Embassy, Av. Salaverry 3240, San Isidro, Lima 27, T 624090.
Swedish Embassy, Centro Comercial Camino Real, Torre El Pilar (piso 9), Av. Camino Real 348, San Isidro, T 406700.
Norwegian Consulate, Canaval Moreyra 595, T 404048.
Finnish Embassy, Los Eucaliptos 291, San Isidro.
Danish Consulate General, Av. El Golf 1124, San Isidro, Lima 27, T 403742.
Netherlands Embassy, Av. Principal 190, Urb. Santa Catalina, La Victoria (Apartado Postal 71). T 721925.
Italian Embassy, Av. G. Escobedo 298, Jesús María.
Argentine Consulate, Pablo Bermúdez 143, T 729920, open 0800-1300.
Bolivian Consulate, Los Castaños 235, San Isidro, T 228231 (0830-1330).
Brazilian Consulate, Cmdte. Espinar 181, Miraflores, T 462635.
Chilean Consulate, Javier Prado Oeste 790, San Isidro, T 407965.
Ecuadorean Consulate, Las Palmeras 356, San Isidro, T 228138.
Colombian Consulate, Natalio Sánchez 125, T 247949, Mon.-Fri. 0900-1230.
Venezuelan Consulate, Av. Salaverry 3005, T 415948.
Dirección General de Migraciones, Paseo de la República 585; if passport stolen can provide new entry stamps.
Intej, Av. San Martín 240, Barranco, can extend student cards, T 774105.
PSNC: Nicolás de Piérola 1002-06, Plaza San Martín. T 283250.
YMCA: Carabaya 664. New building with more facilities on Avenida Bolívar in suburb of Pueblo Libre.
Biblioteca Nacional, Av. Abancay (cuadra 4) y Miró Quesada.
N.B. During the summer, most embassies only open in the morning.

Doctor Dr. Manfred Zapff-Dammert (German), Avenida Primavera 311, T 237129 (private), 350292 (home), highly recommended. Malaria pills from Dr. León on 3rd floor of Ministerio de Salud, Av. Salaverry. **Hospitals** Anglo-American Hospital, Av. Salazar, 3rd block, San Isidro. T 403570 (rec. for injections; stock gamma globulin). Hospital de Niñas, Av. Brasil, vaccination centre at the side. Anti-rabies centre, Chacra Ríos.

Prison Visiting Anyone wishing to visit fellow-countrymen in jail should contact Foreign Prisioners' Fellowship, Church of the Good Shepherd, Av. Santa Cruz 491 (Apartado 5152), Lima 18, T 457-908.

Non-catholic churches The Union Church of Lima (Interdenominational), Av. Angamos 1155, Miraflores. Trinity Lutheran Church of Peru, Las Magnolias 495, Urb. Jardín, San Isidro. Church of the Good Shepherd, Av. Santa Cruz 491, Miraflores (Anglican). First Baptist Church of Lima, Av. Garcilaso de la Vega 1734. Christian Science Society, 1285 Mayta Capac (near Av. Salaverry), Jesús María. English Benedictine Monastery, Jirón Olivares de la Paz, Las Flores (57M minibus from Plaza de Acho); Sunday Mass 0900, weekdays 1900.

Post Offices Central office is on Jirón Junín, west of the Plaza de Armas, hours: Mon.-Sat., 0800-1915, Sun., 0800-1200. On Av. Nicolás de Piérola, opp. *Hotel Crillón*. Poste restante, Camaná 195. Also on Av. Petit Thouars in Miraflores (1 block from intersection of Angamos and Arequipa), open 6 days a week. Express letters can only be sent from the Post Office at the airport. Be careful with the rates charged at this Post Office, they sometimes try to charge more than in the city. For parcels see page 850, **Mail**.

Telecommunications International **phone** calls from Entel office in Edificio Sudamérica on Plaza San Martín. **Cables** Hotels *Bolívar*, *Crillón*, *Miraflores César*, and *Country Club*, also Jirón Lampa 667 and San Isidro. Public telex booths.

Air Freight Emery, in Callao, T 52-3643: to USA US$50 plus US$3 per kg.

Laundry Continental, Cailloma 430, same-day and next-day laundry and dry-cleaning, good. Miraflores, Tarapacá 199 and Inclán, Miraflores. Insist on an itemized receipt. Autoservicio, Porta 198, Miraflores, fast, US$1.20 per machine. Burbujitas, Porta 293, Miraflores, 4 kg. wash and dry for US$1. Av. Petit Thouars 3139, Miraflores, US$2 wash and dry. Lava Velox, Atahualpa 175, Miraflores, US$2 a load, good. Lava Center, Víctor Maurtúa 140, San Isidro, T 403600, US$0.50 per kg. Businessman, A. N. Wiese, fast. Good dry cleaning, but not cheap, at Forty Minutes, Jirón Lampa 1180 in centre.

Cultural Institutions Peruvian-British Cultural Association, Av. Arequipa 3495, San Isidro, with reading room and British newspapers (bus 1, 2, 54A). For other offices, library and film shows, Jirón Camaná 787, T 277927, classes only; theatre, Av. Benavides 620, Miraflores, T 454326. British Council, Alberto Lynch 110, San Isidro 27, T 704-350. Teatro Británico (amateur productions of plays in English), Calle Bella Vista, Miraflores. Peruvian North American Cultural

Institute, Cuzco 446, in centre, with library; branch at Av. Arequipa 4798, Miraflores. Language tuition, US$30 for 4 weeks. American Chamber of Commerce, Juan de Arona, San Isidro. The American Society of Peru, Av. Angamos 1155, Miraflores. Tel: 414545. Goethe-Institut, Ica 426. Mon.-Fri., 1100-2000, library, theatre, German papers, tea and cakes. Alliance Française, Avenida Garcilaso de la Vega 1550, also in Miraflores.

Spanish Classes Centro de Idiomas de Lima, P.O. Box 772, Lima 100 (Av. Manuel Olguín 215, Monterrico, T 350601), 1, 2 and 4-week courses (US$300, 450, 720), accommodation with families can be arranged (room with bath, about US$150 a month). Euroidiomas, Juan Fanning 520, Miraflores 4, 6 and 8 week residential courses (US$480, 890, 1200).

Tourist Offices Enturperú, which administers the State Tourist Hotel chain, is at Av. Javier Prado-Oeste 1358, San Isidro (a 15-min. taxi ride from the centre), open Mon.-Fri., 1000-1900, Sat., 0900-1300 (telex. 20394; P.O. Box 4475), very helpful; rooms in the *hoteles de turistas* may be booked in advance. There are two tourist offices at the airport, which have lists of hotels and will ring to reserve rooms for travellers, or will book taxis—check whether prices are on the free or official rate. Ask for the helpful, free, *Peru Guide* in English. The Fondo de Promoción Turística (Foptur), Unión (Belén) 1066, T 323559 (open Mon.-Fri., 0900-1800, Sat., 0900-1200), highly recommended, many languages spoken, knowledgeable and helpful to budget-minded travellers, sells maps and has free brochures, Cuzco, Puno, Iquitos, etc.
    The Ministerio de Industria y Turismo, Calle 1 Oeste, Corpac, Lima 27, is very helpful regarding complaints and problems connected with travel agencies and touring.

Maps For Lima bus routes you can get a "transit map" from news stands for US$0.50. A good map of the whole country is available from street sellers in N. de Piérola and Plaza San Martín (published by Lima 2000, US$3.50). The Instituto Geográfico Militar (Av. Aramburu 1190, Surquillo, Lima 34), also sells a standard map of Peru (1:2,200,000), US$1.15, department maps, US$0.85 and a 4-sheet map of Peru, 1: 1,000,000, US$8.70, good value, but only available as separate sheets at Av. Aramburu, black-and-white aerial photos available; passport may be required; they are open 0900-1600, Mon.-Fri.; Av. Aramburu open for map sales Mon.-Fri., 0800-1230, 1400-1530. Maps of N and S border areas are not sold. If you submit a letter to the IGM, giving your credentials and adequate reasons, plus a photocopy of your passport, you may be able to obtain maps of the border regions. No accurate maps of the jungle regions have yet been prepared. The Instituto Nacional de Planificación, Avenida República de Chile, also sell a large atlas of Peru, US$25. Petroperú maps for town centres recommended.

South American Explorers' Club Av. Portugal 146 (Breña), Casilla 3714, Lima 100 (telephone 31-44-80), has been formed to bring together all in Peru (and all in Latin America or visiting it) who are interested in activities off the beaten track. Membership is US$25 a year. It produces a magazine, *The South American Explorer*. Don Montague, the editor, 1510 York Street, Denver, CO 80206 (T (303) 320-0388), will provide further information, including trip reports for journeys and the most recent views on where and how to travel safely. Open 0930-1700 Mon. to Fri.; non-members are asked to limit their visits to 30 mins., staff very helpful. The clubhouse is attractive and friendly; it is not necessary to "explore" to feel at home here. They will sell used equipment on consignment (donations of used equipment, unused medicines etc., are welcome), and store luggage for members. Some maps available. Their map of the Inca Trail is good (US$4). They have also recently published an excellent guide to hiking in the Cordillera Huayhuash. They also publish a map of the Cordillera Vilcanota (Ausangate)—1:100,000 (dyeline). There is a good library and they sell travel books and guides (at a discount to members), and some excellent handicrafts. (Also see the Bradts' *Backpacking* book, listed in "Information for Visitors".)

Trekking and Backpacking Percy Tapiá, Casilla 3074, Lima 100, leads treks for groups on the Inca Trail, Cordillera Vilcabamba and Cordillera Blanca. Club Andino Peruano, Las Begonias 630, also helpful. Instituto Nacional de Recreación, Educación Física y Deportes (Inred), have an Andean specialist, César Morales Arnao, at the Estudio Nacional, Tribuna Sur, 3rd floor, T 329177. Trekking and Backpacking Club Peruano, Jr. Huáscar 1152, Jesus María, Lima 11 (T 232515), also at Huarás; free information on Peru and South America, storage and gas cylinders available. Issues a magazine, *El Trekkero*, write for information. Open Mon.-Fri., 1730-1900, phone first at weekends.

The Peruvian Touring and Automobile Club Av. César Vallejo 699 (Casilla 2219), Lince, Lima (T 403270), offers help to tourists and particularly to members of the leading motoring associations. Good maps available of whole country; regional routes and the S. American sections of the Pan-American Highway available (US$2.10).

Tourist Information Best guide to archaeological sites is *Manual de Arqueología Peruana*, by Kaufmann Doig, on sale from stalls and most bookshops, published in Spanish, US$8; an abridged version, *El Perú Arqueológico*, US$2, covering pre-Inca remains, is also available. *Cut Stones and Crossroads: A Journey in Peru*, by Ronald Wright (Penguin Travel Library) is an excellent, modern travel book. Booklet *Lima, City of Treasures and Traditions* by Frances E. Parodi (published by the American Woman's Literary Club, Lima). *Guía "Inca" de Lima Metropolitana* is invaluable for finding less well known, but interesting, parts of Lima, as is the *Guía de Transportes de Lima Metropolitana* (US$1.75) for getting to them. For those interested in architecture, *Itinerarios de Lima*, by Héctor Velarde (in Spanish and English), and *Guía Reparaz del Perú*, by Gonzalo Reparaz Ruiz (Spanish, English and French) are very useful. Also useful is *Guide to Lima* by J. E. Maguiña and *The City of Kings: A Guide to Lima*, by Carolyn Walton (available from major bookshops). Spanish and English news in the lobby of the *Sheraton Hotel*. *Lima Times* publishes a monthly *Peru Guide* and sells some other travel books.

Professional archaeologists should contact the Instituto Nacional de Cultura, Casilla 5247, Lima, or Centro de Investigación y Restauración de Bienes Monumentales del Instituto Nacional de Cultura, Jirón Ancash 769, Lima.

Travel Agents There are many, centred on Plaza San Martín and Av. Nicolás Piérola (Colmena). Sudex S. A. (Gerard Astruck), Sudamérica building, Carabaya 933, Of. 310-317; Lima Tours, Belén 1040, just off Plaza San Martín, American Express agent, slow for money changing, publishes a tourist guide (T 276624). Coltur S.A., Jr. Camaná 868, rec.; Creditio S. A., Schell 319, Oficina 706, Miraflores (T 444200/444727), efficient, helpful, English spoken; Spazio Tours, Juan Fanning 179, Miraflores, T 476451, or PO Box 18-5497, Lima, very helpful, highly rec.; Viajes Universal, Av. Arequipa 2885, San Isidro (T 421111/421112), helpful, contact María del Rosario Berio; Explorandes, Av. Bolognesi 159, Miraflores, rec.; Key Tours (Jorge Gonti Angeles), Av. Nicolás de Piérola 677, Of. 9, T 284311 rec. for swift and efficient arranging of tours throughout Peru and to La Paz. Aventours, Av. La Paz 442, Miraflores, Lima 18, T 441067, trekking, rafting, wildlife tours and more (office in Cuzco, Av. Pardo 505, T 237307).Chávez Tours will arrange drivers to take small groups (or individuals) on trips for US$22 per day. Cecilia Toso Stagi, Turispa, Av. La Paz 1101, Miraflores (T 474903), rec. Julio E. Figueroa Cubas, Fco. Sarmiento de Gamboa 289, Urb. La Colonial, Callao, T 514748, private guide, rec. particularly for non-Spanish speakers, Lima tours, US$5 per hour; also Alfredo Hiromoto, T 312-709 (home), or 441-799 (*Hotel Diplomat*). A good archaeological tour guide is Rolando Peceros, T 276720. To contact the Lima Association of Guides, T 245131. **N.B.** A commission is charged for booking tickets, 20% usual 50% complained of, ask before booking.

Airport The Jorge Chávez airport is 16 km. from the centre of Lima. Taxi, about US$3-8 to centre, US$10 to Miraflores (hang on to your bag if surrounded by taxi touts—if you walk 100 metres outside the airport gate you can probably bargain a much cheaper price from taxis not working the airport route—but not recommended at night). Airport bus to centre (and also colectivos; look for big brown sign) leaves from right-hand end of building as you step out of the door. Municipal blue bus 35 (US$0.10) and colectivo (outside the Air France office), and to and from Plaza Dos de Mayo in the day-time, US$0.50 p.p. and per item of luggage. Minibus every 20 mins., US$0.75, from Calle Serrano, opposite Iberia office. Also, 15 and 35 from the Plaza Dos de Mayo leave for the airport; service about every 30 mins. There is a cheap colectivo service from corner of Av. Tacna with Uruguay (N. de Piérola) 733, from 0400 to 2000, colectivos wait until they have 5 passengers, US0.50 p.p., and US$0.25 for luggage. Buses go from Trans Hotel, Camaná 828 (T 275697, 289812), supposedly 24-hour service, will also collect passengers from hotels (fares range from US$1.75 p.p. with one bag leaving from Camaná office or a hotel nearby, to US$5 if they pick you up from a hotel away from the centre). Passengers report being let down by this service. Also from Miraflores (Avenida Ricardo Palma 280), every 20 min., US$2 p.p. (buses will collect travellers from private houses, US3.20), T 469872. If using this service, book well in advance at Trans Hotel. Hoteltours operate a bus service from the airport to hotels in town for US$4; they have desks near both the domestic and international arrival gates. The big hotels also have their own buses at the airport, and charge about the same. There is a duty-free shop but no duty-free cigarettes. Only official Corpac porters are allowed in the customs area. Airport tax of US$15, payable in dollars, for international flights. Avoid getting left with intis at the airport when leaving; changing them back into dollars at Banco de la Nación can take a lot of time, and you need to show the official exchange slips. Car rental booths in airport may buy intis. Left luggage costs US$1.90 per day, US$0.40 per hour per item. The Prohotel agent at the airport is very helpful with hotel bookings of all classes; there is a second hotel booking agency. Taxi drivers also tout for hotel business, offering discounts—don't let yourself be bullied. Safe to stay all night in 24-hour expresso-snack bar.

Internal Air Services To Andahuaylas, Arequipa, Ayacucho, Bellavista, Cajamarca, Chiclayo, Chimbote, Cuzco, Huánuco, Iquitos, Juanjui, Juliaca, Moyobamba, Piura, Pucallpa, Puerto Maldonado, Rioja, Tacna, Talara, Tarapoto, Tingo María, Trujillo, Tumbes and Yurimaguas. Prices (relatively low in comparison with other countries) and other details are given in text, under names of destinations.

Air Lines Most international airlines have moved out to San Isidro and Miraflores because of bomb threats. Faucett (Plaza San Martín, T 282930), Aeroperú (Plaza San Martín T 317626, domestic, 287825 international). Office hours are usually 0900-1700, Mon.-Fri., 0800-1930, Sat. For Aeroperú, internal flights, Cailloma 818.

Rail Central Railway of Peru maintains passenger and freight service to La Oroya (with an extension N to Cerro de Pasco) and SE to Huancayo (with an extension to Huancavelica): Desamparados station, behind Presidential Palace. (For description of line **see page 820**). Train to La Oroya and Huancayo departs 0740 daily except Sun., arriving La Oroya 1340 and Huancayo 1638. The train from La Oroya to Cerro de Pasco also runs daily, but one cannot buy a through ticket from Lima because the Cerro de Pasco train leaves La Oroya at 1330 before the train from Lima has arrived. If not wishing to go beyond La Oroya, colectivo back to Lima costs US$5.50, 5 hrs., you can make a day trip of it, being back by 2000. You can also return by bus, 7½ hrs., for railway enthusiasts especially. The return from Huancayo is at 0700, arriving Lima 1603. Single, 1st class, US$6, 2nd class, US$4; good cheap breakfast and lunch (US$1) served. (1st class and buffet seats can be reserved for US$0.25—take a torch for the long, dark tunnels; ticket office opens 0700-1200, 1330-1600 Mon.-Fri., 0700-1100 Sat.; tickets can only be bought one day in advance in Lima; in the high season, tickets are often sold out for 1st class by 1200. Sit on the left; remember that the train changes direction at San Bartolomé, so you will be sitting on the right to begin with). Guard your possessions very carefully against pickpockets at the station. Only ticket holders are allowed on the platform. The station is closed on Sundays.

Bus Companies Coastal buses are usually good although liable to delays. Buses in the Sierra, in view of the road surfaces, often break down. The services of the Ormeño group, are generally recommended throughout Peru; Cruz del Sur are also generally well thought of. Tepsa, Paseo de la República 129 (T 321233) run N and S on the coast and to Pucallpa and Arequipa; their services have been improved, but we are told they still tend to drive too fast for safety and that their Lima bus terminal is the scene of many thefts. Expreso Continental (Ormeño) to Trujillo, Piura and Tumbes, rec.; Chinchay-Suyo (northwards), Apurímac 391 and Av. Grau 525; also going north, Perú Express, Pacífico El Norte (to Chimbote), Atahualpa, Jr. Sandía 266, T 275838/287255 (to Cajamarca, Celendín, etc.), good; Sudamericano buses (Av. Nicolás de Piérola 1117) to Tumbes are variable; Roggero are unreliable and slow. Along the South coast route, Ormeño, Av. Carlos Zavala 145, reliable, also to Arequipa and Cuzco; Cruz del Sur, Paseo de la República corner with Almirante Grau (also go to Santiago). To Cuzco: via Arequipa, Cruz del Sur; via Nazca and Puquío, Ormeño, El Cóndor. To Huancayo, Compresa Cáceres, Av. 28 de Julio 2195, and Comité 22 colectivo, Av. Ayacucho 997, T 289082. To Huánuco: León de Huánuco, Av. José Gálvez 1734 (also to Pucallpa not rec., buses in bad condition); Nor Oriente, Luna Pizarro 365. Expreso Intersa, Av. Nicolás de Piérola, 1631; El Trome, Montevideo 949. Colectivos leave for all parts of Peru from Parque Universitario. For prices of routes and more details, see under individual cities in pages following.

International Buses   Tepsa runs a twice weekly service to Santiago, Chile (3 days, 3,500 km.) leaving Lima on Thurs. and Sun. at 1645, fare US$125. Pul Bus Norte to Santiago, US$135. Also connecting twice weekly services to Guayaquil and Quito (although there are no through buses; you can buy through tickets but they are very expensive and give no priority), leaving Lima on Wed. and Sun. at 0845. The trip takes 2½ days; often long frontier delays.

The international trips are much cheaper if one is prepared to take buses to frontier posts only, walk across frontiers, and buy tickets as one goes along. To enter Peru, a ticket out of the country may be required. If you have to buy a bus ticket, be warned: they are not transferable or refundable.

Warning   Luggage is often snatched at terminals. Make sure your luggage is well guarded and put on the right bus. It is also important not to assume that buses leave from the place where you bought the tickets.

In the weeks either side of July 28/29 (Independence), and of the Christmas/New Year holiday, it is practically impossible to get train or bus tickets out of Lima.

Suburbs of Lima   The Avenida Arequipa expressway from the centre of Lima, is a 4-lane highway, 10 km. long, with gardens and a double row of trees in the centre. Parallel to this, a few blocks away, is the Paseo de la República expressway where the large Sears-Todos shopping complex is located. At *San Isidro* is El Olivar, an old olive grove turned into a delightful park (best visited in daylight). Beyond this is the Lima Golf Club where the Country Club is found, primarily a hotel, which incorporates the Real Club with swimming pools, tennis courts, etc. This is an 8 km. taxi ride from the centre of Lima. There are many good hotels and restaurants in San Isidro; see main Lima lists, hotels **page 724** and restaurants **728**. Between San Isidro and Miraflores is the Pan de Azúcar, or Huallamarca, a restored adobe pyramid of the Maranga culture, of about AD 100-500 (Calle Nicolás de Rivera 201, small museum, open daily, 0900-1700, bus 1 from Av. Tacna, or minibus 13 or 73 to Choquechaca, then walk).

The road reaches the sea at *Miraflores,* the largest, most important suburb of Lima, with well stocked shops and many first class hotels and restaurants (see main Lima lists: hotels **page 724**, Youth Hostel, **page 726** and restaurants, **page 728**). There is a handsome park in the middle of the shopping centre and at the end of Avenida Mariscal Benavides, which is commonly called Av. Diagonal, you can get the best view of the whole Lima coastline from Chorrillos to La Punta. The Mariscal Necochea clifftop park overlooks the Waikiki Club, a favourite with Lima surfers. Near Parque Kennedy is the artists' and craftsmens' quarter of L'Ovolo. On no account camp on Miraflores beach; it is extremely dangerous as well as pebbled and dust-blown because of cliff erosion. (In fact, any of the beaches near Miraflores are unsafe regarding theft, especially during school holidays.) You can see sealions at close quarters, but the fishing seabirds are not so numerous as they were.

Buses to Miraflores   No. 2 from Plaza de Armas or Plaza San Martín, Nos. 2 and 53 from Emancipación and Tacna; others from Tacna and Huancavelica (US$0.12). Taxi-colectivos recommended, from Plaza San Martín in front of Ciné Colón, US$0.15.

The road passes through *Barranco* (not to be confused with Barranca, 200 km. N of Lima), with an attractive plaza and nearby the interesting *bajada,* a steep path down to the beach, where many of Lima's artists live and exhibit their work; many old houses are under restoration. (Take bus No. 2 to Miraflores and Barranco beaches from Plaza San Martín, for US$0.15.) The next development on the coast is at *Chorrillos,* a fashionable resort (*Café Suizo* overlooking beach) with a cliff promenade, and boating. At Hacienda La Villa, an old Spanish *hacienda* worth visiting, there is occasionally open air dancing to *salsa* music. Near Chorrillos is the Playa de los Pescadores with seafood stalls, Playa Agua Dulce (a clean beach), and the Club Regatas de Lima. Beyond Chorrillos is *La Herradura,* another bathing resort with several restaurants. The private Club Unicornio is open to tourists. Some of the beaches round Lima are none too clean; La Herradura, however, is a welcome exception. A beach road runs round the entire bay; the main access to it is either at the end of the Paseo de la República in Barranco or by the Bajada de Balta, which is at the end of Av. Diagonal in Miraflores. Bathing at all points, but be careful of the currents.

Avenida Costanera passes through a run down seaside resort, *Magdalena del Mar,* served by a separate road and bus route from Lima. A little inland, along this route, is *Pueblo Libre,* where the

Museum of Anthropology and Archaeology, the Museum of the Republic and the Rafael Larco Herrera Museum are found (see under Museums, page 720), as well as the old church of Magdalena Vieja (1557), which was unfortunately heavily damaged in the 1974 earthquake.

Callao Passengers coming to Peru by sea usually land at Callao (now contiguous with Lima). It handles 75% of the nation's imports and some 25% of its exports.

Callao's maritime terminal or inner harbour covers 100 hectares, and the largest vessels go alongside. Population, 411,200. San Lorenzo island, a naval station, protects the roadstead from the S; inland stretches the Rímac valley. It is a commercial place with no architectural beauty. Lima is reached by road (20 mins. by car or bus, US$0.12). Passengers are expected to be on board half-an-hour before the vessel's departure. (Some have been attacked and robbed just outside the dock gates.) There are some interesting shops in the area between Calle Constitución and Av. Sáenz Peña, and a market between Sáenz Peña and Buenos Aires. "The Club", the oldest English club on the W coast, is at Pasaje Ronald, Calle Constitución, Callao; there is an English cemetery.

History Drake and others raided Callao in the 16th century. An earthquake wiped it out in 1746. On November 5, 1820, Lord Cochrane boarded and captured, after a bloody fight in which he was wounded, the Spanish frigate *Esmeralda*. The Real Felipe fortress (1774), last stronghold of the Royalists in S. America, withstood a siege of a year and finally surrendered after terrible sufferings in 1826. It is still a military post, and tourists are allowed to visit it. The Military Museum (**see page 721**) is in the old barracks. The railway to Lima, opened May 17, 1851, was one of the first in S. America.

Leading Restaurant *El Chalaquito*, Calle Constitución. A number of good fish restaurants can be found on Av. Sáenz Peña. There are a number of reliable bars in the Pasaje Ríos and Calle Constitucíon.

Taxis In Callao use taxis recommended by U.S. Embassy or port authorities—for safety's sake. About US$15 for 3 hrs.

Addresses British Vice-Consulate, Sáenz Peña 154. P.S.N.C., Calle Independencia 150 (Casilla 368), T 299040.

Cables Pasaje Ronald y Constitución 258. Sáenz Peña 160; T 29-0117 (Public Telex booth).

Tourist Office Foptur, Terminal Marítimo-Guardia Chalaca s/n, T 299210.

The Naval College is at *La Punta*, just beyond Callao, served by municipal buses and colectivos through Callao from Lima. La Punta is on a spit of land stretching out to sea; once a fashionable beach, but water is cool. A new yacht club has been built on the N side. The walk along the seafront between Callao and La Punta has its charms.

The road from Callao to Lima is lined by factories. Shipyards, far from sea, load the fishing vessels they build on huge lorries and launch them into the ocean at Callao. San Marcos University (founded May 12, 1551) has now been transferred to a new University City, near the Naval Hospital.

On Avenida Marina between Lima and Callao, a turn-off opposite the entrance to the Feria del Pacífico grounds leads to the Parque Las Leyendas (**see page 723**).

There are bathing, tennis, and a yacht club at *Ancón*, 30 km. NW of Lima, reached by a double-lane asphalted highway. It is the only real seaside resort in Peru, but no hotels apart from *Restaurant Cinco Luches*, which has rooms, E. Beaches are very small. Crowded Jan.-March holidays, good for fish. On the way to Ancón is the pleasant Santa Rosa beach (entrance fee). Beyond Ancón is a Chancay cemetery, from which has come much Chancay weaving and pottery (as seen in the Amano Museum). There are also Inca ruins at Maranga and Chuquitanta, near Lima; unfortunately the latter cannot be visited at present.

Excursions *Pachacámac* is in the Lurín valley, 31 km. from Lima. When the Spaniards arrived, Pachacámac was the largest city on the coast. The ruins encircle the top of a low hill, the crest of which was crowned with a Temple of the Sun, a large pyramid built in 1350 of sun-baked bricks. (There are also a reconstructed Temple of the Virgins and the ancient temple of the Creator God.) Hernando Pizarro, brother of Francisco, came to Pachacámac in 1533; he destroyed images, killed the priests and looted the temples. The setting is marvellous, but the restoration has been criticized and vandals have been at work. Bus or colectivo from Lima, caught at the Plaza Santa Catalina, near the

Parque Universitario at the crossing of Puno with Andahuaylas. The buses (US$0.25, 1 hr.) and colectivos (US$0.50) go by way of Miraflores and Chorrillos, but tell the driver you are going to the *ruinas* or he will land you in Pachacámac town further on. Taxi, 3 hr. trip, US$40. Closed Mon. and May 1, open 0900 to 1700. Entrance US$0.40.

Pucusana, 50 km. from Lima, Silencio, Santa María and Cerro Azul, 90 km., are fishing villages with beaches that are much cleaner than those near Lima. Robbery is common on the beaches and you are advised to sit on your clothes and other possessions. Do not leave anything unattended when swimming.

Also to the South, up the Omas valley beyond Coalla are the Inca adobe structures at Los Gentiles (on the right, well before Omas) and, nearer Omas, Pueblo Viejo, Yampa and Viracocha. Take a colectivo from Plaza Santa Catalina, Jr. Puno (2 blocks from Av. Abancay), Lima to Mala, then hitch, or taxi, via Asia to the sites.

A second excursion is to Chosica, 40 km. up the Rímac valley. In the residential district of **Chaclacayo**, just before Chosica, are the **Huampani Hotel**, C, modern, attractive, good meals, swimming pool (US$0.40), run by the Government's hotel chain, and **Residencial La Casa de los Olivos**, at Los Ficus 373 y Los Olivos, with restaurant and ten rooms. An excellent chicken meal at the **Granja Azul** (take bus 88M or 204 from Parque Universitario) and there are several other places on the road from Lima to Chosica. The **Hotel El Pueblo** has swimming pool, horse riding, tennis, a beautiful garden, entrance, US$3, used heavily for conventions. Try restaurant and campground of **Puerto del Sol**, owned by Sr. Italo de Neqzi Herreros. A delightful place for dinner and dancing is the restaurant **Fiesta**, at km. 6 on the Central Highway. At km. 33 is **El Bosque** Country Club (anyone may enter on payment of US$85), private lake, 4 swimming pools, tennis and ball courts, riding stables, bull ring, etc. Colectivos for Chosica leave from just W of Parque Universitario, near the Ministry of Education building. Buses, 204, 1M.

On the way to Chosica a diversion may be made at Km. 4½ to **Puruchuco**, to see the reconstructed palace of a pre-Inca Huacho noble; with small museum (ceramics, textiles, etc., from the lower Rímac or Lima valley) and a selection of indigenous plants and animals, open 0900-1700, Tues.-Sun. (closed May 1 and July 28). Entrance US$1; Chosica bus or colectivo from Parque Universitario. One km. from Puruchuco are Huaquerones and Catalina Huaca sites now being restored. Nearby, at Chivateros, is a quarry said to date from 10,000 BC. The large adobe pre-Inca city of **Cajamarquilla** may also be visited, for which the turnoff (left, at Huachipa) is about 6 km. on from the Puruchuco turn. The site is difficult to find—you can't see it from the road—but look for a sign "Zona Arqueológica" in the middle of a brick yard. Keep on driving through the yard, and you will find Cajamarquilla at the end of an ill-kept dirt road. Open every day, 0900-1700. Beyond the Huachipa turn-off for Cajamarquilla, along the main road, there are precolumbian ruins at San Juan de Pariache and Huaicán-Tambo, 13½ and 16½ km. respectively from Lima.

Chosica (40 km.), the real starting place for the mountains, is at 860 metres, and is a popular winter resort because it is above the cloudbank covering Lima from May to October. One train a day and frequent buses and minibuses. Beyond the town looms a precipitous range of hills almost overhanging the streets. Up picturesque Santa Eulalia valley off the Rímac valley are the Central Fruit Culture Nurseries. There is some dramatic scenery on the road up the valley, fairly good as far as the hydroelectric station at Callahuanca, but the road is afterwards quite nasty in places, narrow and rocky. Population: 31,200.

Hotels *Residencial Chosica*, D; *Residencial San Jorge*, Av. Lima Sur 401, with hot water, rec., restaurant and bar.

Bus from Lima, No. 204, from 18th block of Calle Ayacucho (US$0.50); also 1M. Colectivos leave from near Education Ministry, just W of Parque Universitario.

Beyond Chosica, near the Santa Eulalia river (80 km. from Lima), is **Marcahuasi**, a table mountain about 3 km by 3 km at 4,200 metres, near the village of San Pedro de Casta (accommodation in a cold shelter only, less than US$1). The *meseta* has been investigated by Daniel Ruzo: there are 3 lakes, a "monumento a la humanidad" (40 metres high), and other mysterious lines, gigantic figures, sculptures, astrological signs and megaliths which display non-American symbolism. Ruzo describes this pre-Incaic culture in his book, *La Culture Masma*, Extrait de l'Ethnographie, Paris, 1956. Others say that the formations are not man-made, but the result of wind erosion. Truck to San Pedro de Casta from Chosica, 3 hrs., colectivo 2 hrs (US$1.70). Trail starts behind the village of San Pedro bending to the left—about 2 hours to the *meseta* (guides about US$3 a day, advisable in misty weather). Buses available for US$1.85 from San Pedro de Casta to Lima. Take food as no-one lives on the *meseta*, although there is a hut which provides good basic shelter; nights are cold. Srta. Paquita Castillo, T Lima 275251, arranges group tours.

Beyond Casta is San Juan de Iris, a tiny village, outside of which impressive ruins have been discovered (bus or truck from *Restaurant 41* in Chosica at 0900 if you're lucky, 7 hrs.). If intending to go there, contact Michael Warren in Casta first; he is very knowledgeable and accommodating.

There are the ancient (from 1500 BC) ruins of a small town on the hill of San Pedro de Casta, a fortress on the hills of Loma de los Papas (daily bus from Chosica at 0800), the ruins of Tambo Inca, and an ancient cemetery to the South.

The Central Highway to La Oroya (see page 821) opens up possibilities of excursions by car with attractive stopping places like Matucana (1 hr.), San Mateo and Río Blanco (2 hrs.). The trip to La Oroya takes over 5 hrs., and crosses the Andean divide at 4,843 metres. An excursion may be made to Infiernillo ("Little Hell") Canyon, beyond Matucana, which is well worth seeing. The Lima-Chosica-Santa Eulalia-Huanza-Casapalca trip is the most impressive in the environs of Lima, and can be done in one day.

To the North, up the Chillón valley is Cantamarca. "Beyond Cantamarca one comes (writes John Streather) to the beautiful Abra de la Viuda pass, where one passes through the Bosque de Piedras (rocks in extraordinary shapes and sizes) and the Junín pampa to Cerro de Pasco." In the Chancay valley are Chiprac, Rupac and Añay. John Streather writes: "These extraordinary ruins are very little visited, especially the last two which are more or less perfectly preserved. They have roofs on them and are extraordinarily well built. For Chiprac and Rupac, go with food, tent and sleeping bag to Huaral on the coast (bus from Lima from the Plaza de Acho, by the bullring, over the Puente de Piedra— beware of thieves). From Huaral, get a lift or a bus (one a week) to San Juan up beyond Acos. Best go first to Acos where there is a restaurant and accommodation and wait at the road junction a few km. out of the village for a lift up to San Juan. Chiprac is high above the village and can be reached on one's own; it is a good day's walk there and back with time to take photographs and eat. In San Juan, a man called Chavelo will act as a guide to Rupac, which can be reached via the pretty and deserted town of Pampas—also a day there and back. For Añay, go to Huaral as for the other ruins, then get transport to Huayopampa (basic accommodation) or La Perla whence the visit to the ruins can easily be made; get a guide to show you up from either village." Further on are **Sayán, Oyón and Churín** (near here, at Chinchín, is *Albergue San Camilo*, C, excellent; bus from Lima, US$5 with Espadín y Hnos at Ormeño terminal to Churín, Oyón and Huamahuanca); at Churín, there are hot, sulphurous baths. From Chinchín, there are buses to nearby villages, such as Huancahuasi, where one can buy woven goods, see interesting churches, and spot *vicuña* in lovely surroundings.

NORTH-WEST FROM LIMA (2)

From Lima to Chimbote   Between Lima and Pativilca there is a narrow belt of coastal land deposited at the mouths of the rivers, but from Pativilca to the mouth of the Río Santa, N of Chimbote, the Andes come down to the sea. Between Lima and Pativilca cotton and sugar-cane are grown, though the yield of sugar is less than it is further N where the sunshine is not interrupted by cloud. Cotton is harvested from April to September by Indian migrants from the basins of Jauja and Huancayo. Much irrigated land grows vegetables and crops to supply Lima and Callao. Cattle are driven down from the Highlands to graze the *lomas* on the mountain sides when the mists come between June and October.

The Pan-American Highway parallels the coast all the way to the far N, and feeder roads branch from it up the various valleys. Just N of Ancón, the Pasamayo sand dune, stretching for 20 km., comes right down to the seashore. The old road which snakes along the base beside the sea is spectacular, but is now closed except to commercial traffic. The new toll road (US$0.85), which goes right over the top, is much safer and you get spectacular views over the nearby coast and valleys. **Chancay**, on the coast (no bathing, sea both dangerous and heavily polluted), suffers from severe water shortages, but there is a fresh water source on the beach; *Hostal Villa de Arnedo*, D, clean and friendly, pool and restaurant, rec.; *Hostal Chancay*, F, safe, friendly, can wash clothes; *Restaurant Rebeca*, good.

Turn right 5 km. along road to Sayán where there is a national reserve, Loma de Lachay, which has thousands of snail shells, locust-trees and much bird life. Or continue north, dual carriageway to Km. 101, to the small port of **Huacho**, 132 km. from Lima. It is the outlet for cotton and sugar grown in the rich Huaura valley; a branch road runs up it to Sayán and beyond to Churín and Raura. There is a cemetery near Huacho where mummies may be found. There are cotton-seed oil and other factories. Port and sea are sometimes alive with monstrous jellyfish. Pop.: 35,900.

Hotels   *El Pacífico*, F, safe, dirty, water problems, inadequate clothes-washing facilities; *Italia*; *Grace*; *Hostal Maury*, E, basic but friendly. Camping is possible at El Paraíso beach.

The journey inland from Huacho is splendid (Lima to Huacho by bus: Transportes América S.A., Av. Colonial 129, Lima). Beyond Sayán are terrific rock formations, then road passes through subtropical vegetation around Churín (**see page 739**), which is visited for its mineral springs. There are coal mines. Above 4,000 metres is a chain of lakes which reflect the Cordillera Raura (up to 5,800 metres). Road ends at Raura mine.

Just across the river is **Huaura**, where the balcony is still preserved from which San Martín declared the country's independence from Spain. Try *guinda*, the local cherry brandy. We pass from the wide valley of Mazo through the irrigated valley of San Felipe. There is more desert and then the cotton-fields of San Nicolás lead to **Supe,** a small busy port shipping fishmeal, cotton, sugar and minerals (*Hostal Supe*, G; better is *Hostal Grau*, basic, G, clean, safe, comfortable, laundry, good value, next to which is a good restaurant: *El Norteño*). At Aspero, near Supe, is one of the earliest prehistoric sites in Peru (see History section, **page 714**). We pass through the town of **Barranca** (*Hotel Chavín*, F, nice, with bath, clean, good value, front rooms are noisy, also restaurant on first floor for lunch and dinner (try *arroz con conchas*), breakfast bar and café opens onto street by main entrance; *Pacífico*, F with bath, clean, good value; *Jefferson*, Lima 946, F, clean, friendly; *Hostería Central*, F, basic; many others on main street, and plenty of bars and restaurants, e.g. *Chifa*). The beach is long, not too dirty, though windy. Next is the straggling town of **Pativilca**, at Km. 203, which has a small museum (bus from Lima US$4, 2½ hrs.—*Restaurant Cornejo*, good and cheap) from which a well-paved road turns off for the Callejón de Huaylas and Huarás (**see page 745**). The road is paved to Conacocha (4,080 m.) then in very poor condition to Catac and on to Chavín. 4 km. beyond the turn-off, beside the Highway, are the well preserved ruins of the Chimú temple of **Paramonga.** Set on high ground (view of the ocean), the fortress-like mound is reinforced by 8 quadrangular walls rising in tiers to the top of the hill (admission US$0.25, well worth visiting, taxi from Paramonga and return after waiting, US$4.50, otherwise hitch from Barranca). Not far from the fortress, the Great Wall (La Muralla) stretches across the Andes. Paramonga is a small port, 3 km. off the Pan-American Highway, 4 km. from the ruins and 200 km. from Lima, shipping sugar.

Hotel   There is no hotel at Paramonga. There are several in Barranca; as bus companies have their offices there, buses will stop there rather than at Pativilca or Paramonga. No buses run to the ruins, only to the port.

Bus   from Lima to Paramonga, Compañía Fortaleza or Empresa América recommended. From Lima to Barranca, 3 hrs. US$2, Empresa América, very comfortable. 1st class from terminal on outskirts; Compañía Fortaleza and Comité Cinco (2nd class) go to Barranca from Parque Universitario in Lima. Buses cover the 7-8 km. from Barranca to Paramonga. Bus from Barranca to Casma US$1; Ancash bus to Huarás, 4 hrs., US$3. Truck, Pativilca-Huarás, 5-6 hrs., US$1.70; many buses, first at 1030.

Between Paramonga and Chimbote (225 km.) the mountains come down to the sea. The road passes by a few very small protected harbours in tiny rock-encircled bays—Puerto **Huarmey** (small *Hotel de Turistas*, D, clean and good service, but noisy, being on Pan-American Highway, rebuilt and reopened after earthquake, at Huarmey town, not port), Puerto Casma, and Vesique. Tepsa bus Lima-Huarmey, US$5.10, US$8.50 by colectivo, from Parque Universitario. From Casma a road runs through the **Callán pass** (4,224 metres) to Huarás. A difficult but beautiful trip. Not all buses take this route, so check before leaving. From Casma to the pass (apart from the paved first 30 km.), the road is appalling (many land-slides), but once the Cordillera Negra has been crossed, the road is better (gravel, wide) with spectacular views. About 40 km. before Casma, at Km. 330, is *Restaurant San Miguel*, good and clean, used by Tepsa as meal stop.

Casma The town was largely destroyed by the 1970 earthquake, but has since been rebuilt. A good new food market.

Hotels *Hostal El Farol*, E, ask for cheaper rate in low season, good, with bathroom (no hot water), breakfast and dinner available (and sandwiches and coffee), pleasant garden setting despite crickets and cockroaches in rooms; *Hostal Madeleine*, Plaza de Armas, F, very basic. *Restaurant Tumi*, rec.; *Chifa Tío Sam*, good, off plaza, and *Chifa San Chan*, on Plaza de Armas. Also *Restaurant Libertad*, fair.

Bus From Parque Universitario, Lima, colectivo to Casma, US$8.80. Bus to Lima leaves 1100 daily (Tepsa) US$4.25 also Chinchay-Suyo, on main street, and Turismo Chimbote (main road opp. road on which *Hostal El Farol* is located), 4 a day, US$3.40 (truck, US$3). Bus to Huarás, Chinchay-Suyo, 2300, daily and Moreno, 0700, 10 hrs., US$3.40. It is well worth making this trip in daylight to get the view of the Cordillera Blanca. Bus to Trujillo, Tepsa and Chinchay-Suyo, US$2.40, 3 hrs.

Excursions From Casma, take a truck going to San Rafael and ask for Castillo (departures all day from the garage opposite Huarás bus stop). After alighting, walk 2 km. uphill to a cemetery with pottery on the ground, and a Chimú castle of 4 concentric rings, with 3 towers in the middle, the Castillo de Chanquillo. Further on is a large wall with 13 towers on a ridge. Take water with you. The trucks return all day up to about 1600. There are several other sites around Casma: Sechín Alto, Pallka, Tokán, Mojeque, La Cantina, Tokachi and Huanchay.

Sechín At Km. 370 on Pan-American Highway, shortly before reaching Casma from Lima, watch for a large concrete sign to Sechín on the right. Follow the road indicated for about 2 km. until you reach the ruins (about one hour's walk). Three sides of the large stone temple have been excavated and restored. You cannot see the adobe buildings inside the stone walls, which belong to an earlier period. They were later covered up and used as a base for a second storey which unfortunately has been completely destroyed. Some experts think the temple and surroundings were buried on purpose. Others believe it was engulfed by natural disaster. The latter theory is supported by finds of human skeletons. Tombs have been found in front and at the same level as the temple. A wall of a large adobe building under excavation can be seen and runs round the sides and back of the temple. The site is open to tourists, 0800-1700 (US$0.75, children half price); ticket also valid for Pañamarca (**see page 742**), and there is an attractive, shady picnic garden. The Max Uhle Museum opened in 1984 by the ruins: interesting display of Sechín artefacts. It is quite easy to walk to the ruins from Casma. One must walk about 3 km. S to a well posted sign showing a left turn, then simply follow the road for 2 km. to the ruins. (Frequent colectivos from in front of market in Casma, easy to hitchhike from Casma to Sechín, but leave early in the morning; no buses.) 2 km. further along there are two pyramids of the late Chavín period, but these have not yet been excavated.

Sechín is one of the most important ruins on the Peruvian coast. It consists of a large square temple completely faced with carved stone monoliths—probably over 500 of them—which depict gruesome battle scenes: men being eviscerated, heads with blood gushing from eyes or mouths, dismembered legs, arms, torsos, ears, eyes and vertebrae. The style is unique in Peru for its naturalistic vigour. Within the stone temple is an earlier, pre-ceramic mud temple with painted walls. The temples are pre-Chavín, about 1500 BC. (John Hemming)

Chimbote, 420 km. from Lima, is one of Peru's few natural harbours, ample in area and depth of water. Rapidly growing population of 185,000; a new port has been built to serve the national steel industry: iron ore from Marcona field is shipped from the port of San Juan, 547 km. S of Lima; anthracite comes by railway from the hinterland, and power comes from the hydroelectric station in the Cañón del Pato, 129 km. inland. The steel industry creates heavy pollution; also Chimbote is Peru's largest fishing port; fishmeal is exported and the smell of the fishmeal plants is very strong. Bathing is forbidden on the beach near the hotel. Flocks of brown pelicans and masked boobies may be seen from the beach. Shanty towns have burgeoned around. Small airport, but no commercial flights. Public swimming pool at Vivero Forestal.

Hotels *Chimú*, now a State Tourist Hotel (D, with bath, meals US$3.50, uninspiring), Chimbote's cleanest snack bar, there are some cheaper rooms at the back, must ask, safe parking; *Presidente* (3 star), E, with bath, clean, friendly, hot showers, safe parking, poor snack bar, rec.; *Carabelle*, F, round corner from *Presidente*, hot water doesn't work, but good value; *Rivera*, E, good, clean, hot water, restaurant on top floor with good view but poor food; *María Isabel*, F, dingy, helpful; *El Santa*, E, with bath, clean and good; *Venus*, F, near Roggero bus station, useful if you arrive at 0200; *Augusto*, Aguirre 265, F, with shower and toilet, overpriced, clean, front rooms noisy, water intermittent as everywhere in town; *Felic*, Av. José Pardo, 552, F, noisy.

Restaurants *Pollo Gordo*, Prado y Aguirre, good chicken and cold beer; *San Remo*, Pardo y

Villavicencio, seafood, good and cheap, good pisco sours; *Buenos Aires*, Aguirre near beach, popular lunch place; *Marisquito*, Bolognesi near Palacios, good local food, disco at night; *Franco* and *Venecia*, same block, good seafood. You can eat well and cheaply (US$0.50) in the market.

Tourist Office Av. Bolognesi 465.

Buses To Lima, best is Turismo Chimbote on Pardo, US$4.50, 6-7 hrs. The Santa valley road via Huallanca to the Callejón de Huaylas and beyond has been rebuilt, but is still hair-raising (scenery is superb). Bus leaves Chimbote for Huarás daily at 0800 and 2000, via Carás and Cañón del Pato, US$4.40 (Transportes Moreno, Jr. Manuel Ruiz 288, T 321235, book the previous day), 8 hrs. (12 hrs. in rainy season). Road is unsurfaced to Carás (bus to Carás, US$3.65, 6 hrs., daily); bus to Huallanca, US$3.25. Colectivo to Casma, 0700 and 0830 daily, US$1.25. Buses run Chimbote to Trujillo, US$1.10 (Empresa El Aguila, José Gálvez 317, hourly from 0600-2000), Tepsa at 1600; Colectivo to Trujillo, US$1.90, 2 hrs.

Warning Thefts are common around the Moreno bus station. The town's reputation for danger is stressed.

John Streather tells us that about 25 km. S of Chimbote a paved road leads E to the Nepeña valley, where a sculpted precolumbian tomb and the temple of Cerro Blanco may be found; also ruins at *Pañamarca* (pre-Mochica temple), 10 km. from the crossroads. Pañamarca is a town from the Mochica culture, where buildings and animal sculpture remains can be seen. 20 km. from Pañamarca is the site of Paredones with the "Puerta del Sol", and a stone carving, the "monolito de siete huacas".

From Chimbote a road branches off to the NE and, joining another road from Santa, goes up the Santa valley following the route, including tunnels, of the old Santa Corporation Railway. (This used to run as far as Huallanca, 140 km. up the valley, but was largely destroyed by the 1970 earthquake.) At the top of the valley the road goes through the very narrow and spectacular **Cañón del Pato** (where the road is closed to private vehicles because of fears of guerrilla attacks on the hydroelectric plant, but buses still ply) before reaching the Callejón de Huaylas and going on S to Carás and Huarás. From Carás to Santa can be driven, in normal times, in 3 hours.

Just before the Cañón del Pato is **Huallanca** (where everything closes early) with an impressive hydroelectric plant built into a mountain. This can no longer be visited because of guerrilla activities. *Hotel Huascarán*, F, good and friendly.

Carás, is now almost totally restored after the 1970 earthquake, and is reported a good centre for walking; splendid views of Huandoy and Huascarán. Information on mountaineering obtainable from the director of the Huascarán National Park in Huarás, or the Tourist Office in Yungay. Excellent views of the northern *cordilleras* in July and August; in other months, mountains often shrouded in cloud. One has to cross a river by cable (20 mins.) and go to Pueblo Libre to climb Tunaspampa. Carás has a milder climate than Huarás and is more suited to day excursions but it is difficult to change money there.

Hotels *El Cafetal*, friendly, clean, hot water; *Hostal Carás*, Calle Sucre, F, dirty, hot showers; *Chavín*, just off Plaza, F with bath, new, clean, good value (but no views), said to be "best of a poor bunch"; *Morovi*, just outside town on Yungay road, F, clean, friendly, helpful, with bath and hot water; *Herrera*, F.

Restaurants *Jeny*, on plaza, good food and prices; *La Capullana*, excellent local dishes; *Juventud*, rec.; *La Punta Grande*, on corner of turn-off to Lake Parón, inexpensive local meals. Also, *Esmeralda*, Av. Alfonso Ugarte, cheap, good local food, friendly; *Djurjuri*, good food and atmosphere; *Chifa Lorena*, Jr. Sucre 1021, cheap local and Chinese food; unnamed restaurant at Sucre 1003, good, English spoken. About 1 km. S of Carás, open-air *Restaurant Palmira*, serves excellent trout, reasonably priced (open 1200-1800); follow the sign for trout off the main road and go through German-owned carnation farm.

Buses Bus to Lima 14 hrs., direct 1500, via Huarás (to which the 67-km. road is now paved) 0600. Also frequent buses to and from Huarás, US$1.20 (last at 1900), 2 hrs. Bus to Chimbote, daily, 1000, 2200, 7 hrs., through the Santa Valley, US$3.65; Transportes Expreso Moreno, Jr. Daniel Villar 407, T 2014, through the Cañón del Pato, sit on right for views, US$2, 0930, 7 hrs. Chinchay-Suyo to Trujillo at 1730, stops for dinner at Huarás, US$3.10.

From Carás a narrow, rough road branches E to Lake Parón, nestling right under the snow-capped peak of Huandoy (the water level has been lowered, and the lake is to be used for the Cañón del Pato hydroelectric scheme—taxi from **Carás**, or from Huarás, US$15 return, will wait all day at the lake, pick-up US$3 approx., bargain hard), one can stay at a lodge by the lake, US$1.60 p.p.

LIMA TO CALLEJÓN DE HUAYLAS

(unguarded, and therefore may not be possible, at weekends), or at the houses 1-2 km. before the lake, US$1 p.p. Comité 20 colectivos also go to Lake Llanganuco (see following page), 0730, returning 1200, US$2, US$15 by taxi. For hikes in the Cordillera Negra, a truck leaves from Carás market at 1000 to Huata (dirty hotel, F; 2,700 metres) from where one can climb to the Quebrada de Cochacocha (3,500 metres) at the top of which is the Inca ruin of Cantu, and on to the Inca lookout, Torreón Andino (5,006 metres; also reached from Rocracallán, US$1 by truck from Carás). Take water, food and tent with you. 6 km. down a track off the Carás-Huata road are the Inca ruins of Chonta. Alternatively, Prof. Bernardino Aguilar Prieto (former teacher), San Martín 1143 (T 2161—rooms to let, G), close to *Hotel La Suiza Peruana*, Carás, can advise in evenings on 2-3-day hikes in the Torreón Andino area. One can visit his apiary and sample the honey (sold at his town house) as well as camp for free at his farm, La Fronda, 7 km. from Carás, rooms G but you must bring bedding/food/candles etc., colectivo from Carás, US$0.15. N of Carás are hot springs at Shangol. The ruins of Pashash Cabana and Huandoval are reached from Chuquicara, about halfway along the Santa Valley road.

John Streather writes: A spectacular circuit may be made to Chavín (**page 748**) from Carás (or Huarás). Take a Morenos Hnos. bus to Tres Cruces or Yuracmarca on the other side of the Cañón del Pato. A detour from Yuracmarca is along a frightening road to Corongo (0530 bus from Carás, Empresa Callejón de Huaylas from the main square once a week), but only go in summer, or else you may be stuck for months. Eat at the baker's shop on the square; the baker is very helpful with information about ruins in the area. From Tres Cruces (basic friendly restaurant, but no accommodation) one can take daytime lorries to Pomabamba, passing pre-Inca *chullpas*, Yanac, Tarica (**see page 745**), the mining town of Pasacancha (hotel and restaurant) and the Callejón de Conchucos. The road continues through cold, wild mountains and valleys to Andaymayo and Palo Seco to Pomabamba, "city of the cedars" - where I saw not one cedar tree.

Pomabamba is worth a visit on several counts. There are very hot natural springs there, the furthest are the hottest and the best. The lady of the house also sells delicious orange-blossom honey from her own garden; however, fresh vegetables may be in short supply. Various hotels; the best is in a nameless house on the hill going down to the bridge over which lie the hot springs and the path to Yaino. *Hostal Pomabamba*, on main square, F, basic, safe for luggage; *Altamayo*, plaza, basic; *San Martín de Porras*, off the smaller plaza, basic. The restaurant on the corner of the main square is friendly and good (cold though); *Canela*, rec. There is a small museum opposite which the people in the courtyard offices will open free on request. Victor Escudero, who speaks English, runs One Pyramid Travel, Huaraz 209, T 721283; he specializes in archaeological tours, including some little known, unspoilt places, rec. Several good walks into the Cordillera Blanca start from nearby: via Palo Seco or Laurel to the Lagunas Safuna, from which one can go on, if hardy, to Mt. Alpamayo ("the most beautiful mountain in the world") and down to Santa Cruz and Carás—several days' hard walking. Up to the quite large and extensive, though sadly dilapidated, ruins of **Yaino**, on top of a very steep mountain and visible from the main square of Pomabamba—though still a good 4½-5 hours walk away. Ask directions in the village and on the way too. If in doubt, veer left after about two hours of going fairly straight uphill. The ruins, when one reaches them, are certainly worth the effort. The walls are beautifully built and there are two very large buildings, a square one and a circular one. The site commands far and majestic views of the many peaks of the Cordillera. Again, the hardy could continue their walk (several days) to the two lakes of Llanganuco and so to Yungay in the Callejón de Huaylas, or down to Santa Cruz and Carás on the other side. The walk to Yaino and back to Pomabamba can be done in a day if one starts early. Take a good lunch, and lots of juicy fruit—one gets very dehydrated climbing and perspiring in the thin dry air. It's also very cold high up if the sun goes in, so go with warm, waterproof clothes.

Cóndor de Chavín and Peruano Andino buses run S to Chavín and on to Lima, all at night. Buses to and from Lima via Chimbote are Empresa Marino (Ayacucho 1140, Lima), leaving Lima at 0800, Sun. and Wed., and Pomabamba at 0600 on the same days, 20 hrs.

The main road goes on to **Yungay**, which was completely buried by the 1970 earthquake—a hideous tragedy in which 20,000 people lost their lives. The survivors are housed just north of the old town, which is now recovering, with houses and a concrete market (Thurs. and Sun.). A new church is being built. The site now has a few monuments, and a field of rose bushes.

Bed and Board A hotel without a signboard is on the left of the Carhuás road (F); *El Señor Blanco's Hotel* (past maternity hospital), G, breakfast and dinner US$1.40, rec., luggage can be left safely, but women need to beware of Sr. Blanco's overfriendly attitude; *Hostal Gledel*, Av. Arias Graziani (owned by Sra. Gamboa, who is hospitable and a good cook), F, clean, secure, good, friendly, nice courtyard, rec.; *Hostal Yungay*, on plaza, F, clean; *Alojamiento Acuña*, F, clean, meals available. There is also private accommodation. Good food and drink can be found in the new market, and there is a good restaurant run by the local co-operative; also *Comedor Yungay* (good) and *El Portal*.

Tourist Office on the plaza (rarely open); opposite is *Café El Palmero*, which offers simple accommodation, F. There are several trucks which leave from the café for Lake Llanganuco (provided there are at least 10 passengers, US$2 single or return). A return allows only about an hour at the lake. Times of departure always change, so check at the Tourist Office. A tourist minibus to the lake leaves at 0800 on Sat., 2 hrs.

For trekkers, one of the finest walks (trees, flowers, birds, midges) is over the path by Huascarán and Lake Llanganuco (2 lakes: Orkoncocha and Chinancocha) from Yungay to Piscobamba (Yungay to Lake Llanganuco, trucks on Mon., Wed., Fri., at 0400, US$3, and Sun. from Huarás, no trucks will go unless there are enough passengers, and departure is often delayed; trucks to Llanganuco continue on the new road to the Portachuelo Pass at 4,750 metres, beautiful views of Huascarán; return to Yungay at 1000). It is a 5-6 day hike over a well-travelled route, but don't try it unless you are properly equipped. After 3-4 days you reach Llumpa on the Chavín-Piscobamba road (basic accommodation, unfriendly people), from here there are 2 buses per week to Piscobamba, and 2 per week to Chavín. After Llumpa, the trek to Piscobamba becomes rather boring and tiring. There are 2 buses per week between Piscobamba, Pomabamba (see page 744) and Huarás. (Advice and registration for mountain hut at Llanganuco from National Park office. N.B. If making an excursion to photograph Huascarán and Huandoy, note that they are usually hidden by cloud after midday.

Deservedly the most popular walk in the Cordillera Blanca is from Llanganuco through the Portachuelo Pass to Colcabamba, and then through the Punta Unión (4,750 metres) to Cashapampa, Santa Cruz and Carás. This hike takes 3-5 days and is well-signed. Guides useful, US$5-8 a day, will catch trout for you. Entrance to the National Park costs US$1 a day. Some of the route is on Inca roads (see pages 842-843). The mountain flowers and humming birds at these altitudes are magnificent. The road to the lake (full of trout) continues up to the tongue of the glacier of Cerro Chopicalqui (not suitable for cars, 4,830 metres)—insect repellant needed; take food, warm clothes, tent, sleeping bag and a stove. The early morning trucks from Yungay on a new road running from Llanganuco over the Portachuelo Pass go to Vaquería, the first settlement after the pass; get off the truck at the tin shacks on the left after Vaquería; from there the trail descends on S side of stream to Colcabamba, or crosses a stream below thatched farmhouse to join Colcabamba-Punta Unión trail above Colcabamba. At Yanamá, on the eastern side of the Cordillera Blanca, there is lodging and food; a day's hike to the ruins above the town affords superb views (truck Yungay-Yanamá, US$2.50—ask at plaza in Yungay). At Colcabamba, the Calonge family welcome travellers with good meals and basic accommodation (G), and small shop—no sign but a white flag and red geraniums. Cashapampa, the first village at the bottom of the Santa Cruz valley has basic accommodation; meals at the house of Sra. Zenaida Pajuelo. Bus to Carás leaves at 0500 (US$1), there are also trucks; or follow footpath from Santa Cruz village a few km. further uphill. Above Santa Cruz (very basic accommodation—dirty and for midgets!) are hot springs at Huancarhuás, which are being "developed". Lorries for Santa Cruz and Cashapampa leave Carás market at 1230, US$0.50, 3 hrs.

After Yungay, the main road goes to Mancos at the foot of Huascarán (*Hotel Mancos*, F, lovely setting, but bathroom dirty, water rationing) and at **Carhuás** (daily bus service to Huarás, and to Huallanca via the Cañón del Pato), with fair hotels (*Perú*, F, good restaurant; and *Gran Hotel*, E, pleasant, no hot water; *Hospedaje La Merced*, F, excellent, clean, friendly, hot water, rec.; *Restaurant Palma*, good value) and very good walking in the neighbourhood; precolumbian baths at Vicus and La Merced, ruins at Cuntuyoc, Hualcan, Huacoy, Torojirca, Tuyo and Huamanvilca. Carhuás has a *mestizo* festival on October 24, followed eight days later by an Indian festival. Before Huarás the road goes to Marcará (bus to Huarás, US$ 0.50), where there is a branch road 3 km. to Chancos, another thermal resort (*Hotel Chancos* closed but you can camp in the neighbourhood, 2 restaurants, minibus from Huarás). Further up the Huandoy valley is Vicos, set in superb surroundings with views of Nevados Tocllaraju and Ranrapalca. From Vicos, one can walk through the Quebrada Honda to Chacas (*Hostal Pilar*); a road has been built to Chacas. From Chacas you can get transport to San Luis (see page 842). The main road goes on to Tarica (*Hostal Sterling*, G, no hot water, food, friendly).

The valley's focus is **Huarás** (population 80,000), capital of the Department of Ancash, at 3,028 metres, 398 km. from Lima. The city was half destroyed in the earthquake of May 1970. Reconstruction is well advanced; the Plaza de Armas has been rebuilt, except for the Cathedral, which is being resited elsewhere. The setting, with the peaks of Huascarán, Huandoy, and San Cristóbal in the background, is tremendous. Good panoramic views are to be had from the *mirador* at the cross (visible from Huarás) one hour's walk from the town (turn left past the cemetery and head uphill through a small forest). Huarás is becoming a very lively place, popular with young gringos and Peruvians alike. Market day is Thursday.

Festival Patron saints' day, May 3, parades, dancing, music and fireworks; much drinking and overcharging. Prices shoot up at time of Independence celebrations, end-July. Semana del Andinismo end of May, international climbing and skiing week.

Hotels *Termas de Monterrey*, 7 km. N (½ hr. in bus), run by State Tourist Hotel chain, rec. for walking, swimming in warm springs, E (accepts American Express), with bath, good, meals US$3, swimming pool. Rock climbing behind hotel, but don't be too vigorous at the start; it's over 2,750 metres up. *El Patio*, near *Hotel Termas*, E incl. breakfast, friendly, no restaurant, nicely laid out, rec. In town, *Hotel de Turistas*, Av. Centenario (T 2696), C, large rooms, clean, restaurant poor; *Marañón*, E, new, clean, near market, hot water limited; *El Tumi I*, San Martín 1122, E, with bath, good restaurant, fairly good; *Tumi II*, beside *Tumi I*, F with bath, good value; *Hostal Huandoy-Cusco*, F (triple rooms available), communal bathrooms, good; *Hostal Andino (Chalet Suisse)*, C, Jr. Pedro Cochachín 357 (some way from centre), best hotel, clean, meals served (fondue expensive), safe parking, Swiss run, rec.; beautiful view of Huascarán, climbing and hiking gear for hire; *Hostal Colomba*, Calle Francisco de Zela 210, bungalow, rooms D, plus 21%, family-run (German), garden, friendly, safe car parking, English spoken; *Cataluña*, Av. Raymondi 622, E or F in dormitory, restaurant, somewhat expensive, clean, safe, noisy, hot water; *Raymondi*, Av. Raymondi 820, F, central, bath, hot water (a.m. only in ground floor shower), comfortable, unfriendly, charges for left luggage, with café; *Janett*, Av. Centenario 106, E, friendly, hot water, clean, large rooms, rec.; *Edward's Inn*, Av. Bolognesi 121, E, clean, hot shower, laundry, friendly, food available, highly rec.; popular, Edward speaks English and knows a lot about trekking; under same ownership, *Alojamiento de Quintana*, Juan de la Cruz Romero 593, F, hot shower, laundry facilities, clean, popular with trekkers. *Hostal Premier*, Av. Luzuriaga 651-53, T 721954, E with bath (cheaper without), not very hot showers, clean, modern, English spoken by owners' son, helpful, informative, rec.; *Landauro*, on Plaza de Armas, F, cheap, clean, basic, friendly, good breakfast place downstairs; *Hostal Continental*, 20 de Julio y Luzuriaga, G, clean, hot water, friendly, cafeteria, rec.; *Hostal Los Andes*, Av. Tarapacá 316, F, hot water, clean, friendly, with laundry, attractive but noisy, hard beds and prices shoot up in the peak season; *Albergue El Tambo*, Confraternidad Internacional—Interior—122 B, F, clean, clothes washing, 3 rooms with 12 beds, and cooking facilities, nice people; *Alpamayo*, same street No. 126, F with bath, G without, clean, quiet, rents camping eqpt., laundry (or do it yourself), rec. *Pensión Maguiña*, Av. Tarapacá 643, opposite Rodríguez bus terminal, noisy a.m., F, hot water, rooms single to 4-bed, clothes-washing facilities, breakfast available, rucksack store, clean, English and French spoken, helpful in arranging trekking and equipment hire, rec.; *Alojamiento Galaxia* (de Inés Herrera) Jr. Romero 638, hot water F, friendly, rec.; *Hostal Oscar*, Morales, F with bath, hot water, cheap breakfast, rec.; *Familia Estella*, Jirón Nueva Granada 519, F, hot water very intermittent, friendly, safe, rec.; *Casa de Señora López* (ask near Estadio just off Avenida Bolognesi at Santa river end), F, luke-warm showers, safe, washing facilities for clothes, patio, very friendly, rec. *Alojamiento San Martín de Porras*, Las Américas, T 721061, F, clean, friendly, rec.; *Alojamiento Líder*, Fitzcarrald 233, G, hot showers, friendly, safe, rec. *Albergue Juvenil Los Capulíes*, Jr. Los Capulíes 160, Centenario—Huarás (15 mins., walk from the centre—information from the owner's bodega at San Martín 618), F, clean, friendly, showers, cooking and washing facilities, rec. There are usually people waiting at the bus terminals offering cheap accommodation in their own homes.

Hot Public Showers on Av. Raymondi 904, US$0.25.

Restaurants Restaurant and bar at *Ebony 86*, Plaza de Armas, friendly, clean. *Tabariz*, Av. Centenario y Av. Raymondi, good food. On 28 de Julio is *Oja-Yo*, Chinese, good. *Samuel's*, off Luzuriaga, "very rich salads, wide variety, inexpensive, excellent, but check your bill". *La Familia* at Luzuriaga 431, popular with gringos, vegetarian dishes, impersonal; *Leñador*, Luzuriaga 979, good coffee, snacks, German books. Good breakfast at *San Miguel*, San Martín 1001. *La Cabañita* is also good and cheap, as is *Rivioli*, Av. Guzmán Barrón 244. *Francos Parrilladas*, Luzuriaga 410, good grills; *Pepe's Place*, Raymondi 622 (upstairs from *Hostal Cataluña*), expensive but good; *Ticino*, Luzuriaga 651, good pizzas and pastas; likewise at *Pizzería Mamma Mía*, Luzuriaga 808, excellent and cheap. *Créperie Patrick*, Luzuriaga y Raymondi, excellent crêpes; *Ebenezer*, opposite *Mamma Mía*, good local food, clean and cheap. *Las Puyas*, Morales 535, good cheap meals and breakfasts, popular with gringos; *Pío Pío*, Av. Centenario 329, rec.; *Amadeus*, next to Plaza, good breakfast and reputed best coffee in town. *Tasco bar*, Lucar y Torre, popular with climbers. *Paccha'k Pub*, Centenario 290, folklore shows, local and international food, travel information.

Entertainment There are discotheques at *Tabariz, Bodega*. *Peña El Rizzo*, Luzuriaga 455, shows Thurs., Fri., Sat.; *Imantata*, Luzuriaga 424, disco and folk music; *Tambo*, José de la Mar, folk music daily, rec.

Museum Museo Regional de Ancash, containing stone monoliths and *huacos* from the Recuay culture has been set up in the *Casa de Cultura*. Open 1000-1700, Tues.-Sun., US$0.25, pay to take photographs.

Camping Several shops of the trekking agencies sell camping gaz cartridges. Bodega

Santillana, Centenario 417, good for all supplies. Andean Sport Tours, Av. Luzuriaga 571, T 721612, German-owned, rents or sells camping equipment, incl. camping gaz cartridges; treks, climbing, donkeys for hire, US$2 a day, guides, US$5, tents, US$1.50 a day. Tent hire for five days about US$13. Huarás Classic Tours, Luzuriaga 557, friendly, cheap for all trekking and climbing equipment. All prices standard, but not cheap, throughout town; US$100, or airline ticket, deposit usually demanded.

Car Hire Empresa de Transporte Turismo Huascarán, Av. Raymondi 870, T 310099; VW Beetles for US$18 a day, plus US$0.18 per km., vehicles not up to much.

Exchange Banco Internacional changes travellers' cheques; also behind Banco de la Nación on Plaza de Armas, open till 1800. Quite good rates from travel agents. Street changers on Luzuriaga.

Laundry Fitzcarrel, Fitzcarrald, close to bridge; Lavandería El Amigo, Bolívar y Sucre.

Tourist Office Foptur, Av. Luzuriaga 459 on main Plaza beside post office, for Chavín tour and treks; ask there for Miguel Chiri Valle, English speaking, maps available, good for backpacking in the Cordillera Blanca. Also Pomabamba 415, 1st floor, and ground floor of Palacio Municipal, Plaza de Armas. **Trekking & Backpacking Club**, San Martín 995 (Casilla 112), issues magazine *El Trekkero*, maps and library at office, also hires equipment and organizes tours. Asociación de Guías de Montaña, at Casa del Guía, behind Banco Internacional. Better maps of the area are available in Lima. However, the Instituto de Geología y Minería (Av. Guzmán Barrón 582, open a.m. only) sells useful maps for hikers; *Hostal Andino* also sells IGM maps.

Travel Agencies Explorandes, 28 de Julio y Luzuriaga, adventure travel, good. Pablo Tours, Luzuriaga 501 and Chavín Tours, Av. Luzuriaga 502, organize trips to Chavín (US$6, all day), Llanganuco and the Huascarán park, the latter is more expensive. Azul Tours, Av. Luzuriaga 658, helpful, friendly staff, hires good quality trekking equipment, rec. Montrek, Luzuriaga 640, good for rafting on Santa river. In the main, US$5-10 tours to sites other than Chavín are too short; private arrangements with taxis are preferable.

Climbing and Trekking Huarás, which is the climbing centre of Peru, particularly between May and October, is the headquarters of the Huascarán National Park (entrance US$1 per day). The office is on Av. Centenario 912 (Prolongación Av. Raymondi—5th block), behind the Ministry of Agriculture building, helpful staff. For **organized treks**, contact Percy Tapiá, Casilla 3074, Lima 100: prices range from US$26 (16-20 people), to US$40 (under 8 people) daily. One should also contact Andes Adventures, Jr. Simón Bolívar 925, Casilla Postal 925, T 721646, Telex 46502 PE CP, Huarás, run by a Belgian, efficient, Spanish, English, French, German and Dutch spoken, reasonably-priced; also Eudes Morales Flores (speaks fluent English) at Pyramid Adventures, Casilla 25, office: Av. Luzuriaga No. 530, Huarás, T 721864, rec. On the second floor of the *Hotel Residencial Cataluña*, Av. Raymondi, T 72117, José Valle Espinosa, "Pepe", hires out equipment (pricey), organizes treks and pack animals, sells dried food, and is generally helpful and informative. Carlos Rodríguez, *Tasco Bar de Lucho*, PO box 111, Huarás, for climbing and trekking in the Cordillera Blanca.

Buses, Lima Transportes Rodríguez, 3 a day, leaves from office at Roosevelt 354, Lima (timekeeping and maintenance criticized), and Tarapacá 622, Huarás; Expreso Ancash, 4 a day (rec.), Av. Carlos Zavala 177, Lima, and Raymondi 845, Huarás; Arellano-Intersa, Colmena 1635, Lima, and Raymondi 408, Huarás; El Trome, Montevideo 1049, Lima, and Raymondi 422, Huarás (not rec.); Empresa Huarás, Leticia 655 (T 275260), Lima, and Raymondi 601, Huarás; Empresa Callejón de Huaylas, Leticia 626 (leaves at 0730); Co-op. de Transportes Huarás Ltda, Prolongación Leticia 1059, Lima, and Raymondi 680, Huarás (neither too good). Transportes Tadeo, Arenillas 139, Act. Cda. 4, Av. Zarumilla, San Martín de Porras, Lima (an extremely dangerous area of Lima) and Raymondi 450, Huarás. Return from Huarás to Lima mostly in evenings, 8 hrs., average price US$5. Taxi to Lima, US$70 for 5.

Other Buses To Casma (150 km.) 6¼ hrs. US$3.40. Bus to Chimbote (Moreno, Av. Fitzcarrald 309) at 0930, 2000, US$4.90, 9½ hrs. via Cañón del Pato, overcrowded, often delayed, day travel advised for both safety and views, sit on the right for best and scariest views. Bus to Marcará, US$0.50. Colectivos take visitors to see the Cordillera, and there is also a trip to the Chavín site, Huari and Huascarán. To Trujillo, US$6, only with Chinchay Suyo (Gamarra 736) departs 2030, 10 hrs. via Pativilca. Truck to Pativilca on coast, 5 hrs., US$ 2.75, or buses Intersa (old, poor service) and El Trome. To Barranca, Ancash, US$3, 4 hrs. Bus to Carás, US$1.20, 2 hrs. (Ormeño) colectivo frequent; to Yungay US$1 hourly. Buses Huarás-Carhuás-Yungay-Carás run every ½ hr.

Excursions About 8 km. into mountains is *Willcawain* archaeological site (entrance, US$0.60, students US$0.30), the ruins of a Tiahuanaco-style temple, dating from about AD 1000. The site is now signposted; walk down Av. Centenario and take the signed right turn 1 km. out of town, 2½ hrs. uphill walk; for better views on return, take right fork when passing the school, the main road is reached after 2 km. Alternatively, take a colectivo towards Yungay or

Monterrey, get out 2 stops past the *Hotel de Turistas,* turn right and then left at a house for "pirotécnicas" (fireworks). Bring torch. There are more ruins at the end of the track, which goes on 27 km. to Laguna Llaca, but taxis reluctant to go there because track is very poor. Excursion by taxi to the Parque Nacional de **Huascarán** costs about US$15; in the park, puya plants, which flower only once at the end of a hundred-year lifetime, usually May-August, reach heights of 10 metres; they grow in the Quebrada Pachacoto valley, some 57 km. S of Huarás and 26 km. E of the road; there is no sign for the Park: the turning is 3 km. before Catac and the signpost is marked Huanzala. Carpa can be reached on foot, by truck, or by San Cristóbal bus from Catac (continuing to La Unión). You can see the Park cheaply by getting the early Huarás-Lima bus to Pachacoto·crossing, then hitch a ride on the road through the Park. Chavín Tours to the Huascarán Park includes a visit to the glacier on the Quebrada Pachacota and to ice caves; take gloves and food, rec., 7 hrs., US$5 p.p. Punta Callán, on the Cordillera Negra between Huarás and Casma, may be reached (3 hrs.) by truck from the football stadium; spectacular views of the Cordillera Blanca. Hitch, or walk virtually straight down, 2-3 hrs. Inca ruins in the Huarás vicinity include Jongopampa, Canray Grande, Llasha, Pallasca, and Quequepampa. To the hot springs and sauna at Chancos **(see page 745);** minibuses and trucks go there.

S of Huarás, off the main road, is **Recuay,** a provincial capital (*Hotel Santa,* F, basic) where unusual pottery is sold. There are a museum and the Pueblo Viejo de Catac ruins here. Many buses run from Recuay to Huarás and Catac (for Chavín).

Chavín   The Chavín de Huantar ruins, of a fortress temple built about 600 BC, are about 3½-7 hrs. drive (depending on the bus, 109 km., avoid back seats) from Huarás, reached by a rough and rocky spectacular road branching E from the main Huarás-Catac road. Unesco has proposed that the site be designated a worldwide cultural heritage. Entry US$0.75, students US$0.40, camera permit US$0.50. The 1970 earthquake destroyed many of the underground structures and now only the first few levels can be toured, but work is now in progress to excavate and light the tunnels closed by the earthquake as well as other temple mounds so far unexplored. Open 0800-1600, 1000-1600, Sun. and holidays. The main attraction is the marvellous carved stone heads and designs in relief of symbolic "gourd" figures. The carvings are in excellent condition, though many of the best sculptures are in Huarás and Lima. The famous Lanzón dagger-shaped stone monolith of 800 BC is found inside the tunnel. **N.B.** Entrances to the temple buildings are locked: you must either hire a guide at the gate or get a child from the caretaker's house to open them for you. Sr. Chiri, Foptur, can arrange permission to enter. You cannot rely on the chambers being lit; if they are not, ask for the guard—but anyway take a torch.

John Streather writes: There is only one carved head *in situ* on the walls of Chavín now. The best things are the finely drawn stone reliefs of condors, pumas and priest warriors— by far the finest work in stone of any Peruvian, or indeed any Andean, culture of any period. The lines are outstanding for their fluidity, sinuousness, complexity and precision. Nothing like them seems to have existed either before or after them: the earlier Sechín art is clearly a fount of inspiration, but is very clumsy when compared with the delicate exactitude of the Chavín . . . In many ways it resembles early Chinese art more than anything Andean—in its spirit and manner, though not in its symbolism, which is entirely Andean and American.

There are hot sulphur baths about 2 km. S of Chavín (US$0.15 for a bath, reported filthy; camping possible here). Beware of thieves in Chavín village; children try to sell fossils and stonework, or swap them for ballpens. Electricity 1800-0600.

Hotels   *Gantu,* F (not rec.) and *Inca,* F, bathrooms filthy, basic but friendly; also *Monte Carlo,* main plaza, F, fairly clean, warm at night; *Monterrey,* F; *Casa de Alojamiento Geminis,* Jr. Túpac Yupanqui, F, fork left after bridge just past ruins, basic (no bath or shower, toilet in outhouse), but clean and friendly, all meals extra; *Albergue de Turistas,* D, with bath, modern, clean, breakfast expensive, beautiful setting, 1 km. from the town on road to Huari; *Alojamiento Chavín Turist Shelter,* 17 de Enero-Norte 831, F, basic, clean and friendly. **Restaurants** Good one 1½ blocks from ruins, on road to them. *La Ramade; Chavín Turístico,* cheap and friendly; *Montecarlo,* very slow, indifferent food; *Comedor de Cooperativa de Chavín*, behind church, good but difficult to get in, closed between mealtimes. All eating places appear to close after 1830. (Better hotels in Huari, 44 km. further on.) Nowhere to change money in or near Chavín.

Bus to Chavín Huascarán from Huarás, 1000 daily, returns 1000, US$2 (tickets available from the *Comedor El Sol*). A magnificent 6-hr. scenic journey, passing through the mountains and along the River Mosna gorge; spectacular views of the Yanamarey peaks and of many snow-fed waterfalls, road surface very poor. Trucks US$1.25, 7 hrs., but very cold. Several from Catac, early a.m. and late p.m. Chavín Tours and Pablo Tours (tours about US$6) make daytime excursions to Chavín and other places of interest; collection from hotels at 0900. Taxi, Huarás-Chavín, US$15, 3-4 hrs. return. Direct bus Chavín to Lima, 13 hrs. Peru-Andino, Ayacucho 1152, Lima, Tues. at 1400, Sat. at 1300 to Huarás, returning Mon. and Thurs. The Lima-Chavín bus goes on to Pomabamba or Huari. From Barranca, every second day by truck, US$1.50, 17 hrs., trip is very bumpy and cold.

Hiking For the active, there is the possibility of a 4-day walk from Olleros, reached by bus or truck from the *frigorífico* in Huarás (US$0.25). The Olleros village carpenter, on the square, has a room where one can stay. Enquire at National Park Office about necessary equipment for walk. A good map of the route is available from the Instituto Geográfico Militar in Lima, or the Trekking and Backpacking Club in Huarás, line maps from Don Pepe at *Hotel Cataluña*, Huarás (ask directions from anyone you meet along the way). The first day you go half-way along the meadows to the first, nameless Quebrada; on the second, you climb the first pass and sleep in the next valley; on the third, you pass Punta Yanashallash and camp in the valley somewhere after it, but before Jato; on the last day you reach Chavín. The area is isolated, so be sure to take good camping equipment, extra food and plenty of warm clothing. A longer walk may also be made to the Laguna Verdecocha, a glacier lake; this is recommended for experienced climbers only. On the first day of the walk, one reaches the Quebrada Quilloc: the second day, the Quebrada Otuto and the Punta Yanashallash (altitude: 4,680 metres); several Inca remains may be seen en route. On the third day, the trail dips and rises like a roller coaster, passing through the River Shongo valley (spectacular views of the Huachecsa gorge), finally reaching Chavín. A two-day walk from Huarás to the Laguna de Churup (4,250 metres) a beautiful blue lake in a crater beneath a mountain peak beyond the small village of Pitec is possible; a guide is necessary for the inexperienced (ask for Victor, US$6 per day), or a very good map to find the Laguna. A pick-up is supposed to go half-way there, but it is hard to find. It is 18 km. from Huarás, of which the first 15 km. are easy, in the valleys (locals will advise on the route)—follow Av. Raymondi E out of Huarás. Just before Pitec, turn right at a fork, and in Pitec, turn left, just before a mountain stream. From here it is very hard going, initially with no path, then occasional trail markers—the general direction is NE towards the snow-covered peak. The hike can be done in a day, with an early start; take sun cream and food.

Warning Recent reports suggest that tourists in the Callejón de Huaylas have been attacked, not so much by local people, but by dogs (a stick is most useful— otherwise, throw stones).

Probably the best way to see the Santa Valley and the Callejón de Huaylas, which contain some of the most spectacular scenery in Peru, is to take the paved road which branches off the coast road into the mountains just N of Pativilca (**see page 740**), 187 km. from Lima. (About 15 km after the turnoff is *Restaurant El Viajero*, Panamericana Norte, Km 185, good.) This route also gives a more spectacular view of the Cordillera Blanca. In 120 km. it climbs to Lake Conococha (delicious trout available in Conococha village), at 4,100 metres, where the Santa River rises. After crossing the high level surface it descends gradually for 87 km. to Huarás, and goes on to the Callejón de Huaylas, where it runs between the towering Cordillera Negra, snowless and rising to 4,600 metres, and the snow-covered Cordillera Blanca, whose highest point is the 6,768 metres high Huascarán. Farms appear at about 4,000 metres, but most of the farming is around Huarás. The inhabitants grow potatoes and barley at the higher and maize and alfalfa at the lower altitudes. The valley has many picturesque villages and small towns, with narrow cobblestone streets and odd-angled house roofs. (At weekends and holidays beware of reckless Lima drivers on the roads.)

The alternative routes to the Callejón de Huaylas are via the Callán pass from Casma to Huarás (**see page 740**), and via the Cañón del Pato (**page 742**).

Advice to Climbers: The height of the Cordillera Blanca and the Callejón de Huaylas ranges and their location in the tropics create conditions different from the Alps or even the Himalayas. Fierce sun makes the mountain snow porous and the glaciers move more rapidly. The British Embassy advises climbers to take at least six days for acclimatization, to move in groups of four or more, reporting to Club Andino or the office of the guide before departing, giving date at which search should begin, and leaving telephone number of Embassy with money. Rescue operations are very limited and there are only eight guides with training (by the Swiss). Insurance is essential, since a guide costs US$40-50 a day and a search US$2,000-2,500 (by helicopter, US$10,000).

Robert and Ana Cook (formerly of Lima) write of the *Callejón de Huaylas*: The heavy rainy season lasts from Jan. to Mar., while the dry season is from May to Sept. The mean daily temperature is determined by the altitude and hardly varies throughout the year. For instance, at 3,000 metres (the altitude of Huarás) the mean temperature is $14°C$.

Apart from the range of Andes running along the Chile-Argentina border, the highest mountains in South America are along the Callejón and perfectly visible from many spots. From the city of Huarás alone, one can see over 23 snow-crested peaks of over 5,000 metres, of which the most notable is Huascarán (6,768 metres), the highest mountain in Peru. Although the snowline now stands at the 5,000 metres level, it was not long ago (geologically speaking) that snow and ice covered the Callejón at 3,000 metres. Despite its receding snowline, the Cordillera Blanca still contains the largest concentration of glaciers found in the world's tropical zone. From the retreating glaciers come the beauty and the plague of the Callejón. The turquoise-coloured lakes which form in the terminal moraines are the jewels of the Andes and visitors should hike up to at least one during their stay. At the same time these *cochas* (glacial lakes) have caused much death and destruction when a dyke has broken, sending tons of water hurtling down the canyons wiping out everything in their path. Now government engineers combat this problem by monitoring water flows and dyke stability.

Hilary Bradt writes: The Cordillera Blanca offers the most popular backpacking and trekking in Peru, with a network of trails used by the local people and some less well defined mountaineers' routes. Most circuits can be hiked in five days. Although the trails are easily followed, they are rugged and the passes very high—between 4,000 and nearly 5,000 metres—so backpackers wishing to go it alone should be fit and properly acclimatized to the altitude, and carry all necessary equipment. Essential items are a tent, warm sleeping bag, stove, and protection against wind and rain (climatic conditions are quite unreliable here and you cannot rule out rain and hail storms even in the dry season). Trekking demands less stamina since equipment is carried by donkeys. There are various trekking companies in Huarás.

Backpackers should buy a copy of *Trails of the Cordilleras Blanca and Huayhuash* by Jim Bartle, an excellent book detailing every important trail in the Cordillera, plus much useful background information. The book includes a large map which is the best available on the area. The book may be purchased in Huarás, or from Bradt Enterprises, or from the South American Explorers' Club in Lima.

The South American Explorers' Club publishes a good map with additional notes on the popular Llanganuco to Santa Cruz loop, and the Instituto Geográfico Militar has mapped the area with its 1:100,000 topographical series. These are more useful to the mountaineer than hiker, however, since the trails marked are confusing and inaccurate. Recommended guides through the Cordillera Huayhuash are Catalino Rojas and Cerillio Zambrano, both from the village of Llamac; also Alejandro Kayupe in Chiquián. "Jefe", who sells maps and key chains in Chiquián, is to be avoided.

Apart from the books by the Bradts and Jim Bartle (see "Information for Visitors"), recommended reading includes *Guide to the Peruvian Andes* by John Ricker, and *Randonées dans la Cordillère Blanche*, published by Uniclam (Paris). Librería Studium in Lima have a good selection of books on the Cordillera Blanca.

There are two spectacular transandine routes from Huarás to La Unión (and on to Huánuco for Cerro de Pasco, La Oroya, etc.; **see page 830**). The first is by twice weekly direct bus or bus leaving Huarás at 1100 (Señor Huascarán) to Conococha and from there another bus, via Chiquián to La Unión. At *Chiquián* (Hostal San Miguel, clean, simple) one can walk into the Callejón de Huayhuash. There are two poor bus services Lima-Chiquián: Landano, Ayacucho 1040, Lima, Mon., Wed., Sat. at 1100, returning to Lima Mon., Wed., Fri., 1100; Tubsa, Leticia 633, Lima, Mon., Wed., Fri., 1900 to Chiquián, and in both directions Tues., Thurs., Sat., 1400 (bus Huarás-Chiquián from Av. Tarapaca 133, at 1130; then Chiquián-La Unión with Tubsa, Mon., Wed., Fri. at midnight). Or one can take a truck from the crossroads at Lake Conococha (a very cold place). The second is to take a Comité 5 bus to Catac (US$0.85, 1 hr., frequent service from 0630); ask to be set down at garage on the edge of Catac. Take a taxi or walk the 5 km. to Pachocoto (2 cafés with accommodation if stranded). If you cannot get a truck Pachocoto-La Unión (9 hrs., US$2.30), wait for a truck from Lima going to the mines at Huansalá (take warm clothes). The road passes through the Huascarán National Park and ascends to a high section with most rewarding views of gigantic geological features. From Huansalá, bus, truck or walk to Huallanca (8 km.) and take transport on to La Unión "through an entertaining gorge by a demanding gravel road" (Friedrich Dürsch). There are occasional trucks Huarás-La Unión. Bus Huarás-Huallanca, 3½ hrs., US$2.80.

Warning If travelling this route, beware of armed robbery; at road blocks it is best that drivers do not get out of the car. There has been guerrilla activity in this area. Check conditions in advance.

museo de arte
prehispánico
de méxico

rufino tamayo

Nº 01340

precio $ 8,000.00 morelos 503 oaxaca, oax.

THE NORTHERN OASES (3)

N of the mouth of the River Santa the Andes recede, leaving a coastal desert belt of from 8 to 16 km. wide containing the three great oases of Northern Peru—the areas of Trujillo, Chiclayo and Piura.

N of Chimbote we cross the valleys of Chao and Virú, coming after 137 km. to the first great oasis of northern Peru, Trujillo. In the valley there is an abrupt line between desert and greenery; cultivation requires irrigation ditches which take their water from far up in the mountains. The area's port is **Salaverry,** exporting sugar and minerals, importing consumer goods and machinery. There is an 8 km. road to Trujillo.

The Quiruvilca copper mines are 120 km. inland by road from Salaverry. The concentrating plant at Shorey is connected with the mines by a 3 km. aerial cableway, and with its coal mine by a further 8 km. The ore is then taken by a 40 km. cableway to Samne, whence it is sent by road to Salaverry.

Trujillo, capital of the Department of La Libertad, disputes the title of second city of Peru with Arequipa. Population 750,000. The traveller entering Trujillo is delighted with its surrounding greenness against a backcloth of brown Andean foothills and peaks. Founded by Pizarro, 1536 (and named after his native town in Spain), it has moved with the times, but still retains many old churches, graceful colonial balconies and windows overhanging its modern pavements, of homes built during the reigns of the viceroys. Besides the Cathedral it has 10 colonial churches as well as convents and monasteries. Its University of La Libertad, second only to that of San Marcos at Lima, was founded in 1824.

Near the Plaza de Armas is the spacious 18th century house in which General Iturregui lived when he proclaimed the city's freedom from Spain in 1820. It is now the exclusive Club Central and Chamber of Commerce, at Pizarro 688 (may

TRUJILLO ENVIRONS
NOT TO SCALE
101

To Chicama Valley
Pacasmayo, Chiclayo

Panamerican Highway

Huanchaco

Caballo Muerto

Galindo

Huaca El Dragón

TRUJILLO

Laredo

Chan Chan

Huaca La Esmeralda

To Otusco, Coina, Huamachuco

RÍO MOCHE

Huaca del Sol And Huaca de la Luna

Buenos Aires Beach

PACIFIC OCEAN

Moche

Puerto Salaverry

To Chimbote, Lima

N

TRUJILLO CENTRE
NOT TO SCALE
101

14 To Pacasmayo Chiclayo

To Airport, Huanchaco, Chan Chan

INDUSTRIAL

ESTETE

Plazuela El Recreo

COLON

ESTADIO MANSICHE

DE LA TORRE

AV. MANSICHE

SALAVERRY

JORGE CHAVEL

D.A. CARRION

PEDRO MUÑIZ

ZEPITA

AV. ESPAÑA

SAN MARTIN

INDEPENDENCIA

GAMARRA

PIZARRO

BOLIVAR

JUNIN

AYACUCHO

21

6

24

27

5

12

18

8

13

9

23

19

2

FCO.

3

26

25

10

20

1

16

4

ORBEGOSO

AV. LIBERTAD

CLUB LIBERTAD

15

DIEGO DE ALMAGRO

GRAU

JESUS DE NAZARETH

17

7

11

BOLOGNESI

22

ESPAÑA

AV. ESPAÑA

ALFONSO UGARTE

To Chimbote And Lima

be visited in mornings). Two other beautiful colonial mansions on the Plaza have been taken over by the Banco Central and Banco Hipotecario, which maintain as museums the parts they do not need as offices (they may be visited a.m.). Certain other mansions, still in private hands, may occasionally be visited with the help of Trujillo Tours; they include the magnificent Orbegoso house at Pizarro 316 and the one at Junín 682; also the Casa de los Condes de Aranda, Bolívar y Gamarra; the Casa del Mariscal de Orbegoso in the 5th block of Calle Orbegoso; Casa del Mayorazgo; Casa Ganoza Chopitea, 4th block of Independencia (which has a private museum that can be seen when Sr. Ganoza is in residence); Casa Madalengo, Pizarro y Gamarra; Casa Baanante, in Grau near Almagro.

The focal point is the spacious Plaza de Armas, with a sculptured group to the heroes of the Liberation (note the short legs on the statue, reportedly the result of the Church's plea that it should not be taller than the Cathedral). Fronting it is the Cathedral, with the old palace of the Archbishop next door; the *Hotel Trujillo*; the building in colonial style of the Sociedad de Beneficencia Pública de Trujillo; and the Municipality building. Many churches damaged in the 1970 earthquake. One of the best, La Merced at Pizarro 550, with picturesque moulded figures below the dome, is being restored, but part of the dome has collapsed because of building work next door. El Carmen church and monastery, described as the "most valuable jewel of colonial art in Trujillo", is still closed after the earthquake. Other old churches include La Compañía, near Plaza de Armas; San Francisco on 3rd block of Gamarra; Belén on 6th block of Almagro; Santa Clara on 4th block of Junín; San Agustín on 6th block of Mariscal Orbegoso; Santa Ana on 2nd block of same street; Santo Domingo on 4th block of Bolognesi. There are also two markets, one on Gamarra (with clean showers, abundant water, US$0.10) and the Mercado Mayorista on Calle Roca. The city's water supply is generally poor.

Archaeological Museum, normally open 0800-1300 in Jan.-March and 0800-1200, 1500-1800 the rest of the year, Pizarro 349 (entrance, US$0.60), recommended; it has an interesting collection of pottery. Another place to visit in Trujillo is the basement of the **Cassinelli** garage on the fork of the Pan-American and Huanchaco roads; it contains a superb private collection of Mochica and Chimú pottery. Be sure to ask for a demonstration of the whistling *huacos*; entry, US$1.25, open 0830-1130, 1530-1630. Sr. Cassinelli has plans to construct a larger museum. The University has a Zoological Museum, San Martín, corner with Bolognesi (0745-1300, 1500-1900).

Fiestas   Second half of September or first half of October transport and hotels booked. Other busy periods are around Mothers' Day (in March/April) and the last week of January, when the Nacional Marinera contest is held (dancing by all ages, public participation and viewing welcomed).

Warnings   As with all Peruvian cities, Trujillo is troubled by theft—beware of robbers working in pairs, especially beyond the inner ring road, Av. España, towards the hill and in the Sánchez Carrión district at night.

Hotels   *Turistas*, Plaza de Armas, D with bath (cheaper without), accepts American Express, full of character, rooms on street are noisy, meals US$4, excellent buffet lunch on Sun. (closed for restoration, 1987); *El Golf* (near California district), C, swimming pool, burglars at night; *Los Jardines*, 4 km. from centre, bungalows in garden, buses to town, D; *Turismo*, 7th block of Gamarra, E, occasional hot water, laundry service, restaurant, good; *San Martín*, in 7th block of San Martín, E, with bath (scant hot water), clean but some rooms damp, has more than 100 rooms, no restaurant. *Opt Gar* (5th block Grau), C, with bath, good, friendly, rec., excellent restaurant (try sea food) and snack bar; *Los Escudos*, Orbegoso 676, T 243523, E, with bath and hot water, breakfast, small garden, rec.; *Continental*, Gamarra, opp. market, F, clean, good, safe, restaurant, rec.; *Hostal España*, Jirón Unión 546, F, clean and friendly (near Antisuyo/Quiroz bus

Key to Map of Trujillo
1. Plaza de Armas; 2. Cathedral; 3. La Merced; 4. La Compañía; 5. San Francisco; 6. Santa Clara; 7. Santo Domingo; 8. Casa Iturrégui; 9. Casa de los Condes de Aranda; 10. Casa del Mariscal Obregoso; 11. Casa del Mayorazgo; 12. Casa Ganoza Chopitea; 13. Casa Madalengo; 14. Museo Casinelli; 15. Archaeological Museum; 16. Zoological Museum; 17. Post Office; 18. Foptur, Tourist Office; 19. Immigration; 20. Central Market; 21. Tepsa Office; 22. Tepsa buses; 23. Chincay-Suyo office; 24. Buses Díaz; 25. *Hotel Turistas*; 26. *Hotel Continental*; 27. *Hostal Americano*.

station); *Hostal Monterrey*, Av. Los Incas 256, T 241673, open 24 hrs., F, friendly, comfortable (close to Tepsa, good for late arrivals); 3 blocks down is *Hostal Rayers*, G with bath, hot water, friendly but dirty; *Primavera*, Nicolás de Piérola 872, E, noisy on the street side, modern and cool; *Hostal Americano*, Pizarro 764, is a vast, old building, now refurbished, F, with bath, rooms without bath are noisy (back on to cinema), most rooms without window, occasional warm water, basic, comfortable, many gringos, parking; *Vogi*, on Ayacucho, E with bath, clean, highly rec. *Hostería Recreo*, Astete 647, T 246991, F, clean, friendly, safe, restaurant, rec.; *Hostería El Sol*, E, opened by the late Dr. Kaufmann of Coina (**see page 757**) and now run by his family, castle-shaped, 55 beds, very clean and quiet, 10 mins. from centre by bus to Santa Inés or Huanchaco (US$0.50 by taxi), at Calle Los Brillantes 224, in front of the Parque Ramón Castilla, in Urbanización Santa Inés. For a private *pensión* contact the family Bravo Díaz, Huayna Capac 542, Urb. Sta. María, T 243347, very friendly, cheap (Clara Bravo Díaz is a tour guide); Familia Moreno, Huáscar 247, F, near centre, clean, quiet, safe, or Cotrina Castillo, Pedro Muñiz 792. See also under Huanchaco, **page 756**.

Restaurants *Hotel Opt Gar*, lunch only except for guests, rec.; *Chifa Oriental*, Gamarra 735, rec.; *El Pesquero*, Junín 118, good fish; *Morroco*, Av. Bolívar, smart and cheap; *Santa Inés*, Calle Los Robles, good fish, try the corvina; *Grau* (on Grau), lunch only, good Criollo food.

Vegetarian restaurants: *Salud y Vigor*, Bolívar 787; *Alfa y Omega*, Bolívar 767; *Naturista*, Pizarro 671, very cheap and filling; *Gran Fraternidad Universal*, Bolívar y Colón.

Pollos Bolívar, Bolívar 577, chicken and salad. Excellent local dishes at *Pedro Moriallas* in nearby seaside resort of Buenos Aires. Good Argentine-style food at *Parrillada El Gaucho*. *24 Horas*, Jr. Gamarra, reasonably priced meals for about US$1, always open, as the name implies; *Oasis* (next to *Hotel Turismo*), good fritos. *ABL*, San Martín 427, large, good portions of chicken; *ABC*, on Orbegoso, likewise; *De Marco*, Pizarro 725, good, especially the ice creams, set menu for US$1, desserts and cakes. *La Calesa*, Pizarro 716, good snack bar; *Romano*, opp. *Hotel Americano*, at Pizarro 747, good cheap menu, highly rec.; *El Mesón de Cervantes*, Pizarro, bar-restaurant, polite, good cheap food; *Ceviche del Rey*, Av. Mansiche opposite clinic, seafood, open only until 1800. *Pizzería Valentino*, Orbegoso block 2, very good; another on Pizarro, near *Hotel Americano*, very good. *Subterráneo*, Plaza Murillo, set lunch US$1. New bar, *Las Tinajas*, on Plaza, good. *La Pileta* (next to Tepsa bus office, Astete 472, strongly rec. for good local food) and *El Recreo*, Bolívar 879, good for breakfast. *La Miel*, Jirón Bolívar 600, good breakfasts, poor coffee, friendly. Wholewheat bread at *Panadería Chalet Suizo*, Av. España e Independencia.

Note Tourists may be approached by vendors selling *huacos* and necklaces from the Chimú period; the export of these items is strictly illegal if they are genuine, but they almost certainly aren't.

Taxis Town trip, US$0.45. Chan Chan, Huanchaco, US$2.20. Taxi driver Jorge Enrique Guevara Castillo, Av. del Ejército 1259, Altos 1, rec. By the hour, in town, US$3, outside US$4.

Night Club Granja Azul—country club. Billy Bob's for drinking. Discotheques: Las Rocas, The Drive Inn.

Peruvian-North American Cultural Institute Húsares de Junín y Venezuela, T 245832, 232512.

Laundry Rapilavo, Grau 337, good and cheap.

Camera Repairs Laboratorios de Investigación Científica, San Martín 745, over Fuji shop opp. *Hotel San Martín*, good.

Post Office Corner of Independencia and Bolognesi. Entel for international phone calls: Calle de la Puerta Aranda 680.

Hospital Anglo-American Hospital, good, reasonable fees.

Exchange Banco NorPerú on Pizarro, recommended for changing cheques and cash with no delay, good rates. Banco Popular del Perú, Gamarra, for cheques (a protracted operation). América Tours, Plaza de Armas, cash dollars only at good rates; Ghia Tours, near Plaza, changes travellers' cheques outside banking hours.

Tourist Office Foptur, Independencia 628, T 24-1936; Pizarro 402, very helpful, and at airport. Maps and information also from Touring and Automobile Club, and from Gira Tours on Calle Independencia; maps from Librería Ayacucho, Ayacucho 570. Tourist Police have an office at Pizarro 422 on the corner of Plaza de Armas; they wear white uniforms and are extremely helpful; will even help lone travellers to visit Chan Chan safely.

Travel Agents Sra. Carmen Melly, Trujillo Tours, Gamarra 440 (T 233-069), recommended for knowledgeable guides (Napoleon speaks good English and Italian) and efficient service. San Valentín Tours, Orbegoso 585 (T 232-812), ask for Sr. Jorge Sánchez, good local tours, very reasonable.

Pedro Puerta, an English speaking expert on Chan Chan and former college librarian, who has an office at Km. 560 on the Panamericana Norte, 2½ hr. from the Plaza de Armas, offers interesting tours to Chan Chan, Huaca El Dragón, and Huaca La Esmeralda. He charges US$3 per hour for a 6-7 hr. tour, not including taxi hire and lunch for him and the taxi driver. He also sells prints of Chan Chan reliefs and Mochica pottery motifs, beautiful but expensive. He gives a slideshow at 2000 nightly at the *Hotel Turistas*.

Immigration   Edificio Demarco, 3rd floor, Diego de Almagro 225. Gives 60-day visa extensions (for 90 days proof of funds and onward ticket required). Involves taking forms to Banco de la Nación, and waiting for papers to be stamped—time-consuming.

Air Transport   Faucett, Pizarro 532, and AeroPerú, Junín 537, daily flights from Lima, 1 hr., Faucett from Tumbes. AeroPerú fly to Cajamarca (Mon., Fri., low season), 25 mins. Tarapoto and Juanjui (Tues. and Sat.). Faucett and AeroPerú to Iquitos, change at Tarapoto, US$28. Flights by Faucett to Cajamarca, Chiclayo and points N and to a multitude of small jungle towns. Taxi to airport, US$2.50; or take bus to Chan Chan and get out at airport turn-off.

Buses   To Lima, 551 km., colectivo, 7-9 hrs., US$11, or by bus, 8-9 hrs. US$5.50 with Tepsa (3 a day—station in Trujillo, Av. Almagro, between Avs. España and Grau, tickets Astete 482), Peru Express, Chinchay-Suyo (5 a day, González Prada 337, insist on ticket before you board or you may get charged extra for luggage), Expreso Continental (part of Ormeño), US$6, or Roggero; mostly at night. To Lima, Roggero departs at 0930, Chinchay-Suyo at 1000 and Panamericana at 1100, 2200 and 2330. Try to book your bus to Lima a day in advance: they fill up quickly. Buses to Lima quite frequent but difficult to go north as buses booked for days; try Emtrafesa (Av. Miraflores with España) N to Pacasmayo (US$1, 2½ hrs.), Chiclayo (US$2, 3 hrs.), Piura, Tumbes. To Huarás (via Pativilca) with Chinchay-Suyo, US$6, 10 hrs., depart 2030, daily (Jirón Bolívar 720, book ahead). To get to Huarás by day you no longer have to spend the night in malodorous Chimbote. (El Aguila at 0530 and 0545 should connect with 0800 Moreno bus to Huarás). Chinchay-Suyo and Tepsa have buses to Casma, 3 hrs., US$2.40 and to Tarapoto, departing at 1200 daily. Bus to Chimbote US$1.10, 1½ hrs., Empresa Cajamarca, Av. España 2023-27, Empresa El Aguila, Av. Nicaragua y Moche, Empresa Chinchay-Suyo leaves 1300; Empresa San Pedro, Av. Moche, 3rd block, every 2 hrs.; colectivo to Chimbote, 2 hrs., US$2. Colectivo to Cajamarca US$6.50, daily at 2200, 0500, 8 hrs., with Empresa Cajamarca (very old buses), 2100, 2300 with Díaz bus, Av. N. de Piérola 1059, US$3, El Cóndor buses (Pizarro 789) at night, 6-9 hrs.; US$4.50 (also Etucsa); to Cajamarca in daylight, take Chiclayo bus to La Cruz, turn-off for Cajamarca, and wait there for a collectivo to Cajamarca, US$3, 8 hrs. Colectivo to Piura, 1000 daily, US$10; bus to Piura (Tepsa, 2000, Chinchay-Suyo 1300 and at night), US$5, 6½-9 hrs.; to Chiclayo, US$3, 3-4 hrs. Tepsa to Tumbes, daily at 1930, US$5 and up, Expreso Moderno and Sudamericano (Jr. Montevideo 618), 15 hrs. Bus to Sullana, Sudamericano, also Chinchay-Suyo at 2300, arrive about 0800, poor road surface.

Excursions from Trujillo   About five km. to the crumbling ruins of *Chan Chan,* imperial city of the Chimú domains and largest adobe city in the world.

The ruins consist of nine great compounds built by Chimú kings. The nine-metre high perimeter walls surrounded sacred enclosures with usually only one narrow entrance. Inside, serried rows of storerooms contained the agricultural wealth of the kingdom, which stretched 1,000 km. along the coast from near Guayaquil to Paramonga. Most of the compounds contain a huge walk-in well which tapped the ground water, raised to a high level by irrigation higher up the valley. Each compound also included a platform mound which was the burial place of the king, with his women and his treasure, presumably maintained as a memorial. The Incas almost certainly copied this system and transported it to Cuzco where the last Incas continued building huge enclosures. Chan Chan was taken by the Incas about AD 1450 but not looted; the Spaniards, however, despoiled its burial mounds of all the gold and silver statuettes and ornaments buried with the Chimú nobles. The dilapidated city walls enclose an area of 28 square km. containing the remains of palaces, temples, workshops, streets, houses, gardens and a canal. What is left of the adobe walls bears well-preserved moulded decorations and painted designs have been found on pottery unearthed from the debris of a city ravaged by floods, earthquakes, and treasure seekers. Heavy rain and flooding in 1983 damaged much of the ruins and although they are still standing, many of the interesting mouldings are closed to visitors. The Ciudadela of Tschudi has been reconstructed (15 min. walk from the road), open 0830 to 1600 (but it may be covered up if rain is expected).

A ticket which covers the entrance fees for Chan Chan, the Huaca El Dragón and the Huaca La Esmeralda (for 2 days) costs US$2.75. Minibuses leave from José Gálvez 394, corner of Los Incas, near market, or corner of España and Orbegoso/Mansiche, or from Salaverry, US$0.15, last one returns about 1200; Trujillo-Huanchaco bus, US$0.10 to Chan Chan entrance; these buses are worked by teams of pickpockets; taxi, US$1.20.

Warning If you walk to the ruins from the main road, keep to the path. Do not go to Chan Chan alone or in couples; it is preferable to go with a guide; Oscar has been recommended (normal fee US$1.50), so has Gustavo Prava, who knows his history and produces excellent woodblock prints for sale; so has Clara Bravo Díaz, Huayna Capac 542, T 243347. White shirted, armed police are in evidence. Sgto. José Soto Ríos, T 251489, is a good guide, speaks English. Do not walk on Buenos Aires beach near Chan Chan as there is serious danger of robbery, and being attacked by dogs.

The restored temple, Huaca El Dragón, dating from the Mochica empire of between 800 and 100 BC, is also known as Huaca Arco Iris (rainbow), after shape of friezes which decorate it. It is on the W side of the Pan-American Highway in the district of La Esperanza; Taxi costs US$1; open 0800-1700.

The Caballo Muerto ruins, about 11 km. inland up the Moche valley, are now forbidden to visitors, and the sculptures have been re-buried to protect them from robbers.

The poorly restored Huaca La Esmeralda is at Mansiche, between Trujillo and Chan Chan, behind the church. Buses from Pasaje Agustín, between Orbegoso and Gamarra, 2 blocks from Plaza (not a friendly district).

A few km. south of Trujillo are the huge Moche pyramids, the Huaca del Sol and the Huaca de la Luna (open all the time, entry free, a police hut is manned from 0700 to 1300), taxi US$6 return, colectivo from the Mercado Mayorista, Calle Suárez, US$0.25, marked Moche El Alto or La Compiña if at all, leaves 0800 and 1300, stops right in front of the ruins, alternatively bus marked Salaverry, El Alto or La Compiña, US$0.15 from corner of Zela near Mercado Mayorista, get out at Bodega El Sol on the right hand side of the road; opposite is a huge Sprite sign. Here starts a path to Moche, about an hour's walk; it is inadvisable to walk unless in a large group). The pyramids consist of millions of adobe bricks and are the largest precolumbian structures in South America (they are being restored, and the interior passageways of the Huaca de la Luna can now be seen; the site is under the control of the tourist police). An interesting feature of the site is the innumerable number of ancient pottery shards lying around on the ground.

The small fishing village of **Huanchaco** is worth visiting to see the narrow pointed fishing rafts, known as *caballitos*, made of tortora reeds and used in many places along the Peruvian coast. Unlike those used on Lake Titicaca, they are flat, not hollow, and ride the breakers rather like surfboards. These craft are depicted on ancient Mochica and Chimú pottery. The village is overlooked by a huge church from the belfry of which are superb views. Children sell precolumbian *objets d'art* and beads; beware of eating fish in the hut-like restaurants as they aren't very hygienic. Bus to Huanchaco, US$0.10, from corner of Av. España and Av. Mansiche (regular ringroad bus, every 10 mins.), or, after 1830, Pasaje Agustín, Trujillo, 2 blocks from Plaza about 1 an hour; taxi US$4. Fiestas throughout January and February.

Hotels Hostal Sol y Mar, Jirón Ficus 570, F (more expensive with hot water) some rooms with bath and balcony, kitchen facilities, friendly owner, garden, rec.; *Hostal Bracamonte*, Los Olivos 503, F, friendly, comfortable, good, chalets with private bath, pool, own water supply, emergency generator, rents bicycles, secure, bar nearby, good pies and cakes (beware of monkey when eating lemon meringue pie, he's very fast), English spoken, highly rec.; *Hostal Huanchaco*, Larco 287 on Plaza, also F, clean and friendly, swimmimg pool, cafeteria with home-made cakes, highly rec.; *Hostal Las Palmeras*, Calle Las Palmeras, G-F, 6 rooms, hot water in bathrooms, cooking facilities, clean, American owner has extensive folk-art collection; *Barraca*, F, private showers; *Caballitos de Totora*, E, swimming pool, friendly, nice garden, but rooms not too clean, the owners are to open a vegetarian restaurant and hold cultural events at the hotel; cheap accommodation at the house of Señora Consuelo, about US$0.50 p.p. Accommodation, inc. food, with families, easy to find, US$2-3 a day.

Restaurants Good fish restaurants on the sea front *La Casita de la Playa*, owned by Walter (an American), meals for US$1.25, highly rec.; *Viña del Mar, El Peón, El Erizo* rec.; *Violetta*, a private house (good meals provided) and Familia Flores, popular; *El Tramboyo*, near the pier, good, helpful, friendly. *Lucho del Mar*, excellent sea food; *Piccolo*, 5 blocks from plaza, cheap, friendly, sometimes live folk music; *Mrs Pepsi*, close to Hostal Bracamonte, good and cheap, rec.; *Colonial*

Club, main square, run by Belgians, chicken or meat, US$1-1.50, good. Try picarones, people come from Trujillo especially to eat them.

A visit may be made from Trujillo to one of the sugar estates, say the Hacienda Cartavio, in the Chicama valley (43 km.). At Laredo (bus from Trujillo, near central market, 7 km.), a sugar refinery can be visited—the tour is free; apply to public relations office in administration building; there are also interesting ruins at Galindo, near Laredo. One of the biggest sugar estates in the world, also in the Chicama valley, is the Casa Grande cooperative. It covers over 6,000 hectares and employs 4,000 members. Visits (guided) are only possible before 1200; US$0.70 by bus. The Chiclín museum, once famous for items from Chan Chan, now contains interesting collection of colonial religious paintings and statuary. Ruins in the Chicama valley: Huaca Prieta and Chiquitoy; colectivos from Av. España, change at Cartavio.

132 km. E from Trujillo is the village of **Coina,** at 1,500 metres in the Sierra Alto Chicama, where the late Dr. Kaufmann, from Germany, opened a hospital for Indians and built the *Hostería El Sol,* with glorious views, E, for full board, F, bed only. Walking. English, French and German spoken. Information from the *Hostería El Sol,* at Calle Los Brillantes 224, Santa Inés, Trujillo (T 23 1933). Mail can be forwarded to Apartado 775, Trujillo.

To the NE of Trujillo is Cajamarca, which can be reached either from Trujillo or from Pacasmayo (paved throughout). The old road from Trujillo is poor, taking 12-15 hours (as opposed to 8 hrs. via Pacasmayo), but it is more interesting, passing over the bare puna before dropping to the Huamachuco valley. Off it lies **Otusco,** an attractive Andean town with an imposing but unfinished church and narrow cobbled streets. Further on, at the mining town of Shorey, a road branches off to **Santiago de Chuco,** birthplace of the poet César Vallejo, where there is the annual festival of Santiago El Mayor in the second half of July. The main procession is on July 25, when the image is carried through the streets. The road runs on to the colonial town of **Huamachuco,** 181 km. from Trujillo, which has a huge main plaza and a controversial modern cathedral. There is a colourful Sunday market. A 2-hr. walk (take the track which goes off to the right just after crossing the bridge on the road to Trujillo) takes you to the extensive ruin of a hilltop pre-Inca fortress, Marcahuamachuco (car US$5 p.p.).

Huamachuco Hotels Best is *Hostal San Francisco,* Sánchez Carrión 380, F, clean, hot shower; *La Libertad,* G, rooms fairly clean, bathrooms filthy; also *Sucre,* G. Rec. restaurants: *Caribe,* quite good, and *El Sol* (both on main square), *El Cairo,* Sánchez Carrión 754, good food and service, rec. and *Danubio.* Good snacks at *Salón Venecia,* Carrión near main plaza.

Buses Transportes Quiroz from Trujillo, US$5, 12 hrs., at 1530, 1700, 1800, take warm clothing; Antisuyo to Trujillo three daily, US$4, 10 hrs. There are also colectivos from Trujillo. Buses to Cajamarca, US$1.50; to Casa Grande, US$0.85. Direct bus to Lima, 24 hrs.

From Huamachuco buses (Empresa Huancapata which start in Trujillo) run to Tayabamba (important ruins nearby), on the far bank of the Marañón, passing through the old gold-mining centres of Patáz province, such as Parcoy and Buldibuyo. This journey takes a good 18 hours in "normal" conditions. Not far, but a time-consuming journey on mule-back, from Patáz itself (a friendly gold-mining town, about 100 km. from Huamachuco) are the unique circular ruins of El Gran **Pajatén** (pre-Inca); ask at Tourist Office in Cajamarca for details. A national park, Río Abiseo, incorporating Gran Pajatén, four other sites—La Playa, Las Papayas, Los Pinchudos and Cerro Central—and the surrounding cloud forest, is scheduled to open for visitors in 1991; until then you need a permit (hard to get) from the Instituto Nacional de Cultura in Lima. Also worth seeing in the Huamachuco area are Laguna Sausacocha (with Inca ruins, similar to those of Vilcashuamán, near Ayacucho, nearby) and *haciendas* Yanasara and Cochabamba, deep down in the valley of the river Chusgón, about 2-3 hrs. by truck east of the town. Yanasara, noted for its fighting bulls, is still in the hands of its long-term owner, Francisco Pinillos Montoya, a well-known local character. There is a guest house at Cochabamba, which used to be the Andean retreat of the owners of the Laredo sugar plantation, near Trujillo. The climate, at about 2,300 metres, is mild.

There is a 2-day walk from Bolívar in the NE to Huamachuco, parts of which follow an Inca trail used by Túpac Yupanqui (**see also page 842**). One walks from Bolívar to Bambamarca, then down the stone steps leading to the Calemar trail, which crosses the River Marañón. At Pallar, there are trucks to Huamachuco. Be sure to take food, water, a small kerosene cooker and a compass; this is an arduous trip and not recommended for beginners.

From Huamachuco the road runs on 48 km. through impressive eucalyptus groves to **Cajabamba,** which lies in the high part of the sugar-producing and once malaria-infested Condebamba valley. It has an attractive Plaza de Armas. Several buses daily to Huamachuco; Quiroz, Antisuyo, about 3 hrs., US$1.75, also trucks and lorries. Two direct buses a day from Trujillo, 12 hrs.

The best hotel is the *Flores* (F, with toilet, friendly, clean) on the Plaza de Armas; *Hostal Bolívar*, F, including fleas but without bath; also *Ramal*, F, friendly; *Restaurant Gloriabamba* good.

Cajabamba can also be reached in a strenuous but marvellous 3-4 day hike from Coina (see above). The first day's walk brings you to Hacienda Santa Rosa where you stay overnight. Then you cross the mountains at about 4,000 metres, coming through Arequeda to Cajabamba. The ruins at Huacamochal may be seen en route; the scenery is spectacular. It is advisable to hire a guide, and a donkey to carry the luggage. The cost for both is about US$4 a day. A map of the route is available from the Post Office in Coina.

The road continues from Cajabamba through San Marcos (basic hotel), important for its Sunday cattle market, to Cajamarca. Bus to Cajamarca (124 km.), Atahualpa and Empresa Díaz leaving early in the morning, takes 6 hrs., US$3.

Pacasmayo, port for the next oasis northward, is 100 km. N. of Trujillo on the Pan-American Highway running N to Chiclayo (bus, 2 hrs., US$0.75). Population: 12,300.

Hotel *Ferrocarril*, F, on seafront, quiet and clean, no hot water (ask for water anyway); *Panamericano*, Leoncio Prado 18, F, with private cold shower, good value, friendly, clean, safe, reasonable restaurant downstairs; *San Francisco*, opp. *Panamericano*, F, basic, OK. Several cheap restaurants on the main street.

Pacasmayo is the best starting point for visiting Cajamarca. The new paved 180 km. road to it branches off the Pan-American Highway soon after it crosses the Jequetepeque River. The river valley has terraced rice fields and mimosas may often be seen in bloom, brightening the otherwise dusty landscape. A few km. to N on other side of River Jequetepeque are the ruins of Pacatnamú—pyramids, cemetery and living quarters of nobles and fishermen, possibly built in Chavín period. Evidence also of Moche tribes. At the mining town of *Chilete*, a worthwhile diversion is to take the road N to San Pablo; 21 km. from Chilete are the stone monoliths of the Kuntur Huasi culture, which resemble those of San Agustín in Colombia. There are occasional buses from Chilete to the site, 1½ hrs., then 20 mins.' walk (no signs; you must ask locals), then a long wait for transport back, best to hitch. In Chilete, hotels *Amazonas* and *San Pedro*; restaurant *Montecarlo* serves cheap *cuy* and other dishes. Truck to Chilete from the police control 1 km. from main plaza in Cajamarca, US$0.85. On the road to Cajamarca is Yonán, where there are petroglyphs.

An alternative route from Trujillo to Cajamarca, via Contumazá, passes through the cane fields and rice plantations of the Chicama valley before branching off to climb over the watershed of the Jequetepeque. From Contumazá, an attractive little town, trucks can be taken to Cajamarca, via Chilete.

Cajamarca (pop. 70,000, 2,750 metres), is a beautiful old colonial town and most important town in the northern mountain area. Here Pizarro ambushed and captured Atahualpa, the Inca emperor. The Cuarto de Rescate (not the actual ransom chamber but in fact the room where Atahualpa was held prisoner—closed on Tues. and after 1200 on Sat. and Sun.) can be seen (US$0.50, ticket also valid for nearby Belén church); a red line purporting to be the height of Atahualpa's hand was only recently painted in. (The room was closed to the public for centuries, and used by the nuns of Belén hospital). The chamber also has two interesting murals. The Plaza where Atahualpa was ambushed and the stone altar set high on Santa Apollonia hill where he is said to have reviewed his subjects are also shown. There is a road to the top. The Plaza das Armas has a 350-year old fountain. The Cathedral (San Francisco, seventeenth century, with catacombs) and Belén churches (handicrafts for sale in the cloisters) are well worth seeing; so are San Pedro (Gálvez and Junín), San José (C. M. Iglesias and Angamos), La Recoleta (Maestro and Casanova) and Capilla de La Dolorosa, close to San Francisco. Many belfries were left half-finished in protest against a Spanish tax levied on the completion of a church. The Cathedral, which took 350 years to build, was completed in 1960; it still has no belfry. Next to the Belén church (closed on Tues.) is a hospital (1774) for men and women. The women's hospital is an interesting musuem, one section with well-displayed

NORTHERN PERU

archaeological finds, pots and textiles, and the other showing modern arts and crafts.

Points of interest include the Bishop's Palace, next to the Cathedral, and many old colonial houses with garden patios, and 104 elaborate carved doorways: see palace of the Condes de Uceda, now occupied by the Banco de Crédito on Jr. Apurímac 719; the house of Toribio Casanova, Jr. José Gálvez 938; the house of the Silva Santiesteban family, Jr. Junín 1123; and the houses of the Guerrero and Castañeda families. The Education Faculty of the University has a museum on Jirón Arequipa with objects of the pre-Inca Cajamarca culture, not seen in Lima; the attendant knows much about Cajamarca and the surrounding area. Open 0800-1200, 1500-1700, in winter, and 0800-1200 in summer, US\$0.20 (guided tour). The University maintains an experimental arboretum and agricultural station. The Museo de Arte Colonial, at the Convento de San Francisco, is also worth a visit.

The town is a favourite among Peruvians for holidays, and has an interesting market with some crafts, especially noted for cotton and wool saddlebags (*alforjas*). Bargains of hand-tooled leather goods can be bought from the prisoners at the jail beyond the white arch on Calle Lima (7 blocks from Plaza de Armas). All museums are closed on Tuesdays (shops take a long lunch) but open at weekends. The rainy season is Dec.-April.

Festivals Plenty. Corpus Christi is a favourite. The pre-Lent Carnival has been revived; it is spectacular but includes much throwing of water, oil and paint, which can develop into fights between local youths and gringos. July 28/29, Independence: *fiesta*, with bullfight and agricultural fair; prices shoot up. In Porcón, 16 km. to the NW, Palm Sunday processions are remarkable.

Warning Beware of pickpockets in the Plaza de Armas and in cinemas.

Hotels *Turistas* (60 rooms) in the Plaza de Armas, E, with private bath, meals, rundown, ask to see room before booking. *Continental*, off Plaza, very clean, hot water, D, rec.; *Laguna Seca*, at Baños del Inca, in pleasant surroundings, clean, private hot thermal baths in rooms. *Sucre*, Amalia Puga 815, near Plaza de Armas, G, with toilet and wash basin in each room, sometimes noisy and no water, poor restaurant upstairs; *Amazonas*, Jirón Amazonas 528, modern, medium-priced. *Casa Blanca*, Plaza de Armas, E, room service; *Gran Hostal Plaza*, Plaza de Armas 631, F, old building with handmade wood furnishings, private bath and balcony, poor water supply, with new annex (dirty but is open at 0200 when bus arrives); *San Francisco*, Jr. Belén 570, F, "a bit dirty, but friendly"; *Jusovi*, Amazonas 637, F, comfortable, all rooms with private baths but hot water only in communal bathroom, safe, rec.; *Becerra*, Jr. Arequipa 195 (unsigned), F, intermittent tepid water, rec.; *Hostal Cajamarca*, E, in colonial house at Dos de Mayo 311, clean, hot water, rec. as the best hotel, food excellent, good local guitarists, musicians welcome. The owners also run *Albergue San Vicente*, outside the town, in an old hacienda. *Hostal José Galves*, E, thermal water; *Hostal Atahualpa*, E, private bath, clean, good value, but hard beds, rec. *Hostal Prado*, Calle Lamar, G without bath, rec. Try to get a room in the sun, no heating for the cold nights.

Restaurants *El Sitio*, Jr. Dos de Mayo 311, in *Hostal Cajamarca*, local specialities, friendly, informal, rec., peña in the evening. *Arlequín*, corner of Plaza de Armas, fish only, good; *Salas*, on Plaza, not expensive, good local food; *El Zarco*, Plaza de Armas at Arequipa 170, very highly rec., much frequented by local residents, inexpensive, try the sopa fuchifú, humitas de maíz; *La Namorina*, on edge of town on road to Baños del Inca, opposite Ché service station, renowned for its speciality, cuy frito (fried guinea-pig); *La Taverna*, Plaza de Armas, rec., clean, good variety, but food cold as in most places, reasonable prices, tamales are best in town; *Super Pollo* on Plaza, rec. for its jugo especial (made from algarrobina); *Buen Amigo*, Jirón Lima, good and cheap, rec.; *Playa Azul*, good food, clean, in Magdalena (about 1 hr. from Cajamarca by car); *Capri*, Jirón Lima, good ice cream; *Rescate* has been rec. for its cuy. *Cajamarqueña*, Amazonas 770, very good, not cheap; *Petit Café*, nr. Belén church, good, sometimes live music at night; *El Cumbe*; *Taverna Johnny*.

Tea Rooms *Café Florida* and *Casa Blanca*, both on Plaza de Armas.

Food Specialities Queso mantecoso (full-cream cheese); manjar blanco (sweet); humitas (ground maize with cheese); cuy frito; eucalyptus honey (sold in the market on Calle Amazonas;

Key to Map of Cajamarca
1. Plaza de Armas; 2. Santa Apollonia hill; 3. Cathedral; 4. Belén church and hospital; 5. San Francisco Convent and Museo de Arte Colonial; 6. San Pedro; 7. La Recoleta; 8. Cuarto de Rescate; 9. Casa Silva Santiesteban; 10. Museum of Education Faculty; 11. Post Office; 12. Foptur, Tourist Office; 13. Central Market; 14. *Hotel de Turistas*; 15. *Hostal Cajamarca*.

CAJAMARCA ENVIRONS 102

NOT TO SCALE

Porcón

RÍO PORCÓN

To Hualgayoc and Bambamarca

Cerrillo

Ventanillas de Combayo

Ventanillas de Otusco

To Celendín and Chachapoyas

CAJAMARCA
Layzón

Las Torrecitas

Baños del Inca

RÍO CHONTA

Cumbe Mayo

Ayllambo

Llacanora
To cajabamba

To Pacosmayo

Pariamarca
La Colpa

CAJAMARCA CENTRE 102

NOT TO SCALE

TO AIRPORT

JOSÉ GALVEZ

PISAGUA

TARAPACAZ

LA MAR

APURIMAC

UNION

ATAHUALAPA

CAJAMARCA

SAN MARTIN

HUANUCO

DOS DE MAYO

BELLAVISTA

JUNIN

LIMA

AMALIA PUGA

LA MAR

APURIMAC

AREQUIPA

JOSÉ SABOGAL

S. SALVADOR

BELEN

AMALIA PUGA

ETEN

AMAZONAS

GUILLERMO URRELO

GUADALUPE

CINCO ESQUINAS

SILVA SANTISTEBAN

SOLEDAD

AYACUCHO

ROMERO

SANTA APOLONIA

SAN PABLO

DESAMPARADOS

PELAYTEROS

TO CUMBE MAYO

LA ESPERANZA

TO BAÑOS DEL INCA

said to be a cure for rheumatism). Try the flaky pastries filled with apple or *manjar blanco* from the street sellers.

Exchange Banco Nor Perú, corner of Lima and Tarapacá, exchanges dollars for 1% commission. Banco de Crédito will not even change cash. Some of the hotels and restaurants, e.g. *Hotel Casa Blanca, Rest. Cajamarqueña*, may help out with travellers' cheques if you're eating there.

Addresses Post Office, Jr. Lima 406; Entel Perú, Jr. San Martín 363; Hospital, Av. Mario Urteaga; Guardia Civil, Plaza Amalia Puga.

Tourist Information Foptur, Santisteban 144, T 92-2228, good maps. Ask here for car hire. Also Cajamarca Tours, Dos de Mayo 323, guides do not speak English, despite what they claim. A group of local guides has formed Cumbemayo Tours and Inca Atahualpa Tours, and do good economical trips, e.g. to Cumbe Mayo itself (US$3 p.p.), the pottery workshop at Ayllambo, 3½ km. out, and the Palm Sunday celebrations at Porcón. Aventuras Cajamarca, enquire at *Hotel Casa Blanca*, trips to Kuelap, Jorge Caballero, rec. driver.

Air Service AeroPerú flights to Lima via Trujillo on Tues., Thurs., Sat. mornings (US$75). Cheaper to pay for each stage separately. **Warning:** Delays at Cajamarca are all too frequent.

Buses Daily buses and colectivos to Lima (bus, US$13), Trujillo (7-8 hrs., US$3-4.50 by bus); Chiclayo (US$3, 6-7 hrs. by Empresa Díaz, 1230 and 2100, with El Cumbe, Amazonas 860, US$3, at 1100 and 1500, with Atahualpa—best—at 1430, US$2.50, Comité de Autos 2, and Chinchay-Suyo). Tepsa leaves for Trujillo and Lima at 1800; Empresa Díaz for Trujillo at 0630 and 2000, for Lima at 1800 (1730 from Tourist Hotel, "Presidential service" non-stop) and for Celendín at 1200. Atahualpa to Lima, 15 hrs., US$9, overnight, rec.; to Celendín daily at 1200 (also to Cajabamba, Chota, Cutervo). Expreso Cajamarca, Amazonas 807, Comité de Autos 12 and 40 also go to Trujillo. Also daily to and from Cajabamba (Empresa Díaz, Calle Ayacucho 717 or Atahualpa at 1000), US$3, 6 hrs. (milk trucks will also take passengers to Cajabamba).

Excursions The warm sulphurous thermal springs known as Los Baños del Inca, where there are a public pool and private rooms (US$0.30, excellent) are 6 km. away. Atahualpa tried the effect of these waters on a festering war wound. Nearby can also be seen La Colpa, a *hacienda* which is now a cooperative farm of the Ministry of Agriculture with bulls for breeding and a lake and gardens. At 1400 the campesinos can be seen handmilking the cows, some of which come when called by name. There is a minibus service from the main square, US$0.10.

The surrounding countryside is splendid. Look out for the local building method called Tapial, made of compressed adobe alternating with layers of stones or wood. Other excursions include Llacanora, a typical Andean village in beautiful scenery and Ventanillas de Otusco, part of an old pre-Inca cemetery (minibus from town, US$0.10), with a gallery of secondary burial niches. A good walk, 10 km., is from Baños del Inca on Celendín road to Ventanillas de Otusco (start from the bridge and take the path along the brook), through beautiful countryside. A new road continues to Ventanillas de Combayo, some 20 km. past those of Otusco; these are more numerous and more spectacular, being located in a rather isolated, mountainous area, and are distributed over the face of a steep 200-metre-high hillside. Cumbe Mayo, mountain village (20 km. SW of Cajamarca but no bus service; it is dangerous to go alone, take a guided tour, US$4; taxi US$12). An aqueduct can be followed for several km., very remarkable; also, be sure to take a strong torch; alternatively you can walk and ask local passers-by the way. The trail starts from the hill of Santa Apollonia (Silla del Inca), and goes to Cumbe Mayo straight through the village and up the hill; at the top of the mountain, leave the trail and take the road to the right to the canal. The walk takes 2-3 hours, but is not difficult and you do not need hiking boots. The Indians use the trail to bring their goods to market. On the way to Cumbe Mayo is the Layzón ceremonial centre, the same period as Huacaloma. Other Inca ruins in the area include Tantarica, Torrecitas, and San Pedro de Pacopampa.

North of Cajamarca is Hualgayoc (**see page 768**). Trip with fantastic scenery. There is excellent trout served in restaurant on the way there; easy to find as it is the only place for a long way. Order on your way there to eat on the way back.

South of Cajamarca, through Santa Catalina and Trinidad, are the Inca and pre-Inca ruins of Tantarica, near Cholol.

Cajamarca is the starting point for the northern route to Iquitos. From Cajamarca there are several buses daily to **Celendín** (5 hrs., 112 km., US$2.50), where there are several hotels off the main plaza (*Hotel Jorge Girón*, F; *Amazonas*, F, rec.; *Hostal Celendín*, F, with bath, check room is clean before booking, good restaurant; *Bolívar*, F; *José Galves*, G, basic, but plenty of character; *Restaurant Jalisco* on Plaza de Armas, simple, not cheap) and cock fighting Sunday night in the local arena. Festival July 24 (Virgen del Carmen). There is also an interesting local market on Sunday. The town has electricity until 2400. The road follows a winding course through the northern Andes, crossing the wide and deep canyon of the River Marañón at Balsas after 55 km. (2½ hrs.). The road climbs steeply with superb views of the mountains and the valleys below. The fauna and flora are spectacular as the journey alternates between high in the mountains and low in the rain forest. After rain, landslides can be quite a problem. There are some interesting Inca ruins on the road between Celendín and Leimebamba (146 km.).

N.B. If going to Kuelap, try to be in Celendín on Sunday, Monday or Thursday, as many buses and trucks leave those nights and there's little transport on other days. Ask at the police checkpoint what transport is going.

Leimebamba is a pleasant town with 2 hotels, the better of which is *Escobedo*, G, friendly owner has lots of local information, toilets, cold shower; 3 restaurants, including *Oasis*, just off Plaza de Armas, and *El Caribe* on the Plaza. Trucks park in main square, leave 0300-0600 for Celendín and Chachapoyas; buses run daily to Celendín and Chachapoyas. Of the ruins in the area **La Congona**, a Sachupoyan site, is 2½ hrs. walk away, take the trail at the end of the street with the hotels and climb up (next to police station). The trail levels out and follows round the mountain, then down into a little valley. La Conga, a system of 3 hills can be seen: aim for the right-hand (easterly) conical hill with a visible small cliff. The trail does not go all the way up the hill; you must cross a field and climb through moss forest. This is the best preserved of 3 sites, with 30 decorated round stone houses (some with evidence of 3 storeys) and a watch tower. The other hills have been levelled. It is worth following the trail along the crest beyond these hills, and then to the left, down through rain forest (muddy), eventually to join the main trail. (A good day's walk—Haydn Washington, Australia.)

The road on to Chachapoyas (10 hrs. from Celendín by car, 12 hrs. by bus—daily at 0400—and 16 by truck is poor (dry weather only), but the scenery is magnificent. Food and warm clothing are necessary; usually only chicken and rice is available in the villages. Gasoline may be available in Leimebamba but cannot be relied on. If you want to go through to Iquitos, better to fly.

Chachapoyas, population 50,000, altitude 2,400 m., is the capital of the Department of Amazonas and has been called the friendliest town in Peru. If you have any problems contact the Guardia Civil (green uniforms), very friendly and more helpful than P.I.P., in the town and countryside. Archaeological and anthropological information can be sought from the local anthropologist, Carlos Torres Mas, who is the head of the Instituto Nacional de Cultura, in the 1200 block of Libertad, also advises about walks in the area (will store luggage). Those interested in the abundant archaeological sites in the area should read Gene Savoy's *Antisuyo* (British edition: *Vilcabamba*). There is also a Tourist Office on the Plaza de Armas, the director, Don Segundo Pastor, is helpful, luggage can be stored here (there is a small but good museum in the same building).

Hotels *El Dorado*, Ayacucho 1062, F, hot water, clean, helpful, rec.; *Johumaji*, Jr. Ayacucho 711 (T 138), F, with bath, cheaper without, dirty, safe for luggage; *El Danubio*, Junín 572, F, clean, hot water, safe for luggage, rec., son of owner works for P.I.P.; *Casa Blanca*, F; *Hostal Kuelap*, Jr. Chincha Alta 631, F with bath, cheaper without, hot water; *Continental*, Jr. Ortiz Arreta 437, G. A new tourist hotel is planned at Laguna Pomacocha, 3 hrs. by bus from Chachapoyas.

Restaurants Chacha, on Plaza de Armas, clean, good for bistec apanado, friendly; *Oh Qué Bueno*, limited menu; good pastries also at *Patisserie*, Jr. 2 de Mayo 558; *Kuelap*, same street as *Johumaji*, good; *Chifa El Turista*, Amazonas 575 near post office, is reasonable, friendly and helpful; *Café Bar Mary*, Plaza de Armas, clean, good, cheap; *Monte Carlo*, opp. market entrance, cheap, friendly; *Mio Mio*, near Post Office, good value chicken restaurant; good fruit juices at stall 67 in the market; *Los Michitos*, Jr. de la Merced 604.
   For leatherwork, Zapatería "El Cairo": a pair of boots costs US$27.

Buses To Chiclayo 3 times per week (Olano, US$15, 1000, 1100, on Sat., none on Sun.) via

Bagua and Jaén (18-25 hrs.); trucks more frequent to Bagua (see below). Many buses, 12 hrs., US$3.50, to Celendín 230 km. (not for those without a head for heights), trucks run, 16 hrs., US$2.50. Atahualga runs daily to/from Cajamarca (book 1 day in advance), 6 hrs., US$2. You can alight in Tingo, for Kuelap. Some trucks will take passengers to Moyobamba or Bagua, or Tingo in afternoon; remember most trucks do shortish runs and be prepared to change trucks frequently. *Bagua* (no hotels reported) is a good place to reach by truck (US$3 from Chachapoyas) as Cruz de Chalpón runs an overnight bus service (US$6) from there to Chiclayo. There are two Baguas, Grande and Chica, with about 20 km. between them; each sells half the available bus tickets. Bagua Chica has the better eating places.

Air Service A new airport has been built; AeroPerú, office on main square, fly Lima (US$50)-Chiclayo (US$25)-Chachapoyas on Mon., Weds., Fri. *Camioneta* from AeroPerú office to airport 0700 (20 mins.), US$0.25. Also Wed. flights to Rioja and weekly to Selva. Aeronorte fly to Chiclayo Fri.

The road is now open via Chachapoyas to Mendoza, a five-hour journey from Chachapoyas by *camioneta*, daily at 1000, US$1 (return 0200, sometimes 0700). Mendoza is ethnologically interesting because of a high incidence of very fair people.

Excursions Huancas, which produces unique pottery, can be reached by a 2-hour walk on the airport road; also Inca and pre-Inca ruins.

"Two hours by truck on the road to Mendoza is Molinopampa, which marks the starting point of an adventurous five-day hike to Rioja. Only experienced hikers should attempt this journey, which is very difficult. Food supplies for the whole journey should be purchased at Chachapoyas and a guide, absolutely essential, hired at Molinopampa for about US$5. The steep trail leads through waist-high unbridged rivers, over the cold, high Sierra and then for three days one follows the muddy trail down to the dense and humid jungle. We were accompanied by exotic butterflies, and never a quiet moment with the chattering of birds and monkeys. The whole magic of the jungle—trees, birds, animals and insects—can be seen untouched in their natural surroundings." (Katrina Farrar and Andy Thornton).

Tingo (1,800 metres), 37 km. from Chachapoyas, is reached by driving S up the Utcubamba valley from Chachapoyas (several trucks or *micros*, 0800-0900), US$1, 2 hrs. (trucks infrequent from Celendín US$3.85—leave at 0300, 12 hrs., driver collects you from hotel). There is a new *hostal* over the bridge on left as you enter from Celedín, with water, clean, basic bathrooms, good meals and a cheap *pensión*, at the entrance to the village painted blue and white, F, mouldy, good restaurant; *Restaurant Viajero* has rooms, G, and can arrange horses, US$2 per day, to go to Kuelap; *Hotalito Tingo*, G, friendly, rec.; no electricity in Tingo. A 3-4 hr. steep walk uphill (take waterproof, food and drink, and start early a.m.), leads to *Kuelap* (3,000 metres), a spectacular pre-Inca walled city. Its massive stone walls are as formidable as those of any precolumbian city. There is crude lodging for US$0.50, 8 beds and some mattresses, and food available at the summit to save you the walk down to Tingo—take candles. Entrance fee is US$1 (the ruins are locked; the proprietor of the lodging has the keys and accompanies visitors). At the archaeologists' research station (the last building before the ruins) you can hire cot and bedding for US$1 a night and leave luggage safely. Kuelap is very remote: you are advised not to try to visit the site from the coast unless you have a week to spare: the roads are bad and the public transport spasmodic. The road from Tingo to Kuelap, now almost complete, is very circuitous (1½ hrs. by car from Tingo). A truck may be hired in Chachapoyas for the day. If walking take the mule track off the main road before the bridge, after ½ an hour there is a sign to Kuelap, the track is very steep; a donkey can be hired in Tingo, US$1 per day.

The whole area is full of largely unexplored remains; some of them have been studied by the Swiss archaeologists Henri and Paula Reichlen (who surveyed 39 sites in 1948—see *Récherches archaeologiques dans les Andes du haut Marañón*, in *Journal des Américanistes*, which includes an accurate map), and the American archaeologist Gene Savoy (who went further than the Reichlens-see his book *Antisuyo*); Kaufmann Doig refers to them as the "12 Cities of the Condors"; his map showing their location is in his *Arqueología Peruana*. See also the booklet on Kuelap, available at the Tourist Office in Chachapoyas, very informative. Some scientists have tried to prove that the fair-skinned, blonde people of this area, described by the Spanish chronicles, were Celtic.

Mark Babington and Morgan Davis write: "Kuelap, discovered in 1843, was the last outpost of a lost white race, known variously as the Sachupoyans or the Chachas, who were in retreat from the advancing Inca around the years 1450-1470. Up till now Kuelap and La Congona were the only Sachupoyan ruins to have been explored in any detail whatsoever. The fact is that Kuelap was the final refuge of the Sachupoyans in a region which must have supported at least one million people before the arrival of the Inca. The known area inhabited by the Sachupoyans extends north from Leimebamba to Chachapoyas, and west as far as the Marañón.

"In 1977 a team of three Americans explored the area between the Marañón and Utcubamba

Rivers; they were the first to do so. They left an account of their journey in the American magazine *Outside*. Inspired by their account the two of us decided to retrace their steps. This is surely a region which overwhelms even Machu-Picchu in grandeur and mystery. It contains no less than five lost, and uncharted cities; the most impressive of which is Pueblo Alto, near the village of Pueblo Nuevo (25 km. from Kuelap). It was discovered some 60 years ago by the father of a local farmer, Juan Tuesta, with whom we stayed. By far the majority of these cities, fortresses and villages were never discovered by the Spaniard; in fact many had already returned to the jungle by the time the Spaniard arrived in 1532. The sites are situated in the tropical rain forest, and on the upper slopes of the *puna*. Furthermore many of them are to be found on or near the trails which today still provide the only medium of transport in this heavily populated and agricultural region. On a recent map of the area, with which we were provided in Chachapoyas, no less than 38 sites can be counted; but Ojilcho and Pueblo Alto, for example, are not charted on this new 1977 map in spite of their enormous dimensions. If all this sounds a bit exaggerated and inaccessible, we must add that the local farmers are conversant with the ruins, whether charted or not. It is among these people that one must look for information, provision and hospitality and, most important of all, guides and mules. The area, though well populated, provides virtually no facilities for the traveller. One should be cognizant of the difficulties ahead before attempting this journey, though this is not to say the trip is beyond the ability of most. Hiking gear is essential: sleeping bags, tents and canned goods (and a machete—Ed.). Small gifts are also much appreciated by the local people in return for their hospitality. (Take money in small notes as villagers do not have change for larger.) Water is no problem, unless it is the rainy season (Feb.-May). Travelling at this time is not advised as the mountain passes are shin-deep in mud.

Oscar Arce Cáceres based at "El Chillo" 4½ km. outside Tingo, who owns a farm and knows the area very well, will help the traveller. The trek into this area, like the walk up to Kuelap, starts from Tingo; the way is all mule track. In Magdalena (a 15-minute walk from Tingo), Abram Torres will be happy to provide one with his services as guide, and his mule, for the first leg of the journey as far as Choctamal, about 4 hours away.

Levanto is 2 hrs by new road (*camioneta* at 0600-0700, no scheduled return) or 6 hrs. walk from Chachapoyas. Levanto was the first Spanish capital of the area and the Spaniards built directly on top of the previous Sachupoyan structures. Although, not many years later, the capital was moved to Chachapoyas, Levanto still retained its importance, at least for a while, as it had been one of the seven great cities of the Sachupoyans as described by Cieza de León and Garcilaso de la Vega. The Kuelap East-West Highway starts at Levanto and links with the Inca military highway at Jalca Grande. Nowadays Levanto is a small, unspoilt, and very beautiful colonial village set on flat ground overlooking the massive canyon of the Utcubamba river. Kuelap can, on a clear day, be seen on the other side of the rift. Levanto is a good centre for exploring the many ruins around, being the centre of a network of ancient ruins, fortified redoubts, residential areas and many others. Very close to Levanto are the ruins of **Yalape**, recently cleared under the supervision of Sr César Torres Rojas, a resident of Levanto. Yalape seems to have been a massive residential complex extending over many hectares and including many well-preserved examples of typical Sachupoyan architecture and masonry with quite elaborate and beautiful friezes. Its scale, like that of Kuelap, can be only described as titanic. In fact the whole area is covered in ruins, almost every prominent hilltop in the immediate vicinity has at least a watchtower of some sort. As yet there is no official accommodation as such in Levanto, although plans are being made to build a small *alojamiento*. However, small groups of travellers are very welcome and beds and bedding are provided in the mayor's office and village meeting hall. Sr Torres Mas, in Chachapoyas, will put the traveller in touch with César Torres Rojas, in Levanto, with regard to all the above. César is entertaining and very friendly, as well as being the official guardian and archaeological supervisor of Levanto. There is one small shop and bar in the village. Using Levanto as a staging point, many beautiful and interesting walks can be done in the area." Taxi from Cachapoyas to Levanto and back, including driver waiting while you look around, US$20.

About 65 km. SW of Chachapoyas, the largest ruined complex yet discovered in South America, Gran Vilaya, was found in 1985 by Gene Savoy. There are 80 inter-connected city-type layouts, comprising some 24,000 structures. It faces the Río Marañón at 2,850 metres.

Another Sachupoyan site is Cerro Olán, reached by colectivo to San Pedro (near Tingo), then a ½-hr. walk; here are the remains of towers which some archaeologists claim had roofs like mediaeval European castles.

40 km. from Chachapoyas are the pre-Inca ruins of **Monte Peruvia** (known locally as Purunllacta), hundreds of white stone houses with staircases, temples and palaces (2 hrs. from the town of Lamud). Colectivos leave Lamud for Chachapoyas at 0600, returning around 1200, 2 hrs. One hotel in Lamud, *Kuelap*, G. Nearby, in Luya, are the Pueblos de los Muertos of the same culture, with fantastic burial figures high on a cliff (daily bus from Chachapoyas). "8 km. from Monte Peruvia is Puente de Conica, where you can see precolumbian burial figures in niches on the cliffside, known as the Purumachus de Aispachaca" (John Streather).

From Chachapoyas the next stretch of the road is 2-3 hrs. through more of the beautiful river canyon (US$1, by truck) to a small crossroads, Pedro Ruiz, where you continue on to Yurimaguas or return to the coast. There is basic accommodation there (*Hostal Marginal* with good, cheap restaurant, and one other, both F), but advisable to stay the night if you arrive late as most trucks to Rioja leave at 0500-0700, the road on this stretch is very bad. Pedro Ruiz to Rioja is about 14 hrs., US$5. The road on from Pedro Ruiz to Moyobamba and Tarapoto can be very bad in the rainy season.

From **Rioja** (an attractive, friendly town, 2 hotels, *Hostal San Martín* and *Restaurante Los Olivos* rec.) there is a road to Naranjillo and Aguas Verdes, with a 5-hr. walk to Venceremos, a pleasant way to see the jungle in good weather (don't attempt otherwise), a paved road to Nuevo Catamarca (colectivos every hour, US$0.80, 45 mins.) where you can catch a colectivo (US$10, 10-12 hrs.) to Chachapoyas, and another paved road with plenty of transport (about ½ hr.) to **Moyobamba,** capital of San Martín district (ruins of Pueblo de los Muertos nearby) (915 metres, 14,000 people). Tourists must register with the P.I.P.; tourist office on plaza. Moyobamba is a pleasant town, in an attractive valley. Mosquito nets can be bought cheaply. Baños Termales (4 km. from Moyobamba on Rioja road), and Puerto Tahuisco (2 km.) at Río Mayo, worth a visit. The more adventurous can hike to the Jera waterfalls in the jungle near Moyobamba. Take a truck in the direction of Tarapoto; alight at the restaurant at km. 218. Take a good path through a well-populated valley (cross 2 bridges), then along the river, through dense jungle, with 3 more river crossings (no bridges—dangerous). A local guide is necessary to find the falls. There have been guerrilla and drug activities in this region; take good care.

Hotels   Turistas, E with breakfast, 1 km. from centre, fine situation, pool, good restaurant; *Hostal Inca*, E with bath, new, clean, good but noisy; *Hostal Cobos*, F with bath, good; *Hostal Country Club*, F, clean, comfortable, friendly, nice garden, rec.; *Hostal Los Andes*, F, clean. **Restaurants** *El Sol del Norte*, good and cheap; several others.

Flights   AeroPerú flights from Lima to Chiclayo stop at Rioja (Wed. and Sun.).

Tarapoto (colectivo from Moyobamba, 3½ hrs., US$7.50, truck, 5 hrs., US$5), is a busy town with several hotels. The journey from Rioja to Tarapoto costs about US$5.75 and it is best to carry food because of endless delays and road problems. A through bus service (Chinchaysuyo) runs to Chiclayo, via Moyobamba, Rioja, Bagua and Olmos; and same company runs to Trujillo, US$11, at least 36 hrs.

Hotels   Turistas (E, with bath, excellent meals US$3.50) 1 km. out of town, non-residents can use the swimming pool for US$1; *Tarapoto*, E with fan, clean; *Las Palmeras*, just off PLaza, F; *San José*, 4 blocks from Plaza, clean and friendly, restaurant; *Juan Alfonso*, F, with shower, noisy, Jr. Pedro de Urzúa. *Hostal Residencial Grau*, Plaza de Armas, G, communal, cheap (in both senses of the word), shower. *Edinson*, near Plaza de Armas, E, clean and comfortable; *Hostal Americano*, E, fan and private bath with each room. *El Sereno*, E with shower, clean.

Restaurants   *Río de Janeiro, Sadel, Tiveli, Chalet Venecia, La Pascana* and *Achín* good; *Heladería Tip Top* and *Cream Rica* for ices. *Las Terrazas*, good, rec. Coconut water is recommended as coconuts abundant. Jirón Gregorio Delgado 268 sell excellent liquor at US$0.50 a glass (uvachado and siete raices).

Exchange   Banco de Crédito, Maynas 134, efficient, no commission on travellers' cheques.

Air Transport   US$1.50 per taxi airport to town (no bus service). Flights by Faucett and AeroPerú to Lima (US$40, 50 mins.), Iquitos, Juanjui and Yurimaguas, but book in advance, particularly in rainy season. Those visiting Tarapoto and Iquitos would be advised to visit Tarapoto first, as aircraft leaving Iquitos tend to overfly Tarapoto; possible to be stuck there for days. AeroPerú flies to Tarapoto from Lima, Iquitos, Chiclayo, Trujillo (US$50), Juanjui and Yurimaguas (US$10). Faucett has similar routes, and daily flights to and from Trujillo and Chiclayo. Many smaller airlines operate flights to Yurimaguas (US$6 with Grupo Ocho—Air Force).

Between Tarapoto and Moyobamba a road leads off to **Lamas** (colectivo from Tarapoto, US$1.20, 35 km.), where there is a picturesque Indian community completely unspoilt by tourism; also a small museum, with exhibits on local Indian community (Lamistas), ask at the café opposite if museum shut, and a new restaurant en route, *El Mirador*, recently opened by Tom, an American, and his Peruvian wife. Market in the early morning. Interesting journey also from Tarapoto to Tingo María (**see page 832**), not advisable in the rainy season. From

Tarapoto to Yurimaguas (136 km.) (**see page 833**), the road can be very bad in the wet season, taking at least 13 hrs. for trucks (at 0800 or earlier, US$6), also colectivos, US$8. There is also a daily bus (10 hrs.) A Swiss runs a quick jeep service to Yurimaguas, leaving early a.m., arrives 4 hrs. later, returns at noon same day from Plaza de Armas. About 20 km. from Tarapoto on this road are the 50-metre falls of Ahuashiyacu, which can be visited by tour from Tarapoto (US$12 incl. lunch) or by hiring motorcycle from Grand Prix, corner Shopajo and Raimondi, US$2.50 an hour. At km. 96 (US$4) there is a bridge over the Shanusi river and the small village of Shanusi. It is possible to leave your truck here and take a 4½ hour (US$1.15) boat ride down the river, meeting the Huallaga at Yurimaguas. There is no accommodation at Shanusi, take a hammock, but boats run daily at about 0800. From Yurimaguas on the Huallaga River, launches ply to Iquitos.

Further N from Trujillo are three ports serving the Chiclayo area. The more southerly is **Etén,** an open roadstead 21 km. by road from Chiclayo; Panama hats are local industry; festival of the Divine Child of the Miracle, 2-17 June. **Pimentel,** N of Etén, is larger, a favourite summer bathing place, with a broad sandy beach (very crowded on Sundays). Reached from Chiclayo (14½ km.) by road branching off from the Pan-American Highway. Sea-going balsa rafts (*caballitos de totora*) are used by fishermen and may be seen here and at Santa Rosa. Also worth seeing is **Santa Rosa,** situated between the two; excellent *ceviche* (small hotel, *Perú,* restaurant *Bello Horizonte*). The 3 ports may be visited on a pleasant ½ day trip. A red bus leaves Chiclayo market place every ½ hr. for Pimentel and Santa Rosa. Colectivos run frequently from Pimentel to Santa Rosa, and on to Etén and back to Chiclayo. To avoid paying excess luggage charges for weight above 15 kg, buy ticket in advance, and catch bus outside terminal (no scales!).

Chiclayo, on a plain near the coast, is capital of Lambayeque Department, which is the largest rice producer and the second largest sugar producer in Peru; wheat and cotton are also grown. Population, about 348,000. Nothing much for the tourist to see, but it is the liveliest of all the northern cities, with many parks and gardens. The most interesting spot is the new market place; the market is the best on the coast of Peru; well worth a visit: best buys are saddlebags (*alforjas*), woven goods such as hats, and baskets, and props for the local witch-doctors. The fine modern cathedral (classical interior with some fine woodwork), principal club, and Municipal Palace front the Plaza de Armas. Sunday is the day for horse racing. Hacienda Batán Grande, with its sugar plantations, is worth a visit.

Hotels *Turistas,* Villareal 115, D, with bath; E, without, meals included, some distance from business centre, but there is much traffic noise, swimming pool, dirty, safe car park, cars may be hired for US$15 a day (check their condition first); *Hostal El Sol,* E, Elías Aguirre 115, hot water, rec. (safe car park, and Chinese restaurant on 1st floor); *Costa de Oro,* Balta 399, E, central, good restaurant *Ebony* downstairs; *Royal,* Plaza de Armas, F, old, clean, poor beds, basic; *Mediterráneo,* Balta 635, near Plaza, F, friendly, noisy, check the bill; *Mundial,* Calle Balta, near Plaza de Armas, basic, F, without bath; *Hostal San Ramón,* Héroes Civiles, F, friendly, clean, comfortable; *Inca,* L. González 662, E with bath, clean, new and good; *Europa,* Elías Aguirre, F without bath, good value, clean, friendly, restaurant, some hot water. Several cheap hotels on Calle Balta, near bus offices. Some hotels prohibit clothes-washing in rooms because of the high cost of water.

Restaurants First-class and very reasonable food (especially good breakfast) at *Roma,* Balta 512; *Bristol,* Balta, good and cheap. *Fiestas,* Av. Salaverry 1820 in Tres de Octubre suburb; *Le París,* M.M. Izaga 716, excellent, not cheap; *Ebony,* Balta 399; *Nápoli,* Balta 951, rec.; also *El Tauro,* reasonable prices, and *Cruz de Chalpón* (good breakfasts) on same street; *Cordano,* on Plaza de Armas, good food, reasonably priced, friendly; *El Patio,* excellent regional food, but service can be poor (Leoncio Prado, 1427); *Plaza Real,* between *Turistas* and Plaza de Armas, good food and value; *Las Paisanos* is rec., has take-away service; *Imperial,* Balta; *Maracaibo,* in market, good, cheap; *Las Américas,* on Plaza, good quick meals and snacks; *Chifa Julio,* good Chinese food; *Chifa Mymy,* near *Hostal Europa,* popular, OK; *Don José,* also serves Chinese dishes.

Folklore Peñas at Brisas del Mar, Elías Aguirre; Los Hermanos Balcázar, Lora y Cordero 1150; El Embrujo, Vicente de la Vega.

Exchange Change travellers' cheques at Banco del Norte. Be prepared to wait. The travel agency next to *Hotel Royal* will change cash or cheques at reasonable rates out of banking hours. Several street changers on 600 block of Balta.

Post Office   on Aguirre, 6 blocks from Plaza.

Tourist Office   Foptur, Elías Aguirre 830, T 22-7776; Sáenz Peña 838, helpful.   Touring y Automóvil Club de Perú, Huancavelica 280, of. 406.

Air Service   Coronel Ruiz airport 2 km. from town. Daily Faucett and AeroPerú (except Tues.) jet flights from Lima, US$35; flights to Rioja (Aero Perú, Weds., and Sat., 1130, US$38.15), Tarapoto, and to Iquitos and intermediate stops. AeroPerú flies to Chachapoyas Mon., Wed., Fri.

Buses and Colectivos   To Lima, Nor Pacífico, 2100, US$10. To Trujillo (Empresa Emtrafesa on Bolognesi) leave eight times a day, 0530 onwards, US$2, 3 hrs. Bus to Piura, US$2, 3 hrs., six a day. Micros to Lambayeque leave from 200 block of San José, US$0.10, frequent. Direct bus to Cajamarca, Empresa Díaz and El Cumbe, US$3, several daily. To Chachapoyas, D. Olano company (Vicente de la Vega 101, T 236310), US$15, 1300, except Sun., 18-25 hrs. depending on breakdowns; goes via Olmos and Jaén (see below), thereafter road is appalling to Pedro Ruiz, then O.K. to Chachapoyas. To Tarapoto, Chinchay-Suyo runs via Olmos, Bagua, Rioja (US$14.50) and Moyobamba. Bus to Huancabamba leaves Tues. and Fri., 1500, arrives 0530 next day, US$7.75 (Civa and Tepsa office, Balta 114b)—very rough ride, impossible to sleep. Tepsa to Tumbes, 0100 daily, US$6, 9½ hrs.; also Continental (Ormeño), Roggero (1930), Olano (rec.) and others (Nor Pacífico not rec.), all night buses US$6, 12 hrs., some continue to Aguas Verdes, but foreigners have to get off at Zarumilla for passport control. Trucks going in all directions leave from Calle Pedro Ruiz 948 and from the market.

Excursions   To El Purgatorio about 30 km. N, near the town of Túcume (colectivos from corner of Pedro Ruiz and Luis Gonzáles, or from Manuel Prado y L. Gonzáles) with an unforgettable view from the top of the large adobe pyramid; Apurlec, 60 km. N: stone wall surrounding hill and pyramids dating from Tiahuanaco period, as well as irrigation canals and reservoirs; the system was enlarged during Mochica, Chimú and Inca occupation of the site, and the ruins of the town of Zaña, 51 km. S of Chiclayo, destroyed by floods in 1726, where the main churches are being restored. A minor road runs to **Chongoyape** (bus from Chiclayo, US$0.85, 1½ hrs., leaves from Leticia, just off Balta on N. of Plaza de Armas; hotel, F, near Plaza de Armas, without restaurant; Restaurant Cascada, main street, limited menu), a quaint old town 60 km. to the E. (3 km. west are the Chavín petroglyphs of Cerro Mulato). **Batán Grande**, a site 50 km. from Chiclayo consisting of nearly fifty adobe pyramids where many precolumbian gold artefacts, notably the 915-gram Tumi, were found, is reached by a branch turning left off the Chongoyape road after Tumán, about 30 km. from Chiclayo (colectivos, US$1.20, from Pedro Ruiz—12th block—and Juan Cuglievan). Also near Chongoyape are the aqueduct of Racarrumi, the hill fort of Mal Paso and the ruins of Maguín. The road goes to **Chota**, an attractive town with a fine Sunday market (several hotels, F, Plaza the best, clean; Continental, poor; Hostal Elisabeth, on plaza, cheap rooms with balcony, dirty bathrooms. Restaurant San Juan, good) where weavings are cheaper than in Cajamarca: cheap, friendly shops at 27 de Noviembre 144 and 246. Daily bus to Chiclayo a.m., 12-14 hrs.; bus to Cajamarca Wed., Fri., 9-10 hrs., return Tues. and Thurs. Occasionally buses, and many trucks, run on to **Bambamarca** (Hotel Bolívar, best; Hotel Velásquez, G, Hotel Perú has bugs; Restaurant Pollos a la Brasa, very good) which has an attractive Sunday morning market (truck from Chota US$1; Empresa Díaz to Cajamarca daily at 0600, 9 hrs., frequent stops, US$4, on Sun, there is a 2 hr. stop in Bambamarca for the market, some days also with Peregrino). Two buses a day pass through Chongoyape to Chota, 8 hrs., US$4. From there it goes on to **Hualgayoc** (a beautifully situated, quaint old mining town) and Cajamarca; a very interesting and beautiful journey, but few buses. The stretch from Bambamarca, about 90 km., to Cajamarca is exhilarating; the road climbs to about 4,000 metres through the Andean highlands with beautiful scenery of a puna landscape, nearly uninhabited, no fuel supply; it takes about 6 hrs. in a 4-wheel drive car. The whole trip between Chongoyape and Cajamarca takes about 2 days in a car, the road is particularly bad between Chongoyape and Chota, max. speed 25 kph. The Chiclayo—Chota bus passes through Cochabamba (no hotels, not a friendly place, police searches for drugs), 34 km. from Chota, from where you can hitch in a truck to **Cutervo**, a town of 6,000 people at 2,800 metres in green meadows. Cattle and vegetables are raised here. Hotels: San Juan on plaza, cheap but has bugs; nicer one by Ciné San Juan, several more. Restaurants: Salón Azul, very good; Central, very dirty. A very friendly town which tourists rarely visit—don't be surprised if the local radio station wants an interview. Many trucks to Cutervo, Tues.-Sat., return Mon.-Fri.; bus from Chiclayo Sat., returns Sun. 2000. Local market Thurs. and Sun.

   Branching off the Pan-American Highway to Piura at **Olmos** (885 km. from Lima) is a poor road (being improved) which runs eastwards over the Porciulla Pass (2,150 metres) at km. 257 is a restaurant, but there are better ones at Jaén and Bagua Chica. A road branching from Chamaya, N of Hualgayoc, leads to the towns of Jaén and Bellavista. N of Chamaya, travelling via Aramongo and Oracuza, one finds a symmetrical hill of niche tombs.

   Jaén (population: 3,600), an old settlement, has recently been revived as a rice-growing centre. The annual festival of the patron saint, Our Lord of Huamantanga, is on September 14. Hotels at Jaén: Danubio; Hostal Lima, not rec. A road has been built N from Jaén to San Ignacio (114 km.), near the frontier of Ecuador. It crosses the valley of the Chinchipe, renowned for its lost Inca gold. San Ignacio has a fiesta on August 31. Another branch road from Jaén has been built SE to Chachapoyas, 263 km. from Olmos (**see page 763**), and has now been completed another 359 km. to Yurimaguas, on the Huallaga River (**see page 833**). A road also goes to Aramongo (280 km.), on the Marañón; it has been extended to Nazareth. From Nazareth two roads branch: one to Oracuza, via Puente Huabico and Puerto Delfus, and the other to *Sarameriza*, the most westerly point on the Marañón with a regular boat connection to Iquitos—it is 1 hr. downstream from Puerto Delfus. To reach Sarameriza, take a bus to Bagua (**see page 764**) from Chachapoyas or Chiclayo, US$5.50, 12-15 hrs., from where pick-ups run twice daily to Imasa. Get out at Campamento Mesones Muro, 15 mins. before Imasa (US$2.55, 7 hrs.), where you must register with the police (this can take time). For 150 km. from Mesones Muro to Sarameriza, you must wait for a pick-up (one should be along in 3-6 days) and then be prepared for a 2-3 day journey because of poor roads and missing bridges. The m/n *Fernández* makes the journey from Sarameriza to Iquitos every second week: downstream US$26 (inc. meals), 4 days, only a few cabins (US$2.50 extra), so take a hammock; upstream, US$30, 6 days. If you can't wait for the boat, it is possible with local help to make a raft and sail downstream, camping at night, until the *Fernández* catches you up (Peter Legaard Nielsen and Niels Pedersen, Copenhagen).

Ten km. to the N of Chiclayo is **Lambayeque,** population 20,700, worth a visit. The narrow streets are lined by adobe houses, many retaining their distinctive wooden balconies and wrought iron grill-work over the windows. The town's most interesting feature is the well-known, recommended Bruning Museum, relocated in an impressive modern building. It specializes in Cupisnique, Lambayeque and Vicus cultures, has a fine collection of Mochica and Chimú ceramics, household implements, and gold artefacts. The magnificent treasure from the tomb of a Moche warrior priest, found at Sipán in 1987, is also being displayed here, open 0900-1300 and 1600-1800 on weekdays, 1000-1200, Sat., Sun. and holidays. Admission, US$0.60. A hotel is soon to be opened. Try the famous Alfajor King-Kong (a sweet). At Lambayeque the new Pan-American Highway branches off the old road (which skirts the Sechura desert to the E) and drives 190 km. straight across the desert to Piura. There are a few restaurants along its length. There is also a coast road, narrow and scenic, between Lambayeque and Sechura via Bayovar.

A large area of shifting sands—the Sechura Desert—separates the oasis of Chiclayo from that of Piura. Water for irrigation comes from the Chira and Piura rivers, and from the Olmos and Tinajones irrigation projects which bring water from the Amazon watershed by means of tunnels (one over 16 km. long) through the Andes to the Pacific coast. They will eventually water some 400,000 hectares of desert land. The northern river—the Chira—has usually a superabundance of water: along its irrigated banks large crops of Tangüis cotton are grown. A dam has now been built at Poechos on the Chira river, to divert water to the Piura valley. In its upper course the Piura—whose flow is far less dependable—is mostly used to grow subsistence food crops, but around Piura, when there is enough water, the hardy long-staple Pima cotton is planted. In 1983 the Niño current brought heavy rains and turned the Sechura desert into an inland sea. Damage to crops, roads, bridges and buildings was estimated at around US$1bn.

Piura, an oasis in the parched desert, is a proud and historic city, 264 km. from Chiclayo. Population, 1,125,800. Founded in 1532, three years before Lima, by the *conquistadores* left behind by Pizarro (whose statue is in the Parque Pizarro). There are two well kept parks, Cortés and Pizarro, and public gardens. Old buildings are kept in repair and new buildings blend with the Spanish style of the old city. Its special dish is the delicious *natillas,* made mostly of goats milk and molasses.

A few blocks from the Plaza de Armas, where the cathedral stands (gold covered altar, paintings by Ignacio Merino), is the San Francisco church, where the city's independence from Spain was declared on January 4, 1821, nearly 8 months before Lima. The colonial church of Las Mercedes has ornately carved balconies, three-tiered archway, hand-hewn supports and massive furnishings. San Sebastián, on Tacna near Bolognesi, is also worth seeing. Birthplace of Admiral Miguel Grau, hero of the War of the Pacific with Chile, whose house Casa Museo Grau, on Jirón Tacna opposite the Centro Cívico, has been opened as a museum; it contains a model of the *Huáscar,* the largest Peruvian warship in the War of the Pacific, which was built in Britain. Interesting local craftwork is sold at the Model Market. The museum on the 3rd floor of the modern Municipalidad building is open Mon.-Fri. 0800-1500.

Cotton has been grown mainly on medium-sized properties, which have changed hands frequently in recent years and which now form communal or co-operative farms, sponsored by the agrarian reform programme. Worth seeing as an example of a fine old plantation is the former Hacienda Sojo, in the lower Chira valley, which was the centre of the properties of the Checa family.

Hotels *Turistas*, D, faulty air conditioning, food and service poor, the city's social centre, swimming pool being added, facing Plaza de Armas. *Cristina*, Jr. Loreto between Plaza Grau and Jr. Ica, one block from Plaza, E, pleasant; *Hostal Esmeraldas*, opp. colectivo stop on Loreto, good rooms, E; *Oriental*, clean but noisy, E; *Hostal Las Palmeras*, Jirón Loreto, F, fan, rec., English owner; *San Jorge*, F with bath, clean and good value, Jr. Loreto, 3 blocks from Plaza Grau, rec.; *Tambo*, E, good, clean; *Palermo*, F, with bath, clean, rec.; *Bolognesi*, E, with private bath, near Roggero bus terminal, good. On Pan-American Highway are *El Sol*, Sánchez Cerro 411, E, bath, snack bar, will change travellers' cheques at official rate; *Vicus*, D, with bath, restaurant. *Oriental*, F without bath, E with, clean but very noisy, with TV in reception, Jr. Callao. It is extremely difficult to find a room in the last week of July because of independence festivities. The city suffers from water shortages and there are reports that no hotel has hot water.

Restaurants and Night Clubs *Tiburón*, 2 km. out of Piura on Panamericana Sur. *Ganso Azul*, a group of steak houses just out of town, rec. In town; *Puente Viejo*, Huancavelica 167 (close to *Hotel Turistas*), excellent seafood, reasonable; *Carburmer*, in Centro Comercial, very good but not cheap. *Las Tradiciones*, Ayacucho 579, high quality, reasonable prices, slow service; *La Taverna*, Av. Loreto between Av. Grau and Jr. Ica, excellent for fish; *La Cabaña* serves pizzas and other good food; *Café Concierto*, Cuzco 933, pleasant; *Snack Bar*, Callao 536, good fruit juices. Good little cheap restaurants on Jirón Junín: *Chalán del Norte* at 722, *Bianca* at 732, *El Capri* at 715. A good ice cream shop is *Venezia* on the main square. *La Huerta*, Libertad 801 on corner of Plaza de Armas, sells 19 fresh juices, quesillo con miel (cream cheese and honey) and natillas.

Exchange Banco de Crédito recommended. Banco Continental, Plaza de Armas, changes travellers' cheques with commission.

Post Office on Plaza de Armas, very helpful.

Shopping Fuji film readily available.

Tourist Offices Plaza de Armas, opp. Cathedral; Lima 575, 1st floor, friendly but not very helpful; Av. La Libertad 945-951 and at airport. Touring y Automóvil Club del Perú, Huancavelica 280.

Air Faucett (0830) and AeroPerú (1700) daily jet flights to and from Lima (US$40). Taxi to airport, US$1.25.

Buses Tepsa buses leave daily to Lima, US$8.50, coming from Tumbes. To Trujillo, 8 hrs., buses run day (not a.m.) and night, US$5 (Chinchay-Suyo on Calle Libertad 1117-27, leaves at 2200 and 2400, also at 1300 to Chiclayo-Trujillo-Chimbote-Huarás). To Trujillo in daylight, take through Chinchay-Suyo bus, or 0800 Empresa Chiclayo bus to Chiclayo (US$2, 3 hrs.) then change to Empresa Emtrafesa. To Tumbes, 7½-12 hrs., at least, owing to flood-damaged road, US$4.50 (El Dorado, Sánchez Cerro, 4 a day, Compañía Petrolera, same location, 2130, continues to Aguas Verdes, or Empresa Chiclayo), with Tepsa, leaving at 1200 (coming from Lima, no reservations), or Sudamericana at 0400 (cheaper), colectivo US$9.50; to Chiclayo, US$2.40, 3 hrs., leave 1400; colectivo to Chiclayo US$5.10 each, leaves from near La Terraza, 4 hrs; to Paita, colectivo US$1.50. To La Tina for Ecuadorean frontier, via Sullana, Montero Peña, Roma 369, runs at 0730, US$4, 4½ hrs. **N.B.** To the north of Piura, buses are subject to military checks.

Excursions 12 km. to the SW of Piura is the village of *Catacaos* (colectivos leave from Avenida Tacna, US$0.35, bus US$0.25) famous for its *chicha* (maize beer, be careful, quality not always reliable), *picanterías* (local restaurants, some with music), tooled leather, gold filigree jewellery, wooden articles, the best straw hats in Peru and splendid celebrations in Holy Week. Also from Piura, one can visit *Sechura*, a coastal town with a fine 17th-century cathedral (splendid west front) and the Hospedaje de Dios (usually full of workmen from the oil terminal at Bayovar--forbidden to visitors). One can visit the coastal villages (no accommodation in any of them) of San Pedro (with a huge lagoon, edible crabs, flamingoes, a superb beach and a fierce sun—best visited in the week; take bus or colectivo to the right fork past Vice, then hitch); Yacila (reached also by *camioneta* for Paita; Los Cangrejos beach nearby, where you can rent an apartment from Sr. Belcázar, but little food available), La Tortuga, Parachique, Matacaballo (which has the best beach of these four places); Chullachay (the nearest beach to Sechura), Los Puertos and Angostura. Balsa reed-boats are common on the coast.

Chulucanas, 50 km. SE of Piura and 10 km. off the Pan-American Highway, is the centre of the lemon and orange growing area. *Hotel Ica*, Ica 636, F; *Restaurant Cajamarquino*, Ayacucho 530, good. **Canchaque** (*Hostal Don Félix*, central square, F, just tolerable; otherwise simple clean accommodation for about US$2 on right hand side of church), is a delightfully-situated small centre for coffee, sugar-cane and fruit production. The difficult and tiring road, impossible for ordinary vehicles in the wet season, continues over a pass in the Andes of more than 3,000 metres to **Huancabamba** (*Hotel El Dorado*, F, good, clean, with restaurant, on the main square; also, *Andino*, *Grau* and *Minerva*). Local specialities: *rompope*, a rich and strong drink made of egg, spices and *cañazo* (sugar-cane spirit); roast *cuy* (guinea-pig); and local cheeses. This very pretty town in a wonderful setting has three claims to fame (apart from a certain hostility among the young towards visitors). First, the predominance of European features, due to the fact that it was an important Spanish settlement in colonial times. Second, it is called "the walking town" (*"la ciudad que camina"*) as it is built on irregularly slipping strata which cause much subsidence. Evidence for this includes the fall of the bridge over the Río Huancabamba some years ago. Third, and by far the most remarkable element, it is the base for reaching Las Guaringas, a series of lakes at about 4,000 metres. Around here live the most famous witchdoctors of Peru, to whom sick people flock from all over the country and abroad. Buses to the lakes at 0400 from main square.

Horses to the lakes can be hired, US$5; village of San Antonio below Lake Carmen, village of Salala below Lake Shumbe (*Hotel San José*, G, very basic, take own food).

A bus from Piura to Canchaque and Huancabamba leaves daily at 0900 and 1000, at least 8 hrs. (and returns from Huancabamba 0700 and 1000) from the Civa office, Av. Ramón Castilla 155 (buy ticket early on day before travelling). If driving, take the Pan-American Highway south of Piura for 66 km. where there is a signpost to Huancabamba. Canchaque is about 70 km. along this same road (in miserable condition) and then there are 50 km. more of steep and winding road to Huancabamba.

By lorry from Piura, or bus from Sullana, is **Ayabaca.** John Streather writes: In the Andean summer—roughly the end of May till mid-September—it is worth making the long trip by lorry or bus (about 0600 from Piura market square, enquire the day, or days, before) to Ayabaca, whence many trips can be made to surrounding ruins, caves, petroglyphs and lakes. Mules are usually essential as are guides; mules about US$4 per day, guides the same. The man to contact in Ayabaca is Sr. Celso Acuña Calle, Jr. Cáceres 161. Buy food and medicine in Piura (enough for the guides too) before leaving, as it is in short supply in Ayabaca. The little town is near the Ecuadorean border in a lovely situation, but is unfortunately a centre of cocaine smuggling. Therefore be sure to carry passport and visa on all trips (in a waterproof bag) and, of course, stop whenever asked to by police. In summer one can usually get a lift to the village of Yanchalá where most trips begin. It is a long muleback journey from there to the petroglyphs of Samanga (booklet purchasable at Piura Catholic University), and another long muleback ride to the Inca fortress town of Aypate—large but very overgrown. Other places of interest are: the pre-Inca cemetery of Hualcuy, Inca ruins and good view from Cerro Granadillo; pre-Inca ruins of Potrero de los Chaves; mummies in the pre-Inca cave cemetery of Potrero de los Jiménez at Cerro Pajonal; 4 or 5 days by mule to the Cuatro Lagunas Sagradas—all different colours. Near Chicuate is the Ciudad Encantada which still awaits explorers or indeed any visitors at all, as it is in a very isolated region, beyond Laguna Shimbe, and the few locals are frightened to visit it. It is said to be a ruined Inca town. There are at least three hotels in Ayabaca; the best, nameless, is in the first street parallel to the square and directly behind the Banco de la Nación (which will almost certainly refuse to change money). Various restaurants too: the *Trébol* is probably the best of a mediocre bunch. A torch is essential for trips outside Ayabaca, as there is no electric light in the region. No one should attempt to journey outside Ayabaca without a guide: there is danger from drug smugglers as well as of getting lost in the trackless bush. The way to the lost Inca city of Chicuate is particularly dangerous: lightning in the pass that gives access, and thick fog descending over the 100 metres of narrow road that lead between two lakes. Easier to reach from Chulucanas (see above) is Frías, where there is a pre-Inca cemetery and more caves can be reached if you have enough time (few locals know of them), rough road, no facilities, beautiful countryside.

The port for the area is **Paita,** 50 km. from Piura (colectivos and buses near Plaza Grau, US$1.50), which exports cotton, cotton seed, wool and flax. Population 51,500. Built on a small beach, flanked on three sides by a towering, sandy bluff, it is connected with Piura and Sullana by paved highways. The Paita-Piura road is now good, buses hourly from Parque Cortés, Piura, 45 mins. (get tickets from office on Av. Sullana, facing the park). Fishing and whaling (at Tierra Colorada, 6½ km. S of Paita) are prosperous industries.

One guest-house which must be booked in Lima. Restaurant: *Marino*.

On a bluff looming over Paita is a small colonial fortress built to repel pirates. A short distance up the coast is Colán, a summer resort, reached by driving down a large, sandy bluff; near the base is a striking and lonely church over 300 years old. There is a good beach, but Colán is rather derelict since the agrarian reform; it used to be the favourite resort of the estate-owners.

Bolívar's mistress, Manuela Sáenz, lived the last 24 years of her life in Paita, supporting herself until her death in 1856 by weaving and embroidering and making candy after refusing the fortune left her by her husband.

Sullana (population 151,000), 39 km. N of Piura, is built on a bluff over the fertile Chira valley. **Warning** It has a serious crime problem: robberies of travellers are all too common.

Hotels *Sullana* (rooms with bath), E; *Hostal y Restaurant San Miguel*, opposite bus companies, E, helpful, good showers, staff will spray rooms against mosquitoes. *Hostal Aypate*, Av. José de Lama, E, comfortable, showers; *Buenos Aires*, F, Av. Buenos Aires, 15 mins. from city centre, friendly but bathrooms dirty. *Hostal La Siesta*, Av. Panamericana 400-04 (T 2264), at entrance to town (direction Talara), D, 3-star, hot water, swimming pool, café, laundry.

Bus to Tumbes, US$2.10. Piura, 45 mins., US$0.45 bus, US$0.70 colectivo; Chiclayo, Tepsa, 4 hrs., US$3. Trujillo, Sudamericano, 1430. To Lima with Sudamericano, Tepsa (*presidencial*, US$10, 1820, ordinary, US$7.50, 1830, 16-17 hrs.), Panamericana, US$5, Roggero. Colectivos to Paita, Colán and Esmeralda leave from the main road parallel to the market; buses to Máncora and Talara (Empresa EPPO) from market area.

To Ecuador At Sullana the Pan-American Highway bifurcates. To the E it crosses the Peru-Ecuador frontier at La Tina and continues via Macará to Loja and Cuenca; the road is poor, though marvellously scenic. Many trucks and other vehicles leave at 0630 to the border at La Tina, US$2 p.p., 5 hrs; taxis also go, US$3 per seat, 3-4 hours. No accommodation at La Tina. At the border the officials are polite and friendly—the Peruvian can be found at the nearby *cevichería* if not at his desk—walk over the bridge, pick-ups run from the border to Macará. A bus leaves the Ecuadorean side at 1300 for Loja, so you can go from Sullana to Loja in one day.

The better route is the W road which passes through Talara and Tumbes, crossing the border at Huaquillas and on via Machala to Guayaquil; it is asphalted and has excellent bus services. All but a section of this road between Talara and Los Organos (20 km.) has been rebuilt since the heavy floods in January 1983.

The main centre of the coastal oil area is ***Talara*** (135 km. from Piura, 1,177 km. from Lima), in a desert oasis, which has a State-owned 60,000 barrel-a-day oil refinery and a fertilizer plant. Water is piped 40 km. from the Chira River. The city is a triumph over formidable natural difficulties, but was badly damaged in the 1983 floods and has many shanty districts. Population 44,500. La Peña beach, 2 km. from Talara, is still unspoilt.

Hotels There are 4 hotels, all overpriced and usually full by early afternoon because of the number of oilmen in the town. *Hostal Talara*, clean comfortable, E. If in trouble finding a bed, enquire at the police station.

Restaurants *La Colmena; Club de Golf.*

Transport Airport with daily flights to Lima by Faucett and AeroPerú (not Sat.). AeroPerú has a direct route to Miami; leaves Tues. at 1035, arriving 1500. Return flight departs Miami Tues. at 0130, arriving at 0550.

Paved highways connect the town with the Negritos, Lagunitos, La Brea and other oilfields. Of historical interest are the old tarpits at La Brea, 21 km. inland from Punta Pariñas, S of Talara, and near the foot of the Amotape mountains. Here the Spaniards boiled the tar to get pitch for caulking their ships. Buses run to Máncora (wayside fish restaurants superb, including lobster; *César*, rec.), a small attractive resort with good beaches, water warm enough for bathing. *Punta Ballena*, E p.p., full board, clean, friendly, rec.; 3 km. S, *Las Pocitas Beach Club*, attractive, friendly, fishing and harpooning trips, balsa rafts, food expensive US$9 for main meal, cheaper for full board. Punta Sal about 20 km. to the north has *Punta de Sal Club Hotel*, B p.p. full board, attractive, good beach, rec. Aqua Explorer arranges undersea activities. Camping is reported to be safe along the beach between Talara and Tumbes, Punta Negra, rec.

N of Talara, 51 km., is the small port of ***Cabo Blanco,*** famous for its excellent sea-fishing; scenery spoilt by numerous oil installations. Camping permitted free of charge at Cabo Blanco, by the Fishing Club Lodge, overlooking the sea (at least in the off-season June-December). Fishing Club, D, clean, attractive, rec., likely to be full in New Year period. Hemingway wrote *The Old Man and the Sea* here.

Tumbes, about 141 km. N of Talara, and 265 km. N of Piura, is the most northerly of Peruvian towns; it is a garrison town with 34,000 inhabitants (do not photograph the military or their installations—they will destroy your film and probably detain you). There is a long promenade beside the high banks of the Tumbes River. There are some old houses in Calle Gran, and a colonial public library in the Plaza de Armas with a small museum. The cathedral is 16th century but restored in 1985. There is a sports stadium; cockfights Sat. and Sun. The main products are bananas and rice. The water supply is not good.

Hotels *Turistas*, C, clean, restaurant, parking, has nice garden, provides some tourist information; *César*, E with bath, clean, secure; *Continental*, E; *Roma*, new, E; *Amazonas*, F, Av. Tnte. Vásquez 33, clean, friendly, showers; *Córdova*, J. R. Abad Puell 777, F, with bath, no hot water, safe, clean, friendly; *Hostal Estoril*, 2 blocks from main square, F, good, friendly; *Lourdes*, one block from main square, F with bath, clean, friendly, rec.; *Italia*, Grau 733, E, cold showers, friendly, good; *Florián*, E, near El Dorado bus company, clean, fan, private bath, rec.; *Hostal Tumbes*, Grau 614, F. Many other cheap hotels. Hotels are often fully booked by early afternoon, so try to arrive early, and at holiday times it can be very difficult to find a vacant room.

Restaurants *Bolívar*, cheap, rec. *Pez Espada*, good for fish, as is *Curich* in the Plaza de Armas. *La Blanquita* rec. Good for seafood is *Tito's*, Alfonso Ugarte 212, about 2 blocks from park (will change money), rec. For criollo dishes, *Pekos* acceptable; *Europa*, off main square, is rec., particularly for omelettes. *Brujos* and *Chifa D'Koko*, Piura y F. Navarete, rec. There are other inexpensive restaurants on the Plaza de Armas and near the markets. Try bolas de plátano, soup with banana balls, meat, olives and raisins, and sudado, a local stew.

Exchange Banco Popular, in a new building on the edge of the main square, will change travellers' cheques. Bad rates at the airport.

Tourist office Foptur, Edificio Majestad, Alfonso Ugarte y Mayor Bodero, T 5054.

Buses Daily to and from Lima, 1,330 km. by Sudamericano (US$12, overbooked, often subject to long delays); Expreso Continental (Ormeño group), new buses, a/c, 1130, 1900, 22 hrs., US$13; also Tepsa (often full, leaves 1100, 1600), 26 hrs., comfortable, rec.; for other companies, ask around (e.g. Roggero, not rec.); cheaper ones usually leave 1600-2100, dearer ones 1200-1400. All buses to Lima are very slow because of repeated police checks—no chance of sleep overnight. On the bus to Lima try to get a seat on the right hand side in order to have a good view of the coast. One can get tickets to anywhere between Tumbes and Lima with little difficulty, although buses are often booked well in advance; Piura is a good place for connections. To Sullana, terrible road, US$2.10. To Talara, 176 km., US$1.50 with El Dorado (colectivo US$7). To Piura, 276 km., US$4.50 with Tepsa, Empresa Chiclayo, up to 12 hrs. Colectivo, US$8.10. To Chiclayo, 548 km., US$6 (Tepsa). To Trujillo, 758 km., 5 a day, 12 hrs. from US$6.50. To Chimbote, 15 hrs., US$8 with Sudamericano, 16 hrs. Most buses leave p.m. from Teniente Vásquez. Frequent buses to Aguas Verdes, 23 km., from market at 0600 onwards, colectivo, US$1, 20 minutes. Bus to Machala (Ecuador), US$4. Taxi to Lima US$30 per seat. Hitching slow.

N.B. Travellers who hold a Tumbes-Huaquillas-Guayaquil ticket with Panamericana Internacional (bought outside Peru as an onward ticket) should note that Panamericana does not have an office in Tumbes. However, this ticket can be used for a colectivo (but not a taxi) to the border, caught at corner of Piura and Bolívar; if colectivo is full, you will be transferred to another company. Connection with bus at the border.

Air AeroPerú and Faucett, Lima to and from Tumbes daily 0840, US$20 single. Essential to reconfirm flights 24 hrs. before departure. Taxi to airport, US$1; taxis meet flights to take passengers to border, US$1.20, 2 mins.

Excursions Río Tumbes is navigable by small boat to the mouth of the river, an interesting 2½ hr. trip.

This is the only part of the Peruvian coast where the sea is warm all year. Two good beaches near Tumbes: one at Caleta La Cruz 16 km. SW, where Pizarro landed in 1532. The original Cruz de Conquista was taken to Lima. Easy to get to with regular colectivos (US$0.60 each way); *Motel*, E. *Zorritos*, 35 km. S of Tumbes, heavily damaged by the 1983 flooding but with a good beach (the water is not oily), *Hotel de Turistas*, E (reported closed for renovation), also *Punta Sal Chica*, 2 stars; the better of the 2 restaurants is *Arriba Perú*. Camping recommended. The first South American oil well was sunk here in 1863. Just north of Tumbes is *Puerto Pizarro*, a small fishing beach at the southern limit of the mangrove swamps. Take a boat across the lagoon to reach a good clean sandy beach. Festival of St Peter and St Paul, 29-30 June; colectivo No. 6 from Tumbes (US$0.30). *Puerto Pizarro Motel*, D, no hot water, restaurant dear and slow but food good, swimming pool, which is usually empty; *Restaurant*

Venecia, seafood cheap, beware shellfish which may cause stomach upsets. Plenty of fishing and swimming; ideal for windsurfing and water-skiing but few facilities. The mangrove swamps are full of pelicans and a few tame ones beg for fish on the beaches. Three islands, Isla Hueso de Ballena, Isla del Amor, Isla de los Pájaros may be visited by boat, bargain hard, good for swimming and picnics, take food and water. Remains of Cabeza de Vaca abode cult centre of the Tumpis Indians can be found at Corrales, 5 km. S of Tumbes. They were heavily damaged by 1983 rains; Museo de Sitio nearby. Bosque Nacional de Tumbes (75,000 ha.) wildlife includes monkeys, nutria and crocodiles; Parque Nacional Cerros de Amotape (91,000 ha.) is a dry tropical forest with jaguars and anteaters, a guide essential. Mosquito repellant is a must for Tumbes area.

To Ecuador Small buses and colectivos (some marked "Puente Internacional") leave about every 20 min. and take 30 min. to get to **Aguas Verdes** on the Peruvian side of the international bridge (the Peruvian departure office opens at 0830, is closed at lunch time and after 1800; try not to arrive within ½ hour of the border closing). On the way most of them pass by the airport. By taxi it costs about US$4, colectivo fare is US$1 and bus fare US$0.65. **N.B.** The customs post is at Zarumilla (basic *hostal* on Plaza, F), 3 km. from the border, so do not pay taxi driver until after you have passed through customs. If entering, they may refuse to accept a return ticket from another country as proof of intended exit from Peru; this is an invitation to bribery, be courteous but firm. Colectivos do not wait at customs. Some bus companies from Chiclayo and beyond go to the border, but will stop at Zarumilla for foreigners to get off. Colectivo, Zarumilla to Aguas Verdes, US$0.20, or 15 mins.' walk. Second check at border, then 5 minutes' walk to Ecuadorean immigration and buses. With a pass from the authorities at the border you can spend the day in Huaquillas, the Ecuadorean border town, as long as you are back by 1800. There is nothing much to see there, but Peruvians hunt for bargains. It is a thoroughly unscrupulous border, with chaotic opening hours. Tepsa leave from the border for Lima.

Warnings Porters on either side of the border charge exorbitant prices: don't be bullied. Many "illegal" money changers at the border. The money changers on the Ecuadorean side give a better rate than the banks in Tumbes; always try to check the rate beforehand. If you are going to change cheques into Ecuadorean sucres in Huaquillas, make sure you cross the border in the morning because the bank is closed after lunch. Do not change money on the minibus to Aguas Verdes, their rates are very poor. Relations between Peru and Ecuador are not good: Ecuadorean Customs tends to confiscate guidebooks and maps of Peru because they show as Peru's certain areas claimed by Ecuador.

Checks for goods smuggled into Peru are carried out, especially at Tepsa bus station as well as at Aguas Verdes. Checks are thorough, both of luggage and body. Checks also intermittently on road to Piura.

SOUTH-EAST FROM LIMA (4)

The group of oases south from Lima grow Pima cotton, sugar-cane and vegetables for Lima and Callao, but the more southerly valleys specialize in vines—Ica in particular is well known for this and its port, Pisco, has given its name to the well-known brandy sold all along the coast. The Pan-American Highway runs S from Lima through all the places now to be described to Tacna and Chile, it is 4 lane to Km. 116 and there are extensive repairs and new building as far as Km. 135. There are battery chicken houses all along the beach. At Km. 200 the *garúa* lifts.

The first 60 km. from Lima are dotted with a series of seaside resort towns and clubs, including **Pucusana**, which is a charming fishing village (*Hotel Bahía*, good seafood). Excellent panoramas from the cliffs above the village. Hire a boat for an hour (fix price beforehand and stick to it); don't go in the direction of the only, smelly factory, but to the rocks where you can see seabirds close at hand.

Resort town of **Santa María,** 40 km. from Lima, beautiful *Santa María Hotel*, A, meals included. Taxi to Santa María: US$30 per day.

Cañete (hotels and restaurants), about 150 km. S of Lima, on the Río Cañete, is a prosperous market centre amid desert scenery. There is a road (no buses) to Huancayo (**see page 824**).

At Cerro Azul, 13 km. N of Cañete, is a unique Inca sea fort known as **Huarco**, now much damaged. *La Malla* is an excellent fish restaurant.

35 km. N of Pisco, near Chincha Baja, is **Tambo de Mora,** with nearby archaeological sites at Huaca de Tambo de Mora, La Centinela, Chinchaycama and Huaca Alvarado.

Pisco, population 82,250, the largest port between Callao and Matarani, 237 km. S of Lima, serves a large agricultural hinterland. The town is divided into two: Pisco Pueblo, colonial-style homes with patios and gardens; and Pisco Puerto, which has been replaced as a port by the deep-water Puerto General San Martín, beyond Paracas. In Pisco Pueblo, half a block W of the quiet Plaza de Armas, with its equestrian statue of San Martín, is the Club Social Pisco, the H.Q. of San Martín after he had landed at Paracas Bay. There is an old Jesuit church hiding behind the new one. You can book for trips to the Ballestas Islands (see below) at a kiosk on the main square (open late); cheaper than doing it through a hotel. Pisco is an alternative airport when landing is not possible at Lima. A 364 km. road has been built to Ayacucho, with a branch to Huancavelica (see Tambo Colorado, next page).

Hotels   *Pisco,* on Plaza, E, basic, breakfast good, friendly, clean, disco until 2400 some evenings, can book (hotel provides sandwiches) for Ballestas Islands (US$3), near Ormeño bus station. *Hostal Belén,* Plaza Belén, E, clean, comfortable, no hot water. *Embassy,* E, clean, noisy, security reported suspect, nice bar on roof, has disco in Jr. Comercio just off Plaza de Armas, good, cheap trips to Ballestas Islands; *Hostal San Jorge,* Juan Osores 267, E, hot water, friendly, very clean, rec., arranges excursions; *Cesar,* 2 de Mayo, F; *Comercial,* F, dirty rooms but good restaurant. *Hostal Angamos,* Pedemonte 134, tiny rooms but good beds, clean, friendly, F, economical with water and light. Mosquitoes are a problem at night in the summer. The town is full at weekends with visitors from Lima. At Pisco Puerto, *Portofino,* F, basic, friendly, clean, in slum area on sea front, good seafood, arranges day excursion to Paracas, US$4, but avoid the nearby peña which is poor and can be dangerous.

Restaurants   *La Rinconada* rec. but expensive; *As de Oros,* on the Plaza de Armas, good restaurant, reasonable prices, closed Mons.; *Las Vegas,* on Plaza, very popular; *Roberto's,* always busy, near Plaza, rec.; *Candelabra,* next to *Hotel Embassy,* quite expensive; *Bill More* near *Hotel Embassy,* good, cheap seafood, also at restaurant of *Hotel Portofino; Turistas,* good cheap food. *Bar Piave,* on Plaza, excellent pisco sours, but lone women should beware of the owner. *Piccolo-Bar,* near Plaza, good breakfast and coffee; *El Norteño,* off Plaza de Armas, good, cheap, clean; a number of restaurants around M. de Mancera 160. Seafood restaurants along shore between Pisco and San Andrés, and in San Andrés (buses from Plaza Belén, near *Hotel Perú*) there are *La Estrellita,* rec. and *Olimpia* (Grecia 200), both rec. Good fried chicken place opposite Ormeño: save your foreign cigarette packets for their mural! *Mendoza 2,* in Pisco Puerto, excellent simple fish restaurant.

Exchange   Banco de Crédito on Plaza de Armas gives good rates, but only for Amex and cash.

Transport   Bus to Lima, Ormeño, US$1.75, recommended, many departures, 4 hrs., San Martín, Callao 136, 4 a day, rec.; Roggero, US$2, twice a day. To Ayacucho, US$7.80 with Ormeño, 12 hrs., 1730, often delayed, wear warm clothes as the road reaches 4,600 metres near Castrovirreyna and is very cold at night; Oropesa (Calle Comercial) to Huancavelica, US$7, 0800 daily, 13 hrs., very tiring, many stops; colectivo to Ica US$1, bus to Ica, US$0.75, 2 hrs. (Ormeño, Roggero). To Arequipa direct 1220 with Ormeño, arrive 0300, US$10.75. To Nazca by bus, US$2, Roggero, 1430 (3-4 hrs.), Ormeño, 5 daily, rec. (3½-4 hrs.), colectivos reported to be more reliable. Reservations can be made here at Nazca Tours for flights over the Nazca lines for US$40 p.p.

Fifteen km. down the coast (bus US$0.20) from Pisco Puerto is the bay of *Paracas,* sheltered by the Paracas peninsula. (The name means "sandstorm" - they can last for 3 days.) The peninsula is a National Park (entrance US$3 for 2 days, no less), ask permission to camp, no water; it is one of the best marine reserves, with the highest concentration of marine birds, in the world. There are archaeological and natural history museums about 20 mins'. walk from the residential area along an isolated stretch of beach (no bus), but contents reported less interesting than the Ica museum. A monument on the sands marks the spot where San Martín set foot in Peru. The area has been developed as a resort: a beautiful bay, good sands, bathing (some pollution from local fishing industry, and beware of jellyfish) and fishing and excursions by boat to offshore islands. The Paracas necropolis, the burial place of a civilization which flourished here between 700 and 300 BC, has been buried by shifting sands and archaeologists can no longer visit it. About 17 km. from the museum is the precolumbian "candelabra" traced in the hillside, at least 50 metres long, best seen from the sea, but still impressive from the land. Hitch along paved road which leads to Punta Pejerrey, get off at left fork and you will see a trail (1½ hrs.

walk to Candelabra). La Mina, a small beach 2 km. from Lagunilla, and Punta El Arquillo are also worth visiting.

On the southern side of the peninsula there is a colony of sealions, with many species of birds (such as cormorants, gannets, gulls, terns, pelicans). On the northern side, in the bay, there are flamingoes (in June and July mainly)—only reached on foot from Paracas. Condors may be seen from the (bad) road between Paracas and Laguna Grande. Trips to the **Ballestas Islands** for US$3 upwards can be arranged at a kiosk on the main plaza in Pisco, or (dearer) with the main hotels in Pisco and Paracas. The trip to the islands, which are now a national reserve, takes about 5 hrs. all together, and is highly recommended (although some boats do not have life jackets, and are very crowded). You will see thousands of inquisitive sealions, guano birds, pelicans (the book *Las Aves del Departamento de Lima* by Maria Koepcke is useful); the boat returns past the Candelabra to the bay of Paracas where flocks of flamingoes and pelicans can be seen. Taxi from Pisco to Paracas (return) US$4, but more if arranged by a hotel. Colectivo, one way, US$0.75 or less if you change at San Andrés. Small buses leave frequently from the market place in Pisco to Paracas (US$0.25, US$0.40 with stop at J. C. Tello museum; last bus from museum at 1630). A yellow bus for Enapu workers leaves Pisco main square 2300 for Paracas National Park; it may give you a lift. Good walking in Paracas peninsula, details available from Park Office or ask for "Hoja 28-K" map at Instituto Geográfico Militar in Lima. The Mirador de los Lobos is a cliff overlooking sealion beaches, 20 minutes by car from Hotel Paracas—no public transport and the road peters out after a while (make sure your car is in good repair; crossing salty sand flats and mountains.

Hotels *Paracas*, B, check your bill carefully, good hotel, bungalows on beach (T Pisco 2220 or Lima 464865) good food, not cheap, good buffet lunch on Sun., US$6 low season, US$9 high, fine grounds facing the bay, is a good centre for excursions to the Peninsula and flights over Nazca; it has tennis courts and an open-air swimming pool (US$2 for non-residents); it also houses the Masson ceramics collection (worth seeing). *El Mirador*, E, at entrance to Paracas, rooms spartan, cockroaches, no hot water, slow service, boat trips arranged, meals available. *As de Oros*, Plaza de Armas, excellent tortuga. Excellent fried fish at open-sided restaurants by the fishing boats, e.g. *Rancho de la Tía Fela*, in Lagunilla, where one can sleep for free on the floor. Camping is possible on the beach near the *Hotel Paracas*.

Up the Pisco valley, 48 km. from Pisco on the road to Huaytará and Ayacucho, is *Tambo Colorado*, one of the best-preserved pre-Inca ruins in coastal Peru (entrance US$0.60); apparently a palace with ancillary buildings; the wall paintings have survived from Inca times. Buses from Pisco, 0800, Oropesa US$0.50 (1½ hrs.). Alight 20 mins. after stop at Humay; the road passes right through the site. Return by bus to Pisco in afternoon; for bus or truck back to Pisco wait at the caretaker's house (he will show you his small collection of items found on the site), as the area is dangerous. Taxi from Pisco US$19.50. From Humay, go to Hacienda Montesarpe, and 500 metres above the hacienda is the line of holes known as "La avenida misteriosa de las picaduras de viruelas" (the mysterious avenue of smallpox spots) which stretches along the Andes for many kilometres (its purpose is still unknown).

Huaytará, on the Pisco-Ayacucho road, contains Inca ruins and baths, and the whole side of the church is a perfectly preserved Inca wall with niches and trapezoidal doorways.

From Pisco the Pan-American Highway runs 93 km. S to *Ica*, on the Ica river, population 147,000. The image of El Señor de Lurén in a fine church in Parque Lurén draws pilgrims from all Peru to the twice-yearly festivals in March and October (15-21), when there are all-night processions. The San Jerónimo church at Cajamarca 262 has a fine mural behind the altar. Ica is famous for its *tejas*, a local sweet of *manjarblanco* (sold behind Lurén church); it is also Peru's chief wine centre and has a harvest festival in March. The Bodega El Carmel (on the right-hand side when arriving from Lima) can be visited; it is a pisco distillery and has an ancient grape press made from a huge tree trunk. The Vista Alegre wine and pisco distillery can be also be visited (Spanish essential) and its shop is recommended. Local bus drops you at the entrance, or 10-15 mins. walk on the other side of the river.

The waters of the Choclacocha and Orococha lakes from the eastern side of the Andes are tunnelled into the Ica valley and irrigate 30,000 hectares of land. The lakes are at 4,570 metres. The tunnel is over 9 km. long.

Hotels *Las Dunas,* A plus 13% tax and service, about 20% cheaper on weekdays, highly rec., in a complete resort with restaurant, swimming pool, horseriding and other activities, own airstrip for flights over Nazca, 50 mins.; Lima offices: Ricardo Rivera Navarrete 889, Oficina 208, San Isidro, Casilla 4410, Lima 100, T 424180; *Turistas,* large and modern, with swimming pool, C, with private bath, meals (US$4.50); *Colón,* Plaza de Armas, E (rooms with and without bath, some shared), old, noisy, restaurant; *Siesta II,* Independencia, E, clean, friendly, rec.; *Lima,* Lima 262, basic but quiet, F; *Confort,* 4 blocks from square, F, clean; *Presidente,* E, with bath, clean; *Royal,* and *Ica* (basic, noisy), both friendly, clean, F or G, and on Calle Independencia. *Hostal Viña,* diagonally across from Entel, G, shower, safe, helpful. Several good hotels on Castrovirreyna, *Las Brisas,* D and *Silmar,* D. *El Carmelo,* on the Pan-American Highway S of turn-off for *Las Dunas,* swimming pool. Hotels are fully booked during the harvest festival and prices rise greatly.

Restaurants *Sergio, San Remo, Flor de Canela,* and *La Casona,* good and reasonable, all along Lima; *Siesta,* Independencia 160; *Venecia,* just off plaza, is the best. *Macondo,* Jr. Bolívar 300, fish good, rec. *El Fogón,* Municipalidad 276, good and cheap. Good one at Ormeño bus terminal.

Warning Beware of thieves; there is an increasing amount of theft here.

Museo Regional Bus 17 from Plaza de Armas, open 0745-1900, Mon.- Sat.: Sun. 0900-1300 (US$0.50). Houses mummies, ceramics, textiles and trepanned skulls from Paracas, Nazca and Inca cultures; a good, well-displayed collection of Inca counting strings (*quipus*) and clothes made of feathers. Good and informative displays with maps of all sites in the Department. Behind the building there is a scale model of the Nazca lines with an observation tower, a useful orientation before visiting the lines. The attendant paints copies of motifs from the ceramics and textiles in the original pigments (US$1), and sells his own good maps of Nazca for US$1.65.

The museum on the Plaza de Armas, run by Dr. Javier Cabrera, has a collection of several thousand engraved stones. Open Mon.-Sat. 0930-1230 and 1730-2000 and sometimes open Sun. If visiting in a group T 234363. We are informed that some of these stones are fakes: people have talked to the craftsmen concerned. If authentic, the stones suggest the existence of a technologically-advanced people contemporary with the dinosaurs, but the archaeological establishment seems very reluctant to study them. If interested, contact Ms. Sophia Afford, Le Petit Canadeau, Le Plan du Castellet, Le Beausset, 83330, France, T 94 987241, a geologist who has written several articles on the subject. (There are so many stones that its is impossible to believe they are all fakes. Most are in a recognisably pre-Inca style, but, for instance, kangaroo and a giraffe in the style of a modern children's story book, strain the visitor's credulity. However, Dr Cabrera is an interesting character, worth a visit. Ed.)

Exchange No travellers' cheques.

Tourist Office Av. Grau 150, T 235247, very helpful and courteous. Touring y Automóvil Club del Perú, Manzanilla 523.

Buses To Lima, Ormeño (Lambayeque 180) and Tepsa, US$4.20, 5 hrs.; Roggero 4 a day; colectivo to Lima, US$8.15. Several buses daily in the evening to Nazca, US$1.75, 2-3 hrs. Colectivo to Nazca, US$2.15; to Pisco, US$1; bus to Pisco, US$0.75 (Ormeño or Roggero). Bus to Arequipa, US$10.25 with Ormeño (a very popular route at weekends). Ormeño go to Cuzco Wed. and Fri., leaving 1700, 30 hrs., US$17.25. To Abancay with El Cóndor de Aymaráes at 1600, US$12.20, 20 hrs. (take blankets). Several departures to Tacna, e.g. 1700, arrive 0900.

5 km. from Ica, round a lake, is the attractive summer resort of **Huacachina**, flourishing again after some years of decline. The *Hotel Mossone* (4 hours' drive from Lima), D, full board, is at the eastern end of the lake. Another good hotel is the *Salvatierra* (under renovation). Sleeping in the open is pleasant here, but swimming in the lake can be dangerous because of soft sand. Local bus from the square in Ica to Huacachina, US$0.20, 10-15 mins.

The southern oases, S of Ica to the Chilean frontier, produce enough to support themselves, but little more. The highlands grow increasingly arid and the coast more rugged. There are only thin ribbons of cultivable lands along valley bottoms, and most of these can be irrigated only in their upper reaches. However, there are a few exceptions: the cotton plantations between Ica and Nazca, the orange-growing centre at Palpa, the large and well-watered oasis with Arequipa at its centre, and the smaller oasis of the river Moquegua further S. In several places the Highway is not protected against drifting sand and calls for cautious driving.

Nazca, 141 km. S of Ica by the Pan-American Highway, is a town of 30,000 people set in a green valley amid a perimeter of mountains, 444 km. from Lima. Its altitude of 619 metres puts Nazca just above any fog which may drift in from

SOUTHERN PERU

the sea: the sun blazes the year round by day and the nights are crisp. **Warning** Beware of thieves if you arrive early in the morning off a bus.

The Nazcas had a highly developed civilization which reached its peak about AD 800. Their decorated ceramics, wood carvings and adornments of gold are on display in many of Lima's museums. The Nazca municipality's own museum, on the main plaza, has a small but fine collection (entry, US$0.25, open 0945-1300, 1345-1815). The valley about 35 km. S of Nazca is full of ruins, temples, and cemeteries; the last-named are quite difficult to find, but taxis do excursions for about US$5 p.p.; the trip is worth it, mummies, bones, pottery shards and scraps of textiles may be seen lying in the desert sun, although the best pieces have of course been taken by grave robbers and archaeologists. At the edge of the town is the reservoir of Bisambra, whose water was taken by the Nazcas through underground aqueducts—many still in use—to water the land.

Hotels *Turistas,* C/D, with bath (less without), clean, rooms with private patio, hot water, peaceful, rec., good meals US$2.75, safe car park, swimming pool (guests only), rec. *Hostal Don Agucho,* Paredones y San Carlos (T 209), E, clean, friendly, rec.; *Nazca,* Calle Lima 438, F, warm showers (electric—beware), clean and friendly, parties in courtyard at night, luggage store, helpful (only hotel with good information on tours, they also run cheap tours); *Montecarlo,* D, bungalows at back also D, reported (Jan. 88) no longer offers flights over the Lines plus one night's lodging at US$30, mixed reports; *Lima,* basic but rather good, F; *Konfort,* Calle Lima 587, G, small, clean, safe, intermittent water (as elsewhere), indifferent manager; *San Martín,* Arica 116, G, basic, electric showers; *Hostal El Sol,* E, basic but friendly, hot showers, small, on Jirón Tacna at Plaza de Armas; *Internacional,* Av. Maria Reiche, E, with bath, clean, quiet, cheap, hot water (if they ask for 10% tourist tax, they won't insist if you refuse to pay), rec. but be careful with belongings. *Hostal Alegría* near bus station, F, clean, hot water, helpful; *Posada Guadalupe,* San Martín 480. Hostales opp. airport, *Maison Suisse,* rundown, food expensive, owned by Aeroíca, *Nido del Cóndor,* only for Aerocóndor passengers.

Camping *Wasipunko,* Panamericana Sur, Km 450.

Restaurants *Selva Alegre,* Lima, good chicken; *Oasis,* Arica 213, quite good and cheap; *La Esperanza,* good set lunch, Lima 594; *La Pascana,* Morzesky y Lima, rec.; *Cañada,* Lima 160, friendly, good seafood, reasonable; *Los Angeles,* half-block from Plaza de Armas, good, cheap, try sopa criolla, and chocolate cake. *Chifa Orlando,* on Lima, not original Chinese but cheap and good, 1¼ blocks from *Hotel Nazca* (direction Roggero); *La Taberna,* Jr. Lima 326, excellent seafood, bar, live music, friendly, popular with gringos, worth a look just for the graffiti; also *El Dorado,* Lima, near *Hotel Nazca,* good sopa criolla. *Fuente de Soda,* near cinema, good *almuerzo,* at Cruz del Sur bus terminal, gringo restaurant, changes dollars, expensive food. Seafood is cheaper than beef. Do not drink the water, but the pisco sours are recommended as the best in Peru.

Exchange Difficult to change travellers' cheques, impossible at weekends; bring cash. Banco de la Nación exchanges at poor rate: better from Chinese-owned paint shop opposite Banco del Crédito.

Post and telephone office Lima 816; **police** Av. Los Incas, T 36.

Tourist Office Bolognesi 397. They will organize local tours for you and they sell books about the lines.

Buses To Lima, about US$4.50, 4 hrs., Tepsa 1600, Ormeño (Lima 184) about 8 a day, cheaper. Colectivo to Lima, Comité 3, Montevideo 581, US$8.80. To Arequipa (if possible, travel by day as there have been a number of hold ups), Ormeño, 7 a day (recommended as seats can be reserved, but dearer, and buses coming from Lima may be delayed) Sudamericano also OK (2030, 2400), all companies take about 12 hrs, US$4.50-6.50, Tepsa US$6.25. Book ticket on previous day. Ormeño to Pisco, leaves at 0900, 1130, 1400, rec.; Roggero to Pisco, US$2. Colectivo to Ica, US$2.15. Bus to Ica, US$1.75, 3-4 hrs. Ormeño, 0900, 1830, Tepsa, 2200, Roggero, 2030. Colectivo to Marcona, US$2. Bus to Tacna, US$9; Ormeño leaves at 1730, 2000 and 2300. Lima-Nazca-Cuzco takes 40 hours (can take 70 hrs.); the route is done by Ormeño twice a week, also Hidalgo. Cruz del Sur, Ormeño, Nazca-Cuzco, US$12, 30 hrs.; El Cóndor de Aymaráes to Abancay, Tues., Thurs., Sat., Sun., 21 hrs., from there take bus or colectivo to Cuzco.

Excursions The Fernández family, who run the *Hotel Nazca,* also have details of the Asociación de Guías de Turismo, a group of six guides trained by the Peruvian Ministry of Tourism. They offer three 2-hr. tours to the *mirador* on the pampa, cemetery at Chauchilla and nearby Inca ruins (e.g. the Estanquería—astronomical sighting posts) and aqueducts (US$4 each tour), rec. Also available is a tour to the pyramids of Cahuachi (17 km. W of Nazca on a very bad road), US$6 p.p. Tours only run if 4 people or more. Profesor Josué Lancho, Callao 771, T 327, offers tours in his car and gives lectures. Mario Raúl Etchebarne, T 85, is a well-informed guide with a car; also Juan Tohalino Vera, Jirón Lima 438, T Nazca 85, an official guide, rec. Recommended taxi-guides are Armando Denegri, office on Plaza de Armas by Aeroíca office, and José Barahona Calle, Jr. Bolognesi 282. All guides must be approved by the Ministry of Tourism: ask to see an identity card.

Nazca Lines About 22 km. N of Nazca, along the Pan-American Highway, are the famous Nazca Lines. Cut into the stony desert are large numbers of lines, not only parallels and geometrical figures, but also some forming the shape of a dog, an enormous monkey, birds (one with a wing span of over 100 metres), a spider and a tree. The lines can best be appreciated from the air; it is now forbidden to walk or drive on them. The German expert, Dr Maria Reiche, who has studied the lines (mostly from a step ladder!) for over 40 years, lives in the *Hotel de Turistas*; she maintains that they represent some sort of vast astronomical pre-Inca calendar.

The lines are thought to have been etched on the Pampa Colorada sands by three different groups: the Paracas people 900-200 BC, Nazcas 200 BC-AD 600 and the settlers from Ayacucho at about AD 630. For years Dr Reiche presented a free lecture in the hotel every evening, but she has handed this over to her sister, Dr Renate Reiche. In 1976 she had a platform put up at her own expense, from which three of the huge designs can be seen—the Hands, the Lizard and the Tree (taxi, US$12 return). Her book, *Mystery on the Desert*, is on sale for US$10 at the hotel, or it may be obtained for US$10 from Dr. R. Reiche Grosse, Kohlgarten 7, 8726 Hohenpeisserberg, W. Germany. Another good book is *Pathways to the Gods: the mystery of the Nazca Lines*, by Tony Morrison (Michael Russell, 1978), obtainable in Lima. Another theory is that the ancient Nazcas flew in hot-air balloons; this is supported by the fact that the lines are best seen from the air, that there are burn (launching?) pits in many of the figures, and that there are pieces of ancient local pottery and tapestry showing balloonists, and local legends of flying men (which would be supported by the engraved designs on stones in Ica—**see page 777**) if these are proved authentic. See *Nazca, the flight of Condor 1*, by Jim Woodman, Murray, 1980 (Pocket Books, N.Y. 1977.) Georg A. von Breunig (1980) discounts both the above theories, claiming that the lines are the tracks of running contests. He bases his argument on the asymetrical surface level at curves in the designs and on the triangular fields which accord with human running characteristics, and with a number of runners starting from a straight line, then becoming an extended string of contestants. A similar theory was proposed by the English astronomer Alan Sawyer. Other theories are that the Nazca designs represent weaving patterns and yarns (Henri Stirlin) and that the plain is a map demonstrating the Tiahuanaco Empire (Zsoltan Zelko). *The Nazca Lines—a new perspective on their origin and meaning* (Editorial Los Pinos, Lima 18), by Dr Johan Reinhard, brings together ethnographic, historical and archaeological data on the lines, including current use of straight lines in Bolivia. Taxi-guides to the lines, 0800-1200, cost US$4 p.p., or you can hitch, but there is not always much traffic. Ormeño bus leaves for the lines at 0900 (US$0.60); hitch back, but have patience. Go by an early bus as the site gets very hot. Better still, take a taxi and arrive at 0745 before the buses.

Small planes take 3-6 passengers to see the Nazca Lines; reservations can be made at the airport for flights with Aerocóndor: small planes, 3 passengers, good view (office opposite *Hotel de Turistas*, or can be booked at *Hotel Nazca*), or Aero Montecarlo (from hotel of that name; new planes and experienced pilots, and good). Aeroíca in Jirón Lima and at the airport, also fly over the lines. Price for flight (cheaper if paid in intis) normally about US$40 in high season (July-August) and US$25-28 in low, plus US$2 airport tax (can bargain in low season). Travellers' cheques accepted; or apply at the Aerocóndor office in Lima (basement of *Hotel Sheraton*, T 329050, ext. 150-117; 471253; 453305, 460296). Sra. Fernández from *Hotel Nazca* can arrange flights by joining single travellers into group parties. Flights should last from 30 to 45 minutes, but are sometimes cut to 20, and are bumpy with many tight turns—many people are airsick. Aerocóndor offer the following round trips: Lima-Nazca-Lima, US$144; Lima-Nazca-Ica (lunch at *Las Dunas*) US$100 for 3; Pisco-Nazca-Pisco, US$98; Ica-Nazca-Ica, US$60; all include a flight over the Lines, and other sights of interest (those from Lima involve a change of plane). The best time to fly is early in the morning, to benefit from the horizontal light. (Taxi to airport, US$1.10, bus, US$0.07). Many air companies (especially Aerocóndor) overbook early flights, then keep you waiting until later in the day when the light has deteriorated. For photographs, be careful you do not find yourself in a middle seat (small planes are best). Nanaska Tours does a tour of the Nazca lines on land, operated by Sr. Carlos Santa Cruz and Sr. Josué S. Lancho (both students of ancient culture), recommended.

Nazca to Cuzco A very rough 470 km. road (can be driven in private car in 18 hrs.' driving time) cuts off through Puquío and NE to Abancay (**page 827**) on the Ayacucho-Cuzco road. Many buses from Lima to Cuzco take this route, which is now being paved; it is mostly narrow with a very bad 25-km. stretch between km. 187 and 212 from Abancay, but offers wild scenery; the journey may be broken at **Puquío** (159 km. from Nazca, *Hotel Los Andes*, F, with garage, "grim"; *Hostal Espinosa*, F, basic), although the town has little to recommend it and is freezing cold at night.

Further on is Chalhuanca (*Hostal Zegarra*, dirty and cold, and *Hostal Porvenir*). After the dusty ascent from Nazca, you reach the research station at Pampa Galera, 89 km. E from Nazca, which controls a vicuña reserve currently containing about 37,000 animals; visitors are welcome, accommodation available (3 rooms). From Puquío to Abancay is very hard for private cars: after the ascent from Puquío you reach the pampa and lakes where you can see flamingoes. About 160 km. from Abancay, you descend to the Pachachaca valley, which is followed to Abancay.

From a point 40 km. beyond Nazca along the Pan-American Highway a branch road (39 km.) runs to the ports of San Juan and San Nicolás, built to ship iron ore from the Marcona field, 29 km. inland, and Acarí, 53 km. E again, where a copper deposit is also being worked. San Juan, 553 km. S of Lima, has a beautiful deep-water bay.

After Nazca the Highway returns to the coast at Lomas (*Hotel Machora* with only 3 rooms and *Restaurant Melchorita*; *Capricho de Verano* due open in 1989) and passes by Chala, Atico (*Alojamiento*, G, good and clean) and Ocoña, to Camaná (392 km. from Nazca).

Chala, 173 km. from Nazca, is a fishing village with beaches where condors may be seen. Good fresh fish available in the morning and possibilities of fishing with the local fishermen. Electricity all day. Between Chala and Camaná a missing bridge causes traffic delays on the highway.

Hotels   *Otero*, F, friendly, basic, clean; *Hostal Chala*. No good restaurants.

Excursion 10 km. N of Chala there are large precolumbian ruins on the coast. Go 6 km. N on the Pan-American; just after Km. 606 post is unpaved road on left. Follow this for 2 km., then take right fork another 2 km. to sea (bay with cliffs); on left there are ruins of a fishing village, on right tombs.

Camaná is a picturesque little town, 222 km from Chala, with a good food market and pleasant beaches 5 km. away at La Punta (hourly buses from Camaná); good bathing but little shade. Rice is the principal crop.

Hotels   *Turistas*, E, poor; *Central*, F, just off main square, adequate; *Villa Mar*, F, basic.

Restaurant   *Hong Kong*, Plaza de Armas, good. The fresh-water shrimps are delicious.

Camaná sends its products to the small port of Quilca, S on the Río Quilca, in colonial times the unloading point for goods imported via Arequipa to Potosí (now in Bolivia). Now a seedy harbour. The village of Quilca is further along, perched on a cliff overlooking the Siguas river.

The Pan-American Highway swings inland from Camaná and runs along the top of a plateau with strange crescent-shaped dunes (**see page 784**). The sudden descents into the canyons of the Siguas and Víctor rivers are interesting. Before Repartición a branch to the left leads to Aplao and the valley of the Majes river. From there continue past Coropuna, the highest mountain in southern Peru, to Andagua, a village lying at the head of the valley of the volcanoes (bus from Arequipa, Sun., Wed., Fri., 1530, with Empresa Delgado; basic accommodation at the mayor's house in Andagua). The Arequipa-Andagua bus goes on to Orcopampa, from which the thermal springs of Huancarama can be visited. A mining lorry leaves Orcopampa for Cailloma on the 12th and the last day of each month; this enables one to make a round trip from Arequipa.

At Repartición, 134 km. from Camaná, the Highway bifurcates: one branch runs through Arequipa into the highlands (near Arequipa is a new 39 km. toll road, US$0.25, Camaná-Arequipa, 172 km.); the other leads S to the Chilean border. From this latter road a branch leads off from La Joya W to Mollendo and Matarani.

Mollendo, 14,650 people, has now been replaced as a port by **Matarani**, 14½ km. to the NW. Port workers still live mostly in Mollendo, where the main customs agencies are. Three beautiful sandy beaches stretch down the coast, small beach nearest town is safest for swimming (swimming pool on the beach open Jan.-March). Mollendo now depends partly upon the summer attraction of the beaches and partly upon the 15,000 hectares of irrigated land in the nearby Tambo valley. On the coast, a few km. SE by road, is the summer resort of Mejía.

Mollendo Hotels *Salerno*, 30 rooms, all with bath, excellent seafood. *Aller*, Arequipa 681, E; *Hostal Cabaña*, Comercio 240, F, clean, good; *Royal*, Tacna 155, basic, clean; *Moderno*, Tacna 179, F; *Verana*, Arequipa 337, cheap.

Restaurants *Salerno Bar*, good, excellent food; *Marco Antonio*, good; *Pizzería*, many gringos; *Sea Room*, Pasaje San Francisco, overlooking the Pacific; *Venezia*, Comercio 188; *Chifa Tun Fong*, good and cheap.

Bus to Arequipa (Empresa Agarón), 2 hrs., US$2 twice daily; colectivo to Arequipa, US$ 2.95. To Tacna, 3 hrs., US$3.40.

The Pan-American Highway runs S from La Joya through Moquegua to Tacna and Arica (Chile). *Moquegua* (200 km. from Arequipa), population 10,460, described as "calm and clean", is a small town of winding cobblestone streets at 1,370 metres in the narrow valley of the Moquegua river. The plaza has llama-shaped hedges. The roofs are built with sugar-cane thatch and clay. Most of the valley below the city grows grapes and the upper part grows avocados (*paltas*), wheat, maize, potatoes, some cotton, and fruits. Climate: subtropical. Interesting cacti at Torata, nearby.

Hotels *Turistas* (1 km. from town), swimming pool, E, clean, friendly, hot water, restaurant fair, telephone calls expensive; *Limoñeros*, E, old house, basic rooms, showers, pretty garden, swimming pool (usually empty); *Hostal Comercio*, one block from Plaza, G, safe and friendly.

Restaurants *La Sirena*, rec. for seafood and chicken dishes.

Buses Moquegua-Ilo, US$1, leaves at 1100. Returns from Ilo at 1700. Moquegua-Tacna, 0500, 3 hrs., US$1.25; Moquegua-Puno, San Martín, daily, about 10 hrs., US$5.

Moquegua's exports—avocados and wine—go by an excellent 96-km. road to the port of *Ilo* (population 95,000: *Hotel Turistas*, D, with or without bath, meals US$3.20).

There are three Ilos: Ilo Viejo, in ruins after the earthquake of 1868; Ilo Nuevo, the present town, dirty, with a fishmeal factory, oil tanks, and dusty and sometimes cobbled streets and "half-door" saloons; and the spick and span village built by the Southern Peru Copper Corporation (hospital, cinema, playgrounds, etc.) for its engineers and their families.

The Southern Peru Copper Corporation is exploiting its copper property at Toquepala, at an altitude of 3,050 metres, and is developing its property at Cuajone nearby (good view of valley, which is full of cacti). All exports are through Ilo, along the 183-km. railway and road from Toquepala. The SPCC smelter is on the coast, 18 km. from the port of Ilo. Some 70 km. S of Moquegua a sign points to the Minas de Toquepala (64 km. by a good road); bus service from Tacna. *Toquepala* village, in a hollow, has a guest house (swimming pool), a church, club house and an American school, and is a pleasant place; however, it is a private mining community, and permission from the management must be obtained in advance to visit the village. A nearby cave contains paintings believed to date from 8000 BC, but it is very hard to find. Helio Courier planes reach it from Moquegua (12 min.) and Ilo (26 min.). Taxis from Ilo. In the desert between Moquegua and Tacna, John Streather tells us that engraved stones dating from 10,000 BC have been discovered.

Tacna, at 550 metres, backed by the snow-capped peak of Tacora, is 156 km. S of Moquegua by Pan-American Highway, 42 km. from the Chilean frontier, and 64 km. from the international port of Arica, to which there is a railway. Above the city, on the heights, is the Campo de la Alianza, scene of a battle between Peru and Chile in 1880. Tacna is 1,292 km. from Lima by road, 987 km. by air.

Tacna was in Chilean hands from 1880 to 1929, when its people voted by plebiscite to return to Peru. There are good schools, housing estates, a stadium to seat 10,000 people, an airport suitable for jet planes, many military posts and one of the best hospitals in Peru. Population: 46,250.

Around the city the desert is gradually being irrigated. The local economy includes olive groves, vineyards and fishing. The waters of Laguna Aricota, 80 km. N, are now being tapped for further irrigation and hydroelectric power for industry. The cathedral, designed by Eiffel, faces the main square, Plaza de Armas, which contains huge bronze statues of Admiral Grau and Colonel Bolognesi. The interior is austere but the round stained glass windows, each with a different motif, accentuate the fine, clean lines. The bronze fountain is said to be the duplicate of the one in the Place de la Concorde (Paris) and was also designed by Eiffel. The Parque Locomotiva (near city centre) has a British-built locomotive, which was used in the War of the Pacific. There is a very good railway museum at the station; the museum in the Casa de la Cultura has precolumbian pottery and war relics.

Hotels *Turistas*, Av. Bolognesi, gardens, small swimming pool, tennis court, safe car park, D, with bath, meals expensive, large rooms, clean, can make telephone bookings for other Tourist Hotels; *Central*, C with bath, near Plaza; *Holiday Suite*, with swimming pool and safe car park, 10 minutes' walk from centre, follow Av. Bolognesi to the University, from where it's one block to the left; *Don Quijote*, Leguía 940, E with shower, secure, clean, pleasant, near Chasquitur office for colectivos to Arica; *Camino Real*, D, restaurant OK, discotheque, modern; *Lima*, on main square, E, with bath, bar, good restaurant, friendly, stores luggage; *Hostal Junín*, Junín, F, old house, hot water, good beds, clean. Cheaper hotels rec. are the *Gruta*, E, and *Hostal Comercio*, *Lido* (Calle San Martín, near Plaza, good), *El Dorado Hospedaje*, Calderón de la Barca 476, *Tacna*, *Las Vegas*, and *San Cristóbal*, all F. Accommodation is hard to find in the centre, especially at Christmas-time, because of Chileans on shopping sprees.

Restaurant *Sur Perú*, Ayacucho 80, rec. *Viejo Almacén*, one of the best in Tacna; *Los Tenedores*, San Martín 888, good, clean, expensive; *Hostal Lido*, San Martín 876 A, good value; *El Sameño*, Arias Aráguez, near Ormeño bus terminal, good value fish restaurant. *Helados Piamonte*, 1 block from *Hotel Turistas*, good ice cream.

Club Unión de Tacna. There is an exclusive Casino.

Tourist Office Foptur, San Martín 405, T 71-5352 (good map); Av. Bolognesi 2088 and Complejo Fronterizo Santa Rosa. Touring y Automóvil Club del Perú, Av. 2 de Mayo 55.

Air Faucett daily jet flights to Lima, many cancellations; AeroPerú on Mon., Wed., and Sat. Taxi to town US$1.50 approx., but beware overcharging. No transport direct to border; cheapest way is taxi to town first, then take colectivo.

Buses No bus station, companies are spread out over a 3-block area (colectivo from Arica will drop you at any company office). Tacna-Arequipa, US$3, Ormeño, about 5 hrs., 6 a day, from Aráguez 698 y Grohman. Berrios to Arequipa very slow, 5-6 police stops en route; better companies are harassed less, e.g. Ormeño. Colectivo to Arequipa, US$4.75, leave from plaza, opposite church. Expreso Tacna, San Martín 201, T 2642, will collect from hotel. Several to Lima, tickets can be purchased several days before departure; many passport checks; Tepsa at 1400, US$11.25, Ormeño 5 a day, US$11.25; all take 21-23 hrs. Bus to Ilave, US$5, about 16 hours; Gironda (the best), Río Blanco and Ponce companies, all leave about 1700; seek them out at 0900 on vacant lot at corner of Carretera Tarata and Calle Varcela. Plenty of minibuses on from Ilave to Puno. To Nazca, US$10.65. Bus Moquegua-Tacna, US$1.25, 3 hrs, Ormeño 7 a day, Sur Peruano (office, Jirón Callao 91, T 2802). To Arica, see below.

Warning Tacna is one of the worst towns for robberies, particularly around the bus station at night.

The road E to Bolivia—via Tarata (where Inca terraces are still in use) and Challapalca to Ilave, where it connects with the Puno-La Paz highway—is gravel, not too bad in the dry season, though difficult in the rains.

N.B. Soon after buses leave Tacna, passengers' passports and luggage are checked, whether you have been out of the country or not. Buses to Arica from bus station on Av. Bolognesi; Empresa Adsublata rec. (US$1.50). Plenty of colectivos to Arica, which will deliver you to a hotel; 2 hrs., US$2.50 (reported to incur fewer delays at border than buses and trains as drivers present all documents to officials), Empresa Chasqui and Chiletur, which stop at both Peruvian and Chilean immigration; they leave from terminal area on Calle Coronel Mendoza. We are told that passport-holders in buses can only cross the border between 0900 and 1300; the rest of the day only border-pass holders (residents of Tacna and Arica) can cross. Coming into Peru from Chile, you can only change pesos into intis with street money changers in Tacna (Banco de la Nación will not); the street rate is bad. Money changers line Av. Bolognesi. Better when leaving Peru to change intis to dollars at Banco de la Nación in Tacna and then buy pesos with dollars. You probably get a better rate for intis here than in Chile, but the money changers give a poor rate for pesos. Border closes at 2400, and Peruvian immigration is shut on public holidays.

For those travelling by car between Peru and Chile, ask the taxi drivers at the rank beside the Tourist Hotel for details of border formalities, and buy *relaciones de pasajeros* (official forms) from a bookshop or from booth close to Customs; you will need eight (8) copies.

AREQUIPA—PUNO—CUZCO—MACHU-PICCHU (5)

The Southern Railway no longer carries passengers between Mollendo and Arequipa, but there is a well-paved road from Mollendo to Arequipa via Matarani, about 130 km.

The **ash-grey sand dunes** near La Joya, on the Pan-American Highway and almost half way from the coast to Arequipa, are unique in appearance and formation. All are crescent shaped and of varying sizes, from 6 to 30 metres across and from 2 to 5 metres high, with the points of the crescent on the leeward side. The sand is slowly blown up the convex side, drifts down into the concave side, and the dunes move about 15 metres a year.

Arequipa, with about 850,000 people, 1,030 km. from Lima by road, stands at 2,380 metres in a beautiful valley at the foot of El Misti volcano, a snow-capped, perfect cone, 5,822 metres high, guarded on either side by the mountains Chachani (6,096 metres), and Pichu-Pichu (5,669 metres). The city has fine Spanish buildings and many old and interesting churches built of *sillar*, a pearly white volcanic material almost exclusively used in the construction of Arequipa. It was re-founded on August 15, 1540, by an emissary of Pizarro's, but it had been an Inca city. It is the main commercial centre for the south, and its people resent the general tendency to believe that everything is run from Lima; business travellers should know this. The climate is delightful, with a mean temperature before sundown of 23°C, and after sundown of 14½°C. The sun shines on 360 days of the year. Annual rainfall is less than 150 mm.

Because of the danger of earthquakes the churches are low, the houses have one storey only, patios are small with no galleries. Roofs are flat and windows are small, disguised by superimposed lintels or heavy grilles. In recent years, higher buildings with large windows have been constructed.

Festivals   Interesting Holy Week ceremonies, culminating in the burning of an effigy of Judas on Easter Sunday and the reading of his "will", containing criticisms of the city authorities. Another festival at end-April and beginning-May fills the hotels. On August 14, eve of the city's anniversary, there is a splendid firework display in the Plaza de Armas and a decorated float parade. On Sundays at about 1030 there is a civic and military parade on the Plaza de Armas.

Points of Interest   The twin-towered Cathedral on the Plaza de Armas, founded 1612, largely rebuilt 19th century, remarkable for having its façade along the whole length of the church; La Compañía church, whose main façade (1698) and side portal (1654) are striking examples of the florid Andean *mestizo* style: see the Royal Chapel to the left of the sanctuary, and its San Ignacio chapel with a beautiful polychrome cupola (admission, US$0.10, open 0900-1130, 1500-1730, recommended); Puente Bolívar, designed by Eiffel. Arequipa has several fine seignorial houses with large carved tympanums over the entrances. The Gibbs-Ricketts house (now offices, open to public 1700-2000), with its fine portal and puma-head waterspouts, and the Casa del Moral, or Williams house (Banco Industrial, with museum) are good examples, as is the Casa Govaneche, Merced 201, now an office of the Central Bank (ask the guards who will let you view the courtyard and fine period rooms). One of the oldest districts is San Lázaro, a collection of tiny climbing streets and houses quite close to the *Hotel de Turistas* at Selva Alegre. Behind the cathedral there is a very attractive alley with more handicraft shops. Churches are usually open 0700-0900 and 1800-2000. The churches of San Francisco, San Agustín, La Merced and Santo Domingo are all well worth seeing. Opposite San Francisco is a handicraft centre, housed in a beautiful former prison. Next door is the municipal museum, open 0900-1730, most interesting, US$0.20. The archaeological museum at the San Agustín University has a good collection of ceramics and mummies (it is being restored and a donation is expected for entry); apply to Dr. E. Linares, the Director. La Recoleta, a Franciscan monastery on the other side of the river, is well worth visiting, with museums; open 0900-1300, 1500-1700, entry US$0.60 (guide is not recommended). It contains several cloisters, a religious art

AREQUIPA
107

NOT TO SCALE

N

SELVA ALEGRE

TO AIRPORT CHIVAY, CUZCO

AV. BOLOGNESI

AV. DEL EJÉRCITO

PUENTE GRAU

RIO CHILI

RECOLETA

VILLALBA

SANTA CATALINA

JERUSALEM

AYACUCHO

MELGAR

ZELA

UGARTE

MORAL

BOLÍVAR

SAN AGUSTÍN

PUENTE BOLOGNESI

SAN FRANCISCO

SANTA MARÍA

SAN JOSÉ

MERCADERES

RIVERO

PERAL

AV. SIGLO

COLÓN

O. MUÑOZ N.

PALACIO VIEJO

CRUZ VERDE

SUCRE

VALDIVIA

MORÁN

STO. DOMINGO

TO JULIACA AND PUNO

CONSUELO

TRISTAN

SAN JUAN DE DIOS

N. DE PIÉROLA

SAN CAMILO

PIZARRO

PERÚ

DE LA LUNA

AV. JORGE CHÁVEZ

LIMA

SAN MARTÍN

LA MERCED

EJERCICIOS

28 DE JULIO

N. ALTO

LUNA PIZARRO

AV. ALFONSO UGARTE

SALAVERRY

AV. TACNA

JUNÍN

HUÁSCAR

TO THE SOUTH

T

1. Plaza de Armas
2. Cathedral
3. Santa Catalina Convent
4. La Compañía
5. San Francisco
6. San Agustín
7. La Merced
8. Santo Domingo
9. La Recoleta
10. Municipal Museum
11. Archaeological Museum at San Agustín University
12. Casa del Moral
13. Casa Gibbs-Ricketts
14. Tepsa and other bus offices
15. Tourist Office
16. Post Office
17. Intel, Telephone Office
18. San Camilo Market
19. Hotel de Turistas
20. Hostal Guzmán

museum, an Amazon museum and a library with many rarities. The church itself is open only 0700-800, 1900-2000.

By far the most interesting visit is to Santa Catalina Convent, opened in 1970 after centuries of mystery, the most remarkable sight in Arequipa; excellently refurbished, very beautiful, period furniture, kitchen utensils, and paintings. It is a miniature walled colonial town of over two hectares in the middle of the city; about 450 nuns used to live there in total seclusion, except for their women servants. The few remaining nuns have retreated to one section of the convent, allowing visitors to see a maze of cobbled streets, flower-decked cloisters and buttressed houses. These have been finely restored and painted in traditional white, browns and blues. Open 0900-1800, admission US$2, daily, including Sun.; the free tour they offer you at the entrance is worthwhile. The many pictures of the Arequipa and Cuzco schools are worth seeing. Good Friday evening service particularly recommended. There is a small café, which sells cakes made by the nuns.

The flowered Plaza de Armas is faced on three sides by colonial arcaded buildings, and on the fourth by the Cathedral. The central San Camilo market (between Perú, San Camilo, Piérola and Alto de la Luna) is also worth visiting. At Selva Alegre there is a shady park in front of the *Hotel de Turistas*, which is within easy walking distance of all the famous churches and main plaza. Arequipa is said to have the best-preserved colonial architecture in Peru, apart from Cuzco. A cheap tour of the city can be made in a Vallecito bus, 1½ hrs. for US$0.30; a circular tour going down Calles Jerusalén and San Juan de Dios.

Hotels *Turistas*, Selva Alegre, C, with bath (less without bath), unsafe area, swimming pool (cold), gardens, good meals, pub-style bar, cocktail lounge, tennis court, Wendy house for children; *Portal*, C, Plaza de Armas, excellent, wonderful views, expensive but food and service disappointing, roof top swimming pool; *Maison Plaza*, Plaza de Armas, D, with breakfast, bathroom and TV, clean, friendly, good value; *Jerusalén*, Calle Jerusalén 601 (T 222502/3), E, will change dollars, comfortable, modern with restaurant; next door at No. 605 is *Hostal Florentina*, F, hot water, washrooms a bit smelly; *Crismar*, Calle Moral 107, opposite main Post Office, E, with shower, modern, central, civilized, food good; *Posada del Puente*, Av. Bolognesi 101, T 21-74-44, D, good, restaurant, rec.; *Hostal Las Mercedes*, end of Calle Consuelo, P.O. Box 417 (T 213601), E, clean, safe, restaurant, highly rec. (but do not confuse with *Hostal La Merced*, in Calle La Merced, which is not); *Hostal Premier*, 50 rooms, Av. Quiroz 100, 2-star, restaurant, garage (T 221-791); *Hostal Selva Alegre*, Los Geranios 104, reasonable, clean; *Casa de Familia*, Av. Siglo Veinte 124, E, bed and board; *Villa Baden Baden* (Sra Bluemel de Castro), Manuel Ugarteche 401, Selva Alegre (T 222416), 6 rooms, D (F p.p.), breakfast included, German, French, English spoken, very informative about city's environs and climbing, rec.; *Arequipa Inn*, Rivero 412, modern hotel, D, with bath (US$4.60 for extra bed in room), garage, T 226077, slow service, owner unsympathetic; *Viza*, 3-star, Perú 202, all rooms with bath and phone, reports please. *Guzmán*, Jerusalén 408 (T 227142), F, hot water irregular, friendly, small café, laundry, very helpful, a bit run down; *Hostal Núñez*, Jerusalén 528 (T 218648), F, hot water, laundry, safe, some mixed reports; *Casa de Mi Abuela*, Jerusalén 606, E, very clean, friendly, safe, hot water, laundry, self-catering if desired, English spoken, breakfast on patio or roof terrace, beautiful garden, highly rec.; *El Conquistador*, Mercaderes 409, E, T 212916, clean, safe, lovely colonial atmosphere, credit cards accepted, owner speaks English; *Excelsior*, Mercaderes 106, T 215241, F, clean, 6 rooms with private bath, warm electric shower, central, some rooms noisy, others small, laundry facilities, safe for luggage and person, owner speaks German and English; *Mirador* (on Plaza de Armas), clean bedrooms but sagging beds, F, good, secure for luggage, friendly, some English spoken, intermittent hot water, bathrooms not too clean, but rec.; *Imperio* (by Cathedral), E, hot water, friendly; *Residencia Niza*, Calle Siglo Veinte 122, E (rooms, cabins and apartments), meals served, friendly; *Hostal Royal*, San Juan de Dios, F, hot showers but not enough (some rooms without water), very noisy but clean and friendly; *Hostal Parra Residencial*, Av. Parra 97, T 223787, 5 mins. from station, clean, friendly, laundry facilities, F (some rooms with shower, US$1 more), rec.; *Grau*, Grau 126, E, with bath (F without), hot water, reasonably clean; *Hostal Santa Catalina*, E or F, near Convent, clean, hot water, friendly, light bulbs in short supply (take your own); *Residencial Rivero*, Rivero 420, F, clean, with bath but not always hot water, friendly, helpful, washing facilities; *Crillón Serrano*, Calle Perú 109, F, with bath, hot water a.m., friendly to Germans, mice; *Americano*, Calle Alvarez Tomás (also called Ejercicios on maps), 4 blocks from the plaza, F, hot shower at any time, clean, beautiful geraniums; *Gran Hostal*, Alvarez Tomás, friendly; *Tito*, Perú 105, F, clean, hot water. Also *Metro*, central (Alto de la Luna), E, showers, friendly, clean; *Residencial Bolívar*, Bolívar 202, E, with shower, clean and friendly. On San Juan de Dios are *San Francisco*, F, good, hot showers, washing facilities, clean; and *Hostal Florida*, E, clean, modern, good beds, rec. On Calle Nueva is *Residencial María*, E, clean, hot shower. *Hostal Extra*, Av. Olímpica, F, with bath, friendly; *Hostal El Dorado*, on Piérola, E, bath, hot water all day;

Hostal Tradicional, Sucre, F, family-run, cheap breakfasts downstairs, clothes drying on roof; *Hostal Sucre*, Sucre 407, G without bath, friendly, clean; *Hostal Vallecito*, Av. Lima 200, F, clean, comfortable, friendly staff; *Hostal Fernández*, Quesada 106, E, 10 mins. from centre, beautiful garden with parrot, views of El Misti, family affair, breakfasts, hot water, clean, rec.; *City Hotel*, Consuelo 211, F, quite good; *César's*, Consuelo 429, F with bath, clean, good, friendly, safe; for family accommodation try Familia Ruiz Rosas, Vallalba 426, F, friendly, hot water.

Restaurants   Many tend to close early—2030 or 2100. *Le París*, Mercaderes 228, good international food and local seafood, quite expensive but good, excellent washrooms; *The Royal Drink*, Centro Comercial Cayma, T 20-20A, clean, good local and Italian dishes; *Manolo*, San Francisco 135, clean, good, expensive; *Astoria*, Calle Santo Domingo, local dishes, good service; *Chopería*, vaguely German, beer good, on road to airport, quite expensive; *André de París*, Santa Catalina 207, good food, holds peñas twice a week; *Las Delicias del Carbón*, Villalba 317, near Santa Catalina, good grills, friendly atmosphere; *Aranada*, Santo Domingo, cheap food; *Rodeo*, on O.M.Najar, Argentine-style grill, rec. *1900 Pub Pizzería*, behind the cathedral, excellent pizzas; *Balcón Arequipa*, good view over Plaza, popular with locals, good breakfasts and fruit juice, slow service, corner of Merced and Bolognesi; *Pizzería*, at Mercaderes 232, good; *Pizzería San Antonio*, Jerusalén y Santa Marta, excellent; *Dolce Vita*, Plaza de Armas, good pastries; *Bonanza*, Jerusalén 114, one block from Plaza de Armas, excellent fish, warmly rec., peña group Fri. evenings; *Bagatelle*, Jerusalén, good snacks and sandwiches, courtyard to eat in; *La Nueva Mundial*, Jerusalén 522, popular, local dishes, band playing; *Salón de Té*, Mercaderes, good coffee, cakes, ice-cream; *Monza*, Santo Domingo 1½ blocks from Plaza, good set meal and breakfast; *La Gran Vía*, Calle Bolognesi, cheap and friendly; *Chifa Liura*, Plaza de Armas, rec.; at Pasaje Catedral 108 is a small restaurant that is rec. for its excellent local food. Also Pasaje Catedral, 101, *La Chimenea*, simple, good food. *La Familia Café*, Calle Perú 105A, friendly, meals about US$1; *La Pizza Nostra*, on Plaza de Armas (open for breakfasts), safe dishes but no local ones. We have received a number of reports of robberies at *El Cerrojo*, Portal de San Agustín 111, Plaza de Armas.

Comedor de Gran Fraternidad Universal, Jerusalén 400, cheap, vegetarian food, friendly; *Govinda*, vegetarian food, good, bread and honey, small, friendly, Jerusalén 402; *La Vie Claire*, interesting vegetarian, good brown bread, Pasaje Catedral 111, rec.; vegetarian food also at Calle Nueva 410A, cheap and good.

Rec. café *Monaco*, Calle Mercaderes, cheap and good: *Café Granada*, Calle Santo Domingo, has several different types of coffee. There is a discotheque next door, *Piscín Club*, no entrance fee. *Hospedaje Cuzco*, corner of Plaza, balcony for drinking and watching the world go by, excellent (especially vegetable) tortillas but avoid the *ceviche*; similar place at *Balcón Arequipa*, San Agustín 115 on Plaza; *Aurelius*, San Francisco 125, cheap and friendly. *Harumi* snack bar, San José 216, Chinese, US$1 for set menu. Excellent bread and cakes at *La Canasta*, Jerusalén 115. *Dairy Room*, Plaza de Armas, cakes and pastries, very good coffee; *La Esquina*, Morán and San Juan de Dios, café with good pisco sours; cheapest good pisco sours at *Jumbo Jet*, Colon 221. *Nenovi*, San Juan de Dios 301, good coffee; *Ice Palace*, Mercaderes 230 and Cruz Verde 213, excellent, ice cream.

A score of picanterías specialize in piquant foods; try one called *El Pato;* rocoto relleno (hot stuffed peppers), cuy chactado (seared guinea-pig), papas con ocopa (boiled potatoes with a hot yellow sauce) and adobo (pork stew). Try them in Yanahuara suburb. Arequipeño food also at San Camilo market. Good cheap places down San Juan de Dios, but dodgy area for tourists. A good local speciality is Mejía cheese; try also the queso helado (frozen fresh milk mixed with sugar and a sprinkling of cinnamon), the chocolate (*La Ibérica*), the toffee (e.g. at *San Antonio Pizzería*), and the fruit drinks called papayada and tumbada, local specialities in the market and restaurants.

Warning   Thieves are very active in Arequipa. Beware particularly in market area, especially after dark, and in Calle San Juan de Dios between Plaza and bus offices; keep baggage secured in restaurants. Women travelling without men can expect much harassment here. However, the police have been complimented as friendly, courteous and efficient.

Current   220 volts A.C., 50 cycles.

Clubs   Club Arequipa; Golf Club; North American Cultural Institute; International Club; Club Hípico Los Leones (riding club).

Shopping   Casa Secchi, Mercaderes 111, sells good arts, crafts and clothing; also Artesanías Peruanas, Puente Bolognesi 147. Empresa Peruana de Promoción Artesanal (EPPA), General Morán 120. The covered market opposite the Teatro Municipal in Calle Mercaderes is rec. for knitted goods, bags, etc. Arequipa is noted for its leather work; the street of saddlers and leather workers is Pte. Bolognesi. The handicraft shop in the old prison opposite San Francisco is particularly good for bags. At Fundo del Fierro shop 14, on Plaza San Francisco, alpaca-wool handicrafts from Callalli in the Colca canyon are sold. Sr. Fernando Delange, N-10 Urbanización Adepa, T 233120, repairs all kinds of electrical equipment as well as cameras. Foto Esperanza S. R. Ltda, Mercaderes 132-2, English spoken, cameras mended. Three antique shops in Calle Santa Catalina. Chocolate factory on Jerusalén (NE of Plaza de Armas) gives tours on weekdays only. Supermarkets nr. market sell good bread and yoghurt.

Bookshop   Librerías ABC has a branch in Calle Santa Catalina 217, between the convent and the Plaza de Armas, which has some English books. Codersa, San Francisco 131, has *Handbook*.

Laundry   Lavandería Cayro, Jerusalén 311 and Ejercícios 442. Lavandería del Pueblo, Ejercícios 558.

Taxi Fares   US$0.75 a trip, US$2 an hr. within the town, US$0.30 minimum; US$2.10 in the country; US$2 airport to city (can be shared). US$0.60 railway station to centre.

Car Hire   Dollar Rent-a-Car, Calle Jerusalén.

Entertainment   Bar Romie, Plaza San Francisco, tiny bar with live music, Mon., Tues., *autóctono*, Wed.-Sat., *peña*. Excellent *peña El Sillar* in the cloisters of La Compañía church, minimum charge of US$0.50, plus US$1 for the music, 1930-2300; also at Jerusalén 204 from about 2100 on Fridays. Watch out for the local folk-music group Chachani, said to be one of Peru's best.

Exchange (Beware of thieves.) Banco Internacional, Mercaderes 217, exchanges Citicorp dollar cheques. Banco de Crédito accepts Visa Card and gives good rates, recommended. Others include Banco Popular, Banco Continental (will not change travellers' cheques) and Banco del Sur del Perú (Calle Jerusalén, close to Post Office, will change travellers' cheques, 2-3 % commission, accepts Master Charge). Lima Tours, Santa Catalina 120 (American Express agent), Via Tours, Santo Domingo 114, Ideal Travel, Jerusalén 201, good rates. Diners Club, San Francisco 112. Parallel market down Calle Santo Domingo, Jerusalén near Plaza de Armas, and at Morán y San Juan de Dios.

British Consul   Mr. Roberts, Calle Quesada, Yanahuara.

English Library   at Peruvian-North American Cultural Institute, Melgar 109.

French Consul and Library   Alianza Francesa, Santa Catalina 208.

Post and Cables   At central Post Office, Moral 118 opposite *Hotel Crismar*. The central Post Office also provides a telex service. Letters can only be posted at the Post Office during opening hours. Telephone: Intel, San Francisco y Valdivia.

Doctor   Dr Julio Postigo, Independencia 225. **Dentist** Dr José Corrales, San Juan de Dios 216.

Sports   Two public stadiums, a racecourse, several swimming pools, tennis courts and golf links (18 holes). The Arequipa Golf Club welcomes visitors from abroad. Riding is very popular. There are bullfights, and elaborate occasional firework displays (especially on August 14).

Climbing   Club de Andinismo de Arequipa. Chanchari Tours, Tristán 224, PO Box 2480, T 213186, hires climbing equipment, can provide guide and transport, rec. Sr Zárate, who also runs a camera repair shop, is very helpful with maps and advice.

Tourist Office   Plaza San Francisco, opposite church, next to the old prison. Complaints and suggestions are welcomed, information not always accurate but try to be helpful, open 0730-1500, free street plans. The Librería at Jerusalén 109 sells maps. Police may be contacted for information by phone: 226549, but not at all hours, Tourist police, Jerusalén 317, and at the bus station, are also helpful, Touring y Automóvil Club del Perú, Calle Sucre 209.

Travel Agencies   Tony Holley takes small private groups by 12-seater Land Rover to interesting places in the area such as the Salinas borax lake, Chivay, the slopes of El Misti, cave drawings at Sumbay, the volcanoes Ubinas and Chachani, Caylloma where the Amazon rises, and rural Arequipa. Excursions cost from as little as $20 per person, providing there is a minimum of 6 people on tour. With fewer passengers the cost rises proportionally. Passengers are insured. Mr. Holley's postal address is Casilla 77, Arequipa, and his home address is Urb. Tahuaycani F-28, Umacollo, Arequipa (T 212525, Mon.-Fri. 0730-1600; 224452 daily after 1700, 24 hrs. Sat., Sun., and feast days.) When not on tour, Mr. Holley's car may be found near Santa Catalina between 0715 and 1230.

Turandes, Mercaderes 130, T 22962, specializes in tours, guides and equipment for climbing El Misti and other mountains, and trips to other local places of interest. They have very good maps. Continental Tours, Calle Jerusalén 402, good value, English and French-speaking guides. Conresa Tours, Jerusalén 409, Casilla 563, T 211847/ 223073/215820, specializes in trips to the Colca Canyon, and to the Toro Muerto petroglyphs (US$20 p.p.), Las Salinas and Mejía lakes, and city tours, *South American Handbook* users welcome. Several agencies offer tours (1 or 2 days) to the Colca Canyon: Vlado, Merced 408, cheaper than most; Expreso Turismo y Confort, Peral 304 (US$10); Condor Tours, on Ugarte across from entrance to Santa Catalina; and Santa Catalina Tours (US$13), buses with large windows, recommended. Many agencies, including Happy Travels, Santa Catalina 106, offer tours of the city and surrounding area, T 218592; English spoken. Local office of Lima Tours reported reliable.

Buses   Most companies have their offices in Calle San Juan de Dios (5-6 blocks from Plaza de Armas). To Lima, 1,030 km, colectivos take 18 hrs., rain damage to the road can cause delays;

fare US$12.75 or more. Warning: need to book in advance to and from Lima in Jan.-March holiday season. Buses, de luxe Pullman, air conditioned with hostess, many daily, 16 hours or more, up to US$15.75 (Cruz del Sur, Arequipeño, Tepsa (toilet on board), Ormeño rec.; Sudamericana is cheapest). Few buses stop at Pisco. Trucks to Lima take 3-4 days. To Puno and Cuzco roads and buses are bad, though recent improvements have been noted; the train is better; buses run only at night to Puno, US$4, San Cristóbal cheapest, up to 17 hrs., uncomfortable, cold; colectivo, heavily booked, some by day (1000), fare US$10. To and from Cuzco by bus (680 km.), San Cristóbal, 1600 (18 hrs.) US$8; Cruz del Sur, 21 hrs., US$8.50, 1600, Jacantaya at 1800. Colectivo-taxi to Cuzco US$20. Colectivo to Juliaca US$8.15 (office on Calle Salaverry) leaves 0900. Bus to Juliaca 8½-9½ hrs., US$4.90. Bus to Tacna (about 20 a day), Cruz del Sur (rec.), Ormeño, US$3, 6 hrs.; also Flores Hnos. Colectivo to Tacna, Expreso Tacna, San Juan de Dios 537, T 213281, will collect at hotel, US$4.75, 5 hrs. Moquegua by Angelitos Negros, leaves in the morning, US$2, interesting journey. Buses must be booked 24 hrs. in advance. Bus to Nazca, Sudamericana, 3 a day, US$7, Ormeño, 7 a day, 10 hours, US$6; also with Roggero and Tepsa.

Air Rodríguez Ballón airport, 7 km. from town. To and from Lima, daily air service by Faucett and AeroPerú, about US$20. No direct flight to Iquitos; all go via Lima. To Miami via Lima and Panama; leaves on Wed. at 2340, arrives Miami 2155 folowing day. Return flight from Miami on Wed. at 0130 arriving 1045. To Cuzco, US$18, by Faucett and AeroPerú, daily at 0815 (except Sun.); to Puerto Maldonado with air force (Grupo 8), usually Friday. To Juliaca by AeroPerú daily except Sun., about US$10, 20 mins. (book well ahead). The plainclothes police at the passport desk may arrange a taxi for you. Buses marked "Zamacola" go to about ½ km. from the airport. The offices of both Faucett and AeroPerú are on the Plaza de Armas.

Rail To Puno, at 2100, with connections to Cuzco via Juliaca; day train suspended. Fares: 1st class US$6, 2nd class US$4. Only the Pullman cars (reported now that doors not always locked by guards) are heated—important above 4,000 metres—do not wear too much clothing. If not travelling Pullman, take a blanket. If travelling 2nd class take a cushion as well. Rail trip to Puno and Cuzco is spectacular, if able try to travel this route by day sit on right-hand side. It is also safer in the rainy season than by road. The night train arrives in Juliaca at about 0700, there is then a 3 hr. wait (time enough to visit the market) until the coaches for Cuzco leave; lighting does not always work: take a torch. Fare to Juliaca is US$5 first class, US$3 second class; to Cuzco, US$12 first class, US$8 second class; best to travel in buffet car, food good. If going to Puno, quicker to leave train at Juliaca (restaurant on platform) and get colectivo from there to Puno. The ticket office is open 0630-0830, 1000-1100, 1500-1700, 2000-2100, Sun. and holidays 1500-1800; queue at 1400 for 1st class tickets on day before morning departure, buy tickets for night train on day of travel. Sr. Guzmán of *Residencial Guzmán*, Jerusalén 408, may be able to help with tickets, for a fee US$0.35; Continental Tours charge US$0.60 extra to book for you. Train schedules and ticket office hours change frequently.

If you feel bad on train ask for the oxygen mask at once.

Warning Beware of thieves on Arequipa station and in the train, and especially when leaving the night train from Puno. Padlock your bag to the luggage rack, tie all your belongings to you and keep pockets empty.

Excursions The hillside suburb of *Cayma,* with delightful 18th century church (open only until 1600). It also has many old buildings associated with Bolívar and Garcilaso de la Vega and is the home of contemporary Arequipeño poet, Manuel Gallegos Sanz. The Candelaria festival on February 2 is colourful. Many local buses marked Cayma. *Yanahuara,* also a suburb, with a 1750 *mestizo*-style church (opens 1500), with magnificent churrigueresque façade, all in *sillar*; the Tiabaya valley; thermal baths of Jesús (½ hour by car, on the slopes of Pichu-Pichu), open 0500-1230. *Yura,* 29 km. from Arequipa (bus every 3 hours from San Juan de Dios, US$0.30) in a small, interesting valley on the W slopes of Chachani (*Yura Tourist Hotel*, D, wth bath, meals US$3, and an unsigned hotel opposite, F, good), has thermal baths open Tues.-Sat., morning only. *Socosani* (1½ hrs. by rail and road), now a spa owned by a mining consortium, can only be visited by appointment, 40 km. from Arequipa, in a beautiful small valley SW of Chachani, with a modern hotel providing meals and Socosani water, sports in Socosani include tennis, bowls. *Tingo,* which has a very small lake and 3 ill-kept swimming pools, should be visited on Sun. (bus 7, US$0.15) for local food; *anticuchos* and *buñuelos*. 3 km. past Tingo on the Huasacanche road is *La Mansión del Fundador*, originally a Jesuit foundation but later a *hacienda*, restored as a museum with original furnishings and paintings, entrance fee US$0.75, with cafeteria and bar (and soon to provide accommodation); it is beside the Sabandía river. Molino de Sabandía, built 1600, entrance fee US$0.50, swimming bath and countryside, well worth seeing (taxi, US$6.50

round trip); Yumina (adjoining Sabandía), many Inca terraces which are still in use. The interior of the church at Chiguita is well worth seeing.

Up a passable dirt road running through Cayma, Sumbay (4,150 metres) and Viscachani, between Misti and Chachani, is the village of *Chivay* (regular buses 5 hrs.) lying in the spectacular terraced *Colca Canyon*. Local, very distinctive, costumes still worn by women, and there is a swimming pool fed by hot springs. Water from this river is currently being diverted through a series of tunnels and canals to the desert between Repartición and Camaná, to irrigate the Siguas and Majes pampas. Further down the Colca Canyon, on both sides (bridge—Puente del Inca—at Chivay only) unspoilt Andean villages are to be found, overlooked by the two volcanoes, Hualca-Hualca and Ampato. At one of these, Yanque (good church, where two nuns from the Bronx sell handicrafts), walkers can cross the canyon by a colonial bridge (no vehicles— reached from the main square in Yanque via Av. Santa Rosa) and walk to villages on the other side: Coporaque and Ichupampa (about 2 hrs.), also with good churches; beyond Ichupampa is Lari, also with a fine church. On the opposite side of the river from Lari is Maca, whose church has an interesting interior. Beyond Maca is *Cabanaconde* (*Hotel de la Colca*, G, friendly; *Cruz del Cóndor*, basic, F; several restaurants). Festivals, 25 May: horseriding, dancing; 14-18 July: bullfighting, dancing. There is a path to the Colca Canyon from the main square, 4 hours' walk; it is possible to cross and go up to Tapay. A longer hike, 4 days, crosses the pass (5,000 m.) and reaches Madugal through a red walled valley. 10 km. before Cabanaconde, you reach the Cruz del Cóndor viewpoint, spectacular scenery, condors to be seen early a.m. and late p.m., the bus will stop there on request.

The Colca (or Majes) Canyon, said to be twice as deep as the Grand Canyon was discovered from the air in 1954 by Gonzalo de Reparaz; the first descent was made in 1978 and the first descent by raft and canoe was made in 1981. AeroPerú and Aerocóndor have flights over it. It is possible to visit the canyon in one day, but you will reach Cruz del Cóndor by about 1300, when there will be no condors around, and the return to Arequipa is very long. A short circuit from Arequipa goes via Chivay, Yanque (more thermal baths), Achoma, Maca, Cabanaconde, then on to Huambo and back to Arequipa. A longer route involves going to Callalli (beautiful alpaca-wool work at Centro Artesanal) from Viscachani, instead of to Chivay, then to Sibayo (possible detour to Cailloma), Tuti, and then to Chivay. This route adds an hour to the circuit, permitting views of fine landscapes with vicuña, Andean duck and llama, and a glance at the churches of Callalli and Tuti.

Travel to Colca Canyon   Bus to Cabanaconde from Arequipa (7 hrs.) via Chivay. Transportes Delgado (rec.), leave Arequipa 0600 and Cabanaconde 0500 daily, 7½ hours. Transportes El Chasqui, at Pampita de Zevallos, Antiquilla, leave for Chivay (US$2.50, 5 hrs.) and Cabanaconde Mon., Tues., Thurs., and Fri., 0600; Transandino (no sign), Jerusalén 104 in Cayma, 15 min. walk from centre, leave daily at 0630. Transportes Sur Colca, San Juan de Dios 537, daily at 0530, US$2, 5-6 hours. Via Huambo with Transportes Jacantaya, Víctor Lira 108, T 23258 leaves Arequipa daily at 0900, and Cabanaconde at 0700. No return Cabanaconde-Arequipa same day. Alternatively, a taxi can be hired for a day tour (US$80 for up to 5) at Expreso Chivay (Comité 10), Calle San Juan de Dios (if going by rented car, ask for an extra fuel can; no fuel in Canyon except at Chivay). Arequipa travel agencies run day tours to the Canyon for US$13 (avoid agents who overcharge), but the one-day trip is very tiring and the viewing stops are short. Among the companies are Conresa Tours, Jerusalén 409 (Casilla 563., T 215820/223073), Condor Tours, on Ugarte, Santa Catalina Tours, and Colca Tours; Vlado, at Merced 408, is cheaper than most. Buses leave Chivay for Cabanaconde at 1100, US$0.60, return from Cabanaconde to Chivay 0500. *Pensión* in Chivay (*Hotel Moderno*, G, basic, noisy, upstairs rooms best, no hot water, restaurant below OK, sanitation unmentionable, friendly; best food at unnamed restaurant at Calle Siglo 20 107, just off the plaza). The *Aldea Turística de Colca* (E, bungalows for 6 are C) at Achoma, half an hour from Chivay along the Cabanaconde road, offers breakfast US$1.50, other meals US$2.50, staff unfriendly, only electricity, heating and hot water in valley; book through Receptur in Lima or Arequipa or Ricketts Turismo, Mercaderes 407, Arequipa, T 225-382, open April-Nov. only. Canyon best visited April-November, after rainy season, but never travel in mountains after dark. Whether travelling independently or on a tour, always take warm clothing.

El Misti volcano may be climbed. Start from the hydroelectric plant (first register with the police there), then you need one day to the Monte Blanco shelter (4,800 metres). Start early (take water) for the 4 hrs. to the top, to get there by 1100 before the mists obscure the view. If you start back at 1200 you will reach the hydroelectric plant by 1800. (Erick and Martine Perruche, of Montargis, who took this route, have left a map in the *Hotel Guzmán*). Alternatively, buses leave Arequipa for Baños Jesús, then on to Chiguata, where one can walk to the base of El Misti. Be sure to take plenty of food and water, it takes 2 days to reach the crater, guides may be available at Cachamarca.

The world's largest field of petroglyphs (hard to find on your own) at Toro Muerto (off the Majes canyon) can be reached by taking a bus (San Antonio, Lima 119, 0700, returns Arequipa at 1300) to Corire, 3 hrs., US$4 return; get out 2 km. before Corire and walk 1 hr. to Toro Muerto (entry free). Guide for US$3.

The early morning scene as the day train from Arequipa winds its way up the valley towards Juliaca is enchanting. Winding around Misti and Chachani the train climbs steadily past Yura, Socosani and Pampa de Arrieros; after another 80 km. it reaches Crucero Alto, the highest point on the line (4,500 metres). Lakes Lagunillas and Saracocha are very pretty and both come into sight at the same time from opposite sides of the train, which skirts their margins for nearly an hour. As the descent continues streams become more plentiful. The scene changes in a few hours from desolate mountain peaks to a fertile pampa carrying a fairly populous agricultural community.

The rough road from Arequipa to Juliaca reaches its highest point at Alto de Toroya, 4,693 metres. Train is more comfortable than bus.

Juliaca, 289 km. from Arequipa, at 3,825 metres (cold at night), has a population—mostly Indian—of 100,000. It is reported to be very poor and run down, and therefore lawless; you can buy good alpaca clothing here very cheaply, in the plaza in front of the railway station; fleeces can be purchased at about US$2.50 per kilo, but they sell very fast. On the huge Plaza Melgar (good place to meet local students), several blocks from the main part of the town, is an interesting colonial church. Large market in the square on Mondays, reported cheaper than Cuzco and Puno; there is another daily market in the square outside the railway station, which is more tourist oriented. A first class hospital is run by the Seventh Day Adventists.

Warning   Beware of pickpockets and thieves, especially at the station, where they get on the train.

Hotels   *Turistas,* good, D, but water turned off 2300, meals US$3; *Hostal Royal,* San Román 158, E, clean, decent accommodation, rec., restaurant good. *Hostal Perú,* on main square, D, with bath, E, without, clean, comfortable, hot water sometimes; *Victoria,* F, cold water, clean but simple. *Yasur,* E with bath, F without, clean, safe, friendly, 500 metres from station, rec., small bar and restaurant in evening. *Alojamiento San Antonio,* G, basic but clean. In Juliaca water is available generally only between 0700 and 1900.

Restaurants   *Royal Hotel* (best); *Ressi,* San Martín, good, but not cheap; *El Comedor del Sur,* adequate; Hole-in-the-wall breakfast parlour at corner of plaza opposite station, good.

Transport   Rail to Cuzco, US$6, 1st class, plus US$2 for seat in buffet car where good, reasonably-priced lunches are served, US$3.30, 2nd class; trains leave Mon.-Fri., 0850, Sat., 1025, 8½ hrs. Ticket office for first class tickets to Cuzco opens at 0700—tickets are hard to get. Trains to Arequipa daily at 2155, Tues. and Thurs. at 0835, Sat. at 1055. Jacantaya bus service, which is half the price of other buses, 11 hrs., to Arequipa. Bus to Cuzco, 3 companies, 12 hrs., US$5.50. **Colectivo to Puno** (from plaza outside rail station), US$1.50; US$0.50 bus. Taxi to Puno via Sillustani, US$15 per car. Daily bus to Moho, on east side of Lake Titicaca, from where it is possible to hitch into Bolivia. A private car can get to Cuzco in 7 hrs.

Air   To Lima (US$25), via Arequipa, with Faucett, 2 a day; AeroPerú, daily, except Sun. 20 mins. to Arequipa. Taxi to airport, US$1 (negotiate).

Excursion   to thermal springs at village of Putina, 90 km. from Puno. Bus from Juliaca, US$0.50. About 32 km. NW of Juliaca (76 km. from Puno) is the unspoiled little colonial town of *Lampa,* known as the "Pink City", with splendid church, La Imaculada, containing a copy of Michelangelo's "Pietà", and Kampac Museo, Ugarte 462, musuem with sculptures and ceramics from Lampa and Juli areas, owner lives next door, interesting. The area also has a chinchilla farm and a grove of *puya* plants. About 114 km. NE of Juliaca is the old town of *Azángaro* with another famous church, La Asunción, filled with *retablos* and paintings of the Cuzco school. Stone monoliths may be seen at Taraco and at Hatuncolla. The sheep farm of San Antonio, between Ayaviri and Chiquibambilla, owned by the Prime family (descendants of British emigrants), may be visited by those with a day to spare.

Puno, capital of its Department, altitude 3,855 metres, population 80,000 (with 8,000 at university), on the NW shore of Lake Titicaca, has a fine main square and an interesting, but dirty, lakeside quarter, largely flooded since the rise in the lake's water level. The austere Cathedral was completed in 1657. Puno gets bitterly cold at night: in June-August the temperature at night can fall to -25°C, but generally not below -5°C. Some guerrilla activity; hotels close at midnight, restaurants at 2200.

N.B. The people who invade buses and trains when they arrive seem to have the hotel business sewn up, so don't shrug them off: you may need their help.

Festival   February 1-8, the very colourful Fiesta de la Virgen de la Candelaria, bands and dancers from all the local towns compete on the Sunday; better at night on the streets than the official functions in the stadium. Check in advance on actual date because Candelaria may be moved if pre-Lentern carnival coincides with it. May 3, Invención de la Cruz, exhibition of local art; June 29, colourful festival of San Pedro, procession at Zepita (**see page 795**). Also July 20. November 4-5, pageant on founding of Puno and emergence of Manco Capac from waters of Lake Titicaca.

Hotels   *Isla Esteves* (Tourist Hotel), B, spacious, good views, cold site (you can ask for an electric fire), on an island linked by a causeway 5 km. NE of Puno (taxi US$1.75), is built on a Tiwanaku-period site, with bath, telephone, bar, good restaurant, discotheque, good service, electricity and hot water all day, check bill carefully, camping allowed in car park; *Sillustani*, Jr. Liambayeque 195, T 351881, C, including breakfast and dinner, good service, clean, friendly, hot water, rec. *Ferrocarril*, Av. La Torre 185, opposite station, is modern, D, plenty of hot water, food good (except for breakfast), but good rooms, noisy, live folk music from 1915 in restaurant (food overpriced), central heating adequate, annex (F, not so good) no hot water (accepts many credit cards and changes Bolivian currency); *Hostal Real*, Av. El Sol (½ block S of Av. Titicaca), E-D, very nice, hot water all day; *Hostal Nesther*, Deústua 268 (T 321), F (also 3-bedded rooms) with bath, hot water, 0730-0900, clean rec., except for safety; *Internacional*, Libertad 161, T 25, E, with

1. Plaza de Armas
2. Cathedral
3. Municipal Museum
4. Boat terminal
5. Taxis to Desaguadero
6. Buses to Yunguyo and Desaguadero
7. Buses to Juliaca
8. Post Office
9. Telephone Office
10. Foptur
11. Immigration
12. Market building
13. Hotel Nesther
14. Hostal Monterrey
15. Hotel Italia
16. Stadium

shower (extra bed US$1.50), hot water, clean, secure, central, reservations not always respected. *Roma*, La Libertad 115, F, is passable. *Motel Tambo Titikaka*, B, with half-pension, at Chucuito on the lakeside, 17 km. S of Puno; electricity only between 1800-2300, poor heating, rooms icy after sunset, food indifferent and bill charged in dollars, wonderful view, book in advance (travellers need own transport, local transport is scarce and expensive); *Hostal Embajador*, E, Los Incas 289 (T 592), clean, quiet, hot water, fairly friendly; *Hostal Tumi*, Cajamarca 243, Tel.:147, F (G in low season), negotiable, clean, safe, cold at night, warm water limited (1830-2100), noisy from 0600, rec.; *Continental*, Alfonso Ugarte 161, F, cold water, dirty, friendly; *Don Miguel*, Av. Torre, T 177, E (negotiable), does not always honour reservations, with restaurant, clean, service good, water intermittent; *Bolognesi*, Bolognesi, E-F, friendly, good; *Hostal Italia*, Teodoro Valcarcel 122 (T 640), E-D (negotiable), with shower and breakfast, good, safe, rec.; hot water except in cheap rooms on ground floor, good food, clean, electric heater, staff helpful, esp. Mario Alvarado, and Rubén, who arranges tours to the Uros islands and Sillustani, US$10 each. *Hostal Monterrey*, Lima 447A, T 343, F, "gringo hotel", reasonable, some rooms with bath, a/c, hot water after 1800, fairly clean, secure for luggage (has colectivo service to La Paz); *Los Uros*, Calle Valcarcel 135, T 644, F, hot water at night, plenty of blankets, breakfast available, quiet, safe for luggage (small charge), friendly, often full, close to station and market; *San Carlos*, F, near railway station, no hot water, no bath but nice room; *Europa*, Alfonso Ugarte 112, G, "gringo hotel", luggage may be stored, hot water in the common bathrooms in the evenings, dirty but friendly. *Hostal Posada Real*, Av. Titicaca 156, T 738, F, good, central, clean, friendly, warm water, rooms overlooking lake are also nearest to disco close by, minibus to station. At Av. Circunvalación 470, good accommodation, F, in house of local priest run by Macericio and Nelly Rodríguez. Hotel rooms are difficult to find after trains arrive as everyone else is also looking. Clean public showers near the football stadium. Puno suffers from power and water shortages.

Restaurants Try *Sale Caliente*, Tacna 381, or any of the pollo (chicken) places: ¼ chicken and french fries, US$1. *Ambassador*, Lima 347, rec. for cheap and varied food; reasonable *Bar Café Delta*, good for snacks, on La Libertad, try flan de chocolate; *Hotel Ferrocarril* for pizzas and pasta; *Itos*, Plaza de Armas, good food, US$1, rec.; *Café Internacional*, Libertad 161, 2 blocks from Plaza, "gringo", meals huge and cheap but service variable, thieves around,"take waders if you want to go to the toilet", reasonable prices; *Peña Hostería*, Calle Lima, good music, serves only pizzas. *Club 31* on Moquegua, good cheap café; *Samaná*, Puno 334, inconsistent service, sometimes has live folk music from 2100, open fire and snacks and drinks (no minimum charge). *Ayllu*, Puno, good sandwiches, pastries; *Cafetería Chimú*, Jr. Lima 517, excellent breakfast, set lunches and dinners reasonably priced, run by very friendly German lady, highly rec.; *La Sirena*, in the lakeside quarter, for cheap breakfasts; *Kimano*, Calle Lima one block from Plaza, very good cakes; *Café Copacabana*, Melgar y Av. del Sol, good pastries. Good coffee shop next to *Hotel Monterrey*, Grau y Lima. *Restaurant Monterrey*, behind hotel, good fish, only drink is pisco. *Café Juthma*, Moquegua 153, open 0630, excellent cheap breakfast.

Shopping In the covered part of the market (mostly fruit and veg.) there are model reed boats, and attractive carved stone amulets and Ekekos (Bolivian household gods). Market down road towards lake (Av. Los Incas) is one of the best places in Peru for llama and alpaca wool articles; many are still hand-made, unlike in Cuzco. Artesanías Puno, on Calle Teodoro Valcarcel, has good quality alpaca goods with sizes for large gringos. Uros on same road, higher quality alpaca, but more expensive. Black market next to stadium; good for contraband imports; e.g. film. For good *artesanías*, take a bus to km. 20, Chinchera, where the *Trenza de Oro* has very good quality goods.

Museums The Municipal Museum has been combined with the private museum of Sr. Dreyer, Conde de Lemos 289, open Mon. to Fri. 0700-1800, entrance US$0.50.

Exchange Very difficult to use credit cards anywhere: best not to try. Souvenir shop opp. *Hostal Monterrey*. Good rates in *Cambio*, Lima 447, and *Hotel Uros*.

Post Office Jirón Moquegua 230. **Telephone** Entel, Arequipa y Moquegua, long waits for international calls.

Bolivian Consulate Issues visas same day.

Laundry Lavandería América, Jr. Moquegua 169; Lavandería Lava Clin, Deustua 252, El Sol 431 and Teodoro Valcarcel 132.

Tourist Information Government Tourist Office, Foptur, Jr. Arequipa 314 y Lambayeque (above Farmacía Central), open Mon.-Fri., 1000-1300 (has maps). Check for details of village festivals. Touring y Automóvil Club de Perú, Arequipa 457. The booklet by Pedro Sueldo Nava on Puno, Arequipa and La Paz is informative and reasonably priced (includes maps), also available in Cuzco.

Travel Agencies Viajes El Sol, Jirón Arequipa 401, T 684, Sr. Ronald Zárate; Puno Travel Service, Tacna 254, rec.. Cooperativa de Transportes Turísticos Dos de Febrero, Libertad 111, has received mixed reports. Turismo Titicaca, Libertad, rec.; Kinjyo Travel Service, Calle Arequipa

401. Turpuno next to *Hotel Sillustani* on Lambayeque rec.; also Andrés and Samuel López at *Hotel Don Miguel.*

Railways   There is a 386-km. railway from Puno to Cuzco, via Juliaca. When the Puno-Juliaca section of line is closed, Puno passengers are taken to and from Juliaca by colectivos which leave from Jirón Pardo, 0630, US$1.50 (or by bus, US$0.25), arriving in good time to get Cuzco tickets in Juliaca station. When running, the Puno to Cuzco train leaves 0700 daily except Sun., arriving at 1900, tourist coach US$22, 1st class US$5, buffet US$2.60 extra. Tickets are on sale only an hour before departure, or you can buy them the day before (which is the only way to get them), after the train to Arequipa has departed (ticket office hours are very irregular—check in advance). Tour companies often buy up all the available tickets and you either have to queue for hours (or ask a young boy to do this for you, paying him half in advance), or pay the companies a premium. A magnificent run, with shopping possibilities at stations. Sit on right side on Puno-Cuzco train for best views. Hotel representatives join train near Cuzco to find customers.
Puno to Arequipa leaves 1900, Mon., Wed., Fri., sometimes withdrawn. Buffet US$8, lunch US$3.20, 1st class US$6, 2nd class US$4 (no lighting), 8 hrs. splendid views. Pullman class available (US$2.50 extra). Tickets can be bought in advance, get to the station early to queue; if short of time get them through a travel agent (20% commission, sometimes more). Beware of supposed Turismo class at an exhorbitant price which is actually 1st class.

Warning   The train from Puno to Arequipa is worked by professional thieves; strict measures are needed to ensure the safety of your valuables. The buffet car is usually full of tourists, which lessens the risk of theft. Beware of thieves at Puno station when train arrives. Although it appears that the number of police on the stations and greater security on the trains has improved the situation, great care should be exercised. One large bag is easier to watch than several smaller ones.

A good idea in Puno, Juliaca and other Andean towns, when moving about with heavy baggage, is to hire a 3-wheel cycle cart (about US$0.20 per km.)

Roads and Buses   To Arequipa, road improved: more bridges have been built. Several bus companies leave in the early morning. Transportes San Cristóbal, cheapest, not recommended, 19 hrs. Jacantaya, El Sol 590, opposite the stadium, leaves at 0830, 10-11 hrs., US$4. Sur Peruano leaves at 1000, door-to-door service, about a 10-hr. journey by road. Colectivo (Comité 31 rec.; also Comité 3 Juliaca Express, Jirón Tacna) takes 9 hrs, US$8.50. To Cuzco, road first 44 km. (to Juliaca) and last 85 km. paved, other 260 km. very bad (the stretch Juliaca-Sicuani is appalling and very demanding for drivers of private cars), again several bus companies cover the route, from US$5, Sur Peruano, Transportes San Cristóbal. Cruz del Sur, El Sol 565, (1730), 11 hrs. Colectivo to Cuzco, US$10.75. To Lima, 18 hours, several companies. To Moquegua, for Chile, San Martín bus, US$5, 1800, 10 hrs., very cold, bad road.

Excursions from Puno   The walk from Jirón Cornejo following the Stations of the Cross up a nearby hill (with fine views) has been recommended. Motorboats charging upwards of US$3.25 p.p. take tourists to the *Uros* "floating islands"; prices should not be over US$6. Those furthest from Puno are most worth seeing, but latest indications are that the islands have been totally spoilt by tourism. Boats go about every ½ hour from about 0700, or whenever there are 10 or more people to fill the boat, and take 3-5 hrs. Local boats may also be hired. (Be careful where you walk on the floating islands.) The Uro Indians on the islands have intermarried with the Aymará and no pure Uros exist. The temptation to move ashore may soon deprive the floating islands of all residents. The present Puno Bay Indians still practise some Uro traditions, but Aymará influence predominates. Many tourists report that though the people are friendly, they are very poor and consequently there are constant requests for money. Rather than giving the children money, give them fresh fruit, pencils and paper, and buy their little reed boats.
   A much more interesting island to visit (quiet and hospitable, except at the height of the tourist season) is *Taquile*, some 45 km. from Puno, on which there are numerous pre-Inca and Inca ruins, and Inca terracing (described by Jane Coburn as "lots of local colour, but pricey due to all the gringos watching the local colour"). On the N side of the island is the warmest part of Lake Titicaca. Plentiful accommodation can be found in private houses (G) but best to take warm clothes and a sleeping bag. No previous arrangements can be made; on arrival you walk up a steep path for 30 mins., are greeted by the Indians, sign the guest book and if wishing to stay are "assigned" a family to stay with (for US$0.75). Boats to Taquile leave daily (get ticket in harbour office ½ hr. in advance) at 0800 and 0915 (subject to change), but in low season there is only one a day, at 0830, return 1430, US$3.20 single, US$5 return, 4 hrs.; a day return is not recommended since one does not have enough time to see the island fully. Boats usually stop at one of the floating islands on the way to Taquile, for about 20 mins.; if you ask after the boat's started, they won't charge extra. An entire boat can be hired for about US$50 to take 5-7 people to Taquile: 3 hrs. there, 3 back, 3 hrs. on island, so day trip possible this way. A sailing boat can be taken to Taquile for about US$1.50 p.p., departure time depends on the wind. There is a cooperative shop on the square that sells fine woollen goods. There are several small restaurants on the island; fish is plentiful and the island has a trout farm, but meat is rarely available and drinks often run out. You are advised to take with you some food, particularly fruit (welcomed by the local

children) and vegetables, water, plenty of small-value notes and a torch. Take precautions against sunburn. June 7, July 25, August 1 and 2 are the principal festival days with many dances in between. Ask for Sr. Agustín, a dressmaker, who is very knowledgeable about the island.

Another island supremely well worth visiting, is **Amantaní**. It is very beautiful and peaceful and like Taquile, has ruins on both of the island's peaks: there are temples and on the shore there is a throne carved out of stone. The Indians make beautiful textiles and sell them quite cheaply. There are no hotels or restaurants, but you can stay with local families, who like postcards: take some. The Borda family rec. good food, also Benedicto Guli Calsin, nr. the windmill; for an insight into subsistance living, stay with the shy but interesting Amadeus family, just outside the main village, turn left along beach from port, be sure to pay a fair price for their wicker work, they are liable to undercharge. Take fruit and vegetables as the Indians live on bread, rice and potatoes. Boats go most days at 0800, the cooperatively owned boat *Atún*, will take you for about US$2.50 (4 hours). Also recommended is Benito, who may be found at the docks (establish a price before leaving the dock). Accommodation on the island for about US$1.50-2 p.p.; Ricardo Quispe Mamani, who has bar/restaurant on main square, has been recommended, F plus food. The festivities on New Year's Day have been reported as spectacular, very colourful, musical and hard-drinking. There are daily boats between Taquile and Amantaní, fare about US$2.50.

Anybody interested in religious architecture should go from Puno along the western shore of Lake Titicaca to the churches of *Juli, Pomata* and *Zepita.* The church at Pomata, which is being restored, is spectacular, with beautiful carvings, in Andean *mestizo* baroque, of vases full of tropical plants, flowers and animals in the window frames, lintels and cornices, and a frieze of dancing figures inside the dome (which is unusual in Peru), and alabaster windows (John Hemming). On the road to Juli is *Ilave,* where the road for Tacna branches off. (The Tacna road is unpaved, but in good condition and a worthwhile journey, not only in terms of scenery, but also because road conditions are better than on the alternative Juliaca-Arequipa route to the coast from Lake Titicaca.) Ilave is typical of a gaunt *altiplano* town; has a good Sun. market (woven goods). Many buses go there from Puno (US$1.15); Ilave-Tacna, US$6.50, 13 hrs., leaves at 1400 and 1700 (Transportes Ponce, best, and Transportes Gironda). You pass these places when travelling by road between Puno and La Paz. Near Juli there is a small colony of flamingoes and many other birds can be seen from the road.

Juli Hotels   Only one, *Hostal Tréboles*, F, cold, dirty—best not to arrive in Juli at night looking for somewhere agreeable to stay. Bus Puno to Juli at 1430 from the market.

"Juli has four churches, two of them in ruins, that the visitor should see. The keys to two of these (Santa Cruz and San Juan Bautista) are kept by the couple who look after San Juan Bautista. San Pedro is now designated as the Cathedral. Juli's fourth church is La Asunción, now abandoned and its fine bell tower damaged by earthquake or lightning. The Peruvians have established a school of picture restoration at Juli to restore its mass of paintings" (John Hemming.)

All the Juli churches are being renovated. San Pedro has been extensively restored, it contains a series of superb screens, some in ungilded mahogany and others taken from other churches; also paintings, and a collection of coloured objects in the sacristy. San Juan Bautista has two sets of 17th century paintings of the lives of St. John the Baptist and of St. Teresa, contained in sumptuous gilded frames. San Juan is now a state museum, open a.m. only (US$0.15); it also has intricate *mestizo* carving in pink stone. Santa Cruz is another fine Jesuit church, partly roofless, so that it is easy to photograph the carvings of monkeys, papayas and grapes. La Asunción has an archway and atrium which date from the early 17th century.

Minibus Puno-Juli, 0800, US$1.80 (Colectur). A hydrofoil at 0800 from Juli to Bolivia operates most days as part of a Puno-La Paz package tour. Juli-La Paz costs US$115, lunch included, from Transportes El Sol (Sr. Ronald Zárate).

Pomata Hotel   *Puma Uta*, F, water, electricity.

There are other excursions, near Puno, to the *chullpas* (precolumbian funeral towers) of **Sillustani** (admission, US$0.30) in a beautiful setting on a peninsula in Lake Ayumara, 32 km. (excellent road) from Puno. (Colectivo US$6 p.p. for 3 hrs., mini bus from Puno, Tranextur, Jr. Puno 525, Plaza de Armas, 1400, US$3, 1 hr. at site, taxi, US$15 wait and return or take morning bus to Juliaca from Corrego y La Torre, get off at Sillustani turn, hitch a ride to Atuncolla, traffic frequent, walk 4 km., return in the afternoon by tourist bus US$0.50-1, negotiate. Take water, food and sunscreen.) Museum, reception area and restaurant now built. "Most of the towers date from the period of Inca occupation in the 15th century, but they are burial towers of the Aymará-speaking Colla tribe. The engineering involved in their construction is more complex than anything the Incas built—it is defeating archaeologists' attempts to rebuild the tallest "lizard" *chullpa*. Two are unfinished: one with a ramp still in place to raise blocks; the other with cut stones ready to go onto a very ambitious corbelled false dome. A series of stone circles to the east of the site are now thought to be the bases of domed thatch or peat living huts, rather than having any religious meaning. The quarry near the towers is also worth seeing." - John Hemming. There are local indians at the site, in costume. Take small change or chocolate, matches etc., as small presents if you wish to photograph the indians. Camera fans will find the afternoon light best; desert country, but impressive. There are Inca ruins at Tancatanca and Caluxo and an Inca sundial may be seen near the village of *Chucuíto* (which has an interesting church, La Asunción, a small museum in the church of Santo Domingo, and houses with carved stone doorways); cave paintings at Chichiflope.

Peru to Bolivia (See also under Bolivia, **page 196**). Migration tax (5 intis) payable in intis at border.

By Road: 1. The most remote route is along east side of Lake via Huancané and Puerto Acosta (Bolivia), rec. only on weekends when there is more traffic; after Puerto Acosta, the road is very bad.

2. The most direct route is the Puno-Desaguadero road (paved) passing through Chucuíto, Ilave, Juli and Pomata. Desaguadero is a miserable place (*Alojamiento Internacional*, dirty, F). Many buses to La Paz e.g. Chaski Andina (Sun., 0930). Bus from Titicaca 165 leaves 2000, arrives Desaguadero 0200. Bus from border to La Paz at 1130; advisable to check the day before when buses are running. Puno-Desaguadero by colectivo, US$4, leaving between 0600-0730. Colectivo, Julaxa Express, Puno-La Paz, twice daily, US$15. Offices: Puno, Tacna 298; Arequipa, Salaverry 111; **Cuzco, Ruinas 407**; Juliaca, San Román 129.

3. Transturin of La Paz runs a luxury service Puno-La Paz, for US$80, including hydrofoil and lunch, leaves Puno 0630, arrives La Paz 1800 on Mon. to Fri. stopping at Copacabana. Transturin has offices in both Puno (Jirón Tacna 201, T 737) and Cuzco (Portal de Panes 109, Of. 1, Plaza de Armas, T 222332) where tickets can be booked in advance. There is also a bus-hydrofoil-bus route from Puno to La Paz run by Crillón Tours (the hydrofoil crossing from Juli to Copacabana, calling at the Island of the Sun), leaves Puno 0800, arriving La Paz at 1830. Expensive (US$150, or US$200 with overnight stay and additional sightseeing) but judged worthwhile; all luggage and formalities taken care of. Colectur/Turisbus runs a luxury bus service Puno-La Paz (to *Residencial Rosario*, who give 10% discount for passengers) for US$12; breakdowns not unknown.

4. Puno-Yunguyo-Copacabana-La Paz: by far the pleasanter journey. Colectivos, leaving Puno 0800, ply to La Paz via Copacabana for US$7.50, but often ask you to pay ferry fare, US$0.25, in addition. You can take a bus-Puno-Yunguyo (e.g. Cruz del Sur, leaving 0800, arriving 1000, US$1, colectivo, US$ 1.15), then bus (irregular service, US$0.30), truck, colectivo (plenty) or 11 km. walk to Copacabana for Immigration. There are three buses a day Copacabana-La Paz and you must book one or two days in advance (e.g. Pullman, US$2.50, reserve seats at *Hotel Ambassador*). Alternatively local buses and trucks go from Yunguyo to Copacabana, stopping at the frontier, for US$0.30. There are also direct buses from Yunguyo to La Paz, which stop at the border for both authorities to stamp passports. On Sun. there are many trucks carrying people between the markets. *Yunguyo* itself has improved: privet hedge on main square shows good examples of topiary. Hotel *Amazonas*, G, *Hostal Yunguyo*, also G, clean, but often no water or electricity. Parallel exchange market good. Passport sometimes stamped at Yunguyo, walk across bridge to Kasami—1 km., where passport must be stamped.

A few agencies in Puno, for example Colectur (Jr. Tacna 232, T 697), Tour Latino, Tacna 300, offer minibus services to the Bolivian border, with a lunch stop in Copacabana, stops at all necessary official posts, and at money changers in Yunguyo, with connection to La Paz, for US$7 up (the less expensive do not include lunch, US$2); depart Puno at 0800, arriving at the hotel of your choice in La Paz between 1500 and 1600. If you wish you can break your journey in Copacabana (US$1 bus, US$2.50 daily colectivo—you have to change buses at Copacabana regardless) and make a connection to La Paz next day. Coming into Peru at this point you can get an overnight truck to Puno for about US$1, though these are cold and uncomfortable. Many colectivos leave from the Laykakota market. La Paz-Copacabana-Yunguyo-Puno is possible in one day as a bus (2 de Febrero company) leaves La Paz at 0800 for Copacabana, leaving you time to catch an onward bus to Yunguyo and bus or colectivo to Puno. The road is unpaved from Yunguyo to Straits of Tiquina.

N.B. Delays and consequent expenses have been reported by travellers going from Puno to Bolivia by car. On the **Yunguyo-Copacabana route** immigration, customs and police offices are all at different places on both the Peruvian and Bolivian sides: failure to check in at each usually means several hours wasted. When crossing Peru to Bolivia get an entry stamp in Copacabana (exit stamp in Peru of course). Bolivian authorities may want proof that you have US$10 for each day you intend to spend in Bolivia. There is no need to go to the Bolivian Consul in Yunguyo—he charges US$3 for a 10 day visa, whereas, at the border, a 90 day visa is free. If you go via Desaguadero, there are two Peruvian offices to visit (colectivo drivers know where they are) and three Bolivian—at the frontier. Tuesday and Friday are bad days to cross because they are days for the peasants on both sides of the border to exchange "national natural produce". Smugglers' paradise: keeps the Customs very busy.

By Ferry: 5. In 1985 the passenger ferry service across Lake Titicaca was suspended; in 1989, the ferry and the rail continuation from Guaqui to La Paz were running for freight only.

side going away from the Plaza. The Religious Art Museum in the former Archbishop's Palace is nearby.

San Sebastián, an interesting church with a baroque façade, is in the little village of San Sebastián, 6½ km. from Cuzco.

Visitors' Tickets   It is not possible to purchase individual entrance tickets to the churches and ruins in and around Cuzco; one must purchase a combined ticket for US$20 (US$10 for student with identification), said to be payable only in US$ (but try intis—could be cheaper), valid for five days, which allows entry to: the Cathedral, San Blas, Santa Catalina, Santo Domingo-Coricancha, Museo Histórico, Museo de Arte Religioso, Sacsayhuamán and the 3 ruins (Kenko, Puku Pukará and Tambo Machay—see below) on the way to Pisac, Pikillacta, Pisac, Chincheros and Ollantaitambo. The tickets can be bought at any of the places mentioned or at the tourist office, said to be renewable at Oficina del Boleta Turística, first block of Av. Sol. Students can pay per individual site, as can others with a lot of insistence (but you may be charged US$5 per site). Student cards and IYHA cards (with photographs) are extremely useful around Cuzco. **N.B.** All sites are very crowded on Sun.

Palaces and Mansions   The Palacio del Almirante, just N of the Plaza de Armas, is impressive. Nearby, in a small square, is the colonial House of San Borja, where Bolívar stayed after the Battle of Ayacucho. The Concha Palace (on Calle Santa Catalina), with its finely carved balcony, is now used by the Guardia Civil. The Palace of the Marquis of Valleumbroso (3 blocks SW of the Plaza de Armas) was gutted by fire in 1973 and is being restored. The Archbishop's Palace (two blocks NE of Plaza de Armas) was built on the site of the palace occupied in 1400 by the Inca Roca and was formerly the home of the Marqueses de Buena Vista; it has been opened to the public and contains a fine collection of colonial paintings and furniture, including the paintings of a 17th century Corpus Christi procession that used to hang in the church of Santa Ana. Well worth visiting. Above Cuzco on the road up to Sacsayhuamán, one finds the church of San Cristóbal, built to his patron saint by Cristóbal Paullu Inca and, N of it, the eleven doorway-sized niches of the great Inca wall of the Palace of Colcampata where Paullu Inca set up home. Further up, to the left, is a private colonial mansion, once the home of the explorer (and murderer) Lope de Aguirre. Also visit the palace called Casa de los Cuatro Bustos at San Agustín 400 (which is now the *Libertador-Marriott Hotel*) and the Convento de las Nazarenas, Plaza de las Nazarenas (alias Casa de la Sirena). See the Inca-colonial doorway with a mermaid motif.

Archaeological Museum   House of Jerónimo de Cabrera, Plaza de las Nazarenas, first-rate precolumbian collection, contains Spanish paintings of imitation Inca royalty dating from the 18th century, as well as an excellent collection of textiles. Visitors should ask to see the forty miniature pre-Inca turquoise figures found at Piquillacta and the golden treasures, all kept under lock and key but on display. Open Mon.-Fri., 0800-1200, 1500-1800. Entry US$1.20.

Religious Art Museum   at old Archbishop's Palace in Calle Hatun Rumioc (constructed over temple of Inca Roca), with religious paintings of the Cuzco School and Colonial furniture in beautiful rooms. Open Mon.-Sat., 0930-1200, 1500-1800. Sun. 1500-1800.

Regional History Museum, in the Palacio del Almirante on the street above the Cathedral, tries to show the evolution of the Cuzqueño school of painting. Open Mon.-Fri., 0900-1200, 1500-1800, Sat., 0900-1200. Contains Inca agricultural implements, colonial furniture and paintings and mementos of more recent times. Note the pillar on the balcony over the door, showing a bearded man and a naked woman. Closed after earthquake damage, April 1986.

Hotels   Book more expensive hotels well in advance through a good travel agency, particularly for the week or so around June 24 when the Inti Raymi celebrations take place. Prices given are for the high season in June-August. On the Puno-Cuzco train there are many hotel agents for medium-priced hotels; prices can often be negotiated down to F category, but best to pay agent for one day only and then negotiate with hotel. Agents also provide transport to the hotel, which can be invaluable when arriving at the dimly-lit station. It is cold in Cuzco, many hotels do not have heating. It is worth asking for an "estufa", a space heater which some places will provide for an extra charge.

Best is *Libertador-Marriott* (5-star), in colonial palace (Casa de los Cuatro Bustos) at Calle San Agustín 400, T 232601/231961, A, plus 28% tax, good, especially the service, but in July and August rooms in the older part of the hotel are cold and dark, restaurant poor and overpriced; *Royal Inka*, Plaza Regocijo 299, A, 3-star, bar, dining room, good service, rec., arranges trips to Machu Picchu; *Cusco*, A, Heladeros 150, administered by Sociedad de Beneficencia Pública del Cusco, hot water, largest and best known, "old fashioned, not cheap and a little fusty", central; *Turistas*, B, good but overpriced; *Alhambra*, Av. Sol, B, modern, very good, prices negotiable for groups, but cold, and food disappointing; *Tambo*, Ayacucho 233, D, central, tatty rooms, hot water, restaurant fair; *Savoy*, A, group rate B, recently upgraded to Peruvian 5-star, food poor and expensive, no coffee or food served after 2200, disappointing; *Marqués de Picoaga* on Calle Sta. Teresa, A, 70 rooms, central heating, private bathrooms, dining room, information in Lima T 286 314; *Viracocha*, Plaza de Armas, corner of Mantas, D, clean, hot water, restaurant opens at 0600

(Casilla 502); *Hostal Inti Raymi*, B, Matará 260, T 228401. *Espinar*, Portal Espinar 142, C, rec. but food poor, clean and helpful, and *El Inca*, Quera 251, D, F in low season, good, clean, heating, may have to ask for hot water after 0900 and before 0600, breakfast overpriced, Wilbur speaks English, and is helpful; *Hostal El Dorado* (4-star) on Av. Sol, good but can be noisy in a.m., food good but expensive. *Hostal Garcilaso*, Garcilaso de la Vega 233, C with bath, but in off-season can be negotiated lower (E), safe for luggage, clean, helpful, "historic charm, but service poor", laundry expensive, noisy disco until 0300, overpriced in season, friendly; *Garcilaso III* in same street, E, less good; *San Agustín*, Maruri y San Agustín, T 222322, A, fine interior, clean, friendly, very hot water, restaurant expensive; *Los Marqueses*, Garcilaso 252, E, early colonial house, very helpful and comfortable, but not well kept, has a masseur, Douglas Chapman, rec., clean and convenient; *Hostal Corihuasi*, Calle Suecia, E, 4-room suites, colonial house, laundry arranged, hot water, quiet, rec.; *Qorichaska*, Nueva Alta 458, close to centre, F, clean, hot water, rec. *Qoricancha*, opposite *Inti Raymi*, F, hot shower, rec.; *Internacional* (near San Pedro station), E, with bath (out of season, more expensive in season), good, clean, safe; *Suecia*, Calle Suecia, F, shared rooms, cosy, clean, hot showers, safe, highly rec., can use their bulletin board to arrange groups for the Inca trail; nearby is *Huaynapata*, Huaynapata 369, small rooms, F p.p., very safe, family-run, hot water, stores luggage, friendly. *Trinitarias*, Trinitarias 263, near San Pedro station, E, clean, hot water in shower, friendly, secure for left luggage; also near San Pedro station, *Milán*, Trinitarias 237, F, with unreliable hot water in evening, safe, clean, friendly, a bit noisy; *Imperio*, Calle Chaparro, comfortable new extension, run by Elena and family, also near station, F, hot water, friendly, clean, safe to leave luggage; *Palermo*, San Agustín 287, F, some Inca walls, good breakfast; *Gran Hostal Machu Picchu*, Quera 274, pleasant, friendly, E or F in low season, will store luggage; *Samaná*, Nueva Baja 472, E, colonial mansion, recently redecorated, good rooms with heaters and private baths, safe for luggage, helpful staff, laundry, restaurant slow but good, rec.; *Hostal Cabildado*, E with or without bath, worth bargaining here, safe; *Hostal El Arqueólogo*, E (rooms or dormitory), Ladrillos 425 not far from Sacsayhuamán (T 232569), run by a Frenchman, hot water, highly rec., clean, will store luggage, cafeteria (expensive) and kitchen; accommodation in *Convento Santo Domingo* (down an alley, behind the church), G, a sleeping bag p.p. in double rooms, hot showers, clean, friendly, safe to leave bags, must be in by 2200; *Hostal Familiar*, Saphi 661, E, with bath, cold, clean, attractive flower-filled patios, with good rooms around them (other rooms are not as good), can leave luggage here, with café (owner's sister Gloria works with Kantu Tours), rec., but reported casual with reservations. Boarding house of Sra. de Angulo at Tullumayo 860 near Puno station, E, rec.; *Hostal San Cristóbal*, Quiscapata 250, near San Cristóbal, G/F, cooking and clothes-washing facilities, very nice people, if everywhere full, Sra. Ema de Paredes will let you spread a sleeping bag on the floor, rec.; *Alamo*, Av. Antonio Lorena 18, F, with bath and hot water if you ask for it, reasonably cheap, needs maintenance; *Hostal Familiar Las Esmeraldas* (Sra. Vega de Pineda), Av. de la Infancia 433, E, full board available, clean, hot showers, highly rec.; *Hostal Corona Real*, F, Av. Huáscar 226-228, clean, friendly; *Hospedaje El Peregrino*, Calle del Medio off Plaza, E, clean, secure, quiet. *Raymi*, Pardo 954, E, hot water, carpeting, safe; *Hostal Bellavista*, Av. Santiago 100, F, hot water, very friendly, safe (long walk from centre, not a safe area at night), breakfast available, will store luggage, rec. (particularly, rooms with view towards Estación San Pedro); *Hostal Cahuide*, Saphi 845, E, clean, good laundry service, helpful, convenient for centre; *Hostal Bambú*, on Av. Tullumayo near San Cristóbal bus station, F, hot water, laundry facilities, quiet, clean; *Hostal San Blas*, Cuesta San Blas 526, T 225781, E, basic, a/c, friendly, secure for luggage; *Hostal Cuichinpunco*, Cuichinpunco 231, F, clean, good; *Mantas*, Calle Mantas 115 (near Plaza de Armas), E, rec., friendly, can leave luggage, has laundry service, good meals; *Hostal Tipón*, Calle Tecte, E, friendly and secure. *Posada del Corregidor*, Portal de Panes 151, Plaza de Armas, T 232632, E throughout year, pleasant, clean, central; *Hostal Granada*, Teatro, F, modern rooms on patio better but more expensive, will wash clothes. *Loreto*, Pasaje Loreto 115, Plaza de Armas, E (triples available—always full), will look after luggage while you go to Machu-Picchu, clean, very friendly, rooms with Inca walls and electric heaters rec.; *Residencial Carmen*, Av. Tullumayo 860, no sign (near Puno station), E, hot water, friendly, clean; *Antarki* (ex-*Inti Huatara*), Siete Cuartones 245, F, simple but clean and quiet, stores luggage; *Residencial Las Rejas*, above main tourist office on Plaza de Armas, good value, hot water; *Tambo Real*, Av. Belén, E with bath and hot water, friendly but noisy (not to be confused with *Hotel Tambo*); *Hotel del Procurador*, F, good beds, clean, hot water, secure, will mind luggage, rec. *Central*, San Agustín 251, F, hot shower US$0.20 extra, safe for leaving luggage; *Hostal Residencial Rojas* (ex-*Hotel Tigre*), Tigre 129, F, good value, friendly, safe, clean, hot water. Sra. Rosa de Calderón rents 2-3 rooms for E, full board and warm water, Almagro 131, 2 blocks from Plaza de Armas, very friendly and helpful. Hortensia de Velasco, Av. Pardo, Pasaje España, private accommodation in F range. Also Irma Rodríguez de Alarcón, Zarumilla 2A-101, 15-20 mins'. walk from Plaza de Armas, 2 rooms sleeping 4 people, safe, breakfast, rec.

Camping   Permitted on hill above Cuzco museum, about ½ km. past museum on left; also permitted near Sacsayhuamán ruins, but arrive late and leave early so as not to interfere with the sightseeing. Travel agencies (see below) rent equipment (check tents carefully, and some sell camping gaz). If you use a spirit stove, "alcohol para quemar" can be bought in most pharmacies (bring your own bottle).

Restaurants Mesón de los Espaderos, Espaderos y Plateros, limited choice; *Roma*, on Plaza de Armas (good food, folk music nightly without extra cost). *Paititi*, Plaza de Armas, live music, good fish and also local food, US$7. For a good meal and décor try *Inti Raymi* in the *Libertador-Marriott*, à la carte dinner for US$13. *Korikancha*, opposite Calle Loreto, rec.; *El Fogón de las Mestizas*, Ruinas 463, local food, best in the afternoon less good at night, has roast guinea-pig (cuy, known in Cuzco as conejo—rabbit).

Vegetarian restaurant *Govinda* (Hare Krishna), Espaderos 128, just off NW corner of Plaza de Armas, excellent food and good value, always busy, you can buy bread here which will keep for days, ideal for Inca Trail (but order a day in advance), also samosas, cheese, etc. *Inca*, vegetarian, Garcilaso 270, cheap; *Café Shantam*, Plateros 334, quiet, friendly, good food, cheap (vegetarian), Japanese owner; *La Comida de Dioses*, Procuradores and Huaynapata, vegetarian, slow service. *Qhaliama Warí*, Torda, part of a natural health centre. *Café Varayoc*, Espaderos 142, good meeting place, Dutch connection (excellent coffee, pizzas and cakes). Good juice bar at Sta. Catalina Ancha 427.

There is a good restaurant with stained glass lamps on Procuradores; same street at 365, *Chez Maggy*, good atmosphere, music, pasta, soups, pizzas freshly baked in wood-burning oven, service sometimes slow; also reasonable restaurants (e.g. *Qarawantana* at 347, *El Corsario*, Italian, excellent pasta; *Bar Kukuli*, good and cheap food and interesting local drinks, good music), also on Procuradores, *Los Almarios*, good food, nice atmosphere. *Bucaro*, Av. Sol 567, fair, reasonable service. *Pizzería America*, on Plateros, highly rec.; *Bilboquet*, Herrajes 171A, French crêperie, rec.; *Café Wiphala*, Plaza Regocijo, 0800-2400, good food and atmosphere, highly rec.; *La Gran Esquina*, corner of San Bernardo and Almagro, good Italian and local food, crowded, modern; *Piccolo Bar*, Plaza de Armas, popular and good; *Ayllu*, Portal de Carnes 208, also on Plaza de Armas, Italian, classical/folk music, good atmosphere, has a superb range of milk products and wonderful apple pastries, try lecheasada, good breakfast, quick service; *Chef Victor*, Plaza de Armas, very good food and good value; *Trattoria Adriano*, Calle Mantas y Av. Sol (just off SE corner of Plaza de Armas), Italian food, open for breakfast at 0700, friendly and helpful; *Hobby*, Av. Sol. good and cheap; *Maximum*, on Procuradores, good meal for less than US$1; *El Truco*, on Plaza del Cabildo (Regocijo 247), excellent stuffed green peppers, good trout, folklore some evenings (at 2030), expensive; *Tip-Top*, Palacio 122, good food, reasonable prices; also restaurant of *Hotel Palermo*, San Agustín 287, cheap. Restaurant of *Hotel El Solar*, good suppers for US$1. *Chifa HongKong*, Av. Sol, good, reasonable prices; *La Cabañita* and *Comedor Nacional*, off the Plaza, good cheap food; *Café Restaurant Rick*, opposite *Hotel Conquistador*, dish of the day US$1. *Café-Restaurant Garcilaso*, Garcilaso 265, no sign, rec. for juices and lemon pie; *Hora Antiqua*, Garcilaso, log fire, friendly bar, reasonable prices; *Café de París*, Plaza de Armas, good breakfasts and snacks, cakes and spaghetti rec.; *Café Citera*, Espaderos, good capuccino and cakes, nice atmosphere, not cheap; *Pizzería Michaelangelo*, San Agustín 171,rec.; *Fuente de Soda San Antonio*, Plaza San Francisco, good, cheap, rec.; on same square is *San Agustín*, cheap and good local dishes; good set meal at *El Tronquito* (also peña); *Los Candiles*, Calle Plateros near Plaza, excellent set meals; *Pucara*, Plateros 313, highly rec.; *Café Haylliy* on Plateros has good snacks and "copa Haylliy" - fruit, muesli, yoghurt and honey. *El Tacho*, near San Pedro railway station, for local food, especially soup; opposite *Bolívar* is a café that serves good breakfasts; *Paraíso*, Av. Sol 441, restaurant snack bar, reasonable prices, varied menu, small, friendly; *La Calesa*, Plateros 396, excellent, cheap bar; *Bazar-Cafetín Minka*, Huaynapata 331, craft shop and café (good) run to benefit disadvantaged women; *Posada*, on Plaza de Armas, good. Several restaurants on Plateros do cheap 3-course set lunches (US$0.50). *Cross Keys Pub*, Juan de Dios, run by a Mancunian, darts, great atmosphere; may not be open all year. You can eat cheaply in the market; a saltado (a mixture of meat and vegetables) costs about US$0.25, but be careful. Street vendors at night on Plaza de Armas sell food: stuffed potatoes (papas rellenas) rec.

Local Specialities Roast stuffed guinea pig (cuy). Order in advance at one of the *quintas* (inns in the suburbs). *Quinta Zárate*, Calle Tortera Paccha, rec. A good cheap picantería-chichería is *Mi Casa*, on 100 block of Choquechaca. Also *Quintas Eulalia*, Choquechaca 384. Very rich and exotically spiced. The yoghurt is excellent. Also try *Quinta Tejada* and *Quinta Country Club*. Try the anticuchos (roast beef hearts) cooked in side streets. The local drinks, herb tea with caña and hot milk with pisco, very warming in the cold evenings.

Festivals and Folklore June 24; pageant of Inti Raymi (Indians outnumber tourists) enacted at 1300 at the fortress of Sacsayhuamán. (Try to arrive in Cuzco 15 days before Inti Raymi, there are many festivals, and get to Sacsayhuamán at about 1030 as even reserved seats fill up quickly.) Tickets for the stands can be bought a week in advance from the Town Hall, or for US$6 from travel agents the day before, otherwise standing is free. On Corpus Christi day statues and silver are paraded through the streets; colourful, everyone gets drunk by 1000. The Plaza de Armas is surrounded by tables with Indian women selling cuy and a mixed grill called chiriuchu (cuy, chicken, tortillas, fish eggs, water-weeds, maize, cheese and sausage). One week before the Inti Raymi, there is a dance festival in the village of Raqchi (see also page 809). On the Monday before Easter is the procession of the Lord of the Earthquakes, starting at 1600 outside the Cathedral. A large crucifix is paraded through the streets, returning to the Plaza de Armas around 2000 to bless the tens of thousands of people who have assembled there. On September 8 (day of the Virgin), there is a colourful procession of masked dancers from the church of Alundena, at the SW edge of Cuzco, near Belén, to the Plaza de San Francisco. There is also a splendid fair at Alundena, and a free bull fight on the following day (tourists should be very discreet at these celebrations, as they are not welcome—avoid pickpockets, too). Carnival at Cuzco very basic; flour, water, cacti, bad fruit and animal manure thrown about in streets. **N.B.** Prices shoot up at end-July—Independence celebrations. December 8 is Cuzco day: church and museums close at 1200.

Regular nightly folklore show at Qosqo Native Art Centre, Av. Sol. 604, at 1830 hours, for US$5 (students US$3), also Amanta Dances, Calle Unión 117, and Qoricancha Dances, San Juan de Dios 285 (US$4), 1830-2000. Peña Folklórica in *Hotel Cuzco*, daily, 1830-1930. *La Taverna* bar on Plaza de Armas has folklore music nightly from 2100-0200, very crowded. Folk-dancing and music in the cellar of *Hotel Ollanta*, Av. Sol, nightly, US$2.50 p.p., 1845-2000. Also nightly at *Hotel Savoy*. Folk dancing at Teatro Central, US$4 and at Teatro Inti Raymi, Saphi 605, US$2. There are good peñas at *Qhatuchay*, Portal Confituría 233 on Plaza, very pleasant, *Peña Do Re Mi*, also on Plaza, opp. La Compañía, and folk music at *Restaurant Roma*, evenings. **N.B.** The Centro de Difusión Cultural Wasapay organizes "folklore evenings" in various restaurants which are supposed to be free, but which will be included as 15 % extra on the bill—watch out for this if you don't want a more expensive meal.

Discotheques   *El Muki* (opposite *Hotel Conquistador*) rec. *Kamikaze*, many gringos, some live folk music, on Espaderos next to *Café Varayoc*, near Municipalidad, admission US$1, rec. *El Molino Rojo*, Av. de la Cultura; *El Gran Prise*, Av. Antonio Lorena 14; cheap local bars. Also, *Las Quenas* in the basement of the *Hotel Savoy*, rec.

Local Crafts   In the Plaza San Blas and the surrounding area, authentic Cuzco crafts still survive. Wood workers may be seen in almost any street. Leading artisans who welcome visitors include: Hilario Mendivil, Plazoleta San Blas 634 (biblical figures from plaster, wheatflour and potatoes); Edilberta Mérida, Carmen Alto 133 (earthenware figures showing physical and mental anguish of the Indian peasant), Víctor Vivero Holgado, Tandapato 172 (painter of pious subjects); Antonio Olave Palomino, Siete Angelitos 752 (reproductions of precolumbian ceramics and colonial sculptures); Maximiliano Palomino de la Sierra, Triunfo 393 (festive dolls and wood carvings); Santiago Rojas, near San Blas (statuettes). Museo Inca Art Gallery of Amílcar Salomón Zorrilla, Huancaro M-B—L8, T 231232 (P.O. Box 690), Telephone between 0900 and 2100. Contemporary art.

Shopping   Market opposite Estación San Pedro (which also has the name Santa Ana) is the best Indian market for a variety of goods, but although less self-conscious and less expensive than Pisac is not very interesting. Empresa Peruana de Promoción Artesanal (EPPA), Plateros 359, and another good market on the corner of San Andrés and Quera.

Cuzco is the weaving centre of Peru, and excellent textiles can be found at good value. Alpaca, Calle Ruinas, genuine, 100% alpaca goods, but not cheap. Artesanía La Paloma, Cuesta San Blas 552 and Plazuela Sta. Catalina 211, good but expensive; Rafael Salazar Sucesores, Plateros 305, for good quality alpaca. Sr. Aller, Plaza Santo Domingo 261, sells interesting antiques. Josefina Olivera, Santa Clara 501, sells old ponchos, without usual haggling. There is a good jewellery store beside the Cathedral in the Plaza de Armas and art shop at Instituto Americano de Arte, Av. Sol. Arto Ovaska from Finland and his Peruvian wife Edith have opened Snow Shop, Procuradores 347, for *artesanía*, posters, music etc. The Bazar-Cafetín Minka, Huaynapata 331, sells craft-work made by people with special needs, and also runs a good café (home-made cakes). However, be very careful of buying gold and silver objects and jewellery in and around Cuzco; we have received many reports of sharp practices.

Sauna   corner of San Bernardo and Quera Almagro, dry sauna, Mon.-Sat. 0900-2000, Sun. 0900-1300, US$0.90.

Laundry   Service at Lavamatic, Procuradores 354, min. US$5 for 4 kg. (charges per item). Ironing extra. Lavanderías Splendor, Suecia 328, just off Plaza de Armas (US$1.50 for 2 kg.), will also dry clean items such as sleeping bags, rucksacks etc. There is one on Plateros, reported cheaper and better. Also Lavanderías Superchick (Ana M. Velarde), Pumacurco 435, San Cristóbal, T 235629, US$3 for 5 kg., washed, dried and ironed in 24 hrs.

Bookshop   Near Plaza San Francisco (Mantas 191), a small shop sells used English, French, German and Spanish paperbacks—not cheap, but will trade paperbacks 2 for 1. Librería Studium, Mesón de la Estrella 144, stocks guide books. Los Andes, Portal Comercio 125, Plaza de Armas, large boxes of postcards, low prices.

Taxis   Large cars parked in Plaza are more expensive. Airport-town, US$2 (bus, US$0.12); Railway-town, US$0.50; per hour in town, US$2.25, out of town, US$3. For many excursions, taxis have a fixed rate; ask the driver for a price list. A rec. taxi driver (also school teacher) is José Cuba, Urb. Santa Rosa, Pasaje R. Gibaja 182, T 226179, who is a guide and can organize tours, accommodation as necessary; he parks at the airport during flight hours, and at the station to await train arrival. Another is Angel Salazar, Saguán del Cielo B-11, Cuzco, English speaking, helpful, arranges good tours.

Car Rental Avis, Av. Sol 900, Volkswagens and Toyotas (poor reports on maintenance). Also, National Rentacar, Calle Santa Catalina near main plaza (cheaper). Never leave anything in a hired car, thieves have keys and may strike the same car again and again.

Exchange Photocopy of passport sometimes required for changing travellers' cheques. Banco de Crédito is good for changing travellers' cheques. Banco de los Andes has the best rates and is quickest for international money transfers. Many travel agencies also change money at favourable rates and remain open during civil disturbances. No bank in Cuzco will give out cash on credit cards and their use is not rec.: surcharges are imposed and your account will be charged at official rate. Lavamatic laundry on Procuradores gives good rates as does Original Travels, Portal Comercio 141, Plaza de Armas; cash better than travellers' cheques. Money changers on Plaza, or Av. Sol give a better rate than travel agents. Beware of people watching you when you change money.

Post Office Principal one on Av. Sol, hrs.: 0800-1900, 0800-1200 Sun. and festivals. Telephone and telegrams at Empresa Nacional de Telecomunicaciones, Av. Sol 386. To send packages over 2 kg., go first to Customs, near Plaza San Francisco, open 0900-1200; buy sacking nearby to sew up the package, and then go to main post office. Packages over 2 kg. must be despatched by customs (more expensive).

Consulates US Agent, Olga Villa García, Apartado 949, Cuzco, T 222183. West German, Av. Tullumayo 874. French, Calle Espinar (in a French-run hotel—may let French people leave luggage if going to Machu-Picchu).

Medical Hospital Regional, Av. de la Cultura, rec. If lab tests needed, Lab. Pasteur, Tullumayo 768 is rec. Dr. Oscar Tejada Ramírez (P.O. Box 425, Cuzco, T 238836 day or night) is a member of the International Association for Medical Assistance to Travellers and is prepared to help any visitor in emergency, 24-hr. attention; he charges according to that organization's scales. Dr Gustavo Garido Juárez, Clínica Paredes, Av. Matará 410, or at home, Av. Pardo 510 T 228613, rec.

Warning Thieves are numerous and persistent. Do not wear jewellery, watches or carry credit cards, leave valuables with hotel management. Be very careful when you change money on the streets. Be especially careful in the railway stations, the bus from the airport, the market (otherwise rec.) and at out-of-the-way ruins. More police patrol the streets and stations than in the past, but one should still be on the lookout.

Police Tourist police, Portal de Belén 115, next to Cathedral on Plaza de Armas (T 221961). If you are robbed and the thief has personal items of no commercial value but important to you, go to **Radio Tawantinsuyo**, Av. Sol 806, and place an *anuncio* offering an unspecified reward for their return. Tell the respondent to go through the radio station; do not reveal your hotel. The *anuncio* costs about US$1 a run and about ten times is standard. They will help you write it; there is a standard etiquette (items are "strayed" never "stolen"). The local TV station will also broadcast the *anuncio* a few times free; enquire at your hotel or at the Policía de Turismo. If you need a *denuncia*, a crime report for insurance purposes, the Policía de Turismo will tell you what documents to buy (stamped paper) at the Banco de la Nación. The police now investigate your complaint; you may have to spend 2 days looking for your things around likely spots, with a policeman, before the police will issue a *denuncia*. Stolen cameras often turn up in the local market and can be bought back cheaply; remember the man selling them is not the thief and has got them at about fourth-hand.

Spanish Classes Exel, Plaza San Francisco 303, T 235-298.

Tourist Office Foptur (very helpful), Portal Belén 115, Plaza de Armas, T 237364; at airport (until 1200) and on Av. Sol. Check all train information carefully. Maps available of Cuzco and Inca Trail to Machu-Picchu. Gives opening hours of churches in Cuzco. Safe-deposit facilities available. Other good guides to the area are the booklets by Víctor Angles (*Machu-Picchu, Ollantaytambo, Sacsayhuamán*) in Spanish and the Uniclam *Machu-Picchu* in French. Another office at Tecsecocha 474, 0745-1300 Mon.-Fri.

Motorists beware; many streets end in flights of steps not marked as such. Very few good maps of Cuzco available; that of Cuzco and Puno Region by Zoila L. Vergara Valenza, available on train to Machu Picchu, is reasonable. The map of the Cuzco-Puno-La Paz route sold at the station can be bought more cheaply (US$0.50) in bookshops.

The book *Exploring Cuzco*, by Peter Frost, is very good; the updated and expanded 3rd edition was published by Bradt Enterprises in 1985 (£5.50). Also rec. *Cusco Peru Tourist Guide*, published by Lima 2000 at US$3.50.

Automóvil Club del Perú, Av. Sol, useful for maps.

Travel Agencies Shopping around will always save money. Lima Tours at Av. Sol 567, next to Faucett office (American Express agent). Cooks around the corner from the *Hotel Cusco*. Andean Adventures, Procuradores 332, friendly, reliable (Aurelio is highly rec. mountain guide) also rent equipment, as do Walking Tours, Portal Confituría 257, Plaza de Armas. Expediciones Mayoc, Procuradores 354, Apartado 596, Cuzco, T 232666 organizes river-running and trekking expeditions on the Urubamba, Apurímac, Inanbari rivers, to the National Parks near Cuzco and weekly departures to walk the Inca Trail, also treks to sites round Cuzco on horseback. Tambo Treks organize 7-21 day tours in the region (to Paucartambo, Pongo de Mainique, Salcantay, with local weavers) from US$490. For information write to Tambo Treks, Casilla 912, Cuzco. International Service is a small, friendly organization with tours in and around Cuzco, including Machu-Picchu, their office is at Garcilaso 285, oficina 213. Peru-Bolivian Tours, Santa Catalina Angosta 149 arranges daily trips Cuzco-La Paz via Copacabana or via Desaguadero. Kantu Tours, Portal Carrizos 258, rec. for local tours (though mixed reports), competitive, Gloria Hermosa Tapiá speaks good English. You can pay extra for English-speaking guides. Sigui Tours, Portal de Panes 123, rents camping equipment, sells maps, rec. Snow Tours, Portal de Panes 109, office 204, run by Arto (Finnish) and Edith Ovaska, local tours, camping equipment hired cheaply (check tents carefully); Peruvian Andean Treks, Av. Pardo 575, rec.; Señorial Travel at *Hotel Colonial Palace* has been rec.; Sumac Tours, Ayacucho 236, small, offers good personal attention; APU Expediciones, Plaza de Armas 236, arranges river rafting on the Urubamba, helpful, English spoken; Luzma Tours, Plaza de Armas, Portal de Harinas 191, rec. for white water rafting, English spoken. SAS Travel, Plaza de Armas 109, helpful and efficient; Rio Bravo, Almagro 120 (off Av. Sol), white water rafting and alternative routes to Machu-Picchu; PeruLand Tours, Portal Confituría 273 (Rosa Morote, English-speaking), rec.; Milla Turismo, Ayacucho 161, Aptdo Postal 348, T 231710, Telex 52018, run by Don Carlos Milla Vidal, mixed reports. Explorandes, Procuradores, rec.; Chincheros Tours (registered at the Cuzco Tourist office) is rec. for the Pisac-Urubamba-Ollantaitambo-Chincheros round trip. Transvaal Tours, Triunfo 122, T 236750, rec.

Sra. Luisa Bueno Hermosa offers tours of the Cuzco area at reasonable prices (in Spanish); Sr. Luis Vargas, Calle Triunfo 374, also is a rec. guide. Srta. Juana Pancorbo, Av. Los Pinos D-2, T 227482, is a guide who speaks English, rec. Marco Bustamante, Casilla 720, T 225391, rec. David Choque, T 224-327, English-speaking, good, but insist on itinerary first. Haydee and Tomás Oblitas, Av. Ramón Castilla J-5, Urbanización Bancopata (15 mins.' walk from centre, or take taxi) have been particularly rec. as guides in and around Cuzco. The potter Nicolás Torre is also a good guide US$2 p.p. Raúl Castelo H., Calle Saphi 877B, Interior No. 6 (flute player at *El Truco*) is a good guide, using his own car. José Huaquina Pacheco, Saphi 635, patio 3, trustworthy guide for the Inca Trail, he has a good tent and stove, highly rec.

N.B. Equipment hire prices are often in dollars, so important to agree on exchange rate at time of hire.

Minibuses in front of cathedral take tourists to see the "Sacred Valley" (Pisac, Ollantaitambo and Chincheros), 0800, all-day tour, US$5, drivers are competent guides; also Sacsayhuamán, Quenco and Tambo Machay, 1400, half-day, US$2.50. Other minibuses to these places, and further afield, from Av. Recoleta. An even cheaper "Sacred Valley" trip, at US$4, is given by César Silva Guzmán, T 226-627, who is often to be found in front of the tourist office on the Plaza de Armas.

Roads and Buses To Juliaca, Puno, La Paz, road in poor condition especially in the wet season, many parts are unsurfaced. Cruz del Sur, to Puno, leave at 1900 from Tullumayo, SE of centre, US$5, 12 hrs., rec. A direct bus Cuzco-La Paz, leaving Calle Belén 451 at 2000 on Mon., Tues. and Sat. at US$22, 22-24 hrs. Bus to Juliaca at 0900, US$5.50. To Lima (1,180 km.), road via Abancay, Andahuaylas, Ayacucho, Huancayo and La Oroya is rec. for magnificent scenery and interesting towns, but sometimes closed by guerrilla action. The road is appalling in places and takes from 3 to 6 days by successive buses or colectivos; take a rug for the cold nights, and extra food. Approx. times of journeys from Cuzco: Abancay 8 hrs.; Andahuaylas 14 hrs.; Ayacucho 24 hrs.; Huancayo 36-45 hrs.; Lima 2-3 days. Through fare Cuzco-Lima about US$23. Only Hidalgo run from Cuzco to Ayacucho, 0730 Thurs., US$15, 40 hrs., book well in advance, many passport checks (if required to leave vehicle for a military search remove valuables or they may be missing on return), take sleeping bag and extra food. An alternative road to Lima goes SW from Abancay through Puquío and Nazca; this road is narrow, unpaved but spectacular. Ormeño (office at Plaza de Armas 177, depot, Av. Húascar 128) to Lima via Abancay and Nazca, Mon., Thurs. 0700, to Abancay 7 hrs., Puquío 22 hrs., Nazca 27 hrs., US$12, Lima 34-45 hrs. (US$22), also Hidalgo. Señor de Anima, Belén 537, to Lima via Abancay and Nazca (US$14, advertised as 13 hrs., more like 40, poor meal stops and often stop at night in Abancay (as do Ormeño), Tues., Wed., Fri., Sun., 0600. By bus to Lima via Arequipa, 1,838 km., 3 days non-stop but the stretch Juliaca-Arequipa is poor, passing through a high arid plain at 4,700 metres before descending into Arequipa valley. Cruz del Sur, Av. Tullumayo, daily at 1800 to Lima via Arequipa, daily at 1900 to Puno, US$7, 11 hrs.; Señor de Anima, 50-55 hrs., US$9, good meal stops; San Cristóbal buses are less good (old and overcrowded), US$8, leave Cuzco at 0900, arrive Juliaca about midnight and depart Juliaca at 1000 for Arequipa next day. Ormeño to Arequipa via Tintaya, 18 hrs., Mon. and Thurs. 0800, US$15. Better to take a more expensive minibus from one of the companies on the Plaza de Armas. For buses to nearby towns and villages, see below under their entries.

Rail To Juliaca and Puno from Av. Sol station, daily, except Sun., at 0820 (though delays common and schedules change) arriving at Juliaca 1900 and Puno 2030, sit on lefthand side. To Juliaca, US$6. **To Puno**, buffet car US$7.25, 1st US$5.40, can be purchased on day before leaving, 2nd, US$4, can be booked, tickets on sale before, or from 0630; buffet car, comfortable, is 1st class fare plus US$2.60 (meals extra). The advantage of the buffet car (if you can get on it: group tours sometimes book the whole car) is that no one is allowed into it without a reserved seat ticket. Usually at stations the attendant keeps out vendors and doors are locked for security, although you are allowed out if you want to buy something. **N.B.** beware of thieves in 1st and 2nd class on this train. Be especially careful leaving the train. Check ticket very carefully if booking to Puno, or you may find the ticket only covers the train to Juliaca, although paid for to Puno. Beware agents on train offering accommodation in Puno, pay no money.

To Arequipa, 0800 daily, 23 hrs., 1st class US$12, 2nd class US$8, extra on the train, heated buffet car, US$2. Train to Sicuani leaves at 1510, arriving at 2120 (US$3). To Lima, cheaper to go via Arequipa (bus from there to Lima) but make sure that your carriage does not detach at Juliaca. It is reported that the Juliaca-Puno stretch is sometimes closed; colectivos meet the train at Juliaca. Lighting on train doesn't always work: take torch/flashlight.

To Anta, Ollantaitambo, Machu-Picchu and Quillabamba, **see pages 812, 815 and 817**.

Machu-Picchu trains leave from Estación San Pedro, opposite the market. Check all times as they change frequently, and that trains are running.

Air To Lima, Faucett has daily flights. AeroPerú also has 2 morning flights. From Lima, AeroPerú flies at 0630 and 0705, and Faucett at 0645, 1 hr., US$33. There is a Sat. and sometimes Thurs. military flight to Lima, ask for next scheduled flight with Grupo Ocho de la Fuerza Aérea; book at airport several days in advance, be at airport at 0630 to check in at 0700, US$20, unpredictable in the extreme. Cuzco-Juliaca (for Puno), Fri. AeroPerú and Faucett fly daily to Arequipa, US$24, often delayed. AeroPerú also flies to Iquitos (and on to Miami) Faucett flies to Iquitos, Tues., Thurs., Sat., 0730, US$104, calling at Pucallpa, 2½ hrs. N.B. in summer all flights to Iquitos go via Lima. To Puerto Maldonado: AeroPerú daily; Faucett Tues., Thurs., Sat.; airforce (Grupo 8) usually Thurs., US$18, enquire at office of Grupo Ocho de la Fuerza Aérea in airport. A new airport at Quispiquilla is in use. Taxi to airport, US$2, bus US$0.10, leaves from Tourist Office on Plaza de Armas. Book return well in advance, especially in the busy season and reconfirm 24 hours before departure. Flights between Lima and Cuzco tend to be heavily booked between July 29 and August 11 because of school holidays. Shop around for seats at travel agencies, especially Lima Tours, if the airlines say they are full. The AeroPerú office is on Av. Sol opposite Faucett office at Av. Sol 391. There is no facility for buying tickets at the airport. There is a limited hotel booking service at the airport, which will give you inflated US$-based prices: better to negotiate with hotels yourself. In emergencies, for flights to Lima, try Sra Rossi at Lima Tours, Plaza de Armas; Faucett are unhelpful in this respect. **N.B.** The LAB flight Cuzco-La Paz no longer operates, and there is no air service between Cuzco and Ayacucho.

Warning Cuzco-Lima, high possibility of cancelled flights during wet season; tourists sometimes stranded for several days. Possible for planes to leave early if bad weather. Sit on right side of aircraft for best view of mountains when flying Cuzco-Lima; it is worth checking in early to get these seats. Both Faucett and AeroPerú are unreliable on bookings: you must reconfirm your tickets in the last 24 hrs. but even then you cannot be sure of a seat. Baggage is often lost en route.

There is some magnificent walling in the ruined cult centre of **Sacsayhuamán,** on a hill in the northern outskirts, which is within walking distance (about ½ hr. walk, tiring because of the altitude). Take steps to San Cristóbal church (shorter than via Calle Saphi). The Incaic stones are bigger and even more impressive than at Machu-Picchu; huge rocks weighing up to 300 tons are fitted together with absolute perfection; three walls run parallel for over 360 metres and there are 21 bastions. Sacsayhuamán was thought for centuries to be a fortress, but the layout and architecture suggest a great sanctuary and temple to the Sun, which rises exactly opposite the place previously believed to be the Inca's throne—which was probably an altar, carved out of the solid rock: broad steps lead to it from either side. The hieratic, rather than the military, hypothesis was supported by the discovery in 1982 of the graves of priests: they would have been unlikely to be buried in a fortress. Zig-zags in the boulders round the "throne" are apparently "*chicha* grooves", channels down which maize beer flowed during festivals. Up the hill is an ancient rock slide for children: the Rodadero; near it are many seats cut perfectly into smooth rock. The temple and amphitheatre of Kenko (Quenco), with excellent examples of Inca stone carving, especially inside the large hollowed-out stone that houses an altar, are along the road from Sacsayhuamán to Pisac, past a radio station. On the same road are the Inca fortress of Puku Pukará and the spring shrine of Tambo Machay, which is in excellent condition; water still flows by a hidden channel out of the masonry wall, straight into a little rock pool traditionally known as the Inca's bath, but he would have had to be a pygmy to have used it as such. It seems much more likely that the site was a centre of a water cult.

The gates are manned from about 0700 but you can get in earlier if you wish and definitely try to get there before midday when the tour groups arrive. Carry your multi-site ticket, there are roving ticket inspectors. After seeing 3 sites you can catch truck back along road, 9 km., for US$0.25. Preferably, take the Pisac bus (from Calle Saphi) to Tambo Machay and walk back (downhill) to Cuzco, or taxi US$0.50 to Tambo Machay. If you walk back, don't take short cuts through farmland; you may get chased by packs of dogs. Between Kenko and Puku Pukará is Cusillyuioc; caves and Inca tunnels in a hillside (take a torch/flashlight). Taxis to Inca sites outside Cuzco for 3 hrs. cost US$14, not including entry to the sites, and may be hired in the Plaza de Armas. A tour bus to all 4 sites costs US$4.

Cuzco is at the W end of the gently sloping Cuzco valley, which stretches 32 km. E as far as Huambutío. This valley, and the partly isolated basin of Anta, NW of Cuzco, are densely populated. Also densely populated is the Urubamba valley, stretching from Sicuani (on the railway to Puno, at 3,960 metres) to the gorge of Torontoi, 600 metres lower, to the NW of Cuzco. There are several ruins of Inca buildings and fortresses in the Cuzco valley itself, especially at Piquillacta (also pre-Inca Huari—8th century) on the road to Andahuaylillas (45 mins. by bus from Av. Huáscar and Av. Garcilaso, US$0.10—ask driver to drop you off at the turning), the monkey temple (Templo de los Monos) NW of Piquillacta, the amphitheatre at Moray (three "colosseums", one large, two small, used by the Incas as a sort of plant breeding and acclimatization centre; remote, beautiful and worth visiting—by car to Maras, then 1½-hrs.' walk, or a bumpy 20-km. drive from Chincheros—Urubamba road; it is a 3½-hr. walk from Urubamba), the administrative and storage centre of Colcampata, and Rumicolca, on the shores of Lake Lucre. Interesting textile mill at Lucre village.

Andahuaylillas is a village 32 km. S of Cuzco, with a particularly fine early 17th century church; beautiful frescoes, splendid doorway and a gilded main altar (ask for Sr. Eulogio, good guide, Spanish only). Taxis go there as does Oropesa bus (Av. Huáscar, Cuzco) via Tipón, Piquillacta and Rumicolca. There are other unexcavated ruins just beyond Andahuaylillas.

John Streather has most kindly given us information about more places south of Cuzco with interesting Inca remains and colonial buildings:

Tipón ruins, between the villages of Saylla and Oropesa, include baths, terraces and a temple complex, accessible from a path leading from just above the last terrace. **Oropesa** church contains a fine ornately carved pulpit. **Huacarpay:** ruins of the Inca town of Kañaracy, well-preserved, are nearby, reached from a path behind the Albergue. Also nearby are the ruins of Piquillacta, the monkey temple and the wall of Rumicolca. At Lucre, 3 km. from Huacarpay, there are many unexplored ruins; ask the local history teacher, Sr. Hernán Flores Yávar, for details. **Tinta,** 23 km. from Sicuani, has a church with brilliant gilded interior and an interesting choir vault. Hotel: *Casa Comunal*, dormitory accommodation, F, clean with good food. Frequent buses and trucks to Cuzco. **Huaro** has a church whose interior is covered entirely with colourful mural painting. **Cusipata,** with an Inca gate and wall, is where the ornate bands for the decoration of ponchos are woven; close by is the Huari hilltop ruin of Llallanmarca.

Raqchi is the scene of the region's great folklore festival in mid-June. (A special train leaves Cuzco early in the morning, or take a truck, US$ 1, 4 hours. At this festival dancers come to Raqchi from all over Peru; through music and dance they illustrate everything from the ploughing of fields to bull fights, reported to be most enjoyable.) John Hemming adds: The Viracocha temple is just visible from the train, looking from the distance like a Roman aqueduct. What remains is the central wall (adobe above, Inca masonry below) of what was probably the largest roofed building ever built by the Incas. On either side of the high wall, great sloping roofs were supported by rows of unusual round pillars, also of masonry topped by adobe. Nearby is a complex of barracks-like buildings and round storehouses. This was the most holy shrine to the creator god Viracocha, being the site of a miracle in which he set fire to the land—hence the lava flow nearby. There are also small Inca baths in the corner of a field beyond the temple and a straight row of ruined houses by a square. The landscape is extraordinary, blighted by huge piles of black volcanic rocks. (San Cristóbal bus to Raqchi from Av. Huáscar, Cuzco every hour, US$0.90, 4 hrs. Nearest hotel is in Tinta.)

Pacarijtambo is a good starting point for the 3-4 hr. walk to the ruins of Mankallajta, which contain good examples of Inca stonework. From there, one can walk to Pumaorco, a high rock carved with steps, seats and a small puma in relief on top; below are more Inca ruins. From Pumaorco walk back to the nearby hamlet of Mollepata (bus from Cuzco, US$1) and ask the schoolteacher the way to Pacarijtambo (a 2-3 hr. walk). One may seek lodging for the night in Pacarijtambo at the house of the Villacorta family and leave for Cuzco by truck the next morning. On the way back, one passes the caves of Tambo Toco, where the legend says that the four original Inca brothers emerged into the world.

Acomayo is a pretty village (*Pensión Aguirre*), which has a chapel with mural paintings of the fourteen Incas. From Acomayo, one can walk to Huáscar and from there to Pajlia; a climb which leads one through very impressive scenery. The canyons of the upper Apurímac are vast beyond imagination, great cliffs drop thousands of metres into dizzying chasms and huge rocks balance menacingly overhead. The ruins of Huajra Pucará lie near Pajlia; they are small, but in an astonishing position. John Hemming adds that the church at Checacupe is very fine, with good paintings and a handsome carved altar rail.

Pisac, 30 km. N of Cuzco, is at the bottom of the Urubamba valley; high above it, on the mountainside, is a superb Inca fortress (admission by combined entrance ticket, **see page 801,** the ruins close at 1700). The masonry is better than at Machu-Picchu, the terraces more extensive and better preserved. When you climb it (a must), remember that there are 3 hill fortifications, but the third is the fortress proper, in which the actual temple is built: so go on to it and get the glorious view from the top. There is a 10-km. motor road up to the level of the ruins, upstream from Pisac town and then up a valley to the S of the spur containing the ruins. From the parking lot, enter along Inca roads and through Inca gates, seeing the fine view of terraces (which can be reached quite easily from the town by a footpath, local boys will guide you US$0.50 per couple). Quite a lot of walking is involved. The central part of the ruins is the Intihuatana group of temples and rock outcrops in the most magnificent Inca masonry. Above on the hilltop reached by a path along a vertiginous cliff are residential groups; there is a large Inca cemetery in caves on the valley opposite to the north; the curving group of houses called Pisallacta below the Intihuatana group; and more buildings, some with curious round towers, others of good Inca adobe, on the steep hillside above the town. It takes about 25 minutes to walk down. There is a path going right round the mountain, behind the main ruins; it has two tunnels. It takes 1-2 hours to walk.

Pisac has a Sun. morning market, described as touristy and expensive after the arrival of tourist buses around 1000; it starts at 0900 and is usually over by midday. There are picturesque Indian processions to a Quechua Mass. Pisac has another, less crowded, less expensive market on Thurs. morning. You can take in the market, then take taxi up to ruins, explore them, walk down and get last bus or truck back to Cuzco by 1630. It is reported that transport to the ruins is not always available for those not in a tour group. You can continue the Sun. morning tour to Pisac along the Urubamba to Ollantaitambo, with lunch at the Tourist Hotel in Urubamba (US$4.25) but tours from Cuzco usually allow only 1½ hours at Pisac: not enough time to take it in. Splendid scenery. Apart from Sun. when Pisac is crowded, there are very few tourists. An alternative for lunch is the restaurant on the square in **Yukay** (open-air, good buffet and local dishes). On the N side of the square is the adobe palace built for Sayri Túpac (Manco's son) when he emerged from Vilcabamba in 1558. A pleasant old hotel, the *Alhambra 3,* B, is in Yukay, rather overpriced but very pretty and old. In Yukay monks sell fresh milk, ham, eggs and other dairy produce from their farm on the hillside. The tour by taxi costs US$40-45. Good walks along river to Inca terraces.

Pisac Hotels   *Albergue Chongo Chico*, F, basic, slightly decayed, electricity and water unreliable, friendly; camping allowed in garden. *Turistas*, E, pleasant, English spoken, meals US$5; *Hostal Pisac* on the square, F, above a handicraft shop, comfortable, breakfast only except on Sundays, good ceramics. The woman who owns the flour mill rents rooms for US$1.30 p.p. *Roma*, near the bridge by the Kodak sign, F, basic, quiet, cold shower, dreadful; camping allowed in its grounds for US$0.45 p.p. No good restaurants in town (basic food in café on main square); better to take a packed lunch from Cuzco.

Buses   Cuzco-Pisac road is paved. Early morning buses on Sunday, every ten min., from 0540 to 0700, 1 hr. (queue early in road opposite Puno station or catch them on Huáscar before they fill up), colectivos to Pisac from Cuzco; they return all afternoon until 1715 and are always full, be prepared to return by truck. Fare US$0.70; try and book the previous day if possible. Tourist minibus leaves Cuzco Plaza de Armas outside Cathedral daily for Pisac and Ollantaitambo if there are more than five passengers, US$5 return. Minibus tours also Cuzco, Pisac, Urubamba, Ollantaitambo, US$10; taxi for this route, including Chincheros, US$40. Colectivos to Pisac and Ollantaitambo leave when full from Calle Recoleta, from 0600, Cuzco (past Calle Pumapaccha), to Pisac 45 mins., US$0.40, to Ollantaitambo, 2½ hrs., US$1. Return fare by truck US$0.40, over 1 hr. Taxi fare (return) from Cuzco to the fortress costs US$8 and includes a visit to the market. Tours by agencies to Pisac on Thurs. and Sun. (market days) only. Two buses daily to Urubamba. Bus stops in Pisac are brief, make sure you get on or off the bus quickly. Try hitching opposite the police checkpoint.

Calca   is 18 km. beyond Pisac (Hotels: *Alojamiento Grau*, basic; *Alojamiento Alvarez; Alojamiento Central*, F, basic. Restaurants: *Sondar, Bolívar*, on Plaza; *Moreñitas* and *Café Calqueñita*, near post office). Mineral baths at Minas Maco (½ hr. walk along the Urubamba) and Machacama (8 km. E of Calca). If one continues past Minas Maco, one bears right up a small footpath leading by a clump of trees; the first house one comes to after crossing a small stream and climbing a hill is a precolumbian ruin. 3 km. beyond Machacama is the Inca ruins of Arquasmarca. The ruins of a small Inca town, Huchuy Cuzco, are across the river Vilcanota, and up a stiff climb. There are a two-storey house, paved with flat stones, and a large stone reservoir at Huchuy Cuzco. Bus to Pisac, or to Urubamba, US$0.50; bus to Cuzco, US$0.30. Market day: Sun. It is a two-day hike from Cuzco to Calca, via Sacsayhuamán, Kenko, Puka Pukará, Tambo Machay and Huchuy Cuzco; there are many places to camp, but take water. Between Calca and Quillabamba the road is narrow and subject to landslides.

Zurite   is a little-known village north of Cuzco; Inca terraces of Patapata are only about an hour's walk from the village's main square. The construction of these terraces represents a Herculean effort as all of the earth is said to have been brought from elsewhere. A canal was built to bring water from the mountains. (John Streather.)

John Hemming recommends visiting to the W of Cuzco:

Chincheros; with an attractive church built on an Inca temple; recent excavations there have revealed many Inca walls and terraces. (On combined entrance ticket, **see page 801**.) It has become very tourist-oriented but nonetheless the Sunday market and Indian mass are more authentic than at Pisac (there is a small market on Thurs.). *Hotel Inca*, F, with restaurant; *Albergue Chincheros*, F, basic, clean, friendly. At the market, there is a varied selection of handicrafts, including weaving, pottery and alpaca goods (nothing is cheap). Celebrations are held in Chincheros on September 8 (the day of the Virgin).

A new road Cuzco-Urubamba has been completed, which has cut the travelling time to Chincheros to 40 mins. from Cuzco by bus, leaving about 0700 from Av. Arcopata on Sun. mornings, US$0.25. Also colectivos from Av. Arcopata. Taxi, US$20 for 5-hr. trip. There is also a scenic path to Chincheros from Urubamba, about 4-5 hrs.

76 km. from Cuzco on the Abancay road, 2 km. before Limatambo (accommodation in *Albergue*, F; nice restaurant hidden from road by trees), at Hacienda Tarahuasi, a few hundred metres from the road, is a very well-preserved **Inca temple platform**, with 28 tall niches, and a long stretch of fine polygonal masonry. 100 km. from Cuzco along the Abancay road is the exciting descent into the Apurímac canyon, near the former Inca suspension bridge that inspired Thornton Wilder's *The Bridge of San Luis Rey*. Also, 153 km. along the road to Abancay from Cuzco, near Carahuasi (restaurant on main road into town; camping possible on the football pitch, ask police), is the stone of Sahuite, carved with animals, houses, etc., which appears to be a relief map of an Indian village. (Unfortunately, "treasure hunters" have defaced the stone.) There are other interesting carvings in the area around the Sahuite stone.

For US$40 a taxi can be hired for a whole day (ideally Sun.) to take you to Cachimayo, Chincheros, Maras, Urubamba, Ollantaitambo, Calca, Lamay, Coya, Pisac, Tambo Machay, Kenko and Sacsayhuamán. (If you wish to explore this area on your own, Road Map (*Hoja de ruta*) No. 10 from the Automóvil Club del Perú is an excellent guide.)

Urubamba is N of Chincheros, on a new direct road from Cuzco via Chincheros; pleasant country surroundings. The Machu-Picchu tourist train can be caught at Pachar, about 20 minutes' drive away, at 0830; no fare reduction. Bus Cuzco-Urubamba, US$0.50. Urubamba-Ollantaitambo, kombi, US$0.50.

Hotels and restaurants *Hotel de Turistas*, E, clean, hot water, poor service, bungalows with neglected garden and swimming pool; the *Centro Vacacional Urubamba*, cabins (some with kitchen, must take own stove), sports facilities, 2 pools, E and F; *Hostal Naranjachayoc*, C, with antique furniture and swimming pool, 20 mins. walk from town, rec., friendly, accommodating, will help with any problems, very clean and well-stocked restaurant and bar, even in low-season, car can be parked in locked patio, *Hotel Urubamba*, F, pleasant; *Hostal Reymada*, F, basic, clean, friendly, outdoor pool, rec.; *Hostal Vera*, beyond the Tourist Hotel; and *Hotel Retamanioj*, and *Restaurant Quinta los Geranios*, excellent lunch for US$3 with more than enough food; *Restaurant Norteñito; Comedor Aries* and *Andes*, both on Plaza. *Quinta Galu*, close to Plaza, large, reasonable, friendly, good.

Joanna Codrington writes: 6 km. from Urubamba on the Ollantaitambo road is the village of Tarabamba, where a footbridge crosses the Río Vilcanota. If one turns right after the bridge one comes to Piychinjoto, a tumbled-down village built under an overhanging cliff. Also, just over the bridge and to the left of a small, walled cemetery is a salt stream. If one follows this (there is a footpath) one comes to Salinas, a small village below which are a mass of terraced Inca salt pans, still in operation. A very spectacular sight. Darrell High, from Ware, writes: Moray is well worth a visit: it is quite beautiful. Wait for pickup on bridge on Chincheros road. This will take you near to Maras; walk to Maras (½ hr.) and on through it, bearing left a little, and ask directions to Moray (walk 1½ hrs.). Hitching back to Urubamba is quite easy.

The Cuzco-Machu Picchu train reaches the heights N of the city by a series of switchbacks (beware of thieves boarding train here) and then descends to the floor of the Anta basin, with its herds of cattle. (In Anta itself, *Restaurant Dos de Mayo* is good; bus to Anta, US$0.25., felt trilby hats on sale). The railway goes through the Anta canyon (10 km.), and then, at a sharp angle, the Urubamba canyon, and descends along the river valley, flanked by high cliffs and peaks.

The railway and a 53-km. road go on to *Ollantaitambo,* 70 km., a clean and friendly little town (alt.: 2,800 metres) built on and out of the stones of an Inca town, which is a fine example of Inca *canchas* or corral enclosures, almost entirely intact. The so-called Baño de la Ñusta (bath of the princess) is of grey granite, and is in a small field between the town and the temple fortress. Some 200 metres behind the Baño de la Ñusta along the face of the mountain are some small ruins known as Inca Misanca, believed to have been a small temple or observatory. A series of steps, seats and niches have been carved out of the cliff. There is a complete irrigation system, including a canal at shoulder level, some 6 inches deep, cut out of the sheer rock face. The flights of terraces leading up above the town are superb, and so are the curving terraces following the contours of the rocks overlooking the Urubamba. These terraces were successfully defended by Manco Inca's warriors against Hernando Pizarro in 1536. Manco Inca built the defensive wall above the site and another wall closing the Yucay valley against attack from Cuzco, still visible on either side of the valley. Visitors should also note the Inca masonry channelling the river and the piers of the bridge of Ollantaitambo. Entering Ollantaitambo from Pisac, the road is built along the long wall of 100 niches. Note the inclination of the wall: it leans towards the road. Since it was the Incas' practice to build with the walls leaning towards the interiors of the buildings, it has been deduced that the road, much narrower then, was built inside a succession of buildings. The site opens at 0700.

The temple itself was started by Pachacuti, using Colla Indians from Lake Titicaca—hence the similarities of the monoliths facing the central platform with the Tiahuanaco remains. The Colla are said to have deserted half-way through the work, which explains the many unfinished blocks lying about the site. Admission by combined entrance ticket, which can be bought at the site. If possible arrive very early, 0700, before the tourists. The Sunday following Inti Raymi, there is a colourful festival, the Ollantay-Raymi. The guide book *Ollantaitambo* by Víctor Angles Vargas is available in Cuzco bookshops, and Peter Frost's *Exploring Cuzco* is also useful.

Accommodation   *Parador Turístico,* off main street between Plaza and ruins, for groups by reservation but will sometimes take other groups or couples if not booked up, E-F, all renovated in 1985, good meals at US$5; offers travel info. and horseback/walking tours; for reservations write to Maria S. Martínez, Parador Turístico de Ollantaitambo, Cuzco, Peru or get your Cuzco hotel to phone the Ollantaitambo exchange as the Parador has no phone as yet. Russ Bentley writes: "a veritable oasis of comfort and excellent food (superb Italian cuisine)". *Hostal Miranda,* F with shower, basic, friendly, clean; *Hostal Alcázar,* F with shower, basic, food, clean; *El Tambo,* also known as *Alojamiento Yavar,* 1½ blocks from main square, G, basic, friendly, has information on riding in the area, horses for hire at US$3 a day; *Hotel Panificadora,* G, tantalizing smell of fresh bread, very hard beds, basic, between main plaza and ruins.

Camping   possible in eucalyptus grove, ½ km. from town, and along the river between the town and the railway station.
Horses can be hired for US$3 per day; a rec. trek is to La Marca, a gentle day's ride along the beautiful river valley; ask in the square for details.

Restaurants   *Restaurant Ollantay* on Plaza de Armas, good. *Café Alcázar* opposite *Parador Turístico* good, cheap food; *El Parador,* in converted barn, down from main square towards ruins, good pasta and garlic bread; *Restaurante Tanta Wasi,* by railway, has two rooms to let, run by Jaime and Pilar Paz. In restaurants, check your bill carefully.

Transport   For those travelling by car, it is recommended to leave the car in Ollantaitambo (or the station previous on the road from Cuzco) for a day excursion by train to Machu-Picchu. Park car in front of the local police station at Ollantaitambo. Much safer there than parked in Cuzco for US$1 a day. Check in advance the time trains pass through here. The **tourist rail** car stops here, as do local trains (0800 or 1630, depending which is running). Hourly bus from Calle Recoleta, Cuzco, 2½ hrs., US$1.15, to Urubamba, to Ollantaitambo, also to Pisac. Many colectivos to Pisac on Sunday for market from 0600, 70 mins. Bus to Cuzco on Sat. at 0800 and 1200. Tourist minibus from outside Cuzco Cathedral to Pisac, Ollantaitambo, Cuzco, daily if over 5 passengers, US$10 (taxi tour costs US$40). Taxi to Cuzco, US$12. Bus to Urubamba, US$0.50 (truck US$0.15), from where one can return to Cuzco via Calca.

A major excavation project has been carried out since 1977 under the direction of Ann Kendall in the *Cusichaca* (Qucsichaca) valley, 26 km. from Ollantaitambo (only 9 km. passable by ordinary car) at the intersection of the Inca routes. (The Inca fort, Huillca Raccay, was excavated in 1978-80, and work is now concentrated on Llactapata, a site of domestic buildings).

From Ollantaitambo one can walk to the Inca Trail in about 5 hrs.: follow the railway in the direction of Machu Picchu until you come to a village where you can cross the river; climb up to a path that runs parallel to the river. This is an original Inca trail (still in use) that leads to Llactapata on the Inca Trail. **Warning** Best not to pass a night on this trail: thefts are common because you have to sleep near villages.

Pinculluna, the mountain above Ollantaitambo, can be climbed with no mountaineering experience, although there are some difficult stretches—allow 2-3 hours going up. The path is difficult to make out; best not to go on your own. Walk up the valley to the left of the mountain, very beautiful and impressive, Inca terraces after 4 km.

The **_Inca Trail_** hike to Machu-Picchu, about 33 km., makes a spectacular 3 to 5 day hike (take it slowly to appreciate it fully). It runs from Km. 88, Qoriwayrachi (about 2,600 metres), a point immediately after the first tunnel 22 km. beyond Ollantaitambo station. (Train to Km. 88 is US$1.10 first, US$0.90 2nd. Be ready to get out at Km. 88; easy to pass it.) A sturdy suspension bridge has now been built over the Urubamba River. An entrance ticket (US$8, US$4 for students) for the trail (which also gives you two days at Machu-Picchu if you get it stamped there) must be bought at Km. 88. The trail is rugged and steep (beware of landslides), at one stage traversing a 4,200-metre high pass, but the magnificent views compensate for any weariness which may be felt. It is cold at night, however, and weather conditions change rapidly, so it is important to take not only strong footwear and warm clothing but also food, water, insect repellant, a supply of plastic bags, coverings, a good sleeping bag, a stove for preparing hot food and drink to ward off the cold at night. A stove using paraffin (kerosene) is preferable, as fuel can be bought in small quantities in markets, whereas camping gas is expensive and scarce. **A tent is essential** (if hiring in Cuzco, check carefully for leaks) because walkers who have not taken adequate equipment have been known to die of exposure; caves marked on some maps are little better than overhangs, and are not sufficient shelter to sleep in. The trail is crowded in July and August. In the wet season (November-April) you don't have to worry about taking drinking water. At Puyopatamarca, on the Trail, there is a "tourist bathroom" where water can be collected (but purify it before drinking). Next place with water is Wiñay-Wayna (where there is a newly-built "tourist complex" with bunk beds (G p.p.), showers and a small restaurant, food and drink expensive), and then none till Machu-Picchu, where water supplies are turned off at 1530. A little-used variation to the Trail is to get off the train at Chilca, some 12 km. beyond Ollantaitambo, cross the bridge and walk 10 km. along the Urubamba River to join the trail at a point above Km. 88. This adds a day to the journey, but has the advantage of giving the body an opportunity to acclimatize itself before the very strenuous climb to the top of the first pass. Camping is possible on the bluff overlooking Llactapata (watch your belongings closely) and Km. 88 and this is an ideal starting point for the climb to the first pass, putting several hours between you and the other hikers who reach Km. 88 by train after 0900. **Warning** We have had a number of reports of armed robbery on the Inca Trail (one couple died), the culprits being variously described as Sendero Luminoso or organized gangsters from Cuzco. For this reason alone, do not go singly or in couples (official advice: no fewer than six—post a guard at night), and if possible stay close to a tour group; avoid the July-August high season and the rainy season from November onwards. Camp away from the sites on the main trail, and leave all valuables back in Cuzco (the tourist office has safes).

All the necessary equipment can be rented; see page 805 under **Travel agencies**. Good maps of the Trail and area can be bought from Walking Tours, the tourist office, at the Club Andino, or at Copias Vélez, Plaza San Francisco, Cuzco. Try to get the map prepared by the curator of Machu-Picchu Museum; it shows best sleeping places and drinking water. The guide Alberto Miori from Inca Trails is recommended, with many good reports. Remember there are no houses you can rush to if you get into difficulties; check carefully all equipment you hire before starting out. Robbers in the villages are on the increase.

Susan Whittlesey and Michael Young have prepared an excellent booklet on the Inca civilization and the Inca Trail (including a superb map), which is available for US$4 from Cin Co., 2912 E. 5th Avenue, Denver, Colorado 80206, USA.

The walk to Huayllabamba, following the Cusichaca river, needs about 3 hrs. and isn't too arduous. If planning a 2-4 day trip, carry on past Huayllabamba, which has become notorious for robberies. There is a camping place about an hr. ahead, at Llulluchayoc and another before the ascent to the first pass, Warmiwañuska, about 4 hrs. on in a meadow (highly recommended) 1½-2 hrs. from the summit. From Huayllabamba to the meadows is often discouragingly steep. Following the right path demands intuition more than orienteering knowhow, and the forest is occasionally very thick—but you should emerge towards 1600 hrs.

Leave early next day. The ascent to the first pass (4,200 metres) is the most taxing part of the walk. Afterwards take the path downhill, along left side of valley. You could camp by a stream at the bottom; it is no longer permitted to camp on the way up to the second pass (a much easier climb) at Runkuracay (3,800 metres), an Inca ruin, where there are huts and caves. Magnificent views near the summit in clear weather. Good overnight place is past the Inca ruins at Sayajmarca (3,600 metres), about an hr. on after the top of the second pass.

Muddy jungle terrain leads gently up to the third pass, only about 2-2½ hrs.' walk, the gradient blissfully gentle. Near the top there's a spectacular view of the Urubamba river and the valley to the right. You descend to Inca ruins at Puyopatamarca, well worth a long visit.

From there steps go downhill to Wiñay-Wayna, reached by forking off to the right (it's marked by a sign) near the pylons, 3-4 hrs. or so on from Puyopatamarca. A tourist complex has been built at the fork: there is no road. There is a shop selling drinks and nearby there is a dormitory, F (no electricity). The ruins at Wiñay-Wayna are in an impressive location. The path from this point goes more or less level through jungle. You need about 2 hrs. to walk to the Intipunku (water available from pipe), where there's a magnificent view of Machu-Picchu, especially at dawn, with the sun alternately in and out, clouds sometimes obscuring the ruins, sometimes leaving them clear. Get to Machu-Picchu as early as possible, preferably before 0830 for best views but in any case before the tourist train arrives at 1030.

Four days would make a comfortable trip (though much depends on the weather) and you would not find yourself too tired to enjoy what you see. Walking the Trail has the advantage of putting Machu-Picchu in its true context: not a "lost city", but an integral part of a heavily populated valley. By the same token Machu-Picchu loses some of its uniqueness; the architecture and scenery are often finer at several points along the trail. **N.B** It is not allowed to walk back along the trail, though you may pay US$1.50 at Intipunku to be allowed to walk back as far as Wiñay-Wayna, and you may not take backpacks into Machu-Picchu.

You can walk back from Aguas Calientes to Km. 107, cross the swing bridge from where Wiñay-Wayna can be reached by a switch-back path in 1½ hrs., thence to Machu-Picchu (this may only be done with special permission from the Cuzco tourist office to cross the guarded bridge). This round trip takes 5 hrs. Alternatively, coming from Cuzco, leave the train at km. 107 and walk the last few hours of the trail; you will reach Machu-Picchu just as the day visitors are leaving, but will have to walk the hour down to Aguas Calientes to stay the night. You can also leave the train at the second stop after Km. 88, called Cedrobamba (a brief stop), and walk from there to the swing bridge (1 hr.)

Littering along the Trail is a serious problem as 5,000 people are now using it each year. The Earth Preservation Fund now sponsors an annual cleanup July-August: volunteers should write to EPF, Inca Trail Project, Box 7545, Ann Arbor, Michigan 48107, USA.

Machu Picchu, 42 km. from Ollantaitambo by rail (2,280 metres), is a complete city, set on a saddle of a high mountain with terraced slopes falling away to the Urubamba river rushing in great hairpin bends below. It is in a comparatively good state of preservation because the Spaniards never found it. For centuries it was buried in jungle, until Hiram Bingham stumbled upon it in 1911. It was then explored by an archaeological expedition sent by Yale.

The ruins—staircases, terraces, temples, palaces, towers, fountains, the famous sundial and the Museo de Sitio below the ruins—require at least a day—some say two (take an insect-repellant). The mountain overlooking the site, Huayna Picchu (on which there are also some ruins), has steps to the top for a superlative view of the whole but it is not for those who get giddy (don't leave the path); the walk up takes about 60 minutes but the steps are dangerous after bad weather (it is only possible to walk up in the morning—start early as there is shade then—and you must register at a hut on the trail; guards prevent you after 1300). The other trail to Huayna Picchu, down near the Urubamba, via the Temple of the Moon, in two caves, one above the other, with superb Inca niches inside (sadly blemished by idiots' graffiti), can only be undertaken with a guide to the Temple of the Moon, leaving Machu-Picchu at 0900; he will clear the path and kill poisonous snakes. After the Temple you may proceed alone to Huayna

Picchu; round trip about 4 hours. An almost equally good view can be had from the trail behind the Tourist Hotel. Before doing any trekking around Machu Picchu, check with an official which paths may be used, or which are one way.

Gillian Handyside, of Harefield, Mx., tells us that another Inca site was discovered in 1987 opposite Machu-Picchu. An archaeologist, Moisés, who works on the project stays in the *Albergue* in Aguas Calientes and sometimes shows slides on the subject.

Transport N.B. "Machu Picchu" is the official name for Aguas Calientes station; that for Machu Picchu is "Ruinas". The most convenient way of seeing the ruins is to pay up to US$60 (including poor lunch at Tourist Hotel) to an agency for a 1-day guided trip from Cuzco to Machu-Picchu by tourist train or the later railcar (*autovagón*), which leave at 0700 and 0800 each day, enabling tourists to arrive at Machu-Picchu at about 1015 and 1130, visit the ruins and leave Machu-Picchu at 1000, 1430 and 1730, arriving in Cuzco about 3½ hrs. later. The railcar stops at Ollantaitambo, but not at Aguas Calientes unless requested in advance. A day's round trip, including train and bus return fares and entrance fee, can be booked at the San Pedro station for US$60. Railcar journey takes 3½-4 hours and costs US$20 each way, without lunch. Tickets may be bought one day in advance (returns available); office open 0600-0820, 1000-1100, 1500-1700; make sure you buy a single if staying overnight, or returning on a different type of train.
   Local trains from Cuzco, en route to Quillabamba, pass through Ollantaitambo, Aguas Calientes ("Machu Picchu") and Machu Picchu ("Ruinas"). It is imperative to check departure times in advance; they leave Cuzco at 0530, or 1400, or both, arriving at Aguas Calientes at 1030 or 1830, respectively. In the dry season there is also a night train from Cuzco at 2200, April-December. The fare is US$4 each way first class; price does not include bus ride up to Machu-Picchu and entrance fee. Book one day in advance in morning for the early train only (ticket office hours: 0800-1200, 1600-1700, Mon.-Fri.; 0500-0600, 1200-1430, Sat.; 1200-1430, Sun.). The local train returns at 1500, but is unreliable (on Sunday only the railcar runs). If the 0530 from Quillabamba is running to Cuzco, it passes Machu Picchu at 0815. Take a drinking mug on the train.
   N.B. It is reported that tourists are now refused tickets for the local trains to "Ruinas", but it is possible to book for a station beyond "Ruinas" and get off early. Alternatively, you can get on the train at a station other than Cuzco, e.g. Ollantaitambo. Arrive early at station, and you will have to fight if you want a seat, particularly the left-hand side facing engine going (right on return) which gives a better view. If you can get a ticket for the local train, 1st class seats have reserved numbers on the way up, but not on the way back. Getting onto the 1500 return train is even more of a fight; many are left behind. Beware of thieves (bag-slitting is extremely common), particularly at the switch-backs when they can jump on and off the train (1st class coaches are locked on this stretch), and on the Urubamba stretch where there are many short tunnels. Police presence has been stepped up at the stations and on the trains.
   Buses from the station to Machu-Picchu start at 0800 (0630 buses for workers only) and meet both local and tourist trains, and charge US$3 each way for the trip to the ruins and back. There are theoretically enough seats on the buses for all the train passengers, but in practice you will have to wait for a seat (beware of drivers charging inflated prices). Last bus down to station goes at about 1530 (if you wish to stay longer, demand a single bus ticket). You can walk up in 1½ hrs. to 2 hrs., and down in 1 hr., if you have no luggage; there is a short-cut for walkers, the Camino de Herradura, said to take 45 mins. to 1 hr., some of it almost rock climbing. Luggage can be deposited safely at the site entrance (for US$0.45, open 0800-1500, there is a self-service restaurant) but not at the station, nor at the museum (on opposite side of river from station, open Tues.-Sun. 1030-1530). Cost of entry to the ruins, US$10; they are open 0630-1700. For the student reduction for groups, apply at Casa de Cultura. Post Office at Machu-Picchu station has special franking marks.
   The cheapest way to visit the site is to take the "Indian train" from Cuzco, or a single ticket on

the tourist train, stay overnight at one of the places offering basic accommodation at Aguas Calientes (see below), 1½ km. back along the railway (the town has electricity 24 hrs a day). **Note:** In the rainy season trains are often delayed by landslides.

Permission to enter the ruins before 0630 to watch the sunrise over the Andes, which is a spectacular experience, may be obtained from the Instituto Nacional de Cultura in Colegio San Bernardo, Cuzco (near La Merced), but it is often possible if you talk to the guards at the gate. Sr. Quispe, a guard for many years (and of royal Inca descent), is friendly and informative.

Mon. and Fri. are bad days because there is usually a crowd of people on guided tours who are going or have been to Pisac market on Sun., and too many people all want lunch at the same time. Food is available around the station.

Camping   Not permitted on the site, nor on Huayna-Picchu; may be possible on football field downstream of the station, or Aguas Calientes. Beware of thieves.

Accommodation and Food   In season the Tourist Hotel at the ruins is heavily booked during the week (best rooms for the view are 10, 16, 18, 20, 22); try Sunday night as other tourists find Pisac market a greater attraction. Book well in advance, through a reliable agency, or at the Enturperú office in Lima or Cuzco: in this way you can spend 24 hrs. at the site. Often, however, though reportedly booked up weeks in advance, there are cancellations and you can obtain a room on arrival. Rooms with shower and breakfast (no singles) A, US$5 for meals in poor self-service cafeteria. There is electricity and water 24 hours a day. Service and honesty not always good, but as they state in the English version of the rules card: "The grandeur of nature is such, that the conniving of man is overcome." The Tourist Hotel often does not have intis for exchange, make sure you have enough before setting out for Machu-Picchu; but the hotel will accept American Express travellers' cheques. Only hotel residents may eat in the restaurant; others have to use the expensive self-service counter outside. It is recommended that you take food and soft drinks with you; prices are high.

At **Aguas Calientes**, the *Albergue Juvenil*, constructed by Copesco, the state tourism agency for the region, has 200 beds in dormitories and private rooms, and dining facilities (US$3 for a poor meal), for travellers and family groups, dirty bathrooms reported, comfortable, noisy with students, laundry, rec., F p.p. (no IYHA card needed). *Hostal Caminantes*, with bath, G, basic, but friendly and clean; *Hostal Qoñi Unu* (known as Gringo Bill's, run by William and Margarita Kaiser, who will act as guides to surrounding areas), third house to left of church, F, clean, cheap, hot water, laundry and cooking facilities, money exchange, meals served (including 0530 breakfast), luggage stored, new huts built (if owners are away, get any price changes written down when you book); *Hotel Sucre*, F, cheap and dingy; *Hostal Machu-Picchu*, F, in communal dormitory, clean, safe, rooms also F, quiet, friendly (esp. Wilber, owner's son, with travel info.), 0530 breakfast if required, being extended, grocery store, rec.; *El Refugio*, cheap, good food, also *Aiko*, rec.; *Waiki*, good cheap food, breakfast. At the *pizzería*, very slow service, but reasonable food; *El Mirador*, run by Manuel, "the prince of the primus", near station, good food, friendly staff and cat, open 0500 for early starters to Machu-Picchu; *Huayna Picchu*, good value restaurant beside railway line. Despite reports that the standard of food and hygiene has improved, you are warned to be careful about what you eat and if in doubt about your constitution, take your own food. It may be difficult to get a room, so be prepared to sleep on a floor. Two new swimming pools have been built. The thermal baths (a communal pool), a 15-minute walk from the town, are particularly welcome to those who have walked the Inca Trail; officially they close at 2000 (US$0.40 per bath, no soap, bathing suits required, take torch if going by night, baths murky, but reported cleaner in morning).

From Machu-Picchu one can take the Inca Trail, which climbs up behind the Tourist Hotel, back to (2 hours' walk) the Inca settlement of Wiñay-Wayna, a village of roofless but otherwise well-preserved Inca houses where a basic "Complejo Turístico" for visitors has been opened. On the way, you will have to pay US$1.50 for entry to the Trail. About 30 mins. along a well-marked trail on the other side of Machu-Picchu ruins is the famous Inca bridge. Both walks give spectacular views of the Urubamba River and the thickly wooded mountains, and the butterflies and flowers are beautiful. The tombs at Chaskapata, near Machu-Picchu, have recently been opened.

Note   Advisable to buy paperback edition of *Lost City of the Incas* by Hiram Bingham, in Lima or Cuzco (more expensive), or *A Walking Tour of Machu-Picchu* (rec.) by Pedro Sueldo Nava, available in Cuzco. Choice of guide books in Cuzco much improved. The Tourist Hotel also sells guides, although at a rather inflated price. (The South American Explorers' Club in Lima has detailed information on walks in this area, and so has the Bradts' book.)

The railway goes on 79 km. through Chaullay to **Quillabamba** (24,000 people) in the Urubamba Valley at 1,054 metres, where there is a Dominican mission.

The train follows the Urubamba River much of the way from Machu-Picchu, and the improvised station at Quillabamba is right on the river. One crosses a foot bridge put up by the Lions Club and then climbs up a 100-odd flight of stairs to reach the town. Many *heladerías*, much needed in the heat, the best on the northwest corner of the square. Not many attractions for the tourist, but a place to bask in the sun or take a swim in the river, though ask the locals where the safe stretches are, as the current is quite rapid in places. Clean market building, and a football stadium.

Hotels *Don Carlos*, D-E, good, friendly, good, if limited meals, transport to station extra; *Hostal Alto Urubamba*, F, on Dos de Mayo, clean, good, with bath, or without, restaurant; *Quillabamba* (unmarked entrance next to Autoservicio behind market), roof terrace restaurant, rec., D; *Urusayhua*, near market, F; *Progreso*, near market, F; *Comercio*, Libertad, D, with bath; *Hostal San Antonio*, cheap; *San Martín*, dirty, F; *Thomas*, cheap; *Barrenechea*, cheap; *Turistas* expensive, though nice and modern, opposite the market, without sign. The best restaurants are to be found on Plaza de Armas.

Transport The morning train from Quillabamba leaves at 0530 and arrives at Machu-Picchu about 0815, giving you 2½ hours at the ruins before the invasion from Cuzco starts with the arrival of the tourist train, but you may have to walk up: the buses may not be operating at that hour. Another train leaves Quillabamba at 1305, 6½ hrs. to Cuzco. Check which is running. There is a night train at 2200 in the dry season, which passes Machu-Picchu at 0100, arriving Cuzco 0500. Tickets must be bought one day in advance, from Enafer office off main plaza.

Minibus leaves Cuzco a.m. when full, from Calle General Buendía near Macchu-Picchu station; also trucks go in the daytime, US$2. The road between Ollantaitambo and Quillabamba passes through Peña, a place of great beauty with snowy peaks already appearing on either side of the valley (taxis are very reluctant to go there). Once out of Peña, the climb to the pass begins in earnest—on the right is a huge glacier. Soon on the left, Salcantay begins to appear in all its huge and snowy majesty. After endless zig-zags and breathtaking views, one reaches Puerto Málaga (rudimentary *pensión*). The descent to the valley is alarming, highlighted by a series of dangerous curves. The hillsides are covered in lichen and Spanish moss. At Chaullay, the road meets the railway to Quillabamba, Machu-Picchu and Cuzco. One can drive from Chaullay to Santa Teresa (hot springs, ask the locals) from where the railway goes to Machu-Picchu, and can hike to Lucma and the village of Vilcabamba, from where one can descend to the valley of the River Concebidayoc where one comes to Espíritu Pampa, the site of the Vilcabamba Vieja ruins, a vast pre-Inca ruin with a neo-Inca overlay in deep jungle at 1,000 metres (the disputed last capital of the Incas); the site is reached on foot or horseback from Pampaconas. From Chaullay, take a truck to Yupanca, Lucma or Pucyura: there rent horses or mules and travel through superb country to Espíritu Pampa. Then continue to Cosireni, from where trucks go to Quillabamba.

A permit from the National Cultural Institute is required to visit this area. Without one, you will be turned back at Pucyura. The Institute is not issuing passes (Aug 87) to visit the area between the Ríos Urubamba and Concebidayoc because of guerrilla activity there, but travel to Chaullay, Quillabamba and Kiteni is permitted.

One can also go by boat to Kiteni and then by truck to Quillabamba (at 0400). There are no buses from Quillabamba to Kiteni, but *camiones* leave between 0700-1000, US$2, 7-10 hrs. (*Hotel Kiteni*, F, basic, several restaurants). At Kiteni you must register on arrival with the police station. Take torch, no electricity. Irregular boats to the Pongo de Maynique, where the river goes through the mountain with a rock wall of several hundred meters on either side, before descending into jungle, where you can see many varieties of animals, birds, butterflies, snakes etc. 2 days, from Quillabamba to Pongo. This journey is only possible between April and August (too dangerous at other times). Between Kiteni and Pongo, on the river, is the village of Israelitos, whose inhabitants have been convinced by a missionary that they are New Israelites and that the Messiah will arise there. You can stay in a small hut next to the synagogue, but bring food and supplies—also gifts—from Kiteni. From Pongo you can get down through the jungle to Pucallpa if there is the right amount of water in the river; boats can be arranged at Kiteni. Price varies for number of people in the party, approximately US$15-20 p.p. Beware of overcharging. En route to Pucallpa it is possible to go to Camisea and Sepahua (near where Yaminavak Indians can be visited; they live in constructions made of mud, but have a mini-hotel for passers-through). To hire a car in Cuzco for this area costs about US$50 per day, including insurance, mileage and fuel for about 250 km.

Paucartambo, on E slope of Andes, is NE of Cuzco by a good road (one way on alternate days). In this remote though now popular tourist town is held the Fiesta of Carmen, usually on July 16, 17, 18, with masked dances. (*Fiesta* dates should be checked in Cuzco.) Hotels: *Quinta Rosa Marina*, near bridge, basic, G; *San Martín*, G, dirty, even more basic. Private car hire for round trip on July 16: US$25, or the Tourist Office in Cuzco arranges an overnight trip (you sleep in the bus) for US$10. Minibus from Av. Huáscar, Cuzco, every other day, US$3, 3-4 hrs. (alternate days Paucartambo-Cuzco).

From Paucartambo, in the dry season, you can go 44 km. to Tres Cruces, along the Pilcopata road, turning left after 25 km.; Sr. Cáceres in Paucartambo will arrange trip. Tres Cruces gives a wonderful view of the sunrise in June and

July and private cars leave Paucartambo between 0100 and 0200 to see it; they may give you a lift. One can walk from Paucartambo to the *chullpas* of Machu Cruz in about an hour, or to the *chullpas* of Pijchu (take a guide). You can also visit the Inca fortress of Huatojto, which has admirable doorways and stonework. A car will take you as far as Ayre, from where the fortress is a 2-hour walk.

The ***Manu National Park*** is the biggest nature reserve in Peru, covering 1.5 million hectares of jungle around the river Manu (an area half the size of Switzerland). Charles Munn, a zoologist from Wildlife Conservation International, writes that "No other park on earth can compare with Manu in terms of sheer variety of life forms." Giant otters, crocodiles, tapirs, jaguars and ocelot, and many other animals and birds may be seen. The dry season runs from April to October; July, August and September are the driest months when animals stay close to the river and are most easily seen. Information is available from Asociación y Conservación para la Selva Sur (ACSS), Av. Sol 627, 3rd floor, Cuzco.

The following companies offer 3-8 day tours: Expediciones Manu EIRL, Procuradores 372, Cuzco, T 226671/233190, Telex 52052PE; Manu Nature Tours EIRL, Av. Sol 627-B, oficina 401, Cuzco, T 231549/234793, Telex 52003/4, which owns *Manu Lodge*, the most remote of the 4 lodges in or near the park; it is highly recommended, both for comfort and as an experience of "pure magic" (it's also expensive).

Individual trips can be arranged by the hardy and adventurous. First obtain a permit (free) from the park's office, Calle Laderos, Cuzco, who may send you to Salvación for it (see below). Buy all supplies in Cuzco: camping gear, fishing tackle, food (for the boatmen as well) and gasoline; take finely-woven, long-sleeved and -legged clothing and effective insect repellent (that on sale in Cuzco is no good). On Mon., Wed. and Fri. a truck leaves Calle Huaruropata, Cuzco, supposedly at 0600, for Shintuya, 250 km. through wild scenery, US$5, minimum 30 uncomfortable hours (much longer in the rainy season as there are no bridges). The priest in Shintuya will let you stay in the dormitory rooms at the mission, or you can camp. One restaurant only.

In Shintuya, hire a boat and guide to go down the Madre Dios river and up the Manu (the 4 Moscoso brothers are recommended). A six week trip will cost a minimum of US$350, after bargaining, maximum 10 people, but fewer are better as jungle clearings are small.

At Tres Cruces in the Park there is an empty bungalow that may be used for the night; it has no window-panes, water or electricity. The National Park office at Salvación can also arrange your entry permit and with luck you might catch a lift in with park staff, or they will know of other people going in (*Hostal Salvación*, F, clean, basic bathrooms, swimming pool). Transport to Shintuya infrequent but possible although most boats are already fully laden and rarely carry tourists. *Quinta Erika*, small jungle lodge run by Sra. Gerlach, a German woman who has lived in the jungle since 1951, tranquil, few bugs, good food, animals, boat trips can be arranged with prior notice, transport from Cooperativa landing, 3 km. from Salvación.

From Shintuya, it is 5½ hrs by boat to Boca Manu, then 4½ hrs to Romero where there is a park checkpoint and a park entry fee of US$10 is charged. Three lakes (cochas) can be visited from Romero, Wasi, Otorongo and Salvador. After your trip you can return to Cuzco via Shintuya, or take a colectivo boat from Boca Manu to Colorado (US$6—6 hrs.), then another to Laberinto (US$4—12 hrs.), from where buses run to Puerto Maldonado (US$1.50—1½ hrs.).

THE SOUTH-EASTERN JUNGLE (6)

From Urcos, near Cuzco (bus US$0.50), a spectacular 484-km. road has been constructed over the Eastern Cordillera to Puerto Maldonado in the jungle. No buses, but several trucks do the journey every day. 47 km. after passing the snow-line Hualla-Hualla pass (4,820 metres) the **super-hot thermal baths** (US$ 0.05) of Marcapata provide a relaxing break. From here the road continues its descent through a tropical rain forest well stocked with orchids. 82 km. from Urcos, at the base of Mount Ausangate (6,600 metres), is the town of **Ocongate**, which has two hotels on the Plaza de Armas. The air force (FAP) provides a weekly air service from Cuzco and Puerto Maldonado to **Quincemil**, 240 km. from Urcos, a centre for alluvial gold-mining with many banks (*Hotel Toni*, F, friendly, clean, cold shower, good meals); ask the food-carriers to take you to visit the miners washing for gold in the nearby rivers. Quincemil marks the half-way point and the end to the all-weather road. Gasoline is scarce because most road vehicles continue on 70 km. to Masuco, another mining centre, where they fill up with the cheaper gasoline of the jungle region. Thirty more km. of sloshing mud and cascading waterfalls brings one out of the mountainous jungle and into the flat plains, for the 141 km. straight run to Puerto Maldonado.

Owing to the present gold rush on the Madre de Dios river, there are many trucks from Cuzco to Puerto Maldonado: 50-55 hr. journey; US$8-11 in the back, US$13 up front. As trucks pass each other, watch out for the exchanges of fire with fruit as the ammunition. The road has been widened. Times by truck: Urcos—Ocongate 6 hrs. (US$2), Ocongate—Quincemil 12 hrs. (US$5), Quincemil—Masuco—Puerto Maldonado 15-20 hrs. (US$5).

Puerto Maldonado is capital of the jungle Department of Madre de Dios. (Altitude, 250 metres.) Overlooking the confluence of the rivers Tambopata and Madre de Dios, this frontier town is the centre for development of Peru's southern jungle. The Plaza de Armas is very pleasant, and nearby is a new Banco de la Nación built to accommodate (and reflect) the prosperity that gold has brought. However, Puerto Maldonado is an expensive town and because of the gold mining and timber industries, much of the jungle (including most of the mahogany trees) has been destroyed. The temperature normally is between 30°-37°C during the dry season (May to October) and 28°-33°C in the rainy season (November to April); but *friajes* (cold winds that roll northwards along the foothills of the Andes from the South Atlantic region) can send the temperature plummeting, to about 7°C. Insect and reptile activity is greatly reduced; warm-blooded animals survive. Because of this climatic phenomenon, the fauna of the Madre de Dios include many unusual species not found in other jungle areas. Also unique to this area is the *rayo blanco* (white rainbow) that can be seen at sunset on the Madre de Dios River.

Madre de Dios has three superb jungle reserves, among the best in the world: Manu National Park, 1.5 million hectares to the N of the department (**see page 818**); Tambopata Wildlife Reserve, 5,500 hectares, 40 km. up the Río Tambopata; and Río Heath Pampas Sanctuary, 100,000 hectares between the Río Madre de Dios and the Río Heath. A pair of binoculars is essential equipment for this area.

Hotels (1988 prices) *Cuzco Amazonic Lodge (Albergue Cuzco Amazónico)*, A, 45 mins. by boat down the Madre de Dios River, jungle tours and accommodation US$140 for 3 days, 2 nights, good food negotiable out of season; avoid in February when everyone goes on holiday including the mechanic. (Book at Av. Arequipa 4964, Lima, T 462775, or Procuradores 48, Cuzco, T 5047.) *Explorers Inn* (best booked through Peruvian Safaris, Garcilaso de la Vega 1334, Casilla 10088, T 313047 Lima, or through Peruvian Safaris, Plaza San Francisco 168, T 235342 Cuzco—post to Puerto Maldonado is very bad but local office is Fitzcarrald 136), A, located in middle of Tambopata wildlife reserve, 58 km. from Puerto Maldonado: an authentic jungle experience, a 4 hr. ride on Tambopata river (2 hours return, in early a.m., so take warm clothes), take food and drink for the journey, probably the best place in Peru for seeing jungle birds (547 species have been recorded here), butterflies (1,100-plus species), dragonflies (over 150 species) as well as tree species and mammals (including a giant otter) recommended more for serious naturalists than average tourists, all guides are graduate biologists (all vegetables and salads washed in iodised water), US$150 for 3 days, 2 nights (depending on season, 1 day spent actually in the reserve), extra day US$45, flight from Puerto Maldonado not included; naturalists' programme at US$45 a night (minimum 6 nights). *Tambo Lodge*, bungalows 8 km. out on opposite bank of Río Madre de Dios, 2-day jungle programme US$70, 3-day US$90, 4-day US$115, rec., book through Cusco-Maldonado Tour, Portal de Panes 109 (T 222-332), Cuzco. *Turistas*, on the bank of the Tambopata River, D, with private bath, electricity and water sometimes cut, restaurant quite good.

In town: *Wilson*, D with bath, E without, well run, clean, no hot water, trucks coming from airport stop here; *Rey Port*, F with shower, secure, rec.; *Cross*, clean, generally rec.; *Toni*, *Central*, F and *Moderno*, G, (very clean but noisy, safe for luggage, no hot water). *Tambo de Oro*, F. As there are many miners in Maldonado, it can be difficult to find a hotel room.

Restaurants There are several good restaurants in town. The unnamed restaurant opposite the AeroPerú office has been rec.; so has *Rulman*, good Chinese food and large selection of other dishes, rec. apart from poor addition, round the corner from *Hotel Wilson*. *Kalifa*, Piura, some regional specialities, rec. Look for *pensiones* where meals are served at fixed times (lunch is at 1300). *Café Danubio Azul* on Plaza de Armas is good for information.

Typical Foods *Castañas* (Brazil nuts), try them, chocolate- or sugar-coated. *Patarashca*, fish barbecued in banana leaves. Try *pescado sudado* as an appetizer. *Sopa de motelo*, turtle soup cooked and served in its own shell. *Mazato*, an alcoholic drink prepared from yuca and drunk by the Indians at their festivals. *Sangre de grado*, a thick deep-red sap collected from trees deep in the jungle which is a highly prized cure-all throughout Peru.

Excursions Motorcycles can be hired for local trips for US$4 an hour. Bargain for reductions for longer. A very worthwhile one-or two-day excursion by motorcycle is to boat across the Madre de Dios River and follow the trail towards Iberia (*Hotel Aquino*, F). Along the trail are picturesque *caserios* (settlements) that serve as collecting and processing centres for the Brazil nut. Approximately 70% of the inhabitants in the Madre de Dios are involved in the collection of this prized nut. The beautiful and tranquil Lake Sandoval is a 1-hr. boat ride along the Madre de Dios River and then a 2-km. walk into the jungle. For fishing Lake Valencia, 60 km. away near the Bolivian border, is unsurpassed (2 days). Many excellent beaches and islands are located within an hour's boat ride; however, make sure you have a ride back at the end of the day. For the adventurous a one-or two-day trip can be planned to visit Indians still relatively unaffected by civilization; the Indians living nearer Puerto Maldonado, like those near Iquitos and Manaus, are strictly tourist Indians. Boats may be hired at the port for about US$30 a day to go to Lake Sandoval or visit the Indians. Bargain hard, and don't pay the full cost in advance. Mosquitoes are voracious. If camping, take food and water. Barbara de Cárdenas from San Francisco and her Peruvian husband, Guillermo, organize interesting trips for photography, bird watching and fishing. They can be contacted at Puerto Tambopata, behind the Tourist Hotel (write to Correo Central, Puerto Maldonado). Tambopata Expeditions offer 2-day tours to Lago Sandoval and longer trips, owner is guide, speaks English and is knowledgeable; take binoculars. A recommended guide is Arturo Balarezo Revilla, who charges US$30 p.p. per day for a boat trip; contact him at his house near the Plaza de Armas, at the *Café Danubio Azul* or at the airport. Another recommended guide is Victorio Suárez, Apartado 177, who charges US$25 p.p. per day, all included, and will tailor the trip to his clients' requirements. Contact Sr. Gombringer, who lives beside the plaza (well known) who runs excursions from his house on Lake Victoria, 7 hrs. down river by boat, very good and reasonable, much wildlife. For guides meeting the plane, US$8-10 p.p. per day is a normal fee. Alejandro and Héctor are recommended. **N.B.** All hunting in Amazonia is illegal.

For those interested in seeing a gold rush, a trip to the town of *Laberinto* (one hotel, several poor restaurants) is recommended. The bus leaves Puerto Maldonado at 0900, 1000 and 1100 and returns in the afternoon daily.

Transport It is possible to travel overland from Cuzco (4-5 days). Take a truck from the social security hospital to Pucapata (lodgings basic), or if possible direct to Shintuya; boats leave most mornings for Colorado (10 hrs.); next day take a canoe to Laberinto (8-12 hrs.), from where there is a dirt road to Puerto Maldonado (bus US$1.50, 1½ hrs.). Take food. Flying is cheaper and quicker but not so interesting.

Taxi to airport US$1.70. The airport has a paved runway; flights are often cancelled because of rain. Faucett to and from Lima and Cuzco, Tues., Thurs., Sat.; AeroPerú on the other days, US$38 return to Cuzco; flights to Lima US$97 one way; AeroPerú may cancel flights in Cuzco if not enough passengers. Once a week to Lima and Cuzco (usually Thursday) there is an air-force flight (Grupo Ocho) that goes in all but the worst conditions via Iberia and Iñapari, fare to Cuzco, US$18, to Iñapari, US$10. A weekly flight Arequipa-Puerto Maldonado (US$18 one way) is run by the air force, usually Friday, if demand is sufficient. Office of Grupo Ocho is in the airport at Cuzco. Open 0800-1200.

Flight to *Iñapari* (½ hr.) on the Brazilian frontier, Thursday; this is a cargo flight and you must see the captain about a seat on the day of the flight. From the landing field it is 7 km. to the village (one hostel) where you must seek out the police for border formalities. Wade across the river to Brazil, to the village of Assis Brasil. Private boats can be contracted for travel into Bolivia; to Puerto Heath, at the border (US$28, one day); to Riberalta (US$90-120, 4 days). The trip by boat to Riberalta is very difficult, especially in the dry season. Boats are very few and far between. Some boats only go as far as Puerto Pardo (a Peruvian military post opposite Puerto Heath) for US$2.20, or US$52-64 *expresso*. The wife of one of the officers in Puerto Pardo offers meals for US$0.80. From here one can cross to Puerto Heath, a Bolivian naval post, but boats into Bolivia are just as infrequent here. It should be noted that waiting for sailings in either Puerto Heath or Puerto Maldonado can take a lot of time.

Before leaving for Bolivia from Puerto Maldonado, one must first get a Bolivian visa (if needed) from the consulate (on Jirón Cuzco; very helpful), then a Peruvian exit stamp, before one can get a Bolivian entry stamp. Similarly if going to Brazil; if you have not obtained an exit stamp from the P.I.P. in Puerto Maldonado, you will be turned back at either border. The immigration office is opposite the *Hotel Moderno*.

Books *An Annotated Check List of Peruvian Birds*, by Theodore A. Parker, Susan Allen Parker and Manuel A. Plenge, published by Buteo Books, Vermillon, South Dakota, is particularly useful in this area. Also, *The Birds of Venezuela*, Princeton University, and *The Land Birds of South America*, by John Dunning.

INLAND FROM LIMA (7)

The Central Railway from Lima to La Oroya and on to Huancayo (335 km.) is one of the wonders of Latin America. It reaches its greatest altitude, 4,782 metres, inside the tunnel between Ticlio and Galera, 159 km. from Lima. The ruling grade is about 4½°. Along the whole of its length it traverses 66 tunnels, 59 bridges, and 22 zig-zags where the steep mountainside permits no other way of negotiating it. It is by far the most important railway in the country, and the views during the ascent are beyond compare. This masterpiece was the project of the great American railway engineer, Henry Meiggs, who supervised the construction from 1870 until his death in 1877; it was built by the Pole Ernesto Malinowski, with imported Chinese labour, between 1870 and 1893. Railway buffs may like to know that the last Andes type 2-8-0 steam locomotive No. 206, is still in working order, although usually locked in a shed at Huancayo. It was built specifically for this route in 1953 by Beyer Peacocks of Manchester. The course of the railway is more or less paralleled by that of the Central Highway between Lima and Huancayo.

For a while, beyond Chosica (**see page 738**), each successive valley seems to be greener, with a greater variety of trees and flowers. At **San Bartolomé** (Km. 57, 1,513 metres), the platform is often crowded with local fruit sellers. The train reverses, then passes through tunnels and over bridges to the next canyon. Sometimes the train seems airborne over the valley and the road far below.

Matucana, Km. 84, at 2,390 metres, is set in wild scenery, where there are beautiful walks. At Tamboraque (3,009 metres) is the first of the mountain mines, with its overhead cables and smelter down a gorge. Climbing always, we pass San Mateo (Km. 107, 3,215 metres), where the San Mateo mineral water originates. From San Mateo a spectacular side-road branches off to the Germania mine. Beyond San Mateo is Infiernillo (Little Hell) Canyon, to which car excursions are made from Lima, 100 km. (Hotels: *Ritz,* F, fair, *Grau,* cheap.) Following Infiernillo (only a glimpse seen between tunnels) the train proceeds in rapid zigzags. Between Río Blanco and Chicla (Km. 127, 3,733 metres) the Inca contour-terraces can be seen quite clearly.

Casapalca (Km. 139, 4,154 metres) has more mines; its concentrators are at the foot of a deep gorge. A climb to the dizzy heights beyond ends in a glorious view of the highest peaks. Soon we see a large metal flag of Peru at the top of Mount Meiggs, not by any means the highest in the area, but through it runs Galera Tunnel, 1,175 metres long. Ticlio, the highest passenger station in the world (Km. 157, 4,758 metres), at the mouth of the tunnel, is on one side of a crater in which lies a dark, still lake. At Ticlio the line forks, one through the tunnel to La Oroya; the other line goes 14½ km. to Morococha, where there are important mines. The highest point, 4,818 metres, is reached on this latter line at La Cima. A siding off this line reaches 4,829 metres.
Beyond the tunnel zig-zags bring us down to Yauli (4,142 metres). Left is the ugliness inseparable from mining; right are mountainsides and moors with cold, small mountain tarns and herds of sheep, very few llamas. After La Oroya the railway follows the valley of the polluted river Mantaro.

La Oroya (Km. 208), the main smelting centre, with its slag heaps is full of vitality and here the train fills up. Population: 36,000. It is at the fork of the Yauli and Mantaro rivers at 3,755 metres, 187 km. from Lima by a road which although officially paved throughout, is in poor condition, particularly between the Anticona Pass at 4,843 metres and La Oroya. (For places to the E and N of La Oroya, **see pages 828 and 830** respectively.)

Hotels *Hostal San Martín,* F, clean, friendly, no heating but plenty of blankets; *Wilson; Lima.*

Restaurants *Las Vegas,* rec. *Huánuco,* good, cheap food. *Central,* rec. *El Tambo,* 2 km. outside La Oroya, good trout and frogs.

Railway N to Tambo del Sol and Cerro de Pasco; SE to Jauja and Concepción (**see page 824**), Huancayo and Huancavelica; SW to Lima and Callao. Train to Cerro de Pasco leaving 1330 and arriving 1716; no connection with train from Lima. To Lima at 1005 and Huancayo at 1340. (Local train to Huancayo on Sun.)

Roads and Buses SE to Huancayo, Ayacucho, and Cuzco, paved to Huancayo; N to Cerro de Pasco (US$0.75) and on to Pucallpa; 25 km. north along this road fork E for Tarma (US$1.50 by bus, US$1.85 by colectivo), San Ramón, the Perené colony, and Oxapampa; SW to Lima (6 hrs. by bus, US$2.50, 5 or less, US$2.95, by colectivo). Take taxi from bus terminal in Lima, which is in a dangerous area.

Huancayo, capital of Junín Department, is the main commercial centre for inland central Peru; alt. 3,271 metres; pop. 359,000. The Indians flock in from far and wide with an incredible range of food, and rugs and blankets of llama and alpaca wool, for sale; fleeces can be bought (alpaca, US$2.50 per kilo), but arrive early before 1000, Av. La Marina, 700 block. The Sun. market, Jr. Huancavelica, 3 km. long and 4 stalls wide, sells typical clothes, fruit, vegetables, hardware, handicrafts but especially traditional medicines and goods for witchcraft. Huancayo is a good place to buy carved gourds, reputedly the lowest prices in Peru. Very impressive Good Friday processions. The colourful annual fiesta of the Virgin of Cocharcas starts on September 8 at Orcotuna, and there are a big early morning market and an afternoon bullfight on the same day as the parade of the Virgin; the feasting and dancing last a week. Costumes and dances are then at their best. In Huancayo, ponchos and various alpaca woollen goods are quite cheap, but often factory-made; most goods are reported to be cheaper than in Lima, particularly silver jewellery. Displays of folklore at the Coliseo, Calle Real, certain Sundays. For woven alpaca goods and other *artesanías,* much cheaper, go to outlying villages, such as San Jerónimo, or Hualhuas, 11 km. north of Huancayo (2 km. off the Huancayo-Jauja road, try Familia Meza, Jr. 28 de Julio 293); minibus from Huancayo, US$0.15 from Church of the Immaculate Conception (see Excursions below).

Warning Huancayo has a bad reputation for thieves, especially in the market and at bus stations. In particular, beware of locals who smear mustard (or something worse) on you, and while you are cleaning it off, steal your belongings.

Hotels *Turistas,* D, with bath, old building, some rooms small, quiet, good meals for US$3.50; *Presidente,* Calle Real 1138, T 231736, D, clean, friendly, helpful, safe, breakfast only, rec.; *Confort,* Calle Ancash 298, F, private bath, basic but clean, good; *Santa Felicidad,* Plaza de Armas, F, good; *Hostal Dani,* Giráldez 486 (T 235645/232762), F, small private hotel, hot water, clean, friendly, clothes-washing and cooking facilities, safe, English-speaking landlady Sra. María Carmela Barraza de Babilón, goes out of her way to help travellers with problems, even if they are not staying at her hotel, someone from hotel meets the Lima train; *Acolla,* corner of Antonio Lobato and Real, Tambo district, F, private toilet, hot shower. *Residencial Inca Wasi,* Federico Villareal 106, clean and friendly, F (owner meets Lima train with car); *Residencia Huancayo,* Av. Giráldez, near railway station, G, all rooms with wash basin, hot showers; *Inca,* Calle Loreto, F, with bath (cold water), clean, but noisy; *Pensión Huanca,* Pasaje San Antonio 113, San Carlos T 223956, no sign (young man, Angel, meets Lima train), F, small, English spoken, hot water, friendly, breakfast extra, laundry and kitchen facilities, good food, typical Huancayo dishes, rec.; *Residencia Baldeón,* Amazonas 543, G, with European-style breakfast, hot water, friendly; *Kiya,* Giráldez 107, Plaza de Armas (known nowadays as Constitución), E, with bath, hot water, restaurant does not serve breakfast, 'phones in rooms (avoid noisy rooms on Av. Real); *Universal,* opp. railway station, F, reasonable. *Hospedaje Suizo,* Huancas 473, T 231732, F, 10 mins. walk from railway station, comfortable, hot water, family atmosphere, warmly rec. Luis Hurtado (**see page 824**) has 2 rooms (G including breakfast), with hot water, washing and cooking facilities.

N.B. Prices may be raised in Holy Week.

Restaurants *Inca,* Calle Puno 530, rec. On Av. Giráldez (Plaza de la Constitución) are *Olímpico, Lalo's,* and *Café Giráldez,* all good, Peruvian dishes at *Olímpico,* Av. Giráldez 199, rec. as the best in town. *Bianca* (opposite *Hotel Prince*) is good, as is *Saloon. Caramba,* good for barbecues. *Marisquería Mar Azul,* Ancash 578, excellent cheap seafood, opened 1986. Street vendors sell delicious apple turnovers, and other delights, for about US$0.10. On Calle Real are *Santa Rosa, La Caravana,* for barbecued chicken and the *Panadería-Pastelería Imperial,* all rec. *Chifa Perú,* Puno 518, good and cheap; *Chifa Porvenir,* Jirón Real 417, clean, reasonable. *Restaurant Florida,* Calle Ayacucho, reasonable, good for fish; *Comedor Vegetariano,* cheap. Also vegetarian *Hare Krishna.* Calle Real 356, cheap, good, clean, friendly. *Koky's,* Av. Huancavelica 109, English-speaking owners Adán and Gladys Camargo, good drinks, food, music, friendly, 10% discount to "South American Handbook" owners, information on sightseeing and travel, rec. *José Antonio,* Av. Cuzco, average. Excellent pastries at *Chalet Suizo,* Huancas 473, closed Mon.

Peruvian-North American Cultural Institute, Jirón Guido 740. Intensive Spanish courses, 1, 2 or 4 weeks living with Indian families in villages or Huancayo, organized by Luis Hurtado and Beverly Stuart (see below).

Museum at the Salesian school has over 5,000 pieces, including a large collection of jungle birds, animals and butterflies, insects, reptiles and fossils.

Country Club (very rural) is open to all, in very pleasant surroundings near the Mantaro River, to the north of town.

Crafts Craft market, Calle Piura, behind the Municipalidad, open every day, good but smelly, also sellers along Calle Real in the evening. Visit Kamaq Maki, Centro Regional de Artesanías (the best craft centre in the area), Jirón Brasilia 200 in San Carlos, about 2 km. from centre, an artesans' cooperative (formerly the workshop of Sra. Francisca Mayer), selling woven goods, ceramics, carved gourds and much more; open Mon.-Fri., 0800-1200, 1400-1730, Sat.-Sun., 1500-1700. Take minibus 5, 6, 13 to corner of San Carlos with P. Aurora, then walk. Woven goods available from Arequipa 463. For carved gourds visit Hermanos Leoncio y Pedro Veli Alfaro, Cochas Chicas, Km. 9, also Florencio Sanabria Osores, excellent quality, high prices, Huancayo (Apartado 402); and Nicanor Sanabria Osores, Cochas Grandes, Km. 10, Huancayo (see under Excursions below). Also visit Izcuchaca, 3-4 hrs. from Huancayo by train or truck to see pottery made. Hotel in main square, F, basic. Back-strap weaving of beautiful *fajas* (belts) can also be seen at Víquez, on the road past Wari-Wilka, 1½ hrs. S of Huancayo by colectivo from near the Mercado Modelo.

Discotheques *El Molino,* Calle Huancas, good; *El Dorado* (more Peruvian), *San Diego,* off Tambo (less good). In El Tambo district, three together, *Alpha 2001, El Infinito, El Rincón de los Recuerdos* ("boring romantic music and oldies").

Exchange Banco de los Andes, near main plaza. For travellers' cheques, Sr. Miguel Velit, Calle Real 552, or Sr. Jung (*Chalet Suizo,* no commission).

Tourist Information Foptur information office, Concejo Provincial, 1st floor, Plaza de Armas, very helpful. Huancayo Tours, Calle Real 543, organize tours of the surrounding countryside with English-speaking guides; they handle AeroPerú and AeroPerú. Emturce, Ancash 475, good service. Touring y Automóvil Club del Perú, Calle Ancash 603. Luis Hurtado (see next page) also gives information at his house; if he's on tour, his New Zealand wife Beverly will help. He has maps, photographs of local crafts, slide shows every Sunday, 1900, and travellers may use his phone for national or international calls.

Rail Train to Huancavelica narrow guage 3 ft., daily except Sun., *autovagón* US$2.30, 3½ hrs. 0700 and 1330, tickets from 0600, make sure to get off at second (smaller) station in Huancavelica (Sub Estación), since it is closer to Plaza; ordinary trains leave every day except Sun. 0730 (6½ hrs.). Both leave from Chilca station, which is not the station for Lima. Train from Huancayo to Lima 0700 daily except Sun., 9-12 hrs., 1st class US$4.20, 2nd class US$3.50, lunches in 1st class and buffet, US$1.50 (arrive early to ensure getting a seat, best on right hand side), 1st class and buffet are bookable one day in advance for US$0.50 extra; ticket office open 1000-1200, 1430-1700.

Road Transport Bus to Lima, Etucsa—not recommended although their terminal does have a waiting room (several daily, US$4, 10 hrs.) Mariscal Cáceres (US$5, 8 hrs.), and other lines. Comité 30 and 22 colectivo to Lima, Av. Loreto 351, five a day, US$9, 5-7 hrs. (takes 5 passengers); also Comité 12 (Calle Montevideo 736, T 271283, Lima; Loreto 425, Huancayo), with services to Huanta. N.B. A new road to Lima is under construction, which will shorten the journey time. There is only one morning bus to Ayacucho (Empresa Ayacucho, 0700, not every day, US$5.50, 16-19 hrs.); evening buses go via Pampa; they are run by Molina (1700 and 1800, book in advance), Empresa Ayacucho (1800, 1830) and Etucsa (not rec.) Mon., Wed., Fri. 1630, US$4.50, 12 hrs. if weather is good; if not can be 20 hrs., bus waits until daylight to cross pass. Colectivo to Ayacucho, US$20 p.p. (Comité 30). Daily bus with Nor Oriente (Calle Huancavelica) to Cerro de Pasco and Huánuco at 1500; same company Mon., Wed., Fri., to Tingo María and Pucallpa at 1600. Ucayali bus company for Huánuco, Loreto 973. Direct buses to Tarma (**see page 828**; the departure point for La Merced) twice daily, US$2.40. Note: Huancayo and other towns in the area have a *fiesta* in January when it is impossible to get a colectivo to Ayacucho and buses are fully booked. If driving to Ayacucho, be careful with direction. Only three signposts, all to totally unknown villages.

Buses to Cuzco can be something of a problem; get a seat on a truck if stuck, lovely scenery. This road is often closed during wet season or the journey can take up to three days. Book as far ahead as possible, as buses tend to be heavily overbooked. They also frequently break down. Trucks are cheaper and offer better views—but take blankets against the cold on the mountains. The trip gives a fine view of the Sierra; one passes the site of the last battle against the Spaniards, near Ayacucho, some distance before Abancay one passes a bridge built by the Spaniards. The canyon of the Río Tomás is recommended for a visit. Those who have made this journey describe it as one of the most beautiful in Peru, but the road may be closed if guerrillas are active in the Ayacucho area. As long as you do not leave the main road to visit more remote villages, or take photographs, there should be no problem—apart from finding transport—travelling from Huancayo to Ayacucho and Cuzco.

Air There is one flight a week to Lima, Mon. 0700.

Excursions W of Huancayo, past Chupaca (good Sat. market) and between Pilcomayo and Huayo is the Geophysical Institute of Huayo on the "Magnetic Equator" (12½° S of the geographical equator). Here meteorological, seismic and cosmic-ray observations are made. Six km. (standard taxi fare US$1.50) S of Huancayo the shrine of Wari-Willka (written "Warivilka" on buses), of the Huanca tribe of Inca times, has been reconstructed in a corner of the main plaza of *Wari* (often written ''Huari''). Bus to Wari from Calle Real, US$0.10. Museum in the plaza, of deformed skulls, and modelled and painted pottery of successive Huanca and Inca occupations of the shrine. Open 1000-1200 and 1500-1700, US$0.15 admission. *Hotel Central*, G, good; *Hotel Sol*, G. Take a minibus to Cerrito de la Libertad, walk up hill to Torre Torre to see impressive eroded sandstone towers on the hillside (beware of begging children on the way up). Not far from here is a large park with a depressing zoo but also a beautiful, clean swimming pool (US$0.10, showers and changing rooms).

Another interesting excursion is to Cochas Chicas (beautiful views of Valle de Mantaro) or Cochas Grandes, where gourds are carved, highly recommended. Buses leave Huancayo every ½ hr. from Church of the Immaculate Conception, for 9 km. journey. In the hills beyond Cochas back-strap weaving of *mantas* for carrying babies can be seen. S of Huancayo by colectivo from near the Mercado Modelo. There is a beautiful drive to **Cañete (see page 774**; the road crosses mountain landscape before following the Cañete river basin with its spectacular gorges (see the Instituto Geográfico Militar map). No bus service, trucks only.

Lucho (Luis) Hurtado (to whom thanks for much useful information) at Huancas 209, San Carlos (Apartado Postal 510, Huancayo, T 22-23-95), organizes 5-day and 7-day excursions, using local transport, to Indian villages in the low-lying jungle, with the possibility of living with the Indians, or to his father's farm near Chanchamayo in the high *selva*. He also organizes walking trips of 3 or more days into the mountains, to live with Indians. Trips cost about US$20 a day. Students can also study weaving, the pan flute and Peruvian cooking. He has been highly and repeatedly recommended as a guide. Contact him only at his home (impersonators have been operating). He is English-speaking, has a New Zealand wife, and takes groups of between two and eight people. Take old tennis shoes or something similar for walking in rivers; no other equipment necessary.

22 km. NW of Huancayo is the village of *Concepción* (3,251 metres), which has a market on Sun. as well as a colourful bullfight later in the day during the season. Colectivos to Concepción from near *Hotel Turistas*, US$0.50, 30 mins. Other hotels, *El Paisanito*, 9 de Julio 641, G, clean; *Royal*, on Plaza, warm shower, G, pleasant; *Hotel Huaychulo* is near Concepción and a 2 hr. walk from Ingenio where there is a government trout farm; good restaurants, especially for pastries. From Concepción a branch road (5 km.) leads to the Convent of Santa Rosa de Ocopa, a Franciscan monastery in beautiful surroundings established in 1724 for training missionaries for the jungle, open 1000-1200 and 1500-1700; closed Tues. Tour costs US$0.65 (students US$0.25). It contains a fine library with over 20,000 volumes and a biological museum with animals and insects from the jungle. The convent has a guesthouse, US$2.50 each, hot water. There is also a good restaurant. Bus from Huancayo (change at Concepción) takes 1½ hrs., US$0.35. Near Concepción is the village of *San Jerónimo*, renowned for the making of silver filigree jewellery (Wednesday market). The work of Sra. Nelly Vásquez, Calle Arequipa, 2 blocks from the Plaza de Armas, is particularly recommended; opposite is Sra. Porras, who also produces good pieces. Its fiesta is in August. There are ruins 2-3 hrs. walk above San Jerónimo, but the hike is dangerous in places. Buses from Plaza Amazonas, Huancayo, US$0.10. 45 mins'. walk from San Jerónimo is Hualhuas where beautiful tapestries of alpaca and sheeps' wool are made on rustic looms. (Luis Hurtado arranges day tours to these places, US$3 p.p., not incl. transport and food.)

18 km. beyond Concepción, on the road to La Oroya, is the old town of *Jauja* (3,552 metres), Pizarro's provisional capital until the founding of Lima, where an interesting festival (San Fermín and San Fabián) begins on January 20 and lasts several days, enjoyable (but lone tourists should be careful). Also, a very colourful Wed. and Sun. market. Jauja is a friendly, unspoilt town, in the middle of a good area for walking, with ruins near a lake 3½ km. away. It has the best archaelogical museum in the Mantaro valley for the Wari culture. A modernised church retains 3 fine 17th-century altars. The Cristo Pobre church is claimed to have been modelled after Notre Dame and is something of a curiosity. On a hill above Jauja there is a fine line of Inca storehouses, and on hills nearby ruins of hundreds of circular stone buildings from the Huanca culture (John Hemming). Bus from Huancayo, US$0.50, many daily, also colectivos (US$1). (*Hotel Jauja* and *Hotel Pizarro*, both E; *Hostal Santa Rosa*, on the square, F, some rooms with bath, poor water supply, restaurant, and on north side, *Turistas*, E, near pleasant Laguna de Paca.) Wood carving is practised in the nearby town of Molinas. At Aco, 1½ hrs. walk from Mito on road to Jauja, large ceramic pots are made, take fruit as a gift if you do not intend to buy. The road to Satipo branches off near the Convento de

Sta. Rosa de Ocopa; the village of Paca (2 km. further on) is very pleasant; easy to catch a taxi to Jauja; spectacular scenery, snow-capped mountains in the Paso de la Tortuga, followed by a rapid drop to the Caja de Silva in Satipo. (**See page 829**.)

Huancavelica, capital of its Department (altitude, 3,680 metres; population, 37,500), a friendly and attractive town, was founded over 400 years ago by the Spanish to exploit rich deposits of mercury and silver; it is predominantly an Indian town, and is still a major centre for mining. It is possible to visit the old mercury mine on the hill above the town—a stiff walk, or hire a car. There are beautiful mountain walks in the neighbourhood. The cathedral, located on the Plaza de Armas, has an altar considered to be one of the finest examples of colonial art in Peru. Also very impressive are the five other churches in town: the church of San Francisco has no less than 11 altars. (Sadly most of the churches are closed to visitors.) Lectures on precolumbian history and archaeology are given in the museum, 2nd floor.

Bisecting the town is the Huancavelica River. South of the river is the main commercial centre where fine leather and alpaca products can be purchased (especially on Calle Virrey Toledo). North of the river on the hillside are the thermal baths (US$0.15). There is a daily market. At the Sunday market, the men wear all black, with multicoloured woollen pom-poms dangling from their skullcaps, waists and knees; these are also used to decorate the livestock.

Hotels *Turistas,* D, for room with private bath, reasonable; *Perú,* near railway station, G, clean, good; *San Francisco,* G, basic; *Savoy,* G, clean rooms, adequate bathrooms, but not safe for women alone; *Tahuantinsuyo* near Plaza de Armas, F, clean and well maintained; *Santo Domingo,* F; *alojamiento* at Santa Inés. Little water in cheaper hotels in evenings.

Restaurants *Hotel de Turistas,* food is expensive and only fair. *El Padrino,* expensive, not rec. *Olímpica,* Virrey Toledo 303, good and cheap; good *chifa* in main street; *Cynthia,* cheap; *Fidel. Snake Bar Joy,* also *Ganso de Oro.*

Tourist Office In Correo building on Plaza da Armas, go up stairs from an entrance on the left-hand side of the building.

Transport Daily (except Sun.) to Huancayo (146 km.) are one train (0730, 7 hrs.) and two *autovagones* (US$2.30, 0700 and 1300, 3½ hrs.), and buses (7 hrs. Expreso Huancavelica leaves at 1700, Hidalgo, 0600 and 1500, US$2.50); sit on the right side for the best views. To Lima via Huancayo, US$5.75 (Expreso Huancavelica, 1700). To Pisco (267 km.), buses only, daily, US$7, 14 hrs. (Oropesa service leaves at 0600, but be there by 0530 to get a seat, tickets can be bought the day before); route is via Santa Inés (4,020 metres), where there are ten restaurants. Half-an-hour's walk from Santa Inés are Lakes Choclococha and Orcococha, where llama herds can be seen; beautiful views; be prepared for sub-zero temperatures a.m. as bus passes snowfields, then for temperatures of 25-30°C as bus descends to coast p.m.

Getting to Ayacucho (296 km.) is a problem particularly in the rainy season. Take a bus (Oropesa) to Santa Inés, 0600, 4 hrs., US$2.20, then catch the Ormeño bus from Lima (Santa Inés-Ayacucho, 8 hrs., US$3). Alternatively catch a pick-up truck to Pilpichaca, via Santa Inés, 1330-1730, US$1.50, then a truck from Pilpichaca to Ayacucho, 2000 to 0500, US$2, very cold. The road (very bad) is the highest continuous road in the world, rarely dropping below 4,000 metres for 150 km. Out of Huancavelica one climbs steeply on a road that switchbacks between herds of llamas and alpacas grazing on rocky perches. Around Pucapampa (km. 43) is one of the highest habitable *altiplanos* (4,500 metres), where the rare and highly prized ash-grey alpaca can be seen. 50 km. beyond Santa Inés, the rocks are all colours of the rainbow, and running through this fabulous scenery is a violet river (all caused by oxides). Eleven km. later one encounters Paso Chonta (4,850 metres) and the turnoff to Huachocolpa. By taking the turnoff and continuing for 3 km. one discovers the highest drivable pass (5,059 metres) in the world. Continuing on to Ayacucho one passes some very cold, fish-filled lakes before the road branches to Pisco at km. 77. Seventy km. later the high (4,750 metres) Abra Apachenta is reached, leaving a 98-km. descent into Ayacucho.

Ayacucho, capital of its Department, was founded on January 9, 1539. This old colonial city is built round Parque Sucre with the Cathedral, City Hall and Government Palace facing on to it. The city is famous for its religious processions and its splendid market. There are no less than 33 churches—some long deserted and most closed—and a number of ruined colonial mansions. A week can be spent there and in the surroundings, which include La Quinua, site of the battle of Ayacucho, December 9, 1824, which brought Spanish rule to an end in Peru. Ayacucho has a very active student life. Altitude: 2,440 metres, with gently rolling hills around. A 364-km. road has been built to Pisco on the coast. Population: 75,000.

Visitors are advised to see the 17th century Cathedral (with Museum of Religious Art, closed indefinitely) and churches of San Francisco de Asís, La Compañía de Jesús, Santa Clara, Santo Domingo, and Santa Teresa, all with magnificent gold-leafed altars heavily brocaded and carved in the churrigueresque style. There is a small but surprising Museo Histórico Regional, in the Centro Cultural Simón Bolívar, at the outskirts of town, US$0.35 (many Huari artifacts). Tombs of the Huari nobles are being excavated along the road from Ayacucho to Quinua. The University, founded 1677, closed 1886, was reopened in 1958.

Festivals Semana Santa begins on the Friday before Holy Week with the procession of the Virgen de los Dolores (very beautiful, but the suffering is "symbolised" by the custom of flinging pebbles from slingshots, aimed mainly at youngsters, but also foreigners). A charming Palm Sunday procession, beginning at 1600, of palm-bearing women and children accompanies a statue of Christ riding on a white donkey. There follows one of the world's finest Holy Week celebrations, with candle-lit nightly processions, floral "paintings" on the streets, daily fairs (the biggest on Easter Saturday), horse races and contests among peoples from all central Peru.

Warning Because of guerrilla (Sendero Luminoso) activity in this region, visitors are advised to seek information in advance and check whether a curfew is in force. Entry into the area has on occasion been prohibited for visitors and it is unwise to go outside the city at night.

N.B. Beware of thieves, even in the AeroPerú office.

Hotels *Turistas*, 9 de Diciembre, E, with bath, comfortable (meals, US$3.20, mediocre); *Colmena*, Jirón Cusco 140, just of Plaza de Armas, F, a beautiful building, nice rooms with table, wardrobe, no hot water, not secure, noisy, good restaurant below; *Samari*, Jirón Callao, F, with toilet, very clean, friendly, rec.; *Hostelería Santa Rosa*, Jirón Lima 140, F, with bath, hot water mornings and evenings, friendly, car park, restaurant, rec. *Imperio*, Plaza de Armas, F, 4-bedded rooms; *Wari*, G, hot showers, clean and friendly; *Ayacucho*, just off the Plaza, G, cheap, with shower, basic; *Crillonesa*, near market, G, hot showers, clean, good value; *Magdalena*, F, next to Etucsa bus station, clean, hot water; *Santiago*, near market (1½ blocks from Hidalgo bus), F, rec. *La Sixtina*, Jirón Callao, F, basic but friendly, clean, clothes washing facilities; and the private home of Sra. Ayala de Ruiz, Libertad 539, hot water, laundry facilities, personal attention. It is extremely difficult to find accommodation at Easter.

Restaurants *La Fortaleza*, Lima 169, 3 courses for US$1.20, very good coffee, reasonable meals; *Chalán*, on same street but not as good; *Clarita*, Jirón Grau 221, cheap, clean, good; good coffee and cakes at *El Turco*; *Tradicional*, San Martín 406, popular, good variety and value; *San Agustín Café Turístico*, Plaza de Armas, good food and lemon meringue pie; *El Alamo* (next to *Hotel Colmena*), reasonable, folk music some evenings, and *El Agullo de Oro* for fish. *Tradición*, Vivanco, rec.; *La Casona* behind *Turistas*, rec. Many good small cafés, one inside University buildings; *Cevichería* on block 500 of Grau, behind market, good fish dishes. On the Plaza, *Savory* café and *Los Portales* are good (live, local music at the latter). The airport offers a good breakfast. Try mondongo, a soup made from meat, maize and mint, also ponche, a hot drink made of peanuts, coconut and cinnamon.

Handicrafts Local craftsmen produce filigree silver, often using *mudéjar* patterns; others make little painted altars which show the manger scene, make carvings in local alabaster, manufacture harps, or carry on the pre-Inca tradition of carving dried gourds. However, the most famous goods are carpets and *retablos*. Best quality woven carpets can be bought in the Santa Ana district where you can watch them being made. Edwin Sulca Lagos, Plaza Santa Ana 82, offers weaving courses. His family are internationally renowned and his rugs sell for at least US$90; only natural colours are used. Other weavers are Gerardo Fernández Palomino, Jr. París 105, Santa Ana, Pomataylla on same street and Saturino Oncebay, same street (No. 60). *Retablos* are wooden boxes containing three-dimensional scenes in papier maché; the Jiménez family in Santa Ana, or César Urbano Ch., Av. Perú 308-318, La Libertad, are worth seeking out. In both weaving and *retablos*, scenes of recent political strife have been added to more traditional motifs.

Sport There are public tennis courts in Ayacucho, and games may be booked at the police station.

Exchange Ayacucho Tours. Try *Hotel de Turistas*, *Hostelería Santa Rosa* (good rates), AeroPerú, Morocucho Tours (Plaza de Armas).

Tourist Information Foptur, Portal Municipal 46, on Plaza de Armas next to church, good information, friendly. Also available from Ayacucho Tours, San Martín 406, near market, or from the AeroPerú office (Plaza de Armas, changes US$). State Tourist Information Office, Asamblea 138, has good free leaflets on Ayacucho.

Air To Lima by AeroPerú, 35 minutes, daily at 0720, US$23; no flights Ayacucho-Cuzco; must go via Lima. Much military scrutiny at airport. In the rainy season expect cancellations. Taxi to airport, US$0.50 p.p., buses from 0600 from Plaza de Armas.

Buses Bus Ayacucho-Huancayo, none by day; via Pampas, Etucsa, 16 hrs., US$ 4.50, very cold and uncomfortable. Ordinary bus goes at night (1500 and 1800 daily), no wc on board; Ayacucho Transport, Etucsa and Molina, Calle Grau, do the journey. Bus to Pisco (and Ica), US$7.80 with Ormeño (Jr. Libertad 257), 12-13 hrs.; and to Lima (1300, 1900), US$10.75, also Hidalgo (San Martín 330), at least once a day. Only one bus a week (Hidalgo on Mon.) to Cuzco, 30 hrs.; alternative is to take Ayacucho-Andahuaylas bus (Molina, 19 hrs. daily at 0900, US$6, beautiful scenery) and change in Andahuaylas for Cuzco. Colectivo may be possible.

Excursions Inca ruins at *Vilcashuamán*, to the S, beyond Cangallo; "there is a five-tiered, stepped *usnu* platform faced in fine Inca masonry and topped by a monolithic two-seat throne. The parish church is built in part of the Inca sun temple and rests on stretches of Inca terracing. Vilcashuamán was an important provincial capital, the crossroads where the road from Cuzco to the Pacific met the empire's north-south highway" (John Hemming). Taxi trips can be arranged with Ayacucho Tours and Morocucho Tours, US$30 p.p., alternatively stay overnight; market day is Wed. A good road going N from Ayacucho (trucks from Calle Salvador Calvero) leads to Wari (**see page 824 Huari**), dating from the "Middle Horizon", when the Huari culture spread across most of Peru (US$0.50 by public transport). Trips can be arranged by Ayacucho Tours, rec., who do a tour to Wari, La Quinua village and battlefield for about US$4.65. *La Quinua* village has a charming cobbled main square and many of the buildings have been restored; there is a small market on Suns. There is a huge obelisk to commemorate the battle of Ayacucho. Handicrafts are recommended, guitars and, especially, ceramics; most houses have miniature ceramic churches on the roof. San Pedro Ceramics, at foot of hill leading to monument, and Mamerto Sánchez, Jr. Sucre should be visited. The village's festival is celebrated around October 7-8, lasting 3 days. Beautiful 18 km. walk downhill from La Quinua to Wari, where trucks leave for Ayacucho until about 1700.

San Francisco in the jungle on the Apurímac River (3 basic hotels, *Suria*, E, the best but dirty) can be reached by bus from Ayacucho (junction of Av. Centenario and Av. Cavero) on Sat. (return Mon.), 10-12 hrs. on a very bad road often impassable in the wet season (very cold at night). Trucks travel daily leaving at about 0700 (wait at police control near airport), US$5 in driver's cabin, US$3 on back, or private cars, twice the price, bargain hard. From San Francisco you can take a morning canoe to *Luisiana*, about 2 hrs. upstream, to stay in Sr. Parodi's *Jungle Hotel*, Centro Vacacional de Luisiana, with swimming pool, C, on his large *hacienda*; trips are organized in the jungle but it is only open for 3 months in the dry season and Sr. Parodi is not always there. There is an airstrip at Luisiana with daily connections to Ayacucho, for over five passengers, US$29 single. Details in the Ayacucho Tourist Office. From San Francisco you can make excursions to nearby villages on cargo canoes, but it is very difficult to find transport all the way to Pucallpa unless you have a large group of people and are willing to pay handsomely.

From Ayacucho to Cuzco (Because of guerrilla activity and army counter-measures, public transport is scarcer than it used to be, but travellers will be allowed through if they do not stray from the main road and do not take photographs.) The road to Cuzco goes through *Andahuaylas*, in a fertile, temperate valley of lush meadows, cornfields and groves of eucalyptus, alders and willows. It offers few exotic crafts, no comfortable accommodation (you must register with the army as a condition for getting into a hotel), poor transport, but beautiful, largely undiscovered scenery. Buses (daily) stop between 2100 and 0530 if there is a curfew (very cold on board). No direct buses Andahuaylas-Cuzco; you must take a colectivo to Abancay, then a bus to Cuzco. The road crosses three mountain ranges and is very rough in places but is definitely worthwhile. *Abancay* is first glimpsed when you are 62 km. away by road, nestled between mountains in the upper reaches of a glacial valley (registration with army required, as at Andahuaylas). From Abancay a 470 km. road runs SW through Chalhuanca and Puquío to Nazca on the Pan-American Highway (**see page 780**).

Trucks and buses leave Andahuaylas for Abancay at 0630-0700, take 8 hrs., US$3. There is one Hidalgo bus a week from Ayacucho to Cuzco (Mon. 0800), US$15 (always overbooked); should take 24 hrs. but can take 3 days. The road is appalling in the rainy season. Sit on the left for best views. The bus is difficult to get on; people have been stuck in Ayacucho for days. Book at least 2 days in advance for a seat on the bus from Ayacucho to Cuzco or Andahuaylas; in the high season you have to wait and see if there is a spare seat. Buses from Abancay to Cuzco leave 0500, 0700, and 1400, US$4.55 (196 km., 12 hrs.), minibus from near the market takes 7 hours to Cuzco, leaving 1200, US$5.35, colectivos also leave around 0800, arriving 1700, dramatic scenery especially in Apurímac valley, but most of the road between Abancay and Cuzco is very bad. See page 810 for sites of interest between Abancay and Cuzco, 10 hrs. Abancay to Machu-Picchu: take a truck to Izcuchaca (US$1.75) where the train can be caught to Machu-Picchu.

Andahuaylas Hotels *Turistas*, Jirón Dias Bárcenas 500, D with bath (E without), meals US$3 extra (no money exchange or credit cards accepted); *Gran*, Plaza de Armas, G, basic, and *Restaurant Las Palmeras*, meal for US$0.25, is possible; *Hermanos Chipuna*, G, basic, near bus station; *Delicias*, G, hot showers, basic but rec., only 7 rooms, ask for extra blankets, cold at night; *28 de Julio*, cheap, G, adequate.

Abancay Hotels Discrimination against foreigners reported. *Turistas*, D, with bath, food good, US$3, comfortable, old-fashioned house, safe car park, camping permitted at US$3; *Hostal Gran*

Hotel, F, with bath, clean; *Abancay*, F; *El Misti*, F, fair. *Alojamiento Centenario*, F. **Restaurant:** *Elena*, almost opp. *Hostal Grau*, good, plentiful and cheap portions.

Ronald Berg, of Cambridge, Mass., writes: Around Andahuaylas the old road by the river to Talavera offers some pleasant scenery. San Jerónimo is another picturesque town nearby. Most worth seeing is Pacucha, an hour's ride by truck from Andahuaylas. Pick-ups leave from the centre of Andahuaylas daily, most frequently on Sun., which is market day. Pacucha (pop. 2,000) is the largest of six villages on the shores of a large scenic lake, with a view of mountains to the NW. In the plaza, where the trucks stop, women sell bread, coffee and hot lunches, the only food for 16 km. There are dirt roads around the lake and the circumference can be done in an afternoon (but be back in Pacucha before dark to ensure transport back to Andahuaylas). The wildlife includes many types of wild duck and other birds, sometimes including flocks of green parrots and swallows. Opposite Pacucha, some 2km. past the lake, are the ruins of a Chanka fortress called Zondor. The trails into the jungle beyond the lake are not recommended: the area is very desolate. Except for Andahuaylas itself, this is a mainly Quechua-speaking region. It is one of the poorest parts of Peru, but as long as you do not display your wealth or eat in public, the people tend to be friendly to foreigners.

East of La Oroya   The 60-km. surfaced road to Tarma follows the Cerro de Pasco road for 25 km., then branches off to rejoin the old road quite near Tarma, which is 600 metres lower than La Oroya.

Tarma, population 105,200; altitude 3,050 metres, was a nice little flat-roofed town, founded in 1545, with plenty of trees. It is now growing, and there are garish modern buildings, but it still has a lot of charm. It has a very colourful Easter Sunday morning procession in main plaza; Indians make fine flower-carpets. The surrounding countryside is beautiful.

Hotels   *Turistas*, D, with and without bath, acceptable meals US$3.20, rather run down; *Plaza*; *Vargas*; *Ritz*; *Acahuantinsuyo*, G, basic; *Gran Hotel El Dorado*, E, with bath, warm water in a.m., secure; *América*, opp. market, F, clean and friendly but noisy; *Galaxia*, on square, E, with bath, modern, highly rec.;

Restaurants   *Don Vale*, Jr. Callao, highly rec.; *Tradición*, Jr. Moquegua 350, also good. *Acobamba*, outside Tarma, rec.; *Chavín Café*, beneath *Galaxia* hotel, on square, trout rec. The manjarblanco of Tarma is famous.

Tourist Office Jr. Dos de Mayo 775.

An Englishman, Mr. V. J. Barnes, an authority on the area east of Oroya, would welcome visitors seeking information at his home in Lima. (T 287800).
      Direct bus service, Huancayo-Tarma, twice daily 0600 and 1600, US$2.15. Daily colectivos from Jirón Huánuco 439 run almost hourly to Huancayo, US$2.40, 2½ hrs, bus to Oroya, US$1.50, colectivo, US$1.85; bus to La Merced, US$1.45; colectivos often leave for Chanchamayo, US$2.15. Passes over high limestone hills with caves. Visit the Grutas de Huagapo, 4 km. from town of Polcamayo—bus twice daily from Tarma US$0.20. Cave guide, Modesto Castro, lives opposite caves and is a mine of information. The precolumbian ruins of Tarmatamba, Shoguemarca, Yanamarca, Huayipirca, Cachicachi, Pichgamarca and Huancoy also lie nearby.

Eight km. from Tarma, the small hillside town of *Acobamba* has the futuristic Santuario de Muruhuay, with a venerated picture painted on the rock behind the altar. Festivities all May.

Dr. David Snashall writes: A road from Tarma via Acobamba goes through the village of Polcamayo to the Gruta de Huagapo (*"la boca que llora"*: the cave that weeps). Even without a guide you can penetrate the cave for some way with a torch. The road continues from Polcamayo (no buses, 3-hr. walk) to *San Pedro de Cajas*, a large village whence most of the coloured sheep-wool weavings for sale in Lima come. You can buy them here for half the price from the weavers themselves. 2 restaurants; no shops. The road continues on to rejoin the one from La Oroya to Cerro de Pasco below Junín.

Hotels   *Oskanoa* in San Pedro de Cajas, F, basic but friendly. Two *alojamientos* (Doña Norma's near plaza, G, is basic but clean and friendly). Daily buses to Tarma, La Oroya (US$0.50) and Huancayo; 3 buses a week direct to Lima (Coop. San Pedro).

Beyond Tarma the road is steep and crooked but there are few places where cars cannot pass one another. In the 80 km. between Tarma and La Merced the road, passing by great overhanging cliffs, drops 2,450 metres and the vegetation changes dramatically from temperate to tropical. A really beautiful run.

Some 11 km. before La Merced is **San Ramón** (population 7,000). Ask at the airport about journey to Pampasilva and Puerto Ubirique (see below).

Hotels   *Chanchamayo*, fairly cheap, *Selva*. *Conquistador*, E, with shower, parking, on main street. There is a rec. *chifa* on the main street, and the *Hawaii* is good for juices. *La Estancia*, Tarma 592, local specialities.

La Merced, population 10,000, lies in the fertile Chanchamayo valley. Sometimes Campa Indians come to town selling bows and arrows, and there is a small but interesting market selling snake skins, hides, armadillo shells, etc. Festival in the last week of September.

Hotels   *Rey* and *Christina*, good, E, with bath; *San Felipe*, F, dirty; *Chuncho*, basic; *Cosmos*, opp. police station, E, fair, probably quieter than others; *Hostal Mercedes*, F, with bath, hot water, clean, rec.; *Romero*, Plaza de Armas, T 2106, F, good but noisy and water in evenings only. Best **restaurant** is *Shambari-Campa*, off Plaza de Armas; *Hong Kong*, restaurant; plenty of bars patronized by the coffee workers, who spend 6 months in the mountains each year.

Note that San Ramón and La Merced are collectively referred to as *Chanchamayo*. Many buses, both from Lima (e.g. Transportes Chanchamayo, best; Av. Luna Pizarro 453, La Victoria, Lima; Los Andes, Arellano, good, 10 hrs., US$4.85) and from Tarma (US$1.45, 3 hrs.). Bus La Merced-Puerto Bermúdez, 8 hrs., US$4, 1000 (Túpac Amaru). To get to Pucallpa, take a launch from Puerto Bermúdez to Laurencia (8 hrs., or more, US$4.50, be prepared for wet luggage), then truck to Constitución, 20 mins., thence colectivo to Zungaro, 1½ hrs., US$2. From Zunzaro, colectivos take 4½ hrs., to Pucallpa, US$3. Alternatively, you can take a truck from La Merced to Pucallpa, 3 days, but between 0830 and 1400 each day you will probably be drenched by rain.

From La Merced you can take the Carretera Marginal de la Selva (a grandiose edge-of-the-jungle project of the mid-1960s, of which some parts have been built) to the jungle town of **Satipo** (Lobato or Los Andes buses from La Merced US$4.50 at 0800; *Hostal Majestic*, D, with bath, no clothes-washing facilities, electricity 1900-2300 only; many smaller hotels, all very basic, the best being *Palmero*, E, with bath, not very clean. Try *Dany's Restaurant*, surprisingly good food for such an out-of-the-way place). A beautiful trip. Halfway between La Merced and Satipo is Pichinaki, which has a good hotel, F, ideal for breaking one's journey (bus La Merced-Pichinaki, US$2.15). There are daily buses direct from Satipo to Huancayo (check whether tunnels are open) and Lima at night, very cold, US$6, 12 hrs., Los Andes and Lobato, so no need to return from Satipo via La Merced. Satipo can also be reached from Concepción, following the Santa Rosa de Ocopa road (see page 824), and from Pucallpa by air.

About 22 km. beyond La Merced is San Luis de Shuaro, but 3 km. before it is reached a road, right, runs up the valley of the Perené river. The Perené colony, a concession of 400,000 hectares, nine-tenths of it still unexplored, has large coffee plantations. The altitude is only 700 metres. Saturday and Sunday are colourful market days for the Indians. Beyond San Luis de Shuaro a branch road runs right to Villa Rica. It is no longer possible to take motorized canoes from Pampasilva on the River Perené to Puerto Ubirique, since the building of the new road.

The road has been extended from San Luis de Shuaro over an intervening mountain range for 56 km. to **Oxapampa,** 390 km. from Lima, in a fertile plain on the Huancabamba river, a tributary of the Ucayali. Population, 5,140; altitude, 1,794 metres. Logging, coffee, cattle are local industries, colectivo service from La Merced. A third of the inhabitants are descendants of a German-Austrian community of 70 families which settled in 1859 at **Pozuzo**, 80 km. downstream, and spread later to Oxapampa. There is much livestock farming and coffee is planted on land cleared by the timber trade. 25 km. from Oxapampa is Huancabamba, from where it is 55 km. to Pozuzo; the whole road between La Merced and Pozuzo is very rough, depending on the season, 30 rivers to be crossed. Sr. Luis Orbeza's *mixto* leaves from Oxapampa, opposite *Hotel Bolívar*, to Pozuzo at 0300, returning 1200, US$4.50, Tues., Thurs., Sat. Downstream 40 km. from Pozuzo is Nuevo Pozuzo (local air service, or two-day walk); Padre Pedro has a collection of insects, weapons and stones in his office. There is a family near Padre Pedro's house who welcome guests for dinner (US$1), German spoken.

Oxapampa Hotels   *Bolívar*, basic, good restaurant; *La Isabela*, F, cheap and clean, opposite church.

Pozuzo Hotels *Hostal Tirol*, E, full board, clean, rec.; *El Oriente*, basic.

There is an "air-colectivo" service from La Merced to **Puerto Bermúdez** on the Río Neguachi, US$10.50 single, 10 kg. baggage allowance, US$5 per kg. of excess luggage. The service continues to Atalaya, Satipo, Puerto Inca (**see page 837**) and Pucallpa. Bus service, La Merced-Puerto Bermúdez (see below). Air-colectivos go to Lima and to most places in the jungle region where there is an airstrip; flights are cheap but irregular, and depend on technical factors, weather and good will. Aero-taxis can be chartered (*viaje especial*) to anywhere for a higher price, maximum five people, you have to pay for the pilot's return to base. In Puerto Bermúdez there is accommodation (*Hostal Tania*, opposite dock where motorized canoes tie up, F, clean), an eating house opposite the airstrip; boat passages possible from passing traders.

North of La Oroya A railway (also a paved road) runs 130 km. N from La Oroya to Cerro de Pasco. It runs up the Mantaro valley through narrow canyons to the wet and mournful Junín pampa at over 4,250 metres, one of the world's largest high-altitude plains: an obelisk marks the battlefield where the Peruvians under Bolívar defeated the Spaniards in 1824. Blue peaks line the pampa in a distant wall. The wind-swept sheet of yellow grass is bitterly cold. The only signs of life are the youthful herders with their sheep and llamas. The line follows the E shores of Lake Junín. The town of **Junín**, with its picturesque red-tiled roofs, stands beside its lake, whose myriads of water birds have made it famous for its shooting. At Smelter, the coal washing plant, the track branches to Goyllarisquisga, while the main line goes to the long-established mining centre of **Cerro de Pasco** (population 29,810, altitude 4,330 metres), 130 km. from La Oroya by road. It is not a pleasant town, having many beggars and thieves and much unemployment. The nights are bitterly cold. Copper, zinc, lead, gold and silver are mined here, and coal comes from the deep canyon of Goyllarisquisga, the "place where a star fell", the highest coal mine in the world, 42 km. N of Cerro de Pasco. A fine new town—San Juan de Pampa—has been built 1½ km. away (*Gran Hotel*, noisy, no hot water, poor service). A recommended excursion is to the precolumbian funeral towers at Cantamasia, reached on muleback. At Morococha (alight from train at Tuctu) is the Centromín golf course, welcoming to playing visitors, which at 4,400 metres disputes the title of the world's highest with Malasilla, near La Paz, Bolivia.

Hotels *Gran Hotel Cerro de Pasco*, Av. Angamos in San Juan suburb, E, shower, little hot water, poor service, noisy; *América*; *Centromín Hotel*, emergency only; *El Viajero*, on the plaza, F, clean but no hot water; *Santa Rosa*, F, basic, very cold; *Restaurant Los Angeles*, near market, rec. Local specialities, trout and fried frog.

Train Through tickets to Cerro de Pasco can no longer be bought at the Desamparados Station in Lima; there is no longer a connection on the same day at La Oroya. The train leaves La Oroya for Cerro de Pasco at 1330; it arrives at 1716. The return train for La Oroya leaves at 0500 from Cerro de Pasco station, which is 20 min. out of town on foot; on the return journey there should be a connection at La Oroya: the train from Cerro de Pasco arrives there at 0825 and the train for Lima leaves at 1006. The *churrasco* served for breakfast on the train is a welcome defence against the cold.

Buses Bus to Lima, departs 0830 and 2000, 9 hrs., US$5. To La Oroya, bus from Plaza Arenales, 0900 and later, US$0.75; cars go when there are passengers, US$6. To Huancayo, US$2.95. Colectivos to Huánuco, US$4.50, from the central plaza. Buses to Huánuco leave between 0800 and 0900 from Plaza de Armas (5 hrs., US$1.20). A bus, connecting with the train from Lima, to Huánuco takes 3 hrs., at night.

CERRO DE PASCO TO IQUITOS (8)

The Central Highway There are two roads from Lima to Cerro de Pasco. One goes via **Canta** (3 buses daily to and from Lima, US$2.25—El Canteño company, San Román 151-153, Lima). Two hotels and one good restaurant in Canta, from where one can visit the pre-Inca ruins of **Cantamarca**—many of the buildings still have roofs, supported by pillars; it is a 2-3 hour walk up to the ruins, from where there are extensive views. Continuing through the beautiful high pass of La Viuda (4,748 metres), one goes to the mines of Alpamarca (truck from Canta, 0200, take warm clothes, blanket, camping gear, food). From here there are 2-3 buses per week to Huallay, where there is the Bosque de Piedras (an outcrop of weathered limestone pinnacles which look from a distance like plantations of conifers). Thence to Cerro de Pasco.

The other road, the Central Highway, accompanies the Central Railway, more or less, over the Anticona Pass (4,843 metres) to La Oroya. From there it crosses the Junín pampa to Cerro de Pasco (130 km.), never far from the railway. From Cerro de Pasco it continues NE another 528 km. to Pucallpa, the limit of navigation for large Amazon river boats. The western part of this road (Cerro de Pasco-Huánuco) has been rebuilt into an all-weather highway (**see map, page 834**, for its contour). Buses run daily between Lima and Pucallpa, 847 km., taking 32 hrs., but ask about the state of the road during the rainy season from November to March, when the trip may take a week.

The sharp descent along the nascent **Huallaga River** (the road drops 2,450 metres in the 100 km. from Cerro de Pasco to Huánuco, and most of it is in the first 32 km.) is a tonic to travellers suffering from *soroche*, or altitude sickness. From the bleak vistas of the high ranges one drops below the tree line to views of great beauty. The only town of any size before Huánuco is Ambo (ask at the *dulcería* for Ricardo, who speaks English; he can arrange to take you to the beautiful village of Huacar where Sr. Tiburcio has a water-mill and distillery and keeps a small zoo).

Huánuco, on the Upper Huallaga (population: 82,240), is an attractive Andean town with an interesting market and the two old (but much restored) churches of San Cristóbal and San Francisco (16th century paintings). There is a small but interesting natural history museum at General Prado 495, called Museo de Ciencias; many of the displays have multiple language signs. Entrance, US$0.50. Watch locals catch fish from the river in their teeth! Visit ruin 5 km. on road to La Unión: Kotosh, the Temple of Crossed Hands, the earliest evidence of a complex society and of pottery in Peru (from 2000 BC). You must ford a stream to get there, and beware of the vicious black flies. The ruin has been sadly neglected since the original excavation in 1963. Main industry: sugar and rum; take Cisne bus from Jirón Ayacucho, 15 mins., in a.m. to visit Cooperativa Vichaycoto, rum for sale. Altitude 1,812 metres.

Hotels   Turistas, D, with bath, no hot water, meals US$6; *Hostal Residencial Huánuco,* Jirón Huánuco (near Plaza de Armas) T 2050, F, with bath, hot water, more expensive than others in this range but excellent value, highly rec.; *Las Vegas*, on plaza, rec., has good restaurant; *Real*, on Plaza, C, overpriced, has extensive café; *Nacional,* cheap but adequate; *Bella Durmiente,* near market square, cheap; *Cuzco,* near market, F, with bath, no hot water, expensive restaurant; *Astoria,* F, cheap and clean; *Imperial,* Ayacucho 581, F, with cold shower (intermittent water), reasonable value, clean, quiet; *Kelin,* F, clean; *La Cabaña,* F, friendly, safe but bathrooms dirty, *Internacional,* F, hot water in the common bathroom in the morning, good, clean and cheap. Hotels are often fully booked; arrive early.

Camping   Camp by river, near stadium.

Restaurants   *Las Palmeras,* good and cheap. *Tokio* and *El Imán,* off main square, both good. *El Café,* in the plaza is cheap and good. Chinese restaurant also in plaza.

Tourist Information   Foptur, General Prado 714, Plaza de Armas, opp. Post Office, T 2124. Huánuco Tours, Jirón General Prado 691.

Buses   To Lima, US$7 with León de Huánuco, 10 hrs., 3 a day in early evening, slow; colectivo to Lima, US$12.75, leaves 0400, arrives 1400; book the night before at General Prado 607, one block from the main square, rec. Etposa also runs to Lima. Daily buses to Cerro de Pasco, La Oroya and Huancayo, 0830, 1600, with Nororiente or Ucayali, Constitución 638, 11-12 hrs., US$4.60. "Mixto" Huánuco-Cerro de Pasco, half bus, half truck, departs 0400, 3 hrs., US$2.25; colectivo 1 or 12, US$ 4.50 at 0500. Frequent buses and colectivos to Tingo María, 3 hrs. (colectivo, US$2, many start from near river bridge, two blocks from main plaza). Bus to Pucallpa, US$7, La Perla del Oriente (Etopsa), 0800 and 1600, rec. 10 hrs. plus; buses make stops for meals but some of them are widely spaced; in any case it is wise to take your own food in case of breakdowns. To Huancayo, 10 hrs., US$3.

Air   Huancapallac airport, 8 km. from town; AeroPerú (office at the Tourist Hotel) flights to and from Lima, Tues. and Sun.

To the north-west of Huánuco is **Tantamayo** (3,600 metres), a farming village in the Central Sierra; it is surrounded by precolumbian ruins which can be reached on foot (3-4 hrs., guides available) called Piruru, Susupillu, Japallan, and Castilla de Selinin; pictures and information from Huánaco Post Office. Hotel: Turística, where Don Cristián Ocaña and his Swiss wife, Theresa, offer full board, D (F without food), they are very helpful, and Sra. de Ocaña speaks German, French, Italian and English. Bus from Huánuco, US$4.25, 12-14 hrs., departs 1800; returns at night. Tantamayo can also be reached by taking a truck to Tingo Chico, US$1.70, then another to Chavín de Pariarca (US$0.75) where there is a basic hotel (US$0.75 p.p.) and restaurants, then walk. This route, like the walks to the ruins, is arduous; take warm clothing, a hat, suntan lotion.

From Huánuco, a road leads to **La Unión**, capital of Dos de Mayo district a friendly town, but electricity can be a problem (it gets very cold at night); 2 buses daily between 0700 and 1000, including Acosta, 2 blocks from the market, returns to Huánuco about midnight, US$3, 8-9 hrs., truck, 10½ hrs., leaves late morning. La Unión-Tingo Chico, US$1.70. Hostal Turista and Hostal Dos de Mayo, at La Unión (G). Neither safe for left luggage. Restaurant El Danubio, near market, good home cooking, lots of garlic.

On the pampa above La Unión are the Inca ruins of **Huánuco Viejo**, a 2½ hr. walk from the town, a great temple-fortress with residential quarters. To get there, take the path starting behind the market and climb towards the cross, which is at the edge of a plateau. Continue straight through the village on the wide path (the locals are friendly, but some of their dogs are nasty); the views of the pampa, surrounded on all sides by mountains, are beautiful. Seemingly at the foot of a mountain, in front and to your right, is a silvery metalic roof of a little chapel, behind which are the ruins (about a 20-min. walk through herds of cattle). Take warm clothing and beware of thunderstorms. (Karin Kubitsch, West Germany).

Bus to Lima daily, crowded. Also possible to get to Callejón de Huaylas by taking 1600 bus to Conococha (US$3.25, 9 hrs.) and waiting there for a truck to Huarás (2-3 hrs.— **see page 745**). The wait is very cold, at 4,100 metres. La Unión-Huarás direct is very difficult because most transport does the route La Unión-Chiquián-Lima. You can take a truck from La Unión to Huansalla, then another to Pachacoto (some wait till 0100 for passengers), and from there it's 1 hr. to Huarás. The San Cristóbal bus to Lima at 1100 goes a few km. S of Catac; from there connections are easy to Huarás (1 hr.) and Chavín (via Catac). Salazar bus to Lima (3 a week at 1000-more like 1100), takes 9 hrs. To Conococha, US$4; this is supposed to connect with a Lima-Huarás bus at 1900-2000; if you miss it, hitch in the cold and dark (2 hrs., US$1.50 to Huarás). A night bus from Lima passes at 0300, but the restaurant at the Conococha crossroads closes at 2230.

The journey to Tingo María, 135 km., is very dusty but gives a good view of the jungle. Some 25 km. beyond Huánuco the road begins a sharp climb to the heights of Carpish (3,023 metres). A descent of 58 km. brings it to the Huallaga river again; it continues along the river to Tingo María. (The road is now paved from Huánaco to Tingo María, including a tunnel through the Carpish hills.) Landslides along this section are frequent and construction work causes delays.

Tingo María is on the middle Huallaga, in the Ceja de Montaña, or edge of the mountains, isolated for days in rainy season. Climate tropical; annual rainfall 2,642 mm. Population, about 20,560 and very mixed. The altitude (655 metres) prevents the climate from being oppressive. The Cordillera Azul, the front range of the Andes, covered with jungle-like vegetation to its top, separates it from the jungle lowlands to the E. The mountain which can be seen from all over the town is called La Bella Durmiente, the Sleeping Beauty. The meeting here of Sierra and Selva makes the landscape extremely striking. Bananas, sugar cane, cocoa, rubber, tea and coffee are grown. The main crop of the area, though, is coca, grown on the chacras (smallholdings) in the countryside, and sold legitimately and otherwise in Tingo María—there have been several shoot-outs between the police and the drug entrepreneurs. As in many other places in Peru, watch out for gangs of thieves around the buses and do not leave luggage on the bus if you get off. A small university outside the town, beyond the Hotel Turistas, has a little museum-cum-zoo, with animals of that zone, and botanical gardens in the town, entrance free but a small tip would help to keep things in order. 6½ km. from Tingo is a fascinating cave, the Cueva de las Lechuzas, reached by car via the new bridge (or colectivo from garage, US$0.80); take a torch, and do not wear open shoes; the Cave can be reached by boat when the river is high. There are many nocturnal parrots in the cave and many small parakeets near the entrance. 13 km. from Tingo is the small gorge known as Cueva de las Pavas (no caves or turkeys, but good swimming).

Hotels   Turistas, D, with and without bath, meals US$6 extra, including taxes, very good, swimming pool US$0.75, some way out of town; *Viena*, F, good value with private bathrooms, clean, near *Café Rex*; *Royal*, E, bed and private showers; *Marco Antonio*, E, clean, laundry service; *Imperial*, E, with bath, pleasant; *La Cabaña*, G, the cheapest, tolerably clean, good restaurant; *Cuzco*, G, clean and good; *Raimundo*, G (not to be confused with *Raimondi*, which is dirty, flea-ridden, and not rec.); *Palacio*, G, shower, but basic and not very clean; *Gran Hotel*, G. Hotels are often fully-booked. Rooms available at Av. Benavides 263, F, also meals; *Pensión* at Jr. Monzón 284, with 3 meals a day for US$ 1.50.

Restaurants *Pensión González*, expensive, but nice setting; *Café Rex*, Avenida Raimondi 500, cakes and ice cream, but rather run down; *Gran Chifa Oriental*, Chinese restaurant, on main street, cheap. Also 2 other restaurants of the same name elsewhere in the town— beware, they're not so good. Restaurant at *La Cabaña Hotel* good.

Transport Flights from Tingo María to Lima and Pucallpa. Normally 5 to 6 flights a week to Tingo María by Faucett and AeroPerú, but times often change. 4-seater plane flies to Juanjui, US$17.20 p.p. + US$0.35 for every kilo of luggage over 10 kilos. From Tingo María on, several transport services are run; the road is narrow and stony. Landslides and mud can be a problem. Some construction work is going on. Many Lima-Pucallpa buses go via Tingo, for example, Arellano, Av. Raimondi, whose buses leave between 0700 and 0900. Bus takes 18 hrs. From Tingo to Pucallpa, US$5, 8 hrs. Seats are hard to get on buses to Pucallpa; there are 4 booking offices: Huallaga, Tepsa, Arellano, Nororiente. Bus to Aguaytía, 3 hrs., US$1.70. León de Huánuco bus Tingo María-Huánuco takes 5-6 hrs., 0930, US$1.40; colectivos take 3 hrs. but beware of unauthorized colectivos, which charge the same as authorized ones but are smaller, slower and sometimes get into trouble with the police, US$2.

The Huallaga river winds northwards for 930 km. The Upper Huallaga is a torrent, dropping 15.8 metres per kilometre between its source and Tingo María. The Lower Huallaga moves through an enervation of flatness, with its main port, Yurimaguas, below the last rapids and only 150 metres above the Atlantic ocean, yet distant from that ocean by over a month's voyage. Between the Upper and Lower lies the Middle Huallaga: that third of the river which is downstream from Tingo María, upstream from Yurimaguas. The valleys, ridges and plateaux have been compared with Kenya, but the area is so isolated that less than 100,000 people now live where a million might flourish. The southern part of the Middle Huallaga centres upon Tingo María; down-river, beyond Bellavista, the orientation is towards **Yurimaguas,** which is connected by road with the Pacific coast, via Tarapoto and Moyobamba (**see page 766**). There is a fine church of the Passionist Fathers, based on the Cathedral of Burgos, Spain, at Yurimaguas; population 25,700. Market from 0400-0700. Tourist information from Consejo Regional building on main Plaza. Interesting excursions in the area include the gorge of Shanusi and the lakes of Mushuyacu and Sanango. **Warning:** there has been guerrilla activity in the Yurimaguas region; visitors can expect attention from the police.

Hotels *Yurimaguas*, E, with shower, toilet and fan, clean, reliable; *Estrella*, F, and shower, rec.; *Floríndez*, E, shower, air conditioning US$1.50 extra; *Camus*, no sign, Manco Capac 201, F, cheap; *Mache*, F, with bath and fan, rec.; *Leo's Palace*, E, Plaza de Armas 104-6, good, friendly, reasonably-priced, restaurant; *Heladería*, round corner from *Estrella*, serves good cheap lunch and dinner. Rec. restaurants, *Leo's Palace*, *El Aguila*, *Chifa Coni*.

Exchange Interbanc only; poor rates.

Air Yurimaguas, flights to Lima, Tarapoto and Iquitos, AeroPerú, Thurs. and Sun. When Yurimaguas-Tarapoto road is impassable, Grupo Ocho flies for civilians. Flights also to Juanjui. Faucett flights to Tarapoto and Lima on Mon., Thurs. and Sat. (highly unreliable). Planes may not land in rain.

River Travel Yurimaguas-Iquitos by regular ferry *Jasmin* or *La Libertad*, 60 hrs., US$15 on upper deck with meals (upstream takes longer). Ask at the harbour for smaller boats, which can take up to 10 days. You can break the journey at Lagunas (*Hostal La Sombra*, Jr. Vásquez 1121, G with shared bath, friendly, good food), where you can ask the Indians to take you on a canoe trip into the swamps; you will see at very close range crocodiles, monkeys and a variety of birds, but only on trips of 4 days or so. Señor Lapiz has been rec. as a good guide; he seems to be well-known. Also Edinson Saldaña Gutiérrez, Sargento Flores 718 and Norberto Flores Rengifo, Jáuregui 703. Typical cost for party of 5 for 12 days is US$200, with 2 guides and 2 boats. One person for 5 days with one guide is charged US$45. Take water purifier and mosquito repellant on excursions that involve living off the land. Hotel *Montalbán* on the plaza (no sign), also accommodation at the Farmacia. The 45-foot river launch *Constante* plies to Lagunas 2-3 times a week, 12 hrs. downstream from Yurimaguas; from there US$10 to Iquitos if you can get a

LA OROYA TO PUCALLPA 115

Elevation of Road LIMA - PUCALLPA

connection. A boat, *La Rosita*, runs regularly but stops at every village of any size. *Alfert* has been rec., cabins, good food. Times of boats to Iquitos and Pucallpa very vague. The boats pass by the villages of Castilla and Nauta (*Residencial Olguita*, basic), where the Huallaga joins the Ucayali and becomes the Amazon. You need a hammock, mosquito net, water-purification tablets, extra food and a good book.

At Tulumayo, soon after leaving Tingo María, a road runs N down the Huallaga past La Morada, successfully colonized by people from Lima's slums, to Aucayacu (*Hotel Monte Carlo*, E with bath; one other hotel, both poor) and Tocache (accommodation at *Hostal San Martín*, F; *Hostal Sucre*, F; one other). The road is paved to 20 km. past Aucayacu, thereafter it is good gravel. Colectivos run; Tingo-Tocache US$8.25 (4½ hrs.) or bus US$6 (6 hrs.). The road has been pushed N to join another built S from Tarapoto (Tarapoto-Tocache, US$4.65 by colectivo) and has now been joined at Tarapoto to the Olmos-Bagua-Yurimaguas transandine highway to the coast at Chiclayo. Colectivos and taxis run from Tocache to Yurimaguas (serviceable unpaved road); daily *camioneta* Tarapoto-Yurimaguas, US$4.90, 6 hrs. The Juanjui-Tocache road has five bridges, but the last one across the Huallaga, just before Juanjui, was washed away in 1983 to be replaced by an efficient ferry (US$9.20 per vehicle); Juanjui-Tarapoto by colectivo US$7.80. For the river journey, start early in the morning if you do not wish to spend a night at the river village of Sión. No facilities, but night is not cold. The river runs through marvellous jungle with high cliffs. Boats sometimes run aground in the river near Sión. Take food and water purifier. Many rafts of balsa wood. Also, a small plane flies between Tocache and Juanjui, US$16 (25 mins.).

From Tingo María to the end of the road at Pucallpa is 288 km., with a climb over the watershed—the Cordillera Azul—between the Huallaga and Ucayali rivers. When the road was being surveyed it was thought that the lowest pass over the Cordillera Azul was over 3,650 metres high, but an old document stating that a Father Abad had found a pass through these mountains in 1757 was rediscovered, and the road now goes through the pass of Father Abad, a gigantic gap 4 km. long and 2,000 metres deep. At the top of the pass is a Peruvian Customs house; the jungle land to the E is a free zone. Coming down from the pass the road bed is along the floor of a magnificent canyon, the Boquerón Abad: luxuriant jungle and ferns and sheer walls of bare rock punctuated by occasional waterfalls into the roaring torrent below. E of the foot of the pass the all-weather road goes over flat pampa with few curves to the village of **Aguaytía** (gasoline; *Hostal San Antonio*, F, clean; 2 restaurants). On to Pucallpa (160 km.—5 hrs. by bus, US$2.70); the last half has no service stations.

Pucallpa, a rapidly expanding jungle town, is on the Ucayali River, navigable by vessels of 3,000 tons from Iquitos, 533 nautical miles away. Population has increased to about 90,000 (district 130,000). It is the capital of the new Department of Ucayali. The newer sections have paved streets, sewers and lights, but much of the frontier town atmosphere still exists. Small but attractive zoo at the brewery (tours on Sat. but far out of city). The economy of the area is growing fast; sawmills, plywood factories, a paper mill, oil refinery, fishing and boat building are all thriving; timber is trucked out to the Highlands and the coast. A newly constructed floating dock for freight promises a great expansion in trade. Large discoveries of oil and gas are being explored, and gold mining is underway nearby. The local drugs problem is becoming serious. The Ganso Azul oilfield has a 75-km. pipeline to the Pucallpa refinery. From Tingo María, 286 km. (gravel road); from Lima, 847 km.

All jungle towns are expensive, but bargains can be found. The floating port of La Hoyada and Puerto Italia are worth a visit to see the canoe traffic and open-air markets. Care should be taken when arranging jungle trips from street vendors in Pucallpa or at the ports. The climate is tropical: dry season in July and August, rainy seasons October-November, February-March; the town is hot and dusty between June and November and muddy from December to May. The centre of Pucallpa is now paved, but both the port and new commercial harbour, about 5 km. away, are reached along dirt roads. Expect plenty of police searches as this is a narcotics area. Also expect plenty of thieves.

Hotels   *Turistas*, C with bath (taxes included), swimming pool, good restaurant; *Mercedes*, E, good, but noisy with good bar and restaurant attached; *Inambu*, C, with good value restaurant, a/c; *Komby*, E, comfortable, swimming pool, excellent value; *Sun*, Ucayali, F, without bath, clean, good value next to *Komby*; *Comfort*, E, clean, *Sisley*, E, adequate, both on Coronel Portillo; *Perú*, Raymondi, E (try bargaining), dirty and not rec., basic; *Europa*, at river end of 7 de Junio, F, dirty, unsafe; *Barbtur*, F, Raymondi 670 (T 6377), friendly, clean, central, opp. bus stop, good beds; *Alex*, F, private bath, dirty; *Hostal Mori*, Jr. Independencia 1114, G, basic; *Hostal Los Angeles*, on Ucayali, E, clean, communal shower, but noisy; *Tariri*, F, with fan, food cheap and good, Coronel Portillo, near Calle Frederico Basadre. If holidaying, better to stay at Lake Yarinacocha (see next page).

Restaurants   Two *chifas* (Chinese restaurants) downtown, both said to be good: *Chifa Pucallpa* and *Chifa Hongkong*, Raymondi 650. *Jugos Don José*, quite cheap; *Restaurant San Isidro* rec., also *Sabores Perú*, good food, poor service; *Jaricho*, under *Hotel Sun*, good; *Escorpión Cebichería*, Jr. Progreso, good, eat in rear garden; *Los Rosales*, expensive; *Puerto de Carlos*, best in the downtown area, expensive; *Jíbaros*, near *Hotel Amazonas*, good food and value; *Embutidos La Favorita*, Cnl. Portillo, good, cheap, friendly, US$1 for all 3 meals; *El Establo*, steak house on road to airport, excellent; *Sandwich Roma*, corner of Portillo and Ucayali, good snack bar. *La Baguette*, good bakery, cheap bottles of pisco. The local beer "San Juan" has been rec.

Small **motorcycles** for hire from Jr. Raymondi 654 and 7 de Junio 864, about US$1.50 per hour plus gasoline.

Bookshop   Librería La Verdad and La Brisa Lodge have collections of English books on loan; a boon for stranded travellers.

Exchange   Banco Continental, no commission. Importaciones Gutiérrez Padilla, Jr. Ucayali, Raymondi 601 (also good ice cream). Try also the owner of the *Barbtur Hotel*, and Textiles Universales, Postillo y Ucayali.

Tourist Office Foptur, Saénz Peña 298, T 5008.

Air   AeroPerú and Faucett to and from Lima daily in the afternoons, US$26, 1 hr. Flights to Iquitos daily (except Fri.) with AeroPerú, 1500, US$52 (US$35 for Peruvians), try different agencies for lower price ticket (e.g. Pucallpa Tours, Jr. Coronel Portillo 747, T 6081); to Tarapoto on Thurs. and Sun. (US$33). Some seats are assigned, you need to arrive early. Departures must be confirmed 24 hrs. in advance. AeroPerú jet flights to and from Lima and Iquitos in the afternoon. Reconfirmation of tickets can only be done with any certainty at the office in town. Float plane from the airforce base at Yarinacocha, Sat, 0900 to Iquitos (check in Fri., be there at 0700), US$20. Grupo Ocho fly to Esperanza, San Ramón, Sepahua, Atalaya, with passengers—office in Pucallpa. The road to Brazil has not yet been opened. For connections by river **see page 404** in Brazil section. SASA fly to Cruzeiro do Sul, US$35, minimum 4 passengers, if plane has no passengers booked for return, you'll have to pay US$70, very unreliable. Airport to town, bus US$0.25; taxi US$3.60.

N.B.   Before entering Peru at Pucallpa by air from Cruzeiro do Sul check thoroughly that immigration facilities have been set up at Pucallpa. If you arrive and cannot get a stamp, the PIP in Pucallpa will (or should) send you back to Brazil; if they don't, you'll be in for a lot of hassles further on in Peru, including the possibility of arrest. To leave Peru from Pucallpa, you must get a special exit visa from the PIP in town or at the airport.

Buses   Much of the Pucallpa-Lima road is now paved (rough stretch for 80 km. E of Tingo María) and there are regular bus services to Lima (check in advance that the road is open). Huallaga, Arellano, Perla del Oriente and León de Huánuco (at 1730) from Lima to Pucallpa (US$10, 24 hrs. in good weather) via Huánuco (10 hrs., US$7 with León de Huánuco (slow)—1300 from Pucallpa, US$6.50 with La Perla del Oriente, 1200). From Pucallpa Nororiente goes to Tingo María, US$5, 10-11 hours. Advised to take travelling rug or blankets as the crossing of the Cordillera at night is bitterly cold. Try to pick a bus crossing the mountains by day as the views are wonderful. It is also possible to get to Lima by truck.

Excursions   The Hospital Amazónico Albert Schweitzer, which serves the local Indians, and Summer School of Linguistics (callers by appointment only) for the study of Indian languages are on picturesque Lake **Yarinacocha**, the main tourist attraction of the area. Yarinacocha is 20 mins. by colectivo or bus (line 6) from the market in Pucallpa (US$0.25), 15 mins. by taxi (US$3.60). The Indian market of Moroti-Shobo is a must. *Hotel La Cabaña*, C (price rises in high season), German owner, plane excursions (for instance to Indian villages). Next door to *La Cabaña* is *La Perla* lodge, good and much cheaper. *La Brisa Lodge*, D, 5 rooms sharing 2 bathrooms, or 4-person bungalows, US-run (Connor and Mary Nixon), recommended, free information on jungle excursions and maps, plus their own excursions (3-day and 10-day); *Los Delfines*, F, rooms with bath, clean, noisy; *EL Pescador*, in Puerto Callao, F, cheap, friendly, restaurant, best buy for budget traveller, but mixed reports recently. Some small houses for rent on weekly basis.

Restaurants: *La Brisa Lodge,* excellent but not cheap; *El Cucharón,* good food; *Grande Paraíso,* good view; local specialities include *tamales, humitas* (maize patties with meat and herbs), *junies* (rice with chicken and spices), *tacutacu* (banana and sauces). Here is bathing in clean water, but there is a lot of weed. It is a pleasant change after the mud of Pucallpa and the Amazon; you can camp, though there are no facilities and it is hot and insect-ridden. Motor canoes can be hired for about US$17 a day with guide, but guide not mandatory for lake trips. Trips into the canals and out to the river need a guide (Sr. Antonio has been rec.). Two types of excursions down river, recommended three days, can be arranged from the port in Yarinacocha directly with the boat owners, prices vary but approximately US$20 per boat a day, you buy food and some supplies. Boats hold up to 8 at reduced price. Recommended boats: *Veloz, Akito* (of the García family, who also have accommodation, rec., trustworthy), Thierry Giles, good English, has two boats called *Delfín,* rec. Beware, many boats are used for drug-running and tourists have come to grief. List of guides, maps and information available in *La Brisa Lodge.* Recommended guides Daniel Saavedra (B/M *Progreso*), Roberto C. Cenepo, Jorge Rucoba (navigator), who offer fishing, hunting, walks in the jungle along the rivers Aguaytía, Callena and Ucayali, and rivers and canals (especially the Chanchaguaya region of Contamaná). Also special excursions to Iquitos from Pucallpa. None of them speaks English, but they can be found at Lake Yarinacocha, Puerto Callao, ask for B/M *Progreso,* prices are competitive. Also rec. for tours, Jorge Matos Grijalva of Selva Tours, also an English teacher and bar owner, great local character and most helpful, Coronel Portillo, next to *Hotel Amazonas.* **Note:** down-river trips visit numerous villages but much of the jungle is cultivated; up-river trips visit fewer villages but mostly virgin jungle. Certain sections of Lake Yarinacocha have been designated as a reserve.

River Service   Bus Line 1 to the port, La Hoyada. In the dry season boats dock 3 km. from the bus stop, along dusty walk, taxi US$2. To Iquitos, some better than others; only 3 boats with cabins, but don't count on getting one (hammocks are cooler): *Madre Selva,* clean, friendly, rec.; US$10 with cabin, 6 days. Travellers to Iquitos may need confirmation from the PIP that their documents are in order, this must then be signed by the Capitanía otherwise no passenger can be accepted on a trip leaving Pucallpa. No such clearance is necessary when returning to Pucallpa. Passenger services are in decline owing to competition by air and priority for cargo traffic; it may be better to make journeys in short stages rather than Pucallpa-Iquitos direct. There's a risk of illness on the river, and public transport can be extremely uncomfortable. River water is used for cooking and drinking: tinned food, mosquito netting, hammock and fresh water are necessary purchases, fishing line and hooks advisable. Take lots of insect repellant (local brand, Black Flag, is not effective), water purifier and tummy pills. The smaller boats call often at jungle villages if you want to see them, but otherwise because the river is wide, the shores can only be seen at a distance. Average time: 5 days. Boats leave very irregularly. When conditions are bad they leave in convoy: none may leave afterwards for 4 to 6 weeks. Avoid boats that will be loading en route, this can take up to 6 days. The fare is about US$20 (bargain) a head with "cabin", rice, meat and beans. It is possible to hire a small boat from Pucallpa to Iquitos for US$89. Try at the north section of the port, but take care not to hire a boat running drugs. Further down the Ucayali river are Contamaná and Requena, from which launches sail to Iquitos, taking 12 hrs., US$7. Roroboya, a small Shipibo Indian village about 12 hrs. downstream from Pucallpa, should not be missed, as most other villages down to Iquitos are *mestizo.* You can go to Puerto La Hoyada and Puerto Italia (smaller boats) to find a boat going to Iquitos; the Capitanía on the waterfront may give you information about sailings, but this is seldom reliable. Do not pay for your trip before you board the vessel, and only pay the captain. (Captains may allow you to live on board a couple of days before sailing.) Boats going upstream on the Amazon and its tributaries stay closer to the bank than boats going down, which stay in mid-stream.

From Pucallpa to Cruzeiro do Sul overland requires plenty of time and money to organize, and even then is difficult. You can take a boat to Abojao (10 days), then walk to Brasiléia, from where buses go to Cruzeiro. Boats and guides are very expensive.

You can take a colectivo from Pucallpa S to Zungaru (US$3), where a boat (30 mins.) can be taken to **Puerto Inca** on the Río Pachitea, about 120 km. N by air from Puerto Bermúdez (**see page 830**) and close to the Carretera Marginal (under construction). It is a gold-rush town, expanding quickly, with two hotels (Don José's *Alojamiento,* G, clean, safe, laundry, big rooms, rec.).

Iquitos, capital of the Department of Loreto and chief town of Peru's jungle region, is a fast-developing city of 350,000 people on the W bank of the Amazon, with Padre Isla island (14½ by 3 km.) facing it in midstream. It has paved streets and plenty of vehicles (including taxis) but roads out of the city go only a little way: Iquitos is completely isolated except by air and river. Some 800 km. downstream from Pucallpa and 3,200 km. from the mouth of the Amazon, it has recently taken on a new lease of life as the centre for oil exploration in Peruvian Amazonia. As one might expect from its use by the oil industry and its remoteness, it is an expensive town, but compensates by being a friendly place.

There is an iron house in the Plaza de Armas, designed by Eiffel for the Paris exhibition of 1898. It is said that the house was transported from Paris by a local rubber baron (the rubber boom lasted until 1912); it is constructed entirely of iron trusses and sheets, bolted together and painted silver.

Belén, the picturesque, friendly waterfront district, is lively, but not safe at night. Most of its huts are built on rafts to cope with the river's 10-metre change of level during floods. *Pasaje Paquito* is a bar with typical local drinks as is *La China*. The main square has a bandstand made by Eiffel. (Canoes may be hired on the waterfront to visit Belén, US$3 per hour; do not try paddling yourself as the current is very strong.) See in the city the Market, at the end of the Malecón, or riverside walk. Note that the principal street Jirón Lima has been renamed Jirón Próspero. Recommended guide with a good car and two boats is Jorge Chávez, T 231532 or through *Hostal Caravel*.

The University of Amazonia of Loreto (1962) specializes in engineering and agriculture. Of special interest are the older buildings, faced with *azulejos* (glazed tiles). They date from the rubber boom of 1890 to 1920, when the rubber barons imported tiles from Portugal and Italy and ironwork from England to embellish their homes. Werner Herzog's film *Fitzcarraldo* is a *cause célèbre* in the town; Fitzcarraldo's house still stands on the Plaza de Armas, and Herzog's boats are moored in the port.

A short drive S of the city is beautiful Lake **Quistococha** in lush jungle, with a fish hatchery at the lakeside. Recommended is a visit (US$1) to the Parque Zoológico de Quistococha (with aquarium) on the lake (closed Mon.). At the entrance are pictures and texts of local legends, the tourist office will supply a map of the zoo. Take bus (tends to be crowded and dirty) from corner of Próspero and Gálves; also a truck (with pink frame, not green) from Abtao and Grau to the zoo and Quistococha, US$0.20; taxi US$2.25. We have heard that the animals (and particularly the fish) often depend on food from visitors to survive. See particularly the *paiche*, a huge Amazonian fish whose steaks (*paiche a la loretana*) you can eat in Iquitos' restaurants.

Warnings   As elsewhere, beware of thieves, especially of handbags, watches, jewellery, etc. Secondly, locals sell necklaces made with red and black rosary peas (Abrus pecatorius), which are extremely poisonous. Do not give them to children. They are illegal in Canada, but not in the U.S.A. If possible, avoid visiting Iquitos around Peruvian Independence Day (July 27 and 28) and Easter as it is very expensive and crowded and excursion facilities are overloaded. Avoid the "headhunters" at the airport who try to steer you to travel agents for a commission: cheaper to go straight to the agents, who are all on Calle Putumayo near the Plaza.

Hotels   *Amazonas*, previously *Holiday Inn*, on Abelardo Quiñónez, 3 km. out of town (taxi US$1.75), A, plus 19% tax and service, swimming pool (free bus service hourly from airport), designed for air conditioning but not working, a 5-star hotel only in price; *Turistas*, Malecón Tarapacá, C, with bath, meals US$4.50, with many good air-conditioned rooms US$1.50 extra (a few second-hand English books available in reception), does not accept travellers' cheques; *Hostal Caravel*, Próspero, B, a/c, very clean, friendly; *Hostal Acosta*, Ricardo Palma 252, A, hot and cold running water, shower, air conditioning, refrigerator in room, very good café, central, rec.; also *Acosta 2*, C, almost same standard plus good restaurant and swimming pool; *Isabel*, Brasil 174, E with bath, very good, clean (but plug the holes in the walls!), secure, often full; *Hostal Safari*, Napo 126, D, a/c, hot showers, restaurant; *Hostal La Pascana*, Pevas 133, E with shower, clean, breakfast available, rec.; *Lima*, Próspero 549, E (triple rooms available), with bath and fan, café good; *Perú*, Próspero 320, F (triples available), fan, clean, bathroom, café downstairs, good value; *Hostal Residencial Alfert*, García Sanz 03, E, with bath, basic, friendly; *María Antonia*, Próspero 616, C, clean, air-conditioned, noisy; *Hostal Europa*, Brasil 222, very good, very helpful, D, a/c (cheaper with fan), shower; *Hostal Tacna*, Tacna 516, T 232839, F, rec.; *Hostal Residencial Ambassador*, Pevas 260, C, with shower, air-conditioning and snack-bar, rec.; *Hostal Residencial Loreto*, Jr. Próspero 311, E, with shower and air-conditioning (cheaper without air conditioning); *Hostal Karina*, Av. Putumayo 467, F, good value, central, friendly, laundry, cheap food, but poor water supply; *Maynas*, Próspero 388, E (triples available), with private shower and fan, very clean and friendly; *Residencial Wagner*, Coronel Portillo 687, opposite the Capitanía, F, friendly, cheap meals available, jungle tours of up to 6 days with groups of 4-6 people, US$ 40 p.p. a day. Cheapest: *Hostal Económico*, Moore 1164, G, very clean, good water supply, quiet, rec.

Restaurants   The best are on or near Plaza Veintiocho (28) de Julio, e.g. *El Dorado Inn*, Calle Huallaga, good value and good menu; *Gran Chifa Wai Ming*, San Martín 462/6, good but quite expensive; *El Tropical*, Av. Quiñónez 39, 1½ km. from centre, owned by Paul Hitschler (German), reasonable, rec.; *El Shupihui*, Calvo de Araujo y Castilla, typical restaurant, highly rec.; *El Mesón*, Jirón Napo, fish rec.; *Maloca*, opposite *Hotel Turistas* on riverbank, excellent, average meal US$5, good fish, really good view, highly rec. Chinese restaurants include *Gran Chifa Central*, Av. Almirante Grau 1133; *Gran Chifa Chung Wa*, on the corner of Arica and San Martín. *Chifa Pekin*, Av. Almirante Grau 837. *La Favorita*, Próspero Morona; *Ebony*, on Próspero, good and cheap; *Blue Moon*, on Morona, also good and cheap; *Tucunaré*, Putumayo 157, good for fish (try paiche); restaurant of Kaya Tours at Putumayo 139, good; the *Cocoroco* chain has a *Pollo a la Brasa* restaurant on the corner of Plaza Veintiocho de Julio. Café beneath *Res. Internacional*, Jr. Próspero, good, cheap. For chocolate cake and ice cream, *Lamborghini*, close to Plaza de Armas. Pineapples are good and cheap. Try the local drink chuchuasi, made from the bark of a tree, which is supposed to have aphrodisiac properties and jugo de cocona, and the alcoholic vete bajando, cola de mono, rompe colzón and siete raices. You can eat cheaply, especially fish, at the three markets. Palm heart salad (churro) excellent; also try inchicapi (corn and peanut soup) and cecina (fried dried pork).

Current   220 volts, A.C.

Clubs   Club Social Iquitos, overlooking Plaza de Armas; Military Casino, for all classes; Centro Internacional.

Shopping   Empresa Peruana de Promoción Artesanal (EPPA), Putumayo 128; Mercado Artesanal de Productores, 3 km. from the centre in San Juan district, take colectivo; La Cocamita, Putumayo 120; Mocahua Juárez, Arica 1083. All sell handicrafts. Pharmacies: Del Correo, Arica 398; D'Onudio, Próspero 541; El Loretano, Próspero 355. Small selection of secondhand English books at the travel agent on Putumayo 184.

Discotheques   The best are said to be *Puma's Club* or *Tropicana Club*, both in Putumayo. *Costa Azul*, Requena 274; *La Pantera Rosa*, Moore 434; *Disco Pub Chich*, Condamine 771. *Pax*, Napo y Condamine; *St Chomas*, Condamine.

Motorcycle Hire   US$15 a day, Carlos del Prado Bawer, Brasil 530, T 239147.

Museum   Municipal Museum, has a large, old collection of stuffed Amazonian fauna which is rather disappointing. It has been incorporated into the Parque Zoológico.

Exchange   Banco Popular cashes travellers' cheques. Banco de Crédito, Plaza de Armas, good rates. Banco Amazónico changes cheques at the official rate without charging a commission or asking for a copy of your passport. Importaciones Lima on Próspero, and shops selling foreign electrical goods offer good rates of exchange.

Post Office   Entel Perú, corner of Calle Arica with Morona, near Plaza de Armas.

Consulates   Brazilian, Sgto. Lores 363; Colombian, Malecón Tarapacá 260; Spanish, Moore 249.

Tourist Office   Foptur, Jr. Próspero 163, on E side of Plaza de Armas, T 238523; Arica 122, and at airport: useful town maps, maps of the Quistacocha zoo and literature from the main jungle tour operators. Good information from Edith (speaks English and French), Three Roses Travel, Próspero 246, very helpful. Other agencies recommended for city and surroundings Belén Viajes y Turismo, Arica 1233, and Fénix Viajes, Pevas 216. Town map also from Librería Mosquera, Jr. Próspero.

Jungle Tours   All agencies are under control of the local office of the Ministry of Tourism on Calle Arica: if you think you're being overcharged, ask for Sra. Lastenia Rodríguez, who will show you the operator's file, in which route and price must be recorded. (Not worth while for booking bus or air tickets). They arrange one-day or longer trips to places of interest with guides speaking some English; package tours cost US$125-180 for three days when booked in Lima; it is much cheaper to book tours in Iquitos. Launches for river trips can be hired by the hour or day (prices are negotiable, about US$10-15 per hour); many tour operators are located on Jirón Putumayo near the Plaza de Armas. Explorama Tours (rec. as the most efficient), Putumayo 150, has three sites: *Explorama Inn*, 40 km. (1½ hrs.) from Iquitos, hot water, comfortable bungalows in a jungle setting, good food, attractive walks, rec. jungle experience for those who want their creature comforts; *Explorama Lodge* at Yanamono, 60 km. from Iquitos, US$80 for 2 days/1 night and US$40 for each additional day; *Explornapo Camp* at Llachapa, 140 km. from Iquitos (better for seeing fauna). Amazon Lodge Safaris, Putumayo 165, owns the *Amazon Lodge*, clean, excellent food. Two-day, 1 night stay costs US$80 plus US$7 for lunch on second day, special tours for fishermen, also a smaller lodge for the more adventurous. Paseos Amazónicos Ambassador, Putumayo 124, operates the *Amazon Sinchicuy Lodge* with 2 day, 1 night stays at US$60; they also organize visits to Lake Quistacocha and the zoo; *Jungle Amazon Inn*, about 10 km. further downstream from the *Amazon Lodge*, tour operators on ground floor of Eiffel-built house on corner of Plaza de Armas with Putumayo. Lima Tours offers 3 day, 2 night tours to Iquitos and the Amazon from Lima for US$250 p.p., flight included. Amazon River Tamshiyacu Lodge, S.A., Putumayo 184 or Los Carolinas 121, Miraflores, Lima T 476919, ask for Lucho de Cossio who runs

Tamshiyacu Lodge, US$30 per day, 1 night, small, friendly, highly rec., swimming, jungle walks, night-time canoe rides, the guide, Antonio is very good; their trips include the Yarapa River Inn, Tambo Inn and wilderness expeditions; tourists are met at the airport by Sr. Pedro Alava with information. A new ornithological garden is opening at Tamshiyacu Lodge, entrance US$5. Amazonia Expeditions, Putumayo 139 (Carlos Grández), owns Yarapa river camp near confluence of Marañón and Ucayali 140 km. from Iquitos, US$45 p.p. per night, warmly rec., strong conservationist inclinations. Amazon Selva Tours, Putumayo 133, highly rec.; they use *Selva Lodge* on Río Momón, and *Yarapa Lodge*, excellent food and able guides, US$32 a day. Amazon Camp Tourist Service, Putumayo 196, owns lodge on Río Momón, cheapest at US$20 for 2 days/1 night. Kaya Expeditions, Putumayo 124. For those who are tough, Freddie of Amazon Adventure Tours, Sgto. Lores 220, T 235151, organizes survival courses in the jungle and you learn to build your own camp, find your own food etc. Be warned, however: he has to approve of you and your level of fitness and stamina, not you of him. He speaks fluent English (US$400 for 3 for 5 days; longer would be better). *Amazon Expedition Camp* on a tributary of the River Ucayali is run by Carlos Pérez, US$260 for 2 nights. *Amazon Village* was opened in 1981; tours there are operated by Exprinter; for details contact Amazon Village, c/o Amazon Hotel Iquitos, Miguel Dasso 167A, San Isidro, Lima, T 404-559. It is located on the Río Momón, some hours away from the Amazon itself, so difficult river conditions can easily prevent visits to the Amazon. At the Village there are clean, well-ventilated bungalows and good food. *Amazon Botanical Gardens*, 56 km. from Iquitos on the Amazon (PO Box 105, Jirón Tacna 516, Iquitos, or 4301 Main St., Suite 14, PO Box 10025, Kansas City, Mo. 64111, T 816-931-2840), 3 days, 2 nights, US$175 (or less if more than 1 person), longer stays available.

It is advisable to take a waterproof coat and shoes or light boots on such trips, and a good torch, as well as *espirales* to ward off the mosquitoes at night—they can be bought from drugstores in Iquitos. The dry season is from July to September and September is the best month to see flowers and butterflies. A recommended tour with a difference is the jungle survival excursion of Moisés Torres Viena, Expediciones Jungle Amazónica, Soledad 718—as taught to Peruvian soldiers—not cheap, but you will learn much about jungle botany and how to live off the plants. Artesanías La Chamita, Jirón Putumayo 157, offers week-long trips to different jungle villages. A bus from Jirón Próspero takes you to Nanay river. Launches may do cruises to Leticia (Amazon Lodge Safaris have a 6-day trip to Leticia on the m/n *Adolfo*).

Excursions By bus to the village of Santo Tomás, about 20 km., a favourite week-end retreat of inhabitants of Iquitos; the village has a good restaurant and canoes may be hired. Launches also leave Iquitos for the village of Indiana; get off at the "varadero de Mazán" and walk through the banana plantations to the River Mazán. A trail leads from the village of Mazán through the jungle to Indiana (hotel), about a 2-hr. walk (steamy). Catch the launch back to Iquitos at 1300.

Naturalists should note that the area 50 km. around Iquitos is too inhabited to support much large wildlife; the Napo or Ucayali rivers have more to offer. Similarly the areas around the Lodges; however there is plenty of scope for seeing small fauna and learning about the flora. Trips to see Yagua Indians offer little but a chance to see "a way of life which is not so much in transition as abandoned." (John C. O'Conor, Arlington, Va.)

Air International airport, Francisco Secada Vigneta, T 231501, 233094. Taxi to the airport costs US$2.50 (US$5 at night); *motocarro* (motorcycle with 2 seats), US$1.50; bus, US$0.15, goes to market area, about 12 blocks from Plaza de Armas, taxi from there US$1.50. Automatic 90-day visa given on arrival on international flights. Faucett (Próspero 646) and AeroPerú between them have two daily jet flights to Lima, one direct, the other via Pucallpa or Tarapoto on alternating days. Fare to Lima, US$24. Faucett flies from Iquitos to Pucallpa, Mon., Wed., Fri., Sat. (US$15), to Tarapoto, Tues., Thurs., Sun. AeroPerú (Jr. Próspero 248, T 232513), to Trujillo, change planes at Tarapoto. Iquitos-Cuzco via Lima only, Faucett, also AeroPerú, Iquitos-Yurimaguas. No flights Iquitos-Ecuador. Faucett flies Sat. to Miami. TANS offices: Grupo 42 (for Brazil, Colombia), Sargento Lores 127; Grupo 8 (for Lima US$35, Trujillo US$30, Yurimaguas and Tarapoto US$19), Castilla 353, nr Plaza Sargento Lores; these flights are less than the cost of the commercial flights. TANS DC6 flight to Ramón Castilla, US$13, Tues., Fri., Sun., and across Amazon by motor-boat to Leticia, Colombia, or Benjamin Constant, Brazil, for onward flights to Bogotá and Manaus, respectively. TANS also has a flight to Cabo Pantoja and other villages. TANS to Leticia (Tabatinga), but often booked up 2 months ahead for the aquaplane. The Brazilian airline Cruzeiro do Sul has two weekly flights on Wed. and Sat., at 1230, between Iquitos, Leticia (Tabatinga airport) and Manaus. Varig, Putumayo 188, T 234381 has flights to Manaus on Weds. and Sat., also to Tabatinga, US$75. It is also possible to fly from Tefé (Brazil—**see page 398**) to Iquitos, stopping at Tabatinga for border formalities. (Mark your luggage "Iquitos" or it will be unloaded at Tabatinga.) Flights Leticia-Iquitos on Sun., Wed., Fri., will have a connection flight to Pucallpa (exit tax Leticia airport US$10.), leaves Leticia 0800, leaves Iquitos for Pucallpa 1510; probably delayed (Pucallpa flight does not always operate). Iquitos flights frequently delayed. (Be sure to reconfirm your flight in Iquitos, as they are often overbooked.) Peruvian Air Force flies Pucallpa-Iquitos, US$20, but unreliable as seats in that plane may be requisitioned at short notice, and Iquitos-Leticia, US$12. The Air Force also flies to Andoas, an oil town in the jungle, on the river Pastaza. TANS hydroplane flies NNW along the river to Peneya, opposite Leguizamo in Colombia, or Gueppi, the military frontier post from where you can get to Puerto Asís (Colombia) by boat. On this flight, locals take precedence.

Aircraft for Hire Ask at airport; normal rate US$300 an hour for plane taking 5.

Shipping Upstream. River boats to Pucallpa (2 boats a week in rainy season) or Yurimaguas, at least 4 days (longer if cargo is being carried, which is usually the case), cheap, but beware of overcharging to gringos; fastest boat to Yurimaguas is *Jasmin*, 4 days or so. Information on boats for Pucallpa obtained on wharves, or at Meneses (Jirón Próspero), Bellavista (Malecón Tarapacá 596), Hurtado (Av. Grau 1223) and Casa Pinto (Sargento Lores 164). Cabins are 4 berth and you have to buy both a first class ticket, which entitles you to food (whether you want it or not) and deck space to sling your hammock, and a cabin ticket if you want the "luxury" of a berth. Adequate washing and toilet facilities, but the food is rice, meat and beans (and whatever can be picked up en route) cooked in river water. Stock up on fruit and tinned food in Iquitos. There is a good cheap bar. Take plenty of prophylactic enteritis tablets; many contract dysentery on the trip. Also take insect repellant; one sold locally, called Black Flag, is not effective. *Campeón* to Pucallpa, US$30 with food, 7 days; *Rosa* to Pucallpa, US$19, 7 days.

Downstream. Communications with Manaus by river are unreliable and the journey takes about 15 days (two boats doing this journey are *Clivia*, frequent, good food, and *Almirante Monteiro*, clean, reasonable food). The Hertzog boat, *Juliana*, is the most beautiful; friendly captain, US$15 to Islandia. Best go first to Leticia, Ramón Castilla or Islandia. Ramón Castilla is a village before Islandia, opposite Tabatinga; Islandia itself is just a mud bank with an exchange shop on the Peruvian side of a narrow creek just a few yards from Benjamin Constant in Brazil. No boats from Iquitos go to Benjamin Constant, but all boats for Manaus start from there and a new hotel (*Benjamin*) has been built. Boats Iquitos-Islandia 36 hrs (2 days in other direction), about US$10, inc. food, US$2 extra for cabin.

If a long wait is involved, then Leticia (Colombia) has the best hotels and facilities. Weekly luxury 54-passenger boat, *Río Amazonas*, plies between Iquitos and Leticia, leaves Wed., operated by Amazon Camp, Putumayo 196, Iquitos, T 233931, US$400, US$250 without facilities, for 4 days. Canoes put out from Leticia and will take off passengers from passing boats at another mud bank called Puerto Ancorade, just opposite. There are also ferries from Benjamin Constant to Tabatinga and Leticia, US$0.50, 1½ hrs. The *Huallaga* is highly recommended for river journeys to Ramón Castilla, Leticia or Pucallpa. It is easy to find a boat, but difficult to get it to move, though you can stay on board. Details on exit and entry formalities seem to change frequently, so when leaving Peru, check in Iquitos first (Immigration, Arica 474, office hours 0900-1300); latest indications are that exit stamps are given only at Puerto Alegría, not at Ramón Castilla nor by the Peruvian Consulate in Leticia (0830-1430—the consul is elusive), while tourist cards for entry into Peru are given at Puerto Alegría, 2 hrs. upstream from Islandia, where the boat stops for police checks. Brazilian entry formalities are in Tabatinga, in town, 2 km. from the pier, or at the airport (taxis from riverfront to airport tend to overcharge). Boats to and across frontiers carry many smugglers and thieves.

THE INCA ROAD

We have had great pleasure since 1979 in incorporating an account by Christopher Portway, the explorer and author, of the Andean Inca road. His most interesting book Journey along the Spine of the Andes (Oxford Illustrated Press) was published in 1984. In view of space constraints, we have therefore shortened his account here.

Basically, there were two great roads in the Inca system. One was the royal road between Cuzco and Quito, progressively extended to take in northern Ecuador, southern Colombia, and southwards, Bolivia and northern Argentina. A mind-boggling 5,230 km. in length, its remains have been best preserved (more through remoteness than any preserving agency) in Peru. Much of the 4,050 km. of the coastal road between Tumbes and the River Maule in Chile has been built over by the Pan-American Highway.

The standard width of the royal road varied between 5 and 6 metres (as against the 8 metres of the less-obstructed coastal road). It was unpaved, except where there was unavoidable water or when climbing steep hillsides necessitating the use of stone steps.

A good section, bordered by stone, may be seen some 13 km. east of the village of Shelby, served by the railway from La Oroya to Cerro de Pasco. Its course is marked by the lonely ruins of Bonbón, an Inca community centre only recently identified, which in turn lies close to the modern dam holding back the Mantaro River as it flows out of the northern end of Lake Junín.

But perhaps the most astounding survival of Inca roads is the long stretch, displaying varied construction over differing terrain, between Yanahuanca and Wari (see page 824).

Yanahuanca is situated in the incredibly beautiful valley of the same name. It is rarely entered by foreigners and thus a visitor has to contend with a retinue of a hundred or more curious inhabitants in his passage through the village. Its amenities include a few bars, a simple restaurant and a community social centre, but no hotel.

Two km. up the Yanahuanca Valley a lesser valley cuts northwards between the towering crags. The road, its paving uneven and disturbed by countless horse and donkey convoys, leads up the smaller valley, its course sometimes shared by a stream, to the village of Huarautambo, a community of some 220 people, about 4 km. distant.

This village is surrounded by many pre-Inca remains and the schoolmaster, Sr. Valentín Inga Castro, will be only too happy to show visitors the many ruins of the area, as well as the cave-tomb full of deformed skulls only recently discovered by him, a crop of cave paintings and numerous underground chambers.

For more than 150 km. the *Camino Incaico* is not only in almost continuous existence from the Yanahuanca Valley but is actually shown on the map issued by the Instituto Geográfico Militar. From Huarautambo, in company with lesser tracks, it winds up the head of the Huarautambo valley and across rock-scattered grasslands, over escarpments, following valleys, then veering away to utilize more valleys hidden by saddles over which the road triumphs even if the weary 20th-century traveller wilts along the way. At a spot known locally as Incapoyo, superb views of the Cordillera Huayhuash, with peaks soaring to 6,000 metres and more, are to be seen.

While the road fades from sight or has become muddled with present day tracks the route is marked by the ruins of *tampus*—or Inca rest houses—and, occasionally, larger sites. *Tampus* were official and utilitarian. Some of them consisted of a single structure, others had a series of smaller rooms opening on a large corral where the llamas were stabled. Each was maintained by the local *ayllu* as part of its labour tax.

Between Yanahuanca and Wari pre-Inca *tampus* and other remains provide landmarks for the road. Thereafter traces of the road become fainter though short sections can be identified in the hills behind San Luis, Piscobamba and Pomabamba. Behind Pomabamba, far up upon the final crest of the mountains to the west, the road is revealed by a chain of old forts older than the highway itself, but it is left to such disintegrating edifices to mark the route to Cajamarca and northwards into Ecuador.

Townships and villages along the way include the following: *Tamboccocha* and *Gashapampa*: One single shop with little to offer enlivens these two remote villages. *Pilcocancha*: A few km. north of the township of Baños, this village is notable only for its hot thermal pools lying a kilometre south. *La Unión* (see also page 832): A "double town" with its main residential section across the River Vizcarra in the sheer-sided valley of the same name. Several small hotels, simple but adequate at about US$1 per night but no hot water, a farce of a cinema and half a dozen restaurants. On the grass plateau above the town are the spectacular ruins of *Huánuco Viejo* (see page 832). *Pomachaca*: A small village with a couple of shops at a road and river junction. The roads lead to Wari (Hotel Ideal, F), San Marcos and Llamellín. San Luis: A village in the shadow of the Cordillera Blanca. A few small restaurants and an occasional bus service to Piscobamba, with a basic, but clean hotel with friendly owner, and another, both F, and a few shops and small restaurants.

The staff of the mayor's office are helpful and from behind the town views across the valley are superb. Occasional buses to Pomabamba (see page 744), a pleasant enough town. On both sides of the valley in which Pomabamba stands are pre-Inca ruins of considerable interest. Sihuas: A small township clinging to a hilltop. No hotel, but a couple of restaurants. Huamachuco (page 757). Cajabamba (see page 758), lively little town with a hotel or two and a number of restaurants (not to be confused with the Ecuadorean town of the same name). Ichocán: Pleasant village with an interesting church and a few small restaurants. The council do not object to overnight camping in the plaza with its fountain and trees. San Marcos: Lively little town with a hotel or two. Cajamarca (page 758).

(**Warning** The Andean Inca road in the north of Peru passes through extremely remote mountain territory. Travellers are advised, therefore, to take full precautions against starvation and exposure. There is, apparently, some danger of attack by cattle rustlers and part of the area has been affected by guerrilla activity).

THE ECONOMY

Revitalization of agriculture, which accounts for 14% of gdp and 37% of employment, is a government priority, with credits and improved prices being granted to farmers. While the Costa (which occupies 11% of the land area) has traditionally been the dominant economic region, with excellent crops of cotton, rice, sugar and fruit where the coastal desert is irrigated, the Sierra is being given preferential treatment with a view to restoring the self-sufficiency in food production of Inca times. Irrigation of the coastal region using Andean waters is the key to improved yields of the main export crops, sugar and cotton. The other main export crop is coffee.

Although employing only 2% of the workforce, mining contributes 10% of gdp and the six major minerals and metals account for 40% of total export value. These are copper, iron, silver, gold, lead and zinc. Copper and iron deposits are found on the southern coast, but the principal mining area for all minerals is the Sierra. Low world prices, particularly for zinc and lead, strikes in the copper industry, rising costs and, from 1985 to 1988, a fixed exchange rate have contributed to considerable losses for both public and private mining companies, and to reduced real output.

Peruvian oil accounts for 50% of domestic energy consumption. The northeastern jungle produced an average of 115,500 b/d in 1986, on and off the northwestern coast 55,000-65,000 b/d, while fields in the southern jungle are being explored. No major new reserves have been found since 1976. Local funds for investment have been falling in the 1980s, hence the need for foreign companies to invest in exploration, but in 1985 the García government rescinded the operating contracts of three major foreign firms, adversely affecting investment prospects, despite subsequent new agreements.

Manufacturing contributes 23% of gdp, employing 10% of the workforce. After high growth rates in the early 1970s, industry slumped to operating at 40% of its total capacity as purchasing power was reduced, and the cost of energy, raw materials and trade credit rose faster than inflation. A consumer-led recovery in 1986 led to most of industry working at full capacity, but the boom was followed by a severe slump in 1988. Similarly, construction returned to growth in 1986 as a result of government projects, after three years of recession, but declined heavily in 1988.

Fishing, which accounts for 1% of gdp, suffered a dramatic decline in 1983 as the Niño current forced out of Peruvian waters the main catch, anchovy, whose stocks were already seriously depleted by overfishing in the 1970s. From being the world's leading fishmeal exporter, with exports accounting for 14% of the country's total, fishmeal sales fell to 4% in 1985, recovering in 1986 to 8%. The García government has partially reversed its predecessor's policy of closing fishmeal plants, in conjunction with promoting fish as a domestic food source.

Growing fiscal deficits in the 1980s led to increasing delays in payments of principal and interest on the foreign debt, which was estimated at US$18.4 bn. at the end of 1988. As arrears accumulated to both multilateral agencies and commercial banks, the IMF declared Peru ineligible for further credits in 1986. On taking office, President García limited public debt service payments to 10% of foreign exchange earnings in order to maintain reserves to promote development. The need to import food, the low level of exports and the fall in disbursements of foreign capital in fact caused international reserves to fall. By 1987 the country was bankrupt after the free spending policies at the beginning of the administration and Peru began to make contacts with its creditors again.

	1961-70 (av)	1971-80 (av)	1981-85 (av)	1986-88 (av)
Gdp growth (1980 prices)	5.7%	3.5%	-0.3%	6.8%
Inflation	9.9%	31.9%	104.9%	193.6%
Exports (fob) US$m	659	1,816	3,135	2,600
Copper	163	366	468	544
Petroleum	—	225	335	217
Zinc	33	139	291	243
Imports (fob) US$m	508	1,398	2,274	2,800
Current account balance US$m (cum)	-592	-4,109	-4,375	-4,301

INFORMATION FOR VISITORS

Air Services from Europe Direct flights from Frankfurt, Paris, Amsterdam, Madrid and Lisbon by Air France, KLM, Iberia, Viasa (who offer a cheap youth fare) and Avianca. Cheap flights from London; one way is to go via Madrid with Iberia, or standby to Miami, then fly with Eastern or AeroPerú to Lima, or Faucett to Iquitos, Cuzco and Lima. Flights with Aeroflot to Luxembourg or Zürich, Top Tours cheapest, N. de Piérola near Plaza San Martín, or Setours, Jr. Unión 1011, Lima. Setours also has cheap flights to Brussels fortnightly. Sobelair, the charter subsidiary of Sabena, has flights leaving Brussels Sun., 16 hrs., stopover of 1 hr. in Martinique, return Mon. Tickets available throughout West Germany, France, Belgium and Holland. Aeroflot fly from Frankfurt via Cuba with 3 hr. stopover in Havana including sightseeing. Tickets from Uniclam-Solmatur, La Paz 744, Miraflores, Lima (T 467298, 478764). To avoid paying Peru's 21% tax on international air tickets, take your used outward ticket with you when buying return passage.

From USA and Canada Miami is the main gateway to Peru with flights every day with Eastern and AeroPerú, Third Avenue, Miami (T 800-255-7378). Other direct flights from New York, Los Angeles, Washington, Vancouver, Toronto and Montreal by CP Air, Avianca, Aerolíneas Argentinas, Air Panamá, Varig, Lan Chile and Ecuatoriana. Faucett has an office in Toronto. AeroPerú offers a bargain, US$759 (US$999 1st class) for a round South America air pass, Miami-Miami, 45 days, plus discount flights inside Peru; can be arranged in USA, T 305-591 9420, or 800-327 7080.

From South America Regular flights to all South American countries; in most cases, daily. Lloyd Aéreo Boliviano (LAB, non-IATA) is usually the cheapest airline for flights out of Lima but tickets bought in Peru are more expensive. LAB flies twice weekly between La Paz and Cuzco. Aerolíneas Argentinas and AeroPerú fly from Mexico. Beware of buying Viasa tickets in Peru, they often turn out to be forgeries. See above for AeroPerú's "Around South America" pass.

Trans-Pacific Flights from Tokyo by Varig and CP Air. From Australia and New Zealand to Tahiti by Air New Zealand, Qantas or UTA with a Lan-Chile connection to Lima via Santiago (stopover in Easter Island).

Trans-South Atlantic From South Africa to Rio de Janeiro by South African Airlines or Varig, with immediate connections.

Taxes There is a US$15 airport tax on international flight departures, payable in dollars (unless you have an Aeroflot ticket). Internal airport tax US$7 (if you are working in Peru, carry a letter stating this and insist you are "residente" and pay local tax of US$0.20). There is a 21% tax on economy international flights originating in Peru. There is a 9% tax on domestic flights. Tax should not be charged on an MCO, but 9% often is.

Shipping Services The French Compagnie Générale Maritime (from La Pallice/La Rochelle to Callao, US$1200 -4 weeks of luxury; enquire at Mundy Travel Ltd, 6-7 Rangoon St., London EC3 2PA, or Paseo de la República 3587, Lima). Passenger services from France can be arranged through Continental Shipping and Travel, 179 Piccadilly, London W1V 9DB, T 01-491 4968. Consorcio Naviero Peruano, Paseo de la República 3587 (Piso 9), Lima, carries a few passengers to Le Havre and sometimes Hamburg; to Italy, Lauro, Av. Enrique Canaval Moreyra 328, Lima.

Documents No visa is necessary for citizens of Western European countries, South American countries (except Chile and Venezuela), Canada, the USA and Japan. Australians and New Zealanders must have visas. A Tourist Card (*Cédula C*, obligatory) is obtained free from the immigration authorities on arrival in Peru for visits up to 90 days (insist on getting the full 90 days, at some borders cards valid for 60, or even only 30 days have been given). It is in duplicate, the original given up on arrival and the copy on departure, and may be renewed (see below). Students should get immigration officials to write "Estudiante" on their cards, so as to get into museums etc. half-price. A new tourist card must be obtained for each re-entry or when an extension is given. An International Certificate of Vaccination against smallpox is no longer required. Declaration of foreign currency no longer required. All foreigners should be able to produce on demand some recognizable means of identification, preferably a passport. Officially, an exit ticket is required for entry into Peru to be allowed. At land frontiers, practices vary; an MCO may not be accepted as an onward ticket. One's best bet is a bus ticket Arequipa-Arica (Tepsa, valid for 6 months, sold as an onward ticket at the Ecuadorean border even though Tepsa have discontinued the route, and more expensive than Arequipa-Tacna, Tacna-Arica bus journeys) which may then be exchanged with persistence. Many travellers have reported that they have not been asked for a ticket at Aguas Verdes, Yunguyo or Desaguadero. If you do not have one on arrival at the border, you may be forced to pay US$15 minimum for an out-going bus ticket. Travellers arriving by air report no onward flight checks at Lima airport.

N.B. Tourist visas may be renewed for 60 days at the Ministerio del Interior, Paseo de la República at Av. 28 de Julio, Lima (also, we are told, in PIP offices in certain towns: check). On presentation of the visitor's passport, a valid return ticket to a destination outside Peru, a *solicitud* (written request for an extension) and on payment of US$20 or the equivalent in intis. If you wish to extend your entry permit after 90 days have already elapsed since your entry into Peru this is possible at the discretion of the authorities, but on payment of a fine of US$20. The maximum stay in such a case would be 150 days from the first entry. If you are in the Puno area when your visa expires, it is sometimes quicker and easier to cross the border to Bolivia for a day and return with a new visa, often for 90 days, which you would not get in Lima or Cuzco. To obtain a one-year student visa one must have: proof of adequate funds, affiliation to a Peruvian body, a letter of recommendation from your own and a Peruvian Consul, a letter of moral and economic guarantee from a Peruvian citizen and 4 photographs (frontal and profile). One must also have a health check certificate which takes 4 weeks to get and costs US$10. If your tourist card is stolen or lost, apply for a new one at Dirección General de Migración, Av. 28 de Julio 1118; very helpful.

Students are advised to take an international student's card in order to benefit from the many student reductions available, especially in and around Cuzco. To be any use in Peru, it must bear the owner's photograph. You can sometimes achieve benefits if "student" is on your tourist card as your occupation, but this can mean hours of haggling.

British business travellers are strongly advised to get "Hints to Exporters: Peru", from Export Services Division, Department of Trade, Sanctuary Buildings, Great Smith St., London SW1P 3DB.

Export Ban No object of archaeological interest may be taken out of Peru.

Duty-free Imports 400 cigarettes or 50 cigars or 500 grams of tobacco, 2 litres of alcoholic drinks, new articles for personal use or gifts up to value US$200.

Tourist Information The Fondo de Promoción Turística (Foptur), at Av. Angamos Oeste 355, Miraflores, Lima, T 43-2525, has offices in the main cities of tourist interest: details in text. See also information under Lima, **page 733**.

Warnings An alarming number of reports of robberies in Peru have been received in 1989. Thieves are active in markets, streets, hotels, buses and trains, choosing especially tourists as their targets. Take care everywhere, but especially when arriving in or leaving from a town at night by bus or train; in fact, it is better to travel by day whenever possible. For general hints on avoiding crime, please see the **Security** section on page 17. All the suggestions given there are valid for Peru. In addition, don't pick up money in the street, it is often a ruse to rob you while you are off guard. If possible, lock your luggage when leaving it in your hotel room. Avoid staying in hotels too near to bus companies, as drivers who stay overnight are sometimes in league with thieves. The police presence in Lima, Arequipa, Puno and Cuzco has been greatly stepped up. It is a good idea to inform your Embassy in Lima of your passport data, so that if the passport is stolen delays for replacement are minimized. In general, common sense is the best policy; seek advice from others at all times (fellow travellers, The South American Explorers Club, Foptur, etc.). Outside the July-August peak holiday period, there is less tension, less risk of crime, and more friendliness. A friendly attitude on your part, smiling even when you've thwarted a thief's attempt, can help you out of trouble.

Although certain illegal drugs are readily available anyone carrying any is almost automatically assumed to be a drug trafficker. If arrested on any charge the wait for trial in prison can take a year and is particularly unpleasant. Unfortunately, we have received reports of drug-planting, or mere accusation of drug-trafficking by the PIP on foreigners in Lima, with US$500 demanded for release. **Drugs use or purchase is punishable by up to 15 years' imprisonment**.

Another Warning The activities of the guerrilla movements, Sendero Luminoso and Túpac Amaru, are spreading. Avoid visiting places where they are reported as particularly active: they have no love for foreign tourists. Since Sendero Luminoso has been linked (supposedly) with the drugs trade, police and army searches have increased. Under state of siege legislation, be careful what you photograph. If possible carry an official letter stating your business. At times provinces are under martial law: a curfew (*toque de queda*) may be imposed; remember to make enquiries about this when you arrive in a new place. The Country Officer for Peru, Office of Andean Affairs, Dept. of State, Washington D.C. 20520, T 202-632-3360, will inform US citizens on the advisability of travel.

Police Action If your belongings are stolen: (1) If the value is over US$20, go to PIP International Police (ask for the *Extranjería* section if you encounter difficulties, the *comandante* or his second-in-command), if under US$20 go to the Guardia Civil. Alternatively, in Lima, one can go to the Tourist Police. (2) Make declaration of loss as soon as possible. (3) Buy *papel sellado* (stamped paper) from Banco de la Nación on which to make statement. A small inducement, say US$1, may help them to speed up the documentation process. See also under Cuzco, **page 805**. If you are robbed on a journey and want to obtain a *denuncia* for insurance purposes, say you were robbed when the bus or train was moving. If it was standing at a bus stop or station at the time the offence was committed, you will be sent back to that particular place to make the *denuncia*, and that might be very inconvenient.

A *denuncia*—a statement of a theft signed by police—is valid in place of a student card if student card is taken, and is essential for insurance purposes. If your American Express credit card is stolen apply immediately to American Express in your own country, or to Lima Tours in Lima or Cuzco. For other credit cards, there is now a combined office in Lima, T 461545 (day and night service).

Internal Air Services link towns which are often far apart and can only be reached otherwise with difficulty. Virtually all the air traffic is in the hands of the Cía. de Aviación Faucett (who run bingo on board!) and AeroPerú. Tickets are not interchangeable between the two companies. See under Lima (**page 735**) for towns served, and above for taxes. Faucett and AeroPerú offer cheap unlimited travel within Peru; the ticket costs £ 140 and is valid for 60 days. You must decide which places you want to go to in advance, but you don't have to go to all of them, and you must fly to Peru with Faucett or AeroPerú and purchase the ticket outside South America. In the UK a £99 airpass is available for unlimited travel, but you can only fly standby; there is also a 4-flight, predetermined-itinerary pass for £165, and a 2-month, unlimited pass for £215. If you have a choice, remember timekeeping tends to be better early a.m. than later.

N.B. Both companies are often criticized for frequent cancellations, unannounced route changes, and poor time-keeping. The Andean area is dangerous for flying, and unpredictable weather contributes to poor time-keeping, but companies are also criticized for their passenger service, especially as regards information and overbooking. Note that flights into the mountains may well be put forward 1 hr. if there are reports of bad weather. Neither company has enough aircraft and both are in financial difficulties. Flights to jungle regions are also unreliable. See also warning on **page 807**.

Flights must be reconfirmed 24 hrs. in advance, but 72 hrs. is advised. Twenty mins. before departure, the clerk is allowed by law to let standby passengers board, taking the reserved seats of those who haven't turned up.

Air Freight (Internal) Packages must be insured and secure so rucksacks should be enveloped in a flour sack.

Roads The Pan-American Highway is open from Lima N along the coast (divided-lane for first 100 km.) to Ecuador (the 1983 flood damage has been almost completely repaired), and S to Arequipa and Chile. It is mostly through desert, with occasional valley oases. The Central Highway from Lima goes through La Oroya NE to Cerro de Pasco, Huánuco, Tingo María and terminates at Pucallpa on the Ucayali River (paved much of the way, but interrupted by mud-slides in the Huallaga valley). From La Oroya a good road goes SE to Huancayo, and on (not good) to Ayacucho, Cuzco, Puno on Lake Titicaca, and on into Bolivia. The Puno-Bolivia stretch is now almost entirely paved. The two roads to Cuzco, one by the Central Andes and the other by Arequipa and Puno, make a most spectacular circuit of 2,400 km. possible. Preferably it should be done clockwise: there would be less driving on the outsides of precipices; it would be downhill on the poor stretch between Puno and Arequipa, and the return to Lima would be by a good road. Another road from Lima to the Sierra branches off the Lima-La Oroya highway at Chosica; it goes along the Río Santa Eulalia and joins the road from La Oroya to Cerro de Pasco just beyond Marcapomacocha. (This road is spectacular, but is mainly used for local access; it is not recommended for long-distance driving.) The Puno-Cuzco section has paved stretches at each end. Most of the high Sierra roads are narrow, unsurfaced and liable to landslides; many accidents. Do not drive fast at night; many local vehicles have poor lights. Be sure to check with the Peruvian Touring and Automobile Club regarding road conditions before driving in the Sierra.

Few roads in Peru, except for the Pan-American and Central Highways and the roads connecting Huarás and Carás with Pativilca, and Pacasmayo with Cajamarca, are paved. Paving of the important Puno-Desaguadero road to Bolivia is now complete. Toll roads in Peru include Aguas Verdes-Tumbes, Pativilca-Huarás, Lima-Pucusana, Ica-Nazca, Lima (highway around city), Variante-Pacasmayo, which vary from US$0.15 (for the roads around Cuzco), to US$0.25 for most others. Landslides are frequent, surfaces are usually very rough, and this makes for slow travel and frequent breakdowns.

Buses Services along the coast and to Arequipa (best is Ormeño) are usually quite good; buses in the mountain areas generally are small, old, crowded and offer little comfort; Ormeño and Cruz del Sur thought generally to be the best. We do not mention the services of Morales Moralitos because so many readers have sent us strongly critical reports. For long journey take a water bottle. Blankets and emergency food are a *must* in the mountains. Always possible to buy food on the roadside, as buses stop frequently. If your bus breaks down and you are transferred to another line and have to pay extra, keep your original ticket for refund from the first company. Colectivos not always much dearer; trucks not always much cheaper; they charge ¾ bus fare, but wholly unpredictable, not for long hops, and comfort depends on the load: the ideal is a half load of sugar. Colectivos go almost anywhere in Peru; most firms have offices. Book one day in advance. They pick you up at your hotel or in main square. Always try to arrive at your destination in daylight: much safer.

Note In the preparation of this edition, it has been impossible to verify bus, or other transport schedules with any accuracy. Shortages of spare parts and disruption of services by guerilla action has resulted in conflicting reports of timetables. Similarly, transport prices have fluctuated greatly, according to exchange rate variations and demand for tickets. Consequently, fares may have changed greatly by the time this edition is in use. We hope that travellers will bear with us while unstable conditions exist in Peru.

Motoring The Touring y Automóvil Club del Perú, Av. César Vallejo 699, Lince, Lima (T 403270), with offices in most provincial cities, gives news about the roads and hotels along the way (although for the most up-to-date information try the bus and colectivo offices). It sells a very good road map at US$2.25 (Mapa Vial del Perú, 1:3,000,000, Ed. 1980, reliable information about road conditions) and route maps covering most of Peru at US$0.40 (Hoja de Ruta, detail maps 1:1,000,000, very good but no information on road conditions). AAA maps sold at *Lima Times* office. Buy maps separately or in packages of 8. Cuadernos de Viaje are travel notebooks covering all Peru with valuable information and maps, in Spanish. Other maps can be bought from street vendors in Colmena and Plaza San Martín, Lima. "Westermanns Monatshefte; folio Ecuador, Peru, Bolivien" has excellent maps of Peru, especially the archaeological sites. Gasoline per US gallon: "extra" (84 octane), US$1.20; "importada" (95 octane), US$1.45, found in Lima, the coastal towns and Arequipa. Gasoline is cheaper in the Selva. In Lima never trust the green light; Peruvian drivers tend to regard traffic lights as recommendations, at most. When parking remove detachable accessories and screen wipers. No-parking signs are painted at the roadside: illegally parked cars are towed away.

Roads go to very high altitudes in Peru—make sure that the spark is properly adjusted and consider use of smaller carburettor jets if driving much at altitude. Avoid mountain travel between November and April. Take 2 planks of wood in case car gets stuck in soft soil when allowing other vehicles to pass. Never travel off the main roads without being self-sufficient. Always make sure your gasoline tank is full when branching off a major highway, fill up whenever possible and make sure you do not receive diesel or kerosene. If you need mechanical assistance in the mountains ask for the nearest mining or road construction camp. If you take your own car you are immediately a symbol of wealth and will be liable to have it broken into. Disadvantages of travelling in your own vehicle include the difficulties of getting insurance, theft, finding guarded parking lots, maintenance on appalling roads and nervous exhaustion, which may outweigh the advantages of mobility and independence.

Imported car spares available and cheaper than in neighbouring countries. Makes with well-established dealerships are easiest to obtain (e.g. Volvo, Peugeot, VW). VW Beetles, Toyota Coronas and Datsun Stanzas are assembled in Peru and therefore easier to get spares and service for. There is also a booming black market in motor parts involving both contraband and stolen parts. Must have international driving licence—especially with a number. If you don't have a number on your licence, improvise. (It has been reported that a UK driving licence is acceptable.)

Note for Hitch-Hikers Hitch-hiking is difficult. Freight traffic has to stop at the police *garitas* outside each town and these are the best places to try (also, toll points, but these are further from towns). Drivers usually ask for money but don't always expect to get it. In mountain and jungle areas you usually have to pay drivers of lorries, vans and even private cars; ask the driver first how much he is going to charge, and then recheck with the locals (the Sierra Indians for whom it is normal method of travel). Private cars are very few and far between. Readers report that mining trucks are especially dirty to travel in, avoid if possible.

Taxis In most places taxi fares are fixed before the journey; therefore it is best to ask local advice on average charges before you bargain with taxi drivers. Taxis ordered at hotels are much more expensive than those hailed on the streets.

Railways There are passenger services on the following lines, which are often quicker and more comfortable than buses, though it is necessary to watch your belongings: Lima-La Oroya-Huancayo, La Oroya-Cerro de Pasco, Huancayo-Huancavelica, Arequipa-Juliaca-Puno, Puno-Juliaca-Cuzco, and Cuzco-Machu Picchu-Quillabamba. Details of services in the text.

Walking Serious walkers are advised to see *Backpacking in Peru and Bolivia*, by Hilary and George Bradt. They describe 3-5 day treks in the Cordilleras Blanca, Vilcabamba and Vilcanota (Cuzco region), and in the Cajamarca area. Also Jim Bartle's book: *Trails of the Cordilleras Blanca and Huayhuash of Perú*, Ed. Gráfica Pacific, Lima, 1980 (Jim Bartle has also published a series of excellent postcards of various peaks, sold in many bookshops in Lima). John Richter's *Yurak Yunka* can be obtained from the South American Explorers' Club or from *Lima 2000* bookshop, J. Bernal 271, Lima. Rob Rachowiecki's *Peru, a Travel Survival Guide*, has been recommended most warmly.

Hotels The State Tourist Hotels (commonly known as *Hoteles de Turistas*) are run by Enturperú. They vary considerably but frequently offer the best accommodation in town in terms of cleanliness and reliable food. They provide safe garaging for cars at US$0.65 a night. Reservations can be made at Enturperú, Av. Javier Prado-Oeste 1358, San Isidro, P.O. Box 4475, Lima, T 287815, 282742, 274077, Telex: 20394.

Heating in rooms is often unsatisfactory. Good local maps can usually be obtained at the Tourist Hotels; in some of the smaller towns they function as tourist offices. All de luxe, 1st class and State Tourist Hotels charge a high 25 % in taxes, which includes service charges; lower category hotels charge 20-23 %. Most hotels have this surcharge included in their prices, but best check first. By law all places that offer accommodation now have a plaque outside bearing the letters H (Hotel), Hs (Hostal), HR (Hotel Residencial) or P (Pensión) according to type. A hotel has 51 rooms or more, a hostal 50 or fewer; the categories do not describe quality or facilities. Many hotels have safe parking for motor cycles. Check all bills most carefully. Bargaining is possible outside the peak July-August holiday season; all hotels seem to be crowded at the end of July, independence celebrations. It should be noted, even in the upper categories, that in general hotel standards are low. Also reception areas may be misleading; it is a good idea to see the room before booking.

Note The Peruvian police seem to be sensitive about finding an unmarried Peruvian woman in a foreigner's hotel room after 1900 hours. They will charge her with prostitution, however innocent your intentions. (Non-Peruvian unmarried couples will not be bothered by the police.)

Camping Easy in Peru, especially along the coast. But following a number of attacks in the Andes on campers, it is not wise to camp in lonely places. Camping gaz bottles are available in Peru. Those with stoves designed for lead-free gasoline should use *ron de quemar*, available from hardware shops (*ferreterías*).

Swimming Between December and April the entire coast of Peru offers good bathing, but during the rest of the year only the northern beaches near Tumbes provide pleasantly warm water.

Climate The coast is at its most agreeable from December to April inclusive, but this is the period when most rain falls in the Sierra. Business is more active later, but climate does not interfere much with business. During the cooler months, June to November, there is little or no rain but Lima's humidity is from 90 to 98 % —and there is little sunshine from Paramonga S to Arica. During this period the temperature rarely falls below 13°C, or rises above 27°C. For the high Sierra heavier clothing should be taken—difference between day and night temperatures is great. The jungles beyond are tropical.

N.B. Between mid-July and mid-September, a great many Europeans go to Peru on holiday (also, many young Peruvians are on holiday in July and the first half of August), so it is better to avoid the country at this time: prices rise, transport is difficult, and the Peruvians tend to be less friendly.

Health Drinking water from the tap is generally not safe in the cities of Peru, but bottled water is available everywhere. Ask for drinks "sin hielo" (without ice) as the ice is likely to be made with ordinary tap water. Salads washed in tap water should be treated with caution on arrival in the country, but once accustomed, you are not likely to get "Inca Quickstep" from salads. Food at better hotels and restaurants is fine, even salads, but watch out for the typical dishes seasoned with highly spiced Peruvian peppers. In cases of diarrhoea, take "Colitina", an effective local remedy. There are frequent outbreaks of typhoid in Lima and in many other parts of Peru. Outbreaks of virus hepatitis occur and can be protected against by taking immunoglobulins; be careful when eating in markets. Be careful about buying gamma globulin in Peru as most pharmacists do not keep it under refrigeration, rendering it valueless. Buy a disposable syringe for US$0.25 to obviate risk of hepatitis from the clinic or doctor's needle. In Lima, there is a Centro de Antirabia if you are unfortunate enough to be bitten by a rabid dog; in other cities, hospitals give anti-rabies injections. Because of a TB epidemic, avoid non-pasteurized dairy products.

Altitude is often a problem in the mountain cities. Also, when walking at high altitude, the body needs sugar, which can be carried conveniently in the form of a block of crystallized pure cane sugar, called *chancaca*, and easily found in markets. (See also **Health Information** at front of book.)

Cost of Living Living costs in the Provinces are from 10 to 20 % below those of Lima. Peru is not too expensive for those who want comfort and reasonable food; eat the set meals when possible; they are served more quickly. Hotel prices compare very favourably with those in other Latin American countries.

Tips Hotel 10 % in addition to the 10 % on the bill. Restaurants: medium to luxury class 5 % in addition to bill which includes tax and 10% service unless otherwise stated. Taxi drivers, none (in fact, bargain the price down, then pay extra for good service if you get it). Cloakroom attendants and hairdressers (very high class only), US$0.50-$1. Railway porters, US$0.15 per bag, according to distance carried. Airport porters, US$0.50, or US$1 for 8 bags or more. Note: anyone who as much as touches you bag will expect a tip. Usherettes, none. Car wash boys, US$0.25, car "watch" boys, US$0.10.

Currency The monetary unit used to be the sol; there are still sol notes and coins in circulation, probably to be withdrawn in 1989. On January 1, 1986, the inti was introduced, worth 1,000 soles, but people still think in terms of soles, or of "libras" (pounds) worth 10 soles (used for amounts under 1,000 soles only). The inti is divided into 100 céntimos. Coins are of 1, 5, 10, 25, and 50 céntimos; 1 and 5 intis. Notes are of 10, 50, 100 and 500 intis. It is difficult to change currencies other than US dollars, and Deutsche marks, and other currencies carry higher commission fees. The Banco de la Nación at Lima airport, and at large towns near the frontier, will repurchase intis from departing travellers if you can produce official exchange slips; you will not be able to buy dollars at the frontier itself.

Warning We have been informed that a large number of forged notes are in circulation; check the numbers if possible, and hold notes up to the light to inspect the blank white space for silhouette portrait. We have also been told that there is a shortage of change in museums, post offices, railway stations and even shops, while taxi drivers are notorious in this regard—one is simply told "no change".

Foreign Exchange Since July 1987 casas de cambio have been closed: it is no longer possible to exchange travellers' cheques for cash dollars. All banks change foreign currency at the official rate. They close Sat., Sun., holidays, and June 30 and December 31 for balancing the books, except that the Jorge Chávez Airport branch is open 24 hrs. every day of the year. Always count your money in the presence of the cashier, particularly the "pre-counted" bundles of notes. It is possible to have US$ or DM sent from your home country. Take the cheque to the Banco de la Nación and ask for a liquidación por canje de moneda extranjera. You will be charged 1% commission in US$ or intis. The main hotels and other banks are now allowed to exchange foreign currencies; however, hotels usually only provide this service for their guests, and many commercial banks charge 4%-5% commission. The services of the Banco de Crédito have been repeatedly recommended. US dollars are the most useful currency (take some small bills), but Deutsche marks can be negotiated in all large towns.

American Express state that they will sell travellers' cheques and give out emergency money, but only in Lima. Travel agents are allowed to accept foreign currencies in payment for their services, and to exchange small amounts. Outside Lima, Arequipa and Cuzco changing travellers' cheques can be a long, slow process and a photocopy of your passport may be required. Travellers have reported great difficulty in cashing travellers' cheques in the jungle area, even Iquitos, and other remote areas. Always sign travellers' cheques in blue or black ink or ballpen.
   The parallel market rate, now formally illegal but very much alive, is used by street money changers in the main centres.

Credit Cards Visa—most common—Diners Club, Visa, and Mastercharge (Access) widely accepted, including at State Tourist Hotels; billed, of course, at the disadvantageous official rate. Some shops only accept cards issued in Peru or South America, and we are told that in Puno it is virtually impossible to use any type of credit card.

Telephones Calls to Europe cost US$13 for 3 min., US$3.25 for each extra minute. Collect calls can now be made to North America and Europe (but not Switzerland) at the Entel offices, off the Plaza San Martín in Lima. Deposit for international calls is more in Cuzco than in Lima. Public telephone boxes need a token (ficha, 300 soles/30 céntimos called a Rin), often in short supply (there are street vendors who sell them, as well as news kiosks). Telephone directories found in most hotel rooms have a useful map of Lima and show itineraries of the buses. Telex to UK: US$15 for 3 minutes.

Mail Sending parcels abroad (over 2 kg.) must be done at Centro de Clasificación de Correos, Tomás Valle, block 600, Lima (take bus 128, direction San Germán). Staff in the post office, which itself will only accept parcels up to 2 kg., help with all checking and then sew parcels into sacks for US$1. Try not to have articles sent by post to Peru; pilfering is very serious. Strikes are also very common. Letters to the UK, most European countries, USA and Canada all cost US$0.55; letters over 10 grammes cost US$0.55, increasing in line with weight. Letters of under 10 grammes within South America cost US$0.25 airmail. For a small fee letters can be sent "con certificado", which is recommended.

The metric system of weights and measures is compulsory.

Public Holidays

January 1: New Year.
March or April: Maundy Thursday (pm).
Good Friday.
May 1: Labour Day.
June 29: SS. Peter and Paul.
July 28,29: Independence (when all prices go up).

August 30: S. Rosa de Lima.
October 8: Battle of Angamos.
November 1: All Saints.
December 8: Immaculate Conception.
December 25: Christmas.

N.B. Everything closes on New Year's Eve, Christmas Eve, and other holidays designated "family holidays", especially July-August. At these times, expect prices to rise.

Hours of Business *Shops:* Jan. to March, 0900-1230 and 1600-1900 (0930-1245, 1615-1900 in Lima). Rest of year: 0900-1230, 1530-1900. Some are closed on Sat.; many close later in the evening. *Banks:* Jan. to March, 0830-1130. Rest of year: 0830-1200 (some have introduced afternoon opening). Closed Sat. **N.B.** All banks close on June 30 and December 31 for balancing; if it falls on Sat. or Sun., banks may close one day before or after. *Offices:* Jan. to March, 0830-1130, and 1500-1830. Rest of year: 0830-1230 and 1500-1830. Many now work a through day, 0800-1500, and most close on Sat. *Government Offices:* Jan. to March, 0900-1130, Sat. 0900-1130. Rest of year: 0930-1100, 1500-1700; on Sat. 0930-1130.

The Press Lima has 8 morning papers: *La Prensa, El Comercio, La República* (liberal-left) *La Crónica, Expreso, Ojo, El Diario, La Actualidad* (founded 1987). There is a weekly paper in English, the *Lima Times*, and a monthly economic and political report, the *Andean Report.* The main provincial cities have at least one newspaper each.

Sports Association football is the most popular. Basketball and other sports are also played on the coast, particularly around Lima and Callao. There are many bathing resorts near Lima. Golf clubs and racecourses are mentioned in the text. Riding is a favourite recreation in the Sierra, where horses can be hired at reasonable rates. Cricket is played at the Lima Cricket Club. There is excellent deep-sea fishing off Ancón, N of Lima, and at the small port of Cabo Blanco, N of Talara (see text). In that part of the Andes easily reached from La Oroya, the lakes and streams have been stocked with trout, and fly fishing is quite good. Bullfights and cockfights are held in Lima.

For details about the best rainbow trout fishing in Peru (near Juliaca and in Lakes Arapa and Titicaca) write to Sr. José Bernal Paredes, Casilla 874, Arequipa.

Food The high-class hotels and restaurants serve international food and, on demand, some native dishes, but the taverns (*chicherías*) and the local restaurants (*picanterías*) supply the highly seasoned native food at its best. Generally found that the modest cafés are best value. Soups tend to be very good, and a meal in themselves. In the Lima area the most popular fish dishes are the *cebiche*—raw fish, seasoned with lemons, onions and red peppers; the *escabeche*—fish with onions, hot green pepper, red peppers, prawns (*langostinos*), cumin, hard eggs, olives, and sprinkled with cheese; and *chupe de camarones*, a shrimp stew made with varying and somewhat surprising ingredients. *Parihuela* is a popular bouillabaisse which includes *yuyo de mar*, a tangy seaweed. *Yacu-chupe*, or green soup, has a basis of potato, with cheese, garlic, coriander leaves, parsley, peppers, eggs, onions, and mint. *Causa* and *carapulca* are two good potato dishes; *causa* is made with yellow potatoes, lemons, pepper, hard-boiled eggs, olives, lettuce, sweet cooked corn, sweet cooked potato, fresh cheese, and served with onion sauce. Favourite meat dishes are *ollucos con charque* (a kind of potato with dried meat), *caucau*, made with tripe, potatoes, peppers, and parsley and served with rice; *anticuchos*, hearts of beef with garlic, peppers, cumin seeds and vinegar; *estofado de carne*, a stew which often contains wine; *carne en adobo*, a cut and seasoned steak; *fritos*, fried pork, usually eaten in the morning; *sancochado*, meat and all kinds of vegetables stewed together and seasoned with ground garlic; *lomo a la huancaína*, beef with egg and cheese sauce; *lomo saltado* is a beef stew with onions, vinegar, ginger, chilli, tomatoes and fried potatoes, served with rice; and *sopa a la criolla* containing thin noodles, beef heart, bits of egg and vegetables and pleasantly spiced. Any dish described as *arequipeño* can be expected to be hot and spicy. *Mondonguito* is a boiled small intestine. The best beef is imported from Argentina and is expensive. Duck is excellent. For snacks, Peruvian *empanadas* are good. *Palta rellena* is avocado filled with chicken salad.

Among the desserts and confections are *cocada al horno*—coconut, with yolk of egg, sesame seed, wine and butter; *picarones*—frittered cassava flour and eggs fried in fat and served with honey; *mazamorra morada*—purple maize, sweet potato starch, lemons, various dried fruits, sticks of ground cinnamon and cloves and perfumed pepper; *manjar blanco*—milk, sugar and eggs; *maná*—an almond paste with eggs, vanilla and milk; *alfajores*—shortbread biscuit with *manjar blanco*, pineapple, peanuts, etc.; *pastellillos*— yucas with sweet potato, sugar and anise fried in fat and powdered with sugar and served hot; and *zango de pasas*, made with maize, syrup, raisins and sugar. *Turrón*, the Lima nougat, is worth trying. *Tejas* are sugar candies wrapped in wax paper; the pecan-flavoured ones are tastiest. The various Peruvian fruits are of good quality: they include bananas, the citrus fruits, pineapples, dates, avocados (*paltas*), eggfruit (*lúcuma*), the custard apple (*chirimoya*) which can be as big as your head, quince, papaya, mango, guava, the passion-fruit (*maracuyá*) and the soursop (*guanábana*).

The tea hour starts about 1800 at the good hotels. If asked to a party ask the hostess what time you are *really* expected unless the time is specified on the invitation card as *hora inglesa*—English time; Peruvians tend to ask guests for dinner at 2000, but don't expect them till at least 2130.

A normal lunch or dinner costs about US$4.50, but can go up to about US$25 in a first-class restaurant, with drinks and wine included. Lunch is the main meal: dinner in restaurants is normally about 1900 onwards. There are plenty of cheap and good restaurants around the centre of Lima and most offer a "business lunch" called *menú fijo* for no more than US$2 for a 3-course meal. There are many Chinese restaurants (*chifas*) in Peru which serve good food at reasonable prices. For really economically-minded people the *Comedores Nacionales* in most cities of Peru offer a standard 3-course meal for only US$0.50. Meals at this price, or little more, can be found under name of *menú económico* at many restaurants throughout Peru.

Drinks　The usual international drinks with several very good local ones: *pisco*, a brandy made in the Ica valley, from which pisco sour is made; *chilcano*, a longer refreshing drink also made with *guinda*, a local cherry brandy; and *algarrobina*, a sweet cocktail made with the syrup from the bark of the carob tree, egg whites, milk, pisco and cinnamon. Wine is acidic and not very good, the best of a poor lot are the Ica wines Tacama and Ocucaje; both come in red, white and rosé, sweet and dry varieties. Tacama blancs de blancs and brut champagne have been recommended, also Gran Tinto Reserva Especial. Viña Santo Tomás, from Chincha, is reasonable and cheap. Casapalca is not recommended. Beer is best in lager and porter types, especially the Cuzco and Arequipa brands (lager) and Trujillo Malta (porter). In Lima only Cristal and Pilsener (not related to true Pilsen) are readily available, others have to be sought out. *Chicha de jora* is a maize beer, usually homemade and not easy to come by, refreshing but strong, and *chicha morada* is a soft drink made with purple maize. Coffee is often brought to the table in a small jug accompanied by a mug of hot water to which you add the coffee. If you want coffee with milk, a mug of milk is brought. There are many different kinds of herb tea: the commonest are manzanilla and hierbaluisa.

For doing the updating work on this chapter, we are extremely grateful to Sylvia Brooks. She would like to express her personal thanks to the following for their assisstance during John and Sylvia Brooks' trip to Peru in September/October, 1988: Sra. Da. Carmen Granda de Byrne, Director of Foptur in London, for arranging the trip; Sr. Willy Angulo Miranda and Da. Bertha Quezada Guzmán of Foptur in Lima, also Sra. Dora Huayane Núñez, for transport to and from the airport in Lima at all hours of the day and night. In addition thanks are due to the staff of Foptur and all who made the trip so worthwhile in Ica, Nazca, Tumbes, Cajamarca, Huancayo, Iquitos and Huaraz.

For new information on Peru we should like to thank Miguel A. Chiri Valle (Trekking and Backpacking Club, Huaraz), Lucho de Cossio (Iquitos), Luis and Beverley Hurtado (Huancayo), Aldo Lazo Del Carpio (Lima), Roberto Silva Janssen (Lima) and Betsy Wagenhauser (South American Explorers Club, Lima); also the following travellers: Julian Anderson (Buenos Aires), Lucia L. Armstrong (Ithaca, NY), Ian Atkinson (Hanley Castle, Worcs), Lee Azus (San Francisco), Rupert Baker (Cropredy, Oxon), Dexter Ball (Chicago), Carolyn Bargman (El Paso, Tx.), Cliff and Martin Barker (High Wycombe), Jane Barlow (London NW6), Bruce Barnes (Gloucester, NSW), Robin E Baronas (Pittsburgh, PE), Urs Baumann (Wildberg, Switz), Pierre-Y Berney (Geneva),

Christophe Beusch (Geneva), Niels Boe (Denmark), Rop Bomer and Wilh. ter Haar (Mexico City), Charlotte Bonordi (University of York), Karen Brooks (London N19), Alison Brysk and Mark Freeman (San Francisco, CA), John Burke (Bristol 7) for a particularly useful contribution, Michelle Burrows (Brisbane), Chris Burton (Norwood, S. Aust.), Rachel Cartwright (Nassau, Bah.), Pamela Caunt and Bob Brass (London N1), Duncan Gourlay Cheyne (Glasgow 13), P. Christmas (Newcastle upon Tyne), Peter and Alison Clarke (Leicester), Marion Clemens (Bonn 3), Jane Coburn and Philip Barnes (Thirroul, NSW), John Crane (Sunbury), Simon Crighton (Ifracombe) for much helpful information, a very useful contribution, Ed Culberson (Brevard Motorcycle Safety Institute, Palm Bay, FL), Klaus Därr (Därr Expeditions Service, München 2), Beat Denzler and Nicole Livet (Zürich), Jeroen Dijkgraaf (Eindhoven), Peter Dryden (UK), Paul Eaton (Victoria, BC), Jytte Eckardt and Kurt B. Petersen (Loendborg, Dmk.), John Edmund (Garstang, Lancs), Eva Ekelund and Jim Lindsay (Stockholm), Hanna Elvrum (Cochabamba), Fred and Marianne Emery (London SE26), Andreas Erne (Zürich 8055), Margaret and Martin Evans (Brighton), Sheila and Dennis Fabricant and Matt Linn, Didier Faget and Sabine Fleury (Vernon, Fr.), Thomas Fedrizzi (Horgen, Switz.) for most useful updatings, R. de Fremond, Felicity Gallagher (Saxon, Switz), Anita Gee and Ian Boonin (Ilford), Theodor A. Gevert (Barueri, S.P. Brazil), Dan Golopentia (Seattle), Martin Gorst (London W13), Christina Gräwe (Tautkirchen) and Joachim Hoell (Wernstadt, W.Ger.), Jan Jacob de Groot (Vroomshoop, Neth.), Monika Gwerder (Muotathal, Switz.), Knut Per Hasund (Stockholm), Robert Hauer (Bonn 1), Charles Havekost (Greenbelt, Md.) and Eva Lindholm (Zug, Switz.), Dave Henson (San Francisco, CA), Detlev Hessenbruch (München 40), Thomas Hirsch and Dörte Weischet (Hannover), Christian and Nickolaj Hoff (Holte, Copenhagen), Christoph Hofmeister (Karlsruhe, W.Ger.), Rainer Hostnig (Abancay), Rod House (Melbourne), David K. Howe (Short Hills, NJ), Don Hoyle (London EC2), David Hutchinson and Susie Maddox (London W8), Gretke Moen Johansen (Kolbotn, Norway), Martina Jost and Heinz Eisenhauer (Darmstadt), Anne Junk, Simon Kahn (Los Angeles), Chris Kapolka (London N3), Omer Karchi (Tivon, Israel), Prof. Alexander Kennaway (Ashtead, Sy.), Simon Kennedy and Sally Constable (Melbourne), Susanna Kent (Auckland 3), Martin Ketels (Hamburg 50), Ronen Khayat (Jerusalem), Bernard and Rebeca Kolner (Ramat Hasharon, Israel), Tom Krasner (Miami Beach), Harald Kremer (Stuttgart 40), François Laffely (Montreux), H. Lanters (Maastricht, Neth.), Kenneth and Nancy Leighton (Vancouver), Christian Levin (Kiel, W.Ger.), John Lewis (London NW3), Charles Locher (San Francisco) and Nancy Blackstock (Berkeley, CA), Loving Team (London), Susan MacCallum and Peter Hedvlin (Sydney, Aust.), Adeline Machler, Bjarne Madsen and Gitte B. Andersen (Odense), Robert E. Manley (Cincinnati), Adrian Marchbank (London SE5), Douglas E. Markham (Houston, TX), Christine Marthaler and Jürg Briner (Zürich 8038), Cindy McNamara (Bath), Dr Bruce Means (Tallahassee), Lucy Meikle (Pershore) and Stuart Duncan (Scotland), Wolfgang Meusburger (Dornbirn, Aust.), Kelvin Moody (Stratford, NZ), Melanie Morningstar and Peter Charley (New York 10002), Dimitri Moursellas (Manhattan Beach, CA), Christoph Müller (Zürich 8004), Richard Müller (Bern), Dr Charles Munn (New York Zoological Society), John and Christine Myerscough (Glossop, Derbys), Melanie Newman (with John Pritchard, Ros Harris, Danial Taylor, Carol Finn and Finn Bangshaad Jensen—London W9), Frank O'Connor (London W3), Bertil Olin (Johanneshov, Swed.), Graham J. O'Neil (London SW7), Mark Pangbourne (Hastings), Florence Paratte (Ollon, Switz.), Pia Parolin (Milano), Jim and Pam Pellegrin (Los Gatos, CA), Diego Puls and Rubén Chapp (Amsterdam), Pierre Rambaud (Echirolles, Fr.), Devendra Rana (London NW1), Danny Rapley (NZ), Geoff A Richardson (Barranquilla), Miranda Roberts (London SE3), Viv and Richard Robinson (Tring, Herts.), Gisele Rochat and Jean-Paul Corboz (Neuchâtel, Switz.), Carlos A. Rodríguez (Mérida), Christian Scherlenzky (Villa Ballester, Buenos Aires), Arno Schmid (Hamburg 71), Anne Schnurr (Mainz-Weisenau, W.Ger.), Rolf Schneider (Effretikon, Switz.), Leon van der Schoor (Netherlands), Florian Schulz (Berlin 27), Markus Schulz (Gambach, W.Ger.), Colin Sears and Caroline Richard, Antony Sherlock (Edinburgh 12), Ian Skeet (Winchester), Stanis Smith (Burnaby, B.C.), Robert Spruytenberg (Peymeinade, Fr.), Karl Stanley (Cheam, Sy.), Mr and Mrs Ernest Stead (Pudsey, W Yorks), Doris Stöckli and Christophe Racine (Fislisbach, Switz.), Dolf Straub (Berlin 12), Bob Straiton (Nevada, Iowa), Hal Stufft and Dorothy Young (Imler, PA/Evesham), Ignacio Tapia (Concepción, Chile), Thomas N Taylor (Houston), Judy Thompson (Australia), Barry Tiffen and Lucy Stephens (Torksey, Lincoln), Heather Varden (Fleet, Hants), John Walker, Rob Ward (Sutton, Sy.), Regina Wetzer and Richard C. Brusca (San Diego, CA), Roland Wiemer and Karla Menner (Hamburg 50), Conrad Wiesendanger (Münchenstein, Switz.), Gordon Williams (London W12), Joseph C. Williams (Tokyo 108), Ray Williams (Pwllheli), Alida and Gordon Wilson (San Rafael, CA), Dr Eldon R Wilson (Columbus, Ohio), Wytske Winter and Hans Haringa (Aberdeen), Cecilia Ydell and Jonas Martensen, Stefani Zapf and Wolfgang Gross (Frising, W. Ger.) and Helmut Zettl (Ebergassing, Aust.).

URUGUAY

URUGUAY (area 186,926 square km.) is the smallest Hispanic country in South America, about the same size as England and Wales together, but its population, 2.93 million, is less than that of Wales alone. The rate of population growth at 0.6% pa. over the last seventeen years is low by the area's standards. Uruguay has Brazil to the north, the River Uruguay between it and Argentina to the west, and the wide estuary of the Plate to the south. The Atlantic Ocean washes its shores on the east.

Apart from a narrow plain which fringes most of the coast (but not near Montevideo), and an alluvial flood plain stretching N from Colonia to Fray Bentos, the general character of the land is undulating, with little forest except on the banks of its rivers and streams. The long grass slopes rise gently to far-off hills, but none of these is higher than 600 metres. The Río Negro, which rises in Brazil, crosses Uruguay from NE to SW, where it empties, amid dense forest, into the Uruguay River.

The black soil, rich in potash, produces grasses superior even to those of Argentina. About 90% of the land is suitable for agriculture but only 12% of it is used for arable farming.

History and Settlement The Spanish explorer, Juan Díaz de Solís, sailed up the River Plate in 1516 and landed E of the site of Montevideo, near what is now Maldonado. His second landing was in the present Department of Colonia, where he was killed by the Charrúa Indians. There was no gold or silver in Uruguay, and it was only after about 1580 that the Spaniards showed any interest in it. Military expeditions against the Indians were unsuccessful, but Jesuit and Franciscan missionaries, landing in 1624, founded a settlement on Vizcaíno Island. It is said that cattle were first introduced during an unsuccessful expedition by Hernando Arias in 1607; they were successfully established between 1611 and 1620.

By 1680, the Portuguese in Brazil had pushed S to the Plate and founded Colonia as a rival to Buenos Aires, on the opposite shore. It was the Portuguese who planned, but the Spaniards who actually founded, the city of Montevideo in 1726. It changed hands several times and was actually taken by the British in 1807, but after their failure to hold Buenos Aires, they withdrew altogether. In 1808 Montevideo declared its independence from Buenos Aires. In 1811, the Brazilians attacked from the N, but the local patriot, Artigas, rose in arms against them. In the early stages he had some of the Argentine provinces for allies, but soon declared the independence of Uruguay from both Brazil and Argentina. Buenos Aires invaded again in 1812 and was able to enter Montevideo in June 1814. In January the following year the Orientales (Uruguayans) defeated the Argentines at Guayabos and regained Montevideo. The Portuguese then occupied all territory south of the Río Negro except Montevideo and Colonia. The struggle continued from 1814 to 1820, but Artigas had to flee to Paraguay when Brazil took Montevideo in 1820. In 1825 General Juan Lavalleja, at the

URUGUAY

1. Montevideo.
2. East from Montevideo.
3. Montevideo North-East to Brazil.
4. Montevideo North to Brazil.
5. West from Montevideo.
6. Up the River Uruguay.

1. Plaza de la Independencia.
2. Plaza Cagancha/Bus Terminal.
3. Parque Battle Y Ordóñez.

MONTEVIDEO

head of 33 patriots (the Treinta y Tres Orientales), crossed the river and returned to Uruguay to harass, with Argentine aid, the invaders. After the defeat of the Brazilians at Ituzaingó on February 20, 1827, Britain intervened, both Argentina and Brazil relinquished their claims on the country, and independence was finally achieved in 1828.

The early history of the republic was wretchedly confused by civil war between two rival presidents, Rivera with his Colorados and Oribe with his Blancos; these are still the two main parties today. Oribe, in this ten years' war, was helped by the Argentine dictator, Rosas, and Montevideo was besieged. Rosas fell from power in 1852, but the contest between Colorados and Blancos still went on. A Colorado, Flores, helped by Brazil, became president, and Uruguay was dragged into the war of the Triple Alliance against the Paraguayan dictator, López. Flores was assassinated in 1868 three days after his term as President ended. The country, wracked by civil war, dictatorship and intrigue, only emerged from its long political turmoil in 1903, when another Colorado, a great but controversial man, José Batlle y Ordóñez, was elected president.

Economic Development   There was little Spanish settlement in the early years, but the cattle, once introduced, multiplied exceedingly and were responsible for a long time for the social structure of Uruguay. Groups of nomadic *gauchos* trailed after the herds, killing them for food and selling their hides only. Organized commerce began with the arrival of cattle buyers from Buenos Aires who found it profitable to hire herdsmen to look after cattle in defined areas around their headquarters. By about 1800 most of the land had been parcelled out into large *estancias*. The only commercial farming was around Montevideo, where small *chacras* grew vegetables, wheat and maize for the near-by town.

It was only after independence in 1828 that immigration began on any scale. Montevideo was then a small town of 20,000 inhabitants. Between 1836 and 1926 about 648,000 immigrants arrived in Uruguay, mostly from Italy and Spain, some into the towns, some to grow crops and vegetables round Montevideo. The native Uruguayans never took to agriculture: they remained pastoralists, leaving commercial farming to the immigrants. Unlike Argentina, Uruguay has remained to this day a preponderantly pastoral country, though modern demands have changed the pastoral life. The upgrading of cattle, importing livestock from Britain, made Uruguay second only to Argentina as a meat and meat-product exporter. From the middle of the 19th century high-grade wool, the result of importing pedigree sheep from England, became an increasingly important item in the Uruguayan economy. Jewish, Armenian, Lebanese and other more recent immigrants chose to enter the retail trades, textiles and leather production rather than farming.

Present Social Structure   With the election of José Batlle y Ordóñez as president from 1903 to 1907, and his re-election in 1911, Uruguay became within a short space of time the only "welfare state" in Latin America. The state has not only nationalized the public services but also controls many industries, including cement and chemicals. Its workers' charter provides free medical service, old age and service pensions and unemployment pay. Divorce has been legal for many years; illegitimate children have status and the right to inherit, and the investigation of paternity is obligatory. Education is free and compulsory, capital punishment abolished, and the church disestablished.

However, as the country's former prosperity has ebbed away over the past three decades, the welfare state has become increasingly fictitious. In 1973 the military promised to reduce the massive bureaucracy, spend more on the poor and development, and generally get the country moving again after the social and political turmoil of 1968-1973. In practice they expanded state spending by raising military and security programmes. Real wages fell to less than half their 1968 level. Less than ten per cent of the unemployed received social security payments. Montevideo began to sprout a few small shanty towns, once unheard of in this relatively affluent corner of the hemisphere. One of the most egalitarian countries in Latin America has increasingly come to resemble the rest of the continent, as only the very wealthy benefited from the military regime's attempted neo-liberal economic policies. Nevertheless, the country's middle class remains very large, if impoverished, and the return to democracy in 1985 raised hopes that the deterioration in the social structure would be halted, if not reversed. Almost ten per cent of the population emigrated for economic or political reasons during the 1960s and 1970s: the unemployed continue to leave, but the political and artistic exiles have returned *en masse*.

Allying himself with the Armed Forces in 1973, the elected President decreed the closure of Parliament, and stayed on to rule for the rest of his term as the military's figurehead. Scheduled elections were cancelled in 1976, and a serious wave of political and trade union repression instituted. Unable to convince the population to vote for a new authoritarian constitution in 1980, the military became increasingly anxious to hand back power to conservative politicians. However, moderate politicians refused to accept the harsh conditions the military continued to try and impose. Finally, in August 1984 agreement was reached on the legalization of most of the banned leftist parties and elections were held in November. The euphoria was spoiled by the fact that the strongest opponent of the regime was not allowed to stand. The new moderate government of Julio María Sanguinetti was inaugurated in March 1985 for a five year term of office (elections were due on November 20, 1989). The process of national reconstruction and healing of political wounds began with a widespread political amnesty, but no new radical economic policies. Despite extraordinarily adverse conditions (such as the highest per capita debt in Latin America) Uruguay's former traditions and the innate conservatism of Uruguayans give grounds for hoping that the troubles will not return.

Population The population was 3.06m by mid-1987; just under half live in Greater Montevideo. Only some 15% are rural, and the drift to the towns is 1.6% per year. Both the death rate and the birth rate are low. The people are almost entirely white, mostly of Spanish and Italian stock, for there are no native Indians left, and only a few light-skinned "blacks" in parts of Montevideo and near the Brazilian border. Possibly 10% are *mestizos*. About 96% are literate. The natural population increase is low for Latin America: 0.7% per annum. So is infant mortality, 37.6 per thousand. Gdp per capita is US$2,400.

MONTEVIDEO (1)

Montevideo, the capital and the only large city in the country, was founded in 1726. Population, in and near: 1,246,500 (1985). The original site on a promontory between the River Plate and an inner bay, though the fortifications have been destroyed, still retains a certain colonial atmosphere. The city not only dominates the country's commerce and culture—almost 90% of all the imports and exports pass through it—but is also a summer resort and the point of departure for a string of seaside resorts along the coastline to the E.

A major landmark, the Palacio Salvo on Plaza Independencia, has recently undergone exterior renovation which removed its formerly splendid *art-nouveau* mouldings. It is not open to visitors. On the same plaza, the Victoria Palace hotel has a rooftop restaurant with fine views. Otherwise, the best place to get a view of the city is from the top of city hall (La Intendencia); external glass elevators take you up to a viewing platform, where there is a pastry shop, and an expensive restaurant. Entrance at the back of the building on Soriano, between Ejido and Santiago de Chile.

Set between the old town (Ciudad Vieja) and the new is the grandest of Montevideo's squares, Plaza Independencia with the impressive black marble mausoleum of Artigas in the middle. On most sides it is surrounded by colonnades, and there are three pavement cafés at the eastern end. The other end has been spoiled by rebuilding, particularly to the N and S beside Government House. In 1986 the government of President Sanguinetti moved the executive offices to the Palacio Libertad far from the centre, which the Armed Forces had put up to house the Ministry of Defence. The old government house, known as the Palacio Estévez, is now used for ceremonial purposes only. The long unfinished modern block to the West was originally intended to be the Palace of Justice, then presidential offices, but its future use is in doubt. Just off the plaza to the West is the splendid Solís Theatre, a Museum of Natural History alongside. In the old town, a short distance west of Plaza Independencia, is the oldest square in Montevideo: the Plaza Constitución, also known as the Plaza Matriz. Here on one side is the Cathedral (1790-1804), with the town hall (1804-1810) opposite. Still further west along Calle Rincón is the small Plaza Zabala, with a monument to Zabala, founder of the city. N of this Plaza are four buildings well worth seeing: the Banco de la República (Cerrito y Solís), the Aduana (Rambla 25 de Agosto), and the houses of Generals Rivera (Rincón y Misiones, 1300-1900) and Lavalleja (around the corner in 25 de Mayo, Tues., Wed. and Fri. 1100-1900). Together, the latter two buildings form the National History Museum.

The Avenida 18 de Julio, whose pavements are always thronged, begins at the Palacio Salvo. Along this avenue is the Plaza del Entrevero (with a statue of a group of *gauchos* engaged in battle), between Julio Herrera and Río Negro, a very pleasant place to sit; and the Plaza Cagancha (or Plaza Libertad), with a statue of Liberty and the main tourist office. The Municipal Palace (Intendencia), with the viewing platform, is on the South side of Av. 18 de Julio, just before it bends N, at the statue of the local equivalent of a cowboy (*El Gaucho*). In front of the Municipality is a plaza with a copy of Michelangelo's David in one corner. The road which forks S from the *Gaucho* is Constituyente, and leads to the fashionable beachside community of Pocitos. There are two museums inside the Municipal Palace, entered around the corner in Ejido: Museum of Art History, and Museum of Precolombian and Colonial Art (1700-2100 except Mondays). The latter is the more interesting. Beyond is the University, and nearby are the National Library, the French *lycée*, and the Ministry of Health. The avenue ends at an intersection with Bulevar General Artigas. Here is an obelisk commemorating the makers of the 1830 Constitution, by José Luis Zorrilla de San Martín (born 1891), and here, too, one may enter the Parque Batlle y Ordóñez (see below). The immense Legislative Palace, built of local marble, is reached from Av. 18 de Julio along Av. del Libertador Brig. Gen. Juan Lavalleja (normally known as Av. Libertador, formerly Av. Agraciada), 5 blocks E of Plaza Independencia (buses 150, 173, 175 from Calle Mercedes). (N.B. Calle Ibicuy is now called Hector Gutiérrez Ruiz.)

At the western end of the bay is the Cerro, or hill, 118 metres high (from which Montevideo gets its name), with an old fort on the top, now a military museum (0800-1800, entry US$0.20) with arms, flags and drums. The Cerro is surmounted by the oldest lighthouse in the country (1804). Bus from centre to Cerro: 125 "Cerro" from Mercedes, and others. In the port (which one can visit on Sat.—see Tourist Office), opposite the Port Administrative Building, the ship's bell of H.M.S. *Ajax* has been set up to commemorate the scuttling of the *Graf Spee*. The anchor of the *Graf Spee* was set up at the entrance to the port area in 1964 to commemorate the 25th anniversary of the battle; the wreck itself lies about 3 km. offshore, but is no longer visible as it was dismantled some years ago. However, plates from its bulkheads have been used in the construction of the city stadium. One can still see the *Graf Spee*'s supply ship, listing but still afloat (used in the past as a prison hulk).

Of the many parks, El Prado (about 5 km. from Av. 18 de Julio, along Av. Libertador) is the oldest. Among fine lawns, trees and lakes is a rose garden planted with 850 varieties; also in the Prado is La Diligencia (the stage coach). The two buildings of the Municipal Museums of Fine Art and History are in the grounds. During August, an annual farm show is held in the park. The largest and most popular park is Parque Rodó, on Rambla Presidente Wilson. Here are an open-air theatre, an amusement park, and a boating lake studded with islands. The National Museum of Fine Arts, with works by living artists, and a children's playground are at the eastern end. In Parque Batlle y Ordóñez (reached by a continuation eastwards of Av. 18 de Julio), are several statues: the most

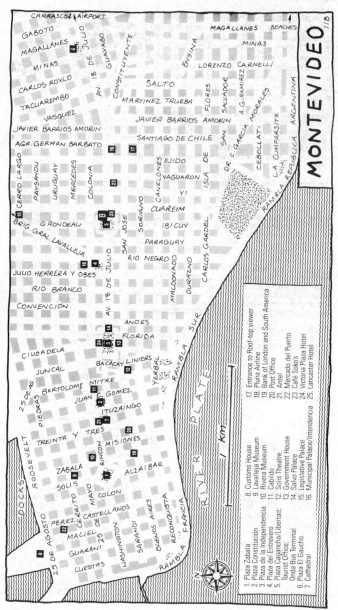

MONTEVIDEO 1/8

1. Plaza Zabala
2. Plaza Constitución
3. Plaza de la Independencia
4. Plaza del Entrevero
5. Plaza Cagancha/Libertad;
   Tourist Office;
   Onda Bus Terminal
6. Plaza El Gaucho
7. Cathedral
8. Customs House
9. Lavalleja Museum
10. Rivera Museum
11. Cabildo
12. Solís Theatre
13. Government House
14. Salvo Palace
15. Legislative Palace
16. Municipal Palace/Intendencia
17. Entrance to Roof-top viewer
18. Pluna Airline
19. Bank of London and South America
20. Post Office
21. Antel
22. Mercado del Puerto
23. Café Soko's
24. Victoria Plaza Hotel
25. Lancaster Hotel

RIVER PLATE

1 km

N

interesting group is the very well-known "La Carreta" monument, by José Belloni, showing three yoke of oxen drawing a waggon. In the grounds is the Estadio Centenario with a seating capacity of 70,000 and the main football pitch (Bus 177 from Av. 18 de Julio) but the 107 or 64 (a trolley-bus) are almost as convenient. There are a field for athletic sports and a bicycle race-track as well. The Zoological Gardens are a few blocks E of this park (open until 2000); in the Gardens is a planetarium, one of the best in South America, displays Tues. 1730, Sat. and Sun. 1730 and 1830. Trolleybus 60 from Aduana (old city) passes the zoo gate. Entrance US$0.80.

Festivals Easter week is also Tourist Week (Fiesta Gaucha), with rodeo-type competitions held in the Parque El Prado (US$1.50 entry—bus 149 from Ejido in centre, or 183 from Pocitos) or Parque Roosevelt (horse-breaking and handicrafts), music (mostly folk). Large barbecues are held in the open air. Christmas Eve and New Year's Eve are celebrated with drummers and firecrackers in the streets. During carnival week and a few days after there are many live shows; especially recommended is the traditional *candombe* singing and dancing in the Barrio Sur in the centre (e.g. at *El Boliche* bar).

The Beaches (See inset map, page 855) Nine sandy bathing beaches extend along almost the whole of the metropolitan water front, extending from Playa Ramírez in the W to Playa Carrasco at the eastern extension of the city. Along the whole waterfront runs the Rambla Naciones Unidas, named along its several stretches in honour of various nations. Bus 104 from Aduana, which goes along Av. 18 de Julio, gives a pleasant ride (further inland in winter) past Pocitos, Punta Gorda and all the beaches to Playa Miramar, beyond Carrasco. The express bus DI leaves from Plaza Matriz (Constitución) in front of the Cathedral and stops at special yellow bus stops; by using this service, which costs slightly more (US$0.40) about 30 minutes are saved on the journey there to Carrasco. The town beaches are reported still to be polluted, despite a major clean-up programme.

Among the main seaside residential areas are Pocitos, well supplied with hotels, restaurants and night-clubs (*boites*), with the reputation of being the "Copacabana" of Montevideo; and Carrasco, a delightful semi-rural place behind the beach of the same name at the end of the Rambla Sur, backed by a thick forest which has partly been turned into a national park. The international airport is nearby. E along the coast is a string of resorts, with much less polluted beaches, which are dealt with later in **East from Montevideo**.

Hotels Below are leading hotels, with average charges per day during the tourist season, when they should be booked in advance. Prices are lower during other seasons. When not included, breakfast usually costs US$1-$2. There is a 12 % value-added tax on hotel bills. Tipping 10 % .

	Single US$	Double US$	Remarks
Hostería del Lago, Arizona 9637	—	—	Luxury, reported best in Montevideo area
Victoria Plaza, Plaza Independencia	48	60	A/c; controlled by interests connected with Mr Moon's Unification Church
Columbia Palace	32	50	Includes breakfast, good restaurant
California	36	50	Including breakfast
Crillón, Andes 1318	35	48	A/c. and including breakfast
London Palace, Río Negro 1278	30	42	Central; garage, parking
Parque, Playa Ramírez	25	35	Including breakfast
Ermitage, Juan B. Blanco 779/83, Playa Pocitos	22	31	

There are a great many hotels, most of them cheaper than the ones listed. In the vicinity of the Onda bus terminal/Plaza Cagancha, and West towards Plaza Independencia are: *Internacional*, Colonia 823, A-L, rec. for business visits; however, no telex. *Alvear*, Yi 1372, C, good service, friendly, also rec. for business travellers. *Gran Hotel Americano*, B, Río Negro 1330 (with telex). *Lancaster*, C, a/c, incl. breakfast and bath, across plaza from bus terminal; *Aramaya*, Av. 18 de Julio 1103, E with bathroom, old, clean, comfortable; *Río de la Plata*, Av. 18 de Julio 937, F, clean, hot water; *Americana*, Av. 18 de Julio 1212, E with breakfast, rec.; *Los Angeles*, Av. 18 de Julio 974, private bath, clean, old-style, friendly, rec., D (reductions for stays of over 3 days); *Balfer*, Cuareim 1328, one block off 18 de Julio, good, safe deposit, excellent breakfast; *Alcalá*, Río Branco 1105, very clean and friendly, C (without bath). Several on Uruguay: *Colonial*, 963, F; *Regencia*, 944, E; *Resid. Arapey*, 925, F. *Mediterráneo*, Paraguay 1486, D with bath, family-run, clean, comfortable converted mansion. Many on Soriano: *Cervantes*, Soriano 868, plain but clean room with bath, C; *Nueva Pensión Ideal*, Soriano 1073, E; *Royal*, Soriano, E, hot showers, clean, friendly; *Hospedaje del Centro*, Soriano entre H.Gutiérrez Ruiz y Paraguay, E with bath, clean, friendly, rec.; *Pensión del Este*, E, Guitiérrez Ruiz y Soriano, hot water, cold rooms, no clothes-washing allowed, nice cat, nosy dueña. *Ateneo*, Colonia 1147, clean, F with bath, friendly. Several along Colonia, between Yí and Florida. *Cifre*, E (10% discount on stays of over 2 weeks) Mercedes 1166, clean. *Libertad*, Ibicuy 1223, E, clean, quiet and food available; *Casablanca*, San José 1039, friendly, E with bath; *Itá*, San José 1160, next to Onda terminal, E, clean and quiet; *Pensión Trinidad*, San José 1220, E, dark and not too clean, though friendly; *Hospedaje Diagonal 2*, Convención entre Av. 18 de Julio y San José, F, clean, friendly.

Plenty of cheap hotels in and near the old city, e.g. *Lavalle*, Bartolomé Mitre 1314, T 962887, F, clean, basic; and *Matriz*, on Ituzaingó, E, clean and friendly, though run down. More expensive, though, are *King's*, just N of Plaza Independencia, C with breakfast, Andes 1491 casi Uruguay, rec.; on Piedras are *Alojamiento Piedras*, No. 272, and *Pensión Universal*, No. 270, both E.

East of Plaza Cagancha: *Arosa*, Constituyente 1917, C, friendly, pleasant. At Carrasco: *Cottage*, B, friendly, no restaurant; *Casino Carrasco*, C with breakfast, good, "ancient splendour, reasonable service"; *Bristol*, E, built in 1926 in Louis XV style, must be seen, pleasant; *Oceania*, Mar Artico 1227, C, near airport (transport service), pleasant view, good restaurant and night club, highly rec..

At the beaches many hotels offer full board only during the season. After April 1 prices are greatly reduced and some hotel dining rooms shut down. For Carnival week, on the other hand, prices are raised by 20%.

Information on hotels from tourist office on Plaza Cagancha (Libertad) and Centro de Hoteles y Restaurantes del Uruguay (Hector Gutiérrez Ruiz, formerly Ibicuy 1213). **Hint**: cheap hotel rooms in Uruguay are invariably gloomy. Bring your own 220V Edison-screw bulbs and hope they don't put too much strain on the wiring. The booking situation at hotels can be found by ringing 90.04.53 (CIHTU) or 90.03.46.

Youth Hostel The headquarters of the Association are at Pablo de María 1583, 8th floor, T 40-42-45, open 1300-1900 Mon.-Fri. Hostel (members only) is at Canelones 935, T 98-13-24. US$1-2.30 p.p. according to season, probably the best bargain, clean, dormitory style, closed 1000-1700. Open all year.

Camping Parque Roosevelt, near Carrasco, about US$2 p.p., free, hot showers, safe, no electricity, 15 km. from centre, open all year, or superb camping in the wild can be had to the west of the Cerro on the flanks of the hill below the fort, amid pine trees. Also, Hugo A. Morante has written to offer to rent a log cabin, 30 km. out in the woods (T 98.93.18/98.11.07). Reports please.

Restaurants The dinner hour is very late, from 2100 to 2400. (Less formal restaurants serve from 1930 onwards.) First-class restaurants at the centre are *El Aguila*, Buenos Aires 694, next to the Solís Theatre; *Morini*, Ciudadela 12-29, serves excellent steaks, simple but not cheap. *Bungalow Suizo*, Andes 1427, very good (about US$22 per head inc. wine). *La Lutèce*, French, excellent, in Mercado del Puerto; *Panorámico*, 24th floor of Intendencia, pricey but worth it for the service and view. Don't miss eating at the Mercado del Puerto, opposite the Custom House, on Calle Piedras, between Maciel and Castellanas (take "Aduana" bus), grills cooked on huge charcoal grates (menus are limited to meat); colourful atmosphere and friendly; *Cabana Verónica* has been particularly rec. There are about a dozen grills open during market hrs. (though now the expanding numbers of grills and bars have largely replaced the market!); at night only *El Palenque* is open. Other good grill rooms (parrilladas) include *Las Tejas*, Av. Brasil, and *Nuevo García*, Calle Arocena, Carrasco. Also for lunch in the old city, *La Crêperie*, Bartolomé Mitre, near Sarandí, in Mercado de Artesanatos, good unusual crêpes and salads, cheap.

In the central Plaza Cagancha/bus terminal district: *La Genovesa* (Spanish), San José 1242, excellent, reasonably priced; *Las Brasas*, San José 909, good typical food, moderate prices; *Viejo Sancho*, San José 1229, restaurant after 2000, excellent, popular, complimentary sherry or vermouth to early arrivals, tearoom by day; Italian restaurant at San José 1166, good; *El Fogón*, San José 1080. *El Gran César*, on Gutiérrez Ruiz, reasonable, rec.. A good cheap place is restaurant on 6th floor of YMCA building, Colonia 1870, open for lunch and 1900-2200, US$2 (two courses) and plentiful with good views too; ask for the Asociación Cristiana de Jóvenes. *Cervecería La Pasiva* on Plaza Independencia, good, cheap; also *La Pasiva*, Ejido y 18 de Julio, rec.. *Los Chivitos*, Río Branco y 18 de Julio, is a good cheap place to eat. *Gran Coco*, on Yí, offers a variety of good meat and vegetable dishes for about US$1.80; *Centro Residentes de Artigas*, San José 885, cheap, clean and friendly; *Antiquario*, Maldonado, atmospheric. In the Barrio Sur, *Bellini*, San Salvador y Minas, with piano music and singing.

Vegetarian: *Alimentación Integral*, Ituzaingó 1478; *Vegetariana*, Yí 1334, esq. Av. 18 de Julio, not very good, also San Juan 1056. *Kombi*, near Onda terminal, lunch Mon.-Fri., cheap, good.

Good cheap breakfasts at *Nuevo Metro*, San José 1200. A good place for lunch is the *Golf Club*, good food, excellent surroundings and grand view.

Many good restaurants in Pocitos including *Doña Flor* (classy French restaurant, limited menu but superb) Blvd. España y Artigas; *Entrevero* (popular with Americans), 21 de Setiembre.

Tea Shops, known locally as *confiterías*. Best is said to be *Sorocabana*, on Plaza Cagancha, traditional atmosphere, cakes and coffee. The most popular are along 18 de Julio, including *Latino, Facal, Manchester, Lusitano, Café del Rex, Lion D'Or, La Puerta del Sol*. Good ones are *Taberna Portofino*, Ituzaingó 1325, and *Oro del Rhin* (0830-2100), Colonia y Convención (ex-Latorre). In Pocitos are *Cakes*, near Villa Beatriz (also in Carrasco), excellent; *Expresso Bar*, J.B. Blanco y Bulevard España, popular meeting place; *Virgilio's Café* at Punta Gorda on Rambla, good views, and many others. At Puerto Buceo Yacht Club, where tourists are allowed in.

Coctelerías Cocktails served with lots of side dishes: *Soko's*, 18 de Julio e Yí, also serves good food; *Bar Hispano*, Av. San José, excellent vermouths with 28 varieties of *hors d'oeuvres* and good food. *Payaso*, Galería Yaguarón, 18 de Julio; *Giorgio's*, Scocería and Rambla, Pocitos. Many others along the Rambla, with good sea views.

Heladerías Ice-cream parlours produce very good, unusual ice creams in the summer, and draw large crowds. Try *La Cigale*, Scocería, Pocitos, on Ejido, or on Brandzen. *Las Delicias*, Carrasco, or *Papitos*, at 18 de Julio 1054.

Discos *People*, on Cuareim; *Eros*, on Boulevard Artigas. The best discotheques, called *boites*, are *Merek* and *Lancelot* in Carrasco (the former at lakeside, with swimming pool and chalet architecture, the latter a castle!); *Zum Zum* and *Privée* (Miguel Barreiro and Rambla) in Pocitos are good too. They admit couples only and have taped music, US$15 a couple, entrance included on 1st drinks. They are open until very late (2230-0500). Reservations are recommended on Sat. night. *Graffiti* is a cheap disco in Carrasco.

Night Clubs The Bar and the Záfiro Room at the *Victoria Plaza* with Tropicana Show US$12 (incl. food), also *Lancaster Hotel*. The delights of the tango are available at *Tanguería del 40* at *Hotel Columbia Palace* or *La Cumparsita* in Calle Gardel (rec.). For music try *Cantores*, Gonzalo Ramírez 1417; there is a *peña* (folk-music show) at *El Templo del Sol*, Blvd. España 2109 (very varied, crowded and hot, similarly *St Elmo's* nearby), or *Pulpería* on Mercedes. In Pocitos, *Ratatouille*, Missini y J. Benito Blanco, Uruguayan, Brazilian and Argentine live music, US$4 incl. first drink; *House of Andrews*, live music, both best after 2300.

Information Dial "214" for the central bureau of information (in front of Onda bus terminal) about communications, the weather, pharmacies on night duty and anything you want to know about streets in the city. Dial "6" for exact time.

Electric Power 220 volts 50 cycles, A.C.

Shopping The main shopping area is Av. 18 de Julio, good for men's business suits. For sheepskin and leatherwork try Casa Mario, Piedras 641. Suede and leather are not as cheap as in Buenos Aires, nor is quality as good; styling is more traditional. Amethysts and topazes are mined and polished in Uruguay and are good buys; see Topaz International, *Victoria Plaza Hotel*. For woollen wall hangings see Manos del Uruguay, which sells floor cushions, crafts, high quality woollen goods, etc. at Reconquista 616, and at San José 1111, and in the shopping centre in Carrasco near the Rambla. Other good craftwork (cheaper) in daily covered craft market on Plaza Cagancha, and Sat. a.m. craft fair in Villa Biarritz. The old city is said to be a good, cheap place to buy antiques. Antique shops on Plaza Independencia. On Sunday morning there is a large, crowded street market on Tristán Narvaja (good for silver and copper, and all sorts of collectibles) opposite Facultad de Derecho on 18 de Julio. Another flea market is held on Plaza Zabala, a couple of blocks behind the cathedral on Saturday mornings. On Sats. there is one at Pocitos for fruit, leather and woollen handicrafts. Also in Galería Diri, 18 de Julio and Río Negro, which now has a branch in New York City. The Montevideo Shopping Center on the E edge of Pocitos (Herrera y Rivera) has wide range of shops including Manos del Uruguay as well as others selling leather goods (bus 141 or 142 from San José).

Cameras and Film Best place for developing films is Photo Martín, Av. Libertador and Uruguay; Delucchi, on Herrera y Obés, good for developing slides; camera repairs by Fotocámara, on Cuareim between Merceded and Colonia. Film developing and equipment is quite expensive in Uruguay; better to bring film from abroad.

Bookshops English and American books: Librería Barreiro y Ramos, 25 de Mayo y J. C. Gómez; Ibana, International Book and News Agency, Convención (ex-Latorre) 1479, specializes in foreign publications. Librería Ingleson, Sarandí 580, specializes in language and children's books. Others include Librería Mosca Hermanos, Av. 18 de Julio 1578; Feria del Libro, Av. 18 de Julio 1308; Paseo del Lector, Av. 18 de Julio y Cuareim; Librería Papacito, Av. 18 de Julio 1415 and Heritage Internacional, Soriano 1610. There is a good one at Tristán Narvaja 1736.

Taxis US$0.30 for first 600 metres, and US$0.02 for each 140 metres afterwards; an additional 20% from midnight to 0600, charge for each hour of waiting, US$3.30. There is a small charge for each piece of luggage. Taxis can be hired, by agreement, by the hour within city limits. Taxis to Carrasco airport from the centre, US$9, also bus US$1.

City Transport City and suburbs US$0.20 (at night it costs a third more). There are many buses to all parts from 18 de Julio; from other parts to the centre or old city, look for those marked "Aduana".

Car Hire without chauffeur, US$50 per 24 hrs., plus extra per kilometre if only hiring for the day; guarantee of US$100 required. Hire for 3-day weekend is US$130. The firms offering this are Hertz and National in Colonia, near Plaza Independencia, Avis at airport, American International Budget and Sudamcar, La Paz 1523, National Fill Service, Rambla Rep. del Perú 815, Esq. 813, self-drive hire is not recommended. With chauffeur, US$35 per 8-hr. day plus US$0.12 per kilometre, and payment for a chauffeur's lunch or supper. Rogelio Martinelli, Canelones 1450; Luis Moro e Hijos, Camino Ariel 4737; Empresa Salhon, Av. 8 de Octubre 4199; F. Miramonte, Magallanes 1446; ARI, 18 de Julio 2142; Hertz, Calle Colonia near Paza Independencia; National, nearby; Snappy, Andes 1363; and Avis.

Casinos Parque Hotel at Playa Ramírez; Hotel Carrasco at Carrasco.

Museums Historical: Casa Lavalleja, Zabala 1464, open Tues., Wed. and Fri., 1100-1900, and Casa Rivera, Rincón 437, open daily 1300-1900. Natural History: Buenos Aires 652, 1400-1800 Tues.-Sat. (has a well-preserved, half-unwrapped mummy). Botanical: 19 de Abril 1179. Art: Museo Nacional de Bellas Artes, in Parque Rodó. Worth a visit for the park alone. Municipal: in large rooms upstairs at the Cabildo. The Intendencia (18 de Julio y Ejido) has occasional exhibitions. Zoological Museum, Rambla Chile 4215, on beach at Puerto Buceo. Gold Museum and Gaucho Museum in the sumptuous Banco de la República building, Av. 18 de Julio 996 (Mon.-Sat. 1300-1830). No entrance fees. The Sociedad de Amigos de Arqueología, Buenos Aires 652 (Casilla 6521) can provide professional advice. Museo Blanes, Millán 4015, has many Pedro Figari paintings, open 1400-1800, Tues.-Fri., free, rec. Automobile museum, Colonia e Yí, 6th floor, open 1700-2000, about 25 old models. Naval museum by the Buceo in Pocitos; air force museum near municipal stadium on Av. Larrañaga. Museum schedules are indefinite: most are open Sun. and Tues. through Fri., but at times are open only in the afternoon, so make sure. Consult the newspaper El Día for current opening times of museums, exhibitions and libraries; also what's on generally.

Theatres Solís, housing the national theatre company and occasional visiting companies, worth seeing inside; cheap concerts on Mondays between March and November (US$0.30). El Galpón theatre company has now returned from exile. The Comedia Nacional plays at Sala Verdi, Soriano 914. Café Teatro "El Reloj"; Circular; Notariado; La Máscara, Río Negro 1180, Teatro del Anglo, San José 1426 (in the same complex free films are often shown, videos of ballet, opera, etc.). The national ballet company Ossodre is said to outperform the Buenos Aires company. Stella d'Italia; Círculo; Centro. All these are more or less professional. Occasionally, small amateur or semi-professional groups put on plays in cinemas or other places.

Cinema-going is very popular. Price is almost the same in all cinemas, at US$1.85-2 (some half-price on Thurs.). Classic films at Cinemateca. Films are released quite soon after the UK and USA, and often before they get to Buenos Aires. At least half Montevideo's cinemas show blue films—marked sexo explícito.

Music Concerts at Solís Theatre (see above). Pop concerts are held in Centenario stadium and Parque Rodó. Jazz at Alíanza Francesa and Alianza Uruguay-Estados Unidos. Brazilian music: Clave de Fu, Pocitos. For tango clubs etc. see above under **Night Clubs**. During the two weeks around Carnival there is a music and dance competition, in the Parque Rodó amphitheatre, in "Murga", a form of satirical revue, 4 hrs. every night, US$0.50 entry, starting at 2100.

Sports The beach is more popular than the water. Uruguay has three important yacht clubs, the Uruguayo, the Nautilus and the Punta del Este. Both the Montevideo Rowing Club and the Club Nacional de Regatas have club houses on the Bay. The German Rowing Club is on the Santa Lucía River. Fishing is becoming popular. Association football is played intensively. Rugby football is also played, and there is a yearly championship. There are two good 18-hole municipal links. There are several lawn tennis clubs, and two for polo. Horse races at Las Piedras (**see page 870**). There is a national lottery. Massage is available at Suomi, Dr. José Scocería 2909.

Schools The British School at Carrasco and some 4 others, 1 French, 1 German, and the Crandon Institute, an American school for children up to 17. All have good scholastic ratings.

Churches The Roman Catholic Cathedral is known locally as the Iglesia San Juan. Anglican Church, Reconquista 522 (a national monument) T 908062 (English Service 1800 Sunday). Methodist services at Christ Church, Carrasco. Holy Trinity Episcopal (British), and the Emanuel Methodist Church (American), hold regular services in English. The German Evangelical Church holds services in German at Calle J. M. Blanco 2. There is a synagogue.

Addresses

British Embassy, Marco Bruto 1073. T 780352/791033.
US Embassy and Consulate, Rambla Wilson 1776. T 409051/409126.
British Chamber of Commerce, Av. Libertador 1641, piso 2°, of.201. T 900936.

American Chamber of Commerce, Bartolomé Mitre 1337, esc. 108. T 906052.

The English Club, Treinta y Tres 1309. T 995605.

The British Council (Instituto Cultural Anglo-Uruguayo), San José 1426, 3° piso. T 908468 (has good library with newspapers, sometimes has free films).

The British Hospital, Av. Italia 2420. T 409011.

Goethe Institut, Canelones 1524. T 405813/404432.

Alliance Française, Soriano 1176 (theatre, concerts, exhibitions in French and Spanish).

The Apostleship of the Sea, Washington 274. T 952421.

West German Embassy, La Cumparsita 1417-35, T 904958.

Spanish Embassy, Av. Brasil 2786.

Swedish Embassy, Av. Brasil 3079, piso 6, Pocitos, T 780088.

Swiss Embassy, Ing. Frederico Abadie 2934-40; T 704315.

Brazilian Consulate, Blvd. Artigas 1257 (Embassy at No. 1328).

Paraguayan Consulate, Blvd. Artigas 1191, open 0900-1200 summer, 1400-1730 winter.

Post Office, Misiones 1328 y Buenos Aires; 0800 (0730 in summer)-1845 Mon.-Fri., 0800-1245 Sat. and holidays (0730-1145 in summer). Also next to Pluna office at Plaza del Entrevero, and under Intendencia at corner of Av. 18 de Julio and Ejido. Closer to tourist area, there is one at Mercedes 929, at Convención.

Telecommunications   All America Cables & Radio Inc., Plaza Independencia; Italcable S.A., 25 de Mayo 400; Western Telegraph Co., Ltd., Cerrito 449; Telégrafo Nacional, Sarandí 478. Public telex booths (open 0700-2300) are available at Antel, Mercedes 884 or Rincón 501 and Treinta y Tres (open day and night also for international phone calls). Antel office at Sarandí 478 is open 24 hrs. a day for international phone calls.

Exchange   Lloyds Bank, Calle Zabala 1500, and 11 city agencies; Citibank, Cerrito 455 (corner Misiones); Banco Holandés Unido, 25 de Mayo 501; and Banco Comercial, Cerrito 400 and Av. Libertador (up to US$1,000 available on Access or Visa card); and Banco Panamericano Uruguayo on Plaza Cajón. American Express, Rincón 403, no commission if buying US$ bills or new pesos with Amex travellers' cheques. Open: 1300-1700, Mon.-Fri. Money-changing is done by banks and hotels. There are exchange houses, especially along 18 de Julio, e.g. Gales, at 1046. (1% commission on travellers' cheques.) However, do shop around for best rates; Exprinter on Plaza Independencia has been recommended. No restrictions on foreign-exchange transactions. i.e. an excellent place to stock up with U.S. dollar bills if travelling onward. Airport bank open every day 0900-2200; so is the Banco de la República exchange office on Plaza Cagancha.

Tourist Commission   Headquarters is at Av. Libertador 1409, fourth floor. Information Centre is on Plaza Cagancha (Libertad); helpful (though little English spoken) but only carries information on Grade D hotels and above. For budget hotels and *pensiones* try Centro de Hoteles y Restaurantes, H. Gutiérrez Ruiz 1213. Also at Carrasco international airport.

Travel Agents   Muritelli, Plaza del Entrevero, JP Santos, Colonia 951, and Jetmar, Plaza Independencia, all helpful. Wagon-Lits (Thomas Cook agents), Av. Gral. Rondeau 1392; Exprinter, Sarandí 700; Turisport Ltda., Mercedes 942 (American Express for travel and mail services, good; sells Amex dollar travellers' cheques on Amex card and personal cheque at 1% commission); Golden Tours, Colonia 1221, T 90 7500, English spoken. Viajes y Turismo, Convención 1343 y 18 de Julio, 4th floor, T 916461, very helpful, English spoken. Turinter, Río Negro 1358, very helpful. Sur Bus does good US$10 day trip to Punta del Este, 0900-1800, transfers from and to your hotel.

Maps   An excellent map is produced by Ancap, the state oil company, US$1.50-2.

Airport   The main airport is at Carrasco, 21 km. outside the city; 30 mins. by taxi (US$ 13-15) to Montevideo or about 50 by bus from Av. 18 de Julio. Buenos Aires-Montevideo by air, US$80 single, plus US$2.50 airport tax. Lapa from Colonia (US$22) is cheaper than the hydrofoil via Colonia, and also lands at Aeroparque (Buenos Aires). Weather permitting, they are also quicker. Internal flights are very cheap, e.g. US$11 to Salto, US$25 to the Brazilian border at Rivera. Pluna will accept credit cards only at its office in Plaza de Entrevero. Tamu, the military airline, offers considerably reduced prices on many internal flights; there are also Tamu flights to Santiago and Rio de Janeiro every other week, civilians are taken for US$15, but service is unreliable (ask at Pluna office in Montevideo, Uruguayan consulates in Santiago or Rio). If exchange facilities closed at airport, buses will accept dollars for fares to town. IBAT, Yaguarón 1318, runs the airport bus, leaves there at 1045 daily and calls at the Pluna office (Plaza Fabini) at 1100. Onda and COT services to and from Punta del Este call at the airport. Pluna airport bus, via Ramblas, starts at Plaza del Entrevero, US$0.75 (free if you hold a Pluna or Tamu flight ticket); Copsa bus goes along Paysandú and Av. Italia, US$0.50. Left luggage, about US$1 a day per item.

Rail   *All passenger services were withdrawn in January 1988.*

Buses within Uruguay   Good services to most towns; to Punta del Este, 2 hrs., US$3.50. Piriápolis US$2 (slow). La Paloma US$4 (slow). Maldonado US$3.25. To La Coronilla US$6.25 (5 hours). Colonia US$3.75, by Onda. During the summer holiday season buses are booked heavily; it is recommended to book in advance (also for Fri. and weekend travel all year round); Carmelo US$5; to Paysandú, US$8, 5½ or 7½ hours, according to route; to Salto, 4 a day, 7½ hrs., US$10. All services out of Montevideo to other parts of Uruguay leave Onda bus terminal on Plaza Cagancha; those to the east make a compulsory stop at Dante 1945/9; others at Terminal Goes, Av. General Flores y Domingo Aramburu. Onda runs services all over the country (the office is just off Av. 18 de Julio). The smaller competing services are just as fast and less expensive; differences in prices can sometimes be large. Services along Route 7 to Tala and San Jacinto are operated by Cita and leave from their office at Av. Libertador 1446. Arco office for buses to Colonia on Plaza Cagancha.

To Paraguay, Brazil, Chile Twice-weekly COT or Brújula bus (Tues. and Fri.) to Asunción, Paraguay (20 hours, US$28) alternatively take bus to Santa Fe, Argentina, via Paysandú bridge, for easy access to Asunción. As the journey involves crossing part of Argentina, British visitors will need a visa. There are very comfortable buses to Porto Alegre (US$21, 12 hrs.) and São Paulo (US$35 daily at 2100) via Onda or TTL company (Plaza Cagancha, opposite Onda), with drinks service on the *coche cama* and luxury service: often booked very early. A cheaper alternative route (which also avoids the risk of being stranded at the border by through-bus drivers) is to Chuy (US$7, 6 hrs.), then catch an onward bus to Porto Alegre (7½ hrs., US$5.50), either direct or via Pelotas. To Santiago (Empresa Gen. Artigas) via Buenos Aires and Mendoza, US$70, 28 hrs., departs Mon. 0800.
N.B. One needs a passport when buying international tickets.

To Argentina: Ferries Argentine immigration officer on ferries. To Buenos Aires: night (2100) service US$14.75 without sleeper and breakfast (US$20 sleeper); restaurant, bar, disco, otherwise three daytime ferries, very convenient either end. Car ferry, about US$37. Buquebus via Colonia, includes cars, four crossings a day, combined bus-ferry ticket US$16, 6 hrs'. journey. See also under Colonia (**page 871**). Travel to Buenos Aires by hydrofoil (*Aliscafo*, Plaza Cagancha 1325, T 904608/905063) 5 sailings a day (3½ hrs.) between 0400 and 1630 from Rinconada de Plaza Libertad, costs US$25. It is cheaper to purchase hydrofoil or Buquebus tickets for Montevideo-Buenos Aires direct, rather than take a separate bus to Colonia and buy ferry tickets there.

Bus Onda, US$17.25 to Buenos Aires; to Tigre via launch from Carmelo, US$15. Buquebus, Río Negro 1400 (Plaza del Entrevero) via ferry from Colonia, 6-7½ hrs., US$15-20, 3-5 times daily (depending on season), fewer on Sun., efficient. Onda, CIT and COT (Sarandí 699—office) have pooled daily service to Buenos Aires, leaving at 2200 and 2300 via Fray Bentos, US$12.50, 10 hrs.

EAST FROM MONTEVIDEO (2)

The beach season is from December to the end of February. This beautiful coastline, over 320 km. long, contains an endless succession of small bays, beaches and promontories set among hills and woods. There is a series of well equipped and modern camp sites all along the coast. Details are published in Friday's edition of *El Día* especially during the tourist season.

Two roads, both paved, go to Punta del Este. The northern branch (no tolls) via Pando and Soca, is Route 8; at Km. 75 Route 8 continues NE towards Minas (**see page 869**); while Route 9 branches off to San Carlos (14½ km. N of Maldonado or 19 km. N of Punta del Este) through beautiful rolling country with views of the Laguna del Sauce and on to Chuy. The "Interbalnearia", runs largely along the coast, with short branches to some of the resorts, and is the one described in the text. There are toll posts (US$0.75) at Arroyo Pando and at Arroyo Solís Grande. There is an alternative road to the Interbalnearia route, running parallel between it and the coast—its use is recommended during heavy traffic periods due to the frequency of dangerous road junctions. Route 9, the road to Chuy, is now completely paved. A spur of the road turn S to La Paloma, and there are secondary roads to some of the resorts further along the coast.

Atlántida (*Rex*, C, is main hotel; *Munday*, C, is clean and friendly; many good *residenciales* charging E off season; some good restaurants—try the *Banzai*), 45 km. from Montevideo, is ringed by fir forest and has a good country club. A short distance beyond, in groves of eucalyptus and pine, is the small and intimate beach of Las Toscas, followed by Parque del Plata, on the Solís Chico river. An *asado* on the beach (with wine) costs about US$12. Shortly before Atlántida, in an old fortress set in pine woods, is *El Fortín de Santa Rosa* hotel and restaurant, 2 mins. from a lovely sandy beach. Small zoo not far off.

At km. 64.5 on the Interbalnearia is Sr. Garabedian's **campsite**. For bookings, telephone Sr. Garabedian at Montevideo 561230.

Crossing by a (toll) bridge we come to **La Floresta** (*Oriental*, highly rec.; *del Parque*), surrounded by woods. The chalets are pretty; the place reminds one of the villages of the Landes, near Biarritz.

About 35 km. on, over a toll bridge, is **Solís** (*Solís Golf; El Chajá*), at the mouth of the River Solís. It has a very long beach, good fishing, delightful river and hill scenery. About 8 km. beyond Solís lies the small village of Las Flores, with a better beach than that at Solís. Accommodation is available at Edén Camping with room at US$3 p.p. or camping at km. 91 site.

Piriápolis, the next resort, 16 km. from Solís, 101 from Montevideo, may be reached either by turning south at the end of the Interbalnearia, and coming through Solís and then along the very beautiful R10, or by taking the original access road (R37) from Pan de Azúcar, which crosses the R93. It has a fine casino hotel and some 50 others, a good beach, a yacht harbour, a country club, a golf course, a motor-racing track and is particularly popular with Argentines. The town, set among hills, is laid out with an abundance of shade trees, and the district is rich in pine, eucalyptus and acacia woods. There are medicinal springs. Six km. to the N is Cerro Pan de Azúcar (Sugar Loaf), crowned by a tall cross with a circular stairway inside; there is only a path up to the cross. Just outside Piriápolis on the side road to Pan de Azúcar (town) by the entrance to the municipal park is a good zoo, containing among other things live specimens of all snakes and most animals native to Uruguay. In the municipal park (La Cascada) is the Museo Castillo de Piriá, open 1300-1700, Fri., Sat., Sun. and holidays. The shortest route from Piriápolis to Punta de Este is by the Camino de las Bases which runs parallel to the R37 and joins the R93 some 4 km east of the R37 junction.

Hotels Most close end-Feb until mid-Dec. *Argentino*, C, with casino, pool open to public for US$2.50, also sauna; *City*, E (off season—otherwise D), with bath, ocean view; *Rex*, next to Onda terminal, C, rec.; *Colón*, open off-season, C; *Centro*, E, rec.; *Colonial*, Rambla de los Ingleses, E with shower, breakfast, heating, clean, rec. *Luján*, C in season, E out of it, rec. The Centro de Hoteles y Anexos de Piriápolis runs a reservation office at Edificio Piriá on Rambla de los Argentinos.

Restaurants *Argentino*; *Don Quijote*, rec. for paella, cheap and good; *Parador Punta Fría*; *Puertito Don Anselmo* (shellfish, excellent and cheap, overlooking sea); *Entrevero*, in which vermouth is offered with about 20 side dishes, described as "a meal in itself".

Youth Hostel Close to beach, behind *Hotel Argentino*, at Simón del Pino 1136, T 0432-2157, US$1 p.p. (open at least Nov.-March), mostly double bedrooms. There is also an international YMCA camp on the slope of Cerro del Toro, double rooms in bungalows, and tents.

Bus to Montevideo, US$2, 1½ hrs. Buses also to Rocha and Gen. José Artigas bridge (Argentina), US$17.

Tourist Information Asociación de Fomento y Turismo, Rambla de los Argentinos 1348.

Portezuelo has good beaches with the Laguna del Sauce and the fine Lussich woods behind. At **Punta Ballena** there is a wide crescent beach, calm water and very clean sand. The *Solana del Mar Hotel* (opens mid-December, payment in dollars cash is demanded unless you protest) modern, is on the beach, A with full board. The place is a residential resort but is still quiet. Casa Pueblo, the house of Uruguayan artist Carlos Páez Villaro, can be visited; it is built in a Spanish-Moroccan style on a cliff over the sea; there are paintings, collages and ceramics on display, and for sale; season: Nov. 1 to April 1. The Arboreto Lussich (only open 1030-1700 in winter) on the West slope of the Sierra de la Ballena (north of R10) contains a unique set of native and exotic trees. At the top of Punta Ballena there is a panoramic road with remarkable views of the coast. From Portezuelo it is possible to drive north towards the R9 by way of the R12 which then continues, unpaved, to Minas.

Maldonado, capital of Maldonado Department, 140 km. from Montevideo; population 6,000. This peaceful town, sacked by the British in 1806, has many colonial remains: the parish church, El Vigia watch tower, and fortifications on Gorriti Island in the semi-circular bay. Gorriti Island, densely wooded and with superb beaches, is an ideal spot for campers. See also the Mazzoni Museum (700 block of Ituzaingó, Tues.-Sat. 1200-1900, Sun. 1400-1900); San Fernando de Maldonado Museum (Sarandí y Rafael Pérez del Puerto, Tues.-Sat. 1300-2000); Museo de Arte Maldonado (José Dodera 648 y Treinta y Tres, private museum, interesting); and the windmill. *Hospedaje Ituzaingó*, E, on Ituzaingó, Irish owner, very friendly, kind and helpful, but makes small charge for water for washing clothes. *Hotel Dieciocho*, on Plaza, E with bath, rec.; *Le Petit Hotel*, Gral. Marco de los Reyes (1st floor), T 23044, E, shower, a/c, clean, rec. Restaurants: *Club Municipal*, *Matias*, *Módena*, 3 de Febrero 642, good fish and meat US$10 p.p. *Ramón Guerra*, Ituzaingó and cheap *parrillada* at 2 Avenida on Santa Teresa. *Círculo Policial*, run by police, good cheap place to eat. Just after crossing the bridges to La Barra de Maldonado is the *Restaurant San Jorge* with its speciality of *torta de mariscos*. Also *La Posta del Cangrejo* (L) has a pleasant terrace, as well as rooms, about US$16 p.p. to eat there; further on is *Rest. Neuhausen*, not too expensive, pleasant. Bus to Montevideo US$3.25; to Piriápolis, US$0.90. Bus to Minas, Coom, 2 hrs., 5 a day, US$2.50. The railway track between Maldonado and Punta del Este has been turned into a road.

Camping Two sites: one free, in Parque El Placer; the other charges.

San Carlos, on Route 8, 14½ km. N of Maldonado, is a charming town, half the size of Maldonado. Buses run from the plaza to Maldonado every 15 mins.; it is a good point for connections to La Paloma, and Chuy on the Brazilian border. Historical museum opposite *Hotel Reyes* (Olivera y Carlos Reyes, E, friendly, "immaculate"); other hotels: *Residencial Plaza*, Treinta y Tres, opposite plaza (E) and *El Amanecer*, Treinta y Tres 634. Free camping, with facilities, in lovely municipal park. 2 *cambios* which exchange travellers' cheques.

Punta del Este   Seven km. on and 139 km. from Montevideo, facing the bay on one side and the open waters of the Atlantic on the other, lies the largest and best known of the resorts, Punta del Este, which is particularly popular among Argentines. Prices seem to have come down since the recession in Argentina. The narrow peninsula of Punta del Este has been entirely built over; it has excellent bathing beaches, the calm *playa mansa* on the bay side, the rough *playa brava* on the ocean side. There are an excellent yacht marina, yacht and fishing clubs, and many beautiful holiday houses. There is good fishing both at sea and in three near-by lakes and the river Maldonado (which the main road crosses at Manantiales by a unique inverted-W-shaped bridge). The rest of the area consists of sand dunes covered with pines. On Isla de Lobos, which is a government reserve within sight of the town, there is a huge sea-lion colony; excursions to it every morning at 0800, return at 1115, US$7 p.p.; ticket should be bought at the harbour the day before. Direct daily Boeing 737 flights from Buenos Aires to Punta del Este airport during the high season. On the land side, Punta del Este is flanked by large planted forests of eucalyptus, pine and mimosa. A large country club (the *Cantegril*) lets cottages and hotel apartments at a high price, or one may hire from an "Inmobiliaria". There are a golf course and two casinos. After the Easter vacation the place is all your own and on sunny days it is still warm enough to swim (even between March 10 and Easter it is quiet). Many of the best hotels and restaurants close after the end of the season in March.

Hotels   Very many, *Palace*, Gorlero y 11, A (B in March, closed in winter), breakfast only (but good restaurant, *El Aguila*, in the hotel), lovely courtyard, colonial style, well kept; *Amsterdam*, El Foque 759, L, ocean view; *San Rafael*, 1½ km. from centre on Atlantic side, B out of season (price doubles in season or with sea view), with breakfast, closed after Easter, luxurious; *Peninsula*, D-C off season, central, with bath, rec., open all year; *Tamaris* (in the woods), very modern but only showers; *Florinda*, Calle 27, A, friendly. Very few low priced hotels but try *Hospedaje Isla de Gorriti*, Calle Isla de Gorriti 884, D; *Residencial Ituzaingó*, Ituzaingó 839, D; both OK and cheapest in town. *Shelton* (but bargain and examine your final bill) and *Charrúa*, near transport terminals. *Puerto*, Muergos 27, 4 blocks from Onda bus station, C, clean and friendly, English spoken; *Tourbillón*, Calles 9 and 12, basic, no hot water, E, in the off season. *L'Auberge*, near golf course, air-conditioned, "lo más refinado". Hotel rates are as much as halved in the winter months. In the high season, cheapest doubles cost about US$18; it is better to find a hotel in Maldonado and commute, or look for a hotel that is rebuilding, so that you can negotiate on prices. To stay at a hotel in the woods you will need a car; no public transport to beach or town.

Restaurants   The most expensive restaurants are *La Floreal* (in the woods), *La Bourgogne*, excellent, French-run, Pedragosa Sierra, with gourmet shop in basement, about US$60 a head and *La Lutèce*, also French cuisine, Los Souces casi Pedragosa Sierra. *Bleu Blanc Rouge*, Calle 9 y 12, very good, US$25 p.p.; *Mariskonea*, one of the oldest established, US$25 p.p.; *Bungalow Suizo*, Av. Roosevelt y Parada 8, expensive but very good; *El Mastil* (behind port), charming atmosphere, open all year; *La Pomme*, Calle 11 esq. 12, Belgian-run, good; *El Ciclista*, Calle 20, 801, inexpensive Italian cooking; *El Metejón*, Gorlero y 17, steak, US$6, simple; *Forte di Makalle*, Calle 8-828 y 11, US$10, rec.; *Cala Mayor*, Calle 11 y 10, US$16, well rec.; *Los Caracoles*, Calle 20 y 28, excellent seafood, in centre; *El Cacique*, Calle 28, No. 620; *El Sargo*, on Av. Gorlero; *Stromboli*, Gorlero y 17, rec., not cheap. On main street, *La Fragata*, open 24 hrs. all year, a good meeting place; one block up main street from bus station, at Gorlero y 30, is *Country Cook*, US-owned, good, cheap, wholesome; *Blue Cheese*, overlooking yacht harbour, for steaks and unlimited salads. *Andrés* on a terrace at the Edificio Vanguardia, about US$13 p.p. Many enticing ice-cream parlours, such as *Confitería Gorlero* or *Concorde* in Gorlero. A good disco is *New Faces*, Calle 20.

Crafts   Manos del Uruguay in front of the Casino Nogaró. Best sweaters from San Carlos.

Museum   Foundation museum of Contempory Latin American Art, Barrio Beverly Hills, T 83477, open Dec. to end of Holy Week, Tues.-Sun. 1000-1400. Worth a visit but car needed to get there.

Tourist Information Liga de Fomento, Parada 1, or Onda at Av. Gorlero and Calle 27, T 40023.

Exchange Both Amex and Diner's Club have offices. Best rates of exchange from Banco de la República, which opens earlier and closes later than the other banks. Also *casas de cambio*.

Buses New terminal on Calle Sarandí (served by local bus No. 7). To Montevideo, COT, Sur Bus or Onda (rec.) buses, US$3.50, less than 2 hrs., plenty of buses in the summer; to Piriápolis, US$1.50. To San Carlos (US$1.50) for a connection to Porto Alegre (US$30) or Onda services. Direct to Chuy, 4 hrs., US$5. To Gen. José Artigas bridge (Argentina) US$20. Local bus fare about US$0.20.

Airport El Jagüel (full customs facilities) as well as the airport on the southern shore of the Laguna del Sauce, Capitán Curbelo, which handles the Pluna and Aerolíneas Argentinas flights to Buenos Aires, US$66. Pluna to Porto Alegre and São Paulo. Airport tax US$2.50 and bus to town US$1.50. Exchange facilities, but no tax-free shopping yet.

Near Punta del Este, to the E, *Playa San Rafael,* where there is an 18-hole golf course, is growing rapidly. (*Casino San Rafael,* L high season (20/12-1/3), B low season, no credit cards, no a/c or balconies, much used for conferences, Telex 28035, T 042-82161; *San Marcos,* B, very pleasant; *Hotel Porto Beri,* new; *L'Auberge,* A). 30 km. from Punta del Este is the quiet fishing village of Faro José Ignacio, with lighthouse and the well-known restaurant *Parador Santa Teresita,* where seaweed omelette is a speciality. Further E are Punta del Diablo, with a beautiful beach, camping and a picturesque fishing village, and Cabo Colonia, which may be reached by horse-drawn carriage (look for signs on the road), or by bus from La Paloma and 1¾ hrs. walk.

Rocha is 211 km. from Montevideo and 28 km. from the sea at La Paloma. Population: 20,000. Two casinos located at *Costas del Mar* and *Cabo Santa María* hotels. *Hospedaje Plaza* on the plaza, budget, D/E (3 rooms only). Cheap food at *Las Vegas* on Ramírez. Groves of palms dotted about the fields give the area an unusual beauty.

Hotels at Rocha: *Arrate; Trocadero,* C; *Roma; Municipal,* very good and cheap.

Camping Sites at Parque Andresito, Rocha, and Rancho Pucará, Barra de Valizas. There are also cabins for rent at US$6 (4 beds).

La Paloma (Hotels del Cabo; Barceló; Viola; Trocadero; Bahía, B; Embeleco, B, friendly, English spoken; Parque, E, clean; Puertas del Sol, C. Youth Hostel at Parque Andresito, G, clean, friendly, good meals available, kitchen facilities, book at Montevideo office; thatched cabins for rent in woods near beach for US$15 per day with maid and kitchen—sleep 4-6, Dec.-April only. Restaurant Trattoria di Luigi, highly rec., superb views.) A good port for yachts as it is protected by two islands. There is attractive scenery and good sea and lake fishing. Buses run between La Paloma and Rocha. An oil refinery is in operation, and a fishmeal plant can smell bad, if the wind is in the wrong direction. Horses can be hired. Some 10 km. beyond Paloma near the sandy beach is the *Hotel La Pedrera,* D, with swimming pool, tennis and comfortable rooms, rec.

Beyond Rocha lies the colonial fortress (converted into a museum) of Santa Teresa, begun by the Portuguese and finished by the Spaniards in the 1750s. (It was the other way round with the fortress of San Miguel—see below— neither smelt battle.) It is set in the Parque de Santa Teresa, with avenues of palms, a bird sanctuary, and fresh-water pools to bathe in. The fortress is very impressive; free admission. Open 0800-2000, closed Tuesdays. There are cottages to let for the summer season, beside the sea and excellent "wild" camping in the north of the park, so get off the bus at the Fortaleza steps, *not* at the main entrance. There is a small supermarket, a butcher's and a bar in the commercial area where campers are expected to register. Nine km. beyond and 15 km. S of Chuy is the bathing resort of *La Coronilla* with excellent ocean fishing for sharks, skate and black *corvina* from the rocks: there is an annual competition in January. Tour by taxi or Onda bus (US$9, daily) from La Coronilla to the Santa Teresa fortress and the strange and gloomy Laguna Negra, and the collection of native and exotic plants under glass. The beach stretches for many km., but there are too many waves for swimming.

Hotels   *Gure-Exte*, B, on beach, small and very pleasant; *Parador La Coronilla*, C; *Costas del Mar*, C, on beach, rec., swimming pool; *Oceanía*, C (highly rec.), family runs restaurant close by; *Las Palmas*, open all year, D with shower (electric), clean, helpful, restaurant; both *Rivamar* and *Las Cholgas* claim to have heating. Preferable to stay here rather than Chuy.

Restaurants   *Buretche* (rec.) and *Las Cholgas*, less good.

From the road between La Paloma and Castillos one can walk down to many pleasant fishing villages along the coast; accommodation is very basic. Visits to the islands of Castillos and Wolf can be arranged. Look out for the sea-lions and penguins along this coast, for instance at Cabo Polonia (2 buses a day, US$5 return, 1¾ hr. walk from road across dunes and through woods). Local buses do not run at weekends.

At *Chuy*, a run-down town half in Uruguay (many duty-free shops) and half in Brazil, 340 km. from Montevideo (*Hospedaje Iramar*, F, rec., modest, shared bathrooms, damp; *Pensión Frontera*, E, *Internacional*, D (incl. own bath); *Hotel Plaza*, D; *Hotel Chuy*, E; *Hospedaje Vitoria*, F, basic, clean, friendly), the road branches off towards the elongated Laguna Merín; the frontier is along its middle. Buses stop to allow immigration formalities. On the Uruguayan side, overlooking the lagoon, stands the fortress of *San Miguel*, set in a park in which many plants and animals are kept. (Bus from Chuy, US$0.35, entry US$0.20, open Thurs.-Sun. only.) A casino, open until 0400, operates nearby. There is an excellent hotel, the *Parador San Miguel*, and good bathing on the sea-shore of the nearby Barra del Chuy; buses (US$0.38) every two hours, bathing excellent, many birds. Tourists arriving from Uruguay may cross the border to the Brazilian side of the town, and purchase a certain amount of Brazilian manufactured goods without formalities (but see below). At present it is better to eat in Brazil and pay for everything in new cruzados.

Transport   Uruguayan taxis are allowed 25 km. beyond the frontier, and vice versa. Onda runs an excursion bus daily from La Coronilla to Barra del Chuy beach, and Chuy to San Miguel fort, US$9 (4 hrs. trip). Bus Chuy-Porto Alegre, 2 a day, 7½ hrs., US$5.50 or 8 express. Bus, Onda or Cita, to Montevideo US$9, cheapest by Ruta del Sol, US$7, 6 hrs., frequent stops. To Maldonado, US$5. To La Paloma, US$3, 3¾ hrs.

The coastal road, now excellent, goes on to Pelotas and Porto Alegre, in Brazil. Ordinary (not international) buses ply the route. The border runs down the middle of the main street in Chuy. Passengers from Montevideo are set down at the bus company's office. You can immediately get passport clearance at the Uruguayan immigration, over one km. back on the way to Montevideo. Money exchange not far from hotel (no facilities on Sunday), bank won't change travellers' cheques. All except one restaurant (on the Uruguayan side) close at 2030; the one closes at 2300. The Brazilian immigration office is about 2 km. from Chuy on the road to Pelotas. Buses from Chuy to Santa Vitória or Pelotas stop at Brazilian customs; alternatively take a taxi. The office for the Pelotas bus is across the road from the hotel, one block inside Brazil, by the *Hotel Quarain*. Make sure your passport is stamped, or you may have difficulty in leaving Brazil. Getting a car into Brazil is no trouble. There is even less hassle if driving a car not registered in Brazil or Uruguay.

MONTEVIDEO NORTH-EAST TO BRAZIL (3)

The Pan-American Highway, 486 km. long, runs NE into the hills away from the coast. Route 8 is paved to about 30 km. beyond Minas, 120 km. from Montevideo; beyond it is all-weather.

Minas, with 34,000 inhabitants, is a picturesque small town set in the beautiful wooded hills, which supply granite and marble. Juan Lavalleja, the leader of the Thirty-Three who brought independence to the country, was born here (equestrian statue), and there is an equestrian statue to Artigas, said to be the largest such in the world, on the Cerro Artigas just out of town. The church's portico and towers, some caves in the neighbourhood, and the countryside around are worth seeing. The Parque Salus, on the slopes of Sierras de las Animas, is only 8 km. to the S and very attractive; take the town bus marked "Cervecería Salus" from plaza to the Salus brewery, then walk 2 km. to the mineral spring and bottling plant (*Parador Salus*, acceptable; reasonable set lunch.) The Cascada de Agua del Penitente waterfall, about 11 km. out of town, off the Minas-Aigue road, is interesting and you may see wild rheas (protected) nearby. It is difficult to get to the falls in the off-season. In March and April you can buy *butea* palm fruit, which is grape size, orange and tastes bitter-sweet. Good confectionery is made in Minas; the largest firm, opposite *Hotel Verdun*, shows tourists round its premises. Museum in the Casa de la Cultura.

Hotels *Verdun*, main plaza, clean, E; *Ramos*, 18 de Julio near bus station, basic, clean, E (discount for IYHA members); *Residencia Minas*, 25 de Mayo 502 on main plaza, clean, E.

Restaurants *San Francisco*, 25 de Mayo 586, is recommended as is *El Portal*, Aníbal del Campo 743, for parrillada. The best pastry shop is *Irisarri*, Calle Treinta y Tres 618, known for yemas (egg candy) and damasquitos (apricot sweets).

Exchange Lloyds Bank and national banks, open 1300-1700 Monday-Friday.

Youth Hostel Route 8, Km. 145, in small village of Villa Serrana, US$1.80 a night, 28 km. beyond Minas on road to Treinta y Tres; most attractive, but take plenty of food and drink as the last shop has now shut. Direct bus from Montevideo or Minas, ask driver to set you down and walk 3 km. to Villa Serrana; essential to book through Montevideo office.

Air Service Daily flight by Tamu from Montevideo.

Bus To Montevideo, US$2.25, COT (4 a day) and many others, 2½ hrs. To Maldonado, Coom, US$2.50, 5 a day, 2 hrs.

The next centre of any importance, 286 km. from Montevideo, is

Treinta y Tres, 15,000 people, picturesquely placed a little way from the Olimar River. Some 20 km. beyond, a dirt road, left, runs 19 km. among and over hills to a rocky region with small streams—the Quebrada de los Cuervos— now a beautiful and quite unspoilt national park. Free camping and swimming at Municipal Park at Río Olimar. Main plaza has all the main restaurants and grills.

Hotel *Central*, and pensions *Jorgito* or *Mota*.

Air Service Daily by Tamu from Montevideo.

The road goes on through **Melo** (111 km. from Treinta y Tres; *Hotel Internacional*, acceptable) to the border town of **Río Branco,** 88 km. from Melo, founded in 1914, on the Yaguarón River. The 1½ km.-long Mauá bridge across the river leads to the Brazilian town of Jaguarão.

Hotel *Italiano*, D, with bath.

Restaurant *Oasis*, good, pollo a la brasa.

This is where most international traffic used to cross the frontier; now the road via Chuy is better. Customs officials are at the international bridge, passport officials at the police station at Jaguarão. From Jaguarão buses run several times daily to Pelotas and Porto Alegre. There is usually a better rate of exchange at Melo than at the frontier.

MONTEVIDEO NORTH TO BRAZIL (4)

The 509 km. road from Montevideo to the border town of Rivera runs almost due north, at first over rolling hills through cattle country, vineyards, apple orchards, orange, lemon and olive groves. Further N, hilly cattle-range land is crossed.

Las Piedras, 24 km. from Montevideo, in vineyard country, has a Gothic Chapel of the Salesians. Race meetings (pari-mutuel betting) Thurs., Sat. and Sun.

Exchange Lloyds Bank, Calle General Artigas 652. Open 1300-1700, Mon.-Fri.

Canelones, 45 km. from the capital, is a typical small town of 10,000 people in a grain growing area. Travellers then pass through the pleasant country towns of Florida, Durazno, **Paso de los Toros** (close to the huge lake created by the Rincón del Bonete dam on the Río Negro; *Hotel Onda*, F, not very clean; beautiful camping by the river) and Tacuarembó. There is a toll on Route 5, going north, 67.8 km. from Montevideo; the road is dual carriageway as far as Canelones. E of Paso de los Toros (1½ hrs by Onda bus at 1700) is San Gregorio, cheap camping and bathing in Río Negro. Bus returns to Paso de los Toros 0245.

Florida Famous for a folklore festival on Independence Day each year.

Hotel *Español*, D.

Rivera is a town of 40,000 people, on the Brazilian frontier. It is divided by a street from the Brazilian town of Santa Ana do Livramento, which has a good golf course, and a daily bus to Porto Alegre. Points of interest are the park (free camping facilities), the Plaza Internacional, and the dam of Cañapirú. There are an airport and a casino, and many duty-free shops.

Hotels *Casablanca*, Sarandí 484, T 3221, E, shower, breakfast, a/c, clean, pleasant. *Mabé* (near station); *Casino; Nuevo*.

Bus to Montevideo, US$10 or less, there is also a service to Fray Bentos and Durazno, US$1.50.

WEST FROM MONTEVIDEO (5)

There is a toll on Route 1 (Montevideo-Colonia) at the Santa Lucía bridge (Km. 22.5). There are no tolls on Routes 2 to Fray Bentos and 3 to Paysandú and Salto.

Route 1, part of the Pan-American Highway, runs from Montevideo westwards for 177 km. to Colonia del Sacramento. There is a nice beach near the disused bull-ring, which is passed by regular buses. Much traffic from Argentina flows along this busy road; the surface has continued to deteriorate.

About 114 km. from Montevideo, a 5 km. branch leads N to **Colonia Suiza**, originally a Swiss settlement, with some 4,500 people. The Swiss national day is celebrated on August 1 with considerable zest. There are several hotels, the *Bungalow Suiza* restaurant and a Youth Hostel. Quite near is Nueva Helvecia, where the tourist can buy locally made Swiss musical boxes. At 120 km. along the main road, and just S, is **Colonia Valdense,** another colony, this time of Waldensians, who still cling to some of the old customs of the Piedmontese Alps. There is little for the budget traveller in either Nueva Helvecia or Colonia Valdense. Bus Montevideo-Colonia Valdense US$2.50; Colonia Valdense-Colonia Suiza US$0.50; Colonia Suiza-Colonia, US$1.20.

Hotels at Colonia Suiza *Nirvana*, A, restaurants, sports facilities, run down but good; *Hospedaje Comercio*, 18 de Julio 1209, E with bath and a/c; *Del Prado* (Youth Hostel), T 0522-4169.

Hotels at Colonia Valdense *Brisas del Plata; Parador los Ceibos*.

About 6½ km. further on, a paved main road branches off right to Rosario (5 km.), Mercedes (164 km.), and Fray Bentos (34 km. further). **Rosario** is a typical agricultural town given over to dairying and grain production. Its port, Juan Lacaze, lies 22 km. SW. Population: 8,000.

Hotels *Ricardi* and *Riviera*, E, good.

Clubs Club Cyssa, a social, cultural and sporting club, with a stadium, football field and basketball ground. Two fishing clubs.

Colonia (del Sacramento), a charming small town with an interesting historic section jutting into the River Plate, was founded by Portuguese settlers from Brazil in 1680. It contains rebuilt city walls and quite a number of colonial buildings and narrow streets in the older part of the town; all the more interesting because there are few such examples in this part of the continent. Worth seeing are the Parochial Church, the Municipal Museum in the old house of Almirante Brown (open Thurs. to Sun. 0800-1330), opposite it on the plaza (and with same hours) is the Museo Portugués; the Mansion of the Viceroy, the house of General Mitre, and the Farola (lighthouse). The plaza is particularly picturesque. The tourist office at Flores y Rivera offers good maps. Buenos Aires, to which there is a ferry service, is only 50 km. A "free zone" has been created here (no consumer goods). Pop.: 10,000. At Real San Carlos, just out of town (take the blue bus from the centre) are the racecourse (Hipódromo) and bull-ring (out of use). The best beach is Playa Ferrando, with campsite, 2 km to the east. In the third week of January, festivities are held marking the founding of Colonia.

Hotels *Posada del Gobernador*, 18 de Julio 205, A, bed and breakfast, no dining room, charming, rec.; *El Mirador*, L, Av. Roosevelt, Km. 176½; *Royal*, General Flores 340, B, comfortable, rec.; *Beltrán*, Gral. Flores, E, shared bath, clean; *Rincón del Río*, E, clean (with shower); *Español*, Manuel Lobo 377, friendly, restaurant, rundown. Under same ownership: *Los Angeles*, small rooms, no restaurant, but clean and friendly, English spoken; *Leoncia*, Rivera 216, modern, good; *Esperanza* (Cral. Flores 237, clean, charming), all D. *Posada de la Ciudadela*, Washington Barbot 164, E, clean, pleasant, a/c, simple; *Italiano*, F without bath, friendly, clean, rec. Several cheap *hospedajes* near the Plaza. *Hospedaje* at General Flores 311, F, no bath but clean, friendly, rec.

Restaurant *Esperanza* (at hotel) and *Yacht Club* (at harbour) are good; several good *parrilladas* along 18 de Julio. *Los Faroles*, rec., friendly; *La Casona* (coffee bar). *Canta Rana*, Comercio y Santa Rita, opened 1988, good and cheap, open weekends only off season, daily in Jan.-April.

Camping Site at Playa Ferrando.

Ferries Four ferries a day to Buenos Aires, three hours crossing, US$12 p.p., clean and comfortable. To Tigre (Argentina) by ferry costs US$13 and takes about 4 hours; leaves 4 times daily. Bus to ferry at Real San Carlos from town, US$0.50. The Argentine consulate is reported unfriendly to the British; best to use the one in Montevideo.

Hydrofoil 4-6 daily services, each way, to Buenos Aires (4 hours), US$25 (limited luggage allowance). It is substantially cheaper to buy ticket at the port than from a tourist agency. The company runs buses to their port in Colonia from Punta del Este, Piriápolis, *Carrasco Hotel* (Carrasco), and Montevideo (Plaza Libertad).

Air Service Lapa to Aeroparque, Buenos Aires, 3 times a day, US$22. It is generally quicker than the hydrofoil.

Bus to Montevideo, US$3.75 (2½ hrs.), Onda and COT, five a day each. US$1.50 to Carmelo, three times daily. To Salto, one a day, US$8, 8 hrs.

UP THE RIVER URUGUAY (6)

The road swings N and NW to reach the sleepy resort town of **Carmelo,** 74 km. from Colonia, on the shores of Las Vacas river. Population: 15,000. Across the bridge is a white restaurant on the left-hand side of the road: friendly, recommended. The port harbours several hundred yachts during the season. There is a free zone at the port. There is a launch service to Tigre, across the delta, a most interesting ride past innumerable islands (leaves Mon.-Sat. 1100, 1030, Sun. 1200, 1400, 1500, 4 hrs., US$7.15: Movilan S.A., Constituyentes 263, T 418, office in Montevideo, Plaza Cagancha 1326, T 910755). You can pay at the Onda bus station in Montevideo for both bus and launch, US$10. Bus to and from Montevideo US$5.

Hotels *Casino Carmelo; Comercio; La Unión*, Uruguay 368, E, very good value. *Centro*, next door, E. The bank will only exchange bills and not travellers' cheques. **Bus** to Fray Bentos and Salto from the main square at 1500.

Some 30 km. up the river, by road, is **Nueva Palmira** (population 3,500). Worth visiting in the vicinity are the Pirámide of Solís (8 km. out of town), the Calera, the Camacho, and the Capilla de la Concepción and the Convento de la Reducción Jesuítica (1780 - both in poor condition, 12 km. from town, and 3 km. off the road). A free zone at the port.

Some 20 km. away is the historic beach of La Agraciada, famous for the landing of the Thirty-Three patriots on April 19, 1825, which led to Uruguayan independence. On the beach is a statue to General Juan Lavalleja, leader of the Treinta y Tres. A festival is held on each anniversary.

The road continues through the small river port of **Dolores** (population 13,000), 32 km. up-river from the confluence of the Río San Salvador with the Río Uruguay, to

Mercedes, a livestock centre and resort best reached by road from the main

Colonia-Montevideo highway (275 km.). It is set on the S bank of the Río Negro, 48 km. above its confluence with the Río Uruguay. This pleasant town of 34,000 inhabitants is a yachting and fishing centre during the season.

The charm of the town derives from its Spanish-colonial appearance, though it is not as old as the older parts of Colonia. There is a pleasant *costanera* (riverside drive).

Hotels *Brisas del Hum,* C; *Comercio; Petit Hotel,* D; *Himalaya,* D, with bath; *Martín,* D; *Universal,* D, rec. *Hospedaje Hotelcito,* Giménez 703, E. Good food at *La Brasa,* Calle Castro y Careaga, and at *Círculo Policial,* Calle 25 de Mayo.

Camping Site at Mercedes, and beside Rivers Negro and Uruguay (US$0.45 p.p.).

Museums Palaeontology and Natural Sciences; the Museum of Eusebio Giménez, with a gallery of paintings.

Tourist Office Artigas 215, T 2733.

Bus to Paysandú, 2½ hrs., US$4.

Excursions To the islands in the Río Negro—the largest has an inn. To the small town of **Santo Domingo** (Soriano), first town to be founded in Uruguay, to see a fine colonial church and an old house. Difficult to do this trip easily in one day.

The road continues westwards (34 km.) to

Fray Bentos, a port on the Uruguay River, 193 km. above Buenos Aires. An international bridge has been built across the Río Uruguay to Puerto Unzué (Argentina); toll US$2.10 per car, 3 buses a day to Gualeguaychú, Argentina, 0700, 1230, 1800. Main industry: meat packing and canning. Population: 14,000.

Hotels *Colonial,* close to main Plaza and ETA bus office, hot water, E; *Gran Plaza* (satisfactory). **Restaurant** *Club Armonía.*

River Boats Launch services four times a week to Gualeguaychú.

There is an ETA bus service to Rivera.

Paysandú, on the E bank of the Río Uruguay, 122 km. by good paved road from Fray Bentos (Route 2), and 480 by paved road via Trinidad from Montevideo (Route 3), has a population of about 80,000. Temperatures in summer can rise as high as 42°C. There is a golf club, and a rowing club which holds regattas. The cathedral is 19th century; the attached Salesian college has an interesting museum, opens 1700. The cemetery on the outskirts is worth a look. Also worth a visit is the Museo de la Tradición, with *gaucho* articles, at the Balneario Municipal beach, north of town. A historical museum has been opened at Florida 930. There is an international bridge to Colón (Argentina) (US$1.90 per car for crossing). It is about 8 km. to Colón. Airport with daily Tamu flights to Montevideo.

Hotels *Gran Hotel Paysandú,* D, 18 de Julio y 19 de Abril, T 3400, a/c, best; *Onda,* D, "super suites", good restaurant (one can reserve through Onda in Montevideo), rec.; *Pensión Popular,* E, with shower; *Concordia,* 18 de Julio, E, clean; *Rafaela,* 18 de Julio 1181, E, large rooms, modern and friendly, electric showers, no food but surrounded by cafés; *Lobato,* Leandro Gómez 1415, E, good. A good hotel, but not in the centre, is *Bulevar* at Bulevar Artigas and República Argentina. *Victoria,* 18 de Julio 979, F, highly rec., cheapest, very friendly

Youth Hostel Liga Departamental de Fútbol, Gran Bretaña 872, T 4247, US$1 p.p., neither clean nor well-maintained. Cabins for 5 or more people.

Camping Free facilities available in a municipal park by the river.

Restaurant *Artemio,* Plaza de Constitución, 18 de Julio, "best food in town", but closed in winter. *Parrillada de Asturias,* good and cheap. *Don Diego's,* 19 de Abril, serves cheap *parrillada,* good value. *Pipan,* 2 blocks S of Cathedral, good and cheap.

Tourist Bureau Plaza de Constitución, 18 de Julio 1226.

Travel Agency Viñar Turismo, Artigas 1163, helpful.

Bus to Montevideo, 7½ hrs., US$8, by Onda, four buses daily. Other lines (Chadre, Agencia

Central) are just as good. To Salto US$3. To Paso de los Toros 1430 (return 0430), US$4. For drivers, Route 3 via Mercedes is only 38 km. longer than the direct Route 2 via Trinidad, but in much better condition.

Excursions　To the waterfalls of the River Quequay, a few km. to the N; the Termas del Guaviyú thermal springs 50 km. away (1½ hrs. by bus) with cheap camping, and to the Meseta de Artigas, 90 km. N of Paysandú, 13 km. off the highway to Salto. The Meseta, where General Artigas lived (statue), is 45 metres above the Uruguay river, which here narrows and forms whirlpools at the rapids of El Hervidero. A terrace commands a fine view, but the rapids are not visible from the Meseta. The statue, with the general's head topping a tall shaft, is very original. There are some pleasant, somewhat primitive, chalets available from Erwin Frey, 90 Estación Chapieny, Dept. Paysandú. Early booking recommended. Bus to Km. 462 on Paysandú-Salto road.

Salto, 120 km. by paved road N of Paysandú, has a population of 80,000. It is a centre for oranges and other citrus fruit and now processes them. See the beautiful park of Solari, the Parque Harriague with an open air theatre and a well-kept zoo (closed Mon., US$0.15—7 blocks from centre, feeding time 1400-1500); the fine-arts museum in the donated mansion, French style, of a rich *estanciero*, Uruguay 1067, opens at 1700, well worth a visit (the locals are justifiably proud of it); and the promenade along the River Uruguay. Across the river is Concordia, in Argentina, to which there are 5 ferries (US$1.10, 15 mins.) on weekdays, 4 on Sat. but none on Sun.

Hotels　*Gran Hotel Salto,* Plaza Artigas, best; *Los Cedros,* a/c, D, Uruguay 657 (T 3989); *Plaza,* Plaza Treinta y Tres, near bus station, simple, clean, good food, E. *Pensión 33,* Treinta y Tres 269, F, basic, central. *Concordia,* Uruguay 749, E, shower, a/c, central, clean, friendly; *Pensión Santa Catalina,* Brasil 1633 or *Pensión Las Tres Fronteras,* General Rivera 1155, cheaper, basic, E; *Artigas Plaza,* Plaza 18 de Julio next to Onda bus station, E with bath, hot water, very clean; *Pensión Pocholo,* 18 de Julio opp. hospital, F, friendly but basic, others nearby at same price.

Youth Hostels　Club de Remeros Salto (by the river) T 0732-3418, or Club de Leones, Uruguay 1626, if you can find a student to sign you in.

Camping　Site at Salto.

Restaurants　*Chef Restaurant,* Uruguay 639; *Sigo* at La Rueda, in the E, for parrillada, 10 blocks from the cathedral; *Club de Remeros de Salto. Club de Uruguay,* Uruguay, good breakfast and good value meals; *Club Bancario,* Brasil 765, lunch US$2, good.

Tourist Office　Calle Uruguay 1052, free map.

Exchange　Lloyds Bank, two agencies: Uruguay 585 and Blandengues y 8 de Octubre. Open 1300-1700, Mon.-Fri. (cashes cheques into dollars without commission). National banks. Cambio Pensotti has been recommended as helpful. The *cambio* at Uruguay 800 is open until 2000, Mon.-Sat.

Anglican Church　Calle República de Argentina, close to Calle Uruguay.

Bus　to Montevideo, US$10 (Onda); to Termas del Arapey, 2 hrs., daily, US$3.50. Paysandú, US$3.65, four a day. To Rivera, US$8.50. To Colonia by Agencia Central, 0555, 8 hrs., US$8.

Air Service　Daily to and from Montevideo via Paysandú, by Tamu, US$15 single. To Buenos Aires.

Excursions　A favourite excursion from Salto is by launch to the Salto Chico; another is to Salto Grande, where a ranch-style guest house for anglers is run by the Tourist Commission. Nearby is the resort *Hotel Horacio Quiroga,* B, sports facilities, staffed by nearby catering school. The most popular tourist site in the area is the large *Salto Grande* dam and hydroelectric plant 20 km. from Salto, built jointly by Argentina and Uruguay; a 2-hr. free tour can be arranged with the CTM (office on corner of *Hotel Gran Salto*). A road runs along the top of the dam. Medicinal springs at Fuente Salto, 6 km. N of the city. Bus No. 4 runs from Calle Artigas (US$0.15) to *Termas de Daymán*; beautifully laid out and eight swimming pools, with Youth Hostel on Route 3, Km. 490, T 0732-4361, restaurant, souvenir shop and campsite (entry to baths US$0.35, towel US$0.50, locker US$0.10).

The road to **Termas del Arapey** branches off the partially paved highway to Bella Unión, 61 km. N of Salto, and then runs 35 km. first E and then S. Pampa birds, rheas and metre-long lizards much in evidence. Termas del Arapey is on the Arapey river S of Isla Cabellos (Baltazar Brum). The waters at these famous thermal baths contain bicarbonated salts, calcium and magnesium. There is a new hotel with pool (*Hotel Termas del Arapey*, A), also a motel (very small bungalows with kitchens, no sheets provided), a nice swimming pool and a very simple *parador* (meals only). Book ahead in Salto or Montevideo. Camping US$2 p.p.

The road (148 km.) runs N to the little town of **Bella Unión**, 5,000 people, (with free campsite, ask at Prefectura Naval, insect repellant needed), near the Brazilian frontier.

There is also a road from near Bella Unión E to **Artigas**, a frontier town in a cattle raising and agricultural area (excellent swimming upstream from the bridge). There is a bridge across the Río Cuaraí to the Brazilian town of Quaraí opposite. Population: 14,000.

Hotels *Concordia; Oriental. Pensión Uruguay* and *Hawaii*, basic but clean.

Camping US$0.25 p.p. a day, or at Agua Corriente—chance of camping at the yacht club on the river.

Youth Hostel Club Deportivo Artigas, Pte. Berreta and L.A. de Herrera, T 0642-2532.

Restaurants *Maricarmen*, Calle Lecueder 302, and *Municipal*, Lecueder y Berreta.

Bus service to Salto, 225 km. **Airport** at Bella Unión.

THE ECONOMY

Although accounting for only 13% of gdp (less than either manufacturing or commerce and catering), agriculture is the dominant sector of the economy, as a supplier and a consumer. It employs 17% of the workforce. 90% of the land area is suitable for farming, and only about 3% of that is unused. Over three-quarters is given over to livestock rearing, the rest for crop production.

In the early 1980s, the beef-cattle sector suffered from low world prices and high interest rates, with the result that much of the herd was slaughtered. Slaughtering, domestic consumption and exports all declined in the 1983-85 period, but picked up thereafter, exports particularly in response to increased Brazilian demand in 1986. The number of sheep has risen in the 1980s, despite increased demand for exports of live and slaughtered animals. This reflects the lower prices for meat than for wool, of which Uruguay accounts for about 3% of total world production. Livestock and its manufactures contribute the major proportion of exports: in 1988, raw wool and manufactures' share was 25%, beef 11%, and hides and skins 6%. The only cereal exported is rice, accounting for 7% of the total. Others grown are maize and wheat. Also important are oilseeds (sunflower and linseed) and citrus fruits, of which oranges and tangerines are the main crops. The fishing industry has been expanded in the 1970s and 1980s, but catches and exports have fluctuated.

Manufacturing, which contributes 25% to gdp and employs 23% of the workforce, is concerned largely with agroindustrial activities. The most important of these are meat packing, drinks, tobacco, textiles, clothing and footwear. There are also some medium-technology industries such as oil refining, plastics, rubber products, electrical appliances and motor vehicle assembly. Import substitution behind tariff barriers encouraged growth until the 1960s, to be followed by stagnation until more export-oriented policies were introduced in the late 1970s. Various factors have contributed to mixed results in the 1980s, not the least of which have been economic problems in Argentina and Brazil. Construction accounts for 3% of gdp and 6% of employment. In the late 1970s, it benefitted from Argentine investment, which was curtailed as the Uruguayan peso appreciated against its Argentine counterpart. The financial sector's fortunes also fluctuate according to the economic health of Argentina and Brazil. Uruguay has been called the Switzerland of Latin America, and is the repository of much of the region's flight capital.

Uruguay has no major mining industry, apart from the extraction of marble and various construction materials. It also has no known reserves of oil or natural gas. Its coal deposits are of poor quality and are not suitable for commercial mining. Almost 100% of electricity generation comes from hydroelectric plants, of which there are four. The combined installed capacity of their 14 turbines is 1,890 MW.

Like many Latin American debtors, Uruguay became unable to service its debts normally in the 1980s and had to reschedule its loans to commercial bank and government creditors in the context of an IMF stabilization programme. IMF targets were successfully met and when the agreement expired in 1987, it was replaced by enhanced surveillance. By the late 1980s Uruguay's external position had strengthened and net new borrowing from multilateral and commercial creditors took place on a voluntary basis, raising total external debt to US$6.2bn.

	1961-70 (av)	1971-80 (av)	1981-85 (av)	1986-88 (av)
Gdp growth (1980 prices)	1.8%	3.1%	-3.0%	3.9%
Inflation	34.2%	63.2%	45.9%	68.4%
Exports (fob) US$m	182	519	1,013	1,224
Meat	51	111	194	155
Wool	82	106	187	251
Hides	18	28	69	81
Imports (fob) US$m	160	607	939	1,040
Current account balance US$m (cum)	-0.1	-1,709	-988	-109

INFORMATION FOR VISITORS

Flights from Europe By air: direct flights by Pluna (Madrid), Air France, Iberia, KLM, Lufthansa and Varig. Flying by other carriers, a change must be made at Rio or Buenos Aires.

From the USA Pan American World Airways (2 a week), Varig, and Lan-Chile, and (as far as Buenos Aires) by Canadian Pacific Airlines, Avianca and Aerolíneas Argentinas.

From Argentina Ferry services (Montevideo and Colonia to Buenos Aires), hydrofoil services (Colonia to Buenos Aires) and launch services (Carmelo to Tigre) are given in the text. Aerolíneas Argentinas and Pluna have several flights a day between Aeroparque in Buenos Aires and Carrasco Airport. Service intensified during holiday period. Also frequent flights to Punta del Este from Buenos Aires. Lapa flies between Colonia and Buenos Aires. From Colonia there is a fast bus service by Onda to Montevideo. Foreign airlines connect Carrasco with the Buenos Aires international airport at Ezeiza. Buses run across the Paysandú and Fray Bentos bridges. Direct bus between Buenos Aires and Montevideo by one of these routes takes about 10 hours. Ferries cross the Río Uruguay between Salto and Concordia.

From Brazil Direct connection between Brazil and Uruguay by all the international airlines landing at Montevideo. Varig flies 3 times a week from Rio de Janeiro to Montevideo, via Buenos Aires. Cruzeiro do Sul has daily flights Rio de Janeiro, São Paulo, Porto Alegre and Montevideo. By road: the Pan-American Highway runs 2,880 km. from Rio de Janeiro to Montevideo and on to Colonia. It is poorly surfaced in parts. There are several bus services.

From Chile Only KLM direct; Lan-Chile flies thrice a week and Avianca and Pluna twice. Lan-Chile flies between Santiago, Buenos Aires and Montevideo and between Montevideo and Lima.

From Paraguay Twice weekly by Pluna, thrice weekly by Líneas Aéreas Paraguayas (LAP) and weekly by Iberia. Twice-weekly buses Asunción-Montevideo.

Airport Tax of US$2.50 on all air travellers leaving Uruguay for South American republics or Mexico; US$7 for all other countries, and a tax of 3% on all tickets issued and paid for in Uruguay.

Documents A passport is necessary for entry except for nationals of other American countries, who can get in with national identity documents. Visas (about US$10) are not required by nationals of American and Western European countries, Israel and Japan. Tourist cards are valid for 3 months, extendable for a similar period. For extensions go to Migraciones office in Calle Misiones. A small fee is charged. Duties are not usually charged on a reasonable quantity of goods (such as tobacco and spirits), brought in obviously for the traveller's own use: 200 cigarettes or 50 cigars or 3 small packets of tobacco are admitted duty-free; so is 1 bottle of alcoholic drink, 3 little bottles of perfume and gifts up to the value of US$5.

The Ministry of Tourism sells a "pasaporte turístico" at points of entry, about US$10, valid 30 days, which entitles the holder to discounts of 10%-20% for cash purchases of a wide range of goods and services from establishments listed (of limited value).

Hours of Business Most department stores generally are open 0900 to 1200, 1400 to 1900, but 0900 to 1230 on Sat. Business houses vary but most work from 0830 to 1200, 1430 to 1830 or 1900, according to whether they open on Sat. Banking hours are 1300 to 1700 in Montevideo; there are special summer hours (Dec. 1-March 15) in Montevideo (1330-1730), in the interior (0730-1130) and in Punta del Este (1600-2000); banks are closed on Sat. Government departments, mid-March to mid-November, 1300 to 1830 from Mon. to Fri.; rest of the year, 0700 to 1230, but not Sat.

British business travellers are strongly advised to read "Hints to Exporters: Uruguay", obtainable from the Department of Trade, Sanctuary Buildings, 16-20 Great Smith Street, London SW1.

Best times for visiting Most tourists visit during the summer (December-mid March), though hotels have to be booked in advance. Business visits can be paid throughout the year, but it is best to avoid the tourist months. In June, July, and August, orders are placed for the winter season 12 months ahead.

Security Personal security offers few problems in Uruguay to travellers who are reasonably prudent.

Roads There are 45,000 km. of roads, 80% of them paved or all-weather. The Comisión Nacional de Turismo will help to plan itineraries by car. Onda buses radiate into the interior from Montevideo, using comfortable American (they even use the Greyhound logo) long-distance coaches; other companies do not run the same extensive network, but are often cheaper and as fast. All hotels display Onda timetables. Hitch-hiking is fairly easy, along the coast, but difficult in the interior because the population is sparse; it is reportedly fairly safe for women to hitch alone. Gasoline prices are very high at US$3 a gallon for super. Route 5 as far as Canelones is now dual-carriageway.

Motoring Carnet required. Vehicles do not stop, nor is there a right of way, at uncontrolled intersections. Traffic manners in Montevideo have improved recently, but the pace is slow because there are so many ancient cars (1920s and 1930s models are called *cachilas* and skilled mechanics keep them on the road); all the same, driving standards are reckoned to be the most suicidal in South America. Insurance is not required by law. Uruguay is said to be much better than Argentina or Brazil to ship a car to.

Maps Automóvil Club del Uruguay, Av. Libertador General Lavalleja (ex Agraciada) 1532, Montevideo, publishes road maps of the city and the country at large, and so do Esso and Ancap at about US$2 each. Official maps are issued by Instituto Geográfico Militar, Abreu y 8 de Octubre, open 0800-1230, T 816868.
Land-Rover garage in Montevideo at Cuareim 2082, near old railway station.

Railways All passenger services were withdrawn in January 1988.

Internal Flights Internal air transport is provided by Tamu, an arm of the air force, which uses Brazilian "Bandeirante" and Fokker "Friendship" F-27s. Tickets from Colonia 1021, Montevideo. Provincial airports are mentioned in the text.

Climate Temperate, if somewhat damp and windy, and summer heat is tempered by Atlantic breezes, but there are occasional large variations. In winter (June-September), when the average temperature is 10° to 16°C, the temperature can fall now and then to well below freezing. It is generally humid and hardly ever snows. Summer (December-March), with an average temperature of 21° to 27°C, has irregular dry periods. There is always some wind and for the most part the nights are relatively cool. There are normally 120 sunny days in the year. The rainfall, with prolonged wet periods in July and August, averages about 1,200 mm. at Montevideo and some 250 more in the N, but the amount of rain varies markedly from year to year.

Youth Hostels Asociación de Alberguistas del Uruguay, Calle Pablo de María 1583 (open 1300-1900), Montevideo (T 404245) operates hostels (IYHA members only) at Montevideo (Canelones 935), Artigas, Paysandú, Piriápolis, Salto, La Paloma, Colonia Suiza, and Villa Serrana, near Minas. A 10% rebate is available on Lapa plane tickets between Colonia and Buenos Aires—obtainable at the Onda terminal in Montevideo, and rebates have also been reported (10-20%) for bus fares and hotel prices.

Camping Several good sites in Montevideo and outside; see references in main text.

Shopping Bargains See under Montevideo, **page 862.**

Food and Drink Beef is eaten at almost all meals; it is good and now always available. The majority of restaurants are *parrilladas* (grills) where the staple is beef. *Asado* (barbecued beef) is popular; the main cuts are *asado de tira* (ribs);

pulpa (no bones), *lomo* (fillet steak) and entrecote. To get a lean piece of *asado*, ask for *asado flaco*. *Costilla* (chop) and *milanesa* (veal cutlet) are also popular; usually eaten with mixed salad or chips. *Chivitos* are Uruguayan steak burgers; *chivitos canadienses* are sandwiches filled with slices of meat, lettuce, tomato, egg, etc. (normally over US$2—very filling). Two other good local dishes are *puchero* (beef with vegetables, bacon, beans and sausages) and the local varieties of pizza, fast becoming a staple. Other specialities are barbecued pork, grilled chicken in wine, *cazuela* (or stew) usually with *mondongo* (tripe) or sea foods (e.g. squid, shark—*cazón*, mussels—*mejillones*). The sausages are very good and spicy (*chorizos, morcillas, salchichas*). *Morcilla dulce*, a sweet black sausage, made from blood, orange peel and walnuts, has been highly praised; so has the *morcilla salada,* which is savoury. For snacks, *media lunas mixtas* are a type of croissant filled with ham and cheese, either hot or cold; toasted sandwiches are readily available; *panchos* are hot dogs, *húngaros* are spicy sausage hot dogs. *Preparación* is a selection of crisps, nuts, vol-au-vent, etc. An excellent dessert is *chajá,* a type of sponge-cake ball with cream and jam inside—very sweet; others are *messini* (a cream sponge) and the common lemon pie. Pastries are very good indeed, and crystallized egg-yolks, known as *yemas,* are popular sweets. Ice cream is excellent everywhere.

The local wines are very varied: the Editor recommends a fair red, Santa Rosa Cabernet, and an good one, Santa Rosa Anticuario, also known as "The Old Museum". Herbert Levi, a connoisseur from Buenos Aires, recommends Castel Pujol, Cabernet Sauvignon and Rosé. The beers are good. Imported drinks are freely available in Montevideo, e.g. whisky, US$2.50-3.00 and Chilean wines. *Mate* is a favourite drink between meal hours. The local spirits are *caña* and *grappa;* some find the locally-made whisky and gin acceptable. In the Mercado del Puerto, Montevideo, a *medio medio* is half still white wine, half sparkling white (a must! Elsewhere a *medio medio* is half *caña* and half whisky). *Espillinar* is a cross between whisky and rum. Try the *clérico,* a tasty mixture of wine, fruit juices and fruits. Coffee is good: a *cortado* is a strong, white coffee, *café con leche* is milk with a little coffee. Milk is always available, either in bottles or plastic sacs. The dinner hour is late, usually from 2100 to 2400.

Health   Milk and fresh water can be drunk and fresh salads eaten fairly freely throughout the country. Medical services are not as good as they used to be, and they are expensive; so are medicines and drugs. Many reports of hepatitis from injections and visits to the dentist. The British Hospital in Montevideo is recommended.

Tipping   Normally all hotel and restaurant bills include a percentage service charge plus 20 % value-added tax, but an additional small tip is expected. In other cases give 10 % of the total bill. Porters at the airport expect about US$0.20 per piece of luggage; although there is an official rate of tips for porters at seaports, the actual charges are mostly higher. Taxi drivers are tipped 10 % of the fare. Tips at cafés are about 10 %. Cinema ushers get a small tip, as do cloakroom attendants and hairdressers (10 % - 15 %).

Local Information Centres   The Comisión Nacional de Turismo central office, at Plaza Cagancha, Montevideo, issues tourist literature. It has built a number of good guest houses at the various resorts and gives information about them at the Information Office. There is a good information kiosk at Montevideo's main bus station. The local papers publish "what's on" columns on Friday evenings and on Saturdays. Tourist section in Friday's *El Día.*

Media   Of the 20 colour-TV stations, 4 transmit from Montevideo (channel 12 is the most popular). There are also 35 radio stations (8 private FM) in Montevideo and 65 in the rest of the country.

There are 6 Montevideo newspapers: *El País, El Día, La República* and *La Mañana,* and *El Diário* and *Mundo Color* which come out in the evening. *Búsqueda* is published weekly. The town of Paysandú has the *Telégrafo.* At noon the main Buenos Aires papers can be had in Montevideo.

Holidays   Jan. 1, 6; Carnival (see below); Easter week; April 19; May 1, 18; June 19; July 18; August 25; October 12; November 2; December 8, 25.

Carnival Week   is officially the Monday and Tuesday immediately preceding Ash Wednesday, but a great many firms close for the whole of the week.

Business comes to a standstill also during Holy Week, which coincides with La Semana Criolla (horse-breaking, stunt riding by cowboys, dances and song). Department stores close only from Good Friday. Banks close all week. Easter Monday is not a holiday.

Currency   Bank notes issued are for 50, 100, 200, 500, 1,000, 5,000 and 10,000 new pesos, and coins for 10, 20 and 50 centésimos and 1, 2, 5 and 10 new pesos. Any amount of currency can be taken in or out.

Exchange   Rates change frequently because of a floating exchange rate and inflation differentials against the US dollar; see the "Latest Exchange and Inflation Rates" table near end of book. Many banks and exchange houses *(casas de cambio)* will give you US$ cash for US$ travellers' cheques with no commission charged (some charge 1%), and US$ cash against a credit card. Dollars cash can be purchased when leaving the country. Exchanges from Brazilian and Argentine currency receive much worse rates than straightforward deals between dollars and pesos. Banks are closed on Saturday throughout the year; hours Monday-Friday 1300-1700.

Credit Cards   Argencard is a member of the Mastercard organization, so one may use Access at outlets displaying their sign. Many shopkeepers are unaware of this but a phone call will confirm it. Also American Express, Diners Club and Visa.

Weights and Measures   Metric units alone are legal. Odd fact: the timber trade still uses inches for the cross section of lengths of timber.

Postal services are very unreliable; all items should be registered and sent by air mail to avoid delay (probably better to go direct to airport, avoiding chaos of the sorting office). Rates are low, e.g. US$0.25 for postcard, US$0.30 for a letter to Europe; US$2 for 1 kg. surface-mail package, US$3.50 for 1 kg. air-mail package (but best not to send parcels at all—if they do arrive they will probably have been opened).

Telecommunications   Telex from most Antel centres, some 24 hrs.; cheaper than telegrams. Western Telegraph Co. Ltd. (British), ITT Comunicaciones Mundiales S.A., and Italcable provide communication with all parts of the world through their cable stations at Montevideo.

The Government-owned Cerrito station supplies international radio-telegraph communication service. Press wireless service is provided by Press Wireless Uruguaya Ltda. Radio-telephone conversations with the United States and Europe, etc., are routed through Buenos Aires. The telephone service still has a poor reputation. Direct dialling abroad is possible. Collect calls only available to UK, USA, Spain, Italy and Canada. Cost: to USA about US$4 a minute; to Europe US$4.50; to New Zealand, US$5. Phone calls are cheaper by 20% between 2200 and 0700.

We should like to acknowledge the help given in revising the Uruguay section by Lena and Hans Bengtsson (Gothenburg), Jens Borchers (Herzberg/Harz) and Michael Franz (Sieber, W. Ger.), Alison Brysk and Mark Freeman (San Francisco, Ca.), Mariann Johnsen (Brandbu, Norway), Herbert Levi (Buenos Aires), Dimitri Moursellas (Manhattan Beach, CA), Wulf Peters (Querenhorst, W. Ger.), Regina Wetzer and Richard C. Brusca (San Diego, CA), and Helmut Zettl (Ebergassing, Aust.).

VENEZUELA

WHEN the Spaniards landed in Venezuela in 1498, in the course of Columbus' third voyage, they found a poor country sparsely populated by Indians who had created no distinctive culture. Four hundred years later it was still poor, almost exclusively agrarian, exporting little, importing less. The miracle year which changed all that was 1914, when oil was discovered near Maracaibo. Today, Venezuela is said to be the richest country in Latin America and is one of the largest producers and exporters of oil in the world. The oil revenues have been used to rebuild Caracas and Maracaibo and other cities, and to create the best network of roads on the continent. In view of recent new discoveries and the cutback of production, at the present rate of extraction oil reserves will last for at least 40 years. Vast investments have been poured into state industry and agrarian reform and into tackling the problems of education, housing and unemployment.

Venezuela has 2,800 km. of coastline on the Caribbean Sea, and 72 islands. To the east is Guyana, to the south Brazil, and to the west Colombia. Its area is 912,050 square km., and its population exceeds 18 million. It was given its name— "Little Venice" - by the Spanish navigators, who saw in the Indian pile dwellings on Lake Maracaibo a dim reminder of the buildings along Venetian waterways.

The country falls into four very different regions: the Venezuelan Highlands to the west and along the coast; the Maracaibo Lowlands around the fresh water lake of Maracaibo; the vast central plain of the Llanos of the Orinoco; and the Guayana Highlands, which take up over half the country.

The Venezuelan Highlands are an offshoot of the Andes. From the Colombian border they trend, at first, towards the NE to enfold the Maracaibo Lowlands. This section is known as the Sierra Nevada de Mérida. Beyond they broaden out into the Segovia Highlands N of Barquisimeto, and then turn E in parallel ridges along the coast to form the Central Highlands, dipping into the Caribbean Sea only to rise again into the North-Eastern Highlands of the peninsulas of Paria and Araya.

The general outline of each area will reveal that natural obstacles to farming, cattle breeding, and communications are formidable. It explains why the country was poverty-stricken for so long.

History At the beginning of the 16th century, Venezuela was inhabited by various tribes of Caribs and Arawaks, who could make no effective resistance against the Spaniards. The first permanent Spanish settlement was at Cumaná, in 1520. Soon afterwards settlers reached Coro, at the foot of the Paraguaná Peninsula. Indian slaves were used to mine and pan for gold, but the results were disappointing and the settlers turned to agriculture, forming settlements at

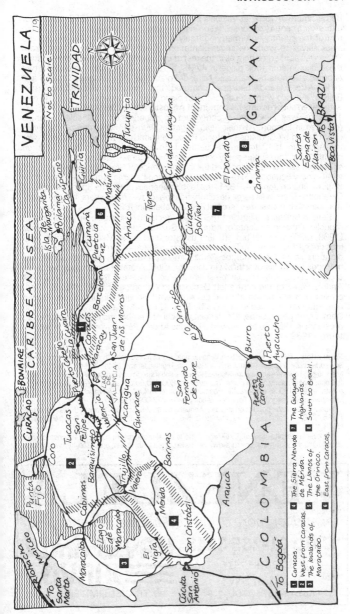

VENEZUELA

Not to Scale

CARIBBEAN SEA

TRINIDAD

GUYANA

COLOMBIA

BRAZIL

1 Caracas.
2 West from Caracas.
3 The lowlands of Maracaibo.
4 The Sierra Nevada de Mérida.
5 The Llanos of the Orinoco.
6 East from Caracas.
7 The Guayana Highlands.
8 South to Brazil.

Barquisimeto in 1552, at Valencia in 1555, and at Caracas in 1567. It was not until after a century of consolidation in these areas that they began to occupy the rest of the country, intermarrying freely with the Indians and later introducing black slaves to work the sugar plantations. Centralized colonial control from Spain was as irksome here as in the rest of Latin America: three risings reflecting these discontents took place in 1749, 1775 and 1797, and there were two abortive attempts by Francisco Miranda to achieve independence in 1806 and 1811. After Miranda had been captured, the movement was led by Simón Bolívar, a *criollo* with a touch of Indian blood, born in Caracas in 1783. He met with mixed success until his capture of Angostura, now Ciudad Bolívar, in 1817. There he was joined by a contingent of experienced Peninsular veterans recruited in London. At their head, together with the horsemen of the *llanos* commanded by Gen. José Antonio Páez, he undertook a dramatic march over the Andes in 1819 to win the battle of Boyacá and capture Bogotá. Three months later, the revolutionary congress at Angostura—with most of Venezuela still in Spanish hands— declared the independence of Gran Colombia, a union of what is now Ecuador, Colombia, Venezuela, and Panama. Bolívar returned from Bogotá, and on June 24, 1821, the revolutionaries routed the Spanish forces at Carabobo. There was some desultory fighting for two more years, but the last of the Spanish forces surrendered at Puerto Cabello in 1823.

Before Bolívar's death in 1830 Páez declared Venezuela an independent republic. Other presidents of note were Guzmán Blanco, Juan Vicente Gómez (1909-1935), a brutal but efficient dictator, and Isaías Medina Angarita, who introduced the oil laws. There was much material progress under the 6-year dictatorship of Gen. Marcos Pérez Jiménez (1952-58), but his Gómez-like methods led to his overthrow in January 1958. A stable democracy has been created since, with regular presidential elections every five years. Sr. Carlos Andrés Pérez of the centre-left Democratic Action party took office in 1974, presiding over a period of rapid development following the first great oil-price rise, and was succeeded in 1979 by Sr. Luis Herrera Campins of the Christian Democratic party, Copei. Dr. Jaime Lusinchi of Democratic Action was elected president in 1983, to be followed by Carlos Andrés Pérez, who began his second term in 1989.

Population   53 % are under 18. A large number are of mixed Spanish and Indian blood. There are some pure Indians, mostly in the Guayana Highlands and in the forests west of Lake Maracaibo. There are some pure-blooded Africans and a strong admixture of African blood along the coast, particularly at the ports. The arrival of 800,000 European immigrants since the war, mostly in the 1950s, has greatly modified the racial make-up in Venezuela. One in 6 of all Venezuelans is foreign born. Total population was 18,272,000 in 1987.

About 79 % of the population is urban. Annual growth: 2.9 %; urban growth: 3.3 %. Birth-rate (1985) 33.0; mortality per 1,000 inhabitants: 5.6; expectation of life, 69 years. Gdp per capita is US$3,300.

Venezuela, despite its wealth, still faces serious social problems. About 12 % are unemployed; about 10 % are illiterate. Many rural dwellers have drifted to the cities; one result of this exodus is that Venezuelan farmers do not provide all the food the nation needs and imports of foodstuffs are necessary, even for items such as beans and rice.

Education Elementary schools are free, and education is compulsory from the age of 7 to the completion of the primary grade. Primary school enrolment is 76 %, secondary school registration 21 % and university entries 3 % of the total.

Government Venezuela is a federal republic of 20 states, a Federal District, and two territories. The current Constitution is dated January 23, 1961. Voting is now compulsory for all over 18.

CARACAS (1)

The capital, Caracas, and the cities of Valencia and Maracay are in the Central Highlands, the most important upland area in Venezuela. The mountains here rise abruptly from a lush green coast to heights of from two to three thousand metres. Caracas, lies in a small basin, a rift in the thickly forested mountains which runs some 24 km. east and west. This historic colonial town has been transformed into one of the most astonishing modern cities in Latin America.

Caracas, founded in 1567, now has a population of around 4 million. It lies at 960 metres, but the southern parts of the city are 120 metres lower. Temperatures are moderate (a maximum of 32°C in July and August, and an occasional minimum of 9°C in January and February) and it is always cool at night.

A comparatively low pass (1,040 metres) in the mountains gives Caracas access by road to its port, La Guaira, and its international and domestic airports nearby at Maiquetía. The distance by a magnificently engineered road is 28 km. or 30 mins. by car (toll US$0.10 when going down; going up is free). Much longer should be allowed, however, for anyone with a plane to catch, as there are often delays arising from heavy traffic.

The proportionate growth of Caracas since the war has been greater than that of any other Latin American capital. Colonial buildings have given way to modern multi-storeyed edifices, many of which are architecturally impressive. Excellent examples are the University City, the twin towers of the Parque Central, the Centro Simón Bolívar, and the Círculo Militar.

Starting in Catia, an industrial area in the W where both roads from La Guaira enter, Avenida Sucre goes past the 23 de Enero workers' flats to join Av. Urdaneta between Palacio Miraflores and the Palacio Blanco, housing government offices. Later come the Post Office and Santa Capilla Church, looking like a wedding cake by a Parisian master pastrycook. Turn right here for Plaza Bolívar and the Capitol (the National Congress, do not take photographs in the vicinity or you may be arrested), or carry straight on down the Av. Urdaneta to San Bernardino (Colonial Museum). Here, we enter Av. Andrés Bello, which passes just below the cable railway station to join Av. Libertador to the Country Club and the E, or we can turn down the Av. La Salle to the eastern end of Los Caobos park, with the fine mahoganies which give it its popular name. From the Plaza Venezuela intersection at the eastern end of the park, the Avenida Abraham Lincoln leads E through Sabana Grande and continues as the Avenida Francisco Miranda to the residential section of Altamira, with its fine plaza and obelisk (unfortunately a construction site for a new Metro station). Sabana Grande, a modern shopping, hotel and business centre, is now a pedestrian mall closed to vehicular traffic: a very popular place to take a stroll.

Alternatively, forking right out of Avenida Sucre and crossing the viaduct, we reach El Silencio, and thence pass through the Centro Simón Bolívar, with its twin skyscrapers and underground parking and shopping centre (with an interesting mosaic at the lowest level), and finally along the Avenida Bolívar past Nuevo Circo bullring towards University City, the Sports Stadium, the *Tamanaco Hotel* and La Casona, residence of the President. S of the Nuevo Circo is the Helicoide, planned as a commercial centre under the Pérez Jiménez regime but left uncompleted at his fall in 1958. From the viaduct, we can also take Av. Universidad past the National Library (former University), Capitol and San

Francisco church. Two corners later, we glimpse, left, Bolívar's birthplace, before continuing to the Art Museum and on round Los Caobos park, or by the Av. Libertador, to the east.

Another west-east route is along the Avenida Boyacá from Avenida Baralt in the west to Petare in the east, connecting with the main road east to Barcelona (Route 9), which skirts the Cordillera de la Costa, including Avila mountain, and gives fine views along the length of the city. Towards the E end is a monument commemorating the battle of Boyacá, and a viaduct strides majestically over the recently remodelled park in Los Chorros suburb, to which access is signposted.

To the SW from El Silencio the Avenida San Martín leads towards the factories of Antímano. This area can also be reached direct from Catia by the Planicie tunnel. In the SW is also the older residential section of El Paraíso.

The shady Plaza Bolívar, where sloths can be seen in the trees, with its fine equestrian statue of the Liberator and pleasant colonial cathedral, is still the official centre of the city, though no longer geographically so. In fact, several centres (Plaza Bolívar, Plaza Venezuela, Sabana Grande, Chacaíto, La Floresta, Boleíta) are strung along the valley with residential areas between.

Parks Jardín Botánico, near Plaza Venezuela, entrance by Ciudad Universitaria (free), is quite small, disorganized and noisy. Parque Los Caobos is being extended; it is peaceful and has a cafetería in the middle. By the entrance in Av. México is the cultural centre, Ateneo de Caracas, with a theatre, art gallery, concert rooms, bookshop and the imposing Teresa Carreño theatre complex. Parque Nacional del Este has a zoo and is a peaceful place to relax, except at weekends, entrance US$0.10, closed on Mon. There is a boating lake and playground for children; many of the birds fly freely and there is an interesting collection of exotic flora. The Parque Caricuao is at the end of the Metro line, quite heavily wooded; it has the city's main zoo (the metro station is called Zoológico). Parque El Pinar also has a large zoo (Av. José Antonio Páez, El Pinar). The Parque Los Chorros at the foot of the mountain has impressive waterfalls, also recommended; El Calvario, west of Plaza O'Leary, is quiet and pleasant with a good view of Centro Simón Bolívar. A new park, Parque Vargas, is to replace the Nuevo Circo bus station. **See page 892** for El Avila National Park.

National Monuments

Panteón Nacional   Open Mon.-Fri., 0900-1200 and 1430-1730, Sat.-Sun., 1000-1300 and 1400-1700. This was designed as the resting place of Bolívar, the Liberator, and Miranda, the Precursor of Independence. The remains of Bolívar lie there, but the tomb of Miranda, who died in a Spanish prison, has been left open to await the return of his body. There is a small military ceremony at 1430 daily.

Capitolio Nacional   The Elliptical Salon has some impressive paintings by the Venezuelan artist Martín Tovar y Tovar and a bronze urn containing the 1811 Declaration of Independence. One of the paintings on the ceiling shows a British regiment fighting in the Battle of Carabobo, and the names of the officers appear on the wall; in acknowledgement of this assistance Bolívar granted the British armed forces the right to march through any city in Gran Colombia (Colombia, Ecuador, Panama and Venezuela) with bayonets fixed, drums beating and flags flying.

Museums

Museo de Bellas Artes, Plaza Morelos in Parque Los Caobos: open Tues.-Fri., 0900-1200, 1500-1730, Sat.-Sun., 1000-1700. Pictures include an El Greco among works by mainly Venezuelan artists. Adjacent is the Galería de Arte Nacional, which also houses the Cinemateca Nacional.

Museo de Ciencias Naturales, also in Plaza Morelos in Parque Los Caobos; open 0900-1200, 1500-1730 except Mon.

Key to map

3. Central Post Office; 5. Capitol; 6. National Library; 7. Bolívar's House and Historical Museum; 8. Cathedral; 9. Centro Simón Bolívar; 10. Road to University; 12. Museo de Bellas Artes; 13. Museo de Ciencias Naturales; 14. Plaza Bolívar; 15. Plaza Candelaria; 16. Parque Carabobo; 17. Plaza Miranda (minibus station nearby); 18. Plaza La Concordia; 19. Road to Museo de Arte Colonial (Quinta Anauco).

Museo de Arte Colonial, Quinta Anauco, Av. Panteón, San Bernardino: open Tues.-Sat. 0900-1200, 1400-1700, Sun., 1000-1700. Admission by guided tour only. A delightful house built in 1720. Chamber concerts most Saturdays at 1800. The beautiful suburb of San Bernardino glories in tropical flowers and whole avenues of forest trees, smothered in blossom in season.

Casa Natal del Libertador   Open 1000-1300 and 1400-1700 daily except Mon. The present house is a reconstruction of the house where Bolívar was born. The first, of adobe, was destroyed by an earthquake. The second became a stable, and was later pulled down. The present building of stone was built by order of Gómez (whose birthday was the same as Bolívar's) in the early 1920s; it contains interesting pictures and furniture.

The Museo Bolivariano is alongside the Casa Natal and contains the Liberator's war relics.

House of Arturo Michelena, four blocks north of Miraflores palace, in the La Pastora section, is a typical 19th century home, now a museum. Open 0900-1200 and 1500-1700 (closed Mon. and Fri.).

Museo de Transporte, Parque Nacional del Este, includes a large collection of locomotives and old cars, as well as a fascinating series of scale models of Caracas a century ago. Open Wed., Sat., Sun., 0900-1800. Admission US$0.50.

In the Parque Central, between Av. Lecuna (E end) and the elevated section of Av. Bolívar there are four museums in a complex which includes 2 octagonal towers (56 floors each) and four large apartment buildings with shopping below.

Museo de Arte Contemporáneo, Parque Central, Cuadra Bolívar, near the Caracas Hilton, very good, European and Venezuelan painters represented. Open Tues.-Sun. 1000-1800.

Museo de los Niños, Parque Central, next to East Tower, is open to the public Wed.-Sun. and holidays, 0900-1200, 1400-1700, otherwise is for school visits; a highly sophisticated modern science museum, well worth a visit and extremely popular, US$0.75 (adults). Book a day or so in advance in school holidays or August. Also in the Parque Central complex, **Museo Audiovisual,** Tues.-Fri., 0900-1700, US$1, includes a library of Venezuelan television programmes, a practice TV studio, and **Museo del Teclado** (keyboard instruments).

Museo Histórico Militar, near Metro Gato Negro.

The Ministry of Foreign Relations contains pictures mostly of national heroes and historical events.

The Concejo Municipal (City Hall) on Plaza Bolívar contains three museums: a collection of the paintings of Emilio Boggio, a Venezuelan painter; the Raúl Santana Museum of the Creole Way of Life, a collection of miniature figures in costumes and poses characteristic of Venezuelan life, all handmade by Raúl Santana and extremely realistic; Francisco Pizarro's battle standard, presented by him to Sucre after the battle of Ayacucho and then given to Bolívar is shown here; and the Sala de Arqueología Gaspar Marcano, exhibiting ceramics, mostly discovered on the coast. All three open Tues.-Fri., 0930-1200, 1500-1800; Sat. and Sun., 0930-1800. Informative guides are available.

Those with a deeper interest in archaeology might like to contact the Junta Nacional Protectora y Conservadora del Patrimonio Histórico y Artístico de la Nación, Palacio de Miraflores, Av. Urdaneta.

Churches   The Cathedral should be seen for its beautiful façade, and pictures including alleged Rubens and Murillo. San Francisco should be seen for its colonial altars. Santa Teresa, between La Palma and Santa Teresa, just SE of the Centro Simón Bolívar, has good interior chapels.

N.B.   Check museum schedules in *El Universal, El Nacional* or the *Daily Journal* (which also have details of events for children). Many museums and most religious buildings will refuse entry to anybody wearing shorts.

Modern Caracas   Visitors should see the Avenida de los Próceres with its twin monoliths and other monuments to the heroes of independence (it also has flowers and gardens); the magnificent Officers' Club on the same avenue, the Cuadra Bolívar near the *Caracas Hilton;* and the University City, an enormous and coherent complex of great buildings in which paintings, sculpture and stained glass are completely integrated with the architecture (which is now showing signs of wear).

Warning   It is advisable not to arrive in Caracas at night and not to walk down narrow streets after dark. Fighting frequently breaks out and thefts and attacks are common, on tourists and residents alike. Police searches are becoming more common, especially in airports; if you have entered overland from Colombia, you can expect thorough investigation (once you've left the airport, better to say you flew in).

Hotels   Prices are no longer high, in view of the 1983 devaluation. Cheap *pensiones* are usually full of long-stay residents and have very few rooms available for travellers. Hotels marked with an asterisk (*) are bookable through Fairmont International (see next page).

Recommended hotels not in the centre: The *Tamanaco* is the best hotel in Caracas, but it is difficult to get rooms as it is normally fully booked, changes travellers' cheques for guests only (poor rate), L (US$135d + 10% tax).   *Hotel Paseo de las Mercedes,* C, Las Mercedes is almost next door to the *Tamanaco. Nostrum,* Av. Orinoco con final Calle París, Las Mercedes (near *Paseo*), T 92-76-46, 92-66-46, a/c, hot water, clean, rec., E. The *Caracas Hilton*, L (US$97-135d + 10% tax), is more central but noisy (traffic and air conditioning) and although the rooms are excellent and clean, the service has also been criticized; connected with the *Hilton* are the *Residencias Anauco Hilton*, Parque Central, an "apartotel", B, bad reports received about the travel agency at this hotel; another apartment hotel is the *CCT Venantur* in the Centro Ciudad Comercial Tamanaco, luxury, C; furnished flats also at *Crillón*, Av. Libertador, between Las Acacias and Los Jabillos, D; *Ribot,* Av. Andres Eloy Blanco, La Mansión Fte. Viasa, La Candelaria (nr. *Hilton*), F, T 5713433/5713244. The *Ávila* is on Av. Jorge Washington in San Bernardino on the higher levels of the city (T 515128/515173, Telex: 21637 Avila), set in park-like gardens and very pleasant, C, swimming pool, "most agreeable", food good; *Aventura*, Av. Fco. Fajardo, San Bernardino, B; *Waldorf,* Av. Industria, San Bernardino, Bellas Artes metro, E, a/c, shower, restaurant, French, German and English spoken, rec. *La Floresta*, Av. Avila, Sur Plaza Altamira, T 2844111, D, clean, friendly, helpful, but restaurant not very good. Also good, *Continental Altamira*, D, Av. San Juan Bosco (there is also *Altamira,* Av. J. F. Sosa, D). *Beethoven,* Av. Beethoven, Colinas de Bellomonte (½ block from Sears), D with bath, TV, good, clean; *Centro Uslar,* 2a Av., Calles 1 y 2, Sector B, Urb. Montalbán, C, good but a long way from centre; *El Paseo,* Av. Los Ilustres, Urb. Los Chaguaramos, T 661-3438/3547/3315, D, good, clean. In the E of the city, *El Marqués,* Av. El Samán esq. Yaruari, El Marqués, medium-priced, comfortable, quiet, good restaurant.

Cheapest hotels can be found around the Nuevo Circo bus terminal: e.g. *ABC,* F, Av. Lecuna, 2 blocks from Nuevo Circo, with shower, very noisy (less so on higher floors, which are good value); *Center Park,* Av. Lecuna 20, T 5418619, F, clean, safe; *Urupagua,* Av. Lecuna, F; but this area is unpleasant and unsafe for women. Better to go several blocks WSW to a quieter area, e.g. *Príncipe,* Av. Sur 3, Gobernador a Pinto, G without bath; *Pensión San Marcos,* Hoyo a Santa Rosalía, T 5453723, G, basic; *Avenida,* Calle Sur 4 (nr. Capitolio), T 426440, E, hot water, a/c, safe, rec.; *La Neve,* Pilita a Glorieta No. 126—Sur 4, nr. Metro Capitolio, F, a/c or fan, bath, good, clean, safe. For other cheap hotels look on Calle Sur 2.

In the downtown area: *Inter*, Animas a Calero on corner of Av. Urdaneta, E, very clean, shower and toilet with each room, friendly, English spoken, very popular so be sure to make a reservation, the queues for rooms begin before 0700 and the hotel is full by 0800, poor restaurant; *Ausonia,* Bolero a Pineda, D, with bath, hot-water, TV, central, clean; *Mara,* E, *Conde,* D, and *Veroes,* D, Av. Urdaneta, are in the centre, convenient for banks and business houses, but noisy; also *Cervantes,* Av. Urdaneta, Norte 5, F, cheap but spartan, safe, very noisy. *Plaza Catedral*, Blvd. Plaza Bolívar, next to Cathedral, D, a/c, TV, phone, excellent, some English spoken, stays limited to 2 nights; *Caroni,* 2 blocks from Capitolio, near Cathedral, E, popular, good value, safe but a bit noisy; *Hospedaje Torreiro,* San Agustín, Sur 11 Bolívar, E, clean, friendly, safe, rec.; *Grand Galaxie*, Truco a Caja de Agua, between Av. Baralt and Norte 4 on Salas Sta. Bárbara, T 83-90-11/83-90-44, D, deluxe, a/c, TV, phone, restaurant, central, comfortable.

If you arrive in Caracas in doubt, ask a taxi driver to take you to Las Acacias in Sabana Grande, where you can choose a hotel from the very large number in that area. There are various grades all close together so you can walk from one to another until you find one suitable. However, many of the numerous small hotels on Av. Las Acacias do not cater for singles or for couples staying more than a few hours. (The weekend is not a very good time to look for a room.) If not using a taxi, take metro to Sabana Grande (for example). On Av. Las Acacias are *Bruno*, D, TV, air conditioning, fair, Peruvian restaurant with live entertainment, unremarkable; *Everest,* D; *Myriam,* E, few single rooms, off-street parking, clean but noisy; *Embassy* (rec. by Tourist Office); *Tanausú*, E. On Av. Casanova are *Luna*, D rec. (with Calle El Colegio); *Capri-Casanova*, D, spartan but clean and friendly; *Broadway*, No. 4, convenient for Chacaíto metro station, D, private bathroom, TV, friendly, clean, a bit noisy, Italian specialities in restaurant. Others in Sabana Grande include *El Cóndor* (3a Av. Las Delicias), D, TV, air conditioning, businessmen on their own need to take suites because single rooms have no desks; *Plaza Palace*, Av. Los Mangos, Las Delicias, very good, friendly, good atmosphere, B; *Las Américas*, Los Cerritos, end of Casanova, D, warm water, food passable but unexciting; *City* (Av. Bolivia, Los Caobos), E, all rooms have TV and private bath; *Ritz*, Av. Las Palmas y Av. Libertador, E, with bath, a/c, secure free parking; *Madrid*, F, Av. Chacaíto, small, hot water, showers in all rooms; *Capri*, F, Calle Las Flores, clean; *The King's Inn Hotel*, D, Calle Olimpo, near Av. Lincoln; *Tampa*, Av. Francisco Solano López, D; *Savoy*, Av. Francisco Solano López, Las Delicias, C, without food, good, efficient, clean, secure vehicle park. *Critsal*, Plaza Venezuela, Av. Colegio, E, a/c, convenient, disco at weekends, good cheap Chilean food.

The weekend is not a good time to look for a room; in the centre, all cheap hotels take only short-stay customers on Fri. p.m.

Hotel Reservations Fairmont International, Torre Capriles, Planta Baja, Plaza Venezuela, Caracas, T 782 8888, Telex 21232 SNRHO, will book hotel rooms in Caracas and also in 102 hotels in the rest of the country. The airport tourist office is very helpful and will book hotel rooms. Finding a hotel, particularly in the middle-price range, is always difficult. If you book from abroad (e.g. Thomas Cook in England) make sure you receive confirmation before beginning your journey or you may turn up and find yourself without a room. **Economy tip**: most hotel rooms have a TV set for which you will be charged; if you don't want it, ask for it to be removed. For apartment rental, consult *El Universal* daily paper, small ads. columns.

Restaurants There is such a profusion of eating places in Caracas that we give the following general advice, with a mention of just a few places currently reported reliable, rather than attempt the impossible task of keeping up to date with all the changes. Don't be shy about asking the price before you order in a bar as beer in one will cost three times as much as in another, and a modest portion of manchego cheese will cost more than a good steak. Food on display in a bar is free with your drink if they offer it as a pasapalo, but will be charged for if offered as a ración. You can save on the service charge by eating at the bar and not at a table. Coffee in a café is at government-controlled price if taken at the counter, but not if served at a table. Milk is subsidized and is cheaper than soft drinks. By decree, restaurants must put up a list of prices on or near the front door, and are prohibited from charging for place settings (cubiertos) or bread, butter, condiments etc. (guarnición). For dining out, there is a selection of good restaurants around Avenida Urdaneta (*Bar Pas de Calais* for paella, *Mesón de Cervantes*—friendly multilingual manager, Nelson, *El Parador* and *Politena*), La Castellana (*La Estancia*), Plaza Altamira (*Mayfair Station*), Las Mercedes (*Piccolo Mundo*, *Hereford Grill*, *Farms Grill*, *Mr Ribs*, Av. Valle Arriba, barbecued ribs etc., very fashionable; *Era de Acuario*, vegetarian, open for dinner), El Rosal (*La Barba Roja*, Calle Venezuela, *El Jabaguero*, Calle Pichincha, both seafood) and Sabana Grande (see below). There are plenty of eating places around Plaza Bolívar. In the Parque Central (Edificio Anauco—basement) is *El Parque*, good food and service; *Tarzilandia*, 10th Transversal Altamira, San Juan Bosco, international food; *Dog and Fox Pub*, Río de Janeiro, Las Mercedes, British-owned, cheap, good music, popular with European residents and travellers; *El Granjero del Este*, Rio de Janeiro, T 916619, traditional barbecues, excellent arepas. Very good Mexican/Peruvian dishes at *El Tizón*, CC Bello Campo, Sótano Local 80, T 316715/2613485. Excellent pastries and cheese from *Panadería y Pastelería Madona*, Av. Sur, near corner with Camejo (0800-2300). The *Sol y Sombra*, Sur 1 No. 110 at Velásquez, doubles as a betting shop on race days. Guides to eating are published in the VAAUW Guide to Caracas and the magazine "Ve Venezuela". Also "Gourmet Dining out in Caracas", available at travel agencies and good hotels. Advertisements appear in the "Daily Journal" and the Yellow Pages of the telephone directory.

Although it is not practicable to cover the whole of Caracas, the following description of the Sabana Grande area will give an idea of what is available. Breakfast in your hotel is likely to be poor (poor bread or none, insipid coffee and orange juice which is half artificial). It is better and cheaper in a fuente de soda, and cheaper still in a pastelería or arepería. (One correspondent recommends *La Ermita* on Plaza Venezuela.) Tables in the open air on the boulevard, however, are expensive, e.g. US$0.40 for a batido which costs US$0.25 down a side street or US$0.20 at a greengrocer, yet it is exactly the same fruit drink. (The boulevard waiters overcharge. Check prices on the displayed list.) Mid-day is the most economical time to eat the main meal of the day and about the only opportunity to find fresh vegetables. Look for "menú ejecutivo" or "cubierto", which is a three-course meal for US$1.50, e.g. at *Ventas de Madrid* on San Gerónimo and *O' Gran Sol* on Villa Flor between Casanova and Sabana Grande (excellent paella, reasonable prices).

Good, economical meals in the evening at *Sorrentino* and *Jabillos* on Francisco Solano, *Coraveña* (next to *La Bússola*, one block east of Torre La Previsora), *La Soledad* (next block south on Casanova) and *Tropical Room* (two blocks east on Casanova). For business and similar occasions: *La Bússola* (see above—try carpaccio), *Rugantino* in Hotel Tampa (speciality cartuccio), *El Chicote* behind La Previsora, and *Villa D'Este* in Hotel Cóndor. For variety: *Floridita* in La Previsora and *Esquina de Tejas* in Hotel Kursaal (both Cuban), *Le Coq d'Or*, Av. Los Mangos

(French), *Hotel Bruno* (Peruvian), *Mario's* on Casanova (Brazilian—noisy), *Dragón Verde*, Ciné París, Av. Maturín (Chinese), *Berlín*, top floor, Centro Comercial Unico, Chacaíto Metro exit (German), and *Buffet Vegetariano*, Av. Los Jardines. Other vegetarian restaurants are *El Acuarino*, Truco a Caja de Agua; *Super Bueno*, esq. Chorro a Dr Paúl, Edif. Plaza El Venozolano and in front of El Conde Hotel; *Chalet Naturista*, nr. Sabana Grande metro station; these four are not open for dinner. Roast lamb at *La Taberna*, Torre Capriles, Plaza Venezuela. Fast foods: there is a plethora of burger and pizza places, as well as the ubiquitous hot dog stalls of doubtful hygiene (when the police don't close them down).

Clubs   There are 3 country clubs in Caracas, all of which have excellent restaurants. The Country Club in the eastern part has an 18-hole golf course. The Social Centre of the British Commonwealth Association, Quinta Alborada, Avenida 7 with Transversal 9, Altamira, Caracas, with bar and swimming pool; British and Commonwealth visitors only; entry fee according to length of stay; T 261-30-60. Membership of the better clubs is by the purchase of a share, which can run to thousands of dollars. An exception is the sports club run by the *Tamanaco Hotel*, open to non-guests and suitable for people staying a short time. The Military Club (Círculo de las Fuerzas Armadas) is well worth seeing and, if the visitors are soberly dressed, permission to view the premises is often granted. Flying Club, at La Carlota, near *Tamanaco Hotel*, mixed reports. Robert and Daisy Kunstaetter of Richmond Hill, Ontario (call sign VE300G) tell us the Radio Club Venezolano is a very welcoming, efficient organization of amateur radio operators which is eager to meet amateurs from around the world (address: P.O.Box 2285, Caracas 1010-A, T 781-4878, 781-8303—Av. Lima, Los Caobos; branches around the country).

Shopping   For gems and fine jewellery, visit the H. Stern shops at the Hotels *Hilton* and *Tamanaco* and at the International Airport. Pro-Venezuela Exposición y Venta de Arte Popular, Gran Avenida at Calle Olimpo, between Plaza Venezuela and beginning of Av. Casanova (opp. Torre La Previsora), for Venezuelan crafts. Indian and Andean crafts can be found at the market in Las Mercedes. The CCCT shopping centre is worth a visit. From Chacaíto, along Av. Abraham Lincoln, Sabana Grande, to Plaza Venezuela, is a pedestrian precinct, with good shops, handicrafts for sale, street traders and cafés.

Bookshops   English language ones include: *English Bookshop*, Concresa, Prados del Este; *Lectura*, Centro Comercial Chacaíto, and *Steele's Bookstore*, Calle Baruta, Sabana Grande. *Librería del Este*, Av. Francisco de Miranda 52, Edif. Galipán, *Librería Multilingua*, Concresa, and *Librería Unica*, Centro Capriles, ground floor local 13N, Plaza Venezuela, all have foreign language books. A French bookshop is *Librería La France*, Centro Comercial Chacaíto, Italian bookshop, *El Libro Italiano*, Pasaje La Concordia (between Sabana Grande pedestrian street and Av. Fco. Solano López), and for German books, *Librería Alemana* (Oscar Todtmann), Centro El Bosque, Avenida Libertador.

Buses and Taxis   Starting from the bus station at Nuevo Circo (being replaced in 1989— **see page 891**), there are many buses, overcrowded in the rush hours, urban fare usually US$0.07 (the correct fare helps to speed things up). *Por puesto* minibuses running on regular routes charge between US$0.08 and US$0.15 depending on the distance travelled within the city; fares rise to US$1.40 for journeys outside. Many *por puesto* services start in Silencio. Taxis are required by law to instal and use taxi-meters. The initial flag fee is US$0.25 plus US$0.10 for each km. and US$0.05 for each 30 seconds of the ride (hourly rate US$3). Taxi drivers are authorized to charge an extra 20% on night trips after 2200, on Sun. and all holidays, and US$0.45 for answering telephone calls. After 1800 drivers are selective about where they want to go. Beware of taxi drivers trying to renegotiate fixed rates because your destination is in "a difficult area". There are pirates, however, with possibly a taxi sign, but without yellow licence plates/registration-number plate, which are to be avoided. If you get in a taxi with no meter you must negotiate the price in advance.

The Metro, opened in 1983, operates 0600-2300, Sun. 0900-1800, and costs US$0.07 for journeys up to 5 stations, US$0.10 for 6-8 stations, US$0.15 for 9-12 stations, and US$0.17 for 13-16 stations (20-journey tickets available). It is air-conditioned, clean, well-kept and more comfortable and quicker than any other form of city transport; no smoking, no large bags. There are 2 lines: Line 1 W to E from Propatria to Chacaíto and beyond; Line 2 SW from El Silencio to Las Adjuntas, Caricuao and Parque Zoológico. There is an interconnecting metro/bus service between La Paz and Capitolio, US$0.10. Guide: *La Practiguía del Metro*, published by Practiguía Azul.

Driving   Self-drive cars (Hertz, National, Avis, Volkswagen, Budget) are available at the airport and in town. They are cheaper than guided excursions for less than full loads. Driver's licence from home country accepted. Major credit card or US$210 cash deposit required. The Government has fixed the rates and the cheapest available is US$19 per day plus US$0.19 per km. for a Volkswagen Beetle or Brasilia or a Ford Fairmont or Cherry Nova. For medium-priced cars, Hertz, National, Avis, US$21 per day plus US$0.21 per km. National Car Rental offers 10-15% discount with Amex credit cards. Auto and personal insurance strongly recommended as you will be lucky to survive two or three days as a newcomer to Caracas traffic without a dent or a scrape. Carry spare battery water, fan belts, the obligatory breakdown triangle, a jack and spanners. Some cars have a security device to prevent the engine being started and this is recommended. Don't run out of fuel; you can incur a Bs.500 fine by so doing. Beware of potholes even in the best roads and avoid driving fast, particularly at night; a nationwide speed limit of 80 kph was imposed in 1982. The best road map can be bought from CVP petrol stations (US$1); it shows the distances between towns and is generally reliable. Many roads may be marked as dirt tracks but have been paved since the map was produced. The Guía Progreso map is very detailed but not very accurate, especially S of Orinoco. **Beware of the traffic-reduction system in Caracas**, under which the Government has prohibited the use of cars with number plates ending in 1 or 6 on Mondays, 2 or 7 on Tuesdays, 3 or 8 on Wednesdays, 4 or 9 on Thursdays, 5 or 0 on Fridays, between the hours of 0700 and 2000.

Motorcycles   may not be ridden in Caracas between 2300 and 0500. Pillion passengers are only permitted if of the opposite sex from the driver.

Garage   Yota-Box, 3a Transversal Mis Encantos, Quinta Morava, No. 1 15, Chacao, T 313772/331035, owner Gerardo Ayala, rec., especially for Toyota.

Night Clubs   Caracas is a lively city by night, and there are many and varied discotheques and night clubs. Caraqueños dine at home around 2000, and in restaurants from 2100 to 2300, so night clubs don't usually come to life until after 2300, and then go on to all hours of the morning. Naiguatá (*Hotel Tamanaco*), expensive; best show in town. El Greco, Av. Principal de Macaracuay (also restaurant in same building). Hipocampo, Plaza Chacaíto. Mon Petit, Plaza Altamira Sur (there are many small clubs, restaurants and bars on Plaza Altamira Sur). México Típico, on Av. Libertador, said to be excellent, a Mexican band alternates with a Venezuelan band: no cover charge and drinks only double normal bar prices. The "Noches Caraqueñas" show put on by the *Hilton* each Mon. evening makes a pleasant introduction to Caracas night-life. Juan Sebastian Bar, Av. Venezuela, El Rosal, is a jazz club (closed Sun.) and Feelings, Av Tamanaco, El Rosal, is a popular *salsa* club. *Cervecería Nueva Esparta*, Av. los Marquitos (Sabana Grande) is cheap, provides good music, but is another couples-only venue. Two gay clubs are Ice Palace at Altamira Sur (not exclusively gay, non members admitted for US$4) and Zigzag restaurant and piano bar, Av. Libertador, Ed. La Línea.

Discotheques   Water Point, Centro Comercial, El Parque de Los Palos Grandes, and Blow-up, Plaza Altamira Sur, have been rec.; also Teorema, La Jungla, Eva, The Flower, and many others. Couples only seems to be the norm.

Sports and Recreations   Golf, tennis, riding, fishing, horse-racing every Sat. and Sun. at La Rinconada (a truly magnificent grandstand), bull fights (in season; go to the *Bar-Restaurant Los Cuchilleros* on Av. Urdaneta next to Plaza Candelaria to meet bullfighters and *aficionados*; tickets sold there on bullfight Sunday mornings, ticket sales end 1400, bar closes 1530, bullfight starts 1600), baseball (October-January), football, swimming, etc. Horse-racing commences at 1300, admission price to grandstand US$1.10. Several buses go to La Rinconada. There are numerous cinemas (US$1-half price Mon.). Parque del Este (Av. Francisco Miranda) has a planetarium and a good jogging track. For flying try Halcón, Centro Comercial San Luis, T 987 1834. The recreational event of the year is the two days of Carnival.

Cultural Events   There are frequent Sun. morning concerts in the Teatro Municipal, 1100, usually US$2.25. Concerts, ballet, theatre and film festivals at the Ateneo de Caracas, Paseo Colón, Plaza Morelos; and similar events, including foreign artists, at the Complejo Cultural Teresa Carreño, on Paseo Colón, just E of *Caracas Hilton* (an interesting building, too). For details of these and other events, see the newspapers, *El Universal*, *El Nacional* and *Daily Journal*, and the Sunday issue of *El Diario de Caracas*.

Exchange   Banco de Venezuela and local banks; Banco Royal Venezolano; Citibank; Banco Unión for Visa transactions. For exchange go to Italcambio offices: esquina Veroes and Urdaneta, Av. Casanova (Sabana Grande), Av. L. Roche (Altamira Sur) Simón Bolívar Airport. Cambios Caracas in Torre Capriles, Plaza Venezuela. Confinanzas, Centro Comercial Paseo Las Mercedes, Local PA-CI, open 0800-1200, 1400-1700. Commission of US$0.04 charged per US$1 changed in travellers' cheques. American Express cheques, Banco Consolidado, Av. San Francisco, Edif. Torre California, floor 9, Urb. Colinas de La California; AmEx rep is Turisol, Centro Comercial Tamanaco, level C-2, Chuao suburb, T 927922, also in *Hotel Tamanaco*.

Addresses   In the centre of Caracas, each street corner has a name, and addresses are generally given as, for example, "Santa Capilla a Mijares", rather than the official "Calle Norte 2, No. 26". Maps can be bought at *Caracas Hilton*, and Lagovén service stations. Good street maps of Caracas can be bought in kiosks, or be found at the back of the yellow pages telephone directory.

British Embassy and Consulate, Torre Las Mercedes, 3rd floor, Ciudad Comercial Tamanaco, Chuao (T 911255/916133). Apartado 1246 for letters.
British Council, Edificio Torre la Noria, 6th floor, Las Mercedes. English classes and modest library oriented towards English teaching, literature and fiction.

USA Embassy and Consulate, Av. Francisco Miranda, La Floresta, T 283 5035.
Centro Venezolano-Americano, Av. Las Mercedes, good free library of books in English, and free concerts. Also good for Spanish courses, US$195 for 2 months.
Colombian Consulate, Av. E, Campo Alegre, T 331835/2611358. Open Mon.-Fri. 0800-1130 for visas, can take anything from 2 hrs. to one day.
Anglican Church, Plaza Urape, San Román section of Las Mercedes (near *Tamanaco*; T 914727). The United Christian Church, interdenominational, Av. Arboleda, El Bosque.
Australian Embassy, Torre C, piso 20, Centro Plaza (T 283-34-87).
Canadian Embassy, Edificio Torre Europa, piso 7, Av. Francisco de Miranda, Chacao (T 33-97-76).
West German Embassy, Edificio Panavén, piso 2, Av. San Juan Bosco, Altmira. T 2610181/310144.
Asociación Cultural Humboldt (Goethe Institut), Av. Juan Germán Roscio, San Bernardino, T 527634, library, lectures, films, concerts, Spanish courses.
Danish Embassy, Ed. EASO, 17th floor, Av. Francisco Miranda, nr. Chacaíto metro station, T 9514618/5606.
Finnish Embassy, Torre C, piso 14, Centro Plaza, Av. Francisco de Miranda, T 284 5013.
Brazilian Consulate, Ed. Cen., Gerencial Mohedano, Av. Mohedano, T 2613459/2621649; visas same day if requested at 0900, returned 1800.
Guyanese Embassy, Quinta Roraima, Av. El Paseo, Prados del Este, T 771158, 9732781 (visa US$2.50, 2 application forms, 2 photos required).
Suriname Embassy, 4a Avenida, between 7a and 8a Transversal, Urb. Altamira, T 324490.
Swedish Embassy, Edificio Panavén, piso 5, Av. San Juan Bosco con Tercera Transversal, Altamira, T 2620176.
Swiss Embassy, Torre Europa, piso 6, Av. Francisco de Miranda, Campo Alegre (T 334787/9510159).

Telecommunications are operated by the state company, CANTV, from El Silencio building in West Caracas, Centro Simón Bolívar, or Centro Plaza on Francisco Miranda in the east. Open 24 hrs., latter opens at 0700. **Post Office** Central at Urdaneta y Norte 4, close to Plaza Bolívar. *Lista de correos* costs US$0.04.

Hospital Hospital de Clínicas, Av. Panteón y Av. Alameda, San Bernardino, T 5742011. Instituto Médico La Floresta, near US Embassy, T 2848111.

Tourist Office Information from floors 35-37, Torre Oeste, Parque Central, (metro Bellas Artes is closest). T 507-8726/8814/8815. No maps. There is a smaller office at the airport, which has been highly praised and where English is spoken. **See page 928** for further recommended reading.

Travel Agents BOT Tours, Torre Oeste, Paseo Hilton, Nivel Lecuna, Parque Central (same building as Tourist Office), good. Molina Viajes, Av. Andrés Bello, Edif. San Bosco, Los Palos Grandes, rec., branch director Daniella Harr speaks English, French, German and Italian; Viajes Vintur have staff speaking English, German and Italian, Plaza Altamira Sur, Av. San Juan Bosco, T 324931/35. Turven Tropical Travel, Real Edificio Unión, local 13, Sabana Grande, PO Box 60622, Caracas 1050, T 9511032, varied tours. Venezuelan Travel Advisers, Venezuela, Edif. Policlínica Americana, Local D-PB, El Rosal, T 9514922. Candes Turismo, office in lobby of *Hilton*, T 571 0987; Servicios Colectivos Especiales in lobby of *Tamanaco*, T 283 6506, trips more varied and slightly cheaper.

Airport Maiquetía, for national flights, Simón Bolívar for international flights, adjacent to each other (5 mins.' walk), 28 km. from Caracas, near the port of La Guaira. The Tourist Office at the airport is very helpful; hotel bookings can be made there. *Casa de cambio* open 24 hrs. (Italcambio, good rates, but only changes small amounts at a time, outside duty-free area). Check your change. Always allow plenty of time when going to the airport, whatever means of transport you are using: the route can be very congested. Taxi fares from airport to Caracas cost on average US$4-5.50, depending on part of city but overcharging up to US$9.50 is rife (fares are controlled supposedly—buy ticket from office in the airport if it hasn't "run out"); more by night when a 20% surcharge is added after 2200, also on Sundays and holidays. (Taxis are much cheaper to national terminal.) If you think the taxi driver is overcharging you, make a complaint to Corporturismo or tell him you will report him to the Departamento de Protección del Consumidor. If you walk about 200 metres to the highway you can catch a Caracas or El Silencio *por puesto*, or a bus for US$0.80 will take you to the bus terminal (but they are often unwilling to stop if you have a suitcase). They stop running after 1900. *Por puesto* directly from Gato Negro metro station on Parque Central, US$0.75, but US$0.80 from near Calvario Park (metro Capitolio) in the city to the airport. Another way: Metro to Gato Negro, take the "Macuto Sheraton" bus to La Guaira, then airport bus, or taxi. When checking in, keep 10 bolívar bills handy to pay departure tax levied at most large airports.

Long Distance Buses The Nuevo Circo bus station in the city centre was due to be closed, and replaced in 1989 by two new ones, at the E and W ends of the city (the latter near La Rinconada race track). Long-distance bus travel varies a lot in quality. However, buses from Caracas to Maracaibo, Mérida and San Cristóbal are usually in excellent condition; buses to Guayana are of poorer quality. Frequent service to Maracay, Valencia and Barquisimeto, but buses are often in bad shape; the Panamericana route is not recommended because it takes the old road on which there are many accidents. Aerobuses maintain regular services by air-conditioned coaches with reclining seats between Caracas and the main towns in eastern and western Venezuela, and also to Cúcuta, in Colombia. The fares of other good companies are a third less. The best lines are: to Maracaibo, Expresos los Llanos; to Guayana, Providencial; to the eastern coast, Responsable. Buses stop frequently but there will not always be a toilet at the stop; always take your own toilet paper. Long distance *por puesto* services are twice as expensive as buses, less comfortable, but generally faster. On public holidays buses are usually fully booked leaving Caracas and drivers often make long journeys without stopping. Always take identification when booking a long-distance journey, the tickets only go on sale the day before travel (seats cannot be reserved). Half-price tickets are available for those with a student card but you may need to provide a photocopy. There is a left luggage store at the bus station. To avoid theft it is advisable not to sleep on the buses. Arrive early, buses may start before time.

Journey to Maracaibo, US$4.65, 10 hrs., *por puesto*, US$9; Maracay, US$0.70, 2 hrs., *por puesto*, US$1.40; Valencia, US$1, *por puesto*, US$2; Coro US$3.30 (overnight), *por puesto*, US$6.60; to Barquisimeto US$2.40. Overnight to Valera, US$4.10, 9 hrs. (Aerobuses). Buses to Mérida, Expresos Mérida, US$4.80, 12 hrs., *por puesto*, US$9.60; overnight to Mérida, via Panamericana or Los Llanos (12 hrs.) to San Cristóbal. Expresos Alianzas Caracas to Cúcuta, US$6, 8 hrs., daily at 1900. Get passport exit stamp at San Antonio; bus will stop there. Bus to San Antonio, US$5.40, *por puesto*, US$10.80. To Barinas, US$3.70, 8 hrs. To Puerto La Cruz, US$2.60, 5 hrs., *por puesto*, US$5.15; to Cumaná, US$3.05, 8 hrs., *por puesto*, US$6.10, to Margarita, US$8 including ferry; to Maturín, US$3.60, *por puesto*, US$7.20. To Ciudad Bolívar, US$4.20-4.80, 8 hrs. *por puesto*, US$8.25; Ciudad Guayana, US$4.80, *por puesto*, US$9.20; to Tucupita, US$4.85; Tumeremo, 1800, 14 hrs., US$5.40; El Dorado, US$5.60, 14½ hrs; San Fernando de Apure, US$3. Tepsa agents in Caracas: Rayco, Av. Olimpo, Edf. Anuncia, San Antonio, Sabana Grande, T 782-8276, reported to be very helpful and friendly.

Excursions   The cable railway (*teleférico*) up Mount Avila gives a stupendous view of the city and the coast. The entrance is on Av. Pral. de Maripérez, which runs between Av. Andrés Bello and Av. Boyacá; take *por puesto* from El Silencio to Simón Rodríguez (abbreviated to "SR" or "SRDR"), or take metro to Colegio Ingenieros, *por puesto* for Pinto Salina or Sarría). It operates daily except Monday, 0800-2100 from the city to the summit only—not from the summit to the coast (US$1 for adults, US$0.50 for children—reservations necessary 4 hrs. in advance—on Sundays queues are very long). The future of the *Humboldt Hotel* on the summit has still been decided. It has been refurbished, but not reopened. Camping is possible with permission. At the summit there is a restaurant, horseriding and an ice rink. Look out for 15 cm. moths with wood or leaf camouflage, trapped in corridor up to restaurant. A recommended trip is to take the cable car up and hike back down (note that it is cold at the summit, average temperature 13°C).

Good hiking: the three principal entrances to the **Avila National Park** are (a) 100 metres W of the restaurant *Tarzilandia* in Altamira (the easiest walk up); (b) the car park on the N side of Av. Boyacá above Urbanización Los Chorros (where there is a crude map)—8 hrs. to Pico Oriental, 2,650 metres; and (c) the entrance to Av. Boyacá from El Marqués (this route well signposted)—7 hrs. to Pico Naiguatá, 2,750 metres. A map of the paths (and entrance permit—US$2.85) is available from the Instituto Nacional de Parques at the north entrance to Parque del Este, price US$1. A description of the park is included in *Backpacking in Venezuela, Colombia and Ecuador*, published by Bradt Enterprises. Essential to carry your own drinking water. Serious danger of bush fires in the dry season January-April, so be careful with cigarettes, etc.

Maximum rates for excursions and transport are published by the Ministry of Development's Tourist Department, which solicits complaints in case of non-compliance. The list of published prices should be shown to the driver *before* he quotes the price.

La Guaira is Venezuela's main port, only 20 mins. by road to Caracas, if the volume of traffic permits. Population: 20,775. Mean temperature: 29°C.

In the area are many seaside resorts and residential districts with a total population of about 70,000. There is a small museum (Museo Fundación John Boulton) in Calle Bolívar, open Tues.-Fri., 0930-1200 and 1500-1700, Sat.-Sun., 0900-1200. Old La Guaira is worth visiting and a short bus ride up the hill to the lighthouse gives a fine view of the port and its surroundings. A pleasant drive can be made along the Avenida Soublette eastwards to Macuto, Laguna Beach, Caraballeda and so on to **Los Caracas** (45 km.), a government holiday resort for workers. (All these places can be reached quite cheaply by bus.) Westward, on the way to Caracas, is the international airport. Taxi to airport, US$2.25.

The town of **Maiquetía** is not spoilt by proximity to the airport. *Hotel Salamanca*, Calle Real; *Hotel Senador*, Plaza Los Maestros, both F. The *Avila* is a good restaurant, near Los Maestros.

Macuto is a pleasant seaside resort with a fine, tree-lined promenade (the Paseo del Mar), a splendid yacht marina and a 'pigeon housing estate'. A good place to find some heat and sunshine in the rainy season and an ideal place to stay if "stopping-over" between flights to and from Caracas. A *por puesto* to Macuto from Caracas costs US$0.35 and takes less than 1 hr. The *por puesto* to the airport (domestic terminal) is US$0.40. The taxi fare from the airport is US$4. Anyone wanting to get on a *por puesto* back to Caracas at rush hour (weekend afternoons, etc.) is advised to walk to the *Macuto Sheraton*. Bus from Caracas is caught one street down from Universidad.

Hotels On the coast, not too far from Maiquetía airport: *Macuto-Sheraton**, L, luxury, at Caribe, 7 km. away; *Meliá Caribe**, A, luxury, also has hotel apartment block, good restaurant in main hotel, rec., Caraballeda; *Macuto**, Av. La Playa y Calle 3, Urb. Alamo, T 031-44561/2/3, D, 5 min. walk to beach, comfortable, swimming pool. *Riviera*, Boulevard Caraballeda, D, clean, good food (French); *Hidalgo**, Av. La Playa, D, good; *Las Quince Letras**, D, Av. La Playa, rec.; *Puerta del Sol*, E, bathless on weekdays, but friendly. *Alamo*, Av. La Playa, D (possible to bargain), with shower and fan, clean, good value, good restaurant on the shore, not cheap; *Diana*, D-F, Boulevard Caraballeda (T 031-44278), on the beach, bath, clean, a/c, helpful, safe for motorcycles, rec.; *La Alemania*, Paseo del Mar, E, pleasant; *Isaibel*, corner of Isaibel and Calle 3, 2 mins. from sea, F, small, quiet, good; *Pensión Guanchez*, Calle Guzmania, F with fan, shower and toilet, breakfast US$1, no sign outside. (* = bookable through Fairmont International)

Restaurants Recommended for paella is the *Solimar* in Urb. Caribe-Caraballeda. *Neptuno* also rec. Good cheap restaurant is *La Esquina*, near *Hotel Alamo. Mokambo* and *Apolo 17*, both on beach boulevard, good; many more on Paseo del Mar. *Panadería* Apdo. 8, on Alamo, good.

Beaches Fishing (boats for hire at *Macuto-Sheraton* marina) just N of La Guaira (mostly marlin).

There are three beaches, with all facilities, along 27 km. of Caribbean seashore: one, Catia La Mar, W of La Guaira, and two—Macuto and Naiguatá—E of it. Catia La Mar is not recommended because it is industrial, very littered and the sea is heavily polluted, but it is very convenient for Maiquetía airport, taxi, US$2.25-2.60 depending on time of day. (*Hotel Bahía La Mar*, Av. La Playa, T 031-515940/515935, D with bath, very comfortable and clean, food good, swimming pool, *por puesto* minibus to Caracas 35 metres from door (US$0.30), handy for airport but under flight path; *Scorpio*, F, clean, modern, but cockroaches; *Aeropuerto*, E, shower, a/c, OK). *Balneario Camuri Chico*, 3 good beaches, restaurant, showers, water fairly clean, rec. New beaches are being prepared. The beaches themselves are enclosed by breakwaters as the currents can be very strong. From Caracas, by car, it takes 30 mins. to the 1st, 45 mins. to the 2nd, and 1 hr. to the 3rd, provided there are not too many traffic jams. West of Catia La Mar are beaches at Puerto Carayaca (*Casa Francisco*, hotel and restaurant), Oricao (small, private beach), and Chichiriviche, no hotels or restaurants (not to be confused with the resort W of Puerto Cabello); hitch or take taxis to these beaches. Far better beaches are three or four hrs. by car from Caracas: Cata and Ocumare de la Costa (see page 895), Chichiriviche (see page 897) and several others in the Puerto Cabello area. These more distant beaches are recommended, but a day trip is tiring because of traffic jams, particularly when returning to Caracas.

The overnight trip to **Los Roques** islands, directly N of La Guaira, is well worth it. These islands are truly beautiful, with long stretches of white beaches and mile upon mile of coral reef. There is a small hotel. You can also reach the islands by hitch hiking a lift from the Aeroclub at La Carlota airport. It is best to go in the morning or weekends; several planes leave then and often have spare places if you ask. Helicópteros del Caribe at Maiquetía sells flights at US$30 (one day) and US$60 (more than one day). Be prepared to wait at the airport. You can take a small boat to other islands. Take care for sunburn as there is no shade.

Other Excursions   Further afield, in *Yare*, a celebration is held on Corpus Christi day; the dance before the church of the enormously masked red devils, and of most of the villagers. It lasts the whole day. Yare is about 90 km. from Caracas; the road to it is through Petare and down the Río Guaira as far as Santa Teresa, and then up the Río Tuy. From Santa Teresa a detour may be made to the beautiful and little frequented Guatopo National Park on the road to Altagracia de Orituco, but you must return to Santa Teresa to continue your journey to Yare.

At the Parque Guatopo are various convenient places to picnic on the route through the forest. Take insect repellant. To stay the night in the park a permit must be obtained. There are a number of good nature trails in the park, for instance a 3-km. trail from Santa Crucita Recreation Area (well-signposted).

Another excursion is into the mountains to *Colonia Tovar* (1,890 metres), a village once so isolated that a few of its blond, blue-eyed people still speak the Black Forest German of their ancestors who settled there in 1843. Now it is very touristy. Strawberries, coffee, garlic, rhubarb and flowers are grown for the Caracas market. See the Scandinavian-style ceramics. Ask in Colonia Tovar for the *petroglifos*, rock paintings. The 1½-hr drive from Caracas is delightful. Along the road are small parks where picnic lunch can be taken (now in bad condition), but at weekends there are long traffic queues and you have to be early just to find a roadside spot to picnic and there are similar problems finding accommodation—no such difficulties in the week. Prices can be very inflated.

The road to Colonia Tovar passes through *El Junquito*, a small town with roadside stands selling fruit and barbecued meat (there are also pony stables). You see Caracas from one side of the road, the Caribbean from the other (*Parador Castilla* at Km. 43). 29 km. beyond El Junquito, a paved road with beautiful views winds down the mountain to the sea: it branches right to Oricao (see above), and Catia La Mar, or left to El Limón and Puerto Cruz (nice beach), from where one can go E, or W to Puerto Maya, a beautiful bay with nice swimming (there is another branch right to Puerto Cruz nearer Colonia Tovar). Another road, 34 km. (well-paved, but hair-raising), leads through glorious mountain scenery from Colonia Tovar to La Victoria on the Caracas-Valencia highway (4 buses a day).

Hotels   in Colonia Tovar: *Bergland* (good, cheap breakfasts); *Selva Negra**, *Cabañas Baden*; *Edelweiss* (not rec.), *Freiburg, Kaiserstuhl*, all C; *Alta Baviera*. All serve German-style food in good restaurants. There is said to be a good spot for camping just below the town's cemetery, if you don't mind the company.

It is generally easy to get a lift if there are no buses. Taxi fare for the round trip from Caracas to Colonia Tovar (driver will wait) is about US$10. Bus from Av. Sur 9 y El Rosario, next to Nuevo Circo, to El Junquito (1 hr.), then change for Colonia Tovar (1 hr.). *Por puesto* from Plaza Catia or O'Leary (more frequently), Caracas, 1 hr., US$0.60. Alternatively, take a *por puesto* from Plaza Capuchino to El Junquito, then one from there to Colonia Tovar, US$0.55.

WEST FROM CARACAS (2)

A hundred km. W of Caracas is the great basin in which lies the Lake of Valencia and the towns of Maracay and Valencia. The basin, which is only 450 metres above sea-level, receives plenty of rain and is one of the most important agricultural areas in the country; sugar, cotton, maize, beans and rice are the main crops. In the other valleys and depressions in the Central Highlands are also grown manioc, bananas, cocoa and the superb local coffee.

The Pan-American Highway, which links Caracas by road with the other capitals of South America, follows closely the route of Gómez' Great Andean Highway as far as Lake Maracaibo, though many sections have been widened and straightened. At the start, there is the choice of a direct toll motorway to Valencia (with exit to Maracay), toll US$0.50, or the old road called, familiarly, "La Panamericana" and known for its dangerous bends. (Hotels on "La

Panamericana'': *Colonial*, D, San Antonio de los Altos; *Cutlas*, D, Km. 10; *Panorama*, E, Km. 13; *Las Vegas*, D, Km. 14.) It leaves La Rinconada race course to its left, and climbs steadily but easily towards **Los Teques,** capital of Miranda state (pop.: 44,000, *Alemán*, E, Plaza Miranda, friendly, good food). This passes on its way the park of Las Colinas de Carrizal (collections of local fish and birds, and pleasant paths). Twenty-four km. beyond Los Teques on the way down into the fertile valleys of Aragua, we can either join the Caracas-Valencia tollway or take the older road through several attractive little towns such as La Victoria (see above). The Quinta de Bolívar is at San Mateo, between La Victoria and Maracay. A little nearer Maracay, a good road leads off to **San Juan de Los Morros (see page 909).**

The Panamericana to Maracay should be taken at least once, for views and local colour, but winding up and down the mountains behind slow, smelly trucks is not much fun. The toll road also offers good views.

The new highway avoids city centres, so all that is seen of Maracay, Valencia and Barquisimeto are factories plus the huge concrete Barquisimeto Fourth Centenary Monument. Beyond Barquisimeto there are mountains like slag heaps, until we reach the green of the Andes.

Maracay, capital of Aragua State, has a population of 322,000, and is at an altitude of 495 metres. In its heyday it was the favourite city of General Gómez and some of his most fantastic whims are still there: the former *Hotel Jardín* (now a Government centre) with its beautiful zoo, park and fountain, built for his revels; the opera house opposite; his modest little house for personal use, and the bull ring, an exact replica of the one at Seville. The Gómez mausoleum, built in his honour, has a huge triumphal arch. Maracay is an attractive, peaceful city; it is the centre of an important agricultural area, and the school and experimental stations of the Ministry of Agriculture are worth visiting; it is also important industrially and militarily.

Hotels *Byblos**, D, Av. Las Delicias, high standard; *Maracay**, C, Las Delicias, swimming pool, gymnasium, night club; *San Luis*, Carabobo Sur 13, off the main shopping street, E, clean, showers, friendly; *Caroní*, Ayacucho Norte 197, Bolívar, E, a/c, comfortable, rec.; *Wladimir*, F, Av. Bolívar Este 27, friendly, good restaurant at reasonable prices; *Italo*, E, Av. 6, Urb. La Soledad, service uninterested, ask for quiet side of building; *Pipo**, D, Av. Principal, El Castaño, swimming pool, discotheque, rec. restaurant (parrillas a speciality), in hills above the city; *Pensión Libertad*, Av. 99E y Calle Libertad (105 Sur), F with bath, clean, safe; (*-bookable through Fairmont International).

Restaurants *Tosca El Pescador*, Av. Sucre Norte 75, rec., especially for seafood; *Paella Valenciana*, rec. There are many Chinese restaurants which are reliable.

Exchange Banco Consolidado (American Express), Av. Bolívar y Fuerzas Aéreas.

Tourist Office Ed. Fundaragua, La Soledad, friendly.

Chris and Josephine Walker write: The FAV (Fuerza Aérea Venezolana) Museum in Maracay is open on Sun. from 0800 to 1800. About two dozen aircraft are displayed, including Second World War fighters and bombers, later jets and earlier aircraft from between the wars. The most celebrated plane is **Jimmy Angel's G-2-W Flamingo**, "El Río Caroní", which he landed on top of Auyan-Tepuy mountain on October 9, 1937. It remained there, embedded in a bog, until it was dug out by the FAV in 1970 and restored in Maracay.

Excursions Lake Valencia; to Las Delicias, Gómez' crumbling country house, where he died, with its adjoining zoo. Take an Ocumare bus from the terminal. The huge 1,000-hectare Henri Pittier National Park (a birdwatcher's paradise) stretches from 24 km. N of Maracay to the Caribbean on both sides of the Andes; take a coat, it is cool in the cloud forest. There are no nature trails but many birds may be seen from the road, avoid weekends, best visibility in the morning. A road runs from Maracay over the 1,130-metre high Portachuelo pass, guarded by twin peaks, to three places by the sea: *Ocumare de la Costa*, 37 km. from Maracay; the naval base of Turiamo; and **Cata**, once the most beautiful beach in Venezuela, now overdeveloped, basic cabins for rent on beach, good fish restaurant, run by Pepe (Cuyagua beach, unspoilt, is 10 km. further on). The road was built by Gómez as an escape route if things grew too hot for him. Near the pass is Rancho Grande, the uncompleted palace Gómez was building when he died; it is in the shape of a question mark and is worth visiting. It is now the Rancho Grande Biological Station; permission to visit may be given to serious naturalists. A taxi can be hired at Maracay for a day's outing in the park for about US$12. The nearby town of *Victoria* has the oldest bullring in Venezuela and an interesting old hotel, *Hotel El Recreo*, D, originally a colonial house built in 1724 (also *Omni*, B). In the hills nearby is the *Hacienda San Mateo* formerly occupied by Simón Bolívar and now a museum. There is also a museum of sugar cane. Another excursion to the coast, also through the Henri Pittier National Park, goes over a more easterly pass (1,830 metres), on a paved but winding road (not for timid drivers) to *Santa Clara de Choroní*, a beautiful colonial town (bus from Maracay, US$0.45, 1 hr. 20 mins.). *Hotel Club Cotoperix*, C p.p. for accommodation, T 573 5241, English spoken, full board and drinks in 3 colonial houses converted into guest houses, price also includes boat trips to otherwise inaccessible beaches, recommended. About 10 km. before Choroní are 2 waterfalls known as El Dique, where one can bathe; ask anyone for directions. Just beyond the town is the beach of Puerto Colombia (camping possible on the beach, dirty at weekends), from where launches (US$10) may be taken to the otherwise inaccessible colonial village of Chuao, famous in the past for its cocoa; the bay is very pleasant with a couple of bars.

Fifty km. to the west of Maracay the road reaches Valencia, through low hills thickly planted with citrus, coffee and sugar.

Valencia (population, about 495,000), the capital of Carabobo State, stands on the W bank of the Cabriales river, 5 km. before it empties into Lake Valencia (rather polluted). It is the third largest city in the republic, the centre of its most developed agricultural region, and the most industrialized. Annual mean temperature 24°C; altitude 490 metres; rainfall, 914 mm. a year. The atmosphere of the older and narrower streets is that of old Spain. The interesting 18th century Cathedral (open 0630-1130, 1500-1830 daily, 0630-1200, 1500-1900 Sun.) is on the central Plaza Bolívar. The statue of the Virgen del Socorro in the left transept is the most valued treasure; on the second Sunday in November it is paraded with a richly jewelled crown. See the Capitol, the Municipal Theatre, the old Carabobo University building and the handsome bullring, which holds the world record for takings at a single *corrida*. Also the Museo de Arte e Historia, Calle 98 and Av. 104 (open Tues.-Sun., 0800-1200 and 1400-1730), and the Aquarium de Valencia at the west end of Calle 107 beyond the *autopista*, featuring a dolphin show at 1630 (open Tues.-Sun., 0930-1800, admission US$0.25). There is a small zoo behind the aquarium. Like its Spanish namesake, Valencia is famous for its oranges. There is a nice country club.

Hotels *Residencias Ucaima**, Av. Boyacá, Centro Comercial La Viña, B; *Canaima*, Av. Lara con Branger, D, clean, TV, rec.; *Don Pelayo**, E, in town centre, Av. Díaz Moreno, rec., good restaurant; *Intercontinental Valencia**, A, Av. Juan Uslar, swimming pool, night club; *Astor*, Calle Colombia, E, a/c, bath, clean, safe parking, good; *Central*, F, near main square, nice patio, quiet and clean, English spoken; *Bilboa*, F, Calle 100 (Colombia), 96-10, clean and quiet; *Metrópole*, F, central but dingy, Calle Comercial 103-47; *Palermo*, Calle Colombia, F, clean and friendly with laundry, other *residencias* on same street for the same price (*-bookable through Fairmont International).

Restaurants *Asociación de Ganaderos*; *Mar Chica*; *La Grillade*; *Venezuela*, rec.; *Fego*, Av. Bolívar 102-75, rec.

British Vice-Consul (Hon.): Corporación Mercantil Venezolana, Av. 100, 93-7.

Exchange Banco Consolidado (American Express), Av. Bolívar, Edif. Exterior; Turisol (also Amex); Italcambio, Av. Bolívar, Edif. Talia, Loc. 2.

Buses To Caracas, US$1; to San Cristóbal, 10 hrs., US$4.70; Barquisimeto, US$1.50, 3 hrs.

Excursions At the Safari Caraboco Reserva Animal, on the road from Valencia to Campo de Carabobo, you can see many wild animals, not all of them South American, in well-planned and quite spacious surroundings. Cars with roof racks are not permitted to enter. To the monument on the battlefield of Carabobo, laid out like a park with a *mirador* where Bolívar surveyed the battle, southwards on the road to San Carlos; the battle story is told in bronze: the British soldiers who helped Bolívar are particularly realistic. Buses to the battlefield leave from La Sanidad (Health Centre), US$0.20, 1 hr.

The Caracas-Valencia motorway continues down the mountains, reaching the sea near El Palito (refinery and pier). Here we turn right to Puerto Cabello. 18 km. from Valencia, the road passes Las Trincheras, a decaying spa with the second hottest springs in the world (98 ''C); there are three baths (hot, hotter, very hot), a mud bath and a Turkish bath. Entrance US$1. Hotel* for patients only (D).

Puerto Cabello, 96 km. W of La Guaira, is the port for Valencia, 55 km. away by modern highway; it is in itself a large industrial centre. This, the second most important Venezuelan port, has an excellent harbour with a lighthouse, and a shipyard with dry dock. Average temperature, 28°C; population, 71,200. A standard-gauge 175-km. railway runs to Barquisimeto.

Hotels *Riviera*, with good restaurant. (Other good restaurants are *El Parque, Mar y Sol, Venezuela*, near the harbour and *San Antonio del Mar*.) Best hotels near are the *Cumboto*, D, Av. La Paz, Urb. Cumboto, swimming pool; *La Sultana*, F, Av. Juan José Flores; *El Ejecutivo*, F, good, friendly; *La Hacienda* (good German food).

Exchange Banco Italo de Venezuela.

About half an hour E of Puerto Cabello over a rough road is a beautiful horseshoe-shaped beach shaded by palms called La Bahía. It is well worth the drive, has a refreshment stand, changing rooms, toilet facilities and lifeguards, but take your own lunch. You can buy oysters from little boys who open them for you and douse them with lemon juice.

Puerto Cabello has another beach, Quizandal, with a coral reef, near the naval base. (Taxi fare, US$2.75 but you may find it hard to get one on the way back.) The nearby Country Club also has a beach with coral reefs within reach by boat. There are two Spanish forts at Puerto Cabello, one on the water (which can be reached by a small ferry boat), the other on a hill over the city (in a military zone and it is difficult to get permission to enter).

N.B. The beach to the W of Puerto Cabello is not so attractive; be careful of going beyond the bathing area as the beach is notorious for armed robbery.

Twenty-four km. W of Puerto Cabello, at the junction of the Pan-American Highway and the road to Tucacas, is **Morón**, where there is a state-owned petrochemical plant.

Quite near Morón is the lovely beach of **Palma Sola**, 16 km. long and deserted save at Easter time when Venezuelans camp out there in crowds. The water can be dangerous but the sands and palms are superb. There are hotels, many closed in the off season (*Balneario Canaima*, C, children's swimming pool; *Balneario Caribe*, D), restaurants and changing rooms. A road has been built from Morón to Coro via Tucacas, an hour from Puerto Cabello.

Tucacas (*Hotel Manaure-Tucacas*, E, Av. Silva, a/c, hot water, clean, restaurant; *Hotel Said*, at entrance, E, swimming pool, good; *La Palma*, F; *Centuca*, F) is a small, dirty town of wooden shacks where bananas and other fruit are loaded for Curaçao and Aruba, but offshore is the national park of Morrocoy, where there are hundreds of coral reefs, palm-studded islets, small cosy beaches and calm water for water-skiing, snorkelling, and skin-diving. (The Park is reached on foot from Tucacas; camping allowed, no facilities, crowded at weekends.) The largest and most popular of the islands is Cayo Sombrero. Boats are for hire. Venezuelan skin-diving clubs come here for their contests. This is one of the two main fishing grounds of Venezuela; the other is off Puerto La Cruz.

A few km. beyond, towards Coro, is the favourite beach resort of **Chichiriviche**; the town is dirty but offshore are numerous lovely islands and coral reefs. *Hotel Mario**, B including 3 meals, swimming pool; *La Garza**, B (including 3 meals), or D, pool (both used by Canadian tour groups); *Náutico*, D with breakfast and dinner, friendly, not very clean, fans but no a/c; *Capri*, near docks, E (bargain), shower and a/c, clean, Italian owned, good restaurant and supermarket, bakery opposite. Restaurant *Fregata*, nr. *Capri*, rec. It is possible to hire a boat to any one of the islands; recommended for a weekend away from Caracas. There is no direct bus, but frequent por puestos from Puerto Cabello, US$0.80, or from Valencia. You may camp on the islands, but there are no facilities or fresh water, and you may require a permit from Inparques (National Parks). Nearby is a vast nesting area for scarlet ibis, flamingoes and herons.

From Tucacas it is 177 km. to **Coro** (population 80,000), capital of the State of Falcón (por puesto, US$4), a charming town, with interesting colonial buildings (the town is a national monument), surrounded by sand dunes (médanos). Worth seeing are the Cathedral, the first in Venezuela, built 1531; San Francisco church; the cross of Cristobal Colón, 1527; San Clemente church and monastery; the Casa de Balcón, now the National Experimental University.

There is an interesting xerophytic garden open to the public. Museo Diocesano, Calle Zamora 69 (open Tues. and Sun. 0900-1200, Wed.-Fri., 1600-1900, very interesting), Museo de Cerámica, Calle Zamora 98 (open Tues., 0900-1200, Wed.-Fri., 1600-1900, Sat. 1000-1300 and 1600-1900, Sun., 1000-1300). At Puerto Cumarebo, just before Coro, is a hotel, *Balneario Bella Vista*, E, private bath, restaurant, with beach, but not recommended (dirty, facilities non-operational). From Coro, there is a good but uninteresting road to Maracaibo and another paved road along the isthmus (a National Park) leading to the Paraguaná Peninsula, along whose beaches men fish, 15 to 20 a net. Near the village of La Vela along the Morón road the local handicraft is the production of rocking chairs of all sizes made from cactus wood. Airport (good restaurant on 1st floor, 10 mins. walk from centre) has a direct service to Caracas and Las Piedras. Bus from Coro to Caracas US$3.35; to Maracaibo, US$1.70.

Hotels at Coro   *Miranda* *, D, Av. Josefa Camejo, opposite airport, swimming pool (very dirty, but non-residents can pay to use it); *Arenas*, opp. bus terminal, D, restaurant; *Caracas*, E, Calle Toledo 17, very good, a/c; *Coro*, E, Av. Independencia, friendly, good value; *Venezia*, E, expensive food, but renovated and good; *Valencia*, E, with private shower; *Maracén*, E, with private shower; *Capri* (friendly). The *Bella Nápoli* is good, F; the *Italia* is cheaper, with bath, fan, friendly, patio.

Restaurant   *Don Camilo*, by *Hotel Miranda* and airport, very good food and reasonable prices. *Cafetería El Indio*, Independencia, nr. statue, very good breakfast.

Exchange   Banco Consolidado, Calle Federación con Buchivacoa (for American Express). Exchange is not possible for Thomas Cook or Master Card.

There is a ferry service (Ferrys del Caribe) from La Vela de Coro and Punto Fijo (see below) to Aruba and Curaçao (several a week). The schedules are continually being changed, so apply to the company's offices. Buy tickets on morning of departure. The journey to both Aruba and Curaçao usually takes 4-6 hrs., but the bureaucracy can lengthen this period to 8-12 hrs. Fare to Curaçao US$25 (cabin extra). It is necessary to have ticket out of Curaçao before entering, even if you are Dutch. It is advisable to arrive at the terminal at least 4 hours in advance, because the immigration officers often leave their posts before the boat departs. The tourist office can provide more information. The office for the boat in Coro is at Av. Independencia, beside Supermercado Victoria (T 068-519676); there are also offices in Caracas at Av. Urdaneta esq. Ibárrez, Edificio Riera (T 5611300). *Por puesto* between La Vela de Coro and Coro itself costs US$0.70 per seat, bus costs US$0.15; taxi from La Vela to the ferry dock (3 km.) is US$1.75; *por puesto* from Maracaibo to ferry terminal, US$6.

The **Paraguaná Peninsula** is connected by pipelines with the oilfields of Lake Maracaibo. The Maravén (ex-Shell) and Lagovén (ex-Esso) groups have refineries, the former at Cardón, and the latter at Amuay. The airport, which has services to Maracaibo (30 min.), Coro and Maiquetía, is known as **Las Piedras**, the town itself as **Punto Fijo** (Hotels: *Luigi*, E, Judibana, swimming pool; *Jardín**, D, Centro Comercial Judibana; *Caribe**, E, Calle Comercio 21-112; *Del Este*, F, Av. Táchira; also *Cardón**, D, *Safri*, Av. Colombia 78-15, clean, cheap, central; *Miami*, Calle Falcón No. 21-196). Eventually, all four places will merge into one large town. There is a seaport, Las Piedras-Paraguaná, between Amuay and Cardón, which also serves the town of Coro. The villages on the peninsula have interesting colonial churches, notably that of Santa Ana. There are many good beaches accessible by car, few visitors, good for camping but no facilities. Adicora is a nice little resort where you can rent a house by the week; good seafood restaurants.

The Segovia Highlands, lying N of Barquisimeto, suffer from droughts, and are only sparsely settled along the river valleys. From Morón the Pan-American Highway strikes up into the hills, reaching 550 metres at **San Felipe** (population 30,750), capital of Yaracuy State (Hotels: *Turístico Río Yurubi**, E; *Hostería Colonial**, E, Av. La Paz, pool; *El Fuerte**, E, Av. La Patria; *La Fuente*, E, Av. La Fuente).

If you do not want to go to Puerto Cabello and the coast, a newer section of the Highway from Valencia via Carabobo to just beyond San Felipe is 56 km. shorter.

Barquisimeto, capital of Lara State, has a population of 504,000. Altitude 565 metres, mean temperature 25°C. It stands on one of the alluvial fans so frequent in the Andes, and is Venezuela's fourth largest city, with the University of Lara. The Cathedral, an ultramodern structure of free-form concrete and glass, is very interesting. The Palacio Municipal at Carrera 17 with Calle 25 is an attractive modern building. Across the street is a large well-shaded plaza with a bronze equestrian statue of Bolívar. On Carrera 15 (Av. Francisco de Miranda) between Calles 41-43 there is a charming park, resplendent with lush vegetation, paths, fountains and another bronze statue of Bolívar. There is a road from Barquisimeto to Acarigua **(see page 909)** on the alternative route from Caracas to Mérida.

Hotels The *Motel El Parador*, B, excellent, near El Obelisco, a great roundabout in the northern suburbs of the town in the middle of which stands a tower; *Hilton**, B, Carrera 5, Nueva Segovia; *Hostería El Obelisco**, D, Av. Panamericana, American motel-style, swimming pool, always full; *Gran Hotel Barquisimeto**, E, Av. Pedro León Torres, pool; *Curumato**, E, Av. 20, esq. Calle 34; *Del Centro*, F, Av. 20, between Calles 26-27, good value; *Hevelin*, E, Av. Vargas, between 20-21, with or without a/c; *La Casona*, F, Carrera 17 con Calle 27 near Plaza Bolívar (T 051-315311/317151), a/c, clean, hot water, excellent, parking, restaurant; *Principe**, E, Carrera 19, esq. Calle 23, swimming pool, good; *Yacambú*, E, Av. Vargas, between Carreras 19-20, swimming pool. *Avenida*, F, Av. Vargas, No. 21-124, 2nd floor, clean, economical.

Restaurants *Mesón de la Campaña*, El Obelisco; *Guido's*, good, expensive; *Terminal Vargas*, food average, service good, expensive; railway station restaurant, excellent.

Exchange Banco Consolidado, Av. Vargas entre Calles 20 y 21, also Turisol (T 516743), both American Express.

Transport Railway to Puerto Cabello, and an airport. (No bus from airport, only taxis. There is a single bus terminal on the edge of the city.) Bus to Mérida, only once a day, leaves at 03 15, 8 hrs. via Agua Viva and El Vigía, US$3.35. For renting cars (Volkswagen best), Av. Pedro León Torres y Calle 56, or agency in lobby of *Hotel Curumato*, Calle 34 with Av. 20, also at airport. To Acarigua by bus, US$0.70, one hr.

West of Barquisimeto, about half an hour's drive, is *El Tocuyo* with a good hotel in a delightful colonial setting. La Pasada Sub-growing area. ... restaurant. Between Barquisimeto

About 24 km. SW of Barquisimeto is the small town of *Quíbor*. There is an interesting museum, Centro Antropológico de Quíbor, with exhibits of the Indians who used to live in the region. Stop in the plaza for a *chicha de maíz* or *arroz*, a refreshing traditional drink of the local Indians. About 18 km. from Quíbor is the mountain village of Cubiro (two hotels) which stands at 1,600 metres, ideal for walking. Direct buses from Barquisimeto or change at Quíbor. Turn right a few km. before Quíbor to get to a tiny *rancho* in the village of El Tintoreto where "blankets" are made from local wool. These are in bright coloured stripes or plaids and serve well as colourful rugs, but not as what we call blankets. They are very good value. Near Quíbor is the *Posadas Turísticas de Sahare**, E.

About 60 km. east of Barquisimeto is the little town of *Chivacoa*. Passing sugar-cane fields you reach the mountain of Sorte which is the holy region for the María-Lionza cult (similar to Voodoo) practised throughout Venezuela. Celebrations are held there mostly at weekends with October 12 (Día de la Raza) being the most important day. It is interesting to walk up the mountain when the pilgrims are camping beside the river and waterfalls, but do not go unless you are prepared to take it seriously, and use only the parking lot to park your car; other places are unsafe because of robbery.

Another pleasant excursion from Barquisimeto by bus or car is to *Río Claro*, about 28 km. inland, "where the Andes begin". You follow a lush river valley through the mountains. There are banana plantations in the area and many dirt trails you can follow on horseback or in a 4-wheel drive vehicle. From Río Claro a gravel road (dry season only) goes to Buena Vista and on to Quíbor; good views and pleasant villages.

Some 75 km. past Barquisimeto the Lara-Zulia motorway to Maracaibo forks off to the right (Caracas-Maracaibo 660 km.), through *Carora* (Complejo Turístico Katuca, D; *Motel* and *Restaurant Indio Mara*, F, reasonable; *Motel Posada Madrevieja*, F, both on Av. Francisco de Miranda; *Irpinia*, F, and *Parrilla Italia*, F, both on Av. 14 de Febrero).

THE LOWLANDS OF MARACAIBO (3)

The Lowlands of Maracaibo, lying in the encircling arms of the mountains, are more or less windless and extremely humid. Average annual temperature is higher than anywhere else in Latin America. Rainfall decreases steadily from the foothills of the Sierra Nevada to the coast. In these lowlands is the semi-salt Lake Maracaibo, of about 12,800 square km., 155 km. long and in places over 120 km. wide. It is joined to the sea by a waterway, 3 to 11 km. wide and 55 km. long, at the mouth of which is the bar of Maracaibo.

The area was once dependent on fishing and the transport of coffee across the lake from the Sierra. Since the discovery there of one of the world's greatest oilfields in 1914, there has been a great transformation, both in appearance (a forest of oil derricks covers the shore swamps and some of the lake), and in prosperity. The Lara-Zulia motorway reaches Maracaibo by the beautiful 8-km. long General Rafael Urdaneta bridge, which has the longest pre-stressed concrete span in the world.

Maracaibo, on the north-western shore of Lake Maracaibo, capital of the State of Zulia, is Venezuela's oil capital: 70% of the nation's output comes from the Lake area. Maracaibo, which is 55 mins. by jet from Caracas, is the country's second largest city. Population: 1.7 million. The airport is at La Chinita. The bus terminal is on the edge of the city.

The climate is damp and hot, but healthy. The hottest months are July, August and September, but there is usually a sea breeze from 1500 until morning. The mean temperature of 28°C and average humidity of 78% are most felt at sea level. The new part of the city round Bella Vista and towards the University is in vivid contrast with the old town near the docks; this, with narrow streets and colonial style adobe houses, is hardly changed from the last century (parts, especially around Santa Lucía church—blue and white, facing Parque Urdaneta, have been well-restored). A trip across the lake through the oil derricks is difficult to organize as the oilfields are a long way from Maracaibo. The zone begins at Cabimas (*Cabimas Internacional**, B, luxury, pool, discotheque) on the E shore of the lake and you can get a good view of the oil rigs from there (boat to Cabimas, US$1.40, *por puesto* US$1, semi-lega. take pictures. among the derricks, US$3-5, ask behind the market) and from other towns Lagunillas (*Hotel Lagunillas**, E, pool)—though don't take pictures. asking permission. A tourist taxi from *Hotel del Lago* to see the oil wells costs US$20.

From the port you can take a ferry to Altagracia for US$0.50, the first at 0645, 25 mins., and either return the same way or take a minibus for US$0.45, travelling through exotic scenery for almost an hour and crossing the General Urdaneta bridge.

Hotels It is difficult to obtain rooms without making reservations well in advance. *Hotel del Lago Intercontinental**, El Milagro, Av. 2, T 912167/911868, A, non-residents may use the pool but will be charged US$1.75; *Gran Hotel Delicias**, D, Av. 15 esq. Calle 70, swimming pool, night club; *Motel Granada* (*Mogranca*), D, room service only, outside town on road to La Concepción; *Aparthotel Presidente**, D, Av. 11, 68-50, pool; *Maruma**, Circunvalación No.2, B, old and new sections, hot water, a/c, TV, reasonable restaurant; *Roma*, E, Calle 86, 3F-76, popular with Italians, food is very good; *Kristof**, D, Av. 8 (Santa Rita), swimming pool, night club, poor exchange rates offered; *Londres*, Calle 94, Av. 6, F, with bath; *San José**, E, Av. 3Y (San Martín) 82-29, a/c, bath, good beds, friendly, Italian restaurant, rec.; several others nearby, e.g. *Caribe*, Av. 7, F, good value, a/c and shower; *Yacambú*, F, Av. Libertador, central and clean, fair; *Aurora*, E, Calle 96, near waterfront. *Victoria*, Av. 6, Calle 99, in picturesque old part of town, F, rce.; *Novedades*, Calle 78 (antes Dr. Portillo) No. 9-43, Bella Vista, T 75766, E, a/c, shower, rec., safe, Italian owner Francesco Scherra; other hotels in Bella Vista include *Montevideo* (E), *Falcón* and *Mary* (both F), a US$0.50 taxi ride from bus terminal. *Santa Ana* is the cheapest, G, poor but friendly, opposite Occidente garage near main banking area on Av. 3, between Ciencias and Venezuela; nearby is *Pensión Familiar*, same price (beside *Restaurant La Friulana*).

Restaurants Most are closed on Sunday. *Chez Nicolás*, excellent food, highly rec.; *El Chicote* (seafood), Av. Bellavista (Av. 4), corner with Calle 70; *Rincón Boricua*, Av. 23, between Calles 66 and 67 (good meat); *El Pescadito* (Av. 2, 76-A-209), by lakeside, with agreeable breeze; *Mi Vaquita* (Av. 3H, Calle 76), steak house, very good; *La Carreta del Ché*, Av. 13A, No. 76-54; *Saint George*, Av. 12, No. 75-80, dear; *El Delfín*, Calle 75 and 3H, rec., especially for seafood; *Pizzería Napoletana*, Calle 77 near Av. 4, excellent, closed Tues.; *El Jardín*, Centro Comercial Costa Verde, Av. 4, good lunches; *Central Lunch*, Calle 98 (near the port), Chinese run, good helpings, cheap for Maracaibo, open when other places are shut; also in port district, *Café Comercio*, off Av. 4 and corner of Av. Libertador, good, "Bogart style". *ABC*, Av. Bella Vista near Calle 78, good Chinese, small, clean, open till 2100, closed Sun. *La Habana*, Av. Bella Vista (Av. 4) near Calle 76, good salads and milkshakes. *La Friulana*, Calle 95, Av. 3. for good cheap meal at less than US$2, repeatedly rec. For confectionery, *Café Samemrum*, Av. 5 de Julio between Avs. 10 and 11, and *Kabuki*, Av. 5 de Julio opp. Banco de Maracaibo, more fashionable. Health food store, *Larga Vida*, Av. 13A between Calles 75 and 76.

Taxis   US$1 fixed fare.

Bookshops   Librería Universal, Av. 5 de Julio y Av. 4, maps, stationery, Caracas newspapers; Librería Italiana, Av. 5 de Julio, Ed. Centro América, post cards and foreign publications (inc. US).

Shopping   Fin de Siglo department stores sell handicrafts, records, tapes, posters of local sights. The outdoor market, Las Pulgas, is enormous, take any bus S down Av. 4 (Bella Vista). Centro Comercial Costa Verde, Av. 4 (antes Bella Vista), good new shopping complex.

Exchange   Banco de Venezuela and local banks; Banco Consolidado, Av. Bella Vista con Calle 67 (American Express, also Turisol Amex rep., T 70611); Citibank. All banks shut at 1630 sharp. All Thomas Cook transactions have to be verified in Caracas. *Cambio* at bus terminal will change Colombian pesos into bolívares at a poor rate.

Colombian Consulate   Av. 3Y (San Martín) 70-16 nr. Av. 4/Bella Vista (T 72232), 10 km. from centre, take bus or *por puesto* (Bellavista) out of town on Av. 4 to Calle 70; open Mon.-Fri., 0800-1200, 60-day visa in 5 hrs., no questions, no tickets required (better than Caracas).

Spanish Consulate   Av. 15, No. 84-41, Delicias, T 526513.

British Vice-Consul   Inspecciones C.A., Centro Comercial Villa Real, Calle 72 Local 2 (Aptdo 1352), T (061)73795/74086.

Anglican Church   Christ Church, Av. 8 (Santa Rita) a Calle 74.

Laundry   Lavandería Laza, Calle 72 near Av. 3H, Bella Vista, rec.

Telecommunications   Servicio de Telecomunicaciones de Venezuela, Calle 99, esq. Av. 3. CANTV, Calle 76 near Av. 3E, Bella Vista, open 0700-2330, inc. Sunday.

Doctors   Dr. García, Hospital Coromoto, Av. 3C and Calle 72, T 912222, speaks English, as does Dr. Carlos Febres, a dentist, Av. 8, No. 84-129, Mon.-Fri. 0900-1200, 1500-1800, T 221504.

Air Services   to Maiquetía (US$24), Mérida, Valera, Barquisimeto, Las Piedras (for Amuay and Cardón), San Antonio (US$18, be early to guarantee seat) and other towns. Other airlines connect Maracaibo with Barranquilla (five flights a week), Curaçao, Trinidad, Miami, New York and Europe. (Pan Am Office, Centro Comercial Tamacuary, Av. 22 y Calle 72. T 529826/513199.) The airport is 14 km. S of the town. Taxis have a set fare of about US$3.50, there are no *por puestos*.

Buses   Bus station is 15 mins. walk from centre, 1 km. S of the old town. There are several fast and comfortable buses daily to Valencia (US$3.75 by Expresos del Lago), San Cristóbal (US$3.60, 8 hrs., *por puesto*, US$8), Barquisimeto, 5½ hrs. including police stops and searches (US$2.35) and Caracas (US$4.65, 10 hrs.). Bus lines, other than Aerobuses de Venezuela, rec. are Occidente and Alianza, whose fares are cheaper. To Mérida, 5 hrs. (US$3.35). To Maicao, Expreso Maicao bus, US$3.25, 3 hrs.; taxi US$17 per car (takes 5), 6 police checks en route.

On the W side of the lake, between the rivers Santa Ana and Catatumbo, a large area of swampland is crossed by the road to La Fría. The swamp is inhabited by the Motilones, who, until 1960, refused to have dealings either with white men or other Indians. The southern border of the Motilones' territory, the River Catatumbo, is famed for its almost nightly display of lightning for which there is, as yet, no accepted explanation and which caused it to be known in the old days as "The Lighthouse of Maracaibo". There are various missions you can visit: the easiest to reach is Los Angeles del Tocuco, 51 km. from Machiques, where they welcome visitors; it helps to take a present, such as dried milk. There is a priest at the mission who was attacked, and they now preserve in their museum the arrow head they took from his body. From here you can do a 5-day trek to Picci Cacao, through beautiful scenery to meet Yuspa Indians. Take them rice and blankets if you can carry them. Ask the padre for a guide and mules, take your own food and camping equipment. *Machiques* is on a fast road from San Cristóbal via La Fría to Maracaibo, and has the good *Motel Tukuko*, E.

The best sightseeing trip is north about 1 hr. to the Río Limón (it has another local name). Take a bus (US$0.30) to El Moján, riding with the Guajira Indians as they return to their homes on the peninsula. Another bus or taxi (US$1.40) can be taken to the river. Alternatively, take a Sinamaica bus from the new station, US$0.70 (*por puesto*, US$1.50, shorter delays from police searches make this worthwhile), then a colectivo to Puerto Cuervito, a small port on the Sinamaica lagoon, US$0.20. Hire a boat (bargaining rec. as the price is around US$30 for a boat holding 10 people; fix price, duration and route in advance to ensure full value), and go up the river for an hour to La Boquita (2,500 inhabitants) to see Indians living in houses made of woven reed mats built on stilts; the only place where they can be seen. Return by *por puesto* Sinamaica-El Moján (US$0.30), thence to Maracaibo (US$1.40). Excursions by boat to the Sinamaica lagoon from Maracaibo charge about US$8 for 1½ hrs., but if you think you are being overcharged, ask for *el libro de reclamaciones* which should give the maximum official price. By crossing the bridge over the river you come, in the north, to a paved road that leads to Riohacha, in Colombia, where border formalities are quick and easy, a recommended route, but the Colombian border town, Maicao, has a most unsavoury reputation; best not to stop there. If you enter Venezuela from Colombia at Maicao, you can expect very rigorous searches both at the border and on the way to Maracaibo. It is reported that a visa is essential despite what may be said by Venezuelan Consulates.

Along the way you see Guajira Indians, the men with bare legs, on horseback; the women with long, black, tent-shaped dresses and painted faces, wearing the sandals with big wool pom-poms which they make and sell for US$2, as against the US$7-10 in the tourist shops. The men do nothing: women do all the work, tending sheep and goats, selling slippers and raising very little on the dry, hot, scrubby Guajira Peninsula. If you don't do this trip, you can see these Indians in the Ziruma district of Maracaibo. There is an interesting Guajira market at Los Filuos, a mile beyond Paraguaipoa, where you can buy the local tent-dress (*manta*) for about US$5-10, depending on the quality, but much cheaper than in Maracaibo.

Those who wish to go on to the Sierra Nevada de Mérida or the State of Trujillo should return over the lake and turn sharp right through Cabimas, Lagunillas, Bachaquero and Mene Grande, all unattractive oil towns, to rejoin the Pan-American Highway at Agua Viva. For the Colombian frontier or San Cristóbal we follow the Pan-American Highway.

The Pan-American Highway from Agua Viva is a splendid asphalt speed track, but devoid of much scenic or historical attraction. It runs along the foot of the Andes through rolling country planted with sugar or bananas, or park-like cattle land. At Sabana de Mendoza, 24 km. S of Agua Viva, is a possible stopover—*Hotel Panamérica* (good; air-conditioned). This road has plenty of restaurants, hotels and filling-stations, especially at Caja Seca and El Vigía, both rather new and raw looking towns. At **El Vigía** (*Hotel Gran Sasso*, E; *Hostería El Vigía*, E; *La Suiza*, Av. 15, opposite bus terminal, F, rec.; restaurant, *Armarilla*, try armarilla asado), where the road from Mérida to Santa Bárbara (Zulia) crosses the Río Chama, there is a fine bridge over 1 km. long. Santa Bárbara (56 km. NW) is a milk, meat and plantain producing centre, with air and boat services to Maracaibo and an important annual cattle show.

From El Vigía, the road continues fairly flat until **La Fría,** with a large natural-gas fuelled power station, where it is joined by the road along the west side of Lake Maracaibo and begins to climb to San Cristóbal. La Fría has two hotels; the family-run *Hotel Turística*, F, on main square, basic but clean, is rec.

THE SIERRA NEVADA DE MERIDA (4)

The **Sierra Nevada de Mérida**, running S of Maracaibo to the Colombian frontier, is the only range in Venezuela where snow lies permanently on the higher peaks. Near Mérida itself there are five such snowcaps of almost 5,000 metres. Several basins lying between the mountains are actively cultivated; the inhabitants are concentrated mainly in valleys and basins at between 800 and 1,300 metres above sea level. The three towns of Mérida, Valera and San Cristóbal are in this zone. There are two distinct rainy and dry seasons in the year. Two crops of the staple food, maize, can be harvested annually up to an elevation of about 2,000 metres.

Those who wish to visit the Sierra Nevada should turn left at Agua Viva to **Valera**, the most important town in the State of Trujillo, with a population of 117,000 and an airport with connections to Caracas and La Fría. The bus terminal is on the edge of the town. The US$5.50 trip by *por puesto* to Mérida across the Pico del Aguila pass (5½ hrs.) is well worth taking.

Hotels *Motel Valera**, E, Urb. La Plata; *Haack*, E, with private cold shower; *Victoria*, F, with bath, basic, noisy; *Pensión Lara*, F, good, friendly. *Albergue Turístico*, F, Av. Independencia, good value; *Camino Real*, nearby, E; *Imperial*, E, Av. 4 esq. Calle 14. *Hidrotermal San Rafael*, 4 km. off road between Valera and Motatán, notable for its hot water springs and the thermal bath.

From Valera a visit can be made to the state capital, ***Trujillo*** (43,000 people), at 805 metres; a *por puesto* from Valera costs US$0.45. This politically important town is losing ground commercially to Valera. Trujillo runs up and down hill; at the top, across from the university, is a park (sadly rundown) with waterfalls and paths. The Centro de Historia de Trujillo is a restored colonial house, now a museum. Bolívar lived there and signed the "proclamation of war to the death" in the house. A monument to the Virgen de la Paz was built by the wife of President Herrera Campins in 1983; it stands on a mountain, at 1,608 metres, ½-hr's walk from town; open 0900-1700, good views. (*Hotel Turística*, Av. Independencia 5-65, F with bath and hot water, highly rec.; *Hotel Roma*, F, good, clean, owner's daughter speaks English).

From Trujillo there is a high, winding, spectacular paved road to ***Boconó***, a town built on steep mountain sides. (*Hotel Vega del Río**, F, offers most services and food and is clean; *Colonial*, F, Av. Miranda; *Colina*, near the river at bottom of town, E, motel-style, clean, comfortable, restaurant;   *Italia*, F, Calle Jáuregui.) From there you can continue down to Guanare in the *llanos* via Biscucuy (where a very difficult road through Guárico leads to Barquisimeto).

We are now in the Sierra Nevada de Mérida, the Western Andes of Venezuela. The people are friendly, and very colourful in their red and navy blue *ruanas*. Forty km. beyond Trujillo on a good paved road we come to ***Timotes*** (hotels: *Las Truchas*, D, very nice, good food; *Aliso*), a mountainous little place set high in the cold grain zone. Near Timotes are La Mesa de Esnujape (*Hotel Tibisay**, E; *Miraflores*, F) and La Puerta (*Guadalupe**, D, a fine hotel; *Chiquinquirá*, E, Av. Bolívar 34; *Valeralta*, F, on road to Timotes; *Los Andes*, F, Av. Bolívar), both places hill resorts for Maracaibo and district. The road now climbs through increasingly wild, barren and rugged country and through the windy pass of **Pico del Aguila** (4,115 metres, best seen early in the morning, frequently in the clouds). This is the way Bolívar went ,when crossing the Andes to liberate Colombia, and on the peak is the statue of an eagle. In the pass is the very pleasant little *Restaurant Páramo Aguila* in chalet style. Behind it there is a small road leading up to the antenna and down towards the village of Piñango where there is trout fishing. Horses can be hired for treks to the Virgen del Carmen shrine and to the lake. The breath-taking scenery and the old village are worth the hardship of the 40 km. road; 4-wheel drive vehicles recommended if the road is wet.

The road then dips rapidly through ***Apartaderos***, 12 km. away (*Hotel Parque Turístico*, D, clean, beautiful house; *Restaurant Mifiafi*, beautiful, with exquisite food, gardener will give you seeds from his flowers); over the centuries the Indians have piled up stones from the rocky mountainside into walls and enclosures, hence the name. On Sunday they all stand and watch the tourists; the children sell flowers and fat puppies called *mucuchíes* (a variant of the Grand Pyrené) after a near-by town. Only 3 km. from Apartaderos is Laguna Mucubají, and a 1-hour walk takes you to Laguna Negra in the Parque Nacional Sierra Nevada for trout fishing; there is a campsite near the lake, restaurant and shop by the turn-off from the main road. A further 1½-hr. walk from Laguna Negra is the Laguna Los Patos (very beautiful if the weather is fine). Horses can be hired. Guides (not absolutely necessary) can be found at Laguna Mucubají or at the hotels in Santo Domingo (*Hotel Moruco**, D, food very good, bar expensive, reservations can be made through *Hotel Río Prado* in Mérida; *Santo Domingo*, E, hot water, clean, good restaurant but beware of overcharging; rooms for rent opp. *Restaurante Familia*, F). This quaint little hamlet lies a few km. away on the road which leads off to Barinas in the *llanos* and then on to Valencia. Between Santo Domingo and Laguna Mucubají is the *Hotel Los Frailes**, D, said to be one of the best in Venezuela, dinner is excellent but breakfast is appalling. Book well ahead through Avensa. *Mucubají* restaurant, at the highest point of the road that passes Laguna Mucubají, is very good for trout.

From Apartaderos the road to Mérida leads up to San Rafael de Mucuchíes, at

3,140 metres (Sra Crys, a French artist, will provide meals if you book in advance), from where you can walk up to a high valley where Indians tend cows and sheep (beware of the dogs that protect the houses), then down to **Mucuchíes**, (*Hotel Los Andes*, F, old house above plaza, 4 rooms, clean hot water, shared bathrooms, excellent; *Hotel Faro*) where there is a trout farm. At Moconoque, to the NW there is a hot spring. An old colonial trail, El Camino Real, can be taken from Apartaderos to Mucuchíes (3-4 hrs.), sometimes joining the main road, sometimes passing through small villages; below San Rafael is an old flour mill still in operation. Tabay, 10 km. from Mérida, has a pleasant main square, look out for humming birds. Hotels: *Las Cumbres*, *El Castaño*; restaurant *Cancha de Bolas*. Gasoline here but not higher on Páramo circuit. There are two hot springs. We descend through striated zones of timber, grain, coffee and tropical products to reach level land at last and the city of Mérida. All through this part of the country you see a plant with curious felt-like leaves of pale grey-green, the *frailejón* (or great friar), which blooms with yellow flowers from September to December.

The patron saint of Mucuchíes is San Benito; his festival on December 29 is celebrated by participants wearing flower-decorated hats and firing blunderbusses continuously.

Mérida (173 km. from Valera and 674 km. from Caracas), founded 1558, is the capital of Mérida State. Its white towers are visible from far along the road, and it stands at 1,640 metres (mean temperature 19° C) on an alluvial terrace 15 km. long, 2½ km. wide, surrounded by cliffs and plantations and within sight of Pico Bolívar, the highest in Venezuela (5,007 metres), crowned with a bust of Bolívar. In January-February, the coldest months, and August-September, it rains almost every late afternoon. Mérida still retains some colonial buildings which contrast with the fine modern buildings, such as those of the University of the Andes (founded 1785), which has 37,000 students from all over South America and the Caribbean. The main square with rebuilt Cathedral is pleasant, but is no longer colonial. The *fiesta* is the week of December 8; hotels will only let for the whole week. Mérida is also well known for its Feria del Sol, held on the week preceding Ash Wednesday. Population: 132,000, including students.

Mérida is known for its many parks (thirty three, some very small) and statues: the Parque de las Cinco Repúblicas (Calle 13, between Avs. 4 and 5), beside the barracks, has the first monument in the world to Bolívar (1842) and contains soil from each of the five countries he liberated (photography strictly prohibited). Bolívar is venerated in Venezuela and it is not permitted to cross a square containing his statue, if unsuitably dressed or carrying large bundles. The peaks known as the Five White Eagles (Bolívar, 5,007 m., Humboldt, 4,942 m., Bompland, 4,882 m., Toro, 4,755 m., León, 4,740 m.) can be clearly seen from here. There is a local legend that five Indian girls were transformed into mountains when they refused to submit to the Conquistadores. In the Plaza Beethoven, a different melody from Beethoven's works is chimed every hour (*por puestos* run along Av. 5, marked "Santa María" or "Chorro de Milla", US$0.08). The Museo de Arte Moderno on the same square has a nice small collection with paintings by local artists. The Parque Los Chorros de Milla has a zoo (some cages disgracefully small) in a hilly setting with a waterfall, closed Mon., it is some distance from the centre (minibus, US$0.35). On the way, there is a new chapel, built on the site where the Pope said mass in 1985. The Parque La Isla contains orchids, basketball and tennis courts, an amphitheatre and fountains; Jardín Acuario, besides the aquarium, is an exhibition centre, mainly devoted to the way of life and the crafts of the Andean peasants, admission US$0.10, open 0800-1200, 1400-2000 (*por puestos* leave from Av. 4 y Calle 25, US$0.08, passing airport). There is fishing and mountaineering in the neighbouring Sierra Nevada.

Hotels *Prado Río**, D, Cruz Verde 1, private bath, swimming pool, main building and individual cabins; *Belensate**, D, Urb. La Hacienda, La Punta; *Park Hotel**, Parque Glorias Patrias, C, but out of high season (i.e not Easter, August, Christmas or carnival) D, with discounts offered on car hire, noisy; there is a taxi rank outside. *Caribay**, Final Av. 2, noisy, D, good restaurant but poor service throughout. *Hostal Madrid*, F, Calle 23, Av. 7-8, good value; *La Sierra*, F, Calle 23, No. 2-31, private bath, friendly, clean, good value, parking; *Luxemburgo*, E, Calle 24 (Rangel), between Avs. 6-7, private bath, excellent breakfast, friendly, rec.; *El Andinito*, Plaza Bolívar, clean and friendly, E, good restaurant; *Montecarlo*, Av. 7 with Calles 24 and 25, T 52-66-88, F, clean, safe, parking, hot water, good but restaurant poor (located between teleférico station and Plaza Bolívar); *Teleférico*, beside teleférico station, E, noisy, clean, hot water, good restaurant. *Chama*, E, Av. 4 con Calle 29, private bath, pleasant, friendly, rec.; *Posada La Merideña*, Av. 4 y Calle 16, clean, quiet, charming, E; *Plaza*, Av. 5 between C. 23 and 24, E with bath, good value , noisy (laundromat next door); *Santiago de los Caballeros*, E, Av. 3, between Calles 24-25, private bath; *Italia*, Calle 19 between Avs. 2 and 3, F, with bath, hot water (cheaper rooms available), clean, friendly; *Encanto*, Av. Lora 25-30, entre Calles 25/26, F, friendly, take own lock, popular, cheapest; *Roje's*, Av. 2 y Calle 25, F with bath, clean, good value, English spoken; several hotels on Av. 2 between Calles 17 and 20. *Don Cándido*, Av. 2, F, good but noisy TV; *Mucubají*, Av. Universidad, E, clean and pleasant. It is difficult to get rooms during school holidays and the Feria del Sol. Recommended to book in advance.

Restaurants *Casa Vieja*, decorated as 19th-century Andean home, very good food, moderately priced, expect to pay about US$10 for two people; good food at *Chama Hotel*; *El "13"*, next to *Hostal Madrid*, good value; *Pekín*, Av. 3, good set meal for US$3; *Hong Kong*, Av. 5 y Calle 25, good Chinese, reasonable prices; *La Paellera*, Av. 5, good food, reasonable prices; *Pabellón Criolla*, Calle 18 and Av. 8, good, cheap local food as well as hamburgers; *Pizzería Monte Carlo*, Av. 3, Calle 24, rec.; *Pizzería Club* is opposite, OK. Around the corner from *Roje's Hotel* are *Los Cibeles*, Spanish, good trout, and *La Puerta del Sol*, not so good.

Vegetarian restaurants: *Comida Vegetariana*, Calle 24, No. 8-205, opp. Parque Las Heroínas, excellent; *Fonda Vegetariana*, Calle 29/Av. 4, rec.; *Anfora de Acuario*, Av. 2, Calles 24 and 23, good set lunches; *Arco Iris*, Av. 4 and Calle 19, very nice; *Pizzería Vegetariano*, Av. 5 and Calle 26, good, cheap; *Gran Fraternidad*, Av. 4, Calle 26, *Macro-Mérida*, Av. 4, Calles 18 and 19. Two cheap and filling restaurants are *Los Nevados*, Av. 2, No. 18-57 (rec.) and *Comedor Popular*, Calle 23, No. 6. *Restaurante Estudiantil Cuarta Avenida*, Av. 4 between C. 18 and 19, cheap. Good arepas at *Arepa Andina*, Av. 5, No. 21-46, and *La Arepera*, Plaza Bolívar. *El Lano*, Av. 3, Calles 28-9, excellent breakfast; *La Fresa*, Calle 26 near Av. 5, for desserts. The *Heladería La Coromoto* on Av. 3 offers 292 flavours, 88 choices of ice cream each day, e.g., trout, cornflakes, garlic, spaghetti. Local specialities, trout, pastelitos (savoury); sweetmeats include dulces abrillantados, higo relleno, mantecado de maiz; also try the local drink, calentado.

Museum Colonial Art Museum, Av. 3 No. 18-48, three blocks from Plaza Bolívar (open Tues.-Fri., 0900-1200, 1500-1800, Sat. 1500-1800, and Sun., 1000-1200, 1500-1800). More interesting is the small Archaeology Museum on the main square. Museum of Modern Art, Plaza Beethoven. Instituto Municipal de Cultura, Av. 4, half block from Parque Bolívar, stages poetry readings, art shows etc.

Films One-day service, CA, Calle 23 between 5 y 6, T 527981.

Exchange No bank accepts travellers' cheques, except Banco Internacional and Banco Consolidado for American Express, at the end of Viaducto Calle 26 or Av. Andrés Bello, Centro Comercial Las Tapias, but only 1000 to 1200 at either bank; Banco Unido accepts Visa and Mastercard. Hotels accept travellers' cheques and there is one *casa de cambio* in town, and one in airport arrivals; Turisol, Amex representative, T 631085. On Saturday, try the Latin Travel Agency by the *Park Hotel*.

Colombian Consulate Calle Ciejo, street opp. Night Club Las Vegas, 4 km. West of Centre; take *por puestro* to La Parroquia and ask at the end of the line. Visas free, take 10 mins.

Post Office and Telephones CANTV, Calle 21 between Avs. 4 and 5.

Laundry Lavandería La Vencedora, Av. 2 between Calles 24 and 25, same day service, US$0.75 a load.

Bullfights Mérida is a famous centre; the Feria del Sol in February is the peak time.

Tourist Offices Near the airport (good map for US$0.15) and near *Hotel Mucubají*. At Terminal Sur, helpful, map, hotel list, useful addresses and guide to events. At Oficina de Turismo Aeropuerto, Manuel, is very informative about excursions in the mountains, T 639330.

Travel Agencies Club de Turismo, Calle 24, No. 8-107 (opp. Teleférico), good advice on excursions, ask for Fanny. Occidente Turismo y Viajes, Av. 4 between Calles 18 and 19 for all flight bookings. Montana offers climbing holidays (US$75-125 per day, including transport and equipment), Ed. Las Américas P.B., Av. Las Américas, Mérida, T (074) 631740; Sierra Tours, *Park Hotel*, T 630879, can book teleférico and has a range of excursions. It is cheaper to take a taxi for a day trip, Línea Tibisay, outside *Park Hotel*, T 637930, rec. Nevada Tours at the airport offer interesting trips. They will take non-climbers up the Pico Bolívar, but owing to the altitude and weather conditions, this can be dangerous. Check all equipment carefully.

Air Services Airport is on the main highway, *por puesto* into town US$0.07, taxi US$1. Aeropostal and Avensa. To Caracas 3 flights daily (US$27.50), 1 hr., also to San Antonio at 1730 (US$12.50). In the rainy season planes may be diverted to San Antonio (if they aren't, it's a hair-raising approach). Avensa pay for overnight accommodation or for *por puestos* to Mérida, 3-5 hrs. on winding roads where landslides are common. Sit on left side of plane from Caracas for views. A new airport is being built at El Vigía, 1 hr. from Mérida; much safer as it is on a plain.

Buses The bus terminal is about 3 km. out of town on the W side of the valley, connected by frequent minibus service. To Caracas, US$4.80 (11-15 hrs.), *por puesto*, US$9.60; daily bus to Maracaibo, US$3.35, or *por puesto* service US$7, by Unión de Conductores, T 24364. Bus to San Cristóbal, US$2, 5 hrs., *por puesto* US$4. Buses to Barinas, US$1.50, 6 hrs. *Por puesto* to Apartaderos, US$1.40. Those hitchhiking east from Mérida should take a minibus to Tabay (US$0.20) and try from there. *Por puesto* to Valera, US$5.50 (6 hrs.), sit on the right side for best views.

The world's alleged highest and longest aerial cableway runs to **Pico Espejo** (4,765 metres) in four stages; it was built by the French in 1958. The trip up and down takes three hours and costs US$3.50, children US$1.75, 50% discount for holders of any student card; check beforehand that the cable car is operating; it runs Tuesday to Sunday, except holidays, starting up at 0730, last trip up at 1200, last trip down at 1545 (only 2 rucksacks are allowed in each cabin, very crowded at weekends and children are affected by the thin air, which makes them vomit). Travellers should book in advance, or at the ticket office on 25, or T (074) 525080. At busy times it can be worth booking through an agency or hotel to save queuing (it is booked up several days in advance at these times, and queues start at 0600) for "white" tickets as there is now a quota of 200 people per hour (on previous day at or before 0700). This is a "must", best done early in the morning (before 0830 ideally), before the clouds spoil the view, and from November to June. In summer the summit, with its statue to Our Lady of the Snows (patron saint of mountaineers), is clouded and covered with snow and there is no view. In the station in Mérida one can buy or hire warm jackets, gloves, caps, and climbing equipment, although there is a café at the top which you don't have to leave if you feel the cold—temperatures can be as low as 0°C. A permit is needed to leave the station area on the summit. August is the coldest month on the peaks. The glacier on Pico Bolívar can be seen clearly; so can Picos Humboldt and Bompland, forming the Corona, and to the E, on a clear day, the blue haze of the *llanos*. Electric storms in the mountains are not uncommon. There is a restaurant at La Montaña, 2,442 m.

If the peak is slightly clouded when you start, stop at the Loma Redonda station (4,045 metres) the last station but one. From this station there is a path to Los Nevados (2,711 metres), a pretty little place, plentiful accommodation G, guest house has food (5 or more hours' walking down, not recommended for the inexperienced, 7 hours up; be prepared for cold rain in the afternoon, start very early and rest before walking because of the sudden ascent in the cable car). Mules do the journey Tues.-Sun., US$3, 5 hrs. From Los Nevados you can continue to El Morro or take a jeep to Mérida (2 hrs., very rough). It is possible to get a room to stay overnight. There is also an ice cave with dazzling crystal ice stalactites two hours' rough walk from the last station. Only those in good heart can make this high trip. At Aguada station you can see the *fraileón* plant and throughout the area there is a great variety and quantity of flora. A description of the Sierra Nevada is included in *Backpacking in Venezuela, Colombia and Ecuador*, published by Bradt Enterprises.

Note You need a permit to walk this mountain range, which must be obtained from the Inparques (National Parks) ranger's office next to the *teleférico*, free; a mediocre topographical map is on sale. Permits are not given to single hikers: a minimum of 2 people is required. Camping gas may be bought in Mérida from a household shop near Plaza Bolívar. If camping, remember that the area is between 3,500 and 4,200 metres so acclimatization is necessary as is warm clothing for nighttime. Water purification is also recommended.

Mountain Guides The Andean Club in Mérida organizes trips to the top and guides will provide all equipment; enquire at the *teleférico* station at the end of Calle 24, beyond Av. 8. Carlos Rodríguez C., can be contacted at the vegetarian restaurant of María Guerrero next to the Teleférico (home address Av. Universidad, Edificio María Gracia, Piso 2, Apto. 5); he offers 1 to 7 day trips in the vicinity of Mérida, including in the price transportation, equipment and food.

Excursions 40 km. NW is the Centro de Investigaciones en Astronomía, responsible for the national observatory. Open daily 1030, 1400, 1530, 1900, 2200. There is a library, Mon.-Fri. 0900-1200, 1530-1730, T 791893, 791988. Visits to other resorts near Mérida: to Laguna de Mucubají, Laguna Negra or Pico del Aguila (**see page 903**). Just outside Mérida is Los Aleros, a model of a 1930s Andean village; examples of traditional skills, fascinating collection of old cameras and photographs; a ride in an open-sided bus and other events; very touristy (however, no Coca Cola, only traditional refreshments), rec. as a "must". *Antano* is a good nearby restaurant. **Jají**, 43 km. (good picnic spot en route overlooking Mérida), *por puesto* (US$1, sit on the left), famous for its colonial architecture, including a nice main square. Tourists can get advice from the Club Andino (P.O. Box 66) or Casa del Turista, La Compalla; T 3391. Recommended hotel and restaurant *Posada de Jají*, good food. Continuing for 62 km.—narrow, but mostly paved—beyond Jají, the Pan-American Highway is reached (several gas stations on the way). From La Azulita, between Jají and the Pan-American, one can visit La Cueva del Pirata. Through splendid scenery to Lagunilla, with pleasant lakeside restaurant; San Juan de Laqunillas, believed to be the first site of Mérida, has a striking church and is noted for its craftwork especially weaving. Fiestas from Christmas to Candlemas, 3 weeks in May (14 and 15 the highpoint) and in July. Thirty mins. beyond Lagunila lies the little church of Estanques (seldom open except on Christmas Day) with a stupendous gold colonial altar. Near Estanques is the colonial village of Chiguará with mineral springs (*Posada Colonial Cantarranos*, F, friendly, try *El Merendero* for local delicacies), visited by exchange students; *por puesto* from Mérida, US$0.70. At El Pedregal there are botanical gardens and a good view over the town. Giant cacti in the area are said to be 300 years old.

After Mérida the road passes on through the Chama valley to Lagunilla. Ninety-six km. beyond Mérida comes ***Tovar*** (population 19,000; *Hotel Junín*, F, *Hostería Sabaneta*, E, private bath), a nice little town with pleasant excursions, whence we can rejoin the Pan-American via Zea or tackle the wild and beautiful old mountain road over La Negra to San Cristóbal. 15 km. from Tovar is Bailadores (*Hotel La Cascada*, D, modern— Wilfredo plays electric organ in the bar on Sat. night, and at Mass on Sun. in the beautiful church, entertaining on both occasions); Las Tapias, 2 km. away, has a hot spring. From Bailadores the road climbs up into the mountains. The *Hotel de Montaña*, E, private bath, T 077-82401/2, is rec., 7 km. before La Grita on the road from Mérida. Daily buses between Tovar and La Grita on the old road. ***La Grita*** is a pleasant town, still not entirely Americanized; Hotels: *La Casona*, F, Carrera 2A, No. 6-69; *Capri*, F, Carrera 3, good value, bargain. Hard to find a reasonable restaurant.

San Cristóbal, capital of Táchira State, is on a plateau 55 km. from the Colombian border, at 830 metres. Average temperature 22°C, population 230,000. The city is on three levels, running N-S: a 1½ km. wide level zone along the Torbes river, which flows S into the Orinoco basin, and two terraces, one of them 200 metres above the river, and 5°C cooler. This, and the La Concordia sector to the S, are the "select" suburbs. The city was founded in 1561, and the Spanish colonial appearance—the appearance only—is preserved. The Cathedral, finished in 1908, had its towers and façade rebuilt in colonial style for the 400th anniversary of the foundation. There is a good road over the mountains, with beautiful Andean views, to San Antonio.

Hotels *De Ferias El Tamá**, D, Av. 19 de Abril, overlooking the town, has an Olympic-size swimming pool; *Korinu*, D, Carrera 6 bis, rec., with good restaurant; *Círculo Militar*, Av. 19 de Abril, E, all services including swimming pool and gymnasium; *Machirí*, E, Calle 7 No. 4-30, bath, hot water, clean, friendly, central, rec.; *Hamburgo*, Av. Libertador, F, clean; *Horizonte*, F, Av. 5, iced water provided; *Hospedaje El Almendro*, opp. old bus station, F, cheap and homely, near to *El Amparo* restaurant; *Motel Las Lomas**, E, Av. Libertador; *Ejecutivo*, F, old and basic but clean and central; *Americano*, Calle 8, F, basic and good; *Tropicana*, F, clean, spacious, just across the street behind the old bus terminal (billiard hall next door). There are several cheap hotels on Avenida 6A, just off the central plaza, in F category; *Residencia Hilton*, clean and friendly, is probably the most expensive; opposite is *Internacional*, F, cheaper and better; but neither are as grand as they sound.

Restaurants *Fung Wah*, on lower of 2 main thoroughfares, Chinese, not cheap but worth it.

Exchange Banco Consolidado (American Express), 5a Av., Edif. Torre E.

Launderette in Cada shopping centre next to *Hotel El Tamá*, open 0800-1200, 1400-1800.

Airports for San Cristóbal: at San Antonio (1 hr.) and La Fría (90 mins.).

By Road To Maracaibo, 8 hrs., US$3.60, *por puesto*, US$7.20. To Mérida, US$4 by *por puesto* or bus, US$2. To Caracas, US$5-5.40, 12 hrs. by Llanos and Panamericana routes respectively; similarly to Valencia, US$4.45-4.70. To San Antonio, 2½ hrs. by bus, US$0.25, or *por puesto*, which continues to Cúcuta, US$1, stopping at Immigration in both countries, runs every 20 mins. By taxi to Cúcuta: US$7.50 to San Antonio, US$3.50 to wait at border, then US$4 to Cúcuta. San Cristóbal has a new bus terminal.

San Antonio, the frontier town (not a tourist attraction, although there is an attractive colonial cathedral, also some pleasant parks), is connected by international bridge with Cúcuta, Colombia, distant about 16 km. (bus US$0.50—in bolívares or pesos—to international bridge), whence you can continue by road or air to Bogotá. Be sure to get your Venezuelan exit stamp from the immigration office at the border bridge (building on left, upstairs, closed 1100-1300) or Colombian officials will send you back (unless you are only visiting Cúcuta). Once you are in Colombia go straight to the DAS office in Cúcuta to complete formalities there (see page 546). If driving to Colombia, you must have your *carnet de passages* stamped at both the border and the DAS office. Entry charge, US$1.50. Entering Venezuela from Cúcuta, there is no point in buying a bus ticket to San Cristóbal before going through formalities. Go to DIEX on the other side of San Antonio, 3 blocks down from Carrera 9; entry stamp is only given after passport and visa have been photocopied at another office (US$0.20). 5 km. after San Antonio is a customs post; be prepared to be strip-searched. **N.B.** Venezuelan customs is closed at weekends; it is therefore impossible to cross from Colombia at these times. Entering Venezuela in your own car presents no problems as long as you have obtained a visa and *carnet* in advance. You must visit Immigration in town, pay US$0.20 for a form on which to pay exit tax and have your passport photocopied. Once in Venezuela, you may find that local police are ignorant of documentation required for foreign cars. Thirteen km. N on the Venezuelan side lies the spa of Ureña, with natural hot springs (*Hotel Aguas Calientes**, C, private thermal bath, swimming pool).

Hotels   At San Antonio: *Don Jorge*, F, a/c dining room expensive; *Táchira*, E, with bath, rec.; *Neveri*, E, Calle 3, No. 3-11, esq. Carrera 3, private bath, parking nearby, by border; *La Villa*, F, clean, fan; *Los Andes*, F, cheap; *San Antonio*, F, fan, clean, cheap meals; *Residencial Colonial*, Carrera 11, No. 251, F, clean, cheap restaurant, rec.; many hotels near town centre.

Exchange   at the Banco de Venezuela on main square. *Casas de cambio* near the international bridge will not all change cheques and some will only change Colombian pesos, not even US dollars cash. The exchange rate for changing bolívares to pesos is better in San Antonio than in Cúcuta.

Colombian Consulate   Carrera 6, No. 3-29, for visas, open until 0200.

Bus to Caracas US$5.40.

Airport has exchange facilities. Taxis run to DIEX (emigration) in town, and on to Cúcuta airport. *Por puesto* to airport, US$0.10. Internal flights, Avensa, to Maiquetía, Mérida, Barquisimeto, Coro, Maracaibo and Valencia; international to Aruba, Bonaire, Mexico, Miami, New York and Panama.

THE LLANOS OF THE ORINOCO (5)

This area of flat grasslands, 1,000 km. by 320 km., lies between the Andes and the Orinoco River and is reported to be one of the best places in the world to see birds. It is veined by numerous slow running rivers, forested along their banks. The vast flatland is only varied here and there by *mesas,* or slight upthrusts of the land. About 5 million of the country's 6.4 million cattle, many of the Zebu type from Brazil and India, are in the *llanos,* 30% of the country's area, but holding no more than 13% of the population. When the whole plain is periodically under water, the *llaneros* drive their cattle into the hills or through the flood from one *mesa* to another. When the plain is parched by the sun and the savanna grasses become uneatable they herd the cattle down to the damper region of the Apure and Orinoco. Finally they drive them into the valley of Valencia to be fattened for slaughter.

Parts of the area are coming under cultivation. The Guárico dam has created thousands of hectares of fertile land by controlling flood and drought. The *llanos* State of Portuguesa has now the largest cultivated area of any: rice and cotton are now produced.

There are several roads to the *llanos*. Sixteen km. E of Maracay, a good road leads off to **San Juan de los Morros** where a cock-fighting tournament is held each year (Hotels: *Motel Santa Mónica*, E; *Gran Hotel Los Morros*, E, on Carretera Nacional towards Villa de Cura; *Excelsior*, E, Calle Marino; *Ana*, F). It has natural hot springs. Nearby are mountains with vertical cliffs, on which several climbing routes have been opened. The road divides later: S to the Guárico dam, the *llanos* and San Fernando de Apure, and E to Valle de la Pascua (*Hotel Venezuela*, E, Plaza Bolívar; *San Marcos*, E, Carretera Nacional towards El Socorro; *Gran Hotel Monte Carlo*, opp. bus station, F, a/c, shower) and El Tigre.

Going S, keep an eye open for egrets, which were almost exterminated early in the century for their feathers, once a valuable export. Crossing the bridge over the River Apure at Puerto Miranda we come to San Fernando de Apure. From there towards Puerto Ayacucho the route is only passable in the dry months of Feb.-May, and with a 4-wheel drive vehicle.

Manfred W. Frischeisen recommends a detour from the Guárico dam: San Fernando road, turn left at Calabozo (*Motel Tiuna*, a/c and good restaurant) along a gravel road (being paved) to Paso del Caballo (81 km.). A little trail goes on to Cazorla (85 km.); on the swamps one can see egrets, parrots, alligators, monkeys (and hear howlers). Turn left in Cazorla to Guayabal, back on the main road, 21 km. from San Fernando (there is also a road to the right to Guayabal, very bad, only passable with 4-wheel-drive or a trail bike with effort). From San Fernando, fair, interesting road goes over Guasdualito to San Cristóbal (take spare gasoline). Peter Straub recommends taking the bus from San Cristóbal to Guasdualito, then the mail plane to San Fernando, continuing to Ciudad Bolívar. Most travel agents do not know of this method: insist on seeing the timetables.

San Fernando de Apure is the capital of the western *llanos*. Bus to Caracas, US$3, two a day to Barinas. Hotels: *Boulevard*, Av. Boulevard; *La Torraca*, Paseo Libertador; *La Fuente*, Av. Miranda; *Trinacria*, Av. Miranda; *El Río*, Av. Miranda; *Europa*, Paseo Libertador; all in F/E range with a/c, water spasmodic.

Exchange Banco Consolidado for American Express, Av. Miranda, Res. 19 de Abril.

From San Fernando you can drive W towards Barinas, the road is beautiful between Mantecal and Bruzual. In the early morning, many animals and birds can be seen, and in the wet season alligators cross the road. At Bruzual, just S of Puente Nutrias over the Apure river, there are 3 primitive inns (e.g. *Los Llaneros*, F, you eat with the family). From San Fernando you can travel east to Ciudad Bolívar either by taking a boat (expensive and unreliable and not possible in the dry season) from opposite the airport to Caicara (see below), or by taking a bus to Calabozo and changing there for Valle de Pascua (see above), US$2.65.

Alternative route from Caracas to Mérida

There is a splendid road to the western *llanos* of Barinas, from Valencia through **San Carlos**, capital of Cojedes State (uninteresting, *Hotel Italo*, F, Av. Carabobo, a/c, private bath), **Acarigua**, a thriving agricultural centre (*Motel Payara**, D, on road to Guanare, pool, a/c; *Motel Rancho Grande*, E, on road to San Carlos; *Miraflores*, E, swimming pool) and **Guanare**, a national place of pilgrimage with an old parish church containing the much venerated relic of the Virgin of Coromoto, Patron of Venezuela. Population 32,500 (*Hotel Italia*, D, Carrera 5, No. 19-60, the most expensive; others, all E, include *Coromoto*, swimming pool; *Motel Portuguesa*, a/c, hot water, clean, good restaurant, pool).

After the first appearance of the Virgin, Chief Coromoto failed to be baptized, though he did hedge by getting other members of the tribe baptized. When the Virgin reappeared he made a grab at her and told her gruffly to be gone, but she vanished leaving in his hand a likeness of herself on the inner surface of a split stone now on display in the church. For years little attention was paid to the image, and it was only in 1946 that this Virgin was declared the Patron of Venezuela.

The road continues to **Barinas** (population 92,000), the capital of the cattle-raising and oil-rich State of Barinas. Fishing and game-watching excursions into the *llanos*. The rivers are full of *caribes* (*piranha*) and many kinds of fish good to eat. The local music at *La Terraza* bar near the bus terminal has been rec.; harp *cuatro*, singing, informal and very good.

Hotels *Motel El Cacique*, D, swimming pool; *Bristol**, Av. 23 de Enero, E; *Comercio**, F, Av. Marqués del Pumar, cooking facilities; *Plaza*, E, a/c, shower, good restaurant; *Motel La Gran Avenida*, Av. 23 de Enero, F, cold showers, bar, restaurant, parking, clean, rec.; *Hostería Los*

Guasimitos, F, a/c, clean, good restaurant, standard motel, on road to Guanare, swimming pool; *Suine*, quiet, F, with shower, no hot water, restaurant; *Lisboa*, opp. bus station, F, good.

Exchange Banco Consolidado (American Express), Av. Libertador con Calle Camejo.

Buses   4 a day for Mérida, US$1.50, magnificent ride through the mountains, 6 hrs. *Por puesto* costs US$3. Bus to Caracas, US$3.70, 8 hrs; to San Antonio, US$2.80. To Acarigua, US$1.60, 3 hrs; San Cristóbal, US$1, 4½ hrs. The bus terminal is on the edge of the town.

Airport   with local services and to Caracas (US$22).

From Barinas there is a beautifully scenic road to Apartaderos, in the Sierra Nevada de Mérida (**see page 903**).

Motorists travelling East from Mérida to Ciudad Bolívar can either go across the *llanos* or via San Carlos, El Sombrero, Valle de la Pascua and El Tigre, which route requires no ferry crossings and has more places with accommodation. In the *llanos*, near El Baúl (turn off main road E of San Carlos), is a safari-type lodge at Hato Piñero, including all meals, good room, and guide for bird-and animal-watching trips; address: Hato Piñero, Edif. General de Seguros, Piso 6, Ofic. 6B, Av. La Estancia, Chuao, Caracas 1060, T (2) 912011—contact Ani Villanueva.
There is a route across the *llanos* to Ciudad Bolívar: from Chaguaramas on the road to Valle de la Pascua, turn S through Las Mercedes and flat cattle land to *Cabruta*, 179 km., daily bus to Caracas, US$3, there is no ferry to Puerto Ayacucho, but you can take a barge, US$10, 3-day trip, fix price with boat captain. Ask for Coronel Tefero about travelling on the river. There is a small hotel, infested with rats and cockroaches, but better accommodation in *Caicara*—ferry from Cabruta, about 1 hr., US$2 for car, passengers US$0.35. Hotels: *Diamante*; *Central*, F; *Italia*, F; *Buenos Aires*, F; *Miami*, E; *Venezuela*, F; *Bella Guayana*, F. By bus from Caicara to Ciudad Bolívar, US$3, on a paved road which crosses the rivers Cuchivero (ferry, US$1.50) and Caura (ferry, US$2.50), takes 7 hrs. An all-weather dirt road runs from Caicara to Puerto Ayacucho; interesting for the Indians and the mining nearby. There is a regular jeep service to Puerto Ayacucho, US$4.50. Ask for Asociación Civil de Conductores. There are two flights a week (Wed. and Sat.) to Puerto Ayacucho. Cargo boats take three days to Puerto Ayacucho but are unwilling to take passengers; better from Cabruta (see above).

Puerto Ayacucho is the capital of the Federal Territory of Amazonas, which has an area of 175,000 square kilometres and a population of only 15,000, a large proportion of whom live in Puerto Ayacucho. At the end of the dry season (April), it is very hot and sticky. It is 800 km. up the Orinoco from Ciudad Bolívar, deep in the wild, but no direct boats do the five day journey up river. The town has daily air service. *Hotel Amazonas**, C, good; *Hotel El Tobogán*, Orinoco, T (048) 21320, E, popular, fair, TV; *Italia*, F, with fan, run down; *Residencia Internacional*, Av. Aguerrevere 18, T 21242, F p.p., clean, safe, friendly, laundry; *Residencia Río Siapa*, Av. Orinoco, T 21138, clean, friendly, hard to find; *Maguari*, F, friendly, will store luggage, rec., restaurant; *Gran Sarola*, opp. gas station, clean. There is a good craft shop for souvenirs.
Tobogán Tours, Av. Río Negro 44, Puerto Ayacucho (T (48)21700), owner Pepe Jaimes, arranges trips on the Orinoco, to Indian villages and to the Paraguena river through waterfalls, untouched jungle with fascinating wildlife. A jungle camp is soon to be opened. For tours of the Territorio Federal Amazonas, S of Puerto Ayacucho, a rec. guide is Yamal A. Nasser, Calle Crisanto Mato Coba 33, Barrio Virgen del Valle, Ciudad Bolívar, T 085-48969 (he may be contacted through the Tourist Office in Ciudad Bolívar). Pedro Lucchini, T (048) 21156, in *artesanía* shop to left of Tobogán Tours will advise and arranges some trips. Before setting out you need a permit from the Bureau of Indian Affairs (Orai) in Caracas, or possibly Puerto Ayacucho. Trips involve a bus journey from Ciudad Bolívar to Puerto Samariapo, boat trip and visits to Indian communities, jungle flora and fauna and the Cerro Autana national monument. The cost should be about US$250 a week for 4-5 people (cheaper if you hunt and fish for food). Another guide, Manuel, goes to the Piraroa people, 3 days, 2 nights sleeping in villages (take blanket).
For trips anywhere from Puerto Ayacucho check at the central service station. Other recommended trips include by *por puesto* to Samariapo and waterfalls at Tobogán de la Selva. From Samariapo boat to Isla de Ratán and Santa Rosa; also to Vichada and Santa Rita and thence bus to Villavicencio (Colombia). From Puerto Ayacucho there is a cargo boat to Puerto Páez, 4 hrs., for crossing to Colombia. Check with Guardia Nacional and insist on exit stamp (they are strangely reluctant). Ferry to Puerto Carreño US$0.75. By air to San Fernando de Apure, US$25. Jeep from Caicara, US$6.50.

Beyond Puerto Ayacucho are rapids, but smaller launches on the upper Orinoco can reach the Casiquiare and the Río Negro which flows into the Amazon. It is very difficult to find boats willing to take passengers. For information on travelling by boat to Manaus, ask for Alejandro. In 1955/56 two Americans successfully canoed to Argentina, continuing from the Amazon by way of the Tapajós, Paraguay and Paraná. The trip took about one year. The journey up the Amazon to the Casiquiare and Orinoco has also been successfully negotiated by a hovercraft with a British crew. It is impossible to go without a permit, available only for scientific expeditions. Permits are obtained from the Bureau of Indian Affairs (ORAI) in Caracas, or in Puerto Ayacucho itself. Buy your provisions here: nobody lives on the Casiquiare despite what the maps say. Do not travel alone. If you want to cross the border into Colombia at Puerto Ayacucho or further north at Puerto Carreño, you can expect difficulties with the local authorities. You will probably be asked for proof of how much money you have and where you are going; some travellers have had to obtain Colombian visas to enter the country when only a passport and ticket out of the country were strictly necessary.

EAST FROM CARACAS (6)

The eastern part of the North-Eastern Highlands, with summits rising to 2,000 metres, has abundant rainfall in its tropical forest. The western part, which is comparatively dry, has most of the inhabitants and the two main cities, Cumaná and Barcelona.

Eastern Venezuela, with the Highlands in the NE, the great *llanos* of the Orinoco to the south, and south of the Orinoco again the range of Guayana Highlands, was until quite recently not of much account in the Venezuelan economy. Some coffee and cacao are grown on the eastern slopes of the north-eastern highlands in the tropical forest, but the western slopes are subject to drought. Cattle roam the *llanos*, and the Guayana Highlands produce gold and diamonds. The picture has now been changed, as about 30% of Venezuelan oil now comes from this area. South of the Orinoco vast iron ore deposits are mined.

It is now only five hours from Caracas to Barcelona by road through Caucagua, from which there is a 47-km. road NE to Higuerote, which has a number of beaches, currently the focus of large-scale tourist projects.

Higuerote can also be reached by a road, which is being paved, along the coastal mountain range from Los Caracas (92 km., **see page 893**)—beautiful views, beaches everywhere, 4-wheel drive vehicles rec. (Higuerote hotels: *Campomar*, D; *Sol Mar*, D). One beach is at La Sabana (turn off after 37 km.); private rooms for rent, San Juan drum (*tambores*) festival at end-June. 4 km. beyond is Caruao, rebuilt in an old style (ask for Josefa, who cooks delicious seafood); follow the road for El Pozo del Cura, a waterfall and pool.

14 km. before Higuerote on the road from Caucagua is Tacarigua de Mamporal, where you can turn off to the Laguna de Tacarigua National Park. The road passes a Tunnel of Vegetation (almost 3 km. long), cocoa plantations, the towns of San José and Río Chico (*Hotel Italia*, E, a/c; excellent natural fruit icecream). In the fishing village of Tacarigua de la Laguna (rooms to rent), you can eat delicious *lebranche* fish; an unmotorized ferry crosses the lagoon, which has many water birds (including flamingoes, usually involving a day-long boat trip to see them), to the beach on the Caribbean.

41 km. from Barcelona is Píritu, which has an interesting Franciscan church, and the fishing village of Puerto Píritu (*Casacoima Puerto Píritu**, D).

Barcelona, population 112,000, mean temperature, 27°C, capital of Anzoátegui State, is on the W bank of the Neverí River, 5 km. from the ocean. You can see the ruins of the Casa Fuerte, grim relic of the War of Independence. Teatro Cajigal is a replica of the Teatro Municipal in Caracas. (Hotels: *Barcelona**, E, no restaurant; *Neverí*, D; restaurant *Castillo del Oriente*, unpretentious, not expensive.) Ships from La Guaira call at **Guanta**, 22 km. away, now connected with the 4-lane highway which goes through Puerto La Cruz and an airport with services to Caracas (US$12.50). Oficambio exchange facilities at the airport. Taxi Barcelona airport-Puerto La Gruz, US$4.

Barcelona has been surpassed commercially by **Puerto La Cruz**, 22 km. away by an asphalted highway skirting the pleasant residential and bathing resort of Lechería (*por puesto* US$0.20). Puerto La Cruz, once a fishing hamlet, is now a thriving town of 180,000 with two oil refineries, and famous for its watersports, fishing, diving, water skiing and surfing. Its seaport is also Guanta. Bus to Caracas, US$2.60, 6 hrs.

On the highway from Puerto La Cruz to Barcelona is the Polideportivo sports stadium seating 10,000 people: covered gymnasium, velodrome, tennis, volleyball, and basket-ball courts and two swimming pools. A new Institute of Technology, part of the Universidad del Oriente, is near the stadium.

Hotels at Puerto La Cruz tend to be fully booked with package tours. *Meliá**, B, on Paseo Colón, luxury hotel with all services and facilities; *Doral Beach**, D, swimming pool, beach, nearer Barcelona than Puerto La Cruz; *Europa*, Calle Sucre, esq. Plaza Bolívar, E, good, clean, safe, a/c; *Neptuno**, D, Paseo Colón, a/c, good restaurant; next door is *Margelino*, F with bath, a/c, safe, clean, very good; *San Remo*, D, Calle Simón Rodríguez 55, rec., near bus station; *Tama*, Rómulo Gallegos, showers, a/c, helpful, courteous; *Colón*, Libertad, F with a/c, TV, 2 blocks from beach; *Equus*, Bolívar, E, shower, a/c, clean; *Mi Hotel*, Calle Libertad, E, a/c, showers, comfortable, but slow service; *Sorrento**, E, Av. 5 de Julio, shower, comfortable; *Noray*, Av. Libertad, E with a/c, good, friendly; *Pensión Rancho Grande*, Paseo Colón, F with fan.

Restaurants *El Parador*, Paseo Colón, excellent food and service (Caesar Salad rec.). Also on or near Paseo Colón: *Da Luigi*, Italian, good; *El Chalet*, opposite, good European food; *Marisquería Guatarasco*; *El Tejas*; *La Bella China*, best Chinese; *Reale* for good breakfasts; plenty of others. *Nature*, vegetarian, Constitución 70, lunch and dinner. *Guatacrazo* bar, great fun, all staff in fancy dress, fun, drinks and surprises.

Shopping Vendors of paintings, jewellery, leather, etc. on Paseo Colón in evenings. Good hammocks may be bought, US$6-12. Perfectfoto SA, Carabobo, Fuente Torre Oriente, T 22821 for film processing; also Fotolisto, Paseo Colón, US$1.70 per film without mounts.

Laundry Lavandería Margarita, Bolívar 160.

Exchange Banco Consolidado (American Express), Av. 5 de Julio, Local No. 43; Turisol, Am Ex rep., T 662161/669910. Banco Royal Venezolano. Casa de Cambio: Oficambio Oriente, Calle Maneiro 17, Edif. Latina; also *cambio* in *Hotel Riviera*.

Post Office and Telecommunications Freitas y Bolívar, one block from Paseo Colón.

Travel Agency Viajes Ven-Mex, Av. Alberto Ravell 15, recommended. Venezuelan Travel Advisers, Municipal esq. Freitas, Edif. Montalero, T (081) 660113/669204.

Excursions To the islands of La Plata and La Chimana for swimming: take taxi to harbour, or *por puesto* to Pamatacualito then walk 10 mins. to harbour, then boat (to La Plata US$1, to La Chimana US$5 return). A tourist complex, El Morro, covering 20 sq. km. is being built at Salto La Sirena, 8 km. away in the Guanta valley.

The Coastal Zone Starting east from Puerto La Cruz, the road passes through the most beautiful coastal scenery in Venezuela, the Mochima National Park—a Côte d'Azur without people—to the seaport of Cumaná, 84 km. from Puerto La Cruz. On the way it passes Playa Blanca, by boat US$5 return, excellent snorkelling, take own equipment. The locals cook and sell fish. Playa Arapito, the popular palm-fringed beach at Playa Colorado with its red sands, 26 km. E of Puerto La Cruz; *por puesto* from Mercado Municipal US$1; it is easy to hitch. Boys sell oysters on the beach; there is a restaurant. Camping is allowed for a small fee and there is accommodation to let. Also Playa Santa Cruz further E. From Mochima, a village in the Park, beyond Santa Fe (Sra. Cellita Día lets rooms, F), boats can be taken around the islands and to lonely beaches—very beautiful; fares negotiable, about US$9 per day for 6 people. *Por puesto* to Cumaná, US$6 (45 min.). At Santa Fe, ask for Christoph Realini at the *Restaurant Cochaima*, or try to phone him, 004981 664330; he is Swiss, speaks German, English, Italian and Spanish, and organizes accommodation, boat trips (US$9). Santa Fe is a good place to relax. There is gasoline here.**N.B.** at holiday time, the coast is overcrowded.

Cumaná, population 155,000, capital of Sucre State, founded 1520, is the oldest Hispanic city in South America. It straddles both banks of the Manzanares, 1½ km. from Puerto Sucre. The castle of San Antonio has been fully restored, and there are good walks along the tree-lined Manzanares. San Luis beach, short local bus ride, recommended, but the water is somewhat dirty. Cumaná has an important sardine canning industry. Beware mosquitoes from the stagnant river. The port area is not safe at night. New airport 10 km. from centre (taxi fare US$2.50). Average temperature 27°C. Car ferry to Margarita Island. Famous for its carnival. A museum was built in 1974 to commemorate the 150th anniversary of the battle of Ayacucho; mainly portraits, relics and letters of Bolívar and Sucre. There is also a maritime museum (Museo del Mar) with good exhibits of tropical marine life, at the old airport, Av. Universidad with Av. Industrial, open Fri.-Sun. 0900-1200, 1400-1800.

Hotels *Cumanagoto**, C, Av. Universidad, swimming pool, beach, travel agency for trips to

Angel Falls, etc.; *Los Bordones*, B, Final Av. Universidad, 8 km. from the bus station, rec., beautifully situated on a good beach with good food and a swimming pool; *Villa Mar*, D, Av. Universidad, clean, comfortable, restaurant; these three are a long way from the centre of town. *Gran Hotel**, D, Av. Universidad, beach, mid-way between *Cumanagoto* and town centre; in same area, *Caribe*, on beach, E with bath and a/c, clean, basic, English spoken, no restaurant. *Minerva**, E, clean, modern, Av. Cristóbal Colón, US$1 taxi ride from centre; *Turismo Guaiqueri*, Av. Bermúdez 26 T (093) 24230/663444, E, comfortable, clean, a/c, bath, friendly, no restaurant; *El Río*, F, Av. Bermúdez, a/c, bath, phone, reasonable restaurant; *Residencias Trevi*, E, with bath and fan, on Av. Universidad, 2 km. from San Luis beach. *Regina*, Av. Arismendi, E with bath, a/c, restaurant, good value; *Mariño*, E, near centre on Av. Mariño with Junín, private bath, a/c, clean. Cheaper hotels can be found across the river from those above, around Plaza Ayacucho, especially on Calle Sucre: *Hospedaje La Gloria*, Sucre 31, opposite Sta. Inés church, F with fan and bath; on same street *Astoria*, F with bath, clean and friendly; *Macuto, Cumaná, Colón, Italia*, all reasonably priced.

Restaurants   Good food at *El Colmao* restaurant in the centre as well as *El Teide* (seafood); *Parrilla Ribera* on Av. Las Palomas. *Jardín de Sport*, only outdoor café, good food, rec. *El Ilustre*, Av. Humbolt (opp. Plaza Sucre), for sandwiches, hamburgers, juices; *Pastelería Sucre*, Calle Mariño, breakfasts, cakes, coffee. All central restaurants close Sun. lunchtime.

Exchange   Banco Consolidado, Av. Bermúdez. Perimetral. Edif. Ajounián. Exchange at Oficambio, Calle Mariño, Edificio Funcal.

Panamanian Consulate in a one-way street, next to Grupo Escolar José Silvero Córdova in Parcelamiento Miranda Sector D, T 663525; take a taxi.

Travel Agent Happy Tour, Centro Comercial, La Banca, P.B., Local No. 6, T 24592; also at *Hotel Cumanagoto*, T 653111.

Bus   *Por puesto* to Puerto La Cruz, US$1.20, bus US$0.60, 1¼ hrs. To Güiria (see page 917), US$1.70, *por puesto* US$3.50 (5 hrs.), often stop in Carúpano. To Caracas, US$3 upwards depending on company (7 hrs.), frequent service; many daily to Ciudad Guayana and Ciudad Bolívar (7 hrs.)

Excursion   The Parque Nacional Cueva del Guáchero (see page 918) can be visited from Cumaná by taking a daily bus at 0730 and 1200 hrs. to Caripe (US$2, 4 hrs.) or frequent *por puestos* (US$4, try bargaining, 2 hrs.). 44 km. east of Cumaná is the beautiful beach of Cachamaure , on the Golfo de Cariaco. To the Araya Peninsula, either by road, turning off the Cumaná-Carúpano road at Cariaco: the road on the peninsula soon becomes very rough; last chance to eat at Chacopata; or by ferry Cumaná-Araya (return ferries haphazard and difficult to get on as more cars than spaces). *Hotel Turístico* in Araya, E, with bar, restaurant, discotheque.

ISLA DE MARGARITA

Isla de Margarita and two close neighbours, Coche and Cubagua, form the state of Nueva Esparta.

Isla de Margarita is in fact one island whose two sections are tenuously linked by the 18 kilometre sandspit which separates the sea from the Restinga lagoon. At its largest, Margarita is about 32 kilometres from north to south and 67 kilometres from east to west. Most of its people live in the developed eastern part, which has some wooded areas and fertile valleys. The western part, the Peninsula de Macanao, is hotter and more barren, with scrub, sand dunes and marshes. Wild deer, goats and hares roam the interior, but four-wheel drive vehicles are needed to penetrate it. The entrance to the Peninsula de Macanao is a pair of hills known as Las Tetas de María Guevara, a national monument covering 1,670 hectares.

The climate is exceptionally good, but rain is scant. Water is piped from the mainland. The roads are good, and a bridge connects the two parts. Nueva Esparta's population is over 200,000, of whom about 20,000 live in the main city, Porlamar (which is not the capital, that is La Asunción).

The island has enjoyed a boom since 1983, largely as a result of the fall in the value of the bolívar and the consequent tendency of Venezuelans to spend their holidays at home. Margarita's status as a duty-free zone also helps. Venezuelan shoppers go in droves for clothing, electronic goods and other consumer items. Gold and gems are good value, but many things are not. There has been extensive building in Porlamar, with new shopping areas and Miami-style hotels going up. A number of beaches are also being developed.

Local industries are fishing and fibre work, such as hammocks and straw hats. Weaving, pottery and sweets are being pushed as handicraft items for the tourists. An exhibition centre has been opened at El Cercado, near Santa Ana, on Calle Principal, near the church.

Despite the property boom and frenetic building on much of the coast and in Porlamar, much of the island has been given over to natural parks. Of these the most striking is the Laguna La Restinga. Launches provide lengthy runs around the mangrove swamps, but they create a lot of wash and noise. The mangroves are fascinating, with shellfish clinging to the roots. The launch will leave you on a shingle and shell beach (don't forget to arrange with your boatman to collect you), and you can rummage for shellfish in the shallows (protection against the sun essential). Flamingos live in the lagoon.

There are mangroves also in the Laguna de las Marites reserve, west of Porlamar. Other parks are Las Tetas de María Guevara, Cerro el Copey, 7,130 hectares, and Cerro Matasiete y Guayamurí, 1,672 hectares (both reached from La Asunción).

By boat from Porlamar you can go to the Isla de los Pájaros, or Morro Blanco, for both bird-spotting and underwater fishing. In Boca del Río there is a Museum of the Sea.

Beaches Apart from the shopping, what attracts the holidaymakers from Venezuela and abroad (especially Canada) are the beaches: long white stretches of sand bordered by palms, but rather hot, with little shade (sunscreen essential—local wisdom is that you can burn even when sitting in the shade). Topless bathing is not seen, but the tanga (hilo dental - dental floss) is fairly common.

In Porlamar, the beach by the *Concorde* hotel is excellent: calm shallow water, boats and pedalos for hire, windsurf classes; but that by the *Bella Vista* is crowded with foreign tourists and polluted. For a more Venezuelan atmosphere go northwest to Pampatar, which is set around a bay favoured by foreign yachtsmen as a winter anchorage. A full-scale model of Columbus' *Santa María* is used for taking tourists on trips. (Beach restaurant *Antonio's*, rec.; also *Trimar*.) Pampatar has the island's largest fort, San Carlos Borromeo, and the smaller La Caranta, where the cannon show signs of having been spiked. Visit also the church of Cristo del Buen Viaje, the Library/Museum and the customs house (now the offices of Fondene, the local development agency).

A number of good beaches are being developed on the eastern side. These are divided into ocean and calm beaches, according to their location in relation to the open sea. The former tend to be rougher (good surfing and windsurfing) and colder. Water is uniformly clear and unpolluted. Not all the beaches have local services yet, such as restaurants, though these, *churuatas* (bars built like Indian huts), sunshades and deckchairs are becoming more widespread. (Hire charges are about US$1.30 per item.) It is still possible, even in high season, to find practically deserted beaches.

On the eastern coast are Playa Guacuco, reached from La Asunción by a road through the Guayamurí reserve: a lot of surf, fairly shallow, palm trees, restaurant and parking lot; Parguito: long and open; Paraguachí: some *churuatas*; Playa del Agua: sea very rough for children, but fairly shallow, the fashionable part is at the far end (interesting range of vendors on the beach—quail's eggs, caipirinha cocktails, coconuts, *cachapa* maize buns; *Kiosko El Agua*, helpful, English spoken; *Posada Shangri-Lâ*, rec., and many other good seafood restaurants open till 1900); Manzanillo: water gets deep rather suddenly, fishing huts, fish sold on beach, new apartments under construction, Playa Escondida at the far end; Puerto Fermín/El Tirano (Lope de Aguirre, the infamous conquistador, landed here in 1561 on his flight from Peru), El Caserío handicrafts museum is nearby; Punta Cabo Blanco: attractive limestone outcrop; El Cardón: some development.

The coast road is interesting, with glimpses of the sea and beaches to one side, inland vistas on the other. There are a number of clifftop look-out points. The road improves radically beyond Manzanillo, winding from one beach to the next. Playa Puerto la Cruz adjoins Pedro González, another fashionable spot with a broad sweeping beach, running from a promontory (easy to climb) to scrub and brush that reach down almost to the water's edge (ask for Antonietta Luciani at *Restaurant Pedrogonzález*, she has an apartment to rent, US$40 per day, sleeps 6, well-equipped, rec. as is her restaurant). The next bay is accessible by scrambling over rocks (major building work under way in 1988). One advantage of Pedro González beach is that there is a large lagoon on the other side of the coast road, so it will be impossible to spoil the bay with speculative building. There are a lot of pelicans and sea urchins (harmless).

Further west is Juan Griego bay and town, famous for its sunsets (tours go to see them). The town is marred by a number of cheap clothing bazaars and the beach has little sand, but there are some hotels, *Restaurant Mi Isla* is rec., also the Lebanese restaurant on the beach. Playas Caribe and Galera are less spoilt. Fortín La Galera is worth a visit for the view of Juan Griego and Galera bays; children will breathlessly recite the epic siege fought here during the wars of independence.

South of Juan Griego, the road goes inland to San Juan, then to Punta de Piedra (a pleasant stretch through cultivated land and farms at regular intervals). Near San Juan is Fuentedueño park which has special walks. A branch goes northwest to La Guardia at the eastern end of La Restinga. The dyke of broken seashells stretches to the Peninsula de Macanao: on its right a spotlessly clean beach, on its left the lagoon. At the far end is a cluster of fishermen's huts with landing stages from which the launches make trips into the labyrinth of canals in the lagoon (US$3.50).

The Peninsula de Macanao is quite underdeveloped, although it is hardly an untouched paradise. Construction companies are extracting large amounts of ballast for the building boom in Porlamar, while urban waste is simply being dumped in large quantities along the roadside. Some of the beaches, however, are highly regarded: Manzanilla, Guayaconcito, Boca de Pozo, Macanao, Punta Arenas and El Manglillo.

The capital, **La Asunción** (population 8,000), is a few kilometres inland from Porlamar. It has several colonial buildings, a cathedral, and the fort of Santa Rosa, with a famous bottle dungeon (open Monday 0800-1500, other days 0800-1800). There is a museum in the Casa Capitular, and a local market, good for handicrafts. Nearby are the Cerro Matasiete historical site and the Félix Gómez look-out in the Sierra Copuy.

Between La Asunción and Porlamar are the Parque Francisco Fajardo, beside the Universidad de Oriente, and El Valle del Espíritu Santo. Here is the church of the Virgen del Valle, a picturesque building with twin towers, painted white and pink. The Madonna is richly dressed (one dress has pearls, the other diamonds); the adjoining museum opens at 1400, it displays costumes and presents for the Virgin, including the "milagro de la pierna de perla", a leg-shaped pearl. A pilgrimage is held in early September. Proper dress is requested to enter the church.

Throughout the island, the churches are attractive: fairly small, with baroque towers and adornments and, in many cases, painted pink.

Most of the hotels are at **Porlamar**, 11 kilometres from the airport and about 28 kilometres from Punta de Piedra, where most of the ferries dock. It has a magnificent cathedral and a picturesque market by the sea in the mornings. At Igualdad y Díaz is the Museo de Arte Francisco Narváez. The main, and most expensive, shopping area is Avenida Santiago Mariño; better bargains and a wider range of shops are to be found on Gómez and Guevara.

Ferries go to the Isla de Coche (11 kilometres by 6), which has over 5,000 inhabitants and one of the richest salt mines in the country. They also go, on hire only, to Isla de Cubagua, which is totally deserted, but you can visit the ruins of Nueva Cádiz (which have been excavated).

N.B. August and September are the vacation months when flights and hotels are fully booked.

Hotels at Porlamar *Hilton*, L (+10% tax), new; other top class establishments, *Concorde*, Bahía de El Morro, and *Bella Vista**, Av. Santiago, B-A, swimming pool, beach; *For You**, Patiño y Av. Santiago Mariño, C, rec.; *Caribbean*, Vía El Morro, D, pool, beach; *Vista Mar*, D, Urb. Bella Vista, on the way to El Morro, beach; *Agila Inn*, Narváez, D-E, clean, swimming pool, restaurant, rec.; *Dos Primos*, Calle Mariño entre Zamora y San Nicolás, E, clean and modern, rec.; on the Boulevard, *Brasilia*, San Nicolás, F, quiet, clean, nice new rooms at back; *Cardón*, E, opposite old airport at Playa Cardón, peaceful, good rooms and restaurant, swimming pool, diving and snorkelling trips organized; *María Luisa**, Vía El Morro, E, beach; *Chez David*, F, a/c, on beach, modern; *Evdama*, Bella Vista y Campos, E, helpful, also holiday flats with parking; opposite is *Imperial*, E, clean, comfortable, safe, rec., but restaurant only average; *Tamá*, E (more with a/c, hot water, TV, etc.), very nice, Vía El Morro, beach; *Marítimo*, E, Calle Maneiro Este 6; *Nueva Casa*, F with bathroom and fan, clean and friendly. *La Opera*, Igualdad y Fraternidad, E with bath (just off plaza); *Residencia Don Francisco*, Igualdad, 2 blocks from plaza, F with bath, quiet, good; *Hotel España*, Marino 6-35, F, hot shower, very clean, friendly, rec. Many others round Plaza Bolívar. Cheaper places on Maneiro, e.g. *Res. Javi*, G, very basic, but friendly; *Maneiro*, No. 13-17, F, poor value. For longer stays, Enrique and Elena Ganteaume rent apartments in Porlamar and La Asunción (Av. Principal 41, Urb. Santa Lucía, La Asunción, T 095-619622/618589, friendly, English spoken).

Restaurants *El Peñero*, *Vecchia Marina*, Vía El Morro, both good; *Bahía* bar-restaurant; good breakfast at *Panadería*, Av. 4 de Mayo y Fermín; *Café de París*, outside *Hotel For You*, croissants and enormous ice creams, a good meeting place; also *París Croissant* on Blvd. Santiago Mariño; *Los 3 Delfines*, Cedeño 26-9, seafood, rec.; *Guanaguanara*, pedestrian boulevard by sea, good food and service, reasonable prices. *La Isla*, Mariño y Cedeño, 8 fast food counters ranging from hamburgers to sausages from around the world. *La Cotorrera*, Av. Santiago Mariño, steaks; *El Mandarín*, next to *Hotel Real Flamingo*, Av. 4 de Mayo, excellent Peruvian and Chinese cuisine. *Jardín de Italo*, Calle Campos, French, classy, little atmosphere; *Centro Vegetariano Mariuxu*, Fermín 12-79, yellow and green house, no sign, lunch only, rec.

Entertainment discotheque for singles (the only good one), *Village Club*, Av. Santiago Mariño.

Shopping Besides all the duty-free shops, Del Bellorín, Cedeño, near Santiago Mariño, is good for handicrafts.

Exchange Banco Consolidado (American Express), Guevara y San Nicolás; banks generally slow with poor rates; best at Banco Construcción, Guevara or at *Hotel Contemporáneo* next to Banco Consolidado. *Casa de cambio* at Igualdad y Av. Santiago Mariño. Most shops accept credit cards.

Post Office Calle Arismendi. **Phones** CANTV, Bolívar, between Fajardo and Fraternidad.

Information Tourist Office, Miranda, near cathedral, free city map. An English-language newspaper, *Mira*, is published on the island; the editor/publisher acts also as an inexpensive tour guide; Av. Santiago Mariño, Ed. Carcaleo Suites, Apartamento 2-A, Porlamar (T 095-613351). The best map is available from Corpoven. Tourismo Guaiquerí, Santiago Mariño y Marcano, helpful, English spoken.

Car Hire An economic proposition for any number above one and probably the best way of getting around the island; several offices at the airport, Avis also at *Hotel Bella Vista*, others also on Av. Santiago Mariño. Scooters can also be hired for about US$6.50 a day from Diversion Rentals, Calle Amador Hernández, or Auto Camping Margarita (boats and bicycles also for rent). **N.B.** remember to keep an eye on the fuel guage; there are service stations in towns, but air conditioning is heavy on fuel.

Public Transport *Por Puestos* serve most of the island, leaving mainly from the corners of Plaza Bolívar in Porlamar. Fares: to Punta de Piedra, US$0.70; to La Asunción, US$0.20; to Pampatar, US$0.35; to La Restinga (from La Marina y Mariño), US$0.70, taxi US$6.50; El Agua, US$0.35; Juan Griego, US$0.35.

Communications There are regular flights from Caracas, which in April 1989 cost Bs 320 one way. If you purchase the ticket outside Venezuela, this will cost you something like US$75, but if you wait till you get to Caracas, change your dollars there and pay in local currency. The ticket will be the equivalent of less than US$10 (check exchange rates before going). Viasa, Av. 4 de Mayo, Edif. Banco Royal, Porlamar (T 32273, airport 691137); Avensa and Aeropostal are both on Calle Fajardo, Porlamar, opposite each other (Aeropostal hours 0800-1200, 1400-1800, T 617064, airport 691128; Avensa T 617111, airport 691021). Aeropostal to Port of Spain, Trinidad, US$90 (but US$40 surcharge if credit card or travellers' cheque used). (Airport: General Santiago Mariño, between Porlamar and Punta de Piedras; taxi US$5.50).

Ferry boats leave Puerto La Cruz for the island 4 times a day (4 hrs., cars, about US$6, passengers US$3.20 first class, breezy, or US$2.30 second, US$3.50 (2 times daily); check all ferry times in advance; book in high season, Calle 1600, return 1100 and 2200; the *Gran Cacique II* is a hydrofoil from Cumaná taking only 2 hrs., US$2.15 (0730 and 1600, return 1030 and 1730); the *Gran Cacique I* from Puerto La Cruz takes 2½ hrs., US$3.50 (2 times daily); check all ferry times in advance; book in high season, Calle Marcano, Porlamar, T 616780. Extensive baggage checks when leaving for the mainland. Several bus companies in Caracas sell through tickets (US$6) from Caracas to Porlamar, arriving about midday. By car from Caracas, it takes about 4 hrs., but will be reduced to 2½ when the Sucre motorway is opened.

A ferry sails from Mercado Viejo to Chacopata on the mainland at 1000 and 1200, US$1.20, also takes cars.

The road from Cumaná goes on to the port of *Carúpano,* on the Pariá Peninsula. The coastal route from Cumaná to Carúpano is beautiful, first passing the Gulf of Cariaco, then crossing to the shores of the Caribbean. Carúpano is famous throughout Venezuela for its pre-Lenten Carnival celebrations, and becomes a focus for tourists at that time. Population 80,000; airport.

Hotels *San Francisco*, F, Av. Juncal 87A (try the mussels); *Bologna*, F, a/c, owner speaks German, rec.; *El Yunque*, E, Av. Perimetral, beach; *Lilma*, E, Av. Independencia 161, good restaurant; *Victoria**, E, Av. Perimetral, beach, swimming pool, restaurant.

Bus to Caracas, Responsable de Venezuela, US$3.90, 8 hrs; Cumaná, US$1.

On the coastal drive W of Carúpano are Cereza, famed for its basket-making, and Guaca, where clams packed with peppers are sold. 10 km. E of Carúpano is the fishing village of El Morro de Puerto Santo, in itself not very interesting but in a beautiful setting.

The road continues East for 135 km. to **Güiria**. En route is Irapa, with hotel and restaurant (G with bath, clean). Güiria can also be reached from Maturín by bus, US$2.60, 6 hrs. (Also flights from Isla de Margarita or Tucupita each morning, US$5.50, best booked in advance). Güiria is very hot and dress is more casual than is common elsewhere. (*Hotel Gran Puerto*, E with bath and a/c, best restaurant in town; *Hotel Plaza*, rec.; *Hotel Nayade*, F. The Librería, on Bolívar opposite, is helpful with travel information, including boats to Trinidad. There are a couple of small places to eat on the main square: *Heladería Güiria* or *Exprex*, rec.) In one of the coves E of Güiria (exactly which one is not known) Spaniards of Columbus' crew made the first recorded European landing on the continent on August 5, 1498, and took formal possession the following day.

A good excursion from Güiria is to **Macuro**, a village of 1,000 people on the tip of the Paria Peninsula. It is accessible only by boat, being surrounded on its landward sides by jungle. Boats leave Güiria daily at 1000 (US$2.10, take protection against sun), returning 0530, taking 1½-2 hrs., passing dense jungle which reaches down to the sea, and deserted, palm-fringed beaches. Macuro is friendly, with a good beach, a few understocked shops, one restaurant, but no hotel (easy to camp or sling your hammock somewhere). Eduardo (who speaks English, French and German) is planning to open a museum of the history of the area; he is knowledgeable about trips into the jungle. Boats may be hired to explore the coast and to go to Trinidad. (Moshe Pinsly, Israel).

You can visit the Orinoco delta from Güiria; there are occasional motor boats trading between Güiria and **Pedernales** in the delta. The trip takes about 5 hrs., check for boats at the harbour or the *Hotel Fortuna* (not always open). Pedernales is a small village only a few km. from the south-western point of Trinidad. It is only accessible by boat from Güiria (ask for Andrecito, who lives on N side of small plaza nearest harbour entrance—boats are very hard to find), or from Tucupita (much easier—**page 922**), or boats from Trinidad costing about US$30-60, the more official, the more expensive. Sisiliano Bottini is a shipping agent. (Some cheap boats carry contraband and unless you avoid Trinidadian or Venezuelan immigration controls you will find this method both difficult and very risky: the Trinidadian authorities are reluctant to let even legal boats in for fear of drug smuggling.) Only one hotel, *Gran Arturo*, F, very basic, bar and restaurant, take your own hammock. For a shower, ask Jesús, who runs a fish-freezing business. Only Indians live in the northern part of the village. Boat trip to Tucupita rec. as the boat stops in some of the Indian villages, where you can buy the best hammocks (*chinchorros*) and some beautiful carved animal figures made of balsa wood (**see also page 922**).

From Puerto La Cruz a toll road goes inland, skirting Barcelona. At Km. 52 (where there is a restaurant) a road forks left to (near) Santa Bárbara (airport) and goes on to Jusepín, Quiriquire, and Caripito, all Lagovén oil camps.

In Santa Bárbara can be bought the native *chinchorros*, hammocks made by hand of woven *moriche* palm leaves, decorated with coloured yarn. They can also be found in Tucupita (**see page 922**). They "give" when you lie on them and do not absorb moisture when used on the beach. Very good for camping.

Maturín, capital of Monagas State, an important commercial centre, is 16 km. beyond Jusepín. Population 152,000.

Hotels *El Cacique*, D, Av. Bolívar; *Pensión El Nacional* and *Latino*, both F, are rec. as simple and clean. *Friuli*, F, Carrera 9 with Calle 30; *Trinidad*, F, clean, English speaking, rec.; *Europa*, F, rec. as being as good as the *Trinidad* but with larger rooms; *Astrolobia*, F, good food, near bus station; *Tamanaco*, F, is reasonable; *Mallorca*, F, Calle Mariño, reasonable with good food; *Comercio*, F with bath, not too clean, English spoken, central; *Asturias*, F, with cheap restaurant which serves excellent rice pudding. All hotel rooms have private bathroom and a/c.

Exchange Banco Consolidado (American Express), Av.Raúl Leoni, Edif. D'Amico.

Transport Air services to Caracas (US$20), and to Ciudad Bolívar (Aeropostal, US$12, 20 mins.). Buses leave three times a day for Caracas from the central bus terminal, 2030, 2200 and 2245 hrs. (US$3.60, 8 hrs.); buses for Ciudad Guayana (US$3.60) and El Dorado leave from the terminus near the airport. To Puerto La Cruz or Barcelona, about US$1.65; *por puestos*, US$3.30. Bus only to Ciudad Bolívar, US$2.25. Colectivos Nos. 1, 5 and 6 to and from the airport (US$0.15) with a five-minute walk from the road. Bus US$0.07. Taxis from the Reponsable de Venezuela office will try to charge much more. The bus leaves from the main road outside the airport when going into town.
There are no exchange facilities in the airport except at the Aeropostal desk or the bar in the departure lounge, and they give a very bad rate.

Just beyond Jusepín an unpaved 32-km. road, left, joins the Maturín-Cumaná road (212 km., all paved but twisty; beautiful tropical mountain scenery; accommodation at Cumanacoa, 56 km.

before Cumaná, 2 hotels—E and F). At San Francisco on this road is a branch road running 22½ km. NE to *Caripe*, a small town set in a mountain valley. There is also a paved road between Carúpano and Caripe via Santa Cruz and Santa María, 2 hrs. 12 km. from Caripe is the remarkable *Cueva del Guácharo* National Monument; open 0700-1700 hrs., entrance US$0.25. Also a caving museum, US$0.15, with a good range of publications for sale; *Hotel Guácgaro* nearby. A bus from Cumaná to Caripe - 0730, returns 1300—takes 4 hrs. and costs US$1.70, or take the *por puesto*, 2 hrs., US$3.40; from Maturín, take a *por puesto* from the bus terminal to Caripe, US$2.50, 2 hrs., and ask the driver to carry on to the Cave, only US$0.05 more; if staying in Caripe, take the Caracas bus at 0800 (or at 1800 to see the birds leaving the cave) at *San Francisco Hotel* to the Cave for nothing. The cave was discovered by Humboldt, and has since been penetrated 10½ km. along a small, crystal-clear stream. First come the caves in which live about 30,000 *guácharos* (oil birds) with an in-built radar system for sightless flight. Their presence supports a variety of wildlife in the cave: blind mice, fish and crabs in the stream, yellow-green plants, crickets, ants, etc. For two hours at dusk (about 1900) the birds pour out of the cave's mouth, continously making the clicking sounds of their echo-location system, coming back at dawn with their crops full of the oily fruit of certain local palms. Through a very narrow entrance is the *Cueva del Silencio* (Cave of Silence), where you can hear a pin drop. About 2 km. in is the *Pozo del Viento* (Well of the Wind). No backpacks, torches (flashlights), cameras, etc. allowed in the caves (but tape recorders are permitted). Guides are compulsory (US$0.10); permits and special equipment are needed to go further than 1½ km. into the caves. The streams are now bridged, but there is still quite a lot of water around; wear old clothes, stout shoes and be prepared to take off your shoes and socks. In the wet season it is very slippery with mud and guano (bird droppings); tours into the cave may be shortened. Opposite the road is a path to a 25-metre waterfall, about 30 minutes' walk, guides available (but not necessary); orange and other fruit trees along the way. (Hotels at Caripe: *Samán**, Enrique Charner 29, E, excellent value and atmosphere, restaurant; *Caripe*, F, restaurant; *San Francisco*, F with bath, clean, restaurant; *Las Chaimas*, F, T 51141. New hotel *Venezia*, E, with excellent *Coba Longa* restaurant, owner speaks English. *Humboldt Cabañas*, between Teresén and Caripe, good, clean, sleep 4 for C, full cooking facilities, little hot water.) There is a huge *samán* tree in purple glory when the orchids which cover it bloom in May.

Continuing straight on from Km. 52, the road passes W of **Anaco** (*Motel Bowling Anaco*, E; *Motel Canaima*, E; *Internacional*, E). It has an airport, is an important centre for oil-well service contracting companies. Beyond Anaco a branch road leads to the oilfields of San Joaquín and San Roque.

The main road passes near Cantaura, a market town, and goes on to **El Tigre** (hotels include *Internacional Gran Hotel*, D, swimming pool, night club; *Milelvi*, F with bath, good, clean, parking in courtyard; and *Santa Cruz*, F; nearby Chilean restaurant serves excellent Chilean food and salads), and El Tigrito (*Hotel Rancho Grande*, D); two important trading centres within 20 km. of one another.

About 8 km. along the road is San Tomé (airport), the eastern headquarters of Menevén, the former Mene Grande oil company.

From El Tigre a good asphalt road leads off to Caracas; the one we are following leads, straight and flat, 120 km. over the *llanos* to the Angostura bridge over the Orinoco to Ciudad Bolívar, 282 km. from Puerto La Cruz.

THE GUAYANA HIGHLANDS (7)

These uplands, lying S of the Orinoco River, constitute half of Venezuela. They rise, in rounded forested hills and narrow valleys, to flat topped tablelands on the borders of Brazil. These lands are very sparsely populated; but the savannas (interspersed with semi-deciduous forest), would make better cattle country than the *llanos*. So far, communications have been the main difficulty, but a road has now been opened to Santa Elena de Uairen on the Brazilian frontier (**see page 924**). This road can be followed to Manaus, and thence, by a suitable vehicle, to Brasília and southern Brazil. The area is Venezuela's largest gold and diamond source, but its immense reserves of iron ore, manganese and bauxite are of far greater economic importance.

Ciudad Bolívar, on the S bank of the Orinoco, is 400 km. from its delta and 640 by road from Caracas. Average temperature 29°C, but a cool and refreshing breeze usually springs up in the evening. It still has much colonial building but is changing rapidly. Population 115,000. It stands by the narrows of the Orinoco, with its Cathedral, on a small hill, and the Zanuro hill fort (1902), on another hill in the centre, dominating the city.

The narrows, not more than 300 metres wide, gave the town its old name of

Angostura. It was here that Bolívar came after defeat to reorganize his forces, and the British Legionnaires joined him; it was at Angostura that he was declared President of that Gran Colombia which he had yet to build, and which was to fragment before his death. When the town was still known as Angostura a physician invented the famous bitters there in 1824; the factory moved to Port of Spain in 1875.

There is a floating pontoon dock where ocean-going cargo boats can discharge, but the harbour is now naval. A walk along the river bank is rec. at dusk when the sun is setting. Launches take passengers across the river, but there are no other passenger boat services.

You can buy baskets and items made by the Indians. It is also the best place in Venezuela for anything made of gold. There are beautiful hand-made charms for charm bracelets and, most typical of all, the Venezuelan orchid, made by hand, of red, yellow and green gold. The gold orchid pin or earrings, or a gold nugget (known as *cochano*), are the best souvenirs of Venezuela. There are many jewellers on Pasaje Guayana, which runs off Paseo Orinoco. Gold shops also in Pasaje Gran Hotel Bolívar: for nuggets, Irma Lapeña has the most beautiful and the most expensive—bargain for a good price. A feature is the netting of *sapoara*, a delicious fish 30 to 35 cm. long which pours from the inlets when the river begins to swell in late June at the start of the rainy season and swims up stream to spawn. During its short season this is the favourite dish of the town.

Hotels   *Don Salo**, Av. Bolívar, nr. Av. Táchira, D, very good apart from a disappointing restaurant; difficult to find, though quite near the airport; *Laja Real **, opp. airport, D, swimming pool open to non-residents, nice, *Terraza* café; *Canaima*, Av. Upata (far from centre), E, bath, a/c, clean, noisy; *La Cumbre*, Av. 5 de Julio, good view of town but rather run down, E, without food; *Gran Hotel Bolívar**, Paseo Orinoco, E, a/c, comfortable, good restaurant; *Hotel del Sur*, Plaza las Banderas, T 206241, E, clean, a/c, rec.; *Mimo*, E, on the corner of Paseo Orinoco and Calle Amazonas, not rec. except for superb views of the river, suspension bridge and sunsets; *Residencias Delicias*, Venezuela, F, clean, good value; *Italia*, Paseo Orinoco, F, a/c and bath, a few single rooms with fan, no bath, food excellent, try *dulce de merey* for dessert; *Unión*, Calle Urica, nr. *Italia*, F with a/c (cheaper with fan), clean, safe, good value; *Pensión Panamericana*, Calle Rocía 6, F, shower, a/c, safe, clean, laundry facilities, good restaurant; *Pensión Boyacá*, Calle Babilonia, F, central, basic, friendly, a bit grubby, one shower for all, hourly rentals; *Brasilia*, D, ¾ km. from bus terminal; *Terminal y Adriana*, E, Av. Moreno de Mendoza, near bus terminal, friendly. It is often difficult to find rooms in hotels here. For the cheaper hotels, take a red bus from the airport to Paseo Orinoco; at the eastern end there are many to choose from.

Restaurants   *Alfonso*, Av. Maracay; *Almanola*, Av. Cumaná; *La Cabaña*, Paseo Meneses; *Las Cibeles*, Paseo Orinoco; *La Cumbre*, Av. 5 de Julio; *La Paragua*, Av. La Mariquita; *Mirador*, prettily situated on the Orinoco, relaxed atmosphere, good at the expensive end of the menu; *La Playa*, Paseo Orinoco 84, fish; *Savoy*, Venezuela y Dalla Acosta, good value breakfast and lunch; good restaurant at Venezuela y Igualdad. Chinese restaurant on Av. Upata, opp. *Hotel Canaima*, good, open late. Cheap food at the market at the east end of Paseo Orinoco, need to bargain.

Museum   The Museo Soto, Av. Germania, on the outskirts of the town has works by Venezuela's José Rafael Soto and other artists, open Tues.-Sun. 1000-1800, good. Museum at Casa del Correo del Orinoco, Paseo Orinoco y Carabobo, modern art and some exhibits of history of the city, and a fat precolumbian goddess, including the printing press of the newspaper which spread the cause of independence; Tues. Sat. 0900-1200, 1500-1800, Sun. 0900-1200. Has free town map (poor) and booklet on Ciudad Bolívar.

Taxis   Under US$1 to virtually anywhere in town.

Exchange   Banco Consolidado (American Express), Edif. Pinemar, Av. Andrés Bello, Centro Comercial Canaima; Banco Royal Venezolano (Calle Orinoco 38) and Banco Mercantil y Agrícola (Av. Jesús Soto); most will change dollars cash or travellers' cheques. Banco Unión or Filanbanco handle Visa transactions.

Post Offices   Av. Táchira, 15 mins' walk from centre.

Tourist Offices   On Calle Bolívar, at eastern foot of the hill in old town; provides free map of state and city. The small offices at the airport and the bus station in particular are very friendly and helpful. You will need a map: the town has a rather confusing layout.

Airport   Served by Avensa, and Aeropostal which flies 4 times a week to Sta. Elena de Uairen for connections to Manaus and Brazil. Also flights to Tucupita. Minibuses and buses marked Terminal to town centre. Taxi to Paseo Orinoco US$1.40. Three flights daily to Caracas (US$19). Charter airline, Utaca, is rec.; ask for Jorge, and verify all prices.

Buses   To get to the bus station take a bus marked Terminal going W along the Paseo Orinoco.

Several daily to Caracas 8 hrs., US$4.20-4.80, and to the coast: to Puerto La Cruz, US$1.80, 4½ hrs.; to Cumaná, US$1.80; Tumeremo US$2.80; Tumeremo bus through to El Dorado US$3, 3 daily. To Santa Elena de Uairen direct with Línea Orinoco, Transportes Mundial or Expreso Rápidos de Güiria leave at 0500 and 0600, spectacular views of the Gran Sabana at sunset (book in advance), US$8, 14 hours. To Ciudad Guayana every 30 mins. from 0700 by Expresos Guayanera, US$0.80, 1½ hrs., *por puesto*, US$2, 1½ hrs. Terminal at junction of Av. República and Av. Sucre. Bus to Caicara, 7½ hrs., including 2 ferry crossings.

For an excursion to see gold mining at Río Claro, take a bus to Guri and ask to be set down at the gate to Río Claro. Minibuses run to the mines, where the people are very friendly and will take visitors by boat to the workings. Return with workers going to Ciudad Bolívar.

73 km. E of Ciudad Bolívar is La Encrucijada (junction). To the left is the freeway to Ciudad Guayana (37 km.); straight on is the road to Upata via the Paso Carnachi (Caroní ferry); to the right is the road to Ciudad Piar (97 km.) and the iron ore mountain (Cerro Bolívar—cheaper to visit from Ciudad Bolívar than from Ciudad Guayana). Following this route through typical Guayana landscape you reach the village of La Paragua (107 km.) on a good, paved road. If you like adventure and untouched nature, take two ferries crossing the Río Paragua, towards El Paúl (4-wheel drive vehicles Dec.-May). There is usually transport available. From El Paúl you can get a ride towards the nearest river to Canaima, which you can cross on a *curiara* (passengers only), and from there hike about 15 km. to Canaima. Alternatively, from La Encrucijada, on the right hand road (in the direction of La Paragua) turn left after 8 km., past enormous black rocks, on to an almost hidden trail. After a further 2 km. is the Cueva del Elefante, where precolumbian relics were found and rock paintings can be seen. Following the track (10 km.) one comes to Playa Blanca on the Río Caroní, where miners dive for gold and diamonds. Mario Venarusso does boat trips.

Angel Falls, the highest fall in the world (979 metres) and **Canaima,** a nearby tourist lodge and hotel, are best reached from Caracas or from Ciudad Bolívar. Avensa airline has inclusive charges for tours which leave twice daily from Maiquetía airport (first at 0710). The flights stop at Ciudad Bolívar, which can be the starting point for the trip. A Boeing 727 takes passengers from there to Canaima arriving in the morning, and will fly over the Angel Falls before landing, weather permitting. Trips to the falls may have to be booked weeks in advance in the holiday season. From Caracas the return flight, two nights' accommodation, six meals and a free boat trip around the lagoon costs about US$80; from Ciudad Bolívar the return flight with two nights' accommodation is about US$70 (US$50 for one night and 3 meals). During the rainy season at least two nights are needed to be sure of taking the flight over the falls as they are frequently obscured by cloud. All arrangements are made through Avensa, direct (best in Caracas) or through travel agencies. You cannot board the flight without a voucher from Avensa for at least one night's accommodation at Canaima; obtaining refunds is very difficult if you do not want to stay at the camp (flight alone from Caracas, US$30, from Ciudad Bolívar US$14). One-night trips are possible, as are longer stays (open flights can be booked from Ciudad Bolívar). Reductions are available for parties. At Canaima there are expensive gift shops, but no alternative accommodation or restaurant. Camping is possible with a permit from Inparques in Caracas (there is a representative at Canaima).
   At Ciudad Bolívar airport Aerotaxis Tanca (unreliable) arranges Cessna flights for 3 persons for a whole day at Angel Falls and Canaima, also Aerobol for 5 people; the one-day excursion includes lunch at Canaima, a boat tour of the lagoon and the Falls. The return flight is usually after lunch (US$100 all in). Canaima is on the edge of a tannin-stained lagoon with soft beige beaches; the Río Carrao tumbles over seven splendid falls into the lagoon below. The country is very beautiful. Lodging is in quite comfortable cabins; each is complete with shower and toilet; there are no hardships whatsoever. If travelling independently, one night's accommodation with 3 meals costs about US$25; the meals are basic, self-service, no choice. You could save yourself some money by taking food with you. Drinks are also expensive.
   There are various excursions from Canaima, which are all worthwhile (and usually crowded): upriver to the Angel Falls costs up to US$240; 5 operators organize this trip at short notice, including Isidoro Sandoval of Excursiones Churun-Vena S.R.L. (rec., he has a video of a Japanese expedition which climbed the Falls in 1980), and "Jungle Rudy", the most expensive (he has his own hotel, US$35 with 3 meals, at Campamento Ucaima, just above the Hacha Falls, 2 hrs. walk from Canaima). All curiaras (dug-outs) must have 2 motors, by law, and carry first aid, life jackets, etc. Take wet weather gear, mosquito net for hammock and insect repellant. Trips by boat to the Falls only go June-November, leaving usually in the afternoon, staying the first night at Isla Orquídea, continuing to the Falls next day. Depending on the river, the trip takes on average 3 days (best to go Mon.-Wed. as everything is fully booked at weekends). You can also make walking expeditions into the jungle to Indian villages with a guide (e.g. Tomás), but bargain hard on the price. Recommended Indian guide is Matherson, ask for him at the camp. A highly recommended flight by Cessna 5-seater costs US$45 p.p., takes 45 mins. and does some circuits over and alongside the falls (better than organized flights is to go to the airstrip and ask around the pilots waiting there on business if they will fly over the Falls for the same price as a tour). Other excursions to Mayupa (US$10, half day), to Yuri Falls (US$10, half day); to Isla Orquídea (US$20, full day, good). The flat-topped Auyan-Tepuy, from which spring the Angel Falls, was the setting for W. H. Hudson's *Green Mansions*. The sheer rock face of the Falls, named after Jimmy Angel,

the US airman (**see page 895**) who discovered them in 1937, was climbed in 1971 by three Americans and an Englishman, David Nott, who recounted the ten-day adventure in his book *Angels Four* (Prentice-Hall).

Auyan-Tepuy can also be reached by a 2-3-hr. hike from the village of *Kamarata*, reached only by air from Ciudad Bolívar (with Aeropostal or Utaca, 2½ hrs., book at least a week ahead in Ciudad Bolívar or Caracas, flights 4 times a week). In the dry season you can take a 3-4 day excursion to Kamarata from Canaima by boat. A friendly village with no hotels or restaurants; either camp (mosquito nets necessary) or, when it is not in session, sling your hammock in the mission school. It may also be possible to use the school's kitchen if you have no stove, otherwise ask around for who may sell you dinner. Several good day-long hiking trips; guides to Auyan-Tepuy, waterfalls and the Cuevas de Kavac, US$10.

In Caracas contact *Hotel Tamanaco*, T 914555, or Caribex Tours, T 728271/2, for trips to Falls. Italcambio, T 820611, organizes camping trips up the River Paragua for parties of four at a cost of US$220 for three days, or US$325 four days. The travel agency at the *Caracas Hilton* has also been recommended; also Edgar Belstar, Caracas T 978 4245, 978 0813 or at home 978 1628, friendly. Tours can usually be booked on the spot, with no reservation problems.

Warning   Credit cards are not accepted by the people who take you on excursions, except on some of the flights. Travellers' cheques can be cashed, but at a poor rate.

Another Warning   Necklaces of poisonous red and black seeds (rosary peas) are on sale here.

In an area rich in natural resources 105 km. down-river from Ciudad Bolívar an entirely new metropolis, known as *Ciudad Guayana,* is still being built. It is forging into one the four separate centres of San Félix, Palúa, Puerto Ordaz and Matanzas. Its population is already approaching half of a planned million, on the south bank of the Orinoco and both sides of the Caroní river before it spills into the Orinoco. The mixing of the rivers' waters is like "pouring cream into coffee". East of the Caroní are the commercial port of *San Félix* (extensive work in progress to make a riverside walk and park) and the Palúa iron-ore terminal of the railway from El Pao. Crossing the Caroní by the 470-metre concrete bridge we come to *Puerto Ordaz* (airport), the iron-ore loading port connected by rail with the famous Cerro Bolívar open-cast iron mine (see below). The iron-tinted waterfall, which looks like a beerfall, in the pretty Parque Cachamay is worth a visit. To the west are the government-owned Siderúrgica del Orinoco whose production is being raised to 4.8m tonnes of steel a year, and an aluminium plant, Venalum. Just up the Caroní is the Macagua hydroelectric plant (with a second phase under construction); there are some truly beautiful cataracts called Salto Llovizna as you enter the grounds (known as Parque La Llovizna, reached by boat from *Hotel Intercontinental Guayana*, or by bus from San Félix most of the way, then hitch). Higher up the river is the massive Guri dam and hydroelectric undertaking, **see page 926**. (The trip to Guri takes 90 minutes by taxi; the plant is open daily 0900-1030, 1415-1515, for a conducted tour phone Edelca, Puerto Ordaz 20-80-66 (Relaciones Institucionales del Guri); the area gets very full during holidays, Easter or carnival. *Por puesto* from Ciudad Bolívar, Route 70, US$10 one way; for return, ask at Alcabala Río Claro (gatehouse) if they can get you a free lift.) About 3 km. away, across bare savanna, is an area reserved for smaller industries. The Casa Machupicchu, Calle Guasipati, sells a city map for US$0.70.

Hotels   *Intercontinental Guayana**, Parque Punta Vista, A, all facilities, swimming pool, food and service poor; *Dos Ríos*, México esq. Ecuador, E, shower, a/c, clean, good value, swimming pool; *El Rasil*, C, Centro Cívico, with all comforts, swimming pool, overpriced, rooms good but food and service poor; *Tepuy**, E, a/c, Carrera Upata, Edif. Arichuna; *La Guayana**, F, Av. Las Américas, clean, a/c, no hot water; *Residencias Puerto Ordaz*, Vía Caracas, E with bath; *Jardín*, F, Italian run, friendly, fan, will store luggage, not too safe. Many cheaper hotels in San Félix, the historical town, have been removed or closed down in the restoration works. Only *Aguila* (D) and *Yoli* (F, no hot water, otherwise OK) in San Félix have decent restaurants. It is difficult to find hotels because of the influx of workers, who live in them for lack of other housing.

Restaurants   In Puerto Ordaz: *Hotel Guayana Restaurant*, under different management from hotel, good service but expensive; near *Hotel Guayana* are *Casa del Roti*, Calle Tumeremo, good, inexpensive, *Siria-Lebanon*, Calle Ciudad Piar, Arab food, *Archie's Soda Fountain*, Tumeremo below *Casa del Roti*, and beyond is a Chinese restaurant; the market at the intersection of Tumeremo and Guasipati has many cheap food stalls; two *areperías* on Vía Las Américas above

Hotel Guayana, and reasonable restaurants at corners of Las Américas with Calle Upata and Calle El Palmar, further up the hill. More expensive on Las Américas is *Rincón Bavaria* (German); two steak restaurants on Calle La Urbana (one next to cinema is best); Italian restaurants: *Paolo's*, Calle Guasipati, fair, *Romanino's*, Calle Ciudad Piar, good, family place, and, opposite but cheaper and less good, *Mario's*; *The Key Club*, via Caracas (opp. Banco Royal), good seafood, expensive; good seafood also at *Porrua*, but further from centre.

Car Hire   Hertz, Puerto Ordaz, rents 4-wheel drive vehicles, US$25 a day with unlimited mileage. This is the best way to visit the Cerro Bolívar mine and Guri dam.

Exchange   Banco Consolidado (American Express), Calle Urbana, Edif. Don Andrés, Banco Royal Venezolano and Banco Provincial at Puerto Ordaz. Banco Mercantil. Very difficult to change travellers' cheques. Hotels give poor rates.

Brazilian Consulate   Av. Las Américas, nr. CANTV, can issue visas but there is delay and a charge for authorisation.

Buses   Bus station at San Félix (can be a dangerous place). Bus from Ciudad Guayana to Santa Elena de Uairen, US$8.50 with Líneas Orinoco, 0700 at least 12 hrs., via El Callao, Tumeremo (US$2.75, 5 hrs.), El Dorado and Km. 88; book a day in advance. *Por puesto* to Ciudad Bolívar US$2 (bus US$0.80); to Maturín US$3.30, 3 hrs., 0800 every day (bus US$1.30); to Caracas, US$4.85, 10½ hrs. Minibuses in town are fast, frequent and cheap; fare San Félix-Puerto Ordaz, US$0.15-0.25; buses run until about 2100.

Air Transport   Airport, with daily flights to Caracas (US$23), walk 600 metres to main road for buses to San Félix or Puerto Ordaz; taxi to centre or bus station, US$3.75.

Excursions   To Cerro Bolívar mine, take a *por puesto* (US$3.75) or hitchhike to Ciudad Piar, or go with guided tour organized by Ferrominera Orinoco at their headquarters building in Ciudad Guayana. Tours are free, and leave at 0930 and 1400. To visit industries in the area, ask at the Corporación Venezolana de Guayana, Departmento de Relaciones Públicas.

From San Félix or Puerto Ordaz go down the Orinoco to Los Castillos (either by *por puesto*, 1 hr., US$1, or by bus to Aceiles, US$0.25, ask to be let off where pick-up goes to Los Castillos 0700, 1130, 1530, returns 0830, 1300 and 1700, US$0.60; difficult to get there by boat). It is possible to camp on the beach. Candes Tours run an excursion from Puerto Ordaz but only if there are four people. There are two old forts here: one on a huge rock near the water, the other on top of a hill and both in good condition. A tiny village lies at their feet. It is said to have been here that Sir Walter Raleigh's son was killed in battle while searching for El Dorado. From Los Barrancos, on the N bank of the Orinoco, opposite San Félix, *curiaras* and other boats can be taken to the delta; settle prices before setting out, take hammock, mosquito net and repellant, and canned food (in the rainy season, take a raincoat).

A most interesting side trip can be made to **Tucupita**, a river town in the Orinoco delta. Transport from Ciudad Guayana is available, and the roads are asphalted. Flights are also available from Caracas, Ciudad Bolívar, Porlamar and Güiria with Aeropostal. Taxi from airport to village US$3. *Por puesto* from Maturín or Ciudad Guayana about US$4, 2-3 hrs. Tucupita-Caracas by bus, 10 hrs., 2000, US$4.80; for Puerto La Cruz at 1530, US$3.30, 6 hrs.

Hotels   *Gran Hotel Amacuro*, F, a/c, Calle Bolívar 23; *Delta*, F, a/c, Calle Pativilca 28; Victoria, near Cathedral, F with a/c, cheaper with fan, reasonable; and a few cheaper *hospedajes*. *Pequeña Venezia* campsite, 20 km. from Tucupita, good, with showers; will arrange river trips. Also 1 star hotel and restaurant beside river. Restaurant: *Tucupita*, Calle Bolívar, good.

For a 3-4 day trip to see the delta, its fauna and the Indians, boats may be arranged by asking for help at the information office near Plaza Bolívar, or contact Juan Carrión (all the taxi drivers know him, but he is very expensive), but they are not easy to come by and are expensive except for large groups. The only recognized tours of the delta are run by Delta Tours, about which poor reports received, US$20 p.p. (it is possible to negotiate). Some boat owners may negotiate a price, about US$30 per day minimum. Delta trips can be arranged in Puerto Ordaz at Happy Tours, *Hotel Intercontinental*, T (086) 223257/227748, up-market but good. For shorter excursions by boat, ask at gas station (*bomba*) by the river. Excursions often only travel on the main river, not in the *caños* where wildlife can be seen. To avoid disappointment, check all details before committing yourself. Alternatively, take a *por puesto* from Plaza Bolívar to the village of La Horqueta (US$0.40), where it is easier to get a boat and where there are many Indians. Be warned, if the river level rises after a downpour, arrangements may be cancelled. Take enough food for yourselves, the guide and the Indians, and plenty of water. Hammocks and mosquito repellants are essential. If you go to a *ranchería* take gifts such as fresh fruit, needles, thread, knives and only give them individually. You can buy hammocks and local handicrafts; always ask permission to take photographs. The climate is very humid and Tucupita often suffers from flooding and subsequent loss of electricity. The cafés on the edge of the plaza are rec. and are said to be "especially interesting at night, without electricity, with your feet virtually awash in the Orinoco."

An interesting dead-end village is **Barrancas** on the Orinoco, reached by road from Tucupita, 63 km. (*por puesto* to San Félix US$3.30) or from Maturín. *Hospedaje El Carmen*, F, Calle Carabobo 20, shower, clean, no fan. From Barrancas you can take a boat to Curiapo (Indian village) and Amacuro (near Guyana border), check at the harbour. It is also possible to go to Georgetown from here; ask for boats to Amacuro and then on to Mabaruma (only for the adventurous) or check with the lady at the *librería* on the river at the bottom of the village, she is from Georgetown and travels there occasionally.

SOUTH TO BRAZIL (8)

Travelling South from Ciudad Guayana to the Brazilian border is becoming an increasingly popular excursion for Venezuelan tourists, as well as for overland travellers heading for Manaus and the Amazon. It is no longer an arduous trip; the road to the border at Santa Elena de Uairen is now paved, with all bridges in place. Four-wheel drive is only necessary if one wanders off the main road, particularly in the rainy season. Beyond Tumeremo, only 83 octane gasoline is available; it is forbidden to travel beyond Km. 88 or off the main road without a spare 20 litres of gasoline (spare tanks are available there, but better and cheaper to get one earlier); it is also advisable to carry extra water and plenty of food. There are police checks at the Río Cuyuní and at Km. 126; all driving permits, car registration papers, and identification must be shown.

South from Ciudad Guayana the road goes through Upata (Hotels: *Andrea**, E, credit cards accepted, restaurant, good; *Yocoima, Comercio, Adriático*, F, good and *La Palma*, which also has a restaurant), El Callao (Hotels: *Italia* and *Ritz*, both F, on Calle Ricaurte), which has a good carnival, and is a good place to buy gold nuggets (8 km. away are the underground goldmines of El Perú).

On another 40 km. is **Tumeremo** (Hotels: *Leocar*, 3 blocks from plaza, F, fair, with shower and toilet, fan, restaurant rec.; *Central*, near plaza, good (but may be "full", or again later), bakery and snackbar, clean, F; *Florida*, E, not too good; restaurant *El Esturión*, good, friendly, Calle El Dorado, Edificio Bolívar). There is a chronic water shortage, check when it is available in your hotel. Tumeremo is recommended as the best place to buy provisions, there is Banco de la Unión (which does not change money), and gasoline (all grades) at a normal price (better than El Dorado). 5 km. from Tumeremo towards the Fuerte Tarabay is the beautiful artificial lake of San Pedro with an attractive campsite. From Tumeremo you can go to the Isla Anacoco, on the River Venamo which forms the border with Guyana. A paved road runs through the jungle to San Martín (one military and one police post en route), where you can arrange a visit to the island. Much English spoken in San Martín; in a house opposite the water tank are some stuffed animals. By bus to Santa Elena, US$5.20 (8-10 hrs., Líneas Orinoco, 1100, 2 blocks from plaza near *Leocar*); bus to Ciudad Bolívar, US$3.25, 6 a day, 6½ hrs or *por puesto* (via San Félix and Puerto Ordaz, 5 hrs, US$2.75); *por puesto* to San Félix (Ciudad Guayana), US$4.50; bus Tumeremo-Caracas, US$5.

285 km. from Ciudad Guayana and 108 km. from Tumeremo is **El Dorado,** where stands the regional prison made famous by Papillon's stay there (take a taxi, can't get in without a car, US$5 for an hour, arrange price with official, not driver). Exchange at El Dorado is possible with the gold buyer on the main street; cash only, poor rates. There is a gas station, open 0800-1900 daily. Bus from Caracas to El Dorado, Expresos del Oriente, at 1830 daily, US$5.60, 14½ hrs., return at 1400 (925 km.). The Orinoco bus line connects with Ciudad Bolívar (6 hrs.) and Santa Elena, as does Transmundial (better buses).

Hotels *Cervino*, next to bus stop, E, fan, clean; *El Dorado*, next to gas station, E, fair; *San Agostino*, main plaza; *Hospedaje Portugal*, F, only six rooms, the Portuguese owner also runs the store next door. *Campamento Turístico*, run by Richard Sidney Coles (speaks English and German), F, with bath, basic.

At Km. 83 (from the bridge over the Río Cuyuní which is 6 km. from El Dorado), is Barquilla de Fresa, where tropical fish are bred (Henry Cleve speaks English and German). From Km. 85 (La Clarita, small hotel—another under construction, restaurant; big market for food and gold; safe parking at Las Hermanitas de las Pobres Convent) it's a ½-hr. drive (US$2 by jeep) to the nearest gold-digging village; other villages can only be reached by helicopter (US$15 one way). These villages are built out of oil cans and other rubbish, but are complete with hotels, restaurants, small shops, hairdressers, brothels, etc.

At Km. 88 (also called San Isidro), there is gasoline (rarely 92 octane), a number of eating places and hotels: *La Pilonera*, opp. Vargas store, F with fan, some rooms with bath, restaurant with good fruit drinks, very friendly; *El Parador del Vía*, with restaurant, O.K. Everything is expensive. Gold is sold here; ask Francisco Vargas at the grocery store and restaurant. Bus Km. 88-Caracas, US$7.50. Frequent *por puestos* from El Dorado to Km. 88, 1 hr., US$2. The only reliable public transport out of Km. 88 is the bus from Ciudad Bolívar, which stops at Vargas store at 1400 daily, 6 hrs. to Santa Elena, US$3.25; the alternative is to get a ride with passing jeeps and trucks (very little passes after 1030). The 40 km. beyond Km. 88 up to the Gran Sabana are very steep. At Km.

100 is the huge, black Piedra de la Virgen; from here the steep climb begins up to La Escalera and the beginning of the beautiful Gran Sabana National Reserve. Characteristic of this area are the large abrupt *tepuyes* (flat-topped mountains or *mesas*) and the hundreds of waterfalls.

At Km. 123 a short trail leads to the 40-metre Danto Falls. If you are paying for your ride, try to persuade the driver to make a short stop at the falls; they are close to the road (about 5 mins.' slippery walk) but not visible from it. 4 km. beyond the Monumento al Soldado Pionero (Km. 141) is a popular camping place at Luepa (on right going South, ask permission at the fort); 6 km. beyond is the military checkpoint at Ciudadela. At Km. 148 is an unpaved road leading to Kavanayén, four-wheel drive needed except in dry season (food, lodging, airport); off this road after 25 km. are the falls of Torón Merú (17 km.) and, further on, a left turn to the falls of Chinak-Merú, 100 metres high and very impressive (take the trail to the Río Aponguao and the Pemón Indian village of Iboribó, tip someone to ferry you across the river and walk 30 mins. to the falls; 30-min. boat trips to the falls cost US$15; this trip is reported not to be possible by normal car, take great care near the falls. 18 km. before Kavanayén is a road to the *Hotel Chivaton*, E, good beds but icy water. Beyond Kavanayén a beautiful but risky trail leads along flat-topped mountains to the Karuari-Merú Falls. For the remaining 200 km. to Santa Elena de Uairen few people or villages are seen. The impressive falls at the Kama river should not be missed (Km. 211); there is also a small lake, possible to camp. At Km. 259 is the Río Yuruaní, from where it is a 15-minute hike to the Yuruaní waterfall—leave the main road 250 metres after the crossing, turn left; then comes the Pemón village of San Francisco de Yuruaní (see page 925), then the checkpoint of San Ignacio de Yuruaní (excellent regional food). A trail at Km. 289 leads to the Quebrada de Jaspe where a river falls over red rocks.

Santa Elena de Uairen is a growing, pleasant frontier town. The festival of Santa Elena, August 9-19, features music, dance and handicrafts. There is a bank where you can change US dollars or cruzados (less easy) cash, not cheques; shops in the centre also change money (e.g. the gold shop S of main plaza, which changes travellers' cheques); to obtain better rates for exchange you must wait until Ciudad Guayana, or Boa Vista if going to Brazil. If the service station is dry, ask for Sr. Lucca who sells gasoline out of barrels. Grocery store: *Tienda Mixta El Gordito*, opp. *Hotel MacKing*, English and French spoken. Passports and car documents must be stamped here if leaving or entering the country; the immigration office is on the north edge of the town on a hill opposite the Corpovén gas station (open 0900-1700 except Sun., and holidays). If shut, go to No. 26, uphill from gas station and ask for help.

Hotels and Restaurants *Fronteras**, E with bath (N.B. if you pay a deposit to hire a fan, you may have difficulty in getting the money back when you leave in the early morning to catch the Boa Vista bus), clean amd quiet; *Hospedaje Uairen*, F, good, clean, rec.; *Hospedaje Roraima*, noisy, mosquitoes, not rec.; *Hotel MacKing*, with private bathroom, very clean, and restaurant attached, service slow, F; *Turístico*, Yarimá, F, rec.; *Aurantepuy*, opp. Ciudad Bolívar bus stop, F with bath (cheaper rooms available), basic, clean, rec.; *Mini Hospedaje*, F, 2 blocks from *Fronteras*, clean, basic, friendly, some rooms with private shower. Opposite airport, rooms to let at Sergio's *granja*, friendly, cheap. The best restaurant is *Gran Sabana*; 2 good restaurants on S side of town, *3 Vs* and a *Lonchería*, within a block of each other; *La Perla*, good grill. Rooms are difficult to find during the fiesta (if stuck, ask for Charlie at the *Hotel Fronteras*, he may be able to find you somewhere else to stay).

Leaving by private car may involve a bit of a run-around, up to 2 hrs. **N.B.** U.S. citizens need a visa for Brazil; don't leave it until Santa Elena, it can take 2 weeks to get there. The new road to Brazil links Caracas with Manaus in three days if you drive hard, although it is only a dirt road with gravel on top. The Brazilian section has been described as "that rutted track which has no business being called a road." Be prepared.

Transport to and from Santa Elena All regular transport appears to call at the Immigration office when leaving Santa Elena. There is a daily União Cascavel bus to Boa Vista (Brazil) at 0800, also Eucator, 0730, and Andorinha, 0600-0700, both from *Hotel Fronteras*, 6 hrs., US$8 (cheaper in cruzados; money changers on buses). From Caracas it is best to go to Ciudad Bolívar and take either the Expreso Brazil-Venezuela bus direct to Boa Vista, or the Línea Orinoco bus straight through to Santa Elena, US$8, 13-14 hrs., returns from Santa Elena at 1600, take food. Alternatively take a daily bus to Tumeremo or El Dorado; Transmundial runs from Tumeremo to Santa Elena (US$5.20) and from El Dorado (US$4.65), returning from Santa Elena at 0830. From Tumeremo you can get a bus to San Félix (Ciudad Guayana), 4 hrs., or colectivo to Maturín, 2 hrs., but Líneas Orinoco go direct Santa Elena-Ciudad Guayana (US$8.50, 12-13 hrs.), or Expreso Maturín goes to Ciudad Guayana (US$8.50) and Maturín daily. Aeropostal has flights to Tumeremo and Ciudad Bolívar (US$24), 3 times a week, but the planes may be fully booked in advance in the high season (timetable uncertain, check on arrival). On Wednesdays there is an interesting flight available to Tumeremo via Icabarú and the Indian villages of Uriman, Wonkin, and Kamarata. Book a week in advance.

116 km. W of Santa Elena is Icabarú, a diamond-producing centre (daily jeep from Santa Elena, US$5). 5 km. before Icabarú is *Villa Tranquila*, a well-appointed, more expensive camp. 58 km. from Santa Elena is a Guardia Nacional checkpoint at Parai-Tepuy, with a waterfall nearby. At Km. 68 is Shailili-ko camp, English, Italian and French spoken, rec. At *El Pauji* (Km. 85, US$3 by jeep from Santa Elena, 3 hrs.; ask in Santa Elena for possibility of a lift with families returning after buying supplies), ask for Luigi, an Italian at El Cajón mine (he speaks English). It is in a lovely area, with good walking and bird-watching. A good walk is to the small hill, 2 km. from El Pauji beyond the airfield; views from the crest into El Abismo, a huge valley.

In El Pauji, Danielle operates *El Caminante* tourist camp, just after the bridge, coming from Santa Elena, F p.p., helpful and friendly, camping, trips arranged, restaurant; in the village is the *hospedaje* of Rodrigo and Margarita, near the airstrip and small store, cabins F, no bath, clean, very knowledgeable and friendly place; just before the bridge is *El Merendero* restaurant. At *La Bodega* general store, Victoriano has information on guides for tourists. Jeep hire in El Pauji, US$50 per day. 15 km. from El Pauji, at Solís, Arquimedes and Philippe have a tourist camp; they organize tours. 25 km. from the town is the *Canta Rana* tourist camp with basic accommodation (owners, Alfonso and Barbara Borrero, speak German, English and Spanish); waterfall and lovely surroundings; they have a private plane that collects people from Puerto Ordaz (T 086-22-68-51 or 22-07-09, Sr. Haissan Al Atrache).

Mount Roraima   An exciting trip is to walk to Mt. Roraima (2,810 metres), which it has been suggested was the "Lost World" made famous by Arthur Conan Doyle's novel (although conflicting evidence points to the Brazilian Serra Ricardo Franco near the Bolivian border west of Cuiabá as the site). Supplies for a week or more should be bought in Santa Elena or El Dorado. You can start walking from **San Francisco de Yuruaní**, an Indian village (built of concrete and corrugated iron) on the main road 60 km. north of Santa Elena, and 10 km. north of the San Ignacio police check post (by jeep prices vary from US$2.25 to US$5.50). By law, you must hire an Indian guide in San Francisco de Yuruaní, about US$7 a day; most drive as far as Parai-Tepuy. Coca-cola and biscuits (very little else) can be bought in San Francisco. Follow the virtually unused dirt road to Parai-Tepuy across open savanna with patches of jungle in the river valleys. Parai-Tepuy is the nearest village to the mountain but has no shops. Short cuts can be taken—ask the friendly and interested local people. Beyond Parai-Tepuy, a guide is recommended since it is easy to get lost on the many trails criss-crossing. Looking from the village, Roraima is the mountain on the right, the other massive outcrop on the left is Mata Hui (sometimes known as Mt. Kukenaan after the river which rises within it). The Kukenaan river quickly goes into flood; take a 50 m. rope if not going in a party and be prepared to get wet. It is about a 2-day walk to the jungle at the foot of Roraima and then it is possible to climb to the plateau along the "easy" gully which is the only route to the top.

This gully is the more central of two which run diagonally up the cliff face. The ascent takes 3-5 hrs. and it is possible to camp on the eerie plateau, but beware of lightning from the frequent electrical storms which the mountains attract.

There is plenty of water en route (too much in the rainy season) but no accommodation. Full camping equipment is essential, and wear thick socks and boots to protect legs from snakes, also essential is effective insect repellant. The whole trip can take anywhere between one and two weeks.

THE ECONOMY

Venezuela's economy has been dominated by petroleum, despite its contributing only 8% to gdp. Oil exports have inflated foreign exchange receipts and government fiscal revenues. Oil revenues have shaped the rest of the productive sector, even though employment creation has been minimal, and inter-industry links have been relatively underdeveloped. High earnings from oil have caused a tendency to overvalue the exchange rate, which has discouraged export-based production and hindered import substitution. Non-oil industry and agriculture are now being targeted for expansion as oil's role has diminished since the early 1980s.

Venezuela has vast natural resources, and is especially rich in energy, possessing 55.52 bn barrels of proved oil reserves. Apart from proved and exploitable reserves, there are another 1.2 trillion barrels in potential reserves of very heavy oil in the as yet unexploited Orinoco belt. There are 2.65 trillion cubic metres of natural gas reserves (plus 5 trillion probable), and 500 m tonnes of coal (9 bn estimated) in the provinces of Zulia and Táchira. There is believed to be a hydroelectricity potential (HEP) of 80,000 MW. The new hydroelectric generating capacity around Ciudad Guayana in the east is designed to act as the hub of economic growth. It includes the 10,300 MW **Guri dam project**, the largest complete HEP station in the world, and which in July 1986 provided just over half the country's generating capacity.

Venezuela is Opec's third largest oil producer, with a capacity of 2.6 m barrels a day. Oil production is concentrated in three major sedimentary basins: the Maracaibo, the eastern, and the Apure-Barinas basins. Petróleos de Venezuela (PDVSA), the state-owned oil company created out of the nationalization of oil companies in 1976, has been relatively successful in keeping its market share because of its forward-looking marketing strategy based on forming partnerships with refineries and marketing chains in Europe and the USA.

The mining sector has been probably the most buoyant part of the economy since 1984, and is likely to continue in this vein with important mining ventures in bauxite, iron ore, gold and coal. Venezuela could become the world's leading aluminium producer by the end of the century.

Only about 20% of the land surface is devoted to agriculture, and about three-quarters of this is pasture. Like mining, it is a small sector of the economy, accounting for 8% of gdp and employing 15% of the workforce. The main grain staples are maize and sorghum, while sugar and rice are also important. The main export crop is coffee, with other cash crops being cocoa and cotton.

Venezuela is Latin America's fourth largest debtor, and despite huge foreign reserves of over US$20 bn accumulated by the mid-1980s from oil wealth, the country became unable to service its external debt normally from 1982 because of a bunching of maturities. A US$21 bn debt rescheduling agreement was signed with commercial banks in 1986 but was almost immediately renegotiated, with longer repayment terms and lower interest rates, as falling oil prices that year caused unexpected foreign exchange constraints; oil revenues fell by 44% in 1986. The government avoided taking adjustment measures and chose instead to spend reserves until by end-1988 liquid foreign exchange reserves were exhausted. In 1989 the new administration turned to the IMF and World Bank for support for a comprehensive macroeconomic adjustment programme to rebuild reserves, encourage domestic savings and cut the public sector deficit. Previous policies were reversed with the freeing of interest rates and the exchange rate. Another debt rescheduling package was expected from commercial banks.

	1961-70 (av)	1971-80 (av)	1981-85 (av)	1986-88 (av)
Gdp growth (1980 prices)	6.1%	4.1%	-1.3%	4.7%
Inflation	1.0%	8.4%	11.1%	22.8%
Exports (fob) US$m	2,436	9,228	15,582	10,015
Crude oil and products	2,240	8,743	14,048	8,250
Imports (fob) US$m	1,294	6,307	9,092	9,190
Current account balance US$m (cum)	1,217	5,114	12,685	-7,150

INFORMATION FOR VISITORS

Travel from UK and Europe   British Airways and Viasa fly from London to Simón Bolívar, the international airport for Caracas; the former twice a week each way via either Port of Spain or St. Lucia. Viasa fly via a European city such as Paris or Lisbon. Fares from the Uk range from £400-520 return, depending on season and type of excursion taken. There are also services from Europe by Air France, KLM, Iberia, Alitalia, Lufthansa, Swissair and Avianca. Iberia have a weekly service to Las Palmas, Canary Islands, from where connections can be made to various North and West African countries.

By sea, there appear to be no passenger services from Europe, although there are cargo services.

From North America   By air, passengers may reach Venezuela by Pan American, Viasa, and Avensa. Miami or New York are served by all three (flying time from New York is 4 hours 15 minutes). Viasa fly to both Montréal and Toronto (flying time 7 hours 15 minutes); there are also many charters at holiday times. There are cargo services, some with limited passenger space, from Atlantic and/or Gulf ports by Alcoa, CAVN, P and O, Insco, Lykes & Torm, and from the Pacific by Moore-McCormack.

From Colombia There are direct flights by Viasa, British Airways, Air France and Avianca. Caracas can also be reached from Bogotá by Pan-American Highway, and from the north coast, by the Caribbean coastal highway.

From Argentina, Brazil and Uruguay There are direct air services by Viasa, Aerolíneas Argentinas, Pan American and Varig. By sea, the Argentine State Line maintains a passenger liner service, every two or three weeks. Caracas may now be reached by a very rough road from Brazil, via Manaus, Boa Vista and Santa Elena de Uairen (thence good to Caracas).

Others Lacsa flies from San José (Costa Rica), Panama and Barranquilla (Colombia) to Maracaibo and Caracas. Aeropostal has services to Port of Spain (3 times a week from Caracas or Isla Margarita. Difficulties have been reported in entering Trinidad unless with a UK, US or Canadian passport. Viasa also flies to Bridgetown, Barbados but it is often difficult to get a seat. There is direct air service from Chile (Viasa has a weekly flight with extra flights Dec.–March; connections can also be made via Bogotá on Avianca), Peru (Air France via Bogotá, Viasa—Viasa tickets purchased in Peru should be checked most carefully), Ecuador (Ecuatoriana, Lufthansa and Viasa), Trinidad (BWIA), Santo Domingo (Viasa, Dominicana de Aviación), Puerto Rico (Pan American), Curaçao (KLM, Viasa; Aeropostal, cheaper), Aruba, US$60 from Maiquetía, US$40 from Las Piedras, **see page 898** (1989). As yet, Venezuela has no road connection with Guyana, except through Brazil. Ferry from Curaçao, three times a week; also from Aruba.

Documents Entry is by passport and visa, or by passport and tourist card. Tourist cards (*tarjetas de ingreso*) are valid only for those entering by air and are issued by most airlines to visitors from 25 countries including the USA, Canada, Japan and all Western European countries except Spain and Portugal. They are valid for 60 days with, theoretically, 2 extensions of 30 days each permissible, at a cost of US$40 each. Renew at DIEX offices, take passport and return ticket. If you enter the country overland, you will be required to obtain a visa from a Venezuelan consulate prior to arrival. Visas cost US$10, but free to Danes and US$3 to US citizens; you will need your passport, return ticket and letter of reference from your employer and bank. You must fill in an application form and the visa will take about three working days to come through, sometimes longer if authorization has to come from Venezuela. It appears that you cannot get a visa in advance in the USA or Canada, so to apply for an overland visa in Colombia you need: passport, yellow fever certificate, malaria certificate, one photo and an onward ticket. Coming from Brazil you need all the above except an onward ticket. A tourist card issued by Viasa in Bogotá is only valid for arriving in Caracas by air from Bogotá, not if you travel overland. To extend a tourist visa for one month, in any city, costs US$50; it is best to leave the country (e.g. to Curaçao) and get a new one free. To change a tourist visa to a business visa, or to extend the latter, also costs US$50. A business visa costs about US$25. Visas are valid for one entry only. Transit passengers to another country can stay only 72 hrs.

N.B. Carry your passport with you all the time you are in Venezuela as the police are increasing spot checks and anyone found without identification is immediately detained (carrying a certified copy for greater safety is permissible). A press card as identification is reported to work wonders.

Information for business visitors is given in "Hints to Exporters: Venezuela", issued by the Export Services Division, Dept. of Trade, Sanctuary Buildings, 16-20 Great Smith Street, London SW1. Businessmen on short visits are strongly advised to enter the country as tourists, otherwise they will have to obtain a tax clearance certificate (*solvencia*) before they can leave.

Taxes All non-tourists leaving the country, except nationals of Denmark and transit passengers who stay for 7 days or less (who pay one bolívar), must pay US$4 at the airport or port of embarkation. Minors under seven years of age do not pay the exit tax. There is also an airport tax of US$0.40 for those passengers on internal flights.

Customs You may bring into Venezuela, free of duty, 25 cigars and 200 cigarettes, 2 litres of alcoholic drinks, 4 small bottles of perfume, and gifts at the inspector's discretion.

Shipping a car from the USA From Miami: Venezuelan Line (agent Oceanic Steamship Co.—rec.) and Delta Line, US$500-650 for a VW minibus (in the other direction, Maracaibo-Miami, it costs US$300); no passengers. From New Orleans: Delta Line, VW minibus, US$1,400-1,700, passengers carried, but for US$1,200. Alternatively, agent Hansen and Tiedemann charges same price as Delta for vehicle, but you can accompany it for US$190 p.p. (5 days, including meals). Also recommended: Coordinadora del Caribe Transmodal C.A. (CCT) Calle Veracruz, Ed. Torreón, Piso 7, Las Mercedes, Caracas, T 92-71-33. Also Seaboard Marine, agent in Venezuela, Conavén,

US$650 for a VW Kombi; their route is advertised as La Guaira-Miami, but actually goes to West Palm Beach, 80 miles North of Miami; almost impossible to travel with your vehicle.

On arrival in Venezuela (La Guaira), you must go to the Tourism Department at Simón Bolívar airport where you must obtain a document identifying your car (serial and engine number, registry, etc.). With this you can get your car out of the port.

Motoring   A tourist can bring in his/her car without paying duty, and the only documentation required is a visa for overland entry (this is necessary despite what Consulates may tell you) and a *carnet*. An entry permit for a car costs US$10 and requires one photograph (takes 24 hrs.); ask for a permit for 6 months, or unspecified time. **See also page 908.** For vehicles with Venezuelan registration leaving Venezuela the following documents are required: an Automóvil passport book from the Touring y Automóvil Club de Venezuela, Apartado 68102, Centro Integral Santa Rosa, Locales 11 y 12, Calle A, Av. Principal, Santa Rosa de Lima, Caracas, T 914879; the original car papers; the registration document; a police *revisión* obtained from the Policía Técnica Judicial; and a temporary import/export licence for a vehicle obtainable from the Ministerio de Hacienda, Caracas, or from a customs agent in San Antonio de Táchira (border town) for about US$100. The export/import licence and the passport book must be signed and stamped by the Customs Administrator. If possible, check all details on bringing in/taking out a car in advance.

All visitors to Venezuela can drive if they are over 18 and have a valid driving licence from their own country. It is a good idea to hire a car **(see page 890)**; many of the best places are off the beaten track. If planning to hire a car for any length of time it is worth the trouble to obtain a *licencia temporal para conducir*; for this you require a medical certificate (eye examination, blood pressure, US$2, issued by an authorised medical centre, try Torre Phelps, Plaza Venezuela, Caracas), photocopy of your home driver's licence and two black-and-white passport photos which must be presented at the Ministerio de Transporte y Comunicaciones, Torre Este, Parque Central, Dep. Licencias, full details in Venamcham's *Executive Newcomer's Guide*. If you have an accident and someone is injured, you will be detained as a matter of routine, even if you are not at fault. Be careful of motor cyclists; if you injure one, others will surround you in a threatening and dangerous manner. Motor cyclists also drive very dangerously, sometimes even on the pavements, and are responsible for many assaults on pedestrians. Do not drive at night if you can help it. Carry insect spray if you do; if you stop and get out, the car will fill with biting insects.

In 1982 a nationwide speed limit of 80 k.p.h. was imposed. Venezuelans are aggressive drivers and use their horns whenever possible. The roads in Venezuela are very good, all major routes are fully paved and even the dirt and gravel roads are reliable. There is a "día de parada" in Caracas which prohibits motorists from driving one day a week **(see page 890)**. Other motoring restrictions in Caracas include a ban on parking in front of a bank; motorcycles may not be driven at night; pillion passengers may not be carried on motorcycles if of the same sex as the driver. You are more likely to be penalized for infringing these rules than for driving through a red light; they are designed to improve security for banks and pedestrians. In addition, motorcyclists are obliged to wear a crash helmet but it must not be of a type which obscures the face.

There are 5 grades of gasoline: "normal", 83 octane (Bs.2.55 a litre); 87 octane (Bs.2.62 a litre); 89 octane (Bs.2.65 a litre); 91 octane (Bs.2.68 a litre); and "alta", 95 octane (Bs.2.75 a litre). Service stations are open 0500-2100, Mon.-Sat., except those on highways which are open longer hours. Only those designated to handle emergencies are open on Sun. In the event of breakdown, Venezuelans are usually very helpful. There are many garages, even in rural areas; service charges are not high, but being able to speak Spanish will greatly assist in sorting out problems. Road maps are available for US$1 at most service stations. **Warning**   There is an automatic US$20 fine for running out of fuel.

Hitch-Hiking   (*Cola*) is not very easy but the Venezuelans are usually friendly and helpful if you know some Spanish. The best places to try are Guardia Nacional posts outside cities (may get free bus rides from them).

Tourist Information   may be obtained from Corpoturismo, Apartado 50.200, Caracas, main office for information is floors 35-7, Torre Oeste, Parque Central. A useful publication is the *Guía Turística y Hoteles de Venezuela, Colombia y el Caribe*, published every July by Corpoturismo, which includes not only hotel details, but also road maps and tourist attractions. For businessmen setting up home in Caracas, the Venezuelan American Chamber of Commerce publication, *Executive Newcomer's Guide, Welcome to Venezuela*, is recommended, with useful chapters on housing, employment, schools, services, recreation facilities and legal matters. Also useful is the *Atlas Geográfico y Económico—Venezuela Visualizada* by Levi Marrero, Ed. Cultural Venezolana, 1977, which contains maps, tourist information and statistics of every state, available in all good bookshops. *The Guide to Venezuela* (1981), by Janice Bauman, Leni Young and others, in English (freely available in Caracas) is a mine of information and maps.

For information on the National Parks system, and to obtain necessary permits, visit the Ministerio del Ambiente y de los Recursos Naturales Renovables (MARNR) at Parque del Este in Caracas. The book: *Guía de los Parques Nacionales y Monumentos Naturales de Venezuela*, obtainable in Audubon headquarters, Las Mercedes shopping centre, Las Mercedes, Caracas.

Hotel Reservations   Fairmont International **(see page 888)** will book hotel rooms both in

Caracas and in other towns, where they have 102 hotels on their books, not all of which are mentioned in these pages. Hotels marked with an asterisk (*) are bookable through Fairmont. All, except luxury class hotels, charge officially controlled prices. In 1988 a 10% tourist tax was added to hotel prices, not for the benefit of hoteliers but for the construction and maintenance of tourist amenities.

Students If you possess a valid international student's card you may find the Organización Nacional de Turismo Estudiantil y Juvenil (Ontej) useful; Parque Central, Edificio Catuche, Nivel Bolívar, Caracas, T 572-7621. They will help you with visas, documents and have youth hostel information.

Tipping Taxi drivers are tipped if the taxi has a meter (Caracas only, so far), but not if you have agreed the fare in advance. Usherettes are not tipped. Hotel porters, Bs.2; airport porters Bs.2 per piece of baggage. Restaurants, between 5 and 10% of bill.

Hours of Business Banks are open from 0830 to 1130 and 1400 to 1630. Mon. to Fri., but are no longer open on Sat. Government office hours vary, but 0800-1200 are usual morning hours. Government officials have fixed hours, usually 0900-1000 or 1500-1600, for receiving visitors. Business firms generally start work about 0800, and some continue until about 1800 with a midday break. Shops, 0900-1300, 1500-1900, Mon. to Sat. Generally speaking, the Venezuelan begins his day early, and by seven in the morning everything is in full swing. Most firms and offices close on Sat.

Holidays There are two sorts of holidays, those enjoyed by everybody and those taken by employees of banks and insurance companies. Holidays applying to all businesses include: January 1, Carnival on the Monday and Tuesday before Ash Wednesday, Thursday-Saturday of Holy Week, April 19, May 1, June 24, July 5, 24, October 12, December 25. Holidays for banks and insurance companies only include all the above and also: March 19 and the nearest Monday to January 6, Ascension Day, June 29, August 15, November 1 and December 8. There are also holidays applying to certain occupations such as Doctor's Day or Traffic Policeman's Day. On New Year's Eve, everything closes and does not open for at least a day; public transport runs, but booking offices are not open. Queues for tickets, and traffic jams, are long. Business travellers should not visit during Holy Week or Carnival.

Local: La Guaira: March 10. Maracaibo: October 24, November 18.

Health conditions are good. Water in all main towns is heavily chlorinated, so safe to drink, although most people drink bottled water. Medical attention is good. State health care is free and said to be good (the Clínica Metropolitana in Caracas has been recommended). Some rivers are infected with bilharzia and in some areas there are warning signs; check before bathing. Inoculation against typhoid and yellow fever, and protection against malaria, is recommended for the Orinoco and other swampy or forest regions. Malaria tablets may be obtained from Hospital Padre Machado (left-hand building as you face it), T 61-8211, no charge; or Ministerio de Sanidad y Asistencia Social (MSAS), Torre del Silencio (SW corner of Plaza Caracas), División de Malariología, free, English spoken; alternatively, bring malaria tablets with you. It is as well to carry some remedy in case of gastric upsets.

Climate is tropical, with little change between season and season. Temperature is a matter of altitude. Mean annual temperatures are given in the text. At Caracas it is 20°C, but during the dry season (December to April), there is a great difference between day and night temperatures, and during the whole year there is a burst of heat around mid-day. Rainfall in mm.: Caracas, 762; Maracaibo, 573; Barcelona, 660; Mérida, 1,295; Amazonas and parts of Barinas state 2,540.

Clothing Tropical weight in normal city colours is best for business in Caracas, otherwise clothing is less formal, but smart jackets and ties are required in the most exclusive restaurants and clubs. In Maracaibo and the hot, humid coastal and low-lying areas, regular washable tropical clothing is used. For women: blouse and trousers (shorts quite acceptable on the coast); cotton dresses, with a wrap for cool evenings, and for air-conditioned restaurants and cinemas. Shoes are very good value.

Railways The only passenger traffic of any importance is on the Barquisimeto to Puerto Cabello line. The 110-km. Yaritagua-Acarigua-Turén electric railway line was opened at the beginning of 1983 but was closed after the inaugural run because of damage to the track. It is intended mostly to transport agricultural products.

Road Transport There are excellent (but slow) bus services between the major cities, but the colectivo taxis and minibuses, known in Venezuela as por puesto, seem to monopolize transport to and from smaller towns and villages. Outside Caracas, town taxis are relatively expensive.

Camping is popular, and plenty of equipment is available at Tienda Scout (Las Acacias), Maxy's (ex-Sears) and sports-goods shops in Caracas. Camping in Venezuela is a recreation, for spending a weekend at the beach, on the islands, in the *llanos* and in the mountains. (People pitch their tents on Mount Avila overlooking Caracas.) Camping is not however used by travellers as a substitute for hotels on the main highways, and no special camp sites are yet provided for this purpose. If camping on the beach, for the sake of security, pitch your tent close to others, even though they play their radios loud. For information on hiking, climbing and relevant equipment, telephone Alexander on (02)573-00-56 (Spanish only).

Air Services   Most places of importance are served by Avensa (private) and/or Aeropostal (government-owned, both heavily overbooked always). Aeropostal also has international service (Viasa does not have domestic services). Both internal airlines offer special family discounts and 15% off for students. Beware of overbooking during holiday time, especially at Caracas airport; it is recommended that you check in two hours before departure, particularly at Easter. Internal night-time flights are scarce, and there is no late hour discount. If you travel with Viasa or any other airline for which Viasa is agent, it is possible to check in the day before flying out of Caracas by taking baggage, ticket and passport to their office at Centro Comercial Tamanaco, Nivel C.2, "Predespacho", between 1500 and 2100 (cost US$0.40); take bus from Chacaíto. To avoid overbooking the Government now obliges airlines to post a passenger list, but it is important to obtain clear instructions from the travel agent regarding confirmation of your flight and checking-in time. Passengers leaving Caracas on international flights must reconfirm their reservations not less than 72 hours in advance; it is safer to do so in person than by telephone; 24 hours for national flights (if you fail to do this, you lose all rights to free accommodation, food, transport, etc. if your flight is cancelled). Beware of counterfeit tickets; buy only from agencies. If told by an agent that a flight is fully booked, try at the airport anyway. International passengers must check in two hours before departure or they may lose their seat to someone on a waiting list. Read carefully any notice you see posted with the relevant instructions. Handling charge for your luggage US$0.50. All flights are subject to delays or cancellation. Avensa operates an air-pass system, open only to non-residents and purchasable only outside Venezuela: 23 destinations are included and a 7-day pass costs US$110, 14-day US$125 and 21-day US$139. Passengers are issued with an MCO (Miscellaneous Charges Order) in the country of purchase, this is exchanged in Caracas at Pasajes Avensa, Esq. El Conde. At the same time ask for a timetable of all Avensa flights. (In view of the cheapness of internal flights and the good bus services, the pass may not be worth buying).

Currency   The unit of currency is the bolívar, which is divided into 100 céntimos. There are nickel alloy coins for 25 and 50 céntimos and 1, 2 and 5 bolívares, and notes for 5, 10, 20, 50, 100 and 500 bolívares. The 1,000-bolívares note no longer circulates, because of extensive counterfeiting. In 1989, the official and free rates of exchange were unified: in June of that year the bolívar stood at 38 to the US dollar (all prices in the text are converted at this rate). Change travellers' cheques or US dollar notes in a *casa de cambio* for optimum rates; of the banks, Banco Unión and Banco de Venezuela change cheques and cash, but the latter usually only change money after 1500. The majority of banks do not cash travellers' cheques; in major towns, one or two banks may, but this varies from branch to branch. American Express cheques are widely accepted as is the Visa card (Banco Consolidado is affiliated with American Express, no commission, some branches cash personal cheques from abroad on an Amex card; Banco Unión handles Visa transactions). When changing dollars cash in banks, it is best to go in the morning. If changing money in hotels, do not take sterling or any other European currencies. It is impossible to change sterling in Ciudad Guayana or Ciudad Bolívar. Have money sent to you by telex and not by post, which can take weeks. Rates of exchange in hotels are generally poor.

Popular names for coins: Fuerte. Bs.5; Real, Bs.0.50; Medio, 0.25; Puya or Centavo, 0.05.

Weights and Measures are metric.

Voltage   110 volts, 60 cycles, throughout the country.

Shopping   Goods in shops bear a label "PVP" followed by the price. This is the maximum authorized price; you may be able to negotiate a discount but should never pay more than the PVP price.

Warnings   Cameras and other valuables should not be exposed prominently. The police are increasing spot-checks and may confiscate pocket knives as "concealed weapons" if they find them, although they are sold legally in the shops. Always carry handbags, cameras etc. on the side away from the street as motor-cycle purse-snatchers are notorious and they often even drive up on to the pavement to assault a pedestrian. Motor cyclists are also very adept at snatching chains from necks in Caracas. Hotel thefts are becoming more frequent, even in the best hotels.

Food   Both in Caracas and to a lesser extent in Maracaibo there are excellent restaurants specializing in foreign regional cuisines. Venezuelan beef is comparable with Argentina's and, surprisingly, portions are larger. There is excellent local fish (we recommend *pargo* or red snapper), crayfish, small oysters and prawns, though sole, trout and large oysters are imported. Sometimes there is turtle, though it is a protected species. For those without a conservationist conscience, turtle may appear on menus in the Peninsula de Paraguaná as *ropa especial*. The *Tarzilandia* restaurant in Caracas also serves it. Of true Venezuelan food there is *sancocho* (a stew of vegetables, especially yuca, with meat, chicken or fish); *arepas*, a kind of white maize bread, very bland in flavour; toasted *arepas* served with a wide selection of relishes, fillings or the local somewhat salty white cheese are cheap, filling and nutritious; *cachapas*, a maize pancake (soft, not hard like Mexican *tortillas*) wrapped around white cheese; *pabellón*, made of shredded meat, beans, rice and fried plantains; and *empanadas*, maize-flour pies containing cheese, meat or fish. At Christmas only there are *hallacas*, maize pancakes stuffed with chicken, pork, olives, etc. boiled in a plantain leaf (but don't eat the leaf). The nearest thing to a boiled egg in most places is a *huevo tibio*. It comes without the shell because there are no eggcups. A *muchacho* (boy) on the menu is not a sign of cannibalism; it is a cut of beef. *Ganso* is also not goose but beef. *Solomo* and *lomito* are other cuts of beef. *Hervido* is chicken or beef with vegetables. *Caraotas* are beans; *cachitos* are croissants of bread. *Pasticho* is what the Venezuelans call Italian *lasagne*. The main fruits are bananas, oranges, grapefruit, mangoes, pineapple and pawpaws. Excellent strawberries are grown at Colonia Tovar, 90 minutes from Caracas. A delicious sweet is *huevos chimbos*—egg yolk boiled and bottled in sugar syrup. There is no good local wine though some foreign wines are bottled locally. Local wine is used only in cooking or in *sangría*. There are four good local beers: Polar (the most popular), Regional (with a strong flavour of hops), Cardenal and Nacional (a *lisa* is a glass of keg beer; for a bottle of beer ask for a *tercio*), mineral waters, gin and excellent rum. The citizens of Mérida sometimes drink a cocktail of beer and milk. The coffee is very good (*café con leche* has a lot of milk, *café marrón* much less); visitors should also try a *merengada*, a delicious drink made from fruit pulp, ice, milk and sugar; a *batido* is the same but with water, not milk. A *plus-café* is an after-dinner liqueur. Water is free in all restaurants even if no food is bought. Bottled water in *cervecerías* is often from the tap; no deception is intended, bottles are simply used as convenient jugs. Insist on seeing the bottle opened if you do not want a mouthful of chlorine with your whisky. *Chicha de arroz* is a sweet drink made of milk, rice starch, sugar and vanilla; fruit juices are very good. The Caracas *Daily Journal* (in English) lists many reliable restaurants in Caracas and Maracaibo. Venezuelans dine late. Gin and rum at about US$2 and coffee beans at US$1.50 per kilo are good buys.

Film   Kodachrome (La Trinidad) and Agfa have a regional plant in Caracas and colour-slide film can be developed in 2 days (go direct to the plant). Film is cheaper to buy and develop than in most parts of the continent.

Postal Services   The postal service is extremely slow and unreliable. Air mail letters to the USA or Europe can take from one to four weeks and registered mail is no quicker. Internal mail also travels slowly, especially if there is no P.O. Box number. If you want money sent to you from abroad, have it sent by telex. Avoid the mail boxes in pharmacies as some no longer have collections.

Telephone Service   All international and long distance calls are operated by CANTV from El Silencio building in west Caracas, Centro Simón Bolívar or Centro Plaza on Fco. Miranda near US Embassy in east Caracas, open 24 hrs. Most major cities are now linked by direct dialling (*Discado Directo*), with a 3-figure prefix for each town in Venezuela. Otherwise CANTV offices deal with all long-distance and international calls in the cities outside Caracas. Collect calls unavailable. Calls out of Venezuela are more expensive than calls into it and are subject to long delays. Local calls are troublesome and the connection is often cut in the middle of your conversation; calls are best made from hotels or CANTV offices, rather than from booths. Local calls in Caracas cost US$0.06.

Note   Telephone, fax or telex are far preferable to cables. Ask your hotel for use of its telex or fax machine.

Official Time   in Venezuela is 4 hrs. behind GMT, 1 hour ahead of EST.

Press: Caracas: *El Universal, El Nacional* and *El Diario de Caracas, La Religión, Ultimas Noticias. The Daily Journal* (English), *El Mundo* and *2001* (evening), *Número* (weekly), *Resumen* (weekly), *Elite* (weekly), *Momento* (weekly), *Venezuela Gráfica* (weekly), *Páginas* (weekly), *Semana* (weekly), *Ve Venezuela*, tourist bi-monthly. Maracaibo: *Panorama, La Crítica.* Puerto La Cruz: *El Tiempo.*

Radio   Write to Radio Nacional, Caracas 101, Apartado 3979, for details about their plans for English-language broadcasts.

We should like to thank the following travellers for help in revising the Venezuelan section: Leonhard Ambacher (Kircheim/München), Tim Austin (Shere, Sy.), Eberhard Baer (Koenigsbrunn, W.Ger.), Eric Beauchemin (Hilversum), Renate Becker (Heidelberg), Erika Berger (Moosseedorf, Switz.), Pierre-Y Berney (Gen6va), Erik A. Bloom (New Haven, CT), Michelle Burrows (Brisbane), Pamela Caunt and Bob Brass (London N1), Tim Connell (Ham, Surrey) for a particularly useful contribution, John Crane (Sunbury), Jeroen Dijkgraaf (Eindhoven), Bernd Dralle (Hannover), Dieter Eigenstetter and Yesim Yazicioglu (München 80), Eva Ekelund and Jim Lindsay (Stockholm), Andreas Erne (Zürich 8055), Per Einar Evensen (Bergen), Janet Fox (London), Sharon Franklet (Lima), Christina Gräwe (Tautkirchen) and Joachim Hoell (Wernstadt, W.Ger.), Jan Jacob de Groot (Vroomshoop, Neth.), Rupert Hafner (Wien 1238), Robert Hauer (Bonn 1), Charles Havekost (Greenbelt, MD) and Eva Lindholm (Zug, Switz.), Alison Henry, Christian and Nickolaj Hoff (Holte, Copenhagen), Alan Jones (Santa Cruz de Tenerife), Jerome Keeton (Mérida "Montaña"), Valerie and Verlen Kruger (2-Continent Canoe Expedition), John Lewis (London NW3), Charles Locher (San Francisco) and Nancy Blackstock (Berkeley, CA), Elaine and George McClellan (Danville, CA), Dr Bruce Means (Tallahassee), Albert Meier and Evelyne Ott (Freudwil, Switz.), Lucy Meikle (Pershore) and Stuart Duncan (Scotland), B.E.Miles (N. Baddesley, Southampton), Daniel Morgan (Wellington, NZ), Dimitri Moursellas (Manhattan Beach, CA), Vera Naujak (Heidelberg), Bertil Olin (Johanneshov, Swed.), Karl Olson (New York), Pia Parolin (Milano), William Parton (London SW11), Tim Pozzi (Jersey), Geoff A. Richardson (Barranquilla), Michael Ridley (S. Croydon), Chris Robertson (Stockholm) and Patricia Galvin (Galway), Markus Schulz (Gambach, W.Ger.), Michael R. Scott (São Paulo), Elizabeth and Virginia Segal (London N2), Antony Sherlock (Edinburgh 12), Nicola J. Smith (Kirby Muxbe, Leics.) and Jean-François Morerod (Les Diablerets, Switz.), Rosalind Sutton and Stephen Crocker (Chislehurst, Kt.) for very helpful information, Anna Syriänen and Marko Sorvaniemi (Tampere, Fin.), Erik Thier and Patricia Wessels (Amsterdam), Thorsten Truijens (Haan, W.Ger.), Ronald van Vliet (Haarlem), Roland Wiemer and Karla Menner (Hamburg 50), Ray Williams (Pwllheli) and Mark Wilson (The Crane, Barbados).

WILL YOU HELP US?

We do all we can to get our facts right in *The South American Handbook.* Each chapter is thoroughly revised each year, but Latin America and the Caribbean cover a vast area, and our eyes cannot be everywhere.

Your information may be far more up-to-date than ours. If your letter reaches us early enough in the year it will be used in the next edition, but write whenever you want to, for all your letters are used sooner or later.   Thank you very much indeed for your help.

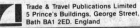 Trade & Travel Publications Limited
5 Prince's Buildings, George Street,
Bath BA1 2ED. England

THE GUIANAS

LIKE the West Indians, the people of the three Guianas, Guyana (formerly British Guiana), Suriname (formerly Dutch Guiana) and French Guyane, are not regarded as belonging to Latin America. The explanation of these three non-Iberian countries on the South American continent goes back to the early days of the Spanish conquest of the New World. There was no gold or any other apparent source of wealth to attract the attention of the Spanish discoverers. This part of the coast, which Columbus had first sighted in 1498, seemed to them not only barren but scantily populated and seemingly uninhabitable. The English, the French and the Dutch, anxious to establish a foothold in this part of the world, were not so fastidious.

All three countries have much the same surface: along the coast runs a belt of narrow, flat marshy land, at its widest in Suriname. This coastland carries almost all the crops and most of the population. Behind lies a belt of crystalline upland, heavily gouged and weathered. The bauxite, gold and diamonds are in this area. Behind this again is the massif of the Guiana Highlands. They reach a height of 3,000 feet in the Tumuc-Humac range, the divide between French Guyane and Suriname, and Brazil, and 9,219 feet (2,810 metres) at flat-topped Mount Roraima (see page 925), where Guyana, Venezuela and Brazil all meet.

N.B. You need to have your own shoe-cleaning equipment; there seem to be no shoeshine boys in any of the Guianas.

Thanks and acknowledgements for help with the Guianas sections will be found at the end of the chapter on French Guyane.

GUYANA

GUYANA has an area of 83,000 square miles, nearly the size of Britain, but only about 0.5% (or 280,000 acres) is cultivated. The population numbers some 988,000, of whom about 91% are literate; less than one-third of the population lives in towns. There has been considerable emigration to the USA, Canada and Britain.

Some 10% of the country is the upland savanna of the Rupununi and Kanaku mountains, in the remote hinterland of the SW. A huge tract of thick, hilly jungle and forest—85% of the country—slopes down from this high plateau towards the sea. The soil is poor and sandy; there is little cultivation, but the bauxite, gold and diamonds are in this area. The rest of the country—3.5%—is a narrow belt, seldom 8 miles deep, running 200 miles along the coast. It contains some 90% of the total population (just under a third of the population work on sugar estates and farms), and grows all the sugar and rice. Much of this belt, which is below sea-level, is intersected by great rivers and suffers from both deluge and drought; it can be maintained only by a complicated system of dykes and drains, a permanent costly burden on agriculture but rather picturesque to travel through. Nearly all the cultivated land is in this belt.

From 80 to 110 inches of rain fall mostly in two well defined seasons: April to August and November to January. Less rain falls as one moves southward; here rainfall is 60 inches a year, mainly between April and September. A little natural

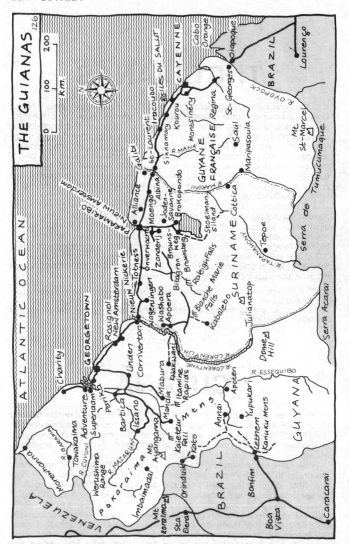

drainage is given by the rivers; the Corentyne, along the Suriname border to the E; the Berbice and Demerara, 30 and 100 miles respectively to the W; and the Essequibo, which drains most of the country and enters the sea midway along the coast. Falls and rapids hinder their use for communication with the interior, but 60 miles of the Demerara river are navigable by shallow-draft ocean craft up to the Mackenzie bauxite mines.

The original Dutch and English settlers at the beginning of the 17th century established posts up-river, in the hills, mostly as trading points with the Amerindian natives. Plantations were laid out and worked by slaves from Africa. Poor soil defeated this venture, and the settlers retreated with their slaves to the coastal area in mid-18th century: the old plantation sites can still be detected from the air. Coffee and cotton were the main crops up to the end of the 18th century, but sugar had become the dominant crop by 1820. In 1834 slavery was abolished. Many of the slaves scattered as small landholders, and the plantation owners had to look for another source of labour. It was found in indentured East Indians, a few Chinese, and some Portuguese labourers from the Azores and Madeira. About 240,000 had come from India by 1914. At the end of their indentures many settled in Guyana.

Sugar and rice are largely dependent for labour on the Guyanese of Indian descent. The Africans, who prefer town life, are outnumbered and will progressively be more so as the population increases. Europeans comprise below 1%, East Indians 51%, blacks 29%, Creoles (mixed race) 13%, and the others 6%. As for religion, 52% are Christian, 34% Hindu, 9% Muslim, 5% others. Unemployment is estimated to be 40%-50%.

Nearly 25% of the population lives in Georgetown or close by. Density per square mile in the coastal belt is over 1,700, compared with 9.87 average over the whole country. Until 1920 there was little natural increase, but the suppression of malaria and other diseases has since led to a large growth of population especially among the East Indians. The country is overpopulated in relation to its readily exploitable resources; whether the interior could support more people if it were opened up is debatable. The few remaining Amerindians, of the Arawak and Carib groups, are rapidly losing their isolation.

History

The country was first partially settled between 1616 and 1621 by the Dutch West India Company, who erected a fort and depot at Fort Kyk-over-al (County of Essequibo). The first English attempt at settlement was made by Captain Leigh on the Oiapoque River (now French Guyane) in 1604, but it failed to establish a permanent settlement. Lord Willoughby, famous in the early history of Barbados, founded a settlement in 1663 at Suriname, which was captured by the Dutch in 1667 and ceded to them at the Peace of Breda in exchange for New York. The Dutch held the three colonies till 1796 when they were captured by a British fleet. The territory was restored to the Dutch in 1802, but in the following year was retaken by Great Britain, which finally gained it in 1814, when the three counties of Essequibo, Berbice and Demerara were merged to form British Guiana. In 1899 a commission arbitrating on a boundary dispute between Britain and Venezuela awarded over half the present territory of Guyana, consisting of the territory to the W of the River Essequibo, to Britain. Venezuela is claiming the land then ceded.

On May 26, 1966, Guyana was granted independence, and on February 23, 1970 it became a co-operative republic within the Commonwealth; the President is Mr. Desmond Hoyte, who took office in August 1985 following the death of his predecessor Forbes Burnham. The bauxite and sugar industries have been nationalized, and the country appears to have been set firmly on a co-operative path. A Prime Minister and Cabinet are responsible to the National Assembly, which has 53 members elected under a single-list system of proportional representation for a maximum term of five years. President Hoyte has been elected unopposed as leader of the governing People's National Congress (PNC) as well as President General of the Guyana Labour Union. The main opposition to the PNC is the People's Progressive Party (Marxist) led by Dr. Cheddi Jagan.

Georgetown, the capital, and the chief town and port, is on the right bank of the River Demerara, at its mouth. Its population is roughly 200,000. The climate is tropical, with a mean temperature of 80.5°F. Georgetown, with 19th-century wooden houses supported on stilts, and charming green boulevards laid along the lines of the old Dutch canals, has a character of its own; protected by a sea-wall and a system of dykes opened at low tide, it is set on an alluvial flat below the high-water mark. All that is seen of it from the sea are the masts of the wireless station, the lighthouse (which may be visited by arrangement with the Harbour Master), the Gothic tower of Stabroek Market, the twin dishes of the radio-telephone system, the tower of the *Pegasus Hotel* and the twin square towers of the Church of the Sacred Heart. Most of the older buildings are of wood and some are shabby; since the disastrous fire of 1945 many concrete buildings have been put up in the commercial centre. Some of the most impressive wooden buildings from the colonial past are: the City Hall (Avenue of the Republic) constructed in 1887 in Gothic style; St. George's Cathedral (North Road) dating from 1892, which at a height of 143 feet is one of the tallest wooden buildings in the world; the Law Courts (High Street), finished in 1878 with mock Tudor framing; the President's residence at Guyana House (Main Street), built in 1852; and the imposing Parliament Building (Avenue of the Republic). Other important public buildings are the Roman Catholic Cathedral (Brickdam); the Bishop's High School; St. Stanislaus College (Jesuit); Queens College; the Technical Institute; the Stabroek Market (Water Street), a focal point of the city; the Public Free Library; the Guyana Museum (Company Path); and several churches. The Playhouse Theatre, seating 216, is in Parade Street. The historical museum opposite the post office no longer has Amerindian exhibits. Modern architecture is represented by the *Pegasus Hotel*, the Bank of Guyana and Telephone House. At the head of Brickdam, a main street, is an aluminium arch which commemorates independence. Across the road is a monument to the 1763 slave rebellion surmounted by a striking statue of Cuffy, leader of the rebellion. Adjacent to the Botanic Gardens on Homestretch Avenue is the new Cultural Centre. This is a magnificent theatre, probably the best in the Caribbean, air-conditioned, comfortable, with a large stage and fine acoustics.

The Georgetown Cricket Club at Bourda, with its pavilions and club rooms, has one of the finest cricket grounds in the tropics. The old Dutch sea-wall (now being rebuilt) is cool in the evening. The mud makes it undesirable to swim in the sea but many locals do so, then go home for a bath. The racecourse has been closed. The international airport is at Timehri, 25 miles S of Georgetown on the first piece of solid ground in the coastlands—a hill rising to the phenomenal altitude of 40 feet. There is an airstrip for local flights at Ogle, six miles from the city.

Things to See The Botanic Gardens (entry free), covering 120 acres, have a fine collection of palms, as well as orchids and ponds of Victoria Regia and lotus lilies. There are thousands of birds in the shrubberies. The Zoo has a fine collection of local animals, including several manatees in lakes surrounding the area. It appears that about half of the gardens is now closed to the public: do not enter or go near the fenced-off part, as you may be attacked by muggers or arrested by the police. The police band gives a free concert on Thursdays, 1730-1830, in the gardens. Entry to Zoo, adults 50 cents, children 25 cents.

The University of Guyana is at Turkeyen, near the city. The Promenade Gardens on Middle Street (entry free) have many beautiful tropical plants and flowers, including the rare cannonball tree (*Couroupita guianensis*), so named for the appearance of its poisonous fruit.

Hotels Air-conditioned, private bathrooms, *Guyana Pegasus*, A, swimming pool (non residents wishing to swim must pay G$50 for a month's bathing), restaurant (G$75, lunch, G$75+ dinner). The following have a/c, and non a/c rooms which are cheaper; all have restaurants: *Tower*, B, run down, swimming pool, also 3-course meals at G$35 p.p., staff courteous and friendly; *Country Pride*, new; *Belvedere*, Camp Street, C, can be very noisy; *Park*,

C with a/c, cold water, good security (new annex rec.); *Penthouse*, D; *La Chalet*, D expensive for what it is; *Le Grille*, 176 Middle Street, P.O. Box 744, T 57593, C, incl. breakfast (beware of robbers); *Demico* (opposite Stabroek Market, over cafeteria, rec.), C, book a month ahead, rec. *Chinese Dragon*, D (a/c and non a/c rooms same price), with restaurant. *Palm Court*, D, with breakfast; *Roma*, C with breakfast; *Waggon Wheel*, E, a bit noisy. *German's*, F, w.c. in every room, flush before use. All in main business area. *C Island Hotel and Disco*, 46 High Street, E, in a rough area of town, meals not available; *Rima Guest House*, Middle Street, D, with breakfast, no a/c, modernized and good; *Water Chris*, D, friendly, good restaurant. Many hotels have a disco. If in doubt, go to a larger hotel for first night and shop around in daylight. Prices are rising rapidly, but using the parallel market can reduce costs.

Restaurants The food situation has greatly improved in the last two years. At *Pegasus* and *Tower* Hotels, good Anglo-American food; the *Pegasus* puts on Sunday lunch for G$120—there is a steel band on Sat. and Sun.; *Palm Court*, quite good; *Belvedere Hotel*, "The Hut", Anglo-American and French; *Qik-Serv*, good and clean self-service; *Arawak Steak House* (US$10) and roof garden (over *Demico Hotel*) with "wild meat" (game) served Thurs. evenings; *Park Hotel* now only serves food upstairs; lunch and dinner must be ordered in advance. A new restaurant for those who can afford the best is *Del Casa*, Middle Street (US$20). *Kwang Chow*, Camp St. and Regent St., good Chinese and *Chinese Dragon*, Robb St. and Av. of the Republic, less good; there are several Chinese places along Sheriff Street (nickname Noodles Boulevard). Indian/Chinese/Creole fare provided at the *Rice Bowl/Doc's Creole Corner* on Robb Street, rec.; also *Country Pride* with excellent fish either fried or curried, and *Aggie's*, good Creole food at 69 Main Street, G$20 for lunch. *Hack's Hallal*, though still serving quality fare, is no longer cheap. Two other rec. Chinese restaurants are *Diamond Food House*, 9 Camp St., Werk-en-Rust, and *Double Happiness* at 88 Sheriff St. near the town centre, which both have the same owners. Chinese restaurant, *Double Dragon*, on Avenue of the Republic, on site of the old *Local*. *Grub Inn*, good cheap Creole food and dancing. Also good for cheap food are *Sip 'n Chat, The Coalpot* (rec., US$8), *Yamin's Eatwell Centre*, Camp St., *King Creole* (fast food) plus a cheap Chinese restaurant in virtually every block.

Tipping Hotel and restaurant staff, 10%; taxis, same; airport porters, 25 cents a bag; hairdressers, 50 cents; cloakroom attendants and cinema usherettes, no tip.

Current 110 volts in the city and 220 volts outside.

Shopping The East Indian shops have a fine assortment of the beaten brasswork commonly known as Benares ware. They sell Indian jewellery, knick-knacks and items made of native hardwood (best buy). Other possible buys are fragrant kus-kus grass, guava jelly, cassava cakes, many Amerindian curios such as bead aprons, bows and arrows, blowpipes, basket work and bright plumed head-dresses. Buy these in souvenir shops in Water Street, Margarita Gift Shop in Middle Street, in the *Tower Hotel* or at the Guyana Crafts Co-operative in High Street or at "Houseproud", 6 Ave. of the Republic, tho' expensive, rec. Woodbine Art Gallery, Woodbine House, 294 Quamina Street, T 68179/58404: modern paintings in a clonial house, worth a visit. Guyana Stores (Amex representative) and Fogarty's (cheaper) are the two big department stores in the centre of town, both have small book sections and are good for clothing. Regent Street is the major shopping area. (Jaigobind rec. for hammocks.) Guyana Stores carries photographic supplies (Kodak), Acme in Regent Street carries Agfa. Developing film takes time and is not always reliable. A more interesting way of getting curios is to go into the Bush (special permit needed) among the Amerindians. Note that Stabroek Market can be dangerous for travellers. Credit cards are accepted at the *Pegasus* and *Tower* hotel shops.

Bookshop Guyana National Trading Corporation on Camp Street. 2nd hand available on Regent Street at "Argosy" and Kharg, some paperbacks. Guyana Stores has some books (Robb St. branch).

Motoring Self-drive from Sankar Bros., Main Street (T 61058), daily charge, then free for 30 miles, then a mileage charge, reported to be rising rapidly. Allied Services, Croal Street (T 63851) and Ammo Taxis, Charlotte Street (T 63687). Try to book one month in advance. Gasoline: G$10 for Imperial gallon of "regular" (G$20 on black market at night). **Beware**: serious gasoline shortages can make this a difficult way to travel.

Taxis Indicated by H on licence plates. G$20 per fare in city limits, double night fares on longer trips. Shared taxis in city during daytime (usually minibuses) cost G$1.00 pp. The system can be difficult to figure out; often impossible to get a seat during rush hours.

Banks National Bank of Industry and Commerce (7 branches); Barclays Bank International (2 branches); The Republic Bank; Bank of Baroda (2); Bank of Nova Scotia; are all good for receiving money from abroad. Guyana Co-operative Bank (10). Open: 0800-1200, but 0800-1100 on Sat. When the amount exceeds G$100 the transaction becomes very time consuming. Amex will hold mail and process loss claims.

Post Office Main one at North Road, open 0730-1600. Overseas postal rates are low.

Travel Agency Guyana Overland Tours, 48 Princes Street, P.O. Box 10173, services reported to be very reduced in 1988; they sell good maps and their guide (G$4.95) is one of the only sources of current tourist information and maps. Extremely helpful. Frandec Travel Service (Main St.), Neil Mendoza (the manager) is very helpful and informative, as is Mrs. Eytle, runs trips to Kaieteur falls. Joe Chin on Main St. is also recommended.

Churches Anglican: St. Georges Cathedral, Christ Church, Waterloo Street; St. Andrews (Presbyterian), Avenue of the Republic; Roman Catholic Cathedral, Brickdam.

Bus Service Plenty of minibuses on all main routes; fewer large buses. Main terminal at Stabroek Market Square. City services run 0600-2200. For New Amsterdam and Springlands; minibus to Rosignol G$20, then G$1 ferry to New Amsterdam, then bus to Springlands, G$20 (2½ hrs). Taxi to Springlands, G$1,200 from *Pagasus*; shared taxi G$80 p.p. or G$480 for vehicle.

Ferries Service reduced since bridge built over Demerara River 4 miles upstream from Georgetown (but the bridge collapsed in March 1988). The *Makouria* crosses the Demerara River between Georgetown's Ferry Stelling and Vreed-en-Hoop on weekdays only (Sunday, bus G$1.50). Single fare: G$1. Weekly ferry direct to Bartica.

N.B. Since 1986 the personal security situation has been much improved and tourists are made welcome; however, care is still necessary at night. Water and power cuts continue, and fuel shortages still occur. Water pressure is low except in the best hotels, and typhoid has become a risk.

Linden (pop. 35,000), the bauxite centre 70 miles S of Georgetown on the Demarara River, is made up of three towns: Mackenzie, Wismar and Christianburg. The latter two are separated from Mackenzie by the river on whose banks they all lie, in secondary jungle. There is a golf club; visitors are welcome. The river is navigable right up to the mine, and it is disconcerting on rounding its bends to meet large ocean-going ships. Linden is the second largest community in Guyana, but accommodation is scarce and expensive (*Mackenzie Hotel*, D, T 04-2183). There are also several other guest houses at a price. There is a bridge across the river, and a road to Georgetown (taxi, about G$30 p.p.). To visit the interior from here you need a permit from Georgetown. Lifts are sometimes available from gold prospectors.

Current 220 volts, 60 cycles. Same at New Amsterdam and Bartica, below.

New Amsterdam, capital of Berbice, the most easterly county of Guyana, is on the right bank of the Berbice River near its mouth. It is 65 miles SE of Georgetown, from which there is a good road to Rosignol, ferry point (95 cents) for New Amsterdam, across the river. Pop. 25,000. The foliage gives the town a picturesque air. Poor roads; water should be boiled before drinking.

Hotels *Penguin* (T 03-2012) B-C, a/c. *Church View Guest House*, D, incl. meals, good. At Rose Hall: *Hotel Embassy*.

Banks National Bank of Industry and Commerce; Barclays Bank International; Bank of Baroda.

Bus To Georgetown, none-direct, but eight ferries a day to Rosignol and then bus (G$20) or taxi (shared) to Georgetown; also to Springlands (G$20 a seat).

Springlands, near the mouth of the Corentyne River (can be smelly), is a small port frequented by sailing vessels. There is a daily ferry (Sf7.50 one-way, Sf12.50 return—counts as onward ticket in both countries) run by Suriname (not Sundays or national holidays of either country) to and from Nieuw Nickerie (Suriname), which involves a 24 hour wait. Booking office open at 0730 Mon.-Sat. in small yellow building 100 feet before ferry; passport and G$2 needed for booking but you can buy the actual ticket on the ferry. If travelling in a group, one member with all the group's passports could travel ahead and book onto the ferry, thus saving time and possibly a wasted trip. Then from 0900 onwards Immigration stamp you out, keeping your passport until about 1200 when you go to Customs with your money declaration. Border formalities at Springlands are very thorough and slow; the waiting list can take a week to clear, and it can take two to ten hours to cross the river. (A new ferry, being installed with EEC funds, was expected to be ready in 1988—but was not.) Before you leave check whether you require a visa to visit Suriname -it can take as long as six weeks to get one. A transit visa on the other hand can be obtained right away. Local advice to save time is to fly. The town is officially referred to as *Corriverton*, as it has been joined with Skeldon to form the Corentyne River Town (population 17,000). The road from Springlands to New Amsterdam has been rebuilt.

Hotels *Ambassador*, close to point for ferry to Nickerie; *Parpark*, E, opposite ferry; *Arawak* (Room 27, the best) honest, opposite ferry, F, good value; *Liberty*; *Mahogany*, with colour TV (Suriname programme), best value. Also *Swiss Hotel* (Pakistani run), rough but helpful. Good Chinese restaurants within a few blocks of town centre.

Banks National Bank of Industry and Commerce; Barclays Bank International. Leaving Springlands for Suriname, change Guyana dollars (undeclared) into guilders on jetty, fairly good rates.

Transport To Georgetown via New Amsterdam, ferry and Rosignol (not a through service) G$40. Shared taxi to Georgetown, G$80 p.p.

Morawhanna (Morajuana to the Venezuelans), on the Waini River near the Venezuelan frontier, is another small port.

Bartica, at the junction of the Essequibo and Mazaruni rivers, is the "take-off" town for the gold and diamond fields, Kaieteur Fall, and the interior generally. Here an Amazonian mass of waters meets, but vastly more beautiful, for they are coloured the "glossy copper" of all Guyanese rivers and not the dull mud-brown of most of the Amazon. Swimming very good.

Ferries A boat takes you between Bartica and *Parika* (36 miles) twice a week on Mondays and Thursdays at 0930, 0815 on Sats., returns a day later at 0800 (1330 on Sats.), G$12.50. Stops at Fort Island, food available, but better to take your own as choice is limited to sweetcorn and pastries. A faster service is available by speedboat G$50. There is a weekly direct ferry to Georgetown. Buses ply between Parika and Vreed-en-Hoop, connecting with the bridge and ferry for Georgetown. (You travel with the *Glory Halleluya*, a wooden boat, at your own risk—it is always overcrowded and has already sunk twice.) Buses also connect with the Parika-Adventure ferry, dep. 1700 daily and 0830 Weds. and Fridays and returning from Adventure 0300 and 1330 Weds. and Fridays. One sailing at 1200 Sunday. From Parika there are 3 ferries a day to Leguan Island (30 minutes, G$1.35) where the new *Hotel President* has opened. Parika-Adventure G$6; Parika-Bartica G$7.20. The m.v. *Malili* plies daily between Parika and Adventure (Essequibo Coast area)—see *Three Singles to Adventure*, by Gerald Durrell.

Hotels *Marin; The Nest* on Fifth Avenue, E, unsafe, very noisy, meals to be had from disco after 1730, or "Robbie's". *Modern*, near ferry, good food. Book ahead if possible. Mrs Payne, near Hospital, basic, clean.

Airstrip Flights on Monday, Wednesday (2) and Saturday to Timehri, Georgetown.

The Essequibo is navigable to large boats for some miles above Bartica. The Cuyuni flows into the Mazaruni 3 miles above Bartica, and above this confluence the Mazaruni is impeded for 120 miles by thousands of islands, rapids and waterfalls. To avoid this stretch of treacherous river a road has been built from Bartica to Issano, where boats can be taken up the more tranquil upper Mazaruni. To visit the diamond fields there are regular air trips by Guyana Airways to Kurupung on the Mazaruni river. From there it is just a walk (with a permit) to the diamond fields.

The **Kaieteur Fall,** on the Potaro River, ranks with the Niagara, Victoria, and Iguazú Falls in majesty and beauty. This Fall, nearly five times the height of Niagara, with a sheer drop of 741 ft., pours its waters over a channel nearly 300 ft. wide. Frandec Travel offer a tour using a boat trip to Bartica, then flight to the Falls. There is a once-a-week air service, most seats reserved for residents but no time for sightseeing. Instead larger groups often charter GAS planes on Sundays, or small parties a light aircraft, for the day. It is rumoured that GAS personnel expect G$30/40 to get you on the scheduled service; the price of a return day trip by air from Georgetown to the Falls is US$140.

The overland route to the Fall takes 7 days and requires a special permit. This takes at least two weeks to obtain from the Secretary of Home Affairs. **N.B.** It was not possible to do this route in early 1989. The first day's journey is from Georgetown to Bartica: either take the ship round the coast and see the island of Leguan (*Hotel President*) at the mouth of the Essequibo or cross the Demerara by bridge or ferry to Vreed-en-Hoop and on by road to Parika, there to join the ship for Bartica at the confluence of the Essequibo and Mazaruni (cost about G$7.)

The second day is a 113-mile journey via Garraway Stream with its fine suspension bridge across the Potaro, over a jungle road to Kangaruma where the night is spent at a government rest house (reservations can be made by radio from Georgetown). The next day a boat is taken to Tukeit (rest house, F, bring your own food) with portages at the Amatuk and Waratuk Falls. There is a rest house at Tukeit and good bathing. The climb to the top of the Kaieteur Fall takes at least two hours (but is worth it) to watch the blue, white and brown water tumbling into a stupendous gorge. There is a rest house at the top of the falls but it has been closed for repairs. Avoid April and October, the dry season, as the flow of the falls is reduced. The height of the wet (June) season should also be avoided if attempting to walk from Mahdia (4-6 days). Alternatively the gold prospectors have boats going up river or one can pay to travel by jeep, or the plane to the Fall leaves on Friday, cost G$25.

The Kaieteur Fall lies within the Kaieteur National Park, where there is a variety of wildlife—tapirs, ocelots, monkeys, armadillos, anteaters, and jungle and river birds. The Pakaraima Mountains stretch from Kaieteur westwards to include the highest peak in Guyana, Mt. Roraima (9,219 feet), the possible inspiration for Conan Doyle's *Lost World* **(see page 925)**.

Kaieteur continues to be where most people want to go, but now that there is very little tinned food available locally, planning five days' food is a headache. The boatman has doubled his hire rates for the 3-day Kangaruma (guesthouse, F)-Tukeit leg and chartering a Britten-Norman Islander costs G$430 each for a return flight to Ogle for eight people. Alternatively in Bartica one can ask around for trucks or prospectors going to the Mahdia area. Even if there is an immediate lift, leave your name at the hotel beside the docks. Other people will be looking to share the cost of transport "down under". The road between Kangaruma and Mahdia is very bad indeed during the rainy season and can take over seven hours, so take sufficient food. The cost of a rented truck for the journey is just over US$200 but divided between six it is reasonable. There are also plenty of gold prospectors above Amatuk falls and they frequently go to Kangaruma and Mahdia. Instead Guyana Overland Tours have suggested Imbaimadai which is accessible, enjoyable and also has a waterfall, not as high but as beautiful a setting. You will also see Mt. Roraima on landing and take-off. Tues. and Sats. by Guyana Airways, try to pick a clear day, book outside Guyana and confirm on arrival in Georgetown.

Precautions Book accommodation at Bartica and the Rest House if at all possible (if not, do not worry too much as few people seem to be visiting the area at the moment), and arrange for boats on the Potaro in advance. Take what food and drink you need, a sleeping bag, a sheet and blanket, a mosquito net, and kerosene for the Tilley lamps.

Rupununi Elizabeth Allen writes: The south-western area of Guyana is known as the Rupununi Savanna. 13,000 sq. km. lie in Guyana and 47,000 sq. km. more in Venezuela and Brazil. The Kanuku Mountains divide the Rupununi from west to east, and rise to 3,143 feet at Mt. Ilamikipang. The savanna is a dry grassland region covered with native grasses, scattered scrub, and termite hills. Since the late nineteenth century it has been settled by cattle ranchers and Jesuit missionaries. It is one of the more densely settled Amerindian areas. Special permits must be obtained to visit, from the Secretary of Home Affairs, 6 Brickdam, Georgetown. Malaria is prevalent and prophylactic should be taken.

Mr J. Dalzell of Guyana Overland Tours writes: There is one major tourist centre in the Rupununi, Karanambu Lodge which is about 40 miles north of Lethem (10 miles north of Yupukari). This was featured in David Attenborough's *Zoo Quest in Guyana* and Gerald Durrell's *Three Singles to Adventure*. It is a cattle ranch, founded by Tiny McTurk in 1926 and now run by his daughter Diane as a ranch and tourist centre. Marvellous situation on the Rupununi River, fishing (including the famous arapaima), hunting, excellent accommodation in small guest houses with running water, showers etc. Food is always superb and the whole place is fabulous. The problem is getting there. The latest arrangement is a package trip involving charter flight from Ogle Airstrip direct to Karanambu, and then returning in a Land Rover (usually via Yupukari) to Lethem, overnight at Manari and back to Georgetown. Wendela Jackson (300 New Garden Street, Georgetown) is Diane's town agent and will make all the necessary arrangements and get permits etc. There is the perennial problem that having made all the arrangements planes aren't always available.

Yupukari is an Amerindian village in the savannah on a breezy hilltop, the centre for Anglican mission work in the Rupununi (begun in 1840). The Alan Knight Training Centre is a theological college for training Amerindians for the Anglican priesthood, and consists of twelve small houses, a thatch and brick library cum-lecture room, wooden church and brick vicarage. It is a unique venture, the first of its kind in the world, and they are always glad to see visitors who may be passing through, and if anyone should get stranded in the savanna will happily provide a bed and food!

Lethem, on the Brazilian frontier in the SW, has no reliable road connection as yet with the rest of the country. Guyana Airways flies Weds. (twice) and Sats. (irregular) from Georgetown, usually direct but sometimes flying via Kato in the Pakaraima Mountains where tomatoes are being produced. The flight takes one hour and costs G$566 return (singles sold). If Guyana Airways flights cancelled, enquire at the Ministry of Regional Development, near Stabroek Market, or at the airport for charter flights which may have room (US$60). To purchase an airline ticket in Lethem one must first complete passport and customs formalities at the police station ½ mile from the airstrip, then buy an open ticket, then make a reservation; the flights are often full as Lethem is where Georgetown's street traders come to get their goods (via Bom Fim and Boa Vista), and flights are generally booked up two or three months in advance. Reconfirmation (repeated) of your flight is therefore essential, and bribes or the right connections may be the only means of getting on. Taxi to Lethem airport from town is unnecessary, the airstrip is practically in town. There are 3 buses a day from Bom Fim to Boa Vista, starting 1½ miles from the Lethem border crossing (G$5 in motorboat). The plane from Georgetown is usually late (it leaves Georgetown at 1430) so an overnight stay in Lethem is often necessary. There are tracks NE to Manari and Annai, and the Takutu river can easily be crossed to enter Brazil (motorboat, or ford in dry season; there is now a vehicle pontoon, G$2 p.p., one way). If you think you have malaria you will be given an injection. Foot-and-mouth dip for boots.

Lethem has a military post, telegraph office and a number of small stores. If you need to cool off, there is a stream 15 minutes out of town on the road with the guest house and the army barracks. It is the centre of the ranching economy (as well as Guyana's parallel economy). The first Jesuit mission to be established in Guyana is at the village of St. Ignatius, about 1½ miles from Lethem— it was founded in 1911 by the famous Jesuit Cary Elwes. There has been an attempt to settle blacks from the coast on agricultural land near Lethem.

Hotels   Mr. Arthur M. Bobb's *Takutu Hotel,* near airfield (he organizes trips into Brazil and will advise and arrange passage to Boa Vista), C, full board, other arrangements possible (very pleasant indeed); *Manari Guest House and Ranch,* 10 km. from airport by jeep, C, with bath and full board, very good, riding, fishing and swimming; Mrs. Irma Matthews' *Cacique Guesthouse,* F (full board available), highly rec. (Cornbread Disco attached to *Guesthouse* may be noisy). Mr. Ching may allow one to stay in the Government rest house (G$6); breakfast G$10. There are food stalls near the airport, 5 bars and "snackettes" (with spotted pigs and guinea fowl roaming freely inside), no beer, only coke, Fanta, rum, vodka and brandy.

Elizabeth Allen writes: The creek at the rear of the ranch-house is safe for swimming, and horses may be hired for riding, and there is good fishing nearby. Day trips can be arranged to the Kanuku Mountains, about 2 hours' drive by jeep, appearing blue, clad in forest and occasional cloud in the distance. A half-day visit can be made to the Moco-Moco Falls to bathe and eat lunch by the cascading river after walking for about a mile through the rich jungle vegetation. G$50 each up to eight people, then G$120. To Manon, same prices.

To visit Indian villages, a special permit must be obtained from District Council (Mr Isaacs), Revolution Square.

Exchange   Mr Jardin, the Portuguese shopkeeper, may change travellers' cheques at a poor rate (technically illegal), and Mr Mahoney gives a better rate for cash, but changing money is best on the Brazilian side.

Border Crossing   Formalities on either side are extremely lax, "you practically have to beg to get a stamp in your passport (ask around for Frank the Immigration Man)". Exit stamp, customs forms and currency declarations and all immigration procedures must be conducted at the police station before leaving Guyana for Brazil. One can hire a taxi and get it to wait while the form filling is carried out. From the police station to the river is about 1½ miles. There are boats there if a flight has come in. The Brazilian military post at Bom Fim is some 1½ miles inside Brazilian territory or 15 minutes walk. It closes at 1800 each evening. The bus leaves at 1700. There is no public transport from the Takutu River crossing to the village; a vehicle costs anything between G$40 and G$120. (Brazilian time at this point is one hour behind Guyanese time.) Beware inebriated immigration officers on Sun.

THE ECONOMY

Apart from instant, temporary prosperity brought about by the brief non-oil commodities boom in the mid-1970s, which raised gdp growth to 10.4% in 1975, Guyana's economy has been in almost permanent recession in the last two decades, despite considerable, unexploited potential in hydroelectric power, minerals and forestry. While Venezuela's long standing claim to the Essequibo region, in which most of these resources are situated, has discouraged investment, other factors are more to blame. Inefficient management in the dominant state sector covering vital sugar and bauxite industries, an investment climate discouraging both domestic and foreign savings, and an acute foreign exchange shortage, have resulted in poor performances from the key agricultural and mining sectors, and a largely moribund manufacturing sector.

Most agriculture is concentrated on the coastal plain, and many sugar plantations are below sea level, necessitating an extensive system of dams, dykes, canals and pumps to prevent inundation. Sugar is the main crop, and has vied with bauxite and alumina as the most important source of export earnings. Rice is the second most important crop, and a useful foreign exchange earner, though significant quantities of rice production are bartered or export proceeds are undeclared through trade with South American neighbours, especially Suriname and Brazil.

Guyana is the world's largest producer of calcined bauxite, the highest grade of the mineral, and currently has roughly half the world market, though competition from China is becoming stronger. Production is currently concentrated at Linden, on the Demarara river, and at Kwakani in Berbice county. No alumina (refined bauxite) has been exported since 1982 because the Linden refinery still awaits investment for refurbishment.

In January 1987 the government devalued the Guyana dollar. This and other adjustment measures proved beneficial both for the current account and for government finances in 1987. Another devaluation was necessary in 1989 as the Government struggled to come to terms with the IMF and other creditors to resume capital inflows. The IMF declared Guyana ineligible for further assistance in May 1985, because of payment arrears, although intermittent policy discussions continued.

	1961-70 (av)	1971-80 (av)	1981-85 (av)	1986-87 (av)(e)
Gdp growth (1980 prices)	3.3%	1.7%	n.a.	n.a.
Inflation	2.2%	10.2%	19.6%	18.1%
Exports (fob) US$m	142	258	242	219
Sugar	47	91	81	82
Bauxite	35	84	96	86
Alumina	22	25	8	n.a.
Rice	16	25	23	13
Imports (fob)US$m	105	247	258	n.a.
Current account balance US$m (cum)	-102 (a)	-602	-677	n.a.

(a) = 1963-70

INFORMATION FOR VISITORS

Air Services: From Europe: flights via Antigua and Barbados (BA recommended route), which connect with British Airways flights to London. Guyana Airways operates 3 times a week to Barbados to connect with the BA London flights; connections from other points via Trinidad (BWIA flights only). Paramaribo is not good for connections with Europe—a night-stop is always incurred.

From North America: by Guyana Airways and Tropical Air from New York taking 5 hrs.; or from Miami (once a week). Connections three times a week via Port of Spain by BWIA (this ticket entitles you to two free stops over on Antigua, St Kitts, St Lucia, Barbados or Trinidad). N.B. BWIA may not accept Guyanese currency in payment for tickets—check in advance.

Regional Services: Georgetown-Paramaribo services are now operated by Suriname Airways. Cruzeiro do Sul flights terminate at Paramaribo. Connecting flights to Paramaribo and Cayenne for Belém leave weekly (Thurs.). Return flights also weekly, leaving Belém on Fri. Cubana fly Havana-Barbados-Trinidad-Georgetown (flight to Trinidad, US$117 plus tax). Guyana Airways has a slightly cheaper link flight to Barbados, Tues., Thurs. and Sat. Boa Vista, Brazil, twice a week. Best to consult your travel agent as flight timetables change frequently. Check over-weight charges in town so as to have enough G$ to pay at the airport. Exchange facilities frequently closed.

Internal Air Services Guyana Airways (next to *Tower Hotel* and across street) has many scheduled and non-scheduled passenger and freight services to airfields in Guyana, which have recently improved. Fuel shortage has lead to curtailment of flights. To Lethem on the Brazilian frontier, daily except Monday and Tuesday, 1145, G$566 return (tickets for this service can only be got at the airline's office and not through travel agents). Try to book as far ahead as possible; local people do it four weeks in advance. Shared taxi (arranged by travel agent with Loy's Taxi Service on booking flight) between Georgetown and airport, G$40 (day/night) per seat; taxi from city G$325 max, from airport officially G$180; bus, G$3.80 (Timehri bus, stops outside airport terminal) uncertain timing, runs sometimes on the hour into town. Do not use pirate taxis as they charge much more. Guyana Airways international bookings are not reliable. Check that the flight you want is operating. Offers in foreign currency can sometimes help clear two-week average waiting lists. Tickets purchased with local currency may not be exchanged abroad. All tickets out of Guyana attract 50% travel tax. Onward tickets after a stop-over if you buy your ticket in Guyana may have to be purchased on arrival. Check with airlines for details.

Exit Tax   Visitors pay a tax of G$50 on leaving, if they stay more than 24 hrs, either to Immigration Officer or the firm with whom booking has been made. On payment of the tax a voucher is issued which must be produced for cancellation at the time of embarkation.

Documents and Customs   All visitors must carry passport and all require visas (US$5), and most must have an interview before travelling with the relevant Consul or High Commission (in London at 3, Palace Court, Bayswater Road. W2 4LP. T 01-229-7684). Take 3 photos when you attend for your visa interview. Visitors without visas lose their passports and have to collect them from Immigration in Georgetown at Camp Street on the next working day before 1030. Travel regulations are liable to change at short notice and visitors are advised to check with their travel agents and Guyanese overseas representatives. Vaccination for yellow fever required by passengers arriving from most tropical countries (check). It is *not* recommended to describe oneself as a journalist as this can entail being ensnared in red tape. Normally the time given at the airport for a visit is 3 days, unless you are staying with friends. Stays can be extended by going to the Home Department with your documents: they will approve the application and send you to have it stamped at Immigration.

A through or return ticket to a destination outside the country is required; a ticket out from Suriname or French Guyane is accepted (a ticket from Georgetown to Lethem is often sufficient for this purpose). In the absence of such a ticket you may be required to pay a deposit. A permit is required from the Home Department at 6 Brickdam to visit Rupununi. (Three weeks' notice is required before an application can be considered.) Tourists may bring in duty free one-sixth of a gallon of spirits and of wine, 200 cigarettes or 50 cigars or half a pound of tobacco; due to shortages, foreign cigarettes and drink are unobtainable and much sought after and surpluses can be easily disposed of. Baggage examination is very thorough but has been speeded up recently. You may be required to show you have enough money for your stay and fill in forms declaring money and jewellery that you may have with you, both when you arrive and when you leave. Keep your copy as you will need it to get your foreign currency out of Guyana. Foodstuffs generally may *not* be imported but one can import food for personal use (any surplus will make very acceptable gifts for hard pressed Guyanese householders). The best place to pay exit tax and obtain a departure card is at the airline office.

Railways   None for passengers. Buses cover the old railway route.

Riverways   The Transport and Harbours Department operates: (1) Ferries across the Demerara (also bridge when working), Berbice, and Essequibo; (2) Georgetown to Morawhanna and Mabaruma, on the Barima and Arika rivers, N.W. District; (3) Georgetown to Adventure on the Essequibo coast; (4) Georgetown to Bartica at the junction of the Essequibo, Mazaruni, and Cuyuni rivers; (5) Georgetown to Pickersgill and other stations on the upper reaches of the Pomeroon river; (6) Parika to Adventure and Bartica; (7) New Amsterdam to Kwakwani, the bauxite town; (8) Launch service from New Amsterdam to Ikuruwa, up the Canje Creek; (9) Daily ferries up Mahaica and Mahaicony creeks. There are 607 miles of navigable river in all. No vehicle ferry across the Corentyne.

Roads   A rebuilt 185-mile road runs along the coast from Springlands on the Corentyne to Charity on the Pomeroon; the Berbice and Essequibo rivers are crossed by ferries and the Demerara by a new bridge (toll G$5 return, but reported collapsed early in 1988). In the interior the road from Bartica to Garraway Stream on the Potaro River (102 miles) links up with the old Potaro road system, leading to the gold fields, and a branch road to Issano, Mazaruni River, gives easy access to the principal diamond areas. The new road from Georgetown to Linden will, if linked with the Ituni road, open a new route to the interior. A very rough old trail runs between Bartica to Mahdia in the deep interior, but the "self-help" road from Mahdia to Annai has reverted to forest. A new road is being built along the Upper Mazaruni river; this will eventually link up with another road being built north along the Essequibo river, which is already open between Wismar and Rockstone. Roads and trails usable by vehicles total

1,810 miles. Motor spares are impossible to come by and people fly out of the country to obtain parts.

Clothes Above all avoid wearing shorts; the locals see this as a remnant of colonialist behaviour.

Food, Drink and Restaurants The variety of races which constitutes the population has led to the emergence of a variety of local food specialities—Indian, Portuguese, African, English and Creole food. Of the latter, the best known is pepper-pot, a meat dish cooked in cassava juice with peppers and herbs. (Guyanese hot pepper sauce is *very* hot.) Most meals are accompanied by rice. There are street traders everywhere, and if you want anything you have to bargain hard. Seafood, found in restaurants near the Stabroek Market in Georgetown, is good, as are the wide variety of tropical fruits such as mangoes, papayas, oranges, bananas, etc. in season.

Rum is the most popular drink. Produced locally it is quite cheap (XM Gold Medal Rum, G$15 a bottle). Other recommended brands are XM Liquid Gold (10 years old) and Eldorado Bonded Reserve. High Wine is a strong local rum. Local gin, vodka and whisky are worth a try. The local beer, Banks, is acceptable. There are about 20 different types of fruit brew; try Mauby, made from the bark of a tree.

Festivals The Mashramani festivals on Republic Day (February 23) are held all over the country; the main event in Georgetown has been compared with the Trinidad Carnival.

Health There is some risk of malaria, especially in the interior. Both types are present. Blood-smear tests are carried out at Georgetown airport. Take prophylactics and sleep under a mosquito net, and vaccinate against typhoid too. Boil milk and sterilize drinking water. Water pressure is very low in Georgetown and there have been outbreaks of typhoid when locals have broken the pipes to increase their supply. Yellow fever vaccination certificate required for landing from Suriname and Venezuela. Medical treatment is free at Georgetown Hospital but the hospital is run-down, understaffed and without equipment. Readers are advised to seek treatment at St. Joseph Hospital run by the Sisters of Mercy (USA), or the small but efficient Davis Memorial Hospital. Doctors expect G$40-G$50 for an appointment. If admitted to hospital you are expected to provide your own sheets and food (St. Joseph's provides all these). Travellers should examine shower pipes, bedding, shoes and clothing for snakes, especially in the interior.

The **climate,** although hot, is not unhealthy. Mean shade temperature throughout the year is 80°F; the mean maximum is about 87°F and the mean minimum 75°F. The heat is greatly tempered by cooling breezes from the sea and is most felt from August to October. There are two wet seasons, from the middle of April to the middle of August, and from the middle of November to the end of January. Rainfall averages 91 inches a year in Georgetown.

Cost of Living Shopping and entertainments are expensive, though you can sometimes get a meal for G$15 in one of the cheaper restaurants.

Hours of Business Shops and offices, 0930-1800; there is some late shopping on Monday and Friday while some stores close half day on Weds. and are open on Saturday afternoon. Banks, 0800-1200 Mon. to Fri., 0800-1100 Sat., Government offices, 0800-1130, 1300-1600 Mon. to Fri., 0800-1200 Sat., British High Commission, 0800-1145, 1300-1615 Mon. to Fri.

Currency The unit is the Guyana dollar (G$) divided into 100 cents. The official exchange rate (April 1989) was G$33 to the US$, though there is a parallel market offering at the time G$53 for US$1 notes. The black market is illegal, but seems to be tolerated as long as one is discreet. Notes: 1, 5, 10, and 20 dollars. Coins: 1, 5, 10, 25, and 50 cents. Only G$40 in local currency may be taken in or out, and money-changing procedures at the banks are laborious because of strict controls. If you have more, only declare the G$40 as the balance can be confiscated. The airport bank is not always open and local currency must be changed back into foreign currency at a named bank. Banks in the city are only open in the mornings 0800-1200. (Travellers' cheques are not recommended as you may only change them into local currency and will have difficulties in getting the balance out of the country.) Few credit cards accepted, and then with a surcharge. A 50% tax on airline tickets for foreign flights purchased locally is in operation, but a good deal on the black market could still save money on a ticket bought locally. Hence the increasing restrictions on the sale of tickets to destinations other than those directly connected with Guyana.

Weights and Measures Electricity: 110v in Georgetown, but some however also have 220 volt 50 cycle A/C. The rest of the country is 110v (50/60 cycles) plug fittings are 2 pin square for radios, lights etc. and 3-pin for heavier apparatus. Guyana went metric in 1982 but the old Imperial system remains in general use.

Telecommunications A radio telephone service connects with a number of Government and private radio telephone stations in the interior. Overseas telegrams are transmitted via Guyintel, Bank of Guyana Building, Georgetown. Cable to UK costs G$0.34 per word up to 22, or G$3.74 for a minimum of 22 words, and G$0.17 for each additional word. Local calls in Georgetown cost twelve cents. There are no longer any functioning telephone booths or post-boxes, and collect calls are not made. Radio telephone calls to the UK cost G$20 for three minutes and G$7 for each additional minute. Telex costs the same.

G.B.C. (state controlled) runs Channels One and Two (radio). Both take commercial advertising. There is no TV service, apart from Suriname's.

Diplomatic Representatives The British High Commission is at 44 Main Street, Georgetown, P.O. Box 10849. T 658814. Telex: GY2221. The US Embassy is at 31 Main Street, T 54900 (new one under construction near *Pegasus Hotel*). USIS Library on main street has a/c, good books, comfortable chairs—a good place to cool off. The following countries also have embassies: Brazil, Canada, China, Colombia, Egypt, West Germany, India, South Korea, Libya, Netherlands, Suriname, Trinidad & Tobago, USSR, Venezuela, Yugoslavia.

Time 4 hrs. behind GMT.

Press *The Chronicle* (state owned) publishes seven days a week, although most locals rely on the *Catholic Standard* (a news sheet), which is sold in all R.C. churches and at 1 Brickdam. *The New Nation* (PNC) and *Mirror* (PPP) are Sunday papers. There are 2 weeklies. The Georgetown Chamber of Commerce issues a monthly *Commercial Review*, and *Caribbean Contact* normally carries extensive reports on Guyana.

Public Holidays

January 1: New Year	Eid ul-Azha
February 23: Republic Day	August 4: Freedom Day
March: Holi Phagwah	October: Deepavali
Easter: Good Friday, Monday	Youm um-Nabi
May 1: Labour Day	December 25: Christmas Day
Eid ul-Fitr	December 26: Boxing Day
July 1: Caribbean Day	

Precise dates for Holi Phagwah and Deepavali depend on specific phases of the moon. The Moslem holidays fall 11 days earlier each year: in 1990 Eid ul-Fitr is April 25, Eid ul-Azha is June 22 and Yaum un-Nabi is October 1. The precise dates should be checked with Consulates or High Commissions during the month preceding a holiday.

SURINAME

SURINAME has a coast line on the Atlantic to the N; it is bounded on the W by Guyana and on the E by French Guyane; Brazil is to the S. Its area is 163,820 sq. km.

The principal rivers in the country are the Marowijne in the E, the Corantijn in the W, and the Suriname, Commewijne (with its tributary, the Cottica), Coppename, Saramacca and Nickerie. The country is divided into topographically quite diverse natural regions: lowland, savanna, and highland.

The northern part of the country consists of lowland, with a width in the E of 25 km., and in the W of about 80 km. The soil (clay) is covered with swamps with a layer of humus under them. Marks of the old sea-shores can be seen in the shell and sand ridges, overgrown with tall trees.

There follows a region, 5-6 km. wide, of a loamy and very white sandy soil, then a slightly undulating region, about 30 km. wide. It is mainly savanna, mostly covered with quartz sand, and overgrown with grass and shrubs.

South of this lies the interior highland, almost entirely overgrown with dense tropical forest and intersected by streams. At the southern boundary with Brazil there are again savannas. These, however, differ in soil and vegetation from the northern ones. A large area in the SW is in dispute between Guyana and Suriname. There is a less serious border dispute with Guyane in the SE.

Population The 1980 census showed that the population had declined to 352,041, because of heavy emigration to the Netherlands. By 1988 it was estimated to have grown to 392,000. The 1980 population consisted of Creoles (European-African and other descent), 35%; East Indians (known locally as Hindustanis), 35%; Indonesians, 15%; Chinese, 3%; Amerindians, and Bush Blacks (retribalized descendants of slaves who escaped in the 17C, living on the upper Saramacca, Suriname and Marowijne rivers), 10%; Europeans and others, 2%. About 90% of the existing population live in or around Paramaribo or in the coastal towns; the remainder, mostly Carib and Arawak Indians and Bush Blacks, are widely scattered. Life expectancy 68 years; birth rate, 29.5 per 1,000; death rate, 6.1 per 1,000; infant mortality 27.6 per thousand; literacy, 80.2%.

The Asian people originally entered the country as contracted estate labourers, and settled in agriculture or commerce after completion of their term. They dominate the countryside, whereas Paramaribo is a predominantly Creole city. One of Suriname's main problems is the racial tension between Creoles and East Indians.

The official language is Dutch. The native dialect, called negro English (Sranan Tongo or Taki-Taki) originally the speech of the Creoles, is now a *lingua franca* understood by all groups, and standard English is widely spoken and understood. The Asians still speak their own languages among themselves.

History Although Amsterdam merchants had been trading with the "wild coast" of Guiana as early as 1613 (the name Parmurbo-Paramaribo was already known) it was not until 1630 that 60 English settlers came to Suriname under Captain Marshall and planted tobacco. The real founder of the colony was Baron Willoughby of Parham, governor of Barbados, who sent an expedition to Suriname in 1651 under Anthony Rowse to find a suitable place for settlement. Willoughbyland became an agricultural colony with 500 little sugar plantations, 1,000 white inhabitants and 2,000 African slaves. Jews from Holland and Italy joined them, as well as Dutch Jews ejected from Brazil after 1654. On February 27, 1667, Admiral Crynssen conquered the colony for the states of Zeeland and Willoughbyfort became the present Fort Zeelandia. By the Peace of Breda—July 31, 1667—it was agreed that Suriname should remain with the Netherlands, while Nieuw Amsterdam (New York) should be given to England. The colony was conquered by the British in 1799, and not until the Treaty of Paris in 1814 was it finally restored to the Netherlands. Slavery was forbidden in

1818 and formally abolished in 1863. Indentured labour from China and the East Indies took its place.

Political System   On November 25, 1975, the country became an independent republic, which signed a treaty with the Netherlands for an economic aid programme worth US$1.5bn until 1985. A military coup on February 25, 1980 overthrew the elected government. A state of emergency was declared, with censorship for press, radio and TV. The military leader, Col. Desi Bouterse, and his associates came under pressure from the Dutch and the USA as a result of dictatorial tendencies. After the execution of 15 opposition leaders on December 8, 1982, the Netherlands broke off relations and suspended its aid programme, which was restored in 1988.

The ban on political parties was lifted in late 1985 and a new constitution was drafted. As a result of these movements towards redemocratization the Dutch Government announced the resumption of partial economic aid early in 1986, but later in that year, guerrilla rebels (the Jungle Commando), led by a former bodyguard of Col. Bouterse, Ronny Brunswijk, mounted a campaign to overthrow the government, disrupting both plans for political change, and the economy. Nevertheless, elections for the National Assembly were held in November 1987. A three-party coalition (the Front for Democracy and Development) gained a landslide victory over the military, winning 40 of the 51 seats. In January 1988, a former agriculture minister, Mr Ramsewak Shankar, was elected President by the Assembly for a 5-year term. Dutch aid was expected to be US$100m in 1989.

Warning: Those caught taking pictures of Fort Zeelandia, the People's Palace, police stations, military installations etc. face confiscation of their film, at least. Be careful also when taking pictures from ferries.

As a result of the civil war which began in 1986, the interior and east of the country were closed to travellers; only the Nieuw Nickerie-Paramaribo route was open. We retain our information on other places in the hope that the situation will improve (peace had not been restored by May 1989).

Paramaribo, the capital and chief port, lies on the Suriname river, 12 km. from the sea. It has a population of about 178,500, mainly Creoles. There are many attractive colonial buildings.

The People's Palace (the old Governor's Mansion) is on Eenheidsplein (formerly Onafhankelijkheidsplein, and before that, Oranjeplein) and many beautiful 18th and 19th century buildings in Dutch (neo-Normanic) style are in the same area. The recently restored Fort Zeelandia used to house the Suriname Museum, but the fort has been repossessed by the military (the whole area is fenced off); very few exhibits remain in the old museum in the residential suburb of Zorg-en-Hoop. Look for Mr. F. Lim-A-Po-straat if you wish to see what Paramaribo looked like only a comparatively short time ago. The nineteenth-century Roman Catholic Peter and Paul cathedral, said to be the largest wooden building in the Americas, is built entirely of wood and is well worth a visit. Much of the old town and its churches have been restored, and date only from the nineteenth century. Other things to see are the colourful market and the waterfront, Hindu temples in Koningstraat, the Caribbean's largest mosque at Keizerstraat and the Synagogue (1854) at Heerenstraat (under renovation and closed in 1988). A new harbour has been constructed about 1½ km. upstream. Two pleasant parks are the Palmentuin and the Cultuurtuin (with zoo)—but the latter is quite a distance from the town and there are no buses to it. National dress is normally only worn by the Asians on national holidays and at wedding parties, but some Javanese women still go about in sarong and klambi. A university was opened in 1968. There is one public swimming pool at Weidestraat, US$0.60 p.p. There is an exotic Asian flavour to the market and nearby streets. Cinemas show US, Indian and Chinese movies, with subtitles.

Hotels   *Krasnapolsky*, (T 74050) A, swimming pool and shops, good breakfast, launderette on 1st floor, and bank (open until 1430); *Torarica*, A-L, swimming pool, casino, nightclub, tropical gardens, fully air conditioned, central, the largest breakfast US$2 (T 71500); *Ambassador*, A (T 77555), Sophie-Redmondstraat, friendly, clean, restaurant, under new management; *Riverclub*, at Leonsberg (8 km. from city), B, many very-short-stay customers, swimming pool; *Lashley*, B-D. All have a/c. Service charge at hotels is 10-15 %.

For budget travellers, best is still the recently refurbished *YWCA Guesthouse* at Heerenstraat 11, D (at official exchange rate), cheaper weekly rates. Best to book in advance but if it's full try the *Graaf Van Zinzendorff-Herberg* at Gravenstraat 100, the same price as the YWCA. Advance booking advisable. Otherwise, try *Continental Inn, Fanna* (Princessestraat 31), *If's Palace*

(Keizerstraat 68), *Blue Moon* or *Au Soleil Levant*; they have more or less similar prices, E. *La Vida* on the way in from the airport is "cheap but nice". *Balden*, Kwathweg 183, 2 km. from centre on the road to Nickerie is probably the cheapest available accommodation; its Chinese restaurant serves cheap meals. Beware: many cheap hotels not listed above are "hot pillow" establishments. The *Salvation Army* will give the hard up a bed for Sf4.50 a night (Saramaccastraat).

Restaurants There are some good restaurants, mainly Indonesian and Chinese dishes. Try a rijsttafel in an Indonesian restaurant, best is *Sarinah* (open-air dining), Verlengde Gemenelandsweg 187. A good restaurant is the *Bali*, Dr J. F. Nassy Laan 5; *Fa Tai*, Maagdenstraat 64, air conditioned; *Tai Toong*, Keizerstraat (good and interesting); *Iwan's*, Grote Hofstraat, for the best Chinese food, but not cheap. Many other Chinese restaurants: *Chi Wan* for its egg foo yung and won ton soup, Keizerstraat and Zwartenhovenbrugstraat 16. The *YMCA Cafeteria* is quite good. Meat and noodles from stalls in the market costs Sf3.00. Along the river there are cheap Javanese foodstalls, lit at night by candles. Try bami (spicy noodles) for Sf1 and petjil (vegetables) for Sf0.50. Especially rec. on Sundays when the area is busiest. In restaurants a dish to try is gadogado, an Indonesian vegetable and peanut concoction, available for about Sf5. Good places for lunch include *Orlando's* opposite the Post Office and *Hola's Terrace*, Domineestraat. For breakfast, try *Lie a Loi*, Heerenstraat, or *Klein Maar Fijn*, Watermolenstraat. A nice place for a drink and dance is *Old Inn Cassiri Club* off the road to Afobakka.

Shopping *Arts & Crafts*, Neumanpad 13a. Amerindian goods, batik prints, carvings, basket work, drums are attractive. Cultuurwinkel, Anton de Kom Straat, bushnegro carvings, also available at *Hotel Torarica*. Carvings are better value at the workshops on Nieuwe Dominee Straat and the Neumanpad.

Bookshops The two main bookshops are Vaco and Kersten, both on Domineestraat, and both sell English-language books. Also Hoeksteen (Gravenstraat 17) and the kiosk in *Krasnapolsky Hotel*. Boekhandel Univers N.V., Gravenstraat 61, is recommended for nature, linguistic and scholarly books on Suriname. Most bookshops sell a large map of Paramaribo, price Sf12.

Taxis generally have no meters. The price should be agreed on beforehand to avoid trouble. A trip inside the city costs about Sf5-6. Fare for one to Zanderij Airport is Sf50; by minibus or shared taxi Sf25. Cheap local buses (route PZB and POZ fairly frequent), but only run in the day, Sf1.50. Try telephoning 79600 (De Paarl) who will arrange pick-up or set down from airport (US$9).

Self-Drive Cars City Taxi charges Sf34 a day plus Sf0.30 per km. after the first 100 km. Other rental agencies with similar prices: Purperhart, Kariem, Intercar, Kentax (T 72078) is open 24 hours a day. All driving licences accepted, but you need a stamp from the local police and a deposit of Sf250-750. Gasoline costs Sf0.84 a litre for "regular" and Sf0.93 for "extra".

Bicycles Can be bought for about Sf80 from A. Seymonson, Rijwielhersteller, Rust en Vredestraat. Recommended rides include to Nieuw Amsterdam, Marienburg, Alkmaar and back via Tamanredjo in the Javanese Commewijne district or from Rust en Werk to Spieringshoek to Reijnsdorp (3½ hours) and return to Leonsberg via ferry, whence it is a 30 minute ride to Paramaribo.

Banks Algemene Bank Nederland (Kerkplein 1), Surinaamse Bank and Hakrin Bank, 0700-1400. Surinaamse branch in *Hotel Krasnapolsky* open 0700-1430; 0800-1200 Sat, the bank charges Sf1.30 flat rate commission on each travellers cheque exchanged.

Current 127 volts AC, 60 cycles.

Church The Anglican Church is St. Bridget's, Hoogestraat 44 (Sunday 0900 service in English).

Golf Club Introduction from a member required.

Tourist Bureau On waterfront, Waterkant 8, T 71163/78421 (P.O.Box 656). Has useful handouts on lodgings in town and rural areas as well as restaurants. Free city map. Sometimes friendly and helpful; organizes tours (4 days at Sf275) and bus journeys.

Tourist Agencies Stinasu, the Foundation for Nature Preservation in Suriname, Jongbawstraat 10, offers reasonably priced accommodation and provide tour guides on the extensive nature reserves throughout the country. One can see "true wilderness and wildlife" with them. (See page 950.) Mrs. W. J. Robles-Cornelissen, Rosenveltkade 34, T 74770, organizes excursions to the interior. Does Travel Service, Domineestraat. Saramaccan Jungle Safaris (John Ligeon), PO Box 676, Zwartenhovenbrugstraat 19, Paramaribo, has been recommended for visits by canoe to Saramaccan Bush Black villages and wildlife tours. Suriname Safari Tours.

Bus services on the 376 km. East-West Highway: E from Paramaribo through the bauxite town of Moengo to Albina, on the French Guyane border (no services 1987-88); and W through Coronie and Wageningen to Nickerie, Sf15 (plus Sf5 per item of baggage), leaves hourly or when full. Transport to Georgetown can take up to five days (night stop at Nieuw Nickerie). Buses to Nickerie leave from Waaldijkstraat and Sophie Redmondstraat (hourly from 0500 to 1300). Get there early for a seat. For all details enquire at Tourist Office. To Afobakka via Brokopondo from

Saramaccastraat (0700 and 0800, Sf3) and to Groningen from in front of Drugstore Singh, Maagdenstraat (0800, 0900, 1100 and 1200, Sf1.25). When someone tells you to take a "numbered bus" they are referring to the "wild buses", *not* the yellow Straat bus.

Most people use so-called "wild buses" running on fixed routes in and around Paramaribo. Not very comfortable, but very cheap (20 cents) and fast. Most towns and villages are served by private buses.

Local Shipping   The three ferries across the main rivers operate only in daytime (the Paramaribo-Meerzorg ferry until 2200). Two bridges have been built. The Suriname Navigation Co. (SMS) has a daily service, leaving 0700, on the Commewijne river (a nice four-hour trip; one can get off—see below—at *De Nieuwe Grond*, a plantation owned by an English couple, and stay overnight). The SMS has a daily service to Reynsdorp, leaving Paramaribo early in the morning. SMS also has infrequent services on other rivers (Wayombo and Cottica). The coastal service to Nieuw Nickerie has been discontinued, but there is a weekly (Mon.) 36-hour run there over inland waterways (**see page 950**).

Airports   The international airport is Zanderij, 45 km. S. of Paramaribo (bus to town Sf15, return Sf20) There is a taxi, US$28, and there is a regular minibus, marked PZB, which leaves from the service station 15 minutes walk from the centre on the south highway, Sf1.25. De Paarl minibus rec. as cheaper.

Airline minibus or shared taxi cost US$5.60 a seat. Money exchange facilities (now compulsory—**see page 954**): Hakrin Bank between Customs and Immigration (closed Sundays). There is a new guest house near Zanderij airport. Internal flights leave from Zorg-en-Hoop airfield in a suburb of Paramaribo; in 1988, local flights were restricted to two destinations: Nieuw Nickerie and Apoera.

Note   It is advisable to check the weather conditions and probabilities of returning on schedule before you set out on a trip to the interior. Heavy rains can make it impossible for planes to land in some jungle areas; little or no provision is made for such delays and it can be a long and hungry wait for better conditions. Check also that entry to the area you wish to visit is permitted.

Excursions   Powaka, about 90 minutes outside the capital, is a primitive village of thatched huts but with electric light and a small church. In the surrounding forest one can pick mangoes and other exotic fruit. By bus (Route 4) or taxi and ferry to Nieuw Amsterdam, the capital of the predominantly Javanese district of Commewijne. There is an open-air museum inside the old fortress (open only in mornings except Fri. 1700-1900), which guarded the confluence of the Suriname and Commewijne rivers. There are some old plantation mansions left in the Commewijne district which are of interest; Mariënburg is the last sugar estate in operation in Suriname. Accommodation for 6-8 persons with own cooking facilities is available on an old citrus plantation, *De Nieuwe Grond*, which is owned by an English couple; details: T 76872, or by mail to Mr. Jenkins, de Nieuwe Grond, district Commewijne.

By private car to ***Jodensavanne*** (Jews' Savanna, established 1639), S of Paramaribo on the opposite bank of the Suriname river, where part of one of the oldest synagogues in the Western Hemisphere has been restored. Small museum. Interesting Amerindian villages nearby. You need permission from the Forestry Department (LBB), in Jongbawstraat, to use the ferry to Jodensavanne. There is a new guesthouse, D (with six rooms), at Blakkawatra, nearby. Accommodation is available through Stinasu (see above) and camping is possible. Near Zanderij Airport there is a resort called Kola Kreek, with swimming area.

By bus (Sf3) or car to Afobakka, where there is a large hydro-electric dam on the Suriname river. There is a government guesthouse, C (including 3 meals a day) in nearby Brokopondo. Victoria is an oil-palm plantation in the same area. The Brownsberg National Park is one hour by car from here.

The narrow-gauge railway, originally built for the Lawa goldfields, between Onverwacht (½ hour from Paramaribo by bus, Sf1, route PBO) and Brownsweg (87 km.) no longer in operation. There is no hotel at Brownsweg, but transport (14 km. up hill) to ***Brownsberg,*** where there is accommodation, can be arranged, Sf30 (T 75845, Ext 34). The return bus is supposed to leave at 1100. Guest house, C. A bus to Paramaribo leaves Brownsweg every morning (price doubles between low and high seasons—**see page 953**).

Stinasu arranges trips to the Brownsberg Park (entry Sf 1) as well as the Raleigh Falls/Voltzberg Nature Reserve on the Coppename river (good swimming), the Wia-Wia reserve on the northeast coast where giant sea-turtles nest, and the Galibi reserve on the Marowijne river, another nesting place for turtles. There is accommodation of sorts in all these places. Soft drinks are generally available from Park offices. See below for more details on Nature Reserves.

Suriname Airways (SLM) has organized tours to **Stoelmanseiland** on the Lawa River (guest house with full board, C, including meals) in the interior, and to the Bush Black villages and rapids in that area. Price Sf240 pp for 3 days (5 persons, minimum). SLM and other airlines (Gonini, GumAir) organize occasional charters to Tepoe, up the Tapanahony river in the S, where one can visit the Trio and Wayana Indians.

Nature Reserves   *Raleighvallen/Voltzberg Nature Reserve* (57,000 hectares) is one of the more accessible rain-forest parks. You can fly via Gum-Air or SLM from Paramaribo (40 mins. Sf555 return) to Foengoe Island in the Reserve. For a more scenic trip, you can take a three-or four-hour car ride from Paramaribo to Bitagron, a colourful Bush-Black village on the Coppename River (swimming good, but do not swim at Moedervallen because of electric fish), where the car can be left with the guard of the Government Geological Service. (Check if this is still possible as the village was reported destroyed in 1987.) From there a four-hour boat trip (Tues. and Fri.) up the Coppename to the reserve costs (round-trip) Sf50 per adult and Sf25 per child. There is no electricity, refrigerator, beds or tents at Voltzberg Camp. However, climbing Voltzberg peak at the sunrise is unforgettable. The camp is 6 km. from the lodge. *Lolopasi Lodge*—with a secluded beach and view of the rapids—accommodates twelve, and can be rented for Sf60-70 per night. The *Foengoe Island Lodge* has accommodation for 64 people with complete kitchen facilities (drinks may be purchased from the manager, but you must bring linen and food), electricity, and shower. Group accommodation with kitchen privileges (twelve people, three rooms) available for US$14 per room; or you may stay for US$1.60 per person per night without kitchen privileges. Bedding is extra. Boat excursions Sf20 per hour (high season) Sf15 (low) and guided tours can be arranged with the manager; otherwise there are huts at Gonini (8 people at Sf65-55), Koejaké (20 persons at Sf140-120 per night) Tamanoea (24 at Sf110-95 per night) or Sonloir, 12 beds at Sf20 p.p. and 10 hammocks, Sf4 per night.

The *Coppename Estuary* is also a national park, protecting many bird colonies.

Only two or three hours by car from Paramaribo is the *Brownsberg Nature Park* (6,000 hectares). Alternative methods of transport from the city include a combination bus and van (schedule irregular, Sf4). In this tropical rain-forest park live giant toads, communal spiders, monkeys, jaguars, peccaries, agoutis, and a variety of birds. Admission for car and driver is US$2 with 57c per extra adult, and 15c per child. Rooms in the *Central Lodge* rent from US$9 to US$15. Group accommodation available for US$2 a night. A cottage or bungalow sleeping eight to ten people—with toilet, shower, and complete kitchen facilities (again, bring your own food)—would be US$58-53. Rates may be slightly higher at weekends and holidays. They are up to one-third cheaper in the low seasons. Hiking maps are available at the Park office, and a guidebook to the birds of Brownsberg can be purchased in the Stinasu office in Paramaribo. A useful contact is Lesley Hattun (English speaking) Stinasu, P.O.B. 436, Paramaribo. T 75845/71856, who is the organization tour organizer. A native canoe (for six people) can be rented for US$25 for fishing and/or sightseeing on the Brokopondo Reservoir.

Two reserves are located on the northeast coast of Suriname. Known primarily as a major nesting site for sea turtles—five species including the huge leatherback turtle come ashore to lay their eggs—*Wia-Wia Nature Reserve* (36,000 hectares), also has nesting grounds for some magnificent birds. The nesting activity of sea turtles is best observed February-July. Since the beaches and consequently the turtles have shifted westwards out of the reserve, accommodation is now at Matapica beach, not in the reserve itself. The turtle nursery was scheduled to close by end-1984 due to lack of funds. (After a visit to the reserves please send any comments to Hilde Viane at Stinasu. Your support is needed to keep the reserve functioning.) There may also be mosquitoes and sandflies, depending on the season. A riverboat leaves Paramaribo daily at 0700, and arrives in Alliance by way of the Commewijne River at 1100. You then transfer to a Stinasu *piaka* (launch) for a one-hour ride to Matapica. The launch holds twelve people and costs US$22.40 per person, round trip. Suitable waterproof clothing should be worn. Two beach huts accommodate five people each at a cost of US$5 per person, high season; bring your own bedding.

The *Galibi Nature Reserve*, where there are more turtle-nesting places, is near the mouth of the Marowijne River. There are Carib Indian villages. From Albina one takes a 3-hour (incl. ½ hr. on the open sea) boat trip at US$4.25 to Galibi where the beach hut holds 12 people at US$9 (high season) per person; or one bed in group accommodation or to Eilanti, US$9 (high season), where the beach hut holds six people at US$2.30 each. Boat travels Fri. and Tues. to Baboensanti and back; there is an extra charge of Sf35 for travel on other days of the week.

Nieuw Nickerie, on the S bank of the Nickerie River 5 km. from its mouth, opposite Guyana is the main town and port of the Nickerie district and is distinguished for its ricefields and for the number and voraciousness of its mosquitoes. The town has a population of more than 8,000, the district of 35,000, mostly East Indian. Paramaribo is 237 km. away by road. Buses leave hourly or when full, Sf15 (plus Sf5 for large bag) and take less time (5 hrs.) with the opening of the bridge than they did before. Sit on the left-hand side of the bus to get the best views of the bird-life in the swamps. SLM has two daily flights to the capital (Sf35). The coastal ferry service has been discontinued, but once a week the SMS company makes an interesting water trip, using inland waterways, to Nieuw Nickerie taking 36 hours; it leaves Paramaribo on Mondays at 0800, departs Nieuw Nickerie 1200 Weds. Food and drink sold on board.

Hotels Blue Hawaii, E, central, reported to overcharge foreigners; *Dorien*, C, bed and breakfast; *Ameerali*, and *De-Vesting*, both similar reasonable quality, B; *Ashoko*, F; *Nickerie Logeergebouw*, B; *Sjiem Fat*, C, without meals; *Luxor*, E-F, among the cheapest; *Oasis* (men only), F, basic. Restaurant: *Tokyo*, rather basic. The *Ajai* (E) guest house is dirty and noisy, but has a balcony for "interesting conversations". Good food at the Asanredjo foodstand (unmarked), ask to be directed, two blocks east of *Ajai*, on Oranjenassaustraat. Cheap filling meals can be obtained on the street for as little as Sf2 p.p.

Banks Algemene Bank Nederland, Hakrin Bank, Post Office Savings Bank, People's Credit Bank, Surinaamse Bank. The bank at the immigration office is reported to close at 1500 Mon.-Fri., whether or not the ferry has arrived.

Ferry to Springlands, Guyana, Sf7.50, Sf12.50 return, 2½ hrs. For the following day's ferry, go to Immigration at 0900, some 200 metres below entry point. It is essential to be in the first 80-100 and the ferry is always crowded. If the police take your passport you are on. Currency declaration forms are handed in at the ferry and you need to change some foreign currency into Suriname guilders (see page 954). Lengthy customs inspection and passport return procedure begins at 0730 and the ferry leaves about 0930. A return ferry ticket to Guyana will suffice as an onward ticket; without one you can be sent back on the next ferry. You reclaim your passport when boarding the ferry. Guyanese entry and currency forms available on ferry, Sf1. No service on Sun., or national holidays of either country; foot passenger service only. The EEC has approved a grant of ECU 12m to finance the provision of a new ferry service to Guyana; a new terminal for the ferry is to be constructed 25 km up river from Nieuw Nickerie; it had not been brought into service by 1988.

Totness is the largest village in the Coronie district, along the coast between Paramaribo and Nieuw Nickerie. There is a good government guesthouse, E. The road (bad, liable to flooding) leads through an extensive forest of coconut palms. Bus to Paramaribo Sf5 at 0600.

Wageningen is a modern little town, the centre of the Suriname rice-growing area. The road from Nickerie has recently been renewed. One of the largest fully mechanized rice farms in the world is found here. (*Hotel de Wereld*, C.) The Bigi-Pan area of mangroves is a bird-watchers' paradise; boats may be hired from local fishermen.

Vast reserves of bauxite have been discovered in the Bakhuis Mountains, in the northern part of Nickerie District. A road has been built from Zanderij to Apoera, but the laterite roads to the Bakhuis Mountains and on to the Kabalebo River, where a large hydro-electric station is planned are now overgrown and almost impassable. Gasoline available at Apoera only. **Apoera** is on the Corantijn and can also be reached by sea-going vessels. **Blanche Marie Falls**, 320 km. from Paramaribo on the Apoera road, is a popular destination. There is a guesthouse, *Dubois*, B, contact Eldoradolaan 22, Paramaribo T 76904/2. Camping is Sf30 tent/day. There is a good guesthouse at Apoera (C, with 3 meals, advance booking from Paramaribo advisable). **Washabo** near Apoera, which has an airstrip, is an Amerindian village. There is no public transport from Paramaribo to the Apoera-Bakhuis area, but many private cars and trucks go there and there are frequent charter flights to the Washabo airstrip. Irregular small boats go from Apoera to Nieuw Nickerie and to Springlands (Guyana). Try to rent a canoe to visit the Amerindian settlement of Orealla in Guyana or Kaboeri creek, 12 km. downstream, where giant river otters may possibly be seen in October or March.

N.B. As a result of civil war since 1986, the road between Paramaribo and Albina has been closed. A special permit is reportedly required to visit Albina, which has been severely damaged and depopulated, and the border was reported still closed in May 1989.

Moengo, 160 km. up the Cottica River from Paramaribo, is a bauxite mining and loading centre for the Suriname Aluminium Company (Suralco) a subsidiary of Alcoa. (*Government Guesthouse,* B, annex D.) Paranam, another loading centre for the Company, is on the left bank of the Suriname River. It can be reached by medium draught ships and by cars. Near Paranam is Smalkalden, where bauxite is loaded by the Billiton company on the road to Paramaribo.

Albina, the eastern frontier village, is 140 km. from Paramaribo, 29 km. from the mouth of the Marowijne River—the boundary with French Guyane. In normal times Albina is the centre for trips by powered dugouts to Amerindian and Bush Black villages on the Marowijne, Tapanahoni and Lawa rivers (about Sf50 plus). It takes 1½-2 days to get to the beautiful Stoelmanseiland (**see Excursions, page 950**). There is a park along the Marowijne river (about 15 minutes walk from the town centre) called Het Park with free hammock places. Opposite Albina, in French Guyane, is St.-Laurent (**see page 957**), with good restaurants and the old penal settlement to see (ferry Sf2, every three hours from 0600).

Hotels *Albina Government Guesthouse,* E; *Marowijne,* E; *Happy Day Inn,* D (swimming and boating); *Albina,* E; *Rorico* (good), D, *Riverside,* D. If these are full, enquire at the police station; they'll let you camp in the park.

THE ECONOMY

Agriculture is restricted to some districts of the alluvial coastal zone, covering about 0.8m hectares and employing about 16.2% of the labour force. At least two-thirds of permanent crop and arable land is under irrigation. Farming accounts for 9.4% of gdp and 10% of exports. The main crops are rice (the staple), sugar cane and citrus fruits, all of which are exported to Europe, along with small quantities of coffee and bananas. Apart from rice, Suriname is a net importer of food; priority is being given to rice and livestock. Between 1981 and 1983, the sector registered annual declines in output, but after 1984, positive growth was restored with the rice and shrimp sectors receiving new incentives. Suriname has vast timber resources, but exports account for only 1.1% of the total and development has been hampered by a lack of investment. There is a small fishing industry, the chief catch being shrimps.

Manufacturing's contribution to gdp is 16.0%, employing 10.6% of the workforce. Import substitution, using both imported goods and local raw materials, is the main activity, with food processing accounting for 60% of the total.

Suriname is the world's sixth largest producer of bauxite, with reserves estimated at 1.9% of the world's total. The country has the capability to process the extracted ore into alumina and aluminium ingot. The bauxite/aluminium industry accounts for 80% of exports, while the mining sector as a whole contributes 6.6% of gdp and employs 4.0% of the workforce. Two companies control the industry, the Suriname Aluminium Company (Suralco), a subsidiary of Alcoa, and Billiton Maatschappij, part of Royal Dutch Shell. Their progressive merging of operations to improve competitiveness on world markets began to yield positive results in 1986 until the industry was severely disrupted by the civil war which started in that year.

Oil production from the Tambaredjo heavy oil deposit, operated by the state oil company, Staatsolie, is about 2,000 bpd. Exploratory wells in the Saramacca district have also yielded oil. Installed electricity generating capacity is 415 MW, of which 54% is thermal, 46% hydroelectric.

Fortunately, Suriname does not have the burden of a high foreign debt, which at end-1985 was US$24m, with a debt service ratio of about 0.5% of exports of goods and services.

	1961-70 (av)	1971-80 (av)	1981-85 (av)	1986-87 (av)
Gdp growth	10.3%	11.5%	2.8%	n.a.
Inflation	4.1%	9.9%	7.3%	35.8%
Exports (fob) US$m	82	298	388	338
Alumina	35	142	217	184
Aluminium	16	44	45	20
Bauxite	40	61	38	20
Imports (fob) US$m	79	266	388	290
Current account balance US$m (cum)	-113 (a)	250	-310	52

(a) = 1965-70

INFORMATION FOR VISITORS

Air Services Zanderij airport is served by SLM (Suriname Airways) and Cruzeiro do Sul. SLM flies to Caracas and Miami (twice weekly) and Belém (weekly), and direct to the Netherlands, twice a week during holiday periods and weekly in low season. Cruzeiro do Sul flies to Cayenne (US$63) and Belém on Mondays, and SLM twice a week, while Guyana Airways provides a twice-weekly flight to Georgetown. This means that there are now only seven or eight flights a week out, and many people now go to Cayenne to take advantage of cheap Air France tickets to Europe as well as increased seat availability. There is an exit tax of Sf30. Internal services are maintained by SLM and two small air charter firms.

Sea Services Three shipping companies have regular sailings to and from Paramaribo: Kroonvlag (former Royal Netherlands Steamship Co., KNSM), Alcoa Steamship Co. and Scheepvaart Maatschappij Suriname (SMS), all with freighters with limited passenger accommodation only. Kroonvlag has a regular service from Europe and from many ports in the Western Hemisphere. Alcoa has sailings from different ports in the USA. SMS has a service to and from New Orleans, via some Caribbean ports. In addition there are many freighters of different companies, which take passengers but have no regular service. Flying is generally cheaper than coming by ship.

Tourism Points of interest are: some colonial architecture, especially in and around Paramaribo; and the tropical flora and fauna in this very sparsely populated country. There are no beaches to speak of; the sea and the rivers in the coastal area are muddy, and mosquitoes can be a worry in places. Hotels and restaurants are rare outside the capital, and you usually have to bring your own hammock and mosquito net, and food. A tent is less useful in this climate. Hitchhiking is not common, but it is possible. The **high seasons**, when everything is more expensive, are March 15-May 15, July-September and December 15-January 15. Travelling is only cheap if you can change cash dollars on the black market, but taking your own hammock and food will reduce costs. Note that travel has been limited within Suriname since 1986, especially eastward to Albina and French Guyane.

Documents Visitors must have a valid passport (issued by any government other than those of the communist countries or Hong Kong), a visa (cost Sf25, valid 30 days—Canadians are exempt) and a through ticket to another country or a return ticket home from any of the Guianas. If the visitor wants to stay longer than 30 days he must report to the Immigration Office in Paramaribo (van 't Hogerhuysstraat, Nieuwe Haven) as soon as he arrives and take with him two passport-size photographs. Any foreign currency must be declared on entry and exit; don't lose the double entry form. No consulate to give visas in Boa Vista, Brazil; nearest is in Caracas. If you require a visa, get it in your home country. All applications have to be authorized in Paramaribo and you will be charged all telex costs.

Customs Duty-free imports include (if declared) 400 cigarettes or 100 cigars or ½ kg. of tobacco, 2 litres of spirits and 4 litres of wine, 50 grams of perfume and 1 litre of toilet water, 8 rolls of still film and 60 metres of cinefilm, 100 metres of recording tape, and other goods up to a value of Sf40. Personal baggage is free of duty. Customs examination of baggage can be very thorough.

Communications There are 2,500 km of main roads, of which 850 km are paved. The main east-west road, 390 km in length, links Albina (inaccessible in 1988) with Nieuw Nickerie. Driving is on the left. Most settlements have an airstrip for the internal air services.

Clothing Except for official meetings, informal tropical clothing is worn, but not shorts. An umbrella or plastic raincoat is very useful.

Climate Tropical and moist, but not very hot, since the north-east trade wind makes itself felt during the whole year. In the coastal area the temperature varies on an average from 23° to 31°C, during the day; the annual mean is 27°C, and the monthly mean ranges from 26° to 28°C, only. The mean annual rainfall is about 2,340 mm. for Paramaribo and 1,930 mm for the western division. The seasons are: minor rainy season, November-February; minor dry season, February-April; main rainy season, April-August; main dry season, August-November. None of these seasons is, however, usually either very dry or very wet. The degree of cloudiness is fairly high and the average humidity is 82%. The climate of the interior is similar but with higher rainfall.

Health No special precautions necessary except for a trip to the malarial interior; for free malaria prophylaxis contact the Public Health Department (BOG). Mosquito nets should be used at night over beds in rooms not air-conditioned or screened. Outside Paramaribo drinking water should still be boiled despite protestations. In some coastal districts there is a risk of bilharzia (schistosomiasis). Vaccinations: yellow fever and tetanus advisable, typhoid only for trips into the interior. Swim only in running water because of poisonous fish. There is good swimming on the Marowijne river and at Matapica beach and on the Coppename river.

Working Hours   Shops: Mon.-Thurs and Sat., 0700-1300 and 1600-1800 or 1900 on Saturday; 0730-1300 and 1700-2000 Friday. Business houses: 0730-1700. Government departments: 0700-1400, but 0700-1130 on Sat. Banks are open 0800-1230 weekdays, 0800-1100 Sat.

Electricity Supply   127 and/or 220 volts AC, 60 cycles. Plug fittings are usually 2-pin round (European continental type). Lamp fittings are screw type.

Post, Telegraph, Telephone   Telegrams can be sent from 0700 until 2200 and from Government Telegraph Service, Gravenstraat, in urgent cases. Night rate Sf7.26 (min). ordinary Sf5.25 (min).
There is a telephone and telegraph office on Vaillantplein. Calls can be made to the US and UK via satellite, Sf18 for 3 mins. The office is open 0700-2000; calls booked before 2000 can be made up till midnight. Censorship is reported to be in operation on telephones and mail.

Currency   The unit of currency is the Suriname guilder (Sf) divided into 100 cents. There are notes for 1, 2½, 5, 10, 25, 100 and 1,000 guilders. Since end-1982 only notes showing the revolutionary symbol have been legal tender: do not accept the old ones. Coins are for 1 guilder and 1, 5, 10 and 25 cents (the 25-cent coin is usually known as a *kwartje*). Suriname's monetary system is quite independent of Holland's; the Suriname guilder is valued against the US dollar at US$1 = Sf1.78 (fixed), which has resulted in the country becoming expensive for the tourist. There has been a crackdown on the black market in cash US dollars (which rose as high as Sf12=US$ in late 1988), which operates mainly from cheap hotel rooms and near the market in Paramaribo. Don't go looking for dealers; they will approach you.

Exchange Regulations   Everybody has to fill out a foreign currency declaration when entering and leaving. On departure, the imported foreign currency can be exported again provided a validated exchange permit is presented. Travellers' cheques can only be exchanged into guilders at banks. Only Sf100 in local currency and up to Sf5,000 (eq) in foreign currency may be imported or exported without currency declaration.
Persons arriving at Zanderij airport and at Nieuw Nickerie are required to exchange money to the equivalent of Sf500 per person at official rates if staying over 10 days. For shorter stays the requirement is to change US$30 per day. At other land borders (or if you say at the airport that you are in transit) the sum may be reduced to Sf300 or Sf30 per day for less than 10 days' stay (or ignored altogether); for children, half these rates. Exchange facilities are now situated at exit-entrance points.

Time   is 3 hrs. behind GMT.

Public Holidays   January 1, New Year; Holi Phagwa (1 day in March); Good Friday; Easter (2 days); May 1 (Labour Day); July 1 (National Unity); November 25 (Independence Day); Christmas (2 days). For Moslem holidays see note under Guyana (page 945).

The **metric** system is in general use.

Newspaper   in Dutch: *De Ware Tijd.*

Broadcasting   There are several stations in Paramaribo and in the districts, broadcasting in Dutch, Hindi, Negro English and Javanese. There is also one state-controlled television station called Surinaamse Televisie Stichting (STVS), transmitting for 4 hours daily in colour on channel 8 (in Dutch).

Embassies   USA (Dr. Sophie Redmondstraat 129, P.O. Box 1821, T 72900), Netherlands, Belgium, Brazil, Cuba, France, Mexico, Venezuela, South Korea, India, Indonesia, Guyana, India, Japan, China (People's Republic), USSR.

Consulates   There are consuls-general, vice-consuls or consular agents for Canada, Denmark, Dominican Republic, Ecuador, Finland, W. Germany, Haiti, UK, Mexico, Norway, Spain, and Sweden—all in Paramaribo.

Visa for Guyana   Nearly everyone now needs a visa and an interview to enter Guyana. The application form costs Sf1 and one needs to show an outward ticket and take three passport photos to the Guyanese Embassy at 82 Gravenstraat to apply.

Information about Suriname can be had from: the Suriname Embassy, Alex. Gogelweg 2, The

Hague, Netherlands or the Tourist Board, Waterkant 8, P.O.B. 656 (T 71163/78421; telex 292 Surair SN), Paramaribo, or Stinasu, Cornelis Jongbawstraat 14, P.O.B. 436 (T 75845). Also from embassies.

GUYANE

GUYANE, an Overseas Department of France, has its eastern frontier with Brazil formed partly by the River Oiapoque (Oyapoc in French) and its southern, also with Brazil, formed by the Tumuc-Humac mountains. The western frontier with Suriname is along the River Maroni-Itani. To the north is the Atlantic coastline of 320 km. The area is estimated at 89,941 square km., or one-sixth that of France. The land rises gradually from the coastal regions to the higher slopes and plains or savannas, about 80 km. inland. Forests cover some 8 million hectares of the hills and valleys of the interior, and timber production is increasing rapidly.

The territory is well watered, for over twenty rivers run to the Atlantic. Besides those named above, there are the Mana, Cayenne, Sinnamarie (with its tributary the Coureibo), Maroni, Oyack, and Approuage. Smaller rivers are the Inini, Ardoua, and Camopi.

The only mountain range of importance is the Tumuc-Humac. Among the higher peaks are Mounts Mitarka, Temorairem, Leblond, and Timotakem; this last in the extreme S on the Brazilian frontier. The mountains reach a height of 800 metres.

The total population is 92,100, the work force 40,500. The basic population consists of Creoles, the descendants of non-indigenous blacks (43%), Asians and whites (24%), and tribal natives (10%). There are an estimated 15,000 migrant workers from Haiti and nearby countries. Their presence has resulted in a rise in the school age population from 13,215 in 1973 to 29,300 by 1986. **The Amerindian villages** in the Haut-Maroni and Haut-Oyapoc areas may only be visited if permission has been obtained from the Préfecture in Cayenne *before* departure to Guyane.

History   Awarded to France by the Peace of Breda in 1667, Guyane was twice attacked, first by the British in 1654 and later by the Dutch in 1676. In the same year the French retook possession and remained undisturbed until 1809. In that year a combined Anglo-Portuguese naval force captured the colony, which was handed over to the Portuguese (Brazilians). Though the land was restored to France by the Treaty of Paris in 1814, the Portuguese remained until 1817. Gold was discovered in 1853, and disputes arose about the frontiers of the colony with Suriname and Brazil. These were settled by arbitration in 1891, 1899, and 1915. By the law of March 19, 1946, the Colony of Cayenne, or Guyane Française, became the Department of Guyane, with the same laws, regulations, and administration as a department in metropolitan France. The seat of the Prefect and of the principal courts is at Cayenne. The colony was used as a prison for French convicts with camps scattered throughout the country; Saint-Laurent was the port of entry. After serving prison terms convicts spent an equal number of years in exile and were usually unable to earn their return passage to France. Those interested should read *Papillon* by Henri Charrière. Majority opinion seems to be in favour of greater autonomy: about 5% of the population are thought to favour independence.

Cayenne, the capital and the chief port, is on the island of Cayenne at the mouth of the Cayenne River. It is 645 km. from Georgetown (Guyana) and 420 km. from Paramaribo (Suriname) by sea. Population 37,100. There is an interesting museum attached to the library on the main square, which it includes paintings of convict life on the Iles du Salut (open daily, Monday-Saturday 0900-1300, additionally Mon. and Thurs. 1630-1830 and Sunday 0900-1200; free admission); the Jesuit-built residence (circa 1890) of the Prefect (L'Hôtel-de-Ville) in the Place de Grenoble; the Canal Laussant built by Malouet in 1777; the Place des Armandiers (also known as the Place Augusto Horth) by the sea; Botanical Gardens; the Place des Palmistes, with assorted palms; a swimming pool; a municipal library and four cinemas. There are bathing beaches (water rather muddy) around the island, the best is Montjoly (no bus), but watch out for sharks.

Excursions Trips by motor-canoe up-river into the jungle can be arranged. Six-and-a-half km. outside Cayenne is a restaurant with paintings of prison life by an ex-convict whose work can also be seen in the church at Iracoubo, between Kourou and St.-Laurent. Ten km. out, near the bridge to the mainland, is an American shrimp-packing plant.

Forty km. away is Ile Connétable, a small offshore island with large frigate-bird colonies; although a restricted area for tourists, some tour operators may take you.

Hotels *Novotel Cayenne*, on beach, A, restaurant, a/c; *Du Montabo*, on Montabo hill, 5 km. out of town, reported closed for remodelling as a Novotel. *Amazonia*, Av. Gen. de Gaulle (100 rooms, central location, T 30-03-02), a/c. *Chez Mathilde*, Av. Gen. de Gaulle, E-C, clean, always full; *Neptima*, Rue F. Eboué 21 (15 rooms), C, best value, breakfast 7.50F, a/c, friendly. *Ket-Tai*, corner of Avs. de la Liberté and Jubelin, C with shower and toilet, mixed reports, but a good view. *Madeleine*, B, a/c, breakfast, will book Raffinel bus to St.-Laurent, 1 km. out of town, friendly (good Surinamese snackbar nearby). About 9 km. from Cayenne is the *Beauregard*, C. Also *Hotel M*, a motel with air conditioned rooms and a small swimming pool; the owner hires out small cars, rec. for businessmen, 15F breakfast, T 35 4100, Telex 010 310. Most hotels do not add tax and service to their bill, but stick to prices posted outside or at the desk (at the end of 1987, none charged less than 100F a night for a double, as expensive as Paris). Great shortage, even in off-seasons: arrive early or book ahead. Amex cards often not accepted but Visa OK.

Restaurants and Bars Main hotels. *L'Auberge des Amandiers*, excellent, good value; *Cap St. Jacques*, Rue Docteur E Gippet, excellent Vietnamese food, reasonable. *Maxim'um*, Av. Estrée. *La Croix du Sud*, Av. de Gaulle; *Le Snack Créole*, 7 Rue Eboué; *Club 106*, about 4 km. outside Cayenne; *Montjoly Bar; Palmiste*, central and spacious; *Frégate*, Av. de Gaulle; *Tatou* (Creole), Av. Pres. Monnerville; *Le Traiteur de la Fôret*, Blvd Jubelin, friendly, good; *Marveen Snack Bar*, Rue Ch. Colombe, near Canal de L'Est, food and staff pleasant, the patrons are very helpful regarding air travel and excursions (the elder of the two is a pilot for the Guyane Flying Club). *Ko Fei*, 18, rue Lallouette, T 312888, good Chinese. Along the Canal Laussant there are Javanese snack bars; try bami (spicy noodles) or saté (barbecued meat in a spicy peanut sauce). Vans around Place des Palmistes in evenings sell cheap, filling sandwiches.

Bookshops Librairie AJC, 31 Boulevard Jubelin, has some stock in English. Also old maps and prints. Current map sold at Librairie Alain Pion, Av. de Gaulle and in most bookshops.

Car Hire R. Desmond & Cie, Hertz International licensee, Route de La Madeleine, BP 148. Cables: Hertzcars. Avis, Esso-Baduel, BP 853. T 31-17-70. Europcar, T 31-16-23. Budget. An international driving licence is required.

Bank Banque de la Guyane, Place Schoelcher. Open 0715-1130 and 1445-1730, and Sat. a.m., but no exchange facilities on Sat., and will only give cash on a Visa card against a personal cheque. American Express at a bank on Place Grenoble. There are no exchange facilities at the airport; if in extreme need on Sat. you may be able to change money at Air France office in Place des Palmistes. Central drugstore may help when banks closed. Buy francs before arrival if possible.

Laundromat Corner of Rue F. Roosevelt and Rue Eboué, US$5 load all in.

Tourist Office Office de Tourisme de la Guyane, located near zoo (open 0900-1200 and 1600-1800) and botanical gardens (T 31-03-56). Free map and tourist guide (Guyane Poche). The SLM manager is reported to be very helpful with advice.

Travel Agent Takari Tour, *Hotel du Montabo*, T 31-19-60 (BP 513). Somarig, Place L. Heder, is reported to be good for South American and European airline tickets. It also sells boat tickets to Ile Royale as well as meal tickets for the Auberge which are recommended.

Post Office, 2 km out from town (15F by taxi or 20 minutes on foot). Poste Restante letters are only kept for one month maximum. Post Office annex opp. Préfecture open a.m. (Place Grenoble).

Bus Only westbound bus is run by Ruffinel & Cie (T 31-17-36) (Kourou 30F, St Laurent 100F) leaves 0530; will pick up at hotel if ticket bought day before. Otherwise transport is by shared taxis (collectifs), which leave from Av. de la Liberté, near the fish market early in the morning (Kourou 40F, St. Laurent 140F.)

International Airport Cayenne-Rochambeau is 16 km. from Cayenne, 20 mins. by taxi. (See Routes to Guyane, page 959.) Local air services: Air Guyane to all main centres, circular flights twice a month. No public transport; only taxis (80F daytime, 100F night, but you can probably bargain or share). No exchange facilities. Cheaper taxi: Richard Lugret, T 31-29-89.

Kourou, 56 km. W of Cayenne, where the main French space centre (Central Spatial Guyanais), used for the European Space Agency's Ariane programme, is located, is referred to by the Guyanais as "white city" because of the number of metropolitan French families living there; its population is about 6,450. It has two excellent hotels and a number of good restaurants, but the project and population have been substantially reduced. Tourist attractions include bathing, fishing, sporting and aero club, and a variety of organized excursions. The space centre occupies an area of about 4 km. deep along some 30 km. of coast, bisected by the Kourou river. It is open to the public on Tues., Weds., and Thurs. 0800-1130. Phone 33-49-19 to reserve a place on the tour of the centre (max 40), often booked up days ahead; closed during Carnival. Kourou has its own port facilities. The port is 4 km. out of town. There are no buses, but one can sometimes hitch a lift with the Space Centre bus to the cross roads 1 km. from the port. *Taxis collectifs* leave for Cayenne at 0600 and 1400 from Shell petrol station. Taxi from Cayenne or from airport, 300F. A bank operates daily.

Hotels *Diamant,* A; *Des Roches* (good restaurants) topless beach, pool, A (incl. breakfast, service and taxes) next to boat dock for Iles de Salut. In the old part of town one can find some rooms for about half the price found in the new.

Restaurants *Guinguette Pim-Pum* (dinner only); *Le Saramacca; Viet Huong* (behind the Church; Vietnamese cooking); *Le Mandarin* (Chinese cuisine); *Le Cactus; Le Bretagne; L'Estrambord; Au Bon Accueil, Resto* and *Le Catouri* (Creole specialities).

The ***Iles du Salut*** islands (many visitors at weekends), opposite Kourou, include the Ile Royale, the Ile Saint-Joseph, and the Ile du Diable. They were the scene of the notorious convict settlement built in 1852; the last prisoners left in 1953. The Ile du Diable ("Devil's Island"), a rocky palm-covered islet almost inaccessible from the sea, was where political prisoners, including Alfred Dreyfus, were held. There is a 60-bed hotel on Ile Royale, *Auberge Iles du Salut,* (address Sothis, 97310 Kourou, T 32-11-00); former guard's bungalow, main meals (excellent) 150-250F, breakfast 30F (ex-mess hall for warders, with good food; bottled water sold). Camping is possible, but suitable sites are limited; take food and water (you can also sling a hammock in the open). You can see agoutis, turtles, humming birds and macaws, and there are many un-owned coconut palms. Paintings of prison life are on show in the tiny church. Boat from next to *Hotel des Roches,* Kourou 120F (130F weekends) return, leaves 0830, returns from island at 1600, 1 hr. each way. Tickets may be obtained from Somarig Voyager, Place L. Heder 1. Four daily crossings (40F return) by small boat from Ile Royale to Ile Saint-Joseph, which is wilder and more beautiful, with a small beach (this island had solitary-confinement cells and the warders' graveyard). Surfing and swimming are possible between Ile Royale and Ile du Diable. Boat owners are very reluctant to visit Devil's Island except around July-August when the sea is calmer.

Between Kourou and Iracoubo, on the road W to St.-Laurent, is ***Sinnamary***, where Galibi Indians at a mission make artifical flowers from feathers, for sale to tourists (Hotels *Sinnarive* and *Eldo Grill*). Scarlet ibis can be seen in numbers on the Sinnamary estuary. A hydroelectric project is under construction on the Sinnamary River.

St.-Laurent du Maroni (population 5,000) is a quiet colonial town 250 km. from Cayenne on the River Maroni, bordering Suriname. (Nearby is St.-Jean du Maroni, an Indian village.) There are three acceptable hotels and several restaurants. *Hotel Toucan,* poor value, E. *Hotel Bacadel,* above *Le Saramarca* restaurant, E, airy; the owner, Mme. Bacadel, is friendly. *Star Hotel* (air conditioned) C. We are informed that the restaurants (*Chez Casimir* near fish market, *Vietnam,* and *Le Point d'Interrogation,* near the hospital) are good, and that the old Camp de Transportation (the original penal centre but now full of squatters) can be wandered round at will (an absolute must if visiting the country), though if you want to see the cells you will have to apply to the local *gendarmerie.* The bank in St.-Laurent will not change Suriname guilders. The brasserie with the orange trim on corner when coming into town from Cayenne has been rec., English spoken, friendly. Normally there is a ferry to Albina (every two hrs.) costs 7.50F or Sf1.70; a dugout can be hired for a bit more. Get your passport stamped at the ferry terminals on both sides of the river. **N.B.** Before trying to cross this border, check that it is open (it was closed in early 1989) and that transport beyond Albina is running again after Suriname's civil war. Possible to fly to Paramaribo on a charter plane. Bus to Cayenne, 100F, 0500 daily; *taxis collectifs* to and from Cayenne, 140F a head, 3½-hr. trip.

There are daily flights from Cayenne to Maripasoula, up the Maroni from St.-Laurent (2-4 day journey up river in *pirogue*). There may be freight canoes which take passengers (200F) or private boats (750F) which leave from St.-Laurent; 5-day tour with Takari Tour US$450 p.p. If going up the Maroni, take malaria prophylaxis.

Jef D Boeke of Boston, Mass., writes: I spent 6 weeks in the Saül area, which I think is interesting. **Saül** (population 52) is a remote gold-mining settlement in the "central massif". The main attractions are for the nature-loving tourist—beautiful undisturbed tropical forests are accessible by a very well-maintained system of 90 km. of marked trails, including several circular routes. The place has running water, a radiotelephone, and electricity. A hostel (*Gîte d'Etape*) is run by Michel Modde (who also runs the tourist office); the price is 50-70F per day with 3 meals. Own hammock and bedding useful but not essential. Air service MWF with Air Guyane from Cayenne or via Maripasoula (215F one way). Try at the airport even if flight said to be full; Air Guyane office in Cayenne very unhelpful. Motor canoe (*pirogue*) from Mana up Mana River; 9-12 days, then one day's walk to Saül. Restaurant: *Chez Joseph*. Tourist Office: Syndicat d'Initiative, 973 14 Saül, Guyane Française.

  40 km north of St.-Laurent du Maroni is **Mana**, a delightful town with rustic architecture (*Gîte d'Etape*, rooms OK, filthy kitchen, mosquitoes, disco next door). 16 km south of Mana along the river (via a single-track access road) is Les Hattes, an Amerindian village: 4 km further on is Les Hattes beach where leather-turtles lay their eggs at night; season April-August with its peak in June-July.

Between St.-Laurent and Mana is the house of Mathieu Witmandt, a Dutch biologist who welcomes visitors to his property in 300 acres of unspoilt tropical rain forest. For a reasonable price you may sling a hammock, buy meals (or bring your own food), and go on expeditions on foot or by boat. From St.- Laurent du Maroni, hitch to the police station 8 km. along the road to Cayenne; turn left here on to the Mana road for 7½ km., then turn left for 1 km. to the house.

Aouara, an Amerindian village with hammock places, is a few kilometres south of Les Hattes. It also has a beach where the leather turtles lay their eggs; they take about three hours over it. Take mosquito nets, hammock and insect repellant.

Off the road SE to Régina and St.-Georges, on an island amid swamps (reached only by boat), is **Kaw**, 83 km. from Cayenne with basic accommodation, where much wildlife, including caymans, can be seen; bring mosquito repellant. 80 km. from Cayenne, on the same road, is **Cacao**, where Hmong refugees from Laos are settled; they are farmers and produce fine traditional handicrafts.

St.-Georges de l'Oyapoc is 15 min. down river from Oiapoque (Brazil) US$2 p.p. (canoe), *Hotel Damas, Hotel Modestina*, E, restaurant, also *Theofila*, lunch US$3, other restaurants and a night club. Several duty-free shops with French specialities. Immigration (*gendarmerie*) ½ km. from docks—French and Spanish spoken. There is nowhere to change dollars into francs; if entering the country here, you must change money before arriving in St.-Georges. There is a beautiful 19 metre waterfall one day up the Oyapoc River at Saut Maripa.

  Air Guyane (office opposite Post Office) has daily flights to Régina and regular flights to and from St.-Georges (US$42, usually booked up a week in advance, but go to the airport if they say the flight is full). If the Air Guyane flights to St.-Georges are fully booked, it is probably cheaper not to wait for a standby (and pay Cayenne prices), but to find 2 or 4 others and take a Cessna from the Guyane Flying Club for US$90 (price includes baggage), 50 minute flight, recommended.

  Camopi is an Indian village 2-3 days up the Oyapoc from St.-Georges (*pirogue*, 600F); to go beyond Saut-Maripa requires a special permit from the Préfecture in Cayenne, which takes 6 weeks and is usually granted only to scientists. Tours from Cayenne, 4,800F p.p. for 6 days.

THE ECONOMY

Guyane has renewable natural riches in its timber forests (about 80,000 sq km.) with 15 sawmills and mineral resources. Farming employs only 13% of the population and the country is very sparsely populated. An estimated 42 million tons of extractable bauxite have been located in the Kaw mountains to the SE of Cayenne by Alcoa and Pechiney. Some 40m tonnes of kaolin have been located at St.-Laurent du Maroni and gold is again being mined.

  Guyane imports most of its foodstuffs and manufactured goods, of which about 50% come from France. The value of exports, mainly shrimps, rum, essence of rosewood, hardwoods and gold, is very low; France buys just over 20% and the USA about 50%.

At end-1982 the French Government announced plans to step up the Department's development in consultation with local parties: the so-called Green Plan (Plan Vert), backed by the Société Financière de Développement de la Guyane. Under the plan local production of basic foodstuffs, such as meat and eggs, was to be raised, and areas of timber plantations doubled to 22,000 hectares. In recent years new building has taken place and facilities for visitors have been much improved.

INFORMATION FOR VISITORS

Routes to Guyane Air France has flights on Wed. and Fri. the year round and on Sat. between Jan. 19 and Oct. 20 from Paris to Quito and Lima (return flight Mondays), via Pointe-à-Pitre (Guadaloupe) and Cayenne. The Air France Vacances flight has been recommended as one of the cheapest flights from Europe. You have to confirm your return trip—which must be within a year. A change of booking may be made once free, thereafter it costs 270F. Cruzeiro do Sul fly to Belém on Mon., Fri. (3 week excursion fares available), also Air France and Suriname Airways. There are Air France 737 flights to Guadeloupe and Martinique twice a week at least. On Monday Cruzeiro do Sul flies to Paramaribo, on Wed. and Fri. Air Guyane, and Mon., Wed. and Thurs. SLM, but there is no boat or bus connection with Suriname. The Compagnie Générale Maritime runs a passenger service to France once a month, via Martinique, and a freight service every three months. **N.B.** Do not accept verbal confirmation of flights from Air France: get a time/date stamped confirmation to avoid later misunderstandings.

Transport There are no railways, and about 1,000 (65% asphalted) km. of road. The main road, narrow but now paved, runs for 130 km. from Pointe Macouris, on the roadstead of Cayenne, to Iracoubo. Another 117 km. takes it to Mana and St.-Laurent. One-to three-ton boats which can be hauled over the rapids are used by the gold-seekers, the forest workers, and the rosewood establishments. There is a twice-a-month shipping service which calls at nearly all the coastal towns of Guyane. Ferries are free except those at the frontier. Internal air services by Air Guyane; bookings are made through Air France. There are 0815 and 1500 Air Guyane flights to St.-Georges—on Sunday it leaves in the afternoon and on Saturday there is only a morning flight. Return flights from St.-Georges 0800 and 1500. These flights are always heavily booked, so be prepared to wait or write or telephone Air Guyane in Cayenne (T 317200).

Transport to Brazil by motorized dugout from St.-Georges to Oiapoque; no customs or immigration post, and foreigners are still sometimes returned to Guyane if their papers and visas are not in order. Be sure to get an exit stamp from Gendarmerie. The other way round is possible (see above, under St.-Georges).

Entry Requirements Passport not required by nationals of France and most French-speaking African countries carrying identity cards. No visa (45F) required for most nationalities (except for those of U.S.A., Guyana, the communist bloc and Asian—not Japan—and other African countries) for a stay of up to 3 months, but an exit ticket out of the country (a ticket out of one of the other Guianas is not sufficient) is essential; a deposit is required otherwise. If one stays more than three months, income tax clearance is required before leaving the country. Inoculation against yellow-fever officially required only for those staying in Guyane longer than 2 weeks, but advisable for all. Travel to certain Amerindian villages is restricted (see page 955). Malaria prophylaxis recommended.

Climate is tropical with a very heavy rainfall. Average temperature at sea-level is 27°C, and fairly constant at that. Night and day temperatures vary more in the highlands. The rainy season is from November to July, with (sometimes) a short dry interruption in February and March. The great rains begin in May. The dry season is from July to mid-November. The best months to arrive are February and March, while trips to the jungle are normally made in the dry season. Tropical diseases, dysentery, malaria, etc., occur, but the country is fairly healthy.

Public Holidays In addition to the feasts of the Church: January 1, New Year's Day and July 14, Fête Nationale. Moslem holidays are observed, but the dates vary because of the shorter Moslem year; see note under Guyana, page 945.

Communications There is telephone communication throughout the territory. International telephone calls via STD to Europe and French Antilles. Foreign telegraph communication is via

Paramaribo or Fort-de-France, from the TSF station at Cayenne. There are about 10,000 TV sets in use.

Consulates British, 16 Av. Monnerville (B.P. 664, Cayenne 97300); Brazilian, 12 Rue L. Helder, at corner of Place des Palmistes, near Air France offices (closed Sats.). Suriname, 38 rue Christophe Colombe.

General The language is French, with officials not usually speaking anything else. The religion is predominantly Roman Catholic. Weights and measures are metric. The currency is the French franc. It is virtually impossible to find a hotel single room under 65F a night or a 3-course meal for under 45F. Food, most of which is imported (except seafood), is very high quality but expensive. Try to bring francs with you as the exchange rate for dollars is always official, and most places demand cash. *La Presse de la Guyane* is the daily paper (circ. 1,500). *France-Guyane-Antilles* is a weekly newspaper with a good information page for the tourist. There is a lack of public transport; car hire can be a great convenience. Gasoline costs 5F a litre and most major car hire firms have an operator in Guyane. It is advisable to arrive in Guyane with a supply of French francs, as many banks do not offer exchange facilities.

The French Government tourist offices generally have leaflets on Guyane; there is a special office in Paris, L'Office du Tourisme des Antilles et de la Guyane, 12 rue Auber, 75009 Paris, T 268-11-07. The Cayenne office is at Jardin Botanique BP 801, 97303 (Telex 910356, 300900). In 1980 there were 5 hospitals with 868 beds, and 11 midwives and 14 dentists as well as 287 nurses.

We are most grateful for updating material to Günter Bechly (Böblingen, W. Ger.) for much detailed information, John J. Chesarek (Billings, Mont.), John Crane (Sunbury), P. Gislain (Cayenne), Karl Olson (New York), J Douglas Porteous (Saturna Island, BC) for some very helpful updatings, Nigel Taylor and Carolyn Johnson (Subiaco, W. Austr.), Roland Wiemer and Karla Menner (Hamburg 50) and Ray Williams (Pwllheli).

FALKLAND ISLANDS ISLAS MALVINAS

(In accordance with the practice suggested by the UN, we are calling the Islands by both their English and Spanish names.)

The Falkland Islands (Malvinas) comprise two groups: East Falkland (Isla Soledad) with its adjacent islands, about 2,600 square miles; and West Falkland (Gran Malvina), with its islands, about 2,100 square miles. Approximately 480 miles northeast of Cape Horn, the Islands lie between latitudes 51° and 53° S and between longitudes 57° and 62° W. Nearly all land combat during the 1982 war was confined to the northern half of East Falkland; its southern peninsula of Lafonia, and West Falkland were little affected. According to the 1986 census, two-thirds of the 1,916 residents are Falklands-born; another quarter were born in the United Kingdom. Slightly more than one-third live and work on sheep farms. During the past decade, land reform through sale and subdivision of traditional large stations has resulted in more broadly based local ownership of pastoral land.

Early History Records of early voyages are ambiguous, but Dutchman Sebald de Weert made the first universally acknowledged sighting in 1598. The Englishman Strong landed in 1690 and named the Falkland Sound for a British peer; this name was later applied to the entire group. The Islands acquired their French appellation, Iles Malouines, from 17th century seafarers from the channel port of St Malo. This in turn became the Spanish Islas Malvinas.

In 1764 France established a small colony of Acadians at Port Louis under Bougainville. Two years later France ceded the settlement to Spain, under which it became a military garrison and penal colony. At about the same time as France, Britain had built an outpost at Saunders Island, West Falkland, whose occupants Spain discovered and expelled in 1770. Restored in the following year after threat of war, the post was abandoned in 1774.

Deserted by Spain in 1811, during the South American wars of independence, the Islands lacked formal authority until 1820, when the United Provinces of the River Plate (later Argentina) raised their flag at Port Louis (Soledad). In 1831, an American warship destroyed a promising colonization project under the auspices of a German-born merchant from Buenos Aires, who had arrested and imprisoned American sealers operating in the area. After British warships expelled a token Argentine force in 1833, the Islands experienced nearly 150 years of stability until April 1982, when Argentina invaded and occupied. Britain's counter-invasion recaptured the Islands by June of that year.

Administration The Islands' Constitution provides for a Governor, appointed from London, an Executive Council composed of appointed and elected members, and an elected Legislative Council. **Education** A Junior and Senior School in Stanley cater to the needs of town children and rural children who board in the School Hostel. Instruction to 'O' Level is available locally, but higher education requires overseas travel, usually to Britain. Rural children receive attention from settlement instructors or travelling teachers. Radio is used to keep in contact with the more isolated farms.

Climate Although the *Sunday Express* once referred to a mutton freezer in the Falklands as a "Colonial Development project near the South Pole" (March 8, 1953), the Islands are in the same latitude South as London is North. Mean monthly temperatures are lower than in London, but London experiences greater extremes. Normal temperature range is 20°F to 70°F, with an annual mean of 42°F. Though not always inclement, weather is very changeable. Persistent westerlies, blowing at an annual average of 14 knots, are the most trying aspect of the climate. Calm is more common in winter than summer. Stanley's annual rainfall of about 26 inches is slightly higher than London's. In the drier camp, outside Stanley, summer drought sometimes threatens local water supplies. Spring, autumn and winter clothing, as used in the United Kingdom, is suitable.

Stanley, the capital, is the major population centre on East Falkland. Its 1,232 residents live mostly in brightly-painted, metal-clad houses. Stanley Harbour, surrounded by rolling moorland, resembles parts of the Hebrides. The outer harbour of Port William is larger but less protected. East Cove, 30 miles southeast of the capital, is the principal port for the new military installations at Mount Pleasant.

Accommodation   Upland Goose Hotel, £31 full board, £20 bed and breakfast; *Emma's Guest House*, £20.50 full board, £14.50 bed and breakfast; *Malvina House Hotel*, 3 Ross Road, £28 full board, £20 bed and breakfast. Prices subject to change. Full meals at all three, with reservations recommended at *Upland Goose* and *Malvina*. Pasties and ice cream at *Poole's* snack bar, John Street. Fish and chips and pizza at *Woodbine Cafe*, Fitzroy Road. *Monty's* bistro, on John Street, recently closed, but may reopen under new management.

At Bluff Cove, midway between Stanley and Mount Pleasant along the new highway, Kevin and Diane Kilmartin have remodeled the farm's former cookhouse and now offer meals and lodging at somewhat lower prices than Stanley. Fred Clark's *Great Britain Hotel*, on the highway near Fitzroy, serves alcoholic beverages and snacks during normal licensing hours.

Stanley has an excellent new civilian-military hospital, replacing the one damaged by fire early in 1984. Dental services are also available. Post Office, Philatelic Bureau, library and some other Government services are in Town Hall, Ross Road. Other Government offices are in the nearby Secretariat. Cable and Wireless operate overseas telephone, telegraph and telex services. There are some fairly well-stocked stores, open mainly Monday to Friday. The few pubs, such as the *Globe*, the *Rose*, and the *Victory* are popular meeting places during their strict drinking hours (Sundays only from 1200 to 1300, the "Glory Hour").

The new Museum at Britannia House, Ross Road West, merits a visit. Mr John Smith, Sparrow Hawk House, Allardyce Street, is knowledgeable on the Islands' maritime history. Government House, the Anglican Cathedral (most southerly in the world, built in 1890), and monuments commemorating the naval battle of 1914 and the 1982 liberation are also worth seeing. Until completion of a new telephone system, most Stanley roads are in disrepair. During the December holidays, the annual sports meeting at the race course attract visitors from all over the Islands. The equally popular West Falkland sports, at the end of the shearing season in February or March, rotate among various settlements.

Travel Agents   Outward Bound Tours, P.O. Box 178, Stanley; Falklands Camp and Tramp, P.O. Box 146, Stanley.

Tourists   For wildlife enthusiasts, especially birders, the Islands are an exceptional destination. Best months to visit are October to March. Make allowance for unpredictable weather. Outside Stanley, the only major road is that to the new airport at Mount Pleasant; elsewhere, tracks require Land Rovers or motorbikes. Off-road driving in the boggy terrain is a skill not easily learned by short-term visitors. Near Stanley and a few farm settlements there are still unexploded mines, but hazardous areas are clearly marked and fenced. Visitors should *never* enter these areas, and should report suspicious objects to the police or military authorities in Stanley. Ordnance Survey maps of the Islands are available from the Secretariat, £2 each for the 1:50,000 sheets; there is also a two-sheet, 1:250,000 map suitable for most purposes.

Travel outside the vicinity of Stanley is mainly by air. The Falkland Islands Government Air Service (FIGAS) operate three Islander aircraft to farm settlements and settled outer islands according to bookings, seat availability, and weather. To book a seat, visitors should telephone FIGAS no later than the morning of the day before travelling; flight schedules are announced that evening on local radio. Although regular service operates only Monday to Friday, it is possible to arrange charter flights to wildlife sites on weekends. Flights leave from Stanley Airport, three miles east of town on the Cape Pembroke peninsula; Stanley Bus Service carries passengers for £1.50. Falkland Islands Tourism, an arm of the post-war Falkland Islands Development Corporation, has recently purchased the 35-metre vessel *Southern Star* to provide passenger service to sites inaccessible by air.

Points of interest   Sparrow Cove, Kidney Cove, and adjacent areas, only a short distance across Stanley Harbour by boat and out into Port William, are good areas to see penguins and other wildlife; dolphins often follow in the wake of your boat near The Narrows. Gypsy Cove, walking distance from Stanley, features a colony of burrowing Magellanic penguins and other shorebirds. Observe minefield fences. At Stanley Common, south of the capital, one can see ground-nesting birds such as dotterels, snipe, and Upland geese.

Kidney Island, a very small island densely covered with tussock grass, is a Nature Reserve. By arrangement in Stanley, it is possible for hardy and dedicated bird lovers to stay in the basic shanty. Rockhopper penguins, King cormorants and many other species nest here. Kidney Island is accessible by boat, 1½ hours from Stanley. Dave Eynon, South Atlantic Marine Services, hires out Land Rovers and his schooner *Penguin*, also arranges diving and fishing trips.

Of particular interest are the hulls of old sailing ships at Stanley and Darwin. Examples at Stanley are the *Jhelum* (built in 1839 for the East India Company) near Government House, the *Charles Cooper* (the last US sailing packet to sail out of New York Harbour; in the Islands since 1866), and the iron-built *Lady Elizabeth* at the far end of the harbour (228 ft long, with three masts still standing). *Snow Squall*, one of the last American clipper ships, was removed by a team of marine archaeologists from Harvard University in 1987. At Darwin are the *Vicar of Bray* (last survivor of the California Gold Rush fleet), and another old iron ship, the *Garland*. Many of these hulls are still used for storage. There are interesting old French buildings and ruins at Port Louis.

Volunteer Point, north of Stanley, is a wildlife sanctuary. Permission to visit must be obtained from the owner, Mr Osmond Smith, at Johnson's Harbour. By arrangement with Mr Smith it is possible to camp at the shepherd's house at Volunteer Point (you must take your own food and sleeping bag). Volunteer contains the only substantial nesting colony of King penguins in the Falklands. Gentoo penguins, Magellanic penguins, geese, ducks, and elephant seals are very tame and easily photographed. An exceptional wildlife hike is along the north coast of East Falkland, from Seal Bay to Volunteer Point. Ask permission of the manager of Port Louis as well, and allow three to four days.

The smaller islands off West Falkland are the most spectacular and attractive for wildlife and scenery. New Island, on the extreme west of the archipelago, is run as a nature reserve, but access is difficult. Enquiries should be addressed to Tony Chater, The Pink Shop, Stanley, or to Ian or Maria Strange. The Island has large colonies of rockhopper penguins, black-browed albatrosses, Gentoo and Magellanic penguins, King and Rock cormorants and many other birds, as well as a fur-seal colony. Saunders Island, besides a representative sample of wildlife, contains the ruins of the 18th-century British outpost at Port Egmont. At nearby Keppel Island are ruins of the South American Missionary Society, which used the site to catechize Indians from Tierra del Fuego during the latter half of the 19th century.

Comfortable tourist lodges at Sea Lion Island and Pebble Island are good bases to view wildlife. Scenic Port Howard's lodge offers excellent trout fishing, a small but interesting war museum, and an opportunity to see the operations of a traditional large sheep station. There is also a new lodge at Salvador, East Falkland, which features fishing and wildlife.

Economy

Since the declaration of a 150-mile fisheries protection zone in 1986, the economy has been transformed. License fees from Asian and European fleets exploiting the Islands' squid, hake, and whiting have quadrupled Government revenue, to about £30 million, in a little over two years. Much of this revenue is being used to fund overdue improvement in education and infrastructure, as well as social expenditures for increased pensions. A new swimming pool is under construction in Stanley.

Most of the camp, as the countryside is known locally, is covered with grass and low heath. Almost all land outside Stanley is devoted to sheep grazing. There are some 600,000 sheep, all of whose wool is exported to the United Kingdom. Native tussock grass, the most valuable fodder, grows to seven feet or more and also shelters wildlife. It has disappeared from East and West Falkland because of grazing pressure, but still abounds on some smaller islands. There are only a few trees, introduced and carefully cultivated at settlements such as Hill Cove.

Entry requirements All travellers must have passports. Only Argentine visitors require advance visas, which are not readily granted. The new airport at Mount Pleasant, 30 miles from Stanley, is built to international specifications. Bob Stewart's Stanley Bus Service transports passengers and luggage to and from the capital for £7 single. Departing passengers should make reservations.

Communications

The RAF presently operates two Tri-Star flights a week from Brize Norton, Oxfordshire, to the new airport at Mount Pleasant (Thursday and Monday, returning to UK Saturday and Wednesday). Standard fare is £1,900 return or £1,180 return on 28-day advance purchase; Falkland Islands residents receive a discount. Enquiries about passages can be addressed to Mrs Allison Dodd, Falkland Islands Government London Office, 29 Tufton Street, London SW1 3QL, T 01-222 5852. For information on organized tours, contact Steve Green, Falkland Islands Tourism, 294 Tadcaster Road, York YO2 2ET.

Unscheduled services of the ferry *Indiana*, carrying passengers and freight between the Falklands and Montevideo, Uruquay, and Punta Arenas, Chile, have been temporarily interrupted. Reluctance to announce itinerary in advance, because of political difficulties in South American ports, makes planning difficult. Passenger capacity is 12. For more details contact Stanley Services Ltd, City House, 190-96 City Road, London EC1V 2QH, T (01) 251 5150. In Punta Arenas, go to Ultragas, Av. Independencia 865. It is hoped that scheduled airline service to the South American continent may begin soon. It is occasionally possible to obtain passage to Montevideo on European fishing boats, but this requires some patience and is undependable.

Cost of living   is about the same as in Britain. Freight adds to the price of imported groceries. Since the construction of a hydroponic market garden near Stanley, fresh produce such as lettuce, tomatoes and aubergines are available year-round. Potatoes and other vegetables are grown in gardens and conservatories for household use, but are not readily purchased.

There is no value-added tax; only tobacco, wine, spirits and beer pay import duty. Small luxury goods on which freight is correspondingly low are sometimes cheaper than in the UK. Colour slide film, which can be scarce, should be brought from Britain.

Currency The local £ is on a par with sterling. Local notes and coins. UK notes and coins also legal tender. Currency from Ascension Island, where the RAF Tri-Star stops for refueling, is not accepted, nor are Falklands notes or coins legal in the United Kingdom. Foreign currency may be changed at Standard Chartered Bank, Ross Road, Stanley.

Mails Since the opening of Mount Pleasant, there is direct and dependable air mail service from the United Kingdom. Heavy parcels come by sea from the UK four or five times a year. Inter-island mail service is carried out by FIGAS and by the vessels *Monsunen* and *Forrest*.

SOUTH GEORGIA

South Georgia, in latitude 54½° S and longitude 36° to 38° W, has an area of about 1,450 square miles, and a small transient population of soldiers and British Antarctic Survey scientists. During the summer months, tourists may book a passage on the merchant supply vessel *Sir Bedivere* at Stanley for £400 return, but weather conditions sometimes prevent passengers from going ashore. Intending visitors must submit a request through the Government Secretary, Stanley. The Island was occupied by Argentina in April-May 1982.

South Georgia is a mass of high, snow-covered mountains and glaciers. Between 1951 and 1980 at King Edward Point, at sea level, snow fell an average of nearly 200 days per annum, but the coastal area is free from snow and partially covered by vegetation in summer. Wildlife consists of most of the same species found in the Falklands, but in much larger numbers. Reindeer, introduced by Norwegian whalers at the turn of the century, have flourished. Other points of interest are several abandoned whaling stations, the little white church, and many sailing-ship hulks.

We are deeply grateful to Wayne Bernhardson, of Oakland, CA, for the complete revision and updating of this chapter; also to Christian Gurney (Thornhill, Ont.) and Dolf Straulo (Berlin 12) for additional information.

MEXICO

CORTES, asked what the country looked like, crushed a piece of parchment in his fist, released it and said: "That is the map of Mexico." This crumpled land is so splendid to the eye, and so exotic to the other senses, that millions, mainly from the USA, visit it each year.

Mexico is the third largest country in Latin America and the most populous Spanish-speaking country anywhere (83.1m. people). Its geography ranges from swamp to desert, from tropical lowland jungle to high alpine vegetation above the tree line, from thin arid soils to others so rich that they grow three crops a year. Over half the country is at an altitude of over 1,000 metres and much at over 2,000 metres; over half is arid and another 30% semi-arid. Only about 30m. hectares (16% of the total land area) can be cultivated, and of these 33% are irrigable.

Mexico has an area equal to about a quarter of the United States, with which it has a frontier of 2,400 km. The southern frontier of 885 km. is with Guatemala and Belize. It has a coast line of 2,780 km. on the Gulf of Mexico and the Caribbean, and of 7,360 km. on the Pacific and the Gulf of California.

The structure of the land mass is extremely complicated, but may be simplified (with large reservations) as a plateau flanked by ranges of mountains roughly paralleling the coasts. The northern part of the plateau is low, arid and thinly populated; it takes up 40% of the total area of Mexico but holds only 19% of its people. From the Bolsón de Mayrán as far S as the Balsas valley, the level rises considerably; this southern section of the central plateau is crossed by a volcanic range of mountains in which the intermont basins are high and separated. The basin of Guadalajara is at 1,500 metres, the basin of México at 2,300 metres, and the basin of Toluca, W of Mexico City, is at 2,600 metres. Above the lakes and valley bottoms of this contorted middle-land rise the

MEXICO

1. Laredo to Mexico City: The Gulf Route.
2. Eagle Pass–Piedras Negras to Mexico City.
3. Ciudad Juárez to Mexico City: the central Highway Route.
4. Nogales – Mexico City: The Pacific Highway.
5. Mexico City.
6. Mexico City–Veracruz–Mexico city.
7. Mexico City–Cuernavaca–Taxco–Acapulco.
8. Pan-American Highway: Mexico City to Guatemala.
9. Yucatán Peninsula.
10. Baja California.

magnificent volcano cones of Orizaba (5,700 metres), Popocatépetl (5,452 metres), Ixtaccíhuatl (5,286 metres), Nevado de Toluca (4,583 metres), Matlalcueyetl or La Malinche (4,461 metres), and Cofre de Perote (4,282 metres). This mountainous southern end of the plateau, the heart of Mexico, has ample rainfall. Though only 14 % of the area of Mexico, it holds nearly half of the country's people. Its centre, in a small high intermont basin measuring only 50 km. square, is Mexico City, with 20 or so million inhabitants.

The two high ranges of mountains which rise E and W of the plateau, between it and the sea, are great barriers against communications: there are far easier routes N along the floor of the plateau to the United States than there are to either the east coast or the west. In the W there are rail and road links across the Sierra Madre Occidental from Guadalajara to the Pacific at the port of Mazatlán; both continue northward through a coastal desert to Nogales. The Sierra Madre Oriental is more kindly; in its mountain ramparts a pass inland from Tampico gives road-rail access to Monterrey, a great industrial centre, and the highland basins; and another from Veracruz leads by a fair gradient to the Valley of México.

South of the seven intermont basins in the south-central region the mountainland is still rugged but a little lower (between 1,800 and 2,400 metres), with much less rainfall. After some 560 km. it falls away into the low-lying Isthmus of Tehuantepec. Population is sparse in these southern mountains and is settled on the few flat places where commercial crops can be grown—subsistence crops are sown on incredibly steep slopes. The Pacific coast here is forbidding and its few ports of little use, though there is massive development of tourism in such places as Acapulco, Zihuatanejo, Puerto Escondido and now Huatulco. Very different are the Gulf Coast and Yucatán; half this area is classed as flat, and much of it gets enough rain the year round, leading to its becoming one of the most important agricultural and cattle raising areas in the country. The Gulf Coast also provides most of Mexico's oil and sulphur. Geographically, North America may be said to come to an end in the Isthmus of Tehuantepec. South of the Isthmus the land rises again into the thinly populated highlands of Chiapas.

Climate and vegetation depend upon altitude. The *tierra caliente* takes in the coastlands and plateau lands below 750 metres. The *tierra templada*, or temperate zone is at 750 to 2,000 metres. The *tierra fría*, or cold zone, is from 2,000 metres upwards. Above the tree line at 4,000 metres are high moorlands (*páramos*).

The climate of the inland highlands is mostly mild, but with sharp changes of temperature between day and night, sunshine and shade. Generally, winter is the dry season and summer the wet season. There are only two areas where rain falls the year round: S of Tampico along the lower slopes of the Sierra Madre Oriental and across the Isthmus of Tehuantepec into Tabasco state; and along the Pacific coast of the state of Chiapas. Both areas together cover only 12 % of Mexico. These wetter parts get most of their rain between June and September, when the skies are so full of clouds that the temperature is lowered: May is a hotter month than July. Apart from these favoured regions, the rest of the country suffers from a climate in which the rainy season hardly lives up to its name and the dry season almost always does.

Population is growing at the rate of 1½ millions a year, or 2.4 %. Birth rate per thousand, 34; death rate, 7. Urban growth is 3.3 %; 50 % of the population is under 20. About 5 % consider themselves pure white and about 25 % pure Indian; about 60 % are *mestizos*, a mixture in varying proportions of Spanish and Indian bloods; some 10 % (mostly in the coastal zones of Veracruz, Guerrero and Chiapas) are a mixture of black and white or black and Indian or *mestizo*. Mexico also has infusions of other European, Arab and Chinese blood. About 12 % are still illiterate; 70 % live in towns or cities; 30 % are rural. There is a national cultural prejudice in favour of the Indian rather than the Spanish element, though this does not prevent Indians from being looked down on by the more hispanicized elements. There is hardly a single statue of Cortés in the whole of Mexico, but he does figure, pejoratively, in the frescoes of Diego Rivera and his contemporaries. On the other hand the two last Aztec emperors, Moctezuma and Cuauhtémoc, are national heroes.

Among the estimated 20 million Indians there are 56 groups or sub-divisions, each with its own language. The Indians are far from evenly distributed; 36 % live on the Central Plateau (mostly Puebla, Hidalgo, and México); 35 % are along the southern Pacific coast (Oaxaca, Chiapas, Guerrero), and 23 % along the Gulf coast (mostly Yucatán and Veracruz): 94 % of them, that is, live in these three regions.

The issue of access to the land has always been the country's fundamental problem, and it was a despairing landless peasantry that rose in the Revolution of 1910 and swept away Porfirio Díaz and the old system of huge estates. Since 1927 the Partido Revolucionario Institucional (PRI), the party which incorporates the social-democratic ideal of the revolution, has been in power. Its accomplishments have been mixed. Life for the peasant is still hard. His minimum wage barely allows him a simple diet of beans, rice, and *tortillas*. His home is still, possibly, a shack with no windows, no water, no sanitation, and he may still not be able to read or write, but something has been done to redistribute the land in the so-called *ejido* system, which does give the peasant either communal or personal control of the land he cultivates, though the purely economic benefit of the system is in doubt. At least the peasant is freed from the landowner, and his family receives some basic health and educational facilities from the state. Gdp per capita is US$2,200.

Constitution Under the 1917 Constitution Mexico is a federal republic of 31 states and a Federal District containing the capital, Mexico City. The President, who appoints the Ministers, is elected for 6 years and can never be re-elected. Congress consists of the Senate, half elected every 3 years on a rotational basis, and the Cámara de Diputados, elected every 3 years. There is universal suffrage, and one Deputy for 60,000 inhabitants. The President for 1988-94 is Carlos Salinas de Gortari.

Local Administration The States enjoy local autonomy and can levy their own taxes, and each State has its Governor, legislature and judicature. The President appoints the Chief of the Federal District.

Religion Roman Catholicism is the principal religion, but the State is determinedly secular. Because of its identification firstly with Spain, then with the Emperor Maximilian and finally with Porfirio Díaz, the Church has been severely persecuted in the past by reform-minded administrations, and priests are still not supposed to wear ecclesiastical dress (see *The Lawless Roads* and *The Power and the Glory*, by Graham Greene).

History Of the many Indian nations in the vast territory of Mexico, the two most important before the Conquest were the Aztecs of Tenochtitlán (now Mexico City) and the Mayas of Yucatán. The Aztecs, a militarist, theocratic culture, had obtained absolute control over the whole Valley of México and a loose control of some other regions. The Mayas (whose early history is given in the Central American chapter) were already in decline by the time the Spaniards arrived. The 34-year-old Cortés disembarked near the present Veracruz with about 500 men, some horses and cannon, on April 21, 1519. They marched into the interior; their passage was not contested; they arrived at Tenochtitlán in November and were admitted into the city as guests of the reigning monarch, Moctezuma. There they remained until June of the next year, when Pedro de Alvarado, in the absence of Cortés, murdered hundreds of Indians to quell his own fear of a rising. At this treacherous act the Indians did in fact rise, and it was only by good luck that the Spanish troops, with heavy losses, were able to fight their way out of the city on the Noche Triste (the Night of Sorrows) of June 30. Next year Cortés came back with reinforcements and besieged the city. It fell on August 30, 1521, and was utterly razed. Cortés then turned to the conquest of the rest of the country. One of the main factors in his success was his alliance with the Tlaxcalans, old rivals of the Aztecs. The fight was ruthless, and the Aztecs were soon mastered.

There followed 300 years of Spanish rule. In the early years all the main sources of gold and silver were discovered. Spanish grandees stepped into the shoes of dead Aztec lords and inherited their great estates and their wealth of savable souls with little disturbance, for Aztec and Spanish ways of holding land were not unlike: the *ejido* (or agrarian community holding lands in common), the *rancho*, or small private property worked by the owner; and that usually huge area which paid tribute to its master—the Spanish *encomienda*—soon to be converted into the *hacienda*, with its absolute title to the land and its almost feudal way of life. Within the first 50 years all the Indians in the populous southern valleys of the plateau had been christianized and harnessed to Spanish wealth-getting from mine and soil. The more scattered and less profitable Indians of the north and south had to await the coming of the missionizing Jesuits in 1571, a year behind the Inquisition. Too often, alas, the crowded Jesuit missions proved as fruitful a source of smallpox or measles as of salvation, with the unhappy result that large numbers of Indians died; their deserted communal lands were promptly filched by some neighbouring *encomendero*: a thieving of public lands by private interests which continued for 400 years.

By the end of the 16th century the Spaniards had founded most of the towns which are still important, tapped great wealth in mining, stock raising and sugar-growing, and firmly imposed their way of life and belief. Government was by a Spanish-born upper class, based on the subordination of the Indian and *mestizo* populations and a strict dependence on Spain for all things. As throughout all Hispanic America, Spain built up resistance to itself by excluding from government both Spaniards born in Mexico and the small body of educated *mestizos*.

The standard of revolt was raised in 1810 by the curate of Dolores, Miguel Hidalgo. The Grito de Dolores: "Perish the Spaniards", collected 80,000 armed supporters, and had it not been for Hidalgo's loss of nerve and failure to engage the Spaniards, the capital might have been captured in the first month and a government created not differing much from the royal Spanish government. But eleven years of fighting created bitter differences. A loyalist general, Agustín de Iturbide, joined the rebels and proclaimed an independent Mexico in 1821. His Plan of Iguala proposed an independent monarchy with a ruler from the Spanish royal family, but on second thoughts Iturbide proclaimed himself Emperor in 1822: a fantasy which lasted one year. A federal republic was created on October 4, 1824, with General Guadalupe Victoria as President. Conservatives stood for a highly centralized government; Liberals favoured federated sovereign states. The tussle of interests expressed itself in endemic civil war. In 1836, Texas, whose cotton-growers and cattle-ranchers had been infuriated by the abolition of slavery in 1829, rebelled against the dictator, Santa Ana, and declared its independence. It was annexed by the United States in 1845. War broke out and US troops occupied Mexico City in 1847. Next year, under the terms of the treaty of Guadalupe Hidalgo, the US acquired half Mexico's territory: all the land from Texas to California and from the Río Grande to Oregon.

A period of reform dominated by independent Mexico's great hero, the pure-blooded Zapotec Indian, Benito Juárez, began in 1857. The church, in alliance with the conservatives, hotly contested by civil war his liberal programme of popular education, freedom of the press and of speech, civil marriage and the separation of church and state. Juárez won, but the constant civil strife wrecked the economy, and Juárez was forced to suspend payment on the national debt. Promptly, Spain, France and Britain landed a joint force at Veracruz to protect their financial rights. The British and the Spanish soon withdrew, but the French force pushed inland and occupied Mexico City in 1863. Juárez took to guerrilla warfare against the invaders. The Archduke Maximilian of Austria became Emperor of Mexico with Napoleon III's help, but United States insistence and the gathering strength of Prussia led to the withdrawal of the French troops in 1867. Maximilian, betrayed and deserted, was captured by the Juaristas at Querétaro, tried, and shot on June 19. Juárez resumed control and died in July 1872. He was the first Mexican leader of any note who had died naturally since 1810.

The distinguished scholar who followed him was soon tricked out of office by General Porfirio Díaz, who ruled Mexico from 1876 to 1910. But Díaz's paternal, though often ruthless, central authority did introduce a period of 35 years of peace. A superficial prosperity followed upon peace; a civil service was created, finances put on a sound basis, banditry put down, industries started, railways built, international relations improved, and foreign capital protected. But the main mass of peasants had never been so wretched; their lands were stolen from them, their personal liberties curtailed, and many were sold into forced labour on tobacco and henequen plantations from which death was the only release.

It was this open contradiction between dazzling prosperity and hideous distress which led to the upheaval of November, 1910 and to Porfirio Díaz's self-exile in Paris. A new leader, Francisco Madero, who came from a landowning family in Coahuila, championed a programme of political and social reform, including the restoration of stolen lands. The reactionaries rose and Madero was brutally murdered, but the great new cry, *Tierra y Libertad* (Land and Liberty) was not to be quieted until the revolution was made safe by the election of Alvaro Obregón to the Presidency. Later, President Lázaro Cárdenas fulfilled some of the more important economic objectives of the revolution; it was his regime (1934-40) that brought about the division of the great estates into *ejidos* (or communal lands), irrigation, the raising of wages, the spread of education, the beginnings of industrialization, the nationalization of the oil wells and the railways. Later presidents nationalized electric power, most of the railways, the main airlines and parts of industry, but at the same time encouraged both Mexican and foreign (mainly US) entrepreneurs to develop the private sector. All presidents have pursued an independent and non-aligned foreign policy.

LAREDO TO MEXICO CITY: THE GULF ROUTE (1)

We are concerned here with the four great road routes from the US border to Mexico City: the Gulf Route from Laredo (by Pan-American Highway), the Eagle Pass/Piedras Negras route, the Central Route from El Paso, and the Pacific Route, from Nogales. The first of these to be opened was the Gulf Route: Nuevo Laredo-Mexico City: 1,226 km. (760 miles).

Traffic from the central and eastern parts of the United States can enter north-eastern Mexico through four gateways along the Río Bravo; at Matamoros, opposite Brownsville (which has 90% Mexican population, despite being in the USA; cheap hotel, *Hotel Bienvenidos*, about 200 metres from Río Grande bridge, D, if you don't want to cross the border at night); at Reynosa (*Hotel San Carlos*, on Zócalo, D, recommended) opposite McAllen; at Ciudad Miguel Alemán, opposite Roma; and at **Nuevo Laredo** (400,000), opposite Laredo—by far the most important of them. The roads from these places all converge upon Monterrey, though there are alternative roads from Reynosa and Matamoros which join the Nuevo Laredo-Mexico City highway at Montemorelos and Ciudad Victoria, respectively: the latter runs along the tropical Gulf coastal plain and then climbs sharply through the Sierra Madre Oriental to Ciudad Victoria, at 333 metres.

Hotels   at Nuevo Laredo, *Dos Laredos*, D, Matamoros and 15 de Junio; many others. *Motels: Hacienda*, Prol. Reforma 5530, A; *Reforma*, Av. Guerrero 822, B; *Texas*, Av. Guerrero 807, D, not bad.

Crafts Shop   Centro Artesanal Nuevo Laredo, Maclovio Herrera 3030. T 2-63-99.

Buses   Buses to Mexico City with Tres Estrellas de Oro, mid-afternoon, from the Nuevo Laredo bus station. Transportes del Norte is generally rec.; 5 buses a day to Mexico City. Buses for Monterrey (4 hrs, US$5.50, leave at 0800), Mexico City (15 hrs., US$25, leave at 1400) and intermediate points. The Nuevo Laredo bus station is not near the border; you need a bus to get there. (Connecting tickets from Houston via Laredo to Monterrey can be obtained at a cost of US$35, 14 hrs. Overland Greyhound bus New York-Laredo, US$85 with as many stops as you want, but only valid for 15 days.) Bus Nuevo Laredo-Tampico leaves at 1600, US$13, arrives in the middle of next day. Bus Nuevo Laredo-Morelia 17 hrs., US$26, leaves at 1730.

If pressed for time, avoid November 20 and other national holidays as there are delays at customs owing to Mexicans visiting the USA in large numbers. Border formalities can take 2 hrs. or more. We have been informed that at the border crossing at Matamoros guards have demanded bribes of from US$5 to US$20 or even US$50, especially from car drivers.

Train   Regiomontano (*servicio estrella*—see page 1029) leaves for Mexico City at 1515, stopping at Monterrey (1900) and Saltillo (0935); it leaves Mexico City at 1800, reserved seat US$21.80, single sleeper, US$41, double US$82. Aguila Azteca to Mexico City from Nuevo Laredo, US$13 *primera especial*, a/c, US$10 1st, US$7 2nd class, daily at 1855, 24 hrs., little difference between 1st and 2nd classes (leaves Mexico City for the border at 0800).

Matamoros (470,000 people), has a bright and unforbidding museum, designed to let a prospective tourist know what he can expect in Mexico. It is well worth a visit. Several lines run first-class buses to Mexico City in 18 hrs. for US$28. Transportes del Norte to Ciudad Victoria for US$6 (4 hrs.). Craft shop: Centro Artesanal Matamoros, Calle 5a Hurtado and Alvaro Obregón (T 2-03-84).

Hotels   *El Presidente*, Av. Obregón 249, A; *Ritz*, Matamoros y Siete, D. There are 4 motels on the road to the beach, all C/B.

Visas can be obtained in Brownsville from the Mexican Consulate at 940, E Washington. About 8 km. outside Matamoros there is an immigration check-point; to cross this point a visa must be shown which must be signed at the bus station by an immigration official. Without this signature you will be sent back.

Rail Tamaulipeco *servicio estrella* train leaves Matamoros at 1400 for Reynosa (opposite McAllen, Texas, arrives 1520) and Monterrey (arrives 1850, US$6).

After 130 km. of grey-green desert, the road from Nuevo Laredo climbs the Mamulique Pass, which it crosses at 700 metres, and then descends to

Monterrey, capital of Nuevo León state, third largest city in Mexico, 253 km. S of the border and 915 km. from Mexico City. The city is dominated by the Cerro de la Silla to the E. Its population now approaches 3 million and is still growing in spite of its unattractive climate—too hot in summer, too cold in winter, dusty at most times—and its shortage of water. It now turns out (using cheap gas from near the Texas border and increasingly from the new gas fields in the South), over 75% of Mexico's iron and steel, and many other products accompanied by an almost permanent industrial smog. Its people are highly skilled and educated, but its architecture is drab. In its main centre, Plaza Zaragoza, there is a pleasant 18th century Cathedral badly damaged in the war against the US in 1846-47, when it was used by Mexican troops as a powder magazine. Plaza Zaragoza, Plaza 5 de Mayo and many surrounding blocks now form the Gran Plaza, claimed to be the biggest civic square in the world; its centrepiece is the Laser Beam Tower. (There is a clean public convenience beneath the Gran Plaza, on Matamoros between Avs. Zua Zua and Zaragoza, near the Neptune Fountain.) Calle Morelos is a pedestrians-only shopping centre. Its famous Technological Institute has valuable collections of books on 16th century Mexican history, of rare books printed in Indian tongues, and 2,000 editions of Don Quixote in all languages. Altitude: 538 metres, and evenings are cool.

Students of architecture should see the remarkable church of San José Obrero built in a working-class district by Enrique de la Mora and his team. The Monterrey Museum is in the grounds of the Cuauhtémoc Brewery, Av. Universidad (beer—in small bottles—is handed out free in the gardens). The Mexican Baseball Hall of Fame is in part of the museum, as is a museum of Modern Art; open Tues.-Fri. 0930-1800, Sat.-Sun. 1030-1730. The Alfa Cultural Centre, in the Garza García suburb, has a fine planetarium and an astronomy and physics section with do-it-yourself illustrations of mechanical principles, etc. In a separate building is a Rufino Tamayo stained-glass window. Reached by special bus from W end of Alameda, hourly on the hour 1500-2000, the centre is open 1500-1920, closed Mon. The Alameda Gardens, between Avs. Aremberri and Washington, on Av. Pino Suárez, are a pleasant place to sit. The Obispado (Bishop's Palace Hill) affords good views, smog permitting. The Palace (1787) is a regional museum; it served as H.Q. for both Pancho Villa and Gen. Zachary Taylor. Take No. 1 bus which stops at the foot of the hill.

Hotels It is difficult to obtain accommodation because of the constant movement of people travelling north/south. *Holiday Inn Crowne Plaza,* Av. Constitución 300 Oriente, near Plaza Zaragoza, A, best, T (91-83) 44-60-00; *Ancira,* Hidalgo y Escobedo, A; *Ambassador,* Hidalgo y Galeana, A; *Río,* Padre Mier 194 Poniente, A; *Colonial,* Escobedo y Hidalgo, B; *Victoria,* E, with shower, hot water only in day time, 2 blocks from railway station, clean, safe, but do not get room opposite station (less 10% if you show student card); *Reforma,* Av. Universidad, 1132, F, one of the better cheap ones; *Mary Car,* opp. bus station, D, clean, a/c; *Nuevo León,* Amado Nervo 1007 Norte con Av. Madero, C with bath (hot water), very clean, pleasant, close to bus station. *Estación,* Guadalupe Victoria 1450, opp. train station, E, bath, reasonable. Many hotels between Colón and Reforma, 2 blocks from the bus station. **Motels** *El Paso Autel,* B, Zaragoza y Martínez, B; several on Nuevo Laredo highway.

Restaurant *La Cabaña,* Calle Pino Suárez, meals and snacks. 23 eating places around the "Pink Zone" and Plaza Zaragoza in the heart of town.

British Consulate (Honorary) Mr Edward Lawrence, Privada Tamazunchale 104, Colonia del Valle, Garza García. T (91-83) 782565/569114.

Tourist Office Infotur on Gran Plaza (W side). Large city maps available at bookshops.

Railways Regiomontano (*servicio estrella*) calls here en route to Mexico City at 1900, and to border at 0800; fares to Mexico City, reserved seat US$17, single sleeper US$31.80, double US$63.70. Tamaulipeco (*servicio estrella*) connects with Regiomontano at 0840 for Reynosa (arr. 1205, US$4.30) and Matamoros (arr. 1330, US$6). To Mexico City (US$6.30 2nd class, US$10.60 1st) and the port of Tampico. Day trains are slow.

Bus Terminal on Av. Colón, between Calzada B. Reyes and Av. Pino Suárez. Monterrey-Mexico

City, US$25, 12 hrs. To San Luis Potosí, US$7. Frequent buses to Saltillo, but long queues for tickets. To Santiago for Cola de Caballo falls, US$0.50.

Airport   Aeropuerto del Norte, 24 km. from centre. Daily flights from Mexico City take 1¼ hrs.

In the hills around are the bathing resort of Topo Chico, 6½ km. to the NW; water from its hot springs is bottled and sold throughout Mexico; and 18 km. away Chipinque Mesa, at 1,280 metres in the Sierra Madre, with magnificent views of the Monterrey area.

W of Monterrey, off the Saltillo road are the García Caves (about 10 km. from Villa García, which is 40 km. from Monterrey). The entrance is 800 metres up, by cable car, and inside are beautiful stalagmites and stalactites. At the foot of the cable car are a pool and recreational centre. A tour of the caves takes 1½ hrs., and it is compulsory to go in a group with a guide. You can take a bus to Villa García, but it is a dusty walk to the caves. On Sun. Transportes Saltillo-Monterrey run a bus to the caves at 0900, 1000 and 1100. Otherwise, take an agency tour, e.g. Osetur (details from Infotur); book at *Hotel Ancira* (on Tues., US$3.50).

Leaving Monterrey, the road threads the narrow and lovely Huajuco canyon; from Santiago village a road runs to within 2 km. of the Cola de Caballo, or Horsetail, Falls. (First-class hotel on the way, and you can get a colectivo, US$1.50, from the bus stop to the falls, and a horse, US$1.50, to take you to the top of the falls, entrance US$0.60; cost of guide US$5.) Our road drops gradually into lower and warmer regions, passing through a succession of sub-tropical valleys with orange groves, banana plantations and vegetable gardens.

At **Montemorelos,** just off the highway, 79 km. S of Monterrey, a branch road from the Matamoros-Monterrey highway comes in. On 53 km. is **Linares** (100,000 people), a charming town. (*Hotel Guidi*, C, nr. bus station; *Escondido Court*, motel, D, clean, air-conditioned, pool and restaurant, rec., 1½ km. N of Linares on Route 855.)

Bus   Linares to San Luis Potosí, US$7.

A most picturesque 96 km. highway runs west from Linares up the lovely Santa Rosa canyon, up and over the Sierra Madre after Iturbide, turn S on top of the Sierra Madre and continue on good road through the unspoilt Sierra via La Escondida and Dr. Arroyo. At San Roberto, N of Matehuala (see page 979) join the Highway 57 route from Eagle Pass to Mexico City.

(Km. 706) *Ciudad Victoria,* capital of Tamaulipas state, a quiet, unhurried city with a shaded plaza and a tiny church perched on the top of a hill. It is often used as a stop-over. Alt.: 336 metres; pop.: 300,000.

Hotels   *Sierra Gorda*, C, garage US$0.70 a night. *Trailer Park,* Libramiento 101-85, follow signs, good service, hot showers. Owner has travel information, US$5 for 2 plus vehicle. **Motels** *Panorámica*, Lomas de Santuario, C; *Los Monteros*, Plaza Hidalgo, downtown, C.

Buses   Omnibuses Blancos to Ciudad Valles (see below) for US$4. Bus Ciudad Victoria-Mexico City 12 hrs., US$23.

After crossing the Tropic of Cancer the road enters the solid green jungle of the tropical lowlands.

Monterrey trains run via Ciudad Victoria to the Caribbean port of **Tampico,** definitely not a tourist attraction, reached by a fine road from (km. 570) El Mante, in a rich sugar-growing area, a deviation of 156 km. Tampico is on the northern bank of the Río Pánuco, not far from a large oilfield: there are storage tanks and refineries for miles along the southern bank. The summer heat, rarely above 35°C, is tempered by sea breezes, but June and July are trying. Cold northerlies blow now and again during the winter. There are two pleasant plazas, Plaza de Armas at Colón y Carranza, with squirrels in the trees, and Plaza de la Libertad, Madero y Juárez. Fishing (both sea and river) is excellent. Huge, interesting market, but watch your possessions carefully. The Playa de Miramar, a beach resort, is a tram or bus-ride from the city, but is reported dirty. If walking there, go along the breakwater (Escollera Norte) on N side of Río Pánuco, for views of the shipping and to see the monument to Mexican merchant seamen killed in World War II. Population: 560,000. The Museo de la Cultura Huasteca in Ciudad Madero, an adjacent town, is worth visiting (Instituto Tecnológico, Av. 1 de Mayo y Sor Juana Inés de la Cruz—in poor condition); take a colectivo, "Madero", from the centre of Tampico to the Zócalo in Ciudad Madero, then another to the Instituto; open 1000-1500, except Mon., small but select collection. Ciudad Madero claims to be Mexico's petroleum capital, with a huge oil refinery.

A second paved road from Tampico joins the Nuevo Laredo-México highway further S at Ciudad Valles. There are direct buses to Brownsville (Texas), leaving at 2400 and 0545, US$12. A splendid new bridge was opened at the end of 1988 to replace the ferry to Villa Cuauhtémoc. Further S, the coast road brings one to Tuxpan, Poza Rica and Veracruz.

Hotels   *Camino Real*, Av. Hidalgo 2000, A; *Impala*, Mirón 220 Pte., B; *Inglaterra*, Mirón y Olmos, A; *Imperial*, Aurora Sur 201, D, clean, shower, fan, but noisy; *Tampico*, Carranza 513, C; several cheap hotels nr. Plaza de la Libertad: e.g. *Sevilla* (always full), *Rex*, F, dirty, no hot water; *América*, nr. market on Olmos, F, dirty but safe. All hotels downtown near market should be treated with discretion; many have a rapid turnover. *Nuevo León*, D, Aduana N. 107, a/c, shower, clean; *Ritz*, on Miramar beach, E, beautiful beach, deserted at night.

Restaurant   *El Diligencias*, Héroes del Canonero Tampico 415 Oriente y Gral. López de Lara, excellent seafood; *Emir*, F.A. Olmos between Diaz Mirón y Madero, good; for breakfast, *El Selecto*, opp. market. To the N of Tampico on the Pan-American Highway, at Soto de Marina, *Colonial*—rec. Also, 4 good Chinese places in town.

West German Consul   Av. Madero, Hon. Consul Dieter Schulze. Postal Address: Apdo. 775, T (91-72) 29784/29817. Also deals with British affairs.

Tourist Office Plaza de Armas, above *Chantal* ice cream parlour on Calle F.A. Olmos, helpful.

Trains To Monterrey at 0845 (2nd class), arrive 1930. To San Luis Potosí.

On the coast S of Tampico we come to Tuxpan, tropical and humid, 12 km. from the sea on the River Tuxpan. Essentially a fishing town (shrimps a speciality). Interesting covered market, but beware of the bitter, over-ripe avocados; fruit sold on the quay. Beach about 2 km. E of town, reached by taxi or bus (marked "Playa"), at least 10 km. long. White sands; hire deckchairs under banana-leaf shelters for the day (US$2). Bus to Mexico City (Terminal del Norte), US$6, 6½ hrs. via Poza Rica. (*Hotel Florida*, Av. Juárez 23, B, clean, hot water; and others.) 45 km. S is *Poza Rica*, an oil town, with paved streets, an old cramped wooden market and great temperament.

Hotels   *Fénix*, basic, E, opposite ADO bus station; *San Román*, 8 Norte 5, E; *Aurora*, Bolívar 4, basic but quiet and fairly clean, E; *Nuevo León*, opp. market, D, rooms quite spacious, fairly clean and quiet, rec. *Poza Rica*, 2 Norte, D, fairly comfortable. *Juárez*, Cortines y Bermúdez, E, average.

Bus   All buses leave from new terminal about 1½ km. from centre (including about 100 a day to Mexico City, 5 hrs., US$5). To Veracruz, 4 hrs., US$6.25. To Pachuca, Estrella Blanca, 4½ hrs., US$2, change in Tulancingo. To Tecolutla (see below), US$1, 1¼ hrs.

From Poza Rica one can visit the Castillo de Teayo, a pyramid with the original sanctuary and interesting carvings on top, buses every ½ hr., change halfway.

Some 20 km. SE of Poza Rica is *Papantla* (280,000 people) which is easily reached from Veracruz, 4 hrs., by ADO bus, US$4.80, good road, Jalapa, by ADO bus, US$2.60, 6 hrs., and Mexico City, via Poza Rica. Men and women come to market in the local costume and there are *voladores* at about 1100 on Sats. in the churchyard. Mariachi bands play in the *cervecerías* near Zócalo on Sundays. Papantla is also the centre of the vanilla-producing zone, and small figures and animals made in vanilla are for sale, as well as the essence.

Hotels   *Pulido*, Enríquez 215, modern, rec. but noisy, clean, E, with bath, parking; *Papantla*, on Zócalo, E, very clean, hot showers, friendly; *Trujillo*, Calle 5 de Mayo 401, E, rooms with basin, but other facilities dirty, friendly; *Tajín*, Calle Dr. Núñez 104, restaurant and bar, D, reasonable. (It is better to stay in Papantla than in Poza Rica if you want to visit El Tajín.)

Restaurant   *Las Brisas del Golfo*, Calle Dr. Núñez, reasonable and very good. *Sorrento*, Zócalo, good, cheap, rec.; cheap breakfasts at *Café Cathedral* on street above Cathedral.

Tourist Office in municipal offices in the Zócalo; it is rarely open, mostly mornings.

About 12 km. away, in the forest, is *El Tajín,* the ruins of the capital of the Totonac culture (6th to 10th century AD) entry, US$0.30, ½ price on Sun. Guidebook US$1.25, available in Museum of Anthropology, Mexico City. At the centre of this vast complex is the Pyramid of El Tajín, whose 365 squared openings make it look like a vast beehive. Traditionally, on Corpus Christi, Totonac rain dancers erect a 30-metre mast with a rotating structure at the top. Four *voladores* (flyers) and a musician climb to the surmounting platform. The musician dances to his own pipe and drum music, whilst the roped *voladores* throw themselves into space to make a dizzy spiral descent, sometimes head up, sometimes head down, to the ground. *Voladores* are now in attendance every day, most of the day, and fly if they think there are enough tourists. There are buses from both Poza Rica marked Martínez or San Andrés, US$0.50, frequent departures near market and Papantla; to reach Tajín from Papantla take a local bus to the crossroads of El Chote (½ hr.) then another local bus (direction Poza Rica) to the ruins (10 mins.); otherwise take a taxi. The tourist office near the Zócalo will show you bus schedules.

E of Papantla and on the coast, on the road to Nautla which divides to Jalapa or Veracruz, is *Tecolutla*, a small resort on the river of that name. *Hotels Playa*, E, good, *Tecolutla*, E, best, and *Marsol* (run down) are on the beach. *Posada Guadalupe* and *Casa de Huéspedes Malena* (F, basic but clean) are on Avenida Carlos Prieto, near the river landing stage. Newer hotels, D, on road to Nautla. *Restaurant Paquita*, next to *Hotel Playa*, rec.

(Km. 548) Antiguo Morelos. A road turns off W to San Luis Potosí (**see page 980**) 314 km., and Guadalajara (**see page 1003**).

(Km. 476) **Ciudad Valles** (200,000), on a winding river and a popular stop-over with many hotels (*San Fernando; Valles*, Carretera México-Laredo, B). Museo Regional Huasteco, Calles Rotarios y Artes (or Peñaloza), open 1000-1200, 1400-1800, Mon.-Fri., centre of archaeological and ethnographic research for the Huastec region. Omnibus Oriente to San Luis Potosí for US$3 (4 hrs.). The road to Tampico (145 km.) goes through the oil camp of El Ebano.

(Km. 370) **Tamazunchale** (alt. 206 metres, 150,000 people), with riotous tropical vegetation, is perhaps the most popular of all the overnight stops. (*San Antonio Hotel; Mirador*, D, good, but passing traffic by night is noisy; *Hotel OK*, F, cheapest but not rec.; *Pemex Tourist Camp*, US$ 2 p.p., nice position, poor plumbing.) The road S of here begins a spectacular climb to the highland, winding over the rugged terrain cut by the Río Moctezuma and its tributaries. The highest point on the road is 2,502 metres. From (km. 279) Jacala there is a dizzying view into a chasm. **Zimapán** (*Posada del Rey*, fascinating but very run down, out on the highway), with a charming market place and a small old church in the plaza, is as good a place as any to stay the night. From (km. 178) **Portezuelo** a paved road runs W to Querétaro (**see page 981**), 140 km. In an area of 23,300 sq. km. N and S of (km. 169) **Ixmiquilpan**, just off the highway, 65,000 Otomí Indians "live the bitterest and saddest life". The beautifully worked Otomí belts and bags may sometimes be bought at the Monday market, and also in the Artesanía shop in the main street almost opposite the government aid offices.

See early Indian frescoes in the main church, which is one of the 16th century battlemented Augustinian monastery-churches; the monastery is open to the public. John Streather writes: "At sunset each day white egrets come to roost in the trees outside the church; it's worth going up on to the battlements to see them swoop down. The church of El Carmen is worth a visit too, lovely west façade and gilded altars inside. There is also a 16th century bridge over the river; beautiful walk along the ahuehuete-lined banks". (*Hotel Diana*, E, rear buildings slightly dearer rooms but much cleaner, rec., safe parking.)

Near Ixmiquilpan are several warm swimming pools, both natural and man-made—San Antonio, Dios Padre, Las Humedades, and near Tephé (the only warm-water bath, clean, entry US$0.40) and Tzindejé (this is about 20 mins. from town). The Otomí villages of La Lagunita, La Pechuga and La Bonanza, in a beautiful valley, have no modern conveniences, but the people are charming and friendly.

Actopán (km. 119) has another fine 16th century Augustinian church and convent. From Actopán a 56 km. branch road runs to one of Mexico's great archaeological sites: Tula, capital of the Toltecs (**see page 1040**).

On the way to Tula there is an interesting cooperative village, **Cruz Azul**. Free concerts on Sun. mornings at 1000 in front of main market. At (km. 85) Colonia, a road runs left for 8 km. to

Pachuca, one of the oldest silver-mining centres in Mexico and capital of Hidalgo state. Pop.: 320,000; alt.: 2,445 metres. The Aztecs mined here before the Spaniards came and the hills are honeycombed with old workings and terraced with tailings. Even today the silver output is one of the largest of any mine in the world. A large number of colonial buildings among its narrow, steep and crooked streets include the treasury for the royal tribute, La Caja, in Calle Cajas (1670), now used as offices; Las Casas Coloradas (1785), now the Escuela Vicente Guerrero; and a former Franciscan convent (1596) on Plaza Bartolomé de Medina, 5 blocks S of the Zócalo at Arista y Hidalgo, now a Regional History Museum displaying chronological exhibits of the state's history. It is known as

the Centro Cultural Hidalgo (open Tues.-Sun., 1000-1400, 1600-1900—may close early on Sun. p.m.). An outstanding photographic museum is in the large cloister on the far side of the convent. In the complex there are a souvenir shop with reproductions of ceramic and metal anthropological items and recordings of indigenous music. Casa de las Artesanías for Hidalgo state is at the junction of Avenidas Revolución y Juárez. In the Plaza Independencia is a huge clock with four Carrara marble figures. The modern buildings include a notable theatre, the Palacio de Gobierno (which has a mural depicting ex-President Echeverría's dream of becoming Secretary-General of the UN), and the Banco de Hidalgo. An electric railway and a road run 10 km. to the large silver-mining camp of Real (or Mineral) del Monte, picturesque and with steep streets. Collective taxis also run frequently from beside La Caja (US$0.40 p.p.).

Hotels *De los Baños*, D, good but unreliable water supply; *América*, F with bath, one block from Zócalo, quiet, rec.; *Colonial*, Guerrero 505, central, E; *Juárez*, Barreda 107, E, with bath, some rooms without windows. just before Real del Monte, in superb wooded surroundings. CREA Youth Hostel at the turn off to El Chico.

Restaurant *Casino Español*, Matamoros 207, 2nd floor, old-time favourite. "Paste" is the local survivor from Cornish miners' days; a good approximation of the real pastie, but a bit peppery!

Transport Bus terminal is outside town; take any bus marked "Central". Train from the capital at 1013 (2nd class, 3 hrs.). Faster service due to start in 1988/89.

Cornish miners settled at Real del Monte in the 19th century; their descendants can be recognized among the people. At each entry to the town is a mural commemorating the first strike in the Americas, by silver miners in 1776. The Panteón Inglés (English cemetery) is on a wooded hill opposite the town (ask the caretaker for the key). Mineral del Chico is a beautiful little town 30 km. from Pachuca in the El Chico National Park. The Park has many campsites and the town weekend homes for the wealthy of Mexico City. There are huge rock formations covered in pine forests; splendid walks. Bus from Pachuca bus station.

N of Pachuca via Atotonilco el Grande, where there are a chapel and convent half-way down a beautiful canyon, is the impressive Barranca de Metztitlán which has a wealth of different varieties of cacti, including the "hairy old man" cactus, and a huge 17th century monastery. Farther N (difficult road) is Molango, where there is a restored convent. 34 km. NE of Pachuca is *San Miguel Regla*, a mid-18th century *hacienda* built by the Conde de Regla, and now run as a resort, fine atmosphere, excellent service. A road continues to Tulancingo, on the Pachuca-Poza Rica road, Route 130. 17 km. from Pachuca, and a further 4 km. off Route 130 to the right is Epazoyucan, a village with an interesting convent. After Tulancingo, Route 119 branches off to the right to *Zacatlán*, famous for its apple orchards and now also producing plums, pears and cider. Its alpine surroundings include an impressive national park, Valle de las Piedras Encimadas (stacked rocks), camping possible. Nearby is *Posada Campestre al Final de la Senda*, a ranch with weekend accommodation, horse riding, walks, D, p.p. full board, T Puebla 413 821 for reservations. Some 16 km. S. of Zacatlán is Chignahuapan (about 1½ hrs. from Puebla), a leading producer of *sarapes*, surrounded by several curative spas.

30 km. from Tulancingo on Route 130 is *La Cabaña* restaurant, of log-cabin construction, cheap; thereafter, the road descends with many bends and slow lorries, and in winter there may be fog. At Huauchinango, an annual flower fair is held in March; 22 km. from here is Xicotepec de Juárez (*Mi Ranchito*, one of the nicest small hotels in Mexico; *Italia*, near main square, E). Along the route are the villages of Pahuatlan and San Pablito, where sequined headbands are made, and paintings are done on flattened *amate* bark. The entire route from desert to jungle is 190 km., taking 5 hours.

A 4-lane highway now runs from Pachuca to Mexico City via (km. 27) Venta de Carpio, from which a road runs E to Acolman, 12 km., and Teotihuacán, another 10 km. Neither of these places should be missed (**see page 1038**); buses are available from Pachuca; get them at the tollbooth on the highway to Mexico City.

At Santa Clara, 13 km. short of the Capital, the road forks. The right-hand fork (easy driving) goes direct to the City; the left fork goes through Villa Madero, where you can see the shrine of Guadalupe.

EAGLE PASS—PIEDRAS NEGRAS TO MEXICO CITY (2)

This route, 1,328 km. (825 miles), is 102 km. longer than the Laredo route, but is very wide, very fast and much easier to drive. It is by now the most popular route, but is far from being the most interesting. Take in enough gasoline at Monclova to cover the 205 km. to Saltillo.

Piedras Negras, pop. 150,000, altitude 220 metres, is across the Río Bravo from Eagle Pass, Texas. (Artesanía shop—Centro Artesanal Piedras Negras, Edificio la Estrella, Puerta México, T 2-10-87.) Beyond (137 km.) Hermanas the highway begins to climb gradually up to the plateau country. Coahuilense *servicio estrella* train leaves for Saltillo at 1300 (arr. 2030), US$8.70 for reclining seat.

Monclova (243 km.) has one of the largest steel mills in Mexico, and 250,000 people. Then comes **Saltillo** (448 km.; alt.: 1,600 metres; population: 650,000), capital of Coahuila state, a cool, dry popular resort noted for the excellence of its *sarapes*. Its 18th century cathedral is the best in northern Mexico and it has a grand market. Local *feria* in first half of August; cheap accommodation impossible to find at this time. Indian dances during May 30 and August 30; picturesque ceremonies and bullfights during October *fiestas*. *Pastorelas*, the story of the Nativity, are performed in the neighbourhood in Christmas week. Good golf, tennis, swimming. College students from the US attend the popular Summer School at the Universidad Interamericana. Good views from El Cerro del Pueblo overlooking city. An 87-km. road runs E to Monterrey. You turn right for Mexico City.

Saltillo Hotels   Several hotels a short distance from the plaza at the intersection of Allende and Aldama, the main streets, e.g. **San Jorge**, Manuel Acuña 240, A; **Metropolí**, E, Allende 436, basic, with shower, a little dark but adequate, quiet. **De Avila**, Padre Flores 211, E, basic, cold water, safe motorcycle parking. Cheaper are **Hidalgo**, on Padre Flores, F, without bath, not worth paying for bath in room, cold water only (hot baths open to public and guests for small fee). **Saade**, Aldama 397, D; **Urdiñola**, Victoria 211, reasonable, D; **Zamora**, Ramos Arzipe (Poniente) 552, F, cheap; also cheap **El Conde**, Pérez Treviño y Acuña. Several good motels in this area, e.g. **Huizache**, Blvd. Carranza 1746, B; **La Fuente**, A, Blvd. Fundadores; **Camino Real**, Carretera 57, Km. 865, A.

Restaurants   **Viena**, Acuña 519, rec.; **Victoria**, by Hotel Hidalgo has reasonable comida; **Dik-Dik**, Aldama 548. Drinks and night-time view can be had at the **Rodeway Inn** on the N side of town; **Kentucky Fried Chicken**, Victoria Pte. 358.

Tourist Office   Near crossroads of Allende and Blvd. Francisco Coss in old railway station, long way from centre. Map with all useful addresses, incl. hotels.

Bus   Terminal is a long way from centre; minibuses to Pérez Treviño y Allende (for centre) will take luggage. To Monterrey and Nuevo Laredo with Transportes del Norte. For Torreón, all buses originate in Monterrey and tickets only sold when bus arrives; be prepared to stand.

Train   Regiomontano (*servicio estrella*) calls here en route to Mexico City at 2130, and to Monterrey and Nuevo Laredo at 0600. Coahuilense (*servicio estrella*) connects with Regiomontano for Piedras Negras 0700 (7½ hrs.). Fares to Mexico City: reserved seat US$15, single sleeper US$28.20, double US$56.40; to Piedras Negras, US$8.70.

(581 km.) San Roberto junction, where a 96-km. road runs E over the Sierra Madre to Linares, on the Gulf Route (**see page 974**).

At about 720 km. we reach **Matehuala** (*Motel Las Palmas*, on the N edge of town, clean, B, English spoken and paperbacks sold, bowling alley and miniature golf, tours to Real de Catorce (see below) arranged; *Hotel Matehuala*, F, rooms shocking pink, full of furniture, adequate), an important road junction; *Motel Palapa*, on highway, C, excellent dining room (*fiesta*, January 6-20).

Chris and Miyuki Kerfoot write: From Saltillo to Matehuala by 2nd class bus, Estrella Blanca, 1½ hrs., US$2 to San Roberto, which is no more than a road junction with a Pemex petrol station, hitch to the junction of Highways 58 and 68 and catch a bus (Transportes Tamaulipas) to Matehuala (US$3, 4 hrs.). From these junctions near Caleana to La Soledad the scenery is worthwhile, as the road winds its way up and down through wooded valleys. The final section to Matehuala passes through undulating scrub country.

Bus   To San Luis Potosí, with Estrella Blanca, 2½ hrs., US$3.50.

56 km. W of Matehuala is one of Mexico's most interesting "ghost towns", **Real de Catorce,** founded in 1772.

Tim Connell writes: Four minibuses a day go there from the agency by the *Hotel Matehuala* (US$3 return, journey 1½ hrs., with 2 hrs. to wander around). A taxi can be hired nearby for US$12.50—economic for 4 people. Tours can be arranged with Turismos del Altiplano, Bustamante 128, T 3-40. (Real de Catorce is also easily reached from Saltillo or San Luis Potosí by train. Jeeps collect passengers from the station (US$8-10 per jeep) and follow a more spectacular route than the minibuses.)

Route: turn left along the Zacatecas road (not signposted) through Cedral. After 27 km. turn left off the paved road, on to a gravel one—which is actually due to be properly paved. The road passes through Potrero, a big centre for nopal cactus. Some people live in the old mine workings and old buildings. Huichol Indians are seen here occasionally. A silver mine is still being worked at Santana.

Real de Catorce is approached through Ogarrio, an old mine gallery widened (only just) to allow trucks through. It is 2½ km. long, and very eerie, with the odd tunnel leading off into the gloom on either side. There is an overtaking bay half way through. A small chapel to the Virgen de los Dolores is by the entrance. The tunnel opens out abruptly into the old city, once a major mining centre with its own mint and nearly 40,000 inhabitants. About 700 people still live here, mainly round the Zócalo, looking for silver. The cockpit and the 16 chapels are worth seeing; the Church of San Francisco is believed to be miraculous. There is a pilgrimage here, on foot from Matehuala, overnight on October 4. The floor of the church is made of wooden panels, which can be lifted up to see the catacombs below. In a room to one side of the main altar are *retablos*, touchingly simple paintings on tin, as votive offerings to the Saint for his intercession. This remarkable city, clustering around the sides of a valley, is so quiet that you can hear the river in the canyon, 1,000 metres below. Next to the church is a small museum (entry US$0.10) showing mining equipment, etc., worth a visit. (Hotels in Real de Catorce: one in the main street, very comfortable with restaurant and bar, expensive, another, *Hotel Real*, in a side street, clean, E.)

Huizache (785 km.) is the junction with the Guadalajara-Antiguo Morelos-Tampico highway. At 901 km. we come to San Luis Potosí.

San Luis Potosí, 423 km. from Mexico City, capital of its state, is the centre of a rich mining and agricultural area, which has expanded industrially in recent years. Alt.: 1,880 metres; pop.: 800,000. Glazed, many-coloured tiles are a feature of the city: one of its shopping streets, the main plaza, and the domes of many of its churches are covered with them. It became an important centre after the discovery of the famous San Pedro silver mine in the 16th century, and a city in 1658. The Cathedral is on Plaza Hidalgo. See the churches of San Francisco, with its white and blue tiled dome and suspended glass boat in the transept (try and get into the magnificent sacristy); Carmen, in Plaza Morelos, with a grand tiled dome, an intricate façade, and a fine pulpit and altar inside (the Teatro de la Paz is next door); the baroque Capilla de Aránzazu, behind San Francisco inside the regional museum (see below); the Capilla de Loreto with a baroque façade; and San Agustín, with its ornate baroque tower. The Palacio de Gobierno, begun 1770, contains oil-paintings of past governors, and the colonial treasury, Antigua Real Caja, built 1767. Other points of interest are the pedestrian precinct in Calle Hidalgo and the Caja del Agua fountain (1835) in Av. Juárez. Plaza de San Francisco is very pleasant. The modern railway station has frescoes by Fernando Leal. The Teatro Alarcón is by Tresguerras (see under Celaya, **page 992**). Locally made *rebozos* (the best are from Santa María del Río) are for sale in the markets. *Feria* is in the second fortnight of August. The University was founded in 1804. A scenic road leads to Aguascalientes airport.

Hotels Many between the railway station and the cathedral. *Panorama,* Av. Venustiano Carranza 315, B; *Gran,* Bravo 235, F without bath, hot water, friendly; *Progreso,* Aldama 415, D. *Jardín,* Los Bravos 530, E, good, restaurant rec.; *María Cristina,* C, with swimming pool on roof (Juan Sarabia 110, Altos); *Nápoles,* Juan Sarabia 120, D, rec. CREA Youth Hostel, Diagonal Sur, on the SW side of the Glorieta Juárez, 5 min. walk from central bus station, F, C.P. 78320, T 26603. **Motels** all along Highway 57: *Hostal del Quijote,* A, five-star, convention facilities, 6 km. S on the San Luis Potosí-Mexico City highway, one of the best in Mexico; *Santa Fe,* B; Cactus, B; all with pools.

Restaurants *Panorama,* roof-garden restaurant, Plaza de la Universidad, good; *Posada del Virrey,* Plaza Hidalgo, clean, pleasant, reasonable; *Tokio,* Los Bravos 510, excellent comida. *La Lonja,* Aldama 300, and *La Virreina,* Carranza 830, both popular eating places; *Café Versalles,* Madero 145, excellent coffee and yoghurt; *El Girasol,* Guerrero 345, vegetarian; good cafeteria at bus station. *Café Florida,* Juan Sarabia 230, *Pacífico,* Juan Sarabia y Manuel José Othon, both good, and many other reasonably-priced eating places at western end of Alameda Juan Sarabia.

Museums   Museo Regional de Arte Popular, open 1000-1300, 1600-1800; Sats. 1000-1300, next to San Francisco church. Nearby is Museo Regional Potosino, archaeological, and a collection of wrought iron work, Capilla Aránzazu on 2nd floor, open Tues.-Fri. 1000-1300, 1500-1800, Sat. 1000-1200, 1000-1300. La Casa de la Cultura on Av. Carranza, halfway between the centre and university, is a converted mansion with frequent art displays and musical recitals. Museo Nacional de la Máscara, in Palacio Federal, has most complete collection of masks in the country, open Tues-Fri. 1000-1400, 1600-1800, Sat.-Sun. 1000-1400. In Parque Tangamanga (still under development S of city) is Museo Tangamanga in an old hacienda, also a Planetarium, observatory and open air theatre (open 0600-1800). In Plaza España, next to the Plaza de Toros, is a Museo Taurino (E of Alameda on Universidad y Triana, Tues.-Sun. 1100-1300, 1730-1930).

Shopping   Local sweets and craftwork at Plaza del Carmen 325, Los Bravos 546 and Escobedo 1030. The famous local painter, Vicente Guerrero, lives in a modest neighbourhood at Plata 407, Colonia Morales (T 3-80-57) where he also has his studio. Markets: head north on Hidalgo and you come to Mercado Hidalgo, then Mercado República, and Mercado 16 de Septiembre.

Post Office Morelos y González Ortega.

Tourist Office   Dirreción Estatal de Turismo, Manuel José Othon 130, opp. Cathedral; Coordinación Regional de Turismo, Jardín Guerrero 14 (Plaza San Francisco), both helpful.

Buses   Station on outskirts of town 1½ km. from centre. Bus to centre US$0.10. Flecha Amarilla to Querétaro, US$3.50, 2 hrs. (50-odd km. of 4-lane highway have been built N of Querétaro, about half the way, and 40 km. have also been completed to the S of San Luis Potosí); to Nuevo Laredo, US$20. To Mexico City, US$6.10, 6 hrs.

Train   to Querétaro, US$2.25 1st class, US$1.20 2nd, supposed to leave at 1015 but arrives full and late from Nuevo Laredo; to Mexico City, 10-11 hrs.; to San Miguel de Allende, 3-4 hrs.

Excursions   Hot springs at Ojocaliente, Balneario de Lourdes and Gogorrón. Balneario de Lourdes (hotel, clean, nice atmosphere, small pool, D) is S of San Luis Potosí. Gogorrón is clean and relaxing, with pools, hot tubs, picnic grounds and campsites. There is a restaurant. A day trip or overnight camp-out is recommended in the lightly wooded hills and meadows near the microwave station (at 2,600 metres) 40 km. E of San Luis Potosí: go 35 km. along the Tampico highway and continue up 5 km. of cobblestone road to the station. Good views and flora.

(1,021 km.) San Luis de la Paz, the junction with Route 110 leading west to three of the most attractive towns in Mexico: Dolores Hidalgo, Guanajuato, and San Miguel de Allende. **(See pages 990-994.)** No one who yields to the temptation of this detour can hope to get back to the main route for three or four days.

Near San Luis is another of Mexico's mining ghost-towns, Pozos, where the population has fallen from 10,000 to 500 in the course of this century. One can explore everywhere in complete tranquillity.

(1,105 km.) Querétaro, pop.: 550,000; alt.: 1,865 metres (can be quite cold at night); 215 km. from the capital, now an important industrial centre and capital of Querétaro state, an old and beautiful city, dotted with attractive squares. (No buses in the centre.) Hidalgo's rising in 1810 was plotted here, and it was also here that Emperor Maximilian surrendered after defeat, was tried, and was shot, on June 19, 1867, on the Cerro de las Campanas (the Hill of Bells), outside the city.

La Corregidora (Doña Josefa Ortiz de Domínguez, wife of the Corregidor, or Mayor), a member of the group of plotters for independence masquerading as a society for the study of the fine arts, was able, in 1810, to get word to Father Hidalgo that their plans for revolt had been discovered. Hidalgo immediately gave the cry (*grito*) for independence. Today, the Corregidor gives the Grito from the balcony of the Palacio Municipal (on Plaza Independencia) every September 15 at 1100 (it is echoed on every civic balcony thoughout Mexico on this date). La Corregidora's home may be visited.

Buildings to see: the Santa Rosa de Viterbo church and monastery, remodelled by Francisco Tresguerras; his reconstruction of Santa Clara, one of the loveliest churches in Mexico, and that is saying much; the church and monastery of Santa Cruz, which served as the HQ of Maximilian and his forces (view from the bell tower); the church of San Felipe, now being restored for use as the Cathedral; the splendid Federal Palace, once an Augustinian convent with exceptionally fine cloisters, now restored with an art gallery containing some beautiful works; the important and elegant Regional Museum on the main plaza, known as the Plaza de Armas or as Plaza Obregón (not all its galleries are always open) which contains much material on the revolution of 1810 and the 1864-67 period; the Teatro de la República, where Maximilian and his generals were tried, and where the Constitution of 1917 (still in force) was drafted; the aqueduct, built in 1726. Several *andadores* (pedestrian walkways) have been developed, greatly adding to the amenities of the city; prices are high here. The *andadores* replace particular roads in places—e.g. Av. 16 de Septiembre becomes Andador de la Corregidora in the centre, and then reverts to its original name. There are local opals, amethysts and topazes for sale; remarkable mineral specimens are shaped into spheres, eggs, mushrooms, and then polished until they shine like jewels (US$10-30, cheaper than San Juan del Río, but more expensive than Taxco). Recommended is Lapidaría Querétaro, Pasteur Norte 72 (Hermanos Ramírez), for fine opals. City tour plus execution site and Juárez monument, excellent value, from museum daily at 1100, US$4.45. There is a *feria agrícola* from 2nd week of December until Christmas; bull fights and cock fights. On New Year's Eve there is a special market and special performances are given in the main street. Try local Hidalgo Pinot Noir wine.

Hotels *Mirabel*, A, Constituyentes 2, good, garage, restaurant; *Corregidora*, Corregidora 138, E, reasonable but noisy; *Del Marqués*, Juárez Norte 104, D, clean; *Plaza*, airy, lovely inner patio, modernized, safe, clean, comfortable, D; *El Cid*, E, Prolongación Corregidora, more of a motel, clean, good value, close to bus station (left out of bus station and first left); *Hidalgo*, near Zócalo, E with bath, quite helpful; *San Agustín*, Pino Suárez 12, E, clean, quiet, rec.; *Avenida*, Invierno 21, F. CREA Youth Hostel, Av. del Ejército Republicano, ex-Convento de la Cruz, F, running water a.m. only, T 43050. **Motels** *Holiday Inn*, near highway junction, A; *La Mansión*, B, 6½ km. S of town, excellent dining facilities, gorgeous grounds; 5 km. on opp. side of highway 3 km. is *Mansión Galindo*, A, exquisite former hacienda, vast; *Flamingo*, on Constituyentes Poniente 138, D, comfortable; *Azteca*, 15 km. N on road to San Luis Potosí, D; *Jurica*, edge of town on road to San Luis Potosí, A, former *hacienda*, with gardens, squash, golf-course; opulent.

Restaurants *Fonda del Camino*, on Highway 57; *Mesón Santa Rosa*, Pasteur 17, good but expensive, restored colonial building; *Fonda del Refugio*, Jardín Corregidora, pretty but food is routine; *La Corregidora*, on the other side of the street, is reportd as greatly superior. *Pizza La Rondine*, Jardín Corregidora; *Flor de Querétaro*, on Plaza Obregón, Juárez Norte 5; *Salón del Valle*, Corregidora 91; *La Cocina Mexicana*, opp. *Hotel San Agustín*, cheap and good, à la carte better value than corrida corrida; *El Mirador*, roadhouse on highway 57, overlooking city, popular.

Tourist Office State office, 5 de Mayo 61 y Pasteur, federal office Pte. de Alvarado 102-A (away from centre).

Post Office Arteaga Poniente 5 (inadequate).

Bus Mexico City (Terminal del Norte) frequently 2nd class with Estrella Blanca or Flecha Amarilla, US$2.90, 3 hrs.; to San Miguel de Allende, 1 hr., hourly with Flecha Amarilla, US$1. To Guadalajara, US$4.45. To San Juan del Río, US$0.70, ½ hr., frequent. To Tula US$2.30. To Guanajuato, US$1.60, 3½ hrs. (Flecha Amarilla); to Pachuca, US$2.20, 4½ hrs. (Estrella Blanca, poor buses).

Rail Constitucionalista (*servicio estrella*) leaves Mexico City for Querétaro 0735, arriving 3 hrs. later (US$5.25); returns to Mexico City at 1800. arr. 2100. At Querétaro, the service divides to San Miguel Allende at 1055 (arr. 1210) and Guanajuato at 1042 (arr. 1345). To Guadalajara US$3 1st class, US$1.80 2nd. Daily fast train from Mexico City at 0700, 1st class US$2.

There is a 4-lane motorway (US$3 a car) from Irapuato past Querétaro to Mexico City. Along it (Km. 1,152) is **San Juan del Río** (*Hotel Mansión Galindo*, A, restored hacienda—apparently given by Cortés to his mistress Malinche—beautiful building; several picturesque hotels, E-D), near where the best fighting bulls are raised; the town is a centre for handicrafts, and also for polishing gemstones—opals and amethysts. There is one friendly and reasonable shop: La Guadalupana, 16 de Septiembre 6; others are expensive and less friendly. Several *balnearios* in San Juan (try *Venecia*, cold water, very quiet mid-week, US$1.30). A branch road runs NE from San Juan to the picturesque town of **Tequesquiapán**, with thermal baths, fine climate, good and cheap hotels (*Los Virreyes*; *El Reloj*, etc.), and between San Juan del Río and Tequesquiapán, a small track leads off the main road 4 km. to the village of La Trinidad, near which lie some of the opal mines which are still in operation. Then at 1,167 km., Palmillas, 153 km. to Mexico City.

Bus San Juan del Río-Tequesquiapán US$0.30, 20 mins.

The Mexico City motorway passes close to Tula and Tepozotlán (**see page 1040**). There are various country clubs along the road: *San Gil Ciudad Turística* 7 km. along the road to Amealco; *El Ocotal; Bosques del Lago.*

CIUDAD JUAREZ TO MEXICO CITY: THE CENTRAL HIGHWAY ROUTE (3)

Ciudad Juárez, opposite El Paso, Texas, to Mexico City: 1,866 km. Buses connect Ciudad Juárez with El Paso hourly (US$1.50) from the Greyhound terminal. Ciudad Juárez is at an altitude of 1,150 metres; Airport.

Hotels *Calinda Quality Inn,* A, Calz. Hermanos Escobar 3515, downtown; *El Presidente,* Centro Comercial Pronas, A; many others in all price ranges.

Restaurants *Denny's,* Lincoln 1345, modern; many reasonable Chinese places.

British Consul (Honorary) Mr C.R. Maingot, Calle Fresno 185, Campestre Juárez, T (91-16) 75791/60750.

Rail Train from Ciudad Juárez to Mexico City (1,970 km.), 36 hrs, US$20.80 1st class. Reverse journey leaves at 1950 from Mexico City. The route is through Chihuahua, Torreón, Zacatecas, Aguascalientes, León, Silao (for Guanajuato), Celaya and Querétaro. Rápido de la Frontera (*servicio estrella*) leaves Ciudad Juárez at 1800 for Chihuahua (arr. 2210, US$8.35).

Road Pemex Travel Club, Chamber of Commerce Building, El Paso. A.A.A. office: 916 Mesa Avenue, El Paso. By bus the trip to Mexico City takes about 26 hrs., US$30. To Chihuahua, 5 hrs., hourly, US$5.

Juárez, like Tijuana on the California border, attracts a nightly horde of tourists to be fascinated by a swarm of bead and spinach-jade peddlers, strip joints, doll shops blazing in magenta and green, dubious book stores, and "native dance" halls, mitigated by nightly bouts of that swift and beautiful ball game, *jai-alai.* It has a famous race course, too. There are pleasant markets. A monument in the form of a giant head of Father Hidalgo, who sparked off the 1810 revolution, surmounts a hill. See the cheerful Museum which acts as a Mexican "shop window" - well worth it for the uninitiated tourist.

The road is wide, mostly flat, easy to drive, and not as interesting as the Gulf and Pacific routes. From Ciudad Juárez, for some 50 km. along the Río Bravo, there is an oasis which grows cotton of an exceptionally high grade. The next 160 km. of the road to Mexico City are through desert; towns en route are Salamayuca (restaurant), at 58 km.; Villa Ahumada (131 km.). *Dunas Motel,* D, scruffy. At 180 km. is Moctezuma (restaurant). The road leads into grazing lands and the valley of Chihuahua. This is the country of the long-haired, fleet-footed Tarahumara Indians, able, it is said, to outstrip a galloping horse and to run down birds.

About 225 km. S of Juárez, near the village of El Sueco (restaurant), is the turnoff to the *Casas Grandes* ruins. Follow paved State Highway 10 for about 105 km. W, then turn NW for about 55. The place is spectacular: pyramids, a large ball court, an irrigation system and a great number of large adobe-brick houses. The ruins are signposted from the plaza in Casas Grandes, about 1 km. (entry US$0.30, guide booklet US$0.45). No accommodation in the Casas Grandes village, but in the nearby Nueva Casas Grandes, *Motel Casa Grande* has air-conditioning, good dining room, fair accommodation; *Hotel California,* C, good looking; *Hotel Juárez,* next to bus stop, E, dirty; cheap hotels between the two bus stations.

Bus There are frequent buses from Nueva Casas Grandes to Casas Grandes village, leaving from near the railway station, one at 0800, US$0.15. Bus Ciudad Juárez-Nuevas Casas Grandes, 4 hrs., US$3.75 with Chihuahuenses. Three bus companies ply from Casas Grandes to Chihuahua, hourly, 5 hrs., US$4.80, passing through pleasant landscapes (especially between Casa Grandes and Madera).

(Km. 1,638) *Chihuahua,* capital of Chihuahua state; alt.: 1,420 metres; pop.: 800,000; centre of a mining and cattle area. Worth looking at are the Cathedral on Plaza Constitución, begun 1717, finished 1789; the old tower of the Capilla Real (in the modern Federal Palace on Calle Libertad) in which Hidalgo awaited his execution; the Museo Regional, Bolívar 401, with interesting exhibits and extremely fine Art-Nouveau rooms: child's room features Little Red Riding Hood scenes; bathroom, frogs playing among reeds, etc.; and the murals in the Palacio de Gobierno. Good Sunday market. The famous Santa Eulalia mining camp is 16 km. away; 8 km. from town is one of the largest smelting plants in the world. Pancho Villa operated in the country around, and once captured the city by disguising his men as peasants going to market; the Quinta Luz, Calle 10 No. 3014, where Pancho Villa lived, is now a museum. Summer temperatures often reach 40°C. Rain falls from July to September. The local hairless small dog has a constant body temperature of 40°C (104°F)—the world's only authentic "hot dog".

Hotels *El Presidente*, Av. Libertad 9, A; *Exalaris Hyatt*, Independencia y Niños Héroes, A; *San Francisco*, Victoria 504, A, restaurant good for steaks; *Victoria*, Juárez y Colón, courtyard, pleasant, D; *Balflo*, Niños Héroes 321, modern, D; *San Juan*, Victoria 823, in old colonial house, D, nice atmosphere, reasonable food, water sometimes scarce; *Victoria*, opp. at No. 218, F; *Plaza*, behind cathedral, Calle 4, No. 206, clean, E, rec.; *Posada Aída*, Calle 10, E, very clean, no hot water in p.m., F. *Maceyra*, Ocampo Antigua 302, F, with shower, simple but clean, despite occasional beetles; *Reforma*, Calle Victoria 809, E, good, friendly, rec.; *El Cobre*, C, Calle 10A y Progreso, with bathroom, beside bus terminal, restaurant, bar and laundry; *Santa Fe*, near bus, friendly, clean, but hourly rentals too. *Turista*, Juárez 817, E, with bath, very clean. *Casa de Huéspedes*, Libertad 1404, F with bath, basic but clean. The cheaper hotels are in Calle Juárez and its cross-streets; the cheapest are behind the cathedral. **Motels** *Mirador*, Universidad 1309, B; *Nieves*, Tecnológico y Ahuehuetes, C.

Restaurants Best: *Los Parados de Tomy Vega*, followed by *La Calesa* and *La Olla*, excellent steaks. *Pam-Pam*, in the centre, rec.; *Orsini's Pizzaría*, 2 locations; *Casita de Paja*, Libertad 402, cheap and good; *Mi Café*, Victoria 807, good, friendly; *La Parrilla*, same building, good steaks. Corn (maize) is sold on the streets, excellent with cheese, lime, salt and chile.

Taxis work on a zone system. Agree price before boarding, to avoid unpleasant surprises.

Tourist Office Sr. Molina at Av. Cuauhtémoc 1800, 3rd floor, is very helpful.

Buses Bus station is out beyond the airport (US$1 shuttle from the centre). To El Paso, Texas, US$7.95 first class, 5 hrs. Change buses at Ciudad Juárez (get a seat number) at Customs. One meal stop. Zacatecas, US$6.45 1st, US$3.45 2nd class, Omnibus de México, several a day, 12 hrs. 2nd class bus, to Hidalgo del Parral, US$4, 5 hrs. To Mexico City, 1,488 km., US$21, 21 hrs., every 2 hours; Silao, US$13. León US$16, Durango, US$7. Bus to Ciudad Cuauhtémoc, 1½ hrs.; this is where the Mennonite order from Germany established its headquarters in 1920.

Airport 20 km. from centre, airport buses collect passengers from hotels, fare US$1.50. Also minibuses.

Chihuahua may also be reached from the border at *Ojinaga* (*Hotel Parral*, cheap; cheap meals at *Lonchería Avenida*, across from bus station) an easy crossing, used infrequently by foreigners. On the way to Chihuahua from Ojinaga is Ciudad Delicias (*Hotel Delicias*, nr. market, several others of similar quality nearby). If leaving Mexico here, make sure they stamp your papers.

Railway There are two railway stations: the station for Ciudad Juárez and Mexico City is 3 km. walk along Av. Niños Héroes, left at Av. Colón, which becomes Av. Tecnológico, past the river and right along Av. División Norte. Train to Mexico City, daily at midnight, US$5.95 2nd, US$9.90 1st class reserved, US$7.40 ordinary first, sleeper US$12.20, plus US$12.20 for bed or US$20 for private cabin, 30 hours, no food provided, soft drinks available, book in advance if you can. Train to Zacatecas about 16 hrs. Rápido de la Frontera (*servicio estrella*) for Ciudad Juárez leaves 0700 (4 hrs., US$8.35).

The station for the 631-km. Chihuahua-Pacífico railway is one block behind the prison (nr. Av. 20 de Noviembre and Blvd. Díaz Ordaz—take bus marked C. Rosario, or walk up Av. Independencia, then right along Paseo Bolívar or Av. 20 de Noviembre). Train journey to Los Mochis is very spectacular and exciting: book seats in advance. Sit on left hand side of carriage going to Los Mochis. As the train weaves through the mountains it crosses over 39 bridges and passes through 86 tunnels. It crosses the Sierra of the Tarahumara Indians, who call themselves the Raramuri ("those who run fast"), and were originally cave-dwellers and nomads. They now work as day-labourers in the logging stations and have settled around the mission churches built by the Spanish in the 17th century. The train stops about 15 mins. at Divisadero Barrancas in the Urique Canyon popularly known as the Copper Canyon and said to be finer than the Grand Canyon in the USA. Deep in the canyon are orange, banana and avocado trees, and jungles inhabited by pumas and parrots. High above, turning green in July, are the rocky mountain sides. The most beautiful part of the trip is between Creel (just east of the Barranca) and Los Mochis. Local women sell their handicrafts at bargain prices. Only *Hotel Cabañas Divisadero*, at Divisadero Barrancas by the station, is on the canyon's edge, B, bookable at Aldama 407-C, Chihuahua, T 12-33-62, reported overpriced and not very clean, full board available; *Posada Barrancas Hotel* has its own stop on the railway between Divisadero Barrancas and San Rafael, good value accommodation and excursions. There are motels at the following places along the railway between Creel and Los Mochis: Temoris, Chinipas, Alamos, Bahuichivo, Cuiteco, and San Rafael.

The *servicio estrella* leaves daily at 0700, supposedly arriving at Creel at about 1130, Divisadero at 1215 and Los Mochis at 1900, local time (reserved seat US$20, all meals included); double check all details as they are subject to frequent change. There is food at 2-3 stations along the way (e.g. Divisadero). An ordinary train to Los Mochis leaves at 0800 (1st and 2nd class, US$10 and US$7; fare to Creel US$5.25), reaching Divisadero at 1700 and Los Mochis at 2300, therefore best part is done in the dark. Recommended places for taking photos, on the engine or between the carriages. There is a freight train (*carguero*), which stops overnight at San Rafael. **N.B.** If you leave the train at Creel you may not get a train back next day, but on most days there are 1 or 2 services to Los Mochis and Chihuahua. No heating on Creel train. The train Creel-Chihuahua may take up to 27 hrs. instead of the scheduled 13; be prepared. Watch your luggage and cameras, thefts occur.(For return journey, and for alternative route to Los Mochis, **see page 997**.) If taking this route with a view to connecting with a train to the North or South buy a ticket to Sufragio (**see page 1112**) not Los Mochis (service in either direction at 2430).

On the Chihuahua-Los Mochis line is *Creel*, at 2,300 metres (very cold in winter), the centre of the Tarahumara region, an important timber centre and tourist resort, colourful and pleasant. Maps of the region (simple) and other good buys (such as excellent photographs of Indians) available at mission, which acts as a quasi-tourist office (none in town, in spite of sign). Several hotels: *Motel Parador La Montaña*, B (full board available), will exchange foreign currency at reasonable rates (horses can be hired here, US$5 and a tip for guides—2 hrs. are necessary to get anywhere; spectacular countryside); *Nuevo*, E, meals overpriced, but nice and clean; *Casa de Huéspedes Margarita*, López Mateos 11, no sign, between two churches, friendly, rec., E inc. good meals, organizes tours to waterfalls and thermal springs, horses can be hired (if full, her sister will put you up for E with dinner and breakfast, enjoyable); *Korachi*, E, opp. railway, not particularly clean, only 1 blanket; *Creel*, F, basic, but friendly, 3 blankets, no running water (jug and basin), buses leave from outside hotel, filthy toilets; *Ejido*, very basic but nice people, F. Cheap meals at *Café El Manzano* next to railway station; other cheap restaurants nearby. A few km. out of town is *Cabaña de las Barrancas de Urique*, B, with 3 meals, with minibus service to and from station. 7 km. out, on lake, Jan Milburn runs *Tarahumara Indian Park*, shared or individual cabins. About 40 mins. drive from station is *Copper Canyon Lodge* (Apdo 3, Creel, Chihuahua, A, full board), which has a minibus to collect travellers, rustic woodstoves and oil-lamps, basic cuisine; set in high grassland near waterfall, considerable distance from canyon. There is a bank in Creel, Serfín, next door to the mission at the railway station, very friendly, changes travellers' cheques between 1030 and 1200; hotels cash travellers' cheques at poor rates. Post Office on W side of main square, large building, no sign. Buses daily at 0700 and 1300, 5 hrs., US$2.50, from *Hotel Creel* to Chihuahua.

N.B. There is a time change (one hour back) between Creel and Los Mochis.

Guachochi, 156 km. from Creel buses from Creel daily exc. Sun. at 0730, Sun. at 1500, 8 hours (check at *Korachi Hotel*); also reached from Hidalgo del Parral. Hotels of questionable quality; try *Hotel Ejidal*, E, clean, friendly, belongs to the Creel-Guachochi bus driver. There is a bank. From Guachochi one can walk 3 hrs. to the impressive Barranca de Sinforosa. Marlen Wolf and Markus Tobler of Switzerland write: "You will reach a point several hundred metres above the Río Verde where you can see an unforgettable extended system of immense canyons, grander than you can see from the Divisadero or on crossing the Barranca del Cobre. You can descend to the river on a path". *San Juanito*, 30 km. NE, a little larger than Creel, dusty, has an annual *fiesta* on June 20-24, one hour away by train; bus from Creel at 0700, returns at 2000, paved roads. The Laguna is a little lake 7 km. S of Creel, but is polluted, hire a truck to get there, horses for hire once there, caves. S of Creel is *Cuzarare* ("Place of the Eagles") 20 km. from Creel with Jesuit church (1767) painted by Indians; *Norogachi* (80 km. away), with Tarahumara school and authentic costumes worn on Sun., typical *fiestas*; El Tejabán (Copper Canyon); *Basihuara* ("Sash") village, surrounded by pink and white rock formations (40 km. from Creel); Puente del Río Urique, spans the Urique canyon, ideal camping climate. *Samachique*, where the *rari-pame* race, consisting of kicking a wooden ball in a foot-race of 241 km. without rest, often takes 2-3 days and nights in September. *Kirare*, 65 km. from Creel and on the road to La Bufa mine, offers sights of Batopilas canyon, of great beauty. At the T junction Creel-Guachochi-Bufa is a small restaurant/hotel, *La Casita*, very primitive and romantic, F.

Batopilas (on a 120-km. dirt road from Creel after La Bufa) is a little town of 600 inhabitants, quiet, palm-fringed, subtropical and delightful, hemmed in by the swirling river and the cactus-studded canyon walls. It is a good centre for walking—the Urique canyon can be reached. Horses, pigs, goats and chickens wander freely along the cobblestone streets; the town now has electricity and accommodation. Hotel Batopilas, G, clean, friendly and pleasant, also *Parador Batopilas*. Basic rooms also at *Restaurant Clarita* (basic accommodation, F) and Sra. Monsé—ask prices first—at plaza (curio shop), rooms with gas lamps, who can give information in English (which she likes to practice on tourists) and can change travellers' cheques at a worse rate than in

Creel. *Carmen's Youth Hostel*, basic accommodation, good food, friendly. In the village there are only basic supplies in shops, no bread or alcohol. Pleasant unnamed restaurant in the top right-hand corner of the little plaza beyond the main Zócalo, fixed, good menu. Bus from Creel, Thurs. and Sat. at 0700, 8 hours, US$4, very crowded, returns Fri. and Sun. (Bring insect repellant against locally-nicknamed "assassin bug" or bloodsucking insect.) There is a 350-year-old, bat-infested church in Satevo, a 7-km. walk from Batopilas along the river, a poor place with 15 houses. The area is inhabited by the Tarahumaras known as Gentiles (women don't look at, or talk to, men). *Chomachi*, famous for its caves, some 10 km. deep, inhabited in the past by Apaches. *Basaseachi*, with highest (over 300 metres) single-jump waterfall in North America. Tours arranged by the more expensive hotels to the places mentioned above require a minimum of 4 people and cost from US$8 p.p. to Cuzarare to US$28 p.p. to places further away such as La Bufa. The Creel-Batopilas bus journey passes through or close to Cuzarare, Basihuare, Urique Canyon, Samachique, Kirare, before awesome 14 km. descent into Batopilas Canyon at La Bufa. The road ends 30 km. later at Batopilas.

Recommended for guided tours deep into the Urique Canyon is Adventure Specialists, Inc. (president Gary Ziegler), Bear Basin Ranch, Westcliffe, CO. 81252 (303/783-2519, 800/621-8385, ext. 648), US$700-800 for 11-day tours from El Paso, vigorous, knowledgeable.

Ciudad Camargo (Km. 1,484), a small cattle town in a green valley, quiet save for its eight days of *fiesta* for Santa Rosalía beginning on Sept. 4, when there are cockfights, horse racing and dancing. Black bass fishing at the dam lake, and warm sulphur springs 5 km. away.

Hotel *Santa Rosalía Courts*. **Motel** *Baca*.

From Ciudad Jiménez (km. 1,225; *Motel Florido*, C, hot water) there are two routes to Fresnillo and Zacatecas: the Central Highway through Durango or a more direct route via Torreón (290 km. from Ciudad Jiménez), passing Escalón (restaurant), Ceballos (*Hotel San José*, F, basic), Yermo (restaurants) and Bermejillo (restaurant), on Route 49.

Torreón is the principal city of La Laguna cotton and wheat district. Population, 700,000. Here is the Bolsón de Mayrán (altitude 1,137 metres) an oasis of about 28,500 square km. which might be irrigated, but only about 2,000 square km. have been developed and much of that is stricken with drought. On the opposite side of the mostly dry Nazas river are the two towns of Gómez Palacio (*feria* first half of August; *Motel La Cabaña*, E, hot water) and Lerdo.

Hotels *El Presidente*, Paseo de la Rosita y Fuentes, A; *Paraíso del Desierto*, Independencia y Jiménez, B, resort; *Río Nazas*, highrise, very good, D, on Av. Morelos y Treviño; *Palacio Real*, Morelos 1280, A; *Galicia*, Cepeda 273, E, good; *Laguna*, Carrillo 333, D; *Princesa*, Av. Morelos nr. Parque Central, F.

Restaurant *La República*, Musquiz 360, abundant comida corrida, cheap; *Kentucky Fried Chicken*, good, 2 locations.

Buses Bus companies all located within 2 blocks of Zócalo. To Chihuahua, 10 hrs.; to Tepic, US$12; to Ciudad Juárez, US$11; about 6 a day to Durango, 4½ hrs. 2nd class. There is also an airport.

From Ciudad Jiménez it is 77 km. to (Km. 1,138) **Hidalgo del Parral,** an old picturesque mining town of 100,000 people with mule waggons in its steep and narrow streets. See the parochial church and one dedicated to the Lightning Virgin (Virgen del Rayo). The Museum of Pancho Villa, which is also the public library, is worth seeing for the many old photos and newspaper clippings related to the 1910 revolution and Villa, who was assassinated in Parral on July 20, 1923 on the orders of Obregón and Calles.

Hotels *Moreira*, Maclovio Herrera 2, D, modern, clean, good value, large restaurant meals for US$2.50, rec. Near the Estrella Blanca terminal are 3 F-range hotels; *Internacional*, *Pinos Altos*, basic, and *La Fe*, *Viajero*, near main square, F. *Fuente*, Herrera 79, F, basic but clean. **Motel** *Camino Real*, Pan-American Highway, C, good restaurant.

Buses Each company has its own terminal. To Durango, Transportes Chihuahuenses US$5.75, 6 hrs. To Zacatecas, Omnibuses de México, US$8, 9 hrs. Also to Guachochi (previous page).

On this road, between Rodeo and Durango, is the "Western landscape" beloved of Hollywood film-makers. Cinema enthusiasts can visit the Western sets of Villa del Oeste (9 km. from Durango) and Chupaderos (10.5 km.), both decaying but smelling authentically of horse (Cía San Juan del

Río buses go there). Between Gómez Palacio and Zacatecas are Cuencame (*Motel la Posta*, F, hot water), Río Grande (*Hotel Río*, F); Fresnillo (*Motel La Fortuna*, E, comfortable, hot water, *Hotel Cuauhtémoc*, F, basic).

(Km. 926) (Victoria de) **Durango,** capital of Durango state: alt.: 1,924 metres; pop.: 600,000; founded in 1563. It is a pleasant city, with parks, a Cathedral (1695) and a famous iron-water spring. Parque Guadiana at W edge of town, with huge eucalyptus trees, is a nice place to relax. Good views of the city from Cerro de Los Remedios: many flights of steps up to a chapel. Presa Victoria can be reached by bus from Durango; one can swim in the lake enclosed by the dam. *Feria* first half of July.

Hotels *Casa Blanca*, 20 de Noviembre 811, C, nice, big old hotel in the centre, unguarded parking lot; *El Presidente*, 20 de Noviembre 257, B; *Posada Durán* (D), *Campo México Courts*, both on 20 de Noviembre, C, good but restaurant service poor; *Reyes*, 20 de Noviembre 220, clean, E; *Gallo*, 5 de Febrero, E, with bath, good. *Oasis*, Zarco between 20 de Noviembre y 5 de Febrero, F with bath, rec.; *Villa*, across roundabout from bus station, D, clean, pleasant, TV; *Karla*, opp. bus station, E, small, clean, friendly but noisy. Cheap hotels: *Patoni*, Patoni entre P.Suárez y 5 de Febrero, *Casa de Huéspedes Buenos Aires*, Constitución 126, Norte, also around the cathedral. CREA Youth Hostel, Av. Heróica Colegio Militar s/n, T 24516/11775, C.P. 34000.

Restaurants *La Bohemia* rec., reasonable food, good breakfasts; good breakfasts also at *Café Salum*, 5 de Febrero y Progreso.

Tourist Offices Hidalgo 408 Sur and 20 de Noviembre y Independencia; both good.

Durango is on the Coast-to-Coast Highway from Mazatlán to Matamoros. The 320 km. stretch of road from Durango W to Mazatlán is through splendid mountain scenery. For a one day trip, go as far as El Salto (96 km.), 7 buses a day, but go early to get ticket. Durango is some 260 km. SW of Torreón.

Buses Bus station out of town: minibus No. 2 to centre, US$0.15. Several buses a day cross the Sierra Madre Occidental to Mazatlán (Transportes Chihuahuenses, 1st class, 7 hrs., US$5.40). This is rec. if you cannot do the Los Mochis-Chihuahua journey, sit on left side. Second class buses for camera buffs stop more frequently. Guadalajara, US$6; Chihuahua, US$7. Second class bus to Hidalgo del Parral, 7 hrs., US$5 with Transportes Chihuahuenses. Zacatecas, Omnibus de México, 4½ hrs., US$4.25. Chihuahua 10 hrs., US$7. Town buses stop running early in evening, so try to arrive before dark if you wish to avoid a long walk or taxi ride to centre.

Rail Centauro del Norte *servicio estrella* to Zacatecas at 1100 (6 hrs. 35 mins., US$7 reserved seat).

Airport 5 km. from centre.

Balneario La Florida on the outskirts is pleasant (take green "Potreros" bus on Calle Pasteur). Between Durango and Zacatecas is Sombrerete, a small colonial mining town with good churches. (Hotels: *Real de Minas, Avenida Real, Hidalgo*).

(Km. 636) **Zacatecas,** founded 1548, capital of Zacatecas state; alt.: 2,495 metres; pop. 180,000; picturesque up-and-down mining city built in a ravine, pink stone houses towering above one another and sprinkled over the hills. The largest silver mine in the world, processing 10,000 tonnes of ore a day or 220 tonnes of silver, is at Real de Angeles. Places to see are the Cathedral (1730-52), the San Agustín church, with interior carvings now being restored, the Jesuit church of Santo Domingo and the little houses behind it, the Pedro Coronel museum on Plaza Santo Domingo, Plaza Hidalgo and its statues, the Casa Moneda (better known as the Tesorería), the Calderón theatre, and the chapel of Los Remedios (1728), on the Cerro de La Bufa (cablecar, US$1.20 return, starts at 1230, crowded Sun.) which dominates the city, through which an old aqueduct runs, the market, and the Museo Francisco Goitia, housed in what was once the Governor's mansion, near the aqueduct and park, with modern paintings by Zacatecans, free admission. La Mina Edén (admission US$0.80) is accessible from the upper end of the Alameda, behind the Seguro Social hospital. Visit also the Chicomostoc ruins 56 km. S by taking the 0930 Línea Verde bus from main terminal to Adjuntas (about 45 mins.), on the Villanueva road. Then walk ½ hr. through beautiful, silent, nopal-cactus scenery to the ruins, which offer an impressive view (may have to hitch back). Admission US$0.20. Women are advised to keep at a distance from the caretaker!

Zacatecas is famous for its *sarapes* and has two delicacies: the local cheese, and *queso de tuna*, a candy made from the fruit of the nopal cactus (do not eat too much, it has laxative properties). Visit the small *tortilla* factories near the station, on the main road. Zacatecas is reckoned by many travellers to be the pleasantest town in this part of Mexico.

Fiesta spreads over most of September, a rainy month here. There are bullfights on Sundays.

Hotels   *Aristos*, Lomas de Soledad, A; *Calinda*, near old bus station, very comfortable, D; the cheap hotels (very few) are all within 5 minutes walk of the old bus station, towards Av. Hidalgo. *Barranca*, F, opp. bus terminal, pleasant, but noisy traffic; *Reina Cristina* on Zócalo, D, run down, with bath, clean; *Posada de La Moneda*, nr. Cathedral, Av. Hidalgo 415, nice and clean, D; *Posada del Conde*, Juárez 18, good-looking, D. *Condesa*, opp. *Posada del Conde*, E, OK. *Baños*, F, with bath, no hot water, at Hidalgo 203. CREA Youth Hostel, Parque del Encantado, T 20223/21891, C.P. 98000, on bus route to centre from bus station, F (no singles). *Insurgentes*, off Plaza del Vivar, E without bath, hot showers extra; *Zamora*, on Av. Independencia off Plazuela del Vivar, F, central, pleasant. **Motels** *Del Bosque*, C, Fortín de la Peña; *Parador Zacatecas*, excellent, C, Pan-American Highway.

Restaurants   *La Parroquia*, beautiful colonial house, excellent food and wines and inexpensive for its class (good meal-stand next door). *La Cuija*, in old Centro Comercial on Av. Tacuba, good food, music, atmosphere; *El Jacalito*, Juárez 18, excellent comida corrida and breakfast. *Don Parroquín*, Av. Hidalgo, good pizzas; *El Fortín*, near Cathedral, good, nice coffee shop. *El Carnerito*, Av. Juárez 110, good and cheap. Several cheap restaurants (corrida for less than US$1.50) along Av. Independencia. *Café Neveria*, good cappuccino. Young people hang out at *La Bohemia*, Av. González Artegú.

Travel Agent   Cantera Tours, Centro Comercial El Mercado, Local A-21, T 29065, tour to Chicomostoc and Jérez at 0930, US$8.50.

Tourist Office   opposite Cathedral friendly, helpful, English spoken, free maps, hotel information. Ask here about language classes at the University. **Post Office**, Calle Allende.

Exchange   Banamex rec.

Trains   San Marqueño-Zacarecano (*servicio estrella*) leaves Mexico City 2130, arrives Zacatecas 1000; returns 0720, via Aguascalientes; reserved seat US$14.80, single sleeper US$29.30, double US$58.65. To Mexico City at 0500 and at 1600, 1st class US$4.90, 2nd US$3.25; to Chihuahua 1030, US$6.45, 1st class, US$3.65, 2nd class to Aguascalientes, 4 hrs. US$1.60 2nd class. To Durango, 1st class US$3, 2nd class US$1.50, very crowded to Pescador (where you change trains), standing room only; after Pescador, train quite empty, 9½ hrs. in all. Also Centauro del Norte *servicio estrella* at 1010 (arr. 1645, reserved seat US$7).

Bus   New terminal 4 km. N of town; yellow No. 8 buses from Plaza Independencia, or white *camionetas* from Av. González Artegú (old bus station on Blvd. A. López Mateos only serves local destinations). To Chihuahua via Torreón, 12 hrs., US$12.50; Jiménez, US$9; San Luis Potosí with Estrella Blanca; Ciudad Juárez 1st class with Omnibus de México at 1930, 11 hrs; to Guadalajara, 6½ hrs., several companies, US$4, but shop around for different journey times. To Mexico City, 8 hrs., US$10.

Airport   25 km. N of city, daily flights to Mexico City and Tijuana.

Beyond Zacatecas lies the Convento de Guadalupe, a national monument, with a fine church and convent, which now houses a museum of colonial religious art; admission US$0.50 (Tues.-Sun. 1000-1700). Next door is Museo Regional de Historia, under development. Frequent buses from old terminal. Jerez is an old colonial town about 65 km. from Zacatecas, worth a visit; frequent buses from new bus terminal.

(Km. 508) ***Aguascalientes**** was founded in 1575 and is capital of its state; alt.: 1,190 metres; pop.: 750,000; its name comes from its many hot mineral springs. An oddity is that the city is built over a network of tunnels dug out by a forgotten people. It has pretty parks, a pleasant climate, delicious fruits, and specializes in drawn linen threadwork, pottery, and leather goods. Places to see are the Government Palace (once the castle of the Marqués de Guadalupe, with colourful murals round inner courtyards), the churches of San Marcos and San Antonio (somewhat odd) and the Municipal Palace.

On items of interest in Aguascalientes, Tim Connell writes:
   Museo de Aguascalientes, Calle Zaragoza 505, is by Church of San Antonio. The José Guadalupe Posada museum is in a gallery, by the Templo del Cristo Negro, close to a pleasant garden—Díaz de León (known locally as the Jardín del Encino). A remarkable collection of prints

by the lithographer Posada, best known for his *cadaveras*, macabre skeletal figures illustrating and satirizing the Revolution and events leading up to it. Admission free, Tues.-Sun. 1000-1400, 1700-2100. Shut Mon. Cultural events in the courtyard on Sat. and Sun. The Casa de las Artesanías is near main square. The Casa de la Cultura, on Venustiano Carranza and Galeana Norte, is a fine colonial building. Display of *artesanía* during the *feria*.

Hacienda de San Blas, 34 km. away, contains Museo de la Insurgencia. Murals by Alfredo Zermeño. The area is famous for viticulture; the local wine is called after San Marcos, and the *feria* in his honour lasts for 3 weeks, starting in the middle of April, with processions, cockfights (in Mexico's largest *palenque*, seating 4,000), bullfights, agricultural shows etc. The Plaza de Armas is lavishly decorated. The *feria*, covered by national TV networks, is said to be the biggest in Mexico. Accommodation can be very difficult and prices double during the *feria*.

Teatro Morelos next to Cathedral; T 5-00-97. The University is ½ hr. from the city centre. Its administrative offices are in the ex-Convento de San Diego, by the attractive Jardín del Estudiante, and the Parían, a shopping centre. The market is not far away. There is carp fishing at El Jocoqui and Abelardo López Mateos.

Hotels   *Francia*, Plaza Principal, A, airy, colonial style; good restaurant (*El Fausto*) for breakfast and lunch; *Praga*, E, with TV, Zaragoza 214, T 5-23-57. *Continental*, Av. 5, No. 307, nr. Zócalo, F with bath, good, cafeteria; another *Continental* at Guatemala y Brasil, F, near bus terminal. At Rep. de Brasil 403, *Casa de Huéspedes*, nr. main square, F, and at No. 602 *Gómez*, E. On main square, *Señorial*, E, helpful lady speaks English; *Maser*, 3 blocks from Cathedral on Montaro, E, *comedor* for breakfast. Cheap hotels around Juárez market (Av. Guadalupe y Calle Guadalupe Victoria), e.g. *Brasil* and *Bahía*, E with bath, *Mexico*, F, no bath or hot water. CREA Youth Hostel, Av. de la Juventud y Rancho del Charro s/n, C.P. 20190, T 80863. **Motel** *El Medrano*, Chávez 904, A; *La Cascada*, Chávez 501, B.

Restaurants   *Mitla*, Madero 220, cheap and clean, good Mexican menu; *Cascada*, main plaza; *Bugambilia*, Chávez 102, quite plush, reasonable menu, but service can be morose. *Café de los Artesanos*, Calle José María Chávez 122, good atmosphere and coffee, friendly owners welcome foreigners.

Market   Main one at 5 de Mayo y Unión, large and clean, with toilet on upper floor.

Post Office Hospitalidad, nr. El Porián shopping centre.

Tourist Office   Next to Cathedral in main square (Plaza de la Patria).

Taxis   There is a ticket system for taxis from the Central Camionera, with the city divided into different fare zones. There is no need to pay extra; a phone number for complaints is on the ticket.

Transport   Trains: San Marqueño-Zacatecano (*servicio estrella*) between Mexico City and Zacatecas calls here at 0740; fare from the capital, US$12.25 for reclining seat, US$24.35 single sleeper, US$48.65 double. Twice a day to Mexico City, due from Ciudad Juárez at 1840 and from Torreón at 0815. Train to San Luis Potosí daily at 0740. Train station at E end of Av. Madero. Bus station about 1 km. S of centre on Av. Circunvalación Sur. Bus: to Guadalajara, 5 hrs. US$3.55 1st, US$3.40 2nd class, but 0900 and 1415 bus take 4 hrs. To Guanajuato US$2.60 with Flecha Amarilla. To Zacatecas: US$1.90. There is an airport. Some 170 km. to the E is San Luis Potosí (see page 980).

Thermal Baths Balneario Ojo Caliente, E end of town beyond train station, at end of Calzada Revolución (Alameda), claims to have been founded in 1808, some private baths and 2 public pools (US$0.45). At end of Alameda fork right to Deportivo Ojocaliente, a large complex with several pools (not so warm water), US$0.65.

Encarnación de Díaz (hotel and restaurant) is halfway to **Lagos de Moreno** (km. 425), a charming old town with fine baroque churches. See the ex-convent of the Capuchins and the Rosas Moreno Theatre. *Feria* last week of July and first of August. A road turns off right to Guadalajara, 197 km. away; the same road leads, left, to Antiguo Morelos via San Luis Potosí. Lagos de Moreno has several hotels (on main plaza: *París*, *Colonial*—both D, *Plaza*, F, and *Victoria*, nr. river, E) and restaurants.

After about 1,600 km. of desert or semi-arid country, we now enter, surprisingly, the basin of Guanajuato, known as the Bajío, greener, more fertile, higher (on average over 1,800 metres), and wetter, though the rainfall is still not more than 635 to 740 mm. a year. The Bajío is the granary of central Mexico, growing maize, wheat, and fruit. The towns we pass through, León, Irapuato, and Celaya, have grown enormously in population and importance.

(Km. 382) **León** (de los Aldamas), in the fertile plain of the Gómez river, is now said to be Mexico's fifth city, with a population of 1.2 million. The business centre is the Plaza de Constitución. There are a striking municipal palace, a cathedral, many shaded plazas and gardens. The Templo Expiatorio has been under construction for most of this century, catacombs open 1000-1300, well worth seeing; the Doblado theatre on Av. Hermanos Aldama; the modernized zoo, reached by the Ibarilla bus. León is the main shoe centre of the country (high quality shoes in the Plaza del Zapato, Hilario Medina, and cheaper ones in places round the bus station), and is noted for its leather work (buy in the shops round the jail, and along Belisario Domínguez), fine silver-trimmed saddles, and *rebozos*. Alt.: 1,885 metres. Frequent buses to Torreón (10 hrs.).

Hotels Rec.: *Estancia*, Blvd. López Mateos, B; *Robert*, Blvd. L. Mateos Oriente 1503, D; *Señorial*, D, near Plaza, and *Condesa*, on Plaza, C; *Tepeyac*, Av. Miguel Alemán, E. Also several cheaper ones near market.

Restaurants Two good and cheap Japanese: *Towaki*, near Plaza, English-speaking owner, and *Eiki*.

Airport San Carlos, 15 km. from centre. Daily flights to Mexico City, Mazatlán and Tijuana, and twice weekly to Houston, Monterrey and Puerto Vallarta. New international airport being built between León and Silao, to be opened 1990.

(Km. 430) Silao (hotel). Between León and Silao, left off Highway 45 at Km. 387 (going S) are the famous swimming pools of Comanjilla fed by hot sulphurous springs (rustic, semi-tropical with hotel and restaurant at moderate rates). Eleven km. beyond Silao, at Los Infantes, a short side road through the picturesque Marfil canyon leads to Guanajuato.

Guanajuato, the beautiful capital of Guanajuato state and a university city, has been important for its silver since 1548. Population, 70,000 in 1880, now 150,000, altitude, 2,010 metres. It stands in a narrow gorge amid wild and striking scenery; the Guanajuato river cutting through it has been covered over and an underground street opened—an unusual and effective attraction. The streets, steep, twisted and narrow, follow the contours of the hills and are sometimes steps cut into the rock: one, the Street of the Kiss (Callejón del Beso), is so narrow that kisses can be—and are—exchanged from opposite balconies. Over the city looms the shoulder of La Bufa mountain. A most interesting building is the massive Alhóndiga de Granadita, built as a granary, turned into a fortress, and now an attractive museum (US$0.35, theoretically closed Mon.). Guanajuato contains a series of fine museums, as well as the most elegant marble-lined public lavatories in Mexico. The best of many colonial churches are San Francisco (1671); La Compañía (Jesuit, 18th century); San Diego (1663) on the Plaza de la Unión; and the splendid church of La Valenciana, one of the most impressive in Mexico, 5 km. out of town and built for the workers of the Valenciana silver mine, once the richest in the world (a local "Valenciana" bus goes to it, US$0.07 from centre, 10 minutes ride; 10 mins. walk between church and mine pit-head; don't believe anyone who tells you a taxi is necessary). A gruesome sight shown to visitors is of mummified bodies in the small Museo de las Momias, arranged in glass cases along one wall (US$0.10—long queues); buses go there ("Momias", US$0.06, 10 mins.), along Av. Juárez, but you can walk; there is a free guide (Spanish-speaking). A new Don Quixote museum was opened in 1987 on Plaza Dr. Enrique Romero: paintings, drawings, sculptures of the Don. The Cathedral (Basilica) and the church of San Roque should also be visited. Local pottery can be bought at the Hidalgo market and along the potters' street. Good bargaining for *rebozos* in the plaza opposite the *Hotel San Diego*. The University was founded in 1732. The painter Diego Rivera was born in Calle de Pocitos; visit the museum there with permanent collection of his drawings, paintings and Popol Vuh collection. On the E side of the city is the Presa de la Olla, a favourite picnic spot; several parks and monuments in the vicinity, frequent buses (US$0.08). The area is being industrialized.

When Father Hidalgo took the city in 1810, the Alhóndiga was the last place to surrender, and there was a wanton slaughter of Spanish soldiers and royalist prisoners. When Hidalgo was himself caught and executed, along with three other leaders, at Chihuahua, their heads, in revenge, were fixed at the four corners of the Alhóndiga. There is a fine view from the monument to Pipila, the man who fired the door of the Alhóndiga so that the patriots could take it, which crowns the high hill of Hormiguera. Look for the "Al Pipila" sign. Steep climb. Local buses go from *Hotel Central*, on the hour, to the Pipila.

Hotels   Bus station very helpful in finding hotels. Check hotel prices, as cheaper central hotels try to put up prices when foreigners appear, and they also try to insist on a room with two beds, which is more expensive than with a double bed. Hotel rooms can be hard to find after 1400. There are frequent water shortages, so that hotels with no reservoirs of their own have no water on certain days. On Jardín de la Unión are *Posada Santa Fe*, No. 12, B, and *San Diego*, No. 1, C, good bar, better run; *Real de Minas*, Nejayote 17 at city entrance, B; *La Abadía*, San Matías 50, C. *El Presidente San Gabriel de Barrera*, C, 2 km. out in Marfil suburb, former hacienda; *Hostería del Frayle*, Sopeña 3, C; *Reforma*, Av. Juárez 113, E, with bath, clean and quiet; *Castillo de Santa Cecilia*, Dolores road, tourist-bus haven, A; *Parador San Javier*, Plaza Aldama 92, opp. side of Dolores road, genuine hacienda style, B; *Central*, Juárez 111, near bus station, restaurant, good value, clean but noisy, E, several others on same street: *El Insurgente* (No. 226) D, pleasant and quiet, good breakfasts; *Posada San Francisco*, Av. Juárez y Gavira, E, on Zócalo, good value but noisy on outside rooms, no hot water, lovely inner patio; *Granadita* (No. 109) clean and friendly, F; *Alhóndiga*, Insurgencia 49, good, E; *Molino del Rey*, Campañero 15, simple and quaint, E. At Calle Alonso 32 is *Casa Kloster*, E, very friendly, rooms for 4 (although few with private bath), very good value, laundry facilities, rec., gardens. Near the bus terminal is *Mineral de Rayos*, Alhóndiga 7, E, with bath, small rooms, clean linen, running down. Very close to the main street is a street full of *casas de huéspedes*. **Motels** Many on Dolores Hidalgo road exit: *Guanajuato*, C, good pool and food, quiet, rec.; *Valenciana*, C; *Villa de Plata*, C; *El Carruaje*, C.   *De Los Embajadores*, Paseo Embajadores, Mexican décor, C, restaurant, famous Sun. lunch. Trailer Park just off the road to Valenciana, clean bathrooms and hot showers, US$1.40 for tent and 2 people. 20 mins.' walk from centre.

Restaurants   Good coffee and reasonable food at *El Retiro*, Sopeña 12, nr. Jardín de la Unión. *Pizza Piazza*, Plaza San Fernando; *Cuatro Ranas*, Jardín Unión 1, most popular; *Casa Kloster* on Calle Alonso, cheap and good value; *La Bohemia*, Calle Alonso, cheap, good sandwiches; *BBQ chicken* on Av. Juárez about 200 metres up from Mercado Hidalgo; *Las Palomas*, near post office, reasonable comidas. *El Granero*, good comida, US$1.50, until 1700. *El Figón*, open after 1830 (closed 2-3 days a week), family run, small, on same street as Teatro Principal, heading towards Teatro Cervantes. *Hamburguesa Feliz*, Sopeña 10, good value. Good small café on N side of Plaza de la Unión.

Entertainment   Sketches from classical authors out of doors in lovely old plazas from April to August. Programme at Teatro Juárez (a magnificent French-type Second Empire building, US$0.25 to view), on Friday and Saturday nights. The Teatro Principal is opposite this. A band plays in Jardín de la Unión (next to the theatre) thrice weekly. Arts festival, the Festival Cervantino de Guanajuato (in honour of Cervantes), is an important cultural event in the Spanish-speaking world, encompassing theatre, song and dance (held in October). *Viernes de las Flores* is held on the Friday before Good Friday—starting with the Dance of the Flowers on Thurs. night at about 2200 right through the night, adjourning at Jardín de la Unión to exchange flowers. Very colourful and crowded.

Laundry   E of Jardín de la Unión, US$2.10 for a load, including drying.

Tourist Office   Excellent, 5 de Mayo y Juárez near bus terminal. They have all hotel rates (except the cheapest) and give away folders. American Express, Georama, Av. Juárez 36.

Bus   San Miguel de Allende, 1st class, US$6, 0700 and 1715, 2 hrs; Flecha Amarilla or Servicios Coordinados, 2nd class, ½ hourly between 0630 and 2300, 2 hrs. via Dolores Hidalgo (most of them go on to Mexico City), US$2; to Guadalajara 1st class US$5.50; via León (US$1) and Lagos de Moreno with Flecha Amarilla, 2nd class, hourly (0550-2235) US$4 (7 hrs.). Also daily at 1500 with Omnibus de México, US$5. Hourly service to Morelia (6 hrs.) US$2.20. To Mexico City, 1st class, Estrella Blanca, 5½ hrs. US$4.80, book well in advance. To San Luis Potosí, US$3. To Querétaro, US$1.60, 3½ hrs. by Flecha Amarilla.

Rail   Constitucionalista (*servicio esrtella*) from Mexico City via Querétaro leaves 0735, arrives 1345; returns from Guanajuato 1430, arr. Querétaro 1350 and Mexico City 1900; fare to the capital, US$8.70. One train a day to Irapuato, at 0820.

Excursions   A very good round trip is through Dolores Hidalgo to San Miguel de Allende, taking in Atotonilco (**see page 994**). See also the three local silver mines of La Raya (you can walk up from town; it is still operating), La Valenciana and La Cata. It is possible to visit the separating plant at La Cata, but visitors are not admitted to mines. At old site of La Cata mine (local bus near market), a church with a magnificent baroque façade, also the shrine of El Señor de Villa Seca (the patron of adulterers) with *retablos* and crude drawings of miraculous escapes from harm, mostly due to poor shooting by husbands. 30 km. from Guanajuato is Cerro Cubilete, with a statue of Christ the King; local buses take 1½ hrs., spectacular view of the Bajío, US$1, hourly from Guanajuato (also from Silao for US$0.60). Dormitory at the site (US$1.50) food available; last bus up leaves at 1600 from Silao and Guanajuato. Visit the *Rancho de Enmedio* midway between

Guanajuato and Dolores Hidalgo. Good dried meat specialities and beautiful scenery. A profusion of wild pears is sold from the roadside by children. Go also to San Gabriel de Barrera with the bus to Marfil, beautiful garden and *hacienda*, 15 patios, quiet. Tours to local sights leave from the main square.

(Km. 315) **Irapuato,** 475,000 people (*Hotel Real de Minas*, overpriced, with equally overpriced restaurant, on Portal Carrillo Puerto, quiet rooms on church side; *Restaurant El Gaucho*, Díaz Ordaz y Lago), noted for delicious strawberries, which should on no account be eaten unwashed.

Divided-lane highway to (Km. 265) **Celaya,** population, 420,000; altitude, 1,800 metres; famous for its confectionery, especially a caramel spread called *cajeta*, and its churches, built by Mexico's great baroque architect Tresguerras (1765-1833), a native of the town. His best church is El Carmen (1807), with a fine tower and dome; see also his fine bridge over the Laja river. (Excellent restaurant, *El Gran Chaparral*, especially for steaks, good service.)

From Celaya to Querétaro, where we join the route from Eagle Pass **(see page 978)**, there is a 56-km. limited-access toll motorway (US$0.40 a car), or the old road through Apaseo el Alto. Between Celaya and San Miguel de Allende is Comonfort; from there go 3 km. N to Rancho Arias: on a hilltop to the W are precolumbian pyramids. Cross the river N of the church and climb to ruins via goat-tracks.

San Miguel de Allende, a charming old town at 1,850 metres, on a steep hillside facing the broad sweep of the Laja River and the distant blue of the Guanajuato mountains, is 50 km. N of Querétaro by paved road. Population, 150,000. Its twisting cobbled streets rise in terraces to the mineral spring of El Chorro, from which the blue and yellow tiled cupolas of some 20 churches can be seen. It has been declared a national monument and all changes in the town are strictly controlled. In recent years there has been a large influx of American residents (now numbering several thousands) and tourists, with a consequent rise in prices.

Social life centres around the market and the Jardín, or central plaza, an open-air living room for the whole town. Around it are the colonial city hall, several hotels, and the parish church, adorned by an Indian mastermason in the late 19th century, Zeferino Gutiérrez, who provided the austere Franciscan front with a beautiful façade and a Gothic tower; see also mural in chapel. The church of San Felipe Neri, with its fine baroque façade, is at the SW end of the market. Notable among the baroque façades and doors rich in churrigueresque details is the Casa del Mayorazgo de Canal, and San Francisco church, designed by Tresguerras. The Convent of La Concepción, built in 1734, now houses an art school, the Centro Cultural Nigromonte, locally known as Bellas Artes; the summer residence of the Condes del Canal, on San Antonio, contains a language school, the Instituto Allende (which has an English-language library; Spanish courses, US$70 a week, US$230 a month, without accommodation, but some rooms can be rented). The Academia América-Española offers full time Spanish courses; Casa de la Luna teaches Spanish less formally. Handicrafts are the traditional pottery, cotton cloth and brasswork. The city was founded as San Miguel in 1542, and Allende added in honour of the independence patriot born there. Local US women's committees run house and garden tours for charity: ask at the hotel. (They start at noon every Sun., and cost US$6.)

Fiestas End-July to mid-August, classical chamber music festival, information from Bellas Artes. One every 10 days or so. Main ones are Independence Day (Sept. 15-16); Fiesta de San Miguel (Sept. 28-Oct. 1, with Conchero dancers from many places); Day of the Dead (Nov. 2); the Christmas Posadas, celebrated in the traditional colonial manner (Dec. 16-24); the pre-Lenten carnival, Easter Week, and Corpus Christi (June).

Hotels Many weekend visitors from Mexico City: book ahead if you can. *Mansión del Bosque*, Aldama 65, B, half-board; *Posada La Aldea*, B, colonial style, clean, quiet, swimming pool, gardens; *Posada de San Francisco*, main square, C; *Parador San Miguel Aristos*, at Instituto Allende, students given priority, D; *Vista Hermosa Taboada*, Allende 11, D, very popular, nice old colonial building, some ground floor rooms dark and noisy; *Rancho-Hotel El Atascadero*, Querétaro road entrance, in an old colonial hacienda, very satisfactory, C; *Posada de las Monjas*, Canal 37, D, with shower, excellent set meals in restaurant, clean and attractive, very good value. *Misión de los Angeles*, de luxe, 2 km. out on Celaya road, colonial style, swimming pool, convenient facilities, C. Near Jardín, on Calle Vinaron, *Posada La Fuente* has a few rooms, good food (by arrangement), D. *San Sebastián*, nr. market, rec., E, large rooms with fireplace, clean, courtyard. *Quinta Loreto*, Loreto 13, modern rooms, swimming pool, pleasant garden, E, splendid value, good food (but beware of mosquitoes); *Hidalgo*, Hidalgo 22, E, hot water, good

SAN MIGUEL DE ALLENDE

/32

Not to Scale

1. Central Plaza (Jardin)
2. Plaza Ignacio Allende
3. Catedral
4. San Felipe Neri
5. San Francisco
6. Centro Cultural Nigromonte
7. Casa del Mayorazgo de Canal
8. Instituto Allende
9. Tourist Office
10. Post Office
11. Market

Hotels:
12. Posada la Aldea
13. Vista Hermosa Taboada
14. San Sebastián
15. Quinta Loreto
16. La Huerta
17. Posada Carmina
18. Sautto.

TO DOLORES HIDALGO & ATOTONILCO

TO RAILWAY STATION

TO CELAYA & GUANAJATO

TO SAN ANTONIO

TO QUERÉTARO & MEXICO CITY

value, but rooms vary in quality. *La Huerta*, E, nice and quiet at the bottom of a dead-end street 4 blocks from the market, "gringo place". *Posada Carmina*, Cuña de Allende 7, D, colonial building, courtyard for meals, rec.; *Mesón San Antonio*, D, Mesones 80, renovated mansion, clean, friendly, quiet; *Sautto*, Dr. Macías 59, E, rustic, pleasant but little hot water. **Motels** *Villa del Molino*, Mexico City road entrance A; *Siesta*, road to Guanajuato, with trailer park, C, gardens; KAO campgrounds further out on same road.

Restaurants *Bugambilia*, excellent, rec.; *Mama Mía*, near main square, jazz evenings, good; *Señor Plato*, Jesús 7, pricey, but has amazing 1920s atmosphere piano bar, and colonial-style patio filled with plants and parrots, excellent steaks, free garlic bread. *Alejandra*, small, near market, all home-cooked food, closed evenings, highly rec.; *El Circo*, Insurgentes by the library, Italian, singing waiters, fancy; opposite library at Insurgentes 74 is *Parroquiazo*, French atmosphere, attractive and not expensive. On Aldama *Posada Carmen*, OK but expensive; *Café Colón*, San Francisco 21, "folksy", great and inexpensive, rec. *Pepe Pizza*, Hidalgo 15, strudel too. *Vegetarian* restaurant at Correo 41/2 (on right-hand side as you walk away from centre), clean, cheap. *Café La Dolce Vita*, excellent coffee, cakes, fruit salads, Italian-owned. Try the licuados (fruit-shakes) in the market; ask for a campechana!

Bookshop El Colibri, near Zócalo, French and English books.

Laundromat on Pasaje de Allende, US$1.50 wash and dry, same day service.

Immigration for tourist card extensions, etc., in Instituto Allende building.

Tourist Office on Plaza, helpful with finding hotels, English spoken.

Transport The *servicio estrella* train, *El Constitucionalista*, leaves 1610 for Mexico City (via Querétaro); leaves the capital 0735, arrives San Miguel 1210 (US$7.40); T 20007 for reservations. The El Paso train stops at Celaya and Querétaro, 1309 (arr. 1920) and 1610 (arr. 2057); also one train to Nuevo Laredo daily. Frequent buses to Guanajuato (2 hrs.) with Flecha Amarilla and Estrella Blanca, via Dolores Hidalgo, US$2. To Dolores Hidalgo, US$0.50. Spectacular scenery between Dolores Hidalgo and Guanajuato as the road corkscrews up to a watershed from which you look down to arid lands on the east and tree-covered slopes on the west. Buses to Mexico City via Querétaro 4 a day before 1200, US$4, 2nd class, crowded but interesting. Buses to Morelia until 2040 daily, 4 hrs., US$3, 2nd class. Bus to Atotonilco US$0.30, plus short walk.

Excursions A good all-day hike can be made to the Palo Huérfano mountain on the S side of town. Take the road to just before the radio pylon then take the trails to the summit, where there are oaks and pines. Twenty mins. away is the small town of **Atotonilco**, where there is a church built around 1740 whose inside walls and ceiling are covered with frescoes done in black, red and grey earth: unrivalled anywhere for sheer native exuberance. There is a spa, the Balneario Taboada (admission US$1.70), between San Miguel and El Cortijo (about 20 mins. bus ride on the way to Dolores Hidalgo very near Atotonilco), a warm and hot pool, a fine swimming pool and good fishing in a nearby lake—very popular. Near the Spa is *Hacienda Taboada* hotel (5-star, large thermal pool, swimming pool, prior booking necessary). *Dolores Hidalgo*, (135,000) the home of Father Hidalgo, is 29 km. on, another most attractive small town; celebrations are held there on September 16. Visit Hidalgo's house, Casa Hidalgo, Morelos 1, entry US$0.30. Traditional Talavera tiles still made there. (*Hotel María Dolores*, between by-pass and centre coming from San Miguel de Allende; *Posada Las Campanas*, Guerrero 15; *Posada locomacán*, on the plaza.)

NOGALES—MEXICO CITY: THE PACIFIC HIGHWAY (4)

From Nogales (across the border from Nogales, Arizona) to Mexico City via Guadalajara is 2,043 km. (1,492 miles).

In summer, west coast drivers prefer the Central Route from El Paso, Texas, unless they love heat. It is dangerous to drive on retread tyres over the hot desert. Do not drive at night and never park or sleep along the road.

The Pacific Highway down the coast to Acapulco and Salina Cruz is completely paved but has military searches in the State of Guerrero (for narcotics and arms). The amount of accommodation along the Pacific Highway has increased greatly in recent years. There are many motels along the whole route, so that each town of any importance has one or more nearby. All available accommodation is listed in the American Automobile Association's *Mexico by Motor*.

From Nogales to Guaymas on the Gulf, the road runs along the western slopes of the Sierra Madre, whose summits rise to 3,000 metres. From Guaymas on to Mazatlán it threads along the lowland, with the Sierra Madre Occidental's bold and commanding escarpment to the E. Like the W coasts of all continents between latitudes 20° and 30°, the whole area is desert, but fruitful wherever irrigated by water flowing from the mountains. Summers are very hot, sometimes rainy, but winters are mild and very dry. Within the Sierra Madre nomadic people hunt the many wild animals; along the coasts available water determines the spots of concentrated settlement and of agriculture. Mexico gets most of its wheat from the southern part of Sonora state, and the irrigated valley bottoms (around Hermosillo) are also used for maize, cotton and beans. Farther S, in frost-free Sinaloa and Nayarit, sugar, rice, winter vegetables, tomatoes, and tobacco are grown. The three coastal states we pass through make up 21% of Mexico's area, but include only 6% of its population.

(Km. 2,403) **Nogales** lies astride a mountain pass at 1,180 metres. It is a mining centre, with walnut groves and cattle ranches. It has the usual border night life. Population, 140,000.

Festival Cinco de Mayo festival, lasting four days, celebrates the defeat of the French army at Puebla on May 5, 1862.

Hotel *Fray Marcos de Niza*, Campillo 91, B, not too good; many others. **Restaurant** *Caverna Greca*, Elias 3, in a cave.

Train Pacific Railway as far as Guadalajara, and on by National Railways of Mexico. Guadalajara, 1,759 km. away, is reached in 29 hrs., at a speed of 60 k.p.h., and Mexico City (after changing in Guadalajara) in 52 hrs. (Mexicali-Mexico City costs US$20, 2nd, US$40, 1st class). Conditions vary in both 1st and 2nd class carriages, several unpleasant experiences reported, e.g. lack of air conditioning, dirt, overcrowding, etc. 1st class trains go only to Guadalajara and journey on to Mexico City has to be made in slower 2nd-class train. 2nd class train to Guadalajara 48 hours, crowded. Train Nogales-Hermosillo, daily at 1000, US$3.50 2nd class, 5 hrs., continues to Mazatlán.

Bus to Mexico City, 42 hrs. with Transportes de Pacífico or Norte de Sonora, US$40, Tres Estrellas de Oro, 36 hrs. To Guadalajara 1st class, US$15, 26 hrs., very clean, fold-down seats, many food stops, leaves 1600, arrives 0700. Bus from Nogales to Tepic, 24 hrs., US$20. Nogales-Obregón via Hermosillo, US$8.50. There is a customs check after Nogales.

The highway passes through the Magdalena Valley. The Cocospera mines are near Imuris and there are famous gold and silver mines near Magdalena, which has a great Indian *fiesta* in the first week of October. Beyond, the cactus-strewn desert begins. At 120 km. from Nogales is Santa Ana, where the road from Tijuana and Mexicali comes in.

From Baja California There is a good road—Route 2—from Tijuana (**see page 1113**), going through Mexicali (**see page 1111**), Sonoita (*Desert Sun Motel; Motel Sono Inn*, E, American style, others nearby; customs inspection and immigration check), and Caborca to Santa Ana, where it joins the West Coast Highway (Route 15) route to Mexico City. Between La Rumerosa and Mexicali, the road descends about 1,200 metres in fantastic, panoramic serpentines from the coastal highland to the desert (organ-pipe cacti in abundance). Between Mexicali and Sonoita is **San Luis Río Colorado** (180,000 people), in the "free zone" and serving cotton country: summer bullfights, small night-life district like those of the old west. Coming from Lukeville, Arizona, make sure you take the road to San Luisito and not San Luis; they are both on Route 2, but 320 km. apart in opposite directions. 9 km. S of San Luis is Pozos, which 40 years ago had 60,000 inhabitants, now only 2,500 and ruins of large buildings, churches, no hotels. Customs stop at Sonoita.

Motel *Naranjo* (first class); *El Rey* and others. Economy hotel: *Capra*.

Between San Luis and Sonoita is the Mexican Sahara, 200 km. with sand dunes and volcanic hills. The desert has interesting vegetation, peculiar formations and few stopping places, but Caborca has the Motel *Posada San Cristóbal*. Sonoita (road off to Puerto Peñasco on the Gulf) is a good place for exploring the famous Kino missions, and there are very interesting archaeological ruins. Transportes Norte de Sonora and Tres Estrellas de Oro have first class services (the former is slightly better). Water and snacks should be carried, the tank kept full and replenished whenever possible. This feeder road can also be entered at Sonoita on the border S of Organ Pipe National Monument (Arizona). The highway from Tijuana to Hermosillo is very good.

(Km. 2,123) **Hermosillo**, capital of Sonora state, is a modern city, a winter resort town, and centre of a rich orchard area. The La Colorada copper mines are to the E. It has a colonial cathedral, a traditional quarter round an old plaza, and houses the University of Sonora. Altitude, 237 metres; population, 675,000. Golf course. Airport.

Hotels Generally poor standard of hotels; *San Andrés*, Oaxaca 14, D, with bath. *Washington*, Dr. Noriega, E, with bath, but gloomy; *Kino*, reasonable, Pino Suárez 151, D; *San Alberto*, Serdán y Rosales, C; *Monte Carlo*, Juárez y Sonora, E; *Royal*, in centre, F, a/c but grubby; *Guaymas Inn*, 5½ km. N, air-conditioned rooms with shower, E. **Motel** *Bugambilia*, Padre Kino 712, C. Two close to railway station.

Restaurants *Henry's Restaurant*, across the road from *Motel Encanto*, nice old house, good.

Bus to Nogales US$3.80, 4 hrs.; 2nd class to Agua Prieta, 7 hrs., US$4; to Los Mochis, 1st class, US$9, 2nd, US$8.50, 7½ hrs. through scrubland and wheat fields. Bus to Tijuana, US$14.50 1st class, 11 hrs. Bus to Mazatlán 10-12 hrs., US$ 12 1st, US$11.50 2nd class. To Guaymas, US$1.60, 1½ hrs. The bus station is on the outskirts.

Train overnight to Mazatlán at 1945, arrives 0730, worth taking a sleeper (US$13).

Excursion A dry-weather road, 106 km., goes W to Bahía Kino, on the Gulf (bus US$1, from Autobuses de la Costa, Calle Plutarco, 1 block from Rosales). The Seri Indians, who used to live across El Canal del Infiernillo (Little Hell Strait) from the port on the mountainous Isla del Tiburón (Shark Island), have been displaced by the navy to the mainland, down a dirt road from Bahía Kino in a settlement at Punta Chueca (no east access). They come into Kino on Sat. and Sun. to sell their ironwood animal sculptures (non-traditional) and traditional basketware (not cheap). They may usually be found at the *Posada del Mar Hotel*. A fine Museo Regional de Arte Seri has opened in new Kino, Calle Puerto Peñasco, 3 blocks from the main beach road. **Camping** on the beaches is possible.

At Km. 1,988 the road reaches the Gulf at the port of *Guaymas* (200,000), on a lovely bay backed by desert mountains; excellent deep-sea fishing, and sea-food for the gourmet. Miramar beach, on Bocachibampo bay with its blue sea sprinkled with green islets, is the resort section. Water sports on May 10. The climate is ideal in winter but unpleasant in summer. The 18th century church of San Fernando is worth a visit; so also, outside the town, is the 17th century church of San José de Guaymas. Excursions to the cactus forests. Some 22 km. N of Guaymas is the Bahía San Carlos, very Americanized and touristy, where "Catch 22" was filmed; there is free camping on a good beach at the end of the runway made for the film; also good fishing. Both Miramar and San Carlos beaches are easily reached by bus. Nice little beach 1 km. past Miramar beach with pleasant cafés, at the end of F bus line. Airport.

Hotels *Club Méditerranée*, end of beach. *Santa Rita*, Serdán and Calle 14, C with bath, a/c, clean, good; *Playa de Cortés*, on Bocachibampo bay, A; *La Posada de San Carlos*, Bahía San Carlos, A. *Leo's Inn* on Miramar beach, C; *Casa de Huéspedes La Colimense*, basic, rooms on the inside best, F, with fan, near bus station; *Ana*, Calle 25 No. 135, near cathedral, a/c, C; *América*, Alemán (Calle 20) y Av. 18, E, a/c, adequate. **Motels** *Flamingos*, Carretera Internacional, C; *El Tular*, D, 15 min. walk from beach, convenient; *Malibu*, D, Carretera Internacional N; *Bahía Trailer Court*, 6 kms. NW of town on Bahía San Carlos road and *Los Playibos*, motel/ restaurant/trailer park, 7 km. N on Highway 15 with pool and all facilities. Those who feel like avoiding high prices in Guaymas and can make Ciudad Obregón, 129 km. S, will find the *Costa de Oro* (see below).

Restaurant *Del Mar*, Aquiles Serdán and Calle 17, excellent seafood, expensive. *Cantón*, Serdán between 20 and 21, good Chinese. Generally, restaurants are overpriced.

Tourist Office Av. Serdán, lots of pamphlets.

Rail *Autovía* from Guaymas to Nogales leaves at 1000, 6 hrs., US$9, daily except Sat.; book in advance.

Ferry Transbordadores sail from Guaymas to Santa Rosalía, Baja California, at 1100 every Sun., Tues. and Thur., and return on the same days at 2300, 7 hr. trip. To La Paz, Baja California Sur, Thur. and Sat. 1500, return Fri. and Sun. 1400, 16 hrs.

Buses 1st class bus to Hermosillo (1½ hrs., US$1.60); Mazatlán, frequent, 12 hrs., US$13; Tijuana, 2nd class, 18 hrs., US$19. To Culiacán, 9 hrs., US$7. Bus to Empalme will allow you to take the train at 1400 (very full at times) coming from Mexicali to Sufragio, to catch the Los Mochis-Chihuahua train the next morning (seats usually no problem).

From Guaymas to Mazatlán is 784 km. First comes *Ciudad Obregón* (*Motel Valle Grande*, *Costa de Oro*, well-kept and pleasant; *Dora*, D, CREA Youth Hostel, Laguna de Sainari s/n, C.P. 85000), mainly important (180,000 people) as the centre of an agricultural region. *Navajoa* (200,000 people) has the *Motel El Rancho* and *Motel del Río* and a trailer park in the N of town on Route 15; 52 km. E into the hills is the delightful old colonial town of *Alamos* (accommodation in short supply; *Los Portales Hotel*, with beautiful frescoes, C, on plaza; *Somar*, on the road into Alamos, E; *Enriques*, F, basic but O.K.) now declared a national monument. (Bus Navajoa-Alamos every hour on the ½ hr. from 0630, about US$0.30, until 1830, 45 mins—bus station can be reached from main bus station by going right out of the front door, again take first right and then walk six blocks to the terminal on the left.) It is set in a mining area fascinating for rock enthusiasts. About 10 mins. by bus from Alamos is Minas Nuevas, once an important source of silver, very photogenic, bus US$0.25. West of Navajoa, on Huatabampo bay, are the survivors of the Mayo Indians; their festivals are in May.

Los Mochis, in a sugar-cane area, is a fishing resort 25 km. from the sea with a US colony. A stairway leads up the hillside behind La Pérgola, a pleasant public park near the city reservoir, for an excellent view of Los Mochis. Km 1,636.5; 200,000 people.

Hotels Book well in advance, especially if arriving late at night. *Santa Anita*, A, Leyva and Hidalgo, comfortable, clean dining room, noisy a/c, not very friendly or efficient, has own bus service to station; *Beltrán*, Hidalgo 281, D, rec., has all travel time-tables; *América*, D, Allende Sur 655, clean, a/c, near bus station, has restaurant with good, cheap sandwiches; *Los Arcos*, Allende (round corner from Tres Estrellas terminal), F, a/c, clean, a bit dingy. *Lorena*, Prieto y Obregón, fair value, a/c, D; *Fénix*, D, safe, clean. *Montecarlo*, D, a/c, Independencia y Flores. **Motel** *Santa Rosa*, López Mateos 1051 N, D.

Restaurants *El Farallón*, Flores and Obregón, good seafood and service; *Los Globos*, near TNS bus station, reasonable. *Las Palmeras*, excellent, reasonably priced.

A railway trip to Chihuahua (**see page 984**) and back from Los Mochis station reached by "*peso*" taxi, US$1.50, 5 mins.; or regular bus from city centre shows you the spectacular scenery of the Sierra Madre and the Urique (or Copper) Canyon. The *servicio estrella* leaves daily at 0700 (arrives 1905, US$20 with all meals, English-speaking hostess). Tickets can be bought at Flamingo Travel (very helpful) the day before, avoiding the queue at the station (but you pay a high commission) and they will try to persuade you into taxis to the station (there is a bus) and into their preferred (expensive) hotels. Find out if you can get a ticket the day before departure at between 1300 and 1600 from the station. An ordinary train, US$10 1st class, US$7 2nd, leaves at 0600 (10 hours) for Chihuahua (this is the cheapest way to see the canyon—the train stops 15 minutes—in daylight; cold as you get to Creel, photographing possible. Train timetables bear little relation to actual departure times, so check at Los Mochis. There is a time change (one hour forward) between Los Mochis and Creel. If you do not want to take the train all the way, go to Bahuichivo (simple hotel, F, a few shops), and return from there. Pick-ups go (5-hr. trip) to Urique (except Sun.) in the Urique Canyon (a bus from the *Misión Urique Canyon* meets the train in Bahuichivo). 2 simple hotels (F) in Urique.

Connection with the Nogales-Guadalajara train at Sufragio, 37 km. from Los Mochis (**see also page 1112**). fare to Mazatlán, US$3.85, 1st class (rec.), US$2 2nd.

Air To La Paz, Baja California Sur.

Bus Mexico City, US$24. Ciudad Obregón, US$6. Tijuana, US$18, several daily up to 24 hrs. Mazatlán US$5, 1st class, leaves 2100, arrives 0345; with Tres Estrellas de Oro or Transport Norte de Sonora. Nogales, 2nd class, US$14, 12 hrs. No reservations can be made for buses N or S at the terminal of Tres Estrellas de Oro and it is difficult to get on buses. Try instead Transportes de Pacífico, 3 blocks away and next to TNS terminal. First class bus to Guaymas 5½ hrs., US$5. To Tepic, Tres Estrellas de Oro, 1st class, US$9, 13 hrs. To Topolobampo, US$0.25, buses leave from lane behind Flamingo Travel.

An hour NE by train from Los Mochis is *El Fuerte* (120,000). This town has recently been renovated and has interesting colonial architecture. The station is a few miles from the town; taxis. *Hotel San Francisco*, good value. Good restaurants, nice plaza.

About half an hour's drive along a side road SW takes us from Los Mochis to **Topolobampo**, on the beautiful bay-and-lagoon-indented coast. It is difficult to find a beach unless one pays for a private launch. Now that a railway— take food with you—has been opened to Ojinaga (**see page 984**), Topolobampo is being developed as a deep-water port.

Hotels *Yacht Hotel*, modern, clean and good food, quiet, C, but seems to close for the winter; *Casa de Huéspedes* not rec.

Ferry Topolobampo-La Paz, Baja California Sur, **see page 1122**.

Some 210 km. beyond Los Mochis (at km. 1,429) is the capital of Sinaloa state, **Culiacán** (950,000 people), chief centre for winter vegetables. No longer a colonial city, but attractive and prosperous; it has a university. The safe beaches of Altata are 30 minutes by dirt road.

Hotels   *Del Valle*, Solano 180, C; *Executivo*, Madero y Obregón, A. *Beltrán*, E, clean, safe, quiet, was once a hospital with appropriate furnishings; *Louisiana*, F with bath and fan, in centre, clean and pleasant. **Motels:** *Los Caminos*, Carretera Internacional, C; *Los Tres Ríos*, 1 km. N of town on highway 15, trailer park, pool, resort style. *Pizzería Tivoli*, good, friendly.

Airport   10 km. from centre.

Transport Culiacán is suitable for connections to Los Mochis (see page 985 for trips to the Copper Canyon). Take one of the several daily Mexico City-Culiacán flights and then rent a plane (US$360 for five), hire a car (3 hrs.' drive), or take a bus. Whichever you do, try to arrive before the train at 2100, as hotel reservations are not always honoured. Bus to Tepic, 8¼ hrs., US$6.80; to Guaymas, 9 hrs., US$7.

Another 208 km. bring us to a roadside monument marking the Tropic of Cancer. Beyond, 13 km. is (km. 1,204) **Mazatlán,** spread along a peninsula at the foot of the Sierra Madre. It is the largest Mexican port on the Pacific Ocean and the main industrial and commercial centre in the W. The beauty of its setting and its warm winters have made it a popular resort, but unfortunately with expansion it has lost some of its attraction. It overlooks Olas Altas (High Waves) bay, which has a very strong current. Tourism is now concentrated on Gaviota beach, which is solidly built up. On one side of the peninsula, the beach is fringed with groves of coconut palm; on the other a promenade overlooks a number of islands. There are more islands in the nearby lagoons, which teem with wild life. A promenade lined by hotels, with a long beach at its foot, curves round the bay; fine for watching the famous sunsets. The local Shrovetide carnival is almost as good as at Veracruz. The best beaches, 3 to 5 km. from the city, are easily reached by taxi. Boats ply between the shore and the island beaches. The lighthouse, on El Faro island, is 157 metres above sea-level. Population, around 800,000. Airport 26 km. from centre. (Taxi, fixed fare US$6.60 airport-Mazatlán.)

Fishing is the main sport (sailfish, tarpon, marlin, etc.). Shrimp from the Gulf are sent, frozen, to all parts of Mexico. Its famous fishing tournament follows Acapulco's and precedes the one at Guaymas. In the mangrove swamps are egrets, flamingoes, pelicans, cranes, herons, and duck. Nearby at Camarones there is "parachute flying", drawn by motorboats. **N.B.** Always check with the locals whether swimming is safe, since there are strong rip currents in the Pacific which run out to sea and are extremely dangerous. There is a free Red Cross treatment station 9 blocks along the avenue opposite the Beach Man on the right. There are bull-fights at Mazatlán, US$4.50 for a general seat in the shade (*sombra*). Good view here, although you can pay up to US$15 to get seats in the first 7 rows—Sundays at 1600. One of the best places in Mexico to buy *huaraches*; seek out the "huarache-man" at one corner of the market.

Firmly rooted and extremely popular in the State of Sinaloa is a type of orchestra known as the Banda Sinaloense or Tamborera, which can be seen and heard at almost any time of day or night in restaurants, dance halls, bars, at family parties or on the street. It usually has from 14 to 16 musicians: 4 saxophones, 4 trumpets, clarinets, tuba, 3-4 men on drums and other percussion instruments, including *maracas, guiro*, and loud, strong voices. It is unabashed, brutal music, loud and lively. One such Banda plays every afternoon at the *Chaparral* bar, opposite the Conasupo market near bus station.

Hotels   Along the northern beach Sábalo-Camarón are: *Los Sábalos*, Health Club facilities; *Playa Mazatlán*, good atmosphere; *El Cid*, with *El Caracol* nightclub; *Camino Real, Oceano Palace, Holiday Inn* all in our A-L range, *Azteca Inn*, C. Along Av. del Mar beach are: *De Cima, Hacienda, El Dorado* all A; *Playamar*, C, with TV, air-conditioned; *Las Brisas*, rec., C, with shower, swimming pool and on sea front, air-conditioned. Along Olas Altas beach are: *Freeman*, old, highrise; *Belmar*, modernized but old, both C. Along Paseo Centenario are: *Olas Altas*, D, efficiently run and clean, but fleas reported. Most of the others are in the downtown area away from the beach front: *Posada Colonial*, N of south docks, D, well-kept, good food; *Del Centro*, J.M. Canizales 705 Pte, modern, E, behind main church; *Roma*, Av. Juan Carrasco 127, very clean and friendly 2 blocks from beach, rec., F, with bath but some rooms noisy; *Zaragoza*, Zaragoza 18, old and pretty, E, with bath; *Posada familiar Sarita*, Mariano Escobedo, F, colonial, nr. beach; *Pensión María Luisa*, Mariano Escobedo, F, no fans, friendly but hot, quiet; *Lerma*, Simón Bolívar 5, near beach, F, friendly, simple, but quiet and cool; *Vialta*, Azueta 2006, three blocks from market, F, with bath, friendly, helpful; *Económico*, E, with bath and fan, noisy, dark but very clean, next to bus station, ½ km. from main beach; *The Sands*, E, pool, a/c, on beach, near bus station.
   Although N of the city there are undeveloped beaches with free overnight camping, they are only rec. if you are in a group for security—travellers have warned against it: e.g. *Isla de la Piedra*, friendly, huts for US$1.50 or camping permitted if you have a meal there, good food. Beware of sandflies! At least 10 trailer parks on Playa del Norte/Zona Dorada and on towards the N, including *Casa Blanca Disco*, F, cheapest, on beach side, dirty. Much better is *La Posta*, ½ block off beach,

with swimming pool and tent space, E, lots of shade. Big hotels rapidly expanding all along N beach seashore to Mármol. **Motels** are strung all along the ocean front: *Las Palmas*, B; *Marley*, C; *Las Gaviotas*, B; *Azteca Inn*, C; *Del Sol*, C. On Highway 15: *Papagayo*, D. Downtown: *Maity*, E; *Mazatlán*, F. *Mar Rosa Trailer Park*, N of *Holiday Inn* on northern beach, F, hot water, safe, rec.

Restaurants *Doney's*, M. Escobedo 610, downtown, good home cooking; *El Bistro*, in craft centre in Zona Dorada, good steaks and seafood; *Shrimp Bucket* and *Señor Frog*, Olas Altas 11 and Av. del Mar, same owners, very famous, popular, good; *Lobster Trap*, Sábalo Camarón, good chicken(!); *Joncol's*, Flores 254, a/c, downtown, popular but deteriorated; *Mamucas*, Bolívar 73, best seafood in town. *La Red*, Av. del Mar 112, reasonable lunches. *Pastelería y Cafetaría Panamá*, several branches for reasonable meals, pastries, coffee. *El Ostión Feliz*, Flores y Villa, seafood; *Pekin*, Juárez 4, good Chinese, inexpensive; *Pizza Hut*, Av. del Mar, good salads too; *Beach Boys Club*, on Malecón nr. fishermans' monument, good value meals, US owned; *Balnearios Mazatlán* and *Miramar*, on Playa Norte, good cheap Mexican fare. *Casa del Naturista*, Zaragoza 809, sells good wholegrain bread. *Amadeus Video Tacos*, a/c, nice bar, occasional live music.

Tourist Office Av. Rodolfo T. Loaizo 100, Local N6; on road to northern beach, past *Señor Frog*. Also Av. Olas Altas 1300, Edificio Bancen, Col. Centro.

Bus Station at Centro Colonia, 10 mins. walk from beach or take yellow bus from centre marked "Insurgentes"; safe luggage store. Bus fare to Mexico City about US$13 (2nd class). Guadalajara, with Transportes Norte de Sonora, several times a day, US$7 (10 hrs.). To crossroads for San Blas, US$3.75; Tepic US$4.25 (5¼ hrs., with Estrella Blanca, efficient, clean buses); bus (frequent) to Los Mochis (7 hrs.), US$6.50 with Transportes Norte de Sonora. To Navajoa, US$5 1st class; 1st class Transportes del Norte bus to Durango, US$5.40, take an a.m. bus to see the scenery; Guaymas, 12 hrs., US$13, 2nd class. Bus to Rosario US$0.80, can then with difficulty catch bus to Caimanero beach, nearly deserted. Terminal Alamos, Av. Oeste Guerrero 402, 2 blocks from market, buses to Alamos every hour on the half hour.

Ferries La Paz (Baja California Sur), daily at 1700, 16 hrs., car (one way), US$17.35-20.00, notorcycle US$2.35. First class (*especial*), US$22.60; tourist class is a small room with two bunks and a sink, US$5.25, rec., cabin class has showers, US$11.35, salon seat US$2.65 in a very crowded room. Children of 2-11, half price. Deck gets wet during the night, toilets quickly get blocked up, so make an early call. Allow plenty of time for booking and customs procedure. Quite a way from centre to dock (take bus marked "Playa Sur"). **N.B.** Ticket office for La Paz ferry opens 0830-1300 only, on day of departure. Don't expect to get vehicle space for same-day departure. Ferry returns from La Paz also at 1700.

Rail Take Insurgentes bus out to Morelos railway station. Train to Guadalajara, 12 hrs., departs 0800, very comfortable, air-conditioned scenic trip with a variety of topography and agriculture. From Tepic it climbs gradually through the hills to 1,650 metres at Guadalajara, passing through some 30 or 40 tunnels. Best travel 1st class US$6 or pullman US$10.50; 2nd class dirty and uncomfortable, US$3, leaves before dawn. Buy tickets at agency in Pasaje Linguna in the Zona de Oro, close to Tourist Office. Train to Tepic, special 1st US$3.50, 2nd class US$2.10, about 6 hrs. 1st class train fare to Mexico City, US$12.50.

Air Daily flights to La Paz and San José del Cabo (Baja California Sur), and the USA.

Excursions to Islas de Piedras, 30 km. of now littered beach. Take a small boat from S side of town from Armada (naval station near brewery), regular service, US$0.20, walk across island (10 mins.). Local *comedores* on beach provide primitive accommodation. Try smoked fish sold on a stick. About 100 km. N of Mazatlán is a turn-off to the town of La Cruz, with two hotels: *Las Palmitas*, F, off the main street, quiet. Few tourists. A boat excursion on the *Yate Fiesta* cruises out at 1000 or 2000 (with dancing), from second last bus stop in the direction of Playa del Sur. Refreshments included, and you can see the wildlife in the day time; US$4.40.

Twenty-four km. beyond Mazatlán, the Coast-to-Coast Highway to Durango (a spectacular stretch), Torreón, Monterrey and Matamoros turns off left at Villa Unión. Heading E, the road reaches Concordia, a pleasant colonial town, then climbs the mountains past Copala, another mining ghost-town (basic hotel). Copala can be reached by tour bus from Mazatlán or by Auriga pick-up truck from Concordia. On this road there is a good German hotel with excellent restaurant. After reaching the high plateau the road passes through pine forests to Durango. The road to Tepic continues S from Villa Unión; before reaching Tepic both road and railway begin the long climb from the lowland level over the Sierra Madre to the basin of Jalisco, 1,500 metres above sea-level. Eleven km. short of Tepic a road on the right descends 900 metres to a pretty South Sea-type beach.

The resort of **San Blas** is 69 km. from Tepic and is overcrowded during US and Mexican summer holidays. It has an old Spanish fortress and a smelly harbour. In August it becomes very hot and there are many mosquitoes, but not on the beach 2 km. from the village (but there are other biting insects, take repellent anyway); few tourists at this time or early in the year. Seven km. from San Blas (bus, taxi US$2 per car) is the beach of Matanchén, good swimming but many mosquitoes. 16 km. from San Blas is the beautiful Los Cocos beach (trailer park). **N.B.** Don't wander too far from public beach; tourists have warned against attacks and robberies.

Hotels *Marino Inn*, Bataillon, a/c, friendly, pool, fair food, A; *Las Brisas*, Cuauhtémoc Sur 106, very clean, B, highly rec., excellent restaurant; *Bucanero*, Juárez Poniente 75, D with bath and fan, frequented by Americans, food good, lizards abound, noisy discos 3 times a week and bar is open till 0100 with loud music; *Posada del Rey*, very clean, swimming pool, excellent value, D; *Posada de Morales* also has a swimming pool, more expensive, ½ block from *Posada del Rey*. *Flamingos*, Juárez Poniente 105, E, clean, friendly; *Vallarta*, very basic with fan, 50 m. from beach, F; *María's*, fairly clean with cooking, washing and fridge facilities, F without bath, E with bath and fan; similar but better is *Hotel/Bungalows Posada*, E for bungalow, clean, pretty, good for long stay. No camping or sleeping permitted on beaches but several pay campsites available. *San Blas Motel*, near Zócalo, D, patio, fans, good value. Sometimes free camping possible behind *Playa Hermosa Hotel*, old house, only partly occupied, occupied rooms clean, 2 km from town, E. Trailer park at town beach. Many apartments for rent.

Restaurants *Tony's* and *La Isla* now said to be best. *Tropicana*, try its *sopa marinera*, fish soup; *La Diligencia*, on Calle Juárez near Zócalo, good food, especially fish, clean, friendly and cheap but slow service; *MacDonald* just off Zócalo. *Bar-Restaurant Torino*, steaks, seafood, pasta, wine by glass, very reasonable. Plenty of seafood restaurants on the beach; e.g. *Las Olas*, good and cheap.

Bank Banamex just off Zócalo, exchange 0830-1000 only. Comercial de San Blas on the main square will change money at 10% commission.

Bus To Tepic, 1st class, US$1.75, 3 a day, 2nd class, 5-6 a day, US$1, 1½ hrs. To Guadalajara, US$5, 1st class, US$3.90 2nd class, 8½ hrs.

It is possible to take a 4-hr. jungle trip in a boat (bus to launching point, US$0.50) to *La Tovara*, a small resort with fresh-water swimming hole and not much else, or walking, to do. Tour buses leave from the bridge 1 km. out of town and cost US$28 for canoe with six passengers. Competition is keen between guides so some bargaining is possible, although official prices are posted. There are coatis, raccoons, iguanas, turtles, boat-billed herons, egrets and parrots. Twilight tours enable naturalists to see pottos and, if very lucky, an ocelot. La Tovara is crowded at midday during the summer. A cheaper 1½-2 hr. cruise is also possible. When arranging your trip make sure you are told the length of journey and route in advance. You can take a bus from San Blas towards Santa Cruz (see below under Tepic) and get off at Matanchén beach (see above). From here, a boat costing US$10 for ½-day hire includes the best part of the jungle cruise from San Blas.

Quaint little towns just off the highway between Mazatlán and Tepic: Acaponeta (turnoff for Novillera beach), Rosario, Tuxpan and Santiago.

(Km. 909) *Tepic*, capital of Nayarit state, altitude 900 metres, population 200,000, founded in 1531 at the foot of the extinct volcano of Sangagüey. The Huichol and Cora Indians of the Sierra come to town in very picturesque dress; their craftwork—bags (carried only by men), scarves woven in colourful designs and necklaces (*chaquira*) of tiny beads and wall-hangings of brightly coloured wool—is available from souvenir shops, but best to let Indians approach you when they come to town. (These handicrafts are reported to be cheaper in Guadalajara, at the Casa de Artesanías.) There are many little squares, all filled with trees and flowers. The Cathedral, with two fine Gothic towers, in Plaza Principal, has been restored. Worth seeing are the Municipal Palace; the Casa de Amado Nervo (the poet and diplomat); the Regional Museum, Av. México 91 Norte (open 1000-1400 and 1700-2000 hrs., closed Mon.); and the Convento de la Cruz, on the summit of a hill close to the centre. The landscape around Tepic is wild and mountainous. Nearby are the Ingenio and Jala waterfalls, good places for picnics. Tombs in cemetery worth seeing.

Hotels *San Jorge,* Lerdo 124, C, very comfortable, good value; *Ibarra,* Durango 297 Norte, luxurious noisy rooms, C, with bath, and slightly spartan, cheaper, cooler rooms without bath, very clean. *Fray Junípero Serra*, Lerdo Poniente 23, A, main square, a/c, good restaurant, friendly, good service; *Casa de Huéspedes Grijalva*, F, on Zócalo, hot water; *Tepic;* E, with bath, Dr Martínez 438, near bus station outside town, clean, friendly but noisy; *Mayo*, near bus station, E, clean and bright; *Corita*, Insurgentes 298, modern, F, free parking in locked yard, good reasonable restaurant, attractive gardens; *Pensión Morales*, Insurgentes y Sánchez, 4 blocks from bus station, F, clean and friendly. *Villa de las Rosas*, Insurgentes 100, C, fans, friendly, noisy in front, good food, but not too clean; *Pensión Marí*, 3 blocks off Zócalo, F, with hot water, friendly, clean, very good value. Others on Zócalo, E. *Juárez*, E, near Palacio de Gobierno, on Juárez 116, for clean room with bath, locks on room doors not very effective, limited parking in courtyard; *Altamirano*, Mina 13 Oriente, near Palacio del Gobierno, E, noisy but good value; *Sarita*, Bravo 112 Poniente, clean, good, E; **Motels** *La Loma*, Paseo la Loma 301 (swimming pool), B, run down; *Cora Motel Apartamentos Koala*, La Laguna, Santa María del Oro, has units for up to 3 people with kitchen and bathroom, and snack bar, US$6.50 per unit. Fishing and waterskiing on nearby lagoon.

Restaurants   Two restaurants in Tepic, both on the outskirts of town, sell carne en su jugo estilo Guadalajara, delicious meat and bacon stew with beans in a spicy sauce, served with stewed onions. *El Tripol*, in mall, near plaza, excellent vegetarian; *Danny O* ice cream shop next door. Restaurant in bus terminal, overpriced. The local huevos rancheros are extremely picante.

Tourist Office   At Convento de la Cruz, Av. México y Calz. del Ejército, English spoken by one employee. Good free map.

Transport   Bus to San Blas from Central Camionera: TNS, US$1, 5 or 6 a day; Tres Estrellas three a day, US$1.75. To Guadalajara, US$3, 1st class, 4-4½ hrs.; Mazatlán, 4½ hrs., US$4.25 (2nd class); to Puerto Vallarta, US$2.55; Mexico City, US$10.50; Torreón, US$12. Culiacán, 8¼ hrs., US$6.80. Train to Guadalajara, US$1.75 (2nd class), US$4.50 (1st) leaves at 1130, arrives at 1800, sit on left-hand side for best views. Train to Mexicali, 22-27 hrs., special 1st class, a/c, US$18; to Nogales, 19-23 hrs., ditto, US$16. (Same train to Benjamín Hill, leaving Tepic 1400, then divides). Airport.

Time Change   There is a time change, forward one hour, between Tepic and most places inland, such as Guadalajara.

Excursions   One can visit Huichol villages only by air, as there are no real roads, takes at least two days. Flight to a village, US$10 return. To various beaches along the coast, some of them off the Nogales highway we have come along. A road runs through Compostela, a pleasant small town with an old church (1539) (1½ hrs. by bus from local bus station at Tepic), to **Santa Cruz**, about 37 km. from Tepic (rocky beach). 2½ hrs. ride by open-sided lorry, US$0.50, difficult to leave the town again, check for transport. No hotels, but accommodation at *Peter's Shop*, F, basic but pleasant and friendly. Simple food available, *Restaurant Belmar*, fish and rice, all reminiscent of the South Seas. (2 buses a day from San Blas to Santa Cruz, US$0.70) From Compostela one can also catch an old bus to **Zacualpan**, 1½ hrs. over a very rough dirt road, to visit a small enclosed park with sculptures that have been found in the area, two blocks from main square. Gate to the park must be unlocked by caretaker: inside there is a small museum. Zacualpan is a pleasant village, knock on a door to ask for the caretaker. Ninety km. (1¼ hrs. by bus) from Tepic on the main road to Guadalajara is **Ixtlan del Río** (*Hotel Colonial*, E, Hidalgo 45 Pte, very friendly, rec.). Two km. out of town along this road are the ruins of a Toltec ceremonial centre. The main structure is the Temple of Quetzalcoatl, noted for its cruciform windows and circular shape. The journey from Tepic to Guadalajara can easily be broken at Ixtlan with a couple of hours' sightseeing: bus on to Guadalajara 3 hours, US$1.60. There are a few souvenir shops and a museum; harvest (maize) festival mid-September; nearby (15 km.) village of Jalán has festival mid-August.

Other beaches between Santa Cruz and Puerto Vallarta include Rincón de los Guayabitos, which is being developed as a tourist resort with hotels, holiday village and trailer park; Chacala, lined with coconut palms and reached by an unsurfaced road through jungle; and Canalán, near Las Varas, reached only on foot, isolated and beautiful.

Puerto Vallarta (population 100,000), is reached by plane from Tepic, Tijuana, Los Angeles and Mexico City. The town is divided by the River Cuale and on one side are the expensive hotels, many shops, the airport and the port where the ferry arrives from San Lucas. On the other side of the river are the bus terminal and some cheaper hotels. Latest reports indicate that every house in the old town has been turned into a tourist trap, speculation is rampant with hotels and timeshare apartments, prices are "US prices and Mexican quality", and taxi drivers are rapacious. It offers aquatic sports, particularly fishing and hunting for sharks. From the public beach you can hire parachuting equipment to be pulled by motor-boat (US$10). The Malecón is the waterfront drive. The beach at Puerto Vallarta is dirty, but there are better ones about 8-10 km. south along the coast, e.g. Mismaloya (reached by bus 02, US$0.30). There is a paved road from Tepic to Puerto Vallarta, continuing down the coast to Barra de Navidad and Manzanillo with excellent *Hotel Careyes*, A, en route, and several cheaper ones, including *El Tecuán* (D) and *Hotel Tenacatita* (A) near the village of the same name (**see page 1008**), and further to Zihuatanejo and Acapulco, and finally to Salina Cruz.

Hotels Puerto Vallarta is divided naturally into 3 sections: N of town are: *Playa de Oro*, A; *Fiesta Americana*, L; *Las Palmas*, A; *Plaza Vallarta*, A; *Bugambilias Sheraton*, L; *Puerto Vallarta Holiday Inn*, Av. de las Garzas, A. In town are: *Buenaventura*, A; *Rosita*, very pleasantly situated, 5 min. bus ride to beaches on other side of town, swimming pool, C; *Cuatro Vientos*, Matamoros 520, C, lots of stairs; *Central*, E, off main square; *Paraíso*, Paseo Díaz Ordaz, on the sea but stony beach, E. South of Río Cuale are: *Camino Real*, L; *Garza Blanca*, Playa Palo María; *Oro Verde*, Gómez 111, A, a/c, rec. as clean, pleasant, friendly; *Posada Río Cuale*, excellent food, Serdán 242, swimming pool, a/c, C; *Fontana del Mar*, Diéguez 171, C, attractive; *Tropicana*, Amapá 227, Mexican families; *Molino del Agua*, Vallarta 130, A, beautiful, beside the new bridge, clean, a/c, good service, pool, rec.; *Playa los Arcos*, Olas Altas 380, B; *Villa del Mar*, Cárdenas 444, E, good; *Ana Liz*, Madero 428, 3 blocks from sea, E, clean, comfortable, secure, small rooms; *Posada de Roger*, C, Badillo 237, good value, near two main city beaches, beware of thieves, popular with students. *Playa de Bucerías*, Carretera Tepic Km. 154, D. Several *casas de huéspedes* in town near bus companies' offices, e.g. *Lima*, F. Cheap apartments: *La Peña*, F, Rodríguez 174.

Camping 8 km. S of Puerto Vallarta at Playa Mismaloya, popular with North Americans travelling by car; not a proper campsite but showers operate during the day, as do toilets, but women's toilets are locked at night. *Chico's Paradise*, in the village of Mismaloya, is a restaurant with cascades forming fresh-water pools where one can swim. Also at fishing village of Yelapa: camp under shelters (*palapas*), about US$4 each.

Restaurants The *Mercado Restaurant* is good and very cheap. *Mismaloya Beach* restaurant, excellent, US$2-4 for dinner (8 km. S of Puerto Vallarta). *Ostión Feliz*, Libertad 177, excellent seafood. *El Coral*, Olas Altas, good breakfast and *comida corrida*. *Carlos O'Brians*, beautifully decorated, popular, young clientèle. *Tony's Please*, Encino y Hidalgo, near bridge, good, reasonable food. Very good ice-cream and frozen yoghurt is sold along the Malecón and at *Bing's* near central plaza. Puerto Vallarta has an active night life, with many bars and discotheques.

Shopping Plaza Malecón, near *Hotel Río*, end of Malecón, has 28 curio shops, restaurant, music, etc.

Tourist Office In the government building on the main square, very helpful.

Ferries To Cabo San Lucas, Baja California Sur, Sun. and Wed., 1600 in each direction (but check in advance), one way fare US$3.35 (reclining seat), US$14.70 (cabin), 18 hrs. Return Fri. and Sun., 1600; Transbordadores, run by Caminos y Puentes Federales. No advance booking for foot passengers; try to pay for cabin or sleeper tickets on board. Poor food. Also to La Paz, Fri. 1200, 21 hrs., back from La Paz Fri. 1200; US$4.05 (reclining seat), US$18.45 (cabin).

Buses By Sonora del Norte, Estrella Blanca and Autobuses del Pacífico, to Mexico City, 15-20 hrs. US$13. Puerto Vallarta to Guadalajara, US$7 1st class, 7 hrs.; to Manzanillo, US$3.55, midnight, Transportes Cihuatlan, Constitución y Francisco J. Madero.

Air Travel International airport 7 km. from centre.

Excursions To Yelapa, Indian village with waterfall, now commercialized; by boat or car.

Warning Those confined to wheelchairs are warned that Puerto Vallarta is a bad place, with its high kerbs and cobblestone streets.

Tequila (58 km. from Guadalajara), on the Tepic-Guadalajara road, is the main place where the famous Mexican drink is distilled, from the *maguey* cactus. Tours of Cuerva (free) and Sauza (small tip) distilleries along the highway. The Sauza distillery has a famous fresco illustrating the joys of drinking tequila. Half-way between Tequila and Guadalajara, in the mountains, is the British-run *Rancho Río Caliente*, 8 km. from the highway, a vegetarian thermal resort.

We have now entered the State of Jalisco. The State's cultural life has been helped by an economy based on crafts, agriculture, and livestock, with fewer pockets of abject poverty than elsewhere in Mexico. Many villages have traditional skills such as pottery, blown glass, shoemaking, and a curious and beautiful form of filigree weaving in which miniature flower baskets, fruit and religious images are shaped from *chilte* (chicle, the raw substance from which chewing-gum is made). The

State is the original home of Mexico's *mariachis:* roving musical groups dressed in the gala suits and *sombreros* of early 19th century rural gentry.

Guadalajara, Mexico's second city and capital of Jalisco state; altitude 1,650 metres, and slightly warmer than at the capital; population, 1,626,000 in 1980, but now reported as up to 4 million, and 696 km. from Mexico City, was founded in 1530. It used to be a fine, clean city, not unlike the towns of southern Spain, but pollution has now grown. Graceful colonial arcades, or *portales,* flank scores of old plazas and shaded parks. The climate is mild, dry and clear all through the year. A pedestrian mall, Plaza Tapatía, has been installed between the Cabañas Orphanage and the Degollado Theatre, crossing the Calzada Independencia, covering 16 square blocks. It has beautiful plants, fountains, statuary, a tourist office, and is designed in colonial style. The best shops are all found in or near the Plaza Mayor (Plaza de los Tres Poderes) and the Avenida Juárez. The Plaza del Sol shopping centre, with over 100 shops, is located at the S end of the city, while the equally modern Plaza Patria, with as many shops, is at the N end near the Zapopán suburb.

The Plaza Mayor is flanked by the Government Palace (1643) where in 1810 Hidalgo issued his first proclamation abolishing slavery (plaque). Orozco's great murals can be seen on the central staircase. In the main University of Guadalajara building, on Av. Juárez Tolsa, is the dome in which is portrayed man asleep, man meditating, and man creating. Other works by this artist can be seen at the University's main Library, at Glorieta Normal, and at the massive Cabañas Orphanage near the Mercado de la Libertad (now known as Instituto Cultural Cabañas, housing, among other cultural attractions, Orozco's "Man of Fire"). The Orphanage is a beautiful building with 22 patios, which is floodlit at night (entry US$0.40). The contents of the former Orozco museum in Mexico City have also been transferred to Guadalajara. Between the Cabañas and the Mercado Libertad is a park, with a fine modern sculpture "The Stampede", by Jorge de la Peña (1982).

On the Plaza Mayor also is the Cathedral, begun in 1561, finished in 1618, in rather a medley of styles; there is no longer admission to the tower (the structure has been declared dangerous), where remarkable frescoes were recently discovered half-way up. There is a reputed Murillo Virgin inside (painted 1650), and the famous La Virgen del Carmen, painted by Miguel de Cabrera, a Zapotec Indian from Oaxaca. NE of the Cathedral is the State Museum (US$0.50, closed Sat.-Tues.) in an old seminary (1700) with a good, prehistoric section (including the complete skeleton of a mammoth found in Jaliso) and interesting display of "hidden" tombs, excellent display of Colima and Jalisco terracotta figures, and possibly the finest display of colonial art in Mexico outside the Museo Virreinal in Mexico City (highly rec.). Two blocks E is the enormous and fantastically decorated Degollado Theatre (1866), half-price for students on Sats. There is an Archaeological Museum of Western Mexico on Plaza Juárez, open Mon.-Sat. 0900-1300 and 1600-1800, free. A school of crafts (ceramics, glass weaving, leatherwork) is on Alcalde and Avila Camacho; and there is also the Albarrán hunting museum, Paseo de los Parques 3530, Colinas de San Javier, Sat. and Sun. 1000-1400, with a collection of rare animals from all over the world.

The best churches are Santa Mónica (1718), with a richly carved façade; El Carmen, with a main altar surrounded by gilded Corinthian columns, San José, a 19C. church with a fine gilded rococo pulpit, San Miguel de Belén, enclosed in the Hospital Civil which contains three fine late 18C. *retablos,* and San Francisco (1550). To the N of this last church is the quite exquisite Jardín San Francisco, and to the W the old and quaint church of Our Lady of Aránzazu, with two fantastic churrigueresque altarpieces (now closed for renovation). There are 3 universities (visit architectural faculty near Parque Mirador, 20 mins. by car from centre, or take bus 45 overlooking Barranca de Oblatos, a huge canyon), a Cultural Institute with contemporary arts displays and a film theatre (US$0.50), and a ticket office for Teatro Azul, and an open-air theatre, Auditorio Gonzalo Cunel. Other sights worth seeing are the Agua Azul park near the Sheraton hotel (swimming pools dirty); dances on Sun. at 1700, flower market, handicrafts

To Aguascalientes & Zacatecas

To Barranca de Oblatos

To Mazatlán

To Mexico City

To Airport and Chapala

1. Plaza Mayor
2. Jardín and Inglesia San Francisco
3. Plaza Juárez
4. Plaza de los Mariachis
5. Cathedral
6. Santa Mónica
7. El Carmen
8. San José
9. Our Lady of Aránzazu
10. Cabañas Orphanage
11. Degollada Theatre
12. Government Palace
13. State Museum
14. Archaeological Museum of Western Mexico
15. Mercado Libertad
16. Post Office
17. Telephone Office
18. Old Bus Terminal
19. Plaza Tapatía and Tourist Offices

shop; and the Parque Alcalde in the middle of the city. The markets, in particular the Libertad (San Juan de Dios) market which has colourful items for souvenirs with lots of Michoacán crafts including Paracho guitars and Sahuayo hats, and delicious food upstairs on the 1st level (particularly goat meat, *birria*, also *cocada*), but expensive soft drinks (check prices before sitting down or you will be grossly overcharged as tourists); the *tianguis* (Indian market) on Av. Guadalupe, Colonia Chapalita, on Fri. is of little interest to foreigners, bus 50 gets you there; the *tianguis* near the University Sports Centre on Calzada Tlaquepaque on Sundays; the Plaza de Los Mariachis, Obregón and Leonardo Vicario, near La Libertad; the Templo Expiatorio, with fine stained glass and intricate ceiling, gothic style, still unfinished after most of a century. There is a new, large park, zoological garden and planetarium just past the bullring going out on Av. Independencia.

Festivals   March 21 commemorates Benito Juárez' birthday and everything is closed for the day. Ceremonies around his monument at the Agua Azul park. At the end of October there is a great *fiesta* with concerts, bullfights, sports and exhibitions of handicrafts from all over Mexico. October 28-December 20, *fiesta* in honour of the Virgin of Guadalupe; Av. Alcalde has stalls, music, fair etc. In December there is one at Parque Morelos and hand-made toys are a special feature.

Hotels   *Fiesta Americana*, López Mateos at Minerva circle, L; *Guadalajara-Sheraton*, 16 de Septiembre, A; *Quinta Real*, Av. México y López Mateos, small, A, good but slow restaurant; *Camino Real*, Vallarta 5005, A, some way from the centre; *Fénix*, Calle Corona 160, reasonable, B, not welcoming; *Francés*, Maestranza 35, B; *Roma*, Av. Juárez 170, B; *El Tapatío*, Bld. Aeropuerto 3275 (in Tlaquepaque, fine view of city), A; *Holiday Inn*, Av. López Mateos opp. Plaza del Sol, A. *Internacional*, C, clean, comfortable, safe, rec. (address please); *Génova*, Juárez 123, D, clean, good service, good restaurant, rec.; *Universo*, López Cotilla 163, D, somewhat run down; *Tres Estrellas*, cheap, noisy, all rooms with bath, restaurant and garage, Calzada Independencia Sur 667 (restaurant closed in January). E. There are many cheap hotels along Calzada Independencia and in the two blocks N of the old bus station, Calle 28 de Enero and Calle 20 de Noviembre (where there is a small market, good for breakfasts) and the side streets (although rooms can sometimes be filthy, so check), and near Mercado Libertad; they include *San José*, *San Carlos*, *Madrid*, *Señorial*, *Central*, *Cónsul*, *Monaco* (rooms on street very noisy), *Emperador de Occidente*, *Praga*, *Celta*, *Lincoln*, all E-F, all rec. *Reno*, Calle Independencia 482, E, clean, front rooms a bit noisy otherwise rec. *Continental*, and *Morales*, both on Calle Corona, E, rec. (but others of similar quality cheaper), often fully booked. *Calzada*, Calzada Independencia Sur, good value but loud TV and electronic games, F; *Hamilton*, F, clean and central at Madero 381; *González*, behind Mercado Corona, 4 blocks W of cathedral, González Ortega 77, good value, E, often full, very friendly, highly rec.; *Posada de la Plata*, López Cotilla y Ocho de Julio, in centre, E, large rooms, shower, clean; *Posada España*, López Cotillo E with bath, nice courtyard, washing facilities, helpful manager; *Casa de Huéspedes Jalisco*, F, very friendly, clean, quiet; *Nueva Galicia*, D, older style, Av. Corona 610; *Pensión Jalisco*, Obregón 833, E, with bath, spotless, comfortable, but in horrible district. *Sevilla*, Prisciliano Sánchez 413, E, good, clean (4 blocks S of cathedral), owner speaks English, good restaurant (not always open). *Pacífico*, Los Angeles 27, nice clean rooms, E. *Lisboa*, Huerta 20, near Mercado Libertad, F, with bath, not clean. *Las Américas*, E, Calle Hidalgo, friendly and clean. *Janeiro*, Obregón 93, by market, clean, F, good value, clean; *Azteca*, 1½ blocks from Mercado Libertad, clean, F; *León*, Calzada Independencia Sur 557, D, clean, shower, ask for room at back. *Casa de Huéspedes Norteña*, Calle 28 de Enero, F, without bath, clean, room to wash clothes in patio. *Nayarit*, F, not very clean, some rooms better than others, Los Angeles 231A; *Manzanillo*, Calle Estadio 2074, F. **Motels** *Rose*, C; *Chapalita*, E; *Del Bosque*, B; *Posada del Sol*, B; *Las Américas*, opp. Plaza del Sol shopping centre, C, a/c, pool, good; *Colonial*, C. There are additional ones at the end of Vallarta: *Vallarta*, C; *Guadalajara*, B; *California*, C; *Real Vallarta*, E. There are 16 more around town. Many along López Mateos near the edge of town, before the *periférico* road.

Youth Hostel   CREA at Prolongación Alcalde 1360, Sector Hidalgo, T 24-62-65, away from centre, dirty, many mosquitoes. Bus from centre: Mezquitera, from bus terminal, No. 133, or No. 216 from Cathedral.

Restaurants   *Gerardo*, on Calle La Paz, main dish about US$5, and *La Vianda*, just off López Mateos Sur by Plaza del Angel, are reported best. *La Concordia*, P. Moreno 1679, good seafood; *El Tío Juan*, Independencia Norte 2246, local meat dishes including goat; Mexican specialities also at *Caballo Blanco*, López Mateos Sur 700; local country fare at *Ahualulco Campestre*, 20 de Noviembre 122A; *Jacques* (in Lafayette Park); *Guadalajara Grill*, López Mateos Sur, excellent meat and music; *El Tirol* on Duque de Rivas, Sector Hidalgo, excellent steak. *Holiday Inn* does grills on Sun., 1300-1700. *Carnes Asadas Tolsa*, Tolsa 510 and Chapultepec 198, rec.; *El Balcón*, smart and reasonable on Juárez 414.

Las Margaritas, one at López Cotilla 1477, and one at Ruben Darío and M. Acuña, good and cheap vegetarian dishes. *Bazar de la Salud,* López Cotilla 608, good vegetarian shop; round the corner on Juárez is *La Naturaleza,* also vegetarian, both closed Sun. Vegetarian restaurant opp. *Hotel Sevilla* on Prisciliano Sánchez; warmly rec. *Zanahoria,* Av. Las Américas 538, for excellent vegetarian food; good vegetarian buffet at *La Pileca,* US$1, Colonias 279, San Javier, open 1000-1730.

Good but expensive Japanese restaurant, *Suchiro. Restaurant and Pastry Shop Suiza,* Vallarta 1519, good breakfast and coffee, rec.; *Don Tomasito,* Vidrio 1688 y Argentina, Jaliscan dishes, very good, unpretentious. *Café de la Parroquia,* Enrique González 25-2, good comidas (US$1.25) and breakfasts. *El Nuevo Polo Norte del Parque,* N side of Parque de la Revolución, excellent chicken, esp. in pepián; *Agora,* in ex-Convento del Carmen, on Juárez, good for fish. *Mesón de Sancho Panza* on park where Calzada Federalismo and Av. Juárez bisect, good five-course meals and Mexican wines. *Las Banderillas* on Av. Alcalde, excellent roast meat, always open, try cerdo adobado (marinated pork) guacamole and cebollitas (onions). Cheap meals at *El Bordo,* Calle Independencia and at the *Fonda Vieja Mexicali* at No. 391 (Sur) of the same street. Many cheap restaurants in the streets near the bus stations, esp. in Calle de Los Angeles, and upstairs in the large market in centre. *Nino's,* Av. México and Manuel, reasonable and good; *Alpes,* Calle López Cotilla, German food, inexpensive. *La Herradura,* Calle Estadio next to *Hotel Terminal* across from bus terminal, good carne asada. In Tlaquepaque, Dayton Herzog runs *El Restaurant sin Nombre,* on Fco. Madero, excellent food and drink out of doors, with singing waiters. Many bars serve snacks, botanas, with drinks between 1300 and 1500, free, e.g. *Pancho S.A.* (best) on Maestranza 179, several blocks from the Libertad market. Most of these bars are for men only, though. **N.B.** The bars in the centre are popular with the city's gay population.

Crafts Two glass factories at *Tlaquepaque* nearby where the blue, green, amber and amethyst blown-glass articles are made; visit the shop of Sergio Bustamante, who sells his own work: expensive but well worth a look. Also, the Casa de los Telares (Calle de Hidalgo 1378), where Indian textiles are woven on hand looms. Potters can be watched at work both in Guadalajara and at Tlaquepaque; you may find better bargains at Tonalá (pottery and ceramics), 15 km. SW of Guadalajara on the road to Mexico City, but no glass there; take bus 110, bumpy ½ hr. journey. Overall, Tlaquepaque is the cheapest and most varied source of the local crafts; best buys: glass, papier mâché goods, leather (cheapest in Mexico), and ceramics. Casa de Artesanías, edge of Agua Azul park, high quality display (and sale) of handicrafts. There is another shop-cum-exhibition at the Instituto de Artesanía Jaliscense, México 54, exhibition of the Avenida Alcalde and Avila Camacho. Look out for leather belts with sewn-on tapestry. Parián is a covered commercial area with a whole variety of restaurants and handicraft shops, Calle Grecia, off Juárez. See also the Tienda Tlaquepaque, at Av. Juárez 267-B, in Tlaquepaque, T 35-56-63.

Car Rental Niños Héroes opp. *Sheraton*: Quick, Budget, National, Avis, Ford and Odin. Others scattered throughout the city.

Entertainment Folk dances every Sun. at 1000 in the Degollado Theatre; concerts and theatre in the ex-Convento del Carmen; concert every Thurs. and Sun. at 1830 in the Plaza de Armas, in front of the Palacio de Gobierno, free. Organ recitals in the Cathedral. *Peña Cuicalli,* Sector Juárez, López Cotilla 1225 with Atenas, opens 2000, small cover charge, food and drink available, fills up fast—local groups perform folk and protest songs. Music also at *La Peña* on Avenida Unión.

Sport Bullfights: October to March; football throughout year; *Charreadas* are held in mid-September at Unión de San Antonio; *Charreada* (cowboy show) near Agua Azul Park at Aceves Calindo Lienzo, Sun. at 1200. Baseball, April-Sept.; golf at: Santa Anita, 16 km. out on Morelia road, championship course; Rancho Contento, 10 km. out on Nogales road; San Isidro, 10 km. out on Saltillo road, noted for water hazards; Areas, 8 km. out on Chapala road.

British Vice-Consul Mr S Cohen, Calz. González Gallo 1987, Apartado postal 32-94, T (91-36) 358295/358927.

Cultural Institutes US at Tolsa 300; British at Tomás V. Gómez 125, Sector Hidalgo, T 160268, closed between 1200 and 1600. Benjamin Franklin Library, Libertad 1492, US papers and magazines.

Post Office V. Carranza, just behind Hall of Justice. Telephone from Teléfonos de México.

Tourist Office Federal tourist office Paseo Degollado 50, Edif. Occidente, Plaza Tapatía; state office Morelos 102, Plaza Tapatía, information on everything, maps, helpful. Instituto Nacional de Estadística, Geografía e Informática, Av. Alcalde 788, T 913614, for maps and information. American Express, López Mateos Norte 477, open Sat. at 0930.

Rail Ticket office in town, Av. Libertad and Colonias, near the US Consulate and some way from centre (but not for trains to Mexico City). National Railways to Mexico City and Manzanillo. Mexico City-Guadalajara Tapatío (*servicio estrella*) leaves the capital 0840, arr. 0810, returns 2055, US$12.65 reclining seat, US$23.85 single sleeper, US$47.65 double. Colimense *servicio estrella* connects with Tapatío at 0900 for Manzanillo (7 hrs., US$7.80), 5½ hrs. to Colima. The ordinary train from Mexico City to Guadalajara leaves at 0945 and 1900 daily, 14-18 hrs., US$6.50 (1st class), US$3.85 (2nd class, which often sells out early; you need to be at the station 4 hours before the train leaves, to be sure of a seat). There is a first and special first class; only the latter is better than 2nd class. Train Guadalajara-Irapuato (US$1.70 2nd class) leaves at 0700, which connects there with the train to Mexico City from the north. Train to Mexicali, 0945 "Pullman", 28 hrs., US$21; ordinary 1200, 44 hrs. Daily trains to Los Reyes (change at Yurécuaro) and Manzanillo. Train to Mazatlán (book well in advance) 1st class and Pullman at 0910, US$3 and US$6 respectively. All classes on 1330 train, 2nd class US$2 (price difference really shows). Journey Guadalajara-Colima, US$1.40, 2nd class, 7 hours, worth taking because scenery between Ciudad Guzmán and Colima is spectacular.

Airport Miguel Hidalgo, 20 km. from town; fixed rate for 3 city zones and 3 classes of taxi: *especial, semi-especial* and colectivo—no tip necessary. Bus No. 71 from 1st class entrance at Terminal de Autobuses, US$0.20; VW buses, Calle Federalismo Sur No. 915, "servicio terrestre", US$2.50 p.p. Eight flights daily to and from Mexico City, 50 mins.

Bus New bus station in outskirts; minibus 04 outside each building goes to centre, one block from San Francisco, US$0.10, taxi officially US$3. To Uruapan, US$3, 2nd class, 6 hrs., with Estrella de Oro before 0900 and at 1500, with Flecha Amarilla about 7 hrs.; departures every hour until midnight; with Norte de Sonora to Mazatlán, 9½ hrs., US$6, Ciudad Obregón, 15 hrs., US$13; Hermosillo, 19 hrs., US$17; Mexicali, 32 hrs., US$25; Tijuana, 36 hrs., US$28 and Ciudad Juárez, US$30, 1st class (15 hrs.) with Omnibus de México; Mexico City, US$7.70 1st class, US$6.80 2nd class, leave every hr., 8 hrs., much of road under repair; Nogales, US$15, 26 hrs.; Zihuatanejo, US$8, 12 hrs. (2nd class); Guanajuato 3 1st class, US$5.50, 2nd class hourly, US$4. To Durango, US$6. To Morelia, every hour until midnight, 1st class US$6, 2nd US$4. Manzanillo, US$5, 6 hrs., Pátzcuaro, US$3.50, 4 a day, otherwise change at Quiroga, 6 hrs. Interesting journey to Zacatecas, but Autobuses de México front window is half painted. To Querétaro, US$5, 7 hrs.; to Colima, US$3, 4 hrs.; to Chapala US$1.

Excursions 8 km. to the canyon of Barranca de Oblatos, 600 metres deep, reached by bus 45 from the market to end of line (admission US$0.05), with the Río Santiago cascading at the bottom (except in dry season). Guides to the bottom. Once described as a stupendous site; now reported made hideous by littering. See especially the Cola de Caballo waterfall and the Parque Mirador Dr All. Park crowded on Sunday; Balneario Los Comachos, a large swimming pool with diving boards set on one side of the Barranca de Oblatos, has many terraces with tables and chairs and barbecue pits under mango trees; drinks and snacks on sale; now descibed as dirty. Entry US$1.30. Also to Barranca de Huentitán, in the canyon of the River Lerma, access via the Mirador de Huentitán at the end of Calzada Independencia Norte, interesting flora, tremendous natural site. 1 hr. to the bottom (no guide needed) and the River Lerma which is straddled by the historic bridge of Huentitán. Buses to Huentitán: 42 "Jonilla Centro" from city centre; 44 "Sevilo C. Médico", stops 100 m. short. An alternative route to Huentitán is bus 133 from Av. Alcalde or 16 de Septiembre, but route 132 takes you back the same way. All buses cost US$0.05. In a NW suburb of Guadalajara are the Basílica de Zapopán, with a miraculous image of Nuestra Señora on the main altar, given to the Indians in 1542, and a museum of Huichol Indian art (agricultural fair in Nov.). Zapopán is reached by taking the system of underground trolley buses, known as the *metro*, which also goes to Tlaquepaque, as far as the Avila Camacho station, then any bus marked Zapopán. En route for Tepic is the Bosque de Primavera, reached by town buses. Pine forests ideal for picnics, although increasingly littered; US$0.50 for a swim.

"From Guadalajara to Irapuato: via Tepatitlán (79 km, on the León road), a small unfinished market town with a *charro* centre, in an impressive setting with steep hills all around; Arandas has a curious neo-gothic church and a pleasant square with a white wrought-iron bandstand; the road then winds tightly up over a range of hills and then down into a long and heavily cultivated valley. Five-hour journey." writes Tim Connell.

Lake Chapala, 64 km. to the south-east, is near the town of Sayula from which D. H. Lawrence took the name when he wrote about Chapala in "The Plumed Serpent" (return 1st class bus fare to the lake US$2, every ½ hr, 1 hr. journey). There is an *Aldea India*, Indian settlement, on the Chapala road, with murals of the history of Jalisco. *Chapala* town, on the northern shore of Lake Chapala (113 km. long, 24 to 32 wide), has thermal springs, several good and pricey hotels, 4 golf courses, helpful tourist office at Hidalgo 227, and is a popular resort particularly with moneyed North Americans. Watch women and children play a picture-card game called *Anachuac*. "The house in which Lawrence wrote his novel still stands at Zaragoza 307, although a second floor and some modernization have been added. The church that figures in the last pages of "The Plumed Serpent" still stands on the waterfront, its humble façade and interior now covered by a handsome veneer of carved stone," writes Robert Schmitz, of Chapala. The lake is set in beautiful scenery. There are boats of all kinds for hire, water-fowl shooting in autumn and winter, sailing, and the lake teems with freshwater fish. Not much swimming because the water isn't very clean. On the Fiesta de Francisco de Asís (Oct. 2-3) fireworks are displayed and excellent food served in the streets. Horses for hire on the beach, bargain.

Hotels *Nido*, only one in town, D, clean, noisy, sparse furnishings, good restaurant, good swimming pool; *Chapala Haciendas*, Km. 40, Chapala-Guadalajara highway, D. Good discotheque, *Pantera Rosa.*

Ajijic, 7 km. to the W, a smaller, once Indian village, has an arty-crafty American colony. *Posada Ajijic* is a pleasant place to stay, from D, some rooms with fireplace, nice garden; *Las Casitas*, apartments, E (just outside Ajijic, at Carretera Puente 20). Try the *Teheban* bar for entertainment. Restaurant: *Italo.* Bus from Chapala, US$0.45. Beyond Ajijic is the Indian town of **Jocotepec**, a sizeable agricultural centre (recently invaded by more cosmopolitan types) on the lake; there is a local *fiesta* on January 11-18. Stay at *La Naranjita*, built 1828 as coaching inn, good food, and an art shop. *Hotel Olmedo*, E, opposite police chief's house. *Casa de huéspedes* on Calle Matamoros 83 (same street as bus station), E, with bath, modern facilities. *Ramón's Bar*, popular drinking place. Jocotepec can be reached from Ajijic or, right, from the Mexico-Guadalajara highway. Bus Chapala-Jocotopec US$1, every hour in each direction. The Indians make famous black-and-white *sarapes*. Nearby is the *Motel El Pescador*. Between Ajijic and Jocotepec lies the small town of **San Juan Cosalá**, with thermal springs at *Balnearios y Suites Cosalá*, which has private rooms for bathing with large tiled baths. Sunbathing in private rooms also possible. Rooms to let at *Balneario Paraíso*, F. Bus service from Chapala.

About 130 km. S of Guadalajara off the road to Sayula and Ciudad Guzmán (*Hotel Flamingo*, nr. main square, D, excellent value, very modern, very clean, and quiet), is **Tapalpa**, very pretty indeed. 3½ hours' drive from Guadalajara. The bus has several detours into the hills to stop at small places such as Zacoalco (Sunday market) and Amacueca. The road up to Tapalpa is winding and climbs sharply; the air becomes noticeably cooler and the place is becoming increasingly popular as a place for weekend homes. The town itself, with only 11,000 inhabitants, shows ample signs of this influx of prosperity. There are two churches (one with a curious atrium) and an imposing flight of stone steps between them, laid out with fountains and ornamental lamps. Tapalpa is in cattle country; the rodeo is a popular sport at weekends.

The main street is lined with stalls, selling *sarapes* and other tourist goods on Sundays and fresh food the other days of the week. The more expensive restaurants have tables on balconies overlooking the square—the *Restaurante Posada Hacienda* (which has a US$1 cover charge) is well placed. Others are the *Buena Vista* (which also has rooms) and *La Cabaña*, and all are visited by the mariachis. Less grand is the *Hotel Tapalpa*, E, but clean and fairly cheap. Some rooms are for hire (*Bungalows Rosita*). The only local speciality is *ponche*, an improbable blend of tamarind and mescal which is sold in gallon jars and rec. only for the curious or foolhardy. If you are planning a day trip get your return ticket as soon as you arrive as the last bus back to Guadalajara (1800 on Sundays) is likely to be full.

Manzanillo has become an important port on the Pacific, since a spectacular 257-km. railway has been driven down the sharp slopes of the Sierra Madre through Colima. The road from Guadalajara is via Jal. 33 to Ciudad Guzmán and on to Manzanillo. Occupations for tourists at Manzanillo (population, 150,000) include deep-sea fishing, bathing, and walking in the hills. There is a bullring on the outskirts on the road to Colima. The best beach is the lovely crescent of Santiago, 8 km. N, but there are three others (San Pedrito beach is oily, convenient, refreshments available). Airport.

Hotels *Roca del Mar*, Playa Azul, vacation centre, A; *Las Brisas Vacation Club*, D, Av. L. Cárdenas, some a/c, good restaurant; *La Posada*, Calz. L. Cárdenas 201, A, US manager. On Plaza: *Savoy*, SW corner, big clean rooms with cold water, good views, F, rec. At Santiago beach: *Playa de Santiago*, B, good but food expensive; *Parador Marbella*, D, including breakfast and dinner; *Club Las Hadas Camino Real*, L; *Anita*, D. At the port: *Colonial*, good restaurant, México 100, C, friendly; also *Colonial*, 10 de Mayo, E; *Flamingos*, 10 de Mayo y Madería, E with bath, quite good; *Emperador*, Davalos 69, E, good value. *Medina*, México 133, E; *Pacífico*, E, with bath, also on Calle México. *Casa de Huéspedes Posada Jardín*, Cuauhtémoc, reasonable, E; *Casa de Huéspedes Corona*, next to bus station, basic, clean, cold water. Camping at Miramar and Santiago beaches.

Tourist Office Juárez 244, 4th floor, helpful.

Transport Bus to Miramar, US$0.20, leaves from J. J. Alcaraz, "El Tajo". Autocamiones del Pacífico bus, 1st class to Guadalajara, US$4, 6 hrs. To Mexico City with Autobus de Occidente, 19 hrs., 2nd class, US$8.80. To Guadalajara, US$5, 6 hrs.; to Barra de Navidad, US$0.80, 1½ hrs.; to Colima, US$1.50; to Tijuana, bus US$48, 1st class, 36 hrs. Down coast to Lázaro Cárdenas and crossroads for Playa Azul (**see page 1063**) by Autobus de Occidente or Galeana, US$4.50, 7 hrs. Bus terminal in Av. Hidalgo outside centre, local buses go there. Train to Guadalajara Colimense *servicio estrella* at 1300 (7 hrs., US$7.80) or daily at 0600, US$1.50.

Another Route to Manzanillo Turn off Mexico City highway 35 km. S of Guadalajara and continue 270 km. S to Melaque bay and the village of **Barra de Navidad** (commercial but still pleasant; *Hotel Barra de Navidad*, with balcony on beach, D, or bungalows, US$6.60, where you can cook (free camping); *Bosantes*, on beach, E with bath, clean, good value; at *Alice's*

Restaurant, E, simple food; *Hotel Jalisco*, E, hot water, safe and clean; ask about camping on beach; fish restaurants e.g. *Antonio* on beach), where there is a monument to the Spanish ships which set out in 1648 to conquer the Philippines. Avoid oil spillages on beach. This road is paved. Pretty seaside villages near Barra de Navidad include La Manzanilla (*Posada del Cazador*) and Tenacatita, with perfect beach complete with palm huts, tropical fish among rocks. *Hotel* (no name) in village near beach, F, or you can sleep on the beach under a palm shelter— but beware mosquitoes. *Melaque* bay is one of the most beautiful on the Pacific coast but has become very commercialized. (Hotels, many, e.g. *Melaque*, too big and very noisy; *Club Náutico*, very pleasant, good value, small swimming pool, good restaurant on beach; *San Nicolás*, E, beside Estrella Blanca bus station, noisy but clean; *Flamingo*, E, Vallarta 19, clean and friendly; *Bungalows Azteca*, 23 km. from Manzanillo airport, D for 4 at Calle Avante, San Patricio, T (333) 7-01-50, with kitchenette, pool, parking.) The road, paved, goes on to Manzanillo. S of Manzanillo is *Tecomán*, (68,000) with delightful atmosphere. Unnamed *pensión* on the corner of the Zócalo, if you face the church it is on your left, F. Try the local deep-fried *tortillas* filled with cheese. The coast road (very dramatic) continues SE to Playa Azul, Lázaro Cárdenas, Zihuatanejo and Acapulco.

A beautiful hilly road runs from Manzanillo to *Colima*, 96 km., capital of Colima state, at an altitude of 494 metres. Colima is a most charming and hospitable town with gothic arcade on main square and strange rebuilt gothic ruin on road beyond Cathedral. Museums: María Ahumada Museun of Western Cultures, Calzada Pedro Galván, in Casa de Cultura complex, Tues.-Sun. 0900-1300, 1600-1800; Museo de la Máscara, la Danza y el Arte Popular del Occidente, Calle 27 de Septiembre y Manuel Gallardo, folklore and handicrafts (items for sale—in the University Institute of Fine Arts). For a change, go to Sr. Francisco Zaragoza's car spare parts business on Jardín Núñez; he has a large collection of dilapidated old cars, mostly US, all stored anyhow (some of his car parts look the same vintage). *Feria*: November. Good tourist office on Hidalgo near Jardín Torres Quintero but no info. on climbing local volcanoes. Post Office, Av. Fco 1. Madero y Gral. Nuñez. Public swimming pool in park on Calle Degollado. Airport.

Hotels and restaurants *Hotel América*, Morelos 162, A, a/c, good restaurant, central, friendly; *Ceballos*, Torres Quintero 16, E, main square, fine building but disappointing rooms, not very clean but good food in restaurant (pricey); *Gran Hotel*, pleasant rooms, Av. Rey Colimán 18, near Jardín Núñez, D with bath, simple, clean, breakfast expensive; *Flamingos*, near Jardín Torres Quintero, not very clean, E; *Núñez*, Juárez 80 at Jardín Núñez, basic, dark, E with bath; *San Cristóbal*, near centre, run down, E. Many *casas de huéspedes* near Jardín Núñez. *Rey de Colimán*, E, on continuation of Medellín on outskirts, large rooms; *Motel Costeño* on outskirts is rec. *Hotel Madero*, basic, F, may not have water. Nice, cheap restaurant *La Fuente* in centre; also *Comedor Familiar El Trébol*, opp. *Hotel Ceballos*, cheap, popular, good food. Good yoghurt and wholemeal bread at *Centro de Nutrición Lakshmi*, Av. Madero 265.Try the local sweet cocada y miel (coconut and honey in blocks), sold in *dulcerías*.

Colima volcano (3,842 metres), one of the most exciting climbs in Mexico, which erupted with great loss of life in 1941, and of El Nevado (4,339 metres) are in the vicinity. They can be climbed from Ciudad Guzmán (formerly Zapotlán), by taking a bus to the village of Fresnito. Bus, Ciudad Guzmán-Colima, Flecha Amarilla, US$1.40, 2 hrs.; train Colima-Ciudad Guzmán, US$0.55, 2nd class, 3 hrs., daily at 1035. Train Colima-Guadalajara at 0830. Comalá is a pretty colonial village near Colima, worth a few hours' visit, bus US$0.10, 20 mins. every ½ hour.

Continuing to Mexico City

We go round the southern shores of Lake Chapala, and after 154 km. come to Jiquilpan (a road leads off, right, to Manzanillo). There are frescoes by Orozco in the library, which was formerly a church.

The State of Michoacán, where the Tarascan Indians live, is a country of deep woods, fine rivers and great lakes. Fruit, game, and fish are abundant. It has some of the most attractive towns and villages in the country. Visitors are attracted by the Tarascan customs, folklore, ways of life, craft skills (pottery, lacquer), music and dance. The dance is of first importance to them; it is usually performed to the music of wooden drum, flute and occasionally, a fiddle. Masks are often worn and the dance is part of a traditional ritual. The dances which most impress outsiders are the dance of Los Viejitos (Old Men; at Janitzio, January 1); Los Sembradores (The Sowers; February 2); Los Moros (The Moors; Lake Pátzcuaro region, *fiestas* and carnival); Los Negritos (Black Men; *fiestas* at Tzintzuntzán); Los Apaches (February 4, at the churches); Las Canacuas (the crown dance; Uruapan, on Corpus Christi). At the weddings of fisherfolk the couple dance inside a fish net. In the local *fandango* the woman has fruits in her hand, the man has a glass of *aguardiente* balanced on his head, and a sword.

Zamora (58 km. beyond Jiquilpan), with 200,000 people, is an agricultural centre founded in 1540. There is an interesting ruined gothic-style church in the centre, several other, fine churches, and a market on Calle Corregidora by the

MEXICO WEST CENTRAL 136

bus station. Nearby is tiny Lake Camecuaro, with boats for hire, restaurants and wandering musicians; popular at holiday times.

Hotels *Fénix*, near bus station, C, run down but clean, swimming pool, pleasant balconies; *Amelia*, Hidalgo 194, E, pleasant. **Motel Jérico**, A, Km. 3 on La Barca road just N of town, swimming pool, restaurant.

On 40 km. is Carapán, from which a branch road runs 72 km. S through pine woods to **Uruapan** ("Place where flowers are plentiful"), a town of 250,000 set among streams, orchards and waterfalls at 1,610 metres in the Parque Nacional Barranca del Cupatitzio, cool at night. The most attractive of its three plazas is the Jardín de los Mártires, with the 16th century church facing it. In the *portales* or at the market can be bought the local lacquered bowls and trays, or the delicate woodwork of the Paracho craftsmen, Patamban green pottery and Capácuaro embroideries. Restored hospital, built by Fray Juan de San Miguel in the 16th century; now a ceramics museum. Adjoining it is a 16th-century chapel now converted into a craft shop. There is also a church of the same period, and a public park, Eduardo Ruiz, 1 km. from the centre, full of streams and waterfalls at the top of Calle Venustiana with a good handicraft shop at the entrance, selling wooden boxes and bracelets. Walk there or catch a bus at the Zócalo marked "El Parque". Airport.

Festivals In the first week of April the Zócalo is filled with pottery and Indians from all the surrounding villages. Around September 16, in nearby village of San Juan, to celebrate the saving of an image of Christ from the San Juan church (see below) at the time of the Paricutín eruption. The two weeks either side of September 15 are *feria* in Uruapan, too.

Hotels *Victoria*, Cupatitzio 13, B, good, quiet, restaurant and garage; *Hernández*, main square, C, older, noisy; *El Tarasco*, Independencia 2, D, pool, lovely; *Oseguera*, main square, E, clean, hot water spasmodic; *Santa Fe*, Constitución 20, F, without bath, adequate, beside open-air food stalls; *Moderno*, main square, E, with bath, dark rooms; *Capri*, Portal Santos Degollado, by market, friendly, E. *Concordia* on main square has nice restaurant, C; *Mirador*, Av. Ocampo 9 (on

Zócalo), F, hot water 0700-1000 and in p.m., rec.; *Económico*, F, 3 blocks from Zócalo, Calle N. Bravo 25. **Motels** *Mansión del Cupatitzio*, on the road to Guadalajara, nice; *Pie de la Sierra*, on N outskirts, C, good moderately-priced restaurant; *Paricutín*, Juárez 295, D, well-maintained. *Las Cabañas*, Km. 1 Carretera a México, near the bus terminal, clean, F, local bus until 2200.

Restaurants One with English menu near bus station at back of church, reasonably priced; *Oriental*, on the Plaza, near *Hotel Moderno*, clean, poor service. Locals eat at open-air food stalls under one roof at back of church, very picturesque. *Typ's*, Madero 16, is quite good, but expensive; *La Puesta del Sol*, supermarket, Juan Ayala, has good meals. *La Palma* behind Cathedral, good and cheap, student clientèle. Local speciality, dried meat, *cecina.*

Laundry Emilio Carranza 51.

Tourist Office close to main square, at 5 de Febrero 17 (T 20633), good map.

Train Two daily to Mexico City: *rápido* at 0635, first class tickets from *Hotel Victoria* and Purepecha (*servicio estrella*) from Mexico City at 2200 (arr. 1010), returning 1915 (arr. 0720) reclining seat US$8.80, single sleeper US$14.55, double US$29.10.

Bus Bus station on the NE edge of town, necessary to get a city bus (US$0.07) into town, finishing at about 2100, or a taxi to the Plaza, US$0.90. To Mexico City, 9¼ hrs., 2nd class, Flecha Amarilla via Toluca leaves 0845 and then every hr., US$6.10, many stops; 1st class less frequent but quicker, US$7.50. Omnibus de México has night buses and Tres Estrellas morning departures. To Morelia, 2nd class (Flecha Amarilla) US$1.60 (2½ hrs.), nice ride. To Colima with Flecha Amarilla US$3.30, 5 hrs. and to Los Reyes, US$0.90, 1¼ hrs. with same company. To Zihuatanejo (Galeana—not rec.—or Occidente) 1st or 2nd class, several a day, 6½ hrs., US$3.50 (2nd) along winding, intermittently wooded road via Nueva Italia and Arteaga, which turns off just before Playa Azul at La Mira and on to Lázaro Cárdenas on the River Balsas. From there, frequent buses to Zihuatanejo (**see page 1062**). Bus to Guadalajara, several companies, US$3, 2nd class, 6 hrs. Bus to Pátzcuaro, Flecha Amarilla every hour, US$ 1.05, 45 mins; also with Galeana.

Excursions Through coffee groves and orchards along the Cupatitzio (meaning Singing River) to the Zararacua Falls—heavily littered; restaurants at bus stop where you can hire a horse for US$2 to the falls. Good camping some 300 metres below the village under the shelter on the top of a rim, with a view down into the valley to the waterfall (1 km. away) and a small lake. A bus (marked Zararacua) will take you from the Zócalo at Uruapan to Zararacua, US$0.30, about every 40 mins. Parque Cholinde, 1.5 km. out of town, swimming pool, US$1.30; Colibrí Nurseries nearby. Balneario Caracha (frequent buses), alight at cross roads by sign, a delightful place, open daily with restaurant, hotel, several pools and beautiful gardens. Tingambato ruins are half way along road to Pátzcuaro, about 2 km. downhill from Tingambato town (pyramid and ball court).

To the volcano of *Paricutín*, 64 km.; it started erupting in the field of a startled peasant on February 20, 1943, became fiery and violent and rose to a height of 1,200 metres above the 2,100-metre-high region, and then died down after several years into a quiet grey mountain surrounded by a sea of cold lava. The church spires of San Juan, a buried Indian village, thrusting up through cold lava is a fantastic sight. If not taking an organized tour (with horses and guides), Paricutín is best reached by taking a "Los Reyes" bus over rough track to Angahuán, US$0.65 return, 1½ hrs., 9 a day each way (from 0700 to 2000) with Galeana; then hire a mule or walk (1 hr.). (Cars suitable for rough terrain can, we are told, also get there.) Sr. José Gómez in Angahuán has mules for hire, but he is expensive; Sr. Juan Rivera and Sr. Francisco Lázaro are recommended, but there are a host of other guides (it is definitely worthwhile to have a guide— essential for the volcano). Up to US$3 per mule, US$1 for a guide—bargain—to San Juan, about 3 hours' journey there and back past a Tarascan village, and if you include also Paricutín the price is US$6.75 in total. Distance Angahuán-San Juan ruins, 3 km., an easy walk: go from the bus stop on the main road, then take right-hand road (with your back to the church) from the plaza, which will lead you to the new hostel, F, from where you can see the buried church. To the peak of the volcano is 12-13 km. Wear good walking shoes with thick soles as the lava is very rough and as sharp as glass; bear in mind the altitude too, as the return is uphill. Chris Kerfoot writes: One can continue on to the volcano itself; it takes about 7 hrs. there and back and costs from US$9 each. The cone itself is rather small and to reach it, there is a stiff 30 min. climb from the base. A path goes around the tip of the crater, where activity has ceased. Take something to drink because it is pretty hot and dusty out on the plains. Best to leave Uruapan by 0800 so that you don't have to rush. Take sweater for evening. Last bus back to Uruapan at 1900 (but don't rely on it).

Past Angahuán and Peribán, after the volcano, over a terrible road is the little town of *Los Reyes*; good swim above the electricity generating plant in clear streams (take care not to get sucked down the feed pipe!). Hotels: *Arias* behind Cathedral, D, best, clean, friendly; *Fénix*, E, clean, between bus station and plaza; *Casa de Huéspedes*, clean, basic, F, lovely courtyard, a little further along the same road as *Villa Rica*, F, often no water; *Plaza*, not as good as *Arias* but nice, clean, D, on street facing Cathedral; *Oasis*, with pool, Av. Morelos 229, good, E. Restaurant: *La Fogata*, in main square. Buses from Uruapan to Los Reyes go via Angahuán (so same frequency as above). Bus to Los Reyes from Guadalajara with Ciénaga de Chapala 4 a day, 14 hrs., US$2.80 2nd class. Train Guadalajara-Mexico City connects at Yurécuaro for Los Reyes, almost no wait, beautiful ride up fertile valley. Bus from Los Reyes, on Av. 5 de Mayo, to Angahuán, US$0.55, 1½-2 hrs.

Paracho, reached by bus from Pátzcuaro, is a quaint, very traditional Indian village of small wooden houses; in every other one craftsmen make guitars worth from US$10 to 1,000 according to the wood used. The town is virtually traffic free. Try local pancakes.

At Zacapu (Km. 400), see Franciscan church (1548). (Km. 357) *Quiroga,* where a road turns off right for Pátzcuaro, heart of the Tarascan Indian country. The town is named after Bishop Vasco de Quiroga, who was responsible for most of the Spanish building in the area and for teaching the Indians the various crafts they still practise: work in wool, leather, copper, ceramics and canework; many Indians, few tourists. Fair and craft exhibitions in December. Good place to buy cheap leather jackets—most shops in town sell them.

Hotels *Quiroga* and *San Diego*, both E, on Vasco de Quiroga; and others inc. motels.

We pass through *Tzintzuntzan,* also touristy, the pre-conquest Tarascan capital; the fascinating ruins just above the town have almost been restored. In Calle Magdalena is a monastery built in 1533 but closed over 250 years ago, which has been restored, but its frescoes have deteriorated badly. The bells of its church, now burnt down, date from the 16th century; a guard will show you round the monastery. A most interesting Passion play is given at Tzintzuntzan. Beautiful and extensive display of hand-painted pottery, very cheap but also brittle. (It is available in other markets in Mexico.) Good bargaining opportunities.

Pátzcuaro is 23 km. from Quiroga; altitude 2,110 metres; population 80,000, one of the most picturesque towns in Mexico, with narrow cobbled streets and deep overhanging eaves. It is built on Lake Pátzcuaro, about 50 km. in circumference, with Tarascan Indian villages on its shores and many islands. The Indians used to come by huge dugout canoes (but now seem to prefer the ferry)

1. Plaza Vasco de Quiroga
2. Plaza Bocanegra
3. Jardín de la Revolución
4. La Basílica/La Colegiata
5. La Compañía
6. El Sagrario
7. San Francisco
8. San Juan de Dios
9. El Humilladero
10. El Hospitalito
11. Museum of Popular Art/Colegio de San Nicolás
12. Casa de los Once Patios
13. Market
14. Post Office
15. Telephone Office

Hotels:
16. Posada San Rafael
17. Gran
18. Misión San Manuel
19. Posada de la Salud
20. El Artillero
21. Posada de la Rosa

PÁTZCUARO
Not to Scale   135

for the market, held in the main plaza, shaded by great trees. There is an interesting *fiesta* on December 12 for the Virgin of Guadalupe; on October 12, when Columbus discovered America, there is also a procession with the Virgin and lots of fireworks.

There are several interesting buildings: the unfinished La Colegiata (1603), known locally as La Basílica, with its much venerated Virgin fashioned by an Indian from a paste made with cornstalk pith and said to have been found floating in a canoe (behind the Basílica there are remains of the precolumbian town and of a pyramid in the precincts of the Museum of Popular Art); the restored Jesuit church of La Compañía (and, almost opposite, the early 17th-century church of the Sagrario) at the top of Calle Portugal. Behind this street are two more ecclesiastical buildings: the Colegio Teresiano and the restored Templo del Santuario; on Calle Lerín is the old monastery, with a series of small patios. (Murals by Juan O'Gorman in the Library, formerly San Agustín.) On Calle Allende is the residence of the first Governor. On Calle Terán is the church of San Francisco; nearby is San Juan de Dios, on the corner of Calle Romero. Visit also the Plaza Vasco de Quiroga. Fifteen minutes' walk outside the town is the chapel of El Calvario, on the summit of Cerro del Calvario, a hill giving wide views; good views also from the old chapel of the Humilladero, above the cemetery on the old road to Morelia.

The very well arranged Museum of Popular Art is in the Colegio de San Nicolás (1540) entrance US$0.40, English speaking, friendly guide: ask there for the Casa de los Once Patios, which contains the local tourist office and boutiques selling handicrafts. See also the attractive Jardín de la Revolución (F. Tena y Ponce de León) and, nearby, the old church of the Hospitalito. Excellent Fri. and also Sat. markets, often much cheaper than shops. Some stalls open daily on the main square, selling handicrafts, and there is a friendly handicraft shop on the road down to the lake, Vicky's, with interesting toys. There is a free medical clinic, English-speaking, on the outskirts of Pátzcuaro.

Fiestas Nov. 1-2: Día de los Muertos (All Souls' Day), ceremony at midnight, Nov. 1, on Janitzio island, but mostly a tourist event, heavily commercialized; Dec. 6-9, Virgen de la Salud, when authentic Tarascan dances are performed in front of the *basílica*. Carnival in February when the Dance of the Moors is done.

Hotels All hotels fully-booked 4 weeks prior to Día de los Muertos. *Posada de don Vasco*, A, attractive, colonial-style hotel on Av. de las Américas (halfway between lake and town), breakfast good, other meals fair; presents the Dance of the Old Men on Wed. and Sat. at 2100, no charge, non-residents welcome but drinks very expensive to compensate; also mariachi band. *Las Redes*, Av. Américas 6, C, near lake, popular restaurant; *Posada La Basílica*, Arciga 6, C, nice restaurant with good views, central; *Mesón del Cortijo*, Obregón, just off Américas, C, rec., but often fully booked at weekends. *Los Escudos*, Portal Hidalgo 74, C, colonial style, good restaurant; *Posada San Rafael*, Plaza Vasco de Quiroga, D, clean, safe, very nice, restaurant, parking in courtyard; *Gran Hotel*, Portal Regules 6, on Plaza Bocanegra, small rooms, good restaurant, C; *Mansión Iturbe*, Portal Morelos 59, restored mansion on main square, E, good food; *Misión San Manuel*, Portal Aldama 12 on main square, restaurant, highly rec., C; these are all central. *Posada Lagos*, Zaragoza 14, E, clean; *Posada de la Salud*, Benigno Serrato, clean, quiet, pleasant, excellent value, some rooms with individual fireplaces, E; *Valmen*, Lloredo 34, E, with bath, charming colonial building but noisy. *El Artillero*, hot water, E, with bath, friendly, near Zócalo, Ibarra 22 (discounts for long stays paid in advance). *Posada de la Rosa*, Portal Juárez 29 (Plaza Chica), F, hot water a.m. only, rec.; next door is *Concordia*, F, good value, clean. There are many *hospedajes* and hotels near the bus station. **Motels** *Chalamu*, Pátzcuaro road Km. 20, trailer park too, C; *San Felipe*, Cárdenas 321, C, trailers; *San Carlos*, Muelle Col. Morelos, C; *Pátzcuaro*, Cárdenas 506, bathrooms but no showers, D, not rec.

Camping Camping and caravan site at *Motel Pátzcuaro*, spotless, lush green grass, flowering trees, showers with hot water, toilets, tennis court and pool, cheap.

Restaurants *El Patio*, on main square, clean, friendly, try pescado blanco (white fish), regional dish, it tends to be expensive; *El Munjo*, main square, reasonable food but slow service. *El Cayuco Café Cantante*, French owner, music Sat. and Sun., open 1600-2300. *Mansión Iturbe*, Portal Morelos 59, good, cheap, delicious coffee. *Hotel Escudos* restaurant, Plaza Quiroga, open till 2130, popular; *San Agustín*, Plaza Bocanegra, friendly, good donuts on sale outside in p.m. Make sure you don't get overcharged in restaurants—some display menus outside which bear no resemblance to the prices inside. *Gran Hotel*, filling comida corrida; good chicken and enchiladas over the market. Several interesting eating places by the jetty for Janitzio.

Tourist Office   West portals of Plaza Vasco de Quiroga.

Transport   New bus station out of town. To Mexico City, Tres Estrellas de Oro and Autobuses de Occidente— ADO (which also runs once a day from Pátzcuaro to Guadalajara; otherwise you change at Quiroga for Guadalajara)—1st (US$8.50) and 2nd class buses. Very enjoyable and cheaper, though slower, train ride around lake and plateau to Mexico City. Train leaves daily at 0655, from Mexico City to Pátzcuaro, arrives at 1920, beautiful views between Uruapan and Acámbaro (*fiesta,* July 4), 1st class US$4. Train to Mexico City at 0905 (*rápido*) and 2140 (Pullman). Take pullover. Trains to Uruapan: 0756, pullman; 1856, *rápido*; 1222, *normal* (slow, 2½ hrs., US$0.40 1st class).

Regular bus service to Morelia, 1 hr., US$1 with ADO and Flecha Amarilla (latter departs every ½ hr.). Buses to Guadalajara go through Zamora, with Occidental US$6.75 1st class, 6 hrs.; no trains to Guadalajara. Local buses from corner of market in town to lakeside.

Excursion   Pátzcuaro-Ario de Rosales-Nueva Italia-Uruapan-Pátzcuaro takes about 6 hrs., beautiful tropical countryside. An excursion can be made into the hills to the village of Santa Clara del Cobre (fine old church), where hand-wrought copper vessels are made. (*Fiesta:* August 12-15.) Nearby is the pretty Lake Zirahuen. Past Santa Clara, on the La Huacana road, after Ario de Rosales, one descends into the tropics; fine views all along this road, which ends at Churumuco. From Pátzcuaro one can also visit Tzintzuntzan and Quiroga by regular bus service. 30 minutes by local bus is Ilhuátzio (US$0.15), on a peninsula 12 km. N of Pátzcuaro. This was the second most important Tarascan City; two pyramids are well-preserved and afford good views of the lake. No entrance fee to the site, but the caretaker expects a tip.

Bus to lake (marked Lago) from corner of market. The best-known island is *Janitzio*, although it has become overrun by tourists and filled with cheap souvenir shops and beggars, which has made its local people hostile and the place lose its charm (45 mins. by motorboat, US$0.75, tickets from dock, including fishermen's show, most picturesque, but an unfortunate monument to Morelos crowning a hill). Winter is the best time for fishing in the somewhat fish-depleted lake, where Indians throw nets shaped like dragonflies. White fish from the lake was a delicacy, but the lake is now polluted, so beware (still plenty of places sell white fish). The Government is planning to improve the lake. On a lakeside estate is the Educational Centre for Community Development in Latin America, better known as Crefal (free films every Wed. at 1930). For a truly spectacular view of the lake, the islands and the surrounding countryside, walk to Cerro del Estribo; an ideal site for a quiet picnic. It is 1½ hrs. walk to the top from the centre of Pátzcuaro. Follow the cobbled road beyond El Calvario, don't take the dirt tracks off to the left. Cars go up in the afternoon, the best time for walking. No buses, 417 steps to the peak.

(Km. 314) *Morelia,* capital of Michoacán state, population 354,000, altitude 1,882 metres, is a rose-tinted city with attractive colonial buildings (their courtyards are their main feature), rather quiet, founded in 1541. The Cathedral (1640), is set between the two main plazas, with graceful towers and a fine façade, in what is called "sober baroque"; there are paintings by Juárez in the sacristy. Other important churches are the Virgin of Guadalupe (also known as San Diego) with a most ornate Pueblan interior, the modernized Iglesia de la Cruz, and the churches in the charming small Plaza de las Rosas and Plaza del Carmen. The oldest of Morelia's churches is the San Francisco of the Spanish Renaissance period, but lacking many of the decorative features of that style.

Even more interesting than the colonial churches are the many fine colonial secular buildings still standing. The revolutionary Morelos, Melchor Ocampo, and the two unfortunate Emperors of Mexico (Agustín de Iturbide and the Archduke Maximilian of Austria) are commemorated by plaques on their houses. The Colegio de San Nicolás (1540) is the oldest surviving institution of higher education in Latin America. (It has a summer school for foreign students.) The fine former Jesuit college, now called the Palacio Clavijero, contains government offices, with a helpful tourist office on the ground floor (corner of Madero Poniente y Nigromante). Also notable are the law school, in the former monastery of San Diego, next to the Guadalupe church; the Palacio de Gobierno (1732-70), facing the Cathedral; the Palacio Municipal; and the Palacio Federal. Visit also the churches of La Merced, with its lovely tower and strange, bulging *estípites* (inverted pyramidal supports), Capuchinas (Ortega y Montaño), which has some Churrigueresque *retablos*, and Santa María, on a hilltop S of the city.

Thursday and Sunday are market days: specialities are pottery, lacquer, woodcarving, jewellery, blankets, leather sandals; in this connection see the Casa de Artesanías de Michoacán, in the ex-Convento de San Francisco, next to the church of the same name; it is full of fine regional products for sale, not

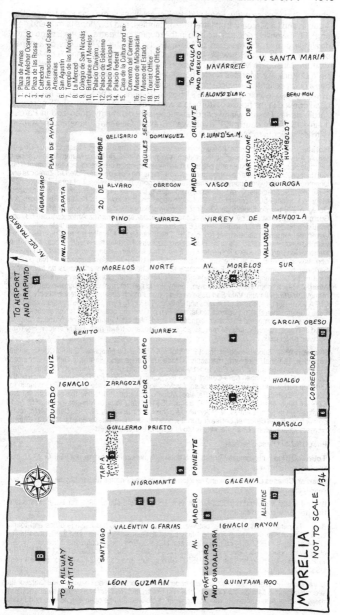

1. Plaza de Armas
2. Plaza Melchor Ocampo
3. Plaza de las Rosas
4. Cathedral
5. San Francisco and Casa de Artesanías
6. San Agustín
7. Templo de las Monjas
8. Colegio de San Nicolás
9. Birthplace of Morelos
10. Palacio Clavijero
11. Palacio de Gobierno
12. Palacio Municipal
13. Palacio Federal
14. Casa de la Cultura and ex-Convento del Carmen
15. Museo de Michoacán
16. Museo del Estado
17. Museo del Estado
18. Tourist Office
19. Telephone Office.

MORELIA

NOT TO SCALE

cheap. Shops close early. Food and drink specialities in the plazas in front of San Agustín and La Merced: fruit jams (*ates*), candies, and *rompope* (a milk and egg-nog). Free weekly concerts are held in the municipal theatre. At the E edge of the downtown area, on the road to Mexico City, are the 224 arches of a ruined aqueduct, built in 1788 (walk 11 blocks W from Cathedral along Av. Madero). Visit the Museo de Michoacán, 3 blocks from the Cathedral, and the new Casa de la Cultura, Av. Morelos Norte, housed in the ex-Convento del Carmen, which has a good collection of local masks, crucifixes and archaeological remains; also at workshops (nominal fee for US$1.55 for 12 weeks). The Museo de Estado has been opened in the house of Iturbide's wife (Casa de la Emperatriz), SE corner of Jardín de las Rosas. Many good language schools. Fairly good zoo in Parque Juárez, S of the centre (25 mins. walk S along Galeana). Planetarium. Airport with daily flights to Mexico City.

Hotels Some of the cheaper hotels may have water only in the morning; check. *Calinda Quality Inn*, A, Av. Acueducto, colonial-style, modern. *Virrey de Mendoza*, Portal Matamoros, A, superb old-style building, poor restaurant, service could be better, could be cleaner, ask for room at front with balcony. Off the Plaza de Armas and much quieter is the *Posada de la Soledad*, Zaragoza and Ocampo, fine courtyards, converted chapel as dining room, B, good value; *Catedral*, Zaragoza 37, close to Plaza, spacious, C, rec.; *Casino*, main square, C, clean, hot water, private bath; *Orozco*, Madero Poniente 507, central, cheerful, soft beds, clean, shower, E; *Posada San José*, Av. Obregón 226 beside Templo de San José, E, rooms like cells, clean; *Posada La Merced*, León Guzmán 50, E, a bit shabby, with bath. *Casa de Huéspedes Margarita*, Antonio Alzate 53, and another next door at 51; *Carmen*, E. Ruiz 673, F, good value, overlooks the Casa de la Cultura, hot water; *del Matador*, same street No. 531, E. Cheap hotels on Morelos Norte: *Colonial*, corner with 20 de Noviembre 15; *Casa de Huéspedes Lourdes*, Morelos Norte 340, 5 blocks E of bus station. *San Jorge*, Madero Poniente 719, E with hot shower, clean; *Plaza*, Gómez Farías 278, opp. bus station, E, clean, friendly, safe, comida for US$1.25 also *Concordia* at No. 328, E; *Señorial*, Santiago Tapía 543, F, also hourly rentals. Cheap *posadas* and *casas de huéspedes* tend to be uninviting. On Santa María hill, S of the city, with glorious views, are hotels *Villa Montaña* (each room a house on its own, run by French aristocrats, very expensive but value for money), *Vista Bella* and *Villa San José* next door and much cheaper (C), reached only by car. CREA youth hostel at corner of Oaxaca and Chiapas, T 33177, 1 km. SW of bus station (walk W to Calle Cuautla, then S along Cuautla to Oaxaca) F, p.p. Camping possible in a forest about 4 km. S of centre on unnumbered Pátzcuaro-signposted road. **Motels** *Villa Centurión*, Morelos road, C, good antiques, pool, TV; *Las Palmas*, Guadalajara road, also trailer park, E; *El Parador*, Highway 45, with trailer park, E.

Restaurants Superb food at the *Villa Montaña* hotel. *La Huacana*, García Obeso behind cathedral, regional, pleasant, mariachis; *Fonda de Cachamay*, Santiago Tapiá y Zaragoza, friendly and interesting; *Rey Sol*, rec. by locals; restaurant of local Woolworth's is in a 17th-century episcopal chapel. *Café Colibri*, close to Zócalo, good local food and music, Dance of the Old Men performed; *Govinda*, vegetarian, Av. Morelos Sur 39, opp. cathedral, delicious lunch for US$1.20. Comidas corridas at the *Paraíso*, Madero Poniente 103 facing the cathedral, and at *Café El Viejo*, Madero Oriente and Quiroga, US$1. *Café Pindaro*, Morelos Norte 150, good breakfasts. On Gómez Farías, N of Av. Madero there is a market for sweets. *Café y Arte*, round corner from *Hotel Catedral*, coffee and drinks, good atmosphere. Reasonable fast food at *Chipps*, on main square. *Mona Lisa* café on Luis Moya, good drinks and sweets.

Post Office in Palacio Federal.

Tourist Office Nigromante 79, has local hotel information list and map, open 0900-2000. Also kiosk at bus terminal.

Spanish Classes Centro Mexicano de Idiomas, Calz. Fray Antonio de San Miguel 173, intensive weekly classes.

Rail Morelia-Mexico City at 2304 (Pullman), US$2.35 2nd class, US$3.90 1st, train starts at Uruapan. Slow train to capital at 1030.

Bus Terminal on Eduardo Ruiz, between Guzmán and Farías, has luggage office and tourist kiosk; 3 blocks W of plaza, then 3 N. Many buses to Guanajuato, 6 hrs., US$2.20. Guadalajara, US$4. Uruapan, US$1.60 2nd class; Irapuato, US$1.80 2nd class, rough ride. Mexico City, 2nd class every hour or ADO, every 20 mins., 6½ hrs., US$4.60. Bus to Acapulco US$14, 15 hrs. Bus to Pátzcuaro every ½ hr., 1½ hrs., US$1. Also about 15 a day to Zihuatanejo on the coast, US$5.50.

Diversion Just after Morelia there is a good road to two villages on beautiful Lake Cuitzeo, the second largest in Mexico. At **Cuitzeo**, the first one (hotel, *Restaurant Esteban*, by post office), there is a fine Augustinian church and convent, a cloister, a huge open chapel, and good choir stalls in the sacristy. From here one can go to Valle de Santiago (*Hotel Posada de la Parroquia*, E), attractive mountain scenery. The second village, 23 km. to the N, **Yuriria**, has a large-scale Indian version of the splendid church and convent at Actopán (**see page 976**). (Before Yuriria is Moreleón, the clothing distribution centre of Mexico—buses empty here.) The road continues to Salamanca (hotel, appalling traffic), where one turns left for Irapuato or right for Celaya and Querétaro.

The road soon climbs through 50 km. of splendid mountain scenery: forests, waterfalls, and gorges, to the highest point at (km. 244) Mil Cumbres (2,886 metres), with a magnificent view over mountain and valley, and then descends into a tropical valley. Between Morelia and Ciudad Hidalgo is Queréndaro, where the pavements are covered in *chiles* drying in the blazing sun, and all the shops are filled with large bags of *chiles* in the season.

Then comes **Zitácuaro**, a quiet and attractive place with a pleasant plaza and a good covered market. Bus to Mexico City, 3½ hrs.,US$1.80; to Guadalajara, 11 hrs., US$6, 409 km.

Hotels   *Rancho San Cayetano*, 3 km. out on Huetamo road, C, chalets, friendly, clean, highly rec.; *Salvador*, Hidalgo Pte. 7, C, clean and pleasant; *Rosales del Valle*, Revolución Sur 56, D-C, near bus station, fair, some rooms hired for very short stays; *Posada Michoacán*, E, main square, fairly clean: *Florida*, E with bath, clean.

Worth a glance are the façade of the 16th century church at **Ciudad Hidalgo** (km. 212, 100,000 people)—*Hotel Fuente*, E, some rooms have no keys, clean, showers, no water in the afternoon; *Restaurant Manolo*, inexpensive, good; and the old colonial bridge and church at **Tuxpan** (km. 193; *Hotel Colón*, reasonable, fan, E, not very quiet, friendly management, can store luggage; *Mara*, E, on main square, adequate; *Hotel Florida*, F, damp rooms, garage US$0.50 a night). At km. 183 a side road runs, right, to the spa of **San José Purúa** at 1,800 metres, in a wild setting of mountain and gorge and woods. The radioactive thermal waters are strong. First-class hotel. Smaller, cheaper hotels lie on the road past the spa and in the town of Jungapeo.

A turning off the main road at Angangueo brings one to a unique site, the wintering grounds of the Monarch butterfly in El Campanario ecological reserve, above the village of El Rosario. It can be reached by taking an hourly local bus (labelled Angangueo) from Zitácuaro (Av. Santos Degollado Oriente) to Ocampo, 1 hr., and from Ocampo another local bus (1¼ hrs., 12 km.) to El Rosario. Entry to the reserve is about US$0.70; it has a small visitors' centre and several trails to see the myriads of large orange butterflies, which migrate every year from SE Canada and NE USA. The reserve can no doubt be reached from other towns nearby, such as Angangueo, Ciudad Hidalgo or Tuxpan, and Aguila Tours, Amsterdam 291-C, Col. Hipódromo Condesa, run tours from early December from Mexico City.

(Km. 86) A branch road, right, goes to the mountain resort of **Valle de Bravo**, a charming old town on the edge of an attractive artificial lake, with another Monarch butterfly wintering area nearby. This area gets the week-end crowd from Mexico City.

Hotels   *Centro Vacacional ISSEMYM*, central, pool, restaurant, satisfactory, Independencia 404; *Refugio del Salto*, Fontana Brava, C; *Los Arcos* (C, but good) is several km. beyond, in pine woods, excellent restaurant. **Motels** *Avándaro*, Fraccionamiento Avándaro, C, pleasant.

If you want to avoid the Mil Cumbres pass take Route 126 from Morelia, via Queréndaro, then turn right 10 km. short of Zitácuaro and join Route 15 (to Toluca and Mexico City) at Huajumbaro. The road is at first flat then climbs and descends again to Maravatio (hotel) and then climbs steeply, towards **Tlalpujahua**, an old mining town with a museum, several churches, and cobblestoned streets, very picturesque among forests and hills. (*Casa de Huéspedes*). There are plenty of places to stop at on the way to Toluca.

(Km. 75) A road branches off to the volcano of Toluca (Nevado de Toluca; 4,583 metres, the fourth highest mountain in Mexico) and climbs to the deep blue lakes of the Sun and the Moon in its two craters, at about 4,270 metres, from which there is a wide and awe-inspiring view. During winter it is possible to ski on the slopes; 5 km. from the entrance is an *Albergue* (US$1) with food and cooking facilities. From here it is 10 km. to the entrance to the crater, where there is a smaller *albergue* (cooking facilities but no food, US$1.50). Trips to the volcano are very popular at weekends; no problem getting a lift to the lakes. If walking remember the entrance to the crater is on the far left side of the volcano. This route, the Mil Cumbres route, is by far the most difficult.

(Km. 64) *Toluca,* population 600,000, altitude 2,639 metres, about 4¾ hrs. from Morelia by bus, is the capital of the state of México. It is known mostly for its vivid Friday market—reportedly less colourful than it used to be— where Indians sell colourful woven baskets, *sarapes, rebozos,* pottery and embroidered goods (beware of pickpockets and handbag slashers). See churches of Tercer Orden and Vera Cruz, convent of Carmen and chapel of S. María de Guadalupe, the new Cathedral, the Palacio de Gobierno, the Museo de Bellas Artes, the botanical garden, called the Cosmo Vitral because of its unique stained-glass decor, Chamber of Deputies, all in centre of city near or on the Zócalo. Also Museo de Arte Popular and Casa de las Artesanías, with excellent display of local artistic products for sale, at corner of Paseo Chamizal and Paseo Tollocán. The new Market is at Calle Manuel Gómez Pedraza Oriente, open daily, big day is Friday. Famous for textiles. (The city is also famous for confectionery and for an alcoholic drink known as *moscos.*)

Hotels   *San Carlos,* Madero 210, C, remodelled; *Morelia,* Hidalgo 615, F without bath, noisy; *Bravo,* Bravo 105, E, near old bus terminal in centre; *Azteca,* Pino Suárez and Hidalgo, F; all the above are in the centre, not many cheap hotels. *Terminal,* adjoining bus terminal, D. **Motels** *Del Rey Inn,* Mexico City road entrance, A, resort facilities.

Tourist Office   Lerdo de Tejada Poniente 101, Edif. Plaza Toluca, 1° piso.

Transport   To Mexico City, US$0.65. Bus to Pátzcuaro, 6 hrs., US$3.10, several daily. Many buses to Tenango de Arista (US$0.25, ½ hrs.), Tenancingo (US$1); also regular buses to Calixtlahuaca US$1.50 (1 hr.) from platform 7. Bus station away from centre. Train from Mexico City 2200, arr. 0025 (Pullman); returns 0509, arr. 0717.

Excursions   A side road runs S of Toluca. Along the road, or reached from it, are a number of most interesting "art and craft" producing villages, all with old churches. The first village is **Metepec,** the pottery-making centre of the valley, 1½ km. off the road to Tenango. The clay figurines made here—painted bright fuchsia, purple, green and gold— are unique. This is the source of the "trees of life and death", the gaudily-painted pottery sold in Mexico. Market is on Mon. Interesting convent. Also off the main highway near Tenango, turning right at La Marquesa, you will come to a sign pointing to Gualupita to the right; just beyond that is the town of *Santiago Tianpuistengo* (38,000). Good *cazuelas, metates,* baskets and *sarapes.* Between July and early November displays of wild mushrooms for sale. Try *gordas* or *tlacoyos,* blue corn stuffed with a broad bean paste. If you are brave try *atepocates;* embryo frogs with tomato and chiles, boiled in maize leaves. Try restaurant *Mesón del Cid,* good regional food, go to kitchen to see choice. Try *sopa de hongos,* mushroom soup. Market day is Tuesday. The town is crowded at weekends.
   The main road descends gradually to *Tenango de Arista* (Toluca-Tenango bus, US$0.25), where one can walk (20 mins.) to the ruins of *Teotenango* (Matlazinca culture, reminiscent of La Ciudadela at Teotihuacán, with 11 ball courts). There is an interesting museum by the ruins of Teotenango; entry to museum and ruins US$0.45; to enter go to the end of town on the right hand side. Restaurant in Tenango: *María Isabel,* cheap, good local food. 48 km. from Toluca the road descends abruptly through gorges to *Tenancingo,* still at 1,830 metres, but with a soft, warm all-the-year-round climate. Nearby is the magnificent 18th century Carmelite convent of El Santo Desierto, making beautiful *rebozos.* The townspeople themselves weave fine *rebozos* and the fruit wines are delicious and cheap. Market day is on Sun. Rec. hotels at Tenancingo are *Lazo,* with clean rooms in annex with shower, E, and *San Carlos,* F, good value. *Hotel Casa Juana* on main plaza, F, good value. There is a small waterfall near the bus station.
   About 11 km. to the E over an improved road is *Malinalco,* from which a path winds up 1 km. to Malinalco (Matlazinca culture, with Aztec additions), certainly one of the most remarkable pre-Hispanic ruins in Mexico, now partly excavated. Here is a fantastic rock-cut temple in the side of a mountain which conceals in its interior sculptures of eagle and jaguar effigies. Visit also the Augustinian convent to see the early frescoes. There is a *fiesta* in Malinalco on January 6. (Camping. Two hotels, one expensive, one cheap. Ester at Ferretería La Provincia in Malinalco arranges accommodation, F, p.p. Swiss-run, open-air restaurant serves local trout, about US$2.50, superb, bring own supplies of beverages, bread, salad.) (Buses Tenancingo-Malinalco, 1 hr.) You can get to Malinalco from Mexico City or Toluca by taking a 2nd class bus to Chalma (see below); Malinalco is the next village along and can be reached by shared taxi for US$0.25 p.p. (Terminal in Mexico City, Central del Poniente, opp. Observatorio, ½ hr. frequency, at least two companies go there.) You can also go to Malinalco from Toluca by leaving the Toluca-Tenancingo road after San Pedro Zictepec, some distance N of Tenancingo, which is gravel surfaced and 28 km. long. Journey will take 45 mins. *Chalma* is a popular pilgrimage spot, and is also where you make connections if coming from Cuernavaca (take a Cuernavaca—Toluca bus to Santa Marta, then wait for a Toluca—Chalma bus).
   On 32 km. from Tenancingo is *Ixtapan de la Sal,* a pleasant forest-surrounded leisure resort with medicinal hot springs. In the centre of this quiet whitewashed town is the municipal spa, adult

admission US$0.55 (massage and facial US$1-4, 20 mins.). At the edge of town is Parque Los Trece Lagos. For the hedonist there are private "Roman" baths, for the stiff-limbed a medicinal hot-water pool, mud baths for the vain, an Olympic pool for swimmers, rowing boats and a water slide for the adventurous. The latter is 150 metres long, prohibited to those over 40 which can lead to plenty of bruises and some nasty clashes with any larger bodies hurtling around (US$1.55 entry, US$0.90 for 2 slides, US$2.20 for slides all day). "The Thirteen Lake Park" is privately run and has a train running around; there are numerous picnic spots. Market day: Sun. *Fiesta*: second Fri. in Lent. *Hotel Ixtapan*, Nuevo Ixtapan, A, food and entertainment included; *Kiss* (*Villa Vergel*), C; *Casablanca*, E; *María Isabel*, good; *Guadalajara*, F, clean, with bath; many others. Plenty of reasonable restaurants on Av. Benito Juárez. Ixtapan de la Sal can also be reached in 2 hrs. by car from Mexico City on Route 55 (turn left off Toluca highway at La Marquesa). The road goes on to Taxco (see page 1057).

From Toluca take bus to pyramids and Aztec seminary of **Calixtlahuaca**, 2 km. off the road to Ixtlahuaca; pyramids are to Quetzalcoatl (circular) and to Tlaloc; they are situated just behind the village, 10 mins. walk from the final bus-stop. Entry US$0.10.

The basin of Toluca, the highest in the central region, is the first of a series of basins drained by the Río Lerma into the Pacific. To reach Mexico City from Toluca—64 km. by new dual carriageway—it is necessary to climb over the intervening mountain range. The centre of the basin is swampy. (Km. 50) Lerma is on the edge of the swamp, the source of the Lerma river. The road climbs, with backward views of the snow-capped Toluca volcano, to the summit at Las Cruces (km. 32; 3,164 metres). There is a good Bavarian restaurant, *La Escondida*, about 100 metres to the left of the Toluca-México road at 38 km., on a beautiful site. There are occasional great panoramic views of the City and the Valley of México during the descent.

MEXICO CITY (5)

Mexico City, the capital, altitude 2,240 metres, founded 1521, was built upon the remains of Tenochtitlan, the Aztec capital, covering some 200 square km. The Valley of México, the intermont basin in which it lies, is about 110 km. long by 30 km. wide. Rimming this valley is a sentinel-like chain of peaks of the Sierra Nevada mountains. Towards the SE tower two tall volcanoes, named for the warrior Popocatépetl and his beloved Ixtaccíhuatl, the Aztec princess who died rather than outlive him: Popocatépetl is 5,452 metres high, and Ixtaccíhuatl (Eestaseewatl) 5,286 metres. Both are snow-capped, but you need to get up early in the morning to see them from the city, because of the smog. To the S the crest of the Cordillera is capped by the wooded volcano of Ajusco.

About 20 million people (one in four of the total population) live in this city, which has over half the country's manufacturing employment, and much of the nation's industrial smog. The last-mentioned makes the eyes of the unaccustomed sore (contact-lens wearers take note).

The city suffers from a fever of demolition and rebuilding, especially since the heavy damage caused by the September 1985 earthquake. Of late years it has burst its ancient boundaries and spread; the new residential suburbs are most imaginatively planned, though there are many appalling shanty-towns. Like all big centres it is faced with a fearsome traffic problem, despite the building of a new inner ring road. The noise can be deafening; Elizabeth Allen tells us that the definition of a split second in Mexico City is the amount of time between the traffic-lights going green and the first horn sounding. To relieve congestion eight underground railway lines are now operating. There is also a large traffic-free area E of the Zócalo.

The 1985 earthquake damage was concentrated along the Paseo de la Reforma, Avenida Juárez, the Alameda, and various suburbs and residential districts. About 20,000 people are believed to have lost their lives, largely in multi-storey housing and government-controlled buildings, including Juárez hospital in which there were about 3,000 fatalities.

Mexico's architecture ranges from Spanish-Baroque to ultra-modern: it is, indeed, fast becoming a city of skyscrapers. The tallest is now the *Hotel de México* in Insurgentes Sur, with a restaurant; US$2.30 just to go up, but the ticket lets you see *son et lumière* in the Siqueiros Polyforum next door (daily exc. Sun., at 1800 in English and 1600 and 1930 in Spanish). The Polyforum includes a

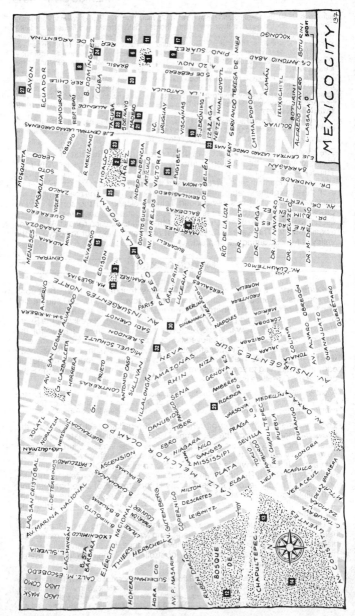

MEXICO CITY 137.

handicraft shop, a "museum of the evolution of man", and huge frescoes by Siqueiros, including the largest mural in the world, inside the huge ovoid dome. Entrance for frescoes, US$1.

Because of the altitude the climate is mild and exhilarating save for a few days in mid-winter. The normal annual rainfall is 660 mm., and all of it falls— usually in the late afternoon—between May and October. Even in summer the temperature at night is rarely above 13°C, and in winter there can be sharp frosts. Despite this, central heating is not common.

Hotels Prices are maximum, including value added tax (but not service), set at Secretaría de Turismo in October 1988 (reductions often available); check if breakfast is included in the room price. Many hotels were destroyed or irreparably damaged by the 1985 earthquake, particularly in the following streets: Paseo de la Reforma, Av. Juárez, Calle Revillagigedo and Calle Luis Moya. Discounts in many hotels if booked through Wagon-Lits México.

Hotels		Double US$ from	Our Price Category
Aristos	Paseo de la Reforma 276	84	L
Camino Real	Mariano Escobedo 700	150	L
Century	Liverpool 152	82	L
Crowne Plaza (Holiday Inn)	Paseo de la Reforma 80	130	L
Diplomático	Av. Insurgentes Sur 1105	42	B
El Stouller Presidente	Campos Eliseos 218	94	L
El Presidente Galerías	Río Tiber	100	L
Fiesta Americana Aeropuerto	Fundidora de Monterrey 89	100	L
Flamingo Plaza	Av. Revolución 333	65	A
Fontan (ex-Purúa Hidalgo)	Colón 27	70	A
Galería Plaza	Hamburgo 195	90	L
Genève Calinda	Londres 130	67	L
Gran Hotel de México	16 de Septiembre 82 (Zócalo)	80	L
Krystal	Liverpool 155	100	L
Majestic	Madero 73	34	B
María Cristina	Lerma 31	67	A
María Isabel Sheraton	Paseo de la Reforma 325	150	L
Nikko	Campos Eliseos 204	139	L
Plaza Florencia	Florencia 61	84	L
Reforma	Paseo de la Reforma y París	130	L
Ritz	Madero 30	38	B
Royal Zona Rosa	Amberes 78	100	L

Motels

Holiday Inn	Blvd. Aeropuerto 502	80	L
Dawn Motor Hote	Mex 57 Highway		B
Park Villa	Gómez Pedraza 68 (near Chapultepec Park)		A

There are fair hotel reservation services at the railway station and at the airport; also services for more expensive hotels at bus stations. A new, rec. good hotel is the *Marco Polo*, on Amberes in the Zona Rosa, A. The *Cortés*, Av. Hidalgo 85, B, is the only baroque-style hotel in Mexico City, a former pilgrims' guest house, with a pleasant patio. *Brasilia*, excellent modern hotel, near Central del Norte bus station, D, on Av. Cien Metros 48-25, king size bed, TV, 24-hr. traffic jam in front. *Bristol*, Plaza Necaxa 17 (T 533-60-60), D, very good; *Carlton*, E, Ignacio Mariscal 32-bis, clean, safe, rec.; *Oxford*, Mariscal 67, E, very clean, radio and TV; *Ejecutivo*, Viena 8, C, staff helpful, rec.; *Hidalgo*, Sta. Veracruz 37, modern, good, D, good 5-course lunch. *Cancún*, Donato Guerra 24, C, safe, clean, rec. *El Romano Diana*, Lerma 237, B; *Fleming*, Revillagigedo 35, D, good value, central; *Palacio Real*, Nápoles 62, apartments, C; *Stella Maris*, Sullivan 69, D; *Versalles*,

---

Key to Map of Mexico City
1. Zócalo; 2. Alameda Central; 3. Plaza de la República; 4. Plaza Ciudadela and market; 5. Templo Mayor; 6. Cathedral; 7. San Fernando; 8. Santo Domingo; 9. Hospital de Jesus Nazareno; 10. Colegio de las Vizcaínas; 11. Palacio Nacional; 12. National Museum of Anthropology; 13. Museum of Modern Art; 14. Castle of Chapultepec; 15. San Carlos Museum; 16. Museum of Popular Arts and Industries; 17. Museum of the City of Mexico; 18. Museum and Monument of the Revolution; 19. Iturbide Palace; 20. Monte de Piedad; 21. Torre Latinoamericana and Casa de los Azulejos; 22. Palacio de la Minería and "El Caballito" statue; 23. Palacio de Bellas Artes; 24. Ministry of Education; 25. Pinacoteca Virreinal; 26. San Juan market; 27. Lagunilla market; 28. Main Post Office; 29. Independence Monument; 30. Monument to Cuauhtémoc; 31. Monument to Colombus; 32. La Madre Monument; 33. Salto del Agua fountain.

G. Prim 59 and Versalles, C; *Prim*, Versalles 46, D, clean, good in all respects; *Catedral*, Donceles 95, behind Cathedral, D, clean, spacious (but bed bugs); *Metropol*, Luis Moya 39, D, touristy, good restaurant, good value, rec.; *Del Valle*, Independencia 35, D, with bath, TV, clean; *Marlowe*, Independencia 17, D, clean, helpful staff, but poor restaurant; *Mallorca*, Serapio Rendón 119, D, clean, reasonable; *Pisa*, Insurgentes Norte 58, E, rec.; *Beverly New York*, Nueva York 301, B, rec.; *Jardín Amazonas*, Río Amazonas 73 (T 533-59-50), C; *Regente*, París 9, D, clean, friendly, noisy at front, restaurant; *Jena*, Jesús Terán 12, D, new, central, rec. (but not the travel agency on the premises). *La Rivera*, Aldama 9, E, with shower, TV and restaurant; *Polanco*, Edgar Poe 8, near Chapultepec, dark, quiet, C, good restaurant; *Sevilla*, Serapio Rendón and Sullivan, C, restaurant, garage, reasonable; *Iberia*, Mina 186 and Zaragoza, F, with private bath, rec., sheets changed every other day, good for buses and trains; *Avenida*, Lázaro Cárdenas 38 (Bellas Artes metro), C with bath, hot water, safe, night porter; *Detroit*, Zaragoza 55, E, very central, clean, rec., has parking.

We have been advised that the best of the cheaper hotels are in the old part of town between the Zócalo and the Alameda, and there are more N of the Plaza República. *Savoy*, Zaragoza, F with shower, clean, good value; *Mayaland*, Maestro Antonio Caso 23, E, with bath, good value, rec.; *Royalty*, Jesús Terán 21, E, clean, phone in room, highly rec.; *Yale*, Mosqueta 200 (near main railway station), E with bathroom, phone and TV, clean and friendly, rec.; *Suiza*, Aldama 99 in Guerrero district, near Delegación de Cuauhtémoc (near bus and railway stations), F, shower, rec., except for noise; *Pontevedra*, Insurgentes Norte opp. railway station, E, clean, helpful, will store luggage; *Isabel la Católica* (street of the same name, No. 63, T 518-12-93) is pleasant, clean, central, quite good restaurant, D, with bath, luggage held; *Gillow*, 5 de Mayo e Isabel la Católica, D, central, large, clean, attractive; *Las Américas*, on Magnolia 61, E, has small free enclosed parking, rates double at weekend; *Santander*, Arista 22, not far from railway station, E, with bath, good value and service, clean; *Buenavista*, Bernal Díaz 34, F, basic, quiet, friendly. *Monte Carlo*, Uruguay 69 (D. H. Lawrence's hotel), clean, friendly owner, E, with bath, good about storing luggage, bit noisy at front, car park inside the hotel premises—small fee, rooms in front noisy, recently renovated; *Concordia*, Uruguay 13, nr. Niño Perdido, excellent, E, lift, phone. *Casa de Huéspedes la Asturiana*, Uruguay 117, in early 17th century house, with cars parked in courtyard, central, near Pino Suárez metro, F, with bath, very good value, cheap 5-course meals for US$2, also good cheap *La Corte* restaurant next door; *Ontario*, Uruguay 87, F, nice exterior but run-down rooms, telephone; on same street, one block away, *Roble*, Uruguay 109 y Pino Suárez, E, with shower, hot water, clean, phone and TV, good; *Casa de los Amigos*, Mariscal 132 (T 705-05-21), near train and bus station, F, use of kitchen, rec., max. 15-day stay, separation of sexes, run by Quakers, breakfast and laundry facilities, safe-keeping for luggage, advance booking recommended; *La Paz*, Mina 141, close to bus stations on Insurgentes, E, with bathrooms. *El Salvador*, Rep. de El Salvador 16, good value E; *Danky*, Donato Guerra 10, E with bath, central, hot water, phone, clean, easy parking (T 546-9960/61), rec.; *República*, Cuba, F, a few blocks from Zócalo, central, clean, pleasant, but not all rooms have windows; *Habana* República de Cuba 77, NW of Zócalo, D, good value; *San Pedro*, Mesones and Pino Suárez, F, clean and friendly, good value. *Congreso*, good, central, F, at Allende 18; *Jardines de Churubusco*, Calzada de Tlalpan 1885, nr. General Anaya metro, excellent value, F; *Antillas*, B. Domínguez 34, E, hot shower, TV, clean, friendly, restaurant. *María Angelo*, Lerma 11, E, with private bath, weekly rates possible, quite pleasant; *Imperio*, Correo Mayor 94, near Zócalo, F, with bath, old fashioned with Mexican residents, sheets changed daily, but noisy early morning and late at night. Near Allende metro are *Rioja*, Av. 5 de Mayo 45, shared or private baths, fairly clean, nosiy at times, well placed, F, rec.; next door (No. 47) is *Canadá*, D, good value; *York* on same street, E, cheaper for longer stays; *Coliseo*, E, with bath, no windows, clean, luggage held, Bolívar 28; *Moderno*, F/E, with bath, clean, not too noisy but not all rooms have windows, on Calle de los Incas 9 (metro Allende) off Honduras 2 blocks from Plaza Garibaldi; *Galicia*, Honduras 11, good; *Galveston*, Insurgentes Sur 50, F, cheap, clean, safe; *Pensión Chacón*, Nayarit and Monterrey, F, clean and good. *Pensión Costa Rica*, Tonalá 260, F, good, friendly; *Hospedaje Estadio* on Coahuila, nr. Insurgentes Sur, F, very clean; *América*, Buena Vista 4 (nr. Revolución metro), E, with bath, clean, good service, rec.; *Londres*, F, Buenavista 5, clean, friendly, occasionally noisy. *Lafayette*, Motolinia 40 and 16 de Septiembre in the Zona 1, E, with bath, and TV, clean, quiet (pedestrian precinct), but check rooms, there's a variety of sizes, watch your luggage; *Buenos Aires*, Motolinia, F, hot shower till 2200, friendly, noisy, cockroaches, will store luggage; *Lepanto*, Guerrero 90, E, set lunch, 6 courses, very good value, modern; *Ambasad*, E, with bath, telephone, TV room, clean, very good value, beside Pino Suárez metro; also nearby *Ambar*, San Jerónimo y Pino Suárez, E, shower, TV, phones in rooms, good service, highly rec. *Meave*, on Meave, 4 blocks from Torre Latinoamericana, F, safe, clean, friendly; *Azores*, Brasil 25, E, helpful, TV, phone; *Casa González*, Lerma y Sena (near British Embassy), D, full board, shower, English spoken by Sr. González, clean, quiet and friendly; *Atlanta*, corner of B. Domínguez and Allende, E, good, quiet, clean and friendly, rec.; *Marina*, opposite, is F, very good; *Patria*, Rep. de El Salvador, nr. Pino Suárez metro, clean, E, but area a bit rough; *Encino*, Av. Insurgentes, 1 block from the railway station, E, clean, private bath; *Managua*, on Plaza de la Iglesia de San Fernando, near Hidalgo metro, E, with bath, phone, TV, good location, car park, very friendly; *Cima*, Av. Alfonso Cevallo 12, 1 street from metro Moctezuma, convenient for Oriente bus terminal, F, clean, shower; *Suites Quinta Palo Verde*, Cerro del Otate 20, Col. Romero de Terreros (Mexico 21 DF) T 554-35-75, C, diplomatic residence turned guest house, near the University; run by German owner/manager, Sr. Günter Böhm, who also conducts personalized tours and expeditions.

Youth Hostels Asociación Mexicana de Albergues de la Juventud, Madero 6, Of. 314, México 1, D. F. Write for information. Mexico City SETEJ hostel at Cozumel 57, Colonia Roma, not far from Chapultepec Park (Sevilla metro, Line 1). Requires Mexican *and* IHS card, very basic, G, not rec. There is a similar organization, CREA, at Of. Oxtopulco No. 40, Col. Oxtopulco, casilla postal 04310. There is a CREA *albergue* (hostel) on Av. Insurgentes Sur y Camino Sta Teresa, Delegación Tlalpan, C.P. 14000, T 573-7740/655-1416. See also Setej, under **addresses** below. Agencia Nacional de Turismo Juvenil on Plaza Insurgentes.

Camp Sites Mexico City has two camp sites, for addresses see American Automobile Association's "Mexico by Motor". There is a trailer-park on Calle Hortensia adjacent to the Av. Universidad, US$4 for 2 plus van, hot water and other facilities. Also *El Caminero*, on Route 99 in the Tlalpan suburb. Or try the parking lot of the Museum of Anthropology.

Restaurants All the best hotels have good restaurants. Note the *Majestic Hotel's* Mexican breakfast, Sat. and Sun. till 1200, excellent, US$5.50, go to terrace on 7th floor, otherwise food mediocre. *Ambassadeurs*, Paseo de la Reforma 12 (swank and high priced); *Prendes*, 16 de Septiembre 12, murals (good European food, moderate); *La Cava*, Insurgentes Sur 2465 (excellent French food and steaks, lavishly decorated as an old French tavern, moderate); *Del Lago*, in exciting modern building in Chapultepec Park, excellent; *Tibet-Hamz*, Av. Juárez 64 (Chinese restaurant specializing in Cantonese and Mexican national dishes, centrally located, nice atmosphere, moderate); *Chalet Suizo*, Niza 37 (very popular with tourists, specializes in Swiss and German food, moderate); *Shirley's*, Reforma 108, real American food, moderate prices, esp. the buffet after midday; *Focolare*, Hamburgo 87 (swank and high priced); *Rivoli*, Hamburgo 123 (a gourmet's delight, high priced); *Jena*, Morelos 110 (deservedly famous, à la carte, expensive); *Sanborn's*, 36 locations (known as the foreigners' home-from-home: soda fountain, drugstore, restaurant, English language magazines, handicrafts, chocolates, etc. try their retsuarnt in the famous 16th century *Casa de los Azulejos*, the "house of tiles" at Av. Madero 17: famous dish is "chilaquiles Sanborns"); *Delmonico's*, Londres 87 and 16 de Septiembre, elegant; *Mesón del Cid*, Humboldt 61, Castilian with medieval menu; *Café Konditori*, Génova 61, Danish open sandwiches; *Mesón del Castellano*, Bolívar y Uruguay, good, plentiful and not too dear, excellent steaks; *Alex Cardini's*, Madrid 21, home of the Caesar Salad. French cuisine at *La Lorraine*, San Luís Potosí 132 (home style), *Les Moustaches*, Río Sena 88, and *La Madelon*, Río Plata 55, home style. *La Marinera*, Liverpool 183, best seafood restaurant in Mexico City. *El Refugio*, Liverpool 166, tourist-oriented, good desserts, check bill carefully.

Reasonable in centre: *Centro Castellano*, Uruguay 16, one flight up; *Café Rosalía*, Eje Lázaro Cárdenas 46. *Reforma*, Reforma 27-1, cheap and good; *Trevi*, Dr. Mora y Colón, at W end of Alameda, good Italian/US/Mexican à la carte and corrida, also cakes and coffee; *Anderson's*, Reforma 400, very good atmosphere, reasonable, excellent local menu. *Sírvase Vd. Mismo*, on Iturbide, near Av. Juárez, fine smorgasbord lunch with choice of 4 hot meals, plus salads and dessert. *Mesón del Perro Andaluz*, Copenhague 26, very pleasant, US$5 for Spanish all-inclusive meal; also in Copenhague, No. 20, *Ginza*, good Japanese. *Centro Catalán*, Bolívar 31, excellent paella (2nd floor). Many economical restaurants in Calle 5 de Mayo: *La Nueva Opera* there has Spanish and Mexican food. *Vasco*, Madero 6, 1st foor and *Español*, Calle López 60, good Spanish food, including roast kid. *Varsovia*, Paseo de la Reforma, Yugoslav food, very good value, also suitable for vegetarians. *Las Fuentes*, Tíber 79 and Liverpool 115, more quantity than quality. *Casa de Húespedes la Asturiana* at Uruguay 117 has enormous corridas at US$2; *París*, El Salvador 91, is good value.

El Vegetariano, Filomeno Mata 13, open 0800-2000, closed Sun., 4-course meal US$3.50. Other vegetarian restaurants: *Comedor Vegetariano No. 4*, Dolores 57, good lunch for US$1. *Chalet Vegetariano*, near Dr. Río de la Loza; *El Bosque*, Hamburgo 15 between Berlín and Dinamarca, rec. Vegetarian restaurant at Motolinia 31, near Madero, is open Mon.-Sat. 1300-1800, reasonably priced. *Yug*, Varsovia 3, excellent and cheap vegetarian, 4-course set lunch US$1.50 (it's worth queuing to get in). Wholewheat bread at *Pastelería Ideal* on 16 de Septiembre 14 (near Casa de Los Azulejos). Health food shop, *Alimentos Naturales*, close to metro Revolución, on P. Arriagal.

Rincón Gaucho, Insurgentes Sur 1162, Argentine food; *La Pérgola*, Londres 107B, in the Zona Rosa, Italian; *Humboldt*, Humboldt 34, off Juárez, friendly and good value; *La Casserole*, Insurgentes Sur near Núcleo Radio Mil building, French; *Rhin*, Av. Juárez, cheap, good, German décor; *Lonchería la Torta*, Av. de la Independencia 16, clean, cheap and very friendly; *El Caminero*, behind *María Isabel Sheraton Hotel*, is an excellent open-air taco restaurant. Many US chain fast-food restaurants. Reasonable *ostionería* (oyster bar) at Bolívar 56, try Baja California Chablis. *Vero's*, Tolstoy 23, Col. Anzures, off Reforma and near Chapultepec Park, very reasonable corridas; many cheap restaurants on Chapultepec, e.g. *El Rico Menudo* at No. 481, comida corrida; *Presente y Futuro*, corner of Independencia and Revillagigedo, good and cheap; also *Anna Capri*, Balderas 91. *Buffet Coyoacán*, on Allende, 50 metres from Frida Kahlo museum, fixed price (about US$4) for unlimited helpings. *Taquería Lobo Bobo*, Insurgentes Sur

2117, mushrooms a speciality; *Beverley Grill*, Reforma 382. *Mr Lee*, Independencia 19-B, Chinese, seafood, good food, value and service; *Victoria*, Bolívar 41, cheap, good Chinese.

San Angel Inn, in San Angel, is excellent and very popular, so book well in advance. (San Angel may be reached by bus from Chapultepec Park or by trolley bus from Metro Taxqueña.) The *Piccadilly Pub*, Copenhague 23, serves British food at its best, especially steak and kidney pie, US$3; very popular with Mexicans and expatriates alike. Similar (and dearer), is *Sir Winston Churchill*, Avila Camacho 67.

Others rec. are *Bellinghausen*, Londres y Niza (Mexican, not German); *Passy*, Amberes 10; *El Nuevo Acapulco*, López 9 (excellent sea food, inexpensive); *Lar*, Río Lerma 86 (opp. British Embassy); *Casa Regional Valenciana*, López 60, 3rd floor; *Ehden*, Correo Mayor 74, 1st floor, open Sun., authentic and reasonably priced Arab food; *Centro Asturiano*, Orizaba and Puebla, Spanish; *Napoleón*, French, and *Viena*, Viennese, in Plaza Popocatépetl; *Café Restaurant Elsa*, Bolívar 44, good vegetable dishes. *La Ya*, Buccarelli, nr. Chinese clock, good value; *Casa Zavala*, on Uruguay between Isabel la Católica and Bolívar, very good, clean and cheap. *El Buen Café*, Sonora 9, has chess sets to lend. *El Reloj*, 5 de Febrero 50, good comida and à la carte; *Pastelería Madrid*, 5 de Febrero 25, one block from *Hotel Isabel la Católica*, good pastries. Also on 5 de Febrero, *Café Blanca*, friendly, reasonably priced food, open till midnight. *Azteca*, Pino Suárez 68, good food. *Fonda del Recuerdo* for excellent mole poblano, Bahía de las Palmas 39A, 17DF, with music. *Club de Periodistas de México*, F. Mata 8, near Calle 5 de Mayo, open to public, OK. More expensive but still good value, *Las Delicias*, Venezuela 41; *El Parador*, Niza 17, good local and international; *La Carreta Rosa*, Hamburgo 96B, good filling meals, reasonably priced; *Lory's de México*, Génova 73, and *La Calesa de Londres*, Londres 102, good meat at both; *Le Gourmet*, Dakota 155, said to be most expensive restaurant in Mexico, and also said to be worth it! Good small restaurants in Uruguay, near *Monte Carlo Hotel*; the *Maple*, next to *Hotel Roble* at No. 109, has been rec. for its comida. Another centre for small restaurants is Pasaje Jacarandas, off Génova: *Llave de Oro* and many others. *Lady Baltimore*, good, cheap and clean, on F. I. Madero. *Francis Drake* on Av. Juárez, reasonable and good. *Gaby*, cheap, friendly, on Calle Palma, near Zócalo. *Lim* on Bucarelli before Morelos, good value comidas. *Grand Chose*, Moya 62, family atmosphere, cheap three-course meals.

A very old restaurant with interesting tile décor and not touristy is the *Café Tacuba*, Tacuba 28; it specializes in Mexican food, very good enchiladas. Cheap cafeterias in Calle Belisario Domínguez. Good breakfasts at *Coliseo*, Bolívar 28. *La Bombi*, corner of Tacuba and Brasil, rec. Typical, non-touristy snack-bar, *Poblanos*, at Heliópolis and Allende in the Tacuba area.

Bars *Opera Bar*, 5 de Mayo near Bellas Artes, good atmosphere, see Pancho Villa's bullet-hole in ceiling. *Bar Jardín*, in the *Hotel Reforma*; *El Colmenar*, Ejido y Eliseo; *Cavalier*, on top of Torre Latinoamericano skyscraper, for sunsets and views at night. *El Morroco*, Club Marrakesh, Calle Florencia.

Cabarets and Night Clubs Every large hotel has one. *El Patio*, Atenas 9; *Passepartout*, Calle Hamburgo, *La Madelon*, Florencia 36; *Gitanerías*, Oaxaca 15, wild gypsy show; *Capri*, on the tourist guided route, to be avoided. *Hotel de Cortés* has Mexican Fiesta incl. meal Sat., entertainment. *El 77*, Calle Londres, Flamenco show. There are many discotheques in the better hotels and scattered throughout town.

Folk Music *Peña El Cóndor Pasa* is a cafeteria, open 1900-0100, closed on Tues., on Rafael Checal, San Angel; it has different folk-music groups every night; get there early. A fine place for light refreshments and music is the *Hostería del Bohemio*, formerly the San Hipólito monastery, near Reforma on Av. Hidalgo 107, metro Hidalgo. Look hard for the entrance: no sign, poetry and music every night from 1700 to 2200, light snacks and refreshments US$1, no cover charge.

Clubs *Sports* Reforma Athletic Club, Hacienda de los Morales, Lomas de Chapultepec; Churubusco Sports Club (golf, tennis, swimming); French Club in San Angel; British, Mexican, and Spanish boating clubs, in Xochimilco, near Mexico City; Polo Club in Lomas de Chapultepec. Club Suiza, Borja 840.

General American Legion, Lucerna 71; Spanish Club, Isabel la Católica 29; YMCA, Av. Ejército Nacional 253; YWCA, corner of Humboldt 62 and Artículo 123 (US$4.80 for single room with bath, good restaurant and laundry); Lions Club, Ures 13; Rotary Club, Londres 15; Automobile Club (Asociación Mexicana Automovilística-AMA), Av. Chapultepec 276; Women's International Club, Humboldt 47; University of Mexico, Paseo Reforma 150; Junior League Library, Iturbide Building, Av. Madero.

Shopping Mexico's "West End", the Zona Rosa (Pink Zone), where most of the fashionable shops and many restaurants are found, is bounded by the Paseo de la Reforma, Av. Chapultepec, Calle Florencia and Av. Insurgentes Sur. Note that most streets in the Zone are called after foreign cities—Londres, Liverpool, Hamburgo, Niza, Amberes (Antwerp), Génova, Copenhague, etc. The handicrafts section is between Liverpool and Hamburgo. There are also many handicraft shops on Av. Juárez. Mexican jewellery and hand-made silver can be bought everywhere. Among the good silver shops are Sanborn's, Calpini, Prieto, and Vendome. There are also good buys in perfumes, quality leather, and suede articles.

San Juan market, Calle Ayuntamiento and Arandas, nr. Salto del Agua metro, good prices for handicrafts, especially leather goods (also cheap fruit); open 0930-1800. The Plaza Ciudadela market (Mercado Central de Artesanías, open 0900-1800 weekdays, Sun. 0900-1400), just off Balderas (metro Juárez), government-sponsored, reasonable and uncrowded, is cheaper, but not for leather, than San Juan; craftsmen from all Mexico have set up workshops here. Mercado Lagunilla on Calle Allende near Plaza de Sta. Cecilia (formerly Garibaldi) has everything from antiques to typical Mexican tourist wares, open Sun. Market in Calle Londres (Zona Rosa) good for silver, but expensive. There is a market in every district selling pottery, glassware, textiles, *sarapes* and jewellery. Try also San Angel market, although expensive, many items are exclusive to it; good leather belts; open Sat. only from about 1100. Mexican tinware and lacquer are found everywhere. Copperware and more in market opp. airmail post office, Aldama 211. Fruit and veg market, Mercado Merced, Metro Merced. Buena Vista craft market, Aldama 187 y Degollado (nearest metro Guerrero), excellent quality. You can bargain in the markets and smaller shops.

Government *artesanía* shop in basement of Siqueiros Polyforum, on Insurgentes Sur. Other sponsored shops: Arts and Crafts of Michoacán and Querétaro, Glorieta del Metro de Los Insurgentes, Locales 14 and 17 (T 525 01 37). Tienda del Arte e Industrias Populares at Juárez 44. Try also Decorask, Pino Suárez 28. Try Fonart, Fondo Nacional para el Fomento de las Artesanías, Av. Patriotismo 691, main office and branches at Av. Juárez 89, Londres 136 (Altos A) in the Zona Rosa, Londres 6 in Colonia Roma, Av. de la Paz 37 in San Angel, Insurgentes Sur 1630 and at Manuel Izaguirre 10 in Ciudad Satélite, with items from all over the country, rec. The Mercado de Artesanías Finas Indios Verdes is at Galería Reforma Norte S.A., F.G.Bocanegro 44 (corner of Reforma Norte, nr. Statue of Cuitlahuac, Tlatelolco); good prices and quality but no bargaining. There is an annual national craft fair in Mexico City, 1st week in Dec. Good selection of onyx articles at the Brunner shop, in Calle Dolores. Víctor, at Av. Madero 10/305, 2nd floor, has genuine, and high quality craft articles. With the extension of the ring roads around the city, hypermarkets are being set up: there are two, Perisur at the extreme S end of the city (with Liverpool, Sears, Sanborn's and Palacio de Hierro), with quite futuristic designs, open Tues.-Fri. 1100-2000, Sat. 1100-2100; and Plaza Satélite at the extreme N end of the city (with Sumesa, Sears and Liverpool), open on Sunday. Luggage repairs (moderate prices) at Rinconada de Jesús 15-G, opposite Museum of the City of Mexico on Pino Suárez, but opening times can be unreliable; better try the shop in Callejon del Parque del Conde off Pino Suárez opp. Hospital de Jesús church.

Handicrafts by Guatemalan refugees are available from the Secretaría de Ayuda a Refugiados Guatemaltecos, Apartado 18-858, T 761-29-98 (please phone or write first). Address is Dr. Arce 25A, Colonia Doctores, near metro Hospital General.

Bookshops   Many good ones, e.g. American Book Store, Madero 25, excellent selection of Penguins and Pelicans, low mark-up, stocks this *Handbook*; Libros, Libros, Libros, Monte Ararat 220, Lomas Barrilaco, T 540-47-78, hundreds of hardback and paperback English titles; Librairie Française, Reforma 250A, for French selection; Librería Británica, Av. de la Paz 23, San Angel; the British bookshop at Serapio Rendón 125 has a second-hand section where you can trade in old books (as long as they're neither even slightly damaged nor "highbrow") and buy new ones, but at poor rates; *Casa Libra*, Monte Athos 350 (Lomas), large stock of second-hand English books; Librería Gandhi, Calle Miguel Angel de Quevedo (metro Quevedo), art books, discs, tapes. Libros y Discos, Madero 1. The *Sanborn* chain has the largest selection of English-language paperbacks, art books and magazines in the country. Second-hand book market on Independencia just past junction with Eje Lázaro Cárdenas has some English books; also Puente de Alvarado, 100 m. from Hidalgo metro, and Dr Bernard 42, metro Niños Héroes.

Photography   Kodak film (Ektachrome, not Kodachrome) is produced in Mexico and is not expensive. Small shops on República de Chile N of Tacuba are cheaper than larger ones S of Av. 5 de Mayo.

Traffic System   The city has two ring roads, the Anillo Periférico around the city outskirts, and the Circuito Interior running within its circumference. In the centre, the system of Ejes Viales has been developed in recent years. It consists of a series of freeways laid out in a grid pattern, spreading from the Eje Central; the latter serves as a focal point for numbering (Eje 2 Poniente, Eje I Oriente etc.). Norte, Sur, Oriente, Poniente refer to the roads' position in relation to the Eje Central. The system is remarkably clear in its signposting with special symbols for telephones, information points, tram stops, etc. Beware of the tram lines—trams, buses, emergency services and plain simple folk in a hurry come down at high speed; and as often as not this lane goes against the normal flow of traffic! Bicycles are permitted to go the wrong way on all roads, which also "adds to the spice of life". **N.B.** Eje Lázaro Cárdenas used to be called Calle San Juan de Letrán.

City Buses   Buses have been coordinated into one system: odd numbers run North-South, evens East-West. Fares 50 pesos, exact fare only. There are 60 direct routes and 48 feeder (SARO) routes. We are informed that thieves and pickpockets haunt the buses plying along Reforma and Juárez. Be careful of your valuables! A most useful route for tourists (and well-known to thieves, so don't take anything you don't require immediately) is No. 76 which runs from Calle Uruguay (about the level of the Juárez Monument at Parque Alameda) along Paseo de la Reforma, beside Chapultepec Park. A new *Peribus* service goes round the entire Anillo Periférico (see Traffic

System). The 100 bus line also insures its passengers: collection of insurance requires presentation of the ticket.

Taxis Taxis are fitted with taximeters, but they are not used now because inflation changes prices so often. Cabs called by radio charge from the time of the call. Fixed-route taxis (VW Kombis) go back and forth on Reforma and its eastern extensions as far as the Zócalo, and on Insurgentes. Number of fingers held out indicates number of seats left. Fares about US$0.10, at driver's discretion. Wave down at special stops on kerb or even from kerb itself. Up to 17 fixed routes. No tip necessary. Fixed-route taxis have to be identified by a lime-green colour, rank taxis by coral and those with no fixed route by yellow.

Agree fares in advance, on basis of time and distance, outside the city. Taxis are very cheap, but the drivers often do not know where the street you want is; try and give the name of the intersection between two streets rather than a number, because the city's numbering can be erratic. When it is raining or dark you may have to agree to pay up to twice the normal amount. There are special tourist taxis, called "Turismo", which are dearer because they have English-speaking drivers, outside the main hotels: arrange the prices beforehand. VW taxis are very cheap, they should be tipped. Unmarked taxis may work out more expensive than marked ones. At all four bus terminals you must buy taxi-tickets at a booth near the door, five persons a taxi. Hired cars with driver are dear.

Metro Maps of the network are usually available from ticket offices at big stations and tourist offices and are displayed at most stations since lines have been extended. There is a metro information service at Insurgentes station on Pink Line which dispenses maps and most interchange stations have information kiosks. (The *Atlas de Carreras*, US$1.65 has a map of Mexico City, its centre and the metro lines marked. Good metro and bus maps at the Anthropology Museum, US$1.25.) All the stations have a symbol, e.g. the grasshopper signifying Chapultepec. There are eight lines in service. 1 from Observatorio (by Chapultepec Park) to Pantitlán in the eastern suburbs. It goes under Av. Chapultepec and not far from the lower half of Paseo de la Reforma, the Mercado Merced, and 3 km. from the airport. 2, from Cuatro Caminos in the NW to the Zócalo and then S above ground to Taxqueña; 3, from Indios Verdes S to the University City (free bus service to Insurgentes); 4, from Santa Anita on the SE side to Martín Carrera in the NE; 5, from Pantitlán, via Terminal Aérea (which is close to gate A of the airport), crossing the green line at La Raza, up to Politécnico; 6, from El Rosario in the NW to Martín Carrera in the NE; 7, from El Rosario in the NW to Barranca del Muerto in the SW; 9 parallels 1 to the S, running from Tacubaya in the W to Pantitlán in the E. Trains are noiseless on rubber wheels. Music is played quietly at the stations. Tickets 50 pesos. If you want to use the metro often, you can buy an *abono* (about US$0.50), which allows you to use the whole system and the 100 bus for 15 days: remember in this case to use the blue entrances to the metro stations, or your *abono* will be lost. Originally a splendidly modern service (virtually impossible to get lost), it is still clean and efficient, although overcrowded at some times. Beware thieves, pickpockets and bag-slashers and women should avoid using the metro when alone between 0800-1000 and after 1630, severe attacks of "roving-hand syndrome" are common—between 1700 and 2100 men are separated from women and children at Pino Suárez, direction Zaragoza. Also beware: no heavy luggage permitted (although at off-peak times the station security guard may allow you on with a back-pack if you carry it in your arms), but medium-sized rucksacks OK. At the Zócalo metro station there is a permanent exhibit about the metro, interesting. At Pino Suárez, station has been built around a small restored Aztec temple. **N.B.** Metro opens 0500 weekdays, 0700 on Sundays. Do not take photos or make sound-recordings in the metro without obtaining a permit and a uniformed escort from metro police, or you could be arrested.

Car Hire Agencies Budget Rent Auto, Reforma 60; Hertz, Revillagigedo 2; Avis, Medellín 14; VW, Av. Chapultepec 284-6; National Car Rental, Insurgentes Sur 1883; Auto Rent, Reforma Norte 604; quick service at Av. Chapultepec 168, T 533-5335 (762-9892 airport); Pamara, Hamburgo 135, T 525-5572—**N.B.** 200 km. free mileage; Odin, Balderas 24-A; and many local firms, which tend to be cheaper. Gasoline is reassuringly cheap.

Entertainments Theatres: Palacio de Bellas Artes (for ballet, songs, dances, also concerts 2-3 times a week), Fábregas, Lírico, Iris, Sullivan, Alarcón, Hidalgo, Urueta, San Rafael and Insurgentes in town and a cluster of theatres around the Auditorio Nacional in Chapultepec Park (check at Tourist Office for details of cheap programmes). Spectaculars (e.g. presidential inauguration) are often staged in the Auditorio Nacional itself. Also in Chapultepec Park is the Audiorama (behind the Castle on the Constituyentes side) where one may listen to recorded classical music in a small open ampitheatre in a charming wooded glade. A request book is provided, for the following day. There may be a free performance of a play in some of the parks by the Teatro Trashumante (Nomadic Theatre). Variety show nightly with singers, dancers, comedians, magicians and ventriloquists, very popular with locals, at Teatro la Blanquita, on Av. Lazaro Cárdenas Sur near Plaza Garibaldi. On Sundays there is afternoon bull-fighting in a vast ring (**see page 1035**) and morning football at the stadium. The balloon sellers are everywhere. Especially rec., the Ballet Folklórico de México, at Palacio de Bellas Artes (**see page 1032**). The Teatro de la Ciudad, Donceles 36 (T 510-2197 and 510-2942) has the Ballet Folklórico Nacional Aztlán.

Cinemas A number show non-Hollywood films in original language (Spanish sub-titles); check *Mexico City News* for details.

Festivals The largest is the Independence celebration on September 15, when the President gives the *grito*: "Viva México" from the Palacio Nacional on the Zócalo at 2300, and rings the Liberty Bell (now, sadly, electronic!). This is followed by fireworks, and on September 16 (0900-1400) there are military and traditional regional parades in the Zócalo and surrounding streets.

Football Sun. midday, Aztec and Olympic stadia (latter has a Rivera mural of the history of Mexican sport); also Thurs. (2100) and Sat. (1700).

Horse Races Hipódromo de las Américas, every Tues., Thurs., Sat. and Sun. almost all the year. Pari-mutuel betting (minimum bet US$0.40). Races begin at 1500, and may be watched from Jockey Club restaurant. Beautiful track with infield lagoons and flamingoes, and plenty of atmosphere. Free entry with a tourist card, just pay the tax.

Jai-Alai Events with the foremost players in the world every day except Friday at the Frontón México across from Monumento a la Revolución, at 1800. It seats 4,000. Theoretically, jackets and ties are needed for admission. The people in the red caps are the *corredores*, who place the bets. Pari-mutuel betting. US$1.

Golf at Chapultepec Golf Club and Churubusco Country Club. These are private clubs, open to visitors only if accompanied by a member. Green fees are high (US$20 upwards).

Hiking Every weekend with the Alpino and Everest clubs. Club de Exploraciones de México, Juan A.Mateos 146, Col. Obrero, DF 06800, T 578-5730, 1930-2400 Wed. or Fri. organizes several walks in and around the city on Sats. and Suns.

Swimming Agua Caliente, Las Termas, Balneario Olímpico, Elba, Centro Deportivo Chapultepec and others.

Charreadas (Cowboy displays), Rancho Grande de La Villa, at very top of Insurgentes Norte (nearest metro Indios Verdes, then walk N beyond bus station and keep asking), Sun. 1100-1500, US$1.30.

Exchange Banks 0900-1330 (closed Sat.); Banco de Comercio (Bancomer, Visa agent), head office at Av. Universidad 1200, also Venustiano Carranza y Bolívar; Banco Nacional de México (Banamex), Av. Isabel la Católica 44 (entrance for exchange on Calle Palmas), said to give best exchange rates (this branch is a converted baroque palace, ask the porter for a quick look into the patio; another worthwhile building is the bank's branch at Madero 17 with Gante); Banca Serfín, corner of 16 de Septiembre y Bolívar; Citibank, Av. Insurgente Sur, for Citicorp travellers' cheques. Apparently many banks carry the Eurocard symbol but do not in fact recognize the card. These include at least some of the branches of the Banco del Atlántico. American Express office at Reforma 234 will change cheques on Sats., 0930-1330, open Mon.-Fri. until 1800; cambio opposite *María Isabel Sheraton*, Paseo de la Reforma, between Niza and Génova, is open weekends; and many others. One can exchange into pesos at the airport from 0400 daily, but only US$500-worth back into dollars after you have passed through customs when leaving. Casa de Cambio Alameda, Londres 118, Zona Rosa, all main currencies negotiable. Impossible to exchange Guatemalan quetzales, Belizean dollars, cruzados and other "exotics".

Addresses Always check location of embassies and consulates; they tend to move frequently. Most take 24 hrs. for visas; check to make sure you have a visa and not just a receipt stamp.
British Embassy, Calle Río Lerma 71. T 207-20-89 (Apartado 96 bis, Mexico 5). Consular Section at Calle Usumacinta 30, immediately behind main Embassy Building. Reading room in main building. Poste restante for 1 month.
British Chamber of Commerce, Río Tiber 103, 6th floor, Cuauhtémoc, T 533-24-53.
Guatemalan Embassy, Explanada 1025, Lomas de Chapultepec, 11000 México DF, T 520-27-94, a.m. only; tourist card costs US$1; visa issued on the spot, must be used within one month from date of issue, now costs US$10 payable only in US currency, no photo for UK passports. Open 0900-1330. No visa required by Canadian citizens.
Nicaraguan Consulate, Nuevo León 144, nr. Parque España, 1st floor, visas for 30 days from date of issue, 2 photographs, US$11, one-day wait. Embassy is at Sierra Villagran, Ahumada 36, T 553-9791.
Honduran Consulate, Calle Alfonso Reyes 220, T 515-6689 (open 1000-1600), visas issued on the spot (no waiting) valid up to one year from date of issue US$3.
Salvadorean Embassy, Paseo de las Palmas 1930, Lomas de Chapultepec, T 596-33-90 (colectivo Las Palmas from Reforma or from Auditorio metro).
Panamanian Embassy, Cincinnati 40, Suite 402, Colonia Nápoles, T 563-9206.
Costa Rican Embassy, Río Póo 113, T 525-7764 (metro Insurgentes).
Belizean Embassy, Thiers, 152-B, Anzures. Delegación Miguel Hidalgo (metro Polanco), México DF, T 203-5642/5960, open 0900-1300 Mon.-Fri., visa US$10, takes a day.
USA Embassy, Reforma 305.
Canadian Embassy, Schiller 529 (corner Tres Picos), nr. Anthropological Museum. T 254-3288.

Australian Embassy, Plaza Polanco Torre B, Jaime Balmes 11, 10th floor, Colonia Los Morales, T 395-9988/9187.

New Zealand Embassy, Homero 229, 8th floor (metro Polanco).

West German Embassy, Byron 737, Colonia Rincón del Bosque. T 545-66-55.

French Embassy, Havre 15, near the Cuauhtémoc Monument, T 533-13-61.

Netherlands Embassy, Monte Urales 635-203 (near Fuente de Petróleos), T 540-7788.

Swedish Embassy, Edificio Plaza Comermex, Blvd. M. Avila Camacho 1-6, T 540-63-93.

Danish Embassy, Tres Picos 45, near Canadian ditto.

Finnish Embassy, Monte Pelvoux 111, 4th floor, 11000, Mexico, D.F., T 540-6036.

Swiss Embassy, Hamburgo 66, 5th floor. T 533-07-35.

Israeli Embassy, Sierra Madre 215.

Colombian Consulate, Reforma 195, 3rd floor, will request visa from Bogotá by telegram (which you must pay for) and permission can take up to a month to come through.

Chief Telegraph Office for internal telegrams, Palace of Communications and Transport, Plaza Senado de la República, off Calle Tacuba. For international telegrams, **see page 1134**.

Mountain Rescue, Socorro Alpino, Eje Lázaro Cárdenas 80-305. Open after 1900 weekday evenings.

American Community School of Mexico, complete US curriculum to age of 12, Observatorio and Calle Sur 136, T 516-67-20.

American Chamber of Commerce, Lucerna 78.

Benjamin Franklin Library, Londres 116.

Anglo-Mexican Cultural Institute (with British Council Library), Maestro Antonio Caso 127. T 566-61-44. Keeps British newspapers.

Instituto Mexicano Norteamericano, Hamburgo 115; 3-week intensive and painless courses in Spanish, US$150, 3 hrs. a day; free, excellent concerts, art exhibits, conversation club, reading-room, bulletin board advertising rooms. Instituto Italiano has the same courses, but less crowded. The Universidad Nacional Autónoma de México (Unam) offers cheap 6-week courses which include history lectures, US$300, 4 hrs. a day.

Goethe-Institut, Tonalá 43 (metro Insurgentes), 0900-1300, 1600-1930.

Instituto Francés de la América Latina, Nazas 43, free films every Thurs. at 2030.

Setej (Mexican Students' Union), Hamburgo 273, Zona Rosa, Metro Sevilla, only office to issue student card, which is required to buy a hostel card, T 514-42-13 or 511-66-91, deals with ISIS insurance. Student cards not available at Setej Youth Hostel on Calle Cozumel 57 (T 514-9230/4210).

International Post Office (Customs) Calle Aldama 218, Colonia Guerrero, near Revolución metro, open until 1800—airmail only (only until 1400 for parcels). Surface parcels can be sent directly from Aduana Postal, Ceylan 468 (open 0900-1300, nearest metro La Raza, then EJ63 Norte buses 11 or 12 along Av. Cuitlahuac to Ceylan, or taxi—US$3).

Spanish Classes See above under *Instituto Mexicano Norteamericano*.

English-Speaking Churches Roman Catholic—St. Patrick's, Calle Bondojito; Evangelical Union—Reforma 1870; Baptist—Capital City Baptist Church, Calle Sur 136; Lutheran—Church of the Good Shepherd, Palmas 1910; Christ Church, Monte Escandinavos 405, Lomas de Chapultepec; First Church of Christ Scientist— 21 Dante, Col. Anzures. Jewish—Beth Israel, Virreyes 1140.

American British Cowdray Hospital, or the ABC, to give it its popular name, on Observatorio past Calle Sur 136. T 277-5000 (emergency: 515-8359); very helpful.

Medical Services C. German, Calle Eucker No. 16-601, T 545-94-34. Dr. César Calva Pellicer (who speaks English, French and German), Copenhague 24, 3° piso, T 514-25-29. Dr Smythe, Campos Elíseos 81, T 547-78-61, rec. by US and Canadian Embassies. For any medical services you can also go to the Clínica Prensa, US$ 1.20 for consultation, subsidized medicines. Hospital de Jesús Nazareno, 20 de Noviembre 82, Spanish-speaking, friendly, US$4 to consult a doctor, drugs prescribed cheaply. It is a historical monument (**see page 1032**). Most embassies have a list of recommended doctors and dentists who speak foreign languages.

Vaccination Centre Benjamín Hill 14, near metro Juanacatlán (Line 1), near Soviet Embassy. Open Mon.-Fri. 0830-1430, 1530-2030, avoid last half hour, also open on Sat. from 0830-1430; typhoid free (this is free all over Mexico), cholera and yellow fever (Tues. & Fri. only) US$2. For hepatitis shots you have to buy gamma globulin in a pharmacy (make sure it's been refrigerated) and then an injection there (cheap but not always clean) or at a doctor's surgery or the ABC Hospital (see above). Malaria prophylaxis and advice free from San Luis Potosí 199, 6th floor, Colonia Roma Norte, 0900-1400. Also from Dr Francisco Biagi, Paseo de las Palmas 403, T 524-96-40, highly recommended.

Pharmacies *Farmacía Homeopática*, Calle Mesones 111-B. Twenty-four hour pharmacy at *Farmacía Arrocha* off the Periférico next to Hospital de Seguro Social. *Sanborn's* chain and *El Fénix* discount pharmacies are the largest chains with the most complete selection.

Laundromat Laundry on Nápoles just off Av. Chapultepec, 3 kg. for US$2. Also on Río Danubio, between Lerma and Panuco and at Chapultepec and Toledo, nr. Sevilla metro. Lavandería Automática Atoyac, Atoyac 69, near Chapultepec Metro station, one block N of Reforma, corner C. Elba. Also at Parque España 14.

Telephones The LADA system provides a range of useful services: Long distance— Dial 91 + town code + the number. There is a 25% discount between 1900 and 2200, and a 50% one between 2200 and 0700. International—Dial 95 for US and Canada. Discounts of 11%-34% are available depending on when you ring and where to. Dial 04 for exact information. Dial 98 for the rest of the world. Other services—92 person to person; 01 Directory enquiries; 02 Long distance; 03 Talking clock; 04 Ex-Directory; 05 Engineers; 09 International and Collect. Calls abroad can be made only from Parque Via 198 from 0800-2130 and at the International Airport.

The **Mexican Secretariat of Tourism** is at Calle Masarik 172, between Hegel and Emerson, Colonia Polanco (reached by bus No. 32), T 250-85-55. Booking of hotels in other parts of the country possible here. There is another office at corner of Londres and Amberes, Zona Rosa. You may refer complaints here, or to the tourist police, in blue uniforms, who are reported to be very friendly. Articles from the various craft displays can be bought. Free maps not always available, but try Mexico City Chamber of Commerce, Reforma 42, which provides maps and brochures of the city; may otherwise be got from Department of Public Works; or buy in bookshops. Bus and metro maps available. Office hours: 0800-1900, closed Sat. and Sun. Information bureau outside Insurgentes metro station. Tourist information can be dialled between 0800 and 2000 (bilingual operator) on 250-01-23. Incidentally, museums are closed Mon., except Chapultepec Castle, which is open daily. A weekly magazine, *Tiempo Libre*, covers what's on in Mexico City.

Maps Centro de Asesoría y Distribución de Información Estadística y Cartografía, Balderas 71 (mezzanine), México 1, D.F. T 585-70-55, ext. 287. Three times a year it publishes an Inventario de Información Geográfica with a list of all maps published. **Instituto Nacional de Estadística Geografía e Informática (INEGI)** sells maps and has information, branches throughout the country and in the Distrito Federal at Insurgentes Sur 795 p.b., Río Rhin 56 and at the airport, Local 61.

Travel Agencies Corresponsales de Hoteles will make reservations for high-category hotels in other Mexican towns, Av. Morelos 20, 7th floor, very friendly. Trailways, Londres 161, No. 48, T 525-20-50; Hadad y Asociados Professionales de Viajes, Miguel Noreña 39, Col. Sn. José Insurgentes, C.P. 03900, T 523-7664/687-0488, arranges mileage tickets; Wells Fargo & Co. Express, Calle Niza 22; Viajes Bojórquez, Av. Juárez 98, very good tours arranged; Thomas Cook, about 11 branches, main office Av. Juárez 88; Uniclam agent in Mexico City is Srta. Rosa O'Hara, Río Pánuco 146, Apto 702, Col. Cuauhtémoc, T 525-53-93. American Express, Reforma 234 y Havre, T 533-03-80, open Mon.-Fri. 0900-1800, Sat. 0900-1300, charges US$3-4 for poste restante if you do not have their travellers' cheques and US$1 if no card or cheques are held for other services. Service slow and you must be firm if you want something. Turistoria, Insurgentes Centro 114, Room 209 (T 535-94-88) takes people to *fiestas* in different parts of the country, tours from ½ day to a few days—speaking Spanish an advantage. Recommended guide, Prof. Juan Cazares López, T 784-58-21, who can be found at the Templo Mayor museum on Sundays. Recommended guide/taxi driver: Raúl Méndez Guerrero, Frontera 80, Dpto. 6, T 536-88-97. For cheap tickets to Cuba, ask round agencies around Hamburgo.

Railways The central station is on Insurgentes Norte, junction Alzate with Mosqueta, nearest metro Revolución or Guerrero. For details of train services, see destinations in text. The *Servicio Estrella*, with reserved reclining seats or in a/c cars, or single and double sleepers, all meals included, has been highly rec. Reservations T 547-3190/4114/5819; information T 547-1084/1097/6593.

International Airport, 13 km. from city. There are five access points: A. Aeroméxico arrivals; B. Departure for internal flights (US$4.50 tax); C. Internal arrivals; D. International departures (US$10 tax); E. International arrivals. The Instituto Nacional de Bellas Artes has a permanent exhibition hall and there is an interesting mural *La Conquista del Aire por el Hombre* by Juan O'Gorman. Telephone calls abroad from booth 19 (0600-2200) and booth 8 (0700-2300). Mexicana bookings in annex by C and Aeroméxico bookings and timetable booklets from near A. Opp. point E, cars are rented. Fixed-price taxis from despatcher's office at exit; about US$4 to Alameda. Buy pesos opp. D and B, open 24 hrs. Near C is a post office, with telegraph and telex. Left luggage on 1st floor. Journey about 20 mins. from town centre if there are no traffic jams. Línea Gris, Londres 166 (T 533-15-40 and 533-16-65), does hotel pick-up service for airport at US$6 per head. (A traveller has rec. Taxi Mex.) Taxi to airport US$10; marked taxis usually cheaper than unmarked. There are regular buses to the airport (e.g. No. 20, along N side of Alameda) but the drawback is that you have to take one to Calzada Ignacio Zaragoza and transfer to trolley bus at the Boulevard Puerto Aéreo (i.e. at metro station Aeropuerto). Buses to airport may be caught every 45 mins. until 0100 from outside *De Carlo Hotel*, Plaza República 35. It takes an hour from downtown and in the rush hour— most of the day—it is jam-packed. But you can take baggage if you can squeeze it in. See under "Metro" on how to get to airport cheaply, if you have no heavy luggage. The Mexican Hotel Association desk at the airport will call any hotel on its list and reserve a room for you, also has a collective taxi which will drop you at your hotel, but it does not open until 1000.

Long-distance Buses   For details of bus services, see destinations in text. Buses to destinations in N. Mexico, including US borders, leave from **Central del Norte**, Avenida Cien Metros 4907 where there is also a tourist information kiosk (Spanish-speaking only, closed at 1630) which at times issues street plans and will make reservations for hotels. The bus station is on metro line 5 at Autobuses del Norte. City buses marked Cien Metros or Central del Norte go directly there. Central del Sur, at corner of Tlalpan 2205 across from metro Taxqueña (line 2), serves Cuernavaca, Acapulco, Zihuatanejo areas. Direct buses to centre (Donceles) from Central del Sur, and an express bus connects the Sur and Norte terminals. It is difficult to get tickets to the S, book as soon as possible; the terminal for the S is chaotic. The Central del Poniente is situated opposite the Observatorio station of line 1 of the metro, to serve the W of Mexico; check luggage in 30 mins before bus departure. You can go to the centre by bus from the "urbano" terminal outside the Poniente terminal (US$0.08). The Central del Oriente is opp. metro San Lázaro (line 1), Calzada Ignacio Zaragoza, for buses to Veracruz, Yucatán and South East, incl. Oaxaca (it has a tourist information office open from 1000). All bus terminals operate taxis with voucher system and there are long queues. It is much easier to pay the driver. However, make sure you don't part with the voucher until you're safely in the taxi. In the confusion some drivers move each other's cabs to get out of the line faster and may take your voucher and disappear. About US$2.20 to Zócalo area, US$3 to Zona Rosa. Advance booking is rec. for all trips, and very early reservation if going to *fiestas* during Holy Week, etc. At Christmas, many Central American students return home via Tapachula and buses from Mexico City are booked solid for 2 weeks before, except for those lines which do not make reservations. You must go and queue at the bus stations; this can involve some long waits, sometimes 2-2½ hrs. Even if you are travelling, you may sometimes be required to buy a *boleto de andén* (platform ticket) at many bus stations.

Bus Companies: (tickets and bookings) Going N: Transportes del Norte, at Av. Insurgentes Centro 137, nr. Reforma (T 5460032 and 5355084); dep. from Central Norte. Omnibus de México, Insurgentes Norte 42, at Héroes Ferrocarrileros (T 5676756 and 5675858). Greyhound bus, Reforma 27, closed Sun.; information at Central Norte from 1100-1500, T 5678444 and 5678426. Going to Central States: Autobuses Anáhuac, Bernal Díaz 8 (T 5468382 and 5910533); Central Norte departures. Going NW: Tres Estrellas de Oro, Calzada de Niño Perdido 19A (T 5789888), Central Norte. Going NE: ADO, Av. Cien Metros 4967 (T 5678364 and 5678076). Going S (incl. Guatemala) Cristóbal Colón, Blvd. Gral Ignacio Zaragoza 38. T 5719128; from Central del Oriente; also ADO, Buenavista 9 (T 5660055 and 5467448). Going SW: Estrella de Oro, Calzada de Tlalpan 2205 (T 5498520 to 29).

Sightseeing in and around the city can easily take up ten days. The main places of interest are listed below.

You will find, as you explore the city, that you use two thoroughfares more than any others. The most famous is Paseo de la Reforma, with a tree-shaded, wide centre section and two side lanes; it runs somewhat diagonally NE from Chapultepec Park. At the Plaza de la Reforma it bends eastwards and becomes Avenida Juárez, still fairly wide but without side lanes. Beyond the Palacio de Bellas Artes this becomes Av. Madero, quite narrow, with one-way traffic. The other and longer thoroughfare is Av. Insurgentes, a diagonal north-south artery about 25 km. long. Reforma and Insurgentes bisect at a *plazuela* with a statue of Cuauhtémoc, the last of the Aztec emperors.

The Zócalo, the main square, or Plaza Mayor, centre of the oldest part barred to wheeled traffic 1000-1700 Mon.-Fri., is always alive with people, and often vivid with official ceremonies and celebrations. On the north side, on the site of the Great Teocalli or temple of the Aztecs, is

The Cathedral, the largest and oldest cathedral in Latin America, designed by Herrera, the architect of the Escorial in Spain, along with that in Puebla; first built 1525; rebuilding began 1573; consecrated 1667; finished 1813. Singularly harmonious, considering the many architects employed and time taken to build it. Restoration work has been completed. There is an underground crypt reached by stairs in the W wing of the main part of the building, open 0900-1330. Next to the Cathedral is the **Sagrario Metropolitano,** 1769, with fine churrigueresque façade. Behind the Cathedral at the corner of Av. Guatemala and Calle Seminario are the Aztec ruins of the **Templo Mayor** or *Teocalli*, which were found in 1978 when public works were being carried out. They are open to the public between 0900 and 1700, a very worthwhile visit, especially since the Aztecs built a new temple every 52 years, and 7 have been identified on top of each other. The sculptured, dismembered body of the Aztec goddess of the moon, Coyolxauhqui, was found here. A **Museum** was opened in 1987 behind the temple, to house various sculptures found there, including the altar of stone of the moon goddess (recommended). On the W side of the Zócalo are the Portales de los Mercaderes (Arcades of the Merchants), very busy since 1524. North of them, opposite the Cathedral, is

The Monte de Piedad (National Pawnshop) established in the 18th century and housed in a

1. Zócalo
2. Chapultepec Park
3. Plaza de las Tres Culturas
4. Basílica of Guadalupe
5. Los Indios Verdes
6. Hipódromo de las Américas
7. Plaza México
8. Villa Obregón
9. Coyoacán
10. Churubusco
11. Anahuacalli
12. University City
13. Olympic Stadium
14. Aztec Stadium
15. Secretariat of Tourism

☐ area of detailed map.

MEXICO CITY
ORIENTATION MAP 137A

16th-century building. Prices are government controlled and bargains are often found. Monthly auctions of unredeemed pledges.

The Palacio Nacional (National Palace) takes up the whole eastern side of the Zócalo. Built on the site of the Palace of Moctezuma and rebuilt in 1692 in colonial baroque, with its exterior faced in the red volcanic stone called *tezontle;* the top floor was added by President Calles in the 1920s. It houses various government departments and the Juárez museum (open Mon.-Fri., 1000-1800), free. Over the central door hangs the Liberty Bell, rung at 2300 on September 15 by the President, who gives the multitude the *Grito*—"Viva México!" The thronged frescoes around the staircase are by Diego Rivera (including *The History of Mexico*). Open daily; guides: ask them for the US$2 booklet on the frescoes. Other murals by Rivera can be seen at the Ministry of Education, four blocks N of Zócalo, on corner of Cuba and Argentina. In the Calle Moneda and adjoining the back of the Palace is the **Museo de las Culturas,** with interesting international archaeological and historical exhibits. Open 0930-1800; closed Suns. Also in Moneda are the site of the first university in the New World (building now dilapidated), the Archbishop's Palace, and the site of the New World's first printing press.

Wax Museum in a remarkable house at Londres 6, 1100-1900 daily.

Museo de Artes e Industrias Populares de México Av. Juárez 44, is reported to be less extensive than it was. Open Tues.-Sat. 1000-1400 and 1500-1800, shop 1000-1800 Mon.-Sat. Free. Operated by Instituto Nacional Indigenista (INI). It has well-arranged permanent exhibitions and the articles are for sale, although you may prefer to find cheaper goods at Ciudadela market (20% cheaper).

Supreme Court, opposite Palacio Nacional, on SE corner of the Zócalo, see frescoes by Orozco.

Palacio de Bellas Artes, a large, showy building, interesting for Art Deco lovers, houses a museum and a theatre, and a *cafetería* at mezzanine level (light, average continental food at moderate prices). Open Tues.-Sun., 1100-1800. Its domes are lavishly decorated with coloured stone. The museum has old and contemporary paintings, prints, sculptures, and handicraft articles. The fresco by Rivera is a copy of the one rubbed out in disapproval at Radio City, New York, and there are spirited Riveras in the room of oils and water-colours. Other frescoes are by Orozco, Tamayo and Siqueiros. Daily, 1000-1730; Sun., 1000-1400. The most remarkable thing about the theatre is its glass curtain designed by Tiffany. It is solemnly raised and lowered—for a fee—on Sun. mornings between 0900 and 1000. The Palace is listing badly, for it has sunk 4 metres since it was built. Operas are performed; there are orchestral concerts and performances by the superb Mexican Folklore Ballet on Wed., Sat. and Sun.—one must book in advance. Tickets from US$5 to US$10 (cheap balcony seats are good value as they provide a good vantage point to see formations from above). Tickets on sale from 1100. Cheap concerts at 1200 on Sun., and also at Teatro Hidalgo, behind Bellas Artes on Hidalgo, at the same time.
Across the road, on the 41st floor of the Torre Latinoamericana, is a good restaurant and bar with splendid views of the city, especially at sunset and after dark (entry fee US$2.20). This great glass tower dominates the **Alameda Gardens,** once the Aztec market and later the place of execution for the Spanish Inquisition. Beneath the broken shade of eucalyptus, cypress and ragged palms, wide paths link fountains and heroic statues. (Much rebuilding going on in this area.)
On the northern side of the Alameda, on Av. Hidalgo, is the Jardín Morelos, flanked by two old churches: Santa Veracruz (1730) to the right and San Juan de Dios to the left. The latter has a richly carved baroque exterior; its image of San Antonio de Padua is visited by those who are broken-hearted for love. A new museum, the **Franz Mayer**, has been opened at the Hospital de San Juan de Dios, next to the church, with fine exhibitions of Mexican decorative arts, paintings and sculpture (open 1000-1700 except Mon., free on Sun.).

Escuela Nacional Preparatoria, N of Zócalo on Calle San Ildefonso, built 1749 as the Jesuit School of San Ildefonso in splendid baroque. There are some exciting frescoes by Orozco and (in the Anfiteatro Bolívar, which you will have to ask a guard to open up for you) by Diego Rivera and Fernando Leal.

Ministry of Education, on Argentina, 3 blocks from Zócalo, built 1922, contains frescoes by a number of painters. Here are Diego Rivera's masterpieces, painted between 1923 and 1930, illustrating the lives and sufferings of the common people.

Plaza Santo Domingo, two blocks N of the Cathedral, an intimate little plaza surrounded by fine colonial buildings: (a) a beautiful palace; (b) on the west side, the Arcades of Santo Domingo, where public scribes and owners of small hand-operated printing presses still carry on their business; (c) on the north side, the church of Santo Domingo, in Mexican baroque, 1737. Note the carving on the doors and façade; (d) the old School of Medicine, where the tribunals of the Inquisition were held (we are told that by standing on tiptoe in the men's room one can see—if tall enough—through the window into the prison cells of the Inquisition, which are not yet open to the public). There is a remarkable staircase in the patio, and striking Siqueiros murals above it. The nearby streets contain some fine examples of colonial architecture.
Two blocks E of Santo Domingo are the church and convent of **San Pedro y San Pablo** (1603), both massively built and now turned over to secular use. A block N is the public market of Abelardo L. Rodríguez, with striking mural decorations.

Church of Loreto, built 1816 and now tilting badly, but being restored, is on a square of the same name, surrounded by colonial buildings. Its façade is a remarkable example of "primitive" or "radical" neoclassicism.

La Santísima Trinidad (1677, remodelled 1755), to be seen for its fine towers and the rich carvings on its façade.

The Mercado Merced (metro Merced), said to be the largest market in all the Americas, dating back over 400 years. Its activities spread over several blocks. In the northern quarter of this market are the ruins of La Merced monastery; the fine 18th century patio is almost all that survives; the courtyard, on Avenida Uruguay, between Calle Talavera and Calle Jesús María, opposite No. 171, is nearly restored.
The oldest hospital in continental America, **Jesús Nazareno**, 20 de Noviembre 82, founded 1526 by Cortés, was remodelled in 1928, save for the patio and staircase. Cortés' bones have

been kept since 1794 in the adjoining church, on the corner of Pino Suárez and República de El Salvador, diagonally opp. Museum of the City.

Avenida Madero leads from the Zócalo W to the Alameda. On it is **La Profesa** church, late 16th century, with a fine high altar and a leaning tower. The 18th century **Iturbide Palace,** Av. Madero 17, once the home of Emperor Agustín (1821-23), has been restored and has a clear plastic roof—wander around, it is now a bank head office. To the tourist the great sight of Av. Madero, however, is the **Casa de los Azulejos** (House of Tiles) at the Alameda end of the street. Now occupied by Sanborn's Restaurant, it was built in the 16th century, and is brilliantly faced with blue and white Puebla tiles. The staircase walls are covered with Orozco frescoes. (There are more Orozco frescoes at Biblioteca Iberoamericana on Cuba between 5 de Febrero and Argentina.) Over the way is the **Church of San Francisco**, founded in 1525 by the "Apostles of Mexico", the first 12 Franciscans to reach the country. It was by far the most important church in colonial days. Cortés' body rested here for some time, as did Iturbide's; the Viceroys attended the church.

Beyond San Francisco church, Eje Lázaro Cárdenas, formerly Calle San Juan de Letrán, leads S towards **Las Vizcaínas,** at Plaza Las Vizcaínas, one block E, built in 1734 as a school for girls; some of it is still so used, but some of it has become slum tenements. In spite of neglect, it is still the best example of colonial secular baroque in the city. Not open to the public; permission to visit sometimes given.

Museo San Carlos, Puente de Alvarado 50 (metro Revolución), a 19th-century palace (open to visitors 1000 to 1700, closed Mon.), has fine Mexican colonial painting and a first-class collection of European paintings. The **Escuela Nacional de Artes Plásticas** at the corner of Academía and Calle Moneda, houses about 50 modern Mexican paintings. There is another picture gallery housing a collection of colonial paintings, the **Pinacoteca Virreinal**, in the former church of San Diego in Calle Dr. Mora, at the west end of the Alameda. (Cheap concerts on Thurs. at 2000.)

Moving eastwards along Av. Hidalgo, before the Palace of Fine Arts, on the right is the **Post Office**, built 1904, open for letters 0800-2400 Mon.-Fri., 0800-2000 Sat., and 0900-1600 Sun. For parcels open 0900-1500 Mon.-Fri. only; parcels larger than 2 kilograms not accepted and difficult to send things other than books, records and cassettes. Mail kept for only 10 days at poste restante window 3, rec. **(see page 1134)**. If they can't find your mail under the initial of your surname, ask under the initials of any other names you may happen to have.

North from the west side of the Post Office leads to the Calle Santa María la Redonda, at the end of which is **Plaza Santiago de Tlatelolco**, next oldest Plaza to the Zócalo, heavily damaged in the 1985 earthquake. Here was the main market of the Aztecs, and on it, in 1524, the Franciscans built a huge church and convent. This is now the Plaza of the Three Cultures (Aztec, colonial and modern): (a) the Aztec ruins have been restored; (b) the magnificent baroque church of Santiago Tlatelolco is now the focus of (c) the massive, multi-storey Nonoalco-Tlatelolco housing scheme, a garden city within a city, with pedestrian and wheeled traffic entirely separate. It sustained serious earthquake damage.

About 4 blocks N of the Post Office off Eje Lázaro Cárdenas is **Plaza Garibaldi**, a must, especially on Saturday night, when up to 200 *mariachis* in their traditional costume of huge sombrero, tight silver-embroidered trousers, pistol and *sarape*, will play your favourite Mexican serenade for US$4. If you arrive by taxi you will be besieged. The whole square throbs with life and the packed bars are cheerful, though there is some danger from thieves and pickpockets. The Lagunilla market is held about 4 blocks NE of the plaza, a hive of activity all week. Inexpensive nearby bar is *Guadalajara*: good drinks (but no soft drinks), dancing to *mariachi* band, entrance US$1, not dear. If very crowded, try *Tenampa*, somewhat dearer. On one side of Plaza Garibaldi is a gigantic eating hall, different stalls sell different courses, very entertaining.

Palacio de Minería, Calle Tacuba 9 (1797), is a fine old building, now restored, and once more level on its foundations. (Cheap concerts on Sun. at 1700, upstairs.) Moved from the Plaza de la Reforma to Plaza Manuel Tolsa opposite the Palacio is the great equestrian statue, "El Caballito", of King Charles IV cast in 1802; it weighs 26 tons and is the second-largest bronze casting in the world.

Museo Nacional de Arte, Tacuba 8, opp. Palacio de Minería, nr. main Post Office. Open Tues-Sun., 1000-1800; paintings, sculptures, objects from pre-hispanic times to modern artists. Entry US$0.20.

Along the S side of the Alameda, running E, is Av. Juárez, a fine street with a mixture of old and new buildings. Diego Rivera's "scandalous" fresco, "Sunday in the Alameda", has been removed from the earthquake-damaged Hotel del Prado and has been mounted in a new museum on the N side of the new Parque de la Solidaridad (on the old Hotel Regis site) at Av. Juárez 77. A stroll down Calle Dolores, a busy and fascinating street, leads to the market of San Juan. The colonial church of Corpus Christi, on Av. Juárez, is now used to display and sell folk arts and crafts. The avenue ends at the small Plaza de la Reforma. At the corner of Juárez and Reforma is the National Lottery building. Drawings are held three times a week, at 2000: an interesting scene, open to the public. Beyond Plaza de la Reforma is the Monumento a la Revolución: a great copper dome, now rather tarnished, soaring above supporting columns set on the largest triumphal arches in the world. Beneath the monument is the **Museo Nacional de la Revolución**, recently opened, dealing with the period 1867-1917, very interesting, lots of exhibits, videos (open Tues.-Sun., 1000-1700, free, but donation expected).

South of this area, on Plaza Ciudadela, is a large colonial building, **La Ciudadela**, dating from 1700. It has been used for all kinds of purposes but is now a library.

The wide and handsome but earthquake-damaged Paseo de la Reforma, 3 km. long, continues to Chapultepec Park: shops, offices, hotels, restaurants all the way. Along it are monuments to Columbus; to Cuauhtémoc and a 45-metre marble column to Independence, topped by the golden-winged figure of a woman, "El Angelito" to the Mexicans. Just before entering the park is the Salubridad (Health) Building. Rivera's frescoes in this building cannot be seen by the public, who can view only the stained-glass windows on the staircases.

Chapultepec Park, at the end of Paseo de la Reforma, with its thousands of ahuehuete trees, is beautiful but is becoming spoiled by constant littering (park closes at 1700). It contains a maze of pathways, a large lake, a marvellous botanical garden, shaded lawns, a zoo with giant pandas (closed Mon. and Tues.), a large amusement park (there is a section for children and another for adults) with huge roller-coasters (open Wed., Sat. and Sun., entry US$0.90, all rides free, except roller-coaster; on Sat. and Sun. only, US$0.22), bridle paths and polo grounds. Diego Rivera's famous fountain, the Fuente de Tlaloc, is near the children's amusement park. Just below the castle and a little to the left are the remains of the famous Arbol de Moctezuma, known locally as "El Sargento". This immense tree, which has a circumference of 14 metres and was about 60 metres high, has been cut off at a height of about 10 metres. In this park too, are the Don Quixote fountain, the Frog's fountain, the Niños Monument, and Monkey Island, a replica of Cacahuamilpa caves. At the top of a hill in the park is Chapultepec Castle, with a view over Mexico Valley from its beautiful balconies, entry US$0.02. It has now become the **National Museum of History,** open 0900-1700. Its rooms were used by the Emperor Maximilian and the Empress Carlota during their brief reign. There is an unfinished mural by Siqueiros and a notable mural by O'Gorman on the theme of independence. Entrance US$0.20; US$0.12 on Sun. Halfway down the hill is the new **Gallery of Mexican History.** On Sun. mornings large numbers of people gather round the lake for open-air extension classes in a great variety of subjects (e.g. hairdressing, artificial flower-making, guitar-playing) organized by the University and open to all.

The crowning wonder of the park is the **Anthropological Museum** built by architect Pedro Ramírez Vásquez to house a vast collection illustrating pre-conquest Mexican culture. It has a 350-metre façade and an immense patio shaded by a gigantic concrete mushroom, 4,200 square metres—the world's largest concrete expanse supported by a single pillar. The largest exhibit (8½ metres high, weighing 167 tons) is the image of Tlaloc the rain god, removed—accompanied by protesting cloud bursts from near the town of Texcoco— to the museum. Open Tues.-Sat., 0900-1900 and Sun., 1000-1800. Only Mexican student cards accepted. Entrance is US$0.25 except Sun. (free), and holidays, when all museums charge US$0.10. Guides in English cost an additional US$0.20; ask for the parts you want to see as each tour only visits two of 23 halls; guided tours in Spanish free. Audio-visual introduction US$0.10. If you want to see everything, you need two days. Permission to photograph (no tripod or flash allowed) US$1.50 from museum office, if you are professionally interested, date must be fixed in advance; otherwise cameras not allowed. The most fanatical museum hater will enjoy this one, particularly the display of folk costumes upstairs. There is an excellent collection of English, French, German and Spanish books, especially guides to Mexican ruins, including maps. Restaurant on site is expensive and not very good.

Warning Be on the lookout for thieves in Chapultepec park, and especially in the underpass between Chapultepec metro and the Archaeological Museum. Sunday is the safest day.

There are now four other museums in Chapultepec Park: the Tamayo Museum, and in the new section the museums of Natural History, Technology and **Modern Art** (US$0.50, students US$0.25). The last shows Mexican art only in two buildings, pleasantly set among trees with some sculptures in the grounds. The smaller building shows temporary exhibitions. The delightfully light architecture of the larger building is spoilt by a heavy, vulgar marble staircase, with a curious acoustic effect on the central landing under a translucent dome, which must have been unplanned; open 1100-1800 daily except Mon. The Gallery of Mexican History has dioramas, with tape-recorded explanations of Mexican history, and photographs of the 1910 Revolution. The **Tamayo Museum's** interior space is unusual in that you cannot tell which floor you are on or how many there are; usually displays Mexican artists, although international modern art is in its possession, situated between the Modern Art and Anthropology Museums, US$0.25 entry, ½ price to students with international card (only place in Mexico). The **Museum of Technology** is free; it is operated by the Federal Electricity Commission, has touchable exhibits which demonstrate electrical and energy principles. It is located beside the roller-coasters.

Natural History Museum Open 1000-1700, Tues to Sun. Entry 2 pesos.

Not far from the Anthropological Museum in Chapultepec Park is the **Sala de Arte Público Siqueiros**, Calle Tres Picos 29, which has a large collection of items associated with the artist in addition to a number of his works. Open Mon.-Fri., 1000-1400, 1700-2100, Sat. 1000-1400, free.

Further places of interest to tourists are as follows:

Museum of the City, on Av. Pino Suárez and República de El Salvador, shows the geology of the city and has life size figures in period costumes showing the history of different peoples before Cortés. In the attic above the museum is the studio of Joaquín Clausell, with walls covered with impressionist miniatures. Free admittance, Tues. to Thurs. Two blocks S on Misioneros from this museum is the **Anglican (Episcopal) Cathedral**, called the Cathedral of San José de Gracia. Built in 1642 as a Roman Catholic church, it was given by the Benito Juárez government to the Episcopal Mission in Mexico. Juárez himself often attended services in it.

Museo Nacional de las Culturas, Moneda 13, open 0930-1800, closed Sun. Exhibits of countries from all over the world and some historical information.

Museo de Arte Carrillo Gil, Av. Revolución esq. Los Leones, near San Ángel; paintings by Orozco, Rivera, Siqueiros and others.

Instituto Nacional Indigenista, Av. Revolución 1297.

Escuela Nacional de Ingeniería, next to the main post office on Calle Tacuba, houses a permanent exhibition of meteorites found all over Mexico (up to 14 tonnes).

Museo Universitario del Chopo, E. G. Martínez 10, opp. metro San Cosme, nr. Insurgentes Norte. Contemporary international exhibitions (photography, art) in a church-like building. Saturday music market, records, cassettes, books, instruments, clothes traded and exchanged, particularly popular with young Mexicans.

Museo Arqueológico del Sitio (ruins of main pyramid of Tenochtitlán), Seminario 4 y Guatemala, open 0900-1800 daily (last tickets at 1700, entry US$0.30).

Museo del Convento de Carmen, Av. Revolución 4, San Ángel, open 1000-1700. **Museo Nacional de Culturas Populares**, Hidalgo 289, focuses on livelihoods in Mexico (open 0900-1600, Tues., Thurs., Sat.; 0900-2000, Weds. and Fri., and 1100-1700, Sun.)

NB For details of other museums, far from the centre, see under Suburbs, **page 1036**, and Teotihuacán, **page 1038**.

Art Galleries Arvil, Cerrada Hamburgo 9, contemporary Mexican and international art; Artmex, Mexican Popular Gallery, Sabino 13; permanent exhibition of over 100 paintings of well-known Mexican artists, open 0900-1900. Central Art Gallery Migrachi, Av. Juárez 4, sculptures, drawings, also Galería de Arte Migrachi, on Génova 20. Galería Lanai, Hamburgo 151. Galería Merkup, Moliere 328. Galerías Rubens, Independencia 68. Galería Tere Haas, important contemporary artists, Génova 2-C. Summa Artis, Hotel Presidente Chapultepec, Campos Elíseos 218, contemporary Mexican art. Val-Ray Gallery, Reforma 412, Zona Rosa.

The Bull Ring is said to be the largest in the world, and holds 60,000 spectators. Bull fights are held every Sunday at 1600 from October through March. The Bull Ring is in the Ciudad de los Deportes (City of Sports), Plaza México, reached by Av. de los Insurgentes. (A little to the W of where Los Insurgentes crosses Chapultepec, and on Av. Chapultepec itself between Calles Praga and Varsovia, are the remains of the old aqueduct built in 1779.) Besides the Bull Ring, the Sports City contains a football stadium holding 50,000 people, a boxing ring, a cinema, a frontón court for jai-alai, a swimming pool, restaurants, hotels, etc.

Modern Buildings On Avenida Insurgentes Norte is a remarkable building by Alejandro Prieto: the Teatro de Los Insurgentes, a theatre and opera house seating 1,300 people. The main frontage on the Avenida consists of a high curved wall without windows. This wall is entirely covered with mosaic decoration, the work of Diego Rivera: appropriate figures, scenes, and portraits composed round the central motif of a gigantic pair of hands holding a mask, worth going a distance to see.

The most successful religious architecture in Mexico today is to be found in the churches put up by Enrique de la Mora and Félix Candela; a good example is the chapel they built in 1957 for the Missionaries of the Holy Spirit, in a garden behind high walls at Av. Universidad 1700. (An excellent Candela church, and easy to see, is the Church of La Medalla Milagrosa, just to the E of Avenida Universidad at the junction of Avenida División Norte, Metro station División del Norte.) "All the churches and chapels built by this team have such lightness and balance that they seem scarcely to rest on their foundations." One of the seminal works of one of Mexico's greatest modern architects, Luís Barragán, is at Los Clubes, Las Arboledas bus from Chapultepec bus station. See also the objet trouvé mural at the Diana cinema in the centre of the city, and Orozco's great thundercloud of composition, the "Apocalypse", at the Church of Jesús Nazareno. Both the Camino Real Hotel and the IBM technical centre were designed by Ricardo Legorreto; very well worth seeing. Consult Max Cetto's book on modern Mexican architecture. In this connection, University City (see next page) is also well worth a look.

Sullivan Park (popularly known as Colonia Park or Jardín del Arte) is reached by going up Paseo de la Reforma to the intersection with Los Insurgentes, and then W two blocks between Calles Sullivan and Villalongín. Here, each Sunday afternoon, there is a display of paintings, engravings and sculptures near the monument to Motherhood, packed with sightseers and buyers; everything is for sale (beware of thieves).

Reino Aventura, S of the city near the Mall del Sur, amusement park for children along Disneyland lines, clean, orderly, popular with families.

The **Basílica of Guadalupe,** in the Gustavo A. Madero district, often called La Villa de Guadalupe, in the outer suburbs to the NE, is the most venerated shrine in Mexico, for it was here, in December 1531, that the Virgin appeared three times, in the guise of an Indian princess, to the Indian Juan Diego and imprinted her portrait on his cloak. The cloak is preserved, set in gold and protected by a 27-ton railing of silver, at the centre of the magnificent altar. A chapel stands over the well which gushed at the spot where the Virgin appeared. The great day here is December 12, the great night the night before. A huge, modern basilica has been built next door, impressive and worth visiting; it holds over 20,000 people. The original basilica is being converted into a museum and was closed in Dec. 1988. Mostly representations of the image on the cloak, but interesting painted tin plates offering thanks for cures, etc., from about 1860s. There are, in fact, about seven churches in the immediate neighbourhood, including one on the hill above; most of them are at crazy angles to each other and to the ground, because of subsidence; the subsoil is very soft. The Templo de los Capuchinos has been the subject of a remarkable feat of engineering in which one end has been raised 3.375 metres so that the building is now horizontal. There is a little platform from which to view this work. Buses marked La Villa go close to the site, or you can go by metro to La Villa (Line 6).

Suburbs of Mexico City

Churubusco, 10 km. SE, reached from the Zócalo by Coyoacán or Tlalpan bus, or from General Anaya metro station, to see the picturesque and partly ruined convent (1762) at Gen. Anaya con 20 de Agosto, now become the Museo Nacional de las Intervenciones (open 0900-2100, closed Mon.). Seventeen rooms filled with mementoes, documents, proclamations and pictures recounting foreign invasions, incursions and occupations since independence. The site of the museum was chosen because it was the scene of a battle when the US Army marched into Mexico City in 1847. There is a golf course at the Churubusco Country Club. Churubusco has the principal Mexican film studios. The new Olympic swimming pool is here. Near enough to Coyoacán (**see page 1037**) to walk there.

Tlalpan, 6½ km. further out, or direct from Villa Obregón (see page 1037), a most picturesque old town on the slopes of Ajusco, an extinct volcano: colonial houses, gardens, and near the main square an early 16th century church with a fine altar and paintings by Cabrera. Reached by bus or trolley bus from the Taxqueña metro station. Two-and-a-half km. W is the village of Peña Pobre, near which, to the NE, is the Pyramid of *Cuicuilco,* believed to be the oldest in Mexico (archaeological museum on site, Insurgentes Sur Km. 16, intersection with Periférico, open 0800-1800, closed Mon.). The pyramid dates from the 5th or 6th century B.C.; it is over 100 metres in diameter but only 18 high. On the road from Mexico City to Cuicuilco there is a pre-classic burial area under the lava flow, at Copilco, which is closed to the public.

Another excursion can be made to *Ajusco,* about 20 km. SW of Mexico City. Catch a bus from Estadio Azteca on Calzada Tlalpan direct to Ajusco (US$0.30). Get out at terminal and ask for directions to Volcán Ajusco, which is very close to the village. It's a 2 hr. walk to the summit, excellent views on a clear day. Foothills are also pleasant.

Xochimilco, to the SE, in the Valley of México. Take metro to Taxqueña (terminus) and catch a colectivo No. 26, or bus No. 140 (US$0.05) to the market. Turn left out of the station to catch the bus. The bus back leaves from the street left of the main church (don't believe taxi drivers who say there is no bus back). The bus stops some distance away beside the market (cheap fruit) in Xochimilco; bad signposting, but often tours from the *embarcaderos* will meet the buses and escort you to the boats. Otherwise keep to the right of the large church on the square, on Nuevo León, carry on until Violeta then turn right for 1 block and then turn left into Embarcadero. Xochimilco has a maze of canals, originally part of the canal system of Tenochtitlán, which wander round fruit and flower gardens. Punts adorned with flowers, poled by Indians, can be hired for about 1½ hrs for US$7-10 weekdays (one per "family", so arrange to join others beforehand) and US$0.25 at weekends only on "public" boats. Make sure you bargain hard before boarding and ensure you get all the time you paid for as many of the boats are punted by boys without watches. At the canal-side restaurants there is music and dancing. The canals are busy on Sundays, quiet midweek. There is a fine market on Saturday; Indians come from miles around. It has a 16th century fortified monastery, San Bernardo, built on Xochimilco's main square by the Franciscans in the 16th century, has escaped heavy-handed restoration. The main altar is a masterpiece of painting and sculpture. Only one hotel, basic, F. Many cheap souvenirs; fruit and flowers sold from boats in canals. Note that it is virtually impossible to get on to the Mexico City-Cuernavaca toll road from Xochimilco.

Ixtapalapa (2 good churches) is at the foot of the Cerro de Estrella, whose top is reached by a bad road or a path for a good view. One of the most spectacular of Mexican passion-plays begins at Ixtapalapa on Holy Thursday.

University City, world-famous, is 18 km. via Insurgentes Sur on the Cuernavaca highway. Perhaps the most notable building is the 10-storey library tower, by Juan O'Gorman, its outside walls iridescent with mosaics telling the story of scientific knowledge, from Aztec astronomy to molecular theory. The Administrative Building has a vast, mosaic-covered and semi-sculptured mural by Siqueiros. Across the highway is the Olympic Stadium, with seats for 80,000, in shape, colour, and situation a world's wonder. Diego Rivera has a sculpture-painting telling the story of Mexican sport. A new complex is being completed beyond the Ciudad Universitaria, including the newspaper library, Hemeroteca Nacional, Teatro Juan Ruiz de Alarcón, Sala Nezahuacoyotl (concerts etc.) and the Espacio Escultórico (sculptures). In the University museum there is an exhibition of traditional masks from all over Mexico. Beyond the Olympic Stadium is also a Botanical Garden which shows all the cactus species in Mexico (ask directions, it's a ½ hr. walk). The University of Mexico was founded in 1551. Bus (marked C.U., one passes along Eje Lázaro Cárdenas; also bus 17, marked Tlalpan, which runs the length of Insurgentes) gets you there, about 1 hr. journey. Another way to the university is on metro line 3 to Copiles station (10 mins. walk to University) or to Universidad station (15 mins. walk). At the University City there is a free bus going round the campus. The University offers cheap 6-week courses.

In the same direction as the University but further out is **Anahuacalli** (usually called the Diego Rivera Museum, open Tues.-Sun. 1000-1800, closed Holy Week). Here is a very fine collection of precolumbian sculpture and pottery, effectively displayed in a pseudo-Mayan tomb built for it by Diego Rivera. View of southern rim of mountains from the roof. In some ways it beats the Anthropological Museum. Reached by bus from the Taxqueña metro station to Estadio Azteca, or take the bus marked División del Norte from outside Salto del Agua metro. Calle Museo crosses Div. del Norte.

Villa Obregón (popularly known as **San Angel**) 13 km. SW, has narrow, cobble-stone streets, many old homes, huge trees, and the charm of an era now largely past. See the triple domes of its church, covered with coloured tiles, and the former Carmen monastery, now a museum (open 1000-1700). See also the beautifully furnished and preserved old house, Casa del Risco, near the market, and the church of San Jacinto and its adjoining monastery. One of the more macabre sights of Mexico is the severed hand of Alvaro Obregón, preserved in a bottle inside his monument on the spot where he was assassinated in 1928. See also the Museo de Arte Carrillo Gil, Av. Revolución 1608, with excellent changing exhibits. In San Angel also, there is a *bazar sábado*, a splendid Saturday folk art and curiosity market, and the Parroquia, a Dominican convent church dating from 1566. Reach San Angel by bus from Chapultepec Park or by metro line 3 to M.A.Quevedo. Excellent restaurants: the *San Angel Inn* is first class. Desierto de los Leones (see below) is reached from Villa Obregón by a scenic road.

Coyoacán, an old and beautiful suburb adjoining Villa Obregón, and also reached via line 3, is the place from which Cortés launched his attack on Tenochtitlán. The Casa de Cortés, now the Municipal Hall, was built 244 years after the Conquest. The rose-coloured house at Francisco Sosa 383 is said to have been built by Alvarado. The San Juan Bautista church and the nearby Franciscan monastery are both early 16th century. Friday market. The Frida Kahlo Museum at Allende y Londres, preserved as lived in by Diego Rivera and Frida Kahlo, is fascinating and well worth an afternoon, reached by metro line 3 to Coyoacán then by Villa Coupe bus/colectivo or 20 mins. walk south. Drawings and paintings by both. Free guided tours Sat. and Sun. at 1100. Nearby, is the Jardín de la Cultura with large statue of Frida Kahlo, on Fernando Leal and Pacífico. Also nearby, Trotsky's house is open at 1100-1400 and 1500-1700, Tues.-Fri., and 1000-1600, Sat.-Sun. (students man it), as a museum at Viena 45 (with Morelos). The Museo Nacional de Culturas Populares, Hidalgo 289, should be seen: open Wed. and Fri. 0900-2000, Tues., Thurs. and Sat. 0900-1500, Sun. 1100-1700. The new market and the remarkable Chapel of Our Lady of Solitude are by Enrique de la Mora and Félix Candela. *El Coyote Flaco* is a good restaurant, as is *La Guadalupana*; night club *Peña Nahuatl*, fine folk singing and poetry readings.

The Pyramid of **Tenayuca,** 10 km. to the NW, is about 15 metres high and the best-preserved in Mexico. The Aztecs rebuilt this temple every 52 years; this one was last reconstructed about 1507; well worth seeing, for it is surrounded with serpents in masonry. The easiest way to get there by car from Mexico City centre is to go to Vallejo, 11 km. N of the intersection of Insurgentes Norte and Río Consulado. Admission US$0.08. By metro, take the line to the Central de Autobuses del Norte (**see page 1030**), La Raza, and catch the bus there. By bus from Tlatelolco; ask driver and passengers to advise you on arrival as site is not easily visible. An excursion to Tula may go via Tenayuca. It is not far from the old town of **Tlalnepantla:** see the ancient convent (ask for the *catedral*) on the Plaza Gustavo Paz and the church (1583), which contains the first image, a Christ of Mercy, brought to the New World. Two-and-a-half km. to the N is the smaller pyramid of Santa Cecilia, interesting for its restored sanctuary.

Los Remedios, a small town 13 km. NW of Mexico City, has in its famous church an image, a foot high, adorned with jewels. See the old aqueduct, with a winding stair leading to the top. It can be reached by car or by taking the Los Remedios bus at Tacuba metro. Fiesta: September 1 to the climax September 8.

At Tlatilco, NW of the city (just outside the city boundary on Querétaro road), pre-classic Olmec-influenced figurines can be seen.

Excursions from Mexico City

Desierto de los Leones, a beautiful pine forest made into a national park, can be reached from Mexico City (24 km.) by a fine scenic road through Villa Obregón. In the woods is an old Carmelite convent, around are numerous hermitages, inside are several subterranean passages and a secret hall with curious acoustic properties. Take a torch.

Take an hour's bus ride from Observatorio metro to La Venta and ask bus-driver where to get off for the path to the monastery (about 4 km. walk). One can either get there via the paved road or via the beautiful conifer-forest path, but the latter sights frequently so stick to what looks like the main path; or take the fire-break road below the row of shops and cheap restaurants near the main road. Food stalls abound, particularly at weekends when it is crowded. We have been advised that kidnap attempts have been made at Desierto de los Leones; do not let children wander out of sight. Do not leave valuables in your car, either.

Acolman has the formidable fortress-like convent and church of San Agustín, dating from 1539-60, with much delicate detail on the façade and some interesting murals inside. Note the fine portal and the carved stone cross at the entrance to the atrium. Closed Fri. Reached by bus from Indios Verdes metro station, or from the Zócalo. It is 42 km. NE of the city.

Teotihuacan, 45 km. from Mexico City, has some of the most remarkable relics of an ancient civilization in the world. The old city is traceable over an area of 3½ by 6½ km. The Pyramid of the Sun (64 metres high, 213 metres square at the base) covers almost the same space as the Great Pyramid of Cheops in Egypt. The sides are terraced, and wide stairs lead to the summit; unfortunately its surface was restored in the wrong materials to wrong specifications around 1910. The Pyramid of the Moon, 1 km. away, is only half its size. There are temples of agriculture, of Tlaloc (the Rain God), of the Plumed Serpent, of Quetzalcoatl (Lord of Air and Wind), and the broad Highway of the Dead. There are subterranean buildings with large halls and coloured decorations, and many superimposed buildings of a later epoch. The pyramids, buildings, courts, etc., are now completely restored and well worth a visit. The Palace of Quetzalpapalotl, where the priests serving the sanctuaries of the Moon lived, has been restored together with its patio. Visit also the cactus garden, with every type of cactus imaginable. Site open 0800-1700. (Entrance near the bus stop only opens at 1000 despite the sign; try entrance near the Pyramid of the Moon.) Entrance, US$0.25, US$0.10 per car. Entrance free on Sundays. Reckon on about 5-8 hrs to see the site properly. Tetitla and Atetelco, two smaller sites to the W of the perimetral road, are worth seeing; they are about 1 km. N of the main entrance from the *autopista*; to get to them from the museum, exit W and walk right up to main road, turning left after crossing stream. NE exit from main site brings you to Tepantitlán, superb frescoes. There is a small museum. Easily reached from the bus station (bus shelter marked for Teotihuacan, platform J) at Indios Verdes metro station (green line 3) where the buses to and from Teotihuacan make a stop (US$0.75, 1½ hrs.), or from Terminal del Norte, Gate 8 (Autobuses del Norte metro), which takes 45 mins. Bus returns from Door 1 at Teotihuacan site, supposedly every ½ hr. *Son et lumière* display, costs US$4 per person (good *lumière*, not so good *son*); lasts 45 mins., 1900 in Spanish, 2015 in English (Oct.-June only) commentary. Shown between January and end-April; take blanket or rent one. You can ride back to town with one of the tourist buses for about US$2. Note that the site is more generally known as "Pirámides" than as "Teotihuacan". Train to Teotihuacan, 2 hrs., US$2.65. Tours to Teotihuacan, picking you up at your hotel, normally cost US$10 or so.

Hotel   *Villas Arqueológicas*, C. **Restaurants** around ruins reported high-priced and service slow.

MEXICO CITY SURROUNDINGS
ROUGH SKETCH

Tepozotlán, about 43 km. NW of Mexico City just off the route to Querétaro, has a splendid Jesuit church in churrigueresque style. There are fine colonial paintings in the convent corridors. The old Jesuit monastery has been converted into a colonial art museum (Museo Nacional del Virreinato, open 1000-1700, closed Mon., entry US$0.40, US$0.20 Sun.) and tourist centre with restaurants.

The *Hostería del Monasterio* has very good Mexican food and a band on Sun.; try their coffee with cinnamon. *Restaurant Artesanías*, opp. church, rec., cheap. Also good food at *Brookwell's Posada.* Bus from Tacuba metro station, US$0.50, 1 hr. ride. Many buses from Terminal del Norte pass the turn-off at "Caseta Tepozotlán" from where one can take a local bus or walk (30 mins.) to the town. (Do not confuse Tepozotlán with Tepoztlán, which is S of Mexico City, near Cuernavaca).

In the third week of December, *pastorelas*, or morality plays based on the temptation and salvation of Mexican pilgrims voyaging to Bethlehem, are held. Tickets are about US$10 and include a warming punch, the play, a procession and litanies, finishing with a meal, fireworks and music. Tickets from Viajes Roca, Neva 30, Col. Cuauhtémoc, Mexico City.

Another one-day excursion is to *Tula,* some 65 km., the most important Toltec site in Mexico; two ball courts, pyramids, a frieze in colour, and remarkable sculptures over 6 metres high have been uncovered. There are four huge warriors in black basalt on a pyramid, the great Atlantes anthropomorphic pillars. The museum is well worth visiting and there is a massive fortress-style church, dating from 1553, near the market. Admission to site and museum, US$0.40 weekdays, free Sun. and holidays. Multilingual guidebooks at entrance. Site is open Tues.-Sun. 0930-1630 (museum open Wed.-Sun. till 1630). The town itself is dusty, however, with poor roads; *Restaurant la Cabaña,* on main square, local dishes, also *Nevería,* with good soup. If driving from Mexico City, take the turn for Actopán before entering Tula, then look for the Zona Arqueológica sign (and the great statues) on your left.

Transport 1½ hrs. by train from Buenavista station; leaves at 0735, returns at 2035, US$2 (excellent breakfast for US$0.65), but sometimes can be several hours late; it follows the line of the channel cut by Alvarado to drain the lakes of Mexico City, visible as a deep canyon (from station walk along track ½ hour to site). One can take bus back, which leaves earlier. It can also be reached by 1st class bus, "Valle de Mesquital", from Terminal del Norte, Avenida de los Cien Metros, goes to Tula in 1½-2 hrs.; US$1.70 each way, 30-min service; Tula bus terminal is 3 km. from the site (badly signposted, an alternative route is: 200m. to the Zócalo, to Calle Quetzalcoatl, to small bridge, sandy road to the right, and opening in the fence). Also bus or car from Actopán, on the Pan-American Highway (see page 976). Tula-Pachuca US$1.30; safe to leave belongings at bus station.

MEXICO CITY-VERACRUZ-MEXICO CITY (6)

By Road A round tour by way of Cholula, Puebla, Tehuacán, Orizaba, Córdoba, Veracruz, Jalapa, Tlaxcala, and Alvarado. Paved all the way (no Pemex service station on road between Puebla and Orizaba, a distance of about 150 km.); total distance: 924 km., or 577 miles. A toll *autopista* (motorway) from Mexico City to Veracruz has been finished as far as Córdoba. From there on you take the regular highway. Our description is a trip along the old road.

We go E along the Puebla road, past the airport and swimming pools, and some spectacular shanty-towns. At (km. 19) Los Reyes, a road runs left into a valley containing the now almost completely drained Lake Texcoco, a valley early settled by the *conquistadores.* Along it we come to *Chapingo,* where there is a famous agricultural college with particularly fine frescoes by Rivera in the chapel. Next comes *Texcoco,* a good centre for visiting picturesque villages in the area. Bus from Mexico City, from Emiliano Zapata 92, near Candelaria metro station. Near Chapingo a road runs right to the lovely village of *Huexotla* (see the Aztec wall and the old church). Another road from Texcoco runs through the very beautiful public park of Molino de las Flores. From the old *hacienda* buildings, now in ruins, a road (right) runs up the hill of Tetzcotingo, near the top of which are the Baths of Netzahualcoyotl, the poet-prince. All the nearby villages are charming to stroll through. Another village worth visiting is (San Miguel de) *Chiconcuac* (road to San Andrés and left at its church), only 4 km. away. Here Texcoco *sarapes* are woven. Tues. is their market day and there is a rousing *fiesta* in honour of their patron saint on September 29.

At km. 29, Santa Bárbara, a road on the right leads to the small town of *Amecameca* (60 km. from Mexico City, Cristóbal Colón 1st class bus every hour, 1-1½ hrs'. journey, US$ 0.70) from the Central del Oriente; if hitching, take the Calzada Zaragoza, very dusty road. By train at 0700, 2½ hr. trip, US$0.20. It is at the foot of the twin volcanoes *Popocatépetl* ("smoking mountain") and Ixtaccíhuatl ("sleeping woman"); the saddle between them, reached by car via a paved road up to the Paso de Cortés (25 km. from Amecameca), gives particularly fine views. On Sats. a pickup truck leaves the plaza at Amecameca, US$1 p.p., for far up the mountain; also taxis for US$4.50-8.50. Just before the pass, cars (but not pedestrians) pay US$0.10 entry to the national park. A road reaches the sanctuary of El Sacromonte, 90 metres above the town (magnificent views), a small and very beautiful church built round a cave in which once lived Fray Martín de Valencia, a *conquistador* who came to Mexico in 1524. It is, next to the shrine of Guadalupe, the most sacred place in Mexico and has a much venerated full-sized image of Santo Entierro weighing 1½ kg. only. Population of Amecameca: 10,000; altitude: 2,315 metres; market day is Saturday. (On the way to Amecameca, see the restored 16th century convent and church at Chalco, and the fine church, convent and open-air chapel of the same period at Tlalmanalco.) Three hotels, E and F, close to Amecameca's main square, and rooms at the *San Carlos* restaurant on the main square, F, clean, good, modern, good food, but no hot water. Several eating-places and a food market.

Popocatépetl is not easy to climb. The best time to climb the volcanoes is between late Oct. and early March when there are clear skies and no rain. From May to October the weather is good before noon; in the afternoons it is bad. Climbers are advised to spend at least a day at *Tlamacas* (3,950 metres) to acclimatize, reached from Paso de Cortés via the paved road which turns right (S), 5 km. on. It is also possible to take a taxi (or hitchhike from the turn-off 2 km. S of Amecameca, morning and early afternoon, best at weekends, no public transport) from Amecameca to Tlamacas, US$5, up to 5 people, 26 km. There are a few houses and a tourist hostel *Albergue de Tlamacas*, catering for day trippers from the capital, with cafeteria (open 0930-1900), limited and expensive food, and a restaurant which opens at weekends. You're not supposed to eat your own food within the hostel; sheets and pillow provided; book in advance, US$1 a night in mixed dormitories (sleeping bag rec.); beautiful house in wooded enclosure, plenty of hot water. 1½ km. below Tlamacas is a camping and picnic area. Minibuses charge US$2 p.p. and run only Sat. and Sun. (from the E to Tlamacas: a bus from Cholula goes as far as San Nicolás de los Ranchos—the remaining 10 km. to Paso de Cortés must be covered on foot or by hitching). From Tlamacas a path goes up to Las Cruces at 4,400 metres (where there was once a refuge) and the snowline; from there it is 3 hours (crampons and ice axe) to the rim of the crater and thence another hour's walk round the rim to the top. Equipment hire US$9 for boots, crampons and ice-axes at the hostel, or in Amecameca, but preferable to hire from Mountain Club in Mexico City. The Brigada de Rescate del Socorro Alpino de México, a.c., in Mexico City (Lázaro Cárdenas 80, T 521 18 13) will provide information and free guides. If you wish to go to the top of Popocatépetl (5,400 metres) leave at 0400, as the ground is more solid early on (take warm clothes and a flashlight, and sunglasses for the snow-glare. Alternative routes from Paso de Cortés: straight down dirt road to reach eventually Puebla; or turn left (N) along another dirt road which leads past TV station for 12 km. to nearest parking to summit of Ixtaccíhuatl. From there you find various routes to summit (12-15 hrs. return) and 3-4 refuges to overnight (no furniture, bare floors, dirty).

Beyond Santa Bárbara our road climbs through pine forests to reach 3,196 metres about 63 km. from Mexico City, and then descends in a series of sharp bends to the quiet town of San Martín **Texmelucan**, km. 91. The old Franciscan convent here has a beautifully decorated interior, and a former *hacienda* displays weaving and old machinery. Market day is Tuesday.

From here a side-road leads NE for 24 km. to the quaint old Indian town of Tlaxcala; a remarkable series of precolumbian frescoes are to be seen at the ruins of **Cacaxtla** near San Miguel de los Milagros, a steep 25-minute climb up from the main highway, between Texmelucan and Tlaxcala. The colours are still sharp and some of the figures are larger than life size. To protect the paintings from the sun they are only shown from 1000-1300 (closed Mon.), admission US$0.20; the whole site is now being roofed in. Then there is **Tlaxcala**, with its simple buildings washed in ochre, pink and yellow, capital of small Tlaxcala state whose wealthy ranchers breed fighting bulls, but whose landless peasantry is still poor. To see: the church of San Francisco, the oldest in Mexico (1521), from whose pulpit the first Christian sermon was preached in the New World—its severe façade conceals a most sumptuous interior; the extremely colourful murals (1966) depicting the indigenous story of Tlaxcala in the Palacio de Gobierno; and the ruins of the pyramid of San Esteban de Tizatlán, 5 km. outside the town. There is an hourly bus from the Central Camionera in Tlaxcala or take a city bus to La Garrita from which the ruins are a 15 min. walk. Most interesting relics are two sacrificial altars with original colour frescoes preserved under glass. The pictures tell the story of the wars with Aztecs and Chichimecs. The annual fair is held Oct. 29-Nov. 15 each year. Population 36,000. Altitude 2,240 metres.

The **Sanctuary of Ocotlán** (1541), on a hill outside the town, described as "the most delicious building in the world", commands a view of valley and volcano. "Its two towers are of lozenge-shaped vermilion bricks set in white stucco, giving an effect of scarlet shagreen, while their upper storeys are dazzlingly white, with fretted cornices and salomonic pillars. . . . A pure-blooded Indian, Francisco Miguel, worked for 25 years on the interior, converting it into a kind of golden grotto." - Sacheverell Sitwell.

(Km. 106) **Huejotzingo** has the second-oldest church and monastery in Mexico, built 1529; now a museum. Market: Sat., Tues. Dramatic carnival on Shrove Tuesday, portraying the story of Agustín Lorenzo, a famous local bandit.

(Km. 122) **Cholula** is a small somnolent town (20,000 people, with the University of the Americas), but one of the strangest-looking in all Mexico. When Cortés arrived, this was a holy centre with 100,000 inhabitants and 400 shrines, or *teocallis*, grouped round the great pyramid of Quetzalcoatl. In its day it was as influential as Teotihuacán. There used to be a series of pyramids built one atop another. When razing them, Cortés vowed to build a chapel for each of the *teocallis* destroyed, but in fact there are no more than about seventy. There is a very helpful tourist office opposite the main pyramid: Cholula map and guide book for US$1; the site is open 1000-1730.

Places to see are the excavated pyramid, admission US$0.45 on weekdays, US$0.23 on Sun. and holidays, guide US$2.25, it has 8 km. of tunnels and some recently discovered frescoes inside, but only 1 km. of tunnel is open to the public, which gives an idea of superimposition. The entrance is on the main road into Cholula; the chapel of Los Remedios on top of it, for the view; the Franciscan fortress church of San Gabriel (1552), in the plaza (open 0600-1200, 1600-1900, Suns. 0600-1900), and next to it, the Capilla Real, which has 48 domes (open 1000-1200, 1530-1800, Suns. 0900-1800).

See also the Indian statuary and stucco work, newly repainted, of the 16th century church of Santa María de **Tonantzintla**, outside the town; the church is one of the most beautiful in Mexico (open 1000-1300, 1500-1700 daily, or get someone to open it for you for a small tip), and may also be reached by paved road from San Francisco **Acatepec** (see its 16th century church also, supposedly open 0900-1800 daily, but not always so) off the highway from Puebla to Cholula. Both these places are easily reached from Cholula or Puebla by the regular bus service between the two.

One can visit Tonantzintla and Acatepec from Cholula main square with a "peso-taxi". Or one can take a bus from Cholula to Acatepec for US$0.25 from junction of Av. 5 and Av. Miguel Alemán. This is 2 blocks from Zócalo, which is 3 blocks from tourist office. You can walk back to Tonanzintla to see church, 1 km., and then take bus Tonanzintla-Puebla US$0.30. John Hemming says these two churches "should on no account be missed; they are resplendent with Poblano tiles and their interiors are a riot of Indian stucco-work and carving." Both churches, though exquisite, are tiny. Some visitors note that regular visiting hours are not strictly observed at Cholula, Acatepec, Tonantzintla and Huejotzingo.

Hotels in Cholula *Villa Arqueológica*, 2 Poniente 501; *Los Sauces*, Km. 122, Carretera Federal Puebla-Cholula; *Motel de la Herradura*, Carr. Federal; *Trailer Park Las Américas*, 30 Oriente 602; *Cali Quetzalcoatl*, on Zócalo, C, clean, expensive restaurant; *Hotel de las Américas*, 14 Oriente, near pyramid, actually a motel, modern with rooms off galleries round paved courtyard (car park), small restaurant, clean, good value, D; *Reforma*, E, near main square, cheapest in town, rec. *Super Motel* on the road from Puebla as you enter town, each room with private garage, very secure, E. *Restaurant Choloyan*, also handicrafts, Av. Morelos, good, clean, friendly.

Buses Second-class bus from Puebla to Cholula from 8 Poniente 713, 9 km. on a new road, US$0.20. From Mexico City, leave for Cholula from Terminal del Oriente with Estrella Roja, every 30 mins. 1st class buses to Mexico City every 10 minutes, US$1, 2½-3 hrs., 2nd class every 20 mins., a very scenic route through steep wooded hills. Good views of volcanoes.

Just before Puebla one comes to the superb church of **Tlaxcalantzingo**, with an extravagantly tiled façade, domes and tower. It is worth climbing up on the roof for photographs.

(Km. 134) **Puebla**, "The City of the Angels", one of Mexico's oldest and most famous cities and the capital of Puebla state, is at 2,060 metres. Unfortunately, its recent industrial growth—the population has risen to 836,000—is rapidly destroying its colonial appearance and filling it with smog, and the centre, though still beautifully colonial, is cursed with traffic jams, except in those shopping streets reserved for pedestrians. On the central arcaded plaza is a fine Cathedral, notable for its marble floors, onyx and marble statuary and gold leaf decoration (closed 1230-1530). There are statues flanking the altar which are said to be of an English king and a Scottish queen. The bell tower gives a grand view of the city and snow-capped volcanoes (open 1100-1200 only). There are 60 churches in all, many of their domes shining with the glazed tiles for which the city is famous. Earthquake damage in 1973. Craft shop sponsored by the authorities: Tienda Convento Sta. Rosa, Calle 3 Norte 1203, T 2-89-04. *Feria* in mid-April for two weeks.

In the Rosario chapel of the Church of Santo Domingo (1596-1659), the baroque possesses a beauty of style and prodigality of form which served as an exemplar and inspiration for all later baroque in Mexico. There is a strong Indian flavour in Puebla's baroque; this can be seen in the 16th century churches of Tonantzintla and Acatepec (see above); it is not so evident, but it is still there, in the opulent decorative work in the Cathedral. Beyond the church, up towards the Fort of Loreto, there is a spectacular view of volcanoes.

Other places well worth visiting are the churches of San Cristóbal (1687), with modern churrigueresque towers and Tonantzintla-like plasterwork inside; San José (18th century), with attractive tiled façade and decorated walls around the main doors, as well as beautiful altar pieces inside; the Congreso del Estado in Calle 5 Poniente, formerly the Consejo de Justicia, near the post office, is a converted 19th century Moorish style town house—the tiled entrance and courtyard are very attractive—it had a theatre inside (shown to visitors on request), and is now the seat of the state government; and the Museum of Santa Rosa has a priceless collection of 16th century Talavera tiles on its walls and ceilings. The Patio de los Azulejos should also be visited; it has fabulous tiled façades on the former almshouses for old retired priests of the order of San Felipe Neri; the colours and designs are beautiful; it is at 11 Poniente 110, with a tiny entrance which is hard to find unless one knows where to look. One of the most famous and oldest local churches is San Francisco, with a glorious tiled façade and a mummified saint in its side chapel. Santa Catalina, 3 Norte with 2 Poniente, has beautiful altarpieces; Nuestra Señora de la Luz, 14 Norte and 2 Oriente, has a good tiled façade and so has San Marcos at Av. Reforma and 9 Norte. The Maronite church of Belén on 7 Norte and 4 Poniente has a lovely old tiled façade and a beautifully tiled interior. Worth visiting is also the library of Bishop Palafox, by the tourist office, 5 Oriente No. 5, opposite the Cathedral.

Besides the churches, the fragile-looking and extravagantly ornamented Casa del Alfeñique (Sugar Candy House), a few blocks from the Cathedral dominating the centre of the town, is worth seeing (entry US$0.40). Nearby is Plaza Parián, with onyx souvenir shops (6 Norte and 4 Oriente). Onyx figures and chess sets are attractive and cheaper than elsewhere, but the *poblanos* are hard bargainers; another attractive buy is the very tiny glass animal figures. A former convent is now the Museum of Santa Mónica; generations of nuns hid there after the reform laws of 1857 made the convent illegal, at Av. Poniente 18, No. 203. The Cinco de Mayo civic centre, with a stark statue of Benito Juárez, is, among other things, a regional centre of arts, crafts and folklore and has a very worthwhile Regional Museum, Natural History Museum, auditorium, planetarium, fairgrounds and an open air theatre all nearby. In the same area, the forts of Guadalupe and Loreto have been restored; they were the scene of the Battle of Puebla, in which 2,000 Mexican troops defeated Maximilian's 6,000 European troops on May 5, 1862 (although the French returned victorious ten days later). Inside the Fort of Loreto (excellent view of the city) is a small museum depicting the battle of 1862. May 5 is a holiday in Mexico.

Other places worth seeing are the church and monastery of El Carmen, with its strange façade and beautiful tile work; the Teatro Principal (1550), possibly the oldest in the Americas; the grand staircase of the 17th century Academia de las Bellas Artes and its exhibition of Mexican colonial painting; a magnificent library, one of the oldest in the Americas, access through the Casa de la Cultura and the Jesuit church of La Compañía, where a plaque in the sacristy shows where China Poblana lies buried. This mythical figure, a Chinese princess captured by pirates and abducted to Mexico, is said to have taken to Christianity and good works and evolved a penitential dress for herself which has now become the regional costume; positively dazzling with flowered reds and greens and worn with a strong sparkle of bright beads. Also worth visiting is the house of Aquiles Serdán, a leader of the Revolution, preserved as it was during his lifetime. The tiled façade of the Casa de los Muñecos, 2 Norte No. 1 (corner of the main square) is famous for its caricatures in tiles of the enemies of the 17th century builder.

The famous Puebla tiles may be purchased from factories outside Puebla, or from Fábrica de Azulejos la Guadalupana, Av. 4 Poniente 911; D. Aguilar, 40 Poniente 106, opposite Convent of Sta. Mónica, and Casa Rugerio, 18 Poniente 111; Margarita Guevara, 20 Poniente 30.

Barrio del Artista The artists' studios are near to *Hotel Latino* and adjoining Mercado El Parián, with tourist shops. Live music and refreshments at small *Café del Artista*. The University Arts Centre offers folk dances at various times, look for posters or enquire direct—free admission.

Museums Museo de Bello—the house of the collector and connoisseur Bello—has good displays of Chinese porcelain and Talavera pottery; the building is beautifully furnished (entry

US$0.40, guided tours, closed Mon.). Museo Regional de Puebla, in the Centro Cívico 5 de Mayo, is open 1000-1700; Museo de Santa Mónica (convent) at 18 Poniente 103, open 1000-1800, closed Mon.; and Museo de la No Intervención, in the Fuerte de Loreto, open 1000-1700, closed Mon.

Hotels *Lastra*, Calz. de Los Fuertes, B; *Royalty*, Portal Hidalgo 8, C, good, central, quiet; *Misión de Puebla*, 5 Poniente 2522, A, delightful; *Del Portal*, Portal Morelos 205, very good, but ask for room away from Zócalo side (noisy), restored colonial, C; *Colonial*, 4 Sur 105, old-fashioned and charming, has excellent restaurant and accepts American Express cards, ask for back room, C, with bath; *Imperial*, 4 Oriente 203, D, basic, shower, noisy, parking; *Cabrera*, 10 Oriente 6, E, with shower and phone, clean, quiet in interior rooms, don't be put off by outward appearance of hardware store; *Latino*, 6 Norte 8, E, with bath, hot water, next ADO bus station, reasonable but noisy; *San Miguel*, 3 Poniente 721, clean and quiet, C; *San Agustín*, 3 Poniente 531, E, basic, clean, quiet; *Victoria*, near Zócalo, 3 Poniente 306, basic, E; *Venecia*, 4 Poniente 716, F, without bath; *Casa de Huéspedes*, 3 Poniente 725, F; several basic *casas de huéspedes*, near market. Very cheap hotel (F), 2 blocks S of train station on 20 de Noviembre, big rooms, hot showers, clean, bus to town. **Motels** Mesón del Angel, A, good, near first Puebla interchange on Mexico-Puebla motorway, possibly best in town. *Panamerican*, Reforma 2114, D, restaurant, bar, rec.

Camping Possible on the extensive university grounds about 8 km. S of centre.

Food Speciality *Mole poblano* (meat or chicken with sauce of chiles, chocolate and coconut). Cheap mole at *Fonda la Mexicana*, 16 Sept. 706; best at *La Poblanita*, 10 Norte 1404-B, and *Fonda Sta. Clara*, 3 Poniente 307, good for local specialities. Also on Zócalo, at *Hostería de los Angeles*, but no dinner. Also good, *Iberia*, Portal Juárez. 101, 1st floor; *La Bola Roja*, 17 Sur 1305. Camotes (candied sweet potatoes) and dulces (sweets). Also nieves—drinks of alcohol, fruit and milk—worth trying, and excellent empanadas bought from a lady just outside the ADO station. Also noted are quesadillas— fried tortillas with cheese and herbs inside.

Other Restaurants *Monza's*, Calle Reforma, reasonable, good food. Cheap comidas at *Las Cazuelas del Chato*, 2 Oriente 209; *Hermilo Nevados*, 2 Oriente 408, good value, rec. *Alianza Francesa*, 2 Poniente, 101-402. Many cheap places between ADO depot and main square with menus prominently displayed. *Hosteria del Virrey*, 11 Sur and 15 Poniente, live music and good atmosphere. *La Chiesa Veglia*, Swiss, good cheese fondue, attached to *Hotel San Pedro*, 2 Oriente, slow service. *Antojitos Aries*, 5 Sur and 5 Poniente, serves a good, cheap comida corrida at lunchtime and à la carte menu for dinner, reasonable. *Teorema* on Reforma and 7 Norte is a cold-store with a cafetería, good.

Tourist Office 5 Oriente 3, Av. Juárez behind the Cathedral, T 46-09-28. Also 3 Sur 1501, 8th floor.

Roads and Buses A 4-lane highway, 70 mins., to Mexico City, toll US$1.30 (ADO buses every 15 mins., seats bookable, 2 hrs.; US$1.50; Mexico City-Puebla buses every 10 mins. but 2½ hr. queue), Estrella Roja from Central del Oriente. 2-lane highway to Orizaba, toll US$1.85. For the road from Puebla S through Oaxaca to Guatemala, **see page 1065**. Bus to Oaxaca costs US$7 (9 hrs.). Bus to Veracruz 1st class, US$3.50. Bus to Jalapa (**see page 1053**) ADO, 4 hrs.

Rail Station is a long way from centre. Trains from Mexico City, 1st class US$2.30, US$1.35 2nd class to Puebla via Cuautla at 0704, a very slow (10-11 hrs.) Puebla train at 0815; train to Oaxaca (1st class), leaves Puebla 0640, US$3, 12 hours. The line weaves through cactus laden gorges recalling the Wild West. On clear days one gets a good view of Popocatépetl. A train from Mexico City leaves at 1730 and stops at 2230 at Puebla on its way to Oaxaca. Train Puebla-Jalapa leaves at 0910, US$1.25, 2nd class, takes 7-8 hrs. The ride to Jalapa is very enjoyable, excellent views, sit on left-hand side.

Excursions Interesting day-trip to *Cuetzalán* market (via Tetela-Huahuaztla) which is held on Sun. in the Zócalo (3 hr walk up.). On October 4 each year dancers from local villages gather and *voladores* "fly" from the top of their pole. Nahua Indians sell cradles (*huacal*) for children; machetes and embroidered garments. Big clay dogs are made locally, unique stoves which hold big flat clay plates on which *tortillas* are baked and stews are cooked in big pots. Also available in nearby Huitzitlán. *Casa Elvira Mora*, Hidalgo 54, cheap, friendly place to stay in Cuetzalán. Women decorate their hair with skeins of wool. You can also go via Zaragoza, Zacapoaxtla and Apulco, where one can walk along a path, left of the road, to the fine 35-metre waterfall of La Gloria.

Direct buses from Puebla (Tezinteco line at Av. 12 Oriente and Calle 4 Norte) leaves 0830. Leaves Cuetzalán at 1520, back at Puebla at 2100. ADO has a night-bus, 1915 arrives 2245; returns 0700, arriving 1030. There are many buses to Zacapoaxtla with frequent connections for Cuetzalán.

15 km. S of Puebla lies Lake Valsequillo, with Africam, a zoo of free-roaming African animals. Entry US$1, open Mon.-Fri. 1000-1730, Sat., Sun. and holidays 0900-1800. Take a bus from Terminal Autobuses Unidos (AU), 4 Norte, Puebla. Information from 11 Oriente, T 460888.

SOUTHERN MEXICO

(Km. 151) *Amozoc,* where tooled leather goods and silver decorations on steel are made, both mostly as outfits for the *charros,* or Mexican cattlemen. Beyond Amozoc lies *Tepeaca* with its late 16th century monastery, well worth a visit; its weekly market is very extensive. An old Spanish tower or *rollo* (1580) stands between Tepeaca's main square and the Parroquia. Beyond Tepeaca, 57½ km. from Puebla, lies *Tecamachalco*: vast 16th century Franciscan monastery church with beautiful murals on the choir vault, in late medieval Flemish style, by a local Indian.

Beyond, the road leads to *Tehuacán* (population 113,000, altitude 1,676 metres), a charming town with a pleasant, sometimes cool, climate. It has some old churches. Water from the mineral springs is bottled and sent all over the country by Garci Crespo, San Lorenzo and Peñafiel, who also have baths at the spas where people come to bathe for health reasons (popular at weekends). From the small dam at Malpaso on the Río Grande an annual race is held for craft without motors as far as the village of Quiotepec. The central plaza is pleasant and shaded; the nights are cool. The government palace is decorated inside and out with murals. From Tehuacán there are two paved roads to Oaxaca: one, very scenic, through Teotitlán (see page 1071 and the other, longer but easier to drive, through Huajuapán (see page 1072). Railway junction for Oaxaca and Veracruz; no passenger trains on line to Esperanza. Wild maize was first identified by an archaeologist in caves nearby. There is an airport.

Hotels *Hotel-Spa Peñafiel,* old "faded glory", reasonable, long term rates, resort facilities (use of pool US$0.90), warmly rec., just out of town, on the way to Puebla; *México,* Reforma Norte and Independencia Poniente, one block from Zócalo, garage, TV, restaurant, renovated colonial building, pool, quiet; *Iberia,* Independencia 211, D, good; *Madrid,* opp. Municipal Library, E, comfortable, good value. Several *casas de huéspedes* along Calle 3 (Norte and Sur) but low standards, and generally a shortage of decent cheap accommodation and restaurants. Cafés on Zócalo serve snacks and drinks, and some meals, but the main meal is served at midday in Tehuacán. Try *Restaurant Santander,* good and inexpensive, and *Peñafiel,* good. No good, cheap restaurants, but excellent taco stands.

Buses ADO bus station on Av. Independencia (Poniente). Bus direct to Mexico City, 3 hrs., US$2.40; to Oaxaca and the Gulf: Autobuses Unidos, 2nd class on Calle 2 Oriente with several buses daily to Mexico City and Oaxaca. Local bus to Huajuapan 3 hrs., US$2; from there, frequent buses to Oaxaca (4 hrs., US$2.50).

Above Tehuacán, in the hills, is the Indian town of Huautla de Jiménez, where the local Mazatec Indians consume the hallucinogenic "magic" mushrooms made famous by Dr. Timothy Leary. Foreigners going up this road are stopped and turned back by the army.

Beyond, our road soon begins to climb into the mountains. At Cumbres we reach 2,300 metres and a wide view: the silvered peak of Citlaltépetl (or Orizaba) volcano to the E, the green valley of Orizaba below. In 10 km. we drop down, through steep curves, sometimes rather misty, to Acultzingo 830 metres below. The road joins the main toll road from Puebla to Orizaba at Ciudad Mendoza, where it has emerged from the descent through the Cumbres de Maltrata, which are usually misty and need to be driven with care and patience. (The toll road Puebla-Orizaba is a much safer drive than the route we have described.)

(Km. 317) *Orizaba,* the favourite resort of the Emperor Maximilian (population 115,000, altitude 1,283 metres), lost much of its charm in the 1973 earthquake, when the bullring, many houses and other buildings were lost, and is now heavily industrialized. In the distance is the majestic volcanic cone of Orizaba. The town developed because of the natural springs in the valley, some of which are used by the textile and paper industries and others are dammed to form small pools for bathing beside picnic areas; Nogales (restaurant) is the most popular, Ojo de Agua is another. The Cerro del Borrego, the hill above the Alameda park, is a favourite early-morning climb. The Zócalo at one time lost much of its area to permanent snack bars, but these have been removed. On the N side is the market, with a wide variety of local produce and local women in traditional dress, and the many-domed San Miguel church (1690-1729). There are several other quite good churches, and there is an Orozco mural in the Federal School on Av. Colón. The Palacio Municipal is the actual cast-iron Belgian pavilion brought piece by piece from France after the famous 19th century Paris Exhibition—an odd sight.

Hotels *De France*, E and US$0.25 for parking in courtyard, clean, comfortable, shower, reasonable if uninspiring restaurant; *Aries*, Oriente 6 No. 265, C (nightclub on top floor). *Trueba*, Oriente 6 and Sur 11, C, resort facilities.

Restaurants *Romanchu* and *Paso Real*, on the main street, have excellent cuisine. Hare Krishna vegetarian restaurant, *Radha's*, on Sur 4 between Oriente 1 and 3, excellent. In the market, try the local morning snack, *memelita picadita*.

A road leaves Orizaba southwards, up into the mountains of Zongolica, a dry, poor and isolated region, cold and inhospitable, inhabited by various groups of Indians who speak Nahuatl, the language of the Aztecs. Zongolica village is a good place to buy *sarapes*; take early bus from Orizaba (ask for direct one) to get clear views of the mountains.

Beyond Orizaba the scenery is magnificent. We descend to coffee and sugar-cane country and a tropical riot of flowers. It is very pleasant country except when a northerly blows, or in the intolerable heat and mugginess of the wet season.

(Km. 331) *Fortín de las Flores,* a small town devoted to growing flowers and exporting them. Sometimes Indian women sell choice blossoms in small baskets made of banana-tree bark.

Hotels *Ruiz Galindo*, now run down (swimming pool, over-elaborate for some tastes). *Posada la Loma*, very attractive, moderately expensive. There are others, slightly cheaper, which also offer tropical gardens for relaxation.
   Near Fortín there is a viewpoint looking out over a dramatic gorge (entry free). The *autopista* from Orizaba to Córdoba passes over this deep valley on a concrete bridge.

Córdoba (population 126,000, altitude 923 metres), 8 km. on in the rich valley of the Río Seco, an old colonial city, is also crazy with flowers. Its Zócalo is spacious, leafy and elegant; three sides are arcaded; two of them are lined with tables. On the fourth is an imposing church with a chiming clock. There are several hotels in the Zócalo, which is alive and relaxed at night. In one of them, the *Hotel Zevallos*, Gen. Iturbide signed the Treaty of Córdoba in 1821, which was instrumental in freeing Mexico from Spanish colonial rule. There is a local museum at Calle 3, 303, open 1000-1300 and 1600-2000. Córdoba has the highest rainfall in Mexico, but at predictable times. The area grows coffee.

Hotels *Hostal de Borreña*, Calle 11, 308, modern, clean, really hot water, some traffic noise but good value, D. *Mansur*, Av. 1 y Calle 3, on square, E, smart. Near the ADO terminal is *Palacio; Marina, Iberia, Trescado* and *Casa de Huéspedes Regis* are all on Avenida 2. *Casa de Huéspedes La Sin Rival* and *La Nueva Querétana* are at 511 and 508 of Avenida 4, respectively. *Los Reyes*, F, warmly rec.

The direct road from Córdoba to Veracruz is lined, in season, by stalls selling fruit and local honey between Yanga and Cuitláhuac. Yanga is a small village named after the leader of a group of escaped black slaves in colonial times. A slightly longer but far more attractive road goes from Córdoba northwards through Huatusco and Totutla, then swings E to Veracruz.

(Km. 476) *Veracruz,* the principal port of entry for Mexico (population 1 million, but recently reported to have risen to 850,000), lies on a low alluvial plain bordering the Gulf coast. Cortés landed near here at the site of La Antigua, now a pleasant little colonial town, on April 17, 1519. The town is a mixture of the very old and the new; there are still many picturesque white-walled buildings and winding side-streets. In spite of the occasional chill north winds in winter, it is generally hot and has become a great holiday resort, and is reported touristy and noisy. Some of the beaches in and around Veracruz are polluted from the many ships.
   The food is good, the fishing not bad, and the people lively: there is much marimba and guitar playing, café life and dancing. (The most famous dances, accompanied by the Conjunto Jarocho, are the Bamba and Zapateado to harp and guitar, with much stamping and lashing of feet.) At night the Malecón is very lively, and sometimes fire-eaters and other performers entertain the public. The

Shrovetide carnival 7 weeks before Easter is said to be Mexico's finest, rivalling those of New Orleans, Brazil and Trinidad.

The heart of the city is Plaza Constitución; make at once for the traditional *La Parroquia* café, cool and tiled. (The newer café of the same name on the Malecón does not have the same atmosphere.) The local craft is tortoiseshell jewellery adorned with silver, but remember that the import of tortoiseshell into the USA and many other countries is prohibited. There are two buildings of great interest: the very fine 17th-century Palacio Municipal, on Plaza Constitución, with a splendid façade and courtyard, and the castle of San Juan de Ulúa (1565), on Gallega Island, now joined by road to the mainland; take bus marked Ulúa. It failed to deter the buccaneers and later became a political prison. Mexico's "Robin Hood", Chucho el Roto, was imprisoned there, and escaped three times. (Entry US$0.45.)

There is a city historical museum with good collection of photographs, poorly maintained and exhibits now visible with difficulty, traces history from Conquest to 1910; it is at Zaragoza 397. The Baluarte de Santiago, a small fort which once formed part of the city walls, is at Francisco Canal y Gómez Farias, open 0900-1800, Suns. and holidays, 1600-1900, closed Tues. On the southern arm of the harbour breakwater is a small aquarium (admission US$0.10). The people are called *Jarochos*, after a preconquest Indian group. Helpful tourist office on Zócalo, in Palacio Municipal, has no hotel price list. Airport at Las Bajadas, 3 flights daily to the capital.

The Zócalo, white-paved, and with attractive cast iron lampstands and benches, and surrounded by the cathedral, governor's palace and colonial-style hotels, comes alive in the evening at weekends. An impressive combination of the crush of people, colour and marimba music in the flood-lit setting.

Culturally, Veracruz is a Caribbean city, home not only to the *jarocho* costume (predominantly white), but also to Mexico's version of the Cuban *danzón* music and the indigenous *música tropical*. Many cultural events can be seen at the Instituto Veracruzano de Cultura, a few blocks from the Zócalo.

The beach along the waterfront, and the sea, are filthy, but a short bus ride from the fish market takes you to Mocambo beach, which has a good swimming bath (with restaurant and bar, admission US$0.40), beach restaurants, Caribbean-style beach huts and the water is quite a bit cleaner through still rather uninviting in colour. There are crabs and mosquitoes. The Gulf is even warmer than the Caribbean. The beach is crowded. At holiday time cars race up and down, there are loud radios, etc. There is little shade near the beach.

NB: Travellers are warned to be particularly wary of thieves in Veracruz.

Hotels *Exalaris Hyatt*, Mocambo 4300, L, fanciest on the entire Gulf coast; *Mocambo*, Boca del Río, B, 8 km. out on Mocambo beach, 1930s palace, good service and food, highly rec.; *Veracruz* on Plaza de Armas, C, a/c with pool and night club; *Emporio*, A, overpriced with pool, swimming pool, inexpensive comida corrida, rather old-fashioned, on Paseo del Malecón; a block before the *Emporio* when approaching from the Zócalo is *Puerto Bello*, good, A; *Impala*, on Orizaba, E, with bath, cold water, mosquitoes but clean, near bus station; *Colonial*, C, on Zócalo, swimming pool, indoor parking, rec.; *Oriente*, on Zócalo, E, secure parking, clean, friendly, balconies, good fans, some a/c, quiet, rec.; *Imperial*, on Zócalo, F, with bath. *Royalty*, E, nice and clean, near beach, 20 min. walk from Zócalo, rec., but noisy as it caters mainly to student groups; *Cristóbal Colón*, one block from *Royalty*, E, smaller, quieter, some rooms with sea-view balconies, clean; *Ortiz*, on Zócalo, good value, F, family-owned; *La Paz*, Av. Díaz Mirón 1242, nr. bus station, E, with bath, highly rec., cheap, clean and helpful; *Casa de Huéspedes Alvarez*, Abasolo 987, F, cold water, fan, clean, friendly. *Mar y Tierra*, on Malecón, F, good value, some rooms with balconies overlooking the harbour. *Central*, Mirón 1412, E, clean, get room at back, esp. on 5th floor, laundering facilities; *Ruiz Milán*, D, Malecón, good; *Príncipe*, Collado 195, F, some distance from centre, very clean with hot shower and toilet; *Vigo*, Av. Landero y Casa, F; many others nearby in port area, reached by bus from the bus terminal. Two more on Miguel Lerdo, near the Portales: *Rías* and *Concha Dorada*. CREA Youth Hostel, Paseo Doña Juana, Municipio de Ursulo Galván.

Trailer Parks Several along the ocean side. Two at Mocambo, side by side, bus marked Boca del Río goes there from corner of Zaragoza and Serdán. *Los Arcos* has hot showers, laundry tubs, lighting and plugs, owner speaks English. The other is *Los Arcos Fiesta*; noisy from main beach road, but good and well supervised, esp. at night. Nearest supermarket is on the road into Veracruz at the modern shopping centre.

Restaurants The local gourmet speciality is *langosta loca* (mad lobster). *La Parroquia* (original) has fans, white tiled walls, cement floors and waiters in white jackets, overlooks town square; wonderful coffee, food not marvellous but place crowded in evenings. Also *El Chato Moya* on the Malecón and the market for excellent fish, opp. is an unnamed restaurant, good seafood, and *El Azteca de Cayetano* where mondongos de fruta (a selection of all the fruits in season) are prepared on one plate. *Torros* are the local drinks made of eggs, milk, fruit and alcohol—delicious and potent. *La Paella*, Plaza Constitución, has its name written into the concrete of the entrance floor, no sign otherwise, good comida corrida. There is a good local fish restaurant, *Olympica*, near the fish market in the street running parallel to Av. 16 de Septiembre, 2 blocks from the Zócalo. Tim Connell recommends two places: *Pescadores*, for fish, on Zaragoza (not evenings); and the steakhouse *Submarino Amarillo*. Good shellfish at Boca del Río.

Exchange Only Bancomer and Banamex, on Independencia change money; hotels are quicker and may use same rate—check at the desk.

US Consular Agent Mr Edwin L. Culp, Juárez 110.

Transport Rail to Mexico City: El Jarocho (*servicio estrella*) leaves Mexico City at 2115, arr. Veracruz 0700; leaves Veracruz 2130, arr. 0737, reserved seat US$7.80, single sleeper, US$25.50; ordinary trains at 0725 via Jalapa, at 0800 and 2130 via Córdoba, 1st class US$5.50 (US$7 reserved seat).

The majority of buses are booked solid for three days in advance throughout summer; at all times queues of up to 2 hrs. possible at Mexico City booking offices of bus companies (best company: ADO, Buenavista 9, Mexico City). Book outward journeys on arrival in Veracruz, as the bus station is some way out of town and there are often long queues. For local buses, get accurate information from the tourist office. Buses to the main bus station along Av. 5 de Mayo. Bus to Mexico City, US$4.30 (6 hrs.), via Jalapa, misses out Orizaba, Fortín and Córdoba; to Villahermosa US$12 (10 hrs.); to Puebla, US$3.50; to Oaxaca, ADO, 9 hrs., US$6.

Connections with Guatemala There are no through buses to Guatemala, but there are connecting services. Train leaves Veracruz 0915 daily for Ixtepec and Tapachula; 2nd class only; not recommended, no light for 30 hrs., so high likelihood of robbery. Take your own toiletries and food. No sleeping accommodation. The connecting railway from the border to Guatemala City no longer carries passengers. Local bus services run Tapachula-border and border-Guatemala City; quicker than the much more mountainous route further N. Alternatively, take ADO bus to Oaxaca, then carry on to Tapachula (11½ hrs.) by bus. Another bus to frontier at Hidalgo, US$0.25. This route allows you to stop at intermediate points of your choice, but has few "comfort" stops. Buy bus tickets out of Veracruz well in advance.

Road very winding from Orizaba so take travel sickness tablets if necessary. Philippe Martin, of the Touring Club Suisse, writes: "The road from Veracruz to Oaxaca is spectacular but tiresome to drive and will take about a day. The road from Veracruz to La Tinaja and Tierra Blanca is good and fast although there are many lorries. From there to Miguel Alemán the road is bad, speed reasonable, still many lorries. The Tuxtepec area has lovely lowland, jungle areas, charming villages, and the traffic is sparser between Tuxtepec and Oaxaca, while there are no more gasoline stations. The road is very bad and winding and the fog only lifts after you leave the pines at 2,650 metres above sea level. After a descent and another pass at 2,600 metres you enter the bare mountainous zone of Oaxaca. Very few eating places between Tuxtepec and Oaxaca." This route is possible by bus but the Tuxtepec-Oaxaca stretch has been reported dangerous because of drug-traffickers.

Excursions Isla de Sacrificios, half an hour from the harbour, beautiful beach (trip US$2.20 return). Trips Sundays and holidays, every hour between 0900 and 1400. Excursion to Zempoala (see page 1053), buses from ADO terminal 1½ hrs. each way, via Cardel, or less frequent direct 2nd class buses. On Sunday, to Mandinga for cheap fresh sea food (big prawns), and local entertainment.

The Papaloapan Region At *Puerto Alvarado* (1½ hrs. S from Veracruz by bus, a modern fishing port, *Hotel del Pastor*, F, avoid next-door restaurant), cross the Río Papaloapan (Butterfly River) by a toll bridge (US$0.50), go along Route 180 into the sugar-cane area around Lerdo de Tejada and Angel R. Cavada. At El Trópico a dirt road turns left to some quiet beaches such as Salinas and Roca Partida. Only at Easter are the beaches crowded: they are normally the preserve of fishermen using hand nets from small boats. In the dry season (Dec.-May) the road is passable around the coast to Sontecomapan.

At Tula, a little further along the main road, is a spectacular waterfall, El Salto de Tula; a restaurant is set beside the falls. The road then climbs up into the mountainous volcanic area of Los Tuxtlas, known as the Switzerland of Mexico for its mountains and perennial greenness.

Santiago Tuxtla, set on a river, is a small town of colonial origin. In the main square is the largest known Olmec head, carved in solid stone, and also a museum (open 0900-1500, Sat.-Sun. 0900-1200 and 1500-1800), containing examples of local tools, photos, items used in witchcraft (*brujería*), and the first sugar-cane press used in Mexico and another Olmec head. (*Hotel Central*, E, cold shower, clean.)

The archaeological site of *Tres Zapotes* lies to the west; it is reached by leaving the paved road south towards Villa Isla and taking either the dirt road at Tres Caminos (signposted) in the dry season (a quagmire from May-Dec.), or in the wet season access can be slowly achieved by turning right at about km. 40, called Tibenal, and following the dirt road north to the site of the Museum which is open 0900-1700 hrs. (If it is closed, the lady in the nearby shop has a key.) There is another Olmec head, also the largest carved stela ever found and stela fragments bearing the New World's oldest Long Count Date, equal to 31 B.C. Not far from Tres Zapotes are three other Olmec sites: Cerro de las Mesas, Laguna de los Cerros, and San Lorenzo Tenochtitlán.

Overlooking Santiago Tuxtla is the hillside restaurant *El Balcón*, which serves excellent langostino (crayfish) for US$4 and *horchata de coco*, a drink made from the flesh and milk of coconut.

15 km. beyond lies **San Andrés Tuxtla** (112,000), the largest town of the area, with narrow winding streets, by-passed by a ring road. This town is also colonial in style and has a well-stocked market with Oaxacan foods such as *totopos, carne enchilada*, and *tamales de elote* (hard tortillas, spicy meat, and cakes of maize-flour steamed on leaves). It is the terminus for trains (daily) from Rodríguez Clara to the south (**see page 1052**) and it is the centre of the cigar trade. One factory beside the main road permits visitors to watch the process and will produce special orders of cigars (*puros*) marked with an individual's name in ½ hr. Near the town centre is the restaurant *La Flor de Guadalajara*; it appears small from the outside but is large and pleasant inside, well rec.; sells *tepachue*, a drink made from pineapple, similar in flavour to cider, and *agua de Jamaica*. Hotels: *Catedral*, nr. Cathedral, F, very nice; *Figueroa, del Parque*, Madero 5, E, a/c, very clean, good restaurant; *Casa de Huéspedes la Orizabana*, in the centre of town, F, without bath, clean hot water, friendly; *Ponce de León*, primitive, pleasant patio, F. (Bus San Andrés Tuxtla-Villahermosa US$5.50, 6 hrs.)

At Sihuapan, 5 km. towards Catemaco, is a turning to the right on to a very bumpy dirt road which leads to the impressive waterfall of Salto de Eyipantla. Bridge toll payable at Comoapan, US$0.10, plenty of small boys offer their services as guides.

Catemaco is a pleasant little town (31,000 people) with large colonial church and picturesque situation on lake, 13 km. from San Andrés Tuxtla. Beware of thieves at all times. At weekends there is a stall selling handicrafts from Oaxaca, and boat trips out on the lakes to see the shrine where the Virgin appeared, the spa at Coyame and the Isla de Changos, and to make a necklace of lilies, are always available (about US$5). The town is noted for its *brujos* (sorcerers) and the Monte del Cerro Blanco to the north is the site of their annual reunion. Catemaco can be reached by bus from Veracruz, changing to a local bus at San Andrés Tuxtla; it is about 120 km. NW of Minatitlán (**see page 1085**). Catemaco is synonymous throughout Mexico with picturesque, vulgar language.

Hotels and Restaurants *Catemaco*, D, excellent food and swimming pool, and *Angel*, a/c, satellite TV, similar prices; both on main square. *Motel Playa Azul*, some km. away, C, modern, a/c; in a nice setting, comfortable and shady, with water-skiing on lake. A number of hotels are situated at the lakeside; *Posada Komiapan* (swimming-pool and restaurant), very comfortable, D; *Brujos*, F, fan, a/c, shower, nice clean rooms, balcony overlooking the lake; *Los Arcos*, E, clean, fan, good value. On the promenade are a number of good restaurants—*María José*, best; *La Julita* (anguilla and tacholgolo), *La Ola* (payiscadas, anguilla, tegogalso, carne de chango, and cesina) built almost entirely by the owner in the local natural materials, and *La Luna*, among others. Best value are those not directly on the lake e.g. *Los Sauces*, which serves mojarra.

The Gulf Coast may be reached from Catemaco along a dirt road (which can be washed out in winter). It is about 18 km. to Sontecomapan, crossing over the pass at Buena Vista and looking down to the Laguna where, it is said, Francis Drake sought refuge. The village of **Sontecomapan** (1,465 pop., *Hotel Sontecomapan*) lies on an entry to the Laguna and boats may be hired for the 20-min. ride out to the bar where the Laguna meets the sea (US$10 return). A large part of the Laguna is surrounded by mangrove swamp, and the sandy beaches, edged by cliffs, are almost deserted except for local fishermen and groups of pelicans. Two good restaurants in Sontecomapan. Beaches are accessible to those who enjoy isolation—such as Jicacal and Playa Hermosa. Jicacal can be reached by going straight on from the Catemaco-Sontecomapan road for 9 km. on a good dirt road to La Palma where there is a small bridge which is avoided by heavy vehicles; immediately after this take left fork (dirt road) for Monte Pío and watch out for a very small sign marked Playa Escondida; road impassable when wet, about 12 km., and then continuing for about 4 km. from there. Playa Jicacal is long and open, the first you see as you near the water. The track reaches a T-junction, on the right Jicacal, to the left Playa Escondida. It is not rec. to sleep on the beaches (assaults and robberies) although at Easter time many people from the nearby towns camp on the beaches.

At **Acayucán** (*Hotel Joalica*, Zaragoza 4, E; *Hotel Ritz*, D, adequate), 267 km. from Veracruz, turn right for Route 185 if you want to go across the Isthmus to Tehuantepec, Tuxtla Gutiérrez and Central America, but continue on Route 180 for Minatitlán, Coatzacoalcos and Villahermosa (Tabasco). The road across the Isthmus is straight but is not always fast to drive because of high winds (changing air systems from Pacific to Atlantic). Gasoline and food on sale at the half-way point, Palomares, where there is a paved road to Tuxtepec (**see page 1052**), 2½ hours' drive. A few kilometres south of Palomares a gravelled road enters on the eastern side; this passes under an imposing gateway "La Puerta de Uxpanapa" where some 24,500 families are being settled on land reclaimed from the jungle. An hour's drive further south the road crosses the watershed and passes across the flat coastal plain to Juchitán (**see page 1074**).

About 15 km. from Alvarado a new bridge replaces the old ferry-crossing at Buenavista over the Papaloapan River and the road heads southwards to the fishing village of **Tlacotalpan** where the Papaloapan and San Juan rivers meet. This town, regarded as the centre of the Jarocho Indian culture, has many picturesque streets with one-storey houses all fronted by stuccoed columns and arches painted in various bright pastel colours. Two churches in the Zócalo, and a Casa de las Artesanías on Chazaro, 1½ blocks from the Zócalo. The Museo Funster contains interesting local paintings and artefacts. There is a famous *fiesta* there on January 31 which is very much for locals rather than tourists (accommodation is impossible to find during *fiesta*). The *Viajero* and *Reforma* hotels are good; so is the *Posada Doña Lala*, D with a/c and TV, restaurant expensive. Excellent *sopa de mariscos* and *jaiba a la tlacotalpina* (crab) at the *Restaurant La Flecha*. Buses go to Veracruz via Alvarado (US$0.35, 45 mins.), to San Andrés, Tuxtla Gutiérrez, Santiago Tuxtla (US$1, 1½ hrs.) and Villahermosa.

Cosamaloapan, some 40 km. beyond Tlacotalpan (103,000 people), is the local market centre with a number of hotels, and the staging point for most bus lines from Veracruz, Orizaba and Oaxaca. One of the largest sugar mills in Mexico is situated just outside the town— Ingenio San Cristóbal—and there is a local airstrip. From Cosamaloapan to Papaloapan the banks on either side of the river are lined with fruit trees. Chacaltianguis, on the east bank of the river, reached by car ferry, has houses fronted by columns.

40 km. beyond Cosamaloapan is a ferry to **Otatitlán,** also on the east bank of the river (it leaves whenever there are sufficient passengers, US$0.08 the ride). The town, also known as El Sanctuario, dates back to early colonial times, its houses with tiled roofs supported by columns, but most interesting is the church. The padre maintains that the gold-patterned dome is the largest unsupported structure of its kind in Mexico, measuring 20 metres wide and 40 high. El Sanctuario has one of the three black wooden statues of Christ brought over from Spain for the son of Hernán Cortés. During the anti-clerical violence of the 1930s attempts to burn it failed, although the original head was cut off and now stands in a glass case. The first weekend in May is the saint's day and fair, for which pilgrims flock in from the *sierra* and from the Tuxtlas, many in local dress. (*Restaurant-Bar Pepe* serves delicious local, but unusual food; *Restaurant-Bar Ipiranga III* also offers excellent cooking; both by embarkation point.)

At **Papaloapan** on the eastern bank of the river, the main road from Orizaba to Rodríguez Clara crosses the main road from Alvarado to Oaxaca; the railway station has services to Yucatán and Chiapas, and to Orizaba or Veracruz. On the west bank is the bus terminal of Santa Cruz (almost under the railway bridge) where all second class buses stop. A passenger ferry may be taken from here to Papaloapan (US$0.08). Although Papaloapan is the route centre for the area the most convenient centre is Tuxtepec, 9 km. further south (see below).

The river basin drained by the Papaloapan and its tributaries covers some 47,000 sq. km.— about twice the size of the Netherlands—and is subject to a programme of regional development by the Comisión del Papaloapan, which includes the construction of two large dams to control the sometimes severe flooding of the lower basin. The lake formed behind Presidente Alemán dam at Temascal is scenically very attractive and boats may be hired to go to Mazatec Indian settlements on the islands or on the other side. There is also a daily ferry passing round the lake. Soyaltepec is the closest settlement, situated high above the water on an island, the peak crowned by a church. **Ixcatlan** lies on a peninsula jutting into the lake on the SE side; it has one hotel and one restaurant, as well as a large beer repository. Ixcatlan may also be reached by dirt road from Tuxtepec, but it is less nerve-racking to take a ferry.

Temascal (Sun. is the most active day) may be reached by taking Route 145 from Papaloapan through Gabino Barreda, Ciudad Alemán (no facilities, centre of the Papaloapan Commission), Novara (petrol and 3 restaurants of varying prices, 1 air-conditioned), as far as La Granja where the turn to Temascal is clearly marked. Route 145 continues paved and straight past Tres Valles (cheap, good regional food; annual fair mid-Nov.), and on to **Tierra Blanca** (hotels *Balun Canán*, cheap, hot, F; *Principal*, E, own shower and fan, clean, just above bus station, noisy; *Bimbis* restaurant by ADO bus station, good; shopping centre, market, car repairs, e.g. Volkswagen agent). Mérida train from Tierra Blanca leaves late although scheduled for 0530 (2nd class, US$2.90, crowded, sleeper for 1—or two small people—US$11) stops at Palenque, 15½ hrs. later. Train also stops at Ciudad Alemán on the way. Route 145 passes under a sign saying "La Puerta del Papaloapan", to join the main Orizaba-Veracruz road (Route 150) at **La Tinaja,** a second-class bus junction, also gasoline, and restaurants (1 air-conditioned at service station). Papaloapan to La Tinaja takes about 1 hr., the road often has a lot of lorries and in the cane-cutting season great care should be taken at night for carts travelling on the road without lights. There are three railway crossings on the road, also poorly marked, two near La Granja and one near Tierra Blanca. The tarmac is often damaged in the wet season (June-Dec.).

From Papaloapan a paved road runs eastwards as far as Rodríguez Clara (planned to continue to Sayula on the Trans-Isthmian road). This road passes through the main pineapple-producing region of Mexico, which has encouraged the development of towns such as **Loma Bonita** (local airstrip, hotels, restaurants and gasoline) and *Villa Isla* (hotels, *La Choca* restaurant good, railway station, ADO bus terminal, and centre for the rich cattle-producing area that surrounds it).

From Villa Isla a good dirt road runs south to *Playa Vicente* (6,974 pop.), another ranching town, located beside a wide river; excellent crayfish may be eaten at the *Restaurant La Candileja*, while the café on the central plaza serves tender steaks. Another dirt road leaves the Villa Isla-Playa Vicente road for Abasolo del Valle (2,000 pop.), but only reaches to within 7 km. The last few kms. can be impassable by vehicle in the wet season. The town is set beside a lagoon and the houses are surrounded by fruit trees (no hotels or restaurants). Gasoline can be bought—ask at a shop who has some to sell.

At the cross-roads of the Papaloapan-Sayula road about 80 km. from Papaloapan, where the S turn is to Villa Isla, the N turn is a paved road which in about ½ hour will take you past two turnings to Tres Zapotes and up to Santiago Tuxtla.

The road from Papaloapan continues E to a point just N of *Rodríguez Clara,* which is reached by branching off S down a dirt road. This is a compact, thriving town, also with a railway station. There are 2 hotels, the better is in the centre of the town, *Hotel Roa,* E; *Restaurant Mexicana* rec. The railway line from Papaloapan is the only all-year means of transport to visit the villages and towns E of Rodríguez Clara.

Tuxtepec is the natural centre for a stay in the Papaloapan area. It is a small market town some 9 km. south of Papaloapan (toll for Caracol bridge, US$0.40). Consequently the streets are alive every day in season with Indians who have come from surrounding villages to buy and sell, and there is a fascinating mixture of the music and exuberance of Veracruz with the food and handicrafts of Oaxaca. The town is built on a meander of the Santo Domingo River and a walk past the main shops in Calle Independencia will allow two halts at viewpoints for the river.

Hotels *El Rancho*, restaurant, bar, evening entertainment, most expensive, accepts travellers' cheques as payment, rec.; *Tuxtepec*, good value; *Sacre*, also good, quiet, F; *Catedral*, Calle Guerrero, nr. Zócalo, E, very friendly, fan and shower; *Miramar*, E, hot showers, safe car park, with view of filthy river. Very good value is the *Avenida* in Independencia round the corner from ADO bus station, E, with bath and ventilator, basic, clean but restaurant below not very good value. *Posada del Sol*, basic and noisy, opp. Fletes y Pasajes bus station, F.

Restaurants *El Estero* across from the street from ADO (fish dishes and local cuisine excellent), *El Mino* (near Fletes y Pasajes bus terminal), *Mandinga* for fish dishes, *Queso Fundido* in Independencia. *Ostionería Pata-Pata*, on the street beside *Hotel Avenida*, good mojarra. *Ronda*, Calle Independencia, cheap and good; *La Mascota de Oro*, 20 de Noviembre 891, very friendly, cheap. Beer from the barrel can be bought from the bar next to the Palacio Municipal, and the best ices are found in *La Morida*.

Transport There are four bus terminals in town, clear street signs for each one. ADO bus services to Mexico City (Thurs., US$7), Veracruz and regular daily minibus (taking 5-6 hrs.) to Oaxaca leaving at 0800 and 1230. AU (Autobuses Unidos, on Matamoros, ½ block from Libertad) daily to wide variety of destinations. AU to Oaxaca, US$4 2nd class, 8 hrs., slow. Fletes y Pasajes to local villages and Juchitán, and a 2nd class, wild journey to Oaxaca, 6 hrs.; Cristóbal Colón, which has its own terminal near the Cultural Centre, sometimes stop by the ADO office to find passengers for Chiapas or Mexico City. The Tuxtepec-Palomares road provides a short cut to the Transístmica; it passes through many newly cleared jungle areas. Bus to Acayucán, ADO, 4 hrs., US$1.50. There are scattered villages, the main halt being at María Lombardo (some 2 hrs. from Tuxtepec where food is sold); Zócalo is attractive. Gas station 4 km. further on at Cihualtepec junction, a village of Indians moved from the area flooded by the Temascal dam.

Excursions To Temascal to see the dam (see previous page); also a visit to the Indian villages of Ojitlán and Jalapa de Díaz (bus leaves from the end of Calle 20 de Noviembre, US$2.20, 2½ hrs.; hotel, F and food stores, good and cheaper *huipiles* from private houses) is well worth the ride; easily reached by car along semi-paved road and also by AU bus service (from Mercado Flores Magón, 20 de Noviembre y Blvd. Juárez, every hour on the half hour). The Chinantec Indians' handicrafts may be bought on enquiry; hotels non-existent and eating facilities limited but some superb scenery, luxuriant vegetation and little-visited area. Ojitlán is best visited on Sunday, market day, when the Chinanteca *huipiles* worn by the women are most likely to be seen. Part of the area will be flooded when the Cerro de Oro dam is finished and the lake will join that of Temascal. Heavily armed checkpoint on the road from Tuxtepec to Tierra Blanca (bus 1½ hrs., US$0.50), non-uniformed men, very officious, do not get caught with any suspicious goods.

The road from Tuxtepec south to Oaxaca (Route 175) is now well paved, and a spectacular route. Many people avoid it; it is said to have become dangerous for travellers because of drug plantations along its length. It takes about 5 hrs. to drive, up Valle Nacional. This valley, despite its horrific reputation as the "Valle de los Miserables" in the era of Porfirio Díaz, for political imprisonment and virtual slavery from which there was no escape, is astoundingly beautiful. The road follows the valley floor, on which are cattle pastures, fruit trees and a chain of small villages such as Chiltepec (very good bathing in the river), Jacatepec (reached by ferry over the river, produces rich honey and abounds in all varieties of fruit, there are no cars at all), Monte Flor (where swimming and picnicking are possible beside natural springs, but very cold water, and an archaeological site) and finally Valle Nacional. (Bus to Valle Nacional from Tuxtepec, 1½ hrs., basic hotel, restaurants, stores, and gasoline available; river swimming.) The road climbs up into the Sierra, getting cooler, and slopes more heavily covered with tropical forest, and there are panoramic views.

San Pedro Yolox lies some 20 minutes' drive W of this route down a dirt road; it is a peaceful Chinantec village clustered on the side of the mountain, while Llano de Flores is a huge grassy clearing in the pine forest with grazing animals and cool, scented air. Wood from these forests is cut for the paper factory in Tuxtepec. Ixtlán de Juárez has gasoline. While houses in the lowlands are made of wood with palm roofs, here the houses are of adobe or brick. From Guelatao (see page 1073) it is about 1½ hours' drive, mainly downhill, to Oaxaca (see page 1066), with the land becoming drier and the air warmer.

By the road followed to Veracruz, the driving time from Mexico City is about 9 hrs. One can return to the capital by a shorter route through Jalapa which takes 6 hrs.; this was the old colonial route to the port, and is the route followed by the railway.

Jalapa, capital of Veracruz state, 132 km. from the port, is in the *tierra templada,* at 1,425 metres. There was a passion for renovation in the flamboyant gothic style during the first part of the 19th century. It is yet another "City of Flowers", with walled gardens, stone-built houses, wide avenues in the newer town and steep cobbled crooked streets in the old. The 18th century cathedral, with its sloping floor, has been recently restored. Population 213,000. Just outside, on the road to Mexico City, is a modern museum (opened Oct. 1986) showing archaeological treasures of the Olmec, Totonac and Huastec coastal cultures. The three colossal heads dating from the 2nd to the 5th centuries A.D., and displayed in the grounds of the museum, are Olmec. Jalapa (spelt Xalapa locally) has a University; you can take a pleasant stroll round the grounds, known as El Dique.

Festival   Feria de Primavera, mid-April.

Hotels   Cheaper hotels are up the hill from the market, which itself is uphill from Parque Juárez (there is no Zócalo). Many hotels are overpriced; no price-lists displayed and not available at tourist office. *María Victoria,* Zaragoza 6, B, good; *México,* Lucio 4, E, clean, with shower; *Salmones,* Zaragoza 24, E, rec. *Amoro,* nr. market, F, no shower but public baths opp., very clean. *Hotel Suites,* by ADO bus station, E with bath, clean, not too friendly; *Continental,* on Enríquez, F, friendly.

Restaurants   *La Parroquia,* Zaragoza 18, rec., good strong coffee; *La Barranquilla,* expensive but good; *Quinto Reyno,* Juárez 67 close to Zócalo, lunches only, excellent vegetarian with health-food shop, very good service. *Chino's,* on Enríquez, very friendly and pleasant; *Enrico,* good value; *El Mayab,* next to *Hotel Regis,* for antojitos and good carne tampiqueña; *La Tasca,* a club, good music, rec.

Theatre   Teatro del Estado, Av. Avila Camacho; good Ballet Folklórico Veracruzano and fair symphony orchestra.

Communications   Radio-telephone available opposite *Hotel María Victoria.* Letters can be sent to the Lista de Correos in Calle Diego Leño, friendly post office.

Airport   15 km. SE, on Veracruz road.

Transport   2nd class bus station, Autobuses Unidos, uphill from Parque Juárez. 1st class buses (ADO) leave from the terminal 1 km. away. Frequent ADO service Jalapa-Veracruz. To Puebla, ADO, 4 hrs. To Villahermosa, ADO, 3 a day, 10 hrs. Railway station on outskirts, buses from near market to get there. Train to Mexico City at 1140, to Veracruz at 1530 (4 hrs.).

Excursions   To ruins of *Zempoala* (hotel, *Chachalaca,* near sea, spotless, rec.), the coastal city which was conquered by Cortés and whose inhabitants became his allies. The ruins are interesting because of the round stones uniquely used in construction. (Entry US$0.40, small museum on site.) Take 2nd class bus to Zempoala via Cardel, which will let you off at the ruins, or take a taxi from the Plaza of Zempoala, US$1.20 return. You can also get there from Veracruz. To Texala waterfalls, some 15 km. away near the neighbouring town of Coatepec, famous for its ice-cream.

Tim Connell writes: "*Naolinco* is ½ hr. ride, 40 km. NE of Jalapa up a winding hilly road,

Restaurant La Fuente serves local food; has nice garden. Las Cascadas, with a *mirador* to admire them from, are on the way into the town: two waterfalls, with various pools, tumble several thousand feet over steep wooded slopes. Flocks of *zopilotes* (buzzards) collect late in the afternoon, soaring high up into the thermals. Baños Carrizal: 8 km. off main road, 40 km. from Veracruz. Chachalacas is a beach with swimming pool and changing facilities in hotel of same name, US$0.70 adults. Thatched huts; local delicacies sold on beach, including *robalito* fish." Also, to El Tajín, **see page 975**.

The road towards the capital continues to climb to Perote, 53 km. from Jalapa. The San Carlos fort here, now a military prison, was built in 1770-77; there is a good view of Cofre de Perote volcano. A road branches N to **Teziutlán** (*Hotel Valdez*, hot water, car park, F), with a Friday market, where good *sarapes* are sold, continuing to Papantla (**see page 975**). The old convent at **Acatzingo**, 93 km. beyond, is worth seeing. Another 10 km. and we join the road to Puebla and Mexico City.

Mount Orizaba   From Acatzingo one can go via a paved road to Tlachichuca (35 km.) and contact the Reyes family to get a four-wheel drive car to go up an appalling road to a hut on Mount Orizaba (Citlaltépetl), the highest peak in Mexico (5,700 metres). There is no hut custodian; it's usually fairly empty, except on Sat. night. No food or light, or wood; provide your own. There is a glacier some 150 metres above the hut. Water close at hand, but no cooking facilities.

MEXICO CITY-CUERNAVACA-TAXCO-ACAPULCO (7)

A 406-km. road, beginning as a 4-lane toll motorway, connects Mexico City with Acapulco. (The 4-lane ends at Iguala, 209 km. from Acapulco.) Driving time is about 6 hrs. The highest point, La Cima, 3,016 metres, is reached at km. 42. The road then spirals down through precipitous forests to (Km. 75):

Cuernavaca, capital of Morelos state (originally Tlahuica Indian territory); at 1,542 metres: 724 metres lower than Mexico City. Population 233,000 and growing (possibly now 400,000) because of new industrial area to the S. The temperature never exceeds 27°C nor falls below 10°C, and there is almost daily sunshine even during the rainy season. The city has always attracted visitors from the more rigorous highlands and can be overcrowded. The Spaniards captured it in 1521 and Cortés himself, following the custom of the Aztec nobility, lived there. The outskirts are dotted with ultra-modern walled homes.

The Cathedral, finished in 1552, known as Iglesia de la Asunción, stands at one end of an enclosed garden. 17th-century murals were discovered during restoration; also, on the great doors, paintings said to have been done by an Oriental convert who arrived by a ship from the Philippines, relating the story of the persecution and crucifixion of 24 Japanese martyrs. The Sun. morning masses at 1100 are accompanied by a special *mariachi* band. *Mariachis* also perform on Sun. and Wed. evenings in the Cathedral. By the entrance to it stands the charming small church of the Tercera Orden (1529), whose quaint façade carved by Indian craftsmen contains a small figure suspected to be one of the only two known statues of Cortés in Mexico. (The other is a mounted statue near the entrance of the *Casino de la Selva* hotel.)

The palace Cortés built in 1531 for his second wife stands by the city's central tree-shaded plaza; on the rear balcony is a Diego Rivera mural depicting the conquest of Mexico. It was the seat of the State Legislature until 1967, when the new legislative building opposite was completed; it has now become the Regional Cuauhnahuac museum, showing everything from dinosaur remains to contemporary Indian culture (closed Thurs., as are other museums in Cuernavaca). The 18th century Borda Gardens, on Calle Morelos, were a favourite resort of Maximilian and Carlota, but have now more or less run wild (small fee). The weekend retreat of the ill-fated imperial couple, in the Acapantzingo district, is being restored. Other places worth seeing are the three plazas, Calle Guerrero, and, some distance from the main plaza, the new market buildings on different levels. The house of David Alfaro Siqueiros, the painter, is now a museum at Calle Venus 7 and contains lithographs and personal photographs. The very unusual Teopanzolco pyramid is to be found near the railway station. Remarkable frescoes have recently been found in the old Franciscan church of La Parroquia. There are occasional concerts at the San

José open chapel. Many spas in surrounding area, at Cuautla, Xocitepec, Atrotomilco, Oaxtepec and others.

Hotels *Las Mañanitas,* Linares 107, L (one of the best in Mexico), Mexican colonial style, many birds in lovely gardens, excellent food. *Hacienda de Cortés,* Atlacomulco suburb, 16th century sugar *hacienda,* magnificent genuine colonial architecture, garden, suites, pool, restaurant, A, access by car; *Posada Jacarandas,* Cuauhtémoc 805, A, garden, restaurant, parking; *Suites Paraíso,* Av. Domingo Diez 1100, family accommodation, B; *Posada Xochiquetzal,* Francisco Leyva 200, near Zócalo, restaurant, pool, garden, A. *Posada San Angelo,* Privada la Selva 100, restaurant, gardens, pool, A; *Casino de la Selva,* A, Leandro Valle 26, with huge mural by Siqueiros on the future of humanity from now till A.D. 3000, shops, restaurant, bars, gardens; *Hostería Las Quintas,* Av. las Quintas 107, A, built in traditional Mexican style, owner has splendid collection of bonsai trees, restaurant, pool, magnificent setting, fine reputation; *Papagayo,* Motolinia 13, 5 blocks from Zócalo, D, incl. breakfast, pool, gardens, clean, convenient, noisy, suitable for families, parking; *Hostería Peñalba,* Matamoros 204, D, beautiful courtyard with exotic birds and a monkey, restaurant with famous Spanish food (long-term guests only), was once Zapata's H.Q. during the Revolution, very atmospheric and friendly but disappointing facilities, much insect life, rooms on street are very noisy; *Casa de Huéspedes,* Morelos Sur 702, good value, D including 3 good meals; for economy, *Roma,* Matamoros 405, E, good value, with hot water 0700-0800 and shower. Probably cheapest is *Casa Blanca,* on Arista, 2 blocks from bus station, simple, F. Rooms from US$75 a month on Calle Degollado 104, quite clean, but heavy bus traffic outside; communal kitchen and bath. Furnished flat US$200 per month. Several cheaper hotels in Calle Aragón y León, rec. is *Colonia,* No. 104, E, clean, friendly, secure; *El Buen Vecino, Casa La Paz, Marilú, Francés,* and *América,* E, noisy (couples only, but clean, basic; some rent rooms by the hour).

Motels *Los Canarios,* Morelos 711, E, old, crumbling; *El Verano,* Zapata 602, C; *Posada Cuernavaca,* Paseo del Conquistador, view, restaurant, grounds, B; *Suites OK Motel* with *Restaurant Las Margaritas,* Zapata 71, special student and long-term rates, apartments, trailer park; swimming pool and squash courts; T (731) 3-12-70. *Torrell,* Jesús Preciado 414, nr. San Antón suburb, student discounts, E.

Restaurants *Las Mañanitas,* beautiful but expensive, Ricardo Linares 107; *Sumiya,* Barbara Hutton's oriental mountain-top retreat, in the suburbs, exquisite decor, must be seen; *Hostería Las Quintas,* Las Quintas 107, excellent; *Harry's Grill,* on Hidalgo, excellent Mexican food, good service and prices; *Los Arcos,* opp. post office in Zócalo, good, prices reasonable, favourite meeting place in a.m., full at weekends. *Casa de Gardenias,* opp. Cortés' palace, open air, food good at US$2 a dish; *Villa Roma* on Zócalo, good chilaquiles for breakfast, good service, pricier; *Château Renee,* Swiss-European cuisine, Atzingo 11, in woods above town. *Mister Grill,* entrance to town, steak house; *Eric Pup,* 2nd floor on main square, German-Mexican food; *Baalbek,* Netzahualcoyotl 300, gorgeous garden, best Lebanese food in town; *Vienés,* Lerdo de Tejada 4, German-Swiss food, very good; *La Parroquía,* main square, very popular, sidewalk café; *Madreterra del Oro,* in pretty patio near Cortés' palace, good vegetarian food. *Portal,* nearby, in Calle Galeana, has good cheap breakfasts. Mexican food at *Los Comales,* Morelos Sur 1321; *Hacienda Los Ocampo,* rec. for *mariachi* music, at 1400 the house-band plays, Av. Plan de Ayala 310 and at No. 616 *Nuevo Comedor Pachuquilla; Mi Ranchito,* Domingo Diez 1518; vegetarian food at *La Remolada* on Matamoros, good, classical music; bar with live music at the *Parrilla Danesa* (guitar); Yucatán specialities at *Merendero Yucateco,* F. Villa 112.

Language Schools There are about 12 Spanish courses on offer. These start from US$45 per week at the University, 4 hrs. daily; private schools charge US$80-125 a week, 5-6 hrs. a day and some schools also have a US$80-100 registration fee. The peak time for tuition is summer: at other times it may be possible to arrive and negotiate a reduction of up to 25%. There is a co-operative language centre, Cuauhnahuac, with Spanish courses, at 1414 Av. Morelos Sur. Intensive courses also at Instituto Panamericano, Morelos Sur 712 (nearest school to centre); Instituto de Idiomas y Culturas Latino Americanas, Dr. Manuel Mazari 100, Col. Miraval; Instituto Fénix, Av. Panorámica 2, Col. Lomas San Antón, which also has excursions and minor courses in politics, art and music; Cale, Nueva Tabachín, 22-A bis, Col. Tlaltenango, friendly; Cemanahuac, Calle San Juan 4, Las Palmas, which includes weaving and pottery classes; Experiencia, which encompasses all these features, Registro Público 16, Colonia Burocrática; Cidoc, Av. Río Balsas 14, Colonia Vista Hermosa; Ideal, Privada de la Pradera 107; and Idel, Las Palmas 101, Colonia Jiguilpan. Staying with a local family will be arranged by a school and costs US$10-15 a day or US$100-250 a month incl. meals; check with individual schools, as this difference in price may apply even if you stay with the same family.

Telephones Long-distance calls can be made at Farmacia Central, on the Zócalo.

Tourist Office Av. Morelos Sur 900, very helpful, many maps also opp. cathedral, on 2nd floor of old office building (with gardens). For cultural activities, go for information to the university building behind the Cathedral on Morelos Sur.

Railway Station on Calle Amacuzac; only passenger service is daily train to Iguala.

Buses Terminal on Av. López Mateos, adjacent to main market. To Mexico City 0600-2200, every 15 mins.: Estrella de Oro, 1st class, US$1.20, Flecha Roja, 2nd class, 2 hr. journey, US$0.65. To Acapulco, 6 hrs. with either. To Taxco, Flecha Roja, 2nd-class buses from Calle Morelos, US$0.80, 1½ hours, fairly comfortable, about every hour, or Estrella de Oro, 1st class, Las Palmas-Morelos Sur. Cuautla (page 1066) via Yautepec every hour, 1 hr., interesting trip; go there for long-distance buses going South.

Warning Theft of luggage from waiting buses in Cuernavaca is rife; don't ever leave belongings unattended.

Excursions To the Chapultepec Park, W end of town, with boating facilities, small zoo, water gardens, small admission charge. To the potters' village of **San Antón**, perched above a waterfall, a little W of the town, where divers perform Sun. for small donations. To the charming suburb of **Acapantzingo**, S of the town, another retreat of Maximilian. To **Tepoztlán**—24 km.—at the foot of the spectacular El Tepozteco national park, picturesque steep cobbled streets, wild view, with Tepozteco pyramid high up in the mountains (US$0.30, open 0900-1700), the climb is an hour long, and strenuous, but the view is magnificent) and a remarkable 16th century church and convent (entry US$0.45, site closes at 1630) the Virgin and Child stand upon a crescent moon above the elaborate plateresque portal; now sporting a noticeably "hippy" population (*Posada del Tepozteco*, a very good inn, C, with swimming pool and excellent atmosphere; *Casa de Huéspedes Las Cabañas*, D, overpriced; budget travellers would do better to stay in Cuernavaca. *Restaurant Carmen*, S of convent, rec.). There is a small archaeological museum behind the church. This was the village studied by Robert Redfield and later by Oscar Lewis. Local bus from Cuernavaca Flecha Roja terminal takes 40 mins., US$0.40; bus to Mexico City, US$0.90.

Near Cuernavaca is Chalcatzingo, where there are interesting Olmec-style rock carvings. Near Jojutla is the old Franciscan convent of Tlaquiltenango (1540), frequent bus service. About 60 km. from Cuernavaca are the Malinoca pyramids, on a temple carved just before the Conquest from solid rock: interesting.

(Km. 100) **Alpuyeca,** whose church has good Indian murals. A road to the left runs to **Lake Tequesquitengo** (*Paraíso Ski Club*) and the lagoon and sulphur baths of Tehuixtla. Near the lake a popular resort—swimming, boating, water skiing and fishing—is *Hacienda Vista Hermosa* (A), Hernán Cortés's original *ingenio* (sugar mill), and several lakeside hotels (also at Jojutla, above). From Alpuyeca also a road runs right for 50 km. to the **Cacahuamilpa** caverns (known locally as "Las Grutas"); some of the largest caves in North America, open 1000 to 1700 (well lit); strange stalactite and stalagmite formations; steps lead down from near the entrance to the caverns to the double opening in the mountainside far below, from which an underground river emerges (entry, US$0.60, up to 1600).

Buses going to Cacahuamilpa from Cuernavaca leave every 20 mins. between 1000 and 1700 (1 hr.); they are usually overcrowded at weekends; enquire about schedules for local buses or buses from Taxco to Toluca, which stop there (from Taxco, 30 km., 40 minutes). Guided tours take you 2 km. inside; some excursions have gone 6 km; the estimated maximum depth is 16 km.

At 15 km. is the right-hand turn to the **Xochicalco** ruins (36 km. SW of Cuernavaca), topped by a pyramid on the peak of a rocky hill, dedicated to the

Plumed Serpent whose coils enfold the whole building and enclose fine carvings which represent priests. The site is large: needs 2-3 hrs. to see it properly.

Xochicalco was at its height between 650 and 900 AD. It is one of the oldest known fortresses in Middle America and a religious centre as well as an important trading point. The name means "place of flowers" although now the hilltops are barren. It was also the meeting place of northern and southern cultures and both calendar systems were correlated here. The sides of the pyramid are faced with andesite slabs, fitted invisibly without mortar. After the building was finished, reliefs 3-4 inches deep were carried into the stone as a frieze. There are interesting underground tunnels; one has a shaft to the sky and the centre of the cave. There are also ball courts, an avenue 18.5 metres wide and 46 m. long, remains of 20 large circles and of a palace and dwellings. Xochicalco is well worth the 4 km. walk from the bus stop; take a torch for the underground part to save employing a guide, entry US$0.10. (Flecha Roja bus to Xochicalco from terminal at Av. Morelos y Arista, marked Las Grutas, passes the turn-off to Xochicalco—same bus schedule as Cacahuamilpa, above.) Alternatively take bus from Cuernavaca to Cuentepec (infrequent), which passes by the entrance gate to Xochicalco ruins. This bus passes through Alpuyeca, which is also easily reached from Taxco by bus.

Leave the toll road at Amacuzac (Km. 121) and take the old road (39 km.) to *Taxco,* a colonial gem, population 76,000, with steep, twisting, cobbled streets and many picturesque buildings. The first silver shipped to Spain came from the mines of Taxco. A Frenchman, Borda, made and spent three fortunes here in the 18th century; he founded the present town and built the magnificent twin-towered, rose-coloured parish church of Santa Prisca which soars above everything but the mountains. Well worth a visit are the Casa Humboldt, where Baron von Humboldt once stayed, and the Casa Figueroa, the "House of Tears" (closed Sun.), so called because the colonial judge who owned it forced Indian labourers to work on it to pay their fines. Museo Guillermo Spratling, behind Santa Prisca, is a fascinating silver museum, entry US$0.20. Large paintings about Mexican history at the Post Office. The roof of every building is of red tile, every nook or corner in the place is a picture, and even the cobblestone road surfaces have patterns woven in them. It is now a national monument and all modern building is forbidden. Gas stations are outside the city limits. The plaza is 1,700 metres above sea-level. A good view is had from the Iglesia de Guadalupe. The climate is ideal, never any high winds (for it is protected by huge mountains immediately to the N); never cold and never hot, but sometimes foggy. Silverwork is a speciality and there are important lead and zinc mines. The processions during Holy Week are spectacular. The most tourist-free part is up from the main street where the taxis can't go; day trippers fill the town in the early afternoon. Wear flat rubber-soled shoes to avoid slithering over the cobbles. Vendors will not bargain. Cheaper silver items can often be found in less touristy towns including Mexico City, but beware of mistaking the cheapish pretty jewellery, *alpaca,* which only contains 25% silver, for the real stuff. By law, real silver, defined as 0.925 pure, must be stamped somewhere on the item with the number 925. The downtown shops in general give better value than those on the highway, but they're still expensive. On the 2nd Sunday in December there is a national silversmiths' competition. Colourful produce market near the Zócalo.

N.B. All silver jewellers must be government-registered. Remember to look for the 925 stamp and, if the piece is large enough, it will also be stamped with the crest of an eagle, and initials of the jeweller. Where the small size of the item does not permit this, a certificate will be provided instead.

N.B. also Beware of handbag snatchers and slashers.

One of the most interesting of Mexican stone-age cultures, the Mezcala or Chontal, is based on the State of Guerrero in which Taxco lies. Its remarkable artefacts, of which there are many imitations, are almost surrealist. The culture remained virtually intact into historic times.

Hotels *De la Borda,* on left as you enter Taxco, largest, all facilities, A, great views; dearest and best, *La Cumbre Soñada,* 1.5 km. or so towards Acapulco on a mountain top, colonial, exquisite, A. *La Hacienda del Solar,* Acapulco exit of town, A, best restaurant in Taxco. *Rancho Taxco-Victoria,* Soto la Marina 15, walk to centre, A; *Posada Don Carlos,* Cerro de Bermeja 6, converted old mansion, restaurant, good view, C; *Los Arcos,* Juan Ruiz de Alarcón 2, magnificently reconstructed 17th century ex-convent, charming, friendly, good restaurant, D; *Posada de los*

TAXCO
ROUGH SKETCH
141

1. Zócalo/Plaza Borda
2. Plaza San Juan
3. Plazuela Ex-Convento
4. Plazuela Bernal
5. Santa Prisca
6. La Santísima
7. San Nicolás
8. San Miguel
9. Navarrieta Church
10. Vera Cruz
11. Museo Guillermo Spratling
12. Casa Humboldt
13. Casa Figueroa
14. Tourist Office North
15. Tourist Office South
16. Telephone Office
17. Social Security Clinic
18. Flecha Roja bus terminal
19. Estrella de Oro bus terminal
20. Market
Hotels:
21. *Posada de los Castillo*
22. *Meléndez*
23. *Agua Escondida*
24. *Los Arcos*
25. *Casa de Huéspedes Arrellano*

TO MEXICO CITY AND CUERNAVACA

CARRETERA NACIONAL

TO HOTEL DE LA BORDA

CALLE DE LA GARITA

JUAREZ

ALTILLO

SIERRA ALTA

LAS CONCHAS

LAS ESTACAS

CHACHALACAS

REFORMA

REDONDO

FAMA

JUAREZ

LA LUZ

LAS DELICIAS

TO GUADALUPE CHURCH

EX-RASTRO

FUNDICIONES

JUAN RUIZ DE ALARCON

CELSO MUNOZ

CALLEJON HUMBOLDT

RAFUL

VERACRUZ

BECERRA

JOHN F. KENNEDY

CHAUHTEMOC

PAJARITOS

TO HOTELS CERRO
LA CUMBRE
SOÑADA AND
RANCHO
TAXCO-VICTORIA

SAN NICOLAS

CERROS OSCUROS

MONTES

DE STA. ANA

FRESNO

OCA

MORA

PILITA

HIDALGO

AV. JOHN F. KENNEDY

SAN MIGUEL

N

CARRETERA NACIONAL

TO ACAPULCO

Castillo, Alarcón 7, off main square, Mexican style, friendly, excellent value, D. *Meléndez*, D, clean, no hot water, somewhat noisy as it is near market, good breakfast, other meals available; *Agua Escondida*, near Zócalo at Calle Guillermo Spratling 4, D, with bath, very good value and nice view; *Casa Grande*, Plazuela San Juan, nr. Santa Prisca church, 2 mins. from Zócalo, small rooms with shower (hot water) ask for top floor, E, good views, rec.; *Posada de la Misión*, Cerro de la Misión 84, Juan O'Gorman mural, restaurant, good, pool, A; *Colina del Sol*, E, clean, nice rooms, on the Kennedy Highway between Estrella de Oro and Flecha Roja terminals. *Casa de Huéspedes Arellano*, Pajaritas 23, by Santa Prisca and Plaza Borda, E with bath (less without), clean, old beds, no soap or toilet paper.

Restaurants *La Ventana* of the *Hacienda del Solar* hotel, renowned. *Alarcón*, overlooking Zócalo, very good meal for US$3.60, with everything included. *Sr. Costilla*, next to church on main square, good drinks and grilled ribs. *Cielito Lindo*, on Zócalo, good food, service and atmosphere; Next door is *Papa's Bar*, a discotheque and a small pizza place in an arcade. *Paco's Bar*, at other end of square for drinks and people-watching. Good drinks at *Berta's Bar*. *Mi Oficina*, straight up hill from where buses from Cuernavaca arrive. Good food at *Los Arcos* and *Victoria* hotels. Argentine *empanadas* at unnamed restaurant opp. Casa Humboldt, cheap, excellent breakfast. *Lonchería Liliana*, Juan Ruiz de Alarcón 13, rec.; *Pozolería Betty*, Mora 20 (below bus station), good food including the local beetle (jumil) sauce. Many small restaurants just near *Hotel Meléndez*, good value. Good snacks in small shop on NW corner of Zócalo. Excellent comida corrida at *Santa Fe*, opp. *Hotel Sta. Prisca*. **Nightclub:** *La Jungla*, set in a jungle-like location (somewhat frightening 15-min. drive out of town), cover charge includes a show and dancing.

Buses Book onward tickets (e.g. to Acapulco) the day prior to departure. (Taxis meet all buses and take you to any hotel, approx. US$0.70.) Taxco is reached from Mexico City from the Central del Sur, Estrella de Oro, 1st class US$2.50, only two stops, quick, no overcrowding, five a day (3 hrs.); also five 2nd class, Flecha Roja, a day for US$2, up to 5 hrs. Buses to Cuernavaca; 1st class buses at 0900, 1600, 1800 and 2000 (Estrella de Oro), 2nd class hourly at a quarter to the hour, but can be erratic. Little 24-seaters, "Los Burritos", take you up the hill from the bus terminal on main road. Spectacular journey from Toluca, missing out Mexico City. To Acapulco 1st class, Estrella de Oro, US$4.75; 2nd class, Flecha Roja, US$2.50, 5 hrs. To Cacahuamilpa for caverns, 40 minutes.

Excursions Visit *Posada Don Carlos*, Bermeja 6, also Ventana de Taxco in *Hacienda del Solar* for view. "Combi" to Panorámica every 30 mins. from Plaza San Juan, US$0.10. Take a funicular just off the Mexico City entrance to town for a spectacular aerial ride. About 20 km. out of Taxco a rodeo is held on Sat., guides available, admittance US$0.50. 12 km. from Taxco to Acuitlapán waterfalls, with colectivo or Flecha Roja bus; hire a horse to travel down 4 km. path to large clear pools for swimming. Taxis about US$4.50 per hour. Visit the villages where *amate* pictures are painted (on display at Casa Humboldt and in the market). Xalitla is the most convenient as it is on the road to Acapulco, take 2nd class bus there. Other villages: Maxela, Ahuelicán, Ahuehuepán and San Juan, past Iguala and before the River Balsa.

Warning Travellers have stressed that people, especially women, should *not* wander alone in isolated places; there have been violent attacks, e.g. in Acuitlapán.

The road descends. The heat grows. We join the main road again at Iguala, 36 km. beyond Taxco. Beyond the Mexcala river, the road passes for some 30 km. through the dramatic canyon of Zopilote to reach **Chilpancingo,** capital of Guerrero state, at Km. 302. Population 98,000, altitude 1,250 metres. The colourful reed bags from the distant village of Chilapa are sold in the market. The Casa de las Artesanías for Guerrero is on the right-hand side of the main highway Mexico City—Acapulco. It has a particularly wide selection of lacquerware from Olinala. Its *fiesta* starts on December 16 and lasts a fortnight. It has a University. Hotel: *La Posada Meléndez*. Not far from Chilpancingo are Oxtotitlán and Juxtlahuaca, where Olmec cave paintings can be seen. The road goes down to Acapulco (about 420 km. from Mexico City). About 20 km. from the coast, a branch road goes to the NW of Acapulco; this is a preferable route for car drivers because it avoids the city chaos. It goes to a point between Pie de la Cuesta and Coyuca, is signed, and has a drugs control point at the junction.

Warning Avoid travelling by car at night in Guerrero, even on the Mexico City-Acapulco highway and coastal highway. Many military checkpoints on highway. *Guerrilleros* have been active in recent years, and there are also problems with highway robbers and stray animals.

Acapulco (population now thought to be over a million) is the most popular resort in Mexico, particularly in winter and spring. During Holy Week there is a flight from the capital every 3 mins. The town stretches for 16 km. in a series of bays and cliff coves and is invading the hills. The hotels, of which there are 250, are mostly perched high to catch the breeze, for between 1130 and 1630 the heat is sizzling; they are filled to overflowing in January and February. It has all the paraphernalia of a booming resort: smart shops, night clubs, red light district, golf club, touts and street vendors and now also air pollution. The famous beaches and expensive hotels are a different world from the littered streets, dirty hotels and crowded shops and buses which are only two minutes walk away. There are some twenty beaches, all with fine, golden sand; deckchairs on all beaches, US$0.50; parachute skiing in front of the larger hotels at US$7 for 5 mins. The two most popular are the sickle-curved and shielded Caleta, with its smooth water and now dirty sands, and the surf-pounded straight beach of Los Hornos. Take local bus to Pie de la Cuesta, 8 km. (now preferred by many budget travellers to Acapulco itself, but becoming commercialized), several bungalow-hotels and trailer parks (see below), nice lagoon and big beaches (warning: the surf is dangerous), where you drink *coco loco*—fortified coconut milk—and watch the sunset from a hammock. Beware at all times of thieves. One can swim, and fish, the year round. Best free map of Acapulco can be obtained from the desk clerk at *Tortuga Hotel*.

Acapulco in colonial times was the terminal for the Manila convoy. Its main defence, Fort San Diego, where the last battle for Mexican independence was fought, in the middle of the city and is worth a visit. (Open 1000-1800, Tues. and Sun. only, free admission.)

Hotels can cost up to US$200 a night double; cheaper for longer stays, but this also means less expensive hotels insist on a double rate even for 1 person and for a minimum period. In the off-season (May-November) you can negotiate lower prices even for a single for one night. The fabulous *Club Residencial de las Brisas*, L, a hotel where the services match the astronomical price. (It begins at sea-level and reaches up the mountain slope in a series of detached villas and public rooms to a point 300 metres above sea-level. Each room has own or shared swimming pool. Guests use pink jeeps to travel to the dining-room and recreation areas.) *Acapulco Plaza*, Costera 22, 3 towers, 2 pools, 5 bars, 4 restaurants, a city in itself, L; *Exalaris Hyatt Regency*, next to naval base, and *Exalaris Hyatt Continental*, at Fuerte Diana, both with all services, L; *Villa Vera Raquet Club*, luxurious celebrity spot, L; *Los Flamingos*, Gran Vía Tropical 73, in the hills, D; *Caleta*, Playa Caleta, remodelled, A; *El Presidente*, Costera near Condesa beach, A; *Elcano*, Costera near golf club, A; *Casa Blanca Tropical*, Cerro de la Pinzona, C, with swimming pool, is rec.; *Condesa del Mar*, Costera at Condesa beach, all facilities, A; *Acapulco Imperial*, Costera 251, B; *Acapulco Tortuga*, A, and *Romano's Le Club*, both on Costera, many groups, A; *Maralisa*, Enrique El Esclavo, B, smallish and elegant, Arab style, rec.; *Tropicano Best Western*, Costera 510, C; *San Francisco*, Costera 219, old part of town, friendly, good value, noisy in front, E; *Maris*, Alemán y Magallanes, B, very good; *Diana*, street beside Costera M. Alemán, B, a/c, clean, quiet, pool. The *Acapulco Princess Country Club*, part of the *Acapulco Princess*, 20 km. away on Revolcadero beach, is highly fashionable. *Vacaciones*, Costera Alemán 63, Caleta zone E, good value. *Jungla*, Miguel Alemán 86, E; *Posada del Sol*, Caleta, friendly, on the beach, pool, good food, C, Playa del Coco opp. new convention centre, thefts from safe-deposit reported; *Playa Hornos*, Calz. Pie de la Cuesta, clean, friendly.

Most cheaper hotels are grouped around the Zócalo, especially Calles La Paz and Juárez; about 15 mins. from the 2nd class bus station (Flecha Roja) on Av. Cuauhtémoc. *Fiesta*, clean and nice, D, with bath, fan, 2 blocks NW from Zócalo. *Misión*, Felipe Valle 12, E, very clean, colonial, close to Zócalo. *Casa García*, E, clean, cold shower, pleasant, 3 blocks SW of Zócalo; *Isabel*, La Paz y Valle, E with fan, reasonable but not too accommodating, near Zócalo; *Sacramento*, E. Carranza y Valle, E with bath and fan, no towel, soap or loo paper, friendly, noisy, OK, purified water, T 20821; *Añorve*, B, Juárez 17, 2 blocks off Zócalo, clean, E, with bath; *Colimense*, E, J.M. Iglesias II, off Zócalo, pleasant; *Santa Cecilia*, Francisco Madero 7, off Zócalo, E, with bath and fan, noisy, but otherwise fine. *California*, La Paz 12, 1½ blocks W of Zócalo, D, good value, fan. Many cheap hotels on La Quebrada, basic but clean with fan and bathroom, including *El Faro* (No. 63, clean, E), *Casa de Huéspedes La Tía Conchita*, Guadalajara, *Casa de Huéspedes Aries* (E with bath, nice); *Amueblados Orozco*, near Quebrada, friendly, clean, E, with shower; *Villa Lucía*, built around pretty swimming pool, with kitchens in rooms, mostly frequented by Mexicans, a/c, one block from sea and one block from *Ritz*. Probably cheapest in town, *La Casa del Río*, 1½ blocks from the 2nd class bus terminal towards Los Hornos beach, cabins with stretchers and sheets, F; and *Betty*, Belisario Domínguez 4, 5 mins. from bus station, F with bath, fan, clean.

María Cristina's, E; in bungalows for 4, clean and comfortable, shower and cooling facilities, at Pie de la Cuesta (Km. 11), near fresh water lagoon and sea; also there is *Villa Rosita*, E for bungalow and primitive accommodation next to *Restaurant Tres Marías*, F. Several other nice places at Pie de la Cuesta, E/D, in clean rooms with shower, *Quinta Karla*, *Quinta Blanca*, *Puesta del Sol*, expensive places for hammocks, *Quinta Dora Trailer Park*, E for hammock, managed by American, helpful.

The student organization Setej offers dormitory accommodation, F, if one has a valid international student card, at Centro Vacacional, Pie de la Cuesta, hours, 0700-2400. For longer (1 month plus) stays, try *Amueblados Etel*, Av. la Pinzona 92 (near Quebrada) for self-catering apartments, cheap off-season (before November), *Apartamentos Maraback*, Costera M. Alemán, D. The Tourist Bureau is helpful in finding a hotel in any price range. **Motels** *Impala, Bali-Hai, Costera, La Joya, Monaco, Playa Suave, Villas del Sol* and *Gran Motel Acapulco* all along the Costera, B-C; *Ofelia, Victoria*, Cristóbal Colón, 1 block behind Costera, C.

Camping *Trailer Park El Coloso*, in La Sabana, small swimming pool, and *Trailer Park La Roca* on road from Puerto Márquez to La Sabana, both secure. *Estacionamiento Juanita* and *Quinta Dora* at Pie de la Cuesta (latter charges US$4 just to sling hammock), *Quinta Carla, Casa Blanca, U Kae Kim*, all US$50 a week upwards, but negotiable.

Restaurants There are a number of variously-priced restaurants along and opposite Condesa beach; many cheap restaurants cluster in the blocks surrounding the Zócalo, especially along Juárez; another group along the Caleta beach walkway; yet another group of mixed prices on the Costera opp. the *Acapulco Plaza Hotel. Antojitos Mayab*, Costera y Avilés, is a favourite for Mexican dishes; *Hong Kong*, near *Ritz Hotel* on Costera, best for Chinese food; *Madeira*, on the hill to *Hotel Las Brisas*, best fixed priced, elegant meal in town, delightful; *San Carlos*, Juárez (near Zócalo), fixed menu lunch, good; opp. is *100% Natural*, mostly vegetarian, other branches on Costera Miguel Alemán (opp. Hyatt Kingsgate), and up the hill from the yacht club. *Carlos and Charlie's*, opp. Condesa beach, 2nd floor, "fun place for the young at heart"; *Emmas*, next to *Playa Suave Motel*, local favourite for chicken; 250 more to select from.

Night Clubs There are dozens of discos including *Baby 'O, Magic, Tiffany's, UBQ*, etc. Every major hotel has at least one disco plus bars; *El Fuerte*, famous Flamenco show; *La Perla*, renowned cliff divers, and at least 3 gay transvestite shows, plus a *Voladores de Papantla* pole dancers' show. Superb varied night-life always.

City Transport Taxis US$8 an hour. Several bus routes, with one running the full length of Costera Miguel Alemán linking the older part of town to the latest hotels, another operating to Caleta beach. Buses to Pie de la Cuesta, 8 km., US$0.15.

British Consul (Honorary), Mr D.B.Gore, MBE, T (91-748) 46605.

Telephones Public offices will not take collect calls; try from a big hotel (ask around—there will be a surcharge).

Tourist Information Costera Miguel Alemán at Hornos beach, helpful, but double-check details.

Buses Mexico City, 406 km., 6½ hours; de luxe air-conditioned express buses, US$8; ordinary bus, about US$6, all-day services from Estación Central de Autobuses del Sur by the Taxqueña metro station, with Estrella de Oro or Flecha Roja (part of Líneas Unidas del Sur). 1st class bus depot at Av. Cuauhtémoc 1490. Taxi to Zócalo, US$2; bus, US$0.12. To Oaxaca by continuation of the scenic highway from the beach and naval base at Icacas, 402 km.: 6 hrs. on main road, 264 km., of which 170 km. unpaved, 6 hrs. on rough dirt road through mountains by bus, change at Pinoteca Nacional; caught close to where highway from Mexico City joins the beach. Several 1st class buses (Estrella de Oro), 5 hrs., US$4.75 and 2nd class (Flecha Rosa) buses a day to Taxco at 1730, US$2.50. Bus to Puerto Escondido every hour on the half-hour from 0430-1630, plus one at 0200 and *directo* at 0915, 2nd class, Flecha Roja, US$7.20, seats bookable, advisable to do so the day before, 7½ hrs.

Air Services Airport, Plan de los Amales, 26 km. from Acapulco. Direct connections with New York, Philadelphia and Toronto, by Aeroméxico. Cancún, 3¾ hrs., via Mexico City. Guadalajara, 55 mins.; Mérida, via Mexico City, 3¾ hrs. Oaxaca, 45 mins. Villahermosa, 2 hrs. Mexico City, 45 mins. Transportación Aeropuerto taxi service charge return trip (*viaje redondo*) when you buy a ticket, so keep it and call for a taxi when required, US$6. Airport bus takes 1 hr., US$2 and *does* exist!

Excursions The lagoons can be explored by motor boats; one, Coyuca Lagoon, is over 110 km. long; strange birds, water hyacinths, tropical flowers. Daily, in the morning and after dark, amazing 40-metre dives into shallow water by boys can be watched from the Quebrada (US$1, 5 times a day, the first at 1300, the last, with torches, at 2200). There is a *jai-alai* palace. At Playa Icacos there is a marineland amusement park *Ci-Ci*, with a waterslide, pool with wave-machine and arena with performing dolphins and sea-lions, US$1.50. Pleasant boat trip across beach to Puerto Marqués, US$ 0.80 return; one can hire small sailing boats there, US$6.50 an hr. Bay cruises, 2½ hrs., from Muelle Yates, US$3, at 1100, 1630 and 2230. Visit island of La Roqueta, glass-bottomed boat, US$2.50 return, 2 hrs., overpriced. Parachute sailing (towed by motor boats), US$6.50 for a few minutes, several operators.

Coast NW of Acapulco

Between Acapulco and Zihuatanejo are Coyuca de Benítez, a lagoon with little islands 38 km. from Acapulco, also a market town selling exotic fruit, cheap hats and shoes. Pelicans fly by the lagoons, there are passing dolphins and plentiful sardines, and young boys seek turtle eggs. 1½ km. beyond Coyuca is a turn-off to **El Carrizal** (7½ km.), a village of some 2,000 people, a little paradise with a beautiful beach (many pelicans) with dangerous waves; *Hotel-Bungalows El Carrizal*, signed simply "Bungalows", E, owned by Armando and Teresa Chávez, very friendly and helpful, swimming pool, access to lagoon, good restaurant opposite; more basic, *Aida*, E, little privacy, Mexican food (good fish). Shops will change dollars (e.g. Doña Joaquina's shoe shop, the video shop), and long-distance phone calls can be made from the *farmacia*. Frequent VW minibuses from Acapulco or Pie de la Cuseta, US$0.25. If driving, take Route 200, direction Zihuatanejo. A couple of km. SE of El Carrizal is El Morro on an unpaved road between the ocean and the lagoon. El Morro is a small fishing village (carp) reminiscent of African townships as it is constructed entirely of *palapa* (palm-leaf and wood). Every other house is a "fish-restaurant". San Jerónimo, 83 km. from Acapulco, has an 18th century parish church, you can make canoe trips up river to restaurants; Tecpan de Galeana, 108 km. from Acapulco, is a fishing village; there is a beach further on at Cayaquitos where a series of small rivers join the ocean and there is a large variety of birds and dense vegetation; three restaurants offer fish dishes, there is a reasonable modern hotel, *Club Papánoa*, with lovely views, and a camping site; and one can also visit the lovely bay of Papanda.

Zihuatanejo is a beautiful fishing port and expensive tourist resort 237 km. NW of Acapulco by the paved Route 200, which continues via Barra de Navidad along the Pacific coast to Puerto Vallarta (see page 1001); 1st class bus from Acapulco, 4 hrs. (This road goes through coconut plantations where you can buy *tuba*, a drink made from coconut milk fermented on the tree, only slightly alcoholic.) There are 3 beaches: one in the natural harbour and one 20 min. walk from centre (Playa de la Ropa) with the *Sotavento* and some beach restaurants. Another is the Playa de la Madera. Las Gatas beach is secluded, a haven for aquatic sports and can be reached by boat from the centre (US$0.75 return) or a 20-min. walk from La Ropa beach over fishermen-frequented rocks. Watch out for coconuts falling off the trees! The chief attraction, apart from beaches, is clam fishing; there is also a small shark-processing factory. The desert islands off the coast may be visited. Difficult to find accommodation in March, and around Christmas/New Year.

Hotels *Las Tres Marías*, very pleasant with large communal balconies overlooking town and harbour, E; *Villa del Sol*, Playa La Ropa, L; *Irma* (Playa la Madera), good hotel but not best location, C; *Catalina* and *Sotavento*, Playa la Ropa, C, same facilities. *Bungalows Capuli*, Playa la Ropa, D; *Posada Caracol, Bungalows Palacios*, on Playa de la Madera, D. Medium hotels: *Casa la Mariana*, pretty, on seafront; *Bahía*, by town pier; *Corona*, in coconut plantation on the road to other beaches; *Casa Lulu*, at end of main beach. *Casa Minam*, clean, E. *Casa Elvira* hotel-restaurant, F, in older part of town, very basic but clean, noisy from 0730, share bath, the restaurant is on the beach front (*the* place to watch the world go by), good and reasonable. Several hotels along the beach, D: try *Del Mar; Playa de la Madera; Safari* (by bus station, expensive); *Casa La Playa*, similar to *Elvira*, E, but not as good; *Belmar*, all rooms face sea; *Sinar-Bahagra*, very good value; *Imelda*, clean, rec., E. CREA Youth Hostel, Av. Paseo Zihuatanejo s/n, C.P. 40880.

Camping on Playa la Ropa (a long walk from town, but beautiful beach nearby), US$0.60 p.p. and US$0.60 per car; US$0.25 to sling hammock (friendly owners with ferocious dogs).

Restaurants On Playa la Ropa, cheap: *Elvi, La Perla*. In Zihuatanejo, *Mi Casita*, in town, rec.; *La Bocana*, favourite for seafood; *Cantamar*, downtown, "cute"; *Cabina del Capitán*, owned by an Englishman, good; *Don Juan*, downtown, English decor, fancy; *Coconuts*, downtown, "Hollywood tropical", nice but somewhat expensive garden restaurant; *Gitano's*, thatched roof beach spots, reasonable; *Kon Tiki*, road to Playa de la Ropa, pizzas and oriental, rec.; *Kapi Kofi*, downtown, a/c, breakfast. *Stall 27* at marketplace is very popular, cheap and good.

Night Clubs *Adán y Eva, Ibiza Disco, Chololo, Captain's Cabin, Joy Disco, Kan Kan.*

Skin Diving US$25 for one, US$35 for two, per day and hire of all equipment and guide from next to tourist office by town pier, lessons also offered. Off Playa de las Gatas is an underwater wall built by the Tarascan king Calzonzin, to keep the sharks away while he bathed; the wall is fairly massive and can be seen clearly while skin diving. Many fish too. US$1 a day for mask, snorkel and flippers.

Exchange Banca Serfín will change travellers' cheques without need to show passport; also lower commission than in banks in hotel district. Good rates at Mario's leather shop.

British Vice-Consul at Zihuatanejo: D. B. Gore, *Hotel Las Brisas*, Aptdo. Postal 281. T (91-748) 4-15-80 and 4-16-50.

Buses and Roads Four direct buses a day from Mexico, Tres Estrellas de Oro, US$10, at Central del Sur (by Taxqueña metro station), a good 12 hrs. 5 times a day from Mexico City via Morelia, by Autobuses de Occidente. Estrella Roja del Sur not rec.: reckless drivers. Bus to Acapulco, US$6.50 1st, US$3.75 2nd class, 4 hrs, at least 20 times a day with Flecha Roja. To Tijuana with Estrella de Oro at 1530, 50 hrs.; to Manzanillo, at 2000 with Estrella de Oro, 16 hrs. To Guadalajara, US$8 overnight 2nd class, 12 hrs., frequent stops and people standing in the aisles, or with Autobuses de Occidente, US$11 at 1320 and 1720. To Morelia (**see page 1014**) at least 15 a day, US$5.50 with Norte de Sonora; connections also to Michoacán at Lázaro Cárdenas (bus from Zihuatanejo US$1.50). To Puerto Escondido, US$4. By road from Mexico City via the Toluca-Zihuatanejo highway (430 km.) or via the Acapulco-Zihuatanejo highway (405 km.).

Airport Frontier Airlines flies from locations in Western USA. Many flights from Mexico City and others from Mazatlán, Guadalajara, Los Angeles, Houston, Albuquerque, etc.

From Zihuatanejo one can drive 5 km. or take a bus (US$0.20) or taxi (US$ 2.50, colectivo, US$0.45) to *Ixtapa*, "where there are salt lakes". The resort, being developed on a large scale, boasts 14 beaches: La Hermosa, Del Palmar, Don Juan de Dios, Don Juan, Don Rodrigo, Cuata, Quieta, Oliveiro, Linda, Larga, Carey, Pequeña, Cuachalate and Varadero. There are turtles, many species of shellfish and fish, and pelicans at El Morro de los Pericos, which can be seen by launch. There is an island a few metres off Quietas beach; boats go over at a cost of US$1.50. Ixtapa has ten large luxury hotels and a Club Méditerranée (all obtain food-supplies from Mexico City making food more expensive, as local supplies aren't guaranteed); a shopping complex, golf course, water-ski/parachute skiing and tennis courts. There are a yacht marina and an 18-hole golf club, Palma Real. Isla Grande is being developed as a nature park and leisure resort. **N.B.** The beach can be dangerous (strong undertow—small children should not be allowed in the sea unaccompanied). Also, there are crocodiles in the beautiful lagoons at the end of the beach.

Hotels All in L-A range: *Camino Real*, spectacular, in a small jungle; *Krystal* (highly rec., book in advance), *Dorado Pacífico*, *Sheraton*, with panoramic lift, *El Presidente*, A; *Aquamarina*; *Aristos*; *Holiday Inn*; *Riviera del Sol*. Taxi between centre and main hotels, US$2.

Restaurants Besides those in every hotel, there are *Montmartre*, *Villa Sakura*, *Villa de la Selva* (rec. for food and views, book in advance), *Baffone*, *Carlos y Charlie's*, *Hacienda de Ixtapa*, all more costly than in Zihuatanejo.

Nightclubs Every hotel without exception has at least one night club/disco and two bars.

Playa Azul, 350 km. NW of Acapulco (bus US$3.50) and 122 km. from Zihuatanejo, is a coconut-and-hammock resort frequented much more by Mexicans than foreigners, with a few large hotels, e.g. *Playa Azul*, C, best value, good but expensive restaurant; *Costa de Oro*, E, clean, with fan, rec. *Posada Marilyn*, clean, run by La Mira schoolteacher, E, cold showers (hard to find; ask in main street). *Hospedaje Casa Silva*, E, very basic but adequate, restaurant around the corner and unnamed *hospedaje* opposite, F with shower. Many small fish restaurants along beach. 40 km. of excellent deserted beaches N of Playa Azul.

  N.B.: Beware of the large waves at Playa Azul and of dangerous currents; always check with locals if particular beaches are safe.

Transport Buses ply up and down the coast road, stopping at the road junction 4 km. from Plaza Azul. Colectivos take you between town and junction. *Lázaro Cárdenas* is the connecting point for buses from Uruapan, Manzanillo and Zihuatanejo (e.g. Galeana to Manzanillo 7¾ hrs. US$4.50; to Uruapán, US$3.50, 6½ hrs; Flecha Roja to Zihuatanejo). Avoid *Hotel Sam Sam* nr. terminal; go to 5 de Mayo for *Capri* or *Costa Azul*, both E with bath, several eating places.

Coast E of Acapulco

Highway 200, E from Acapulco along the coast, is paved all the way to Puerto Escondido; the stretch is known as the Costa Chica (there is a bridge missing about 55 km. from Acapulco, which necessitates a detour inland to Sabana Grande, when you turn off to Pinotepa). "From **Pinotepa** Nacional (*Hotel Carmona*, restaurant, good value but poor laundry service, F), you can visit the Mixtec Indian village of Pinotepa de Don Luis by *camioneta*. These leave from the side street next to the church in Pinotepa Nacional, taking a dirt road to Don Luis. The women there weave beautiful and increasingly rare sarong-like skirts (*chay-ay*), some of which are dyed from the purple of sea snails. Also, half-gourds incised with various designs and used both as caps and cups can be found. The *ferias* of Don Luis (January 20) and nearby San Juan Colorado (November 29-30) are worth attending for the dancing and availability of handicrafts." (Dale Bricker, Seattle)

Puerto Escondido is on a beautiful bay south of Oaxaca (population 25,000) and getting very touristy, good surfing; camping with showers US$1 a day, also trailer facilities. Palm trees line the beach, which is not too clean but well provided with good-quality reasonably-priced restaurants. There are plans afoot to develop the SE end of town, in the words of one developer "to make it the next Acapulco". (Recent travellers report that this aim has already been attained.)

N.B. There can be dangerous waves, and the cross-currents are always dangerous; non-swimmers should not bathe except in the bay on which the town stands. Also, a breeze off the sea makes the sun seem less strong than it is—be careful. Do not stray too far along the beach; armed robbery by groups of 3-5 is becoming more and more frequent, take as little cash and valuables as possible, US$ sought after. Also at La Barra beach 10 km. away.

Hotels   Very crowded during Holy Week. Many cheaper hotels have no hot water. *Viva*, most expensive; *Best Western Posada Real* (ex-*Bugambilias*), very pleasant, A, lovely gardens, pool, path to beach, attentive, a/c, good service, food included (à la carte, also lobster); *El Rincón del Pacifico*, D, very popular, always full, on beach, with restaurant, hot water, much stealing, not always friendly. *Virginia*, D, good views; *Mirador*, on highway into town with good views, D; *Loren*, D, clean, friendly, safe, rec.; *Real del Mar*, nr. bus station, D (cheaper for longer stays), bath, clean, nice view; *Paraíso Escondido*, noisy a/c, not on beach but with own swimming pool, management cool, but rec., C, colonial style; *Nayar*, D, big rooms, views, with bath and fan, restaurant, rec.; opposite is *Bungalows Barlovento*, C/D, very comfortable, highly rec. *La Posada Económica*, one big dormitory, F, attached to restaurant, but also runs hotel across the road, ask for a room opp. the flat; good huachinango; *Alojamiento Las Cabañas* has dormitories with bunks, F, on main road (S side), friendly, very nice, food is good, you will be charged for all beds regardless of whether they are occupied, unless you share the cabin. *Cabañas Coco Beach*, in the town near the church, US$3 per cabin (6 or 7 available), family-run. *Bungalows Villa Marinero*, on beach, at bit run down, own cooking possible, friendly, D, restaurant a little dear but good. Most hotels are on the beach, little air-conditioning. *Cabañas San Diego*, down a sand road just before bridge on road to Puerto Angel, F, safe, nice grounds but few facilities; *Cabañas Neptuno*, F; *Cabañas Cortés*, F for small, basic huts or large, basic huts—in all cases, take mosquito nets.

Camping   If camping, beware of clothes being stolen; 3 sites available. *Carrizalillo Trailer Park*, near old airport on W side of town, on cliff top with path leading down to secluded beach, swimming pool and bar, very pleasant, US$4.45 for 2 plus car, US$1.35 p.p. Campsite for vehicles, tents and hammocks on water front in centre of town, vehicles and tents accepted, swimming pool, US$2.20 p.p. *Las Palmas* (better) and *Neptuno* campsites (with cabins) next to each other on beach US$3.

Restaurants   *Lolys*, cheap and good, try pescado a la parrilla, with sweet onion sauce, and lemon cake after; *Da Ugo*, good pizzas, popular. *Lisa's Restaurant*, nice location on beach but expensive and very poor service. Many restaurants on main street: *San Angel* for fish, *La Posada*, *Disco Macumba*. *Bananas* bar, good, satellite TV, ping-pong, chess, backgammon, Italian-run. Vegetarian at *Hotel Santa Fe*, on beach at end of bay. Good licuados at *Bambú Loco*, also fish. *La Estancia* is good but expensive. *Las Palapas*, good, heading up it is just over the stream (sewer) on the right.

Shopping   Small selection of foreign language books at *Papi's*, souvenir shop 3 doors from Mercado de Artesanías, buy or swap. Local crafts best not bought from vendors on the beach, but in the non-gringo part of town up the hill near where the buses stop.

Banks   Bancomer. Open 0900-1330.

Transport   Bus to Oaxaca, 5 or 6 a day, US$3, advertised as 7 hr. trip, but can take up to 17 hrs, very bad road and many accidents; also Estrella del Valle (1st class, from 2nd class terminal) and Auto Transportes Oaxaca-Pacifico, better, journey through spectacular cloud forest, goes via Pochutla, 10-18 hrs. (depending on roadworks)—leaves at 0700, 2nd class, 2300 1st class; all have bookable seats. Puerto Escondido-Pochutla, US$1.50, and on to Salina Cruz, US$3, Oaxaca-Pacifico company rec. The road to Salina Cruz is now paved (bus US$3.50, about 7 a day. It is now best to go from Oaxaca to Puerto Escondido by the road to Puerto Angel, turning off at Pochutla (see below). The direct highway to Oaxaca is being upgraded. Bus to Acapulco, 2nd class, Flecha Roja (near La Solteca terminal), 7½ hrs., US$7.20, not exciting. The 1030 bus stops for 2 hours' lunch at Pinotepa, 1st class from Acapulco US$11, book tickets at least one day in advance. First bus to Acapulco at 0400, hourly up to 2100 thereafter. Transport to Puerto Angel from Puerto

Escondido consists of VW bus or pick-up truck caught on main road, every hour, 1 hr. to Pochutla, then colectivo/bus.

Flights Airline offices will arrange VW bus to pick you up for your departure when you reconfirm or book your outward flight, US$0.75 p.p. Airport 10 minutes drive from town, orange juice and coffee sold; improvement programme under way. Puerto Escondido-Mexico City, with Aerolíneas Unidas, Wed., Fri. and Sun. at 1710 and 1825 (Mexico City-Puerto Escondido on same days at 1400 and 1515); also Puerto Escondido-Oaxaca, US$40 one way. CV-580 plane, seats 20. Aerolíneas Unidas is at Reforma 157-B, México 5, T 592-57-77.

Also S of Oaxaca (240 km, paved road, but many curves) is **Puerto Angel**, a coffee port on the Pacific with a good safe beach, 69 km. from Puerto Escondido, with road connection but no direct buses; all services involve change at Pochutla. It is 8 hrs. by bus from Oaxaca, nine a day, US$3.50, nearest exchange at Pochutla (bus US$0.25, taxis). Fiesta 1 October.

Luxury hotel on a hill away from the beach, **Angel del Mar**, C, friendly, helpful, bookings not always honoured; for **cabañas** and hammock places ask at **Susanna's Restaurant**, near the football pitch; **Hotel Soraya**, E, fan, bath, very clean; **Anahi**, on road to **Angel del Mar**, F with fan, Indonesian-style wash basins; **Casa de Huéspedes Gladys**, just above **Soraya**, F, owner can prepare food; **Casa de Huéspedes** (Gundi and Tomás López), clean, rooms (E) or hammocks (G), good value, snacks and breakfast (US$0.50-1.25). Similar is the **Pensión Puesta del Sol**, run by Harald and Maria Faerber, F (suite D), very friendly, English and German spoken, situated on road to Playa Panteón, clean, rec. **Noah's Arc**, at the end of the beach, for the "flower-powered"; hammocks at **Gustavos**, F; **Posada Cañón de Vata**, on Playa Panteón, nice, very clean, D, lovely setting, booked continuously; good restaurant **Capís** (has 5 rooms above). **Ma Bell** restaurant, good and cheap; many others. Cabins are being built by Roberto (speaks English) at Estacahuite beach, 1 km. from town. Long distance phone next to **Soraya**; for post office, exchange etc. go to Pochutla.

Three km. N is Zipolite beach (name means "the killing beach" - reached by taxi—US$3.50 for 4—or ½ hr. walk), dangerous for bathing, cabins and hammocks for rent, food available, "may be the last nude paradise in Mexico". The sea is said to be less dangerous at the nudist beach, the trail for which starts at Gloría's (45 min. walk, ask locals). 45 mins. walk N of the nudist beach is another beach and village with a turtle farm. Hammock spot and vegetarian restaurant *Shambala* run by American woman. "About 25 km. from Zipolite (also known as Puerto Angelito) on a dirt road is a sign to Ventanilla beach; follow the rough track until you find a thatched ranch and ask for Hilario Reyes. The beach is long and empty and there are 2 lagoons with fresh water, a lost paradise", writes Janet Westgarth. There are no cabins: you need your own tent (or hammock/mosquito net). Ventanilla beach is also dangerous for bathing.

Restaurant *Suzy*, Playa Panteón, excellent seafood.

You can go to Salina Cruz from Puerto Angel via Pochutla: take bus or taxi (US$2) to **Pochutla** and catch hourly bus to Salina Cruz (US$3, 3½ hrs.), to which a new road is finished. Pochutla-Oaxaca (a safer route than Puerto Escondido-Oaxaca) six 1st class and five 2nd class buses a day, 7 hrs., US$3-4; San José del Pacífico is a pleasant stop on the way, with good restaurant. The bus service between Pochutla and Puerto Escondido (US$0.75) links with the bus to Puerto Angel. Minibus to Puerto Angel, US$0.25. At Pochutla there is a prison; you can buy black coral necklaces made by prisoners very cheaply.

West of Puerto Angel (50 km.) and 112 km. E of Salina Cruz, on the coast road, is the new resort of **Huatulco** being built on about 34,000 hectares around nine bays, for completion around 2020. Several 4- and 5-star hotels are open, including the *Posada Binniguenda* (4-star) and the *Club Méditerranée* (5-star); many to follow. The airport is open with flights from Mexico City. Great care is to be taken to blend the resort into the landscape: about 80% of the total area is to be set aside as a nature reserve.

PAN-AMERICAN HIGHWAY: MEXICO CITY TO GUATEMALA (8)

The National Railway runs daily from Mexico City to Tapachula. Taxi to Talismán, on the Guatemalan border, for bus to Guatemala City (also accessible from Puebla). There is a new bridge which links Ciudad Hidalgo with Tecún-Umán (formerly Ayutla) in Guatemala. Cristóbal Colón bus Mexico City-Guatemala City, 23 hrs., US$24, leave at 1045; at border change to Rutas Lima. Bus Mexico City-Tapachula, 20 hrs., US$15. Bus, Tecún-Umán-Guatemala City US$3.

Note Motorists who know the area well advise that anyone driving from Mexico City to Tehuantepec should go via Orizaba-La Tinaja-Papaloapan-Tuxtepec-Palomares. This route is better than Veracruz-Acayucán and far preferable to the route which follows, via Matamoros and Oaxaca, if drivers are in a hurry. The reason is that between Oaxaca and Tehuantepec the road, although paved throughout and in good condition, serpentines unendingly over the Sierras. But as the Oaxaca route is far more interesting and spectacular we describe it below. For the alternative journey through the Papaloapan region, see page 1049.

This road through southern Mexico is 1,355 km. long. It can be done in 3 or 4 days' driving time. There are bus services from Mexico City along the route through Oaxaca to Tehuantepec and on to the Guatemalan frontier through San Cristóbal de Las Casas to Ciudad Cuauhtémoc or through Arriaga to Tapachula. A road now runs (still rough in places) from Paso Hondo near Ciudad Cuauhtémoc via Comalapa and Porvenir to Huixtla on the S road, and from Porvenir to Revolución Mexicana.

From Cuernavaca to Oaxaca: take Route 160 via Yantepec to the semi-tropical town of **Cuautla** (94,000 people), with a popular sulphur spring (known as *aguas hediondas* or stinking waters) and bath, a week-end resort for the capital. Tourist Cuautla is divided from locals' Cuautla by a wide river, and the locals have the best bargain: it is worth crossing the stream. From Cuautla go to Atotonilco by bus for a swim. Buses from Mexico City to Cuautla from Central del Oriente. Buses from Cuautla at Cristóbal Colón terminal, 5 de Mayo and Zavala, to Mexico City hourly; 2nd class buses to Cuernavaca hourly, 1 hr, US$0.65; to Oaxaca, US$5.80. There is a market in the narrow streets and alleyways around 5 de Mayo. *Hotel Colón* in Cuautla is on the main square, E, good (opp. is excellent *Restaurante Manolo*, Guerrero 53); *Hotel del Sur*, F, rec.; *Hotel Madrid*, Los Bravos 27, F. *Jardín de Cuautla*, Dos de Mayo 94, nr. bus station, modern, clean, but bad traffic noise, pool, C; *Hotel España* in same street No. 22, E. The tourist office is opp. *Hotel Cuautla*, on Av. Obregón, satisfactory. CREA Youth Hostel, Domicilio Conocido Unidad Deportiva, T 20218, C.P. 62040. Try the delicious *lacroyas* and *gorditas*, tortillas filled with beans and cheese. At least 2 good restaurants in main square. A road leads to Amecameca (page 1040). 11 km. from Cuautla, on road to Cuernavaca is the *Hacienda de Cocoyoc*, an old converted *hacienda* with a swimming pool backed by the mill aqueduct. Glorious gardens, 18-hole golf-course, tennis and riding, but isolated, A, AmEx not accepted, reservations at Centro Comercial El Relox, Local 44, Insurgentes Sur 2374, México 01000 D.F., T 550-7331.

Then take Route 140 with long descent and then ascent to *Izúcar de Matamoros* 58,000 people (*Hotel Ocampo*, F, next to bus station, nice and clean), famous for its clay handicrafts, 16th-century convent of Santo Domingo, and two nearby spas, Los Amatitlanes (about 6 km. away) and Ojo de Carbón. A side road leads from Izúcar to Axochiapan (Morelos state), leading to a dirt road to the village of Jolalpan with the baroque church of Santa María (1553). Route 190 heads N from Izúcar to Puebla via Huaquechula (16th-century renaissance-cum-plateresque chapel) and **Atlixco** ("the place lying on the water"), with interesting baroque examples in the Chapel of the Third Order of St. Augustine and San Juan de Dios. There is an annual festival, the Atlixcayotl, on San Miguel hill (*Hotel Colonial* behind parish church, F, shared bath; nearby—20 mins.—are the curative springs of Axocopán). Thence to Acatepec (page 1042) and, 30 km., Puebla. Route 190 S switchbacks to Tehuitzingo (*Hotel Mónica*, F, very basic). Then fairly flat landscape to **Acatlán** (hotel), a friendly village where black and red clay figures, and palm and flower hats are made. Carry on to Petlalcingo (restaurant), then descend to Huajuapan (page 1072) and Tamazulapan (hotel, restaurant). Road climbs slowly at first, then more steeply and eventually flattens to Nocluxtlán (*Hotel Sarita*, E).

The major route from Mexico City first runs generally eastwards to Puebla, where it turns S to wind through wooded mountains at altitudes of between 1,500 and 1,800 metres, emerging at last into the warm, red earth Oaxaca valley.

Oaxaca (population now thought to be over 300,000, altitude 1,546 metres) is 413 km. from Puebla, 531 km. from Mexico City. It is a very Indian town, of airy patios with graceful arcades, famous for its colourful market, its *sarapes*, crafts, dances and feast days. On Sat. Indians of the Zapotec and Mixtec groups come to market near the 2nd class bus station on the outskirts of town, which starts before 0800; prices are rising because of the city's great popularity with tourists. Specialities: black earthenware, tooled leather, blankets, ponchos, shawls, embroidered blouses, the drink *mescal*. Beware pickpockets. The Zócalo with its arcades is the heart of the town; its bandstand has a nice little market underneath. Since the streets surrounding the sides of the Zócalo have been closed to traffic it has become very pleasant to sit there. In the daytime vendors sell food, in the evening their tourist wares and gardenias in the square.

On the Zócalo is the 17th century cathedral with a fine baroque façade, but the best sight, about 4 blocks from the square, is the church of Santo Domingo (reckoned by all to be beautiful) with its adjoining monastery, now the Regional Museum (see below). The church's gold leaf has to be seen to be believed. There is an extraordinary vaulted decoration under the raised choir, right on the reverse of the façade wall: a number of crowned heads appear on the branches of the genealogical tree of the family of Santo Domingo de Guzmán (died 1221), whose lineage was indirectly related to the royal houses of Castile and Portugal. By

OAXACA
NOT TO SCALE 144

1. Zócalo
2. Paseo Juárez
3. Jardín Conzatti
4. Cathedral
5. Santo Domingo
6. La Soledad
7. San Felipe Neri
8. San Juan de Dios
9. San Agustín
10. Regional Museum
11. Rufino Tamayo Museum
12. Teatro Macedonio Alcalá
13. Monument to Juárez
14. 1st Class bus station
15. 2nd Class bus station
16. State Tourist Office
17. Post Office
18. Telephones
19. Abastos Market
20. Craft Market
21. Benito Juárez Market
22. Guelaguetza Stadium
23. Hotel Presidente
24. Hotel Principal
25. Hotel Señorial
26. Hotel Mesón del Angel

TO TEHUANTEPEC

CALZ. NIÑOS HEROES DE CHAPULTEPEC

MORELOS
MARGARITA MAZA DE JUAREZ
QUINTANA
J. DALE VUELTA
GOMEZ FARIAS
ROO
HUMBOLDT
CALZ. DE LA REPUBLICA
PINO
LIBRES
AV. JUAREZ
S MARTIN
ZARATE
SUAREZ

F.G. OLIVERA
COSIJOPI
BERRIOZABAL
CONSTITUCION

QUETZALCOATL
JESUS CARRANZA
A. GURRION
AROSOLO
MURGUIA
5 DE MAYO
REFORMA

CERRO DEL FORTIN
ALLENDE
MACEDONIO ALCALA

To PUEBLA & MEXICO CITY
N. BRAVO
GARCIA VIGIL

FALDAS DEL FORTIN
EL PUNTO
MATAMOROS
TINOCO Y PALACIOS
PORFIRIO DIAZ
AV. INDEPENDENCIA
VALDIVIESO
HIDALGO
GUERRERO

LOS REYES
EL MUERTO
UNION
CRESPO
AV. MORELOS

NEGRETE
CALZ. MADERO
To Train Station
AV. HIDALGO
VALERIO
TRUJANO
COLON

HUZARES
VICTORIA
MIER Y TERAN
GALEANA
DIAZ ORDAZ
ALDAMA
J.P. GARCIA
20 DE NOVIEMBRE
LAS CASAS
MIGUEL CABRERA
C.M. BUSTAMANTE
RAYON

PERIFERICO
ZARAGOZA
MINA

TO AIRPORT AND
PUERTO ESCONDIDO

making a donation (say US$1) to the church you can get the lady at the bookstall to light up the various features after 1800. The Capilla del Rosario in the church is fully restored; no flash pictures are allowed.

The massive 17th century church of La Soledad has fine colonial ironwork and sculpture (including an exquisite Virgen de la Soledad); there are elaborate altars at the church of San Felipe Neri, and Indian versions in paint of the conquest at San Juan de Dios; a museum of religious art behind the church is open in the morning. The church of San Agustín has a fine façade, with bas-relief of St. Augustine holding the City of God above adoring monks (apparently modelled on that of San Agustín in Mexico City, now the National Library).

The Regional Museum (entry US$0.50, US$0.25 on Sun., open 1000-1800, 1000-1700 Sat.-Sun., closed Mon.) has displays of regional costumes, and pottery, glass, alabaster, jewellery and other treasures from Monte Albán, whose jewellery is copied with surprising skill in several home workshops near Oaxaca. Museo Rufino Tamayo, Av. Morelos 503, has a beautiful display of precolumbian artefacts dating from 1250 BC to AD 1100 (1000-1400, 1600-1900, closed Tues.); entry for US$0.25. Teatro Macedonio Alcalá, 5 de Mayo with Independencia, beautifully restored theatre from Porfirio Díaz' time. Visit also the Street of the Little Arches, a picturesque, narrow, cobbled street with archways along the sides. There is a grand view from the monument to Juárez on Cerro de Fortín hill. The house of the Maza family, for whom Bénito Juárez worked and whose daughter he married, still stands at Independencia 1306 (a plaque marks it). Similarly, a plaque marks the birthplace of Porfirio Díaz at the other end of Independencia, in a building which is now a kindergarten, near La Soledad. D. H. Lawrence wrote parts of "Mornings in Mexico" here, and revised "The Plumed Serpent"; the house he rented is in Pino Suárez, a block S of the Llano (the main park), NE corner. The Zapotec language is used by over 300,000 people in the State as a first or second language (about 20% of Oaxaca State population speaks only an Indian language).

Warning Travellers have reported that men asserting they are local Indians sometimes get into conversation, especially near the Zócalo, invite you to a drink, order several things and then claim they have no money and leave the tourist to pay the bill!

The best *mescal* in the region is El Minero, made in Mitla. *Mescal* sours are good at the bar of *Misión Los Angeles*. The poor man's drink is *pulque*. Local *sarapes* are more varied and cheaper than in Mexico City. Buy at the market (which will come down a third) or at Casa Cervantes. The Zapotec Indians, who weave fantastic toys of grass, have a dance, the *Jarabe Tlacolula Zandunga* danced by barefooted girls splendid in most becoming coifs, short, brightly coloured skirts and ribbons and long lace petticoats, while the men, all in white with gay handkerchiefs, dance opposite them with their hands behind their backs. Only women—from Tehuantepec or Juchitán—dance the slow and stately *Zandunga*, costumes gorgeously embroidered on velvet blouse, full skirts with white pleated and starched lace ruffles and *huipil*.

Fiestas Carnival in February. Los Lunes del Cerro, on the first two Mondays after July 16 (the first is the more spontaneous, when Indian groups come to a hill outside the city to present the seven regional dances of the State in a great festival, also known as La Guelaguetza). Hotels book up early. Upper seats free, getting expensive near the front, be there 1½ hrs. in advance to get a good seat, tickets from Tourist Office, Calle García Vigil 105, 3 blocks from the Cathedral (has free maps, brochures and information, open Mon.- Sat. 1000-1300). Nov. 2, the Day of the Dead, is a mixture of festivity and solemn commemoration; the decoration of family altars is carried to competitive extremes (competition in Calle 5 de Mayo between Santo Domingo and the Zócalo on Nov. 1); traditional wares and foods, representing skulls, skeletons, coffins etc. are sold in the market. Ask before photographing. Dec. 6, 7, 8, with fine processions (Soledad), and 23 (Rábanos) with huge radishes carved in grotesque shapes sold for fake money; *buñuelos* are sold and eaten in the streets on this night, and the dishes ceremonially smashed after serving. Night of Dec. 24, a parade of floats (best seen from balcony of *Merendero El Tule*, go for supper and get a window table). Posadas in San Felipe (5 km. N) and at Xoxo, to the S, the week before Christmas. Bands play in the Zócalo every evening except Sat., and there are regional folk dances twice a week.

Hotels *El Presidente/Parador Santa Catalina*, Plazuela Bastida, magnificently restored convent circa 1690, true colonial with all services, street rooms noisy, restaurant greatly improved, A; *Calesa Real*, García Vigil 306, modern colonial but many small dark rooms, good but expensive, *Los Arcos* restaurant, parking, central, slow service, C; *Margarita Courts*, at N entrance to city, good and reasonable, C; *Misión Oaxaca*, San Felipe del Agua, some way out, attractive, C; *Misión de Los Angeles*, Porfirio Díaz 102, A, motel-style, 2 km. from centre, quiet and most attractive, with swimming pool, good food; *Victoria*, A, colonial house turned into hotel, bedrooms with showers built round the garden, many tour groups, but out of town (around 15-min. walk) at Km. 545 on Pan-American Highway; *Hacienda La Noria*, Periférico Con La Costa, C, motel-type, good and convenient; *Santo Tomás*, Abasolo 305, clean, private shower, friendly, kitchen for use of guests, some comfort, washing facilities, D, quiet, rec.; *Francia*, 20 de Noviembre 212, around enclosed courtyard, good food, popular, E; *Plazuela*, La Bastida 115, D, pleasant, friendly; *Plaza*, Trujano 112 (D. H. Lawrence once stayed there), near centre, D with bath, breakfast available, E, reasonable, friendly, book exchange; *California*, Chapultepec 822, near 1st class bus station, D, with bath, friendly, pleasant, restaurant; *Veracruz*, next to ADO bus station, spotless, D. *Del Bosque*, exit road to Mitla, modern, restaurant, D; 2 blocks from the Zócalo at 5 de Mayo 208 is *Principal*, D, colonial house, very clean, private shower with hot and cold water, English spoken, heavily booked (cockroaches too), not suitable for young, single women. *Vallarta*, Díaz Ordaz 309, D, clean, good value, enclosed parking. *María Luisa*, J. García Tinoco 507, F, with bath, good, hot water a.m. only; *Roma*, J.P.García 504 and Aldama, F, fairly clean, a bit noisy (2 blocks from the market), reasonable; *Rivera*, one block from *Roma*, E. *Rex*, Las Casas 308, F, with shower, clean, friendly, secure but not suitable for single women, close to market, narrow entrance; *Linivé*, Periférico 108 y Las Cajas, overlooking bus terminal, clean, shower, F; *Señorial*, Portal de Flores 6, will store luggage, suites or rooms, C, with bath, swimming pool, on main square, some rooms rather noisy, regular folk dance performances are given here, photography permitted, poor restaurant; *Monte Albán*, E, friendly, opp. Cathedral; *Ruiz*, Bustamente 103, just off Zócalo, D, nice and clean, quiet, hot water only very early morning, don't leave valuables lying around, otherwise rec.; *Asunción*, Aldama and García, F, with bath, clean, nr. market; *Pomba*, 20 de Noviembre and Morelos, near Zócalo, E, gringo hotel, hot shower, clean, rec.; *Central*, 20 de Noviembre 104, E, private bathroom, best bet for hot water a.m., good value but very noisy, fills up early, also reports of peeping toms; *Fortín*, Díaz Ordaz 312, nr. south side of main market, clean, some rooms good, others basic, noisy at ground floor level, F, with bath, hot water a.m. only; next door at 316 is *Díaz Ordaz*, F, clean and friendly, similar water problem; many others nearby; *Pasaje*, Mina 302, near market, E with bathrooms, parakeets in patio (Lorenzo is most entertaining), clean, very friendly, free purified water; *Yagul*, F, Mina 103 near market and Zócalo, use of kitchen on request, very clean; *Casa de Huéspedes Arnel*, three blocks to the right of ADO station, Aldama 404, Col. Valatlaco, F, very clean. *Chayo*, 20 de Noviembre 508, F, bath but no fan, clean, friendly and quiet with attractive patio, rec.; *Nacional*, same block, F, clean, quiet. There is also accommodation in private houses which rent rooms (*casas de huéspedes*); *Posada Las Palmas*, Av. Juárez 516, F, without bath, restaurant, rec.; *Del Arbol*, Calzada Madero 131, modern, comfortable, bath, D; *Casa de Huéspedes Farolito*, Calle de Las Casas 508, F, more expensive with bath. *Posada Margarita*, Calle Abasolo, 3 blocks from Zócalo, F, with bath, not clean, friendly. *Villa Alta*, Cabrera 303, 4 blocks from Zócalo, friendly service, F, clean. On the road to Tehuantepec (Km. 9.8), *Hotel Posada Los Arcos*, Spanish-style hotel at San Sebastián Totla, D.

N.B. Hotels near the corner of 20 de Noviembre and Mina are in the red light district. Many other cheap hotels in 400 block of Trujano.

Camping Oaxaca Trailer Park on the N fringe of town (corner of Calles Pinos and Violetas), US$3.50 for 1-2 persons, secure, clothes washing facilities; bus "Carmen-Infonavit" from downtown.

Restaurants *Flor de Oaxaca*, Armenta y López 311, delicious hot chocolate; *Los Arcos*, García Vigil 306 under *Calesa Real* hotel, good but expensive. *Guelatao*, on main square, good for breakfast and snacks, cheap beer; *Portal*, next door, similar to *Guelatao* but better, local dishes US$1-1.50; *Montebello*, good, at Trujano 307; *Colón*, Colón 111; *La Catedral*, corner of Gral. García Vigil and Morelos, 1 block from Cathedral, good for local specialities— steaks, good *tamales*, classical music. *Alameda*, J.P.García between Trujano and Hidalgo, excellent regional food, crowded Sun. *Flamingo*, on Trujano near Zócalo, good cheap comidas.

Vegetarian: *Flor de Loto*, Av. Morelos 509, next to Rufino Tamayo museum, good and new (US$1 a meal); another, dearer, opp. ADO bus station.

Gino's Pizza, pleasant café, inexpensive in Independencia, 500 block; *El Sol y la Luna*, on Murguia, good although not cheap, live music some nights, now open evenings only; *Café Fontana*, excellent, opp. *Hotel Presidente*; *Café ADO*, ADO Terminal; unmarked small restaurant in Calle Abasolo, between 212 and 218, cheap light meals, clean; *Colonial*, 20 de Noviembre, cheap comidas corridas, rec. However, the best Oaxacan food is found in the *comedores familiares* such as *Clemente, Los Almendros, La Juchita*, but they are way out of town and could be difficult to get to; also try *El Bicho Pobre*, Tacubaya y Abasolo, local food, open 1330-1800, excellent value; *El Mesón*, good tacos, clean, quick service, on Hidalgo at NE corner of Zócalo; *Tropical Frutas*, Mina y J.P.García, excellent and cheap. Some restaurants lining the Zócalo are deemed to be overpriced, also very slow service, up to 1½ hrs to get complete order. *Café Tito*, near Zócalo on García Vigil, good value for breakfast; *Cafetería Quickly*, clean, friendly, French, cheap, popular with students; *El Paisaje*, 20 de Noviembre, good, cheap chicken dishes; *El Hipocampo*, Hidalgo 505, cheap, good; *La Piñata*, Hidalgo (just E of Zócalo), good chicken in mole lunches; *La Bougainvillier*, M. F. Fiallo 116 y Hidalgo, good, clean, reasonable prices; *El*

Tecolote, a few blocks from Zócalo, open air eating, good quesadillas and tacos; *Casa de Chocolate*, quiet, pleasant, on Av. Independencia, coffee and home-made cakes; *Cafetería Chips*, Trujano (in 1st block W of Zócalo), good coffee; *Cafetería Alex*, Díaz Ordaz y Trujano, good comida corrida, coffee and breakfasts; *El Patio*, 1 block from Zócalo, has mainly good fish and seafood dishes, moderate prices and good service. Cheap and clean café *Las Palmas* (near *Hotel Pasaje*) on 20 de Noviembre. Good *dulcería* (sweet shop) in the 2nd class bus station.

Entertainment *La Luna y el Sol*, good bar with music.

Doctor Dr Marco Antonio Callejo (English-speaking), Belisario Domínguez 115, T 53-492, surgery 0900-1300, 1700-2000.

Shopping There are endless temptations such as green and black pottery, baskets and bags made from cane and rushes, embroidered shirts, skirts, and blankets; Saturdays are the best for buying woollen *sarapes* cheaply. A group of Zapotecs can be seen weaving on Zaragoza between 20 de Noviembre and Tinoco y Palacios on Saturday, selling wall hangings and *sarapes*. Also daily on Zaragoza and García, between 0800-2000, but more expensive than elsewhere. Unfortunately some of the woven products are of a different quality from the traditional product—more garish dyes and synthetic yarns are replacing some of the originals; but you can still find these if you shop around. *Aripo*, on García Vigil, cheaper and better than most, service good. *Artesanías Cocijo*, interesting collection of handicrafts, a little expensive, English spoken and will ship goods, García Vigil 212. *Pepe*, Avenida Hidalgo, for jewellery; cheap local crafts. Good for silver, *Plata Mexicana*, 20 de Noviembre 209-C. *Yalalag*, Alcalá 104, has good selection of jewellery, rugs and pottery, somewhat overpriced; cheapest and largest selection of pottery plus a variety of fabrics and sandals at *Productos Típicos de Oaxaca*, Av. Dr. B. Dominguez 602; city bus near ADO depot goes there. *Casa Aragón*, J. P. García 503, famous for knives and *machetes*. Fine cream and purple-black pottery (Zapotec and Mixtec designs) available at *Alfarería Jiménez*, Zaragoza 402; further along Zaragoza is a small straw market with all kinds of baskets and bags. Other potteries at Las Casas 614, makers of the Oaxacan daisy design, and Trujano 508, bold flower designs. Many excellent fixed-price bargains to be had at *El Gran Bazaar*, Av. Independencia. Large selection of cotton and wool. Bargain for up 50% reduction. The old market sells fruit, vegetables, meat and some handicrafts (good, cheap meals here); Mercado de Abastos, open daily, which sells mostly food and flowers next to the 2nd class bus station, where the old Saturday market has also moved and caters mainly to the tourist trade. Benito Juárez market, 20 de Noviembre and Las Casas, good tourist items, but bargain hard and watch the quality. Those disappointed with it should go to the Sunday market at Tlacolula.

Library English lending library with very good English books, a few French and Spanish, also English newspapers (*The News* from Mexico City) at Macedonio Alcalá 305—looks like an apartment block on a pedestrian street, a few blocks N of Zócalo (open Mon.-Fri., 1000-1300, 1600-1800). *The News* is also sold round the Zócalo by newsboys, from mid-morning.

Tourist Office 5 de Mayo 200 y Morelos, free map. Tourist Police on Zócalo near Cathedral, friendly and helpful. Federal tourist office Matamoros 105 y García Vigil. Instituto Nacional de Estadistica, Geografía e Informática, Calz. Porfirio Díaz 241A, for maps.

Exchange It's difficult to change travellers' cheques at weekends but if you get stuck try some of the more expensive restaurants in the Zócalo. Bancomer, 1 block from Zócalo, exchanges travellers' cheques, 0900-1330, on García Vigil. *Hotel Señorial* will change travellers' cheques. Amex office on Zócalo said to be unfriendly and unhelpful. *Casa de cambio* at Armenta y López, nr. corner with Hidalgo, 0900-1230, 1600-1900, a.m. only Sat., poor rates.

Washing Self: Baños Reforma, Calle Reforma, US$1.50 for steam-bath for two, same for sauna for two. Clothes: E.L.A., Super Lavandería Automática, Antonio Roldán 114, Col. Olímpica, washes and irons. Another one at Francisco Zarco, off the Periférico, and another in Av. Juárez 900, open until 1900, corner with Niños Héroes de Chapultepec. Good laundry on Calle 20 de Noviembre, 2½ blocks S of the market. All about US$1.50 for 7 lbs.

Local Buses There is a bus marked "Circular" or "Circular Panteón" which connects the first class bus stations on the N of town with the Zócalo, the market, the 2nd class bus station and the railway station.

Railway Station on Calzada Madero at junction with Periférico, 15 min. walk from Zócalo. From Mexico City, 563 km., 17 hrs., take food, magnificent scenery, US$4 1st class, US$3 2nd, at 1720 daily. To Mexico City daily at 1820, not always a sleeper. Tickets must be bought the same day. Seats scarce in 2nd class, quite a scramble! El Oaxaqueño (*servicio estrella*) leaves Mexico City 1900, arr. 0930, leaves Oaxaca 1900, arr. 0920, reserved seat US$7.25, single sleeper US$19.25, double US$38.70. To Puebla 0710, 11 hrs., US$3. Derailments at times.

Buses 1st class terminal is NW of Zócalo on Calzada de Niños Héroes (no luggage office); 2nd class is W of Zócalo on Calz. Trujano, has left-luggage office. Beware of double-booking and short-changing, especially when obtaining tickets from drivers if you have not booked in advance. Cristóbal Colón to Mexico City, 10 hrs., about 8 a day, mostly evenings, US$8, 2nd class by Fletes y Pasajes, 9 hrs., comfortable; about 15 a day with ADO, 10 hrs., US$6. 1st class to Cuautla, US$6 (change there for Cuernavaca); Puebla (1st class, 9 hrs., 2nd class, 11 hrs., US$4, at 0800, 1200 and 1900 with Fletes y Pasajes); to Tuxtepec (2nd class, 6 hrs., US$ 1.20, road regarded as dangerous because of drug plantations) and other towns; Cristóbal Colón to Villahermosa, US$8.50, book well ahead, 13½ hrs., daily at 1200 and 1700 (arrives in time to connect with 0645 bus to Palenque, and good for connecting with ADO buses to Mérida). 1st class; San Cristóbal de Las Casas (US$7.50, at 0700, 12 hrs.) book 1-2 days in advance with C. Colón; and Tapachula, 8-12 hrs., US$9 (2200, Cristóbal Colón). Also Fletes y Pasajes and Transportes Tuxtla (2nd class). Book well in advance as buses often come almost full from Mexico City. To Tuxtla Gutiérrez, 1st class, C. Colón, 3 a day, 9 hrs.; by 2nd class, 11 hrs., US$8 at 1030, 1730 and 2100. To Tehuantepec, scenic, almost every hour, 2nd class US$3, 5 hrs. To Ciudad Cuauhtémoc, US$9, 12 hrs. To Arriaga US$8, 5 a day. To Puerto Escondido, US$3, gruelling 13 hrs. journey (can be longer) at 1300, partly along dirt roads, interesting scenery. Night bus 5 hrs. faster. Probably better to go Oaxaca-Pochutla on new road, 7 hrs., US$3, six 1st-class buses a day, then change for Puerto Angel/Puerto Escondido. Oaxaca-Pacífico has good 2nd class buses (five a day to Pochutla, nine a day to Puerto Angel). Estrella del Valle run 1st class buses from 2nd class terminal, 8-10 hrs., at 0500. Buses to most local villages go from this terminal, too.

Air Services The airport is about 8 km. S, direction Ocotepec. The airport taxis (*colectivos*) cost US$1.50 p.p. Book at Transportaciones Aeropuerto Oaxaca on the Alameda (T 67878) for collection at your hotel to be taken to airport. From Mexico City daily by Aeroméxico in less than an hr., leaves at 0755, or Mexicana four daily and Mon., Fri., and Sun. at 1100 (Tues., Sat. and Thurs. also 1120); Tapachula flights with Aeroméxico, daily, 0820; Aeroméxico also flies daily to Acapulco, 0930, to Villahermosa daily at 1500, 50 mins. and Mérida daily at 1700. Daily flights to Guadalajara with Aeroméxico at 0930 and 1100, 3 hrs., to Ixtapa/Zihuatanejo at 1100, to Chihuahua at 1100 (with Mexicana at 1630), to Manzanillo at 1100; to Mazatlán at 0740 with Mexicana daily (Tues., Thurs., and Sat. at 1500), to Reynosa at 0740, to San Antonio at 0855, to Tijuana at 1100. Mexicana daily to Denver at 0740 (Tues., Thurs., Sat. at 1500), to Los Angeles daily at 0740 via Mexico City and on Fri. at 1100. Daily flights to Puerto Escondido, 40 mins, Aerovías Oaxaqueñas at 1100, returns at 0730 or 1200; Líneas Aéreas Oaxaqueñas fly at 1030 Mon.-Sat. and 0830 Sun. Costs US$40 one way, but all Puerto Escondido planes (DC-3s) break down frequently, and for some days, rough ride back if no plane, 9 hrs. Once weekly flights also to Pochutla. Líneas Aéreas Oaxaqueñas office at Av. Hidalgo 503. T 65362, airport 61280. There is a Mexicana office next to *Hotel Señorial* on the Zócalo, helpful.

Excursions To **Monte Albán** (open 0800-1700) about 10 km. (20 mins.) uphill from Oaxaca, to see the pyramids, walls, terraces, tombs, staircases and sculptures of the ancient capital of the Zapotec culture. The place is radiantly colourful during some sunsets. Beware of fake "antique" sellers. Guide US$1. Take a torch for later visits. Autobuses Turísticos (office at Trujano 607, but departure from behind *Hotel Mesón del Angel*, Mina nr. Díaz Ordaz; bus tickets available from hotel lobby) from Oaxaca hourly on the half-hour from 0930 to 1530 fare US$1.20 return; 2 hrs. at the site, allow not quite enough time to visit ruins before returning (you are allowed to come back on another tour on one ticket but you will not, of course, have a reserved seat for your return). To give yourself enough time, you can walk 4 km. downhill from the ruins to Colonia Monte Albán and get a city bus back from there. Good tours also from *Hotel El Presidente*, US$6 each with excellent guide. Entrance to ruins US$0.10, free on Sun. Most people go in the morning, so it may be easier to catch the afternoon bus. A private museum in an old colonial house was worth visiting. To the right, before getting to the ruins, is Tomb 7, where a fabulous treasure trove was found in 1932; most items are in the Regional Museum in the convent of Santo Domingo. The remarkable rectangular plaza, 300 by 200 metres, is rimmed by big ceremonial platforms: the Ball Court, and possibly a palace to the E, stairs rising to an unexcavated platform to the S, several platforms and temples to the W and one—known as Temple of the Dancers but in reality, probably a hospital—with bas-reliefs, glyphs and calendar signs (probably 5th century B.C.). A wide stairway leads to a platform on the N side. Most of the ruins visible are early 10th century, when the city was abandoned and became a burial place. Informative literature is available at the site. (Recommended literature is the Bloomgarden *Easy Guide* to Monte Albán or *Easy Guide* to Oaxaca covering the city and all the ruins in the valley, with maps. In major hotels or the bookshop at Guerrero 108, and all the ruins.) Restaurant near site is expensive; no food actually at site, but warm drinks. Just before the ruins is a swimming pool, Granja Tita; San Juanito buses take you there.

A paved road leads to **Teotitlán del Valle,** where Oaxaca *sarapes* are woven, which is now becoming rather touristy. If you knock at any door down the street, you will get them only a little cheaper than at the market, but there is greater variety. The best prices are to be had at the stores along the road as you come into town. (Make sure whether you are getting all-wool or mixture.) Buses leave every 2½ hrs. from 0800 from Miguel Cabrera nr. corner with Mina (US$0.30). *Juvenal Mendoza*, Buenavista 9, will make any design any size into a rug to order (daily at 1100). Opposite the turning for Teotitlán, turn right for **Dainzu,** another important ruin recently excavated. Its pyramid contains figures, probably ball players, similar to the Monte Albán dancers. The nearby site of **Lambytieco** is also well worth visiting, to see several fine and well-preserved stucco heads. Only 72 km. from Oaxaca is **Yanhuitlán,** with a beautiful 400-year-old church, part

OAXACA ENVIRONS

NOT TO SCALE

145

of a monastery. NW of Yanhuitlán is **Huajuapan de León,** with *Hotel García Peral*, on the Zócalo, good restaurant, *Hotel Casablanca*, Amatista 1, Col. Vista Hermosa, also good restaurant (just outside Huajuapan on the road to Oaxaca), and *Hotel Bella Vista*, E, and *Colón*, E, very good. 2nd class bus from Oaxaca to Huajuapan, four a day, US$1.75.

To Mitla, paved road, 42 km. from Oaxaca past (1) **El Tule** (12 km. from Oaxaca) which has what is reputed the world's largest tree, a savino (*Taxodium Mucronatum*), estimated at 2,000 years old, 40 metres old, 42 metres round at base, weighing an estimated 550 tons, fed water by an elaborate pipe system, in churchyard (bus from Oaxaca, 2nd class bus station, every ½ hr., US$0.40, buy ticket on bus, sit on the left to see the Tule tree; bus El Tule-Mitla US$0.30); (2) **Tlacochahuaya**, 16th century church, vivid Indian murals, carpets and blouses sold in market nearby, admission US$0.45 to church; and (3) **Tlacolula** (*Hotel Glish Bal*, Zaragoza 3, F, reported clean), with a most interesting Sunday market and the renowned Capilla del Santo Cristo in the church, elaborate decorations and gruesome figures of saints (fiesta 9 October); can be reached by bus from Oaxaca, from the 2nd class bus station every 30 mins. but every 15 mins. on Sun., US$0.25. Taxi costs US$4 each to Mitla for 4 sharing, with time to take photographs at Tule and Mitla and to buy souvenirs at ruins. A band plays every evening in the plaza, take a sweater, cold wind most eves, starts at 1930. Tours (rather rushed) to Tule, Mitla and Tlacolula on Sunday from *Hotel Señorial*, US$5.50, in VW buses. Fletes y Pasajes bus from Oaxaca, 2nd class bus station, every 30 mins. to Mitla, 1 hour, US$0.50; the ruins are 10-min. walk across the village (from the bus stop).

From the main road a turn left leads 4 km. to Mitla (whose name means "place of the dead") where there are ruins of four great palaces among minor ones. Entry US$0.10 (Sun. free), no literature available on site. See in particular the magnificent bas-reliefs, the sculptured designs in the Hall of Mosaics, the Hall of the Columns, and in the depths of a palace La Columna de la Muerte (Column of Death), which people embrace and measure what they can't reach with their fingers to know how many years they have left to live (rather hard on long-armed people); Indians gather on New Year's day to embrace it. There is a soberly decorated colonial church with three cupolas, and a rash of guides and pedlars. Beautiful traditional Indian clothes and other goods may be bought at the new permanent market. Also good *mescal*.

Hotel Mitla, E, clean, local food (comida corrida, US$4.80). *Hotel La Zapoteca*, on road to ruins, E, newer and better than *Mitla*, cheaper food, good, friendly. The University of the Americas has a small guest-house, and runs the small Frissell museum in the Zócalo at Mitla, with very good and clean restaurant, *La Sorpresa*, in a patio; restaurant opp. site, *Santa María*; *María Elena* restaurant

100 meters from site towards village, good comida corrida for US$0.90. The local technical college provides accommodation, showers and a bathroom; good shopping too.

Fletes y Pasajes buses and taxis from Oaxaca go to the ruins of **Yagul** (on the way to Mitla, ask to be put down at the turn-off to Yagul, entry, US$0.05), an outstandingly picturesque site where the ball courts and quarters of the priests are set in a landscape punctuated by candelabra cactus and agave. Yagul was a large Zapotec and Mixtec religious centre; the ball courts are perhaps the most perfect discovered to date; also fine tombs (take steep path from behind the ruins) and temples. You will have to walk some 2 km. from the bus stop to the site, and you can return the same way or walk 3 km. to Tlacolula to catch a bus (signposted). The 2 km.-long side road off the main road is paved.

There are 2 national parks in Oaxaca State: Benito Juárez in the municipality of Huayapan, some 5 km. from the capital, with pine forests, comprising 2,737 hectares; and the Lagunas de Chacacahua (14,187 hectares), including tropical vegetation and a 28-km. coastline on the Pacific, at Tututepec, 57 km. from Pinotepa Nacional.

Friday trips from Oaxaca to market at San Antonio Ocotlán on the road to Puerto Angel, with good prices for locally woven rugs and baskets, also excellent fruit and veg.; buses leave every 30 mins. for San Antonio from the co-operative bus station opposite Oaxaca Mercado de Abastos (½ hr. journey). Stop in San Bártolo Coyotepec to see black pottery (Doña Rosa's—she's been dead for years but her name survives—is a target for tours, but other families are just as good) and don't try to bargain (also red and green ceramics in the village), and in Santo Tomás Jalieza, where cotton textiles are made.

17 km. SW of Oaxaca is **Cuilapan,** where there is a vast unfinished 16th-century convent, now in ruins, with a famous nave and columns, and an "open chapel", whose roof collapsed in an earthquake. The last Zapotec princess was buried at Cuilapan. Reached by bus from Oaxaca from 2nd class bus station, take bus to Zaachila which leaves every 30 mins., then walk to unexcavated ruins in valley. **Zaachila** is a poor town, but there are ruins, with two Mixtec tombs, with owls in stucco work in the outer chamber and carved human figures with skulls for heads inside. Admission US$0.13, no restrictions on flash photography. There is an Indian market on Thursday.

To San Pablo de **Guelatao** (65 km. from Oaxaca), the birthplace of Benito Juárez. The town is located in the mountains NE of Oaxaca and can be reached by bus (3 hrs.) along a paved but tortuously winding road. There are a memorial and a museum to Juárez on the hillside within the village (entry, US$0.17), and a pleasant lake with a symbolic statue of a shepherd and his lambs.

We are approaching a more traditional part of Mexico; Tehuantepec isthmus and the mountains of Chiapas beyond, a land inhabited by Indians less influenced than elsewhere by the Spanish conquest. Only about 210 km. separate the Atlantic and the Pacific at the hot, heavily-jungled Isthmus of Tehuantepec, where the land does not rise more than 250 metres. There are a railway (to be renewed) and a Trans-Isthmian Highway between Coatzacoalcos and Salina Cruz, the terminal cities on the two oceans. Winds are very strong on and near the isthmus, because of the intermingling of Pacific and Caribbean weather systems. Drivers of high-sided vehicles must take great care.

N.B. In southern Mexico the word "Zócalo" is not often used for the main square of a town: "Plaza (Mayor)" is much more common.

Salina Cruz (43,000) is a booming and evil-smelling port with a naval base, extensive oil-storage installations and an oil refinery. Bathing is dangerous because of the heavy swell from Pacific breakers and also sharks. Beware of overcharging in the marketplace.

Hotels *Fuente*, E, bath, basic. *Río*, E, reasonable, nr. Cristóbal Colón bus station. Avoid the *Magda*, overpriced, unfriendly. *Posada del Jardín*, E.

Restaurant *Costa del Pacífico*, hires shower cabin, stores luggage.

Buses The 1130 bus from Salina Cruz to San Cristóbal comes from Oaxaca and is very often full (2nd class, US$5.50); take instead a 2nd class bus to Juchitán, then to Arriaga and from there to Tuxtla and San Cristóbal; a long route. To Coatzacoalcos, US$5, 6 hrs. Salina Cruz-Pochutla, US$3, 3½ hrs.; 2nd class to Puerto Escondido, 6 hrs., slow, US$3.50. Frequent buses to Tehuantepec, 30 mins., US$0.20. To Tapachula, 7½-8 hrs., 0740 and 2030, US$5.60. No luggage storage at bus station.

Ten km. to the S is a picturesque fishing village with La Ventosa beach which, as the name says, is windy. Buses go to the beach every 30 mins. from a corner of the main square. Accommodation: *La Posada de Rustrian*, overlooking the sea, E, with bath in new block, half in old block, poor value; unnamed *pensión*, F, on right of road before asphalt ends. Friendly family at the top of the dirt road coming from Salina Cruz (on the right) and 200 metres after the first path that leads down to the beach, rents hammocks, US$0.20 a night, fried fish US$1. *Champas*, or hammocks under thatch shelters by the beach, US$0.25-US$0.40 a night. The owners serve drinks and food (fish, shrimps, crabs just caught) from early morning on. Prices often high.

Warning   Do not wander too far off along the beach as many people have been attacked and robbed. Do not sleep on the beach or in your car.

(Km. 804) *Tehuantepec* (population 25,000, altitude 150 metres) is 257 km. from Oaxaca and 21 km. inland from Salina Cruz. A colourful place, it is on the bend of a river around which most of its activities are centred and which makes it very humid. The plaza has arcades down one side, a market on the other, and many stands selling *agua fresca*, an iced fruit drink. Houses are low, in white or pastel shades. The Indians are mostly Zapotecs whose social organization was once matriarchal: the women are high-pressure saleswomen, with some Spanish blood; their hair is sometimes still braided and brightly ribboned and at times they wear embroidered costumes. The men for the most part work in the fields, as potters or weavers, or at the nearby oil refinery. Hammocks made in this area are of the best quality. The town is divided into 15 wards, and each holds a *fiesta*, the main one at the end of Holy Week, when the women wear their finest costumes and jewellery. There is another splendid *fiesta* in honour of St. John the Baptist on June 22-25. January and February are good months for the ward *fiestas*.

Hotels   *Oasis* (central and good atmosphere), E, with bath and fan, near Plaza; *Donaji*, Juárez 10, reasonable, fan, nr. market, E; *Posada Villa Real*, E, nice courtyard. A guest house on the same street as Cristóbal Colón bus terminal is basic, but reasonable, friendly, with lovely patio, F.

Restaurants   *Café Colonial*, near the *Hotel Oasis*, and *Kike* under *Posada Colonial* have good comidas corridas for about US$4. Cheap food on top floor of market. The local quesadillas made of maize and cheese are delicious; sold at bus stops.

Bus   There is now a bus station. One bus a day to San Cristóbal at 1230 (7½ hrs., US$6) plus other destinations. To Coatzacoalcos at 0730, 9-10 hrs. Bus to Arriaga at 0600, 0800, 1800 to connect to Tonalá. To Tuxtla Gutiérrez, 1000 and 1500 (6 hrs.) 2nd class at 0130, and Tapachula. Bus to Tonalá (Cristóbal Colón) at 0030 and 0130. To Oaxaca, US$3, 5 hrs., with Fletes y Pasajes every 2 hours or so, or with Istmo at 1000 and 2200; to Salina Cruz, US$0.20. (**N.B.** Some buses from Salina Cruz do not stop at Tehuantepec.)

Train   to Coatzacoalcos daily at 0700, about 11 hrs.

Excursions   To neighbouring villages for *fiestas*. Near the town are the ruins of Criengola, apparently not very accessible.

27 km. beyond Tehuantepec on the road to Tuxtla Gutiérrez is **Juchitán** (*Hotel Don Alex*, F, noisy, *Hotel Casa Río*, has an Indian name, not posted, next to Casa Río shop, F, nr. market, clean; be prepared to bargain in cheap hotels), very old, Indian, with an extensive market, many *fiestas* and a special one on June 19 (2nd class bus Oaxaca-Juchitán, US$3.75, 6 hrs., frequent Juchitán-Tuxtla, 1st class, 4 hrs., US$3). Connect here with train from Veracruz to Tapachula, but Juchitán station is dangerous (at night wait for the train in Ixtepec). A road runs 6 km. N to **Ixtepec** (airport) (Hotels: *Panamericano*, noisy from railway station, F; *San Juan*, F, bath, acceptable; *Colón*) train Ixtepec-Coatzacoalcos at 0800. The Trans-Isthmian highway goes N from Juchitán, with a good hotel at Matías Romero, *Real del Istmo*, a/c, by the road, safe parking. At Las Cruces (restaurant), a road runs right to **Arriaga** (12,000 people; Hotels: *El Parador*, clean with swimming pool; *Juchitán*, E, with bathroom; *Colonial*, next to bus station, F, clean, friendly, quiet; *Restaurant Xochimilco* near bus stations), through **Tonalá**, formerly a very quiet town but now reported noisy and dirty, with a small museum; good market (bus Tonalá-Tapachula, 5 hrs., US$3. Also buses to Tuxtla). At Huixtla, near Tapachula (*Casa de Huéspedes Regis*, Independencia Norte 23, F), there is a good market—no tourists—along the railway line. By Route 200 to **Tapachula** (144,000), a pleasant and neat, but expensive, hot commercial town (airport) and the Talismán bridge to Guatemala. Beyond Tonalá the road is mostly straight, smooth and fast. (North of Arriaga a road is now open paralleling the railway and by-passing Las Cruces, so avoiding dozens of sharp curves on a steep road.) This is by far the better road for travellers seeking the quickest way from Mexico City to Guatemala.

Tonalá Hotels   *Galilea*, D, with bath, air-conditioned, good, basic cheap rooms on 1st floor, balconies, on main square, with good restaurants; *Casa de Huéspedes El Viajero*, Avenida Matamoros, near market, F, with bath, rough but OK; *Faro*, near Plaza, F; *Tonalá*, opposite museum, E; *Sta. Elena Restaurant*, at the S end of town, near Cristóbal Colón bus station on outskirts, good. On the Plaza, *Restaurant Nora*. Numerous Chinese-named restaurants; good breakfast at restaurants on Zócalo.

Tapachula Hotels San Francisco, Av. Central Sur 94, good, air-conditioned, D; *Cinco de Mayo*, E with bath, not very clean, convenient for Talismán colectivos; *Nina*, E, with bath, comfortable; *Colón*, Central Norte Juárez, E, with shower, near bus station; *Casa de Huéspedes Mexicana*, 8a Avenida Norte, F, basic, with a little zoo in the courtyard. Many hotels along Avenidas 4, 6, 8 (near Plaza). *Pensión Mars* (Av. 4) has cheap comidas; *Tayopec*, F, friendly; *Motel Loma Real*, 1 km. N of city, D, operates as a 1st class hotel, use of swimming pool, cold showers. Good restaurant next to Cristóbal Colón terminal.

Travel Agent Viajes Tacaná, operated by Sr Adolfo Guerrero Chávez, 4a Av. Norte, No. 6, T 63502/63501/63245; trips to Izapa ruins, to mountains, beaches and can gain entry to museum when closed. Tourist office on main Plaza not recommended.

Exchange Avoid the crowds of streetwise little boys at the border; exchange is rather better in the town.

Into Guatemala 2nd class buses from Tapachula (taking 50 mins.) include Cristóbal Colón, which leaves at 1245 and 1600 (US$0.60), and Unión y Progreso near the market (1st class leave 0900 and 1100, US$0.80—stating "Col. Juárez" as its destination) to the frontier (open 24 hrs. a day) at the Talismán bridge (8 km.) but no through buses. Kombi vans hourly or so from Unión y Progreso bus station, about US$1.20. Taxi Tapachula-Talismán, US$6, exit tax US$0.45. The Guatemalan customs post is 100 metres from the Mexican one. Exchange cash dollars for quetzales with men standing around customs on the Guatemalan side (but check rates before dealing with them, and haggle; there is a bank on the Guatemalan side, near customs). Crossing into Guatemala by car may take more than 2 hours. If you don't want your car sprayed inside it may cost you a couple of dollars. Guatemalan buses (Galgos) leave Talismán bridge about every two hours for Coatepeque, Quezaltenango and Guatemala City (6 hrs., entry tax 2 quetzales).

There are few buses between the Talismán bridge and Oaxaca or Mexico City (though they do exist); advisable therefore to travel to Tapachula for connection. Buses (Cristóbal Colón) from Tapachula to Mexico City, US$15, five a day, all p.m., take 8-12 hrs. to reach Oaxaca (US$9), and same again to Mexico City. Two additional buses to Oaxaca, 0730 and 1800 may take 10 hrs. Buses from Mexico City all leave p.m. also; the 1545 and 1945 go on to Talismán. The train from Mexico City to Tapachula leaves daily at 2100, it costs US$12.50 1st class but takes 37 hours to complete the journey, changing at Veracruz (Veracruz-Tapachula, 29 hrs., 887 km., US$3.50 2nd class), stops to get food on the way. If travelling in the reverse direction, board train at Tapachula hours in advance of departure to get seats, and guard them. Tickets on sale in Tapachula only at 1630. Train departs daily at 1800 for connection to Mexico City but again requires change at Veracruz and tends to miss evening train to Mexico City. Best to stay overnight at Veracruz and catch morning train. Don't get off at Tierra Blanca to change to the Mérida-Mexico train; you arrive after it has gone. Hitch-hikers should note that there is little through international traffic at Talismán bridge. Tapachula—Salina Cruz, 9 hrs. with Flecha Roja, US$6.40.

Consulates It is possible (but very difficult for Canadians, we are told) to get a visa for El Salvador at the Salvadorean Consulate in Tapachula (Calle 2a Sur, No. 10) without any delay. There is a Guatemalan Consulate in Tapachula at 2 Calle Oriente and 7 Av. S., T 6-12-52, taxi from Colón terminal, US$0.75. (Open Mon.-Fri. 0800-1600; visa US$10, friendly and quick.)

Off the road between Tonalá and Tapachula are several fine-looking and undeveloped beaches (although waves are dangerous) *Puerto Arista* is now being built up and spoiled; bus from Tonalá every hour, 45 mins., US$0.25, taxi US$0.50—one hotel or hammocks on beach, US$0.85 a night (many sandflies), also several guest houses, US$24 a month, 3 or 4 restaurants (closed by 2000) with rooms to rent, e.g. *Restaurant Turquesa*; new small hotel/restaurant 3 blocks down on the right from where the road reaches the beach coming from Tonalá and turns right, next to bakery, no fan, basic, F. Buses also from Tonalá to Boca del Cielo further down the coast, which is good for bathing but has no accommodation, and similarly Cabeza del Toro. *Paredón*, on the huge lagoon Mar Muerto near Tonalá, has excellent seafood and one very basic guest house. One can take a local fishing boat out into the lagoon to swim; the shore stinks because fishermen clean fish on the beach among dogs and pigs. Served by frequent buses. En route for Tapachula one passes through Pijijiapan where there is the *Hotel Pijijilton* (!) next to the Cristóbal Colón bus station. Also *Puerto Madero*, 20 km. from Tapachula (bus US$0.80), worse than Puerto Arista, because built up and stench on beaches from rubbish being burned. Intense heat in summer. (*Hotel Puerto Madero*, accommodation in what are really remains of cement block room, F.) Water defences are being built. Many fish restaurants on beach.

45 km. (16 km. to turn-off) beyond Tapachula, on the way to Guatemala, is *Unión Juárez* (*Hotel Colonial*, E; *Restaurant Carmelita* on the square is modest with fair prices). Visit the ruins of *Izapa* (proto-classic stelae, small museum) on the way to Unión Juárez; the part of the site on the N is easily visible but a larger portion is on the S side of the highway, about 1 km. away, ask caretaker for guidance. These buildings influenced Kaminal Juyú near Guatemala City and are considered archaeologically important as a Proto-Mayan site. In Unión Juárez one can have one's

papers stamped and proceed on foot via Talquián to the Guatemalan border at Sibinal. Take a guide.

A worthwhile and easy hike can be made up the Tacaná volcano (4,150 m.), which takes 2-3 days from Unión Juárez. Ask for the road to Chiquihuete, no cars. Jorge de León will guide you, or the Club Andinista at the Tapachula tourist office can help, on the Plaza Mayor.

Beyond Las Cruces we enter the mountainous Chiapas state, mostly peopled by Maya Indians whose extreme isolation has now been ended by air services and the two main highways. Chiapas ranks first in cacao production, second in coffee, bananas and mangoes, and cattle-grazing is important. Hardwoods are floated out down the rivers which flow into the Gulf.

Mike Shawcross writes: Anyone with a vehicle who has time to visit or is looking for a place to spend the night would find it well worthwhile to make a 4-km. detour. 50 km. beyond Las Cruces a gravel road leads north (left) to the beautiful waterfall El Aguacero (small sign), which falls several hundred feet down the side of the Río La Venta canyon. There is a small car-park at the lip of the canyon. 986 steps lead down to the river and the base of the waterfall.

From Las Cruces to Tuxtla Gutiérez, Route 190 carries on to Cintalapa (restaurant) whence there is a steep climb up an escarpment. Carry on to Ocozocoautla (airport for Tuxtla, hotel, F), make a long ascent followed by descent to

(Km. 1,085) **Tuxtla Gutiérrez,** capital of Chiapas; pop.: 167,000; alt.: 522 metres, 301 km. (183 miles) from Tehuantepec. It is a hot, modern city with greatest interest to the tourist during the fair of Guadalupe, on December 12. The market is worth a look. There is a State Archaeological Museum with a fine collection of Mayan artefacts, open daily, at the E end of town, near the botanical garden (on a wooded hillside near the Teatro de la Ciudad—it has an orchid research station). There is a zoo some 3 km. S of town up a long hill (too far to walk), which contains only animals and birds from Chiapas, wild and in captivity. (It has a respected reseach centre and is said to be the best zoo in Mexico, if not Latin America—good for birdwatchers too (open Tues.-Sun., 0830-1700, free; the buses "Zoológico" and "Cerro Hueco" from Calle 1a Oriente Sur, between Avs. 6a and 7a Sur Oriente, pass the entrance; taxi US$0.50 from centre). Tourist office is about 100 metres E of *Hotel Bonampak*.

The street system here is as follows: Avenidas run from E to W, Calles from N to S. The Avenidas are named according to whether they are N or S of the Avenida Central and change their names if they are E or W of the Calle Central. The number before Avenida or Calle means the distance from the "Central" measured in blocks.

Hotels *Bonampak*, Bld. Belisario Domínguez 180, W end of town, the social centre, C, clean, good restaurant; *Flamboyant*, Bld. Belísario Domínguez 1081, T 29859/29311, comfortable, good swimming pool; *Gran Hotel Humberto*, Av. Central Oriente 180, C; *Posada del Rey*, 2 Av. Norte Oriente 310, C, a/c; *La Mansión*, 1 Poniente Norte 221, D, a/c, bath; all centrally located. *Palace Inn*, Blvd. Belisario Domínguez (on highway just before bypass), C, clean, pool, garden, good value; *Mar-Inn*, D, pleasant, clean, 2a Av. Norte Oriente 347; *Balun Canan*, Av. Central Oriente 922, D. Opp. Cristóbal Colón bus station are *María Teresa*, E, and *Santo Domingo*, F with shower, good if you arrive late, but noisy; *Posada del Sol*, 1 block from Cristóbal Colón buses, F with hot shower, clean, friendly; *Canadá*, near market, F, without bath. CREA Youth Hostel, Calz. Angel Albino Corzo 1800, T 21301/33405, C.P. 29070. **Motels** *Paraíso*, Pan-American Highway, E; *La Hacienda*, trailer-park-hotel, Belisario Domínguez 1197, E, Camping F, owner speaks English.

Restaurants *Los Cazadores,* good, regional, expensive; *Mina,* Av. Central Oriente 525, nr. bus station, good cheap *comidas; Parrilla La Cabaña,* excellent *tacos,* very clean; *Las Pichanchas,* pretty courtyard, *marimba* music between 1400-1700 and 2000-2300, on Av. 14 de Septiembre Oriente 837, worth trying; *Central,* on Plaza, reasonable; many others; *Las Calandrias,* 2a Av. Norte Poniente, 20 metres from Cristóbal Colón terminal, open 0700-2400, good and cheap. Coffee shop below *Hotel Serrano* serves excellent coffee.

Post Office on main square. International phone calls can be made from 1 Norte, 2 Oriente, directly behind post office, 0800-1500, 1700-2100 (1700-200 Sun.).

Travel Agency Carolina Tours, Sr José Narváez Valencia (manager), Av. Central Poniente 1138, T 2-42-81; reliable, recommended; also shop at Av. Central Poniente 230.

Roads and Buses 35 km. E of Tuxtla, just past Chiapa de Corzo (see below), a road runs N, 294 km., to Villahermosa via Pichucalco (**see page 1087**), paved all the way. Cristóbal Colón 1st class bus terminal is at 2 Av. Norte Poniente 268, Transportes Tuxtla 1st and 2nd class terminals are at

2 Av. Sur Oriente 712. Cristóbal Colón has buses daily to Villahermosa at 0620, 1300 and 1730, 8½ hrs., US$6; to Oaxaca at 1100 and 2245, 12 hrs., US$7; 4 a day to Mexico City, US$19, plus frequent buses to San Cristóbal de Las Casas, US$2, superb mountain journey. Tuxtla-Tapachula, US$5, 4 a day; one (1st class) to the Talismán bridge daily at 0300. Oaxaca Pacífico buses to Salina Cruz, from 1st class bus terminal. Take travel sickness tablets for Tuxtla-Oaxaca road if you suffer from queasiness. Transportes Tuxtla has 2nd class buses to Oaxaca, 5 a day, US$8, and 1st class buses to Pichucalco, 6 a day, US$4 (Pichucalco-Villahermosa and Villahermosa-Campeche (6 hrs.) have frequent services); to Villahermosa at 0500 and 1330, US$5; to Mérida at 1330, US$15. The scenery between Tuxtla and Mérida is very fine, and the road provides the best route between Chiapas and Yucatán. There are VW taxis at the bus station but they will not drive to the airport unless they have a full passenger load and may tout hotels before going there.

By Air   The new airport for Tuxtla is way out at the next town of Ocozocoautla, a long drive to a mountain top. It is often shrouded in cloud and has crossroads: there are times when aircraft do not leave for days! Good facilities, including restaurant. Tuxtla Gutiérrez to Tapachula, daily, 35 mins.; to Villahermosa daily, 25 mins.; to Veracruz, Mon. and Fri., 1 hr. 25 mins.; to Monterrey daily via Mexico City, 4 hrs. 15 mins.; to Minatitlán Mon. and Fri., 30 mins.; frequent to Mexico City, direct 1 hr. 15 mins.; to Acapulco daily, 2 hrs. 40 mins.; to Chihuahua daily; to Guadalajara daily; to Ixtapa/Zihuatanejo daily. There is a 40 min. flight by Britten-Norman Islander to Palenque, very exciting, no reservations or tickets available. You must be at the airport before dawn, flights leave at about 0700, Sumidero canyon can be seen during flight.

Excursions   Two vast artificial lakes made by dams are worth visiting: the Presa Netzahualcoyotl, or Mal Paso, 77 km. NW of Tuxtla, and La Angostura, SE of the city. Information from the tourist office. Mal Paso can also be visited from Cárdenas (**see page 1086**). By paved road, which starts at zoo gates (23 km.), in excellent condition, to the rim of the tremendous **Sumidero Canyon**, over 1,000 metres deep (taxi fare US$20 return; minibus daily from 1a Av. Norte Oriente 1121, go at 0900 and hope others turn up to share US$10 cost. Indian warriors unable to endure the Spanish conquest hurled themselves into the canyon rather than submit. Excursions by air to Bonampak and Yaxchilán cheaper from San Cristóbal (see below). Transportes Tuxtla has a 1st class bus from Tuxtla to Palenque at US$6.50 one way, which leaves Tuxtla at 0500; 9-hr. journey via Pichucalco and Villahermosa.

Chiapa de Corzo, 15 km. on, a colonial town of about 7,000 people on a bluff overlooking the Grijalva river, is more interesting than Tuxtla: see a fine 16th century crown-shaped fountain, a church whose engraved altar is of solid silver, and famous craftsmen in gold and jewellery and lacquer work who travel the fairs. Painted and lacquered vessels made of pumpkins are a local speciality. There is a small lacquer museum. The *fiestas* here are outstanding: January 20-23 with a pageant on the river and another, early February. *Hotel Los Angeles*, on Plaza, E, only one, dreadful; make alternative arrangements. Plaza filled with bars playing jukeboxes. Chiapa de Corzo was a preclassic and proto-classic Maya site and shares features with early Maya sites in Guatemala; the ruins are behind the Nestlé plant, and some restored mounds are in a field near modern houses. Ask the householders' permission to climb over the fence as the ruins are on private property. Bus from Tuxtla Gutiérrez, 380 Calle 3C Oriente Sur; several buses a day (1 hr.) to San Cristóbal de Las Casas.

Mike Shawcross tells us: The waterfall at the Cueva de El Chorreadero is well worth a detour of 1 km. The road to the cave is 10 km. past Chiapa de Corzo, a few km. after you start the climb up into the mountains to get to San Cristóbal.

You can take a boat from Chiapa de Corzo into the Sumidero canyon, very impressive, US$25 per boat for a 2-hour trip (or US$5 p.p. if boat has 8 people), much wildlife to be seen.

(Km. 1,170) *San Cristóbal de Las Casas* (population 90,000), 85 km. beyond Tuxtla Gutiérrez, was founded in 1528 by Diego de Mazariegos and was the colonial capital of the region. It stands in a high mountain valley at 2,110 metres. It was named after Las Casas, protector of the Indians, its second bishop. There are many old churches; two of them cap the two hills which overlook the town. Santo Domingo, built in 1547, has a baroque façade, a gilt rococo interior and a famous carved wooden pulpit (see below). Museum in the Convent of Santo Domingo gives a very good history of San Cristóbal, and has a display of local costumes upstairs. Other churches include San Nicolás, with an interesting façade, El Carmen, La Merced, and La Caridad (1715). From the Temple of Guadalupe there is a good view of the city and surrounding wooded hills. Various kinds of craftwork are sold in the new market, open daily, and in the Sunday markets of the local Indian villages. There is a small American colony. July 25 is

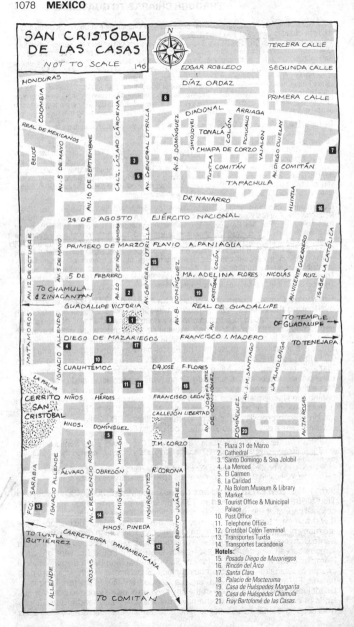

SAN CRISTÓBAL
DE LAS CASAS
NOT TO SCALE 146

1. Plaza 31 de Marzo
2. Cathedral
3. Santo Domingo & Sna Jolobil
4. La Merced
5. El Carmen
6. La Caridad
7. Na Bolom Museum & Library
8. Market
9. Tourist Office & Municipal Palace
10. Post Office
11. Telephone Office
12. Cristóbal Colón Terminal
13. Transportes Tuxtla
14. Transportes Lacandonia

Hotels:
15. *Posada Diego de Mazariegos*
16. *Rincón del Arco*
17. *Santa Clara*
18. *Palacio de Moctezuma*
19. *Casa de Huéspedes Margarita*
20. *Casa de Huéspedes Chamula*
21. *Fray Bartolomé de las Casas.*

fiesta day, when vehicles are taken uphill to be blessed by the Bishop. There is also a popular spring festival on Easter Sunday and the week after. There is a remarkable cemetery on the road to Tuxtla Gutiérrez, 2-3 km. from the centre of town.

Most Indian tribes here are members of the Tzotzil and Tzeltal groups. The Tenejapans wear black knee-length tunics; the Chamulans white wool tunics; and the Zinacantecos multicoloured outfits, with the men exhibiting marital status by the ribbons on their hats; bachelors allow ribbons to flow freely. The Chamula and Tenejapa women's costumes are more colourful, and more often seen in town, than the men's.

N.B. Check on the situation before you visit the surrounding villages. Travellers are strongly warned not to wander around on their own, especially in the hills surrounding the town where churches are situated, as they could risk assault. Warnings can be seen in some places frequented by tourists. Heed the warning on photographing, casual clothing and courtesy (**see page 1082**). Note also: international connections are difficult: only one public trunk telephone line; 30 mins.-2 hrs. wait.

Na Bolom, the house of the archaeologists Frans (died 1963) and Trudi Blom, has become a museum, open 1600-1730 (except Mon. and July 7); address: Vicente Guerrero 33, and a beautiful individual guest house (previous reservation necessary, double room with 3 meals, US$46 a day), with good library, run by Mrs Trudi Blom. It is well worth visiting: beautifully displayed artefacts, pictures of Lacandón Indians, with information about their history and present way of life (in English). Also only easily-obtainable map of Lacandón jungle. At 1600 sharp guides take you round display, rooms of beautiful old house, and garden. Entrance US$0.80. The Na Bolom library opens as follows: Mon., 1430-1800; Tues.-Sat., 0900-1300. We have been told that travellers can sometimes stay there free, in exchange for voluntary work.

Hotels *Motel Alcanfores*, on side of mountain W of city, two-bedroom bungalows (sleep 6), A; *Posada Diego de Mazariegos*, María A. Flores 2, T 8-06-21, 1 block N of Plaza, C, warmly rec., restaurant and bar; *Parador Ciudad Real*, Diagonal Centenario 32, W edge of city; *Bonampak*, Calzado México 5, T 8-16-21, C; *Rincón del Arco*, 8 blocks from centre, friendly, Ejército Nacional 66, D, warmly rec., bar, restaurant, discotheque; *Molino de La Alborada*, Periférico Sur Km. 4, S of airstrip, modern ranch-house and bungalows, D; *Santa Clara*, on Plaza, C, colonial style, clean, good restaurant, rec.; *Palacio de Moctezuma*, Juárez 18, colonial style, D, good Mexican food; *Posada Los Morales*, Ignacio Allende 17, E, cottages with open fires and hot showers, beautiful gardens, rec.; *Real del Valle*, Av. Guadalupe, next to Plaza, E, very clean, friendly, rec., washing facilities on roof, parking; *San Cristóbal*, Independencia near Plaza, E with bath, colonial style, renovated, pleasant; *Parador Mexicano*, Av. 5 de Mayo 38, D, tennis court, quiet and pleasant; *Posada Capri*, Insurgentes 54, near Cristóbal Colón bus terminal, D; 2 *Hoteles Mónica*, larger at Insurgentes 33, E, nice patio, restaurant, bar, rec., and smaller at 5 de Febrero 18, E (also have furnished bungalows to rent on road to San Juan Chamula); *Ciudad Real*, on Plaza, clean, good value, good restaurant, attractive rooms, but noisy parrot talks a lot, D; *Molino de Las Casas*, small bungalows in spacious grounds near Pan-American Highway, D; *San Martín*, Calle Real de Guadalupe 16, near Plaza, E, clean, good value, hot water, left-luggage, check you have enough blankets; *Maya Quetzal*, on Pan-American Highway, adjoining restaurant, E; *Fray Bartolomé de Las Casas*, Insurgentes and Niños Héroes, D, with bath, nice rooms and patio, can be noisy, cold at night but extra blankets available; *Casa de Huéspedes Chamula*, Calle Julio M. Corzo, clean, hot showers, washing facilities, friendly, parking, E, rec.; *Pensión Ramos*, Cuauhtémoc 12, E with bath and hot water, clean, small, rec. *Posada Insurgente*, Av. Insurgentes 5, clean, basic, but cheap F (bargain), one block from C.Colón station; *Casa de Huéspedes Margarita*, Real de Guadalupe 34, E in private room without bath, gringo hotel, free purified water, communal sleeping F, washing and toilets, clean, friendly, hot water, laundry possible, restaurant serves breakfast and dinner, slow service, wholefood, horses and guides arranged for visits to nearby villages or caves in the mountains, US$6 incl. guides for 6 hrs. *Posada Tepeyac*, one block from *Margarita*, friendly, clean, F; *Posada del Caudil*, Mexicanos, F, hot shower, clean, kitchen and washing facilities, good value; *Pensión* at Av. Gen. Utrilla 13, F, rooms vary greatly in quality; *Posada El Cerillo*, F, hot showers, washing facilities, not very clean but nice atmosphere, Av. B. Domínguez 27. *Parador Ciudad Real*, 1 km. from centre, friendly, new, D. *Baños Mercederos*, Calle 1° de Marzo 55, F, shared quarters (apparently Mexicans only), good cheap meals, steam baths ($0.80 extra). (*Baños Torres* next door has no rooms.) At No. 25 and No. 59 of the same street, pleasant rooms with families, quiet, clean, friendly, E, also good food. Several unmarked guest houses.

Camping *Rancho San Nicolás*, at end of Calle Francisco León, 1½ km. E of centre, beautiful, quiet location, is a trailer park (not secure for tent-camping), but do take warm blankets or clothing as the temperature drops greatly at night, hot showers, US$0.80 p.p., rooms available at same price, children free. *La Amistad* trailer park and campground is 27 km. from San Cristóbal (4 km. before Teopisca) on the Pan-American Highway towards Comitán. Hook-ups, hot showers, fresh vegetables, US$2.25 for a VW van plus US$0.45 p.p.; up to US$4 for larger recreational vehicles. "White gas" available at small store on corner across from NE corner of main market (Chiwit).

Restaurants Restaurants close quite early. *La Galería*, S of Plaza at Av. Miguel Hidalgo 3, now rather expensive, also sells quality art-work and handicrafts; frequented by young Americans, coffee shop, carrot cake, German and US magazines to read. *El Fandango*, ex-*Olla Podrida*, US-run and frequented, international menu, rather expensive, slow service, handicrafts, English book exchange, Diego de Mazariegos 24. *El Mural*, Av. Crescencio Rojas, pleasant; *Café Torreón* in Plaza outside La Merced church. *La Plaza*, upstairs, SW corner of Plaza, clean. *La Parrilla*, Av. Belisario Domínguez 35, evenings only, good cheap grills. *Fulano*, on Flores near Plaza, US$3 for excellent set meal. *El Patio*, next to *Posada Diego de Mazariegos*, try their coffee with liqueur, very exotic; *El Unicornio*, Av. Insurgentes 33a, is "gringo place", Italian food, rec. *La Parroquia*, large and airy restaurant, on Guadalupe Victoria nr. 16 de Septiembre, the haunt of the local middle class. *Normita*, Av. Benito Juárez, good Mexican food, open 1300-1500 and for supper, owner plays guitar and his wife and daughter sing, billboard with cheap accommodation. *El Tuluc*, Insurgentes 5 (owner changes money at good rate), good value comida, near Plaza; close by is *Rafaello*, Madero 9, modern, elegant, sells fine Indian weavings; also rec. are *La Peñita* and *Capri* on Insurgentes; *La Casa Blanca*, on Guadalupe, deep sofas, good coffee; *Cafetería San Cristóbal*, Dr José F. Flores near Plaza, very clean, good coffee, rec. *El Punto*, Domínguez y Madero, good pizza. *El Mesón Coleto*, Madero, good and cheap Mexico food; *Los Arcos*, varied menu, on Madero. *Tierra Madre*, Insurgentes (opp. Franciscan church), Anglo-Mexican owned, European dishes, vegetarian specialities, wholemeal breads, popular with travellers; *Familia*, Av. Gen. Utrilla, vegetarian dishes, somewhat "hippie"; *El Trigal*, 1° de Marzo, restaurant and shop, vegetarian, good. Wholemeal bread at health-food shop marked with star-shape near post office. Good cake at *Pan y Arte*, Ignacio Allende 5, amber jewellery for sale. Many others. San Cristóbal is not lively in the evenings: main meeting place is around ponche (local drink) stall on Plaza.

Shopping Part of the ex-convent of Santo Domingo has been converted into a cooperative, *Sna Jolobil*, selling handicrafts from many Indian villages (best quality, so expensive; also concerts by local groups). For local goods try *Miscelánea Betty*, Gen. Utrilla 45, good value. A good place to buy handicrafts is at *Doña Paula*, Calle Real de Guadalupe 25, just off the Plaza (there are craft shops all along the Guadalupe; the farther along, the cheaper) and *El Quetzal* for costumes from local villages. Beautiful handicrafts by Guatemalan refugees are sold in their place in the Seminario, Julio M.Corzo 16B, opposite *Casa de Huéspedes Chamula*; quality high and prices lower than in Guatemala. (If you want to visit the refugee camps, ask the Solidarity committee people in the Seminario). Variety of Mexican and Guatemalan handicrafts at *La Galería* restaurant. (See also under Tenejapa, page 1081). Main market is worth seeing as well. Bookshop *El Sol y La Luna* has good 2nd-hand stock and postcards. Bookshop, good, next to *Hotel San Martín* on Guadalupe.

Laundromat Lava Sec, Av. Rosas near Niños Héroes. Close to Plaza on Calle B. Domínguez, 5-hour service, 3 kg. for US$1.

Exchange *Restaurants El Tuluc*, Insurgentes 5, *Unicornio*, Insurgentes 33A, or *Fulano* will change travellers' cheques at a reasonable rate if the three banks on the Plaza are closed (also into Guatemalan quetzales). Banks (charge commission) are open for exchange between 1030 and 1200 only; this leads to queues. *Casa de Cambio* in Lacantún travel agency, Francisco Madero 192, open daily except Sun., 0800-1730.

Language Schools Roberto Rivas Bastidas, Centro Bilingüe, Insurgentes 19, Int. 22, US$3 an hour for private lessons, rec. In the mornings, Mercedes organizes "non-touristic excursions for tourists who are different, in the villages", about US$7. Universidad Autónoma de Chiapas, Av. Hidalgo 1, Departamento de Lenguas, offers classes in English, French and Tzotzil.

Post Office Cuauhtémoc 13.

Tourist Office helpful, at the Palacio Municipal, W side of main Plaza, some English spoken. Ask here for accommodation in private house. Tours of local villages arranged for US$6.50 p.p. (ask for Mercedes—good guide). Maps of San Cristóbal US$0.35, also on sale at Kramsky, Diego de Mazariaga y 16 de Septiembre, behind Palacio Municipal.

Buses Beware of pickpockets at bus stations. From Mexico City direct, Cristóbal Colón at 1415, 1815, 2300. Cristóbal Colón 1st class bus to Oaxaca, about 12 hrs., at 1645 daily, book well in advance, monotonous trip, US$9.50, 622 km. To do the trip in daytime, you need to change at Tuxtla Gutiérrez (0745 Cristóbal Colón to Tuxtla, then 1100 on to Oaxaca); to Mexico City, via Tuxtepec, about 18 hrs., 1,169 km. at 2200, US$13; to Tapachula, 9 hrs., at 1200, US$6.25, 483 km.; to Puebla at 1400, US$11.25, 1,034 km.; to Tuxtla Gutiérrez, 1½ hrs., 10 a day, US$0.90. Book tickets as far in advance as possible—during Christmas and Holy Week buses are sometimes fully booked for 10 days or more.

Transportes Tuxtla has several 1st (US$2) and 2nd class (US$1.50) buses daily to Tuxtla Gutiérrez, and a 2nd class bus to Tapachula at 1330; to Tapachula via Motozintla: Transportes Tuxtla at 0800 and 0900, 5 hrs., then connections take about 3 hrs. to Tapachula. Cristóbal Colón

1st class; to Villahermosa, 8 hrs., US$4.50; to Arriaga, at 1200 via Tuxtla Gutiérrez, 235 km., US$2.55; to Coatzacoalcos at 0630, 576 km., US$6.25; to Orizaba 845 km.; to Chiapa de Corzo, 64 km., several daily. There is a new 210 km. paved road with fine views to Palenque; Lacandonia 2nd class bus to Palenque from 2nd class bus station on Calle Allende (where the 1st class bus station is also) at 0730 (arrives at 1330), US$3. First-class bus to Palenque, Trans. Tuxtla, 0600 and four others, 5 hrs., US$3.25, essential to book in advance. Same company's 2nd-class buses to Palenque, 0830 and 1600. Other buses leave one at Ocosingo, US$2, 4 hrs. Refunds of fares to Palenque when reaching Ocosingo are not rare, and you then have to make your own way. Transportes Tuxtla has a 1st class service to Palenque via Villahermosa, 0600, 9 hrs., US$8.50, and 2nd class at 0830, 1030 and 1530, but road to Villahermosa described as treacherous.

Into Guatemala Cristóbal Colón, S end of Av. Insurgentes (left luggage facilities open 0600-2000 exc. Sun. and holidays), clean station has several direct 1st class buses to the Guatemalan border at Ciudad Cuauhtémoc, 2½ hrs., US$3, plus US$0.30 to La Mesilla, 87 km., all tickets can be booked up to 4 days in advance (best is 0700 because it originates in San Cristóbal). Cristóbal Colón to Comitán (if you can't get a bus to the border, take one to Comitán and get a pick-up truck there—about US$1), 8 a day from 0700, US$2, 87 km (a beautiful, steep route). Transportes Tuxtla, S end of Av. Ignacio Allende, has several 1st and 2nd class buses, 4½ hrs., to the border daily, though these do not continue through to the Guatemalan customs post (3.7 km., uphill, taxi sometimes available, US$0.65 p.p., minimum 3 people). The 0800 Cristóbal Colón makes connections at the Guatemalan border at 1200 with El Cóndor for Huehuetenango and Guatemala City. Note that it is cheaper to pay initially only to Huehuetenango and buy a ticket onwards from there (no change of bus necessary). Do not buy a ticket at the border until a bus leaves as some wait while others come and go.

Air Services San Cristóbal no longer has an airport; it has been consumed by urban growth. The nearest airport is at Ocosingo (see page 1087) about 50 km. along the Palenque road. To Tuxtla Gutiérrez Tues., Thurs., Sat. at 1345, 84 km. (Tuxtla is the major local airport but see page 1077). Regular daily flights, except Sundays, to Palenque, 0715 (some crashes); booking only at airport. Charter flights to see Lacanjá, Bonampak and Yaxchilán on the Usumacinta River, 7 hrs. in all (US$100 p.p. if plane is full, more if not). All with Aerochiapas at airport. Office in Real de Guadalupe has closed.

Excursions You are recommended to call at Na Bolom before visiting the villages, to get information on their cultures and seek advice on the reception you are likely to get. Photography is resisted by some Indians (see below) because they believe the camera steals their souls, and photographing their church is stealing the soul of God. Many Indians do not speak Spanish. On Sun. you can visit the villages of San Juan Chamula (horses can be hired near Na Bolom, to go here for a morning, at corner of Calle Comitán and Av. Vicente Guerrero, US$6.50 for horse and US$9 for guide, or from Julio González, who may be found at El Recoveco bookshop at 1900 each evening, US$4.50 per horse and the same for a guide, or from *Casa de Huéspedes Margarita*, rather cheaper), Zinacantán and Tenejapa. *Zinacantán* is reached by VW bus from market, US$0.20, ½ hr. journey, sometimes frequent stops while conductor lights rockets at roadside shrines. The men wear pink/red jackets with embroidery and tassels, the women a vivid pale blue shawl and navy skirts. Main gathering place around church; the roof was recently destroyed by fire. Do *not* photograph anywhere or anything in Zinacantán. You can catch a VW bus ride to *Chamula* every ½ hr., last at 1700, US$0.20 p.p. (or taxi, US$4) and visit the local church; a permit (US$0.30) is needed from the village (or the San Cristóbal) tourist office and photographing inside the church is absolutely forbidden. (Two tourists were killed for ignoring the warning, but people are friendly enough if you abide by their rules—see warning below.) There are no pews but family groups sit or kneel on the floor, chanting, with rows of candles lit in front of them, each representing a member of the family and certain significance attached to the colours of the candles. The religion is centred around the "talking stones", and three idols and certain Christian saints. Pagan rituals held in small huts at the end of August. Pre-Lent festival ends with celebrants running through blazing harvest chaff. Just after Easter prayers are held, before the sowing season starts. Festivals in Chamula should *not* be photographed. The men wear grey, black or light pink tunics, the women bright blue blouses with colourful braid and navy or bright blue shawls. Good viewpoint of village and valley from hill SW of village: take road from SW corner of square, turn left towards ruined church then up flight of steps on left. Interesting walk from San Cristóbal to Chamula along the main road to a point one km. past the crossroads with the Periférico ring road (about 2½ km. from town centre); turn on to an old dirt road to the right—not sign-posted but 1st fork you come to between some farmhouses. Then back via the road through the village of Milpoleta, some 8 km. downhill, 5 hrs. for the journey round trip (allow 1 hr. for Chamula). Best not done in hot weather. Also, you can hike from Chamula to Zinacantán in 1½ hrs.: when leaving Chamula, take track straight ahead instead of turning left onto San Cristóbal road; turn left on small hill where school is (after 30 mins.) and follow a smaller trail through light forest. After an hour you reach the road 200 m. before Zinacantán.

The Sun. market at *Tenejapa* (pleasant small *pensión*) is very colourful, mainly fruit and vegetables, excellent woven items can be purchased from the weavers' cooperative near the church (and in San Cristóbal from the house at Calle 28 de Agosto 19). They also have a fine collection of old textiles in their regional ethnographic museum adjoining the handicraft shop. The cooperative can also arrange weaving classes. Buses leave from San Cristóbal market at 0700 and 1100 (1½ hr. journey), and colectivos every hour. We have been warned about threatening behaviour and violence in Tenejapa, but probably OK to visit in daytime if one behaves discreetly. Market thins out by noon. Two other excursions can be made, by car or local bus, from San Cristóbal S on the Pan-American Highway (½ hr. by car) to **Amatenango del Valle**, a Tzeltal village where the women make and fire pottery in their yards, and then SE (15 min. by car) to Aguacatenango, picturesque village at the foot of a mountain. Continue 1 hr. along road past Villa las Rosas (hotel) to **Venustiano Carranza**, women with fine costumes, extremely good view of the entire valley.

SE of San Cristóbal, 10 km., are the Grutas de San Cristóbal, caves with entrance (US$0.20) in a beautiful park.

Get to outlying villages by bus or communal VW bus (both very packed); buses leave very early, and often don't return until next day, so you have to stay overnight; lorries are more frequent. To Zinacantán catch also VW bus from market. Buses from the market area to San Andrés Larrainzar (bus at 1000, 1100, 1400, overnight stay required, return at 0600) and Tenejapa. Transportes Fray Bartolomé de Las Casas, behind Transportes Tuxtla, has buses to Chanal, Chenalhó (US$13 with taxi, return, one hr. stay), Pantelhó, Yajalón and villages en route to Ocosingo. Transportes Lacandonia on Av. Crescencio Rosas also go to the interior villages of Huistán, Oxchuc, Yajalón, on the way to Palenque, Pujiltic, La Mesilla and Venustiano Carranza. If you are in San Cristóbal for a limited period of time it is best to rent a car to see the villages.

Warning Remember that locals are particularly sensitive to proper dress (i.e. neither men nor women should wear shorts, or revealing clothes) and manners; persistent begging should be countered with courteous, firm replies. It is best not to take cameras to villages: there are good postcards and photographs, e.g. at La Galería restaurant. Drunkenness is quite open and at times forms part of the rituals—best not to take umbrage if accosted.

Follow the 170-km. paved road via Teopisca (*pensión*, F, comfortable), past **Comitán** (85 km.), a lively town of 55,000 people at 1,580 metres above sea level with a large, shady Plaza, to the border (buses, kombis and pick-up trucks from Comitán) at Ciudad Cuauhtémoc (not a town, despite its name; just a few buildings and a small restaurant with basic rooms). A road branches off the Pan-American Highway 16 km. after Comitán to a very beautiful region of vari-coloured lakes, the **Lagunas de Montebello**; there are no restaurants or shops, but you can stay in Sra. Gloria's *cabañas*, cheap, pleasant, friendly. Frequent buses and VW Combis from Comitán. Off the road to Montebello, 30 km. from the Pan-American Highway, lie the ruins of **Chinkultic**, with temples, ballcourt, carved stone stelae and *cenote* (deep round lake); from the signpost they are about 3 km. along a dirt road and they close at 1600. Watch and ask for the very small sign and gate where road to ruins starts, worth visiting when passing.

Hotels in Comitán Accommodation inferior in quality and almost twice the price of San Cristóbal. *Robert's*, 1 Av. Poniente Sur, C, restaurant. *Los Lagos de Montebello*, on Pan-American Highway, noisy but good, C; *Internacional*, D, near Plaza, decent restaurant. *Delfín*, on Plaza, E, fairly clean, as are *Hospedaje Santo Domingo*, Calle Central B. Juárez 45, E; *San Francisco*, E, and *Ideal*, 2a Sur Oriente, clean, friendly, E, both centrally located. *Casa de Huéspedes Río Escondido*, next to *Robert's*, F. *Posada Panamericana*, F, basic, and *Posada Maya*, F, both on 1 Av. Poniente Norte.

Restaurants *Nevelandia*, clean, rec., and *Café Casa de La Cultura*, on the Plaza. *L'Uccello*, Italian, 1 Av. Poniente Norte, rec. *Cancún*, 2 Calle Sur Poniente. *Puerto Arturo* on Blvd. Dr. Belisario Domínquez is good. Several small *comedores* on the Plaza.

Exchange It is very difficult to exchange Amex travellers' cheques in Comitán.

Guatemalan Consulate Open till 2000 at 6a Norte Poniente, between 2a and 3a Poniente Norte; visa (if required) US$10, valid 1 year, multiple entry.

Tourist Office 3a Norte Poniente, near 1a Poniente Norte, helpful.

Buses marked Tziscao to the Lagunas de Montebello (60 km. from Comitán, about 2 hrs.), via the Lagunas de Siete Colores (so-called because the oxides in the water give varieties of colours) leave from 2 Av. Poniente Sur between 2 and 3 Calles, 4 blocks from Plaza in Comitán, the buses go as far as Laguna Bosque Azul; *Tziscao* is 9 km. along the road leading right from the park entrance, which is 3 km. before Bosque Azul; five buses a day Comitán-Tziscao, bumpy ride; the last bus back is at 1600 and connects with the 1930 bus to San Cristóbal. (Costs US$0.90.) VW Combis from Comitán bus station take half the time and cost only 10% more. The Bosque Azul area is now a reserve: there are, as well as picnic areas, an *Albergue Turístico* at Lake Tziscao (10 km., F, rooms for 4-6, no hot water, US$2.50 p.p., dirty kitchen facilities, camping US$1.60 per site incl. use of hotel facilities; boats for hire) two very basic food shops in the village, and there are small caves. The area is noted for its orchids and birdlife, including the famous *quetzal*; very crowded at weekends and holidays; better to stay at *Posada Las Orquídeas*, on the road to Montebello near Hidalgo and the ruins of Chinkultic, dormitory or cabin, F, family-run, very basic but friendly, small restaurant. 2 basic shops at Hidalgo.

From Comitán the road winds down to the Guatemalan border at Ciudad Cuauhtémoc via La Trinitaria (restaurant but no hotel). Beyond the Guatemalan post at La Mesilla, the El Tapón section, a beautiful stretch, leads to Huehuetenango, 85 km. This route is far more interesting than the one through Tapachula; the border crossing at Ciudad Cuauhtémoc is also reported as easier than that at Talismán. A tourist card for Guatemala can be obtained at the border, normally available for 30 days, renewable in Guatemala City, US$1. Holders of most European passports do not need visas (note that the British do), only tourist cards. Visas are also available at the border but buses do not wait for those who alight to obtain them. You pay US$0.45 to leave Mexico and 2 quetzales to enter Guatemala, and the border is open until 1900. Have your Mexican tourist card handy as it will be inspected at the Río San Gregorio, about 20 km. before the border. Don't change money with the Guatemalan customs officials: the rates they offer are worse than those given by bus drivers or in banks (and these are below the rates inside the country).

Buses The Cristóbal Colón bus (book seats in advance) leaves Comitán at 0930, 1800 and 2300 daily for the border at Ciudad Cuauhtémoc, fare US$1.50. Frequent 2nd-class buses also by Transportes Tuxtla, US$1.10 (station at 4a Sur Poniente between 3a and 4a Poniente Sur). Another line leaves at 0745 for Ciudad Cuauhtémoc. From here take a taxi to the Guatemalan side and get your passport stamped to allow entry for a month. Cristóbal Colón (terminal on the Pan-American Highway) has 1st class buses to Mexico City at 0900, 1100 and 1600 (which leave the border 2½ hrs. earlier), fare US$24; to Oaxaca at 0700 and 1900, US$14; to Tuxtla Gutiérrez at 0600 and 1600, US$3.50, and to Tapachula (via Arriaga) at 1200 and 1800, US$9. Transportes Tuxtla, 3 Calle Norte Poniente and 1 Av. Poniente Norte, has 6 1st class (US$3.50) and 8 2nd class (US$3.40) buses daily to Tuxtla Gutiérrez; a bus to Tapachula, via Arriaga, at 1100, US$11; to Arriaga at 1215; and 7 buses daily to Motozintla (connections to Tapachula), US$3.30. There are colectivos running between the two border posts.

Airport Flights available from Comitán to Lacanjá, Bonampak, Yaxchilán, contact Capitán Pérez Esquinca, T Comitán 4-91.

Travellers report that the Lacandón Indians at Lacanjá are rude and threatening if one doesn't buy their tourist wares.

N.B. Entering Mexico from Guatemala, it is forbidden to bring in fruit and vegetables; rigorous checking at two checkpoints to avoid the spread of plant diseases.

YUCATAN PENINSULA (9)

Many tourists come to Yucatán, mostly to see the ancient Maya sites and to stay at the new coastal resorts (see below). The places which attract most visitors are Mérida, Palenque, Chichén Itzá and Uxmal. A good paved road (four ferries) runs from Coatzacoalcos through Villahermosa, Campeche and Mérida (Route 180). All the great archaeological sites except Palenque are on or just off this road and its continuation beyond Mérida. An inland road has been built from Villahermosa to Campeche to avoid the ferries; it gives easy access to Palenque. A train from Mexico City to Mérida goes through Palenque; Pullman passengers can make the whole trip without leaving the car in 2 nights. Route 307 from Puerto Juárez and Cancún to Chetumal is all paved and in very good condition; there is very little traffic. Air services from the USA and Mexico City are given under Mérida. Details of the direct road route, with buses, between Guatemala and Yucatán are given on **page 1097**. The state of Quintana Roo is on the eastern side of the Yucatán Peninsula and has recently become the largest tourist area in Mexico with the development of the resort of Cancún, and the parallel growth of Isla Mujeres and Cozumel. **Warning** So many of the tourists coming to the coastal resorts know no Spanish that price hikes and short-changing have

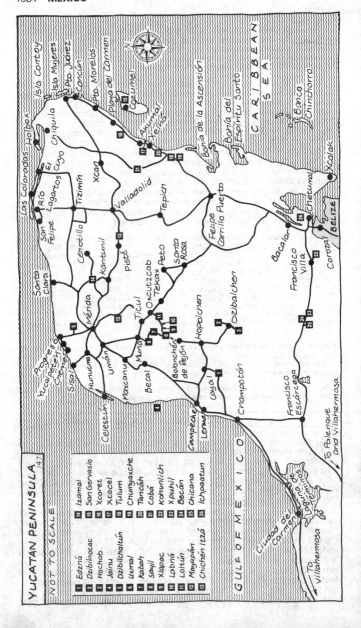

YUCATAN PENINSULA _147_

NOT TO SCALE

1 Edzná	14 Izamal	
2 Dzibinocac	15 San Gervasio	
3 Hochob	16 Xcaret	
4 Jainu	17 Xcacel	
5 Dzibilchaltún	18 Tulum	
6 Uxmal	19 Chumyaxche	
7 Kabah	20 Tancáh	
8 Sayil	21 Cobá	
9 Xlapac	22 Kohunlich	
10 Lobná	23 Xpuhil	
11 Loltún	24 Becán	
12 Mayapán	25 Chicana	
13 Chichén Itzá	26 Ichpaatun	

become very common there, making those places very expensive if one is not careful. In the peak, winter season, prices are increased anyway.

The peninsula of Yucatán is a flat land of tangled scrub in the drier north-west, merging into exuberant jungle and tall trees in the wetter south-east. There are no surface streams. The underlying geological foundation is a horizontal bed of limestone in which rainwater has dissolved enormous caverns. Here and there their roofs have collapsed, disclosing deep holes or *cenotes* in the ground, filled with water. Today this water is raised to surface-level by wind-pumps: a typical feature of the landscape. It is hot during the day but cool after sunset. Humidity is often high. All round the peninsula are splendid beaches fringed with palm groves and forests of coconut palms. The best time for a visit is from October to March.

The people are divided into two groups: the pure-blooded Maya Indians, the minority, and the *mestizos*. The Maya women wear *huipiles*, or white cotton tunics (silk for *fiestas*) which may reach the ankles and are embroidered round the square neck and bottom hem. Ornaments are mostly gold. A few of the men still wear straight white cotton (occasionally silk) jackets and pants, often with gold or silver buttons, and when working protect this dress with aprons. Carnival is the year's most joyous occasion, with concerts, dances, processions. Yucatán's folk dance is the Jarana, the man dancing with his hands behind his back, the woman raising her skirts a little, and with interludes when they pretend to be bullfighting. During pauses in the music the man, in a high falsetto voice, sings *bambas* (compliments) to the woman.

The Mayas are a courteous, gentle, strictly honest and scrupulously clean people. They drink little, except on feast days, speak Mayan, and profess Christianity laced with a more ancient nature worship. In Yucatán and Quintana Roo, the economy has long been dependent on the export of *henequén* (sisal), and chicle, but both are facing heavy competition from substitutes and tourism is becoming ever more important.

The early history and accomplishments of the Mayas when they lived in Guatemala and Honduras before their mysterious trek northwards is given in the introductory chapter on Central America. (**See page 1136.**) They arrived in Yucatán about A.D. 600 and later rebuilt their cities, but along different lines, probably because of the arrival of Toltecs in the ninth and tenth centuries. Each city was autonomous, and in rivalry with other cities. Before the Spaniards arrived the Mayas had developed a writing in which the hieroglyphic was somewhere between the pictograph and the letter. Bishop Landa collected their books, wrote a very poor summary, the *Relación de las Cosas de Yucatán*, and with Christian but unscholarlike zeal burnt all his priceless sources.

In 1511 some Spanish adventurers were shipwrecked on the coast. Two survived. One of them, Juan de Aguilar, taught a Maya girl Spanish. She became interpreter for Cortés after he had landed in 1519. The Spaniards found little to please them: no gold, no concentration of natives, but Mérida was founded in 1542 and the few natives handed over to the conquerors in *encomiendas*. The Spaniards found them difficult to exploit: even as late as 1847 there was a major revolt, mainly arising from the inhuman conditions in the *henequén* plantations.

N.B.: Travellers have found that guards will not permit use of tripods for photography at sites.

Coatzacoalcos, 186,000 people, the Gulf Coast gateway for Yucatán, was 1½ km. from the mouth of its wide river, but now has expanded down to it. It is hot, frantic and lacking in culture, and there is not much to do save watch the river traffic (river too polluted for fishing and swimming—less than salubrious discos on the beach by the pier at the river-mouth; beach is dangerous at nights, do not sleep there or loiter). Ocean-going vessels go upriver for 39 km. to *Minatitlán*, the oil and petrochemical centre (145,000 people; airport), whose huge oil refinery sends its products by pipeline to Salina Cruz on the Pacific. The road between the two towns carries very heavy industrial traffic. The offshore oil rigs are serviced from Coatzacoalcos. Sulphur is exported from the mines, 69 km. away.

Coatzacoalcos Hotels Very difficult as all hotels are used by oil workers. Don't spend the night on the street if you can't find lodging. Prices double those of hotels elsewhere. *Enríquez*, good, A; *Carilla*, F, with shower, basic. *Motel Colima* at km. 5, Carretera Ayucan-Coatzacoalcos, may have rooms if none in Coatzacoalcos; it is clean, in a quiet position, but does have a lot of red-light activity.

Restaurants Meals at *Gloria Café*; *Los Lopitos*, Hidalgo 615, good tamales and tostadas. Cheap restaurants on the top floor of the indoor market near the bus terminal. There is a 24-hr. restaurant in one of the streets just off the main Plaza, good empanadas with cream.

Bus to Mexico City, US$11; to Mérida US$12.25. To Veracruz (312 km, US$3.65, 7¼ hrs.), Ciudad del Carmen (US$7.35), Salina Cruz (US$2); to Minatitlán, to which taxis also ply. To Villahermosa, US$3.

Rail Railway station is 5 km. from town at Cuatro (for Mexico City and Mérida) at end of Puerto

Libre bus route and on Playa Palma Sola route, smelly and dingy, the through train is swept out here; irregular bus services. Better walk about ½ km. to the main road and get a bus there, US$0.10. Train to Tehuantepec takes 13 hrs. (208 km.). Train to Mérida (at 1240). Train to Palenque, 1600. Coatzacoalcos-Campeche at 2030. Another station, in the city centre, serves Salina Cruz, small and dingy. The train to Salina Cruz leaves daily at 0700, costs US$2.50 for the 12 hr. journey 2nd class.

Air Services Minatitlán airport, 30 mins.

Cárdenas 116 km. from Coatzacoalcos and 48 km. from Villahermosa, is headquarters of the Comisión del Grijalva, which is encouraging regional development. Between Cárdenas and Villahermosa are many stalls selling all varieties of bananas, a speciality of the area, and the road passes through the Samaria oilfield. (From Chontalpa there is irregular transport to Raudales on the lake formed by the Netzahualcoyotl dam.) It is very hard to find accommodation in Cárdenas, *Hotel Xol-Ou*, cheapest, E, with bath, a/c, parking, clean, on main plaza.

Villahermosa, capital of Tabasco state, is on the River Grijalva, navigable to the sea. It is a dirty town, very hot and rainy. The Centro de Investigaciones de las Culturas Olmecas is set in a new modern complex with a restaurant, airline offices and souvenir shops, a few minutes' walk S out of town along the river bank. Three floors of well laid out displays of Mayan and Olmec artefacts. Entry US$1, open 0900-2000. The cathedral, ruined in 1973, is to be rebuilt. Paved road to Coatzacoalcos and another S to the railway at Teapa, 50 km.; paved roads to Tuxtla Gutiérrez and Palenque. The tourist office is in the 1st class bus station and there is another close to the La Venta park, at Paseo Grijalva and Paseo Tabasco, both good, closed 1300-1600. Villahermosa is heaving under pressure from the oil boom, which is why it is now such an expensive place. Buses to Mexico City are often booked up well in advance, as are hotel rooms, especially during the holiday season (May onwards). Overnight free parking (no facilities) in the Campo de Deportes. It is hard to find swimming facilities in Villahermosa: Ciudad Deportiva pool for cardholders only. There is a bull ring. There is a warren of modern colonial-style pedestrian malls throughout the central area. Warning: Ash Wednesday is celebrated from 1500 to dusk by the throwing of water in balloon bombs and buckets at anyone who happens to be on the street.

Hotels The price difference between a reasonable and a basic hotel can be negligible, so one might as well go for the former. Best is *Exalaris Hyatt*, Juárez 106, all services, L; *Maya-Tabasco*, on Paseo Tabasco, all services, A; *Manzur*, C, Madero 422, central, slightly faded, good restaurant (accepts American Express card— one of the few that do) nearby parking; many other hotels along Madero. *San Rafael*, Constitución 232, F, with bath, no hot water, clean; *Olmeca*, D, Reforma 304, central, good, fridge in room, restaurant; *El Choco*, Merino 100, C, friendly, clean, a/c; *Sureste*, one block from ADO bus station, D, a/c, small but clean and friendly; *Los Carlos*, Hnos. Basta-Zozoya 624, E, a/c, hot water, from ADO terminal, cross main street, go 2 blocks then left 2 blocks; *Madero*, Madero 301, E, hot water, good value; *María Dolores*, Aldama 104, a/c, D, hot showers, excellent restaurant (closed Sundays). *Caballero*, Lerdo 307, clean, good, E; *San Miguel*, Lerdo 315, good value, but some rooms damp, no hot water p.m., E; *Aurora*, Av. 27 de Febrero 623, F, basic, hot showers, E; *Sofia*, Zaragoza 408, E, central, tolerable but overpriced, a/c. *Viva*, near La Venta, very good, D. There is a CREA youth hostel at the Ciudad Deportiva, but it doesn't accept travellers arriving in the evening (4 km. SW of the bus station).

N.B. Tourists are often wiser to go directly to Palenque for accommodation; cheaper and no competition from business travellers. Villahermosa can be difficult for lone women: local men's aggressive behaviour said to be due to the effect of eating iguanas.

Camping at the old airport, near Parque La Venta, mosquitoes.

Restaurants *El Mural*, highly rec., 4-course lunch with drink included, US$4, dinner US$8, with band; *La Embajada*, good local food, suckling pig is the best, open for lunch only; *La Rueda* serves good local specialities; the *Casino* for odd dishes like turtle steaks and dogfish; *Los Azulejos* serves good lunch for US$2.40; *Restaurant Kathy*, Av. Constitución 204, reasonable prices. Avoid the bad and expensive tourist eating places on and near the river front.

Airport Daily services to Mexico City, Tuxtla Gutiérrez, Mérida, and one to Oaxaca-Acapulco-Guadalajara, from airport 15 km. SE, out along the Palenque road, VW bus to town US$3 p.p., taxi US$7 for 2. Local flights to Palenque and Bonampak.

Local Transport Taxis now mainly on a fixed-route collective system (US$1 per stop), which can be a problem if you want to go somewhere else. You may have to wait a long time before a driver without fares agrees to take you. Bus station (ADO) with restaurant, but very uncomfortable owing to poor ventilation, 20 min.-walk to centre; luggage may be left with Sra. Ana, in minute restaurant/shop at Pedro y Fuente 817, 100 metres from ADO terminal, reliable, open till 2000, cheap. Information office at this station unhelpful and the booking system is complicated, infuriating and best avoided if possible. The 2nd class bus station is only 5 mins. walk from centre and 2½ blocks from 1st class station: usually in disarray and it is difficult to get a ticket. Mind your belongings.

Buses Several buses (1st class) to Mexico City, US$16, 12 hrs., direct bus leaves 1730, expect to wait a few hours for Mexico City buses and at least ½ hr. in the ticket queue. To Jalapa with ADO, 3 a day, 10 hrs.; to Campeche, US$5 (6 hrs.); to Coatzacoalcos, US$2; to Tapachula, US$9, 14 hrs.; to Mérida 8 hrs., 1030, US$6.50 (ADO) (extremely difficult to book, better go 2nd class from Palenque, **see page 1088**) leaves at 0920; to San Cristóbal, US$4.50, 9 hrs.; also 2nd class bus with one change at Tuxtla, leaves 0800, arrives 2100, fine scenery but treacherous road. Cristóbal Colón from ADO terminal to Oaxaca via Coatzacoalcos and Tehuantepec at 0800 and 1900, 1st class, stops at about 7 places, US$10. Bus to Veracruz, US$7, 8 hrs.; to Chetumal, US$8.50, 7 hrs., four buses. To Catazaja, US$2, 1½ hrs. To Palenque (see below), US$2.50, 2½ hrs., Circuito Maya, US$2.60; 1st class 1000 (buy ticket day before) and 1700. To Emiliano Zapata and Tenosique (for Río San Pedro crossing into Guatemala—**see page 1097**), buses 0700, 0800, 1330, 3-4 hrs.

Excursion NW of Villahermosa are the Maya ruins of **Comalcalco**, easily reached by bus (3 a day by ADO, US$1.20, or local Zimillera bus, US$0.90 over dirt roads). The ruins are unique in Mexico because the palaces and pyramids are built of bricks, long and narrow like ancient Roman bricks, and not of stone. From Comalcalco go to **Paraíso** on the coast, frequent buses from town. Interesting covered market, good cocoa. *Centro Turístico* beach hotel, D, clean, no hot water, food and drink expensive. Also hotel in Paraíso main square.

In 1925 an expedition discovered huge sculptured human and animal figures, urns and altars in almost impenetrable forest at La Venta, 96 km. from Villahermosa. Nothing to see there now: about 1950 the monuments were threatened with destruction by the discovery of oil nearby. The poet Carlos Pellicer got them hauled all the way to a woodland area near Villahermosa, now the Parque La Venta with scattered lakes, next to a children's playground and almost opposite the old airport entrance on the edge of town. There they are dispersed in various small clearings. The huge heads—one of them weighs 20 tons—are Olmec, a culture which flourished about 1150-150 B.C. Be sure to take insect-repellant for the visit. It takes 1 hr. to walk around, excellent guides, speak Spanish and English. There is also a zoo of lonely, dispirited and wretched creatures from the Tabasco jungle: monkeys, alligators, deer, wild pigs and birds. Open 0830-1700, entrance US$1, bus, marked "Gracitol", Villahermosa-La Venta from bus terminal US$0.40. Bus Circuito No. 1 from outside 2nd class bus terminal goes past Parque La Venta.

Further Travel If the Villahermosa-Mexico City bus is booked up, try taking the train from **Teapa** (buses run hourly between Teapa and Villahermosa), 1st class pullman fare, US$25. The dining car is good but very expensive. Check in rainy season whether bridges are OK. (It took one passenger 56 hrs. to travel some 950 km. after being diverted). Vendors ply the train with local foods and drinks. Journey 14 hrs. Teapa is a nice, clean little town with several cheap hotels (*Casa de Huéspedes Mija*, F, in the main street) and beautiful surroundings. The square is pleasant, and you can swim in the river or in the sulphur pool, El Azufre and cavern of Cocona (dear). From Teapa, Tapijulapa on the Chiapas border can be visited, beautiful views. Bus to Chiapa de Corzo at 0730, 7 hrs., US$4, lovely, mountainous landscape (**see page 1077**).

80 km. SW of Villahermosa on Route 195 is **Pichucalco**, a very quiet town with some interesting tiles in the main Plaza. *Hotel México*, on left turn from bus station, E, with bath, fan, clean but musty, *Vila*, on Plaza, *Jardín*, F, noisy, *La Selva*. Buses almost every hour to Villahermosa, US$1.50.

Villahermosa to Guatemala by car is by route 195 and 190 to Ciudad Cuauhtémoc via San Cristóbal de Las Casas. Highway 195 is fully paved, but narrow and winding with landslides and washouts in the rainy season, high altitudes, beautiful scenery. If this route is impassable, travel back by route 180 to Acayucan, to 190, via 185 and go to Ciudad Cuauhtémoc or by route 200 to Tapachula.

From Villahermosa you can fly to Campeche, or sometimes by a small plane carrying 3 passengers, to Palenque, which can also be reached by the new paved road from Villahermosa to Campeche (no petrol stations until the Palenque turn-off; if you look like running out, turn left half-way for Macuspana, where there is one). This road has a turning at 117 km. from Villahermosa for Palenque, 26 km. away on a good paved but winding road. (If short of time you can fly Mérida-Villahermosa at 0655, hire car at Villahermosa airport, drive to Palenque and back with 3½ hrs. at ruins, and catch 2205 flight from Villahermosa to Mexico City.) Palenque can also be reached by paved road from San Cristóbal de Las Casas, a beautiful ride via **Ocosingo**, a not particularly attractive place (70,000 people) which has a local airport and many new hotels (two E, of which the best is on the main street across from the Plaza, *Central* on Plaza, F, shower, clean, verandah, and several others F) and clean restaurants. Road to ruins of **Toniná**, 12 km. away, is unpaved but marked with signs once you leave Ocosingo (jeep rec.); well worth visiting the ruins excavated by a French government team. Temples are in the Palenque style with internal sanctuaries in the back room. Stelae are in very diverse forms, as are wall panels, and some are in styles and in subject unknown at any other Mayan site. Ask guardian to show you second unrestored ballcourt and the sculpture kept at his house. (Take drinks with you; nothing available at the site.) Beside the Ocosingo-Toniná road is a marsh, frequented by thousands of swallows in January. The Agua Azul waterfalls (**see page 1090**) are between Toniná and Palenque, on your left. The road to Palenque from San Cristóbal (Route 195) is now reported OK. Excellent road from Campeche, 5 hrs.' drive, only rough stretch about 1 hr. from Palenque; toll bridge US$0.60.

Palenque, 143 km. from Villahermosa (public transport difficult Sun.), is a splendid experience, with its series of Old Mayan hilltop temples in remarkably good condition. It is best to visit the ruins early in the morning. The site is in a hot jungle clearing (with interesting wildlife, mainly birds, but also including mosquitoes) on a steep green hill overlooking the plain and crossed by a clear cascading brook (swimming allowed at pools downstream from the museum). The ruins are impressive indeed, particularly the Pyramid of the Inscriptions, in the heart of which was discovered an intact funerary crypt with the Sarcophagus of the Sun God (you walk from the top of the pyramids into a staircase, descending to ground level, before having to walk up again, very humid; illuminated 1000-1600 only; take flashlight), the temples around, with fantastic comb-like decorations on their intact roofs, and the sculptured wall panels, undoubtedly the most exquisite achievement of the Mayas. Check time of opening of crypt. A path behind the Temple of Inscriptions leads through jungle to a small ruined temple—if you continue for 8 km. the path leads to a friendly village, the only means of access. A small museum at the ruins has some excellent classical Mayan carvings (open 1000—more like 1100—to 1700). Entry to ruins, US$0.20 (Sun. US$0.10), charge for car parking. Special permission required for videos and super-8 cameras. The site opens at 0800 and closes at 1700 (guide, up to 10 people). Beware of thieves at all times. The ruins are 8 km. from the town. A restaurant by the cascades serves a limited range of food, not rec. (stores luggage—compulsory on entering the ruins, no receipt— for US$0.25); shops quick to overcharge. **Warning** The area is very malarial; make sure you're up-to-date with your tablets.

Bus service from station to town, 5 km. goes to local bus stations, but unhelpful, be prepared to wait. Taxi from station to ruins US$1.35 p.p. with 4 people. Taxi, ruins to town US$1.20. Bus to the ruins from bus stations every 2 hrs. from 0600, 20 mins, US$0.25 until 1630. From the village to the ruins: either take a taxi, or a white VW minibus from Pemex station, or corner of Hidalgo and Allende, or the Plaza end of 5 de Mayo, or the Mayan head near bus terminals, US$0.20, 15 mins., from 0600-1800, every 15 mins. or so. Some buses have been seen at 0600, 0930 and 1330 (marked "Ruinas") from *Hotel León* or at Pemex station at the top of the village. It is convenient to stay at hotels near this service station, as they are also nearer the ruins and the bus stations.

Hotels (Prices treble around *fiesta* time.) *Misión Palenque*, far end of town in countryside, complete resort, A, poor food. *Hotel La Cañada*, very rustic but very clean, D, with fan, good value, lovely garden, good restaurant, noisy disco next door, the owner, Sr. Morales, is an expert on the ruins. *Motel Chan Ka Inn*, at Km. 31, closest to ruins, B, swimming pool fed from river, beautiful gardens, perfectly clean, restaurant overpriced; *Centro Turístico Tulijá*, C, car park, satisfactory and convenient; hot water if you get them to turn it on; also bungalows, 10 km. from ruins, first as you enter town; reasonable restaurant; pool, book local flights here; *Hotel and Trailer Park Tulipanes*, Calle Cañada 6, C, basic, a/c, or fan, garage, pool, bar/restaurant next door; *Lacroix*, 2 blocks from Plaza, E, will charge full room price for one or two, fan, no hot water, friendly, dirty, insects, good for motorcyclists; *Palenque*, 5 de Mayo 15, off Plaza, E, with bath, a/c restaurant, vast, rambling menage, poor plumbing and service, has good rooms, pool, night-time robberies reported, usually through bathroom windows, management unhelpful; long-distance telephone office here. *Casa de Pakal*, 1 block from Plaza, E, a/c, good but not very friendly; next door is *Mi-Sol-Ha*, fan, well-booked, with bath, no hot water, E. *Santa Elena*, 2 blocks from ADO terminal, simple and quiet. *Kash'lan*, E with bath, clean, helpful owner; *Avenida*, Juárez 173, opp. 2nd-class bus station above cinema, with restaurant, clean, large rooms, E, but does not display price in rooms so ask for government list to check, no hot showers, some rooms with balcony. *Regional*, 2 blocks from Plaza, E, 100 m. from bus station, no hot showers, but rec. otherwise. *Vaca Vieja*, 5 de Mayo 42, 3 blocks from Plaza, popular with gringos, good value, hot showers, E, cafetería; *Pensión Charpito*, Av. 20 de Noviembre 15, E. *Posada Alicia*, Av. Manuel Velásquez Suárez, E, cheap, mixed reports, rooms on left as you enter are cooler.

Camping *Trailer Park Palenque* nr. entrance to town, good, US$4 p.p. *Trailer Park Mayabel*, a bit scruffy (lots of old-fashioned "hippies"), on road to ruins 2 km. before entrance (bus from town

US$0.20) for caravans and tents, also for rent, US$1 for tent or to sling hammock, palmleaf huts, not very clean toilets and showers, good restaurant; many ticks in long grass (we're told they avoid people who eat lots of garlic!) Watch your belongings. At night, around 0100, one can often hear the howler monkeys screaming in the jungle; quite eerie. Good swimming at *Balneario and Hotel Nututún*, 3 km. along Palenque-Ocosingo road, US$1 camping site per night, rather run down, no tent rentals, showers, toilets, disco bar, at restaurant with laughable service; and beautiful lake and waterfall open to the public for a small fee. Misolhá, 2 km. off same road at km. 19, large paved car-park for camping, good bathing; small cave, with bats, where water flows out.

Restaurants *Maya*, on plaza, fair value; at moderately priced *Tarde*, or rough restaurant *El Jade* in town. Water is often hard to get. There is a good and friendly restaurant on Av. Juárez, *Français*, opp. *Hotel Avenida*, French owner, slow and rather expensive, less on offer than on menu, has tourist information. *El Rodeo*, on main street, does good breakfasts. *Artemio*, Av. Hidalgo, nr. Plaza, good, reasonably-priced food. *Las Carmelitas*, good service, reasonably priced, at Av. Benito Juárez 77. *Chan Ka*, on Plaza, steak about US$3, good atmosphere; *Nicte-Ha* on the plaza, good food and service. *Comedor La Terminada*, off the main street, good value. *Tertulia*, opp. *Hotel Regional*, good steaks, rec. At km. 0.5 on Hidalgo (road to ruins) is *La Selva*, excellent value, live music at weekends. Good juice bar on Plaza in front of *Hotel Palenque*.
N.B. We are told that the large influx of young "hippie-like" people has put off the locals, and visitors may be given misleading information. Also, the Federal police are very strict about tourist cards—*always* keep it with you, even when eating in your hotel. The penalty is searches and jail, with large fines. Visitors should respect the local customs and dress so as not to offend—men should wear footwear and always a shirt; women wearing shorts are unwelcome.

Travel Agencies ATC Tours, Calle Allende y Juárez, local 6, T 50210, and Jiménez y 5 de Mayo (*Hotel Palenque*), run private tours to other Mayan sites (Bonampak, US$50 p.p., Yaxchilán, US$55 p.p.—US$85 to both, also flights, see below, Tikal, US$100, all min. 5 people), local attractions (Agua Azul, Mi Sol Ha waterfall), horseriding in the jungle, etc.

Tourist Office in the municipal offices on plaza, open 0900-1300 and 1700-2000 (maybe). Post Office in the same building, on left-hand side.

Exchange Exchange rate only comes through at 1030, then banks open until 1230. At weekends travellers' cheques will not be changed but the owner at Farmacia Central will change US$ at a reasonable rate.

Laundromat Opposite ADO bus station.

Buses All 3 bus companies have terminals at W end of Av. Juárez. 1st class bus to/from Mexico City, ADO, at 1800, 14 hrs., 1,006 kms., US$ 17. First-class bus from ADO terminal at Villahermosa at 0800, 1200, 1600, 1700, 2½ hrs., US$2.50. Buy return ticket from the ruins on arrival, otherwise the driver may not let you get on for the stretch ruins-Palenque. 1st class to Villahermosa at 1800. 2nd class bus to Villahermosa at 0800 and 1200. Bus 2nd class, to Campeche, US$5, 6 hrs., daily at 1700, overcrowded, arrive early. One direct bus a day from Campeche, leaves 0200, returns from Palenque 1700, US$2 (2nd), but if you wish to travel in the daytime there is a bus to *Emiliano Zapata* 0900 and 1400. *Hotel Ramos*, opp. bus station, F, reasonable restaurant, friendly, bad mattresses. *San Agustín*, 5 de Mayo s/n, E, some a/c, clean and good value; at least 4 other hotels in town, F and E—one by the entrance to town near the Pemex station. No alcohol on Sun.
    From Emiliano Zapata you can make connections to Campeche and Mérida but the bus from Palenque sets you down at the other end of Emiliano Zapata from the bus station: you will have to cross the town (minibus US$0.15). Going to Campeche, it might be easier to change at Catazaja to the Villahermosa-Campeche ADO bus, but this journey cannot be done all in daylight. Daily 1st class bus to Mérida at 1230, US$7, 8hrs. Bus to Mérida via Campeche with Líneas Unidas de Chiapas, leaves Palenque at 1700, daily. (566 km.), numbered seats bookable at least 24 hrs. in advance, US$8.50, 10 hrs., scheduled to arrive at Campeche 2300, arrives in Mérida in the middle of the night; same company runs 1st class bus at 1800 (another possibility is to take 0800 to Villahermosa or 0900 to Emiliano Zapata and travel on from there). (Also to Francisco Escárcega, 3 hrs.)
    To San Cristóbal de Las Casas, good road throughout, 1st class buses at 0700 and 1030, US$2.30; five second class buses a day between 0730 and 2200 (6 hrs.), US$3 via Ocosingo, or 1230 via Pichucalco, 9 hrs.; via Villahermosa by 1st-class minibus, 8 hrs. or more, leaves at 0800 and 1230, US$6. Tuxtla Gutiérrez (no 1st class buses) 5 a day, 377 km., US$3, via San Cristóbal de Las Casas. The San Cristóbal-Villahermosa road has been described as "treacherous". Some buses go 63 km. past ruins to the beautiful Agua Azul waterfalls (see below).
    Palenque-Flores, Guatemala: two routes, one via River San Pedro, the other via the River Usumacinta (see also page 1097) going to Chancalá with the 1200 bus and continuing by bus (evening or early morning) to Frontera Echeverría. From Echeverría boats go up the river in Guatemala, to Sayaxché. No direct bus Palenque-Tuxtepec, but can be done using 7 different buses, staying overnight at, say, Acayucan.

Trains   There are trains daily from Mexico City at 2010, no sleeper, US$10 1st class, US$3.50 2nd (filthy toilets), up to 31 hrs. (book Palenque hotel in advance). Tickets on sale from Estación de Ferrocarril Buenavista on day of departure after a certain hour, no numbered seats; it is apparently impossible to buy 1st class tickets in Palenque for Mexico City but you pay 1st class because from Coatzacoalcos the carriages are treated as 1st class—this is accepted practice. Railway station for Palenque is 10 km. outside town (bus goes from in front of *Posada Alicia* at 2000). Taxi, railway station to Pemex service station US$1 for 2. The slow train from Campeche to Palenque leaves at 2030 (beware of thieves), arrives at 1100. *Rápido* train to Mérida at 0500 hrs., daily, usually late, takes about 11 hrs., keep your luggage with you, US$5, 1st (only one car, no sleeper) very comfortable, US$3, 2nd, dirty and smelly. Tickets on sale one hour before train arrives. The train may be crowded so it may be necessary to stand all the way. It is reported that the train is sometimes unreliable with delays of up to 11 hrs. Slow, 2nd class only train to Mérida at 1400 and 1900, at least 16 hrs., no light (beware of thieves). Make certain you catch the right train as there are two stopping very close together. **N.B.** If returning from Palenque to Mérida on the night train, bear in mind that in Dec. and Jan. it is nearly impossible to make reservations.

Air Travel   Light aircraft Palenque-Ocosingo (for San Cristóbal) (watch for Agua Azul falls 5-10 mins into flight) with Aerochiapas, T 80037, 8 people, supposed to leave at 0715, but more like 0830, provided there isn't a better offer to fly into the jungle. Tickets either at airstrip (shed only), or from Arrendadora de Carros Ik, two doors away from *Restaurante Maya* (on Plaza) in Palenque town. Aviacsa flies from Palenque to Villahermosa and Tuxtla, T 50210.

Other Sites   Flights from Palenque to **Bonampak** and **Yaxchilán** (refreshments), in light plane for 5, US$420 per plane, to both places, whole trip 6 hrs. Prices set, list available; Aviación de Chiapas at Av. Benito Juárez and Allende, open 0800-1330 and 1600-1800, Sat. 0800-1400, to Bonampak; book at airport, best to visit in May—the driest month; Yaxchilán, which is still unexcavated and where there are more howler monkeys around than people, is said to be more interesting. Do not visit ruins at night, it is forbidden. Otherwise hire a jeep at Palenque and drive there yourself, but since there is greater demand than supply of jeeps, make arrangements as soon as possible.

Day tours from Palenque by road for US$20 p.p., but private arrangements with a kombi driver to see both could well be better: US$25 p.p. for a 2-day trip has been quoted, including launch Echeverría-Yaxchilán (US$9 return). Coop Chambalu, Calle Allende, Palenque run all-day tours to Bonampak, leaving 0500, for US$220 for the whole bus, min. 6 passengers. A 2-day trip for US$30 can be arranged next to bus station in Palenque. However you go, take good boots and umbrella for jungle walking. Bonampak is 12 km. from Frontera Echeverría, sometimes known as Frontera Corozal (food, petrol and accommodation; you must register with the Migración office) and can be reached only on foot from the crossroads with the road to Echeverría and then with great difficulty (all maps are inaccurate, directions must be asked frequently). Beware of sandflies, black flies which cause river blindness, and mosquitoes— there is basic accommodation at the site, take hammock and mosquito net. Sturdy boots are needed for the 3½ hr. walk to the ruins. The workers are not to be trusted. There are many new tracks criss-crossing the Selva Lacandona (jungle), most going to Echeverría.

The Río Usumacinta, on the Chiapas border with Guatemala, is being dammed. Three dams are projected just downstream from Piedras Negras ruins. The ruins are accessible only by white water rafts, no road, no airstrip, unspoiled jungle (NW of Yaxchilán). Rafting trips run by Far Flung Adventures.

A German traveller has reported on a journey from Flores (Guatemala) to Palenque along the Pasión and Usumacinta rivers. From Santa Elena to Sayaxché, bus 3 hrs., US$0.75; then private launch (4 hrs, US$60) or trading boat (2 days, US$2) to Pipiles at confluence of Pasión and Usuamacinta, or to Benemérito on the Mexican side of the Usumacinta. Bus on unmade road Benemérito-Palenque, at least 5 hrs., and need to pass Immigration just past bridge over Río Lancantún.

Agua Azul, a series of beautiful waterfalls aptly named for the blue water swirling over natural tufa dams on 7 km. of fast-flowing river, is a popular camping spot reached by a 4-km. paved road from the junction with the paved road to San Cristóbal, 65 km. from Palenque. Best visited in dry season as in the rainy season the water is less blue and it is hard to swim because of the current (don't visit if it was raining the day before). It is extremely popular at holiday time. Some direct buses (and minibuses from Palenque at 0930-1000, returning at 1500) daily, e.g. 0700, 1100, US$1, 2nd class, 2 hours, other buses at 1000 and 1200, though you may be deposited at the junction; otherwise take bus to Ocosingo and get out at the junction (US$0.35, 1½ hours), and walk the 4 km. downhill to the falls. Back from the junction 1500-1600 with Transportes Maya buses. The Palenque minibus stops a few minutes at Mi Sol Ha waterfalls (entry, US$0.75). There are buses between San Cristóbal de Las Casas and Palenque (to 2nd class bus station, Transporte Maya) which will stop there, but a number of others need changing at Temo (over 20 km. away, N of Ocosingo, minibuses require a fair wait. Entrance fee to this *ejidal* park US$1 on foot, more for cars, US$1 per tent for camping, parking a trailer or using a hammock. There are a few restaurants (not very good) and also a *cabaña* for hammocks; if staying there, be very careful of your belongings; thefts have been reported. There is a good campsite, clean, popular and reliable, opposite the parking lot. Coop Chambalu, Calle Allende, Palenque run 5-hr. tours to Agua Azul and Mi Sol Ha for US$5.30, leaving 1000. Other minibuses from minibus terminal (nr. 4 Esquinas) charge for a whole bus holding 10 (1000-1400). The village to one side has, as its main street, the Agua Azul airport runway.

Beware of ticks when camping in long grass, use kerosene to remove them (or eat raw garlic to repel them!). Watch out carefully for thieves; bring your own food, etc. Flies abound during the rainy season (June-November).

Travelling from Villahermosa to Campeche one can follow either the old coastal route, Highway 180, which takes 10 hours to drive and has 4 ferries (total cost for one car US$6.60) or the inland Highway 186, via Francisco Escárcega, with 2 toll bridges (cost US$1.35). Petrol in Champotón, an attractive fishing village where the coastal and inland roads converge.

Ciudad del Carmen (pop. 145,000), on the coastal route, is hot, bursting at the seams since the oil boom, and spoilt by the new conditions. *Fiestas* at the end of July. There is a lot of shipbuilding here now and there are many trawlers in the harbour. The port is to be developed to become one of the biggest and most modern on the Mexican Gulf. The 3.2 km. Puente de la Unión, built in 1982, is considered the longest bridge in Mexico, linking Ciudad del Carmen with the mainland. There is a bull ring.

Hotels *Lli-re*, Calles 32 y 29, near ADO station, best in centre, a/c, expensive restaurant, C; *Acuario*, Calle 51 No. 60, a/c, comfortable, D; *Isla del Carmen*, Calle 20 No. 9, a/c, restaurant, bar, parking, C; *Lino's*, Calle 31 No. 132, a/c, pool, restaurant, C; three others on Calle 22. If you can't find accommodation, there are 3 buses between 2100 and 2200 to Campeche and Mérida. Ciudad del Carmen is renowned for its sea-food: giant prawns, clams, *ceviche* and baby hammerhead shark are all tasty.

Bus To Villahermosa at 1930, arriving 2300-0100; it depends how long one has to wait at the ferry. A connection can be made to Palenque at 2330 or 0400; slow but worthwhile trip.

Campeche, capital of Campeche state, population 200,000, is beautifully set on the western coast of Yucatán. It was the very first place at which the Spaniards landed in 1517. In the 17th century it was fortified against pirates; seven bastions of the old walls and an ancient fort (now rather dwarfed by two new big white hotels on the sea-front) near the crumbling cathedral remain. Some of the bastions house museums: Baluarte Soledad (N of the plaza), a small room of Mayan stelae, free (open Tues.-Sat., 0800-2000), Baluarte San Carlos (NW corner), museum of the fortifications (open Tues.-Sat. 0900-1300, 1600-2000, Sun. 0900-1300, free), Baluarte Santa Rosa (W side), Biblioteca Histórica, open 0830-1400, 1600-1900. The Museo Regional is at Calle 59, No. 35, containing archaeology and history sections, open Mon.-Sat., 0900-2000, Sun. 0900-1300.

There are several 16th and 17th century churches. The most interesting are San Franciscquito (16th century with wooden altars painted in vermilion and white), Jesús, San Juan de Dios, Guadalupe and Cristo Negro de San Román, and there is a historical museum on the Plaza (admission US$0.10). There is also a museum in the former church of San José, which changes its exhibits frequently, near the SW corner of the old town. The old houses are warmly coloured, but the town is now in a sad state of disrepair. The nearest beaches are Playa Bonita (which is no longer fit for swimming and is generally dirty, being next to oil storage tanks, but useful for car parking) and San Lorenzo. The people fish, trawl for shrimp, carve curios and make combs from tortoiseshell. The new market building is attractive. The bathing and fishing resort of Lerma is quite near; take a rickety bus marked Lerma or Playa Bonita; beach strewn with glass and other debris.

Hotels In general, beware of overcharging. *Ramada Inn*, A (5 stars); *Baluartes*, Av. Ruiz Cortines, A, parking for campers, who can use the hotel washrooms, good meal US$2.40-3.20, waiters apt to short-change, pool; *López*, Calle 12, No. 189, D, clean if a bit musty, with bath, better food; *Señorial*, Calle 10, comfortable, D, with bath, no restaurant; *Castelmar*, Calles 8 y 61, colonial style, E, large rooms with bath, recently refurbished, clean, friendly; *Cuauhtémoc*, F, clean (except downstairs rooms which are damp and smelly), with bath, in old house near the square (Calle 57). Several on Calle 10: *América* (No. 252, D, hot water, clean, fans but hot, OK) and *Roma*, E, No. 254; *Posada San Francisco*, No. 331. *Colonial*, clean, good, Calle 14 No. 122, not very friendly, D; *Autel El Viajero*, D, overcharges, but often only one left with space in the afternoon. López Mateos 177. 35 km. S of Campeche is *Hotel Siho*, D, excellent, beautiful setting on Gulf coast, swimming and other facilities but expensive restaurant and nowhere else to eat nearby (bus to Sihoplaya from Campeche US$0.30). CREA Youth Hostel Av. Agustín Melgar s/n, Col. Buenavista, C.P. 24040, T 61802/62164, in the S suburbs, nr. University, bus from market US$0.12, clean and friendly. It is virtually impossible to get hotel rooms around the Mexican holiday period, starting May.

Camping   There is a trailer park with camping signposted in town. Can be reached by taking a Samula bus from the market place. Owner speaks English; US$1.50 p.p.

Restaurants   *Campeche,* good value; cafeteria next door sells good yoghurt and fruit juices; *Miramar* (good seafood, reasonable); *La Perla*, Calle 10 No. 329 (good fish, busy and popular), venison, squid; locals' haunt, sometimes erratic service, off Plaza; *Lonchería Puga*, Calle 8 No. 53, open 0700, rec.; *Pizzería Gato Pardo*, corner of Calle 10 and 49, on Jardín San Martín, outside the wall, excellent pizzas, loud music. Two doors away, *La Cava*. It is hard to find reasonably-priced food before 1800; try the restaurant at the ADO terminal, or *La Parroquia*, Call 59 No. 9, open 24 hrs., good local atmosphere, friendly and clean, rec.

Shopping   Excellent cheap Panama hats (here they are called jipi hats, pronounced "hippie"). Handicrafts are generally cheaper than in Mérida. The new market (just outside the city wall) is worth a visit. Plenty of bargains here, especially Mexican and Mayan clothes, hats and shoes, fruit, vegetables; try ice-cream—though preferably from a shop rather than from a barrow.

Tourist Information   New centre near waterfront (Plaza Moch-Couch Turisplaza, Av. Ruiz Cortines), close to Palacio de Gobierno, good (open 0800-1430, 1600-2030, Mon.-Fri.).

Excursions   Two km. S. of Campeche is the 18th-century fort of San Miguel, containing museums and worth visiting for its archaeological pieces. Entry, US$0.15. Between Campeche and Champotón is Playa Seyba, a fishing village with good camping possibilities (but no facilities) N of the village. Eighty km. N of Campeche is Becal, centre of the panama hat trade. The hats are made in man-made limestone caves, whose coolness and dampness facilitate the weaving.

Maya Sites in Campeche State   About 40 km. beyond Campeche on the road to Uxmal (**see** page 1098), there is a deviation, right, along a white stone road for 20 km. near Cayal to the pyramid of Edzná, worth a visit (entry, US$0.22, bus from Campeche at 0800 but may leave hours later; possible to take 0800 bus to Cayal and hitch from there), but seemingly worth the trouble only for specialists. Restoration is in hand. SE of Edzná are Dzibilnocac and Hochob sites, with elaborately decorated temples and palaces. For these sites you need a car as the bus returns to Campeche almost at once after arrival at Dzibilnocac, and there is nowhere to stay. For those with a car, continue beyond Edzná on Route 261 to the very picturesque villages of Hopelchen and Bolonchen de Rejón.

Dzibalchen, for **Hochob** ruins, is on a road 40 km. from Hopelchen, may be reached by early morning bus from Campeche, 80 km., but again no return buses or accommodation guaranteed. At Hochob (famous for the temple wall, reproduced in the Anthopological Museum in Mexico City) there is another temple (with a serpent's-mouth entrance) about 30 mins. by car and foot from the well-known one: the guard will show you (for a consideration) after closing the main site in the evening. To get to Hochob, ask directions from church in Dzibalchen, which is run by Americans; basically you need to travel 12 km. on a dirt road to a village, Chenko, where the locals will show you the way; remember to bear left when the road forks, then the ruins (very impressive and worth the walk, says Brad Krupsaw, of Silver Spring, Md.) are 1 km. after the fork on top of a hill.

Santa Teresa is a tiny village W of Hopelchen; turn off the main road S for ½ km.; very quiet and simple, excellent bakery with tall beamed ceiling and colourful tiled floor. There are Mayan ruins on the islands of Jainu and Piedra, 3 hrs. by boat off the coast. Written official permission is required to visit as the islands are Federal property and guarded.

Transport   You can go to Mérida by rail, 4 hrs. or by road, 3 hrs., 252 km. (158 miles). First class buses go by the Via Corta, which does *not* pass through Uxmal, Kabah, etc. Take a really quite comfortable 2nd class bus from the same terminal, Via Larga, have 3 hours at Uxmal, and catch the next bus to Mérida, but don't buy a through ticket to Mérida; you'll have to pay again when you board the bus. Check bus times, as there are fewer in the afternoon. Bus Campeche-Mérida direct, US$3.30, 2nd class. Bus Campeche-Uxmal, US$3, 2nd class, 3 hrs., 5 a day (but none between 0900 and 1200). Buses along new inland road to Villahermosa; take posted times with a pinch of salt, 2nd class, 5 a day, US$7, 1st class US$8; 6½ hrs., 2300 bus comes from Mérida but empties during the night. Train Campeche-Palenque, 2nd class, US$2.50, 9½ hrs., leaves at 2310. Bus via Emiliano Zapata (2 hrs. before Villahermosa) to Palenque, change at Emiliano Zapata, **see page 1089**. ADO bus to Mexico City, US$23. Train to Mexico City, 30 hrs., comfortable, US$19 1st class. Mexico City-Campeche train leaves at 2000 daily, very crowded in holiday times.

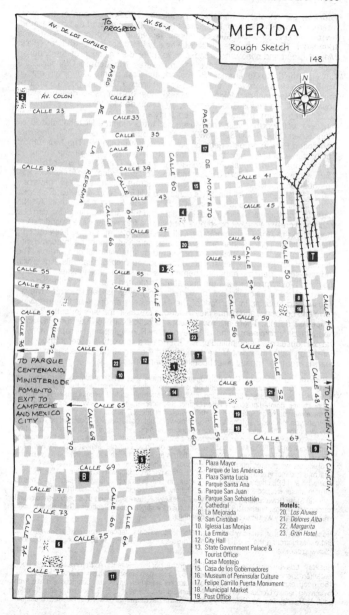

MERIDA
Rough Sketch
148

1. Plaza Mayor
2. Parque de las Américas
3. Plaza Santa Lucía
4. Parque Santa Ana
5. Parque San Juan
6. Parque San Sebastián
7. Cathedral
8. La Mejorada
9. San Cristóbal
10. Iglesia Las Monjas
11. La Ermita
12. City Hall
13. State Government Palace &
    Tourist Office
14. Casa Montejo
15. Casa de los Gobernadores
16. Museum of Peninsular Culture
17. Felipe Carrillo Puerta Monument
18. Municipal Market
19. Post Office

Hotels:
20. Los Aluxes
21. Dolores Alba
22. Margarita
23. Gran Hotel

Mérida, capital of Yucatán state, population 700,000, is one of the most interesting cities in Mexico, but suffers from pollution caused by heavy traffic, narrow streets and climatic conditions favouring smog-formation. It was founded in 1542 on the site of the Mayan city of Tihoo. Its centre is the Plaza Mayor, green and shady; its arcades have more than a touch of the Moorish style. It is surrounded by the severe twin-towered 16th century Cathedral, the City Hall, the State Government Palace, and the Casa Montejo, originally built in 1549 by the *conquistador* of the region, rebuilt around 1850 and now a branch of the Banco Nacional de México (Banamex), open to the public during banking hours. The Casa de los Gobernadores, on Paseo de Montejo, is an impressive building in the turn-of-the-century French style of the Porfirio Díaz era. A small museum well worth a visit, the Museo de Antropología e Historia, closed on Mon. (open 0800-1400 Sun., 0800-2000 all other days, US$0.35), opposite Centenario Park in an old prison on Av. Itzaes with Calle 59. The Museum of Peninsular Culture, run by the Instituto Nacional Indigenista (INI), a contemporary crafts museum, is well worth visiting. There are several 16th and 17th century churches dotted about the city: Tercera Orden, San Francisco, San Cristóbal, and La Mejorada. Along the narrow streets ply horse-drawn cabs of a curious local design. In all the city's parks you will find *confidenciales,* S-shaped stone seats in which people can sit side by side facing each other. All the markets, and there are several, are interesting in the early morning. One can buy traditional crafts: a basket or *sombrero* of sisal, a filigree necklace (a good silver shop is next to *Hotel Panamericana,* Calles 50 and 52), also a good selection of Maya replicas. Tortoiseshell articles are also sold, but cannot be imported into most countries, as sea turtles are protected by international convention. The Mérida market is also particularly good for made-to-measure sandals of deerskin and tyre-soles, panama hats, and hammocks of all sizes and qualities. Some of the most typical products are the *guayabera,* a pleated and/or embroidered shirt worn universally, its equivalent for women, the *guayablusa,* and beautiful Mayan blouses and *huipiles.* In the Park of the Americas is an open-air theatre giving plays and concerts, and bands play in various plazas in the evenings; the Tourist Office has details. There are monuments to Felipe Carrillo Puerto, an agrarian labour leader prominent in the 1910 revolution. Redevelopment is rapid; many of the old houses are being pulled down. Mérida is a safe city in general (though be careful on Calle 58 and near the market), but the large influx of visitors in recent years is creating "mostly quiet hostility" towards them.

In Paseo de Montejo (part of Calle 62), together with many shops and restaurants, there are many grand late 19th century houses. Calle 65 is the main shopping street and the Plaza Mayor is between Calles 61/63 and 60/62. Odd-number streets run E and W, even numbers N and S. In colonial times, painted or sculpted men or animals placed at intersections were used as symbols for the street: some still exist in the small towns of Yucatán. The houses are mostly of Spanish-Moorish type, painted in soft pastel tones, thick walls, flat roofs, massive doors, grilled windows, flowery patios. The water supply, once notorious, is improved. Begging and much molestation from car-washers, shoe-shiners and souvenir-peddlers. All streets are one-way. Free town map at tourist kiosk on the Plaza Mayor, or the Secretaría de Obras Públicas, almost opposite airport at Mérida (cheap bus from centre). Enquire at hotels about the house and garden tours run by the local society women for tourists to raise money for charity. Every Thursday evening there is free local music, dancing and poetry at 2100 in the Plaza Santa Lucía, two blocks from the Plaza Mayor (Calles 55 and 60), chairs provided. The Ermita, an 18th century chapel with beautiful grounds, is full of impressive precolumbian sculpture; a lonely, deserted place 10-15 mins. from the centre.

In the State Government Palace, on the Plaza Mayor, there is a series of superb symbolic and historical paintings, finished 1978, by a local artist, Fernando Castro Pacheco. The Palace is open evenings and very well lit to display the paintings.

Fiesta Carnival on Tuesday before Ash Wednesday. Floats, dancers in regional costume, music and dancing around the Plaza and children dressed in animal suits. **N.B.** Banks closed Monday following carnival.

Hotels *Los Aluxes,* Calle 60 No. 444, delightful, pool, restaurants, A; *Bojórquez,* C, a/c, pool, restaurant, service a little offhand, Calle 58/57, near main square; *Panamericana,* Calle 59, No. 455, good, expensive, with elaborate courtyard in the Porfirian style, very spacious and airy, with swimming pool, 5 blocks from centre, A; *Castellano,* Calle 57, No. 513, modern, clean, friendly, pool, A; *Holiday Inn,* Av. Colón and C.60, L; *María del Carmen,* A, Calle 63, No. 550, breakfast reported poor; *Casa de Balam*, Calle 60, No. 488, A; *Montejo Palace*, Paseo del Montejo 483, B, noisy on 1st floor, lots of cooking smells, pool; *Latino*, Calle 66 and 63, D, with fan and shower (water supply problems), friendly and clean; *Colón*, Calle 62, No. 483, C, good value, pool, being remodelled; *Casa Bowen*, restored colonial house (inside better than out), corner of Calle 66, No. 521-B, and 65, rooms on the main street noisy, stores luggage, near ADO bus station, as is *Posada del Angel*, Calle 67, No. 535, between Calle 66 and 68, D, clean, excellent value (don't bother with the restaurant next door); *Caminante*, also nearby at Calle 64, No. 539, E, clean, friendly; *México*, Calle 60, No. 525, E, good restaurant, attractive; *Milo*, Calle 63, basic but very clean and friendly, E; *Gran Hotel*, Calle 60 No. 496, C, just off the Plaza, is clean, helpful, owner speaks English, recently remodelled; *Caribe*, Calle 59, No. 500 and 60, C, not such good value; *San Luis*, Calle 61, No. 534-68, D, with fan and shower (and US$2.25 for noisy a/c), basic, friendly, patio pool, restaurant; *Gobernador*, on the corner of Calle 59 and 66, D, a/c, big rooms, quite good; *Posada Cristóbal*, about 5 blocks from market on Calle 69, F, with bath, clean and quiet; *Rossana Pastora*, Calle 58, No. 563, E, very clean, excellent value; *Príncipe Maya Airport Inn*, C, noisy from night club, convenient for airport. *Montejo*, Calle 57 and 60, D (bargain), rec.; *Casa de Huéspedes*, E, Victorian showers, will keep luggage for small fee, mosquitoes, so take coils or net, pleasant and quiet except at front, Calle 62, No. 507; *América*, simple, private shower and toilet, noisy, will look after luggage, E, Calle 67, No. 500, between 58 and 60, about 10 mins. from bus station and near centre, rec. *San Fernando*, opp. ADO bus terminal, D with fan and bath, clean; *Posada Toledo*, Calle 58, No. 487, T 3-16-90, C, good, central, in charming old house, has paperback exchange; *Del Mayab*, Calle 50, No. 536A, E, with bath, reasonable, swimming pool and car park; *Flamingo*, Calle 58 and 59, E, near Plaza, with private shower, swimming pool, noisy, so get room at the back; *Peninsular*, Calle 58, No. 519, near Plaza, D, pool, a/c, clean, friendly; *Parque*, Calle 60 No. 495, D, with bath and fan, clean, friendly, rec.; *Alamo*, E, with bath, clean, next to bus station, storage; *Margarita*, Calle 66, No. 506 (with Calle 63), E with shower, clean, friendly, rec.; *Dolores Alba*, Calle 63 No. 464, D, good, pool, clean, cool on 1st floor; *San Jorge*, across from ADO bus terminal, E, clean, but take interior room as the street is noisy; *San José*, E, with bath, basic, restaurant, W of Plaza on Calle 63, one of the cheapest, will store luggage; *Mucuy*, Calle 57, No. 481, between 56 and 58, E, friendly, good, with shower, use of fridge, washing facilities, efficient, nice gardens, highly rec.; *Centenario*, E with bath, friendly, clean, safe on Calle 84, between 59 and 59A; *Farahón*, Calle 65, No. 468 y 59, E, above textile shop near Post Office, big rooms, not too clean, noisy; rooms on Calle 66 Norte, No. 386 (with private bath). *Hospedaje Casbillio*, Calle 56, between 53 and 55, clean and friendly.

Cheaper hotels tend to be S of the main Plaza (odd streets numbered 63 and higher), near the market or bus station: another recommendation is *María Teresa*, Calle 64 No. 529 (between Calles 65 and 67), clean, friendly, safe, central, E with bath. More expensive hotels are on the N side of the city and near the Paseo Montejo. *Maya Paradise Trailer Park*, rec., good pool, pick a site away from the water towers; right opp. the airport. *Trailer Park Rainbow*, Km. 8, on the road to Progreso, US$1.80 for car and US$1.20 for one or two, basic facilities.

Restaurants *Jaraneros Patio*, Montejo Circle, regional food and entertainment from 1600; *Pancho Villa's Follies*, very friendly, try *abalones*, owner speaks English, overpriced; and *Soberanis*, on Plaza with two branches elsewhere, serving delicious fish dishes, seafood cocktails highly rec., but expensive, one on Calle 60, No. 503 between 63 and 65 (slow service), and another on Calle 56, No. 504. *Los Almendros*, Calle 50A, No. 493 at Calle 59, in high-vaulted, whitewashed thatched barn, for Yucatán specialities, rec. but expensive, mind the peppers, esp. the green sauce! *Mesón del Mestizo* (Plaza Sta. Lucía), *Pórtico del Peregrino* (Pop), Calle 57, between 60 and 62, excellent snacks, popular with foreigners, very charming; *Mesón del Quijote*, Calle 62 No. 519, cheap and excellent, try their fish dishes with garlic; the *Patio Español*, inside the *Gran Hotel*, well cooked and abundant food, local and Spanish specialities, moderate prices; *David*, Calle 62, No. 468A (Arab food—closes before 2100); *Café Alameda*, nr. Correos, Arab food, closes at 1900, cheap and good; *Santa Lucía*, Calle 60, good Arab food. *La Prosperidad*, Calle 53 and 56, good Yucateca food, live entertainment at lunchtime; *Los Pájaros*, Calle 69 near ADO bus station, cheap and good; *Yannig*, Calle 62, No. 480, best, cheapest French food. *Cedral del Líbano*, Calle 59 No. 529, good family-style Arabic food. *El Mariachi Hacienda*, Calle 60 No. 466, regional food, loud local music, dancing and cock-fighting, cover charge US$2. *El Faisán y El Venado*, Calle 59 No. 617, inexpensive, regional food, Mayan dance show, near zoo. *El Condado*, Calle 65 opp. Bazaar, good and cheap meals, highly rec. *La Carretera*, Calle 62 and 59, a little expensive but very good. Good food at *Flamingo*, Calle 51; *Leo's*, good value for meat dishes, pleasant, Calle 60, just N of Plaza Santa Lucía; *Café de Guaya*, Calle 60, between 53 and 55, vegetarian; *Pizzería Vito Corleone*, Calle 59 No. 508, near Plaza, good. Cold sliced cooked venison (venado) is to be had in the Municipal Market. *Cafetería La Giralda El Rey*, in the shoe section of the market place, excellent coffee. Good coffee in *Café* on Calle 60, between 65 and 67, traditional coffeehouse where locals meet; *Mil Tortas*, very good and cheap sandwiches, Calle 62 with 65 and 67; *Café Moneho*, Calle 65 between 58 and 60, good, popular, especially for breakfast. *La Pérgola*, warmly rec. (both drive-in and tables), at corner Calles 56A and 43, good veal dishes; also in Colonia Alemán at Calle 24 No. 289A. *Cafetería Erik's*, ½ block from Plaza, meals and snacks. Banana bread and wholemeal rolls at health shop on Calle 59 between 60 and 62, and good juice bar close by. *Jugos California*, good, expensive fruit juices, Calle 60, also in

Calle 65 and at the main bus station; *Jugos de Caña*, Calle 62 between 57 and 59, very good; *Jugos Michoacán*, good milkshakes on Calle 57. *Dulcería Colón*, on Plaza Mayor, for excellent, if expensive, ices.

Shopping   *Guayaberas: Canul*, Calle 59, No. 496; *Genuina Yucateca*, Calle 50, No. 520. At *Mayalandia* on Calle 61, before Calle 48 archway, one can bargain. *Jack* in Calle 59, near Canul, makes *guayaberas* to measure in 4 hrs., expensive.

The best hammocks are the so-called 3-ply, but they are difficult to find, about US$20 (cheaper than in Campeche for cotton, US$7 for nylon); also mosquito nets. Try *Mayoreo de Mérida*, Calle 65, near Post Office; or *Claudia*, Calle 58 and 89 or *Francisco Asís*, Calles 65 and 52. There are three sizes: single, matrimonial and family. *Jorge Razu*, Calle 56 No. 516B, rec.; also *La Poblana S.A.*, William Razu C., Calle 65 No. 492. *La Poblana*, Calle 65, No. 492, is one place to buy (outside the market), fixed prices; and across the street by *El Tigre del 65*; bargain like mad if buying more than one.

Embroidered *huipil* blouses US$3-6. Good panama hats at *El Bombín* next to 511b (tailor's shop) on Calle 67, between 60 and 62. Also *Nipis Becal*, just by market. Sr. Raúl Cervera Sauri has a reasonable souvenir shop on Calle 59, No. 501. *Uncle Sam's* on main square, run by retired American, reasonably priced hammocks, panama hats. Next door to restaurant *Los Almendros* on Calle 59 is the Cordamex (sisal products) outlet—don't go to the factory 8 km. from town as they won't sell there. Good buys in black coral jewellery and tortoiseshell (may not be imported into several countries—check) in the markets, particularly the 2-storey one on Calles 56 and 67. There is a big supermarket, *Blanco*, on Calle 67 and 62, well stocked.

Tourist Office   Corner of Calles 57 and 60, also corner of Calles 61 and 54, and on N side of Plaza Mayor in the Palacio de Gobierno. Has list of all hotel accommodation with prices. Organizes trips to Uxmal. Tourist information from Ministerio de Fomento, Calle 59 opp. Centenario park. Instituto Nacional de Estadística, Geografía e Informática, Paseo Montejo 442, Ed. Oasis, for maps and information.

Travel Agents and Car Hire   Wagon-Lits (Cooks), helpful, Av. Colón 501 (Plaza Colón), T 554-11; Cozumel Travel Service; *Yucatán Trails*, Calle 62, No. 482, is very helpful, run by Canadian, Denis Lafoy. Car reservations should be booked well in advance wherever possible; there is a tendency to hand out cars which are in poor condition once the main stock has gone, so check locks, etc., on cheaper models before you leave town. The all-inclusive cost (inc. gasoline) for a one-day 250 km. trip is about US$50 in a VW. Avis in *Hotel Mérida*; Hertz, Calle 55, No. 479; Budget, Calle 62, No. 588-3; Volkswagen, Calle 60, No. 486; Alquiladora de Autos Sureste, Calle 60, No. 481, and at airport; Mexico Rent-A-Car in the lobby of *Hotel del Parque*, Calle 60, No. 495, has good rates, new VW Beetles; Odin, Calle 59, No. 506-3.

Taxis   We are warned that taxi drivers are particularly prone to overcharge by taking a long route, so always establish the journey and fare in advance.

Exchange   Banamex (passport necessary) in Casa de los Gobernadores on Plaza, at Tourist Office (Calles 57 y 60), and at Calles 56 y 59. Many banks on Calle 65, off the Plaza. *Casa de Cambio*, Calle 56 No. 491 (between 57 and 59) open 0900-1700 Mon.-Sat., but bank's rates better. Jugos California on the main square may change dollars and travellers' cheques at good rates.

Post Office   Calle 65, will accept parcels for sea mail. Generally crowded, use branches at airport (also for quick delivery) or on Calle 58, instead. Telegrams from Calle 56, between 65 and 65A, open 0800-2100.

International Calls   Possible from main telephone exchange at Calle 59 and 64, open until 2200 hrs. Signposted "Larga Distancia", difficult to see; in a small yard.

British Vice Consul   Major A. Dutton (retd), MBE, Calle 58 No. 450, T (91-992) 16799. Postal address Apdo. 89. **US Consulate** Paseo Montejo 453 y Av. Colón (T 255011). **Canadian Consulate** Calle 62, No. 309-D-19.

English-Speaking Doctor   Dr. A. H. Puga Navarrete (also speaks French), Calle 13 No. 210, between Calles 26 and 28, Colonia García Gineres, T 25-07-09, open 1600-2000.

Cameras and Film   Repairs by Señor Riera, Calle 62 Altos, between 65 and 67. Many processors around crossing of Calles 59 and 60.

Laundry   Calle 59 between Calles 72 and 74, at least 24 hrs. *Lavandería* on Calle 69, one block from bus station, about US$1.50 a load. Self-service hard to find.

Trains   Fees for red-capped porters posted at the station (Calles 48 and 57). From Mexico City at 2010. Sometimes only 2nd class available but no 1st class or restaurant car. To Mexico City, Pullman US$37, 1st class US$17.25, 2nd class US$10.30, leaves Mérida at 2200 (37 hrs. but often more like 45 to 72); book ticket from 1100 on same day of departure at station. 2nd class not rec., dirty. Difference between 1st and 2nd class in age of carriages, no seats assigned on either, live animals in 2nd. Even though boarding not supposed to be before 1900, most people get on on arrival of the train, at 1830. Queuing for 2nd class starts hours before. No clean running water, lavatory dirty. Beggars get on at every stop; thieving. Best to take Special 1st Class, reserved seats, comfortable (take blanket, a/c is cold), or Pullman if you can afford it and don't mind small cabins. No food except for vendors at stations, stock up. Many breaks up to Coatzacoalcos. Possible to break journey at Palenque but not on one ticket. Mérida-Palenque (on same train as to Mexico City), takes 12 hrs., no *dormitorio* now available. Old-fashioned 1940 North American coaches, but very comfortable. Track recently improved, train rocks rather than jerks as it did, speed about 50 km. an hour. Air conditioning improves as you leave the station, but not spectacular. Conductor brings drinks round, and coffee and sandwiches early a.m. Fruit near station, bread and cheese a couple of streets away from station, better bought before leaving centre. Mérida-Valladolid at 1510, 5 hrs., US$2. There are two picturesque narrow-gauge railway lines SE of Mérida—one to Sotuta and the other to Peto via Ticul and Oxcutzcab. One train on each line leaves daily at 1400 from Mérida, returns at 0400. The journey takes 5 hrs., covers 150 km., US$0.50 to Peto. You can return by bus from Oxcutzcab (see also page 1099).

Buses Almost all buses except those to Progreso leave from terminal on Calle 69 between Calles 70 and 72. The station has lockers. To Mexico City, US$21.75, 24-28 hrs.; to Coatzacoalcos, US$12. To Puerto Juárez, US$4 1st, US$3.50 2nd class, 5 hrs. Bus to Veracruz, US$18, 16 hrs.; to Chetumal, 1st class, 6 a day, US$6.60, 6 hrs. To Ciudad del Carmen at 0600, 1st class, ADO, US$5, 9 hrs. Three buses to Tulum: at 0500, 1100 and 2300, 10 hrs., US$6.50, drops you off about ½ km. from the ruins. For buses to Uxmal and Chichén Itzá see under those places' names. Regular buses to Campeche (US$3, 4½ hrs.) also pass Uxmal. Last bus from Uxmal to Campeche (US$1.50, 3 hrs.) at 2315 is quite crowded. Buses to Puerto Juárez and Cancún (Autobuses de Oriente) US$4.40 1st class, US$4 2nd, 4½ hrs. Buses to Progreso (US$0.45) passing the road to Dzibilchaltún (see next page), leave from the bus station on Calle 62, between Calle 65 and 67 every 15 mins. from 0500-2100. To Valladolid, US$1.80. One direct bus daily at 1300 via Villahermosa and Pichucalco to Tuxtla Gutiérrez, 8 hrs., US$10. Autotransportes del Sureste de Yucatán, at 0600.

Bus to Palenque leaves 2330 from ADO terminal, arrives 0830, US$8.50, rather a grim proposition, better to travel in daytime via Emiliano Zapata and local bus (see page 1089). Buses to Celestún and Sisal from corner of Calle 50 and 67.

Route 261, Mérida-Francisco Escárcega, paved and in very good condition. Buses.

To Guatemala by public transport from Yucatán, take train from Mérida to Pichucalco (see page 1087); it gets in about 1300. Take a small bus downtown and catch the bus to Tuxtla Gutiérrez. Road is slow, so it is probably quicker to cut across from Coatzacoalcos. Autotransportes del Sureste de Yucatán bus from Mérida to Tuxtla, via Palenque and Ocosingo to either San Cristóbal or Comitán; 2 or 3 changes of bus. Bus from Mérida direct to Tuxtla at 1330 hrs., then direct either Tuxtla-Ciudad Cuauhtémoc or to Tapachula; although the journey may not be as pretty, it saves changing.

Alternatively travel from Villahermosa by ADO bus (0700, 0800, 1330), 4 hrs., or from Emiliano Zapata hourly by ADO, or on the México-Mérida railway line to **Tenosique**, 1 hr. E by train from Palenque, or by colectivo to Catazaja (US$0.10), then bus (US$1.25, 3 a day) *(Hotel Garage*, E, a/c, on main square with restaurant, very clean; *Roma* on main street, E, bath; *Azulejos*, Calle 26 No. 416, E with bath, dirty, hot water, friendly, opp. church, *Casa de Huéspedes La Valle*, Calle 19, G p.p., and others). From Tenosique (pleasant, friendly, but no money exchange except for clothing shop Ortiz y Alvarez at Calle 28, 404), buses leave from Calles 28 and 35 at 0600, 0900, 1300 (one hour) to La Palma on the Río San Pedro, whence boats leave to El Naranjo (Guatemala) at 1400, returning 0700, about 5 hrs., US$12. In La Palma, restaurant and exchange are poor value; Nicolás Valenzuela offers both services, and lodging. Make sure the boat takes you beyond the border, where there is only a customs office. From **El Naranjo** there is a new dirt road through the jungle to Flores; buses leave at 0300 and 1400 for Flores (US$3, 7 hrs.) or hitchhiking apparently possible. Beautiful trip. One can take a boat from La Palma (rather than San Pedro, which is more expensive) and go for US$2.50 to El Martillo.

Road to Belize: paved all the way to Chetumal. Bus Mérida-Chetumal US$6, 2nd class. Leaves at 1200 and takes 7½ hrs. Bus station on corner of Calle 68 and 69.

By Air Mexicana office at Calle 58 and 61. From Calle 67 and 60 bus 79 goes to the airport, marked Aviación, US$0.10. Taxi US$4, voucher available from airport, you don't pay driver direct; colectivo US$2. Mexicana and Aeroméxico both have about 6 flights to Mexico City daily, 1½ hrs., 2½ hrs. from New Orleans; 1¾ hrs. from Miami via Tampa with Eastern Airlines; Aeroméxico Miami-Mérida daily at 1955; 2 hrs. from Mexico City, 960 km. Vega flies every other day to Oaxaca, on to Acapulco. Aeroméxico flies to Acapulco, via Veracruz and Monterrey to Los Angeles, 3 times a week. Acapulco, via Oaxaca and Villahermosa, 3 hrs.; Cancún, 35 mins.; Cozumel, 35 mins.; Monterrey, 1¾ hrs.; Oaxaca, 2 hrs.; Tuxtla Gutiérrez, 2½ hrs.; Villahermosa, 50 mins. (Aeroméxico leaves at 0655 and returns to Mérida at 2205, making it easier to visit Palenque in a rented car in a one-day tour). The airport is splendid. Mexicana to Cuba, Sun. and Wed., US$179 return, payable in pesos. A package tour (one week) Mérida-Havana-Mérida is available, US$213, including flight, hotel and half-board (MAP). For return to Mexico ask for details at Secretaría de Migración, Calle 60, No. 285. The smaller airlines tend to offer cheaper flights, on older aircraft. Food and drinks at the airport are very expensive.

Excursions North-west of Mérida is first Hunucma, like an oasis in the dry Yucatán, about ½ hr. from the Central Camionera bus station, US$0.30. Then about 52 km. (buses), is Sisal beach (frequent buses 0500-1700, from Calle 50, between Calle 65 and 67), with an impressive lighthouse, where one can hire a boat and go to the reef of Los Alacranes where many ancient wrecks are visible in clear water. West of Mérida regular buses (US$1.10) serve Celestún beach, a resort frequented by Meridans, with a huge lagoon with flamingoes; hire a boat (US$18 for one big enough for 6-8). Latest reports are that the place is very dirty and the food in the restaurants cannot be trusted.

Halfway to Progreso turn right for the Maya ruins of **Dzibilchaltún**, open 0800-1700. This unique city, according to carbon dating, was founded as early as 1000 B.C. The most important building is the Temple of the Seven Dolls (partly restored); museum at entrance, where you can buy drinks. The Cenote Xlaca contains very clear water and is 44 metres deep; ruined church nearby. Buses from Mérida to Progreso pass the junction to the ruins, 8 km. from the main road, taxis wait at the bus stop; buses pass in either direction every 15 mins. Apparently one can swim in the *cenote*.

Progreso, the port 39 km. away, is reached by road or railway. Population 14,000; temperatures range from 27° to 35°C. Main export: *henequén*. It claims to have the longest stone-bridge pier in the world. The beach has been cleaned up and plenty of new hotels and houses have been built. It is very popular at holiday times (July-August).

Hotels On beach: *Tropical Suites*, E (more with kitchen), clean, rec.; *Hostal*, E, clean, big rooms; *Posada Linda*, E, clean, kitchen and balcony, rec. Free camping on the beach; huts for hammocks. Good **restaurants** and quite cheap are *Capitán Pescado*, and *Charlie's* expensive but good; *Soberanis; La Terraza*, variable results, expensive. Police permit free beach camping. Many homes, owned by Mexico City residents, available for rent, services included. Sr. A. Morán, at Calle 22 and 27 (speaks English) can arrange furnished accommodation (cheapest unfurnished). Good local market with lowest food prices in Yucatán, esp. seafood. You can buy fresh shrimps cheaply in the mornings on the beach. Bus, Progreso-Mérida US$0.50 every 15 mins. The beach front by the pier is devoted to cafés with seafood cocktails as their speciality. They also have little groups performing every weekend afternoon in summer; and the noise can be both spirited and deafening.

A short bus journey (4 km.) from Progreso are Puerto Yucalpetén and Chelem, a dusty resort. Balneario Yucalpetén has a beach with lovely shells, but also a large naval base. *Fiesta Inn* on the beach. Yacht marina, changing cabins, beach with gardens and swimming pool. Between the Balneario and Chelem there is a nice hotel of small Mayan-hut type bungalows, *Hotel Villanueva* (2 km. from village, hot rooms), and also *Costa Maya*, on Calle 29 y Carretera Costera, with restaurant. Fish restaurants in Chelem, *Las Palmas* and *El Cocalito*, reasonable, also other small restaurants. East of Progreso is another resort, Chicxulub.

Uxmal is 74 km. from Mérida, 177 km. from Campeche, by a good paved road. If going by car, there is a new circular road round Mérida: follow the signs to Campeche, then Campeche via *ruinas*, then to Muna via Yaxcopoil (long stretch of road with no signposting). Muna-Yaxcopoil about 34 km. The Uxmal ruins are quite unlike those of Chichén-Itzá (see below), and cover comparatively little ground. Uxmal, the home of the Xiu tribe, was founded in 1007. Its finest buildings seem to have been built much later. See El Adivino (the Sorcerer, pyramid-shaped, topped by two temples with a splendid view); the Casa de las Monjas (House of Nuns), a quadrangle with 88 much adorned rooms; the Casa del Gobernador (House of the Governor), on three terraces, with well preserved fine sculptures; the Casa de las Tortugas (Turtle House) with six rooms; the Casa de las Palomas (House of Doves), probably the oldest; and the cemetery. Ruins open at 0800, close at 1700, entrance US$1.50 weekdays, free on Sundays. Drinks in the visitors' centre at entrance of ruins, may not be taken inside; also guide books here. Many iguanas (harmless) wandering about, watch out for occasional scorpions and snakes. There is a *son et lumière* display at the ruins nightly—English version (US$0.50) at 2100, Spanish version (US$0.15) 1900 (check for times), highly rec. (but bus leaves at 1400, arriving 1530, thus leaving you only 1½ hrs. to explore the ruins before the site closes). 2nd class bus from Mérida to Campeche ("Via Ruinas") passes Uxmal, US$0.90 one way, can buy tickets on bus, 2½ hr. journey, 2 hrs. just enough to see ruins. Bus stops just under ½ km. from entrance to ruins on main road, follow sign. Return from *Restaurant Bar Nicté-Ha* (open 1230-1900) across the road. From Mérida six 2nd-class buses a day. Return to Mérida after the show is only possible with tourist buses. (There may be spare seats for those without return tickets.) There is, however, a bus to Campeche at 2315. Good service with Yucatán Trails (**see page 1096**). Taxi Mérida-Uxmal US$1.35. For best photographs early morning or late afternoon arrival is essential. Overnight parking for a van US$0.50.

Hotels *Hacienda Uxmal*, 100 metres from ruins, is quite good but very expensive (A, restaurant open 0800-2200). Swimming pool. It has a less expensive dependency *Posada Uxmal*, B, meals in either part cost US$4.35 and US$6 depending on restaurant. *Misión Uxmal*, A, 1-2 km. from ruins on Mérida road. Club Méditerranée *Villa Arqueológica*, A-B, beautiful, close to ruins, good, swimming pool, breakfast US$3 but worth it. *Lapalapa*, A, including meals. New restaurant at ruins, good. From the *Hacienda Uxmal* jeeps visit the four ruins of Kabah, Sayil, X-Lapak and Labná (see below) daily, US$20 p.p., incl. box lunch. **N.B.** There is no village at Uxmal, just the hotels. Camping no longer possible beside the parking lot.

On the road from Uxmal to Mérida (with good restaurant, *Rancho*, a few km. from Uxmal) is **Muna** (15 km. from Uxmal, 62 from Mérida; delightful square and old church), with the nearest railway station to Uxmal. There is a new direct road (Highway 293) from Muna to Bacalar, Quintana Róo, just N of Chetumal.

By the main road a few km. S of Uxmal and often included in tours of the latter (about 5½ km. before the sign for Sayil), are the ruins of **Kabah** where there is a fascinating Palace of Masks, whose façade bears the image of Chac; mesmerically repeated over and over again about six hundred times. The style is classic Puuc. Watch out for snakes and spiders. Bus: Campeche-Kabah, US$2.40.

Further South of Uxmal, about half-way between Mérida and Campeche, a paved road branches off to the left to the **Sayil** ruins (5 km.), **Xlapak** (about 13 km.) and **Labná** (about 22 km.). The palace at Sayil (admission US$0.40) is a good 2 hrs.' walk from the main site. Labná has a most astonishing arch. Both Sayil and Labná are in low, shrubby bush country. From Labná, continue to immense galleries and caves of Bolonchen (bus from Mérida). You *must* take a guide and a powerful torch. If visiting Sayil, Xlapak and Labná, you can take a taxi from the village of Santa Elena at the turn-off (no hotels or restaurants), costing US$20 for 1-3 persons. By hire-car one can continue to Oxcutzcab (see below).

One can arrange to visit Kabah (20 mins.), Sayil (30 mins.), Xlapak (10 mins.) and Labná (30 mins.) with the J. González company Calle 59, No. 476, Mérida (T 10197, 19710, 10865), VW buses, daily round trip at 0900, US$13-20 (admission not included) including Uxmal (90 mins.), often price includes meal and sometimes *son et lumière*. Very tiring, especially since Uxmal last, but soft drinks available at sites. Entry cheaper on Sun. and holidays. Book preferably a day in advance. The ruins of Labná, Xlapak, Sayil, Kabah and Uxmal can now be reached by 2nd class bus from Mérida, 0800-1500, US$7 for the trip (tickets from inside bus terminal). One can connect with the 2nd class bus tours from Mérida from Campeche if one takes the 0600 bus to Kabah. Guided tours from Mérida US$11-13.

Recommended reading for the area: *The Maya*, by M. D. Coe (Pelican Books).

The road from Mérida (and also from Uxmal) to Chetumal is through Muna, *Ticul* (where pottery, hats and shoes are made; *Los Almendros* restaurant, opp. Cinema Ideal, rec.), *Peto* (best avoided, via Tzucacab-Santa Rosa bypass, no restaurant) and Felipe Carrillo Puerto. Between Ticul and Peto is **Oxcutzcab**, with a hotel, F, at W end of town, opp. Pemex station, clean, fan, a little run-down. No beds, hammocks provided, clean, quiet rooms with bath. Also *Hotel Bermujo*, by Pemex station on road to Muna, 4-5 blocks from bus station, F, some a/c, fans, good. Nearby, to the S, are the fantastic caverns and precolumbian vestiges at *Loltún* (supposedly extending for 8 km.). Caves are open Tues.-Sun., admission at 0930, 1130, 1330 and 1500 (US$0.25). Caretaker may admit tours on Mon., but no lighting. Take pickup or truck from the market going to Cooperativa (an agricultural town). For return, flag down a passing truck. Alternatively, take a taxi. Oxcutzcab is a good centre for catching buses to Chetumal, Muna, Mayapán and Mérida. It has a lot of character with a large market on the side of the Plaza and a church with a "two-dimensional" façade on the other side of the square. The area around Ticul and Oxcutzcab is intensively farmed with citrus fruits, papayas and mangos. Between Oxcutzcab and Peto is Tekax with restaurant *La Ermita* serving excellent Yucateca dishes at reasonable prices. From Tekax an unpaved but perfectly acceptable road leads to the ruins of Chacmultun. From the top one enjoys a beautiful view; there is a caretaker. All the towns between Muna and Peto have large old churches. Beyond Peto the scenery is scrub and swamp as far as the Belizean frontier.

Mayapán is a large, peaceful late Mayan site easily visited by bus from Mérida or from

Oxcutzcab, beware of snakes at site; also two large pyramids in village of Acanceh en route. Before Acanceh, on the road to Mayapán, is a restaurant at Kanasin, *La Susana*, to which there are frequent buses. It is known especially for local delicacies like *sopa de lima, salbutes* and *panuchos*. Clean, excellent service and abundant helpings at reasonable prices. Between Acanceh and Mayapán is Tecóh, with the caverns of Dzab-Náh; you must take a guide as there are treacherous drops into *cenotes*.

Chichén-Itzá is 120 km. by a paved road running SE from Mérida. The scrub forest has been cleared from over 5 square km. of ruins. The city was founded in 432, and taken over by the Toltecs in the 10th century; the major buildings in the N half are Toltec. Dominating them is El Castillo, its top decorated by the symbol of Quetzalcoatl, and the balustrade of the 91 stairs up each of the four sides is decorated by a plumed, open-mouthed serpent. There is also an interior ascent to a chamber lit by electricity where the red-painted jaguar which probably served as the throne of the high priest burns bright, its eyes of jade, its fangs of flint (see below for entry times). There is a ball court with grandstand and towering walls each set with a projecting ring of stone high up; at eye-level is a relief showing the decapitation—death was the penalty for defeat—of the losing captain (wall paintings in the temple at the ball court are open 1500-1600, US$0.25, luggage store at entrance). El Castillo stands at the centre of the northern half of the site, and almost at right-angles to its northern face runs the sacred way to the Cenote Sagrado, the Well of Sacrifice. The other *cenote*, the Xtoloc Well, was probably used as a water supply. It requires at least one day to see the many pyramids, temples, ballcourts and palaces, all of them adorned with astonishing sculptures, and excavation and renovation is still going on. Old Chichén, where the Mayan buildings of the earlier city are found, lies about ½ km. by path from the main clearing. The famous observatory (the only one known among the Maya ruins) is included in this group as is the Nunnery. A footpath to the right of the Nunnery takes one to the House of the Three Lintels after ½ hr. walking. Entry to Chichén-Itzá, 0800-1700, US$1.50 (free Sun. and holidays); check at entrance for opening times of the various buildings. Best to arrive before 1030 when the mass of tourists arrives. Entry to see the jaguar in the substructure of El Castillo along an inside staircase at 1130-1300, 1400-1500 and 1600-1700. Try to be among the first in as it is stuffy inside and queues form at busy times. Entry to Cámara de los Tigres at 1000-1100 and 1500-1600. Drinks and snacks available at entrance, also guidebooks, clean toilets. Also toilets on the way to old Chichén, and a drinks terrace with film supplies. The badly translated guide-book of José Díaz Bolio provides useful background comment; the little Bloomgarden booklet is also interesting. The Catholic church has walls built on a boulder and older foundations, and incorporates old Mayan stones, some with carvings (step to the side door); there are even two serpents over one of the doors. *Son et lumière* (US$0.50) at Chichén every evening, in Spanish at 1900, and then in English at 2100; said to be less good than at Uxmal. A tourist centre has been built at the entrance to the ruins; luggage deposit US$0.20.

Into the Cenote Sagrado were thrown valuable propitiatory objects of all kinds, animals and human sacrifices. The well was first dredged by Edward H. Thompson, the U.S. Consul in Mérida, between 1904 and 1907; he accumulated a vast quantity of objects in pottery, jade, copper and gold. In 1962 the well was explored again by an expedition sponsored by the National Geographical Society and some 4,000 further artefacts were recovered, including beads, polished jade, lumps of copal resin, small bells, a statuette of rubber latex, another of wood, and a quantity of animal and human bones. The bottom of the well is paved with the ruins of a fallen temple. There are several tours daily to the Balancanchén caves, 3 km. E, just off the highway (caretaker turns lights on and off, answers questions in Spanish); minimum 3, maximum 15 persons. Worth the trip: there are archaeological objects, including offerings of pots and *metates* in a unique setting, except for the unavoidable *son et lumière* show; it is very damp and you may have to go through narrow openings, so dress accordingly. Not for claustrophobics. Open 0900-1100 and 1400-1600 on the hour, US$2, free Sun. (allow about ½ hr. for the 300-metre descent), closed Sat. and Sun. afternoons.

Hotels All are expensive for what they offer. The only two hotels close to the ruins are *Hacienda Chichén*, A, once owned by Edward Thompson with charming bungalows; *Villas Arqueológicas*, B, 1st class, pool, tennis, poor value. Both are on the other side of the fenced-off ruins from the bus stop; rather than walk through ruins take taxi (US$1-1.50). Others are further away: *Mayaland Hotel*, A, incl. breakfast and dinner, pool, but sometimes no water in it, no a/c, just noisy ceiling fans, but good service and friendly; *Pirámide Inn*, B, with food, swimming pool, US satellite TV, well run; also *Pirámide Inn Trailer Court* (closed for repairs late 1987), 1½ km. from ruins, camping, book swapping facility at desk, clean toilets and showers, lots of trees for hammock hanging (US$2 p.p. per night) and grass space for small tents, electricity and water outlets, US$1.30 p.p., noisy because close to main road, allows use of *Pirámide Inn* swimming pool, watch out for snakes and tarantulas; *Lapalapa Chichén*, B, with breakfast and dinner, a few km. from the ruins, excellent restaurant, modern, park with animals; *Dolores Alba*, small hotel (same family as in Mérida), 2½ km. on the road to Puerto Juárez (bus passes it), good and comfortable, D, with shower; has swimming pool and serves good, expensive meals, English spoken.

Other hotels at **Pisté** about 2 km. before the ruins if coming from Mérida (taxi to ruins US$1.20): *Posada Novelo*, E, near *Pirámide Inn*, run by José Novelo who speaks English, restaurants nearby, not very good value, sanitation in poor condition. *Hotel Cunanchén*, on Plaza, prices negotiable with owner, not rec.; ask to see private *cenote*. *Posada del Paso*, E with shower.

There is a small pyramid in village opp. the *Hotel Misión Chichén Itzá*, A, not easily seen from the road; it has staircases with plumed serpents and a big statue facing N on top; close by is a huge plumed serpent, part coloured, almost forming a circle at least 20 metres long. There is no sign or public path, climb over gate into scrubland, the serpent will be to right, pyramid to left (a traveller believes these to be the remains of a hotel built by a French concern in the 1940s—further reports please!). Bank in Pisté, Banamex. Bus Pisté-Valladolid US$1.40.

Restaurants Mostly poor and overpriced in Chichén itself. *Hotel Restaurant Carrousel* (rooms E); cheap meals at *Las Redes*.

Shopping Hammocks are sold by Mario Díaz (a most interesting character), excellent quality, huge, at his house ½ km. up the road forking to the left at the centre of the village. A few km. from Chichén is Ebtún, on the road to Valladolid. A sign says "Hammock sales and repairs": it is actually a small prison which turns out 1st class cotton or nylon hammocks—haggle with wardens and prisoners; there are no real bargains, but good quality.

Transport If driving from Mérida, follow Calle 65 (off the Plaza) out as far as the dirt section, where you turn left, then right and right again at the main road, follow until hypermarket on left and make a left turn at the sign for Chichén-Itzá.

Chichén-Itzá is easily reached (but less easily during holiday periods) from Mérida by 1st (ADO) and hourly 2nd class buses (US$2 one way), about 1½ or 3 hours' journey; buses now take you direct to the ruins. Tours by 1st-class bus (0800, bus returns 1600) charge about US$3.75 (take 0600 bus to avoid the crowds; no 1st class buses Sat. or Sun.). You can often also negotiate a fare with some of the VW buses that park in the lay-bys off the main road opp. the site entrance. 10 buses a day go to Cancún and Puerto Juárez, last at 1700, US$3.30. The first bus from Pisté to Puerto Juárez is at 0730, 3 hrs. Budget travellers going on from Mérida to Isla Mujeres or Cozumel should visit Chichén from Valladolid (see below). Buses from Valladolid go every hour to the site and you can return by standing on the road at the ruins and flagging down any bus going straight through. Bus Pisté—Tulum, US$3.

On the way back, turn to the right at Kantunil (68 km. from Mérida) for a short excursion to the charming little town of **Izamal** (basic hotel on one of the two main squares, and a restaurant next door), to see the ruins of a great mausoleum known as Kinich-Kakmo pyramid, right at the centre of Izamal, with an excellent view of the town and surrounding *henequén* plantations from the top; a huge old convent, and the magnificent early Franciscan church, built on the ruins of a Mayan pyramid (1553). This church was founded by Fray Diego de Landa, the historian of the Spanish conquest of Mérida.

Train Mérida-Izamal leaves at 0600, returns 1500, US$0.30.

From Izamal one can go by the 1630 bus to **Cenotillo**, where there are several fine *cenotes* within easy walking distance from the town (avoid the one *in* town), especially Ucil, excellent for swimming, and La Unión. From Mérida, take 1530 train to Tunkas, and then bus to Cenotillo. Lovely train ride, US$0.20. Past Cenotillo is Espita and then a road forks left to Tizimín (see below). Take a bus from Mérida (last bus back 1700) to see extensive ruins at Aké, unique structure.

Beyond Chichén-Itzá, and easily reached from Mérida (bus, US$1.80) is **Valladolid** (pop. 37,000), a pleasant Mayan town with another large Franciscan church, on the paved road between Mérida and Puerto Juárez.

Hotels *María de la Luz*, Plaza Principal, T 6-20-71, good, swimming pool (non-residents, US$0.50) and small night-club, poor restaurant, closes at 2230, D; *San Clemente*, Calle 41 and

42 No. 206 (T 62208), D, with air conditioning, has car park, swimming pool, opposite Cathedral, in centre of town. *Mesón del Marqués*, C (air-conditioned), with bath, on square, with good restaurant and shop (helpful for information), excellent value. *Oso Río*, on W side of Plaza, 2 blocks N, small, clean, friendly, E; quiet and excellent is *María Guadalupe*, Calle 44, No. 198, E, with hot water, but uncertain water supply. *Lili*, Calle 44, E, hot shower, fan, basic, safe motorcycle parking, friendly, some G rooms for hammock-slinging; *Don Luis*, Calle 39, (same street as bus station) 1 block E of 26 Calo, quiet, friendly, pool, a/c, D, mosquitoes; *Mendoza*, Calle 39, No. 204C, good, clean, near bus station, E. *Alcócer*, E, with bath if you bargain, fairly clean. *Zaci*, Calle 44, D (E with fan rather than a/c), good. In *Mesón de Caminante*, 6 blocks W from bus station, hammocks US$0.80 a night, "noisy flophouse". **Restaurant** *Los Arcos*, near plaza, set lunch US$1.20; *Los Portales* on main square, very good, try local drink xtabentún. Places serving comida on N side of Plaza.

Post Office   Calle 46, almost opp. bus terminal, 1½ blocks S from square on E side (does not accept parcels for abroad); telegraph office 1½ blocks S on W side of same block.

Bank   Bancomer on E side of square (to the right of church).

Buses   To Chichén-Itzá, take Mérida bus, US$0.80, every ½ hr., 1 hr. ride (taxi US$10), also to Balancanchén caves; many buses go to Mérida, US$2.45; and to Puerto Juárez, US$2.45, from 0800 and Cancún, US$2.45. To Playa del Carmen at 0430 and 1300 (via Cobá and crossing 1 km. from Tulum) US$3; fare to Tulum, US$1.30, 2½ hrs.; to Chetumal, at 0600, 1500 and 2000, 2nd class US$5.30, 5 hrs. Many buses to Mérida. Taxi to Puerto Juárez (160 km.), US$31.10, takes seven passengers. N.B. beware of harassment by beggars at the bus station.

One can swim in the very clean electrically-lit *cenote* of Dzit-Nup (entry US$0.30, open until 1800, taxi, return plus wait, US$3 from Valladolid) outside Valladolid. Also lovely *cenote* at Zací, with a restaurant and lighted promenades, 2 blocks N of *Hotel Don Luis*, but you cannot swim in it because of the algae. Road turns left from Puerto Juárez road a couple of blocks from main plaza.

A paved road heads N (buses) from Valladolid to *Tizimín*, a very pleasant town with a 16th-century church and convent, open squares and narrow streets, and a few hotels, E and F; it has a famous New Year *fiesta*. There is a good restaurant, *Tres Reyes*. There is also a local *cenote*, Kikib. The road continues N over the flat landscape to *Río Lagartos*, itself on a lagoon, where the Mayas extracted salt. (*Hotel Nefertiti*, E, hot shower, also room for hammocks upstairs, fish restaurant.) There are a number of small eating-places. Swimming from island opposite Río Lagartos, where boats are moored. Bus from Río Lagartos to *San Felipe* (13 km.), can bathe in the sea; good cheap seafood at El Payaso restaurant. On a small island with ruins of a Maya pyramid, beware of rattlesnakes. One can also go from Río Lagartos to *Los Colorados* (15 km.) to swim and see the salt deposits with red, lilac and pink water. Boat trips (US$12, expensive, bargain the price before embarking) can be arranged in Río Lagartos to see the flamingoes (often only a few pairs, but apparently thousands in July) feeding in the lagoons E of Los Colorados. Not a lot else here, but if you are stuck for food, eat inexpensively at the *Casino* (ask locals). Road on to El Cuyo, rough and sandy, but passable. El Cuyo has a shark-fishing harbour. Fishermen cannot sell (co-op) but can barter fish—fry your shark steak with garlic, onions and lime juice.

Also N of Valladolid, turning off the road to Puerto Juárez after Xcan, is *Holbox* Island. Buses to Chiquilá for boats, 3 times a day. If you miss the ferry a fisherman will probably take you quite cheaply (say US$2). You can leave your car in care of the harbour master for a small charge; his house is E of the dock. Take water with you if possible. Totally unspoiled, take blankets and hammock (ask at fishermen's houses where you can put up), and lots of mosquito repellant. Best camping on beach E of village (N side of island). Fish expensive but bread very good. Wonderful shell-hunting. Five more uninhabited islands beyond Holbox. Beware of sharks and barracuda, though few nasty occurrences have been reported. Off the rough and mostly unpopulated bulge of the Yucatán coastline are several islands, once notorious for contraband. Beware of mosquitoes in the area.

N.B. The E coast of the Yucatán peninsula suffered damage from Hurricane Gilbert in September 1988.

The famous resort of *Cancún*, near the north-eastern tip of the Yucatán peninsula, is a thriving complex and town with skyscraper hotels, basically for the rich, and many smaller hotels with cheaper accommodation. Prices are higher on Cancún than elsewhere in Mexico because everything is brought in from miles outside. Hotels in Cancún town (or in Puerto Juárez, just 3 km. away) are much cheaper than on the beach and there are buses running every 5 minutes for US$0.05. The population is about 30,000, almost all dedicated to servicing the tourist industry. There is an archaeological museum next to the Convention Centre with local finds, which also houses the Ballet Folklórico shows in air-conditioned splendour. There are 3 supermarkets (one of them, Bodega El Teniente on Av. Tulum, is good place for changing US dollar cash or cheques) and 5 interconnecting shopping malls. Excursion to Isla Contoy daily, once a day,

US$55, including boat, food and snorkelling equipment. The computer which is said to have selected the site seems to have failed in two respects: (a) there are sharks; (b) there are undercurrents. So swimming in the sea is discouraged on several beaches. See free publication, *Cancún Tips*, issued twice a year from Av. Tulum 29, Cancún, QR 77500, Mexico.

Hotels *Camino Real; Sheraton, Exalaris Hyatt, Cancún Caribe* and *Exalaris Hyatt Regency; Fiesta Americana* and *Krystal.* Slightly less expensive: *Aristos, Quality Inn, Club Lagoon Caribe, Viva* (B), *El Presidente* (L), *Miramar Mansion.* Less expensive still: *Caribe Mar* and *Playa Blanca. Novotel,* near bus station, B and up, a/c, pool, rooms on street noisy, but other apartments quiet, clean, secure, cheapest good place. At the far end of the island is the *Club Méditerranée* with its customary facilities. Youth hostel, CREA, Km. 3.2 Blvd Zona Hotelera, T 31337, on the beach, dormitory style, 12 people per room, E p.p. (also possible to put up tent for US$2.50). Hotels in Cancún town: *América, Atlantis, Reifa;* slightly less expensive: *Antillano, Batalo, Carillo, Colonial, Handall, Konvasser* (a Mayan, not German name), *María de Lourdes, Parador, Plaza Caribe, Plaza del Sol, Rivemar, Caribe Internacional, Soberanis, Tulum, Villa Maya,* all C/D. Least expensive but acceptable still: *Arabe, Bonampak, Canto, Coral, Mar y Mar, Marufo, Villa Rossana, Yaxchilán,* and *La Carreta Guest House.* You'll be lucky to find anything below category E.

Camping is not permitted in Cancún town except next to the CREA youth hostel. It is otherwise restricted to a magnificent stretch of beach just past Puerto Juárez.

Restaurants There are about 200 restaurants apart from those connected with hotels. They range from hamburger stands to 5-star, gourmet places. The best buys are on the side streets of Cancún town, while the largest selection can be found on the main street, Av. Tulum. The best is said to be *100% Natural,* in front of *Hotel Caribe Internacional* on Yaxchilán; *Valladolid,* on Uxmal, is reasonable. The ones on the island are of slightly higher price and quality and are scattered along Blvd. Kukulkan, the main island drive, with a high concentration in the 5 shopping centres. The native Mexican restaurants in the workers' colonies are cheapest. Very popular is *El Establo* with *El Granero* disco, just off Av. Tulum on Claveles.

Buses Local bus (Route No. 1), US$0.10 (taxis are exorbitant). Buses along the beach front are crowded with pickpockets. Within easy reach are Chichén-Itzá (bus, 3½ hrs., US$2.75), Tulum, and many lesser known Maya centres such as Cobá and Tablé. The road to Tulum is completely paved. Local bus to Puerto Juárez US$0.25, hourly between 0600-2300. To Chetumal, US$6.45 1st class, 0800-1600 hourly, takes 5 hrs. To Tulum US$1.65, 4 daily 1st class, 5 daily 2nd class, walk 1 km. from bus stop. To Valladolid, US$2.45 1st, US$2 2nd class; To Mexico City, ADO, 1st class at 0615, 1215 and 1815. To Mérida, US$4.40 1st, US$4 2nd class, 4½ hrs.

Puerto Morelos (bus US$0.50), not far S of Cancún. It has 3 hotels, two expensive, one basic, *Amor,* E, near bus stop; also free and paying camping. Popular with scuba divers and snorkellers, but beware of sharks.

Boat Services See Cozumel, below; expensive boats leave from the pier near *Calinda Quality Inn* in Cancún; go instead to Puerto Juárez.

Car Hire Budget Rent-a-Car in Cancún has been rec. for good service.

Air Services Cancún (very expensive shops and restaurant), Cozumel and Isla Mujeres have airports. Aeroméxico, Av. Tulum 3, T 42758; Mexicana, Av. Cobá 13, T 41090; American Airlines, Aeropuerto, T 42947; United Airlines, Centro El Pavaín, T 42340. Mexicana has direct flights Mexico City-Cancún-Miami; also daily flights Mexico City-Cancún-Mérida. From Cancún to Mérida, Monterrey, Mexico City, Houston, Los Angeles, and New York, by Aeroméxico. Flights to Mexico City are heavily booked; try stand-by at the airport, or go instead to Mérida. Aero Quetzal to Guatemala City Mon. and Fri. night (book well in advance, office in Mexico City—can also book this company's Guatemala City-Flores flights here). Lacsa flies Cancún-Costa Rica and on to Panama. Bookable only at *Hotel María de Lourdes,* closed during siesta-time. Nouvelles Frontières fly charter Zürich-Cancún, 66 Blvd. St. Michel, 75000 Paris, France. Many charters from North America. Flight Cozumel-Mexico City via Mérida with Mexicana. Taxi-buses from airport to Cancún town US$2. Irregular bus from Cancún to the airport four times a day. Ordinary taxi US$4.50-5.75.

Puerto Juárez is about 3 km. N of Cancún. *Hotel Caribel,* resort complex, D with bath and fan; *Posada Zuemy,* 100 metres from bus terminal, on road to Cancún, E; another unsigned hotel a bit further along this road, E; *Hotel Los Faroles,* E, with bath, small, hot cabins less good; opp. is *Hotel Jannette,* D, dearer, and better; *Palmeras* is F. *Restaurant Puerto Juárez* at bus terminal, friendly, good value. Camping/trailer park *Almirante de Gante,* hot showers, right on the beach, 4 km. from army camp and 1 km. from Punta Sam. *Cabañas Punta Sam,* clean, comfortable, on the beach, E with bath. Irregular bus service there, or hitchhike from Puerto Juárez. Check to see if restaurant is open evenings. No shops nearby. Take mosquito repellant.

Ferries Tourist kiosk, open 0900-1700, at passenger ferry to Isla Mujeres which leaves from the jetty opposite the bus terminal at Puerto Juárez twelve times a day (at same time each way); can be erratic and sometimes leaves early (US$0.75, 1 hr.). Also small boats, US$0.45. Ferry from Punta Sam to Isla Mujeres, which takes cars (about 75), 5 km. by bus from Cancún via Puerto Juárez (facilities to store luggage), US$0.25; six times a day between 0830 and 2300, returning between 0715 and 2200 (45-min. journey). For early morning ferry from Isla Mujeres, tickets sold anytime from about 0615. Get there early as it is popular. The bus from Mérida (US$4) stops at the ferry and there are hourly buses from Puerto Juárez from 0500. The boat trip across is US$2.20 for car, US$4.45 for trailer, US$0.22 p.p.

Buses go from Puerto Juárez and Cancún to Tulum (see page 1106), Felipe Carrillo Puerto and Chetumal. Bus to Chetumal, 1st class US$7, 2nd class, US$4.80, 5 a day, 6 hrs. To Palenque 2nd class, US$4. To Chichén Itzá, 2nd class, 4 hrs., US$3.30. To Cancún US$0.25. All regular buses from Puerto Juárez stop at Tulum, US$2, 2 hrs. If driving from Puerto Juárez to Tulum, turn right by the Pemex station on to Route 307—it is badly signposted. On the whole it is better to catch outgoing buses in Cancún rather than in Puerto Juárez: there are more of them. You can travel to Emiliano Zapata (40 km. from Palenque) or Villahermosa in a day, taking a launch from Isla Mujeres at 0630, take 0800 bus from Cancún to Chetumal, take 1300 bus from Chetumal to Villahermosa (or later bus at 1430 to Tuxtla Gutiérrez) reach Emiliano Zapata at 1900, good hotels and restaurants; 2nd class buses hourly from E. Zapata to Plaza, at the crossing of the Palenque and Chetumal road.

Isla Mujeres (which got its name from the large number of female idols first found by the Spaniards) once epitomized the Caribbean island: long silver beaches (beware sandflies), palm trees and clean blue water at the N end (although the large *El Presidente* hotel spoils the view there) away from the beach pollution of the town, and the naval airstrip to the SW of the town. There are limestone (coral) cliffs and a rocky coast at the S end. A lagoon on the W side is now fouled up. The island is suffering from competition from Cancún and many hotels are now looking rather run-down. The main activity in the evening takes place in the square near the church, where there are also a supermarket and a cinema. Between December 1-8 there is a fiesta for the Virgin of the island, fireworks, dances until 0400 in the Plaza. If driving, respect speed limits, roads with new gravelling are tricky. The Civil Guard patrol the beaches at night.

There is public transport on Isla Mujeres, i.e. taxis at fixed prices, e.g. US$1.20 to N beach, and US$0.10 bus service. You can walk from one end of the island to the other in 2½ hrs. Worth hiring a bicycle (wonderfully rickety), by the hour, US$0.35, or US$ 2.50 a day (about US$7 deposit), or a Honda 50 hourly or for a day (US$15), to explore the island in about 2 hrs. Do check if there is any damage to the bicycle *before* you hire. Bicycles for hire from several hotels. Try Ciro's Motorrentor by *Hotel Caribe.* You can rent skin and scuba diving equipment, together with guide, from Divers of Mexico, on the waterfront N of the public pier. They can set up group excursions to the Cave of the Sleeping Sharks; English spoken. It is no cheaper to hire snorkel gear in town than on the beach. Deep sea fishing US$89 for 10 in a boat from *Aguamundo.* Diving is not in the class of Cozumel and Mexico Divers, with slapdash attitude to safety, not recommended.

At Garrafón beach, 7 km. (mind your belongings, entry US$0.75) there is a tropical fish reserve (fishing forbidden) on a small coral reef. Take snorkel (rental US$3 a day from shop opp. the ferry or outside entry to Park (need tourist card for security), but US$2 an hour at Park gate and US$0.75 for locker at Garrafón where drinks are twice the price of those in town) and swim among a variety of multicoloured tropical fish—they aren't at all shy. At peak times, however, there can be more snorkellers than fish. Worth walking on from here up a track to the lighthouse. (Taxi to Garrafón US$2.75; there is a bus which goes half-way there.) One can cycle down to the southern end of the island to the curious remains of a pirate's domain, called Casa de Mundaca, a nature reserve with giant turtles at El Chequero, and a little Mayan lighthouse or shrine of Ixtel. It is not signposted—mind you don't walk into the army firing range. Fine views. The island is best visited April to November, off-season (although one can holiday here the year round). It is best to go before 1000. The northern beach has dazzling white sand, so wear sunglasses. **N.B.** Travellers are warned that there is a very dangerous beach on the ocean side near the north with strong undertows and cross-currents; there have been numerous drownings. It is just behind the *Bojórquez Hotel.* Trip to unspoilt Isla Contoy (bird and wildlife sanctuary), US$15, two hours of fishing, snorkelling (equipment hire extra, US$2.50) and relaxing (see also under Cancún). Boats may not leave until full. An experienced diver, Erik Bernesson of Vaxtorp, Sweden, tells us that the underwater scene at Garrafón is much less interesting, and scuba diving more expensive, than at Cozumel or the Laguna Xelhá; Belize, he says, is even better.

Hotels At Christmas hotel prices are increased steeply and the island can heave with tourists, esp. in January. The island has several costly hotels and others, mainly in the D category, and food is generally expensive.

Reasonable hotels to stay at on Isla Mujeres are *Osorio*, E, Medero, 1 block from waterfront, clean, fan, with bath and hot water, rec., excellent bakery nearby. *El Presidente Caribe*, private lagoon, spectacular (changes travellers' cheques), very fancy, L; *Caribe Maya*, Madero 9, central, modern, fans, D; *Carmelina*, Guerrero 9, E, central with bath, rec.; *El Paso*, Morelos 13, D, with bath, clean, facing the pier, 2nd floor; *Posada San Luis*, E, with bath, good, 1 block to ocean side of island in coconut plantation, 4 bungalows; *Xul-Ha*, Hidalgo Norte 33, 1 block to N beach, baths, D, some rooms E, clean and friendly; *Caracol*, E, central, clean, good value; *Rocamar*, C, Nicolás Bravo y Guerrero, Caribbean side, restaurant, sea views, thunderous wave noise (especially at night), clean but overpriced; *Posada del Mar*, Alte. Rueda 15, B (including meals) has pleasant drinks terrace but expensive drinks, restaurant for residents only; *Rocas del Caribe*, Madero 2, D, 100 metres from ocean, cool rooms, big balcony, clean, good service; *Isla Mujeres*, next to church, C/D, with bath, renovated, run by pleasant Englishman; *Berny*, Juárez y Abosolo, C, with bath, good, long-distance calls possible, residents only, but does not even honour confirmed reservations if a deposit for one night's stay has not been made. *Las Palmas*, E, central, Guerrero 20, 1 block from N beach, good, clean. Scrum for a cheap place after the arrival of the morning ferry. There is a trailer park on the island, with a restaurant. At S end of island is *Camping Los Indios* where you can put up your hammock. In town nobody seems to know (or want to know) about this place. **N.B.** If you arrive late, book into any hotel the first night and set out to find what you want by 0700-0800, when the first ferries leave the next morning.

Restaurants Many beach restaurants close just before sunset. *Ciro's*, good, but beware of overcharging; *Caracol*, also good, slightly cheaper; *Super Tortas*, delicious sandwiches served by young Jenny. *Villa del Mar*, rec., delicious but expensive. *Miriti*, opp. ferry, quite good value: *Rolandi's Pizza*, main shopping street, good. At Garrafón Beach: *El Garrafón, El Garrafón de Castilla*, *French Marías*, all 3 cater for tour boats from Cancún, pricey lobster on magnificent tropical beach. *Gomar*, in town, expensive, possible to eat outside on verandah or in the colonial-style interior, popular; *Mano de Dios*, near *Gomar*, probably cheapest on island, quite good. *Eric's*, 1 block inland, very good inexpensive Mexican snacks; *Tropicana*, 1 block from pier, simple, popular, cheap; *Cielito Lindo*, waterfront, open air, good service; *La Langosta*, 3 blocks S, good Mexican dishes, lovely view; *Bucanero*, downtown, steak, seafood, prime rib, classy for Islas Mujeres. *Sergio's* on main square, expensive, very good. *Dhaymeru*, inexpensive, good lentil soup; *Giltri*, in town, good value. Small restaurants round market are good value; try the local Poc-Chuc (pork and vegetables) dish.

Opposite the restaurant *Gomar* is a souvenir shop that sells good stone Maya carvings (copies), macramé hangings and colourful wax crayon "Maya" prints. *El Paso Boutique*, opp. ferry, trades a small selection of English novels.

Paamul, about 90 km. S of Cancún, is a fine beach with chalets and campsites (recommended) on a bay, with good restaurant. Good snorkelling and diving. 2nd-class buses from Cancún and Playa del Carmen pass.

Playa del Carmen is a fast growing tourist centre, with pleasant beaches (though there is litter, there are no sandflies) and many new hotels (but no camping) and restaurants. Apparently old atmosphere has now been lost. It is 68 km. or one hour by bus from Tulum (US$1), but also buses from Mérida, Cancún (US$1, 1 hr.) and Puerto Juárez. From Mérida 1st class buses go via Cancún, 4 a day (co-ordinate with ferry to Cozumel), 2nd class buses 7 a day, 6 hrs. Campsite.

Hotels N of the town is *Blue Parrot*, on beach, B, in bungalow, highly rec. About 6 km. outside are: At km. 297/8, before Playa del Carmen, *Cabañas Capitán Lafitte*, very good, pool, on barren beach, A; at km. 296 and similar, *El Marlín Azul*, A, swimming pool, better food; *Posada Lily*, E, with shower, rec., 1 block from first class bus station; *Hotel Nuevo Amanecer*, B, very attractive, fans, mosquito nets, clean; *Yax-Ha* cabins, Calle 10 Norte, C-A (depending on size and season), excellent. *Sian Ka'an*, Calle Siyan Can, 100 m. from bus station, D, simple, clean, rec. By the T-junction on the outskirts, at Route 307, is reasonable *Hotel Maranatha*, with café next door for breakfast and *Doña Juanita's* restaurant (good, opp. Pemex station). Campsite and *cabañas* close to bus station, US$3-4 per tent, US$2 for hammocks, cabins F p.p. "The Monastery°, 1 block from *Cabaña Banana*, E, free use of kitchen and washing facilities, English spoken, not fancy, but good. *Cabañas La Ruina*, on beach, F, popular, rec. Lots of new places going up, none under US$10 a night. 8 km. from Playa del Carmen you can camp at Xcalacoco for US$2.50 a night (US$15 for cabins). CREA Youth Hostel.

Restaurants *La Nena* and *Pizza Moluscas* (expensive, good service); *Balam*, good breakfasts; *Chac Mool*, good, reasonable, near airstrip. *Máscaras*, on beach, highly rec. *Chateau Las Palmas*, across from school, good, especially breakfast. *El Capitán*, north end, good for fish.

Transport Ferry for Cozumel, US$2.20, 25 mins. journey, 7 a day from 0530-1930, returns between 0400 and 1800. There is also a slower ferry (45-50 minutes). Bus to Tulum and Chetumal

(3½ hrs.), US$4.50 (several between 0530 and 2030); to Villahermosa (coming from Cancún) 1900, 13 hrs. US$10, ADO, seats can be booked in advance.

Cozumel island is not only a marvellous place for snorkelling and scuba diving, but is described as a "jewel of nature, possessing much endemic wildlife including pygmy species of coati and raccoon; the bird life has a distinctly Caribbean aspect and many endemic forms also" - Jeffrey L. White, Tucson, Ariz. A good map, including reef locations, is available from stores and shops. In the shops, dollars are preferred to pesos.

Hotels (prices rise 50% around Christmas) *Maya Cozumel*, clean, friendly, pool, on Calle 7 Sur 4, C; *Aguilar*, 3 Sur 98, C, pool, clean, central, a/c, rec.; *Apartamentos Aguilar*, Calle 10, C, good value; *López*, Calle Sur 7-A, C, hot showers, clean, main square, no meals; *Capitán Candela*, inland, pool, good value, D. The cheapest hotels on the island, all D, are: *Yoli*, Calle 1 Sur 164 close to the Plaza, with bath and fan; *Posada Edén*, Calle 2 Norte, 2 blocks (one N, one E) from Plaza; *Flores*, Adolfo Rosado Salas 7, one block S of Plaza, ½ block E of waterfront, a little more expensive. First class (A-L) hotels include: *Cabañas del Caribe, Cozumel Caribe, El Cozumeleño, El Presidente, La Ceiba, Mayan Plaza*. The first-class hotels on the island charge about US$50-110 d a day and all are directly on the rocky shore except the *Fiesta Americana*, which has a tunnel under the road to the beach. The best public beaches are some way from San Miguel town: in the N of the island they are sandy and wide, in the S narrower and rockier. All the main hotels are on the sheltered W coast. The E coast is rockier and has only one, rustic *Hotel Cupido*, more like bungalows. Swimming and diving on the unprotected side is very dangerous owing to ocean underflows. Camping is not permitted although there are two suitable sites on the S shore. Try asking for permission at the army base.

Restaurants *Las Palmeras*, at the pier (people-watching spot), rec.; *Pizza Rolandi*, waterfront; *Grip's*, waterfront, good; *Morgans*, main square, elegant; *Plaza Leza*, main square, excellent and reasonable; *Café del Puerto*, 2nd floor by pier, South Seas style; *Super Tortas Los Moros*, Av. Juárez and 10 Av. Norte, Mexican, popular; *Costa Brava*, good sea-food and breakfast, good value, rec. *Carlos and Charlie's* restaurant/bar, popular, 2nd floor on waterfront. *Tortas Denny*, Calle 1 Sur close to Plaza, good and reasonable; *Económico*, 10 Av. Norte between Calle 1 Sur and Calle Salas, friendly, good Mexican food.

Nightclubs *Joman's, Scaramouche, Grip's*, all downtown, as well as hotel nightclubs.

Paved road on Cozumel but bus service serves only the expensive hotels N of town; best to hire push-bike (quiet) when touring around the island so one can see wildlife—iguanas, turtles, birds—but if taking motorbike (Rentadora Cozumel not recommended) beware of policemen who take unguarded ones and then claim they were parked illegally; local police are strict and keen on fining so avoid illegal parking, U-turns, etc. The island is famous for the beauty of its underwater environment: snorkel 9 km. S of San Miguel de Cozumel at Parque Chankanaab, with restaurants and hire facilities: equipment US$4 a day. The best reef for scuba-diving is Palacar, reached only by boat. Deportes Acuáticos Damián Piza on Calle 8 Norte, US$40 p.p. includes all equipment, 2 dives with diligent guide separated by a cooked lunch and sunbake on Playa San Francisco—fascinating. There are many diving agencies (Cozumel Divers recommended); the level of charging may vary between US$10 and US$40 a dive, including equipment. Restored ruins of Maya-Toltec period at San Gervasio (7 km. from Cozumel town, then 6 km. to the left).

There are some Mayan ruins on the mainland, unrestored (the Pole ruins) at *Xcaret*, a turnoff left on Route 307 to Tulum, after Playa del Carmen. You can go to a hand-forged chain over a 2 km. bad road and pay whoever comes out of the house an entry fee and proceed down the road a few metres on foot. The ruins are near three linked *cenotes*, to their left; there are also lovely sea water lagoons—one can swim. Pole was the departure point for Mayan voyages to Cozumel. There is a roadside restaurant which despite its looks is very clean (accepts Visa).

Akumal, a luxury resort, is 20 km. N of Tulum, and reached easily by bus from there or from Playa del Carmen (30 mins.) Cove owned by Mexican Skin-Divers Society, 110 km. S from Puerto Juárez. *Hotel Club Akumal Caribe*, L, not very special food (there is a small supermarket nearby at Villas Mayas), poor service, overpriced, no entertainment, excellent beach, linked to two buildings separated by *Villas Mayas*, with coral reef only 100 metres offshore. In addition at *Villas Mayas*, bungalows A, with bath, comfortable, some with kitchens, on beach, snorkelling equipment for hire, US$6 per day, good restaurant with poor service. Recommended as base for excursions to Xelhá, Tulum and Cobá. Not far from Akumal are Chemuyil and Xcacel beaches and campsites down newer roads, with restaurants. Further south, about 8 km. N of Tulum, are the quiet, pleasant *Cabañas Los Arrecifes* on the beach, with cabins all prices from US$4 to US$30 a day, with good fish restaurant. Nearby turtles lay their eggs in July/August, and snorkelling on the nearby reef is good.

Tulum The Tulum ruins, Maya-Toltec, are 128 km. S of Cancún, 1 km. off the main road; they are 12th century, with city walls of white stone atop coastal cliffs (frescoes still visible on interior walls of temples). The temples were dedicated to the worship of the Falling God, or the Setting Sun, represented as a falling character over nearly all the West-facing doors (Cozumel was the home of the Rising Sun). The same idea is reflected in the buildings, which are wider at the top than at the bottom. Open 0800-1700, about 2 hrs. needed to view at leisure (entry US$0.50, half-price for students, Sun. free). Tulum is these days crowded with tourists (fewer p.m.). The village is not very large and has neither a bank nor post office (nearest at Playa del Carmen or Felipe Carrillo Puerto, 132 km. away); there is no accommodation here, so you must leave the bus at the ruins. Shops at the ruins are expensive and locals can be unfriendly. Beaches are beautiful but sometimes dirty, and there is thieving from beach camping spots and *cabañas*, so be careful.

The ruins are just off the paved road, restaurant at turning will store luggage for US$0.40 per bag, between Felipe Carrillo Puerto (*Hotel Carrillo Puerto* has been rec.; *Hotel Esquivel*, just off Plaza, F, not good, dirty, no locks on doors, noisy; *Restaurant Addy*, on main road, S of town, good, simple) and Puerto Juárez (133 km.), and can also be visited by boat from Cozumel.

There is a large car-park at the entrance to the ruins (here you can leave luggage), which is ringed by small shops (selling dresses, etc.) and restaurants of which only one sells beer and liquor and closes at 1700. Soft drinks expensive. There is a newly-laid road linking Tulum with the large but little-excavated city of Cobá (see below) with the turn-off to Cobá about 1½ km. along the main road in the direction of Chetumal, which joins the Valladolid-Puerto Juárez road at Xcan, thus greatly shortening the distance between Chichén-Itzá and Tulum. On the paved road to the right of the parking lot, along the coast, you will find a whole string of beach places with hammock and tent space and rooms with meals, F. Hammock space may also be rented in the village of Tulum, 2 km. from ruins (minibus to ruins at 0900, US$0.50); *Motel Crucero*, E; about 1½ km. from the ruins down the beach is *Santa Fe* where *cabañas* are rented for US$7.50, has poor restaurant, basic toilets, OK but take precautions against theft; again along the beach nearby are *Cabañas El Mirador*, small, quiet, cabins US$10, no sanitation, and *El Paraíso*, very casual, scorpions found, agree rates in advance, electricity only from 1800 to 2100. Mosquito-net supplies are very limited so take good repellant lotion with you. Water at *El Mirador* and *Santa Fe* is bit smelly because well-water is used for washing and suds have spoiled it, but good water at a spot on the road between ruins and the path to the camp sites. Good restaurant at *Cabañas Don Armando* (very unfriendly) between *Santa Fe* and *Paraíso*. One restaurant on the road and two restaurants next to the Navy camp, worth trying. Walk past the restaurants to the shops and main centre (15-20 mins.), where you can stock up on supplies which are cheaper than at the ruins. Continue on the road out of town past the village well and then some beehives, then take a well-worn path to the beach. *Pablo's House* (the village is 3 km. away from Pablo's), is cheaper with own hammocks, meals, no w.c. or showers, only a well, fairly basic, beware of over-charging. Watch your belongings. Trailer Park next door. *Chac Mul*, cheapest place, 3 km. S from ruins, wooden huts, D, good showers, restaurant, nice. You can cook over open fires along the beach about ½ km. from the ruins, so take your own food. A new hotel is being built at crossroads where buses stop to let people off for the ruins, and there is a restaurant there, which will hold luggage while you visit the site. *Hotel Posada Tulum*, 8 km. S of the ruins on the beach, D, has an expensive restaurant and is not served by public transport. About 6 km. from ruins are *Cabañas de Tulum*, D, also with restaurant and camping, Swiss owner; take taxi there (US$2), empty white beaches, no bus to ruins, cabins not clean, well built or well supplied. The road from Tulum to Felipe Carrillo Puerto is paved. Service stations at Cancún, Tulum, Nuevo Xcan and Felipe Carrillo Puerto, but one only between Tulum and Cancún (140 km.). Late arrival at Tulum is not recommended, as everything closes at dusk and it is difficult to find accommodation. Ruins of Chumyaxche, three pyramids (partly overgrown), on the left-hand side of this road, 18 km. S of Tulum, worth a visit.

Parking or camping possible on beach S of lighthouse, whose keeper also rents huts along beach for US$1.20 a day, and at *Cabañas El Mirador*. Good swimming locally; divers bring in lobster from a coral reef about 400 metres offshore.

N of Tulum (12 km.) at km. 245 (bus from Playa del Carmen, 45 mins.) is a beautiful clear lagoon, **Laguna Xelhá**, full of fish, but no fishing allowed as it is a national park (open 0800-1700), entry US$0.60. Snorkelling gear can be rented at US$3.15 for a day, but it is often in poor repair; better to rent from your hotel. Arrive as early as possible to see fish (you need to dive down about a metre because above that level the water is cold and fresh with few fish; below it is the warm, fish-filled salt water) as later buses full of tourists arrive from Cancún. Bungalows being built. Very expensive food. There is a marvellous jungle path to one of the lagoon bays. Xelhá ruins (known also as Los Basadres) are located across the road from the beach of the same name. You may have to jump the fence to visit. Small ruins of Ak are near Xelhá. N of Tulum, at Tancáh, are newly-discovered bright post-classical Maya murals but these are sometimes closed to the public.

Bus from Tulum to Mérida, three daily via Puerto Morelos, 10 hrs.; from Felipe Carrillo Puerto to Mérida via Muna, US$4, 4½ hrs. To Felipe Carrillo Puerto, 1 hr., US$1.50, few buses; to

Chetumal, US$2.90, 4 hrs. (1st class from village only, 4 a day before 1230); to Puerto Juárez, 2nd class; Cancún, US$1.65, 2 hrs.; to Playa del Carmen, 1 hr., US$1. To Cobá at 0600 and 1200, goes on to Valladolid (US$1.30, 2½ hrs.); at 1700 goes only to Cobá; bus to Cobá from Valladolid passes Xcan (no hotel but the owner of the shop where the road branches off to Cobá may offer you a room). (It is easier to reach Valladolid via Cancún than direct.)

Cobá, the ancient political capital of the area, with the largest ruins (entry US$ 0.20), about 50 km. inland from Tulum, still unspoiled, is also being developed; an unusual feature is the network of ancient roads, known as *sacbes*. Hotels: *Villa Arqueológica* (Club Méditerranée), open to non members, clean and quiet, A, swimming pool, good food; *Isabel*, 6 double rooms, F, basic, separate bathrooms (dirty), cool, mosquito-free. Go via Valladolid, Chemax on Puerto Juárez road—or bus from Cancún or daily from Playa del Carmen via Tulum to crossroads 4 km. from Cobá. Bus, Cobá-Tulum, 1500. Few buses, but two daily to Valladolid at 0730 and 1230 (from Valladolid, 0430, 1400, US$1.90, 2 hrs.). Good, cheap restaurant in the village, *El Bocadito* (also has rooms, E), and little grogcery store where you can buy soft drinks and safely leave your luggage. Village is about 1 km. from ruins. Beware of ticks and snakes when rummaging through the brush. 1½ km. from the extensive ruins of Cobá lies a huge pyramid called Nohoch-Mul. The entire archaeological zone encompasses about 6,500 structures and covers many square kilometres.

Villahermosa to Chetumal, on the Belize frontier: Highway 186 (paved), branches off to the SE from *Francisco Escárcega* with interesting ruins (see page 1109) at Chicana (145 km.), Becán (**page 1109**), watch for very small sign—146 km.), X-Puhil (153 km.), via Francisco Villa (217 km.); see below. The road is in excellent condition and there is very little traffic.

Motel Ah Kim Pech, E, reasonable restaurant, nice rooms; good restaurant across from the motel; *Casa de Huéspedes Lolita* on Chetumal highway at E end of town, E, pleasant; *Hotel Bertha*, E, with bath, fairly clean; *Escárcega*, E, good value. Restaurant at ADO terminal is hot, slow and overpriced. Also bank, market and motor repairs. Beside Highway 186, near Km. 231, W of Escárcega (near the turnoff for Candelaria) is a roosting spot for white ibis, known as Ojo de Agua. Bus Escárcega to Palenque at 0430, US$4.75, 3 hrs.; the town is on the Mexico City-Palenque-Mérida railway line. Only train leaves at 0300, crowded. Bus, Escárcega-Chetumal, 3½ hrs. No direct buses to Palenque; need to change from Villahermosa bus at Emiliano Zapata, but ask if your intended bus stops there.

Chetumal, the capital of the state of Quintana Roo, now being developed for tourism (albeit slowly), is a free port with clean wide streets, and a greatly improved waterfront with parks and trees. Good for foreign foodstuffs—cheaper at covered market in outskirts than in centre. Some travellers have warned that there are many drunks roaming the streets; also many mosquitoes and high prices. Airport.

N.B. Now that Quintana Roo is no longer a territory but a state, it is illegal to sell cars and other imported goods there. Visas to Guatemala must be obtained in Chetumal (Consulate, Alvaro Obregón 342, US$10 for 30 days, one entry open) because none in Belize. Hitching is difficult to the Belizean border. Cars with light-green licence plates are a form of taxi.

Hotels (accommodation may be a problem during the holiday season). *Continental Caribe*, Av. Héroes 171, A; *El Presidente*, Héroes de Chapultepec, rather scruffy and poorly equipped, quiet, overpriced restaurant, A; *El Marqués*, Lázaro Cárdenas 121, D, fan, a/c, hot water, restaurant, recommended; *Real Azteca*, Belice 186, C, cheerful, friendly and clean, but no hot shower (top floor rooms best); *Ucum*, Gandhi 4, E (no singles) with fan and bath, clean, good value; *El Dorado*, Av. 5 de Mayo 21, D, hot water, a/c, overpriced (no restaurant); *Brasilia*, E. Aguilar 186, E, "cockroaches paradise"; *América*, E, on Juárez, 1 block from Héroes, basic, but friendly. *Luz María*, Carmen de Merino 204, friendly but not very clean, E, owner speaks English; *Big Ben*, Héroes 48-A, E, clean, pleasant and safe, but a bit overpriced; *Posada Colonial*, F, basic but OK, closest to bus station (left to roundabout, left again for 200 m.). Plenty more. CREA Youth Hostel, F, corner Calz. Veracruz and Obregón, T 23465, C.P. 77000, hot water.

Restaurants bus station, clean and cheap, also one next door to *Hotel Ucum*, which is reasonable. Cheap snacks at *Lonchería Ivette* on Mahatma Gandhi 154. *La Charca de las Ranas Verdes*, opp. bandstand, cheap and good; *Sergio Pizza*, Obregón 182, good pizzas, good but expensive steak meals, a/c, good drinks too. Generally difficult to find restaurants Sunday night. *Caribe*, near park, with bandstand, near water, rec. *Viky* on Isla Cancún, ½ block W of the N side of the market, good local dishes, good value. *Cafetería Don Artur*, nr. market on Héroes, good value breakfasts; *Los Milagros*, Av. Zaragoza and 5 de Mayo, good cheap breakfasts. *Vaticano*, on the same street has good tamales. *Los de Colores*, Zaragoza and Juárez, good fish. Pleasant bar, *La Choza del Huinic*, at Av. Hidalgo 132. Try *Safari* roadhouse in Calderitas suburb for enterprising nightlife.

Shopping Shops are open from 0800-1300 and 1800-2000. For exchange, Banamex (0900-1330) on corner of Juárez and Obregón, may need to wait till 1100 for rates.

Garage Talleres Barrera, helpful, on Primo de Verdad; turn right off main street that passes market, then past the electrical plant.

Tourist Information Av. Héroes, helpful.

Buses Bus station now 2-3 km. out of town at intersection of Insurgentes y Belice; taxi from town US$0.40. You can change pesos into Belize dollars both at bus station and at border. Many buses going to the border, US$0.15; taxi from Chetumal to border, 20 mins., US$4 for two. Autobuses del Caribe to Mexico City, 22 hrs., US$28, leave at 0900, 1300, 2000, 2230 daily via Villahermosa (US$7, 10 hrs.); bus to Francisco Escárcega, 3½ hrs., US$3, 2nd class (2 in the morning, then at 1700, 1945 and 2100); from Chetumal to Palenque, better connections at Emiliano Zapata (bus to there at 0900, 1300, US$6) than Francisco Escárcega, more buses daily, but must take bus from E. Zapata to Catazaja, thence minibus or cheap taxi to Palenque. Bus to Mérida, 6 a day, US$6.60 1st class, about 5½ hrs. To Felipe Carrillo Puerto, US$1.75, 1½ hrs., many, on excellent road. To Cancún, 6 hrs., boring road, about 8 daily, between 0630 and 2400. To Tulum, five (2nd class) a day, 4 hrs., US$2.90.

To Belize Batty Bus and Venus Bus from bus terminal to Belize City (former each even hour, latter each odd hour), taking 3½ hrs. "express", otherwise 5 hrs. on new road, largely paved (0230 or 0400 Batty bus to make direct connection with Guatemalan frontier), US$3.50 in pesos or Belize dollars. Be there in good time; they sometimes leave early if full. Bus Chetumal-Orange Walk, US$1.40. Money checked on entering Belize. Excess Mexican pesos are easily changed into Belizean dollars with men waiting just beyond customs on the Belize side. West German citizens *must* have a visa to enter Belize, obtainable in Chetumal for US$10, open 0900-1300 (see also Belize **Information for Visitors** section). To hitch once inside Belize, it is best to take the *colectivo* from in front of the hospital (1 block from the bus station, ask) marked "Chetumal-Santa Elena", US$0.30. You can change US for Belizean dollar bills in the shops at the border, at a rather poor rate. Note that on the Mexican side border guards can be rather offhand and indolent; money may help to remedy this. **N.B.** If travelling by car be at the border before 1500 to have your papers checked. On entering Belize you must purchase car insurance.

Excursions Just N of Chetumal is Laguna de los Milagros, a beautiful lagoon, and 34 km. N of Chetumal, on the road to Tulum (**page 1106**), is Cenote Azul, over 70 metres deep, with an expensive waterside restaurant serving good regional food and a new and well-equipped trailer park (Apartado 88, Chetumal; other *cenotes* in area). About 3 km. N of Cenote Azul is the village of Bacalar (nice, but not special) on the Laguna de Siete Colores; swimming and skin-diving; minibus service from minibus terminal 2 blocks from the electricity generating plant in Chetumal, US$0.35. There is a Spanish fort there; hotel and good restaurants on the Laguna. *Buk-Halot*, E, and a cheap but comfortable *casa de huéspedes* near the fort on the park. Camping possible at the end of the road 100 metres from the lagoon, toilets and shower, US$0.10, but lagoon perfect for washing and swimming; gasoline is sold in a side-street. N of Bacalar a direct road (Route 293) runs to Muna, on the road between Mérida and Uxmal. About 2 km. S of Bacalar (on left-hand side of the road going towards the village) is *Hotel Las Lagunas*, very good, swimming pool and opp. a sweet-water lake, D; restaurant is, however, overpriced.

From Chetumal one can visit the fascinating Mayan ruins that lie on the way to Francisco Escárcega. Buses leave at 0600 (2nd class) from Chetumal to Francisco Villa and Xpuhil; there is no direct transport to Kohunlich, Becán and Chicana, so from Xpuhil the following journey must be done privately. Just before Francisco Villa lie the ruins of *Kohunlich* (entry US$0.40), about 7 km. S to the main road, where there are fabulous masks (early classic, A.D. 250-500) set on the side of the main pyramid, still bearing red colouring; they are unique of their kind. Seven km. further on from *Xpuhil*, 8th century A.D., (all that remains of one large pyramid, recently restored, beside the road), lies the large Maya site of *Becán*, shielded by the forest with wild animals still wandering among the ruins, surrounded by a water-less moat and a low wall, now collapsed, with vast temples and plazas and a decayed ball court. Two km. further on and 10 mins. down a paved road lies *Chicana*, with a superb late classic Maya temple with an ornate central door which has been formed in the shape of the open-fanged jaws of the plumed serpent. Free camping at both Becán and Chicana. Buses return from Xpuhil at 1300 and 1700. Across the bay from Chetumal, at the very tip of Quintana Roo is *Xcalak*, which may be reached from Chetumal by private launch (2 hrs.), or by a long, scenic (recent) unpaved road from Limones (3½ hrs., 120 km.), suitable for passenger cars but needs skilled driver). Bus runs Fri. 1600 and Sun. 0600, returning Sat. a.m. and Sun. p.m. (details from Chetumal tourist office). Xcalak is a fishing village (250 pop.) with a few shops with beer and basic supplies and one hotel, F. Rent a boat and explore Chetumal Bay and

Banco Chinchorro, unspoiled islands. N of Chetumal are also the unexcavated archaeological sites of Ichpaatun (13 km.), Oxtancah (14) and Nohochmul (20). Do *not* try to walk from Xcalak along the coast to San Pedro, Belize; the route is virtually impassable.

Maps of roads in Quintana Roo are obtainable in Chetumal at Junta Local de Caminos, Secretaría de Obras Públicas. The road from Chetumal through Tulum to Mérida (via Cancún) is paved.

BAJA CALIFORNIA

Baja California (Lower California) is that long narrow arm which dangles southwards from the US border between the Pacific and the Gulf of California for 1,300 km. It is divided administratively into the states of Baja California and Baja California Sur, with a one-hour time change at the state line. The average width is only 80 km. Rugged and almost uninhabited mountains split its tapering length. Only the southern tip gets enough rain: the northern half gets its small quota during the winter, the southern half during the summer. Most of the land is hot, parched deserts, but deserts of infinite variety and everchanging landscapes, clothed in a fascinating array of hardy vegetation. Most visitors find Baja a magical place of blue skies, fresh air, solitude and refuge from the rat race north of the border. Not only the northern regions near the US, but also the southern Cape zone is attracting increasing numbers of tourists. The US dollar is preferred in most places north of La Paz.

Stretching 1,704 km. from Tijuana to Cabo San Lucas, Highway 1 is in good repair, although slightly narrow and lacking hard shoulders. Service stations are placed at adequate intervals along it, but motorists should fill their tanks at every opportunity, particularly if venturing off the main roads. The same conditions apply for Highways 5 (Mexicali-San Felipe), 3 (Tecate-Ensenada-San Felipe road) and 2 (Tijuana-Mexicali-San Luís-Sonoita). Hitch-hiking is difficult, and there is very little public transport off the main highway. The local population has little time to spare for tourists; those from the USA may occasionally find them aloof, but in general the visitor experiences friendliness and hospitality.

There is no immigration check on the Mexican side of the border—the buffer zone for about 70 km. south of the frontier allows North Americans to travel without a tourist card. Immigration authorities are encountered south of Maneadero (theoretically), at Quitovac, 28 km. south of Sonoita (Sonora) on Highway 2, and when boarding the ferries to cross the Gulf. Ferries ply from Pichilingüe (north of La Paz), Santa Rosalía and Cabo San Lucas to various places on the mainland (see text). As a car needs an import permit, make sure you get to the ferry with lots of time and preferably with a reservation if going on the Pichilingüe-Mazatlán ferry. (See under La Paz below.)

Recommended guides The Automobile Club of Southern California's *Baja California*, which contains plenty of information and detailed driving logs for all of Baja's roads; *Baja California: A Travel Survival Kit*, Lonely Planet (1988); and *The Magnificent Peninsula*, by Jack Williams, which includes a km. log to the highways as well as an enormous amount of background detail.

Maps There are only two really comprehensive maps—the road map published by the ACSC, which gives highly detailed road distances (but in miles) and conditions, and which is available only to AAA members; and International Travel Map (ITM) Production's *Baja California 1:1,000,000* (by Kevin Healey Feb. 1989), which includes extra geographical and recreational detail on a topographic base. Many specialist maps and guides are available in book stores in Southern California. Both guidebooks and maps are sadly rare in Baja itself.

The Value Added Tax (IVA) is only 6% in Baja California compared with 15% on the mainland (although costs of food and accommodation are more expensive than the rest of Mexico, but less than in the USA). Tijuana, Ensenada and La Paz all have a good range of duty-free shopping. Stove fuel is impossible to find in Baja California Sur. Beware of overcharging on buses and make a note of departure times of buses in Tijuana or Ensenada when travelling S: between Ensenada and Santa Rosalía it is very difficult to obtain bus timetable information, even at bus stations. Don't ask for English menus if you can help it—prices often differ from the Spanish version. Always check change, overcharging is rife. Note also that hotels have widely divergent winter and summer rates; between June and November tariffs are normally lower than those given in the text below (especially in expensive places). Pemex produce two grades of petrol: *extra*, unleaded, 87 octane (on US sytem), from silver pumps (not easy to find); *nova*, leaded, 80 octane, blue pumps; diesel is in red pumps.

Cortés attempted to settle at La Paz in 1534 after one of his expeditions had become the first Europeans to set foot in Baja, but the land's sterile beauty disguised a chronic lack of food and water; this and sporadic Indian hostility forced the abandonment of most early attempts at settlement. Jesuit missionary fathers arrived at Loreto in 1697 and founded the first of their 20 missions. The Franciscans and then Dominicans took over when the Jesuits were expelled in 1767. The fathers were devoted and untiring in their efforts to convert the peninsula's three ethnic groups, but diseases introduced unknowingly by them and by ships calling along the coasts soon tragically decimated Indian numbers; some Indians remain today, but without tribal organization. Scattered about the Sierras are the remains of about 30 of these well-meaning but lethal missions—some beautifully restored, others only eroded adobe foundations. Most are within easy reach from Highway 1, although 4-wheel drive is necessary for remoter sites such as San Pedro Mártir and Dolores del Sur.

Baja became part of Mexico after the signing of the peace treaty with the United States in 1848, ceded in exchange for Alta California. Battles were fought on the peninsular during the Mexican Revolution. Today's population of about 2.8 million has increased by two-thirds in the past decade through migration from Mexico's interior and Central Pacific coast. The development of agriculture, tourism, industry, migrant labour from California, and the opening of the Transpeninsular Highway has caused an upsurge of economic growth and consequently of prices, especially in areas favoured by tourists.

The Morelos dam on the upper reaches of the Colorado River has turned the Mexicali valley into a major agricultural area: 400,000 acres under irrigation to grow cotton and olives. The San Quintín Valley and the Magdalena Plain are other successful areas where crops have been wrenched from the desert. Industries are encouraged in all border regions by investment incentives; called *maquiladoras*, they are foreign-owned enterprises which import raw materials without duty, manufacture in Mexico and ship the products back to the United States.

Mexicali (pop. 850,000), capital of Baja California state, is not as geared to tourism as Tijuana and thus retains its busy, business-like border town flavour. It is a good place to stock up on supplies, cheap clothing and footware, and souvenirs.

The new Centro Cívico-Comercial, Calzada López Mateos, is an ambitious urban development comprising government offices, medical school, hospitals, bullring, bus station, cinemas, etc. The City Park, in the south-west sector, contains a zoo, picnic area and natural history museum (open Tues.-Fri. 0900-1700; weekend 0900-1800). University of Baja California's Regional Museum, Av. Reforma y Calle L; interesting exhibits illustrating Baja's archaeology, ethnography and missions (Tues.-Fri. 0900-1800; weekend 1000-1500, admission free). Galería de la Ciudad, Av. Obregón 1209, between Calles D y E, former state governor's residence, features work of Mexican painters, sculptors and photographers (Mon.-Fri. 0900-2000). There are *charreadas* (rodeos), held on Sundays during the April-October season, at two separate *charro* grounds on eastern and western outskirts of Mexicali—check times (T 568-2320).

Hotels *Holiday Inn*, A, Blvd. Benito Juárez 2220, a/c, best in town; *Lucerna*, B, Blvd. Juárez 2151, a/c, meeting rooms, bar, nightclub; *Castel Calafia*, B, Calzada Justo Sierra 1495, a/c, plain but comfortable, dining room; *Del Norte*, C, Calle Melgar y Av. Francisco Madero, some a/c and TV, across from border crossing, pleasant. *Rivera*, near the railway station, a/c, best of the cheaper hotels; *Fortín de las Flores*, Av. Cristóbal Colón 612; and *Las Fuentes*, Blvd. López Mateos 1655, both with a/c and TV but noisy, tolerable if on a tight budget, D; *La Siesta*, D, Justo Sierra 899, reasonable, coffee shop. **Motels** *Azteca de Oro*, D/E, Calle Industria 600, opposite the station, a/c, TV, a bit scruffy but convenient. Others around town and in Calexico just across the border around East 4th St.
   Many good night clubs on Av. Justo Sierra, and on your left as you cross border, several blocks away.

Exchange All major banks: currency exchange is only from 0900-1330. *Casas de cambio* in Calexico give a slightly better rate. Several *cambios* near the border post on López Mateos.

Note that the border crossing is only from end of Av, Cristóbal Colón (which parallels the frontier fence); Calzada López Mateos does not go to the border.

Tourist Office State Tourism Office, Calle Comercio, between Reforma and Obregón ("Centro Cívico" bus); better is Tourist and Convention Bureau, Calzada López Mateos y Calle Camelias, helpful, English spoken, open Mon.-Fri. 0800-1900, Sat. 0900-1300. The Procuraduría de Protección al Turista, which provides legal assistance for visitors, is in the same building as the State Tourism office.

Airport 18 km. East, Blvd. Aviación; daily flights to Mexico City. Charter services.

Train The railway station to the S is about 3½ km. from the tourist area on the border and Calle 3 bus connects it with the nearby bus terminal. There is a passport desk at the station. The ticket information office closes at 1230 but there are timetables on the wall. There is no direct service between Mexicali and Mexico City, every trip requires changing in Guadalajara. Slow train (leaves 2145, has regular 1st and 2nd class cars) to Guadalajara and Mexico City takes 57 hrs., fast train 44 hrs. (36 hrs. to Guadalajara) at 1045, has only sleepers and special 1st class (although at times it is as slow as the slow train owing to breakdowns), little price difference. Be sure to take your own food. Make sure you are on the right car as some are disconnected—guards not always reliable. Thorough police luggage searches for drugs and guns possible. Mexicali to Mazatlán, 23 hrs. Toilets in each class are inefficient and therefore unpleasant. There is no air conditioning except in *dormitorio* cabins for 1-2 persons. Price difference between cabins and roomettes minimal, but cabin vastly preferable. If there are dining cars they can run out of food, when there are delays. Very hot and dusty in desert part of trip, though train is cleaned twice. Food and drink sold on station platforms. Passengers not on sleeping cars on fast train change at Benjamín Hill to the train from Nogales which is often very full on arrival (on the slow train only the special 1st class car and the dining car are detached, the rest go all the way to Guadalajara). If you come from the N on the slow train and want to go to Chihuahua you'll arrive at 2005 at the junction, Sufragio (the fast train arrives at 0250). For a hotel, go to San Blas, 5 mins. away by local bus, where there are 3 hotels: *Santa Lucía, San Marco*, both often full; *Pérez* dirty but adequate, F. If the next morning you are refused a ticket because the train is full, try getting in and getting a ticket on the train.

Bus Tijuana, 3 hrs., US$2.35 1st class, US$1.20 2nd class, sit on left for views at the Cantú Grade; San Felipe, 3 hrs., daily at 0800, 1200, 1600, 2000, US$1.50-2.00, Guadalajara, US$27. Mazatlán, US$21. Hermosillo, 10 hrs., US$9. Mexico City, US$36. Ensenada, US$3.75. Santa Rosalía, US$14. La Paz, daily 1630, 24 hrs., US$25. All trips leave from the new central bus station (Camionera Central) on Av. Independencia; four major bus companies have their offices here under one roof. Autotransportes Tres Estrellas de Oro serves both Baja and the mainland. Greyhound from Los Angeles to Calexico (901 Imperial Av.), US$30, 6 hrs. San Diego to Calexico via El Centro, US$15, 3 to 4 hours. Local buses are cheap, about US$0.12. "Central Camionera" bus to Civic Centre and bus station.

Paved Highway 5 heads south from Mexicali 200 km. to San Felipe, passing at about Km. 34 the Cerro Prieto geothermal field and Baja's only volcanically active area. After passing the Río Hardy (one of the peninsula's few permanent rivers) and the Laguna Salada (Km. 72), a vast dry alkali flat unless turned into a muddy morass by rare falls of rain, the road continues straight across sandy desert until entering San Felipe around a tall, white, double-arched monument.

San Felipe is a pleasant, tranquil fishing and shrimping port on the Gulf of California with a population of about 9,000. Long a destination for devoted sportfishermen and a weekend retreat for North Americans, San Felipe has experienced a second discovery by North Americans, with many new trailer parks and the paving of many of the town's sandy streets. A new airport 8 km. south. San Felipe is protected from desert winds by the coastal mountains and is unbearably hot during the summer; in winter the climate is unsurpassed, and on weekends it can become overcrowded and noisy.

A good view of the wide sandy beach can be had from the Virgin of Guadalupe shrine near the lighthouse. Navy Day is celebrated on 1 June with a carnival, street dancing and boat races. Pasqual, "The Clam Man" and self-proclaimed "Official Greeter of San Felipe", can be found in a jumble of shacks by the main road as it enters town.

Hotels *Castel*, A, Av. Misión de Loreto 148, a/c, 2 pools, tennis etc., best in town; *Vagabond Inn*, B, on same street, 3 km. south of town, a/c, pool and beach; *Villa del Mar*, B/C, pool, volley ball court, restaurant; *Fiesta San Felipe*, C, 9 km. south on the airport road, isolated, every room has Gulf view, tennis, pool, restaurant. *Riviera*, C, 1 km. south on coastal bluff, a/c, pool, spa, restaurant. **Motels**   *El Cortés*, B, on Av. Mar de Cortés, beachside esplanade, a/c, pool, palapas on beach, launching ramp, disco, restaurant; *El Pescador*, D, Mar de Cortés and Calzada Chetumal, a/c, modest but comfortable; *El Capitán*, C, Mar de Cortés 298, a/c, some balconies, pool, lovely rancho-style building, hard beds but otherwise OK; *Chapala*, D, some a/c, free coffee, modest but adequate, on beachfront.

Camping Many trailer parks and campgrounds in town and on coast to north and south, inc. *El Faro Beach and Trailer Park*, D, on the bay 18 km. south; *Ruben's, Playa Bonita, La Jolla, Playa de Laura, Mar del Sol*, and the more primitive *Campo Peewee* and *Pete's Camp*, both about 10 km. north. All from US$5-8 per night for two.

Tourist Office Mar de Cortés y Manzanillo, opp. *El Capitán Motel*, helpful, little handout material, open Tues.-Sun. 0900-1400 and 1600-1800.

The coastal road S of San Felipe is being paved as far as Puertecitos, a straggling settlement mainly of North American holiday homes. There is an airstrip, a simple grocery store, a Pemex station and the 8-room *Puertecitos Motel*. Fishing is good outside the shallow bay and there are several tidal hot springs at the south-east point. The road continues S along the coast (graded but rough in places; high-clearance vehicles rec.), leading to the tranquil Bahía San Luís Gonzaga, on which are the basic resorts; the beach here is pure sand, empty and silent. From here, the "new" road heads west over hills to meet Highway 1 near Laguna Chapala, 50 km. S of Cataviña, opening up a circular route through northern Baja California.

The road from Mexicali W to Tijuana runs across barren desert flats until reaching the eastern escarpment of the peninsula's spine; it winds its way up the Cantú Grade to La Rumorosa, giving expansive, dramatic vistas of desert and mountain. La Rumorosa, sited high enough on a boulder-strewn plateau to receive a sprinkling of snow in winter, has a service station. There are three more Pemex stations along Highway 2 before it reaches Tecate after 144 km.

Tecate is a quiet border town of 35,000, without a population centre on the US side. It is a pleasant place to break the journey, especially around the tree-shaded Parque Hidalgo. Brewing beer is an important local industry and the Tecate Brewery runs tours on the first three Saturdays of the month from 0800-1200 (Tecate and Carta Blanca are two of Mexico's most respected ales). The border crossing at Tecate is open 0700-2000 daily. *Motel El Dorado*, C, a/c, central, comfortable; *Hotel Hacienda*, D, Av. Benito Juárez 861, a/c, clean; *Hotel México*, F, Juárez 230, gloomy, rooms with and without baths, said to be a staging post for Mexicans waiting to cross the border illegally.

The highway continues west past the Rancho La Puerta, a spa and physical fitness resort, strictly for the rich, vegetarian meals, petrol station. Leaving the Rodríguez Reservoir behind, Highway 2 enters the industrial suburb of La Mesa and continues into Tijuana as a 4-lane boulevard, eventually to become Av. Revolución, one of the city's main shopping streets.

Tijuana (pop. 1,400,000), on the Pacific, is where 35 million people annually cross the border, fuelling the city's claim to be "the world's most visited city". It came to prominence with Prohibition in the United States in the 1920s when Hollywood stars and thirsty Americans flocked to the sleazy bars and enterprising nightlife of Tijuana and Mexicali. Today, tourism is the major industry; although countless bars and nightclubs still vie for the visitor's dollar, it is duty-free bargains, horse racing and inexpensive English-speaking dentists which attract most visitors. Modern Tijuana is Mexico's fourth-largest city and one of the most prosperous.

Points of interest: Centro Cultural, Paseo de los Héroes y Av. Independencia (museum, handcraft shops, restaurant, concert hall, and the ultra-modern spherical Omnimax cinema, where three films are shown on a 180° screen: English performance at 1400 daily, US$4.50—Spanish version at 1800 costs only US$0.70); Casa de la Cultura, a multi-arts cultural centre with a 600-seat theatre; the Cathedral of Nuestra Señora de Guadalupe, Calle 2. The Jai-Alai Palace (Palacio Frontón) is at Av. Revolución y Calle 7 (games begin at 2000 nightly except Weds.; spectators may bet on each game). Tijuana has two bullrings, the Plaza de Toros Monumental at Playas de Tijuana (the only one in the world built on the sea shore). A few metres away is an obelisk built into the border chain-link fence commemorating the Treaty of Guadalupe Hidalgo, 1848, which fixed the frontier between Mexico and the USA. El Toreo bullring is 3 km. east of downtown on Búlevard Agua Caliente; *corridas* alternate between the two venues between May and September; Sun. at 1600 sharp. Tickets from US$4.50 (*sol*) to US$16 (*sombra*). Horse and dog racing is held at the Agua Caliente track, near the Tijuana Country Club; horse racing Sat. and Sun. from 1200; greyhound meetings Wed.-Mon. at 1945, Mon., Weds., Fri. at 1430. Admission US$0.50, reserved seats US$1. *Charreadas* take place each Sunday from May to Sept. at one of four grounds. Free. Tourism office will give up-to-date information.

There is no passport check at the border, although US freeways funnelling eight lanes of traffic into three on the Mexican side means great congestion, particularly at weekends. A quieter alternative is the Otay Mesa crossing (open 0600-2200) 8 km. east of Tijuana, reached from the US side by SR-117. From the Mexican side it is harder to find: continue on the bypass from Highway 1-D to meet the airport to "Garita de Otay" sign. Those visiting Tijuana for the day often find it easier to park on the San Ysidro side and walk across the footbridge to the city centre. Alternatively, the "San Diego Trolley" is an entertaining way to reach the border, taking visitors from downtown San Diego to "la línea" for US$1.50; departures every 15 mins. between 0500 and 0100. There is a visitor information kiosk at the Trolley's southern terminus.

Hotels   *Fiesta Americana Tijuana*, L, Blvd. Agua Caliente 4500, heated pool, suites, etc., first rate; *Best Western Plaza de Oro*, A, Calle 2 y Av. Martinez, new, a/c, downtown; *Paraíso-Radisson*, A, Blvd Agua Caliente 1 at the Country Club, pool, sauna, bar, a/c, etc.; *Lucerna*, A, Héroes y Av. Rodríguez in new Río Tijuana development, a/c, pool, piano bar, popular with businessmen; *El Conquistador*, A/B, Blvd. Agua Caliente 700, colonial style, a/c, pool, sauna, disco; *Palacio Azteca*, B, Highway 1 south, a/c, modern, cocktail bar, extensively remodelled, in older, congested part of city; *Calinda Tijuana*, B, near the Paraíso-Radisson, a/c, pool, disco, convention centre; *Hotel Caesar*, B/C, Calle 5a y Av. Revolución, a/c, restaurant, decorated with bullfight posters, unique character, good; *La Villa de Zaragoza*, C, behind the Jai-Alai *frontón*, a/c, comfortable; *Nelson*, C, Av. Revolución 502, central, simple clean rooms, coffee shop; *París*, D/E, Calle 5a 1939, adequate, value-for-money budget hotel; *Hotel del Pardo*, D, Calle 5a y Niños Héroes, acceptable, noisy in parts; *Rey*, D, Calle 4a 2021, central, old but comfortable; *Adelita*, E, hot showers, clean, basic, Calle 4a 2770; *Machado*, E, restaurant, basic, reasonable, Calle 1 No. 1724; *San Jorge*, E, Av. Constitución 506, old but clean, basic; *Hotel del Mar*, E, Calle 1a 1448, opposite *Nelson*, central but in a poor section, communal bathroom, good budget hotel. Recommended along Calle Baja California are *Hotel Virrey*, E, and *Pensión Noche Buena*, F; nearby and as good are *Fénix*, Miguel Martínez 355, F; *Chula Vista*, Niños Héroes 380, F, and *Rivas*, on Constitución. *St. Francis*, Benito Juárez 2A, F, recommended, safe and pleasant area. CREA youth hostel T 832680/822760, far from centre, Vía Oriente y Puente Cuauhtémoc, Zona del Río, dirty, not rec., inexpensive cafetería on premises, open 0700-2300. **Motels** *La Misión*, C/D, in Playas de Tijuana near the bullring, modern, a/c, restaurant, pool, popular with businessmen; *Padre Kino* and *Golf* (both D), opposite each other on Blvd Agua Caliente, next to Tijuana Country Club, both OK, *Golf*, an older-type motel.

Restaurants *Capri*, cheap; *Tijuana Tilly's*, excellent meal, reasonably priced. Many more of every category imaginable.

Night Clubs recommended: Flamingos, S on old Ensenada road; Chantecler.

Shopping The Plaza Río Tijuana Shopping Centre, Paseo de Los Héroes, is a new retail development; opposite are the Plaza Fiesta and Plaza del Zapato malls, the latter specializing in footware! Nearby is the colourful public market. Downtown shopping area is Avs. Revolución and Constitución. Bargaining is expected at smaller shops, and everyone except bus drivers is happy to accept US currency.

Exchange Many banks, all dealing in foreign exchange. Better rate than *cambios* but less convenient. Countless *casas de cambio* throughout Tijuana open day and night; commission charged on dollars-for-pesos transactions at *cambios* in San Ysidro—beware!

US Consulate Calle Tapachula, between Agua Caliente racetrack and the Country Club. Mon.-Fri. 0800-1630. T (706) 681-7400.

Tourist Information State Tourism Secretariat, main office on Plaza Patria, Blvd. Agua Caliente, Mon.-Fri. 1000-1900. Branch offices at airport, first tollgate on Highway 1-D to Ensenada, and at the Chamber of Commerce, Calle 1 and Av. Revolución, English-speaking staff, helpful, Mon.-Fri. 0900-1400, 1600-1900; Sat. 0900-1300. Chamber of Commerce also offers rest rooms and first aid facilities to visitors. Procuraduría de Protección al Turista is in the Government Centre in the Río Tijuana development; 0800-1900.

Buses Local buses about US$0.15, "Central Camionera" or "Buena Vista" buses to bus station, downtown buses to border depart from Calle 2a near Av. Revolución. New bus station is 5 km. SE of centre on the airport road at the end of Vía Oriente (at La Mesa). To Mexico City (every couple of hours) 1st class (Tres Estrellas de Oro), about 46 hours, US$34 (Transportes del Pacífico, similar fares and schedules). 2nd class (Transportes del Norte de Sonora), US$31. Other 1st class routes: Guadalajara, 36 hrs., US$27; Hermosillo, 11 hrs., US$10; Mazatlán, 29 hrs., US$21; 2nd class fares: Guadalajara US$24, Hermosillo US$9, Mazatlán US$19. By ABC line: Ensenada, about hourly 0500-2400, 1½ hrs., US$1.50; Mexicali, hourly from 0500-2200, US$2; San Quintín, 7 a day, US$2.75; Santa Rosalía, 1630, direct, US$10; La Paz, 0800, US$16; Tres Estrellas to La Paz, 1030, 1400, 1800, 2200; 24 hours, US$17.50. There are also many services east and south from the old bus station at Av. Madero and Calle 1a (Comercio); this is also the Greyhound depot for departures to San Diego and Los Angeles (US$4 and US$18, about 1 hr. from San Diego). Tijuana is a major transportation centre and schedules are complex and extensive.

International Airport 5 km. east, 20 mins. from San Diego, CA; cheaper flights than from the US. Aero California, daily flights to Los Mochis, US$80, and on to La Paz, US$28. Mexicana: To Acapulco, Veracruz, Zacatecas; direct jet services to La Paz and San José del Cabo, 1½ hours. Taxi to airport should cost US$2-3 but bargaining essential. Mexicoach run from San Diego to Tijuana airport for US$15, combination bus to Plaza La Jolla and taxi to airport.

Flight Bargains from Tijuana airport (20 mins. from San Diego, California); Mexico City and Acapulco, round trip with stopovers in La Paz, Mazatlán, Guadalajara and Puerto Vallarta, or without stop-overs, 30 days, depending on day of departure, by Aeroméxico. Acsa airline offers a round trip to Mérida (Yucatán). Flight to La Paz, 1¼ hrs., leaves at 0950. "Expreso de Lujo" round trip to Puerto Vallarta. Taxi border-airport, US$5; there is also a bus.

A dramatic 106-km. toll road (Highway 1-D) leads along cliffs overhanging the

Pacific to Ensenada; the toll is in three sections of US$0.65 each for cars; total for motorhomes US$4.26. This is the safest route between the two cities and 16 exit points allow access to a number of seaside developments and villages along the coast.

Largest is **Rosarito** (pop. 40,000), a drab resort strung out along the old highway, with numerous seafood restaurants, curio shops, etc. There is a fine swimming beach; horseriding along it is also popular. Many hotels and motels, including: *Quinta del Mar Resort Hotel*, A/B, pool, sauna, tennis, also condos and townhouses with kitchens (L); *Motel Quinta Chico*, B,; *Motel Colonial*, B/C; *Rene's Motel*, D, plain but comfortable; *Motel La Prieta*, D. Best is the *Rosarito Beach Hotel*, B, which was one of the casinos which opened during Prohibition; its architecture and decoration is worth a look.

The coast as far as Cantamar is lightly built-up; there are several trailer parks and many restaurants specializing in local seafood. At Punta Salsipuedes, a *mirador* affords sweeping views of the rugged Pacific coast and the offshore Todos Santos Islands.

Ensenada (pop. 250,000) is Baja's third city and leading seaport. It is a delightful city on the northern shore of the Bahía de Todos Santos, whose blue waters sport many dolphins and underline the austere character of a landscape reduced to water, sky and scorched brown earth. Sport and commercial fishing, canning, wineries, olive groves and agriculture are the chief activities. Tourist activity concentrates along Av. López Mateos, where most of the hotels, restaurants and shops are located. The twin white towers of Nuestra Señora de Guadalupe, Calle 6a, are a prominent landmark; on the seafront boulevard is the new Plaza Cívica, a landscaped court containing large busts of Juárez, Hidalgo and Carranza. The Bodegas de Santo Tomás is Mexico's premier winery, Av. Miramar and Calle 7; daily tours at 1100, 1300, 1500, US$1.50. *Charreadas* are held on summer weekends at the *charro* ground at Blancarte y Calle 2a. A weekend street market is held from 0700-1700 at Av. Riversoll y Calle 7a; the fish market at the bottom of Av. Macheros specializes in "fish tacos" (a fish finger wrapped in a taco!).

Hotels *Punta Morro Hotel Suites*, L, on coast 3 km. W of town, rooms have kitchens and fridges, 2 and 3-bedroom apartments available, pool; *Villa Marina*, A, Av. López Mateos y Blancarte, heated pool, coffee shop; *San Nicolás Resort Hotel*, L, López Mateos y Av. Guadalupe, a/c, suites, dining room, disco; *Las Rosas Hotel and Spa*, L, on Highway 1, 7 km. W of town, suites, spectacular ocean views, pool, sauna, restaurant; *La Pinta*, Av. Floresta y Blvd. Bucaneros (A on Fri.-Sat., B Sun.-Thurs.), TV, pool, restaurant; *Misión Santa Isabel*, A, López Mateos and Castillo, pool, suites; *Bahía*, B/C, López Mateos, balconies, suites, fridges, popular; *Plaza*, D, López Mateos 540, central, plain but clean, rooms facing street noisy. Several cheap hotels around Miramar and Calle 3, e.g. *Perla del Pacífico*, Av. Miramar 229, E, quite clean, hot water. Note that some of the larger hotels have different rates for summer and winter; cheaper tariffs are given above— check first! All hotels are filled in Ensenada on weekends, get in early.
Motels *Ensenada Travelodge*, Av. Blancarte 130, a/c, heated pool, whirlpool, family rates available, restaurant; *Casa del Sol*, A, López Mateos 101; *Cortés*, A, López Mateos 1089 y Castillo; both part of Best Western chain, a/c, TV, pool, comfortable; *El Cid*, A on Fri.-Sat., B on Sun.-Thurs., Av. López Mateos 993, Spanish-style building, a/c, fridges, suites available, dining room, lounge, disco; *Pancho*, Av. Alvarado 211, shabby but clean rooms, opposite the *charro* ground, cheapest habitable motel in town.

Restaurant *Domico's*, Av. Ruiz 283, also Chinese restaurants in same avenue; *Lonchería la Terminal*, opp. bus station, cheap and filling comida, good but basic.

Tourism Office Av. López Mateos y Espinoza, part of the FONART artesan centre, Mon.-Sat. 0900-1900, accommodation literature; the Procuraduría is next door, same hours plus Sun. 0900-1600. Tourist and Convention Bureau, Lázaro Cárdenas y Miramar, Mon.-Sat. 0900-1900, Sun. 0900-1400, helpful; free copies of *Ensenada News and Views*, monthly English-language paper with information and adverts on northern Baja, Tijuana and Ensenada.

Airport 8 km. S; scheduled flights to Tijuana, Guerrero Negro, Cedros Island, La Paz, etc.

Highway 3 east to San Felipe leaves Ensenada at the Benito Juárez *glorieta* monument as the Calzada Cortés. 26 km. out of Ensenada, an 8-km. dirt road branches S for a steep descent to the basic resort of Agua Caliente (*Hotel Agua Caliente*, C, restaurant, bar, closed in winter; adjoining is a campground and large concrete pool heated to 38° by nearby hot springs; access road should not be attempted in wet weather).

At km. 39, a paved road leads off 3 km. to Ojos Negros, continuing E (graded, dry weather) into scrub-covered foothills. It soon climbs into the ponderosa pine forests of the Sierra de Juárez. 37 km. from Ojos Negros, the road enters the Parque Nacional Constitución de 1857. The jewel of the park is the small Laguna Hanson, a sparkling shallow lake surrounded by Jeffery pines; camping here is delightful, but note that the lake is reduced to a boggy marsh in dry seasons and that the area receives snow in mid-winter. A high-clearance vehicle is necessary for the continuation N out of the park to Highway 2 at El Cóndor 15 km. E of La Rumorosa.

At Km. 92½, Ejido Héroes de la Independencia, a graded dirt road runs 8 km. E to the ruins of Mission Santa Catarina, founded in 1797 and abandoned after a raid by the Yuman Indians in 1840; the Paipái women in the village often have attractive pottery for sale.

Highway 3 descends along the edge of the green Valle de Trinidad to the rapidly developing Trinidad. A reasonable dirt road runs S into the **Parque Nacional Sierra San Pedro Mártir** and Mike's Sky Rancho (35 km.), a working ranch which offers motel-style accommodation, a pool, camping and guided trips into the surrounding mountains; rooms about US$8-10 per night, good meals.

After leaving the valley, the highway follows a canyon covered in dense stands of barrel cacti to the San Matías Pass between the Sierras Juárez and San Pedro Mártir which leads onto the desolate Valle de San Felipe. The highway turns E and emerges onto open desert hemmed in by arid mountains. 198½ km. from Ensenada it joins Highway 5 at the La Trinidad T-junction, 148 km. from Mexicali and 50 km. from San Felipe.

Highway 1 S from Ensenada passes turn-offs to several beach resorts. Just before the agricultural town of Maneadero, a paved highway runs 23 km. W onto the Punta Banda peninsula, where you can see La Bufadora blowhole, one of the most powerful on the Pacific. Concrete steps and viewing platform give easy access.

N.B. Tourist cards and vehicle documents of those travelling south of Maneadero are supposed to be validated at the immigration checkpoint on the southern outskirts of the town; the roadside office, however, is not always in operation. If you are not stopped, just keep going.

14 km. S of Colonet a reasonable graded road branches to San Telmo and climbs into the mountains. At 50 km. it reaches the Meling Ranch (also called San José), which offers resort accommodation for about 12 guests. 15 km. beyond San José the road enters the **Parque Nacional Sierra San Pedro Mártir** and climbs through forests to three astronomical observatories perched on the dramatic eastern escarpment of the central range. The view from here is one of the most extensive in North America: east to the Gulf, west to the Pacific, and south-east to the overwhelming granite mass of the Picacho del Diablo (3,096 m.), Baja's highest peak. The higher reaches of the park receive snow in winter. The observatories are not open to visitors.

109 km. from Ensenada **San Quintín**, a thriving market city (pop. 15,000) almost joined to Lázaro Cárdenas 5 km. south. There are service stations in both centres and San Quintín provides all services. Rising out of the peninsula west of San Quintín bay is a line of volcanic cinder cones, visible for many kilometres along the highway; the beaches to the south near Santa María are hugely popular with fishermen, campers and beachcombers.

Hotels   *La Pinta*, A, isolated beachfront location 18 km. S of San Quintín then 5 km. W on paved road, a/c, TV, balconies, tennis, nearby airstrip; *Hada's Rooms*, E/F, just north of Benito Juárez army camp in Láraro Cárdenas, cheapest in town, shabby, basic, sometimes closed when water and electricity are cut off. **Motels**   *Cielito Lindo*, C, 2 km. beyond the *La Pinta Hotel* on S shore of bay, restaurant, cafeteria, lounge (dancing Sat. nights), electricity Mon.-Sat. 0700-1100, 1500-2400, Sun. 0700-2400, modest but pleasant, last km. of access road unpaved, messy after rain; *Molino Viejo*, C, on site of old English mill—part of an early agricultural scheme, modest, on bay 6 km. of W of highway and S of Lázaro Cárdenas, rough access road, restaurant, bar, some kitchenettes, electricity 0800-0900, 1800-2200; *Ernesto's*, D, next door, rustic, overpriced, popular with fishermen, electricity 0700-2100; *Muelle Viejo*, D, between *Ernesto's* and the old English cemetery, restaurant, bad access road, hot showers, bay views; *Chávez*, D, on highway N of Lázaro Cárdenas, family-style, clean rooms, plain but good value.

Camping   *Honey's RV Campground*, 15 km. S and 2 km. W on coast, toilets, showers, full hookups, beach access, US$5 per vehicle, great area for clam-digging. Trailer park attached to Cielito Lindo Motel.

Highway 1 makes a sharp 90° turn at El Rosario (58 km. from San Quintín; *Motel Rosario*, E, small, very clean) and begins to climb into the central plateau; gusty winds increase and astonishingly beautiful desertscapes gradually become populated with many varieties of cacti. Prominent are the stately *cardones*: most intriguing are the strange, twisted *cirios* growing to heights of 6 to 10 m.—they are unique to this portion of Baja California as far south as the Vizcaino Desert, and to a small area of Sonora state on the mainland. At Km. 62 a 5 km track branches S to the adobe remains of Misión San Fernando Velicatá, the only Franciscan mission in Baja, founded by Padre Serra in 1769. 5 km. further on, Rancho Santa Cecília offers meals and refreshments; over the road is an RV park with full hook-ups. The highway is now in the **Desierto Central de Baja California Natural Park** (as yet not officially recognised). About 26 km. north of Cataviña a strange region of huge boulders begins, some as big as houses; interspersed by cacti and crouching elephant trees, this area is one of the most picturesque on the peninsula.

Cataviña is only a dozen buildings, with a small grocery store/*Café La Enramada*, the only Pemex station on the 227-km. stretch from El Rosario to the Bahía de Los Angeles junction, and the attractive *La Pinta Hotel*, A, a/c, pool, bar, electricity 1800-2400, restaurant, tennis, 28 rooms. Attached to the *La Pinta* is the *Parque Natural Desierto Central de Baja California Trailer Park*, flush toilets, showers, restaurant, bar, US$3 per site. 2 km. S of Cataviña is Rancho Santa Inés, which has dormitory-style accommodation (E), meals and a paved airstrip.

Highway 1 continues south-east through an arid world of boulder-strewn mountains and dry salt lakes. At 53 km. the new graded road to the Bahía San Luís Gonzaga (see under San Felipe) branches off to the east. After skirting the dry bed of Laguna Chapala (natural landing strip at southern end when lake is totally dry), the Transpeninsular Highway arrives at the junction with the paved road east to Bahía de Los Angeles; café and gas station at junction, fuel supply sometimes unreliable, best to fill up at Cataviña to be safe.

Excursion The side road runs 68 km. through *cirios* and *datilillo* cactus-scapes and crosses the Sierra de la Asamblea to *Bahía de Los Angeles* (no public transport), a popular fishing town which, despite a lack of vegetation, is one of Baja's best-known beauty spots. The bay, sheltered by the forbidding slopes of Isla Angel de la Guarda (Baja's largest island), is a haven for boating. Facilities in town include: gas station, bakery, stores, two trailer parks and four restaurants, paved airstrip. *Villa Vita Motel*, B, modern, a/c, pool, jacuzzi, boat launch, trailer park, electricity 0700-1400, 1700-2000, bar, dining room; *Casa de Díaz*, C, 15 rooms, restaurant, grocery store, campground, boat rentals, clean, well-run, popular; *Guillermo's Trailer Park*, flush toilets, showers, restaurant, gift shop, boat ramp and rentals; *La Playa RV Park*, on beach, similar facilities and tariff (US$4 per site). La Gringa is a beautiful beach 13 km. north of town, many camping sites, pit toilets, rubbish bins, small fee.

Lynn and Walt Sutherland from Vancouver write: "Bahía de los Angeles (pop. 600) is worth a visit for its sea life. There are thousands of dolphins in the bay June-December. Some stay all year. In July and August you can hear the whales breathe as you stand on shore. There are large colonies of seals and many exotic seabirds. Fishing is excellent. A boat and guide can be rented for US$40 a day; try Raúl, a local fisherman, who speaks English." Camping free and safe on beach.

The highway now runs due south through Villa Jesús María (gas station, store, cafés) to the 28th parallel, the state border between Baja California and Baja California Sur (soaring stylized eagle monument and *Hotel La Pinta*, A, a/c, pool, dining room, bar).

N.B. Advance clocks one hour to Mountain time when entering Baja California Sur, but note that Northern Baja observes Pacific Daylight Saving Time from first Sun. in April to last Sun. in October; time in both states and California is thus identical during the summer.

Guerrero Negro (9,000 people) is 3 km. beyond the state line and 4 km. W of the highway; 714 km. S of Tijuana, 414 from San Quintín, it is halfway point between the US border and La Paz. There are 2 gas stations, bank, hospital, cafés, stores, an airport with scheduled services (just north of the Eagle monument), and the headquarters of Exportadora de Sal, the world's largest salt-producing firm. **Hotel** *Cuartos de Sánchez-Smith*, E/F, Calle Barrera, W end of town, basic rooms, some with showers, cheapest in town. **Motels** *El Morro*, D/E, on road into town from highway, modest, clean; *Las Dunas*, E, few doors from *El Morro*, modest, clean; *Gámez*, E, very basic, near city hall. **Camping** *Malarrimo Trailer Park*, on highway at junction to town, next to *Malarrimo Restaurant*, flush toilets, showers, bar US$4 per vehicle. Good restaurant at bus station.

Whale watching is the main attraction on nearby Laguna Ojo de Liebre, usually known as Scammon's Lagoon after the 18th century whaling captain who first entered it. California Grey Whales mate and give birth between December and February, in several warm-water lagoons on central Baja's Pacific coast, some not departing until as late as May or June. They can be seen cavorting and sounding from the old salt wharf 10 km. NW of Guerrero Negro on the Estero San José, or from a designated "whale watching area" on the shore of Scammon's Lagoon 37 km. south of town, access road branches off Highway 1 8 km. east of junction (if going by public transport, leave bus at the turn off and hitch). Cars are charged US$3 to enter the park. Local personnel collect a small fee for camping at the watching area—this pays to keep it clean. The shores of Scammon's are part of the **Parque Natural de Ballena Gris**. Watch between 0700 and 0900 and again at 1700, saves hiring a boat (US$10 p.p.).

After Guerrero Negro the highway enters the grim Vizcaíno Desert. A paved but badly potholed road leads due east (42 km.) to El Arco, other abandoned mining areas and crossing to San Francisquito on its beautiful bay on the Gulf (77 km.), and to Santa Gertrudis Mission (1752), some of whose stone ruins have been restored, the chapel is still in use. It should be stressed that these minor Bajan roads require high-clearance, preferably 4x4, vehicles carrying adequate equipment and supplies, water and fuel. A new gravel road from Bahía de Los Angeles (135 km.) gives easier road access than from El Arco and opens up untouched stretches of the Gulf coast.

Vizcaíno Peninsula which thrusts into the Pacific south of Guerrero Negro is one of the remotest parts of Baja. Although part of the Vizcaíno Desert, the scenery of the peninsula is varied and interesting; isolated fishcamps dot the silent coast of beautiful coves and untrodden beaches. Until recently only the most hardy ventured into the region; now an improved dry-weather road cuts W through the peninsula to Bahía Tortugas and the rugged headland of Punta Eugenia. It leaves Highway 1 at Vizcaíno Junction (also called Fundolegal, Pemex station, café, market, pharmacy and auto parts store), 70 km. beyond Guerrero Negro and is paved for 8 km. to Ejido Díaz Ordaz. The new road passes Rancho San José (116 km.) and the easily-missed turnoff to Malarrimo Beach (where beachcombing is unparalled). After another bumpy 50 km. is **Bahía Tortugas**, a surprisingly large place (pop. 3,200) considering its remoteness. Many facilities including eating places, health clinic, gas station, airport with services to Cedros Island and Ensenada, and the small *Vera Cruz Motel*, D/E, restaurant, bar, very modest but the only accommodation on the peninsula apart from a trailer park at Campo René, 15 km. from Punta Abreojos. Two roads leave the Vizcaíno-Bahía Tortuga road for Bahía Asunción (pop. 1,600), which has the peninsula's only other gas station, then following the coast to Punta Prieta, La Bocana and Punta Abreojas (93 km.). A lonely road runs for 85 km. back to Highway 1, skirting the Sierra Santa Clara before crossing the salt marshes north of Laguna San Ignacio and reaching the main road 26 km. before San Ignacio.

143 km. from Guerrero Negro is the turnoff for **San Ignacio** (pop. 2,200). Here the Jesuits built a mission in 1728 and planted the ancestors of the town's date palm groves. On the square is the beautifully-preserved mission church, completed by the Dominicans in 1786. The town is very attractive, with thatched-roof dwellings and pastel-coloured commercial buildings; there is limited shopping but several restaurants, service station, mechanical assistance and bank.

Hotel La Pinta, A, on road leading into town, a/c, pool, all facilities, built in mission style, attractive but overpriced; *Cuartos Glenda*, E, with shower, basic but cheapest in town, on highway E. **Motel** La Posada, D, on rise 2 blocks from zócalo, modest, fans, shower, good coffee shop, best value in town, helpful, worth bargaining.

Camping San Ignacio Transpeninsula Trailer Park, Government-run, on Highway 1 behind Pemex station at the junction, full hookups, toilets, showers US$4 per site; two other basic campgrounds on road into San Ignacio, insects, not recommended. West of the mission is La Candelaria, a beautiful palm-shaded camping spot on the edge of a pool—swimming in the middle of the Baja desert!

Loncheria Chalita, on Zócalo, excellent value.

There are many cave painting sites around San Ignacio; colourful human and animal designs left by Baja's original inhabitants still defy reliable dating, or full understanding. To reach most requires a trek by mule over tortuous trails; Oscar Fischer, owner of the *La Posada Motel*, arranges excursions into the sierras (about US$10 per person to Santa Teresa cave). Most accessible is the cave at the Cuesta del Palmarito, 5 km. E of Rancho Santa Marta (50 NW of San Ignacio), filled with designs of humans with uplifted arms, in brown and black; a jeep and guide are required. A better road leads east from the first microwave station past Vizcaíno Junction up to San Francisco de la Sierra, where there are other paintings and petroglyphs in the vicinity.

72 km. from San Ignacio is **Santa Rosalía**, a bustling city of 14,500. It was built by a French mining company in the 1880s, laid out in neat rows of wood frame houses, many with broad verandahs, which today give Santa Rosalía its distinctly un-Mexican appearance. The church of Santa Bárbara (Av. Revolución y Calle C, a block north of the main plaza), built of prefabricated galvanized iron for the 1889 Paris Worlds' Fair from a design by Eiffel, was shipped around the Horn to Baja. It arrived here by mistake! A car ferry leaves for Guaymas at 2300 on Tue, Thur. and Sun. from the small harbour. The tourist office is on the highway a kilometre S of the ferry terminal, opposite the service station. A new Museo de Historia is located off Calle Francesa, 1 km. NE of Santa Bárbara church.

Hotels El Morro, D, on Highway 2 km. S of town, on bluff with Gulf views, modern, Spanish-style, a/c, bar, restaurant; *Francés*, Av. 11 de Julio on the North Mesa, a/c, restaurant, bar, pool not always filled, E, historic 2-storey wooden French colonial building overlooking smelter and Gulf, photos of sailing vessels on walls. *Olvera*, E, on main plaza, 2nd floor, a/c, showers, clean, good value; *Real*, E, Av. Manuel Montoya near Calle A, similar to *Olvera*, rec; *Playa*, F, Av. La Playa between Calles B y Plaza, central, fans, bathrooms, good budget hotel; *Blanca y Negra*, F, basic but clean, Av. Libertad at end of Calle 3. *Panadería El Boleo*, widely noted for its delicious French breads and pastries.

Bus Bus station near tourist office and Pemex station 2 km. S of ferry terminal; stop for most Tijuana-La Paz buses, several per day.

Painted cave sites can be visited from the farming town of Santa Agueda, turnoff 8 km. south of Santa Rosalía then rough dirt road for 12 km. The fishing village of San Lucas, on a palm-fringed cove, is 14 km. south of Santa Rosalía; camping is good and popular on the beaches to north and south. Beside a military detachment is *San Lucas RV Park*, on beach, full hookups, flush toilets, boat ramp, ice, restaurant, US$5 per vehicle. Offshore lies Isla San Marcos, with a gypsum mine at the south end.

Just beyond San Bruno is a reasonable dirt road to San José de Magdalena (15 km.), picturesque farming village dating back to colonial days; ruined Dominican chapel, attractive thatched palm houses, flower gardens. An awful road leads on for 17 km. to Rancho San Isidro, from where the ruined Guadalupe Mission can be reached on horseback.

Mulegé, 61 km. south of Santa Rosalía, is another oasis community (pop. 5,000) whose river enters the gulf as a lushly-vegetated tidal lake. There are lovely beaches, good diving, snorkelling and boating in the Bahía Concepción. The old Federal territorial prison (La Cananea) is being converted into a museum. South of the bridge which carries the highway over the river is the restored Mission of Santa Rosalía de Mulegé, founded by the Jesuits in 1705; good lookout point above the mission over the town and its sea of palm trees. The bank will only change a minimum of US$100.

Hotels   *Serenidad*, B, 4 km. E of town near the river mouth, a/c, pool, dining room, bar, banquet/mariachi band Wed. and Sat. nights, cottages, trailer park; *Vista Hermosa*, B, opp. the *Serenidad*, a/c, pool, restaurant, bar; *Las Casitas*, C, Callejón de los Estudiantes y Av. Madero, central, a/c, showers, restaurant next door, shady garden patio, fishing trips arranged, pleasant older hotel, well-run; *Suites Rosita*, E, Av. Madero near main plaza, a/c, kitchenettes, clean and pleasant; *Terraza Motel*, E, Calles Zaragoza y Moctezuma, in business district, 35 rooms, rooftop bar, basic, clean; *Hacienda*, E, Calle Madero 3, next to *Suites Rosita*; *Casa Nachita*, F with fan, basic and pleasant, hot water in a.m.; next door is *Casa de Huéspedes Manuelita*, sloppily run but reasonably clean, E; *Restaurants Tandil* and *Las Casitas*; *Granny's Goodies*, good breads and pastries, good place for information.

Camping   *The Orchid (Huerta Saucedo) RV Park*, on river south of town, partly shaded, off Highway 1 south of town, pool, boat ramp, fishing, up to US$10.50 for two; *Villa María Isabel RV Park*, on river and Highway east of *Orchid*, pool, recreation area, disposal station, American-style bakery, US$8.50 for two; *Jorge's del Río Trailer Park*, grassy, on river at E end of Highway bridge by unpaved road, US$7.50 per site; *Pancho's RV Park*, next to *María Isabel*, off Highway 1, little shade, US$5 per day; *Oasis Río Baja RV Park*, on same stretch as those above, reasonable, US$6 per site. All the foregoing have full hookups, flush toilets, showers, etc. From here on down the Bahía Concepción coast and beyond are many *playas públicas* (*PP*); some have basic facilities, most are simple, natural camping spots on beautiful beaches where someone may or may not collect a fee. At Mulegé is the Playa Sombrerito (Mulegé US$2) at the hill (site of Mexican victory over US forces in 1847), restaurant and store nearby, US$1 per vehicle.

Beyond Mulegé the Highway climbs over a saddle and then runs along the shores of the bay for 50 km. This stretch is the most heavily-used camping and boating area on the Peninsula; the water is beautiful, swimming safe, camping excellent, varied marine life.

A new graded dirt road branches off Highway 1 to climb over the towering Sierra Giganta, whose desert vistas of flat-topped mesas and *cardón* cacti are straight out of the Wild West; it begins to deteriorate after the junction (20 km.) to San José de Comondú and limps another 37 km. into San Isidro after a spectacular drop into the La Purísima Valley. San Isidro has a population of 1,000 but little for the visitor; 5 km. down the valley is the more attractive oasis village of La Purísima (pop. 800). The road leads on southwards to Pozo Grande (52 km.) and Ciudad Insurgentes (85 km.), paved for the last 26 km. Two side roads off the San Isidro road lead down to the twin towns of San Miguel de Comondú and San José de Comondú (high-clearance vehicles are necessary); both oasis villages of 500 people each. One stone building remains of the mission moved to San José in 1737; the original bells are still at the church. A new graded road leads on to Pozo Grande and Ciudad Insurgentes.

Loreto (pop. 7,300), 1,125 km. from Tijuana, is one of the most historic places in Baja. Here settlement of the Peninsula began with Father Juan María Salvatierra's founding of the Mission of Nuestra Señora de Loreto on 25 October 1697. The Mission is on the Zócalo, the largest structure in town and perhaps the best-restored of all the Baja California mission buildings. It has a gilded altar. The museum beside the church is worth a visit: there are educational displays about the missions, Bajan history and historic horse and ranching equipment, book shop, open Tue.-Sat. 0900-1700. Inscription over the main door of the mission announces: "Mother of all the Missions of Lower and Upper California". Nestled between the slopes of the Sierra Giganta and the offshore Isla del Carmen, Loreto has experienced a tourist revival; fishing in the Gulf here is some of the best in Baja California.

Hotels   *Oasis*, A, Calles de la Playa y Baja California, on bay at S end of Loreto in palm grove, large rooms, pool, tennis, restaurant, bar, skiffs (pangas) for hire, fishing cruises arranged, pleasant and quiet, a/c; *La Pinta*, A/B, on Sea of Cortés 2 km. N of Zócalo, a/c, showers, pool, tennis, restaurant, bar, considered by many the best of the original "Presidente" paradores, 30 rooms, fishing boat hire, recommended; *Misión de Loreto*, C, Calle de la Playa y Juárez, colonial-style with patio garden, a/c, pool, dining rooms, bar, fishing trips arranged, very comfortable, check for discounts; *La Siesta Bungalows*, C, small, manager owns the dive shop and can offer combined accommodation and diving trips; *Villa del Mar*, D, Colina Zaragoza, near sports centre, OK, restaurant, bar, pool, bargain rates, on beach; *Casa de Huéspedes San Martín*, E, Calle Benito Juárez 4, showers, renovated rooms, basic, but poor value. **Motel** *Salvatierra*, E, Calle Salvatierra, on S approach to town, a/c, hot showers, clean, good value. **Camping** *Ejido Loreto RV Park*, on beach a km. S of town, full hookups, toilets, showers, laundry, fishing and boat trips arranged, US\$7.50 per site.

Airport International, 4 km. south; Resorts Airline flights daily to La Paz, San José del Cabo and Los Angeles (John Wayne Orange County Airport) via San Diego; information on other international flights to Loreto welcome.

Bus Bus station at Calle Salvatierra opposite intersection of Zapata; to La Paz 0800, 1000, 1400, 1500 daily, US\$4.25; to Tijuana 1500, 1800, 2100, 2300, US\$13, 17 hrs.

Just south of Loreto a rough road runs 37 km. through impressive canyon scenery to the village of San Javier, tucked in the bottom of a steep-walled valley; the settlement has only one store but the Mission of San Javier is one of the best-preserved in North America; it was founded by the Jesuits in 1699 and took 59 years to complete. The thick volcanic walls, Moorish ornamentation and bell tower are most impressive in so rugged and remote a location. Near San Javier is Piedras Pintas, close to Rancho Las Parras; there are eight prehistoric figures painted here in red, yellow and black.

The highway south of Loreto passes a picturesque stretch of coast. FONATUR, the government tourist development agency, is building a resort complex at Nopoló, (8 km.), which it hopes will one day rival its other resort developments at Cancún and Ixtapa. Campers have been driven out of Puerto Escondido except for the *Tripui Trailer Park*, claimed to be the best in Mexico. There are three lovely *PP*s between Loreto and Puerto Escondido; Notrí, Juncalito and Ligüí—palm-lined coves, which are a far cry from the bustle of the new resort developments nearby. Beyond Ligüí (36 km. south of Loreto) Highway 1 ascends the eastern escarpment of the Sierra Giganta before leaving the Gulf to strike out SW across the Peninsula again to Ciudad Constitución. It passes by Ciudad Insurgentes, a busy agricultural town of 13,000 with two service stations, banks, auto repairs, shops and cafés, then runs dead straight for 26 km. to *Ciudad Constitución*, which has the largest population between Ensenada and La Paz (50,000). Although not a tourist town, it has extensive services of use to the visitor.

Hotels *Maribel*, D, Guadalupe Victoria y Highway 1, 2 blocks S of San Carlos road junction, a/c, TV, restaurant, bar, suites available, clean, fine for overnight stop; *Casino*, E, a block E of the *Maribel* on same street, quieter, 37 clean rooms, restaurant, bar.

Camping *Campestre La Pila*, 2½ km. S on unpaved road off Highway 1, farmland setting, full hookups, toilets, showers, pool, laundry, tennis courts, ice, restaurant, bar, no hot water, US\$10-13 for 4.

Excursion Deep artesian wells have made the desert of the Llano de Magdalena bloom with citrus groves and a chequerboard of neat farms growing cotton, wheat and vegetables; this produce is shipped out through the port of San Carlos, 58 km. to the west of Bahía Magdalena. Known to boaters as "Mag Bay", it is considered the finest natural harbour between San Francisco and Acapulco. Protected by mountains and sand spits, it provides the best boating on Baja's Pacific coast. Small craft can explore kilometres of mangrove-fringed inlets and view the grey whales who come here in the winter season. On the narrow S end of Magdalena Island is Puerto Magdalena, a lobstering village of 400. 7 km. away is a deepwater port at Punta Belcher, used for shipping out the phosphoric sand mined near Puerto Lopes Mateos. On Santa Margarita Island are Puertos Alcatráz (a fish-canning community of 300) and Cortés (important naval base); neither is shown on the ACSC map.

Highway 1 continues its arrow-straight course south of Ciudad Constitución across the flat plain to the village of Santa Rita, where it makes a 45° turn E. 28 km. beyond Santa Rita, a road of dubious quality runs to the remote missions of San Luis Gonzaga (64 km.) and La Pasión (49 km.); it is planned to extend it to the ruins of Dolores del Sur (85 km.) on the Gulf of California, one of Baja's most inaccessible mission sites. There is a service station at the village of El Cien; meals and refreshments are available at the Rancho San Agustín, 24 km. beyond.

La Paz capital of Baja California Sur, is a fast-changing, but relaxed modern city (population 160,000), nestled at the southern end of La Paz Bay (where Europeans first set foot in Baja in 1533). Sunsets can be spectacular. Prices have risen as more tourists arrive to enjoy its winter climate, but free port status ensures that there are plenty of bargains (although some goods, like certain makes of camera, are cheaper to buy in the USA). Oyster beds attracted many settlers in the 17th C. but few survived long. The Jesuit mission, founded here in 1720, was abandoned 29 years later. La Paz became the territorial capital in 1829 after Loreto was wiped out by a hurricane. Although bursting with new construction, there are still many touches of colonial grace, arched doorways and flower-filled patios. The early afternoon *siesta* is still observed by many businesses, especially during summer.

Heart of La Paz is the Plaza Constitución, facing which are the Government Buildings and the graceful Cathedral of Nuestra Señora de la Paz, built in 1861-65 on or near the site of the original mission. The Post Office is a block NE of Revolución de 1910 y Constitución. The street grid is rectangular; westerly streets run into the Paseo Alvaro Obregón—the waterfront Malecón—where the commercial and tourist wharves back onto a tangle of streets just W of the main plaza; here are the banks, City Hall, Chinatown and many of the cheaper *pensiones*. The more expensive hotels are further SW. A must is the Museo Antropológico de Baja California Sur, Ignacio Altamirano y 5 de Mayo (4 blocks E of the Plaza), with an admirable display of peninsula anthropology, history and pre-history, folklore and geology. (The bookshop has a wide selection on Mexico and Baja. Open Tue.-Sat. 0900-1800; entry free.) A carved mural depicting the history of Mexico can be seen at the Palacio de Gobierno on Isabel La Católica, corner of Bravo. There are boat tours from the Tourist Wharf on the Malecón around the bay and to nearby islands like Espíritu Santo.

Hotels *Los Arcos*, A, Paseo Alvaro Obregón 498 at Allende, a/c, pool, restaurant, coffee shop, across the Malecón from the beach, walking distance of centre, fishing trips arranged, excellent value; *Cabañas de los Arcos*, A, opposite with shared facilities, a/c, pool, slightly cheaper; *La Posada*, A, on bay 3½ km. SW of centre, 5 blocks off Highway 1 on Colima, a/c, pool, tennis, bar, restaurant, quiet and relaxing, recommended but away from the centre; *Gran Hotel Baja*, A, "the only high-rise structure south of Ensenada", so easy to find, restaurant, bar, pool, disco, etc, on beach, trailer park adjacent; *Ramada La Paz*, B, 3 km. SW of centre, a/c, pool, beach, tennis, fishing, skin diving, 2 pools, disco, dining room; *El Morro*, B, 3½ km. NE on Palmira Beach, Moorish-style, a/c, TV, fridges, apartments with kitchenettes (1 bedroom US$40, 2 bedroom US$60), pool, restaurant, bar; *Misiones de La Paz*, A, on El Mogote sandspit, isolated, accessible by launch from Hotel La Posada, a/c, showers, pool, restaurant, cocktail bar, quiet; *Palmira*, A, 3½ km. NE of Pichilingüe road, a/c, pool, tennis, restaurant, disco, convention facilities, fishing trips arranged, popular with families; *El Presidente Sur*, A, 6½ km. NE at Caimancito Beach, good location but furthest from town, a/c, pool, restaurant, bar, next door to Governor's mansion; *María Dolores Gardenias*, C, Aquíles Serdán y Vicente Guerrero, a/c, pool, restaurant (good), excellent value; *Hospedaje Marelí*, D/E, Aquíles Serdán 283 y Bravo, a/c, clean, 10 min. walk to Plaza Constitución, pleasant, recommended; *Clark*, D, a/c, with or without bathroom, ½ block from *Mareli* on Bravo, popular with families, best of the budget hotels; *Pensión California*, F, Calle Degollado 209 near Madero, fan, shower, garden patio, basic but popular; similar is *Hostería del Convento*, F, Calle Madero 85, adequate; *Posada San Miguel*, F, Calle Belisario Domínguez Norte 45, near plaza, colonial-style, bathroom, clean, hot water morning and evening, OK; *Palencia*, F, Calle 16 de Septiembre nr. Francisco Madero, central, basic, fans, seedy, not recommended; *Cuartos Jalisco*, Belisario Domínguez 251, F, very basic. *Youth Hostel*, on Carretera al Sur (Highway 1) near S end of Isabel La Catolica, about 20 blocks from centre, dormitory bunk US$1.60 per night, open 0600-2300, good value, "8 de Octubre" bus from market.

Camping *El Cardón Trailer Park*, 4 km. SW on Highway 1, partly-shaded area away from beach, full facilities, US$11 for 2; *Aquamarina RV Park*, 3½ km. SW, 400 m. off Highway 1 at Calle Nayarit, on bay, nicely landscaped, all facilities, marina, boat ramp, fishing, scuba trips arranged, US$17 for 2; *La Paz Trailer Park*, 1½ km. S of town off Highway 1, access via Calle Colima, deluxe, nearest RV Park to La Paz, very comfortable, US$12 for 2.

Restaurants *Palapa Adriana*, on beachfront, open air, excellent service; *Antojitos*, next to *Pirámide* on 16 de Septiembre de 1810, friendly, good value. *La Tavola Pizza*, good value. Vegetarian restaurant *El Quinto*, Independencia y B. Domínguez, expensive (whole wheat bread is half the price at the *panadería* in the market place). Good *lonchería* and juice bars in the market.

Shopping A duty-free port (but see above). *Casa de las Artesanías de B.C.S*, Paseo Alvaro Obregón at Mijares, just N of Hotel Los Arcos, for souvenirs from all over Mexico; *Centro de Arte Regional*, Chiapas y Encinas (5 blocks E of Isabel La Católica), pottery workshop, reasonable prices; *Fortunato Silva*, Highway 1 (Abasolo) y Jalisco at S end of town, good quality woollen and hand-woven cotton garments and articles. Tourist shops are concentrated along the Malecón between the Tourist and Commercial Wharves.

Beaches Many, most popular on the Pichilingüe Peninsula. Going N from La Paz to ferry terminal on Highway 11; Palmira, Coromuel (popular with paceños), El Caimancito, Tesoro. Pichilingüe (bus at 0800 the hourly from 1000-1700, US$0.35 from station at Paseo Alvaro Obregón y Independencia), 100 m. N of ferry terminal is a *PP*, about US$1. Balandra (rubbish bins, *palapas*, US$2), Tecolote (same) and El Coyote (no water or facilities), reached by rough graded road after pavement ends at ferry terminal, ends at a gravel pit at Playa Cachimba (good surf fishing), 13 km. NE of Pichilingüe; beaches facing north are attractive but windy, some mosquitoes. El Comitán and El Mogot, are to SW of La Paz on bay, tranquil, no surf.

Immigration Second floor of large building on Paseo Alvaro Obregón, opp. the pier.

Tourist Office On Tourist Wharf at bottom of 16 de Septiembre, helpful, English spoken, open Mon.-Fri. 0800-1500, Sat. 0900-1300, 1400-1500, open till 1900 high season, will make hotel reservations, some literature and town maps.

Buses Local buses about US$0.15, depot at Revolución de 1910 y Degollado by the Public Market. Central Bus Station (Central Camionera): 5 de Febrero y Valentín Gómez Farías, about 16 blocks from centre, terminal for Tres Estrellas de Oro and Autotransportes Aguila; Autotransportes de La Paz leave from Public Market. Ciudad Constitución 13 departures a day, US$3; Loreto 3 per day, US$4.75; Guerrero Negro 6 per day, US$10; Ensenada US$18.50; Tijuana US$20, Mexicali US$22. To the Cape: San Antonio US$0.85, Miraflores US$2.10, San José del Cabo US$2.75, Cabo San Lucas US$3.10 (all 10 departures per day). Todos Santos, 6 per day, US$1.80; Cabo San Lucas via west loop US$3.

Air General Manuel Márquez de León International Airport, 11 km. SW on paved road off Highway 1. Taxi fare US$3-4, supposedly fixed, but bargain. Mexicana: to Tijuana non-stop, Mexico City, Mazatlán, Guadalajara. Resorts Airline: daily from Los Angeles and San Diego via Loreto. To San José del Cabo daily. Aero California: to Los Mochis, daily 0800, US$30, with connection to Tijuana; city office at Malecón y Calle Bravo. Hughes Air Corporation from Tucson, Arizona.

Ferry Services Modern government-run ferry terminal at Pichilingüe, 21 km. north on paved highway. Make reservations at town office (Ignacio Ramírez y Ejido, on NE edge of town), 3 days ahead if possible. Tourist cards must be valid, allow plenty of time (preferably before 1400) as there are long queues—trucks have loading priority. It should be noted that many motorists have had difficulty getting reservations or having them honoured; the ferry system is becoming increasingly unreliable and fares are rising alarmingly. Vehicles must have car permits, obtainable at ferry ports but best to get at Registro Federal de Vehículos in Tijuana; automobile clubs will provide information. Four classes of service: *salón* (unreserved reclining seat, not particularly comfortable), *turista* (roomette with bunk), *cabina* (bedroom with bathroom), *especial* (suite).
  To Topolobampo Thurs. and Sun., dep. 2000, arr. mainland 0400; dep. Mon. and Thurs. 1000, return to Pichilingüe 1800. Fares (Feb. 1989) *salón*, US$1.60; *turista* US$3.15; *cabina*, US$7.10; *especial*, US$14.40; cars, US$10.75-12.45 (under-over 5 m.); motorhome, US$17.75; motorcycle, US$2.35.
  To Mazatlán Daily dep. 1700, arr. mainland 0900 next day; unclaimed cabins sold off to firstcomers one day in advance at 1500—chaotic queues; stand firm. Fares (Feb. 1989) *salón*, US$2.65; *turista*, US$5.25; *cabina*, US$11.35; *especial*, US$22.60; cars, US$17.35-20.00; motorhome, US$17.75; motorcycle, US$2.35.
  To Puerto Vallarta Fridays only, dep. 1200, arr. mainland 1200 next day. Supposedly a temporary service, schedules change, check. Fares (Feb. 1989) *salón*, US$4.05; *turista* US$8.10; *cabina*, US$18.45; *especial*, US$36.60; cars, US$26.65-29.35; motorhome, US$29.35; motorcycle, US$3.40.
  Bus to ferry terminal from Medrita Travel Agency, Paseo Alvaro Obregón y Calle 5 de Mayo, frequent departures. Reasonable facilities at terminal but crowded; large parking lots—officials may permit RVs to stay overnight while awaiting ferry departures.
  NB On all ferry crossings, delays can occur from September if there is bad weather, which could hold you up for 3 days; fog at the entrance to Topolobampo harbour is often a problem; mechanical breakdowns are not unknown! Keep a flexible schedule if travelling to the mainland.

Excursions 17 km. W of La Paz a paved road branches NW off Highway 1 leading to the mining village of San Juan de la Costa, allowing a closer look at the rugged coastal section of the Sierra de la Giganta. Pavement ends after 25 km., road becomes wide, rolling, regularly graded; OK for large RVs to San Juan, which is a company town of neat-rowed houses; phosphorus is mined and loaded by conveyor and deep-water dock, to be shipped to processing plants for fertilizer production. After San Juan (45 km.), the road is passable for medium-size vehicles to Punta Coyote (90 km.), closely following the narrow space between mountains and coast; wonderful untouched camping spots. From Coyote to San Evaristo (27 km.) the track is poor—rugged vehicle recommended, travel time from Highway 1 about 4½ hours; San Evaristo is a sleepy fishing village on a delightful cove sheltered on the east by the Isla San José. Ideal boating area but as yet undiscovered. Visit the salt-drying operations near San Evaristo or on San José. This is a rewarding excursion for those with smaller, high-clearance vehicles (vans and pick-ups with shells) for the steep final 20 mile stretch.

State Highway 286 leads SE out of La Paz 45 km. to San Juan de Los Planes (pop. 1,350), a friendly town in a rich farming region. A fair road continues another 15 km. to the beautiful Ensenada de los Muertos, good fishing, swimming and "wild" camping. A further 11 km. is the headland of Punta Arena de la Ventana, with a magnificent view of the sterile slopes of Isla Cerralvo. (Hotel Las Arenas, L, resort overlooking Ventana Bay). 6 km. before Los Planes, a graded road leads to the Bahía de la Ventana and the small fishing villages of La Ventana and El Sargento; lovely beaches facing Cerralvo Island.

S of La Paz and its plain, the central mountain spine rises again into the wooded heights of the Sierra de la Laguna and bulges out into the "Cape Region", Baja's most touristically-developed area. The highway winds up to *El Triunfo*, a picturesque village (almost a ghost town); silver was discovered at nearby San Antonio in 1748 and at El Triunfo in 1862. The latter exploded with a population of 10,000 and was for a while the largest town in Baja. The mines closed in 1926 but small-scale mining has resumed in places. *Warning:* present-day miners are using arsenic in the old mine tailings; these areas are fenced and signed. There is a craft shop at the village entrance where young people make palm-leaf objects. 8 km. further on is the lovely mountain town and farming centre of San Antonio (gasoline, groceries, meals), which was founded in 1756 and served briefly as Baja's capital (1828-30) when Loreto was destroyed. 8 km. S of San Antonio was the site of Santa Ana, where silver was first discovered in 1748. It was from this vanished village that the Viceroy and Padre Junipero Serra planned the expedition to establish the chain of Franciscan missions in Alta California.

Highway 1 climbs sharply from the canyon and winds past a number of ancient mines, through the peaceful orchard-farming town of San Bartolo (groceries and meals) and down to the coastal flats around Los Barriles, a small town with fuel, meals and limited supplies. A number of resort hotels are situated near here along the beautiful Bahía de Palmas and at nearby Buena Vista; none is in the "budget" class but all are popular.

The Highway turns inland after Los Barriles (106 km. from La Paz). An "East Cape Loop" turns E off the Highway through La Rivera, following the coast to San José del Cabo. Off Cabo Pulmo, a beautiful headland, is the Northern Pacific's only living coral reef; fishing, diving and snorkelling are excellent (56 km. from Los Barriles). There are many camping spots along the beautiful beaches of this coast.

Santiago is a pleasant, historic little town (pop. 2,000) 3 km. off Highway 1. On the tree-lined main street are a Pemex station, café and stores grouped around the town plaza. A kilometre further W is the Parque Zoológico, the Cape's only zoo—modest but informative, free admission. The Jesuits built their 10th mission in Santiago in 1723 after transferring it from Los Barriles. The town was one of the sites of the Pericué Indian uprising of 1734. (**Hotel** *Palomar*, D, a/c, hot showers, restaurant, bar, on main street, modest, good meals).

3½ km. S of the Santiago turnoff Highway 1 crosses the Tropic of Cancer and runs S down the fertile valley between the lofty Sierra de la Laguna (west) and the Sierra Santa Clara (east), to the Cabos International Airport (direct jet services to California, USA, and Mexico; modern terminal, parking and good transportation to San José del Cabo, 10 km. S).

San José del Cabo, the largest town south of La Paz, has a population of 10,000. Although founded in 1730, it is now essentially a modern town divided into two districts: the resort sectors and new FONATUR development on the beach, and the downtown zone to the north, with the government offices and many businesses grouped near the tranquil Parque Mijares, and numerous shops and restaurants along Calles Zaragoza and Doblado. The N end of Blvd Antonio Mijares has been turned into a "mini-gringoland ... which could have been transplanted from the Main St. of Disneyland" (Scott Wayne). San José also has two service stations, hospital, auto parts and mechanical repairs. The attractive church on the Plaza Mijares was built in 1940 on the final site of the mission of 1730; a tile mosaic over the entrance depicts the murder of Padre Tamaral by rebellious Indians in 1734. Most of the top hotels are located W of San José along the beaches or nearby *estero*; the FONATUR development blocks access to much of the beach near town; best are Playas Nuevo Sol and California, about 3 km. from downtown. Unofficial camping is possible on those few not fronted by resort hotels.

Hotels *Palmilla*, L, one of the top resorts in Baja, 8 km. W at Punta Palmilla (outstanding surfing nearby), some a/c, showers, pool, beach, tennis, narrow access road, restaurant, bar, skin diving, fishing cruisers US$325 per day, skiffs US$125 (daily happy hour allows were mortals to partake of margarita and appetizers for US$3 and see how royalty and film stars live!). *El Presidente*, L, on lagoon S of town, a/c, all facilities, boat rentals, centrepiece of the FONATUR development at San José del Cabo; *Castel Cabo*, A, on beach off Paseo San José S of Town, a/c, another FONATUR hotel; *Posada Real Cabo*, A, next door, a/c, colour TV, showers, pool, tennis, restaurant, bar, gift shop, fishing charters US$90 per day for 3; *Calinda Aquamarina-Comfort Inn*, A, next to Posada Real Cabo, U.S. Comfort Inn chain, a/c, beach, pool, restaurant, bar, fishing, clean and comfortable; *Aston Cabo Regis Resort and Beach Club* (still under construction 1988), in hotel zone on Blvd Finisterra, a/c, colour TV, showers, kitchenettes, private balconies, pool, tennis, golf course, restaurant; *Nuevo Sol*, C, on beach S of intersection of Paseo San José and Highway 1, pool, restaurant, sports facilities, nicely-landscaped, acceptable and good beachside value; *Collí*, D, in town on Hidalgo above Budget Rent-a-Car, fans, hot showers, 12 clean and adequate rooms; *Pagamar*, E, Obregón between Degollado y Guerrero 3½ blocks from plaza, fans, café, hot showers, clean, good value; *Ceci*, E, Zaragoza 22, 1 block W of plaza, fans, hot showers, basic but clean, excellent value, central. CREA youth hostel, Domicilio Conocido Anikan s/n. Motel *Brisa del Mar*, D, on Highway 1, 3 km. SW of town near Hotel Nuevo Sol, 10 rooms, restaurant, bar, pool, modest but comfortable, at rear of trailer park on outstanding beach.

Camping *Brisa Del Mar Trailer Park*, 100 RV sites in fenced area by great beach, full hookups, flush toilets, showers, pool, laundry, restaurant, bar, fishing trips arranged, US$5-10 for 2, popular, good location ("unofficial" camping possible under *palapas* on beach).

Bus Bus station on Calle Manuel Doblado opp. hospital, about 7 blocks W of plaza. To Cabo San Lucas (Tres Estrellas) daily from 0700, US$0.60, ½ hr; to La Paz daily from 0630, US$3.10, 2 hrs.

Regrettably, many of the coastal views and natural camping spots on the 34 km. run from San José del Cabo to Cabo San Lucas are barred to visitors by beachfront developments. These include: *Hotel Cabo San Lucas*, L, *Twin Dolphin*, L+, and *Calinda Cabo Baja-Quality Inn*, L, part of Cabo Bello residential development. At km. 25, just after the *Twin Dolphin*, a dirt road leads off to Shipwreck Beach, with beachside camping area; there is a large ship rotting on the shore. 5 km. before Cabo a small concrete marker beside the highway heralds an excellent view of the famous Cape. The Highway enters Cabo San Lucas past a Pemex station and continues as Blvd Lázaro Cárdenas to the Zócalo (Guerrero y Madero) and the Kilómetro 0 marker.

Cabo San Lucas has grown rapidly in recent years from a sleepy fishing village (pop. 1,500 in 1970) to a bustling international resort with a permanent population of 8,500. There are trailer parks, many cafés and restaurants, condominiums, gift shops, discos and a marina to cater for the increasing flood of North Americans who come for the world-famous sportfishing or to find a retirement paradise. The town fronts a small harbour facing the rocky peninsula that forms the "Land's End" of Baja California. Francisco de Ulloa first rounded and named the Cape in 1539. The sheltered bay became a watering point for the treasure ships from the Orient; pirates sheltered here too. Now it is on the cruise ship itinerary. A popular attraction is the government-sponsored regional arts centre, where distinctive black-coral jewellery is made and sold, located at the cruise liner dock. Post Office is at Morelos y Niños Héroes.

Hotels *Hacienda Beach Resort*, L, at N entrance to harbour, some a/c, showers, pool, tennis, yacht anchorage, various water sports, hunting, horseriding, restaurant, etc., claims the only area beach safe from strong Pacific swells; *Giggling Marlin Inn*, L, central on Blvd Marina y Matamoros, a/c, TV, showers, kitchenettes, jacuzzi, restaurant, bar, fishing trips arranged, lively drinking and poor food in attached cocktail bar; *Finisterra*, L, perched on promontory near Land's End, a/c, TV, shower, pool, steps to beach, poolside bar with unsurpassed view, restaurant, entertainment, sportfishing cruisers US$295 per day; *Marina Sol Condominiums*, L:16 Oct-30 June, A: rest of year, on 16 de Septiembre, between Highway 1 and Bay, full hotel service in 3- and 7-storey buildings; *Solmar*, L, the southernmost development in Baja California, a/c, showers, ocean view, pool, tennis, diving, restaurant, poolside bar, fishing cruisers US$275-295 per day, beach with heavy ocean surf; *Mar de Cortez*, B, on Highway 1 at Guerrero in town centre, a/c, showers, pool, outdoor bar/restaurant, suites US$50; *Marina*, C, Blvd Marina y Guerrero, central, a/c, restaurant, bar, can be noisy, pricey; *Casablanca*, E, Calle Revolución between Morelos y Leona Vicario, central, fan, shower, clean, cheapest in town. Motel *Los Cabos Inn*, C/D, Abasolo y 16 de Septiembre, central, 1 block from bus station, fans, showers, central, modest, good value.

Camping *El Arco Trailer Park*, 4 km. E on Highway 1, restaurant, US$8 per site; *El Faro Viejo Trailer Park*, 1½ km. NW at Matamoros y Morales, shade, laundry, ice, restaurant, bar, clean, out-of-town but good, US$6 for 2; *Vagabundos del Mar*, 3½ km. E on Highway 1, pool, laundry, good, US$15 for 2; *Cabo Cielo RV Park*, 3 km. E on Highway 1; *San Vicente Trailer Park*, 3 km. E on Highway 1, same as Cabo Cielo plus pool, both reasonably basic, rates unknown. All have full hookups, toilets and showers. Several *playas públicas* on coast E of town, inc. Cabo Real, 5 km., showers and restrooms, modest fee; "Barco Barrado" (Shipwreck Beach), 10 km., lovely beach, camping W of shipwreck, showers and restrooms, US$5 per night, popular with RVs.

Tourist Office next to ferry landing, town maps, FONATUR office. Many firms renting aquatic equipment and arranging boating excursions, etc; the beaches E of Cabo San Lucas offer endless opportunities for swimming, scuba diving and snorkelling. Boat trips to Lover's Beach about US$16 for 4; most hotels can arrange hire of skiffs to enable visits to the Arch and Land's End, about US$5-10 per hour.

Bus Bus station at 16 de Septiembre y Zaragoza, central, few facilities. To San José del Cabo, 8 departures a day, US$0.50. To La Paz 6 a day from 0630, US$4.75; Tijuana US$24, 1600 and 1800 daily via La Paz.

Ferry To Puerto Vallarta, Sun. and Wed.; departs 1600 from both destinations, sails from Puerto Vallarta on Sat. and Tues., 18 hours. *Salón* US$3.25, *turista* US$6.75, *cabina* US$14.70, *especial* US$29.35. Vehicle rates (1989): Up to 5 m., US$23, 5 m.-6.5 m., US$25.65; motorhome, US$30; motorcycle, US$2.75. Note again that ferry schedules are subject to change and fares are rising unpredictably—check and reconfirm. Most cabins cannot be reserved and are "released" for sale at 1500 on day before departure at Ferry Office—expect chaos and unbelievable frustration! Reservations should be made three weeks in advance by phoning the Office ((706)843-0079). This service was not running in February 1989.

Ringed by pounding surf, columns of fluted rock enclose Lover's Beach (be careful if walking along the beach—huge waves sweep away several visitors each year), a romantic sandy cove with views out to the seal colonies on offshore islets. At the very tip of the Cabo is the distinctive natural arch ("el arco"); boats can be hired to see it close-up, but care is required because of the strong rips. At the harbour entrance is a pinnacle of rock—Pelican Rock—which is home to vast shoals of tropical fish; it is an ideal place for snorkelling and scuba diving or glass-bottomed boats may be rented at the harbourside.

Highway 19, the western loop of the Cape Region, was not paved until 1985 and the superb beaches of the west coast have yet to suffer the development and crowding of the east. The highway branches off Highway 1 just after San Pedro, 32 km. S of La Paz, and runs due south through a cactus-covered plain to **Todos Santos**, a quiet farming town of 4,000 only a few hundred metres N of the Tropic of Cancer. There is a Pemex station, cinema, stores, cafés, a bank, clinic and market, a museum—the Casa de la Cultura (Calles Topete y Pilar)—and *Misión de Todos Santos Inn*, C, historic brick building near town centre, showers, B&B, other meals available in dining room on request; *Hotel California*, C, Calle Juárez next to Pemex station a block N of Highway 19, fans, showers, pool, restaurant. *El Molino Trailer Park*, off Highway at S end of town, full hookups, flush toilets, showers, laundry, US$8 for 4, better value than the hotels!

Todos Santos was founded as a Jesuit mission in 1734; a church replacing the abandoned structure, built in 1840, stands opposite the Civic Plaza on Calle Juárez. The ruins of several old sugar mills can be seen around the town in the fertile valley. Fishing is also important.

2 km. away is the Pacific coast with some of the most beautiful beaches of the entire Peninsula. Nearest is Playa Punta Lobos, a popular picnic spot; better is the sandy cove at Playa Pedrito (4km SE). Backed by groves of Washingtonia fan palms and coconut palms, this is one of the loveliest camping spots anywhere. Opposite the access road junction is the Campo Experimental Forestal, a Botanical Garden with a well-labelled array of desert plants from all regions of Baja. Here too is the *San Pedrito RV Park*, an open area on the beach, full hookups, flush toilets, showers, pool, laundry, restaurant, bar, US$3 for tent, US$8 for RVs, one of the most beautifully-sited RV parks in Baja, very good value. 11 km. S of Todos Santos is El Pescadero, a fast-growing farming town with few facilities for visitors.

Excursion In the rugged interior E of Todos Santos is the **Parque Nacional Sierra de la Laguna** (under threat and not officially recognized). Crowning peak is the Picacho La Laguna (2,163 m.), beginning to attract a trickle of hikers to its "lost world" of pine and oak trees, doves and woodpeckers, grassy meadows and luxuriant flowers; there is nothing else like it in Baja south of the Sierra San Pedro Mártir. Trail is steep but straight forward; the panoramic view takes in La Paz and both the Gulf and Pacific. Cold at night. Best reached from Todos Santos by making local enquiries; 3-day guided pack trips are also offered by the Todos Santos Inn, US$325 per person.

7 km. S of El Pescadero is *Los Cerritos RV Park* on a wide sandy beach, 50 RV or tent sites but no hook-ups, flush toilets, US$3 per vehicle. Playa Los Cerritos is a *playa pública*; there are several camping areas but no facilities, US$1-2 per vehicle. The succession of rocky coves and empty beaches continues to Colonia Plutarco Elías Calles, a tiny farming village in the midst of a patchwork of orchards. The highway then parallels the coast to Rancho El Migriño, then continues S along the coastal plain; there are no more camping spots as far as Cabo San Lucas. Many now prefer the West Loop to the main highway; it is 140 km. from the junction at San Pedro, thus cutting off about 50 km. and up to an hour's driving time from the Transpeninsular Highway route.

We are deeply grateful to Kevin Healey (Balaclava, Vic.) for rewriting the Baja California section.

THE ECONOMY

Mexico has been an oil producer since the 1880s and was the world's leading producer in 1921, but by 1971 had become a net importer. This position was reversed in the mid-1970s with the discovery in 1972 of major new oil reserves. Mexico is now the world's fourth largest producer, 65 % of crude output coming from offshore wells in the Gulf of Campeche, and 28 % from onshore fields in the Chiapas-Tabasco area in the southeast. Proven reserves of 48.6bn barrels in the mid-1980s were sufficient to last 54 years. Mexico depends on oil and gas for about 85 % of its primary energy supply and exports of crude oil, oil products and natural gas account for a third of exports and about two-fifths of government revenues.

Mexico's mineral resources are legendary. Precious metals make up about 36 % of non-oil mineral output. The country is the world's leading producer of silver, fluorite and arsenic, and is among the world's major producers of strontium, graphite, copper, iron ore, sulphur, mercury, lead and zinc. Mexico also produces gold, molybdenum, antimony, bismuth, cadmium, selenium, tungsten, magnesium, common salt, celestite, fuller's earth and gypsum. It is estimated that although 60 % of Mexico's land mass has mineral potential, only 25 % is known, and only 5 % explored in detail.

Agriculture employs 27 % of the labour force but has been losing importance since the beginning of the 1970s and now contributes only 9 % of gdp. About 12 % of the land surface is under cultivation, of which only about one-quarter is irrigated. Over half of the developed cropland lies in the interior highlands. Mexico's agricultural success is almost always related to rainfall and available water for irrigation. On average, four out of every ten years are good, while four are drought years.

Manufacturing, including oil refining and petrochemicals, contributes a quarter of gdp. Mexico City is the focal point for manufacturing activity and the metropolitan area holds about 45 % of the employment in manufacturing and 30 % of the country's industrial establishments. The government offers tax incentives to companies relocating away from Mexico City and the other major industrial centres of Guadalajara and Monterrey; target cities are Tampico, Coatzacoalcos, Salina Cruz and Lázaro Cárdenas, while much of the manufacturing export activity takes place in the in-bond centres along the border with the USA.

Tourism is the second largest source of foreign exchange, after oil, and the largest employer, with about a third of the workforce. About 4.5m tourists visit Mexico every year, of whom about 85 % come from the USA. The government is actively encouraging new investment in tourism and foreign investment is being welcomed in hotel construction projects.

During 1978-81 the current account of the balance of payments registered increasing deficits because of domestic expansion and world recession. Mounting public sector deficits were covered by foreign borrowing of increasingly shorter terms until a bunching of short-term maturities and a loss of foreign exchange reserves caused Mexico to declare its inability to service its debts in August 1982, thus triggering what became known as the international debt crisis. Under the guidance of an IMF programme and helped by commercial bank debt rescheduling agreements, Mexico was able to improve its position largely because of a 40 % drop in imports in both 1982 and 1983. In 1986, however, the country was hit by the sharp fall in oil prices, which reduced export revenues by 28 %, despite a rapid growth of 37 % in non-oil exports through vigorous promotion and exchange rate depreciation policies. Several debt rescheduling and new money agreements were negotiated during the 1980s with the IMF, the World Bank and the commercial banks. Mexico managed to secure progressively easier terms, helped by the US administration's concern for geopolitical reasons, and debt growth was contained. Prepayment of private debt and debt/equity conversions even reduced the overall level of foreign debt.

	1961-70 (av)	1971-80 (av)	1981-85 (av)	1986-88 (av)(e)
Gdp growth (1980 prices)	7.0%	6.6%	1.6%	−0.5%
Inflation	2.7%	16.6%	60.7%	109.9%
Exports (fob) US$m	1,140	5,097	21,908	19,153
Petroleum	32	2,343	16,536	6,214
Imports (fob) US$m	1,574	7,091	14,347	14,252
Current account balance US$m (cum)	−4,947	−32,139	−9,920	−892

INFORMATION FOR VISITORS

Travel by Air   Several airlines have regular flights from Europe to Mexico City. *Air France* from Paris via Houston; *Iberia* from Madrid non-stop or via Montreal; *Aeroméxico* from Paris and Madrid; *KLM* from Amsterdam via Houston; *Canadian Pacific* from Amsterdam via Montreal; *Lufthansa* from Frankfurt via Montreal to Mérida, Monterrey and Mexico City; also via Dallas; *Pan Am* from Europe via New York, Houston or Miami.

Mexico City from New York, under 4 hrs.; from Chicago, 4 hrs.; from Los Angeles, 3 hrs. with *Mexicana* ("Moonlight Express", cost about 60% of normal); from Houston, 3 hrs.; from Brownsville (Texas), via Tampico, 2½ hrs.; from St. Louis or Washington (by connecting air lines through Houston), 8 hrs. and 9 hrs. respectively. *Mexicana* does a round trip Los Angeles-Guadalajara ("Moonlight Express") nightly. There are direct *Aeroméxico* flights connecting Miami with Mérida, 1½ hrs., and daily connecting New York with Tijuana and Cancún, Miami-Mexico City, 2½ hrs. *Eastern Airlines* flies between Atlanta and Acapulco, Mérida and Cancún. Round-trips Atlanta-Cancún or Mérida-Miami-Cancún. Cheapest way to get to San Diego is to fly from Mexico City to Tijuana, walk across border and take the train to downtown San Diego (15-20 min. journey). Quito-Mexico City with *Ecuatoriana*. *Aerolíneas Argentinas* and *AeroPerú* fly to and from Lima.

Airport Departure Tax   US$10 on international flights; US$4.50 on internal flights (February 1988).

By Sea   All the following shipping services are for cargo, carrying a limited number of passengers.

Mexican Line, from New York to Veracruz, sailing every Fri., 7 days. North-bound ships leave Tampico every Sun. via Philadelphia to New York, 7 days. Commodore Cruise Lines from Miami to Cozumel, sail every Sat. night (November-Spring). Cruise continues on Mon. to Haiti, Jamaica and back to Miami. Naviera Turística Mexicana makes 2 round trips a month between Los Angeles, Mazatlán, and Acapulco.

Hapag-Lloyd, Bremen, 2 to 3 sailings a month from Hamburg, Bremen, Antwerp to Veracruz and Tampico.

Harrison Line: from Liverpool, every fortnight. Sidarma Line: monthly from Genoa to Veracruz. Spanish Line: from Spain to Veracruz. S.A. Armement Deppe: from Antwerp to Tampico and Veracruz.

Norwegian Caribbean Lines occasionally take one-way passengers with about 2 weeks advance booking at a flat rate of US$67 a night.

Overland   Toronto to Mexico City, via Chicago-St. Louis-Dallas-San Antonio- Laredo-Monterrey, with Greyhound bus (74 hrs.) on a 15-day pass. Montreal-Laredo via New York, Washington, Atlanta, New Orleans, Houston and San Antonio, 60 hrs., US$132. Both Greyhound and Trailways provide services from Miami to the Mexican border and on to Mexico City. It's cheaper to make booking outside the US, but the information is hard to come by in Mexico City. Trailways in London, c/o Holiday Inn, Heathrow Airport, Stockley Rd., West Drayton, Middlesex, UB7 9NA. Los Angeles-Mexico City, US$58, 44 hrs.; New York-Mexico City, US$120.50, 70 hrs.; San Antonio-Mexico City, US$27, 20 hrs. If coming from the US it is usually cheaper to travel to the border and buy your ticket in the Mexican border town from the Mexican company.

To Cuba   Return flight to Cuba, Sun. and Wed., with stop at Mérida if plane is not fully booked. Cuba package tours US$285 for seven day all-inclusive stay and return flight from Mexico City or US$213 from Mérida. Ask around Hamburgo in Mexico City for cheap tickets: might pick them up for as little as US$120 or so. If you pay in dollars make sure the fact is noted on the ticket; if you pay in pesos and use the ticket later you may be surcharged if the peso price has risen meanwhile. Visas for Cuba available through Viñales Tours, Melchor Ocampo 469, Colonia Anzures, T 511-30-33; you have to show your return ticket for Cuba.

N.B. VAT is payable on domestic plane tickets bought in Mexico.

Travel in Mexico   Promotional packages for local tourism exist, with 30-40% discount, operated by hoteliers, restaurateurs, hauliers and Aeroméxico and Mexicana (the latter is more punctual). Their tickets are not interchangeable. Aeroméxico has all-inclusive travel (*VTI*) and journey-inclusive hotel (*VHI*) rates; the former includes 3 nights lodging, half-board and return flight, the latter transport and lodging only. Mexicana has similar arrangements with the initials

VIP and *VHP*. Check whether you qualify for the dozen or so destinations. The two local airlines offer 15% discounts to foreigners for their domestic air services; 20% if the foreigners arrive on their own flights. Discounts must be claimed within one week of arrival.

There are three kinds of buses, first and second class, and local. Terminals for each are usually distinct, and may not be in one bus station. Buses in the country will not stop on curves—walk until you find a straight stretch. First-class buses assign you a seat and you may have to queue for 1-2 hrs. to get a ticket. It is not easy to choose which seat or to change it later. No standing, and you may have to wait for the next one (next day, perhaps) if all seats are taken. You *must* book in advance for buses travelling in the Yucatán Peninsula, especially around Christmas, but it is also advisable to book if going elsewhere. Bus seats are particulary hard to get during school holidays, around Easter and August and the 15 days up to New Year when many public servants take holidays in all resorts; transport from Mexico City is booked up a long time in advance and hotels are filled, too. In the north especially, try to travel from the starting-point of a route; buses are often full at the mid-point of their routes. Beware of "scalpers" who try to sell you a seat at a higher price, which you can usually get on a stand-by basis, when somebody doesn't turn up, at the regular price. Sometimes it helps to talk to the driver, who has two places to use at his discretion behind his seat (don't sit in these until invited). Lock your luggage to the rack with a cycle lock and chain. First-class buses often have toilets and air-conditioning which does not work, but are nevertheless recommended for long-distance travelling. If going on an overnight bus, book seats at front as toilets get very smelly by morning. Second-class buses are often antiques (interesting, but frustrating when they break down) or may be brand new; the passengers are invariably more entertaining and courteous than in first-class buses. They call at towns and villages and go up side roads the first-class buses never touch. They stop quite as often for meals and toilets as their superiors do and—unlike the first-class buses—people get on and off so often that you may be able to obtain a seat after all. Seats are not bookable, except in Baja California. In general, it is a good idea to take food and drink with you on a long bus ride, as stops may depend on the driver and also a warm outer garment as air-conditioning on 1st class buses is often turned way down. First class fares are usually 10% dearer than 2nd class ones. Some companies give holders of an international student card a 50% discount on bus tickets; persistence may be required. There seem always to be many buses leaving in the early morning. Buses are sometimes called *camiones*, hence *central camionero* for bus station. A monthly bus guide is available for US$1 (year's subscription) from Guía de Autotransportes de México, Apartado 8929, México 1, D.F.

As for trains, much of the passenger equipment in use dates from the forties or fifties, including a number of *autovías*. There are modern trains between Mexicali and Guadalajara in 36 hours, and overnight good Pullman trains between Mexico City and Monterrey, Guadalajara, Veracruz and Mérida. The *servicio estrella* services (see text for routes) provide good accommodation and all meals, and have been recommended. The railways claim that you can see more from a train than from any other form of transport; this may well be true, but trains tend to be slower than the buses (though cheaper; 2nd class is about one-third of 2nd-class bus fare; they can, however, be very crowded); they sometimes have comfortable sleeper cars with *alcobas* (better berths) and *camarines* (small sleepers). The special first class has air-conditioning and reclining seats and costs about 10% more than the regular 1st class, which costs about twice the 2nd class fare. Tickets are best booked at the stations; agencies tend to add a large commission and the tickets they issue sometimes turn out not to be valid. A condensed railway timetable may be obtained from the Mexican railways' office at 500 Fifth Ave. (Room 2623), New York, N.Y. 10036. (For extensive information about the Mexican railway network consult *Makens' Guide to Mexican Train Travel*, compiled by James C. Makens and published by Le Voyageur Publishing Co., 1319 Wentwood Drive, Irving, Texas 75061, at about US$6.)

If you should get caught during the holiday season try to book a 2nd class train, but this may involve queuing 12 hrs. or more if you want a seat. More first-class tickets are sold than the total number of first-class seats; first-class passengers are allowed on first, so you may still find a 2nd class seat. Some travellers have remarked that the last carriage of a 2nd class train is often half full of soldiers, who might deter would-be thieves from taking one's personal belongings if one shares their carriage. We have received a report of conductors turning out lights on night trains, enabling thieves to operate with impunity; take great care under these circumstances.

Walking Walkers are advised to get *Backpacking in Mexico and Central America*, by Hilary Bradt and Rob Rachowiecki. Do not walk at night on dark, deserted roads or streets.

Hitch-hiking is usually possible for single hikers, but apparently less easy for couples. The most difficult stretches are reported to be Acapulco-Puerto Escondido, Santa Cruz-Salina Cruz and Tulum-Chetumal.

Camping Beware of people stealing clothes, especially when you hang them up after washing. Paraffin oil (kerosene) for stoves is called *petróleo para lámparas* in Mexico; it is not a very good quality (dirty) and costs about US$0.03 per litre. It is available from an *expendio*, or *despacho de petróleo*, or from a *tlalapería*, but not from gas stations. Alcohol for heating the burner can be obtained from supermarkets. Repairs to stoves at Servis-Coliman at Plaza de San Juan 5, Mexico City.

Youth Hostels 21 CREA *albergues* exist in Mexico, mostly in small towns, and generally of poor quality. All US$2.00 with Youth Hostel card, US$2.50 without.

Friends To meet interesting people, it is probably a good idea to visit the Casa de Cultura in any sizeable town.

Documents A passport is necessary, but US and Canadian citizens need only show birth certificate (or for US, a naturalization certificate). Tourists need the free tourist card, which can be obtained from any Mexican Consulate or Tourist Commission office, at the Mexican airport on entry, from the offices or on the aircraft of airlines operating into Mexico, ask for at least 30 days; if you say you are in transit you may be charged US$8, with resulting paper work. N.B. Not all Mexican consuls in USA are aware of exact entry requirements; it is best to confirm details with airlines which fly to Mexico. Some nationalities, including West Germans, appear no longer to need a tourist card. Best to say you are going to an inland destination. (Airlines may issue cards only to citizens of West European countries, most Latin American countries—not Cuba, Chile or Haiti—the USA, Canada, Australia, Japan and the Philippines.) Also at border offices of the American Automobile Association (AAA), which offers this service to members and non-members. There is a multiple entry card valid for all visits within 6 months for US nationals; the normal validity for other nationals is 90 days, but sometimes only 30 days are granted at border crossings; insist you want more if wishing to stay longer. Renewal of entry cards or visas must be done at Secretaría de Gobernación, Dirección General de Asuntos Jurídicos, Av. Juárez 92, piso 2, Mexico City (T 535-2718/5798, C.P. 06500—postal address). There is also a helpful office at Room 78 in the International Airport. Take travellers' cheques as proof of finance. Best to collect visa, not have it forwarded by post. Travellers not carrying tourist cards need visas (Israelis need a visa). Tourist cards are not required for cities close to the US border, such as Tijuana, Mexicali, etc. Businessmen who want to study the Mexican market or to appoint an agent should apply for the requisite visa and permit.

At border crossings make sure the immigration people don't con you to pay a dollar for the card or visa. It is free and the man typing it out is only doing his job. We would warn travellers that there have been several cases of tourist cards not being honoured, or a charge being imposed, or the validity being changed arbitrarily to 60 days or less. In this case, complaint should be made to the authorities in Mexico City. Some border stations do not issue tourist cards; you are therefore strongly advised, if travelling by land, to obtain a card before arriving at the border. Above all, do not lose your tourist card—you cannot leave the country without it and it takes at least a week to replace. If you want to return to Mexico after leaving there to visit Belize or Guatemala, remember that you will need a new visa/tourist card if yours is not marked for multiple entry.

At the land frontiers with Belize and Guatemala, you may be refused entry into Mexico if you have less than US$200 (or US$350 for each month of intended stay, up to a maximum of 180 days). This restriction does not officially apply to North American and European travellers, but we have heard that *everyone* entering Mexico from Belize needs a visa issued by the Mexican Consul in Belize City. (This is presumably an anti-drugs measure; check if still in force.) Persuasion, whether verbal or financial, can sometimes remedy this.

British business travellers are strongly advised to read *Hints to Exporters: Mexico*, obtainable from the Department of Trade, Export Services Division, Sanctuary Buildings, 16-20 Great Smith Street, London SW1P 3DB.

Customs Regulations The luggage of tourist-card holders is often passed unexamined. If flying into Mexico from South America, expect to be thoroughly searched (body and luggage) at the airport. US citizens can take in their own clothing and equipment without paying duty, but all valuable and non-US-made objects (diamonds, cameras, binoculars, typewriters, etc.), should be registered at the US Customs office or the port of exit so that duty will not be charged on returning. Radios and television sets must be registered and taken out when leaving. Tourists are allowed to take into Mexico duty-free 1 kg. of tobacco and 400 cigarettes (or 50 cigars), 2 bottles of liquor, US$80 worth of gifts and 12 rolls of film, also portable TV, radio, typewriter, camera, tent and bicycle. There are no restrictions on the import or export of money apart from gold but foreign gold coins are allowed into the US only if they are clearly made into jewellery (perforated or otherwise worked on). On return to the US a person may take from Mexico, free of duty, up to US$100 worth of merchandise for personal use or for personal gifts, every 31 days, if acquired merely as an incident of the trip. Alcoholic drinks may not be taken across the border from Mexico to California. Archaeological relics may not be taken out of Mexico. US tourists should remember that the US Endangered Species Act, 1973, prohibits importation into the States of products from endangered species, e.g. tortoise shell. The Department of the Interior issues a leaflet about this. Llama, alpaca, etc. items may be confiscated at the airport for fumigation and it will be necessary to return to the customs area on the Mexico City airport perimeter 2-3 days later to collect and pay for fumigation. Production of passport will be required and proof that goods are to be re-exported otherwise they may also be subject to import duties. Duty-free goods from Aeroboutiques at Mexico City, Mazatlán, Puerto Vallarta, Guadalajara, Monterrey, Mérida and Acapulco airports.

Automobiles These may be brought into Mexico on a Tourist Permit for 180 days. Don't overstay—driving without an extension gets a US$50 fine for the first five days and then rises abruptly to *half the value of the car!*. No fee is charged for the permit, and the AAA always writes "free" across the preliminary application form it gives its clients because, apparently, some Mexican border officials tend to forget this fact. If you don't have proof of ownership (certificate or title of registration) you will need a notarized statement that you own the vehicle or drive with the permission of the owner. National or international driving licences are accepted; or you can get a Mexican licence at the International Airport, Mexico City, on presentation of visa/tourist card, signed statement of fitness and ability to drive, and local address. Your US car insurance does not cover you while driving in Mexico, but agencies on both sides of the border will sell you Mexican automobile insurance, so only buy 1-day US insurance if crossing the border. Sanborn's Mexican Insurance Service, with offices in Texas, New Mexico, Arizona and 6 Mexican cities, will provide insurance services (about US$3.20 a day, third party only) within Mexico and other parts of Latin America, and provide "Travelogs" for Mexico and Central America with useful tips. British AA members are reminded that there are ties with the AAA, which extends cover to the US and entitles AA members to free travel information including a very useful book and map on Mexico. Holders of 180-day tourist cards can keep their automobiles in Mexico for that time. Luggage is no longer inspected at the checkpoints along the road where tourist cards and/or car permits are examined. Gasoline is either regular (92 octane, *extra*) or medium (81 octane or *nova*). *Nova* costs about US$0.20 a litre. There are dozens of minor swindles practised at filling stations.

Make sure you are given full value when you tank up, that the pump is set to zero before your tank is filled, that both they and you know what money you've proffered, that your change is correct, that the pump is correctly calibrated, and that your filler cap is put back on. The Free Assistance Service of the Mexican Tourist Department's green jeeps ("*ángeles verdes*°) patrol most of Mexico's main roads. The drivers speak English, are trained to give first aid and to make minor auto repairs and deal with flat tyres. They carry gasoline and have radio connection. All help is completely free. Gasoline at cost price. There is no legal surcharge for service at night, nor additional taxes: two more games frequently tried. Parking: Multi-storey car parks are becoming more common but parking is often to be found right in city centres under the main square.

Motorbikes Grant and Susan Johnson, of Horizons Unlimited, Vancouver, tell us that motor-cycling is good in Mexico as most main roads are in fairly good condition and hotels are usually willing to allow the bike to be parked in a courtyard or patio.

All Japanese parts are sold only by one shop in Mexico City at extortionate prices (but parts and accessories are easily available in Guatemala at reasonable prices for those travelling there). Robert S. Kahn recommends Señor Romano's shop, Av. Revolución 1310, Mexico City, for bike repairs. Sr. Romano, a Belgian-Mexican, speaks French and English. Some motorbike travellers have warned that particularly in Mexico City groups of plain clothes police in unmarked cars try to impound motorbikes by force of arms. Uniformed police are no help here.

Warnings When two cars converge on a narrow bridge from opposite directions, the driver who first flashes his lights has the right of way. Don't drive fast at night; farm and wild animals roam freely. In fact, it is advisable to drive as little as possible at night. Some motorists report that it is better not to stop if you hit another car, as although Mexican insurance is proof of your ability to pay, both parties may sometimes be incarcerated until all claims are settled. "Sleeping policemen" or road bumps can be hazardous in towns and villages as often there are no warning signs; they are sometimes marked "zona de topes", or incorrectly marked as *vibradores*. In most instances, their distinguishing paint has worn away.

On the west coast, the Government has set up military checkpoints to look out for drug-smugglers and gun-runners, almost as far south as Puerto Angel. Papers will be checked at these points and your car searched. The degree of search is apparently linked to general appearance; young people travelling in VW vans can expect thorough searches all the way. Watch searchers carefully; sometimes they try to make off with tools, camping gear and the like, especially if there are two or more of them.

If you are stopped by police for an offence you have not committed and you know you are in the right, do not pay the "fine" on the spot. Take the number of the policeman from his cap, show him that you have his number and tell him that you will see his chief (*jefe*) at the tourist police headquarters instead. It is also advisable to go to the precinct station anyway whenever a fine is involved, to make sure it is genuine.

When entering Mexico from Belize by car point out to the authorities that you have a car with you, otherwise they may not note it and you could be arrested for illegally importing a car.

Tourists' cars cannot, *by law*, be sold in Mexico. This is very strictly applied. You may not leave the country without the car you entered in, except with written government permission with the car in bond.

Assaults The number of assaults is rising, especially in Mexico City. Never carry valuables visibly or in easily picked pockets. Cars are a prime target for theft. Also (and it is very sad having to write this), beware of getting too friendly with young gringos who seem to be living in Mexico permanently—unless, of course, they have jobs. Many of them stay in Mexico for the cheap drugs, and are not above robbery and assault to finance their habit. Couples, and even more, women on their own, should avoid lonely beaches.

Local Information All Mexican Government tourist agencies are now grouped in the Department of Tourism building at Avenida Masarik 172, near corner of Reforma. A few cities run municipal tourist offices to help travellers. The Mexican Automobile Association (AMA) is at Chapultepec 276, México, D.F.; they sell an indispensable road guide, with good maps and very useful lists of hotels, with current prices. The ANA (Asociación Nacional Automobilística) sells similar but not such good material; offices in Insurgentes (Metro Glorieta) and Av. Jalisco 27, México 18 D.F. For road conditions consult the AMA, which is quite reliable. A calendar of *fiestas* is published by *Mexico This Month*.

If you have any complaints about faulty goods or services, go to the Procuraduría Federal de Protección del Consumidor of which there is a branch in every city. Major cities, like Acapulco, also have a Procurador del Turista. The Tourist Office may also help with these, or criminal matters, while the Agente del Ministro Público (Federal or State District Attorney) will also deal with criminal complaints.

Maps The Mexican Government Tourist Highway map is available free of charge at tourist offices (when in stock). If driving from the USA you get a free map if you buy your insurance at AAA or at Sanborn's in the border cities. The official map printers, Detenal, produce the only good large-scale maps of the country.

The Dirección General de Oceanografía in Calle Medellín 10, near Insurgentes underground station, sells excellent maps of the entire coastline of Mexico. Good detailed maps of states of Mexico and the country itself from Dirección General de Geografía y Meteorología, Av. Observatorio 192, México 18, D.F. T 515-15-27 (go to Observatorio underground station and up Calle Sur 114, then turn right a short distance down Av. Observatorio). Best road maps of Mexican states, free, on polite written request, from Ing. Daniel Díaz Díaz, Director General de Programación, Xola 1755, 8° Piso, México 12 D.F. Building is on the corner of Xola with Av. Universidad. Mapas Turísticos de México has Mexican (stocks Detenal maps) and world-maps, permanent exhibition at Río Rhin 29, Col. Cuauhtémoc, Mexico 5, T 566-2177. Maps also available from Instituto Nacional de Estadística, Geografía e Informática (INEGI), which has branches in Mexico City (**see page 1029**) and in 40 other cities around the country. Good road maps of Mexican states also available from Sanborns at US$1.30.

Guidebooks Travellers wanting more information than we have space to provide, on archaeological sites for instance, would do well to use the widely available Easy Guides written by Richard Bloomgarden, with plans and good illustrations. *A Field Guide to Mexican Birds*, Peterson and Chalif, Houghton Mifflin, 1973, has been recommended. 2 books by Rudi Robins: *One-day Car Trips from Mexico City*, and *Weekend trips to Cities near Mexico City*.

Photographs The Instituto Nacional de Antropología e Historia (INAH), Córdoba 44, Colonia Roma, Mexico City, will grant teachers, archaeologists. etc. written permission to take any type of photograph at sites and museums, including photos which general public may not take. Also issue admission discounts.

Hours of Business in Mexico City are extremely variable. The banks are open from 0900 to 1300 from Mon. to Fri. and (head offices only) 0900 to 1230 on Sat. Business offices usually open at 0900 or 1000 and close at 1300 or 1400. They reopen at 1400 or 1500, but senior executives may not return until much later, although they may then stay until after 1900. Other businesses, especially those on the outskirts of the city, and many Government offices, work from 0800 to 1400 or 1500 and then close for the rest of the day. Business hours in other parts of the country vary considerably according to the climate and local custom. In Monterrey they are roughly as in Britain.

Standard Time The same as US Central Standard Time, 6 hrs. behind GMT. In Sonora, Sinaloa, Nayarit and Baja California Sur, 7 hrs. behind GMT; and in Baja California Norte 8 hrs. behind GMT. The states north of the Tropic of Cancer have adopted a summer time (Zacatecas, León, Tamaulipas, Durango, Coahuila, Nuevo León, Chihuahua).

The **best season** for a business visit is from late January to May, but for pleasure between October and early April, when it hardly ever rains in most of the country. August is not a good time because it is a holiday month throughout Central America and most internal flights and other transport are heavily booked (also see above under **Travel in Mexico**).

Hotels Maximum rates are registered with the Government and advertised in the press. There are six rate zones: I: Guadalajara, Monterrey, Mexico City; II: Most seaside resorts, incl. Acapulco; III: Port zones, like Veracruz; IV: State of Yucatán, and several states surrounding the state of México; V: Most border zones, incl. the state of Baja California Sur; VI: The rest, including Chiapas. Rates are set on May 15 and December 15. Complaints about violations to be reported to the Department of Tourism, Presidente Masarik 172, Colonia Polanco, Mexico City. T 250-1964 and

250-8555. English is spoken at the best hotels. The Secretaría de Turismo publishes a *Directorio Nacional de Hospedaje*, with hotel listings (our category D and above), tourist information, maps of the capital of each state, good value at approx. US$6.50 for 680 pages.

Beware of "helpfuls" who try to find you a hotel, as prices quoted at the hotel desk rise to give them a commission. If backpacking, best for one of you to watch over luggage while the other goes to book a room and pay for it; some hotels are put off by backpacks. During peak season (November-April), it may be hard to find a room and clerks do not always check to see whether a room is vacant. Insist, or if desperate, provide a suitable tip. The week after Semana Santa is normally a holiday, so prices remain high, but resorts ar not as crowded as the previous week. When using a lift, remember PB (*Planta Baja*) stands for ground floor. Discounts on hotel prices can often be arranged in the low season (May-October), but more difficult in Yucatán and Baja California.

Motels and Auto-hotels are not usually places where guests stay the whole night (you can recognise them by curtains over the garage and red and green lights above the door to show if the room is free). If driving, and wishing to avoid a night on the road, they can be quite acceptable (clean, some have hot water, in the Yucatán they have a/c), and they tend to be cheaper than respectable establishments.

Airport Taxis   To avoid overcharging, the Government has taken control of taxi services from airports to cities and only those with government licences are allowed to carry passengers from the airport. Sometimes one does not pay the driver but purchases a ticket from a booth on leaving the airport. No further tipping is then required. The same system has been applied at bus stations but it is possible to pay the driver direct.

Tipping   is more or less on a level of 10%; the equivalent of US$0.25 per bag for porters, the equivalent of US$0.20 for bell boys, theatre usherettes, and nothing for a taxi driver unless he gives some extra service. It is not necessary to tip the drivers of hired cars.

Health   The Social Security hospitals are restricted to members, but will take visitors in emergencies; they are more up to date than the Centros de Salud and Hospitales Civiles found in most centres, which are very cheap and open to everyone. There are many homeopathic physicians in all parts of Mexico. You are recommended to use bottled or mineral water for drinking, except in hotels with their own purification system. Tehuacán mineral water is sold all over Mexico; both plain and flavoured are first class. Water-sterilizing tablets can be bought at pharmacies. Raw salads and vegetables, and food sold on the streets and in cheap cafés, especially in Mexico City, may be dangerous. Advisable to vaccinate against typhoid, paratyphoid and poliomyelitis if visiting the low-lying tropical zones, where there is also some risk of malaria; advice and malaria pills from 6th floor, San Luis Potosí 199, Colonia Roma Norte, Mexico City, 0900-1400. Heavy eating and drinking of alcohol is unwise in the capital because of its altitude; so is overdoing it physically in the first few days. Some people experience nose-bleeds in Guadalajara and Mexico City because of pollution; they cease with fresh air. Locals recommend Imecol for "Montezuma's Revenge" (the very common diarrhoea).

Drink   The beer (best brands: Bavaria, Bohemia, XXX, Superior and Tecate) is quite good. Negra Modelo is a dark beer, it has the same alcohol content as the other beers. Local wine, some of it of good quality, is cheap; try (Domecq, Casa Madero, Santo Tomás, etc.—the white sold in oyster restaurants *ostionerías*) is usually good. The native drinks are *tequila*, made mostly in Jalisco and potent, *pulque*, also powerful, and *mescal* from Oaxaca; all are distilled from cactus plants. Also available is the Spanish aniseed spirit, *anís*, which is made locally. Imported whiskies and brandies are expensive. Rum is cheap and good. Remember that drunkenness is detested in Mexico. There are always plenty of non-alcoholic soft drinks (*refrescos*)—try the *paletas*, safe and refreshing (those of Michoacán are everywhere)—and mineral water. Herbal teas, e.g. camomile, are available. There are few outdoor drinking places in Mexico except in tourist spots.

Food   Usual meals are a light breakfast, and a heavy lunch between 1400 and 1500. Dinner, between 1800 and 2000, is light. Many restaurants give foreigners the menu without the *comida corrida* (set meals), and so forcing them to order *à la carte* at double the price; watch this! Try to avoid eating in restaurants which don't post a menu. Meals cost about US$1-2 for breakfast, US$3-5 for lunch and US$4-10 for dinner (about US$7-17 a day on meals, depending on lavishness). In resort areas the posh hotels include breakfast and dinner in many cases.

What to Eat   *Tamales*, or meat wrapped in maize and then banana leaves and boiled. Turkey, chicken and pork with exotic sauces—*mole de guajolote* and *mole poblano* (*chile* and chocolate sauce with grated coconut) are famous. *Tacos* (without *chiles*) and *enchiladas* (with all too many of them) are meat or chicken and beans rolled in *tortillas* (maize pancakes) and fried in oil; they are delicious. Try also spring onions with salt and lime juice in *taquerías*. Indian food is found everywhere: for instance, *tostadas* (toasted fried tortillas with chicken, beans and lettuce), or *gorditas,* fried, extra-thick tortillas with sauce and cheese. Black kidney beans (*frijoles*) appear in various dishes. Try *crepas de cuitlacoche*, best during rainy season—this consists of a pancake stuffed with maize fungus, which has a delicate mushroomy taste— very moreish. In the Pátzcuaro area ask for *budín de cuitlacoche*, with tomato, cream and *chiles*. Red snapper (*huachinango*), Veracruz style, is a famous fish dish, sautéd with *pimientos* and spices. Another excellent fish is the sea bass (*robalo*). Fruits include a vast assortment of tropical types—avocados, bananas, pineapples, *zapotes*, pomegranates, guavas, limes and *mangos de Manila*, which are delicious. Don't eat fruit unless you peel it yourself, and avoid raw vegetables. Try *higos rebanados* (delicious fresh sliced figs), *guacamole* (a mashed avocado seasoned with tomatoes, onions, coriander and *chiles*) and of course, *papaya*, or pawpaw. Mexico has various elaborate regional cuisines. Chinese restaurants, present in most towns, generally give clean and efficient service. Milk is only safe when in sealed containers marked *pasteurizado*. Fried eggs are known as *huevos estrellados*. On January 6, Epiphany, the traditional *rosca*, a ring-shaped sweet bread with dried fruit and little plastic baby Jesuses inside, is eaten. The person who finds a baby Jesus in his piece must make a crib and clothes for Him, and invite everyone present to a *fiesta* on February 2, Candelaria.

Clothing   People are usually smartly dressed in Mexico City. Women visitors should not wear shorts other than at the seaside, though trousers are quite OK. There is little central heating, so warm clothing is needed in winter. Four musts are good walking shoes, sun hats, dark glasses, and flip-flops for the hot sandy beaches. Women are always escorted, except in the main streets of the larger cities. Topless bathing is now accepted in parts of Baja California, but ask first, or do as others do.

Currency   The monetary unit is the Mexican peso, divided into 100 centavos. Owing to the rapid inflation of the past few years both coins and notes are being reissued. The smallest note is for 500 pesos, then 1,000, 2,000, 5,000, 10,000, 20,000, and 50,000 pesos. Coins have all been changed from silver and bronze to strange alloys that have various colours. The tiny 5-peso piece is gold-coloured, as is the 100-peso coin. The 10-peso piece is octagonal; there is a small 20-peso coin as well as an older, larger one, similarly with the 50-peso coins. It is wise to check the number on coins.

Exchange   In the border states such as Baja California Norte, the most-used currency is the US dollar, and the Mexican peso is often accepted by stores on the US side of the border. Travellers' cheques from any well-known bank can be cashed in most towns if drawn in US dollars; travellers' cheques in terms of sterling are harder to cash, and certainly not worth carrying outside Mexico City. The free rate of exchange changes daily and varies from bank to bank even though all are government-owned. Until the new day's rate is posted, at any time between 1000 and 1100, yesterday's rate prevails. Many banks, including in Mexico City, only change foreign currency during a limited period (often between 1000 and 1200), which should be remembered, especially on Fridays. Telegraphic transfer of funds *within* Mexico is not reliable. Beware of short-changing at all times. American Express, Mastercard and Visa are generally accepted in Mexico and cash is even obtainable with these credit cards at certain banks. 25 % tax is payable on the use of credit cards. N.B. An American Express card issued in Mexico states "valid only in Mexico", and is used only for peso transactions. All other American Express cards are transacted in U.S. dollars even for employees living in Mexico. AmEx travellers' cheques are readily accepted.

Weights and Measures   The metric system is compulsory.

National Holidays   Sunday is a statutory holiday. Saturday is also observed as a holiday, except by the shops. There is no early-closing day. National holidays are as follows:

January 1: New Year.	May 5: Battle of Puebla.
February 5: Constitution Day.	September 1: President's Annual Message.
March 21: Birthday of Juárez.	September 16: Independence Day.
Maundy Thursday.	October 12: Discovery of America.
Good Friday.	November 20: Day of the Revolution.

Easter Saturday.   December 25: Christmas Day.
May 1: Labour Day.

Nov. 2, All Souls' Day, and Dec. 12, Our Lady of Guadalupe, are not national holidays, but are widely celebrated.

Press The more important journals are in Mexico City. The most influential dailies are: *Excelsior, Novedades, El Día* (throughout Mexico), *Uno más Uno; The News* (in English, now available in all main cities); *El Universal (El Universal Gráfico); La Jornada* (more to the left), *La Prensa*, a popular tabloid, has the largest circulation. *El Nacional* is the mouthpiece of the Government; *El Heraldo; Uno más Uno* publishes a supplement, *Tiempo Libre*, on Fridays, listing the week's cultural activities. There are influential weekly magazines *Proceso, Siempre* and *Sucesos*, left of centre, nationalistic. The political satirical weekly is *Los Agachados*.

Postal Services Rates are raised periodically in line with the peso's devaluation against the dollar. They are posted next to the windows where stamps are sold. Air mail letters to the US take about six days, and to the UK (US$0.25) via the US one to two weeks. Weight limit from the UK to Mexico: 22 lb., and 5 kg. in the reverse direction. About 3 months to Europe. Small parcel rate cheaper. Parcel counters often close earlier than other sections of the post office in Mexico. As for most of Latin America, send printed matter such as magazines registered. International parcels must be examined by the Customs at Aldama 218, Colonia Guerrero, near Revolución metro, open 0900-1400; or Correo Central at Calle Tacuba, open 0800-1300, window No. 48 from which only books or records can be sent; parcels with books in them must be less than 5 kg. (US$5 air mail to Europe per kg., US$1 surface mail to Europe per kg.) before posting. No more than 3 parcels may be sent at a time; maximum parcel size: 40 cm. X 60 cm.; registered letters received here. Surface parcels from Aduana Postal, Ceylán 468 (open 0800-1300, Mon.-Fri.); Colonia Cosmopólita. Take metro line 2 to Normal station, then a green colectivo No. 106. Bus No. 13 marked "Canal 13-Industrial Vallejo" also goes there. We have heard that the Customs Department at the airport hold up registered parcels coming in from abroad. Many travellers have also recommended that one should not use the post to send film or cherished objects as losses are frequent. A permit is needed from the Bellas Artes office to send paintings or drawings out of Mexico. Not all these services are obtainable outside Mexico City; delivery times in/from the interior may well be longer than those given above. *Poste restante* ("general delivery" in the US) functions quite reliably, but you may have to ask under each of your names; if you wish to use this facilty it is known as *lista de correos*; mail is sent back after ten days. Address "*favor de retener hasta llegada*" on envelope.

Telecommunications Telégrafos Nacionales maintains the national and international telegraph systems, separate from the Post Office. There is a special office at Balderas 14-18, just near corner of Colón, in Mexico City to deal with international traffic (open 0800-2300, Metro Hidalgo, exit Calle Basilio Badillo). There are three types of telegraph service: *extra urgente, urgente* and *ordinario*; they can only be prepaid, not sent collect. A telegram to Britain costs US$0.20 a word, and US$15 for 21 words including flat fee and taxes. Telex US$13-20 for 3 mins, will hold messages. Telephone service to USA, Canada and Europe. There is a telegraph and telex service available at Mexico City airport. There is a heavy tax levied on all foreign long-distance calls originating and paid for in Mexico, so it is better to call collect (dial 09 and ask for operator). Calls to Britain are more expensive per min. from 0500 to 1700, but cheaper per min. from 1700 to 0500 and all day on Sun. It costs US$15 to the US for 3 minutes; US$30 to Europe. Again, not all these services are available outside the capital. Phone services are generally poor.

Cost of Living Manufactured goods and clothing are cheaper than in the USA. Film is reasonably cheap. Food is cheaper. Services are abundant and cheap: there are armies of waiters, waitresses, chauffeurs, maids, gardeners, night watchmen, etc. Doctors' and dentists' services are good, and their fees reasonable. Rent for living quarters outside Mexico City, Guadalajara, border zones and the beach resorts is very low compared to US and European levels.

We are most grateful to Kevin Healey (Balaclava, Vic.) for a thorough revision of Baja California, Daniel Ahumada (Mexicali), Rop Bomer and Wilh. ter Haar (Mexico City), John M. Raspey (Dolores Hidalgo), Jacob de Ruiter (Toluca, Mexico), Sarah Thomas (British Embassy, Mexico) and to the following travellers: Laurence Adelman and Suanne Wiublewski (London), Nils Andersen and Lisbeth Thomsen (Ribe, Dmk), Stephen E. Anderson (Boise, ID), Lucia L. Armstrong (Ithaca, NY), Dr J.R.J. Van Asperen de Boer (Amsterdam), Lee Azus (San Francisco), Rupert Baker (Cropredy, Oxon), Dale Bedford (Auckland 9), Erika Berger (Moosseedorf, Switz.), Christine Blenntoft (Santiago 9), Nataly Bombeck and Christian von Georg (Hamburg 52), J.N. Bowden and K.E. Badgery (Plymouth), David M. Bristor (Palo Alto, CA), Lucy Broadbent and Rick Palmer (Kerikeri, NZ), Karen Brooks (London N19), Tim Connell (Ham, Surrey) for a particularly useful contribution, John Crane (Sunbury), Richard Davies (Great Bookham, Sy.), Thomas Fedrizzi (Horgen, Switz.), Karsten Feucht (Berlin 61), Paul Foulkes (London E11), Buckhardt Franz, Arthur Glickman (Arcata, CA), Christiane Goettel (Annweiler, W.Ger.), Harold Goldstein and Janet Young (Washington DC), Dr Charlie Granger and Jill Wickenden (Manchester M14), Joseph C. Grasmick (Niagara Falls, NY), Jan Jacob de Groot (Vroomshoop, Neth.), Paul Gurn (Waterbury, Conn.), Monika Gwerder (Muotathal, Switz.), Yaakov Haron (Ramat Gan, Israel), Arthur Harris (Arlington, Vermont), Rony

Hermans (Deurne, Bel.), John Higham (Antigua, Guatemala), Wendy Jackson (Crowborough, E. Sx.), René Jung (Winterthur, Switz.), Barbara Kämpf and Martín Männer (Zurich), Omer Karchi (Tivon, Israel), Shirley Kiss (Lively, Ont.), Joel Kumove (Don Mills, Ont.), Dr Rudolf Kurth (Deming, NM), R.W. Le Sueur (Jersey), John Lewis (London NW3), Nanna Lyby (Farum, Dmk.), James Maas (Bocas del Toro, Panama), Bjarne Madsen and Gitte B. Andersen (Odense), Philippe Martin (Swiss Touring Club, Geneva), Anne McLaughlan (San Salvador), Lucy Meikle (Pershore) and Stuart Duncan (Scotland), Daniel Morgan (Wellington, NZ) for very helpful information, Emilie Müller and Eckart Friebis (Freiburg, W.Ger.), Fitz Paul, Bill Potter (Herford, W.Ger.), Jineke Puister and Jan van Dalfsen (Groningen), Diego Puls and Rubén Chapp (Amsterdam), Ms C.R. Pyle (York), Wolfgang Reichert and Annette Karling (Kulmbach, W.Ger.), Geoff A. Richardson (Barranquilla), George M. Ridenour (New York 10016) for a most useful contribution, Varina Rood (Wageningen, Neth.), Gerhard Schweiger (Tamsweg), Joanne Scott and Sheryl McEwen (NZ), Karl Stanley (Cheam, Sy.), Peter van der Stoop and Karin Strooij (Haarlem, Neth.), Anna Syriänen and Marko Sorvaniemi (Tampere, Fin.), John Tippett (Harbord, NSW), Paul Tommassen and friends (The Hague), Dan Toporoski (San Diego, CA), David L Trahlee (Port Aransas, TX), Felix Walter (Bern), Jan Weyers (Beveren, Belg.), Paul Whitehouse (Cleckheaton) and Julia Booker (Havant, Hants) and Marilyn Zecker and B.B.Riefner (Rockville, MD).

CENTRAL AMERICA

CENTRAL AMERICA comprises the seven small countries of Panama, Costa Rica, Nicaragua, Honduras, El Salvador, Guatemala and Belize (formerly British Honduras). Together they occupy 544,700 square km., which is less than the size of Texas. The total population of Central America in 1987 was about 27 million and it is increasing by 2.8% each year.

The degree of development in these countries differs sharply. Costa Rica and Panama have the highest standard of living, with two of the highest rates of literacy in all Latin America. At the other end of the scale, Honduras has one of the lowest standards of living.

Geographically, these countries have much in common, but there are sharp differences in the racial composition and traditions of their peoples. Costa Ricans are mostly white, Guatemalans are largely Amerindian or *mestizo*; Hondurans, Nicaraguans and Salvadoreans are almost entirely *mestizo*. Panama has perhaps the most racially varied population, with a large white group. Most of these countries also have a black element, the largest being found in Panama and Nicaragua.

Early History   The best known of the pre-Conquest Indian civilizations of the area was the Maya, which is thought to have evolved in about A.D. 100 in the Pacific highlands of Guatemala and El Salvador. After 200 years of growth it entered what is known today as its "classic" period when the civilization flourished in Guatemala, Belize and Honduras, and in Chiapas, Campeche and Yucatán (Mexico). This period lasted until A.D. 900-1000, after which time the Mayas, concentrated into Yucatán after a successful invasion of their other lands by non-Maya people (this is only one theory: another is that they were forced to flee after a peasants' revolt against them), came under the influence of the Toltecs who invaded that area. From that time their culture declined. The Maya civilization was based on independent and antagonistic city states, including Tikal, Uaxactún, Kaminal Juyú, Iximché, Zaculeu and Quiriguá in Guatemala; Copán in Honduras; Altún Ha in Belize; Tazumal and San Andrés in El Salvador; and Palenque, Bonampak (both in Chiapas), Uxmal, Chichén Itzá, Mayapán, Tulum and the Puuc hill cities of Sayil, Labná and Kabah (all on the Yucatán peninsula) in Mexico.

The cities were all meticulously dated. Mayan art is a mathematical art: each column, figure, face, animal, frieze, stairway and temple expresses a date or a time relationship. When, for example, an ornament on the ramp of the Hieroglyphic Stairway at Copán was repeated some 15 times, it was to express that number of elapsed "leap" years. The 75 steps stand for the number of elapsed intercalary days. The Mayan calendar was a nearer approximation to sidereal time than either the Julian or the Gregorian calendars of Europe; it was only .000069 of a day out of true in a year. They used the zero centuries in advance of the Old World, plotted the movements of the sun, moon, Venus and other planets, conceived a cycle of more than 1,800 million days, achieved paper codices and glyphic writing, were skilled potters and weavers and traded over wide areas, though they had not discovered the wheel and had no beasts of burden. Their tools and weapons were flint and hard stone, obsidian and fire-hardened wood, and yet with these they grew lavish crops, hewed out and transported great monoliths over miles of difficult country, and carved them over with intricate glyphs and figures which would be difficult enough with modern chisels.

The Mayan cities were principally ceremonial centres controlled by a theocratic minority of priests and nobles in whom was vested the entire cultural activity of each state. The Toltecs, who had firm control in Yucatán in the 10th century, gradually spread their empire as far as the southern borders of Guatemala. They in turn, however, were conquered by the Aztecs, one of whose revolutionary principles was the private ownership of land, but they did not penetrate into Central America.

At the time of the coming of the Spaniards there were several other isolated groups of Indians dotted over the Central American area: they were mostly shifting cultivators or nomadic hunters and fishermen. A few places only were occupied by sedentary agriculturists: what remained of the Maya in the highlands of Guatemala; a group on the south-western shores of Lakes Managua and Nicaragua; and another in the highlands of Costa Rica. The Spanish conquerors were attracted by precious metals, or native sedentary farmers who could be christianized and exploited. There were few of either, and comparatively few Spaniards settled in Central America.

It was only during his fourth voyage, in 1502, that Columbus reached the mainland of Central America; he landed in Panama, which he called Veragua, and founded the town of Santa María de Belén. In 1508 Alonso de Ojeda received a grant of land on the Pearl Coast east of Panama, and in 1509 he founded the town of San Sebastián, later moved to a new site called Santa María la Antigua del Darién. In 1513 the governor of the colony at Darién was Vasco Núñez de Balboa. Taking 190 men he crossed the isthmus in 18 days and caught the first glimpse of the Pacific; he claimed it and all neighbouring lands in the name of the King of Spain. But from the following year, when Pedrarias replaced him as Governor, Balboa fell on evil days, and he was executed by Pedrarias in 1519. That same year Pedrarias crossed the isthmus and founded the town of Panamá on the Pacific side. It was in April 1519, too, that Cortés began his conquest of Mexico.

Central America was explored from these two nodal points of Panama and Mexico. Cortés' lieutenant, Alvarado, had conquered as far south as San Salvador by 1523. Meanwhile Pedrarias was sending forces into Panama and Costa Rica: the latter was abandoned, for the natives were hostile, but was finally colonized from Mexico City when the rest of Central America had been taken. In 1522-24 Andrés Niño and Gil Gonzales Dávila invaded Nicaragua and Honduras. Many towns were founded by these forces from Panama: León, Granada, Trujillo and others. Spanish forces from the north and south sometimes met and fought bitterly. The gentle Bartolomé de Las Casas, the "apostle of the Indies", was active as a Dominican missionary in Central America in the 1530s.

Settlement The groups of Spanish settlers were few and widely scattered, and this is the fundamental reason for the political fragmentation of Central America today. Panama was ruled from Bogotá, but the rest of Central America was subordinate to the Viceroyalty at Mexico City, with Antigua Guatemala as an Audiencia for the area until 1773, thereafter Guatemala City. Panama was of paramount importance for colonial Spanish America for its strategic position, and for the trade passing across the isthmus to and from the southern colonies. The other provinces were of comparatively little value.

The comparatively small number of Spaniards intermarried freely with the local Indians, accounting for the predominance of *mestizos* in Central America today. In Guatemala, where there were the most Indians, intermarriage affected fewer of the natives, and over half the population today is pure Indian. On the Meseta Central of Costa Rica, the Indians were all but wiped out by disease; today, as a consequence of this great disaster, there is a buoyant community of over 2 million whites, with little Indian admixture, in the highlands. Blacks predominate all along the Caribbean coasts of Central America; they were not brought in by the colonists as slaves, but by the railway builders and banana planters of the nineteenth century and the canal cutters of the twentieth, as cheap labour.

Independence and Federation On November 5, 1811, José Matías Delgado, a priest and jurist born in San Salvador, organized a revolt in conjunction with another priest, Manuel José Arce. They proclaimed the independence of El Salvador, but the Audiencia at Guatemala City quickly suppressed the revolt and took Delgado prisoner.

It was the revolution of 1820 in Spain itself that precipitated the independence of Central America. When on February 24, 1821, the Mexican general Iturbide announced his Plan of Iguala for an independent Mexico, the

Central American *criollos* decided to follow his example, and a declaration of independence, drafted by José Cecilio del Valle, was announced in Guatemala City on September 15, 1821. Iturbide invited the provinces of Central America to join with him, and on January 5, 1822, Central America was declared annexed to Mexico. Delgado refused to accept this decree, and Iturbide, who had now assumed the title of Emperor Agustín the First, sent an army south under Vicente Filísola to enforce it in the regions under Delgado's influence. Filísola had completed his task when he heard of Iturbide's abdication, and at once convened a general congress of the Central American provinces. It met on June 24, 1823, and established the Provincias Unidas del Centro de América. The Mexican republic acknowledged their independence on August 1, 1824, and Filísola's soldiers were withdrawn.

The congress, presided over by Delgado, appointed a provisional governing *junta* which promulgated a constitution modelled on that of the United States on November 22, 1824. The Province of Chiapas was not included in the Federation, for it had already adhered to Mexico in 1821. No federal capital was chosen, but Guatemala City, by force of tradition, soon became the seat of government.

Breakdown of Federation The first President under the new constitution was Manuel José Arce, a liberal. One of his first acts was to abolish slavery. El Salvador, protesting that he had exceeded his powers, rose in December, 1826. Honduras, Nicaragua, and Costa Rica joined the revolt, and in 1828 General Francisco Morazán, in charge of the army of Honduras, defeated the federal forces, entered San Salvador and marched against Guatemala City. He captured the city on April 13, 1829, and established that contradiction in terms: a liberal dictatorship. Many conservative leaders were expelled and church and monastic properties confiscated. Morazán himself became president of the Federation in 1830. He was a man of considerable ability; he ruled with a strong hand, encouraged education, fostered trade and industry, opened the country to immigrants, and reorganized the administration. In 1835 the capital was moved to San Salvador.

These reforms antagonized the conservatives and there were several risings. The most serious revolt was among the Indians of Guatemala, led by Rafael Carrera, an illiterate *mestizo* conservative and a born leader. Years of continuous warfare followed, during the course of which the Federation withered away. As a result, the federal congress passed an act which allowed each province to assume what government it chose, but the idea of a federation was not quite dead. As a result, Morazán became President of El Salvador. Carrera, who was by then in control of Guatemala, defeated Morazán in battle and forced him to leave the country. But in 1842, Morazán overthrew Braulio Carrillo, then dictator of Costa Rica, and became president himself. At once he set about rebuilding the Federation, but was defeated by the united forces of the other states, and shot on September 15, 1842. With him perished any practical hope of Central American political union.

The Separate States Costa Rica, with its mainly white population, is a country apart, and Panama was Colombian territory until 1903. The history of the four remaining republics since the breakdown of federation has been tempestuous in the extreme. In each the ruling class was divided into pro-clerical conservatives and anti-clerical liberals, with constant changes of power. Each was weak, and tried repeatedly to buttress its weakness by alliances with others, which invariably broke up because one of the allies sought a position of mastery. The wars were rarely over boundaries; they were mainly ideological wars between conservatives and liberals, or wars motivated by inflamed nationalism. Nicaragua, for instance, was riven internally for most of the period by the mutual hatreds of the Conservatives of Granada and the Liberals of León, and there were repeated conflicts between the Caribbean and interior parts of Honduras.

Of the four republics, Guatemala was certainly the strongest and in some ways the most stable. While the other states were skittling their presidents like so many ninepins, Guatemala was ruled by a succession of strong dictators:

Rafael Carrera (1844-1865), Justo Rufino Barrios (1873-1885), Manuel Cabrera (1898-1920), and Jorge Ubico (1931-44). These were separated by intervals of constitutional government, anarchy, or attempts at dictatorship which failed. Few presidents handed over power voluntarily to their successors; most of them were forcibly removed or assassinated.

Despite the permutations and combinations of external and civil war there has been a recurrent desire to reestablish some form of *la gran patria centroamericana*. Throughout the 19th century, and far into the 20th, there have been ambitious projects for political federation, usually involving El Salvador, Honduras and Nicaragua; none of them lasted more than a few years. There have also been unsuccessful attempts to reestablish union by force, such as those of Barrios of Guatemala in 1885 and Zelaya of Nicaragua in 1907.

Rapid change is now coming to Central America. During colonial times the area suffered from great poverty; trade with the mother country was confined to small amounts of silver and gold, cacao and sugar, and cochineal and indigo. During the present century the great banana plantations of the Caribbean, the growing coffee and cotton trade and industrialization have brought some prosperity, but its benefits have, except in Costa Rica and Panama, been garnered mostly by a relatively small landowning class and the middle classes of the cities. Nicaragua is now a case apart, with extensive and radical reforms carried out by a left-leaning revolutionary government. Poverty, still the fate of the great majority, has brought about closer economic cooperation between the five republics, and in 1960 they established the Central American Common Market (CACM). Surprisingly, the Common Market appeared to be a great success until 1968, when integration fostered national antagonisms, and there was a growing conviction in Honduras and Nicaragua, which were doing least well out of integration, that they were being exploited by the others. In 1969 the "Football War" broke out between El Salvador and Honduras, basically because of a dispute about illicit emigration by Salvadoreans into Honduras, and relations between the two were not normalized until 1980. Despite the handicaps to economic and political integration imposed by nationalist feeling and ideological differences, hopes for improvement were revived in 1987 when the Central American Peace Plan, drawn up by President Oscar Arias Sánchez of Costa Rica, was signed by the Presidents of Guatemala, El Salvador, Honduras, Nicaragua and Costa Rica. The plan proposed formulae to end the civil strife in individual countries, but with the exception of Nicaragua, there has been little progress.

We are most grateful to Janet Krengel of Lloyds Bank Group Economics Department for updating the Central America section. For help with material for the revision we should like to thank: Nils Andersen and Lisbeth Thomsen (Ribe, Dmk), Lucia L. Armstrong (Ithaca, NY), Dr. J.R.J. Van Asperen de Boer (Amsterdam), Ruha'mah Baguette (Caribbean Charter Services), Dale Bedford (Auckland 9), J.N. Bowden and K.E. Badgery (Plymouth), Lucy Broadbent and Rick Palmer (Kerikeri, NZ), Jaina Chaplin (Laytonville, CA), John Crane (Sunbury), Jan Van Dalfsen and Einelle Puister (Groningen, Neth.), Dr. Anthony Daniels (Papworth St. Agnes, Cambs.), Thomas Fedrizzi (Horgen, Switz.), Tim Germain (London) and Marín Conchi (Barcelona), John Gilchrist, Dr Charlie Granger and Jill Wickenden (Manchester M14), Peter Hackenberg (Bielefeld, W.Ger.), Rony Hermans (Deurne, Bel.), John Higham (Antigua, Guatemala), Toby Lanzer (Surrey), Kenneth and Nancy Leighton (Vancouver), R. W. Le Sueur (Jersey), James Maas (Bocas del Toro, Panama), Anne McLaughlan (San Salvador), Daniel Morgan (Wellington, NZ), Michael Mortensen (Oelstykke, Dmk.), Jock Munro (Freeport, Bah.), Mike Niman (San José, CR), Varina Rood (Wageningen, Neth.), Dr. Andreas Siraa and Tanya Siraa (Miami, FL), Karl Stanley (Cheam, Sy.), Regula Stirnemann (Stuttgart), Doris Stöckli and Christophe Racine (Fislisbach, Switz.), Jacqueline Trenbath (London), Rob Ward (Sutton, Sy.), Jan Weyers (Beveren, Belg.), Ray Williams (Pwllheli) and Eric Zolov (Hartsdale, NY).

Travellers who have made particularly valuable contributions to updating individual Central American country sections are listed at the ends of the sections concerned.

GUATEMALA

GUATEMALA (109,000 square km., 8.43 million people), is the most populous of the Central American republics and the only one which is largely Indian in language and culture. It still has large areas of unoccupied land, especially in the north; only about two-thirds is populated. Two-thirds of it is mountainous and 62% forested. It has coastlines on the Pacific (240 km.), and on the Caribbean (110 km.). The population of Guatemala City amounts to 1,500,000, more than ten times as large as that of any other town.

A lowland ribbon, nowhere more than 50 km. wide, runs the whole length of the Pacific shore. Cotton, sugar, bananas and maize are the chief crops of this lowland, particularly in the Department of Escuintla. There is some stock raising as well. Summer rain is heavy and the lowland carries scrub forest.

From this plain the highlands rise sharply to heights of between 2,500 and 3,000 metres and stretch some 240 km. to the N before sinking into the northern lowlands. A string of volcanoes juts boldly above the southern highlands along the Pacific. There are intermont basins at from 1,500 to 2,500 metres in this volcanic area. Most of the people of Guatemala live in these basins, drained by short rivers into the Pacific and by longer ones into the Atlantic. One basin W of the capital has no apparent outlet and here, ringed by volcanoes, is the splendid Lake Atitlán. The southern highlands are covered with lush vegetation over a volcanic subsoil. This clears away in the central highlands, exposing the crystalline rock of the E-W running ranges. This area is lower but more rugged, with sharp-faced ridges and deep ravines modifying into gentle slopes and occasional valley lowlands as it loses height and approaches the Caribbean coastal levels and the flatlands of El Petén.

The lower slopes of these highlands, from about 600 to 1,500 metres, are planted with coffee which is some 40% by value of the total exports. Coffee plantations make almost a complete belt around them. Above 1,500 metres is given over to wheat and the main subsistence crops of maize and beans. Deforestation is becoming a serious problem. Where rainfall is low there are savannas, where water for irrigation is now drawn from wells and these areas are being reclaimed for pasture and fruit growing.

Two large rivers flow down to the Caribbean Gulf of Honduras from the highlands: one is the Río Motagua, 400 km. long, rising among the southern volcanoes; the other, further N, is the Río Polochic, 298 km. long, which drains into Lake Izabal and the Bay of Amatique. There are large areas of lowland in the lower reaches of both rivers, which are navigable for considerable distances; this was, and may be again, the great banana zone.

To the NW, bordering on Belize and Mexico, in the peninsula of Yucatán, lies the low, undulating tableland of El Petén, 36,300 square km. of almost undeveloped wilderness covered with dense hardwood forest. Deep in this tangled rain-forest lie the ruins of Maya cities such as Tikal and Uaxactún. In the Department of Petén, almost one-third of the national territory, there are only 200,000 people. In some parts there is natural grassland, with woods and streams, suitable for cattle, and large scale tree-felling has begun in the south and east of El Petén.

Settlement When the Spaniards arrived from Mexico City in 1523 they found little precious metal: only some silver at Huehuetenango. Those who stayed settled in the intermont basins of the southern highlands around Antigua and Guatemala City and intermarried with the groups of native subsistence farmers living there. This was the basis of the present *mestizo* population living in the cities and towns as well as in all parts of the southern highlands and in the flatlands along the Pacific coast; the indigenous population—more than half the total—is still at its most dense in the western highlands and Alta Verapaz. They form two distinct cultures: the almost self-supporting indigenous system in the highlands, and the *ladino* commercial economy in the lowlands. At first sight the two seem to have much in common, for the Indian regional economy is also monetary, but a gulf opens between the two systems when it is realized that to an Indian trade is seen as a social act, not done out of need, and certainly not from any impulse to grow rich.

N.B. The word *ladino*, used all over Central America but most commonly in Guatemala, applies to any person with a "Latin" culture, speaking Spanish and wearing normal Western clothes, though he may be pure Amerindian by descent. The opposite of *ladino* is *indígena;* the definition is cultural, not racial.

The scenery of the Indian regions W of the capital is superb and full of colour. In the towns and villages are colonial churches, some half ruined by earthquakes but often with splendid interiors. The Indians speak some 20 languages and 100 or more dialects. The coming of the Spaniards transformed their outer lives: they sing old Spanish songs, and their religion is a compound of image-worshipping paganism and the outward forms of Catholicism, but their inner natures remain largely untouched.

Their markets and *fiestas* are of outstanding interest. The often crowded markets are quiet and restrained: no voice raised, no gesture made, no anxiety to buy or sell; but the *fiestas* are a riot of noise, a confusion of processions, usually carrying saints, and the whole punctuated by grand firework displays and masked dancers. The chief *fiesta* is always for a town's particular patron saint, but all the main Catholic festivals and Christmas are celebrated to some extent everywhere.

Indian dress is unique and attractive, little changed from the time the Spaniards arrived: the colourful head-dresses, *huipiles* (tunics) and skirts of the women, the often richly patterned sashes and kerchiefs, the hatbands and tassels of the men. It varies greatly, often from village to village. Unfortunately a new outfit is costly, the Indians are poor, and denims are cheap. While men are adopting western dress in many villages, women are slower to change.

Cochineal and indigo were the great exports until 1857, when both were wiped out by synthetic dyes. The vacuum was filled by cacao, followed by coffee and bananas, and essential oils. The upland soil and climate are particularly favourable to coffee.

Only coffee of the Bourbon variety is planted below 600 metres, and until 1906, when bananas were first planted there, the low-lying *tierra caliente* had been used mostly for cane and cattle raising. The first plantations of the United Fruit Company were at the mouth of the Motagua, near Puerto Barrios, then little more than a village. Blacks from Jamaica were brought in to work them. The plantations expanded until they covered most of the *tierra caliente* in the NE—along the lower Motagua and around Lake Izabal.

In the 1930s, however, the plantations were struck by disease and the Company began planting bananas in the Pacific lowlands; they are railed across country to the Caribbean ports. There are still substantial plantations at Bananera, 58 km. inland from Puerto Barrios, though some of the old banana land is used for cotton and *abacá* (manila hemp). Despite the fall in banana exports, overall exports have increased greatly, because of the growth of other export lines such as coffee, cotton and sugar. As a result of the increase in cotton-growing, many Indians are now moving from the highlands to the *ladino* lowland cotton areas; other Indians come to the southern plains as seasonal labourers whilst retaining their costumes, languages and customs and returning to the highlands each year to tend their own crops.

The equitable distribution of occupied land is a pressing problem. The Agrarian Census of 1950 disclosed that 70 % of the cultivable land was in the hands of 2 % of the landowners, 20 % in the hands of 22 %, and 10 % in the hands of 76 %—these figures corresponding to the large, medium and small landowners. A quarter of the land held by the small owners was sub-let to peasants who owned none at all. There were 531,636 farms according to the 1979 census, of which 288,083 (54 %) were of less than 1.4 hectares, 180,385 (34 %) were of under 7 hectares, while 482 (less

GUATEMALA

NOT TO SCALE

Legend:
1. Guatemala City and Antigua.
2. Guatemala City to the Caribbean.
3. El Petén.
4. Guatemala City to San José.
5. West from Guatemala City.
6. western Guatemala.

than 1%) were of more than 900 hectares. Between 1955 and 1982, 665,000 hectares were redistributed (compared with 884,000 between 1952 and 1954 under Jacobo Arbenz—see below), but it was estimated that in 1982 there were 420,000 landless agricultural workers. Under the present government a peaceful movement of *campesinos* (farm labourers) was formed in 1986 to speed land distribution.

Roads   There are now 18,000 km. of roads, 2,844 of which are paved.

Railways   The only public-service railway links the Caribbean seaboard with the Pacific, running from Puerto Barrios up the Motagua valley to Guatemala City and on to the port of San José. From Santa María a branch line runs W through Mazatenango to the port of Champerico and the Mexican frontier. From Zacapa, half-way from Puerto Barrios to the capital, a branch line runs S to San Salvador (no passenger services). There are 867 km. of public service railways and 290 km. of plantation lines.

Population   Birth rate: 42.7 per 1,000 (60% born to unmarried mothers); infant mortality, 57 (1986); population growth: 2.9%; urban growth: 3.5%. Some 65% of the people live at elevations above 1,000 metres in 30% of the total territory; only 35% live at lower elevations in 70% of the total territory. Gdp per capita is US$1,030. About 43% of the population are illiterate.

Government   Guatemala is administratively divided into 22 Departments. The Governor of each is appointed by the President, whose term is for 5 years. The latest constitution was dated May 1985.

Recent History   For early history see the introductory chapter to Central America. Jorge Ubico, an efficient but brutal dictator who came to power in 1931, was deposed in 1944. After some confusion, Juan José Arévalo was elected President and set out to accomplish a social revolution, paying particular attention to education and labour problems. He survived several conspiracies and finished his term of six years. Jacobo Arbenz became President in 1950, and the pace of reform was quickened. His Agrarian Reform Law, dividing large estates expropriated without adequate compensation among the numerous landless peasantry, aroused opposition from landowners. In June 1954, Colonel Carlos Castillo Armas, backed by interested parties and with the encouragement of the United States, led a successful insurrection and became President. For the following 29 years the army and its right-wing supporters suppressed left-wing efforts, both constitutional and violent, to restore the gains made under Arévalo and Arbenz; many thousands of people, mostly leftists, were killed during this period. In August 1983 General Oscar Mejía Víctores took power; he permitted a Constituent Assembly to be elected in 1984; among its major tasks were to draw up a new constitution and to work out a timetable for a return to democratic rule. This proceeded successfully, with presidential elections held in December 1985. The victor was Vinicio Cerezo Arévalo of the Christian Democrat party (DC); he took office in January 1986. The return to elected government has not as yet greatly reduced the influence of the armed forces, narrowed the huge gap between rich and poor, or brought to an end the civil war being fought in parts of the country (the Arias Peace Plan notwithstanding).

Note   Although security in general has improved, conditions in the northern territories of Quiché, Alta Verapaz and El Petén should be checked prior to travelling because of sporadic guerrilla and military activities. Chichicastenango and Tikal, however, are safe.

GUATEMALA CITY AND ANTIGUA (1)

Guatemala City, at 1,500 metres, was founded by decree of Charles III of Spain in 1776 to serve as capital after earthquake damage to the earlier capital, Antigua, in 1773. The city lies on a plateau in the Sierra Madre. The lofty ranges of these green mountains almost overhang the capital. To the S looms a group of volcanoes. Population, 1,500,000.

The climate is temperate, with little variation around the year. The average annual temperature is about 18°C, with a monthly average high of 20° in May and a low of 16° in December-January. Daily temperatures range from a low of 7°C at night to a high of about 29° at midday. The rainy seasons are from late April to June (light), September to October, with an Indian summer (canicula) in July and August; the rain is heaviest in early September. It averages about 1,270 mm. a year, and sunshine is plentiful. The city has a serious smog problem.

The city was almost completely destroyed by earthquakes in 1917-18 and rebuilt in modern fashion or in copied colonial; it was further damaged by earthquake in 1976. A plaza called Parque Central lies at its heart: it is intersected by the N-S running 6 Avenida, the main shopping street. The E half has a floodlit fountain; on the W side is Parque Centenario, with an acoustic shell in cement used for open-air concerts and public meetings. To the E of the plaza is the Cathedral; to the W are the National Library and the Banco del Ejército; to the N the large Palacio Nacional. Behind the Palacio Nacional, built of light green stone, is the Presidential Mansion.

Guatemala City is large. Any address not in Zona 1—and it is absolutely essential to quote Zone numbers in addresses—is probably some way from the centre. Addresses themselves, being purely numerical, are easy to find. 19 C, 4-83 is on 19 Calle between 4 and 5 Avenidas.

Many of the hotels and boarding houses are in the main shopping quarter between 2 and 11 Avenidas and between 6 and 18 Calles, Zona 1. The railway station is in the southern part of Zona 1, at 10 Av., 18C, facing the Plaza named for Justo Rufino Barrios, to whom there is a fine bronze statue on Av. las Américas, Zona 13, in the southern part of the city. To see the finest residential district go S down 7 Avenida to Ruta 6, which runs diagonally in front of Edificio El Triángulo, past the Yurrita chapel (Zona 4), into the wide tree-lined Avenida La Reforma. Just south are the Botanical Gardens (open Mon.-Fri., 0800-1200, 1400-1800) and the Natural History Museum of the University of San Carlos at Calle Mariscal Cruz 1-56, Zona 10 (same hours as the Botanical Gardens). Admission free. Parque El Obelisco (also known as Próceres or Independencia), with the obelisk to Guatemalan independence, is at the S end of the Avenida. La Aurora international airport, the Zoo (free, newer areas show greater concern for the animals' well-being), the Observatory, the Archaeological and the Modern Art Museums and racetrack are in Parque Aurora, Zona 13, in the southern part of the city.

Museums   The National Museum of Archaeology and Ethnology, Salón 5, Parque Aurora, Zona 13, contains stelae from Piedras Negras and typical Guatemalan costumes, and good models of Tikal, Quiriguá and Zaculeu, and other Mayan items. (Open 0900-1600, Tues.-Sun.) Admission US$0.40, Sun. free for Guatemalans only. Contains sculpture (including stelae, murals, etc.), ceramics, textiles, and a collection of masks. Its excellent jade collection is closed at weekends.

   The Museum of Modern and Contemporary Arts has replaced the National Museum of History and Fine Arts in Parque Aurora, "modest, enjoyable collection". Open Tues.-Fri., 0900-1600, Sat. 0900-1200, 1400-1600, US$0.12.

   Museum of Natural History, collection of stuffed birds and animals as well as butterflies, geological specimens etc., in Parque Aurora, 7 Av. 6-81, Zona 13; open Tues.-Sun., 0900-1530, free; rebuilt and reorganized in 1983.

   National Museum of Arts and Popular Crafts, 10 Av. 10-72, Zona 1, small exhibition of popular ceramics, textiles, silversmiths' work etc. Hours Tues.-Fri. 0900-1530, Sat. and Sun. 1000-1200, 1400-1600 (US$0.12).

   Museo Ixchel del Traje Indígena, 4 Av. 16-27; Zona 10, has a collection of over 4,000 examples of Indian costumes. Open Mon.-Sat., 0900-1730, entrance US$0.35; get off bus at Av. La Reforma and 16 C.

   Popol Vuh Museum of Archaeology, Edificio Galerías Reforma, Av. La Reforma 8-60, Zona 9

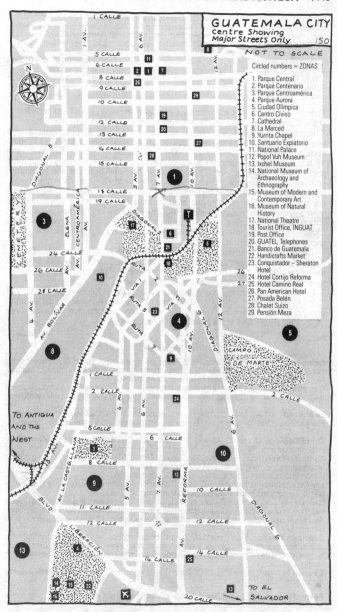

GUATEMALA CITY
centre showing
Major Streets Only

150

NOT TO SCALE

Circled numbers = ZONAS

1. Parque Central
2. Parque Centenario
3. Parque Centroamérica
4. Parque Aurora
5. Ciudad Olímpica
6. Centro Cívico
7. Cathedral
8. La Merced
9. Yurrita Chapel
10. Santuario Expiatorio
11. National Palace
12. Popol Vuh Museum
13. Ixchel Museum
14. National Museum of Archaeology and Ethnography
15. Museum of Modern and Contemporary Art
16. Museum of Natural History
17. National Theatre
18. Tourist Office, INGUAT
19. Post Office
20. GUATEL, Telephones
21. Banco de Guatemala
22. Handicrafts Market
23. Conquistador – Sheraton Hotel
24. Hotel Cortijo Reforma
25. Hotel Camino Real
26. Pan American Hotel
27. Posada Belén
28. Chalet Suizo
29. Pensión Meza

(6th floor, T 318921). Extensive collection of precolumbian and colonial artefacts; said to be best archaeological museum in Guatemala. Has a replica of the Dresden Codex, one of only 3 Mayan parchment manuscripts in existence. Open Mon.-Sat., 0900-1730. Admission US$1.20 (students US$0.40, children US$0.10-20). US$1 charge to take photographs. The research library of FLAAR (**see page 1151**) is on long-term loan to the Popol Vuh Museum.

National Museum of History, 9 C. 9-70, Zona 1 (Mon.-Fri., 0830-1400), US$0.12, historical documents, and objects from independence onward; and colonial furniture and arms.

N.B. Each museum has a sign in 4 languages to the effect that "The Constitution and Laws of Guatemala prohibit the exportation from the country of any antique object, either precolumbian or colonial". The USA in fact prohibits the import of such items and penalties are severe.

There is a magnificent view all the way to Lake Amatitlán from Parque de Berlín at the S end of Av. las Américas, the continuation of Av. La Reforma.

In the northern part (Zona 2) is the fine **Parque Minerva**, where there is a huge relief map of the country made in 1905 to a horizontal scale of 1 in 10,000 and a vertical scale of 1 in 2,000 (open 0800-1700). Buses 1 (from Av. 5, Zona 1) and 18 run to the park, where there are basketball and baseball courts, swimming pool (filled at weekends only, and then used for washing!), bar and restaurant and a children's playground (it is reported to be unsafe for women at night).

The most notable public buildings built 1920-44 after the 1917 earthquake are the National Palace (the guards have keys and may show you round the rooms of state), the Police Headquarters, the Chamber of Deputies and the Post Office. The modern civic centre includes the City Hall, the Supreme Court, the Ministry of Finance, the Banco de Guatemala, the mortgage bank, the social-security commission and the tourist board.

The National Theatre dominates the hilltop of the W side of the Civic Centre. An old Spanish fortress provides a backdrop to the Open Air Theatre adjoining the blue and white mosaic-covered National Theatre; open Mon.-Fri. (unaccompanied tours not permitted in the grounds).

On the W outskirts in Zona 7 are the Mayan ruins of Kaminal Juyú (Valley of Death). About 200 mounds have been examined by the Archaeological Museum and the Carnegie Institute. The area is mainly unexcavated, but there are three excavated areas open to the public, and a sculpture shed.

Churches

Cathedral Begun 1782, finished 1815, damaged by the 1976 earthquake. Paintings and statues from ruined Antigua. Solid silver and sacramental reliquary in the E side chapel of Sagrario. Next to the Cathedral is the colonial mansion of the Archbishop.

Cerro del Carmen A copy of a hermitage destroyed in 1917-18, containing a famous image of the Virgen del Carmen, situated on a hill with views of the city, was also severely damaged in 1976.

La Merced (11 Av. and 5 C, Zona 1), dedicated in 1813, which has housed beautiful altars, organ and pulpit from Antigua as well as jewellery, art treasures and fine statues, also damaged in 1976.

Santo Domingo church (12 Av. and 10 C, Zona 1), 1782-1807, is a striking yellow colour, reconstructed after 1917, image of Our Lady of the Rosary and sculptures.

Santuario Expiatorio (26 C and 2 Av., Zona 1) holds 3,000 people; colourful, exciting modern architecture by a young Salvadorean architect who had not qualified when he built it. Part of the complex (church, school and auditorium) is in the shape of a fish.

Las Capuchinas (10 Av. and 10 C, Zona 1) was another victim of the earthquake. It has a very fine St. Anthony altarpiece, and other pieces from Antigua.

Santa Rosa (10 Av. and 8 C, Zona 1) was used for 26 years as the cathedral until the present building was ready. Altarpieces again from Antigua (except above the main altar). Now damaged.

San Francisco (6 Av. and 13 C, Zona 1) has a sculpture of the Sacred Head, originally from Extremadura.

Capilla de Yurrita (Ruta 6 and Vía 8, Zona 4), built in 1928 on the lines of a Russian Orthodox church as a private chapel. It has been described as an example of "opulent 19th century bizarreness and over-ripe extravagance." There are many wood carvings. Seldom open but worth seeing.

Carmen El Bajo (8 Av. and 10 C, Zona 1) built in the late 18th century; façade severely damaged in 1976.

Festival December 7, Devil's Day, hundreds of street fires are lit, any old rubbish burnt so the smell is awful, but it's spectacular.

Warning Thieves and handbag snatchers operate openly around 7 Av. and 18 C (18 C., between 4 Av. and 8 Av. is bad all the way). Do not park on the street, either day or night, or your car may well be broken into. There are plenty of lock-up garages and parking lots (*estacionamientos*).

Hotels (Av.=Avenida; C.=Calle). More Expensive. Zona 1: *Ritz Continental*, 6 Av. "A" 10-13, C; *Pan American*, 9 C. 5-63, D, central and rec. as quiet and comfortable with good and reasonable food (US$1.25 and US$2 for the set meals), parking; *Maya Excelsior*, 7 Av. 12-46, D, crowded, noisy and commercial.

Zona 2: *La Gran Vía*, Av. Simeón Cañas 7-23, C, fully-equipped apartments.

Zona 4: *Conquistador-Sheraton*, Vía 5, 4-68, A, luxurious, good; *Motel Plaza*, Vía 7, 6-16, D, outdoor pool, squash court, satisfactory.

Zona 9: *Cortijo Reforma*, Av. La Reforma 2-18, A, rec.; *El Dorado Americana*, 7 Av. 15-45, A; *Villa Española*, 2 C., 7-51, T 65417, restaurant, bar, parking, colonial atmosphere, C, rec.

Zona 10: *Camino Real*, Av. La Reforma and 14 C., A; *Guatemala Fiesta*, 1 Av. 13-22, A; *Residencial Reforma*, Av. La Reforma 7-67, near American Embassy, C; *Alameda Guest House*, 4 Av. 14-10, C.

Medium price, all in Zona 1 unless otherwise stated: *Posada Belén*, 13 C. "A" 10-30, with bath in a colonial-style house, C, quiet, good laundry service, extremely friendly, Francesca and René Sanchinelli speak English, highly rec., good dining room (T 29226, 534530, 513478); *Hogar del Turista*, 11 C. 10-43, E, clean, friendly, highly rec.; *Brasilia*, 2 Av. 4-20, D, with bath (10% discount if staying a week or more); *Colonial*, 7 Av. 14-19, D, reasonable restaurant, quiet and rec., although ground floor rooms are small and poorly ventilated, ask for 2nd floor; *Casa Shaw*, 8 Av. 12-75, D, with bath, rec.; *San Juan*, 16 C. 2-51, E, with bath, clean, quiet, convenient; *International Boarding House*, next door, a little cheaper; *Posada Real*, 12 C. 6-21, E, OK, but beware overcharging; *Hernani*, 15 C. 6-56, E, no restaurant, clean, friendly, safe to leave luggage while travelling, the Spanish owner is severe in manner but noble in spirit! *Maya Quiché*, 10 Av. y 12 C., very friendly, many families use it, good restaurant attached.

Inexpensive, all in Zona 1 unless otherwise stated: *Ritz*, 6 Av. 9-28, 2nd. floor, E, central, hot water, friendly; *El Virrey*, 5 Av. 13-52, F, meals US$1.25; *El Virrey 3*, 7 Av. 15-46, F, downstairs clean, communal baths, upstairs no water, but cheaper; *13 Calle Inn*, 13 C. 9-08, 2nd. floor, F, clean; *Spring*, 8 Av. 12-65, E, with shower and hot water, cheaper without, rec.; *Bristol*, 15 C. 7-36, F, shared bath, pleasant, back rooms are brighter; *Bilbao*, 8 Av. 15 C., F, clean, some English spoken, shared showers, good toilets; *San Diego*, 15 C. 7-37, E, with bath (cheap breakfast and meals, annex opp., F, good value, full by 1000); *Diligencia*, 14C, 7-36, F, reasonable but unfriendly; *CentroAmérica*, 9 Av. 16-38, E, with 3 meals, US$1 extra with bath, clean, bright; next door is *Albergue*, F, courtyard, friendly, pleasant except for bathrooms; *Capri*, 9 Av. 15-63, F, with shower, a bit noisy, clean, hot water, rec.; *Le Petit Parisien*, 2 C. 6-77, E, with bath, clean, friendly; *Chalet Suizo*, 14 C. 6-82, E, with or without shower, (US$ 2.25 for extra bed) popular, often crowded, friendly, locked luggage store US$0.10/day; *Fénix*, 7 Av. 16-81, F, some rooms with bath, clean, safe, corner rooms noisy, good meals US$1.25 and 1.50; *Pensión Meza*, 10 C. 10-17, F, popular, helpful staff, hot electric showers, noisy, inhabited mainly by young travellers, basic, beware of petty theft; *Meza Annex*, 13 C., 10 Av. 'A', G; *Hostal Biskaia*, 8 Av. No. 16-14, F, hot shower a.m. only, very pleasant, safe, will store luggage, couples preferred, Basque owners; *Ajau*, F, 8 Av. 15-62, convenient for El Petén and El Salvador buses; on 7 Av. *Santa Ana No. 2*, G, hot water, friendly; *Tranquilidad*, 14 C. 9-59, F, without shower, quiet, hot water, poor service; *Karen Inn*, 17 C. 8-58, F, reasonable; *Pensión San Antonio*, 19 C. between 8 and 9 Av. (near Rutas Orientales), G, or F in new block (rooms with bath, good). *Venecia*, 4 Av. 'A', 6-90, Zona 4, very comfortable, E, with bath, reasonable meals.

N.B. The water supply in hotels tends to be spasmodic, and water for showering is often unobtainable between 1000-1800. At the cheaper hotels it is not always possible to get single rooms. Most hotels charge a 10% room tax. There are many other cheap *pensiones* near bus and railway stations and market; those between Calles 14 and 18 are not very salubrious.

Camping For campsites within easy access of Guatemala City **see page 1168** under Amatitlán. Parking is available free at the Airport from 1900-0700. Camping-gas cartridges not hard to find (they are stocked at Almacén Orval, 11 C. y 8 Av., Zona 1).

Electric Current 110 volts AC, 60 cycles.

Restaurants (Restaurants at hotels. Food prices vary less than quality.) In the capital, the tourist can easily find everything from the simple national cuisine (black beans, rice, meat, chicken, soup, avocado, cooked bananas—plátanos—and tortillas with everything) to French, Chinese, Italian and German food (and pastries). A simple, but nourishing, three-course meal can be had for US$1 at any *comedor*. For local food served in 14 different "menus", try *Los Antojitos*, 15 C. 6-28, Zona 1, with music. Fashionable places, such as *Hola* (French and Italian), Av. Las Américas, Zona 14, *Romanello* (Italian), 1 Av. 13-38, Zona 10, *Estro Armonico* (French), Vía 4, 4-36, Zona 4, *Puerto Barrios* (seafood), 7 Av. 10-65, Zona 9, or *Grischun* (Swiss), 14 Av. 15-36, Zona 10, charge on average US$10 for a three-course meal. Wine and other alcoholic drinks are expensive, beer good and inexpensive. *Peña de los Charrangos*, 6 Av. 13-62, Zona 9, reasonable prices, live music weekends; *Palo Alto*, 14C, 4 Av. Zona 10, superb but dear. *Europa* (German and Austrian), 11 C. at 5 Av., Zona 1, English and German spoken, is rec. as is *Tany*, 12 C. 6-23, Zona 1 (Italian), for good 3-course lunch. Fast food is available in all parts of the city, and is relatively safe; e.g. *Picadilly*, 6 Av., C. 12, good; *Las Cebollines*, several locations in Zona 1, Mexican, inexpensive, good. A rec. pizza chain is *A Guy from Italy* (in Zona 1, 12 C. 6-33 and 5 Av. 5-70). Rec. vegetarian restaurants: *El Arbol de la Vida*, Ed. Reforma Montúfar, 12 C. y Av. Reforma, Zona 9; and *Comida de Vegetales* chain, several branches, also take-away.

The best cafeterias for pies, pastries and chocolates (German, Austrian and Swiss styles) are *Zurich*, 4 Av. 12-09, Zona 10; *Los Alpes*, 10 C. 1-09, Zona 10; *Jensen*, 14 C. 0-53, Zona 1. The *Pastelería Lins* chain (4 or 5 in Zona 1) has been rec. *American Doughnuts*, 5 Av. 11-47, Zona 1, and several other branches in the capital. (With thanks to Rainer Gruss of Guatemala City, and other travellers' recommendations.)

Clubs   The American Club (introductions can be arranged for temporary membership). Lions Club. Rotary Club. Von Humboldt (German). Italian Club.

Shopping   The Central Market was destroyed in the 1976 earthquake but a new one has been opened, from 7 to 9 Av., 8 C., Zona 1; one floor is dedicated to native textiles and crafts, and there is a large, cheap basketware section on the lower floor. Of the markets, the one likely to be of most tourist interest is behind the Cathedral, between Avs. 8 and 9 and Calles 6 and 8 in Zona 1 (underground), selling mainly native textiles and crafts. Apart from the Mercado Terminal in Zona 4 (large, watch your belongings), there is the Mercado del Sur, 6 Av. 19-21, Zona 1, primarily a food market though it has a section for popular handicrafts. There is also a new *artesanía* market in Parque Aurora, near the airport, where marimba music is played, and which is strictly for tourists. *La Placita* by the Church of Guadalupe at 18 C. and 5 Av. is good for conventional clothes, leather suitcases, etc. Silverware is cheaper at the market than anywhere else in Guatemala City, but we are told that a better place for silverware is Cobán. The market is, however, rec. for all local products. Bargaining is necessary at all markets in Guatemala. Also, 4 Ahau, 11 C. 4-53, Zona 1, very good for *huipiles*, other textiles, and crafts and antiques; hand-woven textiles from *Miranda* factory, 8 Av. 30-90, Zona 8; *La Tinaja*, 12 C. 4-80, Zona 1; *El Patio*, 12 C. 3-57, Zona 1; *Rodas Antiques*, 5 Av. 8-42, Zona 1 and *Barrientos Antigüedades*, 10 C. 4-64, Zona 1, have high priced silver and antiques. *Mayatex*, 12 C. 4-46, good choice, wholesale prices. *Maya Exports*, 7 Av. 10-55, credit cards accepted. Opposite is *Sombol*, Av. Reforma 14-14 and Calle 7-80, good for handicrafts, dresses and blouses. *La Momosteca* has a stall in Plaza Barrios and a shop at 7 Av. 14-48, Zona 1, and sells both textiles and silver. Pasaje Rubio, 9 C. near 6 Av., is good for antique silver charms and coins. Shop hours 0830-1230, 1500-1930 weekdays; may open all day on Sats.

Bookshops   *Arnel*, Edificio El Centro No. 108, 9 C.y 7 Av., Zona 1, excellent selection (T 24631); *Geminis*, 6 Av. 7-24, Zona 9 (good selection); both have new English books; *La Plazuela*, 12C. 6-14, Zona 9, large selection of 2nd hand books (very poor resale value, better to buy); *Vista Hermosa*, 2 C. 18-48, Zona 15, (English, German, Spanish); *El Palacio de las Revistas*, 9 Av. 10-14, Zona 1, and 7 Av. 7-16, Zona 4, has limited selection of magazines and US newspapers. Museo Popol Vuh bookshop, Av. La Reforma 8-60, Zona 9, has a good selection of books on precolumbian art, crafts and natural history; also bookshop of *Camino Real* hotel. Librería Bremen, Pasaje Rubio, 6 Av. between 8 C. and 9 C., Zona 1, has material in German plus old books on Guatemala. Instituto Guatemalteco Americano (IGA), Ruta 1 and Vía 4, Zona 4 (also library).

Car Rental   *Hertz*, 19 C. 7-07, Zona 1, T 510202; *Avis*, 12 C. 2-73, Zona 9, T 316990, US$205 all inclusive, unlimited mileage for a week, Nissan March, but US$162 if reserved in advance in N America; *Budget*, Av. Reforma y 15 C., Zona 9, T 316546; *National*, 14 C. 1-42, Zona 10, T 680175; *Dollar*, Av. "A" 10-13, Zona 1, T 23446 (at *Hotel Ritz*, rates as for Avis); *Tikal*, 2 C. 6-56, Zona 10, T 316490; *Ambassador*, 6 Av. 9-31, Zona 1, T 85987; *Tabarini*, 2 C. "A" 7-30, Zona 10, T 316108 (have Toyota Land Cruisers); *Jerry*, 7 Av. 14-60, Zona 1, T 536238 (also rent motorcycles, US$10 a day); *Tally*, 7 Av. 14-74, Zona 1, T 514113 (have Nissan and Mitsubishi pick-ups). The last two offer the lowest rates (US$13 a day + mileage), but these vehicles are not always available. Insurance rate (extra) varies from US$4-6 a day.

Local Buses   in town, US$0.05 per journey. Not many before 0600 or after 2000.

Taxis   are from US$0.50 for a short run to US$3 for a long run inside the city. Hourly rates are from US$4 to US$5. Taxis of the Azules, Concordia and Palace companies rec. Agree fares in advance; no meters. Taxis always available in Parque Central and Parque Concordia (6 Av. and 15 C., Zona 1) and at the Trébol (the main crossroads outside city if coming from Pacific or Highlands by bus, convenient for airport).

Traffic   Traffic lights operate only between 0800 and 2100; at all other times Avenidas have priority over Calles (except in Zona 10, where this rule varies).

Night Clubs   *La Quebrada*, 6 Av. 4-60, Zona 4; *Plaza Inn*, Motel Plaza, Vía 7, 6-16, Zona 4; *Brasilia* in *Hotel Ritz Continental*. Discothèques: *After Eight*, Ed. Galerías España, Zona 9; *Kahlúa*,

1 Av. 13-21, Zona 10; *Manhattan*, 7 Av. opp. *Hotel El Dorado*, Zona 9; *El Optimista*, Av. La Reforma 12-01, Zona 10; *La Petite Discothèque*, La Manzana, Ruta 4, 4-76, Zona 4. *El Establo*, Av. La Reforma 11-83, Zona 10, is a bar with excellent music.

Guatemala (with southern Mexico) is the home of marimba music. The marimba is a type of xylophone played with drum sticks by from one to nine players. Up country the sounding boxes are differently sized gourds, the *marimbas de tecomates*. The city ones are marvels of fine cabinet work.

Theatres National Theatre. Teatro Gadem, 8 Av. 12-15, Zona 1; Antiguo Paraninfo de la Universidad, 2 Av. 12-30, Zona 1; Teatro Universidad Popular, 10 C. 10-32, Zona 1; Teatro Artistas Unidos, 3 Av. 18-57, Zona 1. Occasional plays in English, and many other cultural events, at Instituto Guatemalteco Americano (IGA), Ruta 1 and Vía 4, Zona 4. List of current offerings outside Teatro del Puente, 7 Av. 0-40, Zona 4, and in local English-language publications and city newspapers.

Cinemas are numerous and often show films in English with Spanish subtitles. Prices are US$2. Alianza Francesa, 4 Av. 12-39, free film shows on Mon., Wed. and Sat. evenings; other activities on other evenings, rec.

Concerts Concerts of the Philharmonic Orchestra take place in the Teatro Nacional, Civic Centre, 24 Calle, Zona 1. During the rainy season at the Conservatorio Nacional, 5 C. and 3 Av., Zona 1, and occasionally in the Banco de Guatemala.

Sports There is an 18 hole golf course at the Guatemala Country Club, 8 km. from the city, and a 9 hole course at the Mayan Club. The Guatemala Lawn Tennis Club and the Mayan Club are the chief centres for tennis.

Swimming Pools Apart from those at the Parque Minerva (**page 1146**) there are pools at Ciudad Olímpica, 7 C., 12 Av., Zona 5 (monthly membership only, US$2.50 a month—photograph required; you may be allowed in for a single swim); Piscina Ciudad Vieja, Zona 15; Baños del Sur, 13 C. "A" 7-34, Zona 1, has hot baths for US$0.50, saunas for US$1.50. Try the hotels and the campsites near Amatitlán also.

Bowling Ten-pin variety and billiards at Bolerama, Ruta 3, 0-61, Zona 4, 2 blocks from *Conquistador-Sheraton* hotel.

Exchange Lloyds Bank International (8 Av. 10-67, Zona 1); agencies at Plazuela 11 de Marzo, 7 Av. 4-87, Zona 4; Autovía Mixco 4-39, Zona 11 and C. Marti 14-57, Zona 6. Open weekdays, 0900-1500. Banco de Guatemala (7 Av. and 22 C., Zona 1) open Mon.-Thurs. 0830-1400, Fri. 0830-1430, will change foreign cash and travellers' cheques after 1000. Banks now change US dollars into quetzales at the free rate. Bank of America cashes its own cheques into dollars for Q0.03 per dollar. There is a bank open 7 days a week at the airport, weekdays 0730-1830, Sat., Sun. and holidays 0800-1100, 1500-1800 (only place to change foreign banknotes—but not quetzales back into foreign currencies). When shut, try airport police or porters who may be able/willing to change US$ cash for quetzales. All banks mentioned above cash travellers' cheques, although some travellers have experienced difficulties. Try also the Banco Industrial (which sometimes advances quetzales on Visa cards, on Av. 7, nr. Central Post Office), Banco Internacional, or Bandesa, 9 C. between 9 and 10 Avs., Zona 1. American Express at Banco del Café, Av. La Reforma, 9-00, Zona 9 (bus 2 or 14 from centre), T 311463, open 0830-1530, 1500 on Fri. (3% commission for cashing cheques into dollars cash).

The legal street exchange for cash and cheques may be found on 6 Av., 12-14 C. near the Post Office (Zona 1), although it is better to go direct to the exchange offices to avoid paying the street dealers' commission (for example, in the basement of the big shopping centre between 6 and 7 Av. behind the car park, opp. Post Office). Good place for exchange, *Le Point* shoe shop, C. 14 between Avs. 4 and 5. When changing travellers' cheques, always keep the receipt. Be careful when changing money on the street; never go alone. Quetzales may be bought with Visa or Mastercard in the basement of Av. 7, 6-22 (open until 2000, Mon.-Fri.).

Embassies and Consulates Addresses change frequently.

USA, Av. La Reforma 7-01, Zona 10 (T 311541-55). *Canada*, Galería España, 7 Av. and 12 C., Zona 9. *Mexico*, Consulate, 13 C. 7-30, Zona 9 (closes 1430 for tourist cards). *El Salvador*, 12 C. 5-43, Zona 9, T 629385, 0800-1400, for visa take passport photo, letter of recommendation, visa costs US$20 and you will be charged for telex to San Salvador, may take a week. *Honduras*, 16 C. 8-27, Zona 10. *Nicaragua*, Av. 14-72, Zona 10 (open Mon.-Fri. 0900-1300, visas in 24 hrs.). *Costa Rica*, Edificio Galerías Reforma Oficina 320, Av. Reforma, 8-60, Zona 9, T 325768. *Panama*, Edificio Maya, Vía 5, 7 Av., Suite 717, Zona 4 (T 325001/320763).

Argentina, 2 Av. 11-04, Zona 10. *Bolivia*, 12 Av. 15-37, Zona 10. *Brazil*, 18 C. 2-22, Zona 14, T 37-09-49. *Colombia*, Edificio Gemini 10, 12 C., 1 Av., Zona 10, unhelpful, T 320603/4. *Chile*, 13 C. 7-85, Zona 10. *Ecuador*, Diagonal 6, 13-08, Zona 10 (T 316119). *Paraguay*, 7 Av. 7-78 (8th floor), Zona 4. *Peru*, 2 Av. 9-48, Zona 9 (T 318409). *Uruguay*, 20 C. 8-00, Zona 10. *Venezuela*, 8 C. 0-56, Zona 9.

Israel, 13 Av. 14.07, Zona 10 (T 371303). *Japan*, Ruta 6, 8-19, Zona 4. *South Africa*, 10 Av. 30-57, Zona 5 (T 62890).

Austria, Trade Council, 6 Av. 20-25, Zona 10; Consulate, 6 Av. 11-00 (T 64314, 0900-1100). *Belgium*, Av. La Reforma 13-70 (2nd floor), Zona 9. *Denmark*, 7 Av. 20-36 (Apartment 1, 2nd floor), Zona 1. *Finland*, 10 C. 6-47, Zona 1. *France*, 14 C. 5-52, Zona 9, T 66-336. *West Germany*, 6 Av. 20-25, Edificio Plaza Marítima 2nd floor, Zona 10, T 370028, 370031 (bus 14 goes there). *Netherlands*, Consulate General, 15 C.10-91, Zona 10 (open 0900-1200). *Italy*, 8 C. 3-14, Zona 10. *Norway*, Vía 5, 4-50 (4th floor), Zona 4. *Portugal*, 5 Av. 12-60, Zona 9. *Spain*, 10 C. 6-20, Zona 9. *Sweden*, 8 Av. 15-07, Zona 10, T 680621. *Switzerland*, Edif. Seguros Universales, 4 C. 7-73, Zona 9 (T 65726, 31-3725); *British Embassy*, Ed. Centro Financiero, Torre 11, 7th floor, 7 Av. 5-10, Zona 4 (T 321601/02/04/06).

Immigration Office   12 C and 8 Av., Zona 1 (for extensions of visas, take photo to "Inspectoria").

Central Post Office   7 Av., 12 C., Zona 1. 2nd floor for overseas parcel service. Watch your belongings when standing in queues here. This is the only post office in country from which parcels over 2 kg. can be sent abroad. Poste restante keeps mail for 2 months (US$0.03 per letter). Open Mon.-Fri. 0800-1630. Free marimba concert at post office every Fri. at 1500. Alternative: American Express, for its customers only.

Telecommunications   Empresa Guatemalteca de Telecomunicaciones (Guatel), 7 Av. 12-39 Zona 1, and 8 Av. 11-83 Zona 1 for international calls; 24-hr national and international telephone service. Local telegrams from central post office.

Non-Catholic Churches   Episcopalian Church of St. James, Av. Castellana 40-08, Zona 8, and the Union Church of Guatemala (Plazuela España, Zona 9). Sun. morning service in English at the first: 0930; at the second: 1100.

Synagogues   7 Av. 13-51, Zona 9. Service at 0930 Sat.

Health   Centro Médico Hospital, 6 Av. 3-47, Zona 10, private, but reasonably priced, all senior doctors speak English; very helpful. Dr Mariano A. Guerrero, 5 Av. 3-09, Zona 1, German-speaking, understands English (US$10 for treatment). Dr. Manuel Cáceres, 6 Av. 8-92, Zona 9, 1600-1800, speaks English and German. Dentist: Dr Freddy Lewin, Centro Médico, 6 Av. 3-69, Zona 10, T 325153 (German, English).

Spanish Classes   Instituto Guatemalteco Americano (IGA) offers 6-week courses, 2 hours a day, for US$60. Several other schools in the city.

Laundromats   Lava-Centro Servimatic, Ruta 6, 7-53, Zona 4 (opposite Edificio El Triángulo) sometimes has hot water; Express (dry cleaners), 7 Av. 3-49, Zona 4; El Siglo (dry cleaners), 7 Av. 3-50, Zona 4, 11 Av. 16-35, Zona 1, and 12 C. 1-55, Zona 9. 4 Av., just up from 13 C., Zona 1. Dry cleaner also at Vía 2, 4-04, Zona 4, open Mon.-Fri., 0730-1830.

Car Insurance for Mexico   Granai y Townson, 7 Av. 1-82, Zona 4.

Car Repairs   Christian Kindel, 47 Calle 16-02, Zona 12. Honda **motorcycle** parts from F.A. Honda, Av. Bolívar 31-00, Zona 3; general manager and chief mechanic are German, former speaks English. In Guatemala City, parts available for most motorcycles.

Camera Repairs   Sertecof Panamericana, 10 C. 9-68, Zona 1, Edif. Rosanza, Of. 105, T 537-533, 537-613, expensive but work guaranteed 3 months.

Tourist Information   Inguat, 7 Av. 1-17, Zona 4 (Centro Cívico); T 311333/47. Very friendly. Hotel lists, will ring hotels. Open Mon.-Fri. 0830-1800, Sat. 0830-1200, accurate map of city, other maps, information, major tourist attractions and will book tours. Information on nature from Inafor, 7 Av. 13 C. Zona 9, T 325064.

   Travellers wishing to get to know Guatemala should contact Yvonne Martínez, 11 Avenida, 25-04, Zona 12, who very kindly offers to provide information and a meeting place for young visitors.

Maps   Good maps of all sorts can be bought from the Instituto Geográfico Nacional, Av. Las Américas 5-76, Zona 13, open 0800-1630 Mon. to Fri., closed Sat. and Sun.; some of the more detailed maps can only be obtained by post, and permission must be obtained from the Ministry of Defence before buying maps of "sensitive areas". Those that cannot be bought may be copied by hand from the book containing all the 1:50,000 and 1:250,000 maps of the country. Also good map of city on back of map of country, from Hertz at airport.

Travel Agents   Clark Tours, 6 Av. y Vía 7, no exchange, in Edificio El Triángulo, Zona 4, very helpful, tours to Copán, Quiriguá, etc; Setsa Travel, 8 Av., 14-11, very helpful, tours arranged to Tikal, Copán, car hire; Aire, Mar y Tierra, Plaza Marítima, 20 C. y 6 Av., Zona 10, and Ed. Herrera, 5 Av. y 12 C., Zona 1; Tourama, Av. La Reforma 15-25, Zona 10, both rec., German and English spoken. Servicios Turísticos del Petén, 3 C. 10-58, Zona 10, trips to Flores and Tikal (owns *Hotel Maya Internacional*, Flores).

Archaeological Tours Anyone interested in genuine archaeological (or botanical, ornithological and zoological) expeditions should contact Foundation for **Latin American Anthropological Research (FLAAR)**, 6355 Green Valley Circle, No. 213, Culver City, CA 90230 and Apartado Postal 1276, Guatemala City. (There is no Guatemalan research centre; the foundation's library is on long-term loan to the Popol Vuh Museum.) This organization runs trips to well-known and almost unknown areas of interest (including Yaxchilán, Piedras Negras, Toniná, Comalcalco, El Tajín, Xochicalco, and all of Yucatán, Campeche and Quintana Roo, and the archaeology of Belize). FLAAR, formerly EPANS, has published *Tikal, Copán Travel Guide*, by Nicholas Hellmuth, on all the Mayan sites in Central America and Mexico. It costs US$25 (available from the Popol Vuh museum, the museum at Tikal, and from California address above) and gives useful tips on how to get to each of the sites. Turismo Kim'Arrin, Edificio Maya, Office No. 103, Vía 5, 4-50, Zona 4, and Panamundo Guatemala Travel Service also arrange tours to Maya sites.

Airline Agents Local airlines: Aviateca, 10 Calle 6-30, Zona 1, and at airport; Aerovías, 18 C., Zona 13 (T 81463/316935); Tapsa at airport. In Edificio El Triángulo, 7 Av. and Ruta 6, Zona 4, are offices of Copa, SAM and Avianca. Agencia de Viajes Mundial, 5 Av. 12-44, Zona 1, is very good. PanAm, 6 Av. 11-14, Zona 1, Iberia (Ed. Galerías Reforma, Av. La Reforma, 8 C., Zona 9), Mexicana, KLM (20 C. and Av. 6, Zona 10—bus 2, black or 14 from Av. 10, Zona 1, open 0900-1700) and the Central American airlines all have offices, so has Lufthansa, Plaza Marítima, 6 Av. 20-25, Zona 10.

Airport At La Aurora, 8 km. S; restaurant with cheap "meal of the day" (more appetizing than it looks); all prices marked up in the shops. Taxi to town, US$2.50 one way, US$5 return (airport tourist office supplies official taxi-fare chits—drivers may try to charge new arrivals US$8 to town). Nos. 5 (in black not red) 6 and 20 buses from 8 Av., Zona 1, and the Zona 4, 4 Av., 1 C, bus terminal, run the ½ hour's journey between airport and centre (US$0.05). (Bus 20 runs from Centro Cívico to Aeropuerto Local.) There is also a bus to 7 Av., C. 18 (US$0.08 at night). Domestic flights to Flores (**see page 1163**) leave from the international airport. All other domestic flights must be chartered. N.B. The airport is closed from 2100-0400, so you cannot stay the night there.

Rail Guatemalan Railways to Puerto Barrios, 0645, Tues., Thurs., Sat. 13 hrs., US$1.50 (an excellent, if slow, opportunity to get a first impression of the country, trains are usually delayed). Trains to Tecún Umán (290 km.) 0715 Tues., Thurs. and Sat., arr. 1900, US$1.40 via Escutlán (arr. 1300) and Retalhuleu (arr. 1500). No cooked meals are served in trains, although sandwiches and light refreshments, iced beer and soft drinks can be bought at inflated prices. Station at 18 C. 9 and 10 Av., Zona 1, on east side of Plaza Barrios (T 83031/39). No passenger connections to El Salvador.

Buses *International connections*. To San Salvador: Inter-Futuro Express, 8 Av. 15-69, Zona 1, daily at 0600, 5 hrs., US$2.50 (not rec.; may desert you at the border). With this service one arrives in San Salvador early enough to catch a bus to the El Salvador-Honduras border. (Don't trust phone reservations) Transportes Centroamérica, 9 Av. 15-06, Zona 1, T 23432 (minibus service to hotel on request), daily, 0730 after all passengers have been collected. Melva, 4 Av. 1-20, Zona 9, 2 buses daily from 0800, US$2.50, Pezzarossi 6 departures daily, 6 hrs.; both rec., own terminal in Zona 4 (office at 4 Av. 1 C., Zona 9, at edge of bus station at 4 Av. 7 C., no advance reservations—all except Pezzarossi go also to Santa Ana). To Honduras avoiding El Salvador, take bus to Esquipulas (see below), then minibus to border. To Mexico: Moreliana (from bus terminal) to Talismán, US$2.50, from 0600 to 1600, also to Tecún Umán; Galgos, 7 Av. 19-44, and Rutas Lima, 8 C. 3-63, both Zona 1, have several buses daily to Talismán, US$3.25, connections with Cristóbal Colón bus line— rebookings at the border may be necessary (local buses to Talismán take 7 hrs., involve 3 changes, and cost US$2.50). El Cóndor, 2 Av. 19 C., Zona 1, has several buses daily to La Mesilla, connections with Cristóbal Colón. Unión Pacífica, 9 Av. 18-38, Zona 1, go to El Carmen and Tecún Umán; at both one can get connections to Tapachula, 0630, 0845, 1245 daily. No Guatemalan bus goes into Mexico. Through tickets to Mexico City are available, but don't be tempted to buy one; purchase tickets as you go along because of poor connections and full buses from the border into Mexico.

To Flores (for Tikal and Belize), Fuente del Norte, 17 C. 8-46, Zona 1, 5 a day before 0900, book the day before, first on the list is first on the bus, US$5.40 (from 12 to 20 hrs. over dreadful roads via Morales and Modesto Méndez; La Pinita runs via Sayaxché "no timescale"). To Huehuetenango, El Cóndor (5 a day, US$2.60), Los Halcones, 15 C. 7-66, Zona 1 (reliable, reserved seats) 0700, 1400. To Quezaltenango, Marquesita, 21 C. 1-56, Zona 1, 0430 and 0630, US$2, Rutas Lima, 4 a day, US$2; Galgos, 5 a day, rec., US$2.25. To Panajachel, Rebuli, 20 C. 3-42, Zona 1, terminal C.1 and C.4, Zona 9, take city bus No. 17, hourly 0500-1600, US$1.25 (3 hrs., 1st class). To Chichicastenango, Reina de Utatlán, bus terminal, throughout the day, US$1.50 (3½ hrs.). To Puerto Barrios, Litegua, 14 C., 10-40 Av., Zona 1, hourly 0600-1700, US$4, 6 hrs.; Fuente del Norte, Unión Pacífica y Las Patojas, 9 Av., 18-38, Zona 1 (Zona 4 terminal), 4 a day, US$2.50. To Esquipulas, via Chiquimula, Rutas Orientales, 19 C, 8-18, Zona 1, every ½ hr., 0400-1800, 4 hrs. (US$2.65 "Pullman"). Transportes Guerra to Chiquimula, US$1.25, 3½ hrs., 0700 (Rutas Orientales, US$2.15 pullman, 3 hrs.). To Santa Cruz del Quiché, via Los Encuentros and Chichicastenango, Reyna de Utatlán, Zona 4 bus terminal, 0600 to 1600, 4 hrs., US$1.60. To Cobán (US$2.45) and San Pedro Carchá (US$2.75), Cobanerita and Monja Blanca y Escobar, book a day in advance; take a Cobán bus for the Biotopo del Quetzal, US$1.90.

The Zona 4 bus terminal between 1-4 Av. and 7-9 C. serves the Occidente (West), the Costa Sur (Pacific coastal plain) and El Salvador. The area of 19 C. 8-9 Av. Zona 1, next to the Plaza Barrios market, contains many bus offices and is the departure point for the Oriente (East), the Caribbean zone, Pacific coast area toward the Mexican border and the north, to Flores and Tikal. First class buses often depart from company offices in the south-central section of Zona 1.

To Antigua, the shortest route is 45 km. via San Lucas by paved double-lane highway passing (25 km. out) El Mirador (1,830 metres), with fine view of the capital. Road then rises to 2,130 metres and gradually drops to 1,520 metres at Antigua.

Antigua was the capital city until it was heavily damaged by earthquake in 1773. Population today: 30,000. Founded in 1543, after destruction of a still earlier capital, Ciudad Vieja, it grew to be the finest city in Central America, with a population of 60,000, numerous great churches, a University (1680), a printing press (founded 1660) and famous sculptors, painters, writers and craftsmen. Centre of the city is the Parque Central, the old Plaza Real, where bullfights and markets were held. The Cathedral (1534) is to the E, the Palace of the Captains-General to the S (1769), the Municipal Palace (Cabildo) to the N (all have been repaired since the 1976 earthquake) and an arcade of shops to the west. Alvarado was buried in the Cathedral, but whereabouts is not known. All the ruined buildings, though built over a period of three centuries, are difficult to date by eye, partly because of the massive, almost romanesque architecture against earthquakes: cloisters of the convent of Capuchinas (1736), for example, look 12th century, with immensely thick round pillars (entrance, US$0.12). The most interesting ruins (apart from those mentioned) are of the monastery of San Francisco, the convent of Santa Clara (1723-34, entrance US$0.12), El Carmen, San Agustín (the last two may only be viewed from outside), La Compañía de Jesús (being restored with a Unesco grant), Santa Cruz, Escuela de Cristo church, La Recolección (1703-17) off the road, set among coffee groves, Colegio y Hermita de San Jerónimo (Real Aduana), open every day except Mon., 0800-1700, La Merced (being restored, said to have largest fountain in the New World), the Hospital (badly damaged by 1976 earthquake, and no longer functioning), and the Museum. John Streather tells us that other ruins, such as Santa Isabel, San Cristóbal, El Calvario and San Gaspar Vivar, all south of the town, are well worth visiting. Many sculptures, paintings and altars have been removed to Guatemala City. The Casa Popenoe, 1 Av. Sur, between 5 and 6 C. Oriente, is a restored colonial house with a few original 16th-century parts (the kitchen, herb garden), contains many old objects from Spain and Guatemala; guided tours only, 1500-1600, 1600-1700 (it's still a private house), entry US$0.45.

Antigua is so restored that only convents and churches are in ruins, and San Francisco church has been rebuilt. The old cobblestones are being replaced in the original pattern. Indian women sit in their colourful costumes amid the ruins and in the Parque Central. Most picturesque. Good views from the Cerro de la Cruz, 40 mins'. walk N of town (beware of theft).

Orientation Agua volcano is due S of the city and the market is to the W. Avenidas are numbered upwards running from East (Oriente) to West (Poniente), and Calles upwards from Norte to Sur. Avenidas are Norte or Sur and Calles Oriente or Poniente in relation to the central Plaza; however, unlike Guatemala City, house numbers do not give one any clue towards how far from the central Plaza a place is. There are authorized guides whose tours of Antigua and surroundings are good value.

Fiestas Holy Week. The most important and colourful processions are those leaving La Merced at 1500 on Palm Sunday and 0800 on Good Friday, and Escuela de Cristo and the Church of San Felipe de Jesús (in the suburbs) at 1630 on Good Friday. Gay carpets, made of dyed sawdust and flowers, are laid on the route. The litter bearers wear purple until 1500 on Good Friday afternoon, and black afterwards. Only the litter bearing Christ and His Cross passes over the carpets, which are thereby destroyed. Holy Week in Antigua is claimed to be one of the finest in the New World. Also July 21-26 and Oct. 31-Nov. 2 (All Saints and All Souls, in and around Antigua).

Hotels In the better hotels, advance reservations are advised for weekends and Dec.-April.

Antigua (best), 5 Av. Sur and 8 Calle (4 blocks S of Parque), beautiful gardens, pool (see **Bathing** below); *Ramada Antigua*, 9 C. Poniente and Carretera Ciudad Vieja, B, pool (see below), riding, tennis courts, discotheque, sauna; *Posada de Don Rodrigo*, 5 Av. Norte 17, D, very agreeable, good food, in colonial house (Casa de los Leones), rec., marimba music p.m.; *Aurora*, 4 C. Oriente 16, D (breakfast available, the oldest hotel in the city, rec.); *El Rosario*, 5 Av. Sur and 9 C., pleasant apartment lodge motel complex in a coffee and orange farm round the corner from the *Antigua*, small pool, E, proprietress speaks English and will tell you all about the area, house-keeping apartments by the month US$150-160, not as secure as it claims; *El Descanso*, 5 Av. Norte 9, 2nd floor, F, with private bath, clean, pleasant; *Casa de Santa Lucía*, Alameda de Santa Lucía 5, near bus terminal, highly rec., F (no singles), with bath, hot water, good value; close by, *Hospedaje El Pasaje*, Alameda de Santa Lucía 3, F, clean, quiet, friendly, washing facilities, rec.; *Posada Colonial*, 2 C. Poniente 2, picturesque, F, with or without bath, cheaper rates for longer stays, homely, clean (beware of dog); *Las Rosas*, 6 Av. Sur 8, F, clean, comfortable, hot water; *Posada El Refugio*, 4 C. Poniente 28, F, with bath, or full board, G, without, showers, no hot water, serves good cheap meals, popular, cooking facilities; *Posada La Antigüeñita*, 2 C. Poniente, F, clean; *Pensión y Comida Angélica Jiménez*, 1A C. Poniente 14A, central, cheap, clean; *Posada de Doña Angelina*, 4 C. Poniente 33, F, with shower, G without (rooms in new part more expensive but good), near market. *Placido*, Calle del Desengaño, 7 blocks from Parque Central, F, good, not all rooms have hot water, beautiful courtyard, cooking facilities. Rooms, from about US$50 per month, and houses, from about US$150 per month, are sometimes advertised in the Tourist Office and in Doña Luisa's café. Rec. is Familia Juárez Méndez, 5 Av. Norte 33, For room rental also contact sculptor José Tinoco (speaks English), 7 Av. Norte No. 64; for weekly stays Juan Cuéllar (fire chief) at *Zeus* or *Madison Rock* stores, 4 C. Poniente 23, or Candelaria 38, US$50 for room and board. The buses are often met by men who ask to show you around the unmarked *pensiones* for a tip of about US$0.25. Good accommodation in Jocotenango, 15 mins.' walk, 5 mins. in kombi (on road to Chimaltenango), Doña Marina's, 13 Calle 1-69, Colonia Los Llanos. During Holy Week hotel prices are generally double.

Restaurants In several of the more expensive hotels. *El Sereno*, 6 C. Poniente 30 (T 0320-073), well-prepared meals in beautifully-reconstructed colonial-style house, open 1200-1500, 1830-2200 Wed. Sun. highly rec., reservations advised, especially Sun. lunch (children under 8 not served), chamber music recitals often on Mon. and Tues., art exhibitions, handicrafts and old books on display and for sale. *Portada del Palomar*, 5 C. Oriente, opp. south side of Cathedral, rec. *Panadería y Pastelería Doña Luisa Xicotencatl* ("*Doña Luisa's*"), 4 C. Oriente 12, 1½ blocks E of the Plaza, a popular meeting place, serves superb pies and bread, breakfasts, chile con carne, etc.; *Café de las Américas*, 4 C. Oriente (a few blocks E of *Doña Luisa's*), best cakes and chocolates in town. Near Plaza are *La Estrella*, 5 C. Poniente No. 6, Chinese and other food, rec., and *El Churrasco*, steakhouse, 4 C. Poniente. *Welten*, 4 C. Oriente 21; *El Mesón Panza Verde*, 5 Av. Sur 19, both expensive. *Zen* (Japanese), closed Weds. after 1200, 3 Av. Sur, No. 3, popular, rec., has mail service for travellers; *Fonda de la Calle Real*, 5 Av. Norte No.5, speciality is queso fundido, guitar trio on Sun. evenings, good but not cheap; *Emilio*, on 4 C. Poniente, and *Gran Muralla* opposite, both sell reasonable Chinese food; *Casa de Café Ana*, adjoining *El Rosario* lodge, serves all meals, and sells fine ice-cream, closed Weds.; *San Carlos*, on main square, sells good set meals; *Café Jardín*, on W side of main square, nice atmosphere; *Café Mistral* (close to *Doña Luisa's*), good licuados, juices and snacks. *Comedor Veracruz* in the market, good; *Lina*, near market on Alameda de Santa Lucía, serves good, cheap meals; *El Prado*, in San Felipe, 2 km., limited menu, good food, pleasant atmosphere; *El Capuchino*, 6 Av., between C.5 and 6, excellent Italian food and salads, friendly English-speaking owner. *Pastelería Okrassa*, 6 Av., C. 1-2, for meat and fruit pies.

Bars *Mío Cid*, 3 Av. Sur, Canadian owned, good food and music, meeting place for foreigners.

Market There is an extensive daily market, particularly on Mon., Thurs. and Sat. (best) next to the bus terminal at end of 4 Calle Poniente, W of Alameda de Santa Lucía. Good handmade textiles, pottery and silver.

Shopping Mercado de Artesanías is at 7 Av. between 4 and 3 Calles. Casa de Artes for traditional textiles and handicrafts, antiques, jewellery, etc. 4 Av. Sur. Casa de los Gigantes for textiles and handicrafts and Concha's Footloom, both opposite San Francisco Church. Fábrica de Tejidos Maya, 1 Av. Norte, C. 1-2, makes and sells good cheap textiles, wall hangings, etc. The Utatlán cooperative on 5 Av. Norte specializes in good handicrafts and antiques (expensive). Doña María Gordillo's sweet (candy) shop on 4 C. Oriente is famous throughout the country. There are many other stores selling textiles, handicrafts, antiques, silver and jade on 5 Av. Norte and 4 C. Oriente (*Ixchel* on 4 C. Oriente sells blankets from Momostenango). Galería Klaske, 5 Av. Sur 34, next to San José El Viejo. A number of jade-carving factories may be visited, e.g. Jades, S.A., 4 C. Oriente 34, open 0900-1700, La Casa de Jade, 4 C. Oriente 3 or J.C. Hernández, 2 Av. Sur, 77. Jade is sold on the Parque Central on Sats. more cheaply. Painted ceramics can be obtained from private houses in 1 Av. del Chajón (C. San Sebastián) near C. Ancha, and glazed pottery from the Fábrica Montiel, N of Calle Ancha on the old road to San Felipe. Various local handicrafts at Hecht House in the same area. Ceramic birds at handicrafts shop in the Posada de Don Rodrigo (see under Hotels above). Calzado Fase, 6 Av. Norte 61, makes made-to-measure leather boots.

Bookshops *Casa Andinista*, 4 C. Oriente 5A, sells books in Spanish and English (including *South American Handbook*), photographs, posters, rubbings, maps, postcards, cards, waevings from Ixil Triangle, camping gear for rent (opp. *Doña Luisa's*, which sells *Time* and *Newsweek*), has photocopying machine, repeatedly recommended. *Un Poco de Todo*, on W side of Plaza, sells English language books, postcards, maps. *Librería Pensativo*, 5 Av. Norte 29, good for books in Spanish about Central America.

Bathing Non-residents may use the pool at the *Hotel Antigua* for a charge of US$2.20 (US$12/month); also, at *Ramada Antigua* for US$2 a day, US$35 a month. Both hotels have special Sunday prices of US$3.75 for buffet lunch, swimming and marimba band (the *Ramada* also has children's shows). At the latter, weekly and monthly rates for use of sports facilities can be negotiated. Also *El Viejo Club*, 1 Av. Sur. US$0.75 per session, also has table tennis, same price per hour. Warm mineral springs (public pool and private cubicles) at San Lorenzo El Tejar; Chimaltenango bus to San Luis Las Carretas (about 8 km.) then 2½ km. walk to "Balneario". Public saunas US$0.75, massage US$2.50, health foods, medicinal herbs in Jocotenango, 2 km. N and at the Institute in Santa Lucía Milpas Altas, 500 metres to the left at Km. 35 (10 km. out of Antigua) on the way to Guatemala City. Open Sun.-Thurs., 0730-1730.

Museums Colonial museum in the old University of San Carlos Borromeo (1680), facing Cathedral, includes colonial sculptures and paintings. US$0.12 to get into museum (open 0900-1200, 1400-1800) and other ruins around the town. Museo de Santiago in municipal offices to N of Plaza, contains replica of 1660 printing press (original is in Guatemala City), old documents, collection of 16th-18th-century books (1500 volumes in library, open afternoons), and representations of the colonial way of life, and the Museo de Armas weapons collection. Open Mon.-Fri. 0900-1600, Sat. and Sun. 0900-1200, 1400-1600. Admission US$0.12 (free Sundays). Also small museum in Convento de Capuchinas. Museum of Indian Music, K'Ojam, Calle de Recoletos 55, next to churchyard behind market, Mon.-Sat. 0930-1230, 1430-1800, US$0.25.

Cinemas Los Capitanes on 5 Av. Sur. Showings several days a week. English films with Spanish subtitles often shown. US$0.20.

Concerts Music festival in November, excellent. The Alianza Francesa, 3 C. Oriente 19, has French music on Fridays between 1600 and 2000, also French newspapers.

Exchange Lloyds Bank International, 4 C. Oriente 2 on NE corner of Plaza, Mon.-Fri. 0900-1500; Banco del Agro, N side of Plaza, same times; Banco de Guatemala, W side of Plaza, Mon.-Thurs. 0830-1400, Fri. 0830-1430. Try also 4 Av. Sur 1, good rates. US dollars not obtainable.

Spanish Language Schools There are about 32 in all, consequently Antigua is full of foreigners learning Spanish. Those of which we have received favourable reports are: Proyecto Lingüístico Francisco Marroquín, 4 Av. Sur 4, T 320-406, Apartado 237, Antigua. This school provides up to 7 hrs. individual tuition a day and places students with local families. The fee for one week incl. 7 hrs. study, board and lodging is Q250 (it is more expensive than the other schools). Maya, 5 C. Poniente 20, fees, Q165 for first week, reduction of Q10 for each consecutive week up to 4 (6 hr. day)—must be paid in advance; Tecún Umán, 6 C. Poniente 34, good individual tuition, rec. (rates from US$250-400 per month, depending on number of hours per day); Español Dinámico, Q75 for 30 hrs., Q35 extra for accommodation with a family; Jiménez, near La Merced, 1 C. Poniente 41, small, 5 teachers, US$70 a week staying with family. Cooperativa de Lengua Española Antigua, rec.; contact Vinicio Muñoz, Colonia Candelaria 9; Instituto Antigüeño de Español, small, friendly, US$44.50 for 5 days, 4 hrs. a day; US$25.50 for board and lodging with family. Casa San Sebastián, C. San Sebastián; El Quetzal, 5 Av. Sur 11, US$50 per week, 6 hrs. per day, accommodation with a family costs an additional US$20 per week (20 % of profits go to local hospital); Arcoiris, 7 Av. Norte 2. Marco Tulio's Centro Lingüístico Antigua, 6 Av. Norte 25, (T 320-388) has received mixed reports, US$65 for 5 days, tuition and lodging. The Professional Spanish Language School, 7 Av. Norte 82, T 320-161, opened in early 1989 under the directorship of Roberto King, author of *Spanish, An Easy Way*; the school offers individual tuition for 2, 4 or 6 hrs. a day for any number of weeks, with a change of teacher each week so that students get used to different tones and rhythms of speech (profits go to the Shawcross Aid Programme for Highland Indians). Highly rec. private teacher, Julia Solís, 5 C. Poniente 36. Also check advertisements in Doña Luisa's and the Tourist Office for private lessons (about US$1 per hour). There are guides who take students around all the schools and charge a commission; avoid them if you don't want this extra cost.

Post Office, Telephone, Cables International cables in Guatel building, 5 Av. Sur. Post office at Alameda de Santa Lucía and 4 C., near market (local cables from here); lista de correos keeps letters for a month, air mail parcel service. Boxes of books up to 5 kg. can be sent from the post office, but other packages weighing more than 2 kg. must be posted from Guatemala City (do not seal parcels before going to the capital). The Pink Box (52 Av. Norte No. 14, near the main square) advertizes fast, secure shipping of all parcels, but we have received numerous unfavourable reports.

Research Library The Centro de Investigaciones Regionales de Mesoamérica (Cirma), 5 C.

Oriente 5, offers good facilities for graduate students and professional scholars of Middle American history, anthropology and archaeology.

Public Library On E side of Plaza, open evenings only. The Banco de Guatemala library, on W side of Plaza, is open to the public, Mon.-Fri. 1000-1200, 1400-1900.

Doctor Dr. Julio R. Aceituno, 2 C. Poniente, No. 7, T 0320-512, speaks English.

Tourist Office E corner of Palace of the Captains-General, S side of Plaza, is helpful (free street plan available); English and a little German spoken. Open: 0900-1600 (Monday a.m. only). The tourist office can arrange guides for visits to monuments for between US$3 and US$6 per day. Ask here for campsite details (there are no caravan parks).

Guide Book *Antigua, Guatemala, City and Area Guide*, by Mike Shawcross.

Travel Agent Agencia de Viajes above art gallery on W side of the main square.

Buses Half-hourly from Guatemala City, from 0700 to 1900, US$0.40, 45 mins, from 15 C., 3-37, Zona 1 and from 18 C. and 4 Av. Zona 1 (at least 10 bus lines). Buses to Guatemala City leave from Alameda de Santa Lucía near the market, with the same time and schedules as buses to Antigua. To Chimaltenango, on the Pan-American Highway, hourly, US$0.25, for connections to Los Encuentros (for Lake Atitlán and Chichicastenango), Cuatro Caminos (for Quezaltenango) and Huehuetenango (for the Mexican border). To Escuintla, US$0.45. Buses and minibuses also to nearby villages.

Buses Inter-Hotel y Turismo run a transfer service (1 hr.) from Antigua to La Aurora airport for US$7.50, at 0440, 0900 and 1500, starting at *Ramada*, calling at *Antigua Hotel*, *Posada Don Rodrigo*, *Doña Luisa's* and *Hotel Aurora*; for tickets T 320011/15.

Excursions To *Ciudad Vieja*, 5½ km. SW at the foot of Agua volcano. In 1541, after days of torrential rain, an immense mud-slide came down the mountain and overwhelmed the city. Alvarado's widow, newly elected Governor after his death, was among the drowned; you can see the ruins of the first town hall. Today it is a mere village (*Hospedaje Shigualita*, cheap, at S end of village), but with a handsome church, founded 1534, one of the oldest in Central America. *Fiesta:* December 5-9. Small early market, busiest Sundays; bus US$0.10. At **San Juan del Obispo**, not far, is the restored palace of Francisco Marroquín, first bishop of Guatemala, now a convent. The parish church has some fine 16th century images.

Behind San Juan del Obispo, on side of Agua volcano, is the charming village of **Santa María de Jesús**, with a beautiful view of Antigua. In the early morning, there are good views of all 3 volcanoes 2 km. back down the road towards Antigua. Beautiful *huipiles* are made and sold in the houses. Frequent buses from Antigua on main market days, US$0.10 (Mon., Thurs, Sat.). *Fiesta* on Jan. 10, accommodation at *municipalidad* for US$0.30; *Hospedaje y Comedor El Oasis* on road to Antigua has clean, pleasant rooms, F.

About 9 km. SE of Antigua (bus service, US$0.10) is **San Antonio Aguas Calientes**, a village with many small shops selling locally made textiles. Carmelo and Zoila Guarán give weaving lessons for US$1 per hr., as do Rafaela Godínez, very experienced, and Felipa López Zamora, on the way to the church, 30 metres from bus station (bring your own food and she will cook it with you), US$2 daily. *Fiestas:* first Sunday in January; June 13; November 1.

Volcanoes The three nearby volcanoes provide incomparable views of the surrounding countryside and are best climbed on a clear night with a full moon or with a very early morning start. Altitude takes its toll and plenty of time should be allowed for the ascents. Plenty of water must be carried and the summits are cold. Descents take from a third to a half of the ascent time. There have been reports of robberies on the volcanoes (taking a guide reduces the risk). Tourist Office in Antigua helpful. There is a volcano-climbing club: Club de Andinismo, Chicag, Volcano Tours, Daniel Ramírez Ríos, 6 Av. Norte, No. 34, Antigua; members are informative, enthusiastic, will act as guides for a small fee, and Daniel speaks English.

Agua Volcano 3,760 metres, the easiest of the three, is climbed from Santa María de Jesús (directions to start of ascent in village). Crater (with football field) with small shelter and 5 antennae at top. Fine views of Volcán de Fuego; 3 to 5 hours' climb. To get the best views before the clouds cover the summit, it is best to stay at the radio station at the top. Bus from Antigua to Santa María de Jesús at 0530 allows you to climb the volcano and return to Antigua in one day. Guided tours on Sats., return Sun., US$6; information from *Zen* restaurant.

Acatenango Volcano 3,976 metres. The best trail (west of the one shown on the 1:50,000 topographic map) heads south at La Soledad (15 km. west of Ciudad Vieja on Route 10) 300 metres before the road (Route 5) turns right to Acatenango (good *pensión*, G, with good cheap meals). A small plateau, La Meseta on maps, known locally as El Conejón, provides a good camping site two-thirds of the way up (3-4 hrs.). From here it is a further 3-4 hrs. harder going to the top. There is a shelter on the col between the 2 summits. Excellent views of the nearby (lower) active crater of Fuego. To reach Acatenango, take a bus heading for Yepocapa or Acatenango (village) and get off at Soledad, or from Antigua to San Miguel Dueñas, and then hitch to Soledad. Alternatively, take an early bus to Ciudad Vieja from where you can hitch to Finca Concepción

Calderas (bus Ciudad Vieja-Calderas 0645 Sat. only), then 1 hr. walk to La Soledad. Be sure to take the correct track going down (no water on the way up, hut at top in reasonable repair).

Fuego Volcano   3,763 metres, for experienced hikers only. Can be climbed either via Volcán de Acatenango (sleeping on the col between the two volcanoes), up to 12 hrs. hiking, or from Finca Capetillo in village of Alotenango, 9 km. from Antigua. One hour to reach base of mountain, then 7 hrs. ascent with an elevation gain of 2,400 metres. A very hard walk, both up and down, and easy to lose the trail. Steep, loose lava slopes in places. Danger of eruptions and sulphur fumes.

At the village of San Felipe (US$0.05 by bus, or 15 min. walk from Antigua) is a figure of Christ which people from all over Latin America come to see. *Restaurant El Prado* is rec. There is a small silver workshop which is worth visiting.

Three Indian villages N of Guatemala City are easily reached by bus. At Chinautla (9½ km.), the village women turn out hand-made pottery. Eight km. beyond is another small village, San Antonio las Flores: good walking to a small lake (70 mins.) for bathing. Santo Domingo Xenacoj can be reached by bus from the Zona 4 terminal, Guatemala City. It has a fine old church and produces good *huipiles*.

At *San Lucas Sacatepéquez*, the Fábrica de Alfombras Típicas Kakchikel at Km. 29½, Carretera Roosevelt (usually known as the Pan-American Highway) will make rugs for you. Restaurants: *La Parrilla*, *La Cabaña*, *Nim-Guaa*, *La Diligencia*, and *El Ganadero*, all good for steaks; *Delicias del Mar* for seafood. 5 km. beyond San Lucas is Santiago Sacatepéquez, whose *fiesta* on Nov. 1 is characterized by colourful kite-flying.

A most interesting short trip by car or bus from the capital is to *San Pedro Sacatepéquez,* 22½ km. NW. Good view over Guatemala valley and mountains to the N. Its inhabitants, having rebuilt their village after the 1976 earthquake, are returning to the weaving for which the village was renowned before the disaster. The Cooperative (a member of Artexco, the Federation of Artisans' Cooperatives) is San José Caben. Bus from Guatemala City, Zona 4 bus terminal, US$0.20, 1 hr.; bus to Rabinal, 5½ hrs., a beautiful, occasionally heart-stopping ride. *Hotel Samaritano*, near Plaza, F with bath, clean, hot shower. *Fiestas:* Carnival before Lent; June 29 (rather rough, much drinking) and great ceremony on March 15 when passing the Image of Christ from one officeholder to the next, and in honour of the same image in May.

6½ km. beyond, through flower-growing area, is **San Juan Sacatepéquez**, where textiles are also made.

San Raimundo beyond is a friendly town. Buses go N through Rabinal to Cobán (see page 1158).

28 km. N of San Juan Sacatepéquez is *Mixco Viejo,* the excavated site of a post-classic Mayan fortress, which spans 14 hilltops, including 12 groups of pyramids, but was badly damaged by the earthquake. It was the 16th century capital of the Pokomam Maya; there are a few buses a day from the Zona 4 bus terminal in Guatemala City, departures at 1000 and 1700. The bus goes to Pachalum; ask to be dropped at the entrance to the site—it's an 8 km. walk from the main road (the area is quite remote, take provisions).

The village of *Rabinal* was founded in 1537 by Las Casas as the first of his "peaceful conquest" demonstrations to Emperor Charles V. It has a handsome 16th century church (under reconstruction), Sun. market interesting; brightly lacquered gourds, beautiful *huipiles* and embroidered napkins, all very cheap. The local pottery is exceptional. (*Pensión Motagua*, F, friendly, has bar attached).

The town of *Salamá* can be reached from the capital direct, or from San Juan Sacatepéquez and Rabinal through San Miguel Chicaj along another road which offers stunning views (Rabinal-Salamá US$1, ½ hr.). Its church contains carved gilt altarpieces. Market day is Monday; worth a visit. *Hotel Tezulutlán*, best, E with bath, cheaper without, good restaurant but service a bit slow, 7 Av. Zona 1, just off plaza; *Pensión Verapaz*, 3 C. 8-26 and *Hospedaje Juárez*, 5 C. 8-98, both F p.p. with bath, cheaper without.

Another popular excursion is to the still active *Pacaya* volcano (last major eruption January 1987). Tours are available for US$8. It can be reached by private car, the road from Antigua is unpaved, but suitable for all vehicles. Alternatively take a bus from the central bus station in Zona 4 to **San Vicente de Pacaya** (US$0.35); then one must walk to San Francisco (1½ hrs.), and walk up 1 hr. to the TV station at the first ridge. In early 1988 it was not possible to go to the old cone (2 hrs.) above the active cone because of the continuing eruptions, which could be seen clearly from the first ridge. Check the situation in advance in San Francisco for both climbing and camping (if safe, take torch, warm clothing and a handkerchief to filter dust and fumes). A few buses go to both villages from the turn-off on the Guatemala City-Escuintla road. Last bus back from San Vicente is at 1630. There is also a bus from Palín (see page 1168), US$0.15. If you miss the last bus back to Palín or San Vicente, you can stay overnight with Luis the Mexican in San Francisco (a good guide), or you can sleep in the porch at the school in El Cedro, the village below San

Francisco, or in a house at the entrance to San Vicente (US$1). **Warning:** There have been several reports of armed robbery and equipment being stolen from campsites on the slopes of Pacaya volcano.

Guatemala City to San Salvador

The paved Pan-American Highway through Fraijanes, Barberena and Cuilapa keeps to the crest of the ridges most of the way to the border, 166 km. Beyond Cuilapa it crosses the Río de los Esclavos by a bridge first built in the 16th century. Fifty km. on is Jutiapa (population 9,200). Beyond, it goes through the villages of Progreso and Asunción Mita, where another road runs to Lake Güija. Before reaching the border at Cristóbal it dips and skirts the shores (right) of Lake Atescatempa, an irregular sheet of water with several islands and set in heavy forest. From the border to San Salvador is 100 km.

A right turn after Cuilapa towards Chiquimulilla (road No. 16, with old trees on either side, some with orchids in them) leads after 20 km. to a sign to Ixpaco. A 2-3 km. steep, difficult and narrow road (no problem in a jeep) goes to the Laguna de Ixpaco, an impressive, greenish-yellow lake, boiling in some places, emitting sulphurous fumes, set in dense forest. There is a bus service.
   The quickest way of getting to San Salvador is to take a paved highway which cuts off right from this route at Molino, beyond the Esclavos bridge. This cut-off goes through El Oratorio and Valle Nuevo to Ahuachapán and San Salvador. (Try *Motel Martha*, 15 km. from frontier on Guatemalan side, F, excellent breakfast, swimming pool.) A third paved road, in less good condition, runs from Guatemala City through Escuintla and Guazacapán to the border bridge over the Río Paz at La Hachadura, then through the coastal plain to Sonsonate and on to San Salvador, 290 km. in all; this road gives excellent views of the volcanoes. At Pedro de Alvarado (formerly Pijije) there are several *hospedajes* (all G, basic). If stuck at La Hachadura (the last bus for Sonsonate leaves at 1800), you can get food at the service station restaurant and there is a very basic *hospedaje*, G, nearby—not recommended for lone women.

5 km. W of Guazacapán, at Taxisco, is a turn-off to the coast and the Nature Reserve of Monterrico (operated by the University of San Carlos and Inguat); it combines estuarine and coastal ecosystems with a great variety of waterbirds, turtles, mangroves and other aquatic plants. It is also on the migratory routes of North and South American birds.

GUATEMALA CITY TO THE CARIBBEAN (2)

The Atlantic Highway from Guatemala City to the Caribbean port of Puerto Barrios is fully paved and gives access to the Honduran border, Cobán and the Petén. Note that the distances between filling stations are greater than in other parts of the country.

At km. 54 a paved, winding branch road, 203 km. long, runs through fine scenery, E by way of San José Pinula, Mataquescuintla, Jalapa, San Pedro Pinula, San Luis Jilotepeque, and Ipala to Chiquimula **(see page 1159)**. It was the route to the great shrine at Esquipulas, but visitors now use the Atlantic Highway to Río Hondo and the new road to Honduras past Zacapa **(see page 1156)** and Chiquimula.

Jalapa, capital of Jalapa Department, 114 km. from Guatemala City, is set in an attractive valley at 1,380 metres. The capital can also be reached by bus to Jalapa station on Guatemalan Railway and thence by train, but this route takes longer. Population 42,000.

Hotel *Pensión Casa del Viajero*, F.

The branch road to Cobán is at El Rancho, Km. 85; this is a better alternative to the route through Rabinal and Salamá **(see page 1156)**.

Between Cobán and Guatemala City at Km. 163, 4 km. S of Purulhá and 53 km. from Cobán, is the **_Biotopo del Quetzal_**, a reserve established by San Carlos university for the preservation of the quetzal bird and its cloud-forest habitat; camping (free, good, lots of mosquitoes) and beautiful trails in the jungle. (Bus Cobán-Purulhá, US$0.50; from Guatemala City, take a Cobán bus and ask to be let out at the Biotopo; more difficult to get a bus back to the capital; bus El Rancho-Biotopo, US$0.80, 1 hr.).

Mike Shawcross writes: "I saw my first quetzal late in 1980, and consider the sighting a highlight of all my time here; it really is an incredibly beautiful bird. A series of trails, taking up to 3 hrs. to cover on foot, lead more than 300 metres up the mountainside. At Km. 156 is the new hotel and restaurant *Posada Montaña del Quetzal*, D, highly rec., café, bar, swimming pool, gardens (T 31-41-81 in Guatemala City for reservations, book in advance, especially at weekends). Free camping at entrance. 100 metres N of the entrance to the Biotopo is the *Hospedaje Los Ranchos*, F in 10-bed cabins, fairly basic, limited restaurant; take own food. The *Hospedaje* is a good place to see the bird. The *farmacía* at Purulhá has rooms to let, G. *Comedor San Antonio* in Purulhá, simple meals.

Tactic, on the main Guatemala City-Cobán road, is famous for beautiful *huipiles* and for its "living well", in which the water becomes agitated as one approaches. (Ask for the Pozo Vivo; it is along a path which starts opposite the gas station on the main road—now reported dirty and disappointing.) Colonial church with Byzantine-influenced paintings, well worth a visit. *Fiesta* 3rd week in August. (*Hotel Sulmy*, G, nice, clean, meals, US$0.75; *Pensión Central*, G, clean, hot showers, cheap meals; and *Hospedaje Cocompchi*, less good, G.) Doña Rogelia sells *huipiles* made in the surrounding area, and the silversmith near her shop will make silver buttons etc. to order. Market days are Thursday and Sunday (very few people now wear traditional costume). To the W of Tactic is *San Cristóbal Verapaz*, which has a large colonial church with interesting altar silver and statue of San Joaquín (*Pensión Central* and *Pensión Torres*, both G). The lake is popular for fishing and swimming. Markets: Tuesday and Sunday; festival July 21-26. From Tactic the road (paved) runs 25 km. N to Cobán, past Santa Cruz Verapaz, which has a fine old 16th century church and a festival May 1-4. (*Tico's Hotel and Restaurant*, opp. turn off to Santa Cruz on road to Cobán, E, hot showers, English spoken, good food, rec.)

Cobán, capital of Alta Verapaz Department, is the centre of a rich coffee district. Population 59,307, altitude 1,320 metres, climate semi-tropical. Road S to El Rancho (buses), on Guatemalan Railway and the highway to Guatemala City. Founded by Apostle of the Indies, Las Casas, in 1544. See church of El Calvario (1559), now completely renovated, original façade still intact. Daily market (local costume no longer in evidence). *Fiestas:* Holy Week (which is said to be fascinating) and August 3 (procession of saints with brass bands, pagan deer dancers and people enjoying themselves), followed by a folklore festival, August 22-28.

Hotels *La Posada*, 1 C., 4-12, D, full board available, reasonable; *Central*, 1 C., 1-79, F, with hot shower, good restaurant entered through *Café San Jorge*; *Oxib Peck*, 1 C., 12-11, F, with bath; *Pensión El Portillo*, very good, F; *Hospedaje Maya*, opp. Ciné Norte, F, hot showers, friendly, rec.; *Valenciana*, G (you can sleep on the balcony for US$0.50), basic; *El Carmen*, on main square, G, clean; *La Paz*, 6 Av. 2-19, F, with extension which is rec.; *Monterrey*, next door, G, rec.; *Pensión Familiar*, Diagonal 4, 3-36, Zona 2, 1 block N of Parque Central, G, warm water, fairly basic, friendly; nameless *pensión* at 1-12 Av. Estado (near *Hotel La Paz*), clean. Accommodation is hard to find in August.

Restaurants *Comedores Chinita, El Refugio* (Parque Central, good comidas corridas), *Café Norte* (good fast food), and *Las Delicias* serve meals for less than US$1; *Restaurant Chapín*, good.

Electric Current 110 volts. It has been recommended not to use standard electrical appliances in Cobán as the voltage is high.

Buses from Guatemala City: US$2.45. Transportes Monja Blanca y Escobar, 8 Av. 15-16, Zona 1 (hourly till 1700, 4 hrs.); Transportes La Cobanerita, ordinary buses every other day from 9 C. 11-46, Zona 1. The bus from El Estor takes 9 hrs., 3 services a day (0600, 0800, 1000). Return buses leave at 0400 and 0800. The trip from the capital via Rabinal, along an old dirt road, takes about 12 hrs. (change buses in Salamá). Cobán can also be reached from Sacapulas and Quiché (page 1175) and from Huehuetenango (page 1180).

Excursions Near Cobán is the old colonial church of San Juan Chamelco, well worth a visit. *San Pedro Carchá* (5 km. east of Cobán, bus US$0.10, 15 mins. frequent; *Hotel Shanghai*, F; *Delgado*, G; *Pensión Central*, G, cheap, basic, dirty, serves good meals—all close at 2200) used to be famous for its pottery, textiles and wooden masks, and silver, but only the pottery seems to be available at the Tuesday market. Truck to Sebol (see page 1166), 7 hrs., US$1.20. Good swimming and walks at Balneario Las Islas, just outside the village, well signposted; crowded at weekends, good camping.

From Cobán a rough road runs 70 km. to *Lanquín* cave, in which the Lanquín river rises. If you want to visit the cave ask at the police station in the village (2 km.) to turn the lights on (this costs US$5, however many, or few, people in the group); the entrance fee is US$0.50 (a guide costs

US$2.50). The cave is very slippery, so wear appropriate shoes and take a torch for additional lighting. Outside the cave you can swim in the deep, wide river, and camp or sling a hammock under a large shelter. From Lanquín one can visit the natural bridge of *Semuc Champey* stretching 60 metres across the Cahabón gorge, 10 very hard km. walk, 4 hrs., along a new road which runs to the footbridge over the river, 20 minutes from Semuc Champey. At the end of the road, which is very steep in places, is a car park (quite a few cars, lifts possible). A steep track heads down to the new bridge half-way along the road (the route is not signposted so ask frequently for the shortest route). There are a number of shortcuts between Lanquín and this spot, any locals walking this way will be taking them. The natural bridge has water on top of it as well as below, and the point where the river Cahabón goes underground is spectacular. One can swim in the pools on top of the bridge. At Semuc Champey is a place where you can camp. If planning to return to Lanquín the same day, start early to avoid the midday heat. At Lanquín there is *Hospedaje Mary*, pleasant, G, cheap, basic, and small restaurants. The church has fine images and some lovely silver. Bus from Cobán at 0530, 4 hrs., US$0.75 including breakfast stop en route; returns at 0700; also to and from San Pedro Carchá, 0530 (you can try hitching from San Pedro Carchá, from the fumigation post, where all trucks stop, to the turn-off to Lanquín, then 12 km. walk—very little traffic). There are buses at 0500 and 0730 from **Lanquín to Pajal** (12 km., 1 hr., US$0.30) from where one can go to **Sebol**, US$0.75, 5½ hrs. (**page 1166**); Pajal is just a shop. Pick-up Lanquín-Sebol, US$1.

From Tactic, a reasonable and very beautiful unpaved road runs down the Polochic valley to El Estor, quite easy to hitch (**see page 1163**). Tamahú (12 km.) and Tucurú (28 km.) produce fine *huipiles;* market days are Thurs. and Sat. and there are interesting images in the Tucurú church. 47 km. beyond Tucurú is a turnoff to **Senahú**, (the journey from Cobán takes 8 hrs., Autotransportes Valenciano, departures from Cobán at 1030, US$1.25, particularly crowded on Sundays, difficult to hitch to Senahú). Climb to the cemetery for good views. (*Pensiones* at Senahú: *González*, G, good meals for US$0.60, at entrance to village, *Gladys*, near main square, G, meals for US$0.55, and another in centre, G with full board, rec.). Walking in the Senahú district is magnificent. It is possible to cross the mountains to the village of Cahabón (24 km. E of Lanquín), which will take a full day, or, if you can get a lift to Finca Volcán, only 6 hrs. (either way is quicker than by road). Beyond the turn-off to Senahú, the road continues to Telemán (bus from Senahú at 0300), **Panzós** (pick-up from Telemán; guest house; bus to El Estor p.m. and 2030) and Cahaboncito (6 km. from Panzós). Here you can either carry on to El Estor, or take an appalling road (ave. speed 10 kmph) to Cahabón and Lanquín. Trucks take this road, passing the turning at about 0800, on Fri. and Sun., and possibly Thurs., otherwise no traffic (the alternative is to go back to Cobán and go from there to Lanquín).

To the W of Cobán is Nebaj which can be reached by taking the Huehuetenango bus to Sacapulas (preferable to ride on the roof) and either hitching from there or waiting for the bus from Quiché. **See pages 1176 and 1182** for places en route to Sacapulas, Nebaj and Huehuetenango.

At Río Hondo, 138 km. from Guatemala City (town 1-2 km. from the Atlantic Highway), a road runs S to **Zacapa**. Population 15,000, altitude 187 metres. Sulphur springs for rheumatic sufferers at Baños de Agua Caliente, well worth a visit (closed on Mon.); tobacco grown. It is an attractive town with a colourful market, 148 km. from Guatemala City. Climate hot and dry. *Fiestas:* June 29, Dec. 1-8. April 30-May 1, small local ceremony. Just outside the town is Estanzuela (minibus, US$0.30), a village whose museum houses a complete skeleton of a prehistoric monster.

Hotels *Wong*, F, with bath; *De León*, F; next to station is *Ferrocarril*, D; other *pensiones* (basic) opposite; *Pensión Central*, opposite market, F, clean, friendly, very good, delightful setting. *Posada Doña María*, E of Zacapa at Km. 181 on road to Puerto Barrios, F, with bath, rec.

Exchange Banco Granai y Townson, near central market, changes travellers' cheques.

Transport Bus from Guatemala City to Zacapa, US$1.25 with Rutas Orientales, every ½ hr., 3½ hrs. Train to Quiriguá and on to Puerto Barrios 1330, Tues., Thurs., Sat., usually late.

From Zacapa there is a road S to Chiquimula and Esquipulas. **Chiquimula** (21 km.), capital of its Department, population 42,000, has a colonial character; see church ruined by 1765 earthquake. Bus from Zacapa US$0.12, from Quiriguá, US$0.55, and from Cobán via El Rancho (where a change must be made) US$1.65. Daily market. The town has a historic ceiba tree. A road, 203 km., runs W through splendid scenery to the capital (**see page 1157**). *Fiestas:* August 12-18, Virgen del Tránsito, December 12.

Hotels *Posada del Oriente*, few blocks from centre, restaurant, E, rec.; *Pensión Hernández*, F, rec., good cheap food; next door is *España*, G; *Chiquimuja*, E, with bath; *Casa de Viajeros*, G, basic but clean; *Dória*, 8 Av., 4-40, ½ block from main square, F, with or without bath, rec. *Pollo Frito* for a good meal. The town's water supply is often cut off.

Exchange possible at Banco de Guatemala, corner of main square, Mon.-Fri. 0830-1400, or at Almacén Nuevo Cantón on the Plaza, will change quetzales into lempiras.

At Vado Hondo (10 km.) on the road to Esquipulas, 51 km. from Chiquimula, a good-quality dirt road branches E to the great Mayan ruins of Copán (see Honduras section, **page 1240**). It goes through the small town of *Jocotán* (*Pensión Ramírez*, G, showers, pleasant, very friendly; *Pensión Sagastume*, bus will stop outside, good meals on request; meals at the bakery; exchange at *farmacia*, with 10% commission, *fiesta* July 25) which has hot springs 4 km. from town, and to the border at *El Florido,* where there is now a good bridge. From El Florido to Copán there is a 14-km. dirt road; fording the many streams after heavy rain can be hazardous. The drive to Copán (by car) takes 4-5 hrs. from Guatemala City, or 2 from Vado Hondo, including the frontier crossing.

To Copán There is a through bus from Chiquimula to El Florido at 0600 and 1100 (Transportes Vilma, US$1, 2½ hrs.). At 0900, 1430, 1730 a bus goes as far as Jocotán (no connection to border on last bus). Bus Jocotán to the border, US$0.50, taxi, US$5. Transportes Rutas Orientales buses from 19 C. 8-18, Zona 1, Guatemala City run to Chiquimula from 0530, hourly (US$1.50, US$2 Pullman), any before 0730 should make this connection, but if you take the 1100 bus to the border, you won't get to Copán until 1530, and the ruins close at 1600. Also Transportes Guerra from Guatemala City to Chiquimula. There is a Vilma bus from Zacapa to the border at 0530, US$1, which will enable you to spend 2-3 hours at Copán and return the same day. From the border to Copán there are minibuses, US$1 (leave when full—if no minibus, it may be possible to hire a pick-up for US$15 to take you to the ruins and collect you later to go back to the border if only staying one day). Those travelling by bus will find that it is impossible to visit Copán from Guatemala City in one day. It is best to spend the night in Copán village. Bus to border at 0800, which is met by a pick-up truck to Jocotán (last bus from Copán to El Florido 1300 for connecting bus from Jocotán to Chiquimula at 1700). Through bus border-Chiquimula 0900 and 1400. Last bus Chiquimula-Guatemala City at 1800. Taxi Chiquimula to the border, US$10 (there may be colectivos for US$2); Chiquimula to Copán and back in same day, US$20.

If you are coming in to Guatemala at this point you must carry a visa or tourist card as there are absolutely no facilities for obtaining one. There is no transport from the border after 1700. If returning to Guatemala remember that you must have a new visa or tourist card (**see page 1186, Documents**). However the Guatemalan border official will give a 72-hr. exit pass to visit Copán, stapled into passport (this avoids having to get a new visa or tourist card to reenter), but if you try to reenter at a different border post, the pass may not be recognized. If you do have undue difficulties at this crossing, ask to speak to the *delegado*. Make sure that the customs official stamps your papers. You have to pay all exit and entry taxes: Q3 to leave Guatemala, and a Q3 (re)entry charge, plus a 10 lempiras entry/exit charge for Honduras. Motorists crossing this border are asked for all sorts of "fees"; ask for a receipt or bargain! Unfortunately the border officials of the two countries do not keep the same hours: Guatemalan hours are 0800-1200, 1400-1800; Honduran hours 0800-2100. If you leave Guatemala outside business hours there is an extra charge of US$0.50. You can sometimes get a lift to Guatemala City with tourist agency guides whose minibuses are not full—cost about US$2. Travel agents do a one-day tour from Guatemala City to Copán and back, for about US$35 p.p.

To visit the Mayan ruins of El Petén, take a bus from Chiquimula to Río Hondo (US$0.35, 1 hr.) to connect with the 0730 bus from Guatemala City to Flores which leaves Río Hondo at 1030, cost US$3.

Esquipulas (population: 7,500) is a typical market town in semi-lowland, but at the end of its 1½-km. shabby street is a magnificent white basilica, one of the finest colonial churches in the Americas. In it is a black Christ carved by Quirio Catano in 1594 which draws pilgrims from all Central America, especially on January 27-30 and during Lent and Holy Week. The image was first placed in a local church in 1595, but was moved in 1758 to the present building.

The Benedictine monks who look after the shrine are from Louisiana and therefore speak English. They show visitors over their lovely garden.

Hotels Plenty of hotels, *pensiones* and *comedores* all over town. Near the basilica are *Payaquí*, E p.p., hot water, swimming pool; *Los Angeles*, E; *El Angel*, E with bath, cold water; *Pensión Santa Elena*, F, behind market; near the Rutas Orientales bus stop, *Santa Rosa* (1 block opposite), E, hot water; *San Francisco*, F; *París*, 10 C., 1 Av., G. 2 km. south on road to Honduras is *Posada del Cristo Negro*, C p.p., motel style, swimming pool, restaurant, good.

Honduran Consulate   in the lobby of the *Hotel Payaquí*, very helpful.

Transport   Buses from the capital every 30 mins. US$2.65 (4-5 hrs), Rutas Orientales and Rutas Guatesqui. The road goes on to Atulapa, on the Honduran border (minibuses when full, US$0.25-40, plus US$0.25 across border), and continues to the Honduran town of Nueva Ocotopeque and S to San Salvador.

El Salvador may be reached from Guatemala City by leaving the Esquipulas bus at the Padre

Miguel junction, from where colectivos run to Anguiatú on the border, or from Esquipulas by taking the road to Concepción Las Minas and then on to Anguiatú. From there a good road goes to Metapán.

Part of the Department of Chiquimula falls within the International Biosphere "La Fraternidad", a reserve of cloud forest and its surroundings in the Montecristo range. The reserve will be administered jointly by Guatemala, Honduras and El Salvador.

On the Atlantic Highway, at Km. 126 is *Motel Longarone*, D (higher prices for a/c), good service, swimming pool, in a delightful setting.

Quiriguá is about 4 km. from some remarkable Mayan Old Empire remains: temple, carved stelae, etc. In 1975 a stone sun-god statue was unearthed here. The tallest stone is over 8 metres high. Many of the stelae are now in a beautiful park (but all have shelters which makes photography difficult), where refreshments are served. Open 0800-1800.

From main highway to ruins, ride on back of motorbike, US$0.50, walk or take a taxi. *Hotel Royal*, F, with bath, clean, mosquito netting on all windows, good meals US$1.60; camping in car park of the ruins, US$0.50. Reached by road from Guatemala City to Los Amates, then a 3½-km. dirt road (ask to be put down at the "ruinas de Quiriguá", 10 km. after Los Amates), Velázquez bus at 0700, US$1.25, 3½ hrs. If driving the road branches off the Atlantic Highway at Km. 207. Train to Zacapa, 1030, Wed., Fri., Sun. Take insect-repellant. The best reference book is S. G. Morley's *Guide Book to Ruins of Quiriguá*, which should be obtained before going to the ruins.

Puerto Barrios, on the Caribbean (population 23,000), 297 km. from the capital by the Atlantic Highway (toll, free for motorcycles) and with rail connections also, has now been largely superseded as a port by Santo Tomás. It is the capital of the Department of Izabal. The beach of Escobar on the northern peninsula is recommended. Toll, US$0.25. The launch to Livingston leaves from here, and one can take a boat to Puerto Modesto Méndez, on the Sarstún river.

Hotels *Del Norte*, 7 C. and 2 Av., "rickety old wooden structure" on sea front, E (rooms 5 and 7 have bath), "an absolute must", clean, rec., huge breakfasts, mainly seafood dinners, US$2.50 (but not every night); *San Marcos*, 7 C. 7 Av. 63, F, with bath, 3 good meals, US$4.25; *El Dorado*, 13 C. between 6 and 7 Av., F, with bath, clean, friendly; *Europa*, 8 Av., 8 and 9 C., new, clean, F, with bath, restaurant; *Español*, 13 C. between 5 and 6 Av., E with bath, clean, friendly; *Caribeña*, 4 Av., between 10 and 11 C., F, rec., close to boat and bus terminals; *Hotel Xelajú*, 9 C. between 6 and 7 Av., G, clean, friendly, by market and bus station, noisy; *Pensión Xelajú*, 8 Av., between 9 and 10 C., quiet, clean, G. There are other cheap hotels on 7 and 8 Calles between 6 and 8 Avenidas (e.g. *Canadá*, 6 C., between 6 and 7 Av., F), and on and near 9 Calle towards the sea.

Restaurants Most hotels. *Cafesama*, 8 C., and 6 Av., open 24 hours. reasonable. *Ranchón La Bahía*, reasonable prices but watch the bill; *Guana Chapi*, on 9 C. near landing stage for Livingston ferry, very cheap and good. *Copos* and *Frosty* ice-cream parlours, 8 C. between 6 and 7 Av., both good and clean. Numerous others, undistinguished, in centre and on 9 Calle. *Monte Carlo* has a floor show.

Market In block bounded by 8 and 9 C. and 6 and 7 Av. Footwear is cheap.

Exchange Lloyds Bank, 7 C. and 2/3 Av., open 0900-1500, Mon.-Fri. (will not cash American Express travellers' cheques). Banco de Guatemala on seafront, opens and closes ½ hr. earlier (will cash Amex cheques).

Post Office 3 Av. and 7 C., behind Bandegua building.

Cables / Telephones Guatel, 10 C. and 8 Av.

Buses to capital, 6 hrs., US$4, first class, Litegua office, 6 Av., 9-10 C, hourly, first at 0100, last at 1600. Unión Pacífica y Las Patojas has 4 2nd-class buses a day to capital, and one semi-pullman a day, with luggage on top, to Pacific coast (US$5). Bus to El Rancho (turn-off) for Biotopo del Quetzal and Cobán, US$2.40, 4 hrs. There are good road connections to the Honduran frontier, but one must go as far south as Copán to cross into Honduras by car, though there is a walking route to a border crossing near Puerto Barrios (passable only in the driest of weather). **Train** to Guatemala City Wed., Fri., Sun. 0700, arr. 1900. Fare US$1.50 single. Apparently a passenger coach is sometimes coupled to freight trains to the capital, with a fare of US$0.25, but it would be as quick to walk all the way.

Santo Tomás de Castilla, a few km. S of Puerto Barrios on Santo Tomás bay, is now the country's largest and most efficient port on the Caribbean. It handles 77% of the exports and half the imports as well as 20% of El Salvador's imports and 10% of its exports. Cruise ships put into Santo Tomás. Apart from *Hotel Puerto Libre* (see below), no good hotel or eating place as yet, and no shops, and nothing to do save sea bathing.

Hotel   *Puerto Libre*, 25 rooms, at highway fork for Santo Tomás and Puerto Barrios, D, a/c and bath, TV, phone for international calls, restaurant and bar, swimming pool.

Shipping   A motor-boat service is maintained with Livingston and Puerto Cortés (Honduras). To ship a car to New Orleans costs US$300-400, depending on size of car.

Transport   To Guatemala City one has either to take a local bus to Puerto Barrios to connect with the train, or to Puerto Barrios or the highway fork by the *Hotel Puerto Libre* to catch the Pullman bus.

Puerto Barrios to Río Dulce   Launch to **Livingston** (22½ km.), at mouth of Río Dulce, leaves daily, 0700, 1000, and 1700, arrive 1 hour in advance to ensure a seat, cost US$0.40 (private dugout, US$4-8). (Launch returns at 0500, 1300, 1700.) Very quiet, now little trade save some export of famous Verapaz coffee from Cobán, and bananas. Population: 3,026, mostly blacks of Jamaican origin, a few English-speaking. Beach is reported to be dirty; many young travellers congregate here. Some hotels will change travellers' cheques, as will the Chinese shop. No phone service between 2000 and 0700.

Warning Don't stroll on the beach after dark as there is a risk of rape and robbery.

Hotels   at Livingston: *Tucán Dugú*, A (Fri.-Sun., less in week—all rooms with bath), new, sea view, swimming pool (US$4 for non-residents), restaurant, bars, laundry service, mini zoo, to book, T 0-481-572/588, or Guatemala City 321259, Telex 5139; *Casa Rosada*, 300 metres first left from dock, 5 thatched cabins for 2-3 persons each on the beach, E, breakfast and bar, boat trips to Río Dulce or just for swimming can be arranged, rec., call Guatel in Livingston for reservations, hotel will call back, American owner, Jean Swanson. *African Place*, F with bath, clean, pleasant, restaurant, left on paved road at top of hill; *Caribe*, 100 metres first left from dock, F with bath, cheaper rooms without, good; *Ramón's Place* (no proper name), very basic, sling your hammock for US$1. *Flamingo*, Playa de París D-823, E, with garden, clean, comfortable cottages, safe, German owner. Camping is said to be good around Livingston. Beware of theft from hotel rooms.

Restaurants   *El Malecón*, 100 metres from dock, on right, reasonable. Near *African Place*, *Café Margoth*, rec. *La Cabaña*, good but a little pricey. Good meals can be obtained in private houses; try *New York Greenhouse* where Peter serves delicious meals that must be ordered one day in advance. **N.B.** Coconut bread, although delicious, can cause constipation.
   Río Blanco beach can be reached by *cayuco*, and *Los Siete Altares*, beautiful waterfalls and pools during the rainy season, some 6 km. from town, on foot or by *cayuco*. Beware of theft when leaving belongings to climb the falls. Also paddle up the Río Dulce gorge. *Cayucos* can be hired near Texaco station, US$2.50 per day.

Boats   Government passenger boat to Punta Gorda, Belize, Tues. and Fri. 0830, starting from Puerto Barrios, US$5; return same days at 1500. 20 seats for this boat are sold in Livingston. Ticket office and immigration on Calle 9, near landing; immigration opens 0700, then buy ticket (can be done day in advance). **N.B.** There are immigration offices in both Livingston and Puerto Barrios: to avoid confusion, get your exit stamp in the town from which you intend to leave Guatemala. Similarly, specify which port you will disembark at when arriving in Guatemala. Puerto Barrios immigration at least tries to charge Q10 entry, which is not necessary, only Q3 at customs—be warned. There is a service on Sat. and Sun. Puerto Barrios-Livingston-Río Dulce, US$4.25 one way (it will not leave Puerto Barrios if there aren't enough passengers; it should arrive at Livingston about 0900). Return from Río Dulce to Livingston at 1400. One can get the mail boat from Livingston up to the new bridge at Río Dulce at 1030, Tues. and Fri. (0600 in the other direction) but schedules subject to change, US$1.50—2.50 depending on number of passengers. Boats may be hired for Livingston-Río Dulce trip for about US$30.

Near **Río Dulce**, 23 km. upstream at entrance to Lake Izabal (site of new bridge, toll US$1), is *Turicentro Marimonte*, 500 metres to right at Shell station, C for bungalows (phone Guatemala City 324493/334511 for reservations), restaurant, pool; camping site US$3, use of showers and pool; *Hotel Izabal Fiesta*, D, new; *Marilú*, El Relleno on N side, F with bath, but rooms are sheds full of holes, uncertain water supply, no electricity late p.m., beware of overcharging; *Hospedaje* at Río Dulce bus stop is not rec. (dirty, unsafe, F). The US-owned *Catamaran*, C, in bungalows, pool, meals about US$2, is reached by outboard canoe (US$1.50 from Río Dulce, 2 km. or 10 mins. downstream, phone 324-829, Guatemala City, for reservations). *Hotel Del Río*, a few km. downstream, B, incl. 3 meals (Guatemala City 310-016 for reservations). There are yachting facilities at Río Dulce.

At the entrance to Lake Izabal, 2 km. upstream, is the old Spanish fort of San Felipe in an attractive setting (boat from El Relleno, Río Dulce— below the new bridge—US$2.50 return for one, US$0.50 p.p. in groups; it is a 5 km. walk, practically impossible after rain). (*Hotel Don Humberto*, at San Felipe, E; also basic *pensión*, G.) Lake Izabal is a habitat for the manatee (sea cow). A reserve, the Biotopo del Manatí, has been set up halfway between San Felipe and Livingston at El Golfete. It covers 135 sq. km., with both a land and an aquatic trail. (The Park, like the Biotopo del Quetzal, is run by Centro de Estudios Conservacionistas—Cecon—and Inguat.) Sr. Cambell in Livingston runs boat trips to the reserve (and up rivers) for about US$12 for 6 people—bargain. On the NW shore is *El Estor*—its name dates back to the days when the British living in the Atlantic area got their provisions from a store situated at this spot—where nickel-mining has begun. We have heard that one can hire a boat from Río Dulce to El Estor, which can be alternatively reached by taking two buses to Mariscos on the south side of Lake Izabal, then crossing on the afternoon boat (1300) to El Estor, to which there is no direct road. *Hotel Los Almendros*, F; *Hospedaje El Milagro* G, and *Santa Clara*, G (friendly), others at similar prices. Also restaurants (*Ranchow Mery*, fish and beer only, big helpings, delicious; a very good one at ferry point for Mariscos).

A ferry leaves El Estor at 0600 for Mariscos (US$1, 1 hr. 50 mins., returns 1300) from where there are buses to *Bananera* (officially called *Morales*) US$0.60 and Puerto Barrios, US$1; from Bananera there are buses to the Río Dulce crossing (road paved, 30 km.), Puerto Barrios and the Petén (US$3.50, 10 hrs. to Flores; return buses from Río Dulce to Bananera start at 0600; train to Guatemala City is supposed to leave at 0915). At Bananera, *Hospedaje Liberia*, *Simon's*, both G and basic but OK. Cauca (dory) trips can be arranged to Livingston, via San Felipe, from Mariscos, 5 hrs., US$18 for 3 people. At *Mariscos*, *Hospedaje Karilinda*, G (per room, regardless of number of occupants), rec., good food; *Cafetería/Hospedaje Los Almendros*, G, good. For the routes from El Estor to Cobán via either Panzós and Tactic, or Cahabón and Lanquín, **see page 1159.**

EL PETEN: THE MAYA CENTRES AND THE JUNGLE (3)

El Petén Department in the far N, which was so impenetrable that its inhabitants, the Itzáes, were not conquered by the Spaniards until 1697, is now reached by road either from km. 245, opposite Morales, on the Atlantic Highway, or from Cobán, through Sebol and Sayaxché, or by air. The local products are chicle and timber (the tropical forest south of Flores is being rapidly destroyed)—and mosquitoes in the rainy season; take plenty of repellant, and re-apply frequently.

Driving from Guatemala City or from Puerto Barrios, the road from the Atlantic Highway is paved to Modesto Méndez. Never drive at night. Some drivers suggest driving in front of a truck and, if you break down, do so across the road, then you will be assured of assistance. Alternatively after rain, it is advisable to follow a truck, and do not hurry. A new bridge has been built over the Sarstún River, then 250 km. along narrow, winding, dusty or muddy potholed road.

Flores, the Department's capital, lies in the heart of the Petén forests, and is built on an island in the middle of Lake Petén Itzá. It is linked by a causeway with Santa Elena (airport). Its population is 5,000. From Flores the ruins of Tikal and other Mayan cities can be reached. (For description of Maya culture **see page 1136**). There is a collection of stelae, altars, etc., from Naranjo and other remote Mayan sites, in a park W of the airport; no labels or guide book. *Fiesta*: January 1-14.

Hotels in Flores: *Yum Kax*, E, with bath and a/c, comfortable, restaurant; *El Itzá*, F, basic, no hot water (the owner is a good doctor); *Petén*, T 0811-392, F with cold water, E with hot, clean, friendly, rec., breakfast a little extra, helpful travel agency; *Petén Anexo* (formerly *Santana*), F, poor restaurant; *Pensión Universal*, near Banco de Guatemala, down an alley towards the water, F, pricey, cold shower, friendly, washing facilities; *Tziqui Na Ha*, near airport, C, a/c, new, pool; *El Jade*, F, clean, basic, just by the dyke leading to Flores.

At Santa Elena; *Maya Internacional*, E + tax, tepid water, beautifully situated, good restaurant, used by package tours from the capital; *Diplomático*, F with shower, basic; *Monja Blanca*, E; *Ahauna-Ula*, G, good restaurant; *San Juan* at the Pinita bus stop and Aviateca office, G without bath, F with, noisy, uncooperative.

Restaurants *El Jacal*, on road to left of causeway, good regional dishes; *Gran Jaguar*, pleasant, very good; *La Jungla*, reasonably priced, rec.; opposite is *Arco Iris*, simple but friendly; *Restaurant Típico*.

At Santa Elena, *El Rodeo*, 2 C. y 5 Av., excellent, reasonable prices; *Cafetería Oriental* is said to be good and cheap, as is *Comedor Los Angeles*. Santa Elena market, well-stocked, 2 blocks from *Hotel San Juan*, just off Guatel road.

Dugouts can be hired to paddle yourself around the lake (US$0.50 per hour from Don Rosso, house before *Hotel Petén*). You can swim from "Radio Petén" island, the small island which used to have a radio mast on it, US$0.12 by boat. Petenito (La Guitarra) island in the lake is being developed for tourism (known as "Paradiso Escondido"); there is a small zoo of local animals, birds and reptiles (unfavourable reports received), 3 water toboggan slides, and plant-lined walks, rec., but popular at weekends. Dugout to island, US$3 p.p. Boat tours of the whole lake cost about US$10 per boat, calling at these islands, a lookout on a Mayan ruin and *Gringo Perdido* (see page 1166); whatever you may request, the zoo will almost certainly be included in the itinerary.

San Benito, a US$0.05 (US$0.10 after 1800) ride across the lake, has some small restaurants (e.g. *Santa Teresita*), which are cheaper but less inviting than those in Flores. *San Juan*, G, clean; *Hotel Rey*, G, friendly, untidy, noisy; *Hotel Miraflores*, F, good, private showers. A dirty village. Regular launch service from San Benito across the lake to San Andrés (US$0.12) and San José (US$0.15) on NW shore. *Hospedaje El Reposo Maya*, at San Andrés, G.

Car Hire at airport, mostly Suzuki jeeps; Jade rec.

Exchange Flores is the only place in the Petén where one can reliably change travellers' cheques. Banco de Guatemala open Mon.-Thur. 0830-1400, Fri. 0830-1430. Banks close December 24-January 1. The major hotels change cash and travellers' cheques.

Airport 4 companies fly from Guatemala City to Flores: Aviateca, Aerovías, Aero Quetzal and Tapsa, US$84 return. The schedules appear to change frequently, but all but Aviateca fly daily about 0700; Aviateca flies Fri. and Sun. at 1600. If returning from Flores by plane, reconfirm flight on arrival, flights back leave between 1600 and 1700, but check. Don't buy air tickets at *Hotel San Juan*; they add on all sorts of extras, but they do have a free minibus from airport to hotel. You must have passport (or identity documents) to pass through Santa Elena airport: all bags will be searched and all fruit confiscated. Taxi airport-Flores, US$0.80 p.p., or *San Juan* bus to Santa Elena village then walk. Airport to Flores is 3 km.

Buses The Flores bus terminal is in Santa Elena, a 10-min. walk from Flores (taxi, US$0.40 by day, US$0.80 at night). Daily Fuente del Norte buses leave Guatemala City in the early morning for the 13-22 hr. run via Morales-Río Dulce-Puerto Modesto Méndez to Flores (US$11 for service with reserved seat, no standing, US$5.40, 1st class; one way, take food); return buses to Guatemala City at 0500, 1100, 2100 from centre of Santa Elena; Pinita to Guatemala City from *Hotel San Juan 1* (don't believe them if they tell you Pinita is the only company to the capital), 1100, not as good. Bus Flores to Río Dulce, US$3.50, Fuente del Norte, 8 hrs. Bus between Flores and Quiriguá (see page 1161), US$5, 11 hrs. In the rainy season the trip can take as much as 28 hrs., and in all weathers it is very uncomfortable and crowded (flights warmly rec.).

Mayan ruins fans wishing to economize can travel to Copán by bus from Flores to Río Hondo, then from Río Hondo to Chiquimula, then from Chiquimula to El Florido (see page 1160) and finally from there to Copán. La Pinita also has a service to Flores from Guatemala City via Sebol, El Pato and Sayaxché, see below.

Those who wish to break the journey could get off the bus and spend a night in Morales, Río Dulce, San Luis (*Pensión San Antonio*, G, nice; *Comedor Oriente*, cheap, good) or Poptún. **Poptún** is 100 km. from Flores; 5 minibuses a day from Flores, US$2 or take Fuente del Norte bus, US$1.15, 4 hrs; bus Poptún-Guatemala City at 0900, 11 hrs. take this bus also for Cobán, alight at the turn-off to Sebol, 5 km. before Modesto Méndez, hitch to Fray Bartolomé de las Casas (see page 1166), then take 0500 bus to Cobán. Poptún can be reached by air for US$16. *Pensión Isabelita*, F, clean, rec. but no electricity at night; *Pensión Gabriel*, G. *Restaurant Gil-town*, best. Also at certain times of the year delicious mangoes are on sale in this area. Good view of the town from Cerro de la Cruz, a 15-minute walk from the market.

3 km. S of Poptún is *Finca Ixobel*, a working farm owned by Mike and Carole De Vine, here one may camp for US$1 p.p., rec. ("a paradise"). There are shelters, showers, free firewood, swimming, farm produce for sale; family-style meals available, and there is a small guest house, F, travellers' cheques exchanged; they have a restaurant-bar (also called *Ixobel*, excellent too, with *hospedaje* next door) in the centre of Poptún where the buses stop. Three cave expeditions are organized, the most spectacular being a 3-day mule hike to the Cueva de las Inscripciones, once used by Maya; inside are marvellous glyphs (US$10). Bus travellers should alight at the large signpost on the main road.

24 km. N of Poptún, 8 km. NE of Dolores, is the small Mayan site of Ixcún, unexcavated, with a

number of monuments (some carved), and a natural hill topped by the remains of ancient structures. The access road is impassable in the rainy season.

In 1982, the Cerro Cahui Conservation Park was opened on the northern shore of Lake Petén Itzá; this is a lowland jungle area where one can see 3 species of monkeys, deer, jaguar, peccary, some 450 species of birds; run by Cecon and Inguat.

Tikal   The great Mayan ruins of vast temples and public buildings are reached by plane to Santa Elena, from where buses run (see below). Tikal lasted from the 4th century A.D. until the tenth. An overall impression of the ruins (a national park) may be gained in 4-5 hrs., but you need two days to see everything. Guides are available near the Plaza Mayor. A Land Rover trip through the ruins costs US$2.50. Marvellous place for seeing animal and bird life of the jungle. There is a secluded part, called "El Mundo Perdido", in which wildlife can be seen. *Birds of Tikal* book available at the museum. Wildlife includes spider monkeys, howler monkeys (re-established after being hit by disease), three species of toucan (most prominent being the "Banana Bill"), deer, foxes and many other birds and insects. Mosquitoes can be a real problem even during the day if straying away from open spaces (use repellant and cover up).

Hotels   Note: It is advisable to book a hotel room or camping space as soon as you arrive—in high seasons, book in advance. *Jaguar Inn*, B, full board, triple room D (without board: E), will provide picnic lunch at US$1.30. Its electricity supply is the most reliable (1800-2200); will store luggage, very friendly. *Tikal Inn*, E p.p. in rooms, to C for 2 in good bungalows, cheap accommodation without electricity also available, meals said to be good (US$1 for dinner); *Posada de la Selva* (Jungle Lodge— reservations may be made at Edificio Villa Real, 6 Av., in the capital), from E p.p. (communal shower) to D with bath, full board available (food fair, but service slow; roofs of cheapest accommodation leak badly) has its own campsite where you can sling your hammock for US$0.50. Jungle Lodge's Tikal tours (US$5) have been rec.; runs bus to meet incoming flights, US$2.50 one way. Three comedores, *Comedor Tikal*, *Corazón de Jesús*, and *Imperio Maya* (opens 0530). Economical travellers are best advised to bring their own food (but not fruit, which will be confiscated), and especially drink. Everyone should take drinking water.

Wear light cotton clothes, a broad-brimmed hat and take plenty of insect repellant. The nights can be cold, however; at least one warm garment is advisable. There is one campsite (US$1.85, by the airstrip, good, rents small hammocks for US$3.70. Mosquito netting is rec. Take your own water as the supply is very variable, sometimes rationed, sometimes unlimited, depending on season. Bathing is possible in a pond at the far end of the airstrip (check first). Beware of jiggers in the grass. Soft drinks are available near the Plaza Mayor and Temple IV (US$0.25). No banking services available. Ruins (open 0600-1730) charge US$1.85, and museum US$0.75 (open Mon.-Fri. 0900-1700, Sat. and Sun. 0900-1600). Extended passes to see the ruins at sunrise/sunset (until 2100) are easy to obtain from the Inspectoría office on the slope by the path to the ruins (especially good for seeing animals). It is best to visit the ruins after 1400 (fewer tourists). There is nowhere to store luggage at Tikal while you are visiting the ruins. Recommended guide book is *Tikal*, by W. R. Coe, with essential map, price US$4.20 in the capital or US$3 at Casa Andinista, Antigua, or slightly more at the Tikal Museum. Without a guide book, a guide is essential (Clarence has been rec.), as outlying structures can otherwise easily be missed. Take a torch, electricity at Tikal is only available 1800-2200. It is now possible to visit Tikal in a day: take 0600 minibus from Santa Elena (Flores), arrive by 0700, return at 1300, allowing 6 hrs. at the site. You may hitch back with a tourist bus 1 hr. later if it is not full. Tour from *Hotel Maya Internacional* in Santa Elena: dep. 0800, return 1600, transport only US$7.50, guided tour US$18 (time may be reduced to accommodate people catching flights). *Hotel Petén* also runs tours from 0600-1700. Aviateca and Aerovías have a weekend tour, flying to Flores on Friday, stay the night at *Maya Internacional* or *San Juan* hotels, Saturday at Tikal, Sat. night back at the hotel, Sunday at Tikal if you wish before flight back to the capital, US$95 inclusive.

Buses leave Santa Elena for Tikal from *Hotel San Juan* daily at 0630 and 1300, US$1.30 one way (63 km., 2½-3 hrs. on good paved road). Buses return at 0600 and 1300 (Pinita). Several hotels, including *San Juan* and *Petén*, run minibuses to Tikal for US$4 return (singles available), leaving between 0600 and 1000, returning between 1300 and 1700, 1 hr.; reservations should be made day before. *Jungle Lodge* minibus from Tikal at 1400. Minibuses meet Guatemala City-Flores flights to take visitors to Tikal. Taxi to Tikal costs US$16 (per vehicle), or US$24 waiting for return.

Note   Heavy rains and flooding can close the roads between Tikal and Flores.

To Belize   There are 4 buses daily from Flores to *Melchor de Mencos* (US$1.15) on the border (take the 0500 Pinita bus from *Hotel San Juan 1*—they promise to wake you up, but don't count on it, to be sure of making a connection in San Ignacio for Belize City). This can be caught at El Cruce if coming from Tikal. The 0630 or 1300 bus from Tikal gives you a 1 hr. wait at El Cruce (US$0.50) for the Flores-Melchor de Mencos bus, one leaves El Cruce at 1500 (El Cruce-Melchor de Mencos,

US$1). Pinita bus to Flores leaves Melchor de Mencos 4 times a day (first at 0330—best for Tikal connection 0930), with a 2-4 hr. wait at El Cruce for the bus to Flores, argue price; to Tikal (some Flores-Tikal buses do not stop for passengers at El Cruce; it may be easier to get a ride in a taxi). Journey takes about 3 hrs. and the bus tours town, including the border, for passengers. Pick-up Melchor de Mencos-Flores, US$3.85; taxi from the border to Flores, argue price; to Tikal, US$35 for up to 6 passengers. About 3 km. from El Cruce on the Tikal road, if one turns off to the left along the north shore of Lake Petén-Itzá, is *El Gringo Perdido*, with a restaurant, cabins, camping (US$0.55 a night) and good swimming in the lake, meals available at US$1.25. The road from El Remate to *El Gringo Perdido* is often flooded. For onward connections, it is best to take a taxi from the border to San Ignacio (Cayo), BZ$3. From there you can catch a bus to Belize City. Hitching is not easy as there is little traffic on these roads. Taxis to Belize City can be hired, about US$10 p.p. Banco de Guatemala at the border, when open, gives better rates than money changers; also black market in Belizean dollars. If driving from Flores/Tikal to Belize, be prepared for police checks (watch out for drugs being "planted" in your vehicle) and take spare fuel. **N.B.** If you need a visa to enter either Belize (other than transit) or Mexico, get it before crossing from Guatemala at this point.

Hotels   at Melchor de Mencos: *Maya*, G (sells bus tickets and acts as bus stop, small rooms); *Zacaleu*, G, clean, good value, shared toilets/showers; *Mayab*, F, clean, comfortable, shared showers and toilets, hot water, rec., safe parking. Tienda Unica will change travellers' cheques. *Restaurant Damarco*, very good, US$1 for meal, usually closed in evening; *La Chinita*, 1 block from *Maya*, good dinner under US$2.

To Mexico   From Flores or Tikal to Chetumal in a day is possible if the 0500 bus Flores—Melchor de Mencos, or 0630 from Tikal (change at El Cruce) connects with a bus at 0920 from the border to Belize City, from where you can take an afternoon bus to Chetumal. 72-hour transit visas for Belize can be obtained at the border, but make sure you have all necessary documentation for Mexico before leaving Belize City.

A rough, unpaved road runs 160 km. to **El Naranjo** on the San Pedro River—a centre for oil exploration, unfriendly—on the Mexican border. There are daily buses from Santa Elena at 0500, 1230 and 1500 from *Hotel San Juan* (US$3, 5½ hrs. at least; bus from El Naranjo to Flores at 0300 and 1400). At *Posada San Pedro*, G, basic, (under same ownership as *Maya Internacional* in Santa Elena) there is information, group travel, guides, and arrangements for travel as far as Palenque; reservations can be made through travel agencies in Guatemala City. One other basic hotel, also G; the restaurant by the dugouts is expensive, others in town better value. Also bungalows in El Naranjo, which has an immigration office. On arrival in El Naranjo, your luggage will be searched; next morning, go to immigration and have your passport stamped (if not travelling alone, make sure everyone gets a stamp). From El Naranjo, daily boat leaves at 0700 for La Palma in Mexico (US$12, 7 hrs.), from where buses go to Tenosique and on to Palenque. Mexican tourist cards can be obtained at the border. Expect thorough searches on both sides of the border.

A third route to Mexico is to take a bus from Santa Elena to Sayaxché (see below), then take a boat down the Río de la Pasión to the military post at Pipiles (exit stamps given here) or to the town of Benemérito on the Río Usumacinta (trading boat US$2, 2 days; private launch US$60, 4 hrs.). If stuck at Pipiles, a farmer who lives 800 metres upstream may take you to Benemérito in his launch. From Benemérito, buses go at 0600, 0700 and 0800 to immigration just past the Río Lacantún (or hitch in a truck); 5 hrs. by bus Benemérito-Palenque (more in the wet). Allow 7 days Flores-Palenque; get Mexican tourist card in advance to avoid offering bribes at border. Take also hammock, mosquito net, food and insect repellant; there are no hotels between Sayaxché and Palenque and dollars cannot be exchanged. Yaxchilán and Bonampak in Mexico can be visited from the road Benemérito-Palenque.

Sayaxché is a good centre for visiting the Petén, whether your interest is in the wild life or the Mayan ruins. The *Hotel Guayacán*, known locally as *Hotel de Godoy* after the owner Julio Godoy, is a good source of information on the area, F, beware of theft, expensive food and drink, on S bank of river, close to ferry; *Hotel la Montana*, G, has its own separate restaurant (at which Carlos is very informative); *Hotel Mayapán*, S bank near ferry, F, no water or electricity after 2200; or *Hotel Sayaxché*, G, basic, dirty, food not bad. *Comedor Delphi*, opposite market, good. If travelling south, stock up with fruit-in the market. No money-changing facilities. *Viajes Don Pedro* runs launches to El Ceibal, Petexbatún and Aguateca, 4 hrs., and 2-day trips to Yaxchilán.

There are buses to and from Guatemala City via Sebol, and to and from Santa Elena, Flores, 0600, 1300 (US$0.80, 3 hrs.); La Pinita has a through bus, Guatemala City-Flores, via Sayaxché (no transport south in the rainy season). On August 24, all-night mass is celebrated in **Sebol** (free food at 0100) with games played on the church lawn in the daylight hours. 10 km. from Sebol (no accommodation) is **Fray Bartolomé de Las Casas** (*Hospedaje Ralios*, F, shared bath, OK, and 2 others; restaurants), a pleasant village which has a *fiesta* (parade and rodeo) on May 1. A rough dirt road links Sebol with Sayaxché via *Raxruhá* (*Pensión Aguas Verdes*, G, basic, pleasant; good *pensión* nr. bridge, G p.p., *comedor* opp.; many *comedores*, e.g. *El Ganadero*, quite good) and *El Pato* (2 *comedores* and 1 basic *pensión*, G). Besides the direct Guatemala City-Sebol-Sayaxché-Flores bus, local transport connects most of these towns: Sayaxché-Raxruhá, by pick-up only, 0600, 0900, 1100, 1300, 4 hrs., US$2.60, bad road; El Pato-Raxruhá (minibus 0500 daily);

Raxruhá-Sebol, occasional bus, US$0.40, pick-up more common, US$0.75 (very bad road, 2 hrs. for 25 km.) or El Pato-Sebol; Fray B. de Las Casas-Cobán, 0500, 9 hrs., US$1.50 (Cobán-Sebol at 0530). You can also go from Lanquín to Sayaxché via Pajal, Las Casas, Sebol and Raxruhá (see page 1159) (not rec. as a 1-day journey, better to rest in Raxruhá).

From Sebol, there is an 0300 bus to Poptún (see page 0), via Fray Bartolomé de Las Casas and San Luis (on the Morales-Río Dulce-Poptún-Flores road). This route is impassable in the rainy season. From San Luis there is an 0630 bus to Flores, stopping at Poptún (4½ hrs.). It is easy to get a ride on one of the many trucks which run on all these routes.

Downriver from Sayaxché is **El Ceibal**, where the ruins were excavated by Peabody Museum and Harvard. Some of the best preserved *stelae* are found in a jungle setting. There is now a difficult road linking Sayaxché with El Ceibal—impassable in the wet (leave bus at El Paraíso on the main road—local pick-up from Sayaxché US$0.20.—then walk to the ruins, a further 12 km., 1½ hrs.) so the trip can be made either by road or by river (launch hire US$25, 2 hrs.—*pensión* G). You can sling a hammock at El Ceibal and use the guard's fire for making coffee if you ask politely—a mosquito net is advisable, and take repellant for walking in the jungle surroundings. From Sayaxché the ruins of the Altar de Sacrificios at the confluence of the Ríos de la Pasión and Usumacinta can also be reached. Further down the Usumacinta river is Yaxchilán, just over the border in Mexico (temples still standing, with sculptures and carved lintels— see page 1090). Still further down the Usumacinta in the west of Petén department is **Piedras Negras**, with little standing architecture, and most sculpture removed to the National Museum in Guatemala City (imagination needed), which can be reached by special rafts suitable for light rapids, at some considerable expense (can be arranged through FLAAR, see page 1151). The Usumacinta river has been dammed by Mexico below Piedras Negras; so no longer are river trips possible.

The Río de la Pasión is a good route to visit other, more recently discovered Maya ruins. From Laguna Petexbatún (46 km.), a fisherman's paradise, which can be reached by outboard canoe from Sayaxché (US$10 or more for 6 people and luggage) excursions can be made to unexcavated ruins: these include Arroyo de la Piedra (a small site with a number of mounds and stelae, between Sayaxché and Dos Pilas), **Dos Pilas** itself (many well-preserved stelae), **Aguateca** (excursion over only known Mayan bridge and down into huge chasm) and **Itzán**—discovered in 1968. Lagoon fishing includes 150-lb. tarpon, snoek and local varieties. Many interesting birds, including toucan and *guacamayo*. On W side of Laguna Petexbatún is the *Posada del Mundo Maya*, set in a jungle wilderness. Rooms F (E incl. 3 meals). Camping US$0.50 per day. Hire of hammock US$0.50 per day. Meals US$1.25 each. (Enquire at Sayaxché for the *posada*. Reservations through the owner Ana Smith, Panamundo Travel Agency, or *Hotel Camino Real*, Guatemala City, where she is manager.) Jungle guides can be hired for US$1.50-2.50 per day.

(On the foregoing information, Mr. John Streather comments that the ruins are spread over a large area and that the non-specialist could well content himself with seeing El Ceibal and, possibly, Dos Pilas.)

About 30 km. from Flores, on the road towards the Belize border, is Lake Yaxhá. On the northern shore is the site of **Yaxhá**, the third-largest known classic Maya site in the country, accessible by causeway (little excavation has yet been done). In the lake is the site of Topoxte. (The island is accessible by boat.) The site is unique since it flourished between the 12th and 14th centuries, long after the abandonment of all other classic centres. Twenty km. further north lies **Nakum**, with standing Mayan buildings. It is possible to drive part of the way (dry season, April-May) only, or else to walk, but since there are numerous forks in the track, it is essential to hire a guide (no overland transport or flights in the off-season).

The largest Maya site in the country is at **El Mirador**, 36 km. direct from Carmelita, very many more by jungle trail from Flores (a 2-4 day trek—a guide is essential, take plenty of food). The larger of the two huge pyramids, called La Danta, is probably the largest pyramid in the world. There are paintings and other treasures; guards at the site will show you around if no one else is on hand. Camping is possible. Tom Courtenay-Clack (of New York City) writes: Permission, in the form of a letter from the Governor of El Petén, is required. He is to be found at the FYDEP complex on the mainland near Flores. Free water purification tablets for the trip can be obtained at the pharmacy of the army barracks by the airport. Drive or hitch-hike to Carmelita (no bus service); a hard 35 km. that can take 5 hrs.—after rain four-wheel drive, a winch and shovel are necessary. At Carmelita, ask around for space to sling your hammock or camp. Also ask for guides who go with mules to El Mirador (Victor is rec.; the one who lives next to the doctor is not, he doesn't take mules and is unreliable): US$40 with mule. Allow 2 days each way unless you want a forced march. Take water, food, hammocks, mosquito nets, tents and torches; cooking gear is not essential because guides will make a fire and the guards may let you use their kitchen if you're polite (they also appreciate gifts, e.g. a giant can of peaches).

20 km. north of Tikal is **Uaxactún**, which has a stuccoed temple with serpent head decoration. Uaxactún is one of the longest-occupied Maya sites. There is a direct bus from Flores (same times as for Tikal), US$2 return. The hardy might consider walking the 24 km. through the jungle from Tikal, as the dirt road is impassable to vehicles from June to February, but December to April it can be driven by a standard vehicle. Guides ask about US$8 for a 2-day trip from *Posada de la Selva* in Tikal. Tour from *Hotel Maya Internacional*, US$40 for transport, guide and lunch. No *pensiones*, but the signalman at the airfield will let you sling your hammock in his home for US$0.25. Nearby is **El Zotz**, another large site, reachable by a reasonable dirt road. In the far north of El Petén is **Río**

Azul, which has impressive early tomb murals and Early Classic standing architecture (seasonally being studied). The road to Río Azul goes via Dos Lagunas, beyond which it is very bad (the army sometimes restricts travel north of Dos Lagunas). All the sites are accessible by jeeps and FLAAR runs tours to them in the dry season.

GUATEMALA CITY TO SAN JOSE (4)

Amatitlán is 37 km. by rail and 27 by road SW of the capital, on attractive Lake Amatitlán, 12 by 4 km. (but diminishing in size as a result of sedimentation in the Río Villalobos which drains into it—caused by deforestation). Fishing and boating; bathing is not advisable, as the water has become seriously contaminated. Sunday boat trips cost US$1, or less, for 45 mins.; beware of people offering boat trips which last no more than 10 minutes. The thermal springs on the lake side, with groves of trees and coffee plantations, feed pools which *are* safe to bathe in. Lake surrounded by picturesque chalets with lawns to the water's edge. Altitude 1,240 metres, population 12,225. Grand view from the United Nations Park, 2½ km. N, above Amatitlán. A road goes round the lake; a branch runs to the slopes of Pacaya volcano, US$0.15 by bus **(see page 1156)**. The town has two famous ceiba trees; one is in Parque Morazán. Buses from Guatemala City (every ½-hr. US$0.20) go right to the lakeside.

Fiesta   Santa Cruz, May 2-3.

Hotel   *Rocareña*, E, pay in advance as prices may go up overnight, unfriendly; *Pensión Karla*, F, clean, friendly, family-run; *Hospedaje y Comedor Kati*, F, clean, pleasant dining room.

Camping   The by-road to the UN Park (turning at 19½ km. from Guatemala City) ends at camping sites and shelters; it is rather steep and narrow for caravan trailers. View, US$0.12 entrance fee. On the main highway S of Amatitlán, accessible by any bus going to Palín, Escuintla or beyond, is Automariscos (km. 33.5, T (0)330479), English-speaking owner, electric and water hook-ups, large warm swimming pool (thermal), hot jacuzzi, baby pool, good toilets, entry US$1, restaurant. A second, next door in the direction of Escuintla, is La Red, which has swimming pools fed by volcanic springs (US$0.60 each); restaurant/bar and good toilet facilities (camping US$1). Bus, Guatemala City to any of these 3, US$0.25.

Road continues S to the Pacific port of San José through Palín; rail continues W to Tecún Umán.

Palín, 14½ km. from Amatitlán, has a Sunday Indian market in a square under an enormous ceiba tree. Grand views to E, of Pacaya, to NW, of Agua volcano, to W, of Pacific lowland. Power plant at Michatoya falls below town. Road runs NW to Antigua through Santa María de Jesús **(see page 1155)**. See old Franciscan church (1560). *Fiestas:* December 8, first Sunday January, June 3, and movable feasts of Holy Trinity and Sacred Heart. Textiles here are exceptional, but are becoming hard to find. *Pensión Señorial*, G, basic.

Escuintla, 18 km. from Palín on the road to San José, is a market town in a rich tropical valley at 335 metres. Population 62,500. Famous for its medicinal baths and fruits. There is a large market on Sunday, and a daily market over 2 blocks. Agua volcano looms to the N. Road N to Antigua. Beyond Escuintla a railway branches W at the station of Santa María to Mexico (no passengers).

The Pacific Highway to the Mexican border at Tecún Umán (paved all the way, 200 km.) and E to El Salvador (first 25 km. bad, then only fair) runs through Escuintla. As a route to Mexico, it is shorter, faster and easier to drive, but much less picturesque, than the El Tapón route to the N. There is a meat packing plant. *Fiesta:* December 8 (holiday) to 12. Many buses to the capital (US$0.38, Veloz Porteño) also direct to Antigua at 0730 and 1500, US$0.50 (poor road).

Hotels   (each with acceptable restaurant)   *Motel Sarita*, km.59, CA2 road, E; *Motel Texas*, km. 59, CA9 road, E. *Hospedaje San Vicente*, G; *Pensión México*, G; *Hospedaje El Aguila*, G; *Mansión La Paz* and *Pensión Marina*, both G, on Calle 10; *Hospedaje Comodidad*, near market, G; *Shing Chi Rest*, G; *Restaurant Deliciosas Tony*, meals for US$0.75; also several Chinese restaurants.

Exchange   Lloyds Bank (agency) 7a Calle 3-09, Zona 1. Open 0830-1200, 1400-1600.

The Department of Escuintla, between the Pacific and the chain of volcanoes, is the richest in the country, producing 80% of the sugar, 20% of the coffee, 85% of the cotton, and 70% of the cattle of the whole country.

Between Escuintla and Santa Lucía *Cotzumalguapa* is *La Democracia* (7 km. off the Pacific Highway), where sculptures found on the Monte Alto and Costa Brava estates (*fincas*) are displayed. These are believed to date from 400 BC or earlier and have magnetic navels or temples. Visit the Museo del Pueblo on the main square. At Cotzumalguapa (an unfriendly town which charges tourists for the privilege of visiting) is the 9th century site of Bilbao (or Cotzumalguapa), which shows Teotihuacán and Veracruz influences. El Baúl, a pre-classic monument (stelae) which dates back to Izapán, is 6 km. from Cotzumalguapa: cross bridge, keep left and follow the road to the timberyard where numerous interesting stelae are displayed. From this early art, the classic Mayan art developed. El Castillo, between Bilbao and El Baúl, has some small sculptures dating back to Mayan times. On the Las Ilusiones and Finca Pantaleón estates are ruined temples, pyramids and sculptures, and there are other stelae to be found in the area. More detailed information and a map can be obtained from FLAAR in Guatemala City (page 1151).

Hotels at Cotzumalguapa: *El Camino*, E; *Galeano*, *El Carmen*, both G. Hotel at La Democracia, *El Reposo*, F. Buses from the Zona 4 terminal in the capital run to both places.

San José, 52 km. beyond Escuintla, 109 km. by road (fully paved, bus US$ 1.50, Reyna del Pacífico) and 121 by rail from the capital, is the country's second largest port; it handles nearly half the imports. Population 8,000. Hot climate. Fishing, swimming, though beware the strong undercurrent. *Fiesta:* March 19, when town is crowded and hotel accommodation difficult to get. Interesting trip can be taken through Chiquimulilla canal by launch from the old Spanish port of *Iztapa,* now a bathing resort a short distance to the E. At Iztapa you can camp on the beach (dirty), but as it is only possible to get there by launch, one cannot take a car.

Hotels at San José *Casetas San Jorge*, F p.p.: *Viñas del Mar*, on the beach, E, with bath, run down, unfriendly; *Turicentro El Coquito*, D, on the road to Escuintla; *Motel La Roca*, at km. 71, F; *Veracruz* (Calle Principal), G, clean. *Posada Roma Linda*, G, extra for sheet), no shower, basic, good fish meals with family. At Iztapa *Santa María*, E with swimming pool; basic *hospedaje*, F.

Bus San José-Guatemala City hourly from 0600; from Iztapa to San José US$0.12. To Escuintla, US$0.50. Reyna del Pacífico to the capital, US$1.25.

Beyond San José is the smart resort of *Likin,* which fronts on both the Chiquimulilla canal and the Pacific. (Hotel: *Turicentro Likin*, C, per bungalow, clean, a/c, transfer by boat to hotel, secure parking, acceptable restaurant.) Further on is the less expensive resort of Monterrico.

WEST FROM GUATEMALA CITY (5)

The Pacific Highway goes W from Guatemala City to Tapachula in Mexico. The Pan-American Highway (fully paved) cuts off NW at San Cristóbal Totonicapán and goes into Chiapas by the El Tapón, or Selegua, canyon. This is a far more interesting route, with fine scenery.

A railway also runs through south-western Guatemala from Guatemala City to the Mexican frontier.

Some 6½ km. W of the capital a road (right) leads to San Pedro Sacatepéquez (see page 1156) and Cobán (see page 1143). Our road twists upwards steeply, giving grand views, with a branch to Mixco (16½ km. from Guatemala City). About 14 km. beyond, at San Lucas Sacatepéquez, the road to Antigua turns sharp left. *Sumpango,* which is a little over 19 km. beyond this turn-off, has a Sun. market, and *huipiles* can be bought from private houses; they are of all colours but preponderantly red, as it is believed to ward off the evil eye. Good font in church. At *Chimaltenango,* another road runs left, 20 km., to Antigua; this road is served by a shuttle-bus (US$0.25 or US$0.40 in minibus), so Antigua can be included in the Guatemala-Chichicastenango circuit. Chimaltenango is the capital of its Department (*Pensión La Predilecta*, G, pleasant rooms with bath, rooms without bath not so nice, poor water supply, unfriendly, tends to overcharge, rebuilt since the earthquake). Excellent views at 1,790 metres, from which water flows one side to the Atlantic, the other side to the Pacific. Thermal swimming pool at San Lorenzo El Tejar, which can be reached by bus from Chimaltenango. *Fiesta:* January 18-20. Buses to Antigua pass the famous park of Los Aposentos, 3 km. (lake and swimming pool). Bus to Panajachel, US$1.20. At San Andrés Itzapa (2 km. off Antigua road, 4 km. from Chimaltenango) there is a very interesting chapel to Maximon (San Simón) which is well worth a visit. Shops by the chapel sell prayer pamphlets and pre-packaged offerings.

A side-road runs 21 km. N to San Martín *Jilotepeque* over deep *barrancas*; markets on Sun., Thurs. Bus from Chimaltenango, US$0.50. *Fiesta:* November 11. Fine weaving. Striking *huipiles* worn by the women. Ten km. beyond Chimaltenango is Zaragoza, former Spanish penal settlement, and beyond that (right) a road (13 km.) leads N to the interesting village of **Comalapa:** markets 1000-1430, Mon.-Tues. bright with Indian costumes. Fine old church of San Juan Bautista (1564). *Fiestas:* June 24, Dec. 8, 12.

There are several local artists working in Comalapa; no studios, so best to ask where you can see their work (Artexco cooperative, *Figura Antigua*). There is a *pensión* here, G.

Six km. beyond Zaragoza the road divides. The southern branch, the old Pan-American Highway, goes through Patzicía and Patzún to Lake Atitlán (see below), then N to Los Encuentros. The northern branch, the new Pan-American Highway, much faster, goes past Tecpán and over the Chichoy pass, also to Los Encuentros. From Los Encuentros there is only the one road W to San Cristóbal Totonicapán, where the new road swings NW through El Tapón and La Mesilla to Ciudad Cuauhtémoc, the Mexican border settlement; and the old route goes W through Quezaltenango and San Marcos to Tapachula, in Mexico.

The northern road to Los Encuentros: from the fork the Pan-American Highway runs 19 km. to near **Tecpán,** which is slightly off the road at 2,287 metres. It has a particularly fine church: silver altars, carved wooden pillars, odd images, a wonderful ceiling which was severely damaged by the 1976 earthquake. The church is being slowly restored: the ceiling is missing and much of its adornment is either not in evidence, or moved to a church next door. The women wear most striking costumes. Market: Thursdays. *Fiestas:* May 3 (Santa Cruz), October 1-8, and December 8. *Hotel Iximché; Restaurant de la Montaña,* 1 km. after the road to Tecpán; the owner of *Zapatería La Mejor* has a guest house, G. Buses from Guatemala City (Zona 4 terminal), 2¼ hrs., every hour; easy daytrip from Panajachel.

Near Tecpán are the very important Mayan ruins of *Iximché,* once capital and court of the Cakchiqueles, 5 km. of unpaved road from Tecpán, open 0900-1600 (admission US$0.20). Iximché was the first capital of Guatemala after its conquest by the Spaniards; followed in turn by Ciudad Vieja, Antigua and Guatemala City. There is a museum at the site.

Beyond Tecpán the road swings up a spectacular 400 metres to the summit of the Chichoy pass. The pass is often covered in fog or rain but on clear days there are striking views. Some 14 km. from Tecpán, at km. 101, is the *Café Chichoy,* with cheap accommodation (rec.); 58 km. from the fork is Los Encuentros (and the road to Chichicastenango) and 3 km. further on the new northern road joins the old southern one from Sololá. 12 km. before Los Encuentros is a new road to Godínez (see below); no buses run along it, but it's worth taking if in a car; the paved road down to the lake has many small potholes.

Sololá, at 2,113 metres, 11 km. from the junction, has superb views across Lake Atitlán. Population 4,000. Fine Monday, Tuesday and Friday markets, to which many of the Indians go. Good selection of used *huipiles*. Note costumes of men. Great *fiesta* around August 15. Hot shower 500 metres from market on Panajachel road, behind Texaco station, US$0.18.

Tightly woven woollen bags are sold here: far superior to the usual type of tourist bags. Prices are high because of nearness of tourist centres of Panajachel and Chichicastenango.

Hotels *Tzoloj-yá,* near main square, F, hot shower, good, comfortable; *Letona*, G, communal, cheap food, not clean, outdoor washing facilities; *Posada Santa Elena*, G; *Pensión Paty*, on road to Panajachel, very basic, G. Also good cheap restaurant, *Santa Rosa; Flipper* store near market sells food all day.

Bus   to Chichicastenango US$0.35, 2 hrs. Bus to Panajachel, US$0.25, or 1½-2 hour walk; to Chimaltenango, US$0.25. Colectivo to Los Encuentros, US$0.15.

From Sololá the old Pan-American Highway drops 550 metres in 8 km. to Panajachel: grand views on the way. Take the bus up (US$0.25, they stop early in the evening), but quite easy to walk down (the views are superb), either direct by the road or via San Jorge La Laguna. The walk is highly recommended. You can return to Panajachel from San Jorge along the lake, if you take the southern road from the plaza, go through the woods and down to the flats. Ask permission at the house on the lake shore to follow the trail; a 3-hour walk.

The southern road to Los Encuentros (much more difficult than the northern, with a very poor surface, steep hills and hairpin bends, bus, US$0.35) goes through **Patzicía,** a small Indian village founded 1545 (no accommodation). Market on Wed. and Sat. *Fiesta* for the patron, Santiago, on July 23-26. The famous church, which had a fine altar and beautiful silver, was destroyed by the 1976 earthquake; some of the silver is now in the temporary church. Fourteen km. beyond is the small town of **Patzún**; its famous church, dating from 1570, was severely damaged; it is still standing, but is not open to the public. Sun. market, which is famous for the silk (and wool) embroidered napkins worn by the women to church, and for woven *fajas* and striped red cotton cloth. *Fiesta:* May 17-21 (San Bernardino). Lodgings at the tobacco shop, G, or near market in unnamed *pensión.*

Road (very bad, with many robberies) descends, then climbs to Godínez, 19 km. W of Patzún, where there is a good place for meals (no bus Patzún-Godínez). A branch road runs S to village of San Lucas Tolimán and continues to Santiago de Atitlán; both can be reached by a lake boat from Panajachel. The high plateau, with vast wheat and maize fields, now breaks off suddenly as though pared by a knife. From a viewpoint here, there is an incomparable view of Lake Atitlán, 600 metres below; beyond it rise three 3,000-metre-high volcano cones, Tolimán, Atitlán and San Pedro, to the W. The very picturesque village of San Antonio Palopó is right underneath, on slopes leading to the water.

Occasional guerrilla activity and armed robbery have been reported in this area.

Lake Atitlán, 147 km. from the capital via the northern road and Los Encuentros, 116 km. via the southern road and Patzún, and 1,562 metres above sea-level, about 7-10 km. across and 18 km. long, is one of the most beautiful and colourful lakes in the world. It changes colour constantly— lapis lazuli, emerald, azure— and is shut in by purple mountains and olive green hills. Over a dozen villages on its shores, some named after the Apostles, house three tribes with distinct languages, costumes and cultures. The lake is the only place in the world where the *poc,* a large flightless water grebe, may be seen (**see page 1173**). Beware of robbers (armed) at the lake.

Six hotels are actually on the lakeshore: *Atitlán, Visión Azul, Monterrey, Del Lago, Playa Linda* and *Tzanjuyu.* Apart from them, visitors to the lake stay at or near **Panajachel,** 1 km. from the lake; the main attraction is the scenery. (Visitors planning to travel round the lake should be warned that the only bank is here.) The town is a popular tourist resort and inhabited by many *gringos* ("Gringotenango"). The main tourist season is the second half of November to February. There is water-skiing (at weekends), private boating (kayaks for hire) and swimming in fresh clear water (but the beach is dirty). Good market on Sun. mornings, especially for embroidery; you are expected to bargain (despite the amount of tourism, prices are reasonable). Visit La Galería (near *Rancho Grande Hotel),* where Nan Cuz, an Indian painter, sells her pictures which evoke the spirit of village life. The village church, originally built in 1567, was restored, only to be badly damaged by the 1976 earthquake. *Fiesta:* Oct. 2-6.

Hotels   *Del Lago,* luxury hotel on lakeshore, A, pool, rec.; *Atitlán,* C, 3 meals US$10, 1 km. W of centre on lake, excellent; *Tzanjuyu,* C, 3 meals US$10, a bit disappointing, balconies and private beach; *Monterrey,* E, discounts for longer stay, 3 meals US$9, restaurant fair; *El*

Aguacatal, near *Hotel del Lago*, has bungalows, C, for 4, T 0621482; *Turicentro Los Geranios*, also near *Hotel del Lago*, has fully-equipped new bungalows which sleep 6, B, on Sat. and Sun., C, on other days, outdoor pool; *Bungalows Guayacán*, beautifully located among coffee bushes 700 metres from centre on road to Santa Catarina Palopó, D; *Rancho Grande*, cottages in charming setting, 4 blocks from beach, popular for long stay, good, simple food, D, includes breakfast, rec.; *Cacique Inn*, D (full board available), swimming pool, garden, English spoken, good food, rec.; *Regis*, E, well-kept house, friendly, rec.; *Playa Linda*, above public beach, D, slow service in restaurant; *Visión Azul*, near *Hotel Atitlán*, D, and *Mini Motel Riva Bella*, bungalows, E, with bath, rec.; *Galindo*, on main street, D, with bath, dirty, thin walls, check for bedbugs, nice garden and good set meal, US$1.50; *Fonda del Sol*, on main street, E, with bath, occasional hot water, or F without, noisy but comfortable, good restaurant; *Mayan Palace*, on main street, E, with shower, clean; *Del Camino*, next to Texaco, E with bath, clean, comfortable; *Del Viajero*, on main street, F, basic; *Viajero Annex*, F, camping US$0.75 p.p.; *Panajachel*, near market, simple, F, hot water rarely, clean, lots of other travellers; *Rooms Santa Elena* (N of main road), G, with bedding, beds uncomfortable, cheaper without, all facilities charged extra, friendly, clean, rec.; has annex (off Guatel road) which is OK; 2nd-hand English books on sale. There are a number of cheap *pensiones* on same road to the beach as Guatel building, including *Santander*, F, clean, friendly, lovely garden, rec.; *Villa Martita*, G, friendly, rec.; *Hospedaje Ramos*, close to lake shore, F, run by an Indian family, friendly, safe, repeatedly rec. (despite loud music from nearby cafés); nearby *Bungalows El Rosario*, E, safe, clean, run by Indian family, hot water 0700-1100; *Hospedaje García*, same street as *Last Resort*, opp. *Galería*, G, clean, hot showers extra; *Hospedaje Mi Chosita*, just beyond *Last Resort*, G, clean, friendly, family atmosphere; *Pensión Londres*, G; *Mario's Rooms*, F, T 621313, with garden, clean, hard beds, laundry, hot showers US$0.20 (sheets US$0.35, good breakfast US$0.55), *Vista Hermosa*, on road to *Monterrey*, basic, but very pleasant family, hot showers, G. For long stay, ask around for houses to rent; available at all prices from US$10-75 a month; but almost impossible to find in November and December. The water supply is generally bad, with water usually only available 0630-1100.

Camping No problem, but campsites (US$0.50 p.p.) are dirty. Camping on the lakeshore is currently allowed in a designated area.

Restaurants Many of the higher priced hotels have restaurants open to the public, as does *Fonda del Sol* (large varied menu, reasonable prices). *La Fontana*, where main streets meet, good but expensive. *The Last Resort*, on left after Guatel building, "gringo bar", good breakfast, bar (open 1800). *Blue Bird*, on side street to market, specials rec. US$0.75, good yoghurt and fruit salad (closed Thursdays). *El Cisne*, opposite *Hotel del Lago*, good cheap meals; also nearby *Tres Hermanas*, good pies, slow service. *Brisas del Lago*, good meals at reasonable prices, on lake shore; a number of others on beach front. *El Paraíso*, large meals, inc. vegetarian, in lane, off main street to lake. *Atitlán Fiesta* near market. On the street to the market are a number of vegetarian restaurants: *Comedor Hsieh*, nearest to market, great variety of dishes, rec.; *Casa de Pays* (pie shop, also known as *La Zanahoria*), good food, good value, clean and friendly (shows English language videos in evening US$0.60). *El Unico Deli*, coffee shop, dear, but nice food. *Copo's*, opposite Texaco station, has ice-cream. Go to *Panadería San Martín* at 1500 for fresh brown and banana bread. On Guatel road: *Villa Martita*, rec., and *Ranchón Típico Atitlán*. *El Bistro*, Swiss-owned, "overpriced, bland food", near beach on same road as Guatel; *Restaurant Sicodélico*, next to *Rooms Santander*, is pleasant (good yoghurt and *crêpes*); next door is *Amigos*, US-run, very good. The yoghurt dishes at *Mario's* restaurant are highly rec., but slow service. *Jebel* (same management as *Blue Bird*), good yoghurt, avocado omelette, rec. *Munchies*, good snacks, chocolates and cakes.

Entertainment *Posada del Pintor*, bar and restaurant, cheap beer and steaks, owners are a Swiss couple; *Shell Station Bar*, on site of old gas station, often has live music and dancing, and films on TV *Past Ten* discotheque, open till 0400, Q3 entry. Opp. *Hotel del Lago*, *Circus Bar*, good live music; *The Last Resort*, bar and restaurant, popular, table tennis, foreign magazines; next door, *Los Techos*, above *Cakchiquel* restaurant, English language films on video twice daily. *Video Bar*, on the Guatel road, has US cable TV, US news nightly at 1800, and video films, entry US$1.

Shops Many small stores selling local handicrafts including *Tomás Xon*, on Guatel road, and *Mundo Real* which has jewellery and authentic weaving (they also buy, sell and swap used books), and *Caramba*, both on main street. Also on road to San Andrés Semetebaj is the *Idol's House*, an antique shop where you must bargain. (Indians sell their wares cheaply on the lakeside.)

Bicycle Hire US$2-3 a day.

Health There are good clinics at Santiago Atitlán and San Lucas Tolimán, which specialize in treating dysentery. Amoebic dysentry and hepatitis are less common than in the past. Treatment free, so a donation is appropriate.

Exchange Bank open Mon.-Thurs. 0900-1500. Fri. to 1530. Exchange after 1000. Prefers to change smaller denomination travellers' cheques (if at all). Better rates at Toro Pinto exchange office (0900-1800) opp. Texaco station. The barber's shop near the bank will change travellers' cheques.

Post Office   Will not arrange for parcels to be sent, or received from, abroad.

Tourist Office   Open Wed.- Sun., 0800-1200 and 1400-1800, Mon. 0800-1200, Tues. closed; has maps. (Sells flight tickets for Flores.)

Bus   Rebuli, first class to Guatemala City, 3 hrs. US$1.25; several to the capital daily. There are direct buses to Los Encuentros on the Pan-American Highway (US$0.40). To Chichicastenango direct, supposedly 3 before 0900 and on Sun. at 0730 (US$1), but more reliable to go to Los Encuentros, where you can change for other buses to Guatemala City, Chichicastenango, or Quezaltenango. Direct bus to Quezaltenango 0600. There are direct buses to Cuatro Caminos, US$0.50 (**see page 1177**) from 0530, for connections to Totonicapán, Quezaltenango, Huehuetenango, etc. (No buses from Los Encuentros to Panajachel after 1830). Bus to Chimaltenango (for Antigua), US$1.20. Bus to Sololá, US$0.25. Best to wait for buses by the market, not by the Guatel road to the lake.

Excursions   To *Santiago Atitlán* by mail boat from the pier at the *Hotel Tzanjuyu* at 0845 and 1135 daily (check at hotel for times of services), US$1.25 single (for which you may have to compete), US$2 return, 1-1½ hrs., back to Panajachel at 1200 and 1700. From the beach, many between 0900-0930, returning between 1200 and 1700, US$1 single. By bus to San Lucas Tolimán, and from there by bus, US$0.65. The road is very rough for private cars after San Lucas. The women wear fine costumes and the men wear striped, half-length embroidered trousers. There is an Artexco cooperative: *Flor del Lago*. There is a daily market, best on Friday, *Fiesta*: June 5 and July 25. The Franciscan church dates back to 1568. Nearby were the ruins of the fortified Tzutuhil capital on the Cerro de Chuitinamit (nothing now to see). *Pensión Rosita*, near the church, F, dirty. *Brisas del Lago*, on way to market, G (pay extra US$1 for sheets); *Hospedaje Chi-Nim-Ya*, G, problematic water supply (good café opposite). Houses can be rented, but be extremely careful to check for, and protect against, scorpions and poisonous spiders in the wooden frames. *Santa Rita* restaurant good and cheap. Bus to Guatemala City, US$1.50 (5 a day, first at 0300). Buses back to Panajachel at 0600, 4 hrs. 16 km. rough dirt road from Panajachel, OK for private cars in dry season (about 1 hr.).

2 km. N of Santiago Atitlán is the Parque Nacional Atitlán which has a small reserve for the *poc* (press reports at the end of 1987 said the bird was extinct, but a traveller saw it in early 1988; only about 65 specimens are said to be left). Safe camping, take food and water; the guards may put you up in their cabin. Also in the reserve is a tame *pavo del cacho* (a big black bird with a red horn on its head). To get there, go by canoe from Santiago (US$0.65), with the reserve workers, or on foot, about ½ hr. on the San Lucas Tolimán road, but ask directions.

At *San Lucas Tolimán*, on the southern tip of the lake, there is cheap accommodation at *Pensión Las Conchitas*, G p.p. in 4-bedded rooms (good vegetarian food and yoghurt, parking), and *Hospedaje El Exito*, G, all rooms single, good value, clean. *Pensión Central*, E with private bath, F without, hot water, meals US$1, opened in 1989. Restaurants: *Comedor Victoria*, Guatemalan food; *Café Tolimán*, home made yoghurt and local dishes; *Restaurant El Buen Gusto*, varied menu. Motor boats can be hired for US$9.25 per hour. There is a market on Tues., Fri., and Sun. From San Lucas the cones of Atitlán, 3,535 metres, and Tolimán, 3,158 metres, can be climbed. Warm clothing and sleeping gear are essential, as the climb takes 2 days (less if you are very fit); maps are not available at present, ask in hotels for advice on routes and safety vis à vis guerrilla activity. Bus to San Lucas from Panajachel at 0630 and 1600 daily, 1 hr., US$0.50. A bus leaves San Lucas to Panajachel, 0700 and 1800; to Santiago, hourly between 0900 and 1800, 1 hr., returning hourly between 0300 and 1300. Bus San Lucas to Quezaltenango, US$1.50, 0430 and 0600. Between Santiago and San Lucas is Cerro de Oro, a small village on the lake.

Ferries leave from *Hotel Tzanjuyu* at Panajachel for *San Pedro La Laguna*, daily at 0400, Tues., Fri. and Sun. at 1500, returning on Mon., Wed., Sat., and at 1630 daily (US$0.75 one way). There is a ferry from Santiago to San Pedro at 1200 and 1700 (45 mins., US$0.75) locals pay less (ferry to Santiago at 0700 and 0800). 0300 bus to Guatemala City, US$1.50, 7 hrs. San Pedro is at the foot of the San Pedro volcano (which can be climbed in 4-5 hrs., guide necessary, but after 1000 the top is usually smothered in cloud) and is surrounded by coffee plantations. Canoes are made here (hire, US$0.50 a day) and a visit to the rug-making cooperative on the beach is of interest. Backstrap weaving is taught at some places, about US$0.50 per day. Market days Thurs. and Sun. (better).

There are many *pensiones*, including two on the public beach, at about US$0.50. (*Pensión Balneario*, G, good, *Pensión Chuazanahi*, G (known as the Colonel's Place), bedding US$0.50 p.p., boating and swimming, you can sling your hammock for US$1, reasonable meals; *Johanna*, near landing stage for Panajachel mail boat, G, nice rooms without bath, cold water only, friendly, also *cafetería*; all are basic; houses can be rented on a weekly basis for US$2.50). Good food is available at *Restaurant Chez Michel*, for US$0.75 (some French spoken), turn right from landing stage along beach road, past *Pensión Chuazanahi*; *La Carolina*; good food but slow service at *Comedor Francés* on lake shore. Village café, meals US$0.30. Dugouts can be hired for US$0.50 per day.

From San Pablo (on the way to San Pedro) you can walk to San Marcos and Santa Cruz (a difficult track), where there is a 16th century church, you can get beautiful views of the lake and volcanoes in the early morning light. Sisal bags and hammocks are made at San Pablo. If hiking around the lake, the only hotel between San Pedro and Panajachel is the bungalow accommodation of Wolfgang Kallab and Annegret Kallab-Welzel in Santa Cruz, E (Aptdo. Postal 39, Panajachel), with small restaurant and budget facilities; boat to Panajachel about 1000, or 2½ hrs.' walk.

Warning   Not a safe area for women to go walking alone; rape is not uncommon. Beware of theft, including of clothes hanging out to dry, in the Lake Atitlán area. Also beware of overcharging on private boats crossing the lake: practices include doubling the price half-way across and if you don't agree, out you get.

Santa Catarina Palopó is within walking distance of Panajachel (about 1 hr., path goes from Vista Santa Caterina in Panajachel through many tiny farms, very friendly and pleasant; truck US$0.12). The town has an attractive adobe church. Reed mats are made here, and you can buy *huipiles* (beautiful, green, blue and yellow) and men's shirts. Must bargain for articles. (Houses can be rented here.) From Santa Catarina you can walk to the Mirador de Godínez for views.

San Antonio Palopó (3 km. beyond Santa Catarina), 1 hr. walk, has another splendid church; it lies at the head of the lake in an amphitheatre formed by the mountains behind. The village is noted for the costumes and headdresses of the men, and *huipiles* and shirts are cheaper than in Santa Catarina. You will be charged for photography—whether you take pictures or not. *Fiesta*: June 14. The Artexco cooperative is called by the name of the village. *Hotel Casa de don Félix* (or *Casa del Lago*), superb views and good bathing, E, only a few rooms but gradually being expanded, good restaurant; you can stay in private houses (e.g. Don Tiedera nr. the Post Office) or rent rooms (take sleeping bag). A good hike is to take the bus from Panajachel to Godínez, walk down from there to San Antonio Palopó (1 hr.) and then along the new road back to Panajachel via Santa Catarina Palopó (3 hrs.).

San Andrés Semetabaj, about 6½ km. from Panajachel, has a beautiful ruined early 17th-century church. Market on Tues.
All the villages around the lake can be reached by bus or car, on rough roads.

Los Encuentros The old and new Pan-American Highways rejoin 11 km. from Sololá. 3 km. E is Los Encuentros, the junction of the Pan-American Highway and the road 18 km. NE to Chichicastenango. Altitude 2,579 metres. (Very poor accommodation available, G, if you miss a bus connection, easy to do as they are all full.)

Chichicastenango (also known as Santo Tomás) is the hub of the Maya-Quiché highlands, and is very popular with tourists. Altitude 2,071 metres, and nights cold. About 1,000 *ladinos* in the town, but 20,000 Indians live in the hills nearby and flood the town, almost empty on other days, for the Thursday and Sunday markets. The town is built around a large square plaza of 180 metres a side, with two churches facing one another: Santo Tomás parish church and Calvario. Santo Tomás is now open again to visitors, although restoration work is still going on; photography is not allowed, and visitors are asked to be discreet and enter by a side door. Groups burn incense and light candles on steps and platform before entering. Inside, from door to high altar, stretch rows of glimmering candles, Indians kneeling beside them. Later they offer copal candles and flower-petals to the "Idolo", a black image of Pascual Abaj, a Mayan god, on a hilltop 1½ km. SW of the plaza (beware of armed robbery on the way), boys act as guides for US$1; be very respectful at the ceremony and do not take photographs. Next to the church are the cloisters of the Dominican monastery (1542) where the famous Popol Vuh manuscript of Mayan mythology was found in 1690; Father Rossbach's jade collection can be seen in the municipal museum on the main square and is well worth a visit (open 0800-1200, closed Tues.), and so is the house of a mask-maker on the way up to the "Idolo", who rents masks and costumes to the dancers and will show visitors the path to the idol. This is a little difficult to find even then, and clear instructions should be obtained before setting out.

Derivation of town's name: *chichicas*—a prickly purple plant like a nettle, which grows profusely—and *tenango*, place of. The town itself is charming: winding streets of white houses roofed with bright red tiles wandering over a little knoll in the centre of a cup-shaped valley surrounded by high mountains. Fine views from every street corner. The costumes are particularly splendid: the men's is a short-waisted embroidered jacket and knee breeches of black cloth, a gay woven sash and an embroidered kerchief round the head. The cost of this outfit, over US$200, means that fewer and fewer men are in fact wearing it. Women wear *huipiles* with red embroidery against black or brown and skirts with dark blue stripes. The Sun. market is more colourful than the one on Thurs.: more Indians, brighter costumes and dancing to marimba bands, but it certainly becomes very touristy after the buses arrive from Guatemala City (bargains may be had after 1530 when the tourist buses depart). In fact the markets begin, and are better, on the previous p.m. You must bargain hard. Good value handicrafts at Cooperativo Santo Tomás, opp. *Mayan Inn* on market place.

Fiestas Santo Tomás, December 17-21: processions, dances, marimba music (well worth a visit—very crowded); Holy Week; November 1; January 20; March 19; June 24 (shepherds). There is also a *fiesta* at the end of May.

Hotels *Mayan Inn*, C, seen better days, breakfast, US$2, bar, marimba music, laundry service; *Santo Tomás*, B with beautiful colonial furnishings (a museum in itself), often full at weekends, very good, friendly service, helpful owner (Sr. Magermans), good restaurant and bar, marimba music p.m., same day laundry, old building with nice patio, meals US$2.50; nearby *El Salvador*, 10 C. 4-47, 2 blocks from main square, F with sheets and bath (G without), friendly, noisy; *Maya Lodge*, 6 C. 4-08, E with bath and up, with breakfast, good; *Martita*, F, with bath and sheets (G without either); *Pensión Chiguilá*, 5 Av. 5-24, clean, good, E, with bath and breakfast, F without, meals another US$3.85 (some rooms have fireplaces, wood costs US$0.90 a day extra). *Pensión-Restaurant Katokok*, F, without sheets, serves good meals; *Posada San Antonio*, F (less without sheets), good but basic; *Cantina Claveles*, G, for a poor room, but US$0.35 for a good meal. There is a bakery attached. *Pensión Girón*, F (G without sheets), opp. vegetable market, good, ample parking. Local boys will show you other cheap lodgings, G.

Restaurants *Tapena*, 5 Av. 5-21, clean, a bit expensive; *Las Marimbitas; El Samaritano* (reasonable).

Exchange Banks do not change money at holiday times; *Mayan Inn* will exchange cash, *Santo Tomás* cheques and cash at those times.

Buses Rutas Lima bus leaves Guatemala City four times daily for Quezaltenango, connecting at Los Encuentros for Panajachel (US$0.35) and Chichicastenango. The slower Reyna de Utatlán bus from the capital, 4 hrs. (Zona 4 Terminal) costs only US$1.50, several daily. For return, take local bus (US$0.35) to Los Encuentros where you can pick up another for the capital. One direct bus to Panajachel on Sun. at 1330 from *Hotel Santo Tomás*, US$1, and others in week (supposedly—better go to Los Encuentros). For Antigua, change at Chimaltenango. Beware of overcharging on buses in the Panajachel/Chichicastenango area. To Huehuetenango, via Los Encuentros, US$1.75. 2 weekly buses Chichicastenango-Nebaj, US$1, may have to change at Sacapulas, otherwise take a bus to Quiché and change there.

The Quiché Region (see note on page 1143.) 19 km. N by road from Chichicastenango is Santa Cruz del **Quiché**, a quaint town at 2,000 metres, colourful market on Sun. and Thurs. There are few tourists here and prices are consequently reasonable. Good selection of local cloth. Quiché's speciality is palm hats, which are made and worn in the area, best quality and prices from shop facing the bus terminal. Population 7,750. Remains 3 km. away of palaces of former Quiché capital, Gumarcaj, sometimes spelt Kumarkaah and known also as Utatlán, destroyed by Spaniards; the ruins consist of adobe mounds, their chief attraction being the setting. They can be reached on foot (¾-hr. walk W along 10 Calle from bus station) open 0700-1800, entry US$0.20. *Fiestas:* about August 14-20 (but varies around Assumption), May 3. Serious earthquake damage.

Hotels are reluctant to open doors late at night. *San Pascual*, 7 C. 0-43, F, with hot showers, clean, quiet, locked parking; *Hospedaje Hermano Pedro*, F, friendly, clean, private shower, close to bus terminal so arrive early; *Posada Calle Real*, 2 Av. 7-36, parking, F, clean, friendly, rec.; *Pensión Santa Clara*, G, hot water, plus US$0.50 for good meals; *Centroamérica*, G without bath, very basic; *Tropical*, 1 Av. 9 C., G. Basic accommodation near bus terminal. Restaurant: *Lago Azul*, 2 Av. 6-45, quite good, pricey; *Musicafé* and one next to it, with bookshop, reasonable; most are dirty. Thermal baths at Pachitac, 4 km. away, and beside the market building.

Electric Current 220 volts.

Cinema 3 Av. y 6 C.

Exchange Banco de Guatemala, 3 C. y 2 Av.

Post Office on 3 C., Zona 5; **Guatel**, on 1 Av. Zona 5.

Bicycle Hire 4 Av. y 5C., Zona 1 or 4 Av. y 2 C., Zona 5.

Buses Terminal at 10 C. y 1 Av. Reyna de Utatlán from Guatemala City (US$1.60). ½ hr. from Chichicastenango, US$0.30, every ½ hr. from *Pensión Chigüilá*. At 0930 to Nebaj, US$1.25, 5 hrs.; a rough but breathtaking trip (may leave early if full). At 1000, 1130 and 1330 to Uspantán, 5 hrs., US$1.25. Bus to Joyabaj, 0930 daily, US$0.50, 1½ hrs. 0300 bus Uspantán to Cobán and San Pedro Carchá, about 5 hrs., the best part is done in darkness. If going to Momostenango for the market, take the bus at 0400 as the 0800 one arrives too late (6 hr. journey).

There is a paved road E from Quiché to (8 km.) Santo Tomás Chiche, a picturesque village with a fine rarely-visited Indian Sat. market (*fiesta*, December 21-28). Buses and vans (US$0.25) run from Quiché. (There is also a road to this village from Chichicastenango. Although it is a short-cut, it is rough and should be attempted in dry weather only, and even then only in a sturdy vehicle.)

On 32 km. from Chiche is **Zacualpa,** where beautiful woollen bags are woven. There is an unnamed *pensión* near the square; on the square itself is a private house which has cheap rooms and meals. (Mosquito coils are a must.) Market: Sun., Thurs. Church with remarkably fine façade. On another 11 km. is **Joyabaj,** where women weave fascinating *huipiles*; there is nowhere to stay, but the mayor may have some ideas. This was a stopping place on the old route from Mexico to Antigua. During *fiesta* week (the second in August) Joyabaj has a *palo volador*—two men dangle from a 20-metre pole while the ropes they are attached to unravel to the ground. The villages of San Pedro and San Juan Sacatepéquez (**see page 1156**) can be reached from Joyabaj by a dry-season road suitable only for strong vehicles. The scenery en route is spectacular (Joyita bus, Guatemala City 3-4 Av. 7-9 C. Zona 4, to Joyabaj, US$1.50).

Road N from Quiché, 48 km., to **Sacapulas,** 1,220 metres, at foot of Cuchumatanes mountains, highest in the country. Bus from Quiché, at 0930, very crowded, US$1, 3 hrs. for rough journey; 6 buses to Quiché. Bus to Huehuetenango via Aguacatán (see below), at 0500, 4½ hrs, road can be closed in rainy season. Remains of bridge over Río Negro built by Las Casas. Primitive salt extraction. Market under large ceiba tree on Thursday and Sunday. The only *pensión* is *Comedor Gloris* near the bridge (G), which is basic, cheap and friendly, poor meals, US$0.65. British travellers are made very welcome at *Comedor Central* near the market. Colonial church with surprising treasures inside, built 1554, and there are communal hot springs.

The road E to Cobán from Sacapulas is one of the most beautiful, if rough, mountain roads in all Guatemala, with magnificent scenery in the narrow valleys. Truck to Cobán, 5 daily a.m., US$1.25, 5 hrs. There is no direct bus to Cobán; instead, take one of the three Quiché-Uspantán buses (passing Sacapulas at about 1230, 1400, 1600) to Uspantán, *fiesta* May 6-10 (US$0.60) stay the night at the *Viajero* (3 blocks E of Plaza, basic, G, clean, pleasant), then take early morning bus (0300-0400, you can spend the night on the bus before it leaves) or hitch-hike to Cobán. (Truck Uspantán-San Cristóbal Verapaz, US$1.25.) Buses to Quiché at 0530, 0700, 1530. A morning bus starts at 0200 in Quiché, with a change at Cunén (*fiesta* February 5-7, with dancing with silver deer masks, especially interesting at night; *Tienda y Comedor Rech Kanah María*, next to church, good; ask at *farmacia* where to stay). The road W of Sacapulas, through Aguacatán, to Huehuetenango is also beautiful.

Branching off this road, about 13 km. N of Sacapulas, is a spectacular road to the village of Nebaj (see below). It is easy enough to get by truck to Nebaj (US$0.50) and there is a daily bus from Quiché. It is not so easy to get to the other two villages of the Ixil Triangle, Chajul and Cotzal, though there is a bus to Chajul occasionally, and a small, basic *pensión* there, as well as a small *comedor*. Cotzal is now reported to have a *hospedaje*. There are no lodging or restaurant facilities in other small villages and it is very difficult to specify what transport facilities are in fact available in this area as trucks and the occasional pick-up or commercial van (probably the best bet—ask, especially in *Las Tres Hermanas*, Nebaj) are affected by road and weather conditions. For this reason, be prepared to have to spend the night in villages, even though there may be no accommodation. Chajul has a pilgrimage to Christ of Golgotha on the second Friday in Lent, beginning the Wednesday before (the image is escorted by "Romans" in blue police uniforms!) Also hunting with blowpipes. Chajul has market Tues. and Fri. In Cotzal it is possible to stay in the monastery, market Sat.

Nebaj has *Las Tres Hermanas*, G (friendly, full of character, but very basic), good food available for about US$0.50; *Las Gemelitas*, nice, basic, G without bath, rec.; *Hospedaje El Mundo*, Cantón Batzbacá, at road junction to Acul/Cotzal (look for sign to *hospedaje* and coffin maker, 18 metres), G without bath. Alternatively you can get a room in a private house for slightly less. *Comedor de Olimpia Irene Moreno*, 1 block S from square, painted blue-green, good. There is also an army camp. *Huipiles* may be bought from María Santiago Chel (central market) or Juana Marcos Solís (Cantón Simacol), who gives weaving lessons from 1 day to 6 months. This village has a very good Sun. market (also on Thurs.). Nebaj has a *fiesta* on August 15. There are magnificent walks from Nebaj along the river or in the surrounding hills. Although the weather is not very good at this altitude, the views of the Cuchumatanes mountains are spectacular. From Nebaj, bus to Sacapulas and Quiché 0100, 0300, and on Sun. 0800, 2½ hrs. to Sacapulas (US$0.60), a further 3 to Quiché.

There is good walking West of Nebaj, and the roads are better in this direction than to Chajul and Cotzal since there a number of "model villages" resettled by the government. These include Acul (1½ hrs. walking up-and-down from Nebaj, starting 2 blocks from *Las Tres Hermanas*, or 2½ hrs. walking along the road); there is a good cheese farm 1 km. before the village; Tzalbal, 2½ hrs. walking; Salquil Grande, 26 km. NW of Nebaj (several hours walk); La Pista, where the airstrip is. None has accommodation or restaurants; there is no public transport, only pick-ups. Las Violetas, 15 mins. walk from the centre of Nebaj, is a squatters' village where people who have come down from the mountains live when they arrive in Nebaj.

WESTERN GUATEMALA (6)

The stretch of Pan-American Highway between Los Encuentros and San Cristóbal Totonicapán runs past **Nahualá,** at 2,470 metres, a most interesting Indian village where *metates*, or stones on which maize is ground to make *tortillas*, are made. The inhabitants wear distinctive costumes, and are considered by other Indians to be somewhat hostile. Good church. Market on Thursdays and Sundays, at which finely embroidered cuffs and collars are sold, also very popular *huipiles*, but check the colours, many run. No accommodation except perhaps in Indian families at a small cost. *Fiesta* (Santa Catalina) on November 25. Population 1,369.

There is another all-weather road a little to the N and 16 km. longer, from Los Encuentros to San Cristóbal Totonicapán. In 40 km. it reaches Totonicapán.

Totonicapán, 14½ km. E of Cuatro Caminos (see below), is the capital of its Department, at 2,500 metres. Population 52,000, almost all Indian. There are sulphur baths, but they are dirty and crowded. Market (mind out for pickpockets) considered by Guatemalans to be one of the cheapest, and certainly very colourful, on Tues. (small), and Sat. (the main market noted for ceramics and cloth-very good); annual fair September 26-30; *fiestas* on September 29 and July 25. The school of handicrafts in the centre of town is well worth a visit. *Chuimekená* cooperative is at 3 C. between 7 and 8 Avs., Zona Palín. Frequent buses to Quezaltenango along a paved road (fine scenery), US$0.35, and there are buses from Quiché at 0400 and 0500 daily on a little-travelled but spectacular route (bus returns at 1030, US$1, 4 hrs). Bus to Los Encuentros, US$1.50.

Hotels On 4 Calle: *Pensión Rosario*, G, basic and dirty; *Hospedaje San Miguel*, 2 blocks from town square, F, clean, comfortable.

San Cristóbal Totonicapán, 1 km. from the **Cuatro Caminos** road junction (Pan-American Highway, with the roads to Quezaltenango, Totonicapán, Los Encuentros and Huehuetenango; *Hotel y Restaurant Reforma*, F, T 066-1438) has a huge church, built by Franciscan friars, of which the roof has recently been renovated. The silver lamps, altars and screens, all hand-hammered, and Venetian glass altars are worth seeing. Noted for textiles (and *huipiles* in particular) sold all over Guatemala; they are cheap here because the town is off the main tourist circuit. Also well known for ceramics. Market, Sunday, on the other side of the river from the church (only 2 blocks away), spreading along many streets. Annual fair, July 20-26. Altitude 2,340 metres, population 3,186. Two hotels. Bus service to Quezaltenango.

Excursion Two km. W of the Cuatro Caminos junction a road runs N to San Francisco El Alto (3 km.) and Momostenango (19 km.). *San Francisco El Alto,* at 2,640 metres (also reached by a new paved road 5 km. W of Cuatro Caminos, at Km. 151), stands in the mountain cold, above the great valley in which lie Totonicapán, San Cristóbal and Quezaltenango. Church of metropolitan magnificence. Crammed market on Friday; Indians buying woollen blankets for resale throughout country, and fascinating cattle market. An excellent place for buying woven and embroidered textiles of good quality, but beware of pickpockets. Colourful New Year's Day celebrations. It is a pleasant walk from San Francisco down to the valley floor, then along the river to San Cristóbal. There is a bus from Totonicapán at 0800 on Fri. Bus from Quezaltenango on Fri., 20 mins., from market terminus, US$0.35 (go early if you wish to avoid staying overnight).

Hotel *Hospedaje Central San Francisco de Asís* on main street near market, G. *Buena Vista,* F, clean but cold, no hot water.

Momostenango, at 2,220 metres, is the chief blanket-weaving centre. Indians can be seen beating the blankets on stones to shrink them. The Feast of the Uajxaquip Vats (pronounced "washakip") is celebrated by 30,000 Indians every 260 days by the ancient Mayan calendar. Frequent masked dances also. Momostenango means "place of the altars", and there are many on the outskirts but they are not worth looking for; there is, however, a hilltop image of a Mayan god, similar to the one outside Chichicastenango. There are said to be 300 medicine-men practising in the town; their insignia of office is a little bag containing beans and quartz crystals. Outside town are three sets of *riscos:* eroded columns of sandstone with embedded quartz particles, which are worth visiting. The most striking are the least accessible, in the hills to the N of the town. The town is quiet except on Wed. and Sun., the market days (the latter being larger, and interesting for weaving; also try Tienda Manuel del Jesús Agancel, 1 Av., 1-50, Zona 4; on non-market days, ask for weavers' houses). It has a spring-fed swimming pool; also a sulphur bath (5 in all) at Palo Grande, near town; the water is black, but worth experiencing. Bus service from Cuatro Caminos (US$0.35) and Quezaltenango, US$0.45.

Accommodation *Hospedaje Roxane,* G, bad; *Hospedaje Paclom,* G, basic, hot water, cheap meals. *Comedor Tonia,* friendly, cheap.

At San Cristóbal the old and the new routes of the Pan-American Highway, which joined at Los Encuentros, part again. The new route to the Mexican border at Ciudad Cuauhtémoc (not a town, despite its name: just a few buildings) goes NW, by-passing Huehuetenango before entering the Selegua canyon stretch, known as El Tapón, now in very good condition. The old route, running W to Tapachula, in Mexico, reaches, 5 km. from San Cristóbal, the small *ladino* town of

At *Salcajá,* jaspé skirt material has been woven since 1861. Yarn is tied and dyed, then untied and warps stretched around telephone poles along the road or along the riverside. Many small home weavers will sell the lengths—5 or 8 *varas*—depending on whether the skirt is to be wrapped or pleated. The finest, of imported English yarn, cost US$40. The Artexco cooperative is *San Luis,* Calle Capitán Juan de León y Cardona, Zona 2. Market, Tues.; it is early, as in all country towns. The church of San Jacinto behind the market is 16th century and also worth a visit. (Good restaurant, *Cafesama.*) The taxi rate is US$2.50-3 per hour. Several minibuses a day from new commercial centre, 10 Av. and 8 C.

Quezaltenango, 14½ km. SW of Cuatro Caminos, over 100,000 people, is the most important city in western Guatemala. Altitude 2,335 metres, and climate decidedly cool and damp (particularly November to April, and there is no heating anywhere). Set among a group of high mountains and volcanoes, one of which,

Santiaguito, the lower cone of Santa María (which can be easily climbed), destroyed the city in 1902 and is still active sometimes. A modern city, but with narrow colonial-looking streets and a magnificent plaza (between 11 and 12 Av. and 4 and 7 Calle). Especially interesting is the stately but quaint Municipal Theatre (14 Av. and 1 C.). There is a modern gothic-style church, the Sagrado Corazón, on the Parque Juárez near the market; other churches include San Juan de Dios on 14 Av. and La Transfiguración, from which there is a good view. The cathedral is modern with a 17th-century façade. A National Artisan Park has been built but is almost abandoned; there are a textile museum, warehouses, a craft school, showrooms, shop and restaurant. Festivals March 30-April 5, Sept. 12-18 and Holy Week (very interesting). There is a museum on the S side of the Parque Central, open Mon.-Fri., 0900-1700 (closed in December). A good centre for buses to all parts of the Indian highlands. Airfield. Tourist cards (free) for Mexico can be obtained from the Mexican consulate at the *Pensión Bonifaz*. (All addresses given are in Zona 1, unless otherwise stated.)

Warning   Local people always call the town by its old name of Xelajú, or "Xela" (pronounced "Shayla").

Hotels   At Easter, September 12-18 and Christmas, rooms need to be booked well in advance. *Pensión Bonifaz*, 4 C. 10-50, B, 3 meals US$7, good restaurant (really not a *pensión* but an excellent hotel), clean, comfortable, US cable TV in all rooms, quiet, lounge with fireplace (good for taking afternoon coffee); *Del Campo*, at city limits (4 km.) on road to Cuatro Caminos, C, good meals (European and Chinese), rec.; *Los Alpes*, Zona 3, Swiss-owned, private bath, rec.; *Centroamérica Inn*, Boulevard Minerva 14-09, Zona 3, D; *Modelo*, 14 Av. 'A', 2-31, D, good, with good restaurant; *Kiktem-Ja*, 13 Av. 7-18, E, all with bath, rec.; *Radar 99*, 13 Av. near C. 4, F with bath and hot water, cheaper without bath, friendly; *Canadá*, 4 C. 12-22, F, helpful, reasonable value; *Casa del Viajero*, 8 Av. 9-17, F, with bath, hot water, limited but good restaurant, English-speaking manager, helpful, rec.; *Pensión Altense*, 9 C. and 9 Av., F with bath (cheaper without), new part rec., meals US$0.75, good, hot water extra; *El Aguila*, 12 Av. and 3 C., F, friendly, hot water extra; *Residencial*, nearby, F, good.

Restaurants   *Bikini*, 10 C., behind municipal offices, Chinese restaurant next to *Hotel Canadá*; *Kopetin*, 1 block from *Hotel Canadá*, friendly, good, meat and seafood dishes; *Maruc*, near brewery, good but expensive; *Taberna de Don Rodrigo*, 14 Av. 2-42, hamburgers and beer, cakes and coffee; *Pizza Ricca*, 14 Av. y 3 C., fair; *Café Marzia*, 14 Av. y 3 C., pleasant; *Delicadezas La Polonesa*, 14 Av. 'A' 4-71, snacks, cold meats, sausage, etc.; *Ut's Hua*, Av. 12 y C. 3, good typical food; *La Rueda*, by University in Zona 3, good steaks, somewhat expensive; *Buena Vista* on square, reasonable; *El Portalito*, Av. 12 just above the square, good, cheap; *Coffee Center*, 4 C. 13-3, good cheap meals and coffee; *Pollo Chivo*, US$1 for chicken meals; *Pollos 24 Horas*, 13 Av. y 6 C., for bad but early food; *Hotel Modelo* restaurant (open earlier than most others); *La Oropendola*, 3 C., good light meals; *Bombonier*, 14 Av. 2-20, new, snacks, excellent pastries and ice-cream.

Shopping   *Artexco*, the National Federation of Artisans' Cooperatives, has its headquarters at 7 Av. 15-97, Zona 5, and at Local No. 12, Centro Comercial Municipal, very good value. For local items better to try the markets of which there are 4: main market at Templo de Minerva at Western edge of town (take local bus, US$0.04), has craft section; at the SE corner of Parque Centro América (central park) is a shopping centre with craft stalls on the upper levels, food, clothes, etc. below; another market at 2 C. y 16 Av., Zona 1, S of Parque Benito Juárez. Fine small boutique selling local handicrafts, handmade textiles and traditional costumes of excellent quality in *Los Mangos* restaurant. *Curiosidades La Chivita* makes up locally produced woollen blankets into jackets.

Laundry Minimax, Av. 14, No. C-47, 0730-1930, US$0.75, wash and dry.

Exchange   Many banks on the central plaza. Banco de Guatemala, W side, Mon.-Thurs. 0830-1400, Fri. to 1430.

Cinemas   Cadore, 13 Av. and 7 C., Roma, 14 Av. 'A' and Calle 'A'; from US$0.15.

Communications   Post and Telegraph Office, 15 Av. and 4 Calle, Telephone (Guatel) 15 Av. 'A' and 4 Calle.

Spanish Language Schools   KIN (a cooperative); another cooperative, English Club and International Language School, 3 Calle, 15-16, Zona 1, rec., also offers Maya classes. International School of Spanish, 8a. Avenida 6-33, Zona 1, Aptdo Postal 265 (T 061-4784), cost for 5 hrs': tuition, room and 3 meals a day: 2 weeks US$195, 3 weeks, US$285, 4 weeks, US$375. Proyecto Lingüístico Xelajú, 1 C, 16-87, Zona 1, T 2631.

Tourist Office SW corner of the Plaza, Mon.-Fri., 0900-1200, 1430-1700. Helpful. Free maps of city. Ask here for the Club de Andinismo for information on mountain climbing in the area.

Buses Rutas Lima, 4 a day to Guatemala City (US$2, 3½ hours). The 0800 bus has connections to Chichicastenango, Panajachel and Sololá (US$1.50, 2½ hrs.). Galgos, near La Rotonda, below *Hotel La Posada*, 1st class buses to Guatemala City, 5 a day (US$2.25, 4 hrs; will carry bicycles.). For Antigua, change at Chimaltenango (Galgos, US$2). Rutas Lima to Huehuetenango 0500 and 1530, US$0.75; to frontier at La Mesilla, 0500, US$2.25 (cheaper if change at Huehuetenango); to frontier at Talismán bridge 0500 via Tecún Umán (US$2.25, 5 hrs.). Rutas Lima to San Pedro **(see page 1183)** at 1200. Regular buses from 10 Av., 8 C. to Cuatro Caminos US$0.75 (where buses for Guatemala City and Huehuetenango stop on the highway; bus Guatemala City-Cuatro Caminos, US$1.65), Totonicapán, 1 hr. (US$0.35) San Francisco El Alto (US$0.35) and Momostenango (0600, US$0.45). Also many second class buses to many parts of the country from Zona 3 market (13 Av. 4 C.° A"), e.g. Transportes Velásquez to Huehuetenango, US$0.65; to Malacatán, US$1.25; to Los Encuentros, US$1.20; to Chichicastenango, US$0.65, 1200, 2 hrs.; to Zunil, US$0.30; also to La Mesilla at 0800.

Excursions Many places of interest around on roads N to Huehuetenango, W to San Marcos and Mexico, S to Ocós and Champerico. Six km. SE is *Almolonga,* which is noted for its fine 16th-century church and beautiful costumes, especially skirts, which are hard to buy. There is also an interesting vegetable market. *Fiesta* June 29. Good swimming pool (entrance, US$0.25). About 1 km. further on are the thermal baths of Cirilo Flores (US$0.50 for large pool, US$1 to soak for an hour, hot, soothing water but heavily used— frequently cleaned) and El Recreo (entrance, US$0.30); bus from Quezaltenango, US$0.15. The Fuentes Georginas hot springs, 15 km. from Quezaltenango, are mentioned under Zunil **(page 1184)**. Take picnic or barbecue equipment, but it might be best to avoid Sundays when the Guatemalans descend on the springs. There are also hot steam baths at Los Vahos, reached by a dirt road to the right (3 km.) on the outskirts of town on the road to Almolonga; a taxi will take you there and back with a one-hour wait for US$1.50. El Baúl, a hill to the E, may be reached by winding road, or direct trail to the top where there is a cross (visible from the city), monument to Tecún Umán. To reach the Santa María volcano take bus to Llano del Piñal (every 30 mins. or when full from the Shell station on Av. 9; last bus back from Llano del Piñal leaves at 1830). Get off at cross roads and follow dirt road until it sweeps up to the right, where you should take the footpath on left; bear right at the saddle where another path comes in from left—look carefully, it is easily missed. A rough 4½-hr. climb (1,435 metres) but worth it for the superb views of the Pacific and to watch the still active crater, Santiaguito, on the Pacific side. The volcano can also be reached from Retalhuleu **(see page 1184)** by bus to Palajunoz, from where it is also a 4½-hr. climb.

Travellers to Huehuetenango normally go via Cuatro Caminos and the Pan-American Highway, but there is a direct road N through mountainous farmland.

According to folklore, at Olintepeque, an Indian town 6 km. from Quezaltenango (on a road parallel to the main road, ½ day's good walk), the greatest battle of the conquest was fought, and Alvarado slew King Tecún Umán in single combat. Its river is still known as Xequizel, the river of blood. Market, Tuesday; *fiestas*, June 24, August 29 (beware of theft). The local idol, San Pascual Baillón, has its own little church. The direct road climbs 18 km. to San Carlos Sija, at 2,642 metres, with wide views. The Spanish strain is still noticeable amongst the inhabitants, most of whom are tall and fair. A climb through conifers for another 10 km. to Cumbre del Aire, with grand views behind volcanoes, and ahead of Cuchumatanes mountains. Another 25 km. to the junction with the Pan-American Highway.

From Cuatro Caminos the Pan-American Highway climbs for several km. before dropping down past the *ladino* town of Malacatancito (48 km.) and swinging NW through the **Selegua (El Tapón)** gap to Mexico.

A 6½ km. spur from this road leads to **Huehuetenango,** a mining centre in farming country, with Indians from remote mountain fastnesses coming in for the daily market, and particularly Thurs. and Sun. Fair, July 12-18. Racecourse. Population, 20,000; altitude, 1,905 metres. The Honorary Mexican Consul at the Farmacia del Cid (5 Av. and 4 C.) will provide you with a Mexican visa or tourist card for US$1; Huehuetenango is the last town before the La Mesilla border post, on the Pan-American Highway into Mexico.

Hotels *Centro Turístico Pino Montano*, at Km. 259 on the Pan-American Highway, 2 km. past the fork to Huehuetenango on the way to La Mesilla (swimming pool); *Zaculeu*, poor food in restaurant, 5 Av., 1-14, Zona 1, E, clean; *Gran Shinula*, 4 C., E with bath, negotiate for cheaper rate, restaurant; *Mary*, 2 C. 3-52, Zona 1, F with bath, cheaper without; *Pensión Astoria*, 4 Av., N of Plaza, F, good meals; *Palacio*, 2 C. 5-49, E, incl. 3 meals; *Central*, 5 Av., 1-33, G, communal baths, basic, meals available, washing facilities; *Auto Hotel Vásquez*, 2 C. 6-67, 2 blocks W of Plaza, F, with bath, clean; *Maya*, 3 Av., 3-55, F, with bath, hot water, clean, good value; *Hospedaje El Viajero*, 2 C., 5-20 Zona 1, G, basic but friendly. There are a number of cheap *pensiones* on 1 Av., by the market, including **Pensión San Román**, G, basic, friendly, convenient for bus stations; near market, **Tikal 2**, G, friendly, hot shower extra; **Tikal**, G (reasonably clean), **San Antonio**, next door, G, and **Centroamericana**, 1 Av., 4-85, G. N.B. The cheap *hostales* (F and under) are not rec. for single women.

Camping   at Zaculeu ruins, or further on the same road at the riverside.

Restaurants   All hotel restaurants are open to the public. **Los Alpes**, 2 C., good; **Superlyckoss**, 2 C., quite good; **L'Emperador**, 2 Av. near 2 C., excellent; **Las Magnolias**, 4 C. and 6 Av. are best of the central restaurants; **Cafetería Las Palmeras**, very good, close to Plaza; **Pizza Hogarena**, 6 Av. between 4C and 5C, rec.; **Damasco**, 4 Av., N of Plaza; **Taberna del Conquistador**, ½ km. S of town, peaceful location; **Snoopy's Helados**. **Tienda Santa Marta**, 6 C. is good café; **Rico Mac Pollo**, 3 Av., for chicken; numerous cheap **comedores** on E side of market including **Ideal**, and W side of Plaza; **Doña Estercita's**, 2 C., coffee and pastries, rec.

Shopping   Artexco, Local No. 10, Centro Comercial Xinabajul. In the Huehuetenango area are two Artexco cooperatives: *La Jacaltequita*, at Jacaltenango, and *La Guadalupana*, at San Miguel Acatán.

Cinema   Lili on 3 Calle, W of Plaza, often has films in English.

Swimming Pool   Known as Brasilia, entry US$0.50, ½ hr. walk SE of town.

Exchange   Banco de Guatemala, 4 C. and 5 Av., Mon.-Thurs., 0830-1400, Fri., 0830-1430, will exchange Mexican pesos for quetzales. Several local banks, some open Sat. a.m. Cambio at travellers' cheques. Try also the hairdresser near Banco Café for good rates for pesos. Cambio at bus station, touts will find you.

Post and Phones   telephone in Guatel office on SW corner of Plaza; cable service at post office, Av. 15, C.4.

Spanish Language Schools   Most operate in the summer months only. Casa Xelajú, Aptdo. Postal 302, 6 C., 7-42, Zona 1, runs classes all year, US$185 for first week, or US$675 for first month, reduced rates thereafter, accommodation, meals, laundry with family, individual tuition, 5 hrs., a day, films, seminars, field trips included.

Buses   To Guatemala City (about 5 hrs.): US$2.60. Los Halcones, 7 Av., 3-62, Zona 1, 0700, 1400, reliable; El Cóndor, 5 a day. To Zaculeu, 3 Av. 5-25, 0600 and 1500. Los Flamingos, S side of market, 0445. To La Mesilla: (2 hrs.), buses hourly, US$0.50; US$0.75 Pullman); Los Verdes, 1 Av. 1-34, 0500 and 1330, US$0.50; Osiris, 1 Av. and 3 C., 0430, 1030, 1230, US$0.50; López, 4 C. 2-39, 0630, US$0.50. To Cuatro Caminos, for Quezaltenango, Momostenango and Totonicapán, US$0.50; to Los Encuentros, for Lake Atitlán and Chichicastenango, US$1.50; to Sacapulas, US$0.75, 1200 (Rutas Zaculeu, returns 0600); direct bus to Nebaj at 1200; to Nentón, Cuilco and other outlying villages, enquire on 1 Av. near market. Beware of touts at the bus station who tell you, as you arrive from the border, that the last bus to wherever you want to go is about to leave; it's probably not true.

Car Insurance   for Mexico and Guatemala can be arranged at Granai & Townson, next door to Mexican Consulate (see above).

Ruins of **Zaculeu,** old capital of the Mam tribe, pyramids, a ball court and a few other structures, completely reconstructed, concrete stepped forms, devoid of any ornamentation (museum), 5 km. NW on top of a rise ringed by river and *barrancas* (admission US$0.50, closes 1600). Yellow Alex bus runs at 1030, 1330 and 1530 as long as at least 5 people are going (fare US$0.05) and regular minibuses (US$0.15) to the ruins from *Hotel Maya*. It is possible to walk to the ruins in about 60 mins.

Chiantla, 5 km. N of Huehuetenango, has a great pilgrimage to the silver Virgin of La Candelaria on February 2. Another *fiesta* on September 8. Daily market, largest on Sun. Buses leave regularly from 1 Av. and 1 Calle. Road runs N 117 km. to **San Mateo Ixtatán**, at 2,530 metres, in the Cuchumatanes mountains. The *huipiles* made there are unique and are much cheaper than in Huehuetenango. The road passes through San Juan Ixcoy, Soloma (*Mansión Katty* rec.; *Hospedaje San Ignacio*), and Santa Eulalia (*Nuevo Hotel Río Lindo*, D-E with bath, hot water, parking; rec.; *Hospedaje El Cisne*, G). San Mateo itself (very basic *pensión*, G, bring own sheets or sleeping bag) is a colourful town, with an interesting old church and black salt mines nearby. Bus from Huehuetenango to San Juan Ixcoy, Soloma, Santa Eulalia, San Mateo Ixtatán and Barillas leaves at 0200, very crowded, be early and get your name high up on the list as passengers are called in order. The bus returns to Huehuetenango from San Mateo (at least 5 hrs.) at 1330, but it is advised to take two days over the trip. Solomerita buses (1 Av. and 2 C.) run as far as Soloma, at 0500 and 1300. 5 km. beyond the turn off to Todos Santos Cuchumatán the road becomes rough, narrow and steep; north of Santa Eulalia it is impassable for passenger cars.

After San Mateo the road runs 27 km. E to Barillas (several cheap *pensiones, Terraza* rec., G): a fine scenic route. Some 13 km. N of Chiantla is a viewpoint with magnificent views over mountain and valley.

The village of **Todos Santos Cuchumatán** (*Hospedaje Tres Olguitas*, G, friendly, basic, cheap meals; *Hospedaje La Paz*, F, better, but fleas and cold, enclosed parking, shared showers; *Katty* is the better of the two cheap *comedores*) is very interesting (3,481 metres); some of Guatemala's best weaving is done there, and fine *huipiles* may be bought in the cooperative on the main street and possibly at the makers' huts. There are also embroidered cuffs and collars for men's shirts, and colourful crotcheted bags made by the men. There is an Artexco cooperative, *Estrella de Occidente*. A fair selection of old woven items can be bought from a small house behind the church. The Sat. market is fascinating. One can learn backstrap weaving here; a rec. teacher is Srta. Santa Jiménez J. *Fiesta:* Nov. 1, characterized by a horse race in which riders race between two points, having a drink at each turn until they fall off. Market bus from Huehuetenango at 1100, 2½ hrs., US$0.65, crowded on Fri. (return at 0500 and 1200). Sat. bus at 1100 arrives after market has finished, and there is no afternoon return. The drive is spectacular, ascending to 4,381 metres (according to the sign), but much of the land has been overgrazed and there is much soil erosion.

From Todos Santos, one can walk to San Juan Atitán, 5 hrs. (more interesting costumes; Artexco cooperative *Atiteca* and from there the highway, 1 day's walk). Also, walk to San Martín (3 hrs.), or Santiago Chimaltenango (7 hrs., stay in school, ask at Municipalidad; the Artexco cooperative here is *Flor de Pascua*), then to San Pedro Necta, and on to the Pan-American Highway for bus back to Huehuetenango. **N.B.** Remember the warning on violence in this region.

The views are fine on the road which runs between Huehuetenango and Sacapulas. **Aguacatán** at 1,670 metres is 26 km. E of Huehuetenango, 36 km. from Sacapulas (*Pensión La Paz*, G; unsigned *Hospedaje*, 2 blocks E of market and 1 North, G). Aguacatán has an interesting market on Sunday (beginning Saturday night) and Thursday (excellent peanuts). The women wear beautiful costumes and head-dresses.

The source of the Río San Juan is about 2 km. past the centre of Todos Santos town (signposted); there is a small admission charge to the park, which is a delightful place for a freezing cold swim. Camping is permitted. Los Verdes, 1 Av. 2-34, has buses to Aguacatán at 1300 (last return bus at 1500, 3½-hr. journey), US$0.50, and buses for **Sacapulas**, Quiché, Nebaj and Cobán pass through the village. There are jeeps, Huehuetenango-Aguacatán. Zaculeu, 1 Av. 2-53, to Sacapulas, 1400, 2 hrs. US$1 (truck at 1630, arrives 2000, US$1), and from the same place Alegres Mañanitas has a bus to Quiché at 0415. Bus to Chichicastenango from Aguacatán 0400, very crowded, or take a truck. The Campo Alegre company has buses to Nebaj from the *Hospedaje San José*, 1 Av. and 4 C. 'A', and buses for Cobán leave from the same area.

The Pan-American Highway runs W to La Mesilla, the Guatemalan border post, and on 3.7 km. to Ciudad Cuauhtémoc (just a few buildings), the Mexican border point, a very good and interesting route. Rooms at Ciudad Cuauhtémoc and La Mesilla (both very basic); best to avoid having to stay at either, by leaving Huehuetenango early. There is nowhere to change dollars into pesos at the border and on the Mexican side, quetzales cannot be changed into pesos; coming into Guatemala, the peso-quetzal rate is better than the dollar-quetzal rate (don't change dollars until Huehuetenango or, better still, Guatemala City). The Guatemalan authorities charge Q3 exit tax. Outside the hours of 0800-1200, 1400-1800, an extra US$0.50 is charged. A US$0.20 "bridge tax" (!) may also be demanded. Mexican visas are unobtainable at the border. From Ciudad Cuauhtémoc, Cristóbal Colón and Transportes Tuxtla buses go to Comitán and San Cristóbal de Las Casas. There is a taxi, US$0.40 p.p., between the border posts during the day; Mexican officials charge exorbitant fees for transport between the border posts.

Buses from La Mesilla to Huehuetenango US$0.50 or US$0.75 (first class). Express buses go to Guatemala City. Change at Los Encuentros for Lake Atitlán and Chichicastenango, and at Chimaltenango or San Lucas for Antigua.

Quezaltenango W to Mexico   Eighteen km. to San Juan Ostuncalco, at 2,530 metres, noted for good twice-weekly market and beautiful sashes worn by men. *Fiesta*, Virgen de la Candelaria, Feb. 2. See below for road S to Pacific town of Ocós. The road, which is paved, switchbacks 60 km. down valleys and over pine-clad mountains to a plateau looking over the valley in which are San Pedro and San Marcos, also known as La Unión. Interesting town hall, known as the Maya Palace. *San Marcos,* at 2,350 metres, is 2 km. or so beyond San Pedro. *San Pedro* has a huge market every Thurs. Its Sun. market is less interesting. The Indian women wear golden-purple skirts. (Weaving lessons from Rosa Cruz, who is good and patient, US$1). Tajumulco volcano, 4,200 metres (the highest in Central America), can be reached by taking the road from San Marcos to San Sebastián; after the latter, several km. on is the summit of a pass at which a junction to the right goes to Tacana, and to the left is the start of the ascent of Tajumulco, about 5 hours' climb. Once you have reached the ridge on Tajumulco, turn right along the top of it; there are two peaks, the higher is on the right. The one on the left is used for shamanistic rituals; people are not very friendly, so do not climb alone. Tacana volcano may be climbed from Sibinal village. About 15 km. W of San Marcos the road begins its descent from 2,500 metres to the lowlands. In 53 km. to *Malacatán* it drops to 366 metres, one of the toughest stretches in Central America—even for 4-wheel drive vehicles. It is a tiring ride with continuous bends, but the scenery is attractive.

Hotels   At San Marcos: *Pérez*, with good dining room, G, meals US$0.50; *Palacio*, G, without bath; *Pensión Minerva*, G, basic. At San Pedro: *El Valle*, G, said to be good. *Bagod*, G. At Malacatán: *América*, F, lunch, US$1, good; *Pensión Santa Lucía*, G; *Hospedaje Santa Emilia*, G; *Hospedaje La Predilecta*, G; *Hospedaje Rodríguez*, G, good.

The international bridge over the Suchiate river at Talismán into Mexico is 18 km. W of Malacatán. Beyond the bridge the road goes on to Tapachula; most of the motor traffic from Mexico comes down this road. From Quezaltenango to Tapachula: take 1200 Rutas Lima bus from Quezaltenango to San Pedro; from bus terminal on 4 Av. in San Pedro, frequent local buses from 0430 to 1630 to Malacatán, from where colectivos will get you to the border with ease, arriving Tapachula about 1800.

There is a Mexican consular service at the border, and at Malacatán (closed after 1300). Travelling by bus to Mexico is quicker from Quezaltenango than from San Marcos. Most traffic seems to go via Coatepeque and Quezaltenango and not via San Marcos; the former road is longer but is reported very good. There is one direct bus from the border to Quezaltenango in the early morning (Rutas Lima, US$2). Otherwise you must make your way to Malacatán (only one bus a day, at 1500, US$0.15) from where there are 3 buses a day to Quezaltenango. Beware of overcharging on buses from the border to Quezaltenango. Bus Talismán-Guatemala City, US$3.25, 6½ hrs. because of checkpoints.

Quezaltenango to Ocós   After San Juan Ostuncalco (see above) S for 1½ km. to *Concepción Chiquirichapa,* one of the wealthiest villages in the country. It has a small market early every Thursday morning. 5½ km. to *San Martín* (sometimes known as Chile Verde; this village appears in Miguel Angel Asturias' *Mulata de Tal*), in a windy, cold gash in the mountains. *Huipiles* and shirts from the cottage up behind the church. Accommodation next door to the Centro de Salud (ask at the Centro), US$0.50. Food in *comedor* opposite church, US$0.20. Indians speak a dialect of Mam not understood by other Maya tribes, having been separated from them during the Quiché invasion of the Guatemalan highlands. The men wear very striking costumes. *Fiesta*, November 11 (lasts 5 days). Ceremonies of witchdoctor initiation held on May 2 at nearby Lake Chicabel, in crater of volcano. The walk to the lake from San Martín takes about 2 hrs; there are two paths. The last bus to Quezaltenango leaves at 1900. Road descends to lowlands. From Colomba a road branches S (28 km.) to Retalhuleu: the road to Ocós runs 21 km. W from Colomba to *Coatepeque,* at 700 metres, with a population of 13,657; one of the richest coffee zones in the country; also maize, sugar-cane and bananas, and cattle. Fair, March 10-15.

Hotels   at Coatepeque: *Europa*, 6 C., 4-01, E; *Virginia*, at km. 220, E; *Beachli*, 6 C., 5-35, E; *Posada Santander*, 6 C., 6-43, F. Bus from Quezaltenango, US$0.38.

Both railway and paved Pacific Highway go to

Tecún Umán, 34 km. W, on the Mexican frontier, separated by the Suchiate river from the Mexican town of Suchiate. This is an alternative crossing point to the Talismán bridge and many buses run to it from Guatemala. It is quite a quick border crossing. Buses run from the Mexican side of the border to Tapachula, ½ hr., cheap (beware of overcharging). (Be warned, however, that you have to walk across a very long bridge (toll, US$0.20) over the river between the two border posts.) The bus to the capital costs US$3.25. Colectivo from Coatepeque, US$0.50. Trains to Guatemala City, Wed., Fri. and Sun., depart 0700, arrive 1800, US$1.40. Road N to Malacatán for international road bridge into Mexico. Population 4,250. Hotels: *La Perla; Pensión Rosita.*

Ocós, a small port now closed to shipping, is served by a 22-km. road S from Tecún Umán. Across the river from Ocós is *Tilapa*, a small resort; buses from Coatepeque and ferries from Ocós (*Pensión Teddy*, G, friendly, but said to have deteriorated). The swimming is good, but both here and at Ocós there are sharks, so stay close to the shore.

Quezaltenango to Champerico, via Retalhuleu: a 53-km. link between the old Pan-American Highway and Pacific Highway, paved all the way. A toll (Quezaltenango-Retalhuleu, US$0.25) is collected. The first town (11 km.) is *Cantel*, which has the largest textile factory in the country. There are three Artexco cooperatives: *Ixchel*, at Xecán; *Monja Blanca*, Barrio Centenario Antiguo; *Copavic*, a cooperative of glassblowers. Market, Sunday; *fiestas*, August 15 and a passion play at Easter.

Nine km. from Quezaltenango is *Zunil*, picturesquely located in canyon of Samalá river. Market, Mon., Fri. for vegetables (beware pickpockets); *fiesta*, November 25, and a very colourful procession on Palm Sunday. Striking church, inside and out. The local idol is San Simón, described by a traveller as a plastic tailor's dummy, dressed in ski wear: ski hat, scarf, gloves and sunglasses; the statue is lodged in a 2-storey green house on the left uphill from the main plaza. Behind the church is a cooperative (*Santa Ana*, a member of Artexco) which sells beautiful *huipiles*, and shirt and skirt materials. Zunil mountain, on which are the thermal baths of Fuentes Georginas 6 km. to the E (entrance US$0.50; rooms for night with individual hot spring baths, E), in attractive surroundings. They can be reached either by walking the 8 km., uphill (300 metres' ascent; take right fork after 4 km.) to south of Zunil, a beautiful route, or by truck (US$2.50 to hire). Alternatively, take the bus from Quezaltenango to Mazatenango, but get out at the sign to Fuentes Georginas, from where it is 8 km. to the springs. The springs are 13 km. from Almolonga (see page 1180).

The road descends through Santa María de Jesús (large hydro-electric station) to *San Felipe*, at 760 metres, 35 km. from Zunil. Tropical jungle fruits. Spur line to Mulua, on Guatemalan Railways. Beyond, 3 km., is San Martín, with a branch road to Mazatenango. The thermal baths of Aguas Amargas are also on Zunil mountain, below Fuentes Georginas; they are reached by a road E before Santa María de Jesús is reached. **N.B.** The main road by-passes San Felipe, which has a one-way road system (delays of up to 1½ hrs. if you go through the town).

Mazatenango, 18 km. from San Martín, is chief town of the Costa Grande zone. Altitude 380 metres, population 21,000. Chitalón airfield 3 km. away. The Pacific Highway passes through. Road paved to Quezaltenango.

Hotels *Jumay*, G; *Alba*, E; *La Gran Tasca*, F; *Roma*, F; *Costa Rica*, G; *Pensión Mejía*, G, without bath. **Motel** *Texas.*

SW 11 km. from San Martín is *Retalhuleu*, at 240 metres, a town of 42,000 people on the Pacific Highway and on Guatemalan Railways to border with Mexico. It serves a large number of coffee and sugar estates. *Fiesta*, December 6-12.

Hotels *Astor, Modelo*, both on 5 C. and 4 Av, and both F; *Pacífico*, G, next to new market; *Posada de Don José*, 3 Av. "A", 5-14, E. **Motel** *La Colonia* (swimming pool), 1½ km. to the N, is good, E.

Trains to the capital on Wed., Fri. and Sun. at 0900.

N.B. Retalhuleu is normally referred to as "Reu", both in conversation and on bus signs.

Champerico, 43 km. SW of Retalhuleu by a paved road, once the third most important port in the country, is little used now. Population 4,500. Good beach, though the sand is black and there is a strong undercurrent; good fishing.

Hotels *Martita*, F, without private bath; *Miramar*, F; *Posada del Mar*, E on outskirts of town; *Hospedaje Recinos*, G, and *Hospedaje Buenos Aires*, G, are both very basic.

Post Office two blocks behind *Hotel Martita*, in direction of port.

Buses Last bus to Quezaltenango departs at 1700. Every 30 mins. to Retalhuleu. Direct bus to Guatemala City, 0300 and 0600, 4-5 hrs.

THE ECONOMY

In international trade the accent is still heavily on agriculture, which accounts for some 65% of total exports. Coffee accounts for about 40% of exports, followed by bananas and cotton about 7% each, but sugar, soya, sorghum and cardamom are also important crops. There has been an attempt to diversify agricultural exports with tobacco, vegetables, fruit and ornamental plants, and beef exports are increasing.

The industrial sector has been growing steadily; the main activities, apart from food and drink production, include rubber, textiles, paper and pharmaceuticals. Chemicals, furniture, petroleum products, electrical components and building materials are also produced. Local industries, encouraged by tax remissions and tariff barriers, are gradually eliminating the need for imported consumer goods. Guatemala's exports (mostly industrial) to the other Central American countries account for about 25% of its total exports.

Petroleum has been discovered at Las Tortugas and Rubelsanto in the Department of Alta Verapaz. The Rubelsanto find is estimated to have proven and probable reserves of 27.3 m barrels, with production from this field and from West Chinajá running at 6,600 bpd. A pipeline to transport oil from Rubelsanto to the port of Santo Tomás de Castilla has been completed. Exploration is continuing in both the Rubelsanto area and in the nearby department of El Petén. New wells, for prospects are good, are at Yalpemech, Xan and Caribe. Offshore exploration has so far been unsuccessful. In order to lessen imports of petroleum, five hydroelectricity projects have been developed. Aguacapa (90 Mw) and Chixoy (300 Mw) are already completed and could satisfy electricity needs until the 1990s.

Guatemala's poor growth record in first half of the 1980s was attributable to the world recession bringing low agricultural commodity prices, particularly for coffee, and political instability both at home and in neighbouring Central American countries. The return to democracy and economic restructuring brought confidence and higher rates of growth as inflows of foreign funds were renewed. Other factors improving the balance of payments included moderate imports, rising exports, a rebound in tourism and selective debt rescheduling arrangements.

	1960-71 (av)	1971-80 (av)	1981-85 (av)	1986-88 (av)
Gdp growth (1980 prices)	5.5%	5.6%	-1.3%	2.5%
Inflation	0.8%	9.6%	7.5%	20.3%
Exports (fob) US$m	198	804	1,149	1,042
Coffee	81	283	364	172
Sugar	6	57	71	23
Cotton	30	100	81	12
Imports (fob) US$m	195	848	1,128	1,228
Current account balance US$m (cum)	-265	-974	-1,819	-925

INFORMATION FOR VISITORS

By Air From London, fly British Airways, Pan Am, Continental or Virgin Atlantic to Miami, and Eastern and Pan Am fly from Miami daily to Guatemala

City. Other carriers from the USA: from Miami: Aviateca, Taca (via San Salvador), Sahsa (via Tegucigalpa); from Houston: Aviateca, Taca (via San Salvador), Sahsa (via Tegucigalpa); from New Orleans: Aviateca, Taca (via San Salvador), Sahsa (via Tegucigalpa); from Los Angeles: Pan Am, Taca, Lacsa, Mexicana; from San Francisco: Pan Am, Taca; from New York: Lacsa, Eastern. From Europe, KLM fly to Guatemala from Amsterdam (via Netherlands Antilles, and San José); Iberia from Madrid via Santo Domingo and Panama.

Carriers from Central America/Caribbean: from San Salvador: Taca, Copa, Pan Am. From Tegucigalpa: Taca, Sahsa. From San Pedro Sula: Sahsa. From Mexico: Aviateca, Mexicana, Aeronica. From Belize: Taca (via San Salvador), Sahsa (via Tegucigalpa). From Managua: Copa, Aeronica, Taca (via San Salvador). From San José: Lacsa, SAM, Copa, Mexicana. From Panama: Copa, Iberia, Taca (via San Salvador). From Kingston (Jamaica): Copa (via Panama). From San Andrés: SAM. Carriers from South America: flight connections through Panama/San José, e.g. Barranquilla (Lacsa), Caracas (Copa), Medellín (Copa), Cartagena (Copa) etc. **N.B.** You will have to have an outward ticket from Colombia to be allowed a visa; round trip tickets Guatemala-Colombia are stamped "Refundable only in Guatemala", but it is possible either to sell the return part on San Andrés island—at a discount—or to change it to an alternative destination. There are no direct flights to Peru or Ecuador; connections via Panama or Colombia. Round-trips Miami-Guatemala are good value, and useful if one does not want to visit other Central American countries. MCOs are not sold in Guatemala.

By Sea   There are passenger services between Antwerp, Göteborg and Stockholm and Puerto Quetzal, and between Rotterdam, New York (6½ days) and New Orleans (4 days) and Santo Tomás de Castilla. None of the freight lines represented in Guatemala City makes passenger reservations; the only way to get passage on a freighter is to see the captain.

Taxes   There is a 15% ticket tax, single or return, on all international tickets sold in Guatemala. A stamp tax of 2% is payable on single, return, baggage tickets and exchange vouchers issued in Guatemala and paid for in or out of the country. A US$5 tourism tax is levied on all tickets sold in Guatemala to Guatemalan residents for travel abroad. There is also a US$7 (Q20) airport departure tax, and an entry tax of Q1/US$1 and a departure tax of Q3/US$3 if travelling overland. An additional US$0.50 is charged outside official working hours (0800-1200, 1400-1800).

British Business Travellers   should read "Hints to Exporters: Guatemala", obtainable from Dept. of Trade, Export Services Division, Sanctuary Buildings, 16-20 Great Smith St., London SW1P 3DB.

Business and commercial offices are open from 0800-1200, and 1400-1800 except Saturdays. Shops: 0800-1200, 1400-1800, but 0800-1200 on Saturday. Banks in Guatemala City: 0900-1500. In the interior banks tend to open earlier in the morning and close for lunch, and be open later. Government offices open 0700-1530.

Documents   Necessary, a passport and a tourist card, issued free by the airlines or at the border (best to get it in advance, though), or a visa issued before arrival, but very few nationalities need a visa. Among those that do are the UK, Canada, Ireland and Australia (valid for 30 days, US$10, must be used within 30 days). It is advised that identification should always be carried. Tourist cards (US$1) are valid for 30 days from day of issue, then 6 months from entry into Guatemala (they allow the tourist to leave the country and return once provided that the time outside Guatemala is not more than 30 days). They must be renewed in Guatemala City after 30 days at the Migración office, on the corner of 12 C. and 8 Av., Zona 1, open weekdays 0800-1630. This office extends visas and renews tourist cards on application (before noon) for 30 days at a time (up to 90 days maximum)—takes 1 day. Renewing a visa takes 14 days, costs US$10, fingerprints and photograph required, and you may not be given the full 90 days. Those wishing to make more than one visit should try to get a multiple-entry visa (there are, apparently, no multiple-entry tourist cards). If experiencing obstruction in renewing a visa, it is easier to leave the country for 3 days and then come back.

If you wish to stay longer than 90 days, you must have a Guatemalan guarantor whose financial resources must be vouched for. Tourist cards are not issued to nationals of communist countries, nor to black people unless they are citizens of the USA. Visitors staying less than 30 days, and holders of tourist cards, do not need an exit permit, which costs US$2.50. There is a fine of US$10 per day for overstaying a visa, payable as you leave the country.

Borders are open 24 hours, but outside the official border crossing hours 0800-1200, 1400-1800, weekdays and 0800-1200 Sat., a surcharge of US$0.50 is charged. Although not officially required, some airlines may not allow you to board a flight to Guatemala without an outward ticket (e.g. SAM in Colombia). Bribery is rife at border crossings; the Government is trying to eliminate overcharging for tourist cards and entry and exit taxes. Always ask for a receipt and, if you have time and the language ability, do not give in to corrupt officials.

Tourists can get an entry permit from the customs to take their cars into Guatemala for 30 days (US$10 or Q10), renewable at the Aduana, 10 C. 13-92, Zona 1. There is an exit tax for cars of US$1.50, and to take a car across the Mexico-Guatemala border costs US$5.50. There is also a charge of US$2.50 when the whole car is fumigated on entry. Spare tyres for cars and motorcycles must be listed in the vehicle entry permit, otherwise they are liable to confiscation. It is better not to import and sell foreign cars in Guatemala as import taxes are very high.

You are allowed to take in, free of duty, personal effects and articles for your own use, 2 bottles of spirit and 80 cigarettes or 100 grams of tobacco. Once every 6 months you can take in, free, dutiable items worth US$100. Temporary visitors can take in any amount in quetzales or foreign currencies; they may not, however, take out more than they brought in. The local equivalent of US$100 per person may be reconverted into US dollars on departure at the airport, provided a ticket for immediate departure is shown.

Warning Be prepared for frequent police checks between the Mexican border and Quezaltenango. See also under **Clothing** below.

Information Instituto Guatemalteco de Turismo (Inguat), 7 Av. 1-17, Zona 4, Guatemala, provides bus timetables, hotel and camping lists and road maps. Tourist information is provided at the Mexican border for those entering Guatemala. Recommended reading: Loraine Carlson, *A Traveller's Guide to Yucatán and Guatemala*, Paul Glassman's *Guatemala Guide*, and *Guatemala for You* by Barbara Balchin de Koose. Maps include Belize as Guatemalan territory. Roads marked in the Petén are inaccurate.

Road Travel The paved roads are very bad in places and generally poor, and the dirt roads are often very bad. Identification should be carried at all times. Stopping is compulsory: if driving your own vehicle, watch out for the "ALTO" sign. When driving, keep at least 200 metres in front of, or behind, army vehicles; their drivers are concerned about attacks on military personnel. Most buses are in a poor state of repair and breakdowns can be expected; they are always overloaded. Although recent government legislation has reduced problems of overcrowding, it is still difficult to get on buses in mid route. The correct fare should be posted up; if not, ask your neighbours. Hitchhiking is comparatively easy, but increasingly risky, especially for single women, also beware of theft of luggage, especially in trucks. The only way to retrieve "lost" luggage is by telling the police the vehicle registration number. Gasoline costs US$1.10 "normal", US$1.15 "extra" for the U.S. gallon. All Japanese motorbike parts and accessories are available at decent prices in Guatemala. Guatemalan driving is atrocious.

Hired cars may be taken into neighbouring countries except Mexico; rental companies charge US$7-10 for the permits and paperwork. Only credit cards accepted for car hire. Tourists involved in traffic accidents will have to pay whether the guilty party or not. If someone is injured or killed, the foreigner will have to pay all damages.

Note Many long names on bus destination boards are abbreviated: Guate = Guatemala City, Chichi = Chichicastenango, Xela = Xelajú = Quezaltenango, Toto = Totonicapán, etc. Buses in the W and N are called *camionetas*. Regarding pronunciation, "X" is pronounced "sh" in Guatemala, as in Yucatán.

Railways The railways operate from Atlantic to Pacific and to the Mexican border. Service is neither luxurious nor reliable but very cheap and less crowded than buses.

Walkers should get a copy of *Backpacking in Mexico and Central America* by Hilary Bradt and Rob Rachowiecki. **N.B.** If walking in the Quiché, Huehuetenango or Totonicapán regions, it is advisable to get a letter of permission from the army or civil defence in the main town; in outlying areas you may have difficulty without it.

Clothing Men and women should wear dark clothes in the evening. Trousers are OK for women. It is illegal to bring in, or wear, military-style clothing and equipment; such items will be confiscated.

Shopping Woven goods are normally cheapest bought in the town of origin, or possibly even cheaper at big markets held nearby. Try to avoid middlemen and buy direct from the weaver or from a member-cooperative of Artexco, to be found in all main towns. Guatemalan coffee is highly recommended, although the best is exported.

Kerosene is called "Gas corriente", and is good quality, US$0.80 per U.S. gallon; sold only in gas stations.

Film is very expensive, and film for transparencies is very hard to find (it is available at Calle 9, 6-88, Zona 1, Guatemala City, US$15 for 36 exposures).

Health Guatemala is healthy enough if precautions are taken about drinking-water, milk, uncooked vegetables and peeled fruits; carelessness on this point is likely to lead to amoebic dysentery, which is endemic. In Guatemala City the American, Bella Aurora, and Centro Médico hospitals are good. Herrera Llerandi is a good private hospital. Most small towns have clinics. At the public hospitals you may have an examination for a nominal fee, but drugs are expensive. There is an immunization centre at Centro de Salud No. 1, 9 C., 2-64, Zona 1, Guatemala City (no yellow fever vaccinations). In the high places avoid excessive exertion. If going to the Maya sites and the jungle areas, prophylaxis against malaria is strongly advised; there may also be a yellow fever risk.

Hotels   The tourist office in Guatemala City will deal with complaints about overcharging if you can produce bills etc. Room rates should be posted in all registered hotels. Hotel rooms are subject to 7% sales tax and 10% tourism tax. Most budget hotels do not supply toilet paper, soap or towels. Busiest seasons, when hotels in main tourist centres are heavily booked, are Easter, December and the European summer holiday (July-August).

Tipping   Hotel staff: bell boys, US$0.25 for light luggage, US$0.50 for heavy. Chamber maids at discretion. Restaurants: 10%, minimum US$0.25. Taxi drivers: US$0.25 to US$0.50, according to time and distance. Airport porters: US$0.25 per piece of luggage. Cloakroom attendants and cinema usherettes are not tipped.

Climate,   which depends upon altitude, varies greatly. Most of the population lives at between 900 and 2,500 metres, where the climate is healthy and of an even springlike warmth—warm days and cool nights. The pronounced rainy season in the highlands is from May to October; the dry from November to April.

Currency   The unit is the *quetzal,* divided into 100 centavos. There are coins of 25, 10, 5 and 1 centavos. The paper currency is for 50 centavos and 1, 5, 10, 20, 50 and 100 quetzales. If you have money sent to Guatemala, you will only be given half in US dollars. In January 1985, the Banco de Guatemala authorized the establishment of exchange houses, effectively legalizing the black market, but not preventing street-trading in dollars. In May 1989, the authorized parallel exchange rate of the quetzal against the dollar, at which prices in the *Handbook* have been converted, and which is used by banks, was about Q2.75 to the US$. Rates vary around the country; the best being in the capital, the worst in Livingston, Puerto Barrios, Tikal and Panajachel. Miami airport is sometimes a good place to buy quetzales at favourable rates. **Warning:** Torn notes are not always accepted, so avoid accepting them yourself if possible. There is often a shortage of small change.

The quetzal, a rare bird of the Trogon family, is the national emblem. A stuffed specimen is perched on the national coat of arms in the Presidential Palace's ceremonial hall and others are at the Natural History Museums in Guatemala City, Quezaltenango and in the Historical Exhibit below the National Library. (Live ones may be seen, if you are very lucky, in the Biotopo on the Guatemala City-Cobán road, or in heavily forested highlands.)

Cecon (Centro de Estudios Conservacionistas) and Inguat are setting up Conservation Areas (Biotopos) for the protection of Guatemalan wildlife (the quetzal, the manatee, the jaguar, etc.); 3 have been opened (see text), more are planned. Those interested should see Thor Janson's book *Animales de Centroamérica en Peligro.*

Weights and Measures   The metric system is obligatory on all Customs documents: specific duties are levied on the basis of weight, usually gross kilograms. United States measures are widely used in commerce; most foodstuffs are sold by the pound. The metric tonne of 1,000 kg. is generally used; so is the US gallon. Old Spanish measures are often used; e.g. *vara* (32.9 inches), *caballería* (111.51 acres), *manzana* (1.727 acres), *arroba* (25 lbs.), and *quintal* (101.43 lbs.). Altitudes of towns are often measured in feet.

Public Holidays

January 1.	October 12: Discovery of America.
January 6: Epiphany	October 20: Revolution Day.

Holy Week (4 days).
May 1: Labour Day.

June 30.
August 15 (Guatemala City only).
September 15: Independence
    Day.

November 1: All Saints.
Dec. 24: Christmas Eve: from
    noon.
Dec. 25: Christmas Day.
Dec. 31 (from noon).

October 12 and Christmas Eve are not business holidays. During Holy Week, bus fares may be doubled.

Although specific dates are given for *fiestas* there is often about a week of jollification beforehand.

Time   Guatemalan time is 6 hours behind GMT; 5 hours during Summer Time (May-August).

Posts and Telecommunications   Urgent telegrams are charged double the ordinary rate. Sea mail from Europe takes about 40 days. Airmail to Europe takes 6-12 days (letters cost 30 centavos for first 5 grammes, 15 centavos for each additional 5 g). Telephone calls to other countries can be made any day at any time; to Europe, these are slightly cheaper between 1900 and 0700 (personal calls to Europe cost Q64.20 for minimum 3 mins., plus Q16.05 for each extra minute; station to station calls to Europe Q45). Collect calls may be made only to Central America, Mexico, USA (including Alaska), Italy, Spain, Sweden and Japan. All telephone services and the international cable service are in the hands of Guatel, but local telegrams are dealt with at the post office.

Mail to the US and Canada on average takes twice as long as to Europe. Airmail parcel service to the US is reliable (4-14 days); 2-3 months by boat. Parcels sent abroad must be checked before being wrapped for sending; take unsealed package, tape and string to office 119 at the Central Post Office between 0800 and 1530. Parcels by air to Europe cost about US$4.75/kg.; a good service. Note, though, that parcels over 2 kg. may only be sent abroad from Guatemala City (except 5 kg. of books from Antigua); in all other cities, packets under 2 kg. must be sent registered abroad. Mail from Mexico is specially slow. **N.B.** The Lista de Correos charge US$0.03 per letter received. Correos y Telégrafos, 7a Av. 12 C., Zona 1; Guatel next door. Also, no letters may be included in parcels: they will be removed.

Press   The main newspapers are *Prensa Libre* and *El Gráfico* in the morning; *La Razón* and *La Hora* in the afternoon (best).

For information on Guatemala we are grateful to Joseph Laure (Guatemala City) and Mike Shawcross (Antigua) and to the following travellers: Karl Alchorn (NB, Canada), Stephen E. Anderson (Boise, ID), Rupert Baker (Cropredy, Oxon), Erika Berger (Moosseedorf, Switz.), Nataly Bombeck and Christian von Georg (Hamburg 52), Rop Bomer and Wilh. ter Haar (Mexico City), David M. Bristor (Palo Alto, CA), for a particularly useful contribution, Richard H. Ebright (North Brunswick, NJ), Per Einar Evensen (Bergen), Karsten Feucht (Berlin 61), Buckhardt Franz, Arthur Glickman (Arcata, CA), Hans Gottzmann (Mississauga, Ont.), Jan Jacob de Groot (Vroomshoop, Neth.), Monika Gwerder (Muotathal, Switz.), Yaakov Haron (Ramat Gan, Israel), Verena Henauer (Olten, Switz.), Gerald Islebe (Villingen, W.Ger.), Omer Karchi (Tivon, Israel), Joel Kumove (Don Mills, Ont.), Nanna Lyby (Farum, Dmk.), Judith Pollard, Jineke Puister and Jan van Dalfsen (Groningen), Ms C.R. Pyle (York), Wolfgang Reichert and Annette Karling (Kulmbach, W.Ger.), Bob Rice (S. Euclid, Ohio), John Roberts (Dunedin, NZ), Jörg Singer (Bonn 2), Adam Stapleton (London EC4), Felix Walter (Bern), Paul Whitehouse (Cleckheaton) and Julia Booker (Havant, Hants), Roland Wiemer and Karla Menner (Hamburg 50), Conrad Wiesendanger (Münchenstein, Switz.) and Beverley A Woodbridge (Ashland, OR).

WILL YOU HELP US?

We do all we can to get our facts right in *The South American Handbook*. Each chapter is thoroughly revised each year, but Latin America and the Caribbean cover a vast area, and our eyes cannot be everywhere.

Your information may be far more up-to-date than ours. If your letter reaches us early enough in the year it will be used in the next edition, but write whenever you want to, for all your letters are used sooner or later.

Thank you very much indeed for your help.

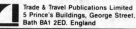

Trade & Travel Publications Limited
5 Prince's Buildings, George Street,
Bath BA1 2ED. England

BELIZE

BELIZE, formerly known as British Honduras, borders on Mexico and Guatemala, and has a land area of about 8,900 square miles, including numerous small islands. Its greatest length (N-S) is 174 miles and its greatest width (E-W) is 68 miles. Forests occupy some 65 % of the area.

The coastlands are low and swampy with much mangrove, many salt and fresh water lagoons and some sandy beaches. In the north the land is low and flat, but in the south-west there is a heavily forested mountain massif with a general elevation of between 2,000 and 3,000 ft. In the eastern part are the Maya Mountains, not yet wholly explored, and the Cockscomb Range which rises to a height of 3,681 ft. at Victoria Peak. To the west are some 250 square miles of the Mountain Pine Ridge, with large open spaces and some of the best scenery in the country.

From 10 to 40 miles off the coast an almost continuous, 150-mile line of reefs and cayes (meaning islands, pronounced "keys") provides shelter from the Caribbean and forms the longest coral reef in the Western Hemisphere (the second-longest barrier reef in the world). Most of the cayes are quite tiny, but some have been developed as tourist resorts. Many have beautiful sandy beaches with clear, clean water, where swimming and diving are excellent. (However, on the windward side of inhabited islands, domestic sewage is washed back on to the beaches, and some beaches are affected by tar.)

The most fertile areas of the country are in the northern foothills of the Maya Mountains: citrus fruit is grown in the Stann Creek valley, while in the valley of the Mopan, or upper Belize river, cattle raising and mixed farming are successful. The northern area of the country has long proved suitable for sugar cane production. In the south bananas and mangoes are cultivated. The lower valley of the Belize river is a rice-growing area as well as being used for mixed farming and citrus cultivation.

Climate Shade temperature is not often over 90°F on the coast, even in the hotter months of February to May. Inland, in the W, day temperatures can exceed 100°F, but the nights are cooler. Between November and February there are cold spells during which the temperature at Belize City may fall to 55°F.

There are sharp annual variations of rainfall—there is even an occasional drought—but the average at Belize City is 65 inches, with about 50 inches in the N and a great increase to 170 inches in the S. Hurricanes can threaten the country from June to November, but there have been only four in the past thirty years. An efficient warning system has been established and there are hurricane shelters in most towns and large villages.

The **population** is estimated at 176,000. About 40 % of them are of mixed ancestry, the so-called Creoles, a term widely used in the Caribbean. They predominate in Belize City and along the coast, and on the navigable rivers. 33 % of the population are mestizo; 7 % are Indians, mostly Mayas, who predominate in the north between the Hondo and New rivers and in the extreme south and west. About 8 % of the population are Garifuna (Black Caribs), descendants of the Black Caribs deported from St. Vincent in 1797; they have a distinct language, and can be found in the villages and towns along the southern coast. The remainder are of unmixed European ancestry (the majority Mennonites, who speak a German dialect, and are friendly and helpful) and a rapidly growing group of North Americans. Birth rate (1985), 40.1 per 1,000; death rate, 4.0; annual population growth, 2.8 % ; adult literacy 90 % . Free elementary education is available to all, and all the towns have secondary schools.

About 75 % speak mostly "Creole" English. Spanish is the mother tongue for about 15 %. About 30 % are bilingual, and 10 % trilingual. Spanish is widely spoken in the northern and western areas.

History Deep in the forests of the centre and S are many ruins of the Old Mayan empire, which flourished here and in neighbouring Guatemala from the 4th to the 9th century and then somewhat mysteriously emigrated to Yucatán. It has been estimated that the population then was ten times what it is now.

The first settlers were Englishmen and their black slaves from Jamaica who came about 1640 to cut logwood, then the source of textile dyes. The British Government made no claim to the territory but tried to secure the protection of the wood-cutters by treaties with Spain. Even after 1798, when a strong Spanish force was decisively beaten off at St. George's Cay, the British Government still failed to claim the territory, though the settlers maintained that it had now become British by conquest.

When they achieved independence from Spain in 1821, both Guatemala and Mexico laid claim to sovereignty over Belize as successors to Spain, but these claims were rejected by Britain. Long before 1821, in defiance of Spain, the British settlers had established themselves as far south as the river Sarstoon, the present southern boundary. Independent Guatemala claimed that these settlers were trespassing and that Belize was a province of the new republic. By the middle of the 19th century Guatemalan fears of an attack by the United States led to a *rapprochement* with Britain. In 1859, a Convention was signed by which Guatemala recognized the boundaries of Belize while, by Article 7, the United Kingdom undertook to contribute to the cost of a road from Guatemala City to the sea "near the settlement of Belize"; an undertaking which was never carried out.

Heartened by what it considered a final solution of the dispute, Great Britain declared Belize, still officially a settlement, a Colony in 1862, and a Crown Colony nine years later. Mexico, by treaty, renounced any claims it had on Belize in 1893, but Guatemala, which never ratified the 1859 agreement, renews its claims periodically.

Belize became independent on September 21, 1981, following a United Nations declaration to that effect. Guatemala refused to recognize the independent state, but in 1986, President Cerezo of Guatemala announced an intention to drop his country's claim to Belize. A British military force has been maintained in Belize since independence.

Communications Formerly the only means of inland communication were the rivers, with sea links between the coastal towns and settlements. The Belize river can be navigated by light motor boats, with enclosed propellers, to near the Guatemalan border in most seasons of the year, but this route is no longer used commercially because of the many rapids. The Hondo River and the New River are both navigable for small boats for 100 miles or so. Although boats continue to serve the sugar industry in the north, the use of waterborne transport is much diminished.

Some 400 miles of all-weather roads, with bus and truck services, connect the eight towns in the country. There are road links with Chetumal, the Mexican border town, and the Guatemalan border town of Melchor de Mencos.

The road system has been upgraded in the interests of tourism. There are no railways in Belize.

Government There is a National Assembly, with a House of Representatives of 28 members elected by universal adult suffrage, and a Senate of 8: 5 appointed by the advice of the Premier, 2 on the advice of the Leader of the Opposition, 1 by the Governor-General after consultation. General elections are held at intervals of not more than 5 years. Dr. Minita Gordon was named Governor-General of the new state in 1981. Mr. George Price, of the People's United Party, who had been reelected continuously as Prime Minister since internal self-government was instituted in 1964, was defeated by Mr Manuel Esquivel, of the United Democratic Party, in general elections held in December 1984 (the first since independence). General elections were due in 1989.

Nature Conservation has become a high priority, with nature reserves sponsored by the Belize Audubon Society, the Government and various international agencies. "Nature tourism" is Belize's fastest growing industry. The reserves (some of which are described below) are: Half Moon Caye, Cockscomb Basin Wildlife Sanctuary (the world's only jaguar reserve), Crooked Tree Wildlife Sanctuary (swamp forests and lagoons with wildfowl), Community Baboon Sanctuary, Blue Hole National Park and Guanacaste Park. All information from the Belize Audubon Society, 49 Southern Foreshore, Belize City, T (02) 7369. A private reserve is the Shipstern Butterfly Farm, near Sarteneja in the N (Paul and Zoe Walker, P.O. Box 1158, Belize City).

N.B. A wildlife protection Act was introduced in 1982, which forbids the sale, exchange or dealings in wildlife, or parts thereof, for profit; the import, export, hunting or collection of wildlife is not allowed without a permit; only those doing scientific research or for educational purposes are eligible for exporting or collecting permits. Also prohibited are removing or exporting black coral, picking orchids, exporting turtle or turtle products, and spear fishing in certain areas or while wearing scuba gear.

Belmopan is the new capital; the seat of government was moved there from Belize City in August 1970. It is 50 miles inland to the west, near the junction of the Western Highway and the Hummingbird Highway to Dangriga (Stann Creek Town)—very scenic. It has a National Assembly building (which is open to the public), two blocks of government offices (which are copies of Mayan architecture), police headquarters, a public works department, a hospital, over 700 houses for civil servants, a non-governmental residential district to encourage expansion, and a market. The Department of Archaeology in the government plaza has a vault containing specimens of the country's artefacts, as there is no museum to house them. Guided tours are offered on Mon., Wed. and Fri. (prior appointment advisable). The city can be seen in a couple of hours (break Belize City-San Ignacio bus journey, storing luggage safely at Batty Bus terminal). Recent additions have been a cinema and a civic centre. The Western Highway from Belize City is now good (one hour's drive), continuing to San Ignacio, and an airfield has been completed.

Hotels and Restaurants   *Belmopan Convention Hotel*, Bliss Parade (opp. bus stop and market), A-L, a/c, hot water, swimming pool, restaurant, bars; *Circle A Lodgings*, 35/37 Half Moon Avenue, C-B, a/c and fans available, despite sign, friendly, breakfast is extra, dinner also served, and bath (laundry BZ$3.75); *Bull Frog Hotel*, 23/25 Half Moon Avenue, D-B, a/c, restaurant, laundry (these 2 are a 15-minute walk S of the market through the Parliament complex). There are two restaurants (*Caladium*, next to market, limited fare, moderately priced, small portions; *Bullfrog*, good, reasonably priced); there is a *comedor* at the back of the market, which is very clean. Local food is sold by vendors, 2 stands in front sell ice cream (closed Sat. and Sun.), fruit and vegetable market open daily, limited produce available Sun. Shops close 1200-1400. No cafés open Sun.

Buses   Batty Bus service to San Ignacio, 45 mins.—1 hr., BZ$1.50 (28 miles), daily every hour between 1430 and 1730, plus Sun. 1330. Novello's hourly between 1100 and 1700 Mon.-Sat. (to 1500 on Sun.) to San Ignacio and Benque Viejo; also Transportes del Carmen. Buses to Dangriga, Punta Gorda, see under Belize City. Bus to Belize City, 1 hr., BZ$2.75, Mon.-Sat. 0800, 0930, 1030, 1130, Sun. hourly between 0800 and 1200.

Exchange   Barclays Bank International (0800-1300, Mon.-Fri., and 1500-1800 Fri.).

British High Commission.

Excursion   13 miles from Belmopan along a bad road is the Blue Hole (Mile 45 on the Hummingbird Highway). This is a natural pool which lies about 100 ft. below the road. It can be reached by steps and swimming is possible. 2 miles SW of the Blue Hole are St. Hernan's Caves, which are magnificent (they are ½ mile off the road from the Blue Hole to Belmopan along a dirt track). A torch is essential; you can walk for more than half a mile underground. At Mile 41 on the Western Highway is the small but excellent Belize Zoo (The Place), open daily 1000-1700, BZ$5, many local species, tours, T-shirts, postcards on sale. At the junction of Belmopan road and the Western Highway is the Guanacaste Park, which is along the Belize River: 4.8 km. of trails, birds and a large guanacaste tree.

Belize City is the old capital and chief town. Most of the houses are built of wood, with galvanized iron roofs; they stand for the most part on piles about seven feet above the ground, which is often swampy and flooded. Ground-floor rooms are used as kitchens, or for storage. A sewerage system has been installed, and the water is perfectly safe to drink. For the tropics the climate is both cool and healthy. Humidity is high, but the summer heat is tempered by the NE trades. The population—42,000—is just over a quarter of the total population, with the African strain predominating. The Anglican Cathedral and Government House nearby are interesting; both were built in the early 19th century. In the days before the foundation of the Crown Colony the kings of the Mosquito Coast were crowned in the Cathedral. In the Cathedral, note the 19th century memorial plaques which give a harrowing account of early death from "country fever" and other tropical diseases. There is an attractive memorial park on the sea front.

Coming in by sea, after passing the barrier reef, Belize City is approached by a narrow, tortuous channel. This and the chain of mangrove cayes give shelter to what would otherwise be an open roadstead.

Belize is the nearest adequate port to the State of Quintana Roo (Mexico), and re-exports mahogany from that area.

Note   Hurricane Hattie swept a 10-ft. tidal wave into the town on October 31, 1961, and caused much damage and loss of life. Hattieville, 16 miles from Belize City on the road to Cayo, originally a temporary settlement for the homeless after the hurricane, still has from 2,000 to 3,000 people. In 1978, Hurricane Greta caused extensive damage.

Warning   Take good care of your possessions. Cars should only be left in guarded carparks (such as Budget Store in N. Front St., BZ$10 a night; cars can enter at any time—no sleeping in parked vehicles allowed—but can only be collected between 0800-1630). Do not trust the many self-appointed "guides" who also sell hotel rooms, boat trips to the Cayes, drugs, etc. Local advice is not even to say "no"; just shake your head and wag your finger if approached by a stranger. Street money changers are not to be trusted either. The Government is making every effort to improve the security in the city in the interests of tourism; nevertheless, be careful at night, especially in side streets.

The whole city closes down on Sunday.

Hotels   All hotels are subject to 5% government tax. *Fort George Hotel,* 2 Marine Parade (P.O.Box 321, T 77400, Telex 220), has much the same tariff as luxury Caribbean hotels, and rooms are air-conditioned, L, helpful staff, reservations must be made, safe parking, good restaurant, good pool (non-residents may use pool for BZ$5). Other hotels: *Villa*, 13 Cork St., L, a/c, TV, good restaurant, bar; *Bellevue*, 5 Southern Foreshore (T 2290), A, including 2 meals, a/c, and private bath, nice bar with live music Fri. and Sat. nights, good entertainment; *El Centro*, 4 Bishop St., B (T 2413), a/c, restaurant, good; *Venus*, Magazine Rd., at Venus Bus Station, D; *Bliss*, 1 Water Lane (T 3310), B with a/c, C without, rooms without a/c have ceiling fans, and are quieter and lighter, private bath, clean, safe; *Mopan*, 55 Regent Street (T 3356), B, with bath, breakfast, a/c, very clean, in historic house, has restaurant and bar (owners Tom and Jean Shaw), a bit overpriced; *Belize Guest House*, 2 Hutson St., T 77569, B, nice balcony, helpful owner, rec.; *4 Fort Street* (address as name), C, charming, excellent but expensive restaurant; *Mom's Hotel and Restaurant* (formerly *Mom's Triangle Bar*), 11 Handyside St., P.O. Box 332, C; *Glenthorne Manor*, 27 Barracks Rd. (T 4-4212), C, with or without bath, colonial-style, meals available, highly rec.; *International Airport Hotel*, at Ladyville, 9 miles on Northern Highway, 1½ miles from airport, B, restaurant and bar; *Chateau Caribbean*, 6 Marine Parade (T 2813), from D to A, a/c, with bar, rec., restaurant and discotheque, parking; *Golden Dragon*, 29 Queen St., D, with bath and a/c, cheaper rooms with bath and fan, cheaper still without bath, hot water, good, clean but noisy; *Simon Quan's "Luxury" Hotel*, 24-26 Queen St. (T 4-5793), E with fan, and D, private shower, hot water, a/c, good value, clean; *North Front Street Guest House*, 1 block N of Post Office, 15 mins. walk from Batty bus station, 124 North Front St., E, no hot water, fan, book exchange, TV, clean, friendly, good fish dinners, keep windows closed at night and be sure to lock your door; *Riverview*, 25 Regent St. West, E, basic; *Mar's Riverside Resort*, 44 Regent St. West, F, no fan, friendly, basic; *Bon Aventure*, Pickstock and Front Sts., E, dirty but helpful, Spanish spoken, good meals at reasonable prices, safe to store luggage here; *Marin Travel Lodge*, 6 Craig St., E, good, fans, shared hot showers, safe, laundry facilities; *Golden Star Guest House*, 114 New Rd., D, fan, clean, shower, simple, facilities leave something to be desired, not very friendly; *Freddie's*, 86 Eve St., E, with shower and toilet, fan, hot water, clean, very nice; *Han's Guest House*, 53 Queen St., E, little or no English spoken by Chinese owners, basic, noisy but clean; *Sea Side Guest House*, 3 Prince Street, E, comfortable, quiet, very helpful owners, German spoken, meals, highly rec.

Warning   Self-appointed tourist guides will offer to take you to a hotel, then demand payment.

Camping   In the city is the *Caribbean Trailer Court*, at the end of Eve St., caravan park with 2 dilapidated showers and toilet, cold drinks available; some supervision, but no fence, beware of thieves; BZ$3 p.p., BZ$5 per car plus BZ$2 per extra person. Caribbean Charter Service, Mile 5 North Highway, short and long stay trailer parking and camp site. Camping on the beaches, in forest reserves, or in any other public place is not allowed. **N.B.** Camping Gaz is not available in Belize and there are no campsites for tents.

Restaurants   *Golden Dragon*, Queen St., expensive; *Macy's*, 18 Bishop Street (T 3419), rec. for well-prepared local game, different fixed menu daily, charming host; *Barracks Restaurant and Bar*, 136 Barracks Rd.; *Grill*, Barracks Green (a short taxi ride), new; *DIT's*, King St., good, cheap; *Caribbean*, 36 Regent St., creole and Chinese; *Hong Kong*, 50 Queen St., Chinese, reasonably priced; *China Village*, 46 Regent St., lunch specials; *Shek Kei*, 34 Freetown Rd., Chinese, good; other Chinese (fair): *Yin Kee*, 64 Freetown Rd.; *Taiwan*, 93 Cemetery Rd.; *New Chon Saan*, 55 Euphrates Av., take away. *Edward Quan Fried Chicken*, New Rd., take away, good. *Big Daddy's*, Pickstock St. (2 blocks from N Front St.), good, vegetarian food available, eat in or take-away, rec.; *H & L Burgers*, 4 locations; *Play Boy Restaurant*, King St., good sandwiches; *Pizza House*, King St., closed Mon., inexpensive, good also for juices and shakes. *Blue Bird*, Albert St., cheap fruit juices; *Admiral Burnaby's Coffee Shop*, Regent St.; *Babb's Saloon*, Queen and Eve Sts., good pastries, meat pies, juices, friendly. Lots of bars some with juke boxes and poolrooms. *Privateer*, Mile 4½ on Northern Highway, on seafront, expensive drinks but you can sit outside. Try the local drink, anise and peppermint, known as "A and P"; also the powerful "Old Belizeno" rum. The local beer, Belikin, is good, as is the "stout", strong and free of gas.

Clubs and Discos   *The Pub*, North Front St., bar and disco, admission charged, taped music, frequented by British soldiers; *The Big Apple*, same street, live music at weekends, good; *Bellevue Hotel* has live music at weekends, respectable, rec. The *Old Louisville Democratic Bar*, though rec. by Richard West of *The Spectator*, has been described as dangerous by a woman visitor.

Electricity   110/220 volts single phase, 60 cycles for domestic supply.

Shopping   Handicrafts, woodcarvings, straw items, are all good buys. Try the gift/souvenir at Caribbean Charter Services, Mile 5, North Highway (see below); Cottage Industries, 26 Albert Street. The Book Centre, close to bridge and Catholic church, very good. Belize Bookshop, Regent

St. (opp. *Mopan Hotel*), sells *South American Handbook* (also available in some expensive hotels). Zericote (a type of tree found only in Belize) wood carvings can be bought in Belize City, for example at Brodies Department Store, which also sells postcards, the *Fort George Hotel*, or from Egbert Peyrefitte, 11a Cemetery Road. (At the Art Centre, near Government House, the wood sculpture of Charles Gabb, who introduced carving into Belize, can be seen.)

Taxis have green licence plates (drivers must also have identification card); within Belize, BZ$3 for one person; for 2 or more passengers, BZ$2 p.p. There is a taxi stand on the corner of Collet Canal Street and Cemetery Road. Outside Belize City, BZ$2 per mile, regardless of number of passengers. Check fare before setting off. No meters. No tips necessary.

Car Hire Caribbean Charter Service (see below under **Tourist Information**); Pancho's, 18th St., T 02-2813; National, near airport, T 025-2114. Smith & Sons, 125C Cemetery Road, T 02-3779; Elija Sutherland, 127 Neal Pen Road, T 02-3582; S & L Tours, 69 West Collet Canal, T 02-3062. Rates US$50/day; some offer tours. Land Rovers at about BZ$90 a day (BZ$400 deposit, no credit cards) at Belize. It is impossible to hire a car with insurance.

Exchange All banks have facilities to arrange cash advance on Visa card. The Belize Bank is particularly efficient and modern; also Barclays Bank International, with some country branches. Bank of Nova Scotia. Banking hours: 0800-1300 Mon.-Thurs., 0800-1200, 1500-1800 Fri. It is easy to have money telexed to Belize City. Guatemalan quetzales are very difficult to obtain. American Express at Global Travel, 41 Albert Street (T 7185/7363/4). All banks charge 2% commission. Money changers at Batty Bus terminal just before departure of bus to Chetumal (the only place to change Mexican pesos). The black market is not recommended.

Baron Bliss Institute Maya remains (3 stelae), and public library.

Churches There are an Anglican Cathedral, a Catholic Cathedral, a Methodist and a Presbyterian church. The Baptist Church on Queen St. is interesting for the sermons (very vivid).

Cinemas Two; films and prices change according to popularity.

Consulates USA, 20 Gabourel Lane; Canada, South Foreshore; Mexico, 20 North Park St. (open 0900-1100, Mon.-Fri.; if going to Mexico and requiring a visa, get it here, not at the border); Honduras, Front St., above *The Pub*; El Salvador, 11 Handyside St.; Panama, Cork St.; Belgium, Eve St.; Norway and the Netherlands, 22 Regent St. No Guatemalan Consulate; Guatemalan visas must be obtained in Chetumal (Calle Alvaro Obregón 342), Mexico.

Post Office Letters, Queen St. and N. Front St.; parcels, Church St. Letters held for one month. Beautiful stamps sold.

International Telecommunications Telegraph, telephone, telex services, Belizean Telecommunications Ltd, Bishop Street, just off Albert Street.

Tourist Information Belize Tourist Bureau, 53 Regent Street, Belize, P.O. Box 325, T 02-77213 (open 0800-1200, 1300-1700 Mon.-Thurs., and till 1630 Fri.), provides complete bus schedule as well as list of hotels and their prices. Also has a list of recommended taxi guides and tour operators, and free publications on the country and its Mayan ruins, practical and informative. Excellent maps of the country for BZ$4 (or US$3 including postage). Mon.-Fri. 0800-1200, 1300-1700. Suggested reading is *Formerly British Honduras* (Setzekorn), or *Hey Dad, this is Belize*, by Emory King, a collection of anecdotes, available in bookshops. Maps (BZ$6), books on Belizean fauna etc. available at Angelus Press, Queen St.

Caribbean Charter Services, Mile 5 North Highway, P.O.Box 752, Belize City, T (011-501-2) 4-5841, Telex 263 Rebco Bz. is a tourist information centre with good maps of Belize City (BZ$6) and of the country. Also agency for boat charters, inland resorts and other facilities including excellent guarded car and boat park and tent sites. Car hire at good rates; open 7 days a week, 0700-1800 in tourist season. The owners (Americans George and Ruha'mah Baguette) operate M.V.s *Princess, Toucan, Jaguar, Le 'Beau* and *Hickatee* for fishing, diving and sightseeing trips to the Cayes.

Tours S and L Guided Tours, 69 W. Collet Canal, recommended group travel in Land Rovers; International Zoological Expeditions, 210 Washington Street, Sherborn, MA 01770, USA, offer guided trips to the rainforests and coral reefs of Belize. Personalized Services (Beth La Croix), P.O. Box 1158, Belize City, T (011-501) 2331. Cunningham Tours, T 7-8016 or (agent) 4-5841, have been highly recommended.

Transport There are bus services to the main towns. To Chetumal, Mexico (**see page 1108**), several daily each way between 0400 and 1800 (there is an express Batty Bus at 0600 stopping at Orange Walk and Corozal only), BZ$7, 3-4 hrs., with 2 companies: Batty Bus, 54 East Collet Canal, T 2025, and Venus, Magazine Rd., T 3354. Batty Bus to Belmopan and San Ignacio, 4 hrs., BZ$3.75, Mon.-Sat. 0630, 0800, 0900, 1000, Sun. 0630, 0730, 0830, 0930, 1030. The 0630 bus goes on to Melchor de Mencos, Guatemala. To San Ignacio and Benque Viejo via Belmopan, Novello's, West Collet Canal, BZ$4.25 to Benque, hourly Mon.-Sat., 1100 to 1700 (to 1600 on

Sun.); Transportes del Carmen, Pound Yard Bridge, to Benque, Mon.-Sat. 1200, 1400, 1600, Sun. 1400. To Dangriga, via Belmopan and the Hummingbird Highway. Z-line, from Venus bus station, daily, 1000, 1100, 1500, 1600, plus Mon. 0600, US$8 to Dangriga (the 1000 bus connects with the 1530 Z-line bus to Punta Gorda); James Bus Line, Pound Yard Bridge (Collet Canal), unreliable, slow, "a real adventure", 10-12 hrs., BZ$16.50, to Punta Gorda via Dangriga and Mango Creek, Tues., Wed., Fri. 0600, Mon., Sat. 0900. Within the city the fare is BZ$1. Take a taxi to town from the bus stations at night: Trucks are cheap (enquire near the market) but the government forbids them to transport travellers to any area served by buses.

Airport   There is a 10-mile tarmac road to the Belize International Airport; collective taxi BZ$25; make sure your taxi is legitimate. Any bus going up the Northern Highway passes the airport junction (BZ$1), then 1½ mile walk. There is a municipal airstrip for local flights. To Corozal, 30 mins., BZ$62; to Punta Gorda, BZ$60; to San Pedro, BZ$35; Caye Chapel, BZ$25; Dangriga, BZ$36.

Airline Offices   Taca (Belize Global Travel), Albert St.; Sahsa/TAN, just off Queen St. Maya Airways, 6 Fort St., T 02-77215. Eastern and Continental Airlines now also fly to Belize. Tropic Air, T 02-45671.

Shipping   The only boat to Guatemala goes from Punta Gorda. Obtain all necessary exit stamps and visas before sailing (remember, nearest Guatemalan consulate is in Chetumal). For Dangriga and Punta Gorda boats must be chartered. To Puerto Cortés, Honduras, BZ$720, 2-4 days, for 8 people.

Fishing   The rivers abound with tarpon and snoek. The sea provides game fish such as sailfish, marlin, wahoo, barracuda and tuna. On the flats, the most exciting fish for light tackle—the bonefish—are found in great abundance.

Skin Diving   The shores are protected by the longest barrier reef in the Western Hemisphere. Old wrecks and other underwater treasures are protected by law and cannot be removed. Spear fishing, as a sport, is discouraged in the interests of conservation. The beautiful coral formation is a great attraction for scuba diving. Boats can only be hired for diving, fishing or sightseeing if they are licensed for the specific purpose by the government. This is intended to ensure that tourists travel on safe, reliable vessels and also to prevent the proliferation of self-appointed guides.

The Cayes off the coast are most attractive. They are used by holiday campers from February to May and in August. From many of the holiday villas stretch pens or "crawls" to protect the bather from sharks or barracudas, and to keep the water clean.

There are 212 square miles of cayes. St. George's Caye, 9 miles NE of Belize, was once the capital and was the scene of the battle in 1798 which established British possession. The larger ones are Turneffe Island and Ambergris, Caulker, and English Cayes. Fishermen live on some cayes, coconuts are grown on others, but many are uninhabited swamps. The smaller cayes do not have much shade, so be careful if you go bathing on them. Sandflies infest some cayes (e.g. Caulker), the sandfly season is December to beginning of February; mosquito season June, July, sometimes October. On Big Caye Bokel, at the southern end of the Turneffe group, are 3 "Caribbean Lodges" for big-spending fishermen and skin-divers, each holding 12 guests (*Turneffe Island Lodge*, bar, restaurant, diving and snorkelling trips, very good; *Turneffe Island Flats*, less expensive). Caye Chapel has a large hotel and a private airstrip, and Caye Caulker several guest rooms and hotels.

Travel by boat to and between the islands is becoming increasingly regulated (see above) and the new licensing requirements will probably drive the cheaper boats out of business. In general, it is easier to arrange travel between the islands once there, than from Belize City. All authorized boats leave from the Shell station on North Front Street. Cargo boats are no longer allowed to carry passengers, too many have capsized with tourists on board, causing loss of life.

On Caye Chapel is the *Pyramid Island Resort*, A without a/c, L with, American or European Plan available, diving packages, air transfers to Belize City (P.O. Box 192, Belize City, T 4-4409). Caye Chapel is free of sandflies and mosquitoes and there are several beaches, cleaned daily. 40 mins. by boat from Belize City. There is also a landing strip used by army helicopters and Maya Airlines.

Ambergris Caye   This island, with its village of San Pedro, is being rapidly developed as a tourist resort and is expensive. *Ramon's Reef Resort*, a diving and beach resort, US$85 p.p. per day for double room, all meals and all diving, highly recommended even for non-divers (fishing, swimming, boating, snorkelling), very efficient. Hotels: *San Pedro Holiday Hotel*, L, including meals; *Journey's End*, P.O. Box 13, T (501) 026-2173, L, resort facilities including meals; *Coral Beach*, A, incl. meals; *Royal Palm*, A-L; *San Pedrano*, C without, to A with meals; *El Pescador*, on Punta Arena beach, L, a/c; facilities for sailing, diving etc. *Tomas Hotel*, D (more if reserved in advance) with bath, clean, trips to reef; *Spindrift Hotel*, has been rec., B, 30 rooms, 4 apartments, trips up the Belize River, a/c, comfortable, restaurant. There are other expensive hotels, several in the BZ$20-45 range, and some basic hotels. *Big Daddy's Disco*, rec. The *San Pedro Grill* is a good place to meet other travellers and swap information on boats etc. At Coral Beach, the Forman, Gómez, González and Paz families provide rooms and meals for BZ$18 each. At Sea Breeze, the Paz and Núñez families offer the same accommodation at the same price. In the same building complex as the *Spindrift* is a branch of the Atlantic Bank, a post office and a chemist. Several flights daily to and from Belize City with Tropic and Maya Air, BZ$35 one way, BZ$60 return. Boats, irregular, between Ambergris and Caye Caulker, no set fare. One cannot in practice walk N along the beach from San Pedro to Xcalak, Mexico.

Caye Caulker A lobster-fishing island, which used to be relatively unspoilt, but the number of tourists is now increasing and the shoreline has become dirty (some services are reported to have deteriorated, and theft and unpleasantness from some mainlanders who go to the cave with tourists occurs). There are no beaches, but you can swim at the channel ("cut") or off one of the many piers. Boats leave from behind Jan's Shell Station on North Front Street, for Caye Caulker, at about 0930 daily except Sun. (BZ$12 p.p., payable only on arrival at Caye Caulker—otherwise you'll be swindled), BZ$24 return, 45 mins. one way (boats depend on weather and number of passengers), return boats at 0700 (if booked in advance at *Edit's Hotel*, BZ$10). Jerry Pacheco's *Blue Wave*, Emilio Novelo's *Ocean Star* and "Chocolate's" *Soledad* are the currently authorized boats.

Hotels *Tom's Hotel*, E, with fan, basic, clean, friendly, excellent value, laundry service US$5, barbeque; Tom's boat trips cost BZ$7. *Mira Mar*, E p.p., bargain if staying longer, helpful owner Melvin Badillo, he owns liquor store, his family runs a pastry shop and grocery store; *Shirley's Guest House*, E, south end of village, very relaxing; *Reef Hotel*, D (formerly *Martínez Caribbean Inn*), under new management in 1989; *Edits*, F per bed in room (whether occupied or not), good; *Marin*, F, with bath, rec. (the proprietor, John Marin, will take you out for a snorkelling trip on the reef for BZ$10), good meals; *Riva's Guest House*, E, basic accommodation. Their reef trips in an attractive schooner are the longest; snorkelling equipment hire, BZ$3; *Daisy's* (or *Deisy's*), E with shower, toilet and fan, reductions for longer stays, cash travellers' cheques, good. *Vega's Far Inn* rents 7 rooms, all doubles, E with ceiling fan and fresh linen, flush toilets and showers (limited hot water) shared with camping ground, which is guarded, has drinking water, hot water, clean toilets, barbecue, can rent out camping gear (camping costs BZ$5.30). *Ignacio Beach Huts*, small huts or hammocks just outside town, E for a hut for 3-4, rec., camping space (Ignacio's reef trips cost BZ$4); *Rainbow Hotel*, on the beach, 10 small bungalows, D, with shower. Beach houses can also be rented for BZ$100-300 a month. Camping on the beach is forbidden.

Restaurant For dinner, seek out Mrs. Rodríguez, who serves meals at 1700/1730 for BZ$7-8 for 2, very good (limited accommodation available). *Melvin's*, excellent lobster meals (opp. *Riva's*); *Tropical Paradise* for excellent seafood. Cakes and pastries can be bought at houses displaying the sign, rec. are *Daisy's*, *Jessie's* (open 0830-1300, 1500-1700, behind *Riva's*); *Emma*, on path to co-op, sells delicious lobster pies, and chocolate-coconut pies. Many private houses serve food.

International telephone connections available on Caye Caulker. The island also boasts two book swaps. Good nightlife at the *Black Coral* disco, very busy Fri. and Sat.

A reef museum has opened with enlarged photos of reef fish, free for school parties, tourists are asked for a US$2 donation to help expansion.

Reef trips (see also above, under Hotels), BZ$6-8 each for 3-7 hours as long as there are 3 or more in a group. Protect against sunburn on reef trips. Mervin, a local man, is reliable for snorkelling trips, he will also take you to Belize City for BZ$10. Also Gamoosa, who will spend all day with you on the reef (BZ$10 for a day's snorkelling, BZ$20 for a trip to San Pedro; his boat leaves at about 1100) and then invite you to his house to eat the fish and lobster you have caught, prepared deliciously by his wife; she also offers a healthy breakfast of banana, yoghurt, granola and honey for BZ$3.50. Also recommended is Alfonso Rosardo, a Mexican, reef trips for up to 6 people, 5-6 hrs., BZ$9, sometimes offers meals at his house afterwards. Also recommended is Lawrence (next to Riva's Guest House) and Obdulio, BZ$6 p.p. for 3 hr trip (or BZ$40 for a full day's fishing, inclusive). Lobster fishing and diving for conch is also possible. Mask, snorkel and fins for BZ$3-6 (for instance at the post office). Wind-surfing equipment hire: BZ$8 an hour, BZ$20 ½ day, BZ$40 a day, lessons, BZ$10 exc. equipment. Frank and Janie Bounting (P.O.Box 667, T 44307, ext. 143 mainland side, past the football pitch) charge US$32 for 2 scuba dives, good value; they also offer a 3-day PADI certificate course, recommended. For sailing charters, Jim and Dorothy of "Sea-ing is Belizing", who also run scuba trips to Goff's Caye Park and the Turneffe Islands (5-10 days). There is a sailing school, charging BZ$60 for a 5-hr., solo beginner's course. It may be possible to hire a boat for 6-8 people to Chetumal. There are also boats leaving for Honduras from Caye Caulker, but be sure to get exit stamps and other documentation in Belize City first.

English Caye, 12 miles off Belize City, is beautiful, with no facilities; take a day trip only. It is part of the reef so you can snorkel right off the beach.

Half Moon Caye at Lighthouse Reef, 45 miles E of Belize City, is the site of the Red-Footed Booby Sanctuary, a national reserve. The Belize Audubon Society, 49 Southern Foreshore, maintains the sanctuary; there is a lookout tower and trail. A lighthouse on the caye gives fine views of the reef. No facilities: take all food, drink and fuel. Bobby takes passengers by sailing boat to Half Moon Caye and the Blue Hole at Lighthouse Atoll for US$25 p.p. inc. food (bring own tent and sleeping bag). To charter a motor boat costs about US$50 p.p. if 10 people are going (6 hr. journey).

Other Excursions Bargain with local drivers for a visit to Tikal ruins, in Guatemala (**page 1165**). Mr. Richard Smith has his own station waggon. There are buses from Belize to the Guatemalan border; for connections to Flores **see page 1200** under Benque Viejo.

The Mayan remains of **Altun Ha,** 31 miles N of Belize City and 3 miles off the old Northern Highway, are worth a visit (insect repellant necessary); they are deserted after 1800 hours. Since there is so little transport on this road, hitching is not rec., best to go in a private vehicle. A vehicle does leave Belize City in the early afternoon, but does not return until 0500 next day; camping not permitted at the site. No accommodation in nearby villages. Tourist Board provides a good booklet on the ruins for BZ$2, and a guide book for BZ$12. The largest piece of worked Mayan jade ever found, a head of the Sun God weighing 9½ pounds, was found here in 1968. It is now in a bank vault in Belize City.

Truck transport at 1230 from George St. goes to Bermudian Landing, a small Creole village 25 miles from Belize City (beyond Burrell Boom); here is the Community Baboon Sanctuary (the local name for howler monkeys). Boats can be hired from the warden for river trips to see monkeys and birds. Booklet (US$3, excellent) from the Audubon Society, 49 Southern Foreshore.

Two main roads penetrate the country from Belize City: one to the N and other to the W. The Northern Highway, well paved to the Mexican border, forks just beyond Sand Hill, the quicker route heading direct to Orange Walk, the older road looping N then NW, passing near Altun Ha. The new highway runs to (66 miles) Orange Walk, centre of a district where about 17,000 Creoles, Mennonites and Mayan Indians get their living from timber, sugar planting, general agriculture and chicle bleeding. In the Orange Walk District is a large Old Mayan ceremonial site, **Nohochtunich**; enormous masonry slabs were used in a stairway up one of the pyramids.

The population of **Orange Walk,** a bustling agricultural centre, is 8,500. A toll bridge (BZ$1) now spans the New River. Spanish is the predominant language. It is a centre for refugees from other parts of Central America. Despite government action against drug-trafficking in this area, travellers still describe it as "a dodgy little town after dark."

Hotels Chula Vista Hotel, at gas station just outside town, safe, clean, helpful owner, D. Mi Amor, 19 Belize-Corozal road, E with shared bath, and more expensive rooms, restaurant; Jane's, Market Lane, E; La Nueva Ola, 73 Otro Benque Rd., E; Paradise restaurant, very expensive; Rocky's Restaurant, rather dear; Julie's, nr. police station, good, inexpensive creole cooking; similarly at Baker's. Several Chinese restaurants.

Exchange Bank of Nova Scotia; same hours as Belize City (**see page 1195**).

Bus All Chetumal buses pass Orange Walk Town (hourly); Belize-Orange Walk, BZ$3.50.

The Northern Highway continues to Corozal (96 miles from Belize) then for 8 miles to the Mexican frontier, where a bridge across the Río Hondo connects with Chetumal. Border crossing formalities are relatively relaxed. Driving time, Belize-frontier, 3 hours, Belize City-Chetumal, 4 hrs. including the border stop. (Taxi, BZ$8 Corozal-border, BZ$17 Corozal-Chetumal, bus, Belize City-Chetumal BZ$7). One can no longer acquire a tourist card at the border; you must get one at the Mexican Consulate in Belize City. If entering Belize for only a few days, you can ask the Mexican officials to save your tourist card for you (but don't depend on it). If you want a new tourist card for a full 30 days you must get it in Belize City. It is possible to buy pesos at the border with either US or Belizean dollars (outside office hours, try the shops). If coming from Mexico it is best to get rid of pesos at the border. Bargain for good rates of exchange at the border (there is a small bank near customs, so compare rates), better here than with money changers in Orange Walk Town or Corozal.

Corozal, with a population of 7,000, is the centre of the growing sugar industry. Like Orange Walk Town it is economically depressed because of low world sugar prices; there has been a greater dependence on marijuana as a result. Corozal is much the safer place. It is open to the sea with a pleasant waterfront.

Hotels At Consejo Shore, Adventure, C with no meals, to L full board, 7 miles from town, bar and restaurant (no public transport); Maya, South End, E; Nestor's Hotel, 125, 5th Av. South (T 04-2354), E with bath and fan, very good value, refrescos available, very helpful owner (Jake); Capri, 14 Fourth Ave., run down, E. Two motels: Caribbean, South End, C, basic, restaurant; Tony's, South End also, D (C, with a/c), clean but unfriendly, restaurant overpriced. Other restaurants:

Club Campesino, decent bar, good fried chicken after 1800; *Rexo*, North 5th St., Chinese; also Chinese: *Bumpers* (rec.); *King of Kings*; *Hong Kong*.

Camping *Caribbean* Motel and Trailer Park, on Barracks Road, camping possible but not very safe, (US$1.50 p.p.), shaded sites, good restaurant, beach.

Exchange Barclays Bank International, Bank of Nova Scotia, open same hours as Belize City (see page 1195).

Buses There are 15 buses a day from Belize to Corozal by Venus Bus, Magazine Road, and Batty Bus, 54 East Collet Canal, 3½-5 hrs., BZ$6. Both continue to Chetumal where there is a new bus terminal on the outskirts of town; because of the frequency, there is no need to take a colectivo to the Mexican border unless travelling at unusual hours (BZ$5). The increased frequency of buses to Chetumal and the number of money changers cater for Belizeans shopping cheaply in Mexico—very popular, book early. Through tickets can be bought from Corozal to San Ignacio (see below), via Belize City, but you must get a new seat number at the Batty Bus counter in Belize City. For those coming from Mexico who are more interested in Tikal than Belize, Batty Buses leaving Chetumal at 0230 and 0400 go straight to the Guatemalan border.

Excursion 8 miles N of Corozal, on the road to Chetumal, is 4 Miles Lagoon, about ¼ mile off the road (buses will drop you there). Clean swimming, better than Corozal bay, some food and drinks available; it is often crowded at weekends.

The Western Highway runs from Belize City to Belmopan and on through savanna, pine ridge and high canopied forest to **San Ignacio** (capital of Cayo District, 72 miles) and the Guatemalan frontier. About 60 miles along this road is Ontario Village. There is camping space and a trailer to rent. San Ignacio, known locally as Cayo, has a population of about 5,600. It stands at 200-250 feet, with a pleasant climate, and is a good base for excursions into the Mountain Pine Ridge, some 120 square miles of well-watered, undulating country rising to 3,000 feet. (Bus to Belize City, Mon.-Fri., 1330, 1530, plus 1230 on Mon., Sat., and Sun., 1300, 1400, 1500, 1600 BZ$3.75, with Batty Bus; also Novello's, 4 daily Mon.-Sat., 1030 on Sun.)

Hotels and Restaurants *Central*, 24 Burns Ave., E with bath; *Hi-Et Hotel*, 12 West St., E, noisy, no fans, low partition walls, clothes washing permitted; *San Ignacio Hotel*, on road to Benque Viejo, C, with bath, fan, hot water, clean, helpful staff, swimming pool, excellent restaurant, highly rec., disco at weekends, bar opens at 1000 (good place for meeting British soldiers); around the corner is *Piache Hotel*, 18 Buena Vista Rd., E-D in either thatched cottages with bath or room without bath, cold water, basic, bar in p.m. Doña Elvira Espat serves meals at her house (inc. breakfast), advance notice required, good, friendly (no sign, corner of Galvez Street and Bullet Tree Road). *La Fuente*, Eve St. and West St., good juices and pastries; *The Place*, small pastry shop on Burns Ave., good; *Maxim's*, Bullet Tree Rd. and Far West St., Chinese, good food, poor service. George, at the *Club Shangrila*, makes a good cup of tea, and offers assistance of all sorts. Also informative is Bob at *Eva's Bar*, Burns Ave. (good, inexpensive local dishes). *Farmers Emporium*, Burns Ave., a shop selling wholewheat bread, raisins, juices, fresh milk. Fruit and vegetable market every Sat. a.m. Note that all shops and businesses close 1700-1900.

Exchange Venus Stores, 23 Burns Av. (09-2186) gives better rates of exchange for quetzales than you can get at the border with Guatemala.

Tours Jungle View Tours, No. 26 18th St., San Ignacio, T 092-2012, recommended. Local taxis which offer tours of Mountain Pine Ridge in the wet season probably won't get very far; also, taking a tour to Xunantunich is not really necessary. Mountain Equestrian Trails, Mile 8, Mtn. Pine Ridge Rd., Cayo District, or P.O.Box 752 Belize City (T 4-5841), offers ½-day, full-day or 7-8 day adventure tours on horseback in western Belize.

The British Army's Holdfast camp is about 12 miles from the border.

San Ignacio is on the eastern branch of the Old, or Belize River, known as the Macal, navigable almost to the Guatemalan frontier. The river journey of 121 miles from Belize, broken by many rapids, needs considerable ingenuity to negotiate the numerous "runs".

Places to Stay *Chaa Creek Cottages*, on the Macal River, 5 miles upstream from San Ignacio, has rooms from B (b. and b.), to L (all meals), set on a working farm in pleasant countryside, highly rec. Trips on the river, to Xunantunich, to Tikal, to Mountain Pine Ridge, nature walks and jungle safaris organized; also joint vacations arranged with *Rum Point Inn*, Placencia. If coming by road, turn off the Benque road at Chial; hotel will collect you by boat from San Ignacio (US$25 for 4), or from international airport (US$90); reservations P.O. Box 53, San Ignacio, T 092-2037.

Nabitunich Cottages, turn off the Benque road 1½ miles beyond Chial, offers spectacular views of Xunantunich and another, unexcavated Mayan ruin, jungle trails, horse riding, canoeing; book through agent, P.O. Box 752, Belize City, T 4-5841.

Maya Mountain Lodge (Bart and Suzi Mickler), also on the Macal River, ¾ mile from San Ignacio at 9 Cristo Rey Road (taxi from town US$2.50, C-B, most welcoming, highly rec., special weekly and monthly rates and for families, **also discounts on lodging (50%) and food (20%) to backpackers with *South American Handbook*,** T 092-2164 (The Farm Store), P.O. Box 46, San Ignacio, restaurant, laundry, postal service, swimming, hiking, riding, canoeing, fishing. Explore Belize Tours in the region and beyond; also "Parrot's Perch" social and educational area with resident naturalist and ornithologist.

Jungle View Campground, 2½ miles on Mountain Pine Ridge road (leave Western Highway at the community of Santa Elena, near Hawksworth Bridge), popular, Mayan and American-run, local tours and to Tikal. *Barton's Creek* is a Mennonite community, from which one can buy produce. Five miles away is *Georgeville*, where one can try the Mennonites' ice cream and cheese. **N.B.** Between January and June, the risk of fire in the reserve is very great, please take extra care; camp fires are strictly prohibited.

El Indio Perdido, a farm/guest house (rec.), is 1½ miles N of the Western Highway (turn-off 5 miles from San Ignacio, 2 from Benque Viejo), D with shared shower, C with shower, B with private bath, meals US$3-7.50; activities include swimming, boating (US$5-15), riding (US$5-15), walking, trips to Xunantunich, Tikal (Sats.), the Caves and Mountain Pine Ridge. The farm is on the Mopan River, near Xunantunich. Address: Marco and Colette Gross, Benque Viejo del Carmen, Cayo District, Belize, T 092-2025 or VHF 8450.

Nine miles up-river from San Ignacio is **Benque Viejo del Carmen,** near the Guatemalan frontier (road not sealed, very dusty in the dry season). Population, 2,500. Visas and tourist cards can be obtained at the border. Exchange rates for buying quetzales are better either in the central square in San Ignacio or the Banco de Guatemala on the Guatemalan side of the border (travellers' cheques changed) than with the Belizean money changers at the border.

Hotels *Okis*, George St., E, and *Hotel Maya*, E, 11 George St., opposite the bus station, are the least bad. (Hotels on Guatemalan side of the border are better.) Meals at *Riverside Restaurant*, on main square; *Restaurant Los Angeles*, Church St.; *Hawaii*, on main street, rec.; or at one of picturesque huts.

Three miles away, at **Xunantunich,** now freed from heavy bush, there are Classical Mayan remains in beautiful surroundings. The views from the roof of the spectacular main temple (reportedly the highest man-made structure in Belize) are magnificent. (A leaflet on the area is available from the Archaeological Dept. for BZ$0.25.) Xunantunich can be reached by walking along the Cayo road for about 10 mins. until you reach the landing stage for a ferry; this will take you across the river (free, does not run 1200-1400), then there is a strenuous 1½ hr. walk uphill, not rec. for cars; motorcyclists may find the hill impossible after rain; taxi from San Ignacio, BZ$3. On the far side turn right for Xunantunich (open 0800-1700, entry, BZ$3).

South of San Ignacio is the rediscovered Mayan city of Caracol, "six times the size of ancient Rome in the classic period".

Transport Novello's and Transportes del Carmen run daily buses from Belize City to Benque Viejo; frequent buses from San Ignacio to Benque Viejo, or colectivo from central square, BZ$3 (or BZ$3 to Melchor de Mencos in Guatemala, 30 minutes). To Guatemala from Benque Viejo by taxi, BZ$3 or BZ$1 by colectivo. Free passage of border only weekdays (or if your stay in Belize was 24 hours or less), 0800-1200 and 1400-1700; at other times a fee is charged (US$1). The bridge over the Río Mopán has been rebuilt. On far side someone will carry the luggage to Melchor de Mencos (hotels, and money change possible—see page 1165), where there is a landing strip (flights to Flores). There is also a road (very rough) on to Santa Elena, for Flores (a bus leaves the border for Flores at 1130, US$1, or 4 daily buses from Melchor de Mencos, 3½ hrs., US$1, leave Belize City before 0930 to catch the 1400 bus); it is not possible to get to Tikal by bus without first going to Flores. Taxi from the border to Tikal, US$35 (takes 6); to Flores, US$7.50.

Some 48 miles from Belize City, near Belmopan, the good but narrow 52-mile Hummingbird Highway branches off SE from the Western Highway, through beautiful jungle scenery to **Dangriga** (chief town of the Stann Creek District), some 105 miles from Belize City and 1¾-2½ hours drive from Belmopan. Dangriga's population is 2,500. In this, the most fertile area in the country, are grown citrus fruits, bananas, cassava, and general food crops. The town is on the seashore, and has an airstrip and cinema. Houses built of wood, on piles. Mosquitoes and sand flies are a nuisance.

Local Holiday   Nov. 18-19, Garifuna, or Settlement Day, re-enacting the landing of the Black Caribs in 1823. Dancing all night and next day; very popular. All transport to Dangriga is booked up a week in advance and hotel rooms impossible to find.

Hotels   *Riverside,* 135 Commerce St., D, not always clean, *Pelican Beach,* outside town (P.O. Box 14), on the beach, L, with private bath and a/c; both have good restaurants. *Cameleon,* 119 Commerce St., E, good and friendly (close by, towards the bridge) is an excellent Chinese restaurant. Cheaper lodgings in *Catalina,* 37 Cedar St., E, good, and in private homes (basic). Unfurnished houses are rented out for BZ$40-60 a month.

Restaurants   *Ten kitchen,* next to Z-line bus office, good. At Mile 25.5 on the Hummingbird Highway, N of Dangriga, is *Hummingbird Café,* owned by Ron and Louise Lines (Canadians—mailing address P.O. Box 120, Belmopan); excellent meals and very helpful.

Exchange   Bank of Nova Scotia; Barclays Bank International. Same hours as Belize City. (**See** page 1195.)

Bus from Belize City, Z Line, Magazine Street, daily at 1000, 1100, 1500 and 1600, plus 0600 Mon., returning daily 0500, 0600, 0900, 1000, Sun. at 0900, 1000, 1500, BZ$8, 4 hrs. (buy ticket in advance to reserve seat), or truck, BZ$2. Two buses daily to Punta Gorda, one is the James Line bus from Belize City and the other (Z line), at 1530, 4-5 hrs., BZ$8.50 (very crowded), stops at Independence, near Mango Creek.

Placentia (also spelt Placencia), a quiet, unspoilt little resort S of Dangriga, reached by dugout, BZ$10 each way, 3 hrs., or, now that the road from Dangriga is finished, by bus (leaves Dangriga at 1530, 1½ hrs., BZ$7). Maya Airways fly 3 times a day Belize City-Dangriga-Placencia/Big Creek (dugout Placencia-Big Creek arranged at *Sonny's;* flight tickets are sold at Placencia's new post office), BZ$63 one way.

Accommodation (note that rooms may be hard to find in p.m., e.g. after arrival of the bus from Dangriga) *E-Lee Placencia,* E, full board BZ$15 extra (single meals available), creole cooking, run by Dalton Eiley and Jim Lee; they offer reef fishing, snorkelling, excursions to the jungle, Pine Ridge, Mayan ruins and into the mountains. If arriving by air at Big Creek, first contact Hubert Eiley, 3 Richard Sidewalk, Belize City (T 3567) who will arrange for a boat to take you to Placencia; *Ran's Travel Lodge,* E, shared shower, toilet, friendly, fresh coconut bread baked next door (1000-1100); *Maya Beach Tropical Lodge,* C no meals—L full board (P.O. Box 23, Dangriga); *Placencia Cove,* A, and *Rum Point Inn* (L, latter T 06-2017); *Hilltop,* F; Miss Jackson rents rooms, E-F, BZ$7 for 3 meals (book in advance if non-resident), cooking facilities, friendly (contact Bill, an American, here, for trips to the reef); Mrs. Leslie at the Post Office rents houses at BZ$40 per day (4-6 people, fridge and cooker); she also has hammock space for 3, BZ$5 per night (noisy); Mrs Leslie's son Charles makes all arrangements for the boat to Puerto Cortés, Honduras (see below), and occasionally changes travellers' cheques; he also organizes trips to the reef, etc. Mr. Clive rents 2 houses, one at BZ$4.50, one at BZ$5 p.p. per day; Mr. Zabari's house (rented by Mr. Leslie), BZ$20 per day, 3 large rooms, all facilities. Rooms for rent behind *Galley* restaurant, very basic but cheap, friendly owner. Camping on the beach or under the coconut palms.

There are three restaurants: *The Galley,* rec., especially the seaweed punch, order meals 2-3 hrs. in advance, information on fishing and snorkelling; *Jennie's*—ask here for lodgings at *Seaspray,* F, without bath, good value, by post office; *Jene's* and *Jayl's* opposite each other, both OK; *The Stone Crab* (sign nr. volleyball court), good seafood; and *Sonny's,* at least 5 shops (fresh fruit and vegetables supplied to *The Market* once a week, mostly sold out the same day), a video-cassette movie theatre, four bars (*Cosy's* is rec., disco every night, good hamburgers), the fishing cooperative, open Mon.-Sat., a.m., sells fish cheaply, and supplies the town's electricity.

There is a police station. The people are very friendly and excursions can be made to the coral reef, 16 km. off-shore (US$75-100 for 6 people). The only 'phone is at the Post Office (good source of information on boats). Nearest bank in Mango Creek (Bank of Nova Scotia) open Fri. only 0900-1200, but shops and market change travellers' cheques. Visa extensions obtainable in Mango Creek.

Mango Creek is a banana exporting port, 20 miles S of Dangriga. Bus Belize City-Mango Creek, Southern Transport, James Bus Service, from Pound Yard Bridge, Tues., Wed., Fri. at 0600, Mon., Sat. at 0900; return Sun., Fri. at 1300, Sun., Tues., Thurs. 0600. BZ$13 (insect-repellant imperative). 1000 Z-line bus from Belize City to Dangriga connects with another Z-line bus to Mango Creek, 2 hrs, BZ$5. Hotel above *People's Restaurant,* F; food better at the white house with green shutters behind it (book 2 hrs. in advance if possible); *Hello Hotel* (at Independence) run by Antonio Zabaneh at the shop where the Z-line bus stops, F, clean, comfortable, helpful. Motorized canoe from Mango Creek to Puerto Cortés, Honduras, no fixed schedule, but mostly Thurs.-Sun. (Antonio Zabaneh at his store—phone 06-2011— knows when boats will arrive), US$50 one way, 7-9 hrs. (rubber protective sheeting is provided—hang on to it, usually not enough to go round, nor lifejackets—but you will still get wet unless wearing waterproofs, or just a swimming costume on hot days; it can be dangerous in rough weather). Remember to get an exit stamp (preferably in Belize City), obtainable at the police station in Mango Creek, not Placencia (the BZ$20 departure tax demanded here is not official). Glover's Reef, about 45 miles off Dangriga, is an atoll with beautiful diving, cottages for rent (BZ$10-25 p.p., bring own food); boats BZ$40-80.

The Southern Highway branches off the Hummingbird Highway, 7 miles before Dangriga, and runs 100 miles from Dangriga S, past Mango Creek, to **Punta Gorda,** port of the Toledo District (the road is unpaved, but good all-weather surface). Population 2,500. Rainfall is exceptionally heavy: over 170 inches. The coast, which is some 10 feet above sea-level, is fringed with coconut palms. The main products are beans, rice, cattle and pigs.

Hotels *St. Charles Inn,* C, with or without bath, good; *Foster's,* 19 Main St., E; *Lux Drive Inn,* 17 Front St., D with bath, often full, cockroaches, noisy, damp, good food; *Mahung's Hotel,* 11 Main St., E; *Mira Mar,* 95 Front St., C-A, overpriced, noisy disco, restaurant. If you arrive too late to find a hotel, try asking around for Ched (a friendly American), who has a house to rent near the church, BZ$30, only one bed but plenty of space to sling hammocks, clean, quiet, cold shower. The town has a cinema.

Bus from Belize, 10-12 hrs., BZ$16.50, daily except Thurs. and Sun. (times as for Mango Creek); returns (Z-line) 0500 daily (James Bus Service) Sun., Fri. 1300, Sun., Tues., Thurs. 0600, with a 1700 bus on Fri. for passengers from Guatemala ferry. To Dangriga, Z-line daily at 0530, arriving in time to catch 1000 bus to Belize City.

Ferry to Guatemala The ferry has superseded all the dugout passages to Livingston and Puerto Barrios, Tues. and Fri. at 1430-1500, 4½ hrs. to Puerto Barrios, ticket must be purchased before 1400, costs BZ$11 (US$5.50) or Q6 (US$2.50); the Tuesday boat tends to be faster, perhaps because there is more demand for the Friday boat (queuing for tickets starts at 0800, sales not till 0930) and it is therefore heavier. Ferry ticket agent is on Middle Main Street (open a.m. only, in a shop 2 blocks from *Hotel Mira Mar*); he will insist that you have a visa for Guatemala. If you do not need a visa, insist on being sold a ticket without one; if you do need a visa, the nearest place to obtain one is Chetumal, Mexico. Police station for exit stamp is near the ticket office. Leaving Belize City by 0600 bus on Tues., Wed. or Fri., theoretically you can be in Guatemala on the same day, but with changes of bus in Dangriga and delays it is usually impossible; besides it's a tiring journey (to make sure, fly to Punta Gorda). In the other direction, two days are needed.

As there are few places to change Belizean dollars into quetzales in Guatemala, try Vernon's or other grocery stores in Punta Gorda (travellers' cheques or cash).

About 9 miles N of Punta Gorda, about ¾ mile off the Southern Highway, is the Mayan site of Nimli Punit.

There is a road inland to two villages in the foothills of the Maya mountains; **San Antonio** (21 miles), with Maya ruins of mainly scientific interest (*Hotel Indita Bonita,* with *comedor,* good, clean; picturesque accommodation at Tacho's, BZ$2; may be allowed use of an army hut); medical centre here. About 3 miles along the road to San Antonio is a branch to **San Pedro Colombia,** a Kekchi village. (Kekchi is a sub-tribe of Maya speaking a distinct language.) The Maya and Kechki women wear picturesque costumes. There are many religious celebrations, at their most intense (mixed with general gaiety) on San Luis Rey day (August 5). No bus; pick-up vans for hire in Dangriga, or get a ride in a truck from the market or rice co-operative's mill in Punta Gorda (one leaves early p.m.); alternatively, go to the road junction, known as Dump, where the northern branch goes to Independence/Mango Creek, the other to San Antonio, 6 miles, either hitch or walk. Transport daily from San Antonio to Punta Gorda at 0500, 0530 punctually; if going to Dangriga, take the 0500, get out at Dump to catch 0530 Z-line bus going N.

Turn left, just after crossing the new bridge at San Pedro Colombia, for one mile to reach the Mayan remains of **Lubaantum,** excavated by Cambridge University in 1970 and found to date from the 8th to 9th centuries A.D., late in the Mayan culture and therefore unique. According to latest reports, however, the site is fast reverting to jungle. Local food at a hut and swimming in a river nearby. If hiking in the jungle in this area, there are plenty of logging trails and hunters' tracks, but do not go alone.

THE ECONOMY

Belize's central problem is how to become self-sufficient in food: imports of food are still some 25% of the total imports. Necessity is forcing the people to grow food for themselves and this is gathering pace. One difficulty is that the territory is seriously under-populated and much skilled labour emigrates. Three immigrant Mennonite communities have already increased farm production, and new legislation provides for the development of lands not utilized by private landowners.

Agriculture is by far the most important sector of the Belizean economy, employing more than half the population, and bringing in 75% of the country's total foreign exchange earnings. The main export crops, in order of importance, are sugar, citrus and bananas. Maize, beans and rice are grown, and attempts are also being made to increase the cattle herd.

Forests cover about 65% of the country, and timber is extracted during the first six months of the year. Forest products were for a long time the country's most important export, but their relative importance has fallen. Fish is an important export item, though some of the traditional grounds have been overfished and restrictions necessary for conservation are enforced.

The Government is encouraging the development of tourist facilities. There is also some light industry; items of clothing have been exported. Oil was discovered, near the Mexican border, in April 1981; the search for oil is being intensified.

The slowing down of economic growth at the beginning of the 1980s was attributable to decline in the sugar industry and pressures on Belize's international accounts. Prudent financial policies in the mid-1980s led to the elimination of external debt arrears and the increase of foreign exchange reserves.

	1971-75 (av)	1976-80 (av)	1981-85 (av)	1986-88 (av)(e)
Gdp (1980 prices)	3.9%	4.4%	1.0%	3.9%
Exports (fob) US$m	37.7	76.1	94.3	96.0
Imports (fob) US$m	50.0	100.1	120.0	120.0

INFORMATION FOR VISITORS

How to get there There is no regular sea passenger service (but see under Belize City). There is a first-class airport, 10 miles from Belize, served by Eastern, TAN Airlines and Taca International from Miami (reached by British Airways, Pan Am, Continental or Virgin Atlantic). Other US points served: New Orleans, Houston (both by Continental, Taca, Sahsa) and Los Angeles (Taca). Also daily flights to San Pedro Sula (Sahsa, Eastern) and Tegucigalpa (Sahsa) and less frequent flights to San Salvador, Managua, San José, and Panama (Taca). Sahsa has connections to Managua via Tegucigalpa. Tropic Air flies to Guatemala and Cancún (Mexico).

Documents and Customs All nationalities need passports, as well as sufficient funds and an onward ticket, but visas are usually not required from nationals of the UK, Commonwealth, USA and Canada. Visas can be obtained from the Belizean Consulate in Chetumal, Mexico, for US$10 (may also be charged the price of a telex to Mexico City, US$40). Visas may not be purchased at the border. Free transit visas are available at borders (for 24 or 48 hours). It is possible that a visa may not be required if you have an onward ticket, but check all details at a Consulate before arriving at the border. Those going to other countries after leaving Belize should get any necessary visas in their home country. Visitors are initially granted 30 days' stay in Belize; this may be extended every 30 days up to 6 months at the Immigration Office, Barrack Rd., Belize City. At the end of 6 months, visitors must leave the country for at least 24 hours. Visitors must not engage in any type of employment, paid or unpaid, without first securing a work permit from the Department of Labour; if caught, the penalty for both the employer and the employee is severe. Travellers should note that the border guards seem to have complete power to refuse entry to people whose looks they do not like. There have also been reports that tourists carrying less than US$30 for each day of intended stay have been refused entry.

Motorists should carry their own driving licence and certificate of vehicle ownership. Third party insurance is mandatory, and can be purchased at any border (BZ$25 a week). Valid International Driving Licences are accepted in place of Belize driving permits.

Clothing and articles for personal use are allowed in without payment of duty, but a deposit may be required to cover the duty payable on typewriters, dictaphones, cameras and radios. The duty, if claimed, is refunded when the visitor leaves the country. Import allowances are: 200 cigarettes or ½ lb. of tobacco; 20 fluid ozs. of alcohol; 1 bottle of perfume. Visitors can take in any amount of other currencies. No fruit or vegetables may be brought into Belize; searches are very thorough.

Sellers of American cars must pay duty (if the buyer pays it, he may be able to bargain with the customs official), but prices are quite good particularly in Orange Walk (ask taxi drivers in Belize City).

Departure tax of BZ$20 on leaving from the international airport, but not for transit passengers who have spent less than 24 hrs. in the country. There is a land departure tax of BZ$1 except for those who have spent less than 24 hrs. in the country and for children under 12.

Language English is the official language, but Spanish is widely spoken. Radio Belize devotes about 40 per cent of its air-time to the Spanish language. A Low German dialect is spoken by the Mennonite settlers, and Mayan languages and Garifuna are spoken by ethnic groups.

Internal Transport Traffic drives on the right. When making a left turn, it is the driver's responsibility to ensure clearance of both oncoming traffic and vehicles behind; generally, drivers pull over to the far right, allow traffic from behind to pass, then make the left turn. Many accidents are caused by failure to observe this procedure. All major roads have been, or are being, improved.

Maya Airways flies daily to each of the main towns (see under Belize City) and offers charter rates to all local airstrips of which there are 25. 5 other companies have charters from Belize City to outlying districts. (Belize Aero Company, T 44102; Cari Bee Air Service, T 44253; Flight Service Ltd, T 7049; National Air Service, T 3727; Tropical Air Service, T 7049). Charter rates: Cessna 3-seater, BZ$240; 4/5-seater, BZ$320; 9-seater, US$560.

Passenger transport between the main towns is by colectivo or bus, and trucks also carry passengers to many isolated destinations, although they are no longer allowed to carry passengers to places served by buses. Enquire at market place in Belize City. By law, buses are not allowed to carry standing passengers; some companies are stricter than others. Hitch hiking is very difficult as there is little traffic.

Health Europeans leading a normal life and taking common precautions find the climate pleasant and healthy. Malaria is reportedly under control, but seek advice on prevailing conditions before leaving your home country. It is advisable to carry mosquito repellent. Inoculation against yellow fever and tetanus is advisable but not obligatory. Out-patients' medical attention is free of charge.

Official time is 6 hrs. behind GMT.

Clothing The business dress for men is a short-sleeved cotton or poplin shirt or *guayabera* (ties not often worn) and trousers of some tropical weight material. Formal wear may include ties and jackets, but long-sleeved embroidered *guayaberas* or bush jackets are commoner. Women should not wear shorts in the cities and towns; acceptable only on the cayes and at resorts.

The **monetary unit** is the Belizean dollar, stabilized at BZ$2=US$1. Currency notes (Monetary Authority of Belize) are issued in the denominations of 100, 20, 10, 5, and 1 dollars, and coinage of 50, 25, 10, 5 and 1 cent is in use. Notes marked Government of Belize, or Government of British Honduras, are only redeemable at a bank. The American expressions Quarter (25c.), Dime (10c.) and Nickel (5c.) are common, although 25c. is sometimes referred to as a shilling. There is a 2% charge for cashing travellers' cheques. Good rates for Mexican pesos in Belize. Best rates of exchange at the borders.

Weights and measures Imperial and US standard weights and measures. The US gallon is used for gasoline and motor oil.

The **Cost of Living** is high. Retail shops are open 0800-1200, 1300-1600 and Fri. 1900-2100, with a half day from 1200 on Wed. Small shops open additionally most late afternoons and evenings, and some on Sundays 0800-1000.

Government and commercial office hrs. are 0800-1200 and 1300-1600 Mon. to Fri.

Public Holidays

January 1: New Year's Day.	Sept. 21: Belize Independence Day.
March 9: Baron Bliss Day.	Oct. 12: Pan American Day.
Good Friday and Saturday.	(Corozal and Orange Walk).
Easter Monday.	Nov. 19: Garifuna Settlement Day.
May 1: Labour Day.	December 25: Christmas Day.
May 24: Commonwealth Day.	December 26: Boxing Day.
Sept. 10: St George's Caye Day.	

Warning Most services throughout the country close down Good Friday to Easter Monday; banks close at 1130 on the Thursday, buses run limited services Holy Saturday to Easter Monday, and boats to the Cayes are available. St. George's Caye Day celebrations in September start 2 or 3 days in advance and require a lot of energy.

Telephone and Cable There is a direct-dialling system between the major towns and to Mexico and USA. Belize Telecommunications Ltd., open 0730-2100 Mon.-Sat., closed Suns. and holidays, has an international telephone, telegraph and telex service. To make an international call from Belize costs far less than from neighbouring countries. BZ$26.25 for 3 min. to UK and Europe (a deposit of BZ$30 required first); BZ$15.75 to most of USA and Canada; BZ$10.50 to Florida and US South-East; BZ$8 per min. to Australia. Collect calls to USA, Canada, Australia and UK only.

Airmail Postage to UK 4-5 days. BZ$0.75 for a letter, BZ$0.45 for a postcard; BZ$0.60 for a letter to U.S.A, BZ$0.25 for a post card.

Press Belize: *Belize Times; Amandala, Beacon, Reporter* (weekly).

We are most grateful to Mr Ricardo Osorio of the Belize Tourist Bureau and Mrs Ruha'mah Baguette (Caribbean Charter Services, Belize) and Stephen E. Anderson (Boise, ID), Rupert Baker (Cropredy, Oxon), Naty Bombeck and Christian von Georg (Hamburg 52), Kath Bücken (Stolberg, W.Ger.), Jeanette Ellis (Cremorne, NSW), Hans Gottzmann (Mississauga, Ont.), Glen Kane (San Antonio, TX), Wolfgang Reichert and Annette Karling (Kulmbach, W.Ger.), Gerhard Schweiger (Tamsweg), Mason Singer and Sarah Lee Terrat (Montpelier, VT), Sarah Thomas (British Embassy, Mex.), Ronald Wright (Port Hope, Ontario) and Simon Zisman (Cambridge).

EL SALVADOR

EL SALVADOR is the smallest, most densely populated, most industrialized and most integrated of the Central American republics. Its intermont basins are a good deal lower than those of Guatemala, rising to little more than 600 metres at the capital, San Salvador. Across this upland and surmounting it run two more or less parallel rows of volcanoes, 14 of which are over 900 metres. The highest are Santa Ana (2,365 metres), San Vicente (2,182), San Miguel (2,129), and San Salvador (1,893). One important result of this volcanic activity is that the highlands are covered with a deep layer of ash and lava which forms a porous soil ideal for coffee planting.

The total area of El Salvador is 21,040 square km. Guatemala is to the W, Honduras to the N and E, and the Pacific coastline to the S is 321 km. or so.

Lowlands lie to the N and S of the high backbone. In the S, on the Pacific coast, the lowlands of Guatemala are continued to just E of Acajutla; beyond are lava promontories till we reach another 30-km. belt of lowlands where the 325 Km. long Río Lempa flows into the sea. The northern lowlands are in the wide depression along the course of the Río Lempa, buttressed S by the highlands of El Salvador, and N by the basalt cliffs edging the highlands of Honduras. The highest point in El Salvador, Cerro El Pital (2,730 metres) is part of the mountain range bordering on Honduras. After 160 km. the Lempa cuts through the southern uplands to reach the Pacific; the depression is prolonged SE till it reaches the Gulf of Fonseca.

The population of 5.33 million is far more homogeneous than that of Guatemala. The reason for this is that El Salvador lay comparatively isolated from the main stream of conquest, and it had neither the precious metals nor the agriculturally active Indians that acted as magnets for the Spaniards. The small number of Spanish settlers intermarried with the Indians to form a group of mestizos herding cattle in the valley of the Lempa and growing subsistence crops in the highlands. There were only about half a million people as late as 1879, but soon afterwards coffee was planted in the highlands; easy access to the coast made this crop profitable. The population grew quickly and the prosperity of the coffee planters fertilized the whole economy, but the internal pressure of population has led to the occupation of all the available land. Several hundred thousand Salvadoreans have emigrated to neighbouring republics because of the shortage of land and the concentration of landownership, and more lately because of the high level of violence.

Of the total population only some 10% are purely Indian; less than 10% are of unmixed white ancestry; the rest are *mestizos*. Birth rate: 38; death rate, 10.8 per 1,000; infant mortality, 77 per 1,000 live births. Annual growth rate 1.2% (1981-87); urban growth: 2.4%; and 47.7% live in the towns. Expectation of life at birth, 57 years.

With a population of 234 to the square km., El Salvador is the most densely peopled country on the American mainland. Health and sanitation outside the capital and some of the towns leave much to be desired, and progress has been very limited in the past few years because of the violence. The illiteracy rate is 33%. Education is free if given by the Government, and obligatory. There are 14 universities, one national and the others private or church-affiliated, and a National School of Agriculture. Roman Catholicism is the prevailing religion. Gdp per capita is US$930.

El Salvador is fortunate in that its temperatures are not excessively high. Along the coast and in the lowlands it is certainly hot and humid, but the average for San Salvador is 23°C with a range of only about 3°. March, April, May are the hottest months; December, January, February the coolest. There is one rainy season, from May to October, with April and November being transistional periods; there are only light rains for the rest of the year: the average is about 1,830 mm. Occasionally, in December and March there is a spell of continuously rainy weather, the *temporal*, which may last from two or three days to as many weeks. The pleasantest months are from November to January. From time to time the water shortage can become acute.

Recent History   On October 16, 1979, the President, General Carlos Humberto Romero, was overthrown in a military coup and replaced by a reformist civilian-military junta. In December 1980 a civilian member of the Junta, the Christian Democrat Sr. José Napoleón Duarte, was appointed President (he was elected to the post in May 1984). A decline in popular support and the founding of an opposition front, the Frente Democrático Revolucionario (FDR), and attempted reforms to shift power away from the landowning and banking families, increased political tension to the proportions of civil war. In addition to the deaths caused by confrontation between the army and guerrillas, 40,000 non-combatants were killed between 1979 and 1984, mostly by right-wing death squads. Among the casualities was Archbishop Oscar Romero, who was shot while saying mass in March 1980. The leftist guerrilla forces (the Farabundo Martí National Liberation Front—FMLN) maintained their strength, but neither exploratory meetings between the guerrillas and President Duarte (the FDR and FMLN have consistently boycotted elections), nor the president's signing of the Central American Peace Plan (drawn up by President Arias of Costa Rica, in August 1987) brought any positive results. The war continued in stalemate until 1989, by which time an estimated 70,000 had been killed. The Christian Democrats' inability to end the conflict, either by victory or agreement, to reverse the economic decline, or to rebuild after the 1986 earthquake led to a resurgence of support for the right-wing Nationalist Republican Alliance (Arena). After 1986 Arena gained support at both congressional and municipal level, and the Arena candidate, Alfredo Cristiani, won comfortably the presidential elections held in March 1989.

Note   At the time of writing it is safe to travel around the country, to the beaches, lakes and mountains, particularly in the West and South West. However, care is advised when travelling to North, East and South East, in departments such as Chalatenango, Morazán, La Unión, Cabañas and Usulután.

Cities and Towns

San Salvador, the capital, is in an intermont basin at 680 metres, on the Río Acelhuate in the Valle de las Hamacas and with a ring of mountains round it; the population is 456,000. It was founded by Pedro de Alvarado in 1525, but not where it now stands. The city was destroyed by earthquake in 1854, so the present capital is a modern city, most of its architecture conditioned by its liability to seismic shocks. However, in the earthquake of October 10, 1986, many buildings collapsed; over 1,000 people died. As a result, many government offices and public services have been temporarily relocated until reconstruction has been completed. Even in 1988/89, the centre was still in a very bad condition, with many people not yet returned to proper housing. The climate is semi-tropical and healthy, the water supply pure. Days are often hot, but the temperature drops in the late afternoon and nights are always pleasantly mild. Since it is in a hollow, the city has a smog problem, caused mainly by traffic pollution.

Four broad streets meet at the centre: Av. Cuscatlán and its continuation Av. España run S to N, Calle Delgado and its continuation Calle Arce from E to W. This principle is retained throughout: all

the *avenidas* run N to S and the *calles* E to W. The even-numbered *avenidas* are E of the central *avenidas*, odd numbers W; N of the central *calles* they are dubbed Norte; S of the central *calles* Sur. The even-numbered *calles* are S of the two central *calles*, the odd numbers N. E of the central *avenidas* they are dubbed Oriente, W of the central *avenidas* Poniente. It takes a little time to get used to this system.

Nearly all the more important buildings are near the main intersection. On the E side of Av. Cuscatlán is Plaza Barrios, the heart of the city. A fine equestrian statue looks W towards the Renaissance-style National Palace (1904-11). To the N is the new cathedral which is, however, unfinished. To the E of Plaza Barrios, on Calle Delgado, is the National Theatre (which has been magnificently restored and is now open). If we walk along 2a Calle Oriente we come on the right to the Parque Libertad; in its centre is a flamboyant monument to Liberty looking E towards the rebuilt church of El Rosario where José Matías Delgado, father of the independence movement, lies buried. The Archbishop's Palace is next door. The big building on the S side of the square is the Municipal Palace. Not far away to the SE (on 10a Av. Sur) is another rebuilt church, La Merced, from whose bell-tower went out Father Delgado's tocsin call to independence in 1811.

Across Calle Delgado, opposite the theatre, is Plaza Morazán, with a monument to General Morazán. Calle Arce runs W to the Hospital Rosales, in its own gardens. SW of the Hospital, along Av. Roosevelt, is the National Stadium. On the way to the Hospital, if you turn S opposite the great church of El Sagrado Corazón de Jesús, you come after one block to Parque Bolívar, with the national printing office to the S, and the Department of Health to the N.

Festivals At the edge of the city (to the N along Avenida España and W along 9a Calle Poniente) is the Campo de Marte, a large and popular park where the Palacio de Deportes has been built, and through which runs the Avenida Juan Pablo II. During Holy Week, and the fortnight preceding August 6, is held the Fiesta of the Saviour ("El Salvador"). As a climax colourful floats wind up the Campo de Marte. On August 5, an ancient image of the Saviour is borne before a large procession; there are church services on the 6th, Feast of the Transfiguration. On Dec. 12, Day of the Indian, there are processions honouring the Virgin of Guadalupe in El Salvador (take bus 101 to the Basilica of Guadalupe, half-way to Santa Tecla, to see colourful processions).

N.B. The city centre is considered unsafe after dark. In general, robberies, particularly on crowded city buses, have increased of late; pickpocketing and bag slashing are common. Women are advised not to wear expensive jewellery on the street.

Hotels *El Salvador Sheraton* (not part of the Sheraton chain), 89a Av. Norte on the slopes of a volcano on the outskirts, A, outdoor pool; *Presidente*, San Benito, A, pool, garden, very pleasant, good buffets (US$8); *Siesta*, on Autopista Sur, off Pan-American Highway, west of the city, C. *Novo*, 61 Av. N (in cul-de-sac), rooms with bath and kitchen US$650/month (shorter periods possible), mini swimming pool, garden, pleasant; *Ramada Inn*, 85a Av. Sur, Calle Juan José Cañas, C; *Alameda*, 43a Av. Sur and Alameda Roosevelt, C; *Camino Real*, Blvd. de los Héroes, A; *Escalón Apartments*, 3689 Paseo General Escalón at Av. 71 Sur, US$300 per month double. *Panamerican*, 8 Av. Sur 113, E, with cold shower, closes early (but knock on door), meals from US$2 and parking space, rec. *American Guest House*, 17 Av. N 119, C, friendly, helpful; *Ritz Continental*, 7a Av. Sur 219, D-C; *Terraza*, 85a Av. Sur, Calle Padre Aguilar, C-B; *Hospedaje Izalco*, Calle Concepción 666, E; *Florida Guest House*, Blvd. Los Héroes y Pasaje Los Almendros 115, D; *Casa Austria*, 1a C. Poniente 3843 (between 73 and 75 Av.), small, quiet, family atmosphere, D, rec., English- and German-speaking owner; *Family Guest House*, 1a C. Poniente Bis 925, D, safe, clean, expensive meals available; *Imperial*, Calle Concepción 659, friendly, serves reasonable meals and has car park, E, with toilet and shower, can be noisy. *Custodio*, 10a Av. Sur 109, F, without bath, basic, clean and friendly but noisy; *Bruno*, 1 Calle Oriente, between 8 and 10 Av., F with bath, cheaper without, not very clean, quite safe (but not a safe area of town). *San Carlos*, Calle Concepción 121, E with bath, early morning call, cold drinks available, good; *Hospedaje Yucatán*, Calle Concepción 673, F with bath, basic, friendly, noisy; excellent restaurant (*Rosita*—vegetarian food good) downstairs; on Blvd. Venezuela west of Occidente bus terminal is *Occidental*, clean, friendly. Prices are without meals unless otherwise stated. Hotel tax: 10%. **Motels** *Boulevard*, E, with shower, very clean, with parking, 2 km. from centre, but good bus service. Several motels on all main roads leading out of the capital.

Restaurants At hotels. All close between 2000 and 2100. *Siete Mares*, Paseo Escalón, very good seafood; *Diligencia* (for good steaks) and *El Bodegón* (Spanish style) both on Paseo Escalón, are excellent; also on Paseo Escalón: *La Ponderosa* (famous for steaks with *chirimol*, near Plaza

Beethoven), *Le Mar* (seafoods), *Beto's* (Italian), *Pip's Carymar* (also in Santa Tecla—good, cheap typical food), *Rancho Alegre* (cheap, also opp. Metrocentro shopping mall), and tacos and pupusas at Redondel Masferrer, good view over city, lively atmosphere, mariachis, but be alert at night for fights and drug dealing on the less well-lit side of the Redondel. *Texas Meats*, Calle La Mascota, good for steaks; *Doña Mercedes*, Blvd. Los Héroes, 3 blocks north of Metrocentro, is another good steakhouse. *München*, Av. Roosevelt, German; opp. is *China Palace*, excellent value (oldest Chinese restaurant in San Salvador); *Romano*, Av. Roosevelt 45 y 47 Av. Norte; *El Café Don Pedro* (drive-in in Av. Roosevelt); *Pupusería Margot*, opp. Estado Mayor on the road to Santa Tecla, good. *Rosal*, El Mirador, near *Sheraton*, Italian, good; *Pizza Capri*, Italian-owned, behind *Hotel Camino Real*.

Restaurants in the Zona Rosa, Blvd. Hipódromo are generally very good, but expensive. These include: *Marcelino's, Mediterráneo* (good ceviche), *La Ola, Chili's, Paradise* (all popular); *Basilea/Schäffer's*, also in Zona Rosa, restaurant and excellent cakes, nice garden atmosphere. Branches of *MacDonalds* and *Biggest* (hamburgers, fast food); *Pollo Campero* (branches throughout the city, good); *Don Paro's*, Calle Arce is especially good for breakfast; *Café Don Alberto*, Calle Arce y 15 Av. Norte, good and cheap.

Vegetarian restaurants: *La Zanahoria*, Calle Arce 1199, *Kalpataru*, 100 m. N of Redondel Masferrer, nice atmosphere; *El Tao*, 21 Av. Norte y Calle Arce, and Centro de Gobierno, 19 Calle Poniente; *Actoteatro*, 1 Calle Poniente (between 15 and 13 Av. N), good atmosphere, patio, music, good buffet lunch, cheap, central. Good pupusas at a cave restaurant in Puerta del Diablo. Good cheap *comedores* in Occidente bus terminal. *Victoria*, bakery, good for pastries. The food market, one of the biggest and cleanest in Latin America, has many stalls selling cheap food. *Pops*, near *Bruno Hotel* on 1 Calle Oriente and Av. 4, is a good ice-cream parlour; there is another branch on Escalón, near the British Club (and at Metrocentro). Coffee shops: *Shaw's*, chocolates and coffee; *Flashback*, Blvd. Hipódromo (Zona Rosa), good coffee.

Electric Current 110 volts, 60 cycles, A.C. (plugs are American, 2 flat pin style).

Clubs Club Salvadoreño, admits foreigners, owns a fine Country Club on Lake Ilopango called Corinto (with a golf course), and has a seaside branch at Km.43 on the coast road, near La Libertad, much frequented during the dry season, November to April. The Automobile Club of El Salvador has a chalet for bathing at La Libertad. British Club (Paseo Escalón 4714—approx), has British newspapers and swimming pool. (Temporary visitors' cards if introduced by a member.) The Country Club Campestre (Paseo Escalón), admits foreigners with cards only. Club Náutico, at the Estero de Jaltepeque, famous for its mud boat races.

Shopping Mercado Cuartel, crafts market, 8 Av. Norte, 1a C. Oriente, a few blocks E of the National Theatre. One can buy towels here with various Maya designs. A large new shopping precinct with ample parking (Metrocentro) is on Boulevard Los Héroes, NW of city centre. Metrocentro and the Zona Rosa have handicraft shops, but at least twice as dear as Mercado Cuartel.

Bookshops at the Universidad Centroamericana (UCA) and Universidad de El Salvador (UES); Nuevo Mundo, 67 Av. Sur 144; Clásicos Roxsil, 6 Av. Sur 1-6, Santa Tecla. A few English books at Librería Quixaje, Calle Arce, and a few at Shaw's chocolate shop, 1 block past Parque Beethoven on Paseo Escalón.

Local Buses Flat fare of US$0.06.

Taxis Plenty (all yellow), none has a meter, ask fare before getting in. Fares: from centre to outskirts or *Hotel El Salvador Sheraton*, US$3; central runs, US$2. Double fare after dark. Taxis from Acontaxis (T 223361, 223268, 223294), Acomet (T 259114, 259576), Acosat (T 244015) and Dos Pinos (T 222321). Self-drive cars cost US$6 to US$16 per day or US$40 to US$80 per week according to size of car plus a rate per km. of US$0.08. **Rentals** from Avis, 42 Av. Sur 137, nr. *Hotel Alameda*; Budget, 85 Av. Sur 220, in the front of *Hotel Terraza*; Hertz, Calle Los Andes behind *Hotel Camino Real*.

Complaints Director General of Police, 6a Calle Oriente. T 71-4422.

Night Clubs All leading hotels have their own night club. *Mario's* on Blvd. Hipódromo, Zona Rosa, with good live music; *Faces on the Top*, double-disco, Calle El Mirador, near *Sheraton*. *Club M*, also near *Sheraton*. *Memories*, Paseo General Escalón; *Luzeiro*, Calle El Mirador; *My Place*, Paseo General Escalón and 83 Av. Norte.

Entertainments Many cinemas, with Cinerama at the Grand Majestic (best quality cinemas cost US$2, films in English with sub-titles), or ballet and plays at the National Theatre of Fine Arts, and music or plays at the Cámara Theatre. Bowling at Bolerama Jardín and Club Salvadoreño. Football is played at the Stadium on Sun. and Thurs. according to programme at the Cuscatlán and Flor Blanca Stadiums. Motor racing at new El Jabalí autodrome on lava fields near Quezaltepeque. Basketball, tennis, international swimming, fishing, target shooting, wrestling, boxing and boat and sailing boat races, but in private clubs only.

Museums Museo Nacional David J. Guzmán, 1 block W of Feria Internacional on Av. de la

Revolución, has a small but good archaeological exhibition. Open Tues.-Sun. 0900-1200 and 1400-1700. Natural History Museum, end of C. Los Viveros, Col. Nicaragua, Wed.-Sun. 0930-1630.

Exchange Citibank, in Torre Roble, Blvd. de los Héroes; and national banks. Open 0900-1300, 1345-1500; some banks have a late night counter until 1900. Banks charge 1 colón for changing money and cheques; cashing travellers' cheques involves lengthy paperwork. Credomatic, for obtaining funds with either Visa or Mastercard, Edificio Cidema, Alameda Roosevelt y Calle 51. Foreign currency is difficult to obtain. Black market can be found outside the Centro Gobierno, near the Post Office, and on the W side of Parque Infantil for dollars cash, travellers' cheques and quetzales (safe).

Immigration Department In the Ministry of Interior Building, Centro de Gobierno, T 22-6090, open Mon.-Fri. 0800-1600.

Embassies British, Paseo General Escalón 4828, T 240473. **US,** 25 Av. Norte, 1230, in front of Fuente Luminosa, T 267100. **Dutch,** Of. La Curazao, Edif. Lotisa 2° piso, Final C. La Mascota y Av. Masferrer (T 23-4000, 0800-1200, 1330-1630). **Guatemalan,** 15 Av. Norte 135 y C. Arce (0900-1200). **Panamanian,** Col. San Francisco, C. Los Bambúes y Av. Bugambilia 21, T 98 0773; **Nicaraguan,** 27 Av. Norte No. 1134 (T 25-7281, 0900-1400); **Honduran,** 7 C. Poniente 4236, T 23-3856; **Mexican,** Paseo Gral. Escalón 3832 (T 24-0162, 0900-1400); **Belizean,** 15C. Poniente 4415 (½ block behind *Sheraton*, T 23-5271, 0830-1200); **West German,** 3a C. Poniente 3832, Col. Escalón (T 23-6173, 0800-1400); **French,** 1a C. Poniente 3718 y 73 Av. Norte, Col. Escalón (T 23-0728, 0900-1200).

Post Office In Centro do Gobierno; branches at Almacenes Simón Librería Hispanoamérica, Centro Comercial Gigante (Col. Escalón), Supermercados Todo's Escalón, Mercado Central Local No. 3, Mercado Modelo, 1st floor above PHL stationer on Plaza Morazán. Open Mon.-Fri. 0730-1730, Sat. 0730-1600. *Lista de correos,* Mon.-Fri. 0800-1200, 1430-1700.

Churches Anglican Centre (St. John's Episcopal Church), 63 Av. Sur and Av. Olímpica, services on Sun., 0900 in English, 1000 in Spanish; American Union Church, C. 4 off Calle La Mascota; has services in English on Sun., at 1000, and also has a gift shop (local crafts and textiles) and an English paperback library (both open Weds. and Sat.). Synagogue, 23a Av. Norte 215.

International Industrial Fair, held in November, every two years (even dates), in Calle Santa Tecla, near the Monument of the Revolution. Site is also used for other functions such as the traditional August fair.

Tourist Office Instituto Salvadoreño de Turismo, Calle Rubén Darío 619. T 22-8000 (Mon.-Fri. 0800-1600, Sat. 0800-1200, closed Sun.). They will advise on the security situation in the country. They give away a map of the country and city, but the Texaco and Esso maps (obtainable from their respective service stations) are more accurate. The office is very helpful. Also "Advice to Tour Guides", a rec. booklet. Good map of the country (about US$6) is available from the Instituto Nacional de Geografía, Av. Juan Bertis, 59 and Librería La Ibérica, 1 Calle Oriente, 127. The tourist office at the International airport is open 0800-1630 all year round except Dec. 25 and Jan. 1, T 39-9454, 39-9464.

Tourist Agents El Salvador Travel Service, 23 Av. Sur 201. Avia, la Calle Poniente, at junction with 73a Av. Norte in Colonia Escalón, are rec. Tour operators include: Alpha Tours, Alameda Roosevelt y 55 Av. Norte, T 24-6928; Joanesa, 41 Av. Sur 518, T 22-1920; Rinsa, 67 Av. Sur, Pas. 2-3 E-69, T 24-4863; and others.

Airport The new international airport at Comalapa is 44 km. from San Salvador, near Costa del Sol beach, reached by 4-lane highway. Acacya minibus to airport from 3 C. Poniente and Av. Norte in front of Shell gas station, T 71-4937, 0600, 0700, 1200, 1500, US$3 one way (leave from airport when full, on right as you go out). Taxi Acacya US$18 one way. The airport tax is US$9, plus US$1 boarding tax. The old airport is at Ilopango, 13 km. away. It is primarily used by the air force. However, from Ilopango small planes fly to San Miguel (30 mins., good, US$25), Usulután, Santa Rosa de Lima and La Unión; tickets from the civilian traffic offices (TAES, Taxis Aéreos El Salvador, or Gutiérrez Flying Service). No regular internal air lines but charter flights are easily arranged. The prices in the gift shops at the airport are exorbitant; there is a post office at the tourist office.

Rail There are no passenger services.

Long-Distance Buses Terminal del Occidente, down an alleyway off Boulevard Venezuela, opposite No. 2963 (dangerous area; take city buses 4, 27 or 34). Most international buses pass through if not starting from here. About 12 buses a day to Guatemala City (5 hrs.). Single, US$3. By car to Guatemala City takes 4 hrs. From Terminal del Occidente: Melva y Pezzarossi (T 24-2953) 8 a day between 0500 and 1430 (be at terminal ½ hr. before departure); Centroamérica (T 24-4258), 0600—home pick-up at 0530, US$7; Taca (T 24-3236), 0930; El Cóndor (T 24-6548),

0530, 0800, 1330; Transsesmer (T 24-1965), 1300; Futuro Express (13 Av. Sur y Pasaje Alcaine, T 22-4272) run a home pick-up service at 0530, US$6; Mermex (Ed. Corfinca Local 3, 11 Av. Sur y Pasaje Costa Rica, T 22-1258), 0600 at office, or 0700 at Terminal del Occidente. El Cóndor also runs daily from Terminal del Occidente to Talismán, on Mexico-Guatemala border, 0700 and 1000, US$7. To Tegucigalpa, Transportes El Salvador, 7a C. Poniente y 14 Av. Norte 322, on Mon., Thurs. and Sat. at 0530 from office, 0600 from Terminal del Oriente, US$6 (unreliable). The only way to Managua and further S is by taking the Tegucigalpa service to Jícaro Galán, or more frequent local buses beyond San Miguel or Santa Rosa from Terminal Oriente, end of Av. Peralta (take city buses 7, 33 or 29): hourly, first at 0400, then to the border, thence to Choluteca and on to Nicaragua.

N.B. The Honorary British Consul in El Salvador advises, "If buses are running regularly, the route is probably reasonably safe." Bus routes most frequently attacked by guerrillas are the Troncal del Norte to Chalatenango and El Poy and the eastern Pan-American Highway between San Vicente and San Miguel, and San Miguel and Goascarán.

A good **sightseeing tour** of from 2 to 3 hrs. by car is along Av. Cuscatlán, past the Zoo (which though small, is quiet and attractive—open Wed.-Sun. 0930-1630) and the Casa Presidencial and up to the new residential district in the mountain range of Planes de Renderos. This place, reached by bus 12 from the centre, is crowned by the beautiful Balboa Park (good view of city from El Mirador at foot of Park). From the park a scenic road runs to the summit of Cerro Chulo, from which the view, seen through the Puerta del Diablo (Devil's Door), is even better. The Door consists of two enormous vertical rocks which frame a magnificent view of the San Vicente volcano. At the foot of Cerro Chulo is Panchimalco (see below). There are local buses (12, US$0.20 and 17, and 12 minibus marked "Mil Cumbres") to Puerta del Diablo about every hour. There are reports that mugging is increasingly common at Cerro Chulo; it is unsafe to make the trip alone. The Teleférico on the hill overlooking the city and Lake Ilopango has good views, cafeterias and a children's funfair. Reached by 9 bus from centre, US$1.60. Open Fri., Sat., Sun. only, 0900-1900.

For a quick "taste" of San Salvador, Taca airlines take passengers in transit through San Salvador to the *Sheraton Hotel* from the airport, provide a free lunch, and a room for US$5 (this generally applies to flights between Managua/San José and Tegucigalpa/Guatemala City, which involve an 8-hour wait in El Salvador for connecting Taca flights).

Excursions can be made by road to Panchimalco and Lake Ilopango; to the crater of San Salvador volcano; and to the volcano of Izalco (1,910 metres) and the near-by park of Atecosol, and Cerro Verde (**see Sonsonate, page 1216**); to the garden park of Ichanmichen (**see Zacatecoluca, page 1215**); to Lake Coatepeque (lunch at *Hotel del Lago*) and to Cerro Verde in 90 minutes. The excavated site of San Andrés, on the estate of the same name, 32 km. west of San Salvador, is unimpressive (take bus 201 from Terminal del Occidente). Bus 495 from the Terminal del Occidente goes to Costa del Sol, a developing seaside resort with beautiful beaches and luxury hotels (e.g. *Tesoro Beach*, pleasant apartment style rooms, large swimming pool, expensive, T 71-2111). Sihuatehuacán and the pyramid of Tazumal (**page 1218**) are reached by bus 202. There are swimming pools at Los Chorros (bus 79 from Calle Ruben Darío—see below). Buses from the Oriente terminal go to Quezaltepeque, near which is La Toma, a popular inland resort, to Amapulapa, where there are gardens and a swimming pool, and to Lake Apastepeque (**see page 1214**).

Panchimalco is 14½ km. S by a paved road. Around it live the Pancho Indians, pure-blooded descendants of the original Pipil tribes; a few have retained more or less their old traditions and dress. Streets of low adobe houses thread their way among huge boulders at the foot of Cerro Chulo (rolled down the hill to repel the Spaniards, according to local legend). A very fine baroque colonial church with splendid woodcarvings in the interior and a bell incised with the cypher and titles of the Holy Roman Emperor Charles V. An ancient ceiba tree shades the market place (disappointing market). Bus 17 from Mercado Central at 12 Calle Poniente, San Salvador, every 45 min., US$0.30, 1½ hrs.

Lake Ilopango A 4-lane highway, the Ilopango Boulevard, runs E for 14½ km. from San Salvador to Ilopango airport, quite near Lake Ilopango, 15 km. by 8, in the crater of an old volcano, well worth a visit. Pre-Conquest Indians used to propitiate the harvest gods by drowning four virgins here each year. There are a number of lakeside cafés and bathing clubs, some of which hire dug-outs by the hr. *Hotel Vistalgo*, D. A number of private chalets make access to the lake difficult, except at clubs and the Turicentro. Bus 15, marked Apulo, runs from the bus stop on 2a Av. Norte y Plaza Morazán to the lake (via the airport), 70 minutes, US$ 0.30. Entrance to the Turicentro camping site costs US$0.18 and is rec.; showers and swimming facilities. The water is reported to be polluted.

Santa Tecla, 13 km. W of the capital by the Pan-American Highway, is 240 metres higher and much cooler, in a coffee-growing district. Population, 63,400. The huge crater of San Salvador volcano (known as Boquerón by the locals)—1½ km. wide and 543 metres deep—can be reached from Santa Tecla, road starts 1 block E of Plaza Central, going due N (very rough). Bus (101) leaves 3 Av. Norte, near the junction with Calle Ruben Darío, San Salvador, every ten mins. for Santa Tecla (US$0.12). There is a bus (103) from there to Boquerón hourly, last one back at 1500 (US$0.30) and from there you must walk the last 1½ km. to the crater. A walk clockwise round the crater takes about 2 hrs.; the first half is easy, the second half rough (the path is used by soldiers and guerrillas). The views are magnificent. The inner slopes of the crater are covered with trees, and at the bottom is a smaller cone left by the eruption of 1917. The path down into the crater starts at the westernmost of a row of antennae studding the rim, 45 mins. down (don't miss the turn straight down after 10 mins. at an inconspicuous junction with a big, upright slab of rock 20 metres below), 1 hr. up. There are a number of army checkpoints on the way to the summit. A road further North leads also to San Salvador volcano through extensive coffee plantations. Santa Tecla, also known as Nueva San Salvador, has a training school for factory technicians, set up with British funds and technical help.

At *Los Chorros,* in a natural gorge 6 km. N of Santa Tecla, there is a beautiful landscaping of 4 pools below some waterfalls. The first pool is shallow, and bathers can stand under the cascades, but there is good swimming in the other three. Visit at night for the lighting effects. Entry, US$0.15. Car park fee: US$0.40. Camping is allowed, US$1 for two people. There is a trailer park at Los Chorros, with restaurant and showers.

Just before Santa Tecla is reached, a branch road turns S for 24 km. to

La Libertad, 37 km. from San Salvador, now only a fishing port. Population 22,800. It is also a popular seaside resort during the dry season, with good fishing and surf bathing, but watch out for undercurrents and sharks. The beaches are black volcanic sand; they are dirty but the surf is magnificent (watch your belongings). (The Automobile Club and the Club Salvadoreño have beach chalets.) Bus 102 from San Salvador leaves from 4 Calle Poniente, 17 Av. Sur, US$0.62. Bus from Santa Tecla, US$0.30.

The Costa del Bálsamo (the Balsam Coast), stretching between La Libertad and Acajutla (see page 1216), is now rather a myth, but on the steep slopes of the departments of Sonsonate and La Libertad, scattered balsam trees are still tapped. The pain-relieving balsam, once a large export, has almost disappeared. Bus along the coast to Sonsonate at 0600 and 1300, about 4 hrs.

Hotels Hotels charge for 12 hrs. only. Many in C range, overpriced. *Don Rodrigo*, C; *Don Lito*, D; *Nuevo Amanecer*, 1 C. Poniente No. 24-1, F, safe, clean, rec.; *Pensión Peace and Love*, F, very basic and friendly; *Bar Gringo* on the beach front lets rooms, F, so does the *Miramar* restaurant (E, negotiable). **Motel Siboney**, nearby, good.

Restaurant Food is good in the town, especially at *Punta Roca* (American-owned, by Don Bobby), try the shrimp soup, and *Altamar* for seafood. *Pupusería*, specializes in snacks, rec. *Los Mariscos*, good, reasonable prices, popular, closed Mons. *The Fisherman's Club*, excellent seafood, bar, swimming pool, tennis court, private beach, entry fee US$2. Cheap restaurants near the pier; also cheap food in the market.

Excursions To the large village of Jicalapa, on high rockland above the sea, for its magnificent festival on St. Ursula's day (October 21). 8 km. to the west is **Zunzal,** which has superb surf (*Hospedaje El Pacífico*, F, 1 km. towards La Libertad; buses 102 and 192, from La Libertad. 15 km. away is the *Atami Beach Club*, with pool, private beach, restaurant, 2 bars, gardens, a beautiful place; tourists may enter for US$2, prices are reasonable. Bus to San Diego beach (from road parallel to La Libertad beach), US$1, ½ hourly, nice but deserted. To the Salto y Cueva Los Mangos: walk along the 2 km. trail almost opposite *Motel Siboney* to a 60 m. waterfall; a little further downstream is the Salto San Antonio (50 m.), best reached by bus 287 from La Libertad to San Antonio quarry (just before San Diego beach), then walking 1 km. upstream.

Eastern El Salvador

E to La Unión / Cutuco   There are two roads to the port of La Unión/Cutuco on the Gulf of Fonseca: (i) the Pan-American Highway, 185 km., through Cojutepeque, San Vicente (road being repaved either side of this city), the 15 de Septiembre dam (since the destruction of the Cuscatlán bridge) and San Miguel; (ii) the Coastal Highway, also paved, running through Santo Tomás, Olocuilta, Zacatecoluca, and Usulután. The roads have frequently been cut by guerrilla action against bridges (most rivers are now crossed by Bailey bridges or dry fords).

By Pan-American Highway   Some 5 km. from the capital a dry-weather highway branches N to Tonocatepeque, Suchitoto, and Chalatenango.

Tonocatepeque, 13 km. from the capital, is an attractive small town on the high plateau, in an agricultural setting but with a small textile industry. There has been some archaeological exploration of the town's original site, 5 km. away.

Suchitoto is quite near the Lempa River, and the Cerrón Grande reservoir, under which is the old road to Chalatenango. The new road to Chalatenango branches right off the Troncal del Norte beyond the Cerrón Grande (**see page 1219**). There has been much guerrilla and counter-insurgency activity in this northern area: visitors are advised to take care.

Continuing along the Pan-American Highway: a short branch road (about 2 km. beyond the airport) leads off right to the W shores of Lake Ilopango. The first town is *Cojutepeque,* capital of Cuscatlán Department, 34 km. from San Salvador. (Reached by bus 113 from Oriente terminal in San Salvador, US$0.75.) Population 31,300. Lake Ilopango is to the SW. Good weekly market. The town is famous for cigars, smoked sausages and tongues, and its annual fair on August 29 has fruits and sweets, saddlery, leather goods, pottery and headwear on sale from neighbouring villages, and sisal hammocks, ropes, bags and hats from the small factories of Cacaopera (Dept. of Morazán).

Hotels   *Turista,* 5 C. Oriente 130, F; *Motel Edén,* E, with shower; *Comedor Toyita,* good value.

Cerro de las Pavas, a conical hill near Cojutepeque, dominates Lake Ilopango and gives splendid views of wide valleys and tall mountains. Its shrine of Our Lady of Fátima draws many pilgrims.

Excursion   From San Rafael Cedros, 6 km. E of Cojutepeque, a 16-km. paved road N to Ilobasco has a branch road E to Sensuntepeque at about Km. 13. *Ilobasco* has 48,100 people, many of them workers in clay; its decorated pottery is now mass-produced and has lost much of its charm. The area around, devoted to cattle, coffee, sugar and indigo, is exceptionally beautiful. Annual fair: September 29. An all-weather road leads from Ilobasco to the great dam and hydroelectric station of Cinco de Noviembre at the Chorrera del Guayabo, on the Lempa River. Bus to Cojutepeque. Another road with fine views leads to the Cerrón Grande dam and hydroelectric plant; good excursion by bus or truck. Permission is given in normal times to enter the dam area and one can climb the hill with the Antel repeater on top for a view of the whole lake created by the dam. The whole Lempa valley is now a security zone and there has been much guerrilla activity there.

Four km. further S along the Pan-American Highway at San Domingo (km. 44 from San Salvador) an unpaved road leads in 5 km. to *San Sebastián* where colourfully patterned hammocks and bedspreads are made. You can watch them being woven on complex looms of wood and string, and can buy from the loom. The 110 bus from the Oriente terminal runs from San Salvador to San Sebastián (US$1.50). There are also buses from Cojutepeque.

Sensuntepeque, 35 km. E of Ilobasco, is a pleasant town at 900 metres, in the hills S of the Lempa valley. It is the capital of Cabañas Department, once a great source of indigo. There are some interesting ceremonies during its fair on December 4, the day of its patroness, Santa Bárbara. It can be reached from the Pan-American Highway from near San Vicente. Population: 45,000.

N.B.   San Vicente and San Miguel have been the centres of intense guerrilla activity in Eastern El Salvador and consequently there is a strong military presence.

San Vicente, 61 km. from the capital, is a little SE of the Highway on the Río Alcahuapa, at the foot of the double-peaked Chinchontepec volcano, with very fine views of the Jiboa valley as it is approached. Population: 56,800. Its pride and gem is El Pilar (1762-69), most original church in the country. It was here that the **Indian chief, Anastasio Aquino,** took the crown from the statue of San José and crowned himself King of the Nonualcos during the Indian rebellion of 1833. In its main square is the *tempesque* tree under which the city's foundation charter was drawn up. Bus 116 from Oriente terminal, San Salvador. Carnival day: November 1.

Hotels *Pensión Vicentina,* E. Better is *Casa Romero,* which is near the bridge but has no sign, so ask for directions, E; good meals for US$0.80. *Hospedaje Viajero,* F; *Hospedaje Rivoly,* E, good food.

Two km. E of the town is the Balneario Amapulapa, one of a number of recreational centres developed by the National Tourist Board. There are three pools at different levels in a wooded setting. Small entry and parking charges. Reached by bus 174 from San Vicente.

Excursion Lake Apastepeque, near San Vicente off the Pan-American Highway, is small but picturesque. The Tourist Board has built a pier and bathing cabins. Hotel: *París.*

The Highway (in poor condition after San Vincente) used to cross the Río Lempa by the 411-metre-long Cuscatlán suspension bridge (destroyed by guerrillas in 1983). It now crosses the 15 de Septiembre dam at the San Lorenzo hydroelectric plant, and goes on to

San Miguel, 136 km. from San Salvador, capital of its Department, founded in 1530 at the foot of the volcanoes of San Miguel (Chaparastique—which erupted in 1976, and Chinameca). It has some very good parks and a bare 18th century cathedral. Some silver and gold are mined. It is an important distributing centre. Population, 161,000. Bus 301 from Oriente terminal, San Salvador (US$1.40, return every ½ hr. from 0500 to 1630). Fiesta of the Virgen de la Paz: November 20. There is a charming church with statues and fountains in its gardens about 16 km. away at Chinameca.

Hotels Very few in centre, most on the entrance roads: *Trópico Inn,* C, clean, comfortable, reasonable restaurant; *Hispanoamericano,* 6A Av. Norte B, F, with toilet and shower, air-conditioned (cheaper in older rooms without a/c); *Motel Milián* (pool), D, rec., good food; *Central,* G, English spoken. *Pensión El Carmen,* F; *San Luis,* G, clean and quiet. Plenty of cheap places near the bus station. *Comedor Divina Providencia* for good meals; 3 Chinese restaurants.

Exchange Local banks. Open: 0830-1200, 1430-1800.

From San Miguel a good paved road runs S to the Pacific Highway. Go S along it for 12 km., where a dirt road leads to Playa El Cuco, a pleasant long beach; a small motel 1 km. from El Cuco village. There are lots of *pensiones* in the village quite near the bus stop, E/F. Bus 320 from San Miguel, US$1. The climate in this area is good. A mainly paved, reasonable road goes to San Jorge and Usulután: leave the Pan-American Highway 5 km. W of San Miguel. The road goes through hills and coffee plantations with superb views of San Miguel volcano. Accessible only by private car from San Miguel is **Laguna de Alegría** in a crater of an extinct volcano and fed by both hot and cold springs; good swimming. To the N are the Indian ruins of **Quelapa** (bus 326).

San Francisco Gotera, the capital of Morazán Department, can be reached from the Oriente terminal in San Salvador, or from San Miguel. It is the last stop for foreigners on Route 7 to the Honduran border (Upper Morazán has been completely controlled by the FMLN and the road is closed). 2 places to stay: *Hospedaje San Francisco,* Av. Morazán 23, nice garden and hammocks, F; *Motel Arco Iris,* next door. Beyond San Francisco, the road runs to Jocaitique (there is a bus) from where an unpaved road climbs into the mountains through pine forests to Sabanetas, near the Honduran border. Accommodation at both Jocaitique and Sabanetas. (This trip is not possible while guerrilla activity continues.)

It is another 42 km. from San Miguel to the port of La Unión/Cutuco. Before it gets there the Pan-American Highway turns N for the Goascarán bridge to Honduras. Bus San Miguel-Goascarán, US$0.80, 2½ hrs. (may be disrupted by guerrillas). There is a tourist office at the border (El Amatillo)—border closes 1700.

To save time when travelling eastwards, take the Ruta Militar NE through (34 km.) Santa Rosa de Lima to the Goascarán bridge on the border with Honduras, 56 km. (There are plenty of money changers, accepting all Central American currencies and travellers' cheques, but beware of short-changing on Nicaraguan and Costa Rican currencies.)

Santa Rosa de Lima (27,300 people) is a charming little place with a wonderful colonial church, set in the hills. There are gold and silver mines. Don't miss the excellent *sopa de apretadores* (crab soup, the best in El Salvador), near the town centre—everyone knows the place. *Hospedaje Mundial*, nr. market, F, basic, friendly; *Hospedaje Florida*, Ruta Militar, F, clean, friendly. Unnamed *comedor* on the Pan American Highway, good and cheap. Buses to the Honduran border half-hourly.

La Unión/ Cutuco, on the Gulf of Fonseca, is the only port in El Salvador except Acajutla at which ships can berth. Population, 43,000. The port handles half the country's trade. The whole coast is a military zone. Bus 304 from Oriente terminal, San Salvador.

Hotels *Centroamérica*, C, with fan, more with a/c; *Miramar*, G, good; *Hospedaje Annex Santa Marta*, F, with shower and fan, not bad; opposite, a bit further away from square is a hotel, F, friendly, noisy, basic, but OK; *San Carlos*, opposite railway station, E, good meals available; *Hospedaje Santa Rosa*.

Restaurant *La Patia*—fish; *Comedores Gallego* and *Rosita* rec. *Comedor Tere*, Av. General Menéndez 2.2, fairly good.

Exchange at *Cafetín Brisas del Mar*, 3 Av. Norte y 3 Calle Oriente. Black market sometimes in centre.

Customs 3 Av. Norte 3.9; **Immigration** at 3 Calle Oriente 2.8.

Ferry There is no longer a ferry to Puntarenas (Costa Rica). It may be possible to take a cargo boat to Costa Rica; ask the captains in Cutuco. It is not possible for foreigners to travel by boat to Potosí (Nicaragua). There is reportedly a boat to Honduras, but it is easier to go by land.

Buses Terminal is at 3 Calle Poniente (block 3); to San Salvador, US$1.75, 4 hrs., many daily, direct or via San Miguel, one passes the harbour at 0300. Bus to Honduran border at El Amatillo, No. 353, US$0.50.

Excursions To Conchagua to see one of the few old colonial churches in the country; Conchagua volcano can also be climbed and a hard walk will be rewarded by superb views over San Miguel volcano (good bus service). One can take an early morning boat to the islands in the Gulf of Fonseca: to Zacatillo (about 1 hr.) and Meanguera (more), where there are many secluded little beaches. Take plenty of provisions, as afternoon boats can be uncertain and one may have to spend the night in a fishing hut. To El Tamarindo (bus 383, US$0.25, service not good so best start early), a small, attractive fishing village with beautiful white beaches. No accommodation, but the place is popular and huts to sling a hammock are US$2 a day. Check if the military will allow excursions to the coast. Also from La Unión, the ruins of Los Llanitos can be visited.

By Coastal Highway This is the second road route, running through the southern cotton lands. It begins on a 4-lane motorway to Comalapa airport at Cuscatlán. The first place of any importance after leaving the capital is (13 km.) Santo Tomás. There are Indian ruins at Cushululitán, a short distance N.

Beyond, a new road to the E, rising to 1,000 metres, runs S of Lake Ilopango to join the Pan-American Highway beyond Cojutepeque.

Ten km. on from Santo Tomás is ***Olocuilta,*** an old town with a colourful market on Sunday under a great tree. Good church. (Both Santo Tomás and Olocuilta can be reached by bus 133 from San Salvador.) From the airport, the road becomes a 2-lane toll-road, going E across the Río Jiboa to

Zacatecoluca, capital of La Paz Department, 56 km. from San Salvador by road and 19 km. S of San Vicente. Bus 133 from Occidente terminal, San Salvador. José Simeón Cañas, who abolished slavery in Central America, was born here. Population, 81,000.

Hotels *América*, E. *Hospedajes América* and *Popular* clean, E. *Comedor Margoth* (beware high charging).

Near the town is the garden park of Ichanmichen ("the place of the little fish"). It is crossed by canals and decorated with pools: there is, in fact, an attractive swimming pool. It is very hot but there is plenty of shade.

Between Olocuilta and Zacatecoluca, a road branches N to the small towns of San Pedro Nonualco and Santa María Ostuma (with an interesting colonial church and a famous *fiesta* on February 2); both are worth visiting, but not easy to get to. Bus 135 from Terminal del Occidente goes to San Pedro. If you get off this bus at the turn off to San Sebastián Arriba, you can walk to the Peñón del Tacuazín (or del Indio Aquino), 480 metres above sea level, which is 4½ km. N of Santiago Nonualco. A cave at its summit was used as a refuge by Anastasio Aquino (see page 1214), before his execution in April 1833.

Both road and railway cross the wide Lempa River by the Puente de Oro (Golden Bridge) at San Marcos. (The road bridge has been destroyed; cars use the railway bridge.) A branch road (right) leads to tiny Puerto El Triunfo on the Bay of Jiquilisco, with a large shrimp-freezing plant. About 110 km. from the capital is

Usulután, capital of its Department. Population, 69,000. Bus 302 from San Salvador.

Hotels   *Hotels and Restaurant España*, on main square, rec., nice patio, bar and discotheque. *Millions*, D; *Motel Usulután*, D; *Central*, E.

A road branches NE from Usulután, some 45 km. to San Miguel (see page 1214) On this road is Lake Jocotal, a national nature reserve supported by the World Wildlife Fund, which can be visited by arrangement with the warden.
   The Coastal Highway goes direct from Usulután to La Unión/Cutuco.

Western El Salvador

The route from the capital S to La Libertad has already been given. Both a paved road and the railway connect San Salvador with Sonsonate and the port of Acajutla. The road goes W through Santa Tecla (see page 1212) to Sonsonate, and then S to the port. 6 km. W of Santa Tecla on the main road is Los Chorros (see under Santa Tecla); 3½ km. beyond, the Pan-American Highway (good) runs NW past Lake Coatepeque to Santa Ana.

Acajutla, Salvador's main port serving the western and central areas, is 85 km. from San Salvador (bus 207 from Occidente terminal, US$2.80), 58 km. from Santa Ana (it is 8 km. S of the Coastal Highway). It handles about 40% of the coffee exports and is a popular seaside resort (good surfing) during the summer, though not an attractive town. Population: 36,000.

Hotels   *California*, E. *Brisas del Mar*, F. Good, cheap *pensión* at back of La Campana store.

The nearby beaches at Metalio and Barra de Santiago are rec., but Los Cobanos is dirty, expensive and unsafe.

Sonsonate, 19 km. N on the road to the capital (64 km.) produces sugar, tobacco, rice, tropical fruits, hides and balsam. An important market is held each Sun. Sonsonate is in the chief cattle-raising region. Population: 60,900. It was founded in 1552. The beautiful El Pilar church is strongly reminiscent of the church of El Pilar in San Vicente. The Cathedral has many of the cupolas (the largest covered with white porcelain) which serve as a protection against earthquakes. The old church of San Antonio del Monte, just outside the city, draws pilgrims from afar. Capital to Sonsonate by bus 205, US$1.50, 90 mins.

Hotels   *Sonsonate*, 6 Av. Norte with Calle Obispo Marroquín, D, with a/c, meals available; *Orbe*, D; *Centroamericano*, near centre, E; *Florida*, beside bus terminal, G, basic, manager speaks English; *Hospedaje Taplán*, near bus station, G, basic; *del Viajero*, opposite bus station, F.

Restaurants   *Milkbar; Comedor Santa Cecilia*.

Roads   N to Santa Ana, 39 km., a beautiful journey through high, cool coffee country, with volcanoes in view; NW to Ahuachapán, 40 km., and on to Guatemala (road paved from Ahuachapán through Apaneca and passes through some spectacular scenery); S and W to the Guatemalan frontier points of La Hachadura and Ciudad Pedro de Alvarado at the bridge over the Río Paz. Border crossing is straightforward, but if in a private vehicle requires a lot of paperwork (about 2 hrs.). Many buses ply between La Hachadura and Sonsonate, US$0.60 to Ahuachapán, US$0.50, 4 hrs.

At the foot of Izalco volcano, 8 km. from Sonsonate, is the town of *Izalco* (population 43,000), which has resulted from the gradual merging of the *ladino* village of Dolores Izalco and the Indian village of Asunción Izalco. Festivals, August 8 to 15 and during the Feast of St. John the Baptist from June 17 to 24. Near Izalco, on the slopes, is the spacious swimming pool of Atecozol, in the middle of a beautiful park with a restaurant. The park is shaded by huge mahogany trees, palms, aromatic balsam trees and *amates*. There is a battlemented tower; a monument to Tlaloc, god of the rain; another to Atonatl, the Indian who, on this spot, shot the arrow which lamed the *conquistador* Pedro de Alvarado; and a statue to the toad found jumping on the spot where water was found. Izalco village and Izalco volcano are not directly connected by road. A paved road branches from the highway 14 km. from the turning for Izalco village (about 22 km. from Sonsonate) and goes up towards Lake Coatepeque (see below); when you reach the summit, an all-weather road branches for *Cerro Verde* with its fine views down into the Izalco crater. A camping ground and car park at 1,980 metres overlook the crater. To climb Izalco: a path leads off the road (signposted) just below the car park on Cerro Verde. In 20-30 minutes descend to the saddle between Cerro Verde and Izalco, then 1-1½ hrs. up (rather steep, but manageable). A spectacular view from top. For a quick descent, find a rivulet of soft volcanic sand and half-slide, half-walk down in 15 mins., then 45 mins. to 1 hr. back up the saddle.

The road to Cerro Verde has fine views of Lake Coatepeque; ¾ of the way to Cerro Verde, a track branches off to the right to Finca San Blas (also can be reached on foot from Cerro Verde car park, 20 mins.). From there it is a 1 hr. walk straight up Santa Ana volcano. There are four craters inside one another; the newest crater has a lake and fuming columns of sulphur clouds. You can walk around the edge and down on to the ledge formed by the third crater (beware of the fumes). The main paved road goes on to the lakeshore. The fine *Hotel Montaña* (C) at the top of Cerro Verde was originally built so that the international set could watch Izalco in eruption; unfortunately, the eruptions stopped just as the hotel was completed. Good food is provided at fairly reasonable prices. There is a US$0.25 charge for parking, but none for camping, although permission must be obtained first from the Departamento de Bienestar, Ministerio de Trabajo on Blvd. Ejército east of Ilopango airport. There is a bus (No. 248) twice daily from Santa Ana to a junction 14 km. from the top of Cerro Verde (US$1). From Sonsonate to the turn-off for Cerro Verde costs US$0.30; from there it is easy to hitch a lift (tip expected).

In the Sonsonate district are a number of waterfalls and other sites of natural beauty: near the village of Santo Domingo de Guzmán (bus 246 from Sonsonate) are the falls of El Escuco, Tepechapa and La Quebrada, all within walking distance of Santo Domingo and each other. Near Caluco (which has a colonial church and a ruined Dominican church, bus 432 from Sonsonate) are Las Victorias Falls, just past the Atecozol Turicentro, with 2 caves above the falls, the meeting of hot and cold streams at Los Encuentros to form the Shuteca/Aguas Calientes river, and La Chapina pool and springs. Bus 219 goes to Cuisnahuat, from where it is 2 km. S to the Río Apancoyo, or 4 km. N to Peñón El Escalón (covered in balsam trees) and El Istucal Cave.

Between Sonsonate and Ahuachapán (see below) is the Indian village of *Nahuizalco*. The older women still wear the *refajo* (a doubled length of cloth of tie-dyed threads worn over a wrap-round skirt), and various crafts are still carried on, although use of the Indian language is dying out. Beyond is Jauyúa, with Los Chorros de la Calera 2 km. N (bus 205 from Sonsonate). From San Pedro Puxtla (bus 246) you can visit the Tequendama Falls on the Sihuapán river. (Details on these and other sites from the Instituto Salvadoreño de Turismo.)

The Pan-American Highway runs through Santa Tecla to Santa Ana. A new dual carriageway road parallels the old Pan-American Highway, bypassing Santa Ana; toll: US$0.40. (Keep your ticket if turning off to Coatepeque, as it serves for the return.) The road, with turnoffs for Sonsonate and Ahuachapán, carries on to San Cristóbal on the Guatemalan frontier.

There is an archaeological site at San Andrés, half-way between Santa Tecla and Coatepeque. Exhibits from it and from Tazumal are at the National Museum.

Some 13 km. short of Santa Ana a short branch road leads (left) to *Lake Coatepeque,* a favourite week-end resort with good sailing, swimming, and fishing near the foot of Santa Ana volcano. There are good hotels, restaurants, and lodging houses. The surroundings are exceptionally beautiful. (Bus 201 from San Salvador to Santa Ana, where one changes to a 220 (hourly) for the lake, or take a bus from San Salvador to El Congo on Pan-American Highway, US$1, then another to the lake, US$0.20.) Cerro Verde is easily reached in 90 mins. by good roads through impressive scenery.

Tourists are put up free in cabins with mattresses and showers at Balneario Los Obreros (a resort for workers). When you reach the lake shore from the rim of the crater follow the road a little. Permission to stay must be obtained from the Departamento de Bienestar, Ministerio de Trabajo, Blvd. Ejército, San Salvador. Restaurant and supervised swimming. Otherwise, water difficult to reach because of the number of weekend homes.

Hotels Hotels charge per 12 hrs. *Del Lago* (try the crab soup), D, overpriced; *Torremolino*, E, noisy, unfriendly (*Comedor Janet* opposite is good); *Lido*, E.

Santa Ana, 55 km. from San Salvador and capital of its Department, is the second largest city in the country (bus 201 from Terminal del Occidente, San Salvador). The intermont basin in which it lies at 656 metres on the NE slopes of Santa Ana volcano is exceptionally fertile. Coffee is the great crop, with sugar-cane a good second. The city is the business centre of western El Salvador. There are some fine buildings, particularly the classical theatre, the neo-gothic cathedral, and several other churches, especially El Calvario, in colonial style. Population: 208,322.

Hotels *La Libertad*, near cathedral, C with bath, good meals for about US$2; *Roosevelt*, E, good meals for US$1.60; *Florida*, room with bath, E, rec., serves excellent meals for US$2; *Internacional-Inn*, 25 C. Poniente y 10 Av. Sur, E with bath, TV, not the most conventional of hotels; *Hospedaje Carao*, Av. José Matías Delgado, F, with bath, basic, quite clean; *Pensión Lux*, on Parque Colón. *Colonial*, F, 8 Av. Norte 2, clean, helpful, good breakfasts for less than US$1, a little noisy; *Hospedaje Livingston*, 10 Av. Sur, 29, F, with bath, clean, friendly, good value; *Pensión Monterrey*, F, without bathroom, and *Hospedaje El Santaneco*, F, without bath, basic, on same street. Restaurants are expensive so it is best to eat in *comedores*, or at the market in front of the cathedral. Everything closes at about 1900.

Exchange Local banks. Open 0830-1200, 1430-1700. Black market around the banks.

The border with Guatemala is 30 km. by paved road from Santa Ana (the fastest road link from San Salvador to Guatemala City is via the Santa Ana bypass, then to Ahuachapán and on to the border at Las Chinamas—tourist office here). Buses (Melva) leave from the *Pensión Lux* on the east side of Parque Colón for Guatemala City, US$3, 5½ hrs. including meal and border stops. Also Inter Futuro Express, Transportes Centroamérica, and Mermex, US$5, unreliable. Alternatively there are local buses to the border for US$0.30; they leave from the market. Bus 406 from the capital (Terminal del Occidente), goes direct to the frontier at Las Chinamas.

Excursions To Lake Coatepeque, 19 km. (220 bus to *Hotel del Lago* US$0.40). *Chalchuapa,* 16 km. from Santa Ana, on the road to Ahuachapán, population 34,865, is at 640 metres. President Barrios of Guatemala was killed in battle here in 1885, when trying to reunite Central America by force. There is some good colonial-style domestic building; the church of Santiago is particularly striking. See the small but picturesque lake; the very interesting church, almost the only one in El Salvador which shows strong indigenous influences, and the *Tazumal* ruin just E of Chalchuapa, built about A.D. 980 by the Pipil Indians but with its 14-step pyramid now, alas, restored in concrete. The site has been occupied since 5000 B.C. and in the simple museum are the artefacts found in the mud under the lake. There are very interesting bowls used for burning incense, intricately decorated with animal designs. The ruin, which is open 0900-1200 and 1300-1730, is free of entry and only 5 minutes' walk from the main road. Minibus (No. 218) from Santa Ana, 20 mins., US$0.30. On the west of the town is the El Trapiche swimming pool. Bus 51 or 55 goes to *Turicentro Sihuatehuacán*, on city outskirts; US$0.13 admission to pools, café, park, etc.

Hotel at Chalchuapa: *Gloria*, E.

Guatemalan consul in Chalchuapa (Av. Club de Leones Norte, between Primero and Calle Ramón Flores—unmarked blue house, knock for attention).

Ahuachapán, capital of its Department, is 35 km. from Santa Ana, at 753 metres. Population, 63,500. It is a quiet town with low and simple houses, but an important distribution centre. Coffee is the great product. Like many places in the area, it draws the mineral water for its bath-house from some hot springs near the falls of Malacatiupán, near-by. Power is from the falls of Atehuezián on the Río Molino, which cascade prettily down the mountain-side. See also the *ausoles*—geysers of boiling mud with plumes of steam and strong whiffs of sulphur, which have been harnessed to produce electric power. A road runs NW through the treeless Llano del Espino, with its small lake, and across the Río Paz into Guatemala. Ahuachapán is 116 km. from the capital by bus 202 from San Salvador (US$2.75). Buses direct to the border, US$0.80.

The *ausoles* are interesting—an area of ground which is warm to the touch. They are used for generating electricity; only the smallest remains uncovered by drums and pipes. One can take a bus from Ahuachapán to El Barro, take a taxi or walk the 5 km. to the area. Permission to visit the power station can be obtained from the office in town, near the police station.

Hotel *Astoria*, E; *La Ahuachapaneca* guest house, E; *Hospedaje San Juan,* E. One can get good meals at *Restaurant El Paseo*.

Between Ahuachapán and Sonsonate are two small lakes, Laguna Verde and Apaneca, whose crater-like walls are profusely covered in tropical forest, in the Cordillera de Apaneca, part of the narrow highland belt running SE of Ahuachapán; they are popular with tourists. It is possible to swim in the former, but the latter is too shallow and reedy. Local buses run some distance away, leaving one with a fairly long walk. Laguna Verde can also be reached by road via Cantón Tulapa, from a turn off on the CA-8 road east of Apaneca. S of here is the Cascada del Río Cauta (take bus 216 from Ahuachapán towards Jujutla, alight 3 km. after the turn-off to Apaneca, then walk along trail for 300 m.).

Metapán (32 km. N of Santa Ana) is about 10 km. NE of Lake Güija. Its colonial baroque cathedral is one of the very few to have survived in the country. The altarpieces have some very good silver work (the silver is from local mines) and the façade is splendid. Lots of easy walks with good views to the lake. There are many lime kilns and a huge cement plant. Population: 51,800.

Hotels *Gallo de Oro*, G; *Ferrocarril*, G. Restaurant *Rincón del Pelon*, best in town, helpful, friendly.

A mountain track from Metapán gives access to Montecristo National Nature Reserve, El Salvador's last remaining cloud forest. There is an abundance of protected wildlife; permits to visit have to be obtained in San Salvador (and are not given during the breeding season, thought to be Feb. to May). This now forms part of El Trifinio, or the International Biosphere "La Fraternidad", administered jointly by Guatemala, Honduras and El Salvador.
   A good paved road runs from Metapán to the Guatemalan frontier.

Lake Güija, on the Guatemalan border, 16 km. by 8, is very beautiful and dotted with small islands, but it is not easy to reach. A new dam at the lake's outlet generates electricity for the western part of the country.

Northern El Salvador

There has been much guerrilla and counter-insurgency activity in the northern areas; visitors have to pass through an "internal border" before the Río Lempa bridge on the Troncal del Norte, where "official El Salvador" meets "FMLN El Salvador". If the region is not safe, foreigners will not be allowed beyond this point, but usually there is no problem or danger.

The Troncal del Norte is paved throughout, and runs due North through Apopa (junction with a good road to Quezaltepeque) and Aguilares to the western extremity of the Cerrón Grande reservoir. A branch to the right skirts the northern side of the reservoir to Chalatenango, capital of the department of the same name. **Chalatenango,** 55 km. from San Salvador, is a delightful little town with an annual fair and *fiesta* on June 24. (Bus 125 from Oriente terminal, San Salvador, US$0.55.) Population, 30,000. It is the centre of an important region of traditional livestock farms. Good market. 2 *hospedajes*: El Nuevo Amanecer, F, good views of the Cathedral from the 2nd floor; one unnamed, G. If walking in the countryside, you may meet FMLN guerrillas who are interested in meeting foreigners, but you also run the risk of meeting army patrols who may arrest you.

The main road continues north through Tejutla to **La Palma,** a charming village set in pine clad mountains, and well worth a visit. It is famous for its local crafts, particularly the brightly-painted wood carvings and hand-embroidered tapestries. There are a number of workshops in La Palma where the craftsmen can be seen at work and pictures made. (The products are also sold in San Salvador.) Buses run from San Salvador to La Palma (No. 119, US$1).
   The road continues north to the frontier at El Poy, for western Honduras (at least 5 buses a day—No. 119—from Terminal del Oriente in San Salvador, frequent military checks, 3-4 hrs. in all). 2 km. before El Poy is *Hotel Cayahuanca*, F, clean, friendly. Travellers' cheques exchanged at El Poy. Exit tax 3 colones, plus a 5 colones "tourist tax" (stamp affixed to passport—don't try to leave without it, you will be turned back).

THE ECONOMY

Agriculture is the dominant sector of the economy, accounting for 75% of export earnings as well as employing some 30% of the population. Coffee and cotton are the most important crops, but attempts have been made at diversification and now sugar and maize are becoming increasingly important as foreign exchange earners. Land ownership has been unevenly distributed with a few wealthy families owning most of the land, while the majority of agricultural workers merely lived at subsistence level; this led to serious political and social instability despite attempts at agrarian reform by successive governments, of which the latest (and most determined) was in 1980.

With the expansion of the industrial sector in recent years, there has been a rapid growth in the middle and industrial working classes. The most important industry is textiles: others include shoes, furniture, chemicals and fertilizers, pharmaceuticals, cosmetics, construction materials, cement (and asbestos cement), food and drink processing, rubber goods. A small quantity of petroleum products, including asphalt, is also produced. Exports of manufactured goods, mostly to other Central American countries, account for some 24 % of foreign exchange earnings.

There are small deposits of various minerals: gold, silver, copper, iron ore, sulphur, mercury, lead, zinc, salt and lime. There is a gold and silver mine at San Cristóbal in the Department of Morazán. In 1975 a geothermal power plant came into operation at Ahuachapán, with capacity of 30 mw. The plant was expanded by 60 mw in 1978. Hydraulic resources are also being exploited as a means of generating power and thermal plants have been shut down, thus affording an even greater saving in oil import costs.

The country's agricultural and industrial production, and consequently its exporting capability, have been severely curtailed by political unrest. In 1986 further economic and social damage was caused by an earthquake; damage to housing and government property alone was estimated at US$311m, while the total, including destruction and disruption of businesses was put at US$2bn. El Salvador is heavily dependent upon aid from the USA to finance its budget. Total US assistance was estimated at US$2.5bn in 1979-86 and US$800m a year thereafter.

	1961-70 (av)	1971-80 (av)	1981-85 (av)	1986-88 (av)(e)
Gdp (1980 prices)	5.6 %	3.2 %	-2.1 %	1.3 %
Inflation	0.7 %	10.7 %	14.7 %	25.5 %
Exports (fob) US$m	182.1	662.9	743.1	660.0
Coffee	90.2	346.9	435.3	421.0 (a)
Cotton	26.5	64.8	39.9	5.0 (a)
Imports (fob) US$m	175.5	623.3	897.9	928.0
Current account balance US$m (cum)	-131.7	-452.2	-572.3	-307.0

(a) = 1986-87

INFORMATION FOR VISITORS

Warning   Prices in El Salvador are sometimes quoted in US dollars. Make sure which currency is being used.

How to get there   From London: To Miami with Pan Am, Continental, British Airways or Virgin Atlantic, thence to San Salvador with Eastern or Taca (direct). Other connecting cities in the USA with flights to San Salvador are: Houston (Continental, Taca), New Orleans (Taca), Los Angeles (Pan Am, Taca, Lacsa, Continental), San Francisco (Pan Am, Continental, Taca), New York (Continental) and Orlando (Eastern). Taca flies to all Central American capitals and to Mexico City (also served by Lacsa and Aeronica). Copa flies to the other Central American capitals, except Belize City and Tegucigalpa (which, together with San Pedro Sula, are served by Sahsa). Pan Am flies to Guatemala City, Lacsa to San José and Copa to Panama, with connection to Kingston (Jamaica). From Europe, San Salvador can be reached with Taca connecting flights from Guatemala City, to which Iberia and KLM (both twice a week) fly. Alternatively, go to Miami and connect from there. Connections for South America through San José or Panama.

Royal Netherlands Line, the Johnson Line, Royal Mail Lines, Hapag-Lloyd and Marina Mercante Nicaragüense operate cargo-passenger services between North Sea ports and El Salvador.

By sea from the USA: from New Orleans, a United Brands cargo boat on to Santo Tomás (Guatemala). This company also plies from New York and Philadelphia to Santo Tomás; it also has a service from New Orleans to the Panama Canal, where transshipment is made to the ports of El Salvador.

N.B. There is a 10% tax on international air tickets bought in El Salvador and a US$1 boarding tax. There is also an airport tax of US$9 if staying more than 6 hours. MCO tickets can be bought.

Documents A passport is necessary for nationals of all countries. Citizens of most countries require a visa, e.g. USA, Canada, Australia, New Zealand, Israel, France. Citizens of other West European countries do *not* need visas, but this is subject to change and it is best to apply in your own country. Visas cost US$20/£8 and take 48 hrs. at a consulate, or up to a week in bordering countries, for a stay of only 8 days. Visas can be renewed for up to 30 days at Immigration in San Salvador, at cost of US$2.48.

Travellers doing business directly in the country must get an ordinary (non-immigrant) visa and visit the Immigration Bureau (Centro de Gobierno) within 48 hours of arrival and get a permit to stay for 30 days. It costs US$4. They must get an exit permit from the same place, at the same price, before they leave the country. Business travellers are sometimes assessed for income tax during their stay. Border formalities tend to be relatively brief, although thorough searches are common. A baggage charge of 2 colones is made at borders. There is an entrance tax of, and an exit tax of 6 colones. There are restrictions on entry by citizens of Belize and Cuba.

All personal luggage and goods up to a value of US$100 are allowed in free of duty. Also allowed in free: 1 kg. of tobacco products, or 100 cigars or 600 cigarettes, and 2 bottles of liqueur. There are no restrictions on export or import of any currency except Nicaraguan córdobas. All animal products are prohibited from importation, with the exception of boned, sterilized and hermetically sealed meat products. Fruits are inspected carefully and destroyed if necessary. Hide, skins and woollen goods will be fumigated against disease. Animals must be free of parasites, fully inoculated and have a vetinary certificate and import permit.

"Hints to Exporters: El Salvador" can be obtained from Dept. of Trade, Export Services Division, Sanctuary Buildings, 16-20 Great Smith Street, London SW1P 3DB.

Warning Do not try to enter El Salvador carrying literature that may be regarded as subversive or left-wing, for example books from Nicaragua, or by Russian authors. At best, it will be confiscated, or you may be refused entry. Furthermore, it is advisable not to say that Nicaragua is on your itinerary. Army-style clothing will also be confiscated. It is wise not to camp out, but generally travellers report no problems; just be prepared for plenty of police checks and body searches on buses. It is best not to mention politics.

Motoring At the border, after producing a driving licence and proof of ownership, you are given a permit to stay for 15 days at the Customs Office and Police Department. This can be extended at the Dirección General de la Renta Aduanas, near the Terminal de Oriente in San Salvador. In any case the formalities for bringing in a car involve considerable paperwork. There is a 4.50 colones charge for compulsory tyre fumigation. There is also a 2-colón quarantine charge and a 5-colón transit fee for cars. Insurance is not compulsory in El Salvador, but you should arrange cover. A good map, both of republic and of capital, can be obtained from Texaco or Esso, or from the Tourist Institute. Petrol costs 7.50 colones a US gallon.

Local Information can be got from the National Tourist Institute, Calle Rubén Darío 619, San Salvador. The Tourist Institute provides a small map of the country with the main beaches and the 15 "Turicentros" marked on it.

The **best months** for a business visit are from February to May, when there is least rainfall and most business. August is the holiday season. Business is centralized in the capital, but it is as well to visit Santa Ana and San Miguel.

Language Spanish, but English is widely understood. Spanish should be used for letters, catalogues, etc.

Clothing White suits and white dinner jackets are not worn.

Food Try *pupusas*, stuffed *tortillas* in 3 varieties (*chicharrón*—pork; *queso*—cheese; *revueltas*), typical, tasty and cheap; also *garobo* (iguana) and *cusuco* (*tatou*—armadillo). They are sold at many street stalls and in fact are better there than in restaurants. On Sat. and Sun. nights local people congregate in *pupuserías*.

Tips at hotels and restaurants: 10%, but 15% for small bills. Nothing for taxi drivers except when hired for the day; airport porters, "bionas rojas", US$1 a bag; haircut, US$0.20, not obligatory.

Health The gastro-enteric diseases are the most common. Visitors should take care over what they eat during the first few weeks and should drink *agua cristal* (bottled water). Specifics against malaria should be taken if a night is spent on the coast. Warning of dengue fever has been reported from that part of the main road running north from San Salvador between Suchitoto and Tejutla, where a large area of land has been flooded for the Cerrón Grande dam. The San Salvador milk supply is good.

Internal Transport Buses are excellent (if sometimes crowded). San Salvador has plenty of taxis. Hitchhiking is comparatively easy. There are no longer any rail passenger services.

Currency The unit is the colón (¢), divided into 100 centavos. Banknotes of 1, 2, 5, 10, 25 and 100 colones are used, and there are nickel coins for the fractional amounts. The colón is often called a peso. The official rate in April 1989 was 5 colones to the US dollar. The black market rate is a little better; trading is done in the street. Credit card payment are subject to 5% commission and are charged at the official rate. When leaving El Salvador, one may only change US$40-worth of colones back into dollars on presentation of boarding pass and passport at the airport bank. Money sent to El Salvador will be paid out in colones only. **N.B.** Change all colones before entering Guatemala or Honduras, where they are not accepted or changed anywhere (except at borders).

The **metric system** of weights and measures is used alongside certain local units such as the *vara* (836 millimetres, 32.9 inches), *manzana* (7,000 square metres, or 1.67 acres), the *libra* (0.454 kilogramme, about 1 English pound), and the *quintal* of 100 *libras*. Some US weights and measures are also used. US gallons are used for gasoline and quarts for oil.

Posts and Telegraphs Air mail to Europe takes up to one month; from Europe about 15 days, from the USA, 1 week. The correct address for any letter to the capital is "San Salvador, El Salvador, Central America". The main post office is at the Centro de Gobierno. Letters to Europe 0.60; parcels 12 half kilo, 30, kilo; surface mail, 15 each kilo.

The charge for a local telephone call is 0.10 for 3 mins. A private telephone call or telex to Europe costs US$20 for first 3 minutes, US$5 per extra minute (if made from the state telecommunications company, Antel, Centro de Gobierno, Calle Rubén Darío y 5 Av. Sur). Calls made from hotels cost US$6-7 per minute. Direct dialling is available to Europe, USA (US$2 per min.) and other parts of the world. No collect calls to Europe.

Radio Inc. communicates with all parts of the world through local stations. Public telex at Antel. British businessmen can use the telex system at the Embassy.

Time in El Salvador is 6 hrs. behind GMT.

Hours of Business 0800-1200 and 1400-1800 Mon. to Fri.; 0800-1200 Sat. Banks in San Salvador 0900-1300, 1345-1500 Mon. to Fri.; different hours for other towns given in text. Government offices: 0800-1600 Mon. to Fri.

Public Holidays The usual ones are January 1, Holy Week (3 days, government 10 days), April 14, 17, May 1, 10, Corpus Christi (half day), August 5-6, September 15, October 12, November 2 and 5 (half-day), December 24 (half-day), and Christmas Day. Govenment offices are also often closed on religious holidays. Little business in weeks ending Easter week, the first week of August, and the Christmas-New Year period. Banks are closed for balance June 29, 30, and December 30, 31.

Press In San Salvador: *Diario de Hoy*, *La Prensa Gráfica*, every day, including Sunday (both right wing). *Diario Latino* and *El Mundo*, afternoon papers, but not on Sunday. There are provincial newspapers in Santa Ana, San Miguel and elsewhere. Weekly bilingual newspaper (English and Spanish, right wing), *El Salvador News Gazette*, available from most hotels which take foreigners. *Semana*, weekly magazine for El Salvador and Central America (liberal).

Most of the 39 radio stations cover the whole country, and all accept advertisements. There are 3 commercial television stations, all with national coverage, and two government-run information channels.

We are most grateful for Salvadorean information to Rubens Calderón (Instituto Salvadoreño de Turismo, C.Rubén Darío 619, San Salvador) for many important updatings, Ronald J. Miller (San Salvador), and to other travellers whose names are listed in the general Central America section.

HONDURAS

HONDURAS is larger than all the other Central American republics except Nicaragua, but has a smaller population than El Salvador, less than a fifth its size. Bordered by Nicaragua, Guatemala, and El Salvador, it has an area of 112,088 square km.—rather less than England. It has a narrow Pacific coastal strip, 124 km. long, on the Gulf of Fonseca, but its northern coast on the Caribbean is some 640 km. long.

Much of the country is mountainous: a rough plateau covered with volcanic ash and lava in the S, rising to peaks such as Cerro de las Minas in the Celaque range (2,849 metres), but with some intermont basins at between 900 and 1,400 metres. The volcanic detritus disappears to the N, revealing saw-toothed ranges which approach the coast at an angle; the one in the extreme NW, along the border with Guatemala, disappears under the sea and shows itself again in the Bay Islands. At most places in the N there is only a narrow shelf of lowland between the sea and the sharp upthrust of the mountains, but along two rivers— the Aguán in the NE, and the Ulúa in the NW—long fingers of marshy lowland stretch inland between the ranges. The Ulúa lowland is particularly important; it is about 40 km. wide and stretches southwards for 100 km. From its southern limit a deep gash continues across the highland to the Gulf of Fonseca, on the Pacific. The distance between the Caribbean and the Pacific along this trough is 280 km.; the altitude at the divide between the Río Comayagua, running into the Ulúa and the Caribbean, and the streams flowing into the Pacific, is only 950 metres. In this trough lies Comayagua, the old colonial capital. The lowlands along the Gulf of Fonseca are narrower than they are along the Caribbean; there is no major thrust inland as along the Ulúa.

The prevailing winds are from the E, and the Caribbean coast has a high rainfall and is covered with deep tropical forest. The intermont basins, the valleys, and the slopes sheltered from the prevailing winds bear oak and pine down to as low as 600 metres. Timber is almost the only fuel available. There is a little coal near the capital but no oil has been found. In the drier areas, N and E of Tegucigalpa, there are extensive treeless savannas.

The Spaniards, arriving in the early 16th century, found groups of Indians of the Mayan and other cultures. Pushing E from Guatemala City they came upon silver in the SE, and in 1578 founded Tegucigalpa near the mines. The yield was comparatively poor, but enough to attract a thin stream of immigrants. Settlement during the ensuing century was mostly along the trail from Guatemala City: at Gracias, La Esperanza and Comayagua. Gradually these settlements spread over the S and W, and this, with the N coast, is where the bulk of the population lives today. The Spaniards and their descendants ignored the northern littoral and the Ulúa lowlands, but during the 19th century US companies, depending largely on black workers from the British West Indies and Belize, developed the northern lowlands as a great banana-growing area. Today the second largest concentration of population per square mile is in the Department of Cortés, which extends northwards from Lake Yojoa towards the Caribbean; it includes the major portion of the river basins of Ulúa and Chamelecón, also known as the Sula valley: the most important agricultural area in the country, with San Pedro Sula as its commercial centre and Puerto Cortés as its seaport. The Atlantic littoral consumes two-thirds of the country's imports, and ships the bananas which are half the country's exports.

Even today, land under some form of cultivation is only 22.4% of the total; 45% of Honduras is forest. Rugged terrain makes large areas unsuitable for any kind of agriculture. Nevertheless, there are undeveloped agricultural potentials in

HONDURAS 161

the flat and almost unpopulated lands of the coastal plain E of Tela to Trujillo and Puerto Castilla, in the Aguán valley southward and in the region NE of Juticalpa. The area further to the NE, known as the Mosquitia plain, is largely unexploited and little is known of its potential.

Population There are very few pure-blooded Indians, and fewer (less than 1%) of pure Spanish ancestry. The largest proportion of Indian blood is found from Santa Rosa de Copán westwards to the border with Guatemala (Chorti is still spoken in this region). The population is 90% *mestizo*, and was estimated at 4.7 million in 1987; death rate 10.1 per 1,000; birth, 44; annual population growth: 3.6%; urban growth, 5.7%, but only 41.4% are urban; 40.3% are illiterate. Some 53% are peasants or agricultural labourers, with a relatively low standard of living. Education is compulsory, but half the rural children do not go to school. The middle class is small, and the purchasing power of the people low. The majority of the population is Catholic, but there is complete freedom of religion.

Communications The railways are in the N, and since 1975 the 595 km. in operation belong to the Ferrocarril Nacional de Honduras.

A light aeroplane is the only way of getting to large areas of the country, but the road system has improved rapidly in recent years. Total road length is now 17,022 km., of which 2,042 are paved. The main paved roads are the Northern Highway linking Tegucigalpa, San Pedro Sula and Puerto Cortés; the road W from Puerto Cortés along the North Coast, through Omoa, to the Guatemalan frontier (although one bridge is missing, necessitating 2 hrs. travel on foot); the highway from Tegucigalpa to Olancho, passing through Juticalpa and Catacamas; the Pan-American Highway in the SW between El Salvador and Nicaragua, and the Southern Highway which runs to it from Tegucigalpa; the North Coast Highway joining San Pedro Sula with Progreso, Tela and La Ceiba, and on to Trujillo; the Western Highway linking San Pedro Sula with Santa Rosa de Copán, Nueva Ocotepeque and the Guatemalan and Salvadorean frontiers, with a branch from La Entrada to Copán ruins; the road linking Choluteca on the Pan-American Highway with the Nicaraguan frontier at Guasaule; and the Eastern Highway linking Tegucigalpa, Danlí, El Paraíso and Las Manos (Nicaraguan frontier). Travel is still by foot and mule in many areas. Tegucigalpa, La Ceiba and San Pedro Sula all have international airports.

Government The Legislature consists of a single Chamber. Deputies are elected by a proportional vote. Executive authority rests with a President, elected for 4 years. No President may serve two terms in succession. The Constitution was revised by a Constituent Assembly elected in April 1980.

Throughout Honduras' history most of its rulers have been military men, often coming to power as leaders of *juntas* and subsequently being elected President. In April 1980, elections for a new Constituent Assembly were won unexpectedly by the Liberal Party. The successor to General Paz García the last military ruler, as President was Dr. Roberto Suazo Córdoba of the Liberal Party, elected in November 1981. Elections, held in November 1985, brought José Simón Azcona del Hoyo, also of the Liberal Party, to the Presidency. Elections were due to be held in November 1989. Honduras is a signatory to the Central American Peace Plan, drawn up by President Arias of Costa Rica in 1987, but US military personnel and Nicaraguan "contra" rebels have not yet been asked to withdraw from Honduran soil, as required by the provisions of the Plan.

The National University is centred in Tegucigalpa though it also has departments in San Pedro Sula and La Ceiba. Also in Tegucigalpa is the Universidad José Cecilio del Valle; there is also a university in San Pedro Sula.

Cities and Towns

Tegucigalpa, the capital, a city of over 800,000 inhabitants, stands in an intermont basin at an altitude of 975 metres. No railway serves it. It was founded as a mining camp in 1578: the miners found their first gold where the N end of the Soberanía bridge now is. The name means "silver hill" in the original Indian tongue. On three sides it is surrounded by sharp, high peaks. It comprises two towns: the almost flat Comayagüela and the hilly Tegucigalpa built at the foot and up the slopes of El Picacho. A steeply banked river, the Choluteca, divides the two towns, now united administratively as the Distrito Central. Tegucigalpa has not been subjected to any disaster by fire or earthquake, being off the main earthquake fault line, so retains many traditional features. Many of the stuccoed houses, with a single heavily barred entrance leading to a central patio, are attractively coloured. However, the old low skyline of the city has now been punctuated by several modern tall buildings.

Its altitude gives it a reliable climate: temperate during the rainy season from May to November; warm, with cool nights, in March and April, and cool and dry, with very cool nights, in December to February, although hot breezes can make the atmosphere oppressive. The annual mean temperature is about 74°F (23°C).

The Carretera del Sur (Southern Highway), which brings in travellers from the S and from Toncontín Airport, 6½ km. from Plaza Morazán, runs through Comayagüela into Tegucigalpa. It goes past the obelisk set up to commemorate a hundred years of Central American independence, and the Escuela Nacional de Bellas Artes, with a decorated Mayan corridor and temporary exhibitions of contemporary paintings and crafts.

The market in Comayagüela is interesting. In Colonia Palmira, Tegucigalpa, is the Boulevard Morazán, an elegant shopping and business complex, with restaurants, cafeterias, discotheques, etc. (worth a visit on Fri. or Sat. evening). You can get a fine view of the city from the Peace Monument on Juana Laínez hill, near the football stadium.

Crossing the river from Comayagüela by the colonial Mallol bridge, on the left is the Presidential Palace (1919). Calle Bolívar runs through the area containing the Congress building and the former site of the University, founded in 1847. Calle Bolívar leads to the main square, Plaza Morazán (commonly known as Parque Central). On the eastern side of the square are the City Hall, and the domed and double-towered Cathedral built in the late 18th century. (See the beautiful gilt colonial altarpiece, the fine examples of Spanish colonial art, the cloisters and, in Holy Week, the magnificent ceremony of the Descent from the Cross).

Av. Paz Barahona, running through the northern side of the square, is a key avenue. On it to the E is the church of San Francisco, with its clangorous bells, and (on 3a Calle, called Av. Colón) the old Spanish Mint (1770), now the national printing works. If, from Plaza Morazán, we go along Av. Paz Barahona westwards towards the river, by turning right along 4 Av. we come to the 18th century church of Virgen de los Dolores. Two blocks N and 3 blocks W of the church is Parque Concordia with copies of Mayan sculpture and temples (open only Sun. and holidays, but people climb the fence anyway).

Back on Av. Paz Barahona and further W are the Ministerial Palace, the National Theatre, with a rather grand interior (1915) and, across the square, the beautiful old church of El Calvario. If we cross the bridge of Carías (quite near the theatre) we can visit Comayagüela's market of San Isidro.

One is always conscious, in Tegucigalpa, of the summit of El Picacho looming up to the N (at the top is a zoo of mostly indigenous animals, open Thurs.-Sun., US$0.25). From Plaza Morazán go up Calle 7a and the Calle de la Leona to Parque Leona, a handsome small park with a railed walk overlooking the city. Higher still is the reservoir in El Picacho, also known as the United Nations Park, which can be reached by number 9 bus from behind Los Dolores church (in front of Farmacia Santa Barbara), Sun. only, US$0.15; camping is allowed here. Parque La Libertad in Comayagüela (where one can find cheap enjoyable entertainment in the evening) is also pleasant.

N.B. If you have anything stolen, report it to Dirección General de Investigación Nacional, DIN, ½ block N of Los Dolores church.

Hotels in Tegucigalpa: *Honduras Maya*, Av. República de Chile, Colonia Palmira, T 32-31-91, L, rooms and apartments, casino, swimming pool (US$2.50), bars, cafeterias (*Cafeteria 2000*), restaurant (*El Candelero*), conference hall, view over the city (only from uppermost rooms); *Alameda*, Blvd. Suyapa (some distance from centre), A, comfortable, pool, good restaurant *Le Chalet* (T 32-69-20). **Downtown:** *La Ronda*, 6 Av, 11 C., 5 blocks from cathedral (T 37-8151/55), a/c, TV, rec., A/B, cafeteria (*Rondalla*) and night club; *Plaza*, in Av. Paz Barahona (T 37-0182/84), A; *Papagallo* restaurant. *Prado*, Av. Cervantes, 7 y 8 Av., A/B, *La*

Posada restaurant; *Istmania*, 5 Av., 7 and 8 Calle (T 37-1638/39, 37-1460) near Church of Los Dolores, A-B, *Versalles* restaurant; *Marichal*, 5 Av., 5 Calle, D/E (T 37-00-69) (ask for a back room), noisy, clean, centrally located; *Nuevo Boston*, Av. Jérez No. 313, T 37-9411, E, hot water, central, clean, laundry, run by an ex-truck driver from Missouri, constant (free) coffee and biscuits available, highly rec.; *MacArthur*, 7 Av., 1225, D/E, good, reasonably-priced restaurant; *Nuevo Hotel MacArthur*, C, expensive, 8C., 4 y 5 Av., under same management; *San Francisco*, Av. Cervantes, D, fan, TV, restaurant, bar, T 37-71-01; *Imperial* (opposite *Istmania*) E, with or without bath, good value, Chinese run; *Fortuna*, 5 Av., near Los Dolores church, E with or without bath. *Granada*, Av. Gutemberg 1401, Barrio Guanacaste, E (hot water on 2nd floor only), good, table tennis, T 37-23-81, annex 1½ blocks uphill, turn right at sign for Cinés Tauro and Aries, also E (but a bit more than old building), better beds, hot water in all rooms.

Comayagüela is convenient for buses to the North and West and there are many cheap *pensiones* and rooms. It is noisier and dirtier than Tegucigalpa, and many establishments are unsuitable for travellers. *Ritz*, 4a C., and 5 Av., E-D, cold shower, clean but noisy; *Centenario*, 6 Av., 9-10 Calles, E-D (T 37-1050), rec.; *Real de Oro*, Av. Cabañas, 11 and 12 C., D/E, clean, friendly; *Regis*, 4a Av., 1 and 2 Calle, E, rec., clean, friendly; *París*, C.4 between Avs. 3 and 4, F for single with bath, café, cheap, good meals, family style; *San Pedro*, Calle 9, Av. 6, D with bath, E without or with private cold shower, popular, clean, restaurant; *Jupiter*, Av. 5, 5 and 6 Calles 509, E-D, clean and comfortable; *Moderna*, Av. 7a, Calle 3a-4a, F, good service; *Ticamaya No. 1*, Av. 6, Calle 9, D, quiet, restaurant, open to non-residents, breakfast from 0600; *Ticamaya No. 2*, Av. 7a, 4 and 5 Calle, E, clean, friendly, noisy, restaurant below; *Teleño*, Av.7, F, clean, friendly; there are 5 *Hospedajes El Nilo*, No. 4 is clean, but the rest are to be avoided; *Royal*, Av. 7, nr. market, F, noisy but cheap; *Hotel Richard No. 1*, 4a Calle, 6 and 7 Av., F/E, "laundry" on roof; *Hotel Richard Nos. 2, 3, 4* and *5* on 5a Calle, all between 5 and 7 Av., fewer facilities, all F, with or without bath. *Hospedaje 515*, Av. 6, No. 536, F, quiet, clean; *Hospedaje Familiar*, Av. 6, No. 812, F, clean, noisy.

A 5% sales tax is added to hotel bills.

Restaurants A meal in a good restaurant costs betweem US$5-10; for hotel restaurants, see above. International food: *El Arriero*, Av. República de Chile, near *Honduras Maya*, good steaks and seafood; *Kloster* and *Bugalow*, Blvd. Morazán; *Marbella*, 6 C., 3-4 Av., central. Seafood: *Hungry Fisherman*, Av. República de Chile 209, Col. Palmira. Italian: *Café Allegro*, Av. República de Chile 360-B, Colonia Palmira, excellent coffee, "Time" magazine, warmly rec. (*South American Handbook* sold here); *Roma*, near Av. Rep. de Chile, Col. Palmira; pizzerias: *Tito*, Callejón Los Dolores, and Blvd. Morazán, Col. Palmira, both branches rec.; *Pizza Deli*, Blvd. Morazán; *Vicente*, near *Honduras Maya*. Spanish: *Mesón de Castilla*, Av. Rep. de Chile 1802, Col. Palmira; *Rincón Español*, Blvd. Morazán. French: *Jardín de París*, Blvd. Morazán, highly rec. Latin American: *Gauchos*, Av. de La Paz, near US Embassy, Uruguayan. Chinese: *La Gran Muralla*, Barrio Guanacaste, good; *Pekín*, 3 C. No.525, Barrio San Rafael, 1 block from *Hotel Maya*; *Mei-Mei*, Pasaje Midence Soto, central, rec.; *Ley-Hsen*, Pasaje Fiallos Soto, also central and rec. *Govinda*, Av. Juan Lindo, Col. Palmira, Indian. Meat: *El Patio 2*, Blvd. Morazán; *La Granja*, and *Jack's Steak House*, same street. Burgers: *2 Burger Hots*, 2 C. north of Parque La Merced, and Centro Comercial Los Castaños. *Totem*, Av. República de Chile, popular US-style bar with satellite TV; *Don Pepe's Terraza*, near Bancahsa, downtown, cheap, noisy orchestra but typical Honduran atmosphere. *Café de Pie*, Edificio Fiallos Soto, downtown; *Al Natural*, behind Cathedral, nice garden atmosphere. *Pops*, ice cream. *Dunkin Donuts*, several outlets. *Pastelería Francesa*, opp. French embassy, rec. Many cheap restaurants on 2 Av., Comayagüela and near market. Fried chicken is sold at small lunch counters all over Honduras, providing an excellent, cheap meal.

Institutes Alliance Française, end of 4 Av., Barrio Abajo, cultural events Fri. p.m., French films Wed. 1730, T 37-04-45; Centro Cultural Alemán, 8 Av., Calle La Fuente, German newspapers, cultural events, T 37-15-55; Instituto Hondureño de Cultura Interamericana (IHCI), Calle Real de Comayagüela has an English library and cultural events, T 37-75-39. **School** American and Elvel School, on US lines with US staff.

Fair at Comayagüela Fair of La Concepción, December 7 to 24.

Market Mercado Colón or San Isidro, Avenida 6 at Calle 1, Comayagüela; many things for sale; food available. Saturday is busiest day. Good supermarkets: La Colonia, Sucasa, Plaza Más x Menos.

Souvenir Shops Candú, opp. *Hotel Maya*, and in Av. República de Chile; Carmen, 1½ blocks S of *Hotel Maya* on Av. República de Chile; Amano, at begining of Blvd. Morazán, good quality.

Bookshops Book Village, Centro Comercial Los Castaños, Blvd. Morazán, English books, both new and secondhand, for sale or exchange. Librería Panamericana, 6a Av., 2a Calle, stocks English books and magazines, expensive. Books in Spanish on Honduras and Central America, Editorial Guaymuras, Av. Miguel Cervantes 1055. Secondhand bookstalls in Mercado San Isidro (Av. 6 y 2 Calle, Comayagüela), good value. There is an English weekly called *Tegucigalpa This Week*; to submit news and ads. write to: Aptdo 1312, Tegucigalpa, T 315821.

Pharmacy *Farmacia Rosna*, in pedestrian mall off Parque Central, T 370605, English spoken, rec.

Car Rentals Car rentals Avis, T 32-00-88; Toyota, Col. El Prado, T 33-52-10; at Toncontín airport: Molinari, T 33-13-07, Blitz, Budget, T 33-51-70, National, T 33-49-62.

Car Repairs Emil Bohnet, 1 Av., Comayagüela. Metal Mecánica, 4 blocks above U.S. Embassy.

Taxis About US$2.50 p.p. (no reduction for sharing, but bargaining possible); more after 2000.

Local buses Cost US$0.10, stops are official but unmarked.

Cinemas Plaza 1, 2 and 3 in Centro Comercial Plaza Miraflores; Regis and Real at Centro Comercial Centroamérica, Blvd. Miraflores; Alfa and Omega in Av. de La Paz (all have good US films). In city centre, double cinemas Lido and Palace, Clamer and Variedades.

Entertainment *Casino Royal* in *Hotel Honduras Maya*, all types of gambling. In front of the National University is a *peña*, where people dance and sing; also a discotheque and restaurant. Backstreet pub; *Copas* discotheque; *Metro Disco*, Blvd. Morazán, good; *Tulipán*, same street; Boulevard Morazán has plenty of choice in night life.

Museum Museo Nacional Villa Roy, in home of a former President, has an exhibition of archaeological finds. It is situated on a hilltop above the beautiful Parque Concordia (entry US$0.50, open 0830-1540, closed Mon.—due to be moved to the old university building on Parque Merced).

Exchange Banco de Londres (Lloyds Bank) 4a Calle y 5a Av. Tegucigalpa. Open 0900-1500; closed Sat. Banco Atlántida, 5C. in front of Plaza Morazán; Banco de Honduras (Citibank), Edif. Midence Soto, Tegucigalpa; Banco de Ahorro Hondureño, 5C. in front of Plaza Morazán; Banco Ficensa, Blvd. Morazán, does Visa advances. All accept American Express travellers' cheques, and cash travellers' cheques which are accredited to them, but not for US$. Visa cash advances and travellers' cheques, Credomatic de Honduras, Blvd. Morazán. American Express: main office Av. República de Chile, opp. *Honduras Maya*, Colonia Palmira; agency at Transmundo Tours, Calle 5a, Costado Norte Ministerios, usually redirect you to main office, otherwise good. Black market outside *Hotel Plaza*, at bus stations, in the office opp. Supermarket Más x Menos and, for both cash and travellers' cheques, at the Rivas and Co. department store.

Embassies UK (also *Belize*), Edificio Palmira, 3rd floor, opp. *Hotel Honduras Maya* (Apartado Postal 123); *USA*, Av. La Paz (0800-1100, Mon.-Fri.—take any bus from Parque Central in direction "San Felipe", T 32-31-20); *Canada*, Edificio Comercial Los Castaños, piso 6, Blvd. Morazán; *West Germany*, Ed. Paysen, Blvd. Morazán. *France*, Av. Juan Lindo 416, Colonia Palmira. *Guatemala*, Calle Juan Lindo 419, Colonia Palmira, Mon.-Fri., 0900-1300; *El Salvador*, Colonia San Carlos—one block from Blvd. Morazán, friendly, helpful; *Nicaragua*, Colonia Lomas del Tepeyac (T 324290), 10 blocks SE of Blvd. Morazán (or take "Alameda" bus from Parque La Merced, alight 1 block above "Planificación de familia", walk left up side street and turn up 4th street on right, a dirt road, with the consulate on a steep hillside on the right), 0800-1200, visa takes 24 hrs., issued after 1100; has to be used within 4 weeks of issue; *Costa Rica*, Colonia Palmira, Primera Calle Casa 704, T 32-1054 (Near Mas x Menos supermarket); *Mexico*, 3 Av., 2 C. No. 1277, Col. Palmira; *Spain*, Col. Matamoros 103; *Israel*, Ed. Palmira, opp. *Hotel Maya*; *Italy*, Col. Reforma; *Netherlands* (also *Portugal*), Carretera a Suyapa, desvío a Lomas del Mayab; *Switzerland*, consul at Oficina de Coordinación de Cooperación al Desarrollo, T 328261 (emergencies only). *Jamaican* consul, Mr George Schofield, *Hotel Boston*, Calle Jérez. To get to Colonia Palmira where most Embassies are, take buses marked "San Miguel" and "Lomas". Take "San Felipe" bus from Central Park for the following consulates: Costa Rica, Guatemala, USA and El Salvador.

Immigration Dirección General de Migración, Edificio Viera, 6 C., 11-12 Av., Tegucigalpa.

Post Office Av. Miguel de Cervantes y Calle Morelos, 4 blocks from Parque Central.

Telephone, Telex Hondutel, Calle 5 and Av. 4, Tegucigalpa.

Laundry Lavaflex, Calle la Salud y Blvd. José C. del Valle, open daily (bus, direction Prado). Lavandería Maya, 3 Av. nr. *Honduras Maya*, 0700-1900, Mon.-Sat.

Churches Episcopal Anglican (Col. Florencia—take Suyapa bus) and Union Church, Colonia Lomas del Guijarro, with services in English. Catholic mass in English at the chapel of Instituto San Francisco at 1000 every Sunday.

Peace Corps has an office with library and photographic dark room, on Av. República de Chile, up hill past *Hotel Honduras Maya*; open Mon.-Fri. 0800-1600.

Tour Operators Trek Honduras, Edificio Midence Soto 217, downtown, tours of the city, Bay Islands, Copán, San Pedro Sula, Valle de Angeles and Santa Lucía. Mindirama, Ed. Ciicsa, Av. República de Chile, 100 m. S of *Hotel Maya*.

Tourist Office Under Congress Building (Plaza La Merced), opp. Banco Central, also at Tocontín airport. Provides lists of hotels and sells posters, postcards and slides. Information on cultural events around the country from Teatro Manuel Bonilla, better than at regional tourist offices. The best map of the country is produced by the Instituto Geográfico Nacional and may be bought from the Institute on production of passport and map request, typed, in triplicate (it is a long process, involving a trip to the Treasury). Open weekdays 0730-1200, 1230-1530. Texaco also do a good map of the country, available at Texaco stations.

National Parks The Asociación Hondureña de Ecología (Aptdo. T-250, Toncontín, Tegucigalpa, office in Centro Comercial Centroamérica, Nivel 2, T 32-90-18) has drawn up a list of over 70 natural reserves in Honduras which it hopes will be developed as national parks or reserves, and 56 plant, animal, bird and aquatic species in danger. Its book *Areas silvestres de Honduras* gives all details (US$7.50). It also publishes *Ecosistemas terrestres de Honduras* (US$3.50) and *Mamíferos silvestres de Honduras* (US$6); *Aves de Honduras* was due for publication in 1989. The parks system is in its infancy, but all support and interest is most welcome. Parks in existence are La Tigra, outside Tegucigalpa (see next page), and the Biosphere of the Río Plátano (**see page 4217**). Under development since 1987 are Mount Celaque (**page 4218**), Cusuco (**page 1238**) and Pico Bonito (**page 1233**—by 1989, these 3 parks are expected to have visitors' centres, hiking trails and primitive camping), and the following have been designated national parks by the government: Montecristo-Trifinio (**see page 1240**), Cerro Azul (Copán), Santa Bárbara, Azul Meambar (Cortés and Comayagua), Pico Pijol (Yoro), Montaña de Yoro, Agalta (Olancho) and Montaña Comayagua. Some of these sites have Peace Corps Volunteers, who would be a good source of information.

Motorists Tegucigalpa is appallingly badly signposted and is a nightmare for motorists. Motorists leaving Tegucigalpa for San Pedro Sula or Olancho can avoid the congestion of Comayagüela market by driving N down to Barrio Abajo, crossing the river to Barrio Chile and taking the motorway up the mountainside, to turn right to Olancho, or left to rejoin the northern outlet to San Pedro Sula (at the second intersection, turn right for the old, winding route, go straight on for the new, fast route).

Airport Toncontín, 6½ km. from the centre. Checking-in takes a long time; restaurant, souvenir shop. Buses to airport from Comayagüela, Loarque Rutas No. 1 and No. 11, on 4a Av. between 6 and 7 Calle, or opp. Ciné Palace in downtown Tegucigalpa; into town US$0.10, 20 mins. from left-hand side outside the airport; yellow cabs, US$6, smaller colectivo taxis, US$3.20.

Airlines For national flights: Aero Servicios, Toncontín airport, T 33-12-69 (private); Lansa, Toncontín, Tel.; 33-18-14; TAN/Sahsa, Toncontín, T 33-10-10, in town, T 37-86-74. SAMi, T 33-85-49, for daily flights to Puerto Lempira/Mocorón. Taca International, Blvd. Morazán, T 32-08-08; Pan Am and Lacsa, Ed. San Miguel, Barrio La Plazuela, T 37-01-57; Alitalia, Centro Comercial Los Castaños, Blvd. Morazán, T 32-18-82; Iberia, Ed. Palmira, opp. *Honduras Maya*, T 31-52-53; KLM, Edificio Ciicsa, Av. República de Chile, Col. Palmira; Lufthansa, Ed. Midence Soto, 5 piso, No.503, T 37-69-00.

Buses To San Pedro Sula on Northern Highway: 4½ hrs. (6 companies including Sáenz, 12 Calle, 7 and 8 Av., El Rey, Av. 6, Calle 9, Comayagüela, Hedmán Alas, 13-14C., 11 Av., Comayagüela, T 377143, 7 a day, and Norteño, all charge US$3.50, except Hedmán Alas, US$4, excellent, first bus leaves at 0630, the 6 more). Mi Esperanza, Av. 6, Calle 23 or 26, Comayagüela, to Choluteca, 3 hrs., US$2.50, 0400 onwards; to San Marcos de Colón for Nicaraguan border at El Espino, 4 a day from 0730, and direct to frontier at 0400, US$3.50, 4 hrs. (0730, 0900 buses to San Marcos best for onward connections). To La Esperanza, Empresa Joelito, 4 Calle No. 834, Comayagüela, 8 hrs, US$3.50. To Comayagua, US$1.50, Transportes Catrachos, Comayagüela, every 30 mins., 1½-2 hrs. To Guatemala, go to San Pedro Sula and take either Impala or Congolón to Ocotepeque and the frontier at Agua Caliente, or take the route via Copán (**see page 1240**). To San Salvador, via San Miguel on Tues., Fri. and Sun., Transportes El Salvador, US$10, book 2 days in advance, 0700 from opp. *Hotel Calle Real*, Calle Real (Av. 2a), Comayagüela; direct bus to border at El Amatillo, US$2.50, 3 hrs., several daily; alternatively from San Pedro Sula via Ocotepeque and El Poy. If you prefer to avoid El Salvador when travelling N, take a bus to San Pedro Sula, and from there go to Guatemala.

For travellers leaving Tegucigalpa, take the "Villa Adela" bus in Calle Jérez, by Cine Pálace, and alight in Comayagüela at Cine Centenario (Av. 6a) for nearby Empresa Aurora buses (for Olancho) and El Rey buses (for San Pedro Sula or Olancho); 3 blocks S is Ciné Lux, near which are Empresas Unidas and Maribel for Siguatepeque (to town centre, US$0.50 cheaper but 1 hr. slower than San Pedro Sula buses which drop you on the main road, a US$0.50 taxi ride from Siguatepeque). By the Mamachepa market is the Norteño bus line for San Pedro Sula; also nearby are buses for Nacaome and El Amatillo frontier with El Salvador. "Villa Adela" bus continues to Mi Esperanza bus terminal (for Choluteca and Nicaraguan frontier). Take a "Belén", "Garnisal" or "Santa Fe" bus from Tegucigalpa for the hill ascending Belén (9a Calle) for Hedman Alas buses to San Pedro Sula and for Comayagua buses (to town centre, cheaper but slower than main line buses to San Pedro Sula which drop passengers on main road, a taxi ride away from the centre).

Excursions Eight km. NE to the church at Suyapa, which attracts pilgrims to its wooden figure of the Virgin, a tiny image about 8 cm. high set into the altar. Excursions to Copán (1 hr. by air, US$295 for a plane taking 5 passengers), visits to **the Agricultural School at Zamorano**, and sight-seeing tours of Tegucigalpa and Comayagüela are arranged by several tour operators. It is about a ½ hour drive to *Valle de Angeles*, 1,310 metres, 6,635 people (old mines, many walks possible in surrounding forests, picnic areas, swimming pool; *Hotel y Restaurante Posada del Angel*, rec., moderate prices; *Hotel San Francisco*, F; *Comedor La Abejita*, rec.; several others. Hospital de los Adventistas, in the valley, a modern clinic, sells vegetables and handicrafts; there are many handicraft shops in town—a visit to the Artisans' School is recommended) and on to San Juan de Flores (also called Cantarranas) and San Juancito, an old mining town. (Bus to Valle de Angeles hourly, US$0.50, leaves from Av. de los Próceres, around the service station—take a Colonia 21 de Octubre bus from Parque Central to Mercado San Pablo in Barrio El Manchen, 10 mins.; to San Juan de Flores 1000, 1230, 1530.) On the way to Valle de Angeles take a right turn off to visit the quaint old mining village of *Santa Lucía* (4,230 people), perched precariously on a steep mountainside overlooking the wide valley with Tegucigalpa below. The town has a beautiful colonial church with a Christ given by King Philip II of Spain in 1592; there is a festival in the 2nd and 3rd weeks of January. Delightful walk down old mule trail across pine-clad ridges to the city (1½ hrs.). Bus to Santa Lucía from Mercado San Pablo, US$ 0.40. Weekend tours to Valle de Angeles and Santa Lucía leave from Av. La Paz, Tegucigalpa, opp. Ciné Presidente.

There are bracing climbs to the heights of Picacho; take right fork at summit to El Hatillo and on 24 km. to visit the rain forest (small buses from north of Parque Herrera, Tegucigalpa). To San Juancito (*Hospedaje Don Jacinto*; simple meals in the village), above which is *La Tigra* rain forest, a National Park (a stiff, 1-hr. uphill walk to park offices and trail, Sendero Bosque Nublado); a few quetzal birds survive here, but do not leave paths when walking as there are precipitous drops; there is accommodation on a first come, first served basis (no problem on weekdays, can be cold at night), and a restaurant. Bus leaves from San Pablo market, Tegucigalpa, from 1000, 1½ hrs., US$1 for San Juancito; passes turn-off to Santa Lucía and goes through Valle de Angeles.

From Parque Herrera a bus at 1200 goes to the village of El Peleguín; a delightful 40-min. walk down the pineclad mountainside leads to El Chimbo (meals at *pulpería* or shop—ask anyone the way), then take bus either to Valle de Angeles or Tegucigalpa.

A half-hour drive from Tegucigalpa to *Ojojona*, another quaint old village (6,670 people); turn right 24 km. down Southern Highway. The village's pottery is interesting (but selection reported to be poor). There is a small museum. *Fiesta* Jan. 18-20. There are 3 well preserved colonial churches in Ojojona (notice the fine paintings), plus two more in nearby Santa Ana which is passed on the way from Tegucigalpa. Ojojona is completely unspoiled; *Pensión Joxone*, comfortable; *comedor*. (Bus every 15-30 mins. from Calle 4, No. 825, Comayagüela, US$0.50, 1 hr.) From same location, buses go to Lepaterique ("place of the jaguar"), another colonial village, over an hour's drive through rugged, forested terrain. Distant view of Pacific on fine days from heights above village.

Minas de Oro, on a forested tableland at about 1,060 metres, is a centre for walking in wooded mountains, 3-hrs. bus ride with Transportes Díaz-Donavil, 10 Av. 11 C. Barrio Belén, Comayagüela at 0630 and 1300 (US$ 2.50). It is a picturesque old mining town, 73 km. N of Talanga, which is on the Olancho highway. Several *pensiones*, incl. *Los Pinares* (F, meals US$1) and *Hospedaje Mi Esperanza* (F, clean, basic). Robert Millar writes: Climb Cerro Grande (beware of snakes); walk to Malacatán mountain and Minas de San Antonio; follow old mule trail to San José Potrerillos. Strenuous climb, 3 hrs., over forested mountain range to lovely old colonial village of *Esquías*, with church, *cabildo* (town hall), tree-shaded plaza; bus from Esquías to Tegucigalpa (irregular), otherwise hitch from Minas de Oro or Comayagua (via Rancho Grande). Also nearby are the villages of San Luis, San José del Potrero, and Victoria and the Montana de la Flor, in a remote area, inhabited by the Xicaques tribe. Bus Minas de Oro-Comayagua (daily) passes through *Cedros*, one of Honduras' earliest settlements, dating from Pedro de Alvarado's mining operations of 1536. It is an outstanding colonial mining town, with cobbled streets, perched high on an eminence, amid forests. The festival of El Señor del Buen Fin takes place in the first two weeks of January.

Swimming at thermal springs of Balneario San Francisco Támara; 32 km., along road to San Pedro Sula, turn off right 8 km. N of Támara. **Parque Aurora**, midway between Tegucigalpa (about 50 km. N) and Comayagua, has a small zoo and picnic area among pine-covered hills, a lake with rowing boats (hire US$1 per hour), a snack bar and lovely scenery. Camping US$0.50 p.p.; admission US$0.75.

At km. 17 on Zamorano road (at summit of range overlooking Suyapa church) take dirt road left to TV tower. From here a delightful 2-hour walk over forested ridges leads to Santa Lucía. At km. 24 on Zamorano road, climb the highest peak through the Uyuca rain forest, information from Pan-American Agricultural School at Zamorano from their office in the Edificio Guillén in Tegucigalpa. The school has rooms for visitors. On the NW flank of Uyuca is the picturesque village of Tatumbla.

The North Coast

Puerto Cortés, at the mouth of the Ulúa river, is 58 km. by road and rail from

San Pedro Sula, 333 from Tegucigalpa, and only two days' voyage from New Orleans. About half of Honduran trade passes through it. The climate is hot, tempered by sea breezes; many beautiful palm-fringed beaches nearby; rainfall, 2,921 mm. It has a small oil refinery, and a free zone was opened in 1978. Population 60,500. Festival, in August, including "Noche Veneciana" on 3rd Saturday.

Hotels *La Playa*, on outskirts, hotel complex, good fish dishes in restaurant; *International Mr. Ggeerr*, Barrio El Centro, B, hot water, a/c, bar, video, satellite TV, rec.; *Hotel-restaurante Costa Mar*, Playas de la Coca Cola, T 55-15-39/55-13-67, new, pleasant. *Los Piratas*, F, basic but friendly; *Colón*, F, basic, noisy, in red-light district; *Formosa*, F, dirty, but good food.

Restaurants *Café Vienna*, on Parque, good, reasonably priced; *Chun Wah*, on Parque, good, big comidas; *Restaurant-Cafe Kalúa* in centre of town. *Restaurant Formosa*, expensive, but good. *La Roca*, Av. Ferrocarril; *Príncipe Maya* on road to Omoa.

Protestant Church Anglican/Episcopal.

Exchange Banco de Londres (agency), 2a Av. y 3a Calle; Banco Atlántida and other local banks. Banco de Comercio cashes travellers' cheques. Banco de Occidente, Calle Principal; Bancahsa, 2 Av. 2 Calle. Open 0800-1130, 1330-1600; Sats. 0800-1100.

Shops There are two souvenir shops in the customs house at the entrance to the National Port Authority, which sell hand-embroidered clothes. A shop on the main street sells mahogany wood carvings and the market in the town centre is quite interesting.

Rail Daily train departs 0815 to San Pedro Sula and Potrerillos, 95 km., 1.067 metres gauge. Two daily trains to Tela, change at La Junta, one at 0700 (US$1, second class, US$1.75 first).

Road To San Pedro Sula and Potrerillos and on to the capital. Bus service hourly to San Pedro Sula, US$1, 45 mins., Citul and Impala lines.

Shipping No regular passenger sailings to New Orleans, or Santo Tomás de Castilla (Guatemala). A goleta (canoe) leaves Pueblo Nuevo, Puerto Cortés, for Mango Creek, Belize, US$20, 7 hrs., no fixed schedule; can be dangerous in rough weather. Remember to get your exit stamp. The Immigration Office is near the Plaza Central (it is not noted for its efficiency—exit stamps cost US$2.50-US$5, depending on the official). If entering Puerto Cortés by boat, one must go to Immigration immediately. Passports are sometimes collected at the dock and you must go later to Immigration to get them; you must pay US$1 entry fee, make sure that you have the stamp. This is the only official payment; if asked for more, demand a receipt.

Excursions W to Tulián, along the bay, for picnics and freshwater bathing. Minibuses (US$0.35 each way) ply along the tropical shoreline past Tulián W to Omoa (or 3-hr. walk—15 km. from Puerto Cortés), with its restored 18th century castle (admission, US$0.25). There is a paved road through Omoa, continuing to the Guatemalan border. (Hotel in Omoa, *Acantilados del Caribe*—Caribbean Cliff Marine Club, Chivana, Omoa, B, good food, nice atmosphere.) Other buses go E to beaches of coconut palms and white sands at Travesía, Baja Mar, etc., which are beautiful, and unspoilt. Café at Travesía, but none at Baja Mar. The black fishing communities are very friendly. Beware of sunburn, and mosquitoes at dusk. From November to May, because of tourist ships arriving two or three times a week, there are tours to La Lima to visit the banana plantations, trips to Copán to visit the Mayan ruins and tourist parties at the Ustaris Hacienda.

Tela, another important banana port some 50 km. to the E, is reached from Puerto Cortés by sea, rail, road, or from San Pedro Sula by rail and by bus service via El Progreso. It is pleasantly laid out, with a magnificent sandy beach (not as safe as it used to be). Population 67,890. *Fiesta*: San Antonio in June.

Hotels *Villas Telamar*, a complex of wooden bungalows, set on a palm-fringed beach, rooms A, villas from A-L, restaurant, bar, golf club, swimming pool, service disappointing; *Paradise Hotel*, in a palm grove about 3 km. W of Tela, beside magnificent beach, cabins, C-B, restaurant, insecure; *Tela*, Calle El Comercio, E, good, with restaurant; *La Playa*, E (singles more), friendly, English-speaking owner, good value, next door is *Atlántico*, D, a/c, E without, both on beach); *Mar Azul*, on same street, E with fan and bath. The *hospedaje* owned by Doña Sara is quite good, Calle Leonicio D. Herrera (on beach, east end of town), E with bath, F without, has 3 cabins priced according to number of occupants; *Hotel Robert*, F, rec., in red light district, noisy, close to bus and railway stations. *Balderach*, in Central Park, old, basic, cheap. Plenty of cheap *hospedajes* near railway station, e.g. *Valencia*, rec. (on R-hand side of tracks as you arrive). *Gina Boarding House*, E, with bath and fan, parking. *Pensión Muñoz* on beachfront, F, meals extra, basic; *Pensión Iris*, both budget. During Easter week, the town is packed; room rates double and advance booking is essential.

Camping   at municipal site next to beach, US$1. Also possible, but not safely, on beach.

Restaurant   *Northern Lights (Luces del Norte)*, Canadian owned (Slim Jim), one block towards beach from Parque Central, excellent value, very popular, also English book exchange; *César's*, on the beach, serves good seafood, beware of short-changing. *Bahía Bar/Restaurant*, overpriced. *China*, on main street. *Bambo Bar*, Av. México. *Maribú Inn*, opp. Colegio San Antonio.

Hondutel and Post Office both on 4 Av. N.E.

Protestant Church   Anglican.

Exchange   Banco Atlántida, Bancahsa, Banadesa.

Buses   Cati or Tupsa lines from San Pedro Sula to El Progreso (US$0.60) where you must change to go on to Tela (3 hrs. in all) and La Ceiba (last bus at 1900). Bus from Tela to El Progreso every 30 mins., US$1.25; to La Ceiba, 2½ hrs., US$1.75.

Rail   The National Railways 1.067-metre gauge line W to Puerto Cortés; two trains per day US$1 2nd class, 4 hrs. A branch of this line runs south along the eastern bank of the Ulúa River to Progreso and Potrerillos. Train to San Pedro Sula with change at Baracoa, at 1345 (in theory) 4¼ hrs.: Mon. and Thurs. direct to Baracoa, other days change at La Junta to Puerto Cortés train. Fare to San Pedro Sula, US$1.50 1st class, US$0.70 2nd.

Excursions   To the tropical experimental farm at Lancetilla (established 1926), 5 km. inland; open Tues.-Fri., 0730-1530; Sat., Sun. and holidays 0830-1600, admission US$0.50. *Hospedaje* and *comedor*, full at weekends, and camping facilities. Either take employees' bus from town centre at 0700, or local bus to entrance from where tours run frequently the 4 km. to the botanical gardens (first at 0900, last at 1400, 1 hr. tour). Ask for Víctor Gámez for a good guided tour.

Local buses and trucks from the corner just E of the market go E to the Black Carib village of *Triunfo*, site of the first Spanish settlement on the mainland, in a beautiful bay, in which a sea battle between Cristóbal de Olid and Francisco de las Casas (2 of Cortés' lieutenants) was fought in 1524. Bus to Triunfo, US$0.40 (about 5 km.- if no return bus, walk to main road where buses pass). Also, W to the Carib villages of Tornabé and San Juan (4 km. W of *Villas Telamar*), worth a visit, beautiful food (fish cooked in coconut oil). Further NW, along palm-fringed beaches and blue lagoons, is Punta Sal, a lovely place.

El Progreso, on the Río Ulúa, an important agricultural and commercial centre (no longer just a banana town) is less than an hour's drive on the paved highway SE of San Pedro Sula en route to Tela. Population, about 106,550. Local *fiesta*: Las Mercedes, end of September. Visit the Santa Elizabeth handicraft centre, where women are taught wood carving.

Hotel   *Municipal*, Calle de Comercio, E to C with a/c and bath, clean, comfortable restaurant. *Honduras*, F p.p. with bath, run down, meals US$1.25; *Imperador*, attractive, F with bath; other cheap *pensiones*.

Restaurants   *Maya*, 1 Av., 4-5 C.; *La Posta*, Calle del Comercio.

Exchange   Bancahsa, Banco Atlántida, Banco del Comercio, Banco Sogerín, Banadesa.

The highway is paved 25 km. S of El Progreso to Santa Rita; if one continues towards the San Pedro Sula-Tegucigalpa highway, one avoids San Pedro Sula when travelling from the N Coast to the capital. The highway is paved from Santa Rita to Yoro. (**See also page 1244**.) 10 km. S of El Progreso on the paved highway to Yoro or Santa Rita, at the village of Las Minas, is El Chorro (1 km. off the highway), a charming waterfall and natural swimming pool. A rugged hike can be made into the mountains and on to El Negrito from here.

La Ceiba, the country's busiest port for the export of bananas and pineapples, is 100 km. E of Tela, from which it is reached by sea or road. The capital of Atlántida Department, it stands on the narrow coastal plain between the Caribbean and the rugged Nombre de Dios mountain range, crowned by the spectacular Pico Bonito (2,435 metres—see below). The climate is hot, but tempered by sea winds. There are some fine beaches nearby (La Barra and Miramar are the most popular), though some are dirty. Beyond La Ceiba is the old colonial village of Jutiapa. The Bay Islands are usually visited from La Ceiba. Population 80,160. *Fiesta*, Feria Isidra (National Carnival), third week in May; main day is the 3rd Saturday of the month (live music from dawn till dusk).

Hotels   *Gran Hotel París*, C, a/c, with good cafeteria, swimming pool (open to non-residents for US$2), parking, and small night club; *Partenos Beach* (Greek-owned, family apartments), swimming pool, restaurant, T 43-04-04; *Ceiba*, Av. San Isidro, 5 C., D with fan and bath, C with bath and a/c, restaurant and bar; next door is *Iberia*, D, a/c, clean, quiet, comfortable, ample hot water, good value; one block down from the *Iberia* is *Dorita*, D with bath, friendly, clean. *Los Angeles*, Av. La República, E, good value; *Príncipe*, 7 Calle, E, with bath, better than average; *La Isla*, next to bus station, F, nice rooms, fans, clean; *El Paso*, Av. La República, F; *Royal*, same Av., 2-3 C., E. Many cheap hotels beside railway line leading from central plaza to pier: *Arias*, F without bath, good value. **Camping** at the airport for US$ 0.20.

Restaurants *Maxim's*, Av. San Isidro; *Atlántico*, Av. 14 de Julio; *Deportivo*, Blvd. Las Américas; *Le Petit Café* (*Gran Hotel París*); *Ricardo's* (American-owned), good food, garden setting and a/c tables. *Mini Café* (near *Pensión Tegucigalpa*), reasonable, helpful owner; *Toto*, Av. San Isidro, one block south of main square, good pizzería. *Hotel San Carlos'* cafetería is assembly point for the predominantly European Bay Islands (money exchange outside). Numerous small, cheap eating places.

Rent a Car Molinari.

Discotheques Leonardo's; D'Lido; Black and White; Scaramouche; all popular.

Non-Catholic Churches Anglican, Methodist, Mennonite, Evangelist and Jehovah's Witnesses, among others.

Exchange Banco de Londres, Av. San Isidro y 10a Calle; Banco Atlántida; Bancahsa, 9 C., Av. San Isidro; Bancahorro, Av. San Isidro, 7 C.; Banco Sogerín, Av. San Isidro. Open 0830-1130, 1330-1600; Sats. 0800-1200.

Tourist Office Calle 1, 2 blocks east of the pier.

Buses Most leave from a central terminal, 8 blocks from centre (taxi US$0.50). Regular bus service to San Pedro Sula, US$4 (7 a day from 0530, 3 hrs.). Alternatively, take bus to Tela (2 hrs.), then another to El Progreso, then another to San Pedro Sula, cost in all US$3.10, but much slower. To Trujillo, 5-8 hrs., US$5; to Olanchito, US$4, 3 hrs.; also regular buses to Sonaguera, Tocoa, Jutiapa, Balfate, Isletas and Iriona and San Esteban.

Airport Golosón, with direct jet services to Miami and New Orleans as well as internal destinations. Sahsa flies to Tegucigalpa, also flights to Roatán, Utila, and Guanaja (Bay Is.). To Puerto Lempira, Isleña (Ed. Hermanos Kawas, T 42-01-79), Tues. and Sun., Lansa on Sun. US$93 return, both booked up 2-3 weeks ahead (T 42-26-83). Taxi to town US$6 per car, share with other passengers, also buses.

The *Pico Bonito* national park (674 sq. km.) is the largest of the 11 new parks designated in 1987. It has deep tropical hardwood forests which shelter, among other things, jaguars and three species of monkey, deep canyons and tumbling streams and waterfalls (including Las Gemelas which fall vertically some 200 metres). Access is limited to the fringes of the range, and to the Río Cangrejal, which cuts through a gentler section, and which is bordered by the old, unpaved road to Olanchito from La Ceiba. As of 1987, Pico Bonito itself had only been climbed by four expeditions, the shortest of which took nine days. The preferred route is along the Río Bonito, starting 10 km. from La Ceiba, and from there up a ridge which climbs all the way to the summit. Expertise in rock climbing is not necessary, but several steep pitches do require a rope for safety; good physical condition is a necessity. Poisonous snakes, including the fer-de-lance (*barba amarilla*) will probably be encountered en route.

A Peace Corps volunteer stationed in La Ceiba is working on the development of Pico Bonito national park and would be a good source of advice on access. Maps at US$2 should also be available. (Leon Kolankiewicz)

The Hog Islands (Cayos Cochinos), with lovely primeval hardwood forests, are NE of La Ceiba (two small islands and a number of palm-fringed cays): privately owned with reserved accommodation at Cayos del Sol. On the Isla de Cochino Grande is a dive resort; very beautiful. The owner of the largest island, Bobby Griffith, permits camping, especially if you can give him a news magazine or two. Take a bus from the stop 1 block from La Ceiba market to Nueva Armenia (US$2), then try to hitch on a dugout, or charter one (about US$10).

The **Bay Islands** (Islas de la Bahía) lie in an arc which curves NE away from a point 32 km. N of La Ceiba. The three main islands are Utila, Roatán, and Guanaja. At the eastern end of Roatán are three small ones: Morat, Santa Elena, and Barbareta; there are other islets and 65 cays. Their total population is 21,550. The main industry is fishing, mostly shellfish, with fleets based at French Harbour. Boat-building is a dying industry. Apart from fish, trade is mostly in coconuts, bananas and plantains. There are some blacks and Black Caribs; the majority are fair-skinned people originally of British stock and still English-speaking. The culture is very un-Latin American. Columbus anchored here in 1502, on his fourth voyage. In the 18th century the islands were bases for English, French and Dutch buccaneers. They were in British hands for over a century but were finally ceded to Honduras in 1859. The government schools teach in Spanish, and the population is bi-lingual. The islands are very beautiful, but beware of the strong sun (the locals bathe in T-shirts) and sand gnats and other insects, especially away from the resorts.

The underwater environment is rich and extensive; reefs surround the islands, often within swimming distance of the shore. Caves and caverns are a common feature, with a wide variety of sponges and the best collection of pillar coral in the Caribbean. The islands are destined to become a major diving centre within a few years.

Utila (population 1,515) is only 32 km. from La Ceiba and is low lying, with only one hill. On it there are caves to which you can hike. One of the caves is reputed locally to have been a hideout for Henry Morgan. There is some evidence of Paya Indian culture. The main town is known locally as East Harbour. Utila is the cheapest of the islands to visit. Take plenty of insect repellant in the rainy season. Do not pick coconuts, even in the remotest places; you may well be fined. Sunbathing and swimming are not particularly good. Snorkelling and diving equipment for hire; a popular snorkelling spot is by the airport.

A 40-minute boat ride from East Harbour are the Cays, a chain of small islands populated by fisherfolk off the S coast. On the main Cay, a few families live; they are very friendly to foreigners, but there is nowhere to put a tent. 3 islands further out is Water Cay where you can camp, sling a hammock or, in emergency, sleep in the house of the caretaker; take food and fresh water. It is a coconut island with "white holes" (sandy areas with wonderful hot bathing in the afternoon) and some of the most beautiful underwater reefs in the world. To hire a *dony* (big motorized canoe) costs US$30 for four; many boatmen go and will collect you in the evening.

Hotels and restaurants on Utila *Captain Spencer*, E-D, with bath, and restaurant; *Trudy's*, C, dear, E without bath, good meals, diving equipment and boats for hire. *Gran View Gallery*, owned by Günter, an Austrian, exotic jewellery from the sea, diving expeditions (equipment for rent, US$25) and plenty of information. *Grant's Cabins*, US$15 for 4 people, cooking facilities, good value. Nearby is the *Manhattan Restaurant*, cheap, good, clean. Good, reasonable food from *Yellow Light Restaurant* (who organizes good picnics on the Cays, US$2 p.p. and US$1.50 for food, "unforgettable"). *Monkey Tail Inn*, F, quite good, cooking facilities, water all the time (beyond the *Bucket of Blood Bar*, the owner of which is Mr Woods, a mine of information on the history of Utila and the Cays). There are plenty of houses and rooms for rent, from US$2.50 a person: e.g. at Willis Bodden, US$12 for 3 people (runs a boat trip to the Cays, US$25); Ronald Janssen (a Dutchman at Cross Creek), US$12 a day, US$50 a week for 4-person house, has scuba diving equipment for hire, US$30 if four people go (T 45-31-34).

There is a bank for changing dollars, but dollars are accepted, a post office and a good clinic. The discotheque is very busy on Saturdays. Local crafts include wood-carving (see Marc Coburn, called Tom).

Transport Isleña, Sosa and Lansa fly from La Ceiba for US$15 one way (at the official exchange rate). The first two have three regular flights, at 0600, 1200 and 1600. Check all flight times in advance. Sometimes air fares are reduced if there is competition from a boat. No need to take a taxi from Utila airport to town; US$2 for 300 metres.

A boat leaves every Tuesday around 1100 (ask in *Hotel San Carlos*). The *Caribbean Pearl* usually sails to Utila from La Ceiba on Mon., US$4 single, 3 hrs., and returns overnight to Puerto Cortés (bunks available), US$5, times posted in main street. Take food and torch. Captain Juni Cooper sails from La Ceiba to Utila from Mon. p.m. to Tues. a.m., US$4 for the 2½-3 hr. trip. He sails to Roatán a day or so later. From Utila to Roatán he charges US$5, 3½ hrs., irregular sailings. Two boats a week between Puerto Cortés and Utila, no regular schedule, US$10, continuing to Roatán.

It is a few hours' sail to *Roatán,* the largest of the islands (population 10,245). The capital of the department, Roatán (locally known as Coxen's Hole), is on the south-western shore. Port Royal, towards the eastern end of the island, and famous in the annals of buccaneering, is now almost deserted. Archaeologists have been busy on the islands but their findings are very confusing.

From Coxen's Hole it is 2 hours' walk to Sandy Bay, or US$1 by bus; airport employees try to charge US$12, beware: it should only be US$2 from airport. West End, on the opposite coast, can be reached by a stiff walk over the hills (3 hours, bus US$1.50). There are many buses on the unmade roads, but those that charge US$1-1.50 on set routes daily at nightfall or on Sunday charge US$10 for express journeys. Frequent bus service from Coxen's Hole to French Harbour (US$1.50), with its shrimping and lobster fleet. At Brick Bay, just before French Harbour, the Caribbean Sailing Club has a modern hotel (A with breakfast) and rents a fleet of 30 sailing boats for US$200 per day. From French Harbour to Oak

Ridge by bus, on a rough road, is US$1.50; Oak Ridge, situated on a cay (US$0.50 crossing in dory), is built around a deep inlet. Hire a boat for an hour's sail up the coast to Port Royal (also reached by good road from Oak Ridge); old British gun emplacements on Fort Cay. No regular bus from Port Royal to Oak Ridge, and it's a tough 3-hr. walk. Note the Black Carib village of Punta Gorda on the north coast (probably the first non-Indian settlement on the islands). Beaches excellent but expensive, twice as dear as the mainland.

Hotels on Roatán At West End, *Roberts Hill*, D, with meals, diving, etc., good value; *Lost Paradise of the West End*, C, full board (D without), delicious meals, snorkelling equipment, transport back to airport; there is no food to be bought at West End. At Sandy Bay, *Anthony's Key Resort*, L (US$75 full board), glorious situation, launch and diving facilities (US$20, US$40 non-residents); *Pirate's Den*, D-A, full board, poor service, beware of overcharging (well named); *Bamboo Inn*, D, clean and good (nice restaurant next door, reasonable prices); *Quinn's*, reasonable. At French Harbour, *Coral Reef Inn*, E-D; *Caribinn*, D; *French Harbour Yacht Club*, C-B; *Buccaneer Inn*, C-A; *Fantasy Island Beach Resort*, 80 rooms, luxurious on a cay; *Hotelito*, E, sometimes no water, in the village; unnamed hotel just before *Buccaneer Inn*, E with fan, very good value.

At Brick Bay: *Island Garden*, good European-run guest house (contact Drs. E. and B. Free, Englewood, Co 80112); *Romeo's Marina*, B, good.

At Oak Ridge, *Reef House Resort*, B-L, inc. meals and boats. *San José Hotel*, D, clean, pleasant, good value, good food, English-speaking owner, Louise Solórzano; *Gran Hotel Ronnie*, cafeteria nearby; *Clear View Hotel*, B.

At Port Royal, *Camp Bay Resort*, A; *Roatán Lodge*, Port Royal, L, accommodation in cabins, hosts Brian and Lisa Blancher provide scuba diving and snorkelling expeditions; *Miss Merlee's Guest House*.

At Coxen's Hole: *Central*, E, basic but rec., run by a doctor; *Coral*, E; *Solbod House*, D; *Airport View*, C (D without bath or a/c); *Cay View*, C (E without bath or a/c); *Comedor Isleña*, good, cheap and *Cafetería El Punto*.

At Punta Gorda, *Spyglass Hill Resort*, overlooking village, L, lodge or bungalow accommodation, 1 hr.'s walk from Oak Ridge. There are other, cheaper, places to stay (for example, Miss Effie's, near *Anthony's Key Resort*) and houses to let (at West End, Half Moon Bay, or Punta Gorda).

At Coxen's Hole are a post office, tourist information, travel agencies, a supermarket and souvenir shops.

Barbareta Beach Club on Barbareta Island; excellent diving, but expensive. The adjacent Pigeon Cays are ideal for snorkelling, shallow scuba, picnics. There are stone artefacts on the island, and you can hike in the hills to caves which may have been inhabited by Paya Indians. The island was once owned by the descendants of Henry Morgan. The island, plus its neighbours Santa Elena and Morat, are part of the proposed Barbareta National Marine Park.

Transport Take a plane to Coxen's Hole (airport is 20 mins. walk from town, taxi US$1.50) and launch up coast to French Harbour and Oak Ridge. Flights to La Ceiba with Sahsa or Lansa, several daily (US$20 one way); Lansa flies frequently to Utila and Guanaja. Also flights San Pedro Sula-Roatán (airport has been extended to take jets).

Boats go irregularly from Puerto Cortés to Roatán, US$10 plus US$0.50 dock charge for tourists. Boats most days at 1400 for La Ceiba, US$12. *Caribbean Pearl* sails irregularly from Puerto Cortés, via Utila, to Roatán; also fishing boats for US$10 p.p. Charter sailing yacht *Lusanda*, US$900 for 4 people for 4 nights/3 days, with transport to and from La Ceiba by air.

Columbus called **Guanaja**, the easternmost of the group, the Island of Pines, and the tree is still abundant. The island was declared a forest reserve in 1961, and is now designated a national marine park also. The locals call the island Bonacca. Much of Guanaja town, covering a small cay off the coast, is built on stilts above sea water: hence its nick-name, the "Venice of Honduras". The island's population is 4,120. Bathing is made somewhat unpleasant by the many sandfleas.

Hotels on Guanaja *Bayman Bay Club* (beautiful location) and *Posada del Sol* (on an outlying cay), both A-L; *Miller*, D-C (cheaper without a/c or bath); *Harry Carter*, E-D. *Club Guanaja Este*, A, full board, many aquatic activities, and horseriding and hiking, reservations and information P.O. Box 40541, Cincinnati, Ohio 45240 or travel agents. *Casa Sobre El Mar*, on Bound Key, T 45-41-80 (31-05-95 in Tegucigalpa), offers all-inclusive packages for US$75 per person. *Comedor Punch a Penny*, good and cheap.

There are 3 banks.

Transport An airport on Bonacca Island, boat to Guanaja, US$1; Lansa flight from Roatán daily except Sun. at 0930, 1430; also to La Ceiba.

The *Suyapa* sails between Guanaja, La Ceiba and Puerto Cortés. The *Miss Sheila* also does the same run and goes on to George Town (Grand Cayman). Cable Doly Zapata, Guanaja, for monthly sailing dates to Grand Cayman (US$75 one way). Irregular sailings from Guanaja to Trujillo, twice a week, 5 hrs., US$10. Irregular but frequent sailings in lobster boats for next to nothing to Puerto Lempira in Caratasco Lagoon, Mosquitia, or more likely, only as far as the Río Plátano (**see page 1248**).

A roundabout railway and a direct road run from La Ceiba to *Olanchito,* a prosperous but hot and ugly town in the hills to the SE. It was founded, according to tradition, by a few stragglers who escaped from the destruction of Olancho el Viejo, between Juticalpa and Catacamas, then a wealthy town. They brought with them the crown made of hides which the image of the Virgin still wears in the church of Olanchito. Population: 12,200. Festival: 2nd week of September, Semana Cívica.

Hotels *Colonial*, Calle del Presidio; *Valle Aguán y Chabelito*, E.

Exchange El Ahorro Hondureño.

Bus To La Ceiba, 2½ hrs., US$4 via Jutiapa and Savá (Cotol 7 times a day; Cotrail); to Trujillo, 3 hrs., US$5 via Tocoa and Savá (Cotol).

Trujillo, 90 km. to the east again, is a port and former capital. The population is 23,760. The town was founded in 1525 (the oldest in Honduras) by Juan de Medina; Hernán Cortés arrived there after his famous march overland from Yucatán in pursuit of his usurping lieutenant, Olid. It was near here that William Walker (see under Nicaragua) was shot in 1860 (a commemorative stone marks the spot); the old cemetery where he is buried is interesting, giving an idea of where early residents came from. El Castillo (Santa Bárbara), a ruined Spanish fortress overlooking the Bay, is worth a visit. Ask the caretaker to show the relics found there. To the S, and E to the Río Segovia, lies a huge territory of jungled swamps and mountains lived in by a few Indians and timber men (**see page 1247**). Nearby is Guaymoreto lagoon, which has a bird island (Isla de Pájaros) and monkeys. Flying in is best—Lansa has flights to La Ceiba. The town can be reached by bus from San Pedro Sula, Tela and La Ceiba now that a road (paved for 123 km. from La Ceiba, through Savá, Tocoa, to Corocito) has been built from La Ceiba (a dull journey, 5 hrs. via Tocoa, 3 direct buses early a.m. from Trujillo, US$5). Public transport also to San Esteban and Juticalpa (pick-up from plaza 0730, US$10, all day ride—**see page 1247**). In this area, many people speak English, so if answered in English, do not continue in Spanish.

Local holiday: San Juan Bautista in June, with participation from surrounding Garifuna (Black Carib) settlements.

Hotels *Villa Brinkley*, T 44-44-44, B, private beach, swimming pool, good view, rec.; *Colonial*, D with bath, near plaza, opp. El Castillo, good; *El Castillo*, has overpriced restaurant; *Central*, E, with bath, basic, no water during the day (*Rubens Restaurant*, good, in the hotel). *Emperador*, E, small but comfortable rooms, friendly; *Imperial*, E, basic, noisy. Excellent seafood at *Cocopando*, set in a coconut grove on western beach (room for rent); *Comedor Albita*, near telephone office, good; *La Cueva del Pirata*, beside airstrip, excellent restaurant and bar, cabins F-C. Also good food in the market. Many fish restaurants along the beach; *pan de coco*, delicious, is baked almost daily.

Exchange Banco Atlántida.

There are interesting villages of Black Caribs (Garifuna) at Santa Fe, 10 km. W of Trujillo (US$1 by bus), San Antonio and eastwards at Limón. At Puerto Castilla near Trujillo, Columbus landed in 1502 and the first mass on Central American soil was said. It is a meat-packing station and active shrimping centre; a new port is being built. A military training centre operates here. The beach between the port and the spit of land that forms Trujillo Bay is deserted. There are some pleasant beaches around the magnificent Bay. Twenty minutes' walk from Trujillo plaza is Riveras de Pedregal (known as *la piscina*), a series of swimming pools filled from the Río Cristales. The owner, Sr. Rufino Galán, has a collection of precolumbian, colonial and modern artefacts and curios. The pools are usually open at weekends and holidays, but not during the Nov.-Feb. rainy season.

San Pedro Sula

San Pedro Sula, 58 km. S of Puerto Cortés by road and railway, the second largest city in Honduras, is a centre for the banana, coffee, sugar and timber trades, a focal distributing point for northern and western Honduras, and the most industrialized centre in the country. Its business community is mainly of Arab origin. The population is 319,740.

The city was founded by Pedro de Alvarado in 1536 but there are no old buildings of interest. The large neo-colonial-style cathedral, started in 1949, is now completed. San Pedro Sula is situated in the lush and fertile valley of the Ulúa (Sula) river, beneath the forested slopes of the Merendón mountains and, though pleasant in the cooler season from October to March, reaches very high temperatures in the summer months with considerable humidity levels.

The higher and cooler suburb of Bella Vista with its fine views over the city affords relief from the intense heat of the town centre. The cafeteria and foyer swimming pool of *Hotel Sula* provide a cool haven for visitors. The city's main festival, San Pedro, is in the last days of June.

Hotels *Gran Hotel Sula* (the best), 1 C., 3 and 4 Av., A/L, pool, restaurant (upstairs, very good, reasonably priced) and café, also good, 24-hr. service; *Copantl Sula*, very modern, A/L in Col. Las Mesetas, free bus to city centre, Telex IT5584; *Bolívar*, 2a C., 2 Av., N.O., D/A, cabins beside pool, with a/c, restaurant; *San Pedro*, 3 C., and 2 Av., S.O., F-D, with bath and a/c, also cheaper rooms, inexpensive restaurant; *Manhattan*, 7 Av. 3-4 C., E-D, with a/c; *Terraza*, C with a/c, E without, dining room rather dark and grimy, friendly staff, 6 Av., 4-5 Calle S.O.; *Colombia*, 3 Calle, 5-6 Av., E/D, with a/c, E without; *Colombia Annex*, a few blocks away, E without bath, pricey; *Moderno*, 7 Av., 5-6 C., E, opp. Empresa el Rey buses; *Brisas del Occidente*, a 5-storey building on Av. 5, E, with fan, friendly, comfortable, rec. (do not confuse with nearby *Brisas de Copán*, a dive which rents rooms by the hour); *Siesta*, 2 Av. S.E., 7 C. (T 522650), E, cheaper without bath, clean, safe, rec., but noisy; *Monte Cristo*, 2 Av. 7C., F, clean, fan, safe; *París*, near bus station for Puerto Cortés, F, shared bath, clean but noisy. Cheap hotels between bus terminals and downtown market. 5 km. south, on the road to Tegucigalpa, is *Tropical*, a good stopping place for motorists.

Restaurants *Touché*, good food, but expensive and slow service; *Le Petit France*, French, good but expensive; *Pat's Steak House*, good food and service; *La Espuela*, Av. Circunvalación N.O., good grilled meats; *La Cascada*, Centro Comercial La Carreta, Av. Circunvalación N.O., rec.; *Don Udo's*, in *Hotel Suites Los Andes*, same Avenida, restaurant and café-bar; *Motel Vitanza* and *Mesón Español* (near *Hotel Manhattan*), good typical dishes available; *Madrid* on Plaza, good; *Pizza Don Corleone*, several throughout the city; *Italia*, near *Gran Hotel Sula*, good; *Vicente* and *Nápoli* restaurants, centre of town, Italian, reasonable; *Salón Marte*, near market, good, cheap light meals in evening; *La Cesta*, good for chicken; *Pops* and *Ka-Boom* for ice cream. Many good fried chicken stands in market.

Discotheques Fondo del Recuerdo and Sancho Panza, good; Don Quijote; San Fernando (small).

Theatre The Círculo Teatral Sampedrano puts on plays at the Centro Cultural Sampedrano, 3 Calle N.O., No. 20, which also has an art gallery and an English and Spanish library. There are five air-conditioned cinemas.

Shopping Excellent wood and leather products are sold at CDI, in the old US Consulate building.

Taxis Cheap; ask the price first and bargain if necessary (US$1-1.50 per journey).

Exchange Banco de Londres at 4a Av. S.O. 26, between 3a and 4a Calle; Banco Atlántida; Banco de Honduras (Citibank); Banco de Ahorro Hondureño, has a beautiful mural in its head office, 5 Av., 4 Calle S.O. Bancahsa, 5 Av., S.O., No. 46; and all other local banks. Open 0830-1500, closed Sat. Black market at *Hotel Gran Sula*. Rates are better in some shops; they will also accept travellers' cheques.

Belize Consulate Sr. Antonio E. Canahuati, Edif. Plásticos Sula, Km. 5, T 52-61-91, open 0800-1100, 1300-1600. **Guatemalan Consulate**, 8 C., 5-6 Av. No. 38.

Schools and Institutes La Escuela Internacional (English-speaking), on US lines with US and some British staff. Alianza Francesa, Ed. Bermúdez, 5 Calle S.O. No. 38, T 53-11-78, has a library, French films on Wed., and cultural events on Fri.

Churches Episcopal Church, round corner from Sports Stadium, English service, Sun., 1000. High Mass on Suns., 1030, at Orthodox church at Río Piedras is picturesque and colourful.

Telphone, Telex and Cables from Hondutel.

Tourist Office Edificio Inmosa, 3-4 C., 4 Av., N.O., and at airport, road maps US$1.50.

Airport Ramón Villeda Morales, 13 km. from city centre, US$7.50 p.p. by taxi; US$3 by colectivo. Buses do not go to the airport terminal itself; you have to walk the final 1½ km. from the La Lima road (bus to this point, US$0.30). Flights to Tegucigalpa (35 mins.) 4 times daily. Twice daily to La Ceiba and to Belize. Direct flights every day to Guatemala, New Orleans and Miami. Irregular flights to other Honduran cities and to the Copán ruins.

Buses To Tegucigalpa, 4½ hrs., 250 km. by paved road. Main bus services with comfortable coaches and terminals in the town centre are Hedmán Alas, 7-8 Av. N.O., 3 C., Casa 51, T 53 1361 (US$4), which is the best, and Transportes Sáenz (Av. 9 y 10, C.9 y Av. S.O.), El Rey, Av. 7, Calle 5 y 6 (all US$3.50), last bus at 1900. Small friendly buses run by El Norteño. Other services operate with less comfortable buses. The road to Puerto Cortés is paved; a pleasant 1-hr. journey down the lush river valley. Train journey takes two hours at least to cover the same distance and there are two or three trains a day. Buses run N to Puerto Cortés (Empresa Impala, 2 Av., 4-5 C., several each hour, US$1), E to La Lima, El Progreso (US$0.60), Tela and La Ceiba (Tupsa, 2 Av. N., 5-6 Calle, 12 a day, from 0530, US$4, 2½-3 hrs.), S to Lake Yojoa and Tegucigalpa, and SW to Santa Rosa and then through the Department of Ocotepeque with its magnificent mountain scenery to the Guatemalan border (US$4.50 to the border by bus). Transportes Impala, 2 Av., 4-5 Calle S.O. No. 23, has 6 buses a day to Nueva Ocotepeque and Agua Caliente on the Guatemalan border (first at 0330, last 1500); Empresa Torito and Transportes Copanecos go to Santa Rosa de Copán every 45 mins. from 0445 to 1715 (6 y 7 Avs., 6 C.S.O., T 54-19-54/53-49-30, and 6 C., 4-5 Av. S.O., respectively). Road paved all the way.

Train To Tela at 0625 changing at Baracoa, US$1.50 1st class, US$0.70 2nd.

Excursions One can take a taxi up the mountain behind the city for US$1-1.50; good view, a restaurant, and interesting vegetation on the way up. Lake Ticamaya, near Choloma, is worth visiting between June and December. The head office of the former United Brands subsidiary is at *La Lima* (45,000 inhabitants), 15 km. to the E by road (bus frequent, US$0.25), where the banana estate and processing plants can be seen. There is a club (golf, tennis, swimming) which takes members from outside. A little to the E, near the Ulúa river, is Travesía (not the Travesía near Puerto Cortés, which can also be reached for a day out at the beach), where Mayan pottery remains have been found, but no ruins as such. Buses run E to El Progreso and on N to Tela on the coast, and to La Ceiba. (The train to Tela goes via Baracoa at 1500, 3 hrs.) A bus from 2 Av. goes to Las Vegas-El Mochito mine where there is a cheap *pensión* (F) and walks along W side of Lake El Rincón.

The waterfall at Pulhapanzak is on the Río Lindo, off the main San Pedro Sula-Tegucigalpa road; by car it's a 1½ hr. drive, longer by bus. Take a Mochito bus from San Pedro Sula (hourly 0500-1700) and alight at the sign to the falls, US$1.25. Alternatively stay on the bus to Cañaveral (take identification because there is a power plant here), and walk back along the Río Lindo, 3-4 hours past interesting rock formations and small falls. The waterfall (42 metres) is beautiful in, or just after the rainy season, and in sunshine there is a rainbow at the falls. There is a picnic area and a small overpriced restaurant, but the site does get crowded at weekends and holidays; there is a small admission charge (US$0.50). *Pensión* at Peña Blanca, 4 km. from the falls.

Twenty Km. west of San Pedro Sula, the cloud forest national park of **Cusuco** is under development (access by dirt road from Cofradía, on the road to Santa Rosa de Copán).

Copán and Western Honduras

The Western Highway (171 km.) runs from San Pedro Sula SW along the Río Chamelecón to Canoa (from where there is a paved road S to Santa Bárbara and Santa Rosa de Copán); it goes on to San Salvador. *Santa Bárbara* (23,000 inhabitants) is 32 km. W of Lake Yojoa, in hot lowlands. Panama hats and other goods of *junco* palm are made in this pleasant town. Carlos Rivera, director of the high school, speaks English and has much information on the area. In the vicinity the ruined colonial city of Tencoa has recently been rediscovered. The road goes on to join the Northern Highway S of Lake Yojoa (being paved).

Hotels *Herrera, Santa Marta,* both on La Independencia, F; *Hospedaje Rodríguez,* F, with bath, rec.; *Pensión Moderno,* E, with hot shower, reasonable dining room. **Restaurants** *Brasero,* the best; also *Majestic* and *Oasis; Comedor Estudiantina,* for good, cheap, basic meal.

Exchange Banco Atlántida.

Bus from Tegucigalpa, Tues., Thurs., Sat. at 0600, return Mon., Wed., Fri., at 0500, US$4.50, 7 hrs. (passing through remote villages in beautiful mountain scenery); from San Pedro Sula, 3½ hrs., US$2.50, 7 a day between 0500 and 1630.

A branch road from the road to Santa Bárbara goes to **San Luis**, a coffee town in beautiful scenery. *Hospedaje San José*, F, clean, friendly; *Hospedaje San Isidro*. Several *comedores*. Bus from San Pedro Sula, US$2.50, twice daily. (Electricity 1800-2130 only.) Near Santa Bárbara is Ilama (7,000 people) with one of the best small colonial churches in Honduras (no accommodation).

In the Department of Santa Bárbara is an area known as El Resumidero, in which are the Quezapaya mountain, and six others over 1,400 metres, and a number of caves (Pencaligüe, Los Platanares, El Quiscamote, and others). From Santa Bárbara, go to El Níspero and thence to El Quiscamote; or go to San Vicente Centenario (thermal springs nearby), and on to San Nicolás, Atima, Berlín, and La Unión, all of which have thermal waters, fossils, petrified wood and evidence of volcanic activity.

Santa Rosa de Copán, 153 km. by road from San Pedro Sula, is the centre of a rich agricultural and cattle-raising area. Altitude 1,040 metres, population 28,865. Much maize and tobacco is grown in the area. Excellent *sombreros de junco* (Panama hats) are made here. Santa Rosa is a colonial town with most attractive narrow cobbled streets. The central plaza and church are perched on a hilltop. It holds a festival in the last 10 days of August.

Hotels *Elvir* (the best), Calle Real Centenario O, 2 Av. O, D, all rooms have own bath, good meals in cafeteria or restaurant; nearby: *Hotel Maya* (not to be confused with *Hospedaje* Maya, see below), 1 C. N.O. y 3 Av. N.O., F, *Rosario*, 3 Av. N.E. No. 139, E with bath, F without; next door is *Hospedaje Guillén*, F, No. 193; *Hospedaje Santa Rosa*, 3 Av. N.E. No. 119, F, simple, clean; *Copán*, 3 Av. N.E. y 4 C. N.E., E with bath, F without, clean, and next door, *Hospedaje Maya*, F. *Hospedaje Calle Real*, Real Centenario y 6 Av., F, clean, quiet, friendly, sometimes water failures, good cheap meals; *Hispano*, on main square, 1 C. N.E. y 1 Av. N.E., F; *Hospedaje Santa Eduvigis*, 2 Av. N.O. y 1 C. N.O., F, with reasonable restaurant; *Erick*, 1 C. N.E. No. 362, E with bath. *Mayaland*, opp. bus station on Carretera Internacional, E p.p., parking, restaurant; *El Rey*, also opp. bus terminal, F p.p., rooms with bath, restaurant, parking.

Restaurants *Danubio Azul*, 1 Av. S.E., No. 040, 1 block from Plaza; *Las Haciendas*, 1 Av. S.E., varied menu, filling comida corriente. *Miraflores* in Col. Miraflores.

Exchange Banco de Occidente and Atlántida, both on main plaza. Banadesa, Calle Real.

Bus from Santa Rosa to Tegucigalpa via San Pedro Sula leaves at 0400 from main square, US$4.50, 7-8 hrs. 4 buses daily 0930, 1130, 1300, 1600, 2½ hrs., US$2. To San Pedro Sula, US$2, 4 hrs. every 45 mins. (Empresa Torito, and Transportes Copanecos), bus to La Entrada, 1 hr., US$0.75. Copanecos bus San Pedro Sula-La Entrada-Santa Rosa de Copán every 90 mins. Frequent service S to Nueva Ocotepeque (US$2, 3 hrs.). Local bus from bus station (on Carretera Internacional, below town) to centre ("El Urbano"), US$0.10, very slow, goes all around the houses; taxi US$0.50.

Excursions Robert Millar writes: There is a bus from Santa Rosa at 1000 and 1400, west to the small town of Dulce Nombre de Copán (US$0.65). Hardy hikers can continue west through forested mountains to stay at the primitive village of San Agustín (take hammock or sleeping bag), continuing next day to emerge a few kms. from Copán ruins. From Santa Rosa there is a 3-hr. bus ride to Lepaera (17,775 inhabitants, cheap, simple *pensión* and *comedores*) perched on a lovely mountainside (also reached from Gracias). One can scale the peak or descend on foot by an old mule trail heading back to Santa Rosa, crossing the river on a swingbridge (*hamaca*), then hitch-hiking.

Numerous daily buses go to Corquín (US$1, 2 hrs.)—2 good *pensiones*, one with a charming garden. From here take a rough, dusty, 2½-hr. ride in a pick-up truck (US$1) to Belén Gualcho, 1,850 metres up in mountains, amid coffee plantations. There are 3 simple *pensiones* (F, cheap meals); it is a fine centre for walking in the dense rain forests of the Celaque mountains; colourful Sunday Indian market. A steep descent east from Belén by mule trail leads in 5 hrs. to San Manuel de Colohuete, with a magnificent colonial church whose façade is sculpted with figures of saints. There is an equally fine colonial church 5 hrs. to the south-west at San Sebastián, continuing then by mule trail via the heights of Agua Fría to reach the bus route near the frontier at Tomalá. Alternatively, one can walk 5 hrs. east from San Manuel to La Campa (colonial church) where there is irregular transport to Gracias.

There are buses from Santa Rosa to Mapalaca and villages bordering El Salvador.

From San Pedro Sula there are regular buses via Santa Rosa south to **Nueva Ocotepeque** (6 hrs., US$4.50); road is well paved. From Nueva Ocotepeque, buses to San Pedro Sula stop at La Entrada (US$2.25), first at 0030, for connections to Copán. There are splendid mountain views. The Salvadorean border S of Nueva Ocotepeque is open again. Colectivos to El Poy on border, US$0.50, and several buses daily from El Poy to San Salvador. You can cross into Guatemala at Atulapa, just after Agua Caliente (tourist office here). There are several buses a day from San Pedro Sula to Agua Caliente, first at 0300 (e.g. Congolón, Impala; US$4.50, 6-7 hrs.; money changers get on the bus between Nueva Ocotepeque and the border, poor rates; the Honduran and Guatemalan migration offices are about 2 km. apart, minibuses do the trip for US$0.30). Minibuses then go to Esquipulas (US$0.25), from where first class buses run to Guatemala City. You can get into El Salvador via Esquipulas, Guatemala (see page 1160). About 25 km. before Nueva Ocotepeque (at the junction to San Marcos Ocotepeque) there is a police checkpoint. Make sure all documents are in order and to hand. There are Guatemalan consuls in San Pedro Sula and Nueva Ocotepeque from whom visas or tourist cards may be obtained (preferable to trying to get one at the border). There is an old colonial church, La Vieja (or La Antigua) between Nueva Ocotepeque and the border. The **Montecristo** national park forms part of the Trifinio/ La Fraternidad project, administered jointly by Honduras, Guatemala and El Salvador.

Hotels in Nueva Ocotepeque   *Gran*, F-D; *Ocotepeque*, F (by Transportes Impala); restaurant *La Cabaña.*

The magnificent Mayan ruins of **Copán** are 225 km. by air from Tegucigalpa or 186 by air from San Pedro Sula (also a paved road), and 1 km. from the village, called Copán Ruinas (population 22,185). The road from San Pedro runs SW for 125 km. to La Entrada, where it forks left for Santa Rosa and right for Copán, 60 km. away. Copán can also be reached by road from Guatemala City. The Honduran immigration office is now at the border; one can get exit stamps there. For the most direct route from Guatemala, **see page 1160.**

How to get there   One can charter flights from Tegucigalpa and Guatemala City. There are also regular buses (Copanecos, Impala or Torito lines) from San Pedro Sula to La Entrada, US$2 (2 hrs.); from La Entrada to Copán, US$2 by bus, US$3 by minibus (2½-3 hrs.), from 0600 hourly (or when full) till 1600, stops at entrance to ruins. Last minibus from village to La Entrada at 1630. If going by bus from San Pedro Sula, and returning, it is impossible to see Copán in one day. But if going on to Guatemala, one can take the 0445 San Pedro-La Entrada bus, 0600 La Entrada-Copán, arriving 0900, then the 1300 bus from Copán to the border; minibus Copán-border or vice-versa, leave when full, US$1. Etumi bus from San Pedro Sula direct to Copán, at 1030 and 1300, 5-6 hrs. Direct bus also from 6 Av. S. O. y 7 C. S. O., at 1100 daily, US$2.50, 5-6 hrs. Return to San Pedro Sula direct at 0400 and 0500. 3 early a.m. buses from Copán to Santa Rosa, 4 hrs., US$2.50. To return to San Pedro Sula, minibuses will collect you from your hotel and take you to La Entrada, from where buses go to San Pedro Sula.

La Entrada is a hot, dusty little town (*Hospedaje Copaneco*, 1 Av. No. 228, F; *Hospedajes Alexandra, Mejía; Hotel Tegucigalpa; Hospedaje María*, F, clean, good, limited food also; eat in the market or at the bus station). There is a small archaeological museum on main street next to Banco Atlántida (US$0.50). This bank won't cash travellers' cheques, but Banco Sogerín will. A few km. beyond is the small town of Florida (24,100 inhabitants, primitive accommodation). The owner of the gas station here will advise archaeologists about the many Maya ruins between Florida and Copán. There are a number of hilltop stelae between the border and Copán. At Jihua, 3 km. to the left from Km. 4 from La Entrada, is a restored colonial church.

To enter (or return to) Guatemala an alternative route is via Nueva Ocotepeque (see above and page 1160 for transit into Guatemala); every 40 mins. a bus leaves Copán for La Entrada (US$2, 2½-3 hrs., longer in rain). From there, there are several buses a day to Santa Rosa (US$0.75, 1 hr.). Buses run from Santa Rosa to Nueva Ocotepeque.

Exit tax from Guatemala is Q3, entry to Honduras US$2.50. If you are leaving Honduras make sure to get your passport stamped at the police check point just outside Copán on the road to the border. The nearest Guatemalan consulate is in San Pedro Sula, so if you need a visa, you must get one there.

Hotels in Copán   *Maya Copantl*, E, with bath, restaurant; *Marina*, on the Plaza, E, with bath, hot water, meals US$3, breakfast US$1.50, cheaper annex, F, excellent value (but rooms on street noisy); *Hotelito Brisas de Copán*, F p.p. without bath, quiet, rec.; *Hospedaje Los Gemelos*, F, without bath, nice, good value, use of kitchen on request; *Hotelito Peña*, F, clean. *Pensión Honduras*, F, food available, clean, friendly, good; *Hotel-Restaurante Paty*, friendly, under the same ownership as one of the minibus companies, has good meals (a bit dear) and 10 clean rooms, G p.p. without bath, E in newer rooms with bath. *Paty* and *Honduras* are noisy from buses after 0400. *Restaurant El Sesteo*, opposite *Brisas de Copán*. *Comedor Isabel* near the plaza, good, cheap; *La Llama del Bosque*, 2 blocks W of central Plaza. Good meals at the market. There is a cinema (films at 1930, daily except Tues. and Wed.), which leaves much to be desired. Horses for hire near the square, US$1 per day (if you look around and bargain).

Travellers' cheques may be changed at the bank (0830-1200, 1400-1600, Mon.-Fri., 0800-1100 Sat.). Guatemalan currency is rarely accepted at Copán; it is possible to change quetzales near where buses leave for the border. Change dollars at the better hotels. Post office next to museum; stamps sold at corner shop opposite. There is a service station at Copán.

N.B.   There is a signposted path beside the road from the village to the ruins, passing stelae en route (1 km., no need to take a minibus). It is advisable to get to the ruins (open 0800-1600) as early as possible, or late in the day; this way you will miss the guided tours. However, the site is crowded only at weekends. There is a cafeteria by the entrance to the ruins, and also a shop. Guided tours available all year. There is a tourist office in the Parque Arqueológico, next to the shop, where luggage can be left for no charge (clean toilets here, too). Entry to ruins US$1.50 and museum (on town square open 0800-1600) with photographs of the excavation work, a maquette of the site and explanations of the glyphs, US$0.50 for foreigners.

When Stephens and Catherwood examined the ruins in 1839, they were engulfed in jungle. In the 1930s the Carnegie Institute cleared the ground and rebuilt the Great Stairway, and since then they have been maintained by the Government. Some of the most complex carvings are found on the 21 stelae, or 3-metre columns of stones on which the passage of time was originally believed to be recorded, and which are still in their original sites among the buildings. Under each stela is a vault; some have been excavated. The stelae are deeply incised and carved with faces and figures and animals. (John Streather tells us that the stelae are not chronologies but in fact "are royal portraits with inscriptions recording deeds and lineage of those portrayed as well as dates of birth, marriage(s) and death".). (Some of the finest examples of sculpture in the round from Copán are now in the British Museum or at Boston.) Ball courts were revealed during excavation, and one of them has been fully restored. The Hieroglyphic Stairway (now covered for protection) leads up a pyramid, with mythical creatures rearing from the steps; the upper level supported a temple. Its other sides are still under excavation.

The last stela was set up in Copán between A.D. 800 and 820, after less than two centuries of civilized existence. That no further developments took place is attributed by one theory to revolt by the common people against an increasingly distanced nobility and priesthood, rather than outside invaders. The nearby river has been diverted to prevent it encroaching on the site when in flood. 1 km. from the main ruins (in the opposite direction from the village) is an area called Las Sepulturas, a residential area where ceramics dating back to 1000 BC have been found. A tomb from the site is on display in the museum (entry US$0.50). Also near the ruins is a nature trail through the jungle to the minor ball court (called Sendero Natural); take mosquito repellant if you intend to stand still. (See general account of Maya history on page 1136..)

South from San Pedro Sula to Tegucigalpa

Potrerillos (Hotel Alvarez), the railhead, is 37 km. S of San Pedro Sula. From Potrerillos the paved Northern Highway (288 km.) climbs some 37 km. from the hot lowlands to **Lake Yojoa,** 600 metres high, 22½ km. long and 10 km. wide, splendidly set among mountains. To the W rise the Jicaque mountains; to the E some lower hills, with Los Naranjos and other villages along the shores or set back towards the hills. Pumas, bears and jaguars range the forests and pine-clad slopes. The road follows the eastern margin to the lake's southern tip at Pito Solo, where sailing boats and motor boats can be hired. The road is mostly out of sight of the lake: the side-road to the lake itself is not signposted and can be easily overlooked. (Bus to Lake from San Pedro Sula, US$1.50, 1½ hrs.; bus from Lake to Tegucigalpa, US$3, 3½ hrs.).

Accommodation Hotel Los Remos has cabins and camping facilities at southern end of the lake, C and up; Motel Agua Azul (at N end of lake), B, meals for non-residents; facilities for swimming and boating; bus waits at junction with the main road to take people to the hotel. Comedores on the road beside the lake serve the bass that is caught there. Buses between Tegucigalpa and San Pedro stop to let passengers off at Los Remos, and at Peñas Blancas, 5 km. from the turning for Agua Azul. At Peña Blanca Córtez on N side of Lake is Comedor El Cruce, very good home cooking. 10 km. N of the lake is the turn off for the village of Santa Cruz de Yojoa, and at 24 km. is the El Cajón hydroelectric project (to visit the dam, apply at least 10 days in advance by phone—22-21-77, or in writing to Oficina de Relaciones Públicas de la ENEE, 1 Av., Edificio Valle-Aguiluz, Comayagüela, D.C.) Accommodation can be booked at El Mochito mine of the American Pacific Holdings Company, near Lake Yojoa.

Thirty-two km. beyond Pito Solo is **Siguatepeque**, a town (population 39,165) with a cool climate. It is the site of the Escuela Nacional de Ciencias Forestales and, being exactly half-way between Tegucigalpa and San Pedro Sula, a collection point for the produce of Intibucá, La Paz and Lempira departments. The beautiful Cerro and Bosque de Calanterique, behind the Evangelical Hospital, is ¾ hour's walk from town centre.

Hotels and Restaurants Hospedaje Gómez, E with bath, clean, use of kitchen on request; Boarding House Central, F, reasonable; Versalles, F; both have restaurants; Mi Hotel, 1 km. from main road, E, with bath, parking, restaurant. Cafetería Ideal, hamburgers and light lunches; China Palace, Chinese and international; Pizzería y Restaurante Fiallos, clean, varied menu, or eat in the market; on the Northern Highway there are several restaurants, best are Nuevo and Antiguo Bethania, good, abundant, inexpensive meals.

Exchange Bancahsa, Banco Atlántida, Banco de Occidente.

Bus to San Pedro Sula, ½ hourly, US$2.50; Tegucigalpa with Empresas Unidas or Maribel, US$2, 3 hrs. (Tegucigalpa-San Pedro Sula buses do not go into town, but leave passengers at junction 2 km. from town, easy to hitch); to Comayagua, Transpinares, US$0.75, 45 mins.

From Siguatepeque through lovely forested mountainous country, 5 buses daily go SW to **La Esperanza** (98 km.), capital of Intibucá Department, at 1,485 metres (bus from La Esperanza to Tegucigalpa 0500 (Cobramil, also to San Pedro Sula) and 0530 (Joelito, 5½ hrs., US$3.50), to Siguatepeque 0700, 0900, last at 1000, US$2, 3 hrs.; bus, La Esperanza, Siguatepeque, Comayagua at 0600, buses from La Esperanza to the Salvadorean border; bus stops by market. This old colonial town set in a pleasant valley has an attractive church in front of the park, and there are simple but pleasant *pensiones* (e.g. *Hospedaje Mina*, F, adequate, 1 block E of market; *Hotel Solís*, 1 block E of market, E (hot water extra), restaurant, rec.; *Rosario*, on road to Siguatepeque; *San Cristóbal*, F; *San José*, 4 Av. Gen. Vásquez No. C-0005, F; *La Esperanza*, F; *Pensión Mejía Paz Batres*, 1 block W of Plaza, E with bath, F without, hot water, overpriced; *San José*, in same building as Farmacia La Esperanza, 2 blocks S of Plaza, F; *Hotel y Comedor San Antonio*, F). Market: Sun., at which Lenca Indians from nearby villages sell wares and food, including *junco* blankets. Nearby is Yaramanguila, an Indian village. The area is excellent for walking in forested hills, with lakes and waterfalls. In Dec.-Jan. it is very cold.

An unpaved road, bus 1 hr. 20 mins., runs from La Esperanza E to **Marcala** (1,300 metres— population 10,770), Department of La Paz (a paved road has been completed to La Paz). *Ideal*, E; *Hospedaje Margoth*, E; *Hotel y Cafetería La Sureña*, E; *Motel Montana*, E. Daily bus to Tegucigalpa (0400, US$3.50), via La Paz (bus from Tegucigalpa at 1000, except Sun., Empresa Lila, 4-5 Av., 7 C., No. 418 Comayagüela); bus to La Paz only, 0800. Plenty of *comedores*. The Marcala region is one of the finest coffee-producing areas of Honduras. Cosude (Cooperación Suiza al Desarrollo) has different projects in the area, includung support to Lenca Indian ceramic production. There are caves nearby on Musula mountain; the Cueva de las Animas in Guamizales and Cueva de El Gigante in La Estanzuela with a high waterfall close by. Transport goes to La Florida (stay with priest, who has a collection of Indian artefacts) where there is good walking to Indian village of Opatoro and climbing Cerro Guajiquiro.

NW from La Esperanza a very bad road runs to **Gracias** (population 19,380). It is one of the oldest and most historic settlements in the country, dominated by the highest mountains in Honduras, Montañas de Celaque. There are 3 colonial churches, San Sebastián, Las Mercedes, San Marcos (a fourth, Santa Lucía, is 2½ km. SW of Gracias), and a restored fort, with two fine Spanish cannon, on a hill in the outskirts (the fort is being converted into a museum which will probably house military historical exhibits currently in Omoa). Some 5 km. from Gracias swim in hot, communal thermal pools in the forest, Agua Caliente (1 hrs. walk by a path, 1 hr. 20 mins. by the road, ask anyone, rec.).

Gracias was the centre from which Montejo, thrice Governor of Honduras, put down the great Indian revolt of 1537-38. Cáceres, his lieutenant, besieging Lempira the Indian leader in his impregnable mountain-top fortress at Cerquín, finally lured him out under a flag of truce, ambushed him and treacherously killed him. When the Audiencia de los Confines was formed in 1544 Gracias became for a time the administrative centre of Central America.

From Gracias buses go through coffee plantations to San Rafael (makeshift accommodation) from where one can walk to El Níspero (*pensión*) and catch a bus to Santa Bárbara. A strenuous 6-hr. hike east from Gracias by mule trail through a wilderness of forest and mountain leads to La Iguala, a tiny village attractively set between 2 rivers, magnificent colonial church. Irregular transport from/to Gracias.

It takes a whole day to climb the summit of Mount Celaque from Gracias. The trail begins from behind the visitors' centre being prepared for the **Celaque National Park**; it is recommended to carry a compass for the last part as it is hard to keep one's bearings in the dense cloud forest canopy (the most impressive in Honduras). Packhorses, and possibly a guide, may be hired from the Villa Verde community ½ hr. below the visitors' centre (animals cannot climb the last half of the trip). It is worthwhile just walking up to the visitors' centre, but the completion of trails higher up should make for beautiful hiking.

For all information, contact Enrique López or Roy Romero at the Cohdefor (forestry) office just off the square in Gracias; or ask for the Peace Corps volunteer working on the project.

Hotels in Gracias *Erick*, hospedaje and shop, 1 block from square, opp. Escuela Normal in same street as bus office, F p.p., rec.; *Herrera*, G, clean, basic; *Hospedaje San Antonio*, on main street, N edge of town, F, good, clean; *Pensión Girón*, 2 Av. No. 76, F, basic; *Iris*, 2 Av. 40, opp. San Sebastián church, E, with restaurant and disco. Many *comedores* and cafeterias. *Comedor Elizabeth*. *La Nasa*, at bottom of the hill, O.K.; *Odiseo 2000*, one block from plaza, good, cheap, friendly; excellent *tacos* ½ block from main square.

Exchange Banco de Occidente, changes money.

Hondutel and Post Office 1 block S of square.

Buses One post bus per day to La Esperanza, wakes you at your hotel (0300, in theory); bus La

Esperanza-Gracias at 1400 daily, US$2.30, 7 hrs. An alternative to La Esperanza is to take the daily 0530 bus to San Juan (collects you from your hotel), get off at El Crucero checkpoint (3 hrs.), 1 km. from San Juan, then hitch (police at the checkpoint will help), or rides can be taken on pick-up trucks for US$2; a plane trip costs US$8. There is also a bus service from Gracias to Santa Rosa de Copán, US$2, 0430, 0700, 1030, 1530, 2½ hrs. (see page 1239); beautiful journey through majestic scenery. Cotral office is 1 block N of Plaza. A new road is under construction between Siguatepeque, La Esperanza, Gracias and Santa Rosa de Copán; it is due for completion in 1991.

Alban Johnson of Sandy Bay, Tasmania, and Jorge Valle-Aguiluz write: Roughly half way between Gracias and La Esperanza is San Juan del Caite, from where a rough track runs 45 km. S to **Erandique** (Pensiones, of Reginaldo Muñoz, and Doña Bárbara Cruz, F; meals at the house of Doña María Felix de Inestroza). Set high in pine-clad mountains not far from the border with El Salvador, Erandique is a friendly town, and very beautiful. Lempira was born nearby, and was killed a few km. away. The third weekend in January is the local fiesta of San Sebastián. Best time to visit is at the weekend. Each of the three barrios has a nice colonial church. For the visitor there are lakes, rivers, waterfalls, springs and bathing ponds; you need to ask around. Nearby is San Antonio where fine opals are mined and may be purchased. There is only one road in the area, and it is impassable from July to October; transport to the many hamlets in the surrounding mountains is on foot or by horse (beware, it is very easy to get lost on the multitude of tracks). Despite what people say, there are minibuses to Erandique, but most people go by truck from Gracias or La Esperanza (US$3, very dusty).

Thirty-two km. beyond Siguatepeque the road dips into the rich Comayagua plain, part of the gap in the mountains which stretches from the Ulúa lowlands to the Gulf of Fonseca. In this plain lies

Comayagua, a colonial town of 59,535 people at about 300 metres, 1½ hrs.' drive N from the capital. It was the capital for 333 years until Tegucigalpa, 120 km. away, displaced it in 1870. It was founded in 1537 on the site of an Indian village by Alonzo de Cáceres, Francisco de Montejo's lieutenant, and there are many old colonial buildings: the former University, the first in Central America, founded in 1632, closed in 1842 (it was located in the Casa Cural, Bishop's Palace, where the bishops have lived since 1558); the Cathedral (1685-1715); the churches of La Merced (1550-58) and La Caridad (1730); San Francisco (1584); San Sebastián (1585). San Juan de Dios (1590, destroyed by earthquake in 1750), the church where the Inquisition sat, is now the site of the Santa Teresa Hospital. El Carmen was built in 1785. The most interesting building is the Cathedral in the Central Park, with its square plain tower and its decorated façade with sculpted figures of the saints, which contains some of the finest examples of colonial art in Honduras. The clock in the tower was originally made over 800 years ago in Spain; it was given to Comayagua by Philip II in 1582. At first it was in La Merced when that was the Cathedral, but moved to the new Cathedral in 1715. There are two colonial plazas shaded by trees and shrubs. A stone portal and a portion of the façade of Casa Real (the viceroy's residence) survives. It was built 1739-41, but was damaged by an earthquake in 1750 and destroyed by tremors in 1856. The army still uses a quaint old fortress built when Comayagua was the capital. There is a lively market area.

There are two museums nearby: the ecclesiastical museum (a small contribution is expected) and the anthropological museum (housed in the former presidential palace) with Indian artefacts (closed Monday). The latter is the less interesting of the two.

The US military base (recently renamed Soto Cano Airbase) at Palmerola, 8 km. from Comayagua, exerts a strong socio-economic and cultural influence over the entire Comayagua Valley, and the city itself. The base has English-language radio and TV stations.

Hotels   Libertad, on Parque Central, E-D, much choice of room size, noisy, clean, Libertad Annex, E with bath, F without, as good as main hotel; Emperador, E-C, good but overpriced, cafeteria, on the boulevard leading into town from the Tegucigalpa-San Pedro Sula highway; Imperial, Barrio Torondón, E with bath and fan, attractive, parking; Boulevard, F, small, clean, economic, dark rooms; Motel Quan, 8 C. N.O., 3 y 4 Av., excellent, E, with private bath, popular; Quan Annex, E; Motel Puma, off the same Boulevard, garage parking, hot water, E with bath (catering for short-stay clientèle).

Camping   possible 2 km. N of town, beside the stream; beware of sandfleas.

Restaurants   Central Park is surrounded by restaurants and fast food establishments. Casa Vieja, near new cinema, good but overpriced; China, 3 blocks W of Plaza, good, but beware of the overpriced "tourist" menu; *Gran Muralla* on park, Chinese and international food, good; *Restaurant Central* (good, not the cheapest), *Sayvic* and *Flipper* in the central park serve ice cream, tacos, etc.; *Pájaro Rojo* on main boulevard, expensive, food reasonable; *Urbano's*, private house, 4 blocks SW of façade of the Cathedral, excellent meals and value. *Cafetería Central* (not to be confused with *Restaurant* on central park), *Palmeras*, S side of Central Park; some food in the market. In the Centro Turístico Comayagua is a restaurant, bar, disco, and swimming pool; good for cooling off and relaxing; on the road to the stadium.

Exchange Banco Atlántida, Banco de Occidente, Bancahsa, Bancahorro, Banco Sogerín.

Bus To Tegucigalpa, US$1.50, every 45 mins., 2 hrs. (Catrachos—or walk 1¼ km. to highway and catch a quicker San Pedro Sula-Tegucigalpa bus); to Siguatepeque, US$0.50 with Transpinares. To San Pedro Sula, either catch a bus on the highway or go to Siguatepeque and change buses there.

Excursion To the coffee town of La Libertad (hourly bus, 2 hrs., US$1), several *hospedajes* and *comedores*; a friendly place. Before La Libertad is Jamalteca (1½ hrs. by bus US$0.75), from where it is a 40-minute walk to a large, deep pool into which drops a 10 metre waterfall surrounded by lush vegetation. Here you can swim, picnic or camp, but it is on private property and a pass must be obtained from the owner (ask at Supermercado Carol in Comayagua). Best to avoid weekends, when the owners' friends are there.

A paved road runs S of Comayagua to **La Paz,** capital of its Department in the western part of the Comayagua valley. Population: 19,900. From the new church of the Virgen del Perpetuo Socorro, on the hill, there is a fine view of the town, the Palmerola military base, and the Comayagua Valley. A short road runs E from La Paz to Villa San Antonio on the highway to Tegucigalpa. 5 km. from La Paz is Ajuterique, which has a fine colonial church. Bus from Comayagua, Cotrapal (opp. Iglesia La Merced), every hour from 0600, passing Ajuterique and Lejamaní.

Hotels in La Paz: all F: *Córdoba* (with restaurant), *Pensión San Francisco* (cheaper, but nicer). *Hotelito Alí* (5 rooms), eat at *Alí's Restaurant*.

Exchange Bancahsa, Banco Atlántida, Banadesa.

A paved road runs SW from La Paz to Marcala (see previous page). Along this road lies **Tutule,** the marketplace for the Indians of Guajiquiro (one of the few pure Indian communities in Honduras). Market: Thurs. and Sun. There are two minibus services a day from Marcala (US$1).

We are grateful to Robert Millar for the following description of the road from **San Pedro Sula to Tegucigalpa**: 46 km. S of San Pedro there is a paved road leading E through banana plantations to Santa Rita, thence either E to Yoro, or N to Progreso and Tela, thus enabling travellers between Tegucigalpa and the North Coast greatly to shorten their route by avoiding San Pedro Sula. An unpaved road right, at Caracol, leads up to Ojo de Agua (a pretty bathing spot), then on to El Mochito, Honduras' most important mining centre. This same turnoff at Caracol, marked "Río Lindo", also leads to Peña Blanca and Pulhapanzak with some unexcavated ceremonial mounds adjacent. On the northern shore of Lake Yojoa (**see page 1241**) a paved road skirts the lake for 5 km. and a further 11 km. (unpaved) to Pulhapanzak. The main highway S skirts the eastern shore of the lake. 16 km. S of the lake at Taulabé is the turnoff northwest of a road (being paved) to Santa Bárbara (**see page 1238**).

1 km. S of Taulabé uphill on the highway South are the caves of Taulabé (illuminated and with guides, open daily). The road now ascends an enormous forested escarpment of the continental divide to reach cool, forested highlands around Siguatepeque (**see page 1241**). Proceeding S, the highway descends to the vast hot valley of Comayagua, skirting the old capital of Honduras with its colonial churches. At the southern end of the valley the road ascends another forested mountainous escarpment. After about 5 km. climb a track leading off to the left (ask for directions), with about half-an-hour's climb on foot to a tableland and natural fortress of Tenampua where Indians put up their last resistance to the *conquistadores,* even after the death of Lempira. Visitors last century rated Tenampua of equal importance archaeologically with Copán, but sadly it has now been looted of its treasures, except for an interesting wall and entrance portal.

The road continues its ascent through lovely forested heights to Zamorano and Parque Aurora (**see page 1230**)—this spot would be perfect for caravans, which need to avoid the narrow streets and congestion of Tegucigalpa. The road then descends to the vast intermont basin of Támara; a turning right at the village leads to San Matías waterfall, another delightful area for walking in cool forested mountains. There is another entry to San Matías when the road S has once more climbed about 9 km. north-east of the capital.

From Tegucigalpa to the Pacific

A paved road runs S from the capital through fine scenery. Just off the highway is Sabanagrande, with an interesting colonial church. Further S is **Pespire,** a picturesque colonial village with a beautiful church. At **Jícaro Galán** (92 km.) the road joins the Pan-American Highway, which enters Honduras from El Salvador over the Santa Clara bridge at Goascarán and runs through **Nacaome,** where there is a 16th-century colonial church, to Jícaro Galán (40 km.). A temporary pass can be purchased in Honduras for US$1.50 for a visit to the Salvadorean village of El Amatillo for an hour or so (many Hondurans cross to purchase household goods and clothes; towels are the best buy. Bus Tegucigalpa—El Amatillo, US$2.50, 4 hrs.). This border is very relaxed, with good rates of exchange with money changers. Border closes 1700. On the Pacific coast nearby is **San Lorenzo,** on the shores of the Gulf of Fonseca (21,025 people). The climate on the Pacific littoral is very hot, but healthy.

Hotels   The only good modern hotel is the *Miramar* at San Lorenzo, 26 rooms, 4 air-conditioned, E. Also *Paramount*, E, and *Hospedaje Perla del Pacífico*, F, very basic. There are hotels of a sort at Goascarán (pop.: 2,190), Nacaome (pop. 4,474). At Jícaro Galán (pop.: 3,007) is *Oasis Colonial*, B, and an unnamed, basic guesthouse. Restaurants at all these places.
   Frequent service of small *busitos* from Tegucigalpa to San Lorenzo (US$1) and to Choluteca (US$1.50).

The Pacific port of **Amapala** (7,925 people), on Tigre Island, has been replaced by Puerto de Henecán in San Lorenzo, reached by a 3.5 km. road which leaves the Pan-American Highway on the eastern edge of San Lorenzo. Amapala has a naval base, but otherwise it is moribund. Fishermen will take you—but not by motor launch—to San Lorenzo at a low charge: the trip takes half a day. It is possible to charter boats to La Unión in El Salvador. There is an airport, and a plane for the capital (35 mins.) can be chartered. The deep-sea fishing in the gulf is good. There is a passable bathing beach. *Hotel Internacional* on the harbour, F, pleasant; *Tino's Restaurant,* owned by Sr. Tino Monterrosa who has recently opened two bungalows (US$25 for 4, rooms at D); he also arranges fishing trips. Swimming at beautiful Playa Grande. The hill on the island may be climbed, best early in the day.

There is a daily direct bus service between Tegucigalpa and Tigre Island, except on Sunday, with Transportes CHE; leaving Tegucigalpa at 1130, 3-4 hrs. A new 31 km. road leaves the Pan-American Highway 2 km. W of San Lorenzo, signed to Coyolito. It passes through scrub and mangrove swamps before crossing a causeway to a hilly island, around which it winds to the jetty at Coyolito (no facilities). Motorized dugouts and a small car ferry cross to Amapala. Return journey starts at 0400 from Tigre Island.

The Pan-American Highway runs SE from Jícaro Galán past Choluteca to the Nicaraguan border at El Espino, on the Río Negro, 111 km., and NW from Jícaro Galán to the Salvadorean border at Goascarán, 40 km.: a total of 151 km. in Honduras.

Choluteca, 34 km. from San Lorenzo in the plain of Choluteca, has a population of 87,889, expanding rapidly. Coffee, cotton and cattle are the local industries. The town was one of the earliest foundations in Honduras (1535) and has still a colonial centre. The church of La Merced (1643) is now the Casa de la Cultura. The local feast day, of the Virgen de la Concepción, is December 8. The climate is very hot; there is much poverty here.

Hotels   *Pierre*, Av. Valle y C. Williams, T 82-0676, C, with bath and a/c, D, with fan, central, free protected parking, cafeteria, very central, English-speaking owner (Glyn M. Harris), credit cards accepted; *Lisboa*, Av. Rosa (by Transportes Mi Esperanza), E (some with bath), rec., laundry facilities, clean, good restaurant; *Pacífico*, also near Mi Esperanza terminal, outside the city, clean, quiet, E, breakfast US$1.50; *Tomalag*, moderately priced with bath and fan; *La Fuente*, Carretera Panamericana, C, with bath, rec., swimming pool, a/c, meals; *Rosita*, E, with bath, basic, friendly, good food; *Camino Real*, road to Guasaule, D, good steaks in restaurant; *San Carlos*, F with shower, pleasant, Paz Barahona 757, Barrio El Centro; *Hibueras*, F, with bath and fan, clean, purified water, *comedor* attached; Av. Bojorque; *Motel Fraternidad*, E, on Panamericana. Local specialities are the drinks *posole* and *horchata de morro*.

Banco de Honduras is close to market, as are Post Office (US$0.15 per letter for post restante; telephone collect calls to Spain, Italy, USA only) and Banco Atlántida. Good rates of exchange on the black market at Choluteca bus station (a fascinating place!). There is also a black market in

Jícaro Galán. The Texaco service station, which is known as *Gringa Patricia's*, is very helpful in case of car trouble. Laundry, groceries and propane on sale. The campsite here is run by a Canadian, Elvin; shaded camping, showers, swimming pool, peaceful, pleasant, safe water supply, US$1. Mosquito repellant or netting may be needed.

Bus or taxi to El Espino from Choluteca, US$1.50, 1 hr., 0700. Mi Esperanza buses regularly to Tegucigalpa (US$2.50); bus station is 5 blocks from market. Taxis will wait at the border post as you go through the formalities and then take you into Nicaragua.

An hour's drive from Choluteca over an excellent road leads to Cedeño beach, very basic accommodation (inc. *Hotel Coco*) and meals. A lovely though primitive spot, but avoid public holiday crowds. In the dry season, there is little fresh water, often none for bathing. Turning for Cedeño is 13 km. W of Choluteca. Hourly bus from Choluteca, US$1 (1¼ hrs.). A turn off leads from Choluteca- Cedeño road to Ratón beach, also lovely, bus from Choluteca early p.m., returns early next morning.

Beyond Choluteca is a long climb to San Marcos de Colón, 915 metres in the hills (a clean, tidy town of 9,570 people with plenty of eating places). 3 *pensiones* in San Marcos: *Colonial*, E, friendly, clean; a shabby *hospedaje* next door, F; *Hospedaje Flores*, F, friendly, clean, washing facilities, breakfast and dinner, exchange. Bus from Choluteca at 0700, US$1, 1½ hrs., one bus back at 1130; bus from Tegucigalpa, Mi Esperanza, 6 Av. 23 or 26 C., Comayagüela (office in San Marcos near Parque Central), from 0730. 6 km. beyond San Marcos the road enters Nicaragua at El Espino—a ghost town—(altitude 890 metres); immigration is 100 metres from the border. Taxis/minibuses run from Choluteca to the border. Entry and exit tax in Honduras, US$2.50, but on Sat. and Sun. officials may try to charge extra: ask for a receipt and/or bargain. Border closes between 1600 and 0800 (open till 1700 on the Nicaraguan side). Exchange is easy at the border for dollars, córdobas, Costa Rican colones, even Salvadorean colones, but the rate for buying córdobas is better on the Nicaraguan side, where you are obliged to change US$25 (cash or travellers' cheques) if in transit, or US$60 if staying longer in Nicaragua. Border formalities tedious at El Espino, do not allow yourself to show irritation at the Honduran officals' personal questions. Officials on the Nicaraguan side are more friendly. Americans and Europeans travelling N through Central America are advised to check with their embassies in San José, Costa Rica, to see if there are any restrictions on entering Honduras from Nicaragua. **N.B.** After floods in May 1982, the border bridge at Guasaule was washed away and the road Choluteca-Chinandega (Nicaragua) is closed.

East of Tegucigalpa

A good paved road runs E from Tegucigalpa to Danlí, 121 km. away, in the Department of El Paraíso. Some 40 km. along, in the Zamorano valley (**see page 1230**), is the Pan-American Agricultural School run for all students of the Americas with US help: it has a fine collection of tropical flowers. At Zamorano turn off up a narrow winding road for about 5 km. to the picturesque old mining village of **San Antonio de Oriente**, much favoured by Honduran painters such as Velásquez (it has a beautiful church). A little further along, an unpaved road branches S to **Yuscarán**, in rolling pine-land country at 1,070 metres (*Hospedaje Monserrat*, F, good value). The climate here is semi-tropical. Yuscarán was an important mining centre in colonial days and is a picturesque, typically Spanish colonial village, with cobbled streets and houses on a steep hillside. The Yuscarán distillery is considered by many to produce the best *aguardiente* in Honduras (tours possible). Cardomom plantations are being developed here. The Montserrat mountain which looms over Yuscarán is riddled with mines; the disused Guavias mine is about 4 km. along the road to Agua Fría, 10 km. to the SE by a steep, narrow, twisting and very picturesque road. Population, 9,270. For information, ask the lady who owns the *comedor* opposite the church in Yuscarán. From Zamorano, a road goes to Güinope (one hotel, F, several *comedores*) famed for its oranges and jam. Good walking in the area.

Danlí (100,800 people), a pleasant town, grows sugar for making *aguardiente* and is a centre of the tobacco industry. There are 7 cigar factories; visit the Honduras-América S.A. factory (opposite Ciné Aladino) and purchase export quality cigars at good prices. Its *fiesta* at the last weekend of August (Fiesta del Maíz, with cultural and sporting events, all-night street party on the Saturday) is very crowded with people from Tegucigalpa. One road continues from Danlí to Santa María, crossing a mountain range with panoramic views. Another goes S to **El Paraíso** (124 km. from the capital, hourly bus, US$1.80, 2 hrs.; 27,291 people), from which a connecting paved road links with the Nicaraguan road network at Las Manos/Ocotal.

Hotels at Danlí *La Esperanza*, Gabriela Mistral, E, adjoining restaurant; *Danlí*, Calle del Carral, E; *Apolo*, del Canal, E, with bath; *Maya Ejecutivo*, C, with bath; *Regis*, F, with bath, basic. **Restaurants:** *Pepy Lu's*, very good food at reasonable prices; *McBeth's*, snackbar, good ice cream. *Nan-kin 2*, Chinese.

Hotels at El Paraíso *Eva*, E; *Florida*, F; *Recreo*, F.

Exchange in both towns, Bancahsa, Banco Atlántida, Banadesa, and other local banks.

Buses To Danlí, from near Mercado Jacaleapa, Colonia Kennedy, Tegucigalpa, 2 hrs., US$2, Emtra Oriente, Comayagüela, runs at 0830, 0910, 1230 and 1630 to El Paraíso, 2½ hrs., US$2.25; buses from El Paraíso to Las Manos.

North-east of Tegucigalpa

The Carretera de Olancho runs from the capital to the Río Guayape, 143 km., and continues another 50 km. to *Juticalpa* (capital of Olancho department), at 820 metres above sea-level in a rich agricultural area, herding cattle and growing cereals and sugar-cane. There is a gravel road N to Olanchito and a paved road NE through the cattle land of Catacamas to the coast at Cabo Camarón. Population 74,000. Airfield.

Hotels at Juticalpa *Antúñez*, Barrio El Centro, D with bath, E without; *Las Vegas*, E; *Boarding House Honduras*, F.

There is an adventurous bus service from Juticalpa to Trujillo (**see page 1236**), via San Francisco de la Paz and San Esteban (*Hotel San Esteban*, F, expensive but clean; *Hospedaje Henríquez*), the last part being on a good, unpaved road; it passes through interesting scenery. The road is being paved; it passes through San Jerónimo, the setting of Paul Theroux's *The Mosquito Coast*
    Bus Tegucigalpa to Juticalpa/Catacamas, Empresa Aurora (8C. 615, Av. Morazán) 8 times a day, 3½ hrs. to Catacamas, US$3.50. Bus Catacamas-Dulce Nombre de Cumli (see below), 3 hrs., US$1.75, several daily; bus Juticalpa-San Esteban from opp. Aurora bus terminal at 1200, 6 hrs., US$3, very difficult in rainy season. Pick-up Juticalpa-Trujillo, US$10, whole day's journey.
    The route by road from Tegucigalpa to Trujillo through Olancho is 413 km. via Talanga, San Diego (restaurant *El Arriero*), Los Limones and Juticalpa (fill up with fuel here as there is none available until Trujillo). After Juticalpa, take the turn off, where the paved road ends, to San Francisco de la Paz. Beyond San Francisco is Gualaco, which has an interesting colonial church; from here to San Esteban you pass Agalta mountain and some of the highest points in Honduras, and the waterfalls on the Babilonia river. The road from San Esteban to Bonito Oriental (via El Carbón, a mahogany collection point with Paya Indian communities in the vicinity) is being paved. The final 38 km. from Bonito Oriental to Trujillo are paved, through Corocito.

Mosquitia is the name given to the region in the far NE of the country, which is forested, swampy and almost uninhabited, but well worth visiting. Apart from the one road that stretches 100 km. from Puerto Lempira to Leymus and a further 100 km. to Ahuasbila, both on the Río Coco, there are no roads in the Honduran Mosquitia. The Government has still to build the last stage of the Tegucigalpa-Puerto Lempira road, between Catacamas (*Hotel Moderno*, F, excellent value) and Mocorón. SAMi flies from Tegucigalpa to Puerto Lempira and Mocorón daily in 9-seater planes (T Tegucigalpa 33-85-49; Setco flies to both places Mon., Tues. and Fri. at 0800, US$125 return (N side of Toncontín airport entrance, T 33-17-11/12). Osmán Paz (private pilot) also flies twice a week (may be contacted through Glenda at World Relief, Tegucigalpa, T 327667/326139/324578). The UN High Commission for Refugees (called ACNUR in Honduras) has daily flights (usually full); it is a good place to get information on flights, and if going to Mocorón a permit from ACNUR is essential (T Tegucigalpa 321995). Lansa flies from La Ceiba on Wednesday, and Isleña on Friday (cheaper, US$46, 1¼ hrs.), to Ahuas, Brus Laguna and Puerto Lempira. Coastal vessels leave several times a week from La Ceiba to Brus Laguna and Puerto Lempira and back (2-3 day journey), carrying passengers and cargo. There are also refugee boats which are quicker. Essential equipment: torch.
    Communication between Honduras and Nicaragua is not possible in Mosquitia due to the Río Coco border area was reported safe to visit in 1988, but as well as an ACNUR permit, one must also be obtained from the army battalion outside Mocorón. This village is largely populated by refugees (*Chaly's*, accommodation F p.p., basic, meals for US$1.25, agent for Setco and Osmán Paz; ACNUR will find lodging for those staying a long time). Rus Rus may be visited with difficulty (in terms of getting permits and transport—any vehicle will give a lift); a beautiful, quiet village (accommodation at Friends of America hospital's house; meals from *Capi's* next door, ask Friends about transport out).
    Robert Millar writes (with additional information from Grace Osakoda of Hawaii): Numerous

large *cayucos* (canoes) with outboard motors cross the large **Caratasco Lagoon from Cauquira to Puerto Lempira** for about US$2.50. *Pensión Modelo,* F (good, friendly, electricity 1800-2230), and inferior *Pensión Santa Teresita,* F, at **Puerto Lempira;** *La Perla* restaurant, next to dock, fish meals US$1.75; *Restaurant Quinto Patio,* good breakfasts and information on refugee boats; generous meals at Doña Marina's for US$1.25 (Isleña flight tickets for La Ceiba may be bought here; Lansa tickets at *La Perla).* Contact helpful Reverend Stanley for almost daily flights in tiny Moravian mission plane to the Evangelical hospital at Ahuas; a 15-minute (US$15) scenic flight above Caratasco Lagoon and grassy, pine-covered savannas to **Ahuas,** one hour's walk from the Patuca River (fabled for gold). *Hospedaje y Comedor Suyapa,* F, basic, no electricity, meals, US$1.25; mosquito repellant and coils absolutely essential here. Irregular *cayucos* sail down to **Brus Laguna** (Brewer's Lagoon) for US$ 2.50, at one mouth of the Patuco River, or US$12.50 (15-mins.) scenic flight in the mission plane. George Goff rents rooms (good but basic, no electricity, F,) and has meals for US$1, he speaks English and runs the Lansa agency (flights to La Ceiba—he will also help with mission-plane flights). Behind his house is a *hospedaje* being built by the "Medio-Francés" (who speaks English, German, French, "Scandinavian" and Spanish); he plans to operate tours. Meals with Sarah de Eden, but plague of mosquitoes for all but 5 months of the year (winter and spring). Two tiny hilly islands near the entrance to the wide lagoon were hideouts where pirates once lurked. It is better to fly direct from Ahuas for US$15 via Brus and the mouth of the **Plátano River** to mosquito-free **Cocobila** (Belén), picturesquely situated on a sandspit between the ocean and huge, sweetwater Ibans Lagoon. (Nicaraguan refugee settlements S of here may be visited). Excellent meals (US$1.25) with Miss Erlinda, and room with Alfonso Molina who has a motor boat for **Paplaya** at the mouth of the Río Negro or Sico (bad mosquitoes), or walk the distance in over two hours along the beach. Malaria is endemic in this area; take anti-malaria precautions. Room and meals with Doña Juana de Woods at Paplaya. Boats to La Ceiba (US$11), or up the Río Sico (US$5) to Sico. Paplaya is the western terminal of the Honduran Mosquitia. Plátano village at the mouth of the Río Plátano can be reached by lobster boat from Guanaja or by the supply ships from La Ceiba to Brus Laguna (in all cases *cayucos* take passengers from ship to shore); Plátano-Brus Laguna, 1½ hrs., US$ 2.50, Plátano-La Ceiba, US$17.50.

The **Río Plátano Preserve** was established by the U.N. and the Honduran government in 1980 to protect the outstanding natural and cultural resources of Río Plátano valley and environs. The tropical jungles that still cloak the landscape here shelter a number of endangered birds, mammals, and fish, among them scarlet macaws and harpy eagles, jaguars and tapirs, and the cuyamel, a prized food fish going extinct throughout Honduras. In addition, there are a number of archaeological sites about which little is known, and the fabled lost White City of the Maya is said to be hidden somewhere in the thick jungles of the Plátano headwaters.

Miskito and Paya (who call themselves "Pech") Indians living along the lower Plátano cultivate yuca, bananas, rice, corn, and beans, as well as hunting and fishing. The upper (southern) portion of the Plátano watershed was virgin jungle until quite recently, but is being quickly populated by *mestizo* immigrants from the poverty-stricken south of Honduras. These new residents are cutting down the forest to plant crops, hunting wildlife mercilessly, and using homemade dynamite in a very destructive form of fishing. Given the pressure the Preserve is under, it is recommended to visit it sooner rather than later.

To get there, you can fly or take one of the boats that periodically leave from La Ceiba and Trujillo to either Palacios, Cocobila, Belén or Barra Río Plátano, the main villages in the vicinity of the river mouth. Expect to pay perhaps US$15-20 for passage from Ceiba. There are, however, regular daily commercial flights on Sosa and Isleña from La Ceiba to Belén, for US$40. From Belén to the Biosphere headquarters in Kuri it is a 45 min. walk or 10 min. ride (US$2). The staff are friendly and can probably put you up for the night free. They can also help you contract with a *tuk-tuk* (motorized dug-out canoe) to carry you upriver as far as Las Marías, the Miskito-Pech village that is the limit of upstream settlement. The cost is about US$70 one way, regardless of the number of passengers (up to 6) and takes 6-8 hours (3-4 downstream).

Once in Las Marías, it is possible to contract villagers for trips upstream in a *pipante.* This is a shallow dugout canoe manoeuvered with poles called *palancas* and paddles (*canaletes*): remarkably graceful. Each *pipante* can carry up to two passengers and their gear, plus three villagers who pole it upstream. The cost per day to rent *pipante* and crew is about US$12.50 per passenger (negotiable).

The rainy season is from June-December: it is harder to advance upriver then.

Palacios, situated in the next lagoon west of Paplaya, is mosquito-free; cannons are relics of an old English fort. Room for US$2.50 with Felix Marmol and meals for US$1. Lansa's Wednesday 6-seater plane (often booked up) flies for US$ 28 to La Ceiba or East to Brus/Puerto Lempira. When sea is calm, irregular sailings of the *Baltimore* or *Douglas,* US$11, go to La Ceiba. One can also cross the lagoon by *cayuco* (US$0.50) from Palacios to Black Carib village of Batalla, from which it is 112 km. W along beach to Limón where, in dry months March to May, there are buses to Tocoa, Trujillo and La Ceiba. The beach route is gruelling, past *morenales,* or Black Carib villages (honest, friendly) of Tocamacho (Reverend Donald Grable is a godsend to benighted travellers), Sangrelaya (Catholic mission), Siraboya (dry weather walk from here across forested mountain to Sico River, and downriver to Sico village); further W along the beach to Iriona Casuna and interminable stretch of 48 km. along the beach to Limón (this stretch is now inadvisable because of recent murders and robberies when crossing the beautiful forested headland at Farellones). One can take a picturesque *cayuco* trip from Paplaya up the Río Sico for US$4-5 to Sico village (possible food and meals with Edmund Jones—insist on paying him). A strenuous 32 km. walk from Sico (only in dry months from March to May) up forested Río Paulaya Valley to stay with Ray Jones, who has mined gold here for 60 years (insist on paying him too). One can also descend the Paulaya River from Dulce Nombre de Culmi, Olancho (*Hospedaje Tania*, G, very basic, on main street; several *comedores* on main square), 34 km. in the pick-up of "el Indio", then on foot or muleback over the Cerro de Will, staying en route with the *campesinos*, arriving in about three days at Mr. Ray's. (Local police say there is a footpath in the dry season from Dulce Nombre de Cumli to San Esteban).

THE ECONOMY

Honduras has the poorest economy in Central America and one of the lowest income rates per head in all Latin America (US$830). Unemployment is about 25% of the working population, owing to low investment, and poor harvests and labour disputes in the agricultural sector. Inflation has dealt less severely with Honduras than with some other Central American countries: the rate has been less than 10% a year in the 1980's.

About 75% of the population live by the land: coffee and bananas are the main export crops. Cotton, once important, is now far less so. Tobacco, maize, beans, rice and sugar are grown mostly for domestic use but small quantities are sometimes exported. Cattle raising is important and exports of both meat and livestock are growing. Some 45% of the land is forested and timber is the third leading export; it is to become more important as the development of forestry reserves in the Department of Olancho is carried out. This project includes the installation of a vast paper and pulp complex and is expected to have a considerable impact on the whole economy, once implemented.

Honduras has considerable reserves of silver, gold, lead, zinc, tin, iron, copper, coal and antimony, but only silver, gold, lead and zinc are mined and exported. Considerable offshore exploration for petroleum is in progress. There is an oil refinery at Puerto Cortés and exports of petroleum derivatives are becoming significant. The US$600m. hydroelectric scheme at El Cajón was expected greatly to reduce the country's oil bill.

Local industries are small, turning out a wide range of consumer goods, besides being engaged in the processing of timber and agricultural products. The more important products are furniture, textiles, footwear, chemicals, cement and rubber.

Honduras' total external debt amounts to some US$3.2bn, over three times merchandise exports. From 1982 the government held negotiations to reschedule its debt with commercial banks but failed to sign any agreement. Arrears mounted and in 1989 the negotiating committee disbanded to allow banks individually to recover their debts as best they could.

	1961-70 (av)	1971-80 (av)	1981-85 (av)	1986-87 (av)(e)
Gdp growth (1980 prices)	5.0%	4.8%	0.9%	3.3%
Inflation	2.3%	8.1%	6.9%	3.3%
Exports (fob) US$m	129	446	748	900
Bananas	57	123	217	250
Coffee	18	107	162	300
Imports (fob) US$m	127	473	834	900
Current account balance US$m (cum)	-194	-1,186	-1,315	-300

INFORMATION FOR VISITORS

How to get there From London: British Airways, Pan Am, Continental or Virgin Atlantic to Miami, then Eastern Airlines (via San Salvador) or TAN to Tegucigalpa. Also from Miami, Taca via San Salvador; to Tegucigalpa from New Orleans and Houston with Sahsa, Taca (via San Salvador) and Continental; Lacsa flies to San Pedro Sula from New York, and Eastern flies to Tegucigalpa from Orlando. Sahsa flies from Tegucigalpa to all Central American capitals, and to San Andrés Island, and to San José from San Pedro Sula (also Lacsa on this route direct); TAN flies to Mexico

City and Belize City direct while Taca flies to Mexico City and Guatemala as well as to San Salvador. Eastern connects Belize and San Pedro Sula, and San Salvador and Tegucigalpa. Tapsa flies between San Pedro Sula and Guatemala City 3 times a week. Connections with Curaçao are made at Guatemala City (KLM/Taca). From Europe: Iberia twice weekly to Guatemala City, connecting with Sahsa; KLM have the same connection; alternatively, fly to Miami and on from there.

There are airstrips in the larger and smaller towns. Sahsa, Aero Servicios, Lansa, SAMi and Isleña have daily services between Tegucigalpa, San Pedro Sula, La Ceiba, and the Caribbean coastal towns and islands.

There is an airport tax and hospital tax of 3 % on all tickets sold for domestic journeys, and a 10 % tax on airline tickets for international journeys. There is an airport departure tax of US$10 and a customs tax of US$3 (neither charged if in transit less than 9 hrs.). Note that the border offices close at 1700, not 1800 as in most other countries; there is an extra fee charged after that time.

N.B.   If you are flying from Honduras to a country that requires an onward ticket, Sahsa will not let you board their planes without it.

By Sea   The French Line sails regularly from London, the Hapag-Lloyd, the Royal Netherlands Steamship Co. and others run regular cargo vessels with limited passenger space from North Sea ports to the Atlantic ports of Honduras; 3 or 4 weeks. Hapag-Lloyd, N.G. Lloyd and Johnson Line have cargo/passenger services from North Sea ports to Amapala, on the Pacific coast of Honduras. The United Brands Line and the Standard Fruit Co. have services from continental and US ports.

Documents   Visa not required, nor tourist card, for nationals of West European countries (except France, West Germany—tourist card only, Austria—visa, and Portugal) and Japan. Citizens of the USA, Australia, New Zealand require a visa and a tourist card which can be bought from Honduran consulates for US$2-3. Holders of the card must show proof of nationality. The price of a visa apparently varies per nationality, and according to where bought.

Practice varies as to whether a visa can be bought at the border. For this reason it is imperative to check entry requirements in advance at a consulate. (For instance, Canadians do not officially require visas, but may have trouble without one.) 2-day transit visas costing US$5, for any travellers it seems, are given at the El Florida border for visiting Copán, but you must leave at the same point and your right of return to Guatemala is not guaranteed since Guatemalan visas are valid for one journey only.

Officials at land borders and airports allow only 30 days for visitors, regardless of arrangements made prior to arrival. Make sure border officials fill in your entry papers correctly and in accordance with your wishes. Extensions of 30 days are easy to obtain (up to a maximum of 6 months' stay, cost US$5). There are immigration offices for extensions at Tela, La Ceiba, San Pedro Sula, Santa Rosa de Copán, Siguatepeque, La Paz and Comayagua, and all are more helpful than the Tegucigalpa office. A valid International Certificate of Vaccination against smallpox is required only from visitors coming from the Indian subcontinent, Indonesia and the countries of southern Africa. A ticket out of the country is necessary for air travellers (if coming from USA, you won't be allowed on the plane without one); onward tickets must be bought outside the country. Proof of adequate funds is normally asked for at land borders. An entry and exit tax is charged to all but travellers in transit, US$2.50 each (and sometimes requested in dollars). An additional US$1 "baggage inspection charge" is levied on bus passengers. Customs charge US$3.50 for "special Sunday service". It is advisable always to carry means of identification, since spot-checks have increased. Charges for motorists appear to be: on entry, US$2 for provisional permission from the police to drive in Honduras, US$1 (official minimum) for car papers, US$1 baggage inspection; on exit, US$1 to return permission, US$1 to have papers stamped and US$2 more for registration, etc. Bicycles must pay the same entrance taxes as motor vehicles. No fresh food is allowed to cross the border and the interiors of cars are fumigated (US$2 on entry, with receipt). There is a fair amount of bribery at border crossings.

N.B.   To enter, you must *not* have in your passport a stamp from a communist country (i.e. one with which Honduras does not have diplomatic relations; this includes India); there is no official regulation concerning this, it is left to the individual judgement of border officials and therefore treatment may vary according to entry point. If going on to Nicaragua and needing a visa, do *not* get it before Tegucigalpa, otherwise you may have to pay US$25-40 for custodial transit through Honduras. If coming from Nicaragua, all literature and maps concerning that country, even Nicaraguan produce, will be confiscated; if you have spent more than a month in Nicaragua you may not be allowed into Honduras. There have been cases of tourists being deported for carrying left-wing literature.

There are no Customs duties on personal effects; 200 cigarettes or 100 cigars, or ½ kg. of tobacco, and 2 quarts of spirit are allowed in free.

British business travellers planning a visit should get a copy of "Hints to Exporters: Honduras", on application to Dept. of Trade, Export Services Division, Sanctuary Buildings, 16/20 Great Smith Street, London SW1P 3DB.

Hours of Business Mon. to Fri.: 0900-1200; 1400-1800. Sat.: 0800-1200, and some open in the afternoon. Banks in Tegucigalpa 0900-1500; 0800-1100 only along the N coast on Sat. In San Pedro Sula and along the N coast most places open and close half an hour earlier in the morning and afternoon than in Tegucigalpa. Post Offices: Mon.-Fri. 0700-2000, Sat. 0800-1200.

Language Spanish, but English is spoken in the N, in the Bay Islands, by West Indian settlers on the Caribbean coast, and is understood in most of the big business houses. Trade literature and correspondence should be in Spanish.

Tipping Normally 10% of bill.

Electric Current generally 110 volts. US-type flat-pin plugs.

Internal Transport Buses tend to start early in the day; very few leave late afternoon or evening, which may make onward connections difficult. Hitch-hiking is relatively easy. If hiring a car, make sure it has the correct papers, and emergency triangles which are required by law. Petrol costs over US$2 per US gallon. **N.B.** There are frequent police searches on entry or exit from towns and villages. You must stop at Puestos de Tránsito, indicated by "Alto Repórtese" signs (usually in smaller letters than the Coca Cola or other *refresco* advert on the sign).

Climate Rain is frequent on the Caribbean littoral during the whole year; the heaviest occurs from September to December inclusive. In Tegucigalpa the dry season is normally from November to April inclusive. The coolest months are December and January but if a traveller visits the Caribbean littoral he should avoid these months because heavy rains impede travel; the best months for this area are April and May, though very hot.

Clothing Western; suits optional for most businessmen; on the north coast, which is much hotter and damper, dress is less formal. Laundering is undertaken by most hotels.

Health Dysentery and stomach parasites are common and malaria is endemic in coastal regions, where a prophylactic regime should be undertaken and mosquito nets carried. Inoculate against typhoid and tetanus. Drinking water is definitely not safe; drink bottled water. Salads and raw vegetables must be sterilized under personal supervision. There are hospitals at Tegucigalpa and all the larger towns. Excellent ointments for curing the all-too-prevalent tropical skin complaints are Scabisan (Mexican) and Betnovate (Glaxo).

Currency The unit is a lempira. It is divided into 100 centavos and its par value is half the United States dollar. There are copper coins of 1 and 2 centavos and nickel or silver coins of 5, 10, 20, and 50 centavos. US visitors will find that many coins are exactly the same size and material as US coins of equivalent value; hence the 20 centavos is a "dime". A *real* is 12½ centavos (there are no coins of this value, but the term is much used). Bank notes are for 1, 2, 5, 10, 20, 50 and 100 lempiras. **Any amount of any currency can be taken in or out. N.B.** US dollars are quite hard to obtain in Honduras. There is a parallel market, particularly active at borders (but poor rate for travellers' cheques), which fluctuated between L3.20 and L3.70 to the US$ in May 1989.

The metric system of weights is official and should be used. Land is measured in *varas* (838 mm.) and *manzanas* (0.7 hectare).

Shopping The best articles are those in wood: straw baskets, hats, etc., are also highly rec. Leather is cheaper than in El Salvador and Nicaragua, but not so cheap as in Colombia. The coffee is good. Note that film is expensive.

Food Cheapest, meals are the *comida corriente* or (sometimes better prepared and dearer) the *comida típica*; these usually contain some of the following: beans, rice, meat, avocado, egg, cabbage salad, cheese, *plátanos*, potatoes or yuca, and always tortillas. Pork is not rec. as pigs are often raised on highly insanitary swill. *Carne asada* from street vendors, charcoal roasted and served with grated cabbage between tortillas is good, though rarely sanitarily prepared. *Tajadas* are crisp, fried *plátano* chips topped with grated cabbage and sometimes meat; *nacatamales* are ground, dry maize mixed with meat and seasoning, boiled in banana leaves. *Sopa de mondongo* (tripe soup) is very common.

Cheap fish is best found on the beaches at Trujillo and Cedeño and on the shores of Lake Yojoa. While on the north coast, look for *pan de coco* (coconut bread) made by *garifuna* (Black Carib) women.

Soft drinks are called *refrescos*, or *frescos*, the name also given to fresh fruit blended with water; *licuados* are fruit blended with milk. *Horchata* is rice water and cinnamon. Coffee is thick and sweet. (Don Moore, ex-Peace Corps volunteer, Bellefonte, Pa.). There are 4 brands of beer, Port Royal Export, Nacional, Imperial and Salvavidas (more malty than the other 3).

Air Mail takes 4 to 7 days to Europe and the same for New York. Airmail costs 85 centavos for a letter to N America (1 lempira to Europe), 60 centavos for a postcard (80 centavos to Europe); aerograms (not easy to find), 75 centavos.

Telephones Hondutel provides international telephone and telex services from stations at Tegucigalpa, San Pedro Sula, Puerto Cortés, Tela, La Ceiba, Comayagua, Siguatepeque, Santa

Rosa de Copán, Danlí, Choluteca, Juticalpa, La Paz, La Lima, El Progreso, Valle de Angeles, El Paraíso, Catacamas and Marcala.

Telephone service between Honduras and Britain costs about L40 for a 3-min. call; calls to USA L22 for 3 mins. Local Standard Time is 6 hrs. behind GMT. Collect calls to N America and Europe can be made from Hondutel office in Tegucigalpa.

The principal **newspapers** in Tegucigalpa are *El Heraldo* and *La Tribuna*. In San Pedro Sula: *El Tiempo* and *La Prensa* (circulation about 45,000). None is of very high quality.

There are 6 television channels and 167 broadcasting stations.

Public Holidays Most of them feast days of the Roman Catholic religion and also

January 1: New Year's Day.
April 14: Day of the Americas.
Holy Week: Thurs., Fri., and Sat.
before Easter Sunday.
May 1: Labour Day.

September 15: Independence Day.
October 3: Francisco Morazán.
October 12: Discovery of America.
October 21: Army Day.

We are most grateful to Jorge Valle-Aguiluz (Tegucigalpa), Bruce Gunn (USPCV, Gracias), Leon Kolankiewicz (USPCV), Ronald Janssen (Utila), George W. Gorman (Ft Lauderdale, Fl.) and Kurt Rumler (APO Miami); also to other travellers whose names are listed in the general Central America section.

NICARAGUA

NICARAGUA (148,000 square km.), the same size as England and Wales, is the largest Central American republic. It has 541 km. of coast on the Caribbean and 352 km. on the Pacific. Costa Rica is to the S, Honduras to the N. Only 8% of the whole country, out of a possible 28%, is in economic use and population density is low: 12.2 persons to the square km., as compared with El Salvador's 157.3. Nine-tenths of its 3.5m. people live in the west. An odd feature for a country so slightly industrialized is that 57% of its people live in towns.

There are three well-marked regions. (1) A large triangular-shaped central mountain land whose apex rests almost on the southern border with Costa Rica; the prevailing moisture-laden NE winds drench its eastern slopes, which are deeply forested with oak and pine on the drier, cooler heights. (2) A wide belt of eastern lowland through which a number of rivers flow from the mountains into the Atlantic. (3) The belt of lowland which runs from the Gulf of Fonseca, on the Pacific, to the Costa Rican border south of Lake Nicaragua. Out of it, to the E, rise the lava cliffs of the mountains to a height of from 1,500 to 2,100 metres. Peninsulas of high land jut out here and there into the lowland, which is from 65 to 80 km. wide along the Pacific.

In this plain are two large sheets of water. The capital, Managua, is on the shores of Lake Managua, 52 km. long, 15 to 25 wide, and 39 metres above sea-level. The river Tipitapa drains it into Lake Nicaragua, 148 km. long, about 55 km. at its widest, and 32 metres above the sea; Granada is on its shores. Launches ply on the Río San Juan which drains it into the Caribbean.

Through the Pacific lowland runs a row of volcanoes. The northernmost is the truncated zone of Coseguïna, overlooking the Gulf of Fonseca; then the smoking San Cristóbal, the highest of them all; a number of smaller volcanoes, of which Cerro Negro was built up during its last eruption in 1971; and the famous Momotombo, which normally smokes a little and now has a geothermal power station at its foot. Around Managua, even in the city centre, there are small craters, but none is active. Further south is the twin cone of Masaya/Santiago, which stopped smoking in late 1986. In Lake Nicaragua is the beautiful Concepción, the second highest, on the Isla de Ometepe, on which also stands the extinct Las Maderas. The volcanic chain continues northwest into El Salvador and to the south into Costa Rica. The volcanic ash makes rich soil for crops.

The wet, warm winds off the Caribbean pour heavy rain on the Atlantic coastal zone, especially in the southern basin of the San Juan river, with more than six metres annually. While the dry season on the Atlantic coast is only short and not wholly dry, the Pacific dry season, or summer (November to April), becomes very dusty, especially when the winds begin to blow in February.

Settlement   The Spanish *conquistadores* reached the lowland from Panama as early as 1519. On the south-western shores of Lake Nicaragua they found an area comparatively densely settled by peaceful Indians, who lavished gold ornaments on them. Five years later another expedition founded colonies at Granada and León, but the flow of gold soon stopped and most of the Spaniards moved elsewhere. In 1570 both colonies were put under the jurisdiction of Guatemala. The local administrative centre was not rich Granada, with its profitable crops of sugar, cocoa, and indigo, but impoverished León, then barely able to subsist on its crops of maize, beans and rice. This reversal of the Spanish policy of choosing the most successful settlement as capital was due to the ease with which León could be reached from the Pacific. In 1858 Managua was chosen as a new capital.

Nine in ten of the people of Nicaragua live and work in the lowland between the Pacific and the western shores of Lake Nicaragua, the south-western shore of Lake Managua, and the south-western sides of the row of volcanoes. It is only of late years that settlers have taken to coffee-growing and cattle-rearing in the highlands at Matagalpa and Jinotega. Elsewhere the highlands, save for an occasional mining camp, are very thinly settled.

The densely forested eastern lowlands fronting the Caribbean were neglected, because of the heavy rainfall and their consequent unhealthiness, until the British settled several colonies of Jamaicans in the 18th century at Bluefields and San Juan del Norte (Greytown). But early this century the United Fruit Company of America (now United Brands) opened banana plantations inland from Puerto Cabezas, worked by blacks from Jamaica. Other companies followed suit along the coast, but the bananas were later attacked by Panama disease and exports today are small. Along the Mosquito coast there are still English-speaking communities in which African, or mixed African and indigenous, blood predominates.

Ports and Communications   The main Pacific ports are Corinto, San Juan del Sur and Puerto Sandino. The two main Atlantic ports are Puerto Cabezas and Bluefields. The **roads** have been greatly extended and improved. The Pan-American Highway from the Honduran border to the borders of Costa Rica (384 km.), is paved the whole way and so is the shorter international road to the Honduran frontier via Chinandega (though the frontier here is closed); the new road between Managua and Rama (for Bluefields) is almost all paved and in good condition. There are now 14,576 km. of road, 1,604 paved and 1,300 km. all-weather. There is only one **railway**, the Ferrocarril del Pacífico, 349 km. long, single track, with a gauge of 1.067 metres.

The People   Besides the *mestizo* intermixtures of Spanish and Indian blood (69%), there are pure blacks (8%), pure Indians (4%), and mixtures of the two (mostly along the Atlantic coast). A small proportion is of pure Spanish and European blood. Death rate is 9.7 per 1,000; birth rate, 44.2; infant mortality, 61.7; life expectancy, 60 years. Annual population growth: 3.4%; urban growth: 4.7% (Managua 7%). Gdp per capita is US$680. Illiteracy is being rapidly reduced by a determined government campaign: 88% of the population, it is estimated, can now read and write.

Roman Catholicism is the prevailing religion, but there are Episcopal, Baptist, Methodist and other Protestant churches. Education at the Universidad Nacional Autónoma de Nicaragua at León, with 3 faculties at Managua, and the private Jesuit Universidad Centroamericana (UCA) at Managua is good (with strong Sandinista links).

History   For Nicaragua's early history, see the introductory chapter to Central America. The country became an independent state in 1838. The famous (or infamous) filibustering expedition of William Walker is often referred to in the text. William Walker (1824-1860) was born in Nashville, Tennessee, graduated at the University in 1838, studied medicine at Edinburgh and Heidelberg, was granted his M.D. in 1843, and then studied law and was called to the bar. On

October 5, 1853, he sailed with a filibustering force to conquer Mexican territory, declared Lower California and Sonora an independent republic and was then driven out. In May 1855, with 56 followers armed with a new type of rifle, he sailed for Nicaragua, where a belligerent faction had invited him to come to its aid. In October he seized a steamer on Lake Nicaragua belonging to the Accessory Transit Company, an American corporation controlled by Cornelius Vanderbilt, He was then able to surprise and capture Granada and make himself master of Nicaragua. Rivas was made President, with Walker in real control as Commander of the Forces. Two officials decided to use him to get control of the Transit Company; it was seized and handed over to his friends. A new Government was formed and in June 1856 Walker was elected President. On September 22, to gain support from the southern states in America he suspended the Nicaraguan laws against slavery. His government was formally recognized by the US that year. A coalition of Central American states, backed by Cornelius Vanderbilt, fought against him, but he was able to hold his own until May 1857, when he surrendered to the US Navy to avoid capture. In November 1857, he sailed from Mobile with another expedition, but soon after landing near Greytown, Nicaragua, he was arrested and returned to the US. In 1860 he sailed again from Mobile and landed in Honduras. There he was taken prisoner by Captain Salmon, of the British Navy, and handed over to the Honduran authorities, who tried and executed him on September 12, 1860. Walker's own book, *The War in Nicaragua*, is a fascinating document. (A film based on his life, by Alex Cox, was released in 1988.)

In 1911 the United States pledged help in securing a loan to be guaranteed through the control of Nicaraguan customs by an American board. In 1912 the United States sent marines into Nicaragua to enforce the control. Apart from short intervals, they stayed there until 1933. During the last five years of occupation, nationalists under General César Augusto Sandino waged relentless guerrilla war against the US Marines, who failed to suppress it. In November 1932 the American high command appointed Anastasio Somoza García supreme commander of the Nicaraguan National Guard. General Sandino was killed by Somoza's men in February 1934. American forces were finally withdrawn in 1933, when President Franklin Roosevelt announced the "Good Neighbour" policy, pledging non-intervention. From 1932, with brief intervals, Nicaraguan affairs were dominated by General Anastasio Somoza until he was assassinated in 1956. His two sons both served a presidential term and the younger, Gen. Anastasio Somoza Debayle, dominated the country from 1963 until his deposition in 1979; he was later assassinated in Paraguay.

The 1978-79 revolution against the Somoza government by the Sandinista guerrilla organization (loosely allied to a broad opposition movement) resulted in extensive damage and many casualties (estimated at over 30,000) in certain parts of the country, especially in Managua, Estelí, León, Masaya, Chinandega and Corinto. After heavy fighting General Somoza resigned on July 17, 1979, and the Government was taken over by a Junta representing the Sandinista guerrillas and their civilian allies. Real power was exercised by nine Sandinista *comandantes* whose chief short-term aim was reconstruction. A 47-member Council of State formally came into being in May, 1980; supporters of the Frente Sandinista de Liberación Nacional had a majority. Elections were held on November 4, 1984 for an augmented National Assembly with 96 seats; the Sandinista Liberation Front won 61 seats, and Daniel Ortega Saavedra, who had headed the Junta, was elected president. The Democratic Conservatives won 14 seats, the Independent Liberals 9 seats and the Popular Social Christians 6 (the Socialists, Communists and Marxists/Leninists won 2 seats each). The failure of the Sandinista government to meet the demands of a right-wing grouping, the Democratic Coordinating Board (CDN), led to this coalition boycotting the elections and to the US administration condemning the poll as a "sham".

Despite substantial official and private US support, anti-Sandinista guerrillas (the "contras") could boast no significant success in their war against the Government. In 1988, the Sandinistas and the contras met for the first time to discuss the implementation of the Central American Peace Plan drawn up by President Oscar Arias Sánchez of Costa Rica, and signed in August 1987. To comply with the Plan, the Nicaraguan government made a number of political concessions. By 1989 the contras, lacking funds and with diminished numbers, following a stream of desertions, appeared to be a spent force; some were expected to participate in general elections due to be held on 25 February 1990. The Sandinista government has brought major improvements in health and education, but the demands of the war against the contras and a complete US trade embargo has done great damage to the economy as a whole.

Cities and Towns

Managua, the nation's capital and commercial centre since 1858, is on the southern shores of Lake Managua, at an altitude of between 40 and 150 metres. It is 45 km. from the Pacific, but 140 km. from the main port, Corinto, though a new port, Puerto Sandino (formerly Puerto Somoza), is only 70 km. away. Managua was destroyed by earthquake in March 1931, and part of it swept by fire five years later; it was completely rebuilt as an up-to-date capital and

MANAGUA
ROUGH SKETCH SHOWING ONLY
MAJOR ROADS AND STREETS
166

NOT TO SCALE

LAKE MANAGUA

CARRETERA NORTE

BLVD. BUENOS AIRES

PISTA JOSÉ ANGEL BENAVIDES

PISTA P.J. CHAMORRO

PISTA LARREYNAGA

STO. DOMINGO

10 DE JUNIO

EL CHIPOTE

PISTA DE LA SOLIDARIDAD

CARRETERA A MASAYA

AV. EL GUERRILL-ERO

BUITRAGO

JULIO

DUPLA SUR

DUPLA NORTE

EL TRIUNFO

R. BERMÚDEZ

C.A. ESPINOZA

R. IBARRA

B. ZELEDON

SALVADOR ALLENDE

PASEO DE LA RESISTENCIA

AV. VARGAS BATRES

PISTA DE LA RESISTENCIA

CARRETERA SUR

KEY:
1. Plaza España
2. Parque Luis Alfonso Velásquez & Inturismo Kiosk
3. Laguna de Tiscapa
4. Laguna de Assossca
5. Laguna de Ahuacalinca
6. Cathedral
7. Museo Nacional
8. Museo de la Revolución
9. Museo de la Alfabetización
10. Teatro Ruben Darío
11. Ministerio de la Cultura
12. Universidad Centroamericana
13. Eduardo Contreras/Ricardo Huembes Market & bus station
14. Iván Montenegro/Oscar Benavides Market & bus station
15. Israel Lewites Market & bus station
16. Immigration
17. Telcor

Centros Comerciales:
18. Camino Oriente
19. Metrocentro
20. Ciudad Jardín
21. Zumen
22. Managua
23. Bello Horizonte
24. Mercado Oriental
25. Martha Quezada/Ticabus/cheap hotel district

Hotels:
26. Intercontinental
27. Estrella
28. Fiedler
29. Palace
30. King's Palace
31. El Pueblo

Restaurants:
32. Sandy's
33. Los Gauchos
34. Naturales Margarita

commercial city (population 850,000) but the centre was again completely destroyed, apart from a few modern buildings, by another earthquake in December 1972. There was further severe damage during the Revolution of 1978-79.

The Government has now decided that it will rebuild the old centre, adding parks and recreational facilities (one such has opened E of Avenida Central, the tourist office is located here), although it is anticipated that this project will take years to complete. Present-day Managua has no centre as such, but rather consists of a series of commercial developments in what used to be the outskirts of the old city. No street names are in evidence, and the overall effect can be disconcerting. Directions are given according to landmarks; in place of cardinal points, the following are used: Al Lago (N), Arriba (E), Al Sur (S), Abajo (W).

The principal commercial areas of Managua are now situated on the Masaya road and the two bypass roads S of the city. These centres contain a wide variety of shops, modern cinemas and discotheques.

In the old centre of Managua, one can still see examples of colonial architecture in the Palace of the Heroes of the Revolution (previously the National Palace) and the Cathedral. The Cathedral is open, although its interior is in ruins, and its exterior cracked. These buildings are situated on the Parque Central and provide a striking contrast with the modern Ruben Darío theatre on the lake shore (good plays and musical events, entry US$1.50; also Teatro Experimental) and the Banco de América building in the background. At the Iglesia Santa María de los Angeles a Catholic/secular/revolutionary mass is held each Sunday at 1730 (very popular); it is recommended to attend, to savour the atmosphere of present-day Nicaragua.

Points of Interest There are several volcanic-crater lakes in the environs of Managua, some of which have become centres of residential development and also have swimming, boating, fishing and picnicking facilities for the public. Among the more attractive of these lakes is Laguna de Xiloá, situated about 16 km. from Managua just off the new road to Léon. At Xiloá a private aquatic club (El Náutico) has recently opened; here boats can be rented; bathing possible. On Sat. and Sun., the only days when buses run, Xiloá gets very crowded, but it is quiet during the week, when you must walk there. You can camp there. Take bus 113 to Piedracitas for bus to Xiloá; admission US$0.50. Other lakes within a 45-min. drive of Managua are the Laguna de Apoyo and Laguna de Masaya (**see page 1266**), situated respectively at Kms. 35 and 15 on the Masaya road.

The Huellas de Acahualinca are Managua's only site of archaeological interest. These are prehistoric animal and human footprints which have been preserved in tufa, located close to the old centre of town, near the lakeshore at the end of the South Highway. Bus No. 102 passes the site, on which there is also a small museum which exhibits a variety of prehistoric artefacts.

A 10-km. drive down Carretera Sur—this is the Pan-American Highway— through the residential section of Las Piedracitas takes us by the US Ambassador's residence to Laguna de Asososca, another small lake (the city's reservoir) in the wooded crater of an old volcano. Piedracitas Park is to one side of the lake: there is a beautiful 3½-km. ride, playgrounds for children, a café, and splendid view of Lake Managua, two smaller lakes—Asososca and Xiloá—and of Momotombo volcano. Beyond again is the little Laguna de Nejapa (medicinal waters). The Pan-American Highway to Costa Rica passes through Casa Colorada (hotel), 26 km. from Managua, at 900 metres, with commanding views of both the Pacific and of Lake Managua, and a delightful climate (but no trees because of poisonous gases from Santiago volcano, **see page 1266**).

Boats can be hired on the shores of Lake Managua for visiting the still-smoking Momotombo and the shore villages (**see also page 1264**). At its foot lies León Viejo, which was destroyed in 1609 and is now being excavated. It was in the Cathedral here that Pedrarias and his wife were buried. Near the large volcano is a smaller one, Momotombito. A fine drive skirts the shores of the lake. Do not swim in Lake Managua, as it is polluted in places.

Fiesta Santo Domingo is the patron saint of Managua. His festival is held at El Malecón from August 1 to 10: church ceremonies, horse racing, bull-fights, cock-fights, a lively carnival; proceeds to the General Hospital. August 1 (half day) and August 10 are local holidays.

Voltage 110 volts AC, 60 cycles.

Hotels Hotel bills must be paid in US dollars, except where indicated. Several hotels have been built along the highway that bypasses the old part of the city, but there is still a shortage. Try to choose a central hotel (i.e. near *Intercontinental* or Plaza España) since transport to the outskirts is so difficult. There is regular water rationing and most hotels do not have large enough water tanks. The government stipulates a small additional charge for rooms with a telephone (whether used or not).

Intercontinental, just N of Calle Colón, L, service poor, sauna, use of swimming pool for non-residents on Sunday, US$3, do not take photographs in vicinity as it is surrounded by military areas; *Casa Serrano*, 3 streets N of Sears (T 2-52-64), C b. and b., a/c, pleasant, friendly; *Las Cabañas*, B, nr. Plaza 19 de Julio, good; next door, *Casa San Juan*, D, shared bath, clean; *Ticomo* at Km. 8½, Carretera Sur, has parking facilities, rents apartments, a/c, with maid service and kitchenette, C, breakfast extra, good for longer stay; *Estrella*, Pista de la Solidaridad, A, a/c, swimming pool, with breakfast, long way from centre, book in advance as it's very popular; *Casa de Fiedler*, 8a Calle Sur-Oeste 1320, C, with bath and a/c or fan, comfortable, good breakfasts; *Palace*, Av. Pedro A. Flores, C, with a/c and bath, comfortable, helpful, TV lounge, quiet and good value; at Km. 3.5 on Carretera Sur is *Hotel D'Lido*, C + 10%, use of swimming pool by non-residents, US$1; *Tres Laureles*, C with bath, fan, clean, rec.; *Carlos*, nr. Ticabus, D, friendly, clean; *Colón*, near Sirca bus terminal and road to Masaya, D, with bath and fan, a bit run down, secure, good restaurant.

For accommodation in our E range or below: *El Pueblo*, in the old centre, F with bath, good; *Hospedaje Oriental*, nr. Mercado Oriental, F, clean; *Royal*, near railway station, F (payable in córdobas), shared shower and toilet, nice family, always full; *Sultana* (basic) E, noisy, clean, rec., if full, staff will arrange for you to stay at *Mi Siesta* (E on the other side of town (E with bath and a/c, F no a/c), good, friendly, laundry facilities; *Mascote* also accepts córdobas, F, opp. Mercado Huembes, often full; *Hospedaje Fuente*, 2 blocks behind this hotel, G (córdobas accepted), friendly, safe.

Many cheap hotels W of *Intercontinental Hotel* in the Barrio Martha Quezada and nr. the Ciné Dorado; most have very thin walls and are therefore noisy. This district, which also has a number of good eating places, is where many gringos congregate. *Casa de Huéspedes Santos*, on street leading to *Intercontinental Hotel*, F, basic, friendly, clean; one block away on same street is *Hospedaje Meza*, (T 22046) G p.p., very basic, TV, friendly, popular; *Hospedaje Quintana*, F p.p., large rooms with fan, shared shower (cold), laundry, friendly; *Casa de Huéspedes Gladys*, in same area, F; *El Colibrí*, single-storey, thatched, clean, with shower, good value, often fully-booked, E, 4 blocks from *Intercontinental*; *Pensión Norma*, F, shared rooms, basic, friendly, popular. *El Dorado*, 8 blocks from *Intercontinental*, F, clean, basic, safe but noisy (good breakfast next door); *El Chepito*, close to *Hotel D'Lido* (see above), G, with bath, basic but friendly, safe, much "passing trade". Many others in same area, e.g. *Azul* (blue doors, no sign), east of terminal; nearby is *El Portal*, F, shower, cheap.

Camping 13½ km. from the centre, W of Managua on Route 12 is the Nica Trailer Park. Another 5 km. N of Nica, 2½ km. after the junction with Ruta 2. Free, good camping at Laguna de Xiloá.

Restaurants The *Hotel Intercontinental* serves enormous breakfasts (0600-1100) for US$2.50 (plus 20% tax and service), and an excellent lunch between 1200 and 1500, US$7 for as much as you want (best to dress smartly).

In the *Intercontinental*/Plaza España/Barrio Martha Quezada area: *Antojitos*, opp. *Intercontinental*, Mexican, a bit overpriced, interesting photos of Managua pre-earthquake, good food and garden (open at 1200); a good piano bar next door; *Costa Brava*, N of Plaza España, excellent seafood; *La Terraza*, 300 m. S of Plaza España, good; *La Ronda*, quite good; *Pizza Boom*, Plaza España; *Cafetería Bolonia*, next to *Panadería* on Plaza España, a/c, good; *Yierba Buena*, Pista Benjamín Zeledón, 2 blocks E of Plaza España, open 1700-2400 except Sun., coffee house, good recorded music and chocolate cake; 2 good *sorbeterías* on the street N of Plaza España. 3 blocks towards the lake from *Intercontinental*, a thatched-roof restaurant run by Salvadorean refugees, good, handicrafts shop nearby, information on cooperatives in Estelí region. *Comedores Sara* and *Victoria*, cheap, popular with gringos; other cheap *comedores* in the area. *Eskimo* ice cream, W of *Intercontinental* and 2 opp. Ciné Dorado (you can eat at the factory at Km.3 on Carretera Sur).

Also on Carretera Sur: *The Lobster's Inn* (Km. 5.5), good for guess what; *Los Ranchos* (Km. 3); *El Tucán* (Km. 7.5), rec., and another at Km. 8.5.

On Carretera a Masaya: *La Carreta* (Km. 12), rec.; *Lacmiel* (Km.4.5), good value, real ice cream; *El Chaguite*, just S of Pista de la Resistencia; *Los Gauchos*, steaks; *El Coliseo* (Km.8), Italian; *Pizza Deli* (Km.6); *La Marseillaise*, Colonia Los Robles, French, excellent. Vegetarian:

Soya Restaurant, just off the Carretera on Pista de la Resistencia; *Naturales Margarita*, several blocks towards lake from casa de cambio, also does other dishes, good refrescos (closed Tues.).

Other recommendations: Cheap meals at Mercado Huembes. *Mirador Tiscapa*, overlooking Laguna Tiscapa, good food, slow service, live music 2000-2400 (0200 Sat., closed Wed.); health food bakery near Tiscapa (E from *Intercontinental*, turn R at drycleaners, after 2 blocks turn L, bread sales at 1100, get ticket at 1000, max. 4 loaves p.p.). In Bello Horizonte, *La Botija*, and pizza bars on La Rotonda. In Camino Oriente entertainment centre, *El Ternero* and *La Fonda* (also has a bad local version of *MacDonalds*, cinemas, discos and bowling alley). *El Rincón Español*, Av. Monumental, old Managua, Spanish; *Los Nopales*, good food and service; *Faisán Dorado*, Ciudad Jardín L-3.

Shopping   Some handicrafts (goldwork, embroidery, etc.) are available in the Centro Comercial de Managua; good general shopping here and at Mercado Huembes (also called Eduardo Contreras), very good for crafts, both on Pista de la Solidaridad (buses 110 or 119). Good shopping also at Metrocentro, Pista de la Resistencia. Best bookshops at the Ministry of Culture (near Plaza España), which also sells records and maps, the Centro Sandinista de Trabajadores, Ho Chi Minh Way, and in the Centro Antonio Valdivieso, Calle José Martí, near *Mirador Tiscapa* (also sells records). Most ordinary shops are in private houses without signs. Dollartienda (formerly Diplotienda), opp. *Los Gauchos* restaurant on Carretera a Masaya, offers Western-style goods, take your passport, accepts dollars and travellers' cheques if to value of purchase (another Dollartienda is under construction). At the Mercado Oriental you can get just about anything, on the black market.

Local Transport   Bus service in Managua is cheap and as good as can be expected under the circumstances. All buses are packed. Last services begin their routes at 2200; buses are regular but it is difficult to fathom their routes. Beware of pickpockets on the crowded urban buses particularly those on tourist routes (e.g. No. 119). A map from the Tourist Office (poor), and a couple of days riding the buses will help you orient yourself. Taxis can be flagged down along the street, but they run mostly on set routes, so you have to know where you're going. Most taxis are colectivos, charging at most US$0.20; bargain on those that aren't (fares range from US$0.40-US$1.50). One pays per zone.

Car Hire   Hertz, Avis and Budget. Rates are US$25 per day plus US$0.25 per km., or US$60 per day with unlimited mileage— only foreign exchange or credit cards accepted; special weekend rates available. Given the poor public transport and the decentralized layout of Managua, renting a car is often the best way to get around. Alternatively hire a taxi for long-distance trips, about US$1.50-2 per hour for the car; for journeys out of Managua, taxis need a special permit from an office opp. *Hotel Intercontinental* (opens 0930).

Entertainment   Discotheques: Lobo Jack, La Nueva Managua, Frisco Disco, Casa Blanca, Pantera Rosa. 2 discos, cinemas, restaurants in Camino Oriente centre (bus 119 or 117). Live music is offered at La Vista, Torre Blanca, Tiffany's Saloon and El Arroyito. Plaza 19 de Julio, Pista de la Resistencia opp. Universidad Centroamericana, some live bands, crowded, festive, great dancing. Jazz club at *Cafetería de la ASTC* in El Carmen, from 2000, inexpensive, good food. **Ballet** Ballet Tepenahuatl, folkloric dances in the ruins of the *Gran Hotel*.

Cinemas   Most films in English with Spanish sub-titles (US$0.50). Cinemateca, on Av. Bolívar (behind Cine González), Government theatre with good programmes (only US$0.20 on Sun. a.m.).

Sport   Baseball—between Plaza de España and Plaza 19 de Julio on Sunday mornings (the national game), basketball, cockfighting and bullfighting (but no kill), swimming, sailing, tennis, golf.

Museums   The National Museum is near the lakeshore, to the E of the railway station (closed Sun.). Museo de la Alfabetización (closed Mon.) near Parque Las Palmas in W section of city commemorates the Sandinista Government's literacy programme. Museum of the Revolution, behind bus station near Mercado Eduardo Contreras; fascinating collection of photographs, weapons and documents from 1880s to the struggle against the Somozas (open Tues.-Sat., 0900-1200, 1400-1700; admission free). Centro Cultural Ruinas del Gran Hotel, near Palacio Nacional, permanent display of "revolutionary" art and visiting exhibitions; small cafeteria (expect to have to deposit your bag at the door).

Exchange   Banco Central de Nicaragua, Km. 7, Carretera del Sur (not for exchange). Local banks all nationalized in July 1979. Banco Nicaragüense del Interior y Comercio at Plaza España changes both bank notes and travellers' cheques. *Casas de cambio* behind Ed. Oscar Pérez Cazar at Km. 4.5 on road to Masaya, opp. *Sandy's* restaurant (Bus 119), takes Master Card, open 0900-1200, 1400-1600; at terminal for Granada buses, several in Ciudad Jardín; much quicker than banks (ask taxi drivers). If stuck buy postcards or a snack at the *Intercontinental* with a travellers' cheque and change will be given in córdobas, but normally the hotel only changes dollars for residents. It is advisable to change money in Managua as it is very difficult elsewhere. Cred-o-matic, Camino Oriente on Carretera a Masaya. The illegal "parallel" market offers far better rates of exchange; ask discreetly for the "coyotes" in Ciudad Jardín suburb. Otherwise change money at the parallel rate at the Costa Rican or Honduran border. Beware of short-changing. (**See page 1275.**)

Immigration Pista de la Resistencia, approx. 1 km. from Km. 7 Carretera del Sur, bus No. 118, open till 1400.

Customs Km. 5 Carretera del Norte, bus No. 108.

Embassies USA, Km. 4½ Carretera del Sur (T 23881); W. German, off Plaza España; French, Km. 12 Carretera del Sur, T 26210/27011; British, El Reparto, "Los Robles", Primera Etapa, Entrada Principal de la Carretera a Masaya, Cuarta Casa a la mano derecha, T 70034, Telex 2166, Apdo Aéreo 169, it is located on a R-turn off Carretera a Masaya; Honorary British Consul at Viajes Griffiths, No. C8, Centro Comercial San Francisco, T 72365/74785; letters to Apdo. Postal 13, Managua; Swiss, in emergency, at Hungarian Consul, T 74173; Swedish, from Plaza España, 1 block W (Abajo), 2 blocks to the Lake, ½ block W (Abajo), Apartado Postal 2307, T 60085; Danish Cosulate General, Iglesia del Carmen, 2 cuadros al Oeste No. 1610, T 23189; Panamanian Consulate, near UCA, Plaza 19 de Julio; Costa Rican, Pista Benjamín Zeledón, nr. Plaza España, 1 block to the south. Honduran Consulate, Carretera del Sur, Km. 15, Colonia Barcelona, open Mon.-Fri., 0800-1400 (bus 118 from Hotel Intercontinental); Guatemalan, just after Km. 11 on Masaya road, visa US$10 (for British citizens, cash only), fast service.

Spanish Classes and thorough introduction to Nicaragua: Casa Nicaragüense de Español, Km. 11.5 Carretera Sur (835 Broadway, Suite 1105, New York 10003); accommodation with families. Universidad Centroamericana has Spanish courses which are cheaper, but with larger classes.

General Post Office 3 blocks W of Palacio Nacional and Cathedral, 0700-1600 (closed Sat. p.m.). Separate entrance and exit, luggage searched on entry. Wide selection of beautiful stamps. Poste Restante (Lista de Correos) keeps mail for 1 month.

Cables Telcor, same building as Post Office. Mercado Roberto Huembes (Eduardo Contreras), on bus route 109 from Hotel Intercontinental.

Tourist Information Inturismo occupies a kiosk in Parque Luis Alfonso Velásquez (behind the Biblioteca Infantil), just N of the Banco de América building. Hours: 0800-1700, Mon.-Fri. (Adminstration office, 1 block E of Hotel Intercontinental, gives information reluctantly, enter by side door.) Standard information available. Maps of Managua (almost up-to-date), with insets of León and Granada and whole country on reverse, US$4 (paid in dollars). Inturismo will help with finding accommodation with families, with full board. Post cards for sale at Tourist Office, Ministry of Culture and Intercontinental Hotel (more expensive); also at Tarjetas Gordión. Nicatours Turnica, Av. 11 S.O., 2 mins. from Plaza España, sells maps of Managua and of the country.

Airlines Around Plaza España: Sahsa, Aeronica (international flights; internal information at airport), Aeroflot, Iberia (MCOs only), KLM (300 metres E.); in Colonia Los Robles (Carretera a Masaya), Copa, Taca, Cubana (E of Plaza 19 de Julio, turn right on road opp. Restaurant Lacmiel, T 73976). Foreigners have to pay in dollars for all flight tickets.

Airport César Augusto Sandino, 12 km. E of city, near the lake. Take bus 105, very crowded so may be better to take a taxi, US$3 from main road, US$6 from terminal, or US$8, Taxis Unidos, regardless of number of passengers. Be early for international flights since formalities can take 2 hours. X-ray machines reported not safe for film. Internal flights to Puerto Cabezas, Bluefields and the Corn Islands with Aeronica (difficult to get seats, flights are cancelled frequently, US$80 return; air-taxi flights to Bluefields cost US$200, to Corn Islands US$275). Hotel Las Mercedes, near airport, has swimming pool open to non-residents (free).

Rail Station behind the Cathedral; to Granada (45 km.), via Masaya, 0800, 1330 and 1730 (1 hr. 25 mins., US$0.60), to Masaya one a.m., one p.m. Trains on the continuation to Jinotepe, Masatepe, San Marcos and Diriamba run only a few times a year for tourists. Trains daily to León (90 km.) at 0730, 1100 and 1800, 3 hrs., US$0.30; one or two trains continue on the branch line to El Sauce (90 km.) and Río Grande. The León-Chinandega-Corinto section of the Pacific Railway has been out of service since 1982, but was expected to be open again in 1989. Be 30 minutes early to get seats. Always very dusty in the dry season, and there are no windows to close.

Roads to León and Chinandega and then (when frontier bridge is repaired) to Choluteca in Honduras; to Masaya and Granada; Pan-American Highway N to Honduras (to Tegucigalpa is 444 km.), and SE to Costa Rica. Good paved roads from Casa Colorada to Masachapa, Managua to Granada and Nandaime, to Boaco and Rama.

Buses Good connections by bus or taxi between city centre and bus stations. The Comandante Casimir Sotelo bus station by the Mercado Roberto Huembes (adjacent to Mercado Eduardo Contreras), by Museo de la Revolución, on Pista de la Solidaridad, is for Granada, Masaya, Estelí, Somoto, Matagalpa, etc., and all destinations in the N. Take bus 109, which runs past Hotel Intercontinental and terminates near railway station, or bus 118 and alight at San Juan Bosco church and walk 2 blocks. Bus to Granada, Ruta 4, 0530-2200, every 10 minutes, US$0.20, 1 hr.

(luggage extra). To Masaya, US$0.12. To Somoto, 0430, 7½ hrs., US$0.50. To Ocotal US$2 (with Lestram). To Estelí US$0.60, every 20 mins, 3 hrs. For León, Corinto and Pacific Coast, Chinandega and Rivas, the terminal is beside Mercado Israel Lewites, Pista de la Resistencia, on SW side of city (bus 118). To get from the first to the second, take bus 109, then change at *Intercontinental* to bus 118. Bus to León, US$0.80, 1½ hrs., or take Interlocal taxi from bus station, 1½ hrs., US$1.60; to Rivas, 3 hrs., US$0.80, 1400; to Peñas Blancas on Costa Rican border, 3½-4 hrs., US$1.60; to Chinandega, 3 hrs., US$1.20. Buses to Boaco, Juigalpa and Rama leave from the Mercado Oscar Benavides/Ivan Montenegro, on Pista José Angel Benavides, in the east of the city.

International Buses Look in *El Nuevo Diario* for buses running to San Salvador, Tegucigalpa and Guatemala City. Ticabus to San José and Panama (Tues., Thurs., Sat., US$25 single, US$40 to Panama City, US$ only), and to Honduras and Guatemala (US$35 return to Guatemala City, 36 hrs., singles not sold, return section valid for 3 days only); terminal is in Barrio Martha Quezada. Sirca Express leaves 0600 Mon., Wed., and Fri. or Sat. for Costa Rica (office near *Sandy's* restaurant, taxi for 0600 departure very expensive, US$5). Sirca Bus to San José, US$12, 12-15 hrs. (inc. 4-6 at border); Sirca office and terminal in Altamira, Av. Eduardo Delgado, behind Plaza de Compras, T 73833/75726. A very cheap way (US$4) of travelling to San José is to take a bus Managua-Rivas, then colectivo to border and another between the border posts, then take local bus to San José; takes 15 hrs. altogether. International buses are always booked-up many days in advance and tickets will not be sold until all passport/visa documentation is complete.

Tours of city by private car, 1 or 3 persons, about US$10. All-day tour to Granada and León, US$30. A 2-day round trip by bus and riverboat from Managua to Bluefields costs US$50. Bus tours are available Managua-Tegucigalpa-Copán-Guatemala City for US$28. All must be paid in US dollars. Few tours of the country are available.

Beaches There are several beaches on the Pacific coast, about an hour's drive from Managua. The nearest are **Pochomil and Masachapa** (54 km. from Managua, side by side, regular bus service from terminal in Israel Lewites market) and Casares (69 km. from Managua, dirty, thorns on beach; one hotel—*Casino Casares*, clean, simple—and 2 restaurants). A few km. from Casares is La Boquita, visited by turtles from Aug. to Nov. Because of their proximity to the capital, these are very popular during the season (Jan.-April) and tend to be somewhat crowded. Out of season, except at weekends, Pochomil is deserted (don't sleep on the beach, mosquitoes will eat you alive); it is clean and being developed as a tourist centre with hotels and restaurants. Masachapa is cheaper but dirtier; hotels on beach, G (but *Terraza* not rec.). Very slow bus journey from Managua. A visit to the broad, sandy El Velero beach (turn off at Km. 60 on the old road to León and then follow signs) is recommended despite the US$3.50 entrance charge. All facilities controlled by the INSSBI, for the benefit of state employees, and at weekends is fully booked for weeks in advance. You may be able to rent a cabin (F for 2) in the week, pay extra for sheet and pillows. You can eat in the restaurant (*Pirata Cojo*), at the INSSBI cafeteria (bring your own utensils, buy meal ticket in advance, or take your own food). However, the beach itself is beautiful, and the sea is ideal for both surfing and swimming. El Tránsito is a beautiful, undeveloped Pacific beach; bus from Managua at 1300 (from end of No. 107 bus route behind Ciné México), return at 0600 or 0700. Good cheap meals from Sra Pérez on the beach (possible accommodation); *Restaurant Yolanda*; beach flats for 4-6 people normally available mid-week at N end (Centro Vacacional de Trabajadores, good value).

Pan-American Highway from Managua to Honduras:

214 km., paved the whole way. Also paved are the branch roads to Matagalpa and Jinotega. The first stretch of 21 km. to Tipitapa is along the southern edge of Lake Managua. **Tipitapa**, on the SE shore of the lake, is a tourist resort with hot sulphur baths, a casino, a colourful market, and a *fiesta* of El Señor de Esquipulas on January 13-16. Swimming in El Trapice park, US$0.50. (The border with Honduras on the more easterly route, by road from Ocotal via Las Manos to Danlí, has been reopened, but the more westerly Chinandega-Río Guasaule-Choluteca link is closed.)

Hotel *Aguas Calientes*, F with shower; the thermal bath is under reconstruction.

Restaurant *Salón Silvia*, unpretentious. Slightly cheaper, but good, is the a/c restaurant attached to the thermal baths.

Bus from Managua (minibus), US$0.20. Bus to Estelí, US$1.

At San Benito, 45 km. from Managua, the Atlantic Highway branches E, paved all the way to Rama. Shortly after Teustepe, a paved road goes NE to Boaco. A turn-off, unpaved, goes to Santa Lucía, a village inside a crater, with a women's handicraft shop. **Boaco** (15,000 people) has several *hospedajes* and its specialities are white cheese and cream. From Boaco, unpaved roads go N to Muy Muy and Matagalpa, and S to Comoapa (4,000 people). The Atlantic Highway continues through *Juigalpa* (30,000 people; 109 km. from Managua). Here is one of the best museums in Nicaragua, with a collection of idols resembling those at San Agustín, Colombia. Lodging at Hotel Mayales, G, close to Cathedral, best of a bad lot, or on the main road beside a restaurant. Small zoo in the valley below town. A gravel road goes to La Libertad, a goldmining town at 600 metres (4,000 people, *hospedaje*), and on to Santo Domingo. The main road goes S to Santo Tomás (10,000 people, several *hospedajes*) and smaller villages (including La Gateada, turn-off to Nuevo Güinea, centre of cacao production), to Cara de Mono (*hospedaje*), on the Río Mico, and finally to Rama, on the Río Escondido or Bluefields River, 290 km. from Managua. River boats ply from Rama 100 km. downstream to Bluefields (see page 1270). 25 km. S of Juigalpa an unpaved road turns off to Acoyapa (7 km., 5,000 people, *hospedaje*), El Morrito, San Miguelito and San Carlos on Lake Nicaragua (see page 1268).

The Pan-American Highway goes N through Tipitapa to Sébaco, 105 km. Fourteen km. before reaching Sébaco is Ciudad Darío (off the main road, turning N of town, is not signposted), where the poet Ruben Darío was born; you can see the house, which is maintained as a museum (Hotel: *Grande*). E of the Highway is Esquipula, 100 km. from Managua, 2½ hrs. by bus, a good place for hiking, fishing, riding; Hotel Oscar Morales, G, clean, shower, friendly.

From Sébaco a 24-km. branch road leads (right) to *Matagalpa* at 678 metres, in the best walking country in Nicaragua, population 70,000. Matagalpa has an old church, but it is about the only colonial style building left; the town has developed rapidly in recent years. It was badly damaged in the Revolution, but is undergoing reconstruction, retaining much of its original character. The birthplace of Carlos Fonseca is now a museum, 1 block E of the more southerly of the 2 main squares; off the northerly square (with the Cathedral) is a Galería de los Héroes y Mártires; N of the Cathedral is the Centro Popular de la Cultura, with murals on the outside. The town is safe, but visitors can expect frequent police checks. There is a small zoo in the northern suburbs along the river. The main occupation is coffee planting and there are cattle ranges; the chief industry is the Nestlé powdered-milk plant. A 32-km. road runs from Matagalpa to the Tuma valley. September 24, Día de La Merced, is a local holiday.

Hotels *Selva Negra*, at 1,200 m., 10 km. on road to Jinotega, F, good, but poor restaurant (reserve in advance at weekends by telegram); *Soza*, opp. river, E, basic; *Ideal*, E, with bath, same range without (but C for those not on a work brigade), good but expensive restaurant; *Bermúdez*, reasonably clean, friendly, no meals; *Hospedaje Plaza*, on main plaza, G, clean, quiet; on other side of square, *Hospedaje Colonial*, G, basic; round, brick hostel with communal rooms, nr. *Hotel Bermúdez*, no sign, basic, inexpensive.

Restaurants *Comedor San Martín*, main street, good breakfasts; *San Diego*, opp. cinema near plaza, good; *Comedor* in park near church (built with assistance from Tilburg, Neth.), rec.; *Comedor Vicky*, S of cathedral, good breakfast and lunch (closed p.m.); *Sorbetería* 1 block E of square with Fonseca quotes, on a corner, rec.; *Chinatown*, Chinese, 1 block E, 1 block N of plaza; *Lanchería Marcia*, opp. fire station, excellent value lunch; *Los Pinchitos Morenos*, near the centre, good and cheap.

Exchange Banco Nacional de Desarrollo.

Shopping Mercado del Norte, close to northern highway; Mercado del Oeste, 2 blocks W of *Royal Bar*; Dollartienda to open. Bookshop: Fundacíon Manolo Morales, 1 block N, ½ block E of plaza, Spanish editions of international literature and stamps.

Buses every half hour to Managua, 127 km., take 2½ hrs. (US$1.20) (express at 1100 and 1500, queue from 0900). Buses for the local area leave from Guanuco, a long way from the centre in the E suburbs.

There is a fine 34-km. highway from Matagalpa to *Jinotega*, and on another 80 km. (unpaved), via the picturesque villages of San Rafael del Norte and Yalí (check if safe to visit now), to join the main highway at Condega, 51 km. from the Honduran border (*pensión*, F). Jinotega (altitude 1,004 metres) is served by buses from Managua and Matagalpa. Population 20,000; famous images in church. The Somoza jail has been converted into a youth centre. Excellent coffee grown here and in Matagalpa. Road (18 km.) to El Tuma power station; another to Estelí.

The 134-km. section from Sébaco to the border at El Espino is through sharp hills with steep climbs and descents, but reasonably well banked and smooth.

A road (very poor in places) leads off the Pan-American Highway 10 km. N of Sébaco, near San Isidoro, to join the Pacific Highway near León (110 km.). This is an attractive alternative route to Managua through the Chinandega cotton growing area, past the spectacular chain of volcanoes running W from Lake Managua, and through León. (Bus Estelí-San Isidoro, US$0.20, San Isidoro-León, 2½ hrs., US$0.80). On this road, 12 km. N of the intersection with the Chinandega-León road, is San Jacinto; 200 metres to the west of the road is a field of steaming, bubbling mud holes (approach carefully, the ground may give, and scald your legs).

The Pan-American Highway goes through *Estelí* (839 metres), a rapidly developing departmental capital of about 20,000 people (heavily damaged during the Revolution of 1978-79). It is the site of prehistoric carved stone figures (in park in front of tourist information office). Worth visiting are the Casa de Cultura and the Salvadorean cooperative for crafts (off main square). Also ask at the Reforma Agraria Office (above Banco de América) if you wish to see any local farming cooperatives. Tourist information at Cathedral Plaza. Bus Estelí-Managua, first at 0400, express at 0600, none after dark, every 30 mins., US$0.60 plus a charge for luggage.

Hotels *Mesón*, 1 block N of Cathedral and plaza, E with shower, good value, but not very clean, restaurant; *Hospedaje El Chepito*, clean, friendly, G; *Mariela*, F behind bus station, clean, safe, washing facilities; *Bolívar*, unmarked, 2 blocks S on main street from *Restaurant La Plancha*, good, G; *Moderno*, F, with shower, good, safe parking, slow service in restaurant; *3 hospedajes* on Av. Bolívar, all G: *La Florida* (not rec., but has space for car), *Juárez*, and *San Francisco*; *Barlop*, Av. Bolívar, opp. bus station, 5 blocks from main square, 12 rooms, 6 of which good, 6 basic, former have hot showers, T (071) 2486, E, good; *Galo*, Nicaragua y Central, F, accepts córdobas.

Restaurant Opp. *Sorbetería Estelí*, is *Colectivo de Soja* vegetarian restaurant; *El Mesero*, on street which joins main street at hospital, opp. an open field, popular and very good despite appearance. *Chupis* ice cream, next to *El Faisán* restaurant on Calle Bolívar; about 3 blocks N of park on same street *Panadería España*, good but pricey. Dollartienda.

Spanish Classes Nuevo Instituto de Centro América (NICA), 5-week programme of Spanish tuition and courses on Nicaragua, including meetings with people, volunteer work, visits to cooperatives, etc. Apply at least a month in advance; charge is 5% of your annual income, or minimum US$950. All accommodation is with local families. Details from NICA, PO Box 1409, Cambridge MA 02238, USA, or Apartado Postal 50, Estelí.

Exchange Banco Nacional de Desarrollo.

Bathing near Estelí at Puente La Sirena, 200 metres off the road to Condega, or Salta Estanzuela, 5 km. S of Estelí, a waterfall of 25 metres, with a deep pool at the bottom, surrounded by trees and flowers (inc. orchids—only worth it in the rainy season), at least 5 km. off the Managua road, four-wheel drive recommended. Take the dirt road, starting ½ km. S of Estelí on Pan-American Highway, through San Nicolás.

A new gravel road from Estelí runs to Achuapa and El Sauce **(see page 1265)**; there is a poor, direct road Estelí-El Sauce.

The Highway then goes to Condega (5,000 people) and to Somoto (7,000 people), centre of pitch-pine industry, thence to El Espino (20 km.), a ghost town 5 km. from Honduran border at La Playa. The Nicaraguan passport control and customs are at El Espino in the ruined customs house, 100 metres from the Honduran border (customs used to be carried out 5 km. from the border); US$60 to be changed into córdobas, proof of US$200 when entering Nicaragua. Minibuses run between Somoto and the border (US$0.20, plus US$0.40 per bag), and 3 or 4 buses daily between Somoto and Estelí (US$0.40); Somoto-Managua, 5 hrs., US$0.50 plus extra for luggage, 0400 and 0600 only (private car Somoto-Managua, US$25). The border opens at 0800 on each side, Nicaraguan side closes at 1530, and 1200-1300 for lunch (if you arrive at the border after 1530, there are no buses back to Somoto and nowhere to stay in El Espino). (There is a food bar on the Nicaraguan side.)

Hotels 2 *pensiones*, G, in Somoto; restaurant *Zetaponat* in Somoto, good value but little choice; *Somotillo*, F (7 km. from frontier, no sign, on right just before sign on left to Cine Karla), communal showers, adequate, meals.

Just before reaching Somoto a road leads off from Yalagüina right (18 km.) to *Ocotal*, a clean, cool, whitewashed town of 3,863 people at 600 metres on a sandy plain (well worth a visit). It is near the Honduran border, to which a road runs N (bus marked Las Manos); this border is open again; bus Ocotal-Somoto, US$0.20. Close by, at San Albino, there are many gold mines and gold is washed in the river Coco (bus only from Ciudad Sandino—formerly Jícaro, 50 km. from Ocotal; a dangerous area). Friendly, helpful Tourist Office 2 blocks from main square, opposite the market. Bus Estelí-Ocotal, US$0.20, 2 hrs., beautiful views.

Hotels at Ocotal *El Portal*, G, reasonable; *El Castillo*, G, basic, quiet; *Segovia*, cheap, basic, OK; *Pensión Centroamericana*, G, not as dirty as most others. For eating, *Restaurant La Cabaña*; *El Deportivo*, excellent value comida corriente, friendly; *Brasilia*, very good, ask for directions.

Exchange Banco Nacional de Desarrollo.

Managua to Corinto 140 km. The first city of note along the railway is León, 88 km. from Managua, reached in 2¼ hrs. The Pacific Highway between the two cities follows the shore of Lake Managua and goes on to Chinandega; it has been continued to Corinto and to the Honduran border (border bridge destroyed by floods early in 1982, and frontier crossing closed). The old, paved road to León crosses the Sierra de Managua, offering fine views of the lake (it is no longer than the Pacific Highway, but is very bad in places).

About 60 km. down the new road to León lies the village of La Paz Centro. It is from here that one can gain access to the volcano **Momotombo**, which dominates the Managua skyline from the West.

One now has to have a permit from Empresa Nacional de Luz y Fuerza in Managua to climb Momotombo; they have built a geothermal power station on the volcano's slopes; alternatively ask police in León Viejo for a permit (very difficult to get).

León, with a population of 130,000, was founded by Hernández de Córdoba in 1524 at León Viejo, 32 km. from its present site, at the foot of Momotombo. It was destroyed by earthquake on December 31, 1609 (the ruins can be reached by boat from Managua), and the city moved to its present site the next year. It was the capital from its foundation until Managua replaced it in 1858; it is still the "intellectual" capital, with a university (founded 1804), religious colleges, the largest cathedral in Central America, and several colonial churches. It is said that Managua became the capital, although at the time it was only an Indian settlement, because it was half-way between violently Liberal León and equally violently Conservative Granada.

The city has a traditional air, its colonial charm unmatched elsewhere in Nicaragua: narrow streets, roofs tiled in red, low adobe houses and time-worn buildings everywhere. The old Plaza de Armas, in front of the Cathedral, is now Parque Jérez; it contains a statue of General Jérez, a mid-19th century Liberal leader.

The Cathedral, begun in 1746 and not completed for 100 years, is an enormous building. It has a famous shrine, 145 cm. high, covered by white topazes from India given by Philip II of Spain, which is kept in a safe in the vestry, and the bishop holds the key; a very fine ivory Christ; the consecrated Altar of Sacrifices and the Choir of Córdoba; the great Christ of Esquipulas, a colonial work in bronze whose cross is of very fine silver; and statues of the 12 Apostles. At the foot of one of these statues is the tomb of Rubén Darío, the 19th-century Nicaraguan poet, guarded by a sorrowing lion.

The western end of the city is the oldest, and here is the oldest of all the churches: the parish church of Subtiava (1530) where Las Casas, the Apostle of the Indies, preached on several occasions. It has a fine façade, the best colonial altar in the country and an interesting representation of the sun ("El Sol") revered by the Indians. Near the Subtiava church are a small town museum (entrance free) and the ruins of the parish church of Vera Cruz, now crumbling. Other churches well worth visiting include El Calvario (beautifully decorated ceiling), La Recolección (fine façade), La Merced, San Felipe, Zaragoza, San Francisco and El Laborío. There is a pleasant walk S across the bridge, past the church of Guadalupe, to the cemetery. The house of Rubén Darío, one of the greatest Latin American poets, the famous "Four Corners" in Calle Rubén Darío, is now the Museo-Archivo Rubén Darío; he died in 1916 in another house in the NW sector marked with a plaque. The Holy Week ceremonies are outstanding. Visit the Casa de Cultura in the suburb of Subtiava.

León was the centre of heavy fighting during the 1978-79 Revolution; much of the damage has still to be repaired (a public works programme was promised in 1988), but there are also many monuments from that time in the city (descriptions of León's fight against the Somoza régime can be found in *Fire from the Mountain: The Making of a Sandinista* by Omar Cabezas). Visitors can see El Fortín, the ruined last stronghold of the Somocista national guard (a commemorative march goes there each July, from 1 block E of Cathedral, go straight S over river for 2 km., then up a hill, best in early a.m.); El Veinte Uno, the national guard's 21st garrison, also ruined, with the jail around the corner converted into a garden (3 blocks S of cathedral); statue of Luisa Amanda Espinoza, the first woman member of the FSLN to die (in 1970), after whom the women's organization (AMNLAE) is named (7-8 blocks N of market behind Cathedral, in Barrio San Felipe); 2 blocks W of La Merced church is the Centro Popular de la Cultura (frequent exhibitions and events); Galería de Héroes y Mártires, a museum just W of main square. In the blocks N of the Cathedral is a commemorative park with portraits of Sandino, Carlos Fonseca and Jérez.

Local Holidays June 20 (Liberation by Sandinistas), September 24, November 1 (All Saints' Day).

Hotels *Europa*, 2 blocks S of railway station, best, E (córdobas accepted), with bath, F without, excellent, good breakfasts (US$0.35); *América*, Av. Santiago Argüello, 2 blocks E of central market, F, with bath and fan, clean and friendly, restaurant (good breakfast); *Telica*, F with shower, clean, good breakfast, 4 blocks N of railway station; *Hospedaje de la Primavera*, Calle 9N, 3½ blocks W of railway station, F with shower, pleasant but women travelling alone should take one of the more expensive rooms close to reception as drunken men are a problem here, also has rats; Several cheap *pensiones* near the railway station.

Restaurants *La Cueva del León*, good seafood and steaks, two blocks N of Parque Jérez, slow service; *El Filete*, 4 blocks N of Parque Jérez, good fish, pricey; *Los Angeles* and *Dragón de Oro* (Chinese), ½ block N of Parque Jérez; *Central*, Calle 4 Norte, good comida corriente. *Cuerva*, Av. 1 Poniente, good value; *Metropolitano*, 1 block W of Post Office, good steaks. *Capricornio*, nr. Central University, good comida corriente, interesting atmosphere; good value comida corrida at *Comedores Emu* (nr. La Recolección church) and *La Cucaracha* (1 block S of *Hotel América* on opp. side of street, no sign); *Sacuanjoche*, Calle Darío several blocks W of Cathedral, expensive but good; *Lacmiel*, 5 blocks S of Cathedral, good food, live music, open air, rec.; *Los Pescaditos*, nr. Subtiava church, good fish. Excellent ice cream parlour on corner of central square.

Shopping The old market (dirty) is in the centre, and the new market is at the bus terminal, 5-6 blocks E of railway station. Good bookshop next to city hall at Parque Jérez. Dollartienda planned.

Cinemas 3 in centre. 2 discotheques at weekends.

Exchange Banco Nacional de Desarrollo.

Post Office and Telephones Telcor, Parque Jérez, opposite Cathedral. Phone calls abroad possible. Small Telcor office on Darío about 10 blocks from main plaza, open till 2200, less crowded.

Buses From bus station at new market: Managua-León, Route 12, 1½ hrs., US$0.80 (fight for a ticket and place). Colectivo, US$1.60; to San Isidro, US$0.80 to Chinandega and Corinto hourly between 0500 and 1900.

Train Managua-León, US$0.30, 3 hrs.; train from León to Managua departs 0430 (good views of Momotombo at sunrise) 0900, 1540; rough, dusty (in dry season), colourful, real experience! Trip gives good view of lakes and volcanoes. A branch railway runs to Malpaisillo and *El Sauce*, 90 km., 3-4 hrs., once or twice a day, where there is a large 19th century church, and a riotous fair in February. (*Hospedaje Diana*, G, clean, basic; *Hospedaje Viajero*, noisy, dirty; *Restaurant Mi Rancho* and others); regular trucks to Estelí, on a very rough road.

There is a road (20 km.) to the sandy Pacific beach (large waves, strong currents, very dangerous) at *Poneloya* (Hotel *Lacayo*, basic, G, meals, beware of insects at night, bring coils; good fish restaurant down the road); bus 101 from centre of León (US$0.25, 50 mins., last at 1700) finishes at Las Peñitas at the S end of Poneloya beach (swimming much safer here; several small restaurants). It gets crowded at weekends; camping possible on the beach.

Chinandega is about 35 km. beyond León. Population 37,000. This is one of the main cotton-growing districts, and also grows bananas and sugar cane. Horse-drawn cabs for hire, and a crocodile in the fountain in the main square. Not far away, at Chichigalpa, is Ingenio San Antonio, the largest sugar mill in Nicaragua, with a railway to its own port on the Pacific. From Managua, by road, 3 hrs.,

US$1.20. Hourly buses to Managua from main square from 0500. From León, 1 hr. by bus, US$0.50. Local holiday: July 26.

Hotels   *Glomar*, F (shower extra), friendly, safe, may be closed Sun. p.m., owner (Filio) will change dollars; *Salón Carlos*, F, with breakfast, share shower; *Pensión Cortés*, S of Parque Central, G, basic. *Pensión Urbina*, G, basic; *Hospedaje Aguirre*, G. On the road to Honduran border, *Cosigüina*, 50 rooms, 2 restaurants, shops, cinema and discotheque.

Restaurants   *Corona de Oro*, Chinese, 1½ blocks E of Parque Central, T 3511; *Central Palace*, same street; *Caprax Pizza*, one block E of Parque Central. Dollartienda planned.

Exchange Banco Nacional de Desarrollo.

Post Office   in new building opp. *Caprax Pizza*.

A road runs NE to Puerto Morazán. This passes through the village of El Viejo (US$0.20 by bus from Chinandega, 5 km.) where there is an old church. (Restaurant: *El Retoño*, on main street, N of market; bars close to market.) Puerto Morazán (hotel), 26 km. from Chinandega (bus at 1030 and 1600, 1½ hrs., US$0.20), is a modern town on a navigable river running into the Gulf of Fonseca. From Chinandega there is a bus at 1400 daily to Potosí, at least 3 hrs., US$0.40 (return 0330). *Comedor Adela*, 24-hr. service, cheap. You can sling your hammock at the *comedor* 150 metres past immigration for US$0.50. Ask Héctor for permission to stay in the fishing cooperative. The fishermen are very friendly. The passenger ferry from Potosí to La Unión (El Salvador) has been suspended.

It is a 4-hour hike to the cone of Cosigüina volcano. On January 23, 1835, one of the biggest eruptions in history blew off most of the cone, reducing it from 3,000 metres to its present height of 870 metres. Michael Tesch and Leone Thiele of Cape Paterson, Australia, tell us: There are beautiful views of the lake inside the cone and over the islands of Honduras and El Salvador. There is plenty of wildlife in the area, including poisonous snakes, so take a machete. There are pleasant black sand beaches; the sea, although the colour of *café con leche*, is clean. In the centre of the village are warm thermal springs in which the population relaxes each afternoon.

From Chinandega a paved road goes to the Honduran border at Somotillo, on the Río Guasaule, where it is continued by an equally good road to Choluteca, Honduras. **N.B.** The bridge over the Río Guasaule was washed away in floods in May 1982 and the bridge over the Río Negro was destroyed by guerrillas in the same year. The border here was closed at the time of going to press (1989).

Jiquilillo beach, 42 km. from Chinandega, is reached by a mostly-paved road branching off the El Viejo-Potosí road. It lies on a long peninsula; small restaurants (e.g. *Fany*) and lodgings.

Corinto, 21 km. from Chinandega, is the main port of entry, and the only port at which vessels of any considerable size can berth. About 60% of the country's commerce passes through it. The town itself is on a sandy island, Punto Icaco, connected with the mainland by long railway and road bridges. There are beautiful old wooden buildings with verandahs, especially by the port, but photography near the port is forbidden. (Entry to the port is barred to all except those with a permit.) Population: 10,000. On the Corinto-Chinandega road is Paseo Cavallo beach (*Restaurante Buen Vecino*). Dollartienda planned.

Hotel   *Hospedaje Luvy*, G, fan, dirty bathrooms, 2 blocks from plaza.
Restaurants   *Meléndez*, on main square, good but pricey; *El Imperial*, evenings only; cheapest meals in market, but not rec.

Managua to Granada   There are two routes, one by rail and one by a 61 km. paved road with a fast bus service; both run through Masaya.

Santiago Volcano   The entrance to Masaya National Park is at km. 23. The road is paved up to the crater (6 km.). The volcano is double-crested, but half (Masaya) is dormant. The other crater (Santiago) collapsed in late 1986, and the resulting pall of sulphurous smoke made the soil in a broad belt to the Pacific uncultivable. There is a beautiful picnic area half-way up and a fine but expensive restaurant (next door is a good science museum). Take something to drink. There is no public transport, although you can alight from the Managua-Masaya bus at Km. 23. Park rangers may give you a lift. Luggage may be left at the gate lodge safely. Drivers have to pay US$1 to get their cars in; pedestrians 1 centavo. The Park is open 0700-1700.

Masaya (population 38,000), 30 km. SE of Managua, is the centre of a rich agricultural area growing tobacco. Small **Laguna de Masaya** (at the foot of Masaya volcano, water too polluted for swimming), and Santiago volcano are near the town. Interesting Indian handicrafts and a gorgeous *fiesta* on September 30, for its patron, San Jerónimo. (Indian dances and local costumes.) The market (Sunday at railway station) is reportedly commercialized now, but good for snake-, iguana-, and alligator-skin items. There is a new Centro de Artesanías, near the hospital and overlooking Laguna de Masaya; big selection, high quality (closed Sun.). Nearby is *Taller de Tapices Luis* where brightly coloured straw mats can be bought more cheaply than in the market. Doña Luisa (near church) sells good woven articles. The best place for Indian craft work is Monimbo, and 15 minutes from Masaya is Villa Nindirí, which has a rich museum and an old church with some even older images. There are horse-drawn carriages, some very pretty and well-kept. A branch railway runs SW to Jinotepe and Diriamba in the small highland between the two lakes. The town suffered severely in the Revolution of 1978-79. Visit the Museo de Héroes y Mártires.

Hotels *Motel El Nido*, D, expensive, not too good. *Regis*, Sergio Delgado (main street), F, clean, basic, breakfast (other meals if ordered), helpful owner; *Victoria*, G; *Rex*, G, dark, dirty but friendly, near the church; *Cailagua* (Km. 29.5, Carretera a Granada), clean, F with bath (cold water), good, very friendly, meals available (but breakfast only by arrangement), reasonably priced. *Pensiones* are hard to find, and dirty when you've found them.

Restaurants *Chema*, Arturo Velazques, no sign (except *Nueva Bar*), very good food, service and value; *El Jade*, near 2nd market, good Chinese food. *Alegría*, nr. main square, good, expensive; *El Arabe* at station; *Mini 16*, W end of town, nr. hospital.

Exchange Banco Nacional de Desarrollo.

Transport from Managua, 2 trains daily, Managua-Masaya, 1½ hrs. (0800, 1300, return 0930, 1400); tourist trains to Jinotepe occasionally. By car to Managua, ½ hr.; taxi, US$10; bus every 10 mins., US$0.12; bus and train to Granada, US$0.15. Entering Masaya by bus, do not wait for the end of the line as there are no hotels near the market terminal.

Excursions Just outside Masaya, on the road from Managua, is an old fortress, Coyotepe, also called La Fortillera. It was once a torture centre, and is now deserted, eerie "with a Marie Celeste feel to it" (take a torch).

To Niquinohomo, Sandino's birthplace. James N. Maas writes: Take a bus from Masaya (or Granada) to San Juan de Oriente, a colonial village with an interesting school of pottery (products are for sale). It is a short walk to neighbouring Catarina, and a 1 km. walk uphill to El Mirador, with a wonderful view of **Laguna de Apoyo** (very clean, quiet during week but busy at weekends—swimming, drinking, drowning—entrance fee US$0.20; get out of bus at Km. 38 on Managua-Granada road, walk 1½ hrs. or hitch—easy at weekends), Granada and Volcán Mombacho in the distance. Follow the Jinotepe branch railway down to Masaya.

Another 18 km. by road and rail is *Granada*, on Lake Nicaragua, the terminus of the railway from the port of Corinto (190 km.). It is the third city of the republic, with a population of 45,200, and was founded by Hernández de Córdoba in 1524 at the foot of Mombacho volcano. The rich city was three times attacked by British and French pirates coming up the San Juan and Escalante rivers, and much of old Granada was burnt by filibuster William Walker in 1856, but it still has many beautiful buildings and has faithfully preserved its Castilian traditions. The Cathedral has been rebuilt in neo-classical style; also of interest are the church of La Merced (1781-3), the church of Jalteva in the outskirts, and the fortress-church of San Francisco: its chapel of María Auxiliadora, where Las Casas, Apostle of the Indies, often preached, is hung with Indian lace and needlework. Horse-drawn cabs are for hire (bargain over the price), there are many oxcarts and a fine cemetery. The lake beach is popular, but dirty; marimba bands stroll the beach and play a song for you for a small charge. Launches to the islands on the lake leave from a pier about 3 km. from the city centre. The island vegetation is unusual and different, so are the Indian idols found there on display in the Instituto Nacional del Oriente, next door to the San Francisco church; most of the idols come from one of two larger islands, Isla Zapatera. (The Instituto is a school; teachers will open the door for you.) Worth visiting.

Fiestas Holy Week: Assumption of the Virgin, August 14-30; and Christmas (masked and costumed mummers).

Hotels *Alhambra*, Parque Central, T 2035, pleasant, comfortable rooms with bath, B (dollars only), large restaurant serves good food, often has good, live music, parked cars guarded by nightwatchman; *Granada*, Calle La Calzada (opp. Guadalupe church), B, new, luxury, swimming pool, a/c, breakfast only served, very good, only US$ accepted, T 2974. *Pensión Cabrera*, Calle Calzada, F without bath, clean, pleasant; opposite and of same standard is *Pensión Vargas*, G, basic, mixed reports. These three hotels are on the road from the main square to the wharf. *Pensión Cigarro*, G (short stay, thieves). There is a shortage of hotels and restaurants in Granada (do not arrive after 2300).

Restaurants *Pingüín*, good, expensive; *Drive Inn El Ancla*, opp. *Hotel Granada*, clean, rec.; *Interamericano*, road to Masaya next to Esso, clean, dear. *La Cabaña Amarilla*, on lakeshore. *Asia*, rec., a/c, good food, friendly, dollars changed; *Chupi's Ice Cream Parlour*. A tourist complex on the lakeside (S of Plaza España) includes 2 expensive restaurants and bars. 1 km. further along the beach are 3 restaurants which have launch trips for US$2.50 p.p. for an hour to some of the islands. Good breakfasts at the market. Dollartienda near *Hotel Alhambra*.

Exchange Banco Navional de Desarrollo.

Post Office, telephones Telcor in moorish building on Parque Central, left of Cathedral.

Buses leave from an area 200 metres beyond the market, except those going S (e.g. to Rivas) which leave from a "fenced lot uptown". Many fast minibuses to Managua, US$0.20, 1 hr. (these do not stop in Masaya). Bus to Nandaime, US$0.25. Bus to Masaya, US$0.15, 15 mins. Express bus to Rivas, 1130, 1½ hrs., US$2, other, slower buses every ½ hr., US$0.20. To Costa Rican border: if you ask around the Cathedral you may find someone to drive you to the border for US$10: note, taxis are not allowed out of town. Sirca Bus from Granada or Masaya to San José 3 times a week; Tica from Granada to San José.

Rail To Managua, via Masaya, 3 a day, US$0.60, journey times vary from 1hr. 25 mins., to 2 hrs. 5 mins.; ½–¾ hr. to Masaya, US$0.15.

Lake Nicaragua, the "Gran Lago", 148 km. long by 55 at its widest, is a fresh-water lake abounding in salt-water fish, including sharks, which swim up the San Juan river from the sea and later return. Terrapins can be seen sunning themselves on the rocks and there are many interesting birds. There are about 310 small islands, Las Isletas (most of them inhabited), which can be visited either by hired boats or motor launches, from *La Cabaña Amarilla*, about 3 km. along the beach from Granada (turn right at the wharf, taxi from city centre, US$0.40), for US$1 p.p. for 1½ hour. Alternatively, take the morning bus from Granada to Puerto de Aseses (pleasant restaurant with fine view) and hire a rowing boat for US$1.50 per day. (No buses back p.m. though.)

The largest island, Ometepe (population 20,000), has two volcanoes, one of them a perfect cone rising to 1,610 metres. There are two villages on the island: *Moyogalpa* (population 4,500) and Alta Gracia, which are connected by bus (1 hr. US$1.50). Boat from Granada to Alta Gracia, US$2, 4½ rough hrs., the public service is on Tues. and Thurs., at 1000; returning the following days. Boat Moyogalpa-Granada, Sun. a.m. Moyogalpa is pleasanter than Alta Gracia (which has several unnamed *hospedajes* of varying quality); *Pensión Aly*, friendly, clean, helpful and *Pensión Moyogalpa*, both G, rec., cheap. Cheaper, *Pensión Jade*. Cock-fights in Moyogalpa on Sunday afternoons. One can stroll to the base of Volcán Concepción for good views of the lake and the company of howler monkeys (*congos*).

Moyogalpa can be reached from *San Jorge* on the lake's SW shore; boats at 1100 and 1500, US$0.20, returning at 0600 and 1350, 1¼ hrs., schedules can be checked at the Tourist Board in Managua (1330 boat is too late for last bus Rivas-Granada). From San Jorge a road runs through Rivas (bus service every 10 mins., US$0.12, 30 mins.) to the port of San Juan del Sur. The Río San Juan, running through deep jungles, drains the lake from the eastern end into the Caribbean at San Juan del Norte. Launches ply down the river irregularly from the lakeside town of *San Carlos* (15-20,000 people) at the SE corner of the Lake. Much of the town was destroyed by fire in 1984, but some rebuilding has been done. Several boats run from Granada to San Carlos: three slow passenger/cargo boats leave on Mon., Wed. and Fri. at 1400, taking 15-20 hrs.; they start the return journey next day. Fare is US$4 (plus US$1.20 for a hammock— be early; tickets from near the pier). Two fast boats a week leave Granada, 8 hrs. returning next day, costing US$15 (a noisy trip, anything left on deck will get wet). Tickets must be bought from the office by *Hotel Granada*, open at 0800 but be there earlier. The slower boats stop at San Miguelito (pop. 8,000, one primitive *pensión*). (Bus Granada-San Miguelito, Mon., Tues., Wed., Thurs. 0830 from the pier, 8 hrs.)

At San Carlos are the ruins of a fortress built for defence against pirates (*Restaurant Río San Juan*, good meals, rooms for rent, G, dirty, noisy); also *San Carlos* and 2 more basic *pensiones*: vacancies hard to find; exchange at Banco Nacional de Desarrollo). Some 6 hrs. down river (9 hrs. back, US$1) are the ruins of another Spanish fort, Castillo Viejo (*Pensión Merlot*, G, no sign). This is the furthest point down the Río San Juan that non-military travellers are allowed to go (a permit needed nonetheless).

Boats also run from San Carlos to the *Solentiname Islands* in the Lake. A special permit is required to visit this area, **see page 1274**. The only hotel on the islands is *Hotel Isla Solentiname*, on San Fernando island, safe, acceptable but basic (you wash in the lake), cost including meals D (at official rate); on Mancarrón island, the largest, is a library and an interesting church. Ernesto Cardenal (the poet and Minister of Education) lived and worked here. The islands are home to many renowned primitive painters and are pleasant to hike around.

About 40 km. S of San Carlos, on the Río Frío, is Los Chiles, over the border in Costa Rica (**see** also page 1290). Until 1988, no foreigners were allowed into this area, but some reports say it is possible now to cross into Costa Rica from San Carlos. Check with the police in advance for the latest position.

Warning The lake is not only shark-infested but dirty, even contaminated in some places, so do not swim in it. Swimming is possible in nearby Laguna de Apoyo (see page 1267).

By Pan-American Highway from Managua to Costa Rica: 148 km.; bus services all the way to San José de Costa Rica. The road, in good condition, runs into the Sierra de Managua, reaching 900 metres at Casa Colorada, 26 km. from Managua. Further on, at El Crucero, a paved branch road goes through the Sierra S to the Pacific bathing beaches of Pochomil and Masachapa (see page 1261. The Highway continues through the beautiful scenery of the Sierras to *Diriamba,* 42 km. from Managua, at 760 metres, in a coffee-growing district. Population 26,500. Hotel: *Diriangén,* G with bath. Good fish at restaurant *2 de Junio.* Its great *fiesta* is on January 20. There is a 32-km. dirt road direct to Masachapa (no buses), and another NE to Masaya, on the Managua-Granada highway. Being on a through route, it is impossible to get on buses to Managua or Rivas.

Five km. beyond Diriamba is *Jinotepe,* capital of the coffee-growing district of Carazo, joined also by railway with Diriamba and Masaya. It has a fine neo-classical church with modern stained glass windows from Irún, in Spain. The *fiesta* in honour of St. James the Greater is on July 24-26. Altitude 760 metres; population 17,600; *Hospedaje San Carlos,* G, no sign, ask around for it; local holiday, July 25. Banco Nacional de Desarrollo for exchange.

From *Nandaime,* 21 km. from Jinotepe, altitude 130 metres, a paved road runs N to Granada (bus US$0.25). Nandaime has two interesting churches, El Calvario and La Parroquia (1859-72). About 45 km. beyond Nandaime (US$0.40 by bus) is *Rivas,* a town of 21,000 people. The Costa Rican national hero, the drummer Juan Santamaría, sacrificed his life here in 1856 when setting fire to a building captured by the filibuster William Walker and his men. The town has a lovely old church. (In the dome of the Basilica, see the fresco of the sea battle against the ships of Protestantism and Communism.) Rivas is a good stopping place (rather than Managua) if in transit by land through Nicaragua. The road from the lake port of San Jorge joins this road at Rivas; 11 km. beyond Rivas, at La Virgen on the shore of Lake Nicaragua, it branches S to San Juan del Sur.

Buses to the frontier: every 2 hrs.: 0545 and 0700 good for connections for buses to San José (US$0.20, 1 hr.) (taxis available, about US$4.50), or try to get on the Sirca bus which stops at the Sirca office about 0830, Mon., Wed. and Fri. or Sat. (N.B. Tica bus stops in Rivas, but only to let people off). Bus to Managua, from 0400 (last one 1700), 3 hrs., US$0.80; taxi, US$25. One fast bus to Granada, US$2; other, slower buses, frequent. Regular bus to San Jorge on Lake Nicaragua (taxi to San Jorge, US$0.40).

Hotels *Nicaragua,* on street behind bank on main square, G p.p. (accepts córdobas), E, clean, well-equipped, good restaurant but pricey (cinema next door); *Pensión Primavera,* F, basic; *El Coco,* G, near where bus from frontier stops; *Hospedaje El Mesón,* basic; *Hospedaje Delicia,* on main Managua-border road, G, basic and dirty, friendly; several on Highway, *Hospedaje Lidia,* near Texaco, F, clean, noisy, family-run. (At the Texaco station, Lenín, who speaks English, is very helpful.) *Restaurant Chop Suey* on Parque Central; *Rinconcito Salvadoreño,* on Parque Central, open air, charming.

Exchange Banco Nacional de Desarrollo.

San Juan del Sur is 34 km. from Rivas (regular minibus from market, crowded, 45 mins., US$0.20), 93 from Granada. There are roads from Managua (a 2½-hr. drive) and Granada. Population 4,750. It has a beautiful bay with a sandy beach and some rocky caves reached by walking round the point past the harbour. Best beaches (Playa del Coco, Playa del Tamarindo) are 15 km. away on the road to Ostional. Sunsets here have to be seen to be believed. Check tides with officials at the Customs Office, who will give permission to park motor-caravans and trailers on the wharves if you ask them nicely.

These vehicles may also be parked on Marsella beach, about 5 km. from San Juan; coming S, turn right on entering San Juan, by shrimp-packing plant.

Hotels *Barlovento,* Government-owned on hill above town, B p.p., restaurant, accepts only

US$ for room bill but meals can be paid for in córdobas, tax free shop (US$ only) for toiletries, radios etc. *Estrella*, on Pacific, F, with balconies overlooking the sea, breakfast extra, partitioned walls, take mosquito net, toilet facilities outside, rooms must be shared as they fill up; *Irazú*, one block from beach, some rooms with bath, very run down; *Buengusto*, opposite, F, OK. *Hospedaje Casa No. 28*, 40 metres from beach, near minibus stop for Rivas, G p.p., shared showers, kitchen and laundry facilities, clean, juices and meals available. 2 other *casas de huéspedes* near market.

Restaurants *Salón Siria*, good. *Soya*, vegetarian, good and cheap. AMNLAE (national women's organization) has a good vegetarian restaurant, one block from beach; good *panadería* on same street. Good cafés along the beach for breakfast and drinks. Breakfast and lunch in market. Food in the evening from a stall in street running W from the market; *Lago Azul*, good fish restaurant at N end of bay beyond the river; *Rancho Miravalle*, good for fish. Dollartienda planned.

Exchange Banco Nacional de Desarrollo.

Post Office 2 blocks S along the front from *Hotel Estrella*.

The road reaches the Costa Rican boundary at Peñas Blancas, 37 km. beyond Rivas (no gasoline for sale between border and Rivas; no hotels at the border). It is easy to exchange money on the Costa Rican side of the border, which is closed from 1200-1300 and 1800-0800. Nicaraguan side closes 1200-1300 and 1600-0800. It is 3½-4 hrs. by bus to Managua, 4 to San José, but through journeys are longer because of slow border formalities (last bus to Liberia, 1715). Minibuses run the 4 km. from the Nicaraguan border offices at Sapoá to the Costa Rican border posts every 20 mins., US$1.20, otherwise you must walk or hitch. When the Tica or Sirca bus passes through, the queues are long; if not on a Tica or Sirca bus, arrive at border before 0800 to miss the queues. This border presents no problems for motorists, but remember that it is compulsory to buy insurance in Costa Rica (seepage 1304).

The Caribbean Coast (Autonomous Atlantic Region) was given the status of a self-governing region in 1987. These tropical lowlands have heavy rainfall between May and December. The economy is based on timber, fishing and mining.

Warning Indian guerrilla groups have been active since 1981 and although fighting has been reduced since 1986, movement is restricted for tourists to the urban centres. Overland travel can be dangerous. Permits are needed; see page 1274.

The area, together with about half the coastal area of Honduras, was never colonized by Spain. From 1687 to 1894 it was a British Protectorate known as the Miskito kingdom. It was populated then, as now, by Miskito Indians, but today there is strong African influence. Other groups are Sumu, Rama and Garifuna, as well as Spanish-speaking *mestizos*. English is widely spoken. The Sandinista revolution was met with mistrust, and many Indians engaged in fighting for self-determination. About half the Miskito population fled as refugees to Honduras, but most have returned since 1985.

Bluefields, the most important of Nicaragua's 3 Caribbean ports, gets its name from the Dutch pirate Abraham Blaauwveld. It stands on a lagoon behind the bluff at the mouth of the Bluefields river (Río Escondido), which is navigable as far as Rama (96 km.). From Rama a paved highway runs through Santo Tomás and Juigalpa to Managua, 290 km. away. Bananas, cabinet woods, frozen fish, shrimps and lobsters were the main exports until the hurricane in 1988 (see below). Population 17,700. Flights with state airline Aeronica from Managua (1 hr.) daily (except Sun.), US$80 return (double-check bookings).

Tragically, in October 1988, Huricane Joan detroyed virtually all of Bluefields and it is not recommended to the casual visitor. Rama still has some hotels working, although many houses were swept away when the river rose 16 metres above normal height. The Corn Islands also suffered extensive damage and, although some hotels survived, be prepared for very basic conditions and severe food shortages.

N.B. To visit Bluefields, the Corn Islands and the Atlantic Coast, a permit is required in Managua. See page 1274. Immediately on arrival in Bluefields you must present your permit at Migración.

From Managua to Bluefields Take a bus from Mercado Ivan Montenegro/Oscar Benavides, Managua to *Rama* (pop. 12,000) along the now-completed road (in poor condition near Rama), 6-7 hrs., leaves 0500, to connect with boat to Bluefields at 1300, Sat. or Sun., Tues., Thurs. (both legs US$2, book 24 hrs. in advance). You have to show your permit to get on the boat. Take your own food and drink. On other days 4 or 5 buses from Managua and a fast boat can be hired for US$17 or hitch on a fishing boat. Return from Bluefields: boat at 0500, bus to Managua 1300 (combined tickets available, ticket office at Encab, nr. dock). Or take your car and park it in the compound at the Chinaman's store at Rama (opposite *Hotel Amy*) for US$0.50 a day. Buses back to Managua leave Rama from 0300 onwards. *Hotels Amy* and *Johanna* both F, neither has showers, *Amy* cleaner and quieter, near main jetty.

Corn Islands (Islas del Maíz), in the Caribbean opposite Bluefields, are two small beautiful islands fringed with white coral and slender coconut trees, though sadly many were blown down by the hurricane. The larger is a popular Nicaraguan holiday resort; its surfing and bathing facilities make it ideal for tourists (best months March and April). For fishing (barracuda, etc.), contact Ernie Jenkie (about US$5/hour). If you climb the mountain, wear long trousers, as there are many ticks. The language of the islands is English. There is no regular boat service. It is possible to hitch a lift on a fishing boat, enquire at Inpesca at the port. Air services twice a week, US$16, book well in advance and book return immediately on arrival. Also, check your reservation continually; there is a waiting list and your chances depend on the size of the plane (either 22- or 26-seater). Return flights to Bluefields at 0930; on Wed. to Managua, US$80; timetable seems to change weekly, so check. Local industries: coconut oil, lobsters, and shrimp-freezing plants.

Hotels and Restaurants *Isleño*, F, Government-owned, beach huts, clean, good, running water (except afternoons), rec., restaurant; *Residencia Bryan*, F, with shower, clean, friendly, meals on request; *Hotel de la Punta*, F; *Marisol*, F; one can find rooms for about US$2 (rec. is Miss Florence's house—*Casa Blanca*—at Playa Coco). The chief problem in all the hotels is rats, which may not be dangerous, but neither are they pleasant. Miss Maree's house, near airstrip, for good food. Sally Beaches, US$1 per meal. Doña Quita's *comedor* on the quay. Good restaurant next to *Coco Playa*. Ask around for where meals are available. Try banana porridge and sorrel drink (red, and ginger-flavoured). There is a severe shortage of food, water and most drinks (except rum). Dollars are widely used and there is a dollartienda. In general, the islands are expensive. Disco opp. airport office; also *Artistas*, nicer.

The best beach for swimming is Long Beach on Long Bay; walk across the island from Playa Coco.

Boat Mon., Wed., Fri. from Bluefields at 0600 to Laguna de las Perlas, US$5, 5 hrs.; permission needed from Migración in Bluefields, may be hard to obtain. Army launches take passengers for free. One fairly small *pensión*, private lodging, discotheque, electricity.

At El Bluff, on the headland opposite Bluefields (regular boats from market, US$0.50, 15 mins.), a deep-sea port is under construction. There are beaches nearby. San Juan del Norte on the Costa Rican border has been destroyed and is now a military base. Visits are not possible to the region S of Bluefields.

Puerto Cabezas (Bilwi in local language) is N of the Río Grande. Population: 22,000. There are air services daily (except Thur. and Sun.) at 0800 from Managua (US$95 return). Permit needed. Aeronica flies from Bluefields on Thurs.; every fortnight there is a cargo boat from Bluefields. The port is run down and heavily militarized; visitors are not allowed outside the town without special invitation. There are severe food shortages. At Bocana is a nice beach with a fresh water lagoon behind.

Hotels and Restaurants *Hospedaje Rivera* is better than *Descanso del Viajero* which is filthy and full of mosquitoes. Several restaurants: *Atlántico* (best); Doña Sergia opposite does good, cheap meals; *Ma Weh*; *Linda Vista*. 3 lively discos, the best being *Scorpio* and *Blue Beach*.

Exchange Banco Nacional de Desarrollo.

Note The dialogue between government and Indian guerrillas means there are often armed guerrillas in the streets of Puerto Cabezas. Roads outside town are frequently mined; there is no access to the Honduran border, nor to the mining towns of Rosita, Siuna and Bonanza. A Nicaraguan press card may gain access to these areas.

THE ECONOMY

Nicaragua's economy showed a fairly stable annual growth rate over the two decades up to 1977, despite sharp fluctuations from year to year as agricultural production and world commodity prices varied. The economy is based on agriculture, principal export items being cotton, coffee, sugar, beef, seafood and bananas. The Government is encouraging a diversification of exports, and exports of tobacco and other agricultural products are gaining in importance. At present agriculture constitutes 24% of gdp but employs 48% of the economically active population and is responsible for by far the largest proportion of exports. Land reform has been actively undertaken by the Sandinistas. In the 1970s however, substantial industrialization developed, mainly through foreign investment. Main industries are food processing (sugar, meat, shrimps), textiles, wood, chemical and mineral products. There are few mineral resources in Nicaragua: although gold, copper and silver are mined, they are of little importance to the overall economy.

Since the late 1970s gdp has fallen, starting with a decline of 29% in 1979, although there have been a few years of growth. The huge variations have been caused by guerrilla insurgency, fluctuations in Central American Common Market trade, floods, drought and changing commodity prices. Growth has usually been led by agriculture when weather, international prices and political conditions have been favourable.

Inflation, which had been traditionally low, has been a problem since the 1972 earthquake; it rose to 84.3% in 1979 as a result of the civil war, moderating to an average of 30% in 1980-84. As an effect of insurgency and other difficulties, the rate shot up to an estimated 750% in 1986, 1,200% in 1987 and 24,000% in 1988. In 1988 a new currency was introduced as part of an anti-inflation package which realigned prices of the dollar and basic goods, but neither this nor subsequent economic packages succeeded in controlling hyper-inflation; at the time of going to press the cost of US$1 had risen by 68,000% since the new currency's introduction. Nicaragua is dependent upon foreign aid, which has averaged US$600m a year since 1980, of which the USSR is believed to have granted nearly half. The EEC and Canada are the other major donors. There have been no new investment projects for several years and consumption fell by 42% in 1984-86. The government aims to manage carefully the distribution and rationing of scarce resources and increase production and productivity, but until peace is firmly established, inflation and other economic problems will continue and the black market will persist. Nicaragua's foreign debt, including arrears, amounts to some US$7bn, but reduced foreign exchange earnings in the mid-1980s (partly because of the US blockade) made it impossible for the government to service the debt.

	1961-70 (av)	1971-80 (av)	1981-85 (av)	1986-88 (av)(e)
Gdp growth (1980 prices)	6.9%	1.1%	1.2%	-2.7%
Inflation	n.a.	17.8% (a)	54.4%	12,617%
Exports (fob) US$m	133	436	406	242
Cotton	46	99	110	46
Meat	12	46	23	8
Coffee	22	105	132	125
Imports (fob) US$m	130	468	803	820
Current account balance US$m (cum)	-280	-976	-3,064	-2,620

(a) = 1973-80

INFORMATION FOR VISITORS

Air Services   From London: British Airways, Virgin Atlantic, Continental or Pan Am to Miami and connect to Taca for Managua, via San Salvador; Taca also flies from Houston, New Orleans and Los Angeles; Lacsa flies from Miami. Aeronica flies to Mexico City direct, Guatemala City, San Salvador, San José and Panama City; Taca to Belize City as well as San Salvador; Sahsa flies to Tegucigalpa, and Copa flies to Guatemala City, San José, San Salvador and Panama. From Europe, with Iberia to Managua on Tues., or connect with KLM in San José. Aeroflot and Cubana (once a week) fly to Havana, and Aeroflot continues via Shannon to Moscow. Aeronica flies from Managua to Puerto

Cabezas, Bluefields and the gold-mining centres of Siuna and Bonanza (when permitted); also to the Corn Islands. All flight tickets purchased by non-residents must be paid in US dollars.

All passengers have to pay a sales tax of US$5 on all tickets issued in and paid for in Nicaragua; a transport tax of 1% on all tickets issued in Nicaragua to any destination; and an airport tax of US$10 on all departing passengers (except on Aeroflot and Cubana flights).

By Sea   There are good shipping services from the United Kingdom to Cristóbal (14 to 16 days), including those of the PSNC and Royal Mail Lines (no passengers). The port of Corinto, on the Pacific Coast, is served by vessels from Cristóbal, and also from San Francisco and Los Angeles.

Both the Royal Netherlands Steamship Company and the local Mamenic Line run monthly services from Europe to San Juan del Sur, Corinto or Puerto Sandino: the former from Amsterdam and the latter from Antwerp. The Mamenic Line also serves most other central and north American ports.

Documents   Visitors must have a passport with 6 months validity (at least), and proof of US$200 (or equivalent in córdobas) in cash or cheques for their stay in the country (according to the Nicaraguan Consulate in London—but see below). No visa is required by nationals of Central American countries, USA, Canada, Belgium, Denmark, Liechtenstein, Luxembourg, Netherlands, Norway, Finland, Spain, Sweden, Switzerland or the United Kingdom for a 90-day stay. Citizens of all other countries need a visa, which should be bought before arriving at the border, is valid for arrival within 30 days, and for a stay of up to 30 days (90 days if working in an International Brigade); it costs US$25; 6 months validity on passport, 2 passport photographs and an onward ticket are required. Visas can take 24 hrs. to be processed. Extensions are difficult to obtain. W. Germans can obtain visas (DM 70) from Generalkonsulät von Nicaragua, 2 Hamburg, P.O. Box 32 33 54, or in Central America. Ensure that your visa runs from the day you enter the country, not from the day of issue: ask the Generalkonsulät to give a written statement, in Spanish, to this effect. Commercial travellers should carry a document from their firm accrediting them as such. Only those visitors who have no tourist cards and require visas for entry need an exit permit. 72-hour transit visas cost US$20, from embassies, but apparently not at borders. A transit visa, obtained at a land border, cannot be converted into a full visa within the country. An air ticket can be cashed if not used, especially if issued by a large company, but bus tickets are sometimes difficult to encash. It is reported, however, that the Nicaraguan Embassy in a neighbouring country is empowered to authorize entry without the outward ticket, if the traveller has enough money to buy the ticket. Also, if you have a visa to visit another Central American country, you are unlikely to be asked to show an outward ticket (this applies to all Central American countries: be two visas ahead!). An exit stamp costing US$10 is required for visitors who have stayed over 30 days in the country.

In 1983, a regulation was introduced stating that all visitors, whether arriving by air or land, *must* change US$60 into córdobas at the official rate (US$25 for transit-visa holders). If turned back from Honduras or Costa Rica for any reason, get your Nicaraguan exit stamp cancelled, not a new entry stamp, otherwise you will have to change another US$60. Motorists and motorcyclists must pay US$20 in cash on arrival at the border (bicyclists pay US$2); allow plenty of time for border facilities (especially when coming from Honduras)—average is 4 hours—because vehicles not cleared by 1700 are held at customs overnight. Make sure you get all the correct stamps on arrival, or you will encounter all sorts of problems once inside the country. You will also be asked on arrival to show that you have US$200 to cover your stay in Nicaragua and fill in a declaration on the amount of money and valuables you are bringing in. Hotel bills must be paid in dollars in Managua and a few more expensive places elsewhere.

Warning   Nicaraguan customs and border formalities can take up to 8 hours (but sometimes much less).

Customs   Duty-free import of ½ kg. of tobacco products, 3 litres of alcoholic drinks and 1 large bottle (or 3 small bottles) of perfume is permitted.

Much detailed commercial information is given in "Hints to Exporters: Nicaragua", obtainable on application to the Dept. of Trade, Export Services Division, Sanctuary Buildings, 16-20 Great Smith Street, London SW1P 3DB.

Motoring   Low octane gasoline costs US$1.50 a US gallon (shortages frequent). Cars will be fumigated on entry, for which there is a US$2 charge. For motorcyclists, the wearing of crash helmets is compulsory. Petrol is only available with coupons, which are obtained at Petronic offices in all cities and at borders (open Mon.-Fri. 0830-1630; service stations close at 1700-1800). Beware when driving at night, the national shortage of spare parts means that many cars have no lights.

Climate and Dress   There is a wide range of climates. According to altitude, average annual temperatures vary between 15°C and 35°C. Mid-day temperatures at Managua range from 30° to 36°C, but readings of 38° are not uncommon from March to May, or of 40° in January and February in the West. It can get quite cold, especially after rain, in the Caribbean lowlands.

Maximum daily humidity ranges from 90% to 100%. Dress is informal; business men often shed jackets and wear sports shirts, but shorts are never worn. The wearing of trousers is perfectly OK for women. The dry season runs from December to May, and the wettest months are usually June and October. Best time for a business visit: from March to June, but December and January are the pleasantest months.

Warnings Visitors to Nicaragua must carry their passports (or a photocopy) with them at all times. Border officials do not like army-type clothing on travellers, and may confiscate green or khaki rucksacks (backpacks), parkas, canteens. They also inspect all luggage thoroughly on entering and leaving Nicaragua. Do not photograph any military personnel or installations.

Pickpocketing and bagslashing has increased greatly in Managua, especially in crowded places, and on buses throughout the country.

The whole of the Atlantic Coast, almost all the Honduran and Costa Rican border zones and the Solentiname Islands are **"special regions"** (i.e. fighting is possible). To visit them (and this includes the towns of Bluefields, the Corn Islands, Puerto Cabezas and San Carlos), you must apply to Turnica, Ho Chi Minh Boulevard, 2 blocks from Plaza España, taking your passport (or photocopy), entry stamp and visitor's card; the special permit takes 3 days to issue and must be used within 15 days. It costs US$8, payable in dollars only. To visit places outside towns in these regions, you must apply to the local Migración office.

The standard form of address is "compañer-o/-a", rather than "señor/-a".

Working in Nicaragua Volunteer work in Nicaragua is a good way of meeting the people. Most international brigades are coordinated through the Comité Nicaragüense de Solidaridad entre los Pueblos (CNSP, near Plaza España, Managua), but this office is unlikely to find work for individual travellers. Better to go to Centro Sandinista de Trabajadores (CST, Barrio Martha Quezada, Managua) or organizations such as local Comités de Defensa Sandinista (CDS), UNEN (the students' organization), UNAG (the agricultural union), AMNLAE (women's organization) or Irena (Instituto Nicaragüense de Recursos Naturales y del Ambiente). If you wish to help with harvests, go to Matagalpa for coffee, León for cotton, or Chinandega for sugar cane. Alternatively, just ask on the gringo grapevine or at the Thursday morning demonstration outside the US Embassy (0700-0800). Another option is to teach English, since there is a great shortage of teachers of the language. In all cases, a letter of introduction from an appropriate political or professional organization at home is a good idea.

Internal Transport Hitchhiking is widely accepted—offer to pay ("pedir un ride"), even with military vehicles. Local buses are the cheapest in Central America, but are extremely crowded owing to a lack of vehicles and fuel. Baggage that is loaded on to the roof or in the luggage compartment is charged for, usually twice the rate for passengers.

Health The usual tropical precautions about food and drink. Tap water is reasonably safe but avoid uncooked vegetables and peeled fruit. Intestinal parasites abound; if requiring treatment, take a stool sample to a government laboratory before going to a doctor. Malaria risk especially in the wet season; take regular prophylaxis. Treatment in Centros de Salud, medical laboratories and dispensaries is free, even for foreigners. Private dentists are better-equipped than those in the national health service (but no better trained).

Food There is still a food shortage in some parts of the country, and it can be difficult to find items such as eggs and rice outside Managua. Sugar and salt are rationed to one packet each per purchase. Note the government-owned *Colectivo de Soja* which encourages the use of soya as an alternative source of protein; vegetarian restaurants of this chain in San Juan del Sur, Rivas, Masaya, Managua, León, Granada and Estelí.

Tipping in Nicaragua: 10% of bill in hotels and restaurants (many restaurants add 10% service and 15% tax to bills); US$0.50 per bag for porters; no tip for taxi drivers.

Hours of Business 0800-1200, 1430-1730 or 1800. Banks: 0830-1200, 1400-1600, but 0830-1130 on Sat. Government offices are not normally open on Sat. in Managua, or in the afternoon anywhere.

Standard Time Six hours behind GMT.

Cost of living Since the realignment of prices and revaluation of the córdoba in February 1988, a *comida corriente* costs between US$3 and US$5, including drinks, a coke US$1.50, a beer

US$2-3. These economic measures have made Nicaragua a much more expensive country to visit than hitherto, although the rapid decline in the currency's value still makes it very cheap for anyone with US dollars. There are shortages of various items such as toilet paper, toothpaste, batteries and film. A 15% tax is levied on all hotel and restaurant bills, nevertheless, outside Managua, hotel accommodation is extremely cheap. An extra 10% service charge is often added to restaurant bills.

Currency The unit is the new córdoba (C$), divided into 100 centavos. In February 1988 the córdoba was revalued at C$10 to the US$; by May 1989 it had fallen to C$6,800=US$1.

Exchange controls are fairly stringent. The **black market** for exchange, which is illegal and therefore dangerous, can be found with difficulty in Managua, in **Ciudad Jardín**, or in Granada. Money changers are called *coyotes* (but some are government officials). Visa card is hardly accepted anywhere (in banks only), but Master Card is used and, to a lesser extent, Cred-o-Matic and Diners Club.

Remember, when changing money at the border, that hotel bills in Managua, and in larger hotels outside, are in most cases charged in dollars; so do not overstock with córdobas.

Weights and Measures The metric system is official, but in domestic trade local terms are in use; for example, the *medio*, which equals a peck (2 dry gallons), and the *fanega*, of 24 *medios*. These are not used in foreign trade. The principal local weight is the *arroba*=25 lb. and the *quintal* of 101.417 English lb. Random variety of other measures in use include US gallon for petrol, US quart and pint for liquids; *vara* (33 ins.) for short distances and the lb. for certain weights.

Mail By Sea: from the UK to Nicaragua is sent via Panama, and takes 4 to 5 weeks. There are delays in forwarding between the western ports and the interior owing to poor communications. Air-mail to Europe takes 2-4 weeks, from Europe 7-10 days. Sea mail must be passed through customs at Telcor building, Managua.

Telegraph and Telephone lines are owned by the Government (Telcor). Rather unreliable automatic telephone services between Managua, León, Chinandega and Corinto. Plenty of public telephones in Managua of the Brazilian "big-ear" type (they take 1 córdoba coins). There are wireless transmitting stations at Managua, Bluefields and Cabo Gracias a Dios, and private stations at Puerto Cabezas, El Gallo, and Río Grande.

Telephone calls from Managua to Europe: in any major town at the Telcor office, open 0700-2200. International phone calls are usually paid in córdobas, but dollars may be asked for in Managua; price increases, though steep, have not kept pace with currency decline and calls are therefore very cheap in dollar terms, e.g. 15 mins. to US, US$2.50. You may have to wait a long time for a line, except for early in the morning on weekdays. Collect calls to the USA are easy ("a pagarse allá"), also possible to Europe.

Telex As with telephones, prices have been greatly increased.

Press Managua: *La Prensa* (anti-government), *Nuevo Diario* (the best—close to government line). *La Barricada*, official organ of the Sandinista Front (has a fortnightly international edition). León: *El Centroamericano. La Gaceta* is the official gazette. *Ya Veremos*, monthly, covering international subjects. *Revista Conservadora* is the best monthly magazine. Other magazines: *Envío* (monthly, English and Spanish editions, Jesuit); *Pensamiento Propio* (current affairs, monthly); *Soberanía* (Nicaraguan affairs, Spanish/English bilingual). *El Pez y la Serpiente* is a monthly magazine devoted to the arts, poetry and literature.

Public Holidays January 1: New Year's Day. March or April: Thursday of Holy Week and Good Friday. May 1: Labour Day. July 19: Revolution of 1979. September 14: Battle of San Jacinto. September 15: Independence Day. November 2: All Souls' Day (Día de los Muertos). December 7 and 8: Immaculate Conception (Purísima). December 25: Christmas Day.

Businesses, shops and restaurants all close for most of Holy Week; many companies also close down during the Christmas-New Year period. Holidays which fall on a Sunday are taken the following Monday. Local holidays are given under the towns.

Broadcasting There are about 50 radio stations, and 2 television channels of the Sistema Sandinista de Televisión.

In addition to those travellers listed in the general Central America section we should like to thank the following for new information on Nicaragua: Tina Borgmann and Mette Christopherson (Copenhagen), Gunter Frentz (Miami), Chr. Stuven Hellmuth (Roskilde, Dmk.), Nanna Lyby (Farum, Dmk.), Steve Morris (St John, NB), Charlie Nurse (Twickenham), Jens Stockmarr and Dorte Dahl Johansen (Hellerup, Dmk.).

COSTA RICA

COSTA RICA is the smallest but one—El Salvador—of the Central American republics, and only Panama has fewer inhabitants, but it is known throughout Latin America as the continent's purest democracy. The Army was abolished in 1949, though it should be stressed that there is a very efficient-looking khaki-clad Civil Guard. Costa Rica has the highest standard of living in Central America, the fastest population growth and the greatest degree of economic and social advance. Area, 51,100 square km. Population in 1988 was 2.8 million—a density of 55 to the square kilometre.

Costa Rica lies between Nicaragua and Panama, with coastlines on both the Caribbean (212 km.) and the Pacific (1,016 km.). The distance between sea and sea is from 119 to 282 km. A low, thin line of hills between Lake Nicaragua and the Pacific is prolonged into northern Costa Rica, broadening and rising into high and rugged mountains in the centre and S. The highest peak, Chirripó Grande, SE of the capital, reaches 3,820 metres. Within these highlands are certain structural depressions; one of them, the Meseta Central, is of paramount importance. To the SW this basin is rimmed by the comb of the Cordillera; at the foot of its slopes, inside the basin, are the present capital, San José, and the old capital, Cartago. NE of these cities about 30 km. away, four volcano cones rise from a massive common pedestal. From NW to SE these are Poás (2,704 metres), Barba (2,906 metres), Irazú (3,432 metres), and Turrialba (3,339 metres). Irazú and Poás are intermittently active. Between the Cordillera and the volcanoes is the Meseta Central: an area of 5,200 square km. at an altitude of between 900 and 1,800 metres, where two-thirds of the population live. The north-eastern part of the basin is drained by the Reventazón through turbulent gorges into the Caribbean; the Río Grande drains the western part of it into the Pacific.

There are lowlands on both coasts. The Nicaraguan lowland along the Río San Juan is continued into Costa Rica, wide and sparsely inhabited as far as Puerto Limón. A great deal of this land, particularly near the coast, is swampy; SE of Puerto Limón the swamps continue as far as Panama in a narrow belt of lowland between sea and mountain.

The Gulf of Nicoya, on the Pacific side, thrusts some 65 km. inland; its waters separate the mountains of the mainland from the 900-metre high mountains of the narrow Nicoya Peninsula. From a little to the S of the mouth of the Río Grande de Tárcoles, a lowland savanna stretches NW past the port of Puntarenas and along the whole north-eastern shore of the Gulf towards Nicaragua.

Below the Río Grande the savanna is pinched out by mountains, but there are other lowlands to the S. From Puerto Quepos, built by the United Fruit Company (now United Brands), 188 km. of railway run through banana-growing lowlands, which are not now as productive as they were. Small quantities of African palm and cacao are now being grown in these lowlands. In the far S there are swampy lowlands again at the base of the Peninsula of Osa and between the Golfo Dulce and the borders of Panama. Here there are 12,000 hectares planted to bananas; 317 km. of railway run to the United Brands banana port of Golfito. The Río General runs through a southern structural depression almost as large as the Meseta Central; this is now being occupied.

Altitude, as elsewhere in Central America, determines the climate, but the *tierra templada* and the *tierra fría* start at about 300 metres lower on the Pacific than on the Atlantic side. The Pacific side is the drier, with patches of savanna among the deciduous forest; the Atlantic side has heavy rainfall— 300 days a year of it—and is covered far up the slopes with tropical forest: about two-fifths

of Costa Rica is forested. On the Cordillera Talamanca, the average temperature is below 16°C.

National Parks   Tourists will particularly enjoy the many well-kept and well-guarded national parks and nature reserves which protect some samples of the extraordinarily varied Costa Rican ecosystems. Some of the last patches of dry tropical forest, for instance, can be found in the Santa Rosa National Park, and other parks protect the unique cloud forest.

The first step is to visit the **Servicio de Parques Nacionales (SPN)** in San José (Calle 17 y Av. 9; write in advance to Apartado 10094, or T 33-50-55), to get permits if necessary. Persistence may be sometimes needed to get permits, particularly in the case of the Corcovado park, where visitors' facilities are officially considered inadequate. To contact park personnel by radio link, T 33-54-73.

Bird watchers and butterfly lovers have long flocked to Costa Rica to see some of the 900 species of birds (the whole of the United States counts only about 800 species) and untold varieties of butterflies. All of these can be best seen in the parks, together with monkeys, deer, coyotes, armadillos, anteaters, turtles, coatimundis, raccoons, snakes, wild pigs, and, more rarely, wild cats and tapirs. Bird lists can be purchased in San José from the Organization for Tropical Studies (in San Pedro, near the University; take the "San Pedro" bus from Av. 2 and Calle 1 and get off in San Pedro at the church—on the left—, the OTS is 2 blocks S and 3 blocks E); they will have a breakdown by park. You can also get plant and butterfly lists from them, and other valuable natural history information as well. Good field guides are Petersen, *Birds of Mexico* and *Birds of North America*; Ridgely, *Birds of Panama*; Golden Guide, *Birds of North America*; Daniel H.Janzel, *Costa Rican Natural History*; Philip J. de Vries, *Butterflies of Costa Rica*. Cheap maps and all information for the parks are available at the CIDA office of the SPN in Parque Bolívar (the zoo), Av. 11 just E of Calle 7, open Mon.-Fri., 0800-1530 (on Mon. ask zoo guard to let you in as zoo grounds are closed Mon.) The map annex to the SPN office in San José has all the parks marked in the excellent Instituto Geográfico maps, and the latter can be purchased at various places.

Nature guides can be found at The Bookshop in San José, and there is also available an illustrated book, *The National Parks of Costa Rica*, by Mario A. Boza (1986), which gives a good impression of what the different parks are like. (Descriptions of the individual parks will be found in the text.)

Settlement   Costa Rica was discovered in September 1502, during Columbus' last voyage. Rumours of vast gold treasures (which never materialized) led to the name of Costa Rica (the Rich Coast). The Spaniards settled in the Meseta Central, where there were some thousands of sedentary Indian farmers (whose numbers were soon greatly diminished by the diseases brought by the settlers). Cartago was founded in 1563 by Juan Vásquez de Coronado, but there was no expansion until 145 years later, when a small number left Cartago for the valleys of Aserrí and Escazú. They founded Heredia in 1717, and San José in 1737. Alajuela, not far from San José, was founded in 1782. The settlers were growing in numbers (many farmers emigrated from northern Spain) but were still poor and raising subsistence crops only. Independence from Spain was declared in 1821 whereupon Costa Rica, with the rest of Central America, immediately became part of Mexico. This led to a civil war, during which, two years later, the capital was moved from Cartago to San José. After independence, the government sought anxiously for some product which could be exported and taxed for revenue. It was found in coffee, introduced from Cuba in 1808, which Costa Rica was the first of the Central American countries to grow. The Government offered free land to coffee growers, thus building up a peasant landowning class. In 1825 there was a trickle of exports, carried on mule-back to the ports. By 1846 there were ox-cart roads to Puntarenas. By 1850 there was a large flow of coffee to overseas markets: it was greatly increased by the opening of a railway from San José and Cartago to Puerto Limón along the valley of the Reventazón in 1890.

From 1850, coffee prosperity began to affect the country profoundly: the birth rate grew, land for coffee was free, and the peasant settlements started spreading, first down the Río Reventazón as far as Turrialba; then up the slopes of the volcanoes, then down the new railway from San José to the old Pacific port of Puntarenas.

Much of the Caribbean coastland, more especially in the N, is still unoccupied. Bananas were first introduced in 1878; Costa Rica was the first Central American republic to grow them. Labour was brought in from Jamaica to clear the forest and work the plantations. The industry grew and in 1913, the peak year, the Caribbean coastlands provided 11 million bunches for export, but the spread of disease lowered the exports progressively. The United Fruit Company then turned its attentions to the Pacific littoral especially in the S around the port of Golfito. However, although some of the Caribbean plantations were turned over to cacao, *abacá* (Manilla hemp) and African palm, the region has regained its ascendancy over the Pacific littoral as a banana producer (the Standard Fruit Company is an important redeveloper of the region).

On the Pacific coastlands a white minority own the land on the *hacienda* system rejected in the uplands. About 46 % of the people are *mestizos*. To the N, most of the country's cattle come from the large estates of the savannas, and timber is exploited along the northern coast. The mountainous Peninsula of Nicoya is an important source of coffee, maize, rice and beans. Its population has risen sharply. Rainfall is moderate: 1,000 to 2,000 mm. a year, but there is a long dry season which makes irrigation important.

Population In all provinces save Limón over 98 % are whites and *mestizos* but in Limón 33.2 % are blacks and 3.1 % indigenous Indians, of whom only 5,000 survive in the whole country. Although officially protected, the living conditions of the indigenous Indians are very poor. But even in Limón the percentage of blacks is falling: it was 57.1 in 1927. Many of them speak Jamaican English as their native tongue. Some 50 % are urban. Population growth rate is 2.7 %; urban growth rate 4.4 %. Illiteracy, at 10 %, is among the lowest in Latin America. Gdp per capita is US$1,680. Contact with the rural population is easy: the people are friendly and enjoy talking. (The national adjective, *costarricense*, is rather a mouthful: the universal short form is *tico/a*.)

Roads Costa Rica has a total of 29,095 km. of roads. The route of the Pan-American Highway (now wholly paved) is described on page 1299. A new highway is being built from San José to Caldera, a new port on the Gulf of Nicoya which has replaced Puntarenas as the principal Pacific port, and another has been completed from San José via Guápiles and Siquirres to Puerto Limón. Also a new road is being built to improve access to the Pacific beaches, from Playas de Jacó to Puerto Quepos and Puerto Cortés. All 4-lane roads into San José are toll roads (US$0.03-0.10).

Railways There are 1,286 km., all of 1.067-metre gauge; 967 km. are plantation lines—336 km. of the Northern Railway and 631 km. of the United Brands Company. The formerly British-owned Northern (Atlantic) Railway has 525 km.: its main line is between Puerto Limón and San José (166 km.), and it has a branch line (21 km.) between San José and Alajuela. The government-owned Ferrocarril Eléctrico al Pacífico between San José and Puntarenas has 132 km. of track; this line has been lengthened by the new branch to Caldera. New track has been laid in the Río Frío banana plantation zone; these trains are electric. Plans exist for electrification of the entire Atlantic railway.

Constitution and Government

Legislative power is vested in a Legislative Assembly of 57 deputies, elected for four years. Executive authority is in the hands of the President, elected for the same term by popular vote. Men and women over 20 have the right to vote. Voting is secret, direct and free. The President from 1986 (until May 1990) is Sr. Oscar Arias Sánchez of the Liberación Nacional party (Social Democrat). He won the Nobel Peace Prize in 1987 for the Central American Peace Plan, drawn up by him, and signed by all five Central American republics in that year. Presidential and legislative elections are due to be held in February 1990.

Main Towns

San José, with a population estimated at over one million, stands in a broad, fertile valley at an altitude of 1,150 metres, which produces coffee and sugar-cane. It was founded in 1737 and is a pleasant mixture of traditional Spanish and modern. The climate is excellent, though the evenings can be chilly. The lowest and highest temperatures run from 15° to 26°C. Slight earthquake shocks are frequent. Rainy season: May to November. Other months are dry.

Streets cross one another at right-angles. Avenidas run E-W; the Calles N-S. The three main street are Av. Central, Av. 2 and the intersecting Calle Central: the business centre is here. The best shops are along Av. Central. It is best not to take a car into San José between 0700 and 2000; traffic is very heavy. Many of the narrow streets are heavily polluted with exhaust fumes. Seven blocks of the

Av. Central, from Banco Central running east to Plaza de la Cultura, are closed to traffic.

Avenidas to the N of Av. Central are given odd numbers; those to the S even numbers. Calles to the W of Calle Central are even-numbered; those to the E odd-numbered. The Instituto Costarricense de Turismo has an excellent map of the city, marking all the important sights and business houses. **N.B.** Few buildings have numbers, so find out the nearest cross-street when getting directions (200 metres means 2 blocks).

Sightseeing   Many of the most interesting public buildings are near the intersection of Avenida Central and Calle Central. The Teatro Nacional (1897)—marble staircases, statuary, frescoes and foyer decorated in gold with Venetian plate mirrors—is just off Av. Central, on Calle 3 (US$0.75 to look around). Functions (ballet, concerts, etc.) take place most Tuesdays. Closed on Sundays. It has a good coffee bar. Nearby is Plaza de la Cultura, Av. Central, C. 3/5. The Palacio Nacional (Av. Central, Calle 15) is where the Legislative Assembly meets; any visitor can attend the debates. Along Calle Central is Parque Central, with a bandstand in the middle among trees (bands play on Sun. mornings). To the E of the park is the Cathedral; to the N are the Raventos and Palace theatres, interesting; to the S are the Rex Theatre and a branch of the Banco Nacional. N of Av. Central, on Calle 2, is the Unión Club, the principal social centre of the country. Opposite it is the General Post and Telegraph Office. The National Museum, with a good collection of precolumbian antiquities, is in the reconstructed Vista Buena barracks, E along Av. Central (open 0900 to 1700; closed Mons.). Facing it is the new Plaza de la Democracia, constructed to mark the November 1989 centenary of Costa Rican democracy. Two blocks N of the National Museum is Parque Nacional, with a grandiloquent bronze monument representing the five Central American republics ousting the filibuster William Walker (see Nicaraguan chapter) and the abolition of slavery in Central America. There is also a statue donated by the Sandinista Government of Nicaragua to the people of Costa Rica. To the N of the park is the National Library.

Still further N is Parque Bolívar, now turned into a recreation area, with zoo (sloths in the trees), entrance, US$0.30. Along Av. 3, to the W of Parque Nacional, are the four gardens of Parque Morazán, with another bandstand at the centre. On Sun. there is an art market here. A little to the NE, Parque España—cool, quiet, and intimate—has for neighbours the Casa Amarilla (Yellow House), seat of the Ministry of Foreign Affairs, and the Edificio Metálico, which houses several of the main schools. In Parque Carrillo opposite the church of La Merced is a huge carved granite ball brought from the archaeological site at Palmar Norte.

The attractive Paseo Colón continues the Av. Central W to the former La Sabana airport (now developed as a sports centre, which is worth visiting) with a colonial-style building with frescoes of Costa Rican life in the Salón Dorado, on the upper floor. Further W is La Sabana, which has the National Stadium, seating 20,000 spectators at (mainly) football matches, basketball, volleyball and tennis courts, a running track, lake and swimming pool.

Local Holiday   December 28 to 31. Festivities last from December 18, with dances, horse shows and much confetti-throwing in the crowded streets. Also parades during Easter week in the streets.

Warning   Pickpockets are on the increase in San José, especially in the centre, in the market and on buses—the same applies throughout the country; be careful. We have also received reports of travellers (in particular backpackers) being detained or harassed by the police in a drive against illegal immigration, although few explanations are given. You must carry your passport with you at all times and make sure your papers are in order. To report theft: Policía Judicial-Detectives, Av. 6, C. 17/19.

Hotels

	Address	Tel.	US$ Single	Price Double	Range
Alameda	C. 12 Av. Ctl	23-63-33	18	22	C
Ambassador	C. 26 P. Colón	21-81-55	30-35	40-45	B
L'Ambiance	C. 13 Av. 9-11	22-67-02	62	85	A-L

*Amstel**	C.7 Av.1	22-46-22	28-31	33-36	B
Aurola Holiday Inn†	C.5 Av.5	33-72-33	90	100	L
Balmoral	C.7 Av.Ctl	22-50-22	42	51	A
Bougainvillea‡†	Barrio Tournon	33-66-22	35-45	40-50	B-A
Cariari‡	Near Airport	39-00-22	95	105	L
Club Paso Fino‡	Santa Ana	49-14-66	18	25	C
Corobici†‡	Sabana Norte	32-81-22	75	85	A
Gran Hotel Costa Rica	C.3 Av.2	21-40-00	39-42	52-57	A
D'Galah‡	San Pedro	34-17-43	18-23	23-28	C
Diplomat	C.6 Av.Ctl-2	21-81-33	12-21	18-24	D-C
Europa†	C.Ctl Av.3-5	22-12-22	36-46	45-57	B-A
Royal Dutch	C.4 Av.Ctl-2	22-10-66	41-43	52-54	A
Royal Garden	C.Ctl. Av.2	57-00-23	30	35	B
Sheraton Herradura‡†	Near Airport	39-00-33	80-90	90-98	L
Irazú††	La Uruca	32-48-11	41-48	47-57	A
La Gran Vía	C.3 Av.Ctl	22-77-37	25	33	C
Posada Pegasus‡†	S.Antonio de Escazú	28-41-96	14-17	19-23	D
Plaza	C.2 Av.Ctl	22-55-33	20	30	C
President	C.7-9 Av.Ctl	22-30-22	40	50	C
Talamanca	C.8-10 Av.2	33-50-33	21	24	C
Torremolinos†	C.40 Av.5	22-52-66	45	50	C
Tennis Club‡	Sabana Sur	32-12-66	36-54	45-62	B-A

Apartotels (With kitchen, etc.)

Apartotel San José	C.17 Av.2	22-04-55	28	35	C-B
Apartotel Los Yoses‡†	Los Yoses	25-00-33	28-36	32-40	C
Apartotel Conquistador‡†	Los Yoses	25-30-22	26	31	C
Apartotel Castilla‡	C.24 Av.2-4	22-21-13	25	30	C
Apartotel Lamm§	C.15 Av.1	21-49-20	26	29	C
Apartotel Ramgo‡	Sabana Sur	32-38-23	25	33	C
Apartotel María Alexandra‡	Escazú	28-15-07	35	35	B
Apartotel Napoleon	C.40 Av.5	23-32-52	25-28	30-33	C
Apartotel Villas de Cariari‡	Cariari	39-26-72	75 per day		
			900 per month		
Apartotel Res. de Golf‡	Cariari	39-10-20	70 per day		
			1,200 per month		
Gran Hotel Costa Rica Anexo	C.9 Av.1	21-72-72	275-440 per month		

* Food recommended, book in advance †Swimming pool
‡ Out of town § 10 % discount given for monthly stays

These rates are per day, without food and exclusive of 13.3 % tax (April 1989). The *Gran Hotel Costa Rica* has been reported as noisy, but otherwise rec. The *Ambassador* is rec., clean, modern, TV and phone in rooms, travel agency next door, restaurants and cinemas opposite; *Bougainvillea* (rooms facing the street are noisy from traffic) and *Amstel* also rec. The *Herradura Sheraton*, on the other hand, has had some unfavourable reports, about reliability in particular.

Don Carlos, C. 9, Av. 7/9, T 21-67-07, B with bath and breakfast, clean, comfortable, convenient; *Park*, C. 2/4, Av. 4, B, clean, with bar (T 21-69-44); *Ritz*, C. Central, Av. 8 and 10, T 224103, D with bath and hot water, friendly, manager helpful, good breakfast, 2nd-hand book exchange, clothes washing facilities, rec.; *Pensión Centro Continental*, Av. 8-10, C. Central (T 33-17-31), E without bath, Japanese hospitality, clean, friendly, laundry, helpful, coffee available, rec.; *Boston*, C. Central, Av. 8 (T 21-05-63), E, with or without bath, good, but noisy; *Roma*, C. 14, Av. Central and 1, T 23-21-79, uphill from Alajuela bus station, E, clean, safe, good value but windowless rooms; *Johnson*, C. 8, Av. Central (T 23-76-33), E, clean, restaurant and bar, popular with Peace Corps; *Napoleón*, C. 6, Av. 3-5 (T 21-06-94), E, bath, friendly, small rooms, free safe parking for motorcycles; *Lido*, C.3, Av. 8-10, F, clean, laundry, quiet; *Residencial Balboa*, Av. 10, C.6, F, safe, cold shower, thin walls, basic, cheap.

Pensiones are: *Araica*, Av. 2 No. 1125, T 22-52-33, F without bath, clean, dark, thin walls, friendly; *Americana*, C. 4, Av. 2, F, without bath, clean, friendly, luggage store, washing facilities; *Reforma Hilton*, C. 11, No. 105, E with bath, T 21-97-05, restaurant; *Moreno*, C. 12, Av. 6-8, T 21-71-36, E with bath. *Astoria*, Av. 7, No. 749, T 21-21-74, F, clean, hot showers, uncomfortable beds, thin walls, noisy; *Poás*, Av. 7, Calles 3-5, F, friendly, hot water, laundry facilities, *soda* attached; *Managua*, C. 8, Av. 1/3, F, small rooms, cold showers, rec.; *Boruca*, C. 14, Av. 1/3, T 23-00-16, F without bath, clean, laundry service, popular with Peace Corps, restaurant; *Musoc*, C. 16, Av. 3/5 (T 22-94-37), E, with private bath (F without), very clean, hot water, luggage stored, near to (and somewhat noisy because of) bus stations, but rec.; *San José*, C. 14 and Av. 5, E, with shower, clean, friendly, near bus station; *Asia*, C. 11 No. 63N (between Avs. Central and 1), T 23-38-93, E, clean, friendly, but paper-thin walls, lots of noise from rapid turnover, hot showers, Chinese-run, English spoken; *América*, Av. 7, C. 4, F, clean, good value; *Corobicí*, Av. 1, between C. 10 and 12, F, clean, cold showers; *Pensión Otoya*, C. Central, Av. 5-7 (T 21-39-25) F, pleasant, popular with foreigners, English spoken; *Pensión Familiar* (also called *Hotel Delca*), Av. 6, C. 6-8, F, bath, clean, good value; *Rialto*, Av. 5 and C. 2, F, bath, clean, hot water, noisy, good value.

Near Tica Bus terminal are: *Illimani*, C. 9/11, Av. 2, T 22-06-07, F, friendly, will change money; *Avenida 2*, Av. 2, C. 9-11, F, clean, friendly, shared hot showers; *Nicaragua*, Av. 2, No. 1167, F, clean, friendly, safe to leave luggage, partitioned rooms. *Ticalinda No. 1*, Av. 2, No. 553, F, friendly, noisy, very dirty, little privacy, cheap laundry, good information, "gringo" place, often full; *Ticalinda No. 2*, C. 1, No. 858, Avs. 8 and 10, G, shared rooms, quieter but no food (neither *Ticalinda* is signed). There are several hotels near the various markets, such as the *España*, Av. 3/5, C. 8, F, run by a Spanish family; *Comerciante* annex (C. 10, Av. 3/5) and *Valencia* (C. 8, Av. 1, T 21-33-47, in F range) which are quite clean. Cheaper hotels usually have only wooden partitions for walls, so they are noisy. Also, they often rent only by the hour. *Toruma Youth Hostel*, Av. Central between Calles 29 and 33, spacious, kitchen, clean, rec., hot water not always available, F p.p. more expensive for those who do not hold International Student Identity Card (which can be purchased here); music, free for guests, on Fri. and Sat. nights; a good place for meeting other travellers to arrange group travel (ask for Fred Morris, editor of *Meso America* journal). Students are taken in as guests in private houses at low rates.

Electric Current   110, 60 cycles, A.C.; (U.S. flat-pin plugs).

Trailer Park Belén, in San Antonio de Belén, 2 km. W of intersection at Cariari and San Antonio, 4 km. from airport, US$60/month, US$4/day, American-owned, shade, hot showers, laundry, good bus service to San José.

Restaurants Apart from the hotels, the best ones are the *Bastille*, French type (limited choice), on Paseo Colón; *Ile de France*, C. 7, Av. Central and 2 (T 22-42-41), good French chef; next door is *La Hacienda Steak House*, expensive but good; *Salón París*, Av. 3, C.1/3, rec.; *La Tranquera* (parking space) on the highway to Cartago at Curridabat, 6-8 km. E of San José, serves good steaks and other foods (orchestra for dancing at weekends). On N side of old La Sabana airport on Av. 3 and about C. 50 are two good restaurants, *El Chicote* (country-style; good grills) and *El Molino*, in Escazú area, grills; also *Il Tula*, very good, same area; *Las Cascadas de Pavas*, 3 km. from centre, very good. *El Chalet Suizo*, Av. 1, C. 5-7 (T 223118), good food and service, international. *La Flecha*, Centro Colón Building, Paseo Colón, superb; *Lobster Inn*, Paseo Colón, C. 24, seafood, large choice, expensive; *La Casa de los Mariscos*, Los Yoses; *Italiano*, Carretera a Sabanilla, 1 block N. of Av. Central; *Goya*, Av. 1, C. 5/7, Spanish food (in the centre). *Casa de España*, in Bank of America, C. 1, good lunches; *Gourmet*, C. Central, Av. 3/5, lunches US$2, good value, menu changes daily; *Masia de Triquell*, Av. 2, Calle 38/40, Barra 1, Catalan, warmly rec. *Piccolo Roma*, Av. 2, Calle 24, highly rec.; *Los Lechones*, Av. 6, C. 11 and 13, good food, live music Fri. and Sat., reasonable prices; *Antojitos*, on Paseo Colón and in Centro Comercial Cocorí (road to suburb of San Pedro), serves excellent Mexican food at moderate prices; *La Perla* (name on doormat), C. Central y Av. 2, 24 hr., rec.; *El Balcón de Europa*, Av. Central y C.1, Italian, good, especially the cheeses.

Chinese: *Kuang Chaou* on C. 11 between Av. Central and Av. 2; *Kiam Kon*, C.Central and Av. Central-2, good, large helpings; *Kaw Wah*, Av. 2, C. 5-7, rec.; *Fortuna*, Av. 6, C. 2-4; *Lung Mun* on Av. 1, between C. 5 and 7, reasonably priced. Also rec., *Kung Fu*, Av. 5, C. 1; *Fu Su Lu*, C. 7, Av. 2, Chinese, Korean, very good; *Tin Hao*, Av. 10, C. 4, T 21-11-63, good; and *Kam King*, Av. 10, C.19-21.

Vegetarian: *La Mazorca*, in San Pedro, near University of Costa Rica (Rodrigo Facio site), vegetarian and health foods; *Macrobiótica*, C. 2, Av. 3/5, vegetarian and take-away; *Shakti*, Av. 8, C. 13, excellent.

MacDonald's, Av. Central, C. 4, near Banco Central, opp. Plaza de la Cultura, and in Sabana, and Guadalupe, also for hamburgers; *Kentucky Fried Chicken*, Paseo Colón, Calle 32, also Av. 2, C. 6, and Av. 3, C. 2, and Los Yoses, Av. Central; *Pollo Obay*, Av. 10, 6 C., good fried chicken; *La Fánega*, in San Pedro, for excellent hamburgers, folk music some nights; *Orléans*, also in San Pedro, serves crêpes; *Churrería Manolo*, Av. Central, C. Central and 2, good sandwiches and hot chocolate; *El Floridito*, Av. 1, just E of post office, good, clean, inexpensive, excellent breakfasts; *Don Taco*, Av. 1, C. 2, Mexican food in MacDonald's style; *José Taco*, Av. 1, C.3-5, Mexican fast food, plato del día US$1.50; *Corona de Oro*, Av. 3, excellent value midday meals; *Comedor* beneath "Dorado" sign, C. 8, Av. 4-6, very cheap; *Las Condes*, Av. Central/1, C. 11, inexpensive; *Café H.B.*, C.2, Av. 5 for breakfast; *Lido Bar*, C.2, Av. 3., for casado. *Soda Malagaly*, Av. Central, C.23, nr. Youth Hostel, good, cheap; *Soda Coliseo*, Av. 3, C. 10-12, next to Alajuela bus station, rec.; *Soda Amon*, C.7, Av. 7-9, good, cheap casados; *Soda Nini*, Av. 3, C. 2-4, cheap; *La Geishita*, C. Central, Av. 14, cheap casado; *Soda Maly*, Av. 4, C. 2-4, Chinese and tico, good.

Restaurants are decidedly expensive in San José; the budget traveller is advised to stick to the bars W of C. 8, i.e. in even-numbered Calles with a number larger than 8. Food bars in restaurants in the Mercado Central (C.6/8) are good for breakfast and lunch, high standards of sanitation. At lunchtime cheaper restaurants offer a set meal called a casado, US$1-1.50, which is good value; e.g. in the snack bars in the *Galería* complex, Av. Central-2, C. 5-7. Try *Chicharronera Nacional*, Av. 1, C.10/12, very popular, or *Popular*, Av. 3, C.6/8, good casado.

Ice cream, confectionery, etc.: *Helados Rena*, C.8, Av. Central, excellent; also *Helados Boni*, C. Central, Av. 6-8, home-made ice cream; *Pops*, near Banco Central, and other outlets, for ice cream (excellent); also for ice cream *Mölnpik*, Av. Central, C. Central. *Las Cuartetas*, 2 C., 1 block N of Post Office, excellent pastries and expresso; *Spoon*, Av. Central, C. 5-7, good coffee and pastries; *Fudge*, Centro Comercial Los Lagos, Escazú, coffee and pastries; *Heladería Italiano*, excellent ice cream; *El ABC*, Av. Central between Calles 11 and 9, self-service, good, clean, cheap. *La Selecta* bakeries rec.; *Le Croissant*, Av. Central, C.33, good French bakery. *Café del Teatro*, reasonably priced, belle époque interior, popular meeting place for poets and writers.

Bars Quiet places to have a drink include *Key Largo*, Av. 3, C. 7, a bar with live music, expensive; *El Cuartel de la Boca del Monte*, Av. 1, C.21-23, rec., nice atmosphere.

Shopping Market on Av. Central, Calles 6/8, open 0630-1800 (Sun. 0630-1200), good leather suitcases and wood. Mercado Borbón, Avs. 3/5, Calles 8/10, fruit and vegetables in abundance. More and more artesanía shops are opening, e.g. Mercanapi (C. 11, Av. 1) and Mercado Nacional de Artesanía (C. 11, Av. 4), and others on Av. Central, C. 1 and 3. La Casona, a market of small artesanía shops, Av. Central-1, C. Central. In Moravia (8 km. from centre) El Caballo Blanco and H.H.H. are good for leather work. The leather rocking chairs (which dismantle for export) found in some artesanía shops are cheaper in Sarchí. Coffee is good value and has an excellent flavour (although the best quality is exported). Automercados are good supermarkets in several locations (e.g. C.3, Av. 3). Cosiña de Leña, new shopping centre (good regional food available).

Bookshops The Bookshop, Av. 1, Calle 1 and 3 (T 21-68-47), good selection of English language books (double US prices), also in Pavas, opp. new American Embassy under construction; Universal, Av. Central, Calles Central and 1, for Spanish books and maps. Lehmann, Av. Central and C. 3, maps, Spanish, a few English and German books; Librería Italiana/Francesa, C. 3, Av. Central/1, English, French, Italian books, German magazines; Staufer, nr. Centro Comercial, Los Yoses, also in San Rafael de Escazú and Plaza del Sol shopping mall in Curridabat, English and German books; Apple, Barrio California; Airport shop; Casey's, C. Central between Av. 7 and 9, second-hand books and book exchange (1 new for 2 old), English only, good.

Photography 1 hr. colour processing available at all IFSA (Kodak) branches (15 % discount for ISTC cardholders), poor reports received. Fuji processing in 1 hr. at Universal stores. Minor camera repairs undertaken. Camera repairs, Taller de Equipos Fotográficos, 120 metres E of kiosk Parque Morazán, Av. 3, C. 3-5, T 23-11-46. Film prices are similar to Europe.

Fares Bus fares in San José: large buses: US$0.10, small: US$0.15 from the centre outwards. Hand baggage in reasonable quantities is not charged, but no trunks of any kind are taken.

Taxis Minimum fare US$0.60 for first km. Taxis are red and now have electronic meters (called "Marías"); make sure they are used.

Car Rentals Check your vehicle carefully as the rental company will try to claim for the smallest of "damages". International driver's licence and credit card generally required. Insurance cost US$10 per day extra; basic prices: compact car US$18 (plus US$0.17/km.), or US$32 free km.; jeep US$26 (plus US$0.26/km.), or US$45 free km.; minibus same rate as jeep. Avis, Sabana Norte (T 32-99-22); Budget, C. 30, Paseo Colón (T 23-32-84); Dollar, C. Central, Av. 9 (T 33-33-39); National, C. 38, Paseo Colón (T 33-44-06); and many local ones. Various companies at airport, including Santos (T 41-30-44).

Night Clubs Grill La Orquídea at the Hotel Balmoral; Les Moustaches in Centro Colón, Paseo Colón, C. 38, expensive. Many restaurants and bars with varying styles of music at El Pueblo centre on road to San Francisco (take "Calle Blancos" bus from C. 1, Av. 5-7, alight 500 m. after river); also 3 discos here, Cocoloco, Infinito and La Plaza (very luxurious and expensive). Discos in the centre: Kamakiri, on the way to Tibas; Top One (US rock music); La Rueda (for the over 30's). Other nice, less expensive dance spots downtown: El Túnel del Tiempo, Talamanca and Disco Salsa 54. Night spots W of Calle 8 are in the red light district.

Theatres All are closed on Monday. Teatro Carpa, outdoor, alternative; plays, films, C. 9, opp. Parque Morazán. Teatro Tiempo (also called Sala Arlequín), C. 13 between Av. 2 and Central. Compañía Nacional de Teatro. Teatro del Angel, Av. Central, between C. 13 and 15. Teatro Nacional, Av. 2, C. 3/5, behind it is La Plaza de la Cultura, a large complex. 3 modern dance companies. All good.

Cinemas Many excellent modern cinemas showing latest releases. Prices, US$1.40. See La Nación for films and times.

Swimming Pools The best is at Ojo de Agua, 5 minutes from the airport, 15 minutes from San José. It is open up to 1700 hours; direct bus from Parque Carrillo, Av. 2, C. 14, US$0.65 or take bus to Alajuela via San Antonio de Belén. There is also a pool in La Sabana (at western end of Paseo Colón), entrance US$3, open 1200-1400, about 2 km. from the city centre. Open air pool at Plaza González Víquez (south-eastern section of city).

Museums   Museo Nacional, Calle 17, Av. Central and 2, very interesting, partly under reconstruction, open Tues.-Sun., 0900-1700; replicas of precolumbian jewellery may be bought at reasonable prices (entrance, US$0.20). Gold Museum in the Plaza de la Cultura complex adjoining the Teatro Nacional, Av. Central, C.3/5, excellent, open Sat.-Sun. only, 1000-1700, free 1½-hr. bilingual guided tour available (get ticket in advance); Museo de Arte Costarricense at the end of Paseo Colón, Calle 42, in La Sabana park in the old airport building (Tues.-Sun. 1000-1700, US$0.20). In the INS building, Av. 7, C. 9/11, is the Jade Museum on the 11th floor (Tues.-Sun. 1000-1800), with jade carvings, very interesting, a "must", and a beautiful view over the city. Museo de Ciencias Naturales, Colegio La Salle, Mon.-Fri., 0730-1500; US$0.10 (in the grounds of the Ministry of Agriculture; take "Estadio Sabana" bus from Av. 2, C.2/ Central to the gate). Entomology Museum, in School of Agronomy of the University of Costa Rica, Mon.-Fri. 1300-1800, many beautiful insects, only museum of its kind in Central America. Museo Criminológico, 2nd floor, Supreme Court Building, Av. 6, C. 17-19, Mon.-Fri. 0800-1600, "pretty grisly".

Zoo   There is a small zoo in Parque Simón Bolívar (Av. 11, just E of C.7), near INS building. Entrance US$0.40, open 0830-1530, Tues.-Fri., 0900-1600, Sat. Go down C. 11 about 3 blocks from Av. 7.

Exchange   Opening times: Mon.-Fri., 0900-1500 Banco Nacional, head office, Av. 3, C. 2/4; office in Plaza de la Cultura for changing dollars on weekdays and at weekends (0900-1500, Sat., 0900-1300, Sun. and holidays); Banco de Costa Rica, Av. Central, C. 4., changes travellers' cheques for colones and for dollars, but must present a ticket out of Costa Rica—take passport. Banco de San José, C. Central, Av. 3-5. Money can be sent through Banco de San José or Banco de Costa Rica at 4% commission. Banco Anglo Costarricense, Av. 2 near Teatro Nacional, very good service for travellers' cheques. Credit card (Visa, Mastercharge) holders can obtain cash advances from Banco de San José in colones or US dollars; minimum cash advance: US$50. Banco Crédito Agrícola de Cartago, 9 branches, also makes advances on Visa, no limits. Since August 1986, banks may charge whatever commission they please on foreign exchange transactions and other services: shop around for the best deal. Dollars are available at banks but a commission is payable when cashing any cheque and there is a maximum limit of US$50-worth (much paperwork and at least 1-hr. wait involved; you have to show your ticket out of the country and the dollars can only be obtained when you are leaving). All casas de cambio have been closed down, and exchange transactions on the street, the centre for which is the corner of Av. 2, C.2 (beware fake notes), are now illegal. Most hotels will change dollars (cash or travellers' cheques) into colones, but only for guests; hotels cannot sell dollars, however.

Embassies and Consulates   British, Centro Colón, 11th floor, end of Paseo Colón with C. 38 (Apartado 10056), T 21-55-66 (also serves Nicaragua); West German, Sabana Oeste, Aptdo 4017, T 32-55-33; Swiss, Paseo Colón, Centro Colón, 4th floor, Calles 34/36, T 21-48-29; Canadian, Av. Central, C. 3, Cronos Building, 6th floor, Aptdo 10303 (T 23-04-46), US, Av. 3, C. 1, 2nd floor, T 22-55-66, open Mon.-Fri. 0800-1130, 1230-1500 (a new embassy is under construction in the western suburb of Pavas—the consulate will remain at present address); Colombian, corner Av. 5 and C. 5, La Viña building, 2nd floor, T 21-07-25 (Mon.-Fri. 0800-1230) issues free tourist cards for Colombia, but onward ticket must be shown and 2 photos provided. Venezuelan, 1 block S of Automercado de Yoses (on Av. Central, C.35/37), consulate open Mon.-Fri. 0900-1230, T 25-13-35, visa takes 48 hrs.; French, Curridabat, 200 metres S, 25 metres W of Indor Club. T 25-07-33. Belgian, C. 35-37, Av. 3, T 25-62-55; Dutch, Los Yoses, C.35-37, Aptdo 10285, Mon.-Fri. 0900-1200, T 34-09-49; Italian, C. 29, Av. 8-10, T 25-20-87; Spanish, Paseo Colón, C. 32, T 21-19-33; Japanese, Bo. Rohrmoser, T 32-12-55. Nicaraguan, Av. Central, Calles C.25-27, Mon.-Fri., 24-hr. wait for visa; Salvadorean, Los Yoses, opposite Venezuelan Embassy; Guatemalan, Embassy and Consulate, Colonia del Río (T 22-89-91), visa given on the spot, US$10 (dollars only); Panamanian, La Granja (100 metres S of Banco Popular), San Pedro district (T 25-34-01), none further south; Honduran, Av. 5, C. 1, T 22-21-45; Mexican, Consulate, Av. 7, C. 13-15, open 0800-1000, 1400-1500; Ecuadorean, Av. 2, C. 19-21, T 23-62-81; Brazilian, Av. Central-1, C. 4, T 23-43-25. Argentine, Av.6, C.21-25 (T 21-34-38); Austrian, Av.2, C.2-4 (T 23-28-22); Belizean, Curridabat (T 53-96-26); Danish, Sabana Este (T 22-13-07); Peruvian, Los Yoses (T 25-91-45); Paraguayan, Los Yoses (T 25-28-02).

Immigration   Irazemi Building, C. 21, Av. 6-8; you need to go here for exit visas, extensions, etc. (or a travel agent can obtain them).

Churches   Protestant, in English: The Good Shepherd, Av. 4, Calles 3-5 (Anglican), Union Church, Moravia; free bus service from downtown hotels; times and locations given in Friday Tico Times. International Baptist Church, in San Pedro, 150 metres N from Banco Anglo Costarricense corner, on San Pedro or Periférico bus route, English services at 0900 on Sun., Sunday school at 1100, nursery provided, Chinese services at 1100 on Sun. Cariari Christian Fellowship (Hotel Cariari), Sun. 1630; Escazú Christian Fellowship (Country Day School campus), Sun. 1800; Victory Christian Centre (125 metres W of Tennis Club, Sabana Sur), Sun. 1000. Roman Catholic services in English at Sheraton Herradura Hotel, 1600 every Sun. Centro de los Amigos para la Paz, Quaker, English books, US periodicals, information, T 21-03-02.

Libraries   Centro Cultural Costarricense Norteamericano (Calle Negritos—good films, plays, art exhibitions and English-language library), University of Costa Rica (in San Pedro suburb), and National Library (opp. Parque Nacional; has art and photography exhibitions), all entry free. Alianza Franco Costarricense, Av. 7, C. 5, French newspapers, French films every Thursday evening, friendly.

Language Schools   Conversa, Apartado No. 17, Centro Colón (T 21-76-49), 12 monthly programmes. Centro Cultural Costarricense Norteamericano, C. Negritos, T 25-93-47; Instituto Lengua Española, San Francisco suburb, T 26-92-22. Instituto de Idiomas, Av. 3, C. 3-5, Edif. Victoria, piso 3, T 23-96-62, Spanish lessons and lodging with Costa Rican families. Intensa, C. 33, Av. 5-7, Barrio Escalante, T 25-60-09, P.O. Box 8110, 1000 San José.

British School   San Pedro, Av. Central, C. 33 (T 34-22-66).

Post Office   Av. 1 and 3, C. 2; charges 10 colones for receiving letters.

Cables   Internal, from main post office, abroad from Compañía Radiográfica Internacional de Costa Rica, Av. 5, C. 1, 0730-1000, collect calls available from special booths.

Hospitals and Inoculations   Social Security Hospitals have good reputations (free to social security members, few members of staff speak English), free ambulance service run by volunteers: Dr Calderón Guardia (T 22-41-33), San Juan de Dios (T 22-01-66), México (T 32-61-22). The Clínica Bíblica C. 1, Av. 14, (T 23-64-22) and Americana (C. Central-1, Av. 14 (T 22-10-10) have been rec.; both offer 24-hr. emergency service at reasonable charges and have staff who speak English; better than the large hospitals, where queues are long. Bíblica also has addresses for emergencies it cannot handle. Yellow fever inoculation, Ministerio de Salud (Av.4, C.16), Departamento de Enfermedades Epidémicos, Dr. Rodrígo Jiménez Monge, or at his private clinic, C.5, Av.4, T 21-66-58. Free malaria pills also from Ministerio de Salud, from information desk in office to left of ministry.

Dentist   Clínica Dental Dr. Francisco Cordero Guilarte, T 323645, Sabana Oeste, opposite Colegio La Salle. Take bus marked Sabana Estadio. Dra. Fresia Hidalgo, corner C. 10, Av. 15, 1400-1800, English spoken, reasonable prices, rec. (T 22-16-53).

Laundromat   Washing and dry cleaning at Centro Comercial San José 2000, 0730-2000,

US$3.75 for large load. Sixaola, branches throughout San José, 2-hr. dry cleaning available, expensive.

Travel Agencies Swiss Travel Service, *Hotel Corobici*, T (506) 31-40-55, P.O.Box 7-1970, with branches in *Hotels Sheraton, Irazú, Amstel* and *Balmoral*, large agency, good guides, much cruise business, railway excursions, warmly rec. Tikal, Av. 2, C. 7-9, T 23-28-11, rec. Panorama Tours, C. 9, Av. Central/1, P.O. Box 7323, Greyhound agent; Viajes Rodan, Calle 1, 75 yards (*varas*) S of American Embassy. French-speaking owner. American Express, TAM, only open Mon.-Fri., Edif. Alde, 2nd floor, Calle 1, Av. Central/1, good service. Costa Rican Expeditions, Av. 3, C. Central/2, offer tropical forest adventure tours, white water rafting, etc. (P.O. Box 6941), T 23-99-75; Mundo Acuático, 200 metres N of *Mas X Menos*, San Pedro, rents snorkelling gear. Tursa, *Gran Hotel Costa Rica*, T 336194/214000, all types of tour offered.

Tourist Office Instituto Costarricense de Turismo, information office: below Plaza de la Cultura, C. 5, Av. Central/2, T 23-1733, ext. 277, and 22-1090 (Mon.-Sat. 0900-1700, closed Sun.). Also at Juan Santamaría airport (very helpful) and borders. Head office is at Av. 4, C. 3/5 (open at 0900). Excellent service. Free guide: *Gran Pequeño Guía de San José*, good. **Otec, youth and student travel office** and cheap lodgings, Edif. Victoria, 2nd floor, Av. 3, C. 3-5, T 22-08-66, for ISTC and FIYTO members (has discount booklet for shops, hotels, restaurants; also good fares on Aeronica and flights to Guayaquil, Caracas-Miami, Orlando, or Luxembourg. Beware, however, booking Panama-Bogotá, Air Panama does not accept Otec tickets; no discounts on international flights in Dec.-Jan. high season, though). The Instituto Geográfico, Av. 20, C. 9/11 at Ministry of Public Works and Transport, supplies very good topographical maps for walkers (which can easily be bought at Librerías Universal and Lehmann). The national park service (SPN, office: Calle 17, Av. 9) can provide very interesting material on the flora and fauna of the parks, brochure with descriptions and how to reach the parks, US$0.50 from its CIDA information office in the zoo grounds at the N end of Av. 11 **(see page 1278)**. American Express office has good, free maps of San José. **N.B.** It is much cheaper to take tours aimed at the local rather than the tourist market.

Airports The Juan Santamaría international airport is at El Coco, 16 km. from San José by motorway (5 km. from Alajuela). Minibus from Av. 2, C. 10/12, or Av. 2, C. 12/14, every 10 mins., US$0.30, or by Alajuela bus via the motorway from C. 14, Av. 5 and 7. Taxi to airport, US$10; Taxis Unidos run a colectivo for US$1-2 each. Sansa runs its own bus service to the airport. If catching an early flight it is a good idea to stay in Alajuela **(see page 1293)**, taxis run all night from the main square to the airport. Bank at the airport open 0800-1600; at other times try car rental desks, or the restaurant cash desk. X-ray machines reported unsafe for film. Light aircraft use the Tobias Bolaños airport at Pavas, about 5 km. W of San José.

Airlines Addresses (and telephone numbers) of major airlines: Copa, Av. 5, C. 1-3 (23-70-33); SAM, Av. 5, C. 1-3 (33-30-66); Lacsa, Av. 5, C. 1 (31-00-33); Aeronica, Edif. Cristal, Av. 1, C. 1-3 (23-02-26); Sansa, Paseo Colón, C.24 (21-94-14); Sahsa, Av. 1-3 (21-55-61); Taca, Av. 3, C. 1 (22-17-90); Mexicana, Av. 2-4, C. 1 (22-17-11); Varig, Av. 5, C. 3-5 (57-00-94); Viasa, Av. 5, C. 1 (23-34-11); TWA, Av. 1-Central, C.2 (22-13-32); Pan Am, Av. 3, C. 5 (21-89-55); Eastern, Paseo Colón, next to *Ambassador Hotel*, C. 26, T 22-56-55 (to cash an MCO takes 6 weeks, must be sent to Miami); British Airways, Paseo Colón (23-56-48); Iberia, Paseo Colón, C.40 (21-33-11); KLM, Av. Central, C. 1 (21-30-81); Lufthansa, Av. 3-5, C. 5 (22-73-11); Air France, Av. 1, C. 4-6 (22-88-11); Swiss Air, Av. 1-3. C. Central (21-66-13). Singapore Airlines, Av. 1, C. 3-5 (55-35-55).

Internal Flights Sansa operate internal flights throughout the country at reasonable prices from Juan Santamaría airport, Mon.-Sat. only. Check-in is at Sansa office on Paseo Colón at C.24 one hour before departure (free bus to and from airport); reservations here, or from Super Viajes. Check schedules on 21-94-14 or 33-27-14. If you made reservations before arriving in Costa Rica, confirm and collect tickets as soon as possible after arrival. Flights operate Tues., Thurs. and Sat. to Barra del Colorado (US$10), Golfito 0600 daily (US$12), Puerto Quepos 0800 daily and 1300 on Mon., Wed. and Fri. (US$9), Coto 47, daily (US$12), Palmar Sur, Mon., Wed. and Sat. (US$12) and Tamarindo and Sámara on Mon., Wed. and Fri. (both US$12).

Railway Services On the NE side of Parque Nacional is the main station of the Northern Railway to the Atlantic port of Limón and to Heredia and Alajuela in the Meseta Central, Av. 3, C. 21 (T 26-00-11). The main station of the Ferrocarril Eléctrico al Pacífico to the Pacific ports of Puntarenas and Caldera is in the extreme S of the city C. 2, Av. 20, T 26-00-11 (take bus marked Paso Ancho). The two 1.067-metre gauge lines are connected. The trains are slow, noisy and dusty, but comfortable; rec. for beautiful views.

There is one train a day from San José to Puerto Limón (156 km.) at 1000, ticket office opens at 0900; train from Limón to San José at 0600. Journey takes about 7-8 hrs. to Limón (on a good day) and 9 back. Fare: US$1.15. Train times should be checked in advance: the timetable varies. Light refreshments are served on all trains except the local service, which operates once a day between San José, Heredia and Alajuela on the Northern Railway. A luxury, 1st class coach may be taken to Puerto Limón for US$55 (bookable through Swiss Travel Service).

The journey to Limón is one of the most beautiful railway journeys anywhere. On the way to Limón, sit on the right-hand side. From the continental divide near Cartago the line follows the narrow, wooded Reventazón valley down past Turrialba and Siquirres (2 hrs. from Limón). One can shorten the journey by transferring to a bus at Siquirres. The 40 km. of line in the lowlands near Limón cost 4,000 lives during building in the 1870s, mostly from yellow fever. The last 16 km. into Limón run along the seashore, amid groves of coconut palms. Train splits at Siquirres, front half to Puerto Limón, rear to Guápiles. Beware of robberies on trains after dark and in the crush while boarding.

Between San José and Puntarenas there are two trains daily, this also is a very scenic journey; from Puntarenas to San José (116 km.) leaving at 0600 and 1600 and from San José to Puntarenas leaving at 0600 and 1500 (the timetable changes sometimes). Journey takes about 4 hrs. Fastest trains (*directo*) 3 hrs. Fare US$1 one way. Last return train on Sundays is overcrowded. Passengers can buy light refreshments at wayside stations and stops. There are also services to the new port of Caldera.

Buses   There are services to most towns. *Cartago*, every 15 mins., 0500-2300, *Turrialba* buses start from the Parque Nacional. *Puntarenas* every hour from 0600 to 1900 (US$1.40), Av. 7-9, Calle 12. *Heredia*, every 30 mins., Av. 5, Calle 1. Minibuses from Av. 6, C. 14. *Alajuela* (including airport), 30 mins., (US$0.30) Av. 2, Calle 12-14 every 15 mins., to Sarchí, change at Alajuela, to Poás Volcano, change at Alajuela's central park where bus leaves, Sun. only, 0830. *Quepos*, from Coca Cola bus station, Calle 16, Av. 1-3, 4 buses daily, 3 hours. Direct bus to Manuel Antonio, 0600, 1200, US$4, 3½ hrs., from Coca Cola station. Many buses for nearby towns and others to the west of San José leave from the main Coca Cola bus station or the streets nearby (eg: *Santa Ana, Escazú, Acosta, Puriscal, Santa María Dota, San Marcos, San Ramón*). *Escazú* minibuses from Av. 6, Calle 14; buses from front of Coca Cola terminal. *San Isidro de El General*, regular buses, near Coca Cola. *Liberia, Nicoya, Sta. Cruz, Cañas* buses, Empresa Alfaro, Coca Cola bus station. *Grecia*, bus Calle 6, Av. 5-7. *San Carlos* bus at Coca Cola terminal. *Guápiles*, Calle 2, Av. 7-9. *Monteverde* (Mon.-Thurs. 1430, Sat.-Sun. 0630, US$3.50) and *Puerto Viejo*, by Puntarenas terminal, Av. 7-9, Calle 12. *Siquirres*, Av. Ctl, Calle 11-13. *Limón*, hourly service, 0600-1800, 2½ hours, good views, leaving on time, you may buy ticket the day before. US$1.55, Calle 19-21, Av. 3 Transportes Unidos/ Coop Limón. *Paso Canoas* (US$5.25), *Golfito, Ciudad Neily* (Zona Sur) buses, Tracopa, Calle 2-4, Av. 16 (21-42-14). Direct to *Sixaola* (via Puerto Viejo, Cahuita and Bribri), C.1 Central, Av.11, 0600 and 1430, 5 hrs., US$3.

Minibuses run on most routes to nearby towns offering better service, never crowded like the regular buses. Fares about US$0.20-0.25.

International Buses   Sirca (Av. 2, Calle 11, T 22-55-41) runs a scheduled service along the Pan-American Highway from San José to Peñas Blancas, on the Nicaraguan frontier, and on to Managua (US$7), dep. 0500 (Wed., Fri., Sun.; schedules appear to change frequently), reports of unreliability with this company (book on Fri. for following week). Tica buses run to David, Panama City and Managua; the terminal is at Calle 9-11 and Av. 2 (T 21-89-54). It is here that all refund claims have to be made (take 10 days and have to be collected in person). Ticabus to Managua leaves at 0700, Mon., Wed., Fri., US$8. The Ticabus journey from San José to Panama City (with at least 3 hrs. at the border) US$19 (at official exchange rate and much cheaper than in Panama), leaves at 0500 daily and arrives at 2400 (book at least 3 days in advance); by Ticabus to David, US$18. To get a Panamanian tourist card one must buy a return ticket. Tracopa, opposite Pacific railway station on C.2/4, Av.18 (T 21-42-14), goes as far as David, US$7 (buses daily at 0700, 9 hrs.); fare to border US$6; book in advance. A bus to Changuinola via the Sixaola-Guabito border post leaves San José at 1000 daily, from outside the *Hotel Cocori*, Calle 16, Av. 3, US$5 payable on board in colones, best to arrive 1 hr. before departure; the bus takes the splendidly scenic, fast new road through the Braulio Carillo National Park to Guápiles and Siquirres and is the quickest route to Limón. The journey from San José to Changuinola takes 6-7 hrs.

Excursions   San José is a good centre for excursions into the beautiful Meseta Central. The excursions to the Orosí valley and volcano of Irazú are given under Cartago. Poás volcano (described on **page 1293**) can be visited from Alajuela. Enquire first about the likely weather when planning a visit to Poás or Irazú. To reach Barba take a bus to San José de las Montañas (**see page 1292**). A road runs NE of San José to (11 km.) San Isidro de Coronado, a popular summer resort (bus from Terminal Coronado, Av. 7, C. Central and 1); its *fiesta* is on February 15. Those interested in medical research can visit the Instituto Clodomiro Picado snake farm, open Mon.-Fri. 0800-1600 (snake feeding, Fri. only 1330-1600), take Dulce Nombre de Coronado bus from C.3, Av. 5/7, 30 mins., or San Antonio Coronado bus to end of line and walk 200 metres downhill. The road goes on through fine countryside to Las Nubes (32 km.), a country village which commands a great view of Irazú. For horseback excursions, *Finca Ob-la-dí Ob-la-dá*, 17 km. W of San José, Villa Colón, offers 1-day and longer tours (1-day trip, including transport from your hotel, lunch and all tack, costs US$59).

From San José to the Atlantic Coast

Cartago, 22½ km. from San José, stands at 1,439 metres at the foot of the Irazú volcanic peak and is encircled by mountains. It was founded in 1563 and was the capital until 1823. It has a population of only 25,000, though the neighbourhood is densely populated. Earthquakes destroyed it in 1841 and 1910, and it has been severely shaken on other occasions. That is why there are no old buildings, though some have been rebuilt in colonial style.

The most interesting church is the Basilica, rebuilt 1926 in Byzantine style, of Nuestra Señora de Los Angeles, the Patroness of Costa Rica; it houses La Negrita, under 15 cm. high, an Indian image of the Virgin which draws pilgrims from all over Central America because of great healing powers attributed to it. The feast day is August 2, when the image is carried in procession to other churches in Cartago and there are celebrations thoughout Costa Rica. In the Basilica is an extraordinary collection of very finely-made silver and gold images, no larger than 3 cm. high, of various parts of the human anatomy, presumably offered in the hope of being healed. Worth seeing is the old parish church (La Parroquia), ruined by the 1910 earthquake and now converted into a delightful garden retreat with flowers, fish and humming birds. There is an impressive procession on Good Friday.

Hotels *Casa Blanca* in Barrio Asís, E, *Pensión El Brumoso*, C.5, Av. 6-8, F, *Valencia*, F, clean, are among the very few NOT in the red light district; *Familiar Las Arcadas*, at railway station, F (rents rooms hourly late into the night).

Restaurants *Salón París*, very good food; *Ambientes* in front of La Parroquia, is also very good; *City Garden*, Av. 4, C. 2-4; *Puerta del Sol*, in front of the Basilica. Restaurants, among other places, are closed on the Thursday and Friday of Holy Week, so take your own food.

Shopping Bookshop at Librería Cartago, C.1, Av. 2-4. High quality Costa Rican clothes at Boutique Belinni International, in front of post office. There is a market facing the train station. The main **post office** is at C.1, Av. 2-4, near the park.

Buses The main terminal is at Av. 4, C.2-4, but buses to most destinations, including Turrialba, make a stop at the Cartago ruins on Av. 3.

Excursions Best is by a road (40 km., paved) to the crater of Irazú (3,432 metres). Michael J. Brisco of Cambridge writes: Irazú crater is a half-mile cube dug out of the earth, and all around is desolate grey sand, with little wildlife other than the ubiquitous Volcano Junco, a bird like a dunnock, and the few plants which survive in this desert. The phrase "it's like the surface of the moon" describes Irazú quite well. Entrance to Irazú in season, US$0.10, out of season free. There is a small museum. Cartago buses to Irazú from 1 block N of Cartago ruins at 0700 and 1300 on Mon. and Thurs. and 0700 on Sun. (but check in advance if bus is running), 1¾ hrs. up, the first bus arrives long before the tour buses and private cars, but returns after about 30 minutes, so you must either hitch down, or wait until the afternoon bus goes down at about 1500, US$2 return; taxi is US$24 return (it is very difficult to get taxis to return for you in the morning if you have stayed at the crater overnight). Since it can be difficult to find a hotel in Cartago that is not rented hourly (and therefore very expensive for a full night) it may be easier to take one of the guided tours leaving from San José, about US$40. The clouds come down early, obscuring the view. Alternatively you can take a bus from Cartago to Sanatorio. Ask the driver at the crossroads just outside the village. From there you walk to the summit. 16 km.; on the way up are the *Hotel Montana* (D inc. 3 meals) and the *Bar-Restaurant Linda Vista*. 1½ km. from the crater a road leads to Laguna Verde and a camping site; the road is paved, but steep beyond the Laguna. If driving from San José, take the road signed "Plantel M.O.P.T. Cartago, 3 kms.", just after Río Taras, which goes directly to Irazú, avoiding Cartago. The walk down, on a dirt road through Pinchas, is also rec. On Sat. and Mon. a bus goes from Cartago to San Juan, 12 km. from the summit (0630 and 1300); *Hotel Gran Irazú*, E, comfortable, clean.

National Park rules forbid visitors to walk around the crater: on the tourist track on the North side is a "Prohibido pasar" sign, which can be passed only at your own risk, there are some very dangerous drops, and the rim is cracking (we advise obeying the rules). There is an easier walk on the southerly side, which ends before the high crest; J. Douglas Porteous of the University of Victoria, B.C., writes: "Stupendous views: you look down on mountain tops, clouds, light aircraft. Wear good shoes and a hat, the sun is strong. Those with sensitive skins should consider face cream if the sulphur fumes are heavy. By 1300 (sometimes by even 0900 or 1000) clouds have enveloped the lower peaks and are beginning to close in on Irazú; time to eat your picnic on the far side of the crater before returning to the tourist side."

Mike Marlowe, of Blacksburg, Virginia, writes: "In the afternoon the mountain top is buried in fog and mist or drizzle, but the ride up in the mist can be magical, for the mountainside is half-displaced in time. There are new jeeps and tractors, but the herds of cattle are small, the fields are quilt-work, handcarts and oxcarts are to be seen under the fretworked porches of well-kept frame houses. The land is fertile, the pace is slow, the air is clean, there is no poverty. It is a very attractive mixture of old and new. Irazú is a strange mountain, well worth the two-plus hours' bus ride up."

Aguas Calientes is 4 km. SE of Cartago and 90 metres lower. Its *balneario* (warm water swimming pool) is a good place for picnics. 4 km. from Cartago on the road to Paraíso is the Jardín Lancaster orchid garden (run by the University of Costa Rica), 10 mins.' walk from the main road (ask bus driver to let you out at Campo Ayala—Cartago-Paraíso bus); the best display is in April. Open 0830-1530, entry usually on the hour, US$0.50. 1 km. further on is Parque Doña Ana (La Expresión), a lake with picnic area, basketball courts, exercise track and bird watching, open 0900-1700, US$0.50. Get off bus at Cementario in Paraíso and walk 1 km. south. **Ujarrás** (ruins of a colonial church and village) is 6½ km. E of Cartago by a road which goes from Paraíso through a beautiful valley to the small town of **Orosi**, in the enchanting Orosi valley, down which flows the tumultuous Reventazón (*Motel Río*, D, and *Restaurant Río Palomo*). Bus from Cartago, US$0.15. Here are magnificent views of the valley, a 17th century mission with colonial treasures, and just outside the town two *balnearios* (bathing, US$1.60) and restaurants serving good meals at fair prices. The *miradores* of Ujarrás and Orosi both offer excellent views of the Reventazón valley. There are buses from Cartago to all these places. A beautiful one-day drive from Cartago is to Orosi, then to Ujarrás, and on to Cachi where there is a dam with artificial lake (very popular with residents of San José, Charrarra buses from 1 block N of Cartago ruins, several daily). The Charrarra tourist complex, with a good restaurant, swimming pool, boat rides on the Orosi river and walks, can be reached by direct bus on Sun., otherwise ½-hr. walk from Ujarrás.

12 km. beyond Orosi is the Tapanti Wildlife Refuge (Refugio Nacional de Vida Silvestre Tapanti, run by the Forest Service), on the headwaters of the Reventazón. It is a 6,000 hectare reserve of mainly cloud forest and pre-montaine humid forest with over 300 species of birds, 3 of monkeys, orchids and ferns. There are picnic areas, a nature centre with slide shows (ask to see them) and good swimming in the dry season (Nov.-June), and trout fishing (April 1 to October 31). Open daily 0600-1600, US$0.10. From June to Nov.-Dec. it rains every afternoon. To get there take 0600 bus from Cartago to Orosi which goes to Puricil by 0700, then walk (5 km.), or take any other Cartago-Orosi bus to Río Macho and walk 9 km. to the refuge, or take a taxi from Orosi (ask for Julio who, for US$7 round trip, will take 6 passengers). By the refuge is the *Pensión Tapanti* with 8 beds (E p.p.), meals included, reserve in advance (T 51-34-52), U.S.-owned. discounts for group reservations and biologists doing research (address: David Lockshin, Pensión Tapanti, C.P. 7107, Orosi, Cartago, Costa Rica).

The Turrialba volcano may be visited from Cartago by a bus to the village of Pacayas, where horses may be hired to take you to the top (fine view and a guesthouse).

Turrialba (57 km. from San José, 40,000 people, altitude 625 metres), on the railway between Cartago and Puerto Limón, has the Centro Agronómico Tropical de Investigación y Enseñanza (CATIE) and many fine coffee farms. CATIE covers more than 2,000 acres of this ecologically diverse zone, has one of the largest tropical fruit collections in the world and houses an important library on tropical agriculture; visitors welcome. The railway runs down to Limón on a narrow ledge poised between mountains on the left and the river on the right.

Hotels *Wagelia*, Entrada de Turrialba (T 56-15-96), D with bath, best; *Albergue La Calzada*, F; *Central*, F with restaurant, no bath; *Interamericano*, F with bath (all opp. railway station); *Pensión Primavera*, F, 1 block away; opp. is *Restaurant Kingston*, reasonable, cheap food. About 22 km. from Turialba is the *Rancho Naturalista Lodge*, A with bath, gourmet meal, horse riding, transfers from San José and airport, 6 rooms only so reservations essential—write P.O. Box 6951, 1000S San José; 7-14 night programmes organized for birdwatchers and naturalists.

From Turrialba you can get to the village of Moravia del Chirripó, where guides and horses can be hired for an excursion into the jungled, trackless area of the Talamanca Indians, where there are legends of lost goldfields (bus from Turrialba takes 4 hrs., only certain in dry season; in wet season go to Suiza and get out at Gran d'Oro, from where it's one hr. walk—no accommodation in Moravia, stay put at *pulpería* in Gran d'Oro). About 30 km. E of Turrialba, near Guayabo, an Indian ceremonial centre has been excavated and there are clear signs of its paved streets and stone-lined water-channels. This area is now a National Park. There are buses daily at 1100 from Turrialba (US$0.45) to Guayabo (*Albergue y Restaurant La Calzada*, E, T 56-04-65) from where it is a 1½ hour walk to the site (several buses each day pass the turn-off to Guayabo, the town is a 2-hr. walk uphill). It is possible to camp at the park (water and toilets, but no food); entry US$0.05. Further along this road (1½ hours' drive) is Santa Cruz, from which the Turrialba volcano can be reached. Bus from Cartago to Turrialba, 1 hr., US$0.60.

Puerto Limón, on a palm-fringed shore backed by mountains, is the country's most important port. It was built on the site of an ancient Indian village, Cariari, where Columbus landed on his fourth and last voyage. Much of the population is black. Visitors should see the palm promenade and tropical flowers of the Parque Vargas (where sloths live in the trees); the nightlife is good, particularly for

Caribbean music and dancing. A new highway to the capital (190 km.) has been built. Population 49,600. Some 2.8 million bunches of bananas are exported each year. New docks are being built. Moín, just outside Puerto Limón, has docks for tankers, container and ro-ro ships, and is also the departure point for barges to Tortuguero and Barra del Colorado (8 hrs.). There is now much drilling for oil around Puerto Limón.

Warning   Beware of theft at night.

Hotels   *Maribu Caribe*, A, T 58-45-43, bungalow accommodation, swimming pool; *Acón*, C. 3, Av. 3, T 58-10-10, C with bath, a/c, clean, safe, good restaurant, discotheque *Aquarius; Puerto*, C. 7, Av. 5/6, D, a/c, restaurant, bar; *Lincoln*, Av. 5, Calle 2-3, F, with bath, excellent value; *Tete*, C.4-5, Av. 3 (T 58-11-22), D with bath; *Pensión Los Angeles*, Calle 6-7, Av. 7, F, with bath, cheap, average; *Fung*, E, by market, modern; *Pensión Hotel Costa Rica*, 1½ blocks E of central park, F, pleasant, spacious rooms; *Pensión El Sauce*, one block from main square, F, reasonably clean; *Paraíso*, C. 5, Av. 5-6, F, no bath, clean, noisy; *Hong Kong*, on main street, F, clean but noisy; *Nuevo Oriental*, F, nice, cold showers; *Centro*, E, clean, basic, noisy, cold showers; *Pensión Dorita*, C. 3-4, Av. 4, fairly clean, friendly, basic, close to bus stop for Cahuita; *Ng*, T 58-06-47, F with bath. *Balmoral*, near market, G, basic; *Caballo Blanco*, 2 blocks from market coming from railway station, F, basic, quite clean but noisy; *Linda Vista*, Parque Vargas, F, basic, friendly, noisy.

On the road to nearby Portete, *Las Olas*, C, a/c, bath, with pool and sauna, set on rocks in the sea (buses every 1½ hr.), own water supply, no protection against insects, expensive restaurant; in Portete *Matama*, Playa Bonita, T 53-65-28, B, bath, a/c, restaurant, tennis, pool, boats for rent to Tortuguero; *Cabinas Getsemaní*, cabins, C, bath, a/c, restaurant, pleasant (T 58-11-23).

Restaurants   Several Chinese restaurants. *Park Hotel*, C.1-2, Av.3, does good meals, US$2.25; *American Café Springfield* (try the tortuga). *Restaurant La Chucheca* serves good comidas and breakfast. *La Hacienda*, for steaks, cheap. *Soda/Restaurant Mares*, on main square, clean; *Soda/Restaurant Roxie*, opp. hospital, some way out of town, good value casado. *Harbour Restaurant*, good value meal of the day. *Mölnpik* for good ice cream; *Milk Bar La Negra Mendoza* at the central market has good milk shakes and snacks. Casados in market in the day, outside it at night. Cheap food at the corners of the Central Park.

Swimming   Japdeva, the harbour authority, has a 25-metre pool open to the public for a small fee in the harbour area.

Exchange   Banco Nacional de Costa Rica, and also Banco Anglo Costarricense next to Limón-San José bus terminal.

Post Office out of town (take "Pueblo Nuevo" bus).   **Cables**   Radiográfica maintain offices in Limón.

Protestant Church   Baptist, with services in English.

Hospital   Social Security Hospital.

Rail   One train daily to San José, 0700, US$1.15 (sit on left); the new station is on the edge of town (bus from centre, US$0.03).

Buses   Town bus service is irregular and crowded. Service to San José with Transportes Unidos del Atlántico, every hour on the hour between 0600 and 0800; leave from the street between central plaza and Parque Vargas (ignore the old signs for the departure point), US$1.55, 3-4 hrs. To Cartago, US$1.50.

The Atlantic Coast   The Río San Juan forms the border between Costa Rica and Nicaragua; the frontier (closed since 1981) is not in mid-river but on the Costa Rican bank. *Los Chiles* has cheap accommodation (F range) and restaurants; the principal traffic is on the river, but a road has been built to Los Chiles (bus to Quesada, US$1). English is spoken widely along the coast.

Northward from Limón, past *Siquirres* (a clean, friendly town: hotels include *Colerón, Wilson, Idamar, Garza, Cocal* and *Vidal*, all E), trains run to *Guápiles*, centre of the new Río Frío banana region. One flight daily from San José to Río Frío. The new San José-Limón highway passes Guápiles, only 1 hr. from the capital. Standard Fruit have built about 75 km. of new railway lines on from Guápiles (Hotels: *Keng Wa* and *As de Oro* (with bath, both E; *Hugo Sánchez Cheng, Cariari* and *Alfaro* (with bath, above noisy bar), all F; *Hospedaje Guápiles*, F, good—T 71-61-79). On the coast N of Limón is Playa Bonita (littered, strong currents); buses every ½ hr. from Limón; train from San José.

6½ km. N of Limón is *Moín*, with a pleasant beach and *Hostal Moín* (F, T 58-24-36, 15 mins. from railway and docks—runs 24-hr. service), buses run every 40 minutes from 0600-1740, ½ hr., US$0.10. From Moín one can go to *Tortuguero*, a 52,129-acre National Park protecting the Atlantic green turtle egg-laying grounds and the Caribbean lowland rain forest inland. The turtles lay their eggs at night from July to September (the eggs start hatching in the second week of

September), but before going to watch, contact the National Park administration, or the scientists at Casa Verde (very helpful), Km. 0.6, for instructions, otherwise you may disturb the protected turtles (take a torch if going at night). No permission is needed to enter the park. There are several hotels: *Tortuga Lodge*, A, T 71-68-61 (owner Costa Rica Expeditions, packages available from San José, B); *Mawamba Lodge*, B, comfortable, fans, restaurant, canal and egg-laying turtles in front of property; *Cabinas Tortuguero Tatane*, D; *Sabina's Cabañas*, F, good food is limited, but good at *Miss Juni's* with Mona Lisa painting (book in advance) and at *Tío Leo's*. Don't dally on arrival if you want cheap accommodation. San José travel agencies offer 3 day/ 2 night excursions from US$75 inc. meals, bus/boat and accommodation. The main tours are Mawamba Boats, US$125 inclusive, accommodation at *Mawamba Lodge*, T 33-99-64, or Limón 58-49-15, P.O. Box 10050 San José, and Miss Caribe, US$100 inclusive, T 33-01-55. For students and young people, Otec's (**see page 1286**) 3-day tour, US$68, is rec.

Park rangers are friendly and make trips into the jungle waterways; particularly recommended for viewing tropical rain forest wildlife (birds, crocodiles, tapirs, jaguars, ocelots, peccaries, anteaters, manatees, sloths, lungfish); their trips are quite short, about US$2 p.p. for 3-4 hr. trip. Canoe and guide can be rented for US$3 p.p. per hour. There are several boats for rent from Tortuguero, ask at the *pulpería*. Take insect repellant against the ferocious mosquitoes, ticks and chiggers. From Moín, a regular boat goes to Tortuguero, Thurs., 0700, Sat., 1030, returning Fri., 0600 and Sun., 1000, US$6 one way, 7 hrs. (locals are always given preference, ask one to get tickets for you; the boat is noisy and often out of order, take protection against rain). Other boats (every 2 days or so) go to Barra del Colorado and take 9 hrs. through the natural canals to Tortuguero. If excursion boats have a spare seat you may be allowed on. A road is under construction from Guápiles.

Michael J. Brisco writes: "The canals pass many small settlements, and for many of them the barge is their only means of communication. The canals are part artificial, part natural; they were originally narrow lagoons running parallel to the sea, separated from it by ¾ km. of land. Now all the lagoons are linked, and it is possible to sail as far as *Barra del Colorado*, in the extreme NE of Costa Rica, 25 km. beyond Tortuguero." The area is world famous for fishing. The passenger launch from Moín to Tortuguero continues to Barra del Colorado on Thurs., returning early Fri. a.m. There is a luxury hotel lodge operated by Swiss Travel Service; *Río de Colorado Lodge*, C p.p. inc. 3 meals and fishing with guide, reservations rec., T 71-88-92; *Isla de Pesca*, D with bath (T 71-67-76); *Hotel Pesca Casa Mar*, with bath (T 41-28-20); *Cabinas New Tropical Tarpon* with bath (T 27-04-73). Flight San José-Barra del Colorado with Sansa Tues., Thurs. and Sat., 0600 (returns 0645), US$10 one-way.

Southward from Limón, travellers can catch a train to Penshurst or can drive; the road is paved. Here the road branches to Valle de Estrella, a large Standard Fruit banana plantation; camping is easy in the hills and there are plenty of rivers for swimming. Small buses leave Limón (C. 4, Av. 6) for Valle de Estrella/Pandora at 0500, 0700, 0900, 1100, 1300, 1500, 1800, 1½ hrs. (returning from Pandora at similar times).

From Penshurst it is 11½ km. to **Cahuita**; this stretch of the road is paved to the edge of Cahuita. There is a bus service direct from San José (Av. 11, C. 1-Central), 0600 and 1430, 4 hrs., returning 0930, US$3, and from Puerto Limón, in front of Radio Casino (0500, 1000, 1300, 1700, return 0600, 1000, 1200, 1730, US$0.60, 1-3 hrs., both continuing on paved road to Bribri, two basic *residencias*, and on to Sixaola on the Panamanian border (US$1, 2 hrs.). The Cahuita National Park has a narrow strip of beach (1,780 hectares) and a unique coral reef off shore; an old Spanish wrecked ship may be seen, although the water can be very cloudy at times (both can be reached without a boat; take snorkelling equipment, but the undercurrent is strong). The Park extends from Cahuita town to Puerto Vargas further SE. Best access to the Park is from Puerto Vargas where there are the Park headquarters, a nature trail, camping facilities, drinking water, toilets (take the bus to Km. 5, then turn left at the sign; the road from the Cahuita-Bribri road to Puerto Vargas is muddy; take a torch if walking it after dark). The length of the beach can be walked in 2 hrs., passing endless coconut palms and interesting tropical forest, through which there is also a path, including fording the shallow Perezoso River, which is brown with tannin (it is hot and humid, but a wide range of fauna can be seen, including howler monkeys, white face monkeys, coatimundis, snakes, butterflies and hermit crabs—torch essential if walking at night, assaults and rape have been reported on the path and some of the jungle has been cleared for safety reasons). No permission is necessary from SNP to enter the Park.

The bus drops you at the crossing of the 2 main roads in Cahuita; at the corner is *Hotel Victoria* (above a noisy bar). On the street parallel to the sea, towards the Park entrance are *Cabinas Vaz*, E, friendly, cold shower, fan, T 58-15-15 ext. 218, and *Hotel Cahuita*, D, friendly, expensive restaurant, T 58-15-15 ext. 201 (opp. is *Soda Sol y Mar*, rec.). A little road from the bus stop goes straight to the seafront, passing *Cabinas Palmer*, E (T 58-15-15, ext. 243), clean, helpful; carry on to the sea, and on left is *Jenny's Cabinas*, (same phone, but ext. 256), E, clothes washing area, rustic, basic, running water, rec. On the road from Limón to Cahuita, km. 22, is *Club Campestre Cahuita*, C with bath, fans, swimming pool, T 55-61-76, isolated and difficult to get to Cahuita National Park from here. For cheaper rooms, walk 15 mins. N to Playa Negra: *Pepe's Place*, pleasant owner, but beware of theft; *Grant's Cabins*, F, good water service, Señorita Letty Grant (blue house on right of track to black beach) rents rooms (F) and *cabañas*, clean, nice, friendly; *El Atlántido*, next to football ground, nice gardens but cabins are dirty, E with bath, fan, mosquito screen, pleasant, free safe parking for cars and motorcycles (also known as Canadian John's); *Cabinas Surf Side*, *Cabinas Black Beach*, both E, clean and well situated; *Samwell's*, F, clean, friendly, rec. There are also empty rooms to let, so take a hammock or sleeping bag. Camping: US$0.25 p.p., good facilities but no meals. *Daisy's Café*, for breakfast and dinner, 100 metres past ball ground, good view of beach, good service, also book exchange and snorkelling equipment hire, very expensive. Other restaurants: *Sands*, cheap, *Típico*, good, Winston is very helpful but not always accurate.

On public holidays Cahuita is very crowded; the remainder of the year it is a favourite resort of backpackers (don't bathe or sun-bathe naked). Money can be changed in the store in same building as *Bar Vaz*. Tony Mora runs glass-bottomed boats over the coral reef. The National Park services have warned against muggings in the park at night; also beware of theft on the beach.

The beaches at **Puerto Viejo**, 13 km. from Cahuita, unpaved (bus from San José—en route to Sixaola—4½ hrs., US$3, ½ hr. from Cahuita), are also worth a visit. Hotels: *Rafa's*, dearest, *Maritza*, E, clean, friendly, English spoken; *Cabinas Manuel León*, F with bath, T 58-08-54; *Maiti*, cheapest, best of several restaurants; electricity 24 hrs., also rooms to let. It is possible to walk along the beach from Puerto Viejo to Cahuita in one day; there is a bus, US$0.45. Take road from Cahuita to Hone Creek where one road (dirt) goes to Puerto Viejo and another (paved) to Bribri, one of the villages at the foot of the Talamanca range, which has been declared an Indian Reserve.

From Limón, Aerovías Talamaqueñas Indígenas fly cheaply to Amubri in the Reserve (there is a *Casa de Huéspedes* run by nuns in Amubri). Villages such as Bribri, Chase, Bratsi, Shiroles and San José Cabécar can be reached by bus from Cahuita. (For a good introduction to the Talamanca mountains, read *Mamita Yunai* by Fallas, or *What Happen* by Palmer.) Continuing S from Cahuita is **Sixaola**, on the border with Panama. 2 hotels just before the bridge: *Central*, Chinese run with good restaurant, and *Pensión Doris*, F. There are no banks in Sixaola, but it may be possible to change money in one of the shops before the bridge. A narrow-gauge railway runs to Almirante (Panama) from Guabito, on the Panamanian side (shops will accept colones). Remember to advance watches by 1 hr. on entering Panama. If crossing to Panama take the earliest bus possible to Sixaola (see page 1326). Direct Sixaola-San José bus, 5 hrs., US$3 (T Sixaola 58-15-72), 0600 and 1430; also 4 a day to Puerto Limón via Cahuita.

From San José to the Pacific Coast

A paved road and a railway run from the capital to the two other main towns of the Meseta: Heredia and Alajuela.

Heredia, capital of its province, 10 km. from San José, is a great coffee and cattle centre. It looks a little like the towns of southern Spain: church towers above red-tiled roofs, iron grilles at the windows, and bright gardens set among whitewashed adobe and stone walls. The main church was built in 1797. There is a statue to the poet Aquileo Echeverría (1866-1909). The Tourist Institute will arrange a visit to a coffee *finca*. Altitude 1,137 metres, population 23,600.

Hotels *Bougainville de Santo Domingo*, A, spectacular mountain setting; *Herediana*, E, Calle 6; *Colonial*, C.4-6, Av.4, G; *El Verano*, C.4, Av.6, F.

Excursion Beautiful views from road across mountains to town of **Puerto Viejo de Sarapiquí** (*Selva Verde Lodge*, Chilamate on Río Sarapiquí, B, T 71-64-59; *Para Avis Lodge*, B, rustic cabins, T 53-08-44; *Cabinas Monteverde*, T 71-69-01, ext. 236, F with bath; Hotels *El Antiguo*—ext 205—and *Santa Marta*, both G; pensiones *Las Brisas* and *González*, both G, *Pip's* restaurant, good) on river with good fishing. There is a spectacular waterfall near here. There is a bus service from San José, C. 12, Avs. 7-9, via Heredia, US$2.50, at 0600 and 1400, returning at 0730 and 1230. Buses from Puerto Viejo to Río Frío and San Carlos. Nearby is the Organization of Tropical Studies station at Finca La Selva on the Río Sarapiquí. To visit, phone in advance to book, T 71-85-27. Visitors are provided with maps of the superb primary rain forest and a bunk in a co-ed dormitory; rates are US$60 a day inc. all meals for ordinary visitors, US$30 for students, researchers or interested journalists (proof required). Try to avoid the rainy season. To get there by car, take Route 9 from San José, 2 hours' driving; park at the suspension bridge then walk. Buses run from Puerto Viejo. The river flows into the San Juan, which forms the northern border of Costa Rica. River trips on the Sarapiquí and on the Río Sucio are beautiful (US$15 for 2 hrs.). In the mountains near Heredia is **San José de la Montaña** (hotels with beautiful views across the Meseta Central: *El Pórtico*, T 37-60-22, rec., *Cabinas Montaña Cypresal*, T 37-44-66, *Cabinas Las Ardillas*, T 37-60-22, all D with bath).

Braulio Carrillo National Park. This large park was created to protect the high rain forest north of San José from the impact of the new San José-Guápiles-Puerto Limón highway and it also includes Barba volcano. The latter is only accessible from Heredia, there is no entrance from the new highway; take a bus to **San José de la Montaña**; from there it is 4 hrs.' walk to Sacramento, but some buses continue towards Sacramento, halving the walk time (otherwise walk, hitchhike, or arrange a ride with the park director). Ranger station nearby, from which 3 km. of easy climb to the top. Good views; no permit needed here. Easter Week is a good choice. The views down the Patria River canyon are impressive. Bird watchers will also get their fill. The park is also widely known among (illegal) birdcatchers. Alternatively, you can take one of many buses to San Jerónimo de Moravia (1 hr. from San José).

Alajuela, 13 km. beyond Heredia (5 km. from Juan Santamaría international airport), capital of its province, stands at 952 metres, and is a midsummer resort for people from the capital. It is famous for its flowers and its market days (Sat. market is good value for food); an interesting craft cooperative provides pictures in relief metalwork; the unusual church of La Agonía in the E part of town has murals done from life. The national hero, Juan Santamaría, the drummer who fired the building at Rivas (Nicaragua) in which Walker's filibusters were entrenched in 1856, is commemorated by a monument. The Museo Histórico Juan Santamaría (Tues.-Sun. 1000-1700) tells the story of this war. Just outside the town is the Ojo de Agua swimming pool (good restaurant) in beautiful surroundings: a popular bathing and boating resort. Entrance, US$0.60 p.p., plus US$0.80 per vehicle. The gushing spring which feeds the pool also supplies water for Puntarenas. Population 28,700.

Hotels *Alajuela,* C. 2, Av. Central and 2 (T 41-12-41), E, with shower, clean, friendly (best to book in advance). *El Real,* C.8, Av. 1-Central, clean, F, opp. bus terminal; *Moderno,* same street but other side of railway; *El Americano,* at Turrucares (T 48-71-92), F with bath.

Restaurants *Antarcha,* Av. 2, C. 2 and Central, good; *El Cencerro,* on Parque Central, good meat, especially steaks.

Language School Centro Lingüistico Latinoamericano, Apartado 151, T 41-02-61, recommended (located in San Antonio).

Excursion From Alajuela a paved road runs to 2,704-metre volcano *Poás* (57 km. by road from San José). In the National Park of Poás, the still-smoking volcano is set in beautiful tropical forest. The crater is 1½ km. across (said to be the second largest in the world). Within part of its sharp-sided walls is a lake of very hot water. In another area geysers may throw steam 600 metres or so. One km. away is a still, forest-fringed lake in another crater. A 30-min. jungle trail to the crater starts from the car park. **Clouds often hang low over the crater** after 1000 permitting little to be seen. Entrance to Park, US$0.40. The volcano can be reached by car from San José. (Tours from San José, US$40, are not worth it since they tend to arrive after the cloud has come down and include neither lunch nor the entrance fee.) On Sunday there is a regular excursion bus from the main square of Alajuela right up to the crater, leaving at 0830, connecting with bus from San José (from Av.2, C. 12-14); be there early for a seat, extra buses run if necessary, the area gets very crowded, US$3 return. The bus waits at the top with ample time to see everything, returning at 1500. Daily bus Alajuela-Poasito 1200 (US$1). From Poasito hitch a lift as it is a 10 km. walk. The visitors' centre offers shelter, electricity outlets and good water even when closed (hours claim to be Mon.-Fri. 0800-1200, 1300-1500, Sat., Sun. and holidays 0800-1600); further up the road are good toilets. There is a restaurant near the parking area. If you spend the night there, a ranger might take you down to the water's edge on a clear night to watch and listen to the dome. The volcano is very crowded on Sun., go in the week if possible.

Hotel *Country Club Monte del Mago,* Carrillo de Poas (T 61-24-10), D with bath, swimming pool, restaurant. **Campsite** Trailer park nearby, with hookups: the *Inca.*

Beyond Alajuela the Pan-American Highway divides into a toll highway and a *vía libre,* which is the old road. Though it is rough, the latter passes through attractive countryside and the towns of Naranjo, Sarchí and Grecia.

San Carlos, also known as Villa Quesada, lies some 25 km. from the Pan-American Highway and can be reached by a road which branches off the highway near Naranjo. It is the main town of the lowland cattle and farming region. Between San Carlos and the Highway is the mountain town of Zarcero, known for its beautiful park and church. There are buses every hour from San José (US$2.50).

San Carlos Hotels *El Tucán Country Club,* B, thermal pools, sauna, T 46-18-22; *Balneario Carlos,* E with bath, swimming pool (T 46-07-47); *La Central,* E, with bath, restaurant; *Conquistador,* E with bath; *El Retiro,* E with bath; *Lily, Cristal, Diana, Ugalde, París, Los Fernandos,* all F; *La Terminal,* G.

1 hour from San Carlos by bus (US$0.60) is **Venecia** (3½ hrs., US$2.50 by bus from San José); one hotel, F, clean, friendly. Nearby is Ciudad Cutris, precolumbian tumuli (a good road goes to within 2 km. of Cutris, from there walk or take 4-wheel drive vehicle; get a permit to visit from the *finca* owner). A difficult road goes from San Carlos to **La Fortuna** (3½ hrs. US$1.50). At the base

is a thermal pool with bar/restaurant (*Balneario Tabacón*; plans are underway to build cabins). Free camping is encouraged at the site, which is 10 km. from La Fortuna on the road to Tilarán (at night you can see red hot lava bursting out into the night sky). Buses from San Carlos or Tilarán daily (limited service Tues. and Wed.); several cheap hotels in La Fortuna (*Pensión San Bosco*, E with bath; *La Central*, F, clean, quiet, cold showers, friendly; *Restaurant El Jardín*, good food, public phone with international access).

Arenal volcano can be reached by taking the road S for 20 km. (buses every 1-2 hrs. from San Carlos, or at 0800 from *Hotel Central*, La Fortuna); here are the lake and dam for hydroelectric power and irrigation. Hot baths near the dam. The volcano can be climbed, but is very dangerous because it is active with flying white-hot rock, jets of steam and explosive noises (only for the adventurous). The S side of Lake Arenal is very difficult to drive, with many fords; the longer N side is paved for all but 3 km. From San Carlos there are buses to the Río Frío district and to towns on the San Carlos and Sarapiquí rivers (incl. Puerto Viejo) where launches can be taken via the Colorado river to the Canales de Tortuguero and Moín, about 10 km. by road and rail from Puerto Limón.

At **Sarchí** one may visit the factory that produces the traditional painted ox-carts, which are almost a national emblem. Also, hand-made cowhide rocking chairs and wooden products may be purchased at Fábricas de Carretas; there are many shops at the roadside (prices are half those in San José). Travel agents in San José charge US$20 or more; Tuasa buses every 15 mins. from Alajuela bus station. The pink-painted church in Sarchí is especially attractive at sunset. **Grecia** is the centre for the pineapple-growing area (*Cabaña Los Cipreses*, D per cabin; *Complejo Trailer y Cabinas Los Trapiches*; *Pensión Quirós*, G with bath). Two very attractive towns in this region are **San Ramón** (76 km. from San José—*Hotel Nuevo Jardín*, E, with bath, hot water; *El Viajero*, F; *Restaurant Tropical*) and, 7 km. beyond, Palmares (one hotel). (The people in this region are friendly and like talking to foreigners.)

Puntarenas (population 50,000) is on a 5-km. spit of land thrusting out into Nicoya Gulf and enclosing the Estero lagoon. It is hot (mean temperature 27°C), the beaches are dirty, and are crowded on Suns. There is a new public swimming pool on the end of the point (US$ 0.35 entrance). Good surfing off the headland. Across the gulf are the mountains of the Nicoya Peninsula. In the gulf are several islands, the Islas Negritos, to which there are passenger launches. The chief products around Puntarenas are bananas, rice, cattle, and coconuts. Puntarenas is connected with San José by a road (1½ hrs,. by hourly buses), and a railway (116 km.; 4 hrs., **see page 1287**). It is being replaced as the country's main Pacific port by Caldera.

Hotels *Tioga*, Barrio El Carmen (T 61-02-71), near beach, C with bath, including continental breakfast, swimming pool, very good indeed. *Colonial*, Calle 72-74, Av. Central, C, a/c, swimming pool, with breakfast, T 61-18-33; *Porto Bello*, Calle 68 y 70, Av. Central, next door, C with bath, a/c, pool, quiet, clean, gardens, excellent food, helpful Italian owner, T 61-13-22; *Cayuga*, Calle 4, Av. Central, E, with shower, a/c, restaurant. Others are *Las Brisas*, on the waterfront, C.31-33, Av. 4, C, good restaurant, swimmimg pool; *Chorotega*, Calle 3, Av. 3, E, with bath and fan, clean, central, rec. (one block east of river); *Viking*, C. 32, Av. 2, new, on the beach, D; *Río*, Av. 3, C. Central/2, near market, F, with shower, basic and noisy, but clean and friendly; *Cabinas Thelma*, very good, friendly (ask at Holman Bar, Calle 7); *Pensión Familiar los Jardines*, nr. bus station on beach, F with fan and shared showers, clean, safe. Many *cabinas* on Av. 2. Apartments for rent from Jacob Puister, Contigua Casino, Central, 2° piso, T 61-02-46, US$37 for 2 weeks. *Cabinas Orlando* at San Isidro de Puntarenas, with bath and kitchen, D; *Villa del Roble*, by the sea 18 km. E (T 63-04-47), B, 5 rooms, quiet, charming; *Río Mar Hotel* at Barranca, 15 km. from Puntarenas, D with bath, restaurant, good, pricey. Accommodation difficult to find Dec.-April, especially at weekends.

Restaurants Next to *Hotel Tioga* is *Aloha Restaurant* (good). *Mariscos Kahite Blanco*, downtown, excellent seafood. A number of Chinese restaurants on the main street (e.g. *Mandarín*, good value). *Soda Parada* and *Soda La Nación* are both good, as is *Soda Internacional*. *Fonda Brisas del Pacífico*, near wharf, good value casado. There is a lively night life in the cheaper bars. On the beach, *Bierstube*, good for sandwiches, hamburgers and spaghetti. Recommended bars: *Pier 14*, near wharf, good pizza and hamburgers made by Captain Ed from Mobile (Alabama) and his wife; *Yate Bar*, friendly, English-speaking owner (no girls at either).

Ferry to Nicoya Peninsula (see page 1297) To Playa Naranjo (*Salinero*), US$1 p.p., US$7 per car, 1½ hrs., crossings Mon.-Fri. 0700 and 1600, returning 0900 and 1800; Sat. and Sun. 0700, 1100 and 1600, returning 0900, 1400 and 1800 (T 61-10-69). Buses meet the ferry for Coyote,

Bejuco, Nicoya and Jicaral. Launches to Paquera (for Cóbano, Playa Montezuma, etc.) daily 0600, 1500, returning at 0900 and 1800, 2 hrs., US$1.20). Take bus "Barrio Carmen" from centre for ferry.

Cables   ICE and Radiográfica.

Warning   Thieves abound on the beach.

On the San José-Puntarenas railway, near the new port of Caldera, is *Mata de Limón*, which has a beach. It is on a lagoon surrounded by mangroves, peaceful. Bus from Puntarenas market every hour (marked to Caldera); train back to Puntarenas passes through at about 1615. (Hotels: *Casablanca*, E, full board available, or cabins; *Manglares*, E, reasonable, good restaurant; *Dormitorios de Mata de Limón*, F, next to railway.)

Monteverde   The site of a 1,600-hectare private nature reserve, mainly primary cloud forest with hundreds of species of birds (including the quetzal, best seen between January and May, which are the dry months, especially near the start of the Nuboso Trail, and the three-wattled bell-birds), monkeys, reptiles, amphibians (including orange toads) and orchids and other flowers. Too many visitors have frightened most of the wildlife out of sight. Entry, US$2.50 (students US$1.65); a 7-day pass costs US$15; limited camping space, less than US$1. At any time of year protective rainwear and boots are a must; also take food and drink. The entrance is at 1,500 metres, but the maximum altitude in the Park is over 1,800 metres. The best months to visit are January to May, particularly March and April. There are two rather run down shelters in the reserve, 2 and 2½ hrs.' walk from the office (US$2.50 for their use, take sleeping bag). A free map is available from the office. An experienced guide to the reserve is Gary Diller, Apdo. 10165, 1000 San José (T 61-0903); he charges US$10 p.p. for half-day tours, US$25 for a full, 6-hr. day. Donations to the reserve can be made at the park centre, or to the Tropical Science Centre, C. 1 No. 442 (apply here for information), Apdo. 8-3870, San José.

Take bus which runs from Puntarenas, opposite the bus station, to *Santa Elena*, one a day, 1415 (2½ hrs., US$1.20) which is about 4 km. from Monteverde. Bus from Santa Elena to Puntarenas at 0600 only. From San José, take any bus in the direction of Tilarán, Las Cañas or Liberia to the turn off to Santa Elena, at Río Lagartos, about 150 km. from the capital (US$1.50 from turn off to San José). From here you can take a bus at about 1530 (Puntarenas-Santa Elena) to Santa Elena (hitching is difficult). A direct bus, The Monteverde Express, runs from San José (4 hrs., US$3.50) Mon.-Thurs. 1430, Sat.-Sun. 0630, returning Tues.-Thurs. 0630, Fri.-Sun. 1500. *Pensión Quetzal*, C, with or without bath, full board only, American-run (very popular so reservations must be made, T 61-09-55; Apdo. 10165, 1000 San José). Also *Pensión Flor Mar*, E, full board (less without food), excellent value, very friendly and helpful, American owner, rubber boots for hire; it is 3 km. from Santa Elena, 4 km. from Monteverde, Arnold's jeep meets Puntarenas bus, taxi US$4.70, 2 km. from Monteverde; for bookings, T 61-09-09. *Hotel de Montaña*, between Santa Elena and Monteverde, B, restaurant, horses for hire (US$2-3 per hr.); located just outside Santa Elena, excellent birdwatching around the hotel (reservations T 61-18-46); *Bel Mar*, C, Swiss-chalet style, beautiful views, good, T 61-10-01; *Albergue Reserva Biológica de Monteverde* (T 22-62-41), F. *Pensión Santa Elena*, in Santa Elena, F, pleasant (except room 8—very hot), cheap, clean, good food; and *Pensión de Franklyn Vargas*, F, with shower, clean; *Restaurant Irene*, opp. church, good *casado*. *Restaurant Iman*, opp. bus stop, will let you eat your Quaker cheese on its toast; under same ownership, *Pensión Iman*, inexpensive, clean, spartan, room 6 has shower. In Santa Elena there is a cooperative gift shop, Casem, which sells embroidered shirts, T-shirts, wooden and woven articles and baskets. Also Banco Nacional which changes travellers' cheques.

The settlement at Monteverde was founded by American Quakers in the 1950s; it is essentially a group of dairy farms and a cheese factory run by a cooperative. Excellent cheeses of various types can be bought; also fresh milk and *cajeta* (a butterscotch spread) are sold. The land has only been partially cleared. The Quakers have an English library at Monteverde. A number of Christian sects can be found at Santa Elena.

From Puntarenas a road runs to the Pan-American Highway at *Las Cañas*. (5 buses daily from Coca Cola terminal, San José. Hotels: *Cañas*, C, 2, Av. 1, E with bath; *El Corral*, C. 4, Av. Central, E with bath; *Guillén*, C. Central, Av. 2, F; also *Luz* and others; a good restaurant is *Rincón Corobicí*, clean and pleasant.) From there are buses to Tilarán (and from San José, 0730, 4 hrs.). (Hotels *Grecia*, F with shower, cheaper without, *Cabinas El Sueño*, both 1 block from bus station, and other *Cabinas*.) Two buses leave each afternoon for Arenal on the N side of the lake formed by the new Arenal dam (check return times if you want to go back same day). Further round the lake are the villages of the Guatuso Indians near the Nicaraguan border, Upala and Caño Negro. There is now a direct bus from San José to Upala (from Av. 5, C. 14 at 1445, 4 hrs., US$2.80), where there are the *Hotel Rigo*, *Pensión Isabela*, *Pensión Buena Vista*, basic, F, food available. 5 km. N of Las Cañas is a very good campsite and hotel, *La Pacífica*, D, French-run, with restaurant, cottages, cabins, pool, small zoo, medical service, workshop, spare parts, etc., T 69-00-50. There is free camping along the river. Good camping is also reported at a beach 2 km. north of Brasilito.

Also S of San José one can visit Aserrí, a village with a beautiful white church; further along the same road is the *Mirador Ram Luna*, a restaurant with a fine panoramic view. At the end of the road is San Ignacio de Acosta, again with a good church containing life-size Nativity figures.

Some 155 km. S of San José, in Puntarenas province, is **Puerto Quepos,** built by United Brands as a banana exporting port, but now rather run down. The road is beautiful and paved until beyond Santiago; the last hour goes through United Brands' palm oil plantations (between Santiago and the plantations is difficult on a motorbike because of the loose surface). There are 4 buses a day from the capital, book a day in advance, 3 hrs., US$2.50, and there is one daily a.m. flight and an afternoon flight on Mon., Wed., Fri. (Sansa, US$9) to the international airport, 20 mins., US$7. *Hotel Viña del Mar,* D with bath, fan, restaurant; *Hotel Quepos,* E with bath; *Linda Vista,* F with bath, OK but noisy; *Luna,* E with bath. *América,* G p.p., basic, clean; *Ramuz* (E with bath) and *Allan,* F. Accommodation is impossible to find on Sats., Dec.-April. The *Jardín Cervecero Los Arcos* sells good food; *El Gran Escape,* central, good food, cheap, slow service; *Soda Nido* and *Restaurant Ana,* cheap *casados.*

A few km. E of Quepos (½ hr.) lie the 3 beautiful beaches of **Manuel Antonio** which have been declared a National Park (entrance US$0.40, good hiking in the area; camping, US$0.25 p.p., beware of theft); the beach on which the hotels stand has dangerous rip tides, the 2 inside the park are safest (all littered and crowded at weekends). The Park is of 490 hectares with swamps as well as beaches, and a rich variety of bird life. No permit is needed to enter. A paved road runs from Quepos to Manuel Antonio and to a pleasant beach at Dominical, which has simple cabins for rent. There is a regular bus service from Quepos, 6 a day (US$0.25); taxi, US$2.50), and a twice daily bus from San José, 3½ hrs (0600, 1200). Minibuses meet flights at Quepos airport, US$1.25.

Accommodation Hotel Manuel Antonio, C, restaurant; there are many new sets of *cabinas;* the *Cabinas Ramírez* (T 77-05-10), E, without bath, food and bar, friendly, generous owners; contact Sr. Ramírez (hammocks and camping free), guests can help with cooking in exchange; *Vela-Bar,* B with private bath, large rooms, fans, safes, good restaurant, 150 m. from beach, organizes fishing and other trips, also has a fully-equipped house to rent (77-04-13, or write to Rosa, Apt. 13 Quepos); *Manuel Antonio Cabinas,* E without bath in house behind beach, F p.p. in small dirty rooms at back, no hot water, or D-C for family cabin on beach, gets very damp in rainy season; *Costa Linda,* cheapest, F, quite noisy; very basic rooms behind *Soda El Grano de Oro; Karahue,* C, friendly, clean; *Los Almendros,* good fish restaurant, has rooms for 1-4 people, E, quiet, pleasant. On beach, just S of *Ramírez,* is a shop renting surf boards, selling drinks and light meals, has a collection of English novels to read in the bar. Also, **Hotel Mariposa,** 3 km. from Manuel Antonio on way to Quepos, L, exclusive (no guests allowed under 15), but non-residents may use restaurant, good meals (book in advance), and swimming pool for US$1; nearby are the cabins of John and Mavis Beisanz (T 49-15-07), also expensive but very good. Also nearby is *Barba Roja* restaurant/bar, US-style, popular, not cheap (closed Sept.- Nov.). Take a torch when walking on roads at night; there are snakes, reportedly poisonous.

SW of San José is the Santa Ana valley, which includes the popular weekend centre of Lagos de Lindora. The road (being paved) goes on through lovely scenery to Puriscal and Puerto Quepos. Before Quepos, at Parrita, is a fine beach, Playa Palma; Hotels *El Nopal* (F) and *Memo* (E, with bath). W of Parrita is the beach at Esterillos Este (*Hotel El Delfín,* A, swimming pool, good moderately-priced restaurant, T 71-16-40); other *cabinas).* Further on is the beach at *Jacó* (with many small pebbles and rip tides, 50 km. from Quepos, 40 km. paved), which now has a good hotel *Jaco's Beach,* B, *El Jardín,* D with bath, pool, other hotels and many *cabinas,* including *Antonio* (E), *Cabinas Heredia,* E with bath, can be reached from San José (bus service, from Coca Cola terminal, 1500 daily plus 0845 at weekends, US$1.60) by taking the highway via Alajuela and turning off at Atenas to Orotina and the Río Tárcoles (bridge) and then on to Jacó. A coastal road is being built from Esparta (on the Pan-American Highway) through Orotina, Jacó, Quepos, Playa Dominical and thence on to San Isidro de El General. Paving was expected to be done and bridges in place by 1989 between Dominical and San Isidro.

To get to the Panamanian border from Puerto Quepos take the direct bus to San Isidro de El General at 0430 and 1330 daily from the cinema (5-5½ hrs.), hard ride on the unpaved coastal section, landslides can make the paved section (from Dominical) hazardous. Motorists can do a round trip from San José via San Isidro de El General and the Pacific Coast in a day in the dry season. (Turn-off on the coast road to San Isdro is near Baru.)

Isla del Coco is a thickly-wooded island and National Park of 24 square km., 320 km. off the Peninsula of Osa, in the S. It has a 2-man outpost. Contact Michael Kaye of Costa Rican Expeditions for reasonably priced tours; also Otec in San José, see page 1286. Arrangements for reaching it by chartered boat can be made in Puntarenas, after a permit has been got from the Government, or you can now take a luxury "adventure" cruise on the *Okeanos Agressor,* 10 days, two sailings a month, T 32-05-72 ext. 60. "It was at one time a refuge for pirates, who are supposed to have buried great treasure there, though none has been found by the 500 expeditions which have sought it. Treasure seekers make an initial cash payment, agree to share any treasure found with the Government, and are supervised by Costa Rican police. The offshore waters are a fisherman's paradise.

Isla San Lucás is a prison island, but you may visit its beautiful beaches on Sunday. The prisoners are friendly and sell arts and crafts very cheaply. You can buy them or exchange them for items such as toothpaste, soap, etc. There is a shop selling refreshments. Launch leaves Puntarenas Sun. 0900, but arrives by 0800; returns 1500, US$1.50.

Guanacaste Province, in the NW, includes the Peninsula of Nicoya and the lowlands at the head of the gulf. The Province, with its capital at Liberia, has a distinctive people, way of life, flora and fauna. The smallholdings of the highlands give way here to large *haciendas* and great cattle estates. Maize, rice, cotton, beans and fruit are other products, and there is manganese at Playa Real. The rivers teem with fish; there are all kinds of wildlife in the uplands.

The people are open-handed, hospitable, fond of the pleasures of life: music, dancing (the Punto Guanacasteco has been officially declared the typical national dance), and merry-making (cattle and jollity often go together). There are many *fiestas* in January and February in the various towns and villages, which are well worth seeing. There are no hotels worthy of the name, and the lowlands are deep in mud during the rainy season. From San José to Nicoya, one can go via Liberia; or one can take the Pan-American Highway to a point between Puntarenas and Cañas, at a sign to Río Tempisque ferry. After crossing on this ferry (hourly 0600-1800, US$0.50) one can drive to Nicoya. A third route is: San José to Puntarenas, then take the ferry *Salinero* across the Gulf of Nicoya to Playa Naranjo (see below). Buses ply along the road from Playa Naranjo (due W across the Gulf from Puntarenas) to Nicoya (40 km. unpaved, 30 km. paved road, crowded), US$1.25, 2¼ hrs. and to Sámara, US$1.30. At Nicoya there are connections for Liberia (US$1.30, 2 hrs., US$6 from Playa Naranjo) on the Pan-American Highway. All the beaches on the Nicoya Peninsula are accessible by road in the dry season.

Nicoya, on the Peninsula, is a pleasant little town distinguished by possessing the country's second-oldest church. 5 buses a day to San José, and to nearby towns. Daily buses to Liberia.

Hotels At Nicoya: *Curime*, D with bath, restaurant; *Las Tinajas*, near bus station, E with bath, modern, clean, good value; *Chorotega*, E with bath (F without), very good; *Jenny*, E with bath; *La Elegancia*, F; *Ali*, F, both with bath; *Pensión Venecia*, opp. old church, F, good. A good restaurant is *Chop Suey* (Chinese).

Beaches on the Nicoya Peninsula At Playa Naranjo is *Playa Oasis del Pacífico*, D, a/c, bath, and at Playa Nandayure are *El Banco*, F, and *Hotel San Marcos*, F. On the Gulf of Nicoya is Jicaral (*Hotel Guamale*, F with bath, restaurant). At Playa de El Ocotal is *Hotel El Ocotal*, A, T 66-01-66. The beaches of Tambor and Cóbano can be reached by road from Nicoya or launch from Puntarenas market to Paquera, 1½ hrs. (daily 0615 and 1515); Cóbano can also be reached by bus from Paquera ferry terminal, 1½ hrs., and buses meet the launches from Puntarenas (not the ferry), US$1.50; *La Hacienda* at Tambor, C, built around a cattle farm, excellent, good restaurant, the beach is 14 km. long, grey sand, rolling surf, 1½ hrs. on a boneshaking road from ferry; *Hotel Playa de Tambor* at Cóbano, C (other *pensiones*, F). From Cóbano it is a ½-hr. ride by taxi (US$4.50, or hitch) to *Montezuma*, a small village on the sea. *Hotel Montezuma*, D, large rooms, clean, own shower (cold), *Cabinas Mar y Cielo*, D, both with restaurants; several restaurants, 2 small shops, vegetarian car comes to Montezuma Thur. and Sun. *La Casita de Doña Karen*, F—out of season G, tiny, cosy clean cottage with kitchen; Doña Marta next door has the key. Doña Karen, who lives 1½ km. N, is Danish, speaks English, is very friendly. She and her late husband established Costa Rica's first national park; the income from renting rooms goes towards the upkeep of her 170-acre private nature reserve, which has lots of monkeys. After her death it will be a national park too. There are beautiful walks along the beach, sometimes sandy, sometimes rocky, always lined with trees. Close to the village, 20 mins. up the Montezuma river, is a beautiful, huge waterfall with a big, natural swimming pool (it's beyond a smaller waterfall). Horses for hire from the hotels.

The beach at *Sámara*, 37 km. from Nicoya, is recommended as probably the safest major bathing beach in Costa Rica. Tourists are spoiling this, and other beautiful beaches, by leaving litter. Bus from Nicoya, US$1.15, 2 hrs., twice daily (bad road, poor bus). *Brisas*, B with a/c, pool, expensive restaurant, German-owned; *Cabinas Milena*, F, clean, safe, restaurant; *Cabinas Los Almendros*, on beach, E, restaurant, disco Sat.; *Cabinas Punto Sámara*, E. Camping on the beach possible. North of Sámara is Nosara (one bus daily from Nicoya, US$2, 2 hrs., 31 km.), with 2 beaches, Guiones, which is safe for swimming, and Peladas; a colony of North Americans has formed the Nosara Association, to protect its wildlife and forests, and prevent exploitation. There is the *Hotel Playa de Nosara* (D), expensive restaurant, *Pensión Estancia Nosara*, E, and a condominium. 12 km. S of Nosara is *Hotel Villaggio Aquario Morada*, at Punta Guiones de Garza, A, a luxury beach hotel (30 bungalows, Italian restaurant, club house, bars, pool, disco, T 68-07-84).

A number of beaches are reached by unpaved roads from the Nicoya-Liberia road. They can be reached by bus from the Liberia bus station. *Playa de Panamá* and *Playa Junquillal* are reached by taking a bus from Liberia to Santa Cruz (on the Nicoya road), then bus at 1000 or 1415 from Guillermo Sánchez store to Paraíso (US$0.80), from where it is a 4 km. walk to Playa Junquillal, or take a car from one of the *cantinas* (*Hotel Antumalal*, C with bath, pool, T 68-05-06; *Villa Serena*, D, T 68-07-37; *Junquillal*, F, nice, friendly, good food; *Tortuga Inn*, 2 rooms for rent, F, restaurant, all meals, US$1/3, tent, and hammock space, run by Californian Bill Lauer who has plenty of information for travellers, also riding, fishing, hiking, surfing—and beautiful sunsets) glorious camping and a good beach. At Playa de Panamá is *Los Bananos*, cabins, restaurant and bar, D with bath, friendly, English spoken, good hiking, swimming, horseriding can be arranged, rec. (address is Apdo. 137, Liberia, Guanacaste); *Cabinas Vallejo*, F, with bath; camping possible on beach, a few basic fish restaurants, one *pulpería*—a peaceful place. Buy food inland in **Santa Cruz**, NW of Nicoya. Hotels in Santa Cruz: *Palenque Diria*, D, bath, restaurant; *Sharatoga*, D, bath (T 68-00-11); *Agente Viajero*, E, T 68-02-39. Cheap *pensiones*, G and basic: *Santa Cruz, Isabel. La Tortillera* tortilla factory is an excellent place to eat. Bus San José-Santa Cruz, 0730 direct, US$2.80; bus Santa Cruz-Tamarindo at 1500, US$0.85; Santa Cruz-Nicoya, US$0.30. Another good beach is *Playa Tamarindo*, which has an airport (plane Mon., Wed., Fri., US$12, to San José), and is served by several buses from Liberia. *Hotel Tamarindo Diria*, A with bath, excellent; *Pozo Azul*, cabins, D (all rooms), cooking facilities, clean, good; two small *pensiones: Cabinas Zullymar*, E, rec. (free, protected camping nearby), and *Dolis Bar*, E, basic. *Tamarindo Diria* has a good restaurant and there are several bars and a good restaurant, next to *Zullymar. Boutique New York*, good French clothing and waffles. The beaches go on for many km. (one, to the left is covered in small shells). At Playa Hermosa is *Playa Hermosa Cabinas*, run by an American couple, D, clean, good reasonably-priced food; also cheaper cabins (F p.p.); 3 small restaurants on the beach. Also *Condovac La Costa*, A (T 67-02-67), luxury. Walking either to the left or the right you can find isolated beaches with crystal-clear water. At Playa Flamingo (white sand) are *The Presidential Suites*, L (T 68-06-20/-04-44), *Flamingo Beach Condo Rentals* and *Club Playa Flamingo.* At Playa Potrero (black sand), *Hotel Potrero*, D, T 68-06-69; bus from Santa Cruz at 1030 and 1430. Popular (noisy and very dirty) is **Playa del Coco** in an attractive islet-scattered bay hemmed in by rocky headlands; to reach it one should leave the bus at Comunidad. There are bars, restaurants and one or two motels along the sandy beach: *Hotel Flor de Itabo*, B, T 67-00-03; *Casino Playa del Coco*, E with bath and cockroaches; *Luna Tica* E, also has a dormitory, F (friendly, clean), both usually full at weekends. Bus to San José 0800 (Arata company), US$4, 4 hrs., bus from San José (Calle 14, Av. 1-3) at 1000 and from Liberia at 1230 (US$0.50).

Barra Honda National Park   Small park in the midst of the Nicoya Peninsula. No permit required. Created to protect some caves (in particular Terciopelo) on a *mesa* and small remainders of dry tropical forest at the *mesa's* foot. First go to Nicoya (frequent buses from Liberia, or take the Tempisque ferry if you come from San José). There are several buses a day to Quebrada Honda, a settlement one hour away. The park office is there, at the foot of the *mesa*, and there are two different trails to the top; two hours hiking. Also noteworthy are the *cascadas*, bizarre limestone fountains built by sedimentation on a seasonal riverbed. You'll need a guide to get here, as the trails are hopelessly muddled by cowpaths; arrange in advance for the visit to the cave. Avoid coming in the rainy season (May to November), but the dry season is exceedingly hot in the open fields. Bring your own food from Nicoya.

Also on the Nicoya Peninsula, is the **Palo Verde National Park** of marshes and many water birds. Getting there is rather complicated.

Liberia (pop.: 13,700) is a neat, clean, cattle town with a church in the most modern style and a small meticulous market. There is a tourist office at the junction of the Pan-American Highway and the road leading to the town. There are regular buses (7 a day, US$2.30) to and from the capital. A well paved branch road leads SW into the Nicoya Peninsula.

Hotels   *La Siesta*, Calle 4, Av. 4-6, D with bath, clean, swimming pool, helpful owner who speaks English; *Las Espuelas*, 2 km. South, C, expensive but good, swimming pool, American Express accepted (T 66-01-44); *La Ronda* (T 66-04-17), E with bath, restaurant; *El Sitio*, just off highway on road to Nicoya, C, bath, a/c, good; *Intercontinental*, D, new, good; *Bramadero Motel*, E/D, not all rooms have bath, good, open air restaurant and bar but somewhat noisy, swimming pool; *Liberia*, 50 metres from main square, F with shower (less without), noisy, reasonable; *Margarita*, F, basic but OK, friendly; *Boyeros* (also has swimming pool) D, bath, restaurant; *Oriental*, F, bath, restaurant; *Motel Delfin*, 5 km. N of Liberia on the Pan-American Highway, E, with bath, run down, large swimming pool.

Good Chinese **restaurants:** *Pekin, Cuatro Mares* (just off main square), *Cantón. Elegante* restaurant opp. *Hotel Liberia.* On the west side of the Plaza is *Soda Las Finajas*, which specializes in *refrescos.*

There is also a photographic studio.

37 km. north of Liberia, about half-way to the Nicaraguan border, is the **Santa Rosa National Park** (entry US$0.35; camping US$0.55). Together with the Murciélago Annex, which lies north of the developed park, it preserves some of the last dry tropical forests in Costa Rica, and shelters abundant and relatively easy-to-see wildlife. During the dry season, the animals depend on the water holes, and are thus easy to find (except at the end of the season when the holes dry up). Santa Rosa (16,000 hectares) is easy of access from San José, as it lies west of the Pan-American

Highway, about one hour north of Liberia. Any bus going to Peñas Blancas (from Libreria, US$0.80, 1½ hrs.) on the Nicaraguan border will drop you right at the entrance. There is a pleasant campground about 7 km. from the entrance with giant strangler figs that shade your tent from the stupendously hot sun, and very adequate sanitary facilities, picnic tables, and so forth. Bring your own food, although meals available for US$3 from kitchen at administration; a tent is useful—essential in the wet season. Bring a mosquito net and insect repellant against gnats. (If the water is not running, ask at Administration. Administration hires horses for US$1.50 per hour; if you want to make a one-way journey, ask for a *vuelvo automático*, horse which will make its own way home.) In the park is the Santa Rosa *hacienda* (*Casona*), at the start of the nature trail and close to the camp. There the patriots repelled the invasion of the filibuster Walker, who had entrenched himself in the main building.

Michael Tesch and Leone Thiele of Cape Paterson, Australia, write "Playa Naranjo (3 hrs.' walk or more) and Playa Nancite (20 mins. further) are major nesting sites of Leatherback and Ridley sea turtles. The main nesting season is between August and October (although stragglers are seen up to January regularly) when flotillas of up to 60,000 Ridley turtles arrive at night on Playa Nancite. Females clumsily lurch up the beach, scoop out a 2-foot hole, deposit and bury an average of 100 ping-pong-ball sized eggs before returning exhausted to the sea." Playa Nancite is a restricted access beach; you need a written permit to stay there free, otherwise, US$1 per day to camp, or US$1.50 in dormitories. Permits from SPN in San José.

Rincón de la Vieja National Park (20,000 hectares, NE of Liberia) was created to preserve the area around the Volcán Rincón de la Vieja, including dry tropical forest and various geothermal curiosities: mudpots, hot sulphur springs, hot springs of various other kinds. The ridge of which the volcano is the highest peak can be seen from a wide area around Liberia; it is often enshrouded in clouds. The area is cool at night and subjected to strong, gusty winds and violent rains; in the day it can be very hot, although always windy. These fluctuations mark all of the continental divide, of which the ridge is a part. To get there: a bumpy 2-hr. ride from Liberia in a truck leaving at irregular hours; alternatively, inquire when the park's truck will visit Liberia; a frequent occurrence. You can stay for free in an old, spacious, refurbished *hacienda* 2 km. inside the park. Bring your own food and bedding. From the old *hacienda* you can hike to the boiling mudpots and come back in the same day; the sulphur springs are on a different trail and only 1 hr. away. Horses can be rented from the park for US$0.60 per hour. The climb to the volcano requires camping near the top (need a tent) in order to ascend early in the morning before the clouds come in. Permission required from the SPN for visiting the park. Warning: millions of tiny ticks can be picked up in a short time of strolling in the apparently innocuous grass. Bring masking tape and a flashlight for those midnight tick hunts.

The Pan-American Highway to the Nicaraguan border, 332 km., completely paved and good. From San José it leads past El Coco airport, Heredia and Alajuela, on a new dual-carriageway section, to San Ramón (79 km.) in the middle of a coffee area, where there are good hotels (**see page 1294**). From San Ramón to Cañas, now resurfaced, is 98 km.; this stretch includes the sharp fall of 800 metres from the Meseta Central between San Ramón and Esparza (34 km.). (Beware of fog on this stretch if driving or cycling.) Beyond Esparza there is a left turn for Puntarenas. From Esparza through Cañas to the frontier (198 km.) the road runs through the low hills of northern Guanacaste Province; the likeliest stopover is Liberia (**see page 1298**), 119 km. from Esparza and 79 from Peñas Blancas on the Nicaraguan border. (Bus Liberia-Peñas Blancas, US$1.25, usually very crowded at 0900, very few between late a.m. and late p.m., third and last bus Peñas Blancas-Liberia at 1700. Bus Peñas Blancas-San José, Tracopa, 1030 and 1500, from San José—Coca Cola terminal—at 0445 and 0745, 6 hrs, US$2.50.) The last town before the border is La Cruz, with eating places and 3 small hotels (*El Faro*, F, clean), lovely views over the bay. At Peñas Blancas there are a duty-free shop, a bank which changes travellers' cheques and a thriving black market for córdobas. There is a good bar and restaurant adjoining the Costa Rican immigration offices; a good map of Costa Rica is available from the tourist office at the border (the desk opposite the counter where one pays entry tax). It's a 5 km. walk from Costa Rican immigration to the Nicaraguan side of the border. The Costa Rican border offices and the Nicaraguan border are closed 1200-1300. Crossing to Nicaragua can be a slow process (up to 6 hrs.). If you have no outward ticket for Costa Rica, you can buy a cheap bus ticket back to Nicaragua at the border (valid for 1 year).

The Pan-American Highway to the Panama border runs 352 km. from San José (frequent rockslides during rainy season). First to Cartago (toll road, US$0.10), and southwards over the mountains between Cartago and San Isidro de El General (124 km.). (This is a spectacular journey. The climate is ideal for orchids.) At Cartago begins the ascent of Cerro Buena Vista, a climb of 1,830 metres to the continental divide at 3,490 metres; this is the highest spot on the Highway (with an interesting *páramo* ecosystem). Those unaccustomed to high altitude should beware of mountain sickness brought on by a too rapid ascent—see Health Information, page 30. For 16 km. it follows the crest of the Talamanca ridge, with views, on clear days, of the Pacific 50 km. away, and even of the Atlantic, over 80 km. away.

5½ km. S. of the highest point (at Km. 95, 3,335 metres, temperatures below zero at night) is *Hotel Georgina*, E, a bit primitive but good food; before you get there a side road leads off to the peaceful mountain villages of **Santa María de Dota** (Hotel Santa María, E with bath) and San Marcos de Tarrazú (Hotels: Marilú, F, restaurant; Continental, E with bath; Zacateca, F with bath). Santa María is quiet, and beautifully situated; it is in a good area for walking, and 8 km. away is a small lake where many waterbirds nest. From Santa María one can hike (10 hrs.) to the Pacific coast of the Puerto Quepos district, or go by road (3 hrs. in a 4-wheel drive vehicle).

The road then drops down into **San Isidro de El General**, 760 metres above sea-level in a fertile valley in the centre of a coffee and cattle district. The town is growing fast and now has several hotels: **Amaneli**, with restaurant, and **Manhattan**, both E with bath; **Lala**, F, cheap, shared bath; poor ventilation; **Astoria, Del Sur**, D with bath, comfortable, swimming pool, good restaurant; **Hotel Balboa** in the centre, F, with bath; **Hotel Chirripó**, E with bath, near bus office, modern, clean, good; **El Jardín** hotel, F (good value), and good restaurant (especially the breakfast); **Restaurant Wu Fu** is good, as are **Kong Kong**, across the park from **Hotel Chirripó**, and **Soda El Parque**, one block from Parque Central, reasonable prices; **Restaurant El Tenedor**, not bad. Club de Montañismo Kabata (part of Asociación Costarricense de Conservación de la Naturaleza) meets 1st and 3rd Fri. of each month at 1900, 25 metres from main square, sign on 2nd floor balcony next to dentist.

From San Isidro de El General one can go to the highest mountain in Costa Rica, Cerro El Chirripó (3,820 metres) in the middle of the **Chirripó** National Park (at 72,000 hectares, the second largest), including the highest peaks of Costa Rica and a considerable portion of cloud forest. Splendid views from the mountaintops; interesting alpine environment on the high plateau.

At San Isidro de El General, get food and take the Pueblo Nuevo bus to San Gerardo (0500 or 1400; be early; it leaves from the NE corner of the central plaza, but enquire carefully or you may miss it). Highly interesting trip up the Chirripó River valley; San Gerardo offers no lodging and little food; but it is situated in a cool, pleasant landscape at the confluence of two rivers. You can camp at or near the park office, 500 metres further up the road from the bus stop. Horses can be rented. There is a hot spring 1 km. from San Gerardo. Start in the early morning for the 8- to 10-hr. hike; no special skills are needed. The first shelter, where the horses will take you, is barely adequate and located in a windy spot; the second, 40 min. away, is better built, larger, and more convenient for reaching Cerro Chirripó the next morning before the clouds come in. Plan for at least two nights on the mountain, and bring warm sleeping bags and clothing. It can be hot in the daytime, though. In the rainy season trails up the plateau are uncomfortably slippery and muddy, and fog obscures the views. Time your descent to catch the 1530 bus to San Isidro. Permission from SPN necessary for this park.

Near the border is the town of **San Vito**, built by Italian immigrants among denuded hills; it is a prosperous but undistinguished town. **Hotel Pitier**, 2 blocks off main street, new, clean, E with bath; **Las Mirlas** in same range; and **El Ceibo** without bath. Tracopa bus from San José, 0630 daily, book previous day. Hotels also in the nearby village of Cañas Gordas. At Las Cruces there is a botanical garden run by an American couple, in an old coffee plantation, 8 km. from San Vito. It consists of 50 hectares of tropical plants, orchids, other epiphytes, and tropical trees. Many birdwatchers come here. It is possible to spend the night here if you arrange first with the Organization of Tropical Studies in San José. Buses to Ciudad Neily 0700, 1730, or easy to hitch; from San Vito at 0530 and 0700; return buses pass Las Cruces at 1510.

Thirty-two km. N of the border a road (26 km.) branches S at Río Claro to **Golfito**, the former banana port (fuel available at the junction on the Pan-American Highway). Many of the banana plantations have been turned over to oil palm, others are diseased, so much of Golfito's business has disappeared. Golfito is really two towns—the banana company community and the town itself—about 2½ km. apart. (Hotels: **Costa Rica Surf**, D; **Delfina**, G; **Golfito**, E with bath; **Miramar**, F with bath; **Cabinas El Tortugo**, C, with good restaurant (**Las Gaviotas**) on waterfront; **El Uno**, above restaurant of same name, G, basic, friendly.) About 6 km. (1½ hr. walk) from Golfito is the Playa de Cacao and Captain Tom's place, where you can sling your hammock or camp for US$5 a day (he also has accommodation: boat, caravan or shed—the cheapest—and sells pricey drinks), but take your own food as local shopping is poor. A taxi boat from Golfito will take you there for US$0.50 (1½ km.), or you can drive (if it hasn't rained too heavily) along an inland road, starting at the left of the police station in Golfito, and left again a few km. later. 0630 bus from San José (US$3.50) with Tracopa; from San Isidro de El General, take 0730 bus to Río Claro and wait for bus coming from Ciudad Neily. Daily flights San José-Golfito, US$12. Bus Golfito-Paso Canoas, US$0.70.

At the southern end of the country is the **Osa Peninsula**, reached by public boat from Golfito. A boat leaves at 0700 and 1200 for **Puerto Jiménez**, the only town on the Peninsula (1 hr., US$1; returning 0500 and 1000, all times subject to the tide). At the same time a smaller boat leaves for Rincón (boat is called Rincón, 4 hrs., US$1.75). Accommodation in Puerto Jiménez: best is **Cabinas Los Manglares**, small, cold showers, D, restaurant, T 78-50-02 for reservation; **Cabinas Brisas del Mar**, F with bath (T 78-50-12); **Pensión Quintero**, G p.p., clean, good value. Also on the Peninsula: Estación Biológica Marenco (information, P.O. Box 4025, San José, T 21-15-94). Plenty of deserted beaches (tide goes out a long way, plenty of sandflies at high tide). Puerto Jiménez is full of North Americans because of the gold mines near Carate on the Pacific coast and elsewhere on the Peninsula. Several buses a day to Dos Brazos to see the gold mines; ask for the road which goes uphill, beyond town, for the mines. Last bus back from Dos Brazos at 1530 (often late). Rubber boots advisable as a precaution against poisonous snakes. To reach

Puerto Jiménez from the Pan-American Highway (70 km.), turn R at the restaurant about 30 km. S of Palmar Sur; the road is newly paved to Rincón, therafter best tackled with four-wheeled drive as a few rivers have to be forded (high clearance essential). Bus Puerto Jiménez-Ciudad Neily 0500 and 1400, 3½ hrs., US$2.50. There is a police checkpoint 47 km. from the Pan-American Highway. Trucks, called "taxis" run daily between Puerto Jiménez and La Palma (several, 1 hr., US$1.50); from the small settlement of La Palma an all-weather road goes to Rincón.

From Agujitas boats go to the **Corcovado National Park**. Including the Isla del Caño, it comprises 86,000 hectares, making it the largest park in the system. It consists largely of tropical rainforests, and it includes swamps, miles of empty beaches, and some cleared areas now growing back. It is located at the western end of the Osa Peninsula, on the Pacific Ocean. The SPN plane will fly you in (Wednesdays US$47 round trip) if they have room. Reserve well in advance. You may also arrange to eat meals and lodge at Sirena (where the plane leaves you). There is a reasonable fee for these services; lodging is US$1.20, in the open and relatively cool attic of the main building at Sirena; bring mosquito netting.

From Sirena you can walk north along the coast to the shelter at Llorona (adequate; plenty of water—waterfalls, in fact), from which there is a trail to the interior with another shelter at the end. From Llorona you can proceed north through a forest trail and then along the beach to the station at San Pedrillo on the edge of the park. You can stay here, camping or under roof, and eat with the friendly rangers, who love company. From San Pedrillo you can take the park boat (not cheap) to Isla del Caño, a lovely park outpost with 2 men. New tourist facilities at Bahía Drake, close to Isla del Caño include: *La Paloma Jungle Lodge*, L with bath, meals, T 39-29-11. *Drake Bay Wilderness Camp*, B with meals per person, pleasant family atmosphere, canoeing, ocean fishing, horse riding facilities, large reductions for children, rec., T 71-74-36; *Cabinas Isla Fantasma*, E. Continue north to the village of Agujitas (*Cabinas Sir Francis Drake*, B with bath per person, meals, T 71-24-36), outside the park. Frequent trips with the park boat from San Pedrillo to Agujitas. From Agujitas you can get a boat (road under construction) to Sierpe on the Sierpe River (4 hrs.; perhaps 2 boats a week; boat from Sierpe to Bahía Drake, 1½ hrs., US$60 return p.p.); Sierpe is connected by bus with the town of Palmar (flights from San José, US$11) on the Pan-American Highway. Also from Sirena you can walk along the beach to Madrigal on a southern direction (excellent tidepools on the way; 2 hrs. walking) and continue along the coast to Carate.

You can head inland from Sirena on a trail past three conveniently spaced shelters to the park border (6 hrs. of walking); then, crisscrossing the Río Rincón to La Palma, a settlement near the opposite side of the Peninsula (six more hours); from which there are several "taxis" making the one-hour trip to Puerto Jiménez. An offshoot of this trail will lead you to a raffia swamp that rings the Corcovado Lagoon. The lagoon is only accessible by boat, but there are no regular trips. Caymans and alligators survive here, sheltered from the hunters. Horses can be rented cheaply at Sirena. Chiggers (*coloradillas*) infest the horse pastures and can be a nuisance; bring spray-on insect repellant.

Avoid the rainy season. Bring umbrellas (not raincoats—too hot), because it will rain. Shelters can be found here and there, so only mosquito netting is indispensable. Bring all your food if you haven't arranged otherwise; food can only be obtained at Puerto Jiménez and Agujitas in the whole peninsula, and lodging likewise. The cleared areas (mostly outside the park, or along the beach) can be devastatingly hot. Get the Instituto Geográfico maps, scale 1:50,000. Remember finally that, as in any tropical forest, you may find some unfriendly wildlife, like snakes (fer-de-lance and bushmaster snakes may attack without provocation), and herds of wild pigs.

At **Palmar Sur** (gas station), 99 km. from the border, a banana plantation has stone spheres, 1½ metres in diameter and accurate within 5 mm., which can also be seen in other places in Costa Rica. They are of precolumbian Indian manufacture, but their use is a matter of conjecture; among recent theories are that they were made to represent the planets of the solar system, or that they were border markers. Flights San José-Palmar Sur on Mon., Wed., Sat., US$12. 96 km. from the border at Río Claro is *Cabinas Pérez* (F with bath). At *Ciudad Neily*, about 18 km. from the border, are the *Motel Rancho*, F with bath; *Hotel Musuco*, E with bath, F without, fan, good, clean, quiet; 4 sets of *cabinas* (all E with bath) and *pensiones* in F range. 6 km. from the border is the *Camino Real* where it is possible to camp. Here and there on the road *cantinas* sell local food. Bus Ciudad Neily to border, US$0.25. Daily bus to San José, Tracopa, from main square, US$2.70, 7 hrs. (on Sunday buses from the border are full by the time they reach Ciudad Neily). The road goes (plenty of buses, 20 mins.) to **Paso Canoas** (Azteca, E, *Cabinas Interamericano* E, *Evelyn*, F, and *El Descanso* F, all with bath) on the Panama border. No fruit or vegetables can be taken into Panama. At Paso Canoas shops sell luxury items brought from Panama at prices considerably lower than those of Costa Rica (e.g. sunglasses, stereo equipment, kitchen utensils, etc.); banks either side of border close at 1600. No difficulty in getting rid of surplus colones with money changers. Bus San José-Paso Canoas, US$5.25, Tracopa terminal Av. 18, C. 4 at 0500, 0800 and 1700, not all buses go to border; Paso Canoas-San José at 0700 and 1400. Those motoring N can get insurance cover at the border for US$6 ensuring public liability and property damage. Border open 0700-1130, 1300-1700, 1800-2200. **N.B.** If you need a tourist card only to enter Panama, you are strongly advised to get it before the border, as Panamanian border officials often do not have them (**see page 1333**).

THE ECONOMY

The country's economy is based on the export of coffee, bananas, meat, sugar and cocoa. The Meseta Central with its volcanic soil is the coffee-growing area: here too are grown the staple crops: beans, maize, potatoes and sugar cane, and the dairy farming is both efficient and lucrative. Some 22% of the land area is planted to crops, 36% to pasture and 40% is forested. The country's timber industry is very small and its resources have yet to be commercially utilized.

High growth in the industrial sector has led to considerable economic diversification, and industry accounts for about 20% of gdp, compared with 21% in the case of agriculture. Industry is largely concerned with food processing but there is also some production of chemicals (including fertilizers—also exported), plastics, tyres, etc. Current major industrial projects include aluminium processing, a petrochemical plant at Moín, and a tuna-fish processing plant at Golfito.

There are small deposits of manganese, mercury, gold and silver, but only the last two are worked. Deposits of iron ore are estimated at 400m. tons and sulphur deposits at 11m. tons. Considerable bauxite deposits have been found but have not yet been developed. In 1980, the Arenal hydroelectric plant was opened; when operating at full capacity it can supply 98% of the country's electricity needs. The Government is presently involved in developing the Corobicí and other hydroelectric complexes as well as improving the port of Caldera on the Pacific coast and encouraging manufacturing through the state agency Codesa. Oil companies are interested in offshore concessions in the Pacific. There is an oil refinery at Puerto Limón.

Despite several IMF-supported austerity programmes, the Costa Rican economy still suffers from large public sector deficits, partly because of a high level of government spending on social welfare. The country is burdened with a large foreign debt, which including accumulated arrears, amounts to nearly US$5bn and is one of the highest per capita in the developing world. In the late 1980s, Costa Rica turned to the IMF and the World Bank for help in adjusting its economy, and proposed several radical means by which it could service its debt to commercial banks and other creditors.

	1960-71 (av)	1971-80 (av)	1981-85 (av)	1986-88 (av)(e)
Gdp growth (1980 prices)	6.1%	5.6%	0.2%	4.8%
Inflation	2.3%	10.8%	34.8%	16.4%
Exports (fob) US$m	137	601	922	1,132
Coffee	52	180	255	353
Bananas	35	126	231	226
Beef	79	45	53	60
Imports (fob)m	164	765	959	1,184
Current account balance US$m (cum)	-407	-2,823	-1,503	-766

INFORMATION FOR VISITORS

Air Services From London: British Airways, Pan Am, Continental, or Virgin Atlantic to Miami, then by Eastern Airlines, Lacsa, Pan Am (all non-stop), or Taca (via San Salvador) to San José. Carriers from the USA are: from Houston, Sahsa (via Tegucigalpa), Taca (via San Salvador); from San Francisco, Taca (via San Salvador); from Los Angeles, Taca, Lacsa, Eastern (via Miami), Mexicana; from New Orleans, Lacsa, Taca, Sahsa; from New York, Pan Am, Lacsa, Eastern (via Miami); from Los Angeles, Lacsa, Eastern (via Miami). From Canada: Fiesta Sun, from Toronto (once a week—Sat.—non-stop charter), and from Vancouver (twice a month, Mon.). Lacsa flies to the following Central and South American destinations (other airlines on these routes in brackets): Mexico City (Mexicana, Taca, Aeronica), Cancún, Guatemala City (Mexicana, Copa, SAM, Aeronica, Taca), Managua (Aeronica, Copa, Sahsa), San Pedro Sula (Sahsa), San Salvador

(Taca, Aeronica, Copa), Panama City (Copa, Taca, Aeronica), San Juan (Puerto Rico—Iberia), Bogotá (SAM) and Barranquilla (Copa), Maracaibo and Caracas. Varig flies from Quito/Guayaquil, Rio de Janeiro, São Paulo (once a week). Aeronica excursion from Panama City, US$200 including 3 free nights in a good hotel and free airport transfers. Other connections from San José: Belize City (Sahsa, Taca), Tegucigalpa (Sahsa), San Andrés Island (SAM), Kingston, Jamaica (Copa via Panama), Lima (Iberia, once a week, Fri., March to October only). From Europe: KLM from Amsterdam twice a week via Curaçao and Guatemala; Iberia from Madrid via Santo Domingo or San Juan, twice a week, with a once-weekly flight to Lima.

There is an airport tax of US$6.50 for tourists. There is an 8% tax on airline tickets purchased in the country. For cheap flights for students **see Otec, page 1286.**

Shipping Services   The quickest and cheapest freight route from the United Kingdom is by vessels of the Pacific Steam Navigation Co., with transshipment at Cristóbal: thence by local service to Limón or through the Canal to Puntarenas. Hapag-Lloyd and the Horn Line have services from European ports to Puntarenas and Puerto Limón. Shipping a vehicle from Puerto Limón to Guayaquil costs US$1,500 in a container (virtually impossible to travel with your car on the ship); arrange through an Agente de Vapores (look in Yellow Pages), US$200-500 for agents' fees and "miscellaneous charges."

Documents   A passport is required. For visits of up to 90 days the following do not need visas: nationals of most Western European countries, Canada, Israel, Japan, Yugoslavia, Romania, Argentina, Colombia, Panama and South Korea. The following also do not need a visa, but visits are limited to 30 days: citizens of the USA, Australia, New Zealand, Eire, Belgium, Switzerland, Iceland, Monaco, Brazil, Mexico, Ecuador, Guatemala and Honduras. US and Canadian citizens may enter with a tourist card, which can be purchased at airline counters for US$2 on proof of identity. Extensions may be arranged for US$1.20, but they involve a lot of red tape. All other nationalities need a visa, costing US$20, valid for only 30 days.

Extensions for visas are very costly, about US$30; they are valid for 30 days. With any extension, you have to get an exit visa when you leave (US$12). Alternatively you can just get an exit permit, which is valid for one month. This involves going to Tribunales in San José to declare that you are leaving no dependants in Costa Rica. There is an emigration tax of US$2. For longer stays ask for a Prórroga de Turismo at Migración in Puntarenas. For this you need 3 passport photos, an airline or bus ticket out of the country and proof of funds (e.g. travellers' cheques); you can apply for an extension of 1 or 2 months, 175 colones per month. The paperwork takes three days. If you leave the country, you must wait 72 hours before returning, but it may be cheaper and easier to do this and get a new 30-day entry. Travel agents can arrange all extension and exit formalities for a small fee.

An onward ticket (a bus ticket—which can be bought from the driver on Tica international buses—a transatlantic ticket or an MCO will do) is asked for, but cashing in an air ticket is difficult because you may be asked to produce another ticket out of the country. Also, tourists may have to show at least US$300 in cash or travellers' cheques before being granted entry (especially if you have no onward ticket). Half a kilo of manufactured tobacco and 3 litres of liquor are allowed in duty-free. Any amount of foreign or local currency may be taken in or out. Always carry a passport, or photocopy, for presentation at spot-checks. Failure to do so may mean imprisonment.

N.B.   If you have been more than a few days in Nicaragua (for example, working on a brigade), you may be refused entry into Costa Rica. Nicaraguan literature is likely to be confiscated. If entering from Nicaragua, you will be forced to take a blood-test for malaria at the border point, and if you are not carrying anti-malaria tablets, officials may oblige you to swallow some in their presence. There have also been cases of tourists with stamps from Eastern bloc countries in their passports being refused entry.

N.B. also   Entrance and exit taxes, by air or land, and legislation regarding visa extensions, are subject to frequent change and travellers should check these details as near to the time of travelling as possible.

Warnings   Those arriving by air from Colombia can expect to have their persons and baggage carefully searched because of the rampant drug traffic in the area. In Costa Rica, particularly on the Atlantic coast, do not get involved with drugs: many dealers are undercover police agents.

There has been much illegal immigration into Costa Rica: this explains why Migración officials sometimes grill visitors in their hotels.

The information offices of the **Instituto Costarricense de Turismo** are by the Plaza de la Cultura, entrance on C. 5, Av. Central/2, San José (T 22-10-90). There is a branch office at Cartago. All tourist information is given here. Take complaints about hotel overcharging to the

Instituto. There is a free weekly magazine, *The San José Gourmet*, dealing with tourism and restaurant news.

Shopping Best buys are wooden items, ceramics, leather handicrafts and coffee.

British business travellers going to Costa Rica are strongly advised to get a copy of "Hints to Exporters: Costa Rica" from Export Services Division, Dept. of Trade, Sanctuary Buildings, 16-20 Great Smith Street, London SW1P 4DB.

Business Hours 0800 or 0830 to 1100 or 1130 and 1300 to 1700 or 1730 (1600, government offices), Mon. to Fri., and 0800 to 1100 on Sat. Shops: 0800 to 1200, 1300 to 1800 Mon. to Sat.

Standard Time is 6 hrs. behind Greenwich Mean Time.

The climate varies from the heat and humidity of the Caribbean and Atlantic lowlands to warm temperate on the Meseta Central and chilly temperate at the greater heights. There are dry and wet seasons: the dry runs from December to April, the wet from May to November, when the rainfall in the Meseta Central averages 1,950 mm. and roads are often bogged down. The hottest months are March and April. Between December and April is the best time to visit.

Clothing Strapless sun-dresses are never worn in San José, but trousers are quite OK for women. Shorts are only acceptable at the beach or country club, especially for women. Women need hats only for weddings and official functions.

Health Drinking water is safe in all major towns; elsewhere it should be boiled. Intestinal disorders and Chagas disease are prevalent in the lowlands although malaria has to a great extent been eradicated; malaria prophylaxis is advised for visitors to the lowlands, all the same; in Costa Rica it is available only from the Ministerio de Salud in San José (free). Uncooked foods should not be eaten. The standards of health and hygiene are among the best in Latin America. Ice cream, milk, etc. are safe.

Food Stefaan Platteau, resident in San José, tells us: *Sodas* (small restaurants) serve local food, which is worth trying. Very common is *casado*, which includes rice, beans, stewed beef, fried plantain and cabbage. *Olla de carne* is a soup of beef, plantain, corn, yuca, *ñampi* and *chayote* (local vegetables). *Sopa negra* is made with black beans, and comes with a poached egg in it; *picadillo* is another meat and vegetable stew. Snacks are popular: *gallos* (filled tortillas), *tortas* (containing meat and vegetables), *arreglados* (bread filled with the same) and *empanadas*. *Pan de yuca* is a speciality, available from stalls in San José centre. A *soda* in Moravia (8 km. from San José), *Soda San Martín*, is highly rec. for local fare. Best ice cream can be found in *Pops* shops in San José. *Schmidt* bakeries are highly rec.; they also serve coffee. Also *La Selecta* bakeries. Eating in Costa Rica is cheap on the whole.

There are many types of cold drink, made either from fresh fruit, or milk drinks with fruit or cereal flour whisked with ice cubes. The fruits range from the familiar to the exotic; others include *cebada* (barley flour), *pinolillo* (roasted corn), *horchata* (rice flour with cinnamon), *chan*, "perhaps the most unusual, looking like mouldy frogspawn and tasting of penicillin" (Michael J. Brisco). All these drinks cost the same as, or less than, bottled fizzy products. Excellent coffee.

Motoring Car hire firms are not covered by tourist regulations and many complaints have been made to the authorities concerning their operations. If hiring a car, be very cautious. Tourists who come by car pay US$10 road tax and can keep their cars for an initial period of 30 days. This can be extended for a total period of 6 months at the Instituto Costarricense de Turismo, or at the Customs office if you take your passport, car entry permit, and a piece of stamped paper (*papel sellado*) obtainable at any bookshop. Cars are fumigated on entry (50 colones). It is now mandatory for foreign drivers to buy insurance stamps on entry for a minimum of 3 months; e.g. motorcycle, US$6 and car, US$6. If you want to travel on from Costa Rica without your car, you should leave it in the customs warehouse at the international airport at San José. For a longer period than 60 days, however, it is necessary to leave it in a private bonded warehouse. The cost is about US$10 a week, plus US$60 to arrange it through a customs agent, plus a considerable amount of paperwork. San José is the best place to get Land Rover spares. To sell a car in Costa Rica you must pay a duty which is equivalent to four times the market value of the car. **Important Note:** Only regular-grade gasoline is available (but of good quality), US$0.40 per litre; high-compression engines need to be adjusted before entering Costa Rica. Tyres without rims are confiscated and burnt by the Customs. It is illegal to ride in a car or taxi without wearing seatbelts. Motorcyclists must wear crash helmets. Gas-oil is available, as are spares for Japanese makes in San José.

Cycling John Gilchrist tells us that cycling is easier in Costa Rica than elsewhere in Central America; the asphalted roads are better, there is less heavy traffic and it is generally "cyclist friendly". The prevailing wind is from the north-east, so if making an extensive tour, travelling in the direction of Panama-Nicaragua is slightly more favourable. Be prepared for a lot of rain. It is perfectly possible to travel light, without tent, sleeping bag or cooking equipment.

Hitch-hiking is easy by day in the week. Walkers should obtain a copy of *Backpacking in Mexico and Central America* (1982), by Hilary Bradt and Rob Rachowiecki.

Currency The unit is the colón, sub-divided into 100 céntimos. The old coins of 5, 10, 25 and 50 céntimos and 1 and 2 colones, and notes of 5, 10 and 20 colones are being phased out. New coins in use are for 25 and 50 céntimos and 1, 2, 5, 10 and 20 colones. Public telephones now use 2, 5, and 10 colón coins. Paper money in use: 50, 100, 500 (new, orange-coloured) and 1,000 colones. (5,000 and 10,000 colon notes have not yet been issued, although they are planned).

Exchange of US dollars (etc) must be effected in a bank, and for bank drafts and transfers commission may be charged (set by the banks themselves). Most tourist and first class hotels will change dollars for guests only. A small black market exists although it is illegal to exchange in the street, and is hardly worth the risk. In May 1989 the official exchange rate was 80.50 colones per US$. It is almost impossible to exchange any other major currency in Costa Rica; only the Banco Lyon, S.A., will do so (e.g. Barclays sterling cheques) but at very poor rates.

Tips A 10% service charge is automatically added to restaurant bills, as well as 10% government tax. Ten colones per bag for porters; same for hairdressers. Taxis and cinema usherettes, nil; 10% at hotels, restaurants, cafés, bars; Ten colones for cloakroom attendants.

Mail by sea from the UK takes from 2-3 months and 3 to 5 days by airmail. Airmail letters to Europe cost 24 colones; to North/South America, 18 colones; to Australia, Africa and Asia, 28 colones. "Expreso" letters, 17 colones extra, several days quicker to USA and N. Europe. Registered mail, 30 colones extra. All parcels sent out of the country by foreigners must be taken open to the post office for clearance (packaging available from The Bookshop in San José). Lista de Correos charges 8 colones per letter, and will keep letters for 4 weeks.

Cable Offices and long-range radio-telephone service are run by the Instituto Costarricense de Electricidad and by Cía. Radiográfica Internacional de Costa Rica, whose HQ is at San Pedro. Local cables, though, are sent from the main post office in San José, Av. 1/3, C. 2. A telephone system connects San José with the country's main centres. The Government's wireless station at San José communicates with Mexico, Guatemala and El Salvador. A Radio and Telephone Ground Satellite Station was opened at Aserrí in January 1982. Calls abroad can be made from phone booths; collect calls abroad may be made from special booths in the telephone office, Av. 5, C. 1, San José. A daytime telephone call to the UK costs US$3 a minute, US$2 Fri. 1900 to Mon. 0700; to USA and Canada, US$1.60-3.80 per min., US$0.65-1.50 at night (2200-0700) and weekends, depending on to which state or province; to Australia, Africa, Asia, US$5 per minute. Public telex booth at Radiográfica S.A., Av. 5, C. 1 (telex CR 1050); the telex must show your name and Tel. no. or address for them to advise you; also public FAX service, to receive, 100 colones (FAX +506-231-609 or +506-337-932); to send, US$5.50 per page to Europe, US$4 per page to USA. There is a public telex service run by Canon Copying Centres (Av. 2, C. 11/13—Telex No. CR 2913) who charge US$1 for receiving; telex to UK, US$3 per minute.

For Customs the metric system of **weights and measures** is compulsory. Traders use a variety of weights and measures, including English ones and the old Spanish ones.

Public Holidays

January 1: New Year's Day	August 2: Virgin of Los Angeles.
March 19: St. Joseph.	August 15: Mothers' Day.
Easter: 3 days.	September 15: Independence Day.
April 11: Battle of Rivas.	October 12: Columbus Day.
May 1: Labour Day.	December 8: Conception of the
June: Corpus Christi.	Virgin
June 29: St. Peter and St. Paul	December 25: Christmas Day.
July 25: Guanacaste Day.	December 28-31: San José only.

N.B. During Holy Week, nearly everyone is on holiday. Everywhere is shut on Fri., Sat., and Sun., and most of the previous week as well (in San José and Cartago only a small percentage of businesses and services close Mon.-Wed. and Sat. of Holy Week; almost all transport stops on Good Friday only).

Association football is the **national sport** (played every Sunday at 1100, May to October, at the Saprissa Stadium). There are golf courses at San José and Puerto Limón. There is sea-bathing on both Atlantic and Pacific coasts (see text). The Meseta is good country for riding; horses can be hired by arrangement directly with owners. Most *fiestas* end with bullfighting in the squares, an innocuous but amusing set-to with no horses used. Bullfights are held in San José during the Christmas period. There is no kill and spectators are permitted to enter the ring to chase, and be chased by, the bull. Much wildlife in the Guanacaste and northern jungle areas. There is good sea-fishing off Puntarenas and in the mouth of the Río Chirripó, on the Caribbean side near the Nicaraguan border; inland river-fishing has been ruined by dynamiting.

Newspapers   The best San José morning papers are *La Nación* and *La República*. *La Prensa Libre* is a good morning and evening paper. *Libertad*, weekly newspaper (socialist). *El Debate* is another good weekly. *La Gazette* is the official government weekly paper. *Tico Times* (Fri.) in English.

Broadcasting   6 local TV stations, many MW/FM radio stations throughout the country. Local Voz de América (VOA) station. Many hotels and private homes receive one of the 4 TV stations offering direct, live, 24-hr TV from the USA (Canal 19, Supercanal, Cable Color and Master TV-channels 56, 58, 60—all US cable TV can be received in San José on the 2 cable stations).

We are most grateful for a complete review of the Costa Rica section to Simon Ellis (San José), Jim Cilch (USPCV, CR), Lee Azus (San Francisco), Dexter Ball (Chicago), Russell Blaauw (Springfield) for a most useful contribution, Mary B. Clark (USA), Henry Z.M.Corman (Halifax, N.S.), Dr Burkhard Dressler (Thornhill, Ont.), Eva Ekelund and Jim Lindsay (Stockholm), Prof. Richard Heller (London NW3), Vivien Isaacs (Berlin 27), Martina Jost and Heinz Eisenhauer (Darmstadt), Alan Mishael (Miami), Huberth Monge (Costa Rican National Parks Service SPN), Steve Morris (St John, NB), Leon van der Schoor (Neth.) and Rachel Wood (Newbury, Berks); also to other travellers whose names are listed in the general Central America section.

PANAMA

THE S-SHAPED ISTHMUS OF PANAMA, 80 km. at its narrowest and no more than 193 km. at its widest, is one of the great cross-roads of the world. Its destiny has been entirely shaped by that fact. To it Panama owes its national existence, the make-up of its population and their distribution: two-fifths of the people are concentrated in the two cities which control the entry and exit of the canal. Panama covers 82,860 square km. The Canal Area, formerly Zone, is being gradually incorporated into Panamanian jurisdiction; this long process began in 1964, when Panama secured the right to fly its flag in the Zone alongside that of the USA, and is due for completion, with Panamanian operation of the Canal, by 2000.

Only about a quarter of the country is inhabited and most of it is mountainous, with shelvings of lowland on both its 1,234 km. of Pacific and 767 km. of Atlantic coastlines. The country's axis is, in general, SW to NE, but the mountain chains do not conform to this and run NW to SE. At the border with Costa Rica there are several volcanic cones, the boldest of which is the extinct Barú, 3,383 metres high. The sharp-sided Cordillera de Talamanca continues SE at a general altitude of about 900 metres, but subsides suddenly SW of Panama City. The next range, the San Blas, rises E of Colón and runs into Colombia; its highest peaks are not more than 900 metres. A third range rises from the Pacific littoral in the SE; it, too, runs into Colombia and along the Pacific coast as the Serranía de Baudó.

Good fortune decreed a gap between the Talamanca and San Blas ranges in which the divide is no more than 87 metres high. The ranges are so placed that the gap, containing the Canal, runs from NW to SE. To reach the Pacific from the Atlantic we must travel eastwards, and at dawn the sun rises over the Pacific.

Rainfall is heavy along the Caribbean coast: more than 3,800 mm. a year in some places, with huge but brief downpours between April and December. Temperature in the lowland ranges from 21°C (70°F) at night to 32°C (90°F) by day. The result is deep tropical forest along the coast and up the sides of the ranges of Panama, though little remains forested. The rain begins to shade off towards the crests of the mountains (10° to 18°C), and is much less along the Pacific, though there is no scarcity of it anywhere. At Balboa it is only 1,727 mm. a year, and the tropical forest gives way to semi-deciduous trees and converted areas of savanna between the Pacific and the mountains.

Most of the rural population live in the 6 provinces on the Pacific side, W of the

Canal. Only 16% of the total land area is farmed; 7.3% is pasture, nearly all of it in the 6 provinces; 3.1% only is under crops, almost all in the same provinces. There are some very large estates but the land-reform process has begun. There is only one rural population centre of any importance on the Caribbean: in Bocas del Toro, in the extreme NW.

Population The population (2.28 million in 1987) is mostly of mixed blood but there are communities of Indians, blacks and a few Asians. About 51% are urban dwellers. Annual population growth is 2.2%. Gdp per capita is US$2,340. Of the sixty Indian tribes who inhabited the isthmus at the time of the Spanish conquest, only three have survived: the Cunas of the San Blas Islands, the Guaymíes of the western provinces and the Chocóes of Darién.

The birth-rate is 28.0 and the death-rate 5.4 per thousand; 14% are illiterate; 65.5% of the children are born to unmarried mothers. In Bocas de Toro half the population speaks Spanish, half speaks English. Only a few of the indigenous Indians can speak Spanish.

Numbers of African slaves escaped from their Spanish owners during the 16th century. They set up free communities in the Darién jungles and their Spanish-speaking descendants can still be seen there and in the Pearl Islands. The majority of Panama's blacks are English-speaking British West Indians, descended from those brought in for the building of the railway in 1850, and later of the Canal. There are also a number of East Indians and Chinese who tend to cling to their own languages and customs.

Education is compulsory up to the age of 14. English is the compulsory second language in the schools.

Communications There are now about 9,535 km. of roads, of which 3,050 km. are paved. Road building is complicated by the extraordinary number of bridges and the large amount of grading required. The road running from Colón to Panama City is the only paved one crossing the isthmus, and the Pan-American Highway connecting Chepo and Panama City with the Costa Rican border is paved throughout.

The **Constitution** of 1972 provides for a president, a vice-president, and an Assembly with 505 Representatives. Panama is divided into nine provinces and one autonomous Indian reservation. Provincial governors and mayors of towns are appointed by the central authorities. Power was held by General Omar Torrijos from 1968 until his death in an air accident in 1981. Elections were held in May 1984, resulting in a narrow (and contested) victory for the government candidate, Nicolás Ardito Barletta, who took office in October 1984 for a six-year term but was removed from office by military pressure in September 1985. He was replaced by Eric Arturo Delvalle. Sr. Delvalle's attempts to reduce military influence in government, concentrated principally in the hands of General Manuel Antonio Noriega, led to his own removal by General Noriega in February 1988. Sr. Manuel Solís Palma was named president in his place. Elections were held in May 1989 but the civil unrest which immediately followed led to their annulment by the military; both the ruling party and an opposition coalition had claimed an overwhelming majority of votes.

History The history of Panama is the history of its pass-route; its fate was determined on that day in 1513 when Balboa first glimpsed the Pacific. Panama City was of paramount importance for the Spaniards: it was the focus of conquering expeditions northwards and southwards along the Pacific coasts. All trade to and from these Pacific countries passed across the isthmus.

Panama City was founded in 1519 after a trail had been discovered between it and the Caribbean. The Camino Real (the Royal Road) ran from Panama City to Nombre de Dios until it was re-routed to Portobelo. An alternative route was used later: a road built from Panama City to Las Cruces, now swallowed up by Gatún Lake; it ran near Gamboa on the Culebra Cut, and traces of it can still be seen. Las Cruces was on the Chagres river, which was navigable to the Caribbean, particularly during the rainy season.

Intruders were early attracted by the wealth passing over the Royal Road. Sir Francis Drake attacked Nombre de Dios, and in 1573 his men penetrated inland to Las Cruces, captured its treasures and burnt the town. Spain countered later attacks by building strongholds and forts to protect the route: among others San Felipe at the entrances to Portobelo and San Lorenzo at the mouth of the Chagres. Spanish galleons, loaded with treasure and escorted against attack, left Portobelo once a year. They returned with European goods which were sold at great fairs held at Portobelo, Cartagena and Veracruz. There was feverish activity for several weeks as the galleons were loaded and unloaded. It was a favourite time for attack by enemies, especially those with political as well as pecuniary motives. Perhaps the most famous was the attack by Henry Morgan in 1671. He captured the fort of San Lorenzo and pushed up the Chagres river to Los Cruces. From there he descended upon Panama City, which he looted and burnt. A month later Morgan returned to the Caribbean with 195 mules loaded with booty. Panama City was re-built on a new site, at the base of Ancón hill, and fortified. With Britain and Spain at war, attacks reached their climax in Admiral Vernon's capture of Portobelo in 1739 and the fort of San Lorenzo the next year. Spain abandoned the route in 1746 and began trading round Cape Horn. San Lorenzo was rebuilt: it is still there, tidied up and landscaped by the US Army.

A century later, streams of men were once more moving up the Chagres and down to Panama City: the forty-niners on their way to the newly discovered gold fields of California. Many perished on this "road to hell", as it was called, and the gold rush brought into being a railway across the isthmus. The Panama Railroad from Colón (then only two streets) to Panama City took four years to build, with great loss of life. The first train was run on November 26, 1853. The railway was an enormous financial success until the re-routing of the Pacific Steam Navigation Company's ships round Cape Horn in 1867 and the opening of the first US transcontinental railroad in 1869 reduced its traffic.

Ferdinand de Lesseps, builder of the Suez Canal, arrived in Panama in 1881, and decided to build a sea-level canal along the Chagres river and the Río Grande. Work started in 1882. One of the diggers in 1886 and 1887 was the painter Gauguin, aged 39. Thirty km. had been dug before the Company crashed in 1893, defeated by extravagance and tropical diseases (22,000 people died). Eventually Colombia (of which Panama was then a Department) authorized the Company to sell all its rights and properties to the United States, but the Colombian Senate rejected the treaty, and the inhabitants of Panama, encouraged by the States, declared their independence on November 3, 1903. The United States intervened and, in spite of protests by Colombia, recognized the new republic. Colombia did not accept the severance until 1921.

Before beginning the task of building the Canal the United States performed one of the greatest sanitary operations in history: the clearance from the area of the more malignant tropical diseases. The name of William Crawford Gorgas will always be associated with this, as will that of George Washington Goethals with the actual building of the Canal. On August 15, 1914, the first passage was made, by the ship *Ancón*.

The former Canal Zone was a ribbon of territory under US control extending 8 km. on either side of the Canal and including the cities of Cristóbal and Balboa. The price paid by the United States Government to Panama for construction rights was US$10m. The French company received US$40m. for its rights and properties. US$25m. were given to Colombia in compensation for the transfer of the French company's rights. The total cost at completion was US$387m. Panama long ago rejected the perpetuity clause of the original Canal Treaty. In April 1978 a new treaty was ratified and on October 1, 1979 the Canal Zone, now known officially as the Canal Area, was formally transferred to Panamanian sovereignty, including the ports of Cristóbal and Balboa, the Canal dry docks and the trans-isthmus railway, but the US still retains extensive military base areas. Until the final transfer of ownership in 2000 the Canal administration is in the hands of the Comisión del Canal, on which the USA retains majority representation.

Landfall on the Caribbean side for the passage of the Canal is made at the twin cities of Cristóbal and Colón, the one merging into the other almost imperceptibly and both built on Manzanillo Island at the entrance of the Canal; the island has now been connected with the mainland. Colón was founded in 1852 as the terminus of the railway across the isthmus; Cristóbal came into being as the port of entry for the supplies used in building the Canal.

Cristóbal   Ships usually dock at Pier No. 9, five mins. from the shops of Colón. Vehicles are always waiting at the docks for those who want to visit Colón and other places. Cristóbal Yacht Club has a good restaurant.

Colón, population 68,000, the second largest city in Panama, was originally called Aspinwall, after one of the founders of the railway. Despite its fine public buildings and well-stocked shops, it has some of the nastiest slums in Latin America, and is generally dirty. It has been described as having a "rough, but wonderful honky-tonk atmosphere." Annual mean temperature: 26°C.

Warning Mugging, even in daylight, is a real threat in both Colón and Cristóbal. We have received repeated warnings of robbery in Colón, often within 5 minutes of arrival. The two main streets and some of the connecting ones are guarded by armed Panama Defence Force men; you are strongly recommended not to leave their range of sight.

There is a Free Zone at Colón which offers facilities for the importing, free of duty, of bulk goods for re-export to neighbouring countries after packaging; it is not possible to take your purchases out of the zone; you must arrange for them to be taken to the airport before you leave (or you must smuggle them out). The zone is closed on Saturdays and Sundays. (If with your own car, pay a minder US$1 to look after it while in the zone).

There are good roads to Coco Solo nearby, to France Field, and to Fort Davis and the Gatún Locks, some 11 km. away.

The tourist should see the Cathedral between Herrera and Av. Amador Guerrero (open afternoons only), and the statues on the promenade known as the Paseo Centenario (Av. Central). The historic *Hotel Washington* is worth a look. For local products, try Isthmian Curio Shop, between Calle 10 and 11, and Sombrería Aldao, on Front Street, for panama hats.

The beach drive round Colón, pleasant and cool in the evening, takes less than 30 minutes.

Hotels *Washington*, A, there is a small casino; *Carlton*, B, is the next best hotel; *Sotelo*, B, also has casino; *Andros*, C; *Plaza*, C; *García*, C; *Astor*, D. These rates are without meals, whose average price is US$5-8. *Pensión Plaza*, Av. Central, is clean, cheap, D. *Pensión Acrópolis*, E, clean and comfortable; *Pensión Andros Annex*, E, comfortable and safe; *Pensión Kingston*, E. If destitute try the Salvation Army.

Principal Restaurants *Cristóbal Yacht Club*; *La Nueva China*, Av. Central and Calle 8, a/c; good Chinese food also at *La Fortuna*, Av. Central, is clean, cheap, D. *VIP Club* in Front Street; YMCA restaurant, right across from the railway station; *Tarpon Club*, at the Gatún Spillway.

Taxi Tariffs vary, but are generally not high and may be agreed on in advance. Most drivers speak some English.

Cabarets Club 61, Av. Bolívar. No cover charge. Three shows nightly at 2000, 2300 and 0100. Club Florida, 3 shows nightly. Café Esquire.

Cinemas Teatro Lido, across from YMCA on Bolívar, and Teatro Rex, Calle 5 and Av. Central.

Clubs Golf (18 holes) at Brazos Brook Country Club. Rotary Club, weekly lunches.

Cables Tropical Radio Telegraph Co., Av. Roosevelt.

Post Office In Cristóbal Administration Building, on corner of Av. Bolívar and Calle 9.

Exchange Chase Manhattan Bank; Citibank; Banco Nacional de Panamá; Caja de Ahorros; Lloyds Bank International (Bahamas)—ex BOLSA—agency in Colón Free Zone, at Calle 15 & D. Open 0800-1300, Mon. to Fri.

British Consulate P.O. Box 1108, Cristóbal. T 7-3075.

Shipping a vehicle to Colombia, see page 1330. To the USA costs between US$1,800-2,600.

Bus Service At least every hour to Panama City: US$1.75, 2 hours, from bus terminal at Calle 13 and Av. Bolívar, including express bus.

Trains On weekdays there are 4 trains a day and on Sat and Sun. and holidays 3, to Panama City from Colón. Journey time 1 hr. 25 mins., US$1.25. Colón station is at Calle 11 and Front Street, near the shopping area. The journey is interesting, with intermittent views of Canal, ships and jungle.

Air Services Local flights to Panama City: Mon.-Fri. at 0700 and 1600 from the France Field Airport.

Trips from Colón: *Portobelo* is 48 km. NE of Colón by sea or by road. Colombus used the harbour in 1502 and it was a Spanish garrison town for more than two centuries. Drake died and was buried at sea off the Bay of Portobelo. Three large stone forts face the entrance to the harbour. There can be seen old Spanish cannon, and the treasure house where gold from Peru brought over the

Las Cruces trail from Panama City was stored until the galleons for Spain arrived. There are ruins of various forts, a waterfall, and mountain views (no information available locally). In the Cathedral is a statue of the Black Christ; it was being shipped from Spain to the Viceroy of Peru, but the ship was wrecked in the bay and the statue salvaged by the natives. The image is carried through the streets at 1800 on October 21; afterwards there is feasting and dancing till dawn. Local rainfall, 4,080 mm. a year. Population 1,980.

Buses from Colón to Portobelo, every hour from 0700; leave from Calle 13 and Av. Bolívar, US$1.30 single. Portobelo can be visited from Panama City in a day by taking an early train to Colón, then go straight to the bus for Portobelo: on the return, take a bus from Portobelo to Sabanitas, at the junction with the Transisthmian Highway (US$1) and catch a bus back to Panama City (US$0.90)—take this bus route from Panama City if you wish to avoid Colón. Many beaches on the way from Colón, such as Cangrejo, about 8 km. Playa Langosta, 17 km. from Portobelo, is also recommended (toilets, bar, restaurant). María Chiquita beach has a bathing pavilion managed by the government tourist bureau, 45 minutes from Colón, US$0.60.

From Colón, visit also the old French canal, modern Canal township of Margarita, Gatún Locks (one hour). The locks are open to visitors every day 0800-1600; they can enter the lock area and take photographs, while guides explain the Canal operation. (Bus from Colón to Gatún locks, US$0.20.) Visitors can cross the locks at Gatún, and also ride through virgin jungle where wild pigs, iguanas, land crabs and snakes scuttle across the road.

Fort San Lorenzo, on the other side of the Canal at the mouth of the Chagres river, is a 16th-century fort with 18th-century additions, reached from Gatún locks by road to Fort Sherman in the Canal Area. From Fort Sherman one must drive, hitch-hike or walk 10 km. to the fort; the 18th-century part, on the top of cliffs, commands a fine view of the mouth of the Chagres river and the bay below. It was sacked by Henry Morgan and by Admiral Vernon; one of Vernon's cannon with the GR monogram can be seen.

Isla Grande, just off the coast, can be reached by boats hired from a car park, and a bus service; there are two hotels: *Isla Grande,* A p.p. in huts scattered along an excellent sandy beach, meals extra, and *Jackson's,* cheaper, also huts. The island is a favourite of scuba divers and snorkellers.

San Blas Islands An interesting trip can be made to the San Blas archipelago, which has 365 islands ranging in size from tiny ones with a few coconut palms to islands on which hundreds of Cuna Indians live. The islands, off the Caribbean coast E of Colón, vary in distance from the shore from 100 metres to several kilometres.

The Cuna are the most sophisticated and politically organized of the country's three major groups. They run the San Blas Territory virtually on their own terms, with internal autonomy and, uniquely among Panama's Indians, send their representative to the National Assembly. They have their own language, but Spanish is widely spoken. The women wear gold nose-and ear-rings, and costumes suggestive of ancient Egyptians. They are outside the Panamanian tax zone and have negotiated a treaty perpetuating their long-standing trade with small craft from Colombia. Many men work on the mainland, but live on the islands.

Photographers need plenty of small change, as set price for a Cuna to pose is US$0.25. *Molas* (decorative handsewn appliqué for blouse fronts) cost upwards of US$5 each (also obtainable in many Panama City and Colón shops). Agencies run trips to El Porvenir where the planes land, Wichub Huala, Nalunega and Corbisky, all close to each other (hotels on first 3, one-day tour US$85, US$100 for weekend, one night at *Hotel Anai* on Wichub Huala, US$40 for each additional night), bookable at the major Panama hotels. These trips are inclusive of food and sightseeing. Take your own drinks, beer costs US$1. Flight leaves Paitilla airport at 0600, returning next day at 0630; if you can collect 9 people to fill the plane, you can leave at 0800 and return next day at 1600. The airline serving the islands, Aviones de Panamá (T 64-1677), can provide further information, and also runs trips to the Chocó Indians of the Darién jungle. Ansa flies at 0800, returning same day at 1630, US$49.35.

There are occasional boats to the San Blas islands from Colón, but there is no scheduled service and the trip can be rough.

Through the Canal to Panama City

As the crow flies the distance across the isthmus is 55 km. From shore to shore the Canal is 67½ km., or 82 km. (44.08 nautical miles) from deep water to deep water. It has been widened to 150 metres in most places. The trip normally takes 8 or 9 hours for the 42 ships a day passing through.

About 10 km. from Cristóbal, up the Chagres river, is the Gatún Dam, built to impound its waters. The 422 square km. Gatún Lake serves as a reservoir to hold sufficient water in the channel and for use in the locks during dry spells. A high level reservoir, Lake Alajuela (formerly the Madden Dam), feeds the lake and maintains its level, 26 metres above the sea. A ship ascends into Lake Gatún in three steps or lockages. Each of the twin chambers in each flight of locks has a usable length of 305 metres, a width of 33½ metres, and is about 21 metres deep. The flights are in duplicate to allow ships to be passed in opposite directions simultaneously. Passage of the Gatún Locks takes about an hour. Gatún may be reached by bus or train from Colón.

The largest section of the Canal is in Gatún Lake. In the lake is **Barro Colorado** island, to which the animals fled as the basin slowly filled. It is now a biological reserve for scientific research. Visits can be arranged with the Smithsonian Institute in Ancón, US$10 including boat, audio-visual display and lunch; take a Gamboa Summit bus from near Plaza 5 de Mayo (0605 or 0630) to the Dredging Division dock at Gamboa (US$0.65), from where the boat leaves. Trips go on Mondays only for 5 people. The excursion is highly recommended for seeing wildlife, especially monkeys. For longer stays, write to the Director, Smithsonian Tropical Research Institute, Box 2072, Balboa, Panamá. Administration, T 62-30-49. hours 0800-1145, 1315-1515.

We travel over the lake for 37 km. and then through the narrow rock defile of the Gaillard or Culebra Cut for 13 km. to Pedro Miguel Locks, where the descent to sea-level is begun. Culebra Cut can be seen from Contractor's Hill, reached by car (no buses) by turning right 3 km. past the Bridge of the Americas, passing Cocoli, then turning left as signed. The first stage is a descent into Miraflores Lake, 16½ metres above sea-level. The process is completed at the Miraflores Locks, 1½ km. further on. The road beyond Cocoli goes on to Posa, where there are good views of the locks, the cut and former Canal Zone buildings. Opposite Miraflores Locks is a swing bridge which only operates when traffic is heavy (e.g. on long weekends). The Canal channel takes us on to Balboa and the Pacific. An odd fact is that the mean level of the Pacific is some 20 cm. higher than the Atlantic, but the disparity is not constant throughout the year. On the Atlantic side there is a normal variation of 30 cm. between high and low tides, and on the Pacific of about 380 cm., rising sometimes to 640 cm.

Most people are surprised by the Canal. Few foresee that the scenery is so beautiful, and it is interesting to observe the mechanics of the passage. Since no tourist boat runs the length of the canal, and since the Panama City-Colón train journey does not afford full views, travellers are advised to take a bus to the Miraflores Locks (open 0900-1700, best between 0600-1000 and

1430-1800 if you want to see shipping—the museum and model of the canal, formerly in the Department of Transport at Ancón, is being moved here). If travelling by train, get out at Pedro Miguel (no station at Miraflores), and take a bus from there, US$0.35. About 250 metres past the entrance to the Locks is a road (left) to the filtration plant and observatory, behind which is a picnic area and viewing point. Bus from Panama City to Miraflores Locks leaves from near Plaza 5 de Mayo (direction Paraíso or Gamboa), 15 mins., US$0.65 Ask driver to let you off on the main road, from where it's a 10-min. walk to the Locks. Taxi to the Locks, US$10 per hour. Another good way to see the Panama Canal area is to rent a car (but the very best way is by boat, see below).

It is possible to traverse the canal as a linehandler (no experience necessary) on a yacht; the journey takes two days. Yachts are allowed through the canal on Tues. and Thur. only. The yacht owners need 4 linehandlers. Go to the Yacht Club in Balboa, and ask people hanging around the bar. The Club offers good daily lunch special for US$ 2.15. Good place to watch canal traffic. 50 metres R of the Club is a small white booth which has a list of boat departures for the next day; ask here if you can go to the dock and take the motor boat which shuttles out to yachts preparing for passage. Ask to speak to captains from the launch and see if they'll let you "transit".

Balboa   The ship usually berths at Pier 18. Panama City is about 3¼ km. from the docks, an average of 10 minutes by taxi.

Balboa stands attractively between the Canal quays and Ancón hill, which lies between it and Panama City. It has been described as an efficient, planned, sterilized town, a typical American answer to the wilfulness and riot of the tropics.

The Canal administration building (with fine murals on the ground floor) and a few official residences are on Balboa Heights. At the foot of Balboa Heights is Balboa, with a small park, a reflecting pool and marble shaft commemorating Goethals, and a long parkway flanked with royal palms known as the Prado. At its eastern end is a theatre, a service centre building, post office and bank. Farther along Balboa Road are a large YMCA (where only male employees of the Canal Company can stay, but where all comers may eat; in the same building is Chadwick's Travel Agency, excellent, English spoken), various churches and a Masonic temple.

Banks   Citibank; Chase Manhattan Bank.

Telegrams   INTEL; Tropical Radio & Telegraph Co. Public Telex booth.

Post Office   Av. Balboa and El Prado.

Excursions   There is a launch service to **Taboga Island,** about 20 km. offshore (return fare US$5). Taboga is reached in about an hour from Pier 17-18 in Balboa (check the times in advance). There are 2 boats daily during the week and 3 boats on Sat. and Sun. The island is a favourite year-round resort; its pineapples and mangoes have a high reputation and its church is the second oldest in the western hemisphere (admission to beach US$0.50, covered p.oicnic huts extra).

Hotels   *Taboga* and *Chu*, B, beautiful views, own beach and bar.

The trip out to Taboga is very interesting, passing the naval installations at the Pacific end of the Canal, the great bridge linking the Americas, tuna boats and shrimp fishers in for supplies, visiting yachts from all over the world at the Balboa Yacht Club, and the 4-km. Causeway connecting Fort Amador on the mainland with three islands in the bay. Part of the route follows the channel of the Canal, with its busy traffic. Taboga itself, with a promontory rising to 488 metres, is carpeted with flowers at certain seasons. There are few cars in the meandering, helter-skelter streets, and only one footpath as a road. Swimming is fine, though you may have to pay US$0.50 to use the beach in front of the hotel.

The first Spanish settlement was in 1515, two years after Balboa's discovery of the Pacific. It was from here that Pizarro set out for Peru in 1524. For two centuries it was a stronghold of the pirates who preyed on the traffic to Panama. Because it has a deep-water, sheltered anchorage, it was during colonial times the terminal point for ships coming up the W coast of South America. El Morro, at low tide joined to Taboga, is at high tide an island; it was once owned by the Pacific Steam Navigation Company, whose ships sailed from there. For a fine view, walk through the town and up to the top of the hill with a cross at the summit, to the right of the radar station (there is a shady short cut, ask locals). When surveying the view, don't miss the pelican rookery on the back side of the island; it is an easy walk down.

It is a longer trip by launch—some 75 km.—to the **Pearl Islands,** visited mostly by sea-anglers for the Pacific mackerel, red snapper, corvina, sailfish, marlin, and other species which teem in the waters around. High mountains rise from the sea, but there is a little fishing village on a shelf of land at the water's edge. There was much pearl fishing in colonial days. **Contadora,** one of the smallest Pearl Islands, has become quite famous since its name became associated with a Central American peace initiative; it has *El Galeón Hotel,* A, and the very luxurious chalet complex known as *César Park Contadora Resort and Casino,* L, nice location on beach, T 50-4033. Return air ticket from Paitilla, US$12.75 by Aeroperlas, T 69-4555. Good skin-diving and sailing, 3-hour boat trip. Beware the sharks. Three day package tour to Contadora, US$150 for 2, recommended. Argonaut Steamship Agency, Calle 55 No. 7-82, Panama City, T 64-3459, runs launch cruises.

Ancón curves round the hill N and E and merges into Panama City. It has picturesque views of the palm-fringed shore. The following walk, proposed by Andrew M. Smith of Panama City, takes in the sights of Ancón: walk to the top of the hill in the morning for views of the city, Balboa and the Canal (conveniences and water fountain at the top); the entrance is on Av. 4 de Julio (Av. de los Mártires). Return to Av. 4 de Julio and take a clockwise route around the hill, bearing right on to Balboa Road (Av. Estado de Jamaica), passing YMCA, Chase Manhattan and Citibank, until you reach Stevens Circle where Cuna Indians sell *molas.* Here is the Post Office and a cafeteria. Then walk down the Prado lined with royal palms to the Goethals Memorial and up the steps to the Administration Building to see the murals of the Construction of the Canal (entrance free, identity must be shown to the guards). Follow Heights Road until it becomes Gorgas Road. You will pass the headquarters of the Smithsonian Tropical Research Institute (where applications to visit Barro Colorado Island are made) and, among trees and flowers, the famous Gorgas Hospital for tropical diseases. Gorgas Road leads back to Av. 4 de Julio, but look out for the sign to the Museo de Arte Contemporáneo (open Mon.-Fri. 0800-1230, 1430-1800, Sat. 0800-1200), before Av. 4 de Julio. 2 libraries are open to the public: that of the Smithsonian Tropical Research Institute in the Canal Area, opp. Plaza 5 de Mayo, and that of the Panama Canal College, underneath the Bridge of the Americas.

At the foot of Ancón Hill stands the Instituto Nacional on the 4-lane Avenida 4 de Julio (Tivoli). The University City is on the Transisthmian Highway. Opposite the campus is the Social Security Hospital.

Panama City, capital of the Republic, has a population of 1.2 million. It was founded on its present site in 1673 after Morgan had sacked the old town, now known as Panamá Viejo, 6½ km. away by road. Most of Panama City is modern; the old quarter of the city—the part that Spain fortified so effectively that it was never successfully attacked—lies at the tip of the peninsula; both it and Panamá Viejo are being extensively restored.

Note Some of the street names have recently been changed, which may make finding your way around a little difficult. The locals are likely still to refer to the streets by their old names, so if in doubt ask. Also, few buildings display their numbers, so try to find out the nearest cross street.

Panama City is a curious blend of old Spain, American progress, and the bazaar atmosphere of the East. It has a polyglot population unrivalled in any other Latin American city. For the sober minded, the palm-shaded beaches, the islands of the Bay and the encircling hills constitute a large part of its charm. The cabarets and night life (very enterprising) are an attraction to those so inclined.

Most of the interesting sights are in the old part of the city and can easily be reached by foot, taxi, or bus. A good starting place is the Plaza de Francia, in the extreme S. In this picturesque little Plaza, with its red poinciana trees, is a memorial obelisk (topped by a cock) to the French Canal pioneers, and a monument to Carlos Finlay, the Cuban who discovered the cause of yellow fever. Facing the Plaza are several colonial buildings and the Palace of Justice, where the Supreme Court meets. Behind it runs part of the old sea wall—Las Bóvedas (The Dungeons)— built around the city to protect it from pirates. There are steps up this old wall to the promenade—the Paseo de las Bóvedas—along its top, from which there is a fine view of the Bay of Panama and the fortified islands of Flamenco, Naos, and Perico. Beyond are Taboga and Taboguilla, tinged with blue or violet. Just beyond the end of the promenade is the Club de Clases de la Guardia Nacional, a barracks, previously the Club Unión, the city's leading club, which is now housed in a new building in the residential area.

Flush under the wall, at the side of the Palace of Justice, are the old dungeons, with thick walls, arched ceilings and tiny barred windows looking on to the Bay (they have been converted into art galleries and a handicraft centre by IPAT, the tourist authority). Behind the French monument, in a

PANAMA CITY orientation map   173A

Key to Panama City Orientation Map
1. Fuerte Amador; 2. Docks; 3. Balboa; 4. Ancón; 5. Santa Ana; 6. Caledonia; 7. La Exposición; 8. Bella Vista; 9. Paltilla; 10. El Cangrejo; 11. Atlapa Convention Centre; 12. Ruins of Panamá Viejo. .... area of detailed map.

recess in the walls, is a series of large tablets recording, in Spanish, the early attempts to build the Canal. The French Embassy faces the Plaza.

A little way from the Club de Clases, along Av. A and to the right, are the ruins of Santo Domingo church, which has been restored and is now open to the public at times. Its flat arch, made entirely of bricks and mortar, with no internal support, has stood for three centuries. When the great debate as to where the Canal should be built was going on, a Nicaraguan stamp showing a volcano, with all its implications of earthquakes, and the stability of this arch—a proof of no earthquakes—are said to have played a large part in determining the choice in Panama's favour. At the Santo Domingo site is the interesting Museum of Colonial Religious Art, open Tues.-Sat. 1000-1530, Sun. 1500-1730 (adults US$ 0.50, children US$ 0.25, closed for extensive rebuilding in 1987).

Panama City's main street, the Av. Central, runs NW from the old city, then turns N and (less than 2 km. further) NE and sweeps right and almost parallel with the shore through the whole town (its name changes to Av. España and finally to Vía España). On the right, at the intersection with Calle 3, is the National Theatre, built in 1907, and recently restored. Up Calle 3 on the right is San Francisco church (colonial, but modernized), and the Instituto Bolívar, where the Liberator proposed a United States of South America during the Bolivarian Congress of 1826. On Av. Norte, running along the Bay, is the President's Palace (La Presidencia), the most impressive building in the city. It is locally known as Palacio de las Garzas, or herons, which are kept in a fountain area there. It was the residence of the Spanish Governor during colonial days. Av. Norte goes on to the colourful public market, on the waterfront. On Av. Norte are the wharves where coastal boats anchor and fishermen land their catches.

Av. Central runs on to the Plaza Independencia, or Plaza Catedral. This Plaza, with busts of the Republic's founders, is the heart of the colonial city. Facing it

PANAMA CITY
SHOWING MAIN STREETS ONLY
NOT TO SCALE

173

BAHÍA DE PANAMÁ

1. Plaza de Francia
2. Plaza Independencia/Catedral, with Cathedral, Cabildo/Post Office, Archbishop's Palace, Museo de Historia de Panamá, and *Hotel Central*
3. Plaza Santa Ana
4. Plaza 5 de Mayo, with Museo del Hombre Panameño
5. Plaza Herrera
6. Santo Domingo and Museo de Arte Colonial Religioso
7. National Theatre, San Francisco and Instituto Bolívar
8. San José
9. Palace of Justice
10. Presidential Palace
11. Las Bóvedas
12. Santo Tomás Hospital
13. Social Security Hospital
14. Gorgas Hospital
15. Balboa Monument
16. University
17. INTEL
18. Market
19. Main banking district
20. Canal Administration
21. Buses to the West and Chepo
22. Buses to Colón
23. Ticabus and *Hotel Ideal*
24. *Holiday Inn*
25. *Hotel El Panamá*
26. *Hotel Acapulco*
27. *Pensión América*

are the Cathedral, the old Cabildo (which has now become the Central Post Office), the venerable *Hotel Central* and the Archbishop's Palace. The Cathedral has twin towers and domes encased in mother-of-pearl. The Post Office was the headquarters of the French during their attempt to build the Canal. Also in the Plaza Catedral (in the town hall) is the Museo de Historia de Panamá from colonial times to Torrijos' days in power, US$0.25 (open Tues.-Fri., 1000-1600, Sun. 1500-1800, closed for lunch). Beyond the Cathedral, Calle 8a runs S to the church of San José, which has a famous organ and a magnificent golden baroque altar, originally installed at a church in Panamá Viejo; the golden walls were resourcefully covered in mud by nuns to disguise them during Morgan's famous raid.

On Av. Central, to the right, in the second block beyond the Cathedral, is the church of La Merced, burnt in 1963 and now completely restored. It was near here that the landward gate of the fortified city stood. Further along the now curving Av. Central is the small Plaza Santa Ana, a favourite place for political meetings. Its church is colonial. Not far away is Sal si Puedes, "Get out if you can", a narrow street swarming with vendors, and Panama's Chinatown; don't linger round here late at night, best before 1930.

Some blocks E is the Caledonia district, where live the descendants of the British West-Indian blacks brought in to build the railway and the Canal. Caledonia is the Harlem of Panama City, exotic and unassimilated; whites are said to be unwelcome. Mugging is very frequent, even in daylight.

Much further along Av. Central, on Plaza 5 de Mayo (at Calle 22A Este), is the old railway station, now the Museo Nacional del Hombre Panameño, with a good display showing the origins of the populations of Panama (Tues.-Sat., 1000-1530, Sun. 1500-1730, US$0.50), and almost opposite is the Plaza De Lesseps. This part of the city is known as La Exposición because of the International Fair held here in 1916 to celebrate the building of the Canal. Calle 35 Este leads down to the Av. Balboa along the waterfront. The Santo Tomás hospital is here and on a promontory jutting out from this popular promenade is a great monument to Balboa, who stands on a marble globe poised on the shoulders of a supporting group, representing the four races of man. Many of the best hotels are in Bella Vista, also one of the main business areas, and the chief restaurant area is, appropriately, El Cangrejo ("the crab").

On Independence Day, November 3, practically the whole city seems to march in a parade lasting about 3½ hours, centred in the old part of the city. Colourful, noisy, spectacular. Another parade takes place the following day.

Hotels

	Address	Telephone	US$ Single	Double	Our Price Range
El Marriott Panamá	Vía Israel	26-4077	110	120	L
El Panamá	Vía España, 111	23-1660	78	89	L
El Continental*	Vía España	64-6666	55-81	88	L
Europa	Vía España y Calle 42	63-6911	45	52	A
El Ejecutivo	Calle Aquilino de la Guardian	64-3333	65	70	A
La Siesta	Near Tocumen airport	20-1400	50	55	A
Gran Hotel Soloy	Av. Perú	27-1133	65	70	A
Granada	Av. Eusebio Morales	62-4900	65	71	A
Internacional	Plaza 5 de Mayo	62-1000	45	54	A
Roma	Av. Justo Arosemena	27-3844	38	44	B
Centroamericano	Av. Ecuador	27-4555	32	36	B
Gran Hotel Lux	Av. Perú	25-1950	33	38	B

*noisy till 2230 from organ music

Note a 10% tax on all hotel prices. All hotels are air-conditioned. *Vera Cruz*, Av. Perú, B, without breakfast, new, clean, good, but rooms at front noisy; *Doral*, Calle Monteserín (T 62-5144), B, a/c, TV, cold water, rec. as safe, although not in safe area, cheaper commercial rates available;

Colón, Calle 12, Oeste and Calle "B", C with shower (cheaper without), a/c, erratic water supply; *Acapulco*, Calle 30 Este (near *Hotel Soloy*), T 25-3832, between Avs. Perú and Cuba, C, a/c, clean, comfortable, TV, private bath, restaurant, conveniently located, rec.; also around corner from *Soloy*, *Residencia Turístico Volcán*, Calle 29, D with shower, a/c, clean; *California*, Vía España y C.43, C with bath, a/c, TV, restaurant (breakfast US$1.75); *Central*, Plaza Catedral (22-6080), D with bath, E shared bath, safe motorcycle parking, good cheap meals in restaurant, lots of South American travellers; *Caracas*, Plaza Santa Ana, C, with bath, a/c, TV, central, convenient, unprepossessing area at night; *Riazor*, Calle 16 Oeste, near *Ideal*, D, a/c with bath, good value, cheap restaurant downstairs. *Herrera*, Plaza Herrera, basic, noisy but quite clean, E, good meals in restaurant downstairs at about US$1.50 p.p. Ten mins. from airport (nearest) on right is *El Continental*, D, air conditioned, shower, bar, excellent and easy to reach from the city, the docks, or Panamá Viejo, free bus service to airport; *Parador*, 5 km. from airport at first traffic lights, D, clean. Apartments for rent at *Las Vegas Apartotel*, write to Aptdo. 7186, Panama 5, T 64-2424/6024.

Cheaper accommodation can be found in *pensiones*: *América*, Av. Justo Arosemena and Av. Ecuador, D-C, back rooms best to avoid street noise, communal bathrooms, safe, clean and pleasant (airport bus stops outside); *Las Palmeras*, Av. Cuba between C.38-39, T 250811, E, safe, clean; *Foyo*, Calle 6, No. 825, near Plaza Catedral, clean (but there are mice—hang up food), E, noisy on street but good and central (reduced rates for weekly or monthly stays); the restaurant nearby is OK and cheap but closes at 1700 and on Sun.; *Panamá*, Calle 6, 8-40, E, fan, noisy, reasonable (best rooms have balcony overlooking street), safe, but cockroaches. *Mi Posada*, Calle 12 y Av. Central (Plaza Santa Ana, dangerous area), F, cheap, OK; many (unlisted here) on Av. México; *Nacional*, Av. Central 22-19, near Plaza 5 de Mayo, E with fan, basic, no hot water, many permanent residents; *Pacífico*, Calle Carlos Mendoza (dangerous area), E, fans, laundry facilities; *Vásquez*, Av. A, 2-47, close to the Palace of Justice, quiet, friendly, nice rooms and view of ocean and sand, E; *Rivera*, Av. Calle 11 Oeste, 8-14, off Av. A, pleasant and friendly, but noisy, E (monthly rates available).

N.B. It may not be easy to find accommodation just before Christmas, as Central Americans tend to invade the city to do their shopping, nor during Carnival. In the higher parts of the city, water shortages are common in summer, and electricity cuts are common in late summer everywhere.

Warning Thieves abound, and muggings are frequent. It is not safe to walk on any streets alone after dark (i.e. after 1730). Keep valuables in money belt, or otherwise hidden, and don't carry a bag of any sort if possible. Also you shouldn't take a taxi which has 2 people in it already. Be careful when putting luggage into a car. (All the same, most Panamanians are friendly and helpful.) Marañón (around the market), El Chorillo (W from Santa Ana to Ancón hill) and Caledonia can be particularly dangerous; never walk there at night and take care in daylight, too. For this reason, be very careful when booking into a hotel or *pensión* between Calles 9 and 30, i.e. W of Plaza Herrera (where most of the cheap ones are to be found).

Camping There are no official sites but it is possible to camp on some beaches or, if in great need (they agree, but don't like it much) in the Balboa Yacht Club car park. It is also possible to camp in the Hipódromo grounds (11 km. E of the city, on Vía España) where you can use the swimming pool showers; this is allowed if you are waiting to ship your vehicle out of the country. Also possible, by previous arrangement, at La Patria swimming pool nearby, and at the Chorrera (La Herradura) and La Siesta beaches on the Pan-American Highway.

Electricity In modern homes and hotels, 220 volts. Otherwise 110 volt 3 phase, 60 cycles A.C.

Restaurants (apart from hotels). Good are: *Pana China* (Chinese and international food), Vía España; *Lesseps*, Vía España y C. 46, La Cresta, French restaurant and bar; *Sarti's* (Italian food), Calle Ricardo Arias 5; *Panamar*, end of Calle 50, specializes in seafood; *Pez de Oro* (Peruvian) superb *mariscos*, and fish, and good wine, Calle 2, El Cangrejo; *Las Rejas*, Vía Brasil, just off Vía España; *Las Américas*, Calle San Miguel, Obarrio. *La Casa del Marisco* (sea food) on Av. Balboa, is open-air. *Cocina Vasca* (sea food) Calle D, in El Cangrejo, really excellent, US$18-20 for a full meal. Also in El Cangrejo, *El Cortijo*, between Eusebio A. Morales and Vía Argentina on Calle D; *Tinajas*, on Calle 51, near *Ejecutivo Hotel*, Panamanian food and entertainment, rec. Two French restaurants: *Casco Viejo*, nr. Plaza Francia, behind French embassy, and a luxurious one in Las Bóvedas dungeons (US$15-20 a head). *Le Bistrot*, Centro Comercial La Florida, Calle 53, expensive.

Other restaurants include: *El Trapiche*, Vía Argentina, Panamanian food, good; *Manolo*, Vía Argentina; *Piscolabis*, Transisthmian Highway, Vista Hermosa district, local food, reasonable; *El Jorrón*, Vía Fernández de Córdoba, Vista Hermosa district, local food, reasonable and good; *La Tablita*, Transisthmian Highway, Los Angeles district, reasonable; *Nápoli*, Av. Estudiante, corner with Calle 16, Italian, good and cheap, and many other good Italian places. *1985*, C. Eusebio A. Morales, Swiss; *Madrid*, Vía España near UK Consulate, Spanish and local food, comida daily for US$ 2.60; *Marbella*, Av. Balboa y Calle 39, Spanish, small; *La Cascada*, Av. Balboa and Calle 25, seafood, rec., enormous helpings, open air; the same management runs *Las Costallitas* on Vía

Argentina, same menu (which takes ½ hr. to read!), same reasonable prices; *El Dorado,* Calle Colombia 2, good service, excellent seafood, rec.

Many good Oriental places. *Matsuei,* Japanese, excellent, pricey; *Mandarin,* Chinese, excellent, fair prices; *Kwang Chow,* in the Sal si Puedes area of Av. Balboa, sells Tsingtao beer, rec.; *Gran China,* Av. Balboa, between Calles 26 and 27, Chinese, good value; *Palacio Imperial,* C.17 above Ticabus terminal, Chinese, good and cheap; *Bajwa's Shamiana,* Galerías Marbella, Paitilla, T 63-8586, Indian, US$15 p.p., fair. *Jimmy's,* Paseo Cincuentenario just beyond Atlapa Centre, Greek; *Chipré,* Av. Central y C. 11 Oeste, rec.

Krispy, Macdonalds, Frutilandia, Dairy Queen, Hardee's, Burger King and *Kentucky Fried Chicken* all have their branches; *La Viña,* corner C. 6 Oeste and Av. A (no sign), behind Post Office, good, cheap; also *La Esquina,* Av. A y C. 12 Oeste; *Cafetería Jaime,* Plaza Santa Ana; *La Conquista,* Calle J, up Av. Central. *La Cresta* (good food from US$1), Vía España and Calle 45. Two good restaurants on Avenida Central are *A & P* and *Yimy,* the first opposite the National Museum, the second near Chase Manhattan and Bank of America. *Café El Exagerado* serves very good meals at reasonable prices; *Markany,* Av. Cuba y Av. Ecuador, good snacks. *Café Coca Cola,* Av. Central and Plaza Santa Ana, pleasant, reasonably-priced; *Café Jaime,* corner of Calle 12 and Av. Central, for good *chichas* (natural drinks). There are good pavement cafés along Av. Balboa.

Shopping The most expensive shops are on Vía España; Av. Central is cheaper but less safe. *Casa Salih,* Av. Central 125, try local perfume Kantule from San Blas islands; *Casa Fastlich,* Av. Central at Plaza 5 de Mayo, good local jewellery; *Nat. Méndez,* Calle Jota 13, near Av. Tivoli, for Colombian emeralds and pearls; *Curiosidades Típicas de Panamá,* Av. 4 de Julio y Calle J. B. Sosa, for local craft work; *Mercado Artesanal Gago,* next to Gago supermarket on corner of Vía España y Vía Brasil, competitive prices; *Curiosidades Panameñas,* Calle 55 near *Hotel El Panamá,* local crafts; *Panamá Típico,* Via España y Calle La Perejil, same again; *Indutípica,* Av. A y Calle 8 Oeste (opp. San José church), for *artesanía,* friendly. *Inovación* is a gift shop in the *Hotel El Panamá* complex on Via España, has wide selection of new and used *molas; Crossroads,* Calle E. A. Morales, by *Granada Hotel,* more "typical" goods; *Joyería La Huaca,* Av. Central y Calle 21, genuine precolumbian ojects for sale upstairs. Good selections also in main hotels. Gago, El Rey, Super 99 and Machetazo (on Central) supermarkets are said to be the best. Mercado Público, near Presidential Palace, for all general items (bargain for everything except food). There is a store (Army-Navy) on Av. Central, near Plaza 5 de Mayo, which sells camping and hiking equipment. There are many laundromats around Plaza Catedral, where wash and dry will cost about US$2.

Duty-free imported luxuries of all kinds from all nations (technically only for US military personnel). Panamanian items include *molas* (embroidered blouse fronts made by Cuna Indians, e.g. Emma Vence, T 61-8009); straw, leather, wooden and ceramic items; the *pollera* circular dress, the *montuno* shirts (embroidered), hats, the *chácara* (a popular bag or purse), the *chaquira* necklace made by Guaymí Indians, and jewellery; good selection at Artesanías Nacionales, in Panamá Viejo.

Bookshops English books at Librería Argosy, Vía Argentina y Vía España; Menéndez, Av. Justo Arosemena y C. 36, good selection, some in English; Gran Morrison shops, Vía España (near Calle 51 Este and *Hotel Continental,* Av. 4 de Julio, Transisthmian Highway, El Dorado, limited selection of English books. National University Bookshop, on campus between Av. Manuel Espinosa Batista and Vía Simón Bolívar, very good, wide selection (including some in English).

Photographic Equipment Camera Center, on Tivoli at 4 de Julio (P.O. Box 7279); Foto Internacional, on main street. Panafoto, Av. Central by Plaza 5 de Mayo. Foto Enodi, Vía Porras, Kodak slides developed in a day. Developing in one day in Foto El Halcón, Calle 55 alongside the *Hotel El Panamá.* In some places you will get a free film.

Local Transport Taxis have no meters; charges are according to how many "zones" are traversed (about US$0.75-US$2). Try to settle fare beforehand if you can. Note that there are large taxis (*grandes*) and cheaper small ones (*chicos*). Taxis charge US$12 for a 2½-hr. tour to Miraflores locks and the Canal Area. The adventurous will board one of the numerous small buses nicknamed *chivas* (goats). These charge US$0.15, are not very comfortable but run along the major streets (e.g. Av. Central as far as Calle 12, Av. Perú and Av. Justo Arosemena; all buses go to Bella Vista—the business section—except those marked Tumba Muerta or Transístmica). Travel into the suburbs costs more. Yell "*parada*" to stop the bus.

Car Rental At the airport (Hertz, Avis, Econorent); rates about US$30/day, special rates if reservations made abroad (e.g. Toyota, 1 day, unlimited mileage, US$13 inc. insurance). Cars in good condition. Other offices on Vía España.

Motorcycle Club Road Knights, at the Albrook Air Force base (T 86-3348), very welcoming; allows international motorcyclists to stay for free for up to 2 weeks, has repair and maintenance workshop.

Cabarets and Discotheques Hotels *Holiday Inn* and *El Continental;* Playboy de Panamá, Calle 55, El Cangrejo; Bunny Club, Jerónimo de la Ossa; Oasis, Vía Brasil; Los Cuatro Ases, Calle L.

Recommended discos: *Open House*, near Ejecutivo Hotel, *Bacchus*, Vía España and *Magic*, Calle 81; Las Molas, entrance to Chase Manhattan Bank, Vía España, Los Angeles district, small band, rural decor, drinks US$1.50; Unicornio, Calle 50 y R. Arías 23 is night club with discothèque and gambling; reasonable prices, will admit foreigners for US$3 a week. El Bon Ton and Camelot, Río Abajo. La Parrillita, Av. 11 de Octubre in Hato Pintado district, is a restaurant in a railway carriage. El Pavo Real, off Calle 50 Oeste in Campo Alegre, hard to find, pub selling British beer (at a price), darts board, popular with expats.

Theatres and Cinemas   There are occasional performances at the National Theatre (folklore sessions every other Sun., 1600, check dates). Atlapa Convention Centre. The usual air-conditioned cinemas (US$2.50 except Balboa cinema, near Stevens Circle, US$2). National University cinema, US$1.50 for general public, wider variety than in city cinemas. Foreign films must, legally, have Spanish sub-titles.

Casinos   In the main hotels, at Unicornio on Calle 50, and at airport.

Bathing   Piscina Patria (the Olympic pool), take San Pedro or Juan Díaz bus, US$0.15. Piscina Adán Gordon, between Av. Cuba and Av. Justo Arosemena, near Calle 31, 0900-1200, 1300-1700 (except weekends to 1700 only). Admission US$0.50 (take identification), but beards and long hair frowned on (women must wear bathing caps). Hotels *El Continental, Ejecutivo, Holiday Inn, Granada* and *La Siesta* have pools. Many beaches within 1½ hours' drive of the city. Fort Kobbe beach (US$0.50, bus from Canal Area bus station US$0.40) and Naos beach (US$1, Amador bus from same station, US$0.30, then 2 km. walk along causeway) have been rec.; both have shark nets, but at low tide at the former you must go outside it to swim! Vera Cruz beach is not recommended as it is both dirty and dangerous (all are dangerous at night).

Golf   Panama Golf Club; courses at Summit, Amador and Horoko; Coronado Beach Golf Club (open to tourists who get guest cards at Coronado office on Calle 50).

Horse Races   (pari-mutuel betting) are held Sat., Sun. and holidays at the Presidente Remón track (bus to Juan Díaz, entry from US$0.50 to 2.50). Cockfights are held on Vía España, near the road that leads to Panamá Viejo, every Sun., same bus but get out at crossing with Calle 150.

Instituto Panameño de Arte, Av. de los Mártires near Palacio Legislativo, art gallery. Open 0900-1200, 1500-1800 except Sun.

Exchange   The Chase Manhattan Bank (US$0.65 commission on each cheque); Citibank; Lloyds Bank International (Bahamas) Ltd. (ex-BOLSA) Calle Aquilino de la Guardia y Calle 48, Bella Vista (also El Cangrejo agency), offers good rates for sterling (the only bank which will change sterling cash, and only if its sterling limit has not been exhausted); Bank of America; Banco de Colombia; Swiss Bank Corporation. Thomas Cook travellers' cheques only exchangeable at Banco Sudameris and Algemene Bank Nederland; Deutschmarks exchanged at Deutsch-Südamerikanische Bank. Panamanian banks, open 0800-1300, closed Sat., except for Banco General which takes Bank of America and Thomas Cook travellers' cheques. American Express, Banco Union building, 12th floor, Av. Samuel Lewis, T 635858, Mon.-Fri. 0800-1700 (US$0.10 commission on each cheque). **Note:** many banks closed down their Panamanian operations in 1988; if requiring banking services from your own country, check in advance which institutions still have offices in Panama.

If travelling N stock up on dollars as they are hard to obtain, but essential for exchange, in the rest of Central America.

Free market for almost all currencies, and good rates for all South American currencies. *Cambio* on Av. Central near *Hotel Internacional*. The US dollar is the normal circulating medium in Panama.

Embassies and Consulates: British, Torre Swiss Bank, Calle 53, Zona 1, T 690866, Fax (507) 230730, Apartado 889. **US**, Av. Balboa and Calle 37; P.O. Box 1099. T 27-1777. **French**, Plaza Francia. T 22-0024. **W. German**, Edificio Altamira, piso 11, Vía Argentina 5. Tel: 23-0202. **Netherlands**, Vía Argentina y Erick del Valle, T 64-6793. **Swedish**, Edificio Melinda, Vía Argentina 25, Panama 5, T 64-7655. **Swiss**, Av. Samuel Lewis y C. Gerardo Ortega, Ed. Pronasa, T 64-6731/64-7115, P.O. Box 499. **South African**, Edificio Las Vegas, P.O. Box 7010, T 23-1834. **Colombian**, Calle 52 (E. A. Morales) No. 5, 1 block from Vía España and Calle 52, open 0800-1200; the **Chilean, Ecuadorean** and **Israeli** embassies are housed in the same building. **Guatemalan**, Vía España 128, about Calle 55, open 0800-1300. **Costa Rican**, Edif. Plaza Regency, Piso 2, Vía España, T 642980. **Salvadorean**, Vía España 125. **Nicaraguan**, Av. Federico Boyd y Calle 50, T 23-0981.

Customs   for renewal of permits and obtaining exit papers for vehicles in Ancón, off Curundu Road, near Albrook U.S. airbase.

Hospitals   Gorgas Hospital, Balboa is only for US military personnel, except in emergency. The private clinics charge high prices; normally visitors are treated at either the Clínica San Fernando or the Clínica Paitilla (both have hospital annexes). For inoculations buy vaccine at a chemist, who will recommend a clinic; plenty in La Exposición around Parque Belisario Porras. Dentist: Dr. Daniel Wong, Clínica Dental Marbella, Ed. Alfil (Planta Baja), near Centro Comercial Marbella, T 63-8998.

Post Office   Plaza Catedral, Calle 6 and Avenida Central. Also Calle 30 E, nr. Av. Balboa, and at the University. Parcels sent "poste restante" are delivered to Encomiendos Postales Transístmicos, behind the Sears store on Simón Bolívar; tax has to be paid on the value of the goods. If asked for a tip, feign inability to understand!

Cables   All America Cables & Radio, Inc., Calle 228, No. 12-17; Tropical Radio Telegraph Co., Calle Samuel Lewis. T 3-7474. Intel, Edificio Avesa, Vía España (close to *Hilton*, open 0700-2300 weekdays, from 0800 Sat and Sun.) Public telex booth available TRT office. Excellent long-distance telephone by Intel and Tropical Radio. Charges can be transferred to UK.

Worship   Services in English at St. Luke's Episcopalian Cathedral, Ancón. Bahai temple, 11 km. out on Transisthmian Highway, in the Ojo de Agua district. Modern; worth seeing for its architecture. Taxi round trip for US$5, with an hour to see the temple, can be arranged.

Travel Agency   Viajes Panamá S. A., Av. Justo Arosemena 75, T 25-1838/4466, 27-4166, repeatedly rec., English spoken, helpful with documentation.

Tourist Bureau   Information office of the Instituto Panameño de Turismo (IPAT), in the Atlapa Convention Centre, Vía Israel opp. *Hotel Marriott* (0900 to 1600) issues good list of hotels, *pensiones*, motels and restaurants, and issue a free *Focus on Panama* guide (available at all major hotels, and airport). Best **maps** from Instituto Geográfico Nacional Tommy Guardia (IGNTG), on Vía Simón Bolívar, opp. the National University (footbridge nearby, fortunately), take Transístmica bus from C. 12 in Santa Ana: physical map of the country in 2 sheets, US$3.50 each; Panama City map in many sheets, US$1.50 per sheet (travellers will only need 3 or so). At the back of the Panama Canal Commission telephone books are good maps of the Canal Area, Panama City and Colón.

Buses   Ticabus, with office on ground floor of *Hotel Ideal*, Calle 22 B, run air-conditioned buses to San José, about US$30; also to Managua (3 a week, US$40, overnight stop in San José where you must reserve seat to Managua). Air conditioners rarely work. (Tickets are refundable; they pay on the same day, minus 15%.) Impossible to do Panama City-San José in one day on public transport. Buses going north tend to be well booked up, so make sure you reserve a seat in advance, and never later than the night before you leave. Buses to the W of the country (and also Chepo) leave from a terminal at the corner of Av. A and Av. Balboa (Av. 6 Sur), behind a 13-storey block of flats (no sign). Buses to all Canal Area destinations (Balboa, Summit, Paraíso, Kobbe, etc.) leave from Canal Area bus station (SACA), behind Plaza 5 de Mayo. Bus Panamá-Chepo US$1.20. Panamá-Colón 1¾ hrs., US$1.75, from Calle 26 Oeste y Av. Central in Caledonia, opp. San Miguel church. To Kobbe Beach by bus ½ hr., US$0.40 on US military territory (Pacific side). Panamá-David, 6 hrs., US$10.60, express US$15, 5 hrs. 1200 and 2400. (Transchiri, from Calle 17 Este and Balboa).

Rail   Four trains daily (at 0440, 0645, 1520, 1740—the 0645 train is best for seeing shipping), except 3 on Sat. and Sun., and holidays (0830, 1230, 1630), to Colón from Panamá. Station now on Av. de los Mártires, 1 km. NW of Plaza 5 de Mayo, not a pleasant area at night. Comfortable steel-car trains run roughly parallel to the Canal, of which there are excellent views, especially of Gatún Lake, crossed by a causeway. Journey takes 1 hr. 25-50 mins. Single costs US$1.25. For information, T 52-7720.

Airport   Omar Torrijos, at Tocumen, 27 km. Taxi fares about US$20, colectivo US$8 p.p. (if staying for only a couple of days, it is cheaper to rent a car at the airport, e.g. from Econorent). For about US$3 (should only be US$1.20) driver takes you by Panamá Viejo, just off the main airport road. Travellers wishing away hours at the airport can visit the delightful nearby village of Pacora, a few km. off the Pan-American Highway. Bus marked Tocumen, every 15 mins., from Plaza 5 de Mayo, US$0.35, one hour's journey. Bus ("El Chirrillo") to Panama City from the crossing outside the airport (US$0.30), 45 mins. There is a 24 hour left-luggage office near the Avis car rental desk for US$1 per article per day (worth it, since theft in the departure lounge is common). There are duty-free shops at the airport but more expensive than those downtown. There is a small airport at La Paitilla (take a number 2 bus going to Boca La Caja, from Av. Balboa at Calle 40), nearer Panama City, for domestic and private flights.

Excursions   A visit is usually paid, along the beachside highway, to **Panamá Viejo** and its ruins, 6½ km. away. On the way you can visit the Justo Arosemena Institute in the Paitilla district. Panamá Viejo, founded in 1519 by Pedrarias, was the point where gold from Peru was unloaded and kept in the King's store-house. There it was loaded on to mules and transported across the Isthmus to Nombre de Dios and Portobelo for shipment to Spain. In January, 1671, Henry Morgan looted and destroyed the city. Because the old site was hard to defend, the city was refounded on its present site.

Today the visitor can wander among the ruins of the Cathedral, its plaza with moss-covered stone pillars and what remains of the old government buildings. The King's Bridge, the starting point of the three trails across the Isthmus, still stands. Past the Plaza and near the sea is what remains of San José, where the golden altar and walls were. At one side are the dungeons. The whole area is attractively landscaped and floodlit. Taxi from the centre, US$1.50; bus US$0.15 from Vía España or Av. Balboa, Nos. 1 and 2.

In Panamá Viejo is the Artesanía Nacional shop, for handicrafts (more expensive than elsewhere). There is also a free display of folk dancing on six Saturdays in the dry season, which is well worth seeing.

See Balboa (page 1313) for trips to Taboga Island and Pearl Islands. A good excursion—a 2-hr. drive through picturesque jungle—is to Lake Alajuela (formerly Madden Dam). The drive runs from Balboa along the Gaillard Highway and near the Canal. Beyond Fort Clayton there is a fine view of the Pedro Miguel and Miraflores locks. Beyond Pedro Miguel town a road branches off to the left to Summit (Las Cumbres), where there are experimental gardens containing tropical plants from all over the world (closed Mondays) and a small zoo containing native wild life. (The trip to Summit may be made by buses marked Gamboa, every 1-1½ hrs., from near Plaza 5 de Mayo, US$0.35; the Paraíso bus will also take you to the Miraflores and Pedro Miguel locks.) The road to Lake Alajuela (37 km.) crosses the Las Cruces trail (old cannon mark the spot), and beyond is deep jungle (if walking the trail, take machete and compass and arrange boat across the Chagres river at the end of the trail well in advance). A large area of rain forest between Gatún Lake and Lake Alajuela has been set aside as Parque Nacional Soberanía (trails for walking). The Park has an information centre at the Summit Garden. For excursion to Portobelo, **see page 1310**.

The Madden Dam (Lake Alajuela) is used to generate electricity. A trip through part of the Canal by launch *Fantasía del Mar* costs US$16 for adults, US$8 for children, and lasts about 4 hours. A trip to Lake Alajuela by taxi is only worth while if there are enough people to fill the taxi.

The return from Lake Alajuela to Panama City can be made by the Transisthmian Highway. In Las Cumbres the restaurant *La Hacienda* serves native dishes.

West from Panama City

The Pan-American Highway runs westwards from Panama City through Concepción to the Costa Rican border (489 km.), and is well graded and completely paved. The Highway begins at the Puente de las Américas across the Canal at the Pacific entrance. The bridge, 1,653 metres long and high enough to allow all ships to pass under it, has 3 lanes, a 4-lane approach from Panama City and a pedestrian pavement all the way (muggings have occurred on the bridge in broad daylight, so be careful!).

Where the road W crosses the savannas, there are open pastures and fields where clumps of beautiful trees—largely mangoes and palms—alternate with grass.

The first place you reach, 23 km. from Panama City, is the small town of Arraiján (2,200 people). On 21 km. by 4-lane highway (toll US$0.50) is La Chorrera (26,317 people); an interesting store, Artes de las Américas, has items in wood, etc. A branch road (right) leads 1½ km. to a waterfall. On 20 km., among hills, is the old town of Capira (12,744 people). We pass through the orange groves of Campana (where a 10-km. road climbs to Cerro Campana National Park; no lodgings), and then twist down to Río Sajalises (bathing) and the low-level plains. On through Bejuco and Chame to the town of **San Carlos** (7,289 people; Hotels: *Playa Coronado*; *Río Mar*, C; *El Palmar*, B), near the sea; good river and sea-bathing. Not many restaurants in San Carlos, but there are plenty of shops where food can be bought. Near San Carlos are the Nueva Gorgona (*Cabañas Ocean Blue*, C) and Coronado (*Golf Club* villas, B) beaches, both with restaurants. The Coronado beach is between San Carlos and Chamé and is the most popular in Panama, even so it is never crowded (it is about 4 km. from the main road). Minibus Panama City-San Carlos, US$2.70, San Carlos-David, US$9.30. Beyond San Carlos is the Río Mar beach, with a good seafood restaurant.

Five km. on a road (right) leads after a few km. to a climb through fine scenery to the summit of Los Llanitos (792 metres), and then down 200 metres to a mountain-rimmed plateau (7 by 5½ km.) on which is comparatively cool **El Valle**, a small summer resort. 4 km. before El Valle is a parking spot with fine views of the village. (*Hotel Campestre*, C; *Cabañas El Potosí*, friendly; *El Greco Motel*, D; *Pensión Niña Delia*, E, no single rooms; private houses nearby rent rooms, F with meals; accommodation hard to find at weekends.) Soapstone carvings of animals, and straw birds, for sale. The town's Sunday market has become touristy and expensive, but the town itself is a good example of what life away from the cities is like. Gold coloured frogs can be seen here, including at the main hotel. There are many good walks in the vicinity, for instance to the cross in the hills to the W of town.

We leave Panamá Province at La Ermita and enter Coclé, whose large tracts of semi-arid land are used for cattle raising.

Santa Clara, with its famous beach, 115 km. from Panama City, is the usual target for motorists: fishing, launches for hire, and riding (Hotels: *Muu Muu,* B; *Vista Bella,* A, per cabin, for weekend). About 13 km. beyond is Antón (20,561 people): it has a special local type of *manjar blanco.* There is a crucifix here which is reputed to be miraculous. (*Hotel Rivera,* D, Km. 129.; *Pensión y Restaurante Chung,* on Highway, F with bath, basic, friendly, moderately-priced food.) On 20 km. is the capital of Coclé: **Penonomé** (30,913 people), an old town even when the Spaniards arrived. An advanced culture here, revealed by archaeologists (things found are in National Museum, Panama City, also Museo Conte here), was overwhelmed by volcanic eruption (*Hotel Dos Continentes,* C with shower, a/c, restaurant; *Pensión Los Pinos,* on left of Highway to Panama City, E with bath and fan (D with a/c); *Pensión Motel; Pensión Ramírez,* E with bath, Calle Juan Arosemena near church and Parque; *Pensión Dos Reales,* Calle Juan Vásquez, E, basic, noisy). Just under a km. N of town is Balneario Las Mendozas, on street of the same name, an excellent river pool for bathing in deep water. In another 18 km., we come to *Natá* (9,318 people), an important place in colonial days; old church (Iglesia de los Caballeros, 1522) and other colonial buildings. A few km. beyond we enter the sugar area and come to (10 km.) *Aguadulce,* 30,000 people (bus from Panamá, US$4.50); native pottery for sale; large salt-beds nearby. Hotels: *El Interamericano* (D, a/c); *Pensión Sarita,* E p.p., and others (it may be possible to sleep by the fire station). On the way to (22½ km.) Divisa, just beyond the large Santa Rosa sugar plantation, a road leads off right to the mountain spa of Calobre, 37 km. from Aguadulce; the hot springs are, however, a good hour's drive away, on a very rough road; grand mountain scenery.

From Divisa a road leads (left) into the Azuero Peninsula through Parita (25 km., 6,554 people; colonial church), and **Chitré** (40 km., 14,635 people), capital of Herrera Province (bus from Panama City, US$6, 4 hours; from Divisa, US$1, ½ hour); Herrera museum in centre of town.

Hotels *El Prado,* D, friendly; *Rex,* D (good restaurant next door), on main plaza; *Pensión Azuero,* Calle Manuel Correa, F, usually full; *Pensión Granada,* E (bargain), on road to Los Santos, basic; *Pensión Lilly,* E with bath, road to Monagrillo; *Toledo,* C. *Restaurant Popular,* Manuel Correa, good, cheap; *Restaurant Las Tejas,* on main square, small, good juices. Swimming pool on road to Monagrillo, US$0.25 (closed lunchtime). Tourist agencies in Panama City can arrange trips to La Arena, ¾-hr. walk from the centre of Chitré, which is the centre for Panamanian native pottery.

Los Santos (13,999 people), an old and charming town in Los Santos Province, has a fine church containing many images. The History Museum on plaza is small but interesting, in lovely house and garden. *Feria de Azuero,* held late each April, is worth seeing. (*Pensión Deportiva,* E, no single rooms, private showers; *Hotel La Villa de Los Santos,* C, a/c caravans, with swimming pool and good restaurant.) *Las Tablas* (19,323 people), capital of Los Santos (Hotels: *Oria,* out of town, C; *Piamonte,* C; *Pensión Mariela,* opposite, Calle Belisario Porras, E, basic, O.K.; *Pensión Marta,* E; swimming pool near National Guard barracks, US$0.25), has a picturesque and famous *fiesta* at Carnival time, just before Lent. Bus from Chitré, US$1, ½ hour (bus Las Tablas-Panama City leaves at 0930, US$6, 4½ hrs.). From Divisa to Las Tablas is 67 km.; the road runs on nearly 13 km. to the port of Mensabé. From Las Tablas it is possible to take a bus to *Pedasí* (leaves when full, US$2, 1½ hrs., very bad road) which has beautifully empty beaches with crystal clear sea 3 km. from town. *Pensión Moscoso,* E with shower, good, friendly (only place in town), meals arranged by owner at nearby bar. Most things in Pedasí, a peaceful colonial town, are run by the Moscoso clan, including, it seems, a charming wild fowl reserve near the beach, with storks and herons. You can drive from Las Tablas to Pedasí by an inland route: take the unsigned road to Flores, a small tropical village (no hotel), after which the road deteriorates to Tonosí and thence to Cañas. Between Cañas and Pedasí the road is good again; a sign points to the black-sand beach of Puerto Venado (small restaurant). After Pedasí, heading back to Las Tablas, a right turn at a white house goes to a beautiful, quiet beach (cross currents can make swimming dangerous, however).

About 53 km. W of Chitré, by road into the mountains, is *Ocú* (12,722 people), an old colonial town whose inhabitants wear traditional dress during the *fiesta* for its patron saint, San Sebastián, January 19-24.

Hotel *Posada San Sebastián,* E.

Travel Ocú can be reached from David (see below) by taking a bus to the Ocú turning on the Pan-American Highway (US$4) and a colectivo from there (US$0.50). One bus a day to Chitré, and several minibuses from Chitré to Panama City, US$6. From Chitré, a bus can be taken to Las Minas in the mountains, and then another to Ocú, stay the night and take a bus on to Santiago.

The road from Divisa to Santiago, the next town, 37 km., runs across the Province of Veraguas, the only one which has seaboards on both oceans. It is very dry in the summer. *Santiago* (28,866 people), capital of the Province (bus from Penonomé, US$3, from Aguadulce, US$2), is well inland; one of the oldest towns in the country, in a grain-growing area (very good—and cheap— macramé bags are sold in the market here). Nearby is San Francisco; it has a wonderful old church with wooden images, altar pieces and pulpit.

Hotels in Santiago: *Motel Gran David,* on Pan-American Highway, D, a/c, TV, shower, clean, rec.; *Pensiones Continental, Central* and *Jigoneva,* all on Av. Central, close together, all E; *Pensión San José,* Av. Central, (edge of town on Panama City road), E with bath and fan, good (good *pizzería* next door); *Santiago* near the Cathedral, clean, D with a/c, T.V. and shower. *Fortuna,* D, Chinese-run, safe, a little unfriendly. Swimming pool near town centre, US$0.75.

W of Santiago is La Mesa, with a beautiful, white colonial church. The bad road through Soná (43 km., 19,372 people) in a deep fertile valley to Guabalá, near Remedios (4,809 people), the country's largest stock-raising centre, has been replaced by a direct paved highway from Santiago to Guabalá. This saves a couple of hours. From Guabalá to David is 92 km.

17 km. W of Guabalá, on the highway, is a hotel just outside Las Lajas, D, with restaurant. No hotels in Las Lajas itself. *Hotel Playa Corona,* 2½ km. S of Pan-American Highway at 100 km., has camping (secure, clean, showers, pleasant beach, bar, US$5 for 2; also has good seafood restaurant). Las Lajas has good beaches (no facilities, 2 bars, costly shade for cars—shark-infested waters). To get there take a bus from David to the turn off (US$2), then walk 3 km. to the town, from where it is 10 km. to the beach (taxis only, US$5).

David, 45,000 people, capital of Chiriquí Province, rich in timber, coffee, cacao, sugar, rice, bananas and cattle, is the third city of the Republic. It was founded in colonial times and has kept its traditions intact while modernizing itself. The town has a fine park and beautiful neighbourhoods. Airport (flights to Panama City and Changuinola). International fair and *fiesta,* March 19.

Hotels *Siesta Motel,* on edge of town on the Pan-American Highway, rec.; *Fiesta,* B, on Pan-American Highway, good pool (US$2 for non-residents); *Nacional,* C, restaurant, pizzería, swimming pool (US$2 for non-residents), tennis court; *Pensión Fanita,* a/c rooms with bath, F, clean, noisy, basic, food fair. *Iris* in central square, D with bath and fan (a/c more), rec.; *Pensión Chiriquí,* Av. 4 Este, W of Calle Central, clean, but very noisy, E; *Pensión Colonial,* clean, E; *La Fortuna,* ½ block from plaza, F, cold showers, fairly clean; *Hotel Valle de la Luna,* E, reasonable food; *Pensión Costa Rica,* E with shower, toilet and fan, ask to see room first, some are very small; *David* and *Madrid* also E. Most cheap hotels are on Av. 5 Este.

Restaurants Many around central Parque Cervantes. *Parriada El Portal,* excellent but expensive; *J.C. Car Rental,* opp. *Hotel Nacional,* rec.; *McPato,* fast food; *Las Brasas,* café. *Don Dicky,* very good 24-hr. café, meals, friendly. Good cheap food at *Rocío,* Av. 5 Este. A few cheap places round bus station and the market. *Balneario Risacua,* on the Pan-American Highway, N end of town (follow Av. 6 Este to the river), has restaurant, very nice.

Entertainment Discotheques: Brandy and Wine, Av. 5 Este, nr. Fuerzas de Defensa building, young clientèle; Jorón Sebede, more national music, older set, both rec. Plaza and Imperial cinemas, by Parque Cervantes.

Car Hire Fecar, T 75-3246, reasonable.

Local Transport Urban buses US$0.20; agree taxi fares in advance.

Museum Regional and national history at Av. 8 Este, entry US$0.25.

Costa Rican Consulate above Citibank.

Post Office Calle C Norte, 1 block from Parque Cervantes. **Cables** Intel, Calle C. Norte, telex and long-distance telephone.

Immigration just off Av. Central.

Tourist Office IPAT, 1st floor office at Av. 4 Este, adjacent to Parque Cervantes; ask for details of hot springs in the vicinity.

Bus from Panama City: apart from Ticabus, ordinary buses, US$10.60 (7 hrs.), about every hour from 0700 to 1900, plus express buses at 1200 and at midnight, 5½ hrs., US$15 (try Transchiri, Calle 8, 7A-23). The municipal bus terminal is in Av. 3 de Noviembre. An alternative way to Panama City is to Santiago (US$6) and then to Panama City (US$6). There is a bus to San Isidro (Costa Rica) at 0600 and 1300, 6 hrs., US$8, and to San José (Costa Rica), five buses a day from 0500 to 1430, US$10, that leave from outside the *Pensión Costa Rica*. Regular minibus to Boquete from bus station (US$1.20) 1 hr., Frequent "*frontera*" buses, US$1, 1½ hrs. Bus station in north of town.

Note: If driving S, stock up with food in David: it is much cheaper than in Panama City. It is difficult to change Costa Rican colones in David, but the Store Romero in main square gives a good rate of exchange.

Inland from David are the sparsely forested highlands of Chiriquí, rising to 3,383 metres at the extinct Barú volcano. The region favours coffee, fruit and flowers and is very beautiful, with mountain streams for bathing and fishing. A great variety of wildlife flourishes in the area. There is some camping. There is a road from David, through Dolega (swimming pool, good carnival 4 days before Ash Wednesday), to the mountain village of ***Boquete***, at 900 metres, on the slopes of Chiriquí. It enjoys a spring-like climate the year round and has many attractions: good lodging and board, excellent river bathing, fishing, riding, and mountain climbing, but it is an expensive place. Around is a beautiful panorama of coffee plantations, orange groves, and gardens which grow the finest flowers in the country. Plenty of good walks, including paved road to summit of Barú volcano. It is possible to cash travellers' cheques in the small bank in plaza.

Hotels *Panamonte*, A, full board, in very attractive surroundings, rec. Cheaper hotels: *Fundadores* and *Central*, both D; *Pensión Marilos*, D, English spoken, very clean and well run with excellent, cheap food; *Pensión Wing*, F; *Pensión Virginia*, F for cheapest rooms, clean, friendly, English spoken, good and cheap restaurant downstairs. *Coffee Bean*, a café on road into town, very friendly, English-speaking owner (they have a lioness—Elsa—caged!) Plenty of cheap eating places.

After David, a dirt road turns off to the right to Las Palmas, a pleasant orange-growing village which welcomes tourists. Just before the village is a waterfall where a single column of water falls into a pool, delightful for swimming and camping.

The road and a railway go from David to ***Concepción*** (24 km.; 6,532 people—*fiesta* end of January), from where one can visit the beautiful Highlands to the N (US$11 bus fare—Transchiri—from Panama City, US$0.50 from David). A road runs 29 km. N to **El Hato del Volcán** (Hotels: *Dos Ríos*, C; *California*, D; *Pensión Omaya*, E; *Pensión Hung Wang*, F—no singles. Plenty of cheap eating places) and on to Río Sereno (*Hotel Los Andes*, D, good; private cars can cross into Costa Rica here, immigration at frontier post) or to ***Cerro Punta*** (*Hotel Cerro Punta*, B, good, attractive restaurant; *Pensión La Primavera*, E-D, no singles; several restaurants). There are mountain lakes nearby. Bus David-Volcán, US$2.30. At Bambito there is a luxury hotel which serves good but expensive meals, it has swimming pool, horse-riding, trout farm (in the off-season very good bargains can be had here). From Volcán to Cerro Punta (US$0.95 by bus) the road follows the Chiriquí Viejo river valley. Just beyond Cerro Punta lies the Finca Rogelio Rodriguez Argüello (only a 4-wheel drive vehicle can get to it), where Sr. José will show you the haunts of the quetzal; see the quetzal also at the Finca Fernández in the Volcán National Park, to which there is a good asphalt road. Cerro Punta itself, in a beautiful valley at 2,130 metres devoted to vegetables and flowers, has many fine walks in the crisp mountain air. One such is a 6-8 hour hike, mostly downhill after an initial climb, to Boquete (the track is clear in places and there are a few signs showing the direction and time—ambitious—to Boquete); the last part is down the Río Caldera canyon. Don't hike alone, take a machete and sufficient provisions for 2 days in case of mishap, wear ankle boots, and notify someone before leaving and on arrival. This hike is also recommended for bird watching. Concepción is 30 km. from the Costa Rican border at Paso Canoas by road (the border is open 0700-1200, 1400-1800, 1900-2200— remember Panama is 1 hr. ahead of Costa Rica).

Chiriquí Railway, S from Concepción to Puerto Armuelles, with passenger trains, one a day in each direction, irregular. There is also a "Finca Train," 4 decrepit, converted banana trucks, leaving at 1500 for the banana *fincas,* returning, by a different route, at 1800. No charge for passengers. Minibuses also leave all day for the *fincas.* Freight service only to David and to Pedregal.

Puerto Armuelles (10,712 people), is the port through which all the bananas grown in the area are exported. Puerto Armuelles and Almirante (Bocas del Toro) are the only ports in Panama outside the Canal area at which ocean-going vessels habitually call and anchor in deep water close inshore; there is now an oil transit pipeline across the isthmus between the two places.

Hotels *Pensión Balboa,* on waterfront, E, pleasant; *Pensión Trébol,* E, 1 block from waterfront. Plenty of cheap eating places, e.g. *Enrique's,* Chinese, good; *Club Social,* on water, ask any taxi, chicken and rice dishes.

Across the Cordillera from David, on the Caribbean side, are the once thriving but now depressed banana ports of *Bocas del Toro,* on the SE tip of Colón Island, and Almirante, on the SW side of Almirante Bay, the central office of the Chiriquí Land Company (the Panamanian subsidiary of The American Banana Company). Some of the plantations, destroyed by disease, have been converted to *abacá* and cacao, but are now being planted again, especially near *Changuinola* (airport with bank, open on Sat. till 1200). Unlike Almirante, which is a busy port, dirty and disorganized, Bocas del Toro deserves a visit (*fiesta* end September): clean, peaceful, quiet, English spoken by most of the black population. The protected bay offers all forms of water sport and diving, beautiful sunrises and sunsets, and, on land, tropical birds, butterflies and wild life. For information on tours; Ligia (Lee) Paget, Turismo y Artesanías Bocatoreñas, Apdo Postal 5, Bocas del Toro (T 78-9309/9248), or Wilberto Martínez, Panama Nature Tours, Box 1223, Cristóbal, Colón (T 42-1340).

Boat Almirante-Bocas del Toro, Tues., Thur., Sat. 0725, 1¼ hrs., US$0.50, *Isla Colón.* From Almirante, take ferry or *Almirante* launch (Mon., Wed., Fri. 0930) to Chiriquí Grande, 5 hrs. if lucky, US$7.50, from where a spectacular road runs over the mountains, passing the Cricamola Indian Reservation and the Fortuna hydroelectric plant, to connect with David, bus 3 hrs., US$6 (ferry Chiriquí Grande-Almirante Tues., Thurs., Sat. 1100, 5 hrs., US$0.80; *Hotel Buena Vista* in Chiriquí Grande, E; other accommodation on seafront). Alternatively Bocas del Toro and Changuinola can be reached by Aeroperlas, Alas Chiricanas, Aviones de Panamá both from Paitilla Airport (US$41) and David (US$21). There is a road from Changuinola to Almirante (buses every ½ hr. till 2000, US$1); a road is planned from Almirante to Chiriquí Grande.

Hotels At Bocas del Toro; *Bahía* (D); *Pensión Peck,* F (Miss Peck is a charming hostess); *Botel Thomas,* on the sea (postcards for sale). At Changuinola: *Changuinola,* D, near airport; restaurant near market has rooms, also D; restaurant *El Caribe,* nr. airport, rec.; also nightclubs (*54* best), cinema and theatre. At Almirante: *Hong Kong,* D with a/c, cheaper without, *San Francisco,* E with bath, both very clean; *Pensión Colón,* E, basic, overpriced, uncertain water supply, friendly English-speaking owner; *Viajero,* E, secure—all hotels noisy. Bocas del Toro province is about 25% more expensive than the rest of Panama.

Railways The banana railways provide links between Guabito on the Costa Rican frontier, Changuinola and Almirante. Trains leave Almirante 0735 and one later, for Changuinola (US$0.40, 45 mins., rec.), but only one on Thur., and one Sat. continuing to Guabito. Train stops often.

On Thurs. and Sun. the *Isla Colón* ferry leaves Bocas del Toro at 1300 for Bastimentos Island, a small community of blacks with a marvellous beach; good snorkelling about ½-hr. walk from the jetty. Return 1800, no charge.

Entering Panama from Costa Rica The border at Sixaola-Guabito is open 0700-1100, 1300-1700, but only on Mon.-Thurs. can you guarantee with any certainty that officials will be on hand. Malaria test on entering Panama, entry charge US$10 (receipt given), 30 days given if you already have a visa, 5 days' entry card if not, US$2 (extensions at Changuinola airport immigration, opens 0830—5 passport photos, photographer nearby charges US$7 for 6). Advance clocks 1 hr. entering Panama.

No accommodation in Guabito; bus to Changuinola US$1, ¾ hr (every ½ hour until 2000). If seeking cheap accommodation, cross border as early as possible in order to get as far as Almirante.

How to get to Colombia

By Land The Pan-American Highway runs E 60 km. from Panama City to the sizeable town of

Chepo, full of friendly blacks. From Chepo the Highway has been completed to Yaviza, 240 km. from Panama City; it is gravel from Chepo until the last 30 km. which are of earth (sometimes impassable in rainy season). 35 km. E of Chepo it crosses the new Lago Bayano dam by bridge (the land to the N of the Highway as far as Cañazas is the Reserva Indígena del Bayano). The road will eventually link Panama with Colombia. (Bus to Chepo from Panama City leaves from Plaza 5 de Mayo.)

Darién East of Chepo is Darién, almost half the area of Panama and almost undeveloped. Most villages are accessible only by air or river and on foot. At Bahía Piñas is the *Tropic Star Lodge,* where a luxury fishing holiday may be enjoyed on the sea and in the jungle for over US$1,000 a week. (Information from *Hotel El Panamá.*)

The Darién Gap road will not be open for some years, so the usual way of getting to Colombia is by sea or air. It is possible to go overland: the journey is in fact more expensive than going by air, and while still challenging, the number of travellers going overland is increasing. The main villages (Yaviza, Pucuro, Paya and Cristales) have electricity, radios and cassette decks, canned food is available in Yaviza, Pucuro and Paya (but no gasoline), only the Chocó Indians and the Cuna women retain traditional dress. Prices are rising steeply and friendliness is declining. Venturers are advised to get *Backpacking in Mexico and Central America* (Bradt Publications), which contains special maps covering the whole route and background information on Indians, fauna and flora. Maps of the Darién area can be purchased from the Ministro de Obras Públicas, Instituto Geográfico Nacional Tommy Guardia, in Panama City (US$5, reported to contain mistakes). The best time to go is in the dry months (Jan.-mid April); in the wet season (from May) it is only recommended for the hardy. Organized jungle tours to Cuna Indians, Chocó Indians and the Río Bayano costing from US$65 to over US$300 can be purchased through Mar Go Tours, Aptdo 473, Balboa. The journey as described below takes about 7 days to the first house in Colombia.

There are 5 buses from Panamá to Yaviza between 0600 and 1200, US$15, 10 hrs. Alternatively there is an irregular boat, about three times a week. The only sleeping accommodation is the deck and there is one primitive toilet for about 120 people. The advertised travel time is 16 hours, but it can take as much as 28. There is only one hotel at **Yaviza** (*Three Américas,* E, basic, meals available but not very sanitary; there is a TB clinic run by a Canadian (who appreciates classical music), and a hospital. Crossing the river in Yaviza costs US$0.25. From Yaviza it is an easy walk, with two river crossings by dugout, US$1 each, to Pinogana, 2 hrs on foot (small and primitive) and by motor dugout from Pinogana to Boca de Cupe (US$60). Or you can take a boat from Yaviza to El Real (US$10), stay at the Touricenter of Gringo Gery (very nice and friendly people) and from there a motor dugout to Boca de Cupe (if possible, take a banana dugout, otherwise bargain hard on boats). There are also boats from Panama City (at the harbour by the market in the old town) to El Real for US$12 p.p. inc. meals. Boats from El Real are not very frequent and may only go as far as Unión de Chocó or Pinogana.

Stay the night at **Boca de Cupe** with a family; food and cold beer on sale here. You can go with Chocó Indians to Unión de Chocó, stay one or two days with them and share some food (they won't charge for lodging). Chocós are very friendly and shy, better not to take pictures (US$5 after bargaining). In Boca de Cupe get your exit stamp and keep your eye on your luggage. Lodging in Boca de Cupe with María (meals available). From Boca de Cupe to Pucuro, dugout US$30 (bargain), to Paya (if river level high enough) US$60; Pucuro-Yaviza by canoe, US$100-150, 8 hrs.

Pucuro is a Cuna Indian village and it is customary to ask the chief's permission to stay (he will ask to see your passport). Visitors usually stay in the assembly house. People show little interest in travellers there; stop with your luggage. From Pucuro you can walk through lush jungle to Paya, 5-6 hrs. (guide costs US$20, not really necessary, do not pay in advance), which was the capital of the Cuna empire. From Pucuro to Paya you have to cross the river 4 times.

In ***Paya*** you may be able to stay in the assembly house at the village, but it is mandatory to go 2 km. away eastwards to the barracks. You can stay there, too. (passport check and baggage search), and for a small fee you will get meals. The Cuna Indians in Paya are more friendly than in Pucuro. Paje is a similar village, with a chief (be sure to ask his permission on everything).

From Paya, the next step is a 4-6 hr. walk to Palo de las Letras, the frontier stone; at every bifurcation, take the left-hand trail. On reaching the left bank of the Tulé river (in 3 hrs., no water between these points), you follow it downstream, which involves 7 crossings (at the third crossing the trail almost disappears, so walk along the river bed—if possible—to the next crossing). About ½ hr. after leaving this river you cross a small creek; 45 mins. further on is the abandoned camp of the Montadero, near where the Tulé and Pailón rivers meet to form the River Cacarica. Cross the Cacarica and follow the trail to the Inderena (Colombian National Parks) hut at Cristales (7 hrs. from Palo de las Letras). Guides Paya-Cristales (they always go in pairs), US$50. If you insist on walking beyond Montadero, a machete, compass and fishing gear (or extra food) are essential; the path is so overgrown that it is easier, when the river is low, to walk and swim down it (Cristales is on the left bank, so perhaps it would be better to stick to this side). The rangers at Cristales (friendly) may sell you food, will let you sleep at the hut, cook, and will take you by dugout to Bijao (or Viajado), 1½ hrs., for US$5 (they will try to charge US$30). At Bijao ask for the Inderena station, where you can eat and sleep (floor space, or camp). From Bijao a motor dugout runs to Cacarica (also called Puerto América) for US$30 (3 hrs.), from where motorboats go to Turbo for US$10 (in scheduled boat—if it stops; if not it'll cost you about US$130 to hire a boat). One *residencial* and a shop in Cacarica. There is nowhere to get your Colombian entry stamp in Turbo; you will probably have to wait until Cartagena and then explain yourself in great detail to DAS there.

The **Katíos National Park** (**Warning:** entry by motorized vehicle is prohibited), extending in Colombia to the Panamanian border, can be visited with mules from the Inderena headquarters in Sautatá (rangers may offer free accommodation, very friendly). In the park is the Tilupo waterfall, 125 metres high; the water cascades down a series of rock staircases, surrounded by orchids and fantastic plants. Also in the park are the Alto de la Guillermina, a mountain behind which is a strange forest of palms called "mil pesos", and the Ciénagas de Tumaradó, with red monkeys, waterfowl and alligators.

Dr Richard Dawood, author of *Travellers' Health: How to Stay Healthy Abroad*, and photographer Anthony Dawton, crossed the Darien Gap at the end of the wet season (November). We are pleased to include Dr Dawood's health recommendations for such a journey: **Heat** Acclimatization to a hot climate usually takes around 3 weeks. It is more difficult in humid climates than in dry ones, since sweat cannot evaporate easily, and when high humidity persists through the night as well, the body has no respite. (In desert conditions, where the temperature falls at night, adaptation is much easier.) Requirements for salt and water increase dramatically under such conditions. We had to drink 12 litres per day to keep pace with our own fluid loss on some parts of the trip.

We were travelling under extreme conditions, but it is important to remember that the human thirst sensation is not an accurate guide to true fluid requirements. In hot countries it is always essential to drink beyond the point of thirst quenching, and to drink sufficient water to ensure that the urine is consistently pale in colour.

Salt losses also need to be replaced. Deficiency of salt, water, or both, is referred to as heat exhaustion; lethargy, fatigue, and headache are typical features, eventually leading to coma and death. Prevention is the best approach, and we used the pre-salted water regime pioneered by Colonel Jim Adam and followed by the British Army; salt is added to all fluids, one quarter of a level teaspoon (approx 1 gram) per pint—to produce a solution that is just below the taste theshold. Salt tablets, however, are poorly absorbed, irritate the stomach and may cause vomiting; plenty of pre-salted fluid should be the rule for anyone spending much time outdoors in the tropics.

Sun Overcast conditions in the tropics can be misleading. The sun's rays can be fierce, and it is important to make sure that all exposed skin is constantly protected with a high factor sun screen—preferably waterproof for humid conditions. This was especially important while we were travelling by canoe. A hat was also essential.

Food and Water Diarrhoea can be annoying enough in a luxurious holiday resort with comfortable sanitary facilities. The inconvenience under jungle conditions would have been more than trivial, however, with the added problem of coping with further fluid loss and dehydration.

Much caution was therefore needed with food hygiene. We carried our own supplies, which we prepared carefully ourselves: rather uninspiring camping fare, such as canned tuna fish, sardines, pasta, dried soup, biscuits and dried fruit. In the villages, oranges, bananas and coconuts were available. The freshly baked bread was safe, and so would have been the rice.

We purified our water with 2 per cent tincture of iodine carried in a small plastic dropping bottle, 4 drops to each litre—more when the water is very turbid—wait 20 minutes before drinking. This method is safe and effective, and is the only suitable technique for such conditions. It is also worth travelling with a suitable antidiarrhoeal medication such as Arret.

Malaria Drug resistant malaria is present in the Darien area, and antimalarial medication is essential. We took Paludrine, two tablets daily, and chloroquine, two tablets weekly. Free advice on antimalarial medication for all destinations is available from the Malaria Reference Laboratory, T (01) 636 8636 in the UK. An insect repellent is also essential, and so are precautions to avoid insect bites.

Insects Beside malaria and yellow fever, other insect-borne diseases such as dengue fever and leishmaniasis may pose a risk. The old fashioned mosquito net is ideal if you have to sleep outdoors, or in a room that is not mosquito-proof. Mosquito nets for hammocks are widely available in Latin America. An insecticide spray is valuable for clearing your room of flying insects before you go to sleep, and mosquito coils that burn through the night giving off an insecticidal vapour, are also valuable.

Ticks It is said that ticks should be removed by holding a lighted cigarette close to them, and we had an opportunity to put this old remedy to the test. We duly unwrapped a pack of American duty-frees that we had preserved carefully in plastic just for such a purpose, as our Indian guides looked on in amazement, incredulous that we should use these prized items for such a lowly purpose. The British Army expedition to Darien in 1972 carried 60,000 cigarettes among its supplies, and one wonders if they were for this purpose! The cigarette method didn't work, but caused much amusement. (Further discussion with the experts indicates that the currently favoured method is to ease the tick's head gently away from the skin with tweezers.)

Vaccinations A yellow fever vaccination certificate is required from all travellers arriving from infected areas, and vaccination is advised for personal protection.

Immunization against hepatitis A (with gammaglobulin) and typhoid are strongly advised.

Attacks by dogs are relatively common: the new rabies vaccine is safe and effective, and carrying a machete for the extra purpose of discouraging animals is advised.

In addition, all travellers should be protected against tetanus diptheria and polio.

You can get some food along the way, but take enough for at least 5 days. Do take, though, a torch/flashlight, and a bottle of rum for the ranger at Cristales. It is highly recommended to travel in the dry season only, when there is no mud and fewer mosquitoes. If you have time, bargains can be found.

Taking a motorcycle through Darién is not an endeavour to be undertaken lightly, and cannot be recommended. Ed Culberson (who, in 1986 after two unsuccessful attempts, was the first to accomplish the feat) writes: "Dry season passage is comparatively easy on foot and even with a bicycle. But it simply cannot be done with a standard sized motorcycle unless helped by Indians at a heavy cost in dollars...It is a very strenuous, dangerous adventure, often underestimated by motorcyclists, some who have come to untimely ends in the jungle." Culberson's account of his Journey (in the October 1986 issue of *Rider*) makes harrowing reading, not least his encounter with an emotionally unstable police offical in Bijao; the 29-mile "ride" from Pucuro to Palo de las Letras took 6 days with the help of 6 Indians (at US$8 a day each).

By Sea There are about two boats a week from Colón for San Andrés Island (see page 560), from which there are connections with Cartagena; the *Johnny Walker* takes 30 hours, costs US$20, including food, but the service is very irregular and travellers have sometimes waited over a week in vain. Boats also leave, irregularly, the Coco Solo wharf in Colón (minibus from Calle 12, 15 mins., US$0.30) for Puerto Obaldía, via the San Blas Islands. There is also a light plane at 0600 from Panama City to Puerto Obaldía 3 times a week (Mon., Wed., Fri.) for US$37 single, Aerolíneas Nacíonales (SAANSA, T 26-78-91, book well in advance). There are boats from Puerto Obaldía (after clearing Customs) to Turbo, on the Gulf of Urabá (see page 559), US$15 p.p., 10-18 hrs. (take shade and drinks), from which Medellín can be reached by road. Walk from Puerto Obaldía to Zapzurro for a dugout to Turbo, US$10. It seems that most of the boats leaving Puerto Obaldía for Colombian ports are contraband boats. There are also (contraband) boats from Coco Solo, Colón, to the Guajira Peninsula, Colombia. 70 tough hours (minimum). 3-day journey, US$25, uncomfortable, and entirely at your own risk; captains of these boats are reluctant to carry travellers (and you may have to wait days for a sailing—the customs officials will let you sleep in the wind-shadow of their office, will watch your luggage and let you use the sanitary facilities). Once in Colombia, it's a 6-7 hr. ride on top of a truck to Maicao, where you must take a US$0.85 colectivo ride to the Venezuelan border to go through Colombian entry formalities. A passenger travelling in a contraband boat had some problems in the DAS office about getting an entrance stamp: they wanted official papers from the boat's captain showing that he brought him in. You have to bargain for your fare on these boats. Accommodation is a little primitive. There is a good *pensión* in Puerto Obaldía: *Residencia Cande*, nice and clean (E) which also serves very good meals for US$1.50. Book in advance for meals. Also in Puerto Obaldía are shops, Colombian consulate, Panamanian immigration, but nowhere to change travellers' cheques until well into Colombia (not Turbo). Alternatively one can get from Puerto Obaldía to Acandi on the Colombian side of the border, either by walking nine hours or by hiring a dugout or a launch to Capurgana (US$60), thence another launch at 0715, 1 hr., US$3. Several *pensiones* in Capurgana. To walk to Capurgana takes 3-4 hrs., guide not essential (they charge US$20); first to go to La Miel (2 hrs.), then to Zapzurro (20 mins.), where there are shops and cabins for rent, then 1-1½ hrs. to Capurgana. Most of the time the path follows the coast, but there are some hills to cross (which are hot—take drinking water). From Acandi frequent but irregular boats go Turbo (US$8, 3 hrs.).

Dale De Graaf of Grand Rapids, Minn. and Paul K. Kirk of Stockton, Calif. have sent us details of an **alternative route** through the Darién Gap to Colombia: Although not quick, it is relatively straightforward (spoken Spanish is essential). Take a bus from Panama (Plaza 5 de Mayo) to Santa Fe, a rough but scenic 6-8 hours (US$8, 3 a day, check times). In Santa Fe it is possible to camp near the national guard post (no *pensiones*). Then hitch a ride on a truck (scarce), or walk 2 hrs. to the Sabanas River at Puerto Lardo (11 km.) where you must take a dugout or launch to La Palma, or hire one (US$5, 2 hrs.; also reached by boat from Yaviza, US$3, 8 hrs.—bank changes travellers' cheques in La Palma). **La Palma** is the capital of Darién; it has one *pensión* (friendly, English-speaking owners, F, pricey, with cooking and laundry facilities, or see if you can stay with the *guardia*). Wait for a flight to Jaque (US$25, you may have to return to Panama City with the plane first—no one seems to know), near Puerto Piña, 50 km. N of the Colombian border. Alternatively, at the Muelle Fiscal in Panama City (next to the main waterfront market, near Calle 13), ask for a passenger boat going to Jaque.

The journey takes 18 hours, is cramped and passengers cook food themselves, but costs only US$10. Jaque (pop. 1,000) is only reached by sea or air (the airstrip is used mostly by the wealthy who come for sport fishing); there are small stores with few fruit and vegetables, a good *comedor*, one *hospedaje* (but it is easy to find accommodation with local families), and camping is possible anywhere on the beautiful 4 km. beach. The guard post is open every day and gives exit stamps. Canoes from Jaque go to Jurado (US$20) or Bahía Solano (US$45, 160 km., with two overnight stops) in Chocó. The first night is spent in Jurado (where the boat's captain may put you up and the local military commander may search you out of curiosity). There are flights from Jurado to Turbo.

Bahía Solano is a deep-sea fishing resort with an airport and *residencias*. Get your Colombian entry stamp here. Flights from Bahía Solano go to Quibdó, US$18, connecting to Cali, US$30 (with Satena), or Medellín (all flights have to be booked in advance; the town is popular with Colombian tourists). On this journey, you sail past the lush, mountainous Pacific coast of Darién and Chocó, with its beautiful coves and beaches, and you will see a great variety of marine life.

N.B. It is not easy to get a passage to any of the larger Colombian ports as the main shipping lines rarely take passengers. Those that do are booked up well in advance. The Agencias Panamá company, Muelle 18, Balboa, represents Delta Line and accepts passengers to Buenaventura (US$90). Anyone interested in using the Delta Line ships should book a passage before arriving in Panama. The only easy way of getting to Colombia is to fly. Copa, SAM and Avianca fly to Medellín, Cartagena and Barranquilla.

Shipping agencies have not the authority to charge passages. Many travellers think they can travel as crew on cargo lines, but this is not possible because Panamanian law requires all crew taken on in Panama to be Panamanian nationals.

Colombia officially demands an exit ticket from the country. If you travel by air the tickets should be bought outside Panama and Colombia, which have taxes on all international air tickets. If you buy air tickets from IATA companies, they can be refunded. Copa tickets can be refunded in Cartagena (Calle Santos de Piedra 3466—takes 4 days), Barranquilla—2 days, Cali or Medellín. Refunds in pesos only. Copa office in Panama City, Av. 3 Sur, Calle 39 Este. One traveller has told us that the Colombian consulate at Panama City required him to buy a Miscellaneous Charges Order (US$100) which was not required at Cali airport (Colombia). Those who do not want to go to Panama can fly from San José (Costa Rica) to San Andrés and on to Cartagena cheaply.

Shipping a Vehicle from Panama to Colombia is not easy or cheap. The cheapest we have heard of is US$500, but this was arranged in the home country (Netherlands). Inair, T 66-11-98, are very helpful and offer a variety of destinations, e.g. Curaçao (US$2,000 for Land Rover and driver). The following agencies can be contacted: Agencia Motonaves (Colón); Prudential Line; Litres; Pacific Ford; French Line; Lauro Line. The Italian Line takes vehicles but tends to be booked well in advance. It has an office opposite the Post Office in Cristóbal, or you can book through a travel agent. The Grancolombiana line charges US$60 per square metre for shipping a car from Cristóbal to Cartagena, plus US$100 for paperwork and "bribes", reported to be a safe route. If going on one of the large lines it is recommended to ship to Guayaquil rather than Buenaventura, thereby avoiding the hassles of Colombia's paperwork, also taxes make it more expensive to ship to Colombia. Cheaper than the Italian line is the Unif. Trading Company in Colón (contact Captain Gilberto Pavis, T 47-3867). (For the return journey contact the Remar Agency in Buenaventura.) With a great deal of luck you might get one of the sugar boats bringing cargo to Aguadulce (page 1323) to ship you and your car to Colombia. One traveller was lucky and it cost him only US$100.

Sometimes, if enough vehicles are collected together, it is possible to charter a boat to Buenaventura from the Zócalo (Nuevo Panamá). One secret here is to go to the Hipódromo in Panama City because there are usually enough cars there to form a party at least once a month. The groups will then rent a local freighter (a customs agent is necessary for the group, and this is included in the price). It is considered the best way to go south, and drivers and cars arrive at the same time. The regular shipping companies are not interested in this business, so they raise prices to discourage customers. In addition to freight charges there are, of course, handling charges of about US$25. Very few lines take passengers; if you do succeed in getting a passage it may cost as much as US$180. (A plane ticket to the port of arrival can cost up to US$150.) Lykes Line (head office: New Orleans) runs a fortnightly ship to Cartagena (preferable—car costs US$1,520) and Barranquilla in Colombia. Lykes takes passengers but it is more expensive than flying.

A cheaper alternative to the above-named lines is to try to ship on one of the small freighters that occasionally depart from Pier 3 in Colón, which allow you to travel with your car. Obviously there is a considerable element of risk involved though the financial cost is far lower. In Balboa shipping arrangements can be made at Agencias Panamá, whose office is located just outside the entrance to Pier 18; they act as agents for most shipping lines. It is possible to sleep in your car when loading at Pier 18; there is a good and cheap restaurant inside the dock.

Once you have a bill of lading, have it stamped by a Colombian consulate. The consulate also provides tourist cards. They require proof, in the form of a letter from your Embassy (or the Embassy representing your country in Panama) that you do not intend to sell the car in Colombia, though this requirement is usually dispensed with. Then go to the customs office in Panama City (Calle 80 and 55) to have the vehicle cleared for export. After that the vehicle details must be removed from your passport at the customs office at the port of departure. In Colón the customs office is behind the post office. The utmost patience is needed for this operation as regulations change frequently, so do not expect it to be the work of a few minutes.

Some small freighters go only to intermediate ports such as San Andrés, and it is then necessary to get another freighter to Cartagena; a couple had to wait for a week in San Andrés to make the connection. From Colón to San Andrés takes 2 days and from San Andrés to Cartagena takes 3 days. There are two boats plying regularly between Colón (Pier 3) and San Andrés that are big enough for vans, but there is no schedule; they leave when they finish loading. There are also two regular boats between San Andrés and Cartagena; each stays in port about 15 days, but it can be longer.

Customs formalities at the Colombian end will take 1-3 days to clear (customs officials do not work at weekends) even if you have a *Carnet de Passages*. Make sure the visa you get from the Colombian consulate in Colón is *not* a 15 day non-extendable transit visa, but a regular tourist visa, because it is difficult to get an extension of the original visa. Clearance from the Colombian consul at the Panamanian port of embarkation may reduce the bureaucracy when you arrive in Colombia, but it will cost you US$10. In Colombia you can pay an agent US$15 to deal with the paperwork for you, which can reduce the aggravation if not the waiting time. It is understood that Cartagena is much more efficient (and therefore less expensive) as far as paperwork is concerned.

Do not ship or fly your vehicle to Ecuador without the *Carnet*, or you may be held up for up to two weeks at customs, and only allowed to continue to Peru with a police escort!

Warning The contents of your vehicle are shipped at your own risk—generally considered to be a high one! One reader who escaped theft had chained two padlocked, wooden boxes to the car seats.

Air-freighting a Vehicle: Most people ship their vehicles from Panama to South America but some find air-freighting much more convenient. Generally it is faster and avoids many of the unpleasant customs hassles, but is more expensive. Prices vary considerably. The major carriers (Avianca, Ecuatoriana) charge about US$3,000 for a VW bus, US$1,500 for a 4-wheel drive Subaru station wagon, but the cargo lines and independents can offer more reasonable prices (US$800 to US$1,250). Prices and availability change from month to month depending on the demand by regular commercial shippers. You are generally not allowed to accompany the vehicle. Taking a motorcycle (BMW R100RS) from Panama to Medellín by Copa: driver US$110, bike US$0.62 per litre (charged either by volume or by litre). Drain oil and gasoline, and remove battery before loading; the bike goes in with just an inch to spare so you must expect a scratch or two. Mr Barham at the Copa office is most helpful. Having bought your passenger ticket, and checked bike in at Copa Cargo, old Tocumen airport, go to customs in Ancón (**see page 1320**) with your entry permit and freight papers, and pay US$4.20 to have stamp cancelled in passport. Then take your airweighbill to the Colombian Consulate for stamping 3 hrs. before flight time. Allow 2 days in Panama. Retrieving the bike in Colombia, although costing very little, will take from 0900 to 1630 for paperwork.

THE ECONOMY

Panama's economy has traditionally been founded on income derived from services rendered to incoming visitors, taking advantage of its geographical position, its banking centre, and Canal employees and US military personnel spending money in the Republic. However, this contribution is lessening proportionately as the country develops new sources of income: tourism, industry, copper, etc.

Apart from the Canal, the other traditional mainstay of the Panamanian economy is agriculture, which contributes about 10% of gdp. About 25% of the population works in agriculture. Agrarian reform has begun, and has brought the post-1968 governments much support from tenant-farmers and squatters. Most of the land is forested, and development here could also bring added wealth into the country, at the same time helping to reduce the country's dependence on services. Recently the Government has taken a more significant role in industry and now owns sugar mills and cement plants. The main industry is food processing and there are textile and clothing concerns and chemicals, plastics and other light industries. Petroleum products are the only industrial export.

Vast deposits of copper have been found at Cerro Colorado and if fully developed the mine could be the largest in the world. There is also copper at Petaquilla, Cerro Chorca and Río Pinto. Large coal deposits have been found at Río Indio. The country also has gold and silver deposits. So far no oil has been discovered, but exploration is taking place.

One of the most dynamic sectors of the economy is banking. Since 1970 offshore banks have increased from 20 in number to 130 with the establishment of liberal conditions and the abolition of currency controls. In the mid-1980s, total assets amounted to over US$40bn, while deposits were around US$35bn. However, in 1987-88, political uncertainties severely affected the international banking centre. Loss of confidence led many banks to close their offices and move to other offshore centres such as the Bahamas or the Cayman Islands, the level of assets declined, and deposits fell by up to 25%.

Following a rapid accumulation of foreign debt by the public sector in the late 1970s and early 1980s, the debt service burden became intolerable. Panama received assistance after 1983 from the IMF and the World Bank in support of its fiscal and structural adjustment programme, while commercial banks have both rescheduled existing loans and provided new money on easier terms. As a result of the 1988 financial crisis, Panama fell into arrears to all its creditors; consequently, capital inflows were halted and the World Bank cut off loan disbursements. Moreover, the US economic blockade which began in 1988 directly caused a 24 % fall in gdp that year.

	1961-70 (av)	1971-80 (av)	1981-85 (av)	1986-88 (av)(e)
Gdp growth (1980 prices)	7.7%	5.5%	2.6%	-7.0%
Inflation	1.3%	7.0%	3.2%	0.3%
Exports (fob) US$m	94	451	2,052	2,381
Bananas	40	63	72	80
Shrimp	8	26	39	62
Sugar	3	26	36	10
Imports (fob)m	211	933	2,759	2,746
Current account balance US$m (cum)	-295	-1,836	203	764

INFORMATION FOR VISITORS

Air Services From London: British Airways, Pan Am, Continental or Virgin Atlantic to Miami, then by Eastern Airlines, Pan Am or Air Panamá to Panama City. Other airlines flying to Panama from Miami are Ecuatoriana and Lloyd Aéreo Boliviano. From elsewhere in North America: New York City, Eastern, Pan Am, Ecuatoriana; from Los Angeles, Varig, LAN-Chile, Taca (via San Salvador); from Houston, Taca; from Boston, Eastern. From Mexico, Air Panamá, Taca, Aeronica. From Central America, Taca, Iberia (Guatemala City; also to Santo Domingo), KLM (Guatemala City and to the Netherlands Antilles), Copa, Lacsa (to San José, to connect with its Central American network and Los Angeles/Mexico/Miami/New Orleans routes), Sahsa and Aeronica (to Managua, San Salvador, Mexico, San José). Copa also flies to Kingston, Port-au-Prince, Santo Domingo and San Juan (Puerto Rico). From South America, Eastern, Air Panamá, Lacsa (Barranquilla, Maracaibo, Caracas), Copa, LAN-Chile, Avianca, Ecuatoriana, Varig, Avensa, Lloyd Aéreo Boliviano, SAM, Aerolíneas Argentinas, LAP, AeroPerú. From Europe, Iberia, KLM.

There are local flights to most parts of Panama by the national airlines Copa and Adsa. There is a service between Paitilla airport (Panama City) and the Comarca de San Blas by Sasa. To Barranquilla, Cartagena and Medellín by Copa, who also fly to Port-au-Prince, Santo Domingo and Kingston, Jamaica. To Bogotá via Medellín by SAM, it leaves Panama City at 1230 and arrives Bogotá 1430, but be at airport very early because it can leave before time; also to Cali with SAM. Student flights Panama-Bogotá or Guayaquil for those with valid student cards, US$88, are a cheap way to South America, but are only available through Otec in San José, Costa Rica (see page 1286).

An airport tax of US$15 has to be paid by all passengers, except those in transit who do not pass customs. If you stay for a short period (9 hrs. maximum), make sure you put "transit" on your arrival card, so as to avoid the airport tax; foreign residents must pay US$30. There is a 4 % tax on air tickets purchased in Panama.

Shipping Services From Panama there are frequent shipping services with the principal European and North American ports; with the Far East, New Zealand, and Australia, with both the E and W coast ports of South America and Central America, regularly with some, irregularly with others. Freighters carrying a limited number of passengers operate in all trades. The Italian Line serves Cristóbal from Mediterranean ports. For service from France contact Continental Shipping and Travel, 179 Piccadilly, London W1V 9DB, T 01-491 4968 (passengers taken).

The Hamburg South America Steamship Co. operates a scheme called "workaway" (subject to captain's approval) whereby unskilled labour (cleaning, painting, etc.) is exchanged for a free passage (medical insurance, doctor's certificate and returnable US$400 bond required); it functions between Australia/New Zealand and the US east and west coasts via the Panama Canal and the Caribbean, also from European ports. Panama agent is: Fermi and Co., T 62-2019.

Documents Visitors must have a passport, together with a tourist card (issued for 30 days and renewable for another 60) or a visa (issued for 90 days). Holders of visas require exit permits unless they stay in Panama less than 48 hrs.; holders of tourist cards (US$2 from Panamanian consulates, Ticabus or airlines, valid 30 days, renewable in Panama City) do not need exit permits. **Customs at Paso Canoas**, at the border with Costa Rica, have been known to run out of tourist cards. If not entering Panama at the main entry points (Tocumen airport, Paso Canoas), expect more complicated arrangements. Neither visas nor tourist cards are required by nationals of Costa Rica, the Dominican Republic, El Salvador, Western Germany, Honduras, Spain, Switzerland and the UK, but if the stay in Panama exceeds 30 days they must obtain an exit permit from the authorities in Panama City. The procedure is: take your passport to the Ministerio de Hacienda y Tesoro, Av. Perú y Calle 35 E, to obtain a *Paz y Salvo* form (US$0.25); then go to Oficina de Migración, Av. Cuba y Calle 28 E, where the *Paz y Salvo* will eventually be stuck into your passport, and you are given an exit stamp covering the week beginning on the date you went to the office.

US and Japanese citizens need a visa (free to the former, US$20 for the latter, produced in the same day); Australians need a visa (US$10) and Canadians need one (US$15). Tourist cards may not be issued to citizens of Communist countries, India and Pakistan, who must have visas. Onward tickets are required, with the exception of travellers in their own vehicles (hitch-hikers in vehicles may get away without being checked). Once in Panama, you cannot get a refund for an onward flight ticket unless you have another exit ticket. Copa tickets can be refunded at any office in any country (in the currency of that country). **Note:** You may be asked to show that you have at least US$150, or US$10 for each day of intended stay if that exceeds 15 days, before being allowed in. (However, several people have told us that the Panamanian customs are not always that strict in this respect. On the other hand, young Europeans have been strip-searched on arrival by air.)

Customs Even if you only change planes in Panama you must have the necessary papers for the airport officials. Cameras, binoculars, etc., 500 cigarettes or 500 grams of tobacco and 3 bottles of alcoholic drinks for personal use are taken in free. The Panamanian Customs are strict; drugs without a doctor's prescription and books deemed "subversive" are confiscated. In the latter case, a student's or teacher's card helps. **Note:** Passengers leaving Panama by land are *not* entitled to any duty-free goods, which are delivered only to ships and aircraft.

Motoring Coming in by car from Costa Rica, passport is stamped for 3 days for a car or motorcycle at frontier (passengers get 30 days). Then go to David for extensions. Entry costs US$4.05, plus US$1 for fumigation. Exit calls for 4 papers which also cost US$4.20 (obtainable, as are extensions for entry permits, from Customs in Ancón, off Curundu Road, near Albrook air base. Low octane gasoline costs US$1.90 per gallon, super grade US$1.98. For motorcyclists, note that a crash helmet must be worn. **Note** that you may not take dogs into Panama by car, though they may be flown or shipped in if they have general health and rabies certificates; dogs and cats now have to spend 40 days in quarantine after entry.

Warning It is virtually impossible for a tourist to sell his car in Panama unless he can show (with help from his Consulate) that he needs the money for his fare home. He will in this case have to pay import duty on the sale. The only alternative is to sell the car in Costa Rica, but the level of tax incurred is very high. It is also impossible to leave a vehicle in Panama while travelling on.

British business travellers are advised to get "Hints to Exporters: Panama", on application to the Export Services Division, Department of Trade, Sanctuary Buildings, 16-20 Great Smith Street, London SW1P 4DB.

Hours of Business Government departments, 0800-1200, 1230-1630 (Mon. to Fri.). Banks: open and close at different times, but are usually open all morning, but not on Sat. British Embassy: 0800-1330 and 1430-1630 Mon. to Fri. Shops and most private enterprises: 0700 or 0800-1200 and 1400-1800 or 1900 every day, including Sat.

Business interests are concentrated in Panama City and Colón.

Climate The Isthmus is only 9°N of the equator, but prevailing winds reduce the discomfort, especially in the cool evenings of the dry season, though the humidity is high. The mean temperature in the city is 26°C with a maximum temperature record of 36°C and a minimum of 17°. The average rainfall in the area is 1,524 mm. a year (the wet season is called *invierno*—winter, the dry *verano*—summer).

Clothing Light weight tropical type clothes for men, light cotton or linen dresses for women, for whom the wearing of trousers is quite OK. The dry season, January-April, is the pleasantest time. Heavy rainfall sometimes in October and November.

Health No particular precautions are necessary. Water in Panama City and

Colón is safe to drink. It is currently very difficult to obtain chloroquine in Panama; stock up before arrival.

Language   Spanish (hard to understand), but English is widely understood.

Living   is costly, although food is much the same price as in Costa Rica. Military personnel buy their supplies at low prices in special stores. These facilities are not available to tourists. The annual average increase in consumer prices fluctuates in line with US trends.

Festivals   The *fiestas* in the towns are well worth seeing. That of Panama City at Carnival time, held on the four days before Ash Wednesday, is the best. During carnival women who can afford it wear the *pollera* dress, with its "infinity of diminutive gathers and its sweeping skirt finely embroidered", a shawl folded across the shoulders, satin slippers, tinkling pearl hair ornaments in spirited shapes and colours. The men wear a *montuno* outfit: native straw hats, embroidered blouses and trousers sometimes to below the knee only, and carry the *chácara*, or small purse. There is also a splendid local Carnival at Las Tablas, west of Panama City.

At the Holy Week ceremonies at Villa de Los Santos the farces and acrobatics of the big devils—with their debates and trials in which the main devil accuses and an angel defends the soul—the dance of the "dirty little devils" and the dancing drama of the Montezumas are all notable. The ceremonies at Pesé (near Chitré) are famous all over Panama. At Portobelo, near Colón, there is a procession of little boats in the canals of the city.

There are, too, the folk-tunes and dances. The music is cheerful, combining the rhythms of Africa with the melodic tones and dance-steps of Andalusia, to which certain characteristics of the Indian pentatonic scale have been added. The *tamborito* is the national dance. Couples dance separately and the song— which is sung by the women only, just as the song part of the *mejorana* or *socavón* is exclusively for male voices—is accompanied by the clapping of the audience and three kinds of regional drums. The *mejorana* is danced to the music of native guitars and in the interior are often heard the laments known as the *gallo* (rooster), *gallina* (hen), *zapatero* (shoemaker), or *mesano*. Two other dances commonly seen at *fiestas* are the *punto*, with its promenades and foot tapping, and the *cumbia*, of African origin, in which the dancers carry lighted candles and strut high.

The Guaymí Indians of Chiriquí province meet around February 12 to transact tribal business, hold feasts and choose mates by tossing balsa logs at one another; those unhurt in this contest, known as Las Balserías, are allowed to select the most desirable women.

What to Eat   Best hors d'oeuvre is *carimañola*, cooked mashed yuca wrapped round a savoury filling of chopped seasoned fried pork and fried a golden brown. The traditional stew, *sancocho*, made from chicken, yuca, dasheen, cut-up corn on the cob, plantain, potatoes, onions, flavoured with salt, pepper and coriander. *Ropa vieja*, shredded beef mixed with fried onions, garlic, tomatoes and green peppers and served with white rice, baked plantain or fried yuca. *Sopa borracha*, a rich sponge cake soaked in rum and garnished with raisins and prunes marinated in sherry. Panama is famous for its seafood: lobsters, corvina, shrimp, tuna, etc. Piquant *seviche* is usually corvina or white fish seasoned with tiny red and yellow peppers, thin slices of onion and marinated in lemon juice; it is served very cold and has a bite. *Arroz con coco y tití* is rice with coconut and tiny dried shrimp. Plain coconut rice is also delicious. For low budget try *comida corriente* or *del día* (US$1.50 or so). Corn (maize) is eaten in various forms, depending on season, e.g. *tamales*, made of corn meal mash filled with cooked chicken or pork, olives and prunes; or *empanadas*, toothsome meat pies fried crisp. Plantain, used as a vegetable, appears in various forms. A fine dessert is made from green plantain flour served with coconut cream. Other desserts are *arroz con cacao*, chocolate rice pudding; *buñuelos de viento*, a puffy fritter served with syrup; *sopa de gloria*, sponge cake soaked in cooked cream mixture with rum added; *guanábana* ice cream is made from sweet ripe soursop.

Tipping   at hotels, restaurants: 10% of bill. Porters, 15 cents per item. Cloakroom, 25 cents. Hairdressers, 25 cents. Cinema usherettes, nothing. Taxi drivers don't expect tips; rates should be arranged before the trip.

Currency   Panama is one of the few countries in the world which issues no paper money; US banknotes are used exclusively, being called balboas instead of dollars. There are silver coins of 50c (called a *peso*), 25c, 10c, nickel of 5c (called a *real*) and copper of 1c. All the silver money is used interchangeably with US currency; each coin is the same size and material as the US coin of equivalent value. You can take in or out any amount of foreign or Panamanian currency.

Both metric and the US system of weights and measures are used.

Foreign Postage   Great care should be taken to address all mail as "Republic of Panama" or "RP", otherwise it is returned to sender. Air mail takes 3-5 days, sea mail 3-5 weeks from Britain. Rates (examples) for air mail (up to 15 grams) are as follows: Central, North and South America and Caribbean, 30c; Europe, 37c up to 10 grams, 5c for every extra 5 grams; Africa, Asia,

Oceania, 44c; all air letters require an extra 2c stamp. Parcels to Europe can only be sent from the post office in the El Dorado shopping centre in Panama City (bus from Calle 12 to Tumba Muerta).

Telecommunications The radio station at Gatún is open to commercial traffic; such messages are handled through the Government telegraph offices. The telegraph and cable companies are given under the towns in which they operate.

Telex is available at the airport, the cable companies and many hotels. Rate for a 3-minute call to Britain is US$14.40, and US$4.80 for each minute more.

Telephone calls can be made between the UK and Panama any time, day or night. Minimum charge for 3 min. call: US$10 station to station, but person to person, US$16 on weekdays, US$12 on Sun. plus tax of US$1 on each call. To the USA the charge is US$4 for 3 mins. Difference in time: GMT minus 5 hrs. Phone to Australia costs US$16 for 3 mins. (US$13 on Sunday).

Inter-continental contact by satellite is laid on by the Pan-American Earth Satellite Station. The local company is Intercomsa.

Public Holidays

Jan. 1: New Year's Day.
Jan. 9: National Mourning
Shrove Tuesday: Carnival.
Good Friday.
May 1: Labour Day (Republic)
Aug 15: (Panama City only, O)
Oct. 11: National Revolution Day
Nov. 1: National Anthem Day (O)
Nov. 2: All Souls (O)

Nov. 3: Independence Day.
Nov. 4: Flag Day (O).
Nov. 5: Independence Day (Colón only).
Nov. 10: First Call of
Independence.
Nov. 28: Independence from
Spain.
Dec. 8: Mothers' Day.
Dec. 25: Christmas Day.

O=Official holiday, when banks and government offices close. On the rest— national holidays—business offices close too. Many others are added at short notice.

Press *La Estrella de Panamá* and *La República*, (Spanish) are the largest daily newspapers. Other papers are: *Crítica*, and *Matutino* (daily Spanish); *Colón News* (weekly—Spanish and English).

We are most grateful for Panamanian information to

Ed Culberson (Brevard Motorcycle Safety Institute, Palm Bay, FL) and Dr. Richard Dawood (London) for valuable contributions on crossing the Darién Gap, Harald Fischer (Linz, Austr.), Dr. Alan K. Hogenauer (Port Washington, NY), David K. Howe (Short Hills, NJ), Don Hoyle (London EC2) and Kurt Rumler (APO Miami); also to other travellers whose names are listed in the general Central America section.

CUBA

THE ISLAND OF CUBA, 1,250 km. long, 191 km. at its widest point, is the largest of the Caribbean islands and only 145 km. S of Florida. Gifted with a moderate climate, afflicted only occasionally by hurricanes, not cursed by frosts, blessed by an ample and well distributed rainfall and excellent soils for tropical crops, it has traditionally been the largest exporter of cane sugar in the world. The population is about 10.38 million.

About a quarter of Cuba is fairly mountainous. To the W of Havana is the narrow Sierra de los Organos, rising to 750 metres and containing, in the extreme W, the strange scenery of the Guaniguánicos hill country. S of these Sierras, in a strip 145 km. long and 16 km. wide along the piedmont, is the Vuelta Abajo area which grows the finest of all Cuban tobaccos. Towards the centre of the island are the Escambray mountains, rising to 1,100 metres, and in the E, encircling the port of Santiago, are the most rugged mountains of all, the Sierra Maestra, in which Pico Turquino reaches 1,980 metres. In the rough and stony headland E of Guantánamo Bay are copper, manganese, chromium and iron mines. About a quarter of the land surface is covered with mountain forests of pine and mahogany. The coastline, with a remarkable number of fine ports and anchorages, is about 3,540 km. long.

History Cuba was discovered by Columbus during his first voyage on October 27, 1492, and he paid a brief visit two years later on his way to the discovery of Jamaica. Columbus did not realize it was an island; it was first circumnavigated by Sebastián de Ocampo in 1508. Diego Velázquez conquered it in 1511 and founded several towns, including Havana. The first African slaves were imported in 1526. Sugar was introduced soon after but was not important until the last decade of the 16th century. When the British took Jamaica in 1655 a number of Spanish settlers fled to Cuba, already famous for its cigars, made a strict monopoly of Spain in 1717. The coffee plant was introduced in 1748. The British, under Lord Albemarle and Admiral Pocock, captured Havana and held the island in 1762-63, but it was returned to Spain in exchange for Florida.

The tobacco monopoly was abolished in 1816 and Cuba was given the right to trade with the world in 1818. Independence elsewhere, however, bred ambitions, and a strong movement for independence was quelled by Spain, in 1823. By this time the blacks outnumbered the whites in the island; there were several slave rebellions and little by little the Creoles (or Spaniards born in Cuba) made common cause with them. A slave rising in 1837 was savagely repressed and the poet Gabriel de la Concepción Valdés was shot. There was a ten-year rebellion against Spain between 1868 and 1878, but it gained little save the effective abolition of slavery, which had been officially abolished since 1847. From 1895 to 1898 rebellion flared up again under José Martí and Máximo Gómez. The United States was now in sympathy with the rebels, and when the US battleship *Maine* exploded in Havana harbour on February 15, 1898, this was made a pretext for declaring war on Spain. American forces (which included Colonel Theodore Roosevelt) were landed, a squadron blockaded Havana and defeated the Spanish fleet at Santiago de Cuba. In December peace was signed and US forces occupied the island. The Government of Cuba was handed over to its first president, Tomás Estrada Palma, on May 20, 1902. The USA retained naval bases at Río Hondo and Guantánamo Bay and reserved the right of intervention in Cuban domestic affairs, but granted the island a handsome import preference for its sugar. The USA chose to intervene several times, but relinquished this right in 1934.

From 1925 to 1933 the "strong man" Machado ruled Cuba as a dictator. His

EAST OF HAVANA
NOT TO SCALE

CUBA 174

downfall was brought about by Fulgencio Batista, then a sergeant. Corrupt, ineffectual governments held office in the 1940s, until Batista, by then a self-promoted general, staged a military coup in 1952. His harshly repressive dictatorship was brought to an end by Fidel Castro in January 1959, after an extraordinary and heroic three years' campaign, mostly in the Sierra Maestra, with a guerrilla force reduced at one point to twelve men.

From 1960 onwards, in the face of increasing hostility from the USA, Castro led Cuba into communism. All farms of over 67 hectares have been taken over by the state. Rationing is still fierce, though less so than formerly, and there are still shortages of consumer goods. However, education, housing and health services have been greatly improved. Considerable emphasis is placed on combining productive agricultural work with study: there are over 400 schools and colleges in rural areas where the students divide their time between the plantations and the classroom. Education is compulsory up to the age of 17 and free.

Before the Revolution of 1959 the United States had investments in Cuba worth about 1,000 million dollars, covering nearly every activity from agriculture and mining to oil installations; it took 66.8% of Cuba's exports and supplied 69.8% of the imports in 1958. Today all American businesses, including banks, have been nationalized; the USA has cut off sugar imports from Cuba, placed an embargo on exports to Cuba, and broken off diplomatic relations. Cuba's sugar is today sold largely to Communist countries, although in recent years sugar sales to non-communist countries, for instance Japan, have increased appreciably. It was hoped that relations with the USA might soon be normalized. Promising moves in this direction were given renewed impetus in 1988 by the termination of Cuban military activities in Angola under agreement with the USA and South Africa.

Government   In 1976 a new constitution was approved by 97.7% of the voters, setting up municipal and provincial assemblies and a National Assembly of 481 members, elected by the members of the municipal assemblies. As a result of the decisions of the First Congress of the Communist Party of Cuba in December 1975, the number of provinces was increased from six to fourteen. Dr. Fidel Castro was elected President of the Council of State by the National Assembly and his brother, Major Raúl Castro, was similarly elected First Vice-President.

The People   Some 73% of Cubans register themselves as whites: they are mostly the descendants of Spanish colonial settlers and immigrants; 12% are black, now living mostly along the coasts and in certain provinces, Oriente in particular; about 1% are Chinese; the indigenous Indians disappeared long ago. Some 70% live in the towns, of which there are 9 with over 50,000 inhabitants each. The population is estimated at 10,380,000; a third lives in Havana province, a fifth in Havana itself. It is claimed that illiteracy has been wiped out.

Communications   Cuba has 14,835 km. of railway and over 20,000 km. of roads. An 8-lane highway along the length of the island, between Pinar del Río and Santiago, is being built. Internal flights link Havana with other main towns. Tourism, which had long been more or less confined by the authorities, in practice, to Havana and environs, is being extended to other parts of the country.

Carnival During July, carnivals are held in Havana and Santiago, reaching fever pitch with the 26 July festivities. Similar events are held in all Cuban cities and large towns at different times during the summer months. They generally last one-two weeks.

Havana, the capital, was before the Revolution the largest, most beautiful and the most sumptuous city in the Caribbean. Today it is rather run-down, but thanks to the Government's policy of developing the countryside, it is not ringed with shantytowns like so many other Latin American capitals. With its suburbs it has 1,996,000 people, half of whom live in housing officially regarded as sub-standard. Many buildings are shored up by wooden planks. Some of it is very old—the city was founded in 1515—but the ancient palaces, plazas, colonnades, churches and monasteries merge agreeably with the new. The old city is being substantially refurbished with Unesco's help, as part of the drive to attract tourists.

The oldest part of the city, around the Plaza de Armas, is quite near the docks.

HAVANA
Orientation Map
Not to Scale 175A

1. Plaza de Armas
2. Parque Central
3. Plaza de la Revolución
4. Cathedral
5. El Príncipe Castle
6. Monument to General Antonio Maceo, and Torre San Lázaro
7. Napoleonic Museum
8. Decorative Arts Museum
9. Philatelic Museum & Ministry of Communications
10. University of Havana
11. Airline Offices
12. Habana Libre building
13. Hotel Capri
14. Hotel Nacional
15. Hotel Deauville
16. Hotel Caribbean

Area of Old City Map

Here are the former palace of the Captains-General, the temple of El Templete, and La Fuerza, the oldest of all the forts. From Plaza de Armas two narrow and picturesque streets, Calles Obispo and O'Reilly, go W to the heart of the city: Parque Central, with its laurels, poincianas, almonds, palms, shrubs and gorgeous flowers. To the SW rises the golden dome of the Capitol. From the NW corner of Parque Central a wide, tree-shaded avenue, the Paseo del Prado, runs to the fortress of La Punta; at its northern sea-side end is the Malecón, a splendid highway along the coast to the western residential district of Vedado. The sea crashing along the seawall here is a spectacular sight when the wind blows from the north. Calle San Lázaro leads directly from the monument to Gen. Antonio Maceo on the Malecón to the magnificent central stairway of Havana University. A monument to Julio Antonio Mella, founder of the Cuban Communist Party, stands across from the stairway. Further out, past El Príncipe castle, is Plaza de la Revolución, with the impressive monument to José Martí at its centre. The large buildings surrounding the square were mostly built in the 1950s and house the principal government ministries. The long grey building behind the monument is the former Justice Ministry (1958), now the HQ of the Central Committee of the Communist Party, where Fidel Castro has his office. The Plaza is the scene of massive parades and speeches marking important events.

From near the fortress of La Punta a tunnel runs eastwards under the mouth of the harbour; it emerges in the rocky ground between the Castillo del Morro and the fort of La Cabaña, some 550 metres away, and a 5-km. highway connects with the Havana-Matanzas road.

The street map of Havana is marked with numerals showing the places of most interest to visitors.

1. Castillo del Morro was built between 1589 and 1630, with a 20-metre moat, but has been much altered. It stands on a bold headland; the flash of its lighthouse, built in 1844, is visible 30 km. out to sea. The castle is open to the public, Tues.-Sun., 1000-1800, as a museum. On the harbour side, down by the water, is the Battery of the 12 Apostles, each gun named after an Apostle. It can be reached by bus through the tunnel to the former toll gates. In 1989 restoration work was in progress.

2. Fortaleza de la Cabaña, built 1763-1774. Fronting the harbour is a high wall; the ditch on the landward side, 12 metres deep, has a drawbridge to the main entrance. Inside are Los Fosos de los Laureles where political prisoners were shot during the Cuban fight for independence. Visitors are no longer allowed inside La Cabaña as it is used as a barracks; there are plans to convert it into a hotel.

The National Observatory and the railway station for trains to Matanzas are on the same side of the Channel as these two forts.

3. Castillo de la Punta, built at the end of the 16th century, a squat building with 2½-metre thick walls, is open to the public, daily 1400-2200. Opposite the fortress, across the Malecón, is the monument to Máximo Gómez, the independence leader.

4. Castillo de la Fuerza, Cuba's oldest building and the second oldest fort in the New World, was built 1538-1544 after the city had been sacked by buccaneers. It is a low, long building with a picturesque tower from which there is a grand view. Inside the castle is the Museo de Armas, open Tues.-Sat., 1300-1900, Sun., 0900-1200. The downstairs part is open in the mornings for art exhibitions. *Note:* There are two other old forts in Havana: Atarés, finished in 1763, on a hill overlooking the south-west end of the harbour; and El Príncipe, on a hill at the far end of Av. Independencia (Av. Rancho Boyeros), built 1774-94, now the city gaol. Finest view in Havana from this hill.

5. The Cathedral, built in 1704 by the Jesuits, who were expelled in 1767. On either side of the Spanish colonial baroque façade are belltowers, the left one (W) being half as wide as the right (E). There is a grand view from the latter. The church is officially dedicated to the Virgin of the Immaculate Conception, but is better known as the church of Havana's patron saint, San Cristóbal, and as the Columbus cathedral. The bones of Christopher Columbus were sent to this cathedral when Santo Domingo was ceded by Spain to France in 1795; they now lie in Santo Domingo (see page 1368). The bones are in fact those of another Columbus. The Cathedral is open Mon-Fri. 0900-1130 and Sat. 1530-1730.

6. Plaza de Armas, has been restored to very much what it once was. The statue in the centre is of Céspedes. In the NE corner of the square is the church of El Templete; a column in front of it marks the spot where the first mass was said in 1519 under a ceiba tree. A sapling of the same tree, blown down by hurricane in 1753, was planted on the same spot, and under its branches the

HAVANA
OLD CITY
Not to Scale
175

GULF OF MEXICO

CHANNEL

TUNNEL

BAY

MALECÓN

SAN LÁZARO

(PRADO)

CÁRCEL

GENIO

REFUGIO

COLÓN

ZULUETA

MORRO

ESPADA

CUARTELES

CHACÓN

TACÓN

AV. C.M. DE CÉSPEDES (DEL PUERTO)

INDUSTRIA

CONSULADO

ÁNIMAS

PASEO DE MARTÍ

AV. DE LAS MISIONES

TEJADILLO

EMPEDRADO

VIRTUES

NEPTUNO

PROGRESO

O'REILLY

CUBA

SAN IGNACIO

MERCADERES

BOULEVARD

BRISTOL

AMISTAD

AV. MONSERRATE

BERNAZA

VILLEGAS

AGUACATE

OBISPO

OBRAPIA

LAMPARILLA

AMARGURA

TENIENTE REY (BRASIL)

AGUIAR

SAN PEDRO

MURALLA

DRAGONES

S. BOLÍVAR

MÁXIMO GÓMEZ

CORRALES

EGIDO (AV. DE BÉLGICA)

ZULUETA

CARDENAS

ECONOMIA

COMPOSTELA

HABANA

SOL

LUZ

ACOSTA

JESÚS MARÍA

MERCED

PAULA

INQUISIDOR

OFICIOS

REVILLAGIGEDO

SUÁREZ

APODACA

GLORIA

MISIÓN

ESPERANZA

SAN ISIDRO

DESAMPARADOS

ÁGUILA

GENIO

supposed bones of Columbus reposed in state before being taken to the cathedral. This tree was cut down in 1828, the present tree planted, and the Doric temple opened. There are paintings by Vermay, a pupil of David, inside.

7. On the W side of Plaza de Armas is the former palace of the Captains General, built in 1780, a charming example of colonial architecture. The Spanish Governors and the Presidents lived here until 1917, when it became the City Hall. It is now the Historical Museum of the city of Havana (open Tues.-Sat., 1430-2130; Sun. 0900-1230). The arcaded and balconied patio is well worth a visit (open in the morning). The former Supreme Court on the N side of the Plaza is another colonial building, with a large patio.

8. The church and convent of San Francisco, built 1608, reconstructed 1737; a massive, sombre edifice suggesting defence rather than worship. The three-storeyed tower was both a landmark for returning voyagers and a look-out for pirates. Having been restored to the Franciscan order, it is now open to the public on Sunday mornings or at other times immediately after services. Most of the treasures were removed by the government and some are in museums.

9. The Corinthian white marble building on Calle Oficinas S of the Post Office was once the legislative building, where the House of Representatives met before the Capitol was built.

10. The Santa Clara convent was built in 1635 for the Clarisan nuns. The quaint old patio has been carefully preserved; in it are the city's first slaughter house, first public fountain and public baths, and a house built by a sailor for his love-lorn daughter. You can still see the nuns' cemetery and their cells.

11. La Merced church, built in 1746, rebuilt 1792. It has a beautiful exterior and a redecorated lavish interior.

12. The Palacio de Bellas Artes now called the National Museum of Fine Arts. It also has a large collection of relics of the struggle for independence, sculptures, classical paintings (most of them copies), and a fine array of modern paintings by Cuban and other artists. It also has temporary exhibitions. Open Tues.-Sat. 1330-2030, Sun. 1600-2000.

13. Parque Fraternidad, landscaped to show off the Capitol, N of it, to the best effect. At its centre is a ceiba tree growing in soil provided by each of the American republics. In the park also is a famous statue of the Indian woman who first welcomed the Spaniards: La Noble Habana, sculpted in 1837. From the SW corner the handsome Avenida Allende runs due W to the high hill on which stands Príncipe Castle (now the city gaol). The Quinta de los Molinos, on this avenue, at the foot of the hill, once housed the School of Agronomy of Havana University. The main house now contains the Máximo Gómez museum (Dominican-born fighter for Cuban Independence). Also here is the headquarters of the young writers and artists (Asociación Hermanos Saiz). The gardens are a lovely place to stroll. N, along Calle Universidad, on a hill which gives a good view, is the University.

14. The Capitol, opened May 1929, has a large dome over a rotunda; it is a copy, on a smaller scale, of the US Capitol in Washington. At the centre of its floor is set a 24-carat diamond, zero for all distance measurements in Cuba. The interior has large halls and stately staircases, all most sumptuously decorated. Entrance for visitors is to the left of the stairway. The Capitol now houses the Museum of Natural Science, which is open Tues. to Sat. 1400-2130, and Sun. 0900-1230.

15. Parque Central.

16. Gran Teatro de la Habana.

17. Presidential Palace (1922), a huge, ornate building topped by a dome, facing Av. de las Misiones Park; now contains the Museum of the Revolution. Open Tues.-Sat. 1300-2000, Sun. 1000-1300, 1400-2000 (allow plenty of time to see it all). A bit of the old city wall is preserved in front of the front entrance. The yacht *Granma*, from which Dr Castro disembarked with his companions in 1956 to launch the Revolution, has been installed in the park facing the S entrance.

18. The Church of El Santo Angel Custodio was built by the Jesuits in 1672 on the slight elevation of Peña Pobre hill. It has white, laced Gothic towers and 10 chapels, the best of which is behind the high altar.

19. Museo de Arte Colonial, Plaza de la Catedral (in the former Palacio de los Condes de Casa Bayona), Tues.-Fri. 1330-2030, Sat. 1500-2000, Sun. 0900-1245, contains colonial furniture and other items, plus a section on stained glass.

20. Birthplace of José Martí, opposite central railway station (Tues.-Sat. 1300-2000, Sun. 0900-1300).

21. Carlos J Finlay Museum of Medicine, Calle Cuba 460 (Mon.-Fri. 0800-1200, 1300-1700).

Other Museums Museo Nacional, Palacio de Belles Artes, Animas y Zulueta; Museo de Alfabetización, Plaza de la Catedral, Tues.-Sat. 1015-1300, 1415-1845, Sun. 0900-1300; Napoleonic Museum, Calle Ronda (Tues.-Sat. 1300-2100; Sun. 0900-1300), houses paintings and other works of art, a specialized library and a collection of weaponry; Decorative Arts Museum, 17th and E Streets, Vedado (Tues.-Sat. 1330-2000; Sun. 0900-1300); Postal Museum, Ministry of Communications, Plaza de la Revolución (Mon.-Fri. 1000-1800, Sat. 1000-1400); also Numismatic Museum. Vintage Car Museum, Oficios y Jústiz (just off Plaza de Armas), Arab Museum (with restaurant) opposite, on Oficios; Africa Museum, on Lamparilla between San Ignacio and Mercaderes. Admission to all museums, galleries etc. free. Always check opening times in advance.

Hotels (Payment for hotels used by tourists is in US$). Foreign tourists should obtain a reservation through an accredited Cubatur agent (see **Travel Agencies** at the end of this chapter). On arrival at José Martí International Airport, you must go straight to the Cubatur Individual Desk where pre-booked accommodation vouchers will be exchanged for Cubatur vouchers. If accommodation has not been pre-booked, it must be arranged at the Cubatur desk before you are allowed through immigration and customs. Always tell the hotel each morning if you intend to stay on another day. Do not lose your "guest card" which shows your name and room number. Tourist hotels are a/c, with "tourist" TV (US films, tourism promotion), restaurants with reasonable food (*Riviera* does a good breakfast), but standards are not comparable with Europe and plumbing is often faulty.

	Address	No. of rooms	Tele-phone	Rates (US$) Single	Double
Capri	21 y N, Vedado	220	32-0511	53	70
Riviera	Paseo y Malecón, Vedado	360	30-5051	55	73
Nacional	21 y O, Vedado	525	7-8981	47	63
Habana Libre	L y 23, Vedado	568	30-5011	64	85
Victoria	19 y M, Vedado	32	32-6531	53	70
St. John's	O, entre 23 y 25, Vedado	96	32-9531	30	40
Vedado	Calle O, No. 244	120	32-6501	40	53
Colina	Calle 1			26	35
Deauville	Galiano y Malecón	140	61-6901	33	44

The Vedado hotels (the best) are away from the old centre; the others reasonably close to it. Other "dollar" hotels are *Sevilla*, Trocadero y Zulueta, T 6-9961, D, good restaurant; *Lincoln*, in Central Havana on Italia, down from *Deauville*, B; *Caribbean*, Paseo Martí 154 (bus 82 from Vedado), D, popular with travellers, clean, old city, rec.

The cheaper hotels are usually hard to get into; often full. The *Lido* reception (on Consulado) says that the hotel "takes only socialists, no capitalists", but if you can get in it's good, D. To pay in pesos at cheaper hotels involves presenting yourself in the morning to be listed at the hotel selected and then going back in the afternoon to collect a registration card. Some are reserved for Cuban tourists, most have two rates, one for nationals and another (higher) for foreigners. (We have recently been told that it is quite impossible for tourists to stay in "peso hotels" in Havana.)

Restaurants are not cheap. The choice of food is limited except in "dollar" restaurants. Book a table between 2200 and midnight the evening before, if you can, in the main ones, where meals are about US$10-15, usually paid in US dollars. Check the bill carefully as overcharging is common in some Havana "dollar" restaurants, also the bill may not record what you actually ate. **NB** Mealtimes in most peso "peso" restaurants are limited 1130-1400 (the best dishes are gone by 1200) and from 1800-2030 (when the food runs out). The *Bodeguita del Medio*, Empedrado, near the Cathedral, made famous by Hemingway and worth a visit if only for a drink (mojito—rum, crushed ice and mint—is a must), and *The Patio*, Plaza Catedral, nearby, are rec. for national dishes. *La Mina*, on Plaza de Armas, traditional Cuban food; nearby, *El Arabe*, lamb dishes; and *Don Giovanni*, Italian (all "dollar"). *Las Ruinas* in Parque Lenín, Cuba's most exclusive restaurant—and aptly named for its prices—is most easily reached by taxi; try to persuade the driver to come back and fetch you, as otherwise it is difficult to get back. Visit *Dulcería Doña Teresa* (end of Obispo) for the caramel pudding. Reasonable cafeteria-style meals are available at *Wakamba*, opposite *St. John's* hotel; nearby is the *Pizzería Milán*; *Budapest*, near Parque Central, expensive but not rec. In Vedado, *El Cochinito*, Calle 23 (national criollo dishes); *El Conejito*, Calle N, and *La Torre* (at top of Edificio Fosca), are quite expensive. *Lafayette* (Aguiar, entre O'Reilly y San Juan de Dios), alone of the better restaurants, accepts pesos from tourists. *Daytona*, Calle Amistad off San Rafael, good, opens 1200 and 1900, is a good "peso" restaurant; also *Los Parados*, corner of Neptuno and Consulado. Good cheap restaurant, which accepts pesos from tourists, in Calle Trocadero near *Caribbean Hotel*. In the *Habana Libre Hotel*, try *El Barracón*, traditional Cuban with good fish and seafood and restaurant and bar on the 25th floor (spectacular views of Havana but restaurant open only from 1900). Also expensive, "*1830*" on Malecón. Along and near La Rampa there are some cheaper pizzerias and self-service restaurants. At Miramar beach there are also some cheaper bars and restaurants.

A visit to the *Coppelia* ice-cream parlour, 23 y L, Vedado, is recommended. It tends to be very crowded in the evenings as it and La Rampa are very popular with young people. To get an ice-cream (0.50-1.50 pesos), pay first, collect a dish and then the ice. This process can take more than an hour, so it might be best to sample the Coppelia ice-cream in the tourist hotels and restaurants.

Rincón Criollo and the nearby *Tabernita* are just past Santiago de las Vegas, east of the airport (tourist taxi from *Habana Libre* US$15 one way). Both serve national dishes with uncertain menus. It is possible to take a bus to Santiago de las Vegas and take a taxi from there, but best to get there by rented car.

Bars Visitors often find that ordinary bars *not* on the tourist circuit will try to charge them in dollars. There is no need to argue—just pay them in pesos. You can tell whether the bar is on the "dollar" circuit simply by looking at the patrons.

The best bar in Old Havana is *La Bodeguita* (see above), where tourists and Cubans, dollars and pesos, receive the same treatment. *La Casa del Agua La Tinaja*, on SW corner of the Plaza de Armas is a nice place selling drinking water for 5 cents (either type).

Shopping Local cigars, cigarettes and rum are excellent. Original lithographs and other works of art can be purchased directly from the artists at the Galería del Grabado, Plaza de la Catedral (Mon.-Fri. 1400-2100, Sat. 1400-1900). Just opposite this is the Galería de Arte (Mon.-Fri. 1030-1800, Sat. 1700-2200), where a variety of works of art are on sale. On Saturday afternoons there are handicraft stalls in the Plaza. There is a special boutique in the old mansion at Calle Cuba 64 where the largest selection of Cuban handicrafts is available; the artisans have their workshops in the back of the same building (open, Mon.-Sat. 1230-1930). The "Intur-shops" in tourist hotels and elsewhere, which sell tourists' requisites and other luxury items, require payment in US$ (or credit cards: Masterchage, Visa) and will generally cash travellers' cheques and give change in US$ cash. Large diplomatic store at Marianao accepts all foreign currencies (no pesos) and has a variety of goods at prices way below the government Intur dollar shops. The large department stores are along Galiano (Av. Italia) near San Rafael and Neptuno. Rationed goods are distinguished by a small card bearing the code number and price but a great deal is now sold freely and these articles bear only the price. Most stores are open only in the afternoon. International bookstore at end of El Prado, near Parque Fraternidad and Capitol, English, French, German books. Other good bookshops near Parque Central and on Calle Obispo (books are very good value). Universal (San Rafael) and El Siglo de las Luces (Neptuno), both near Capitolio, are good places to buy *son*, *trova* and *jazz* (rock) records.

Night Club The *Tropicana* (closed Mon.) is a must; book with Cubatur or through a tourist hotel, US$25-31 depending on seat, for 2 shows and 2 cocktails or one bottle of rum between 6 people (2030-0200). Despite being toned down to cater for more sober post-revolutionary tastes, it is still a lively place with plenty of atmosphere. Admission is free, but the drinks are expensive: minimum charge is 5 pesos a head; payment in dollars. Bringing your own bottle seems acceptable. Foreigners showing their exchange paper at the door may be admitted without booking if there is room. All the main hotels have their own cabarets. Best to reserve through Cubatur.

Theatres *Teatro Mella*, Vedado, specializes in modern dance; more traditional programmes at *Gran Teatro de la Habana*. Havana has some very lively theatre companies.

Jazz *Maxim Club*, Calle 10, T 33981, 7 pesos, music starts at 2100; *Coparrun*, Hotel Riviera (big names play there).

Cinemas Best are *Yara* (opposite *Habana Libre* hotel); *América*, Galiano 253; *Payret*, Prado 505.

Culture In Havana, a weekly guide (Cartelera) appears every Thursday, with listing of concerts, theatre programmes, art exhibitions, etc. It also carries the names, addresses and programmes of the Casas de Cultura and Casas de la Trova, houses where traditional Cuban music can be heard for free, thoroughly recommended (in Havana: San Lázaro between Belascoaín and Gervasio).

In Vedado, the National Folklore Company, Calle 2 entre Calzada y 5ta, sometimes stage "Rumba Saturday" at 1400.

Festivals of dance (including ballet), theatre, jazz, cinema and other art forms are held frequently—tickets (in dollars) from lobbies of the major hotels.

Outside Havana, ask in hotels for detailed information.

NB Last-minute changes and cancellations are common.

Zoo Av. 26, Vedado (open Tues.-Sun. 0900-1800).

El Bosque de la Habana is worth visiting. From the entrance to the Zoo, cross Calle 26 and walk a few blocks until you reach a bridge across the Almendares. Cross this, turn right at the end and keep going N, directly to the Bosque which is a jungle-like wood.

Aquaria National Aquarium, Calle 60 and Av. 1, Miramar, specializes in salt-water fish and dolphins (open Tues.-Fri. 1300-1730, Sat. and Sun. 1000-1730) while the Parque Lenín aquarium has fresh-water fish on show.

Banks Banco Nacional and its branches. (See also under **Currency** below.)

Post Office There is a post and telegraph office in the *Hotel Habana Libre* building.

Telephones A fire badly damaged the Havana central exchange in November 1988 and all telephones beginning with 6 or 61 (including the British Embassy) were put out of service. Repairs are not expected to be complete until mid-1990. **Other cable offices** Calle Obispo 351. T 6-9901/5; Telegraph in *Habana Libre* building. Ministerio de Comunicaciones, Plaza de la Revolución, T 70-5581.

Embassies British is on the 8th floor, Edificio Bolívar, Carcel 101-103 (just off Prado), Havana. Telegraphic address: Prodrome, Havana. Canadian, Calle 30 (No. 518) and Av. 7, Miramar (T 2-6421); Mexican, Calle 12, 518 and Av. 7, Miramar; West German, Calle 28 No. 313, Miramar, T 222560; Swiss, Av. 5 No. 2005 between 20 and 25; T 2-6452/4; US Interests Section, on the Calzada, Calle L and M, Vedado, T 320551 and 329700; Swedish, Av. 31 No. 14A, Miramar, T 292871; Finnish, Av. 5, No. 9202, Miramar, T 224098; Danish, Paseo de Martí 20, T 616610/611496.

Transport A fleet of white "Turistaxis" has been introduced for tourists' use; payment in US$. Some ordinary taxis are only allowed to operate in a restricted area (indicated by a sign in the window). If you want to go further afield look for one without a sign. The newer taxis have meters which should be set at No. 1 during the daytime and at No. 2 at night (2300-0700). Normal charge: 60 centavos per person for 500 metres, then 10 centavos for each 300 metres thereafter. In the older taxis there are no meters and there is normally a fixed charge between points in or near the city. The fare should be fixed before setting out on a journey. Ordinary taxis are not allowed to accept US dollars, so be sure to have pesos on you. Beware of unofficial taxis at the airport arrival gate who will overcharge.

Town buses are frequent and cheap (10 centavos flat rate fare), though crowded, and run hourly through the night as well. Destinations are sometimes indicated above or behind windshield. There are long queues for all buses; you must get a waiting number at the starting point. The local word for bus is *guagua*.

The out-of-town bus services (reconfirm booking 30 mins. before departure) leave from the Terminal de Omnibus Interprovinciales, Av. Rancho Boyeros (Independencia), buses nos. 67 and 84 go there from the hotel area, and No.47 from Prado and Animas near *Hotel Caribbean*. See **Information for Visitors** for advance booking addresses. Trains leave from the station in Av. Monserrate (de Bélgica), Havana, to the larger cities. Trains for Pinar del Río leave from the West (Occidente) station. It is sometimes easier to get a seat on a train than on a bus (though there are waiting lists for buses), but all public transport out of Havana is heavily booked in advance and difficult to get on. It might be easier to take a local bus to a nearby town, such as Santa Cruz, where buses can be caught to Matanzas. For details of services, **see page 1351.**

The peso taxi base is beside the Interprovincial bus terminal (see also below).

Airport José Martí, 18 km. from Havana. No departure tax. Turistaxi to airport, US$12; peso taxi about 7-8 pesos.

Suburbs The western sections of the old city merge imperceptibly into Vedado. W of it, and reached by a tunnel under the Almendares river, lies Miramar, some 16 km. W of the capital, and easily reached by bus. Miramar was where the wealthy lived before the Revolution; today there are several embassies and government buildings, and also many old, abandoned villas.

The Cuban pavilion, a large building on Calle 23, Vedado, is a combination of a tropical glade and a museum of social history. It tells the nation's story by a brilliant combination of objects, photography and the architectural manipulation of space.

The National Arts College, located in the grounds of the former Havana Country Club in Cubanacan, SW of Miramar, houses schools for different arts and was designed by Ricardo Porro. Architects will be interested in this "new spatial sensation".

Pabexpo completed in January 1989, a sprawling new facility SW of Havana, past Lenin Park, near the botanical gardens, features a score of pavilions showing Cuba's achievements in industry, science, agriculture and the arts and entertainment. Open weekdays Wed.-Fri. 1400-1600 and Sat.-Sun. 1000-1800 (times subject to change). Special trains leave from main terminal in Old Havana. Information on times (and special buses) from hotels.

Beaches The beaches in Havana, at Miramar and Playa, reached by No. 132 bus, are generally very crowded in summer. Those to the E, El Mégano, Santa María del Mar and Bacuranao, for example, are much better. Buses going along the Vía Blanca to these places leave from near the central railway station in the old city. To the W of Havana are Arena Blanca and Bahía Honda, which are good for diving and fishing but difficult to get to unless you have a car.

Short ferry rides across Havana Bay to Casablanca and Regla (10 centavos) are fun and a good way of looking at these "across the bay" villages and Havana itself from a different perspective. The best view of Havana is from Morro Castle.

An easy excursion is to Cojimar, the seaside village featured in Hemingway's *The Old Man and the Sea*. Take local bus (65 and others). *La Terraza* is a seafood restaurant ("dollars") with a pleasant view (mixed reports, the cheap dishes are said to be better).

Guanabacoa is 5 km. to the E and is reached by a road turning off the Central Highway, or by the Hershey Railway, or by No. 162 bus or by launch from Muelle Luz (not far from No. 9 on the map) to the suburb of Regla, then by bus direct to Guanabacoa. It is a well preserved small colonial town; sights include the old parish church which has a splendid altar: the monastery of San Francisco; the Carral theatre; and some attractive mansions. The Historical Museum of Guanabacoa, a former estate mansion, has an unusual voodoo collection in the former slave quarters at the back of the building. Open: Tues.-Sun., 1600-2200.

A delightful colonial town, **Santa María del Rosario,** founded in 1732, is 16 km. E of Havana. It is reached from Cotorro, on the Central Highway, or by 97 bus from Guanabacoa, and was carefully restored and preserved before the Revolution. The village church is particularly good. See the paintings, one by Veronese. There are curative springs nearby.

Hemingway fans may wish to visit the house in San Francisco de Paula where he lived from 1939 to 1960 (called the Museo Hemingway). Bus 23 from Vedado to Virgen del Campo, then bus 7 to San Miguel de Padrón (ask to be let out at the place—all the passengers will oblige). Open Tues.-Sat. (closed Mon. and on rainy days) 0900-1200 and 1300-1700, Sun. 0900-1300. There is a bust of the author in the village of Cojimar.

Some 60 km. E of Havana is **Jibacoa** beach, which is excellent for snorkelling as the reefs are close to the beach. To get there take bus 70 to Santa Cruz del Norte and from there either a 126 or "La Matancera" - be warned, though, that the journey takes some time. From the bus stop walk to the beach. Peso taxi Santa Cruz del Norte-Havana, 13 pesos. (*Camping de Jibacoa*, D for a cabin for four, F for 2. Food is rather expensive: 1.40 pesos for breakfast, 5 for lunch; 5 for dinner).

The old provincial town of **Matanzas** lies 104 km. E of Havana along the Vía Blanca, which links the capital with Varadero beach, 34 km. further E. There are frequent buses but the journey via the Hershey Railway is more memorable (six trains daily—3 hrs., 1.03 pesos—from the Casablanca station, which is reached by public launch from near La Fuerza Castle, 0.50 peso). Those who wish to make it a day trip from Havana can easily do so.

In Matanzas one should visit the Pharmaceutical Museum (Mon.-Sat. 1400-1800, 1900-2100), the Matanzas Museum (Tues.-Sun. 1500-1800, 1900-2200), and the cathedral, all near Parque La Libertad. There is a wonderful view of the surrounding countryside from the church of Montserrat. Bellamar Cave is only 5 km. from Matanzas.

From Matanzas one can continue on to **Varadero**, 144 km. from Havana, Cuba's chief beach resort with all facilities. It is undergoing large scale development of new hotels and cabins. In Varadero all hotels, restaurants and excursions must be paid in US dollars; pesos only for local bus rides and the cinema. Book excursions at *Hotel Internacional*, Av. Las Américas. Each November a festival is held in Varadero, lasting a week, which attracts some of the best artists in South America. Entrance US$2-10 per day. From Varadero it is possible to explore the interesting town of **Cárdenas**, where the present Cuban flag was raised for the first time in 1850. Another excursion is to Neptune's Cave (thought a more appealing name than the old one, Cepero), which is south of the town of Carboneras, half-way between Matanzas and Varadero. It has an underground lagoon, stalagmites and stalagtites, evidence of Indian occupation and was used as a clandestine hospital during the war of independence.

Hotels and Restaurants (All prices high season, double.) *Los Cactus* (L); *Kawama*, A; *Internacional*, L; *Oasis*, A; the *Siboney*, L; *Caribe*, B. *Pullman*, B, best value for the independent traveller; *Ledo*, Av. Playa, B, not rec.; *Villa La Herradura*, Av. Playa, B; *Los Delfines*, Av. Playa, B. *Solymar Cabines* (near *Hotel Internacional*), A, rec., pool and restaurant; more will be ready during 1989 and 1990. *Rincón Francés*, campsite 10 km. from town, hourly 220 bus, E for *cabaña*, many mosquitoes. Good restaurants: *Bodegón Criollo* and *Mi Casita* (book in advance).

A cheap, recommended method of getting to Varadero is to take the train to Matanzas (see above), then a taxi to Matanzas bus terminal (3 pesos) from where you catch a bus, 0.40 pesos, about 1 hour (state destination, take ticket, wait for bus and then your number to be called, and run for the bus). About 5½ hours in all.

Santa Clara, 300 km. from Havana and 196 km. from Varadero, is a pleasant university city in the centre of the island. It was the site of the last battle of the Cuban Revolution before Castro entered Havana, and the Batista troop train captured by Che Guevara can be seen near the cathedral. There are two "dollar hotels", *Motel Los Caneyes* (outside the city), B and *Santa Clara Libre* (central, on Plaza Vidal), C; and three "pesos hotels" *Modelo*, *América* (Calle Mujica) and *Central* (Calle Cuba), all D-E.

Trinidad, 133 km. south of Santa Clara is a perfect relic of the early days of the Spanish colony. It was founded in 1514 as a base for expeditions into the "New World"; Cortés set out from here for Mexico in 1518. The five main squares and four churches date from the 18th and 19th centuries; the whole city, with its fine palaces, cobbled streets and tiled roofs, is a national monument. Four museums (Humboldt, Architecture, Archaeological and Romantic) are on the Plaza Mayor, now Martí). Nearby are the excellent beaches of La Boca (6 km) and Ancón (13 km).

Accommodation Hard to find, particularly in summer. *Motel Las Cuevas*, C, on a hill near the centre; *Hotel Ancón*, at Ancón Beach, B, and *Costa Sur*, good value, 10 km. out of town, C, all "dollar hotels". The "peso hotels" are *Hotel Canadá*, E, and *Hotel La Ronda*, E, both on Parque Central. Campsites at Ancón beach and La Boca (5-bed apartments for 10 pesos a night). Camping at Base Manacal in the mountains: tent or small hut for US$5 per day; take No. 10 bus from Cienfuegos.

Transport from Havana: a/c buses at 0335 (arrive 0905) and 1220 (arrive 1750), 8 pesos; train from Estación Central 1301; taxi to Cienfuegos, 20 pesos per person, from base beside Interprovincial bus terminal, then on to Trinidad.

Cienfuegos, on the S coast, is an attractive seaport and industrial city 80 km. from Trinidad and 70 km. from Santa Clara. Interesting colonial buildings around the central Parque Martí. There are one "dollar hotel", *Jagua*, A, and 3 "peso hotels", *Perla del Sur*, *San Carlos*, and *Ciervo del Oro*, Calle 29, No. 5614 (entre 56 y 58), T 5757, E. Many of the hotels are out of town or booked solid by Cubans. *Hotel Pasacaballo*, B and *Rancho Luna*, C, are seaside complexes with cafeteria etc.

From Cienfuegos take a taxi to Playa Girón and the Bay of Pigs (26 pesos, 1½ hours). Ask the driver to wait while you visit the beach and tourist complex, and the site of national pilgrimage where, in 1961, the disastrous US-backed invasion of Cuba was attempted. Further west from Girón is the Zapata Peninsula, an area of swamps, mangroves, beaches and much bird and animal life. Access from Playa Larga or Guamá, inland.

The Museo Ignacio Agramonte in the large city of **Camagüey**, half-way between Santa Clara and Santiago, is one of the biggest and most impressive museums in the country. *Hotel Camagüey*, Carretera Central, T 8834/6218; *Puerto Príncipe*, Av. de los Mártires y Andrés Sánchez, La Vigía (in town), T 7575/78; *Gran Hotel*, Maceo 67, T 2093/4, all same price range, B, are the "dollar" hotels; "peso hotels": *Colón*, República 472, T 2553 and *Isla de Cuba*, San Esteban y A. Popular, both E.

Holguín, a provincial capital in the E, near Santiago, has the *Hotel Pernik*, B; *Motel El Bosque* and *Motel Mirador de Mayabe*, both C.
    From Holguín the Atlantic resort of Guardalavaca (*Hotel Guardalavaca*, pool, rec., "dollar hotel", C), with good beach, can be reached by bus.

Santiago de Cuba, near the E end of the island, 970 km. from Havana and 670 km. from Santa Clara, is Cuba's second city and "capital moral de la Revolución Cubana". It is a pleasant colonial Caribbean city, with many balconies and *rejas* (grills). Of the several museums, the best is the Colonial Museum located in Diego de Velázquez' house (the oldest in Cuba), at the northwest corner of Parque Céspedes. It has been restored after its use as offices after the Revolution and is in two parts, one 16th century, one 18th century (each room shows a particular period; open Tues.-Sat. 0800-2200, Sun. 0900-1300, Mon. 0800-1200, 1400-1800, free). On the south side of Parque Céspedes is the Cathedral, and on the north side the Alcaldía. Two blocks east of the Parque, opposite the Palacio Provincial is the Museo Bacardí (exhibits from prehistory to the Revolution downstairs, paintings upstairs), open Mon. 1400-1800, Tues.-Sat. 0800-2145, Sun. 0900-1300. Also visit the Moncada barracks museum and the house of Frank País (General Bandera 226), leader of the armed uprising in Santiago on November 30, 1956, who was shot in

July, 1957. The national hero, José Martí, is buried in Santa Efigenia cemetery, just W of the city. Another historical site is the huge ceiba tree in the grounds of the *Leningrado* hotel, beneath which Spain and the USA signed the surrender of Santiago on July, 16, 1898; at the Loma de San Juan nearby are more monuments of the Hispano-Cuban-American war (only worth visiting if staying at the *Leningrado*, or going to the zoo and amusement park behind the hotel).

The Festival de Caribe runs from 16 to 19 April, with traditional African dancing and beautiful costumes. There is singing every weekend at the Casa de la Trova on Calle Heredia (but hope that there is no modern music at the Casa de Estudiantes Josué País García next door to drown out the real thing).

Hotels   *Motel Versalles*, between airport and town, A; *Leningrado* (too far out of town, turistaxi US$3.95, a complex with cabins, pool, bar and several restaurants for which there are always queues), C; *Las Américas*, B, not so far out of town (turistaxi US$2.35), poor food; and *Balcón del Caribe*, next to Castillo del Morro, C, overlooking the sea, nightclub, are the "dollar hotels". The "peso hotels" are *Casa Granda* (where you will probably have to pay dollars,   but it's the best place to stay), on Parque Céspedes, D, restaurant (book at the office 20 metres from corner of hotel, alongside cathedral, not at the Tourism Bureau at the corner of the same street); *Imperial*, José A. Saco 261; *Libertad*, Aguilera 658; *Rex*, Av. Garzón 10 (cheapest); *Venus*, San Félix 658, all E.

Telephones   For calls outside Santiago, Centro de Comunicaciones Nacional e Internacional, Heredia y Félix Pena, underneath the cathedral.

Train   Santiago-Havana, leaves 18.15, 16.80 pesos, 12-20 hours at night (longer by the day).

Excursions   Excellent excursions can be made to the Gran Piedra (26 km. inland—a viewpoint from which it is said you can see Haiti and Jamaica on a clear day, more likely their lights on a clear night) and along the Ruta Turística to the Castillo del Morro, a clifftop fort with a museum of the sea, piracy and local history (open all week, but only morning on Monday). Turistaxi to El Morro, US$5.50-6 round trip with wait. The road passes the ferry to the resorts of Cayo Granma and La Socapa in the estuary (5 cents each way). Also to Playa Bacanao, a wonderful amusement park and beach. There are buses Nos 14, 35 & 62 to the public beaches. From Santiago, it is possible to visit El Cobre where the shrine of Cuba's patron saint, the Virgen de la Caridad del Cobre, is located; and to El Caney, famous for its fruit.

Hire a Turistaxi for US$25 for the day to visit La Granjita, El Valle Prehistórico (with lifesize replicas of dinosaurs), an old car and trailer museum and the Daiquirí Beach and Hotel (arrange for the driver to collect you later).

Baracoa, 150 km. E of Santiago, close to the most easterly point of the island, is an attractive place surrounded by a fruitful countryside. "Dollar hotel" *Castillo*; "peso hotel" *Plaza*, E.

Guantánamo 80 km. from Santiago on the Baracoa road, is close to the US base of the same name (which cannot be easily visited from Cuba). "Dollar hotel" *Guantánamo*, C; "peso hotel" *Brasil*, E.

West from Havana a dual carriage highway has been completed almost to *Pinar del Río*, the major city W of Havana. At the eastern entrance to the city is the modern *Hotel Pinar del Río*, swimming pool, night club etc., B; also the *Vuelta Abajo*, D, rec., and the *Hotel Occidente*, Calle Gerardo Medina, clean but old, D. For travel to Pinar del Río, train from Havana's West station, rather than bus, is recommended (leaves Havana 0512, leaves Pinar del Río 1702, arrives Havana 2206, 3.30 pesos each way); slow but comfortable.

If travelling by car on this route, you can make a detour to *Soroa* in the Sierra de Rosario, 81 km. southwest of the capital. It is a spa and resort in luxuriant hills. As you drive into the area, a sign on the right indicates the Mirador de Venus and Baños Romanos. Past the baths is the *Bar Edén* (open till 1800), where you can park before walking up to the Mirador (25 minutes). From the top you get fine views of the southern plains, the palm-covered Sierra and the tourist complex itself; lots of birds, butterflies, dragonflies and lizards around the path; many flowers in season.

The road continues into the complex where there is an orchidarium with over 700 species (guided tours between 0830-1140, 1340-1555 daily) and the Castillo de las Nubes restaurant (1130-2200), a mock castle. At the resort are cabins (B high season), restaurant El Centro (quite good), disco, bar, olympic swimming pool, bike rental, riding nearby and handicrafts and dollar shops. Despite the ugly, gloomy cabins, it's a peaceful place and would be more so without the loud juke box.

Nearer Pinar del Río another detour north off the main road is to the spa of San Diego de los Baños, also in fine scenery in the Sierra de los Organos.

North of Pinar del Río, on a road which leads to the north coast and eventually back to Havana is *Viñales*, a delightful small town in a dramatic valley. Stands of palm and tobacco fields with their drying barns (*vegas*, steep, thatch-roofed buildings which you can enter and photograph with ease) lie amid sheer and rounded mountains reminiscent of a Chinese landscape, especially at dawn and dusk. These massifs were part of a cave system which collapsed millions of years ago and, on some, remnants of stalactites can still be seen.

6 km beyond Viñales is the Cueva del Indio which can be approached from two ends, neither far apart. Inside, though, you can travel the cave's length on foot and by boat (1 peso, or a dollar for foreigners), very beautiful. There is a restaurant at the cave (also at a smaller cave nearer Viñales).

Viñales itself is a pleasant town, with trees and wooden colonnades along the main street, red tiled roofs and a main square with a little-used cathedral and a Casa de Cultura with art gallery.

Hotels *Motel Los Jazmines*, 3 km. before the town, in a superb location overlooking the valley, C, restaurant, bar, shops, rec. apart from garish swimming pool and loud music which detract from the overall effect; *La Ermita*, C, 3 km. from town with good view, pool, good food, rec.; *Rancho San Vicente*, near Cueva del Indio, C.

Turistaxi from Havana to *Motel Los Jazmines* takes 2½ hours, 57 pesos, but a bus back to the capital is easy to catch, 3½ hours, 2.70 pesos.

From Viñales to Havana along the coast road takes about 4 hours by car. It is an attractive drive through sugar and tobacco plantations, pines, the mountains inland, the coast occasionally visible. All the small houses have flower gardens in front. You pass through La Palma, Las Pozas (which has a ruined church with a boring new one beside it), Bahía Honda and Cabañas; many agricultural collectives along the way. After Cabañas the road deteriorates; either rejoin the motorway back to the capital, or take the old coast road through the port of Mariel to enter Havana on Av. 5. Off this avenue is the Marina Hemingway tourist complex, with *El Viejo y El Mar* and *Hotel Tritón*, A (Havanautos office).

In the Gulf of Batabanó is the *Isla de la Juventud*, 97 km. from the main island, reached by daily Cubana flights or ferry from Surgidero de Batabanó. At about 3,050 square kilometres, it is not much smaller than Trinidad, but its population is only 60,000. It gets its present name from the educational courses run there, particularly for overseas students. Columbus, who discovered it in 1494 called the island Evangelista and, until recently, it was called the Isla de Pinos. From the 19th century until the Revolution its main function was as a prison and both José Martí and Fidel Castro served time there. Today the main activities are citrus-growing, fishing and tourism. There are several beaches and ample opportunities for water sports. The capital is Nueva Gerona, with a museum in the old Model Prison (El Presidio) and four others. Main tourist hotel is *El Colony* (L high season).

Cayo Largo, east of Isla de la Juventud, is a westernized island resort reached by air from Havana (US$49 return), or by light plane or boat from Juventud. It has pleasant *cabañas* at L for 2, half board, not much cheaper than the main hotel (*Isla del Sur*, half board high season, L). Hotel expansion is planned to cater for water sport tourism. Cayos Rosario and Avalos, between Juventud and Largo, have not yet been developed.

THE ECONOMY

Following the 1959 revolution, Cuba adopted a Marxist-Leninist system. Almost all sectors of the economy are state controlled and centrally planned, the only significant exception being agriculture where some 12% of arable land is still privately owned by 192,000 small farmers. Cuba assumed full membership of the Council for Mutual Economic Assistance (Comecon) in 1972.

The Government has made diversification of the economy away from sugar the prime aim of economic policy. Some progress towards this has been made. The overwhelming reliance on sugar remains and there is little expectation of achieving balanced and sustained growth in the foreseeable future. Aid from the USSR is estimated at about 25% of gnp. Apart from military aid, economic assistance takes two forms: balance-of-payments support (about 84%), under which sugar and nickel exports are priced in excess of world levels and oil and other imports priced below world levels; and assistance for development projects. There is, however, a trend towards more trade credits, which are repayable, rather than trade subsidies.

Construction and industry have been the main growth motors in recent years; the sugar industry (70% of export earnings) has consistently failed to reach the targets set. Cuba's dream of a 10m tonne raw sugar harvest has never been reached. Cuba is expected to remain the world's second-largest producer after Brazil and will probably retain its position as the world's leading exporter. Cuba has no difficulty in selling its sugar to the Comecon countries; it receives subsidized prices, but is paid in inconvertible roubles or by barter.

The largest source of dollars was the resale of unneeded supplies of Soviet-supplied crude oil, which amounted to US$574m in 1985 but to only half that in 1986. The USSR's production difficulties, combined with the collapse of the oil price in early 1986, increase Cuba's incentive to save energy. The use of sugar cane bagasse helped to cut total energy consumption by 2.1% in 1985: the economy now uses 20% less in oil-based energy imports than in 1980.

Cuba became a member of the International Coffee Agreement in February 1985, and was allocated an export quota of 160,000 bags of 60 kg (1985/86). In that period production was 375,000 bags; exports were 250,000 bags. Citrus has become the second-most important agricultural export. Annual production rose from 289,000 tonnes average in 1976-80 to 743,500 tonnes in 1985.

Tourism is set to expand considerably with the construction of 5,000 new hotel rooms. In 1987, 250,000 tourists visited Cuba, mostly from Western countries, bringing earnings of US$120m. Annual tourist arrivals were expected to reach 350,000 by 1990.

In 1987 90% of Cuba's foreign trade was with centrally planned economies. Commercial relations with market economies deteriorated because of lack of progress in debt rescheduling negotiations.

Cuba's foreign debt in convertible currency is about US$5.5bn including substantial arrears to banks and suppliers. Cuba's first US$125m (eq) repayment to the USSR, originally due in 1986, has been rescheduled to 1990. The debt with the USSR is a secret: estimates range from US$8.5bn (eq) to US$34bn (eq).

Foreign Trade (US$m)

	1981	1982	1983	1984	1985
Exports (fob)	1,799	1,627	1,431	1,283	1,356
Imports (fob)	-1,435	-900	-919	-1,201	-1,283

	1961-70(av)	1971-80(av)	1981-85(av)
Global social product at constant prices (%)	2.8	5.7	6.7

INFORMATION FOR VISITORS

Documents   Visitors from the majority of countries need only a tourist card to enter Cuba, as long as they are going solely for tourist purposes. A tourist card may be obtained from Cuban embassies, consulates, or approved Cubatur agents (price in the UK £10). Nationals of other countries without visa-free agreement with Cuba, and those visiting on other business must check what visa requirements pertain. US citizens wishing to visit Cuba should contact Marazul Tours, 250 West 57th Street, Suite 1311, New York City, 10107 New York, T 212-582-9570, or Miami T 305-232-8157 (information also from Havanatur, Calle 24 No. 4314, La Sierra, Havana, T 29-3555). In the USA, the Czechoslovak Embassy in Washington, D.C. will process applications for visas for US$5. Visas can take several weeks to be granted, and are apparently difficult to obtain for people other than businessmen, guests of the Cuban Government or Embassy officials. When the applicant is too far from a Cuban consulate to be able to apply conveniently for a visa, he may apply direct to the Cuban Foreign Ministry for a visa waiver. Visitors may stay in Cuba for 72 hours in transit without tourist card or visa.

Visitors travelling on a visa must go in person to Cubatur or the Immigration Office for registration the day after arrival. The office is on the corner of Calle 22 and Av. 3, Miramar. (Bus 132 from the old city centre, get off at second stop after the tunnel; also bus 32 from La Rampa or Coppelia ice-cream parlour in Vedado, alight at same stop.) When you register you will be given an exit permit.

Travellers coming from or going through infected areas must have certificates of vaccination against cholera and yellow fever.

Some Latin American countries will not admit anyone carrying a passport stamped by the Cuban authorities but the Cubans will not insist on stamping your passport in and out if you ask them not to.

British business travellers should get "Hints to Exporters: Cuba", from the Dept. of Trade, Export Services Division, Sanctuary Buildings, 16-20 Great Smith Street, London SW1P 4DB. US citizens on business with Cuba should contact Foreign Assets Control, Federal Reserve Bank of New York, 33 Liberty St., NY 10045. Another useful leaflet "Tips For Travelers to Cuba" is available from the Passport Office, US Dept. of State, Washington DC 20524.

How to Get There Cubana, Iberia, Aeroflot, and Interflug have direct flights to Havana from Madrid, Brussels, Basle, Moscow, Prague and East Berlin, and intending travellers should contact these airlines for further information. Cubana also fly from Paris-Orly Saturdays. Aeroflot takes on passengers at Shannon (Eire) 9 times a week—said to be cheapest way from UK (410 Irish punts in early 1989, excursion return).

Cubana operates two flights weekly between Havana and Mexico City. Cubana also flies weekly to Barbados, Georgetown, Panama City (twice), Managua, Lima, and Jamaica (Thurs., US$162). Cubana has one weekly flight to Buenos Aires. Cubana also has two weekly flights to Montreal; Air Canada flies between Toronto and Havana.

Mexicana de Aviación flies from Mexico to Cuba calling at Mérida (Yucatán), and organizes package tours (see **Travel Agencies** below for ticket sellers). From Mérida, 7 nights in Havana (tourist class) US$275-335, good value, 4 nights (first class). Similar from Mexico City (US$407, or US$463 with single room supplement). Unitours (Canada) run package tours to Cuba for all nationalities. Eastern charters fly Miami-Havana twice a week (US$150 one way).

It is advisable to book your flight out of Cuba before actually going there as arranging it there can be time-consuming. Furthermore, it is essential to reconfirm onward flights as soon as you arrive in Cuba, otherwise you will lose your reservation.

No passenger ships call regularly.

Internal Air Services Cubana de Aviación services between most of the main towns. Camagüey (US$38 one way), Cienfuegos, Holguín ((US$44), Baracoa, Guantánamo, Manzanillo (US$44), Moa, Nueva Gerona (US$12) and Santiago (from Havana, US$50 one way) all have airports. Tourists must pay airfares in US$; it is advisable to prebook flights at home as demand is very heavy.

Airline Offices All are situated in Havana, at the seaward end of Calle 23 (La Rampa), Vedado: e.g. Cubana, Calle 23 esq., Infanta, T 7-4916; Aeroflot, Calle 23, No. 64, T 76-6138; C.S.A., Calle 23, No. 74, esq. P, T 70-1777.

Buses From Varadero: to Havana 3 pesos (2 hrs.); to Santa Clara 2.50 pesos (4 hrs.). From Santa Clara to Santiago 13.20 pesos. From Holguín to Santiago 3.85 pesos (six departures daily, there are four to Havana). There are buses at 1330 and 0130 from Camagüey to Santiago. The 20-hour journey from Santiago to Havana costs 27.50 pesos, and leaves daily at 0500 and 1930. (It is best to travel on weekdays and at night.) From Havana to Santiago 1320 and 1930. Havana to Matanzas (1.35 pesos), 2 hrs.; Havana-Cienfuegos (6.50 pesos); Santa Clara to Cienfuegos (0.60 peso), 2 hrs.; Cienfuegos to Trinidad (1.20 pesos), 2 hrs.; Trinidad to Sancti Spiritus (0.90 peso), 2 hrs.; Sancti Spiritus to Santiago (13.20 pesos), 10 hrs.; Santiago-Guantánamo (1.10 peso); Guantánamo-Baracoa (2.30 pesos). The urban bus fare throughout Cuba is 10 centavos.

Bus Reservations Tickets between towns must be purchased in advance from: Oficina Reservaciones Pasajes, Calle 21, esq 4, Vedado; Plazoleta de la Virgen del Camino, San Miguel del Padrón; Calzada 10 de Octubre y Carmen, Centro; Terminal de Omnibus Nacional, Boyeros y 19 de Mayo (all in Havana).

Trains Recommended whenever possible. See the text above for details.

N.B. In major bus and train terminals, ask if there are special arrangements for tourists to buy tickets without queuing; payment would be then be in dollars. Trains and some buses are air-conditioned—you may need a warm jersey.

Peso taxis For independent travellers who do not have the time to queue for buses, or reservations on transport out of Havana or the other major cities, peso taxis are an interesting and relatively easy way to travel. They take as many passengers as can be crowded in; if you are travelling in a group, you can hire the taxi for yourselves, but this is only viable if you are using black market pesos. They are generally found in main squares; ask for Taxi Servicios Especiales and their base, where they can be booked in advance. Bear in mind that the taxi is liable to turn up at the agreed pick-up point up to two hours late. Some examples of fares: Havana-Viñales, 57 pesos, 2½ hours (ask for Rafael at the Havana taxi base—address above); Trinidad-Santiago de Cuba, 140.90 pesos, 8 hours; Trinidad-Cienfuegos, 20 pesos, 1¼ hours; Santa Clara-Cienfuegos, 16.50 pesos, 1¼ hours.

Car Hire Through Havanautos at a caravan in the car park of the International Airport, *Hotels Capri* and *Triton* in Havana and at Varadero; vehicles can be returned to any depot. Minimum US$35 a day (or US$40 for a/c) plus US$0.20 each km. after the first 100 km., and US$5 a day insurance. Visa and Mastercharge accepted for the rental, or US$100 deposit; you must also present your passport and home driving licence. Petrol coupons must be purchased, in 20 litre amounts, when you rent the car, so work out how much you'll need; unused coupons are returnable. Recommended, in view of difficulties of getting seats on buses and trains.

Excursions Cubatur, the national tourist office, offers day trips to Soroa, Viñales, Trinidad, Cienfuegos, Varadero (particularly recommended) and Guamá as well as tours of colonial and modern Havana. It is also possible to go on a "Vuelta a Cuba", 7-day round-trip of the island, travelling by bus to Santiago and returning by air. Details from the Cubatur office.

Customs Personal baggage and articles for personal use are allowed in free of duty; so are 200 cigarettes, or 25 cigars, or 1 lb. of tobacco, and 2 bottles of alcoholic drinks. Many things are scarce or unobtainable in Cuba: take in everything you are likely to need other than food (say razor blades, medicines and pills, tampons, reading and writing materials and photographic supplies).

Shopping Essentials—rent and most food—are cheap; non-essentials are very expensive. Compared with much of Latin America, Cuba is expensive for the tourist (you can make it cheaper by using the black market—see below), but compared with many Caribbean islands it is not dear. Even if you don't want to use the black market for money, you can get Cuban cigars very cheaply this way.

Hotel Reservations It is advisable to book hotel rooms before visiting any of the provinces. This can be done abroad through accredited Cubatur agencies, or through the Cubatur office, Calle 23, No. 156, Vedado, La Habana 4; telex 051-243; telephone 32-4521, or through Turismo Buró desks in main hotels. It is imperative to book the first night's hotel at the airport on arrival, if you have not done so beforehand (see under Havana **Hotels**). Cubana give a one-night hotel voucher to their passengers. Cubatur will inform you only about the main hotels, where you have to pay in dollars. On arrival in a town, check if there is a dollar hotel booking office for making reservations. You have to find the cheaper places, where you can pay in pesos, independently, but you may find it very difficult to get a room. "Peso hotels" may demand payment in dollars. It's also a good idea to book hotel rooms generally before noon. In the peak season, July and August (carnival time) and December to February, it is essential to book in advance. Prices given in the text are high season; low season prices are about 17% lower.

Camping Official campsites are opening up all over the island, charging 5-8 pesos a night (in pesos); they are usually in nice surroundings and are good value.

Note Cuba is geared more to package tourism than to independent visitors. It is impossible to lodge with local families and camping out on the beach or in a field is forbidden. Because of rationing it is difficult to buy food in the shops. Do not take photographs near military zones. Also be prepared for long waits for everything: buses, cinemas, restaurants, shops etc.

Eating out Visitors should remember that eating is often a problem and plan ahead. It is generally impossible to have an evening meal and go on to a concert or the theatre (performances start at 2030 or 2100 in Havana).

Breakfast can be particularly slow although this is overcome in the larger hotels who generally have buffets (breakfast US$3, lunch and dinner US$10-12). Look out for the *oferta especial* in small hotels which gives guests a 25% discount on buffet meals in larger hotels. Also, the "all-you-can-eat" vouchers for buffets in tourist hotels do not have to be used in the hotel where bought. Breakfast and one other meal may be sufficient if you fill in with street or "dollar shop" snacks.

Tipping Tipping customs are currently in a state of flux after a period when visitors were not allowed to tip in hotels and restaurants. It is now definitely recommended. Tip a small amount (not a percentage) in the same currency as you pay for the bill (typically US 1-2 on a US$25 meal, 1 peso on amount over 6-7 pesos). At times taxi drivers will expect (or demand) a tip. Tourist taxis are not tipped. If you want to express gratitude, offer a packet of American cigarettes.

Language is Spanish, with local variants in pronunciation and vocabulary. Little English is spoken.

Security Visitors should never lose sight of their luggage or leave valuables in hotel rooms (most hotels have safes). Do not leave your things on the beach when going swimming. Pickpocketing and pursesnatching on buses is quite common in Havana and Santiago. Visitors should remember that Cuba's dual (peso-dollar) economy means that the local population will often do anything to get hard currency, from simply asking for money or dollar-bought goods, to mugging.

Health Sanitary reforms have transformed Cuba into a healthy country, though tap water is generally not safe to drink; bottled and mineral water are recommended.

Medical service is no longer free for foreign visitors in Havana and Varadero, where there are clinics that charge in dollars. Visitors requiring medical attention will be sent to them. Emergencies are handled on an ad hoc basis. Check with your national health service or health insurance on coverage in Cuba. Fees are generally lower than those charged in western countries. According to latest reports, visitors are still treated free of charge in other parts of the country, with the exception of tourist enclaves with on-site medical services.

The Cira García Clinic in Havana (payment in dollars) sells prescription and patent drugs and medical supplies that are often unavailable in chemists.

Between May and October, the risk of sunburn is high—sun blocks are recommended when walking around the city as well as on the beach. In the cooler months, limit beach sessions to 2 hours.

NB The summers are unbearably hot and travel between Havana and Santiago is extremely difficult during Carnival (July) and also during the Christmas-New Year period.

Climate NE trade winds temper the heat. Average summer shade temperatures rise to 30°C (86°F) in Havana, and higher elsewhere. In winter, day temperatures drop to 19°C (66°F). Average rainfall is from 860 mm. in Oriente to 1,730 mm. in Havana; it falls mostly in the summer and autumn, but there can be torrential rains at any time. Hurricanes come in June-October. The best time for a visit is during the cooler dry season (November to April). In Havana, there are a few cold days—8°-10°C (45°-50°F)—with a north wind. Walking is uncomfortable in summer but most offices, hotels, leading restaurants and cinemas are air-conditioned. Humidity varies between 75 and 95 %.

Dress is generally informal. Summer calls for the very lightest clothing, such as cotton or cotton-terylene mixture. Cuban men mostly wear the *guayabera* (a light pleated shirt worn outside the trousers). Men should not wear shorts except on or near the beach. Trousers are quite OK for women, if preferred. A jersey and light raincoat or umbrella are needed in the cooler months.

Hours of Business Government offices: 0830-1230 and 1330-1730 Mon. to Fri. Some offices open on Sat. morning. Banks: 0830-1200, 1330-1500 Mon. to Fri., 0830-1030 Sat. The Banco Nacional de Cuba is the only bank in the country. Shops: 1230-1930 Mon. to Sat.

Time zone Cuban time is 5 hrs. behind Greenwich Mean Time.

Holidays January 1: Liberation Day. January 2: Victory of Armed Forces. May 1: Labour Day. July 26: Revolution Day. October 10: Beginning of War of Independence.

Currency The monetary unit is the peso, US$1=0.75 peso. There are heavy penalties for Cubans caught exchanging money on the black market, though a tourist will frequently be approached, especially on the east side of La Rampa, in front of the *Hotel Caribbean*, in the Parque Central and along the Malecón in Havana (beware muggers); also in Santiago, Trinidad and Cienfuegos. The going rate is US$1 = 5-7 pesos: watch out for pre-1962 notes, no longer valid. There are notes for 1, 3, 5, 10, and 20 pesos, and coins for 5, 10, 20, and 40 centavos and 1 peso. You must have a supply of 10 centavos coins if you want to use the local town buses. The 20 centavo coin is called a *peseta*. US dollars are accepted by hotels and other official institutions. Major credit cards (but not AmEx) are acceptable in most places.

Currency Control The visitor should be careful to retain the white exchange paper every time money is changed officially; this will enable Cuban pesos remaining at the end of the stay to be changed back into foreign currency (to a maximum of US$10 equivalent).

Travellers' cheques expressed in US or Canadian dollars or sterling are valid in Cuba. Travellers' cheques issued on US bank paper are generally not accepted, so it is best to take Thomas Cook. Don't enter the place or date when signing cheques, or they may be refused.

The Oficina de Turismo Individual suggests changing only US$10 per week at hotel rates, but this will make your stay expensive. While changing money in a hotel is the easiest method, using the black market will ensure that you have pesos for doing things off the tourist route, particularly outside Havana and Varadero, and at better value. Note that US$10 changed on the street will be plenty for a week if not going far from the cities. If needing more pesos, for long-distance peso taxis for example, do heed the warnings given above.

Sale of Possessions As in the Soviet Union, tourists willing to take risks can earn extra spending money by trading along consumer goods to sell to Cubans. Any foreigner sitting in the Parque Central with a flight bag at his side is soon approached by buyers. One can usually get about 3 times what was paid for the articles, but every visitor will have to change at least some money legally as most hotels, tourist restaurants, and bars insist on seeing an exchange paper which covers the amount of the bill. It's inadvisable to bring in too many of a single item or you may have trouble at Customs. (David Stanley).

Post, Telegraph and Telephone When possible correspondence should be addressed to post office boxes (Apartados), where delivery is more certain. Telegraphic services are adequate. You can send telegrams from all post offices in Havana. Telegrams to Britain cost 35 centavos a word. The night letter rate is 3.85 pesos for 22 words. Local telephone calls can be made from public telephones for 5 centavos. A telephone call to Britain costs US$15 for the first 3 mins. "Collect" calls are not permitted. Air mail rates to Britain are 31 centavos for half an ounce and 13 centavos to Canada. All postal services, national and international, have been described as appalling. Letters to Europe, for instance, take at least 4-5 weeks.

Weights and Measures The metric system is compulsory, but exists side by side with American and old Spanish systems.

Electric Current 110-230 V. 3 phase 60 cycles, A.C.

Newspapers *Granma*, mornings except Sunday; *Trabajadores*, Trade Union daily; and *Juventud Rebelde*, evening paper. No foreign newspapers are on sale, but *Granma* has a weekly English edition.

Travel Agents In the UK, agents who sell holidays in Cuba include Thomson Worldwide, Melia Travel, 12 Dover Street, London W1X 4NS, T 01-491 3881, Progressive Tours, 12 Porchester Place, Marble Arch, London W2 2BS, T 01-262 1676 and Regent Holidays, 13 Small Street, Bristol BS1 1DE, T 0272-211711. Recommended agents in Eire for assistance with Aeroflot flights are Smurfit Travel, 38 Dane Street, Dublin 2, T 774211, fax 01793436, and Concorde Travel, T Dublin 763232. See above under **Documents** for Marazul Tours in the USA. If travelling from Mexico, Cuba-Mex SA, Calle 63 No 500, Depto D, Edificio La Literaria, Mérida, Yucatán (Apartado Postal 508, CP 97000; T 23-91-99/23-97-25, Telex 753806 Cumeme), or Manzanillo No 123 D 104, esq Baja California, Colonia Roma Sur, Mexico City, DF, T 574-08-13/584-24-65/584-68-14, CP 06760. Also Celeste Tours, Aguascalientes 191, Mexico City.

Tourist Information The main Cubatur office is at Calle 23, No. 156 between N and O, La Rampa, Vedado (open Mon.-Fri. 0800-1700, Sat. 0800-1200), and reservations for all Cuban hotels, restaurants, and night clubs can be made here. The Oficina de Turismo Individual is in the *Hotel Habana Libre* building, on entrance floor, open 0830-1215, 1315-1730; all problems with pre-booked accommodation, transport, etc. should be dealt with here. Sr Justo is very helpful. Most tourist hotels have a Turismo Buró, which will arrange bookings, etc. Cubatur also has offices in: Canada, 440 Blvd Dorchester Ouest, Suite 1402, Montréal, T (514) 857-8004/5; 55 Queen St E, Suite 705, Toronto, T (416) 362-0700/2; Spain, Paseo de la Habana No. 28 4B, T 411-3297; France, 24 rue de 4 Septembre, Paris 75002, T 742-5415; West Germany, Steinweg 2, D-6000 Frankfurt am Main 1, T (069) 288322; Mexico, Insurgentes Sur 421 y Aguascalientes, Complejo Aristos, Edificio B, Local 310, México D.F. 060100, T 574-9454.

Maps Mapa Turistico de la Habana, Mapa de la Habana Vieja, and similar maps of Santiago de Cuba, Trinidad, Camagüey, Varadero are helpful, but not always available.

Ben Box would like to thank Pat Smith in Havana for her hospitality in October, 1988, and Suzanne Durbridge of Progressive Tours for assisting with travel arrangements and information; thanks also to Noll Scott for his help. We are most grateful to Margarita Zimmerman in Havana for a complete revision of the *South American Handbook* Cuba chapter and, for valuable updating material, to Christina Gibbons of Regent Holidays, and to the following travellers: Tina Borgmann and Mette Christopherson (Copenhagen), Gerald D. Featherstone (Hounslow) for much important information, Thomas Fedrizzi (Horgen, Switz), Alan Jones (Santa Cruz de Tenerife), John Purkiss (London SW7) for a very helpful contribution, R.W. Le Sueur (Jersey), James Maas (Bocas del Toro, Panama), Anna Syriänen and Marko Sorvaniemi (Tampere, Finland) and Roland Wiemer and Karla Menner (Hamburg 50).

HISPANIOLA

One might expect that a relatively small island such as Hispaniola (from Spanish "Isla Española" - the Spanish island) lying in the heart of the Caribbean would be occupied by one nation, or at least that its people should demonstrate ethnic and cultural similarities. This is not so. Hispaniola, with an area of just over 76,900 square km., not much more than half the size of Cuba, is shared by two very different countries, the Dominican Republic and Haiti. The original indigenous name for the island, Quisqueya, is still used in the Dominican Republic as an "elegant variation". Hispaniola is mountainous and forested, with plains and plateaux. Haiti, with 27,750 square km., has a population of just over 5.5 million increasing at an annual rate of 1.8 %. The Dominican Republic is much larger in area, about 48,420 square km., but its population is not larger to the same degree at 6.7 million, growing at 2.9 % a year.

Columbus visited the north coast of Hispaniola, modern Haiti, on his first visit to the West Indies, leaving a few men there to make a settlement before he moved on to Cuba. Columbus traded with the native Arawaks for trinkets such as gold nose plugs, bracelets and other ornaments, which were to seal the Indians' fate when shown to the Spanish monarchs. A second voyage was ordered immediately. Columbus tried again to establish settlements, his first having been wiped out. His undisciplined men were soon at war with the native Tainos, who were hunted, taxed and enslaved. Hundreds were shipped to Spain, where they died. When Columbus had to return to Spain he left his brother, Bartolomé, in charge of the fever-ridden, starving colony. The latter sensibly moved the settlement to the healthier south coast and founded Santo Domingo, which became the capital of the Spanish Indies. The native inhabitants were gradually eliminated by European diseases, murder, suicide and slavery, while their crops were destroyed by newly-introduced herds of cattle and pigs. Development was hindered by the labour shortage and the island became merely a base from which to provision further exploration, being a source of bacon, dried beef and cassava. Even the alluvial gold dwindled and could not compete with discoveries on the mainland. Sugar was introduced at the beginning of the sixteenth century and the need for labour soon brought African slaves to the island. In 1512 the Indians were declared free subjects of Spain, and missionary zeal ensured their conversion to Christianity.

The Haitians are almost wholly black, with a culture that is a unique mixture of African and French influences. Haiti was a French colony until 1804 when, fired by the example of the French Revolution, the black slaves revolted, massacred the French landowners and proclaimed the world's first black republic. Throughout the 19th century the Haitians reverted to a primitive way of life, indulging in a succession of bloody, almost tribal wars. Even today, nowhere else in the Caribbean do African cults, particularly voodoo, play such a part in everyday life. The standard of living is the lowest in the New World (gdp per capita is US$360).

The Dominicans are a mixture of black, Amerindian and white, with a far stronger European strain. Their culture and language are hispanic and their religion Roman Catholic. Economically, the country is much more developed, despite a stormy political past and unsavoury periods of dictatorship, particularly under Generalissimo Trujillo (1930-61). Nevertheless, in a material sense the country prospered during the Trujillo era and the standard of living is much higher than it is in Haiti (gdp per capita is US$840).

The climate is tropical but tempered by sea breezes. The cooler months are between December and March.

HAITI

The Republic of Haiti occupies the western third of the island. French and Creole are the official languages (and knowledge of either is virtually essential for the visitor), though the common speech of all classes is Creole. (It is not a patois, but a language.) Nine-tenths of the people are of African descent, and the remainder are mulattoes, the descendants of French settlers. Haiti means "high ground"

and indeed it is the most mountainous country in the Caribbean. There are three mountain ranges, the main one stretching right across the northern peninsula. In this range the highest peaks are in the Dominican Republic, about 3,000 metres above sea-level (the highest being Pico Duarte). In Haiti, the highest is Pic Laselle, at 2,684 metres. The once luxuriant forest cover of Haiti's mountains is being rapidly destroyed for fuel and building.

History By the eighteenth century Saint Domingue, as Haiti was then called, was regarded as the most valuable tropical colony of its size in the world and was the largest sugar producer in the West Indies. However, that wealth was based on slavery and the planters were aware of the dangers of rebellion. After the French Revolution, the issue of slavery led eventually to violence, with shifting alliances and mutual hatred between white, mulattoes and black slaves.

Out of the chaos rose a new leader, an ex-slave called François-Dominique Toussaint, known as Toussaint L'Ouverture. When France and Spain went to war, he joined the Spanish forces as a mercenary and built up a troop of 4,000 negroes. However, when the English captured Port-au-Prince in 1794 he defected with his men to join the French against the English. After four years of war and disease, the English withdrew, by which time Toussaint was an unrivalled leader among the black population. He then turned against the mulattoes of the west and south, killing 10,000 in 1800. By now Toussaint was politically supreme. In 1801 he drew up a new constitution and proclaimed himself governor general for life. Napoleon did not approve and in 1802 a French army defeated Toussaint and shipped him to France where he died in prison. The news that slavery had been reintroduced in Guadeloupe, however, provoked another popular uprising which drove out the French, already weakened by fever.

This new revolt was led by an African-born ex-slave, Dessalines, who had risen to power in Toussaint's entourage. In 1804 he proclaimed himself Emperor of the independent Haiti, changing the country's name to the Taino word for 'mountainous'. Dessalines died in 1806 and the country divided between his rival successors: the negro Christophe in the north, and the mulatto Pétion in the south. The former's rule was based on forced labour and he managed to keep the estates running until his death in 1820. Pétion divided the land into peasant plots, which in time became the pattern all over Haiti and led to economic ruin with virtually no sugar production and little coffee. Revolution succeeded revolution as hatred between the blacks and the ruling mulattoes intensified; constitutional government rarely existed in the nineteenth century.

At the beginning of the twentieth century, the USA became financially and politically involved for geopolitical and strategic reasons. By the 1930s the strategic need for occupation had receded and the expense was unpopular in the USA. In 1934 the USA withdrew, leaving Haiti poor and overpopulated with few natural resources.

In 1957 François (Papa Doc) Duvalier, a black nationalist, was elected president and unlike previous autocrats he succeeded in holding on to power. In 1964 he became President-for-Life, a title which was inherited by his 19-year-old son, Jean-Claude (Baby Doc) in 1971. The Duvaliers' power rested on the use of an armed militia, the "Tontons Macoutes", to dominate the people. Tens of thousands of Haitians were murdered and thousands more fled the country. However, repression eased under Jean-Claude, and dissidence rose, encouraged partly by US policies on human rights. Discontent began to grow with the May 1984 riots in Gonaïves and Cap Haïtien, and resurfaced after the holding of a constitutional referendum on 22 July, 1985, which gave the Government 99.98% of the vote. Several months of unrest and rioting gradually built up into a tide of popular insistence on the removal of Duvalier, during the course of which several hundred people were killed by his henchmen. The dictatorship of the Duvaliers (father and son) was brought to a swift and unexpected end when the President-for-Life fled to France on 7 February 1986.

Government The removal of the Duvaliers has left Haitians hungry for radical change. The leader of the interim military-civilian Government, Lieutenant-General Henri Namphy, promised presidential elections for November 1987, but they were abandoned because of violence on polling day. New elections were held on 17 January 1988, and Professor Leslie Manigat of the centrist Rassemblement National des Democrates Progressistes was elected president for a 5-year term. A number of leading contenders boycotted the election. Professor Manigat was ousted after 5 months in office by a military coup, after which General Namphy was named president. About seven months later, another coup deposed Namphy and the presidency was given to Lieutenant-General Prosper Avril. Dissatisfaction within the army resurfaced in April, 1989, when several coup attempts were staged within quick succession. The country is awaiting democratic elections which have been promised for the early 1990s.

Festivals Carnival in Haiti takes place on the three days before Ash Wednesday. It is not nearly as lavish as the Brazilian or Trinidadian carnivals. On Sunday afternoons before carnival there are practice parades in the main streets and the atmosphere is exuberant. Carnival attracts many tourists: it is best to book a flight and hotel well in advance if you plan to visit Haiti at this time. Independence is celebrated on January 1-2. Voodoo and Christianity exist side by side, each borrowing elements from the other. It is, however, voodoo which attracts most attention and which colours a large part of Haitian life. It is basically a spirit religion, involving *loas* (gods), and the ceremonies which maintain the harmony between them and the individual. It is not black magic, nor is it any different from the retention of African religions in black communities elsewhere in the Caribbean or Brazil. Visitors are not usually allowed to go to ceremonial centres (*péristyles*); you must be accompanied by a Haitian if you want to see a priest (*houngan*). The National Tourist Office publishes a list temples which may be visited, but tours are only a facsimile of the real thing. If you do consult a *houngan*, he will probably say that the god wants a large amount of dollars (say US$45, which may be bargained down).

Haiti is especially fascinating for the tourist who is avid for out-of-the-way experience. In order that you may make the most of your visit, we offer the following hints. Although it is one of the poorest countries in the world, most of whose citizens suffer from one kind of oppression or another, Haiti is proud of having been the only nation to have carried out successfully a slave rebellion. Haitians at all levels are very sensitive to how they are treated by foreigners, commonly called "blanc". If you treat them with warmth and consideration, they will respond with enthusiasm and friendship. There is no hostility towards "blanc"; if you feel threatened it is probably the result of a misunderstanding.

It is assumed that each "blanc" is wealthy and therefore it is legitimate to try to separate you from your riches. Such attempts should be treated with humour, indignation or consideration as appropriate.

Guides Young men and boys offer their services as guides at every turn and corner. It seems that it's worthwhile taking one (for about US$10 a day) just to prevent others pestering you. If you hire a guide you can also visit places off the beaten tourist track and avoid some of the frustrations of the public transport system. However, if you take guides you must realize that they expect you to buy them food if you stop to eat.

Secondly, and more important, the guides are often "on commission" with local shop- and stall-keepers, so that even if you ask them to bargain for you, you will not necessarily be getting a good price; nor will they necessarily go where you want to go. If you don't want a guide a firm but polite "non, merci" gets the message across. It is best to ignore altogether hustlers outside guesthouses, etc, as any contact makes them persist.

Port-au-Prince, capital and chief port of Haiti, population 457,000, is set at the end of a beautiful deep horseshoe bay, with high mountains behind and a small island across the bay protecting it from high seas and tidal waves. The town, with its fascinating "gingerbread" houses, is built in the form of an amphitheatre. In the lower part, at sea-level, is concentrated the business section, with a palm-shaded sea-front known as the Exposition which unfortunately has become very dirty. On the heights are the private houses, generally surrounded by shady gardens. The heat is some degrees less at several summer resorts easily reached from the city. Port-au-Prince is a friendly place, but it is very poor, apart from a few "swank" areas. The centre of the town is quite small and nearly everything of interest is within walking distance.

The Protestant Episcopal Cathedral of Sainte-Trinité has naive biblical murals painted by Haitian artists. The Musée du Panthéon National is in the former presidential mansion in the Place des Héros de l'Indépendence (213 Av Jean Paul, Turgeau, T 5-5647). It houses Haitian relics, early costumes, paintings and historic documents and also boasts the anchor of Columbus' ship, the *Santa María* (usually open 0830-1200 Monday to Friday). The Musée d'Art Haitien du Collège St-Pierre (or Le Centre d'Art), 56 rue 22 Septembre (T 2-2018), off rue Capois, contains the works of Haiti's leading artists. It also has exhibitions, a shop selling handicrafts and a restaurant with simple Asian fare at lunchtime (museum open 0900-1700 Monday to Friday, 0900-1300 Saturday). The Musée Defly, rue Légitime (T 2-4081), is a restored and refurnished gingerbread mansion dating from the turn of the century (open till 1200).

Hotels Check all rooms in advance; service may leave something to be desired. *Castel Haiti*, St Gérard, T 2-0624, most rooms air-conditioned, swimming pool, A, room only; *Oloffson*, Rue Capois, St Gérard, swimming pool, gardens, from A for standard room to L for suite; *Plaza Holiday Inn*, and *Park*, both Rue Capois near Place des Héros, former L. *Royal Haitian Club*, Carrefour, A. Cheaper are *Splendid*, Rue N, off J C Duvalier (swimming pool), B, recommended,

TO ST MARC,
CAP HAÏTIEN

TO
AIRPORT

AV. ST. MARTIN

RUE DES REMPARTS

RUE TIREMASSE

RUE MACAJOUX

RUE DES CESARS

RUE DES FRONTS FORT

RUE BONNE FOI

RUE DES MIRACLES

RUE PAVÉE

RUE DES CASERNÉS

RUE DU CENTRE

RUE DU CHAMP DE MARS

RUE D'ENNERY

RUE ST. HONORÉ

RUE CARBONNE

RUE JOSEPH JANVIER

RUE CHARERON

RUE OSWALD DURAND

RUE DR. DE HOUX

TO LÉOGANE
JACMEL

BLVD. LA SALINE

BOULEVARD DU QUAI

RUE COURBÉ

AVENUE MARIE JEANNE

BOULEVARD HARRY TRUMAN

RUE MAGASIN DE L'ETAT

GRAND RUE

RUE D'ENTERREMENT

RUE DE LA RÉUNION

RUE JN. MARIE GUILLOUX

RUE COURTE

RUE DR. AUBRY

RUE DES PUCELLES

RUE MONTALAIS

RUE GEFFARD

LAMARRE

RUE CAPOIS

AV. JOHN BROWN LALUE

TO
PÉTIONVILLE

R. ROMAIN

BLVD. J.J. DESSALINES

CIMETIERE
EXTÉRIEURE

N

1. Place des Héros de
   l'Indépendance
2. Place des Nations Unies
3. Place Ste Anne
4. Cathedral
5. Cathedral of Sainte-Trinité
6. Musée Nationale
7. Musée d'Art Haïtien
8. Palais National
9. Hôtel de Ville
10. Customs House
11. Iron Market
12. Teleco Telephone Office
13. Post Office
14. Tourist Office
15. Banque National de Paris
16. Agence Citadelle

and *Prince*, Rue 3, B, small and friendly; *Palace*, rue Champ-de-Mars 55, C; *Central*, rue du Centre 78, D, central, very basic; good cheap restaurant below.

Guest Houses Coconut Villa, Delmas 19, T 6-1691, B, room only; *Hillside*, Ave M L King, C; on same street *Le Triangle* is recommended, food available, possible to leave luggage, D; *L'Auberge Port-au-Prince*, rue du Centre, D, near Iron Market, basic but clean, cheap restaurant downstairs; *Hotel Acropolis*, on road S, electric fan, swimming pool, D; *Haiti Chérie*, near supermarket en route for airport, D, run by Haitian/American couple; *Villa Carmel*, Ave J C Duvalier 40, D, meals available, swimming pool. Other guest houses recommended as both cheap and good: the *Santos Guest House*, rue Pacot, colonial building with excellent view, highly recommended, C, including 2 good meals; *La Griffonne*, Rue Jean-Baptiste 21, Canapé Vert (T 5-4095), C, including 2 meals, in the hills above the main part of the town and so slightly cooler, yet within walking distance of the centre, and near to *publique* run to centre, swimming pool, clean, comfortable, friendly and recommended; *May's Villa*, Debussy district, over B for a/c room, including taxes and 2 meals, clean, swimming pool and panoramic view of the city. There are a number of other guest houses; most are priced in the US$ 15-30 range.

Note There is a 10% service charge and 5% tax added to all hotel bills. Most hotels and guest houses do not have full air-conditioning, so aim for the A range if you want something cool. Also, an energy charge of US$1.50-2.50 may be made.

Restaurants There are some very good but very expensive eating places in Port-au-Prince. *Aux Cosaques* (local food, good business special for US$5); *Le Carillon* (local food); several restaurants on both sides of Grand' Rue to S have meals for US$1; *Château Caprice*, at Mousseau (Continental and American food); *Chez Noelle*, rue Pavée; *Chez Tony*, rue Ponce in town centre, good, cheap meals (nearest thing to fast food).

Clubs The Turgeau Club; society clubs such as the Bellevue and the Port-au-Princien; the American Colony Club at Bourdon and sports clubs. Pétionville Golf Club (T 7-1437), also at Bourdon, 9-hole, clubs for rent.

Art Centres Commercial galleries include the Néhémy, Nader's (92 Place Geffrard) and Issa's (17 rue Chile), very good quality for buyers. Local art can be seen at the Cathedral of Saint Trinité, the Airport, and Exposition buildings, and in the principal hotels. Olivier has a gallery near the *Hotel Oloffson* and is very knowledgeable about local artists. There is a gallery at 29 rue Champs de Mars, run by Raoul Michel, which is one of the least expensive and has a good variety of work.

Recommended **craft shops** include: Gingerbread, rue Lamartinière, antiques, voodoo-inspired craft, woven wall-hangings, etc (Taggart, of Cap Haitien—see below—exhibits here); Zin d'Art, Ave John Brown, wall-hangings, basket-ware, woven goods, tablecloths, painted trays, jewellery, and more; Pericles' Gallery, 46 rue Geffrard, T 2-0059, for good copper jewellery.

Warning Watch out for pickpockets in the market and bus-station areas.

Taxis *Publiques*, shared taxis, charge US$0.20 a trip (double after 1900). They are identified by a red cloth or ribbon tied to the inside rear-view mirror. *Camionettes* (Peugeot station wagons) charge the same. *Tap-tap* (open-sided truck) fares are US$0.20 anywhere in town; they are dificult to manage with luggage. Taxis charge per car, about US$1.50 within Port-au-Prince, but prices rise when going uphill and at night. They are scarce early in the morning, in the evening, and along the rue Dessalines. Outside the capital, it costs US$25 for 1-4 people to Ibo Beach, US$38 for 1-2 people to beaches near St Marc. Taxis may also be hired, with driver, by the hour, half- or whole day: US$25 for 3 hours in the capital; US$40 for 3 hours to Kenscoff, etc.

Night Clubs *La Lambie*, just S of Port-au-Prince (take a taxi, or *tap-taps* run past until about midnight), good national food and music, open to the ocean.

Cinemas Cheap and interesting: the best are Imperial (a/c), Delmas; Théâtre Triomphe (a/c), Champs de Mars; Capitol (a/c), 53, rue Lamarre; Rex, Place des Héros de l'Indépendence; Paramount, Champs de Mars. Popular foreign films (British, US, French) are shown; non-French films are dubbed into French.

Banks Banque Nationale de Paris, Ave John Brown, First National City Bank, route de Delmas, Bank of Nova Scotia; Banque de Boston, rue des Miracles, and others, including local banks. Banque d'Haiti (which has branches throughout the country) reported to have best rate for £.

Library Alliance Française, opposite Pan Am, open 0830-1200, 1430-1900 except Monday and Saturday afternoon.

Travel agents Agence Citadelle (American Sightseeing of Haiti and American Express), PO Box 41, 36 place du Marron Inconnu, T 2-5900; Chatelain Tours (Gray Lines Sightseeing of Haiti), rue Geffrard, T 2-4469, PO Box 1056; Continental Travel, PO Box 1010, T 2-0604; Southerland Tours, Ave Marie Jeanne, PO Box 851, T 2-1600. Tours offered by agencies or through hotels include to Kenscoff mountains (3 hours), city and shopping in Port-au-Prince (3 hours), beaches, voodoo (see above), Cap Haitien (2 days) and Jacmel. Agencies can also handle travel documentation, car rental, travel and hotel reservations, cruises, etc.

Tourist Office   Avenue Marie Jeanne, Cité de l'Exposition (T 2-1729) provides maps of the city and is very helpful. It is worth checking bus and taxi fares to avoid being overcharged. Maps of Haiti available at US$1.50 from Carlos' shop opposite Tourist Office, and from bookshops. The Budget Rent-a-Car
sketch map of the city contains a lot of useful information.

Internal Air Services   Mission Air (MAF—Mr Bruce Smith), General Aviation, Delmas, near Delmas 60, T 7-3086, has daily flights to Cap Haitien (Except Sunday—twice a day Monday and Friday), US$25, 3 a week to Jérémie (US$35) and once a week to Port-au-Paix (US$35).

Excursion   A few km. out in Port-au-Prince harbour is Sand Cay, said to be one of the most beautiful coral reefs in the world. To visit it, go with Romi Roy (T 7-4846), who owns a 16-foot catamaran and takes day trips to any local destination, lunch included.

A paved road leads to (10 km.). ***Pétionville***. There is a track (45 minutes walk) from near the Baptist church to the 19th century Fort Jacques, from where there is an excellent view across Port-au-Prince harbour (*publiques* from Pétionville turn round at the junction). At Boutilliers/La Boule, about 5 km. outside Pétionville, visit the Jane Barbancourt Castle. One can sample an unlimited quantity of the company's 17 differently-flavoured rums, which include coffee, mango, coconut, orange. Rum is sold at US$3.50 a bottle. From the castle one can visit the bottlers and get an excellent view of Port-au-Prince. (Taxi from Port-au-Prince, US$16 for 1-2 people, US$3 for extra person.)

If you have time, a drive through the fertile Cul-de-Sac plain, about 30 km. each way, is well worthwhile for those interested in agriculture and local life.

Hotels Hotels include: *Montana*, rue Cardoza, between the capital and Pétionville (PO Box 523, T 7-1920/21), A/B with breakfast, US$14 for dinner, all rooms a/c with view, pool, tennis; *Villa Créole*, off Ave Panamericaine (PO Box 126, T 7-1570), L with breakfast, extra 2 meals supplement US$15, also with pool, tennis, a/c rooms, smart; *El Rancho*, elegant, "Mexican-style" hotel, same location and facilities as *Villa Créole*, good, A/L B & b, supplement for 2 extra meals (PO Box 71, T 7-2080/1/2/3/4); *Kinam*, Place St Pierre (T 7-0462), B upwards for double, a/c, restaurant, bar, pool, based on a gingerbread mansion; *Ibo Lélé*, on street of same name, same price range, recommended.
 Guest houses: *Doux Séjours*, 10 rue Magny (T 7-1560), C with breakfast, delightfully eccentric, 460 metres above sea-level; *Villa Kalewes*, 99 rue Gregoire (T 7-0817), B with breakfast, nice, conveniently situated.

Restaurants An excellent sea food restaurant is *La Recife* in Route de Delmas; also good is *Le Plantation*, Impasse Fouchard, Bois Moquette, T 7-0979 (French, US$30 per person for 3 course meal). Other French restaurants: *Le Chalet*, rue Kenscoff (US$20), *La Viole* (US$25); French/Creole: the moderately-priced *Belle Epoque*, and *Chez Gerard*. Caribbean cuisine at *Le Pote*, 43 rue Maeny, T 7-4141, US$25 a head. *Le Bolero* serves pasta/pizza and French food, US$10-15, popular. Asian food at *Le Gregoire*, rue Gregoire, US$25, very good. *Le Bato Fou* at 52 Rue Foubert is a disco/restaurant, T 7-0131 (French, dinner with wine costs US$10-15 per head). Institut Français, 19 rue Lamarre, has excellent restaurant *Café des Arts*; several other good ones. Lots of informal pizza places in and around town, about US$10 a head.

Shopping There is a market here every Tuesday and Friday which is well worth a visit. Good quality local crafts can be purchased at the Baptist Church. Galérie Monin for Hiatian art; Boutique Marassa, a variety of painted articles. United Sculptors of Haiti, on the road to Kenscoff. Mountain Maid Shop Artisanal, Fermanthe, sells wooden plates and clothes at very reasonable prices (good snack bar attached).

Transport   *Publique* from Iron Market to Pétionville, US$0.30. *Publiques* in Pétionville run along the Rue des Miracles, US$0.20 any distance.

A good paved road, 16 km. runs from Pétionville to the holiday resort of *Kenscoff*, 1,370 metres above sea-level, where the climate is excellent all the year round. (*Hotels Dereix, Florville; Restaurant Altitude 1300*, open Sunday only, local cuisine served out of doors, cool, very nice, US$15 per person. *Publique* from Pétionville market, US$0.40.) Furcy is a mountain town nearby in a pleasant setting; worth a day's excursion for horse riding, or a picnic.

South of Port-au-Prince Take a Léogâne *tap-tap* west from Port-au-Prince, get off west of Gressier at the sign for Guilou beach (¼ km. walk), clean and tidy with all amenities, entrance US$1. When available, food and drink on the beaches is expensive. Further to the southwest are Taino and Sun beaches, near Grand Goâve, while by Petit Goâve is the beautiful Cocoyer Beach. (*Le Relais de l'Empereur* hotel in Petit Goâve—B and up, room only, other meals US$15 each—has boat service to Cocoyer, US$9, including beach tariff; drinks on beach US$2, or US$3 for alcohol. The hotel itself was the residence of Emperor Faustin I— 1849-56.)

Jérémie, an attractive place with colonial buildings, can be reached from Port-au-Prince by bus (every other day, US$10, 8-10 hours), or *tap-tap*, or by weekly overnight boat (US$6 incl. bunk in bridge-house), no food, dirty and crowded. Mission Aviation (MAF) flies from the capital Monday, Wednesday and Friday, US$35. (Hotels: *Trois Dumas*, overlooking town, shady garden; *Pension Frankel*, both D with food.) Road to Les Cayes may be impassable after rain. One *tap-tap* a day goes to the fine beach of Anse d'Hainault (take plenty of food and drink), which can also be reached by boat from Port Salut, see below (arrange at *Bar-Restaurant Le Sable*).

Les Cayes is a pleasant town with several hotels including *Concorde* and *Pension Mme Bayard*, D with 2 meals. In Cayes Bay is Vache Island (Henry Morgan's base for his 1670 attack on Panama), which can be visited by taking the boat leaving between 1600 and 1700 and spending the night there or by hiring a motorboat for a day (about US$30). There are several beaches on the island. Buses leave Port-au-Prince for Les Cayes every morning (US$3-5), but no buses from Jacmel. The road to Port-au-Prince has recently been paved and is very good.

About 1½ hours drive from Les Cayes (2 buses a day) is **Port Salut,** with beautiful beaches (eg Pointe Sable). There are 2 Swiss-owned hotels here: *Arada Inn*, known as *Deck's*, and *Pension Sylvie*, not always open, both over US$50 including 2 meals; basic rooms, at *Bar-Restaurant Le Sable*, 2 km. outside town. The St. Dominique and Althania bus companies go to Port Salut from Port-au-Prince.

A trip round this south-western corner of Haiti is recommended for the adventurous. From Les Cayes you can get transport to see Les Anglais and thence walk through the attractive town of Tiburon to Les Irois; alternatively it is possible to get on one of the sloops which sail from port to port round the coast. From Les Irois the road goes to Dame Marie (on Jérémie road, cheap hotel) and Jérémie, and from there a spectacular but rugged mountain route takes you back to Les Cayes. The round trip can take about 5-7 days; the missionaries in the larger villages sometimes have accommodation.

Jacmel, a port on the S coast, is 2-3 hours by *tap-tap* on a new road from Port-au-Prince—seat by driver US$2.50, in back US$2, they leave from behind the customs house on the corner of Rue du Quai and Rue des Césars, every hour. The road takes you through some spectacular scenery. The town itself has some interesting old architecture and many buildings are being restored. The town's Congo beach has black sand and although it is free, it is rather dirty. A new and expensive hotel has been built on the beach. Saturday is market day and at weekends local bands play on the beach in the evening.

Hotels The luxury *La Jacmélienne sur Plage*, 30 rooms, Haitian cuisine (T 2-4899). *Guy's Guesthouse*, Ave François Duvalier 52 (T 8-3421), friendly and clean; *Pension Craft*, B with 2 meals, quaint and clean, recommended; *Manoir Alexandra*, also recommended, opposite, cheaper, C including 2 good meals; *Chez Madame Luc*, E. Several discothèques, including *La Ruine*.

Near Jacmel, Raymond-les-Bains has a good beach and near the village of Cayes Jacmel is a beautiful white-sand beach (*tap-tap* from Jacmel, US$0.20). Cyradier Cove has a small but protected white sand beach. It is best to take your own provisions with you to the beaches. A visit to the Bassin Bleu is well worthwhile. Horses are provided for the day's excursion; choose one that looks sound as part of the journey is steep and rocky. You have to walk the last kilometre and climb down a rope to the first waterfall. From there you can see a series of other cascades and enjoy the view out across the Bay of Jacmel. The cost is US$5 for the horse and US$2 per person for the guide.

To the N of Port-au-Prince is Ibo beach (very touristy, entrance fee US$2). Lee Sharon at Ibo (T 6-1271) takes private deep-sea fishing trips. To get there, either go by boat (pay on board), or take the *tap-tap* from the Hachot factory to St Marc and tell the driver where you want to get off (you will probably have a half-hour walk from the turnoff). The same *tap-tap* will take you to Kyona beach, about 1 hour from Port-au-Prince (entrance US$2.50, good diving) and Kalico Beach Club, where you can hire scuba and snorkelling equipment, or take reef excursions (entrance US$5—US$2.50 for the beach, the remainder for a drink). Kalico Dive Shop, T 2-5773/2-6530, rents snorkelling and diving equipment, offers dive trips and lessons. The fare to Kalico is US$1. Further on still are Ouanga bay, Joly (US$2.50), Moulin-sur-Mer (US$3, in beautiful surroundings among the restored ruins of a sugar mill), and Amani-Y (very beautiful).

The highway from the capital to Cap Haïtien, from which all the above beaches can be reached, is fairly new, with some hair-raising bends, but also affording breathtaking views. It passes through Duvalierville (Km. 35) and the historic little port of St Marc (Km. 98). After St Marc, the road crosses the Artibonite valley and an area known as La Savane Désolée before climbing to **Gonaïves** (Km. 152). Here General Dessalines proclaimed the independence of Haiti in 1804. There is a motel, *Chez Frantz*, C, with restaurant, 3 km. past the town; *Pension Elias*, Rue L'Ouverture, clean, friendly and safe. The restaurant in town lets rooms above. Bus from Port-au-Prince, US$2, no fixed schedule. Most leave between 0700 and 1200. Buses from Gonaives to Cap Haïtien also leave mornings only.

190 kilometres from the capital you cross Puylbroreau hill and enter the greener northern region. At Plaisance (Km. 204) there is a police checkpoint; at Limbé (Km. 227) the hospital of Le Bon Samaritain (founded by an American missionary).

Cap Haïtien, 258 km. from the capital, is the second city, locally known as Le Cap. Population 70,500. It is on the north coast. On entering the town, you have to register with the police at the checkpoint; keep an eye on your papers. The city is poor and scruffy, but not without interest.

Hotels *Mont Joli*, north of town (PO Box 12, T 3-20300/20326, Telex 2030 300), L 2 extra meals, a/c, pool, free tennis, bars, restaurant, night club, private beach 3 minutes from hotel; in the same area, on beach, *Brise de Mer*, A, 2 meals included, excellent food, private bathroom, pleasant atmosphere, but not very safe. *Roi Christophe* (patronized by Pauline Bonaparte Leclerc while her own home was being built near Port-au-Prince), in town (PO Box 34, T 2-0414, Telex 3490300), B, beach close by, pool, restaurant, mini casino; *Beck*, a long way from centre, but has a pool and attractive grounds, B, quite good, may be amenable to bargaining. In cheaper categories are: *Le Gite*, rue 11, E, restaurant attached; *Pension Colon*, on seafront opposite Post Office, E, without food (not recommended); *Dupuy*, D, very pleasant; *Bon Dieu Bon*, E, reasonably priced restaurant; *A à Z*, on main square opposite Cathedral, E, rambling, delightful colonial building with and good views from the balcony, but amenities and staff poor; *Universal*, rues D et 14, good restaurant. Mme Manoir runs an unmarked *pension* in a rambling old colonial house on Av. E between rues 24 and 25, D, including 2 meals, rather run down.

Restaurants *Sacade*, rues 18 et B, near *Pension Dupuy*; *San Raison*, near market, cheaper; *Universelle*, 2 blocks from *Sacade*, bakery with restaurant, friendly, cheap and good value. Unnamed restaurants on corner of 6 and I and on 11 between F and G, cheap meals. *Ti Paradis*, rues D et 15, good. Fresh and cold fruit juices served on Av. A, between rues 23 and 24.

Shopping Taggart Artilliers, T 03-2-1931, make excellent Haitian crafts; run by Mme Ginette Taggart (she is building 2 houses on her property, which were expected to be available for rent by end-1989).

Exchange Banque Union Haïtien changes travellers' cheques, open until 1800.

Travel agent Cap Travel, 84 rue 23A, T 2-0517. **Tourist bureau** Rue 24, Esplanade.

Rent-a-Bike Cap Rent-a-Bike at 11-D-D (Tel.: 3-8831) rent bicycles and motorcycles. The cost is US$15-20 per day.

Transport Tap-taps and *camionettes* leave from the Mahogany Market, near the waterfront in Port-au-Prince, usually about 0630. The journey to Le Cap can take as little as 4 hours but usually it is much longer, even as much as 10 hours. Fares vary as to whether you sit in the front or back. Public transport stops short of the town, at the police checkpoint, and from there it is an easy 15 minute walk. The official bus fare is US$5. Mission Aviation (MAF) have flights from the capital daily except Sunday at 0830 and 1500 Monday and Friday, US$25.

Beaches There are many beautiful beaches near Le Cap but most are difficult to get to. The *Mont Joli* hotel has a beach at Rival (with glass-bottom boat trip daily at 0830) which is about 15 minutes walk from the public beach near the *Brise de Mer* hotel. *Cormier* beach (admission US$2) is 9 km. from Le Cap (*Hotel Cormier*, L, inc. 2 meals, bungalows, boat trips with diving, tennis) and can be reached by the hotel bus (get your hotel to phone the *Hotel Cormier* to arrange transport) or taxi (US$15-20). You may be able to get a lift back in the hotel minibus. At Cormier, where boats are built, you can buy freshly-caught lobster very cheaply and you can hire someone to row you to *Labadie*, a fine, deserted beach from where there is excellent snorkelling over coral reefs, or you can walk there from Cormier in 30 minutes. The village of Labadie itself is worth a visit and bungalows can be rented there for about US$7. Coco Beach, close to Labadie, is a new resort utilized at times by cruise ships (admission US$3, US$20 if in use by cruise passengers). Fishermen on the beach near the *Brise de Mer* hotel can be hired to sail you to beaches further afield.

Labadie Pointe St Honoré is now a beautiful, US$5-million project belonging to Royal Caribbean Cruise Lines, which is used several times a week. The public may use all the facilities, such as watersports and restaurants, for a US$20 admission fee. On the days when no ship docks, the point is empty and facilities, except for one public lavatory, are locked. At these times, the premises may be entered for US$3. Nearest accommodation is at the villages of Labadie or Cormier Plage, each a few minutes away.

15 minutes beyond Cormier and Labadie is Belli Beach, small, with white sand and a basic hotel (E). Meals are excellent (lobster, etc), but take your own ice box with ice and bread and butter. From here you can hire small boats, with or without outboard motor, for a nominal fee which must be arranged in advance. Beautiful secluded beaches can be discovered this way, and the locals are charming and helpful.

Excursions   The Citadelle is a vast ruined fortress built for Roi Henri Christophe between 1804 and 1817. 20,000 people were involved in its construction. With 4-metre thick walls, it covers 10,000 square metres on the summit of Pic La Ferrière. It was designed to protect the island from French invasion and its garrison of 5,000 soldiers (plus the royal family, their staff, etc) could have resisted siege for a year. Haitians claim that it is the eighth wonder of the world and it is indeed very impressive and has breathtaking views. Restoration work is being carried out. To get there take a *publique* or *tap-tap* from Le Cap to *Milot*, the fares being US$1 and US$0.30 respectively. (*Tap-taps* leave from outside the *Hotel Bon Dieu Bon* in the morning.) From Milot it is an interesting two-hour walk on the steep road to the fortress. You can however hire a horse and with it two men—one to push and one to pull!—for about US$4 (in wet weather it is too dangerous for horses). Guides are also available. The men expect, if not a drink at each stage of the journey, then at least a tip. If you have your own transport you can drive 5-6 km. along a very rough road from Milot to a parking area and thence have a much shorter walk up to the fortress. Admission to the Citadelle (including Sans-Souci) costs US$1.25. It is advisable to take refreshments with you: prices charged at the Citadelle are exorbitant. It is also essential to go protected against the sun and to wear stout shoes.

In Milot itself are the ruins of the Sans Souci Palace which was built in the early 19th century to rival Versailles. Even though it has been devastated by an earthquake (in 1842), it is well worth a visit. Admission is US$1.25. Try to avoid visiting the Citadelle and Sans Souci when cruise ships are in Le Cap. If intending to see both sites, you must arrive before 1300 as they close at 1700 and you will not have enough time. Also, there are no buses or *tap-taps* back to Le Cap after 1700.

Inland from Le Cap is Hinche with the nearby waterfall of Bassin Zim. Hinche can be reached from Port-au-Prince (by bus 5½ hrs.; also by *tap-taps* for US$11 round trip) but from Le Cap the journey is more difficult: there are buses to Pignon (US$1.50) and from there you can take seats in a truck to Hinche. The waterfall is a 3-hour walk from Hinche but it is also possible to hire horses. There is a guesthouse, *Centre d'Acceuil*, D, behind the church in the main square in Hinche, but no accommodation in Pignon.

THE ECONOMY

Haiti is the poorest country in the Western hemisphere and is among the thirty poorest countries in the world. It suffers from overpopulation, lack of communications, lack of cheap power and raw materials for industry, and mountainous terrain that cannot provide an adequate living for the farming population. Life expectancy at birth is only 54 years and the infant mortality rate 11%. Haiti's recent economic problems have been caused by historical low productivity in the vital agricultural sector, compounded by the world recession which depressed commodity prices and therefore export earnings, and the continuing effects of hurricane damage. Deforestation has seriously damaged agriculture and watersheds, in the south in particular: some 70% of all fuel needs are met by charcoal.

Agriculture provides about a third of gdp and employs two thirds of the workforce. Coffee is the most important crop, providing over a quarter of total exports and a livelihood for 2m people. Production of sugar and sisal has been declining because population pressure has encouraged many farmers to plant subsistence crops.

The industrial and commercial sectors are small and are heavily concentrated in the Port-au-Prince area. There are assembly operations producing baseballs, electric and electronic parts and clothing for export to the USA, and domestic operations producing vegetable oils, footwear and metal products. Manufacturing wage rates average below US$3 a day and manufactured goods make up a third of total exports.

Business was seriously disrupted after the fall of the Duvalier regime, but the new government managed to reduce its fiscal deficit and achieve a balance of payments surplus in the 1985-86 fiscal year, although gdp declined by about 2%. The continuing political unrest meant that in 1987-88 overseas aid donors withdrew US$100m of aid, leading to a foreign exchange shortage and a slide in the parallel exchange rate.

	1961-70 (av)	1971-80 (av)	1981-85 (av)	1986-87 (av)(e)
Gdp growth (1980 prices)	1.1%	4.7%	-1.0%	0.0%
Inflation	2.8%	10.7%	9.1%	-7.0%
Exports (fob) US$m	37	101	190	194
Imports (fob) US$m	39	151	353	305
Current account balance US$m (cum)	-44	-296	-659	-76

INFORMATION FOR VISITORS

Documents All visitors apart from North Americans need passports, and visas are required for all except nationals of Austria, Belgium, Denmark, Israel, Liechtenstein, Luxembourg, Netherlands, Switzerland, West Germany and the UK; US and Canadian visitors need only proof of citizenship. (It is however advisable to check this information.) Visitors must have an onward ticket. All visitors, except cruise ship passengers, must complete an embarkation/disembarkation card on the plane; this is valid for 90 days, and may be extended. It is no longer necessary to have a *laissez-passer* before visiting the interior, but you must have some form of identification to satisfy the many police controls. It may also be wise to obtain a letter from the Tourist Office or police in Port-au-Prince confirming that you are a tourist.

Regulations regarding travel to the Dominican Republic seem to change constantly. The best place for discovering the latest requirements is the Community Liaison Officer, American Embassy, J J Dessalines, Cité de l'Exposition, Port-au-Prince, T 2-0200, ext 276 (open 0800-1630 Monday and Tuesday, 0800-1200 Wednesday, 1230-1630 Thursday). The Consulate of the Dominican Republic is at 84 rue Geffrard, Port-au-Prince, T 2-9574.

Customs Baggage inspection is thorough and drug-enforcement laws are strict. There is no restriction on foreign currency. You may bring in one quart of spirits, and 200 cigarettes or 50 cigars. There are no export limitations.

How to get there: by Air From USA: Air France, Eastern Airlines, American Airlines, and ALM all fly direct from New York or Miami, or San Juan, Puerto Rico. ALM also flies from Curaçao (4 times a week), Kingston and Aruba; Dominicana flies from Santo Domingo. BWIA flies to Kingston (as does Air Jamaica, using BWIA planes—check which airline has your reservation carefully); BWIA also connects Haiti with Puerto Rico, Antigua, Barbados and Trinidad. Air Canada flies direct from Montreal. Haiti can often be reached by making a stop-over between Miami and South America; no extra charge, depending on the routing of the ticket. Copa flies the route Panama City-Kingston-Port au Prince twice weekly. Travellers to Haiti report problems with flights, so check thoroughly.

Airport 13 km outside Port-au-Prince. Arrival can be pandemonium, especially if more than one flight is being accommodated at once. Knowledge of French helps; just get on with your affairs and try not to be distracted. The so-called "supervisors" at the airport are in fact taxi-drivers, touting for business. Porters charge US$0.50 per bag. Once through the squash inside you emerge into a squash outside, of taxi drivers and people awaiting friends. Taxi into town, US$10, or a seat in a *tap-tap* (open-sided truck), US$0.20.

Tourist bureau at the airport is very helpful, but the snackbar is expensive and service unfriendly. Upstairs are the duty free and handicraft shops.

There is an airport tax of US$15, payable in gourdes or dollars. If in transit (under 24 hours), you are exempt from this tax, but you must get a transit paper from immigration or the Information Office.

Airlines Pan Am, Cité de l'Exposition (T 2-3675) or the airport (T 6-2300); American Airlines at same locations (T 2-4300 or 6-0100); Air Canada, airport, T 6-0441; Air France, Champ de Mars (T 2-1700); BWIA, Madson Import/Export (T 2-0563), airport (T 6-0949/7).

Shipping Cruise traffic has fallen off because of travellers' reaction to the incessant begging, among other reasons, and only Royal Caribbean call at present.

Internal Transport Public transport services between towns are mainly operated by collective taxis known as *publiques* (they have a "P" on registration plate) and by open-backed pick-up trucks, known as *tap-taps*. *Camionettes* are a type of minibus (actually Peugeot station wagons) with fares similar to *publiques*. Timetables are normally ignored in the urge to fill up the conveyance with as many people as possible.

Chauffeurs-Guide Used like regular taxis, or hired by the hour, half-day, day or for a tour, these vehicles are found around hotels and the airport. The drivers usually speak French and a little English. They can be booked through Association des Chauffeurs-Guide, 18 Blvd Harry Truman, Port-au-Prince, T 2-0330.

Car Rental There are numerous car rental firms, with all the major companies represented. Many have agencies at the airport. The hours there are 0800-2000 whereas offices in town tend to close earlier. The major firms offer a/c small cars, such as a Hyundai Pony, for about US$45/day, US$373/week. Hertz rents cars and trucks. There is no car rental agency in Cap Haïtien, but there is in Pétionville.

Driving in Haiti is extremely impulsive, and it is not easy to get fuel outside Port-au-Prince. The capital's streets are very busy.

Foreigners may use a national driving licence for 3 months in Haiti, then a local permit is required.

Hitchhiking Foreigners do not normally hitch. There are many young Haitian men who stick out a thumb asking for a "roule libre", especially from foreigners. Use your discretion.

Air charter See under Port-au-Prince for Mission Aviation's internal services. Plane rental and charter is limited to 2 private aircraft that are kept at General Aviation. The owners are willing to negotiate any arrangements. Documents for flight within Haiti are to be obtained from the Security Department at the International Airport.

Camping Camping in Haiti is an adventure. The dramatic scenery is very enticing but access to much of it is over rough terrain and there are no facilities, leaving exploring to the rugged. Campers have to take everything and create, or find their own shelter.

Peasant homes dot the countryside and it is almost impossible to find a spot where you will be spared curious and suspicious onlookers. It is best to set up camp or lodging before dark. To prevent misunderstanding, it is important to explain to the locals your intentions, or better yet, talk to the local elder and ask assistance or protection. Creating a relationship with the locals will usually ensure cooperation and more privacy.

Entertainment Until the mid-1980s, Haiti used to be a very good place for night spots. With the drop in tourism and Haitians hesitating to be out late at night in uneasy times, many places have had to shut or curtail their level of entertainment. Those that survive offer a good evening's enjoyment and plenty of personality. Following French custom, entertaining starts late in the evening, about 2030-2100. Night clubbing starts around 2330 and continues into the small hours.

Eating Out Restaurants offer mostly Créole dishes which have a characteristic piquant sauce and/or French cuisine. There is a good selection of places which have great food and atmosphere. Fast food in the US sense does not exist.

Good local specialities are lobster, pepper steak, griot (deep fried pieces of pork), lambi (conch), tassot, rice and beans, rice with local djon-djon.

Babancourt rum is excellent and is widely available in hotels and leisure spots; rum punch is a favourite drink. Prestige is the local beer and imported varieties are also available.

Haiti's wide range of micro-climates produces a large assortment of fruits and vegetables. It is popular to buy these in the regions where they grow and are freshest (prices can be bargained 40% below shop prices). The French influence is obvious in butcher shops where fine cuts of meat, cold cuts, paté and cheeses can be bought. The bakeries sell fabulous French pastries, baguettes and croissants, together with Créole bread and meat pasties. American influence is felt in the supermarkets. Most common are US-brand foods along with smaller amounts of Haitian, French and Middle Eastern brands.

Tipping Budget travellers, particularly outside Port-au-Prince, are a rarity. Expect to be the subject of much friendly curiosity, and keep a pocketful of small change to conform with the local custom of tipping on every conceivable occasion. Even cigarettes and sweets are accepted. Hotels generally add 10% service charge. Baggage porters at hotels usually get 50 cents per bag. Nobody tips taxi, *publique*, *camionette* or *tap-tap* drivers, unless exceptional service has been given.

Shopping Haiti is very rich in its arts and crafts. You can find excellent examples of sewn, woven and embroidered textiles, mahogany ware, basketry, pottery, copper jewellery and cut-out metal wall hangings. Any would be a good buy. Many crafts are functional yet involve much inventiveness of design. For those who enjoy discovering the personality of a nation, negotiating with the street vendors and artists is quite an animated experience. There is, however, a lot of junk to go through before finding a special item. The Iron Market, the largest in Haiti, is situated in the filthy heart of Port-au-Prince. It is the place to get just about anything and witness a slice of Haitian life. For shops with the best choice of handicrafts, see **Art Centres** and **Shopping** sections above.

There are many tourist shops in Port-au-Prince, but be warned that they charge high prices for items which can be bought for far less in the market. In the craft shops and stalls, many of the products are of high quality. Many good bargains still to be had at the Iron Market, but it is said to be getting more and more touristy. People always ask for a discount in shops, except at food shops. All handicrafts can be bought at a discount. See above under **Culture** for best buys, and under towns for individual establishments.

Film processing services are the same as in the USA, but the price of film is high; transparency developing is considerably less.

Security Crime seems to be confined to the Port-au-Prince area, usually in the form of petty theft. Carry handbags securely and do not leave belongings in sight in a parked car.

Should there be any political unrest during your stay it is advisable to limit your movements in the daytime and not to go out at night. Foreigners are not normally targeted at such times, but seek local advice.

Health Prophylaxis against malaria is essential. Tap water is not to be trusted (drink only filtered or treated water) and take care when choosing food. The local herb tea can help stomach troubles.

Good professional advice is available for the more common ailments. Ask friends, associates, or at the hotel desk for referrals to a doctor suited to your requirements. Office hours are usually 0730-1200, 1500-1800. A consultation costs about US$10-15.

Hospital care and comfort varies. Availability of medical supplies is not a problem in hospitals, clinics or at doctors' surgeries. Pharmacies/chemists can fill out prescriptions and many prescription drugs may be bought over the counter.

Recommended hospitals (all in Port-au-Prince) are Canapé Vert, rue Canapé Vert (5-1052/3/0984); Adventiste de Diquini, Carrefour Road (T 4-2000/0521), Hospital Français de Haiti, rue du Centre (T 2-2323); St Francois de Salles, rue de la Révolution (T 2-2110/0232).

A note on prostitution: there are no laws in Haiti to suppress it. Activity seems to be evident only at night with the commonly known areas being along the main roads in Carrefour and street corners in Pétionville. After hours the women move into the dive-type joints, targeting foreigners. With regard to casual sex, there is a red alert in Haiti over Aids.

Climate The climate is generally very warm but the cool on-and off-shore winds of morning and evening help to make it bearable. In coastal areas temperatures vary between 20° and 35° C, being slightly hotter in April-September. The driest months are December-March. In the hill resorts the temperature is cooler.

Clothing As in most other countries in the Caribbean beachwear should not be worn away from the beach and poolside. Dress is casual but never sloppy; Haitians appreciate good manners and style. Above-the-knee hems for women are considered risqué but acceptable. Men always wear a shirt, but a tie is not necessary in the evening.

Time Zone Eastern standard time, GMT—5 hours.

Public Holidays January 1-2 (New Year and Glorification of Heroes), Mardi Gras (the 3 days before Ash Wednesday), April 14 (Americas Day), Good Friday, May 1, May 18 (Flag and University Day), May 22 (Sovereignty Day), August 15 (Assumption), October 8 and 17 (Deaths of Henri Christophe and Dessalines), October 24 (United Nations Day), November 1 (All Saints), November 18 (Armed Forces Day), December 5 (Discovery of Haiti), December 25, Corp... and Ascension are also public holidays.

Hours of business Government offices: 0700-1200, 1300-1600 (0... October-April); banks: 0900-1300 Monday to Friday; shops and offices... October to April).

Currency The unit is the Gourde, divided into 100 centimes... exchangeable on demand and without charge at the fixed rate of 5 g... the legal black market, it changes at a 20-25 % premium. Coins in ci... 50 centimes, notes for 1, 2, 5, 10, 25, 50, 100, 250 and 500 gour... circulate with local currency. Always double-check whether you are... There is no exchange control. Travellers' cheques are widely accepte... Express, Visa, Master Card, Diners Club) are accepted in most hotels...

See under towns above for **banks**. Note that a commission is charged on the exchange of currencies other than the US dollar.

Weights and measures The metric system is used. **Electricity** 110 volt, 60 cycle AC.

Media There are radio broadcasts in English from 1100 to 1400 on 1,035 KHz, MW. 6 daily newspapers, 4 weeklies, and one English monthly.

Embassies and Consulates France, Champs de Mars (Tel.: 2-0963); British Consulate, 21 Ave Marie Jeanne, P.O. Box 1302 (Tel.: 2-1227, Telex RCA 32911, and ITT 349001), diplomatic representation is in Kingston, Jamaica; Netherlands, Rue D Destouches (Tel.: 2-1321); West Germany, Cité de l'Exposition (Tel.: 2-0663); USA, Blvd Harry Truman, Port-au-Prince, T 2-0354/0368; Canadian Embassy, c/o Bank of Nova Scotia, Route de Delmas, PO Box 826, Port-au-Prince, T 2-2358.

Tourist Office Ave Marie Jeanne (on the corner of Rue Roux), Port-au-Prince, T 2-3076/2-1729, gives information on hotels, guest-houses and transport, also has maps (very helpful); open Monday-Friday 0800-1400. Hotel and Tourist Association, *Hotel Montana*, rue Cardoza, Pétionville, T 71920, ext 483 (varying hours, best try in the morning). In Paris: Office du Tourisme d'Haïti, Ambassade d'Haïti, 10 rue Théodule Ribot—75017 Paris, T 4763 4778. In other countries, go to the Haitian embassy or consulate.

We are deeply grateful to Robert Simpson (Edmonton) for useful information on Haiti.

DOMINICAN REPUBLIC

The Dominican Republic occupies the eastern two-thirds of Hispaniola. Its population is mostly a mix of black and white, and is Spanish-speaking. The country is mountainous, though less so than Haiti, with large sugar plantations and widespread food production.

Government The Republic has the conventional type of presidential system, with separation of powers, but in practice for many years anarchy alternated with dictatorship. Though President Trujillo was killed in 1961, his associates retained power until 1978, except for a few months in 1963. In 1978 and again in 1982 the Dominican Revolutionary Party won free elections. President (1986-90): Dr. Joaquín Balaguer.

The Dominican Republic is building up its tourist trade, and has much to offer in the way of natural beauty, old colonial architecture and native friendliness. The climate is tropical. The rainy months are May and June, September to November. The temperature shows little seasonal change, and varies between 18° and 32°C.

Santo Domingo, the capital and chief seaport, population now about 1.6 million, was founded in 1496 by Columbus' brother Bartholomew and hence was the first capital in Spanish America. For years the city was the base for the Spaniards' exploration and conquest of the continent: from it Ponce de León sailed to discover Puerto Rico, Hernán Cortés launched his attack on Mexico, Balboa discovered the Pacific and Diego de Velázquez set out to settle Cuba. In the old part of the city, on the W bank of the River Ozama, there are many fine early 16th-century buildings: some of them have been restored by the Government and others are in ruins. Of the greatest interest are:

·edral Basílica Menor de Santa María, Primada de América, Isabel La Católica esq. ' the first cathedral to be founded in the New World. First stone laid by Diego Columbus, son ⁀topher, in 1514. Architect: Alonzo Rodríguez. Finished 1540. Alleged remains of ⁀r Columbus found in 1877 during restoration work. In 1892, the Government of Spain ⁀omb in which the remains now rest, behind the high altar.

·naje inside Fortaleza Ozama, reached through the mansion of Rodrigo Bastidas ⁀of Santa Marta in Colombia) on Calle Las Damas, which is now completely restored and has a museum/gallery with temporary exhibitions. Oldest fortress in America, constructed 1503-07 by Nicolás de Ovando, whose house in the same street has been restored and turned into a splendid hotel.

Museo de las Casas Reales, on Calle Las Damas, in a reconstructed early 16th-century building which was in colonial days the Palace of the Governors and Captains-General, and of the *Real Audiencia* and Chancery of the Indies. It is an excellent colonial museum (often has special exhibits); entry US$0.50; open 0900-1200, 1430-1730; closed Mon.; entry US$0.80.

Alcázar de Colón at the end of Las Damas, constructed by Diego Colón (Columbus' son) 1510-14. For six decades it was the seat of the Spanish Crown in the New World. Sacked by Drake in 1586. Now completely restored, it houses the interesting Viceregal Museum (Museo Virreinal). Open 0900-1200, 1430-1730; Alcázar closed Tues., Museum closed Mon.; entry US$0.80.

Casa del Cordón, Isabel La Católica esq. Emiliano Tejera, built in 1509 by Francisco de Garay, who accompanied Columbus on his first voyage to Hispaniola. Named for the cord of the Franciscan Order, sculpted above the entrance. Now the offices of the Banco Popular; free guided tours during working hours.

Monasterio de San Francisco (ruins), Hostos esq. E. Tejera, first monastery in America, constructed in the first decade of the 16th century. Sacked by Drake and destroyed by earthquakes in 1673 and 1751.

Reloj de Sol (sundial) built 1753, near end of Las Damas, by order of General Francisco de Rubio y Peñaranda; by its side is

Capilla de Nuestra Señora de Los Remedios, built in the early 16th century as the private chapel of the Dávila family. It has recently been restored.

La Ataranza, near the Alcázar, a cluster of 16th-century buildings which served as warehouses. Now restored and contains shops, bars and restaurants.

Hospital-Iglesia de San Nicolás de Bari (ruins), Hostos between Mercedes and Luperón, begun in 1509 by Nicolás de Ovando, completed 1552, the first stone-built hospital in the Americas. Sacked by Drake. Probably one of the best constructed buildings of the period, it survived many earthquakes and hurricanes. In 1911 some of its walls were knocked down because they posed a hazard to passers-by; also the last of its valuable wood was taken. It is now full of pigeons.

Convento de San Ignacio de Loyola, Las Damas between Mercedes and El Conde. Finished in 1743, it is now the National Pantheon. Restored 1955 and contains memorials to many of the country's heroes and patriots. It also contains an ornate tomb built before his death for the dictator Trujillo, the "Benefactor of the Fatherland", but his remains do not lie there.

Iglesia de Santa Bárbara, off Mella to left near Calle J. Parra, near end of Isabel La Católica. Built in 1574. Sacked by Drake in 1586, destroyed by a hurricane at the beginning of the 17th century. Reconstructed at the beginning of the 17th century. Behind the church are the ruins of its fort, where one can get good views.

Convento de los Dominicos, built in 1510. Here in 1538 the first university in the Americas was founded, named for St.Thomas Aquinas; it now bears the title of the Universidad Autónoma de Santo Domingo. It has a unique ceiling which shows the medieval concept that identified the elements of the universe, the classical gods and the Christian icons in one system. The Sun is God, the 4 evangelists are the planetary symbols Mars, Mercury, Jupiter and Saturn. The University itself has moved to a site in the suburbs.

Iglesia de la Regina Angelorum, built 1537, contains a wall of silver near one of its altars.

Iglesia del Carmen, built around 1615 at side of Capilla de San Andrés, contains interesting wooden sculpture of Christ.

Puerta del Conde (Baluarte de 27 de Febrero), at the end of El Conde (now a pedestrian street) in the Parque Independencia. Named for the Conde de Peñalva, who helped defend the city against William Penn in 1655. Restored in 1976, near it lie the remains of Sánchez, Mella and Duarte, the 1844 independence leaders.

Puerta de la Misericordia, Palo Hincado and Arzobispo Portes. So named because people fled under it for protection during earthquakes and hurricanes. It forms part of the wall that used surround the colonial city, into which are now built many of the houses and shops of Ci Nueva. It was here on February 27, 1844 that Mella fired the first shot in the stru independence from Haiti.

Capilla de la Virgen del Rosario, on the other side of the Río Ozama, ne Dominicanos at the end of Av. Olegario Vargas. It was the first church constr restored in 1943.

Museo Duartiano, Isabel La Católica 308. Contains items linked with the independence struggle and Duarte, the national hero, whose home it was.

Other old buildings are the Iglesia de las Mercedes, dating from 1555; the Puerta de San Diego, near Alcázar; the Palacio de Borgella, Isabel la Católica, near Plaza Colón; the ruins of Fuerte de la Concepción, corner Mella and Palo Hincado, built in 1543; the ruins of Fuerte de San Gil, Paseo de Pte. Billini, near end of Calle Pina; and the ruins of Iglesia de San Antón, off Mella, near V. Celestino Duarte.

To mark the 500th anniversary of Columbus' first journey to the Americas, the Dominican Republic is planning a number of celebrations under the title of "The First of the Firsts". It is hoped that the Pope and King Juan Carlos of Spain will visit in 1992, that many of Santo Domingo's unrestored colonial monuments will be repaired and that the gigantic Columbus Memorial Lighthouse, being built in secrecy on the E bank of the Río Ozama, will be complete.

The modern city is very spread out because, until recently, there was no high-rise building. The outer city has fine avenues, especially Av. George Washington (also known as the Malecón), Av. Independencia, Av. Bolívar, Av. Abraham Lincoln and Av. Winston Churchill. Among the attractive parks are the Central Olímpico in the city centre, with excellent athletic facilities, Parque Independencia (a peaceful haven amid all the traffic), Parque Colón and Parque Mirador (Paseo de las Indios at Mirador Sur), the Botanical Gardens at Marmolejos (open Tues.-Sun. 0900-1200, 1400-1800) and the National Zoo (Zoodom) at Arroyo Hondo (open 0900-1800). Admission to the Botanical Gardens and the Zoo is US$0.15; children US$0.10; for information call 566-8151. The Botanical Gardens are highly recommended (the Japanese Garden especially); horse-drawn carriages and a small train tour the grounds. The 1955/56 World's Fair buildings now house the Senate and Congress and other government offices. The national museum collection, which includes a wonderful display of Taino artefacts, has been moved to the Museo del Hombre Dominicano (closed on Mon.), which forms part of a new cultural centre also including the ultra-modern national theatre and national library; there are also the Gallery of Modern Art, Museo de Historia Natural and Museo de Historia y Geografía. The Museum of the Dominican Family is housed in the Casa de Tostada (Calle Padre Billini, esq. Arzobispo Meriño), an early 16th century mansion. On the Carretera Duarte (km. 4½) the Fundación García Arévalo has an exhibition of pre-hispanic art and civilization. For archaeologists there is the Instituto de Investigaciones Históricas, José Reyes 24. At the entrance to the airport is La Caleta museum with its display of Taino and Arawak artefacts. The new pink stone National Capitol is worth seeing, as is the spectacular monument to Fray Antón de Montesinos at the E end of Av. George Washington.

Three bridges cross the Río Ozama: the nearest to the sea is Mella (nicknamed La Bicicleta because it is so narrow), next is Duarte, and further inland Sánchez. On the road to the airport are the Tres Ojos de Agua, two water-filled caves and a sunken lake which are worth a visit. To reach the last-named you must take the raft across the second cave (1 peso p.p.); it is supposed to have two crocodiles in it, put there by the Botanical Gardens , but they didn't reproduce (no one bothered to check their sex). There is excellent scuba diving at La Caleta, a small beach near the turn-off to the airport, on the Autopista de las Américas.

Tours There are several tours of the city, taking in the duty-free shops, nightlife, etc. Particularly recommended (from 2100 to 0200) is the ritual *paseo* along the Malecón.

Hotels (prices are high season)

	Address		Price Range
		Lincoln	L 316
Dominican	Av. Anacaona	Abraham Lincoln	L
Concorde†	Calle El Conde		L 220
Santo Domingo†	...ez 16		L 260
Sheraton†	Las Américas 96		D 165
Hispanà*†	Av. Tiradentes 22		B 75
...tes*†	Av. Máximo Gómez y 27 de Febrero		B 100
...an Gerónimo*†	Av. Bólivar 193		60
El Nuevo Jaragua†	Calle Cervantes 202		C 36
	Av. Independencia		A
*Convenient to centre † Swimming pool and fully air-condition...	Av. George Washington 2		L 105 / B 200 / B ...

SANTO D.
OLD CITY

The Domitel chain throughout the country has excellent, good value establishments: Isabel la Católica 165, Santo Domingo, T 689-9191; prices vary through the year, and are more expensive for foreigners. *Hostal Nicolás de Ovando*, a restored 16th-century mansion in the oldest part of the city, is warmly rec. for comfort, quiet, food and atmosphere. *Gran Hotel Lina* is also highly rec. and has a good restaurant, and has recently been enlarged. Other hotels include: on Av. George Washington, *Napolitano*, B*†; and *Neptuno*, C; also *Caribe 1*, C/B, pool, Italian restaurant, good. In the old city, *Hostal Nicolás Nader*, Duarte y Gral. Luperón, C.

Cheaper hotels include: *Aida*, El Conde and Espaillat, D, fairly quiet (but record shop below may be noisy in day), well run, good value; *Estrella*, Isabel La Católica 59, near cathedral, looks basic but is central for old city, at E, among the cheapest accommodation available, rec.; *Villy Guest House*, Pasteur 4, very good value; *Independencia*, Estrella casi esq. Arz. Nouel, near Parque Independencia, recently renovated, E, soap, towels etc. provided, rec., also has a club, bar, language school (across the street), a roof terrace and art exhibitions. *Señorial*, Vinicio Burgos 58, friendly, clean and informal, and famous for its "Hemingway" atmosphere. *Tres Gigantes*, E, at eastern end of Mella. There are dozens of cheap hotels, especially around the Mercado Modelo; have a good look round them before making any decision.

Note There is a 10% service charge and 5% government tax added to all room bills. The newspaper *Listín Diario* advertises rooms or apartments to let by the week or month.

Restaurants *Lina* and *Las Palmas* at *Hotel Santo Domingo* (both rec.) and other main hotels; *Vesuvio I* on Av. George Washington and also *Vesuvio II* on Av. Tiradentes, Italian and international cuisine; *Mesón de la Cueva*, Mirador Sur, near *Hotel El Embajador*, situated in a natural cave, good steaks, dancing, very popular so reserve in advance; *Cantábrico*, *Jai-Alai*, and *La Mezquita Taverna* on Av. Independencia for excellent seafood; *El Bodegón*, *Il Buco* (Italian, Arz. Meriño 152A, reserve on 685-0884), and *Chez François* on Arzobispo Meriño and Padre Billini near the Cathedral are rec. Many good ones, but usually expensive, on the Malecón (Av. George Washington) along the seafront, including *Le Café*, *El Gaucho*, good value for steaks, and 3 blocks east of *Hotel Napolitano*, *Llave del Mar*, which has a stuffed dolphin hanging outside, a weird and wonderful collection of curios inside and serves good seafood at reasonable prices. *Fonda La Ataranza*, in La Ataranza, popular for creole and international cuisine; *Gerd's Hofbrauhaus*, Palo Hincado, unpretentious, good German food; *Lucky Seven*, Av. Pasteur, good for seafood and steaks, popular haunt for baseball fans. Also worth visiting are *Veneto Ice Cream* on Av. Independencia; *Italiano 1*, Av. Winston Churchill; *La Fromagerie*, on Av. Pasteur, *Cafe St. Michel* on Av. Lope de Vega (French cuisine). *Mesón de Castilla*, on Dr. Báez near the National Palace; and *Juan Carlos*, Gustavo Mejía Ricart (Spanish cuisine). For good Chinese food try *Marios* on Calle Mercedes opposite Parque Independencia, very popular, *La Gran Muralla*, Av. 27 de Febrero, or *Comedor Buen Sabor*, Av. Duarte 32, upstairs, very good. For local food at reasonable prices try *El Buren* on Padre Billini, *Pacos Café*, *Comedor Independencia* and *Freidura Nacional*, all near Parque Independencia. For the local dish mofongo (see under **Food and Drink** below), *Palacio del Mofongo* on the Malecón, or *Casa del Mofongo*, 27 de Febrero (a long way from the centre).

Two good vegetarian restaurants are *Ananda*, Casimiro de Maya 7, and *Vegetariano*, Calle Luperón 9 (open 0800-1500). Also *El Terrenal*, Malecón y Estrelleta, some vegetarian dishes. *Vita Naturaleza*, Mercedes 255, sells health products (by small park at junction with Luperón).

There are numerous pizzerias whch are good value; also try a chimichurri (spiced sausage) from the stalls along the Malecón. *La Plaza Argentina* near the Cathedral, *Drakes Pub* opposite the Alcázar. Many good restaurants, of all cuisines, on or very near Plaza Colón, *Raffles Pub*, *Mesón de Bari* and *The Village* in Calle Hostos, opposite the ruins of Hospital San Nicolás de Bari, are good places for snacks and drinks in a pub-type atmosphere, in the colonial city; and so is *La Taberna* (classical music) at Padre Billini with Las Damas.

Shopping Duty free at Centro de los Héroes, La Ataranza, shops in *Embajador*, *Sheraton* and *Santo Domingo* hotels; departure lounge at airport; all purchases must be in US dollars. Mercado Modelo, on Av. Mella esq. Santomé, includes gift shops; you must bargain to get a good price. There are also "speciality shops" at Plaza Criolla, 27 de Febrero y Máximo Gómez. The native amber is sold throughout the country. Larimar, a sea-blue stone, and red and black coral are also

Key to Map of Santo Domingo
1. Plaza Colón; 2. Parque Independencia; 3. Cathedral; 4. Monasterio de San Francisco (ruins); 5. Capilla de Nuestra Señora de los Remedios; 6. Santa Bárbara (fort and church—ruins); 7. Convento de los Dominicos; 8. Iglesia del Carmen; 9. Iglesia de la Regina Angelorum; 10. Iglesia de las Mercedes; 11. Iglesia de San Antón (ruins); 12. Convento San Ignacio de Loyola/Panteón Nacional; 13. Hospital de San Nicolás de Bari (ruins); 14. Alcázar de Colón; 15. Casa del Cordó 16. Palacio de Borgella; 17. Casa de Tostada/Museo de la Familia Dominicana; 18. Ca Francia/Teatro Nacional; 19. Museo de las Casa Reales; 20. Museo Duartiano; 21. T Homenaje and Fuerte Ozama; 22. Fuerte de la Concepción (ruins); 23. Fuerte de San Gi Puerta del Conde; 25. Puerta de la Misericordia; 26. Puerta de San Diego; 27. Su Sol); 28. Monument to Fray Antón de Montesinos; 29. La Ataranza; 30. Hostal de 31. Casa Bastidas; 32. Central Post Office; 33. Mercado Modelo; 34. Parque F

available. Calle El Conde, now reserved to pedestrians, is the oldest shopping sector in Santo Domingo; Av. Mella at Duarte is a good spot for discount shopping and local colour. In contrast are the modern complexes at Plaza Naco and the new US style shopping mall at the corner of Av. 27 de Febrero and Av. Abraham Lincoln. Shops in the capital are open 0830-1200 and 1430-1800/1830.

Buses Public transport buses (Onatrate), commonly called *guaguas*, run throughout the city, fares are 25 centavos, but the service is very limited therefore crowded. Exact change is needed. Private companies (e.g. Caribe Tours) operate on some routes, charging 50 centavos.

Taxis *Carros públicos*, or *conchos*, are shared taxis normally operating on fixed routes, 24 hours a day, basic fare US$0.40, though more on longer routes. *Públicos* can be hired by one person, if they're empty, and are then called *carreras*. They can be expensive (US$2.30-3.25, more on longer routes); settle price before getting in. Fares are higher at Christmas time. *Públicos* also run on long-distance routes; ask around to find the cheapest. Many private cars now operate as *públicos* as owners try to earn supplementary income. You can get to just about anywhere by bus or *público* from Parque Independencia, but you have to ask where to stand. Radio taxis are cheaper and safer than street taxis, call about 20-30 minutes in advance: Taxi Fácil, 533-8489/7640; Taxi Radio, 562-1313/1101; Taxi Carro Radio, 541-2777/2474 (fare to airport US$8). Most hotels have a taxi or limousine service with set fares throughout the city and to the airport. There are motorcyclists who offer a taxi service; they raise the noise level (in most towns) very considerably.

Car Rentals Many places at the airport, on the road to the airport and on Malecón. Avis, Budget, Hertz, Rentauto, Toyota, National, Dial, City, Econo-Car, and others; McDeals, Av. George Washington 105, has the most reasonable rates, the staff are friendly, but the cars are in poor condition. Car hire costs from US$35 a day (including insurance) and is on a free mileage basis. Pueblo Renta Car, rec., on Av. Independencia (esq. *Jaragua* hotel), also provides the best road map of the country. Thrifty Rent-a-Car on Av. Bolívar has also been rec. Avoid going for the cheapest: it is better to pay more with a well-known agency. Credit cards are widely accepted; cash deposit is usually twice the sum of the contract. Minimum age 25; maximum period for driving 90 days.

Library Instituto Cultural Dominico-Americano, corner of Av. Abraham Lincoln and Calle Antonio de la Maza. English and Spanish books. Biblioteca Nacional, in the Plaza de la Cultura, has a fine collection and is a good place for a quiet read.

Concerts and other cultural events are often held at the National Theatre, the Casa de Francia, corner of Las Damas and El Conde, where Cortés lived for a while (run by the French Embassy—also art gallery and library, open to non-members), and the Casa de Teatro on Arzobispo Meriño.

Theatres Teatro Nacional, Plaza de la Cultura, Av. Máximo Gómez; Palace of Fine Arts, Av. Independencia and Máximo Gómez; Casa de Teatro, small drama workshop, Arzobispo Meriño.

Night Clubs *Embajador, Napolitano, San Gerónimo, Sheraton* (El Yarey); *Dominican Concorde, Santo Domingo* and *Comodoro* hotels all have nightclubs; José Night Club, Av. George Washington; Maunaloa, Centro de los Héroes; Le Petit Chateau, Autopista 30 de Mayo; La Voz de Santo Domingo; Mesón de la Cueva. The Safari is the best place to see locals dance and to listen to leading *merengue* bands; The Herminias, a colourful nightclub, is best left to the sophisticated male visitor. **Bars:** La Pipa; Moulin Rouge; El Bodegón Bar-Lounge, Arz. Meriño 152, live jazz Monday nights.

Discotheques in Hotels *Sheraton* and *Hispaniola*, also *Jet Set*, Av. Independencia 184; *Alexanders*, Av. Pasteur; *Opus*, Av. Independencia. *Bella Blue*, next to *Vesuvio I* on George Washington. New ones: *Tops* and *Luigi's*.

Casinos in *Hotels Dominican Concorde, San Gerónimo, Sheraton, El Embajador, Naco, Jaragua, Lina* and Maunaloa, Centro de los Héroes.

Sports Golf: Country Club Santo Domingo; *Casa de Campo Hotel* in La Panamana; some hotels including the *Santo Domingo* can arrange guest passes. Polo matches at weekends at Sierra Prieta, Santo Domingo. Baseball (the national sport) at Quisqueya stadium, water skiing/deep-sea fishing at Náutico Club, Boca Chica beach. Demar Beach Club, Andrés (Boca Chica, T 523-4365) for fishing, sailing, diving and water skiing charters, windsurfing, snorkelling and canoeing. Basketball, boxing and wrestling matches can also be seen in Santo Domingo. Snorkelling and scuba-diving tours are operated by Mundo Submarino at Gustavo Ricart 99, and by Bucco Dominicano, Av. A. Lincoln 960. Tennis at Country Club.

Exchange Officially possible only in banks, many along Isabel La Católica, but check which banks accept which traveller's cheques. Banco de la Reserva is next to the Palacio de las Comunicaciones on Isabel La Católica. The largr hotels are also permitted to change dollars and ~~pen till 2100. Banco Popular, Ataranza y Emiliano Tejera, opp. Alcázar de Colón is supposedly open 0830-1730 Mon.-Sat.; Banco de la Reserva in the main post office is open 0900-1600, dollars only.

Post Office Calle Emiliano Tejera, opp. Alcázar de Colón. Open 0700-1300, 1400-1600, Mon.-Fri. Also certain hours on Sat. There is a post office on the 2nd floor of the government building El Haucal, tallest building in the city, and in *Hotel Embajador*.

Telephones International and long distance, also Telex and Fax: Codetel, Av. 30 de Marzo 12, near Parque Independencia, and 7 others throughout the city (open 0800-2200). The Palacio de las Comunicaciones next to the Post Office (at Isabel La Católica y Emiliano Tejera) does not handle phone calls.

Episcopal Church Av. Independencia 253. Service in English, 0830 Sunday.

Health Clínica Abreu, Av. Independencia and Beller, and adjacent Clínica Gómez Patiño are rec. for foreigners needing treatment or hospitalization. Fees are high but care is good. 24-hour emergency department.

Tourist Office Centro Dominicano de Información Turística, now at Av. George Washington (Malecón) near the Obelisk, friendly, helpful though some brochures are old. Gives Texaco map free and publishes *La Cotica* Tourism Guide. Also in arrival area at airport, and on Arzobispo Meriño, opposite the cathedral. City and country map available in bookshops for US$1.55.

National Parks Office Casa de Bastidas. There are 5 parks in the republic: Armando Bermúdez and J. del Carmen Ramírez (pine forests and mountains in the Cordillera Central), Isla Cabritos in Lago Enriquillo, Los Haitises (S coast of Samaná Bay), and Parque Nacional del Este (the peninsula S of San Rafael del Yuma and the Isla Saona).

Travel Agents Viajes Internacionales, El Conde 15; Servicios Turísticos, Av. George Washington 67; Metro Tours, Av. Winston Churchill; Santoni, José Joaquín Pérez 6. Amber Tours and Prieto Tours, Av. Francia 125, both offer a variety of sightseeing tours around the country. Thomas Tour, Pedro Henríquez Ureña 170-E 1, T 688-2562; Cesintur, Av. Independencia 301, T 685-4655 (highly rec., near *Hotel Cervantes*). Consult your hotel reception or yellow pages for others.

Airport Aeropuerto La Américas, 23 km. out of town. Immediately on arrival there is a tourist office on your right, and just past that an office selling tourist cards (a blackboard indicates who needs a card—see **Documents** in Information for Visitors). You must check if you need a card, otherwise the long queue to get through immigration will be wasted. Just beyond immigration is a bank for exchanging dollars. In the departure area are lots of duty free shops, one small café (dollars only) and limited seating. The X-ray machines are not safe for film.

Taxi or minibus to town US$10 (can be shared) or less if you bargain with drivers in the car park (though this is not easy) or telephone Radio Taxi in advance. Bus or *público* to town from *Restaurante La Caleta*; turn right out of airport compound along main road; cross over main highway; turn left to restaurant (about 25 mins. walk). Buses pass every ½ hr., but are infrequent in p.m., or walk down the airport road to the highway, Avenida de Las Américas, and flag down anything that passes! To get to the airport cheaply take a *público* at Av. Duarte and París (to Savanna Larga). Get off before the car turns on to Savanna Larga, walk 50 metres and there are *carros* to the airport, US$4-7. Various tour agencies also run minibuses to the airport; check with your hotel. Herrera airport for internal flights to Santiago, Puerto Plata, Barahona and La Romana (allow plenty of time). Departure tax US$10.

Long-Distance Buses See page 1383.

To the north of Santo Domingo, along the Carretera Duarte, is **Bonao** (Hotels: *El Viejo Madrid*, D; *Yaraví Rooms*, D; *Jacaranda*, D, *Elizabeth*, G, with bath, and other cheap hotels near the market such as *Mi Provincia*, F, and *San Juan*, G). Further N is **La Vega**, a quiet place in the heart of the Cibao valley. (Hotels: *América*, D; *Guaricano*, D; and *Royal*, *San Pedro*, and *Astral*, all F.) Further along the road from La Vega on the right is the turn for Santo Cerro. From there one can get a view of the valley of La Vega Real. If one continues along the road to the other side of the hill and into the valley the ruins of La Vega Vieja can be seen. It was founded by Columbus but destroyed by an earthquake in 1564; it is presently undergoing restoration. (*Hotel Mariza*, E, very basic with fan; *Pensión Ana*.)

Further along the highway, on the left, is the turn for **Jarabacoa.** The road winds through some beautiful pine forests to the town itself, which is a popular summer hill resort with warm days and cool nights. *Público* from La Vega, US$1.25; bus from Santo Domingo, US$2.50. (Hotels in Jarabacoa: *Nacional*, D, friendly and clean; outside town, *La Montaña*, D, some km. out, friendly,

To Airport & San Pedro de Macoris

SANTO DOMINGO
Orientation Map
Main Streets Only
Not to Scale

179A

1. Plaza Colón
2. Parque Independencia
3. Parque Enriquillo
4. Tourist Office
5. Capilla de la Virgen del Rosario
6. Iglesia de San Lorenzo
7. Palacio Nacional
8. New Cultural Centre
9. Tres Ojos de Agua
10. Botanical Gardens
11. Zoo
12. Parque Mirador

13. Parque Infantil
14. Central Olímpico
15. Ciudad Universitaria
16. Caribe Tours
17. Terrabus
18. Autobuses Metro.

RIO OZAMA

Puente Sánchez

Puente Duarte

Puente Mella

AV. DE LAS AMERICAS

AV. ESTADOS UNIDOS

AV. ESPAÑA

CARIBBEAN SEA

CALLE CASTELLANOS

DUARTE

AV. NICOLAS DE OVANDO

AV. PEDRO LIVIO CEDEÑO

AV. SAN MARTIN

AV. MAXIMO GOMEZ

AV. PTE. JOHN F. KENNEDY

FTE. A. GARCIA

27 DE FEBRERO

30 DE MARZO

AV. MELLA

EL CONDE

BOLIVAR

INDEPENDENCIA

MALECON

AV. GEORGE WASHINGTON

AV. TIRADENTES

AV. ABRAHAM LINCOLN

AV. WINSTON CHURCHILL

27 DE FEBRERO

AV. BOLIVAR

AUTOPISTA DUARTE

RESTAURADORES

AV. DE LOS CACIQUES

MIRADOR DEL SUR

To San Cristobal

To Santiago, Puerto Plata and the North.

clean, highly rec. and *Pinar Dorado*, C, which has cottages. *Lina*, E, dirty; *Continental* is short-stay only; *Dormitorio*, basic, clean, friendly, with a good *comedor*, *Carmen*, nearby. The town has several restaurants; try the *Rincón Montañés* on Calle El Carmen; other good-value ones are run by shopkeepers.) There are several clubs offering golf, tennis and riding, and the good *balneario* (swimming hole) of La Confluencia is nearby (nice campsite, crowded at holiday times). Further along the road which goes to Jarabacoa is **Constanza,** where the scenery is even better than in Jarabacoa, with rivers, forests, waterfalls, etc. The valley is famous for its strawberries, mushrooms and ornamental flowers. (Hotels: *Nueva Suiza*, C; *Mi Cabaña*, F, good. *Margarita* and *Casa de Huéspedes*, both on Calle Luperón, latter F but poor; *Brisa del Valle*, G, simple, acceptable, meals available.) Constanza can be reached by taking a bus to Bonao from either Santo Domingo or Santiago, then two *públicos*, the last one making the rough 1½ hr. trip to the town through the finest scenery in the Republic. *Público* from Jarabacoa, US$3.50.

In the Cordillera Central near both of these towns is **Pico Duarte**, at 3,075 metres the highest peak in the Caribbean. Before climbing it one must obtain the permission of the army in Jarabacoa. (When doing this you will be told that mules are necessary at 6 pesos daily for the ascent, but it can be done without them.) The climb takes two days and the walk from the tropical rain forest of the National Park through pine woods is pleasant. There are two huts on the path, which is clearly marked; they are lacking in "facilities". Take adequate clothing with you; it can be cold and wet. The last *carro* leaves Manabao for Jarabacoa at 1600, so aim to climb the peak well before lunch on the second day. The National Park itself is a 4 km. walk from La Ciénaga, which is reached by a road passing through some magnificent scenery from Jarabacoa. In La Ciénaga you can purchase a permit for the Park for US$10.

Santiago de Los Caballeros is the second largest city in the Republic and chief town of the Cibao valley in the north-central part of the country. It is much quieter, cleaner, cooler and "slower" than Santo Domingo, from where it is easily reached by bus **(see page 1383)**. Places worth visiting are the Universidad Católica Madre y Maestra (founded 1962), the new tobacco museum (opposite the Cathedral), the Catedral de Santiago Apóstol, and the Monumento a 'los Héroes de la Restauración. The Instituto Superior de Agricultura is in the Herradura on the other side of the Río Yaque del Norte (km. 6). A carriage ride around the city should not be missed.

Hotels *Camino Real*, B, Del Sol and Mella, has good restaurant and night club, no parking facilities; *Don Diego*, B, Av. Estrella Sadhalá, has restaurant and night club; *Ambar*, C, also on Av. Estrella Sadhalá; *Matun*, B, Las Carreras (altos) has night club. Also *Corona*, C, away from centre. *Mercedes*, Calle 30 de Marzo, central so a bit noisy, but rec., D. A rec. *pensión* is the *Diri*, F (Las Carreras and Juan Pablo Duarte). Many cheap hotels around Plaza Valerio.

Restaurants The best are the *Pez Dorado* (Chinese and international), the restaurant of the *Hotel Don Diego; Oriente*, Calle 30 de Marzo, good; *El Dragón* (Chinese). Excellent sandwich and pizza places are *Olé* (Av. Juan Pablo Duarte, esq., Independencia), *Dinós* (Del Sol). *Don Miguel*, Autopista Duarte opp. Catholic University, good local, Cuban and US food, popular. Others include *Las Antillas* (Parque Duarte), meals from US$4 upwards; *El Mexicano* (Ensanche El Ensueño); *Yaque* (Restauración), US$4 plus for a good meal; and *La Suiza*.

Buses in Santiago US$0.20 (very restricted service). *Públicos* charge US$0.50 in the city; *carreras*, US$2.40. Transporte del Cibao, Restauración casi esq. J.P. Duarte, runs buses up to Dajabón in the north-west near the Haitian border.

There is a Tourist Office on the 2nd floor of the Town Hall (Ayuntamiento), Av. Juan Pablo Duarte; it has good maps and brochures. The markets are located at Del Sol and España, Av. J. Armando Bermúdez and near the lower part of 16 de Agosto.

To the SW of Santiago is the pleasant town of San José de las Matas (Hotels, *Oasis* and *La Modenza*, F.). To the NW of Santiago a road runs through the Yaque del Norte valley to Mao (*Hotel Cahoba*, D) and on to **Monte Cristi**, a dusty little town on the coast. One can visit the house of Máximo Gómez, a Dominican patriot who played an important role in the struggle for Cuban independence and in the Dominican Restoration. Very near Monte Cristi is a peak named El Moro which has a beach (very rocky) at the foot of its east side. There are a couple of decent hotels there (*Montechico*, on Bolaños beach, E; *Roalex*).

Puerto Plata, the chief town on the Atlantic coast (which is also known as the Amber Coast) was founded by Columbus and has some fine colonial architecture. It is reached by bus from Santo Domingo (US$6 by Metrobus) or by *público* (US$10). The older scenic road from Santiago to Puerto Plata is now in excellent condition. A visit to the colonial San Felipe fortress, at the end of the Malecón is recommended. The *teleférico* which goes some 1,000 metres up behind the town to the summit of Isabel de Torres (with a statue of Christ, craft shops, a café and some fine gardens with a view of the coast and mountains) has been out of action for years. The Museum of Dominican Amber, Duarte 61, houses a collection of rare amber; open Mon.-Sat. 0900-1700. The town is already a stop for cruise-ships, thus attracting hordes of beggars and overly persistent small boys. There is a tourist office on the Malecón (No. 20) which has plenty of useful information. Fishing: contact Santiago Camps (T 586-2632) for equipment and boat hire. A new international airport (taxi from town, US$5) has been built to serve the area (flights Mon., Fri. and Sun to San Juan; also to USA— probably a better entry point than Santo Domingo). At the E end of town is Long Beach, 2 km. from centre, US$0.15 by bus, but it is crowded at weekends and rather dirty. To the W is the new Costambar resort area (cottages, sports facilities) and Cofresí beach (cabins, US$30 p.p. and more at weekends). Further W is Punta Rucio which has a beautiful beach not yet developed for tourism.

Hotels *Montemar,* on beach, B, all facilities; *Dorado Naco,* EP, A (add US$20, MAP) T 586-2019. *Castilla,* in centre of town, D, splendid atmosphere, toilets not rec.; *El Condado,* Av. Circunvalación Sur, D. *Caracol,* on sea front, C, modern; *Costatlántica Resort,* on the seafront, B; *Palacio,* Av. J. F. Kennedy, D, bar and restaurant below, friendly, good value; *Ilra,* Calle Villa Nueva, T 586-2337, good food, E; *Alfa,* E, friendly, safe, clean; *Andy's Guest House,* E, rec., one of many of similar price range, breakfast US$1 extra; some houses also available from US$22 a week. Ask in the *Wienerwald* restaurant, Long Beach, about cheap (E/F) rooms.

Restaurants *Los Pinos,* international cuisine; *Pizzería Portofino,* Hermanas Mirabel; *La Isabella* (Hotel Montemar); *La Carreta,* Calle Separación; *Oceánico* on sea front; *El Canario,* 12 de Julio; *Hotel Castilla* restaurant, all have good food at relatively low prices. *Valter,* on a side street leading to casino, good food and service, US$10 p.p. *China,* Av. Hermanas Mirabel; *D'Amico,* Luis Ginebra 150; *El Sombrero,* Autopista Santiago-Puerto Plata; *Terraza La Carpa,* Av. John F. Kennedy; *Madrid,* very good value; *Cafetería Los Bonilla,* La Javilla, highly rec., *merengue* players visit it most evenings. *La Canasta,* 2 blocks N of main square, good for lunches; *Pepe Postre* bakery chain in Puerto Plata/Sosúa area, good breads, yoghurt, etc. Also rec. are *Café Terminus* (where you can get info. on horseback safaris), *El Cable; La Paella; Wienerwald, Infratur* and the *Beach Club Restaurant,* all at Long Beach.

Motorcycle hire, US$9 a day, from Trixxy Rent-a-Car.

Just E of Puerto Plata is the new beach resort of **Playa Dorada** with an exceptional golf course. *Jack Tar Village* hotel, L, all inclusive, T 586-3800, US style and US prices; *Playa Dorada* (use the Club Playa snack bar next door to save money), *Dorado Naco Resort,* L; *Villas Doradas Resort Hotel; Villas Caraibe,* L. Further E is Cabarate, with rooms, D, for rent above restaurants, good restaurant *Tipi del Indio de Pluma Roja,* and fine windsurfing, frequented by French Canadians.

Still further E is **Sosúa,** which has an excellent beach in a small bay, very good for diving and water sports (but latest reports say the beach is dirty); *público* from Puerto Plata, US$1. Also popular among Europeans and French Canadians. The unusually European atmosphere stems from the Jewish refugees who settled here in 1940.

Hotels *Sosuamar,* in the hills overlooking Sosúa; *Club Náutico; Sosúa Caribbean Fantasy; Casa Marina Beach Club,* C, ocean views, pool, private beach, restaurant, excellent value. *Playa Chiquita Beach Resort,* Batey, D (Domitel chain), highly rec. for food, accommodation and service, but not close to a beach; *One Ocean Place,* A, El Batey; *Sosuasol,* D, in El Batey.

Restaurants *La Roca, El Coral, El Oasis, Pizzería Roma III, Sosuasol* in El Batey and *Le Bistró* in Charamicos (where you still can find accommodation in the D range).

At one point the old road passes La Cumbre, which used to be a Trujillo mansion, but is now the property of the Secretariat of Agriculture. Still further to the east is **Río San Juan,** a friendly town with a lagoon called Gri-Gri and the fine Playa Grande beach. *Público* from Puerto Plata, US$2.50. Best hotel *Río San Juan,* C, on main street, also has a good restaurant (price includes a donkey tour; hotel also offers boat trips on the lagoon, with caves and rocks, rec.). Cheaper hotels: *San Martín* and *Caridad.* **Playa Grande,** 60 km. from Puerto Plata, is another beautiful new resort which is being developed, in conjunction with Playa Dorada, at a cost of many millions of dollars. Between Playa Grande and Samaná, on the coast, is **Nagua** (*Hotel-Restaurant China; Hotel Corazón de Jesús,* F). *Público* from Río San Juan to Nagua, US$1.50. The scenery along the northern coast from Sosúa to Samaná is exceptionally beautiful. The road is in good condition, apart from the stretch between Nagua and Sánchez (a pleasant, unspoilt little place with some basic accommodation).

On the peninsula of **Samaná** is the city of the same name. Santa Bárbara de Samaná was founded in 1756 with families expressly brought from the Canary Islands. The recently reconstructed city shows no evidence of this past, with its modern Catholic church, broad streets, new restaurants and hotels, and noisy motorcycle taxis. A new airport for the peninsula was recently opened (a long way from town).

Hotels *Bahia Beach Resort,* B, on a hill overlooking the bay, swimming pool, reservations: World Travel Center, Av. Bolivar 260, Santo Domingo, T 687-5053/5033; *Tropical Lodge,* on E exit along Malecón, B; *Nilka,* Santa Bárbara y Colón, E with a/c (less without downstairs), all with bath, popular; *Kiko,* behind Malecón, E with fan and bath, basic; *Casa de Huéspedes Tete de Casado,* Duarte 4, very friendly, good value (owner is a teacher). Some cheaper hotels (e.g. *Fortuna*) near the market.

Restaurants Going E along Malecón: *Típico El Coco, L'Hacienda,* grill and bar; *Le Café de Paris,* pizzeria, crêperie, cocktails; *La Mata Rosada, Camilo* (on corner of Parque), local and not-so-local food, reasonable (takes credit cards)—some are closed out of season. Chinese restaurant on the hill above *Kiko.* At the dock, *El Marino* and *La Serena.* Between the Malecón and market: *Quioli, Le Belge; Salt and Pepper.*

Other services Petrol station at the dock, open 0700-2200. Banco Hispano Dominicano on Malecón. Post Office behind *Camilo,* just off Parque; Codetel, Calle Santa Bárbara, 0800-2200 daily. Tourist information at Richard Tours at *Samaná Sam* sandwich bar and Samaná Information Service, both on Malecón, and closed out of season.

Communications with the capital either by bus direct, 4½ hrs. via San Francisco de Macorís (10 min. stop), Nagua and Sánchez (return bus to capital, Caribe Tours on Malecón, 0630, 0900, 1400), or by bus or *público* to San Pedro de Macorís, then another to Sabana la Mar (*Hotel Brisas de la Bahía,* E), and cross by boat (3 return trips a day, US$0.80 one way) from Sabana to Samaná; boats to Sabana from Samaná at 0700, 1000 and 1500. Road from Sabana la Mar to Hato Mayor is bad, but from Hato Mayor to San Pedro de Macorís (see below) it is excellent.

Excursions There are several beautiful offshore islands. Cayo Levantado is a popular picnic place, especially at weekends when the beach is littered. The white sand beach is nice, though, and there are good views of the bay and the peninsulas on either side. The hotel on the island is shut; drinks and fish lunches (not worth it) are for sale. Public boats go there from the dock in Samaná (US$0.65); alternatively, take a *público* out of town (US$0.50) to where two companies, Transportes José and Simi Báez, run boats to the island and will pick you up later for US$6.35 (the latter company also does fishing and whale-spotting trips). At the eastern end of the peninsula is Playa Galeras, 26 km., worth a visit. The whole peninsula is beautiful, but many beaches are accessible only by boat (and the Samaná boatmen charge the earth). Others are reached by a dirt road, negotiable by ordinary cars.

Visits to the Parque Nacional de Haitises, across the bay, can be arranged by launch.

On the north coast of the peninsula is **Las Terrenas,** a fine beach from which, at low tide, you can walk out to coral reefs to see abundant sea life. Note, though, that robberies have taken place here. Insect repellent is necessary at dawn and dusk to combat the sandflies. Many people go there by private plane, but it is reachable by private car from Sánchez. No petrol beyond Sánchez, but houses sell it in gallon jugs for US$0.80. **Hotels** *Punta Bonita,* C-A; *El Portillo Beach Club,* secluded, clean (part of Domitel chain), A full board with drinks included, good value; *Modus Vivendi,* D; *Las Palmas,* E; *Diny,* on the beach, E, with restaurant and dancing; bungalows to right of *Diny* as you face the sea are only a little more expensive (French-owned). Both *Chez Paco* and *Club Las Terrenas* are outstanding seafood restaurants on the beach.

About 25 km. E of Santo Domingo is the beach of Boca Chica, the principal resort for the capital. It is a reef-protected shallow lagoon, and has an excellent restaurant, *L'Horizon*. The Guayacanes and Embassy beaches, further E, are also popular, especially at weekends. Further E again is Juan Dolio (*Palmas de Mar*, US$60-80 for chalets; *Punta Garza* bungalows, B; *Hotel Playa Real*, B). Buses going to **San Pedro de Macorís,** a quiet town on the coast which is now being developed for tourism (*Hotel Macorís*, D, *Hotel Brisas de Higuamo*, central, dirty, noisy, poor) will drop you, and pick you up again, at the turn-off to the beaches. E of San Pedro is **La Romana** (*Casa de Campo*, hotel, villas and country club with many sporting facilities in 7,000 acres, prices start at US$95, low season; *Club Dominicus*, a 2,000-acre beach resort with cottages, villas and sports facilities; cheaper is the brand-new *Puerto Laguna*. *Hotel Romana*, A; *Roma*, much cheaper, E; *Pensión de Aza*, Parque Duarte; *Pensión Verónica*, Calle Santa Rosa). Nelly Veerman from Volendam, Holland says that the village of Bayahibe is well worth a visit. La Romana can be reached by air and by bus from Santo Domingo (US$2). An international artists' village in mock-Italian style has been established at Altos de Chavón, near La Romana, in a spectacular hilltop setting; there is a free bus every 15 minutes from *Casa de Campo*. There are a hotel here, and two restaurants. Further E is **Boca de Yuma,** an interesting fishing village which is the scene of a deep-sea fishing tournament every year. A recently repaved road runs from Boca de Yuma inland to Higüey; along this, about 2 km. N of San Rafael de Yuma, is the restored residence of Ponce de León (1505-1508).

Higüey has the Basílica de Nuestra Señora de la Altagracia (patroness of the Republic), a very impressive modern building to which every year there is a pilgrimage on Jan. 21; the old 16th-century church is still standing. Plenty of cheap hotels on Calle Colón. Due E from Higüey, on the coast again, is **Punta Cana** which has some beautiful beaches; there is a Club Méditerranée, A, and the whole resort is almost complete. Continuing round the coast, there are many other beaches to be visited, with white sand and reef-sheltered water. Another new resort on the eastern tip, Bávaro Beach, has been opened, to which charter flights go (e.g. from Manchester, UK). Hotel rates A-L in high season, half board. Take a taxi from Higüey. If exploring the eastern tip, Spanish is essential. A road runs W from Higüey to Hato Mayor, via El Seibo; its first 30 km. to the El Pintado junction with the road from La Romana is dusty and in poor condition (unpaved). From here to El Seibo (16 km.) is good.

To the west of Santo Domingo is Haina, the country's main port. Further W one can visit **San Cristóbal** in the interior, the birthplace of the dictator Trujillo. Trujillo's home, the Casa de Caoba (now rapidly disintegrating, but open 0900-1700) may be reached by a Land-Rover bus from behind the market, though you may have to walk the last km., uphill. Nearby are La Toma pools for scenery and swimming. Hotels: *San Cristóbal*, D; *Constitución*, E.

From San Cristóbal the road runs W to Bani, "a much richer town than any other in Santo Domingo". Cheaper hotels to be found near the market on Máximo Gómez. Don't bother with the beach, better to carry on to Las Salinas and Barahona. At **Barahona** *Hotel Guarocuya* is particularly rec., being cheap, clean and on the beach, E for double room with fan, D with a/c; also *Hotel Barahona* on Calle Jaime Mora, *Cacique*, E, nice, and *Fenicia*, *Palace* and *Victoria*, all F; *Hotel Caribe*, E, basic, with an excellent open-air restaurant (*La Rocca*) next door. Those with a car can visit other, more remote, beaches from Barahona (public transport is very basic): all along the southern coast are many white sand beaches which offer the best snorkelling and scuba diving in the Republic. One such is San Rafael (about 40 mins. from Barahona) where there is a fresh-water swimming hole in the river at the end of the beach. There is a small, pleasant restaurant on the beach and it is possible to camp there. At weekends it gets very crowded. There are cool, fresh-water lagoons behind several of the other beaches on this stretch of coast. One must explore for oneself: the area is not developed for tourism, yet. It is scheduled for development when Punta Cana is finished. A new road S of Barahona is being built.

Inland from Barahona, near the Haitian border, is the salt-water, below-sea-level **Lake Enriquillo** with a wealth of wild life including crocodiles (best seen in the morning), iguanas and flamingoes. The iguanas can, however, only be seen on the largest island in the lake, the Cabritos National Park. To visit the lake it is best to have a car, though it is possible to get there by bus from Santo Domingo to Jimaní (US$5, La Experiencia and Riviera companies, the journey takes 8 hours) and getting off either at Los Ríos or at La Descubierta. From these places walk or hitch a lift to the lake. At Jimaní there are *Hotel Jimaní*, E, a bit run down, *Hotel Quisqueya*, F, shared bath, basic but clean, *Mellizos* facing the park, with bath, and 5-6 basic, low cost *dormitorios*.

For drivers, the road S of the Lake is under reconstruction while that to the N is reported bad. **La Descubierta**, at the NW end, is larger than Jimaní, has several *dormitorios*, a disco, and a celebrated *balneario* (swimming hole—highly rec.). It is the best place to stay for visiting the Lake. To get to the Isla Cabritos National Park, drive 4 km. SE of the town to La Zofrada. Below the road on a curve is a building where arrangements can be made (US$15 for 4 people). Bathe in the sulphur springs while you wait, or on the way back.

William E. Rainey, of Berkeley, Calif., writes: "The highway south from Barahona deteriorates considerably after Baoruco but is passable by passenger car. Between Baoruco and Enriquillo there is wet tropical forest with rushing mountain streams and fruit stands in little roadside settlements. At Enriquillo you enter the Barahona Peninsula lowlands and the terrain grows markedly drier. Continuing west from Oviedo to Pedernales the road is in good condition and the surrounding habitat, particularly near Pedernales, is tropical thorn scrub with abundant cacti growing on karstic limestone.

"The entire country is dotted with checkpoints adjacent to roadside military installations; at most of these the traffic is simply waved through. At checkpoint in Pedernales (perhaps because gringos were an anomaly there) there were brief interrogations each time we passed (with automatic weapons pointed at us by uniformed teenagers). The last time we passed this point, one of them initiated a detailed search of our gear. Fortunately, this entertainment was cut short by a senior officer who apologized. It was, on balance, a minor aggravation, but one likely to be experienced by travellers near the Haitian border."

San Juan de la Maguana is further from the Haitian border (*Hotel Maguana*, D). Visit the Corral de Los Indios, an ancient Indian meeting ground several km. north of the town.

NB The staff of the *Santo Domingo News* recommend visiting the many swimming holes, *balnearios*, both in the towns and surrounding countryside. Among others try *Bayaguana* about 1 hr. NE of Santo Domingo; *La Descubierta* north of Lake Enriquillo near the Haitian border; *Loma de Cabrera* south of Dajabón; and *La Confluencia* in the attractive town of Jarabacoa in the centre of the island.

THE ECONOMY

The land area is 4.8m hectares, of which 12% is forest and woodland, 30% arable land and 44% pasture. Agriculture provides work for about 42% of the labour force, compared with 20% in manufacturing and 3.5% in construction. About 25% are unemployed. There are six main agricultural regions: the north, the Cibao valley in the north central area, Constanza and Tiero, the east, the San Juan valley, and the south. Cibao is the most fertile and largest region, while the eastern region is the main sugar producing area. Sugar is the main crop and largest export item. Until 1984, the US import quota system, of which the Dominican Republic was the largest beneficiary, provided a preferential market for over half the country's sugar exports as well as a cushion against the slump in world sugar prices. Major adjustments in US consumption patterns, particularly the switch by Coca Cola and Pepsi to High Fructose Corn Syrup, prompted the USA to cut quotas drastically. By 1988, the Dominican Republic's quota had been cut to 25% of previous levels. The Government is encouraging diversification of some cane lands to other crops.

Since 1975 gold and silver mining has been of considerable importance. The Pueblo Viejo mine's oxide ores are expected to be exhausted by 1990, but there are undeveloped reserves of sulphide ores, believed to contain 60m tonnes of gold-bearing ore. The country also produces ferronickel, which is the third largest export earner. Reserves are estimated at 10% of total world deposits.

The largest foreign exchange earner nowadays is, however, tourism, with annual receipts of over US$550m. New hotel projects brought the number of hotel rooms to 15,000 in 1988, compared with 11,000 in 1987 and this was expected soon to rise to 22,000 rooms. Stopover arrivals rose by 20% in 1987 to 940,000.

In the first half of the 1980s, a combination of fiscal and external account problems brought about a sharp decline in the rate of gdp growth and led the Government to turn to the IMF for financial assistance. The Government agreed to reduce its fiscal deficit and take a number of other austerity measures, including a gradual devaluation of the peso. It failed to meet targets, so the programme was suspended in early 1984. Government measures to remove subsidies, as part of the austerity package agreed with the IMF, led to riots in Santo Domingo in April 1984. Negotiations with the Fund were finally resumed and a one year standby loan facility worth SDR78.5 m was approved in April 1985 but not renewed because of political opposition. The Government renegotiated its debts to foreign commercial banks, although persistent low world prices for its major export commodities made debt servicing commitments increasingly burdensome.

	1961-70 (av)	1971-80 (av)	1981-85 (av)	1986-88 (av)
Gdp growth (1980 prices)	5.0%	6.9%	1.5%	5.1%
Inflation	1.9%	10.4%	16.2%	20.6%
Exports (fob) US$m	170	657	869	770
Sugar	88	262	318	140
Doré	-	100 (a)	156	110
Imports (fob)m	165	747	1,307	1,480
Current account balance US$m (cum)	-419	-2,158	-1,521	-600

(a) = 1975-80

INFORMATION FOR VISITORS

How to get there   American, Eastern, Pan Am and Dominicana fly to Miami and New York Dominicana (US$89 return), American (US$110) and Eastern fly to San Juan, and Iberia, Viasa, Copa and Dominicana fly to Central and South America. Iberia flies to Madrid 6 times a week; Lufthansa flies from Frankfurt twice a week (once via Antigua, continuing to San Juan); Air France from Paris twice a week (via Martinique or Guadeloupe). From the new international airport at Puerto Plata there are flights to Miami, New York and Puerto Rico by American, Continental and Dominicana, also to Toronto, Turks and Caicos, Haiti and Caracas. Many charters from Montreal and Toronto; also from Italy. ALM flies to the Netherlands Antilles six times a week (Aruba Air twice a week to Aruba). There are cargo and passenger shipping services with New York, New Orleans, Miami and South American countries. Many cruise lines from USA, e.g. Commodore Cruise line from Miami. A daily ferry from San Pedro de Macorís to Mayagüez, Puerto Rico was due for reintroduction at the end of 1988.

Documents   Citizens of the following countries do not need a tourist card to enter the Dominican Republic: Argentina, Costa Rica, Curaçao, Denmark, Ecuador, Israel, Italy, Japan, Spain, Sweden, Switzerland, Uruguay, UK, West Germany. All others need a tourist card, which costs US$10, purchased either from airlines or at the airport on arrival. Extensions obtainable from Immigration, Huacal Building. Citizens of communist countries need a consular visa, which takes time to get. Check all entry requirements in advance if possible.

All visitors should have an outward ticket. The airport police are on the lookout for illegal drugs. There is a departure tax of US$10.

Currency   The effective rate of exchange of the Dominican peso (RD$) to US dollar was US$1 = RD$6.40 in May 1989. In 1988, new legislation outlawed all exchange transactions except those in banks and large hotels approved by the Central Bank. You will be given a receipt and, with this, you can change remaining pesos back into dollars at the end of your visit. Most European currencies can be changed at the Banco de la Reserva (and some other banks). Illegal exchange houses still operate, but no receipt will be given, and money changers on the street approach foreigners (do *not* use them). The Dominican peso is the only legal tender.

Travel To Haiti   No special permit is needed, just a passport or visa (check if you need one, US$12, takes a day). Haitian Embassy, Calle Scout 11 Sd, Santo Domingo, T 562-3519. By plane to Port-au-Prince takes ½ hr., US$50 approx; by bus US$40 from *Hotel San Tomé*, Calle Santomé, beside Mercado Modelo, Santo Domingo (T 688-5100, ask for Alejandro).

Internal Travel Agencia Portillo offers air taxi services to Puerto Plata and Punta Cana, US$32 including transfers and a meal, Herrera airport, T565-3927/0832. Hitchhiking is perfectly possible, though bus (*guagua*) services between most towns are efficient and inexpensive.

There are usually fixed *público* rates between cities, so inquire first. Many drivers pack a truly incredible number of passengers in their cars, so the ride is often not that comfortable. If travelling by private taxi, bargaining is very important.

Buses Autobuses Metro operates from Av. Winston Churchill and Hatuey, near 27 de Febrero and has buses to La Vega, Santiago, Puerto Plata, the airport, Nagua, Azua, San Juan and other points. Terrabus, Plaza Criolla, Av. 27 de Febrero y Máximo Gómez (also Restauración y Juan Pablo Duarte in Santiago, and 30 de Marzo y Duarte in Puerto Plata) offers the most luxurious service for only slightly higher fares; their service to Santiago offers hostesses and refreshments (US$6). A third company, Caribe Tours, operates from Av. 27 de Febrero at Leopoldo Navarro (and Av. Sadhalá in Santiago); most of their services (cheaper than Metro) are in air-conditioned buses, recommended (US$2.25 Santo Domingo-Santiago); they run to all parts except E of Santo Domingo. In the capital buses leave from Parque Enriquillo (Av. Duarte and Ravelo) for the east: Higüey (US$1.50), Nagua, San Francisco de Macorís, Miches, etc. Expresos Moto Saad, Av. Independencia near Parque Independencia runs 12 daily buses to La Vega.

Driving A valid driving licence from your country of origin or an international licence is accepted. Dominicans drive on the right. The speed limit for city driving is 60 kph and on main roads 80 kph. Service stations close at 1800. Cars driven by tourists can expect to be stopped by the police at the entrance to and exit from towns (normally brief and courteous). Local drivers can be erratic; be on the alert. There are tolls on all principal roads out of the capital. Road signs are very poor: a detailed map is essential, plus a knowledge of Spanish for asking directions. Look out for unmarked "sleeping policemen" in all towns.

Customs Duty-free import of 200 cigarettes or one box of cigars, plus one opened bottle of alcoholic liquor, is permitted. Military-type clothing and food products will be confiscated on arrival. Currency in excess of US$5,000 may not be taken out of the country without special permission.

Health It is not advisable to drink tap water. All hotels have bottled water. It is also advisable to avoid the midday sun.

Electricity 110 volts, 60 cycles A.C. current. There are frequent power cuts, so take a torch with you when you go out at night. Many establishments have their own (noisy) generators.

Tipping A 10% service charge is added to all hotel and restaurant bills, however it is customary to give an extra tip in restaurants, depending on service. Porters receive US$0.50 per bag; taxi drivers, *público* drivers and garage attendants are not usually tipped.

Note In Santo Domingo, on the beaches and at other tourist attractions, visitors will be approached by unofficial guides, sellers of rum, women or black market pesos. The last three are undoubtedly a rip-off and probably the only value in taking an unofficial guide is to deter others from pestering you (similarly, hiring a lounger on the beach). Be prepared to say "no" a lot.

Beware of drug-pushers on the Malecón in Santo Domingo.

Food and Drink Local beers, Presidente, Bohemia and Quisqueya, are excellent. There are also many good rums. Imported drinks are very expensive. Local dishes include *sancocho* (a type of stew made of local meats and vegetables, often including *plátanos*, *ñame* and *yautia*), *mondongo* (a tripe stew), *mofongo*, ground *plátano* with garlic and *chicharrón* (crackling), usually served with a soup, a side dish of meat and avocado (very filling), *cocido* (a soup of chickpeas, meat and vegetables), *chivo* (goat). The salads are often good; another good side dish is *tostones* (fried and flattened *plátanos*). *Quipes* (made of flour and meat) and *pastelitos* (fried dough with meat or cheese inside) can be bought from street vendors; can be risky. Also try *pipián*, goats' offal served as a stew. The traveller should be warned that Dominican food is rather on the greasy side; most of the dishes are fried. Local food can often be obtained from private houses, which act as *comedores*. Basic prices, US$3-6. There are excellent cigars at very reasonable prices.

Music and Dance The most popular dance is the *merengue*, which dominates the musical life of the Dominican Republic; other dances are the *mangulina*, the *salve* and the *carabiné*. The traditional *merengue* is played by a 3-man group called a *perico ripiao* which consists of a *tambora* (small drum), a *guirra* (a percussion instrument scraped by a metal rod) and an accordion. There is a *merengue* festival in the last week of July and the first week of August, held on the Malecón in Santo Domingo, great fun.

Banks Bank of Nova Scotia at Santo Domingo, Santiago, and Puerto Plata. The Chase Manhattan Bank, Santo Domingo and Santiago. Citibank, Santo Domingo and Santiago; Banco Universal, Banco Popular, Banco de la Reserva, nationwide.

Business Hours Shops: 0830-1200/1230; 1430-1800/1830, or 0930-1730 Mon.-Fri.; 0800-1300 Sat. Banks: 0800-1730 Mon.-Fri. Government offices 0730-1430.

Newspapers The best daily papers are *Listín Diario, El Caribe* and *Hoy*, the afternoon tabloids *Ultima Hora* and *Nacional* have the widest circulation. There are 9 daily papers in all. English-language *Santo Domingo News*, published every Wednesday and available at hotels.

Broadcasting There are many local radio stations and 5 television stations. Also 2 cable TV stations broadcasting in English.

Maps Publicaciones Triunfo has map of the Dominican Republic, with plans of Santo Domingo, Santiago, Puerto Plata and Sosúa. Texaco also produce a good (Rand McNally) map of the country, capital and Santiago. A set of five (US$11) covering the whole country can be got at Instituto Geográfico Universitario, El Conde with Las Damas.

US Embassy and Consulate, César Nicolás Penson; T (embassy) 682-2171; (consulate) 689-2111; **UK**, Independencia 506, T 682-3128; **West Germany**, J.T. Majía y Calle 37, T 565-8811; **France**, George Washington 353, T 689-2161; **Netherlands**, John F. Kennedy, T 566-1111.

Public Holidays Jan. 1: New Year's Day. Jan 6: Epiphany. Jan 21: Our Lady of Altagracia. Jan 26: Duarte Day. Feb. 27: Independence Day. Good Friday. Corpus Christi (60 days after Good Friday). May 1: Labour Day. Aug 16: Restoration Day. Sept 24: Our Lady of Las Mercedes. Dec. 25: Christmas.

Fiestas Santo Domingo, Carnival between Feb. 26 and 2 March; Year-end celebration Dec. 22-Jan. 2.

Churches Roman Catholicism is the predominant religion. There are also Episcopalian, Baptist, Seventh Day Adventist, Presbyterian and Methodist Churches in the main towns. There is a synagogue on Av. Sarasota, Santo Domingo; call Israeli Embassy (533-7359) for details of services. Voodoo, technically illegal, is tolerated and practised mostly in the western provinces.

Postal Services Don't use post boxes, they are unreliable. Postcard to Europe, 1 peso; recommended to use *entrega especial* (special delivery, with separate window at post offices), for 2 pesos extra, on overseas mail.

Telephones are operated by the Compañia Dominicana de Teléfonos. All local calls and overseas calls to the Caribbean, US and Canada may be dialled directly from Santo Domingo. For 'phone boxes you need two 5-centavo coins or one 10-centavo coin. Phone calls to the USA cost US$7.85, to Europe US$8.50 and to Australia US$9.60.

Weights and Measures Officially the metric system is used but business is often done on a pound/yard/US gallon basis.

We are most grateful to Lic. Leoncio Crespo, Director of International Relations, Secretaría de Estado de Turismo, and Sabrina Cambiaso of the Tourist Office for their assistance in the preparation of this chapter. Ben Box would also like to thank Dania Goris of *Ultima Hora* for her help and hospitality in Santo Domingo in October 1988. Thanks are also due to the following travellers: Ulrich Bähringer (Krefeld, W. Ger.), Michael Beck (Schweinfurt, W. Ger.), Blair Federico Bertaccini (Southbury, CT), Teresa H. Castro (San Francisco, CA), Jan Jacob de Groot (Vroomshoop, Neth.), James Maas (Bocas del Toro, Panama), Wolfgang Reichert and Annette Karling (Kulmbach, W. Ger.), Florian Schulz (Berlin 27), Martin Schützler and Pauline and David Tither (Silver Spring, Md) for most useful information.

PUERTO RICO

THE COMMONWEALTH OF PUERTO RICO, the smallest and most easterly island of the Greater Antilles, is the first Overseas Commonwealth Territory (defined as a "free and associated State") of the USA. Spanish is the first language but the citizenship is US and English is widely spoken. Puerto Rico lies about 1,600 km. south-east of Miami between the island of Hispaniola and the Virgin Islands, which give it some shelter from the open Atlantic, and is between longitudes 66° and 67° west and at latitude 18°30 north.

Almost rectangular in shape, slightly smaller than Jamaica, it measures 153 km. in length (east to west), 58 km. in width, and has a total land area of some 8,768 square km.

Old volcanic mountains, long inactive, occupy a large part of the interior of the island, with the highest peak, Cerro de Punta, at 1,325 metres in the Cordillera Central. North of the Cordillera is the karst country where the limestone has been acted upon by water to produce a series of small steep hills and deep holes, both conical in shape. The mountains are surrounded by a coastal plain with the Atlantic shore beaches cooled all the year round by trade winds, which make the temperatures of 28-30°C bearable in the summer. Temperatures in the winter drop to the range 21-26°C and the climate all the year round is very agreeable.

The population is 3.3 million; half of them live in urban areas. The country is a strange mixture of very new and very old, exhibiting the open American way of life yet retaining the more formal Spanish influences. The people are very friendly and hospitable but there is crime, probably because of economic difficulties and unemployment.

History   Puerto Rico was discovered by Columbus, accompanied by a young nobleman, Juan Ponce de León, on November 19, 1493. Attracted by tales of gold, Ponce obtained permission to colonize Borinquén, as it was called by the natives. In 1508 he established the first settlement at Caparra, a small village not far from the harbour of San Juan. A year later the Spanish Crown appointed him the first Governor. In 1521, however, the settlement was moved to the present site of Old San Juan as the former site was declared unhealthy. In that year Ponce de León was mortally wounded in the conquest of Florida.

Because of Puerto Rico's excellent location at the gateway to Latin America, it played an important part in defending the Spanish empire against attacks from French, English and Dutch invaders. After the Spanish-American war, Spain ceded the island to the United States in 1898. The inhabitants became US citizens in 1917, with their own Senate and House of Delegates, and in 1948, for the first time, they elected their own Governor, who is authorized to appoint his Cabinet and members of the island's Supreme Court. In 1952 Puerto Rico became a Commonwealth voluntarily associated with the United States.

Government   The Governor (1988-92) is Sr Rafael Hernández Colón of the Popular Democratic Party, which favours the island's existing Commonwealth status. The other main party is the New Progressive Party, which favours Puerto Rico's full accession to the USA as the 51st state. Pro-independence groups receive little support. Puerto Ricans do not vote in US federal elections, nor do they pay federal taxes, when resident on the island.

Flora and Fauna
Although less than 1% of the island is virgin forest, there are several forest reserves designed to protect plants and wildlife. In El Yunque tropical rain forest there are an estimated 240 types of plants and trees, including 1,000 year-old redwood trees, tiny wild orchids, bamboo trees, giant ferns, and trumpet trees. It is also home to the Pueto Rican parrot, which has been saved from extinction. Mangroves are protected in Aguirre Forest, on the south coast near Salinas, and at Piñones Forest, east of San Juan. The largest number of bird species can be found at Guánica

PUERTO RICO
Not to Scale 180

Forest, west of Ponce, which is home to several unique and endangered species. Most of the trails through these and other forests are unmarked, so it is advisable to contact the wardens for directions before wandering off. One of the most notable creatures on Puerto Rico is the inch-long tree frog called a *coquí*, after the two-tone noise it makes at night.

San Juan   Founded in 1510, San Juan, the capital (population about 1 million) spreads several km. along the North coast and also inland. The nucleus is Old San Juan, the old walled city on a tongue of land between the Atlantic and San Juan bay. It has a great deal of charm and character; the Institute of Culture restores and renovates old buildings, museums and places of particular beauty. The narrow streets of Old San Juan, some paved with small grey-blue blocks which were cast from the residues of iron furnaces in Spain and brought over as ships' ballast, are lined with colonial churches, houses and mansions, in a very good state of repair.

Some of the restored and interesting buildings to visit include La Fortaleza, the Governor's Palace, built between 1533 and 1540 as a fortress against Carib attacks but greatly expanded in the 19th century (open 0900-1600 Mon-Fri; guided tours in English every hour, in Spanish every half-hour, T 721 7000 ext 2211); the Cathedral, built in the 16th century but extensively restored in the 19th and 20th, in which the body of Juan Ponce de León rests in a marble tomb (open daily 0630-1700); the tiny Cristo Chapel with its silver altar, built after a young man competing in 1753 in a horse-race during the San Juan festival celebrations plunged with his horse over the precipice at that very spot (open Tues. 1000-1600); San Felipe del Morro, built in 1591 to defend the entrance to the harbour, and the 11-hectare Fort San Cristóbal, completed in 1772 to support El Morro and to defend the landward side of the city, with its five independent units connected by tunnels and dry moats, rising 46 metres above the ocean (open daily 0800-1800, admission US$1, children free); the Dominican Convent built in the early 16th century, later used as a headquarters by the US Army and now the office of the Institute of Culture, with a good art gallery (Chapel museum open Wed.-Sun., 0900-1200, 1300-1600; Popular Arts Museum open Mon.-Sat., 0915-1615, T 7240700); the 16th-century San José church, the second oldest church in the western hemisphere and once the family church of Ponce de León's descendants, Ponce was buried here until moved to the Cathedral in the 20th century (open Mon.-Fri., 1000-1600, Sun. 1130-1600, Sun. mass at 1200); the early 18th century Casa de los Contrafuertes, believed to be the oldest private residence in the old city, now has periodic art exhibitions on the second floor (open Wed.-Sun., 0900-1200, 1300-1600, T 724 5949); the Casa Blanca, built in 1523 by the family of Ponce de León, who lived in it for 250 years until it became the residence of the Spanish and then the US military commander-in-chief, and is now a historical museum which is well worth a visit (open 0900-1200, 1300-1630, except Mon.); guided tours Tues.-Sat., T 724 4102); the Alcaldía, or City Hall, built 1604-1789 (open Mon.-Fri. 0800-1600 except holidays, T 724 7171 ext 2391); the Intendencia, formerly the Spanish colonial exchequer, a fine example of 19th century Puerto Rican architecture, now houses Puerto Rico's State Department (open Mon.-Fri. 0800-1200, 1300-1630, T 722 2121); the naval arsenal was the last place in Puerto Rico to be evacuated by the Spanish in 1898, exhibitions are held in three galleries (open Wed.-Sun., 0900-1200, 1300-1600, T 724 5949); and the Casa del Callejón, a restored 18th-century house containing two colonial museums, the architectural (Tues.-Sun., 0900-1200, 1300-1600, T 725 5250) and the Puerto Rican Family (closed for restoration). The university campus has beautiful gardens and architecture.

Museums   Apart from those in historic buildings listed above, there are the Pablo Casals Museum beside San José church, with Casals' cello and other memorabilia (Tues.-Sat. 0930-1700, Sun. 1200-1700, T 723 9185); the San Juan Museum of Art and History, built in 1855 as a marketplace (open Mon.-Fri., 0900-1200, 1300-1700, Sat.-Sun., 1000-1200, 1300-1700); the Casa del Libro in an 18th century house, has a collection of rare books, including some over 400 years old (Mon.-Sat. 1100-1630, T 723 0354); and the Museum of the Sea on Pier One, with a collection of maritime instruments and models (open when the pier is open for cruise ships, T 725 2532).

OLD SAN JUAN
Not to Scale 181

Other museums include a military museum at Fort San Jerónimo (open Wed.-Sun., 0900-1200, 1300-1630, T 724 5949); the Ponce de León Museum at Caparra, Puerto Rico's first Spanish settlement, which has many exhibits from the period when the Taino Indians inhabited the place (open 0900-1700, closed Sun.); and the Adolfo de Hostos archaeological museum behind the Tapiá theatre on Plaza Colón (in the old public baths, open Tues.-Sat. 1000-1700, Sun. 1200-1900).

The metropolitan area of San Juan includes the more modern areas of Santurce, Hato Rey, and Río Piedras. Río Piedras was founded in 1714 but became incorporated into San Juan in 1951. On the edge of Río Piedras, the gardens and library of the former governor, Luis Muñoz Marín, are open to the public, with a museum showing his letters, photos and speeches.

The University of Puerto Rico at Río Piedras is in a lovely area. The University Museum (open Mon.-Fri., 0900-2100, weekends 0900-1500, T 764 0000, ext 2452) has archaeological and historical exhibitions, and also monthly art exhibitions. The Botanical Garden at the Agricultural Experiment Station has over 200 species of tropical and sub-tropical plants, a bamboo promenade, an orchid garden, and a lotus lagoon (open Tues.-Sun., 0900-1630, T 766 0740).

Hato Rey is the financial district of San Juan, nicknamed "the Golden Mile". The Sacred Heart University is in Santurce, as is the modern Fine Arts Centre, opened in 1981, which has theatres and halls at the corner of De Diego and Ponce de León (T 724 4751). The residential area Miramar has several moderately priced hotels as well as some expensive ones. Miramar is separated from the Atlantic coast by the Condado lagoon and the Condado beach area, where the luxury hotels, casinos, night clubs and restaurants are concentrated.

Directions Up until the 1950s tramcars ran between Río Piedras and Old San Juan along Avs Ponce de León and Fernández Juncos. To this day directions are given by Paradas, or tram stops, so you have to find out where each one is.

Excursions A ferry ride crosses every half-hour, 0615-2200, US$10, to Cataño where you can catch a *público* (US$1 pp) to the Bacardi rum distillery. There are free conducted tours around the plant Mon.-Sat., 0930-1530, travelling from one building to the next by a little open motor train.

On Sun. and holidays at 1430 and 1630 there are trips around the bay lasting 1½ hours, adults US$2.50, children US$1.25. The boat passes the city wall, the San Juan gate and La Fortaleza. Another boat trip is around the Torrecilla Lagoon, which takes 2 hours and shows passengers the mangrove forests and the bird sanctuary. *La Paseadora* launch carries 30 passengers and has tours on weekends and holidays beginning at 1200 (T 791 0755).

On Route 2, shortly before Bayamón, is the island's earliest settlement, Caparra, established by Ponce de León in 1508. Ruins of the fort can still be seen and there is a Museum of the Conquest and Colonization of Puerto Rico (open Mon.-Fri. 0900-1700 and weekends 1000-1800, T 781 4795).

Isla Grande, to the west of Miramar, was once a US naval base but now houses government offices, an airport and the Club Náutico. There are also many migratory and sea birds.

The Interior

Out of the metropolitan area "on the island" are a variety of excursions; as it is a small island it is possible to see forested mountains and desert-like areas in only a short time. However, because the public transport system is rather limited, it is difficult if not impossible to visit some places without your own car. The cool climate in the mountains has caused resort hotels to be built in several towns inland.

An interesting round trip through the eastern half of the island, starting E from San Juan, is as follows: San Juan-Río Piedras (there are *públicos* between these two places, US$1.85)-Fajardo-El Yunque-Vieques-Culebra-Humacao-Yabucoa-Guayama (again it seems that you can get from Humacao to Guayama by a series of *públicos*, the whole journey costing about US$2.50)-Cayey-Aibonito-Barranquitas-Bayamón-San Juan. A variant between San Juan and El Yunque takes you on Route 187 from Isla Verde, outside San Juan, to Loíza along an unspoilt stretch of the N coast.

Fajardo is a boating centre with several marinas and a public beach at Seven Seas. Offshore is an uninhabited, but much visited, coral island, Icacos. You can camp at Seven Seas Beach, but call T 722 1551 first.

El Yunque (also called the Caribbean National Forest) is a tropical forest of 11,200 hectares with some 240 varieties of trees. The whole area is a bird sanctuary. Trails (very stony) to the various peaks: El Yunque (The Anvil) itself, Mount Britton, Los Picachos. In view of the heavy rainfall, another name for the forest is Rain Forest. Visitors need not worry unduly, as storms are usually brief and plenty of shelter is provided. (No buses through the national forests, unfortunately; El Yunque is reached via Route 3 from San Juan towards Fajardo, and then right on Route 191.) A narrow-gauge steam railway offers a different mode of travel from Fajardo to El Yunque on Sun., taking an hour for the return journey. Adults US$1.75 and children US$1.25.

The quiet, unspoilt offshore islands of ***Vieques*** and ***Culebra*** can be reached daily by air from Isla Grande airport, San Juan, ½ hour, about US$15,—by air from Fajardo, 10 minutes., US$10, or by launch from Fajardo beach, 1¾ hours, US$2.50. On Vieques the main settlement is Isabel Segunda, with an attractive square and the last fort built by Spain in the Americas. There are fine beaches. The public beach of Sun Bay has picnic and camping areas. Blue Beach on the south coast is good for snorkelling. Motorcycles can be hired. Culebra's main village, Dewey (called Pueblo by the locals) is attractively set between two lagoons, with *Seafarer's Inn*, and houses to let; bicycles can be hired at US$2 a day; there are also good beaches. A visitor's information centre is in the City Hall. Prices rise steeply at weekends. The Culebra National Wildlife Refuge protects large colonies of sea birds, particularly terns and boobies. The islands can also be reached from the US Virgin Islands.

One of the prettiest parts of Puerto Rico, which should be visited, lies S of Humacao, between Yabucoa and Guayama. Here are the villages of Patillas (*público* from Guayama, US$0.50) and Maunabo (*público* from Patillas, US$0.65 and from Yabucoa, US$0.65) where you can camp on the beach. There is a bar which sells good, cheap food.

A round trip through the western half of the island would take in Ponce, the second city (reached by motorway from San Juan via Caguas), Guánica, Parguera, San Germán, Boquerón, Mayagüez (the third city), Aguadilla, Quebradillas and Arecibo, with side trips to the Maricao State Forest and fish hatchery, the Río Abajo State Forest and Lake Dos Bocas (launch trips all day), the precolumbian ceremonial ball-park near Utuado (open 0900-1700, free), and the Arecibo observatory (open Sun. pm, but there is no public transport, so you have to hitchhike from Arecibo).

Off the motorway which runs from San Juan to Ponce is Baños de Coamo, which was once the island's most fashionable resort. (Take Route 153 and then 546 from the motorway.) It has been redeveloped by Paradores Puertorriqueños and still has a thermal bath. About 45 minutes southeast of Coamo is Salinas, a fishing and farming centre. There are several good seafood restaurants on the waterfront.

Ponce has a very fine art museum, donated by a foundation established by Luis A. Ferré (Governor 1968-72) in a modern building now famous. It contains a representative collection of European and American art of the last five centuries. (Open 1000-1200, 1300-1600, Mon. and Wed.-Fri., 1000-1600 Sat., 1000-1700 Sun. and holidays, closed Tues.; entry US$2.50 for adults, US$1.50 for children under 12.) The cathedral is also worth a look, and so is the polychromatic fire-station, built for a fair in 1883 and now used by the information office. *Público* to Guayama, US$2.50. The walkway next to the Yacht and Fishing Club is a good place to be at the weekend: good atmosphere.

A short drive away on Route 503 is the Tibes Indian Ceremonial Centre. There is an ancient Indian burial ground, seven ball courts and two dance grounds, a replica of a Taino village and a small museum, open Tues.-Sun. 0900-1630. Admission US$1.00 for adults, US$0.50 for children; bilingual guides.

Going W from Ponce is Parguera, a fishing village, and nearby is Phosphorescent Bay, an area of phosphorescent water, occurring through a permanent population of minescent dinoflagellates, a tiny form of marine life, which produce sparks of chemical light when disturbed. One hour boat trips round the bay depart between 1930 and 0030, hourly departures, the experience is said to be rather disappointing, however. Further W is Guánica, the place where American troops first landed in the Spanish-American war. It has an old fort from which there are excellent views.

Mayagüez has fine botanical gardens, at the Tropical Agricultural Research Station, near the University of Puerto Rico: well worth visiting, free admission, open Mon.-Fri., 0730-1630. The city also has an interesting zoo; open Tues.-Sun., 0900-1630, adults US$1, children US$0.50. *Públicos* leave from a modern terminal in Calle Peral. The tourist office is in the Municipalidad on Plaza Colón.
Mona Island, 50 miles west of Mayagüez, is fascinating for historians and nature lovers, but can only be reached by chartered boat or plane. Originally inhabited by Taino Indians and then by pirates and privateers, it is now deserted except for its wildlife. Here you can see three-foot iguanas, colonies of sea birds and bats in the caves. 200-foot high cliffs are dotted with caves, ascending to a flat table top covered with dry forest. The island is managed by the Department of National Resources (T 722 1726), who have cabins to rent with prior permission. Camping is allowed at Sardinena Beach, US$1.00 per night. There are no restaurants or facilities. Take all your food and water with you and bring back all your rubbish.

San Germán has much traditional charm; it was the second town to be founded on the island and has preserved its colonial atmosphere. The beautiful little Porta Coeli chapel on the plaza contains a small museum of religious art. (Open 0900-1200, 1400-1600.) A university town: it can be difficult to get cheap accommodation in term time.

As there is a large forest area, there are several excursions to various countryside resorts. The Maricao State Forest (Monte del Estado) is open from 0600 to 1800, and is a beautiful forest with magnificent views. Also the views are marvellous at the Toro Negro State Forest, open from 0800 to 1700, and further north-east at Río Abajo State Forest (open 0600-1800) where there is a swimming pool and various picnic spots. It is approached through splendid views of the karst hills and the Dos Bocas Lake. Free launch trips are offered on this lake at 0700, 1000, 1400 and 1700; they last two hours and are provided by the Public Works Department. The Caguana Indian Ceremonial Park, near Utuado, dates from about 1100 AD, and contains Taino ball courts and monoliths. It is believed to be a site of some religious significance and has been restored with a museum in the landscaped park. On route 111, Km. 12.3, open 0900-1700, admission free. Nearby, the Rio Camuy Cave Park, on Route 129, Km. 19.8, is a fascinating cave network with sinkholes, an underground river and a cave developed for visitors. There are fine examples of stalactites, stalagmites, and of course, plenty of bats: very impressive. Admission US$4 for adults, US$2.50 for children, T 756 5555 because entry is limited. A private devlopement is the Cueva de Camuy, on Route 486, Km. 11.1, popular with children because there are ponies, go-carts and a pool. Admission US$1 for adults and US$0.50 for children, guided tours; open Mon.-Fri. 0900-1700, Sat. 0900-1800, Sun. 0900-2200 (T 898 2723).

On the southern side of the W coast is **Boquerón** which has a good beach; there are cottages for rent and restaurants serving the local speciality, oysters. This is one of the cheapest spots on the island. Going N from here, through Mayagüez, you come to **Rincón**, on the westernmost point of the island. Here the mountains run down to the sea, and the scenery is spectacular. The town itself is unremarkable, but the nearby beaches are beautiful and the surfing is a major attraction. Several international windsurfing championships are held here. Humpbank whales visit in winter. There are cottages to rent and there is also accommodation in Rincón and the neighbouring village of Puntas (see below). There are also some small bars and restaurants, including *Danny's Café* in Rincón, a health food restaurant in Puntas and a pizzeria just N of Puntas. Rincón can be reached by *público* from Mayagüez or (less frequent) from Aguadillas. Public transport is scarce at weekends.

Hotels Most of the large San Juan hotels are in Condado or Isla Verde and overlook the sea, with swimming pools, night clubs, restaurants, shops and bars. The summer season runs from April 16 to December 14 and is somewhat cheaper than the winter season, for which we give rates where possible. A 6 % tax is payable on rooms costing more than US$5 a day. A full list is given in the monthly tourist guide, *Qué Pasa*, published by the Puerto Rican Tourism Company, but listed below is a selection. To get value for money, it may be advisable to avoid the luxury hotels on the sea front. There is plenty of cheaper accommodation within walking distance of the beaches. *Howard Johnson's*, 1369 Ashford, L; *Caribe Hilton*, Ocean Front, Puerta de Tierra, L, set in 17 acres of gardens, many sporting facilities; *Dutch Inn*, 55 Condado Av, Condado, L; *Du Pont Plaza*, 1309 Ashford Av, Condado, A; *Joffre*, Condado, cheaper, C, swimming pool, a/c, 2nd floor particularly noisy, reasonable bar and restaurant; *Condado Plaza Holiday Inn*, 999 Ashford Av., Condado, L; *Caribbean Beach Club*, Loíza and Jupiter, Isla Verde, A; *El San Juan*, Ocean Front, Isla Verde, A; *The Duffy's*, 9 Isla Verde Road, popular for its pub-like bar, B; *El Palmar*, Route 187, km. 0.3, Isla Verde, B, swimming pool. *La Casa Mathieson*, Uno Este 14, Isla Verde, near airport, B, swimming pool, cooking facilities, friendly, free transport to and from airport; *El Patio*, Tres Oeste 87, Bloque D-8, Villamar, swimming pool, use of kitchen, A, rec.; *Green Isle*, 36 Uno Este, Isla Verde, B, airport transport service. *Capri*, Fernández Juncos 902, basic and not very safe.

In Old San Juan, *El Convento*, a converted Carmelite nunnery, is a charming hotel with a Spanish atmosphere and the dining room is in the former chapel, L. Try Calle Luna for cheap accommodation: one block on the corner of San Justo has rooms that can be rented from US$40 a week (noisy from disco bar); enquire at the launderette next door. Guest house at Calle San Francisco 260, US$50 per week, T 723-3973. Information from Joyería Sol, Tanca 207. Fan, cooking and washing facilities, friendly and helpful. Also in Old San Juan are *La Fortaleza*, Fortaleza 252, B and *Central*, Plaza de Armas, C, quiet, satisfactory. *Linda*, Calle Tetuán, cheap, D; *La Bahía Guesthouse*, Sol 320, most rooms rented by the month but empty rooms can sometimes be taken on a daily basis, E, clean, hot water, rec. (telephone first, 722-4050). *San Francisco Inn*, San Francisco 263, C, popular among gays, small, friendly, clean and quiet. *Buena Vista Guesthouse by the Sea*, Gral Valle 2218, Sta Teresita, English, French spoken, A-B, near beach, airport pickup for US$1.

In Miramar, *Borinquén*, Fernández Juncos 725, Miramar, A; *Villa Firenze*, Avenida Miramar, C, much cheaper if rooms taken on a weekly basis, basic and not very clean, but runs good Italian restaurant; nearby, *El Toro*, C, good value, there is an airport limousine to *El Toro*.

In Santurce, *Los Dos Hermanos*, clean, bathroom shared with one other room, D, cheaper weekly rates. Several hotels around Plaza de Armas are in cheaper D range. There is a guesthouse on Calle Tetuán, near the bus station, which charges B per week, basic but share kitchen and bathroom.

In Ponce, *El Coche* and *Hotel Meliá*, rec. (both A), also the *Ponce Holiday Inn*, L, where there are tennis courts, pools, and golf arrangements made. Cheaper hotels round main square; *Hotelito Argentino*, Calle Luna, D, basic; *Hospedaje Mi Hogar*, F, very basic. *Sta Bárbara Guesthouse*, Calle Cristina, E. To the W of Ponce, at Guánica, *Cycle Center Youth Hostel*, E, cooking facilities.

At Barranquitas the *Barranquitas Resort Hotel*, 700 metres above sea level, offers a quiet mountain setting with golf, tennis, horse riding and swimming in a heated pool, B. In San Germán, *Oasis Hotel*, a parador, F; for room on top of Giuseppi's shop on main plaza, F. In Parguera, *Posada Porlamar*, a/c, kitchen facilities, B, good.

On Vieques, *Sportsman's House*, a former hacienda with pool and riding, and *La Casa del Francés*, near Esperanza, A; *Ocean View Guesthouse*, US-type motel, B, balconies on seafront; *Carmen*, C, very clean; *Alvarez*, D, and *Depakos* also reasonable.

On Culebra, *Seafarer's Inn*, B; *Posada La Hamaca*, C, well-kept; *Doña Coral* has four rooms, C.

On the E coast, *Palmas del Mar Hotel*, A, swimming pools and other sports. At Guayama, *Caribe*, E, clean; *España*, near square, F, noisy, dirty and very little privacy. At Arecibo, *El Cid*, D, about cheapest of all the hotels and guesthouses which are situated around the main square.

At Mayagüez, *Hilton*, casino, pool, L; *Palma*, on Méndez Vigo, B; *Sol*, 9 S R Palmer Este, B; *Las Américas*, cheap but adequate, on road from *público* terminal to main square; *Colón*, Plaza Colón, E, no bath, ask for a quiet room. *Hospedaje San Vicente*, Calle San Vicente, F, very basic.

At Rincón, *Parador*, *Villa Antonio*, A, pool, beach, tennis courts. At Puntas, Carmen's grocery store has rooms, basic, F, cooking facilities.

At Utuado, *Riverside*, D, bargain with the manager.

There are Paradores Puertorriqueños to put you up while touring, some old, most new, with prices starting at B: one is at Baños de Coamo (A) where there are thermal water springs, rec., and another is the *Hacienda Gripiñas*, an old coffee plantation house, which lies in the mountains near Jayuya, North of Ponce, B. Reservations can be made through Paradores Puertorriqueños, 301 San Justo St., PO Box 4435, Old San Juan Station, San Juan, Puerto Rico 00905, T (809) 721 2400.

Camping Camping is permitted in the Forest Reserves; you have to get a permit (free) from the visitor centres. Camping is also allowed on some of the public beaches, contact the Recreation and Sports Department (T 722 1551 or 721 2800 ext 225). There are tent sites at Añasco, Cerro Gordo, Luquillo, Sombé and Punta Guilarte, cabins at Boquerón, Punta Guilarte and Punta Santiago, tent and trailer site at Seven Seas.

Restaurants   All major hotels. In old San Juan: *Galería, Fortaleza*; for Puerto Rican cuisine, *La Fonda del Callejón*, Fortaleza 319; *Bacardi*; *La Mallorquina*, San Justo 207, the oldest restaurant in the Caribbean, rec.; *La Zaragozana*, San Francisco 356, some Spanish and Cuban specialities, highly rec.; *La Posada de San Luis Rey*, Fortaleza 317; *La Danza*, corner of Cristo and Fortaleza; *La Bombanera*, San Francisco (in the 200s). *Sole Mio*, Av Ponce de León 655, good, cheap Italian food; on same street *El Miramar*, good and cheap. *Taza de Oro*, Luna 254, near San Justo. *Atena*, on corner of Luna and San Justo. Excellent ice-cream parlours on Plaza Colón in Old San Juan. *Cecilia's Place*, Rosa St., Isla Verde. In Mayagüez the *Cacique Restaurant* is rec., as is the *Drive-In Restaurant*. The best of the restaurants in small towns and villages are denoted by a knife and fork emblem, which is part of a government-sponsored association of restaurants. They are moderatley priced and offer local dishes.

Nightclub   Jazz at The Place, Calle Fortaleza in old San Juan, no admission charge, drinks about US$2.

Warning   Female tourists should avoid the Condado beach areas at night if alone. Take precautions against theft from your person and your car, wherever you are on the island.

Sports   All the hotels provide instruction and equipment for water skiing, snorkelling, boating and day trips to areas of aquatic interest. At Puerta de Tierra, near the Caribe Hilton, is the sports complex built for the 1979 Pan-American Games.

Beaches and Watersports Swimming from most beaches is safe; the best beaches near San Juan are those at Isla Verde in front of the main hotels; Loquillo to the E of San Juan is less crowded and has a fine-sand beach from where there are good views of El Yunque. The north coast Atlantic sea is rougher than the southern waters, particularly in winter. There are 13 *balneario* beaches round the island where lockers, showers and parking places are provided for a small fee. *Balnearios* are open Tues.-Sun. 0900-1700, in winter and 0800-1700 in summer. The shallow waters are good for snorkelling but scuba divers need to take a boat out to deeper water. There are many companies offering equipment rental and diving instruction, including The School of Aquatics (T 723 4740), Caribbean Divers: The Fun Boat (T 724 3292), Coral Head Divers (T 850 7208), Cueva Submarina Training Centre (T 872 3903), Mundo Submarino (T 791 5764) and also at some of the larger hotels. There are also semi-deserted beaches.

Boating   Puerto Rico's coastline is protected in many places by coral reefs and cays which are fun to visit and explore. Sloops can be hired at US$35 a day, with crew, and hold six passengers.
There are three marinas at Fajardo, the Club Náutico at Miramar and another at Boca de Cangrejos in Isla Verde (both in San Juan) and one near Humacao. The first phase of an ambitious marina project at Puerto del Rey, Fajardo, opened late 1988.

Deep-sea Fishing   is popular and more than 30 world records have been broken in Puerto Rican waters, where blue and white marlin, sailfish, wahoo, dolphin, mackerel and tarpon, to mention a few, are a challenge to the angler. Fishing boat charters are available. You can also fish in the many lakes out on the island. Contact the Department of Natural Resources (T 722 5938) for details.

Surfing   The most popular beaches for surfing are the Pine Beach Grove in Isla Verde (San Juan) and Punta Higuero, Route 413 between Aguadilla and Rincón on the west coast, where several international surfing competitions have been held. The Condado Lagoon is popular for windsurfing, as is Boquerón Bay and Ocean Park beach.

Other sports Golf There are 10 golf courses around the island. The *Cerromar* and *Dorado Beach* hotels in Dorado have excellent 36-hole championship golf courses, there are several 18-hole courses, and in Ponce the *Hotel International Ponce* makes arrangements for guests to play at a nearby country club's 9-hole course. **Tennis** Over 100 tennis courts are available, mostly in the larger hotels. There are also 17 public courts in San Juan's Central Park, open daily. The Dorado del Mar Country Club has 6 courts and the Palmas del Mar resort, at Humacao, has 20 courts. **Cockfighting** The season is from November 1 to August 31. This sport is held at the new, air-conditioned Coliseo Gallístico in Isla Verde, near the Holiday Inn, Wed. and Fri. 2030; Sat. and Sun. 1400. Admission from US$4 to US$10. **Horse Racing** El Comandante, Route 3, Km. 5.5, is one of the hemisphere's most beautiful race courses. Races are held all the year round (Wed., Fri. and

Sun.). First race is at 1415. Wed. is ladies' day. Children under 12 not admitted at any time. **Riding** Rancho Borinquén, at Carolina, near San Juan, rents horses by the hour, or half-day, free transport from San Juan. Rancho Criollo at El Yunque near the rain forest, rents horses by the hour every day except Sun. At Palmas del Mar, Humacao, there is an equestrian centre which offers beach rides and riding and jumping lessons. Other places include Ranchos Guayama, at Guayama; Hacienda Caraboat. Beach Trails at Río Grande; Parador Guajataca and Vistamar, at Quebradillas; Hacienda Rosas at Utuado; La Casa del Francés, on Vieques Island.

Car Hire There are 13 car rental agencies, including Hertz (T 791 0840), Isla Verde International Airport; National (T 791 1805), 1102 Magdalena Ave.; Budget (T 791 3685) have a bus service from the airport to their office. A small car may be hired for US$32 (including collision damage waiver) for 24 hours, unlimited mileage (national driving licence preferred to international licence). The Rand McNally road map is recommended. Avoid driving in the San Juan metropolitan area as traffic can be very heavy.

Taxis Lease Division Caribe Motors, 519 Fernández Juncos; Metro Taxicabs, Km. 3.3, Route 3, Isla Verde; Metropolitan Taxi Cabs, 165 Quisquella. University Taxi, Río Piedras. All taxis are metered and charge US$0.40 for initial charge (US$0.80 in San Juan) and US$0.10 for every additional ⅓ km.; US$0.25 is charged for a taxi called from home or business. Taxis may be hired at US$6 an hour unmetered. Taxi drivers sometimes try to ask more from tourists, so beware, insist that the meter is used, and avoid picking up a taxi anywhere near a cruise ship. There are also shared taxis (*públicos*) which have yellow number plates with the letters P or PD at the end and run to all parts of the island. Most of them leave from Río Piedras. They do not usually operate after about 1900. A service referred to as *línea* will pick up and drop off passengers where they wish. They operate between San Juan, and most towns and cities at a fixed rate. They can be found in the phone book under Líneas de Carros.

Airport There are airport limousines to a number of hotels. There is also a bus service (T1), US$0.25 to and from Plaza Colón and the airport; note that people take precedence over luggage if the bus is full. The taxi fare to old San Juan is US$10-12; the Airport Limousine Service shared taxi is US$2.75, but seems to run very seldom.

Buses *San Juan*: There is a city bus (*guagua*) service with a fixed charge of US$0.25. They have special routes against the normal direction of traffic and the bus lanes are marked by yellow and white lines. Bus stops are marked by yellow posts or signs marked "Parada de Guaguas". The central terminal is at Plaza Colón and there is another at the San Juan main post office (for *públicos*). No 10 passes near all the main hotels; No 1 to the University of Puerto Rico. (No change given; make sure you have right money.) City buses are not very frequent, however; they run to a 30-, or 45-minute schedule and many do not operate after 2200. *Interurban*: Puerto Rico Motor Coach company has daily scheduled services between San Juan, Arecibo (US$2.50), and Mayagüez (6 per day, US$8, 4 hour drive) through Caguas and Cayey or through Salinas. Hitchhiking is possible, but slow. From Old San Juan buses Nos 1 and 2 run to the Río Piedras bus station. Walk to the Plaza Colón for other buses. *Público* to Ponce takes 7 hours (US$5-7).

The Economy Income per head is high at over US$4,700. Life expectancy is now 71 years, and illiteracy has been reduced to about 10%. Great social and economic progress has been made in the past thirty years, as a result of the "Operation Bootstrap" industrialization programme supported by the US and Puerto Rican governments, which was begun in 1948. Accordingly manufacturing for export has become the most important sector of the economy, in place of agriculture. Until 1976, US corporations were given tax incentives to set up in Puerto Rico and their profits were taxed only if repatriated. Industrial parks were built based on labour intensive industries to take advantage of Puerto Rico's low wages. In the mid-1970s, however, the strategy changed to attract capital intensive companies with the aim of avoiding the low wage trap. Nowadays about 70% of manufacturing income is repatriated; manufacturing produces half of total output, but only 20% if remittances are excluded, about the same as in the 1950s. Investment has also fallen recently to 17% of gdp, having risen from 15% in 1950 to 30% in 1970.

The principal manufactures are textiles, clothing, electrical and electronic equipment and petrochemicals. Dairy and livestock production is one of the leading agricultural activities; others are the cultivation of sugar, tobacco, coffee, pineapples and coconut. Tourism is another key element in the economy. Despite the progress made to industrialize the country, the economy has suffered from US budget cuts. Some 30% of all spending on gnp originates in Washington and high unemployment is possible because of food stamps and other US transfers. Migration is a safety valve, and there are more Puerto Ricans living in New York than San Juan. Inflation is low, averaging only 1.1% a year in 1982-86.

INFORMATION FOR VISITORS

How to get there *International*: British Airways; Aeropostal; COPA; Lacsa; Lufthansa; Viasa; Virgin Air; BWIA (T 791 1190); Iberia (T 725 5630); Liat (T 791 1190); Mexicana Aviación (T 725

5450); Dominicana (T 725 9393); Air France (T 724 0500); ALM (T 724 3013). *Domestic*: American Airlines (T 725 8484); Delta (T 724 5221); Eastern (T 725 3131); TWA. Several local airlines operate services within Puerto Rico and between the islands, including Antilles Air Boats, Air BVI, Air Jamaica, Virgin Islands Seaplane, Caribair, Prinair, Air Best, Culebra Aviation, Crownair, Air Indies, Aero Virgin Islands and Vieques Air Link, and they all have offices at the Luis Muñoz Marín International Airport. There are cheap Eastern and American Airlines night flights between New York and San Juan, and hourly flights between San Juan and Ponce (US$15). One of the cheaper ways of getting from Mexico to the Caribbean is to fly from, say, Mérida to San Juan and there get a connection. Lacsa and Iberia fly between San Juan and San José (Costa Rica). Some charter or inter-island flights leave from the Isla Grande airport.

Shipping There is a daily hydrofoil service, the *Caribbean Princess*, from Pier 6, Old San Juan to St Thomas, US Virgin Islands, at 0800, 2½ hours, returning 1630, fare US$65 adults, US$32.50 children one way (T 793 7159). From Fajardo Beach to Vieques, 1 hour 20 minutes, US$2 adults, US$1 children, daily 0915-1630, return ferry 0730-1500. Fajardo-Culebra, 2 hours, US$2.25 adults, US$1 children, Tues.-Sat. 1600, Sat., Sun. and holidays 0900, Mon. 0915 via Vieques; return ferry Tues.-Sat. 0700, Sat. 1500, Sun. 1600, Mon. 1330 via Vieques. Vieques-Culebra, 2 hours, US$2 adults, US$1 children, Sat.-Sun. 1330, Mon. 1100, return Sat.-Sun. 1100, Mon. 1300. There are no boats to other Caribbean destinations, apart from cruise ships.

Documents All non-US residents need a US visa. (Canadians may not need one: check.)

Tourist Information can be obtained from the Puerto Rico Tourist Bureau, PO Box 4435, San Juan 00905, with offices also at the international airport, Convention Center Condado (T 723 3135); the Puerto Rico Tourism Company, San Justo 301, old San Juan, Hato Rey, San Juan (GPO Box BN, San Juan PR 00936), with offices in New York, Chicago, Los Angeles, Philadelphia, Houston, Dallas, Miami, Atlanta, Toronto, Geneva, Madrid, Mexico City and Frankfurt/Main. In London, write for brochures to The Puerto Rico Tourism Company, PO Box 15, Coulsdon, Surrey, CR3 2UZ (T 01-589 5216), or call at the USTTA office, 22 Sackville Street, London W1. The office at the cruise dock is open for normal office hours. The Caribbean Travel Service, Av Ashford 1300, Condado, are happy to help. Out in the country, tourist information can be obtained from the town halls, usually found on the main plaza.

Qué Pasa, a monthly guide for tourists published by the Tourism Company, can be obtained free from the tourist office. It is very helpful, and we wish here to acknowledge our debt to it.

The Puerto Rico Tourist Zone Police are at Vieques Street, Condado (T 722 0738 and 724 5210).

Health Dengue fever is endemic; any "common cold" syndrome should be investigated. Avoid swimming in rivers: bilharzia may be present.

Shopping Puerto Rico is a large producer of rum, with many different types ranging from light rums for mixing with soft drinks to dark brandy-type rums. Hand-made cigars can still be found in Old San Juan and Puerta de Tierra. The largest shopping mall in the Caribbean is Plaza las Américas in Hato Rey, others include Plaza Carolina in Carolina, Río Hondo in Levittown, Plaza del Carmen in Caguas and Mayagüez Mall in Mayagüez. There are more traditional shops in Old San Juan. Imported goods from all over the world are available. Local artesanías include wooden carvings, musical instruments, lace, ceramics, hammocks, masks and basketwork. There are several shops in San Juan, but it is more interesting to visit the workshops around Puerto Rico. Contact the Centro de Artes Populares (T 724 6250) or the Tourism Artisan Office (T 721 2400 ext 248) for details.

There are a number of bookshops in the metropolitan area, and the Librería Sociedad de Autores Puertorriqueños is in the Casa de los Contrafuertes, Plaza San José, Old San Juan (Wed.-Sat. 1000-1700).

Food and Drink Two good local dishes are the mixed stew, *asopao*, and a splendid risotto known as *yuquiyú*, a mixture of rice, sausage, pineapple, peppers, etc, cooked in a pineapple husk. Black bean soup is another local speciality. Corona beer is good and many restaurants pride themselves on their *piñas coladas*. *Maví* is a drink fermented from the bark of a tree and sold in many snack-bars.

Currency United States currency. Most international and US credit cards are accepted.

Newspapers and Periodicals *San Juan Star* is the only daily English paper. There are two Spanish daily papers of note, *El Mundo* and *El Día*.

Public Holidays New Year's Day. January 6: Three Kings' Day. January 11: De Hostos' Birthday. February 22: Washington's Birthday. March 22: Emancipation Day. Good Friday. April 16: José de Diego's Birthday. May 30: Memorial Day. June 24: St John the Baptist. July 4: Independence Day. July 17: Muñoz Rivera's Birthday. July 25: Constitution Day. July 27: Dr. José Celso Barbosa's Birthday. September 1: Labour Day. October 12: Columbus Day. November 11: Veterans' Day. November 19: Discovery of Puerto Rico. November 25: Thanksgiving Day. Christmas Day.

Everything is closed on public holidays. One of the most important is June 24, though in fact the capital grinds to a halt the previous afternoon and everyone heads for the beach. Here there is loud *salsa* music and barbecues until midnight when everyone walks backwards into the sea to greet the Baptist and ensure good fortune.

Churches Roman Catholic, Episcopal, Baptist, Seventh Day Adventist, Presbyterian, Lutheran, Christian Science and Union Church. There is also a Jewish community. At the Anglican-Episcopal cathedral in San Juan there are services in both Spanish and English.

Medical Services Government and private hospitals. Hospital charges are high. Ambulance, T 343 2500.

Banks Banco de Ponce; Banco de San Juan; Banco Mercantil de Puerto Rico; and branches of US and foreign banks.

Postal Service Inside the new Post Office building in Hato Rey, on Av. Roosevelt, there is a separate counter for sales of special tourist stamps. In Old San Juan, the Post Office is in an attractive old rococo-style building.

Telephone Operated by Puerto Rico Telephone Co, state-owned. Overseas calls can be made from the former ITT office at Parada 11, Av. Ponce de León, Miramar, and from the airport. Three minutes to New York, US$2.35 and to the UK, US$14. The blue pages in the telephone book are a tourist section in English, divided by subject.

Broadcasting Two radio stations have English programmes.

Tipping Fixed service charges are not included in bills and it is recommended that 15-20% is given to waiters, taxi drivers, etc.

We are most grateful to Jan Jacob de Groot (Vroomshoop, Neth.) for some most valuable updating.

CLIMATIC TABLES

The following tables have been very kindly furnished by Mr. R. K. Headland. Each weather station is given with its altitude in metres (m.). Temperatures (Centigrade) are given as averages for each month; the first line is the maximum and the second the minimum. The third line is the average number of wet days encountered in each month.

MEXICO, CENTRAL AMERICA & CARIBBEAN

	Jan.	Feb.	Mar.	Apr.	May	June	July	Aug.	Sept.	Oct.	Nov.	Dec.
Acapulco, Mex.	29	31	31	31	32	32	32	32	31	31	31	31
3m.	21	21	21	22	23	24	24	24	24	23	22	21
	0	0	0	0	2	9	7	7	12	6	1	0
Guatemala City	23	25	27	28	29	27	26	26	26	24	23	22
1490m.	11	12	14	14	16	16	16	16	16	15	14	13
	2	2	2	5	8	20	17	16	17	13	6	2
Havana	26	27	28	29	30	31	31	32	31	29	27	26
49m.	18	18	19	21	22	23	24	24	24	23	21	19
	6	4	4	4	7	10	9	10	11	11	7	6
Kingston	30	29	30	30	31	31	32	32	32	31	31	30
7m.	22	22	23	24	25	25	26	26	25	25	24	23
	3	2	3	3	5	6	3	6	6	12	5	3
Managua, Nic.	30	30	30	32	32	31	31	31	31	31	30	30
46m.	23	24	26	28	27	26	26	25	26	24	24	24
	0	0	0	0	6	12	11	12	15	16	4	1
Mérida, Mex.	28	29	32	33	34	33	33	33	32	31	29	28
22m.	17	17	19	21	22	23	23	23	23	22	19	18
	4	2	1	2	5	10	11	12	13	7	3	3
Mexico City	19	21	24	25	26	24	23	23	23	21	20	19
2309m.	6	6	8	11	12	13	12	12	12	10	8	6
	2	1	2	6	9	14	19	18	17	8	3	2
Monterrey, Mex.	20	22	24	29	31	33	32	33	30	27	22	18
538m.	9	11	14	17	20	22	22	22	21	18	13	10
	3	3	3	4	4	4	4	3	8	5	4	4
Nassau	25	25	27	28	29	31	31	32	31	29	28	26
10m.	17	17	18	20	22	23	24	24	24	22	20	18
	6	5	5	6	9	12	14	14	15	13	9	6
Panama City	31	31	32	32	31	30	30	31	30	30	29	30
36m.	21	21	22	23	23	23	23	23	23	22	22	23
	4	2	1	6	15	16	15	15	15	16	18	12
Port-au-Prince	31	31	32	33	33	35	35	35	34	33	32	31
41m.	23	22	22	23	23	24	25	24	24	24	23	22
	3	5	7	11	13	8	7	11	12	12	7	3
Port of Spain	30	32	31	32	32	31	31	31	32	31	31	30
12m.	20	21	21	21	23	23	23	23	23	22	22	21
	11	8	2	8	9	19	23	17	16	13	17	16
San José, Costa Rica	24	24	26	27	27	27	26	26	27	26	25	24
1172m.	14	14	15	16	16	16	16	16	16	15	15	15
	1	0	1	4	17	20	18	19	20	22	14	4
San Juan, PR	27	27	27	28	29	29	29	29	30	30	28	27
14m.	21	21	22	22	23	24	24	24	24	24	23	22
	13	7	8	10	15	14	18	15	14	12	13	14
San Salvador	30	31	32	32	31	30	30	30	29	29	29	29
700m.	16	16	17	19	19	19	18	18	18	18	17	16
	0	3	2	5	12	20	21	20	18	14	4	1
Santo Domingo	28	28	29	29	30	30	31	31	31	31	30	29
14m.	20	19	20	21	22	23	23	23	23	23	22	21
	7	6	5	7	11	12	11	11	11	11	10	8
Tegucigalpa, Hond.	25	27	29	30	30	28	28	28	29	27	26	25
935m.	14	14	15	16	18	19	17	17	17	17	16	15
	4	2	1	3	14	18	10	10	17	16	8	4
Willemstad	28	29	29	30	30	31	31	31	32	31	30	29
23m.	24	23	23	24	25	26	25	26	26	26	26	24
	14	8	7	4	4	7	9	8	6	9	15	16

CLIMATIC TABLES (Cont.)

SOUTH AMERICA

	Jan.	Feb.	Mar.	Apr.	May	June	July	Aug.	Sept.	Oct.	Nov.	Dec.
Arica, Chile	26	26	25	23	21	19	19	18	19	21	22	24
29m.	18	18	17	16	14	14	12	13	13	14	16	17
	0	0	0	0	0	0	0	0	0	0	0	0
Asunción, Par.	34	34	33	28	25	22	24	25	27	29	31	33
64m.	22	22	21	18	14	13	14	14	16	17	19	21
	7	6	9	7	5	4	4	4	6	5	6	7
Bariloche, Arg.	21	21	18	14	10	7	6	8	10	11	16	18
825m.	8	8	6	4	2	1	0	0	1	3	5	6
	2	3	5	7	11	13	11	11	8	6	4	4
Barranquilla, Col.	31	31	32	33	34	33	33	33	33	32	32	30
12m.	22	22	23	24	25	25	25	25	25	24	24	23
	0	0	0	1	4	8	5	6	8	11	6	4
Belém, Braz.	31	30	30	31	31	32	32	32	32	32	32	32
24m.	23	23	23	23	23	23	22	22	22	22	22	22
	24	26	25	22	24	15	14	15	13	10	11	14
Belo Horizonte	27	27	27	27	25	24	24	25	27	27	27	26
857m.	18	18	17	16	12	10	10	12	14	16	17	18
	15	13	9	4	4	2	2	1	2	10	12	14
Bogotá	21	21	21	20	20	19	19	19	20	20	20	21
2560m.	7	7	9	10	10	9	8	8	8	9	8	7
	9	7	10	18	16	10	6	10	13	18	16	13
Brasilia	27	28	28	28	27	26	26	28	30	29	27	27
912m.	18	18	18	17	15	13	13	14	16	18	18	18
	19	16	15	9	3	1	0	2	4	11	15	20
Buenos Aires	30	29	26	22	18	15	15	16	18	21	25	29
25m.	18	17	15	12	9	6	6	6	8	11	13	16
	5	5	6	6	4	4	5	6	5	7	7	7
Caracas	26	26	28	28	28	27	26	27	28	27	27	26
1035m.	15	15	16	17	18	18	17	17	17	17	17	16
	4	3	2	4	8	13	13	11	11	11	8	6
Córdoba, Arg.	32	31	28	25	21	19	19	20	23	26	28	31
425m.	17	16	14	11	7	4	4	5	8	11	13	16
	8	9	9	6	4	2	2	1	3	7	9	10
Cuzco	20	21	21	22	21	21	21	21	22	22	23	22
3310m.	7	7	7	4	2	1	-1	1	4	6	6	7
	18	13	11	8	3	2	2	2	7	8	12	16
Guayaquil	31	31	32	31	31	29	28	29	30	29	30	31
6m.	22	22	23	23	22	21	20	20	20	21	21	22
	12	13	15	10	4	1	0	0	0	1	0	2
La Paz, Bol.	18	18	18	19	17	17	17	17	18	19	19	19
3632m.	6	6	6	5	3	2	1	2	3	5	6	6
	21	18	16	9	3	2	2	4	9	9	11	18
Lima	25	26	26	24	21	19	17	17	17	19	20	23
137m.	19	20	19	18	16	15	14	13	13	14	16	17
	1	0	0	0	1	1	1	1	2	1	0	0
Manaus	30	30	30	30	31	31	32	33	33	33	32	31
48m.	23	23	23	23	23	23	23	24	24	24	24	24
	20	18	21	20	18	12	12	5	7	4	12	16
Montevideo	28	28	26	22	18	15	14	15	17	20	23	26
22m.	17	16	15	12	9	6	6	6	8	9	12	15
	6	5	5	6	6	5	6	7	6	6	6	7
Porto Alegre, Braz.	31	30	29	25	22	20	20	21	22	24	27	29
10m.	20	20	19	16	13	11	10	11	13	15	17	18
	9	10	10	6	6	8	8	8	11	10	8	8
Punta Arenas, Chile	15	14	13	9	6	4	3	4	7	10	12	14
28m.	7	7	6	4	2	1	1	1	2	3	4	6
	6	5	7	9	6	8	6	5	5	5	5	8
Quito	21	21	20	21	21	21	21	22	22	21	21	21
2818m.	8	8	8	8	8	7	7	7	7	7	8	8
	9	11	11	15	10	9	3	3	8	13	13	7

SOUTH AMERICA (Cont.)

	Jan.	Feb.	Mar.	Apr.	May	June	July	Aug.	Sept.	Oct.	Nov.	Dec.
Recife, Braz.	30	30	30	30	29	28	27	27	28	29	30	30
56m.	24	25	24	23	23	22	21	21	22	23	24	24
	7	8	10	11	17	16	17	14	7	3	4	4
Rio de Janeiro	30	30	29	27	26	25	25	25	25	26	28	28
30m.	23	23	23	21	20	18	18	18	19	20	20	22
	13	11	9	9	6	5	5	4	5	11	10	12
Salvador (Bahia)	29	29	29	28	27	26	26	26	27	28	28	29
8m.	23	23	24	23	22	21	21	21	21	22	23	23
	6	9	17	19	22	23	18	15	10	8	9	11
Santa Cruz, Bol.	30	31	30	28	25	23	24	28	29	30	31	31
437m.	21	21	20	19	16	15	15	16	19	20	20	21
	14	10	12	9	11	8	5	4	5	7	8	11
Santiago de Chile	29	29	27	23	18	14	15	17	19	22	26	28
520m.	12	11	9	7	5	3	3	4	6	7	9	11
	0	0	1	1	5	6	6	5	3	3	1	0
São Paulo	28	28	27	25	23	22	21	23	25	25	25	26
792m.	18	18	17	15	13	11	10	11	13	14	15	16
	15	13	12	6	3	4	4	3	5	12	11	14

Sources:—H.M.S.O. Meteorological Reports
K.L.M. Climatic Data Publication

TEMPERATURES CONVERSION TABLE

°C	°F	°C	°F	°C	°F	°C	°F
1	34	11	52	21	70	31	88
2	36	12	54	22	72	32	90
3	38	13	56	23	74	33	92
4	39	14	57	24	75	34	93
5	41	15	59	25	77	35	95
6	43	16	61	26	79	36	97
7	45	17	63	27	81	37	99
8	46	18	64	28	82	38	100
9	48	19	66	29	84	39	102
10	50	20	68	30	86	40	104

The formula for converting °C to °F is: °C x 9 ÷ 5 + 32 = °F.

STANDARD TIME ZONES

(Expressed as hours behind Greenwich Mean Time)

Argentina	3	Nicaragua	6
Falkland Islands	4	Costa Rica	6
Bolivia	4	Panama	5
Brazil	3*(2* 1)	Cuba	5
Chile	4(3†)	Haiti	5
Colombia	5	Dominican Republic	4
Ecuador	5	Puerto Rico	4
Paraguay	4(3†)	Jamaica	5
Peru	5	Barbados	4
Uruguay	3	Trinidad & Tobago	4
Venezuela	4	Leeward Islands	4
Guyana	3¾	Windward Islands	4
Suriname	3½	Bahamas	5(4**)
Guyane	3	Turks & Caicos Islands	5
Mexico	6‡	Cayman Islands	5
Guatemala	6	Bermuda	4
Belize	6	Virgin Islands	4
El Salvador	6	Netherlands Antilles	4
Honduras	6	French Antilles	4

*Standard time, except for Fernando de Noronha (2); Amazonia W of the Jari and Xingu rivers and E of the Tabatinga-Porto Acre line, and the States of Mato Grosso and Mato Grosso do Sul (4); and Amazonia W of the Tabatinga-Porto Acre line (5).
†Summer time, October-March.
‡Standard time, except for Baja California Sur, Sonora, Sinaloa and Nayarit (7); and Baja California (8).
**Summer time, May-October.

WEIGHTS AND MEASURES

Metric	British and U.S.

Weight:

Metric	British and U.S.
1 kilogram (kg.) = 2,205 pounds	1 pound (lb.) = 454 grams
1 metric ton = 1.102 short tons	1 short ton (2,000 lb.) = 0.907 metric ton
= 0.984 long ton	1 long ton (2,240 lb.) = 1.016 metric tons

Length:

Metric	British and U.S.
1 millimetre (mm.) = 0.03937 inch	1 inch = 25.417 millimetres
1 metre = 3.281 feet	1 foot (ft.) = 0.305 metre
1 kilometre (km.) = 0.621 mile	1 mile = 1.609 kilometres

Area:

Metric	British and U.S.
1 hectare = 2.471 acres	1 acre = 0.405 hectare
1 square km. (km²) = 0.386 sq. mile	1 square mile (sq. mile) = 2,590 km²

Capacity:

Metric	British and U.S.
1 litre = 0.220 Imperial gallon	1 Imperial gallon = 4.546 litres
= 0.264 U.S. gallon	1 U.S. gallon = 3.785 litres

(5 Imperial gallons are approximately equal to 6 U.S. gallons)

Volume:

Metric	British and U.S.
1 cubic metre (m³) = 35.31 cubic feet	1 cubic foot (cu. ft) = 0.028 m³
= 1.31 cubic yards	1 cubic yard (cu. yd.) = 0.765 m³

N.B. The *manzana*, used in Central America, is about 0.7 hectare (1.73 acres).

LATEST EXCHANGE AND INFLATION RATES

This information updates that given in the "Information for Visitors" sections of the country chapters.

	Exchange for tourists: Units per US dollar	Inflation: % increase in cost of living over last 12 months	
	End-May 1989	Latest month	1989
Argentina	175 (250)	April	460.8
Bolivia	2.59 (2.59)	March	20.4
Brazil	1.14 (3.10)	April	991.4
Chile	255.00 (278)	April	13.2
Colombia	373.00 (378)	April	24.8
Ecuador	515.00 (541)	April	93.2
Paraguay	1,075.00	March	22.2
Peru	2,025.00 (2,765)	April	4,328.0
Uruguay	556.00 (560)	April	78.1
Venezuela	38.30	April	94.0
Mexico	2,418.00 (2,445)	April	19.2
Belize	2.00	December (88)	2.0
Costa Rica	79.20 (81)	February	20.2
El Salvador	5.00 (5.20)	October (88)	19.4
Guatemala	2.70 (2.70)	October (88)	8.9
Honduras	2.00 (2.70)	February	8.9
Nicaragua	7,400.00 (8,500)	December (88)	23,997.0
Panama	1.00	December (88)	−0.2

Black ("parallel") market rates in brackets.

WILL YOU HELP US?

We do all we can to get our facts right in *The South American Handbook.* Each chapter is thoroughly revised each year, but Latin America and the Caribbean cover a vast area, and our eyes cannot be everywhere. A new highway or airport is built; a hotel, a restaurant, a cabaret dies; another, a good one is born; a building we describe is pulled down, a street renamed. Names and addresses of good hotels and restaurants for "budget-minded" travellers are always very welcome. We would especially like to receive diagrams of walks, national parks and other interesting areas to use as source material for the Handbook and other forthcoming titles.

Your information may be far more up-to-date than ours. If your letter reaches us early enough in the year it will be used in the next edition, but write whenever you want to, for all your letters are used sooner or later.
Thank you very much indeed for your help.

Trade & Travel Publications Limited
5 Prince's Buildings, George Street,
Bath BA1 2ED. England

INDEX TO PLACES

Now arranged alphabetically under countries

INDEX TO TOWN AND REGIONAL MAPS

INDEX TO ADVERTISERS

Page

THOMAS COOK MASTERCARD TRAVELLERS CHEQUES REFUND ASSISTANCE POINTS

Visitors to South and Central America should telephone MasterCard New York 212-974-5696 (collect) – 24 hour service – or during normal business hours, contact one of the following Thomas Cook Travellers Cheque offices:-

BUENOS AIRES
25 de Mayo 195-G Piso   Tel: 30-7192, 8610, 8371
1002 Buenos Aires
Argentina

CARACAS
Edificio "Cavendes"   Tel: 2-284-3866, 3255
Piso 7, Ofc 701
Ave. Francisco de Miranda
Los Palos Grandes
1060 Caracas
Venezuela

MEXICO CITY
Campos Eliseos 345-1 Piso   Tel: 596-7839, 8430
Col Polanco
11560 Mexico City
Mexico

SAO PAULO
Rua Haddock Lobo 337-2-Andar   Tel: 259-3022
01414 Sao Paulo
Brazil

Customers will be provided with full details of the nearest convenient local agent.

Visitors to the Caribbean area should also telephone MasterCard New York 212-974-5696 (collect) 24 hour service for assistance.

In many Latin American countries there is a vigorous parallel (black) market for both travellers cheques and U.S. Dollar notes. (This may be with or without Government permission). Rates are usually slightly better for notes but travellers cheques are obviously safer, which is especially important when theft is becoming more common.

You should shop around for rates since these may vary considerably. Hotel rates in particular tend to be poor.

Do not take currencies other than U.S. Dollar. If accepted at all, the rate will be poor.

In some countries, only specific bank branches may deal in foreign exchange and you may have difficulty obtaining local currency when far from capital cities.